D0340342

Contributors

ALAN CACKETT
HANNAH CHARLTON
JOHN CHILD
DONALD CLARKE
DEMITRI CORYTON
FRED DELLAR
RONNIE GRAHAM
MICHAEL HEATLEY
PATRICK HUMPHRIES
KEN HUNT
ROBIN KATZ
JOHN MARTLAND
SUE STEWARD
JOHN TOBLER
CLIFF WHITE

THE PENGUIN ENCYCLOPEDIA OF
Popular Music

EDITED BY DONALD CLARKE

VIKING

VIKING

Published by the Penguin Group
27 Wrights Lane, London W8 5TZ, England
Viking Penguin Inc., 40 West 23rd Street, New York, New York 10010, USA
Penguin Books Australia Ltd, Ringwood, Victoria, Australia
Penguin Books Canada Ltd, 2801 John Street, Markham, Ontario, Canada L3R 1B4
Penguin Books (NZ) Ltd, 182–190 Wairau Road, Auckland 10, New Zealand

Penguin Books Ltd, Registered Offices: Harmondsworth, Middlesex, England

First published 1989
10 9 8 7 6 5 4 3 2

Filmset in Plantin Typeface
By C.R. Barber & Partners Ltd, Wrotham, Kent TN15 7DN.

Printed in Great Britain by Richard Clays Ltd, Bungay, Suffolk

A CIP catalogue record for this book is available from the British Library

ISBN 0-670-80349-9

To my father, Donald E. Clarke,
who taught me, not with words but by his
example, to do the best I could;
to Joe and Sol Hoffmann, for much
the same reason;
and in memory of Joseph Hollingsworth Igo
and Elmer Hugo Reuss –
all Wisconsin men, good and true

Introduction

I began listening to all kinds of music several decades ago, on my mother's kitchen radio. I heard bits of Bizet played by a swing band; playing in my grandma's farmhouse living room, I heard WGN's Barn Dance while she made popcorn in an iron skillet; when I was old enough, I twiddled the dial on the radio myself, and listened to rhythm and blues from the south side of Chicago, as well as Randy Blake and his Suppertime Frolic, with Hank Williams, Roy Acuff and the Chuck Wagon Gang. Later, when Elvis Presley happened, I was almost the only kid in my school who wasn't astonished.

I listened to 'popular instrumentals' (searching, though I didn't know it, for classical music); the best of Percy Faith's arrangements hold up well to this day. When I discovered that the public library had records, I found Louis Armstrong's Hot Five (and became a Mahler fan long before that composer's day finally arrived).

Usually I was to be found slightly outside the mainstream. I had pawed through my parents' stack of 78s, and looked behind Glenn Miller to find Benny Goodman, then Fletcher Henderson; but there weren't any Henderson records anywhere. Similarly, a little later on, Dave Brubeck was all right, but I was curious about Art Tatum and Thelonious Monk. I heard about records on labels called Riverside, Prestige and Blue Note, but the record shops in my home town couldn't afford to stock them, because I couldn't afford to buy them. The steadily rising standard of living in the early '50s was based on keeping up with the Joneses, and the Joneses had cloth ears.

That was a long time ago. Then, as now, popular music seemed to be floundering; then, as now, there were a lot of interesting things happening, if you knew where to look. The difference is that I am not alone any more: nowadays there are a lot of people who listen to lots of different kinds of music, and there are more records available than ever before. Hence the book.

Popular music has always been a great mainstream with many tributaries; we have tried to compile entries for all the most important contributors to it, rather than confine ourselves to this or that minority music. There are nearly 3,000 entries, mostly for performers, but also for songwriters, producers and record labels; there are potted histories of the tributaries, such as Minstrelsy, Ragtime, Jazz, Blues, Rhythm & Blues, Country Music, Rock 'n' Roll and so forth; for the first time in a book of this type the Latin American scene is covered, and there are also entries for African acts, as well as Tex-Mex, Cajun, Zydeco and others. There is an entry for 'Recorded Sound, History of'. The entries for the major record labels document the history of the business through wars, depressions, innovations and mergers.

This book is for people who enjoy buying records. We have listed the most important albums by each artist (all the albums, in many cases), without regard to whether they are in print or not, giving the year of original release and the label, so that fans can look for them second-hand, or hope for their reissue. In the case of jazz albums, the date given is usually the date of recording; in other genres it is the date of issue. Where two labels are named, usually one is British and one is American; the label in the country where the music originated should come first. We have ignored Christmas albums, comedy albums and many of the greatest hits compilations. In the case of country music, the lists of albums are selective because in that genre the practice has been to issue a large number of albums, each titled after the current hit.

We have quoted a great many chart placings because these are of interest, and the further back in the decades we look, the more fun the 'hit parade' seems to be. (There is an entry for 'Charts' that goes into this subject.) For the most part we have ignored gold or platinum status, because the sales necessary to achieve precious metal change from time to time and are different in each country.

The names in small capital letters within the entries are cross-references to other entries, and there is also an index: if your favourite sideman, songwriter or teen queen doesn't have an entry of his/her own, the index allows access to information about many more individuals. The alphabetical order in the book treats Mc as though it were Mac: hence McGuire, Machito, McHugh, McIntyre, Mack, McKenzie. Stage names are usually alphabetized thus: LITTLE WILLIE JOHN, ROCKIN' JIMMY, RATTLESNAKE ANNIE, etc.; but there are exceptions: WATERS, Muddy; WOLF, Howlin'. Where the individual's true surname is used, the entry will be found there: MONTGOMERY, Little Brother. Many fine performers have given up on the mainstream record industry and are doing it themselves; there is a list of useful addresses at the back of the book, and we welcome information from other do-it-yourselfers for the next edition.

I have largely allowed the judgements of my various contributors to stand; Michael Heatley, for example, is far more qualified than I am to tell you that this or that heavy metal band is somewhat less unimaginative than another. Where I have passed some judgements of my own is in the entries for genres, nearly all of which I wrote myself. I have to be grateful to a large number of people, not least to my contributors, but every word has passed through my keyboard: any mistakes which may have got through are mine.

There are 13 Johnsons, 14 Kings, 18 Joneses, 20 each of Browns and Williamses and 30 Smiths (not counting The Smiths). I hope you enjoy using this book, or just browsing in it, as much as I have enjoyed preparing it: it has been, for me, a voyage of discovery and rediscovery. If you find any mistakes or if I've outraged your sensibilities in some way, let me know; I welcome information from performers about themselves, and from anybody who wants to tell me what should be in the next edition.

Acknowledgements

About 35 years ago my mother and I sent to WFOX in Milwaukee for a pamphlet with smudgy pictures and thumbnail biographies of Perry Como, Guy Mitchell and the rest; that was my introduction to reference books, which became an abiding addiction, so I suppose its anonymous compiler should get some credit/blame for the less wieldy tome you hold in your hands.

Much more recently, in London, I was lucky to rent a room from Dr Paul Auerbach, whose friendship and sense of humour belie the description of economics as the 'dismal science'. He is the sort of fellow, like me, who might come home from a record shop with Schönberg and Dolly Parton in the same bag; indeed, his idea for a book called *Dolly Parton and the Future of Western Music* may have planted the seed of this project.

John Denny, in 1983 an editor at Penguin, was first to see the possibilities of it and offered me a contract, for which I shall always be grateful. I thought I had him on a hook the first time I talked to him, but it was the other way round: he let me twist in the wind until I proved I could condense my prose and round up a team of contributors. I rang up Angela Errigo, an old friend who knew a thing or ten about the pop world; she gave me a list of names and telephone numbers, among them Robin Katz, who was Britain's authority on the Jackson Five and the Brill Building, and John Tobler, who had already published umpteen books: *The Guitar Greats* and *The Great Producers* (co-written with Stuart Grundy) had become BBC radio series. The number I had for John was out of date and Robin couldn't take a big part in the project, but she saw John and mentioned it to him; he rang me up and came from North London to South London to see me (and if you don't think that's impressive, you've never driven through London).

John introduced me to Patrick Humphries, who has written books about Fairport Convention and Paul Simon, and whose current project is a book (with John Bauldie) about Bob Dylan; and to the world's foremost authority Fred Dellar, whose latest book (with Roy Carr and Brian Case) is *The Hip – Hipsters, Jazz and the Beat Generation*. Fred brought along John Martland, who, like Fred, somehow unearthed information about well-loved mainstream artists who are rarely included in reference books, until the demands of his day job as a carpenter forced him to quit.

Tobler had to bow out; after ten years as a full-time freelance music journalist, he'd had enough of the wolf slavering at the door and wanted to look for a real job: he was then unable to stay away from the music world, but meanwhile had recruited Michael Heatley to replace himself. Michael had been editor of the Orbis part-work history of rock and is responsible for a large number of the rock and pop entries here; he did more and better work in less time than anyone else I have met in fifteen years of working in publishing.

Alan Cackett is a contributor to *Country Music People*, Britain's foremost country monthly; he did most of the entries for country music artists – in fact, the third largest number of entries after Donald Clarke and Michael Heatley.

Sue Steward began to help with the African and Latin American entries, and through her I found John Child and Ronnie Graham. John is one of those rare fans who turn out to be better journalists than many who belong to the union: thanks to what must be an unbelievable record collection, he was able to tell me more about calypso and salsa than I needed to know; he wrote virtually all the entries in those areas, with some help from his friend Gordoni Bramaz. Ronnie Graham, who did the African entries, is one of those fans who does it as well as talking about it: the latest release on his own label is an exquisitely produced compilation of charming hi-life 78s by E. T. Mensah.

Through Michael I met Demitri Coryton, who contributed the material on the major record labels; they add an extra dimension to the book, and someone should hire Demitri to write an entire volume about the history of the record business. With complete access to the EMI archives, which go back almost a hundred years, he is writing the official history of the company. He is also working on a revised multi-volume edition of Joseph Murrell's *Million Selling Records.* Ken Hunt, whose wonderful little magazine *Swing 51* appears now and then, wrote excellent entries on international and British folk and other areas. Hannah Charlton, Robin Katz and Cliff White wrote little gems on their areas of special interest. Peter O'Brien, whose *Omaha Rainbow* is also a priceless periodical, responded to many a query.

Len Joseph, taxi driver, accountant and *bon vivant,* is also a country music fan: access to Len's record collection was of great value. He has relocated to Austin, Texas, which is lucky to have him; we miss Len and Sue very much, but dispatches from the heart of the country have kept us abreast of one of the most satisfying scenes in popular music today.

My father, after whom I am honoured to be named, provided a great many clippings from American newspapers, each monthly envelope full of valuable current information. I am grateful to Chuck Nessa for reading virtually all the manuscript and making many valuable suggestions, to Jon Riley and Elizabeth Bland at Penguin, for guiding the book around the patches of quicksand found in any big publishing office and to David Duguid for his sterling editorial work.

On behalf of all my contributors, the following individuals and agencies have our thanks for putting up with our letters, phone calls and endless questions: Alan Bates at Black Lion, Moira Bellas and her staff at WEA (especially Barbara Charone), Rod Buckle and his staff at Sonet UK, Chrissie Cremore at A&M, Mike Carr, Michael Cuscuna, Mrs Anna Davis, Bill Dixon, Richard Dobson, Cathy Gardener and her staff at EMI, Martha Glaser, Bob Golden at Teresa Gramophone Co. Ltd, Vanya Hackel, Terry Hinte at Fantasy in Berkeley, Tim Hodgekinson, Terry Hounsome, John Humphries at Music Master, Colin Lazzerini, Gene Lees, Terry Lickona at the Southwest Texas Broadcasting Council, Lloyd Maines, Eugene Manzi at London Records, Dan

Morgenstern, Peter Nicholls, Chris Parker, Sue Parr,
Paul Pelletier, Eddie Prevost, Ronnie Pugh at the
Country Music Foundation in Nashville, Judy Reynolds
at the much lamented Import Music Service, Tony Rice
at Recommended Records, John Storm Roberts, William
Schwann, Bobby Scott, Peter Stampfel, David Suff,
Dave Walters, Cliff White at Charly, Richard Wootton,
Robert Wyatt, Jeff Young at MCA; also Island Records
(Deborah Walker and Rob Partridge), RCA (Keith
Shadwick and Lee Simmonds, and formerly Dave
Lewis), Virgin Records (Mike Soutar) and Books (Jane
Charteris), and the anonymous folks who manage the
acts, such as the Fabulous Thunderbirds, Roomful of
Blues and many others; and all those we are forgetting to
thank: you know who you are, and we are grateful. A
great many artists were interviewed; it was great fun to
meet and to talk to Guy Clark, Chico Freeman, Keith
Copeland, Donald Harrison, Terence Blanchard, Butch
Hancock, Terry Allen, Fred Krc, Rattlesnake Annie and
many, many others.

I am grateful to Tony Hughes at The Den in
Teddington for selling me my Kaypro II computer (a
machine so sturdy I am afraid it will eat my desk) and
for his follow-up service; and to Small Turnkey Systems
for excellent computer services; and to Yamaha UK for
lending me a compact disc player (I grew so attached to
the CDX-700 that I had to buy it).

And finally, most of all, to my wife, Ethne, without
whom I could do nothing, and who has put up with this
for five years; and to my son, David, who has missed too
many snowball fights because Dad was too busy.

D.C.
Norfolk, England, 1988

A

AACM Association for the Advancement of Creative Musicians, Chicago black music collective formed May '65. Departure of SUN RA band to NYC had left void in local music scene; AACM grew out of Experimental Band led by Muhal Richard ABRAMS. About three dozen musicians gathered at home of trumpeter Phil Cohran in May; other early members incl. Charles CLARK, Steve McCall, Thurman BARKER, Anthony BRAXTON, Fred ANDERSON, members of later groups ART ENSEMBLE OF CHICAGO, AIR. Modest aim of opportunities to play soon enhanced by quality of music: held concerts and open rehearsals exploring free jazz, original music only, composers writing for anyone wanting to play. Co-ops had failed in NYC, but earlier work in idiom had been 'energy music': now Chicago musicians produced more thoughtful, lyrical work. Drew talent from outside Chicago (e.g. Leo SMITH); inspired similar groups (Black Artists Group, St Louis; Strata, Detroit; many others around the world). Played together more often and more freely, under less commercial pressure than peers in the East; dominance of NYC lessened (Art Ensemble moved on to Paris instead of New York), though Abrams (and others) have since moved there, to 'follow up some of the business we've generated'. With example of AACM, musicians seek 'self-employment amongst themselves, instead of waiting for somebody to hire them' (Roscoe MITCHELL). AACM also operates music school, free for inner city youth. 20th anniversary marked by 10 concerts in Chicago May '85. Air's Henry THREADGILL formed Sextett, albums on About Time and RCA/Nexus labels mid-'80s: infl. of AACM continues to be felt.

A&R Artists & Repertoire. Through the '50s, A&R people at record companies decided who should record what in pop music, buying in songs from publishers or commissioning them from composers; many A&R people were arrangers (Percy FAITH, Paul WESTON, Hugo WINTERHALTER, Mitch MILLER); many had served apprenticeships during the Big Band era. They were effectively producers, working on sessions with recording engineers; power often went to their heads: in a well-known story (perhaps apocryphal, but has the ring of truth) an A&R man is said to have asked Frank SINATRA to bark like a dog on a recording. The A&R situation altered (along with much else) in the '60s; the BEATLES and others changed the rules, wrote their own material anyway. The great producers of R&B acts, such as Ralph BASS, Jerry Wexler at Atlantic, etc. had more sympathy for the artists under their control and were a big influence on the next generation. One of the first to become famous as a producer was George MARTIN ('the fifth Beatle'); during a transitional period, the dead hands of Hugo Peretti and Luigi Creatore at RCA were evident in Sam COOKE's records: his singles were big hits, but the studiobound accompaniment now seems stilted compared to his *Live At The Harlem Square Club* '63, which has the timeless quality of all great performances. Record companies have A&R staff negotiating contracts, overseeing promotion etc. but in making records they work with producers who are often freelance and often chosen with the approval of the artists involved. Today's producers often began as engineers or musicians; with so much technology available the problem now is how to avoid over-producing: mavericks like Bill LASWELL and widely experienced people like Michael CUSCUNA usually manage it so that the music can breathe.

AARONSON, Irving (*b* 7 Feb. 1895, NYC; *d* 10 May. '63, Hollywood, Cal.) Pianist, songwriter, bandleader. Played theatre piano at 11; formed group The Versatile Sextet; then a band called The Crusaders: obsolescent vertical-cut 78s at its first recording

1

session for Edison ('26; *see* RECORDED SOUND); changed name to Commanders, label to Victor same year, later on Columbia until '35. Played theatres, vaudeville, arr. by Chummy MacGregor (later pianist for Glenn MILLER); also employed Artie SHAW, Claude THORNHILL, Gene KRUPA, Tony PASTOR. Aaronson was later a dir. of music at MGM.

ABBA Swedish pop group formed '73: Bjorn Ulvaeus (*b* 25 Apr. '45, Gothenburg), Benny Andersson (*b* 16 Dec. '45, Stockholm), Agnetha Faltskog (*b* 5 Apr. '50, Jonkoping), Anni-Frid 'Frida' Lyngstad (*b* 15 Nov. '45 Narvik, Norway). The girls attained fame in Sweden as solo singers, Bjorn in Hootenanny Singers and Benny with Hep Stars ('Swedish Beatles'). The boys made album together (single 'People Need Love', '72); by then Benny & Anni-Frid and Bjorn & Agnetha were couples; formed group using initials as acronym. Quickly popular in Europe; more fame when 'Waterloo' won '74 Eurovision Song Contest, no. 1 UK single, made USA top 10. Eurovision stigma held them back for a year; then followed a remarkable run of 18 consecutive top 10 UK singles (eight at no. 1), eight no. 1 albums: first LP *Waterloo* no. 28 UK LP chart '74; *Abba* no. 13 '75; *Greatest Hits* made no. 1 and stayed in chart 130 weeks, *Arrival* also no. 1 '76. Subsequent LPs all no. 1: *The Album* '78, *Voulez-Vous* and *Greatest Hits Vol. 2* '79, *Super Trouper* '80, *The Visitors* '81, 2-disc set *The Singles – The First Ten Years* '82. *Spanish Album* (aka *Gracias por la Musica*) issued '81. Records on Epic in UK, Atlantic USA. Less dramatic success in USA incl. hit LPs and 10 top 40 singles ('Dancing Queen' no. 1 '76). Formed Polar Music Company, acquired property, became valuable share on Swedish market. Tours were costly because slick production was difficult to duplicate live; also the girls disliked them (first international tour '77, USA tour '79); even so they were the most successful group since The BEATLES, resembling them with self-written material and good production; their sound was also redolent of The MAMAS AND THE PAPAS. 'I Have A Dream' (no. 2 UK '79) typical of clever writing, folkish sound carrying almost mawkish sentiment. Group faded as couples divorced (Bjorn & Agnetha '79;

Benny & Anni-Frid '81). Phil COLLINS prod. Frida's solo LP *Something's Going On* '82; single 'I Know There's Something Going On' no. 43 UK; Agnetha's 'Can't Shake Loose' prod. by Mike Chapman, no. 29 USA '83. Boys collaborated with Tim Rice on musical *Chess*, recorded London '84, staged '86; they wanted to do something on their own, but do not rule out reunions. They also prod. LP *Gemini* '86 (duo of Karin & Anders Glenmark), etc.

ABC UK pop/rock group formed '81; original lineup: Martin Fry (vocals; *b* 9 Mar. '58, Manchester), Mark White (guitar; *b* 1 Apr. '61, Sheffield), Stephen Singleton (sax; *b* 17 Apr. '59, Sheffield), Mark Lickley, bass; and David Robinson, drums. Fry got Eng. Lit. degree from Sheffield U., founded fanzine *Modern Drugs*, interviewed White and Singleton, both from local band Vice Versa. They invited him to join as vocalist, but he persuaded them to change band's name and direction (more poppish). Lickley, Robinson recruited; they were signed by Phonogram UK and given own Neutron label. First single 'Tears Are Not Enough' reached UK top 20 late '81; Fry asked Trevor HORN to prod. 'Poison Arrow' which made top 10 as did the next two. Lickley, Robinson left; drummer David Palmer (*b* 29 May '61, Chesterfield) joined; debut LP *The Lexicon of Love* no. 1 UK four weeks '82, helped by impressive if overblown tour. Second LP *Beauty Stab* '83 self-prod. with ROXY MUSIC backing musicians: muscular funk but no hit singles. By '84 songwriters Fry and White were the only remaining original members: *How To Be A Zillionaire* '85 was cartoon pop with little of *Lexicon* sheen, but USA chart hit with 'Be Near Me'. Fry developed Hodgkin's Disease, a form of cancer, and recovered; *Alphabet City* '87 said to be more realistic, less dreamy than *Lexicon* but with good pop songs incl. 'When Smokey Sings', 'King Without A Crown'.

ABDUL-MALIK, Ahmed (*b* 30 Jan. '27, Brooklyn NY) Primarily bassist; also tuba, piano, violin, cello, Eastern instruments. Father Sudanese; grad. High School of Music and Performing Arts, played with Art BLAKEY, Don BYAS (late '40s), Sam Taylor, Randy WESTON, T. MONK,

ODETTA (*Odetta And The Blues* '62 on Riverside). To South America and Africa '60-61; increasingly interested in oriental music from late '50s, returned to formal study in mid-'60s. Own LPs incl. *Jazz Sahara*, Riverside '58; an RCA set '59 with 11 pieces incl. Lee MORGAN, Curtis FULLER, Johnny GRIFFIN, Benny GOLSON, plus African instruments; *Music Of* '61 and *Sounds Of Africa* on New Jazz; *Eastern Moods* '63 on Prestige; *Spellbound* '64 on Status. Played oud '77 on Hamiet BLUIETT LP *Orchestra, Duo & Septet*.

ABENI, Queen Salawa (*b* '65, Nigeria) Singer-composer in Waka style (*see* FUJI); a prodigy, establishing local reputation by age 8, first LP *The Late Murtala Mohammed* '77. Gained fame singing in Yoruban, hard-edged vocals against typical backing (by New Waka Group) of talking drums and percussion; 12 LPs followed on Leader label, the most recent *Ikilo, Challenge Cup* '82, *Adieu Alhaji Haruna Ishola* widely available outside Nigeria. Backing group then called the Waka Modernisers left her for rival Kubarat Alagagbo; she bounced back same year with hit LP *Indian Waka* '84.

ABIODUN, Dele (*b* '55, Bendel State, Nigeria) Singer-composer, guitarist. Experimented with various styles, opted for cool, spacey sound of JUJU, though not a Yoruban himself. Left Nigeria for Ghana with school tuition fees to study in school of music established by Nkrumah; played bass in Ghanaian HIGHLIFE bands; returned to Lagos, formed own outfit Sweet Abby and the Tophitters '69, playing mixture of juju, highlife and rock; next year introduced own style called Adawa ('independent being'), fusion of juju and Afro-beat. During '70s released more than 20 LPs on Olumo label; toured UK '74 at a time when very few Nigerian records were available outside the country; during tour began using Hawaiian steel guitar, introduced it to juju. On return to Nigeria fans nicknamed him Admiral. Firmly established in top rank, released impressive *Beginning Of A New Era* '81, then split with Olumo; less impressive LPs *E O Fura* and *1,000 Miles* '82 followed by return to Olumo and successful *Ma Se'ke* '83. More recently has followed Sunny ADE and

Ebenezer OBEY in acquiring distribution in Europe: Earthworks in UK distribute mini-LP *Confrontation*, album *It's Time For Juju Music*; new Nigerian LP was juju/funk/soul *Oro Ayo* '85.

ABRAMS, Muhal Richard (*b* 19 Sep. '30, Chicago) Piano, reeds, etc.; composer, leader. Four years of music college; professional debut at 18. Gigged with visiting musicians incl. Miles DAVIS, Sonny ROLLINS, Dexter GORDON, many others; formed Experimental Band '61, incl. Eddie HARRIS; founder/dir. of Association for the Advancement of Creative Musicians (AACM). Moved to NYC '76, joined loft scene there. An influence by virtue of imagination and attitudes as well as hard work and musical skills: in Joseph JARMAN's famous remark, when he met Abrams 'I was like all the rest of the "hip" ghetto niggers; I was cool, I took dope, I smoked pot . . . In having the chance to work in the Experimental Band . . . I found something with meaning/reason for doing.' Infl. on the new music was vast, encouraging creative collaboration between composer and improvisor: 'Now I can take eight measures and play a concert' (J. Litweiler). Own LPs incl. *Levels And Degrees Of Light* '67 (plays clarinet on own title comp.), *Young At Heart, Wise In Time* '69, *Things To Come From Those Now Gone* '70, all on Delmark. Other work: *Afrisong* '75, now on India Navigation; *Sightsong* '75, duet with Malachi Favors (first of many LPs on Black Saint); *Duet 1976* (with Anthony BRAXTON); *1-OQA+19* '77 (with Braxton); *Lifea Blinec* '78, sextet; *Spiral/Live At Montreux 1978*, solo on Arista; *Spihumonesty* '79; *You Can't Name Your Own Tune* '77, with Barry ALTSCHUL; *Mama And Daddy* '80; *Duet* '81, two pianos with Amina Claudine Myers; *Blues Forever* '81; 'Nutturno' on *Amarcord Nino Rota* '81 (other tracks by Jaki BYARD, Steve LACY, etc.); *Rejoicing With The Light* '83, with big band; *View From Within* '85 with octet incl. Thurman BARKER; *Roots Of Blue* '86 on Enja is duo with Cecil MCBEE; *Colours In Thirty-Third* '86 on Black Saint a sextet with Dave HOLLAND, Andrew CYRILLE, Fred Hopkins, John Blake on violin, John Purcell on reeds. Also plays on Jarman's *As If It Were The Seasons* '68, *Fanfare For The Warriors* '74 with ART ENSEMBLE, etc.

ABSHIRE, Nathan (*b* 27 June '13, Gueydan, La.; *d* 13 May '81, Basile, La.) CAJUN accordionist, vocalist, composer of seminal influence: illiterate, he translated everyday concerns into memorable songs which placed him among the greatest of the genre. Began very early, playing local functions at age 8, self-taught (though both parents could play); also dabbled with fiddle at one time. First recordings for Bluebird '33 (initially misspelled as 'Nason Absher'); his 'Pine Grove Blues' on O.T. '49 was a huge success and has few rivals for its importance to the genre. Career and status went into temporary decline '50s but he bounced back with a series of singles that proved he could still cut the mustard; he starred in PBS documentary *Good Times Are Killing Me* '75 (based on catchphrase, also emblazoned on his battered accordion case). Recordings are scattered over many labels; excellent LPs compile tracks from Khoury, Lyric, O.T., Swallow days, as well as more recent work: *The Good Times Are Killing Me, Pine Grove Blues, Nathan Abshire & The Pinegrove Boys*, all on Swallow; *The Cajuns* (backing by the BALFA Brothers) and *Good Times Killin' Me* on Sonet.

ABYSSINIANS, The Jamaican vocal trio formed late '60s, led by Bernard Collins. Support singers were Donald and Linford Manning, brothers of Carlton Manning, lead singer with rock steady group CARLTON AND THE SHOES. The Abyssinians recorded only sporadically but were influential; first release was 'Declaration Of Rights', made at Studio One; Collins soon formed his own Clinch label and recorded their seminal 'Satta Amassa Gana' and similarly inflected 'Yis Mas Gan', both titles quoting from the ancient Ethiopian Amharic language. In mid-'70s they released LPs *Forward On To Zion* and *Arise*, showcasing their understated style; Collins lived in the UK late '70s, but nothing more was heard of the group.

AC/DC Hard rock band formed Australia '74; original lineup: Ronald Belford 'Bon' Scott (vocals; *b* 9 July '46, Kirriemuir, Scotland; *d* 19 Feb. '80, London), Angus Young (lead guitar; *b* 31 Mar. '59, Glasgow), Malcolm Young (guitar; *b* 6 Jan. '53, Glasgow), Phil Rudd (drums; *b* 19 May '54, Melbourne), Mark Evans (bass; *b* '57, Melbourne). The Youngs emigrated in '60s with older brother George (*see* EASYBEATS); AC/DC formed in Melbourne around them and Scott, another immigrant, but rhythm sections came and went before Rudd and Evans fit in. George helped get record deal; first two LPs big Aussie hits; compilation of these became first UK/US release '76, supported by long tour of small UK venues; fans won by general outrageousness of act and energy of Angus, who dressed as schoolboy in short trousers onstage. LP *Let There Be Rock* reached UK top 20 '77; Evans left, replaced by Cliff Williams (from group Home; *b* 14 Dec. '49, Romford, London); *Powerage* album charted '78; *Highway To Hell*, produced by 'Mutt' Lange, charted strongly in USA as well '79; then Scott died from alcoholic indulgence. Replaced by Brian Johnson (from Geordie; *b* 5 Oct. '47, North Shields, near Newcastle). Next LP *Back In Black* made no. 1 in UK charts; early Australian material issued in USA (album titled *Dirty Deeds Done Dirt Cheap*) made no. 3 there '81; *For Those About To Rock* '81 no. 3 UK, no. 1 USA. Simon Wright (*b* '63) replaced Rudd. Remain a big act but excitement had peaked. *Fly On The Wall* '85 cited by L.A. mass murderer Richard Ramirez as inspiration; album *Who Made Who* '86 for soundtrack of Stephen King movie *Maximum Overdrive* has three new tracks incl. two instrumentals, six oldies; new album *Blow Up Your Video* '88 celebrated survival against the odds.

ACE, Johnny (*b* John Marshall Alexander Jr, 29 June '29, Memphis, Tenn.; *d* 24/25 Dec. '54, Houston, Texas) Singer. US Navy in WWII; played piano in Albert Duncan band, which incl. Bobby BLAND; formed Beale Streeters with Bland late '40s. Recorded on Duke label '52; first release 'My Song' topped R&B chart, several follow-ups also hits. 'Pledging My Love' reached top 20 on pop chart '55, but like so many early rockers a gun nut; he had died on tour in a backstage Russian roulette accident. First notable casualty of rock'n'roll era and probably one of the most talented. Best work in *Johnny Ace: Memorial Album* on Ace.

ACID ROCK Rock music inspired by or related to drug-induced experience, term more or less interchangeable with psychedelic rock. THIRTEENTH FLOOR ELEVATORS released first LP in Austin, JEFFERSON AIRPLANE in San Francisco, 'Psychotic Reaction' reached top 5 by its writers the Count Five (San Jose quartet, lead singer Ken Ellner *b* '48 in Brooklyn, N.Y.), all '66. Encouraged by DJs; musicians were said to record under the influence, used fuzztone, feedback, synthesisers, sheer volume etc. mimicking supposed mind-expanding properties of marijuana, LSD (acid). Success of genre centred in San Francisco; Airplane was biggest success, but S.F. had hundreds of bands going. The GRATEFUL DEAD (first LP '67) allegedly performed while stoned; it took them a while to tune up. If there was a difference between acid rock and psychedelia, the latter was a softer, colourful phenomenon, related to fashion, poster and record sleeve design etc. as much as music, mainly West Coast and British (BEATLES *Sergeant Pepper* '67 the fad's peak) with drug references more or less restricted to 'soft' drugs; acid rock attempted more: on East Coast the VELVET UNDERGROUND treated heroin as a serious doom-laden subject rather than a hippy joke. Acid rock contributed musical infl. to HEAVY METAL, though HM is mostly about adolescent frustrations rather than drugs. Songs assumed to refer to drugs were recorded by BEATLES, Bob DYLAN, Van Dyke PARKS, Jimi HENDRIX, many others. Infl. was also heard in art rock, e.g. GONG, VAN DER GRAAF GENERATOR etc., perhaps the ultimate in psychedelia; and electronic/experimental (often European) bands TANGERINE DREAM, CAN, KRAFTWERK etc. Series of *Nuggets* compilations on Rhino c.'80 revived interest in CHOCOLATE WATCH BAND, Elevators etc. as well as collecting some of the most amusing bits.

ACKLES, David (*b* 20 Feb. '37, Rock Island, Ill.) Singer/songwriter. From showbusiness family; child star of B movies. Began composing in college (Edinburgh, S. Cal.); worked as TV writer, signed to Elektra late '60s; intellectual element (interesting lyrics) made first two LPs critical successes but commercial failures. Julie Driscoll, Brian AUGER had minor hit with 'Road To Cairo' '68; *American Gothic* '72 produced in England by Bernie Taupin; made no. 167 on Billboard LP chart. Switched to Columbia; *D.T. Ackles Five and Dime* '73 notable for mournful quality rather than humour (e.g. 'Surf's Down'). Nothing more has been heard, but infl. persists: Elvis COSTELLO praised work in '84 interview.

ACTION, The UK group formed '63. Lineup: Reg King, vocals; Alan 'Bam' King, guitar; Pete Mason, lead guitar; Mike Evans, bass; Roger Powell, drums. Formed in north London as 'Mods' but achieved only cult status, despite having five singles Oct. '65 to June '67 produced by George MARTIN. Reg King has made solo LPs; Watson left music; Alan King, Evans and Powell formed Mighty Baby, folded '71; Bam later founder member of Ace. Complete Action with unreleased tracks on Edsel '80, notes by Paul Weller.

ACUFF, Roy Claxton (*b* 15 Sep. '03, Maynardsville, Tenn.) Singer, fiddler, bandleader. Grand old man of American music, gaining worldwide fame with traditional style through decades of change in country music. Father was fiddler, lawyer, Baptist minister; Roy grew up on tenant farm in Smoky Mountains; high school in Knoxville; attended NY Yankees baseball summer camp in Florida, but sunstroke ended sports career. Joined medicine show; on radio '33; record contract with ARC (later Columbia) through Art SATHERLEY '36. Some early records on pop side, but soon elected trad. mountain style; two biggest hits came from first session: 'Great Speckled Bird', based on Jeremiah 12:9, using trad. tune ('I'm Thinking Tonight Of My Blue Eyes', recorded by CARTER family), sung in Southern churches; 'Wabash Cannon Ball' (also sung by Carters) is train song in 'Big Rock Candy Mountain' tradition: the train will take the hobo to promised land; sold a million copies, one of the most famous country records ever made. Acuff went to Grand Ole Opry '38, became its most famous star and helped establish singer rather than string band as main attraction, though his band remained traditional: called Tennessee Crackerjacks, then Crazy Tennesseans, finally Smoky Mountain Boys, they wore casual clothes or country overalls, no cowboy outfits. Acuff played fiddle (not often enough: lacked confidence on instrument); band incl. bass fiddle, five-string banjo, rhythm guitar, mandolin, accordion, harmonica; distinctive sound was that of the dobro or Hawaiian guitar, fitting the wailing, high-lonesome mountain music sound, played by James Clell Summey (1914-76, *b* Tenn.; later with Pee Wee KING one of the first to play steel guitar on the Opry, still later became comic Cousin Jody). After '38 Beecher 'Pete' Kirby played dobro for Acuff, also playing banjo, singing high harmony; became comic (Bashful Brother Oswald). From mid-'40s Howard 'Howdy' Forrester, Jimmy Riddle played harmonica and accordion. After two years on Opry Acuff hosted show's first network hookup, starred in film *Grand Ole Opry* '40; other films incl. *Hi Neighbor* '42, *My Darling Clementine* '43, *Cowboy Canteen* and *Sing, Neighbor, Sing* '44, *Night Train To Memphis* '46. Acuff co-wrote many songs, e.g. 'The Precious Jewel', another big hit; formed Acuff-Rose Publications in Nashville with Fred ROSE '42, eventually becoming wealthy. Scores of hits incl. 'Wreck On The Highway', 'Fireball Mail' '42, 'Night Train To Memphis', 'Pins And Needles', 'Low And Lonely' '43. Sincerity never in doubt, the most important asset of any country artist: he sometimes wept at his own performance. Wartime return to trad. values confirmed popularity; widely circulated story (said to have originated with correspondent Ernie Pyle) was that Japanese troops in South Pacific shouted battle cry 'To hell with Roosevelt! To hell with Babe Ruth! To hell with Roy Acuff!' (Wartime hit: 'Cowards Over Pearl Harbor'.) Postwar poll of Armed Forces Network saw Acuff beat Frank SINATRA as most popular vocalist. Opened Dunbar Cave Resort near Clarksville, Tenn., '48, became folk-music park; same year ran for governor of Tenn. as Republican, made good showing in Democratic state. Refused to change style as sales fell off; left Columbia, hopped to Decca, MGM, Capitol; started Hickory with Rose, '57. Entertained troops in Berlin during blockade '49, later Korea, Dominican Republic, Vietnam; touring slowed down after serious car crash in '65. Entertained returned POWs at White House '72; gave yoyo lessons to Nixon at opening of new Opryhouse in Nashville '74. First living artist elected to Country

Music Hall of Fame '62; last country chart hit: remake of 'Freight Train Blues' '65, nearly 30 years after first recordings. With Kirby on *Will The Circle Be Unbroken*, 3-disc set with the NITTY GRITTY DIRT BAND '73. LP reissues incl. Hickory LPs now on Elektra: *Greatest Hits* (2 vols.), *Sings Hank Williams, Back In The Country*; *Best Of* on Capitol; *Roy Acuff* '85 in Columbia Historical Edition series from Country Music Foundation '85 incl. hits from '36-51.

ADAMS, Bryan (*b* '59, Vancouver) Singer, guitarist, songwriter. Co-writes with Jim Vallance; hits for Ian Lloyd in Canada, Prism USA; formed own five-piece band. Success outside Canada came when group supported FOREIGNER; led to USA top 20 hits 'Cuts Like A Knife' and 'Straight From The Heart'. Act with 'outlaw' overtones *à la* Bruce SPRINGSTEEN popular on MTV video channel. LP *Cuts Like A Knife* '83, *You Want It, You Got It* '84; *Reckless* hit LP USA and UK '85. Wrote 'Tears Are Not Enough' for Canadian BAND AID disc; toured with Tina TURNER '85. As *Reckless* had sold 7m copies he played London's famous Marquee club on 48 hours' notice in June '87 (with co-star second guitar Keith Scott): keeping his hand in, close to his roots.

ADAMS, George Rufus (*b* 29 Apr. '40, Covington, Ga.) Tenor sax; also flute, bass clarinet. Scholarship to Clark College, Atlanta; studied reeds with Wayman CARVER. R & B experience with Howlin' WOLF, Lightnin' HOPKINS, Bill DOGGETT, others; supported singers Sam COOKE, Hank BALLARD; to NYC '68, worked with FLAMINGOS, Art BLAKEY; played and recorded with Roy HAYNES, Gil EVANS; then with Charles MINGUS. Albums with Mingus incl. *Mingus Moves* '73 (incl. own comp. 'Flowers For A Lady'); *Mingus At Carnegie Hall* '74; on *Changes One*, *Changes Two* LPs '74, wonderful solo on Mingus's 'Duke Ellington's Sound Of Love', delightful vocal on 'Devil Woman' created while playing opposite then-new MANHATTAN TRANSFER at Max's Kansas City: Mingus began playing a blues, said 'You might as well go on out there and sing.' Other LPs incl. *Paradise Space Shuttle* '80, quintet on Dutch Timeless label; *Sound Suggestions* '79 sextet on

ECM with Dave HOLLAND, Kenny WHEEL-ER, Jack DEJOHNETTE; *Hand To Hand* '80, *Gentlemen's Agreement* '83, quintet LPs with Dannie RICHMOND, Jimmy KNEPPER, Hugh Lawson, Mike Richmond on bass; *More Sightings* with Marvin 'Hannibal' Peterson made live in Zurich '84. Worked with Don PULLEN, Dannie Richmond in Rome '75, made two LPs there incl. *Suite For Swingers*; formed George Adams-Don Pullen Quartet with Richmond, Cameron BROWN '79: albums *All That Funk* and *More Funk* '79, made in Milan for Palcoscenico label; *Don't Lose Control* '75 on Soul Note; *Earth Beams* and *Life Line* '80, *City Gates* '83 on Timeless; two vols. of *Live At The Village Vanguard* '83 on Soul Note; *Decisions* '84, *Live At Montmartre* '85 (with John SCOFIELD on guitar) on Timeless, *Breakdown* '86 on Blue Note. Quartet works 10-20 weeks a year, touring Europe, Japan, playing mix of hard bop, R&B: consistently satisfying drive, swing, wit. Adams's technique incl. seamless upper-register arpeggios that make tenor sound almost like clarinet; tracks incl. Adams's powerful title tune from *City Gates* LP; Pullen comps. 'Samba For Now' (lovely ballad); 'The Necessary Blues' (or 'Thank You Mr Monk') pays dues to Thelonious, tips over into free jazz, always with soul. Adams/Pullen made duo LP *Melodic Excursions* '82 on Timeless; Adams worked with Gil EVANS, went to Japan with him '76 after Mingus's death, played on Evans LPs '84-5. Planned new quartet Phalanx with James Blood ULMER; toured Europe '86 with him.

ADAMS, Johnny (*b* '32, New Orleans) Singer. Known as The Tan Nightingale. One of 10 children; sang in gospel groups for years (The Soul Revivers, The Consolators); then to R&B '59 for Ric records. 'Losing Battle' reached top 30 in R&B chart '62. Signed to Shelby SINGLETON's SSS International '68; reached pop top 100 with 'Release Me' that year, top 30 with 'Reconsider Me' the next. 'I Can't Be All Bad' also a hit in '69; but then Singleton switched to country music; Adams joined Atlantic, had only four singles released in two years '71-2. Only regional hits with Chelsea, Ariola, other labels; then came excellent LP on Rounder label: *From The Heart* '83 incl. songs by Tony Joe WHITE, Sam COOKE, Doc POMUS

and Percy MAYFIELD; even scat singing on 'Why Do I'. A superior singer on wide range of material. Collection *Heart & Soul* '78 on Charly '78.

ADAMS, Pepper (*b* Park Adams, 8 Oct. '30, Highland Park, Mich.; *d* 10 Sep. '86, NYC) Baritone sax; became Harry CARNEY fan age 12. Served in Korean war; worked in Detroit with Lucky THOMPSON, Kenny BURRELL, others; recorded in '55 with John COLTRANE, Paul CHAMBERS, Curtis FULLER; to NYC '56; with Stan KENTON, Maynard FERGUSON, Benny GOODMAN, Donald BYRD; nicknamed 'The Knife' for authoritative attack: could not play uninteresting solo. Played on darkly beautiful John Coltrane-Mal WALDRON album *Dakar* ('57: wrote 'Mary's Blues' and 'Witches' Pit', featured solo on 'Cat's Walk'); in Thad JONES-Mel LEWIS band from '65 incl. tours, records; worked with David AMRAM. Own quintet LPs incl. *Pure Pepper* '57; *10 to 4 at the 5 Spot* '58, with Byrd; *Out Of This World* '61, with Byrd and Herbie HANCOCK, later reissued under their names; *Pepper Adams Plays Mingus* '63 has octet on some tunes. Other LPs: *Mean What You Say* '66, with Jones, Lewis, Ron CARTER; *Encounter!* '68, with Carter, Zoot SIMS, Elvin JONES, Tommy FLANAGAN; *Ephemera* '73 and *Reflectory* '78, both with Roland Hanna, the latter nominated for Grammy '80; quartet LPs *The Master* '80, with Flanagan; *Urban Dreams* '81 with Jimmy ROWLES. Also plays on LPs led by Byrd; on Amram's *Triple Concerto* '71; on Mingus LPs *Blues & Roots* '58, *Me, Myself An Eye* '78, many others. Plays bassoon on LPs *Julian, Twelfth And Pingree* '75 on Enja.

ADDERLEY, Julian Edwin 'Cannonball' (*b* 15 Sep. '28, Tampa, Fla.; *d* 8 Aug. '75, Gary, Ind.) Alto, later soprano sax, composer. Nickname said to be from 'cannibal', reference to capacity for food as a teenager. From musical family; directed high school band in Florida '48-56 and US Army bands c.'50-3; signed first record contract '55 (2-disc set *Spontaneous Combustion* on Savoy reissues debut recordings with Paul CHAMBERS, Kenny CLARKE, others). Formed first combo with brother Nat '56; made quintet LP *Somethin' Else* on Blue Note '58, with Miles DAVIS, Art BLAKEY; then played and recorded with Davis sextet with John COLTRANE '58-9, incl. seminal album *Kind Of Blue*. Toured late '59 with George SHEARING, then re-formed with Nat: this combo one of the most popular in the history of jazz. The quintet first incl. Bobby TIMMONS on piano; after some changes, Joe ZAWINUL for some years. Became sextet with addition of Yusef LATEEF in '61, replaced by Charles LLOYD '63; became quintet again mid-'65. Personnel remained constant from mid-'60s with Roy McCurdy (*b* 28 Nov. '36, Rochester, NY), drums and Vic Gaskin (*b* 23 Nov. '34, Bronx, NY), bass; Gaskin replaced '69 by Walter Booker (*b* 17 Dec. '33, Prairie View, Texas). Zawinul succeeded by George DUKE '71. First LP to make pop chart featured Nancy WILSON on Capitol '62, then *Jazz Workshop Revisited* '63 on Riverside, then LP and single 'Mercy, Mercy, Mercy!' '66 (Zawinul comp.) made no. 11 on USA pop single chart, 13 on album chart; album still available in UK and USA 20 years later. Next album live recording *Why Am I Treated So Bad!* also did well '67: title comp. by Roebuck STAPLE; with Zawinul's electric piano, definitely a pretaste of jazz-funk. Other chart albums incl. 2-disc live *The Price You Got To Pay To Be Free* '71; in all band had five singles in Hot 100; of 12 LPs charted '62-75 in USA, eight were live recordings. Others incl. *Accent On Africa* '68 (now on Affinity), with additional brass and reeds, female voices; Adderley played alto, electric alto and soprano: may have been arr. and cond. by mystery man H. B. BARNUM. Adderley's style rooted in tradition of his generation – infl. by Charlie PARKER, Benny CARTER – but also receptive to contemporary commercial taste, communicated with rare skill; like anyone making money in jazz he was accused of selling out, but made friends for the music and kept the flame burning. Toured overseas, made albums with Coltrane (*In Chicago* '59), Bill EVANS '61, Ray BROWN, JATP, others; produced LPs by Bud POWELL, Wes MONTGOMERY, others; active in music education. Film work incl. Clint Eastwood's *Play Misty For Me* '71; even dabbled in acting. At height of career suffered a stroke; died a few days later. Among compositions: *Big Man* on John Henry legend; LP with Joe WILLIAMS released after his death. About 20 LPs in print in mid-'80s, incl. live Japanese concerts, sextet records with Lateef, Zawinul from early '60s.

ADDERLEY, Nathaniel 'Nat' (*b* 25 Nov. '31, Tampa, Fla.) Cornet, composer. Started on trumpet '46 infl. by father and brother Cannonball (*see above*); switched to cornet '50; also plays mellophone, French horn. Worked in late '50s with Lionel HAMPTON, in brother's combo, with J. J. JOHNSON, Woody HERMAN; rejoined brother late '59, shared combo's success until Cannonball's death in '75. LPs as leader, mostly on Riverside in quintet context, incl. *Work Song, That's Right*, both '60; four albums on Atlantic '64-6 incl. versions of 'Sermonette' and 'Work Song', his best-known tunes; *The Scavenger* (Milestone '68) followed by *Comin' Out Of The Shadows* on A&M with strings same year; *Soul Zodiac* on Capitol '70 was 2-disc set with narration, made Billboard LP chart '72; *Soul Of The Bible* '72 also two discs. Other LPs incl. *Double Exposure* on Prestige '74 (large group incl. Julian); *A Little New York Midtown Music* on Galaxy '78 (quintet with Johnny GRIFFIN, Ron CARTER). *On The Move* and *Blue Autumn* '83 on Teresa have quintet live at Keystone Korner.

ADE, King Sunny (*b* Sunday Adeniyi, '46, Oshogbo, Ondo State, Nigeria) Singer/composer, guitarist. Son of Methodist church organist. Joined comedy group in Ibadan as teenager; drifted to Lagos, joined Moses Alaiya and his Rhythm Dandies, popular HIGHLIFE band; but in '64 inspired by music of I. K. DAIRO, joined legendary JUJU pioneer Tunde Nightingale. Formed own band the Green Spots '66; had first hit 'Challenge Cup' (football song), first LP *Alanu Loluwa* on Song label '67. 12 LPs on that label '67-74; contract disputes led to forming his own Sunny Alade Records linked with Decca in London; changed name of band to African Beats. Style characterised by tight vocal harmony, exquisite guitar work; not reluctant to introduce new sounds to trad. ensemble: Demola Adepoju joined '77, one of the first Africans to play steel guitar. Since '74 over 40 LPs each added to stature as leading exponent of juju, lyrics often concerned with Nigerian social problems; many records available outside

Nigeria, backed by tours of Europe, Japan, USA. Albums incl. *E Kilo F'Omo Ode* '74, *The Late General Ramat Mohammed* '76, *Synchro Chapter I* '77, *The Golden Mercury Of Africa* '78, *The Royal Sound* '79. Link with UK Island label '82 in attempt to crack international market: LPs *Juju Music*, *Synchro System* '83 (incl. remixes as well as new tracks), *Aura* '84 promoted on tours; though first two charted on Mango label in USA sales were not up to Island's hopes, dropped him '84. Dissension in band after Japanese tour '84; formed new band the Golden Mercury, back to domestic market with albums *Explosion, Togetherness, Gratitude, Otito*, regaining title 'Minister of Enjoyment'. Owns and operates the Ariya Club in Lagos; compilation *Vintage Sunny Ade* distributed in UK; toured USA '87.

ADEWALE, Segun (*b* '55, Oshogbo, Nigeria) Singer-composer, guitarist. Born into a Yoruba royal family; infl. by father's amateur guitar playing, but ironically left home after secondary school to pursue music because his father disapproved. To Lagos; became apprentice with Chief S. L. Atolagbe and his Holy Rainbow; learned some composition and arranging from I. K. DAIRO. Formed own band the Superstars '73; LP *Kogbodopa Finna-Finna*; band collapsed. Bounced back '74 as singer-composer with top JUJU band Prince Adekunle and the Western Brothers, which toured UK '76; left '77 to form Shina Adewale and the Superstars International with close friend Sir Shina Peters: juju duo lasted three years, seven LPs in *Verse* series on Welkadeb label; despite growing success and popularity, band with two leaders was untenable; split '80; Segun kept name Superstars International, formed own record label, was managed by Ola Kazzim, owner of Mutt-Mokson Records. Completed *Verse* series with two more vols. and started new chapter with album *Ope Ye Baba* '81, incl. single hit 'Olugbala Salabomi', which consolidated reputation. Polished, progressive LPs incl. *Boomerang* '82, *Endurance* and *Ase* '83; signed with Sterns Records in London for *Play For Me* '83. Played shows and Channel 4 film *Repercussions* '84 UK with 20-strong Superstars: own brand of juju called Yopop is fusion of juju, jazz, Afro-beat and reggae: also called kick and start music, without

slow introductions favoured by many juju stars. Several more albums in Nigeria; compilation *Ojo Je* released in UK; toured UK '85 incl. three consecutive nights at Edinburgh International Festival.

ADLER, Larry (*b* 10 Feb. '14, Baltimore, Md.) Mouth organist, composer. Studied piano; discovered harmonica (prefers term mouth organ: plays chromatic as opposed to blues harpist's diatonic instrument), was vaudeville trouper while still teenager. Played Ravel's *Bolero*, GERSHWIN's *Rhapsody In Blue*; appeared in *Ziegfeld's Smiles* '31; films: was accompanied by Duke ELLINGTON in *Many Happy Returns* '34 (on soundtrack only, because Guy LOMBARDO was star of film); appeared in *St Martin's Lane* '38, *Music For Millions* '44 etc. Big hit in London '34, made first records there ('Smoke Gets In Your Eyes' backed with 'The Continental' was a hit); played, broadcast with AMBROSE, Henry HALL; henceforth better known in British Empire than USA. Records in UK '35-6-7-8, in Paris with Django REINHARDT '38. Act with dancer Paul Draper performed in theatres, etc. Supported Progressive candidate Henry Wallace for President '48, blacklisted by anti-Communist witch-hunters, thereafter lived mostly in London. Entertained USA troops during WWII with Jack Benny; after blacklisting played for British troops instead; toured Israel with Draper after visit to South Korea, was picketed by Israeli Communist Party. On TV USA with Dizzy GILLESPIE '59; has also played duets with Sonny TERRY, Lord Mountbatten, Malcolm MacDonald (Australian Commissioner-General) etc. Also journalist from '41, writing dispatches for *Chicago Post* from Africa; later replaced Humphrey LYTTELTON as restaurant critic for *Harpers And Queen* until magazine involved in libel suit; London's *What's On* until it folded. Remark on radio that having a vasectomy means never having to say you're sorry got into *Penguin Book of Modern Quotations*; letters to *Private Eye* are more amusing than the magazine. Established mouth organ as serious instrument: first music especially composed for him '36 by Cyril Scott, then Arthur Benjamin, Ralph Vaughan Williams, Darius Milhaud, Malcolm Arnold etc. Own film scores incl. *Genevieve* '53 (took percentage because he liked script but producers had no money, made more than the actors: score nominated for Oscar with someone else's name on it), *High Wind In Jamaica* and *King And Country* '64, *The Great Chase* (anthology of film comedy). Grand Prix du Disque for 'Le Grisbi', tune from French film *Touchez-pas au Grisbi*. LPs in USA on London and Audio Fidelity labels; also *Discovery* '67 on RCA with Morton GOULD (first recordings of obscure songs by Gershwin, Cole PORTER etc.). Published *Jokes And How To Tell Them* '63; autobiography *It Ain't Necessarily So* '84 packed with good stories.

ADLER, Lou Pop music entrepreneur, notable since late '50s when he managed JAN & DEAN in partnership with Herb ALPERT. Also wrote songs under name of Barbara Campbell ('Only Sixteen', for Sam COOKE). Worked for Screen Gems (music publisher), Colpix, Dimension (labels), involved with Shelley Faberes (beach party actress, later his wife), Carole KING, Steve Barri, and P. F. Sloan. Using the last two as songwriter/producers, launched Dunhill Productions (later a record label) in '64; oversaw hits by MAMAS & PAPAS, Barry McGUIRE (whose '65 no. 1 'Eve Of Destruction' was written by Sloan). Also produced non-Dunhill acts such as Johnny RIVERS and Jan & Dean. Sold label to ABC '66; involved with Monterey Pop Festival and launched Ode label '67. Ode's first hit was 'San Francisco (Flowers In Your Hair)' by Scott McKENZIE. Other acts incl. SPIRIT and Carole King; produced songwriter turned performer King to huge fame in early '70s. Less active after mid-'70s.

ADLER, Richard (*b* 23 Aug. '23, NYC) Composer, lyricist, producer/director. Met Jerry Ross '50 (*b* 9 Mar. '26; *d* 11 Nov. '55); they signed with Frank LOESSER music publishing company; 'Rags to Riches' big hit for Tony BENNETT '53; that year wrote most of the songs for revue *John Murray Anderson's Almanac*, with Hermione Gingold, Billy DeWolfe, Harry BELAFONTE. On Loesser's recommendation George Abbott hired them to write the score for *The Pajama Game* '54; hit songs incl. 'I'm Not At All In Love', 'Steam Heat', 'Hernando's Hideaway', 'Hey There' (no. 1 hit: Rosemary

CLOONEY). *Damn Yankees* '55 another hit ('Heart', 'Whatever Lola Wants'). Each show ran more than 1000 performances on Broadway and was transferred to London; both were filmed ('57 and '58 respectively; *Yankees* was called *What Lola Wants* in UK). After Ross's death Adler wrote music and lyrics for *Kwamina* '61, *A Mother's Kisses* '68, also TV adverts; produced and staged galas for Democratic party '62-5, dir. Sammy CAHN one-man show '74.

AD LIBS, The Pop vocal group from N.J., USA, hitmakers for short-lived but influential label Blue Cat, formed (with Red Bird) by LEIBER & STOLLER with George Goldner. Incl. Mary Ann Thomas and Hughie Harris (alternating lead vocals), Danny Austin and David Watt. Biggest hit: 'The Boy From New York City', USA top 10 '65.

ADVERTS, The UK punk rock group formed '77. Original lineup: Tim 'T.V.' Smith, vocals, guitar; Gaye Advert, bass; Howard Pickup, guitar; Laurie Driver, drums. Smith moved from Cornwall to London inspired by punk movement, formed group with Advert. First single for Stiff: 'One Chord Wonders'; signed with Anchor; biggest hit 'Gary Gilmore's Eyes' made UK top 20 late '77. First LP *Crossing The Red Sea* briefly made UK top 40 '78; Driver left, replaced by John Towe (ex-Generation X), himself replaced by Rod Latter. Tim Cross (keyboards) joined for final LP '79, group broke up. Smith did solo work, founded short-lived T.V. Smith's Explorers.

AEROSMITH USA rock group formed '70. Original lineup: Steven Tyler (vocals; *b* 26 Mar. '48, NY), Joe Perry (guitar; *b* 10 Sep. '50, Boston), Brad Whitford (guitar; *b* 23 Feb. '52, Winchester, Mass.), Tom Hamilton (bass; *b* 31 Dec. '51, Colorado Springs), Joey Kramer (drums; *b* 21 June '50, NY). Formed New Hampshire, spotted at Max's Kansas City (NYC), signed to Columbia '72. Accused at first of being ROLLING STONES rip off; early records successful but third LP *Toys In The Attic* '75 huge success. Enjoyed major USA stardom until competition from New Wave, making US top 40 with five singles '75-8. LP *Rocks* '76 was biggest hit at no. 3; then *Draw The Line* and 2-disc *Live! Bootleg* '77-8; after *Night In The Ruts* '79 Perry left, formed Joe Perry Project, replaced by Jimmy Crespo; Rick Dufay replaced Whitford '81. After *Rock In A Hard Place* '82 Aerosmith switched to Geffen for *Done With Mirrors* '85, *Permanent Vacation* '87.

AFRICAN BROTHERS INTERNATIONAL BAND Ghanaian band and concert party formed '63, led by Nana Kwame Ampadu (*b* Kwahu, eastern Ghana). Top HIGHLIFE electric guitar band of up to 12 musicians: four guitarists make criss-cross network of sound, backed by percussionists, vocalists and 'Ancient' Amuah on keyboards. First big hit '67 with single 'Ebi Tie Ye' ('Some Are Sitting Well'), followed by single hits until first LP '71 marked them as one of most popular bands in Ghana, Ampadu as leading singer, guitarist, arranger, composer, with entertaining, thoughtful lyrics full of social commentary, also active in musicians' union and defender of highlife heritage. Over 50 LPs and 70 singles since '67 maintained popularity with variety of new dance beats incl. Locomotive, Afro-reggae, Afro-hili and Odonson highlife. Growing international reputation led to albums becoming available in UK and USA (on Makossa) incl. *Agatha* '81, *Me Poma* '84, *Obi Doba* '85. Appeared in Channel 4 TV film UK *Repercussions* '84 playing both in London and Ghana; also tours in recent years of USA, Europe. Eddie Donkor, rhythm guitarist and founder member, left mid-'70s to form own group the Simple Seven, had dance hits e.g. 'Jemima Medley', 'Asiko Darling', 'Destiny'.

AFRO-CUBAN MUSIC Cuban music has had an important influence on international popular music for a hundred years, and still does so despite a cultural embargo between the USA/Cuba since the Castro revolution '59; much of its essence comes from the ceremonies of Afro-Cuban religious cults, which struck a compromise between African and Catholic religious beliefs. In general the African side came from the people of the Niger River, who were either Yoruba or Lucumie; the deities were called Orisha and Oricha respectively. One of the best-known of all Afro-Cuban songs was 'Babalu', an invocation to the god of illness (Catholic equivalent San Lazaro: Lazarus), written by Margarita Lecuona (*see* Ernesto LECUONA), introduced in USA by Xavier CUGAT, sung for many years by the popular Cuban singer Miguelito Valdes (also in a less authentic version by Desi ARNAZ). The internationally popular salsa singer Celia CRUZ recorded the invocations 'Babalu Aye' and 'Chango' in her early years (on Panart LP *Santero*) and continued to sing dozens of songs from the genre (Chango is the god of virility and strength, thunder and lightning, master of fire and war, etc.; Catholic equivalent San Barbara). The Afro-Cuban songs adapted by Cuban dance orquestas generally fall into categories of invocations (others are 'Ochun', 'Ecue'), cradle songs ('Oggere', 'Lacho'), popular sayings ('Facundo') and romantic songs ('Negra Trista', 'La Cumparsa'). The rhythms have been even more influential than the songs: the MAMBO, others came from the religious ceremonies; the legendary Afro-Cuban drummer Chano POZO influenced generations of jazz and pop recording sessions (*see* CUBOP). Dizzy GILLESPIE among jazzmen was especially receptive of Cuban rhythms.

AFTER THE FIRE UK group formed '77. Peter Banks (*b* Isle of Wight) formed band on sometime basis '72, Andy Piercy (*b* Guildford) joined on guitar '74, Ivor Twidell (from Luton) on drums '77. Band released first album on own label, after which bass player left, Piercy moved to bass and John Russell (from Guildford) joined on guitar. Initial major label interest muted owing to band's Christian beliefs, thought commercially unviable; but after signing with CBS 'One Rule For You' made UK top 40 '79; LP *Laser Love* '79. did not excite. Twidell left because of ill health '80, replaced by Pete King; third LP *Batteries Not Included* early '82 dismissed as 'easy listening'; unexpected success in USA of '83 single 'Der Kommissar' (title cut of late '82 LP) came too late to stop King, Banks, Russell leaving Piercy sole original member of group, by now sometimes known as ATF.

AHLERT, Fred E. (*b* 19 Sep. 1892, NYC; *d* 20 Oct. '53, NYC) Composer. Trained as lawyer, took job with music publisher;

worked as arranger, wrote special material for vaudeville performers and Fred WARING's Glee Club, began writing some of the best Tin Pan Alley (non-show) songs of the period. 'I'll Get By' '28 written with Roy Turk; has featured in at least six films incl. *Follow The Boys* ('44, with Dinah SHORE) and *I'll Get By* ('50, with June Haver); also made UK top 20 twice (Connie FRANCIS '58, Shirley BASSEY '61). 'Mean To Me' '29, also with Turk, became a standard and was incl. in Ruth ETTING biopic ('55, Doris DAY). 'Walkin' My Baby Back Home' ('31, with Turk and Harry Richman) was Johnnie RAY hit in '52 (both UK and USA); 'Where The Blue Of The Night (Meets The Gold Of The Day)' '31, with Turk and Bing CROSBY, became Crosby's theme. Others: 'I Don't Know Why' '31, 'Love, You Funny Thing' '32, 'The Moon Was Yellow' '34, 'I'm Gonna Sit Write Down And Write Myself A Letter' (hit for Fats WALLER '36, Billy WILLIAMS Quartet '57).

AIR Black music trio formed in Chicago '71 to play in theatrical production: Henry THREADGILL, saxophones, flutes, hubkaphone; Fred Hopkins, bass; Steve McCall, percussion; all alumni of AACM: free jazz style with wit and energy, displaying deep roots in all forms of black music, as well as Eastern influences. They went to NYC '75, toured internationally; contributed 'USO Dance' to '76 Wildflower project. They did not get enough work but managed to make albums incl. Japanese releases now on India Navigation, excellent first release in USA *Airtime* '78 on Nessa; live sets: *Live Air* '76 and '77, both on Black Saint; *Live At Montreux 1978* on Novus/Arista; *Air Lore* '79 on that label examined ragtime/early jazz roots (CD came out on Bluebird '87 after RCA changed hands); *Air Mail* '80 was on Black Saint; *80° Below* '82 on Antilles. McCall left c.'83; name changed to New Air with Pheeroan akLaff on Black Saint: *Live At Montreal International Jazz Festival* '83, *Air Show Vol. 1* '86 (said to be their best since *Air Lore*, vocalist Cassandra Wilson on half the tracks; her LP *Point Of View* on JMT). Threadgill's Sextett makes fine albums incl. members of Air.

AIR SUPPLY Australian group formed '76. Lineup: Russell Hitchcock (vocals; *b* 15 June '49, Melbourne), Graham Russell (guitar, vocals; *b* 1 June '50, Nottingham, England), Frank Esler-Smith (keyboards; *b* 5 June '48, London), David Moyse (lead guitar; *b* 5 Nov. '57, Adelaide), David Green (bass; *b* 30 Oct. '49, Melbourne), Ralph Cooper (drums; *b* 6 Apr. '51, Coffs Harbour, Australia). Hitchcock and Russell met in Aust. production of *Jesus Christ Superstar*; mus. dir. Esler-Smith helped them make demos. Debut single 'Love And Other Bruises' went high in Aust. chart; group then went to USA as support for Rod STEWART tour. In '80 Rex Goh (guitar; *b* 5 May '51, Singapore) had joined and Russell provided vein of hit songs: 'The One That You Love' no. 1 '81 USA; seven other top 10 hits '80-3; hit LPs in same period show remarkable AOR consistency: *Love And Other Bruises, Lost In Love, Now And Forever, The One That You Love, Greatest Hits*.

AIRTO (*b* Airto Guimorva Moreira, 5 Aug. '41, Itaiopolis, Brazil) Percussionist, singer. On radio age 6; studied guitar and piano late '40s, later formed own groups, played all over Brazil, collecting and studying many instruments. To USA '68 with his wife, vocalist Flora PURIM; to NYC c.'70, records with Miles DAVIS; worked with Lee MORGAN '71; became busy freelance, recording with Stan GETZ, Cannonball ADDERLEY, Gato BARBIERI, Al DiMEOLA, WEATHER REPORT, many others; original member of Chick COREA's Return To Forever. Own LPs incl. *Fingers* '73 on CTI; *Virgin Land* '74 on Salvation, with Purim, Stanley CLARKE, George DUKE, others; *Identity* '75, *Promises Of The Sun* '76 on Arista; *Brazilian Heatwave* on Accord; *see also* entry for Purim. Band with Purim appeared in London June '86; Dave Gelly wrote in the *Observer*, 'I doubt whether anyone else could get away with sending the band off for a breather, getting a packed crowd yelling with excitement with a tambourine and a whistle.'

AITKEN, Laurel (*b* Cuba) Ska singer who emigrated first to Jamaica, then to UK early '60s. He made the first Jamaican recording issued in the UK, 'Boogie In My Bones'/'Little Sheila' '58, and the first release on the Bluebeat label, 'Boogey Rock' '60. Earliest efforts were in two styles: jump

R&B on titles such as 'Railroad Track', 'More Whisky', 'Back To New Orleans', 'Bartender'; and revivalist tunes like 'Judgement Rock', 'Zion City Wall', 'Mighty Redeemer', 'Brother David'. Singing ska and later REGGAE, he recorded through the '60s-early '70s, issuing hundreds of sides on many labels, subjects ranging from social commentary ('Landlords And Tenants') and vagaries of sound system life ('Blues Dance' and 'Woppi King'), love songs ('You Left Me Standing'), risqué items ('Pussy Price', still a staple of stage act). The most popular of these were collected on *The High Priest Of Reggae* early '70s; he teamed with female singer Girly for *Scandal In Brixton Market*, though mostly concentrating on singles. In the 2-Tone era he enjoyed a small revival; still performs now and then with his band The Full Circle.

AKENDENGUE, Pierre (*b* '44, Port Gentil, Nandipo, Gabon) Singer-composer, guitarist, poet. From musical family; songs performed on radio by age 14. To France '64; baccalaureate at Orleans, degree in literature at Caen, studied psychology at Sorbonne, went blind; returned to Gabon, became outspoken critic of government and forced to leave '72. First LP *Nandipo* '74 established uniquely wide range of modern and trad. instruments and techniques, combining music and poetry, parables and politics. *Africa Obota* '76 coincided with MIDEM award for best Francophone songs; presidential pardon '77, invited back to represent Gabon at FESTAC in Nigeria. *Eserengila* '78 won the Maraccas d'Or as best African record of '79; LPs *Owende* and *Mengo* confirmed reputation. *Awana W'Afrika* '81 showed modern, dance-oriented aspects of music; *Mando* '83 released on CBS; *Réveil de l'Afrique* '84 on own NYTE label; *Nandipo* and *Obota* reissued '85 on Saravah.

AKIYOSHI, Toshiko (*b* 12 Dec. '29, Manchuria) Piano, highly regarded composer/arranger. Went to USA '56; made album with her then husband Charles MARIANO *Toshiko-Mariano Quartet*; returned to Japan with him '61; back to USA; with Charles MINGUS '62. Long stays in Japan, visits to Europe '60s; with J. J. JOHNSON '64, at Newport Jazz Festival same year. Own radio show NYC; Town Hall debut '67 as leader, pianist, composer. Toured with husband Lew Tabackin (reeds, flute; *b* Lewis Barry Tabackin, 26 May '40, Philadelphia, Pa.) in quartet; they formed workshop big band which became Akiyoshi-Tabackin big band, won Downbeat polls. Band LPs *Kogun*, *Top Of The Gate* hits in Japan early '70s. Solo Monterey Jazz Festival '73; with big band at Playboy Jazz Festival L.A., Carnegie Hall '80. Albums incl. quartet, trio sets on Verve, other labels in '50s; many LPs in Japan; *Tales Of A Courtesan* '75 on RCA; *Notorious Tourist From The East* on Inner City, *Tribute To Billy Strayhorn* on Jam, trio *Finesse* on Concord Jazz, all '78; trio *Interlude* '87 on Concord Jazz; quintet *At The Top Of The Gate* '86 on Denon; big band albums incl. *Long Yellow Road* '75 (won record of the year awards in *Downbeat*, *Stereo Review*); *Road Time* '76 (2-disc set); *Farewell To Mingus* '80, *Tanuki's Night Out* on Jam; *Wishing Peace* '86 on their Ascent label.

AKKERMAN, Jan (*b* 24 Dec. '46, Amsterdam) Highly rated guitarist (electric, acoustic), also plays lute. First LP *Talent For Sale* '69 on Dutch Imperial; sextet *Profile* '72 for EMI; served time with bands Friendship Sextet, Johnny & the Cellar Rockers, Brainbox; then jazz/rock band Focus (with Thijs Van Leer, *b* 31 Mar. '48, Amsterdam, organ, flute, occasional vocals; Martin Dresden on bass, various drummers, other occasional personnel incl. Philip CATHERINE on guitar '76; LP with P. J. PROBY and Catherine '78). Akkerman played on their first six LPs, hit singles '70s; left '76, formed Eli with Kaz Lux (vocals), drummer Pierre Van der Linden (*b* 19 Feb. '46), both ex-Brainbox (Van der Linden also played on a couple of Focus LPs). Played on pianist Jasper van't Hof's *Fairy Tale* '78 on MPS with Kenny WHEELER; own albums incl. *Aranjuez* '78 on CBS with Claus Ogerman, *Jan Akkerman Live* '79 and *Jan Akkerman 3* '80 on Atlantic, octet *Pleasure Point* '81 on Dutch WEA; rejoined Focus '85 for *Focus: Jan Akkerman & Thijs Van Leer* on Vertigo. Also quartet *It Could Happen To You* '82 on Polydor, reissued on Charly UK along with compilations *Complete Guitarist* and *Can't Stand Noise* '85-6.

ALABAMA USA country-rock group formed '69 as Wild Country; changed name '77. Jeffrey Alan Cook (*b* 27 Aug. '49), Randy Yeull Owen (*b* 13 Dec. '49), guitars; Teddy Wayne Gentry (*b* 22 Jan. 52), bass guitar, cousins from Fort Payne, Ala., began playing with Gentry still in school; others in day jobs. All three sing; another cousin, Jackie Owen, was first drummer. Backed visiting stars and played dances; turned to music fulltime '73; signed to GRT records '77; 'I Want To Be With You' minor hit. To Dallas label MDJ '79, worked with Nashville prod. Harold Shedd; new drummer Mark Joel Herndon joined (*b* 11 May '55, Springfield, Mass.); 'I Wanna Come Over' '79 made country chart top 40; 'My Home's In Alabama', written by Owen and Gentry, made top 20 '80. To RCA '80; string of big hits followed: 'Tennessee River' and 'Why Lady Why' '80; 'Old Flame', 'Feels So Right' and 'Love In The First Degree' '81; 'Mountain Music' and 'Close Enough To Perfect' '82; 'The Closer You Get' and 'Dixieland Delight' '83; 'When We Make Love' and 'Roll On Eighteen Wheeler' '84; '40 Hour Week' '85. Crossovers to pop chart began with 'Feels So Right', 'Love In The First Degree' making pop top 40 '81-2. Named Country Group of the Year '80 to '84; RCA LPs hits: *My Home's In Alabama, Feels So Right, Mountain Music, The Closer You Get, Roll On, 40 Hour Week* '85, *Just Us* '87. Started trend for country group sound, paving way for Atlanta, Bandana, etc., transition of pop group Exile to C&W success.

ALADDIN R&B label founded on West Coast early '46 as Philo, by Leo, Edward and Ida Mesner. Began jazz oriented, demonstrating superficial influence of bop on pop: Helen HUMES made 'Be-Baba-Luba' for Philo (same time as Lionel HAMPTON, Tex BENEKE hit with 'Hey! Ba-Ba-Re-Bop'); also recorded Nat COLE trio, Lester YOUNG, Jay McSHANN, but soon had R&B success with torch-ballad style of Charles BROWN; first to record Lightnin' HOPKINS '46; began recording Amos MILBURN '46, who had a classic series of barroom hits. Also on booze theme was Peppermint Harris (*b* Harrison Nelson, c.'25, probably Texas), had no. 1 hit 'I Got Loaded' '50. Vocal quartet The Five Keys (Rudy and Bernie West, Ripley and Raphael Ingram, from Newport News, Va.)

had no. 1 '51 with 'The Glory Of Love'; also brought dark sound to white ballads 'Red Sails In The Sunset', 'These Foolish Things': more hits later on Capitol, but Aladdin singles are collectors' items. Label's hits infl. pop music directly with Thurston Harris and SHIRLEY & LEE. Though Shirley & Lee's 'Let The Good Times Roll' was banned by some deejays, Harris's simple plea was far more erotic: 'Little Bitty Pretty One' (no. 5 R&B, no. 6 pop '57), written by Bobby DAY. Aladdin sold to Imperial late '50s; label name revived '75 but original catalogue is owned by EMI. Harris compilation is *Little Bitty Pretty One* on EMI America; see entries for Milburn, Shirley & Lee.

ALAIMO, Steve (*b* Dec. '40, Rochester, NY) Singer. Forsook medical career for music, forming The Redcoats at Miami U. late '50s. Worked on *American Bandstand*; then for Miami record distributor, while performing locally at night. Biggest hit: 'Everyday I Have To Cry Some', made USA top 50 in '63. Had eight other minor hits by '72, but gave up performing for production, usually working with black artists.

ALARM, The UK rock band formed Summer '81 South Wales. All four had been 17-year-olds in band called 17: Mike Peters (*b* 25 Feb. '59, vocals, guitar); Dave Sharp (*b* 28 Jan. '59, guitar); Eddie MacDonald (*b* 1 Nov. '59, bass); Nigel Twist (*b* 18 July '58, drums). Signed by Miles Copeland (POLICE manager) to his IRS label; single '68 Guns' '83 set the tone: loud 'revolutionary' rock drew comparisons with early CLASH. Less bombastic second single 'Where Were You Hiding When The Storm Broke?' reached top 30. First album *Declaration* '84 had melodic aspects, acoustic bias and empty rhetoric. They began to incl. acoustic treatment of Welsh poem 'The Bells Of Rhymney' in '84 shows, demanding comparison with the BYRDS of 20 years before; pompous rock appealed to audiences unaware of 'protest' music of '60s or political aspects of '70s punk. Second LP *Strength* '85 was no advance.

ALBAM, Manny (*b* Emmanuel Albam, 24 June '22, Dominican Republic) Composer/arranger, sax. Went to USA as an infant.

Played alto and baritone in NYC from '40 and wrote for many bands in that decade, incl. Muggsy SPANIER, Boyd RAEBURN, Bobby Sherwood, Sam DONAHUE, Charlie BARNET. From '50 a fluent, successful Swing Era-based freelance arranger. *Drum Suite* '55 on RCA is typical of his best work: he wrote half the arrangements (rest by Ernie Wilkins); band incl. Al COHN, Joe NEWMAN, Conte CANDOLI, other excellent sidemen; drummers Osie Johnson, Gus Johnson, Don Lamond (*b* 18 Aug. '20, Okla.), Ted Sommer (*b* 16 June '24, NYC) providing tasteful punctuation: no loud solos, just beautiful swing. Much TV and film work; visited the UK, recorded with Tubby HAYES; many albums as leader are now out of print on RCA, Dot, Solid State, Coral (*The Jazz Greats Of Our Time*, two vols. of original comps. with all-star sidemen; *West Side Story, Sophisticated Lady,* '57-8). Wrote and recorded with Curtis FULLER, Stan GETZ, Coleman HAWKINS ('La Vie en Rose', '56), Gerry MULLIGAN, Buddy RICH, Clark TERRY; wrote 'Afro-Dizzyac' for Dizzy GILLESPIE, 'Country Man' for Dakota STATON, etc. He taught at the Eastman School of Music during the '70s.

ALBANY, Joe (*b* Joseph Albani, 24 Jan. '24, Atlantic City, N.J.; *d* 11 Jan. '88) Piano, songwriter. Important bop pianist, modern execution not obscuring deep feeling for blues. Overlooked by critics for many years, partly because he walked out of jobs (e.g. with Charlie PARKER) over musical differences. Worked in '40s with Georgie AULD, Benny CARTER, Stan GETZ; recorded with Lester YOUNG '46, L.A.; quartet LP with Warne MARSH *The Right Combination* '57; wrote songs recorded by Anita O'DAY '59; worked with Charles MINGUS NYC '63. Own albums incl. *Joe Albany At Home* '71; *Proto-Bopper* '72 on Spotlite; trio set *Birdtown Birds* and *Two's Company* with bassist Niels-Henning Ørsted Pedersen, both on Steeplechase, made in Copenhagen '73-4; in Italy '74 with Joe VENUTI, solo sets *This Is For My Friends, Plays George Gershwin & Bruce Lane* made in Paris '76, *The Albany Touch* '77 in Cal.; trio *Bird Lives!* NYC '79. *Portrait Of An Artist* '81 on Elektra with George Duvivier, Charlie Persip, Al Gofa on guitar.

ALBERTO Y LOST TRIOS PARANOIAS Comedy band from Manchester, England '76-8. C. P. 'Chris' Lee (vocals, guitar), Bob Harding (vocals, guitar, bass), Bruce Mitchell (drums), Tony Bowers (guitar, bass), Jimmy Hibbert (vocals, bass), Les Pryor (vocals), Simon White (guitar). Sent up some of the more ridiculous aspects of popular music, especially in '77 EP *Snuff Rock* and '78 LP *Skite*. Single 'Heads Down No Nonsense Mindless Boogie' made no. 47 UK chart '78. They broke up; splinter group Mothmen appeared for a while; Hibbert made obscure solo LP; Lee occasionally wrote for the music press, did one-man show *M'Lords & Ladies* ('82; *see* Lord BUCKLEY); Pryor died of an incurable disease c.'80.

ALBION BAND UK folk rock band. Various lineups have fractured history, but have been responsible for much of the best music in genre for past 25 years. Albion Country Band formed '71 by Ashley Hutchings (*b* Jan. '45, London), bass, founder member of both FAIRPORT CONVENTION and STEELEYE SPAN. Well-received album *Morris On* '72 incl. Richard THOMPSON, Dave Mattacks (both ex-Fairport). Immediately suffered Fairport malaise of fluctuating lineup, but incl. '71-3 such people as Martin CARTHY, John Kirkpatrick, Sue Harris; made excellent LP *Battle Of The Field* ('73, not released till '76). Hutchings then oversaw documentary song and dance LPs *The Compleat Dancing Master* '74, *Rattlebone & Ploughjack* '76. Next project was low-key Etchingham Steam Band, with Shirley COLLINS, then his wife; acoustic outfit worked mainly in Sussex, didn't record. Uncredited *Son Of Morris On* '76 was in fact new Albion Dance Band, which lasted '75-8, also made *The Prospect Before Us* '77. Hutchings made generally disappointing solo album *Kicking Up The Sawdust* '77; then another name-change: as The Albion Band, made *Rise Up Like The Sun* '78, perhaps the best English folk rock since halcyon days of Fairport 10 years earlier. Lineup incl. ex-Gryphon guitarist Graeme Taylor, laconic singer/songwriter/narrator John Tams, former SOFT MACHINE violinist Ric Sanders. Now began fruitful association with National Theatre, becoming virtual house band at the Cottesloe, most intimate of the three theatres on London's South Bank, appearing in and providing music for productions *The Passion, The World Turned Upside Down, Lark Rise*. LP *Lark Rise To Candleford: A Country Tapestry* '79 was effective souvenir of show. Band tied to theatre carried on as The Home Service; Hutchings left, keeping Albion name, recruiting former Fairport colleague Simon Nicol, Cathy LeSurf (from one-hit wonders Fiddlers Dram: 'Day Trip To Bangor' no. 3 UK '79). With multi-instrumentalists Jean-Pierre Rasle and Dave Whetstone, debut album of this edition, *Light Shining* '81, contained Hutchings-Whetstone comps. (e.g. 'Always Chasing Rainbows', 'Wolfe') as good as anything genre had seen for a decade. *Shuffle Off!* '81 was return to stylisation of *Compleat Dancing Master*. Next 'official' Albion LP incl. lineup of Hutchings, LeSurf (vocals), Phil Beer, Doug Morder (guitars), Trevor Foster (drums) on *Under The Rose* '84; *The Christmas Album* '86 was followed by Hutchings solos *An Hour With Cecil Sharp* '86 (his stage act, about pioneer English song collector), *By Gloucester Docks I Sat Down And Wept* '87.

ALCAPONE, Dennis (*b* Dennis Smith) Jamaican toaster, the most popular to emerge in the wake of U Roy in the early '70s, with a distinctive microphone style. Made his name with the El Paso sound system and went on to make scores of sides for most of the island's leading producers, incl. Studio One, Treasure Isle, Keith Hudson, Upsetter, Prince Tony, Dynamic. His Studio One titles were compiled on seminal album *Forever Version*, the label's first DJ set. Other early LPs incl. his first UK set *Guns Don't Argue* plus a selection of his Treasure Isle recordings on an LP shared with Lizzie, *Soul To Soul DJ's Choice*, another with U Roy *Version Galore Vol. 2*; he also featured on various-artists set *Version To Version*. The mid-'70s saw the emergence of more Ras Tafari-infl. toasters and a reversal of Alcapone's fortunes. Following his arrival in UK he made *Belch It Off* for producer Sydney Crooks, followed it up with *Dread Capone*, both received with indifference. He teamed with Bunny Lee on *King Of The Track, Investigator Rock* and *Six Million Dollar Man*, but faded from the scene towards the end of the decade.

ALDEBERT, Monique (Dozo) (*b* 5 May '31, Monaco) Sings with jazz infl. in French or English, solo or duo with husband Louis J. (*b* Egypt, 24 Jan. 24, also piano, composer). Gigged in Paris '50s; with group Double Six of Paris '60s, toured Canada and visited USA; when group broke up '66 played year in Las Vegas, moved to L.A. Much TV and film work; wrote many songs, vocal arrs. of jazz instrumentals (e.g. Django REINHARDT's 'Nuages'). Albums on European labels arr. by Quincy JONES, Michel LEGRAND.

ALEXANDER, Alger 'Texas' (*b* c.1880, Leona, Texas; *d* c.'55, Texas) Blues singer. Worked at itinerant music and at odd jobs; made records '27-34 (with King OLIVER NYC '28); imprisoned for murder early '40s, sang with his cousin Lightnin' HOPKINS in streets, on city buses in Houston late '40s-early '50s; recorded in Houston '50. One of the purest stylists in genre, his work based on shouts, work songs, field hollars.

ALEXANDER, Arthur, Jr (*b* '40, Sheffield, Ala.) Singer/songwriter. Wrote early '60s pop/soul classics 'You Better Move On' (his first record; made no. 24 on US pop chart '62; one of first hits out of Muscle Shoals studios), 'Anna' (no. 10 R&B chart '62), etc. Initiated use of word 'girl' in song lyrics, as in 'Go Home, Girl'. Songs were covered by Tina TURNER, BEATLES, BEE GEES, ROLLING STONES, etc. Less active in '70s ('Everyday I Have To Cry' no. 45 pop chart '75; recorded duets with Carl PERKINS '79), but songs still being covered (e.g. 'Go Home, Girl' by Ry COODER '79). Compilation album on Ace '82.

ALEXANDER, Monty (*b* Bernard Montgomery Alexander, 6 June '44, Kingston, Jamaica) Piano. To Florida '62, NYC c.'70. Led own trio; with Milt Jackson and Ray Brown early '70s; played Concord, San Diego, Monterey jazz festivals; albums on several labels. Unique laid-back style, slightly behind the beat and with Caribbean influence. Many albums recorded in Europe for MPS, others, incl. solo set *So What?* '79 on French Black & Blue label. Other LPs incl. *Now's The Time* '74 (MPS, on Pausa in USA), *Montreux Alexander Live* on MPS

'76, *Soul Fusion* with Milt Jackson on Pablo, '77. Albums on Concord Jazz: *Facets* '79 with Ray Brown, Jeff Hamilton on drums; *Trio* '80 and *Triple Treat* '82 with Brown and Herb ELLIS, no drums; *Overseas Special* (recorded '82, released '84) with same trio; *Reunion In Europe* is trio with Hamilton on drums and John Clayton, bass; *Ivory And Steel* (on Concord Picante) has bass, drums, percussion and steel drum. *Full Steam Ahead* '85 on Concord is a trio with Brown, drums.

ALEXANDER, Willie, & the Boom Boom Band USA punk/R&B band formed c.'77. Lineup: Willie 'Loco' Alexander (*b* '43) vocals, keyboards; Billy Loosigian (aka Mercer), guitar; Severin Grossman, bass; David McClean, drums. Alexander, veteran of Boston area groups (The Lost '64-6; briefly post-Lou REED VELVET UNDERGROUND '71), organised Boom Boom Band for local talent show, which they won. Appeared on *Live At The Rat* (compilation of Boston acts, '77); signed by MCA: two LPs late '70s.

ALI, Rashied (*b* Robert Patterson, 1 July '35, Philadelphia, Pa.) Drummer. Played with local groups; drove taxi for two years; to NYC '63. Worked with Pharoah SANDERS, Don CHERRY, Paul BLEY, Bill DIXON, Archie SHEPP, SUN RA, did rock'n'roll work; with John COLTRANE in important two-drummer experiment (with Elvin JONES) until Trane's death, then with Alice Coltrane trio. The only Coltrane sideman who did not go on to make LPs of his own, allegedly blackballed by record industry for independent stance. Toured Europe '68, jazz festivals, Carnegie Hall '70. Also recorded with Marion BROWN. Formed own Survival label '72, made LPs for it '73-5, with Frank LOWE, James Blood ULMER, etc. Opened loft Ali's Alley '73. Important figure in free jazz, determined to maintain integrity.

ALICE COOPER USA group/leader. Original lineup: Alice Cooper (*b* Vincent Furnier, 4 Feb. '48, Detroit), vocals; Glen Buxton (*b* 17 June '47, Washington DC), lead guitar; Dennis Dunaway (*b* 15 Mar. '46, Cal.), bass; Michael Bruce (*b* 21 Nov. '48, Cal.), keyboards, guitar; Neal Smith (*b* 10 Jan. '46, Washington), drums. Cooper

brought up in Phoenix; formed first band Earwigs '65 with Buxton, Dunaway and two others who left as Bruce joined and group changed name to The Spiders. Had local hit; Smith joined and name changed to The Nazz (no connection with later group of that name). Moved to L.A. late '60s; Alice Cooper as name of both group and leader: this ambiguity may have appealed to Frank ZAPPA, reportedly impressed by their ability to empty a local club with their performance; he signed them to his label Straight. Two albums later switched to WB '71, prod. Bob Ezrin: LP *Love It To Death* contained first USA hit single 'I'm 18'; belated success paid off huge debts group had incurred. Notorious at the time for excess (theatrical gore); LP *School's Out* '72 was biggest hit; title track made USA top 10, no. 1 in UK; great chart success in UK – three singles (all from '73 album *Billion Dollar Babies*) made top 10. Cooper then recruited ex-Lou REED and Mitch RYDER sidemen (original group later worked as Billion Dollar Babies without success). Subsequent Cooper releases used session musicians. Son of clergyman who once shocked with androgyny, chopped-up doll babies had TV special '75, became game-show guest; had ballad hits '76-7. Also had well-known alcohol problem; exorcised it in *From The Inside* '78, with some lyrics by Bernie Taupin. Contributed to film *Roadie* '80. LPs *Flush The Fashion* '80; *Zipper Catches Skin, Live In Toronto* '82; *Hold Up Your Fist And Yell* '88.

ALIX, May (*b* Liza Mae Alix, 31 Aug. '04, Chicago, Ill.) Singer. Worked in Chicago with Jimmie NOONE, Carroll Dickerson; sometimes billed as 'Queen of the Splits'. One of Louis ARMSTRONG's favourites, recorded 'Big Butter And Egg Man' '26 with his Hot Five: good example of cabaret style of the period. Toured Europe late '20s; worked in Chicago and NYC until ill health forced retirement '40s.

ALLAN, Johnnie (*b* John Guillot, 10 Mar. '38, Rayne, La.) Cajun rock guitar, singer. Rhythm guitar in local band age 13; changed to steel guitar and joined accordionist Lawrence Walker's band, which split '57; nucleus incl. pianist-fiddler U. J. Meaux, cousin of Huey Meaux, became rock'n'roll outfit The Krazy Kats. Minor hit

'Lonely Days And Lonely Nights' '59 issued on Jin, later on MGM. Next single heavily infl. by Fats DOMINO: 'Angel Of Love' (Jin/Mercury) with members of Jivin' Gene and Gene Terry bands did well but not well enough. Had been schoolteacher in Lafayette but led own band from '60; quit teaching '61 to concentrate on music. Records created regional popularity, never broke nationally. Back to college '67, obtained master's degree, became vice-principal Lafayette's Arcadian Elementary School; gigged locally. Became UK cult hero '74 when Charlie Gillett heard Cajun-tinged cover of Chuck BERRY's 'Promised Land', issued it on Oval label to general acclaim: single and several LPs available UK '85 incl. compilation on Ace.

ALLANSON, Susie (*b* 17 Mar. '52, Minneapolis, Minn.) Country singer. Made start in musicals *Hair* '67, *Jesus Christ Superstar* '71; also *Superstar* LP, film '73. Married record producer Ray Huff, started her in country music as background vocalist (later divorced). Signed to his Oak label, made C&W chart with debut single 'Baby, Don't Keep Me Hangin' On' '77. Switched to Warner/Curb for 'Baby, Last Night Made My Day' '77; 'Maybe Baby', 'We Belong Together' '78; to Elektra with 'Words', 'Two Steps Forward And Three Steps Back' '79. Joined Liberty records '81; now based in L.A.

ALLEN, Henry 'Red' (*b* Henry James Allen, 7 Jan. '08, New Orleans, La.; *d* 17 Apr. '67, NYC) Trumpet, singer. To NYC with King OLIVER, '27; first records with Clarence WILLIAMS. Recorded for Victor '29-30 as 'Henry Allen Jr and his Orchestra' (father led well-known New Orleans brass band); came to wider attention with Luis RUSSELL's band '29-32. With Fletcher HENDERSON '33-4; made small-group records with Coleman HAWKINS '33, reissued c.'80 by Smithsonian Collection: made quickly, cheaply for juke boxes, among the most delightful pop music of the time, turning ordinary tin-pan-alley songs into pearls. Worked for Lucky MILLINDER; briefly subbed with Duke ELLINGTON; with Louis ARMSTRONG '37-40, residencies with own sextet (incl. J. C. HIGGINBOTHAM) at clubs across USA until '52; dixielandish combo

work NYC. Newport Jazz Festivals beginning '57; CBS-TV *The Sound Of Jazz* same year; first visit to Europe '59 with Kid ORY band; several visits to UK '60s, last just a few weeks before death from cancer. Always underrated, partly because compared to Armstrong; in fact he was link between New Orleans and later jazz, while Armstrong's style never really changed after late '20s; at '58 reunion with Hawkins ('Mean To Me', 'Lonesome Road') he sounded as much like Miles DAVIS as Armstrong, but lovely muted horn also evoked King Oliver. He was unique.

ALLEN, Jules Verne (*b* Waxahachie, Texas) One of the first singing cowboys, when they were real cowboys and songs were still folk songs. Worked as cowboy from Rio Grande to Montana 1893-'07; sang on radio '20s-30s ('Longhorn Luke' in San Antonio). Tracks on out-of-print RCA Vintage series LP *Authentic Cowboys And Their Western Folksongs*.

ALLEN, Lee (*b* 2 July '26, Pittsburgh, Kansas) Tenor sax. Took up music while in school in New Orleans. Quit school to get married; worked with Paul GAYTEN band and singer Annie Laurie in late '40s. In the right place at the right time, he worked for Gayten and Dave BARTHOLOMEW on records and became studio stalwart, recording with LITTLE RICHARD, Fats DOMINO, Amos MILBURN, Lloyd PRICE, Etta JAMES, many others: kids danced to his rocking sax all through the '50s. First solo record with Aladdin '56: 'Rockin' At Cosmo's' '56; *Walkin' With Mr Lee* '58 LP went gold, title track made pop chart; 'Tic Toc' also minor hit same year. Made some records for Ember, toured with Domino and Little Richard; from '65 worked in West Coast aircraft factory, but kept playing; with Domino again in '75; sessioned with BLASTERS early '80s. LP collection: *Down On Bourbon Street*.

ALLEN, Rex, (*b* 31 Dec. '24, Willcox, Arizona) Singer, songwriter. One of the few singing cowboys who was real cowboy, better actor and singer than most. Highly rated rodeo performer, studied electronics in California, on radio in New Jersey '44, Chicago '45-50 (National Barn Dance). Own

TV show '50, reportedly seventh in national ratings. Cheap films for Republic studio for years; feature roles in other films; narrated documentaries, often for Walt Disney. 'Crying In The Chapel' no. 4 in country chart '53 (not his song), other hits in '60s. Owns hotel in Mexico, ranch in California; various awards and honours; continued to perform in rodeos for many years; published more than 300 songs.

ALLEN, Rex, Jr (*b* 23 Aug. '47, Chicago, Ill.) One of four children of singing cowboy star (*see above*); raised in Cal.; travelled with father on rodeo tours as a child. Formed bands in school, appeared on TV; US Army service, to Nashville and more TV late '60s. Success came with WB contract '73: country chart entries incl. 'The Great Mail Robbery', 'Goodbye', incl. in first album *Another Goodbye Song*, all '74. More of the same '75; co-written 'Can You Hear Those Pioneers' made top 30 '76. Own comp. 'With Love' and co-written 'It's Time We Talk Things Over' top tens '78. Now a headliner, incl. Grand Ole Opry; half a dozen more chart singles '80-1. LPs incl. *Singing Cowboy* on WB; also *On The Move* on Moon Shine label '85.

ALLEN, Rosalie (*b* Julie Marlene Bedra, 27 June '24, Old Forge, Pa.) Country singer. Queen of the yodellers; popular radio star in USA Northeast '30s-40s. Recorded for RCA '40s; biggest success with 'He Taught Me How To Yodel'; also duets with Elton BRITT. DJ at WOV NYC; had record shop in New Jersey.

ALLEN, Steve (*b* Stephen Valentine Patrick William Allen, 26 Dec. '21, NYC) Comedian, TV personality, also songwriter and selftaught pianist (playing by ear). DJ in L.A.; back to NYC '51, became famous TV host (*Tonight* show from '54, etc.). A likeable unpretentious man, saw wacky humour in everyday situations. Own albums incl. *Jazz For Tonight* '55, with Milt HINTON, Urbie Green, others; album of his songs arr. and recorded by Manny ALBAM '58. Used first-class talent on TV shows (e.g. Les BROWN band; Skitch HENDERSON, Steve LAWRENCE and Eydie GORME). Hosted first networked TV programme on jazz, NBC '57; narrated 3-disc historical jazz album

'59; portrayed GOODMAN in '59 biopic *The Benny Goodman Story*. Helped career of Jerry Lee LEWIS, who named a son after him.

ALLEN, Terry (*b* 7 May '43, Wichita, Kansas) Singer/songwriter, pianist. Well known as sculptor and painter, increasing cult fame in music. Raised in Lubbock, Texas; art school in L.A. '62. First LP *Juarez* '75 is a concept album of story songs recorded in San Francisco; the rest of his work was recorded on trips to Lubbock. Sprawling *Lubbock (On Everything)* '78 is a 2-disc set of cleverly observed songs with recitations, strings here and saxes there, about loneliness, memories of '50s ('Pink And Black Song'), being an art teacher, etc.; 'Thirty Years War Waltz' is about meeting Jo Harvey Allen at high school dance; iconoclastic humour of delivery complements irony in material. 'New Delhi Freight Train', 'Amarillo Highway' covered respectively by LITTLE FEAT, Bobby BARE. *Smokin The Dummy* '80 has band with Lloyd, Kenny and Donnie MAINES, guests Ponty Bone, Joe ELY and others now called Panhandle Mystery Band; provided tough, driving delivery of superb set of songs about places, coming/going in USA: 'The Heart Of California' (highway song dedicated to Lowell George), 'Whatever Happened To Jesus (And Maybelline)?' (partly a good cover of Chuck BERRY classic), also 'Cajun Roll', 'Cocaine Cowboy', 'The Night Cafe', 'Texas Tears', more. *Bloodlines* '83 more of the same, with 'Gimme A Ride To Heaven Boy', savage antiterrorist 'Ourland'; also usefully revives 'Cantina Carlotta' and 'There Oughta Be A Law Against Sunny Southern California' from *Juarez*. Last three albums on Fate Records, Chicago. Wrote music for film *Amerasia* '86. Rare appearances in London Apr. '86 covered by TV's *Whistle Test*; 'Gimme A Ride To Heaven Boy' broadcast.

ALLIGATOR Label formed in Chicago by Bruce Iglauer '71, an important blues label in line of Chicago's CHESS and DELMARK, with help of world-wide distribution by Swedish based Sonet, successful beyond expectations. Like Chuck NESSA Iglauer once worked at Delmark; he was Hound Dog TAYLOR's manager and driver; his theory that young white fans would buy LPs by modern blues artists proved correct: first release was first Taylor LP '71, carried on with Koko TAYLOR (won Alligator's first Grammy), Son SEALS, Lonnie Brooks ('Guitar Jr' *b* 18 Dec. '33, Dubuisson, La.); Iglauer rescued Albert COLLINS from years of neglect, his straightforward prod. with good sound and no gimmicks resulting in series of splendid LPs incl. *Showdown* with Collins, guests Johnny COPELAND and Robert CRAY, one of four Alligator LPs in Billboard charts '86. Also manages many acts, personal attention and full-time interest avoiding mistakes of labels that get too big. Good-time music continued with Big Twist and the Mellow Fellows (Larry 'Big Twist' Nolan, *b* 23 Sep. '37): *Playing For Keeps*, then *Live From Chicago! Bigger Than Life!!* '87 with excellent nine-piece band incl. horns (also two earlier LPs on Flying Fish, incl. *One-Track Mind* on Red Lightnin' UK). Signed white legends Lonnie MACK, Johnny WINTER, Roy BUCHANAN, whose careers were in danger of terminal slowdown; latest discoveries incl. L'il Ed and the Blues Imperials: L'il Ed Williams, guitar and vocals (*b* 8 Apr. '55); James 'Pookie' Young, bass; Dave Weld, guitar; Louis Henderson, drums: Williams and Young are nephews of the late J. B. HUTTO, had never recorded before, came to Streeterville Studios to cut one track for an anthology and didn't stop until they'd had a party, made LP *Roughhousin'* '87. Little Charlie and the Nightcats' *All The Way Crazy* '87 was made on West Coast, where they are local legend in Sacramento Valley: guitarist Charlie Baty (counts Cray among fans), plus Rick Estrin on harmonica and vocals; Jay Peterson, bass and backing vocals; Dobie Strange on drums. Anthology *The New Bluebloods* '87 incl. an extra track by L'il Ed, nine other fine Chicago acts.

ALLISON, Luther (*b* 17 Aug. '39, Mayflower, Arizona) Blues singer. One of 12 children; toured with The Southern Travelers gospel group, late '40s; went to high school in Chicago, learned guitar. Worked in band of his brother Ollie Lee, '54; later formed The Rolling Stones with another brother, Grant; later renamed The Four Jivers, this band played The Bungalow in Chicago '57-8. Gigged with Jimmy

DAWKINS, LITTLE RICHARD, MAGIC SAM, Chuck BERRY, etc., also with own units. Went to West Coast late '60s, played Ann Arbor Blues Festivals '70-4; Motown recording contract '74. Montreux, Antibes Jazz Festivals; several successful European tours, e.g. London's 100 Club, summer '76. Heard on film soundtrack *Cooley High* '76; has recently played around 300 dates a year. Albums incl. *Blues Nebulae, Love Me Mama* on Delmark; live *Southside Safari*.

ALLISON, Mose (*b* 11 Nov. '27, Tippo, Miss.) Singer/songwriter, leads piano trio; white child infl. by blues on filling-station juke box. US Army service '46-7; formed trio '49. Played with Stan GETZ, Gerry MULLIGAN, Al Cohn, Zoot Sims late '50s; toured Europe '59. *Back Country Suite* '57 10 short vignettes on one side of Prestige LP; other side of debut confirmed blues-based cabaret style. Played on LPs with Al Cohn/Zoot Sims late '50s, others; as his work matured, cynical, witty songs were covered by The WHO ('A Young Man Blues'); John MAYALL ('Parchman Farm'), Georgie FAME, Bonnie RAITT and others. Six LPs on Prestige '57-9; recorded for CBS '59-61; Atlantic LPs incl. *Mose Alive* (charted UK '66), *I've Been Doin' Some Thinkin'* '68, *Hello There, Universe* '69, *Western Man* '71, *Mose In Your Ear* '72, *Your Mind's On Vacation* '76. LPs on Elektra '82: *Middle Class White Boy* made in L.A., *Lessons In Living* at Montreux, with Lou DONALDSON, Eric Gale, Jack Bruce, Billy COBHAM. *Ever Since The World Ended* '88 on Blue Note has guests incl. Arthur BLYTHE, Kenny BURRELL.

ALLMAN BROTHERS Southern rock band formed '68. Original lineup: Duane Allman (*b* 20 Nov. '46, Nashville; *d* 29 Oct. '71, Macon, Ga.), guitar; Gregg Allman (*b* 8 Dec. '47, Nashville), keyboards, guitar, vocals; Richard 'Dickie' Betts (*b* 12 Dec. '43, West Palm Beach, Fla.), guitar; Berry Oakley (*b* 4 Apr. '48, Chicago; *d* 11 Nov. '72, Macon, Ga.), bass; Jai Johanny Johanson, aka Jaimo (real name John Lee Johnson, *b* 8 July '44, Ocean Springs, Mo.), Butch Trucks (*b* Jacksonville, Fla.), drums. Duane and Gregg worked in various Fla. bands, then formed Allman Joys (pun on a USA chocolate bar) with Bob Keller (bass),

Manard Portwood or Billy Canell (drums); after two LPs re-formed with Paul Hornsby (keyboards), Johnny Sandlin (drums), Mabron McKinney (bass); moved to Hollywood '67, replaced McKinney with Jesse Willard Carr, renamed band Hour Glass, cut two LPs '67-8, they still didn't sell. Allmans returned to Fla. '68, briefly joined 31st of February, folk-rock trio of Scott Boyer, guitar, vocals; David Brown, bass and Trucks, who made one album. (Five-piece LP later issued early '70s as *Duane And Gregg Allman*.) This band folded; Gregg obliged to cut album for Liberty (Hour Glass's label), not released at the time; Duane became notable session man at Fame Studios, Muscle Shoals, playing for Wilson PICKETT, Boz SCAGGS, KING CURTIS, Aretha FRANKLIN, others, also cutting unreleased LP with Hornsby, Sandlin and Oakley; met Betts, who had played with Oakley in group The Second Coming. After jamming with Betts, Oakley, Trucks and Johanson decided to form band; Gregg came to complete it. In this original form, band made excellent albums *The Allman Brothers Band* '69, *Idlewild South* '70, *Live At The Fillmore East* '71; then Duane killed in motorcycle accident while recording 2-disc album *Eat A Peach*. Band decided to continue without replacing Duane; both *Live* and *Peach* made top 10 album chart. Chuck Leavell added on keyboards, '72; while making *Brothers And Sisters* Oakley killed in accident similar to Duane's. Completed LP made no. 1; single 'Ramblin' Man' made top 3 with Les Dudek (guitar) and Lamar Williams (bass, *b* '47, *d* Jan. '83, L.A.). Gregg made solo album, as did Betts (*Highway Call* '75); band's *Win, Lose Or Draw* '75 followed by live albums '75-6; Gregg briefly married to CHER, album *Allman And Woman* with her; band broke up after he testified in drug case against road manager. Betts formed Great Southern (*Dickie Betts And Great Southern* '77, *Atlanta Burning Down* '78), while Gregg formed Gregg Allman band; Trucks, Leavell, Johanson, Williams and Jimmy Nails (guitar) formed Sea Level. In '78 Allman Brothers re-formed with Allman, Trucks, Jaimo, Betts, Dan Toler (guitar) and David Goldflies (bass) from Great Southern. LP *Enlightened Rogues* '79 was good seller; Jaimo left, Mike Lawler (key-

boards) and David Toler (drums) joined; LP *Brothers Of The Road* '81. Leavell rejoined '82; state of flux continued. Best years between formation and *Brothers And Sisters*; they were the most important of the southern 'boogie' genre, though Duane never satisfactorily replaced. He can also be heard on classic *Layla* LP (Derek and the Dominos; *see* Eric CLAPTON) and two vols. of *Duane Allman – An Anthology*, incl. both session and band tracks.

ALLYN, David (*b* Albert DiLello, '23, Hartford, Conn.) Singer. From musical family, father played in Hartford Symphony Orchestra; Allyn recorded with Jack TEAGARDEN at 17 (reissues on Savoy '86). Saw action in WWII, wounded in North Africa, introduced to pain-killing drugs: joined legendary Boyd RAEBURN band '45 ('Forgetful', 'I Only Have Eyes For You') but by then was heroin addict. Imprisoned mid-'50s, came out clean but forgotten. LPs with arranger/conductor Johnny Mandel now reissued on Discovery: *Sure Thing* (songs of Jerome KERN), *In The Blue Of The Evening* (unreleased then), *Yours Sincerely* with Bill Holman, *I Only Have Eyes For You* with Mandel again '57-9; *Don't Look Back* '75 with excellent Detroit pianist Barry HARRIS on piano now also reissued on Xanadu. With *Soft As Spring* on Audiophile almost everything is in print, but the singer who got even better as he got older and had been highly praised by Frank SINATRA and Alec WILDER had left music, worked managing a hardware store (also drug counselling). Heard one of his own records on the radio in Minneapolis early '80s, rang up DJ to say thanks, did an interview and ended up back on the bandstand: to NYC and new album on Discovery with pianist Clare Fischer.

ALMEIDA, Laurindo (*b* 2 Sep. '17, São Paulo, Brazil) Spanish acoustic guitar, composer. To USA '47; played with Stan KENTON, own trio in L.A.; recorded with Bud SHANK on flute (two '54 LPs *Laurindo Almeida Quintet*); also Herbie MANN, FOUR FRESHMEN, etc.; became famous with bossa nova style: *Viva Bossa Nova* album no. 13 on USA chart '62. Played with MODERN JAZZ QUARTET '63, toured Europe with them '64. Also fine classical guitarist, pursuing concert career since late '60s, often with his wife, soprano Deltra Eamon. Recorded own *First Concerto For Guitar And Orchestra* '79 on Concord. Composed and conducted albums for other artists; worked on many films, incl. underscoring for *Viva Zapata* '52, Downbeat poll winner in film music category for *The Old Man And The Sea* '58, etc. Long-popular album *Braziliance* with Shank reissued USA on Pausa; *Guitar From Ipanema* '64 with eight pieces (two flutes), rhythm, vocalist Irene Kral on Capitol won Grammy. Solo LPs incl. *Suenos* (Dreams) '65 on Capitol, *Concierto de Aranjuez* '78 on East Wind (Japan). Also on Concord: Shank and Almeida's *Selected Classical Works For Guitar And Flute* '82; *Chamber Jazz*, trio with bass and drums; *Brazilian Soul* '80 and *Latin Artistry* '82 both with Charlie BYRD; *Artistry In Rhythm* '83, trio; in addition nine LPs by L.A. Four (*see* entry for Ray BROWN).

ALMOND, John (*b* 20 July '46, Enfield, Middlesex, England) Reeds, keyboards, vibes. Played with John MAYALL '69; own LP *Hollywood Blues* made in Hollywood '69: group called Johnny Almond and the Music Machine was lucky to incl. Curtis AMY, Joe PASS. Formed band with guitarist Jon Mark: Mark-Almond Band made lightweight vocal jazzrock LPs '70s, anticipating New Age music, first on Blue Thumb, then *Other People's Rooms* on A&M, *Rising* on Columbia, *To The Heart* on ABC.

ALMOND, Marc (*b* Peter Marc Almond, 9 July '57, Southport, Lancs., England) Singer, songwriter. Studied performance art at Leeds Polytechnic, cabaret act became Soft Cell, duo with Dave Ball (*b* 3 May '59, Salford) on synthesisers late '79. Released EP independently, had track on *Some Bizzare* compilation LP with DEPECHE MODE, BLANCMANGE, The The (*see* Matt JOHNSON). Effeminate, diminutive Almond and stolid mustachio'd Ball made odd couple; Ball's staccato synth interjections and Almond's piping tenor made classic pop for New Romantics on cover of Gloria Jones's 'Tainted Love', no. 1 in 17 countries incl. UK, top 10 USA. Almond's camp sense of humour made for strange videos, such as 'Sex Dwarf', sending up video nasties. Ten

top 40 hits, four more in top 5 by end of '82; albums *Non Stop Ecstatic Dancing* '82, *The Art Of Falling Apart* '83; went separate ways. Ball issued instrumental solo LP *In Strict Tempo* '83; Almond had formed Marc & the Mambas (LP *Torment And Toreros* '83), did solo LP *Vermin In Ermine* '84, duet with BRONSKI BEAT on cover of Donna SUMMER's 'I Feel Love', UK top 5 hit '85; *Stories Of Johnny* '85 on Some Bizzare label had top 20 UK hit title track; *A Woman's Story* '86 on Virgin incl. big pop ballads from PROCOL HARUM's 'Salty Dog' to Johnnie RAY's 'Little White Cloud That Cried'; *Mother Fist And Her Five Daughters* '87 by Marc Almond with the Willing Sinners incl. Martin McCarrick on cello and accordion: perhaps his most successful, knitting together trademarks of flamenco, torch song and Jacques BREL style in songs about lust and broken dreams.

ALPERT, Herb (*b* 31 Mar. '35, L.A.) Trumpet, composer, arranger, producer. With Lou ADLER managed JAN & DEAN; they also prod. no. 15 novelty hit 'Alley-Oop' '60 by Dante and the Evergreens (Hollywood Argyles had no. 1); later Alpert allegedly said that he and Adler had been Dante and the Evergreens. Had played trumpet in US Army; overdubbing experiments with song 'Twinkle Star' (comp. Sol Lake) led to quasi-Mexican sound, with bullfight/crowd noises dubbed; record prod. for $200 retitled 'The Lonely Bull' '62, went gold. Formed A&M records with Jerry MOSS; LP of same title also sold a million by end of '67. Successful novelty style dubbed 'Ameriachi'; had 13 chart singles '62-7, 15 LPs in USA charts in 10 years; five no. 1 albums incl. *Whipped Cream (& Other Delights)* '65, helped by saucy sleeve photo of pretty girl dressed in whipped cream. In UK 14 LPs charted '66-79, nine singles '63-80; long since abandoned ersatz Mexico for MOR. His vocal on 'This Guy's In Love With You' re-entered UK chart three times. Alpert is a first-class entertainer who enjoys his success; Dave FRISHBERG told Whitney Balliett about 'two wonderful, funny first-class-all-the-way years' working for him. *Wild Romance* '85, *Keep Your Eye On Me* '87 are dance LPs using the latest studio technology, latter half vocal, half instrumental, incl. top 10 'Diamonds', written by

Jimmy Jam and Terry Lewis, who wrote hit LP *Control* for Janet Jackson.

ALPHONSO, Roland Jamaican tenor saxophonist and founder member of the Skatalites Ska instrumental outfit, with whom he was featured soloist on scores of records in the '60s, mostly at Studio One but also for Treasure Isle and others. Some of his best known sides are 'Hully Gully Rock', 'Blackberry Brandy', 'Blockade', 'Sandy Gully', 'The President', 'Crime Wave', 'Hot Rod', 'Nuclear Weapon', 'Downbeat Special', 'VC10', and the big club hit 'Phoenix City' '66. In addition he sessioned for virtually every Jamaican artist who cut a record during the ska and Rock Steady eras. He brought a revamped Skatalites to UK to play at Sunsplash '84. His solo work can be heard on Studio One albums *Best Of* and *King Of Sax*, as well as his *Brighter Shade Of Roots* and the more recent *Roll On* session for NYC REGGAE specialist label Wackies.

ALTERED IMAGES Scottish group formed '79. Clare Grogan, vocals; Tony McDaid and Jim McInven, guitars; Johnny McElhone, bass; 'Tich' Anderson, drums. Signed by Epic on potential of Grogan, star of cult films *Gregory's Girl, Comfort & Joy* (as C. P. Grogan). Debut LP *Happy Birthday* produced by Steve Severin except title track by Martin Rushent, which made UK top 3 late '81. Rushent produced next two hit singles; McInven left, Anderson replaced by Steve Lironi; third LP *Bite* produced half by Mike Chapman, other half by Tony Visconti. Images dissolved by '84, leaving compilation album *Collected Images*.

ALTSCHUL, Barry (*b* 6 Jan. '43, Bronx, NYC) Drummer. With Jazz Composer's Orchestra late '60s. Versatile musician has played, recorded with Paul BLEY and Chick COREA trios, Anthony BRAXTON, bluesman Buddy GUY, also Julius HEMPHILL (*Coon Bid'ness* '75). Worked in Europe with Johnny GRIFFIN, Steve LACY, etc. Own LPs incl. *You Can't Name Your Own Tune* '77, with Sam RIVERS, George LEWIS, Muhal Richard ABRAMS, Dave HOLLAND; *Another Time/Another Place* '78; *For Stu* '79, all on Muse; *Brahma* '80, trio set with bass, trom-

bone on Sackville; *Irina* '83, *That's Nice* '85 on Soul Note.

AMAZING RHYTHM ACES USA country-rock band formed '74. Original lineup: Russell Smith, lead vocals, guitar, harmonica; Butch McDade, vocals, drums; Jeff Davis, bass; Billy Earhart, keyboards; all *b* Tenn. Main songwriter Smith began as DJ in his hometown of Lafayette; some members played back-up for Jesse WINCHESTER early '70s, Davis had played with Otis RUSH. Smith song 'Third Rate Romance' recorded by others incl. Winchester: band got serious, adopted name, added James Hooker (vocals, keyboards), Barry 'Byrd' Burton (guitar, mandolin, dobro, steel guitar, vocals). Didn't want to play heavy rock or disco, so played what they wanted: music ultimately unsuccessful despite respectable sales (incl. country charts) because not easy to categorise: too much diversity, live sound more R&B than on records. LPs on ABC began with *Stacked Deck* '75: 'Third Rate Romance' no. 14 pop hit; 'Amazing Grace (Used To Be Her Favorite Song)' also charted that year; then *Too Stuffed To Jump* and *Toucan Do It, Too* '76 (incl. 'The End Is Not In Sight', no. 42 pop, won Grammy for best country vocal). Oldest member Byrd left to session in Nashville, tired of the road; replaced by Duncan Cameron. *Burning The Ballroom Down* '78 followed by *Amazing Rhythm Aces* '79, prod. in Muscle Shoals by Jimmy Johnson; appeared first on ABC, then on Columbia; perhaps best LP but mix of R&B style, country songs didn't sell well. Switched to WB for *How The Hell Do You Spell Rhythm* '80; gave up. Smith made single 'Honky Tonk Freeway', solo album for Capitol '82.

AMAZONES, Les All-female dance band, founded '61 in Guinea. Has long remained prominent African outfit despite many personnel changes; large group plays mixture of Congo and trad. music with guitars, percussion, vocalists, full horn section; has toured West Africa, France, Germany. Best work on LPs *Au Coeur de Paris*, followup *Sons de la Savanne* '84, showcasing lead vocalist Sona Diabate.

AMBROSE (*b* Bert Ambrose, 1897, London; *d* 12 June '73, Leeds, England) Violinist, bandleader. Led one of the best British dance bands of '30s-40s, employing top musicians, singers, arrangers. Played violin age 5; went to NYC in teens, playing at Reisenweber's Restaurant, then sixth violin at Club de Vingt, became leader in six months, stayed three years. Back to London '20, led band at Embassy Club in Old Bond Street, the most glamorous of night spots: no society hostess in London gave a party on Thursday, which was the night everybody went to the Embassy. For the Prince of Wales, Ambrose played a waltz slowly at first, speeding up the tempo when the Prince was successfully whirling: Edward thought it was the best band in the world. After another briefer visit to NYC (lured back by a telegram: 'Come back, we need you. Edward P') he added USA musicians, began recording, got £10,000 a year to go to the Mayfair Hotel '27 with Anglo-American band incl. trumpeter Henry 'Hot Lips' Levine (later NBC staff NYC). His most famous band incl. Ted HEATH; Max Bacon, drums; Joe Crossman, alto sax; USA clarinettist Danny Polo (1901-49) joined '29; band first to be signed by Decca UK. Added trombones Lew Davis, Tony Thorpe, made formidable section with Heath; also Max Goldberg, trumpet; Billy Amstell, reeds; Joe Branelly, guitar; singers Elsie Carlisle, Sam Browne; arrangements by Lew STONE, later reedman Sid Phillips. Own weekly radio show live from Mayfair gained large following. Returned to Embassy Club '34-5; then to Ciro's, Café de Paris; with George CHISHOLM, singer Evelyn Hall; Vera LYNN got first break with this band. Last dates at Mayfair '39; went on tour, used octet in stage shows, recorded with bands drawn from available stars; used singer Anne SHELTON. Returned to clubs after WWII; formed classy big band early '50s to record for MGM, arrangements by Laurie Johnson; further records on Parlophone and Philips of less interest: strict tempo for dancing. Led small group at Café de Paris; then moved into management, concentrating on singer Kathy Kirby, whom he discovered at Ilford Palais '57. High social standing in heyday; great favourite with British royal family. Theme was 'When Day Is Done'. Many compilation LPs, both USA and UK; e.g. *The Golden Age Of Ambrose And*

His Orchestra EMI UK, with notes by Brian Rust.

AMBROSIA Rock group formed L.A. '71 by schoolmates David Pack, guitar; Joe Puerta, bass; added Christopher North, keyboards; Burleigh Drummond, drums. All *b* '52, all accomplished vocalists and multi-instrumentalists whose ability brought date with L.A. Philharmonic and '73 debut of Leonard BERNSTEIN's *Mass* in heyday of classic/rock fusion: all before a record contract. LP *Ambrosia* '75 incl. first of occasional hit singles, 'Hold On To Yesterday' (no. 17). *Somewhere I've Never Travelled* followed the next year, and all but North also played on Alan Parsons LP *Tales Of Mystery And Imagination*. North not on *Life Beyond LA* ('78; no. 3 hit 'How Much I Feel'); next LP *One Eighty* ('80) did even better, with 'You're The Only Woman' (no. 13), 'Biggest Part Of Me' (no. 3). Surviving trio are excellent musicians with session credits (mostly as vocal team) with Chris Rea, Kerry Livgren of KANSAS, Al STEWART; nice harmonies brought AOR hit singles USA only; nothing since '82 LP *Road Island*. Pack prod. *Patti Austin* LP, sessions.

AMEN CORNER Pop group formed Cardiff, Wales, '66. Andy Fairweather-Lowe (*b* '48), vocals, guitar; Neil Jones, guitar; Blue Weaver, keyboards; Clive Taylor, bass; Dennis Byron, drums; Allen Jones and Mike Smith, saxes. First charted '67 with 'Gin House Blues', first of four UK top 30 hits on Deram label; biggest was 'Bend Me Shape Me' ('68, cover of hit by AMERICAN BREED). Switched to Immediate, topped chart '69 with '(If Paradise Is) Half As Nice'; label collapsed, stunting success. Reformed '70 without horns as Fairweather, made top 5 with 'Natural Sinner', then folded. Weaver and Bryon worked with BEE GEES during '70s, Weaver briefly in STRAWBS. Fairweather-Low embarked on solo career.

AMERICA Folk-rock trio/duo formed England '69. Original lineup: Gerry Beckley (*b* 12 Sep. '52, Texas), Dan Peek (*b* '50, Fla.), Dewey Bunnell (*b* 19 Jan. '52, Yorkshire, England). All sing, play guitar. Sons of US servicemen, attended school in London, began playing, writing together; discovered by pop music entrepreneurs Ian Samwell and Jeff Dexter, cut debut LP in London; single 'A Horse With No Name' reached top 3 in UK, no. 1 USA '72. Two more top 10 USA hits '72; sequence of easy-listening folk-rock LPs, seven of which had titles starting with letter 'H': *Hat Trick* '73, *Holiday* '74, *Hearts* '75, etc. many prod. by George MARTIN, but few big hits. Peek became born again Christian, left '77 for solo career on religious label; Beckley and Bunnell changed from WB to CAPITOL '80. 'You Can Do Magic' made USA top 10 '82; much work written by Russ Ballard (ex-ARGENT). Best work of trio on greatest hits *History* '75.

AMERICAN BREED Pop group formed Chicago '66. Lineup: Gary Loizzo (*b* 16 Aug. '45), vocals, guitar; Al Ciner (*b* 14 May '47), guitar; Charles 'Chuck' Colbert (*b* Aug. '44), bass; Lee Graziano (*b* 9 Nov. '43), drums. All born in Chicago, regionally popular as Gary & the Nite Lites, one flop single; changed name and label and had five hits '67-8; biggest 'Bend Me Shape Me', USA top 5. Group then augmented by Kevin Murphy (keyboards) and Andre Fischer (drums), who left '72 to form Rufus with Chaka KHAN.

AMERICAN FLYER Folk-rock quartet formed '76. Lineup: Craig Fuller, Eric Kaz (*b* '47, Brooklyn), Steve Katz (*b* 9 May '45), Doug Yule. All sang, played guitar except Yule, bass. Two notable songwriters in Fuller (ex-Pure Prairie League) and Kaz (ex-BLUES MAGOOS, solo LPs), plus Katz (ex-BLOOD, SWEAT & TEARS, Blues Project), and Yule (ex-VELVET UNDERGROUND); debut LP to be produced by George MARTIN: high expectations not satisfied, genre out of fashion anyway. Second LP *Spirit Of A Woman* '77 also unsuccessful.

AMES BROTHERS USA vocal quartet: Ed, Gene, Joe, Vic, all *b* Malden, Mass. Vic (*b* Urick) *d* 23 Jan. '78 aged 51. 23 top 40 hits '49-60 began with 'You, You, You Are The One' '49 followed by 2-sided no. 1 'Rag Mop'/'Sentimental Me' '50. Top 10 hits continued with 'Undecided' '51 (with Les BROWN), then switched from Coral to RCA for 'You You You' '53, 'The Man With The Banjo' and 'The Naughty Lady Of Shady Lane' '54 (latter was only UK chart entry), 'Tammy' and 'Mélodie d'Amour' '57. Own TV show '55, mixing comedy with distinctive vocal style (like close-harmony baritones). Split up late '50s; Ed pursued solo career, made top 10 with 'My Cup Runneth Over' from Tom Jones/Harvey Schmidt musical *I Do, I Do*; 'Who Will Answer' made no. 19, both '67. Ed's LP *Hits Of Broadway And Hollywood* incl. popular version of 'Try To Remember' from long-running off-Broadway Jones/Schmidt show *The Fantasticks*.

AMM Band of UK musicians playing original music that defies categorisation, incl. group improvisation, prepared piano, maybe a transistor radio, altering the sound of the electric guitar by bowing the strings or inserting foreign objects, etc., the idea being to create a sound world of shifting colours incl. every conceivable timbre, often sounding like a much larger group. Formed '65 as a free jazz group by percussionist Eddie Prévost (*b* '42), Keith Rowe (*b* '40) on guitar and electronics, Lou Gare (*b* '39) on tenor sax; Lawrence Sheaff (*b* '40) joined on cello and accordion and Cornelius Cardew (1936-81) on piano for first LP *Amm Music* '67 on Elektra. Cardew was a composer who had founded the Scratch Orchestra at about the same time, improvisations and compositions by people of no great skill, the idea being that everyone could be a musician (which of course is the case in 'primitive' societies); he was the best-known member of AMM (at one point mistakenly labelled the Cornelius Cardew Quintet); he found his Maoist theory shaken by the need for absolute freedom in the music, but Prévost wrote that Cardew's 'The Tiger's Mind' was 'the description-cum-composition to come nearest to . . . the AMM experience.' (They haven't recorded it.) Among AMM's aphorisms: 'AMM started itself. It was there a few minutes before we thought of it,' and 'The reason for playing is to find out what I want to play.' Sheaff left; Christopher Hobbs (*b* '50) joined on percussion; *Live Electronic Music* '68 on Mainstream had Musica Electronica Viva on the other side, a group mostly of Americans living in Italy at the time. *The Crypt – 12th June 1968* released '80 on Matchless; Hobbs left; Cardew left '72 (later killed in car crash). *At The Roundhouse* '72 is on Incus, *To Hear And Back Again* '74 on Matchless, both by AMM II (duo of Gare and Prévost); Gare left '77; *It Had Been An Ordinary Enough Day In Pueblo, Colorado* '79 on Japo was AMM III (Rowe and Prévost); John Tilbury (*b* '36) joined on piano '79, had worked with Cage, Morton Feldman, Cardew etc.; *Generative Themes* '82 on Matchless was a trio. Rohan de Saram (*b* '39) joined on cello '85, an international concert artist who studied with Gaspar Cassado, Pablo Casals, worked with composers from Kodaly to Berio. Ian Mitchell (*b* '48) joined on clarinet '87; *The Inexhaustible Document* '87 released on Matchless. Rowe played with Mike WESTBROOK and Cardew's Scratch Orchestra, interprets Cardew's *Treatise*, a synthesis of graphics and notation; Prévost leads a free jazz quartet, also plays in Supersession (with Rowe, saxophonist Evan Parker, bassist Barry Guy). An AMM performance usually consists of 90 minutes of continuous improvisation, '. . . something like having one's free associations . . . turned into sound' (*New York Times*). Was influential on other improvisors and avant-garde pop groups.

AMMONS, Albert (*b* '07, Chicago; *d* there 5 Dec.'49) Piano. Playing from age 10; drove taxi in Chicago c.'24, as did Meade Lux LEWIS; appeared around town with various groups, residencies in Chicago clubs '34-8; became more famous when blues-based genre boogie-woogie became national fad late '30s. First records '36 on Decca as Albert Ammons' Rhythm Kings. To NYC '38; appeared Carnegie Hall with Pete JOHNSON and Lewis; trio recorded 'Boogie Woogie Prayer' that year. Accidentally cut tip off a finger while making sandwich '41, later suffered paralysis in both hands, but recovered. At Café Society, etc. often in duo with Johnson. Recorded nine solos, two duets with Lewis, five sides with Port of Harlem Jazzmen for Blue Note, '39; later on other labels, incl. Commodore '44 with Don BYAS, Vic DICKENSON, Hot Lips PAGE and others; later on Mercury, with Sippie WALLACE and with son Gene (see below). Toured USA, played President Truman's inaugural in '49. Complete Blue Notes reissued in limited edition on Mosaic '83.

AMMONS, Gene (*b* 14 Apr. '25, Chicago; *d* there 23 July '74) Tenor sax. Son of Albert AMMONS; aka 'Jug'. Came to prominence with Billy ECKSTINE band '44-7; own group '47-8; then replaced Stan GETZ in Woody HERMAN band. Beginning '50 often teamed with Sonny STITT for friendly hard-blowing tenor contests. Led combo early '60s with tenor and organ; served jail term '62-9 on narcotics charge; resumed tours with rhythm section; died of pneumonia. Veered from straight jazz to R&B honking and back again; always popular and always a fine ballad player: 'This Foolish Heart' made top 10 of R&B chart '50; incl. in 2-disc compilation *Early Visions* ('48-51 material from Chess, released UK '85). More than 40 LPs in print in USA, incl. reissue/compilations: *Gene Ammons Story – 78 Era* '50-5, *Organ Combos* '60-1, *Gentle Jug* '61-2, *Jug & Dodo* (with Marmarosa), all 2-disc sets; five sets with Stitt, from '50s *Blues Up* to *Together Last Time*, '73; all on Prestige except '73 Enja set recorded *In Sweden*.

AMNESTY INTERNATIONAL ALBUMS Amnesty International is a worldwide non-profit organisation that 'works impartially for the release of prisoners of conscience: men and women, detained anywhere for their beliefs, colour, ethnic origin, sex, religion or language'. Won Nobel Peace Prize '77; that year also released first Amnesty benefit LP *Frolics At The Mermaid*, with comic contributions from John Cleese, Peter Cook, Peter Ustinov; musical from Pete ATKIN, Julie COVINGTON. *The Secret Policeman's Ball* '79 incl. solo tracks by Pete Townshend, John WILLIAMS, Neil Innes, Tom ROBINSON. *The Secret Policeman's Other Ball* '82 drew other stars out of their usual orbits: STING performed solo versions of 'Roxanne', 'Message In A Bottle'; BOOMTOWN RAT Bob Geldof sang 'I Don't Like Mondays' to solo piano; Phil COLLINS soloed on 'In The Air Tonight', 'Roof Is Leaking'; Jeff BECK and Eric CLAPTON appeared for the first time together, playing 'Farther On Up The Road' and 'Crossroads'. Amnesty have adopted Bob DYLAN's 'I Shall Be Released' as their anthem; DIRE STRAITS donated their South African royalties; SIMPLE MINDS gave proceeds from 'Ghostdancing'; *Conspiracy Of Hope* '86 incl. tracks by Peter GABRIEL, Paul

McCartney, Dire Straits, Elton John. Planned to launch own label in '87.

AMRAM, David Werner III (*b* 17 Nov. '30, Philadelphia, Pa.) French horn, flute, piano; composer. Played horn in orchestras; jam sessions in own NYC flat, sometimes with Charlie Parker, Dizzy Gillespie. With US 7th Army Symphony '52-4; with Sonny Rollins, Charles Mingus etc. '50s; played horn on quintet LP recorded in Paris '55; several instruments on quartet LP with George Barrow tenor sax NYC '57. Incidental music for stage, TV and films from '56; mus. dir. Lincoln Center, own group Amram-Barrow Quartet at the Five Spot '63-5; led own TV opera *The Final Ingredient*, about Passover ceremony in Nazi camp ABC-TV '65; first composer-in-residence with New York Philharmonic '66-7; own quartet with Pepper Adams '70. Many compositions from late '50s incl. Piano Sonata '60 (tribute to T. Monk and Bud Powell); String Quartet '61; opera *Twelfth Night* '68; Triple Concerto For Woodwinds, Brass, Jazz Quintet, Orchestra '70 (recorded '77 for Flying Fish with Pepper Adams, Rochester Philharmonic); *Native American Portraits* for violin, piano and percussion '76; Violin Concerto '80. Biography *Vibrations* '68; NET documentary *The World Of David Amram* '69. Main infl. are black jazz; minorities, esp. American Indian; own Jewish background. A musical ambassador everywhere: free concerts for children, NYC; travel to Kenya, Central America, Middle East. *En Memoria de Chano Pozo* '77 first heard in Cuba, where Amram troupe was the first USA group to be heard there since '61; piece is incl. in Flying Fish LP *Havana/New York* '77, *Latin-American Jazz Celebration* '82 on Elektra-Musician. Also on Flying Fish: *No More Walls* '78, *At Home/Around The World* '80. All these LPs feature first-rate jazz sidemen; has made 'classical' records as well.

AMY, Curtis Edward (*b* 11 Oct. '29, Houston, Texas) Reeds, flute. Played tenor sax in backing group on single by singer Hubert Robinson, Houston '47; degree in music ed. from Kentucky State College '52; to L.A. '55. LPs on Pacific Jazz with varying personnel incl. *Blues Message* '60 with Les McCann; *Groovin' Blue* '61 with Bobby

Hutcherson; *Meeting Here* '61; *Way Down* '62 with Roy Ayers and Victor Feldman; *Tippin' On Through* '62 with Ayers. *Katanga!* '63 (now on Affinity UK) is fine example of West Coast post-bop jazz, also noteworthy for presence of mysterious Dupree Bolton. *Mustang* on Verve '66 has Kenny Barron on piano (*b* 9 June '43; at Rutgers U. in '73). Amy also played soprano sax on last two LPs, sessioned on pop LPs (Doors *On The Soft Parade*, Carole King's *Tapestries*, etc.).

ANDERS & PONCIA Singers/songwriters, producers Peter Andreoli, Vincent Poncia, both New Yorkers, with intertwined careers. Both members of The Videls, who scored minor hit with 'Mr Lonely' '60; contract writers for Hill & Range music publishers, then with Phil Spector, writing Ronettes hits 'Do I Love You', '(The Best Part Of) Breaking Up', also for Darlene Love, early single by Cher under name of Bonnie Jo Mason. Formed production company, recorded as The Trade Winds ('New York's A Lonely Town', 'Mind Excursion' hits '65-6), The Innocence ('There's Got To Be A Word', 'Mairzy Doats', '67). Signed with WB late '60s, cut *The Anders & Poncia Album*, produced by Richard Perry, and split up. Anders made eponymous solo album '72; Poncia worked with Perry, on six Melissa Manchester LPs, several by Ringo Starr incl. *Bad Boy*, two by Kiss and solo LP by Peter Criss, plus work with Fanny '74, Lynda Carter, Mary Travers both '78, Ellen Foley '83, etc.

ANDERSEN, Arild (*b* 27 Oct. '45, Oslo) Bass. Toured France, Africa with Stan Getz '70; to USA; worked with Sam Rivers, Paul Bley, own group '74; *Flexible Flyer* with Roswell Rudd. Own LPs incl. *Clouds In My Head* '75, *Shimri* '76, *Green Shading Into Blue* '78, *Lifelines* '80 (with Kenny Wheeler), *A Molde Concert* '81, all on ECM.

ANDERSEN, Eric (*b* 14 Feb. '43, Pittsburgh, Pa.) Singer-songwriter in folk style; plays guitar, harmonica. Raised in upstate New York, dropped out of college early '60s; discovered by Tom Paxton '63 sharing a bill with Janis Joplin in San Francisco; soon working Boston area with Joan Baez, Phil Ochs, Judy Collins, etc. Expected to assume mantle of Bob DYLAN when Dylan went electric, he just carried on being Eric: writing songs, touring, occasional album; best-known song probably 'Thirsty Boots'. Signed with Vanguard '64; first LP *Eric Andersen* '65 (aka *Today Is The Highway*) followed by *'Bout Changes And Things, Take 2, More Hits From Tin Can Alley, Country Dream* '66-9, plus 2-disc Vanguard *Best Of*. Switched to WB '69 for LPs *Eric Andersen, Avalanche*; to Columbia for *Blue River* '72, which made Billboard Top Pop Albums; then masters of material for second Columbia LP were lost. Switched to Arista for *Be True To You* '75 which charted, *Sweet Surprise* and *The Best Songs* which did not. Sometimes added electric bass guitar to act from mid-'70s, but emphasis always acoustic; published *Eric Andersen Songbook*, formed music publishing company Wind And Sand which distributes latest albums in USA: *Midnight Sun, Tight In The Night*, film soundtrack *Istanbul* mostly made in Europe; latter to be retitled *Movin' With The Wind* for LP. USA tour late '85 incl. party at NYC Cat Club for 1000 friends: foresees recording other artists, publishing song books, fiction: 'I'm interested in people who really care about what they're doing.' Long-term hard-core fans still being rewarded.

ANDERSON, Alistair (*b* 18 Mar. '48, Wallsend, UK) Concertina and Northumbrian pipes player, composer; learned from pipes masters such as Billy Pigg, in turn passing on knowledge to younger musicians. Began playing blues with schoolmates incl. Dave Richardson (now with Boys of the Lough); took up English concertina '63; part-time with High Level Ranters from '64; LPs with them incl. *Northumberland Forever* '68 on Topic, then *The Lads Of Northumbria* '69 and *Keep Your Feet Still Geordie Hinnie* '70 (Tyneside music hall songs) on Leader. Went full time after first solo LP *Plays English Concertina* '72 on Trailor, followed by *High Level* '72, *A Mile To Ride* '73, all on Leader; LP plus book *Concertina Workshop* '74 on Topic. Other Ranters LPs incl. *The Bonnie Pit Laddie* '75 (2-disc set of mining songs), *Ranting Lads* '76, *Four In A Bar* '79, all on Topic. His own trad. LPs began to incl. own music; good examples of late work are *Traditional Tunes* '77, *Corby Crag*

'78, *Dookin' For Apples* '79 (on Front Hall USA), tradition-based 'linked series' of tunes *Steel Skies* '81 (Flying Fish), all on Topic in UK; the last his masterpiece, showing range of ideas, accommodation of original music in trad. idiom. Also prod. LPs of various Northumbrian pipers on Topic *Cut & Dry, Cut & Dry II* late '70s; worked with Kathryn Tickell on her *Borderlands* on Black Crow and anthology of Northumberland music and poetry *From Sewingshields To Glendale* on MWM, both '86. festival administrator (Rothbury from '76, South Bank Summer Folk from '83); wrote and performed music for Sargasso Sea segment of Anglia TV's *Survival* nature series. *The Grand Chain* '87 on Black Crow has two sets of musicians: a Geordie hootenanny on one side, more like *Steel Skies* on the other.

ANDERSON, Bill (*b* James William Anderson, 1 Nov. '37, Columbia, S.C.) Singer, songwriter; aka 'Whispering Bill'. Guitar at 12; BA in journalism U. of Georgia/Athens; worked as newspaper sportswriter and broadcaster, led semi-pro C&W band The Avondale Playboys; initial impression as songwriter with hits for Ray PRICE ('City Lights'), Jim REEVES ('I Missed Me'), Hank LOCKLIN ('Happy Birthday To Me'), etc. Signed to Decca '58, had 20 years of USA C&W hits: joined Grand Ole Opry '61. After success of 'Po' Folks' '61, formed band The Po' Boys with front man Jimmy Gateley (*b* 1 May '31, Springfield, Mo.; also singer/songwriter, e.g. 'The Minute You're Gone', pop hit for Cliff RICHARD '64); Sonny Garrish, noted steel guitar session man, also in band for 10 years. Singles 'Still', '8×10' crossed to pop chart '63. Duet hits with Jan HOWARD '66-71 incl. no. 1 'For Loving You', top 5 'If It's All The Same To You', 'Someday We'll Be Together', 'Dissatisfied'; also discovered Mary Lou Turner, duet partner in '70s ('Sometimes', 'I Can't Sleep With You'). When records slumped mid-'70s turned to country-disco sound ('I Can't Wait Any Longer', 'Three Times A Lady'); in '80s became TV personality, game-show host (*Mister And Mrs*, Nashville TV's *Fandango*). His second LP since leaving MCA was *A Place In The Country* '87 on his own Whispering label. One of country's most prolific songwriters with more than 1000 to his credit; other hits incl. 'Happiness' (Ken DODD), 'Five Little Fingers' (Frankie McBride), 'Cold Hard Facts Of Life' (Porter WAGONER), 'Tips Of My Fingers' (Roy CLARK).

ANDERSON, Cat (*b* William Alonzo Anderson, 12 Sep. '16, Greenville, S.C.; *d* 29 Apr. '81, Cal.) Trumpet. Raised in orphanage; acquired nickname beating up a bully. With Sunset Royals '38-41 (*see* Doc WHEELER), Erskine HAWKINS, then Lionel HAMPTON '42-4; then Duke ELLINGTON from '44 until '71 except for two short breaks (own band '47). Already known for high notes, playing parts an octave higher than written (originally because the high-note artist got the girls), he was Duke's nonpareil specialist: e.g. 'Jam With Sam' '50; capped famous version of 'Diminuendo in Blue/Crescendo in Blue' at Newport '56; decorated 'Tourist Point Of View' '66 (*Far East Suite*) etc. More versatile than that, however, at his first Ellington rehearsal he played lead parts, later fine plunger mute e.g. on 'A Gatherin' In A Clearing' '46, which he co-wrote, and Billy STRAYHORN's 'Charpoy' '67. 'The Eighth Veil' '50 written for him by Ellington-Strayhorn. To California early '70s; TV and film work, toured with Ice Capades show '74-5, gigs with own groups, Ellington alumni, etc. Own LPs incl. *Cat Speaks* on Classic Jazz label (Paris '77); eponymous set on Inner City.

ANDERSON, Ernestine Irene (*b* 11 Nov. '28, Houston, Texas) Jazz singer, persistently underrated. Began in Russell Jacquet band, Texas '43; then with Eddie HEYWOOD; record 'K.C. Lover' with Shifty Henry's band '47; with Johnny OTIS '47-9; Lionel HAMPTON '52-3; club work NYC; records with Quincy JONES '53, Gigi GRYCE '55; Swedish tour summer '56, with all-stars (Cecil PAYNE, Duke JORDAN, etc.) led by Swedish-American trumpeter Rolf Erickson. Asked to stay on, headlining own dates; made LP *Hot Cargo* with Harry Arnold Orchestra: released USA on Mercury to critical acclaim. LP *Ernestine Anderson* with Pete Rugolo '58; won Downbeat critics New Star award '59; more LPs for Mercury, others; lived in Europe for a while. Back in USA sang 'He Says He Loves Me' for soundtrack of Sidney Poitier film *The Lost Man* '69, but

had been largely forgotten; returned home to Northwest. Sang at Turnwater Conservatory backed by bassist Red Kelly, Select Jazz Weekend at Qualicum Beach B. C. '75, attracting attention of Ray BROWN, who became her manager; hit at Concord Jazz Festival '76, leading to contract with new Concord label: first album in many years *Hello Like Before* '76, with Brown, Hank JONES, Jimmie Smith, led to more: *Live From Concord To London, Sunshine, Never Make Your Move Too Soon* (nominated for Grammy '81), *Big City* '83, *When The Sun Goes Down* '84, *Be Mine Tonight* '87 with Benny CARTER; sings on *Live At The Alley Cat* '87 with CAPP-PIERCE big band.

ANDERSON, Fred (*b* 22 Mar. '29, Monroe, La.) Tenor saxophone. Played with piano as a small child; to Evanston, Ill. age 10, took up saxophone; infl. by Lester YOUNG, Gene AMMONS, Charlie PARKER, but went his own way, developing a 'metallic cocaine bebop' (J. B. Figi). Encouraged by Von FREEMAN, another Chicagoan with a unique tone; in turn employed young Chico FREEMAN in one of his groups. Then he heard Ornette COLEMAN: 'I didn't feel like I was alone, 'cause they were laughin' at *him*.' Founder member of AACM '64; plays on Joseph JARMAN's *Song For* '67; made LP *Accents* '77 with Austrian pianist Dieter Glawischnigg on EMI; own LPs incl. quintet *Another Place* '78 on Moers Music, with trombonist George Lewis, made live at Moers; quartet sets *Dark Day* '79 on Australian Message label, made at Chicago Museum of Contemporary Art, and *The Missing Link* '79 on Nessa. First two incl. longtime Chicago collaborator Bill Brimfield on trumpet; all feature Hamid Hank Drake, a younger drummer, born in Monroe.

ANDERSON, Ivie (*b* 10 July '05, Gilroy, Cal.; *d* 28 Dec. '49, L.A.) Singer. Also sometimes 'Ivy'. Dancer, singer at Cotton Club '25; toured in review *Shuffle Along*; worked with Paul Howard, Anson WEEKS; toured Australia '28; with Earl HINES '30, then from '31 with Duke ELLINGTON. One of the best girl singers of the era: warm, distinctive vocal colour, excellent pitch and diction, great respect for lyrics, rapport with audiences. Sensation at London Palladium with 'Stormy Weather', '33; sang 'All God's

Chillun Got Rhythm' in Marx Bros film *A Day At The Races* '37. Among dozens of fine records with Ellington: 'It Don't Mean A Thing', '32; 'I'm Satisfied', '33; 'Rose Of The Rio Grande' and 'A Lonely Coed', both '38; 'Rocks In My Bed', '41; 'I Don't Mind', '42. Asthma forced retirement from fulltime music to operate restaurant in L.A. Made last recordings '46 with 'all-stars' incl. Charles MINGUS, Willie SMITH.

ANDERSON, John (*b* 13 Dec. '54, Apopka, Fla.) Country singer in trad. '50s honkytonk style. To Nashville after high school; contracts first as songwriter, then singer; to WB label, began with small hits: 'I've Got A Feelin' (Somebody's Stealin')' '77; 'Whine, Whistle Whine' and 'The Girl At The End Of The Bar' '78; 'My Pledge Of Love' and 'Low Dog Blues' '79; then bigger hits: 'Your Lying Blue Eyes' '79; '1959' '80; 'I'm Just An Old Chunk Of Coal' '81; 'I Just Came Home To Count The Memories' '82. Hardcore country blues 'Swingin' this' crossed over to pop chart '83; 'Black Sheep' '84 'Eye Of A Hurricane' '85 were further country hits. LPs since early '81: *Wild And Blue, I Just Came Home To Count The Memories, All The People Are Talkin', Greatest Hits, Eye Of A Hurricane*; then *Tokyo, Oklahoma* '85, *Countryfied* '86; *Blue Skies Again* '88 on MCA.

ANDERSON, Laurie (*b* Laura Phillips Anderson, 5 June '50) Violinist, composer, singer, performance artist. Resident of lower Manhattan loft scene early '70s; began as sculptor, presented 12-hour long audio-visual experience *The Life And Times Of Joseph Stalin* at Brooklyn Academy of Music '73. Eight minute single 'O Superman' (from LP *Big Science*) voted 'most likely to clear dance floors' by brain-damaged disco generation in UK, but reached no. 2 there '82. EP *Mr Heartbreak* expanded to LP '83; it is a good introduction to her work for the fainthearted. Most of her work is part of the spectacular *United States* (recorded live in four parts – transportation, politics, money, love – in Brooklyn '84, issued on five discs, four tapes; picture-book published '83: 76 titled sections contain multi-tracking, synthesisers, accordion, visual puns, bagpipes, digital electric violin, backing vocalists and much

else; compelling or repelling, depending on the listener. Her work reflects the difficulty of portraying the modern USA; she is also interested in the other mysterious 20th-century place: a visit to the USSR with Harry BELAFONTE and Leonard BERNSTEIN was cancelled in '84. 'There are numerous themes in Anderson's work but no arguments. She appears to be obsessed by the passing of time, about dreams, technology and its threat, communication, language, and about her status and function as an artist.' Concert/soundtrack LP *Home Of The Brave* '86 co-prod. by Nile Rogers; 'Each song, according to Anderson, is as much about camera movement and artistic effect as it is about music' (quotes from Robin Denselow in the *Observer*). Single from *Home Of The Brave*, 'Language Is A Virus From Outer Space', has its title taken from novelist William S. Burroughs.

ANDERSON, Leroy (*b* 29 June '08, Cambridge, Mass.; *d* 18 May '75, Woodbury, Conn.) Composer, arranger, conductor. Graduated with honours from Harvard, '29; choirmaster, organist, bass player with orchestras; arranger with Arthur Fiedler's Boston Pops from '35. Clever little orchestral works often introduced by Fiedler; under own name 'The Syncopated Clock' written '46 no. 12 hit USA '51; lovely 'Blue Tango' in charts 38 weeks '51, reached no. 1. 'Forgotten Dreams' charted UK '57. Comps. incl. 'Sleigh Ride', 'Fiddle Faddle'. Compilation LP on MCA. Wrote score of Broadway musical *Goldilocks* '58.

ANDERSON, Liz (*b* Elizabeth Jane Haaby, 13 Mar. '30, Roseau, Minn.) Country singer, songwriter. Husband Casey Anderson (they married '46); daughter Lynn ANDERSON. Worked as secretary; initial success as songwriter, with 'Pick Of The Week', Roy DRUSKY '64; '(My Friends Are Gonna Be) Strangers', Drusky and Merle HAGGARD '65; 'Guess My Eyes Were Bigger Than My Heart', Conway TWITTY '66; 'Ride, Ride, Ride', Lynn Anderson '66; 'The Fugitive', Haggard '67. Own records on RCA from '64; made several LPs, single hits 'Mama Spank' '66, 'Tiny Tears' '67, 'Husband Hunting' '70; signed to Epic label '72 but no more hits.

ANDERSON, Lynn (*b* Lynn Rene Anderson, 26 Sep. '47, Grand Forks, N.D.) Country-pop singer, daughter of Liz ANDERSON. Attended schools Cal., worked as secretary, signed to Chart label Nashville '66, hit 'Ride, Ride, Ride' that year written by Liz; 'If I Kiss You', 'Promises, Promises' '67; 'No Other Time' '68; 'That's A No-No' '69. Married producer/writer Glenn Sutton '68; signed with Columbia '70; single 'Stay There Till I Get There' was in C&W top 10 as she appeared at second Wembley Country Festival, London. Recording of Joe SOUTH song '(I Never Promised You A) Rose Garden' '71 crossed over to no. 3 on pop chart, won gold disc, Grammy for best female vocal; then further country hits: 'You're My Man', 'How Can I Unlove You' '71; 'Listen To A Country Song' '72; 'Keep Me In Mind', 'Top Of The World' '73; 'What A Man, My Man Is' '74; 'I've Never Loved Anyone More' '75; 'Wrap Your Love All Around Your Man' '77; 'Isn't It Always Love' '79. Divorced mid-'70s, remarried, retired to concentrate on riding horses; back to Wembley '84. LPs *Greatest Hits*, *Rose Garden*.

ANDREWS, Chris (*b* '42, Romford, Essex) UK singer-songwriter, producer. Served musical apprenticeship in pre-BEATLE Hamburg; in Jack Good's *Oh Boy!* on UK TV late '50s; formed Chris Ravel and the Ravers for stage work. Regular at London's R&B Flamingo Club early '60s. Wrote Mersey-styled 'The First Time' for Adam FAITH (UK no. 5, '63); next year teamed with Faith discovery Sandie SHAW to produce and often write series of varied hits '64-6, incl. 'Girl Don't Come'; bouncy no. 1 'Long Live Love', allegedly written in five minutes; 'Message Understood'. Charted in his own name '65 with 'Yesterday Man', a song Shaw rejected: made no. 3 UK, went gold in Germany; and 'To Whom It May Concern', no. 13 hit. Shaw and Andrews got back together after her 'Puppet On A String', '67 Eurovision win with writers/producers Bill Martin and Phil Coulter; his own 'Pretty Belinda' was good worldwide seller '69, though not a UK hit. They faded in early '70s. 'Puppet' Euro winner had a calypso-derived 'oom-pah-pah' style cloned from Andrews' 'Yesterday Man'; next year's Martin-Coulter Euro hit (Cliff RICHARD's 'Congratulations') established it as Euro sound, a legacy Andrews didn't deserve. He worked in Europe; returned to UK '77 with Faith as manager, made Epic LP *Who Is This Man*, without much success. Robert WYATT did good cover of 'Yesterday Man' '77.

ANDREWS, Julie (*b* Julia Elizabeth Wells, 1 Oct. '35, Walton-on-Thames, Surrey, UK) Actress, singer. Performed in music halls as a child in Ted and Barbara Andrews' family act. In London show *Starlight Roof* '47; on radio late '40s-50s especially in series *Educating Archie*, starring with ventriloquist Peter Brough's dummy. Very English voice ideal for typical British musical roles: played Polly Brown in NYC prod. of *The Boy Friend* '54, then major triumph in LERNER & LOEWE's *My Fair Lady* NYC '56, London '58, introducing songs 'Wouldn't It Be Loverly', 'I Could Have Danced All Night'. Played Queen Guinevere in their *Camelot* '60. Ignored by casting dir. when *My Fair Lady* filmed '64 (in favour of Audrey Hepburn, whose singing voice had to be dubbed by Marni Nixon); gained lead same year in Walt Disney film *Mary Poppins*, won Oscar for Best Actress. Many other films incl. *Sound Of Music* '65 (one of the biggest grossers of all time), *Thoroughly Modern Millie* '67, *Star!* '68 (playing Gertrude LAWRENCE), *Darling Lili* '69, etc. ABC-TV variety series flopped '73; had hit Las Vegas night club act '76. Second husband, dir. Blake Edwards, once described her image as so sweet that people think she probably has violets between her legs; she challenged image by appearing nude in film *S.O.B.* '81, then played woman passing as female impersonator in *Victor, Victoria* '81. Once wore badge 'Mary Poppins is a Junkie'. Became country singer '83 with LP *Love Me Tender* (title cut duet with Johnny CASH). CBS LP *Broadway's Fair Julie* '62 reissued on Cameo UK '84; album *Love, Julie* '87 on USA, backed by quintet.

ANDREWS SISTERS Close harmony vocal trio from Minneapolis, Minn. LaVerne (*b* 6 July '15; *d* '67), Maxene (*b* 3 Jan. '18) and Patti (*b* 16 Feb. '20), who sang lead. Went on RKO theatre circuit c. '31 in show with 55 people; learned a lot and decided to stick with it. Maxene sang high harmony, LaVerne was a contralto. First record was 'Why Talk About Love?'/'A Simple Melody' '37; struck it rich with 'Bei Mir Bist Du Schön'. Took up where BOSWELL SISTERS left off and are still biggest girl group ever, said to have sold 60 million records. Big hits incl. 'Pistol Packin' Mama' '43 (with Bing CROSBY), 'Rum and Coca Cola' '44 (considered sexy at the time), 'Don't Fence Me In' '44 and 'South America, Take It Away' '46, (both with Bing), 'Winter Wonderland' '47 (with Guy LOMBARDO). Many other hits, some with Danny KAYE, Judy GARLAND, Les PAUL, Russ MORGAN, Carmen MIRANDA; cashed in on boogie-woogie fad with 'Rhumboogie', 'Beat Me Daddy Eight To The Bar', etc. Appeared in films incl. *Buck Privates* and *Hold That Ghost* '41 with Abbott & Costello, *Hollywood Canteen* '44, *Road To Rio* '47 (with Crosby and Bob Hope). Sound, along with that of Glenn MILLER, Vera LYNN, causes wartime nostalgia for millions; like Miller, they had hits with American chestnuts ('Beer Barrel Polka'), covers of hits by others: Fats WALLER's 'Hold Tight', Orrin TUCKER's 'Oh Johnny'. Patti had own hit 'I Can Dream, Can't I?' '49, with Gordon JENKINS. Though semi-retired from late '50s, Patti appeared in film *The Phynx* '69, with Maxene in Broadway show *Over Here* '74-5, as well as occasional TV spots, etc. Bette MIDLER hit 'Boogie Woogie Bugler Boy' '73 was cover of theirs. Maxene had heart attack '82 after 11 concerts in Chicago, followed by heart by-pass operation; made first solo LP '85 arr. by Arnold Goland. Midler wrote sleeve note for *Maxene* on Bainridge label: incl. medley of sisters' hits, new songs (e.g. 'I Suppose', written by Nancy Goland).

ANDY, Bob (*b* Keith Anderson) Jamaican singer, songwriter whose exquisitely crafted *Songbook* album for Studio One, compiling sides made for that label in the mid-'60s, is considered to be among the finest works in the island's brief history of recording. After a short stint with rock steady vocal group the Paragons, he went solo mid-'60s and almost immediately made his mark with the diasporic 'I've Got To Go Back Home', with Peter Tosh, Bunny Wailer on harmony vocals. Other hits incl. 'Let Them Say', 'Experience', 'Going Home', 'Born A Man'; in

'70 he teamed with former Studio One labelmate Marcia Griffiths for duet on Nina SIMONE's 'Young Gifted And Black' for Harry J, an international hit. Duet LP of the same name was soon followed by the duo's *Pied Piper*; after one of his periodic bouts of inactivity came solo set *The Music Inside Me* '75, *Lots Of Love And I* c.'77; he retired again, came back mid-'80s with tours and new LPs *Friends* and *Retrospective* on his own I-Anka label.

ANDY, Horace (*b* Horace Hinds) Prolific Jamaican singer and guitarist, with an unusually distinctive choking tenor voice. After first recording '66, he retired to perfect his vocal technique, came back in '70 to make hits at Studio One: *Skylarking* LP contained title track, 'See A Man's Face', 'Just Say Who', 'Love Of A Woman'; further sessions were collected on the label's *Best Of* album later in the decade. Left Brentford Road early '70s to freelance on local labels such as Derrick Harriott's Crystal and Leonard Chin's Santic, as well as Randy's, Ja-Man, Channel One; producers like Keith Hudson, Niney, Yabby You, Phil Pratt, and in '73 with Bunny Lee's Jackpot label for a few dozen singles, LPs *You Are My Angel* and *Sings For You And I*. Emigrated to the USA, settled in Connecticut, set up own Rhythm label, released singles like 'Control Yourself', 'Good Vibes' and a cover of Delroy Wilson's 'Won't You Come Home'. Returned briefly to Jamaica '80 and teamed with Tapper Zukie, who prod. his biggest hit so far, 'Natty Dread A Weh She Want', and LP of that name. He has remained busy and estimates that he's written over 300 songs, many found on LPs like *Showcase*, *In The Light*, *Pure Ranking*, *Dance Hall Style*, *Exclusively*, *Confusion*, electronic set *Elementary* '86.

ANIMALS British R&B band, formed Newcastle '60 as Alan Price Combo: Price (*b* 19 Apr. '42, Co. Durham), vocals, keyboards; Hilton Valentine (*b* 2 May '43, North Shields), guitar; John Steel (*b* 4 Feb. '41, Gateshead), drums; Bryan 'Chas' Chandler (*b* 18 Dec. '38, Newcastle), bass. Wild stage act after Eric BURDON recruited as lead singer, suggested new name. Worked in northeast backing visiting USA blues artists (gig with Sonny Boy WILLIAMSON issued on

LP in '70s); to London early '64, as demand for British R&B, created by success of ROLLING STONES, became competition for 'Mersey' sound of BEATLES and others. Produced by Mickie MOST, Animals raided Bob DYLAN's first LP for 'Baby Let Me Follow You Down' (retitled 'Baby Let Me Take You Home') and trad. 'House Of The Rising Sun'; on the latter, crisp pop production of Price's rolling organ and Burdon's gritty vocal (more 'authentic' sound than Jagger) made transatlantic no. 1 despite its length: over four minutes for a single unheard of then. LPs *Animals* '64, *Animal Tracks* '65 limited to repertoire of blues workouts, but singles consistent winners: Most's shrewd choice of material brought six top tens in UK by end '65; all hits in USA too: e.g. 'Don't Let Me Be Misunderstood' (Nina SIMONE), 'Bring It On Home To Me' (Sam COOKE), 'We Gotta Get Out Of This Place' (MANN-WEIL). Price's departure that year hastened split from Most and pursuit of bluesier approach on records; Price was replaced by Dave Rowberry (*b* 4 July '40, Newcastle, ex-Mike Cotton Sound). After two more hit singles, change of labels, third LP *Animalisms* '66, band split up, Burdon taking recently acquired drummer Barry Jenkins (ex-NASHVILLE TEENS) to start new group under same name (see separate entry for Burdon). Price became MOR pop star; Valentine made solo LP *All In Your Head* '69, found religion, left the scene; Chandler entered management with Jimi HENDRIX, later with SLADE, Steel his assistant. Subsequent reunions incl. '68 Xmas concert at Newcastle, lacklustre LP *Before We Were So Rudely Interrupted* '76 on Chandler's Barn label. POLICE manager Miles Copeland inspired world tour, LP *Ark* on his IRS label '83; by this time only Burdon still had the stage presence that gave them their name. Original schizoid melange of pop and R&B mirrored mixture of personalities but singles remain '60s classics.

ANKA, Paul (*b* 30 July '41, Ottawa) Singer-songwriter, entrepreneur; teen idol proved to be more than just a pretty face. Syrian parents; first disc 'I Confess' '56 on local label after he buttonholed record execs while on Hollywood holiday; paid off when ABC's Don COSTA signed him up. 'Diana' no. 1 USA '57; worldwide hit sold 9 million by '61, said to have been written for baby-sitter five years his senior. Precocious teen followed up with other hits, provided clean-cut alternative to Elvis PRESLEY ilk. Buddy HOLLY recorded his 'It Doesn't Matter Any More' '58; 'Puppy Love' '60 (no. 2 USA) typical mawkish ballad, dedicated to Anka's then girl-friend ANNETTE. Made several screen appearances, notably D-Day epic *The Longest Day* '62 (also wrote title song). Left ABC for RCA as newer stars eclipsed him, but shrewdly bought his own masters (since periodically reissued). TV, cabaret work along with writing; wrote 'Johnny's Theme' for Carson *Tonight* TV show; translation of French singer-songwriter Claude François' lyric gave Frank SINATRA (and Sid Vicious, many others) 'My Way' '68. Legacy in teen stars Donny OSMOND, David CASSIDY, etc. who covered early sentimental hits; but continues to do well on his own: 32 USA top 40 hits '57-83 incl. no. 1 '74 with 'You're Having My Baby', no. 7 with 'One Man Woman'/'One Woman Man', duets with Odia Coates, produced in Muscle Shoals; further top 10 hits 'I Don't Like To Sleep Alone' and 'Times Of Your Life' '75; latest top 40 entry 'Hold Me 'Til The Mornin' Comes' '83; LP *Walk A Fine Line*.

ANNETTE (*b* Annette Funicello, 22 Oct. '42, Utica, NY) Singer, actress. Family moved to West Coast '46. Became Mouseketeer on Mickey Mouse Club, Disney kiddie TV show, '55; most Mouseketeers were retired at a certain age, but Disney turned her popularity into recording career: she had four top 20 singles '59-60, beginning with 'Tall Paul'. Three LPs charted, incl. *Annette's Beach Party*, '63; her prettiness featured in movies (*Bikini Beach*, *Muscle Beach Party*) playing opposite Tommy Kirk or Frankie AVALON. Arrival of BEATLE's first movie *A Hard Day's Night* '64 caused instant demise of genre. Later did TV ads; turns up on American Bandstand anniversary shows.

ANN-MARGRET (*b* Ann-Margret Olsson, 28 Apr. '41, Valsjobyn, Sweden) Singer, dancer, actress. Came to USA '46. Runner-up at 16 on Ted Mack's *Original Amateur Hour*. Pro debut '58 with band in Kansas City; graduated high school '59; to Northwestern U., joined combo called Suttletones, went solo. Hired by George Burns for Vegas Xmas show '60; signed to RCA. Top 20 single 'I Just Don't Understand' '61; well-crafted LPs *And Here She Is* '61, *On The Way Up* '62, *Bachelor's Paradise* '63, *Beauty And The Beard* (with Al HIRT, '64). Broke into films: singing roles incl. *State Fair* '62; *Bye Bye Birdie* '63, *Viva Las Vegas* '64 (co-starred with Elvis PRESLEY). More films; typecast as big-bosomed sex symbol; two Sour Apple awards from Hollywood's Women's Press Club for lack of cooperation '60s, but *Carnal Knowledge* '71 brought Oscar nomination. Fell 22 feet from stage Hotel Sahara, Lake Tahoe '72; nearly killed, but soon back in action. Played Roger Daltrey's mother in film of The WHO's *Tommy* '75; much-praised role in *Return Of The Soldier* '82; has continued singing.

ANT, Adam (*b* Stuart Leslie Goddard, 3 Nov. '54, London) Punk rock/new wave star of early '80s; art student/semi-pro bassist inspired by '76 punk explosion to form band The Ants. Small part in Derek Jarman's *Jubilee* movie ('78, with TOYAH), remained little-known; Nazi references in lyrics and six different lineups from Apr. '77-Oct. '79 didn't help. LP *Dirk Wears White Socks* (on Do It, '79) made UK independent chart, but break came with appointment of ex-SEX PISTOLS manager Malcolm McLaren as 'consultant'. He poached Ants – Dave Barbe, drums; Matthew Ashman, guitar; Lee Gorman, bass – to back protégé Annabella Lwin in BOW WOW WOW, but left Adam 'noble savage' image of facepaint and frills. Updating Gary GLITTER double-drum kit sound with dash of Burundi rhythms, Adam and writing partner Marco Pirroni (ex-Models) hit chord with sated punk audience; whole UK soon followed suit: seven top 10 hits '80-1 incl. 'Prince Charming' and 'Stand And Deliver' at no. 1. With CBS marketing muscle *Kings Of The Wild Frontier* '80 no. 1 LP; *Prince Charming* made no. 2. Inventive videos directed by Mike Mansfield (later by Adam himself) depicted him as highwayman, pirate, armoured knight, and captured even more fans. Sacked band Spring '82 (final lineup was Gary Tibbs, bass; Chris 'Merrick' Hughes and Terry Lee Miall, drums), retained guitarist Pirroni for disappointing solo LP *Friend Or Foe* '82; though

rockabilly-infl. single 'Goody Two-Shoes' made no. 1, follow-up flopped; with advent of new teen idols (Culture Club, WHAM!) LP *Strip* '83 only made no. 20. Spent next year in USA, where videos had become belated MTV cable channel success. Despite one-off single hit 'Apollo Nine' late '84, star was on the wane. Music described by *Stereo Review* USA as 'profoundly defiant drivel', but dropout design student a millionaire at 30. Appeared at Live Aid '85, LP *Vive Le Rock* same year; tour cancelled owing to poor ticket sales; *Hits* video/LP collection '86 as he went into acting.

ANTHONY, Ray (*b* Raymond Antonini, 20 Jan. '22, Bentleyville, Pa.) Trumpet, leader. Played '40-2 with Glenn MILLER, Jimmy DORSEY, then own band with unusual line-up: 1 trumpet, 1 French horn, 5 saxes, 3 rhythm. US Navy '42-6, led band in Pacific; own post-war band, conventional good dance band. Eight singles charted '50-4; biggest hit was 'Dragnet', TV cop show theme; Anthony also co-writer of pop novelty 'The Bunny Hop'; single 'Dancing In The Dark' won award as best dance band record c.'53. Was married to actress Mamie Van Doren. Extensive tour of colleges '53; TV work with Helen O'Connell, Bob Eberly same year; film appearance in *Daddy Long Legs* '55; further TV work, reviews, clubs; bought Billy MAY band '54, hired Sam DONAHUE to front it. Disbanded, formed combo for club work; band in Las Vegas '80; founded Big Bands '80s to furnish sound to schools, radio. Capitol albums *Plays For Dream Dancing, Swingin' On Campus, Houseparty Hop* reissued '84-5 by EMI UK (the first was no. 10 LP USA '56).

AOR Music business merchandising term, originally FM radio in USA: 'Album Oriented Rock', 'Album Oriented Radio', then 'Adult Oriented Rock'. A good idea in early '70s when 'progressive' rock was 'underground' music: playing longer cuts from LPs was move away from singles mentality at a time when more LPs were being sold and singles were less important. Soon became a formula, sold by consultants to stations that couldn't do it themselves; now regarded as boring because pop music has acquired sameness, but also because FM radio has reached big commercial success:

DJs are not allowed to exercise personal choice, which is where we started from. Now stands for 'All Over the Road' (or same as MOR, 'middle of the road', another merchandising term).

APHRODITE'S CHILD Greek pop trio formed '63: Demis ROUSSOS, Evangelos Papathanassiou (*b* 15 June '47, Velos) and Lucas Sideras (*b* 5 Dec. '44, Athens). All came from musical families and played several instruments. Greece was more resistant to Anglo-USA pop style at this time than any other country in Europe; on their way to London '68 they were signed to Philips by Pierre Sberre in Paris, who produced 'Rain And Tears'; 17th-century German song sung in English was a massive hit in France, no. 2 in Italy, no. 3 in Turkey, made top 10 in Belgium, Netherlands, Spain, Lebanon; no. 30 UK; did not make Greek top 20; nothing in USA. Hits in Southern Europe followed, incl. 'It's Five O'Clock' and 'Spring, Summer, Winter And Fall' (both '70). *666* 2-disc album did well on the Continent, but UK success eluded them. Split in mid-'70s; Roussos became successful solo; Evangelos teamed with Jon Anderson (*see* YES) as Jon and Vangelis: LPs *Short Stories* and *Friends Of Mr Cairo* '80-1; singles 'I Hear You Now' and 'I'll Find My Way Home' both top 10. He then became composer of synthesised film music as Vangelis: theme single and soundtrack LP from *Chariots Of Fire* topped many charts '81 incl. USA. He was sued by EMI on behalf of Stavros Logarides over similarity of *Chariot* theme to latter's TV theme 'City Of Violets'; EMI lost '87. His other UK hit LPs incl. *Heaven And Hell* and *Albedo 0.39* '76 on RCA, *Soil Festivities* and *Mask* '84-5, like *Chariots*, on Polydor.

APOLLO THEATRE NYC mecca for black artists '34-'80. Former Hurtig & Seamon's burlesque theatre closed as authorities cracked down on risqué shows; owner Sidney Cohen closed another smaller theatre, took its name for 125th Street Apollo, opened 26 Jan. '34; established Wednesday as amateur night. As battle shaped up between Cohen and Frank Schiffman (formerly operated the Lafayette, then the Harlem Opera House), Cohen died: Schiffman took over larger venue, better location '35, turning Opera House over to films; made Apollo premier location for black entertainment, called Mother Church or 'uptown Palace' (downtown Palace was top venue for white vaudeville); variety shows incl. comics, dancers, bands, singers; chorus line best in the business (but not highest paid) until phased out early '40s on grounds of cost. White comics Milton Berle, Joey Adams etc. came to steal jokes; white acts successful at Apollo incl. Charlie BARNET band, others; but every black act wanted to try for unique success with Harlem audience: largest black community in the world had no political power, escaped from racism, welfare queues to see its own great talent at the Apollo and gave short shrift to acts that didn't make it but bestowed instant fame on those who did. Winners of amateur night going on to stardom incl. Lena HORNE, Pearl BAILEY, Sarah VAUGHAN, Ruth BROWN, Sam COOKE, KING CURTIS, Marvin GAYE, many more. Second balcony was called Buzzard's Roost: act which died onstage got bones metaphorically picked, but fans in ecstasy jumped from balcony, allegedly inspiring arr. for Earl HINES band 'Second Balcony Jump'. Seminal vocal group the ORIOLES late '40s were smash harbinger of things to come; during '50s variety lost out: there were gospel nights, African ballet, off-Broadway plays, but mainly R&B/soul acts with hit records dominated Apollo in its last two decades (Elvis PRESLEY paid visit months before his own stardom). Schiffman's son Bobby kept unique relationship with black stars, but success of blacks in charts, on TV caused Apollo to lose importance: last show was George Clinton's PARLIAMENT/FUNKADELIC in March '83. Officially designated New York City landmark, reopened as theatre/cable TV centre for 50th anniversary. *Showtime At The Apollo* '85 by Ted Fox tells full story.

APPICE, Carmine (*b* 15 Dec. '46, Staten Island, NY) Veteran rock drummer. With seven years' experience and three of formal training, joined East Coast group The Pigeons late '66; group renamed VANILLA FUDGE, almost alone defined heavy metal genre with sound based on Appice's bedrock style, series of LPs on Atlantic. Formed Cactus with bassist Tim Bogert and ex-Amboy Dukes Rusty Day in Feb. '70, then 'supergroup' Beck, Bogert and Appice Aug. '72 ('69 plans had been thwarted by Beck's car crash). This group split '74; Appice joined even shorter-lived KGB (Ray Kennedy, Mike BLOOMFIELD, Rick Grech) '76 for two LPs, joined Rod STEWART (another ex-Beck sideman) '77. Co-wrote '78 transatlantic no. 1 'Da Ya Think I'm Sexy' with Stewart, but wrangle with Brazilian singer Jorge Ben over tune marred success; royalties donated to UNICEF. Solo LP *Carmine Appice* '81, with Stewart band members Danny Johnson, guitar; Jay Davis, bass; Duane Hutchings, keyboards (this had also been final Cactus lineup). By '84 replaced in Stewart's group by Tony Brock (ex-BABYS). Short stint backing Ozzy Osbourne ended acrimoniously with ego clash. With wide experience of styles, having played with Stanley CLARKE, Bo DIDDLEY, Ted NUGENT etc. Formed new band King Kobra '85, LP *Ready To Strike*. Younger brother Vinnie also drums; sometime member of BLACK SABBATH.

ARDOIN, Amadé (*b* before 1900, l'Anse Rougeau, La.; *d* '30s, Pineville, La.) Name also spelled Amédé, Amadie. Cajun accordionist, vocalist; cited by Nathan ABSHIRE, Clifton CHENIER, Leo SOILEAU, Iry LeJune, Austin Pitre as a major influence; his importance to the genre is like that of Robert JOHNSON in the BLUES and as with Johnson, details of his life are shrouded in mystery: most of what we know comes from the memory of fiddler Dennis McGee (*b* 26 Jan. 1893, Eunice, La.), who worked with him from '21. He is supposed to have died in the state mental hospital at Pineville, yet the Louisiana State Bureau of Vital Statistics has no record of his birth or death: his memorial is his body of work. His colour was evidently no hindrance to entertaining white audiences; he was a gifted musician, adept at spontaneously improvising songs and lyrics, very much with a blues heart yet in the Cajun idiom, drawing on African songs and hollers as well as trad. Acadian and Old French material. He and McGee were popular around Eunice, recorded independently and together late '20s/early '30s; pieces from Ardoin's repertoire incl. 'Eunice Two-Step', 'La Valse à Abe', 'Les Blues de la Prison', 'Madame Etienne' have

become standards. Records incl. *Amadé Ardoin – Louisiana Cajun Music Vol. 6* on Old Timey; anthology *The Early Recordings Of Dennis McGee* on Morning Star incl. some Ardoin accompaniment.

AREA CODE 615 Country-rock group formed Nashville '69, named after local telephone code: Charlie McCoy (*b* 28 Mar. '41), harmonica, vocals; Mac Gayden, guitar, vocals; Weldon Myrick, steel; Kenny Buttrey, drums; Bobby Thompson, banjo, guitar; Wayne Moss, guitar; Buddy Spicher, fiddle; Norbert Putnam, bass; Ken Lauber, keyboards. Ace session men capitalised on media focus on Nashville after Bob DYLAN's LP *Nashville Skyline*, on which long-time Dylan sidemen McCoy and Buttrey played. First LP *Area Code 615* predictably faultless in execution; Lauber replaced by David Briggs on next LP *Trip In The Country* '70, incl. 'Stone Fox Chase': harmonica instrumental became theme for BBC-TV's *Old Grey Whistle Test* through '70s. Most members returned to more lucrative session playing; Gayden went solo; Moss formed Barefoot Jerry: several LPs '70s on which many of the others have played, incl. Gayden on debut *Southern Delight* '71. Putnam and Briggs are producers in Nashville.

ARGENT, Rod (*b* 14 June '45, St Albans) UK rock keyboardist. Success came early with first group ZOMBIES winning talent contest straight out of school, transatlantic hit with second song 'She's Not There' '64. Resisted alleged six-figure offers to revive band after posthumous USA success, formed Argent instead, with Russell Ballard (*b* 31 Oct. '47, Waltham Cross), guitar, vocals; Jim Rodford (*b* 7 July '45, St Albans), bass; drummer Robert Henrit (*b* 2 May '46, Broxbourne). Argent (with ex-Zombie Chris White) and Ballard (ex-Roulettes, Unit 4+2) wrote the songs; Henrit, Argent's cousin, recruited from Unit 4+2. (Argent and White formed songwriting/production partnership Nexus Productions; they guided early '70s solo career of their former colleague Colin BLUNSTONE.) Zombie-esque LP *Argent* '70, heavier *Ring Of Hands* critically well received; *Ring* provided 'Liar', USA hit for THREE DOG NIGHT. Breakthrough came with *All Together Now*, hit single 'Hold Your Head Up', no. 5 in UK and USA. *In Deep* '73, live LP *Encore* and *Nexus* '74 followed by Ballard's departure, allowing Argent's pseudo-classical pretensions full rein; replacements John Verity (*b* 2 May '44), vocals, rhythm guitar, and John Grimaldi (*b* 25 May '55), lead guitar, couldn't redress balance: music declined in welter of synthesisers and band split '76 after two more LPs. Commercial edge which set band apart from YES, EMERSON, LAKE & PALMER etc. was only present in mid-period work; original lineup promised more than they delivered. Verity, Rodford and Henrit recorded unsuccessfully as Phoenix before Rodford joined KINKS; Verity then had own band, Henrit went into musical instrument retailing. Argent played numerous sessions (Chris Rea, WHO etc.), founded retail keyboard shop in London. Returned to records on MCA '78 with jazz-influenced LP *Moving Home*; all-star group incl. Phil COLLINS, Al Johnson of WEATHER REPORT, but chosen genre limited success compared to earlier work. Has done session, film, TV, prod. work; close to Andrew LLOYD WEBBER; played on his *Variations* '78. Recorded with Barbara THOMPSON '83-4; re-formed own group for charity appearance after fire at Bradford City Football Club '85.

ARLEN, Harold (*b* Hyman Arluck, 15 Feb. '05, Buffalo, NY; *d* 23 Apr. '86, NYC) Songwriter. Fell in love with jazz, played piano in cafés at 15, led a jazz band; played in pit band for *George White's Scandals Of 1928*; had songs published '28 ('The Album Of My Dreams' recorded by Rudy VALLEE) but never intended to be a songwriter. Hired by Vincent YOUMANS to play rehearsal piano for *Great Day!* '29, began to write tune on introductory vamp, Will Marion COOK advised him to publish it before somebody stole it: result was his first big hit 'Get Happy' (with words by Ted Koehler, *b* 14 July 1894, Washington DC). Were signed to write songs for COTTON CLUB revues (replacing Jimmy McHUGH and Dorothy Fields, who were busy on Broadway); they wrote 'Between The Devil And The Deep Blue Sea', 'I've Got The World On A String', 'Kickin' The Gong Around' and 'Minnie The Moocher's Wedding Day' (for Cab CALLOWAY), 'Stormy Weather' (always

associated with Ethel WATERS), 'As Long As I Live' (introduced by Lena HORNE at age 16), plus many more, all '31-4. They also wrote 'I Gotta Right To Sing The Blues' for *Earl Carroll's Vanities Of 1932*, 'It's Only A Paper Moon' for a flop show same year, 'Let's Fall In Love' for their first film (of that title) '34. Arlen also collaborated with Yip HARBURG ('Last Night When We Were Young'), Ira GERSHWIN, and Johnny MERCER: 'Blues In The Night', 'Come Rain Or Come Shine', 'That Old Black Magic' (for film *Star-Spangled Rhythm* '42), 'One For My Baby' (for *The Sky's The Limit* '43). Arlen shows incl. 'Bloomer Girl' '44 with Harburg, all-black musical *St Louis Woman* '46 with Mercer, *House Of Flowers* '54 for Pearl BAILEY, *Jamaica* '57 for Horne. His other films incl. *Here Come The Waves* '44 with Mercer ('Accent-tchu-ate The Positive'); and most unforgettably of all, *Wizard Of Oz* '39 with Harburg ('Over The Rainbow' etc.) and *A Star Is Born* '53 with Ira Gershwin ('The Man That Got Away'), both for Judy Garland.

ARMATRADING, Joan (*b* 9 Dec. '50, St Kitts, West Indies) Singer/songwriter. To Birmingham, England '56; London early '70s. During touring production of *Hair* met Pam Nestor; partnership resulted in *Whatever's For Us* '74 (on Cube, later issued on A&M) followed by A&M contract, solo *Back To The Night* '75: these caused a stir; *Joan Armatrading* '76 was described by prod. Glyn JOHNS as best he ever worked on, made no. 12 UK, incl. top 10 hit 'Love And Affection', 'Down To Zero', delightful 'Water In The Wine'. She has always chosen good sidemen, e.g. from FAIRPORT CONVENTION, LITTLE FEAT, E Street Band; acoustic-based music is tinged with jazz and hard rock. Her stage presence was criticised at first (she is very shy); it improved markedly. Five more chart singles '76-81; albums *Show Some Emotion* '77, *To The Limit* '78 charted (both with Johns). *Me, Myself, I* '80 prod. by Richard GOTTEHRER; contained title single, 'All The Way From America', 'When You Kisses Me'. *Walk Under Ladders* '81 and *The Key* '83 (incl. hit single 'Drop The Pilot') prod. by Steve Lillywhite; *Track Record* was 'best of' compilation '83. Attended

St Kitts independence celebration; HRH Princess Margaret became the first member of Royal Family to appear in a pop video. *Secret Secrets* '85 (prod. by Mike HOWLETT) has arr. with brass and strings; *Sleight Of Hand* '86 was another hit, followed by *The Shooting Stage* '88. The singer/songwriter genre lost favour during '70s mainly because few new ones were as good as Armatrading: her excellent lyrics and tunes appeal to both wistful romantics and the women's movement.

ARMENTEROS, Alfredo 'Chocolate' (*b* c. '26, Ranchuelo, Santa Clara, Las Villas, Cuba) Trumpet, flugelhorn, bandleader, composer, arranger, producer. Nicknamed both for sweet musical style and handsome sepia complexion. He played and recorded with Conjunto Los Astros, formed '48 by singer/composer René Alvarez (10 tracks from '48-50 compiled on *Dejame Tranquilo* '74 on Cariño), worked with Arsenio RODRIGUEZ, led brass section of Beny Moré's band '53-6, did radio and TV staff work, recorded with many more Cuban artists incl. Sonora Matancera, and played in the band accompanying Nat COLE on album *Rumba à la King*, made in Cuba. USA debut late '50s in NYC's Palladium Ballroom with José FAJARDO; soon took up residence there and worked for Puerto Rican bandleader César Concepción; played and recorded with MACHITO, Johnny PACHECO, both Eddie and Charlie PALMIERI, Mongo SANTAMARIA, Joe Quijano and Ismael Rivera (*see* Rafael CORTIJO), the Tico All Stars, etc. Debut on LP as leader (of small conjunto Los Contemporarios), co-arranger (with pianist Javier Vázquez) and composer of three tracks was *Chocolate Aquí*, early '70s on Carib Musicana label, with vocals by Cuban veteran Marcelino Guerra, younger compatriot Justo Betancourt. A leading exponent of the septeto trumpet style (*see* SON), he recorded in this format with Grupo Folklorico y Experimental Nuevayorquino and Armando Sanchez y su Septeto Son de la Loma (*Caliente Hot* '77 on New World); fronted a conjunto on *Chocolate . . . En el Rincón* '76 on Salsoul, with two trumpets (himself doubling on flugelhorn), two trombones (co-arr. with Brazilian trombonist José Rodrigues), wrote two tracks. He re-

created the trumpet style of '30s-40s Trinidad calypso, backing veteran Growling TIGER on Rounder album *Growling Tiger – Knockdown Calypsoes* '79. He once more fronted the band on three tipico (means typical, traditional) Cuban LPs prod. by Roberto TORRES for his SAR label: *Prefiero El Son* '80 had similar frontline (with Rodrigues) plus Charlie Rodriguez on tres, pianist Alfredo Valdés Jr (another co-arranger), vocalist Tony Divan; *Y Sigo con Mi Son* '80 had one trombone (Rodrigues), Fernando Lavoy as lead vocalist and Valdés Jr doing all the arr. (extended versions of classic Cuban son montunos); *Chocolate Dice* '82 had second trombone restored, Afro-Cuban virtuoso Alfredo Rodriguez on keyboards, trombonist Lewis Khan (from Larry HARLOW band) and vocalist Charlie Romero, Valdés Jr again arranging. He was house musician with SAR and related Guajiro and Toboga labels, recording with Torres, Papaito, Henry FIOL, many others incl. SAR All Stars; then went to new Caimán label for own instrumental sextet sets *Chocolate en Sexteto* '83 and *Rompiendo Hielo!* '84, with pianist Sergio George (from Conjunto Cache), Dominican saxist/flautist Mario Rivera, percussionist Mario Grillo (Machito's son), with George doing the arranging incl. Chocolate tunes and LECUONA's classic 'Siboney' on the second LP. He made three LPs on the Dutch Timeless label '82-3 with the Machito Salsa Big Band, appearing with it in historic London gigs '82-4; the crossover oriented Caimán LP *Super All-Star* featuring Chocolate has been a steady seller there since being released in '84. Also popular is *Pionero del Son* '84 by veteran singer Alfredo Valdés, who was vocalist with the Septeto Nacional, formed '20s in Cuba by Ignacio Piñeiro (1888-1969); five of eight tracks are Piñeiro tunes, and the LP was another opportunity for Chocolate to play in the Cuban septeto format. He has also recorded with Israel 'Cachao' LOPEZ, Lou Perez y su Conjunto Tipico, and the veteran Cuban group Los Guaracheros de Oriente; he appeared in London at the Bass Clef late '86 for five nights with the London-based nine-piece Robin Jones' King Salsa band. *Oye Listen!* '87 on Globe-Style UK is a compilation of Caimán tracks featuring Chocolate, many others.

ARMSTRONG, Frankie (*b* 13 Jan. '41, Workington, Cumbria) UK folksinger, social worker. Began singing '50s, infl. by USA trad. music, especially the WEAVERS; joined skiffle group Ceilidh Singers '60; music interests gradually returned to England. Recorded *The Bird And The Bush* '66 with A. L. LLOYD and Anne Briggs, first solo LPs *Lovely On The Water* '72, *Frankie Armstrong* '75, all on Topic. Continued as social worker, repertoire frequently reflecting concerns; *Out Of Love, Hope, Sufferin'* '74 (Bay), *Nuclear Power* '81 (Pläne) covered some of these issues, latter with topical songwriters Roy Bailey, Leon Rosselson. Often works solo, but occasionally with Bailey or Rosselson, recently with eclectic instrumental group Blowzabella, with whom she recorded *Tam Lin* (Plant Life), long work based on folktale.

ARMSTRONG, Lil (*b* Lillian Hardin, 3 Feb. 1898, Memphis, Tenn.; *d* 27 Aug. '71, Chicago, Ill.) Piano, singer, leader. To Chicago '17; own band '20; played with King OLIVER on and off '21-4; married band's second cornet, Louis ARMSTRONG, '24; urged him to leave Oliver. Led own Chicago band while Louis was with Fletcher HENDERSON; then to NYC; both returned to Chicago, he worked in her band '25. She played on his Hot Five and Hot Seven discs '25-7; toured with Freddie KEPPARD; gained degree, teacher's diploma in music; separated from Louis '31 (divorced '38). Led all-girl and all-male bands, radio broadcasts, appeared solo in revues; was house pianist at Decca late '30s. Mostly solo from '40s; had long residencies at clubs in Chicago, Milwaukee; toured Europe and worked in Paris '52, continued playing dates in midwest USA and Canada, '50s-60s. She died during memorial concert for Louis.

ARMSTRONG, Louis (*b* 4 Aug. '01, New Orleans, La.; *d* 6 July '71, NYC) Cornet, trumpet; vocalist, leader (aka 'Dippermouth', 'Satchmo', 'Satchelmouth', 'Pops'). A baptismal certificate discovered in '88 confirmed this birthdate. The first and still perhaps greatest solo star in jazz; the most infl. musician of the century and one of the best-known, best-loved entertainers in the world. Sent to Colored Waif's Home after firing a pistol in the air, c.'12; learned to play cornet there. Worked at odd jobs and in various bands; married first wife, '18; replaced King OLIVER in Kid ORY's band early '19; joined Fate MARABLE's riverboat band a few weeks later; returned to New Orleans, '21. Joined Oliver in Chicago on second cornet, '22; that band made the first great jazz records, '23. Married band's pianist Lil Hardin, '24 (*see* Lil ARMSTRONG, above); she encouraged him to leave Oliver. With Fletcher HENDERSON band for a year, influenced it profoundly, but also recorded with Sidney BECHET, others in small groups directed by Clarence WILLIAMS (Blue Five, Red Onion Jazz Babies); accompanied singers Bessie SMITH, 'Chippie' Hill, Ma RAINEY and others (Jimmie RODGERS in '30): all these records are of great historical interest, as well as containing much beauty: the best record we have of what the music sounded like in New Orleans taverns and brothels. With wife's band in Chicago '25; then began making series of records known as Hot Fives and Hot Sevens, with small groups assembled for studio only. Hot Five incl. Ory, Johnny DODDS, Johnny St Cyr, banjo, as well as Louis and his wife; they cut 33 sides in about two years from Nov. '25. Now matured as an artist, gradually abandoning collective improvisation of New Orleans style, doing it all himself: other musicians astonished at complete mastery, demonstrating all the self-expression possible in jazz. Had clear, accurate, beautiful tone; first to improvise freely in lower registers of instrument; technical skill allowed him to place notes as he wished, bending a note or placing emphasis within it, playing around the beat: could swing entire group himself. As improvising melodist, went further than anyone in recomposing a song. Didn't invent stop-time chorus (in which band played 1 beat in 1 or 2 bars, leaving soloist to do as he wished) but first to take fullest advantage of that freedom; solos perfectly constructed, yet obviously improvised in their ebullience; he sang the same way: seemed to have invented scat singing, he did that, too, with such freedom. Among the Hot Five's best recordings: 'Cornet Chop Suey', 'Heebie Jeebies' (for scat singing), 'Struttin' With Some Barbecue', 'Big Butter And Egg Man' (with vocal by May ALIX), 'Hotter Than That' (for fine series of solo choruses). During Hot Five series switched from cornet to brighter trumpet; Hot Seven began to record, adding Pete Briggs, tuba, Baby DODDS, drums; John Thomas (1902-71) for Ory on trombone. 'Wild Man Blues', 'Gully Low Blues', 'Potato Head Blues' are mostly solos, last famous for stop-time chorus. 'Chicago Breakdown' made by Louis Armstrong and His Stompers, group he worked with in Chicago café: 11 players incl. Earl HINES, piano. Savoy Ballroom Five made 18 sides in '28; had no New Orleans players except Zutty Singleton, drums; included Hines, one of the few Armstrong ever worked with who was his equal: 'West End Blues' famous for perfect architecture, also contained basic elements identifying popular music for decades, especially in vocal. Also made classic duet with Hines, 'Weather Bird'. Beginning '28 Armstrong fronted larger bands, directed by Luis RUSSELL, Carroll Dickerson (1898-1951), Les HITE (1903-62), Zilner Randolph (*b* 1899); in his prime at end of silent film era he was primarily a singer and theatre entertainer: seen as a star by audiences caring little about jazz itself, he often played more than 100 consecutive high notes at end of hackneyed show-stoppers such as 'Shine' or 'Tiger Rag'; also made beautiful records: 'Stardust', 'Between The Devil And The Deep Blue Sea', 'The Peanut Vendor', many more. Always suffering from insecurity due to racial prejudice and extreme poverty of his youth, he was managed at first by Tommy Rockwell, recording director of Fives and Sevens, but then by Johnny Collins, a small-time gangster. Sometimes booked 365 nights a year; had never acquired proper embouchure and began to suffer chronic lip problem. Went to Europe '33, was idolised there, rested. Not content with stealing from Armstrong, Collins abandoned him in London without passport. On return to USA put affairs in hands of Joe Glaser (*d* '69), then small-time booking agent; Glaser was ruthless businessman and no music lover, but at least understood the value of his property, even travelling with the band in its early years. Armstrong began appearing in better films (*Pennies From Heaven*, '36; made more than 50 eventually) finally had financial security. Armstrong's bands often not very good; jazz fans disappointed by emphasis on entertainment, but Louis was grateful to his public:

always gave full measure. He said his favourite band was Guy LOMBARDO's, appalling some people: his point was that Lombardo's 'sweet' band was reliable and impeccable musically. Made charming pop records, recording with Bing CROSBY, MILLS BROS, others; had hits (e.g. 'Blueberry Hill' '49, with Gordon JENKINS). Band's function was to back star, who continued to innovate long after '30: too good a musician to stop creating: '38 broadcast aircheck exists with Fats WALLER, Bud FREEMAN, Al CASEY, Jack TEAGARDEN, and Willmore 'Slick' Jones (1907-69; Waller's drummer at the time): priceless for singing of the introduction to 'Jeepers Creepers' alone. Finally big band era was over; in May '47 Armstrong played Town Hall NYC with Teagarden, Bob Haggart, Peanuts Hucko, Sid CATLETT, Bobby HACKETT, others; new small-group format was critical and public success (French RCA issued complete concert on two LPs, '83). For rest of his life led small-group All-Stars. Always played contemporary material, but now criticised for playing pop songs, mugging, clowning, mopping face with white handkerchief; but presented personality his audience wanted. At first All-Stars incl. Hines, Teagarden, Barney BIGARD; it is a great shame that this group ('48-52) made only a handful of commercial recordings while Louis recorded for Decca with Gordon JENKINS, etc.: personnel changed and was not always first rate, especially in later years. Best LPs incl. *Satchmo At Symphony Hall* '51, *Satch Plays Fats* '55 (both made no. 10 on USA LP chart). Band in mid-'50s incl. Bigard, Billy Kyle (1914-66), piano; Arvell Shaw (*b* '23), bass; Barrett Deems (*b* '14), drums; Trummy Young; Velma Middleton sang and did splits. 4-LP set *Satchmo: A Musical Autobiography* ('56-7, prod. by Milt Gabler) is relaxed attempt to capture All-Stars at their best: booked for a change into studio as though into club, instead of coming in exhausted from engagements. *Ambassador Satch* '56 recorded on European tour, with Edmond HALL for Bigard, *sans* Middleton. Armstrong became American ambassador of good will, touring amid adulation nearly every country in the world, often sponsored by US State Dept. Criticised during civil rights era as Uncle Tom, but as Billie Holiday said, 'Pops toms from the heart.' Then he exploded at sight on TV '57 of black children being spat on when Alabama's Gov. Faubus used state's National Guard to prevent integration of schools; abandoned talk about tour of the USSR: 'Because of the way they are treating my people . . . the government can go to hell'; he accused President Eisenhower of having 'no guts', allowing Faubus (a 'plow-boy') to run country: sensational words helped force federal government to uphold the law. Eight hits in UK singles charts '52-68, incl. one EP, one re-entry, and three at no. 1; in USA 'Blueberry Hill' charted when reissued '56, 'Mack The Knife' same year; 'Hello, Dolly!' made no. 1 '64. Began by defining jazz, pointing out its direction; no singer or player of consequence failed to acknowledge debt to Pops: yet at the end of his life fans were surprised to read in obituaries that the world-famous entertainer was also one of the most important innovators in music. Selection of Hot Fives, Hot Sevens long available on four LPs *The Louis Armstrong Story* on Columbia USA; other USA compilations and more complete collections from European CBS also available. Red Onion Jazz Babies/Blue Five material available in compilations incl. 2-disc set from Smithsonian Collection. Many LPs of big band items on CBS, RCA, MCA; All-Star LPs as recommended above. Often recorded with other artists (Dave BRUBECK, Duke ELLINGTON, DUKES OF DIXIELAND); these experiments usually unsuccessful, but LPs with Ella FITZGERALD on Verve (*Ella & Louis*) are magic pop ballad singing; they also made songs from *Porgy And Bess*, first Armstrong set to be issued on compact disc. Publications: *Swing That Music* '36 (ghost-written autobiography); *Satchmo: My Life In New Orleans* '55 (valuable but unreliable); interview from *Time-Life* '61 published '71 as *Louis Armstrong – A Self Portrait*; pioneering biography *Louis* '71 by John CHILTON and Max Jones now superseded by *Louis Armstrong* '83 by James Lincoln Collier. When widow Lucille died, she left their house to New York City; Queen's College now oversees meticulously collected library of tapes, etc. maintained by Louis for decades.

ARNAZ, Desi (*b* Desiderio Alberto Arnaz y de Acha III, 2 Mar. '17, Cuba; *d* 2 Nov. '86) Singer, bandleader, actor, TV executive. His mother's father was one of the founders of Bacardi Rum, but the family lost everything in the revolution of '33; he went to the USA and cleaned birdcages in Florida. Formed band, sang rumbas in Miami La Conga club, credited with helping to make the conga a national fad; big break touring with Xavier CUGAT at 19. Through Cugat met RODGERS & HART, who cast him in *Too Many Girls* on stage '39: he did the conga, also played in film version '40 co-starring Lucille Ball (married her '40; divorced '60); minor roles in other films. Like Cugat, Arnaz was a popularizer of Cuban dance music; inferior version of Margarita LECUONA's 'Babalu' was minor hit '46 from 10" LP *Cuban Carnival*. Others incl. 'Green Eyes' (with Cuban pianist Rene Touzet), 'Rumba Matumba', 'Le Conga en Nueva York', etc. He was also mus. dir. of Bob Hope radio show after WWII; he played Ball's TV husband Ricky Ricardo '51-9 in massively successful series *I Love Lucy*, still being re-run; they formed TV prod. company Desilu; 'Cuban Pete' (from low-budget film of same name) was minor hit after the series began. He will be remembered more for introducing the TV sitcom three-camera production technique (which is still in use today) than for his music. Autobiography *A Book* was published in '76.

ARNHEIM, Gus (*b* 11 Sep. 1897, Philadelphia, Pa.; *d* 19 Jan. '55, L.A.) Bandleader, composer. Co-wrote 'I Cried For You', '23; 'Sweet And Lovely', '31. Had top West Coast dance band late '20s-30s, popular with film folk; gave Bing CROSBY start as solo star, also employed Woody HERMAN, Russ COLUMBO. National fame with broadcast remotes for Lucky Strike '31; on Crosby radio show '34; updated band in Chicago mid-'30s, arrangements by Budd JOHNSON; later Stan KENTON as pianist-arranger. Big hits '30s on Victor incl. 'Them There Eyes' '30 with Crosby, MILLS Bros; 'I Surrender, Dear' '31 helped Crosby to get radio network contract; 'Sweet And Lovely' '31 was no. 1 hit with vocal by Donald Novis; 'So Rare' '37 was no. 2 with vocal by Jimmy Farrell (song written by Jerry Herst and Jack Sharpe): Jimmy DORSEY revived it '57 for another no. 2 hit.

ARNOLD, Billy Boy (*b* William Arnold, 16 Sep. '35, Chicago, Ill.) Blues singer, guitar, harmonica. Worked as a child with Bo DIDDLEY washboard trio at parties, etc.; with Johnny SHINES, Otis RUSH, Diddley, Earl HOOKER, Howlin' WOLF, Muddy WATERS, LITTLE WALTER during '50s; recorded in Chicago '54-5, '64, '70; toured Europe '75, '77, incl. concerts and broadcasts; in *The Devil's Music: A History Of The Blues,* BBC TV (segment taped in Chicago); recorded in England '77. UK Red Lightnin' label has issued compilation LPs *Blow The Back Off It* (2 tracks with Diddley), *Sinner's Prayer* (early '70s sessions), *Checkin' It Out, Superharps* (7″ EP, 2 tracks each by Arnold and Little Walter); *It's Great To Be Rich* (5-track 12″ EP incl. '82 cut by Diddley).

ARNOLD, Eddy (*b* 15 May '18, nr Henderson, Tenn.) Country singer who became one of the most popular recording artists of all. Left high school to help on family farm; later accurately billed as 'The Tennessee Plowboy'. Radio debut '36 in Jackson, then to Memphis, St Louis; travelled with Grand Ole Opry's Camel Caravan '41-2 entertaining servicemen; back in Jackson '42, RCA record contract '44. First manager was Tom Parker, later Elvis PRESLEY's manager. Hits began in '46; in '48 incl. 'Texarkana Baby', 'Any Time', 'A Heart Full Of Love', 'Bouquet Of Roses'; 70 top 20 entries in Billboard country chart '49-69, incl. number ones: 'Don't Rob Another Man's Castle', 'I'm Throwing Rice At The Girl That I Love' '49; 'There's Been A Change In Me', 'Kentucky Waltz', 'I Want To Play House With You' '51; 'Easy On The Eyes' '52; 'Eddy's Song' '53; 'Cattle Call' '55; 'What's He Doing In My World', 'Make The World Go Away' '65; 'I Want To Go With You', 'Somebody Like Me' '66; 'Lonely Again', 'Turn The World Around' '67; 'Then You Can Tell Me Goodbye' '68. Star of country radio (incl. Opry) but always smooth balladeer, co-writing many songs; cross-over hits began '48 when 'Bouquet Of Roses' made top 40 of pop chart; also 'One Kiss Too Many' '49; 'I Wouldn't Know Where To Begin' '56; 'Make The World Go Away' '65; 'I Want To Go With You', 'The Last Word In Lonesome Is Me' '66; three singles charted in UK '66. RCA said '47 that 2,700,000 Arnold records had been sold; by '70 sales were 60 million; by end of the '70s, 70 million. Of dozens of LPs in the '50s-60s, many top 10 hits; in '67 Billboard named him no. 1 country-album artist, with five LPs in charts at once; following year he was tied with Glen CAMPBELL. Left RCA for MGM mid-'70s; came back '76, hits continued. Had own TV series on NBC, then ABC, then a syndicated show; hosted *Kraft Music Hall* on TV many times, as well as summer series *Country Fair* for Kraft; he was guest host on Johnny Carson show (mark of show-biz success in USA), co-hosted *Mike Douglas* show; played Carnegie Hall twice, often performed with symphony orchestras. When elected to the Country Music Hall of Fame '66 there were grumbles: with perversity endemic in music business Arnold was accused of selling out; in fact he made friends for the values in country music. LPs in print in USA '86 incl. 'Best Of', 'Greatest Hits' sets on RCA, MGM; *Legendary Performances (1944-71)* is 2-disc specially priced set on RCA; in UK *20 Of The Best* on RCA International.

ARNOLD, James 'Kokomo' (*b* 15 Feb. '01, Lovejoy, Texas; *d* 8 Nov. '68, Chicago, Ill.) Blues singer, guitar. Worked mostly outside of music in New York State and Chicago; made two sides for Victor '30 in Memphis under the name of Gitfiddle Jim, more for Decca in Chicago and NYC '34-8. Acquired nickname from 'Old Original Kokomo Blues' '34 (Kokomo was brand of coffee, as well as town in Indiana). Highly regarded by critics and collectors; made comeback in Chicago at height of folk-blues revival (Gate of Horn club, '62).

ARNOLD, P. P. (*b* Pat Arnold, '46, L.A.) Soul singer. Sang in church choirs from age 4; joined Ikettes (Ike & Tina TURNER's backing group); visited London '66, decided to stay, forming impressive three-piece backing group; signed to Andrew Oldham's Immediate label, immediately hit with Cat STEVENS song 'First Cut Is The Deepest' (UK no. 18, '67). Album *First Lady Of Immediate* same year was produced by Mick Jagger/Mike Hurst; next LP *Kafunta* '68 by Jagger and Steve Marriott (of SMALL FACES). Labelmate Marriott also wrote her flop single 'If You Think You're Groovy'; she in turn sang on his group's 'Tin Soldier'. After second top 30 entry 'Angel Of The Morning', starred in Jack GOOD production *Catch My Soul* '69, then *Jesus Christ Superstar* '70, by which time her former backing group had found fame as The NICE. Returned to USA '70s for film/TV work (*Fame, Knots Landing, T.J. Hooker*, etc.); toured with re-formed Small Faces, '78; contributed to *Electric Dreams* soundtrack '84, returned to London same year to star in Andrew LLOYD WEBBER's *Starlight Express*; recording for 10 Records '85. First-rate talent has never hit the really big time, but has had a successful career for all that.

ART ENSEMBLE OF CHICAGO Black music quintet: Roscoe MITCHELL, Joseph JARMAN, reeds; Lester BOWIE, trumpet, flugelhorn; Malachi Favors (*b* 22 Aug. '37, Chicago), bass; Don Moye (*b* 23 May '46, Rochester, NY), percussion. All but Moye members of AACM. Jarman had led informal group with Charles CLARK, Thurman BARKER (drums), Christopher Gaddy (*b* 8 Apr. '43, Chicago; *d* there 12 Mar. '68; piano); with others they made LPs *Song For* and (after Gaddy's death) *As If It Were The Seasons*; Mitchell made sextet LP *Sound* which incl. Bowie, Favors (all on Delmark '67-8). Mitchell's Art Ensemble made *Old/Quartet* in May '67 with Bowie, Favors, Phillip Wilson: released '75 on Nessa, it is their 'basement tapes' (but well recorded, in Mitchell's home, by Terry Martin); good introduction to their casual brilliance, full of soul roots. Chuck Nessa had been a producer at Delmark; first release on his own label was *Numbers 1&2* '67, under Bowie's name, with Bowie, Mitchell, Favors; sleeve shows Mitchell's painting of Wilson, Bowie, Favors: 'returns Picasso's *Three Musicians* to their African source' (G. Giddins), but Wilson had left group. *Congliptuous* '68 on Nessa as Roscoe Mitchell Art Ensemble, with Robert Crowder (*b* 22 Oct. '46, Atlanta), drums; first side of LP has unaccompanied solos for bass, alto sax and trumpet. Deaths of Gaddy and Clark, brilliant and much-loved colleagues, stirred group to action: formed cooperative and went to Paris, where they recruited Moye '69 (he had played with Steve LACY, Pharoah SANDERS, others; recorded with Randy WESTON; on Hamiet BLUIETT trio LP *Bars*, '77; own

LP: *Sun Percussion*, '75). Quintet became best-known group playing what some might call avant-garde jazz, but which defies labels, except for 'Great Black Music'. Mitchell and Jarman are main composers, but entire group contributes; all play 'little instruments': steer horns, whistles, gongs, drums, rattles, sirens, etc. inspired by African music. Their work swells and roars with collective improvisation, contains essences of black music, plus marches, dada, drollery, silence. Theatrical act incl. painted faces, sometimes recitation, mime etc., providing levels of reference and invoking community spirit. *People In Sorrow* is a tone poem recorded in Boulogne (leased by Nessa): tape ran out before they stopped playing, but like the story it tells the piece was not finished anyway; heard again at London's Roundhouse 12 years later its richness was still developing: like all good music, theirs is a live art, a record only a souvenir. *A Message To Our Folks* displays roots: 'Old Time Religion', 'Rock Out', Charlie PARKER's 'Dexterity', as well as group comp. 'Brain For The Seine'; these and several more LPs made '69 in a burst of urgency (many now on Affinity in UK). *Les Stances à Sophie* (film soundtrack with Fontella BASS, also on Nessa) made in Boulogne; *Certain Blacks, Go Home, Chi Congo* made in Paris, all '70; back in the USA ('We missed the stimulation of the ghetto,' said Bowie) they allegedly made fun of traditional blues singers at Ann Arbor Blues Festival '72: this was theatre, with the advantage of outraging young white trendies. Festival LP *Bap-Tizum* was their first release on a major label, prod. by Michael CUSCUNA, as was *Fanfare For The Warriors* '73, both on Atlantic. Among many other albums: *Live At Mandel Hall* '72 on Delmark (2-disc set) recorded on U. of Chicago campus; Muhal Richard Abrams plays on live album from Montreux Jazz Festival *Kabalaba* '74 (also plays on *Fanfare*); *Nice Guys* '78, *Full Force* '80 are on ECM: on the latter Jarman and Bowie play 12 reed and woodwind instruments (and little ones), Favors contributes comp. 'Magg Zalma', Jarman's 'Old Time Southside Street Dance' precedes the 'Full Force'. *Urban Bushmen* '80 is two LPs of shamanism, perhaps best example on record of live act, in Jarman's words ' . . . flowers blooming through concrete, gong with trumpet announcing the present . . . ' *Among The People* '80 made live in Italy. Shared bill with rock act at London's Royal Festival Hall late '84, were poorly served by sound: no subtlety in earsplitting volume. Album *Third Decade* '84 on ECM raised hope of continuing evangelism; then *Live In Japan* '84, return to form on *Naked* '85-6, both on DIW. Film *Art Ensemble Of Chicago* made in Chicago '83 by Bright Thoughts Company for UK's Channel 4 TV.

ARTWOODS UK R&B band formed c.'63 from Red Bludd's Blusicians, after departure of Don 'Red Bludd' Wilson (bass), Reg Dunnage (drums). Lineup of new group: Art Wood, vocals; Derek Griffiths, guitar; Malcolm Poole, bass; Jon Lord, keyboards; Keef Hartley, drums. Frontman Wood was vocalist in Alexis KORNER's Blues Incorporated and elder brother of future ROLLING STONE Ron Wood; classically trained Lord came from Bill Ashton Combo. Popularity on disc never equalled that in London clubs. *Art Gallery* LP released '64 on Decca (eponymous compilation issued '73, Spark). Split in summer '67 when rampant psychedelia forced name change to St Valentine's Day Massacre; Griffiths to sessions, Hartley to John MAYALL, Lord to Flowerpot Men, thence DEEP PURPLE. Remembered more for connections than for music.

ASABIA (*b* Eugenia Asabia Cropper, '57, Ghana) Singer, saxophonist. Born into musical family; at 18 sang with her elder brother in groups in and around Accra. Sessioned with Ghanaian musicians working in Togo; audience response persuaded her to turn pro. Returned to Accra, joined the Sweet Talks, leading Ghanaian band of mid-'70s, sang with them for two years; established contacts while touring Ivory Coast; when contract ran out joined the Black Hustlers, went with them to Ivory Coast; spotted and signed by Ivorian label Disco Stock. Polished act and selected material for two years; debut LP *Wamaya* early '80s inspired by Ko Nimo, incl. brother Sammy Cropper on guitar: 'refined highlife' LP now on American Makossa label became much sought-after in Africa. Now living in Abidjan, in demand as live act; has toured Germany but stays close to her roots.

ASCAP American Society of Composers Authors and Publishers; first and still largest of American performing rights societies, which collect and distribute royalties to members from use of their music. Founded '14 following Victor HERBERT's lawsuit against NYC restaurant which was using his music (played by a small orchestra); historic decision of United States Supreme Court decided that whether or not use of music helped the restaurant to make a profit 'the purpose of employing it is profit, and that is enough'. From 182 members in '14 ASCAP grew to more than 33,000 by '81. First deal with National Association of Broadcasters (NAB) '32; affiliated with societies in 40 other nations; makes such annual awards as Nathan Burkan Memorial Competition for law school essays on copyright law (since '38, honouring one of the founders) and the ASCAP-Deems Taylor Awards for writing about music (since '68). ASCAP strike against broadcasters resulted in formation '39 of Broadcast Music Inc.; ASCAP settled for less than its former rate. Society of European Songwriters Authors and Publishers (SESAC) also founded, '31.

ASHER, Peter Former popstar, now US-based manager/producer. Success as half of PETER AND GORDON mid-'60s; appointed head of A&R at BEATLES' Apple label; demonstrated skill by signing James TAYLOR, singer-songwriter then living in London. Moved with Taylor to L.A. '69 when flop of debut LP coincided with Allen Klein's purge of Apple staff (one of the problems with the Apple label was that if the record wasn't the Beatles nobody played it). After helping Taylor through a bout of mental illness, prod. his first three LPs for WB; *Sweet Baby James* '70 and *Mud Slide Slim* '71 both went platinum. Also managed the Section, Taylor's backing musicians, who made three low-key LPs in the '70s. Found Midas touch with former Stone Poney Linda RONSTADT, prod. her LPs from *Don't Cry Now* '73 onwards. Svengali infl. similar to '60s pairings of George MARTIN/ Cilla BLACK, Chris ANDREWS/Sandie SHAW, Mickie MOST/LULU; yielded long series of platinum LPs with his choice of material (from EVERLY Bros '74 to Elvis COSTELLO '78) crucial in maintaining her popularity. Also prod. Ronstadt's one-time beau John

David SOUTHER, Bonnie RAITT, John STEWART, others; gathered many awards for production, notably '77 Grammy for work with Ronstadt. Exerted consistent influence on '70s West Coast pop, which is not unlike an update of the Peter and Gordon sound.

ASHFORD & SIMPSON USA vocal duo, songwriters, producers: Nickolas Ashford (*b* 4 May '42, Fairfield, S.C.), Valerie Simpson (*b* 26 Aug. '46, Bronx, NYC). Husband and wife soul team met '64 at Harlem gospel meeting when she sang with the Followers, married '74. Recorded as Nick & Valerie, '60s but first success as writers ('Let's Go Get Stoned' top 40 hit for Ray CHARLES '66). On staff at Sceptor/Wand wrote hits for Maxine Brown, Chuck Jackson; to Tamla/Motown as writers, developed into prod. work; hits incl. top 10 duets by Marvin GAYE and Tammi Terrell '68 ('Ain't Nothing Like The Real Thing', 'You're All I Need To Get By'); soft soul approach used with launch of Diana ROSS as solo: 'Reach Out And Touch Somebody's Hand', 'Ain't No Mountain High Enough' (also no. 19 for Gaye/Terrell). Valerie had two underrated solo LPs: *Exposed!* '71, *Valerie Simpson* '72; duo LP *Keep It Comin'* '73, reissued '77; left Motown for WB '73: succession of duo LPs saw fame grow: *Gimme Something Real* '73, *I Wanna Be Selfish* '74, *Come As You Are* '76, *Send It* '77, *Is It Still Good To Ya* '78, *Stay Free* '79, *A Musical Affair* '80, 2-disc *Performance* '81; then on Capitol: *Street Opera* '82, *High Rise* '83 (title track top 10 USA black chart), *Solid* '84 (title track world-wide hit '85). Still in demand as prod./writers, e.g. Chaka KHAN no. 21 hit 'I'm Every Woman' '78, worked with former labelmates Ross (*The Boss* '79), Gladys KNIGHT (*About Love* '80).

ASHTON, Tony (*b* 1 Mar. '46, Blackburn, Lancs.) UK keyboardist/vocalist. Played piano in local groups from age 15, then in '60s beat scene: backed Cilla BLACK, Chris FARLOWE among others, toured UK as member of Mike Hurst and the Method. Joined mid-'60s Liverpool band Remo Four, which backed Brian EPSTEIN protégé Tommy Quickly; took drummer Roy Dyke (*b* 13 Feb. '45, Liverpool) with him to back P. P. ARNOLD on European tour (with Steve Howe; *see* ASIA), then formed Ashton,

Gardner and Dyke '68, with Kim Gardner (*b* 27 Jan. '46, London; ex-Birds, ex-Creation). Released three LPs '69-72, supplied soundtrack to *The Last Rebel* '71, but failed to make real impact despite superstar help (George HARRISON produced a track on eponymous '69 debut album). Sole hit 'Resurrection Shuffle' '71 (no. 3 UK) typified Ashton's barrelhouse piano and gruff vocal style. At end of AG&D Dyke formed Badger with ex-YES organist Tony Kaye (Gardner joined later), while Ashton augmented FAMILY for their last year '73. He produced, sessioned and arranged through the '70s, teamed with DEEP PURPLE's Jon Lord for *Last Of The Big Bands* '74 (LP/concert project); after Purple's end, with Ian Paice of that group formed shortlived Paice, Ashton and Lord (album *Malice In Wonderland*, '77). Became TV music show host early '80s (UK Channel 4) with Rick Wakeman; flop remake 'Resurrection Shuffle' seemed to indicate low level of remaining musical ambition.

ASHWORTH, Ernie (*b* Ernest Bert Ashworth, 15 Dec. '28, Huntsville, Ala.) Country singer, hits in '60s. Worked in civil service, on radio Huntsville '48-9, Nashville '50-5. Member of Tune Twisters '48-50, Tennessee Drifters '50-5. Signed to MGM '55 without much success; joined Decca '60, had hits 'Each Moment', 'You Can't Pick A Rose In December'; switched to Hickory for 'Everybody But Me' '62; 'Talk Back Trembling Lips', no. 1 C&W chart '63; 'I Love To Dance With Annie' '64; 'The DJ Cried' '65. Joined Grand Ole Opry '64; entertains tourists in Pigeon Fork, Tenn. when not on the road. LP *Greatest Hits* on Starday.

ASIA UK AOR supergroup formed Jan. '81 by Steve Howe (*b* 8 Apr. '47, London), guitar; Carl Palmer (*b* 20 Mar. '51, Birmingham), drums; John Wetton (*b* 12 July '49, Derby), bass, vocals; Geoff Downes, keyboards. All refugees from UK progressive boom of '70s. Palmer, ex-EMERSON, LAKE & PALMER, had been unable to sustain career with own band PM (Mar. '79-June '80), so linked with former YES-men Howe and Downes and much-travelled Wetton (who started in Mogul Thrash '69, then passed through FAMILY, King Crimson, ROXY MUSIC, URIAH HEEP before going solo).

Critics derided the new quartet as irrelevant even before eponymous '82 debut LP was heard, but tailored-for-radio sound with lush harmonies backing Wetton's smoky vocals found wide acceptance in USA; LP spent nine weeks at top of chart, spawned two top 20 singles ('Heat Of The Moment' no. 4; 'Only Time Will Tell' no. 17). But with MTV-assisted influx of more vital, younger UK bands, second LP *Alpha* (recorded in Canada) peaked late '83 at no. 6; promo tour cancelled halfway through owing to poor ticket sales. In UK, where *Asia* had made no. 11, second LP did much better. Wetton replaced by Greg Lake (*see* EMERSON etc.), with whom band made attempt on MTV audience with live Dec. '83 broadcast to 20 million in Japan and USA titled *Asia In Asia*; then Wetton, who'd replaced Lake in early incarnation of King Crimson, rejoined Asia, replacing him again. Though Asia's conservatism is antithesis of what rock is fondly supposed to be about, few begrudge them cashing in on AOR phenomenon that their earlier collective work helped to create, but they may lack confidence: they rejected a 'family tree' commissioned for tour booklet: it revealed their ages. New LP *Astra* '85.

ASLEEP AT THE WHEEL USA western swing band formed West Coast late '60s. Ray Benson (*b* 16 Mar. '51), guitar, vocals; Lucky Oceans (*b* Reuben Gosfield, 22 Apr. '51), pedal steel (both *b* Philadelphia). Moved to Paw Paw, W.V.; added girl singer Chris O'Connell (*b* 21 Mar. c.'53, Williamsport, Md.); to San Francisco; pianist Floyd Domino joined. Debut LP *Comin' Right At Ya* for United Artists '73; moved to Austin, Texas; LP *Asleep At The Wheel* on Epic '74; signed with Capitol, had biggest single 'The Letter That Johnnie Walker Wrote', string of critically acclaimed albums: *Texas Gold* '75 was top 10 C&W LP, also made pop chart; *Wheelin' And Dealin'* '76; *The Wheel* '77; *Collision Course* '78. Voted top touring band by ACM '77; Grammy '78 for best country instrumental ('One O'Clock Jump'). Other LPs incl. *Framed* (MCA), *Live* (Capitol). Among those who've played with the band or passed through: Pat 'Taco' Ryan (reeds; *b* East Texas, 14 July '53); Danny Levin (fiddle, mandolin, piano; *b* Philadelphia, '49); Link

Davies (reeds, accordion; from Port Arthur, Texas); LeRoy Preston (rhythm guitar); Fran Christina (drums); Dean Demerritt (bass); Johnny Gimble (fiddle); others. Size of band cut from 11 to 8 early '80s. Revival of western swing revived interest in music of Bob WILLS; as usual in the genre, music contains jazz, humour, originality. *Pasture Prime* released '85, on Demon in UK; has duet with Benson, Willie NELSON on 'Write Your Own Song'. '74 LP *Jumpin' At The Woodside* reissued '86 on Edsel, one of their best, with Gimble on most tracks.

ASMUSSEN, Svend (*b* 28 Feb. '16, Copenhagen, Denmark). Violin. Toured for years with group called Swe-Danes (The Three Danes), with Alice BABS until '61; reunited with Babs off and on, touring Brazil with her '74. Also plays classical music. Regarded as a comic entertainer in Scandinavia, in fact plays first-class jazz violin, later experimenting with amplifiers. LPs incl. *Yesterday And Today*, with Toots THIELEMANS; *European Encounter* with John LEWIS, *Violin Summit* with Stuff SMITH, Stephane GRAPPELLI, Jean-Luc PONTY; *Duke Ellington's Jazz Violin Session*, with Ray Nance and Grappelli; also with David GRISMAN on *Swinging With Send* '88.

ASSOCIATES Scottish new wave group formed in Dundee by Billy MacKenzie (vocals) and Alan Rankine (guitar, bass, keyboards) who met '76 in cabaret group the Ascorbic Ones. MacKenzie's high, pure singing so BOWIEesque that choice for first (privately released) single, recent Bowie composition 'Boys Keep Swinging', was a natural one. Added Michael Dempsey, bass (ex-CURE) and Australian John Murphy, drums; first LP *The Affectionate Punch* ('80). After string of independent singles (collated '81 as *Fourth Drawer Down*) original duo signed to WB; 'Party Fears Two' no. 9 single, then two more top 30 hits. Volatile relationship split group early '83 despite top 10 hit 'Sulk'. After a solo single ('Ice Cream Factory'), MacKenzie readopted group name with new personnel: Steve Reid and Ian Mackintosh, guitars; L. Howard Hughes, keyboards; Roberto Soave, bass for *Perhaps* '85. Combination of abrasive sounds with MacKenzie's soaring voice now turned to seamless '80s pop; more commercial but less innovative. He is also heard on B.E.F./Heaven 17 all-star *Music of Quality And Distinction* '82, still one of new wave's most promising vocalists.

ASSOCIATION US soft-rock/harmony group formed '65 by Russ Giguere (*b* 18 Oct. '43, New Hampshire), guitar; Brian Cole (*b* '44, Tacoma, Wa.; *d* 2 Aug. '72 of drug overdose), bass; Terry Kirkman (from Kansas), winds; Gary Alexander (Chattanooga, Tenn.), guitar; Jim Yester (Birmingham, Ala.), guitar, sax; Ted Bluechel (San Pedro, Calif.), drums. All shared vocals; many were multi-instrumentalists. Lush harmony of L.A.-based group brought US hits '66 with first two singles on small Valiant label; 'Along Comes Mary' made no. 6 despite allegation that it was a paean to marijuana; determinedly non-controversial 'Cherish' reached no. 1 and won three Grammies. WB label took over Valiant, reissued first two LPs *And Then . . . Along Came Association* '66, *Renaissance* '67; 'Windy' was second no. 1, 'Never My Love' no. 2. Opened at Monterey Pop Festival June '67; Larry Ramos (from Hawaii) replaced Alexander '68. They made soundtrack for *Goodbye Columbus* '69; Richard Thompson replaced Giguere, who went solo '70; but hits dried up: 'Everything That Touches You' was last big hit (US no. 10, '68). Alexander returned from sabbatical in India, but band called it a day after several label changes and little further success. Songs are still staples on easy-listening radio. Perhaps a cult band that peaked too soon: group's success may have stifled a sense of humour similar to that of Yester's brother Jerry's group, the LOVIN' SPOONFUL, evident in '66 single 'Pandora's Golden Heebie Jeebies', album *Waterbeds In Trinidad* '72.

ASTAIRE, Fred (*b* Frederick Austerlitz, 10 May 1899, Omaha, Neb.; *d* 22 June '87, L.A.) Dancer, singer, actor; one of the best-loved entertainers of the century. Pro debut at the age of 5; starred with sister Adele in dancing act on vaudeville until '16, on Broadway until '32 when she retired to marriage. Their biggest hit was George GERSHWIN's *Lady Be Good* '24, which was written for them; they also did his *Funny Face* '27, *The Band Wagon* '31 (by Arthur Schwartz and Howard Dietz); solo stardom in Cole PORTER's *The Gay Divorce* '32 led to famous screen test ('Can't act, slightly bald . . . can dance a little'). *Dancing Lady* '33 starred Joan Crawford; second film *Flying Down To Rio* '33 established dance team with Ginger Rogers: smash hit in films *The Gay Divorcée* '34, *Roberta* and *Top Hat* '35, *Follow The Fleet* and *Swing Time* '36, *Shall We Dance?* '37, *Carefree* '38, *The Story Of Vernon And Irene Castle* '39, and reunion *The Barkleys Of Broadway* '49. Also danced with Vera Ellen, Cyd Charisse, later Barrie Chase on TV, others; later films incl. *You Were Never Lovelier* (with Rita Hayworth) and *Holiday Inn* '42, *Ziegfeld Follies* '44, *Yolanda And The Thief* '45; he announced his retirement, came back to do *Easter Parade* '48 with Judy GARLAND, because Gene KELLY wasn't available. Other films: *Three Little Words* '50, *Daddy Long Legs* '55 (with Leslie Caron); another retirement was followed by *Funny Face* '56, *Silk Stockings* '57; he gave up retiring. *Finian's Rainbow* '68 was his last musical; straight roles incl. *On The Beach* '59, *The Towering Inferno* '75 (Oscar nomination as supporting actor; received a special honorary Oscar '49). Also wrote a few songs (e.g. 'I'm Building Up To An Awful Letdown' '35 with Johnny MERCER), had own radio series in '30s, many appearances on TV incl. series *It Takes A Thief* and *The Over The Hill Gang*, plus highly acclaimed specials '58, '60. In the most charming escapist films of the Depression era his dancing was superb, but personality won affection: as actor and singer he got the girl because he was a nice guy who could dance; some of his later films were not great films, but they were better because he was in them: not only a fine actor, but regarded as among the finest interpreters of great songs by critics and songwriters: Irving BERLIN said he would rather hear Fred Astaire sing his songs than anyone; among songs associated with him are 'Lady Be Good', 'Fascinating Rhythm', 'Dancing In The Dark', 'Night And Day', 'The Way You Look Tonight', 'I Won't Dance', 'They Can't Take That Away From Me', 'A Foggy Day', 'A Fine Romance', 'I Guess I'll Have To Change My Plan', more incl. Richard RODGERS' beautiful 'Waltz In Swingtime' (no words). Songs by Fred and Adele from *Lady Be Good* '26 reissued on Monmouth Evergreen, from *Funny Face* '27 on EMI UK (piano solos by Gershwin). Fred's Brunswick discs from '32-8 compiled on CBS 2-disc set *Fred Astaire* in USA; Deccas from '40s on *The Very Best Of Fred Astaire* MCA/UK. In '53 he made 4-disc Mercury album *The Fred Astaire Story* of songs associated with him, using superb studio sidemen; at about the same time *Swings And Sings Irving Berlin*; *The Berlin Songbook* issued '87 on Verve with Oscar PETERSON, Ray BROWN, Charlie SHAVERS. Several film soundtrack LPs were available late '40s-early '50s on MGM. Last screen role in *Ghost Story* '81; autobiography *Steps In Time* '60.

ATCHER, Bob (*b* Robert Owen Atcher, 11 May '14, Hardin County, Ky.) Popular country singer of '30s, '40s. Father was popular local fiddler. Sang on radio in Louisville, Atlanta, Charleston; to Chicago and fame '35: signed to Columbia, had hit versions of 'I'm Thinking Tonight Of My Blue Eyes', 'Broken Vows', 'Cool Water', 'You Are My Sunshine' '36-40. Made transition from radio to Chicago TV early '50s. Albums on Columbia incl. *Early American Folk Songs*, *Songs Of The Saddle*, *Dean Of The Country Singers*; also *Saturday Night At The Old Barn Dance* for Kapp label, '65. Businessman in home base of Schaumburg, Illinois.

ATILLA THE HUN (*b* Raymond Quevedo, 24 Mar. 1892, Trinidad; *d* there 22 Feb. '62) Calypsonian. Mother Trinidadian, father Venezuelan. Won a scholarship which would have prepared him for higher education overseas, but chose CALYPSO instead, then regarded as disreputable. First sang in public '11. Atilla and Roaring Lion (Hubert Raphael Charles, later Raphael de Leon) were first local artists sent to NYC to record '34 by local businessman Edward Sa Gomes; 16 sides for Brunswick made with Gerald Clarke's orchestra: Bing CROSBY and Rudy VALLEE attended sessions; Vallee featured Lion on his network radio show, heard in Trinidad; records shipped sold out there, but distributor got all the royalties. More followed: 'Good Will Flyers' and 'Women Will Rule The World' '35 and 'Intercolonial Tournament' '37 were issued in UK '38 on Brunswick, after WWII 'His-tory Of Carnival' '35 and 'Roosevelt In Trinidad' '37 (the last on Decca). Suffered early from censorship: songs 'Mrs Simpson' '37, 'The Banning Of Records' '38 were rejected. Recorded in Keskidee Trio with Lord Beginner (Egbert Moore) and Growling TIGER; others. From '46 combined music with political career as City Councilor in Port of Spain, later deputy Mayor, etc.; had reputation as defender of the poor, fought for recognition of calypso as folk art, also for its trad. role as poor people's newspaper. Charged '49 with infringement of the Theatre and Dance Halls Act of 1934, accused of permitting a calypso to be performed in his tent which subjected a member of the community to ridicule: case decided in his favour on a technicality. Elected '50 to Legislative Council of the colonial government, moving an amendment to the Act '51: defeated, but alternative government amendment regarded as improvement. Worked with John La Rose '56-8 on a history of calypso, published as *Atilla's Kaiso: A Short History Of Calypso* '83. Records in Folkways compilations: *The Real Calypso* incl. 'Five Year Plan', 'Miss Bombilla Brown', 'Louis – Schmeling Fight' with Lion, 'War' with Lion and others; *Send Your Children To The Orphan Home: The Real Calypso Vol. 2* incl. 'Good Will Flyers', 'If I Won A Sweepstake'.

ATKIN, Pete, and Clive James Songwriting team. Atkin (*b* Cambridge, England) sang and played guitar; James (from Sydney, Australia) wrote lyrics. Met at Cambridge U. mid-'60s, sharing a love for elegance and wit of songwriters such as Cole PORTER, best of modern pop. In Cambridge Footlights Review with Julie COVINGTON (who made LP of their songs, *The Beautiful Changes*, '71). Own first LPs were folk-based: *Beware Of The Beautiful Stranger*, *Driving Through Mythical America* reissued by RCA '73; more ambitious *A King At Nightfall* ('73) incl. 'Screen Freak', on James's film obsessions. Collection of parodies *Live Libel* savaged Leonard COHEN, James TAYLOR, STEELEYE SPAN, Marc BOLAN. Songs sometimes too clever, but welcome in arid, pretentious early '70s. *The Road Of Silk* and *Secret Drinker* were other sets; *The Essential Pete Atkin* was 14-track collection incl. haunting 'Girl On A Train', catty 'Wristwatch For A Drummer'. Split up mid-'70s. James was popular TV critic for Sunday *Observer*, published doggerel, literary/film criticism, volumes of autobiography, a 'novel'. Atkin had a play produced by the Royal Shakespeare Company; became producer for BBC Radio 4.

ATKINS, Chet (*b* Chester Burton Atkins, 20 June '24, Luttrell, Tenn.) Guitarist: named outstanding instrumentalist by Cashbox magazine 14 years in a row '51-65; also prod., RCA executive. Son of music teacher; his older half-brother Jim played guitar with Fred WARING, Les PAUL. Began as fiddler with Dixieland Swingers on Knoxville radio '42; toured with Archie Campbell, Bill CARLISLE, playing fiddle and guitar. To Cincinnati's radio WLW '44; married singer Leona Johnson there '46. Sang on first records for RCA '47 (later had masters destroyed!). Toured with Maybelle CARTER; to Nashville '49. Recorded as guitarist, appeared on Grand Ole Opry, assisted RCA A&R man Steve Sholes, organising recording sessions; first LP *Chet Atkins' Gallopin' Guitar* '53 followed by over 100 more, in many genres (*Finger Style Guitar* '56, *Three Dimensions* '64, *Picks On The Beatles* '65), but own playing stayed the same: bass rhythm with the thumb, melody picked with three fingers. Became assistant prod. to Sholes '52; took over when he moved to NYC '57; uncanny knack for finding talent, matching material to artist resulted in credit for the 'Nashville sound': prod. records for Jim REEVES, Don GIBSON, Charley PRIDE, Waylon JENNINGS, Hank SNOW, Jerry REED, Dottie WEST, EVERLY BROTHERS, Elvis PRESLEY, Trini LOPEZ, Perry COMO, many more; an RCA vice-president '68 until retirement '79. During '60s teamed with Floyd CRAMER, Boots RANDOLPH and others for Masters Festival, occasional concert series. Elected to Country Music Hall of Fame '73. Albums incl. *The Night Atlanta Burned*: attempt at country string quartet based on arr. for mandolin orchestra discovered in instrument case dating from Civil War; *Chester And Lester* '75 (duet with Les Paul, one of several Grammy winners); also *Picks The Best, Legendary Performer, Great Hits Of The Past*, 2-disc *This Is Chet Atkins* (all RCA-USA); *Solid Gold Guitar, Best Of*, 2-disc *Famous*

Country Music Makers (all RCA UK); *Guitar Pickin' Man* (Cambra UK). To Columbia '83; *Work It Out* that year, *Stay Tuned* '85 with Earl KLUGH, George BENSON, Mark Knopfler, Larry Carlton.

ATLANTA RHYTHM SECTION Smooth southern rock group formed '70 in Doraville, Ga. by session players. Original lineup: J. R. Cobb (*b* 5 Feb. '44, Birmingham, Ala.) and Barry Bailey (*b* 12 June '48, Decatur, Ga.), guitars; Dean Daughtry (*b* 8 Sep. '46, Kinston, Ala.), keyboards; Paul Goddard (*b* 23 June '45, Rome, Ga.), bass; Robert Nix, drums. Cobb and Daughtry ex-CLASSICS IV; all met at Roy ORBISON recording session (most had been in Candymen, Orbison's backing group). Manager/prod. Buddy Buie responsible for slickness, had also handled Classics IV. Eponymous debut LP '72 on MCA had vocals by Rodney Justo (also Candyman); replaced by Ronnie Hammond (*b* Macon, Ga.). *Back Up Against The Wall* '73 followed by move to Polydor for *Third Annual Pipe Dream* '74, *Dog Days* '75, *Red Tape* '76; touring built following and *A Rock And Roll Alternative* '77 made no. 11 USA LP chart (incl. top 10 hit 'So In To You'); first two LPs reissued by MCA '77; Nix left, replaced by Roy Yeager (*b* 4 Feb. '46, Greenwood, Ms.); *Champagne Jam* was peak: no. 7 LP incl. top 10 'Imaginary Lover'. Others incl. *Underdog*, live 2-disc *Are You Ready!* '79, *The Boys From Doraville* '80, then *Quinella* '81 on CBS; apparently quit after good innings.

ATLANTIC Record label formed NYC Oct. '47 by Herb Abramson (formerly recording dir. for National Records), Ahmet Ertegun (son of Turkish ambassador to USA). Initial jazz releases (Erroll GARNER, Tiny GRIMES, etc.) but moved into R&B after first hit by Stick McGhee ('Drinkin' Wine Spo-Dee-O-Dee' was no. 3 '49). Became the most important R&B label in '50s with Ray CHARLES, Ruth BROWN, Joe TURNER, LaVern BAKER, Chuck WILLIS, the CLOVERS, Clyde McPHATTER and the DRIFTERS, Little Esther, etc. Ex-Billboard R&B reviewer Jerry Wexler joined as prod./talent scout '53. Ahmet's brother Nesuhi Ertegun, formerly lecturer in jazz/folk at UCLA, set up jazz division '56, signed MODERN JAZZ QUARTET, Charles MINGUS, John COLTRANE, Ornette COLEMAN, Rahsaan Roland KIRK, Mose ALLISON, others; also in '56 LEIBER & STOLLER signed independent songwriting/ prod. deal, created string of crossover hits for the COASTERS. Signed distribution deal with Memphis-based Stax label '60; Wexler sent stars to record there and to Fame Studios at Muscle Shoals, Ala., then distributed Fame label; thus the Atlantic group was at forefront of SOUL (*which see*), roster incl. those named above plus Otis REDDING, Solomon BURKE, SAM & DAVE, Percy SLEDGE, Don COVAY, Joe TEX, Eddie FLOYD, Arthur CONLEY, etc. Bobby DARIN on Atco was the only big success '50s with a white act, but in '60s the group signed BUFFALO SPRINGFIELD, IRON BUTTERFLY, the RASCALS, later LED ZEPPELIN, CROSBY STILLS NASH & YOUNG, YES, EMERSON LAKE & PALMER, Eric CLAPTON etc.: became second only to giant Columbia in pop music of decade: having evolved from specialist independent to major label, was taken over '68 by Warner Communications to become part of Warner – Elektra – Atlantic (*see* WEA). Signed distribution deal with Rolling Stone label early '70s; issued first LPs on major label by ART ENSEMBLE OF CHICAGO; continued pop/soul successes incl. Roberta FLACK, CHIC, MANHATTAN TRANSFER, Bette MIDLER, Sister Sledge. Other subsidiary companies incl. Cat, Clean, East-West labels, Progressive Music (publishing).

ATWELL, Winifred (*b* '14, Tunapuna, Trinidad; *d* Feb. '83, Sydney, Australia) UK pop pianist. Began playing age 4, recitals at 6. Degree in chemistry; played piano in spare time, later studying in London, NYC. Making no headway in classical music, moved into pop; successful appearance at London Casino charity concert mid-'40s led to variety, cabaret, first broadcast '47, contract with Decca UK '51. Second single 'Jezebel' did well; 'Black And White Rag' big hit (written '08 by ragtime composer George Botsford, 1874-1949), established gimmick of tinny 'old-time' piano sound: the 'other piano' became part of the act. Played London Palladium, Royal Command performance, had top 10 hit 'Brittania Rag' '52; 'Coronation Rag', 'Flirtation Rag' and 'Let's Have A Party' (knees-up medley) all

made top 10 '53. Concert with LPO at Royal Albert Hall followed; tours of Australia, New Zealand, USA; charted '54 with Rachmaninov's '18th Variation On A Theme Of Paganini', then had first no. 1 with 'Let's Have Another Party'. More top 20 hits, tours, classical concerts ('56 with Andre KOSTELANETZ) made her one of UK's best-paid stars. Appeal faded in the '60s; by '72 she lived in Australia; last performance '80.

AUDIENCE UK art-rock group c.'70. Howard Werth, vocals; Trevor Williams, bass, keyboards; Keith Gemmell, sax; Tony Connor, drums. Debut LP *Audience* '69 (on Polydor) all but ignored; after playing support to LED ZEPPELIN at London Lyceum signed to Tony Stratton-Smith's emerging Charisma label, along with similar quirkily English GENESIS. Intelligent rock of LPs *Friend's Friend's Friend* '70, *House On The Hill* '71, *Lunch* '72 (with session musicians) never widely appreciated in UK; cult following in USA after tour with FACES. Also made film soundtrack *Bronco Bullfrog* '70. Last shortlived lineup saw Gemmell replaced by Patrick Neubergh; Nick Judd on keyboards; split '72. Prod. of last two LPs Gus Dudgeon went on to work with Elton JOHN *et al.*; Connor joined long-running popsters HOT CHOCOLATE; Gemmell to Stackridge and reggae sessions; Williams to Jonathan Kelly. Werth recruited most of Hookfoot (and Dudgeon) to record *'King Brilliant* '75 as Howard Werth and the Moonbeams; on Demon with *Six Of One And Half A Dozen Of The Other* '82, but luck did not improve.

AUGER, Brian (*b* 18 July '39, London) Keyboards, leader. Voted best new jazz artist by *Melody Maker* '64; switched to R&B that year. First group incl. the future Mahavishnu players Rick Laird, bass; John McLAUGHLIN, guitar; disbanded end '64 to form Trinity with Rick Brown, bass, Mickey Waller, drums. Name of group changed to Steampacket after adding singers Long John BALDRY and Rod STEWART from Baldry's Hoochie Coochie Men; Vic Briggs, guitar, Julie Driscoll, vocals, joined. Driscoll was secretary of manager Giorgio Gomelsky, who also managed YARDBIRDS; Auger played harpsichord on their 'For

Your Love' '65. Steampacket's vocalists showcased separately on stage, as was Auger with his own instrumentals; his distinctive, distorted organ sound was produced by playing the Hammond through a guitar valve (tube) amplifier. Predictable ego problems split group mid-'66, Baldry to Bluesology, Stewart to Shotgun Express; Driscoll stayed on to make 'This Wheel's On Fire' for Gomelsky's Marmalade label; DYLAN song made no. 5 UK '68. She quit on US tour, leaving *Streetnoise* LP as group's final testament. Back to Trinity, which finally split '70; final lineup had Dave Ambrose, bass; Gary Boyle, guitar; Clive Thacker, drums. Auger joined US-based jazz rock group Oblivion Express with everchanging personnel incl. Jim Mullen (of MORRISSEY-MULLEN), Robbie McIntosh and Steve Ferrone (Average White Band); group's output overshadowed by re-releases of old material, but *Closer To It* '73 successful LP from Oblivion. '78 saw reunion with Driscoll for LP *Encore*; '84 brought Blues Reunion aggregation with Spencer DAVIS, guitar, and Pete York, drums; also Colin Hodgkinson, bass (ex-Back Door). Anthology of Auger and Driscoll *London 1964/67* issued '77; *Jam Session* with Jimmy PAGE and Sonny Boy WILLIAMSON in '82, both on Charly. Like John MAYALL, Auger is remembered as much for who he played with as for his music.

AUGUST, Jan (*b* Jan Augustoff, c. '12, NYC; *d* 17 Jan. '76) Pianist. Self-taught; played Greenwich Village clubs as teenager; later played xylophone with Paul WHITEMAN, Ferde Grofe. Cocktail piano in clubs, records on Mercury; accent on pseudo-Latin beat then considered sophisticated ('Malaguena', 'Oye Negra', 'My Shawl', etc.). 'Misirlou' biggest hit '47 (Greek song from '34); 'Bewitched' (with HARMONICATS) '50, 'Theme From Three Penny Opera' ('Moritat') under Richard Hayman's name '56 also hits.

AULD, Georgie (*b* John Altwerger, 19 May '19, Toronto) Saxophones. To NYC '29; had started on alto, switched to tenor infl. by Coleman HAWKINS. Worked with Bunny BERIGAN, Artie SHAW, Jan SAVITT, Benny GOODMAN, Shaw again '37-42. Best known recordings with Goodman sextet '40-41 re-

veal fine swing era soloist with big tone, already slightly boppish ideas (plays on about half the tracks in CBS Charlie CHRISTIAN compilation *Solo Flight*). Served in US Army; own big band after WWII played clubs with arrs. by Manny ALBAM, Al COHN, Neal HEFTI; featured at various times Sarah VAUGHAN, Erroll GARNER, Sonny BERMAN, Dizzy GILLESPIE, Billy BUTTERFIELD, Freddie Webster. Broke up '46; from then on mostly small groups; commercial and studio work in Las Vegas, L.A.; mus. dir. for Tony MARTIN, '67. Many USA LPs as leader. Tours, albums in Japan in '70s. Acted on Broadway (*The Rat Race* '49); played bandleader, dubbed soundtrack tenor for Robert DeNiro in *New York, New York* '77, Martin Scorsese film set post-war. Reissues incl. big band sets on Musicraft label ('45-6 tracks), *Homage* '59 on Xanadu; in UK *Jump Georgie Jump* on Hep, *I've Got You Under My Skin* '56 on Jasmine.

AUSTIN, Gene (*b* Eugene Lucas, 24 June 1900, Gainesville, Texas; *d* 24 Jan. '72) Singer. Ran away at 15 to join the circus; US Army in Mexico and WWI; started in vaudeville '23, first records for Victor March '25, became famous with 'My Blue Heaven' '27. It may have sold 5 million copies, astonishing when a hit song normally sold more sheet music than discs; it was one of the biggest hits of the entire era before '55, and 'Ramona' was almost as big '28. Altogether *Pop Memories* lists 55 hits '25-34 incl. nine at no. 1. A genial man who enjoyed his success; did radio, film work; co-wrote flapper-era standards 'How Come You Do Me Like You Do', 'When My Sugar Walks Down The Street', 'The Lonesome Road'. He had good taste in entertainers; among his friends were Jimmie RODGERS and Fats WALLER; he recorded with Waller '29, crooning Waller's 'Your Fate Is In My Hands', again '39: 'Sweet Sue', 'I Can't Give You Anything But Love'. Featured guest on radio series '36-8; had own California club My Blue Heaven '40s; appeared on Merv Griffin TV show '71.

AUSTIN, Lovie (*b* Cora Calhoun, 19 Sep. 1887, Chattanooga, Tenn.; *d* 10 July '72, Chicago, Ill.) Blues pianist. Worked in Knoxville, Nashville; vaudeville tours; led

Blues Serenaders, recording for Paramount '24-6. Directed own shows, playing Club Alabam NYC with *The Lovie Austin Revue* '26; settled in Chicago and led band at Monogram theatre for 20 years. As house pianist for Paramount, backing Ma RAINEY, Louis ARMSTRONG, Ethel WATERS, others, she wrote many songs ('Graveyard Blues' recorded by Bessie SMITH). Defence work during WWII; resumed theatre activities, played Jimmy Payne's Dancing School for many years; last recordings '61 on Prestige: *Albert Hunter With Lovie Austin And Her Blues Serenaders.*

AUSTIN, Patti (*b* 10 Aug. '48, Cal.) Soul singer. Made stage debut age 3 singing 'Teach Me Tonight' at Apollo theatre during Dinah WASHINGTON act, appeared on Sammy DAVIS Jr TV show; more TV, theatre dates; worked on stage in *Lost In The Stars* and *Finian's Rainbow*, went to Europe age 9 with bandleader/arranger Quincy JONES. Toured with Harry BELAFONTE age 16; established as studio performer at 17, session credits with Paul SIMON, Billy JOEL, Frankie Valli, George BENSON, Roberta FLACK, etc. Returned to spotlight with jazz-infl. LPs on CTI '76-80: *End Of A Rainbow, Havana Candy, Live At The Bottom Line, Body Language*; incl. own songs. Sessioned with MARSHALL TUCKER, STEELY DAN, Blues Brothers (John Belushi, 1949-82; Dan Aykroyd) all in '80; then linked again with Jones (who calls her 'the daughter I don't remember asking for'). Sang lead on his '81 smash 'The Dude', won Grammy '82; title track hit single from debut LP *Every Home Should Have One* '81 on Jones's Qwest label; LP also incl. duet with James Ingram 'Baby Come To Me', became theme on TV soap opera *General Hospital*, made no. 1 USA, no. 11 UK '83. Second duet 'How Do You Keep The Music Playing' from film *Best Friends* nominated for best song Oscar. Second solo album on Qwest called *It's Gonna Be Special* in USA '84, eponymous *Patti Austin* in UK; then *Getting Away With Murder* '85. Has still to gain stardom she deserves.

AUSTIN, Sil (*b* Sylvester Austin, 17 Sep. '29, Dunnellon, Fla.) Tenor sax, leader. Won talent show at Apollo theatre '46 with 'Danny Boy'. Worked for Roy ELDRIDGE '49, Cootie WILLIAMS '49-52, Tiny BRADSHAW '52-4. Composed a song called 'Ping-Pong'; his favourite solo of his own was on Bradshaw's record of it; Ella FITZGERALD recorded it, bestowed nickname Ping-Pong on Austin. Formed own band, signed with Mercury, had several R&B hits; 'Slow Walk' made no. 3 R&B, no. 17 pop chart '56. His ambition was to start a BASIE-ish big band, but he was born too late for that.

AUTRY, Gene (*b* Orvon Autry, 29 Sep. '07, Tioga Springs, Texas) Most successful of singing cowboys. Father Baptist minister. Played sax; preferred singing, switched to guitar. Worked as railway telegrapher in Oklahoma; sang for a stranger sending a wire who encouraged him; turned out to be humorist Will Rogers. Went to NYC on free rail pass, auditioned for Victor, told to go away and practise on radio; own radio show in Tulsa; then to WLS Barn Dance in Chicago and success '30-34. Sears & Roebuck catalogue carried full-page ad for his records; songbooks, guitars carried his name. Like others began as Jimmie RODGERS imitator, singing Rodgers songs; also 'A Gangster's Warning', 'You Are My Sunshine', 'My Old Pal Of Yesterday', and one of the biggest sellers of all time, 'That Silver-Haired Daddy Of Mine', co-written with Jimmie Long; sold 30,000 copies in three months (EVERLY BROTHERS revived it on '58 LP *Songs Our Daddy Taught Us*). Another famous Autry record 'The Death Of Mother Jones' was labour movement song, his disc available on at least seven labels from ARC conglomerate. In '34 producer Nat Levine, looking for someone who could ride, sing, act for Western B movies settled for Autry, who was no actor, knowing that films were aimed at same small-town audience that heard him on radio. First solo epic was 12-part sci-fi serial *Phantom Empire* (sang 'Silver-Haired Daddy' in eight episodes); then made over 100 movies for Republic, Monogram (*Boots And Saddles* '37, *Under Western Stars* '38, *Carolina Moon* '40, etc.). The songs became more cowboy-flavoured ('Tumbling Tumbleweeds', 'Mexicali Rose' '36); comic sidekicks (first Smiley Burnette, then Pat Buttram) were popular with kids the world over; visit to Dublin '39 allegedly brought a million people into the streets: Champion became a very famous horse. Jimmy WAKELY, Johnny BOND among those who came to Hollywood as members of Autry organisation. Became wealthy, but stopped own career by volunteering during WWII, spent flying in Burma: Roy ROGERS took his place as king of the Saturday matinee. Autry's hits postwar were seasonal money spinners: 'Rudolph The Rednosed Reindeer', 'Here Comes Santa Claus' came out '49, annually in charts for years; also 'Frosty The Snowman', 'Here Comes Peter Cottontail'. Continued as TV cowboy Saturday mornings with Buttram. Owned hotels, petrol and radio stations, TV production company, even baseball team (Los Angeles Angels). Elected to Country Music Hall of Fame '69. Compilations have incl. original hits, material from films, *Melody Ranch* radio show; *All American Cowboy/South Of The Border* on his own Republic label; several others available from Country Music Hall of Fame incl. *Sounds Like Jimmie Rogers*. Bond wrote unpublished biography.

AVALON, Frankie (*b* Francis Thomas Avallone, 18 Sep. '39, Philadelphia, Pa.) Singer. Played trumpet as a child; guest spots on TV as a prodigy, instrumental single on RCA's X label. Formed group Rocco and the Saints with future rival Bobby RYDELL, but did not record again until '57, signed by music publishers to new Chancellor label; with constant access to locally based American Bandstand TV show, became big stars in teen idol genre: 24 hits '58-62. Third single 'De De Dinah' no. 7 USA owing to Avalon's pinching nose to make distinctive sound. 'Venus' no. 1 for five weeks in USA, reaching no. 3 in UK; syrupy song with Avalon singing flat is contender for all-time worst hit. 'Why' '60 also no. 1; that year he was eclipsed by Rydell, better singer on rival Cameo label. Appeared in films incl. beach party epics; later Alan Ladd's last, *The Carpetbaggers* '62 (role too small to be mentioned in film reference books). Disco remake of 'Venus' surprise top 50 hit '76; floated up in *Grease* '78; *The Idolmaker* '80 profiled Chancellor's Bob Marcucci, who with Peter DeAngelis pulled strings for Avalon and FABIAN. Attends Bandstand anniversaries; '85 tour with Fabian and Rydell as 'The Golden Boys of Bandstand'.

AVERAGE WHITE BAND UK soul/funk band formed '72 with group of Scottish musicians, named after their collective obsession with black music. Original lineup: Alan Gorrie (*b* 19 July '46, Perth), bass, vocals; Onnie McIntyre (*b* 25 Sep. '45, Lennoxtown), guitar; Robbie McIntosh (*b* '50; *d* 23 Sep. '74 L.A.), drums; Roger Ball (*b* 4 June '44, Dundee), sax, keyboards; Malcolm 'Molly' Duncan (*b* 24 Aug. '45, Montrose), sax; Mike Rosen, guitar, trumpet. McIntosh ex-Brian AUGER; last three worked together in Mogul Thrash, later freelanced as Dundee Horns; Rosen ex-Eclection. Added Hamish Stuart (*b* 8 Oct. '49, Glasgow) on guitar/vocals as Rosen left: Stuart and McIntyre had been in Dream Police (late '60s Glasgow). Band caught attention warming up Eric CLAPTON Rainbow Theatre comeback concert Jan. '73. False start with LP *Show Your Hand* on MCA '73; switched to Atlantic, famed house producer Arif Mardin (Aretha FRANKLIN, Wilson PICKETT, etc.) resulted in no. 1 LP *AWB* '74 which remains their best work: strong songs incl. disco instrumental 'Pick Up The Pieces' (no. 1 USA; no. 6 UK), cover of ISLEY BROS 'Work To Do'. McIntosh died in drug accident; replaced by another Auger sideman Steve Ferrone (*b* 25 Apr.'50, Brighton), ironically first black member of the band. Relocated to US West Coast after *Cut The Cake* went gold; title track remake of 'Pieces' with vocals, just missed UK top 30 but made USA top 10, confirming success of coals-to-Newcastle approach. LPs less satisfying from then on despite recording and touring with former DRIFTER Ben E. KING (*Benny And Us*, '77); split with Mardin following year didn't help. Brief reprise with *Shine* '80 (hit single 'Let's Go Around Again') prod. by David Foster; then public was confused by switch of producer to disco king Dan Hartman and guest guitarist Richie Stotts with Mohican hairstyle, recruited from New York punks Plasmatics for *Cupid's In Fashion* '82. Band members sessioned, esp. Dundee Horns; Gorrie's first solo LP *Sleepless Nights* '85 signalled end for band that got good mileage out of what was ultimately a musical cul-de-sac.

AXTON, Hoyt (*b* 25 Mar. '38, Commanche, Oklahoma) Singer, songwriter, actor. Mother Mae Boren Axton wrote 'Heartbreak Hotel' (Elvis PRESLEY), hits for Faron YOUNG, Hank SNOW, Jean SHEPARD; also worked as publicist for Snow, Jim REEVES, etc. Hoyt made first record in Nashville '57, served in US Navy, moved to West Coast: worked bars, coffee houses, made folk, blues records for Vee Jay. Wrote hits 'Greenback Dollar' (KINGSTON TRIO '63), 'The Pusher' (STEPPENWOLF '64), 'Joy To The World', 'Never Been To Spain' (THREE DOG NIGHT '71-2), 'Snowblind Friend' (Steppenwolf '71), other songs recorded by Waylon JENNINGS, Glen CAMPBELL, John DENVER, Ringo STARR ('The No-No Song', '75). Signed to Columbia '69 (LP *My Griffin Is Gone*), Capitol '70, A&M '72: hit singles 'When The Morning Comes' '74, 'Flash Of Fire' '76; LPs on A&M incl. *Fearless, Southbound, Life Machine, Road Songs, Less Than The Song* using excellent backing: Linda RONSTADT, James BURTON, John HARTFORD, Nicolette Larson, the Miracles, Joe Sample, Larry Carlton, others. Moved to MCA '77; minor country hits 'You're The Hangnail In My Life', 'Little White Moon'; LPs *Snowblind Friend, Free Sailin'*. Set up own Jeremiah label '78, named after the bullfrog in 'Joy To The World'; had biggest hits with 'Della And The Dealer', 'Rusty Old Halo' '79. Became actor with TV guest parts (*McCloud, Bionic Woman*), films *The Black Stallion* '79, *E.T.* '83, *Gremlins* '84. Current LPs: *Live!, Where Did The Money Go, Pistol Packin' Mama, A Rusty Old Halo, Everybody's Goin' On The Road*, last two on Young Blood label in UK.

AYERS, Kevin (*b* 16 Aug. '45, Herne Bay) UK singer/songwriter, born in Kent but raised in Malaya. Formed Wilde Flowers in Canterbury '63; combination of soul, R&B, jazz, qualify it as one of the first progressive outfits. Formed SOFT MACHINE '66 but quit after tiring six-month USA tour supporting Jimi HENDRIX to write songs in Majorca. Returned to sign with new EMI progressive label Harvest: LP *Joy Of A Toy* with Soft Machine plus keyboardist/arranger David Bedford; then formed Whole World with Bedford, Lol COXHILL on sax and Mike OLDFIELD, guitar and bass. Continued tradition of quirky, philosophical lyrics but was always too far left of rock mainstream to attract large following; no apparent wish

to chase success. Following *Shooting At The Moon, Whatevershebringswesing* '72 and *Ban An Amour* '73 he switched to Island for *The Confessions Of Dr Dream* '74 with guitarist Ollie Halsall, linked with new labelmates NICO, John CALE, Brian ENO for *June 1, 1974* same year, retired '75 to recharge his batteries; success of reissues incl. compilation of singles, out-takes in *Odd Ditties* '76 led to new Harvest LP *Yes We Have No Mañanas* '76, recording again with Halsall, Zoot MONEY and future POLICEman Andy Summers, but unwillingness to work regularly meant changing lineups. Spell under Elton JOHN manager John Reid in the late '70s threatened commercial breakthrough (*Rainbow Takeaway* '78); retired again to spend '80s in sunny Majorca. Has recorded there with Spanish musicians, Halsall; tracks released UK on Roadrunner as *Diamond Jack And The Queen Of Pain* '83. Deep baritone voice, quintessentially English lyrical content an acquired taste; compilation *The Kevin Ayers Collection* '83 on Charly is opportunity for those who missed him first time around; new LP *As Close As You Think* '86 on Illuminated.

AYERS, Roy E., Jr (*b* 10 Sep. '40, L.A.) Vibes, singer. Played piano as a child; at age 5 met Lionel HAMPTON, who gave him a pair of mallets. LPs with Curtis AMY early '60s; co-led group with Hampton HAWES; with Herbie MANN '66-70; also own quartet mid-'60s. Own LPs incl. *West Coast Vibes* '63 on United Artists; to Atlantic with variety of good sidemen, increasing range of musical interest: *Virgo Vibes, Stoned Soul Picnic; Daddy Bug And Friends* '69 incl. Laura NYRO song 'Emmie' with string quartet, woodwinds; LP features Ron CARTER, Herbie HANCOCK, Fred Waits, Mickey Roker, others. LPs on Polydor by fusion group Roy Ayers Ubiquity used Latin percussion, etc.; incl. *Ubiquity* '70; *He's Coming* '71 with Carter, Billy COBHAM; *Live At Montreux* '72, *Red Black And Green* '73. Wrote music for black sexploitation movie *Coffy* '73. More LPs: *Virgo Red* and *Change Up The Groove* '74, *A Tear To A Smile* and *Mystic Voyage* '75, *Everybody Loves The Sunshine* and *Vibrations* '76. Some success with single 'Running Away' '77, LP *Life Line*; dropped 'Ubiquity' name of group. More LPs: *Starbooty, Let's Do It, You Send*

Me, Step Into Our Life '78; single 'Get On Up, Get On Down' reached UK top 50. With trombonist Wayne Henderson (*see* CRUSADERS) had UK top 50 single 'Heat Of The Beat' '79; *Fever* LP '79 followed by third UK hit 'Don't Stop The Feeling' '80, LP *No Stranger To Love*. LPs continue with *Africa, Center Of The World* '81, *Feeling Good* '81; to CBS for *In The Dark* '84, *I'm The One (For Your Love Tonight)* '87. Eight Ayers LPs '76-9 in top 100 albums chart.

AYLER, Albert (*b* 13 July '36, Cleveland, Ohio; *d* 25 Nov. '70, NYC) Tenor sax. Played with Cecil TAYLOR, NYC; toured Europe with brother Don (trumpet; *b* Cleveland 5 Oct. '42); began recording NYC often with Sunny MURRAY, also collaborating with Don CHERRY. Burst upon 'new thing' or free jazz scene with honks, yelps and screeches of early '50s JATP or R&B, but with obvious technical command and using starting points from Mexican or folk music rather than post-bop; totally confused critics and fans who use pre-printed stick-on labels. In era of 'black power', racial pride he frightened people, trying to forge a new thing by himself: in retrospect his music is much gentler than it seemed at the time, with investment in tonal beauty, unfashionably wide vibrato. LPs incl. *First Recordings*, made in Stockholm '62, now on GNP label; *My Name Is Albert Ayler* '63 made in Copenhagen, on Debut; *Swing Low, Sweet Spiritual* and *Spirits* on Debut apparently made the same day Feb. '64: *Spirits* on Arista and Freedom was called *Witches And Devils*. *Prophecy* and *Spiritual Unity* are by a trio with Murray and Gary PEACOCK; *New York Eye And Ear Control* added Cherry, Roswell RUDD, John Tchicai to make a sextet (all '64 on ESP). *Vibrations* '64 with Cherry revealed romanticism ('Mothers'); *Spirits Rejoice* '65 featured collective improvisation; live concerts and fragments from '66-7 have been issued; *Love Cry* '67 was a respite and a reworking of favourite themes ('Bells', 'Ghosts') with Don Ayler and a harpsichord. *New Grass* '68 was a rock LP that didn't work. *Music Is The Healing Force Of The Universe* and *The Last Album* '69 on ABC-Impulse incl. bagpipes; a French concert from '70 has been issued. Then he was found floating in the East River, his death never explained. 2-disc

sets *Paris 1966* on Hat Hut, *Village* on MCA have been compiled.

AZIMUTH UK trio: Norma Winstone (*b* 23 Sep. '41, London), vocals; John Taylor (*b* 25 Sep. '42, Manchester), piano; Kenny WHEELER on trumpet. Winstone highly regarded jazz singer, worked with Mike WESTBROOK, John DANKWORTH; Taylor, her husband, was regular at Ronnie SCOTT's club '77, then formed this trio. LPs on ECM incl. *Azimuth* '77, *The Touchstone* '78, *Départ* '79 with Ralph Towner, guitar; *Azimuth 85*. Original compositions described as 'voice weaving with horn, ecstatic piano rhapsodies'. Winstone and Taylor had worked with Wheeler before; Taylor also recorded with Wheeler and Dave HOLLAND '83. Winstone albums incl. *Edge Of Time* '72; for *Somewhere Called Home* '87 on ECM (accompanied by Taylor and Tony COE) she wrote words to tunes by Wheeler, Towner, Egberto Gismonti, Bill EVANS, Fran Landesman. Taylor and reedman Stan Sulzmann made instrumental duet LP of Wheeler songs *Everybody's Song But My Own?* '87 on Loose Tubes label.

AZNAVOUR, Charles (*b* Shahnour Aznavurjan, 22 May '24, Paris, France) Singer, songwriter, actor. Family had fled Turkish massacre of Armenians '15; mother actress, father musician; operated restaurant but remained poor. First audition at age 9: landed part of Caucasian soldier in play. Restaurant closed following German occupation of Paris; began acting on tour. Voice at the time such that 'I became the best newspaper-caller on the Boulevards.' Teamed with actor Pierre Roche by nervous announcer, who introduced them as double act; they began writing songs during nine-year partnership. First hit 'J'ai bu' ('I Have Drunk') sung by George Ulmer, followed by flood of songs recorded by Mistinguette, Maurice CHEVALIER, Edith PIAF, etc. Went to USA '48 without visa; 'We owed our entry permit to the Judge's love of *Finian's Rainbow*' (which Aznavour had translated into French). Appeared at Café Society NYC, 40 weeks in Canada; Aznavour since toured North America several times. Went solo '50, encouraged by Piaf, others to interpret own songs; resumed acting, which had brought little work because 'I was too small, too ugly.' Long refused film offers, but small part in *La Tête Contre les Murs* '58 won Crystal award from French film academy; then in *Shoot The Pianist* '60, *Passage du Rhin* '61. Single 'La Mama' '63 no. 1 for 12 weeks in France; Matt Monro cover was no. 36 UK '64. More films: *Cloportes* '65, *Candy* '68, *The Adventurers, The Games, Un Beau Monstre* all c.'70. First UK hit 'The Old Fashioned Way' '73; no. 1 UK with 'She' '75, written for TV series *The Seven Faces Of Woman*. Films *And Then There Were None* '75, *Sky Riders* '76, etc. Among other songs: 'Yesterday When I Was Young', 'All Those Pretty Girls', 'Le Temps'. Warmth and angst in onstage performance called epitome of French romance; sings in both French and English ('Venice Blue' translated/adapted by Gene LEES). LPs incl. *A Tapestry Of Dreams, Charles Aznavour 1965, Son passé au présent*, three vols. of *Sings Aznavour*, all on French Barclay label. Autobiography *Aznavour par Aznavour* Paris '70.

AZTEC CAMERA Scottish band built around songwriting skill of Roddy Frame (guitar, vocals; *b* '64), with Malcolm Ross, guitar; Campbell Owens, bass; David Ruffy, drums. '79 band Neutral Blue did covers of CLASH, VELVET UNDERGROUND tunes; as Aztec Camera on Glasgow label; debut LP on Rough Trade *High Land, Hard Rain* '83 brought attention, along with praise for Frame from Elvis COSTELLO as most promising songwriter. Contract and LP taken over by WEA; single 'Oblivious' reissued on new label was a hit, 'Walk Out To Winter' also successful. Acoustic-based music marked by Frame's edgy melodies and florid, sometimes obscure lyrics. Second LP *Knife* '84 was debut on WEA; lavish production by Mark Knopfler threatened to obscure things further. 'All I Need Is Everything' from the LP skirted the charts; 12" version carried bonus: live cover of VAN HALEN's 'Jump!' Album's other tracks incl. cynical 'Just Like The USA', touching 'Birth Of The True', as well as over-

ambitious nine-minute title track. *Love* '87 was a Frame solo LP in all but name, hightech studio prod. threatening to swamp his fragile talent.

AZYMUTH Brazilian jazz trio formed '72: José Roberto Bertrami (aka 'Ze Roberto', *b* 21 Feb. '46, near São Paulo), keyboards, writer, producer; Ivan Conti (*b* Ivan Miguel Conti Maranhao, aka Mamao, 16 Aug. '46, Rio), percussion; Alex Malheiros (*b* Jose Alexandre Malheiros, 19 Aug. '46, Rio), bass. Bertrami worked in São Paulo nightclubs mid-'60s with singer Flora PURIM, percussionist AIRTO playing 'progressive' bossa novas. To Rio '67, formed samba trio, played in popular nightclub Canecao; met Mamao playing in rock band the Youngsters; they found Malheiros playing in bowling alley. Gigged, sessioned separately for five years (with Brazil's top musicians e.g. Milton Nascimento, Jorge Ben, DEODATO; Bertrami in Elis Regina's band for two years) while working on style described as *samba dioda* (crazy samba): blend of Brazilian rhythms and jazz-funk infl. by Bill EVANS, Gene KRUPA, Scott LA FARO. First Azymuth LP was film soundtrack *O Fabuloso Fittipaldi* '73, written by Bertrami; *Limite Horizonte* '74 and *Agui Nao Come Mosca* (Eagles don't eat flies) consolidated success. Appeared at Montreux Jazz Festival '77, toured South America; toured USA '78 with Purim and Airto; Bertrami arranged, played on Sarah VAUGHAN LP *I Love Brazil*. Solo LPs incl. Malheiros' *Atlantic Forest*, Conti's *The Human Factor* (incl. Brazilian rhythms, electronic percussion, synthesisers), Bertrami's *Blue Wave* '84, *Dreams Are Real* '86, all on Milestone, as are Azymuth LPs *Light As A Feather, Outubro, Telecommunication* '81 (incl. in first CD release from Fantasy group), *Cascades* '82, *Rapid Transit* '83, *Flame* (incl. Purim). *Spectrum* '85 incl. several famous Rio samba drummers, baiao rhythms of north-east Brazil, covers of songs by Marvin GAYE, Antonio Carlos Jobim, single 'Jazz Carnival' (hit in UK).

B

BABS, Alice (*b* Alice Nilson, 26 Jan. '24, Kalmar, Sweden) Singer; film and TV star in Europe. Toured with trio incl. Svend ASMUSSEN, early '60s. No. 43 UK hit '63 with 'After You've Gone'; made album *Serenade To Sweden* with Duke ELLINGTON in Paris '63, sang in his Sacred Concerts '65 NYC, '73 London; also Newport Jazz Festival '75. Ellington said, 'Alice Babs is a composer's dream, for with her he can forget all the limitations and just write his heart out.'

BABYS, The UK pop group formed '76. Lineup: John Waite (*b* 4 July '55, London), bass, vocals; Wally Stocker (*b* 27 Mar. '54, London), guitar; Mike Corby (*b* 3 July '55, London), keyboards, guitar; Tony Brock (*b* 31 Mar. '54, Bournemouth), drums. Demonstrated media awareness by circulating video (directed by Mike Mansfield) instead of demo tape, showcasing teen appeal confirmed by teenybop adulation at Spring '77 NYC concert debut. First LP *Babys* '76 prod. by American Bob Ezrin; after success of next LP *Broken Heart*, single 'Isn't It Time' (USA no. 13, '77) concentrated on USA, UK remaining apathetic; tailored-for-radio pop, cute image scored in USA, where media hype continued: band 'kidnapped', manager called in FBI to rescue them. Added bass Ricky Phillips for third album *Head First* '78, so Waite could concentrate on moves; Jonathan Cain then replaced Corby. More USA hits: 'Every Time I Think Of You' (no. 13 '79), 'Back On My Feet Again' (no. 33 '80), but formula wore thin; after *On The Edge* '80 they split '81. Waite's dalliance with Britt Ekland drew more headlines than musical career for a while; solo effort *Ignition* (made with Patti SMITH and friends) was false start; better luck with *No Brakes* '84, POLICE-derived 'Missing You' (USA no. 1/UK 9), 'Tears' (USA top 40), *Mask Of Smiles* '85.

BACHARACH, Burt (*b* 12 May '28, Kansas City, Mo.) Songwriter, pianist, arranger, conductor. To NYC as a child; studied with composers Milhaud, Martinů, Cowell; after US Army service '52-4 was accompanist/arr. for Polly Bergen, Steve LAWRENCE, AMES Bros, Vic DAMONE, then toured with Marlene Dietrich '58-63. At Paramount studios '57 met Hal David (*b* 25 May '21, Brooklyn), younger brother of lyricist Mack David; Hal wrote 'The Four Winds And The Seven Seas' with Don Rodney '49, 'American Beauty Rose' with Lee Pokriss, 'Broken-Hearted Melody' with Sherman Edwards '58-9. Bacharach wrote 'Baby, It's You' (hit by the SHIRELLES '61, covered on BEATLES' first LP) with Mack, but first hit with Hal was 'The Story Of My Life' (USA top 20 for Marty ROBBINS, '57); then 'Magic Moments' (Perry COMO top 5, '58). Bacharach became distinctive '60s composer, catchy tunes concealing complicated rhythms and changes. Wrote 'Tower Of Strength' with Bob Hilliard (no. 1 UK for Frankie VAUGHAN; no. 5 USA by Gene McDANIELS); David wrote words for Henry MANCINI ('Baby Elephant Walk', from film *Hatari!* '62), but Bacharach/David was the great team: 'Wives And Lovers' ('63, Jack JONES), 'Twenty Four Hours From Tulsa' ('64, Gene PITNEY), 'Make It Easy On Yourself' ('65, WALKER BROS), 'There's Always Something There To Remind Me' ('64, Sandie SHAW), 'I Just Don't Know What To Do With Myself' ('64, Dusty SPRINGFIELD), 'What The World Needs Now' ('65, Jackie DeSHANNON), 'Close To You' ('70, The CARPENTERS) all made major pop impression; but their ideal interpreter was Dionne WARWICK, with 'Don't Make Me Over' '63, 'Anyone Who Had A Heart' and 'Walk On By' '64, 'I Say A Little Prayer' and 'Alfie' '67, 'Do You Know The Way To San Jose?' '68, 'This Girl's In Love With You' '69. Cilla BLACK also scored in UK with 'Anyone Who Had A Heart' and 'Alfie'. In '65 they wrote film score *What's New, Pussycat?*, Woody Allen/Peter Sellers comedy; Tom JONES had hit title song.

Same year Bacharach with chorus and orchestra had no. 4 hit UK with 'Trains And Boats And Planes'. In '68 they wrote their only Broadway score, for Neil Simon's *Promises, Promises*, based on Billy Wilder film *The Apartment*, incl. hit 'I'll Never Fall In Love Again'; it ran for over 1200 performances, won a Tony. Won two Oscars '69 for film score *Butch Cassidy And The Sundance Kid*, song from film 'Raindrops Keep Fallin' On My Head'. Film musical *Lost Horizon* '73 flopped; team with David had run out of steam and requirement to prod. Warwick sessions ran into trouble when they couldn't come up with material; Bacharach entered a lean period as pianist, conductor, singing in what record company called 'rumpled and earnest baritone'. No top 10 hits '71-81: LP *Women* '78 with Houston Symphony Orch. flopped; marriage to actress Angie Dickinson failed; remarried to singer/songwriter Carole Bayer SAGER, they co-wrote '81 Oscar winner 'Arthur's Theme (Best That You Can Do)' with Christopher CROSS; performed at White House together; wrote songs for Neil DIAMOND, Roberta FLACK; then reunited with Warwick (and guests Elton JOHN, Stevie WONDER, Gladys KNIGHT) on 'That's What Friends Are For', also 'On My Own' for Patti LABELLE and Michael McDonald, both no. 1 hits '86; also songs for new LPs by Knight and Natalie COLE. David became president of ASCAP '80, worked with others, e.g. Albert Hammond ('To All The Girls I've Loved Before', hit for Julio IGLESIAS and Willie NELSON '84).

BACHMAN-TURNER OVERDRIVE Canadian hard-rock band formed early '70s by Randy Bachman, after leaving first group GUESS WHO at height of fame '70. Solo LP *Axe* same year; illness prevented planned linkup with ex-NICE keyboardist Keith Emerson (later EMERSON, LAKE & PALMER); Bachman turned to production, working on LP for original Guess Who singer Chad Allan; duo made two LPs as Brave Belt for Reprise label with drummer brother Robbie Bachman (*b* 18 Feb. '53, Winnipeg), bass C. F. 'Fred' Turner (*b* 16 Oct. '43, Winnipeg). As group changed name, label (to Mercury), yet another brother Tim replaced Allan. Group's gearwheel logo, name borrowed from a trucking magazine led to 'working-

class rock' label. New outfit's first (eponymous) album released '73; took six months to chart in USA; single 'Let It Ride' took a year to reach no. 23; meanwhile *Bachman-Turner Overdrive 2* issued. By *Not Fragile* '74, guitarist Blair Thornton (*b* 23 July '50) recruited to replace would be producer Tim Bachman; his visual appeal helped band to promote LP to platinum sales. Same year saw hit singles 'Takin' Care Of Business' (USA no. 12), 'You Ain't Seen Nothin' Yet' (no. 1); Townshend-like power chords took latter to no. 2 UK. Anthemic 'Roll On Down The Highway' last UK hit at no. 22 (14 USA), but six top 40 hits to '76 some measure of stateside popularity; '75 LP *Four Wheel Drive* went platinum. As Randy Bachman left in '77, workmanlike guitar-boogie formula was worn out, though more LPs released as BTO rolled to a halt: total incl. *Head On* '75; *Freeways* '77, Jim Clench replacing Bachman; *Street Action, Rock'n'Roll Nights* '78, *Best Of* '76. Randy Bachman did unsuccessful second solo LP *Survivor* '78, returned to BTO sound with Ironhorse: two LPs *Ironhorse* '79, *Everything Is Grey* '80 did poorly; struck up songwriting partnership with Carl Wilson of BEACH BOYS, wrote two songs on their *Keeping The Summer Alive* LP '80; reformed Guess Who for nostalgia gigs in Canada '83; by then other Overdrivers had driven off the highway.

BAD COMPANY UK blues-rock group named after '72 western movie. Formed '73 by ex-FREE members Paul Rodgers (*b* 12 Dec. '49, Middlesbrough), piano, vocals; Simon Kirke (*b* 28 July '49), drums; recruited Mick Ralphs (*b* 31 Mar. '48, Hereford), guitar, piano, from MOTT THE HOOPLE; Boz Burrell (*b* Raymond Burrell, *b* '46, Lancs.), bass, ex-KING CRIMSON, to form 'supergroup'. They played everything except sax and some backing vocals on own LPs; even had luxury of leadsinger-turned-bassist Burrell singing harmony. Eponymous first LP manifesto for straight-ahead macho-rock swagger; titles like 'Can't Get Enough' (single no. 5 USA, no. 15 UK), 'Ready For Love' epitomised approach, LP went platinum USA. Steady rather than spectacular success with shrewd management of LED ZEPPELIN supremo Peter Grant, on whose label Swan Song they came out in USA; world tours associated with new LPs (on Island in UK) took band through decade. Next two LPs *Straight Shooter* '75, *Run With The Pack* '76 also platinum in USA, transatlantic top 5 album entries. 'Feel Like Makin' Love' from *Shooter* second and last UK top 20 single, but maintained more singles success in USA. Progressively more predictable, with none of Free's rough edges, but band always good on stage; three-year gap to *Rough Diamonds* suggests band felt played out. Appearance of Rodgers solo *Cut Loose* '84 on Atlantic confirmed split; he teamed with Led Zep guitarist Jimmy Page in another supergroup The Firm; Kirke played in little-known Wildlife; Burrell sessioned, notably with ex-FAMILY man Roger Chapman; Ralphs went back to the bars with own band: Ralphs solo *Take This* '85 was followed by Bad Company hits compilation *Ten From Six* '86; re-formed group with ex-Ted NUGENT Brian Howe replacing Rogers made *Fame And Fortune* '86.

BADFINGER UK pop group formed S. Wales mid-'60s as the Iveys: Pete Ham (*b* 27 Apr. '47, Swansea; *d* 23 Apr. '75, Weybridge), David Jenkins, guitars; Ron Griffiths, bass; Mike Gibbons (*b* c.'49, Swansea), drums. Spotted '66 by former jazzband leader Bill Collins (son Lewis, now actor, played in Mojos); he introduced the band to the BEATLES' Apple organisation through long-time friendship with Paul McCARTNEY's musician father, Jim. First single 'Maybe Tomorrow' cut '68 with new guitarist Tom Evans (*b* 21 June '47, Liverpool; *d* 23 Nov. '83, New Haw, Surrey) replacing Jenkins; made no. 60 in USA chart but LP of same name (released Europe only) flopped '69. McCartney lookalike guitarist Joey Molland (*b* 21 June '48, Liverpool) replaced Griffiths (Evans moving to bass) same year; this coincided with name change to Badfinger, patronage of McCartney himself; version of his 'Day After Day' (with Paul on piano) transatlantic top 10 hit, while rehash of much of first album into *Magic Christian Music* as soundtrack to Ringo STARR/Peter Sellers film also did well. String of Beatle-sounding hits followed: 'No Matter What', 'Day After Day' (produced by George HARRISON) both USA/UK top 10 hits, 'Baby Blue' USA no.

14; strong vocal harmony pop lapped up by fans bereaved by breakup of Beatles. Derivative style masked talent of Ham/Evans songwriting team; they wrote NILSSON's '72 transatlantic no. 1 'Without You'. Group prospered as Beatle connection continued: sessions for Harrison (*All Things Must Pass*), LENNON (*Imagine*), Ringo ('It Don't Come Easy'); appearance at '71 all-star Concert for Bangla Desh. But disintegration of Apple label, management problems took toll: *Badfinger* '74 (first LP on WB) much inferior to *No Dice* '70, *Straight Up* '71 (prod. by Todd RUNDGREN); had to compete with *Ass*, Apple LP released after their departure. WB withdrew *Wish You Were Here* '74 pending investigation of alleged management problems; group split. Ham hanged himself in fit of depression. New projects of Molland (Natural Gas), Evans (Dodgers) failed; duo re-formed '78 with Tony Kaye (keyboards), Peter Clarke (drums) for two more LPs, USA Hot 100 hit 'Hold On' '81. Suicide of Evans, reportedly after battle over royalties on 'Without You', brought down curtain. Good pop group might have had longer career if short-cut to fame had not been available.

BAD MANNERS UK ska revival band, formed London '80: rose to fame on back of 2-Tone dance-music movement, although did not record initially for label of that name. First lineup: Buster Bloodvessel (*b* Douglas Trendle, 6 Sep. '58), lead vocals; Gus 'Hot Lips' Herman, trumpet; Andrew 'Marcus Absent' Marson and Chris Kane, saxes; David Farren, bass; Winston Bazoomies (Alan Sayag), harmonica; Brian Chew-it (Tuitt), drums; Louis Alphonzo (Cook), guitar; Martin Stewart, keyboards. Together since schooldays, band's appeal centred around Trendle, shaven-headed heavyweight whose cartooned head became band's logo; his penchant for outrageous costumes (e.g. ballet dancer's tutu), being photographed in vat of baked beans etc. soon brought press attention. Signed to Magnet label, hit with typically ridiculous 'Ne-Ne Na-Na Na-Na Nu-Nu' (no. 28 UK) followed by 'Lip Up Fatty' (no. 15), 'Special Brew' (no. 3, ode to Carlsberg lager), 'Lorraine' (no. 21, to blow-up doll), all '80. Tight ensemble of good musicians carried on with four top 40 hits '81, incl. 'Can Can' (no. 3), semi-serious 'Walking In The Sunshine' (no. 10), also most successful LP *Gosh It's Bad Manners* (no. 18 LP chart). Only top 40 hit '82 was sex-changed revival of Millie's '64 hit 'My Girl [Boy] Lollipop' (no. 9); novelty faded and ska unfashionable once more. Finally appeared on 2-Tone label on '81 *Dance Craze* soundtrack album; hits anthologised on TV-advertised *The Height Of Bad Manners*. Toured Europe, Middle East, USA; despite lack of record company support and previous albums not released in USA, drew 3000-plus to gigs there; ska revival in USA (Untouchables, etc.) resulted in contract with Portrait (CBS subsidiary), new LP '85: fun never goes out of style for long. Only MADNESS of that era's UK groups have lasted longer; though Bad Manners have yet to show comparable musical diversity, garrulous Trendle may outlast his band.

BAEZ, Joan (*b* 9 Jan. '41, Staten Island NY) Folk-rock singer. Sang in folk clubs/coffee houses, Greenwich Village, Boston, Newport '59. First eponymous solo LPs accompanying herself on the guitar among first successes of folk boom '60-1; silvery voice, unfussy treatment of trad. ballads were revelation after long neglect of folk music in USA. Next two LPs live concerts (more of this material released '84); fourth incl. Pete SEEGER song 'We Shall Overcome': became anthem of civil rights/anti-war movements. Eighth LP *Joan* '67 was unwise attempt at art-song treatment, with arr. by Peter Schickele. An early advocate of her friend Bob DYLAN, introduced him at concerts; tenth album *Any Day Now* '68 was 2-disc set of his songs: should have been edited to one, some songs needing his emotionally naked delivery rather than her precision, but incl. e.g. nice treatment of 'Don't Think Twice, It's All Right'. She founded Institute for the Study of Non-Violence '65; became active opponent of Vietnam war, arrested at demo; published journal *Daybreak* '68; married student leader David Harris '68 (later jailed for resisting the draft; son Gabriel born '69; they separated '71). Single 'The Night They Drove Ol' Dixie Down' (song by Robbie Robertson) no. 5 USA '72, from 2-disc *Blessed Are*; 2-disc *Ballad Book* '72 was compilation of first five Vanguard LPs. Part of *Where Are You Now, My Son?* '73

taped in Hanoi; then after string of LPs loaded with political content she returned to commercial product (confessing frankly that she needed the money); changed labels to A&M; *Diamonds And Rust* '75 incl. electric band, dubbed strings, own comps. and songs by sister Mimi FARINA, Jackson BROWNE and others. Title song a good one – single hit, own comp. about relationship with Dylan – but album was uneven; version of Dylan's 'A Simple Twist Of Fate' rashly imitated his style with ridiculous result. Toured with band, issued live 2-disc set *From Every Stage*; *Gulf Winds* contained entirely own comps. all '76. Joined Dylan's Rolling Thunder tour, appeared in his overlong home movie *Renaldo And Clara*; switched labels to Portrait (a mistake, she admitted later): LPs incl. *Blowin' Away* '77, *Honest Lullaby* '79, live *European Tour* '81. Conservatives hated her, but only fools doubted her integrity. When the Daughters of the American Revolution would not rent their hall in Washington DC to Baez for a concert '60s, as they had refused it to black contralto Marian Anderson during the Roosevelt era, she appeared on Irv Kupcinet's Chicago talk show, saying hardly a word while liberal Republican Senator Chuck Percy tonguelashed an inarticulate D.A.R. chairperson: Baez was a heroine of terrible times without even trying. With no record contract for several years, she denied being blacklisted for politics in Reagan era: 'I don't think they would care whether I was a communist or a fascist if I would commit myself to making platinum singles.' Sang at Farm Aid, Amnesty International tour '86, songs by U2, TEARS FOR FEARS, PINK FLOYD. First USA LP in eight years *Recently* '87 on Gold Castle Records has songs by U2, DIRE STRAITS, Peter GABRIEL: 'I haven't been a folk singer for 15 years.' Autobiography *And A Voice To Sing With* '87.

BAHULA, Julian (*b* '38, Mamelodi, South Africa) Drummer. Played drums as a child, then drum kit in dance bands, but returned to African drums, with Philip Tabane and Abe Cindi forming legendary group Malombo, South African jazz band which toured widely; albums incl. *1964 Jazz Festival Winners* on Gallo. Tabane left '65; band carried on attracting international attention with LPs such as *Sangoma* and *Pele Pele*. Bahula went to UK '73 with multiracial band Joburg Hawk, which made one LP before splitting; then formed own band Jabula, with Lucky Ranku and Ernest Mothle: they had immediate success with LPs on Caroline, *African Soul* and *Soweto My Love*. The band toured extensively in Europe before Bahula settled in London and started promotion company Tsafrica for African music, regular Friday evening gig at 100 Club in Oxford Street expanding into larger festivals, bigger venues. Album *Jabula With Me* released '82 on Pläne; following year Bahula helped organise the Nelson Mandela's Birthday Festival, from which came excellent compilation album *African Sounds For Mandela*. He then reformed his band, renaming it Jazz Africa, now among the most active musical units in London. Also wrote theme music for Channel 4's series *Africa* presented by historian Basil Davidson.

BAILES BROTHERS Country-gospel group of late '40s-early '50s: Johnny, Kyle, Homer, and Walter Butler Bailes (*b* 17 Jan. '20, North Charleston, W. Va.). Appalachian-based style with guitar, mandolin, dobro; vocally suggestive of Pentecostal Holiness. Began on local radio in West Virginia, moved to Grand Ole Opry, later to Louisiana Hayride in Shreveport, La. Recorded for Columbia, King. Wrote gospel, sentimental love songs some of which became classics of their kind: 'Dust On The Bible', 'Give Mother My Crown', 'Oh So Many Years'. Former members of their band incl. Red SOVINE, Little Jimmy DICKENS, Shot Jackson, Molly O'Day, Jimmy Osbourne; they were also major infl. on Carl BUTLER.

BAILEY, Benny (*b* Ernest Harold Bailey, 13 Aug. '25, Cleveland, Ohio) Trumpet. Soloist and leadman with roots in bop; played with Dizzy GILLESPIE, Lionel HAMPTON, Quincy JONES; mostly in Europe since late '50s. Member of CLARKE-BOLAND big band; played on Les McCann-Eddie HARRIS LP *Swiss Movement* from '69 Montreux Jazz Festival; own LPs made in Sweden, Germany since '56 incl. *Soul Eyes* with Mal WALDRON '68; *Serenade To A Planet* with Kenny CLARKE '76; *East Of Isar* with Sal Nistico '76; *Grand Slam* made NYC '78

with fine cast: Charlie ROUSE, Billy Hart (*b* 29 Nov. '40, Washington DC), drums, Richard Wyands (*b* 2 July '28, Oakland, Cal.), piano, Sam Jones (*b* 12 Nov. '24, Jacksonville, Fla.), bass. Co-led working band Upper Manhattan Jazz Society with Rouse; LP of that title '81 with Al Dailey, Buster Williams, Keith COPELAND released on Enja '85.

BAILEY, Deford (*b* 1899, near Nashville, Tenn.) Harmonica. Polio age 3 left slight deformities. Came second in harp contest with 135 others; played on radio, became popular regular on WSM Barn Dance '25 at a time when USA popular music still contained minstrelsy element. Led off a '27 show with his *Pan American Blues* following broadcast of classical concert when George D. Hay rechristened show Grand Ole Opry. Appeared on 49 of 52 Opry broadcasts in '28; got $5 a performance; crudely dismissed '41, alleged unwilling to learn new tunes. For many years he remained the only black ever to have appeared on the show. Records incl. eight sides for Victor '28, mostly blues; he may have been the first artist to record in Nashville.

BAILEY, Derek (*b* 29 Jan. '30, Sheffield, Yorkshire) Guitar, composer. From musical family; served apprenticeship '52-65 in theatres, dance hall, recording sessions, etc.; began improvising '65, became major artist on European contemporary scene: listeners persevering with his demanding, abstract music are rewarded with considerable drama and wit. He also plays a 19-string guitar, crackle-box, ukelele. Worked with Spontaneous Music Ensemble (two discs of *Eighty-Five Minutes* recorded '74, issued '87 on Emanem, with John STEVENS, Evan Parker, Kent Carter, Trevor Watts). Formed Incus Records '70 with Parker and Tony Oxley, first independent in UK owned by musicians; formed Company '76, ensemble with changing personnel, but has mostly played solo or duo with selected company such as Parker, Steve LACY, Tony COE; Book *Improvisation: Its Nature And Practice In Music* '80 has been translated into several languages. More than 50 LPs since '68 incl. *Music Improvisation Company* '70, *Improvisations For Guitar And Cello* '71 with Dave HOLLAND on ECM; solo

61

Domestic And Public Pieces '75-6 on Quark, *Improvisation* '75 on Cramps, *New Sights, Old Sounds* '78 on Morgue; also *Duo And Trio Observations* '78 on Kitty with Japanese musicians, *Yankees* '82 on Celluloid, with George LEWIS, John ZORN on reeds; *View From Six Windows* '82 on Metalanguage nominated for a Grammy, solo except for one vocal by Christine Jeffrey. On Incus: *The London Concert* with Parker, *Duo* with cellist Tristan Honsinger, *Company 1* with Parker and two others, *Company 2* with Parker, Anthony BRAXTON, *Company 3* with Han Bennink on several instruments; *Company 4* with Lacy, all '75-6; *Company 5* with Honsinger, Parker, Lacy, Braxton, Leo SMITH, bassist Maarten van Regteren-Altena, *Company 6* and *7* with Lol COXHILL, Bennink, Steve Beresford, all '77; *Fictions* '77 with Coxhill, several others; *Time* '79 with Coe, *Fables* '80 with Lewis, Parker, Holland; solo *Aida* '80, others.

BAILEY, Mildred (*b* Mildred Rinker, 27 Feb. '07, Tekoa, Wash.; *d* 12 Dec. '51, Poughkeepsie, NY) Singer, bandleader. Part American Indian. Unique high-pitched range; accuracy and jazz-infl. phrasing made her one of the best girl singers of the '30s-40s, a favourite with musicians. Played piano in cinema, music store; brother Al was one of Paul WHITEMAN's Rhythm Boys trio with Bing CROSBY; she worked for Whiteman from '29, became famous on records, radio. Married Red NORVO, who was in the band; they co-led excellent band '36-9 billed as Mr and Mrs Swing, with arr. by Eddie SAUTER. With Benny GOODMAN '39; solo in '40s, own radio show '44-5. Serious car crash '32 led to inactivity, weight problem which stayed with her, contributed to poor health later. *Her Greatest Performances* is CBS 3-disc compilation from '29-46, full of beauty.

BAILEY, Pearl (*b* 29 Mar. '18, Newport News, Va.) Singer, actress. Born in same town same year as Ella FITZGERALD; brother of dancer Bill Bailey. Moved to Washington DC; won amateur night contest age 13; later another at Apollo. Worked as dancer with Noble SISSLE; singer with Edgar HAYES, Cootie WILLIAMS '43-4; lifelong friendship with Don REDMAN began: he wrote arr. for Williams/Bailey, e.g. 'Get Up, Mule'. NYC nightclub debut at Village Vanguard '44; eight months at Blue Angel: a natural cabaret artist, developed throwaway style, full of asides, raps. Toured with Cab CALLOWAY replacing Sister Rosetta THARPE. On stage in Harold ARLEN/Johnny MERCER show *St Louis Woman* '46 (songs 'A Woman's Prerogative', 'Legalise My Name'; received Donaldson Award for acting debut). Impact in first film *Variety Girl* '47 singing 'Tired' (song became her first record). Other films: *Isn't It Romantic?* '48, *Carmen Jones* '54, *That Certain Feeling* '56, *St Louis Blues* '58 (with Nat COLE), *Porgy And Bess* '59, *All The Fine Young Cannibals* '60, *The Landlord* '69, *Norman Is That You?* '76. On stage: *Arms And The Girl* '50, *Bless You All* '50, lead in Arlen's *House Of Flowers* '54; smash in all-black cast of *Hello Dolly* '67. TV special '65 had guest Ethel WATERS; own series '70 featuring band of third husband Louie BELLSON (married '52); sang at White House church service '71, Concord Jazz Festival '74. Redman was her mus. dir. '50s. Records incl. bluesy duet with Frank SINATRA 'A Little Learnin' Is A Dangerous Thing' '47; delightfully comic version of Louis JORDAN's 'Saturday Night Fish Fry' with Jackie 'Moms' Mabley '49; sexy hit 'Takes Two To Tango', no. 7 USA pop chart '52. LPs: *Pearl's Pearls* (RCA); on Roulette mid-'60s: *Back On Broadway, Cole Porter Songbook*, LPs of songs by Arlen, Jimmy Van Heusen, LP with Bellson, tastefully wicked *Pearl Bailey Sings For Adults Only*. Hits compilation *Hello, Pearlie May* on MCA/UK; autobiography *The Raw Pearl* '68.

BAILEY, Razzy (*b* Erastus Bailey, 14 Feb. '39, Five Points, Ala.) Country/pop singer. Grew up on farms in Alabama, New Mexico, Texas; formed first band in his teens, spent almost 20 years on honky-tonk circuit in Alabama, Georgia, Florida. Made single for Peach in Alabama; Freddy Weller prod. 'Stolen Moments' for ABC '69; signed to Capitol's 1-2-3 label; formed Aquarian label '73, released 'I Hate Hate': became regional hit, issued by MGM made pop charts '74. Worked with prod. Bob Montgomery on Capricorn without success; formed Erastus '76, made no. 99 on country chart with 'Keepin' Rooie Proud Of Me'. RCA artist

Dickey Lee had top 10 country hits with Bailey songs '9,999,999 Tears' '76, 'Peanut Butter' '77, leading to RCA contract and Bailey's first major success with 'What Time Do You Have To Be Back In Heaven' '78, prod. by Montgomery. Further hits: 'If Love Had A Face' '79, 'I Can't Get Enough Of You' '79, 'Lovin' Up A Storm' '80, 'I Keep Comin' Back'/'True Life Country Music' '80, 'In The Midnight Hour' '84. Moved from Lizella, Georgia to Nashville '80. LPs incl. *A Little More Razz, Makin' Friends, Feelin' Right, The Midnight Hour, Greatest Hits* (all on RCA); *Cut From A Different Stone* and *Arrival* '85 on MCA.

BAKER, Arthur DJ in NYC disco scene; became premier mix master, e.g. on New Order's 'Blue Monday' '83, helping pioneer hip hop craze. Like John 'Jellybean' Benitez, he rebuilds songs to make an entirely new mix. Most controversial work was with Bruce SPRINGSTEEN's 'Dancing In The Dark', 'Cover Me'; mixes for dance, radio, blaster outraged Springsteen's basically conservative fans. Best work compared to that of Phil SPECTOR; by mid-'80s he was in demand by artists such as Cyndi LAUPER, HALL & OATES, Diana ROSS, Afrika BAMBAATAA. Worked on Bob DYLAN LP *Empire Burlesque* '85: e.g. spacey prod. on tracks like 'When The Night Comes Falling From The Sky'.

BAKER, Carrol (*b* Bridgewater, Nova Scotia) Canada's top female country singer. Father was well-known old-time fiddler. Success came on Gaity label early '70s; went to RCA '76, had string of hits incl. two at no. 1 on Canadian charts. Popular in UK: appeared at International Festival of Country Music (Wembley, London) '77-8; UK tour with Slim WHITMAN '79. RCA LPs incl. *Carrol Baker, Sweet Sensation, If It Wasn't For You, All For The Love Of A Song, Hollywood Love.*

BAKER, Chet (*b* Chesney H. Baker, 23 Dec. '29, Yale, Okla; *d.* 13 May '88, Amsterdam) Trumpet. To California '40; played in US Army bands '46-8, '50-2; with Charlie PARKER, national fame with Gerry MULLIGAN quartet '52, own groups from '53; in Europe '59-64. Light, wistful tone, laid-back lyricism was at centre of West Coast 'cool jazz'

scene. Baker's singing popular in early days with some (female) fans, derided by others; edited out of some reissued LPs; *Chet Baker Sings* '54 on Pacific Jazz was a 10″ LP, tracks added '56 to make a 12″, rhythm guitar by Joe PASS added '60s to make stereo LP (Pacific Jazz did that sort of thing). Recorded in Europe late '50s-early '60s; several albums on Prestige mid-'60s; played flugelhorn late '60s. Dogged by narcotics habit; beaten by San Francisco hoodlums '68, lost teeth; comeback mid-'70s incl. Mulligan reunion; ill health still a problem, but recent LPs issued, early ones out again: cf. tasty ballad set *Chet*, made Mar. '59 on Riverside, with Pepper ADAMS, Bill EVANS, others. Limited edition compilations on Mosaic incl. 5-disc *Original Gerry Mulligan Quartet With Chet Baker*, 4-disc sets of *Complete Pacific Jazz Chet Baker/Russ Freeman*. *Trumpet Artistry of Chet Baker* '52-3 now on Pausa; several LPs made in Europe late '70s-early '80s; recent work incl. *You Can't Go Home Again* '77, *This Is Always* and *Touch Of Your Lips* '79, *Peace* and *Chet Baker, Jim Hall & Hubert Laws* '82, *Blues For A Reason* '84 with Warne MARSH, *Chet's Choice* '85 with just bass, guitarist Philip Catherine; trio set *Candy* on Sonet, studio *Chet's Choice* on Criss Cross and *Strollin'* on Enja (live at Munster), all '85. Russell Donald Freeman (*b* 28 May '26, Chicago) toured with Baker on piano '53-4; also recorded with Shelly MANNE, André PREVIN, own trio on World Pacific, etc.; worked in A&R for Pacific Jazz, went into studio work and was mus. dir. for *Laugh In* on TV.

BAKER, Ginger (*b* Peter Baker, 19 Aug. '39, London) UK rock drummer. Played trumpet in youth; learned theory and notation early. Switched to drums to play trad with Acker BILK, Terry Lightfoot. Met bassist Jack Bruce in Bert Courtley band; sat in with Blues Incorporated; played '63 with Bruce in Graham BOND Organisation. Style reached peak on *Sound Of '65* LP, incl. stage workout on 'Oh, Baby'. Baker's lively drum sound at odds with period practice; style of attack promoted him from mere timekeeper to featured musician. Founder member of powerhouse trio CREAM '66 with Bruce, Eric CLAPTON; played major part in group whose success depended on improvisation, musical ability. Solo on

'Toad' (album *Fresh Cream*) inspired generation of rock drummers; 15-minute live 'Toad' on *Wheels Of Fire* inevitably seemed self-indulgent on record. Member of short-lived, song-oriented supergroup BLIND FAITH; turned bandleader with Airforce, 10-piece outfit with three drummers, containing famous and not-so-famous people, perhaps reaction to supergroups: incl. Rick Grech, Stevie WINWOOD from Blind Faith, Denny LAINE, Chris Wood, drummers Remi Kabaka, Phil Seamen. After two cluttered, uninspired LPs *Airforce*, *Airforce 2* (both '70), opened recording studio in Nigeria, played host to local, international talent (Paul McCARTNEY band Wings made *Band On The Run* there, '73). Made own *Stratavarious* '72 on Polydor with Fela KUTI, recorded with Nigerian band Salt; back to UK to form Baker-Gurvitz Army with bros. Paul and Adrian Gurvitz (ex-Gun). Trio in Cream mould made undistinguished albums *Baker-Gurvitz Army* '74, *Elysian Encounter* '75, *Hearts On Fire* '76, then split. After an unimpressive solo effort *11 Sides Of Baker*, he left music to breed polo ponies but returned in '79 to form Energy, played briefly with heavy metal trio Atomic Rooster, space-rockers Hawkwind, Ginger Baker's Nutters; like most rock drummers was not a good leader, seeming unable to see projects through. Emigrated again '82 to Italy with second wife, ran drum school, played old Cream tunes with young Americans. Sought out by producer Bill LASWELL; played on LP by PUBLIC IMAGE LTD '86, made *Horses And Trees* on Celluloid, with Laswell, L. SHANKAR on violin; also *African Force* on ITM.

BAKER, Harold 'Shorty' (*b* 26 May '14, St Louis, Mo.; *d* 8 Nov. '66 NYC) Trumpet. Played with a large number of bands incl. Don REDMAN '35-7, Teddy WILSON '39-40; Andy KIRK '40; he was married to Mary Lou WILLIAMS and played with her '42; was with Duke ELLINGTON '38, '43-51, '57-9; then freelanced NYC. Played lead as well as solo. A version of 'Mood Indigo' on LP *Ellington Indigos* '59 was almost entirely a lovely muted Baker solo because, Ellington said, 'Shorty loves to play it.'

BAKER, Josephine (*b* '06, St Louis, Mo.; *d* '75, Paris) Dancer, singer. Drew attention to herself clowning in chorus line of SISSLE and BLAKE's *Shuffle Along*; to Paris '25 with USA blacks in show *La Revue Nègre*, became European superstar. She had rubber legs and fine comic timing, but exotic looks helped during 'Jazz Age' in Europe. Adopted by prod. Jacques Charles, artist Paul Colin, conductor Wal-Berg, composer Vincent Scotto (wrote her theme song 'J'ai Deux Amours'); posters helped make her famous, countless magazine covers. Starred at Folies-Bergère '26 (famous for jungle dance wearing only bananas); worked in Berlin (Nazi hecklers made life difficult); had own club Chez Josephine, pet leopard on a leash; starred in revival of Offenbach's *La Créole* '34. During WWII sang all over North Africa for Allied troops; allegedly worked in Resistance (nobody knows what she did, but as exotic celebrity she may have made an ideal courier): she escaped stigma of collaboration suffered by other French stars; received Légion d'Honneur from De Gaulle, then even rarer Médaille de la Résistance. Trips to USA not successful; suffered racial discrimination at the Stork Club NYC '50s: actress Grace Kelly noticed her courage. Retired to chateau in Dordogne '56 to look after 'Rainbow Tribe', 12 adopted children, all different nationalities, but had to go back to work; evicted '69, rescued by Princess Grace: Rainiers gave her villa in Monaco, helped put on show *Josephine* '75: celebrated 50 years in Paris, still dancing Charleston, with a dozen costume changes; died in her sleep after 14 triumphant performances. First records '26 for Odéon ('Dinah', 'Sleepy Time Gal' etc.) revealed tremulous voice, but high notes soon took on silver purity; had enough power at her peak to sing without a microphone. Compilation albums: *Josephine Baker* on Monmouth; 2-disc set *50 Years Of Song* from EMI France.

BAKER, LaVern (*b* 11 Nov. '29, Chicago) Rhythm and blues singer. Began at 17 as 'Little Miss Sharecropper'. Spotted by bandleader Fletcher HENDERSON, signed to Columbia, 'When I'm In A Crying Mood' a local hit; with Todd Rhodes band ('Trying' on King '52); signed to Atlantic: 15 R&B hits '55-65 incl. eight top tens; 18 Hot 100 pop entries same period incl. several 2-sided hits. 'Tweedle-Dee' '55 (no. 4 R&B, no. 14

pop) beaten in pop chart by Georgia GIBBS cover (no. 2; also covered by Frankie VAUGHAN for UK top 20); 'I Cried A Tear' '58 (no. 2 R&B, no. 6 pop) was only top 10 pop entry; 'Jim Dandy' (no. 3 R&B, no. 17 pop) only other top 20. Also had minor duet hits with Jimmy Ricks ('You're The Boss' '61; Ricks *d* 2 July '74), Jackie WILSON ('Think Twice' '66 on Brunswick). She later moved to Japan. *Real Gone Gal* is a good compilation on Charly UK. She is said to have taught Johnnie RAY how to sing the blues; whether true or not the story adds to the legend: she had a profound infl. on pop music, and was one of those who suffered most from being covered by white artists in early days of rock'n'roll. Another story had her meeting Gibbs at an airport and telling her that she should take out insurance in case she (LaVern) was killed in a crash.

BALDRY, Long John (*b* 12 Jan. '41, London) UK R&B singer. Owes nickname to height of 6'7"; big voice to match. Started career in folk clubs late '50s; toured Europe with Ramblin' Jack ELLIOTT, '57-61. Turned to R&B, joined Alexis KORNER's embryonic Blues Incorporated, appeared in seminal *R&B At The Marquee* LP. After spell in Germany, joined fellow Blues Inc. refugee Cyril DAVIES in All Stars, proving at home with Davies' Chicago blues style as in Korner's more jazz-oriented music. On Davies' death '64 formed Hoochie Koochie Men from band; first LP *Long John's Blues* issued same year. Most celebrated member of band, Rod STEWART, followed Baldry to Brian AUGER's supergroup Steampacket; expected success didn't happen; went solo, took over Bluesology for backup with Reg Dwight (later became Elton JOHN) on keyboards, turned to straight pop. Soaring ballad style ideal for his voice; showcased on 'Let The Heartaches Begin' (no. 1 UK '67); Royal Command Performance, MOR hits followed: 'Mexico' (no. 15), 'When The Sun Comes Shinin' Through' (no. 29, both '68), 'It's Too Late Now' (no. 21, '69). Dropped easy-listening style when hits dried up; former colleagues John and Stewart each produced a side of LP *It Ain't Easy* '71, but USA Hot 100 single from this 'Don't Try To Lay No BoogieWoogie On The King Of Rock'n'Roll' was his only hit of the '70s. Sporadic work interrupted by spell in psy-

chiatric hospital; '80s saw him (now a naturalised Canadian) belting out his big hit in Toronto clubs. One of the fathers of British rock.

BALFA BROTHERS Family of Cajun musicians who helped preserve trad. Louisiana music; the 'Balfa Brotherhood' consisting of Dewey (*b* 20 Mar. '27, Mamou, La.), Burkeman, Harry, Rodney, Will; Rodney and Will were killed in car crash Feb. '79. They learned old songs from their father Charles, became accomplished on accordion, fiddle, guitar, harmonica, *petit fer* (triangle) and spoons, trad. Cajun instrumentation. 'My father, grandfather, great-grandfather all played the fiddle, and you see, through my music, I feel they are still alive,' as Dewey put it. 'I think of the Balfa Brothers band as a brotherhood of musicians, not just as three or four blood brothers.' Further influences were Harry CHOATES, Leo SOILEAU, Bob WILLS; they played and recorded extensively with Nathan ABSHIRE as well as on their own. Despite their importance in the genre, Dewey runs a furniture business as his main livelihood. They made film *Blues des Balfas* (Flower Films). Best LPs incl. *The New York Concerts, Balfa Brothers Play Traditional Music* and *More Traditional Music* (with Marc Savoy) on Floyd Soileau's Swallow label; *Underneath The Green Oak Tree* (with Savoy, D. L. Menard) on Arhoolie; *Cajun Days* on Sonet; *J'ai Vu le Loup, le Renard et la Belette* on Rounder.

BALL, Kenny (*b* 22 May '30, Ilford, Essex, UK) Trumpet, leader. Own band with dixieland line up (Kenny Ball and his Jazzmen) late '58; appeared at Albert Hall, London (Festival of Jazz), made TV debut, '59; toured Continent, signed record contract, did well in UK trad. fad of the period. 14 singles charted in UK '62-7, incl. three top tens; 'Midnight in Moscow' also reached no. 2 in USA. *Golden Hits* album charted UK '63. Toured USSR '85.

BALLARD, Hank (*b* 18 Nov. '36, Detroit, Mich.) Soul singer, songwriter. Raised in Alabama; worked on Ford assembly line in Detroit; infl. as a child by gospel and by Gene AUTRY: 'I heard him singing "I'm Back In The Saddle Again" when I was a

65

little kid, and I said, "Man, we got us a singing cowboy now!" ' Picked at 16 to join Royals, doo-wop group that had incl. Levi Stubbs (later FOUR TOPS), Jackie WILSON. Ballard replaced Lawson Smith; others were Sonny Woods, Henry Booth, Charles Sutton; Alonzo Tucker played guitar. First session yielded R&B top 10 'Get It' '53; renamed Midnighters to avoid confusion with the Five Royales, labelmates on King; Tucker replaced by Arthur Porter, then Cal Green. '54 saw three million-sellers: 'Work With Me Annie', 'Sexy Ways', 'Annie Had A Baby'. Original 'Annie' helped by controversy over sexually explicit lyric (for the time): e.g. 'Annie please don't cheat/Give me all my meat', banned from radio. Johnny OTIS wrote answer lyrics 'Roll With Me Henry' for Etta JAMES; watered-down-for-whites version 'Dance With Me Henry' was no. 1 pop '55 by Georgia GIBBS, one of the first big rock'n'roll-pop hits; Otis, James, Ballard split royalties. Following decreasingly successful rehashes of 'Annie', Ballard invented dance craze 'The Twist' (derived from Clyde McPHATTER '55 R&B hit 'What'cha Gonna Do'); released on B-side of first Hot 100 pop chart entry 'Teardrops On Your Letter' '59 (no. 4 R&B; group now called Hank Ballard and the Midnighters); 'Twist' became hit; group invited to appear on American Bandstand; Ballard failed to turn up and host Dick CLARK had unknown Chubby CHECKER cover disc note-for-note. Checker had no. 1 pop hit, but original made no. 28 '60, hard on heels of no. 7 hit 'Finger-Poppin' Time'. Ballard now says, 'We did "Twist" first, but the best thing that ever happened to me was Chubby Checker doing it . . . I didn't really cross over until "The Twist" and "Finger-Poppin' Time".' 'Let's Go, Let's Go, Let's Go' at no. 6 made pop top-40 hat trick, but after four lesser hits in '61, fortunes waned. Midnighters '60s lineup incl. Norman Thrasher, Frank Stanford, Wesley Hargrove. Ballard's career faltered despite patronage of James BROWN, whose style he had infl. and with whose band he sometimes recorded; stayed with King until '69 ('How You Gonna Get Respect' by Hank Ballard and the Dapps made no. 15 R&B chart '68), then label-hopped (e.g. novelty 'Let's Go Streaking'). *What You Get When The Gettin' Gets Good* '85 on Charly compiles work massively influential

when R&B still stuck in ghetto. Touring now thanks to '50s revival: 'Don't sit down on me, I tell 'em. My biggest thrill is watching people dance to my music.' 2-disc *Hank Ballard Live At The Palais* '87 on Charly UK was recorded at Hammersmith venue late '86; should keep fans on their feet.

BALLEW, Smith (*b* 21 Jan. '02, Palestine, Texas) Bandleader, singer. Handsome man with good voice, in demand for pop sessions because he did't need special arrangements: sang in any key. Attended U. of Texas; fronted various bands; made records '29-36 with Ben POLLACK, many others; with Duke ELLINGTON as 'Billy Smith' Nov. '30: 'Ten Little Miles From Ten-Ten-Tennessee'. Own band early '30s with Ray McKINLEY, Glenn MILLER; broke up when they left. Freelanced as vocalist, became singing cowboy; voice may have been used when Monogram Pictures tried to make singing cowboy of John Wayne '33-5. Film *Palm Springs* '36, also low-budget Westerns as late as '46; quit show business '50, lived in Texas.

BAND, The USA rock band, easily most infl. of late '60s-70s: Jaime 'Robbie' Robertson (*b* 5 July '43), guitar; Garth Hudson (*b* 2 Aug. '37), organ; Richard Manuel (*b* 3 Apr. '43; *d* 4 Mar. '86), piano, vocals; Rick Danko (*b* 29 Dec. '42), bass, vocals; Levon Helm (*b* 26 May '43), drums, vocals. All Canadians except Helm, from Arkansas. Hired as backup for rockabilly Ronnie HAWKINS (also from Ark.) who promised them not much money but 'more pussy than Frank Sinatra'. Association lasted on and off until c.'63. Then called themselves the Hawks, Levon and the Hawks, the Crackers, the Canadian Squires; played all over North America, soaking up the culture: one gloomy dance hall turned out to be owned by Jack Ruby. Spotted in Canada by blues singer John HAMMOND, son of CBS producer; met Bob DYLAN working in Greenwich Village: he was moving from pure folk to electric backing group, hired band for '65-6 world tour (Mickey Jones replaced Helm on drums). Antagonism meeting Dylan's new sound captured on bootleg album *Live At The Albert Hall*. After Dylan's near-fatal motorcycle accident July '66, retired with him to rural house 'Big Pink' near Woodstock NY;

rehearsal of new songs resulted in rock's first important bootleg, 2-disc *Great White Wonder* (from plain sleeve), aka *The Basement Tapes*, title when issued by Columbia '75: mellower side of Dylan possibly infl. by Robertson's growing confidence as writer (Dylan praised him as 'a mathematical guitar genius'). Word-of-mouth rumour from George HARRISON, Eric CLAPTON prepared fans for release of The Band's astonishingly assured debut of maturity, *Music From Big Pink* '68, incl. Dylan's 'I Shall Be Released', Dylan-Manuel collaboration 'Tears Of Rage', Dylan-Danko 'This Wheel's On Fire', folkish C&W 'Long Black Veil'; instant classic Robertson comp. 'The Weight'. Next LP *The Band* '69 incl. all Robertson comps. except Manuel's 'Whispering Pines': 'Up On Cripple Creek', 'Rag, Mama, Rag', 'Across The Great Divide' and one of his best, 'The Night They Drove Old Dixie Down', written for Helm to sing: Robertson said they could have called LP *America*; earned designation 'the only band that could have warmed up the crown for Abraham Lincoln'. Long experts at playing old rock'n'roll hits that dancers wanted to hear in taverns, but a *band*, not a collection of egos, able to switch instruments, vocals; thanks perhaps to spark provided by Dylan they had learned what to do with technique. Lyrics tell mysterious stories, cannot always be understood: it may be 'the instinct of the American artist . . . to tell his tale from the shadows, probably because that is where he finds it' (G. Marcus). *Big Pink* had not been massive hit (no tour to promote it); second LP not released when they played first gig, in San Francisco '69, discovered how much was expected: crowd had come from all over the West. First night was disaster; recovered the next, but called third LP *Stage Fright* '70 (another story, that title track was about Dylan's reclusiveness, does not ring true); more Robertson comps. incl. 'Shape I'm In'. *Cahoots* '71 excellent LP from anyone else, began slow decline for this group; but still incl. Manuel co-comp. with Van MORRISON '4% Pantomime', Dylan's 'When I Paint My Masterpiece', Robertson's 'River Hymn', 'Life Is A Carnival'. 2-disc set *Rock Of Ages* '72 is definitive souvenir of group's live work; *Moondog Matinee* '73 tribute to Alan FREED radio show, covers of favourite rock'n'roll songs of '50s-60s. Public appeal undeniable; steeped in trad. values, with none of prevalent psychedelia, effortlessly reproducing studio sound after years on the road; at Watkins Glen Festival '73 (with GRATEFUL DEAD), 600,000 fans made history as largest ever rock gathering. Both Band, Dylan now received new impetus: first official LP together *Planet Waves* '73 usually denigrated in Dylan canon, but good group of new songs and Band's backing made it his best set since '68. Was with him on first tour in eight years; 2-disc live tour set *Before The Flood* '74 is rich collection of treatments of classics: the fire still burned. But *Northern Lights, Southern Cross* '75, first new Band collection in four years, and *Islands* '77, last official LP, had many qualities yet disappointed. With intimations of mortality after 16 years on the road, called it quits Thanksgiving Day '76 with massive gig at Winterland, San Francisco, where they had 'stage fright' in '69. Hawkins, Clapton, Dylan, Morrison, Ron Wood, Ringo STARR, Joni MITCHELL, Neil YOUNG, Muddy WATERS, Neil DIAMOND, Mac REBENNACK were all present, most had guest spots; dinner served to invited audience; filmed by Martin Scorsese, with specially made segments (e.g. 'The Weight' with The STAPLE SINGERS, Robertson's 'Evangeline' sung by Emmylou HARRIS); *The Last Waltz* is easily the best rock concert film yet made: movie, 3-disc album released '78. Robertson has done film work: starred in *Carny* '80, scored Scorsese's *King Of Comedy* '83, contributed to *The Sound Of Money* '87; he prod. Diamond LPs '76-7; *Robbie Robertson* '87 on Geffen was his first solo LP, with nine of his own new songs, horns on one track arr. by Gil EVANS, guests incl. Peter GABRIEL, U2, the BoDeans (quartet from Waukesha, Wis. with acclaimed LPs *Love & Hope & Sex & Dreams* '86, *Outside* '87 on Slash/WB). Danko made eponymous LP '79; Helm made solo *American Son* '78, sessioned, acted in film *Coal Miner's Daughter* '80 with Sissy Spacek, with Sam Shepard in *The Right Stuff* '83; Helm/Danko gigged as duo. Critics wrote that The Band without Robertson was like *Hamlet* without the Prince; others played reunions late '83 with the Cate Brothers, late '85 with Jimmie Wieder on guitar; sold out gigs at restaurant lounge in Winter Park, suburb of Orlando,

Fla. early '86; Manuel apparently hanged himself next day: Clapton dedicated 'Holy Mother' on *August* '86 to him. The Band had two top 40 singles in USA, two different ones in UK; they became a living legend with LPs. *Anthology* is 2-disc compilation.

BAND AID Charity projects undertaken by Bob Geldof (BOOMTOWN RATS) after he saw BBC documentary of Ethiopian famine, '84. Contacted Midge Ure (ULTRAVOX); they booked array of stars, studio time; on a Sunday in Nov. recorded 'Do They Know It's Christmas?', written by Geldof and Ure, prod. by Ure. Biggest ever UK single, with worldwide sales over 7 million. Among those involved: Sting, Paul Weller, George Michael, BOY GEORGE, Phil COLLINS, Paul YOUNG, members of U2, DURAN DURAN, SPANDAU BALLET, STATUS QUO. Spoken messages from David BOWIE, Paul McCARTNEY, FRANKIE GOES TO HOLLYWOOD on the B-side. Event compared to '71 Bangla Desh concert, but unlike George HARRISON's well intentioned charity effort, this one had Geldof talking record companies, printers, distributors and the press into working for nothing; saw that profits from related projects (T-shirts, video, etc.) went to the famine victims. Only the UK government of the day refused to waive its sales tax. Geldof visited Ethiopia '85, then arranged huge simultaneous concert, linking Wembley Stadium (London), Philadelphia by video, Concorde airliner: 16 hours of Live Aid (13 July '85) televised to most countries, even featured a Soviet group; the money raised by all this said to be £60 million mid-'87. Geldof nominated for Nobel Peace Prize by British MP, seconded by Irish Prime Minister. Meanwhile 'American Band Aid' (USA FOR Africa) made 'We Are The World' released 1 Apr. '85, written by Lionel RICHIE, Michael JACKSON; stars taking part incl. Bob DYLAN, Bruce SPRINGSTEEN, Paul SIMON, Stevie WONDER, Billy JOEL, Diana ROSS, Willie NELSON, Waylon JENNINGS, Cyndi LAUPER, Harry BELAFONTE, Ray CHARLES, held together by Quincy JONES. LP of that name incl. unreleased tracks by Springsteen, POINTER SISTERS, Linda RONSTADT, PRINCE. Other projects incl. Welsh, Canadian Band Aid singles; 2-Tone 'starvation' single with members of UB40, the SPECIALS, the Pioneers; BRAFA (British Reggae Artists Appeal), incl. Matumbi, Misty in Roots, Aswad. Dylan made remarks during Live Aid broadcast about plight of American farmers losing homesteads under Reaganomics; Nelson had talk with Illinois Governor J. Thompson about it, result was Farm Aid, hoping to make $40m: 12-hour country music festival broadcast from U. of Illinois by cable company Nashville Network mid-'85, with Dylan, Neil YOUNG, Ry COODER, many country stars. Also in '85, Emmylou HARRIS hosted Nashville songwriters event Bread'n'Jam 1, with Gail DAVIES, many others, on behalf of USA For Africa and Second Harvest Food Bank. Geldof has sparked off social concern missing from music scene for many years: he asked Eurocrats in Brussels Oct. '85 why they maintain a grain mountain courtesy of EEC taxpayers while Africans starve; answer came there none. He helped with Sports Aid '86, received honorary knighthood: honorary because he is Irish, not British, but (unusually) bestowed by Queen Elizabeth II instead of UK Foreign Secretary partly because Geldof had severely criticised Sir Geoffrey Howe's speech at the UN. Sir Bob's autobiography *Is That All?* was a bestseller in UK '86. He went back to pop career, refused to try to cash in on charity fame.

BANDY, Moe (*b* 12 Feb. '44, Meridian, Miss.) Honky-tonk country singer, also half of Moe & Joe duo. Father played guitar, mother piano; grandfather worked on railroad with Jimmie RODGERS. Family moved to farm near San Antonio, Texas; Moe's father started a band '50. Moe tried rodeo riding, following several falls turned to music; TV series with own band The Mavericks in San Antonio. Went solo '72; with Ray Baker (formerly with Jim REEVES), recorded self-financed single 'I Just Started Hatin' Cheatin' Songs Today' on GRC label, made country top 20 '74. Further hits '74-5: 'Honky Tonk Amnesia', 'It Was Always So Easy To Find An Unhappy Woman', 'Doesn't Anybody Make Love At Home Anymore', 'Bandy The Rodeo Clown'. Moved to Columbia; 'Hank Williams, You Wrote My Life' made no. 2 on country chart. Toured with band The Rodeo Clowns nearly 250 days a year; more hits '76-7 incl. 'Here I Am Drunk Again', 'She Took More Than Her Share', 'I'm Sorry For You My Friend' (Hank WILLIAMS song), 'That's What Makes The Juke Box Play'. Named top new male vocalist by ACM '76; widely hailed for straight country presentation. Following appearance with Joe STAMPLEY at Wembley (London) they recorded duets: LP *Just Good Ol' Boys*, no. 1 country singles with title track and 'Holding The Bag' '79. *Hey Joe! Hey Moe!* LP followed; both ACM, CMA named them vocal duo of the year '80. Moe's hits continued: 'It's A Cheating Situation', 'Following The Feeling' (duet with Judy Bailey), 'Yesterday Once More' '80. After 10 years with Ray Baker, switched prod. to Blake Mevis for hits 'Motel Matches', 'The Horse That You Can't Ride'. LP with Joe *Alive & Well* had no. 1 hit 'Where's The Dress', spoof on Culture Club's 'Karma Chameleon'; they dressed in drag for shows and TV promotion. Many single hits are title tracks of LPs; other albums incl. *I Still Love You In The Same Ol' Way*, *Sings The Songs Of Hank Williams*, *Devoted To Your Memory* on CBS; *20 Great Songs Of The American Cowboy* on Warwick in UK '82. Moe & Joe: *Live From Bad Bob's In Memphis* on CBS '85.

BANGLES, The Pop group formed L.A. '81: Susanna Hoffs and Vicki Peterson, guitars; Debbi Peterson, drums; Michael Steele, bass; all sing. One of the West Coast USA 'paisley underground' bands. Had local fans, then toured with The BEAT, Cyndi LAUPER; guided by POLICE manager Miles Copeland. Hoffs' tracks on *Rainy Day* ('83 compilation LP of West Coast music) incl. good version of DYLAN's 'I'll Keep It With Mine'; band's eponymous EP on Independent Records Syndicate (IRS, Copeland's label) well received; then proper debut LP *All Over The Place* (CBS, '84) revealed good singing and playing. *Different Light* '86 was no advance, incl. bubblegummish 'Walk Like An Egyptian', hit with 'Manic Monday', written by PRINCE.

BANKS, Billy (*b* c.'08, Alton, Ohio; *d* 19 Oct. '67, Tokyo) Jazz singer; impressive aptitude for happy scat. Signed by manager Irving Mills, made Victor test pressing 'Sleepytime

Down South' Apr. '32, other sides same month for Banner-Perfect with band incl. Eddie CONDON, Henry ALLEN, Pee Wee RUSSELL, Joe SULLIVAN, Gene KRUPA, Al Morgan (*b* 19 Aug. '08, New Orleans; *d* 14 Apr. '74, L.A.), bass, Jack Bland (*b* 8 May 1899, Sedalia, Mo.), guitar; appeared that year at Connie's Inn NYC. Records by interracial recording bands under names of Eddie Condon and his Rhythmakers, Chicago Rhythm Kings, Jack Bland and his Rhythmakers, Harlem Hot Shots, etc.: e.g. The Rhythmakers incl. Condon, Allen, Bland, Russell, Fats WALLER, Zutty Singleton, Jimmy Lord (*b* 28 Nov. 1889; *d* 27 Apr. '70, Calif.), clarinet; George Murphy 'Pops' Foster (*b* c.1892, McCall, La.; *d* 30 Oct. '69, San Francisco), bass, recorded 26 July '32 NYC for American Record Company group: 'I Would Do Anything For You', 'Mean Old Bed Bug Blues', 'Yellow Dog Blues', 'Yes Suh!'. Banks returned to Cleveland '33 during Depression, helped to run family business; joined Noble SISSLE band '34; then resident at Billy ROSE's Diamond Horseshoe club NYC: played 7,151 dates there from Dec. '38 to June '48. Toured Europe '50s; settled in Japan.

BANNON, R. C. (*b* 2 May '45, Dallas, Texas) Country singer, songwriter; duet team with wife Louise MANDRELL (*m* Feb. '79). Sang in choir of Pentecostal church; during high school in rock, soul bands; worked club circuit across Texas, then DJ, singer in Seattle. Opened shows for Marty ROBBINS '73, who advised him to move to Nashville. Unsuccessful Capitol records followed by move to Nashville '76; worked as DJ at Smuggler's Inn; became friends with songwriter Harlan Sanders, led to contract as writer with Warner Brothers Music: hits for Ronnie MILSAP ('Only One Love In My Life' no. 1 country chart '78), Charly McCLAIN ('Women Get Lonely' '80). Signed by Columbia '77; debut LP *R.C. Bannon Arrives* '78, with sleeve note by Robbins; single hit 'Somebody's Gonna Do It Tonight' same year. Duet hits began with 'Reunited' '79, 'We Love Each Other' '80, LP *Inseparable* '80. R.C. also arranger, sound engineer for TV series Barbara MANDRELL and the Mandrell Sisters '80. Solo hits '80 incl. 'Lovely Lonely Lady', 'Never Be Anyone Else'. R.C. and Louise signed to RCA '81, scored with 'Where There's Smoke There's Fire' '81, 'Our Wedding Band' '82. Duet LPs *Love Won't Let Us Go* '81, *Me And My R.C.* '82, *(You're My) Superwoman, (You're My) Incredible Man* '83, *Best Of* '84, plus Louise's successful solo career on RCA.

BANTOUS DE LA CAPITALE Dance band formed in Brazzaville, Congo, '59; became one of the longest established acts in African music as leading interpreters of Cuban RUMBA. Co-led by saxophonists Dieudonne (Nino) Malapet and Jean Serge Essous; made local impact followed by ambitious tour of West Africa '60. Best early work on series of singles, reissued on Africain label LPs *Les Merveilles du Passé 1962-4* (3 vols.). Launched new dance and new sound Le Boucher '65, seen as renewal, revitalisation of rumba; then soukous '66: successful dance became generic name for Congolese music. Then changes: after recording trip to Paris Essous decided to stay there (but remained member of band), Malapet took over leadership; more personnel changes with proclamation of official cultural policy 'Authenticitie' '67. Carried on '70s with tight, exciting rhythms, virtuoso soloists, and singers: Kosmos (Come Mountouari), Pamelo Mounk'a, Tchico; Nedule Papa Noel and Samba Mascott on guitars; saxes of Malapet and Essous. The musical wheel turned full circle when the band toured Cuba '74. Best '70s material issued on compilations *Les Bantous de la Capitale* (2 vols. '76); then celebrated with 2-disc set *Special 20th Anniversaire* '79. Like other great African outfits, established own distinctive sounds while also training new generation of young musicians; solo LPs backed by band incl. *Samba Mascott And The Bantous* '81, *Philosophie* and *Lily Germaine* '83 by Essous, outstanding *Mokilimbembe* '84 by Malapet. One of the biggest African LPs of '85 was *Nono*, with guitar wizardry of Papa Noel.

BARBER, Chris (*b* 17 Apr. '30, Welwyn Garden City, Hertfordshire, UK) Trombone, leader. Own band briefly, '50; joined Ken COLYER band, took it over '54. First UK combo to appear on Ed Sullivan TV show in USA, '59. Three singles charted during trad fad. in UK '59-62; 'Petite Fleur' no. 3, no. 5 in USA. Ironically Barber did not play on solo vehicle for clarinettist Monty Sunshine, who used pretty vibrato similar to that of song's composer (in '52) Sidney BECHET. Sunshine (*b* 8 Apr. '28, London) and Barber played in films incl. *Look Back In Anger* '59; three Barber albums charted UK '60. LPs incl. *Chris Barber Band Box* '60, *Elite Syncopations*, both on EMI/Columbia; *Best Of* on Ace Of Clubs, all '60; *Chris Barber In Budapest* '68 on Storyville. Other *Best Ofs* on Pye also featured Acker BILK, Kenny BALL.

BARBER, Glenn (*b* 2 Feb. '35, Hollis, Okla.) Country singer, songwriter. Raised in Pasadena, Texas, played guitar from age 6, won talent contests, moved to Nashville early '60s; recorded for Sims ('How Can I Forget You' '64), Starday ('If Anyone Can Show Cause', 'Stronger Than Dirt' '64). Contract with Acuff-Rose; wrote for Roy ORBISON, Don GIBSON, Roy ACUFF, Sue Thompson. On Hickory records '67; had own hits 'Don't Worry 'Bout The Mule' '68, 'Kissed By The Rain, Warmed By The Sun' '69, 'She Cheats On Me' '70, 'I'm The Man In Susie's Mind' '72, 'Daddy Number Two' '73. On Groovy Records '77, then Century 21 and made comeback with 'What's The Name Of That Song' '78, 'Love Songs Just For You' '79. Since recorded for MMI '79, Sunbird '80, KIK '81 without much success. Painter in spare time, specialises in portraits.

BARBIERI, Gato (*b* Leandro J. Barbieri, 28 Nov. '34, Rosario, Argentina) Tenor sax, composer. Clarinet and alto sax; played in Lalo SCHIFRIN band '53, switched to tenor '53. Went to Brazil, to Rome '62, Paris '65, met Don CHERRY there, made LPs with him in NYC, e.g. *Complete Communion* '66 on Blue Note with Ed BLACKWELL, Henry Grimes (*b* '35 Philadelphia) on bass. Also recorded with Steve LACY, Dollar Brand; then began mixing South American rhythms with free jazz, e.g. LP *Third World* '69 with Charlie HADEN, Roswell RUDD; won Grammy for film soundtrack *Last Tango In Paris* '72 (also appeared in film); formed group of South American musicians '73, several LPs on Impulse in mid-'70s followed popular groove of hip predictability. *Tropic Appetites* with Carla BLEY demonstrated value for him of collaboration with others.

BARBOUR, Dave (*b* 28 May '12, NYC; *d* 11 Dec. '65, Malibu, Cal.) Guitar, songwriter. Played and recorded during swing era with Red NORVO '35, Benny GOODMAN '42-3; married Goodman's singer Peggy LEE '43; they co-wrote 'I Don't Know Enough About You', 'Manana', 'It's A Good Day', etc. Own hit 'Mambo Jambo' '50. LP *BBB & Co.* with Benny CARTER '62; otherwise retired after divorce from Lee '52.

BARCLAY JAMES HARVEST UK rock band. Lineup: John Lees (*b* 13 Jan. '48 Oldham, Lancs.), guitar; Melvyn Pritchard (*b* 20 Jan. '48, Oldham), drums; Les Holroyd (*b* 12 Mar. '48), bass; Stuart 'Woolley' Wolstenholme (*b* 15 Apr. '47, Oldham), keyboards. Lees and Wolstenholme formed band Blues Keepers at school; Lees also played recorder, flute, clarinet; Wooly 12-string guitar. Pritchard and Holroyd veterans of local bands Heart and Soul, The Wickeds; BJH formed Sep. '66, turned pro '67, rehearsing in farmhouse provided by local businessman. First single 'Early Morning' on Parlophone; others on EMI's new 'progressive' Harvest label. Tour with full orchestra to promote first LP *Barclay James Harvest* '70 was financial disaster; this with critical indifference (in sharp contrast to labelmates PINK FLOYD) caused lower profile (though orchestra reappeared for '71 festival in Weeley, Essex). Best of early singles and first three LPs (*Once Again, Other Short Stories* both '71) compiled as *Early Morning Onwards* '72. Band slogged around UK college circuit, released two more LPs; Pritchard thought of joining FAIRPORT CONVENTION. Change of label to Polydor brought reward when 2-disc *Barclay James Harvest Live* '74 became first top 40 LP. *Time Honoured Ghosts* recorded in USA; charted '75. From experimental feel of early discs, band's sound had coalesced into mellotron-based rock (derived from orchestral period) with Floyd-like lead guitar, breathy harmonies not unlike MOODY BLUES (comparison was resented: 'Poor Man's Moody Blues' on '77 LP *Gone To Earth* was answer to critics'). LPs continued to chart in UK, sold well in Europe: *Gone To Earth*, released in heyday of punk, was

big hit in Germany. Musical stagnation was illustrated by late release of Lees '73 solo LP *A Major Fancy* because of lack of perceived demand; promoted four years later to cash in/recoup losses. Former label also released three more best-of compilations. Wolstenholme left '79 (the first personnel change in 13 years); did solo *Maestoso* '80, while band replaced crucial keyboard contribution with sessionmen Kevin McAlea (ex-Bees Make Honey, Kate BUSH), Colin Browne, later Bias Boshell. *Eyes Of The Universe* '79 failed to chart in UK; enthusiastic reception in Europe led to concentration on market: repaid German support 30 Aug. '80 with historic free concert on steps of Reichstag near Berlin Wall: *A Concert For The People (Berlin)* was not only biggest UK hit LP (no. 15) but film, video, simultaneous TV/radio broadcast. Continued into '80s defying fashion with conservative musical policy (despite titles of LPs *Turn Of The Tide* '81, *Ring Of Changes* '83), reaping benefits of European following (German sales now well over 3 million) while consistently charting in UK; label switches in USA failed to bring sales there. Annual tours with spectacular laser shows similar to '70s YES extravaganzas.

BARE, Bobby (*b* 7 Apr. '35, Ironton, Ohio) C&W singer, songwriter. Struggled in local bands, recorded own song at own expense weeks before joining US Army, sold 'All American Boy' to Fraternity label for $50, became no. 2 pop hit credited to 'Bill Parsons'. On discharge did songs for Chubby CHECKER film, signed to RCA as solo artist; own first top 40 entry was 'Shame On Me' '62, top 20 next year with his own 'Detroit City' (Grammy '64); other pop crossovers were '500 Miles Away From Home', 'Miller's Cave' '63-4. Starred in film *A Distant Trumpet* '64, decided to continue with music despite Hollywood offers; to Nashville, soon became one of town's biggest stars, more than 50 country hits to his name: 26 top 40 entries in Billboard C&W chart '62-71, not counting duets: top 10s 'Have I Stayed Away Too Long', 'Four Strong Winds', 'It's Alright', 'The Streets Of Baltimore', '(Margie's At) The Lincoln Park Inn', 'How I Got To Memphis', 'Come Sundown', 'Please Don't Tell Me How The Story Ends'. Not only writes prolifically, has ear for other talent: championed work of Kris KRISTOFFERSON, Waylon JENNINGS, Ian Tyson, Shel SILVERSTEIN, Rodney CROWELL, Guy CLARK. Made over 40 albums; best of '50s-60s work in RCA 2-disc *Famous Country Music Makers - Bobby Bare* '79, incl. 'Last Dance At The Old Texas Moon', 'Dropkick Me Jesus (Through The Goal Posts Of Life)'. Switched to Mercury '70s: 2-disc set of Silverstein songs was *Bobby Bare Sings Lullabies, Legends And Lies*; *Singing In The Kitchen* '74, *Hard Time Hungries* '75 well received; to Columbia late '70s; LPs incl. *Down And Dirty*, also *As Is* '81, prod. by Crowell, incl. Clark's 'Let Him Roll', Tyson's 'Summer Wages'. Hits '80s incl. 'Numbers', 'Have Another Tequila, Sheila', 'Food Blues', etc. *Biggest Hits* compilations on RCA, CBS; RCA duet LPs with Skeeter DAVIS.

BARKER, Thurman (*b* '48, Chicago) Drummer, composer, leader. Infl. by Cozy COLE hit 'Topsy' '58, later records by Roy McCurdy (with Cannonball ADDERLEY), Louis Hayes (with Oscar PETERSON), Tony WILLIAMS, Elvin JONES; played professionally while still in high school, attended rehearsals of Muhal Richard ABRAMS' Experimental Band, second meeting of AACM. First record with Joseph JARMAN (*Song For* '67; then *As If It Were The Seasons*, two LPs by Abrams, Kalaparusha's *Humility In The Light Of The Creator*, all on Delmark); was 'house drummer for the new music'. Invited to join ART ENSEMBLE in Paris, but had gig playing in show *Hair*: continued at Chicago's Schubert Theatre '68 to '80. Also studio work; gigged behind Bette MIDLER (with Barry MANILOW on piano), Marvin GAYE; toured and recorded with Sam RIVERS, Anthony BRAXTON '78-9; three more LPs with Abrams, *The Maze* on Nessa with Roscoe MITCHELL, others; moved to NYC. Replaced Steve McCall in AIR for European tour; played with Leroy Jenkins, Henry THREADGILL; began composing and formed his own small group. He has been too busy working to seek star billing, but when he makes albums as a leader more fame may be forthcoming, perhaps like that of Threadgill in the mid-'80s.

BARLOW, Randy (*b* Detroit). Country singer. Studied clinical psychology at Western

Kentucky U. To Cal. mid-'60s; toured with Dick CLARK's Caravan of Stars singing pop and rock'n'roll; to Capitol records '74, minor country hit with 'Throw Away The Pages'. String of hits with Fred Kelly's Gazelle label incl. 'Goodnight My Love', 'Lonely Eyes', '24 Hours From Tulsa', all '76; 'Kentucky Woman', 'California Lady' '77. To Republic label for LP *Fall In Love With Me*, hits 'Slow And Easy', 'No Sleep Tonight', 'Fall In Love With Me Tonight', all '78. Appeared London Wembley Country Festival '79. Hits continued with 'Sweet Melinda', 'Lay Back In The Arms Of Someone' '79. To Paid label for LP *Dimensions*, hits 'Willow Run', 'Dixie Man', 'Love Dies Hard', all '81. Single on short-lived Jamex label 'Love Was Born' '82, then re-formed Gazelle with Kelly and was back in the charts with 'Don't Leave Me Lonely Loving You' '84.

BARNES, Kathy (*b* Henderson, Kentucky) Child prodigy, later country singer. Sang with brother Larry; signed to RCA late '50s and recorded under guidance of Chet ATKINS; to Cal. and signed to Gene AUTRY's Challenge label mid-'60s; finally broke in country charts on MGM with 'I'm Available (For You To Hold Me Tight)' '75. Move to Autry's Republic label led to bigger hits with 'Someday Soon' '76, 'Good'n'Country' '77. Albums: *Someday Soon* (Republic '76), *Body Talkin'* (UK London '77), *Sings Gene Autry* (Republic '78).

BARNET, Charlie (*b* Charles Daly Barnet, 26 Oct. '13, NYC) Saxophones, bandleader, sometime vocalist. Infl. by C. HAWKINS on tenor, J. HODGES on alto; led reed sections on soprano. Blatant admirer of Duke ELLINGTON; one of the most musical and faithful to jazz of white leaders in BIG BAND ERA. From wealthy background, refused to become lawyer; led band on ocean liner age 16, others from '32 incl. Eddie SAUTER, Tutti CAMARATA trumpet/arrangers. With Artie SHAW, Teddy WILSON in Red NORVO small group '34; hired black musicians as early as '37 (Frankie Newton, John KIRBY). Ray NOBLE's 'Cherokee' big hit for Barnet '39; became enduring jazz standard and favourite of bop musicians; same year Billy MAY joined as trumpet/arranger and Palomar ballroom (L.A.) burned down: band lost instruments, music; Barnet said, 'Hell, it's better than being in Poland with bombs dropping on your head!' and recorded 'We're All Burnt Up'. Ellington and Benny CARTER lent him scores. Three top ten hits '40-1 in first Billboard pop charts: 'Where Was I?', 'Pompton Turnpike', 'I Hear A Rhapsody'; other titles: 'The Count's Idea', 'The Duke's Idea', 'The Right Idea', 'The Wrong Idea' – the last a send-up of 'sweet' bands; subtitle poked fun at Sammy KAYE billing: 'Swing and sweat with Charlie Barnet'. 'Redskin Rhumba' followed 'Cherokee' (not an ASCAP tune: written to be used during society's ban on broadcasts). Always a great talent scout, made four sides with Lena HORNE '41 incl. 'Good For Nothin' Joe'. Next year hired Neal HEFTI, Buddy DeFRANCO, Dodo Marmarosa (b Michael Marmarosa, 12 Dec. '25, Pittsburgh; brilliant bop-infl. pianist later suffered from ill health); later Kay STARR, Ralph BURNS, Trummy Young, Barney KESSEL, Oscar PETTIFORD and Clark TERRY; a late band had arrangements by Gil FULLER, Manny ALBAM. More than 25 chart hits '36-46 incl. 'Skyliner' '45, written by Barnet. Disbanded '49; settled on West Coast, led mostly smaller groups; assembled big band '66-7 for specific gigs; made TV concert tape, album Big Band '67 issued (now on Creative Sounds). Married 6, 10, 11 times, depending which book is consulted; lives life to the full, as did those who worked for him. Complete '39-45 recordings on several Bluebird 2-disc sets (RCA-USA). Autobiography Those Swinging Years with Stanley Dance '84.

BARNUM, H. B. (b '36, Houston, Texas) Producer, arranger, multi-instrumentalist. Moved to L.A. age 4, attended UCLA, studied law. Sang with the Robins (later became the COASTERS) while in high school; later said that the first record he produced was their 'Riot On Cell Block No. 9' (credited to LEIBER & STOLLER). Own initial success 'Pink Shoe Laces', '59 US no. 3 single by Dodie Stevens. Then to Motown, worked with the Miracles ('Shop Around'), SUPREMES, MARVELETTES, Martha and the Vandellas, etc. About to produce RCA session for Jesse BELVIN, heard of Belvin's death and did it himself: album The Big Voice Of Barnum, hit single 'Baby, Baby,

Baby' '60, Everybody Loves H.B. '62. Arranger for Lou RAWLS '66-8; success with OSMONDS, JACKSONS, Johnny BRISTOL, TEMPTATIONS, Junior WALKER, Gladys KNIGHT, CHAIRMEN OF THE BOARD, Nancy WILSON, Frank SINATRA, Count BASIE, Sammy DAVIS Jr. Claims to be responsible for around 100 gold LPs and 160 gold singles, and still at it.

BARRETT, Syd (b Roger Barrett, 6 Jan. '46, Cambridge, England) Singer/songwriter, then legend. Founder member of PINK FLOYD, contributed 10 of 11 songs on their debut album Piper At The Gates Of Dawn '67; left April '68 with well-publicised personal and drug-related problems. Solo work done in two bursts: unique The Madcap Laughs '70, then Barrett, zealous psychedelia married to nursery-rhyme vision; beguiling quality now missing from Floyd in 'Baby Lemonade', 'Effervescing Elephants'; work also incl. setting of James Joyce's 'Golden Hair', chilling 'She Took A Long Cold Look'. Did a few shambolic gigs, then totally withdrew. Legend kept alive by critical and public fascination; UK fanzine Terrapin incl. monthly reports on activity (or lack of it). Surfaced briefly at mixing of Floyd's Wish You Were Here '74, largely about his crack-up; solo albums issued in set on Harvest that year, charted in USA; David BOWIE, others allegedly approached him to resume recording; remains inactive. Tracked down by French journalists '82 at mother's home, said he no longer played guitar but preferred watching TV. Rumours of third solo issue as bands such as the Shamen, TV Personalities etc. made From The Wildwood '87, an album of his songs.

BARRETTO, Ray (b 29 Apr. '29, Brooklyn, NYC of Puerto Rican family) Conga drummer, bandleader, songwriter, arranger. Began playing while in US Army in Germany; jammed with jazz musicians in NYC, turned pro and joined Eddie Bonnemere's Latin Jazz Combo, then two years with José Curbelo band; to Tito PUENTE replacing Mongo SANTAMARIA, stayed four years. He sessioned on R&B singles; as sideman with Red GARLAND, Gene AMMONS, Lou DONALDSON '57-8; Riverside jazz label decided to do a Latin album '61 and asked

Barretto to form a CHARANGA: *Pachanga With Barretto* was his first LP as a leader, tracks written by Hector Rivera. This was an adventurous move by label boss Orrin Keepnews; the album didn't sell very well partly because Riverside and the Latin market were unfamiliar with each other, but Barretto used many of the sidemen forming own band Charanga Moderna: follow-up LP was *Latino* '62, incl. guests 'El Negro' Vivar on trumpet, José 'Chombo' Silva on tenor sax, Alfredo Valdés Jr on piano; tracks incl. 'Carnaval' (from film *Black Orpheus*), GERSHWIN's 'Summertime'. (LPs reissued '73 as 2-disc *Carnaval* on Fantasy.) Sessioned with Kenny BURRELL '63, Freddie HUBBARD '67, Cal TJADER '68, also George BENSON, the ROLLING STONES, BEE GEES, AVERAGE WHITE BAND in the '70s, many others, but his most important work has been for Latin audience: he retained authenticity while updating the charanga with inclusion of brass. *Charanga Moderna* '62 on the Tico label was on the market for several months before track 'El Watusi' took off and reached top 20 USA pop chart '63: that crossover success was short lived but blamed on poor management. Other LPs on Tico were *On Fire Again*, *The Big Hits Latin Style* (crossover attempts with 'If I Had A Hammer', etc.), *La Moderna de Siempre* (straight charanga), *Guajira y Guaguanco* (with jam session flavour, incl. Pedro 'Puchi' Boulong on trumpet), compilation *Lo Mejor de Ray Barretto*. Went to UA hoping for better distribution, became a 'little artist in a huge bowl'; LPs incl. *Viva Watusi!* (incl. 'Watusi '65'), *Señor 007* (movie themes), *El Ray Criollo*, *Latino con Soul* (lead singer Adalberto Santiago). Joined Fania '67: *Acid* was logical experiment with R&B fusion and brought major popularity with Latin audiences for the first time, tracks incl. 'Espiritu Libre', 'Acid', soul sound of 'Teacher Of Love'. Personnel in two-trumpet conjunto incl. Rene Lopez and Roberto Rodriguez, with Orestes Vilato on timbales and vocalist Santiago. *Hard Hands* '68 (incl. 'Abidjan') had trumpeter Joseph 'Papy' Roman replacing Lopez, who'd been drafted; Tony Fuentes joined on bongos and the LP gave Barretto a new nickname. For *Together* '69 (incl. 'Tin Tin Deo', CUBOP classic written for Dizzy GILLESPIE by Chano POZO and Gil Fuller)

Andy Gonzalez joined on bass; *Head Sounds* was compilation incl. most of those named above plus 'Drum Poem (Free Spirit) For Ray Barretto', a poem by Victor HernanDez Cruz spoken over Latin percussion. On *Power* Lopez returned (three trumpets); on *The Message* '71 Barretto co-produced, Johnny Rodriguez replaced Fuentes on bongos; *From The Beginning* was another compilation. *Que Viva la Musica* '72 was prod. by Barretto, with Dave Perez replacing Andy Gonzalez on bass; Barretto's tune 'Cocinando' was theme of film *Our Latin Thing (Nuestra Cosa)*. Some personnel incl. Santiago left at this point to form TIPICA 73. *The Other Road* '73 was an instrumental Latin jazz set incl. 'Abidjan Revisited'; *Indestructible* '73 was prod. by Barretto; new personnel incl. Manuel Duran doubling on trumpet/flugelhorn and Art Webb on flute, lead vocalist Tito Allen. *Barretto* '75 was his biggest hit LP so far, nominated for a Grammy, incl. hit single 'Guarare'. Rubén Blades shared lead vocals with Tito Gomez, wrote two songs incl. hit 'Canto Abacua'. Barretto was tired of gigging in clubs, pessimistic about reaching larger audience with pure salsa; his band carried on as Guarare and Fania issued compilation *Energy To Burn* '77 (he prod. their LP *Guarare* '79 with lead vocals by Ray de la Paz). Meanwhile formed large jazz/rock/Latin fusion group, recorded for Atlantic: *Live/-Tomorrow* was made May '76 at NYC's Beacon Theatre with two trumpets, a trombone, two reeds and Blades. Indifferent fusion LPs were *Eye Of The Beholder* '77 (prod. by the CRUSADERS; Joe Sample and Wilton Felder played on it) and *Can You Feel It* '78. He was voted the best conga player '75-6 by *Latin NY* and Musician of the Year '77. *Gracias* '79 on Fania was live LP, probably from the Beacon concert; versions of earlier hits incl. Santiago on side two. He prod. Guarare's eponymous '79 LP on Inca, with Ray de la Paz on lead vocals and pianist Oscar Hernandez. *Rican/Struction* '79, new Fania LP with Santiago, was return to progressive and intense salsa bringing Latin poll awards '80: best conga player, Musician of the Year, Album of the Year: horn lineup was three trumpets, trombone, tenor and soprano sax, with pianist/arranger Hernandez, Ralph Irrizary joining on timbales and de la Paz in the chorus, who sang lead on *Giant Force/Fuerza Gigante* '80. All-star fusion LP made in '79 was released as *La Cuna* '81 on CTI, Tito PUENTE on timbales, Charlie PALMIERI on piano, singer Willie Torres, Joe Farrell on reeds and Steve GADD on drums; it was a good seller and 'Pastime Paradise' was UK club hit. *Rhythm Of Life/Ritmo de la Vida* '82 with de la Paz was nominated for a Grammy; *Tremendo Trio!* '83 incl. Celia CRUZ and Santiago; Hernandez and Irrizary left to join Blades' Seis del Solar; *Todo Se Vá Poder* '84 incl. many new younger musicians, lead singers Cali Aleman (who'd replaced de la Paz at Barretto's UK appearance mid-'82) and Ray Saba. Barretto toured and recorded with the FANIA ALL STARS from '68 well into the '80s; was mus. dir. of *Bravisimo* TV show '84; appeared in anti-apartheid video and LP *Sun City*. London appearance '86 incl. many of the personnel from *Todo Se Vá Poder*, with Ray Saba singing lead; Aleman had left for Eddie PALMIERI band. *Aquí Se Puede* '87 on Fania featured lead vocals by Saba and Carlos Ferrer; compilation *We Got Latin Soul!* '87 on Charly's Caliente label UK incl. Barretto tracks from the '60s.

BARRISTER, Sikiru Ayinde (*b* Sikiru Ayinde, '48, Lagos, Nigeria) African singer-composer, a Yoruban who originated FUJI style which now threatens to overtake JUJU as favourite recreational music of the Yoruban: nicknamed 'Barrister' by fans. Attended Muslim school, then Yaba Polytechnic '61, but since age 10 had sung in *were* competitions (a Yoruban Muslim vocal style performed mainly during Ramadan). Lack of funds forced him to leave school; worked briefly as stenographer; joined Nigerian army; during civil war '67-70 kept up music studies, gaining knowledge of trad. instruments. Resumed musical career managed by Nigeria-African Songs Ltd, releasing many records; through '70s struggled to perfect style with band the Supreme Fuji Commanders, working from a base incl. elements of juju, apala and trad. Yoruban blues: result now called fuji has criss-cross of amplified percussion, commercial appeal in what had been purely Islamic music; he describes it as percussion conversation. By '80s Barrister and 25-strong Commanders established as a top Nigerian act; best sell-

ing recent LPs incl. *Iwa, Ise Logun Ise* and *E Ku Odun* '82; *Ijo Olomo, Nigeria* and *Love* '83; *Military* '84, most recently *Fuji Vibration* '84-5, *Destiny* and *Superiority*. Success resulted in competition: another Barrister, Wasio Ayinde Barrister, sprang up '84 with his Talazo Fuji Commanders; LPs incl. *Elo Sora* and *Tala Disco '85*.

BARRON, Blue (*b* Harry Friedland, 22 Mar. '11, Cleveland, Ohio) Bandleader, trombonist. Booking agent; started own sweet band. Gimmick was to have vocalist sing first phrase of each song, introducing it. First hit was 'At A Perfume Counter' '38; Geo. T. Simon says band had a tuba playing oompah beat in '39, but also an electric guitar, unusual then. More hits incl. vocals by Russ Carlyle, Clyde Burke; also no. 1 '49 with 'Cruising Down The River', the year's smash piece of nostalgia: Russ MORGAN also had no. 1; 'Are You Lonesome Tonight' '50 had narration by Chicago late-night DJ John McCormick.

BARRON KNIGHTS UK Comedy/vocal quintet formed '60. Original lineup hasn't changed through 6000-plus performances: Duke D'Mond, vocals; Peter Langford, guitar; Butch Baker, drums; Barron Anthony Osmond, bass; Dave Ballinger, drums. Formed in Leighton Buzzard, Bedfordshire as straight pop group; played tours with BEATLES, ROLLING STONES etc.; got greater audience response with humour: vocal talent allowed passable irreverent imitations of big names. First hit 'Call Up The Groups' (no. 3 UK '64) parodied Beatles, Dave CLARK 5 and FREDDIE AND THE DREAMERS, all then in vogue; policy of alternating 'straight' songs with parodies abandoned after relative flop of 'Come To The Dance' (no. 42). Notched four more top 40 hits incl. 'Pop Go The Workers' (no. 5), Xmassy 'Merry Gentle Pops' (no. 9, both '65). When novelty wore off, ideally suited for cabaret circuit, especially abroad; switched to CBS '77 from EMI; found new audience parodying next generation of pop stars with 'Live In Trouble' '77, 'A Taste Of Aggro' '78; 'Never Mind The Presents' '80 was second Yule-related hit; by this time they aped Shakin' STEVENS, Adam ANT, Cliff RICHARD ('Blackboard Jumble' '81), even rubik cube fad ('Mr Rubik'). Albums have been heavy going, though belated first chart entry *Night Gallery* '78 reached no. 15, went gold. Despite accusations of banality from trend-obsessed critics, talent and nose for topicality has kept them going much longer than contemporaries.

BARRY, Jeff USA prod./songwriter. Began as a singer. First major hit as writer was classic '60 'death' song 'Tell Laura I Love Her'. Met and married Ellie GREENWICH; they were one of the most successful songwriting teams in pop music (*see* entry for Greenwich). Divorced '65 but continued writing together until he moved to Cal., worked in Don Kirshner world of BUBBLEGUM: wrote and prod. '69 mega-hit 'Sugar Sugar' for the Archies, studio creation led by Ron Dante with Barry, Tony Wine, Andy Kim (*b* Andrew Joachim, Montreal; had five top 40 hits on Barry's Steed label '68-70; then no. 1 'Rock Me Gently' '74 on Capitol). Later Barry prod. at A&M, worked in film music.

BARRY, Len (*b* Leonard Borrisoff, 12 June '42, Philadelphia, Pa.) Soul singer. Began with Boss-Tones (minor hit 'Mope-Itty Mop' '58); high tenor equipped him to follow in Philly teen idol trad.; bigger hits with the Dovells: 'Bristol Stomp' no. 2 USA on Parkway label '61, infectious oft-revived dance-craze number followed by similar 'Do The New Continental', 'Bristol Twistin' Annie', 'Hully Gully Baby' (all top 40 '62), 'You Can't Sit Down' (no. 3 '63). Solo career brought major hits: '1-2-3' (no. 2 USA, 3 UK '65, prod. by Leon Huff), 'Like A Baby' (no. 27 USA, 10 UK '66), 'Somewhere' (no. 26 USA). Left Decca for RCA, toned down James BROWN-styled stage act as cabaret beckoned '70s. Hits matched pleasant voice with memorable songs, but fame was surprisingly brief.

BART, Lionel (*b* Lionel Begleiter, 1 Aug. '30, London) Composer, lyricist. Stint at art school, RAF service; formed pop group The Cavemen '56 with Mike Pratt, Tommy STEELE; trio provided Steele with first chart entry '56 'Rock With The Cavemen'; Bart and Steele turned to musical stage: *Tommy Steele Story* won Ivor Novello Awards for complete score, 'A Handful Of Songs', 'Water, Water'; Bart's name on 10 others.

'Living Doll' no. 1 for Cliff RICHARD '59; 'Little White Bull' for Steele's film *Tommy The Toreador* won another award; recognised for 'Outstanding Personal Services To British Popular Music'. Wrote scores *Lock Up Your Daughters* (Mermaid Theatre), *Fings Ain't Wot They Used To Be* (Theatre Royal, Stratford East; transferred to West End for two years). 'Do You Mind' no. 1 for Anthony NEWLEY '60, but that year pulled off trick then believed impossible: internationally successful British musical. *Oliver!* had score, lyrics, book by Bart, based on Dickens's *Oliver Twist*; Ron Moody as Fagin, Georgia Brown as Nancy; score incl. 'Where Is Love', award-winning 'As Long As He Needs Me'; over 2500 performances, revived '67, again '71 and ran for almost three years. Filmed '68; won six Oscars. *Blitz* '62 ran over a year; *Maggie May* '65 did reasonably well; *Twang* '65 was flop; *La Strada* '69, based on '54 Fellini film, closed opening night NYC. Always rumoured to have new projects hatching.

BARTHOLOMEW, Dave (*b* 24 Dec. '20, Edgard, La.) Trumpet, bandleader, singer, songwriter, producer, arranger. In vanguard of rhythm & blues explosion in '50s. Began on trumpet with Fats Pichon's river boat band; formed own first band '46, playing frat dances, school hops around New Orleans and worked for Aladdin, De Luxe labels (own hit 'Country Boy' '49); then Specialty and Imperial: discovered Fats DOMINO; initial prod. successes were Domino's first hit 'The Fat Man' '50 for Imperial (no. 6 R&B chart), Lloyd PRICE's 'Lawdy Miss Clawdy' '52 on Specialty (no. 1), SHIRLEY & LEE's 'I'm Gone' '52 on Aladdin (no. 2): Imperial wisely signed him to long-term contract. Prod. all of Domino's hits, co-wrote many of them incl. the biggest; 'I'm Walkin' '57 had Domino's version in top 5 of pop chart, Ricky NELSON's in top 20, both on Imperial; Domino's 'Walkin' To New Orleans' '60 had adventurous use of strings for the time. Also responsible for 'I Hear You Knockin' ' (hit by Smiley LEWIS '52, no. 1 in UK by Dave EDMUNDS '70), much else. Used cream of local talent in studio, drawn on by other local artists such as LITTLE RICHARD: Earl Palmer on drums, saxes Lee ALLEN, Alvin 'Red' Tyler (*b* 5 Dec. '25, N.O.; tracks as Alvin and the

Gyros compiled on Ace as *Rockin' And Rollin';* own LPs *Heritage* '86 and *Graciously* '87 on Rounder); etc. Imperial was sold to Liberty '63; Bartholomew turned down offer to move to West Coast, still lives in New Orleans.

BARTON, Eileen (*b* c.'28, Brooklyn, NY) Singer. Parents vaudevillians; debut age 2; spots on Eddie CANTOR, Rudy VALLEE, Milton BERLE radio shows; understudied in Broadway musical Best Foot Forward '41; worked with Frank SINATRA '44, Berle again '45; club work. Smash no. 1 international hit '50 with inane novelty 'If I Knew You Were Comin' I'd've Baked A Cake', co-written by Bob Merrill, sold for $300 to Chicago publisher who got it a spot on local Breakfast Club radio show; that day NYC publishers were bidding for it. Lyric changed by schoolboys to 'baked a bomb' in those pre-terrorism years. Barton then got better club, TV spots; recorded for Coral: standards ('You Brought A New Kind Of Love To Me'), covers (Johnnie RAY's 'Cry', Dean MARTIN's 'Sway', Perry COMO's 'Don't Let The Stars Get In Your Eyes'); top 20 '53 with version of 'Pretend'.

BARTZ, Gary (*b* 26 Sep. '40, Baltimore, Md.) Reeds, also keyboards; composer, singer. Father ran jazz club; studied at Juilliard at 17; played with Art BLAKEY '65-6, Max ROACH '68-9; organised own combo Ntu Troupe (Bantu word meaning unification of physical and spiritual), then went with Miles DAVIS '70-1 (Live-Evil album). Own records: *Libra* '67, *Another Earth* '68, *Home!* '69, *Harlem Bush Music: Taifa* and *Uhuru* '70-1, all on Milestone; *Juju Street Songs* '72, *Follow The Medicine Man* '72, *I've Known Rivers And Other Bodies* '73, *Singarella: A Ghetto Fairy Tale* '73-4, *The Shadow Do* '75, all on Prestige; *Music Is My Sanctuary* '75 on Capitol, *Ju Ju Man* '76 on Catalyst with vocals by Syreeta Wright, *Love Affair* '78 on Capitol, *Bartz* '80 on Arista.

BASCOMB, Dud (*b* Wilbur Odell Bascomb, 16 May '16, Birmingham, Ala.; *d* 25 Dec. '72, NYC) Trumpet; underrated and influential. Last of 10 children; 2 older brothers were musicians; began on piano, switched to trumpet in elementary school: 'Louis was

my only influence.' Brother Paul (*b* 12 Feb. '10) played tenor sax with 'Bama State Collegians, Dud left high school to play with them '32: became Erskine HAWKINS band, Dud stayed till '44, then joined Paul's combo, which became 15-piece band until '47; short spells with Duke ELLINGTON; led combo for over three years at Tyler's Chicken Shack near Rahway, N.J., Milt JACKSON, Sonny STITT, others came to jam. Then one-night stands, recording work; LP for Savoy '60 with nine pieces, never issued; sessioned with the SHIRELLES, Isley Bros ('Twist And Shout'), James BROWN ('It's A Man's World'), etc. Played in clubs with Dinah WASHINGTON, others; toured Japan several times mid-'60s. Most famous work on record is muted solos with Hawkins band: first solo on 'Swingin' On Lenox Avenue', 'Gin Mill Blues', second on 'Tuxedo Junction', etc. Dizzy GILLESPIE compared Bascomb's harmonies with those of Clifford BROWN; in his autobiography *To Be Or Not To Bop* rated him an influence: 'My solos started taking on a quality where there were long runs and . . . where the playing was sort of behind the beat. Sort of like the style of Dud Bascomb . . .' Good chapter on Bascomb in Stanley Dance's *The World Of Swing*.

BASIE, 'Count' (*b* William Allen Basie, 21 Aug. '04, Redbank, N.J.; *d* 26 Apr. '84, Hollywood, Fla.) Piano, organ, for 45 years one of the best-loved American bandleaders. Nicknamed by radio announcer: Benny GOODMAN was billed as the 'King of Swing', there were 'Duke' ELLINGTON, 'Earl' HINES; he was called 'Count' and the name stuck. Tuition on cinema organ from teenaged Fats WALLER; accomp. vaudeville acts; stranded in Kansas City when circuit troupe folded; played piano in cinema, joined group led by Walter PAGE '28-9, incl. Jimmy RUSHING, folded; joined Bennie MOTEN, featured on Moten's 'Prince of Wails'. Moten died '35; Basie took best men for own group. Playing KC Reno Club with nine pieces; John HAMMOND heard them on radio in Chicago carpark, wrote about the band, told Goodman about it; booking agent Willard Alexander signed Basie, who hired more men, went to Chicago, then NYC. Rough-hewn music unsuccessful at first; men were not good readers, did not play in tune: too poor to buy decent horns. Opened at Famous Door '37; filled small club with big swing: Basie had lost lead alto Buster SMITH, who would not leave KC; Oran 'Hot Lips' PAGE lured away in hope of rivalling Louis ARMSTRONG; but band soon incl. Buck CLAYTON, trumpet; equal but opposite tenor stylists Lester YOUNG and Herschel Evans (*b* '09, Denton, Texas; *d* 9 Feb. '39, NYC); Dicky WELLS, Benny MORTON, trombones; and most famous rhythm section in history of jazz: Walter PAGE, bass; Jo JONES, drums; Freddie GREEN, guitar. Basie led band from keyboard, like Ellington, with economic accuracy. By this time the BIG BAND ERA well under way: the rhythm section sounded modern, swung like a light, well-oiled machine; arrangements were by Eddie DURHAM, Don REDMAN, Jimmy MUNDY, Redman's pianist Don Kirkpatrick (*b* 17 June '05, Charlotte, N.C.; *d* 13 May '56, NYC), or 'heads', devised on the bandstand. KC style of riffing, unfancy blues-based swing was like fresh air, and the band became world famous within a year. Signed bad contract with Decca (musicians' union helped to obtain royalties); before first Decca records Hammond prod. a session with Basie, Young, Page, Jones, trumpeter Carl 'Tatti' Smith (*b* Texas, c.'08; to South America after WWII) as Jones-Smith Incorporated (Chicago, Oct. '36): 'Shoe Shine Boy' and 'Lady Be Good' are first recorded solos by Young, important innovator; 'Boogie Woogie' and 'Evenin' ' have Rushing vocals (all on 2-disc CBS anthology *Super Chief*). At first Decca recording session (Jan. '37) the band incl. Smith, Clayton, Joe Keyes, trumpets; George Hunt, Dan Minor, trombones; Jack Washington, Coughey Roberts, aito saxes; Evans, Young, tenors; Claude Williams, guitar; Jones and Page. (Washington also played baritone.) Records for Decca incl. 'One O'Clock Jump' (head arr. originally called 'Blue Balls', became band's theme), 'Roseland Shuffle', 'Honeysuckle Rose'; 'Jumpin' At The Woodside', 'Every Tub', 'Cherokee' (2-sided 78) all feature Young; 'Blue And Sentimental', 'John's Idea' (named for Hammond) star Evans, who also wrote 'Texas Shuffle', 'Doggin' Around'. Rushing vocals incl. 'Sent For You Yesterday And Here You Come Today', 'Good Morning Blues', 'Pen-

nies From Heaven'; Helen HUMES sings 'Dark Rapture', 'Blame It On My Last Affair', 'My Heart Belongs To Daddy'. Basie made 10 blues sides with rhythm section, incl. 'The Fives', 'Boogie Woogie', 'The Dirty Dozen' etc. Signed with CBS group '39-46; recorded 'Taxi War Dance', 'Lester Leaps In', Young comp. 'Dickie's Dream', many more. Billie HOLIDAY sang with band '37, but could not record with it for contractual reasons; is heard on broadcast air checks ('They Can't Take That Away From Me'). Basie recorded with small groups: Goodman sextet ('40; 'Wholly Cats', 'Breakfast Feud', etc.), Kansas City 7 ('44; 'Lester Leaps Again'); changed labels to Victor '47-50. Evans had died of heart trouble; Young had been fired '40, Clayton had left. Swing era was almost over; band recorded some novelties: Basie's record of Jack MCVEA's 'Open The Door, Richard', with 'vocal' by Harry EDISON, made no. 1 on USA pop chart '47. As well as 'Sweets' Edison on trumpet there were Emmett BERRY, Clark TERRY, Joe NEWMAN; and Buddy TATE, Paul GONSALVES, on tenor. Irving Berlin's 'Cheek To Cheek' had pretty arrangement; Don Redman did 'Just An Old Manuscript'; Moten's 'South' got subtle, gentle update. Basie comps. incl. 'Swingin' The Blues', 'Basie's Basement'. Recorded small group sides early '50 ('Rat Race', 'Sweets'), disbanded, led small group incl. Terry, Wardell GRAY and Buddy DE FRANCO; made short film with Holiday '50, then started all over: formed band to record for Norman GRANZ's Verve label '52 and stayed the course. New accent on arrangements, with Neal Hefti ('Sure Thing', 'Why Not?', 'Two For The Blues', 'Two Franks', etc.). Yet there were fine soloists: 'Two For The Blues' was duet for two Franks, Wess (*b* 4 Jan. '22, K.C.) and Foster (*b* 23 Sep. '28, Cincinnati, Ohio); both left Basie '64, have been busy, highly regarded freelancers ever since; Wess wrote 'Basie Goes Wess', Foster 'Shiny Stockings', 'Down For The Count' and 'Blues Backstage'. Ernie Wilkins (*b* 20 July '22, St Louis) was a third reedman/composer (later with Clark Terry big band, A&R staff at Mainstream Records, etc.); he wrote 'Blues Done Come Back', 'Sixteen Men Swinging'. Band incl. Henry Coker (*b* 24 Dec.'19, Dallas; *d* 23 Nov. '79, L.A.), trombone; Newman and Thad

JONES, trumpets; Marshall Royal (*b* 5 Dec. '12, Sapulpa, Okla.), clarinet, alto; Charlie Fowlkes (*b* 16 Feb. '16, NYC; *d* 9 Feb. '80, Dallas), baritone; Gus Johnson (*b* 15 Nov. '13, Tyler, Texas), drums; later Lucky THOMPSON, Paul QUINICHETTE, others. Late '54 singer Joe WILLIAMS joined; band's future was safe: big, smooth, handsome blues voice made ladies squirm and jazz fans happy. Album *Count Basie Swings – Joe Williams Sings* '55 is one of the best LPs of the decade: Sonny Payne (*b* '26, NYC), drums, Eddie Jones (*b* '29 Red Bank, lived two doors from Basie home) on bass made important contribution to music drenched in blues: 'Please Send Me Someone To Love', by Percy MAYFIELD; 'The Comeback' and 'Every Day (I Have The Blues)' by MEMPHIS SLIM, 'In The Evening (When The Sun Goes Down)' by Leroy CARR; Williams's own 'My Baby Upsets Me'; 'Teach Me Tonight' (by Sammy CAHN) made erotic plea by Williams; three more, six arr. by Foster. 'Every Day' was no. 2 on R&B chart, first Basie chart hit for years; band still with KC roots swung the blues authoritatively, easily: swing era survivors had paid their dues, would be mainstream stalwarts for years to come. Small group LP (sextet, nonet) *The Swinging Count* c.'55 had Count on both organ, piano, with Buddy RICH, drums; music reminiscent of Smith-Jones in '36, but more relaxed. Metronome all-star session yielded 'Party Blues', Williams and Ella FITZGERALD scat duet: the ultimate in high spirits. 'April In Paris' charted '56. Toured Europe '56, UK Apr. '57, first black big band to play Waldorf-Astoria Hotel NYC, June-Sept '57, back in UK that fall: first USA band to play royal command performance. Changed to Roulette label; album *The Atomic Mr Basie* '57 all Hefti comps, incl. 'Li'l Darlin': band could swing at slow tempo, with lovely muted trumpet solo from leadman Wendell Culley (*b* 8 Jan '06, Worcester, Mass.). (Poor early stereo master usually reissued; PRT UK issued excellent mono engineered by Teddy Reig instead '84.) Benny CARTER wrote albums *Kansas City Suite* and *The Legend* ('60-1, now in cheap 2-disc set), these perhaps the band's last masterpieces: crisp ensemble playing, KC spirit intact. 2-disc set *The Count Basie Story* '61 incl. 23 stereo versions of hits of '30s-40s, with

Leonard Feather booklet. Freelanced on various labels; *Kansas City Seven* ('62, Impulse) suffers if compared to similar, earlier essays; *On The Sunny Side Of The Street* ('63, Verve) with Ella, arr. by Quincy JONES, is better. Often on Frank SINATRA's Reprise label; *Hits Of The 50s And 60s*, *Sinatra – Basie* both charted '63. The band recorded with Tony BENNETT, Teresa BREWER, Billy ECKSTINE, MILLS BROS, Sammy DAVIS Jr etc. in '60s. Nistico cousins joined Basie: in '65-7 Sal Nistico played tenor; in '68 Sam Nestico arranged (both *b* Salvatore Nistico: Sal *b* c.'38, Syracuse, NY; played with Woody HERMAN, Don ELLIS; Sam *b* 6 Feb. '24, Pittsburgh; did total of 20 years in US military, retiring '68 from US Marine Band; wrote *Basie Big Band* LP on Pablo). Album *Afrique* '70 arr., conducted by Oliver NELSON; had flute, harmonica, electric bass; comps. by Albert AYLER, Pharoah SANDERS, Basie title comp. in 7/4 time: good LP in its own right, but getting pretty far from Kansas City. Personnel had changed completely by now; there were times band still snapped, but time was running out; at London's Royal Festival Hall '75 it sounded like a Las Vegas hotel band, but public affection long since secure. Basie was in a wheelchair by then; many LPs on Granz's Pablo label, incl. tasty small-group settings: *Trio (First Time!)*; trio with Ella and Joe PASS; *Basie Jam* albums. Band appeared in several films, incl. film music send-up: spoof *Blazing Saddles* (Mel Brooks, '74) had band playing all by itself in the middle of the desert (in real life the desert would have been full of Basie fans). The Count Basie Orchestra still tours, sounding good, led '85 by Thad JONES, then by Frank Foster; Johnny COLES played in band, Freddie Green still there for a while (accepted a Grammy for the band, '85), as well as young talent incl. singer Carmen Bradford, featured on '86 LP on Denon written by Foster. *Diane Schuur & The Count Basie Orchestra* '87 was Green's last recording; Schuur's fourth LP on GRP; she is a vocalist with excellent technical equipment.

BASIL, Toni US choreographer, video pioneer turned singer. Association with music began '60s; choreographed some *Shindig* and *Hullabaloo* TV shows in USA, also MONKEES' cult movie *Head* '69, *American*

Graffiti '74. As rock shows became fancier, advised David BOWIE ('77 Diamond Dogs tour), Linda RONSTADT, Tina TURNER, Bette MIDLER, others. Moved into video with TALKING HEADS, co-directing with singer David Byrne, continuing parallel dance career with own troupe the Lockers; into musical performance when new Radialchoice label came up with video album, for club patrons to look at and dance to at the same time. Result was *Word Of Mouth* '81, with (uncredited) contributions from Members of DEVO, Brand X's John Goodsall, ex-Seatrain violinist Richard Greene. Drawback was Basil's voice, like Kate BUSH with laryngitis; became wearing on mixed bag of material incl. BACHARACH/David's 'Little Red Book', Devo's 'Be Stiff'. Though project didn't work commercially, subsequent 30-minute TV show generated interest: CHINN & CHAPMAN's 'Mickey' no. 1 USA late '82, nine months after being no. 2 UK. Record described by *Rolling Stone* as 'cheerleading vocals and a backing track that merges Eighties funk to Sixties garage-rock' remained Basil's only top 40 entry. LP *Toni Basil* '83 on Chrysalis.

BASS, Fontella (*b* 3 July '40, St Louis, Mo.) Singer, pianist, organist. Daughter of one of Clara Ward singers; first public appearance late '50s with St Louis Gospel-Blues Show. Spotted by soul singer LITTLE MILTON, joined his band early '60s, signed with Chess/Checker: two duet hits with Bobby McClure and five solo hits '65-6 in R&B chart almost all also made pop Hot 100: 'Don't Mess Up A Good Thing' with McClure and her own 'Rescue Me' were both top 5 (McClure's solo hit 'Peak Of Love' also made Hot 100). Trombonist Joseph Bowie was her mus. dir.; she married his brother Lester BOWIE, has since performed with ART ENSEMBLE OF CHICAGO: exciting singing on 'Thème de Yoto' from film soundtrack *Les Stances à Sophie* '70 on Nessa; also *The Art Ensemble Of Chicago With Fontella Bass* '72 on Prestige; sang back-up on title cut of Bowie's *The Great Pretender* '81 on ECM.

BASS, Ralph (*b* 1 May '11, NYC) Producer. R&B pioneer, described by Peter Guralnick as a 'flamboyant, white jive-talking hepcat'. Played violin in high school; became inter-

ested in jazz, moved to L.A., became DJ; joined Black & White Records '44, prod. T-Bone WALKER, Lena HORNE; first big hit was Jack MCVEA's 'Open The Door Richard' (see McVea entry for that story). Went on to prod. Charlie PARKER, Charles MINGUS, Dizzy GILLESPIE, Erroll GARNER, others. Became West Coast A&R man for Savoy, prod. three of top 10 biggest R&B hits '50 with Johnny OTIS, Little Esther, Mel Walker. Took his Federal label to join King '51, recorded the DOMINOES ('Sixty-Minute Man'), Hank BALLARD and the Midnighters ('Work With Me Annie'); helped the PLATTERS, lost them; discovered James BROWN. Moved to Chess '60, worked on hits by Muddy WATERS, Howlin' WOLF, Ramsey LEWIS, Etta JAMES, Sonny Boy WILLIAMSON, indeed the whole roster. Long quotes in valuable *Honkers And Shouters: The Golden Years Of Rhythm & Blues* '78 by Arnold Shaw.

BASSEY, Shirley (*b* 8 Jan. '37, Tiger Bay, Cardiff, Wales) Singer. First pro job at age 16 in a touring revue *Memories Of Al Jolson*. Discovered in variety at Astor Club '55 by Jack HYLTON; he put her in revue *Such Is Life* with Northern comic Al Read. Top 10 UK hits began with 'Banana Boat Song' '57, 'Kiss Me Honey Honey Kiss Me' no. 3 '58; first no. 1 'As I Love You' '59; no. 2 in '60 with 'As Long As He Needs Me' from *Oliver*; 'You'll Never Know' no. 6, 'I'll Get By' no. 10, 'Reach For The Stars'/'Climb Every Mountain' no. 1, all '61. Her real talent was on stage, with dynamic singing, extravagant gestures, often backless, sideless, strapless gowns keeping audience in suspense. Smash hit in Persian Room NYC '61 established her as live act in USA, but only top 40 entry there was theme from Bond film *Goldfinger* (no. 8 '65). UK hits continued: 'What Now, My Love' '62; 'I (Who Have Nothing)' '63. 'Big Spender', Cy COLEMAN-Dorothy FIELDS hit from *Sweet Charity*, reached no. 21 '67, became memorable body-grinding moment in live act; later record was found effective, played very loud, in clearing pigeons from runways at Liverpool airport. Moved to Switzerland '69, leading to LP *Does Anybody Miss Me*. In '70s hits slowed; George HARRISON's 'Something' made no. 4 '70, 'For All We Know', 'Never, Never, Never' made top 10;

another Bond theme 'Diamonds Are Forever' did well, but by mid-'70s record hits had stopped. Concert and cabaret appearances still a hot ticket; played Carnegie Hall '72-3-4; live album from there '73; in early '80s she talked of semi-retirement. Superb on UK TV '83, with guests Richard CLAYDERMAN, Robert GOULET; more serene and mature, extravagant only on specialties such as the Coleman-Fields tune 'Nobody Does It Like Me'. Many compilation LPs; 40 greatest hits collected on *Shirley Bassey 25th Anniversary* 2-disc set '78. Public sympathy on daughter's death by drowning '85; UK tabloid papers sold issues with implication of neglect.

BATAAN, Joe (*b* '42, Spanish Harlem NYC of Afro-American and Philippine parents). Singer, bandleader. Teenaged gang leader; spent time in reform schools, prison, began to study music. Formed band in BOOGALOO era, joined new Fania label '67. First LP was *Gypsy Woman*, with own hit title song and 'Ordinary Guy', described in sleeve note as Latin soul; then *Subway Joe* '68 with title hit; then *Riot!* '68, with 'My Cloud'. 'Gypsy Woman' and 'Subway Joe' crossed over onto black radio. He featured on *Fania All-Stars Live At The Red Garter* '68 (2 vols.), on Vol. 2 singing Marvin GAYE's 'If This World Were Mine'. Other LPs on Fania c.'69-71 incl. *Poor Boy, Singin' Some Soul, Mr New York And The East Side Kids, Sweet Soul*. LP *Salsoul* '73 was on Mericana label, incl. hits 'The Latin Strut', 'Johnny's No Good'; got airplay outside Latin stations through contact with DJ Frankie Crocker, sold 20,000 first week. Prod. own *Afrofilipino* on Mericana's new Salsoul subsidiary incl. 'La Botella', instrumental version of Gil SCOTT-HERON song 'The Bottle'. Bataan's soft soul sound derived from infl. of doo wop; set him apart from fellow Hispanics, made work more acceptable to non-Latin audience. Left Salsoul mid-'70s owing to disagreements; LP *LaSo* (as in Latin Soul) '76 used Brazilian rhythms in disco-soul-Latin fusion. *Mestizo* '80 incl. dance hit 'Rap-O-Clap-O', early cross of Latin with rap; involved with the new HIP-HOP scene through working with young offenders; then he was spending more time mid-'80s teaching kids in the Bronx than on music. UK compilation *We Got Latin Soul!* '87 on Caliente incl. *Riot!* title track.

BATT, Mike (*b* 6 Feb. '50) UK singer, songwriter, arranger, producer; best known for bringing Wombles to life. Cuddly residents of Wimbledon Common in books by Elizabeth Beresford got TV series; Batt wrote theme, other tunes: Wombles had eight UK top 40 hits '74-5, with session men like ace guitarist Chris Spedding sweating in hairy costumes. Pop credibility rose with prod. of LPs: STEELEYE SPAN's *All Around My Hat*; KURSAAL FLYERS' *Golden Mile* (both '75). Own solo career sporadic; 'Summertime City' no. 4 UK '75, but solo LPs poorly received. More success as songwriter: 'Bright Eyes', for film *Watership Down*, no. 1 UK by Art Garfunkel '79; other hits incl. 'A Winter's Tale' (David ESSEX), 'Ballerina' (Steve Harley), 'Run Like The Wind' (Barbara DICKSON), 'I Feel Like Buddy Holly' (Alvin STARDUST). *The Hunting Of The Snark* '86 on Starblend is an adaptation of the Lewis Carroll nonsense poem two years in the making, with Julian LENNON, Cliff RICHARD, Art Garfunkel, Captain Sensible, Roger Daltrey, incl. 'Children Of The Sky'.

BAUZA, Mario (*b* 28 Apr. '11, Havana) Trumpet, reeds, arranger. Began on bass clarinet in Havana Philharmonic, then played clarinet in nightclubs. Met MACHITO in Havana; they played together in teenage orchestra Jovenes de Redención. To USA '30, joined Chick WEBB band as lead trumpet '33, music dir. '34; helped discover Ella FITZGERALD. Married Machito's sister Graciela; left Webb '38; briefly with Don REDMAN, Fletcher HENDERSON, then Cab CALLOWAY '39: became close friend and infl. on Dizzy GILLESPIE, who knew and loved Latin music. Joined Machito's Afro-Cubans '40, reorganising and expanding band (*see* CUBOP), combining Cuban rhythm section with jazz-oriented brass writing, non-Latin guest-star jazzmen: one of those rare original musical ideas. Graciela sang with the band; with Bauza as mus. dir. redefined the Latin sound as hot Cuban music, as opposed to bands like that of Xavier CUGAT, which played polite style for white hotels. Co-prod. Graciela's LP *Esa Soy Yo, Yo Soy Asi* '74, *Dizzy Gillespie y*

Machito: Afro-Cuban Jazz Moods '75, both with Chico O'FARRILL, latter nominated for a Grammy; but Bauza and Machito split after 35 years early '76: Bauza was replaced by Machito's son Mario Grillo. LP *La Botanica* '77 with Graciela; continued guesting on Latin and jazz LPs such as Rafael CORTIJO's *Caballo de Hierro* '78; *Afro-Cuban Jazz With Graciela, Mario Bauza And Friends* '86 incl. some former members of Machito band, e.g. Victor Paz on trumpet, Patato Valdez on congas; Mario/Graciela also incl. in *Rica Charanga* '86 on Caiman by veteran vocalist Rudy Calzado.

BAXTER, Les (*b* 14 Mar. '22, Mexia, Texas) Conductor, composer. Began as concert pianist; sang in Mel TORMÉ's Mel-Tones, '45; mus. dir. on radio shows, incl. Bob Hope; arranged for singers incl. Nat COLE; staff producer at Capitol with own top 10 hits: 'Because Of You' '51; 'April In Portugal', 'Ruby' '53; 'The High And The Mighty', 'Unchained Melody' no. 1 (USA), no. 10 (UK) '55; 'Wake The Town And Tell The People' no. 5 USA same year; 'Poor People Of Paris' (instrumental; French title *La Goulante du Pauvre Jean*) no. 1 USA for six weeks '56. Composer of descriptive pieces for orchestra, often with jungle/ exotic flavour: 'Coffee Bean', 'Sunshine At Kowloon' 'Le Sacre du Sauvage' etc. LPs issued late '60s, GNP Crescendo label: *Brazil Now, Love Is Blue, African Blue, Moon Rock.*

BAY CITY ROLLERS Scottish teenybop group '70s, formed Edinburgh late '60s as the Saxons by brothers Derek (*b* 19 Mar. '55, drums), Alan Longmuir (*b* 20 June '53, bass). Manipulated by danceband leader Tam Paton into moneyspinning UK teen idols. Band renamed by sticking pin into map of USA; with original singer Nobby Clark, had no. 9 UK hit '71 with 'Keep On Dancing', cover of '65 USA hit by Gentrys, prod. by Jonathan KING. Umpteenth follow-up 'Remember (Sha-La-La)' finally hyped into UK top 10 '74 by sending pics to 10,000 addresses lifted from teen magazines; image of short-trousered, tartantrimmed, spikey-haircut group had undisputed two years' dominance of bubble-gum market. Lineup stabilised '74 with

Longmuirs, Stuart 'Woody' Wood (*b* 25 Feb. '57), Eric Faulkner (*b* 21 Oct. '55), guitars; Les McKeown (*b* 12 Nov. '55), vocals (all from Edinburgh). Had nine UK top 10 hits '74-6, incl. two at no. 1: 'Bye Bye Baby', 'Give Me A Little Love'; plundered '60s songbooks for covers – 'Bye Bye Baby' from FOUR SEASONS, 'I Only Wanna Be With You' from Dusty SPRINGFIELD; admitted not playing on some records. Pressure told: Faulkner and Alan Longmuir attempted suicide; 'bad boy' McKeown in court cases; Alan left group '76, returned two years later. USA no. 1 'Saturday Night' early '76 led them to concentrate on USA, Japanese market; lost home following by '77; McKeown replaced by South African Duncan Faure '78; Paton left '79; then it was over. Comeback attempts '80s underlined silliness, but they were so hot at one point that Nick LOWE cut novelty cash-in 'We Love The Rollers'.

BEACH BOYS, The USA vocal/instrumental group formed '61. Original lineup: Brian Wilson (*b* 20 June '42), bass, keyboards; Carl Wilson (*b* 21 Dec. '46), guitar; Dennis Wilson (*b* 4 Dec. '44; *d* 28 Dec. '83), drums, keyboards; Mike Love (*b* 15 Mar. '41) vocals; Alan Jardine (*b* 3 Sep. '42), bass, guitar. All sang. Wilson bros. from Hawthorne, Cal., near L.A.; Love is their cousin: boys liked harmonising, graduated from simple two-part EVERLY BROS. arr. to more complex FOUR FRESHMEN style. Wilsons' father Murry amateur songwriter; mother Audree occasionally made fifth voice until Jardine joined: schoolmate of Brian's, interested in folk music, was best musician in their early days. When Wilson parents left boys home while on long holiday, they used food money to rent instruments, formed group called Carl and the Passions (later title of '72 LP); also called themselves the Pendletones at one point. Only Dennis was interested in surfing, but persuaded Brian and Mike Love to write songs about West Coast pastimes: surfing, cars, girls. Hite Morgan, prod. friend of Murry's, wanted folk-song demo made; Murry recommended Jardine, group went to Morgan's studio, played primitive first song 'Surfin'. Released on small label late '61 with group renamed Beach Boys, became regional hit, no. 75 nationally. Played first gig New

Year's Eve, after which Jardine left for a year to study dentistry, replaced by David Marks on bass (friend of Carl's), who moved to rhythm guitar as Brian took over bass. Group cut three more songs by Brian and Love; Murry took them to Capitol, who signed them '62. Brian Wilson a consummate writer of teenage anthems, perfected surf music blend of Chuck BERRY rhythms, Freshmen harmonies, adolescent interests: 24 top 50 hits '62-6, incl. eight 2-sided hits, 13 top tens, three at no. 1 ('I Get Around' '64, 'Help Me Rhonda' '65, 'Good Vibrations' '66). 'California Girls' (no. 3 '65) used for UK airline commercial '80s ('Caledonia Girls'); still among group's best known records, along with 'Surfin' USA', 'Little Deuce Coupe', 'Surfer Girl', 'Be True To Your School' (all '63). Brian, who suffered deafness in one ear, also worked with JAN & DEAN, co-writing their '63 no. 1 'Surf City' with Jan Berry; prod. the HONEYS, girl vocal trio (married Marilyn); began to sample 'mind-expanding' drugs, had nervous breakdown '64; no longer enjoyed playing live gigs after mid-'60s but wrote and worked in studio. Surf-and-car genre worn thin by '65; more grown-up songs continued to be hits. Although group did the singing, often used session musicians in studio, where Brian played, arr. and prod. hits; replaced on stage by session player Glen CAMPBELL, then permanently by Bruce Johnston (b 24 June '44, Chicago), who had previously recorded with Terry MELCHER as Bruce & Terry and as the Rip Chords. Group continued to tour world to acclaim, almost the only major USA act to survive British Invasion of '64. Brian recorded masterpiece *Pet Sounds* LP '66, pre-dating BEATLES' *Sergeant Pepper* in use of advanced studio technique: critically acclaimed but sales small, in spite of hit singles 'God Only Knows', 'Wouldn't It Be Nice'. Following smash success of hi-tech 'Good Vibrations' (no. 1 both USA/UK) next attempt 'Heroes And Villains' reached no. 12 USA, no. 8 UK: first release on own Brother label (Brother issues on Capitol UK, then Warner/Reprise). Began work on album provisionally titled *Smiles*, collaborating with lyricist/boy wonder Van Dyke PARKS: intake of psychedelic substances may have led to over-elaboration; legendary LP never finished (though bootlegged in '80s). Brian now abdicated, though writing a few songs for various LPs; group largely absent from top 40 after '67. Personnel changes incl. addition of Ricky Fataar, bassist/guitarist Blondie Chaplin, both ex-South African group the Flames who had been signed to Brother; on drums, Fataar replaced Dennis, who had injured his hand. Daryl Dragon (later of CAPTAIN & TENNILLE) added on keyboards; brother Dennis Dragon sometimes augmented stage act on percussion (Dragons sons of classical conductor Carmen Dragon; Daryl also worked as group's arr.). Few significant LPs early '70s except *Surf's Up* '71, *Holland* '72; group had relocated to Holland under then-manager Jack Rieley; Johnston left because of personal differences with Rieley; group regarded as washed up. Compilations of early hits *Endless Summer*, *Spirit Of America* were enormous sellers (both 2-disc sets; former no. 1 album USA '74); for new album *15 Big Ones* '76 Brian persuaded to rejoin on part-time basis, causing the most media interest in 10 years (LP named for band's anniversary and number of tracks; made no. 8 USA). Johnston rejoined '78 as they changed labels to Caribou; single 'Lady Lynda' (written by Jardine for his then wife) made top 10 UK. Releases thereafter sporadic: Fataar, Chaplin, Dragons left; Carl and Dennis cut solo LPs; Johnston prod. for his own Johnston label; everyone seemed to be waiting for Brian to recover lost genius when Dennis drowned while swimming after heavy drinking. In spite of problems of individuals with drugs and alcohol, band's image clean-cut: deep public affection ensured by nostalgia for sun-drenched all-American subject matter of songs; when US Secretary of the Interior James Watt tried to prevent them playing at '83 4th of July celebrations on the Mall, Washington DC, wanting Las Vegas entertainer Wayne NEWTON instead, he was laughed out of court. Band made first original LP in five years with Culture Club prod. Steve Levine; album *The Beach Boys* '85 no more inspired than its title, but they were already an established legend. TV special *The Beach Boys: 25 Years Together* '87 taped in Hawaii with guests Campbell, Ray CHARLES, EVERLY Brothers; Brian beat various addictions, lost 120 pounds and made solo *Love and Mercy* '88.

BEAT

BEAT, The UK ska revival/pop group. Birmingham-based multi-racial outfit formed late '78 by Dave Wakeling (*b* 19 Feb. '56), vocals, guitar; Andy Cox (*b* 25 Jan. '56), guitar, both from B'ham; David Steele (*b* 8 Sep. '60, Isle Of Wight). Played first dates Feb. '79 with drummer Everett Morton (*b* 5 Apr. '51, St Kitts, W. Indies) who'd played with Joan ARMATRADING. Picked up 'black punk' Ranking Roger (*b* 21 Feb. '61, B'ham), former drummer turned vocalist; saxophonist Saxa (*b* c.'31, Jamaica), onetime Prince Buster sideman. Broke out of clubs on back of 2-tone ska explosion; toured with SPECIALS, recorded cover of Smokey ROBINSON's 'Tears Of A Clown' for 2-Tone label: off-beat interpretation, echoey sax, contrasting vocal styles of Wakeling, Roger brought no. 6 UK chart success and custom label, Go-Feet. Next 2 singles also top 10; debut LP *I Just Can't Stop It* '80 made no. 3; American Dance Company called it 'too fast to dance to' but mixture of up-tempo, contemporary lyrics made it good party record. Political edge, too; 'Stand Down Margaret' aimed at Thatcher; royalties donated to Anti-Nuclear Campaign. Group went off the boil somewhat with reggae-tinged 'Wha'appen' '81; by '82 LP *Special Beat Service*, constant touring in USA (as English Beat) had turned them into another new wave pop group. With Saxa semi-retired on health grounds, added Wesley Magoogan (*b* 11 Oct. '51) from Hazel O'CONNOR's Megahype, further augmented with former road-manager David 'Blockhead' Wright on keyboards. Lack of chart success led Arista (who'd signed them for UK only) to drop group and label (which had released few other artists). Mid-'83 split coincided with biggest chart hit: cover of Andy WILLIAMS hit 'Can't Get Used To Losing You' made no. 3 UK, taken from first (best) LP. Wakeling and Roger formed USA-oriented General Public, while Steele and Cox formed Fine Young Cannibals with vocalist Roland Gift (eponymous LP, UK hit 'Johnny Come Home' '85). With MADNESS, Beat were brightest and longest-lived of '79 2-tone explosion; first LP, singles remain high-class pop.

BEATLES, The UK pop group formed '59 Liverpool, all born there: John Winston LENNON (*b* 9 Oct. '40; *d* 8 Dec. '80, NYC), rhythm guitar; James Paul McCARTNEY (*b* 18 June '42), rhythm guitar, then bass; George HARRISON (*b* 25 Feb. '43), lead guitar; Ringo STARR (*b* Richard Starkey, 7 July '40), drums. Lacked steady drummer until joined by Pete BEST Aug. '60; Best sacked 17 Aug. '62 in favour of Ringo. Lennon had started skiffle group The Quarrymen (after Quarrybank school) '56; asked McCartney to join summer '57; Harrison added late '57. Close friend art student Stuart Sutcliffe (*b* 23 June '40, Edinburgh; *d* 10 Apr. '62) joined '58 on bass; couldn't play at first but had money from sale of painting, needed to upgrade group's equipment. Changed name of group to Johnny and the Moondogs, then Silver Beatles, then Beatles. Played four tours in tough Hamburg clubs, perfecting covers of Chuck BERRY, LITTLE RICHARD etc.; EVERLY BROTHERS had been infl. on Lennon for harmony, softer rock style; Buddy HOLLY (because unlike Elvis PRESLEY Holly played guitar, wrote his own songs). Lennon and McCartney wrote songs together from the beginning; from Jan. '61 played hundreds of dates at Liverpool's Cavern Club between Hamburg trips. Sutcliffe left group to paint, settle with photographer Astrid Kirchherr in Hamburg '61 (died of brain tumour, possibly caused by hooligan's kick in the head after '60 English gig); Astrid inspired much of Beatle style in dress, haircuts which left deep imprint on the period. Recorded back-up as The Beat Boys for pop singer Tony Sheridan on Polydor; Brian EPSTEIN saw them at Cavern, became manager; turned down by many labels, then got audition with George MARTIN at Parlophone, then label for EMI residue, comedy records. Best played at audition, Martin advised Epstein to replace him; 'Love Me Do' re-recorded with Ringo on 11 Sep. '62, hit UK top 20; second single 'Please Please Me' no. 2 early '63; UK LP of same name completed in marathon session; third single 'From Me To You' was no. 1: press coined term 'Merseybeat' to describe phenomenon incl. other groups from Liverpool (on river Mersey: the SEARCHERS, GERRY AND THE PACEMAKERS, etc.). Beatlemania began; group could not appear in public without police protection. 'She Loves You' was biggest single in UK history late '63; they toured Europe; played Royal

84

Command Performance (Lennon told royals to rattle jewellery instead of applauding). Candour, style, insouciant humour evident in interviews; something new had happened: they were real, not a press-agent's creation; Lennon and McCartney became one of the most successful song-writing teams in history. Next came British Invasion of USA. EMI's USA outlet Capitol had refused to handle the records; first USA issues on Vee Jay. Fourth single 'I Want To Hold Your Hand', second UK LP *With The Beatles* (*Meet The Beatles* in USA) issued by Capitol none too soon as group landed in NYC to mob scenes 7 Feb. '64; millions saw two appearances on Ed Sullivan TV show (music could not be heard for screaming); in Apr. 'Can't Buy Me Love' became first single to top USA and UK charts simultaneously. First film *A Hard Day's Night* opened in USA August, made $1.3 million first week: dir. by Richard Lester in monochrome, realistic style, good actors in support (Wilfred Bramble as lecherous grandfather), still probably the best pop film ever made. *Help!* '65 co-starred Victor Spinetti; dir. by Lester and well-received but (prophetically) more self-indulgent. They received MBE (Member of the British Empire) honours at Buckingham Palace from HM Queen Elizabeth II 26 Oct. '64: the 'gongs' are recommended by politicians, in this case Prime Minister Harold Wilson, who wanted credit for 'Swinging London'. Songs improved in craftsmanship, lyrics became more adventurous; 'Day Tripper', 'Paperback Writer' '65-6 broke new ground: some were puzzled, esp. in USA, by UK idioms, but records sold automatically. With soundtrack LPs and *Beatles For Sale* '64 they had five straight no. 1 LPs UK, five slightly different no. 1 USA issues; *Help!* incl. McCartney's lovely 'Yesterday', with string quartet (covered since about 2000 times) and Lennon's Bob DYLAN-infl. 'You've Got To Hide Your Love Away'. They no longer wrote together (though by mutual agreement songs published under both names), so that John's acerbity, Paul's prettiness no longer complemented each other. *Rubber Soul* '65 made full use of 4-track studio techniques, polished layer by layer by Martin, called 'fifth Beatle'. LP incl. John's boredom ('Nowhere Man'), sadness of anonymous lust ('Norwegian Wood',

with Harrison on sitar), Paul's too-pretty 'Michelle'. *Revolver* '66 plunged further afield; Harrison allowed three songs: 'Taxman' (mentioned rapacious interchangeable UK politicians by name), 'Love You To' with sitars, 'I Want To Tell You'; LP incl. upbeat 'Good Day Sunshine' as well as Paul's 'Eleanor Rigby' (sung alone with string octet); stunningly simple 'Here, There, and Everywhere'; powerful, brassy 'Got To Get You Into My Life'; title song from *Yellow Submarine*, '68 cartoon by Heinz Edelman, still delighting children; John's quirky 'I'm Only Sleeping', 'And Your Bird Can Sing', mysterious 'Tomorrow Never Knows'. Single 'Penny Lane'/'Strawberry Fields Forever' was first not to be no. 1 UK (no. 2 '67); snapshots of Liverpool childhood were too good: 'Penny Lane' was Paul's, 'Fields' had John's surreal lyrics. Best songs to date intended for new LP but released because they took so long to make and new single was needed. UK LPs had seven songs on each side; because of the way royalties were paid and the price structure in American market, American LPs had only six (hard-core fans bought the imported editions); the Beatles changed that, too: *Sgt Pepper's Lonely Hearts Club Band* '67 was identical everywhere (it cost $1 more in USA than previous Beatles sets): concept album was carnival of pure entertainment of highest quality. Overture, mixture of music hall, old theatre posters ('For The Benefit Of Mr Kite'), engaging nonsense ('Lovely Rita'), psychedelia ('Lucy In The Sky With Diamonds', LSD mnemonic), Paul's sentimentality ('When I'm Sixty-Four'), Ringo's jolly singing on 'With A Little Help From My Friends', all strained Martin's then state-of-the-art equipment to its limits: hurdy-gurdy effect in 'Mr Kite' obtained by mixing taped bits of steam-organ music at random; last track 'A Day In The Life' began with leftover lyrics, ended with 40-piece orch. playing long improvised chord like a coffin lid, followed by a 20,000 Hz sound only dogs could hear. Collage on sleeve art-work also set fashions, featured marijuana plants (unknown to EMI) amid jungle/jumble. Twenty years later people remembered where they were when they first heard the album, which worked partly because drug-induced bonhomie brought Fab Four closer together than they had been for a long time or would be again: they had conquered the world but not seen it, prisoners in hotel rooms. Seen in world-wide satellite broadcast '67: 200 million people saw them sing 'All You Need Is Love' two weeks after Arab-Israeli war. They now extended interest in Eastern music to philosophy, following Maharishi Mahesh Yogi; at retreat with him in Wales Aug. '67 heard about Epstein's death (probably drug induced by accident, but enormous fortunes being made had begun to haunt them all). They decided to make improvised film; left London on bus Sep. '67 without Epstein to organise everything for them, followed by crowds and snarled traffic; forgot to book studio time and had to shoot interiors in disused aircraft hangar: *Magical Mystery Tour* was like a sequence of early experimental pop videos, shown on BBC 26 Dec. '67 and trounced by critics; USA TV deal was cancelled: first Beatle failure. 2-disc 7" 45 EP soundtrack album reached no. 13 UK singles chart; in USA it filled LP side, recent singles the other. Meanwhile tax/financial problems to be sorted out by investment in company which became Apple Corps Ltd, to be operated in hippie 'peace and love' fashion, creativity unstifled by businesslike methods: Dutch design team The Fool commissioned to run Apple boutique in Baker Street, became shoplifters' heaven; Apple Electronics run by incompetent 'Magic Alex', who never invented anything; also Apple Music, Retail, Foundation for the Arts, record label: a few long-time friends worked hard for little reward, hangers-on and people off the street helped themselves with no one in charge: a fortune saved from taxman by throwing it away. As disaster was getting under way, Beatles went to India with Maharishi; Liverpudlians still hardheaded enough quickly to tire of trying to levitate, but used time to write songs: sessions for *The Beatles* '68 (aka 'White Album') marred by John's romance with Yoko ONO, who was constantly present, carelessly in the way; but group was disintegrating anyway. 2-disc set had no sleeve artwork at all: incl. scribbles, scraps among flashes of old brilliance: Lennon's 'Julia' to his long-dead mother, rocker 'Back In The USSR', charming market-place romance 'Ob-La-Di, Ob-La-Da'. Martin begged them to edit it to single LP; the only

thing they agreed on was not to do that. First batch bore serial numbers: a 'limited edition' of 2 million. Apple label nearly successful: single 'Hey Jude' sold 3 million; label signed Mary HOPKIN ('Those Were The Days' no. 1 UK, no. 2 USA), James TAYLOR, Jackie LOMAX, MODERN JAZZ QUARTET; but empire was collapsing. Beatles wanted industry shark Allen Klein to sort it out, except Paul, who wanted NYC lawyer John Eastman, soon-to-be father-in-law; Klein won; sweep-out of Apple Corps began. *Yellow Submarine* soundtrack album '69 was very short weight. *Abbey Road* '69 had famous sleeve photo of four crossing road to EMI studio; absurd rumour started, still peddled today, that Paul was dead, lookalike replacement had been hired. LP contrasted Paul's nursery-rhymish 'Maxwell's Silver Hammer' (which John hated), Ringo's vocal on 'Octopus's Garden' with 'Come Together', 'She Came In Through The Bathroom Window' (hit for Joe COCKER '70). Last LP *Let It Be* released '70 after final split; sessions saw hundreds of songs recorded; some went back to Quarrymen ('One After 909'); 'Get Back' was best thing on it. They could not finish it; John wanted to release the chaos: 'It'll tell people, This is us with our trousers off, so will you please end the game now?' LP handed over to Phil SPECTOR; when Paul could not stop what Spector had done to his 'Long And Winding Road' (dubbed strings, etc.) he too knew group was finished. Film for LP completed Jan. '69 with rooftop concert at Savile Row headquarters; sound in the sky was enough for neighbours, who called police: decade and Beatles ended with John saying, 'I'd like to say thank you very much on behalf of the group and myself and I hope we passed the audition.' The self-contained group creating its own material had temporarily turned the music business upside down, giving popular music back to the people who made it; clever lyrics often contained puns, but critics and public tried too hard to read secrets: when lines from Shakespeare were thrown into Lennon's sound-collage 'I Am A Walrus' (from *Magical Mystery Tour*), critic Rex Reed (in *Stereo Review*) thought they were mocking a priest in the confessional; when psychopathic murderer Charles Manson claimed to be inspired by

'Helter Skelter' (a Lennon scribble on the White Album) everybody rushed to listen. Excitement was overdone in '66 when Lennon said, 'We're more popular than Jesus now,' a banal piece of social comment which some clergymen admitted might be true. He wanted sleeve illustration on USA compilation LP that year featuring chopped up dolls, fake blood in butcher shop; said it was 'as relevant as Vietnam': nobody laughed. First issues of Beatle albums on compact disc early '87 were revealing: the first was recorded all in one day in mono; Martin had only a two-track machine to work with, putting instruments on one track, voices on the other; mixing down a mono master was a breeze. David Sinclair in *The Times* wrote of the second LP, revealed by digital technology in all its strangeness: 'Did George intend the guitar intro to "Roll Over Beethoven" to sound like a rubber band? Did Paul forget to plug in his bass during "Hold Me Tight"?' And were the Beatles really such a barber shop vocal unit as the . . . versatile harmonies, so prominently mixed, suggest?' They were, and unlike other 'beat' groups, they went on from there to get better. They spent four months and $75,000 making *Sgt Pepper*; less talented groups later spent far more making flops: the Beatles were blamed. Tony Palmer wrote in the *Observer* '69 that Lennon and McCartney were 'the greatest songwriters since Schubert'; Fritz Spiegl described them in BBC weekly the *Listener* as doing more damage than anyone in history of music: thus the media contributed to the nonsense, while the Beatles were no more or less than a deeply loved pop group who made people laugh (except when they were being serious), and whose original, essentially English music contained a large element of seaside postcard and music hall: among their many saving graces was that they knew and cheerfully acknowledged that the mystery of their popularity was greater than the sum of their parts. *Shout!* '81 by Philip Norman tells their story in detail; see also entries for individuals.

BEAU BRUMMELS USA pop group formed '64. Lineup: Sal Valentino (*b* Sal Spampinato, 8 Sep. '42, San Francisco), vocals; Ron Elliott (*b* 21 Oct. '43, Haddsburg, Cal.), Ron Meagher (*b* 2 Oct. '41, Oakland), guitars; Declan Mulligan (*b* Eire), bass; John Petersen (*b* 8 Jan. '42, Rudyard, Mich.), drums. Was one of the first Bay area bands with Sopwith Camel, Country Joe, Big Brother to break nationally. Signed by pioneer FM DJ Tom Donahue to his labels; hits prod. by Sylvester Stewart (later became SLY STONE). BEATLES-infl. 'Laugh Laugh' made USA no. 15, established band as answer to British Invasion; even name chosen to be British-sounding. '65 hat-trick completed with 'Just A Little' (no. 8), 'You Tell Me Why' (no. 38), but couldn't sustain it. Label bought by WB; band became album band as fashion dictated. Petersen had left to join HARPERS BIZARRE; Mulligan departed (later sued band for share of loot). Voguily progressive LP *Triangle* '67 (with guest guitar Van Dyke PARKS), country-rock *Bradley's Barn* '68 (with session men soon-to-be AREA CODE 615) failed to shake Beatle-suited harmony image. Split after '68; Valentino made solo singles, formed Stoneground; Elliott did solo LP *The Candlestick Maker* '69, then sessioned widely (Randy NEWMAN, Van MORRISON, LITTLE FEAT), formed shortlived Pan. Original lineup re-formed '74 with guitarist Dan Levitt made eponymous LP for WB; split '75; Mulligan, Valentino re-formed '84. Rhino label reissues '80s. Derivative bandwagon-jumping left them a curiosity; some say that their 12-string-and-harmony SEARCHERS-soundalike period infl. early BYRDS: Roger McGuinn isn't talking.

BEBEY, Francis (*b* '29, Douala, Cameroon) African singer-composer, poet, novelist, guitarist, musicologist, film-maker. Son of clergyman; attended French school, learned French and religious songs. B.S. in Maths at Douala; to France '50s to study modern languages at Sorbonne; began playing guitar infl. by Segovia. Worked briefly as radio journalist in Ghana; to NYC '61 to study broadcasting; devoted full-time energy to African music from '64: toured continent performing, researching; continued to write, publishing first novel *Agatha Moudious' Son* '68 (won Grand Prix Littéraire de l'Afrique Noire); since then nine novels, vols. of poetry incl. *Ashanti Doll, King Albert*; also *African Music: A People's Art*, widely considered best book on subject. First LP on Philips *Concert Pour un*

Vieux Masque '69; 14 LPs '75-85 on Ozileka label incl. *African Sanza* '82 (also released in USA and as Vol. 5 of African Dance series), *Super Bebey* (2 discs), *New Track*. Has won international awards for music sung in English, French, Douala, styles incl. trad., rumba, Makossa, pop.

BE-BOP DELUXE UK rock group formed '72 by Bill Nelson (*b* Wakefield, Yorkshire), who had previously made limited edition LPs *A To Austr* and *Astral Navigations* with local group Gentle Revolution, *Northern Dream* '71 later reissued on Butt. Original Be-Bop lineup incl. Nelson, guitar and vocals; Nick Chatterton-Dew, drums; Robert Bryan, bass; Ian Parkin, guitar; Richard Brown, keyboards. All except Brown on *Axe Victim* '74, after patronage of DJ John Peel helped secure EMI contract. After touring with Cockney Rebels Nelson revamped band with ex-Rebels Paul Avron Jeffries (bass) and Milton Reame-James (keyboards) plus ex-Hackensack drummer Simon Fox; but more stable lineup of Nelson, Fox, New Zealand Maori Charlie Tumahai on bass made LP *Futurama* '75. Music a pastiche of David BOWIE's futuristic rock, guitar-led heavy metal: ended up sounding more like 10CC's vapid pop. UK no. 23 hit 'Ships In The Night' from LP *Sunburst Finish* '76 pleasant enough, but Nelson lacked distinctive vocal ability. Three more LPs (plus posthumous *Best Of*) before project laid to rest after failure to find hoped-for USA success. *Hot Valves* EP UK no. 36 '76 was Be-Bop's last success at home, where energy of punk soon swamped Nelson's comparatively half-baked ideas. Returned with DEVO-esque *Red Noise* '79, retaining keyboardist Andrew Clark (joined Be-Bop after *Futurama*), added Ian Nelson, sax; Rick Ford, bass; Steve Peer, drums; disbanded after *Sound On Sound* '79. Nelson continues to record under own name (notably *Quit Dreaming And Get On The Beam* '81, top 10 LP in UK); could be compared to Todd RUNDGREN in having fair-sized cult following, making occasional commercial record without producing work of consistent quality. Has also moved into prod. (e.g. FLOCK OF SEAGULLS).

BECHET, Sidney (*b* 14 May 1897, New Orleans; *d* 14 May '59, Paris) Clarinet, soprano sax. With Louis ARMSTRONG, Johnny DODDS, King OLIVER, one of the greatest of all New Orleans musicians. Sat in with Freddie KEPPARD as a child; toured South, song-plugging with Clarence WILLIAMS, '14-6; Played with Oliver '16, went to Chicago, then NYC; with Will Marion COOK's Southern Syncopated Orchestra '19, went to Europe. Swiss conductor Ernest Ansermet wrote, 'I wish to set down the name of this artist of genius; as for myself, I shall never forget it – it is Sidney Bechet . . . who is glad one likes what he does, but who can say nothing of his art save that he follows his "own way" . . . perhaps the highway the whole world will swing along tomorrow . . .' The rediscovery of this article more than a decade later helped spark off the New Orleans revival (*see* JAZZ). Bought straight model soprano in London, played in Paris till '21, deported from England (fight with prostitute), back to NYC '21. First records with Williams; with Armstrong (Red Onion Jazz Babies, '24), accompanied singers; played briefly with Duke ELLINGTON, James P. JOHNSON at Kentucky Club '25 and had the same effect as Armstrong's on NYC musicians who were not yet playing jazz. He toured with shows, revues; to Europe with Josephine BAKER, Claude HOPKINS '25; left show, toured Russia '26. To Berlin; toured Europe '27; joined Noble SISSLE Paris '28; jailed there 11 months (shooting incident '29). Toured New England with Ellington '32; organised New Orleans Feetwarmers with Tommy LADNIER, made first recordings for Victor '32. Ran tailor shop with Ladnier '33. Played all over the East (Springfield, Ill. '43; New Orleans with Armstrong '44) but mostly NYC; to Europe '49, made home in France, becoming famous and well-loved entertainer there. Visits to USA '49, '51, '53; UK, Argentina, Peru '57; Brussels International Exhibition '58; extended works *Nouvelle Orléans, The Night Is A Witch* performed late '50s; autobiography *Treat It Gentle* published '60. *Sidney Bechet: The Wizard Of Jazz* '87 by John CHILTON is authoritative. He made more than 36 sides with Victor '32-41; various groups incl. drummers from New Orleans veteran Baby DODDS to bopper Kenny CLARKE, but Bechet always dominated. Most famous dates with Port of Harlem Jazzmen on Blue Note '39: 'Blues

For Tommy' (Ladnier), 'Summertime', etc. followed by more Blue Note sessions through '55. Recordings in France incl. 'Les Oignons' ('The Onions', '49, with Claude Luter, clarinet, leader, *b* '23, Paris) said to have sold a million copies by '55; comp. 'Petit Fleur' '52 (hit for Chris BARBER '59). Bechet's heavy vibrato was instantly recognisable; he was the only jazzman until Steve LACY and John COLTRANE to concentrate on the soprano, but his lyricism was a profound infl. on Johnny HODGES, who played soprano until '40 as well as alto sax. He never altered his pure New Orleans lyricism, even when some thought it was old-fashioned; it belonged to him: on 'Wild Man Blues' '40 he played solos and breaks in the styles of both Armstrong and Johnny DODDS on their classic recording of '27, but made them his own. 2-disc set *Master Musician* on Bluebird (RCA USA) has '38-41 material; '39 *Port Of Harlem Jazzmen* issued by Mosaic '84, also complete Blue Note recordings (13 recording sessions) in 6-disc box '85; also 2-disc *Armstrong & Bechet In New York 1923-5* from Smithsonian Collection, '45-6-7 material on Storyville *Sidney Bechet Sessions*.

BECK, Jeff (*b* 24 June '44, Surrey) UK rock guitarist. Gave up early piano lessons, made own guitar; dropped out of art school to join Tridents, local R&B group; replaced Eric CLAPTON in YARDBIRDS; unpredictable behaviour led to split '66. Made commercial singles prod. by Mickie MOST while attempting to assemble hard-rock unit for album work: 'Hi Ho Silver Lining' no. 14 UK '67, 'Tallyman' no. 30 '67, instrumental version of Paul Mauriat Euro-hit 'Love Is Blue' no. 23 '68: expressed distaste for the last by playing sharp. Original supergroup with Jet Harris (ex-SHADOWS), Viv Prince (ex-PRETTY THINGS) unstable; after interim lineups made album *Truth* '68, with Rod STEWART, vocals; Nicky HOPKINS, piano; Mickey Waller (*b* 6 Sep. '44, London), drums; Ron Wood (*see* ROLLING STONES) on bass: something of a classic, incl. raunchier version of Yardbirds' 'Shapes Of Things', two Willie DIXON covers, version of Rose/Dobson's 'Morning Dew' (Beck not a prolific composer). On second LP *Beck-Ola* '69 Tony Newman replaced Waller on drums; provided more of the same: high-

light was version of PRESLEY hit 'All Shook Up' with startling slide guitar: Beck was fast and inventive, but Most's pop prod. unsuitable to material. Most also prod. DONOVAN, who made one-off single with group: 'Goo Goo Barabajagal' effective despite silly title, made no. 12 UK/36 USA '69. Beck planned to link with VANILLA FUDGE rhythm section of Carmine APPICE and Tim Bogert, plus Stewart, but was hospitalised after car smash. Stewart joined FACES; Beck's next group had Bobby Tench, vocals; Max Middleton, keyboards; Clive Chaman, bass; Cozy Powell, drums; made two LPs: *Rough And Ready* '71, *Jeff Beck Group* '72 lacked good songs, as did long-awaited Beck-Bogert-Appice outing when their eponymous debut released '73; vocals not strong either: singer Kim Milford (ex-*Jesus Christ Superstar* stage show) dropped from BB&C before recording. They incl. first recording of Stevie WONDER song 'Superstition' on LP but were scooped by Motown release of Wonder's single (Beck played on Wonder LP *Talking Book* '72). Beck resolved vocalist/material problem by turning to jazz-rock fusion music composed spontaneously in studio. *Blow By Blow* '75 had new (studio only) lineup: Richard Bailey, drums; Phil Chen, bass; Middleton. LP was Beck's biggest chart success yet in USA, where all albums except *Rough And Ready* had made top 20: *Blow* made no. 4 and excited curiosity by incl. voice-tube rendition of BEATLES' 'She's A Woman': technique of channelling guitar sound through tube to be 'voiced' by guitarist's mouth long-favourite Beck trick on stage. Fifth Beatle George MARTIN prod. *Blow*; retained for *Wired* '76, which saw the first of the collaborations with ex-MAHAVISHNU keyboardist Jan Hammer; stormy partnership resulted in tour (*Jeff Beck With The Jan Hammer Group Live* '77), further LP *There And Back* '80. Though jazz-rock showed off technique, many fans disappointed that he refused invitation to join Stones when Mick Taylor left late '74; link warmly welcomed with Robert Plant (ex-LED ZEPPELIN) and former Yardbird colleague Jimmy Page to record R&B standards as The Honeydrippers; LP of that name charted strongly '84; then linked with Stewart again for cover of IMPRESSIONS soul classic 'People Get Ready' and more rock-oriented LP *Flash*, both '85.

Beck is certainly flash; and exciting when he gets it together. Also well-known for collection of classic American Ford cars.

BEE GEES, The UK vocal trio: Barry (*b* 1 Sep. '46), Robin and Maurice Gibb (both *b* 22 Dec.'49). Family originally from the Isle of Man; sons of bandleader Hugh Gibb made debut in Manchester cinema when record they were to mime as pre-matinee attraction broke. Emigrated to Australia '58; spotted by driver Bill Gates singing for change at speedway track; named Bee Gees for Gates, local DJ Bill Goode, and/or for Brothers Gibb. Successful on Festival label in pre-BEATLE period, but decided to head home early '67; sent on demos to Brian EPSTEIN's NEMS concern, 5-year management contract followed. Australians Colin Peterson on drums, Vince Melouney on guitar were added to Barry on rhythm guitar, Maurice on bass. NEMS dir. Robert Stigwood launched them Apr. '67 on £50,000 budget; first single 'New York Mining Disaster 1941' introduced keening harmony to UK audience, who made it no. 12 hit. 'To Love Somebody' flopped; dirge-like 'Massachusetts' no. 1 Oct.; all three written jointly by boys, marked them all-round talent in Beatles mould. Subsequent releases lacked Beatles' depth; 'World', 'Words', 'I've Got To Get A Message To You', 'First Of May', 'Don't Forget To Remember' all were top 10 hits, all ballads after bluesy 'Jumbo' only made no. 25. Melouney left '68, craving more varied musical diet; success assured as long as brothers stuck together, but marriages (Maurice to singer LULU), problems adjusting to fame caused breakup and lawsuits (drummer Peterson claimed rights to group name!). Polydor released *Best Of* LP, Robin had no. 2 solo UK hit 'Saved By The Bell', Barry and Robin made pointless rockstar film *Cucumber Castle*; late '70 reunion failed to capture imagination in UK. Apart from no. 1 single in USA 'How Can You Mend A Broken Heart' next four years virtually hitless: became oldies act. Rescued by link with Atlantic soul producer Arif Mardin after that label (which distributed their records in USA) rejected new LP *A Kick In The Head Is Worth Eight In The Pants*. New partnership started with transitional *Mr Natural* '74, blossomed with *Main Course* '75, in which Mardin encouraged

R&B feel. New band with Alan Kendall, guitar, Dennis Byron on drums and Blue Weaver on keyboards (both ex-Amen Corner) provided missing backbone: songs like 'Jive Talkin'' (their second US no. 1) improvised in studio from instrumental base, while 'Nights On Broadway' (later hit for black singer Candi Staton, a compliment indeed) saw Barry unleash falsetto that became trademark in third career. Trio had unwittingly presaged disco boom, so after consolidating approach with *Children Of The World* '76 (platinum LP incl. no. 1 single 'You Should Be Dancing') they were commissioned by Stigwood to write score for disco movie *Saturday Night Fever*: soundtrack album broke sales records worldwide, in excess of 30 million; top of US LP chart 24 weeks (a record for a 2-disc set), as well as yielding three US no. 1 singles ('How Deep Is Your Love', 'Stayin' Alive', 'Night Fever' nos. 3, 4 & 1 respectively in UK). (Meanwhile, brother Andy – *b* 5 Mar. '58 in Brisbane, *d* 10 Mar. '88, Fla. – launched own career with three straight no. 1 singles, all written or co-written by older brothers.) Repeated disco formula with variations in *Spirits Having Flown* '79, LP incl. three more US no. ones in 'Too Much Heaven', 'Tragedy' (also no. 1 UK), 'Love You Inside Out'. *Living Eyes* '81 not so successful, but they were passing golden touch to others: with Karl Richardson and Albhy Galuten (team that took over from Mardin when Stigwood left Atlantic mid-'70s), Barry prod. *Guilty* '81 for Barbra STREISAND, *Heartbreaker* '82 for Dionne WARWICK, both no. 1 LPs, and *Eyes That See In The Dark* '83 for Kenny ROGERS, which only went platinum. Other films following *Fever* were sequel *Stayin' Alive*, disaster *Sgt Pepper's Lonely Heart's Club Band* '78 with Peter FRAMPTON; Barry's solo effort *Now Voyager* '84 indicated hiatus in trio's recordings, but it was clear that his touch could sell records. They co-wrote 'Chain Reaction' ('85 hit for Diana ROSS), came back with LP *ESP* '87 after image of *Fever* had finally died down: career much longer than outsiders predicted isn't over yet.

BEGUINE Dance rhythm emerging around the turn of the century in French-speaking Caribbean islands of Guadeloupe and Martinique; *orchestras antillais* recorded in Paris from '29; LP *Jazz And Hot Dance In Martinique 1929-1950* has six beguines made in Paris. The rhythm comes in fast triplets and could be described as a calypso-rumba; clarinets and trombones were featured solo instruments. When Cole PORTER stayed at the Waldorf Astoria NYC where Xavier CUGAT had a residency, the meeting resulted in 'Begin The Beguine' '35, a popularised beguine which became an international hit '39 with recordings by Artie SHAW (instrumental swing treatment), Joe LOSS in UK (Latin-flavoured dance beat with vocal by Chick Henderson); also Fred ASTAIRE in film *Broadway Melody Of 1940*. The beguine is now a strong element in CADENCE, a successful Latin style emerging in the '80s.

BEIDERBECKE, Bix (*b* Leon Bix Beiderbecke, 10 Mar. '03, Davenport, Iowa; *d* 6 Aug. '31, Queens, NYC) Cornet, piano, composer. First great white jazz musician; became distorted legend after death (alcoholism), a 'young man with a horn'. Began learning piano age three; brother brought home records incl. ORIGINAL DIXIELAND JAZZ BAND's 'Tiger Rag'. Fascinated by improvised music, Bix slowed turntable speed to pick out cornet part on piano; soon took up cornet. Played in high school band; expelled from military academy '22; gigged in Chicago, played Lake Michigan excursion boats, joined Wolverines '23, made first records '24. Continued studying piano; first important jazzman to be infl. by contemporary 'classical' music. Technique unorthodox, intonation perfect; never read music well, but had faultless ear; knew little about the blues, but was a lyrical, linear soloist; unlike Louis ARMSTRONG, he avoided bravura, experimenting harmonically from the start; but like Louis was a natural melodist, one of the first to be able to solo for 32 bars using logically compatible phrases, recomposing as he went along rather than improvising close to melody. Unusually beautiful tone: contemporaries said his notes sounded like they had been struck, as with a mallet on a bell. First white jazzman significantly to infl. blacks. Wolverines were not a great band, poorly recorded; his sound described as piercing a curtain of fudge; recommended by Hoagy CARMICHAEL the

band played Indiana U., became a sensation on campuses. To NYC; Bix hired away by Jean GOLDKETTE. Made two sides with Sioux City Six, incl. Frank TRUMBAUER, Miff Mole; lost Goldkette job because of poor reading, but returned, made many records for Goldkette, later with Paul WHITEMAN. Many Goldkette records were spoiled by label's choice of songs and singers; Whiteman's was a big, precise band that played very little jazz; records are distinguished only by a few solos. Yet the legend is not true that Bix was frustrated by his position in that band: he was at the top of his trade and knew it; Whiteman kept a chair open for him until the end. Best records made with small groups from '27 led by Trumbauer; often incl. Eddie LANG, J. DORSEY, Adrian ROLLINI; most famous 'I'm Comin' Virginia', 'Singin' The Blues'. Compositions incl. 'In The Dark', 'Candlelight', 'Flashes', 'In a Mist' (recorded the last as piano solo). Had first breakdown with delirium tremens '29. Despite personal success, never had confidence in himself or in value of his work; he sent copies of his records home, but family did not open the parcels. Admiration of Armstrong was mutual: Louis allegedly lent Bix his horn so he could sit in, never did that for anyone else. He infl. Red NICHOLS, Bobby HACKETT, who infl. Roy ELDRIDGE and Miles DAVIS respectively; Eldridge was the greatest infl. on Dizzy GILLESPIE. Some scholars find links between his advanced harmonic thinking and that of Charlie PARKER; the beauty of his tone and phrasing can stand alone. Carmichael's songs 'Stardust', 'Skylark' may have been based on Bix solos; Carmichael carried Bix's mouthpiece in his pocket the rest of his life. *Bix: Man & Legend* by Sudhalter and Evans '74 was one of the first great biographies in jazz; documentary film *Bix* c.'82 dir. by Brigette Berman. Compilations incl. *Bix Beiderbecke Story*, three LPs on Columbia USA; volumes in EMI/UK Retrospective series; digital transfers by Robert Parker '87 from BBC reveal as much of his beautiful tone as we are likely to hear.

BEL, Mbilia (*b* Mbilia Mboyo, 30 Aug. '59, Kinshasa, Zaire) African female singer-composer, dancer. Began in chorus of leading Zairean female singer Abeta Masekini;

asked by Tabu Ley to join his chorus, the Rocherettes. After several years and tours with Tabu Ley emerged as solo, taking turns with him fronting Afrisa International: first LPs *Eswi Yo Wapi* and *Faux Pas* '83 on Genidia label; shared honours with Ley on hit 2-disc set *Loyenghe*; success confirmed by *Ba Gerants Ya Mabala* '84, tours of USA, the Far East, Australia. Had first child '85 while maintaining stardom: in poll by Radio France International named Africa's best female singer; excellent LP *Kenya* followed by first UK release *Boya Ye* on Sterns label, recorded in Paris '85: 'Tabu Ley's stage shows are basically step-perfect soul reviews, and Bel is his vivacious dancer-wife in that context . . . but in his music she takes on a strangely otherworldly voice, keening angles and abstraction, and the music dancing round her . . .' (Mark Sinker in *The Wire*).

BELAFONTE, Harry (*b* Harold George Belafonte, 1 Mar. '27, NYC) Singer, actor, producer. Spent 5 years in Jamaica, back to NYC age 13; served US Navy, attended drama workshops, wrapped packages in garment district. Film *Bright Road* and Broadway *Almanac* (incl. singing) both '53; lead in stage, film versions of Oscar Hammerstein musical *Carmen Jones* (based on opera) '54; toured country in revue *Three For The Road* same year. Tried pop singing; restaurant in Greenwich Village; discovered folk music, closed restaurant, had 22-week engagement at Village Vanguard. Signed by RCA '55; singles 'Scarlet Ribbons', 'Shenandoah' attracted attention; first album *'Mark Twain' and Other Folk Favorites* no. 3 in USA album chart, second *Belafonte* no. 1, both early '56; third *Calypso* same year: first LP to sell a million copies (by '59): no. 1 in USA album chart for 31 weeks, and incl. next year's hit singles 'Jamaica Farewell' and 'Banana Boat Song' (aka 'Day-O', 'Star-O'). Other smash hits in '57 incl. LP *Belafonte Sings Of The Caribbean*; singles 'Mama Looka Boo Boo' and Xmas song 'Mary's Boy Child' from album *An Evening With Belafonte*. 2-disc set *Belafonte At Carnegie Hall* ('59) also sold a million. A natural success on TV from '55; appeared on all the talk and variety shows, produced own shows in the '60s. Also recorded with ODETTA (single 'Hole In The Bucket'

charted UK '61); Lena HORNE (*Porgy And Bess* '59); Miriam MAKEBA '65; Nana MOUSKOURI '66. Altogether 24 albums charted '56-70, nine in top 10. Other films incl. *Island In The Sun* ('57; controversial at the time for interracial theme); *The World, The Flesh And The Devil* ('57); *Odds Against Tomorrow* ('59). Active in civil rights movement in '60s: a director of Southern Christian Leadership Conference, etc.; produced Lorraine Hansberry's *To Be Young, Gifted And Black* (NYC '69); many awards, honorary degrees, etc. More films: spoof western *Buck And The Preacher* '72, with Sidney Poitier; *Uptown Saturday Night* '74, with all-star cast of black comics. Signed with CBS: albums *Turn The World Around* '77, *Loving You Is Where I Belong* '81; next album was concept *Paradise In Gazankulu* '88 on EMI with strong African influence.

BELEW, Carl (*b* 21 Apr. '31, Salina, Okla.) USA country singer, songwriter. Worked as plumber; then became regular on Town Hall Party TV show, Compton, Cal. '56. Joined Louisiana Hayride, began writing hit songs: 'Am I That Easy To Forget' (later a big pop hit for Engelbert HUMPERDINCK), 'Stop The World And Let Me Off', 'Lonely Street' (hit for Andy WILLIAMS '59; often credited to Elvis PRESLEY, who never wrote a song in his life, because of reference to 'Heartbreak Hotel' in lyric). Records on Four Star label '55-7, Decca '58-62: own hit with 'Am I That Easy To Forget' '59, also 'Too Much To Lose' '60; on RCA '62-9 for 'Hello Out There' '62, 'In The Middle Of A Memory' '64, 'Crystal Chandelier' '65, 'Boston Jail' '66. Wrote big hits 'What's He Doing In My World' (Eddy ARNOLD '65), 'Don't Squeeze My Sharmon' (Charlie Walker, '67), 'That's When I See The Blues In Your Pretty Brown Eyes' (Jim REEVES, '68). Rejoined Decca '70, teamed with Betty Jean Robinson for duets 'All I Need Is You' '71, 'Living Under Pressure', LP *When My Baby Sings His Song* '72. 'Welcome Back To My World' '74 solo hit on MCA; now works in publishing. LPs incl. *Carl Belew* (Decca '60); *Hello Out There* '64, *Am I That Easy To Forget* '68, *Twelve Shades Of Belew* '68 (all RCA).

BELL, Archie, and the Drells USA soul vocal quartet. Original lineup: Bell (*b* 1 Sep.

'44, Henderson, Texas), James Wise (*b* 1 May '48), Willie Pernell (*b* 12 Apr. '45), all from Houston. Met in high school mid-'60s, entered talent shows, had regional hit 'She's My Woman' '66; signed to Atlantic '67, had nationwide no. 1 with 'Tighten Up', followed by 'I Can't Stop Dancing' (no. 9), 'There's Gonna Be A Showdown' (no. 21), all '68. Lee Bell (*b* 14 Jan. '46, Houston) added '69. Had more danceable hits and remained popular act, but no more top 40 pop chart entries in USA; made no. 11 UK with 'Here I Go Again' '72 whereupon 'Showdown' issued there and reached no. 36 '73. Switched to Philadelphia International, made no. 8 UK '76 with 'Soul City Walk', no. 43 UK '77 with 'Everybody Have A Good Time'. LPs *Tighten Up, There's Gonna Be A Showdown* '68-9, *Dance Your Troubles Away* '76 made Billboard charts; Archie made solo LP *I Never Had It So Good* '81.

BELL, Carey & Lurrie (*b* Carey Bell Harrington, 14 Nov. '36, Macon, Ms.; his son Lurrie Bell, *b* 13 Dec. '58, Chicago) Blues singers. Carey taught himself harmonica from age 8; ran away from home c.'50, to Chicago '56; worked outside music and in Maxwell Street for tips, becoming a premier bluesman player in the great line of Walter HORTON, LITTLE WALTER, etc. Also plays bass, drums, guitar. Recorded with Earl HOOKER on Arhoolie '68, own LP *Blues Harp* on Delmark '69; worked with Muddy WATERS '70, also with Jimmy DAWKINS, many others; recorded with Horton on Alligator '72; on ABC-Bluesway '73; with Bob Riedy's Blues band on Rounder '73, Flying Fish '74; appeared in documentaries *Born In The Blues* '73, *Sincerely The Blues* '75, has toured the world. Lurrie is a fine guitarist and blues singer, his unique vocal colour with traces of Muddy, B. B. KING; in concert '86 his intimate lower register was uncannily like that of the great Junior WELLS. Lurrie visited Berlin with the New Generation of Chicago Blues '77; worked with Koko TAYLOR. Father/son tour as duet, recorded *Son Of A Gun* '82, on Rooster Blues '84; toured UK '86, recorded live and studio tracks on *Straight Shoot* on Blues South West label, backed by sympathetic UK band Junkyard Angels. They are also heard on Rooster LPs

by Eddie C. Campbell and by their cousin Eddy Clearwater. Several of Carey's other sons are stars of the future: young James plays drums on two tracks of *Son Of A Gun*.

BELL, Graeme (*b* '14, Australia) Pianist and leader. The Australian revival scene (trad. or dixieland jazz; see JAZZ) incl. players regarded as superior to some of their counterparts in UK or USA, of whom Bell is best known. Began playing New Orleans style jazz in Melbourne '43, toured Europe; ran an art gallery late '50s, then formed a new band. Records on Swaggie made late '40s-early '50s incl. *Paris (1948)*; eight tracks made '48 in London incl. on *The Great Revival* on Esquire, with brother Roger Bell on trumpet and vocalist 'Lazy' Ade Monsborough, who also played trombone and clarinet (eight tracks by Ken COLYER on reverse).

BELL, Madeline (*b* 23 July '42, Newark N.J.) Singer. Sang in gospel group age 14, UK-based after visit with *Black Nativity* show '62. Became cabaret singer on club circuit '63, signed with EMI; met Dusty SPRINGFIELD at '65 New Year's Eve party for UK TV pop show *Ready Steady Go*; did many sessions, signed with Philips: fine LPs *Bell's A Poppin'* '67, *Doin' Things* '68; single 'I'm Gonna Make You Love Me' was no. 26 in '68 US chart. Joined session group BLUE MINK '69, turned into full-time group on success of first single 'Melting Pot'. Still with them, signed RCA solo contract: *Comin' Atcha* arranged, produced by John Paul Jones '73. One other LP on Pye *This Is One Girl* '76, now on PRT; continued as session singer, and to broadcast with BBC Radio Orchestra/Radio Big Band. Singles with David Martin on Deb: 'East Side West Side', 'I'm Not Really Me Without You' '82.

BELL, Maggie (*b* 12 Jan. '45, Glasgow) Singer. Career started with bet when she went on stage to sing with Alex Harvey for £2. Linked personally/professionally with Harvey's younger brother Les in Kinning Park Rangers and (after spell as dance band singer) Power; this band rescued from Continental gig circuit by Peter Grant, LED ZEPPELIN manager. Lineup: Bell, vocals; Les Harvey (*b* '47), guitar; Colin Allen, drums; Jim Dewar, bass; John McGinnis, keyboards. Power renamed Stone The Crows, signed to Polydor; first two blues-based LPs *Stone The Crows, Ode To John Law* (both '70) highly praised, with Bell's throaty style compared to that of recently deceased Janis JOPLIN. *Teenage Licks* '72 saw Ronnie Leahy and Steve Thompson replace McGinnis and Dewar; Bell cleaned up critics' polls. Harvey's death on stage in Swansea '72, accidentally electrocuted during sessions for *'Continuous Performance,* tore heart out of band; album released same year and most successful so far, reaching no. 33 UK LP chart, spawned (almost hit) single 'Good Time Girl'. Bell had already started session work, duetting with Rod STEWART most effectively on title cut of his *Every Picture Tells A Story* '71; voices similar yet complementary. Solo career failed to take off despite prod. Jerry Wexler for *Queen Of The Night* '73; *Suicide Sal* '75 did no better. One-off hit was theme for TV series *Hazell* (no. 37 UK '78); most recent tilt at stardom as frontperson for Midnight Flyer (eponymous LP released '81 on Led Zep's Swan Song label, renewing association with Grant): lineup was Anthony Glynne, guitar; Tony Stevens, bass; David Dowle, drums; John Cook, keyboards. Bell peaked too early to benefit from vogue for female singers apparent since punk, but with her fine voice should never be short of session work.

BELL, Thom (*b* c.'40, Philadelphia) Soul producer. First records with schoolfriend Kenny Gamble '59 on Heritage label; went on as member of Gamble's Romeos, using classical keyboard training to advantage. Group recorded for Arctic with little success, later formed nucleus of Philadelphia's MFSB (Mother, Father, Sister, Brother) session band. Bell left, replaced by Leon Huff, who later formed Philadelphia International with Gamble. Bell sessioned for local Cameo label, had first success as arr. with Showstoppers' 'Ain't Nothin' But A Houseparty' (no. 87 pop chart USA '68; no. 11 UK that year, re-entered chart three times '71), then concentrated on arr., prod. notably with sweet soul vocal group Delfonics. Cameo folded '68; group and Bell moved to Philly Groove, hit with 'La-La Means I Love You' (no. 4 USA '68, no. 19 UK '71), 'Didn't I Blow Your Mind This

Time' (USA no. 10 '70, UK no. 22 '71), 'Break Your Promise' (USA no. 35 '68), others. Linked again with Gamble/Huff to arr. for Jerry BUTLER '69, but major move in this period was formation of songwriting team with Frenchwoman Linda Creed, who wrote lyrics to Bell's music: soon hit with STYLISTICS ('Betcha By Golly Wow', 'I'm Stone In Love With You' transatlantic hits '71-2), later Spinners after they left Motown (aka Detroit Spinners in UK: 'Could It Be I'm Falling In Love', 'Ghetto Child' '73). Bell's lush orchestral scores stemming from classical training became trademark not easily imitated (Hugo Peretti and Luigi Creatore tried on Stylistics stuff but lacked R&B edge, nod to doo-wop). Bell spread talents wide: arr. for O'JAYS (Gamble/Huff), on his own (Ronnie Dyson, Johnny MATHIS). Later in '70s prod. hit EP *Mama Can't Buy You Love* for Elton JOHN, continued in soul with Phyllis Hyman, Deniece Williams. Disco fad dealt blow to popularity of sweet soul; that Bell's work endures demonstrated by faithful '85 cover of 'Can It Be I'm Falling In Love' by UK singers David Grant and Jaki Graham.

BELL, William (*b* William Yarborough, 16 July '39, Memphis, Tenn.) Soul singer. Began with vocal group Del-Rios at 14, group recorded for Meteor; studied to be a doctor, worked with local Phineas Newborn band, recorded for new Satellite/Stax label early '60s at invitation of Chips Moman, bringing organist BOOKER T with him. First (critics say best) records cut before Stax was successful nationally, but 'You Don't Miss Your Water' was third R&B success, made top 100 of pop chart, while 'Any Other Way' (also '62), 'I'll Show You' '63 showed solid Southern blues/soul vocal stylings: he dropped medical studies, was drafted '63, came back strong and ventured afield as Stax rose to mid-'60s peak: ballads ('I Forgot To Be Your Lover' (no. 45 pop chart USA '69), 'Tribute To A King' (eulogy for Otis REDDING), dance numbers ('Never Like This Before', 'Eloise (Hang On In There)'. 'Tribute' made no. 31 UK '68, duet with Judy Clay 'Private Number' made no. 8 UK (no. 75 USA) same year; did well in R&B chart but none of Bell's Stax-era records made pop top 40 USA. Wrote most of his own output; also wrote for others, often with Booker T (e.g. 'Born Under A Bad Sign' for Albert KING); continued on Stax until its demise '76, but duets with Clay, Mavis STAPLES, Carla Thomas, venture into reggae failed to match 'Number', though several listed in Billboard's Bubbling Under chart. Five LPs on Stax incl. *The Soul Of A Bell* '66, *Phases Of Reality* '72. Recorded for Mercury: *Comin' Back For More, It's Time You Took Another Listen*; scored long-overdue USA top 40 hit '77 with 'Trying To Love Two' (no. 10). Songs still often covered (e.g. 'You Don't Miss Your Water' '85 by Triffids) but he did not have pop success he deserved in soul's golden era. Formed own labels: Peachtree '69-71, Wilbe '84; *Passion* '86 on WRC incl. 'Headline News' which was hit in USA black chart.

BELLAMY BROTHERS (David *b* 16 Sep. '50; Howard *b* 2 Feb. '46; both *b* Fla.) USA pop/country duo. Began in country band with father in Tampa; later in soul band The Accidents, backing touring artists; combo Jericho '68; worked with ALLMAN BROS, BREWER & SHIPLEY. Break came with David's song 'Spiders And Snakes', no. 3 USA hit by Jim Stafford '74. Moved to L.A., contract with WB, no. 1 pop hit (no. 7 UK) 'Let Your Love Flow' '76. 'Satin Sheets' (no. 43 UK), 'Crossfire', 'Bird Dog' in country-rock vein; moved to Nashville '78 to concentrate on country: 'Slipping Away', 'Lovin' On' '78 followed by 'If I Said You Had A Beautiful Body Would You Hold It Against Me', international hit (no. 3 UK, no. 39 USA pop, no. 1 USA country chart). LP *The Two And Only* '79 cemented country following; string of hits: 'You Ain't Just Whistlin' Dixie' '79, 'Lovers Live Longer' '80, 'Do You Love As Good As You Look' '81, 'For All The Wrong Reasons' '82, etc. Other LPs: *The Bellamy Brothers* '76, *Plain & Fancy* '77, *Sons Of The Sun* and *You Can Get Crazy* '80, *When We Were Boys* and *Strong Weakness* '82, *Restless* '84, *Howard And David* '85, *Country Rap* and *Crazy From The Heart* '87. On Warner-Curb label, then MCA-Curb.

BELLAMY, Peter Franklyn (*b* 8 Sep. '44, Bournemouth, UK) Founder member of folk trio the YOUNG TRADITION remains infl. figure on UK folk scene. Solo career

since late '60s incl. LPs *Mainly Norfolk* '67, *Fair England's Shore* '68 on Xtra label while still with group; then *The Fox Jumps Over The Parson's Gate* '70 on Topic, *Won't You Go My Way?* '71 on Argo (collaboration with Louis Killen), *Tell It Like It Is* '75 on Trailor, *Both Sides Then* '79 on Topic (with guests Heather and Royston Wood from Young Tradition), the WATERSONS, Dave Swarbrick, others. His interest in poet Rudyard Kipling, seen by some as Empire jingoist, by others (incl. T. S. Eliot) as major poet, coincided with Kipling reappraisal: *Oak, Ash & Thorn* '70 used poems from Kipling's children's books *Puck Of Pook's Hill* and *Rewards & Fairies*, set to trad. folk tunes; *Merlin's Isle Of Gramarye* '72 similar (both on Argo). Strong friendship with COPPER FAMILY, incl. their songs in act; helped with their 4-disc *A Song For Every Season* on Leader, seminal set of British unaccompanied singing; discovered veteran trad. singer Walter Pardon '73 and helped with his *A Proper Sort* and *Our Side Of The Baulk* on Leader; also Joe Heaney and Gabe O'Sullivan with *Joe & The Gabe*. Wrote and prod. 2-disc ballad-opera *The Transports – A Ballad Opera* '77 (on Free Reed) about convicts sent to Australia; incl. contributions from Martin CARTHY, June TABOR, The Watersons, A. L. LLOYD, others, settings by Dolly COLLINS. Kipling odyssey resumed with *Barrack Room Ballads* '77 (Free Reed UK, Greenlinnet USA) incl. 'Mandalay', 'Gunga Din'; also *Keep On Kipling* '82 on Fellside. Tour with hour-long show on Kipling life, works; made Fellow of the Kipling Society, vice-president '81. *Second Wind* '85 for English Folk Dance & Song Society label: played all instruments, incl. some American songs ('Motherless Child'), Chris Smither's 'Devil Got Your Man'.

BELLOW, Bella (*b* '46, Togo; *d* 10 Dec. '73 in car crash) Singing in the Ewe language, thereby reaching audiences in Togo, Ghana and Benin, released many singles in HIGH-LIFE, agbadza, Congo and trad. styles; biggest hit was 'Rockia'. Made several successful African tours, also appeared in USA, Germany, France, Belgium; only LP *Album Souvenir* '71 incl. help from Manu DIBANGO, with whom she'd worked in Paris: became a classic. Career tragically cut short, but still regarded as one of Africa's finest female vocalists.

BELLSON, Louie (*b* Louis Paul Balassoni, 26 July '24, Rock Falls, Ill.) Drummer, bandleader, composer. Father owned music shop; won contests as amateur. Worked for Benny GOODMAN, T. DORSEY '40s; used two bass drums from '46. Small group with Charlie SHAVERS '50, then Harry JAMES. The 'James Raid' led to Bellson, Willie SMITH, Juan Tizol joining Duke ELLINGTON early '51. A first-class musician, among the few playing listenable, musical drum solos, Bellson helped popularise the Ellington band, at a low ebb in its long history; he wrote and arranged 'The Hawk Talks', at same session (May '51) his cymbals providing elegant shuffle beat on Duke's vehicle for Harry CARNEY, 'V.I.P's Boogie'. Drum features were not in Ellington's line, but Bellson's 'Skin Deep' was early hi-fi spectacular, a post-swing era sensation among those who still thought that drum solos were the whole point. Bellson's skill rendered it palatable, but his subtly menacing contribution to 'The Mooch' on the same album (*Ellington Uptown*) should have been the hit, helping to make it one of the most compelling of all Duke's re-creations of his own works. Married Pearl BAILEY, left Duke '53; mus. dir. for her; to Europe with JATP '55; with a Dorsey Bros. band '55-6; had own big band '58-9; to Sweden with BASIE '62; with a Dorsey band in Japan '64; re-joined Duke '65, James '66; led band and wrote song 'I Need Your Key' on James BROWN album *Soul On Top* '70. Many LPs as sideman with various groups on Norman GRANZ's labels, also own LPs *Explosion* '75, *Sunshine Rock* '77, *Jam*, *Matterhorn* '78 on Pablo; on Concord Jazz: *Louie Bellson's 7* and *Prime Time* with septet, *Raincheck* with quintet, all incl. Blue MITCHELL; *Side Track* '79 with sextet incl. congas; also *150 MPH*, *Dynamite!* and *London Scene* with big band. Comps. incl. a jazz ballet; *The London Suite* (incl. 'Carnaby Street', used as theme for Pearl's TV show); etc. Toured '87 with quartet incl. Don Menza, tenor (*b* 22 Apr. '36, Buffalo, NY); pianist Larry Novak (from Chicago), the excellent John Heard (*b* 3 July '38, Philadelphia) on bass. *Louis Bellson And His Jazz Orchestra* '87 on

Musicmaster has big band and combo tracks.

BELVIN, Jesse (*b* 15 Dec. '32, San Antonio, Texas; *d* 6 Feb. '60, Little Rock) Singer/songwriter. To L.A. age 5, sang in church choir, band singer age 16. First recordings '51 with Big Jay McNEELY; solo cuts for various Hollywood labels followed by US Army, during which he wrote 'Earth Angel', a huge hit for The PENGUINS on R&B chart, also covered by The CREW-CUTS on pop chart. Returned to L. A. after service, recorded with groups and solo on several labels, went to Modern records '56, hit with first single: 'Goodnight My Love' used as closing theme by Alan FREED radio show. Continued to turn up on several labels; then wife/co-writer Jo Ann also became his manager, landing RCA contract late '58. She also wrote 'Guess Who', his first top 40 hit '59. Fine singer whose voice fitted somewhere between Nat COLE and Sam COOKE, he made LP *Just Jesse Belvin* '59, was working on *Mr Easy* when he and wife were both killed in car crash after leaving a gig in Little Rock, Arkansas.

BEMBEYA JAZZ African big band formed Conakry, Guinea '61. As the national orchestra of Guinea played central role in development of nation's modern music. 12-15 musicians incl. trumpets, guitars, singers, percussionists; prod. a blend of indigenous West African and Congo styles with distinct Islamic overtones. Led by Aboubacar Demba Camara, composer, arranger, historian of Guinea trad. until his death in a car crash '73; band under his leadership captured on album *10 Ans de Succès* '71 on Syliphone label. Performed regularly in West Africa, on state occasions in Guinea, European tours incl. visits to Moscow. LPs incl. *Parade Africaine. Le Défi*, *La Continuité*, *Regard sur le Asse*, *Mémoire de Aboubacar Camara*, *Discotèque* '76 (latter compilation with Bembaya on four tracks). Led by guitarist Sekou Diabate on visit to London, Amsterdam '85; recorded songs incl. 'Yekeke' and 'N'kanuwe' on live LP *African Roots: Vol. 3*.

BENATAR, Pat (*b* Pat Andrzejewski '53, Brooklyn, NY) Singer. Studied opera; won NY talent contest '75, signed by Chrysalis

'79, captured AOR with accessible neo-heavy metal material, wide vocal range, use of operatic training: 'permanent wave music' described as 'Wonder Woman produced by ZZ Top'. 'Hit Me With Your Best Shot' no. 9 on US chart; several more singles charted, none in UK. Won Grammies for best rock vocal '80-1; five albums big hits in USA: *Crimes Of Passion*, *In The Heat Of The Night*, *Live From Earth*. *Precious Time* no. 1 USA, also charted in UK as did *Get Nervous* '82. Material (often written by second husband guitarist Neil Geraldo) seemed to slip in commercial appeal; *Tropico* '84 followed by *Seven The Hard Way* '86, *Wide Awake In Dreamland* '88.

BENEKE, Tex (*b* Gordon Beneke, 12 Feb. '14, Fort Worth, Texas) Tenor sax, singer, leader. One of the stars of the Glenn Miller band '38-42; as a tenorist favoured by Miller: played 'chase' exchange with Al Klink on 'String Of Pearls', etc. Likeable and distinctive Texas voice featured in Miller hits incl. 'Chattanooga Choo Choo', 'Don't Sit Under The Apple Tree', 'I've Got A Gal In Kalamazoo'; and in both the band's films. After WWII led Miller band with sanction of the estate, then Millerish ones without it. Post-war top 10 hits incl. 'Hey! Ba-Ba-Re-Bop', 'A Gal in Calico'. Entirely absent from awful biopic '54 *The Glenn Miller Story* despite importance in band's history. Appeared on UK TV with band led by Miller's brother, '84.

BENFORD, Tommy (*b* 19 Apr.'05, Charleston, West Va.) Drummer. With brother Bill on tuba, played in Jenkins Orphanage band, S. Carolina, toured Europe '14. Worked with Edgar HAYES, Fats WALLER, Duke ELLINGTON, most notably on Jelly Roll MORTON's Red Hot Peppers records '28, '30; session of 11 June '28 incl. Bill in band, trio, quartet sides. Back to Europe with Eddie SOUTH '32; recorded there with him, Benny CARTER, Coleman HAWKINS, Joe TURNER, etc. Freelanced NYC; toured Europe again '52, '60-1. Came out of retirement to join pianist Bob Greene (*b* '22, NYC) in World of Jelly Roll Morton concerts, '73-4; album on RCA. He lives in France, and is often interviewed for jazz documentaries.

BENNETT, Boyd (*b* 7 Dec. '24, Muscle Shoals, Ala.) Singer, bandleader. Won talent show with folk songs, Evansville, Ind. age 14; formed high school band Goodlettesville, Tenn. After US Navy service worked as disc jockey, Louisville, Ky. '46, later weekly TV show and own western swing band. Signed to King label; output veered from country to dixieland, finally settling into Bill HALEY rock'n'roll style, calling band the Rockets and sharing vocal duties with 250-lb Big Moe. 'Seventeen' reached no. 5 pop chart, no. 8 R&B; 'My Boy Flat Top' no. 39 pop, both '55, both sung by Big Moe. Version of 'Blue Suede Shoes' made no. 63, '56. 'Seven Nights To Rock', with C&W pianist Moon MULLICAN, gained some cult status; there were also vocals by Rocket's pianist Cecil McNabb. Switched to Mercury; seven singles of which the only hit was 'Boogie Bear', did not make top 40. Early '60s on Kernal; gave up bandleading, operated Thunderbird club in Indianapolis, later moved to Dallas. Compilation LP *Collector's Items* on King.

BENNETT, Cliff (*b* 4 June '40, Slough) UK pop singer. Started Rebel Rousers in West London '59, playing Elvis, Gene VINCENT covers; for next nine years worked steadily in UK, Germany; ever-changing lineup incl. at various times Frank Allen (SEARCHERS), Roy Young, Nicky Hopkins, Chas Hodges. Two-man brass section added late '61, when band prod. by Joe Meek; despite his help first four singles on Parlophone flopped. Fat brass sound lent itself to covers of USA R&B material (Ray CHARLES, Bobby BLAND, Sam COOKE); version of DRIFTERS' 'One Way Love' was Bennett's first success at seventh try, no. 9 (UK) hit followed by 'I'll Take You Home' (no. 42, '65); then Brian EPSTEIN appointed manager: cover of 'Got To Get You Into My Life', written/prod. by labelmate Paul McCARTNEY, made no. 6, '66: lineup at this time Bennett; Sid Phillips, Moss Groves, saxes; Young on keyboards; Hodges on bass, Mick Burt, drums. Young absconded with rest of group, '68; Bennett formed eight-piece Cliff Bennett Band, attempted to clone his hit with 'Back In The USSR'; failed. Late '69 lineup re-emerged as progressive Toe Fat, with future URIAH HEEP sidemen Ken Hensley, guitar; Lee

Kerslake, drums; no luck. Bennett scuffled for five years; with former Pirates/Cliff Bennett Band guitarist Mick Green in group Shanghai (other members Brian Alterman, guitar; Speedy King, bass; Pete Kircher, drums) but punk explosion, record company problems killed LP *Fallen Heroes* '76; after another BEATLE retread in '80 ('Drive My Car'), Bennett left music. Never an innovator, Bennett was nevertheless good value, as '78 EMI *Best Of* shows. DEXY'S MIDNIGHT RUNNERS paid homage with '80 version of 'One Way Love'; brassy arrangement of 'Got To Get You Into My Life' revived '78 by EARTH, WIND AND FIRE.

BENNETT, Tony (*b* Anthony Dominick Benedetto, 13 Aug. '26, Queens, NY) Jazz-infl. pop ballad singer; highly rated by critics and public for more than 35 years. Father was a grocer. Sang since childhood; singing waiter as teenager; after service in US Army appeared on Arthur GODFREY Talent Scout show; discovered '50 by Pearl BAILEY and Bob Hope working under name Joe Bari; Columbia contract that year on strength of demo records incl. 'Boulevard Of Broken Dreams', song revived from '34 film *Moulin Rouge* (with Russ COLUMBO; score by Harry WARREN and Al Dubin): critical interest but no hit. Worried that contract would be dropped; at last scheduled session recorded 'Because Of You' written '40 by Arthur Hammerstein (uncle of Oscar II), Dudley Wilkinson: arr. by Percy FAITH, no. 1 hit '51, was in charts for 31 weeks; flip side 'I Won't Cry Anymore' did well too. 'Cold, Cold Heart' (by Hank WILLIAMS) another no. 1 same year; Hot 100 entries in Billboard almost every year for 16 years: 24 top 40 hits '50-64 incl. 'Rags To Riches' by Richard ADLER and Jerry Ross (no. 1 '53); 'Stranger In Paradise' from show *Kismet*, tune by Russian composer A. Borodin (no. 3 '53); 'There'll Be No Teardrops Tonight', another Williams song (no. 11 '54). Other songs now identified with him incl. 'Just In Time' '56 (from show *Bells Are Ringing*), 'I Left My Heart In San Francisco' '62, 'I Wanna Be Around' and 'The Good Life' '63, 'Who Can I Turn To' '64 (by Anthony NEWLEY), many more. 25 LPs charted '62-72 incl. four with arrangements by Robert FARNON (see his entry); *I*

Left My Heart In San Francisco '62, 2-disc sets *At Carnegie Hall* '62, *All-Time Greatest Hits* '51-72 still in print years later. Pianist Ralph Sharon (*b* 17 Sep. '23, London) has been mus. dir. for many years. Also recorded with Count BASIE (incl. *In Person* '58); also two LPs '75-6 accompanied solo by Bill EVANS. LPs on Improv label USA incl. live *Beautiful Music* with the McPARTLANDS '77 (reissued on DRG '86 as *Make Magnificent Music*), two vols. of *Rodgers & Hart* with Ruby BRAFF; first new LP in 10 years *The Art Of Excellence* '86 on Columbia co-prod. by son Danny, with Sharon trio, strings; incl. 'I Got Lost In Her Arms' from Irving BERLIN show *Annie Get Your Gun*, James TAYLOR's 'Everybody Has The Blues' (duet with Ray CHARLES). 2-disc anthology *Tony Bennett/Jazz* '87 incl. previously unreleased 'Danny Boy' ('64) with Stan GETZ: transmutes gooey song into art; *Bennett & Berlin* '87 had guests George BENSON, Gillespie, Dexter GORDON. He is also a painter under his real name; first exhibition Chicago '77, others in Paris, London, San Francisco, L.A., NYC.

BENNINK, Han (*b* 17 Apr. '42, Zaandam, Netherlands) Percussionist. Played with visiting Americans, with Eric DOLPHY on LP *Last Date* '64, also with John Tchicai, Cecil TAYLOR, Gary PEACOCK, Paul BLEY, Steve LACY, Derek BAILEY etc. in '60s-70s; like Lacy and Bailey now prominent in free improvisation in Europe, a scene with its own integrity, not dependent on American influence. Many LPs as leader, co-leader, sideman on labels incl. ICP, Incus in UK, others. Works in duo with reedman Peter Brötzmann (*b* 6 Mar. '41, Remscheid, Germany); about 12 LPs by duo (10 by Brötzmann as leader, co-leader) on FMP (Free Music Production) alone: FMP is musician's collective which organizes concerts and festivals as well as records. Brötzmann also plays in Last Exit (*see* Bill LASWELL).

BENSON, Bobby (*b* '20s, Ikoredo, Ondo, Nigeria; *d* '83) African composer-singer, guitarist, saxophonist, bandleader. Nicknamed Pa Bobby by fans. Began playing ballroom and swing styles in various Lagos bands; then in early '50s, infl. by several tours of E. T. Mensah and the Tempos, along with many others switched to HIGHLIFE: as style flourished throughout West Africa and began to acquire international reputation, Bobby Benson and his Combo were at the centre: 11-piece band had seven-piece horn section, string bass, guitar, percussion. Like all top bands, Benson's spawned others, helping careers of many musicians; among graduates: Victor OLAIYA, Chief Billy Friday, Zeal Onyia, and King Pagoe, who later joined Sir Victor Uwaifo. Benson also active in musicians' unions: first president of Nigerian Union of Musicians '60; this union split and he was active in healing schism to form Performing Artists Association of Nigeria '81. Civil war '67-70 dealt serious blow to highlife; many musicians left Lagos and JUJU gained strong following in Western Nigeria; along with Olaiya and Roy Chicago, Benson was one of the few who stuck with highlife through '70s. Biggest hits of pre-war period incl. 'Taxi Driver' and 'Freedom, Yes Sir'; album *Caban Bamboos* occasionally available outside Nigeria. After Benson's death tributes incl. album *Bobby* '83 from Sunny ADE.

BENSON, George (*b* 22 Mar. '43, Pittsburgh, Pa.) Guitar, singer. Sang with local R&B bands; began playing guitar in public age 15, sang and played guitar on R&B single for RCA Groove label '54: 'It Shoulda Been Me', 'She Makes Me Mad'. Joined Jack McDUFF quartet at 19; LPs *Benson And McDuff*, *The New Boss Guitar Of George Benson* with McDuff '64, later issued in 2-disc set on Prestige. Met main influence Wes MONTGOMERY '65; albums on Columbia *It's Uptown* '65, *Cookbook* '66, *Benson Burner* '65-6; on Verve *Giblet Gravy* '67 (quintet with Herbie HANCOCK, Ron CARTER), *Goodies* '68 with vocals by The Sweet Inspirations. Turned down chance to join Miles DAVIS, played on one track of *Miles In The Sky* '68. After Montgomery's death his producer, Creed Taylor, signed Benson to A&M (LPs *Shape Of Things To Come*, *Tell It Like It Is*, *Other Side Of Abbey Road*, *I Got A Woman & Some Blues* '68-70), then to Taylor's new label CTI: *Beyond The Blue Horizon* (Feb. '71) followed by single and album *White Rabbit* (Nov.) which got pop play on radio. Material from this period issued on several LPs with various titles incl. *Bad Benson*, *Good King Bad* '74-5 with big bands, strings; *Benson & Farrell* '76 with

Joe Farrell, reeds, flute. Along the way an album written by Cedar WALTON was made but never released because it was 'too good', according to Benson. Had substantial mainstream jazz following, not a lot of financial success; then switched to WB label: *Breezin'* '76 incl. Leon RUSSELL song 'This Masquerade' (no. 10 Billboard pop chart with Benson vocal; instrumental title single also charted), made no. 1 LP chart, won Grammies: septet LP made in studio, 31 strings dubbed for MOR set. Earlier albums reissued in wake of success; Benson resumed singing; four more WB LPs top 10 USA '77-80: *In Flight*, *Weekend In L.A.* and *Livin' Inside Your Love* (both 2-LP sets), *Give Me The Night* (title track no. 4 single). *The George Benson Collection* '81 (also two LPs) no. 14 USA LP chart (incl. no. 5 single 'Turn Your Love Around'); *In Your Eyes* '83, *20/20* '85 good sellers; TV-advertised *Love Songs* no. 1 hit LP UK '85; seven USA top 40 singles '76-83. Jazz fans dismayed by funky crossover style, but Benson has family to support, blames broadcasting, music business: 'If kids can't hear it, I don't care how good it is, you can't sell it to them.' Others feel he plays hits in concert 'with such panache, creation and re-creation . . . that he is in truth a great jazzman' (Derek Jewell). *When The City Sleeps* '86 on WB to be followed by guitar LP with his former protégé Earl Klugh (with many albums on WB and EMI labels), recording of arrangement for large orchestra of ' 'Round Midnight' by Bulgarian-born collaborator Angle Rangelov.

BENTON, Brook (*b* Benjamin Franklin Peay, 19 Sept. '31, Camden, S.C.; *d* 9 Apr. '88, NYC) Soul singer. From gospel music background; sang with Camden Jubilee Singers and delivered milk mornings while still a boy. Trip north at 17 to sell songs; back to gospel with Bill Landford Spiritual Singers and Golden Gate Quartet; next trip north with R&B group The Sandmen; drove a truck on the side, made around 500 demo discs for Nat COLE, Roy HAMILTON, Clyde McPHATTER, many others, with writing collaborator Clyde Otis. First signed as solo to Epic; minor hit 'A Million Miles From Nowhere' released on Vik; then at Mercury with Otis and arranger Belford Hendricks: 'Endlessly', 'It's Just A Matter

Of Time', 'Thank You Pretty Baby' all top 20 hits '59. His warm, golden brown voice appealing to just about everybody, ballad style compared to Nat Cole, SINATRA and Tony BENNETT, he went on to 21 gold discs in five years: 'So Many Ways' '59, 'Kiddio' '60, 'Think Twice' '61, 'The Boll Weevil Song', 'Frankie And Johnny', 'Shadrack', 'Lie To Me', 'Hotel Happiness', all '62. In addition duets with Dinah WASHINGTON incl. successful singles 'Baby (You've Got What It Takes)', 'A Rockin' Good Way', both '60. Chart hits '63-4 incl. 'True Confession', 'I Got What I Wanted', 'Two Tickets To Paradise', 'Another Cup Of Coffee', but none made top 20. Label hopping began, RCA to Reprise to Cotillion; top 5 hit '70 with Tony Joe WHITE's 'Rainy Day In Georgia', but little else: good, black soulful voices were an aberration of quality in the charts; public taste had gone elsewhere. LPs are still in print and being reissued in UK, incl. *Back To Back* (2-disc set with Dinah), *Best Of Brook Benton* ('84) incl. tracks with Dinah; he remained a top attraction (London's Barbican Centre '84).

BERIGAN, Bunny (*b* Roland Bernard Berigan, 2 Nov. '08, Hilbert, Calumet County, Wis.; *d* 2 June '42, NYC) Trumpet, bandleader. Gigged in college bands in Wisconsin; trips to NYC, doubled on violin until '27. Joined Hal KEMP NYC '30 incl. European tour; studio and freelance work and with Smith BALLEW summer '31, Paul WHITEMAN '32-3, Benny GOODMAN '35, Tommy DORSEY '37, own band '37-40. Went bankrupt, led small group, another big band, but alcoholism was killing him: he could no longer play his own best solos. Loved by everyone who knew him, but no businessman; capacity for liquor was legendary. Best solos: 'King Porter Stomp', 'Sometimes I'm Happy', 'Blue Skies' with Goodman; 'Song Of India', 'Marie' with Dorsey; 'Prisoner's Song', 'I Can't Get Started' with own band. 'Marie' was one of the most famous solos of the whole era; 'I Can't Get Started' was recorded twice: second version (RCA, '37) issued on 12" 78, incl. homely vocal, intro modelled after Louis ARMSTRONG's 'West End Blues': one of the biggest hits of the year. Finest white trumpeter of the swing era, perhaps second only to Armstrong in the bravura style, and

like Louis unusually capable in the lower registers. Won a '39 poll with five times as many votes as next best competitor. Armstrong reportedly reluctant to record 'I Can't Get Started', saying it was Bunny's tune. Complete Victor material '37-40 reissued on Bluebird (RCA), 2-disc sets flawed by the fact that the band had to record so many second-rate tunes.

BERLIN, Irving (*b* Israel Baline, 11 May 1888, Temun, Russia) Songwriter; prolific composer of pop songs in Tin Pan Alley, then scores of hits in shows and films. Emigrated from Siberia to NYC as a child, father died young; became singing waiter, song plugger, published hits: printer's error on song 'Marie From Sunny Italy' changed name to Berlin. Became partner in firm with pianist/collaborator Ted Snyder; sang medley of own songs in *Up And Down Broadway* '10 with Snyder accompanying. 'Alexander's Ragtime Band' '11 huge hit when taken up by vaudeville singer Emma Carus; 'Everybody's Doin' It' same year hit for Eddie CANTOR, who also began as singing waiter. Married Dorothy '12, sister of Ray Goetz (*b* 12 June 1886, Buffalo, NY; *d* 12 June '54, Greenwich, Conn.; composer of 'For Me And My Gal' etc.; became Broadway producer): she died five months later; Berlin wrote 'When I Lost You'. Starred at London Hippodrome '13 singing own songs, billed as The King Of Ragtime, which he was not. His special piano was shipped to England with him; had mechanism allowing him to change keys while playing only one he knew: never learned to read or play properly; later employed musical secretary. Wrote 'When The Midnight Choo-Choo Leaves For Alabam', 'I Want To Go Back To Michigan', 'Play A Simple Melody' (for musical *Watch Your Step* with Vernon & Irene CASTLE); drafted '17 into US Army (music press said 'Army takes Berlin!'); wrote show for army '18, left out 'God Bless America', thinking it was over the top (on Armistice Day '38 Kate SMITH sang it on radio from New York World's Fair: moving tribute from successful immigrant to adopted country became second national anthem; royalties given to Scout movement). Wrote 'A Pretty Girl Is Like A Melody' '19, 'All Alone' '24; during '20s began buying back rights to own songs, became publisher; married wealthy Catholic girl Ellin MacKay against her family's wishes '26, as wedding present gave her rights to 'Always' '25. Also wrote 'Remember' '25; 'Blue Skies' '27 (featured by Al JOLSON in first talkie *The Jazz Singer*); 'Marie' '29 later became enormous Swing Era hit by Tommy DORSEY. Wrote 'Puttin' On The Ritz' '30, 'Soft Lights And Sweet Music', 'How Deep Is The Ocean?' and 'Say It Isn't So' all '32 (latter hit for Rudy VALLEE); then 'Easter Parade' '33 (from *As Thousands Cheer*). Initially had used collaborators, later wrote words, music himself: 'Easter Parade' was earlier unsuccessful song with new words. Film work incl. 'Cheek To Cheek', 'Top Hat, White Tie And Tails' in *Top Hat* '35, 'Let's Face The Music And Dance' from *Follow The Fleet* '36, both with Fred ASTAIRE; 'I've Got My Love To Keep Me Warm', 'You're Laughing At Me' from *On The Avenue* '37 with Dick Powell; 'Be Careful, It's My Heart', 'Happy Holiday' and 'White Christmas' from *Holiday Inn* '42 (at '42 Oscar ceremony he said, 'This goes to a nice guy; I've known him all my life' – gave himself the award for 'White Christmas'). Jerome KERN intended to write score for Broadway show *Annie Get Your Gun* '46, but died; producers RODGERS & HAMMERSTEIN hired Berlin, had more hits than any other show ever written: 'They Say It's Wonderful', 'I Got The Sun In The Morning', 'Doin' What Comes Naturally', 'The Girl That I Marry', 'There's No Business Like Show Business' (belongs forever to Ethel MERMAN), others. 'Old Fashioned Walk' from *Miss Liberty* '49, 'You're Just In Love', 'It's A Lovely Day Today' from *Call Me Madam* '50 (also with Merman). Congressional Medal of Honor from President Eisenhower '54; wrote flop musical *Mr President* '62, 'Old-Fashioned Wedding' for revival of *Annie* '66. Medal of Freedom from President Ford; also member of French Legion of Honour, charter member of ASCAP (on first Board of Directors '14-18). 80th birthday marked by star-studded Ed Sullivan broadcast. Biographies with same title *The Story Of Irving Berlin* by Alexander Woolcott, David Ewen; always refused permission for dramatised biography on stage or film. Even his earliest songs were models of their kind, revived for TV celebrations of 100th birthday.

BERMAN, Sonny (*b* Saul Berman, 21 Apr. '24, New Haven, Conn.; *d* 16 Jan. '47, NYC) Trumpet. Played in many bands early '40s; legendary Boyd RAEBURN band '44. Joined Woody HERMAN '45; solos on 'Your Father's Mustache', 'Sidewalks Of Cuba'; played at Herman's '46 Carnegie Hall Concert. A few small-group records from two dates in '46 on Esoteric, Dial; also on Onyx, Spotlight, some with alternate titles under name of Bill Harris. One of the brightest young stars, died of drug-related heart attack.

BERNS, Bert (*b* '29; *d* 31 Dec. '67 NYC) Producer/songwriter. Began as record salesman, session pianist; wrote in NYC early '60s for small labels, then followed LEIBER & STOLLER as resident writer-producer at Atlantic. Set up own publishing company Webb IV, supplying material to acts such as Ben E. KING, The DRIFTERS, Solomon BURKE, Tony ORLANDO. Hits of the '60s for which he was wholly or partly responsible incl. 'Twist & Shout' (ISLEY BROS, BEATLES), 'Here Comes The Night' (THEM, Van MORRISON), 'Hang On Sloopy' (The McCOYS), 'Piece Of My Heart' (Janis JOPLIN), 'I'm Gonna Run Away From You' (Tammi Lynn), 'Everybody Needs Somebody To Love' (Burke, ROLLING STONES). Worked for Decca in London '64, prod. hits for LULU, Them; championed Morrison's solo career with top 10 USA hit 'Brown Eyed Girl' '67, also producing first solo LP, variously titled *Blowin' Your Mind, TB Sheets, This Is Where I Came In* same year (though Morrison was not happy with it). Formed Bang label '65; roster initially incl. Morrison, McCoys, Neil DIAMOND. When he had heart attack the East Coast stranglehold on American pop had been lost, but songs are still remembered, some written under pseudonym Bert Russell.

BERNSTEIN, Elmer (*b* 4 Apr. '22, NYC) Composer, arranger, conductor. Studied at Juilliard; worked as concert pianist; arr. for AAF radio shows WWII. Became one of the most prolific composers of film scores, incl. *Sudden Fear* '52; Frank SINATRA film about drugs *The Man With The Golden Arm* '55 (controversial subject then; Bernstein's recording of the main theme made USA top 20); *Ten Commandments* '56; *Sweet Smell Of*

Success '57; *The Magnificent Seven* '60; *Walk On The Wild Side* '62; *To Kill A Mockingbird*, *Love With The Proper Stranger*, both '63; *Thoroughly Modern Millie* '67 (won Oscar for score of year's biggest money-maker, with Julie ANDREWS); *A Walk In The Spring Rain* '70; *Big Jake*, *See No Evil*, both '71; etc. 'Staccato's Theme' from TV show *Johnny Staccato* made no.4 UK pop chart '59; re-entered following year.

BERNSTEIN, Leonard (*b* 25 Aug. '18, Lawrence, Mass.) Composer, conductor, pianist, lecturer; classical superstar with important Broadway credentials. Early life in Boston; degree at Harvard; scholarship to Curtis Institute of Music, Philadelphia (recommended by Dmitri Mitropoulos). Became star at 25 on podium of NY Philharmonic when Bruno Walter taken ill. Ballet *Fancy Free* choreographed by Jerome Robbins turned into full-blown musical *On The Town* '44, lyrics by Betty Comden and Adolph Green; '49 film, directed by Gene KELLY, Stanley Donen, praised for innovative production, criticised for dropping most of Bernstein's music. Wrote music for TV prod. of *Peter Pan* and one-act opera *Trouble In Tahiti* '50; show *Wonderful Town* '53 adapted play *My Sister Eileen* set in '30s, lyrics by Comden/Green. *Candide* '56 was adapted by Lillian Helman from Voltaire, won New York Critics Award, flopped at box office but remained cult success (revised/revived '74). *West Side Story* '57 was smash hit, with Robbins, librettist Arthur Laurents, lyricist Stephen SONDHEIM (his first big success): update of Romeo and Juliet set among New York street gangs incl. 'Maria', 'Tonight', 'I Feel Pretty', 'Somewhere', agile dancing ('America'), ran for two years; film '61 scooped Oscars incl. best picture. Last show *1600 Pennsylvania Avenue* (White House address), with book, lyrics by Alan Jay LERNER, flopped badly '76. *West Side Story* revived several times (in London '84); Bernstein had never conducted full score; recorded it '84 with Kiri Te Kanawa: it was a best-seller despite miscasting. Also wrote three symphonies (*Jeremiah* '44, *The Age Of Anxiety* '49, *Kaddish* '63, latter with narrator and mezzo soloist); also vocal music *Chichester Psalms* '65, *Mass* '71, *Songfest* '77, other pieces. Admits that the better a conductor he became the harder it was to

compose: full-length opera *A Quiet Place* '87 incl. scenes from *Trouble In Tahiti* used as flashback; critics said the comparison of stronger early work was unfortunate. Score of Marlon Brando film *On The Waterfront* '54 received *Downbeat* award. Taught at Brandeis U. '51-4; lecture/concerts on TV began '54 (lectures on Bach, Beethoven, Ives, jazz still available in Columbia Collectors Series: *What Is Jazz*; *Leonard Bernstein Discusses*). Assistant mus. dir. of NY Philharmonic '57-8 under Mitropoulos; took over '58-69; recordings of Haydn 'Paris' symphonies, Beethoven 3rd & 5th, Mahler 7th, Bartók *Concerto For Orchestra*, Berlioz *Harold In Italy*, many others especially fine; first Shostakovich piano concerto recorded with André Previn, second had Bernstein playing/conducting. Since then conducted the world's great orchestras as freelance. Two eponymous biographies '87: Michael Freedland's is straight panegyric while Joan Peyser's gossip pins down a massive ego; neither has much about the music. His 70th birthday was marked by many new releases and reissues.

BERRY, Chu (*b* Leon Berry, 13 Sep. '10, Wheeling, W. Va.; *d* 31 Oct. '41, Conneaut, Ohio) Tenor sax. One of the finest tenors of the era dominated by the style of Coleman HAWKINS. Played with Benny CARTER, Teddy HILL; Fletcher HENDERSON '35-6; with Cab CALLOWAY '37 till death in car crash. Won polls late '30s; freelance records with Spike HUGHES, own groups Stompy Stevedores '37 (with Hot Lips PAGE, Henderson on piano, reissued on Epic LP), his 'Little Jazz' Ensemble (with Roy ELDRIDGE) '38 and Jazz Ensemble (with Page) '40, last two on Commodore; also duets with Charlie VENTURA and rhythm '41. Among many fine solos on records are 'Krazy Kapers' with Chocolate Dandies, '33; 'Christopher Columbus' with Henderson '36 (Berry is listed as co-writer); 'Hot Mallets' with Lionel HAMPTON; and 'Limehouse Blues' with Wingy MANONE '39; 'Ghost Of A Chance' with Calloway. LP compilations incl. *Chu With Calloway 1936-41* on Columbia Special Products USA; 2-disc *The Indispensible Chu Berry 1936-39* on French RCA incl. all 24 items with Manone, others with Henderson, Calloway, Hampton etc.

BERRY, Chuck (*b* Charles Edward Anderson Berry, 18 Oct. '26, San Jose, Cal.) Guitar; singer, songwriter; R&B superstar, biggest infl. in pre-BEATLES rock. Family moved to St Louis, where he learned guitar, led trio weekends; pianist Johnnie Johnson remained associated with him for many years. Jailed for armed robbery '44; became hairdresser; took demo tape to Chicago '55, sought out Muddy WATERS, was introduced by him to Leonard Chess. A song on the tape, 'Ida Red', was a country song performed R&B style; reworked and retitled 'Maybellene', became no. 1 R&B hit, no. 5 pop same year. DJs like Alan FREED broke it nationally, took co-composer credit. Other side, 'Wee Wee Hours', was slow blues with very fine piano: introduced many a teenager to the genre. Next singles 'Thirty Days', 'No Money Down' failed to cross over; 'Roll Over Beethoven' made no. 29 on pop chart '56; 'Too Much Monkey Business'/'Brown Eyed Handsome Man' made top 10 of R&B chart and remains two-sided classic. Back to formula of 'Beethoven': celebration of rock'n'roll, emphasis on generation gap leaped over entertainment's colour bar, selling to teenagers of all races: 'School Day' no. 3 USA pop chart, 'Rock And Roll Music' no. 8, both '57; 'Sweet Little Sixteen' no. 2, 'Johnny B Goode' no. 8, both '58. 'Carol', 'Almost Grown', 'Back In The USA' also made top 40 '58-9. Rock'n'roll films incl. *Rock Rock Rock* '56, *Mr Rock And Roll* '57; seen on Dick CLARK's American Bandstand '58, Newport Jazz Festival '58 and festival film *Jazz On A Summer's Day*. Opened night club in St Louis '59: fell foul of Mann Act, transporting 14-year-old across state line to check hats. Career took nose dive: first blatantly racist trial thrown out, second sent him to Federal prison '62-3. Marriage to Themetta ('Toddy') faltered but survived (four children; daughter Ingrid Gibson is singer who has worked with him for years). Stockpiled records issued: 'Route 66', 'Come On', 'Down The Road A Piece'; back to liberty and pop top 40 '64 with 'Nadine', 'No Particular Place To Go', 'You Never Can Tell'; paucity of later output suggests these written before incarceration. Back catalogue provided substantial repertoire of groups perpetrating British Invasion of '64: BEATLES covered 'Roll Over Beethoven', 'Rock And Roll Music'; ROLLING STONES chose 'Come On' for first single, recorded four others in their first year; The ANIMALS covered 'Memphis, Tennessee', 'Around And Around'; YARDBIRDS did 'Too Much Monkey Business': at the time some Americans saw them all as rip-off artists. 'If you tried to give rock'n'roll another name, you might call it "Chuck Berry",' said John LENNON later. (Most of Berry's UK top 40 entries achieved at this time; biggest were 'Let It Rock'/'Memphis' no. 6 '63, 'No Particular Place To Go' no. 3 '64.) Royalties rolling in must have been good, but jail embittered him, perhaps blunted creative edge. Toured UK with Carl PERKINS, showed off trademark 'duckwalk' (played in squatting mode, hopping around stage); even then did not use full-time backing band, preferring to hire and fire local musicians in each town: quality of live performance variable. Left Chess label for Mercury late '60s, no worthwhile new stuff; on return to Chess, delivered live/studio set from Coventry and London: live part incl. 11-minute version of salacious nursery-rhyme-styled 'My Ding-A-Ling', long used in stage act; cut to single length made no. 1 both UK, USA pop charts: first no. 1 either side of the pond except for USA R&B chart. In his heyday he not only rocked but wrote memorable lyrics; hits characterised by distinctive 4-bar guitar intro, lyrics could always be understood, incisive guitar breaks moved songs along: like most formulas it became careworn from ham-fisted imitation (but there were memorable covers: Jimi HENDRIX on 'Johnny B Goode'; ELECTRIC LIGHT ORCHESTRA with 'Roll Over Beethoven'). Berry records rarely (*Rockit* '79 on Atlantic his latest); had another brush with the law (income tax '79). Work from '55-65 (a compilation LP is named *Golden Decade*) will endure as long as records are sold. 2-disc *Rock'n'Roll Rarities* issued '86 in USA: stereo remixes, unreleased takes from Chess vaults '57-65. *Chuck Berry: The Autobiography* '87 written without a ghostwriter; rockumentary *Hail! Hail! Rock'n'Roll* same year incl. footage from 60th birthday concert at Fox Theatre in St Louis, with guests Keith Richard (who organised all-star backing band), Bruce SPRINGSTEEN. He promises another book about his love life.

BERRY, Dave (*b* David Grundy, '41, Sheffield, England) Rock'n'roll singer. Changed name to that of idol Chuck BERRY, formed group The Cruisers '61. Sometimes joined onstage by local lad Joe COCKER. Signed to Decca '63; version of 'Memphis, Tennessee' no. 19 UK; cover of Arthur CRUDUP's 'My Baby Left Me' minor hit. Stage presence disguised unexceptional singing: prowled platform shielding his eyes, clad in black leather, trailing microphone cable down his back. Alan Price can be seen explaining Berry's stage act to bemused Bob DYLAN in '65 documentary film *Don't Look Back*. Alvin STARDUST borrowed gimmicks for his act, '70s. Berry switched to brooding ballads after split from Cruisers; 'The Crying Game' no. 55 UK '64; dreary 'Mama' no. 5 '66. Continued on northern club circuit in psychedelic era of late '60s; still seen in British rock'n'roll revival shows. Billy McKenzie of the ASSOCIATES revived 'Crying Game' in concert '85; *This Strange Effect* '86 was Berry hits compilation.

BERRY, Emmett (*b* 23 July '15, Macon, Ga.) Trumpet. Fine swing era soloist, mainstream stalwart thereafter. Played with Fletcher or Horace HENDERSON '36-40, Teddy WILSON '41-2, others; then Count BASIE '45-50, Johnny HODGES '51-4; toured Europe '56, '59, '61; located L.A. '62-5; retired to Cleveland, Ohio '70. Records with Basie, Hodges; prolific freelancing and recording with Illinois JACQUET '46, Sir Charles THOMPSON '53, album *Jo Jones Special* '55; Henderson reunion album '57, many others. Records under his own name incl. the Emmett Berry Five '44 with Don BYAS, reissued on Savoy LP; and small-group tracks made in '56 and '59 issued by EMI.

BERTONCINI, Gene (*b* 6 Apr. '37, NYC) Guitarist. Began at age 9, turned pro at 16, played on children's TV show. Studied architecture at Notre Dame U., returned to music. Worked in TV with Merv Griffin, Skitch HENDERSON; in Metropolitan Opera House orchestra; also accompanied singers (Tony BENNETT, etc.). For the last decade he has worked each year in a duo with Michael Moore, a classical bassist who is also a crossover musician: the duo is perhaps the most difficult of forms, because

the two musicians must be equals and the music must have room for each to breathe as well as support the other: Bertoncini chooses the material and writes the arrangements (often combining classical and pop songs); they play in clubs without much amplification and have the rapport that only those who like to play duets can have. LPs: *Bridges* and *Close Ties* on Omnisound, *O Grande Amor: A Bossa Nova Collection* '86 on Stash.

BEST, Denzil De Costa (*b* 27 Apr. '17, NYC; *d* 24 May '65, NYC) Drummer, composer. Jammed on trumpet, piano at Minton's in early bop era; took up drums '43. with Ben WEBSTER, Coleman HAWKINS, to Sweden with Chubby Jackson '47; George SHEARING Quintet '49-52; later with Artie SHAW, Erroll GARNER, others. Wrote modern jazz standards: 'Dee Dee's Dance', 'Move', others; co-wrote 'Bemsha Swing' with Thelonious MONK.

BEST, Pete (*b* 24 Nov. '41, Madras, India) Drummer. With the BEATLES '60-2. Among earliest Beatle gigs were sessions at the Casbah Club, in basement of Best family home; he was with them for crucial early shows in Germany, on original 'Love Me Do' session at EMI. Sacked by Brian EPSTEIN, primarily because George MARTIN, producer at Parlophone, said he wasn't good enough; replaced by Ringo STARR. Other Beatles were not personally hostile to Best, but agreed that Ringo was better drummer; Best never cut his hair in the early Beatle style, his broody good looks making him group's heart-throb; some speculated about clashes with Paul McCARTNEY. Sacking caused hostility among group's staunch Merseyside fans. Had desultory career in music, quit '68; as the Beatles conquered the world, Best wrapped bread in a factory. Made a suicide attempt, felt silly; then the nightmare was over: now works as a civil servant in Liverpool. Listed as 'technical consultant' on US TV movie *Birth Of The Beatles* '79; autobiography *Beatle!* published '85.

BETANCOURT, Justo (*b* 6 Dec. '40, Barrio La Marina, Matanzas, Cuba) Singer; a leading vocalist in Salsa. Sang with bands Alfonso Salinas, Orlando Marin, Eddie PALMIERI, Sonora Matancera; solo albums on Fania: *El Explosivo* and *El Que Sabe, Sabe!* '71, *Pacheco/Betancourt – Los Dinamicos* with Johnny PACHECO '72, *Pa Bravo Yo* '73, *Justo Betancourt* '74, *Lo Sabemos* '75, *Distinto y Diferente* '77, *Presencia!* '78, *Justo Betancourt* '79, *Legule Ya No* '82; also performed and recorded with FANIA ALL STARS, Larry HARLOW (incl. Latin opera *Hommy*), Mongo SANTAMARIA, *Recordando El Ayer* '76 with Pacheco, Celia CRUZ, Papo Lucca; *Homenaje a Beny Moré Vol. 3* with Cruz and Tito PUENTE.

BETHANIA, Maria (*b* '46, Salvador, Bahia, N. Brazil) Singer, sister of singer Caetano Veloso; began mid-'60s as a protest singer under the infl. of her brother. To Rio '65 as substitute for Nara Leao, then 'Goddess of Bossa Nova'; eponymous first LP same year incl. topical protest songs of the day. She was caught up in student politics; in show *Opinion* (by Caetano and Gilberto Gil) she sang 'Carcara' (became signature tune); but in '66 she sang of love when all around her were protesting, singing Brazilian oldies when others covered BEATLE songs and wrote 'new pop' in style called Tropicalia. First big hit was *Recital: No Boite Barroco* '68, in charts for months. Her appeal lay in dramatic interpretation, emotional rather than technical skill; critics said that she gave the impression of protest even when singing of love. Performing barefoot, she was Brazil's Sandie Shaw, and one of the country's best-loved artists. Popular live show '71-2 on LP as *Drama And Drama, Luz da Noite.* An untypical return to topical material was *Chico Buarque e Maria Bethania* '75, as well as *Passaro Proibido* '76 ('Forbidden Bird'), co-written with her brother; the old team (Maria, Caetano, Gil) did *Doces Barbaros* '76 ('The Sweet Barbarians'), coinciding with tour and revival of '60s songs. *Maria Bethania Alteza* '81 ('Your Highness') was her 21st record in 17 years, simultaneously launched in 21 Brazilian cities via cable TV: show featured songs by various well-loved writers, title by Caetano and Wally Salomão. *Ciclo* '84 was her first self-production, with trio and strings, lush and mellow chamber music.

BEVERLY HILLBILLIES House string band on Beverly Hills, Cal. radio stations late '20s-30s, founded '28 by Zeke Manners. Hit record: 'When The Bloom Is On The Sage'/'Red River Valley', 'My Pretty Quadroon' '30. Promoted by station manager Glen Rice, made debut on KMPC that year and lasted a decade. Stuart HAMBLEN, Elton BRITT were among those passing through.

B-52's USA electro-pop dance band formed in Athens, Ga. '76 by brother/sister Cindy (*b* 28 Feb. '57) and Ricky (*b* '53; *d* 12 Oct. '85) Wilson, vocals, guitar respectively. Recruited drummer Keith Strickland (*b* 26 Oct. '53), vocalist Fred Schneider (*b* '54, Newark, Ga.), Kate Pierson (*b* '48, Weehawken, N.J.) on vocals and keyboards for jam session at friend's house that turned into fulltime hobby. Named after girls' favourite beehive-style hairdos; played first gigs with taped accompaniment, learned fast when someone pulled the plug. Sound relied on heavy drums, synthesised keyboard bass and scratchy guitar over which girls and gangly Schneider wailed and warbled gems like 'Rock Lobster', a meaningless rhyme issued on own Boofant label which together with appearance at NYC club CBGB's saw them signed by WB (USA) and Island (elsewhere). Island boss Chris Blackwell prod. eponymous debut LP '79. Horror movies, fast food and other important subjects informed the album and B-52's fun music attracted a sizeable audience. *Wild Planet* '80 made USA LP top 20 but disappointed; only 'Quiche Lorraine' approached danceability of such first-album gems as '606 0842' and 'Dance This Mess Around': novelty alone was not enough. *Party Mix* '81 attempted to rehash the early songs for disco market but only served to emphasise lack of fresh ideas, as did six-track EP *Mesopotamia* '82, prod. by TALKING HEAD David Byrne, whose sense of humour rivalled their own. *Whammy* '83 followed by Ricky's untimely death (cancer); Schneider recorded eponymous '84 LP with breakaway Shake Society (four girls/two guys, B-52's lookalikes); it seemed they would never bop again, but they re-formed, made *Bouncing Off The Satellites* '86. UK counterparts were HUMAN LEAGUE (boy/girl synth group) and Rezillos (revival chic).

BHUNDU BOYS, The Pop band from Zimbabwe, formed '80, hit singles there since

'82. Lead singer Biggie Tembo was a member of Robert Mugabe's Zanu during the civil war; headed for Harare when war was over with political feelings but trad. roots: music blends Mibira sound of East African village with synthesised 'jit', dance-hall beat relying on throbbing bass (David Mankaba), percussion (Kenny Chitsvatsva). Biggie also plays guitar; all sing, incl. keyboardist Shakie Kangwela (name means Shakespeare Little Crocodile) who became a pop star with 'Hatisitose' (no. 1 at home for three months '84); also guitarist Rise Kagona. LPs: *Shabini* '86, *Tsvimbodzemoto* ('Sticks On Fire') '87 on Discafrique, *True Jit* '87 on WEA incl. single 'Jit Jive', 'Vana (The Children)' (dedicated to those who died in the war, especially Tembo's boyhood friend Theo); the LP thanks Mugabe 'and the others who restored sanity to our country'. First toured UK '86; exhausting '87 tour saw them play almost every town in the country; fans are astonished at their endurance: they are used to playing eight-hour sets. White purist critics are whining about their music, especially now that they're on a major label, but they are a world-class act.

BIGARD, Barney (*b* Leon Albany Bigard, 3 Mar. '06, New Orleans, La.; *d* 27 June '80, Culver City, Cal.) Tenor sax, clarinet. With King OLIVER, Louie RUSSELL, Oliver's Dixie Syncopators, '25-8; then with Duke ELLINGTON, concentrating on clarinet. Solos on scores of Duke's classics from 'Black Beauty' (March '28) to 'Main Stem' (June '42). Beautiful ensemble work, co-composer credit on 'Mood Indigo' '30. Solos often took the form of high-spirited filigree, sailing over riffs or ensembles: 'Jack The Bear', 'Harlem Air Shaft'; but also lovely low register work: 'Across The Tracks Blues' (all '40). Then with Freddie SLACK, Kid ORY, own small groups; with Louis ARMSTRONG's All-Stars '46-55. Freelanced in Las Vegas, L.A. incl. Disneyland; with Cozy COLE '58-9, rejoined Armstrong '60-1. Played Leonard Feather record date *B. B.B. & Company* '62; Armstrong's 70th birthday concert '70; keys to City of New Orleans '72; toured high schools, colleges; Switzerland '75, French TV film *Musical Biography Of Barney Bigard*. Other films: *New Orleans* '47, *St Louis Blues* '57. With Louis

And The Duke: The Autobiography Of A Jazz Clarinetist by Barney Bigard and Barry Martyn, published '85 with introduction by Earl HINES. Records issued under his own name incl. Ellington small-group tracks '36-9 (reissued on Epic, Tax, others) and '40 (classics with Jimmy BLANTON now on French RCA). *Fantasy For Clarinet And Strings* '44 with guitar, bass and string section was two 78s issued in set numbered and signed by Bigard. Various other small-group dates incl. LPs *Bucket's Got A Hole In It* '68 on Delmark with Art HODES; *Clarinet Gumbo* '73 on RCA (aka *Easy On The Ears*); *Barney Bigard And The Legends Of Jazz* '74, *And The Pelican Trio* '76, both on Crescent Jazz Productions; *Giants In Nice* '74 on RCA with Earl Hines.

BIG BAND ERA Term describing popular music during period c.'35-47; also called Swing Era. Big modern dance bands began during WWI. Art Hickman (*b* 13 June 1886, Oakland, Cal.; *d* 16 Jan '30, San Francisco) and his pianist Ferde Grofe began arranging for saxophone choirs: Hickman composed theme 'Rose Room', had big hits on Columbia '20-1 but suffered from ill health; meanwhile Paul WHITEMAN hired Grofe and Bill Challis, another important arranger; another top leader who took on good white jazz soloists was Jean GOLDKETTE (Whiteman raided his band for sidemen). But these were not jazz bands; parts were written out for reed and brass choirs, with solo space in some of them for stars like Bix BEIDERBECKE, but Fletcher HENDERSON and his brother Horace (with arranger Don REDMAN) invented the style later called 'swing', inspired by brief Louis ARMSTRONG stay in Fletcher's band (*see also* SWING IN MUSIC), while Duke ELLINGTON (similarly inspired towards jazz by Sidney BECHET) soon found a unique skill for voicing and tonal colour in the big band mode (and Henderson's was the band he admired). It was Redman who perfected the big band style, writing out parts for reed and brass sections that were like written-down solos, playing sections against one another and leaving space for soloists: while jazz purists did not consider big band jazz to be jazz at all, arrangers like Redman created 'charts' that could swing relentlessly if the right band played them; he did this for

Henderson before going off on his own and Henderson's was the top band of the late '20s. Before the swing era proper began there was also Bennie MOTEN in the Midwest; of white dance bands, the CASA LOMA band and Ben POLLACK's were popular (again, not really jazz bands but had good soloists, some 'hot' arrangements); 'sweet' bands used similar instrumentation, but records by Ted WEEMS, Irving AARONSON, Gus ARNHEIM etc. from the late '20s-early '30s reveal arrangements that were excessively busy and relentlessly cute. Early bands used tuba, banjo in rhythm section; string bass and guitar took over as New Orleans 2/4 beat was superseded by smoother 4/4 late '20s-early '30s. A band might have three trumpets, two trombones, four reeds, four rhythm (bass, drums, piano, guitar); leaders who were arrangers innovated in search for extra voicing: Ellington was first to amplify bass on records late '20s; his and Redman's bands first had three trombones early '30s; Duke had two bassists late '30s, six trumpets '46, insisted that reedmen (sax section) double on clarinet even after clarinet became unfashionable. 'Head' arrangements were improvised (cf. BASIE's 'One O'Clock Jump'). Ellington was a composer, in a class by himself; other top arrangers incl. Don Kirkpatrick, Deane Kincaide, Jerry Gray, Edgar SAMPSON, Billy MAY, Sy OLIVER, Bill Finegan, Eddie SAUTER, Ralph BURNS, Neal HEFTI, Ernie Wilkins, Manny ALBAM, Benny CARTER, *et al.* Section leaders rehearsed attack and phrasing, were not always soloists: men like George Dorman 'Scoops' Carry (1915-70) with Earl HINES '40-7, Langston Curl (*b* 1899) with Redman '27-37, Hilton Jefferson (1903-68) with Claude HOPKINS, Chick WEBB, Carter, Henderson, briefly Ellington, were admired by musicians, less well known to public. Big band era began USA '35: Benny GOODMAN was sudden national success playing Henderson's music; the style then dominated USA music until after WWII. In general, black bands played best music but did not often play in top white hotels/restaurants/dance halls, so did not get radio exposure, did not make big money: Ellington, Henderson, Redman, Hines, Basie, Webb, Jimmie LUNCEFORD, Erskine HAWKINS, Harlan LEONARD, others. The most popular white bands were led by Goodman, Charlie BARNET, Jimmy and Tommy DORSEY, Artie SHAW, Woody HERMAN. Band fronted by singer Bob CROSBY, with key men from New Orleans, played a unique big band dixieland style; small-group Bob Cats were a band-within-a-band (also T. Dorsey's Clambake Seven, Woody's Woodchoppers, Goodman trio, quartet and sextet). Glenn MILLER band was most successful of all, with less jazz content; scores of sweet bands did good business (e.g. Guy LOMBARDO). There were also fine UK bands: AMBROSE, Henry HALL, Jack HYLTON, Carroll GIBBONS, others; Ray NOBLE transplanted successfully to the USA (it is even possible to argue on the basis of the old records that the average white dance band of the '30s in the UK had higher standards than its USA counterpart). Goodman, Barnet, Herman were the most faithful to jazz of the white leaders. Sidemen went off and started their own bands: Harry JAMES and Gene KRUPA from Goodman; Bunny BERIGAN from T. Dorsey, many others. Goodman, Shaw, Krupa, Barnet, others hired black musicians but racism on the road was serious problem. During WWII dance halls closed and bands toured less as petrol was rationed (and public transport in USA was being wrecked by special interests); there was a 20% entertainment tax, not lifted until well into the '50s; record business was hurt as war industries demanded shellac from which 78s were made; from Aug. '42 a long musicians' strike stopped recording (*see* James PETRILLO): the band singers – Doris DAY, Peggy LEE, Jo STAFFORD, Frank SINATRA, Perry COMO, Dick HAYMES, Rosemary CLOONEY, many others – sang *a cappella* (and sang anything out of copyright during ASCAP broadcasting ban); they were glamorous heart-throbs (easier for fans to emulate than instrumentalists), cheaper to record than big bands. They became stars of the following decade. The Dorseys, Shaw, others tried using strings, which raised costs with little musical benefit, while blacks invented BOP partly to get their music back, partly because jazz is an art form, had to evolve; some white musicians were interested in bop (mainly a small-group music), tired of playing the same old stuff, but the bands themselves were partly to blame for their downfall: Herman's was the most up-to-date white band '44; Stan KENTON seemed hip at the time; indeed Billy ECKSTINE, Boyd RAE-BURN, Claude THORNHILL, Dizzy GILL-ESPIE were leading innovative bands, and Ellington never stopped; the music was still becoming more interesting, but dancers were forsaken as arrangements were slowed down to accommodate vocalists or speeded up to show off musical skills. Jan. '47 seen as the end: big-name bands folding that month incl. Herman, James, Goodman, Les Brown, T. Dorsey, Carter, Jack TEA-GARDEN and Ina Ray HUTTON: music business was shocked, but economics of the road had changed. Basie, Ellington, Kenton carried on; Goodman, Herman, Gillespie re-formed from time to time; Lionel HAMP-TON led crowd-pleasers in the '50s; new bands were born, usually died, e.g. CAPP – PIERCE, SAUTER – FINEGAN, Don ELLIS, Gerald WILSON, Carla BLEY, Toshiko AKI-YOSHI, SUN RA; Ted HEATH in England, CLARKE – BOLAND in Europe (perhaps best of all). Arrangers May, Paul WESTON, Axel STORDAHL, Nelson RIDDLE worked for record companies; first-rate sidemen took studio jobs; Albam and Carter formed bands for record dates, jazz festivals; big-money pop music was dominated by white vocalists/studio A&R execs/producers until banality caused pressure released in rock'n'-roll explosion. Big bands remained useful in schools so that young musicians could learn to read arrangements, play in sections, etc. (the National Youth Jazz Orchestra in UK has graduated scores of fine musicians) and have never gone away entirely; Mel LEWIS has played every week at Village Vanguard for 20 years, while Courtney PINE's Jazz Warriors and LOOSE TUBES were drawing fans in the '80s; Louie BELLSON led bands subsidised by other work, and 'ghost' bands of Basie, Ellington, Miller etc. still gigged; North Sea Jazz Festival saw Gillespie, Ray CHARLES, Ike QUEBEC '88.

BIG BOPPER, The (b Jape Richardson, 24 Oct. '30, Sabine Pass, Texas; d 3 Feb. '59, Iowa) Disc jockey in Beaumont, Texas; used name of J. P. Richardson. After army service '55, determined to regain leading position as regional disc jockey: broadcast continuously for more than 122 hours, breaking a record. Wrote songs for friends; 'Running Bear' no. 1 hit for Johnny Preston after

J.P.'s death. Own records under the name Big Bopper: 'Chantilly Lace' no. 6 '58; 'Big Bopper's Wedding' hit chart same year. On tour with Buddy HOLLY, Ritchie VALENS; all killed in plane crash.

BIG COUNTRY Scottish rock group formed '81. Lineup: Stuart Adamson (b 11 Apr. '58), guitar, vocals; Bruce Watson (b 11 Mar. '61), guitar; Tony Butler (b 13 Feb. '57), bass; Mark Brzezicki (b 21 June '57), drums. Following break-up of SKIDS Adamson teamed with Watson, enrolled rhythm section hot from playing on Pete Townshend solo LP *All The Best Cowboys Have Chinese Eyes* '82. Began supporting acts such as ALICE COOPER, U2, JAM; debut single 'Harvest Home' reached charts, but swirling 'Fields Of Fire' established them: no. 10 UK '83. Band always described as 'guitar based': deft guitar work refreshing change from ubiquitous synthesiser duos. Top 20 hits: 'In A Big Country' (also in USA), 'Chance' (both '83); 'Wonderland', 'East Of Eden' ('84). Debut LP *The Crossing* '83, containing four hit singles, consolidated UK success, established them in USA; more of the same, *Steeltown* '84 entered UK chart at the top. They found favour with pop, folk, heavy metal fans with characteristic 'bagpipe' guitar sound. 'Where The Rose Is Sown' in UK chart end of '84; *The Seer* '86 incl. guest Kate BUSH.

BIG DADDY USA '50s pop group emerged early '80s. Lineup: David Starns, Mark Kaniger, Tom Lee, vocals, guitars; Bob Wayne, keyboards, vocals; Gary Hoffman, drums. Otherwise secretive publicity makes them out as the last great unsigned '50s group, entertaining troops in SE Asia, kidnapped by Laotian guerillas who treated them well, having heard that rock'n'roll was a Communist plot. Debut LP *Big Daddy* '83 (year of their rescue) incl. contemporary hits in style of '50s: Barry MANILOW's 'I Write The Songs' sounds like DANNY AND THE JUNIORS; Paul McCARTNEY's 'Ebony & Ivory' like LITTLE RICHARD, EAGLES's 'Hotel California' like Del SHANNON. Top 20 in UK '85 with cheeky reworking of Bruce SPRINGSTEEN's 'Dancing In The Dark' in style of Pat BOONE; they threatened to record Michael JACKSON's 'Beat It' in Gene VINCENT style. Wayne says rumours that they started in oldies bands no further east than L.A. are spread by big record labels, jealous of little Rhino, and by the CIA, embarrassed that their rescue took 24 years.

BIGGS, Barry Mainstream Jamaican singer who had a string of crossover hits in UK charts late '70s, with 'Work All Day', 'Sideshow' '76; 'Three Ring Circus' '77; 'What's Your Sign Girl' '79; cover of Blues Busters' 'Wide Awake In A Dream' '81, all on Dynamic label, as well as LPs *Mr Biggs, . . .With Inner Circle, Sincerely* and *Wide Awake In A Dream* before fading from sight.

BIG MAYBELLE (*b* Mabel Louiee Smith, 1 May '24, Jackson, Tenn.; *d* 23 Jan. '72, Cleveland, Ohio) R&B singer. Big person with voice to match; sang in Memphis '30s, toured with Sweethearts of Rhythm '36 into '40s, with Tiny BRADSHAW '47-50. Records on Savoy and Okeh '50s; appeared in film of '58 Newport Jazz Festival *Jazz On A Summer's Day* '60. Regular at Harlem Savoy '60-7; suffered from increasingly bad health due to diabetes. Compilation album: *The Pure Soul Of Maybelle* on Epic.

BIG THREE Merseybeat trio, claimed to be first beat group in Liverpool, formed from late-'50s Cass and the Casanovas: Casey Jones, rhythm guitar; Adrian Barber, lead guitar, John Gustavson, bass; Johnny Hutchinson, drums. Backed blues singer Duffy Power on package-tour circuit early '60s; dropped Jones, became Big Three '62, so named for 6ft stature of members. Stood out from Liverpool groups in being trio and in lead singer being drummer. Signed by Brian EPSTEIN and sent to Hamburg, where Brian Griffiths replaced Barber. Signed by Decca on return (label had turned down Epstein's BEATLES), released singles: first 'Some Other Guy' no. 37 UK '63; considered by Freddie Garrity (of FREDDIE AND THE DREAMERS) as record that 'really typified the Mersey sound'. Second 'By The Way' no. 22, but poppy sound did not represent loud, hardrocking stage appeal (song written by GERRY AND THE PACEMAKERS songsmith Mitch Murray). Band's inability to go along with Epstein's insistence on image (as Beatles did with suits etc.), unwillingness or inability to develop own ma-

terial held them up. Live act captured on LP *At The Cavern*, incl. covers of Chuck BERRY's 'Reelin' And Rockin' ', Ray CHARLES's 'What'd I Say'. Epstein dropped them; Gustavson, Griffiths left to form The Seniors late '63; Hutchinson carried on with Bill 'Faron' Russley on bass, vocals, Paddy Chambers on guitar (both ex-Faron's Flamingoes); they left within a year; after trying more replacements Hutchinson hung up the drumsticks. Gustavson played with MERSEYBEATS, Hard Stuff, Quatermass; sessioned with ROXY MUSIC, Gene PITNEY, Ian Hunter, Shirley BASSEY, others; played on original cast recording of *Jesus Christ Superstar*; re-formed Big Three for *Resurrection* '73, Merseybeat collection with Griffiths, Elton JOHN sideman Nigel Olsson, drums. Original Big Three tracks collected on Edsel label's *Cavern Stomp*: everything released by group that was well-liked by other musicians but never made lasting impact.

BIG YOUTH (*b* Manley Augustus Buchanan) Jamaican toaster, first to preach an overt Ras Tafari message in his lyrics. Made reputation with the Tippertone sound system early '70s, first hit 'S90 Skank' for singer/prod. Keith Hudson. Featured on Prince Buster's *Chi Chi Run* album; made his own epochal *Screaming Target* '73 for Gussie Clarke. He freelanced, with titles such as 'JA To UK', 'Foreman v Frazier' and 'A So We Stay' with Dennis Brown; also formed his own Negusa Nagast label, releasing 'Sky Juice', 'Daylight Saving Time', 'Dread In A Babylon'; breakthrough came with *Dread Locks Dread* '75 for Prince Tony Robinson, perhaps the most infl. reggae album of that year. He began to prod. himself more or less exclusively and to vary his style, even singing (approximately) e.g. 'Every Nigger Is A Winner' on *Natty Cultural Dread* and a reworking of Ray CHARLES' 'Hit The Road Jack' on the album of that name. His great popularity waned towards the end of the decade, but he continued to prod. work on his label into the '80s: *Isaiah - The First Prophet Of Old, Progress, Rock Holy* and *Reggae Gi Dem Dub*, while retrospectives such as 2-disc *Reggae Phenomenon* and *Everyday Skank (The Best Of)* in UK, *Some Great . . .* in USA fuelled his cult status.

BIKEL, Theodore (*b* 2 May '24, Vienna) Actor, folksinger. Emigrated to Israel, began working in theatre there late '40s. Moved to London to study drama; signed by Laurence Olivier for first European production of *Streetcar Named Desire* '47; first film with Humphrey Bogart, Katherine Hepburn in *The African Queen* '51. Moved to NYC, began recording '55, specialising in folk music of Europe, Israel; solo Town Hall concert '58, signed to Elektra that year. Many albums of folk songs: *Harvest Of Israeli Folksongs* and *Jewish Folk Songs* still listed in USA Schwann catalogue; some work reappeared later on Reprise. One of the hits of Newport Folk Festival '60, along with Joan BAEZ, CLANCY BROTHERS. Concentrated on career as versatile actor: films *The Pride And The Passion* '57, *The Defiant Ones* '58, *My Fair Lady* '64, *The Russians Are Coming* '66, many others as well as TV, stage roles.

BILK, Acker (*b* Bernard Stanley Bilk, 28 Jan. '29, Somerset, England) Clarinet. Took up instrument to pass time while in guardhouse in Egypt '47; formed band '58, played in Bristol, England; German beer cellars; then trad. boom hit: slow blues 'Summer Set' reached no. 5 UK '60. Total of 11 singles, nine albums charted '60-78, incl. many top tens; two albums charted in USA and one single: Bilk comp. 'Stranger On The Shore' (with string arrangement), no. 2 UK '61, no. 1 USA '62; reportedly sold 4 million. 'Acker' is rural English for 'mate' or 'chum'.

BISHOP, Elvin (*b* 21 Oct. '42, Tulsa, Okla.) Blues guitarist. Met Paul BUTTERFIELD at U. of Chicago, played parties as duo; Bishop played in bars south, west sides of city, had been sideman for MAGIC SAM, Junior WELLS, Hound Dog TAYLOR before joining Butterfield's band '65. Stayed until '68, by which time he'd regained lead guitar slot from Mike BLOOMFIELD; last LP with Butterfield *In My Own Dream* '68 incl. first recorded composition, 'Drunk Again'. Formed Elvin Bishop Group: lineup Art Stavro, bass; Steven Miller (ex-Linn County Band, not the famous guitar player), organ; John Chambers (ex-Loading Zone), drums; made first (eponymous) LP '69 for Bill GRAHAM's Fillmore label. Miller stayed

with Bishop to form fluctuating group, incl. at one point POINTER SISTERS. Three LPs for CBS/Epic plus *Best Of* before signing with Phil Walden's Capricorn label. Bishop's material always strong on humour, but guitar prowess not matched by vocal ability; singer Mickey Thomas recruited for Capricorn debut *Let It Flow* '74, impressive result had one rock, one country side (Bishop said, 'My no. one infl. is Hank WILLIAMS'). Mellower direction continued through *Juke Joint Jump* '75, *Struttin' My Stuff* '76, latter yielding gorgeous bluesy ballad 'Fooled Around And Fell In Love' (no. 3 USA, 34 UK). Thomas's departure to JEFFERSON STARSHIP Apr. '79 (after *Raisin' Hell*) spelled end of chapter for Bishop. He adopted alter ego Pigboy Crabshaw when guesting on others' LPs; Capricorn released *Best Of* '79. Little heard from him in '80s, which is a pity.

BISHOP, Stephen USA singer/songwriter (*b* San Diego, Cal.) Gift of brother's electric guitar decided him on songwriting career at age 14 (even then unprepossessing, bespectacled Bishop was not his own idea of a pop idol). Formed the Weeds '67, BEATLE-style quartet who demo'd in L.A., broke up; he searched seven years for solo deal, gave up, becoming staff songwriter for publishing house. Patronage of Art GARFUNKEL etc. found him signed with ABC for highly praised *Careless* '76 and *Bish* '78, very much in Garfunkel mould; both reached top 35 LPs in Billboard, former gaining Grammy nomination for best new male artist, while single 'On And On' (no. 11) nominated for best pop vocal (other hit on *Careless* was 'Save It For A Rainy Day'; also 'Everybody Needs Love' from *Bish*). *Red Cab To Manhattan* '80 had stellar cast of helpers incl. Garfunkel, Eric CLAPTON, Phoebe Snow and Phil COLLINS: many moods and styles, from big band jazz ('This Is The Night') to new Randy NEWMAN-like irony ('Living In The Land Of Abe Lincoln') perhaps kept LP from charting, but pleased fans. Major interest in film music: sang theme from *Tootsie* 'It Might Be You' (no. 25 '83, unusually not his song), wrote/sang theme for *Animal House* and 'Dream Girl' for same film; wrote/sang theme for *China Syndrome* 'Somewhere In Between' and duetted with Yvonne ELLIMAN '80 on 'Your Precious

Love' for *Roadie* soundtrack. Also played parts in *Phantom Of The Paradise*, *Animal House*, *Kentucky Fried Movie*, *The Blues Brothers*, last three courtesy of friend/prod. John Landis. Songs covered by Barbra STREISAND, Chaka KHAN, FOUR TOPS, etc. etc.; sang background on Collins LPs (Collins wants to produce a Bishop LP but record company hassles have prevented it); wrote Collins' hit '86 duet with Marilyn Martin 'Separate Lives' (from film *White Nights*). Beatles remain abiding influence and his best stuff, like theirs, is timeless: '60s-style 'Don't You Worry' on *Red Cab* is tribute to them.

BLACK, Bill (*b* William Patton Black, 17 Sep. '26, Memphis, Tenn.; *d* there 21 Oct. '65) Bass, bandleader. Played stand-up bass in C&W bands; neighbour of guitarist Scotty Moore; they played with Elvis PRESLEY from the beginning ('That's All Right' '54). Went on the road with Presley as a trio, at first sharing money 50-25-25; later drummer D. J. Fontana added; group augmented on RCA records from '56 with session players and vocal group the JORDANAIRES. Moore and Black quit c.'57 because of low pay for arduous touring while Presley was getting rich (Jordanaire Gordon Stoker said, 'Scotty and Bill really got a going over. Nobody will ever know how bad'). Formed own Bill Black Combo '59, now playing electric bass; original lineup: Carl McAvoy, piano; Reggie Young, guitar; Jerry Arnold, drums; Martin Wills, sax; with local Hi label; instrumental work linked pre-rock country music with later bass-heavy Southern soul sounds of the Mar-Keys, then BOOKER T AND THE MGS. First charted with 'Smokie Part 2' late '59 (no. 17 USA), followed by 'White Silver Sands' (no. 9 '60), other top 40 hits 'Josephine', 'Don't Be Cruel', 'Blue Tango', all '60, 'Hearts Of Stone', 'Ole Buttermilk Sky' '61, 'Twist-Her' '62 before Black retired from touring. Received Billboard Most Played Instrumental accolade three times early '60s. Black replaced by Bob Tucker; personnel varied in '60s, at times incl. Bobby Emmons, piano; Ace Cannon, sax. Backed Gene Simmons on no. 11 hit 'Haunted House' '64; continued operating under Black's name after his death from brain tumour. Still active in '80s with Tucker, tending to

straight crowd-pleasing country instrumentals; compilation of original hits on Hi series from Demon in UK.

BLACK, Cilla (*b* Priscilla Marie Veronica White, 27 May '43, Liverpool) Hat-check girl at the Cavern, swept to fame as only girl singer to emerge from Liverpool during BEATLEmania. Signed by Brian EPSTEIN, then to Parlophone label, produced by George MARTIN; first single LENNON-McCARTNEY tune 'Love Of The Loved' made no. 35 UK chart; 'Anyone Who Had A Heart' no. 1 Feb. '64 (Dionne WARWICK had USA hit); 'You're My World' also no. 1 (her only USA hit, made no. 26). Strong rather than subtle voice; string of '60s UK hits: 'Alfie', 'Love's Just A Broken Heart', 'Surround Yourself With Sorrow'. McCartney's 'Step Inside Love' was theme for her '68 BBC TV series. Girl-next-door image stretched career well into '80s, though last chart hit was 'Baby We Can't Go Wrong' '74. *Best Of Cilla Black* contains all the chart hits; *Cilla Sings A Rainbow* '66 probably her best album; she now hosts TV game shows.

BLACK OAK ARKANSAS USA rock band formed '65 by Jim Dandy Mangrum (*b* 30 Mar. '48, Black Oak, Ark.), vocals; Pat Daugherty (*b* 11 Nov. '47, Jonesboro, Ark.), bass; Stanley Knight (12 Feb. '49, Little Rock, Ark.), Rickie Reynolds (*b* 28 Oct. '48, Manilla, Ark.), Harvey Jett, guitars. After three years on road under various names made LP *The Knowbody Else* '69 for Stax under that name (made no impression at the time; reissued '75 as *The Early Years*). Moved to L.A., signed with Atlantic; built reputation by non-stop touring 50 weeks a year. First eponymous LP '70 prod. by ex-IRON BUTTERFLY Lee Dorman and Mike Pinera, incl. 'Memories At The Window'; second (best) album *Keep The Faith* '72 showcased southern blues boogie style typified by Mangrum's longhaired macho barechested stage persona; same year's *If An Angel Came To See You* diversified into mystical swamp rock, was significantly less popular. After *High On The Hog* (first gold album) and *Street Party* '74, Jett replaced by Jimmy Henderson (*b* 20 May '54, Jackson, Miss.), while *Raunch And Roll Live* '75 introduced drummer Tommy Aldrich (*b* 15

Aug. '50, Nashville), followed by *Live Mutha* '76. Band's 3-guitar boogie style pre-dated LYNYRD SKYNYRD, made big live attraction which conquered UK '74 when they supported BLACK SABBATH. Band's breadth broadened considerably when they added Ruby Starr, female vocalist who'd worked with Wayne Henderson (*see* CRU-SADERS) and proved useful onstage foil for Mangrum; first sang with band in studio on 'Jim Dandy To The Rescue': no. 25 USA radio hit helped sell albums. After '76 many changes to lineup: Joel Williams, Greg Reding, Anday Tanas, Jack Holder for Aldridge, Reynolds, Daugherty and Knight; band split '80 after spells on MCA, Capricorn labels, Mangrum's heart attack. He returned with *Ready As Hell* '84, with former lieutenant Reynolds; reportedly nearly joined Black Sabbath as replacement for Ian Gillan. BOA's stage act did not transfer to record well except on live albums; uneven output, uncertain songwriting ability hampered success: but string of gold albums and sellout concerts mid-'70s testified to popularity.

BLACK SABBATH UK heavy metal band, originally formed '68 as Earth by former schoolfriends Tony Iommi (*b* 19 Feb. '48), guitar; Bill Ward (*b* 5 May '48), drums; Ozzy Osbourne (*b* John Osbourne, 3 Dec. '48), vocals; Geezer Butler (*b* Terence Butler, 17 July '49), bass; all from Birmingham. Iommi and Ward ex-Mythology, Osbourne ex-Rare Breed. Earth played jazz-blues fusion in Europe; good reaction to live gigs, no critical acclaim; Iommi briefly flirted with then more successful JETHRO TULL. Renamed Black Sabbath after self-penned song of that name; cranked up volume, simplified formula to sub-CREAM riffing, made much mileage out of tenuous black magic connection to garner press. Eponymous debut LP recorded early '70 in two days on £600 budget, incorporating suitably spooky sound effects; despite obvious formula made no. 8 in UK LP chart, spent three months in USA chart. *Paranoid* '70 had title track marking inclusion of mental illness in band's subject matter, provided first and only hit single, reached no. 4 in UK (14 on reissue '80). Album topped UK chart, spent 65 weeks in USA top 100, signalled arrival as major force. Top 10 LP success

continued in UK; loyal fan following accepted band's concentration on USA market, where sledgehammer rock, satanic overtones found equally ready acceptance. Iommi's guitar dominant, with screaming, crucifix-wielding Osbourne also in evidence; keyboards added to live show (unknown Gerald Woodruffe played in wings so as not to steal any spotlight; keyboards played by Rick Wakeman on *Sabbath Bloody Sabbath* '73). Management problems caused mid-'70s hiatus in relentless album-tour-album schedule: when recording recommenced with *Technical Ecstacy* '76, Iommi's insistence on horn section and still more keyboards precipitated split. Osbourne left temporarily (replaced by ex-SAVOY BROWN, FLEETWOOD MAC vocalist Dave Walker), then quit permanently '79 claiming dilution of successful formula; audience agreed: albums began to slip, while publicity followed Osbourne's solo career. Sabbath dawned anew with recruitment of Ronnie James Dio (*b* 10 July '49, Cortland, NY; ex-Rainbow, Elf) as vocalist, Vinnie Appice (Carmine's brother) replacing ailing Ward on drums. After successful studio LPs (*Heaven And Hell* '80, *Mob Rules* '81) arguments over vocal mix on *Live Evil* '83 split band again. Americans left to form Dio; veteran Ian Gillan filled in on vocals for *Born Again* '83 before DEEP PURPLE reunion caused his sudden departure. Osbourne meanwhile had solo success with Blizzard Of Oz, but biting head off dead bat on stage caused rabies scare (we are not making this up); then guitarist Randy Rhoads killed in air accident. Carried on with changing lineup; showcased old Sabbath songs in '82 live *Talk Of The Devil*; had UK hit singles 'Bark At The Moon' (no. 21 '83), 'So Tired' (no. 20 '84). Formula left little room for development, leading to personnel changes; top 5 success of early material (*Live At Last* '80), Osbourne's solo success suggest that fans regarded first lineup as definitive. Re-formed for Live Aid appearance '85 with Osbourne, who had solo hit 'Suicide Solution' '85, was sued '86 by parents of West Coast teenager who shot himself. Guitarist Rhoads had played with Quiet Riot as well as Osbourne; 2-disc *Tribute* '87 on CBS incl. live tracks with Rhoads and Osbourne, studio out-takes. Osbourne had four hit albums '81-3.

BLACK, Stanley (*b* 14 June '13, London) Pianist, arranger, conductor. Piano at 7, later studied composition, orchestration; had own composition broadcast by BBC SO at 12. Worked in dixieland band at Margate's Dreamland Ballroom age 16; with AMBROSE, Lew STONE etc. through '30s, recording and broadcasting with visiting Americans Coleman HAWKINS, Benny CARTER, Louie ARMSTRONG. Visited S. America '38, found interest in Latin rhythms. Joined RAF '39, in charge of entertainment Wolverhampton area; upon discharge '44 made conductor of BBC Dance Orchestra, broadcast average six times a week for nine years. Work on nearly 200 films incl. *Rhythm Racketeers* '36, *Mrs Fitzherbert* '47, *It Always Rains On Sunday* '47, *Laughter In Paradise* '50, *The Trollenberg Terror* '57, *City Under The Sea* '65, *Crossplot* '69; in '58 became mus. dir. for Elstree Studios. Wrote new signature tune, music library for Pathé News, '60. Score for Cliff Richard movie *Summer Holiday* '62 won joint Ivor Novello award for best musical picture score. Celebrated 25 years as Decca recording artist '70; many LPs incl. *Tropical Moonlight, Gershwin Goes Latin, Broadway Spectacular, Spain, Dimensions In Sound*. Recording of Rimsky-Korsakov's *Capriccio Espagnol* was a *Gramophone* magazine record of the year '65; has conducted all the best orchestras in UK. LP *Digital Music* '79 on compact disc '83; wrote fanfare for Royal Film Performance '84.

BLACKMORE, Ritchie (*b* 14 Apr. '45, Weston-Super-Mare, England) UK heavy metal guitarist, graduated from skiffle. With Screaming Lord SUTCH's Savages '62; then Joe MEEK's Outlaws house band Oct. '62-Apr. '64 (with Chas Hodges, bass; Ken Lundgren, rhythm guitar; Mick Underwood, drums); toured UK behind Jerry Lee LEWIS, Gene VINCENT etc.; short spell with Meek protégé Heinz; spent most of '65-8 in Germany: cut fuzz-guitar-led single 'Getaway'/'Little Brown Jug' for Oriole '65; backed Neil Christian in Crusaders; Sutch again; formed Three Musketeers with Jimmy Evans, drums and Avid Anderson, bass. Returned to UK '68, joined DEEP PURPLE until Apr. '75, leaving because of funk musical direction favoured by Purple's new members; already had solo LP *Rainbow* in

the can, recorded with members of Elf, NYC band contracted to Purple label: ousted Elf guitarist Steve Edwards and renamed band Rainbow. First lineup: vocalist Ronnie James Dio (*b* Ronald Padavona, 10 July '49, Cortland, NY); Mickey Lee Soule, keyboards; Craig Gruber, bass; Gary Driscoll, drums. LP reached no 11 UK/30 USA; at Nov. live debut only Dio left, with drummer Cozy Powell (*b* 29 Dec. '47, Cirencester), Jimmy Bain and Tony Carey on bass and keyboards replacing the others. *Rainbow Rising* '76 first LP by new band, remains Blackmore's best solo work: songs cowritten with Dio remained core of live act for years, showcased on live *On Stage* '77 which also incl. instrumental version of 'Over The Rainbow'. USA chart status waned, but *Rising* equalled predecessor's chart entry in UK; next LP (live and studio) *Long Live Rock'n'Roll* '78 made no. 7 UK, also adding ex-Widowmaker bassist Bob Daisley, ex-Symphonic Slam keyboardist David Stone to ranks. Personnel changes went on: newcomers ousted by former Purple colleague Roger Glover (*b* 30 Nov. '45, Brecon, Wales) on bass and ex-Cozy Powell's Hammer keyboardist Don Airey. Dio left halfway through recording *Down To Earth* '79; ex-Marbles vocalist Graham Bonnet recruited. LP made no. 6 UK yielded two hit singles in Russ Ballard's 'Since You've Been Gone' (no. 6 '79), 'All Night Long' (no. 5 '80). Crisp prod. of *Earth* by Glover made singles success possible. Bonnet's departure to Michael Shenker and Powell to WHITESNAKE taken in stride; repacements Joe Lynn Turner on vocals, Bobby Rondinelli on drums (both Americans) debuted on *Difficult To Cure* '81, which followed trend by having less hard-rock feel than predecessors, had hit single in Ballard-penned 'I Surrender', at no. 3 UK the band's biggest hit. After more LPs (*Straight Between The Eyes* '82, *Bent Out Of Shape* '83) and despite finally cracking USA top 40 with 'Stone Cold', Blackmore called it a day, re-formed Deep Purple, a move he said he'd never make. Rainbow's sound was remarkably consistent depite personnel changes; combined heavy metal fire-and-brimstone with rare commercial appeal and formed missing link between classics of genre *In Rock, Machine Head* and so-called New Wave of British Heavy Metal (IRON

MAIDEN, DEF LEPPARD, etc.). *Best Of* compilation is worthy souvenir.

BLACKWELL, Bumps (*b* Robert A. Blackwell, 23 May '18; *d* 9 Mar. '85) Producer. Assistant to Art Rupe at Specialty label in Hollywood when Rupe sent him to New Orleans '55 to record LITTLE RICHARD: he converted obscene song to rock'n'roll classic 'Tutti Frutti', prod. and arr. many hit sessions, also getting co-author credit on 'Rip It Up', 'Good Golly, Miss Molly', etc.; in fact ignited an era of great studio recording in the city. Recorded first Sam COOKE sessions in Hollywood '56, took them to Keen label and huge hit 'You Send Me' was the result. Made artistic mistake in selling Cooke to white audiences using inappropriate songs; blacks knew better, but commercial success was big on both fronts. Maintained professional relationship with Little Richard off and on for many years.

BLACKWELL, Ed (*b* c.'27, New Orleans, La.) Drummer. Played '40s with Plas JOHNSON, Roy BROWN; to L.A. '51; played with Ornette COLEMAN; with Huey 'Piano' SMITH. Toured with Ray CHARLES '57; to NYC '60, succeeded Billy HIGGINS in Coleman's quartet (LPs *Science Fiction*, *Free Jazz*, others). Played with John COLTRANE and Don CHERRY (LP *The Avant Garde*); duet LPs with Cherry (*Mu First Part*; *Second Part*); recorded with Eric DOLPHY band live at The Five Spot '61; Dewey REDMAN (*Tarik*); also Gato BARBIERI, Archie SHEPP, many others; also Coleman 'ghost band' Old And New Dreams (*see* ECM). His combination of roots and technique made him one of the best-known percussionists in free jazz. Tours of Africa with Randy WESTON mid-'60s. Lived in Morocco '68; back with Coleman '70; teaching at Wesleyan (Conn.) mid-'70s.

BLACKWELL, Otis (*b* '31, Brooklyn NYC) Singer, songwriter, pianist; one of the most successful writers in rock'n'roll, infl. by R&B singers such as Chuck WILLIS, but also by cowboys, such as Tex RITTER. Won talent contest at Apollo theatre; early gigs with Doc POMUS, who encouraged him; early record 'Daddy Rollin' Stone' '53 on Jay-Dee was later revived by the WHO. Sold six songs for $25 each on Xmas Eve '55, incl. 'Don't Be Cruel'; made demo of it playing piano, using cardboard box for a drum. Subsequent Elvis PRESLEY record was no. 1 for nine weeks; the only Presley hit to match it was also a Blackwell tune: 'All Shook Up'. He wrote 'Return To Sender' and 'One Broken Heart For Sale' for Presley, 'Fever' for LITTLE WILLIE JOHN, who took composer credit (song was later a hit for Peggy LEE); 'Great Balls Of Fire' and 'Breathless' for Jerry Lee LEWIS; 'Hey Little Girl' for Dee CLARK; also wrote under pseudonym John Davenport (e.g. 'I Sit By The Window' for the Four Fellows c.'55). Selling part or all the rights to a song was not unusual, and Blackwell admired Presley; but Presley's method at early RCA sessions was to choose a demo that he liked and copy it, arrangement and all: 'Don't Be Cruel' was Presley's first hit with a slick pop song, rather than R&B or country songs; the style was apparently learned from Otis, who recorded for many labels but never had hits of his own. He wrote 900 songs and received overdue recognition '70s: Stevie WONDER acknowledged him '76 when Wonder received a Best Male Vocalist award. Blackwell was writing a score for a biographical film about Presley when Presley died; he recorded 'The No. 1 King Of Rock'n'Roll' on his own Fever label. LPs: *These Are My Songs!* '77 on Inner City, *Singin' The Blues* on Flyright.

BLACKWELL, Scrapper (*b* Francis Hillman Blackwell, 21 Feb. '03, probably N.C.; *d* 7 Oct. '62, Indianapolis, In.) Guitar, piano, blues singer. Made own cigar-box guitar as a child; often worked outside music in '20s; best known for collaboration with Leroy CARR from '28. Recorded solo, with Carr, Chippie Hill, Georgia Tom (Thomas A. DORSEY), etc. '28-31, '35. After Carr's death left full-time music, but recorded '59-61. Shot to death. Eponymous LP on Yazoo; also on Carr's reissues.

BLACKWOOD BROTHERS USA gospel quartet. Original lineup: R.W., Roy, Doyle J. (*b* 22 Aug. '11) and James Webre Blackwood (*b* 4 Aug. '19). From sharecropping family, Choctaw County, Miss. Discovered by music publisher V. O. Stamps. Began mid-'30s on small radio stations in Miss.;

then Shreveport; Shenandoah, Iowa; Memphis, Tenn. by early '50s. Doyle became a record distributor in Memphis. R.W. and bass singer Bill Lyles killed in Memphis plane crash 30 June '54; bass player replaced by youngest brother Cecil Stamps Blackwood (*b* 28 Oct. '34, Ackermann, Miss.), who had gone to Sunday School with Elvis PRESLEY. Recorded for RCA from '54; own records 'The Man Upstairs' '55, 'Keys To The Kingdom' '57, 'The Old Country Church' '59, etc. plus sessions with Hank SNOW, Porter WAGONER, Presley. Won Arthur GODFREY talent shows '54,6, Grammies '67-8. LPs in print incl. *Best Of* (RCA), *16 All-Time Favorites* (Starday), many more on Skylite. J. W. Blackwood Jr (*b* 31 July '43, San Diego, Calif.) leader of the equally famous Stamps Quartet (owned by his father) from '65, with many LPs on Skylite ('65-8), Heartwarming ('67-75).

BLADES, Rubén (*b* 16 July '48, Panama City) Singer-songwriter, bandleader. Father from St Lucia, mother Cuban, both musicians. Began singing in Panama City '66, first recording with Los Magnificos '68, first LP *A las Seis a Nueva York Los Salvajes del Ritmo* '69. LP *De Panama a Nueva York* '70 with Pete Rodriguez band, made on visit to NYC, incl. nine songs by Blades; to NYC to stay '73, worked in mail room at Fania. Joined Ray BARRETTO band '74, sang on his *Barretto* '75; wrote hits for singer Ismael Miranda, bandleaders Ricardo Ray, Bobby Rodriguez; made LP *The Good, The Bad, The Ugly* '75 with Willie COLON, Hector LAVOE; appeared on FANIA ALL STARS' *Tribute To Tito Rodriguez* '76, sang on Barretto's live 2-disc *Tomorrow* same year; appeared on Fania All Stars LPs *Rhythm Machine, Spanish Fever, Crossover, Habana Jam Commitment* '77-80. Work with Colon began in earnest with *Metiendo Mano!* '77, his unconventional (for SALSA) social realist lyrics combined with Colon's eclectic Pan-Latin music; *Siembra* '78 made them a new force, hits 'Plastico' and 'Pedro Navaja' proving that songs need not be odes to love. Had hit with own song 'Paula C' '78 from album *Louie Ramirez y sus Amigos*. 2-disc concept LP *Maestra Vida* '80 mixed songs and narrative in song-poem about lives of ordinary Latin-Americans. *Canciones del Solar de los Aburridos* '81 was followed by

The Last Fight '82, their last collaboration, named after film in which they both appeared. Blades song 'Tu Cariño' appeared in cult hip-hop movie *Beat Street* '84; to Elektra records same year: resurrected format of Joe CUBA Sextet in band Seis del Solar (Six from the Tenement) for LP *Buscando America* '84, juxtaposing DOO WOP, Peruvian folk tunes, pure salsa; standout track 'GDBD' is minimal half-spoken rap against Afro-Cuban percussion. LPs *El que la Hace la Paga* and *Mucho Mejor* on Fania '83-4; he played a young salsa singer in film *Crossover Dreams* '85, wrote songs for soundtrack; *Escenas* '85 on Elektra went further from salsa roots, incl. soul-ballad duet 'Silencios' with Linda RONSTADT, synthesised element incl. Joe JACKSON on 'La Canción del Final del Mundo'; 'Muevete' (Move It!) is Blades adaptation of Cuban song by Los Van Van, infectious danceable call to Latins against USA domination. Appeared in anti-apartheid video and LP *Sun City* '85, was subject of Channel 4 UK documentary by American film-maker Robert Mugge; graduated from Harvard Law School, declared intention of political career in Panama; did historic double act with Los Van Van at Paris Olympia May '86 for finale, a joint version of 'Muevete'; also appeared live in London in June with Seis del Solar. *Agua de Luna* '87 on Elektra (Moon Water) incl. songs based on Gabriel García Márquez; *Doble Filo* on Fania, probably contractual obligation album, incl. his 'El Cantante', written for Lavoe late '70s.

BLAKE, Arthur (*b* c.1890, Fla.; *d* c.'33, Fla.) Guitar, blues singer; aka 'Blind Blake', 'Blind Arthur', etc. Real name probably Arthur Phelps. Itinerant singer, streets, parties, picnics, etc.; lived in Chicago mid-'20s, recorded with Ma RAINEY, others through '20s to '32. Toured in a show *Happy Go Lucky* '31-2. Infl. many: Bill BROONZY, Gary DAVIS, Josh WHITE, Blind Boy FULLER, etc.

BLAKE, Eubie (*b* James Herbert Blake, 7 Feb. 1883, Baltimore, Md.; *d* 12 Feb. '83) Piano, bandleader, composer. Taught by W. Llewellyn Wilson (1887-1950); at one time in '20s all the black music teachers in NYC schools were former Wilson pupils, as well as many entertainers. Long career began

1899 in Baltimore cafés. Teamed with Noble SISSLE '15 in vaudeville; went to Europe with him in James Reese EUROPE's band (which Sissle later led for a while after Europe's death). Blake composed piano rags incl. 'Charleston', recorded piano rolls '17-21; team had hit song ('It's All Your Fault', performed by Sophie TUCKER); then produced musical *Shufflin' Along* in NYC '21. Mounted with difficulty owing to lack of funds; singer, dancer Florence Mills came from chorus to become a star before early death '27; smash hits incl. 'Love Will Find A Way' and 'I'm Just Wild About Harry' (revived '48 for Truman election campaign). Sissle and Blake performed on radio, also contributed to *Elsie* '23, *Revue* '26 (in London); split up until *Shuffle Along Of 1952* as Sissle returned to Europe. Blake worked on *Chocolate Dandies* '24, with Spencer WILLIAMS; *Blackbirds Of 1930* with Andy RAZAF, incl. smash hit 'Memories of You'; *Shuffle Along Of 1932*, Olsen and Johnson's *Atrocities Of 1932*; *Swing It* '37; *Tan Manhattan* '40, with Razaf; *Brownskin Models* '54; *Hit The Stride* '55. Toured as USO entertainer during WWII; joined Sissle in clubs, benefits, LP *Piano Wizard Of The Ragtime Piano* '59; on revival of interest in ragtime came out of retirement: 2-disc set *The 86 Years Of Eubie Blake* '69 prod. by John HAMMOND; started own record company and appeared at jazz festivals '72; honours from ASCAP on 90th birthday. First ride in airplane to piano roll recording date, '73; concerts, festivals, TV shows increased. Illustrated book by R. Kimball, W. BOLCOM *Reminiscing With Sissle And Blake*, '72; TV tape with same title '74; honorary degree in music '74; played at President Carter's White House jazz party '78; continued performing almost until centenary. LPs on own label incl. set with singer Edith Wilson (1896-1981); with Ivan Harold Browning (b 1891, Texas, who originated lead roles in *Shuffle Along*, *Chocolate Dandies*); *Eubie Blake/Live Concert*, *Rags To Classics*.

BLAKE, Ran (b 20 Apr. '35, Springfield, Mass.) Piano, composer. Teamed with singer Jeanne Lee '57; experimented with vocal/piano duo improvisation. Successful tour of Europe '63, but no fame at home. In '70s he did political/academic committee work for music, wrote a book about vocal improvisation. First LP *The Newest Sound Around* '61 on RCA featured Lee, George DUVIVIER on bass, followed by solo albums on several labels: *Ran Blake Plays Solo Piano* '65; *The Blue Potato And Other Outrages* '69; *Breakthru* '75; *Wende* '76; *Open City, Crystal Trio, Realisation Of A Dream* and *Third Stream Recompositions*, all '77. *Take One, Take Two* on Golden Crest (also '77) have different takes of same titles. *Rapport* '78 has one vocal each by Eleni Odoni, Chris CONNOR, some Blake solos, duets with Ricky Ford (b 4 Mar. '54, Boston), Anthony BRAXTON on tenor on one track. *Improvisations* '81 is piano duets with Jaki BYARD. *Film Noir* '80 has many guests, incl. Ted CURSON. Albums on Soul Note: *A Duke Dreams* '81 solo; *Suffield Gothic* '83 incl. medley 'Tribute To Mahalia', Houston Person (b 10 Nov. '34, Florence, S.C.) plays tenor on four tracks; quartet set *Short Life Of Barbara Monk* '86 with Ford. Solo *Vertigo* '84, two '77 solo LPs are on Owl.

BLAKEY, Art (Islamic name: Abdulla Ibn Buhaina) (b 11 Oct. '19, Pittsburgh, Pa.) Drummer, leader. Worked in steel mills, played piano in clubs, switched to drums; went to NYC; played with Mary Lou WILLIAMS '42, Fletcher HENDERSON '43, own band in Boston, Billy ECKSTINE '44-7, own group, Buddy DeFRANCO quartet '51-3. Used name Messengers for 17-piece band, octet called Jazz Messengers '47; led Birdland quintet early '54 with Clifford BROWN, Lou DONALDSON, Curley Russell, Horace SILVER; later that year Blue Note recording artist Silver set up quintet date with Blakey, Kenny DORHAM, Hank MOBLEY, bassist Doug Watkins (b 2 Mar. '34, Detroit; highly rated player later recorded with Mal WALDRON; killed in road crash 5 Feb. '62, Arizona): Horace Silver and the Jazz Messengers invented 'hard bop', with modern harmonies but based on the blues and less uncompromising than BOP itself: the style became Blue Note's mainstay, remains influential to this day. Silver stayed for two years, helped set tone with fine tunes; Blakey has led quintets, sextets called Jazz Messengers ever since (except two-year hiatus with Giants of Jazz tours '71-2, other freelance work): international tours, many LPs on Blue Note, other labels; the message never fails to please.

With Benny GOLSON he composed score for Edouard Molinaro film *Des Femmes Disparaissent* '58; band heard in soundtrack also incl. Lee MORGAN, Bobby TIMMONS, Jymie Merritt on bass (*b* '26, Philadelphia). One of the all-time great talent scouts, over the years Blakey employed the brightest stars in jazz: Freddie HUBBARD, Curtis FULLER, Wayne SHORTER, Donald BYRD, Jackie McLEAN, Johnny GRIFFIN, Junior MANCE, Cedar WALTON, etc. '72 band incl. Mickey TUCKER, Cameron BROWN, Bill Hardman and David Schnitter on tenor (LP on Lotus *Art Blakey & His Jazz Messengers* recorded live in Oslo and Tunis). Other LPs incl. *In This Korner* '78 (with Valeri Ponomarev, trumpet; Bobby Watson, alto sax), *Straight Ahead* '81 (with Watson, Wynton MARSALIS), *Keystone 3* '82 (with both Wynton, Branford Marsalis) '82, all on Concord Jazz; *In My Prime* Vols. 1&2 '77-8, *Reflections In Blue* '78, *Album Of The Year* '81 with W. Marsalis, *Oh, By The Way* '82, all on Timeless. Messengers were strong sextet in '84-5: Terence BLANCHARD, Donald HARRISON, Mulgrew MILLER, Lonnie PLAXICO, Jean TOUSSAINT; LPs incl. *New York Scene* and *Live At Kimball's* on Concord Jazz, *Blue Night* on Timeless; in '86 Toussaint became mus. dir. with new lineup: Wallace Roney on trumpet (*b* 25 May '60), Kenny Garrett on alto (*b* 9 Oct. '60), Timothy Williams on trombone (*b* 17 Sep. '57), Donald Brown on piano (*b* 28 Mar. '54), Peter Washington on bass (*b* 28 Aug. '64): a new unique sound and a new crop of stars-to-be. *Live At Montreux And Northsea* '80 on Timeless incl. Ponomarev, Watson, both Marsalises, Billy Pierce on tenor (*b* 25 Sep. '48, Hampton, Va.; Blakey called him 'the best tenor player I've had since Wayne Shorter': LP as leader *William The Conqueror* on Sunnyside with Keith COPELAND), Kevin Eubanks on guitar (the only guitarist ever featured by Blakey, *b* 15 Nov. '57, Philadelphia; played with Sam RIVERS '82; own LPs on Elektra, GRP). Classic Blakey sets now reissued on Blue Note incl. *A Night At Birdland* (2 vols. with Clifford Brown); *Jazz Connection* '57, with MONK; *Moanin'* '58; *The Big Beat* '60; many more. *The Jazz Messengers At Cafe Bohemia* made live '55 (2 vols. in USA, third was bonus record in Japan only). Bethlehem LP '57 *Art Blakey's Big Band* incl. Al COHN,

John COLTRANE, Ray COPELAND, Walter Bishop, Melba Liston (*b* 13 Jan. '26, Parmele, N.C.) and Jimmy Cleveland (*b* 3 May '26, Watrace, Tenn.) on trombones, many more. Blakey is one of the greatest jazz drummers of all time, combining power, good taste, unique swing: pianist Miller describes him as 'a master of tension and release'. Another side revealed on Giants of Jazz tour London '71; Blakey and bassist Al McKibbon (*b* 1 Jan '19, Chicago) recorded with Thelonious MONK as trio, making chamber music at its best (on Black Lion; complete session now in Mosaic boxed set).

BLANCHARD, Jack, and Misty Morgan Country duo; singers, songwriters. Jack *b* 8 May '41; Mary Morgan *b* 23 May '45; both in Buffalo, N.Y. Married early '60s, teamed professionally late '60s, had huge hit 'Tennessee Birdwalk' '70; 'Humphrey The Camel', 'You've Got Your Troubles, I've Got Mine' hits same year; the first two also entered pop charts and album *Birds Of A Feather* charted. Named vocal duo of the year by *Billboard, Cashbox, Record World*; ASCAP writing award, later BMI citations. Never had another year that good, but still popular act with singles, albums in various charts: also do comedy, had many TV spots, wrote hits for others; Jack has also done newspaper column and comic strip.

BLANCHARD, Terence (*b* 13 Mar. '62, New Orleans, La.) Trumpet. One of the stars of of Art BLAKEY's Jazz Messengers from '82. Compositions incl. title track of *Oh, By The Way* '82 on Timeless label; lovely solo feature on 'Tenderly' in Blakey LP *New York Scene* '84 (which also incl. 'Oh, By The Way'). LPs on Concord Jazz as co-leader with Donald HARRISON: *New York Second Line* '84 incl. current Messengers, except for Marvin 'Smitty' Smith on drums (*b* 24 June '61, Waukegan, Illinois; own septet LP *Keeper Of The Drums* '87); *Discernment* '86 has Mulgrew MILLER on piano, Phil BOWLER on bass and Ralph Peterson Jr on drums, both on Concord; *Nascence* '86 is aptly titled first LP on major label (CBS), followed by *Crystal Stair* '87, *Black Pearl* '88.

BLANCMANGE UK synthesiser duo named after British pudding. Neil Arthur (*b* 15

117

June '58, Darwen, Lancashire), Steven Luscombe (*b* 29 Oct. '54) met at art college '78; both had bands (Luscombe MIRU, Arthur the Viewfinders), got together as L360, drifted apart, regrouped Jan. '79 to record KRAFTWERK-infl. 'Sad Day', instrumental issued on LP *Some Bizzare* '81, compilation of material in New Romantic mode (SOFT CELL, DEPECHE MODE, etc.). Meanwhile made EP mid-'79 *Irene And Mavis* with Laurence Stevens on drums, issued a year later; by then exposure on Bizzare tour led to demos with Martyn Ware of Heaven 17, contract with London. Toured with Depeche Mode, Grace JONES, JAPAN; audacious audio/visuals got attention (e.g. projection screen in front of group instead of rear), gangling Arthur with roots in punk a slightly reluctant frontman contrasting with diminutive accomplished keyboardist Luscombe. Debut LP *Happy Families* contained singles 'Sad Day' (again), 'God's Kitchen', 'Feel Me' and chart breakthrough 'Living On The Ceiling': TALKING HEADS-infl. electro-pop piece made no. 7 UK '82; success followed up with heavily orchestrated 'Waves' (no. 10 '83). Second LP *Mange Tout* '84 recorded with USA remix/dance prod. John Luongo; saw Indian infl. apparent in 'Ceiling' emerge more fully (with Pandit Dinesh on tablas, Deepak Khazanchi on sitar, santour); hits on LP incl. cover of ABBA's 'The Day Before You Came' (no. 22), 'Blind Vision' (no. 10), 'That's Love, That It Is' (no. 33), 'Don't Tell Me' (no. 8). Since earliest gigs with drum machine had built up full band, with backing singers, session guitarist David Rhoads (ex-Random Hold, Peter GABRIEL, Joan ARMATRADING). Third LP *Believe You Me* '85 continued unique mix of pop sensibility and electronics (only two Indian-infl. tracks this time); single 'What's Your Problem' barely reached top 40. They split '86.

BLAND, Billy (*b* 5 Apr. '32, Wilmington, N.C.) Soul vocalist. Began in Southern venues; to NYC late '50s. Fine singles incl. 'Chicken Hop' with Sonny TERRY, then Billboard pop chart hits incl. top 10 'Let The Little Girl Dance', Hot 100s 'You Were Born To Be Loved', 'Harmony', 'My Heart's On Fire' (all '60-1); then faded from pop scene.

BLAND, Bobby 'Blue' (*b* Robert Calvin Bland, 27 Jan. '30, Rosemark, Tenn.) Blues singer. First records '54; 'It's My Life' revealed smooth pop balladeer using blues palette. 37 hits in R&B chart '60-70, incl. 17 top tens; 'I Pity The Fool' '61, 'That's The Way Love Is' '63 made no. 1. Double-sided hit 'That's The Way Love Is'/'Call On Me' made pop chart as well, as did 'Turn On Your Love Light', 'Ain't Nothin' You Can Do'. Three albums charted '62-4; *Call On Me* reaching no. 11. Title song was obvious attempt on pop market, but Bland always faithful to himself; result was classic pop during soul era of early '60s. Many LPs on MCA in USA, incl. *Ain't Nothing You Can Do*, *Early Years* (2-disc set), *Best Of* compilations; in UK on MCA's ABC label, also on Duke *Call On Me/That's The Way Love Is*, on Charly *Foolin' With The Blues*. He's not through yet: *Members Only* '86, *Blues You Can Use* '88 on Malaco among his best.

BLANTON, Jimmy (*b* Oct. '18, Chattanooga, Tennessee; *d* 30 July '42, L.A.) Bass. Played with Jeter-Pillars band, then Fate MARABLE; discovered by Duke ELLINGTON late '39 playing three-string bass in a St Louie hotel. Bought four-string bass on credit, joined Ellington; in the short time before he died of TB he revolutionised the instrument, infl. all who came after him. He was first to utilise bass fully, playing harmony, melody lines as on a solo instrument, while 'pushing' the beat slightly with such graceful swing that the band sounded like it was swinging on tip-toe. He was the capstone of one of Duke's greatest periods; best heard on 'Jack The Bear' with full band, on small-group sessions (e.g. led by Johnny HODGES, incl. 'Squatty Roo'), duets with Duke's piano (all RCA '40-1).

BLASTERS USA rock band. Original '79 lineup: Dave Alvin, guitar; Phil Alvin, vocals; John Bazz, bass; Bill Bateman, drums. Alvin brothers from Downey, Cal. brought up on diet of Sun rockabilly, Chess R&B, local heroes Eddie COCHRAN, BURNETTES, Jack SCOTT. First album *American Music* incl. anthemic title song for local Rolling Rock label, but quality was poor; recut title on proper album *Blasters* '81 on Slash (with 'Marie Marie' – cover by Shakin' STEVENS was top 20 UK and 'Border Radio'. Live EP *Over There* '82 made at The Venue in London, with five covers ('High School Confidential', 'Keep A-Knockin', etc.), one original, as though to exorcise rockabilly leaning. Came to critical attention with *Non Fiction* '83. By this time they were seven pieces: Gene Taylor (keyboards) had turned down early invitation to join in favour of touring with Ronnie HAWKINS, changed mind in time for *Blasters*; band also augmented by Steve Berlin (baritone sax); legendary Lee ALLEN sessioned on *Blasters*, on a live EP playing own tenor sax riffs from LITTLE RICHARD's original '56 'Keep A-Knockin'. *Non Fiction* likened to Bruce SPRINGSTEEN's *Nebraska* in dealing with plight of working class under Reagan: Dave Alvin's songs combined downbeat lyrics with rock'n'roll excitement to great effect: 'Long White Cadillac' is story of death of Hank WILLIAMS; 'Boomtown' and John Fogerty-like 'Jubilee Train' examined hard times in rural USA; 'Red Rose' in romantic vein. *Hard Line* '85 had four pieces plus Taylor (Berlin joined labelmates LOS LOBOS); stripped-down sound had noticeable gospel element (e.g. trad. 'Samson And Delilah'), 'Just Another Sunday' co-written with John Doe (of L.A. punk band X) with whom Dave Alvin had played in Flesheaters, then concurrently in part-time group the Knitters (LP *Poor Little Critter On The Road* '85), signifying some realignment with New Wave instead of rockabilly revival. *Hard Line* furthered anti-Reaganism with 'Common Man': like Springsteen in *Born In The USA*, guitar-based music attempts reconciliation of national pride and social conscience. John MELLENCAMP's 'Coloured Lights' incl. in *Hard Line* as attempted hit at label's request; deserved acclaim anyway. Dave left to join X; guitarist Hollywood Fats (Michael Mann) was recruited, died of a heart attack at 32, Dave rejoined temporarily; Berlin and Phil Alvin toured UK with Blasters early '87 while Los Lobos were also there. Phil's eclectic solo LP *Unsung Stories* '86 on Slash (London UK) incl. backing by SUN RA, DIRTY DOZEN BRASS BAND, Lee Allen, Jubilee Train Singers, etc.; Dave Alvin went solo with *Every Night About This Time* '87 (on Demon UK), a showcase from country flavour to X's '4th Of July': came out on Epic USA as *Romeo's Escape*, incl. Al KOOPER, Lobos's David Hidalgo, other guests.

BLEY, Carla (*b* Carla Borg, 11 May '38, Oakland, Cal.) Piano, composer, bandleader. Worked in club NYC selling cigarettes; married pianist Paul BLEY '57; wrote for him and many others. With Pharoah SANDERS and Charles Moffett '64; entered music full-time. Founder member of Jazz Composers Guild, co-leader of Jazz Composers Orchestra (Town Hall concert '64); to Europe with quintet '65; TV, radio and record work there. Co-founder with Mike Mantler of Jazz Composers Orchestra Association (JCOA); 2-disc album '66; divorced Bley, married Mantler. Wrote *A Genuine Tong Funeral* for Gary BURTON '67; own album *Escalator Over The Hill* '72, with JCO, soloists, vocalists; arr., comp., performed for Charlie HADEN's *Jazz Liberation Orchestra* '69 and *Ballad Of The Fallen* '83. Started Watt record company with Mantler. Other albums incl. *Tropic Appetites* '73-4; *Dinner Music* '76 and *European Tour* '77 with Mantler, Roswell RUDD; *Musique Méchanique* '78; *Social Studies* '80; *Live!* '82; *Mortelle Randonné* (soundtrack) '83; *Heavy Heart* '84; *Night Glow* '85; percussive *Sextet* '87 with no horns. Contributed to A&M tribute LPs prod. by Hal Willner: *The Way I Feel Now* '84 (the music of Thelonious MONK) and *Lost In The Stars* '86 (Kurt WEILL; Bley did title track); plays organ on Steve SWALLOW's *AfterGlow* and *Carla* '86-7; the latter on XtraWatt is effectively her sextet playing his tunes. She seemed to ignore the trad. difficulties of being a woman in music; distinctive and witty pieces recorded by Don ELLIS, Art FARMER, Steve LACY, George RUSSELL, others, though late '80s output tended to MOR vein.

BLEY, Paul (*b* 10 Nov. '32, Montreal) Piano, composer. Led own quartet in a Montreal hotel '45. To NYC, study at Juillard, back to Canada '52. Made jazz film short, worked in TV, returned to NYC c.'54. Debut LP on Debut label: *Introducing Paul Bley* '53 was trio with Charles MINGUS, Art BLAKEY (now on Fantasy); played clubs, colleges '55-9; with Chet BAKER, trio with Billy HIGGINS and Charlie Haden, group with Don CHERRY and Ornette COLEMAN '58.

119

Own quartet NYC '59, with Mingus '60, Founder member Jazz Composers Guild. Toured Europe '60, '65; Japan with Sonny ROLLINS '63. Particular empathy with bassists: Haden, Mingus, Scott LA FARO, Gary PEACOCK. Teamed with singer Annette PEACOCK '70s; they experimented with synthesisers. Trio LPs with Barry ALTSCHUL on various labels incl. *Touching* and *Closer* '65; *Ramblin', Blood, Paul Bley In Haarlem* '66; *Ballads, Virtuosi* '67; *Canada* '68, *Scorpio* '72 (with Dave HOLLAND); Peacock plays bass on *Virtuosi, Mr Joy* '68; Bley plays synths on *Revenge: The Bigger The Love, The Bigger The Hate* '69 (with Annette on Polydor), also *The Paul Bley Synthesiser Show* '70 on Milestone; solo LPs *Alone Again* '74 and *Axis* '77 on Improvising Artists; LPs on ECM incl. *Paul Bley With Gary Peacock* '68 (with Paul MOTIAN), trio *Ballads*; solo *Open To Love* '72, *Fragments* '86 with Motian, John SURMAN, Bill Frisell on guitar (*b* 18 Mar. '51, Baltimore; has played with Carla BLEY, Charlie Haden, Julius HEMPHILL, others; prolific recording as sideman '80s). More Bley albums on Savoy, other labels; trio *My Standard* '73 on Steeplechase on CD '87 with seven more tracks. His playing and composing, like that of Bill EVANS, has influenced NEW AGE music, but his musical integrity and intellectual curiosity have not crossed over to that genre.

BLEYER, Archie Arranger, bandleader. One of the best known writers of stock arrangements for music publishers in '30s; wrote hot arrangement 'Business In Q' for jazz bands, led own dance bands e.g. at Earl Carroll's Club in Hollywood late '30s; recorded for Vocalion. Arranged, conducted for shows; became well-known late '40s-50s as Arthur GODFREY's mus. dir. on popular radio and TV shows; led band on Godfrey's novelty records. Founded Cadence pop label '53 (no connection with today's Cadence Jazz Records). Own top 40 hits 'Hernando's Hideaway' (from *Damn Yankees*), 'The Naughty Lady Of Shady Lane' '54; label had huge hits with CHORDETTES, Julius LaROSA, EVERLY BROTHERS, seminal rock single 'Rumble', by Link WRAY '58. Subsidiary Candid started '60 for jazz, blues; Nat Hentoff in charge, made LPs by Charles MINGUS, Max ROACH, Booker ERVIN, Cecil TAYLOR, Otis SPANN, Lightnin' HOPKINS, Abbey LINCOLN etc.

BLIND FAITH Archetypal '60s supergroup, born and died '69: Eric CLAPTON, Ginger BAKER, Stevie WINWOOD, Rick GRECH. Several influential LPs had appeared with uncredited contributions by contemporary talent: BEATLES *White Album*, Jimi HENDRIX *Electric Ladyland*, ROLLING STONES *Beggars Banquet*; musicians wanted to be free from normal confines of music business. Blind Faith formed on dissolution of CREAM, TRAFFIC, and FAMILY; but supergroup idea resulted in unrealistic public and critical expectations and worse pressure than ever. Group made debut before 100,000 in Hyde Park, London; set off on tour of US stadia where Cream had made their reputation; single LP *Blind Faith* showed promise: incl. Clapton's 'In The Presence Of The Lord', Winwood's 'Can't Find My Way Home', effective reworking of Buddy HOLLY's 'Well All Right'. Quality high, but group split up: Clapton was soured by experience, founded low-key Derek & The Dominoes; Winwood went back to re-formed Traffic; Grech played in Traffic, later with Gram PARSONS; Baker founded cumbersome Air Force.

BLONDIE US new wave group formed by Deborah Harry (*b* 1 July '45, Miami), vocals, Chris Stein (*b* 5 Jan. '50, Brooklyn), guitar. Harry had recorded with Wind In The Willows '68 (LP now collector's item), combining music with stints as barmaid, beautician, Playboy bunny. Recruited Stein '73 for Stilettoes, group with three female singers doing girl-group covers; became Blondie '74 with Stilettoes rhythm section Fred Smith (bass), Billy O'Connor (drums). Made reputation at NYC punk club CBGBs; scantily clad peroxide-blonde Harry made valuable visual impact. Smith left to join TELEVISION before first LP sessions; new rhythm section of Clem Burke (drums), Gary Valentine (bass) added, with obligatory new-wave Farfisa organ provided by Jimmy Destri. That LP *Blondie* used cartoons, B-movies, other ephemera as inspiration was appropriate, as band named after syndicated Chic Young comic strip. Contract bought from small Private Stock label by Chrysalis for $500,000; only success to date was no. 2 single in Australia ('In The Flesh'), but gamble paid off. *Plastic Letters* '78 saw band start to shed '60s overtones for up-to-date pop sheen, though hit 'Denis' had both: cover of 15-year-old hit by Randy and the Rainbows (originally 'Denise') reached no. 2 UK as first instalment on payoff, followed by no. 10 hit '(I'm Always Touched By Your) Presence Dear', still without top 40 hit in USA. Switched prod. from Richard GOTTEHRER to UK pop svengali Mike Chapman (*see* CHINN & CHAPMAN) confirmed direction to mainstream pop. Made most successful LP *Parallel Lines* '78 with new (English) bassist Nigel Harrison, addition of guitarist Frank Infante (who had played on *Letters*); LP incl. four UK hits 'Picture This', 'Hanging On The Telephone', 'Sunday Girl', 'Heart Of Glass', the last two no. 1 in UK, voguishly disco-styled 'Glass' also no. 1 USA, their first top 40 entry there. Media attention on Harry, with endorsement of designer jeans, other high-visibility money-spinning ideas, made it easy to forget that Blondie was a group, not just the lead singer. Chapman-prod. *Lines*-clone *Eat To The Beat* had three more UK top 5 hits ('Dreaming', 'Union City Blue', 'Atomic'), but USA chart placings disappointing. LP released simultaneously as video to capitalise on Harry's visual appeal, as she branched into TV (*The Muppet Show*), films (*Union City, Videodrome*). Group wrangled as Harry/Stein axis called in Eurodisco prod. Giorgio MORODER; in the event he did only transatlantic no. 1 'Call Me'; Chapman returned for *Autoamerican* '80: formula was wearing thin, but two USA no. 1 singles in 'The Tide Is High' (cover of Paragons' reggae hit), 'Rapture' (1 and 5 in UK). Harry pursued musical direction of mock-funk 'Rapture' in disappointing solo LP *Koo-Koo* '81, recorded with CHIC; release of *Best Of* album suggested end of chapter; Infante lawsuit alleging exclusion from group activities confirmed split between Harry/Stein and rest of band, most of whom had taken up session work to fill time while Harry promoted herself. Contractual obligation dictated release of *The Hunter* '82: incl. USA/UK top 40 'Island Of Lost Souls', but a sad parody of former glories. Stein formed Animal Records, Harrison and Burke formed Chequered Past with Harrison's former Silverhead colleague Michael Des Barres; Burke also drummed with EURYTH-MICS. Destri made solo *Heart On The Wall* '82, went into production; Harry had dabbled in underground film; acted in cult movie *Videodrome*, Broadway flop *Teaneck (Trafford) Tanzi*. Retired '83 to nurse Stein through *pemphigus vulgaris*, a rare debilitating disease of genetic origin. New contract '85 with David GEFFEN; single 'Feel The Spin' co-written with its producer 'Jellybean' Benitez, heard in film *Krush Groove* '85; Stein recovered, wrote theme music for Andy Warhol cable-TV show *Fifteen Minutes*, worked on songs for her second solo LP *Rockbird* '86 incl. hit 'French Kissin' '. At its peak Blondie had epitomised post-punk new wave, competent tunesmiths whose image for the video age was right-time-right-place; meanwhile Harry became a very good singer whose material is often not worthy of her talent.

BLONDY, Alpha (*b* Seydou Kone, '53, Dimbokoro, Ivory Coast) Singer-composer. Formed Afro-rock band Atomic Vibrations in high school; to Liberia to improve English, then USA for two years, studying English and trade. Recorded reggae songs in Jamaica but no money to release them. Returned to Ivory Coast; parents put him in psychiatric hospital for two years; continued to sing and make English translations for Ivorian TV. Following own TV appearance '82 album *Jah Glory* released June '83, became massive hit: topped charts all over Africa; West Africa flooded with videos, tapes, T-shirts; some songs became standards copied by other bands. Single 'Rasta Poue', LP *Cocody Rock* on Pathé Marconi also hits '84; played to 60,000 in Paris; now preparing a film of his life. Reggae with strong Rasta appeal in Dioula, French and English. Track 'Apartheid Is Naziism' on LP *Apartheid* '85.

BLOOD, SWEAT & TEARS Jazz-rock group formed late '60s by former DYLAN session man Al KOOPER after leaving Blues Project. Original rock quartet incl. Steve Katz (*b* 9 May '45, NYC; also ex-Project), guitar; Jim Fielder (*b* 4 Oct. '47, Denton, Texas; ex-BUFFALO SPRINGFIELD, Mothers of Invention), bass; Bobby Colomby (*b* 20 Dec. '44, NYC), drums; augmented by four-man horn section: Randy BRECKER, Jerry Weiss (*b* 1 May '46, NYC), trumpets; Dick Halligan (*b* 29 Aug. '43, Troy, NY), trombone; Fred Lipsius (*b* 19 Nov. '43, NYC), sax. First LP *Child Is Father To The Man* '68 (Columbia) mixed brash blues/rock with Maynard FERGUSON-inspired horn arrangements on numbers by Carole KING, Randy NEWMAN, others, Kooper contributing keyboards, vocals. Attempt at fusion lent credibility when 40 overseas officials of US Information Agency required to attend Washington concert '68 as part of programme to acquaint them with 'cultural developments in the homeland'; band later made Iron Curtain State Dept-funded tour. Lost main inspiration when Kooper left, replaced by David Clayton-Thomas (*b* 13 Sep. '41, Surrey, England), naturalised Canadian with big frame, voice to match; trumpets also left, replaced by Lew Soloff (*b* 20 Feb. '44, NYC), Chuck Winfield (*b* 5 Feb. '43, Monessen, Pa.). Against odds, second LP *Blood Sweat & Tears* '69 hit successful formula: seven weeks at no. 1 LP chart, three gold singles: Laura NYRO's 'And When I Die', Brenda HOLLOWAY's 'You Made Me So Very Happy', Clayton-Thomas's own 'Spinning Wheel'; all made USA no. 2, last two now cabaret standards worldwide. Net spread equally wide for material on *Blood Sweat & Tears 3* '70, yielding top 20 single 'Hi De Ho'; loss of producer James William Guercio to rival band CHICAGO was major blow, but LP topped chart none the less, though brass-laden remakes of ROLLING STONES, TRAFFIC material struck some fans as pretentious. More personnel changes ensued; Clayton-Thomas left '72, replaced by bearded lookalike Jerry Fisher, then Bobby Doyle, Jerry La Croix; rejoined '74, but audience had moved on. Sold 35 million records for CBS in heyday; Clayton-Thomas once said 'there are only 20 cities in US with concert halls big enough for us'; soldiered on in '70s with only Colomby remaining from first LP. By *Nuclear Blues* on MCA '80, few were listening.

BLOODSTONE Soul vocal group with Charles Love, Willis Draffen Jr, Roger Durham, Charles McCormick, Harry Williams. Local dates Kansas City c.'62 as The Sinceres while all in high school; after military service to L.A. Moved base to London

'71, making impact in shows with Al GREEN, Percy MAYFIELD; LP *Bloodstone* '72 for London records. Next LP *Natural High* contained UK top 40 title single, also made no. 10 in USA, reviving stateside career. Durham died that year; remainder of group maintained moderate success with ebullient mixture of rock and soul. In '76 film *Train Ride To Hollywood* as The Sinceros; moved to Motown (LP *Don't Stop* '79). Little heard since.

BLOOMFIELD, Michael (*b* 28 July '44, Chicago; *d* 15 Feb. '81, San Francisco) Guitarist. Learned first-hand from legendary Chicago blues greats: haunted clubs at the same time as Elvin BISHOP, Paul BUTTERFIELD, learning from Muddy WATERS, Albert KING, *et al.*; later played clubs with vocalist Nick Gravenites, harmonica player Charlie Musselwhite. Joined Butterfield band '65 playing lead guitar on first two LPs; they played Newport Folk Festival '65, backed Dylan; Bloomfield played on DYLAN hit single 'Like A Rolling Stone', LP *Highway 61 Revisited*. Formed Electric Flag with Gravenites, R&B drummer Buddy Miles (later formed Buddy Miles Express), Barry Goldberg, keyboards; Harvey Brooks, bass; and horns: first LP *A Long Time Comin'* '68 on Columbia helped start trend (*see* BLOOD, SWEAT & TEARS, CHICAGO), but Bloomfield left, overweight group collapsed after next LP. (Bloomfield appeared on one-off reunion *The Band Kept Playing* '74 on Atlantic.) *Super Session* '68 with Al KOOPER, Stephen Stills a hoped-for miracle at the time, now sounds pretentious in excessively laid-back attitude; followed by *It's Not Killing Me* and *The Live Adventures Of Al Kooper And Michael Bloomfield* '69, *Try It Before You Buy It* and *Triumvirate*, last with John HAMMOND Jr and Mac REBENNACK (as Dr John), both '73, all on Columbia; *Mill Valley Session* '76 on Polydor. *KGB* '76 on MCA was last attempt at supergroup, with Goldberg, vocalist Ray Kennedy, Rick Grech on bass, Carmine APPICE: aptly described by Robert Christgau as 'heavy horseshit'. Among best musicians of genre/era, he then gave up stardom: stuck to film soundtracks (e.g. *Steelyard Blues* '72, porn films), string of lower-key LPs: *If You Love These Blues, Play 'Em As You Please* '77 on Guitar Player (magazine) label nominated for a Grammy; also *Analine* and *Michael Bloomfield* on Takoma, *Count Talent And The Originals* on Clouds, all '77; *Between The Hard Place And The Ground*, *Cruisin' For A Bruisin'*, *Living In The Fast Lane*, all '80-1 on Waterhouse. Died of drug overdose.

BLUEBELLS, The Sottish pop group formed '82: Ken McCluskey (*b* 8 Feb. '62), vocals; David McCluskey (*b* 13 Jan. '64), drums; Robert Hodgens (*b* 6 June '59), vocals, guitar; Craig Gannon (*b* 30 July '66), guitar. Came to prominence on enterprising Postcard label of Glasgow; part of trend back to pure pop away from synthesiser sound-alikes. Debut LP *Sister* '84 a long time coming partly owing to litigation with Bluebell Girls of Paris over name, which group won. Chart entries: 'Sugar Bridge', 'I'm Falling', 'Kath'; LP incl. controversial cover of Dominic Behan's 'The Patriot Game', assumed erroneously by some to be a tribute to IRA gunmen. 'South Atlantic Way' is comment on '82 Falklands War. 'All I Am (Is Loving You)' minor hit '85; incl. old Lee Hays union song 'Ballad Of Joe Hill' on other side.

BLUE BOY (*b* Austin Lyons, '55, Point Fortin, Trinidad) SOCA artist, Calypsonian. Parents from Grenada. Played tenor steel pan for six years until '78 with Point Fortin Tornadoes Steel Orchestra, tried unsuccessfully to get into a CALYPSO tent '79; worked at sea and was nicknamed by mates, who described him as 'bluer than black'. First success 'Soca Baptist' written during a layover in Santo Domingo; record shop owner Romeo Abraham sent cassette to NYC-based Trinidadian prod. Rawlston 'Charlie' Charles, who re-recorded for his Charlies label for '80 Trinidad Carnival season. Blue Boy performed it in SHADOW's Masters Den calypso tent; Baptists of Trinidad and Tobago (T&T) objected to it, exerting pressure on Dr Eric Williams, then Prime Minister; he said 'let good sense prevail': broadcast media and Carnival Development Committee banned Blue Boy and his calypso, but he won Road March contest that year (*see* CALYPSO). During off-season (i.e. after Carnival) released 12″ single 'Soca Spirit'; LP *Soca In The Shaolin Temple* made in NYC mid-'80, released for '81 Carnival and was

major hit, 'Ethel' becoming Road March song, 'Unknown Band' (about his former steel band Tornadoes) performed by Catelli Trinidad All Stars, winners of that year's National steel orchestra contest (Panorama). These tracks took him to sixth place in Calypso Monarch final; same year made first UK appearance. LP *Tic Tac Toe* was poorly received in '82 season; off-season released 12″ single 'Hello'; back on form '83 with LP *Super Blue Boy*. Performed with Spektakula calypso tent; 'Rebecca' was performed by WITCO Desperadoes, Panorama winners; he reached third place in Calypso Monarch final with 'Rebecca' and 'Salvation'; that year he was also a member of Committee of Ten, campaigning for reforms to protect and promote interests of the music. *Thundering Soca* '84 on Kalico label inc. 'Lucy' and 'Fete', which took him to third place in Calypso Monarch final; 'Lucy' was Road March runner-up. Handicap in '85 was late release of *The Power Within* on Blue Boy label; problems with producer were reported. Headed calypso tent for the first time, new one called Calypso Palace, but late arriving, didn't appear opening night; unsuccessfully promoted 'Soca Tremor' for Road March; that and 'Retreat' took him into Calypso Monarch finals, but was placed last. Calypso Palace was taken over by musicians because of management's alleged failure to pay them. Led another new tent, the Culture House, '86; released album *Blue Fever* on Culture House label; appeared at Socalypso '86 in London, the largest live soca festival so far staged in Europe; headed Culture House tent '87 but music from LP *Jingay* failed to place in contests because (he said) of its late release. T&T's *Daily Express* asked 'Where's Blue Boy?' 'Is just late I comin',' was answer.

BLUE CHEER USA heavy metal trio formed Boston, Mass. '67. Original lineup: Bruce 'Leigh' Stephens, guitar, vocals; Richard Peterson, bass, vocals; Paul Whaley, drums. Disciples of 'volume is power' school, though term was not yet in use: one of the loudest acts of the late '60s. Associated with San Francisco; remembered mainly for raucous top 20 remake of Eddie COCHRAN's 'Summertime Blues', although suprisingly three LPs made top 100 of USA LP chart:

Vincebus Eruptum (incl. hit, made top 20), *Outside Inside* and *New! Improved!* Personnel changed (because of deafness?): Stephens departed after first LP for solo career, made *Red Weather* '69 for Philips UK, *Cast Of Thousands* '71 on Charisma, backed on both by UK sessionmen such as Nicky HOPKINS, Tony Ashton. His replacement was Randy Holden; keyboardist Burns Kellog added for final albums *Blue Cheer* '69, *Original Human Beings* '70. Subsequently not much heard of. Manager (former Hell's Angel called Gut) said of them that 'They play so hard and heavy they make cottage cheese out of the air.' More recently Stephens said to have joined group called Foxtrot.

BLUE, David (*b* Stuart David Cohen, 18 Feb. '41, Pawtucket, R.I.; *d* 2 Dec. '82, NYC) Singer/songwriter, actor; played guitar, piano. Joined US Navy '58 but soon left to Greenwich Village coffeehouse scene: infl. and/or infl. by Bob DYLAN, Ramblin' Jack ELLIOTT, Luke Faust; best-known song 'Outlaw Man' covered by the EAGLES. Albums on Elektra: *David Blue* '66, *David Blue And The American Patrol* '67; on Reprise: *These 23 Days In September* '68, *Me* '70 (released under name of S. David Cohen); on Asylum: *Stories* '72, *Nice Baby And The Angel* '73, *Comin' Back For More* '75, *Cupid's Arrow* '76. Later LP for WB not released; working on another when he died of heart attack while jogging. Best-known film roles incl. Bob Dylan's *Renaldo And Clara* '78, Wim Wenders' *The American Friend* '78, Neil YOUNG's *Human Highway* '79; TV roles incl. *Studs Lonigan* '75, *The Ordeal Of Patti Hearst, Uncertain Futures* (dir. by his wife, Nesya Blue, and for which he also wrote score). Starred in plays *American Days* '82 dir. by Jacques Levy at Manhattan Theatre Club, *The Leonard Cohen Show* '80 in Montreal.

BLUEGRASS Country music genre representing earliest, trad. style: that of 'hillbilly' string bands, themselves originating in the Appalachian mountains of southeastern USA. Trad. songs with high-harmony vocals were backed by basic instrumentation of fiddle, guitar, mandolin, 5-string banjo and dobro, invented by violin-maker John Dopyera (*b* 1893; *d* 3 Jan. '88), who made a cone of spun aluminium to amplify the guitar mechanically; 'dobro' stood for Dopyera Brothers. Bill MONROE and Blue Grass Boys (after home state of Kentucky) joined Grand Ole Opry '39, added banjo for rhythm '42; Earl Scruggs joined '45 with astonishing banjo technique and almost extinct North Carolina style was reborn, modified by improvisation and inventiveness, instrumental virtuosity infl. by jazz. Monroe was infl. by black music; experimented until he had intricate jazz-infl. mandolin style: indeed one of the best, fastest mandolin players of all time; others such as Frank Wakefield and John Duffey have moved even closer to jazz. Monroe's music began to be called bluegrass around '50, but considered old fashioned, representing a minority interest; Scruggs made solo appearance at first Newport Folk Festival '59; following year as Lester FLATT & Earl Scruggs, with fellow Monroe alumnus on guitar; many bluegrass festivals since mid-'60s have established popularity for roots of country music. The DILLARDS moved from Missouri to L.A., continued developing bluegrass; other West Coast bands (COUNTRY GAZETTE, Kentucky Colonels) attracted fans from '70s rock audience; film *Deliverance* gave shot in the arm to bluegrass, yielding hit single 'Duelling Banjos' (no. 2 '73 USA), played in soundtrack by multi-instrumentalist Eric Weissberg on banjo, guitarist Steve Mandel. Contemporary 'newgrass' won young fans (many jokes about good grass), e.g. Newgrass Revival, led by Sam Bush (banjo, guitar, mandolin), with guitarist Curtis Burch, Courtney Johnson on banjo, Ebo Walker on bass, all singing except Walker (LPs on Sonet, Flying Fish, Paradise, Ridge Runner). Duffey has managed and played in Seldom Scene for 16 years (LPs on Rebel, Sugar Hill; they've appeared at the White House three times). Ricky SKAGGS had bluegrass-infl. country hits. Other bluegrass acts incl. OSBORNE BROS, STANLEY BROS, COUNTRY GENTLEMEN, Greenbriar Boys, Jimmy MARTIN, JIM & JESSE, Bill Clifton, Mac WISEMAN, Don Reno & Red Smiley (Reno and Wiseman were also Monroe alumni; *see also* Vassar CLEMENTS).

BLUE MAGIC Soul vocal group. Vernon and Wendell Sawyer, Richard Pratt, Keith

Beaton and Ted Mills recorded with good studio musicians, arrangers Norman Harris, Vince Montana, producer Bobby Eli, etc. at Sigma Sound (Philadelphia); resulting high-class product was leased to Atlantic. USA top 40 hits incl. 'Sideshow', 'Three Ring Circus', both '74. Compilations on Streetwave in UK, Omni/Atco in USA.

BLUE MINK UK pop group '69-75. Original lineup: Madeline BELL, Roger Cook, vocals; Herbie Flowers, bass; Barry Morgan, drums; Alan Parker, guitar; Roger Coulam, keyboards: all in-demand session musicians, made LP '69 *Blue Mink*. Cook had successful songwriting partnership with Roger Greenaway; took lead vocals with Bell. Surprise no. 3 pop hit with 'Melting Pot', catchy plea for racial harmony; barely had enough material to play at own London reception. Six more Cook/Greenaway top 30 singles '69-73 UK rarely strayed from trite, nursery-rhyme-style lyrics, Eurovision 'boom-banga-bang' formula. Success led to cabaret dates which in turn led to lineup changes: Coulam left for studio work, replaced by Ann Odell; Ray Cooper joined on percussion after a USA tour. Split '75; Bell resumed solo/session career, Cook back to writing, Parker and Morgan sessioned at own Morgan Studios, while Flowers (who wrote actor Clive Dunn's Xmas '70 no. 1 'Grandad') made LP *Plant Life* '75 before joining Sky, John WILLIAMS's classical/rock fusion group; second solo LP *A Little Potty* '80. Cooper now works with Elton JOHN, Odell is highly regarded arranger. Group was never more than part-time project; memory revived when similarly multi-racial Culture Club used 'Melting Pot' as encore in '83-4 tours.

BLUE NOTE USA jazz label founded '39 by Alfred Lion (*b* 21 Apr. '08, Berlin; *d* 2 Feb. '87, Cal.), a jazz fan since age 16, emigrated to USA '38. Began by recording Albert AMMONS and Meade Lux LEWIS, piano solo and duo (recorded Lewis on harpsichord '41); then Port of Harlem Jazzmen in two sessions, first with Ammons, Frankie Newton, J. C. HIGGINBOTHAM, Sid CATLETT, Teddy Bunn (1909-78), guitar, Johnny Williams (*b* '08), bass; then with Lewis instead of Ammons and adding Sidney BECHET, whose 'Summertime' became nearest thing

to a hit. Lion was joined late '39 by fellow Berliner childhood friend Francis 'Frank' Wolff (*d* '71). Recorded Edmond HALL quartet with Charlie CHRISTIAN, Lewis on celeste '41: 'Profoundly Blue' a classic. Label's imaginative, instinctive innovation in production revealed deep sympathy for the music and its players: often cut 12″ 78 sides, rare and uncommercial then, providing more flexibility for musicians; held sessions at night, provided food and drink; attitude helped to obtain quality results. Turned to 'swingtets' led by tenor saxists John HARDEE, Ike QUEBEC, etc. Quebec's 'Blue Harlem' was another hit '44; he became close friend, urged recording of bop: Blue Note recorded Bud POWELL, Thelonious MONK, Miles DAVIS; carried on for decades with characteristic photographic sleeve art supervised by Wolff, quality studio sound (after '53 the work of Rudy Van Gelder, master of jazz recording engineers, who credited Lion with helping to invent his techniques). Label famous for Art BLAKEY and the Jazz Messengers, hard bop classics (forerunners of today's disco-funk) 'Sidewinder' (by Lee MORGAN), 'Maiden Voyage' (Herbie HANCOCK), work of Horace SILVER, Donald BYRD, Bobby TIMMONS, Lou DONALDSON, Bobby HUTCHERSON, early free jazz masterpieces of Cecil TAYLOR, '60s rediscovery of Dexter GORDON, much, much more. After 25 years sold label to Liberty; identity lost, product in and out of print as Liberty acquired by United Artists, then absorbed by giant EMI. Last Blue Note records by Silver, '80, label phased out '81; Japanese and French EMI began reissuing discs with original sleeve art, proving that market was there; EMI London imported French pressings from '84 digitally remastered; disc jockeys rediscovered funk roots, EMI released 12″ single in limited edition of 'Sidewinder' '85; producers Michael CUSCUNA, Charlie Lourie reissued classics on Mosaic: limited edition sets of Monk, Ammons, Lewis, Quebec, Hardee, Tina BROOKS etc. incl. previously unissued material; Blue Note relaunched '85 by Manhattan Records and Capitol Industries (EMI) under dir. of Bruce Lundvall (who had earlier created Elektra/Musician at WEA); Town Hall concert/celebration incl. artists associated with label: Blakey took night off from Feb. dates in London to be there; party was issued on four LPs. Plans incl. LPs by Grover WASHINGTON, George RUSSELL, Stanley JORDAN, Michel PETRUCCIANI; Cuscuna on A&R committee.

BLUE OYSTER CULT USA heavy rock band formed late '60s as Soft White Underbelly; later made two unreleased LPs as Stalk Forrest Group for Elektra. Fluctuating line-up incl. Allen Lanier, guitar and keyboards; Buck Dharma (Donald Roeser), lead guitar; plus college mate Sandy Pearlman, critic at Crawdaddy magazine and band's mentor/prod. together with Murray Krugman through '70s. After various vocalists incl. R. Meltzer, Phil King, Les Bronstein, settled for Eric Bloom, adding Bouchard brothers Joe (bass), Albert (drums, both sing); first eponymous BOC LP released '72. Music basic, riff-dominated; lyrics in mock-occult style paralleling UK's BLACK SABBATH. Cut teeth opening for ALICE COOPER; stage pyrotechnics (lasers, smokebombs) became trademark; *Live Bootleg* EP circulated by CBS '72 showed band at its best live; they've since made live LPs *On Your Feet Or On Your Knees* '75, *Some Enchanted Evening* '78, *ETI* '82. Released an album a year through the '70s, supported by heavy touring. Lanier's girlfriend Patti SMITH contributed songs with rest of band; *Agents Of Fortune* '76 criticised for excessive democracy in songwriting sphere, but incl. USA no. 12/UK no. 16 hit 'Don't Fear The Reaper', menacing BYRDS-style jangler written by Dharma. Album thankfully dropped Nazi-chic imagery first adopted '74 with *Secret Treaties*, but follow-up *Spectres* '77 failed to maintain commercial momentum of *Agents*, which reached no. 29 LP chart: best-selling cult LP yet. Dropped Perlman for CHEAP TRICK prod. Tom Werman on *Mirrors* '79, indicating desire for more polished sound; continued in live shows to dish out rip-roaring rock in grand style. Switched prod. again to British heavy metal maestro Martin Birch (DEEP PURPLE, Rainbow) for *Cultosaurus Erectus* '80, *Fire Of Unknown Origin* '81, both showing return to previous formula. Birch concurrently prod. Black Sabbath; bands toured together under banner of Black and Blue; film of that name in '81 contained concert footage.

First personnel change in a decade when Albert Bouchard replaced by Rick Downey after *Fire*; last LP *Revolution By Night* '83.

BLUE SKY BOYS Brothers Bill and Earl Bolick (*b* 28 Oct. '17 and 16 Dec. '19, Hickory, S.C.) Singers, mandolin (Bill) and guitar. Trad. country act, began on local radio '35 and recording for Victor '36. Popular regulars until '51; refused to add electric guitar to act and left music. Reformed briefly during '60s revival of trad. music; made album for Capitol '65. Compilation LPs in USA on Rounder and Starday labels.

BLUES Genre created by Americans of African descent: with JAZZ one of the few new art forms of modern times, also (paradoxically) a true folk music, its development complete shortly after 1900. Jazz incl. a greater European element, while blues remained relatively unsophisticated, accessible to untrained players and singers, whose art was in subtle but direct communication. Ex-slaves sang as they worked; inexorable rhythm of work songs, with lyrics full of irony, earthy imagery, became a commentary on daily life and love: relief of tension. Classic blues is 12-bar form, three lines of four bars each; lyric is a couplet with first line repeated once: each line of lyric takes about 2.5 bars, the rest of each 4-bar segment being improvised fill, sometimes vocal, usually instrumental on singer's own guitar or piano. The form has been further developed by many artists: 13-bar blues are not uncommon; it used to be said that songs such as W. C. HANDY's 'St Louis Blues' were not really blues; such distinctions now seem unnecessary. Blues are contrary to European musical practice, were therefore frowned upon by educated blacks (we are also taught that polyphonic music was invented in Renaissance Europe; Africans had practised it for centuries). Blues are played not in major or minor but in 'blue mode'; the off-pitch 'blue notes' cannot be played on the piano, are now thought to be more or less direct from African music. First blues published '12 ('Dallas Blues', Handy's 'Memphis Blues'; but Bill BROONZY claimed that some of his blues dated to 1890); first blues recorded '20 by Mamie SMITH: her Okeh record of Perry

BRADFORD's 'Crazy Blues' was a surprise hit and a new market was discovered. Great female blues singers incl. the Smiths (not related: Mamie, Clara, Trixie and Bessie, greatest of all), Victoria SPIVEY, Ida COX, Ma RAINEY, many more, accompanied on piano by James P. JOHNSON, Fats WALLER, Fletcher HENDERSON, many others; Louis ARMSTRONG, other jazz greats were sidemen on records. A pattern of fractured family life resulting from slavery followed by institutionalised racism meant that male blues singers were itinerant, accompanying themselves on guitar, were often recorded in the field by talent scouts, researchers; they led hard lives, often died young. Charley PATTON, Robert JOHNSON, Son HOUSE, Bukka WHITE came from Mississippi delta; Tommy JOHNSON, Blind Lemon JEFFERSON, many more had profound effect on post-war pop music decades after they died, thanks to records. Blind Boy FULLER, Sonny TERRY, Brownie MCGHEE, Gary DAVIS represented the more delicate Piedmont trad. of S.E. USA. Instrumental blues piano enjoyed '40s vogue called BOOGIE-WOOGIE; MEMPHIS SLIM (Peter Chatman) and Roosevelt SYKES played piano, wrote and sang classic songs; with guitarists John Lee HOOKER, Lightnin' HOPKINS became legends in their own lifetimes; many bluesmen like Snooks EAGLIN, Mance Lipscomb, Mississippi John HURT were all-round entertainers, infl. as much by RAG-TIME and other styles as by blues. Leroy CARR played piano and sang a smoother style '30s, also wrote fine songs in a more urban vein, infl. later black styles. The emergence of the Count BASIE band and others from KANSAS CITY late '30s gave a powerful reinjection of blues into big-band jazz of the Swing Era; partly for this reason, BOP had a strong blues element for all its technical sophistication; in '50s-60s small-group 'blowing sessions' from Blue Note, Prestige labels always incl. blues: the blues is not jazz but the best jazz has blues in it. RHYTHM & BLUES began in '40s infl. equally by Swing Era, blues: this black pop/party music was imitated by '50s rock'n'rollers. Muddy WATERS first recorded in Ms. '41-2, went to Chicago '43; urban blues emerged as performers adopted microphones, electric guitars to be heard in noisy taverns: a Chicago scene of great power developed with Waters, Willie DIXON, Walter HORTON, LITTLE WALTER, James COTTON, Otis RUSH, Howlin' WOLF, Otis SPANN, J. B. HUTTO, MAGIC SAM, Johnny SHINES, many others; inspired by country blues artists of '20s-30s mentioned above, their own post-war work in Chicago was imitated in the '60s by new generation of rock bands, singers: tours and imported records inspired London scene that threw up ROLLING STONES (see Alexis KORNER, John MAYALL), thus having profound impact on pop music of the last 20 years. Beginning late '50s whites in USA like Paul BUTTERFIELD, John KOERNER, John HAMMOND, Dave VAN RONK worked hard at playing authentic blues style: at Newport Folk Festival '65 folkies booed Bob DYLAN, appearing with Butterfield's electric band, but accepted the band separately because they had never heard electric blues before; despite a foolishly insulting introduction from Alan LOMAX, Michael BLOOMFIELD's guitar did not fail to impress; the band's LP on Elektra sold steadily and long-overdue commercial success of the modern bluesmen was at hand: from '60s Junior WELLS, Buddy GUY, Jimmy DAWKINS, Hound Dog TAYLOR, others held down Chicago scene; B. B. KING began at Memphis radio station late '40s, worked 'chitlin circuit' for years, emerged as the most highly regarded living bluesman (Albert KING and Freddie KING also highly rated; may or may not have been related). As blues genre was worked to death by rock'n'rollers (leading to HEAVY METAL, whose lack of subtlety is a vulgar antithesis), Texans Albert COLLINS and Johnny COPELAND, in the '80s Robert CRAY (born in Georgia, raised in Washington state) have emerged as new keepers of the flame. Followers of the blues are divided into fans of the more authentic black stuff and those of white guitarists such as Roy BUCHANAN, Johnny WINTER, Stevie Ray VAUGHAN etc. but streams were converging to some extent mid-'80s: Rush was recording again, Earl King was backed on an album by white band ROOMFUL OF BLUES; white bands like the FABULOUS THUNDERBIRDS and Kingsnake (from NY state, LP on Blue Wave) carried on with love for the music, and new talents like Cray and Walter 'Wolfman' Washington (LP on Rounder) transcended category.

Good books incl. classic *Urban Blues* '66 by Charles Keil; *The Devil's Music* by Giles Oakley (with '76 BBC TV series); *The Roots Of The Blues: An African Search* '81 by Samuel Charters; *Blues Off The Record* '85 by Paul Oliver (anthology of 30 years' writing). Blues also infl. COUNTRY MUSIC (*see* Jimmie RODGERS, Hank WILLIAMS, Bill MONROE etc.): the blues, like country music, was originally of rural southern origin.

BLUES MAGOOS USA blues band, then psychedelic pioneers, signed by Mercury '66 after residencies at Café Wha and Nite Owl Café in NYC. Lineup: Ralph Scala (*b* 12 Dec. '47, NY), vocals, keyboards; Ron Gilbert (*b* 25 Apr. '46, NY), bass, vocals; Peppy Castro (*b* Emil Thielheim, 16 June '49, NY), rhythm guitar, vocals; Geoff Daking (*b* 8 Dec. '47, Delaware), drums; Mike Esposito, lead guitar. Debut LP *Blues Magoos* '66; next two went gold: *Psychedelic Lollipop* '66 (first LP to use 'psychedelic' in title, also advising 'play at high volume'), *Electric Comic Book* '67. Adapted previous blues sound – too well, some said – to psychedelic fad for fashionably acid-oriented hits '(We Ain't Got) Nothing Yet' (no. 5 USA), 2-sided 'Pipe Dream' (no. 60) and 'There's A Chance We Can Make It' (no. 81), 'One By One' (no. 71), all '66-7. Stage act featured neon-trimmed suits that lit up at high spots in show, went down well opening for UK bands like HERMAN'S HERMITS and the WHO; but music on record did not live up to live reputation. Lineup split after *Basic Blues Magoos* '68; Castro recruited John Liello (vibes, percussion), ex-Bear Eric Kaz (keyboards, vocals) and sundry others for LPs *Never Going Back To Georgia* '69, electronic *Gulf Coast Bound* '70 on ABC/Probe before the final split. Kaz became a successful songwriter (for Bonnie RAITT, Linda RONSTADT, etc.), formed AMERICAN FLYER. Castro joined Barnaby Bye (with future teen idols Billy and Bobby Alessi); later sessioned, notably for Paul Stanley (of KISS) on his solo LP '78, then emerged as lead singer of Balance alongside Bob Kulick (now with MEATLOAF) and Doug Katsaros on keyboards (LPs *Balance* '81, *In For The Count* '82 on Portrait). Other original Magoos never resurfaced: may or may not be evidence for cynical 'right time, right place' theory of lightweight talents.

BLUIETT, Hamiet (*b* c.'40, Lovejoy, Ill.) Baritone saxophonist (also flute, clarinet) in contemporary black music. Added deep voice to Julius HEMPHILL's *Coon Bid'ness* '75; also plays on long title cut on Lester BOWIE's *The Great Pretender* '81; recorded with Dollar Brand (*African Space Program* '73, *The Journey* '77). 'Tranquil Beauty' recorded by septet incl. Don Moye in May '76 for Wildflower series on Douglas (*see* JAZZ). First own LP *Endangered Species* '76 by quintet with Phillip Wilson on India Navigation label; then six albums '77: *Bars* is trio set with Moye, Marcello Melis on bass, on Musica; *Birthright* is solo blues concert recorded live; *S.O.S.* live quartet set with Moye, Don PULLEN, Fred Hopkins (last two on India Navigation); *Resolution* on Black Saint adds Billy Hart to make quintet; *Orchestra, Duo & Septet* on Chiaroscuro has 11 playing 'Glory (Symphony For World Peace)', duet with Pullen, two pieces for septet. Sextet on *Dangerously Suite* '81 incl. vocalist Irene Datcher; *Ebu* '84 is a quartet, both on Soul Note. Also plays in WORLD SAXOPHONE QUARTET, leads the Clarinet Family, with seven clarinets incl. Buddy COLLETTE, plus Hopkins and Ronnie Burrage in rhythm section; *Live In Berlin With The Clarinet Family* '84 on Black Saint.

BLUNSTONE, Colin (*b* 24 June '45, Hatfield, Herts.) UK singer/songwriter. Learned guitar age 10 from radio; struck gold as lead singer with ZOMBIES, formed with school friends. When they split '68 took job as insurance clerk; tempted back into music by former collaborators (now producers) Rod ARGENT and Chris White: made singles as Neil MacArthur, incl. remake of 'She's Not There' (UK no. 34 '69; same year Zombies' 'Time Of The Season' made no. 3 in USA posthumously). First solo LP *One Year* '71 prod. by Argent/White: ballads, strings showcasing quintessential English chorister's voice; spawned no. 15 hit following year in Denny LAINE's 'Say You Don't Mind'. Recruited band: Pete Wingfield, keyboards; Derek Griffiths, guitar; Jim Toomey, drums; made LPs *Ennismore* '72 (with no. 31 hit 'I Don't Believe In Miracles'), *Journey* '74; but band's rocking approach conflicted with choice of tunes: singer and band split. Left Epic after two more albums for Elton JOHN's Rocket label; fell out of spotlight until one-off single under name of keyboardist Dave Stewart, cover of Motown hit 'What Becomes Of The Brokenhearted?' (top 10 both USA and UK '66 for Jimmy RUFFIN), made no. 13 UK '81, contrasting Stewart's synths to that exquisite voice. Tried to repeat formula with another Motown classic; 'Tracks Of My Tears' (under Blunstone's name) only made no. 60 '82, but link forged with keyboardist Peter Bardens (ex-Them, CAMEL) maintained by formation of session supergroup Keats in '84, with Ex-Pilot members Ian Bairnson, guitar, David Paton, bass, and ex-COCKNEY REBEL Stuart Elliot, drums, all stalwarts of Alan Parsons Project. Blunstone had been featured vocalist on Project's *Pyramid* '78, *Eye In The Sky* '82, *Ammonia Avenue* '84, among numerous session credits; new group based on model of ASIA, playing AOR radio fodder without much imagination, yet it's good to hear Blunstone's pure haunting tones 20 years on from 'She's Not There'.

BLYTHE, Arthur M. (*b* 5 July '40, L.A., Cal.) Alto, soprano sax, composer, aka 'Black Arthur'. Worked with Stanley CROUCH '67-73; their LPs incl. *Now Is Another Time, Past Spirits*. To NYC '74; with Julius HEMPHILL (LP *Coon Bid'ness* '75), Chico HAMILTON, Lester BOWIE, Jack DEJOHNETTE *Special Edition*, others; played in film soundtracks and at black music festivals in L.A. Own LPs began with *The Grip* and *Metamorphosis* on India Navigation, recorded the same day in '77 by a sextet; *Bush Baby* same year is a trio set on Adelphi. Then a series with various combos on Columbia: *Lenox Avenue Breakdown* '78 was an excellent beginning; *In The Tradition* '79, *Illusions* '80, *Blythe Spirit* '81 (quintet tracks, smaller groups, duo with Amina Claudine Myers on organ on 'Just A Closer Walk With Thee'), *Elaborations* '82, *Light Blue* '83 (plays Thelonious MONK) were followed by *Put Sunshine In It* '85, descent into synthfunk with Stanley CLARKE, *Da-Da* '86 was better, but big label's desire to sell black music as pop isn't good enough for the man of whom Gary Giddins once wrote, 'Black Arthur means not having to search for your roots anymore because they are there at your fingertips.' (On the other hand, Blythe once said, 'I

don't want to make records for posterity. I want to make records for prosperity.') New album *Basic Blythe* '87 returned to an acoustic group of pianist John Hicks, Anthony Cox on bass, drummer Bobby Battle, string quartet. Also tours with The Leaders, with Chico FREEMAN, etc. (LP *Mudfoot* on Blackhawk).

BMI Broadcast Music Incorporated, USA performing rights society, chartered Oct. '39 using money pledged by 256 radio stations in expectation of ASCAP strike against broadcasters (for 15% of their income, raised from 5%). Strike began end of '40; ASCAP is still biggest of the societies collecting and distributing royalties for members, but during the strike none of the top 20 songs (sheet music sales) were ASCAP songs; settlement was made end of '41 for 2.8%. Meanwhile some publishers switched to BMI, notably Acuff-Rose, Ralph Peer; BMI helped BLUES, COUNTRY MUSIC artists largely ignored by ASCAP. Broadcasters indirectly encouraged to cultivate minority audiences, publishers serving radio stations subsidised, modern growth of independent record labels began. New business muscle of minority audiences had far-reaching effects: during WWII blacks and 'hillbillies' in armed forces were able to hear their music; other GIs exposed to it for the first time while Big Band Era was passing its peak: in retrospect, post-war NYC-based pop music dominated by trivia; rise of rhythm & blues, crossover hits, rockabilly etc. became inevitable. BMI affiliated with 39 overseas societies, as well as American Composer Alliance ('44): Roy Harris, Walter Piston, Elliott Carter, Charles Ives etc. became BMI composers. Also sponsors awards to student composers since '51; BMI Musical Theatre Workshop (since '59) and recent Alternative Chorus Workshop have best works presented annually to audiences of agents, publishers, producers, record executives.

BOB B SOXX & THE BLUE JEANS US vocal group. Lineup: Bobby Sheen (*b* '43, St Louis, Mo.), Graycha Nitzsche (wife of Jack NITZSCHE), Darlene LOVE, Fanita James. Last two with Jean King were legendary session trio the Blossoms. Collection of black session singers brought together by prod. Phil SPECTOR, initially to be called Bobby and the Holidays. Debut smash no. 8 hit '62 with 'Zip-A-Dee-Doo-Dah', unusual treatment with unique guitar sound, idiosyncratic arr. of song from '48 Disney film *Song Of The South* (not revived until mid-'80s because treatment of Joel Chandler Harris's Uncle Remus stories regarded as racist, but Br'er Rabbit cartoons were brilliant). Lesser hits 'Why Do Lovers Break Each Other's Heart?', 'Not Too Young To Get Married' followed, both '63. Soxx was not the only outlet for reservoir of talent: also recorded as the CRYSTALS and under Love's name. Sheen recorded solo before and after; now tours as one of the COASTERS.

BOBO, Willie (*b* William Correa, 28 Feb. '34, NYC) Latin percussionist. From Puerto Rican family; father a weekend musician, playing cuatro (a 10-stringed guitar). Bobo played bongos at 14, then congas, timbales, trap-drums. Was bandboy for Machito's Afro-Cubans; tutored by Mongo SANTAMARIA '48. Recorded in '50s with Mary Lou WILLIAMS, who dubbed him Bobo. Joined Tito PUENTE '54, replacing Manny Oquendo on bongos; at first gig deputised for Puente – who was late – on timbales; band's percussion unit for duration of Puente's reign as 'The Mambo King' was Ti-Mon-Bo: Tito, Mongo, Bobo. Bobo played timbales during Puente's solos on vibes, also on 'The Shearing Spell', by George SHEARING; appeared on Birdland network radio programme as Willie Boborosa '57 and briefly joined Shearing's group, playing drum kit and timbales with Armando Peraza on congas, Al McKibbon on bass. Albums with Puente incl. *Cuban Carnival, Puente Goes Jazz, Top Percussion*. 'Ti-Mon-Bo' was a hit '57; same year played on Cal TJADER LP *Mas Ritmos Caliente* with Mongo; joined short-lived Puente splinter group Orquesta Manhattan. Also on Tjader albums *Tjader Goes Latin, Latin For Lovers, Demasiado Caliente, Tjader's Latin Concert*. With Mongo again forming La Sabrosa '61, charanga band with decidedly jazz leanings; recording of 'Afro-Blue' became standard. Played timbales on 'Linda Guarjira' on Mongo's *Our Man In Havana*. Formed own small improvisational group using Victor Panoja on congas; made several Latin-jazz and pure Latin LPs. Taught percussion in NYC.

BOGLE, Eric (*b* '44, Peebles, Scotland) Singer/songwriter, one of the most interesting emerging from UK folk scene in the last 20 years. Emigrated to Australia '69 ('The only sensible thing I've ever done'); wrote best-known song 'The Band Played Waltzing Matilda' '72 after watching military parade. June TABOR heard it at UK folk festival, incl. it in '76 LP *Airs & Graces*; also recorded by the CLANCY BROTHERS, the Furies, others; might have been used in Peter Weir film *Gallipoli* '81 but for contractual difficulties. Bogle made first UK appearances in '82 (with partner multi-instrumentalist John Munro); his fascination with WWI continued with 'No Man's Land', incl. in Tabor's *Ashes & Diamonds* '77. Own LPs *Now I'm Easy* '80, *Plain And Simple* '81 incl. 'Leaving Nancy', 'Belle Of Broughton'; *Scraps Of Paper* '82 probably his best album, with characteristically wistful 'If Wishes Were Fishes', 'Big Mansion House', wry observations 'Ballad Of Henry Holloway' and 'He's Nobody's Moggie Now'. Best songs are compared with those of Tom PAXTON and Phil OCHS; they reached a wider audience in 'rogue folk' boom of '84, when bands such as the POGUES and The Men They Couldn't Hang covered 'Matilda' and 'No Man's Land' (aka 'The Green Fields Of France').

BOKELO, Johnny (*b* Bokelo Isenge, Zaire) Guitarist, composer. Began in '50s with Orchestra Congo Success, formed by his brother DeWayon (Paul Ebengo). Honours shared on early Africain LP *L'Afrique Danse Vol. 7*, but Bokelo's virtuoso guitar overshadowed brother for top billing on '66 LP in series. Introduced new dance KiriKiri '67, quickly became a favourite; formed own band Johnny Bokelo and the Congo '68 for string of hit singles; then renamed band Orchestra Congo de Bokelo '70s as stardom faded, challenged by new generation in '70s; but with opening of new 24-track studio in Lome, Togo, Bokelo and several others (Mayaula, Dr Nico) revived careers with records backed by Les Redoubtables d'Abeti: Bokelo LP *Isabelle* was '84 hit on Tabansi label.

BOLAN, Marc (*b* Mark Feld, 30 July '47, London; *d* 17 Sep. '77) Pop singer, songwriter, bandleader. Same primary school as future PROCOL HARUM lyricist Keith Reid; in school group with Helen SHAPIRO. Male model at 15; pursued pop career as Toby Tyler, then single 'The Wizard' as Marc Bowland on Decca earned spot on TV's *Ready Steady Go*; flop followup 'The Third Degree' saw first use of name Marc Bolan. Met Simon Napier-Bell (pop svengali who steered YARDBIRDS, later WHAM! to success). Turned down offer from Yardbirds, joined John's Children '67; reportedly wrote their mini-hit 'Desdemona' in 25 seconds; BBC banned it. Formed acoustic duo Tyrannosaurus Rex with percussionist Steve Peregrine-Took (*b* 28 July '49, London; choked to death '80); fans of Tolkien's Hobbit books, they were stalwarts of London underground scene; disc jockey John Peel read fairy story on their first LP, *My People Were Fair And Had Sky In Their Hair, But Now They're Content To Wear Stars On Their Brows* '68. (Peel wrote '85 in the *Observer* of sitting onstage at Albert Hall reading a 'half-baked story written by the late Mark Bolan, a performance which in a more discerning age would have resulted in serious insurrection . . .') But Bolan's distinctive, quavery vocals had fey charm, e.g. on early single 'Jaspar C. Debussy'. Second album *Prophets, Seers & Sages, The Angels Of The Ages* '69 was wholly acoustic, with childlike poems, delicate guitar, but hippie charm did not hide Bolan's love of classic rock'n'roll (had been Bill HALEY fan age 7-8). Transitional LP was *Unicorn* '70, one side acoustic, one electric, incl. first real hit 'Ride A White Swan' (no. 2 UK). One-off single 'Oh Baby' same year credited to 'Dib Cochran & The Earwigs'; rumoured to be in conjunction with David BOWIE; it wasn't, but they were close friends, shared same prod. Tony VISCONTI. Published book of poetry *Warlock Of Love*. Took left (later joined Pink Fairies; Bolan hired bongo player Mickey Finn (*b* 3 June '47), featured electric instruments on *Beard Of Stars*; shortened name of group to T.Rex, became premier UK pop star with lineup incl. Finn, bassist Steve Currie (*b* 21 May '47, Grimsby; *d* '81), Bill Legend (*b* Bill Fifield, 8 May '44, Essex) on drums, backing vocalists Flo and Eddie (ex-TURTLES Howard Kaylan and Mark Volman), churned out electric boogie for kids: 'Hot Love', 'Get It On' (as 'Bang A Gong' in USA), 'Telegram Sam', 'Metal Guru' were all UK no. ones; albums *Electric Warrior* and *The Slider* '71-2 also no. 1; top 5 hits with 'Solid Gold Easy Action', 'Children Of The Revolution', 'Jeepster'. Music press called T.Rex 'new BEATLES'; headlined gigs with 'T.Rexstacy!' With nonsense lyrics, relentless thumping T.Rex sound, first generation after Beatles had found its idol. Hysteria was captured on film by Ringo STARR in semi-documentary *Born To Boogie* '73; but teenybop fans are fickle; competition was David CASSIDY, the OSMONDS; after 'The Groover' '73 Bolan's star waned: 'New York City' ('75, with line 'Have you ever seen a woman coming out of New York City with a frog in her hand?') was his last top 20 hit. He revamped band with girlfriend Gloria Jones (vocalist who did original version of 'Tainted Love', later SOFT CELL's first hit), Dino Dines (ex-BEACH BOYS) on keyboards, retaining Currie; TV series *Marc* was '77 showcase for emerging punk bands The DAMNED, The JAM, EDDIE & THE HOT RODS, Generation X; Bowie was a guest: punk brought rejuvenation, as many were Bolan fans; he toured with the Damned as support '77, T.Rex now incl. Herbie Flowers on bass, Tony Newman on drums, Dino on keyboards; made proficient LP *Dandy In The Underworld*, started family with Jones, but was killed in car crash near Putney Common, the offending tree still pointed out by everyone who passes. Remembered for enthusiasm, vitality, infl. on punks; songs covered by SIOUXSIE & the Banshees, Bauhaus, '80s 'supergroup' Power Station. Best collection: 3-disc Australian set *20th Century Boy* '81; K-tel LP *Best Of The 20th Century Boy* UK hit '85; Visconti remixed T.Rex hits '87 to mark anniversary of Bolan's death.

BOLCOM, William Eldon (*b* 26 May '38, Seattle, Wash.) Composer, pianist. Discovered recordings of Ives and Stravinsky as a child; later admired Boulez, Berio; found own eclectic style drenched in popular music: string quartet '65 got second prize at Paris Conservatoire instead of first (it alluded to rock'n'roll); second violin sonata '76 has last movement in memory of Joe VENUTI. Wrote piano concerto for USA Bicentennial, etc. Recordings of piano music by Scott JOPLIN and others helped spark early '70s revival of interest in ragtime (LPs on Nonesuch label: *Heliotrope Bouquet, Pastimes and Piano Rags*; also piano music of George GERSHWIN). Wrote own rags (*Plays His Own Rags* on Jazzology); also co-author of book about Eubie BLAKE. On music faculty U. of Michigan, Ann Arbor. Performs and records with his wife, mezzo Joan Morris, songs from 1890s to present; LPs incl. two vols. of RODGERS & HART songs on RCA, Gershwin, Irving BERLIN and LEIBER & STOLLER on Nonesuch, KERN on Arabesque. Morris also has vaudeville collections on Nonesuch *After The Ball* and *Songs Of The Great Ladies Of The Musical Stage*; on RCA *Till The Clouds Roll By* with Max MORATH (songs of P. G. Wodehouse).

BOLDEN, Charles 'Buddy' (*b* 6 Sep. 1877, New Orleans, La.; *d* 4 Nov. '31, Jackson, La.) Cornet, leader. Legendary figure who was probably a link between ragtime and jazz, infl. many New Orleans musicians; allegedly his horn could be heard across Lake Pontchartrain. There is confusion about his biographical details partly because he operated several bands at once, appearing briefly with each (and had a barber shop as well). Committed to hospital, '07; was immortalised in Jelly Roll MORTON's 'I Thought I Heard Buddy Bolden Say'.

BOLERO A universal, sentimental ballad style, rooted in Spanish-derived African-infl. fusion from Cuba, Puerto Rico, Dominican Republic, later Mexico; the Puerto Rican style more closely related to Spanish root than syncopated Cuban. Visit of an Italian opera company to Cuba 1842 is still heard in high, passionate voices of best exponents of bolero; Cuban middle classes exported it back to Europe in slowed-down style which held sway in salons and dance halls for decades, infl. heard in songs by George GERSHWIN, Xavier CUGAT; still traces in USA country music, especially in the work of Freddy FENDER, Linda RONSTADT, Maria MULDAUR. (Maurice Ravel's *Boléro* '27 was an instrumental experiment in dynamics having little to do with the Latin style.) In the '50s Celia CRUZ

and Tito RODRIGUEZ combined the smooth romantic qualities of bolero singing with the improvisational nature of mambos, rumbas etc.; they remain among the foremost exponents on record.

BOLIN, Tommy (*b* '51, Sioux City, Iowa; *d* 4 Dec. '76, Miami) US rock guitarist. Formed band Zephyr in Denver '68; lineup: Candy Givens, vocals, keyboards; David Givens, vocals, bass; John Faris, vocals, sax, keyboards; Robbie Chamberlain, drums (later replaced by Bobby Berge). Appeared on LPs *Zephyr* '70, *Going Back To Colorado* '71 (but not on *Sunset Ride* '72). After a year on the road with blues legend Albert KING, went to NYC and expanding jazz-rock scene. Session credits incl. Billy COBHAM LP *Spectrum* '73, where his work helped convince Jeff BECK to pursue fusion music. Ascribed lightning-fast fingerwork to early work as drummer strengthening wrists and hands. Returned to rock as Joe WALSH's replacement in JAMES GANG recommended by Walsh himself; played on *Bang* '73, *Miami* '74. Mid-'75 replaced another famous axe-man, Ritchie BLACKMORE, in DEEP PURPLE, co-writing seven songs on *Come Taste The Band* '75; went solo when band split '76. First solo LP pre-Purple *Teaser* '75 with Jan HAMMER; then *Private Eyes* '76 with Reggie McBride, bass; Bobbye Hall, percussion; ex-VANILLA FUDGE Mark Stein, keyboards; Norma Jean Bell, sax, percussion; Berge on drums. While on road promoting *Private Eyes* was found dead in hotel room, probably from accidental drug overdose. Versatile, talented player had yet to find niche.

BOLTON, Dupree Trumpet. Extremely fine bop-influenced, West Coast musician about whom nothing is known. The only thing he ever said in an interview was 'When I was 14, I ran away from home.' Two appearances as a soloist on record: *The Fox* '59 by Harold LAND quintet, and *Katanga!* '63 by Curtis AMY sextet (Bolton wrote title tune). Had a warm, fresh vitality that (predictably) made critics reach for the names of Fats NAVARRO and Clifford BROWN.

BOMBA African-derived music and dance style developed in coastal towns of Puerto Rico, especially Loiza Aldea, among large communities of black sugar-cane mill-workers. Traditionally performed at social gatherings with an ensemble of one or two low-pitched barrel-shaped drums providing a fixed rhythmic pattern, an improvisatory higher-pitched one, maracas and a pair of sticks, which tap out a fixed organising rhythmic timeline on the side of a drum or any resonant surface. The woman performs relatively fixed steps while her partner exhibits his dancing skill, 'dialoguing' with the solo drummer; singing is call-and-response between lead singer and chorus, lyrics on topics of everyday interest, local and island history, often improvised about the dancing/music. Modernised in '50s by Rafael CORTIJO (from Loiza Aldea) and his vocalist Ismael RIVERA, who introduced it into the Cuban-infl. conjunto format; Willie COLON took the music increasingly electric in his bands of late '60s, '70s. Now one of many styles comprising pan-Latin SALSA.

BOND, Graham (Graham John Clifton Bond, *b* 28 Oct. '37, Romford, Essex; *d* 8 May '74, London) UK R&B multi-instrumentalist. An orphan, adopted from a Dr Bernardo home. Had music lessons in school; played in a Don Rendell quintet; forsook jazz for R&B, joining Alexis KORNER's Blues Incorporated '62, replacing Cyril DAVIES. Hired on strength of Eric DOLPHY-infl. alto sax playing, but switched to organ. Formed own trio with Jack Bruce, Ginger BAKER; became quartet with John McLAUGHLIN on guitar (later Neil Hubbard, with Dick Heckstall-Smith on sax), name of group changed to the Graham Bond Organization, back to R&B once more. Lack of pedigree on organ led to irreverent innovation: credited with being first to use Hammond organ/Leslie speaker combination in R&B context; first to split keyboard for portability; first to build electronic keyboard; first to use a mellotron, heard on *The Sound Of '65, A Bond Between Us* '66; LPs now considered seminal, but receiving little attention at the time. Bruce and Baker left to form CREAM with Eric CLAPTON; Baker's replacement Jon Hiseman (*b* 21 June '44) left with Heckstall-Smith for John MAYALL, then COLOSSEUM. Bond disbanded, went to USA, wrote and recorded '68 LPs *Love Is The Law, The Mighty Graham Bond* on Pulsar, *Solid Bond*

'70 on WB. With Baker in short-lived band Air Force. He married the American singer Diane Stewart, who shared interest in 'magick'. Several shortlived projects followed incl. Initiation; Bond and Brown (with Stewart and Cream lyricist Pete Brown); made *Two Heads Are Better Than One* '72. Marriage failed; formed group Magus with folksinger Carolanne Pegg; drugs and personal problems led to nervous breakdown '73; he died under London subway train. With Korner and Mayall one of the founders of UK R&B, but promise never fully realised.

BOND, Johnny (*b* Cyrus Whitfield Bond, 1 June '15, Enville, Okla.; *d* 12 June '78, Burbank, Cal.) USA C&W singer, songwriter, film actor. Played country dances around Marieth, Okla. '33-4; first radio work Oklahoma City '34. Joined Pop Moore's Oklahomans '36, Jimmy WAKELY Trio '37 (then called The Bell Boys) with Dick Reinhart; trio joined Gene AUTRY in Hollywood. On Autry's Melody Ranch CBS broadcasts '40-55; appeared as guitar-playing sidekick in films with Autry, Tex RITTER, Roy ROGERS, Hopalong Cassidy, but also main features: *Saga Of Death Valley* '39, *The Tulsa Kid* '40, *Pony Post* '40, *Duel In The Sun* '45, etc. First appearance on Grand Ole Opry '40; Cal. TV Town Hall Party from '53; signed to Columbia (Okeh) '40-58, with hits 'Cimarron' '40, 'I'll Step Aside' '45, 'Rainbow At Midnight' '46, 'Oklahoma Waltz' '48, 'Sick, Sober And Sorry' '51, 'Love Song In 32 Bars' '52, etc. Wrote classic country songs such as 'I Wonder Where You Are Tonight', 'Tomorrow Never Comes', 'I'll Step Aside', 'Your Old Love Letters'. With 20th Century Fox label '59, Autry's Republic label '60-2 (hit 'Hot Rod Lincoln' crossed over to no. 26 on pop chart '60), Starday '62-72: many hits incl. 'Ten Little Bottles' '65, 'Here Come The Elephants' '71. LPs incl. *Wild, Wicked West* '62, *Songs Made Famous By Johnny Bond* '63, *Bottled In Bond* and *Ten Little Bottles* '65, *Branded Stock* '66, *Ten Nights In A Barroom* '67, *Drink Up And Go Home* '68. Published books *The Tex Ritter Story*, autobiography *Reflections*; wrote unpublished biography of Autry. More records mid-'70s: *Rides Again* (Shasta '75), *How I Love Them Old Songs* (Lamb & Lion '76). Compilations on *The Singing Cowboy Rides Again, Return Of The Singing Cowboy* (Country Music Heritage '77).

BONDS, Gary 'US' (*b* Gary Anderson, 6 June '39, Jacksonville, Fla.) Moved to Virginia as a child, sang in church and high school group The Turks. Local record shop owner Frank Guida asked him to join his Legrand label with Guida song 'New Orleans'; smash hit USA, UK '60. Earthy voice brought soul to white pop audience; Guida's deliberately muddy production contributed raunchy sound: 'Quarter To Three' no. 1 '61, three more top 10 hits '61-2; then reduced to small time for 20 years. Bruce SPRINGSTEEN incl. 'Quarter To Three' as encore at concerts; saw Bonds perform in '80; revival happened: Springsteen and Steve VAN ZANDT produced Bonds LP *Dedication* '81; good voice, good songs and lavish production recalled best of Springsteen's E Street Band. Standout tracks incl. Springsteen's title tune and 'This Little Girl', Jackson BROWNE's 'The Pretender', BEATLES' 'It's Only Love', cover of Cajun 'Jole Blon'. Sequel *On The Line* not as successful, though Bonds' singing good, notably on 'Rendezvous'. Concerts in UK '81 were joyous affairs; then less active until self-produced *Standing In The Line Of Fire* '84 got good reviews: satisfying mixture incl. tribute to 'Fred Astaire', revival of Ritchie VALENS' 'Come On Let's Go'. Compilations incl. *The Star* (10″ disc on Charly UK); *Certified Soul* (Rhino).

BONEY M German-based Eurodisco group '70s, created by prod./performer Frank Farian to cash in on European dance sound pioneered by Giorgio MORODER (with Donna SUMMER), others. Having written, recorded typical example of genre in 'Baby Do You Wanna Bump' (hit in Belgium, Holland; synthetic strings, minimal lyrics, relentless drumbeat), needed group to promote it. Advert in trade papers brought two abortive lineups, then stable vocal quartet: Marcia Barrett (*b* 14 Oct. '48, Jamaica), Bobby Farrell (*b* 6 Oct. '49, Aruba, West Indies), lead singer Liz Mitchell (*b* 12 July '52, Jamaica), Maizie Williams (*b* 25 Mar. '51, Monserrat; only survivor of earlier lineups). Farian recorded backing tapes in Munich, road-testing them in discos to gauge

reaction before cutting group's vocals on top. From late '76 when 'Daddy Cool' made no. 6 UK to mid-'79 notched up nine top 10 singles in UK, rivalling ABBA as most successful group of decade: series mixed covers (Bobby Hebb's 'Sunny', old Harry BELAFONTE hit 'Mary's Boy Child') with Farian's own nursery-like chants. Attempt at outrageous image (underwear, bondage etc.) at odds with biggest hit: old Jamaican nursery rhyme 'Brown Girl In The Ring' began as B-side of cover of Melodians' 'Rivers Of Babylon'; became A-side three months after entering chart: 2-sided hit had 40-week run. No. 1 LP from which it came, *Night Flight To Venus*, had four hit singles, was first of three no. 1 LPs (last being TV-promoted *The Magic Of Boney M* in '80s as singles success faded). Apart from sales figures, accomplished notable feat of playing 10 concerts in USSR during boom year of '78. Unlike Summer, failed to sell Eurodisco to USA, where 'Rivers' (no. 30) was sole top 40 hit. Farrell was recording solo in '85; 'Rivers'/'Brown Girl' stood as all-time UK best-seller after Wings' 'Mull Of Kintyre' and BAND AID's 'Do They Know It's Christmas', but Germany's most popular pop export had vanished.

BONNER, Juke Boy (*b* Weldon H. Philip Bonner, 22 Mar. '32, Bellville, Texas; *d* 29 June '78, Houston, Texas) Blues singer, guitarist; also played drums, cymbals, harmonica. Began singing gospel as a child; orphaned at 8, learning guitar from 12; won talent show at a Houston theatre '48, appeared on radio, worked clubs, juke joints; first records on Irma in California '57, worked as one-man band, recorded in Lake Charles, La. '60, in Houston '67-70 (*Going Back To The Country* and *The Struggle* on Arhoolie, *The One Man Trio* on Flyright). Toured Europe, worked festivals, clubs; portion of Royal Albert Hall concert '69 issued on CBS; recorded for Liberty in England '69, for Sonet '72 in California (*Legacy Of The Blues Vol. 5* on GNP/Sonet), for Home Cooking in Houston '75; died of cirrhosis of the liver. Also wrote poetry. Style was influenced by Lightnin' HOPKINS, but with a more driving rhythm; younger than the classic bluesmen, he played a trad. style (but influenced by country music) on electric and acoustic guitars incl. 12-string; his yrics tried harder than trad. blues lines and o some extent he missed both the black audience and white college audiences because his work demanded close listening. The records are still selling.

BONOFF, Karla (b '52, L.A.) USA singer/ songwriter. Former UCLA student formed Bryndle '69 with Wendy Waldman (b '51, L.A.), Andrew Gold (b 2 Aug. '51, Burbank); LP was prod. for A&M by Chuck Plotkin, incl. Kenny Edwards (ex-Stone Poneys bass) but never released. Gold and Edwards formed Rangers, but ended up in Linda RONSTADT's backing band (she also ex-Stone Poneys). Inclusion of three Bonoff songs 'If He's Ever Near', 'Lose Again', 'Someone To Lay Down Beside Me' on Ronstadt's Hasten Down The Wind '76 led to Bonoff signing with Columbia; despite presence of ace West Coast sessionmen (plus Ronstadt, Gold, EAGLES etc.), neither Karla Bonoff '77 (incl. three songs covered by Ronstadt), Restless Nights '79, Wild Heart Of The Young '82 made great impact (despite no. 19 hit 'Personally' '82, ironically not her song). Problem was partly that best songs covered by others, such as Nicolette Larson, Bonnie RAITT (e.g. 'Home' from Sweet Forgiveness '77) so that her own interpretations were heard as covers. Waldman had same problem, her songs recorded by Maria MULDAUR, Judy COLLINS, Kim CARNES, others; Bonoff sang on Waldman's first two Warners LPs '70s, also backed Warren ZEVON (Excitable Boy '78) as well as Ronstadt on Hasten. Unlikely now to become star in own right; L.A. soft-rock scene has became unfashionable.

BONZO DOG BAND London band formed '66, originally Bonzo Dog Doo-Dah Band: Vivian Stanshall (b 21 Mar. '43, Shillingford), vocals; Neil Innes (b 9 Dec. '44, Essex), vocals, guitar; 'Legs' Larry Smith (b 18 Jan. '44, Oxford), drums; Roger Ruskin Spear (b 29 June '43, London), saxes, robots; Rodney Slater (b 8 Nov. '44, Lincolnshire), sax, Sam Spoons (b Martin Stafford), percussion, others. Art students provided light relief in pompous rock scene; early act mixture of Temperance Seven/trad. jazz, Spear's robots running amok, music and lyrics by Stanshall and Innes. Flop singles on Parlophone; switched to Liberty label

for LP Gorilla '67, dadaist riposte to BEATLES Sgt Pepper; Dennis Cowan added on bass (b 6 May '47, London); became more rockish on The Doughnut In Granny's Greenhouse '68, incl. digs at blues boom, concept albums, other vogues. Regulars at Brian EPSTEIN's Saville Theatre '67; seen in Beatle's Magical Mystery Tour; Paul McCARTNEY (as Apollo C. Vermouth) prod. their only hit single (written by Innes) 'I'm The Urban Spaceman' '68 (on LP Tadpoles '69). Featured in adventurous TV show Do Not Adjust Your Set, along with fledgling Monty Python team. Touring was traumatic; especially incongruous USA tour had them supporting SLY AND THE FAMILY STONE. Split after LP Keynsham '69, based on Stanshall's experience of a mental home, though astringent humour was apparent ('Look At Me I'm Wonderful'). Smith and others joined Bob Kerr's Whoopee Band, still a popular London pub act. Stanshall and Innes worked with members of Liverpool Scene and Scaffold in Grimms satirical review; re-formed Bonzos for LP Let's Make Up And Be Friendly '72, incl. C&W parody 'Bad Blood', Beatle send-up 'Straight From My Heart'; also introduced Stanshall's long-running Rawlinson End saga of loony aristocrats: dinner followed by billiards on horseback, or catching the javelin (book, feature film, LPs Sir Henry At Rawlinson End '81, Sir Henry At Ndidi's Kraal '84). Stanshall formed other bands (Human Beans, etc.), helped with film That'll Be The Day '72, did LP Men Opening Umbrellas Ahead '74, worked with Stevie WINWOOD on his Arc Of A Diver '82. Smith appeared on USA tours with Elton JOHN and Eric CLAPTON '74; Spear sporadically turned up with his Kinetic Wardrobe; Slater became a civil servant. Innes formed The World; album How Sweet To Be An Idiot '73 was a collection of various pop styles; he followed a Pythonesque trail with Eric Idle in Beatle parody film/album The Rutles, BBC TV show Rutland Weekend Television, LP Rutland Times '76; toured with Pythons; maintained band Fatso, incl. Rockpile guitarist Billy Bremner. 2-disc History Of The Bonzos issued '74; tradition continued with AL-BERTO Y LOST TRIOS PARANOIAS and in '84 spoof documentary This Is Spinal Tap. Stanshall's Christmas musical Stinkfoot praised by The Times late '85.

135

BOOGALOO Short-lived but infl. dance style '66-9 in NYC, aka bugalú. An adaptation of MAMBO, simplified but sharply accented and with infl. of R&B; English lyrics with Spanish accent and often brash, rough-and-ready music reflected experience of first-generation Cuban, Puerto Rican New Yorkers. Infl. by experiments of bandleader Eddie PALMIERI, with characteristic use of two-trombone lineup, pivotal Latin percussion. Helped to cross over to non-Latin audience with often risqué English lyrics; first recorded boogaloos on Ricardo Ray album *Se Solto* '66, Joe BATAAN's *Gypsy Woman* '67 followed by string of hits: Pete Rodriguez' 'I Like It Like That', Johnny Colon's 'Boogaloo Blues', Hector Rivera's 'At The Party', and first million-selling Latin hit Joe CUBA Sextet's 'Bang Bang'. Bandleader Larry HARLOW mixed boogaloo and R&B-inspired songs with Cuban material; Willie Rosario kept to a purer edge, playing slow mambo style; Ray BARRETTO LP *Acid* drew on R&B, jazz: not strictly boogaloo but not possible without it. First Willie COLON LP *El Malo* '67 incl. boogaloos. Style merged into Latin soul, a minor strand against a major revival of purist Cuban music, epitomised by Bataan's *Salsoul* '73, hinted at in *Gypsy Woman* '67 (described in sleeve note as 'soul' Latin), and *Riot!* '68 (described him as no. 1 Latin soul singer). These fusions led directly into '70s disco, with emphasis on Latin percussion, heartbeat, zany lyrics. Sudden extinction of pure boogaloo left a myth of its demise planned by a jealous older generation of musicians. UK compilation *We Got Latin Soul!* '87 on Caliente incl. Cuba, Barretto, Tito PUENTE.

BOOGIE WOOGIE Blues piano style, combined with infl. of ragtime 'sixteens' and the habañera (New Orleans 'Spanish tinge'). Pianists in eastern USA often had formal training before turning to jazz; elsewhere they taught themselves what they wanted to play and left it at that, like itinerant blues guitarists: 'stride' pianists like James P. JOHNSON, Willie 'The Lion' SMITH and Fats WALLER used more sophisticated harmony, improvising on the best pop songs of a golden era, while boogie woogie, like the blues itself, was a limited genre which depended for its subtlety on the native skill of the player. It began in lumber camps in Texas and Louisiana, where the only entertainment was a barroom piano (the 'bar' was planks laid over barrels, hence 'barrelhouse'); the style used repeated figures in the left hand, often eight notes to the bar with blues improvisation in right hand: the player could keep the beat going while he grabbed a drink or a bite. It did not provide a good living: Jimmy YANCEY was groundskeeper in Chicago baseball park; Meade Lux LEWIS, Albert AMMONS were taxi drivers in early years. Pete JOHNSON, Cow Cow DAVENPORT, Pine Top SMITH, Roosevelt SYKES, Little Brother MONTGOMERY also fine players; Peter Chatman (MEMPHIS SLIM) played, sang, wrote good songs in genre for decades. Ammons and Lewis were 'discovered' by John HAMMOND late '30s, formalised and played too fast, the style became a fad during the Big Band era. Waller had a clause in his contract saying he would not be required to play it. Will BRADLEY had fluke smash hit with 'Beat Me Daddy, Eight To The Bar' '40, then a rash of sequels; Tommy DORSEY had big wartime hit 'Boogie Woogie' '38 (reissued '43 during recording ban), at least credited to Pine Top; in '47, when times were getting hard for big bands, BASIE recorded 'One O'Clock Boogie', 'St Louis Boogie'. Adolescents all over the country pounded out boogie-woogie on parlour pianos – it is superficially easy to play – in pre-echo of adolescent blues guitar playing now called rock. Boogie-woogie infl. heard in R&B shuffle rhythms played by Louis JORDAN *et al.*; in early rock'n'roll through piano styles of Fats DOMINO, Huey 'Piano' SMITH, LITTLE RICHARD, Jerry Lee LEWIS, others; in countless song titles.

BOOKER T AND THE MGs US soul instrumental group formed '61 by multi-instrumentalist Booker T Jones (*b* 12 Nov '44, Memphis, Tenn.) and guitarist Steve Cropper (*b* 21 Oct. '41, Willow Springs, Mo.), then of the MAR-KEYS; Jones had joined Stax '60 as saxophonist; Mar-Keys were Stax house band. Recruited Lewie Steinberg, bass; Al Jackson drums (ex-Roy MILTON band: *b* 27 Nov. '35, Memphis, murdered there by intruder 1 Oct. '75). Instant empathy made hit of debut 'Green Onions', sinuous understated 12-bar instru

mental led by Jones's organ: shot to no. 3
'62. (Mar-Keys reached no. 3 previous year
with own similar 'Last Night'.) While Jones
studied music at Indiana U. band also busy
backing Otis REDDING, SAM & DAVE, Rufus
THOMAS, William BELL, Wilson PICKETT,
other Stax/Atlantic soul legends; notable too
for being interracial, despite blackness of
sound. Steinberg replaced '64 by Mar-Keys
bassist Donald 'Duck' Dunn (b 24 Nov. '41,
Memphis); later band adopted lighter
sound, bringing string of hits: five top 40
singles from '67 incl. 'Hang 'Em High' (no.
9 '68), 'Time Is Tight' (no. 6, no. 4 UK '69).
Sound based on strong foundation of Dunn
and Jackson, whose empathy let Jones's cool
organ, Cropper's original insistent rhythms
swap around on top. Broke up '71 when
Jones married Rita COOLIDGE's sister
Priscilla, moved west; LPs they made as duo
revealed him to have good voice but used
weak material; also went into prod. (e.g.
with Bill WITHERS). Others in demand sessioning with Rod STEWART, Ringo STARR,
Eric CLAPTON, Art GARFUNKEL, many others. Reunion *The MGs* '73 disappointed,
with Carson Whitsett, keyboards, Bobby
Manuel, guitar replacing Jones and Cropper. Jones made solo LP *Evergreen* '75, appeared in film *A Star Is Born* '76 as part of
Kris KRISTOFFERSON's band (had written
score for *Uptight* '68, MGs appearing in
soundtrack). MGs made *Universal Language* '76 for Asylum; both Stax and Jackson were gone: Willie Hall played drums.
Jones with Cropper and Dunn in Levon
Helm group RCO All Stars '77; prod. hit
Willie NELSON LP *Stardust* '79. Cropper,
Dunn guested with Blues Brothers '78, a
loose group assembled to back actors Dan
Aykroyd, John Belushi who were keen to
revive Stax sound: one-off stretched to several LPs and well-received film of same
name. Survivors continue to work in '80s
with John Fogerty, Stephen 'Tin Tin'
Duffy, etc., Jones having minor disco hit
'Don't Stop Your Love' '83. Original ver-
sion of 'Green Onions' has been used in
films, made top 10 UK '79 after exposure in
Quadrophenia, '65 hit 'Soul Dressing' used
on UK TV as theme for cricket broadcasts.
Original MGs LPs incl. *Green Onions* '62,
Soul Dressing '65, *And Now* '66, *Doin' Our
Thing* and *Soul Limbo* '68, *McLemore Avenue*
'70. CD compilations incl. *The Booker T Set*.

BOOMTOWN RATS Seminal Irish punk
band formed '75, led by verbose vocalist
Bob Geldof (*b* 5 Oct. '54, Dublin), with
Johnnie Fingers, keyboards; Pete Briquette,
bass; Gerry Cott and Garry Roberts, guitars.
Top 20 hits during '77-8 incl. 'Looking
After No. 1', 'She's So Modern'; breakthrough came with 'Rat Trap' (no. 1 UK
'78), then controversial 'I Don't Like Mondays' (no. 1 UK/73 USA '79): title was excuse for mindless murders from San Diego
schoolgirl; single also notable for early use
of promo video. LPs *Tonic For The Troops*
'78, *Fine Art Of Surfacing* '79 showed more
'rockist' tendency than among other Punk
acts. Geldof always centre of attention in
live performance, nearest New Wave had to
Mick Jagger figure: ex-freelance on music
weekly *New Musical Express* gave as good as
he got in interviews. Shoddy reggae-infl.
'Banana Republic' (no. 3 '80) saw decline;
Mondo Bongo '81, *Five Deep* '82 and *In The
Long Grass* '84 were perfunctory: Rats had
no more top 20 hits as of early '86; compilation *Ratrospective* '83 incl. all their best
stuff: fine selection of late '70s singles.
Geldof evangelical about group, but diversified into acting; role of Pink in PINK
FLOYD's *The Wall* '82 well received; *No. 1*
'85 (with Ian DURY) less successful; meanwhile worked tirelessly '84-5 on BAND AID
project (*which see*): with ULTRAVOX's Midge
Ure got music people to work together
feeding starving Africans in the most successful charity project in history; toured Africa, saw that the money went to famine
victims, took no nonsense from politicians,
nominated for Nobel Prize, knighted '86; he
organised Live Aid '85, was criticised for
incl. Rats on grounds they were no longer a
big enough name. His work inspired similar
projects around the world; autobiography *Is
That All?* '86 a best-seller, called best-ever
book by a rock star. Having done all he
could for famine relief, went back to music;
solo *Deep In The Heart Of Nowhere* '86 incl.
hits 'This Is The World Calling', 'Love
Like A Rocket', coordinated by Dave Stewart, contributions from Eric CLAPTON,
Lone Justice's Maria McKee, Alison
MOYET.

BOONE, Debby (*b* 22 Sep. '56, Hackensack,
N.J.) Pop/country singer, daughter of Pat
BOONE. Sang on Boone family gospel al-

bums; first solo single was Oscar-winning film song, prod. by Mike Curb: 'You Light Up My Life' also won Song of the Year Grammy '77, 10 weeks no. 1 on pop chart, top 5 country. Named top new vocalist '78 by ACM; country hits incl. 'God Knows' '78, 'My Heart Has A Mind Of Its Own', 'Breakin' In A New Pair Of Shoes' '79, 'Are You On The Road To Lovin' Me Again' '80. LPs incl. *You Light Up My Life, Midstream, Love Has No Reason.* Wrote autobiography *Debby Boone . . . So Far*; starred in musical play from '54 film *Seven Brides For Seven Brothers*, '82: successful on tour but closed on Broadway. Married to Gabriel Ferrer, son of Rosemary CLOONEY.

BOONE, Pat (*b* Charles Eugene Boone, 1 June '34, Jacksonville, Fla.) Singer, said to be direct descendant of frontiersman Daniel Boone. Began professional career while still at North Texas State College; signed to Dot label, first single 'Two Hearts, Two Kisses' first of 38 USA top 40 hits '55-62, incl. 10 top 10 entries, six no. 1. Style distinguished only by smoothness; clean-cut image, trademark 'white bucks' (shoes) made him second most popular singer of the late '50s after Elvis PRESLEY. Many hits were covers of black artists: Fats DOMINO ('Ain't That A Shame', no. 1 '55), Ivory Joe HUNTER ('I Almost Lost My Mind', no. 1 '56); those who favoured originals found watered-down version of LITTLE RICHARD's 'Long Tall Sally' (no. 8 '55) risible. Ballads incl. 'Don't Forbid Me' '56, 'Love Letters In The Sand' '57, 'April Love' '57, 'Moody River' '61, all chart toppers; last top 40 entry was novelty 'Speedy Gonzales' (no. 6 '62). Made films *Bernardine, April Love* '57; *State Fair* '62; had own TV series '57-60. Married to Shirley (daughter of Red FOLEY) '55; had four daughters: Laury, Lindy, Cherry, Debby (*see* Debby BOONE). Fade from pop scene accompanied by bad business investments, marriage trouble; religious beliefs provided strength: Boone family made gospel albums *The Pat Boone Family* (Word, '74), *New Songs Of The Jesus People, The First Nashville Jesus Band, The Family Who Prays*; he continued with *Born Again, S.A.V.E.D., Golden Hymns, Just The Way I Am* (all on Lamb & Lion label, '75-80). Also country hits: 'Indiana Girl' (Melodyland '75), 'Texas Woman' (Hitsville '77); LPs *I*

Love You More And More Each Day (MGM '73), *Country Love* (DJM '77), *The Country Side Of Pat Boone* (Hitsville '77). Other LPs incl. *Best Of* in USA (MCA, two discs); in UK, where he had 27 top 40 hits, one no. 1 ('I'll Be Home', '56), LPs incl. *Friendly Persuasion* (Cambra; title cut no. 5 USA, no. 3 UK '56) and *16 Classic Tracks* (Music For Pleasure).

BOOTHE, Ken Jamaican singer with distinctive style who began recording with veteran Stranger Cole in duo Stranger & Ken (e.g. 'Hush' and 'All Your Friends' '63). Emerged as soloist at Studio One during rock steady era, scored with 'Train Is Coming' and 'Moving Away' '67-8; made some two dozen singles contained on LPs *A Man And His Hits, More Of* and *Mr Rocksteady* up to early '70s. Joining forces with producer Lloyd Charmers c.'71 he became something of a pin-up with teenage girls in the reggae world, especially after militant 'Freedom Street' single, LPs *Black Gold And Green, Let's Get It On.* Cover of David Gates's 'Everything I Own' was UK no. 1 '74, after several months heading the REGGAE chart; LP of same name also incl. no. 11 hit 'Crying Over You'. The advent of more Ras Tafari-oriented singers and groups after the mid-'70s checked his career, though he recorded intermittently into the '80s. Other LPs: *Who Gets Your Love, Got To Get Away, Showcase, Live Good, Mr Boothe* and *20 Greatest Reggae Hits.*

BOOTS AND HIS BUDDIES USA territory band led by drummer Clifford 'Boots' Douglas (*b* 7 Sep. '08, Temple, Texas). Began on drums at 15, formed own 13-piece band popular in Texas and recorded about 40 sides for Bluebird in San Antonio: '35-6 sessions issued complete on a Tax LP, '37-8 on French RCA. Vocalists were Celeste Allen, Israel Wicks, Cora Woods, Henderson Glass. He moved to L.A. '50, left full-time music.

BOP Genre developed by black jazz musicians in early '40s, beginning of modern era in jazz. Short for re-bop or be-bop, onomatopoeic in origin from the music itself, or possibly from scat-singing. Rhythm section playing had become smoother and technical fluency of soloists higher than

ever: infl. by Lester YOUNG, Charlie CHRIS-
TIAN, Jimmy BLANTON, Jo JONES, Art
TATUM and others, younger musicians such
as Charlie PARKER, Dizzy GILLESPIE,
Kenny CLARKE, Thelonious MONK, Miles
DAVIS, Fats NAVARRO, Max ROACH, Curley
Russell, Al HAIG, Clyde Hart jammed at
Harlem clubs like Minton's, where house
leader Teddy HILL was sympathetic. (Jamming was against union rules, because people played free or for tips, but some local
union officials turned a blind eye.) They
improvised on chords instead of melody,
inventing new tunes from chord structures
of standards; used altered chords and higher
intervals; insisted on using a wider range of
notes (a process that has been going on in
classical music for centuries). Tempi were
often furiously fast or very slow (but even
when the tempo was slow the soloist often
played fast, using machine-gun runs of six-
teenth notes). Syncopation finally disappeared; new accents within measures, together with phrases of unusual lengths,
changed even the rhythmic nature of jazz:
intense music was created, full of pride,
sardonic wit, fierce joy; technically brilliant
music not for dancers. Scene accompanied
by attitudes and language incomprehensible
to outsiders (some of this pioneered by
Young; zany wit of Gillespie also important). First bop records made '44-5 by small
groups on independent labels, mainly
Savoy. Bop big bands were led by Gillespie,
Billy ECKSTÍNE, Boyd RAEBURN in late '40s,
but were poorly documented on disc because of musicians' union strikes. Among
older men, Budd JOHNSON was important:
the Texas tenor saxophonist wrote arrangements for Earl HINES, who hired young
boppers, then for Eckstine, Raeburn, Dizzy
Gillespie and Woody HERMAN, all the most
important modern big bands. The chromatic style of Coleman HAWKINS had been influential; he encouraged boppers, hiring
them for record dates; but Cab CALLOWAY
called it 'Chinese music'. Boppers often
flatted the fifth note of a chord, inventing
short routes between keys: Eddie CONDON
said, 'We don't flatten our fifths, we drink
'em.' (But Igor Stravinsky had used flatted
fifths in 1910.) There were white boppers in
black combos (e.g. Red RODNEY, Al Haig)
(but pressure on leaders to practise Crow
Jim sent them into obscurity later; many

made comebacks as bop became repertory
music in the '70s). Some say that 'bop left
jazz in a shambles' but that is nonsense: jazz
content in pop music was decreasing anyway; bop wasn't a revolution, but a further
flowering of an art form already decades
old, towards emancipation of black music
from ballrooms, taverns by making demands on listeners: the orthodoxy is that
bop was not commercially successful because it wasn't dance music; but bop was
fun, and Gillespie regarded it as dance
music. The record business tried to climb
on the bop bandwagon (critic George
Hoefer complained '51 of 'the "Bop for the
People" campaign indulged in by the Capitol and RCA record bigwigs'). Gillespie
formed Dee-Gee label that year and went
broke, but the music he recorded holds up
much better than the pop music of the
period; there is an extent to which the
music business (incl. broadcasters) co-opts
and tries to control whatever it doesn't
understand, as it did rock'n'roll ten years
later. Bop was also very obviously black
music; America c.'50 was not yet ready for
black pride. In any case, the music soon
developed in several directions: sheer beauty resulted from 'modern jazz' in '50s, e.g.
Davis's quintet of '56; composer/arrangers
Tadd DAMERON, Mal WALDRON, George
RUSSELL, Gil EVANS, Benny GOLSON applied their talent to new harmonic ideas;
bop led to 'hard bop', less frenetic but with
modern harmony and strong backbeat, appealed to R&B, club audiences, thus entering the commercial mainstream; this led to
the clichés of jazz-funk '70s, in turn to new
interest in jazz roots of pop. More importantly, it led ultimately to more freedom for
musicians/composers: *see* JAZZ; also CUBOP.

BOP Term for rock'n'roll dance style in '50s
USA, resembling Swing Era jitterbug, with
awkward heel-and-toe movement (hence
e.g. the BIG BOPPER, 'Western bop' term for
rockabilly, etc.). It was obligatory; people
who couldn't do it didn't dance. Dancing
loosened up in the '60s, became more fun.

BOSCO, John Mwendo (*b* '25, Jadotville,
Zaire) Singer-composer, guitarist; virtuoso
maringa and RUMBA musician, pioneer of
Zairean music. A Sanga speaker with urban
roots; received formal education, worked as

clerk in Jadotville; 'discovered' by ethnomusicologist Hugh Tracey on recording trip, using standard steel-strung Spanish guitar; first recording '51. Most enduring song 'Masanga' '52 made him famous, won Osborne award for best African music, theme used by Sir William Walton in *Johannesburg Festival Overture* '56. Bosco released over 80 78 singles '52-62 on South African Gallotone label, incl. second major hit 'Bombalaka'. Dropped into obscurity as amplified music swept Africa '60s; resurfaced briefly for two singles on Decca '74; rediscovered '82 and invited to tour and record in Germany and Austria: two LPs of his songs re-recorded there. 'Masango' also available on Folkways African compilation *Guitars Vol. 1* '76. Bosco lives alternately in Sakanya, near Zambian border, and in Lubumbashi.

BOSSA NOVA Dance rhythm invented late '50s in Rio de Janeiro, a hybrid of samba with the local baiao of Northeast Brazil and imported cool jazz from West Coast of USA, a fashionable music by poets (lyricists) and musicians (mostly of European descent), more infl. by Afro-American music than by indigenous rhythms: 'bossa' is the hump on an ox's back; 'bossa nova' means 'new disturbance'. It combined the samba with a jazz feeling, resulting in one of the most difficult of popular rhythms for a kit drummer, but a beguiling one. Guitarist Joao Gilberto (*b* June '31, Bahia, North Brazil) showed his songs to Antonio Carlos Brasieiro De Almeida Jobim (*b* 25 Jan. '37, Rio), mus. dir. at Odeon: Gilberto recorded his 'Bim Bam', Jobim's 'Chega de Saudade' '58, starting fad; among definitive songs were 'Desifinado' ('Slightly Out Of Tune'), 'One Note Samba', 'Corcovado' etc. many written by Jobim and lyricist Vinisius de Morais (*d* '80). Gene LEES in USA wrote English lyrics for Jobim songs; 'Corcovado' became 'Quiet Night Of Quiet Stars'. During '60s student unrest in Brazil Jobim avoided getting involved; bossa nova was unpopular with the young left, seen as Americanism especially after Carnegie Hall concert Nov. '62 with Gilberto, Jobim, Sergio MENDES, Dizzy GILLESPIE, Charlie BYRD, Stan GETZ; Byrd and Getz made album *Jazz Samba* '62; Laurindo ALMEIDA and Herbie MANN were also active in the

music's sudden international popularity: 'The Girl From Ipenema' (a suburb of Rio) was recorded in Portuguese by Gilberto; sung in English by his then wife Astrud (*b* 30 Mar. '40) with Getz and Jobim on guitar, it was no. 5 hit USA '64; *Getz/Gilberto* was hit LP. Jobim and Vinisius wrote songs for Brazilian film *Black Orpheus* '58 (as did Luiz Floriano Bonfá, *b* 17 Oct. '22, Rio: 'Samba de Orfeu'); his songs were recorded by hundreds of artists, among them Ella FITZGERALD, Sarah VAUGHAN, Miles DAVIS, Dionne WARWICK, Frank SINATRA, etc. He also wrote film soundtrack *Cronica da Casa Assassinada* '72 ('Story Of The Murder House'), *O Tempo e O Vento* '85 (soap mini-series 'The Time And The Wind'); songs paying tribute to Portuguese poet Fernando Passoa, etc. Other exponents were Brazilian guitarist Bola Sete (*b* Djalma de Andrade, 16 July '28, Rio; *d* 14 Feb. '87, Greenbrae, Cal.), who came to USA '59, played at Monterey Jazz Festival '62, worked with Dizzy Gillespie; own albums and others with Vince Guaraldi on Fantasy; also AIRTO and Flora PURIM, who brought bossa feeling (and her unique scat style) to West Coast fusion scene late '60s. The style has entered the currency of 20th-century music; a mini-revival of bossa rhythms in UK early '80s was due to cool associations, boredom with current pop music among young people.

BOSTIC, Earl (*b* 25 Apr. '13, Tulsa, Okla.; *d* 28 Oct. '65, Rochester, NY) Alto sax, leader. With Don REDMAN, Cab CALLOWAY, others; arranged for many bands: 'Let Me Off Uptown' for Gene KRUPA, etc. Own band '41; with Lionel HAMPTON; own groups from '45: recorded for Allegro, Gotham, then King '49-63. Extrovert small combo was highly successful: in the early '50s nearly every juke box in a black neighbourhood had Bostic records on it, and many a white box as well. 'Flamingo' was no. 1 R&B chart '51; 'Sleep' no. 9 same year. Other hits incl. 'You Go To My Head', 'Cherokee', 'Temptation'. Over the years Bostic sidemen incl. Al CASEY, John COLTRANE, drummers Earl Palmer and Specs Wright, guitarist Mickey Baker, Stanley TURRENTINE, Benny GOLSON, Bill DOGGETT, many more. Recorded nearly 400 selections for King; fans trying to collect them all would get confused: many were stereo remakes with different personnel, but King used the same album numbers: e.g. KING LP571, *Bostic Rocks Hits Of The Swing Age*, was recorded in L.A. '57 and in Cincinnati '59 with an entirely different group. He had a heart attack; resumed music part-time '59, elected to all-star band in Playboy poll; made LPs with more jazz content: '63 tracks with Richard 'Groove' HOLMES, Joe PASS on guitar, Al McKibbon on bass incl. LP *A New Sound*. Said to have developed technique at the price of strident tone; but Art BLAKEY said, 'Nobody knew more about the saxophone than Bostic, I mean technically, and that includes Bird.' Compilations: *14 Hits* '45-64 on King, *16 Sweet Tunes Of The '50s* on Starday, *Earl Bostic Blows A Fuse* '46-58 tracks on Charly.

BOSTON USA hard rock band '70s formed by Tom Scholz (*b* 10 Mar. '47, Toledo, Ohio), guitar, keyboards, vocals. Masters graduate of MIT played nights in Boston bar bands, worked days as senior product designer for Polaroid, dabbled in home recording; result (later bootlegged as *We Found It In The Trashcan, Honest*) secured contract with Epic, who promoted band lineup with slogan 'Better music through science'. Sidemen all good enough to gild the lily: Bradley Delp (*b* 12 June '51), vocals; Sib Hashian (*b* 17 Aug. '47), drums; Barry Goudreau (29 Nov. '51), guitar; Fran Sheehan (*b* 26 Mar. '49), bass; all from Boston. First LP *Boston* (on which Hashian's predecessor Jim Masdea also appeared) was remake of demos, fastest selling debut in pop history: entered US charts 25 Sep. '76, ended up no. 3 incl. top 40 singles '77: 'More Than A Feeling' (no. 5), 'Long Time' (no. 22), 'Peace Of Mind' (no. 38), identified by ringing harmonies, twin lead guitars, classy prod. by John Boylan: ideal driving music for US male's in-car cassette deck. In UK LP made no. 11, 'Feeling' no. 22 (regarded as heavy metal classic, LP recharted to no. 58 on budget reissue '81). Band having vaulted from bars to stadiums found success hard to follow: less inspired sequel optimistically titled *Don't Look Back* '78 sold 3.5m to debut's 7.5m. Title track no. 4 USA; 'Man I'll Never Be' no. 31. After a tour all except Sheehan sessioned for Sammy HAGAR; Goudreau made epony-

mous solo LP for Portrait, formed pomp-rockers Orion The Hunter (eponymous LP '84); Scholz spent early '80s working on Rockman, device for obtaining overdriven guitar sound at low volumes for home recording. Seen as a Polaroid band: instant short-lived success; then *Third Stage* '86 on MCA was surprise hit LP, with no. 1 single 'Amanda', Delp still on board, Masdea returning on drums, Scholz doing most of the rest.

BOSWELL, Connie (*b* '07; *d* Oct. '76 NYC) Later Connee. Singer; with sisters Helvetia ('Vet'; *d* '88) and Martha (*d* '58), vocal trio from New Orleans; anticipated ANDREWS SISTERS, McGUIRE SISTERS, other white girl groups. Boswell sisters had middle-class background, grew up listening to blues, spirituals and opera (Connie gave Caruso credit for inspiring breath control); they also played several instruments. Connie did vocal arr. for trio; a victim of polio, she worked in wheelchair. They won local talent show; signed with Victor and made acoustic sides '25: a Connie solo and a trio side were released, but Vet was too young and the act was a duo at first. It was five years before they recorded again, but the record led to vaudeville work, West Coast radio show; played Paramount Theatre NYC '31; then many records on Brunswick (18 tracks '32-4, mostly with the DORSEY Bros, on *You Oughta Be In Pictures* on Conifer), contract with CBS radio, appearance on first public TV transmission in USA; films incl. *The Big Broadcast* '32 (with song 'Crazy People'); *Moulin Rouge* '34; *Transatlantic Merry-go-round* '34 (with 'Rock And Roll'). Made overseas tours, UK '33, '35; recorded with Bing CROSBY, many fine white jazz musicians incl. top black band of Don REDMAN. Regulars '34-5 on Crosby radio show; to new Decca label '35; Martha and Vet retired '36. Connie carried on solo; appeared on Broadway; much radio work '30s, '40s; entertained troops during WWII; films incl. *Artists And Models* '37, *Kiss The Boys Goodbye* '41, *Syncopation* '42, *Swing Parade* '46, *Senior Prom* '59. She could swing, like many white New Orleans musicians; helped evolution from stiff pop singing of earlier years, infl. younger people incl. Ella FITZGERALD. Many records incl. sessions with AMBROSE '35, Bob CROSBY band '36, Ben POLLACK '37, Woody HERMAN '39-40; '37 date produced classic 'Basin Street Blues' duet with Bing; only chart hit was 'If I Give My Heart To You' (no. 20 USA '54). Albums incl. *Connie Boswell & The Original Memphis Five In Hi-Fi* (RCA, '56), with legendary jazz band re-created, led by Billy BUTTERFIELD; same period *Sings Irving Berlin* on Design label. Stopped touring in '50s; frequent TV work '60s, early '70s. Compilation albums on Biograph (USA), MCA (UK).

BOSWELL, Eve (*b* c.'29, Hungary) UK singer. From circus family, toured Europe before WWII; joined Boswell's Circus in S. Africa, married son of owner. Sang in Johannesburg for wounded servicemen, then theatre dates, records, radio; to UK '49, joining GERALDO replacing Doreen Lundy. Contract with Parlophone; first record 'Bewitched', '50. Toured UK theatres; first hit 'Sugarbush', S. African song; version competing with Frankie LAINE/Doris DAY duet. Royal Command Performance '53; series on radio Luxembourg '54; first nationally known singer to sign ATV contract '55, that year had major hit with 'Pickin' A Chicken', S. African winner of songwriting contest, with new words by Paddy Roberts. Song re-entered top 20 twice '56, year of debut album *Sugar And Spice*. More theatre work late '50s, 60s, incl. appearances on Scottish summer show *Five Past Eight*, then semi-retirement. Album *Sugar Bush 76* recorded '75 with arr. by Roland Shaw, also single.

BOWIE, David (*b* David Robert Jones, 8 Jan. '47, Brixton, South London) UK rock singer. Unrivalled success story of '70s; introduced theatrical aspect to pop, but always with substance; mercurial ability to chart trends escaped venom of punk rock movement '76-7; also the most successful of rock stars making separate acting careers. First influence was older step-brother Terry (later mentally ill, *d* '85), who introduced him to Beat poets, jazz, rock'n'roll or the '50s, also was subject of some songs ('All The Madmen', 'Bewlay Brothers', 'Aladdin Sane'). Began with sundry UK beat groups of '60s: King Bees, Manish Boys, Lower Third, The Buzz. Name changed '66 to avoid confusion with MONKEES' Davy Jones; 'Bowie' from Western knife; early

singles later collected on London/Deram LP *Images 1966-67*. Bit work on UK TV; spent time in Buddhist monastery, then Lindsay Kemp mime troupe '69; signed with Mercury: LP *Man Of Words, Man Of Music* contained first top 40 hit 'Space Oddity', inspired by Kubrick film *2001: A Space Odyssey*', coincided with Moon landing of '69. *The Man Who Sold The World* '70 incl. 'All The Madmen'; original sleeve had Bowie in drag, had to be changed in those far-off days. Seemed set as fresh-faced pop star like his friend Marc BOLAN, but serious influences discernable: Jacques BREL, VELVET UNDERGROUND (Anthony NEWLEY a vocal influence, e.g. 'The Laughing Gnome' '67, 'Ashes To Ashes' '80). LP *Hunky Dory* '71 featured players Mick RONSON, Rick Wakeman, incl. important theme 'Changes', tributes to mentors: 'Song For Bob Dylan', 'Andy Warhol', Velvet-ish swagger of 'Queen Bitch'; also 'Oh You Pretty Thing', UK hit for Peter Noone. Change of managers from Ken Pitt to Tony DeFries coincided with USA tour to promote second RCA LP *The Rise And Fall Of Ziggy Stardust And The Spiders From Mars* '72; RCA talked into lavish support of glam-rock monster/persona Stardust; it paid off: stage show a hit (D. A. Pennebaker film of the show released '83, with 2-disc set *Ziggy Stardust: The Motion Picture*); LP big seller, incl. 'Suffragette City', 'Rock'n'Roll Suicide', UK top 10 hit 'Starman'. Bowie, the only important star of glam-rock movement, characteristically threw away Ziggy before he got stale, at '73 London 'farewell' concert. '73 LP *Aladdin Sane* inevitably seemed to disappoint at the time; incl. hits 'Jean Genie' (about Jean Genet/IGGY POP), 'Drive-In Saturday', Bowie histrionics in 'Cracked Actor', 'Time'. *Pin Ups*, also '73, celebrated pop's lost innocence with covers of seminal hits of The WHO, THEM, YARDBIRDS, PINK FLOYD, The Merseys (whose '66 hit single 'Sorrow' was a hit again for Bowie). *Diamond Dogs* was rewritten from adaptation of Orwell's *1984*, thwarted by author's estate; result was patchy '74 LP incl. classic, sleazy 'Rebel, Rebel'. Became less extravagant in 'thin white duke' period; obligatory live 2-disc set now followed; *David Live* was '74 rush job, later disowned by its author. By now he was the biggest act of the era: always good copy, with ambiguous sexuality, tempestuous marriage to Angela Barnett ('70; son Zowie *b* '71), fashion metamorphoses; ideal '70s pop figurehead. Based in L.A. at this time; often appeared on USA TV; *Young Americans* '75 was beginning of 'Plastic Soul' phase; incl. hit title track, also 'Fame', co-written with John LENNON, who played on album. *Station To Station* was transitional; tracks incl. 'TVC15', 'Golden Years'. First substantial film role, as androgynous alien in Nic Roeg's *The Man Who Fell To Earth*, won praise '76; same year's return to UK controversial: he vehemently denied making fascist salute at Victoria Station. Period of reclusiveness in Berlin, collaborating with Brian ENO, Robert Fripp, ended with new leap into avant garde, with trio of electronic/synthesiser LPs: *Low, Heroes* both '77, *Lodger* '79; songs like 'Sound & Vision', 'Warszawa', 'Heroes' helped to launch generation of often imitative synth bands: JOY DIVISION, HUMAN LEAGUE, ORCHESTRAL MANOEUVRES IN THE DARK, etc. He had always experimented, diversified; e.g. in producing LPs for others: Iggy Pop's *Raw Power* '72, *Lust For Life* '77; Lou REED's *Transformer* '72; MOTT THE HOOPLE's *All The Young Dudes* '72. One-off single with QUEEN 'Under Pressure' was no. 1 UK hit '82; did lyrics, vocal for title theme (composed by Giorgio Moroder) for '82 remake of classic horror film *Cat People*; also score for *Christiane F.*, film about young heroin addict (appeared in it '81). 'This Is Not America' recorded by Pat METHENY with Bowie vocal for film *The Falcon & The Snowman*, '85. In his own work, LP *Lodger*, film *Just A Gigolo* were '79 low points, but new decade saw revitalisation: single 'Ashes To Ashes' '80 revived character of Major Tom from 'Space Oddity' for worldwide no. 1; eclectic LP *Scary Monsters (And Super Creeps)* well received that year, as was long Broadway run in play *The Elephant Man*. Starred in Bertolt Brecht play *Baal* on BBC TV '82; had duet Xmas hit with Bing CROSBY, 'The Little Drummer Boy'. RCA contract expired; old recordings savaged for 'new' LPs; in '83 signed with EMI for huge sum, proved value with hit LP *Let's Dance*, incl. four hit singles. Serious Moonlight, first Bowie tour for six years, seen by over two million fans; best film to date rounded off good year:

Merry Christmas Mr Lawrence. Tonight '84, despite guest Tina TURNER, was lacklustre LP with dodgy covers (BEACH BOYS' 'God Only Knows'), but also addition to Bowie canon 'Blue Jean'; *Never Let Me Down* '87 featured guitar of Peter FRAMPTON, was regarded by critics as tired comeback; Bowie acknowledged that PRINCE was logical successor in '80s. Meanwhile duet with Mick Jagger from Live Aid concert 'Dancing In The Streets' released by popular demand '85: instant megahit. Bowie appeared in films *Absolute Beginners* (contributed theme), *Labyrinth* '86 (five new songs incl. top 20 'Underground'); also prod. new Iggy Pop LP. Glass Spider tour '87 incl. Frampton. He rang the changes for nearly 20 years, didn't sell all that many records in his best years; ironically now that he has run out of new images, superstar status guarantees sales. *ChangesoneBowie* '76 and *ChangestwoBowie* '81 are RCA compilations of '70s material; *On Stage* '78 was orthodox tour souvenir; *Rare Bowie* '82 an imaginative compilation. Among many books: Murray and Carr's *David Bowie: An Illustrated Record*; Cann's *David Bowie: A Chronology*; *Stardust: The Life And Times Of David Bowie* '86 by Henry Edwards and Tony Zanetta (ex-President of MainMan, company that managed Bowie for some years).

BOWIE, Lester (*b* 11 Oct. '41, Frederick, Md.) Trumpet, flugelhorn, composer. Worked with R&B bands, with wife Fontella BASS; became founder member of AACM and of ART ENSEMBLE OF CHICAGO. LP under his name *Numbers 1&2* '67 on Nessa was first Art Ensemble LP. To Europe with them '69; wrote and recorded *Gettin' To Know Y'all* on MPS: Baden Baden Free Jazz Orchestra was international 50-piece all-star band incl. Kenny WHEELER, Albert MANGELSDORFF, Jarman, Mitchell. With humour, full dark tone, smears and growls, he is called the 'Cootie WILLIAMS of the avant garde'; describes himself as a 'research trumpet player'. 'Jazz Death?' on *Congliptuous* (Roscoe MITCHELL Art Ensemble, '68) gives solo answer to question 'Is jazz as we know it dead, yet?' Own LPs also incl. *Fast Last* '74, with Julius HEMPHILL, Cecil McBEE, Phillip Wilson, others, and *Rope-A-Dope* '75 incl. Favors, Don Moye, both on Muse; also *Fifth*

143

Power '78 on Black Saint with Arthur BLYTHE; *Duet* '78 with Wilson on Improvising Artists; *The Great Pretender* '81 on ECM with Wilson and others marks affectionate strides deeper into repertory: 16-minute title cut with Hamiet BLUIETT's baritone sax, Bass and Davis Peaston on back-up vocals, is treatment of old PLATTERS hit, album also incl. theme from 'Howdy Doody' ('50s kiddie TV puppet show), Bowie comps. 'Rose Drop', 'Rios Negroes', 'Oh, How The Ghost Sings'. *All The Magic* '82 is 2-disc set with Wilson, Bass, Peaston, others on one disc, solo trumpet on the other; Lester Bowie and his Brass Fantasy made *I Only Have Eyes For You* '85, *Avant Pop* '86 on ECM, *Twilight Dream* '87 on Venture. Guest spots on others' LPs, e.g. with Jack DEJOHNETTE on *New Directions* '78. Brother Joseph Bowie plays trombone on *Fast Last*, *Rope-A-Dope*, Frank LOWE LP *The Flam* '76, etc.; he was founder member of St Louis Black Artists Group (BAG), mus. dir. for Bass; own LPs incl. *In Concert* '76 on Sackville (duets with Oliver LAKE), *I Can't Figure Out* (Watcha Doin' To Me) '79, made in Paris with Luther Thomas Saint Louis Creative Ensemble. Another brother, saxist Byron, was also mus. dir. for Bass.

BOWLER, Phillip (*b* 2 Mar. '48) Bassist. Degree from U. of Hartford (Conn.) '71; with Roland Kirk '76; first LP with him '78: *Boogie Woogie String Along For Real* (Atlantic). With Hugh MASEKELA '80; singer Joe Lee Wilson '81; Wynton MARSALIS '82-3; played on Grammy-winning Marsalis LP *Think Of One*, worked with Slide HAMPTON, recorded *Big And Warm* with Big Nick Nicholas, all in '83. Went freelance late '83, now a rising star. Has played in eight countries on TV; also major jazz festivals; at Ronnie SCOTT's in London and Continental tour with Benny GOLSON quartet, '85. Also leads own groups and teaches privately. Admires Ron CARTER (to the point of feeling that the next Marsalis LP, with Carter, should have won Grammy instead!). Playing has big tone, personality, imaginative use of bow reminiscent of Cecil McBEE's. Fine solo at Scott's on Golson's 'Caribbean Runabout', others.

BOWLLY, Al (*b* 7 Jan. 1898, Lourenço Marques, now Maputo, Mozambique; *d* 17 Apr. 41, London) Singer. Greek father, Lebanese mother; brought up in Johannesburg. Became barber, learned to play ukelele. He toured Africa, India and Java as banjo/guitarist; became resident vocalist with Jimmy Laquime band at Raffles in Singapore. Made first records in Berlin '27, then freelance in London, making 678 sides '30-3, mainly with Roy Fox and Ray NOBLE. Best-known records are Noble comps: 'The Very Thought Of You' ('34) and others also did well in USA; Noble took Bowlly with him to NYC '34, where Glenn MILLER was Noble's arranger; Bowlly sang an early lyric to a Miller tune that later became 'Moonlight Serenade'. Worked at New York's Rainbow Room, had own NBC radio show with Al GOODMAN. Returned to England Jan. '37; headed own Radio City Rhythm Makers on four-week tour; many more records; teamed with Maltese singer Jimmy Messini in Radio Stars With Two Guitars; worked with West Indian bandleader Ken 'Snakehips' Johnson at Café de Paris '40-1. A famous bomb hit café killing Johnson and many others, 8 March; Bowlly was killed by another a few weeks later. Still a much-loved voice, in the UK top 10 LP chart '78 as predominant singer on the *Pennies From Heaven* soundtrack LP. Biography *Al Bowlly* by Sid Colin and Tony Stavacre. Compilation LPs in EMI (UK) Retrospective series, i.e. *Sweet As A Song*, several others; 'The Very Thought Of You' is on *Ray Noble Plays Ray Noble*; also *Al Bowlly With Ray Noble 1931-34* on BBC Records, digitally remastered.

BOWMAN, Don (*b* 26 Aug. '37, Lubbock, Texas) Country comic. Radio DJ in Texas, San Francisco, Minneapolis, Nashville; signed to RCA '63. Hits incl. 'Chit Atkins Make Me A Star' '64, 'Giddyup Do-Nut' '66, 'For Loving You' '68 (duet with Skeeter DAVIS), 'Poor Old Ugly Gladys Jones' '69. Named Best Country Comedian by Billboard '66; albums incl. *Support Your Local Prison* '67, *Best Of Country Comedy* '68, *Whispering Country* '70 (a 'tribute' to Bill ANDERSON), *The All New* '71 (on Mega). Made films *Hillbillies In A Haunted House*, *Hillbillies In Las Vegas* '67-8; on Anderson TV show '68. Comeback on Willy NELSON's Lone Star label: single 'Still Fighting Mental Health', LP *Willon And Waylee* '79.

BOW WOW WOW UK post-punk pop group formed '80. Original lineup: Annabella Lwin (*b* Myant Myant Aye, '66, Rangoon, Burma), vocals; David Barbarossa (*b* '61, Maritius, aka Barbe), drums; Matthew Ashman (*b* '62, London), guitar; Leigh Gorman (*b* '61), bass. Protégés of Malcolm McLaren, who advised Adam ANT's backing group (Ashman, Barbarossa, Gorman) to leave him (Adam became very successful with new Ants). May have intended them to back him, but in event did not start own singing career until later; discovered Annabella singing in dry-cleaning shop, invited her (against mother's wishes) to front group. Typically outrageous McLaren behaviour continued with first single 'C30, C60, C90, Go!' issued only on cassette, recommending obliquely that illegally taping music off the air for playing in personal cassette machines was the future of pop music: predicted London full of teenagers on roller skates with headphones, but also that paedophile sex would become prevalent, which was even less acceptable (Annabella posed nude on record cover at 15). Single made top 40 UK when issued on disc, followed late '80 by *Your Cassette Pet*, cassette EP with eight tracks, made no. 58 on singles chart. After another minor hit on EMI (embarrassed at vaguely promoting cassette revolution when record companies were blaming falling sales on cassettes), group moved to RCA for debut album *See Jungle! See Jungle! Go Join Your Gang, Yeah, City All Over! Go Ape Crazy!*, which made LP chart. Had minor hits '81; early '82 saw 'Wild In The Country' in top 10; success repeated June with remake of Strangeloves' 'I Want Candy'; deal then made allowing issue of EMI LP *I Want Candy*: reached LP chart that summer with RCA title track and old EMI stuff, while RCA issued single 'Louis Quatorze' from EMI cassette. Public got bored despite this ingenuity and Annabela's nubile charms; McLaren tried to control her behaviour by introducing then unknown BOY GEORGE (later led Culture Club) as potential replacement, then dissociated himself from group, which recorded through '83 attracting less and less attention. LPs on RCA in USA: *Wild In The Country, I Want Candy, Last Of The Mohicans, When The Going Gets Tough*; also compilation *12 Original Record-*

ings on Harvest (an EMI label). Annabella left (re-emerged '85 solo); group changed name to Chiefs Of Relief. Band's music was acceptable pop; briefly new sound for UK in using Burundi drumming, like Gary GLITTER, Adam's Ants.

BOXCAR WILLIE (*b* Lecil Travis Martin, 1 Sep. '31, Sterratt, Texas) Country singer who finally hit it big almost 50 years old, aka 'Boxie'. Began semi-pro early '50s as Marty Martin, with day jobs as salesman, mechanic, in bowling alley; became pilot in USAF, then back to music late '60s, adopted hobo guise and new name playing small clubs mid-'70s. Spotted by Scottish promoter Drew Taylor at Possom Hollow club, Nashville '77; booked to tour Scotland; four more tours and '77 appearance at Wembley Festival '79 made overnight star of unknown with train whistle sound. Repertoire based on music of idols Jimmie RODGERS, Hank WILLIAMS, Lefty FRIZZELL; has also written more than 400 songs in trad. style. Breakthrough in USA on Grand Ole Opry; chart single 'Not The Man I Used To Be' '83. LPs incl. *King Of The Road* (Warwick and Spartan), *Boxcar Willie, Daddy Was A Railroad Man, Sings Hank Williams And Jimmy Rodgers, Take Me Home* all '80; *20 Greatest Hits* '81 (all on Big R label, UK); *Good Ol' Country Songs* '82 (K-tel, UK); *Not The Man I Used To Be, Last Train To Heaven* '85 (on Sparton).

BOX TOPS, The White soul group '60s, first called The De Villes. Lineup: Alex Chilton (*b* 28 Dec. '50, Memphis, Tenn.), vocals, guitar; Billy Cunningham (*b* 23 Jan. '50, Memphis), bass; Gary Talley (*b* 17 Aug. '47), guitar; Danny Smythe, drums; John Evans, organ. Signed with songwriting/prod. team Dan Penn and Spooner Oldham, first single 'The Letter' no. 1 USA, written by unknown Wayne Carson Thompson. Follow-up 'Neon Rainbow' flopped by comparison, but third 'Cry Like A Baby', with psychedelic guitar, blue-eyed soul vocal from Chilton made no. 2. Known as Memphis's answer to NYC's Young RASCALS, Box Tops became purely studio creation; Smythe, Evans replaced after second single by Tom Boggs (*b* 16 July '47, Wynn, Ark.) and Rick Allen (*b* 28 Jan. '46, Little Rock), but Chilton often the only band member invited to participate in studio. LPs *The Letter – Neon Rainbow, Cry Like A Baby* (both '68) incl. padding with hits. By late '68 Penn/Oldham had passed prod. duties to Tommy Cogbill and Chips Moman; maintained sporadic presence in top 40 '68-9 ('Choo-Choo Train' no. 26, 'I Met Her In Church' 37, novelty 'Sweet Cream Ladies, Forward March' 28) but recaptured original flavour with another Thompson song 'Soul Deep', no. 18 late '69 and their last big hit (later revived by Gary US BONDS); LP *Dimensions* showed ideas still limited. Chilton quit in mid-performance early '70, unable to take pressure (he had been only 16 at time of first million-seller); group built around his voice disintegrated. He played NYC folk circuit for a year; back in Memphis formed Big Star with Chris Bell (*b* 12 Jan. '51, Memphis; *d* '78 in car crash), guitar; Andy Hummel (*b* 26 Jan. '51, Memphis), bass; Jody Stephens (*b* 4 Oct. '52), drums. Sound heavily infl. by British Invasion; LPs *No. 1 Record* '72 (after which Bell left), *Radio City* '74 got critical praise, but poor sales, collapse of distributor Stax caused disillusion, split before release of third LP. Chilton has recorded, gigged sporadically, sometimes with garage band Panther Burns, also prod. Cramps' first records; despite talent never matched success of 'The Letter' (since covered by Joe COCKER, D-Notice, etc.): two gold discs in first three is a hard act to follow. Chilton compilation on Aura '85.

BOYCE, Tommy, & Bobby Hart USA songwriting team, Boyce (*b* '44, Charlottesville, Va.) and Hart (*b* '44, Phoenix, Ariz.) Provided two '61 hits for Curtis Lee (*b* 28 Oct. '41, Yuma, Ariz.), spotted in Tucson nightclub by Ray Peterson, owner of the Dunes label: 'Pretty Little Angel Eyes' and 'Under The Moon Of Love' were his only hits, both revived by SHOWADDY-WADDY in UK for huge sales late '70s. Boyce & Hart had no. 3 USA hit with JAY AND THE AMERICANS ('Come A Little Bit Closer', '64), wrote for Don Kirshner's Screen Gems (*see* BUBBLEGUM), linked with MONKEES: 'Last Train To Clarksville' was no. 1 '66 (hyped by TV show, ad campaign). Other hits followed, but Monkees threatened to write/prod. themselves, Boyce &

Hart stepped out and became recording duo. LP *Test Patterns* and three top 40 singles on A&M: 'Out And About', 'I Wonder What She's Doing Tonite', 'Alice Long (You're Still My Favorite Girlfriend)' '67-8. But their prolific work outstripped customers: three albums in '68 – *I Wonder What She's Doing Tonite, Which One's Boyce And Which One's Hart?, It's All Happening On The Inside* – were released while progressive rock was overtaking street-smart pop; duo retired to clubs for a while. Monkee Mike NESMITH called 'Valleri' (no. 3 '68) 'the worst record I've ever heard in my life'; Mickey Dolenz and Davy Jones disagreed, went on the road with Boyce & Hart to present a Golden Greats of the Monkees show five years after group split, made LP *Jones Dolenz Boyce & Hart* '76 for Capitol. Boyce then relocated in UK (as coincidentally did Dolenz), with Richard Hartley in new team, prod. LPs for UK doo-wop revivalists DARTS and others, branching into heavier rock with IGGY POP (*Party* '81) and MEATLOAF. *Rolling Stone* claimed Boyce & Hart's 300 plus songs sold over 42 million records.

BOYD, Bill (*b* 29 Sep. '10, Fannin County, Texas) Singer, bandleader. Formed group with younger brother Jim called Alexander's Day Breakers '25, based Greenville, Texas; changed name '28 to Bill Boyd's Cowboy Ramblers: daily radio show on WRR (Dallas) for about 30 years; more than 300 records for Bluebird '34-50 incl. 'The Strawberry Roan' '34, 'Spanish Fandango' '39, 'Lone Star Rag' '49, many instrumentals; biggest hit, '35 fiddle/guitar version of German march 'Under The Double Eagle', became a country classic. Jim also worked in other bands (Light Crust Doughboys); made western films, but should not be confused with actor William Boyd, who played Hopalong Cassidy. Compilation album in RCA Bluebird reissue series, deleted.

BOYD, Little Eddie (*b* Edward Riley Boyd, 25 Nov. '14, Stovall, Ms.) Blues singer, pianist, songwriter; also played guitar, kazoo, organ; aka Ernie Boyd. Raised on a plantation; ran away from home at 15 after sticking a pitchfork in a foreman who was threatening him. Began playing early '30s. Formed Dixie Rhythm Boys '37 Memphis;

to Chicago early '40s, playing with Johnny SHINES trio, Muddy WATERS (his cousin), others; recorded with Sonny Boy WILLIAMSON for RCA. When his first recordings failed he worked in a steel mill, saved money until he could produce his own: 'Five Long Years' was no. 1 R&B hit '52 on J.O.B., followed by hits '24 Hours', 'Third Degree' '53 on Chess. Own band at Flame Club '46-8, recorded for many labels, incl. Chess in '50s; wrote many songs. Toured Europe '65 (LP with Buddy GUY in London); toured Continent several times, with John MAYALL's Bluesbreakers '67; made LP *7936 South Rhodes* on Blue Horizon '68, settled in Paris. Recorded (often in concert) for Euro-labels Philips, Storyville, Blue Beat, etc. *Legacy Of The Blues Vol. 10* '75 on GNP/Sonet prod. by Sam Charters in Sweden with fine boogie band incl. Ed Thigpen on drums, Christer Eckland on tenor sax; 'Black Brown And White' is a sardonic, rocking commentary on the theme 'If you're white, you're all right; if you're brown, stick around; if you're black, get back.' Other albums: *And His Blues Band With Peter Green* on Cross Cut (Bear Family), *Lovers Playground* on Stockholm.

BOYD, Joe (*b* '43, Boston, Mass.) Producer. Part of New England folk and blues scene, early '60s; discovered Paul BUTTERFIELD Blues Band in Chicago, which led to their backing Bob DYLAN at controversial '65 Newport Folk Festival, of which Boyd was production manager. Ran London office of Elektra label; prod. LP *What's Shakin'* '66, incl. early performances by Eric CLAPTON, Stevie WINWOOD. Helped run premier London underground club UFO, showcasing early gigs by SOFT MACHINE, PINK FLOYD. Prod. first Floyd single 'Arnold Layne' '67, but then dropped: label insisted on using house producer Norman 'Hurricane' Smith. Prod. and managed FAIRPORT CONVENTION, INCREDIBLE STRING BAND, formed own Witchseason company, establishing him as underground svengali. Prod. all Fairport LPs until '70, Incredibles' best work; Nick DRAKE's only three albums; Sandy DENNY and her short-lived Fotheringay band. Prod. first film '72, documentary on life and works of Jimi HENDRIX. Formed own Hannibal Records late '70s; prod. Richard & Linda

THOMPSON's *Shoot Out The Lights* '82; Richard's *Hand Of Kindness* '83, *Across A Crowded Room* '85. In '80 prod. film about 2-Tone movement *Dance Crazy*, incl. performances from SPECIALS, MADNESS, etc. Staged S. African play *Poppie Nongena* '83, which transferred to the West End. As legendary figure of '60s, came back into favour in '80s: prod. LPs '85 for new bands REM, 10,000 Maniacs.

BOY GEORGE (*b* George Alan O'Dowd, '61, London) UK pop singer, songwriter, bandleader; trend-setting 'new romantic' in early '80s. Worked picking fruit, dressing windows, as model, as makeup artist for Royal Shakespeare Co.; almost joined BOW WOW WOW early '81; while leading group In Praise Of Lemmings met drummer Jon Moss (*b* 11 Sep. '57, London; ex-DAMNED, Adam ANT); both had links with Malcolm McLaren, but formed band Culture Club '81 free of his infl. with Mikey Craig (*b* Michael Emile Craig, 15 Feb. '60), Roy Hay (*b* Roy Ernest Hay, 12 Aug. '61). LPs, singles prod. by Steve Levine, massive hits '82-3: *Kissing To Be Clever* incl. 'Do You Really Want To Hurt Me' (white reggae, no. 1 UK), 'I'll Tumble 4 Ya'; Motown pastiche 'Time (Clock Of The Heart)' no. 3 '82 UK, no. 2 USA '83; *Colour By Numbers* incl. 'Church Of The Poison Mind', 'Karma Chameleon' (no. 1 USA/UK), 'Victims', 'It's A Miracle', 'Miss Me Blind'. Helen Terry sang with band (e.g. backup on 'Do You Really Want To Hurt Me'; also sang on Lou REED hit 'Walk On The Wild Side' '72), later went solo. George's image in frocks, makeup provocative at first; soon perceived as delight in dressing up: object was to have fun; eclectic music had wide appeal; even parents liked him, with his sense of humour, same persona offstage as on; group headed new British Invasion of USA (Moe BANDY, Joe Stampley had USA top 10 country hit 'Where's The Dress?', spoofing 'Karma'). Finally George was overexposed, musical cleverness seemed to flag: media backlash accompanied by slump in sales relying on image. *Waking Up With The House On Fire* '84 described as forgettable: made no. 26 in USA LP chart (compared to no. 2 for *Colour By Numbers*); single 'The War Song' made no. 2 UK/17 USA, but 'The Medal Song', 'Mistake No. 3' did not make top 20 anywhere. George forgot to shave for a while, then cut hair, confusing image; played '85 Athens European culture festival (promoter Greek Minister of Culture Melina Mercouri, actress best known for *Never On Sunday* '60): crowd threw bricks, bottles. Undaunted, George was an amusing talk-show guest, enjoyed band's popularity in France, USA sales of 7 million LPs: 'If that's not being successful, I don't know what is.' *From Luxury To Heartache* '86 prod. by Arif Mardin: silky modern soul with classy backup singing incl. single 'Move Away'. In mid-'86 his family revealed his heroin problem; musician friends Michael Rudetsky, then Mark Goldring were found dead: no blame attached to George, but 'new romantics' had got old quickly. He recovered; album *Sold* '87 was noticeably more mature, incl. songs by Lamont Dozier: he may be around for a while yet.

BRACKEEN, Joanne (*b* Joanne Grogan, 26 July '38, Ventura, Cal.) Piano, composer. Mostly self-taught. Began copying parents' Frankie CARLE records; then learned by copying solos of Charlie PARKER, Bud POWELL, later John COLTRANE, developing her own rhythmic complexity and an experimental approach to harmony. Worked through '60s with Dexter GORDON, Charles LLOYD, vibraphonist Freddie McCoy (recorded on Prestige), Woody SHAW, many others; joined Art BLAKEY '70-2 (while hearing Blakey in a club: the pianist got lost, Brackeen took over), Joe Henderson '72-5, Stan GETZ '75 (*Getz Gold* on Inner City); LP with Toots THIELEMANS *Captured Alive* '74 on Choice. Own LPs: *Snooze* '75 on Choice, with Cecil McBEE, Billy Hart; *Invitation* with Hart, Clint Houston on bass (*b* 24 June '46, New Orleans) and *New True Illusion* (duo with Houston made the next day), both '76, Holland; *Tring-A-Ling* '77 on Choice with Hart, McBee or Houston, Mike BRECKER on some tracks; *Aft* '77 on Timeless with Houston, Ryo Kawasaki on guitar; *Trinkets And Things* '78 on Timeless, duo with Kawasaki; *Prism* '78 on Choice, duo with Eddie Gomez; solo *Mythical Magic* '78 on MPS or Pausa. *Keyed In* '79 on Tappan Zee or CBS, *Ancient Dynasty* '80 on Columbia (with Henderson on tenor), *Special Identity* '81 on Antilles all with Gomez, Jack

DeJOHNETTE. *Inside The Plane Of The Elliptic* '79 under Houston's name is on Timeless; *Havin' Fun* '85 with McBee and Al Foster and *Fi-Fi Goes To Heaven* '87 on Concord Jazz, the latter her first with two horns: Terence BLANCHARD and Wynton MARSALIS. She also contributed 'Song For Helen' to 2-disc *A Tribute* to Bill EVANS '82 on Palo Alto. All LPs feature her own tunes (except *Havin' Fun*, standards). Married to saxophonist Charles Brackeen (works with Ronald Shannon Jackson), has four children; on the position of women in music she is pragmatic: 'If I want a bass player I want a player at Eddie Gomez's level. What woman can I call?' (quoted by Linda Dahl in *Stormy Weather*).

BRADDOCK, Bobby (*b* 5 Aug. '40, Lakeland, Fla.) Country songwriter. Played piano in various bands; to Nashville '64; with Marty ROBBINS '65-6, wrote his hit 'While You're Dancin'' '65. Signed to Tree Publishing '67, wrote hits 'Ruthless' (STATLER BROTHERS '67), 'D-I-V-O-R-C-E' (Tammy WYNETTE '68), 'Did You Ever' (Charlie LOUVIN & Melba MONTGOMERY '70), 'Golden Ring' (George JONES & Wynette '76), 'He Stopped Loving Her Today' (Jones '80), last named song of the year by ACM, CMA, Nashville Songwriters Association, also won a Grammy. Has also recorded for MGM '67-9 (country charts with 'I Know How To Do It', 'Girls In Country Music'), Elektra '79, RCA '81-5. Albums incl. *Love Bomb* '80 (Elektra), *Hardpore Cornography* '83 (RCA).

BRADFORD, Professor Alex (*b* Bessemer, Ala.) Gospel singer. Title 'professor' from early stint as schoolteacher. Son of ore miner; raised during Depression. Vaudeville debut age 4; took music lessons from pianist Martha Bell Hall; later infl. by The Blue Jays Quartet. Formed own group The Bradfordettes, then to NYC leading group the Bronx Gospelaires. In Army during WWII, sometimes singing blues at camp concerts; after war to Chicago, at various venues; early '50s toured with several groups, formed own all-male Bradford Specials, had '54 million-seller on Specialty 'Too Close To Heaven'. Toured worldwide, with Marion Williams presenting musical gospel play *Black Nativity* during '60s (participant Madeline BELL going on to become UK pop star). On Broadway early '70s with show *Don't Bother Me, I Can't Cope*. Helped launch stream of gospel-turned-pop stars such as Dionne and Dee Dee WARWICK, Judy Clay through association with The Greater Abyssinian Baptist Church of Newark, N.J. Hailed by gospel writer Tony Heilbut as 'Gospel's Little Richard'. LPs incl. *The Best Of Alex Bradford* (Specialty), *Black Nativity* (DJM).

BRADFORD, Bobby (*b* 19 July '34, Cleveland, Miss.) Cornet, trumpet, teacher, composer. Lived in Europe; later teaching in Cal. Played with Ornette COLEMAN (LPs *Science Fiction*, *Broken Shadows* '71), John CARTER, Quincy JONES; own LPs incl. *Flight For Four* '70, on Flying Dutchmen with Carter. *Bobby Bradford & John Stevens: Spontaneous Music Ensemble* '71 made in London with Trevor Watts (alto sax, *b* 26 Feb. '39, York), Ron Herman (bass), Julie Tippetts (vocals, guitar), drummer John STEVENS; session was partly issued on Black Lion, Freedom, etc.; now complete in two vols. on Nessa. *Love's Dream* '73 on Emanem, made in Paris with Stevens; *Lost In L.A.* '83, on Soul Note. Plays on albums by trombonist Michael Vlatkovich, composer Vinny Golia (3-disc limited edition *Compositions For Large Ensemble* '86). *See also* Carter entry.

BRADFORD, Perry (*b* 14 Feb. 1893, Montgomery, Ala.; *d* 20 Apr. '70, Queens, NY) Composer, piano, producer. Worked in minstrel shows '06, worked solo, first visit to NYC '10, toured theatres, began writing. Mus. dir. for Mamie SMITH; wrote and produced first blues record by a black artist: Mamie's 'Crazy Blues' ('21) huge hit for the time, established market for 'race' music. Toured with her, produced many sessions with Louis ARMSTRONG, James P. JOHNSON, etc. Got black artists on radio, started own publishing company; comps. incl. 'You Can't Keep A Good Man Down', 'Evil Blues'. Fell on hard times during the Depression. Bitter autobiography *Born With The Blues* '65.

BRADLEY, Harold (*b* 2 Jan. '26, Nashville) Studio guitar player. With Ernest TUBB band '43, then Eddy ARNOLD, Pee Wee

KING, Bradley KINCAID '46-8, with WSM radio group on Grand Ole Opry, Sunday Down South '48-50. Worked with brother Owen (see below) on sessions; own records for CBS '62-6, incl. LPs such as *Bossa Nova Goes To Nashville* '63, *Misty Guitar* '64, *Guitar For Lovers Only* '65. Mus. dir. Jimmy Dean TV show '65. Formed Forrest Hills Publishing Company '67; toured with Slim WHITMAN '84-5.

BRADLEY, Owen (*b* 21 Oct. '15, Westmoreland, Tenn.) Musician, record producer, studio owner; pioneer of recording in Nashville. Mus. dir. and pianist for WSM radio '40-58; asked by Decca to take over prod. chores: mus. dir. '47-58, A&R dir. '58-68. Prod. early recordings in Nashville by Red FOLEY, Ernest TUBB, Webb PIERCE, WILBURN BROTHERS. Had his first studio '52 in rooms rented from Teamsters' Union, moved when they raised the rent; built the famous Quonset hut '55, recorded Buddy HOLLY there '56; sold it to Columbia when he built studio on 16th Avenue South, now famous as Music Row; there prod. Brenda LEE, Gene VINCENT, Marty ROBBINS, Kitty WELLS, etc. With studio group Owen Bradley Quintet made USA country chart with 'Blues Stay Away From Me' '49; pop chart with 'White Silver Sands' '57, 'Big Guitar' '58. Billboard's Country Music Man of the Year '61. In '64 built studio Bradley's Barn; prod. Loretta LYNN, Bill ANDERSON, Conway TWITTY etc.; it burned down 20 Oct. '80. Elected to Country Music Hall of Fame '74. *Big Guitar* LP on Charly UK '84. Son Jerry (*b* 30 Jan. '40) also in music: began as publisher with Forrest Hills Music, discovered Gary STEWART; later executive prod. at RCA, head of Nashville operations '75 to present.

BRADLEY, Will (*b* Wilbur Schwichtenberg, 12 July '12, Newton, N.J.) Trombone, leader, composer. To NYC '28; met Ray McKINLEY in Milt Shaw's Detroiters (Roseland Ballroom house band); with Red NICHOLS; CBS staff '31-4; with Ray NOBLE '35-6, then more radio work. Approached by booking agent Willard Alexander, formed own band actually co-led by McKinley '39-42; changed name because 'Schwichtenberg' wouldn't fit on marquee. Unusually polished white jazz-oriented dance band, with Peanuts Hucko, Freddie SLACK; records incl. theme 'Strange Cargo', 'Celery Stalks At Midnight'; got bogged down in boogie-woogie fad. Fluke hit 'Beat Me Daddy, Eight To The Bar' no. 2 in pop chart '40, followed by 'Down The Road A Piece' (trio only; piano, bass and drums), then the more tendentious 'Scrub Me, Mama, With A Boogie Beat', 'Bounce Me, Brother, With A Solid Four', 'Fry Me, Cookie, With A Can Of Lard . . .' Bradley was annoyed. Band made wartime records with pickup personnel; he then returned to radio and TV work, composition. Played on Benny GOODMAN set *B.G. in HI-FI* '55.

BRADSHAW, Tiny (*b* Myron Bradshaw, '05, Youngstown, Ohio; *d* Dec. '58, Cincinnati) Singer, drummer, pianist. Majored in psychology at university; sang with Horace HENDERSON's Collegians, Luis RUSSELL; own band, recording contract '34. Switched from Big Band style to R&B mid-'40s; employed such young stars as Sonny STITT, Charlie Fowlkes (1916-80; later with BASIE for many years on baritone sax). Led band until suffered strokes in '50s, incl. USO tour of Japan late '45. Hits in '40s, usually incl. raunchy sax by Red (Wilbert) Prysock, Sil AUSTIN, etc. three top tens in R&B chart '50-3: 'Well, Oh Well', 'I'm Going To Have Myself A Ball', 'Soft'. Once cited as Buddy HOLLY's favourite. Compilation *Breaking Up The House* on Charly UK.

BRADY, Paul (*b* Paul Joseph Brady, 19 May '47, Strabane, Co. Tyrone, N. Ireland) Singer, multi-instrumentalist, songwriter. While still attending school, played piano on summer holidays in Donegal, accompanying patrons; then on rock circuit with Dublin-based groups the Kult and Rockhouse (which he calls his 'formative period'). Member of the Johnstons folk group until '72; lived in USA '72-3 (first of three stays there); joined PLANXTY '74 replacing Christy MOORE: although he did not record with them, this was regarded as one of their best lineups. *Andy Irvine/Paul Brady* '76 on Mulligan showcased Planxty-period repertoire impressively, incl. 'Arthur McBride', 'Lough Erne Shore', 'The Jolly Soldier'. Considerable reputation as interpreter of trad. material culminated in *Welcome Here Kind Stranger* on Mulligan, unquestionably a brilliant folk album, voted best of the year by *Melody Maker* '78: incl. 'Lakes Of Pontchartrain' (derived from Moore's version, itself from Mike Waterson's), which became closely identified with Brady. Sessioned on Kevin Burke's *If The Cap Fits*, *Matt Molloy Paul Brady Tommy Peoples*, Peoples' *High Part Of The Road*, *Andy McGann & Paul Brady* and Irvine's *Rainy Sundays . . . Windy Dreams*. At this point he felt he had 'exhausted all the possibilities of interpreting traditional music'; this was premature, but he was now writing songs himself. He scored an anthology of Sean O'Casey's writings called *The Green Crow Caws* '80 on EMI for various instruments, attracting little publicity; on the strength of demos made early '80, WEA offered him a singles deal and 'Crazy Dreams'/'Busted Loose' was no. 1 in Eire later that year; *Hard Station* '81 was an accomplished debut, incl. new versions of the single, 'Night Hunting Time' (covered by SANTANA on *Shango* '82), and the vehement 'Nothing But The Same Old Story', specifically about British attitudes to the Irish but applicable to the majority's treatment of a minority of whatever persuasion. He opened concerts for DIRE STRAITS and Eric CLAPTON; *True For You* '83 on 21 Records shifted its approach slightly towards radio play and Tina TURNER covered its 'Steel Claw' on her LP *Private Dancer* '84 at the suggestion of Mark Knopfler, with whom Brady collaborated on soundtrack to film *Cal* '84 (LP on Phonogram); Dave EDMUNDS also covered 'Claw'. *Full Moon* '84 on Demon was a live LP, *Back To The Centre* '86 on Phonogram a polished collection of songs, with 'The Island' standing out. He contributed trad. 'Green Fields Of Canada' to *Feed The Folk* '85 on Temple, folk's contribution to Band Aid; wrote 'Paradise Is Here' especially for Turner (on *Break Every Rule* '86); and Bob DYLAN named him as one of five favourite performers in the notes to *Biograph* '85.

BRAFF, Ruby (*b* Reuben Braff, 16 Mar. '27, Boston, Mass.) Trumpet, then mostly cornet from '67. Highly rated for swing, tone, ideas, technique, but came to prominence playing mainstream style in 'modern' jazz heyday: did not become the star he deserved to be, but is now making up for lost time.

Playing, acting role in Rodgers & Hammerstein musical *Pipe Dream* '55-6, then mostly out of work for years. Solos on Benny GOODMAN LP *B.G. in HI-FI* '55; other LPs in and out of print incl. two 10" LPs on Bethlehem '54-5 (reissued on Affinity as *The Mighty Braff*), *Buck Meets Ruby* on Vanguard with Buck CLAYTON; others on Vanguard incl. duet LPs with Ellis Larkins on piano, and a session with Vic DICKENSON, Sam Margolis (*b* 1 Nov. '23, Dorchester, Mass.) on tenor, Nat PIERCE, Walter PAGE, Jo JONES, all '55; *Ruby Braff And The Dixie-Victors* '56 on RCA; '56-7 sessions on Epic, RCA; *Easy Now* '58 on RCA; on WB, Stereocraft and UA '58-9, UA again '61, then a gap till '67, switch to cornet: *Hear Me Talkin'* on Polydor, Black Lion; *On Sunnie's Side Of The Street* '68 live at Sunnie's Rendezvous, Aspen, Colorado, with Mousey Alexander, drums; Milt HINTON, bass; Ralph SUTTON, piano. *Swing That Music* '69 with Red NORVO; on Chiaroscuro: *And Ellis Larkins – The Grand Reunion* '72 (duets), *And His International Jazz Quartet* '73, *Ruby Braff-George Barnes Quartet* '73, *Live At The New School* '74, *Fats Waller's Heavenly Jive* with Dick HYMAN '76; on RCA: *To Fred Astaire With Love* '75; on Concord: *Braff-Barnes Quartet Plays Gershwin, Salutes Rodgers & Hart* '74; *With Ed Bickert Trio* '79 on Sackville; on Concord again: duet *America The Beautiful* (with Hyman on pipe organ), then sextets *A Fine Match* '85, *A Sailboat In The Moonlight* '86; also quintet (no drums) *Mr Braff To You* '86 on Phontastic, last three with Scott HAMILTON. Also *Them There Eyes* '76 and *Pretties* '78 made in NYC for Sonet; *Swinging On A Star – Braff Plays Bing* '78 live at London's Pizza Express.

BRAGG, Billy (*b* 20 Dec. '58, Barking, Essex) Singer/songwriter, guitar. Heard the CLASH, served spell with punk band Riff Raff '78, hit the road with guitar and amplifier, supporting everybody '83-4 from Richard THOMPSON to Dave Gilmour. Dubbed 'one man Clash'; 7-track mini album *Life's A Riot With Spy Vs Spy* drew attention to pungent, topical material, staccato guitar; further songs: 'The Milkman Of Human Kindness', 'A New England' (hit for Kirsty MacColl '85), 'Man In The Iron Mask'. Second album *Brewing Up* had 14

passionate tracks incl. 'St Swithins Day' and 'Island Of No Return', comment on Falklands war. Bragg is dismissive of folk clubs ('They wish it was 1960, er, ideally 1860!') but because of his solo nature is championed by farsighted folkies, and is part of '80s folk mini-revival; throughout UK miners' strike '84-5 did benefit concerts, went on the road with Labour MPs 'Jobs For Youth' tour; Labour party leader Neil Kinnock (life member of Gene VINCENT fan club) climbed aboard. EP *Between The Wars* was surprise chart hit April '85, with title cut, Leon Rosselson's 'World Turned Upside Down' and the old strikers' anthem 'Which Side Are You On?'. Miners' strike ignominiously lost; Bragg went on to be moving force behind Red Wedge tour '86, with Tom ROBINSON, Paul Weller; hit single 'Levi Stubbs' Tears' was incl. in LP *Talking With The Taxman About Poetry* '86; he contributed to anti-apartheid LP *Not Just Mandela* '86.

BRAMLETT, Delaney & Bonnie Delaney (*b* 1 July '39, Randolph, Miss.), Bonnie (*b* Bonnie Lynn, 8 Nov. '44, Acton, Ill.) met, married in L.A. '67. He had been resident member of TV's *Shindig* cast; she was backing vocalist for Fontella BASS, Albert KING, first white member of Ike & Tina TURNER's Ikettes. Early LP on Stax backed by BOOKER T AND THE MGs '68 not released at the time; formed fluctuating group of backing musicians to further aspirations, incl. Leon RUSSELL, keyboards; Carl Radle, bass; Duane ALLMAN, Dave Mason, J. J. CALE, guitars; reputation as hottest act around led to signing with Elektra, LP *Accept No Substitute: The Original Delaney & Bonnie* '69. By this time group called Delaney & Bonnie & Friends, incl. Jim Keltner, drums; Bobby Whitlock, keyboards; Jim Price, Bobby Keys, horns; Rita COOLIDGE, backing vocals: fusion of country, gospel, rock in blue-eyed soul was new at the time. Support on BLIND FAITH USA tour '69 gained patronage of Eric CLAPTON, who set up European tour, joined Friends after Blind Faith split. George HARRISON also guested, issued *Substitute* on Apple in UK to coincide with tour; live LP *On Tour (With Eric Clapton)* made USA top 30; much was expected, but after guesting with John LENNON's Plastic Ono Band, plans for

151

headlining USA tour collapsed: lost Clapton, then Joe COCKER poached Friends for his tour as Mad Dogs and Englishmen. Duo never recovered momentum. Delaney prod. Clapton's debut solo LP '70; *To Delaney From Bonnie* had LITTLE RICHARD guesting on 'Miss Ann'; but this and following LPs never approached excitement of debut. Despite two hit singles in USA '71, 'Never Ending Song Of Love' (no. 13), 'Only You Know And I Know' (no. 20), partnership on wane in both senses. Marriage dissolved '72; Bonnie recorded on Capricorn, became born-again Christian '80, sang gospel; Delaney switched labels through '70s with no real success, despite recruiting Clapton, Harrison and others for *Delaney And Friends: Class Reunion* '77. Critical favourites never found audience; Elektra's failure to promote '69 album properly didn't help.

BRAND, Oscar (*b* 7 Feb. '20, Winnipeg, Manitoba) Folksinger, broadcaster. To NYC; attended Brooklyn College; was section chief of psychology unit in US Army during WWII. Became coordinator of folk music '45 for municipal station WNYC; one of the first revivalists to mix new and trad. songs. He was suspicious of the Communist Party's interest in folk music and made a speech '51 which cost him credibility on the folk scene, refused to testify before the House Un-American Activities Committee and was not subpoenaed. Best known to the man in the street for bawdy songs: 11 LPs on Audio Fidelity in '50s incl. five vols. of *Bawdy Songs And Backroom Ballads*, plus *Bawdy Western Songs*, *College Songs*, *Sea Songs* etc.; others on Elektra, Riverside, Caedmon, ABC, Roulette. Also children's songs (*Come To The Party* for Children's Record Guild), *The Americans* on Pickwick with Kate SMITH, Stephen FOSTER songs on Caedmon with Judy COLLINS, nearly 80 LPs in all. More media work than any other folk artist: credits in 75 films, hundreds of TV appearances, mus. dir. of NBC-TV *Sunday Show*, advisor to panel that created *Sesame Street*, four years as host of Canadian series *Let's Sing Out*, has done weekly *Folksong Festival* on WNYC for 40 years. Curator of songwriters Hall of Fame Museum NYC; has compiled 10 books and manuals of music; has written songs for Ella

FITZGERALD, Doris DAY, Harry BELAFONTE, the Smothers Brothers and the Mormon Tabernacle Choir. Scores for ballet and plays incl. Kennedy Center's Bicentennial musical *Sing America Sing*.

BRANIGAN, Laura (*b* 3 July '57, Brewster, NY) USA singer. Educated at NY's Academy of Dramatic Arts; first break was selection from among 600 as backing singer for Leonard COHEN '77. Club success NYC early '80s led to contract with Atlantic. Albums prod. by Jack White, beginning with *Branigan* '82: in album charts for a year; incl. strident no. 1 USA/6 UK hit 'Gloria' (one of the longest-running singles of decade in USA, Grammy nomination for best pop vocal): English translation of Eurohit by Umberto Tozzi brought big gay following as part of Hi-NRG disco movement, aided by vocal likeness to Donna SUMMER. *Branigan 2* '83 saw diversification of material, incl. the WHO's 'Squeeze Box', no. 7 USA hit 'Solitaire', no. 12 'How Am I Supposed To Live Without You'. Third LP *Self Control* '84 incl. hit title track (no. 4 USA/5 UK): another Eurohit cover, this time of RAF (both in German charts, Branigan no. 1, RAF no. 2): backing was cliché-Eurodisco, but erotic video prod. by William (*Exorcist*) Friedkin aroused interest. LP also incl. US no. 20 'The Lucky One' (from TV programme *An Uncommon Love*), another Tozzi Eurohit from '70s 'Ti Amo'. Friedkin connection led to further collaboration on his film *Live And Let Die In LA*; she was also seen on TV's *Hill Street Blues*, played mud wrestler in *Mugsy's Girl*, sang theme song for *Octopussy*; did 'Hot Night' for *Ghostbusters* soundtrack. Fourth LP *Hold Me* '85. Unlikely to surpass initial success.

BRASS MONKEY UK folk band formed early '81. Original lineup: Martin CARTHY and John Kirkpatrick, both singers and multi-instrumentalists; Howard Evans (*b* 29 Feb. '44, Chard, Somerset) on trumpet; Roger Williams (*b* July '54, Cottingham, Yorks.), Martin Brinsford (*b* 17 Aug. '44, Gloucester), percussion, harmonica, saxophone. Five-piece group grew out of earlier trio, work at London's National Theatre and other antecedents going back to mid-'70s. Carthy and Kirkpatrick were well-established folk performers, Evans and Williams were sought-after theatre and classical brass musicians and Brinsford had played in various folk dance bands, notably The Old Swan band. For several months in '81 Kirkpatrick, Evans and Williams were concurrently members of the First Eleven, which became the HOME SERVICE; the latter two are still members of that band. The quintet built up a strong repertoire mixing CHILD ballads with songs by Richard THOMPSON, Keith Christmas, etc. The album *Brass Monkey* '83 on Topic was a revelation, incl. *tour-de-force* 'The Maid And The Palmer' (previously recorded by a STEELEYE SPAN lineup that incl. 'The Well Below The Valley' by PLANXTY); David LINDLEY in a *Swing 51* interview described the group as 'the most exciting, original thing I've heard in ten years'. In Apr. '84 Richard Cheetham (*b* 29 Jan. '57, Ashton under Lyne) replaced Williams; the new lineup recorded *See How It Runs* '86, also on Topic: inevitably it seemed marginally less accomplished than the first album, but still confirmed their status as one of the most imaginative European folk bands. They guested same year on Loudon WAINWRIGHT's *More Love Songs* (Rounder/Demon). Their significance lay in the way they shook up folk arrangements; demands on them in other spheres caused suspension of group '87.

BRAUD, Wellman (*b* Wellman Breaux, 25 Jan. 1891, St James Parish, Louisiana; *d* 29 Oct. '66, L.A.) Bass. To Chicago, then London ('23), played in reviews, then with Duke ELLINGTON mid-'27 to May '35. Always made sure exuberant style prominently heard on Ellington records in COTTON CLUB era; also used bow effectively. (Later sat in with Duke, '44 and '61.) Own club with Jimmie NOONE in NYC, '35; own trio from '37, played with many bands, left full-time music in '40s, returned to play with Kid ORY from '56 incl. European tour; with Joe DARENSBOURG '60. One of Duke's last compositions *New Orleans Suite* '70 incl. 'Portrait Of Wellman Braud'.

BRAXTON, Anthony (*b* 4 June '45, Chicago, Ill.) Reeds, composer. Studying music age 17, infl. by Roscoe MITCHELL; joined AACM '66; taught harmony. Formed group

Creative Construction Company, to Europe '69; played and recorded there with the group plus Steve McCall, Muhal Richard ABRAMS; also with ART ENSEMBLE OF CHICAGO. Formed Circle NYC '70 with Chick COREA, Dave HOLLAND, Barry ALTSCHUL. Initially interested in scientific (mathematical) aspects of music, all his works have diagrammatic titles; plays standards, ragtime, comps. of Warne MARSH, Charles MINGUS, etc. but his own music is ambitious and unclassifiable, leading to confusion among critics. First LP as leader *Three Compositions Of New Jazz* on Delmark '68, with Leo SMITH, Leroy Jenkins (*b* 11 Mar. '32, Chicago), trio playing about 20 instruments; followed by solo *For Alto Saxophone* on same label. *Silence* made in Paris '69 by the trio; *Anthony Braxton* and *This Time* '69-70 added McCall, are now available on Affinity in UK. Toured USA and Europe; returned from Italy with group playing formal and improvised music '70-1; appeared in London c.'71, recorded with Derek BAILEY (*Live At Wigmore, Duo 1, Duo 2*), Kenny WHEELER. Many albums, mostly on European, some Japanese labels, always with first-class jazz-based sidemen; incl. *Creative Construction Company* (2 vols. '70); *Recital Of Paris, The Complete Braxton* '71; *Circle 1&2* '72; *Dona Lee* '72, *Together Alone* '71 (duets with Joseph JARMAN, on Delmark), *Anthony Braxton Creative Music Orchestra* '72, *Town Hall 1972, Four Compositions 1973; In The Tradition* (vols. 1&2), *Trio And Duet* '74. Michael CUSCUNA brought him back to USA; prod. Arista LPs *New York Fall 1974, Five Pieces 1975, Creative Music Orchestra 1976, Montreux/Berlin Concerts* '77. Contributed '73° −S Kelvin' to Cuscuna's Wildflowers series of LPs on Douglas, '76. Arista albums also incl. *For Four Orchestras*, 3-disc set recorded May '78 at Oberlin, Ohio; nearly two-hour piece is an exercise in spatial textures intended for quadrophonic sound; easy to take but difficult to capture fully with two channels. He does not play on this, nor on *For Two Pianos* '80, but *Alto Saxophone Improvisations 1979* is a solo set (these also on Arista). Other LPs incl. *Live At Moers New Jazz Festival* '74 (one quartet, one solo); *Seven Compositions 1978; Anthony Braxton With The Robert Schumann String Quartet* '79 on Sound Aspects label; *Performance 9-11979; Composi-*

tion 98 '81 on Hat Hut label has both live and studio versions; *Six Compositions: Quartet* incl. Ed BLACKWELL; *Open Aspects '82* is duet with electronics. Most recent LPs are *Six Duets '82, Four Compositions (Quartet) 1983, Composition 113* '84. The last is a solo set, but like much of his music has theatrical aspect: takes place on North African night train. Played sopranino sax on Mitchell's 'Off Five Dark Six' (LP *Noonah*, Nessa '77); percussion with five others on *The Maze* ('78, also by Mitchell on Nessa); *Birth And Rebirth '78, One In Two, Two In One '79* are duets with Max ROACH. Working on *Trillium*, a series of 12 operas; wants to compose for 100 orchestras linked by satellite: colour, shape, ritual, the whole history of music in an urgent attempt to communicate. Like '74's *In The Tradition, Seven Standards 1985* (two vols. on Magenta) is a homage to earlier styles: music of Charlie PARKER, Miles DAVIS, Thelonious MONK etc. backed by a mainstream trio and played superbly: on *In The Tradition* he played Parker's 'Ornithology' on a contrabass clarinet; in the '85 sets he sticks to alto sax; throughout he demonstrates the solid foundation on which the more adventurous work is built. *The Coventry Concert* on West Wind, recorded '86, is a rather nasty bootleg.

BREAD USA soft rock trio/quartet formed '69 L.A. Original lineup: David Gates (*b* 11 Dec. '40, Tulsa, Okla.), vocals, guitar, keyboards, etc.; James Griffin (*b* Memphis), vocals, guitar, etc.; Robb Royer, vocals, keyboards. Gates began in Tulsa trio incl. Leon RUSSELL, then did session work, songwriting; Griffin worked alongside master prod. Snuff GARRETT, was also songwriter (co-wrote 'For All We Know' under name of Arthur James; song won Oscar '70, top three hit for CARPENTERS '71). Gates was prod. of LP by Pleasure Faire for which Griffin had written, Royer was member. Trio signed with Elektra '69, cut eponymous LP same year with session drummer Jim Gordon: critically acclaimed but commercial flop. Drummer Mike Botts (*b* Sacramento; ex-Wes MONTGOMERY sideman) joined to make full-time quartet; LP *On The Waters* '70 incl. USA no. 1 'Make It With You'; Royer left, replaced by Larry Knechtel (*b* Bell, Cal.; ex-Duane EDDY,

played piano on 'Bridge Over Troubled Water' by SIMON & GARFUNKEL); LP *Manna* '71 incl. USA no. 4 'If'; next LP *Baby I'm-A Want You '72* had no. 3 title track. *Guitar Man* same year had no. 11 title played by Knechtel; after 11 top 40 hits by '73 group split for solo, session work; reformed '77 for *Lost Without Your Love* (title track top 10). Superbly musical act suffered tension between Gates (who wrote most of the hits) and Griffin, who wanted more of his songs used. Gates had three top 40 solo hits '75-8; Griffin made an LP with Terry Sylvester (ex-HOLLIES). UK compilation LP *Best Of Bread* was big seller.

BREAKSTONE, Joshua (*b* 22 July '55, Elizabeth, N.J.) Guitarist. Exposed to a wide variety of music at home; saw Jimi HENDRIX dozens of times (his sister worked at Fillmore East); studied with Sal Salvador (*b* 21 Nov. '25, Mondon, Mass.; played with Stan KENTON '50s); played in rock group but quit as they were about to sign contracts: switched to jazz while acquiring several college degrees. Toured Canada with reedman Glen Hall, LP debut on Hall's *Book Of The Heart* '79 on Sonora (with Joanne BRACKEEN, Cecil McBee, Billy Hart); gigging in NYC followed his own albums *Wonderful!* '83 with pianist Barry HARRIS, *4/4=1* '84 with Kenny Barron on Sonora; switch to Contemporary for *Echoes* '86, with Barron, Pepper ADAMS, Keith COPELAND, Dennis Irwin on bass. Fine mainstream post-bop playing infl. by Kenny BURRELL, Grant Green. Adams had not long to live, but *Echoes* was a fittingly happy, swinging date, with tunes by Harris, Bud POWELL, Thad JONES, ballads by RODGERS & Hart.

BREAU, Lenny (*b* 8 Aug. '41, Auburn, Maine; *d* Aug. '84, L.A.) Guitarist; once described by Chet ATKINS as 'the best guitar player in the world today'. He came up through country music infl. by jazz, like Hank Garland and Jerry REED, but added full range of classical technique. Albums *Guitar Sound Of Lenny Breau* '68 and *The Velvet Touch Of* '69 (live at Shelly's Manne-Hole), both on RCA with bassist Don Thompson, drummer Claude Ranger; albums on Adelphi: solo *Five O'Clock Bells* and *Mo' Breau* '78, also *Lenny Breau Trio*, which may be reissue of one of the RCA LPs or of *Now* c.'78, once on Sound Hole label. Tracks for Direct-Disc Labs '79 had Thompson and Ranger, Atkins second guitar on one track. Also *Lenny Breau And Brad Terry*, made privately by clarinettist Terry, on Livingroom Records, Austin, Texas; *Quietude* '83 on Canadian Electric Muse label (duo with bassist Dave Young). A heroin addict, Breau was found strangled in a swimming pool.

BRECKER, Randy and Michael All-round sidemen of the fusion era late '60s-early '70s, both *b* Philadelphia. Mike (*b* 29 Mar. '49) is reedman; Randy (*b* 27 Nov. '45) plays trumpet; both also play drums and piano. Both have played and recorded with Horace SILVER, Billy COBHAM, James TAYLOR, Larry Coryell, Charles MINGUS (*Me Myself An Eye* '78), Mike also with Carly SIMON, on John LENNON album *Mind Games* '73; with Yoko ONO in Japan '74; Randy with BLOOD, SWEAT & TEARS, Stevie WONDER, Art BLAKEY, Janis JOPLIN, Clark TERRY, Duke PEARSON, Larry Coryell, Edgar and Johnny WINTER, MINGUS Dynasty, etc. Opened restaurant (with Kate Greenfield) in NYC '78 where they played with guest artists; at Playboy Jazz Festival '80. LPs together as Dreams on CBS (two LPs '70-3, with John Abercrombie on guitar, Billy Cobham on drums, Will Lee on bass), as the Brecker Brothers on Arista: *The Brecker Brothers*, *Back To Back* '75, live *Heavy Metal Be-bop* '78, *Detente* '79, *Straphangin'* '80. Randy did octet LP *Score* on Solid State, incl. Eddie Gomez, Larry Coryell; led electric band mid-'80s with his wife, keyboardist Eliane Elias (from São Paulo); released *In The Idiom* '87 on Denon. Mike played disco mid-'70s ('The Players Association'); on *Cityscape* '82 on WB with octet arr./cond. by Claus Ogerman; played in house band on *Saturday Night Live* '83-4; with group Steps Ahead from '79: three LPs on Elektra; he began playing Steiner EWI (electronic wind instrument) plugged into synthesiser, adding octaves, sampling etc. but still a wind-driven sound of human origin. First LP as leader on revived Impulse label *Michael Brecker* '87, with Jack DEJOHNETTE, Charlie HADEN, Pat METHENY, Kenny Kirkland; touring with Mike Stern on guitar, Jeff Andrews on bass, Joey

Calderazzo on piano, Adam Nussbaum on drums.

BREL, Jacques (*b* 8 Apr. '29, Brussels; *d* 9 Oct. '78, Bobigny, nr Paris) Singer-songwriter. Taught himself guitar at 15; expelled from school; worked in father's factory four years while writing songs. After military service began singing in French cafés; first pro engagement in Pigalle '53, second billing at Paris Olympia '54; by the early '60s leading French 'troubador' performer, dispensing sensual, sometimes angry, sometimes bitter-sweet songs. USA debut at Carnegie Hall Dec. '65; concert LP for Reprise, USA tour '67. Poet Eric Blau and songwriter Mort Shuman collaborated on *Jacques Brel Is Alive And Well And Living In Paris*, translating 25 songs; show opened at Village Gate NYC '68. Cast (incl. Shuman) sang 'Mathilde', 'Jackie', 'Amsterdam', 'Next', 'Funeral Tango', 'My Death', 'Sons Of', 'You're Not Alone', etc. Brel appeared in his own French version of *Man Of La Mancha* '68, playing Brussels and Paris; also dramatic role in film *Mont-Dragon* '71. Songs were much covered, by Scott Walker (recorded several incl. 'Jackie', UK hit '67), Alex HARVEY ('Next'), 'If You Go Away' (Dusty SPRINGFIELD, Ray CHARLES, Neil DIAMOND, Rod McKuen), 'I'm Not Afraid' (Frank SINATRA and McKuen), Gene LEES translated some songs, McKuen wrote his own lyrics to Brel's tunes. A recluse in later years, Brel emerged in '77 to make his first LP in 10 years: *Brel* sold 650,000 copies on the first day of release, totalled over 2 million. He died of cancer the next year. French records incl. *Music For The Millions*, recorded live '62 at Paris Olympia, and *American Debut* from Columbia Special Products in the USA.

BRENSTON, Jackie Singer, songwriter, saxophonist; one-hit wonder whose one hit is often hailed as first true rock'n'roll record. Played sax with Ike TURNER and his Kings Of Rhythm, then located Clarkesdale, Miss.; wrote jumping car song 'Rocket 88', band recorded it for Sam Phillips's Sun Records in Memphis who leased it to Chess as Jackie Brenston and his Delta Cats (his mother signed contract; he was under age), one of the biggest '51 R&B hits. Brenston fronted band on tour but faded when he parted with them. Song had been sold to Phillips for about $900; country bandleader Bill HALEY switched styles in order to cover it on Holiday label, thus launching new career.

BRESH, Thom (*b* '46, Hollywood) Country singer, actor. Father was photographer at Corriganville Movie Ranch; appeared in first film age 7, worked as actor/stunt man, appeared in episodes of TV's *Gunsmoke*, *Cheyenne*. Friend of the family Merle TRAVIS encouraged music interest; studied theory at college, many instruments. Replaced Roy CLARK in Hank Penny's band '60, with band six years; to Seattle '67; managed restaurant, photographic studio; recording studio for pop artist Merilee Rush, who prod. his first record 'D. B. Cooper, Where Are You?'; song about skyjacker was banned just as it started to take off. Worked clubs, then made commitment to country music; signed with Farr records, made charts with 'Homemade Love' '76, 'Sad Country Love Song' '77; obtained contract release when Farr moved to East Coast, joined ABC-Dot, had hits 'That Old Cold Shoulder' '77, 'Ways Of A Woman In Love' '78. LPs incl. *Homemade Love* '76, *Kicked Back* '77, *Portrait* '78.

BREWER & SHIPLEY Soft-rock duo Mike Brewer (*b* '44, Oklahoma City), Tom Shipley (*b* '42, Mineral Ridge, Ohio), both formerly solo folksingers, teamed as songwriters for A&M '65. After label released unauthorised LP of demos *Down In LA* '68, they moved to Kama Sutra. San Francisco prod. Nick Gravenites used first-class backing musicians such as Nicky HOPKINS, Mike BLOOMFIELD, Jerry Garcia for albums *Weeds* '69, *Tarkio* '70; latter made USA charts with surprise hit 'One Toke Over The Line', despite being banned for blatant drug reference. Folksy style continued on LPs *Shake Off The Demon* '72 and *Rural Space* '73; duo switched to Capitol, then Mercury for sporadic LPs. Set up home with families on farmland in Missouri, not too disturbed at lack of continued commercial success. Last LP *Not Far From Free* '78, with sessionmen from AREA CODE 615 stable; Brewer made solo album *Beauty Lies*.

BREWER, Teresa (*b* 7 May '31, Toledo, Ohio) Pop singer. On radio age 2; won Major Bowes talent show age 5, toured with it seven years. Won another talent show age 15, two-week booking at NYC's Latin Quarter, other clubs, hid when law visited (under age). Signed to London label: 'Music! Music! Music!' worldwide hit '50. Further hits 'Choo'n Gum' '50, 'Longing For You' '51; switched to Coral label for string of top 20 successes: 'You'll Never Get Away' (duet with Don CORNELL) and no. 1 'Till I Waltz Again With You', both '52; 'Ricochet' '53; 'Bell Bottom Blues', 'Jilted', 'Let Me Go Lover' '54; 'Pledgin' My Love', 'Silver Dollar', 'Banjo's Back In Town' '55; 'A Tear Fell', 'A Sweet Old Fashioned Girl' '56, 'Empty Arms' '57 (C&W hit for Sonny JAMES, '71). With advent of crossover hits in mid-'50s, Brewer's spirit and incredibly bright, accurate voice made better covers of country, R&B than most: Fats DOMINO hit 'Bo Weevil' '56; Sam COOKE's 'You Send Me' '57. Also major role in '53 film *Red-heads From Seattle*. Continued with minor hits, touring, playing clubs; contract '70s with Howard Hughes, who owned five Las Vegas venues. Married Bob THIELE '72, who had prod. some of her early hits; he then prod. adventurous series of albums for her with Count BASIE (*Songs Of Bessie Smith*), Duke ELLINGTON (*It Don't Mean A Thing*), Stephane GRAPPELLI (*On The Road Again*), Bobby HACKETT (*What A Wonderful World*), Svend ASMUSSEN (*On The Good Ship Lollypop*), also *Teresa Brewer And Earl 'Fatha' Hines*, *I Dig Big Band Singers*, another with World's Greatest Jazz Band (*see* Bob WILBER). Backed by Oily Rags (CHAS & DAVE) with all-star sidemen on *In London*: LP incl. remake of 'Music, Music, Music', songs by Chas & Dave, Robbie Robertson, Kris KRISTOFFERSON, Chuck BERRY, Van MORRISON, others: well designed to show her off, now on Thiele's Signature label. 2-disc set on his Doctor Jazz: *Live At Carnegie Hall & Montreux* '85, with Dizzy GILLESPIE, Clark TERRY, etc., praised by *Stereo Review*.

BRICE, Fanny (*b* Fannie Borach, 29 Oct. 1891, NYC; *d* 29 May '51, L.A.) Comedienne, Ziegfeld show girl '10 to '36. Mostly sang novelties and dialect songs, but also known for torch numbers: 'I'd Rather Be

Blue', 'When A Woman Loves A Man', 'My Man' backed with 'Second Hand Rose' all recorded for Victor '30s: RCA Vintage series '60s had compilation of Brice on one side, Helen MORGAN on the other. Compilation LP on Audio Fidelity, also out of print. Put on funny voice, played brat Baby Snooks on radio '39-51. Inspired title role of '64 Broadway musical *Funny Girl*, played by Barbra STREISAND in '68 film.

BRIDGEWATER, Dee Dee (*b* 27 May '50, Memphis, Tenn.) Jazz singer. Grew up in Flint, Michigan; father played trumpet; formed trio in high school, sang with father's group; married trumpeter/composer Cecil Bridgewater (*b* 10 Oct. '42, Urbana, Ill.; recorded with Thad JONES-Mel LEWIS band, Max ROACH, Frank Foster, Horace SILVER; album with saxophonist brother Ron: *Generations* on Strata-East); went to NYC with him (later divorced); she was featured singer with Jones-Lewis band '72-4, studied with pianist Roland Hanna; recorded with Jones-Lewis, with Dizzy GILLESPIE, Roach, Roland KIRK; now lives in France, where she originated one-woman show *Lady Day*, brought it to London early '87. Album *Live In Paris* '87 on Affinity.

BRIGADIER JERRY (*b* Robert Russell) Jamaican toaster who emerged as the most acclaimed of mike chanters in early '80s. Along with Josie Wales and Charlie Chaplin he was one of the few to carry on the signifying tradition formerly practised by U Roy and Big Youth. He rarely recorded, but examples of his work were readily available via the reggae network of sound system cassettes recorded in dance halls wherever his set Jahlovemuzik was in session. Like Dennis Brown, Freddie MacGregor and a number of Studio One musicians of the era, he was associated with the Twelve Tribes sect of Ras Tafari; as a result the Brentford Road players featured on his few records, though the Brigadier himself never released any records from Studio One. Among intermittent releases were 'Pain', 'Jamaica Jamaica', 'Horse A Gallop'; but first album *Live At The Controls* was made at a dance in Ocho Rios with Jack Ruby sound system. First studio album

was *Jamaica Jamaica* '85 from USA reggae specialists Ras.

BRIGGS, Anne Patricia (*b* 29 Sep. '44, Toton, Notts.) UK folk singer, songwriter; one of the most infl. of '60s revivalists, affecting acts as diverse as FAIRPORT CONVENTION, Bert Jansch (who learned 'Blackwater Side' on his '66 LP *Jack Orion* from her, in turn appropriated by LED ZEP from him), Christy MOORE and June TABOR. Sang in a decorated style, like many others of the era, but significant for innovation: with her accompanist Johnny Moynihan, their early use of the bouzouki was a direct inspiration for PLANXTY. Involved with Centre 42, financed by UK trade unions to decentralise multi-media arts from London; noticed by A. L. LLOYD, who used her with others on his *The Iron Muse* '63, a major examination of industrial folk music, which led to Briggs EP *The Hazards Of Love* '63, LP *Anne Briggs* '71 on Topic. Also worked with Lloyd on his *The Bird In The Bush* '66 and with Frankie Armstrong. *The Time Has Come* '72 on CBS incl. 'Fine Horseman' (written by Lal Knight); appeared on Lal and Mike WATERSON's *Bright Phoebus* '72 on Trailor (her version of title track already covered by PENTANGLE on *Sweet Child* '68). 'Wishing Well' was co-written with Jansch. Her third LP was never released and she retired to raise a family, also involved in conservation, growing herbs and wild plants. Performed at memorial concert for Lloyd '83.

BRILL BUILDING '60s equivalent of TIN PAN ALLEY: 1619 Broadway NYC was centre of Brill Building sound, which actually began across the street at Aldon Music: Aldon were AL Nevins and DON Kirshner; gathered songwriters eventually recognised as the best of late '50s to mid-'60s, especially husband–wife teams Barry MANN and Cynthia Weil, Gerry GOFFIN and Carole KING, also Neil SEDAKA, Howard Greenfield, Toni Wine, Bobby DARIN, others. Wrote songs in great quantity, but also quality; good tunes fitted with lyrics and phrases meaningful to record buyers at the time were in demand for teen idols to record; but if stars were factory made, songs were not: images of publishers' cubicles furnished with pianos and slaves writing music was greatly exaggerated. Brill Building as a term came to encompass Jeff BARRY and Ellie GREENWICH, Doc POMUS and Mort Shuman, Bert BERNS, even LEIBER & STOLLER, Burt BACHARACH and Hal David. Pop music so fragmented mid-'80s that some would wish for an institution that seemed to work for everyone's benefit.

BRINSLEY SCHWARZ UK pop group formed from remnants of Kippington Lodge, who made flop singles for Parlophone late '60s incl. 'Shy Boy', 'Rumours', 'In My Life'. Lineup: Brinsley Schwarz, guitar, sax; Nick LOWE, bass, vocals; Barry Landerman, keyboards; Pete Whale, drums; the last two replaced by Bob Andrews (*b* 20 June '49), Billy Rankin when band signed to United Artists, management company Famepushers, whose grandiose scheme, flying planeload of journalists to NYC to watch them at Fillmore East, led to adverse publicity: band carried on *Despite It All*, as '70 follow-up to eponymous debut LP was called. Harmonies infl. by CROSBY, STILLS & NASH gave way to country flavour, then chunkier, BAND-infl. sound and New Orleans feeling; sound thickened from '72's *Silver Pistol* onwards by addition of Ian Gomm (*b* 17 Mar. '47, London) on second guitar. Chose to play London pub circuit, perhaps because of early over-exposure; thus no LPs became big sellers: *Nervous On The Road* '72, *Please Don't Ever Change* '73 followed by last LP (except for compilations) *New Favourites* '74, which introduced them to Dave EDMUNDS, who used them as house band for film *Stardust*, later linked with Lowe in Rockpile. Members sessioned widely, backing Frankie MILLER, others as a band; Andrews and Schwarz added freelance saxes to DR FEELGOOD, KURSAAL FLYERS etc. Split Feb. '75; Schwarz and Rankin joined pub-rockers Ducks Deluxe in their final months; Lowe became house prod. at Stiff; Andrews prod. at Stiff after leaving the Rumour, in which he'd backed Graham PARKER with Schwarz and others since '75; Gomm released three low-key but likeable LPs on Albion and had one-off no. 18 single in USA '79 ('Hold On' on Stiff), played live dates fronting Joe JACKSON's band late '70s, then concentrated on songwriting: co-wrote Lowe's 'Cruel To Be Kind', transatlantic hit '79. Unfashionable in their lifetime, like Ducks Deluxe, Kilburn & The High Roads etc. Brinsley Schwarz latterly famed for activity of members in late-'70s new wave: compilation *15 Thoughts* still available; early LPs much sought-after by collectors.

BRISTOL, Johnny (*b* Morgantown, N.C.) Soul singer, songwriter, producer, arranger. Began after service in USAF as half of Johnny and Jackie, boy/girl duo with Jackie Beavers, recording for Tri-Phi label owned by Gwen Gordy (sister of Berry) and husband Harvey Fuqua. Beavers left when Tri-Phi taken over by Motown; Bristol was Fuqua's assistant, then became partner in prod./writing for Edwin Starr, David RUFFIN, Stevie WONDER, Marvin GAYE, others. Bristol wasted nothing; first two Johnny and Jackie singles recycled: 'Someday We'll Be Together' by Diana ROSS and the SUPREMES (no. 1 '69), 'Do You See My Love (For You Growing)' twice by Junior WALKER (first single for Tri-Phi, then no. 32 hit '70). Bristol had persuaded Fuqua to take interest in Walker '62, later toned down rough'n'ready sound of veteran Motown saxophonist to give him no. 4 hit 'What Does It Take To Win Your Love' '69 (Walker's first top 10 since '65). Left Motown '73 when label moved from Detroit to Cal., became prod. for Columbia: worked with Buddy Miles, Boz SCAGGS (*Slow Dancer* '74), O.C. SMITH, Jerry BUTLER (for Mercury). When Columbia rejected him as vocalist, took dusted-off talents to MGM for *Hang On In There Baby* '74: album went gold, title track in vogueish Barry WHITE vein no. 8 USA/no. 3 UK. *Bristol Creme* '76 (Polydor), *Free To Be Me* '81 (Hansa) predictably seamless but not as successful. Continued prod. in soul field with first Tavares LP *Check It Out* '74, venturing into MOR with Johnny MATHIS, Tom JONES. Unsung, behind-the-scenes talent deserves more than one-hit-wonder tag from chartwatchers.

BRITISH INVASIONS UK transformations of USA music scene, two so far. UK acts had been successful in USA in '30s-40s (Ray NOBLE, Vera LYNN, George SHEARING, others), but emergence of rock'n'roll changed the nature of the game. Rockabilly and R&B input into '50s USA charts was exciting, but vested interests in music business damped it down, invented teen idol genre, made stars with little talent. Meanwhile UK had discovered roots of ROCK through imported records, touring USA acts; began playing R&B style in London, writing own material in wake of SKIFFLE fad. USA record company execs at first refused to credit BEATLES but they conquered USA charts '64 and the floodgates opened: ROLLING STONES, Dave CLARK Five, HERMAN'S HERMITS, GERRY AND THE PACEMAKERS, The ANIMALS, SEARCHERS, ZOMBIES, KINKS, Wayne FONTANA & the Mindbenders, PETER & GORDON, FREDDIE & THE DREAMERS all scored. Such was demand for anything British that acts were stars in USA while unknown at home, e.g. CHAD & JEREMY. Ian Whitcomb had one USA hit ('You Turn Me On', '65), none at home, but toured USA in deerstalker cap; became archivist/performer incl. book *After The Ball* '72. The Beatles stopped touring '66; by then USA produced its own stars, especially on hippie-flavoured West Coast, but David BOWIE, Elton JOHN, Rod STEWART effortlessly duplicated UK success in USA early '70s. 'Second British Invasion' early '80s brought energy of UK punk, new wave; shocked sterile and uncertain USA music scene dominated by AOR radio. This time there was no single group as spearhead; UK acts had been infl. by early examples of ALICE COOPER, VELVET UNDERGROUND, NEW YORK DOLLS, etc.; success was largely visual: DURAN DURAN, BOY GEORGE, EURYTHMICS, Adam ANT had pioneered slick videos and became easy hits on MTV cable music channel. Guitar-based bands like BIG COUNTRY, U2 had effect; POLICE and SQUEEZE played big arenas; by mid-'80s Phil COLLINS, WHAM!, Julian LENNON, FRANKIE GOES TO HOLLYWOOD were all hits in USA, where affection had also been retained for The WHO, Eric CLAPTON, PINK FLOYD, Jimmy Page, who were getting a harder ride at home. With video and satellite technology, pop festivals in Brazil and Wham! playing in China, pop music is now international to an extent unimagined 20 years ago; future invasions may be obviated by the worldwide diffusion of roots musics, a reaction against today's overproduced rock and pop. But the shock of '64 will never be forgotten.

BRITT, Elton (*b* James Britt Baker, 7 July '17, Marshall, Ark.; *d* 23 June '72) Country singer, yodeller. Discovered '32 by talent scouts seeking a country yodeller in Oklahoma; worked with BEVERLY HILLBILLIES on Cal. radio for four years, recorded with them and solo on ARC, Decca, Variety; with Victor from '37, association lasted 20 years, 672 records, over 50 LPs. Hits with yodelling songs 'Chimebells', 'Maybe I'll Cry Over You', 'Patent Leather Boots', 'Lorelei'. Wartime 'There's A Star-spangled Banner Waving Somewhere' eventually sold 2 million, resulted in Britt becoming first country singer invited to the White House, late '42. Duet hits with Rosalie ALLEN late '40s incl. 'Quicksilver' '49; solo hits 'Candy Kisses' '49, 'Mockingbird Hill' '50. Made B-films (e.g. *Laramie* '49); many TV spots '50s-60s. Stopped touring late '50s, settled as gentleman farmer near Washington DC but joined ABC-Paramount records mid-'60s, made several LPs: *The Wandering Cowboy* '66, *Beyond The Sunset* '67, *16 Great Country Performances* '68. Rejoined RCA '68, made LP *The Jimmie Rodgers Blues*, country chart entries with LP's title cut and 'The Bitter Taste' '69.

BROMBERG, David (*b* 19 Sep. '45, Philadelphia, Pa.) Ace session man, playing guitar, mandolin, dobro, fiddle. Studied at Columbia U., immersed in Greenwich Village folk scene mid-'60s, friends with Bob DYLAN, Tom PAXTON, Carly SIMON, on whose records he later played, notably Dylan's *New Morning*, '70. Backed Jerry Jeff WALKER four years; solo appearance Isle of Wight festival '70 led to own CBS LPs: *David Bromberg* '72, *Midnight On The Water* '75 well received critically; *Reckless Abandon* '77 showed off eclectic band. Versatility ensured he was in demand; by his own account had played on more than 75 albums by '77, but solo career never took off. With '80 LP *You Should See The Rest Of The Band*, announced that he would quit live work, but plays at NYC's Bottom Line once a year: famous friends in the neighbourhood drop in.

BRONSKI BEAT UK pop group formed London '84: Jimi Somerville, vocals (*b* 22 June '61, Glasgow), Larry Steinbachek (*b* 6 May '60) and Steve Bronski (*b* 7 Feb. '60), keyboards and percussion. Built up strong following on gay circuit, signed to London; to everyone's surprise became pop stars. Debut single 'Smalltown Boy' overtly dealt with gay problems, yet effortlessly took in gay/straight market. Next hit 'Why' typical of sound: synthesiser, drum machine, Somerville's castrato-style vocal; version of GERSHWIN classic 'It Ain't Necessarily So' third hit. Debut LP *Age Of Consent* '84 incl. hit singles; inner sleeve listed homosexual age of consent in various European countries; USA label refused to print it. Donna SUMMER's hit 'I Feel Love' became fourth hit, ironic in view of her hostility to gays: sung as duet with Marc ALMOND, with snatch of '61 John Leyton hit 'Johnny Remember Me' tacked on, made top 5 UK May '85; *Hundreds & Thousands* '85 was hastily compiled alternate mixes from debut. Some critics found Somerville's voice as irritating as enervating; he announced that he was quitting, blaming 'pressures of being a pop star', worked with new group called The Committee, then Body Politic, with saxist Richard Cole; then Communards: eponymous debut LP '86 incl. hit singles 'You Are My World', 'Don't Leave Me This Way' (no. 1 UK). Bronski, Steinbachek and John Foster carried on with original group name in less political direction: *Truthdare, Doubledare* '86 incl. hits 'C'mon, C'mon', 'Hit That Perfect Beat'.

BROOKER, Gary (*b* 29 May '45, Southend, England) Singer, keyboards. Formerly with The Paramounts and PROCOL HARUM; later part of Paul McCARTNEY's Rockestra concept, appeared in all-star lineup at Hammersmith Odeon (London) in Concerts for Kampuchea '79. Solo LP that year *No More Fear Of Flying* prod. by George MARTIN, with mostly own songs (with former King Crimson lyricist Pete Sinfield); also covers of Murray Head's 'Say It Ain't So Joe' and Mickey JUPP's 'Switchboard Susan'. Still a soulful voice, but in post-punk era nobody cared. Second LP *Lead Me To The Water* not better, despite musical help from George HARRISON, Phil COLLINS, Albert Lee, Eric CLAPTON: songs less memorable; followed by *Echoes In The Night* '85. Toured with Clapton '82; appeared at Princes Trust Charity Ball '83.

BROOKMEYER, Bobby (*b* 19 Dec. '29, Kansas City, Mo.) Valve trombone, piano, composer. Played piano with Tex BENEKE '51, others incl. Claude THORNHILL, Woody HERMAN '51, Stan GETZ '53, Gerry MULLIGAN '54-7 incl. European tours, Jimmy GIUFFRE '57-8, Mulligan big band '60, combo with Clark TERRY '61 incl. visit UK '64; visits to Europe with Mulligan '62-3, Japan '64; married lyricist Margo Guryan '64; TV staff (Merv Griffin show) '65, Thad JONES-Mel LEWIS big band late '60s. Moved to California '68, much studio work; festival reunions with Jones-Lewis and Mulligan, '70s; with Terry '80; with Lewis band '82. Often witty mainstream/modern style, always reliable and rewarding, always fits in yet instantly recognisable. First LP '54, quartet with Al COHN; about 25 own LPs as leader, incl. *Traditionalism* '57 with Jimmy Giuffre and Jim HALL; *Street Swingers* '57 with Hall; *The Blues Hot And Cold* '60; *Suitably Zoot* '65 with Zoot SIMS; *Back Again, Small Band* both '78; arr. and comp. *Live At Village Vanguard* '80 with Mel Lewis and the Jazz Orchestra.

BROOKS, Elkie (*b* Elaine Bookbinder, 25 Feb. '45, Manchester) UK singer. Her father was a baker; Elkie the Yiddish equivalent of Elaine. Made pro debut at 15, billed as 'Manchester's Brenda Lee'; moved to London, entered jazz scene with bands led by Eric Delaney, later Humphrey LYTTELTON; first single 'Something's Got A Hold On Me' '64; commenced session career. Personal/professional linkup with guitarist Pete Gage (*b* 31 Aug. '47), ex-Geno WASHINGTON's Ram Jam Band, led to 12-piece jazz/rock group Dada; one eponymous LP for Atco '70 before slimming down to R&B oriented Vinegar Joe. Shared vocals in both bands with Robert PALMER (*b* 19 Jan '49); combination of her huskiness, his urbanity effective, as was her stage appearance with thigh-high skirts *à la* Tina TURNER. Band incl. Steve York, bass; Mike Deacon, keyboards, Pete Gavin, drums; made three LPs for Island: *Vinegar Joe, Rock'n'Roll Gypsies* both '72, *Six Star General* '73 without capturing raunchy live flavour. After Joe disbanded '74, Brooks signed to A&M as a solo. Like Maggie BELL, her only competition as gutsiest female rocker of the era, seemed unlikely to fulfil promise on basis of *Rich Man's Woman* '75. Sudden change to MOR material on *Two Days Away* '77 (prod. by LEIBER & STOLLER) brought UK hit singles in own comp. 'Pearl's A Singer' (no. 8) and 'Sunshine After The Rain' (no. 10). Concentrated on covers of pop material such as Chris Rea's 'Fool If You Think It's Over' (no. 17 '82), MOODY BLUES' 'Nights In White Satin', scoring top 5 marks with LPs *Pearls* '81, compilation named for hit single, and *Pearls II* '82, both big Xmas hits. Only occasional LP tracks, such as Rod STEWART's 'Stay With Me' from *Shooting Star* '78, showed flashes of old fire; *Screen Gems* '84 was first UK pop album released on CD. Then after guiding her into MOR, her label (A&M) regarded her as washed up; she switched to Mike Heap's Legend label for *No More The Fool* '86: back high in the charts with both album and title single, tougher songs by ALICE COOPER ('Only Women Bleed'), Bob SEGER.

BROOKS, Randy (*b* 28 Mar. '17, Maine; *d* 21 Mar. '67, Springfield, Maine) Trumpet, bandleader. Played with Salvation Army band age 6, with Rudy VALLEE early '30s while still in school. Good lead and solos with Hal KEMP '39, Les BROWN '43-4; formed own band '45 as BIG BAND ERA was drawing to a close: had good arrangements by John Benson Brooks (no relation); Stan GETZ joined '46. Recorded for Decca; best records were bop-tinged 'A Night At The Three Deuces', 'How High The Moon' with Getz solo; most were ballads with sweet solos and vocals: 'Tenderly', 'More Than You Know'. Disbanded; married Ina Ray HUTTON and formed new band '49, had stroke '50 which ended musical career. Died in a fire at home. Radio air checks from '45 issued on Joyce label.

BROOKS, Tina (*b* Harold Floyd Brooks, 7 June '32, Fayetteville, N.C.; *d* 13 Aug. '74, NYC) Tenor saxophone. To the Bronx '44; grade-school nickname from 'Teeny', though he grew to 5'7". Began on C-melody sax, had lessons from brother David 'Bubba' Brooks (later with Bill DOGGETT for many years), followed him into R&B work, made first recordings with Sonny Thompson band on King in Cincinnati '51. On the road with Amos MILBURN, then

turned to jazz: joined Lionel HAMPTON '55; became fine solo stylist and writer. Discovered by Blue Note, recorded for that label '58-61 on four LPs of his own and others by Jimmy SMITH, Kenny BURRELL (incl. three tracks live at the Five Spot '59), Freddie HUBBARD (*Open Sesame* partly written/ arr. by Brooks), Jackie McLEAN (*Jackie's Bag*) and pianist Freddie Redd (*b* 29 May '28: made two Blue Note LPs incl. *Shades Of Redd* with Brooks; wrote score for Jack Gelber's off-Broadway play *The Connection* '59, played, acted in stage and film versions; later led own trio in San Francisco). Brooks was understudy for McLean in *The Connection*; played on LP of music from it for Felsted label UK led by Howard McGHEE with Redd, but McLean did '61 film. Brooks' first LP '58 unreleased until Japanese edition *Minor Move* '80; *True Blue* released '60; two LPs made '61 not released although *Back To The Tracks* listed in Blue Note catalogues. A shy, reserved man who had acquired a drug habit; never recorded after '61 and died of kidney failure. All four quintet LPs issued in limited edition set by Mosaic '85 with full notes, discography; Hubbard is quoted: 'He wrote and played beautifully. What a soulful, inspiring cat. I loved him.'

BROONZY, Big Bill (*b* William Lee Conley Broonzy, 26 June 1893, Scott, Miss.; *d* 15 Aug. '58, Chicago) Grew up in Arkansas, to Chicago '20; worked as redcap, had a farm late '30s, janitor late '40s, had a tavern Chicago '54; but recorded regularly from '26 with Cripple Clarence Lofton, Bumble Bee Slim, Memphis Slim, Washboard Sam, many others; solo: the best selling black male blues singer in late '30s. John HAMMOND's *Spirituals To Swing* concerts, '38-9; first visit UK '51, became famous in Europe. Columbia LP *Big Bill's Blues* (c.'56) showed him at informal best: talked about his mother; he sang to her so she would give him his favourite tea-cakes. (Born a slave, she died '57 aged 102.) Set incl. his versions of 'See See Rider', 'Trouble In Mind'; his own 'Texas Tornado', 'Bossie Woman'; gospel songs. Set of five LPs for Verve '57 incl. valuable reminiscence, conversation. Many compilation LPs on Folkways, Yazoo, Biograph; made in Copenhagen for Storyville: *An Evening With* and vol in *Portraits*

In Blues series '56. As-told-to biography *Big Bill Blues* '55.

BROTHERS JOHNSON Session musicians with own band. George (*b* 17 May '53, L.A.), vocals, guitar; Louis (*b* 13 Apr. '55. L.A.), bass. Played first gigs while still at Santa Barbara Transfiguration Catholic High School; formed band Johnson Three Plus One with elder brother Tommy (drums), cousin Alex Weir (rhythm guitar). George joined Billy PRESTON's God Squad '71, Louis joined '72; they quit '74 to work on own material: four songs on Quincy JONES LP *Mellow Madness* '75; toured Japan with Jones. On return he prod. Brothers Johnson debut LP on A&M *Look Out For No. 1*; it sold over a million, incl. hit singles 'I'll Be Good To You' (no. 3 '76), 'Get The Funk Out Ma Face' (no. 30 '76). Jones-prod. sequels *Right On Time* '77, *Blam!* '78, *Light Up The Night* '80 did well, as did singles 'Strawberry Letter 23' (no. 5 '77), 'Stomp!' (no. 7 '80). Singles also charted UK, as did 'Ain't We Funkin' Now' and 'Ride-O-Rocket' '78, 'Light Up The Night' '80, 'The Real Thing' '81. Prod. their own *Winners* '81; failed to go platinum, had no hit singles in USA. Further LPs: *Blast* (a 'best of', incl. hits); *Out Of Control*. Prolific session players; separately or together appeared on records by Patti AUSTIN, George BENSON, CRUSADERS, POINTER SISTERS, Lee RITENOUR, Grover WASHINGTON, many others.

BROWN, Arthur (*b* 24 June '44, Whitby, Yorks.) UK singer. Philosophy student at Yorkshire U.; played in small-time R&B groups; formed Crazy World of Arthur Brown with Vincent Crane, organ; Drachen Theaker, drums (later replaced by Carl Palmer: Theaker later in USA soft-rock LOVE; Palmer in EMERSON, LAKE & PALMER, ASIA). Only big hit 'Fire' '68 (no. 1 UK/ no. 2 USA) took them from residency at London's UFO underground club to worldwide exposure of Brown's act: flowing robes, painted face, helmet (often ignited on stage) made impact owing much to Screamin' Jay HAWKINS. Toured USA after release of eponymous album '68, but split when Crane and Palmer left to form Atomic Rooster. Formed Kingdom Come '70 with Andy Dalby, guitar; Michael Harris,

keyboards; Martin Steer, drums; Phil Shutt, bass; made LPs of rock theatre (*Galactic Zoo Disaster* '72, *Kingdom Come* and *The Journey* '73); group split, Brown toured Middle East solo, returned to play priest in WHO's film *Tommy* ('Fire' had been released on Who's Track label); carried on with LPs *Dance* '74, *Lost Ears* '76, *Chisholm In My Bosom* '78, *Faster Than The Speed Of Sound* '80; by then LPs issued only in Europe, two of synthesiser music: *Requiem, Speaknotech* '80s; lives in Austin, Texas. Great British eccentric, flashing intermittently on the periphery.

BROWN, Buster (*b* 11 Aug. '14, Criss, Ga.; *d* 31 Jan. '76) Blues singer, harmonica player. Played and sang in clubs in the South, then on Bobby Robinson's Fire label NYC from '59. 'Fannie Mae' '60 was no. 1 soul chart, made top 40 pop; revival of Louis JORDAN's 'Is You Is Or Is You Ain't My Baby' made Hot 100 but not soul chart; 'Sugar Babe' just made Hot 100, was top 20 soul, covered in UK by Jimmy Powell. No more hits despite records on five more labels.

BROWN, Cameron (*b* 21 Dec. '45, Detroit, Mich.) Bass; also studied piano, clarinet. Toured Europe summers '65-6; degree from Columbia NYC '69; taught elementary school South Bronx; turned full-time pro '72. Played and recorded with Archie SHEPP more than two years; also worked with Art BLAKEY, Chet BAKER, Art FARMER, others (LP *Art's Break* '72 made in Oslo and Tunis, with Jazz Messengers incl. Bill Hardman, Mickey TUCKER, on Joker and Lotus labels). Toured Europe with Roswell RUDD '75, recorded with Sheila JORDAN that year for Japanese label; original member George ADAMS-Don PULLEN quartet. Excellent sound, drive, interplay with Dannie RICHMOND.

BROWN, Charles (*b* '20, Texas City, Texas) Singer, pianist. Smooth blues stylist, much infl. by Nat COLE and very influential in his turn. Studied classical piano in youth; to L.A. '43; won talent show at Lincoln Theatre with 'Claire de Lune'. With Bardu Ali band, then Johnny Moore's Three Blazers '44, began recording career with them on Aladdin, first date incl. classic 'Driftin' Blues'. Trio on Aladdin '48; R&B hit 'Merry

Christmas Baby' on Modern, '49. Toured in package shows, with Johnny ACE tour '54; records on various labels, no more hits until 'Please Come Home For Christmas' became pop hit on King '61. Toured, played clubs, reviving best tunes, incl. 'Trouble Blues', 'Black Night'. LPs *Sunnyland* (Route 66), *Charles Brown* (Blues Spectrum).

BROWN, Clarence 'Gatemouth' (*b* 18 Apr. '24, Vinton, La.) Singer, guitarist, fiddler. Stetson-wearing bandleader who switches from blues to bluegrass, both live and on record. Learned guitar at 5, fiddle and mandolin at 10; also plays drums, bass, harmonica. Raised in Orange, Texas, son of musician/rancher. Joined Brown Skin Models as drummer in '40s, toured Midwest; service in US Army Engineer Corps; then made solo debut '45 depping for indisposed T-Bone WALKER; played drums with San Antonio-based big band '46. Signed by manager Don Robey, went on the road with 23-piece band; flew to L.A. '47 to record for Aladdin with little success; Robey formed Peacock, first black-owned label, recording Brown with Jack McVEA band: minor hit 'Mary Is Fine', many other Peacock releases were juke box winners; Brown's guitar work was profoundly influential, but he received little reward: claimed that his songs were credited to Robey under his own name or pseudonym D. Malone; offer to buy back his contract for $20,000 was refused. During '50s led both black big band, small white group playing all kinds of venues, continuing to record for Peacock through early '60s, then for several labels. Eclectic big band LP for MCA '78 featured AIRTO (percussion), Jim Keltner (drums), The Memphis Horns, The Mondane Willis Singers, country star Roy CLARK and Garland Craft, then keyboardist with The OAK RIDGE BOYS. One of the great all-round entertainers, Brown has worked both jazz and country festivals, made commercials for Lone Star beer, and was once deputy sheriff of San Juan County, New Mexico. LPs in UK: *One More Mile* (Demon); *San Antonio Ballbuster* ('49-59 compilation on both Charly and Red Lightnin'); *The Duke-Peacock Story Vol. 1* ('49-51, early sessions complete) on Ace in UK; new records and Peacock collections on Rounder in USA.

Pressure Cooker '86 on Alligator is tracks made in Paris '73, some live; followed by *Real Life* '87 on Rounder. Gigged with Hank Wangford UK country band '87.

BROWN, Cleo (*b* 8 Dec. '09, DeKalb, Ms.) Pianist, singer. Father was a clergyman; moved to Chicago '19; heard on Chicago radio '30s, recorded for Decca '35-6 with rhythm section: 18 sides incl. 'Pinetop's Boogie Woogie' (before boogie woogie fad), 'The Stuff Is Here And It's Mellow', 'Me And My Wonderful One' (top 20 hit). She went to NYC to replace Fats WALLER on CBS radio, taught piano, suffered from ill health '40-2, recorded '49 for Capitol, settled in Denver, Col., qualified as a nurse '59. Her first-class technique and strong left hand, vocals in sweet, sexy voice reminiscent of Ethel WATERS were influential; fans incl. Bobby SHORT, Dave BRUBECK, Teddy WILSON; she paved the way for pianist/singers Nellie LUTCHER, Julia LEE, Una Mae CARLISLE, Blossom DEARIE, Shirley HORN. Appeared on Marian McPARTLAND radio show '86. The Decca sides would make a nice reissue.

BROWN, Clifford (*b* 30 Oct. '30, Wilmington, Del.; *d* 26 June '56 on Pennsylvania Turnpike) Trumpet. Played in Philadelphia with Miles DAVIS, Fats NAVARRO '48; scholarship to Maryland State College, '49; hospitalised for months after car crash June '51; toured with R&B group on trumpet and piano '52-3; with Tadd DAMERON, Lionel HAMPTON '53; to California with Max ROACH quintet incl. Harold LAND: albums in '54 on EmArcy (a Mercury label); concerts and live takes released later; no commercial recordings made during most of '55 while quintet was becoming the hottest act in jazz. (*Clifford Brown With Strings* arr. by Neal HEFTI, Jan. '55.) In Dec. '55 Harold Land left and was replaced by Sonny ROLLINS; interplay of the two horns became something unusually fine. Group recorded Jan.-Feb. '56, both live and in studio: 'I'll Remember April' is one of the masterpieces of the era; pianist Richie Powell (*b* 5 Sep. '31, NYC, brother of Bud POWELL) wrote fine tunes; played celeste on 'Time'. Brownie would have been one of the brightest stars of the decades; kept himself conspicuously clean during the heroin plague of early '50s, only to die with Powell in another car crash. Records, incl. then-rare live locations, issued and reissued, incl. *Live At Basin Street April 1956* with Roach quintet. Complete Blue Note and Pacific Jazz sessions '53-4 in Mosaic 5-disc limited edition, incl. live Birdland session with Horace SILVER and Art BLAKEY; much else. *Live At The Bee Hive In Chicago* '55 later issued on Columbia, Japanese Victor; *Pure Genius* '56 on Elektra Musician from the collection of Mrs Brown; 10 LPs in Polygram Classics series USA, half of them with Roach.

BROWN, James (*b* 3 May '28, Barnwell, S.C.) Singer, songwriter, producer/arranger, keyboards, drums: immensely influential in postwar black pop music, both stylistically and in his independence. Raised in Augusta, Ga.; emerged from poverty, prison, southern synthesis of gospel music, vaudeville and infl. of R&B pioneers Louis JORDAN and Roy BROWN; made first records with the FAMOUS FLAMES for King initially on Federal label: first single 'Please, Please, Please' a regional hit and eventual million seller; 'Try Me' '58 a national gold disc. Signed by Universal Attractions booking agency (owner Ben Bart becoming business mentor); recruited backing band (initially led by saxman J. C. Davis), developed the hottest roadshow in USA: became known as 'Soul Brother No. 1', 'Mr Dynamite'. Records incl. 'Think', 'Lost Someone', LP *Live At The Apollo* '60-2. Recorded dance hit 'Do The Mashed Potatoes' in Florida under his drummer's name for no. 8 R&B hit because of King label's obstinacy; formed publishing co. and produced himself, selling tapes to Smash (subsidiary of Mercury); 'Out Of Sight' heralded early 'funky' sound and beginning of international fame. Back on King with a better deal (*see* KING), still recording independently, consolidated sound and success with 'Papa's Got A Brand New Bag' and 'I Got You (I Feel Good)' (both '65); also intense ballads, e.g. 'It's A Man's Man's Man's World' '66. Progressively further removed from mainstream rock'n'roll and already ahead of pop music, he now began to infl. jazzmen e.g. Miles DAVIS, Donald BYRD with records such as 'Cold Sweat', 'Mother Popcorn' and 'Ain't It Funky Now' 67-9. During '60s

band was led first by Nat Jones, then Alfred 'Pee Wee' Ellis (both alto sax); also incl. such notables as Maceo Parker (tenor) and John 'Jabbo' Starks (drums); at the end of the decade most of this band left him, becoming Maceo & All The King's Men. Brown's image confused by political ambiguity; after TV appearances following Martin Luther King murder he was feted both by the White House and by black militants; he responded both ways with 'America Is My Home' and 'Say It Loud, I'm Black And I'm Proud' '68, with personal appearances in Vietnam and West Africa. Returned to singleminded record success with new, young band, The JBs, at first with William 'Bootsy' Collins (bass) and his brother Phelps 'Catfish' (guitar): 'Sex Machine' and 'Super Bad' '70, 'Soul Power' '71. Signed to Polydor with changing lineup of JBs led by Fred Wesley (trombone) and maintained frontline 'funk' status until '74: 'The Payback' and 'Papa Don't Take No Mess'. Since then fewer hits: 'Get Up Offa That Thing' '76, 'It's Too Funky In Here' '79, 'Rapp Playback' '80, 'Unity' '84 (with Africa Bambaataa). With over 100 US hits incl. 56 R&B top tens, 17 no. 1 entries and more than 40 gold discs, his career is legend and his influence is permanent, and he's not through yet: following smash hit 'Living In America' early '86, written by Dan Hartman/Charlie Midnight for film *Rocky IV*, LP *Gravity* on Scotti Brothers label written by the same team, prod. by Hartman with guests Alison MOYET, Stevie WINWOOD. Collections available incl. *Federal Years, Part 1* and *Part 2* ('56-9); *Ain't That A Groove* ('66-9), *Doin' It To Death* ('69-73), *Best Of*. In UK seven LPs reissued by Polydor/King in the original sleeves, covering '62-7: *I Got You, It's A Man's Man's Man's World, Live And Low-Down At The Apollo, Live In New York, Mean On The Scene, Papa's Got A Brand New Bag, Please, Please, Please. Soul Power* '86 is reissue EP incl. early version of 'It's A Man's World'. He became a giant, encountering resistance all the way (King didn't want to release 'Please'); tells all in autobiography *James Brown* '87 with Bruce Tucker.

BROWN, Joe (*b* Joseph Roger Brown, 13 May '41, Lincolnshire, England) Singer, guitar. Moved to London's East End age 2, played in The Spacemen skiffle group as teenager. Friends with and played with Eddie COCHRAN, Gene VINCENT, also backed visiting Johnny CASH, Freddy CANNON. Producer Jack Good put him on TV in the '50s; had 12 chart hits '60-73, incl. top tens with his group The Bruvvers 'A Picture Of You' (also LP of same title), 'It Only Took A Minute', 'That's What Love Will Do' '62-3. Showed affection for Music Hall in 'I'm Henry VIII I Am' (a hit in USA by HERMAN'S HERMITS). Did instrumentals (rare then): 'The Switch' and 'Pop Corn'. Success of BEATLES put pre-Beatle rockers in the shade; Brown switched to contrived pop films such as *What A Crazy World* '63 and *Three Hats For Lisa* '65. One of three hit versions of Beatles' 'With A Little Help From My Friends' '67. Appeared with Anna Neagle in musical *Charley Girl* late '60s; formed country-style group Brown's Home Brew with wife Vicki early '70s; now a familiar face on TV game shows and adverts. Compilation *Collection* '74.

BROWN, Lawrence (*b* 3 Aug. '07, Lawrence, Kansas) Trombone. Grew up in California, studied several instruments; first recorded with Paul Howard and his Quality Serenaders '29 (featured on 'Charlie's Idea'); with Les HITE '31, Duke ELLINGTON '32-51; Johnny HODGES; freelance NYC '55-6; studio work '57; back with Duke '60-70. Featured with Duke on 'Ducky Wucky', 'Slippery Horn' ('32-3); then became famous for legato ballad style. Best known solo: 'Rose Of The Rio Grande', '38. Featured on '45 remake of Duke's classic 'Black Beauty'; composed 'Transblucency' ('46, based on own solo on 'Blue Light' '38); 'Golden Cress', 'On A Turquoise Cloud' ('47). During second stay with Ellington, took over plunger-mute role of 'Tricky Sam' Nanton, played part in 'Mood Indigo' trio, etc. Also recorded with Louis ARMSTRONG, Ruby BRAFF, Rex STEWART, Jimmy RUSHING, Jackie GLEASON; own LPs on Clef (Verve) '56, Impulse '65. Appointed by Nixon to Advisory Committee for Kennedy Center; retired to California '72.

BROWN, Les (*b* Lester Raymond Brown, 14 Mar. '12, Reinerton, Pa.) Bandleader; played reeds but did not solo. Duke Blue Devils formed Duke University early '30s; broke up '37. Arranged freelance, started again '38: 'Les Brown and his Band of Renown' became the most famous and popular white dance band of late '40s-50s. First hit: 'Joltin' Joe DiMaggio', with vocalist Betty Bonney '41, when entire country was following the New York Yankees. Made film *Seven Days Leave* '42; many radio broadcasts for Coca-Cola; Doris DAY was vocalist '40, '43-6; biggest hits: 'My Dreams Are Getting Better All The Time', 'Sentimental Journey' (comp. by band's arranger, Ben Homer) both no. 1 in Billboard chart '45; 'You Won't Be Satisfied (Till You Break My Heart)', no. 5 '46; also 'Doctor, Lawyer, Indian Chief', instrumentals 'I've Got My Love To Keep Me Warm', 'Bizet Has His Day', 'Leap Frog', etc. Quit late '46 to take a year off, settle in L.A. but had forgotten a March '47 ballroom gig; could not get out of it and formed another band. From then on based on West Coast; radio, TV work with Bob Hope (entertained troops for many years), Steve ALLEN shows '59-60; Dean Martin '66 etc. 'Best of' LP: *Sentimental Journey* (Columbia Special Products). Recorded for Coral '51-5; hits with the AMES BROS. Broadcast airchecks issued on Hindsight, Joyce, First Heard labels; 2-disc set on MCA had live concert from the Hollywood Palladium '53; LPs on Capitol '55-8, on Coral, Columbia '59-63; *New Horizons* '72 on Daybreak, *Les Brown Today* '74 on MPS, many others: concert albums made in Japan '83 incl. long-time Brown vocalist Jo Ann Greer, sideman Butch Stone on baritone sax, vocals; guests Rosemary CLOONEY, Georgie AULD, Buddy DeFRANCO. *Digital Swing* '86 on Fantasy celebrated Brown's 50 years as a bandleader.

BROWN, Marion (*b* 8 Sep. '35, Atlanta, Ga.) Alto sax, composer in contemporary black music. Early teacher was Wayman CARVER; played with Johnny HODGES in Atlanta '57; to NYC, worked with Archie SHEPP. With JCOA '64, own group '65; USIA film with Bill DIXON same year. Records with Dixon, John COLTRANE (*Ascension* '65); played with SUN RA, toured Europe, formed duo with Leo SMITH. Entered education, at Wesleyan U. mid-'70s studying ethnic instruments, black fife-and-drum corps in

Southern states. Own records as leader began '65-6 on ESP with *Marion Brown Quartet* followed by 'Jazz Improvisation' on *The East Village Other*, a collage of free playing. Other records incl. some privately made, unaccompanied alto solos on LP *Gesprachsfetzen* '68, made in Munich with Gunter Hampel Quintet; film soundtrack *Le temps fou* '68; also *The Visitor* and *Three For Shepp* '66, with Grachan MONCUR III, Kenny BURRELL, others; *Porto Novo* '67, trio set made in Holland; *Afternoon Of A Georgia Faun* '70 on ECM, with Anthony BRAXTON, Andrew CYRILLE, Chick COREA, etc.; *Soundways* '73, duets with Elliott Schwartz on various instruments at Bowdoin College; *Geechee Reflections* '73, with Smith on Impulse; *Sweet Earth Flying* '74, *Vista* '75, also on Impulse; *Awofofora* and *Zenzile* '76; *La Placita* '77, live in Switzerland; *Solo Saxophone* '77 on Sweet Earth label; *Reeds 'n Vibes* '78 with Hampel; *Passion Flower* '78; *Soul Eyes* '78 with Kenny Barron, Cecil McBEE, Philly Joe JONES; *November Cotton Flower* '79; *Marion Brown Live* '79, *Back To Paris* '80, quartet with Fred Waits. *Recollections: Essays, Drawings, Miscellanea* '84 published in Germany (incl. long interview with Brown); *Marion Brown Discography* '85 in Brussels, by DeCraen and Janssens.

BROWN, Nacio Herb (*b* 22 Feb. 1896, Deming, N.M.; *d* 28 Sep. '64, San Francisco) Songwriter, mainly for films. Raised in L.A.; toured as piano accompanist; started tailoring business and wrote songs. Early success 'When Buddha Smiles' '21 later a Swing Era hit for Benny GOODMAN. Talking films *Broadway Melody* ('You Were Meant For Me'), *Hollywood Revue* ('Singin' In The Rain'), *Untamed* ('Pagan Love Song') made reputation, all '29. Collaborated with lyricists Buddy DESYLVA, Gus Kahn (*b* 6 Nov. 1886, Coblenz, Germany; *d* 8 Oct. '41, Beverly Hills), Arthur Freed (*b* 9 Sep. 1894, Charleston, S.C.; *d* 12 Apr. '73), others. Among many hits: 'You're An Old Smoothie' and 'Turn Out The Lights' '32, 'Temptation' and 'All I Do Is Dream Of You' '34, 'You Are My Lucky Star' '35, 'You Stepped Out Of A Dream' '41, 'Make 'Em Laugh' '52 for film *Singin' In The Rain* dir. by Freed, which revived the title song.

BROWN, Nappy (*b* Napoleon Brown, Charlotte, N.C.) Rhythm & blues singer. Began with local gospel groups; moved to New Jersey and signed with Savoy Records for 25 singles '55-61: 'Don't Be Angry' was no. 2 R&B hit, pop top 40 '55 (also covered by CREW-CUTS); 'Pitter Patter' '56, 'It Don't Hurt No More' '58 were top 10 R&B, made Hot 100 pop; 'I Cried Like A Baby' '61 was last R&B chart entry. Most hits written by Rose Marie McCoy. Resumed recording '69 after spell in prison; '70s with Bell Jubilee Singers on Jewel label; album *Something Gonna Jump Out The Bushes* '88 on Black Top.

BROWN, Oscar, Jr (*b* 10 Oct. '26, Chicago Ill.) Singer, songwriter. First recorded comp: 'Brown Baby', Mahalia JACKSON. Signed by Columbia as singer, mainly of his own work ('60); collaborated with Max ROACH on *Freedom Now Suite* (album *We Insist!*, '60). Lyrics for instrumental jazz comps: 'Dat Dere' (Bobby TIMMONS), *All Blues* (Miles DAVIS), 'So Help Me' (Les McCANN), 'One Foot In The Gutter' (Clark TERRY), etc. MC of TV series *Jazz Scene USA* '62. *Sin & Soul* LP from Columbia period reissued by Special Products division. In recent years he has been back in Chicago, prod. musical revues with his wife.

BROWN, Pete (*b* 25 Dec. '40, London) Poet, lyricist. Active on London jazz-poetry scene early '60s, worked in group with Graham BOND, then with CREAM, writing lyrics for hits 'Sunshine Of Your Love', 'White Room', 'I Feel Free', 'Politician' etc. which he said would pay the rent for the rest of his life. After Cream split '68, continued to work with Jack Bruce on his albums *Songs For A Tailor* '70 (incl. 'Themes For An Imaginary Western'), *Harmony Row* '71; also did *Jazz Poetry* '66, *A Meal You Can Shake Hands With* '69, *Thousands On A Raft* '70; own group Battered Ornaments (with Chris Spedding on guitar), then Piblokto for three LPs incl. *Things May Come And Things May Go, But The Art School Dance Goes On Forever,* '72; then Back To Front c.'77; then odd gigs around London, concentrating on poetry readings. *Before Singing Lessons 1969-77* '87 is 2-disc compilation.

BROWN, Ray (*b* Raymond Matthews Brown, 13 Oct. '26, Pittsburgh, Pa.) Bass. With Dizzy GILLESPIE late '40s; formed own trio; married to Ella FITZGERALD and her accompanist '48-52; with JATP annual tours and Oscar PETERSON trio '51-66. Records with Peterson, JATP, many others; moved to California. Career with Peterson and JATP led to long association with Norman GRANZ's labels: own albums incl. *Bass Hit, This Is Ray Brown* on Verve. As star sideman on Pablo: *Duke's Big Four*; *Milt Jackson/Ray Brown Jam*; *The Big Three* (Jackson, Brown and Joe PASS); *The Giants* (Peterson, Brown and Pass); *Duke's Big Four*; *This One's For Blanton* re-creates 1940 ELLINGTON-Blanton duets '72. Among other own LPs: *Brown's Bag* '75 on Concord Jazz; *Something For Lester* '77 on Contemporary; *As Good As It Gets* '77 (trio), *Trio Live At Concord Jazz Festival 1979* (with Ernestine ANDERSON), *Tasty!* '79 (duet with Jimmy ROWLES), all on Concord; *Summerwind* '80 (quartet with Martin Drew, Johnny GRIFFIN, Monty ALEXANDER). *Moonlight Serenade* (duo with Laurindo ALMEIDA), both on Jeton; *A Ray Brown 3*, with Alexander, Sam MOST, *Overseas Special* with Alexander and Ray Ellis both on Concord; also nine LPs on that label with the L.A. Four: Almeida, Bud SHANK, Brown, Shelly MANNE or Jeff Hamilton, drums: albums incl. *The L.A. Four Scores* '77, *Live At Montreux* '79, *Zaca* '80, *Montage* '81, *Just Friends* and *Executive Suite* '82; two more LPs by this group on East Wind (Japanese label for direct-to-disc records). Brown has prod. Hollywood Bowl concerts, managed Quincy JONES, published instruction books; one of the busiest and most highly regarded of bassists.

BROWN, Roy (*b* 10 Sep. '25, New Orleans; *d* 25 May '81) Rhythm & blues singer. Began with local bands; recorded his own song 'Good Rockin' Tonight' for De Luxe '48, covered by Wynonie HARRIS on King, later by Elvis PRESLEY on Sun. 'Boogie At Midnight' was no. 3 R&B hit '49, then 'Hard Luck Blues' no. 1 '50, followed same year by 'Love Don't Love Nobody' (no. 2), 'Long About Sundown' (no. 8), 'Cadillac Baby' (no. 6); in '51 'Big Town' (no. 8). Signed with King '52 and had less luck, though always a popular act; to Imperial '56,

teamed with Dave BARTHOLOMEW for cover of Buddy KNOX's 'Party Doll' (no. 14 R&B '57; made Hot 100 on pop chart, where Knox had no. 1). 'Let The Four Winds Blow' same year made pop top 40. After period of inactivity joined the Johnny OTIS review; re-formed own band late '70s, toured until sudden death. Performs own hits on compilations on Route 66 and Magnum Force labels.

BROWN, Ruth (*b* 30 Jan. '28, Portsmouth, Va.) R&B/jazz singer. Sang in church; heard Billie HOLIDAY, Ella FITZGERALD; won amateur night at the Apollo singing ballad 'It Could Happen To You' (she'd heard Bing CROSBY sing it); landed a job with Lucky MILLINDER band '48; Blanche Calloway (Cab's sister) became her manager, got audition at Atlantic records. On the way a car crash hospitalised her for months, but contract signed: first record 'So Long' was no. 6 R&B chart '49, 10 more top 10 hits '50-5 incl. no. 1 entries 'Teardrops From My Eyes' '50, '5-10-15 Hours' '52, '(Mama) He Treats Your Daughter Mean' '53, 'Oh What A Dream' and 'Mambo Baby' '54. Hits covered in pop charts by Georgia GIBBS, Patti PAGE; billed as Miss Rhythm, always a star attraction at the Apollo, where she shared a bill late '50s with Miles DAVIS, Thelonious MONK. Pop crossover began none too soon '57 with 'Lucky Lips' (no. 25 pop, no. 12 R&B); song by LEIBER & STOLLER, covered in UK '70s by Cliff RICHARD); 'This Little Girl's Gone Rockin'' '58 (no. 24 pop/23 R&B) featured KING CURTIS on sax; 'I Don't Know' '59 was no. 5 R&B, Hot 100 pop; hits continued through '62 with seven Hot 100 entries, 18 R&B altogether. Lives on Long Island, still performs occasionally at jazz festivals. Atlantic hits compiled on *Rockin' With Ruth* on Charly UK.

BROWN, Walter (*b* 17 Aug. '17, Dallas; *d* June '56, Okla.) Blues singer. Worked in Dallas; Sunset Crystal Palace, Kansas City c. '37; heard by bandleader Jay McSHANN in Vine Street club '40. (McShann later claimed that at initial meeting he gave Brown 50 cents to sing a blues, then borrowed 25 cents back to buy a bowl of chili.) First sides with band incl. 'Hootie Blues'/'Confessin' The Blues' Apr. '41:

'Confessin' written by Brown and McShann, sold 500,000 copies for Decca, became classic; Chuck BERRY sang it in high school, B. B. KING covered it '69, etc. More sides '41-2 incl. 'Lonely Boy Blues', 'The Jumpin' Blues', etc. Toured with the band, sometimes played solo dates; fully solo by '45. Recorded for Queen/King label; club dates with Earl HINES '46; records with Tiny GRIMES Sextet on Signature '47, incl. one of many covers of hit 'Open The Door Richard' (Count BASIE record no. 1 on pop chart '49). With Jay McShann quartet on Mercury '48. Further work in New Orleans, records for Capitol, Peacock; drug problem contributed to early death. Standard McShann compilation LP (on MCA USA; Affinity UK) incl. Brown's hits.

BROWNE, Jackson (*b* 9 Oct. '48, Heidelberg, West Germany) Singer/songwriter. Father was keen jazz pianist, played with Django REINHARDT while in Europe. To L.A. early '50s; began performing, writing early '60s; NITTY GRITTY DIRT BAND recorded songs; to NYC '67, landed residency at Andy Warhol's Dom Club, friendship with NICO, who incl. a song on '67 LP *Chelsea Girls*. By the end of '70s his songs had been recorded by The BYRDS, Tom RUSH, Bonnie RAITT, Linda RONSTADT, the JACKSON 5. Own first single hit 'Doctor My Eyes' '72 (no. 8 USA; hit in UK for Jackson 5 '73); debut LP *Jackson Browne* '72 followed by more successful *For Everyman* '73, incl. 'Take It Easy', hit for the EAGLES, and 'Redneck Friend' on which Elton JOHN played piano (credited as 'Rockaday Johnnie'). Browne worked with Eagles, co-writing hit single 'James Dean', also songs on their '73 concept album *Desperado*. Still a cult figure; '74 LP *Late For The Sky* established him in own right, incl. 'For A Dancer', 'Before The Deluge' (covered by Moving Hearts, '82). Wife Phyllis committed suicide '76, casting dreadful shadow over fine album *The Pretender* that year, prod. by Jon Landau; title track is perhaps his best song ever (covered by Gary 'US' BONDS on '81 comeback LP *Dedication*). Live '78 concept LP *Running On Empty* was patchy, but contained hit singles in title track and cover of Maurice WILLIAMS's 'Stay'. After nuclear scare at Three Mile Island, joined MUSE (Musi-

cians United for Safe Energy), helped stage '79 NYC concert with Carly Simon, James TAYLOR, Bruce SPRINGSTEEN, CROSBY STILLS & NASH; film, triple album *No Nukes* well received '80. Browne remained active; arrested in demonstrations. *Hold Out* in '80 was first album of new material in four years, incl. uncharacteristic 'Disco Apocalypse' as well as hallmark 'Of Missing Persons'. Has prod. LPs by old school friend Greg Copeland, accompanist David LINDLEY, Warren ZEVON; had second top 10 USA single 'Somebody's Baby' '82 (from film *Fast Times At Ridgemount High*); appeared at Glastonbury CND festival UK '82. *Lawyers In Love* '83 had standout title track, 'For A Rocker' (dedicated to Lowell George), 'Tender Is The Night'; epitomises laid-back '70s California sound. He once admitted that his technique was limited to three chords; music press describes him as 'chilled white whine', but best work raises him far above most contemporaries. Album *Lives In The Balance* '86 displayed powers unwaned.

BROWNS, The James Edward (*b* 1 Apr. '34, Sparkman, Ark.), Ella Maxine (*b* 27 Apr. '32, Sampti, La.), Bonnie (*b* 31 July '37, Sparkman). Vocal pop/country trio '54-67, then Jim Ed solo, duo with Helen Cornelius. Began as duo with Jim Ed and Maxine working local functions late '40s; radio series KCLA Pine Bluff, Ark. '50-5. Won talent contest on Barnyard Frolic show in Little Rock; Bonnie joined '54; appeared on Louisiana Hayride '54-6; signed with Fabor label (subsidiary of Abbott); Jim REEVES recommended them to Chet ATKINS: their smooth harmony right for the Nashville sound he was creating. Joined RCA '56 (while Jim Ed did military service, another sister Norma took his place); made charts with 'I Take The Chance'; further country hits 'I Heard The Bluebirds Sing', 'Would You Care', 'Beyond The Shadow' '57-9 preceded no. 1 hit in both pop and country charts '59 with Edith PIAF song 'The Three Bells' (no. 6 UK). Further hits incl. 'Scarlet Ribbons', 'The Old Lamplighter' '60; 'Send Me The Pillow That You Dream On', 'Ground Hog' '61; appeared on Dick CLARK, Arthur Murray, Ed Sullivan TV shows; etc. Went on with country hits such as 'Then I'll Stop Loving You' '64, 'I'd

Just Be Fool Enough' '66, 'Big Daddy' '67; LPs incl. *Sweet Sounds By The Browns, This Young Land, Three Shades Of Brown, When Love Has Gone.* Girls retired '67; Jim Ed had already recorded solo at urging of his sisters: had hit 'I Heard From A Memory Last Night' '65; trying not to sound too much like Reeves, had further hits with 'A Taste Of Heaven' '66, 'You Can Have Her' and 'Pop A Top' '67, 'The Cajun Stripper' and 'The Enemy' '68 (Maxine scored solo that year on Chart label with 'Sugar Cane Country'). Jim Ed's biggest hit 'Morning' '70 covered in UK by Val DOONICAN. Career slumped early '70s; came back to country top 10 with 'Southern Loving' '73, 'It's That Time Of Night' '74; then teamed with Helen Cornelius (*b* 6 Dec. '50, Hannibal, Mo.) for series of duet hits from '76. Helen entered talent contest in Quincy, Ill.; spotted for Ted Mack Amateur Hour; began writing songs; signed to RCA '75, had own hit 'There's Always A Goodbye' '76; their duet 'I Don't Want To Have To Marry You' topped country chart '76, LP of same name '77. Other hits incl. 'Saying Hello, Saying I Love You, Saying Goodbye' '76, 'Born Believer' and 'If It Ain't Love By Now' '77; named country duo of the year by CMA '77; more hits: 'If The World Ran Out Of Love Tonight', 'You Don't Bring Me Flowers' '78, 'Lying In Love With You', 'Fools' '79. They split up '82; Jim Ed teamed up with Dianne Morgan and Christy Russell for new touring band. Also had syndicated TV show *Nashville On The Road*, on which Helen appeared; she has appeared on many other TV shows, leads five-piece band Southern Spirit on state and county fair circuit; about 40 of her songs have been recorded by Lynn ANDERSON, Jeannie C. RILEY, DOTTSY, others; 'Ready To Take My Chances (Of Falling In Love Again)' was a hit by the OAK RIDGE BOYS; had own minor hit 'If Your Heart's A Rollin' Stone' '83. Jim Ed made more than 50 LPs for RCA, incl. *The Best Of The Browns, Born Believer* '78 with Helen; *Jim Ed & The Browns* '86 on MCA/Dot was reunion with sisters.

BRUBECK, Dave (*b* David Warren Brubeck, 6 Dec. '20, Concord, Cal.) Pianist, leader, composer. From musical family, played with local bands age 13; studied with Darius Milhaud, Arnold Schoenberg; recorded with nonet '48, trio '49 with Ron Crotty (*b* '29, San Francisco) on bass, Cal TJADER; quartet became internationally popular '51-67 with Paul DESMOND, alto sax: easily the most successful of West Coast (largely white) school of cool jazz emerging in early '50s. First successes on college campuses '52 (with Lloyd Davis on drums), LPs such as *Jazz At Oberlin College* on young Fantasy label; switched to Columbia '54. Bob Bates (*b* '23, Idaho) played bass '53-5, then brother Norman Bates (*b* 26 Aug. '27); Eugene Wright (*b* '23, Chicago) bass from '58. Joe Dodge (*b* '22, Monroe, Wisc.) played drums '53-6; had earlier played in a group with Desmond. Joe Morello (*b* '28, Springfield, Mass.), partially blind since birth, drummer from '56. Brubeck's style was cerebral, harmonically dense, full of classical devices – block chording, fugues, counterpoint – not unknown in jazz but used rather self-consciously; seemed more innovatory than it was, but group's enormous popularity was valuable at a time when jazz was not otherwise commercially successful. Brubeck's swing was unfairly questioned, but he played lovely solos on ballads ('Stardust' on Fantasy '53); Morello's tasty technique, Desmond's wistful tone were liked even by critics. Quartet played Newport Jazz Festivals '56-8; international tour '58; Brubeck and/or quartet won all the polls, toured the world. Joe Benjamin (*b* 4 Nov. '19, Atlantic City, N.J.) played bass at Newport '58 instead of Wright. First Columbia album, *Jazz Goes To College*, made top 10 of LP chart '54, as did others: *Dave Brubeck At Storyville, Brubeck Time, Red Hot And Cool* (tied to cosmetics promo), all '55; *Jazz Goes To Junior College* '57. Biggest seller was *Time Out* '60, with different time signature on each tune: single 'Take Five' reached no. 25 on USA chart; 'It's A Raggy Waltz', 'Unsquare Dance' also charted in UK; *Time Further Out* '61 was first sequel. Recorded with Louis ARMSTRONG, Trummy Young '59; in '60-1 with Jimmy RUSHING, Carmen McRAE, longtime associate from San Francisco days Bill Smith on clarinet; string orchestra dir. by composer brother Howard Brubeck; Armstrong again; Lambert, HENDRICKS & Ross. Howard's comp. *Dialogue For Jazz Combo And Orchestra* was broadcast '59, recorded '60 by quartet with

NYPO cond. by Leonard BERNSTEIN; wrote *Points In Jazz* '60 for American Ballet Theatre; show *The Real Ambassadors* with lyrics by wife Iola performed at Monterey Jazz Festival '62 with quartet, Armstrong, McRae plus Lambert, Hendricks and Bavan. Disbanded to concentrate on composition; then new quartet '68 for Mexican Festival with Gerry MULLIGAN (with whom Brubeck had appeared at Newport '54); Jack Six, bass (*b* 26 July '30, Danville, Ill.), Alan Dawson, drums (*b* 14 July '29, Marietta, Pa.); trio after '72 except for special engagements. From '74 toured, recorded with sons Danny (*b* 4 May '55, Oakland), percussion; Chris (*b* 19 March '52, L.A.), trombone; David Darius (*b* 14 June '47, San Francisco), piano; act called *Two Generations Of Brubeck* (Atlantic LP '74). Comps. incl. fine tunes 'In Your Own Sweet Way', 'The Duke'; oratorio *The Light In The Wilderness* '68, cantatas, songs etc. with texts by Iola. *Time Out* coupled in 2-disc set with *Time Further Out* in UK, with *Gone With The Wind* ('59) in USA. About 100 albums incl. solo piano LP '56; other quartet LPs incl. 2-disc *At Carnegie Hall* '63, *Jazz Impressions Of Japan, Of New York* '64-5, *Time Changes* '64, *Plays Cole Porter* '65, *Time In* '66, several *Greatest Hits* compilations, all on Columbia; *25th Anniversary Reunion* '76 on Horizon. With Mulligan: *Blues Roots* '68, *Last Set At Newport* '71, others. More recent LPs incl. *The Duets* '75 on Horizon with Desmond; *All The Things We Are* '76 on Atlantic has imaginative quintet organised and prod. by Michael CUSCUNA, with Brubeck, Six, Roy HAYNES, Lee KONITZ, Anthony BRAXTON. LPs on Concord incl. *Back Home* '79, *Tritonis* '80; *Paper Moon* '81 features Chris on trombone, Jerry Bergonzi on tenor sax (both doubling on bass), Randy Jones, drums; *Concord On A Summer Night* '82 and *For Iola* '85 have Brubeck, Chris, Jones and Smith.

BRUCE, Ed (*b* 29 Dec. '39, Keiser, Ark.) Country singer, songwriter, TV actor. Began as rock'n'roller Edwin Bruce on Sun '58; had songs recorded by Jerry Lee LEWIS, Charlie RICH, Johnny CASH, etc. Became used car salesman, continued to write; back to music full-time after 'Save Your Kisses', B-side of Tommy ROE gold disc 'Sheila' '63. Moved to Nashville as background singer and songwriter ('See The Big Man Cry' for Charlie LOUVIN; 'Northeast Arkansas Mississippi County Bootlegger' for Kenny PRICE); signed to RCA and released acclaimed own LP *If I Could Just Go Home* '67. Changed to Monument label, scored minor hits 'Song For Ginny', 'Everybody Wants To Get To Heaven' '69. Early morning TV show on Nashville WSM '69-74; songwriting; TV commercials for United Airlines, Burger King, etc. Big rugged looking man was also hired by the state of Tenn. for adverts promoting tourism. Signed to UA '73, minor hit 'July You're A Woman' '73; dropped from label but re-signed on strength of 'Mamas Don't Let Your Babies Grow Up To Be Cowboys', C&W top 20 '75: revived by Waylon JENNINGS/Willie NELSON '78, became no. 1 country chart and won Grammy. Wrote hits 'Restless' (Crystal GAYLE '74), 'When I Die', 'The Man That Turned My Mama On' (Tanya Tucker '75). Signed to Epic '77; hits incl. 'Star Studded Nights', 'Love Somebody To Death', 'Angeline'; to MCA '80 for biggest hits 'Diane', 'The Last Cowboy Song' (duet with Nelson), 'You're The Best Break This Old Heart Ever Had' (no. 1 '82), 'My First Taste Of Texas' '83, 'After All' '84. Appeared in Brett Maverick TV series '81-2. LPs incl. *Shades Of Ed Bruce* on Monument '69; *Mamas Don't Let Your Babies Grow Up To Be Cowboys* on UA '76; *The Tennessean* Epic '78; *Ed Bruce, One To One, I Write It Down* '82, *You're Not Leavin' Here Tonight* '83, *Tell 'Em I've Gone Crazy* '84 (MCA); *Homecoming* RCA '85. Managed by wife Patsy, who also contributes ideas for songs, some lyrics.

BRUFORD, Bill (*b* 17 May '49, Sevenoaks, Kent) UK art-rock drummer become composer, musician's musician, leading highly rated Fusion groups. Played jazz as an amateur '60s; turned pro '68, toured the world with King Crimson, YES; also with GONG, GENESIS, National Health; made *Feels Good To Me* '78 with Dave Stewart on keyboards, bassist Jeff Berlin, Allan Holdsworth on guitar; with bassist/vocalist John Wetton (ex-FAMILY, King Crimson) he formed group UK for LPs *UK, Danger Money, Night After Night* '78-9, but experiment in leaderless democracy was ultimately unsuccessful; formed quartet Bruford, toured, made LPs *One Of A Kind* '79, *The Bruford Tapes* and *Gradually Going Tornado* '80 (John Clark replacing Holdsworth on some tracks; Berlin vocals on *Tornado*); also compilation *Masterstrokes* '86. Duo with Patrick Moraz made *Music For Piano And Drums* '84, *Flags* '85; new group Earthworks co-led by Bruford and Django Bates with Iain Ballamy (both from LOOSE TUBES) has eponymous LP '87 (entered Billboard jazz chart USA at no. 23), all on EG/Editions EG labels UK. Also recorded with Al DIMEOLA, Jamaaladeen Tacuma, Akira Inoue, guitarist David Torn (*Cloud About Mercury* '87 on ECM), etc.

BRUNSWICK US and UK labels. Piano makers Brunswick-Balke-Collender started Brunswick USA '16; artists incl. conductor Arturo Toscanini and bandleader Isham JONES, whose 'Wabash Blues' was label's big hit in '21. Strong film links: Al JOLSON had first big hit of talking film era with 'Sonny Boy'/'There's A Rainbow Round My Shoulder', both from his second film *The Singing Fool* '28. (Label also made Rudolf Valentino's only record, so bad it was never released.) Bing CROSBY, Fred ASTAIRE were Brunswick stars early '30s. Warner Brothers bought label '30, sold it to American Record Corporation (ARC) '31; it became company's premier label, with stars like MILLS BROS, ANDREWS SISTERS and Harry JAMES, whose version of 'One O'Clock Jump' was label's last big hit before CBS bought group '38, closed Brunswick down in favour of reactivated Columbia, sold Brunswick to Decca (US) '42, who reactivated it '57: label's acts then incl. the CRICKETS, Jackie WILSON and Chicago doo-wop group the CHI-LITES, whose songwriter, producer, singer Eugene Record was responsible for no. 1 soul 'Have You Seen Her' '71, 'Oh Girl' '72. Nat Tarnopol bought Brunswick '69, added it to his Dakar label; Record became A&R vice president; Tarnopol sold label back to MCA '84. In UK Chappell Piano Co. launched Brunswick Cliftophone '23; had success with US import Mound City Blue Blowers (e.g. 'Arkansas Blues' '24). Rights to Brunswick UK passed to Count Antoni de Bosdari '27, Duophone Syndicate '28, Warners '30; in '32 ARC sold UK Brunswick to Decca UK, who used it as outlet for US imports: hence Bill HALEY's

'50s hits were on Brunswick in UK and label acquired the WHO because in '65 only US Decca would give them a contract. In USA MCA bought US Decca in '59, later closed down all labels in favour of worldwide MCA logo; UK Brunswick came to an end when UK Decca's contract with US Brunswick ended '79. When MCA reacquired Brunswick USA in '84 the label was retired there as well.

BRYANT, Anita (*b* 25 Mar. '40, Tulsa, Okla.) Pop singer. Sang on Arthur GODFREY show, was Miss Oklahoma '58, Miss America finalist; recorded for Carlton (formed '59 in NYC by Joe Carlton; also had Jack SCOTT); 10 Hot 100 entries '59-61 incl. top tens 'Paper Roses', 'In My Little Corner Of The World' '60; switched to Columbia, faded. Did orange juice commercials on TV, made headlines with outspoken anti-gay, pro-convention remarks; separated from husband, Miami DJ Bob Green.

BRYANT, Felice & Boudleaux Country-pop songwriters. Boudleaux (*b* 13 Feb. '20, Shellman, Ga.; *d* 30 June '87) studied music, played violin in Atlanta Philharmonic '38, switched to country and jazz; on tour '45 met wife Felice (*b* 7 Aug. '25) operating hotel lift in her home town of Milwaukee, Wis.: they had both been writing lyrics, wrote together for fun, then sent 'Country Boy' to Fred ROSE '49: top 10 country hit for Little Jimmy DICKENS. To Nashville '50, wrote hits for Carl SMITH: top 10 country entries '52-3 incl. 'It's A Lovely, Lovely World', 'Our Honeymoon', 'Just Wait Till I Get You Alone'; 'This Orchid Means Goodbye' co-written by Boudleaux and Smith. 'Hey Joe!' covered by Frankie LAINE '53, made no. 11 on pop chart; 'Back Up Buddy' no. 4 country '54. Wrote 'I've Been Thinking' and 'The Richest Man' for Eddy ARNOLD '55, etc.; then worked with EVERLY BROS: their 'Bye Bye Love' was one of the most exciting pop records of '57, selling huge numbers in advance orders before anyone had heard it: no. 1 country, no. 2 pop; three Bryant/Everly hits all no. 1 pop '57-8: 'Wake Up Little Susie', 'All I Have To Do Is Dream', 'Bird Dog': as modern era in pop music began, country flavour of Bryants' writing bang in the middle of it. Had country hit 'Blue Boy' (by Jim REEVES)

'58; Boudleaux had worldwide hit with instrumental 'Mexico' '61; country top 10 hits in '60s incl. 'My Last Date' (co-written with Skeeter DAVIS), 'Baltimore' (by Sonny JAMES), 'I Love To Dance With Annie' (by Ernie ASHWORTH), 'Rocky Top' (by Buck OWENS); in '70s Felice's 'We Could' (by Charley PRIDE), their 'Raining In My Heart' (by Leo SAYER), many more. *Surfin' On A New Wave* '80 was their own LP, with songs new and old; still going strong '81 with 'Hey Joe, Hey Moe' for Joe STAMPLEY, Moe BANDY. Hits published by own House of Bryant; ran motel in resort area of Gatlinburg, Tenn. Success never changed them: Jack CLEMENT said, 'Boudleaux and Felice are the kind of people you can call up just to say hello and they will believe you.'

BRYANT, Ray (*b* 24 Dec. '31, Philadelphia, Pa.) Piano. Became house pianist at Blue Note Club in Philadelphia, accompanying visiting jazzmen; since late '50s has played solo and in trio format at jazz festivals (Newport '57 with Carmen McRAE; '59 with Jo JONES trio). Own tunes incl. 'Slow Freight', 'Little Susie', 'Cubano Chant', many more; LPs with Jones, Miles DAVIS, Sonny ROLLINS, Benny GOLSON, many others. Own LPs incl. about 16 trio sets on Epic, Prestige, Signature, Columbia, Sue, Cadet, Atlantic, Black and Blue '55-75; big band LP on Columbia '62. Also singles: 'Little Susie (Part 4)' on Signature made no. 12 R&B chart '60; sessions with 5-8 pieces on Columbia '60-2 featuring Harry EDISON, Buddy TATE, etc. yielded R&B hits: 'The Madison Time' '60 also made pop top 40, 'Sack Of Woe' '61; last Columbia single was 'After Hours'/'Tonk' '62 with Al Sears, Kenny BURRELL, Mickey Roker, Jimmy Rowser, bass (*b* 18 Apr. '26, Philadelphia). Cadet LP '67 had piano with orchestra arr., cond. by Richard Evans; also big band set '72. Solo sets *Alone With The Blues* '55 on New Jazz (Prestige); *Alone At Montreux* '72 on Atlantic; *Solo Flight* '76 and *Live At Montreux* '77 on Pablo. Pablo trio sets incl. *Here's Ray Bryant* '76, *All Blues* '78, *Potpourri* '80; *The Best Of Ray Bryant* is a compilation of these. Solo and trio sets reissued '87 on Fantasy and Doctor Jazz. CDs incl *Plays Basie & Ellington* and *Trio Today* with Rufus Reid and Freddie Waits.

BRYSON, Peabo (*b* 13 Apr. '51, Greenville, S.C.) Sweet soul singer. Background in harmony singing from church; joined first group Al Freeman and the Upsetters age 14. Sang pro with Moses Dillard and the TexTown Display '68-73, toured while following parallel career as prod./songwriter for Bang label: group recorded for Curtis MAYFIELD's Curtom and Bang labels. Formed partnership with Mayfield confederate, arr. Johnny Pate, recording *Peabo* mid-'70s for Bang's Bullett subsidiary; team endured for several years. Singles like 'Underground Music' (first release), 'I Can Make It Better', 'Just Another Day' showed strongly in R&B charts '76-77, as did guest shot with Michael Zager on 'Do It With Feeling'. Signed with Capitol on Bang's demise for *Reaching For The Sky* '77; duet LP with Natalie Cole *We're The Best Of Friends* '79 was successful despite lacking a certain consistency: tracks recorded separately. Greatest crossover success as part of team with Roberta FLACK: she lost partner Donny HATHAWAY in tragic circumstances; Bryson cloned him for *Live And More* '80, repeating formula in studio to better effect on *Born To Love* '83, slick selection written/prod. largely by Diana ROSS's songsmith Michael Masser. LP incl. no. 16 USA/2 UK 'Tonight I Celebrate My Love'. After nine albums for Capitol, all of which went gold except for Bullett-era compilation, made *Straight From My Heart* '84, *Take No Prisoners* '85 for Elektra, former incl. no. 10 USA hit 'If You're Ever In My Arms Again'. Underestimated as songwriter; now having competition from soul balladeers like Jeffrey Osborne (*b* 9 Mar. '48, Providence, R.I.; hits on A&M since '82 prod. by George DUKE).

BUARQUE, Chico De Hollanda (*b* '44, São Paulo, Brazil) Guitarist, singer, songwriter. Born into wealthy academic family, became key figure in left-wing Brazilian popular culture: first hit was 'A Banda' ('The Parade'), became carnival classic; many songs were censored and he endured enforced exile in Italy and Portugal. A typical hit was 'A Pesar de Voce' ('In Spite Of You'), about political oppression and censorship, dedicated to the president of Brazil: he was the absent figurehead of the left in the late '60s. Wrote 'Grandola Vila Morena' '75, a hymn to the Portuguese revolution, later adapting the lyrics for Brazil. Album history incl. key sets with Maria BETHANIA, Milton Nascimento, Caetano Veloso. Themes are always social issues, incl. poverty and sexual politics; by the late '70s he was recognised throughout Latin America incl. Cuba, where his songs were covered by Los Van Van; in NYC Willie COLON made covers. His *Opera do Malandra* '79 ('Streetbum') was based on the Brecht-WEILL 'Mack The Knife' theme, also starred Alcione ('The Empress of the Samba') and singer Gal Costa. Visit to Angolan festival '80 with other Brazilian artists inspired 'Morena de Angola' ('Black Girl of Angola') which was no. 1 hit in Brazil; TV documentary *Certas Palavras Con Chico Buarque* '80 ('Some Words With . . .') reflected status; he did film soundtrack *Eu Te Amo* '81. French President Mitterrand gave him a medal '84.

BUBBLEGUM Pop genre originated in USA late '60s. Brill Building mogul Don Kirshner moved into TV with Screen Gems; saw TV's potential for pushing pop and advertised in *Variety* for four actors/musicians to become the MONKEES, whose networked TV show sold millions of singles composed by Kirshner lieutenants BOYCE & HART, played by sessionmen with only Monkees' voices used. Another pioneer act was Tommy JAMES and the Shondells, with writing team of Bo Gentry and Richie Cordell making hits on Roulette. Common to all bubblegum was strong beat, nursery-rhyme lyrics, clever 'hooks' in melody lines: antithesis to sex, drugs, protest endemic in '60s rock. It was taken to its logical extreme by (Jerry) Kasenetz & (Jeff) Katz's Super K production company, which had hits '67 with Ohio Express ('Beg Borrow And Steal', no. 29 on Cameo) and Music Explosion ('Little Bit O' Soul', no. 2 on Laurie); signed with Cameo boss Neil Bogart's new Buddah Records, the production line commenced: first *nom de disque* was 1910 Fruitgum Company (writer/producer Joey Levine as lead voice with session players): 'Simon Says' adapted nursery game for no. 4 USA/2 UK hit, followed by '1,2,3 Red Light', 'Goody Goody Gumdrops', 'Indian Giver', 'Special Delivery' '68-9; a touring band of Chuck Travis, Lawrence Ripley, Bruce Shay, Rusty Oppenheimer and

'Mark' promoted it. Ohio Express was recreated for 'Yummy Yummy Yummy (I've Got Love In My Tummy)', 'Chewy Chewy', more; touring group was Dale Powers, Douglas Grassel, James Pfayler, Dean Kastran, Tim Corwin. Super K with collaborators Levine, Richie Cordell, Artie Resnick virtually defined bubblegum, with Peppermint Trolley Company, Captain Groovy and his Bubblegum Army, the Rock & Roll Dubble Bubble Trading Company of Philadelphia 19141, etc.; some totally spurious, some existing groups sucked into the hit machine. Many combined to make 46-piece Kasenetz-Katz Singing Orchestral Circus, which played Carnegie Hall, scored hit 'Quick Joey Small (Run Joey Run)' '68. Not all crossed over to UK, where Brian POOLE's Tremeloes, MARMALADE etc. were home-grown competition. Ultimate came with the Archies (manufactured by Kirshner; studio lead singer Ron Dante) whose 'Sugar Sugar' (on Calendar in USA) was biggest selling RCA/UK single of all time: that they were cartoon characters sums up the whole thing. By c.'70 genre was being absorbed into pop mainstream (outpost in UK: Mickie MOST's RAK label, with Suzi QUATRO, etc.), but some sounds (e.g. Farfisa organ) remained unfashionable until punk, when kids took over the shop. Kasenetz-Katz carried on producing, notably USA hard-rockers Ram Jam '77. To judge from UK charts, pop music late '80s was a hybrid of bubblegum and DISCO.

BUCHANAN & GOODMAN Bill Buchanan and Dickie Goodman (both *b* c.'35, NYC) enlivened '56 summer with million-selling single 'Flying Saucer Parts 1&2' (no. 3 USA), written with help from Mae Boren Axton (Hoyt AXTON's mother): interview with spacemen was interspersed by their replies lifted from pop songs of the day. Fast paced, well-edited novelty had sequel '57, but idea brought lawsuits, demonstrating pop music's lack of humour where money is concerned.

BUCHANAN, Jack (*b* 2 Apr. 1891, Helensburgh, Scotland; *d* 20 Oct. '57, London) UK actor, song-and-dance man of debonair, man-about-town persona. Introduced songs 'And Her Mother Came Too' (in show *A To Z*, '21); 'Fancy Our Meeting'

(*That's A Good Girl*, '28); 'I'm In A Dancing Mood' (*This'll Make You Whistle*, '36); 'By Myself' (*Between The Devil* '37). To USA with Bea Lillie, Gertrude LAWRENCE in Andre Charlot's Revue '24; many other shows London and NYC; films incl. *Bulldog Drummond's Third Round* '25; *Goodnight Vienna, Yes Mr Brown*, '32; *Brewster's Millions* '33; *The Gang's All Here* '39; with Fred ASTAIRE in *The Band Wagon* '53. Biography *Top Hat And Tails* by Michael Marshall published '78.

BUCHANAN, Roy (*b* 23 Sep. '39, Ozark, Tenn; *d* 14 Aug. '88) Guitarist. Son of Pentecostal preacher; grew up in California. On the road in teens with Dale HAWKINS; cut solo singles, retired to session work early '60s, playing for Freddy CANNON, LEIBER & STOLLER etc. Infl. by both black and white sources, yet established distinctive style; like James BURTON, Steve Cropper identified with Fender Telecaster instrument. Once slashed speakers to get fuzztone in '50s, now relies on harmonics: 'One note can be as effective as dozens.' 'Discovered' early '70s when TV special *Best Unknown Guitarist In The World* screened USA; voted best new guitarist by *Guitar Player* readers '72 before debut solo LP *Roy Buchanan* '72 on Polydor. Early gospel influence revealed on 'Thank You Lord' from *Second Album* '73 (single 'Sweet Dreams' made no. 40 UK '73). Subsequent LPs incl. *That's What I Am Here For* and *In The Beginning* '74, *Rescue Me* '75, *A Street Called Straight* '76, *Loading Zone* '77, *You're Not Alone* '78; most made USA charts (the last three on Atlantic) established him as master of many styles. ROLLING STONES allegedly offered him place of Brian Jones, but his personality would have made a reluctant 'axe hero'; Robbie Robertson calls him 'finest rock guitarist I ever heard'. Records stopped for a while; gigged widely; then *My Babe* '81 on Waterhouse in USA; *When A Guitar Plays The Blues* '85 and *Dancing On The Edge* '86 on Alligator (Sonet UK), latter especially highly praised, with fine Texas singer Delbert McCLINTON.

BUCK & BUBBLES Black song and dance team. Ford Lee 'Buck' Washington (*b* 16 Oct. '03, Louisville, Ky.; *d* 31 Jan. '55, NYC) played piano, also trumpet; John William 'Bubbles' Sublett (*b* 19 Feb. '02, Louisville; *d* 18 May '86) was one of the first rhythmic tap dancers; both sang, danced and clowned. They teamed as children after meeting in a bowling alley c.'17; to NYC '19; soon played at vaudeville mecca The Palace; they were the first blacks to perform at Radio City Music Hall. Toured Europe '31, '36; films incl. *A Star Is Born* '37, *Cabin In The Sky* '43. They made a test record for Victor '27, nine sides for Columbia NYC '30-4 incl. alternate takes, mostly unreleased ('He's Long Gone From Bowling Green' and lovely version of 'Oh! Lady Be Good' later issued on LP anthologies), and six sides for Columbia/EMI in London '36. Broke up '53. Buck recorded with Louis ARMSTRONG '30, Bessie SMITH '33, Coleman HAWKINS '34 (Billie HOLIDAY said that he played on her first records '33; not confirmed by discographies); accompanied comedian Timmie Rogers '54. Bubbles created the role of Sportin' Life in George GERSHWIN's *Porgy And Bess*, later was the first black to appear on Johnny Carson *Tonight* TV show.

BUCKLEY, LORD (*b* Richard M. Buckley, '05, Cal.; *d* '60, NYC) Comedian. A white man who picked up patois of black jazz world well enough to use it in monologues, fashioning an act that castigated organised religion, big business, racial prejudice etc., anticipating Lenny Bruce in many ways. Allegedly won the 'Lord' title in a poker game. Delivery was important and the humour will be flat on the page, but in his Sermon on the Mount, Jesus becomes 'the Nazz' (subsequently used as name of rock groups), and prefaces his miracles with 'What's de matter wid you, baby?'. Shakespeare became 'Willie the Shake', and the soliloquy from *Julius Caesar* transformed: 'Hipsters, flipsters and finger-poppin' daddies, knock me your lobes!' With the rise of iconoclasm in '50s (the beatniks; comedians Bruce, Mort Sahl and others) Buckley enjoyed wider fame before he died; his albums became collector's items. Bob DYLAN used Buckley's 'Black Cross' in early shows; elements of his infl. can be heard in the work of Tom WAITS, others. C. P. Lee, former member of ALBERTO Y LOST TRIOS PARANOIAS, did one-man show *M'Lords & Ladies*

'82 in Buckley's style. *Lord Buckley: Blowing His Mind (And Yours Too), Bad Rapping Of The Marquis de Sade, In Concert* reissued on Demon UK.

BUCKLEY, Tim (*b* Timothy Charles Buckley III, 14 Feb. '47, Washington DC; *d* 29 June '75) Folk-based singer, songwriter. Worked with Jackson BROWNE, Jim Fielder (later of BLOOD, SWEAT & TEARS); signed to Elektra; second LP *Goodbye & Hello* '67 established indefinable stylist, soaking up jazz, folk, rock'n'roll influences; song 'I Never Asked To Be Your Mountain' showed extraordinary range. George HARRISON was early fan; there was talk of signing to Apple. Albums *Happy/Sad* '69, *Lorca* '70 showed him moving towards jazz; ambitious *Starsailor* '71 puzzled fans; *Greetings From L.A.* '72 was more commercial; *Sefronia* '73 and *Look At The Fool* '74 followed. He was concentrating more on writing, acting; at time of death from drug overdose was being considered for role of Woody GUTHRIE in film *Bound For Glory*. *Best Of Tim Buckley* '83 was not, but incl. fine cover of Fred NEIL's 'Dolphins'; group This Mortal Coil (incl. Cocteau Twins) covered 'Song To The Siren' '84.

BUCKNER, Milt (*b* 10 July '15, St Louis, Mo.; *d* 27 July '77, Chicago) Piano, Hammond organ, composer, leader. With McKINNEY'S COTTON PICKERS in Detroit; Lionel HAMPTON '41-8; own big band; Hampton again '50-2; organ with own trio. Pioneered 'locked hands' piano style, both hands playing parallel chords, as early as '34; not his fault that it became a cliché. Wrote 'Hamp's Boogie Woogie', own solo feature; also 'The Lamplighter', 'Count's Basement', many more. Played and toured with Illinois JACQUET, Roy ELDRIDGE, Jo Jones, Hampton again in '71, many others; appeared at Newport, Nice, Monterey Jazz Festivals. Own records began '46-7 on Savoy; Capitol LPs '55-7 incl. *Rockin' Hammond* '56; on Argo '59-61: *Mighty High, Please Mr Organ Player, Mighty Mood*; *The New World Of Milt Buckner* '62 on Bethlehem was followed by many LPs on European labels with varying sidemen incl. Jo Jones, Buddy TATE, Arnett COBB, ex-Ellington drummer Sam Woodyard, many others: *Milt Buckner Plays Chords* '66 on Saba aka *Milt Buckner In Europe* on Prestige; also *Locked Hands* on Saba '68; on Black & Blue: *Midnight Slow* (several vols issued '67-77), *Crazy Rhythm* '67, *Rockin' Again* '72, *Black And Blue Stomp* '73 (with Clarence 'Gatemouth' BROWN; Buckner plays both piano and organ, piano overdubbed), *Blues For Diane* '74, *Green Onions* '75, *Pianistically Yours* '75-6, *Boogie Woogie USA* '77. Also *The Gruntin' Genius* '76 on Dutch Riff label, with Sonny Payne on drums, guests Tate, Jacquet, Kai WINDING; several other LPs on Jazztone, Riverboat, etc. Rocking style made fans happy, had its infl. on pop. Buckner's brother Theodore Guy 'Ted' (*b* 14 Dec. '13; *d* Apr. '76, Detroit) played alto sax in Jimmie LUNCEFORD band '39-43; brother George (*d* '69) played trumpet; distant relative J. E. 'Teddy' Buckner (*b* 16 July '09, Texas) played trumpet with Hampton, Benny CARTER '30s, led small groups on West Coast.

BUCKS FIZZ UK vocal group named '80 by husband/wife management/prod. team of Andy Hill/Nichola Martin after Home County term for champagne and orange juice. Martin protégée of Sandie SHAW manager Eve Taylor; would-be Eurovision star aimed to build vocal group around herself, with ad jingle-writer Hill supplying material. 900 auditioned; end result in image of ABBA of two boys/two girls: Mike Nolan (*b* 7 Dec. '54), Bobby G (*b* Robert Gubby, 23 Aug. '53), Jay Aston (*b* 4 May '61), Cheryl Baker (*b* 8 Mar. '54). Impressed by both girls, Martin stood down as performer. 'Making Your Mind Up' won Eurovision '81 as planned, first UK win since similarly manufactured 2+2 Brotherhood of Man in '76. Performance lent some memorability by gimmick of removing girls' skirts mid-song, borrowed from Martin's Eurovision hopefuls Rags, whose heat of Song For Europe blacked out by technicians' strike. Two subsequent singles in identical style only breached UK top 20; fourth hit 'Land Of Make Believe' performed pantomime style made no. 1 late '81; early '82 'My Camera Never Lies' also made it. Variations on theme – *a cappella*-styled 'Now Those Days Are Gone', reggae-tinged 'If You Can't Stand The Heat' – notably less successful. Fall from

175

top 40 arrested by importing material: cover of Romantics' '83 US hit 'Talking In Your Sleep' restored top 40 UK status '84, saw boys playing instruments in significant image shift towards adulthood. Coach crash Dec. '84 in which Nolan was seriously injured preceded split in ranks: Aston, whose sexy image at odds with cleancut appeal of group, quit mid-'85 for solo career; replaced after more mass auditions by lookalike Shelley Preston (*b* 14 May '64). (Aston's move delighted tabloids with revelations about hanky-panky in group; resulted in lawsuits needed to free her from management contract.) Baker meanwhile became part-time TV show host; Gubby wrote/sang theme to BBC's *Big Deal* sitcom. 'You And Your Eyes So Blue' confirmed group's return to charts mid-'85, also middle-of-the-road musical stance, outside writers (bizarrely incl. former King Crimson lyricist Pete Sinfield) collaborating with Hill. Seem likely to remain favourites in UK variety for years to come.

BUFFALO SPRINGFIELD Early folk-rock group named for a piece of farm machinery, formed c.'65 by Richie Furay (*b* 9 May '44, Ohio) and Steve Stills. After their stint in Au Go Go Singers, Stills went to Canada, met Neil YOUNG, then leading Squires; went to L.A. joined by Furay, Young and Canadian bass player Bruce Palmer; recruited drummer Dewey Martin (*b* 30 Sep. '42, Chesterville, Ontario), became house band at Sunset Strip's Whiskey A Go-Go, exciting interest from BYRDS, others. Signed by SONNY & CHER managers Charlie Green, Brian Stone; made eponymous LP for Atlantic '66. Had good lead singers in Furay, Stills and Young; last two gifted guitarists. First single, Young's 'Nowadays Clancy Can't Sing' lost airplay (contained word 'damn') but Stills' 'For What It's Worth', inspired by alleged police brutality on Strip following student demo previous Nov., went to no. 7 USA Mar. '67. Ringing guitar harmonics and urgent chorus complemented Furay's plaintive lead voice; mixture of electric and acoustic guitars with vocal 3-part harmony presaged successful CROSBY, STILLS, NASH & YOUNG. Personnel problems through '67 blunted band's impact; no further USA top 40 hits resulted, despite excellent material on *Again* '67,

Last Time Around '68 (latter recorded with individuals overdubbing parts so as not to meet in studio). *Again* particularly regarded in retrospect as classic album, with sound collage collaborations between Young and arr. Jack NITZSCHE in 'Broken Arrow' paralleling BEATLES' experiments in *Revolver*. Young left before band's appearance at Monterey (replaced there by David Crosby, then by Doug Hastings before returning later); Palmer replaced by Ken Koblun, Jim Fielder, finally Jim Messina. On band's final disintegration in May '68, Messina formed country-rockers POCO with Furay, Fielder joined BLOOD, SWEAT & TEARS, Young went solo before joining supergroup Crosby, Stills & Nash in summer '69. Too many differing strands in Springfield to make stable outfit, but best music (collected on 2-disc *Buffalo Springfield*, not to be confused with first LP) stands up as transitional music of era, leading to later better-known activities of individuals.

BUFFETT, Jimmy (*b* 25 Dec. '46, Mobile, Ala.) Contemporary country-rock singer/songwriter. Studied journalism, which comes across in his songs. Recorded in Nashville '70 for Barnaby Records: *Down To Earth* LP flopped; follow-up *High Cumberland Jubilee* tapes lost, but mysteriously rediscovered when he hit the big time in '76. Feature writer for Billboard '72; signed to Dunhill records '73 (later ABC, then MCA): highly praised LP *A White Sport Coat And A Pink Crustacean*, country hit 'The Great Filling Station Holdup'. First crossover hit with 'Come Monday' '74 (made no. 30 USA pop chart) from LP *Living And Dying In 3/4 Time*, first to make pop album chart. Songs reflect lifestyle in Florida Keys where he spends much time on his boat, though 'Gulf & Western' country style comes through in songs like 'Brand New Country Star', 'Please Bypass This Heart', 'Cowboy In The Jungle'. 'Margaritaville' no. 8 on pop chart '77, from LP *Changes In Latitudes, Changes In Attitudes*; 'Cheeseburger In Paradise', 'Fins' all made top 40; two LPs went platinum: *Son Of A Son Of A Sailor*, *You Had To Be There* (2-disc live set), both '78. Other albums incl. *A1A* '74 (named for beach access road off US 1 in Florida), *Havana Daydreamin'* '76, *Volcano* '79, *Coconut Tele-*

graph '80, *Somewhere Over China* '81, *One Particular Harbor* '82, *Riddles In The Sand* '84, *Last Mango In Paris* '85, *Floridays* '86. He reported that '85 was his biggest year in concert grosses, reflecting popularity of act: 'I go onstage with the attitude that this is going to be my last concert, so let's all have fun and party till we drop.' He has written unproduced TV scripts for *Miami Vice*, *Amazing Stories*; talks to Michael Nesmith about producing musical/adventure movie *Margaritaville*, 'a rock'n'roll Robinson Crusoe fantasy'.

BULL, Sandy (*b* '41, NYC) Solo artist on guitars, other instruments. Prodigy as teenager, eclectic style infl. by Eastern music, jazz, country. Signed to Vanguard; first LP *Fantasias For Guitar And Banjo* '63 followed by *Inventions* (guitar, banjo, oud, electric guitar and bass) '65; both used drummer Billy HIGGINS: played the rest himself overdubbing. Beautifully played improvised comps. (side-length 'Blend' on *Fantasias*, 'Blend II' on *Inventions*) anticipated psychedelia of late '60s. Also played Bach, Chuck BERRY, Floyd CRAMER's 'Last Date', etc. Other Vanguard LPs: *Demolition Derby*, *E Pluribus Unum* (on which electric signal was split for four different amplifications); *The Essential Sandy Bull* was 2-LP compilation for the price of one. Also recorded for Decca and Buddah. Drugs crimped career from '72; still occasionally plays college circuit.

BULLOCK, Chick (*b* 16 Sep. '08, Butte, Montana; *d* 15 Sep. '81, Cal.) Vocalist; one of the most prolifically recorded of all time, with deep, virile voice; shunned publicity. Made hundreds of records '30-42; sides with Duke ELLINGTON '33 incl. 'Keep A Song In Your Soul'; with Adrian ROLLINI '34: 'A Hundred Years From Today', 'Keep On Doin' What You're Doin' . But studio lineups often given different name at each session: among pseudonyms were Chick Bullock And His Orchestra, Bobby Snyder, Bob Causer or Sleepy Hall And His Collegians, Al Green And His Orchestra, Hollywood Dance Orchestra, Ralph Bennett And His Seven Aces, Hal White And His All-Star Collegians; many really were all-star bands: recorded with sidemen such as T. and J. DORSEY, Muggsy SPANIER, Bunny

BERIGAN, Benny GOODMAN, Jack TEAGARDEN, Eddie LANG; in '34 the Mills Blue Rhythm Band (*see* Irving MILLS). Okeh session '41 incl. Bill COLEMAN, Benny MORTON, Jimmy HAMILTON, Teddy WILSON, J. C. Heard, Al Hall on bass (*b* 18 Mar. '15, Jacksonville, Fla.; staff musician at CBS '43-4, toured with Erroll GARNER, with Eubie BLAKE at Newport '60, with Alberta HUNTER '78, etc.); George James on reeds (*b* 7 Dec. '06, Beggs, Okla.; played with Fats WALLER, Benny CARTER, many others), Eddie Gibbs, guitar (*b* 25 Dec. '08, New Haven, Conn.; played with Edgar HAYES, Luis RUSSELL, Claude HOPKINS, Wilbur DE PARIS). Bullock quit mid-'40s; in real estate on West Coast; appeared on radio tribute to Berigan mid-'50s.

BURDON, Eric (*b* 11 May '41, Newcastle) UK singer who attained fame with The ANIMALS. After '66 split of original group, retained name and drummer Barry Jenkins, went to USA to sample drug culture. Other members of New Animals were Vic Briggs, guitar (ex-Steampacket); John Weider, guitar/violin; Danny McCulloch, bass. Tried like John LENNON to exchange rough'n'ready image for that of hippie prophet; signed to MGM (who'd released Animals in USA), made four good singles espousing peace, love, etc.: 'When I Was Young' (USA no. 15), 'Good Times' (UK no. 20), 'San Franciscan Nights' (USA 9; UK 7) all '67, 'Sky Pilot' (USA 14; UK 40) '68. Quotes like 'the drug experience has taught us that to be deranged is not necessarily to be useless' caused problems; New Animals split after two LPs *Wind Of Change* '67, *The Twain Shall Meet* '68. McCulloch left to make solo LP, Briggs got religion; replacements Andy Summers, guitar (*see* POLICE), Zoot MONEY on keyboards, lasted till Dec. '68; double album *Love Is* signalled end of group. Posthumous 'Ring Of Fire' made USA no. 35 early '69. Reformed original Animals for Newcastle Xmas gig; reappeared '70 as frontman for black band WAR: 'Spill The Wine' from LP *Eric Burdon Declares War* made USA no. 3 '70; partnership survived further LP excruciatingly titled *Black Man's Burdon*. War went on to become funk superstars; Burdon spent '70s in stops and starts, incl. one-off LP with original Animals '76. Only real achievement of note was LP with blues legend Jimmy WITHERSPOON (*Guilty* '71). Abandoned black music for heavy rock LPs *Sun Secrets* '74, *Stop* '75; after two more unsuccessful solos, started Fire Dept with German musicians (his popularity in Germany undiminished through the years), but survived little longer than '80 LP *Last Drive*. Made soundtrack for film *Comeback* '82, about faded rock star; irony was inescapable. Interest in Animals' back catalogue remained, with many covers, hit reissue of 'House Of The Rising Sun' '82; Police manager Miles Copeland persuaded original lineup to re-form once more for tour and album; former mates looked like successful businessmen they had become, while Burdon still looked lean and hungry. Wasted decade did nothing to erode vocal talent; published *I Used To Be An Animal But I'm Alright Now* '86.

BURGESS, Wilma (*b* 11 June '39, Orlando, Fla.) Pop-styled country singer. Left college mid-'60s, moved to Nashville to sing on demo tapes for a friend. Signed to Decca and hit country charts with 'Baby' '65, 'Misty Blue', 'Don't Touch Me' '66, 'Tear Time' '67. Joined Shamon Records '73, made duets with Bud Logan (ex-Jim Reeves's Blue Boys); on RCA '77-8 without much success.

BURKE, Solomon (*b* '36, Philadelphia) Soul singer, ordained minister. Soloist in church choir age 9, had own radio show *Solomon's Temple*, on stage as the Wonder Boy Preacher; later one of the biggest soul stars of the '60s. Recorded religious ballads on Apollo label '55 (formed '42 by Ike and Bess Berman; pioneering gospel list incl. Mahalia JACKSON, Dixie Hummingbirds, also entered R&B market). To Singular label '59, 'Be-Bop Grandma' was picked up by Atlantic: 22 Hot 100 pop entries, 15 soul chart hits on that label '61-8 incl. 'Just Out Of Reach (Of My Two Empty Arms)' '61 (no. 7 soul/24 pop hit with country song may have inspired Ray CHARLES's smash hit 'I Can't Stop Loving You', '62); 'Cry To Me', no. 5 soul/44 pop '62 was covered by the ROLLING STONES. Catholic material incl. 'Down In The Valley' (covered by soul superstar Otis REDDING), 'You Can Make It If You Try' and 'Everybody Needs Some-

body To Love' (both also covered by the Stones). Dubbed the 'King of Rock'n'Soul', as he described own style; live act said to be even better than records. Took on heavier gospel feel c.'64: 'The Price', 'Can't Nobody Love You', 'Goodbye Baby (Baby Goodbye)' oozed fervour. Hits prod. by Bert Berns, Jerry Wexler; after departure of Berns Burke lost some of the power: hits continued, but 'Got To Get You Off My Mind', 'Tonight's The Night' were his last top 10 soul entries. To Bell label '69; prod. own LP *Proud Mary* that year at Muscle Shoals, had no. 45 pop hit (no. 15 soul) in title cover of John Fogerty's song, LP also charted; spent three years with MGM; then to ABC Dunhill (*I Have A Dream* '74 was tribute LP to Martin Luther King); teamed with arr. Gene Page for Barry WHITE-infl. singles 'Midnight And You' (Dunhill), 'You And Your Baby Blues' (Chess). Return to charts seemed likely with 'Sidewalks, Fences And Walls' on Infinity late '79 when label went broke. Since then has recorded gospel on Savoy, toured in Soul Clan revival with Atlantic stablemates Wilson PICKETT, Ben E. KING, Don COVAY, Joe TEX. *Best Of* LP '64 on Atlantic charted; others incl. *Music To Make Love By* '75 on Chess; self-penned hits compiled on *Cry To Me* (Charly UK).

BURNETT, T-Bone (*b* John Henry Burnett, '45, Fort Worth, Texas) Singer/songwriter. Grew up listening to R&B, C&W on radio; busied himself in the Texas record scene, producing albums, e.g. by Delbert McCLINTON. Joined Bob DYLAN Rolling Thunder Review tour '75, appearing on subsequent '76 LP *Hard Rain*, film *Renaldo & Clara*. Formed Alpha Band '77 with Steve Soles and David Mansfield from the Dylan tour for LPs *Alpha Band*, *Spark In The Dark*, *Statue Makers Of Hollywood* '77-8; appeared in film *Heaven's Gate* '80; mini-LP *Trap Door* made stir with laconic lyrics, dry delivery on 'A Ridiculous Man', 'Diamonds Are A Girl's Best Friend'; *Truth Decay* '80 was solo debut, followed by *Proof Through The Night* '83, with Ry COODER, Richard THOMPSON, Pete Townshend, quirky songs touched on Marilyn Monroe ('Fatally Beautiful'), '80s USA ('Hefner & Disney'); good reviews in UK, USA; tour with Thompson; then in '84 with Elvis

COSTELLO: they appeared onstage together as The Coward Brothers, released single 'The People's Limousine' '85. Burnett prod. albums by Los Lobos . . . *And A Time To Dance* '83, *How Will The Wolf Survive* '84; own further mini-LP *Behind The Trap Door* '84 incl. 'Having A Wonderful Time, Wish You Were Her', co-written with U2's Bono; then *T-Bone Burnett* '86, overdue solo LP on MCA prod. by David Minor, incl. Billy Swan, David Hidalgo. Genuinely idiosyncratic artist; accusations of faddism dispelled by small but impressive body of work. Prod. Costello's *King Of America*, assisted debuts of Peter Case, country rocker Steve EARLE '86. New album *The Talking Animals* '88 on Columbia.

BURNETTE, Johnny and Dorsey Rockabilly singers, Johnny (*b* 25/28 Mar. '34, Memphis, Tenn.; *d* in boating accident 1 Aug. '64, Clear Lake, Cal.) and Dorsey (*b* 28 Dec. '32, Memphis; *d* 19 Aug. '79, L.A.) formed trio with guitarist Paul Burlison, former Howlin' WOLF sideman whose buzz-saw guitar sound became group trademark. Early lives similar to Elvis PRESLEY's; even worked at Crown Electric, but unlike Presley turned down by SUN's Sam Phillips. To NYC early '56, won Ted Mack's Amateur Hour three times in a row, signed to Coral label; little success then but mixture of R&B and country now regarded as seminal, often revived: YARDBIRDS picked up 'Train Kept A-Rollin' ', Rod STEWART, many others 'Tear It Up'. Dorsey left late '56, replaced by Bill BLACK's brother Johnny; trio broke up when Burlison left '57, but breakneck live performance captured in Alan FREED film *Rock Rock Rock*. Brothers worked on West Coast writing songs for teen idol Ricky NELSON; recorded as duo and separately, both having chart hits '60-1. Johnny cleaned up image, scored with 'Dreamin' ' (no. 11), 'You're Sixteen' (8), 'Little Boy Sad' (17), 'God, Country And My Baby' (18); Dorsey with 'Tall Oak Tree' (23) and 'Hey Little One' (48). Dorsey had low-key country career until death from heart attack. Burlison had quit music to run construction business, but released '81 tribute LP recorded on Sun's original tape machine with fellow Memphis rockabillies Johnny Black, Charlie FEATHERS. Dorsey's son Billy, Johnny's son Rocky continued in

music; Rocky (*b* 12 June '53, Memphis) was songwriter with Acuff-Rose '67; recorded 'Tired Of Toein' The Line', sent to EMI UK as a B side; became minor hit there '79, re-exported back to USA it was no. 8 '80, but no follow-up.

BURNING SPEAR (*b* Winston Rodney) Jamaican visionary and singer whose lorn vocal style was appropriate to the kind of protest he contemplated. Made early reputation when dub-plates of songs recorded at Studio One were given prominent airing on the island's sound systems, later released on albums *Burning Spear* and *Rocking Time*; even wider acclaim as he joined forces with backup singers Delroy Hines and Rupert Willington on stirring 'Slavery Days' for Jack Ruby, as well as LP *Marcus Garvey*, so popular that its dub incarnation *Garvey's Ghost* was also issued; the preachings of Garvey were a recurrent theme in his work. He embarked on heavy touring schedules, also cutting album after album all in the same basic style; final set for Ruby was *Man In The Hills* '76, then self-produced sets: *Dry And Heavy, Harder Than The Best, Live, Living Dub, Hail H.I.M., Farover, Resistance, People Of The World*.

BURNS, Ralph (*b* 29 June '22, Newton, Mass.) Piano, arranger, composer. New England Conservatory '38-9; worked for Charlie BARNET, Red NORVO early '40s; associated with Woody HERMAN for many years from early '44, played piano initially but also wrote first-class arrangements which, with those of Neal HEFTI, formed the band's character: 'Bijou', 'Lady McGowan's Dream', 'Summer Sequence' (in four parts; part IV later became 'Early Autumn'). 'Head' arrangements also created – 'Apple Honey', 'Northwest Passage' – to which all contributed, 'Ralph and Neal especially', according to Herman. Played with small groups and accompanied singers, toured Europe with Herman '54, wrote vocal arrangements for him '65; studio and commercial work, arranged Broadway shows, etc.

BURRELL, Dave (*b* Herman Davis Burrell II, 10 Sep. '40, Middletown, Ohio) Piano, composer; other instruments. Degrees from Boston Conservatory and Berklee College

179

of Music, later taught at Queen's College NYC '71-3; cross-cultural work on films, books with Haitian, African, Jamaican music; TV work incl. soundtrack for *Witherspoon* (CBS), *Jazz In New York Today* (Rome TV); many arrangements and albums with Archie SHEPP, Pharoah SANDERS, Marion BROWN on several labels; contributed trio track 'Black Robert' to Wildflower project. Own LPs began with trio sets on Douglas '65, Arista '68; *Echo* '69 recorded in Paris, now on Affinity in UK: two tone poems played by septet incl. Grachan MONCUR III, Archie Shepp, Sunny MURRAY. *Teardrops For Jimmy* '77 is solo set; *Lush Life* and *Round Midnight* '78 are solos with bass acc. on some tracks (all on Denon). Other LPs on European, Japanese labels: *La Vie de Bohème* '69 (after Puccini; septet incl. Moncur, singer Eleanor Burrell), *After Love* '70 (quintet with Roscoe MITCHELL), *Dreams* '73 (duo with bass), solo sets *Only Me* '73, *Black Spring* '77; 2-disc solo concert *Windward Passages* '79 on Hat Hut recorded in Basel. A fine American musician without a single album listed in USA Schwann catalogue.

BURRELL, Kenny (*b* Kenneth Earl Burrell, 31 July '31, Detroit, Mich.) Guitar. Music degree Wayne U. Detroit '55. Played with Dizzy GILLESPIE '51, Oscar PETERSON trio '55, Benny GOODMAN '57; also own combos since '51. Internationally popular, in demand for club, concert and studio work as well as college seminars, festivals, etc. First European tour '69, Japan '70; has won innumerable polls, incl. Japan and UK. Recorded on Verve with Astrud Gilberto, Gil EVANS, Stan GETZ, others incl. *Guitar Forms* '64-5 arr. by Evans. About 40 own LPs begin with sets on Blue Note, Prestige, Argo, Columbia, Kapp, Cadet, Verve, Fantasy '56-75; Prestige sets incl. tracks now in 2-disc sets with Coltrane, Mal WALDRON, Coleman HAWKINS, Hank MOBLEY etc.; *The Cats* with Coltrane and Tommy FLANAGAN now in Fantasy's OJC series; *Ellington Is Forever* '75 is two 2-disc tribute sets on Fantasy; *Tin Tin Deo* '77, *When Lights Are Low* are trios on Concord; *Handcrafted, Live At The Village Vanguard, In New York* '78 trio sets on Muse; *Moon And Sand* '79 quartet on Concord; *Heritage* '80 larger group on Audio Source; *Listen To*

The Dawn trio on Muse. *Generation* '87 on Blue Note has three guitarists, with Bobby Broom, Roland Prince.

BURTON, Gary (*b* 23 Jan. '43, Anderson, Ind.) Vibes. Studied piano, composition; self-taught on vibes. Prof. debut Nashville '60; to South America with own group '62; association with George SHEARING '63 led to Japanese tour, Shearing album of Burton compositions '64. With Stan GETZ '64-6, incl. two films and gig at the White House. Unusually rich harmony generated using four mallets. Also in music education; published books on instrument, staff member at Berklee College (Boston), lectures, seminars, etc. 12 LPs on RCA '61-8; 7 on Atlantic '67-71; 12 on ECM '72-82. Has led own groups since '67, initially incl. Larry CORYELL: that year recorded RCA quartet LPs *Duster* (with Roy HAYNES), *Lofty Fake Anagram* (with Bob Moses on drums, *b* 28 Jan. '48, NYC), also *A Genuine Tong Funeral*, written by Carla BLEY, recorded by 10-piece group incl. Bley, Mike Mantler, Coryell, Moses, Jimmy KNEPPER, Steve LACY, Gato BARBIERI, Steve SWALLOW (*b* 4 Oct. '40, NYC): these three issued in box on French RCA. About 20 more incl. *Paris Encounter* '69 with Stephane GRAPPELLI; *Alone At Last*, solo at Montreux '71, won a Grammy; *Gary Burton And Keith Jarrett* '71; first ECM album *Crystal Silence* '72, duo with Chick COREA made in Oslo; *Hotel Hello* '74 is duo with Swallow; *Matchbook* same year with guitarist Ralph Towner; *Dreams So Real* '75 written by Bley for quintet: Pat METHENY, Swallow, Moses, second guitarist Mick Goodrick; *Passengers* '76 incl. Metheney; *Duet* '78 is duo with Corea (other recent LPs under Corea's name as well); *Easy As Pie* '80, *Picture This* '83 are by quartet incl. Swallow, Jim Odgren (alto sax), Mike Hyman, drums; Burton said it was 'one of the best balanced' quartets he has had. *Slide Show* '86 is duet with Towner; *Whizz Kids* '86 features Swallow, newcomers Makoto Ozone on piano, Martin Richards on drums, Scottish saxophonist Tommy Smith (*b* 27 April '67; leads group Forward Motion: LP *Progressions* on Hep UK). Burton makes a habit of discovering new talent; he helped Smith to celebrate his 21st birthday and his contract with EMI '88.

BURTON, James (*b* 21 Aug. '39, Shreveport, La.) Guitarist; with Steve Cropper and Roy BUCHANAN, one of the quietly influential stylists in popular music since late '50s. Served apprenticeship on Louisiana Hayride country radio show, backing Slim WHITMAN, George JONES, etc. before first major work on disc: heavy inventive solo on 'Suzie Q', Dale HAWKINS hit on Checker '57 was early calling card. After short spell backing Bob LUMAN, went with teen idol Ricky NELSON; Burton's picking Sun-style, with shades of Carl PERKINS and Scotty Moore, much in evidence on Nelson's hits such as 'Believe What You Say' and 'Bucket's Got A Hole In It'; helped Nelson graduate to mellower country-rock style; then Burton graduated: left Nelson mid-'60s (though tracks continued to surface until *Another Side Of Rick* '68), selected to form band to back Presley on his comeback to live performance '69; stayed with him until his death, though sessioning the while. Appeared on at least three Hoyt AXTON albums, plus many with Randy NEWMAN, Ry COODER, BUFFALO SPRINGFIELD, Judy COLLINS, countless others. Backed country-rock pioneer Gram PARSONS on *GP* '73, *Grievous Angel* '74; continued with Parsons' sweetheart Emmylou HARRIS after his death as a member of her Hot Band: cemented reputation with whole new generation of fans, touring with Harris when Presley's engagements allowed, played stunning yet supremely tasteful solos such as that on 'Till I Gain Control Again' (*Elite Hotel* '76). Has since worked extensively with John DENVER, following tradition of loyalty to a singer/songwriter over several albums. Like Cropper and Buchanan, Burton is identified with thin, cutting tone of Fender Telecaster (though his collection, stored in safe deposit under guard, numbers 200+ instruments). Has made only two solo albums: *Corn Pickin' And Slick Slidin'* in '60s and *The Guitar Sounds Of James Burton* on A&M in '71, when Presley indisposed. Despite low-key image, Burton's reputation is assured: a prime mover in increasingly important country-rock genre.

BUSCH, Lou (*b* Louis Ferdinand Busch, 18 July '10, Louisville, Ky.; *d* 18 Sep. '79 in car crash) Pianist, arranger, composer. Worked for Hal KEMP late '30s; became staff arranger-A&R man for Capitol late '40s, working with Kay STARR, Dean MARTIN etc. As Joe 'Fingers' Carr he made about 14 solo piano albums, had top 20 hits 'Sam's Song', 'Down Yonder' and 'Portuguese Washerwoman' '50-6. It was inevitable that his would be seen as 'honky tonk' music during the '50s fad for tinny pianos, but he was a serious student of RAGTIME, writing many pieces of his own and inspiring younger players long before the '70s rediscovery of the genre.

BUSH, Johnny (*b* 17 Feb. '35, Houston, Texas) Honky tonk country singer. Learned to play drums because 'drummers work fulltime'. Met Willie NELSON early '50s, became life-long friends; toured with him, then Ray PRICE playing drums. Price recorded his 'Eye For An Eye'. Nelson set up recording session; *Sound Of A Heartache* LP and single attracted attention, then string of 10 hits leased to Stop label '67-71 incl. no. 7 'You Gave Me A Mountain' '69; switched to RCA for more hits; back on small labels late '70s. Minor hit with own song 'Whiskey River' '81, long a staple of Nelson's act. LPs incl. *Bush Country* on Stop, *Here's Johnny Bush* '72 on Starday, *Whiskey River/There Stands The Glass*, *Here Comes The World Again* '73, both on RCA; *Greatest Hits* on Power.

BUSH, Kate (*b* 30 July '58, Plumstead, England) UK singer, composer. Precocious daughter of Surrey doctor; friend of Dave Gilmour of PINK FLOYD, who subsidised her early demos, landed unusual deal with EMI: allowed to take time over material. Scored no. 1 '78 with first single 'Wuthering Heights'; gothic Brontë novel condensed to three minutes remains one of the most original records by a UK female singer. Unique vocal style showcased on Feb. '78 debut album *The Kick Inside*; single 'Man With The Child In His Eyes' proved she was more than one-hit wonder. 'Wow' '79 (no. 14) was her catch phrase (she had been mercilessly satirised on UK TV, sure sign she had arrived). *Lionheart* late '78 followed by several Best Female Singer awards; theatrical sense with mime training made for exceptional live work; *On Stage* '79 was live EP. *Never Forever* '80 entered LP chart at no. 1. Sang on eponymous Peter

GABRIEL LP '80; own third LP *The Dreaming* '82 was the only top 3 LP that year by UK female singer; songs seemed inaccessible to some: she aimed high. Controversial 'biography' by Fred Vermorel published '83. 'Running Up That Hill' '85 followed by concept LP *Hounds Of Love* '86 (with elaborate video): side 2 of UK no. 1 LP inspired by Tennyson's poem 'The Holy Grail'. *The Whole Story* '86 compiles hit singles, incl. latest, 'Experimental IV'; she sang on Gabriel's *So* '86, contributed song to film *Castaway* '87.

BUSHKIN, Joe (*b* 7 Nov. '16, NYC) Piano, songwriter. Mainstream swing era style; played with many small groups from '35; recorded with Eddie CONDON, Lee WILEY, others '36-9; own solo date '40, sextet date '44 on Commodore. With Tommy DORSEY '40; played trumpet in US Army band, worked in *Winged Victory* Air Force show; with Benny GOODMAN '46; on Broadway with Georgie AULD playing, acting in *Rat Race*. Freelanced, played in dixieland groups in the '50s; recorded for Savoy '46, Atlantic '50, Columbia '50-1, Capitol '55-7: nice mood music *Midnight Rhapsody* charted '56. Moved to Hawaii, then raised horses in Santa Barbara, Cal. Town Hall quartet concert with Milt HINTON on Reprise '64; *100 Years Of Recorded Sound* on UA made in Norway and England '77 with Hinton, Jake Hanna on drums, guitarist Johnny Smith, one vocal by Bing CROSBY; *Play It Again, Joe* '86 on Atlantic prod. by Les PAUL, seven sidemen incl. Al Grey, Warren Vaché, Major Holley, Butch Miles on drums, plus strings.

BUSSE, Henry (*b* 19 May 1894, Magdeburg, Germany; *d* 23 Apr. '55, Memphis, Tenn.) Trumpet, bandleader. Came to USA '16; with Paul WHITEMAN '18-28, then formed own dance band. Solo on Whiteman's 'When Day Is Done' '27 started vogue for 'sweet jazz'; he also used mute to great effect, and later used shuffle rhythm as identifying gimmick with his own band. Cowrote 'Wang Wang Blues', 'Hot Lips', recorded with Whiteman and issued back-to-back '20, was big hit for the time and same pairing with own band '35 stayed in print for many years. Recorded as Busse's Buzzards '25; broadcasts from '35-49 issued on Hindsight, Golden Era, Circle.

BUTLER, Carl (*b* Carl Robert Butler, 2 June '27, Knoxville, Tenn.) Honky-tonk country singer, songwriter; also duets with wife Pearl (*b* Pearl Dee Jones, 20 Sep. '30, Nashville, Tenn.; *d* Mar. '88). Began singing in teens, joined Grand Ole Opry '48, Capitol Records '51. Intense, emotional style not very successful on record; to Columbia '53; first success 'Honky Tonkitis' '61. Wrote hits ('If Teardrops Were Pennies' hit for Carl SMITH '51, Porter WAGONER and Dolly PARTON '73); remained popular stage performer. When Pearl did harmonising vocal on 'Don't Let Me Cross Over' '62, started new career as duet partnership, revitalised honky-tonk style. By '71 they had faded from record scene, remained popular stage act until early '80s. Debt to country gospel styles and assistance to Salvation Army Rehabilitation Programme led to Meritorious Service Award '70. *Greatest Hits* LP on Columbia '79.

BUTLER, Jerry (*b* 8 Dec. '39, Sunflower, Miss.) Soul singer. Moved north to Chicago with family at 3; church background typical of many soul giants: met Curtis MAYFIELD with Northern Jubilee Gospel Singers. Both also sang in smaller secular units; Butler in Quails, Mayfield with Alphatones. Butler recruited '57 by the Roosters (Sam Gooden, bros. Richard and Arthur Brooks), recruited Mayfield, renamed group Impressions, scored no. 11 pop hit 'For Your Precious Love' '58: infl. combination of restrained Butler style with sparse background harmonies for haunting neo-doo-wop feel. Falcon label's billing of group as 'Jerry Butler and the Impressions' led to rift; ex-Rooster Fred Cash replaced him (but Mayfield continued to write/arr. for Butler). Vee Jay took over Falcon, signed Butler as single, let Impressions go (in temporary decline); 'He Will Break Your Heart' (no. 7 '60) first fruit of Butler-Mayfield partnership, then 'Find Another Girl', 'I'm Telling You' (top 30 '61), 'Moon River' (no. 11). Henry MANCINI/Johnny MERCER wrote 'Moon River' for film *Breakfast At Tiffany's*, thanked Butler for helping to make it Song of the Year. He wrote solo too, contributing to books of Jackie WILSON, Otis REDDING,

Count BASIE, others. Mellow ballads, cool stage style earned him nickname 'Iceman'; hit touch grew too cold after '64 no. 5 duet with Betty EVERETT 'Let It Be Me'. To Philadelphia '67 on collapse of Vee Jay; worked with GAMBLE & HUFF writing/prod. team, returned to hit form with 'Never Give You Up' (no. 20 '68), 'Hey Western Union Man' (no. 16 '69). LPs *The Iceman Cometh* and *Ice On Ice* (both '69) established Butler in the newly realised black album market, balance of ballads/uptempo numbers. The Gamble/Huff/Butler partnership ended when G&H formed Philadelphia International label; Butler duetted with Gene CHANDLER on *Gene & Jerry – One & One* '71, single with Brenda Lee Eager, leader of his backing group the Peaches ('Ain't Understanding Mellow' no. 21 '72). Signed with Motown '75, series of tasteful LPs sold respectably, incl. duets with Thelma HOUSTON (*Thelma & Jerry* '77); back with Gamble & Huff at end of decade for two LPs; founded Fountain and Memphis labels with singer brother Billy ('I Can't Work No Longer' no. 60 pop chart '65); they ran Butler Music Workshop in Chicago for young singers/musicians/ writers (grads incl. Natalie COLE, Chuck Jackson). Now runs singing career in tandem with business of importing beer: style could be likened to cool glass of lager, refreshing the fans other singers can't reach. Compilation *Only The Strong Survive* '85 on Rhino.

BUTTERBEANS AND SUSIE Black Singing, dancing, comedy team: Susie Hawthorn (*b* 1896, Pensacola, Fla.; *d* 5 Dec. '63, Chicago, Ill.); Jody Edwards (*b* 19 July 1895; *d* 28 Oct. '67). Susie toured as cakewalk dancer with circus '10-16; married Butterbeans '16; worked with Butler 'Stringbeans' May while Edwards served in WW1. They worked revues, theatres, tours; musical comedy *Ease On Down* '30, etc. Recorded for Okeh '24-30; made LP for Festival '60, NYC. She was an underrated singer who sometimes worked solo, e.g. with Trixie SMITH '20, Bessie SMITH (*Hot Stuff Of 1933*, '32), several times with Ethel WATERS from '22 (e.g. in show *Cabin In The Sky*, '40-1).

BUTTERFIELD, Billy (*b* Charles William Butterfield, 14 Jan. '17, Middleton, Ohio; *d* 18 Mar. '88, Fla) Trumpet. Always popular

mainstream stylist: solos with Bob CROSBY '37-40, Artie SHAW '40-1, Benny GOODMAN '41-2, studio work and freelance. Lived in Virginia (worked there with Ernie Caceres), then Florida. Founder member of Worlds's Greatest Jazz Band '68-72. Prolific recording on Capitol, Decca, RCA, Columbia etc. '44-62; '46 big band collected on First Time LP, also *The Uncollected* on Hindsight; *Rapport* '75, duet with Dick WELLSTOOD on 77 label (Dobell's London jazz record shop; used to be at 77 Charing Cross Road), *For Better Blues And Ballads* '75 on Dutch Riff label with Bud FREEMAN, Bob WILBER; *Plays George Gershwin* '77 on Carosello with an Italian band; *Watch What Happens* '77 on Flyright with English sidemen; on Fat Cat's Jazz, mostly from Manassas Jazz Festival: *The Incomparable Butterfield Horn* '77 (big band with Wellstood, Warren Vaché on cornet); *Swinging At The Elks* '78 with Wellstood and Kenny Davern on clarinet; *You Can Depend On Me* '80 with Dill Jones on piano.

BUTTERFIELD, Paul (*b* 17 Dec. '42, Chicago; *d* 3-4 May '87, L.A.) Singer, harmonica player, bandleader. White teenager ventured to Chicago's south side to jam with blues legends Muddy WATERS, Howlin' WOLF, Buddy GUY, Otis RUSH, LITTLE WALTER, MAGIC SAM etc.; as black Chicago blues scene passed its golden age, formed own band '63 with ex-Wolf bassist Jerome Arnold and drummer Sam Lay, adding Mike BLOOMFIELD and Elvin BISHOP on guitars, Mark Naftalin on keyboards; first LP *Paul Butterfield Blues Band* '65 on Elektra followed by Newport Folk Festival appearance with Billy Davenport replacing Lay on drums, after their set backing Bob DYLAN in his controversial first electric performance. Second album stretched out from trad. blues: 13-minute title track of *East-West* '66 featured solos by Bloomfield and Bishop that helped establish modern role of rock guitarists, since abused by many lesser lights. Bloomfield left; *The Resurrection Of Pigboy Crabshaw* '67 and *In My Own Dream* '68 turned in R&B direction, retaining Bishop and Naftalin, with Phillip Wilson on drums, adding horns incl. David SANBORN on alto sax, Charles Dinwiddie (*b* 19 Sep. '36, Louisville, Ky.) on tenor. Other LPs incl. *Keep On Movin'* '69, *Sometimes I*

Just Feel Like Smilin' and 2-disc *Live* '71. In '71 band was eight-piece outfit with only Sanborn and Dinwiddie retained; *Golden Butter – Best Of* '72 was last Elektra release. *An Offer You Can't Refuse* on Red Lightnin' label UK is radio broadcast from '60s with Butterfield and Walter HORTON; he had also played on Muddy Waters' *Fathers And Sons* '69. Disbanded blues band, formed Better Days with original lineup of Billy Rich, bass; Christopher Parker, drums; Ronnie Barron, piano; Amos Garrett and Geoff Muldaur, guitars (Garrett with Elvin Bishop Band '78; duo LP with Muldaur same year). Albums on Bearsville *Better Days* '72, *It All Comes Back* '73 well received; *Put It In Your Ear* '76 was an ambitious failure; too many styles, instruments: Butterfield experimented but never imposed himself to give product identity. Appeared at the BAND's *Last Waltz* party '76; toured with Levon Helm, then with Rick Danko; released *North-South* '81; old albums reissued on Rhino '87.

BUZZCOCKS, The New wave/punk combo, formed Manchester UK '75 by guitarist Pete Shelley (*b* Peter McNeish, 17 Apr. '55) and Howard Devoto (*b* Howard Trafford), who sang and wrote lyrics. Manchester appearance of SEX PISTOLS Mar. '76 inspired them to form band with John Maher, drums, Steve Diggle, bass. Played many late-'76 punk events, incl. Sep. festival at London's 100 Club with Pistols, CLASH, Banshees, DAMNED. *Spiral Scratch*, 4-track EP on own New Hormones label, confirmed promise, but then Devoto left to form Magazine, broke songwriting partnership. Diggle moved to guitar, Garth joined on bass (replaced '78 by Steve Garvey). LP *Another Music In A Different Kitchen* '77 saw Shelley's romantic/adolescent lyrics differ from prevailing social/politicising concerns of punk, yet songs played at breakneck punk pace, like BEATLES at 78rpm. Worked better as singles: 'Ever Fallen In Love (With Someone You Shouldn't Have)' made no. 12 UK chart, was consummate late '70s power-pop, with churning guitars and keening vocals. Four top 40 hits '78-9 incl. reissue of *Spiral Scratch*. Second LP *Love Bites* '78 saw songwriting shared more widely, incl. long, experimental 'Late For The Train', like first LP's 'Moving Away

From The Pulsebeat' reflected Shelley's interest in avant-garde Euro rock e.g. CAN (he wrote sleeve note for Can compilation LP '78). As Diggle took over singles composition, Shelley lost musical direction; third LP *A Different Kind Of Tension* '79 disappointed fans. Despite overt commercialism and signing for Miles Copeland's IRS label in USA, two successful American tours failed to lead to breakthrough; only output was three singles '80 as band fell foul of record company takeover; impetus lost, group disbanded early '81. Shelley had been collaborating with Buzzcocks' prod. Martin Rushent; Diggle and Maher formed Flag of Convenience; Shelley was more successful: *Homosapien* '81 capitalised on groundwork in USA, made no. 1 in Australia; 'Telephone Operator' from album *XL 1* '83 just missed UK chart. LP incl. computer-programmed lyrics to be run on Sinclair, common UK home computer. Despite this ingenuity, has yet to equal Buzzcocks' simple (some would say childish) appeal; follow up was *Waiting For Love* '86. Buzzcock singles compilation is *Going Steady* '79. Diggle formed FOC for *Northwest Skyline* '87 on FOC label.

BYARD, Jaki (*b* John A. Byard Jr, 15 June '22, Worcester, Mass.) Piano, composer, other instruments. Local bands late '40s; Army service; mainstay post-war in Boston area, periods with Earl BOSTIC ('49-50) and Herb Pomeroy (Boston-based leader, teacher at Berklee College, *b* '30). With Maynard FERGUSON '59-62, then Charles MINGUS '63-70. Many LPs with Mingus incl. studio sets on Impulse, concert recordings from Town Hall NYC, Monterey, Paris, other European sets issued since Mingus's death. Has also taught at Berklee, many other places. Said that Mingus hired him for Town Hall Concert because he needed somebody who could play 'old fashioned': plays the blues from the inside to a degree unusual in an East Coast musician, plays first-class stride; but also 'modern' as anybody: communicates with technique, swing, wit. 'Byard's fabled eclecticism . . . has long since yielded an indigenous, insoluble style in which stride and bop and clusters are less bemused affectations than tools to make improvisations engaging and lucid' (Gary Giddins). First own LP was solo set *Blues

For Smoke '60 on CBS/Sony as a bonus disc in Japan. LPs on Prestige from '61 incl. trio sets *Here's Jaki, Hi-Fly, Out Front, Freedom Together, The Sunshine Of My Soul* and six other small-group sets; with sidemen incl. Ron CARTER, Roland KIRK, Ray Nance, Paul CHAMBERS. Billy HIGGINS, Elvin JONES, many others; *Jackie Byard With Strings!* incl. string players Ray Nance, George BENSON, two bassists Ron Carter and Richard Davis. Last Prestige outing was *Solo* '69; also on Prestige LPs by Eric Kloss (*Grits And Gravy, Sky Shadows, In The Land Of The Giants*), DOLPHY; some of Byard's sessions reissued under Roland Kirk's name. On other labels, solo sets incl. *Parisian Solos* '71; *The Entertainer* '72; *There'll Be Some Changes Made* '72 on Muse; *Flight Of The Fly* '76; *To Them – To Us* '81 on Soul Note. Also quartet sets *Live At The Jazz Inn* '71 Paris; *Family Man* '78 on Muse; solos 'Amarcord', 'La Strada' on collection *Amarcord Nino Rota* '81; also *Duet* c.'72 with Earl HINES, duets with Ran BLAKE: *Improvisations* '82. Also leads 20-piece band the Apollo Stompers: LP *Phantasies* '85 on Soul Note was said to fall among several stools, without Byard's usual incisive vision.

BYAS, Don (*b* Carlos Wesley Byas, 21 Oct. '12, Muskogee, Okla.; *d* 24 Aug. '72, Amsterdam) Tenor sax. Own band at college, '30; played with Don REDMAN, Lucky MILLINDER, Andy KIRK, others; well-known with Count BASIE '41 (recorded with small group 'Count Basie And His All-American Rhythm Section' Hollywood '42), Dizzy GILLESPIE '44. To Europe with Redman '46; lived in France, settled '50s in Holland. Visited UK '65, Newport Jazz Festival '70, Japan with Art BLAKEY '71. Of Coleman HAWKINS school, but more modern stylist in rhythmic and harmonic conception; could be described as a link between swing era and bop, but too good a musician for a label. Underrated in the USA but not in Europe. LPs incl. *Midnight At Minton's* '41 with Thelonious MONK on Onyx; 2-disc *Savoy Jam Party* '44-6 (22 tracks by five different small groups; sidemen incl. Slam STEWART, Charlie SHAVERS, Milt HINTON, Max ROACH, etc.); *Don Byas Meets The Girls* on Vogue ('53-5 session with piano trios); *Danish Brew* '59 on

Swedish Jazz Mark label; *A Tribute To Cannonball* '61 on Columbia, with Idrees Dawud Sulieman (*b* 27 Aug. '23, St Petersburg, Fla.) on trumpet, Bud POWELL, bassist Pierre Michelot, Kenny CLARKE; LP made in Paris '62 with Jacques Denjean Orchestra on Polydor; *Anthropology* '63 on Black Lion; *Ben Webster Meets Don Byas* '68, with Al HEATH, drums; Peter Trunk, bass; Tete MONTOLIU, piano. An album with strings '71 was issued on Japanese Polydor; quartet with Montoliu made a radio recording in Holland '72, not issued; EmArcy reissued some European tracks: *Don Byas On Blue Star* issued on CD '88.

BYGRAVES, Max (*b* Walter Bygraves, 16 Oct. '22, London) Entertainer, named 'Max' after imitating legendary UK comedian Max Miller in RAF during WWII. After the war played clubs, music halls, recorded medley of Al JOLSON songs. Minor film roles, e.g. *Skimpy In The Navy* '49, *Tom Brown's Schooldays* '50; played London Palladium several times early '50s, incl. season with Judy GARLAND; on radio with Peter Brough and young Julie ANDREWS in *Educating Archie*. Date in NYC at Palace with Garland '50, later with her in Hollywood. 12 UK top 30 entries in '50s incl. 'Cowpuncher's Cantata', 'Heart Of My Heart', novelty by Dick Manning-Al Hoffman 'Gilly, Gilly, Oscenfeffer, Katzenellen Bogen By The Sea'. His own song 'You Need Hands' '58, recording of Leslie Bricusse number 'Out Of Town' '56 won Ivor Novello awards. Straight film roles *A Cry From The Streets* '58 (NY Film Critics Award), *Spare The Rod* '60. UK top 10 hit 'Fings Ain't Wot They Used T'Be' '60 was his last; after hearing his mother complain about 'beat' music, made LP of standards prod. by Cyril STAPLETON: Medleys *Singalongamax* '71 was first of more than 20 similar gold albums. Did cabaret all over the world, especially popular in Australia; many UK TV series; hosted game show *Family Fortunes* '83. Autobiography *I Wanna Tell You A Story* '76; OBE '82. To a younger generation he represented all that is old-fashioned in music; story is that a thief stole some Max records from a dark room in an old folks home, brought them back when he discovered whose they were: nevertheless, skilfully blended comedy and

185

music made him one of the most popular British entertainers of all time.

BYLES, Junior Jamaican singer who made a series of troubled, ironic and powerful sides during mid-'70s. Earliest efforts were with vocal group the Versatiles for prod. Joe Gibbs' Amalgamated label, 'Just Can't Win' and a dozen others '68-70. Began lucrative association with prod. Lee Perry, scoring big '72 with exuberant 'Beat Down Babylon', LP of that name '73; biggest success with landmark 'Curly Locks' '74, followed by a string of odd, bitter songs such as 'Dreader Locks', 'The Long Way', 'Bur O Boy', others '75. Reports began to be heard of emotional fitfulness; singular work '76 incl. 'Lorna Banana', 'Remember Me', 'Chant Down Babylon', 'I Wish It Would Rain', others; LP *Jordan* with prod. Pete Weston '77; very little since: last side was 'Don't Be Surprised' '78.

BYRD, Charlie (*b* 16 Sep. '25, Suffolk, Va.) Spanish guitar. Prolific recording – about 40 LPs under his own name – places him in 'easy listening' category, but apart from first-class technique he is one of the most versatile on the instrument, playing jazz, classical, South American music in same concerts. Studied with Segovia '54; played with Woody HERMAN '59, etc.; toured South America with combo for US State Dept. On Stan GETZ LP *Jazz Samba* '62, suggesting tunes by Antonio Carlos Jobim; helped spark off much pretty music in Bossa Nova fad. Own LPs began on Savoy '57; also Riverside (*Solo Flight* '65), Offbeat, Milestone; Columbia from '65-9 (*Brazilian Byrd* '65, *Plays Villa-Lobos* '67 (solo), many others. *Great Guitars* '74 first of five LPs on Concord Jazz with Herb ELLIS, Barney KESSEL and rhythm; other LPs incl. *Byrd By The Sea* '74 and *Top Hat* with Nat ADDERLEY '75 on Fantasy; on Concord *Blue Byrd* '78, *Sugarloaf Suite* '79, *Isn't It Romantic* '84 are trio sets with bass and drums; *Brazilian Soul* '80 a quartet with Laurindo ALMEIDA; *Brazilville* '81 a quartet with Bud SHANK; *Latin Odyssey* '83 sextet with Almeida.

BYRD, Donald (*b* 9 Dec. '32, Detroit, Mich.) Trumpet, leader, academic. Fame as member of Art BLAKEY's Jazz Messengers from late '55; freelanced, toured, made films in Europe. LPs beginning '55 on Transition, Savoy, Columbia, Verve, etc.: *September Afternoon* '57 on Discovery, with Claire Fischer, piano (*b* '28, Durand, Mich.), and strings. Blue Note LPs began '58 with *Off To The Races*, with Pepper ADAMS, Jackie McLEAN, Wynton KELLY, Sam Jones (bass), Art TAYLOR; other quintet LPs with Adams: on Bethlehem '60, back on Blue Note *At The Half Note Cafe* '60 (2 vols.); *Chant, The Cat Walk, Royal Flush*, all '61; *The Creeper* '67 is sextet LP with Adams. Among many other Blue Notes, *A New Perspective* '63 incl. 'Christo Redentor', a hymn written, arr. by Duke PEARSON; personnel incl. Hank MOBLEY, Herbie HANCOCK, Kenny BURRELL etc. and Coleridge Perkinson Choir; it began Byrd's moving away from straight Blue Note hard bop. *Electric Byrd* '70 used 12-piece group incl. Adams, AIRTO, Ron CARTER and Pearson on electric piano; *Stepping Into Tomorrow* '74 incl. whistling, synthesiser, background vocals; *Black Byrd* '73, sextet arr. by Larry Mizell, biggest selling album in Blue Note's history; *Places And Spaces* '75, *Caricatures* '76, continued experiments with larger groups, were Byrd's last LPs on Blue Note label, then staggering after changing hands. Meanwhile obtained college degrees, teaching experience, doctorate at Columbia U. '71, also studied law; became leading ethnomusicologist, concerned about black music taken seriously in academia. Own LPs *Thank You For F.U.M.L.* '78, *Love Byrd* '81, *Words, Sounds, Colors And Shapes* '82, all on Elektra Musician; described by a discography as soul music. As Chairman of Black Music at Howard U. started Blackbyrds with students; prod. their LP *Blackbyrds* on Fantasy (didn't play on it); series of funk outings now incl. *Flying Start, City Life, Unfinished, Night Grooves, Action, Better Days*. Byrd is accused by critics of selling out: in every generation for decades blacks have shown whites how to do it; disco-funk etc. is not new in that respect but a spinoff from Blue Note jazz of '50s-60s. Also studied law; taught late '70s at North Carolina Central College; album of straight jazz due '88 with Mulgrew Miller on piano, Kenny Garrett on alto, Rufus Reid on bass, Marvin 'Smitty' Smith on drums.

BYRD, Gary (*b* '50, Buffalo, NY) Soul rapper. Became radio deejay age 15; by '69 youngest deejay in NYC. Regards himself as 'disc journalist', adding rap to music. While working at WWRL received call from Stevie WONDER, for whom he'd written lyrics for 'Black Man', 'Village Ghetto Land' (*Songs In The Key Of Life*, '76); played demo of a song over phone, in L.A. days later recording 'The Crown', 10-minute celebration of black history from Egypt to Malcolm X: Wonder supplied backing and joined in choruses; long track issued on 12″ only, on Wonder's Wondirection (through Motown) in USA, on Motown elsewhere; made no. 6 UK '83, top 10 in Holland, Germany, France, but failed in USA, perhaps owing to Motown switch in distribution. Continues to broadcast on WLIB NYC, hosting talk show and *Star Quiz* programme syndicated in USA; a born-again Christian, Byrd presented *Sweet Inspiration* series of gospel-related programmes for BBC '85 while demoing new musical projects. Contract with Motown has run out, but interesting career could lie in future.

BYRD, Jerry (*b* Jerry Lester Byrd, 9 Mar. '20, Lima, Ohio). Nashville session steel guitarist. Worked as house painter before turning pro '39. Member of Ernie Lee's Pleasant Valley Boys '36-8, Ernest TUBB band '45-7. Signed as soloist for Mercury '49-52; '50s LPs had subdued Hawaiian-infl. style: *Shores Of Waikiki* (Mercury '51), *Hawaiian Beach Party* (RCA '54), *Hi-Fi Guitar* (Decca '58) etc. Led Bobby Lord TV show band '64-8; made several LPs for Monument '58-72. Pioneer of steel, now virtually retired from music.

BYRDS, The USA folk-rock, then country-rock group formed '64 L.A. Original lineup: Jim McGuinn (*b* 13 July '42, Chicago), vocals, guitar; Gene CLARK, vocals, percussion, guitar; Chris Hillman (*b* 4 Dec. '42, L.A.), bass, mandolin, vocals; Michael Clarke (*b* 3 June '43, NYC), drums; David Crosby, guitar, vocals (*see* CROSBY, STILLS, NASH & YOUNG). McGuinn had worked with The Limelighters, Chad MITCHELL Trio, sessioned with Judy COLLINS; Clark with NEW CHRISTY MINSTRELS; Crosby with Les BAXTER's Balladeers; Hillman

with bluegrass groups the Scottsville Squirrel Barkers and the Hillmen (LP on Together label); McGuinn, Clark and Crosby met at Troubador folk club in L.A.; formed trio called The Jet Set, then Beefeaters (flop single on Elektra), then with Hillman and Clarke (who was inexperienced but looked right thanks to Beatle haircut) changed name to Byrds. Early tapes issued '69 in LP *Preflyte*, but major breakthrough came with Bob DYLAN's 'Mr Tambourine Man', no. 1 both UK/USA summer '65. Same year no. 40 USA/4 UK with Dylan's 'All I Really Want To Do', no. 1 USA/no. 11 UK with 'Turn, Turn, Turn', biblical text set by Pete SEEGER; never made top 10 again, but it was the era of a switch in public and critical emphasis from singles to albums: their first four all made top 30 USA album chart, while others which didn't sell particularly well at the time are still selling today. *Mr Tambourine Man* '65 followed by *Turn, Turn, Turn* '66; Clark left early '66 (joined Rodney DILLARD), McGuinn and Crosby taking over lead vocals; *Fifth Dimension* '66 saw move from folk rock to more 'progressive' material (single 'Eight Miles High') often written by McGuinn. McGuinn and Crosby no longer getting along musically, latter left '67; Clarke left, toured with Dillard & Clark, then Flying Burrito Bros (*see* Gram PARSONS), helped form Firefall. McGuinn changed his name to Roger, allegedly for religious reasons. New drummer Kevin Kelley (*b* '45, Cal.) joined for *Younger Than Yesterday* '67 (uneven LP incl. Hillman's 'So You Want To Be A Rock'n-'Roll Star', Dylan's 'My Back Pages'), stayed until '68, as did Gram Parsons, most important Byrd after original members: he was heavy infl. on *Notorious Byrd Brothers*, milestone *Sweetheart Of The Rodeo* (both '68, the last the first country-rock LP), though his work not much in evidence because of contractual commitments; he left for political reasons on eve of South African tour. Hillman left to form Burritos with Parsons, others; McGuinn regrouped with bassist John York (soon replaced by Clyde 'Skip' Battin, *b* 2 Feb. '34, Gallipolis, Ohio, who had pop hit 'Cherry Pie' '60 in duo Skip & Flip), drummer Gene Parsons (*b* '44, L.A.; unrelated to Gram), Clarence White (*b* 6 June '44, Lewiston, Maine; *d* 14 July '73) on guitar: last two from bluegrass group Nashville West, White also from Kentucky Colonels ('60-6). White and Gene Parsons were Byrds late '68 to '73, Battin from late '69 to '73, making this lineup the most stable, but with lower sales: LPs incl. *Dr Byrds And Mr Hyde* and *Ballad Of Easy Rider* (both '69, the last cashing in on McGuinn's vocal contribution to film soundtrack); *(untitled)* '70 was 2-disc half-live, half-studio album incl. McGuinn's highly rated 'Chestnut Mare'; *Byrdomaniax* '71, *Farther Along* '72. Group dissolved '73 as Gene Parsons made solo *Kindling* '73 for WB, joined re-formed Burritos; Clarence reformed Kentucky Colonels early '73, but was killed by a drunken driver July (it was not a good year for ex-Byrds; Gram Parsons died two months later). McGuinn reformed original quintet for *The Byrds* '73 on Asylum (all others CBS) but the magic was gone. With vocal harmony and some good songs their most important contribution (thanks to Gram Parsons) was introducing country feel to pop audience. Compilations incl. *Greatest Hits*, *The Byrds Play Dylan*; plus 2-disc *History Of The Byrds* in UK. Chris Hillman's solo LPs incl. *Cherokee* '71 on ABC, *Slippin' Away* '76 and *Clear Sailin'* '77 on Asylum; Battin made an eponymous LP on Signpost '73; Gene Parsons made *Melodies* '80 on Sierra; McGuinn did *Roger McGuinn* '73, *Peace On You* '74, *Roger McGuinn And Band* '76, *Cardiff Rose* '76 and *Thunderbyrd* '77, all CBS; McGuinn, Clark and Hillman made eponymous LP '79 on Capitol, followed by *City* '80, also *McGuinn And Hillman* '80. *Never Before* on Re-Flyte has unreleased tracks.

C

CABARET VOLTAIRE Electronic group formed Sheffield, England '73-4 by Stephen 'Mal' Mallinder, bass, lead vocals; Richard Kirk, guitar, winds; Chris Watson, electronics, tapes. First recording *a cappella* version of David BOWIE's 'Five Years', but home tapes revealed deeper European infl.: CAN, KRAFTWERK, etc. Live gigs fraught with audience hostility to machine-like rhythms; Mal hospitalised '75 with chipped backbone after incident, but punk movement rendered uncompromising stance acceptable. Music sampled on *1974-1976*, cassette-only release on Industrial label '80; signed with Rough Trade and released EP *Extended Play*: sound collages and distorted vocals took Bowie's electronics of *Low* and *Heroes* to new extremes. Very prolific, with EPs, singles, LPs on Rough Trade, Crepuscule, Paradox Product, Factory. Musical stance carried over to video: used audio techniques of repetition, montage, distortion to create disturbing visual images: Paul Hardcastle's '19' (UK no. 1 '85) noticeably influenced. *Cabaret Voltaire* video on Doublevision '82; film score *Johnny Yes No* (dir. by Sheffield's Peter Care) also on Doublevision. Watson left for TV work '81; others carried on, also did solo material (Mal's compiled as *Pow Wow Plus* '85). Signed with futurist label Some Bizzare; 3-disc set *The Crackdown* '83 betrayed black infl. (though 'scratching' techniques nothing new to Cabs). *The Covenant The Sword And The Arm Of The Lord* '85 (named after USA neo-Nazi cult) most successful album in commercial terms; amazingly their thirteenth; they had long since toured Europe, USA and Japan without major label support. Other albums: *Mix Up* '79, *Live At The YMCA* '80, *Red Mecca* '81, *Hai!* and *2 X 45* '82 (latter made bottom of UK LP chart), *The Voice Of America* '84, all on Rough Trade; *Code* '87 on EMI's Parlophone label. *Golden Moments* compilation on Rough Trade CD '87. Kirk released solo LPs *Black Jesus Voice* and *Ugly Spirit* '86.

CADENCE Dance style in 2/4, played on electric instruments and developed in Martinique and Guadeloupe '70s, derived from the Antillean beguine. The hybrid shows elements of calypso, soca, merengue; also Spanish melodies and strong affinity for West African pop, since two-way exchange with Belgian Congo/Zaire in '70s when guitar bands in Africa were developing own hybrid. Zairean infl. is evident in close-knit guitar parts and insistent hiss of cymbals over other parts of drum kit, though West African pop often relies excessively on studio technology: studio techniques have not yet overcome the freshness of cadence. *Dance! Cadence!* on UK GlobeStyle label is a sampler of eight bands revealing local variations: Group Guad'M, Come Back, Batako, Godzom Son Traditionnel, Makandjia, Eugene Mona, Georges Plonquitte and Georges Decimus, one of the best-known producers/performers. Others incl. popular big band Malavoi, a modernised Martinique string band heard on an eponymous 2-disc album; Dédé St Prix, a player of wooden flutes inspired by local trad. music, also accompanies avant-garde, deep-voiced Martinique singer Jody Bernabé on eponymous two-volume set, a curious mixture of styles: halfspoken intonations like voodoo chants, lyrical backing, and surreal lyrics. Kassav, dir. by Jacob Desvarieux, led by Georges and P. E. (Pierre Edouard) Decimus, reveals the infl. of soul, soca, and even reggae, with heavy conga-drum rhythm patterns. *Jean Philippe Marthely/Patrick Saint-Eloi* is recent LP by a Paris-prod. splinter group from Kassav, revealing an emerging new hybrid of *zouk*, even more pan-Caribbean. Haitian variant is called mini-jazz, bands incl. Tabou Combo, Coupe Cloué: there may be more input from Haiti if the political situation is ever resolved.

CADENCE USA magazine, record label. *Cadence: The American Review Of Jazz And Blues* monthly since Jan. '76; then Bob

Rusch and Tom Lord started label (about 30 releases to date). Magazine is priceless archive of interviews, oral histories, book reviews, more than 12,000 reviews so far of improvised music worldwide; label is separate corporation (records do not always get good reviews in magazine!); issues incl. records by Chet BAKER, reedman Maurice McIntyre, Frank LOWE, newcomers like guitarist Rory STUART, well recorded with natural balance rather than electronic gimmicks; also *Collection* in 2-disc limited edition of Bill DIXON's trumpet solos made '70-6. Cadence is also an important mail-order source for jazz records (and wholesalers to the trade as North Country Records).

CADILLACS, The USA doo wop vocal group formed NYC '53. Original lineup: Earl 'Speedoo' Carroll (*b* 2 Nov. '37), Robert Phillips (*b* '35), Laverne Drake (*b* '38), Gus Willingham (*b* '37). Formed as the Carnations; signed '54 by Esther Navarro, manager/songwriter; changed name, added Papa Clark (*b* '37), cut four songs leased to Jubilee subsidiary label Josie; Willingham, Clark left, replaced by Charles Brooks, Earl Wade. Known for energy, flamboyance; credited with infl. onstage choreography of later Motown acts. Pop chart glory with 'Speedoo' (top 20 '56, no. 3 R&B), 'Peek-A-Boo' (top 30 '59, no. 20 R&B). 'Speedoo' written by Navarro about lead singer Carroll; later covered by Ry COODER ('Well, my friends call me Speedoo/but my real name is Mister Earl'). Carroll left '59 to join the COASTERS; Cadillacs continued, had R&B no. 30 'What You Bet' '61.

CAGE, John (*b* 5 Sep. '12, L.A., Cal.) Composer. Studied with Arnold Schoenberg (*b* 13 Sep. 1874, Vienna; *d* 13 July '51, L.A.) and Adolph Weiss (*b* 12 Sep. 1891, Baltimore; *d* 20 Feb. '71, Van Nuys, Cal.) '35-7; infl. by the 'organised sounds' of Edgar Varèse (*b* 22 Dec. 1883, Paris; *d* 6 Nov. '65, NYC). He has explored the nature of music, consistently challenging assumptions about the way it is presented, as in his '50s 'happenings', inspired by Antonin Artaud's book *The Theatre And Its Double*. From late '30s-50s he experimented with the 'prepared piano' technique, inspired by the earlier work of Henry Cowell (*b* 11 Mar. 1897, Menlo Park, Cal.; *d* 10 Dec. '65,

Shady, NY): foreign objects of metal or wood are placed inside the piano, attached to or placed between strings and soundboard to alter the relationship of the 'note' and the piano's response. *Bacchanal* '38 was intended 'to place in the hands of a single pianist the equivalent of an entire percussion orchestra' (from *For The Birds*); the Sonatas and Interludes of '46-9 were more significant. (The GRATEFUL DEAD's Tom Constanten played prepared piano on *Anthems Of The Sun* '68, having earlier used it in the San Francisco Mime Troupe's Music Now series; Dead bassist Phil Lesh used it in '6⅞ For Bernardo Moreno' early '60s.) The infl. of prepared piano was preempted by the emergence of compact electronics (e.g. synthesisers, etc.). Cage taught at the Chicago School of Design '41-2, then returned to NYC to organise concerts of percussion music; he collaborated with Merce Cunningham on multi-media projects/ballets. He assimilated household sounds into compositions: banging doors, scraping furniture in *Living Room* '40, radio static, pouring water and riffling cards in *Water Music* '52; also exotica such as a roaring lion, conch shells, cricket calls (*Third Construction* '41). He explored the relationship of silence to music, notoriously in *4'53"* '52, in which the pianist(s) sit(s) before an unplayed keyboard for four minutes and 53 seconds. He pioneered the techniques of working with magnetic tape in the '50s; e.g. *Williams Mix* '52 used up hours of intricate splicing and editing work, a practice that became commonplace among rock groups in the late '60s (with more sophisticated and readily available tape recorders). He pioneered 'aleatory' or 'chance' music, in which random factors (rolling dice) or chance (the order in which pages are picked up) introduced variables; this was coloured by his interest in Eastern philosophy: he used the Chinese oracle *I Ching* as an aleatory factor, incidentally revealing old-fashioned values along with his all-embracing modernity: 'The *I Ching* was delighted to be "computerized" (an increase of advantages) and advised modesty, recourse to ancient wisdom' (*For The Birds*). *Variations I* and *II* '58 allowed musicians to choose what to play or do next on the spur of the moment (or 'at the moment of preparation', to be precise): create distorted sounds, write a letter, etc. Later multi-media *Variations V* '65 also used visual effects, as did *HPSCHD* '67-9, co-written with Lejaren Hiller (*b* 23 Feb. '24, NYC), lasting four hours and financed by a grant from the Thorne Music Fund. In *Renga* the composer gave the conductor a free hand to insert pauses and make changes; the piece could be performed separately or simultaneously as a single piece with *Apartment House 1776*, a second piece commissioned by the US Endowment for the Arts for the Bicentennial. In his 60s he used star maps as overlays to arrive at musical notation, as in *Etudes Australes*, a new chance source. He has been derided as a charlatan, also experiencing more gentle derision; Aaron Copland (*b* 14 Nov. 1900, Brooklyn) wrote in *The New Music 1900-60* '68: 'Cage has practically removed himself from the sphere of music' and defined his attraction as being 'for those teetering on the edge of chaos'. This was balanced by the National Institute of Arts and Letters in '49, recognising his achievement in pushing back the 'boundaries of music', by a Guggenheim Fellowship the same year, etc. He has occasionally fallen prey to whimsy and an apparent inability *not* to use an idea, but the wit and invention of his experiments and his teaching have been influential far beyond his own music. Further reading: Richard Kostelanetz (ed.): *John Cage* '70; Calvin Tompkins: *The Bride & The Bachelors: Five Masters Of The Avant-Garde* '73; John Cage & Daniel Charles: *For The Birds* '81; Heinz-Klaus Metzger & Rainer Riehn: *John Cage* '82.

CAHN, Sammy (*b* 18 June '13, NYC) Lyricist. Worked with three main composers. Played violin part-time in band, met pianist Saul Chaplin (*b* 19 Feb. '12, Brooklyn), began writing songs to order for record producers; first hit 'Rhythm Is Our Business' for Jimmie LUNCEFORD band '35, then 'Until The Real Thing Comes Along' for Andy KIRK, also recorded by the INK SPOTS, Fats WALLER, many others. 'Shoe Shine Boy' same year used by Louis ARMSTRONG, MILLS BROS, Bing CROSBY, became jazz classic (*see* Count BASIE). Adapted Yiddish song 'Bei Mir Bist Du Schön' for one of the biggest hits of '30s by ANDREWS SISTERS, Benny GOODMAN. To

Hollywood, reached even greater heights with Jule Styne (*b* 31 Dec. '05, London), who had previously worked with Frank LOESSER; Cahn-Styne hits in '40s incl. 'I'll Walk Alone', 'It's Magic', show *High Button Shoes* '47, much more; 'Three Coins In The Fountain' '54 won an Oscar. Cahn wrote songs for Frank SINATRA with Jimmy Van Heusen (*b* Chester Edward Babcock, 26 Jan. '13, Syracuse, NY) incl. 'The Tender Trap', 'Love And Marriage', 'All The Way', 'My Kind Of Town', 'September Of My Years' (the last winning a Grammy), several more. Van Heusen was also a test pilot during WWII under his own name. Earlier he had worked with bandleader-composer Eddie DeLange ('Darn That Dream' from the flop show *Swingin' The Dream*), then Johnny Burke (*b* 3 Oct. '08, Antioch, Cal.; *d* 25 Feb. '64, NYC): hits for Bing Crosby and Sinatra incl. 'Polka Dots And Moonbeams', 'Swingin' On A Star', many more. Burke also wrote the words for Erroll Garner's 'Misty'.

CAIOLA, Al (*b* Alexander Emil Caiola, 7 Sep. '20, Jersey City, N.J.) Guitar, studio stalwart. Singles on RCA incl. version of international hit 'Delicado' (Percy FAITH had no. 1, '52). Quintet LPs on Savoy *Deep In A Dream*, *Serenade In Blue* '55 featured Hank JONES, Kenny CLARKE. Worked with Hugo WINTERHALTER, Faith, Andre KOSTELANETZ; then United Artists: themes from film *Magnificent Seven*, TV show *Bonanza* were chart hits '61; briefly had own TV show. LPs available in USA: *Italian Guitars*, *Soft Guitars*, *Guitar Of Plenty*.

CAJUN Musical genre indigenous to Louisiana among descendants of French colonialists deported from Acadia after the treaty of Utrecht in 1713: the French ceded the colony to the British, who renamed it Nova Scotia; the cultural group resettling in Louisiana referred to itself as Cadien, then Cajun, speaking a French dialect more distinct from European French than that of French Canadians, differing in grammar and vocabulary. Traditionally they also called themselves Creoles (*créoles*), but English speakers called the whites Cajuns and the French-speaking blacks Creoles; the rural French-speaking blacks developed their own musical variant of ZYDECO (in the past, zodico). Cajun is sung either in Creole or Louisiana French. Legislators forbad the teaching of French in elementary schools; English-language education became mandatory in '16, causing resentment; Nathan ABSHIRE was never taught to write his own name, but was unhindered in creating memorable work. Among the foremost contemporary performers, Zachary Richards articulated bitterness six generations old towards *les goddams* (the English) in his 'Réveille!'. In the main Cajun is a dance music, with a rich repertoire of *contredanses*, cotillions, mazurkas and *valses à deux temps*; its instrumentation, like that of TEX-MEX, altered with the arrival of the diatonic accordion in the 19th century: hitherto the fiddle was the dominant instrument, open-tuned with a double-string bowing technique to produce a drone effect. Other instruments incl. *petit fer* (triangle), guitar and harmonica. Black pioneers like Amadé ARDOIN, Adam Fontenot were important in the music's development before black voicings led to zydeco. Originally played at home as parlour or front-porch music, at *bals de maison* and on church outings or socials, Cajun's audience became larger as the oil boom at the turn of the century provided larger disposable incomes; its market value was recognised in the late '20s/early '30s by labels such as Victor (and Bluebird), Okeh, Decca and Brunswick/-Vocalion, expanding into the 'race' market; the first known Cajun record was made by the fiddlers Dennis McGee (*b* 1892) and Saday Courville (*b* '05; *d* 3 Jan. '88); after the Depression its popularity increased. From mid-'30s, infl. of WESTERN SWING and COUNTRY was felt, as was 'high lonesome' sound of embryonic BLUEGRASS. Leo SOILEAU, Harry CHOATES and the Hackberry Ramblers contributed; Rambler Luderin Darbonne foresaw the potential of amplification, steel guitar and drum kit, pioneering in this direction; Ramblers also recorded country numbers, scoring at least one regional hit with 'Wondering'. Choates also crossed over to some extent, his version of 'Rubber Dolly' comparing well with Western Swing versions (e.g. by the Swift Jewel Cowboys). By the late '40s the French flavour seemed to be waning; in other ethnic groups acculturation grew; Iry LeJune (Ira LeJeune) had a hit '48 with 'La Valse

du Pont d'Amour' which helped redress the balance: his death (hit by a car while mending a flat tyre) cut short a promising future, but musicians like Abshire, Alphonse 'Bois Sec' Ardoin, the BALFA Brothers, Joe Falcon, Austin Pitre and Lawrence Walker stepped into the breach. Unlike other working-class musics such as country and Tex-Mex, Cajun has produced few female artists of standing; Cléoma B. Falcon, Joe's wife, was a rare example: her 'J'ai Passé Devant Ta Porte' and 'Allons à Lafayette' (recorded with her husband) stand out, as does her anthology *A Cajun Music Classic* on Jadfel. Local labels (Jin, Swallow, etc.) supplied home-grown talent as academics impressed upon people the need to counter the stealthy homogenisation process; work for the Library of Congress by Alan LOMAX, and Irene Whitfield's collection *Louisiana French Folk Songs* were part of the ethno-musicological renaissance. Chris Strachwitz (*b* 1 July '31, Gross Reichenau, Lower Silesia) came to the USA '47, later formed the Arhoolie label; after a Mance LIPSCOMB release in '60 he expanded to compile a catalogue of Cajun with few equals; his Old Timey label pioneered compilations of classic Cajun and zydeco; Folkways, Rounder and Sonet have also issued good collections; of special note is *Louisiana Cajun Music Special* '87 on Ace, anthology of Swallow's best tracks incl. Abshire, Pitre, the Balfas, Doris Matte, the Lake Charles Playboys: perhaps the first Cajun collection on CD. English-speaking performers discovered Cajun; 'Jole Blon', Choates' classic hit, was covered not only by Cajuns but other Americans: Waylon JENNINGS recorded it while a DJ in Lubbock, Texas, with Buddy HOLLY and KING CURTIS (reissued in *The Complete Buddy Holly* '78); Gary 'US' BONDS and Bruce SPRINGSTEEN in '81. Musicians as different as Hank WILLIAMS ('Jambalaya'), The BAND, COMMANDER CODY AND HIS LOST PLANET AIRMEN, Ry COODER (especially on *Southern Comfort*, which incl. a *fais do-do* with Dewey Balfa and Marc Savoy), the NITTY GRITTY DIRT BAND, Buck OWENS, SHAKIN' STEVENS and Paul SIMON have drawn on the genre. The slump in oil prices mid-'80s hurt music by affecting the spending power of its supporters, but even at its peak few Cajun musicians have made a liv-

CALLENDER … Cale, J.J. … Cale, John … Calender … Callender Red

ing at it. As older musicians pass on, newer ones such as Richard, Savoy, ROCKIN' DOPSIE, D. L. Menard, Beausoleil, Michael Doucet and Joel Sonnier emerge to keep the flame alive. Recommended: John Broven's *South To Louisiana – The Music Of The Cajun Bayous* (Pelican USA); Barry Jean Ancelot and Elemore Morgan Jr's *Musiciens cadiens et créoles/The Makers Of Cajun Music* (U. of Texas), a bilingual account.

CALE, J. J. (*b* Jean Jacques Cale, 5 Dec. '38, Oklahoma City, Okla.) Singer, songwriter, guitar. In high school bands with Leon RUSSELL, worked with Phil SPECTOR, Delaney and Bonnie BRAMLETT; made single 'Slow Motion'/'After Midnight' '65; with producer Snuff GARRETT formed band The Leathercoated Minds '66, made one LP. Eric CLAPTON covered 'After Midnight' in '70; Cale signed to Russell's Shelter label and his lazy country blues, laid-back singing and impeccable guitar acquired a cult following: he does not exert himself either in concert or on record, but fans get just what they want. LPs include *Naturally*, *Really* '72, *Okie* '74; *Troubador* '76 had another hit for Clapton: 'Cocaine'; *Shades* '81, *Grasshopper* '82 were more of the same; on *No. 8* '83, he was joined by Richard THOMPSON and Mark Knopfler, whose own style owes something to Cale.

CALE, John (*b* 3 Dec. '40, Garnant, South Wales) Vocalist, composer, multi-instrumentalist. Initially studied at Goldsmiths' College, London; fascination with US avant-garde of early '60s led to scholarship to study in NYC with Aaron Copland and Lamont Young. Became founder member with Lou REED of seminal NYC band VELVET UNDERGROUND; classical and avant-garde experiments infl. their first LPs, notably on 'The Gift' and epic 17-minute 'Sister Ray', both on *White Light, White Heat* '67. Left Velvets Sept. '68; first solo LP *Vintage Violence* '69 continued experiments. Worked with composer Terry Riley on *The Church Of Anthrax* '71 and *The Academy In Peril* '72. Solo *Paris 1919* featured contributions from Lowell George, was lavishly prod. by Chris THOMAS, incl. enigmatic 'Half Past France' and 'A Child's Christmas In Wales'. *Fear* '74

was harder-edged rock; *June 1, 1974* found Cale reunited with NICO from the Velvets, as well as Brian ENO and Kevin AYERS. *Slow Dazzle* '75 incl. 'Heartbreak Hotel' and featured Phil Manzanera; *Helen Of Troy* came same year. *Guts* '77 is a Best Of. *Honi Soit* '81 was considered one of his strongest albums; incl. haunting version of cowboy ballad 'Streets of Laredo'. *Music For A New Society* '82 was debut on Ze label; *John Cale Comes Alive* and *Caribbean Sunset* came in '84. Also worked as A&R man and quadrophonic consultant for CBS. A godfather of punk because of his reputation with Velvets and his idiosyncratic solo work; he pre-empted UK punk with prod. of IGGY POP's *The Stooges* '69, Patti SMITH's *Horses* '75 and Jonathan RICHMAN's *Modern Lovers* '76; prod. first SQUEEZE LP, demos by POLICE, Nico album. He casts an influential shadow.

CALENDER, Ebeneezer (*b* '12, Sierra Leone) Composer, guitarist, singer. Began playing gombe drum (a large bass drum); a carpenter by profession, later formed own band Ebeneezer Calender and his Men with gombe drum, frame drums, guitars, flutes, recorders, trumpets and sousaphone; sang in Krio and English, became best known performer of maringa (combination of Caribbean MERENGUE with HIGHLIFE), most popular musician in Sierra Leone '50s-60s. Songs related to daily life, special events, questions of social behaviour; many 78 singles on Decca incl. 'You Cooked Jollof Rice', 'Double Decker Bus', 'Baby Lay On Your Powder Now', 'Do Your Thing, Leave Mine', 'Vulture Has No Certificate'. Worked for Sierra Leone Broadcasting Service '60-84, now Director of Traditional Music for Radio Sierra Leone, working occasionally with the Maringa Band on radio and TV.

CALLENDER, Red (*b* George Callender, 6 Mar. '16, Richmond, Va.) Bass, tuba. Studied in New Jersey, played in Atlantic City while still in high school; went to California with Louis ARMSTRONG (first recording with him, '37). Settled on West Coast, became pioneer studio man as well as jazz session player; sought after in both capacities ever since. With King COLE trio, Lester YOUNG, own trio early '40s; *New*

Orleans film with Armstrong '46; trio in Hawaii late '40s (wrote a symphony there; it was performed but is now lost); R&B records under own name; played with Art TATUM incl. trio, quartet LPs '56 (with long-time collaborator, drummer Bill Douglass, *b* 28 Feb. '23, L.A.). First appeared at Monterey Jazz Festival '59; his tune 'Primrose Lane' was no. 8 in pop chart that year (by Billy Wallace); later used as theme on Henry Fonda TV show; earlier tune 'Pastel' was recorded by Erroll GARNER, Illinois JACQUET. He recorded with Ray CHARLES on tuba, with Charles MINGUS at Monterey '64 on that instrument; with Stan KENTON '65; countless sessions incl. Billy MAY's *Big Fat Brass* '58, Earl HINES album *Hits He Missed* '78, plus albums with Art PEPPER, Shorty ROGERS, Bing CROSBY, Carmen McRAE, Plas JOHNSON, Mel TORMÉ, Pearl BAILEY, Erroll GARNER, Billy ECKSTINE, Buddy COLLETTE, Ry COODER: too many to list. His autobiography with Elaine Cohen *Unfinished Dream* '85 has priceless description of L.A. jazz scene of late '40s – early '50s, otherwise poorly documented; has high praise for under-recorded band led by Lester and Lee Young. Callender was one of the first blacks in studio work, helped integrate musicians' unions in L.A.; also praises TV employers Jerry Fielding, Danny KAYE, Flip Wilson, others, especially the women: Lucille Ball, Carol Burnett, Dinah SHORE, Doris DAY, etc.: they never forgot anybody who worked for them. Active with James Newton Wind Quintet: LP *The Mystery School* '80 on India Navigation with flautist/composer Newton, Bobby BRADFORD, John CARTER, John Nunez on bassoon, Charles Owen on English horn and oboe; also *Dauwhe* '82 on Black Saint, by Carter octet with similar personnel. Callender's own albums incl. *Speaks Low* and *Swingin' Suite*, both '57 on the Bihari Bros' Crown label: the former used in music schools for tuba playing, now reissued on his own RED label; the latter a set of 12 original tunes incl. 'Pastel'. Also *The Lowest* '58 on MGM, *Basin Street Brass* '73 on Legend, *Red Callender-Gerald Wiggins* '83 on Hemisphere, duets with old friend pianist Wig (*b* 12 May '22, NYC; his son, also Gerald Foster Wiggins, *b* 15 Apr. '56, L.A., plays bass, joined Mercer ELLINGTON

'74). Callender is a lucky man and he knows it, but then you've got to be good at music to get Mingus to leave you a bass in his will.

CALLOWAY, Cab (*b* Cabell Calloway, 25 Dec. '07, Rochester, NY) Singer, bandleader: exuberant entertainer, scat-singing, zootsuited Highness of Hi-De-Ho: incalculable influence. Raised in Baltimore, sang in group Baltimore Melody Boys, attended law school, quit to work Chicago club circuit. Toured with sister Blanche Calloway's band (she was a star in late '20s, fine singer who even looked like Cab, but soon eclipsed by his fame, ignored by booking agency in his favour: she employed fine musicians in '30s but went bankrupt. She made about 30 sides '25-35, some issued as 'Fred Armstrong and his Syncopators'. Ironically, she was not used to trade on the name after Cab became famous: brother Elmer did not play or sing but fronted band for promoter; Jean and/or Ruth Calloway was not even related). Cab fronted band The Missourians; appeared in show *Connie's Hot Chocolates* '29; that year fronted band The Alabamians at Harlem's Savoy Ballroom; then Missourians again, changed name to Cab Calloway and Orchestra, followed Duke ELLINGTON into COTTON CLUB, became famous '31-2 as result of broadcasts from club. Films incl. *Big Broadcast Of 1932*, *International House* '33, *Manhattan Merry-Go-Round* '37, *Stormy Weather* '43, *Sensations Of '45* '44, others. Records on Brunswick from '30: 'Minnie The Moocher', 'Kicking The Gong Around', both '31; 'The Scat Song', 'Reefer Man', 'Eadie Was A Lady', all '32; many more. Signed to Victor late '33; pianist was Benny Payne (*b* '07, later accompanist to Billy DANIELS). Toured Europe '34 incl. UK. Band was full of stars: Ben WEBSTER, Shad Collins, Milt HINTON, Chu BERRY, singer June Richmond (1915-62), Dizzy GILLESPIE '39-41 (sacked in famous spitball incident). Act full of physical energy, long black hair flying; made 'hi-de-ho' national catch-phrase, but ballad style underrated. Biggest hit 'Blues In The Night' on Okeh; no. 8 '42. One of the highest-earning bands '30s-40s; when big band money tailed off, disbanded '48, led sextet, visited UK that year; re-formed big band for special engagements, tours of Canada, South America. George

GERSHWIN allegedly wrote part of Sportin' Life in *Porgy And Bess* '35 for Calloway; he finally played it in revival, tour beginning Dallas June '52 (London Oct. that year) until Aug. '54; sometimes played in later productions. Solo tour UK '55. Film *St Louis Blues* '58; occasionally appeared as part of Harlem Globetrotters interval show mid-'60s; with Pearl BAILEY in hit all-black version of *Hello, Dolly!* NYC '67: played Cornelius Vandergelder; daughter Chris played Minnie Fay. Autobiography published *Of Minnie The Moocher And Me* '76. New generation of fans from '80 film *The Blues Brothers* (sang 'Moocher'); guest spot on Muppet TV show; in show *Bubbling Brown Sugar*; portrayed by Larry Marshall in film *The Cotton Club* '84, featured 'Moocher', 'Lady With The Fan', 'Jitterbug', all his own comps. Made TV film *The Cotton Club Comes To The Ritz*, at London hotel, broadcast UK May '85; sang 'Blues In The Night'; *Cotton Club Revisited* toured North America '85 with Chris, who has done club work, was married to Hugh MASEKELA, planned recording sessions '86 inspired by Tina TURNER, Carly SIMON, 'who have given a whole new dimension to this over-35 business'. To say nothing of her father, who has now infl. new jump/jive bands in '80s, Joe JACKSON, etc. LP *The Hi-De-Ho Man* '58 on RCA with big band incl. Hinton, Joe WILDER, Urbie Green on trombone, J. C. Heard on drums (*b* James Charles Heard, 8 Oct. '17, Dayton, Ohio). Other LPs on Coral and Glendale in late '50s; compilations incl. 2-disc *The Hi-De-Ho Man* on Columbia, *Mr Hi-De-Ho* on MCA; in UK: *Jumpin' Jive* on CBS, *Kicking The Gong Around* on ASV/PRT, *Minnie The Moocher* on RCA International. 2-disc *Cab Calloway & Co.* on French RCA has complete '33-4 Cotton Club sessions, '49 sides, six '31 tracks by Blanche and her Joy Boys, two by Billy BANKS incl. Calloway's 'The Scat Song'.

CALVERT, Eddie (*b* 15 Mar. '22, Preston, England; *d* 7 Aug. '78, Johannesburg, S.A.) Trumpet. Played with Northern brass bands; worked with Billy Ternent and GERALDO in the '40s; ran own café units. Solo variety dates '50s, solo spot on Stanley BLACK BBC TV show (playing 'September Song') led to UK no. 1 hits: instrumental version of 'Oh Mein Papa', '53; copy of Perez PRADO USA hit 'Cherry Pink And Apple Blossom White', '55; both also charted in USA. Four more hits in UK incl. two top tens; also heard in soundtracks of films *John And Julie*, *Beyond Mombasa*, both '55. After '58 played clubs; moved to S. Africa '68. EMI 2-disc compilation '85: *The Man With The Golden Trumpet*.

CALYPSO Song form native to Trinidad, originally improvised social commentary and medium of poor people's information, from West African praise singer (trad. recorder of tribal history, commentator, celebrator, satirist). Terms calypso and kaiso used interchangeably in Trinidad, where 'Kaiso!' is often heard in calypso tents as patrons wish to show approval: probably comes from West African Hausa term which depending on context can mean regret, triumph, contempt, etc. Possible derivations of 'calypso' incl. West African 'kaiso', French patois 'carrousseaux', Spanish 'caliso', Virgin Islands topical song 'careso', etc. First appeared 1900 spelled 'calipso'. According to legend, the first 'chantwell', or singer of what became calypso, was a slave, Gros Jean, in the late 18th century. Rhythms and melodies are predominantly African, but melodies infl. by nearby Venezuela: identified early 20th century by terms 'pasillo' or 'paseo', a Venezuelan dance form. Music of French, Irish and English origin has also been incorporated; French was basis of patois or Creole lyrics through 19th century. After 1838, when slave apprenticeships ended, the annual Trinidad Carnival changed from a genteel aristocratic affair to a popular African-dominated festival, incl. masquerade or costumed bands; season begins after Christmas, ends at midnight on Shrove Tuesday. In 19th century, masquerade bands preparing for carnival used practice tents with bamboo supports, roofs of palm leaves, in back yards of Port of Spain (capital of Trinidad); here the chantwell composed songs and practised, with band members providing the chorus; on carnival days he led the band in the streets with the prepared choruses, but also improvising songs of praise, criticism, challenge: prepared to do battle with rivals. At the turn of the century, patois gave way to English, people moved from tent to tent to see what was happening; audiences gathered at rehearsals and tents began to charge admission. Calypsonian and railway ticket collector 'Chieftain' Walter Douglas (1895-1982) made the break in '21, produced first recognisable calypso tent, completed the process of calypso's breaking away from the old masquerade band tradition: he replaced the palm roof with railway tarpaulins, kerosene flambeaux with gas lamps; erected a stage, provided rented chairs; printed tickets, handbills for railway passengers and employees; brought in an orchestra of flute, clarinet, cuarto, guitar, bass, occasionally violin, and chorus. Shows are still called tents, though now using halls, cinemas, other accessible buildings as venues, with sound systems and touring the country during the season. Performers move from tent to tent looking for the best deal. First calypso records made '14 when Victor visited the island; emigrants to USA were recorded there throughout '20s, incl. Johnny Walker, Sam Manning, Wilmoth Houdini (1895-1973); local businessman Edward Sa Gomes sent ATILLA the Hun and Roaring Lion to NYC to record '34; he continued sending artists to NYC annually after each season, expanding and cornering the record market; USA Decca and Bluebird also sent engineers with mobile recording units to Trinidad late '30s. 78s made in NYC were released in UK '38 by Atilla, Lion, Lord Beginner, King Radio, Growling TIGER; did not make much impact. Artists still record in NYC; a stable industry has not been established in Trinidad because of seasonal nature: early '80s there were three recording studios there but in '85 only Coral remained. Most calypso records are released just before or during season, though non-T & T artists will release records the previous year in time for other Caribbean festivals. First known calypso competition was '14, first national Calypso King contest '39; final of competition run by Trinidad and Tobago (T & T) government-run Carnival Development Committee (CDC) at Dimanche Gras shows on Carnival Sunday nights from '58; on inclusion of women contestants '78 title changed to Calypso Monarch. CDC panel of judges visits tents, selects about two dozen semifinalists who compete at Skinner Park in San Fernando a week before the big night; seven finalists compete against reigning Monarch during Dimanche Gras show in Queens Park Savannah in Port of Spain, required to sing two songs, usually choosing one with serious topic, one in lighter vein. Winning still regarded as singular achievement, but there is controversy about the competitive element nowadays. The Road March is the 'people's choice', played by steel bands, brass bands and DJs as accompaniment for parade of costumed bands over the two-day climax of carnival, emphasis on melody rather than lyric. Road March is thought to be derived from kalinda, an early song type which accompanied stick fighting. Watershed year was '56; up to then people like Atilla and Tiger prevailed, since then Mighty SPARROW has more or less dominated and new generation emerged: Calypso ROSE, Black STALIN, Mighty SHADOW, BLUE BOY. Lord KITCHENER began before '56 and continues to present day. During the '70s the modern form of SOCA began to emerge. In '86 for the first time the Young King, Calypso Monarch and Road March titles were held by the same composer/performer: David RUDDER (b c.'53) challenged tradition by using his own name, full-time working band (Charlie's Roots) and by allowing infl. of jazz, soul; threatened to become a hero bigger than the genre by revitalising the island's roots at time of economic and political crisis; records released UK '86 on London. *Port Of Spain Shuffle* and *Caribbean Connection* '87 on Charly's New Cross label are good compilations of calypso hits.

CAMARATA, Tutti (b Salvador Tutti Camarata, 11 May '13, Glen Ridge, N.J.) Trumpet, arranger, bandleader; sometimes 'Tootie'. Studied at Juilliard; arranged for Bing CROSBY radio show, Paul WHITEMAN, Charlie BARNET; greatest success with Jimmy DORSEY: 'Green Eyes', 'Maria Elena' (no. ones '41), 'Yours' (no. 2). Mus. dir. Decca USA mid-'40s, then London (UK '48-50), then back to USA Decca; formed Commanders, brassy big band: LPs *Meet The Commanders, Dance Party*. Late '50s-60s mus. dir. for Walt Disney; LPs *Autumn* '58, *Rendezvous* '61, *Snow White* '63, *35 Disney Picture Melodies* '64. Comps. incl. 'Trumpeter's Prayer', 'Rhapsody For

Saxophone', etc. Hi-Fi spectacular album *Vienna Of J. Strauss* issued '72.

CAMEL UK progressive rock band formed '72 by keyboardist Peter Bardens (ex-Them, Shotgun Express, Village, etc. plus solo LPs *The Answer* '70, *Peter Bardens* '71), Andy Latimer (flute, guitar, vocals), Doug Ferguson (bass), Andy Ward (drums). Had been together as Brew, backed singer/songwriter Philip Goodhand Tait. Similarity of name to ex-Herd heart-throb Peter FRAMPTON's Camel didn't help first two LPs *Camel* '73, *Mirage* '74; third *The Snow Goose*, concept LP suggested by Paul Gallico's children's novel, took them to no. 22 UK LP chart, out of college circuit and into Royal Albert Hall Oct. '75 with LSO: instrumental album reminiscent of Focus, with Latimer's flute much in evidence. After *Moonmadness* '76 Ferguson left; bassist Richard Sinclair (ex-CARAVAN, National Health) joined, his distinctively English vocals marking *Rain Dances* '77; these and *Breathless* '78 made top 30 UK albums, bottom of USA charts; *A Live Record* from same time did not. Saxist Mel Collins (ex-Kokomo, King Crimson) also present during this time. Sinclair replaced by Colin Bass; major upheaval was departure of Bardens: played with Van MORRISON again, also solo LP *Heart To Heart* '79 before joining Colin BLUNSTONE in Keats. Latimer led band through *I Can See Your House From Here* '79 and *Nude* '81 (concept LP about Japanese soldier unaware war was over). Music became noticeably less keyboard-oriented (*The Single Factor* '82) despite addition of ex-Caravan sideman Jan Schelhaas. Lineup in '84: Ton Scherpenzeel, keyboards, Paul Bass, bass; Paul Burgess (ex-10CC), drums; Chris Rainbow, vocals; made *Stationary Traveller* and live LP with Bardens guesting. Never the most distinctive of progressive bands, but survived New Wave vicissitudes.

CAMPBELL, Archie (*b* 17 Nov. '14, Bull's Gap, Tenn.) Country comic. Started out on Knoxville radio's Tennessee Barn Dance, Mid-Day Merry-Go-Round '36-43; own TV show there '52-8; joined Grand Ole Opry '58, RCA records '59. Country hits with serious recitation 'Trouble In The Amen Corner' '60, humorous 'Bleeping Sleauty', 'Ridercella'; 'The Men In My Little Girl's Life' '65 serious again. Duets with Lorene Mann incl. 'Dark Side Of The Street' '68, 'My Special Prayer' '69; named Comedian of the Year by CMA '69. Star of *Hee Haw* TV series early '70s as both writer and performer. LPs incl. *Bedtime Stories For Adults* '66 (RCA), *Live At Tupelo* '77 (Elektra), *Grand Ole Opry's Good Humor Man* '79 (Starday).

CAMPBELL, Cornell Jamaican singer. Began early '60s with love ditties in ska mould like 'Rosabelle', 'Gloria'; sang lead with the Eternals on their classic Studio One titles 'Queen Of The Minstrel' and 'Stars'; Bunny Lee prod. first LP *Cornell Campbell* '73, partnership flourished '75 with thematic 'Conquering Gorgon', 'The Gorgon Speaks', 'Gorgon At The Ginegog' and album *Gorgon*, then similar series of 'Greenwich Farm' lyrics, *Dance In A Greenwich Farm* LP '76. Big solo hit 'The Investigator' '77, still with Lee; also LPs *Stalowatt* and *Turn Back The Hands Of Time*. Later sets incl. *Sweet Baby, Fight Against Corruption, Johnny Clarke Meets Cornell Campbell In A New Style* and *Boxing*, title track of latter a hit '81.

CAMPBELL, Glen (*b* Glen Travis Campbell, 22 Apr. '36, Delight, Ark.) Country/pop guitar, singer; hugely successful late '60s-70s. Started out in his Uncle Bill's Western Band '50; formed group Western Wranglers, played around Albequerque, N.M., Phoenix, Ariz.; to L.A. '58, played on Champs' smash hit 'Tequila', sessioned with Nat COLE, Frank SINATRA, Elvis PRESLEY, MAMAS & PAPAS, Merle HAGGARD, etc. Records on Crest '61 (minor hit 'Turn Around Look At Me'); signed to Capitol '62, had country hit with 'Kentucky Means Paradise'. Made several LPs spotlighting both guitar and singing without much success; deputised for Brian Wilson in BEACH BOYS '65; broke through '67 with John HARTFORD song 'Gentle On My Mind' (country hit, made pop chart next year), Jim WEBB's 'By The Time I Get To Phoenix' (no. 26 pop, no. 2 country); won Grammies incl. 'Phoenix' single, *Gentle On My Mind* LP; named Entertainer of the Year by CMA '68. Once he struck vein of good songs, laid-back sincerity crossed over

197

regularly: 'I Wanna Live', 'Galveston', 'Wichita Lineman' (last two by Webb), many others: 12 gold, 7 platinum LPs '68-72. Appeared in films *True Grit* '69, *Norwood* '70; own TV series early '70s; own golf tournament: Glen Campbell Los Angeles Open. More hits through '70s incl. 'Rhinestone Cowboy', 'Southern Nights', 'Country Boy'; some LPs went back to country roots: *I Remember Hank Williams* '74, *Arkansas* '76, *Highwayman* '80. Affair with Tanya TUCKER made news; toured and recorded together, split up '81. Also duet records with Anne MURRAY, Bobbie GENTRY, Rita COOLIDGE. With Atlantic label '82, LP *Letter To Home* '83. Other current LPs in USA incl. *Southern Nights, Rhinestone Cowboy*, hits compilations; also gospel LP *No More Nights* '85 on Word. Many others in UK (where *Greatest Hits* LP '71 was 113 weeks in charts) incl. *All I Have To Do Is Dream* with Gentry, reissued on budget label. *Still Within The Sound Of My Voice* '88 on MCA described as straight country.

CAMPBELL, Stan (*b* 2 Jan. '62, Coventry, UK) Soul singer. Fronted various local groups; at centre of Coventry's 2-tone scene: with Selector early '80s, then Jerry Dammers' Special AKA (*see* SPECIALS): co-lead vocalist on *In The Studio* '84, lead on hit single 'Free Nelson Mandela'; signed with WEA, eponymous debut LP '87: excellent LP manages not to be over-produced (unusual in mid-'80s) despite several producers; incl. seven originals, covers of ANIMALS' 'Don't Let Me Be Misunderstood', Billie HOLIDAY's 'Strange Fruit'; 'Crawfish' by Ben Wiseman and Fred Wise (from Elvis PRESLEY movie *King Creole*) released as single. Album's fine rhythm sections show strong Latin bent.

CAN German avant-garde electronic rock band formed '68 in Cologne: Irmin Schmidt, keyboards; Michael Karoli, guitar, violin; Holger Czukay, bass, electronics; Jaki Liebezeit, drums, reeds; last three also on vocals. First LP *Monster Movie Made In A Castle With Better Equipment* '70 on UA also had David Johnson, flute, electronics, black USA vocalist Malcolm Mooney: the noise, repetition and distortion that would infl. electro-art rock was still primitive.

They discovered Damo Suzuki singing in the streets in Munich and absorbed more of the infl. of Karlheinz Stockhausen (*b* '28). *Tago Mago* '71, *Ege Bamyasi* '72, *Future Days* '73 followed; Suzuki left and *Soundtracks* '73 collected their work in that medium; *Soon Over Baluma* and *Limited Edition* '74 preceded switch to Virgin label for *Landed* '75, *Opener, Flow Motion* and *Unlimited Edition* '76 (latter reissue of '74 LP with additional material); somewhat funkier *Saw Delight* '77, *Cannibalisms* (on UA) and *Out Of Reach* (on Lightning) '78 added ex-TRAFFIC Rosko Gee on bass, Reebop Kwaku Baah on percussion. 'I Want More' '76 was top 30 single '76 in UK from *Flow Motion*. They split up for various splinter efforts, notably Czukay's *Movies* '80, *On The Way To The Peak Of Normal* '82 (both on EMI), *Snake Charmer* '83 on Island with Jah Wobble & The Edge; also *Der Esten Ist Rot* '84, *Rome Remains Rome* '86 on Virgin (the latter 'rescues the Pope's gently swinging vocals from an obscure Easter performance', wrote a UK critic).

CANALES, Angel (*b* Caracas, Venezuela) Singer, bandleader, composer, producer, label boss; leader of an adventurous salsa band, presenting hard-edged jazz-oriented dance music, replete with solos, with a constant core of trombonists John Torres and Ricardo Montañez, Antonio Tapia on congas, and bongo player Louie Rivera (who left to work with Rubén BLADES '84). First LP was *Sabor* '75 on Alegre, with Torres as mus. dir. (name of band meant 'taste' or 'flavour'); with 'El Cantante y la Orquesta' written by Tapia, two other standout tracks by Canales; leader got top billing on *Angel Canales & Sabor* '76 on TR, with eight of ten tracks by Canales, incl. 'Sandra', unusually sung in English; bassist John Henry Robinson III joined with this LP, coprod. by keyboardist Ricardo Marrero, who also plays now in Blades' band, with Tito Rodriguez II (Tito Rodriguez founder of label). *Mas Sabor* '77 on Alegre again was a stylistic deviation, infl. by the early '70s sound of Eddie PALMIERI, written by pianist Mark 'Markolino' Dimond, known for his work with Willie COLON (he wrote tracks on *The Hustler* and *Guisando – Doing A Job*; played brilliant solo on 'Rompe Saraguey' on Hector LAVOE's *La Voz* '75; also notable mid-'70s solo LP *Beethoven's V* with singer Frankie Dante). The name 'Sabor' fell into disuse; Canales had 'interesting – because new to salsa – mannered, indeed almost decadent edge to his singing,' wrote John Storm Roberts. He soon prod. his first LP, *El Sentimiento del Latino en Nueva York* c.'78 ('The Feeling Of The Latin In New York') on his own Selanac label (Canales backwards), with a respectful cover of Beny MORÉ's 'Soy Del Monte' ('I Come From The Mountain') and Canales' own 'Panama Soberana'. Same line-up made *Angel Canales Live At Roseland* '78 on TR, reworking hits in the famous ballroom; both LPs featured Lesette Wilson on piano, a rare instance of a woman in salsa: she had worked with Yambú (formed '72 to play their version of the sound of El Barrio, a combination of typical and progressive Latin with shades of rock and soul), sang on the track on their eponymous '75 LP on Montuno, and had her own hit on UK dance charts with 'Caveman Boogie' (from her solo LP *Now That I've Got Your Attention* on Headfirst), which made UK soul charts '81. Canales recruited Victor 'Even' Perez on timbales; he appeared on *El Diferente* c.'81 on Selanac, which incl. a driving version of Puerto Rican classic 'Bomba Carambomba', and stand-out track in 'La Vida Es una Caja de Sorpresa'. *El Diferente en 'Vivo' Desde el Poliedro* '82 was made live at Poliedro Stadium in Caracas, issued on Venezuelan GM label. Well-known session player Steve Sacks on flute/baritone sax joined with *Different Shades Of Thought* '82 on Selanac, on which Canales reworked 'Sandra' as 'Baby Please Don't Go', covered another Beny Moré's tune, 'Guantanamo'. Trumpeter/flugelhornist Angel Fernandez arr. several tracks on various LPs; on *Ya Es Tiempo (It's Time)* '85 on Selanac five of the seven tracks were his, incl. his own composition, a long instrumental 'Angel Canales Theme Song', studded with solos. In the '80s members of Canales' band (incl. Perez, Robinson and Sacks) also played with Hector Lavoe's band, adding rawer edge to its sound.

CANDIDO (*b* Candido Camero, 22 Apr. '21, Havana) Latin-American percussion: bongo and conga drums. 12 years on radio and Tropicana Club in Havana; to Miami, then NYC late '52. Played with Billy TAYLOR, Stan KENTON, Dizzy GILLESPIE, own groups; JATP '60; Carnegie Hall with Tony BENNETT '62, etc. Easily the busiest freelance in his field; many TV appearances; has played and recorded with Sonny ROLLINS, Elvin JONES, Randy WESTON, David AMRAM; one side of Columbia LP *Drum Suite* '57 by 'Art Blakey Percussion Ensemble' incl. Candido, congas; Blakey and Jo JONES, drums; Sabu Martinez, bongos; Charles 'Specs' Wright, tympani (*b* 8 Nov. '27, Philadelphia; *d* there 6 Feb. '63); Oscar PETTIFORD, Ray BRYANT. Own LP on ABC-Paramount '56, followed by five more on ABC, Roulette, Solid State; *Beautiful* '70 on Blue Note, *Drum Fever* '73 on Polydor.

CANDOLI BROTHERS Trumpets. Walter Joseph 'Pete' Candoli *b* 28 June '23; Secondo 'Conte' Candoli *b* 12 July '27, both in Mishawaka, Indiana. Pete played with Will BRADLEY, Benny GOODMAN, Charlie BARNET, Woody HERMAN (featured on 'Superman With A Horn' at Herman's Carnegie Hall concert '46), many other big bands in '40s; led own band mid-'50s. Conte studied with brother Pete; played with Herman while still in high school; finished school, rejoined Herman; played with Stan KENTON, Charlie VENTURA, many others; led band in Chicago; played in combo at Lighthouse, Hermosa Beach, Cal. late '50s; with Shelly MANNE '61-6; Monterey Jazz Festival '60 with Herman, European tour '61 with Gerry MULLIGAN, with SUPERSAX '72, etc. Conte is the more aggressive soloist, Pete a talented arranger. Both have been busy freelances, in TV studio bands etc.; both have conducted college music seminars; worked together on film *Bell, Book And Candle* '58. Albums *Brothers Candoli* '57 on Dot, *Bell, Book And Candoli* '58 on Colpix, others. Conte played in T. MONK band cond. by Oliver NELSON '68, Pete for Igor Stravinsky: between them they've played on hundreds of records. Conte's *Fine And Dandy* issued on Affinity '87; mellow sextet LP *Old Acquaintance* '85 on Pausa has Conte and Phil WOODS.

CANNED HEAT White blues band formed '66 by Bob 'The Bear' Hite (*b* 26 Feb. '45, Torrance, Cal., *d* 5 Apr. '81) and Alan

'Blind Owl' Wilson (*b* 4 July '43, Boston, *d* 3 Sep. '70). Hite former record shop manager, mania for blues; Wilson music major at Boston U., formed jug band '65 L.A. with drummer Bob Cook. Recruited ex-Frank ZAPPA sideman Henry Vestine (*b* 25 Dec. '44, Washington DC), ex-Jerry Lee LEWIS bassist Larry Taylor (*b* 26 June '42, NYC) to mix country blues with electric instrumentation. Exposure at Monterey Festival '67 promoted eponymous first LP, made them headliners overnight. Bespectacled Wilson, man-mountain Hite made unlikely looking combination, but Wilson's light tenor was effective contrast with Hite's growl. Replaced Cook with Mexican Adolpho 'Fito' de la Parra (*b* 8 Feb. '46) for *Boogie With Canned Heat* '68, incl. hit singles 'On The Road Again' (USA no. 16/UK no. 8), 'Going Up The Country' (11 USA/19 UK), midtempo chuggers adapted from old blues songs by Jim Oden, Henry Thomas respectively. '69 LPs *Living The Blues*, *Hallelujah* consolidated appeal; then Vestine left to work with Albert AYLER, replaced by Harvey Mandel (*b* 11 Mar. '45, Detroit); played Woodstock that year. Best year was '70, with cover of Wilbert Harrison's 'Let's Work Together' (USA 26/UK 2), classic compilation *Cookbook*, album *Future Blues* with ecological feel. Session with John Lee HOOKER (*Hooker & Heat* released '71) showed legendary black bluesman sympathetic to white disciples. Changes destabilised lineup: Mandel replaced by returning Vestine, Taylor by Antonio de la Barreda (aka Tony Olav); but Wilson's death on eve of band's third UK tour tore heart out of group. Continued in '70s with *Historical Figures And Ancient Heads* '72, *New Age* '73, *One More River To Cross* '74, Hite driving force and only constant factor; his death from heart attack ended story. Initially imitative, at their peak paralleled John MAYALL's Bluesbreakers in UK in producing genuinely moving white blues; Hite, who had 60,000+ blues record collection, left further legacy by helping United Artists compile *Legendary Masters* series.

CANNON, Freddy (*b* Frederick Anthony Picariello, 4 Dec.'40, Lynn, Mass.) Singer; Philadelphia teen star. Played solo guitar on a G-Clefs Hot 100 entry '56; under stage name Freddy Karmon made demo for DJ Jack McDermott of 'Rock'n'Roll Baby' (written by Cannon and his mother); remade as 'Tallahassee Lassie' with prod. Frank Slay and Bob Crewe (latter the force behind the FOUR SEASONS) and name change for singer, became no. 6 hit '59; Cannon quit truck-driving, appeared on American Bandstand. Though covered by home favourite Tommy STEELE, Cannon's record made no. 15 UK. Throaty, rasping vocals with horns, Bo DIDDLEY-style guitar from Kenny Paulson, roaring sax section had more hits: second single 'Okefenoke' made top 50 USA but update of '22 hit 'Way Down Yonder In New Orleans' was no. 3 USA/4 UK, led to LP written around place names; *The Explosive Freddy Cannon* topped LP chart UK '60 (he toured there, unlike some contemporaries). Revival of '50 Red FOLEY hit 'Chattanooga Shoe Shine Boy', 'Jump Over', 'Transistor Sister' made top 40 USA '60-1; next big hit had organ sound: 'Palisades Park' no. 3 USA/20 UK; LP *Freddy Cannon At Palisades Park* charted in USA; he appeared in British film *Just For Fun* '63; switched from Swan to WB for top 20 hits 'Abigail Beecher' '64, 'Action' '65, ending with five top 20 entries in each USA/UK. Was promo man for Buddah; joined oldies revival circuit; had minor comeback '81 with 'Let's Put The Fun Back In Rock'n'Roll'.

CANTOR, Eddie (*b* Edward Israel Iskowitz, 31 Jan. 1892, NYC; *d* 10 Oct. '64, Hollywood) Singer, comedian, actor; aka 'Banjo Eyes'. Parents Russian immigrants; orphaned at 2, raised by grandmother. Never finished primary school; entertained on street corners; appeared at 12 in YMCA summer camp show; won talent contest '08; first appeared in blackface in Gus Edwards's *Kid Kabaret* revue '12; Flo Ziegfeld's *Midnight Frolic* '16; became star in successive shows of *Ziegfeld's Follies* '17-8-9. Sold Liberty bonds during WWI. Shows *Broadway Brevities* '20, *Midnight Rounders* '21; *Make It Snappy* '22; acclaimed for routines in *Kid Boots* '23, incl. songs 'Alabamy Bound', 'If You Knew Susie' (film of that name three years later). Singer of enormous vivacity, with cross-stage movements, handclapping and eye-rolling; also associated with songs 'Dinah', 'Ida', 'My Baby Just Cares For Me', others. Triumph in Ziegfeld production *Whoopee* '28, incl. Gus Kahn-Walter Donaldson hit song 'Makin' Whoopee'. Lost $2 million in Wall Street crash '29; became highest paid star on radio by '36 (*The Eddie Cantor Chase And Sandborn Hour*, sponsored by coffee maker); in routines often dropped remarks about wife Ida and their five daughters. Delightful films, sprinkled with saucy jokes and costumes (before movies censorship began), some featuring early colour process: *Makin' Whoopee* '30, *Glorifying The American Girl* '30, *Palmy Days* '31, *The Kid From Spain* '32, *Roman Scandals* '33, *Kid Millions* '34, *Strike Me Pink* '36, *Ali Baba Goes To Town* '37. Plot of *Roman Scandals* featured populist streak; Cantor speech at NY World's Fair '39 denounced some public figures as fascists: dropped by radio sponsors; made spectacular comeback after USA entry into WWII on NBC's *Time To Smile* show; also film *Forty Little Mothers* '40; on Broadway first time in 12 years in *Banjo Eyes* '41. TV debut on *Colgate Comedy Hour* '50 (Sunday evening show opposite Ed Sullivan, alternated famous comics through most of '50s); still moved at maximum pace, concl. act with blackface medley: 'Susie', 'Whoopee', 'Ma! He's Makin' Eyes At Me!' etc. Helped Dinah SHORE, Eddie FISHER, others early in their careers. Won award for straight role in *Seidman & Son* on TV's *Playouse 90*. Heart trouble caused retirement; brief appearance in film *The Eddie Cantor Story* '53 (portrayed by Keefe Brasselle); Oscar '56 for distinguished service to film industry. Autobiographies *My Life Is In Your Hands*, *Take My Life*; other books *Yoo-hoo Prosperity*, *The Eddie Cantor Five-Year Plan*, *Ziegfeld The Great Glorifier*, *As I Remember Them*, *Since Ma Is Playing Mah Jong*, *Caught Short* (account of '29 losses), others. Wrote lyrics 'Get A Little Fun Out Of Life', 'Merrily We Roll Along', others. Compilation LP *The Best Of Eddie Cantor* on RCA UK; others on Biograph, MCA, Audio Fidelity in USA.

CAPITOL First major USA record label to be located on West Coast. It was formed Hollywood Apr. '42 by record retailer Glenn Wallichs, songwriters Johnny MERCER, Buddy DESYLVA with investment of $10,000. Because of WWII shortage of shellac, bought old records from dealers at 6 cents a pound, converting them to raw material (Mercer reportedly signed not-very-good young bandleader whose father owned a shellac warehouse), soon producing 20,000 records a week, first six releases 1 July '42: 'Cow Cow Boogie', by Ella Mae MORSE and Freddie SLACK, was first no. 1 hit. Union ban on recording '42-3 made survival difficult, but label's innovations kept it growing: first to give records to disc jockeys, record masters on tape, issue records in all three speeds; signed Stan KENTON, Peggy LEE, Nat COLE from '40s; Julia LEE, Nellie LUTCHER and others in black pop; owned seminal Miles DAVIS *Birth Of The Cool* recordings '48-9; made classic Frank SINATRA albums from Apr. '53; by then technical quality of records set standard for industry: made albums, some produced by Dave Cavanaugh, of vintage hits by Duke Ellington, Guy LOMBARDO, Glen Gray and CASA LOMA band, Benny GOODMAN, Fred WARING, in new recordings (e.g. *B.G. in HI-FI* '55), often using pool of swing era veterans now in L.A. studio work. Also in '50s had Dean MARTIN, Les PAUL & Mary Ford, satirist Stan FREBERG; Axel STORDAHL, Billy MAY, Nelson RIDDLE on staff; active in West Coast jazz: recorded Art TATUM, Duke Ellington solo set, much else; hired West Coast country DJ Cliffie STONE to shape country list: hits with Jimmy WAKELY, Ernie FORD, Ferlin HUSKY, Hank THOMPSON, Sonny JAMES, later Buck OWENS, many more. Small but select classical output: Hollywood String Quartet, Pittsburgh S.O. with William Steinberg; etc. Sold to EMI '55; moved to new Capitol Tower on Vine Street '56; success late '50s with Gene VINCENT, BEACH BOYS, KINGSTON TRIO, but Sinatra left to start own label '62; Capitol had to be forced by EMI to issue records by the BEATLES, who then carried company through '60s; invested in rack-jobbing firm, mail-order record club, both lost money; label lost $8m '71: had The BAND, Helen REDDY, GRAND FUNK, PINK FLOYD, many country artists, but innovative label had become clumsy giant; EMI seemed unable to exercise control. Producer Dave Dexter kicked out on short notice after decades of service c.'73; Morse's records have been reissued, and the label (once the most honest as well as innovative) says *she* owes *them* money. (*See* EMI.)

CAPITOLS, The USA vocal trio, earlier called The Three Caps: Samuel George, lead singer, drums (*b* c.'42; *d* 17 Mar. '82), Don Storball, guitar (real name Don Norman); Richard Mitchell or McDougall, keyboards; all *b* in Detroit. Prod. by veteran local entrepreneur Ollie McLaughlin, who also worked with Deon Jackson, Barbara Lewis; he met them '62, cut unsuccessful 'Dog And Cat'; they broke up but came back later with Storball comp. 'Cool Jerk'; released on McLaughlin's Karen label: dance craze/top 10 hit '66, still heard in discotheques. A few more minor hits; broke up again '69. George stabbed to death; Storball is a policeman in Detroit. Compilation LP on Solid Smoke label '84.

CAPP-PIERCE JUGGERNAUT Big jazz band. Frankie Capp (*b* 20 Aug. '31, Worcester, Mass.) was drummer with Stan KENTON, many others, then studio/session player in L.A. for many years; Nat PIERCE is the well-known arranger and rhythm pianist; The Capp-Pierce band was called 'a juggernaut in Basin Street' '76 and the name stuck. Though everybody says big bands are dead, uneconomic and so forth, Concord Jazz sells the records anyway. LP *Juggernaut* followed by *Live At Century Plaza*, then *Juggernaut Strikes Again* '81; *Plaza* has vocals by Joe WILLIAMS, the others by Ernie Andrews. *Live At The Alley* '87 features Ernestine ANDERSON.

CAPTAIN AND TENNILLE Daryl Dragon (*b* 27 Aug. '42, L.A.), keyboards; Toni Tennille (*b* 8 May '43, Montgomery, Ala.), vocals. Tennille (classically trained on piano) co-wrote ecology musical *Mother Earth* with Ron Thronson; Dragon (son of conductor Carmen Dragon) hired to play in it: had been BEACH BOYS sideman, asked her to join tour with them when show closed. Carried on as duo; self-financed 'The Way I Want To Touch You' typical keyboard-based multi-voiced faceless MOR product, local hit; signed by A&M, married '74. First LP's title track, Neil SEDAKA's 'Love Will Keep Us Together', was no. 1 '75, re-released 'Touch You' no. 4. 'Together' won a Grammy, was only song to make

Hot 100 in two languages when they re-recorded LP in Spanish (*Por Amor Viviremos*). Like labelmates CARPENTERS whose sound theirs resembled, mixed originals with hand-picked covers (AMERICA's 'Muskrat Love', Smokey ROBINSON's 'Shop Around', both no. 4 '76). Left A&M as that label embraced New Wave at expense of MOR; first single for Casablanca was no. 1 'Do That To Me One More Time' for total of seven top 10 entries USA, but attempt to change image of that disco-oriented label thwarted by death of its founder Neil Bogart. They hosted ABC variety series '76-7; Tennille hosted TV talk show, made *More Than You Know* '84, solo album of standards on Mirage label with big band, like Linda RONSTADT's *What's New* showing that nothing is.

CAPTAIN BEEFHEART & HIS MAGIC BAND USA avant-garde rock group, formed '64 by Beefheart (*b* Don Van Vliet, 15 Jan. '41, Glendale, Cal.), singer and various instruments. Original lineup had Alex St Claire Snouffer (Snuffy), Doug Moon, guitars; Jerry Handley, bass; Paul Blakely, drums. One of music's great eccentrics, Beefheart was child prodigy who appeared on TV as juvenile sculptor. Lived in Mojave Desert in early teens, played in local bands there and met Frank ZAPPA. To Cucamonga with Zappa '60 to form band, make film *Captain Beefheart Meets The Grunt People*; that fell through, Zappa formed Mothers Of Invention, Beefheart formed above group, cut five heavy-duty R&B tracks for A&M, prod. (somewhat incongruously) by David Gates (later of BREAD). 'Diddy Wah Diddy' was regional hit, played by John PEEL, then DJ at KMEN in San Bernardino; four tracks released on EP '65, but remained obscure for years. Moon, Blakely left, replaced c.'67 by Ry COODER, John French; signed with Buddah; classic *Safe As Milk* '67 prod. by Richard PERRY (whose voice is announcer on 'Yellow Brick Road'). Cooder replaced by Jeff Cotton; live *Mirror Man* (four tracks) released '67; group switched to Blue Thumb for bizarre *Strictly Personal* '68; then to Zappa's Straight label: Bill Harkleroad, Mark Boston replaced Snouffer and Handley for 2-disc *Trout Mask Replica*, teetering on the edge between genius and madness with tracks like 'Hair Pie', 'Old

Fart At Play': remains group's masterwork. Beefheart had renamed everybody: obscure lineup was Antennae Jimmy Semens (Cotton), Zoot Horn Rollo (Harkleroad), Rockette Morton (Boston), Drumbo (French), with The Mascara Snake on bass clarinet and Moon (briefly returned). Semens, Moon left; ex-Mother Arthur D. Tripp III (as Ed Marimba) augmented band for *Lick My Decals Off Baby* '70; to Reprise label for *Clear Spot* '72 on which Drumbo replaced by ex-Mother Roy Estrada, who became Orejon (means 'Big Ear'); for *The Spotlight Kid* Orejon left, Drumbo returned, ex-Mother Eliot Ingber (Winged Eel Fingerling) joined on guitar; Marimba played piano, harpsichord, marimba and drums. To Mercury label (Virgin in UK) for less outrageous *Unconditionally Guaranteed* and *Bluejeans And Moonbeams* '74 with entirely new lineups of session players; Beefheart toured, recorded vocals with Zappa, Cooder song for soundtrack of film *Blue Collar* '78, then his own *Shiny Beast (Bat Chain Puller)* '78 (on WB), *Doc At The Radar Station* '80 (on Virgin), *Ice Cream For Crow* '82 (Virgin UK, Epic USA). A complete original, not for the fainthearted, with 7.5 octave vocal range, ideas tumbling over each other: 'Captain Beefheart has, for 20 years, been the man at the heart of the music that has stirred and excited me; echoes of his work . . . are heard in every radio programme I do' (Peel). His paintings were exhibited in a London gallery Apr. '86; Edsel UK reissued *The Legendary A&M Sessions* and *Mirror Men* '86.

CARA, Irene (*b* NYC) Pop singer found *Fame* by singing title song of film. Father and brother both musicians; first pro work as infant on Spanish-language radio/TV NYC; first Broadway musical *Maggie Flynn* at 8, sang in Madison Square Garden tribute to Duke ELLINGTON with Roberta FLACK, Sammy DAVIS Jr at age 10. Films, TV followed from age 16, incl. part in *Roots* TV series; won part of Coco Hernandez in *Fame* '80, Alan Parker film about New York's High School for the Performing Arts. Title song sung by Cara made no. 4 USA, no. 1 UK two years later; Dean Pitchford/Michael Gore composition nominated for Oscar, won over another nomination from same film: 'Out Here On My

Own', also sung by Cara, made no. 19 USA. Avoided profitable cul-de-sac of spin-off TV series; made first solo LP *Anyone Can See* '82, adding to laurels by writing or co-writing half the songs. Further film and TV roles, but next chart entry was second movie theme 'Flashdance . . . What A Feeling' no. 1 USA, no. 2 UK. Co-written by Cara, Keith Forsey and Eurodisco producer Giorgio Moroder, uptempo dance number reminiscent of latter's previous charge Donna SUMMER; won second Oscar. LP *What A Feelin'* '83 incl. hits 'Why Me?' (no. 13), 'Breakdance' (no. 8), chart entries falling either side of yet another film theme: 'The Dream (Hold On To Your Dream)' from *DC Cab* made top 40.

CARAVAN UK rock band early '70s. Richard Coughlan (drums), Julian 'Pye' Hastings (guitar), David Sinclair (keyboards), Richard Sinclair (bass); all *b* Canterbury, England, played in local band Wilde Flowers '65-6, which also incl. Kevin AYERS, members of SOFT MACHINE. First LP *Caravan* notable for being first product by UK act from USA MGM/Verve label; UK Decca LPs *If I Could Do It All Over Again* '70, *In The Land Of Grey And Pink* '71, *For Girls Who Grow Plump* '73 established fluent purveyors of progressive rock with jazzy touch (usually from flautist/saxophonist Jimmy Hastings). Sinclair brothers left to form Hatfield and the North (named after sign on the M1 out of London); Dave later rejoined briefly; recruited ex-Delivery keyboardist Steve Miller, carried on: LPs *Waterloo Lily* '72, *Cunning Stunts* '75 incl. flashes of brilliance, but as with other acts impact of punk left them regarded as passé. Added Geoffrey Richardson on viola, other instruments, infl. sound; LPs incl. *Blind Dog At St Dunstan's* '76, *Better By Far* '77, *The Album* '80, *Back To Front* '82. Best work on 2-disc compilation *Canterbury Tales* '77; also *The Show Of Our Lives* '81 incl. '70-5 material, *The Collection* '84. Protohippy Neil (*sic*; UK TV phenomenon) incl. their 'Golf Girl' on his *Heavy Concept Album* '84.

CARGILL, Henson (*b* 5 Feb. '41, Oklahoma City, Okla.) Deep-voiced country singer. Worked as deputy Sheriff before moving to Nashville '66. Signed to Monument Records, made no. 1 country, no. 25 pop hit with first single 'Skip A Rope' '68. Signed to Mega '71, Atlantic '73, Elektra '75, Copper Mountain '79. Other country hits incl. 'Row, Row, Row' '68, 'None Of My Business' '69, 'Some Old California Memory' '73, 'Stop And Smell The Roses' '74, 'Silence On The Line' '79. LPs incl. *Coming On Strong* '68, *None Of My Business* '70 (both Monument); *On The Road* '72 (Mega), *Henson Cargill Country* '73 (Atlantic).

CARLE, Frankie (*b* Francis Nunzio Carlone, 25 Mar. '03, Providence, R.I.) Pianist, bandleader, composer. Clung to melody line without alienating jazz-oriented fans; bands were an extension of his piano style, with integrity, lack of pretension. Taught piano by uncle, Nicholas Colangelo. Played in vaudeville, with dance bands as teenager; formed own band but gained fame with Horace HEIDT '39-43, becoming co-leader. Own band again, opened Feb. '44 Café Rouge NYC, arrangements by Al Avola (guitarist, *b* 27 Jan. '14, also with Artie SHAW, T. DORSEY, others); used as theme his own 'Sunrise Serenade', already big hit by Glenn MILLER '38. Singers incl. Betty Bonney (ex-Les BROWN, later called Judy Johnson), Phyllis Lynne; then Marjorie Hughes, Carle's daughter, hired after auditioning many others: changed her name and kept relationship secret for a while. Hits incl. 'Saturday Night Is The Loneliest Night Of The Week' (no. 8 in Billboard chart), 'A Little On The Lonely Side' (both '45); then two no. ones: 'Oh! What It Seemed To Be' (own tune, Marjorie's vocal; pundit Walter Winchell broke story of justified nepotism); 'Rumours Are Flying' (both '46); cover of Francis CRAIG's 'Beg Your Pardon' no. 6 '48. Also wrote 'Falling Leaves', 'Lover's Lullaby', others. Many broadcasts, film *My Dream Is Yours* '49; from '50s sometimes led small combo, continued recording; toured in big band revival shows into mid-'70s. Tracks from '44-6 issued on Circle LP.

CARLISLE, Una Mae (*b* 26 Dec. '18, Xenia, Ohio; *d* 7 Nov. '56, NYC) Singer, pianist, songwriter. American Indian, Afro-American ancestry. Studied piano as a child; shared vocal with Billy BANKS on 'Mean Old Bed Bug Blues' recorded mid-

'32 with Fats WALLER, joined Waller programme on WLW Cincinnati at Christmas, left high school to work and tour with him '33-4, went solo. Joined Blackbirds revue late '30s, toured Europe, also did solo dates and film work there. Recorded 'I Can't Give You Anything But Love' with Waller, '39, singing straight chorus to his wisecracks; recorded solo on Bluebird with all-star back-up band incl. Lester YOUNG, Benny CARTER, etc.: 'Walkin' By The River', 'I See A Million People', two of several hundred songs she wrote. Own radio and TV series late '40s, retired in ill health, '54.

CARLISLES, The Brothers Cliff (*b* 6 May '04, Taylorsville, Ky.) and Bill (*b* 19 Dec. '08, Wakefield, Ky.) Popular hillbilly group '30s-40s, noted for novelty, blues, risqué numbers; both also had solo careers. Cliff began in vaudeville, recording '30 with Wilbur Ball in a yodelling duet; he pioneered use of dobro, accompanying Jimmie RODGERS on records '31. Solo on Gennett, Conqueror, etc. in Rodgers's style with 'The Girl In The Blue Velvet Band', 'Tom Cat Blues', 'Lonely Blue Dreams' etc. Teamed with Bill as The Carlisle Brothers, retired '47. Bill formed The Carlisles, signed with Mercury, joined Louisiana Hayride, Grand Ole Opry; hits incl. 'No Help Wanted', 'Is Zat You Myrtle?' '53. Reunited '59 for LP *Fresh From The Country* on King; Bill carried on solo, had hit on Hickory 'What Kinda Deal Is This' '65, LP *Best Of Bill Carlisle*. Bros. compilations incl. *Maple On The Hill* '64 on RCA; *Old Timey 1&2* '65 on Arhoolie.

CARLOS, Wendy (*b* Walter Carlos, '41) Engineer, composer. Worked with Dr Robert A. Moog (*b* '34; earned PhD in engineering), who switched to musical interests through composing for adverts, built the first synthesiser '64 with team of 20 people incl. composers helping; Carlos persuaded him to put his name on the machine, with musicologist Benjamin Folkman perpetrated album *Switched-On Bach* (prod. by Rachel Ellkind): it was no. 10 pop LP '69, won three Grammies, stayed on 'classical' chart for 310 weeks; *The Well-Tempered Synthesizer* '70, *Walter Carlos' Clockwork Orange* '72 (with sounds from the Kubrick film, also on soundtrack LP) and 2-disc *Sonic Seasonings* '72, all made pop top 200 LPs; *By Request*, 2-disc *Switched-On Brandenburgs*, *Digital Moonscapes* ('suite of ethereal melodies threaded through tape-manipulated environmental sounds') and *Tron* (soundtrack to Walt Disney's computer-game fantasy film) did not. *The Shining* on WB was soundtrack of Kubrick horror film with Jack Nicholson, widely panned. Carlos attempted to get inside the mathematical essence of Bach, not simply sicking synthetic music on us, but there didn't seem to be much reason to throw away our Glenn Gould LPs. Optimists hope that electronic gadgets will become a tool in the composer's workshop rather than a mere source of new (unswinging) sounds; time will tell. The composer in Carlos tries to stay ahead of today's pack of kids with studio toys by digitally synthesising the sounds of the orchestra (digital sounds merged with the London Symphony Orchestra in *Tron*); work-in-progress *Beauty In The Beast* will use 'bent' tunings to combine Western and other modes, perhaps also new sounds, e.g. bowed piano, woodwind glockenspiel, etc. *See also* NEW AGE, SPACE MUSIC.

CARLTON AND THE SHOES Venerated Jamaican vocal trio who were led by Carlton Manning, elder brother of Donald and Linford, who later sang with the Abyssinians. Singles 'This Feeling', 'Love Is A Treasure', 'Love Me Forever', and 'Happy Land' for Studio One '68, not issued on LP until *Love Me Forever* late '70s, with previously unreleased material from the same period. As The Carltons they also made 'Better Days' in early '70s for Lee Perry; Manning resurfaced late '70s, as Carlton and the Shoes, prod. LP *This Heart Of Mine*, providing his own backup vocals. Self-prod. singles 'What A Day', 'Forever And Always', Studio One title 'Let Me Love You' also appeared at this time; then he disappeared again.

CARMICHAEL, Hoagy (*b* Howard Hoagland Carmichael, 22 Nov. 1899, Bloomington, Ind.; *d* 28 Dec. '81, Palm Springs, Cal.) Singer, pianist, bandleader, perhaps the most quintessentially American songwriter. Mother played piano in cinema. Family moved to Indianapolis; went to Indiana U.,

played piano at dances to help pay for education; recorded own song 'Washboard Blues' with Hitch's Happy Harmonists on Gennett label '23; formed campus band '24, met Wolverines same year, befriending cornet star Bix BEIDERBECKE. Graduated '26, practised law. Frankie TRUMBAUER and his Orchestra (with Bix) recorded his 'Riverboat Shuffle'; Red NICHOLS, Paul WHITEMAN recorded 'Washboard'; Carmichael turned to music: formed band, early sides (Carmichael's Collegians) rejected by record company '26, Hoagy Carmichael and his Pals (with T. & J. DORSEY) made Gennett sides released '27. Flourished on records as bandleader late '20s, early '30s, all-star sides on Victor incl. Bix, Dorseys, Bud FREEMAN, Eddie LANG, Bubber MILEY, Joe VENUTI, Gene KRUPA, Benny GOODMAN, Jack TEAGARDEN, etc. And the songs: perhaps best-known, most-recorded song of the century is 'Stardust', which may have been suggested by Bix's horn: an uptempo version recorded '28 by Chocolate Dandies with fine guitar solo by Lonnie JOHNSON; song made more famous in slower versions by Isham JONES, Louis ARMSTRONG ('31, year of publication with Mitchell Parrish lyrics); syrupy versions by Artie SHAW, Glenn MILLER (both '40) good for romantic dancing; began practice of playing it without the lovely introduction to the verse, a revelation when revived by Nat COLE '57. Other songs incl. 'Rockin' Chair' ('30, own lyrics; highlight of famous Town Hall concert '47, sung by Armstrong and Teagarden); 'Georgia On My Mind' ('31, lyrics by Stuart Gorrell; no. 1 hit for Ray CHARLES, '60); '(Up A) Lazy River' ('31, with Sidney Arodin; no. 14 hit '61 for Bobby DARIN); 'Lazybones' ('33, with Johnny MERCER); 'One Morning In May' ('33, Parrish); 'Two Sleepy People' ('38, Frank LOESSER for film *Thanks For The Memory*); 'The Nearness Of You' ('40, Ned Washington); 'Skylark' ('42, Mercer); 'Lamplighter's Serenade' ('42, Paul Francis Webster); 'How Little We Know' ('44, with Mercer, for film *To Have And Have Not*); 'Memphis In June' ('45, own lyrics, film *Johnny Angel*); 'In The Cool, Cool, Cool Of The Evening' ('51, lyrics by Mercer, film *Here Comes The Groom*, song won Oscar); also 'New Orleans' (own lyrics), many more. Wrote songs for Broadway show *The*

Show Is On '37, then own show with Mercer Walk With Music '40; ran only 55 performances. Actor/performer in films, usually played himself: laconic pianist with slightly gritty voice. To Have Or Have Not '44, Canyon Passage '46, The Best Years Of Our Lives '46, Young Man With A Horn ('50, from Dorothy Baker novel perhaps inspired by, but not based on, life of Bix). Contributed songs to films The Stork Club '46, Ivy '47, Gentlemen Prefer Blondes '53, Hatari '62. Part in TV series Laramie '59-62; TV special with Svend ASMUSSEN '68; on Henry MANCINI TV show with Bing CROSBY '71; also straight TV acting role opposite Peggy LEE. Own top 10 hits: 'Ole Buttermilk Sky', 'Huggin' and Chalkin' ' (both no. 2 '46); 'Old Piano Roll Blues' (no. 15 '50, with Cass Daley; song by Cv Loben). LP Hoagy Sings Carmichael, with Art PEPPER, Harry EDISON, arrangements by Johnny Mandel, reissued by EMI UK '85, on Pausa in USA; Georgie FAME/Annie Ross LP In Hoagland '81 inspired by great songs. 1944-5 V-Disc Sessions issued on Totem '86, mostly solo studio session from Aug. '45.

CARNES, Kim (b 20 July '45, L.A.) USA singer, songwriter. Had passed through NEW CHRISTY MINSTRELS, written and sung advert jingles, briefly recorded for Amos label; discovered by A&M singing in L.A. clubs. Albums Rest On Me '72, Kim Carnes '75, Sailin' '76 brought few sales, but songs (often co-written with husband/backing musician David Ellingson) recorded by Anne MURRAY, Frank SINATRA, Barbra STREISAND, Rita COOLIDGE, etc. First artist on new EMI/America label: St Vincent's Court '79 incl. no. 56 hit 'It Hurts So Bad'. Ex-Minstrel Kenny ROGERS made LP Gideon '80 of Carnes/Ellingson songs; duet on 'Don't Fall In Love With A Dreamer' became no. 4 hit. Husky, breathy vocal style compared to Rod STEWART; apparent on first solo hit 'More Love' '80 (Smokey ROBINSON song); but song by Donna Weiss/Jackie DeSHANNON brought fame: 'Bette Davis Eyes' '81, contrasting vocal and electronic percussion, was nine weeks no.1 USA, boosted LP Mistaken Identity into best seller, won deserved Grammy. Remains biggest hit; other, lesser hits overshadowed by rematch with Rogers on 'What About Me' by Rogers and James Ingram:

no. 15 '84. Early material available on A&M Best Of (which isn't); irony remains of successful writer having biggest hits with other people's songs.

CARNEY, Harry (b 1 Apr. '10, Boston, Mass.; d 8 Oct. '74, NYC) Baritone sax, also bass clarinet. Piano as a child, then clarinet, alto sax; played with local bands; joined Duke ELLINGTON age 17 with mother's permission, switched to baritone; worked for Ellington more than 46 years. Credited as co-author of 'Rockin' In Rhythm' '30, band's theme then, again in later years; wrote 'Jenny' '46 (after his mother), but didn't solo on the record. Countless times assigned the opening bars of an arrangement, e.g. 'Jive Stomp' '33; memorably set tone with elegant growl/purr on '40 masterpiece 'Ko-Ko'. Many solos incl. those on 'Slap Happy' '38, 'I Can't Believe That You're In Love With Me' '46, 'Dancing In The Dark' '60. Tunes written especially for him incl. 'Sono' '46 (introduced in Carnegie Hall), 'Frustration' '47 (he recorded these again with strings, '48; another recording of 'Frustration' made '56 in Chicago released on Affinity UK '85, LP Duke Ellington Presents), also 'Serious Serenade' '55. Well-named 'V.I.P.'s Boogie' '51 features Carney; bass clarinet can be heard in ensembles on 'Creole Love Call' '56; also 'Mood Indigo' '62 from LP Duke Ellington Meets Coleman Hawkins: on that album 'Limbo Jazz' is example of Carney establishing character of irresistible, riffing ensemble. Baritone players could be divided into two groups: Carney and the rest; he gave the instrument its place in jazz as his idol Coleman HAWKINS did for the tenor. Ellington's reed voicings, perhaps most important ingredient in band's sound, to a large extent depended on Carney's anchor; he lost valuable sidemen from time to time but his music cannot be imagined without Carney. Also one of Ellington's closest friends; often drove alone together in Carney's Cadillac from gig to gig. Master classes at U. of Wisconsin '73 revealed his modesty and gentleness of spirit, as though he could not believe his good fortune at being the object of so much affection.

CAROLAN (b Turlough O'Carolan, 1670, Newton near Nobber, Co. Meath; d 25 Mar.

1738, Alderford) Irish harper, composer. Blinded by smallpox at 18; patroness enabled him to study harp for three years, then he travelled as a bard, moving from house to house, composing tunes honouring families and homesteads that supported him, as was the custom: unlike that of most contemporaries, his music was preserved; earliest book of his tunes is also the earliest collection of Irish secular music: adapted for many instruments; Derek Bell of the CHIEFTAINS (among others) has recorded them on harp, guitarist Richard THOMPSON one of the most beautiful ('Sheebeg And Sheemore').

CARPENTERS Brother/sister vocal duo, stars of '70s MOR pop. Richard (*b* 15 Oct. '46) and Karen Carpenter (*b* 2 Mar. '50; *d* 4 Feb. '83) both *b* New Haven, Conn.; moved to Cal. '63. He took up piano at 9, seven years later played in semi-pro club trio; she was a drummer; bassist Wes Jacobs joined to make Carpenters a trio; victory in 'battle of the bands' at Hollywood Bowl '66 was to have won RCA contract, but deal fell through; Carpenters formed Spectrum with four Cal State students: John Bettis later became Richard's writing partner, Danny Woodhams their guitarist; at the time progressive rock wiped out their mannered pop. Carried on recording demos; signed to A&M by Herb ALPERT, scored first hit with cover of BEATLES' 'Ticket To Ride': debut LP first called *Offering* '69 quickly retitled to capitalise no. 54 chart entry. Another cover, title track of second album *Close To You* '70 originally written by Burt BACHARACH for Dionne WARWICK, was USA no. 1: showcased trademark boy/girl harmonies, Richard's classical keyboard, immaculate pop sheen courtesy prod. Jack Daugherty: sound was epitome of A&M's corporate 'easy listening' policy; next five singles all USA top 3 entries: 'We've Only Just Begun' written by Paul Williams/Roger Nichols; 'For All We Know' from film *Lovers And Other Strangers*, 'Rainy Days And Mondays' (Williams/Nichols), Leon RUSSELL's 'Superstar', 'Hurting Each Other'. Shrewd mix of covers and Carpenter/Bettis material made hit after hit: 19 top 40s USA, 16 UK in '70s. Albums were bland, but ambitious *Yesterday Once More* '74 with triple gatefold automobile

sleeve and side of golden oldies was brave attempt to break mould. Singles collection *1969-1973* was massive seller (no. 1 in UK, 115 weeks on LP chart), followed by *1974-1978*, both highly recommended for fans. Karen's pure, soaring voice was good mix with brother's baritone; she combined lead/harmony vocals with drumming (in stage act more than studio); top 40 hits ranged from Neil SEDAKA's 'Solitaire' to KLAATU's 'Calling Occupants Of Interplanetary Craft', incl. two more USA no. 1 hits: 'Top Of The World' '73, 'Please Mr Postman' '74. In that year Karen collapsed from 'exhaustion'; she was suffering from *anorexia nervosa*, wasting disease that led to fatal heart attack '83. By this time sales were falling partly owing to relaxation of gruelling album/tour schedule that had obtained until '77, when Richard moved into production. *Voice Of The Heart* '83 released posthumously. Winners of three Grammies, Carpenters, like David Gates's BREAD, claimed fans of all ages.

CARR, Ian (*b* 21 Apr. '33, Dumfries, Scotland) Trumpet, flugelhorn, leader, composer, writer. Self-taught from age 17. Made five LPs as co-leader of quintet with Don RENDELL '63-9, five with New Jazz Orchestra, also played with Joe HARRIOTT, John McLAUGHLIN, Don BYAS, others. Formed fusion group Nucleus '69, influential in Europe: LPs incl. *Elastic Rock* and *Solar Plexus* '70, *Belladonna* '72, *Labyrinth* and *Roots* '73, *Snakehips Etcetera* '75, all on Vertigo (Phonogram); *In Flagrante Delicto* and *Out Of The Long Dark* '77-8 on Capitol, *Awakening* '80 and *Live At The Theaterhaus* '85 on Mood. Also five LPs since '75 with United Jazz And Rock Ensemble. Teaches workshops for teenagers in North London, also at Guildhall School of Music and Drama; a valuable music journalist, contributions to many periodicals; books *Music Outside: Contemporary Jazz In Britain* '73; *Miles Davis: A Critical Biography* '82; co-author of *Jazz: The Essential Companion* '87. Younger brother is Mike CARR (*see below*).

CARR, Leroy (*b* 27 Mar. '05, Nashville, Tenn.; *d* 29 Apr. '35, Indianapolis, Ind.) Piano, blues singer. Teamed with Francis 'Scrapper' BLACKWELL, '28; they toured and recorded together, became famous in the Indianapolis area, then enormously popular in black communities everywhere: Carr's piano, smooth vocal style and songs were important infl. on next generation of urban blues. Of many songs the best known are 'How Long Blues', 'In The Evening When The Sun Goes Down'. Died of the effects of acute alcoholism. CBS compilation *Blues Before Sunrise* has '32-4 tracks, some with Josh WHITE, second guitar; others on Yazoo and Magpie.

CARR, Mike (*b* 7 Dec. '37, Durham, England) Piano and vibes, then electric piano, organ with bass pedals from '66; composer. Self-taught on piano; formed EmCee Five with brother Ian CARR, popular in Newcastle area and made highly praised EP, not revivalists but playing the contemporary jazz of the early '60s, showing that UK jazz existed outside London. Led trios with Malcolm Cecil on bass (later played with Stevie WONDER, Jim HALL), John McLAUGHLIN, others; duo with drummer Tony Crombie became Ronnie SCOTT Trio '71-5 incl. gigs in NYC: 'P&O Blues' (with drummer Bobby Gien on RCA LP *Scott At Ronnie's*) shows why Carr was highly praised for swing by Oscar PETERSON; his Hammond organ with bass pedal made trio sound larger. Other LPs: *Hammond Under Pressure* on EMI, *Mike Carr And Rhythm* on Arps, trio *Live At Ronnie Scott's* on Spotlite, *Loving You* on Fly Productions; also recorded with Prince LASHA for CBS '66. Formed jazz-funk recording group Cargo '80, released singles on labels incl. WEA UK, Atlantic USA; formed own labels: excellent *Bebop From The East Coast* '87 on Birdland contains EmCee Five, trios incl. rare tracks; *Cargo The Album* '87 on Cargo Gold has instrumentals on one side, mixes with backing vocals on the other; soloists on various tracks incl. MORRISSEY-MULLEN, Victor FELDMAN, Don Weller, Danny Moss: less mechanical than most dance music today because less influenced by disco. Gigged on piano '87 with Jean TOUSSAINT in London, again demonstrating his gift for pure jazz, never the best way to earn a living.

CARR, Vikki (*b* Florencia Bisenta de Casillas Martinez Cardona, 19 July '41, El Paso, Texas) Singer. Eldest of seven children; father engineer; grew up near L.A.

Singing age 4, in Latin: 'Adeste Fidelis' at school concert. Played leads in school shows; worked in bank, singing with local bands; won audition with Pepe Callahan Mexican-Irish band, opening as 'Carlita' at Palm Springs Chi Chi Club; later to Reno, Las Vegas, Lake Tahoe, Hawaii. Opened solo act in Reno backed by Chuck Leonard Quartet, signed to Liberty, first single a hit in Australia, toured there. First LP *Color Her Great* '63; TV dates incl. guest shots, 26-week series on Ray ANTHONY show; LPs displayed show-biz crowd-pleasing talent: *Discovery* '64 was first of 12 albums to chart on Liberty, then Columbia. Single 'It Must Be Him' (from French song 'Seul Sur Son Etoile') was no. 2 UK, no. 3 USA '67; other USA top 40s: 'The Lesson', 'With Pen In Hand'; 'Eternity' reached no. 79 (all '68-9). Played '67 Command Performance UK; played White House for Nixon '70, Ford '74. Switched to Columbia '71 for seven LPs; dropped by label. Played hospitals, benefits, set up scholarship foundation for Chicano children. Resumed recording '80: LP *Y el Amor* for Mexican CBS. Other LPs: *Best* (Liberty); *En Espanol*, 2-disc *Love Story/First Time Ever I Saw Your Face* (Columbia).

CARROLL, Jim (*b* '50, NYC) Poet, songwriter, singer. Published book of poems at 16; self-confessed heroin addict who supported habit by hustling and writing about it. Best-known book is *The Basketball Diaries*, collection of teen-age sex-and-drug traumas. To West Coast by '74 where he kicked habit; returned to NYC, collaborated with Patti SMITH on poetry; followed her into rock. Was slated to sign with Rolling Stone Records, whose president Earl McGrath became his manager, but records came out on Atco (USA), CBS (UK): *Catholic Boy* '80 and *Dry Dreams* '82. 'People Who Died' on *Catholic Boy* is powerful catalogue of tragedies of personal friends.

CARS USA New Wave group began with songwriter/guitarist Ric Otcasek (*b* Baltimore, dropped 't' from name), Ben Orr (*b* Benjamin Orzechowski, Cleveland) who met at party in Cleveland: Ric college dropout, Orr session musician (ex-*Upbeat* TV rock show). Formed folk act Milkwood, made eponymous LP '72, then *How's The*

Weather (both on Paramount, with keyboardist Greg Hawkes (*b* Baltimore) who had worked with singer/comedian Martin Mull). Added lead guitar Elliot Easton (*b* Elliot Shapiro); Boston-based group became Cap'n Swing. Catalyst was David Robinson, ex-Modern Lovers/Pop/DMZ drummer: changed name, galvanised them into making demos '77, evolved red/white/black colour scheme to overcome ill-assorted appearance. Played Boston's Rat club Feb., later opened for Bob SEGER at Music Hall (standing ovation); demos played on radio, signed Dec. by Elektra; *The Cars* '78 prod. in London by Roy Thomas Baker (QUEEN, etc.): punchy powerpop instantly successful in wake of punk. LP no. 18 in USA charts, stayed 139 weeks, sold 2 million; singles from it top 40 USA: 'My Best Friend's Girl', 'Just What I Needed', 'Let's Go'; first two made top 20 UK, aided by then-unique picture-discs. *Candy-O* '79 had sleeve artwork by pin-up artist Alberto Vargas; peaked at no. 3 USA, stayed 62 weeks. Ric demanded control of guests and presentation of USA *Midnight Special* TV show Autumn '79, turned it into showcase of favourite bands. After album *Panorama* '80, took a year off: Ric revealed sides of musical outlook, working with singer/model Bebe Buell, avant-garde duo Suicide; *Shake It Up* '81 made with Baker in group's Synchro Sound studio, title no. 4 USA hit; Ric's solo *Beatitude* '83 showed more adventurous approach than band formula (most of group seemed happy to indulge themselves solo so as not to rock the boat); but they showed equal adventure in replacing Baker for Robert John 'Mutt' Lange (AC/DC, DEF LEPPARD, etc.) for *Heartbeat City* '84: most popular singles to date, with 'You Might Think' no. 7, 'Magic' no. 12, 'Drive' no. 3 in USA '84. Latter entered UK chart twice: used as theme for Live Aid famine film footage; Ric donated royalties. 'Tonight She Comes' released '85 with reissue of 'Just What I Needed' on flip: new track incl. in *Greatest Hits* showcase '85. Ric's second solo was *This Side Of Paradise* '86 incl. Tom Verlaine, fellow Cars; Orr made solo *The Lace* '86; *Door To Door* was new Cars LP '87.

CARSON, Fiddlin' John (*b* 23 Mar. 1868, Fannin, Co. Ga.; *d* 11 Dec. '49) Pioneer hillbilly fiddle player, recording artist. Worked as jockey, in cotton mills, house painting; became principal figure at annual Atlanta fiddlers' convention: Champion Fiddler of Georgia seven times. Radio debut on WSB Atlanta '22; first record 'The Little Old Log Cabin In The Lane', recorded by Ralph PEER for Okeh on 14 June '23, thought to be the first hillbilly (country) music ever released. Member of Virginia Reelers '24; group made more than 150 sides for Okeh. More records on Victor from '34; best known tunes incl. 'Boston Burglar', 'Didn't He Ramble', 'The Letter Edged In Black'. Worked as lift operator in Atlanta after '40. Compilation LP *The Old Hen Cackled And The Rooster's Gonna Crow* on Rounder '79.

CARTER, Benny (*b* Bennett Lester Carter, 8 Aug. '07, NYC) Composer, arranger, alto sax; one of the giants of jazz, mainly self-taught. Worked with Horace/Fletcher HENDERSON, Chick WEBB, McKINNEY'S COTTON PICKERS; started own band '33, same year organised all-star band NYC for visiting composer-leader Spike HUGHES (*see also* Chocolate Dandies). To Europe '35; staff arranger for Henry HALL BBC band (e.g. 'I'm Putting All My Eggs In One Basket', 'One, Two, Button Your Shoe', '36-7); recorded with Hall sidemen in BBC studio (*Swingin' At Maida Vale*, UK Decca compilation), in Paris April '37 with Coleman HAWKINS and Django REINHARDT (e.g. 'Honeysuckle Rose', 'Crazy Rhythm'); led interracial, international big band at Dutch seaside that summer. Own band again in USA '38; sextet '41, new band '43 on West Coast; settled there, became freelance writer-arranger in films, TV, jazz festivals, etc. Records under own name almost every year '33-'46 (big band reissues incl. *Somebody Loves Me* '45 on Magic, *Vol. 1 The Deluxe Recordings* '46 on Swingtime); again '53-7 for Norman GRANZ, incl. set with Johnny HODGES and Charlie PARKER '53, quartet set with Art TATUM '54, LPs *New Jazz Sounds*, *The Formidable Benny Carter*, *Cosmopolite* '52. Other LPs in and out of print (often from France) incl. *Benny Carter 1933* (Prestige); *1940-41* (RCA; with typically beautiful reed writing on 'All Of Me'); *Session At Midnight* (Capitol '55). He also played clarinet; fine trumpet on 'I Surrender Dear' and trombone solo on 'All I Ever Do Is Worry' (with Julia LEE), both on Capitol. On alto sax he had no equal in the '30s-40s except Hodges; as arranger very few. Apart from records under his own name he wrote for Henderson '28-37, Ellington ('Jazz Cocktail', '32), others; played on two Lionel HAMPTON small-group all-star dates '38-9, incl. famous version of his best-known tune 'When Lights Are Low'; in '40 on dates with Coleman HAWKINS, Billie HOLIDAY. Studio work has not stopped jazz output: wrote LPs *Kansas City Suite*, *The Legend* for Count BASIE '60-1, among that band's best postwar sets; his own later LPs incl. *Jazz Giant* '57 and *Swingin' The Twenties* '58 on Contemporary, *Aspects* '58-9 on UA; *Further Definitions* '61 on Impulse duplicates the instrumentation and some of the tunes of '37 Paris session: with four reeds incl. Hawk and a rhythm section, the writing is so rich that the group sounds much bigger. *B.B.B. & Co.* '62 with Barney BIGARD, Ben WEBSTER was issued on Prestige; he led an octet at Montreux '75, played on *Basie Jam No. 2*, led quartet at Montreux '77, made sextet LP *The King* and *Benny Carter & Dizzy Gillespie* '76, *Benny Carter 4* at Montreux and *Live And Well In Japan* '77, all on Granz's Pablo label. Other LPs: *Summer Serenade* '80 on Storyville, *Gentlemen Of Swing* '80 on Japanese East Wind with Harry EDISON, Milt HINTON, Teddy WILSON, Shelly MANNE; *Skyline Drive* '82 on Phontastic from Monterey Jazz Festival, with Plas JOHNSON, eight others; his work at Chicago Jazz Festival early '80s was further proof that the iron was still hot. Toured with Swing Reunion group in '80s with George DUVIVIER, Louie BELLSON, Red NORVO, Remo Palmier (guitar, *b* 29 Mar. '23, NYC): 3-disc live set available from Book of the Month Club, also on CD; *Benny Carter's All Stars* '87 on Gazell with Norvo, Nat ADDERLEY, Horace PARLAN; 2-disc *American Jazz Orchestra* '87 from Musical Heritage Society is live set incl. suite *Central Cities Sketches*. *The Deluxe Recordings* from '46 on Swingtime; *Somebody Loves Me* has airchecks from '45; *Meets Oscar Peterson* comes out '88.

CARTER, Betty (*b* Lillie Mae Jones, 16 May '30, Flint, Mich.) Singer; highly regarded critically as one of the few true jazz singers around; also does arrangements. Studied piano at Detroit Conservatory, won amateur show and turned pro singer '46. At first known as 'Betty Be-Bop' Carter; toured with Lionel HAMPTON '48-51, Miles DAVIS '58-9, Japan with Sonny ROLLINS '63, Annie Ross's club in London '64; mainly worked in clubs and theatres but toured colleges in '70s, usually with trio (which incl. Cameron BROWN and pianist John Hicks '79). Albums incl. *Out There* '58 on Peacock with Gigi GRYCE, Ray COPELAND, Benny GOLSON, Wynton KELLY, others; *The Modern Sound Of Betty Carter* '60 and *Ray Charles and Betty Carter* '61 on ABC Paramount. The '58 and '60 LPs were available in an Impulse reissue called *What A Little Moonlight Can Do* '76. Finally, *Now It's My Turn*, *'Round Midnight* are on Roulette; she has also published *Betty Carter 1* (made live '70), *Betty Carter 2*, *The Audience* (2-disc set), *What Ever Happened To Love* on own Bet-Car label: forced to start her own company so fans can buy her work. That she has made so few LPs, most of them out of print, is an indictment of entertainment business: most people get no chance to hear her. At concerts '79 she 'phrased comfortably behind the beat, making every lyric a channel of communication' (G. Giddins); with renewed interest in jazz in '87 she signed with Verve, released *Look What I Got* '88 to rave reviews.

CARTER, Carlene (*b* 26 Sep. '55, Nashville, Tenn.) Singer. Based in London, resists close identification with Nashville, but has impeccable country music pedigree: daughter of June Carter and Carl SMITH; mother married to Johnny CASH; half-sister Rosanne Cash married to Rodney CROWELL; learned guitar from grandmother Maybelle Carter (*see* CARTER FAMILY). Cheerleader at Henderson High School; married at 15; third husband ('79; later separated) was Nick LOWE. Toured as part of Carter family, worked as model; came to London, made debut LP *Carlene Carter* '77 with contributions from Lowe, prod. and backed on record by Graham PARKER's the Rumour: incl. Crowell's 'Never Together, But Close Sometimes', minor UK hit. LP *Two Sides To Every Woman* '79 followed by *Musical Shapes* '80, prod. by Lowe: incl. Cash's 'Ring Of Fire', duet with Dave EDMUNDS on Richard DOBSON's 'Baby Ride Easy', Carter family classic 'Foggy Mountain Top', her own 'Appalachian Eyes', 'Too Bad About Sandy'. Next LP *Blue Nun* '81 not as well received, despite help from members of SQUEEZE; single 'Do It In A Heartache' made USA country chart '80. *C'est Si Bon* '83 incl. members of Rockpile, Lowe's band; live shows always first class, with musicians from Rockpile, Rumour; joined family during Cash's '81 UK tour to sing 'Will The Circle Be Unbroken?'. In London cast of show *Pump Boys & Dinettes* '84; made short film seen at London Film Festival, *Too Drunk (To Remember)*, based on song from *Musical Shapes*; to star in London musical *Angry Housewives* '86, walked out first week of rehearsals.

CARTER FAMILY Vocal and instrumental trio of enormous infl. on American music: A. P. Carter (*b* Alvin Pleasant Carter, 15 Dec. 1891, Mace Springs, Va.; *d* there 7 Nov. '60), aka 'Doc', sang bass lines, played some fiddle, collected songs; wife Sara (*b* Sara Dougherty, 21 July 1899, Wise Co., Va.; married A.P. 18 June '15; *d* 8 Jan. '79, Lodi, Cal.), sang lead, played guitar, autoharp; Maybelle (*b* Maybelle Addington, 10 May '09, Copper Creek, Va.; *d* 23 Oct. '78, Nashville; Sara's cousin, married A.P.'s brother Ezra), sang harmony, played guitar, autoharp. Sara and A.P. had 16 brothers and sisters between them. Trio drove to Bristol, Tenn. with Ezra, made first records for Ralph PEER on 1 Aug. '27, same day as Jimmie RODGERS with ultimate infl. equal and opposite to his: while he established blues, vaudeville elements of country music, theirs was folk component. They emphasised songs (other period groups were instrumentalists whose singing was often incidental); Sara's mastery of the autoharp was mainstay of trad. sound; Maybelle played melody on bass strings of guitar, rhythm on treble: infl. 'Carter style'. A.P. had improvisatory method of coming in with bass harmony when he felt like it; mountain ballads that A.P. collected or wrote (at any rate, copyrighted) often of ancient lineage, still being sung many years later by the WEAVERS ('I Never Will Marry'), Joan BAEZ ('Wildwood Flower',

'Little Moses'), FLATT & SCRUGGS ('Jimmy Brown The Newsboy'), Emmylou HARRIS ('Hello Stranger'), Roy ACUFF ('Wabash Cannon Ball'), many others. 'I'm Thinking Tonight Of My Blue Eyes' has countless recordings; tune adapted by Acuff for 'Great Speckled Bird'. Family made more than 100 sides for Victor '27-35 incl. many country classics: 'My Clinch Mountain Home', 'Foggy Mountain Top', 'Church In The Wildwood', 'Worried Man Blues', 'Diamonds In The Rough', 'Lonesome Valley', 'Keep On The Sunny Side' ('06 pop tune, became their theme), gospel hymn 'Anchored In Love', 'Little Darling Pal Of Mine' (later became bluegrass standard). 'Wildwood Flower' learned orally in the mountains, but published version 1860; may have sold a million, phenomenal for the time: they were paid $75 to record it. Recorded with Rodgers '32. A.P. and Sara separated '33 but recorded together until '43. Original group recorded for Decca, Okeh, ARC '35-40; broadcast from '38 on powerful Mexican border radio: already famous, then reached wider public than ever. Final Victor session '41 raised trio's total to over 250 sides; A.P. and Sara's children began singing; Maybelle's daughter Anita was a pro at 4 in '40, soon joined by sisters Helen, June; original group split '43. A.P. retired; Sara had remarried; Maybelle and daughters formed act, broadcast in several states, recorded for Decca, Columbia: 'Are You Afraid To Remember Me', 'Gold Watch And Chain'; their hymns infl. gospel music: 'Gethsemane', 'Blood That Stained The Old Rugged Cross'. Joined Grand Ole Opry '50, Maybelle regular there until '67 after daughters were on their own; Opry performances included songs she wrote or co-wrote: 'A Jilted Love', 'Don't Wait', 'Walk A Little Bit Closer', 'I've Got A Home In Glory'. Anita had five country hits '68-71. Maybelle and Ezra had faith in Johnny CASH, helped him through troubled time; June married him. Anita, Helen, Maybelle often appeared with June, Johnny on their TV shows late '60s, early '70s. Maybelle appeared at Newport Folk Festival '67, in NITTY GRITTY DIRT BAND album *Will The Circle Be Unbroken*. Carter family never got very rich (became famous without high-powered management), but first group elected to Country Music Hall of

Fame, '70. Maybelle gave Chet ATKINS one of his first jobs, infl. Floyd CRAMER's piano style, etc.; taught grand-daughter Carlene CARTER to play guitar; she was deeply loved for modesty and generosity of spirit. Of many compilations, only *Best* (Columbia) now listed in USA Schwann catalogue; *20 Of The Best* RCA/UK incl. nearly all Victor titles mentioned above. Transcriptions compiled on *The Carter Family On Border Radio* from John Edwards Memorial Foundation, UCLA (based on legacy of Australian country music fan who bequeathed large collection of material to U. of California); Japanese RCA has issued complete *The Original Carter Family 1927-34, 1941* in 10-record set.

CARTER, Fred (*b* 31 Dec. '33, Winnsboro, La.) Top-rated country session guitarist and producer. Said to have played on 90% of country recordings made in Nashville in the '60s, incl. Bob DYLAN's Nashville sessions; one of the creators of the 'Nashville sound'. Later emerged as producer, becoming head of ABC's Nashville office '68-70 and president of Nugget records. Recorded for Monument ('And You Wonder Why' '67) but mainly a behind-the-scenes musical influence.

CARTER, John (*b* John Wallace Carter, 24 Sep. '29, Ft Worth, Texas) Reeds, flute. Gigged around Southwest '40s, '50s in jazz, blues groups; college degrees beginning '49; formed quartet with Bobby BRADFORD '65; has done much educational lecture and concert work. Played with Ornette COLEMAN, cond. orchestra in his music L.A. '65; played in Europe '73. LPs on various labels with Bradford '69, '72 incl. *Seeking, Secrets; Echoes from Rudolph's* '77 is by a different quartet with Melba Joyce vocal on one track. *Variations* '79 is quintet incl. Bradford, Phillip Wilson, with *A Suite Of Early American Folk Pieces for Solo Clarinet* '79 made in Düsseldorf on Moers label. *Dauwhe* '82 is by an octet with Bradford, Red CALLENDER, flautist James Newton; plays on Newton quintet LP *The Mystery School* '80 with similar personnel on India Navigation; also on that label: two vols of *Clarinet Summit* '84, recorded live in NYC with Jimmy HAMILTON, Alvin Batiste, David MURRAY. *Castles Of Ghana* '86

on Gramavision with Bradford and Andrew CYRILLE followed by *Dance Of The Love Ghosts* '87 with Cyrille, Fred Hopkins, others. New Clarinet Summit album *Southern Bells* released '88.

CARTER, Ron (*b* Ronald Levin Carter, 4 May '37, Ferndale, Mich.) Bass, cello, other instruments; leader, composer. Started on cello age 10; took up bass in Detroit high school; led own groups in Rochester while studying at Eastman; played and recorded in school orch. under Howard Hanson. Joined Chico HAMILTON '59. Auspicious LPs '60-1 incl. Eric DOLPHY album *Out There*, with George DUVIVIER, Roy HAYNES; own LP *Where?* with Dolphy, Mal WALDRON; Waldron set *The Quest*, all on Prestige, all later reissued under Dolphy's name. Carter played bass on *Where?*, cello on all three; on *The Quest*, his entry on Waldron's 'Warm Canto' (plucked counterpoint to Joe Benjamin's bass), bowed melody lines on other tunes announced major new voice: time, tone and taste are unique. Infl. by Paul CHAMBERS, followed him into Miles DAVIS band '63-8, many tours and LPs as part of legendary Davis rhythm section with Tony WILLIAMS, Herbie HANCOCK; other tours and LPs (incl. hit Hancock set *Maiden Voyage*, '65); concert tour packages with CTI label stars '70-3 (own CTI LPs '73-6: *All Blues, Blues Farm, Spanish Blue, Yellow And Green*); played piccolo bass in own quartet from '75. Said his aim was 'to reinvestigate acoustic sounds' giving 'a viable listening option' at a time when electronic sounds threatened takeover; was profound infl. on younger generation while still young himself. Wide-ranging work as composer/arranger means that any LP with Carter's name on it is worth investigating: as sideman with Grover WASHINGTON, Roberta FLACK, Michel LEGRAND, Horace SILVER, Milt JACKSON, Jaki BYARD (*With Strings* '68), Chet BAKER (*Once Upon A Summertime* '77), Wynton MARSALIS (*Hot House Flowers*), many others. Own LPs on Milestone incl. *Pastels* '76; *Piccolo, Third Plane* (trio with Hancock, Williams), *Peg Leg* all '77; *A Song For You* and *Pick 'Em* '78; *Parade* and *New York Slick* '79; *Patrio* and *Parfait* '80; *Super Strings* '81 has sextet incl. Jack DEJOHNETTE plus big string orchestra;

Heart And Soul is duo with Cedar WALTON on Timeless; *Carnaval* on Galaxy has Williams, Hank JONES, Sadao Watanabe on alto sax; *Etudes '82* on Elektra has Williams, Art FARMER, Bill Evans, reeds; *Live At Village West* on Concord is a duo with Jim HALL.

CARTER, Wilf (*b* 18 Dec. '04, Gaysboro, Nova Scotia) Canada's first country star. Raised on ranch in Alberta; worked as rancher. Made radio debut '33 Calgary; recorded for RCA Canada from '34. Adopted name Montana Slim on USA debut '37. Wrote more than 500 songs, incl. 'Swiss Mountain Lullaby', 'There's A Bluebird On Your Windowsill', 'I'm Hitting The Trail'. Recorded for Decca early '50s, Starday '60s, back with RCA Canada until retirement '80. Member of Calgary's Horsemen Hall of Fame. More than 40 albums incl. *32 Wonderful Years* '66, *God Bless Our Canada* '68, *Sings The Songs Of Australia* '69, *How My Yodelling Days Began* '70, *40th Anniversary* '74, all on RCA.

CARTHY, Martin (*b* Martin Dominic Forbes Carthy, 21 May '41, Hatfield, Herts.) Singer, arguably the most important in the English folk revival; also a gifted multi-instrumentalist, esp. guitar and mandolin; well-known both for solo work and with the ALBION BAND, STEELEYE SPAN, BRASS MONKEY, the WATERSONS. Worked as assistant stage manager for theatrical companies after leaving school, drifted into performing in London coffee houses, the heavy infl. of SKIFFLE giving way to mainly British repertoire. A Topic EP with Bill Leader was 'conveniently lost' early '60s while he was resident singer at the Troubador club; proper debut on *Hootenanny* anthology on Decca with 'My Baby Has Gorn Dahn The Plug 'Ole' and 'The End Of My Old Cigar' (now sums up this role as 'comic relief'). Played with Thameside Four with Redd Sullivan (sang with him on *Hootenanny*), Marion Gray, Pete Maynard. Open to exotic music, citing a fluke introduction to Indian music taking him to Ravi SHANKAR's first London gig c.'57 (while still at school) and the infl. of Davey Graham's 'She Moves Through The Fair', this period also marking friendship with songwriter Leon ROSSELSON. His stature in clubs grew; first solo LP *Martin Carthy* on Fontana showed embryonic talent at work, incl. arr. of 'Scarborough Fair' (also sung on the early EP): he let Paul SIMON have the words and chording and it became the basis of SIMON & GARFUNKEL's version; Bob DYLAN (then in London for TV play *Madhouse On Castle Street*) based 'Bob Dylan's Dream' on Carthy's version of 'Lord Franklin', also mentioned him in notes to *Freewheelin'* LP. *Second Album* '66 followed by *Byker Hill, But Two Came By, Prince Heathen* '67-9, all with Dave Swarbrick (billing 'with Dave Swarbrick' became a partnership, reversed on *Rags, Reels & Airs* '67 by 'Dave Swarbrick with Martin Carthy & Diz Disley', incl. several tunes which later turned up in FAIRPORT CONVENTION repertoire). Strong development underscores these LPs; title track and 'Arthur McBride And The Sergeant' from *Prince Heathen*, later overshadowed by still stronger performances, show powerful vocal skills, playing becoming sparer, more confident. Good workmanlike LPs *Landfall* '71, *Shearwater* '72 and *Sweet Wivelsfield* '74 overshadowed by masterful *Crown Of Horn* '76: he could do no wrong with erotic 'Bedmaking', intricate 'Bonny Lass Of Anglesey', epic 'Willie's Lady'. *Because It's There* '79 incl. Gilbert O'SULLIVAN's 'Nothing Rhymed', stunning guitar instrumental 'Siege Of Delhi', gruesome 'Death Of Young Andrew'; also the playing of Howard Evans and John Kirkpatrick. *Out Of The Cut* '82 is possibly his most rounded product, having a rare unity and strong political current: his embellishments to 'Rigs Of The Time' (also incl. by Shirly COLLINS in *The Sweet Primeroses*) updated a tale of usury and cheating, while Chartist 'The Song Of The Lower Classes' had timeless lyrics. His side ventures incl. two stints with Steeleye early and late '70s (on LPs *Ten Man Mop, Please To See The King, Storm Force Ten* and *Live At Last*); he was involved with Albion for *Battle Of The Field* and worked with them and Ashley Hutchings in subsequent years (e.g. in National Theatre prod. of Flora Thompson's *Lark Rise To Candleford*); he married second wife Norma Waterson '72, joined her in the Watersons; through work with Kirkpatrick (i.e. on *Plain Capers*, Free Reed label) he met Martin Brinsford, at National Theatre met Evans and Roger Williams:

threads pulled together resulted in jolly quintet vocal-instrumental BRASS MONKEY '83, *See How It Runs* '87 on Topic. Many sessions incl. *The Silly Sisters* for short-term June TABOR-Maddy Prior partnership and several with Rosselson; also Peter BELLAMY's *The Transports*. His mandolin playing is underrated, being the equal of Ry COODER's bluesier style yet remaining distinctively British; the standards he has set in each area have rarely been matched.

CARVER, Johnny (*b* 24 Nov. '40, Jackson, Miss.) Country singer. Featured with house band at Hollywood's Palimino Club '66-7, leading to contract with Imperial Records; initial hits: 'Your Lily White Hands' '67, 'Hold Me Tight' '68, 'Sweet Wine' '69. Wrote songs recorded by Ferlin HUSKY, Connie SMITH, Roy DRUSKY, etc. Recorded for Epic '71-2; joined ABC-Dot '73 and covered pop hits with more success: 'Tie A Yellow Ribbon 'Round The Old Oak Tree' in country top 5 '73; 'Afternoon Delight' top 10 '76, 'Living Next Door To Alice' top 20 '77. Also recorded for Equity '80, Tanglewood '81, Monument '83. LPs incl. *Tie A Yellow Ribbon* '73, *Don't Tell That Sweet Old Lady* '74, *Afternoon Delight* '76, *Best Of* '77.

CARVER, Wayman (*b* 25 Dec. '05, Portsmouth, Va.; *d* 6 May '67, Atlanta, Ga.) Flute and reeds. Worked for Elmer SNOWDEN, Benny CARTER, Spike HUGHES '33, Chick WEBB and Ella FITZGERALD '34-40. Early and very fine soloist on flute (e.g. 'Sweet Sue, Just You', cut with both Hughes and Webb). Taught music at Clark College, Atlanta; dir. school bands and played local dates on clarinet. Pupil George ADAMS called him 'guide to taste and style'.

CASA LOMA ORCHESTRA Dance band formed c.'29. Personnel incl. Glen Gray Knoblaugh (*b* 7 June '06, Roanoke, Ill.; *d* 23 Aug. '63, NYC), saxes, frontman; Harold Eugene Gifford (*b* 31 May '08, Americus, Ga.; *d* 12 Nov. '70, Memphis, Tenn.), guitarist/arranger; Clarence Behrens Hutchenrider (*b* 13 June '08, Waco, Texas), reeds; Kenny Sargent (*b* 3 Mar. '06, Centralia, Ill.; *d* 20 Dec. '69, Dallas, Texas), saxes, vocals; Elmer Louis 'Sonny' Dunham (*b* 16 Nov. '14, Brockton, Mass.), trumpet.

Originally mid-'20s Detroit-based GOLDKETTE band called the Orange Blossoms; George T. Simon says band was named after projected Canadian club that never opened. Formed corporation with Gray (aka 'Spike') elected leader. First records for Okeh '29; also on Victor as Glen Gray and the Casa Loma Orchestra. Pee Wee HUNT was founder member; Gifford joined '29; Dunham early '32; Sargent came from Francis CRAIG; in '40s Herb ELLIS, Red NICHOLS, Bobby HACKETT passed through. It compared better to black bands than any other white group of its era; in early '30s featured romantic ballads for dancing with sweet vocals by Sargent ('For You', 'It's The Talk Of The Town'), but hot arr. such as 'Black Jazz', 'White Jazz', 'Casa Loma Stomp' etc. (many written by Gifford, as was theme 'Smoke Rings') kept flame of jazz alive on college campuses until the BIG BAND ERA proper began. Dunham, Sargent led own bands in '40s; Sargent returned to lead Casa Loma band late '40s, later was late-night Dallas DJ for years. Gifford went freelance '34, made classic small-group sides for Victor '35 with Bunny BERIGAN, Bud FREEMAN, Wingy MANONE. Casa Loma style re-created on Capitol mid-'50s (*Glen Gray in Hi-Fi*); using good studio sidemen, new records had as much snap as originals.

CASCADES, The USA vocal group from San Diego: John Gummoe, Eddie Snyder, Dave Wilson, Dave Stevens, Dave Zabo. Clean-cut sound reminiscent of Rooftop Singers; one-hit wonders whose hit will not soon be forgotten: Gummoe's comp. 'Rhythm Of The Rain' made US no. 3, UK no. 5 early '63, almost the last flourish of pop crooning before onslaught of BEATLES. Bleak song played on teen-age heartbreak syndrome; frequently revived but cries out for sympathetic modern cover. Other minor hits: 'The Last Leaf', 'Maybe The Rain Will Fall'.

CASEY, Al (*b* Albert Aloysius Casey, 15 Sep. '15, Louisville, Ky.) Started on violin age 8, then ukelele, guitar. Pro debut with Fats WALLER and his Rhythm '34; played acoustic guitar on nearly all Waller's subsequent records. With Teddy WILSON '39-40, Waller again through '42, many residencies with own trio across USA from '43, switched to amplified guitar; freelance gigging all over: records under own name on Capitol '45; with Billy Kyle trio '49; on Fletcher HENDERSON reunion LP '57; *Buck Jumpin'* and *Quartet* on Prestige c.'60; with KING CURTIS until '61, etc.; LP *Six Swinging Strings* '81 on JSP. Waller's sidemen were dismissed as unable to shine on their own; in fact they were good craftsmen: Casey's genial mainstream jazz always pleases.

CASH, Johnny (*b* 26 Feb. '32, Kingsland, Ark.) Guitarist, singer, songwriter; giant of country music. Born to cotton-farming parents during the Great Depression; moved to Detroit '50, worked in car factory, swept floors; four years in USAF, stationed in Germany, began writing songs, playing guitar. To Memphis on discharge; signed to Sun Records '55 in heyday of rockabilly, along with Roy ORBISON, Carl PERKINS, Jerry Lee LEWIS, Elvis PRESLEY. Early country hits incl. own 'Cry, Cry, Cry', 'Folsom Prison Blues'; 'I Walk The Line' crossed over to pop chart '56. Distinctive sound of Sam Phillips's studio, Cash's sepulchral voice, the Tennessee Two (Luther Perkins's electric guitar, Marshall Grant's slap-bass style) made sound of early hits unique: LP *Hot And Blue Guitar* '57 captured essence. Fooling around in studio, Cash sang with Lewis, Perkins and Presley old gospel songs they'd all grown up with; result later bootlegged as *The Million Dollar Quartet*. Drummer W. S. Holland added '58 making The Tennessee Three (stayed with Cash 25 years). Version of Jack CLEMENT's 'Ballad Of A Teenage Queen' first country no. 1 (no. 14 pop), 'Guess Things Happen That Way' also country no. 1 (no. 11 pop), both '58. Altogether had 58 top 40 country hits in 25 years, 11 pop. Other country no. 1 entries: 'Don't Take Your Guns To Town' '59 (no. 32 pop), 'Ring Of Fire' '63 (no. 17 pop), 'Understand Your Man' '64 (no. 35 pop), remake of 'Folsom Prison', 'Daddy Sang Bass' both '68, 'A Boy Named Sue' '69 (no. 2 pop), 'Sunday Morning Coming Down', 'Flesh And Blood' both '70. Joined Grand Ole Opry '57; was playing 300 gigs a year early '60s, relying on drugs to keep him going. To Columbia label '58 as golden era at Sun drew to a close; had country hits on both labels '58-61 as Sun scraped vault for unissued sides; Sun reissues made country charts again '69-70. Columbia concept LPs successful: *Ride This Train* '60 was history of USA in train songs; *Bitter Tears* '64 was subtitled *Ballads Of The American Indian*; *True West* '65, *From Sea To Shining Sea* '68 were others; *Trains & Rivers* '71 was a Sun compilation. Friendship with Bob DYLAN led to country no. 4 with 'It Ain't Me, Babe' '64; duet on 'Girl From The North Country' on Dylan's *Nashville Skyline* '69 (wrote LP sleeve note; other duets never released); encouraged younger writers, e.g. Peter Lafarge, Kris KRISTOFFERSON. Marriage to June Carter '68 brought stability, helped him kick pill addiction; he later recovered fundamental Christianity of his youth, worked for evangelist Billy Graham. Duets with June resulted in five top 40 hits in country chart, incl. 'Jackson' '67, 'If I Were A Carpenter' '70, both no. 2; they had highly rated TV show late '60s-70s, other members of CARTER FAMILY also appeared. His concert LP *Johnny Cash At San Quentin* '69 also TV documentary, caught enthusiasm of captive audience; incl. 'Wanted', 'San Quentin' as well as biggest hit 'A Boy Named Sue' (written by Shel SILVERSTEIN). Called 'The Man In Black' after no. 3 '71 country hit, became country's ambassador abroad; toured heavily with June, Perkins, won countless Grammies; member of Nashville Songwriters Hall of Fame. Made film *A Gunfight* '70. Honesty made somewhat mawkish 'A Thing Called Love' big '72 hit; jokey 'One Piece At A Time' crossed over to pop top 40 '76. Nick LOWE, married to June's daughter Carlene, prod. 'Without Love' on excellent LP *Rockabilly Blues* '80; LP incl. Steve GOODMAN's '20th Century Is Almost Over', Cash's own 'Rockabilly Blues (Texas 1955)'. Narrative title track from *The Baron* '81 saw some action as a single; he made TV movie *The Baron And The Kid* '84. *Johnny 99* '83 incl. two Bruce SPRINGSTEEN songs from *Nebraska*: title song, 'Highway Patrolman' both ideally suited. He guested on Emmylou HARRIS LPs, Paul Kennerley's concept LP *The Legend Of Jesse James* '80, etc. Cash, Lewis and Perkins made LP *Survivors* '81, first time together in more than 20 years; they recreated the 'million-dollar quartet' with Orbison on *Class Of '55* '85 (recorded at the old Sun studio, with mobile equipment), incl. guest spots from Dave EDMUNDS, John Fogerty, the JUDDS, Rick NELSON (his last session); *The Highwayman* '85 with Waylon JENNINGS, Willie NELSON and Kristofferson, had no. 1 country single in title track; *Heroes* '86 with Jennings incl. cover of Dylan's 'One Too Many Mornings'. Columbia lost points when it dropped Cash after 28 years; comment from Dwight YOAKUM was 'He paid for their Nashville building.' LP on Mercury '87 (latest of over 100) prod. by Clement, with Jennings, Carter girls, incl. single/video 'The Night Hank Williams Came To Town'.

CASH, Rosanne (*b* 24 May '55, Memphis, Tenn.) Successful pop/country singer; one of four daughters from Johnny CASH's first marriage. Worked for CBS records in London; studied drama; signed to Arista Records Germany '77, switched to American CBS. LP *Right Or Wrong* '79 incl. duet hit with Bobby BARE 'No Memories Hangin' Round'. Married singer/songwriter Rodney CROWELL '79; he prod. her second LP *Seven Year Ache* '81, incl. two no. 1 country singles ('My Baby Thinks She's A Train' had harmony with Rosemary Butler, Emmylou HARRIS), LP went gold and title track made pop top 30. *Somewhere In The Stars* '82 followed by biographical concept album *Rhythm And Romance* '85: had three producers incl. Crowell; she wrote or co-wrote eight songs incl. 'Halfway House' (about drugs), 'Second To No One' (marriage), 'My Old Man' (her father); LP also incl. Tom PETTY/Benmont Tench song 'Never Be You', originally intended for soundtrack of film *Streets Of Fire*; cover of John HIATT's 'Pink Bedroom'. Duet single co-written by Rosanne and Vince Gill 'If It Weren't For Him' country hit '85. Album *King's Record Shop* '87 named after a shop in Louisville, Ky. pictured on sleeve.

CASH, Tommy (*b* 5 Apr. '40, Dyess, Ark.) Country singer; brother of Johnny CASH. Began as DJ on Armed Forces Network in Frankfurt, Germany '60-1; continued as DJ in Memphis, then worked for Johnny's publishing firm in Nashville; wrote 'You Don't Hear' for Kitty WELLS (top 5 country hit '65). Signed to Musicor Records '65, United Artists '66, Epic '69, Elektra '75, UA again '76, Monument '77, Audiograph '83. Big-

gest hits: 'Six White Horses' '69, 'Rise And Shine' and 'One Song Away' '70, 'I Recall A Gypsy Woman' '73. Busy on show dates with band The Tom Cats.

CASSIDY, David (*b* 12 Apr. '50, NYC) TV star, singer; son of actors Jack Cassidy, Evelyn Ward. Followed them into acting on TV's *Marcus Welby MD*, *Bonanza*, *Mod Squad*, others; Screen Gems/Columbia, power behind MONKEES, hired stepmother Shirley Jones to play adult lead in music-oriented kids' show; Cassidy played Keith in *The Partridge Family* of six who made music in their garage, studio creations of Wes Farrell, who also wrote most of material; Cassidy and Jones were the only ones who sang on record. Family's first single 'I Think I Love You' no. 1 '70; unlike Monkees, music was secondary to TV image, but records sold, in decreasing numbers: 'Doesn't Somebody Want To Be Loved' and 'I'll Meet You Halfway' each no. 10 '71; four lesser hits as novelty wore off. But Cassidy had gone solo: safe cover of ASSOCIATION's 'Cherish' was no. 9 debut '71; LP of same title sold a million. Revealed in *Rolling Stone* interview Mar. '72 that he hated Family, liked sex and drugs; three top 40 entries that year reached no higher than 25. Started all over again in UK; with only one hit there before Feb. '72, screening of show brought Family's records to top 20 incl. no. 3 cover of Neil SEDAKA's 'Breaking Up Is Hard To Do'; Cassidy had seven top 20s UK '72-4 incl. 'How Can I Be Sure', 'Daydreamer/The Puppy Song', both at no. 1. Departure from Family late '73 effectively axed show; May '74 teenybopper Bernadette Whelan died at crushed, crowded London show; Cassidy retired from live performance, attempted to create adult image with help of Richie Furay (POCO), Bruce Johnson (BEACH BOYS), Flo and Eddie (TURTLES), others; two more top 20 singles UK '75 but LPs '75-7 uninspired at best: discarded like many teen idols before him. Inspired by hearing POLICE early '80s, returned to music; in Broadway cast of *Joseph And The Amazing Technicolour Dreamcoat*; returned to UK charts with 'The Last Kiss', made LP *Romance* '85. Still has good looks, ordinary voice. Planned collaboration with '80s counterpart George Michael of WHAM! didn't happen.

CASTLE, Lee (*b* Lee Castaldo, 28 Feb. '15, NYC) Trumpet, leader. Pro debut at 18; good swing era sideman with Artie SHAW, Red NORVO, Tommy DORSEY, Glenn MILLER, Jack TEAGARDEN, all '37-9. While with Teagarden in Chicago, June '39, played on small-group freelance date prod. by John HAMMOND with organist Glenn Hardman, Lester YOUNG, Jo JONES, Freddie GREEN (tracks incl. 'Upright Organ Blues'); according to Jones, Castle had been out all night and 'was pretty mussed up. Played OK, though.' Then played with Will BRADLEY, Shaw again, Benny GOODMAN (appeared in films, e.g. *Stage Door Canteen* '43). Changed name to lead own bands early '40s; with Shaw '50, Dorsey brothers from '53. Led Jimmy Dorsey's band during leader's final illness, incl. smash hit 'So Rare' '57; continued leading (and partly owned) Dorsey Bros. band through '70s. Also published transcriptions of Louis ARMSTRONG solos.

CASTLE, Vernon and Irene Dance team. Vernon Blythe was English magician; began career in USA with small parts in shows c.'06; met Irene Foote in show '11; they married and became international sensation, capped in '14 show *Watch Your Step*. Employed first-class talent; James Reese EUROPE led 11-piece band at dance palace Castle House, aka 'Castles in the Air', wrote original music, invented dances Fox Trot, Turkey Trot; they also originated Bunny Hug, Maxixe, Castle Rock, others. Dress and habits were imitated; organised string of dance studios. He joined British flying squad France WWI, did aerial photography; transferred to USA to teach flying, was killed in accident at Fort Worth Flying School '18. Biopic '39 starred Fred ASTAIRE, Ginger Rogers (who else?).

CATHERINE, Philip (*b* 27 Oct. '42, London) Guitarist. Mother English, father Belgian; lived in Brussels after WWII. Turned pro at 17, played jazz-rock; with Jean-Luc PONTY early '70s; studied at Berklee in USA; joined Pork Pie with Charlie MARIANO, pianist Jasper van't Hof (*Transitory* '74, *The Door Is Open* '75); recorded with Larry CORYELL (duos *Twin House* '78, *Splendid* '78, *Live!* '80 on Atlantic and Elektra), Chet BAKER '83; etc. Own LPs: *Stream* '72 on WB with

piano and drums; then *Nairam* '74-5 on WB with Palle MIKKELBORG, *September Man* '74 and *Guitars* '75 on Atlantic, *Sleep My Love* '78 on CMP, all with Mariano, van't Hof, others; *Babel* '80 on Elektra, with children's voices, some strings, etc.; *End Of August* '82 on WEA with Toots THIELEMANS, Mariano, others; duo *The Viking* '83 on Pablo with Niels-Henning Ørsted Pedersen.

CATLETT, Sidney 'Big Sid' (*b* 17 Jan. '10, Evansville, In.; *d* 24 Mar. '51, Chicago) Ace big band drummer, some said the best of all, with Benny CARTER, McKINNEY'S COTTON PICKERS, Jeter-Pillars, Fletcher HENDERSON, Don REDMAN, Louis ARMSTRONG, Benny GOODMAN, others; also small groups, e.g. Commodore sessions: Chu BERRY And His 'Little Jazz' Ensemble '38; Coleman HAWKINS And The Chocolate Dandies '40; Hawkins And Leonard FEATHER's All-Stars '43 (Esquire magazine poll winners). Precise time and good taste made him superior accompanist for soloists; he was so successful with Goodman '41 that Goodman got rid of him. Led own big band briefly '46; at Louis ARMSTRONG's historic Town Hall concert '47; freelanced with Dizzy GILLESPIE, Charlie VENTURA; one of the swing era veterans who made transition to modern jazz. Died suddenly in the wings at theatre gig.

CAVALLARO, Carmen (*b* 6 May '13, NYC) Piano, bandleader. Classical training in teens; took dance band jobs, gaining featured role as flashy stylist (e.g. with Al Kavelin, '33-7). Formed own combo for St Louis hotel gig '39, octet in Detroit '40, then a flood of jobs at swanky hotels. Briefly led swing band '43 but soon returned to cocktail set. No. 3 hit '45: 'Chopin's Polonaise'; no. 1 albums (of 78s) in '46-8. Appeared in films: *Hollywood Canteen* '44, *Out Of This World*, *Diamond Horseshoe* '45, etc. Played soundtrack piano for Tyrone Power in '56 biopic *The Eddy Duchin Story*. Played semi-pop concerts till '60s.

CAYENNE UK salsa band formed London '79 by Robert Greenfield (aka Roberto Campoverde; *b* 14 May '49, Margate, Kent), guitar: ran Hampstead music shop; worked with Crossbreed, with London guitarist John Ethridge (SOFT MACHINE); played on

Incognito LP '81; does music for *The Comic Strip*, UK alternative comedy series. Other founder members: Ron Carthy (trumpeter; with Freddie KING '74-5; also founder of Latin-flavoured disco band Gonzales: 8 LPs incl. USA/UK hit 'Haven't Stopped Dancing Yet' '79); Paul Nieman, trombone (*b* 19 June '50, London; now leads band Elephant); Bud Beadle (alto/soprano sax; *b* Geoffrey Stephen Beadle, 27 Mar. '47, London; worked with Georgie FAME, Ginger BAKER); Roy Davies (piano; *b* 3 Oct. '40, Wales; on Freddy KING LP *Burglar*, Elton JOHN's *Victim Of Love*, with Gonzales, Butts Band). Current lineup: Steve Waterman, trumpet (*b* 8 Sep. '60, Lincolnshire; also plays for Alison MOYET); Fayyez Virgi, trombone (*b* 6 Nov. '60, Tanzania; also composer: witty, swinging 'Mr Crazy Buys Some Manuscript' for Cayenne; also tours with DEXY'S MIDNIGHT RUNNERS); Jody Linscott, percussion (*b* 12 Feb. '53, Boston, Mass.; played on David SANBORN LP *Hideaway*, Pete Townshend's *Chinese Eyes*, Robert PALMER's *Sneaking Sally Through The Alley* and *Some People Can Do What They Like*). Phil Crabe, drums (ex-Cilla BLACK), John Chambers, congas (BBC radio Big Band), Steve Carter, bass. Ace UK session men who've been through or play occasional gigs incl. drummer Marc Parnell (joined Joan ARMATRADING Jan. '85; brother Rick ex-Atomic Rooster; father Jack *b* 6 Aug. '23, drummer with Ted HEATH, became head of music at ATV); Steve Gregory, tenor sax (*b* 4 Sep. '45, London; with Georgie FAME 11 years, has played on records with WHAM!, China Crisis, Alison Moyet all in '85; also works with the Inspirational Choir, black London gospel group recording for CBS). Cayenne played Capital Jazz Festival in London '83, then to Nyon, Switzerland for another gig same evening; in '85 with Nina SIMONE for six weeks at Ronnie SCOTT's club; festival in Ghent, Belgium; back to Scott's supporting Lou DONALDSON, then Gil SCOTT-HERON. First LP '81 incl. original tunes, also Freddie HUBBARD's 'Little Sunflower'; LP and title single 'Roberto Who?' made some UK charts but Groove label folded; LP reissued as *An Evening In Jaffa* '84 on Coda. Has track on Afro-Latin compilation *Live At The Bass Clef* '85 on Wave; new Coda LP made at MADNESS's Zarjazz studio. Excellent rhythm section; tasty writing and playing for brass: Greenfield says, 'I'd rather avoid the hit singles business and make good albums.' Not much chance of hit singles: little radio time for popular music of this quality in UK, which is why most grown-ups don't listen to the radio.

CBS International record label, division of Columbia Broadcasting System, NYC. Early USA radio network United Independent Broadcasters taken over by world-wide British-based COLUMBIA, descended from the oldest record label in the world; network renamed Columbia Phonograph Broadcasting System, then record company pulled out; network dropped the word 'phonograph' to become CBS. In aftermath of rationalisation during Depression, CBS bought control of BRUNSWICK Record Corporation '38, which by then owned rights to Columbia name in USA as well as several other labels (*see* EMI for Columbia in the rest of the world). Of 33 million records sold '38 in USA, BRC had sold only seven million; CBS sold Brunswick, Vocalion names to Decca '42; with CBS behind it, reactivated Columbia label soon became biggest in USA, historic black label colour changed to red; as a result of Depression-era conglomeration the vault CBS acquired for $700,000 was best in the industry: the best recordings of Louis ARMSTRONG; most of the best Duke ELLINGTON, Fletcher HENDERSON, some of the CARTER FAMILY, all of Bessie SMITH, Robert JOHNSON etc. Signed Benny GOODMAN, Count BASIE, other stars of the period; first big hit Orrin TUCKER's 'Oh, Johnny, Oh' '39. Classical recording was revived; price of 12″ discs cut in half '40, RCA forced to follow suit; according to Roland Gelatt, classical sales increased 1500% in USA. CBS introduced long-playing record '48, perfected in their labs by Dr Peter GOLDMARK; dominated USA industry in '50s, with Percy FAITH, Paul WESTON, Mitch MILLER as staff A&R men, stars like Jo STAFFORD, Rosemary CLOONEY, Guy MITCHELL, Johnny MATHIS, Carl SMITH, Lefty FRIZZELL, Ray PRICE, etc. For the jazz market, Miles DAVIS, Thelonious MONK, Dave BRUBECK were signed; product was leased to PHILIPS group for European distribution. The label did well with Broadway original cast albums and film soundtracks, beginning with *South Pacific* OC '49: OC LPs *Kiss Me Kate* '49, *My Fair Lady* '56, *Flower Drum Song* '59 and *Camelot* '61 were all no. 1 on album chart; *West Side Story* OC was no. 5 '58, but soundtrack of *West Side Story* film '61 set a record: no. 1 for 58 weeks, staying in chart for nearly four years. CBS rode high on '60s boom, with Clive DAVIS looking after Bob DYLAN, Janis JOPLIN etc.; began to use CBS label to market own product outside USA. Retrenchment during '70s recession left Davis an obvious target: bounced as a sop to critics of the industry (has done well at Arista). Outrageous hype of latest John HAMMOND discovery Bruce SPRINGSTEEN was initially unsuccessful, but he soon proved his worth. Artists recently signed incl. Alison MOYET, Wynton MARSALIS; Philip GLASS became first living 'classical' composer to be signed to exclusive contract since Igor Stravinsky and Aaron Copland, who were also on CBS. Okeh label has been used in USA by CBS as R&B outlet, Harmony and Odyssey for budget LPs; Epic is important subsidiary. CBS distributed GAMBLE & HUFF Philadelphia International product in '70s; then Epic had the best-selling LP in history: Michael JACKSON's *Thriller* '82 incl. seven top 10 singles (but was no. 1 album 17 weeks fewer than *West Side Story* 20 years earlier). Columbia 78s had been laminated, more break resistant than RCA's but higher in surface noise; 45 singles were made of styrene rather than vinyl for decades: exceptionally quiet surfaces but soon wore out. CBS/USA LPs became highest quality; custom pressing and distribution for other labels important: c.'70 CBS was pressing the majority of LPs in USA. *Billboard* had been reporting since '65 that venerable Columbia name would be dropped in USA for single worldwide CBS logo, but it didn't happen; CBS tried to buy world rights to Columbia name (then not much used in UK) from EMI early '80s but deal fell through, partly because EMI subsidiaries around the world each owned a piece of the name. Then the CBS record division itself was sold as parent company concentrated on TV, coping with falling ratings and other problems; EMI bid for it; Sony (CBS outlet in Japan) offered $1.25 billion, then took the prize for $2 billion '87. Both RCA and Columbia USA, rivals

since the beginning of gramophone records, had now changed hands; the results will probably be beneficial in the rejuvenation of these venerable labels.

CELESTIN, Oscar 'Papa' (*b* 1 Jan. 1884, Napoleonville, La.; *d* 15 Dec. '54, New Orleans) Trumpet, vocals, leader. Played in New Orleans brass bands from '06, led own band at Tuxedo Hall '10-13; from then on, when not working other jobs (e.g. WWII shipyard) co-led, then led various Tuxedo Bands, until his was one of the last trad. New Orleans ensembles. Badly injured by hit-and-run driver, '44. A few records in late '20s, late '40s; some radio and TV work; played in Washington DC for President Eisenhower '53, featured in film *Cinerama Holiday* same year.

CHACHACHA Dance that swept Cuba '53, became fad in USA later: a Cuban derivation of the danzón (itself derived from European contradanza in late 19th century). Invented '48 by violinist Enrique Jorrín (*b* '26) who had played in popular danzónera Arcaño y Sus Maravillas; he was dir. of Orquesta América when he wrote 'La Engañadora' '48: when recorded '53 became a craze. Invented from a passage in final part of the danzón; as dancers adapted to it their feet made a 'chachacha' shuffling sound; instrumentation remained the same as danzónera: strings, piano, bass, congas, timbales, guiro (scraper) and lead flute; Jorrín added unison voices and the effect was a lighter, brighter, sweeter sound. Most significant chachacha bands of the day, which came to be called CHARANGAS, were Orquesta Aragón (still recording in Cuba today) and FAJARDO y sus Estrellas (Fajardo moved to NYC '60s). NYC big bands emphasised horns to suit the city's sound. Tito PUENTE covered Orquesta Aragón's 'Pare Cochero'; other noteworthy chachachas incl. José Curbelo 'El Pescador', MACHITO 'El Campesino'; biggest hit was Perez PRADO's 'Cherry Pink And Apple Blossom White', no. 1 pop chart USA '55 (played as a chachacha by other bands; Prado actually played it as a slow mambo). Non-Latin bands diluted music for American dancers; fad was such that TV scripts joked about mother dragging tired businessman father to dancing lesson: Tommy DORSEY Orches-

219

tra charted '58 with 'Tea For Two Cha Cha' etc.; Stan KENTON's *Viva Kenton* featured three chachachas. Jorrín still leads band in Cuba, using electric instruments; made new version of 'La Engañadora' '70: LP on Cuban state label Areito also on Spanish Fonomusic as *Cha-Cha-Cha/Orquesta de Enrique Jorrín* '85. He featured in performance and interview on BBC 2's Arena programme *What's Cuba Playing At?* '84.

CHACKSFIELD, Frank (*b* 9 May '14, Battle, Sussex) UK pianist, arranger, conductor. Piano at 7, church organist at Salehurst Church, Robertsbridge. Worked as solicitor's clerk, began leading bands in spare time; residencies in Tonbridge '36, Jersey '39. Joined RASC WWII, made first broadcast '43; staff arranger to Stars In Battledress entertainment unit, also for Merry-Go-Round radio show then for radio's Stand Easy '46. Became show's conductor '48 leading Henry HALL band; made first record that year backing singer Frederick Ferrari. Conducted Geraldo band '49; made records under own name for Polygon label, incl. own comp. 'Prelude To A Memory'. Single 'Meet Mr Callahan' successful on Oriole, then top 10 UK hit 'Little Red Monkey' on Parlophone '53. Signed by Decca UK (London label in USA), doing lush string arrangements well recorded with Decca's 'FFRR' system (full frequency range recording), the best technology around at the time. Worldwide hit with theme from Chaplin film 'Limelight' '53; even bigger hit later same year with 'Ebb Tide', no. 2 in USA. Consistent LP seller for many years; also UK single hits 'In Old Lisbon', 'Donkey Cart' both '56; USA chart entry with 'On The Beach' '60. Music adviser to Irish Television Service at its formation; mid-'70s took 40-piece orchestra on 15-date tour of Japan. Typical mood music LPs in print UK; *Stardust* on Pickwick has 'Ebb Tide', 'Limelight'.

CHAD & JEREMY UK vocal duo '60s: Chad Stuart (*b* 10 Dec. '43), Jeremy Clyde (*b* 22 Mar. '44), ex-public schoolboys, met at London's Central School of Speech and Drama; both played guitars and sang; Chad wrote lyrics; Jeremy wrote music, doubled on piano, sitar, tablas, banjo, flute. Folk-based pop far more popular in USA than UK, where they failed to chart higher than no. 37. In USA 'Yesterday's Gone' was no. 21 '64 as anything British was of interest; but their 'soft rock' (like that of PETER & GORDON) was a natural for West Coast scene of the period. USA top 40 hits '64-6 helped by TV appearances on *Hulabaloo*, other shows: 'A Summer Song' (no. 7), 'Willow Weep For Me' (15), 'If I Loved You' (23), 'Before And After' (17), 'I Don't Wanna Lose You Baby' (35), 'Distant Shores' (30). As 'progressive rock' began, they tinkered with formula and lost sales: *Of Cabbages And Kings* '67 incl. 5-movement 'Progress Suite' arr. by Stuart, acclaimed as concept LP but inevitably paled in comparison with BEATLES' *Sgt Pepper*; similarly portentous *The Ark* '68 followed; they split '69 in face of critical and public indifference. Clyde became successful actor, joining National Theatre, doing films (*Silver Bears* '78 with Michael Caine) and TV (title role in *Sexton Blake* '78). Stuart stayed in USA, sang with wife Jill, was MC for Smothers Brothers TV show, wrote musicals (two prod. in Cal.). Duo made comeback LP '84 for USA Rockshire label, which immediately went bankrupt; worked together in London in *Pump Boys And Dinettes*. Having helped to originate soft rock, which USA groups then took over in '70s, reportedly considered new comeback in '85 under different name.

CHAIRMEN OF THE BOARD USA vocal group formed '69 by 'General' Norman Johnson (*b* 23 May '44, Norfolk, Va.). Had been lead singer with Showmen, whose hymn to rock'n'roll 'It Will Stand' was no. 61 USA '61 (re-entered at no. 80 '64), their only hit in seven years of trying (other personnel: Leslie Fenton, Milton Dorsey, Gene Knight). He refused offer of Frankie LYMON's place in the Teenagers, signed '68 with Invictus, new label formed by ex-Motown legends HOLLAND-DOZIER-HOLLAND; recruited Danny Woods (*b* 10 Apr. '44), Harrison Kennedy (*b* Canada; ex-Stoned Soul Children), Eddie Curtis (ex-Huey SMITH & the Clowns) to form Gentlemen, later renamed Chairmen of the Board. Each could handle leads, but Johnson took most; first single 'Give Me Just A Little More Time' (no. 3 USA/UK) heavily infl. by FOUR TOPS, introduced Johnson's 'B-r-r-r' hiccuping vocal delivery to large audience. 'You've Got Me Dangling On A String' (no. 38 USA/5 UK) suggested greater popularity overseas; in fact top 40 tenure in USA lasted only through '70 with 'Everything's Tuesday' (38), 'Pay To The Piper' (13) making 12 and 34 in UK, latter featuring lead voice of Woods (higher, harder sound than General's strangulated tone). Last studio session by original group late '71 (prod. as they all were by Holland-Dozier-Holland), but hits in UK carried on through '73, continuing dance-floor tradition Motown temporarily lost, making conservative UK soul fans happy: five more top 40 hits UK incl. gospelly 'Working On A Building Of Love' (20), 'Elmo James' (21), clarinet-led 'Finders Keepers' (21), reminiscent of Stevie WONDER. But group cast too much in trad. mould: Motown found second wind with orchestrated social comment of TEMPTATIONS, funky soul/rock fusion from Wonder; Chairmen were overtaken by events. Johnson had written for THREE DE-GREES, Freda PAYNE ('Bring The Boys Home'), Clarence Carter (transatlantic smash 'Patches'), now diversified further, writing with prod. Greg Perry for Invictus/ Hot Wax acts like Honey Cone, 100 Proof Aged In Soul; solo albums by Johnson (*Generally Speaking* '72), Woods (*Aries*), Kennedy (*Hypnotic Music*) further slowed group's impetus; Curtis had left '72, then Kennedy; Johnson, Woods carried on until '76 with no new records (*Skin I'm In* '74 was all old tapes), they split after UK tour as duo. Johnson made six flop singles for Arista, eponymous '77 LP; wrote for Martha REEVES (another soul legend out of favour), e.g. title track on her *The Rest Of My Life* '76; reunited with Woods on Surfside '81 for 'Success' as the Chairmen. Meanwhile group had been championed by STYLE COUNCIL's Paul Weller in UK; Kevin Rowland of DEXY'S MIDNIGHT RUNNERS had vocal style distinctly Johnsonesque; acquisition of long-defunct Invictus vault by Holland-Dozier-Holland resulted in *Salute The General* '84, superb compilation on Demon UK. Weller remixed 'Loverboy' for UK hit '86; Johnson active on USA circuits promoting dance fad 'The Shag': Johnson's track from '84 revived a sort of 'dirty boogie' fad from c.'60, also revived in nostalgia film '88.

CHALOFF, Serge (*b* 24 Nov. '23, Boston, Mass.; *d* there 16 July '57) Baritone sax. Mother was music teacher, father played in Boston S.O.; studied piano, clarinet, self-taught on baritone; played with Boyd RAEBURN '45, Georgie AULD, J. DORSEY '45-6; Sonny BERMAN date for Dial '46 incl. 'Nocturne', a striking Chaloff feature; joined Woody HERMAN '47, anchor in 'four brothers' reed section and featured on uptempo 'Man, Don't Be Ridiculous'. As first major bop player on the instrument he displaced Harry CARNEY in *Downbeat* polls three years in a row. Records late '40s on Savoy, Mercer with Al COHN, Red RODNEY, Oscar PETTIFORD, Denzil BEST, other stars of the period; also on Keynote '47 with Rodney, Boston Motiff label '49 with Ralph BURNS. Wrecked career, reputation, health with drugs, as pusher/addict, but music survived: returned to Boston, cleaned up and came back better than ever with local men Boots Mussulli (*b* 18 Nov. '17, Milford, Mass.; *d* 23 Sep. '67, Norfolk, Mass.: reedman and teacher, played with Stan KENTON, Charlie VENTURA, Gene KRUPA, etc.), Herb Pomeroy (*b* 15 Apr. '30, Glastonbury, Mass.; trumpet, leader, teacher; led band at Newport '58, dir. Radio Malaysia Orchestra '62, Montreux '70, etc.): '54 sessions incl. 'The Fable Of Mabel' (on Vogue, then Storyville); *Boston Blow-up* '55 and his masterpiece *Blue Serge* '56 (last with Sonny CLARK, Leroy Vinnegar, Philly Joe JONES) both on Capitol, now Affinity UK. Contracted spinal paralysis; played well mid-'56 at Metronome All-Star session and early '57 at four brothers reunion for RCA/Vik, but died of cancer.

CHAMBER MUSIC SOCIETY OF LOWER BASIN STREET NBC radio 'jazz' band led c.'40 by Henry 'Hot Lips' Levine (*b* '07, London; worked with Original Dixieland Jazz Band '26-7). Broadcasts chiefly notable for Dinah SHORE (a regular), guests LEADBELLY, Jelly Roll MORTON, Sidney BECHET.

CHAMBERS BROTHERS Vocal/instrumental group formed early '60s in L.A., became funk pioneers. George Chambers (*b* 26 Sep. '31) played bass, brothers Willie (*b* 3 Mar. '38) guitar, Lester (*b* 13 Apr. '40) harmonica, Joe (*b* 22 Aug. '42) guitar; all *b*

Miss. Began as gospel/folk quartet, added white drummer Brian Keenan (*b* 28 Jan. c.'44), played Newport Folk Festival '65, rock and soul venues. LPs on Vault label: *People Get Ready* '65, *Chambers Brothers Now* '66, *Shout!* '68, *Feelin' The Blues* '70; on Columbia: *The Times Has Come* (first and biggest of six LPs to chart; title cut first and biggest at no. 11 of five Hot 100 entries '68-70), *A New Time, A New Day*, all '68; *Love, Peace And Happiness* '69 was 2-disc set, one disc live at Fillmore East; *New Generation* '70, *Oh My God!* '72 followed by split. Brothers re-formed '74 for *Unbonded* and *Right Move* '75 on Avco. *Greatest Hits* LPs on Vault and Columbia charted '70-1; later 2-disc *Best Of* on Fantasy represents gospel family period. Sessioned with Maria MULDAUR on Takoma label '80.

CHAMBERS, Joe (*b* Joseph Arthur Chambers, 25 June '42, Stoneacre, Va.) Drums, piano; composer. First job with Eric DOLPHY, also played with Freddie HUBBARD, Lou DONALDSON, Bobby HUTCHERSON, Charles MINGUS, many others incl. Wayne SHORTER, among his best (e.g. *Adam's Apple* '67). Has concentrated on writing; compositions on sextet LP *The Almoravid* '73, also co-led *Double Exposure* '77 (with Larry Young – Islamic name Khalid Yasin – *b* 7 Oct. '40, Newark, N.J.; dubbed 'the Coltrane of the organ' by Jack McDUFF), both on Muse. *Punjab* '78 on Denon is solo piano set. His brother Steven is a contemporary composer (*b* 8 Feb. '40), known since '73 as Talib Rasul Hakim.

CHAMBERS, Paul (*b* Paul Lawrence Dunbar Chambers Jr, 22 Apr. '35, Pittsburgh, Pa.; *d* 4 Jan. '69, NYC) Bass. With Miles DAVIS '55-60; then trio with Wynton KELLY, Jimmy COBB, also freelanced. With Davis a member of the most important rhythm section of the period; subtle time, beautiful tone, all-round technique made him the most influential bassist of the decade. Own all-star small-group LPs incl. '55-6 sessions prod. for reissue by Michael CUSCUNA complete on Blue Note as 2-disc Chambers/John COLTRANE *High Step* '75. Also *Paul Chambers Quintet, Bass On Top*, both Blue Note '57; '59-60 sessions for Vee Jay mostly reissued on Trip as *Just Friends*. As well as Davis albums, played on Sonny

ROLLINS LP *Tenor Madness* '56; *Art Pepper Meets The Rhythm Section*, John Coltrane LPs *Blue Train* and *Traneing In*, J. GRIFFIN's *Blowin' Session*, all '57; Coltrane's *Black Pearls* '58, *Giant Steps* and *Bags And Trane* both '59; also with Bill EVANS, many more.

CHANDLER, Gene (*b* Eugene Dixon, 6 July '40, Chicago) USA soul singer. Lead singer of Dukays; then first chart entry as solo artist was no. 1 both pop and R&B: 'Duke Of Earl' '62 owed much to doo-wop with its 'dook, dook, dook' chorus. Follow-ups on Vee Jay not as sensational; switched to Constellation for string of crossovers '64-5 incl. top 40 'Just Be True', 'Bless Our Love', 'What Now', 'Nothing Can Stop Me'; benefited from writing/prod. skill of Curtis MAYFIELD, who wrote Chandler's signature tune 'Rainbow' (Vee Jay '62), others. Chandler's visual gimmick was ducal outfit incl. monocle, top hat, cane and cloak. Duets with Barbara Acklin ('From Teacher To The Preacher', no. 57 pop '68), Jerry BUTLER ('Ten And Two') very popular in soul market; re-entered pop chart with no. 12 'Groovy Situation' '70 on Mercury, switched to Mayfield's Curtom label '72; had consistent success in late '70s disco boom with chocolate-brown vocals on series of dance records more popular in UK than USA, incl. 'Get Down', 'When You're Number 1' '79, 'Does She Have A Friend' '80, all prod. by Carl Davis on Chi-Sound label (Chandler executive vice-president). Had spent lean years managing/prod. groups on own Bamboo label (hits incl. 'Backfield In Motion' '69 by Mel & Tim, no. 3 soul chart); hectic pace led to drug involvement, served short time in jail '76. New LP *Your Love Looks Good To Me* '85 on Fastfire will be third stab at chart fame, already assured since 'Duke Of Earl'.

CHANNEL, Bruce (*b* 28 Nov. '40, Texas) Pop singer based in country music. Like Elvis PRESLEY, early break came on Louisiana Hayride late '50s; 'Hey Baby' made no. 1 USA, no. 2 UK '62 with plaintive harmonica of Delbert McCLINTON, inspiring John LENNON's style on BEATLES' 'Love Me Do', 'Please, Please Me'. Ironically, Beatles swamped Channel's pop career along with many others, though he had minor hit 'Going Back To Louisiana' '64, worldwide hit with 'Keep On' '68.

CHANNING, Carol (*b* 31 Jan. '21, Seattle, Wash.) Singer, actress: can upstage anybody with vivacious, wide-eyed wackiness. High school in San Francisco, college in Bennington, Vt.; went on stage. Impact as the Gladiola Girl in *Lend An Ear* '47 on Broadway, stardom as Lorelei Lee in *Gentlemen Prefer Blondes* '48, stopping show with 'Diamonds Are A Girl's Best Friends'. Then *Wonderful Town* '54 (replacing Rosalind Russell), *The Vamp* '55; teamed with George Burns playing Las Vegas, nightclub circuit; after *Show Girl* '61 stole *Hello, Dolly!* '63 as Dolly Levi (did 'Hello, Lyndon' for anyone who'd listen during '64 Presidential campaign. *Dolly* was composed and written by Jerry Herman, *b* 10 July '32, NYC, who also wrote *Mame* '66, *Dear World* '69, *Mack And Mabel* '74 about Mack Sennett and Mabel Normand). Channing played in *Lorelei* '73 (sequel to *Gentlemen Prefer Blondes*), then revived *Dolly* on tour for 11 months, eventually taking it back to Broadway '74 for 320 performances. Because of food allergies, takes organic food, bottled water wherever she goes. Films inc. *Paid In Full* '50, *The First Travelling Salesgirl* '56, wonderfully zany *Thoroughly Modern Millie* '67 (with Julie ANDREWS and Beatrice Lillie), *Skidoo* '69 (with music by Harry NILSSON).

CHAPIN, Harry (*b* 7 Dec. '42, NYC; *d* 16 July '81, Long Island) USA singer/songwriter, guitarist. Father was Jim Chapin, Swing Era drummer; brother Tom is also singer/songwriter (latest LP *Let Me Back Into Your Life* '87 on Flying Fish). Harry attended Air Force Academy, Cornell U.; became a pilot, with Jim Jacobs made silent documentary film about boxers *Legendary Champions* which was nominated for an Oscar '69. Involved with music all the while, wrote songs for Chapin Brothers LP on Epic '70; always willing to try something new, he rented an NYC venue for the summer '71 instead of renting himself out as an entertainer (band incl. brother Steve), leading to deal with Elektra: *Heads And Tales* '72 incl. 'Taxi', followed by *Sniper And Other Love Stories* '72, *Short Stories* '73 (incl. 'W', about an ageing DJ); *Verities &*

Balderdash '74 was no. 4 LP incl. no. 1 hit 'Cat's In The Cradle', about a father too busy to give time to his children. *Portrait Gallery* '75, 2-disc *Greatest Stories – Live* '76, *On The Road To Kingdom Come* '76, 2-disc *Dance Band On The Titanic* all charted well in top 100 LPs, but latter concept set was over-ambitious and perhaps suffered from his furious activity: as well as heavy touring he mounted Broadway show *The Night That Made America Famous* '75 (nominated for awards), Hollywood revue *Chapin* '77; also worked supporting politicians not according to party but to what they proposed to do about world hunger. LP *Living Room Suite* '78 was back on form but did not make top 100 LPs; neither did 2-disc *Legends Of The Lost And Found – New Greatest Stories Live* '79. Story-telling folk-rockers were old-hat by then in chart terms, but last LP *Sequel* '80 (on Boardwalk label) was back-up to no. 58, title track a 'Sequel' to 'Taxi'. He was killed in a car crash, still sorely missed for talent and spirit of optimism.

CHAPMAN, Marshall (*b* 7 Jan. '49, Spartanburg, N.C.) Singer, songwriter, guitarist in country rock whose work falls between stools in the marketplace. From upper-class family; lived in France, Boston; back to Nashville '73 (where she had attended Vanderbilt U.), writing songs and meeting 'outlaws' Tompall GLASER, Waylon JENNINGS and his wife Jessi Colter, etc. Signed with Epic for *Me, I'm Feeling Free* '77, *Jaded Virgin* '78, *Marshall* '79; they didn't sell and Epic dropped her. She toured with a rock trio, but songs found some favour in country fraternity: Colter, Glaser, Crystal GAYLE, others covered 'A Woman's Heart (Is A Handy Place To Be)'; other songs were 'Somewhere South Of Macon' (too sexy for country radio), 'Don't Get Me Pregnant', 'Rock And Roll Clothes'. *Pick Up The Tempo* '81 on Rounder was tame by comparison; cassette-only *Dirty Linen* '87 on her own Tall Girl Records was return to strong country boogie incl. steaming cover of 'Daddy Long Legs' (also recorded by Tanya Tucker), good-time workout 'Betty's Bein' Bad'.

CHARANGA The name for both a kind of Cuban music and the bands that play it: a light, elegant, sprightly music; at its most lush and string-laden veering towards kitsch MOR; at its most commercial a light medium for pop covers; at its hardest a virtuosic interplay among overblown flutes, searing strings and percussion. The bands developed out of charangas francesas (19th-C. 'French orchestras') and are characterised by flute lead, legato violins, crisp timbales, bass, piano, unison male voices; they were first called danzóneras, playing danzóns and (from early '50s) chachachas; when composer Eduardo Davidson, flautist/bandleader José FAJARDO, and the Orquesta Aragón introduced the pachanga rhythm, bands were called charangas. Orquesta Aragón was formed by violinist Oreste Aragón in Cienfuegos '39; composer/violinist Rafael Lay (1927-82) was mus. dir., then flautist Richard Egües (b Eduardo Egües Martinez, 26 Oct. '23; a member of the band since '55). They located in Havana mid-'50s, have toured in over 30 countries incl. USA and Japan; '84 lineup incl. 10 pieces plus two vocalists; their many LPs incl. a Monitor LP recorded live in NYC in '83, and on Areito (the main Cuban state label) two vols. made live in Paris '84, one with leading Cuban singer Elena Burke; also *Original de Cienfuegos* ('53-5 tracks, once on RCA) and *La Época de Oro de la Orquesta Aragon Vol. 11* '57-8, both on Cariño. Egües also plays reeds and has recorded with other outfits, incl. Cuban jam sessions on Panart and Areito. The charanga's USA heyday was '60s, led by Charlie PALMIERI's Charanga Duboney (led on flute by Johnny PACHECO) with four violins, infl. by Orquesta Aragón; Ray BARRETTO's Charanga Moderna, Mongo SANTAMARIA's jazz-oriented charanga, Felix 'Pupi' LEGARRETA y su Charanga, and Fajardo, who settled in the USA early '60s. Charanga abated in NYC mid-'60s, most bandleaders eventually swapping strings for brass, but Orquesta Broadway has kept going as popular dance band for 25 years, formed by singer Roberto TORRES early '60s: the Zervigón brothers have been mainstays, Eddy on flute, Ruddy on violin, Kelvin on piano, while Rafael 'Felo' Barrio served as percussionist/vocalist '70s, '80s. They recorded for Musicor (some reissues on SonoDisc), Tico; LPs incl. *Dengue* c.'64 on Gema when that rhythm had been popularised by Perez PRADO;

Pasaporte '76 on Coco with three violins and rumba percussion on one track; *New York City Salsa* '78 on Coco had two more violins and a trumpet; members played on Torres LPs '81; after *Orquesta Broadway Loves New York* '82 on Broadway they came back to unaugmented format with *Ahora Es Cuando Eh!* '87 on Mambo. Barrio led a band with frontline of brass, reed, flute on *Felo Barrio y la Inspiracion* '86 on Musica Internacional. Orquesta Novel (previously called Orquesta Tipica Novel) was led by Afro-Cuban pianist Willie Ellis; recorded for TR, switching to Fania with *Salsamania* '78, adding trombone to lineup on *Que Viva el Son Montuno* '80; aimed *Novel Experience* '80 at crossover market with pop hits in charanga style and sung in English. Charanga came back late '70s; Tico released LPs *Nuestra Herencia* '77 and *De Todo un Poco* '78 by flautist Lou Perez; new bands were Charanga 76, Charanga Casino: former formed '76 led by Cuban güiro player Felipe Martinez, played smooth pop style with singers Hansel Martinez, Raúl Alfonso (aka duo Hansel & Raúl); Charanga Casino was formed '78 as a slick commercial band led by güiro player and composer Felipe Javier Ramos; fourth LP *Charanga Casino* '82 on SAR had Puerto Rican guest Charlie Rodriguez on tres; *Alone Again* '83 featured title cover of Gilbert O'SULLIVAN hit sung in English. (Singers Miguel Martin and Oscar Diaz made duet LPs *Miguel & Oscar: La Fantasia* '85 on Suntan and *Un Regalo de Salsa* '86 on Sonotone, both in Florida backed with brass-led bands.) Ramos renamed his band La Casino, replaced strings with horns, turned singer and producer for *Felipe Ramos y la Casino* '86 on Musica Internacional. Fusion with typical frontline of conjunto trumpets and tres with Colombian vallenata accordion style to create 'charanga vallenata' hybrid in merengue-like 2/4 rhythm was played in '80s by Torres. Revival of charanga incl. LPs '86-7 by Rudy Calzado and Charanga Calé on Caimán, Orquesta Son Primero on Montuno, Miami-based Charanga de la 4 on SAR; Calzado's *Rica Charanga* also issued on Globe Style in UK.

CHARLATANS USA pop group formed San Francisco '65: original lineup had Sam Linde on drums, replaced by Dan HICKS on drums, guitar, vocals; Richard Olsen, on bass; Michael Ferguson, keyboards; Mike Wilhelm, guitar, vocals; George Hunter, vocals. Claimed to be original S.F. hippie band playing country-rock dressed as gold-rush dandies, learning trade in Carson City, Nevada; returned to Haight-Ashbury area to ride wave of drug counterculture: among the first to play at Family Dog, original Fillmore. Bay area DJ Tom Donahue made demos with them; album prod. for Kama Sutra by LOVIN' SPOONFUL alumnus Eric Jacobsen was not released, though '67 single 'The Shadow Knows' came out. Ferguson replaced '67 by Patrick Gogerty, who was replaced '68 by Darrel Devore; Hicks moved to guitar (Terry Wilson played drums), then left '68, as did Hunter, a designer whose visual flair had been all-important. Eponymous LP on Philips '69 had Olsen, Wilhelm, Devore, Wilson; then they split up. Strong visually in histories of the era (Rick Griffin posters, etc.). Hicks formed Hot Licks (see his entry); Wilhelm fronted FLAMIN' GROOVIES, had brief solo career; Olsen sessioned on clarinet for It's A Beautiful Day, then prod./played on *Wilhelm*, '76 LP released by UK fanzine *ZigZag*, for whom mystique had lingered on.

CHARLENE (*b* Charlene Duncan, L.A.) Singer, signed mid-'70s by Berry Gordy; as with Kiki DEE, another white female vocalist on Motown, stay there was brief, acrimonious, unsuccessful: three singles barely made top 100 '77. After an album she retired from music, moved to London; working behind counter of sweet shop there when saccharine ballad 'I've Never Been To Me' revived by DJ Scott Shannon on radio Q105 in Tampa, Fla.; it reached no. 3 USA/no. 1 UK mid-'82; LP of that title no. 20 USA LP chart. Swiftly re-signed by Motown, railroaded by prod. Curtis Nolen into going disco on LP *Hit And Run Lover*, while title cut of *Used To Be* (duet with Stevie WONDER) made no. 46 USA, lyrics allegedly too strong for airplay; LP barely made LP chart at no. 197. Moved back to L.A., has not made chart again.

CHARLES, Bobby (*b* Robert Charles Guidry, '39, Abbeville, La.) Singer, songwriter. Wrote huge Bill HALEY hit 'See You

Later, Alligator', 'But I Do' for Clarence HENRY, 'Before I Grow Too Old' and 'Walking To New Orleans' for Fats DOMINO; made fine records with Paul GAYTEN in New Orleans (compiled on *Bobby Charles* on PRT/Chess in UK '83); later recorded for Imperial incl. some pop but never made charts. Worked with Eddy RAVEN c.'64; turned to country music on Jewel, then Bearsville LP '72 incl. 'Before I Grow Too Old'.

CHARLES, Ray (*b* 13 Sep. '18, Chicago) Composer, arranger, conductor. Leader of Ray Charles Singers: 'easy listening' choral arrangements, many LPs '50-70s on several labels incl. Decca, MGM, Command. Smooth professionalism much in demand as mus. dir. of family TV shows, e.g. Perry COMO in USA, Val DOONICAN UK.

CHARLES, Ray (*b* Ray Charles Robinson, 23 Sep. '30, Albany, Georgia) Piano, organ, singer, composer, also alto sax; aka 'The Genius'. Perhaps the most successful soul artist of all time. Some sources give '30 as year of birth. Blind from accident age 6; went to Florida school for the blind; to Seattle to get as far from the South as possible. Taught himself to arrange and compose by braille. Formed Maxim Trio c.'47 in Nat COLE style; first black act to have TV show in Pacific Northwest; developed more personal style, soaked in Southern blues, gospel feeling, subsequently brought to wide range of material. First records late '40s on Swingtime, hits in R&B chart '51-2; went to Atlantic. Didn't compose or arrange at first but style already evident: 'Losing Hand', 'It Should've Been Me', 'Mess Around' (all May '53). Arrangement of 'The Things I Used To Do' no. 1 R&B hit for GUITAR SLIM early '54; string of originals followed beginning Dec. '53: 'Don't You Know', 'Come Back Baby', 'I Got A Woman' (covered by Elvis PRESLEY), 'This Little Girl Of Mine', 'Hallelujah I Love Her So', others, all R&B hits: sometimes fitted new words to gospel tunes: 'Talkin' 'Bout Jesus' became 'Talkin' 'Bout You'; Clara Ward's 'This Little Light Of Mine' became 'This Little Girl Of Mine'; 'How Jesus Died' became 'Lonely Avenue'. Big Bill BROONZY said 'He's mixing the blues with the spirituals. I know that's wrong . . .

he should be singing in a church.' But the mixture of gospel emotion, secular subject matter and smooth but honest delivery led to comic Bill Cosby's routine about Columbus going to America so he could discover Ray Charles. He used a female quartet, the Raelets; on soulful 'What Kind Of Man Are You?' they carried vocal on their own. First LP *The Great Ray Charles* '57 was a jazz set, with laid-back instrumentals 'Doodlin'' (Horace SILVER comp.), own 'Sweet Sixteen Bars'; first top 40 pop hit 'Sewanee River Rock' same year. Tracks with strings, voices, arrangements by Ralph BURNS, others with BASIE, ELLINGTON sidemen, writing by Quincy JONES, Al COHN, Ernie Wilkins etc. recorded May '59: *The Genius Of Ray Charles* was his first entry (no. 17) in LP chart. Extended arrangement with Raelets 'What'd I Say' was hard-driving gospel-style rock'n'roll hit '59. Switched to ABC '60: contract allowed him to retain ownership of his own recordings at the end of the association, unusual for a black artist then; soon had smash no. 1 hit '60 with down-home vocal on Hoagy CARMICHAEL evergreen 'Georgia On My Mind' (used in soundtracks of Norman Jewison film *In The Heat Of The Night* '69, Arthur Penn's *George's Friends* '82). Film theme 'Ruby' (pop hit '53) recorded with strings '60; played organ on 'One Mint Julep' '61 (from Impulse LP *Genius Plus Soul Equals Jazz*, arranged by Jones); women got upper hand as Raelets told him to 'Hit The Road Jack', second no. 1 single '61. Duet album *Ray Charles And Betty Carter* '61 charted ('Takes Two To Tango', 'Baby It's Cold Outside'), followed by *Modern Sounds In Country And Western Music, Vol. 1* '62, his only no. 1 LP, incl. Don GIBSON's 'I Can't Stop Loving You', top of all three charts: country, soul, pop. (Vol. 2 no. 2 LP same year; *Ingredients In A Recipe For Soul* '63 also no. 2.) Eclectic material upset some critics, yet voted best male singer five times in a row from '61 by international jazz critics in *Downbeat* magazine. First Grammy '61. Formed own company Tangerine, '62, leased records to ABC, recorded Louis JORDAN, others; to Europe, packing huge sports stadium in Paris several nights at height of Algerian crisis; toured the world '64. Walked out of Atlanta gig because audience segregated; played first

ever integrated concert in Memphis municipal auditorium. Took time off '65-6, cured himself of long-term drug addiction; acting role in film made in Ireland, released '66, variously titled *Light Out Of Darkness*, *Ballad In Blue*, *Blues For Lovers*. Hits continued to alternate between straight soul numbers and others with slushy strings setting off blues-flecked vocals and piano. Top 10 entries in pop chart incl. 'You Don't Know Me' and 'You Are My Sunshine' '62, 'Take These Chains From My Heart' (Hank WILLIAMS song) and humorous 'Busted' '63, 'Crying Time' '66 (won two Grammies); 32 top 40 hits altogether '57-71, more than 50 R&B '51-71. LPs *My Kind Of Jazz* '70, *Jazz Number II* '73 on Tangerine label. Heavy tours continued; virtually annual visits to Japan in '70s; 12 countries in '75 plus annual USA tours; London jazz festival appearance taped for TV '83, etc. Among other albums, most out of print: 3 vols. of *The Ray Charles Story* on Atlantic, 2-disc *A Man And His Soul* on ABC (with photos; notes by Stanley Dance) are good compilations; *Soul Meeting* and *Soul Brothers* on Atlantic, both with Milt JACKSON; 2-disc *Ray Charles Live* on Atlantic charted '73: one record recorded at Newport Jazz Festival '58, the other a reissue of *Ray Charles In Person* '60 from Herndon Stadium, Atlanta, '59; *Porgy & Bess* '76 on RCA with Cleo LAINE; *True To Life* '77 on Atlantic. He still rocked with good pick-up bands on tours; *Friendship* '85 on Columbia was duets with 10 country music superstars; *From The Pages Of My Mind* '87 was described as 'commercial Nashville schlock' (*Cadence* magazine). Dance wrote: 'Charles sings from the shadow about the shadow with such compelling authority that everyone . . . can identify with him . . . On stage, he seems to face the realities of life, even to mock the shadow, with a spirit that inspires others to greater resolution.' His legend is secure.

CHARLY/AFFINITY UK record labels. Jean Luc Young (*b* '47, Strasbourg) began as concert promoter, worked for Barclay label, met Jean Karokos: they formed a chain of record shops (Richard Branson came over to look, later formed Virgin). They formed Byg label '67, then the only independent in France: licensed Savoy and built own catalogue of over 60 albums of free jazz, incl. Archie SHEPP, SUN RA, Anthony BRAXTON etc. (most now on Affinity); also founded monthly paper *Actuel*, trendy at the time and still running. Byg went broke '75, partly because of losing money on one of the biggest live festivals Europe ever saw. Young talked Shelby Singleton, owner of SUN Records vault, into switching rights from Phonogram to him, formed Charly in Paris '74, moved it to London '75, soon with Joop Visser as MD (used to work for EMI). Labels licensed incl. Jewel, Vee Jay, Gusto; Sun product incl. original LPs reissued, compilations incl. sumptuous boxes of Johnny CASH, Jerry Lee LEWIS (13-disc box has sold 13,000 copies), 9-disc box *The Blues Years 1950-56* with 44-page illustrated booklet. Other early reissues incl. GONG, YARDBIRDS. Joop formed Affinity '77 for jazz, began with the Byg records; Big Band, Bounce & Boogie series began '85 with reissue of classic MCA compilations of Jimmie LUNCEFORD, Chick WEBB, Count BASIE etc.; carried on with rarities such as Cootie WILLIAMS big band, 2-disc sets of Roy ELDRIDGE and Claude THORNHILL bands, latter with arr. by Gil EVANS; 8-disc Django REINHARDT set. Charly/Affinity catalogue incl. over 350 albums (Johnny ADAMS to ZYDECO, the ART ENSEMBLE to Lester YOUNG): some leasing from King (Earl BOSTIC, Bill DOGGETT), Bethlehem (Mel TORMÉ, Ruby BRAFF, Nina SIMONE), Capitol (Serge CHALOFF); rare stuff like the Flatlanders (*see* Butch HANCOCK), Hardrock Gunter; reissued Robert CRAY's first album, sold 25,000 the first month; albums by almost everybody who was anybody in country or urban blues, R&B, soul, jazz, hillbilly. Offshoot labels incl. Goldband, Decal, New Cross, New Cross Gospel, and budget lines Topline and Atlantis. First in UK with CDs of vintage material (e.g. Duke ELLINGTON from Bethlehem '56), absurdly cheap and generous CD samplers of blues and jazz. Young and Visser were among the first to perceive that all musics were becoming repertory and that as sales of adolescent pop went down, sales of quality reissues would go up. Competition Ace, Edsel/Demon in UK now have similar, smaller catalogues (Ace licensed FANTASY catalogue for the UK '87). Karokos has not been idle: formed Celluloid '76 in NYC, leasing Rough Trade from UK; published Bill LASWELL's music; formed offshoots incl. Moving Target, Mercenary, OAO (Fred Frith, Laswell, Billy Bang, Ronald Shannon Jackson's Pulse, John ZORN, Derek BAILEY, Daniel PONCE etc.).

CHARTS 'The charts' (lists of hit records) have been manipulated illegally, most famously at the time of the payola scandal in the USA late '50s, and a great many of the best records never appear in any charts anyway; yet as the decades go by the charts acquire charm of their own. Music industry weekly *Billboard* was founded in USA 1894, began publishing lists of sheet music hits, top vaudeville songs '13; most-played songs on network radio '34; record companies' lists of best-sellers '35; finally 'Best-Selling Retail Records' '40: changed to 'Top 100' '55, to 'Hot 100' '58; 'Bubbling Under' for singles no. 101-200. Album chart began '45; 'Best Selling Retail Country & Western Records' began '49, abbreviated to 'C&W' '56, changed to 'Hot Country Singles' '63. Top 10 'Harlem Hit Parade' began early '40s; changed to Top 15 'Race Records', then to 'Rhythm & Blues' '49, to 'Soul' '69, later to 'Black'. For 14 months '62 R&B chart was not published: black and white charts were so similar during golden age of soul that the separate chart was not needed. Recent issues of *Billboard* incl. eight album charts (Rock, Black, Jazz, Country, Classical, Hits of the World, Top Pop and Bubbling Under); 13 singles charts incl. three for Black, three for Country; Dance, Disco, Radio Action, Retail Action and so on; Adult Contemporary chart listed singles by Barbra STREISAND (whose first USA top 40 hit was in '64), CHICAGO ('70), and Culture Club ('83): it is not clear what is meant by 'adult'. Also five charts for videos and computer games. Joel Whitburn, record collector since early '50s, began publishing music industry reference books using *Billboard*'s charts '70: books now incl. *Top Pops 1955-1982, Top Pop Albums 1955-85*, others; annual *Music Yearbook* from '83 updates information. *Pop Memories 1890-1954* '86 collates sheet music sales and other lists, charts from *Variety* and other magazines (research by Steve Sullivan) to make a fascinating book, to be followed by *Top Black 1942-1986* and *Top Country 1944-1986* incl.

227

LPs; *Top Videocassettes 1979-1986*. Guinness books of *British Hit Singles, British Hit Albums* in UK are based on charts from *New Musical Express, Music Weekly*. (This encyclopedia quotes, pop, country, black lists, but ignores specialist charts.)

CHAS & DAVE UK trio: Charles Hodges, piano, vocals, guitars (fiddles a little) (*b* 28 Dec. '43, London); Dave Peacock, vocals, guitars (*b* 24 May '45, London); Mick Burt, drums (*b* 23 Aug. '38). Hodges had career in pre-BEATLES pop: playing piano at 18 as stand-in at pub rehearsal, Jerry Lee LEWIS walked in, said 'What the hell do you need me for when you've got him?' Worked with Joe MEEK, Ritchie BLACKMORE in The Outlaws, joined Cliff BENNETT's Rebel Rousers, with Peacock in short-lived band Black Claw '70. Then made 3 LPs with cult band Heads Hands & Feet '70-2; rejoined Peacock in Albert Lee band '75; meanwhile Burt had played in Rebel Rousers, gone back to plumbing: Chas and Dave decided to form group, asked Burt to join. Minor UK hit single 'Strummin' ' '78; then advertising agent heard them doing 'Gertcha' (Gotcha) in a pub, signed them for series of TV adverts for Courage beer: 'Gertcha' made UK no. 20 '79, became utility catchphrase. 'The Sideboard Song (Got My Beer In The Sideboard Here)' minor hit '79; 'Rabbit' also used in Courage advert, became no. 8 hit (cartoonish sendup of talking wives finally outraged feminists who wrote a song called 'Beer Belly'). Had perfected 'Rockney' (Burt's nickname, name of own label, of '78 LP incl. 'Strummin' '): hybrid of basic rock'n'roll, Cockney lyrics (also pioneered by Ian DURY). Wrote, prod. two singles for Tottenham Hotspur Football Club '81. Fine ballad 'Ain't No Pleasin' You' reached no. 2 '82: timeless appeal similar to that of 'You Don't Understand' ('28, recorded by James P. JOHNSON, Bessie SMITH). Albert Lee incl. on '79 cover of Lewis's 'Breathless'. LP list confusing: UK LPs recycled, reissued, retitled; depending on source first album '75 was called *Chas & Dave* or *One Fing And Anuvver*. Others incl. *Don't Give A Monkey's* '79; *Musn't Grumble* '81 incl. 'Lonnie D' (for DONEGAN), 'Don't Anyone Speak English?'; *Live At Abbey Road* also '81; *Gertcha* '83 is hits compilation on budget label;

Greatest Hits is another on different label; also *Chas'n'Dave's Knees Up* (50 singalong tunes and songbook), *Christmas Jamboree Bag* both '83; latter has become annual series. Lent by ATLANTIC in USA to producer Bob THIELE: he made his own LP as *Oily Rags* (Cockney rhyming slang: rags = fags = cigarettes; not allowed to be billed as Chas & Dave) with drummer Ian Wallace, Gerry Hogan on steel guitar; with Lee, Peter FRAMPTON etc. backed Teresa BREWER on *In London*; these now on Thiele's Signature label. Very popular live, TV act (Christmas Day special '82, series summer '83); opened own London pub '85 called Chas & Dave's – a Courage house, of course. Album *Jamboree No. 3* top 30 UK chart Dec. '85.

CHASE, Bill (*b* '34, Boston, Mass.; *d* 9 Aug.'74, Jackson, Minn.) Trumpet, leader. Studied at Berklee in Boston, infl. by faculty member, prominent local bandleader Herb Pomeroy (*b* 15 Apr. '30, Gloucester, Mass.). Attracted to jazz by playing of Maynard FERGUSON; joined his band late '50s, also with Stan KENTON, Woody HERMAN. Worked in Las Vegas, formed own nine-piece jazz-rock band Chase with four trumpets. Debut eponymous LP on Epic voted no. 1 by *Downbeat* readers; hits 'Get It On' (no. 24), 'Handbags And Gladrags' (no. 84), 'So Many People' (no. 81), all in '71. Next two LPs less successful (*Ennea* '72; *Pure Music* '74); split and re-formed with new lineup, but Chase and Wally Yohn (keyboards), John Emma (guitar), Walter Clark (drums) all killed in plane crash.

CHEAP TRICK USA rock band formed '72-4 by guitarist Rick Nielsen (*b* '46), bassist Tom Peterson (*b* '50), both from Rockford, Ill.; first played together in local band Fuse (eponymous LP on Epic '68), previously called Grim Reaper: incl. Craig Meyers, guitar; Joe Sundberg, vocals; Chip Greenman, drums (replaced by Brad Carlson). After short liaison with ex-Nazz vocalist Robert 'Stewkey' Antoni group split; Nielsen and Peterson worked in Europe. Back in Rockford later, Nielsen formed Cheap Trick with Carlson and vocalist Zeno; got Europe-based Peterson to join, claiming band were on the edge of stardom. Zeno fired '74, replaced with Robin Zander (*b* 23 Jan. '52, Loves Park, Ill.) with folk background. Toured midwest as support act; spotted by AEROSMITH prod. George Douglas, signed to Columbia; reinvented image: Carlson became Bun. E. Carlos; Petersson added extra 's' to name to enhance mystique (too many Americans called Peterson). *Cheap Trick* '77, prod. by Douglas, reflected energetic stage act; but next LP *In Color* six months later prod. by Tom Werman, aimed at radio, made USA top 40, as did Werman-prod. *Heaven Tonight* '78; and band had become superstars in Japan, where 10-date tour '78 greeted with adolescent hysteria captured on *Cheap Trick At Budokan* '79. Act unusual: diminutive, rubber-faced Nielsen in baseball cap bounced about stage with collection of guitars (sometimes several at once) while swarthy, bespectacled Carlos sweated behind kit, Zander grew into role of teen heart-throb alongside the almost-as-pretty Petersson. *Budokan* was imported and bootlegged, its possession conferring hipness; platinum when officially released, helped by teenpop no. 7 hit 'I Want You To Want Me'. Studio album *Dream Police* '79 held up by live LP's popularity, disappointed by comparison; after first LP had flopped owning to rough edges, fans wanted raunchy live sound instead of studio pop. Even so three top 40 singles resulted: 'Ain't That A Shame', 'Dream Police', 'Voices'. Nielsen's songs always infl. by first British Invasion (especially YARDBIRDS); he jumped at chance to have *All Shook Up* '80 prod. by BEATLE guru George MARTIN: predictably Fab Fourish result upset Petersson, who left to form group with wife, replaced by Pete Comita, then Jon Brant. Next album rejected by label; *One On One* '82 prod. by Roy Thomas Baker (QUEEN, CARS) was uninspired; on *Next Position Please* '83 mix of prod. by Todd RUNDGREN, Ian Taylor and band, material (incl. cover of Motors song 'Dancing The Night Away') betrayed road-weariness: fizz in Nielsen's songs had gone. *Standing On The Edge* '85 reunited them with Douglas and was partial return to form, moulding power pop with 'heavy metal disco' of ZZ TOP. Back on the road supporting REO SPEEDWAGON, band were hoping to repeat history, but *The Doctor* '86 was poorly received.

CHEATHAM, Doc (*b* Adolphus Anthony Cheatham, 13 June '05, Nashville, Tenn.) Trumpet; first-class lead player and soloist for more than 50 years. To Chicago playing cornet, reeds, mid-'20s, recorded with Ma RAINEY on soprano. With Wilbur DE PARIS '27-8, to Europe with Sam WOODING '28-9, with Cab CALLOWAY '33-9 with intervals; Teddy WILSON, Benny CARTER, Fletcher HENDERSON '39-41; Eddie HEYWOOD '43-5, also teaching NYC; Marcelino Guerra '48-50, Perez PRADO '51-2, other Latin bands; toured with Calloway summer '51, '52-5 mostly in Boston; regular work and records with de Paris through '50s; led own band at International on Broadway NYC '60-5; with Benny GOODMAN '66-7; has toured the world. Many records with Billie HOLIDAY, Heywood on Commodore, Count BASIE, Pee Wee RUSSELL, others; MACHITO on Roulette (LP *Kenya*), de Paris on Atlantic, Buck Clayton jam sessions '74 on Chiaroscuro. Own LPs incl. *Adolphus 'Doc' Cheatham* '72 on Jezebel, two LPs with rhythm section; *Good For What Ails Ya* '77 on Classic Jazz; albums on Canadian Sackville label '76: *Black Beauty* (salute to black songwriters), *Doc & Sammy*, both with Sammy Price (*b* 6 Oct. '08, Honey Grove, Texas: singer, blues and boogiewoogie pianist; house pianist at Decca '30s, made Texas Bluesicians records there early '40s, etc.). Very popular on USA festival circuit late '70s early '80s; LPs continue on Canadian Parkwood label: *It's A Good Life!* and *The Fabulous Doc Cheatham* '84; also *Echoes Of Harlem* '85 on Stash, sextet recorded at NYU; *Too Marvelous For Words* and *I've Got A Crush On You* on New York Jazz made '82 with octet incl. Milt HINTON, Dill Jones on piano, Howard Alden on guitar plus vocalists (latter LP also has duos with just Doc and guitar, with Doc vocalising). Appeared with old boss Calloway on UK TV '85: *The Cotton Club Comes To The Ritz*. Unusually for a brass player, he gets better as he gets older.

CHEATHAM, Jimmy & Jeannie Pianist/blues singer Jean Evans Cheatham, bass trombonist James Cheatham make timeless music: they met '56 on stage in Buffalo, NY, married '59; she sang in clubs, he sessioned on TV, Broadway; with Bill DIXON, Duke ELLINGTON, Lionel HAMP-

TON, Thad JONES, Ornette COLEMAN; mus. dir. for Chico HAMILTON. She began singing in church in Akron, Ohio, studied piano at age of 5; has accompanied Dinah WASHINGTON, Al HIBBLER, Jimmy WITHERSPOON, others. They went to U. of Wisconsin/Madison '72, taught in jazz programme; to West Coast, San Diego '78: he taught at U. of California, she was president of Lower California Jazz Society; they played clubs, organised weekly jam sessions as they've done wherever they were, now in the Bahia Hotel; she was seen in PBS TV's *Three Generations Of The Blues* '83 with Sippie WALLACE, Big Mama THORNTON. Long overdue record deal with Concord Jazz: *Sweet Baby Blue* '85 incl. 'Meet Me With Your Black Drawers On', featured sidemen like Red CALLENDER and guest Charles MCPHERSON, often seen at jam sessions, *Midnight Mama* '86 ('Down-the-middle piano, down-the-decades blues' – Leonard Feather) had guest Lockjaw DAVIS; *Homeward Bound* '87 incl. Callender, Jimmy NOONE Jr, Snooky Young on trumpet, others incl. Eddie 'Cleanhead' VINSON.

CHECKER, Chubby (*b* Ernest Evans, 3 Oct. '41, Philadelphia, Pa.) USA singer. Former chicken-plucker signed to Cameo-Parkway, new name (after Fats DOMINO) at suggestion of Dick CLARK's wife; of first four releases 'The Class' made top 40 '59; then Hank BALLARD didn't appear for recording session for Clark's American Bandstand TV show: Checker's hastily arranged cover of Ballard's 'The Twist' (backed by Bandstand resident group) shot to no. 1 '60, returned there late '61, launched series of dance fads. Checker had been third choice after Ballard, DANNY AND THE JUNIORS; energetic ebullience served him well: 20 top 40 hits '59-64 incl. Don Covay's 'Pony Time' (no. 1 '61), revival of Paul Williams' R&B hit 'The Hucklebuck' (no. 14), 'Let's Twist Again' (8), 'The Fly' (7), 'Limbo Rock' (2), 'Slow Twistin'' (duet with Dee Dee Sharp, no. 3). In UK 'Let's Twist Again' (a better song, easier to dance to) outsold the original; total of nine top 40 entries in UK incl. reissue of 'The Twist' and 'Again' back to back (no. 5 '75). Checker moved to Buddah '69, then Chalmac '71, dropping saxophone-led backing for 'progressive soul'; revival shows

incl. the film *Let The Good Times Roll* '73; yielded to the temptation of disco on MCA ('Running' made Billboard Hot 100 '82).

CHENIER, Clifton (*b* 25 June '25, Opelousas, La.; *d* 12 Dec. '87) Accordionist, vocalist in ZYDECO. Worked as farmhand, then as a truck driver in oil industry; given accordion and lessons by his father, performed at dances, etc. Sang in French patois, Creole and English; later described his music as 'simply the French two-step with new hinges so she can swing': this captures basically CAJUN structure and tradition, but by the time an Elko label talent scout discovered him he'd absorbed infl. from Amadé ARDOIN and Sidney Babineaux to Lowell FULSON and Clarence Garlow, and played the distinctly black zydeco variant, tinged with R&B. His first sides, 'Cliston Blues' and 'Louisiana Stomp', spelled not only a title wrong but his name as well: he was 'Cliston' Chenier. At times he concentrated on the R&B side; he tells the anecdote against himself of the time he played San Francisco's Avalon Ballroom at the height of the psychedelic era, backed by BLUE CHEER, an early heavy metal group: result was a debacle. Search for a wider audience also led to labelhopping: he recorded for Argo, Arhoolie (who also leased singles to Bayou), Crazy Cajun, Checker, Jin, Specialty, Maison de Soul and Zinn. Had lots of regional hits; 'Squeeze Box Boogie' was a '50s hit in Jamaica. He suffered from diabetes; a renal infection '79 led to amputation of part of his right foot; this slowed him down but he remained one of the most important in the genre, having popularised a music barely known beyond the Gulf of Mexico until the '60s. Noteworthy LPs incl. *Bon Ton Roulet* '66, *King Of The Bayou* '70, *Bogalusa Boogie* '75, compilation *Classic Clifton* '80 on Arhoolie; *Boogie & Zydeco* on Maison de Soul/Sonet; *Boogie In Black And White* on Jin with Rod Bernard (an R&B-flavoured excursion). He was nominated for Grammies in '79 and '86 (for *Live At The San Francisco Blues Festival*). Film *Hot Pepper* '73 made in Lake Charles and other towns by Les Blank for Flower Films incl. music, interview with his 108-year-old grandmother, as well as lots of pretty girls and kids.

CHERRY, Don (*b* 11 Jan. '24, Dallas, Texas) Pop singer, golfer. Allegedly took time off from tournament to make records early '50s, at first on Decca; 'Band Of Gold' big hit '55 (no. 4 USA, no. 6 UK early '56), was also first Columbia arrangement by Ray CONNIFF. Other USA top 40 hits: 'Wild Cherry', 'Ghost Town', both '56. Was still recording 10 years later on Monument label, with more time for golf.

CHERRY, Don (*b* 18 Nov. '36, Oklahoma City, Okla.) Trumpet, cornet, other instruments; composer. Came to prominence in Ornette COLEMAN's free jazz quartet, playing small 'pocket' trumpet; also on John COLTRANE quartet LP *The Avant-Garde* '60. Played early '60s with Steve LACY, Sonny ROLLINS; founder-member of New York Contemporary Five '63-4 with Archie SHEPP, John TCHICAI; spent much time in Europe as prominent exponent of improvised contemporary music. Admirer of Bix BEIDERBECKE, played cornet from c. '69; also flutes, bells, gamelon, etc. Own records began '61; untitled originals recorded by trio with Henry Grimes, bass (*b* '35, Philadelphia), Blackwell not then released by Atlantic. Quintet with Gato BARBIERI made *Togetherness* '65 in Paris, now on Inner City; then Blue Note LPs '65-6: *Complete Communion*, quartet with Barbieri, Grimes, Blackwell; *Symphony For Improvisors* added Pharoah SANDERS, two more; *Brooklyn Is Now* is quartet with Sanders, Grimes, Blackwell. *Eternal Rhythm* '69 made in Berlin by octet with Cherry on cornet, also playing three flutes, other instruments; incl. Albert MANGELSDORFF, Arild ANDERSEN, Sonny Sharrock. *Mu First Part, Second Part* '69, duo with Blackwell, issued as set on French Actuel, separate LPs on Affinity UK. Trio set *Live In Ankara* '69 made at US Embassy; *Human Music* '69-70 solo LP made at Dartmouth College; trio set *Don Cherry* made in Paris '71; *The Creator Has A Master Plan* '71 in Sweden by Organic Music Society, 'visitors and friends', some tracks incl. Youth Orchestra. Other LPs mostly on Japanese or European labels incl. trio *Orient* '71; *Don Cherry And The New Eternal Rhythm Orchestra* '71, made at a German festival; *Organic Music* '72, Copenhagen, Stockholm; *Relativity Suite* '73 on JCOA label NYC, with large group incl.

Carla BLEY, Frank LOWE, Haden, Blackwell; *Eternal Now* '73, Stockholm, quintet with harmonium, bells, cymbals, gongs; *Brown Rice* '75 on A&M with Lowe, Haden, Billy HIGGINS, others; *Hear And Now* on Atlantic '76; *The Journey* '77 on Chiaroscuro incl. Hamiet BLUIETT, Dollar Brand, others. *Music/Sangam* '78 is duo with Latif Khan, tabla; *El Corazon* '82 with Blackwell, both made in Europe. Formed quartet Old And New Dreams '78 with Charlie HADEN, Ed BLACKWELL, Dewey REDMAN celebrating original Coleman groups; LPs under group's name: *Old And New Dreams*, *Playing*. Also three ECM LPs '80-2 by Codona, trio with Collin Walcott (*b* 24 Apr. '45, NYC), Nana Vasconcelos playing Eastern instruments.

CHESS USA blues/R&B/jazz label formed by Leonard and Phil Chess, immigrants from Poland who settled in Chicago '28. In '40s they owned taverns on Southside of Chicago; the Mocambo booked artists such as Billy ECKSTINE; seeing lack of local recording facilities, bought into Aristocrat label '47; Muddy WATERS was one of the first to record. Took over label and changed name to Chess '50, first single on new label by Gene AMMONS, soon followed by Howlin' WOLF, Elmore JAMES, Rosco Gordon, Willie DIXON (who was also prod., arr., session bassist; Leonard called him 'my right arm'). Hired A&R man Ralph BASS away from King. Checker subsidiary '53 introduced LITTLE WALTER, LITTLE MILTON, Lowell FULSON, FLAMINGOS. Hung microphone in toilet for echo chamber; sold records out of car boot; leased product from Sun in Memphis (e.g. Jackie BRENSTON's 'Rocket 88'); first recorded Wolf on field trip in Arkansas, with Ike TURNER on piano, James COTTON on blues harp. Greatest years were mid-'50s, when R&B charts were dominated by Muddy, Wolf, Walter, Willie MABON, Jimmy Rogers, the Moonglows; Chuck BERRY on Chess, Bo DIDDLEY and Dale HAWKINS on Checker crossed to pop chart, made label world famous. Also had subsidiary Argo with Ramsey LEWIS trio, Ahmad JAMAL, Wes MONTGOMERY, Ray BRYANT; rock'n'roll, soul markets invaded with Dells, Etta JAMES, Monotones, Clarence 'Frogman' HENRY, others. By late '50s Chess had dropped blues acts except for the biggest (Muddy, Wolf, Walter, Sonny Boy WILLIAMSON, Otis RUSH, Buddy GUY), entered '60s with Sugar Pie Desanto, Koko TAYLOR, Fontella BASS, others. Owned radio stations in Chicago, Milwaukee. Leonard Chess died '69; labels sold to GRT, USA's second-biggest tape company; Leonard's son Marshall stayed on for a while. Product finally owned by MCA; stop-and-start reissue series continue with new one '86.

CHEVALIER, Maurice (*b* 12 Sep. 1888, Menilmontant nr Paris; *d* there 1 Jan. '72) Actor/singer. Café performer early 1900s; dance team with Mistinguette at Folies Bergère '09-13; revue entertainer after WWI. Introduced first of songs identified with him '25: 'Valentine', about charms of a mistress, did not translate well from French. Had made several silent films by this time; went to Hollywood '28, signed Paramount contract for talking pictures. *Innocents Of Paris* '29 incl. 'Louise'; between films he appeared on stage in New York, on one occasion accompanied by Duke ELLINGTON's band. Ernst Lubitsch's *The Love Parade* '29 confirmed stardom; Rouben Mamoulian's *Love Me Tonight* had songs by RODGERS & HART incl. 'Mimi', also 'Isn't It Romantic' in an innovative opening scene: lyrics were so tied to action that Hart rewrote them for song's general release. Chevalier returned to Europe, reconquered Paris on the stage '35, now world-famous. Reluctant during WWII German occupation to perform in Paris; when invited to Germany '41 complied on condition that 10 French prisoners were released (later accused but cleared of collaboration). Developed one-man show late '40s; took it to London and USA. Lived quietly in France early '50s, then back to USA for *Love In The Afternoon* '57, Billy Wilder film with no songs. Next LERNER & LOEWE score *Gigi* '58 with classics 'Thank Heaven For Little Girls' and 'I Remember It Well' (with Hermione Gingold): Oscar that year for 'contributions to the world of entertainment for more than half a century'. *Can Can* followed, with Frank SINATRA and Louis Jourdan '60; *Fanny* '61 was his last characteristic role, though several more films raised total to 44. Boulevardier identity and trademark straw boater are imperishable; he made countless records, compilations still being issued.

CHIC USA disco band formed '77 by Bernard Edwards (*b* 31 Oct. '52, Greenville, N.C.), bass, Nile Rodgers (*b* 19 Sep. '52, NYC). Met in local post office NYC, formed Big Apple Band with ex-Patti LABELLE drummer Tony Thompson, after playing in countless small-time bands: Rodgers had run gamut from folk (New World Rising) to punk (Allah and the Knife-Wielding Punks) as well as Apollo house band. Big Apple briefly backed New York City, vocal group prod. by Thom BELL (e.g. '73 hit 'I'm Doing Fine Now'), but success began when DJ Rob Drake played demos in Night Owl Club, Atlantic picked up on audience reaction. Renamed Chic because Walter Murphy & The Big Apple Band had no. 1 hit '76 (Beethoven disco-style from *Saturday Night Fever* soundtrack); recruited Norma Jean Wright, Alfa Anderson (*b* 7 Sep. '46, Augusta, Ga.: ex-Brown Sugar; sang in *The Wiz* soundtrack) to sing. First single 'Dance Dance Dance' (on LP *Chic* '77) was no. 6 both USA/UK, placed band in vanguard of disco. Wright quit for solo career, replaced by Luci Martin (*b* 10 Jan. '55, NYC; toured with *Hair*, *Jesus Christ Superstar*). Good singers were icing on firm musical cake: upfront pulsing bass of Edwards (most imitated black bassist since Family Stone's Larry Graham) with scratchy, compulsive rhythm guitar of Rodgers, metronomic yet powerful beat from human drum machine Thompson, and strings. Formula brought hit after hit: 'Everybody Dance' (no. 38 USA/9 UK), 'Le Freak' (no. 1 USA/7 UK, 5 million sold, both '78), 'I Want Your Love' (no. 7 USA/4 UK), anthemic 'Good Times' (no. 1 USA/5 UK, both '79). Second and third albums *C'est Chic* '78, *Risqué* '79 both platinum, unusual for disco LPs; compilation *Greatest Hits* '79 two years after formation emphasised whirlwind success: but gradually became faceless as most disco acts, as Rodgers and Thompson responded to demand for their services playing/prod. for others, e.g. on Diana ROSS's *Diana* '80, also for Sheila B Devotion (European dance production), Debbie Harry from BLONDIE, Sister Sledge. Soundtrack *Soup For One* '82 didn't gel; projected LPs with Johnny MATHIS, Aretha FRANKLIN failed to happen; Chic LPs *Real People* '80, *Take It Off* '81 (with horns replacing strings), *Tongue In Chic* '82 confirmed fall from grace; Rodgers and Edwards split up '83. Solo LPs *Glad To Be Here* (Edwards), *In The Land Of The Good Groove* (Rodgers) were mediocre; 'comeback' Chic LP *Believer* late '83 showed promise, but when original Chic fans formed own bands (DURAN DURAN, Kim Wilde, THOMPSON TWINS, MADONNA) their prominence returned: Rodgers prod./remixed those named, Edwards prod. Duran spin-off Power Station's '85 LP with Thompson as drummer, Rodgers prod. David BOWIE's *Let's Dance* '83, again with Thompson drumming. In '85 Thompson played with re-formed LED ZEPPELIN on Live Aid show; Rodgers prod. Mick Jagger's solo LP *She's The Boss*. WHAM! invariably cover 'Good Times' on stage (*the* hedonistic disco anthem), Sugarhill Gang used it as basis for 'Rapper's Delight', QUEEN rewrote it for 'Another One Bites The Dust': Chic's infl. on both black and white music may be as great as that of Chuck BERRY on ROLL-ING STONES; best-selling act ever on Atlantic.

CHICAGO USA jazz-rock band formed Chicago '67 by Terry Kath (*b* 31 Jan. '46; *d* 23 Jan. '78, L.A.), guitar; Peter Cetera (*b* 13 Sep. '44), bass; Robert Lamm (*b* 13 Oct. '44, Brooklyn), keyboards; Danny Seraphine (*b* 28 Aug. '48), drums; James Pankow (*b* 20 Aug. '47) and Lee Loughnane (*b* 21 Oct. '46), brass; Walt Parazaider (*b* 14 Mar. '45), reeds. All except Lamm from city that gave them their name; known as Chicago Transit Authority until '70, originally the Big Thing: Mafia-inspired name dropped at suggestion of prod. James William Guercio (*b* '45; played bass in Dick CLARK road shows, later with BEACH BOYS; prod. and managed them, prod. BLOOD, SWEAT & TEARS; prod. and dir. film *Elektra Glide In Blue* '73 which cast members of Chicago; opened Caribou Ranch studios, recorded Elton JOHN there '74, etc. etc.) who'd studied music at De Paul U. with Pankow, Seraphine, Parazaider, Loughnane; quartet picked up Lamm from cabaret circuit, Cetera joining '66 and Kath '67. Debut *Chicago Transit Authority* '68 2-disc set, like BS&T

mixing horns with rock, though maintaining rockier sound with cohesive rhythm section better able to bear weight of horns. Side 4 of album began with chants of demos from '68 Democratic convention in city, cementing link with Chicago, counterculture. First Columbia act certified platinum (selling a million albums); had top 10 USA singles 'Does Anybody Really Know What Time It Is?', strong cover of Spencer DAVIS Group's 'I'm A Man' '70. *Chicago II, III* '70-1 both 2-discs; *Live At Carnegie Hall* a triple. Rot set in: muscular white soul of first sets became limp-wristed: not surprising at rate of prod., effectively 10 albums in three years. First UK hits '70: 'I'm A Man', '25 or 6 to 4' both top 10; last UK hits for six years, but top 10 hits in USA continued through '77. Lyricist Lamm hit at doubters with 'Critics' Choice' from '73's *Chicago IV*; made solo *Skinny Boy* '74. Personnel changes rare as musical surprises: Brazilian percussionist Laudir De Oliveira added '74; Kath died in firearms accident, replaced by Donnie Dacus (ex-Steve Stills), in turn replaced by Chris Pinnick '79; Bill Champlin additional guitarist/keyboardist from '81. Split with Guercio '77; self-prod. until link with David Foster, when Columbia dropped them and they moved to Full Moon label: second flush of success '76 with lush ballad, no. 1 UK/USA 'If You Leave Me Now'; following this direction had transatlantic top tens 'Hard To Say I'm Sorry' '82 (from film *Summer Lovers*), 'Hard Habit To Break' '84; also USA 'You're The Inspiration' '84: altogether 33 singles in Hot 100 '69-84, 26 in top 40. Latterly have sounded much like former Foster protégés HALL & OATES. Cetera released solo *Full Moon* '81; left band '85 to write with Foster for Julio IGLESIAS, film *Rocky IV*; his vocal interplay with Lamm had become highlight, but with *Chicago 17* '84, *18* '86 they seem likely to continue with ballads. Two *Greatest Hits* sets on Columbia/CBS chart their evolution from anti-establishment to MOR.

CHICKEN SHACK UK blues band, formed Birmingham '65: Stan Webb, vocals, guitar; Christine Perfect, vocals, piano; Andy Sylvester, bass; Dave Bidwell, drums. Along with CREAM, John MAYALL, FLEETWOOD MAC, unearthed obscure USA blues, left room for guitar solos. Among groups parodied by BONZO DOG BAND for earnest white approach to ethnic black music. Considerable success with Etta JAMES's 'I'd Rather Go Blind' (no. 14 UK '69) largely to Perfect's singing; debut LP *40 Blue Fingers, Freshly Packed & Ready To Serve* '68 well received; Perfect again singled out, winning *Melody Maker* poll as Best British Female Singer. Webb was focal point of live act; extended solos using 200 feet of guitar lead were legendary. Perfect married Fleetwood Mac's bassist John McVie by late '69; with him reconstituted that group for its greatest success mid-'70s; Webb persevered. LPs *OK, Ken?* and *100 Ton Chicken* '69, *Accept* '70 consolidated reputation, but band split, re-formed; Webb briefly joined SAVOY BROWN, had band Broken Glass; in '85 Stan Webb's Chicken Shack were regulars on London pub-rock scene, still more popular in Europe. Other LPs incl. *Imagination Lady, Unlucky Boy, Goodbye* '72-4, *Chicken Shack* '79, *Roadies Concerto* '81; compilation with Perfect *In The Can* '80.

CHIEFTAINS One of the most infl. and long-lived Irish folk bands, spearheading a revival of Irish trad. music and remaining cultural ambassadors for over 20 years. Original lineup: Paddy Moloney, uillean pipes, tin whistle; Michael Tubridy, tin whistle, concertina, flute; Seán Potts, tin whistle; Martin Fay, fiddle; David Fallon, bodhrán. First LP *Chieftains (1)* '64 on Claddagh Records, followed by *Chieftains 2* '69, *3* '71; by *4* '73 they consisted of Moloney, Tubridy, Potts, Fay and Pendar Mercier on bodhrán and bones, 'with Derek Bell' on harp, oboe and tionpán, and had actor/comedian Peter Sellers writing their sleeve notes. They made *5* '75, *Bonaparte's Retreat* '76, *Live* '77, *7* '78, *Boil The Breakfast Early* '80, *10* '81, all Claddagh (some were also issued on Island and on Columbia in USA). Bell became a leading light in the band, with extrovert stage antics, patter as well as virtuosity; his solo projects incl. *Derek Bell Plays With Himself*. Film and TV work incl. Zoetrope Studios' *The Grey Fox* '83 (contribution billed as 'traditional Irish music composed and played by the Chieftains'), Stanley Kubrick's *Barry Lyndon*, RTE docudrama *The Year Of The French* '82, National Geographic TV special *The*

Ballad Of The Irish Horse '85 (LP on Shanachie). Among first Western acts to appear in China early '80s (*Live In China*); had one of the largest audiences in history when the Pope visited Phoenix Park '79. Sessioned on various projects incl. with Art GARFUNKEL, Van MORRISON, Gary MOORE, and with flautist James Galway (*In Ireland* '87, joint billing on RCA); also their own *Celtic Wedding* '87 on RCA.

CHIFFONS, The USA vocal group; quintessential '60s 'girl group'. Lineup: lead singer Judy Craig, Barbara Lee, Sylvia Peterson, Patricia Bennett, all *b* '46-7. Like others in the genre an outlet for creative writer/prod. team, in this case doo-wop group the Tokens. Chiffons had minor hit 'Tonight's The Night' '60, then no. 1 '63 both R&B and pop chart with 'He's So Fine'. Other 'fine' hits 'One Fine Day' (no. 5), 'A Love So Fine' (no. 40); then 'I Have A Boyfriend' (no. 36) (also had minor hits as the Four Pennies with 'My Block', 'When The Boy's Happy The Girl's Happy Too'), all '63: then minor hits. 'Nobody Knows What's Goin' On (In My Mind Except Me)' '65 (no. 49) was almost psychedelic; one more top 10 hit '66 with classic 'Sweet Talkin' Guy'. Interest rekindled '71 with litigation over Paul McCARTNEY hit 'My Sweet Lord' (tune similar to 'He's So Fine'); 'Sweet Talkin' Guy' reissued UK '72; surprise no. 4 hit was their biggest UK entry.

CHILD, Francis James (*b* 1 Feb. 1825, Boston, Mass.; *d* there 16 Sep. 1896) Ballad collector, scholar. Son of a sail-maker; ability recognised early: received BA at Harvard '46, became lecturer, then professor; at Harvard all his life except two-year leave of absence to Europe; received D. Phil. from Göttingen '54 despite irregularities in studies, also higher degrees from Harvard '84, Columbia '87. Published *Four Old Plays* 1848; general editor of 150-vol. series *British Poets* from 1853, *Poetical Works Of Edmund Spenser* 1855, paper *Observations On The Language Of Chaucer's Canterbury Tales*; but best known for 10-part (5 vols.) *English And Scottish Popular Ballads* 1882, codifying tales, texts of 305 songs, recovering fragments, comparing variants: work still mined today by folksingers, so highly regarded that ballads are referred to by numbers he gave them. He collected more verses of 'Greensleeves' than anyone wants to sing, as Pete SEEGER humorously pointed out at WEAVERS concerts; Joan BAEZ incl. Child ballads in her first several albums. Bertrand Harris Bronson published *Tunes Of The Child Ballads* (4 vols., 1959).

CHILDRE, Lew (*b* 1 Nov. '01, Opp, Ala.; *d* 3 Dec. '61) Long time Grand Ole Opry star and radio personality. Began in vaudeville; joined Opry '45, working with STRINGBEAN till '48; featured on Red FOLEY TV show '55-9. Billed as The Boy From Alabama, with relaxed, down-home style comedy, picking, singing. Gave comic advice in 'Doctor Lew' routine; performed American standards like 'Alabamy Bound'. LP *Old Time Get Together With Lew Childre* '58 on Starday.

CHI-LITES, The USA soul vocal group with 21 Hot 100 entries USA '69-75. Formed '61 Chicago with Marshall Thompson, baritone and leader; Robert Lester, tenor; Creadel Jones, bass; had regional hit 'Love Bandit' on Daran label; then taxi-driver Eugene Record joined as lead tenor and they signed with Carl Davis, vice-pres. of Brunswick label: first release 'Give It Away' '69 was no. 10 soul, 88 pop; in black power era '(For God's Sake) Give More Power To The People' became first pop top 40 USA/UK; more MOR 'Have You Seen Her' '72 became no. 1 soul, 3 pop USA/UK (co-written by Record and labelmate Barbara Acklin, whose own big hit was 'Love Makes A Woman', no. 3 soul, 15 pop '68). Record's 'Oh Girl' no. 1 soul/pop USA, no. 14 UK (also '72: back-to-back reissue '75 made no. 5 UK). No more top 10 pop hits USA, but 'Homely Girl' and 'Too Good To Be Forgotten' made it in UK '74. Jones and Record left '75, replaced by David Scott and Danny Johnson; Record went solo without much success, was head of A&R at Brunswick; group occasionally reached USA soul chart, then faded.

CHILLI WILLI and the RED HOT PEPPERS UK pub-rock group formed '72 by USA expat Phil Lithman (vocals, guitar) and Martin Stone (guitar). Met early '60s in Junior's Blues Band; Lithman's roots in country music and bluegrass, while Stone

worked with Rockhouse Band '64, Stones Masonry (two tracks on Immediate label sampler), Savoy Brown, Mighty Baby and Uncle Dog; together again to make LP *Kings Of Robot Rhythm* '72 for shortlived Revelation label: backing incl. Bob Andrews, Billy Rankin and Nick LOWE from BRINSLEY SCHWARZ. Then formed Chilli, recruiting Paul 'Dice Man' Bailey, banjo, guitar, sax; Paul Riley, bass; Pete Thomas, drums. Soon became busy outfit, playing Lithman's cheery, undemanding country rock. Made *Bongos Over Balham* '74 for Mooncrest, whose demise together with LP's poor sales made instant collector's item; band settled for status as stalwart pub-rockers, like Ducks Deluxe, Brinsley, etc. filling small venues regularly. Manager Jake Riviera (later founder of Stiff label with Dave Robinson) organised '75 package tour with Kokomo, DR FEELGOOD; latter band broke through to national fame but Willies music seemed derivative (resembling that of COMMANDER CODY, Flying Burrito Brothers), lacked visual appeal of Feelgood's Wilko Johnson as stage act. Split up '75: Stone continued nomadic career, joining Pink Fairies, having old Stones Masonry track ('Jump For Joy') on Stiff sampler *A Bunch Of Stiffs* '77; back in USA Lithman emerged '80s as Snakefinger on the Residents' Ralph label with experimental electronic music; Riley sessioned with Dave EDMUNDS, Kirsty MacColl, etc.; Riley, Bailey played on early Graham PARKER demos. After two-year USA exile with folk-rocker John STEWART, Pete Thomas rescued by Riviera to join Elvis COSTELLO's Attractions. Chilli's records now sought after because of posthumous notoriety as part of scene that threw up Punk/New Wave: at the time you couldn't give them away.

CHILTON, John (*b* 16 July '32, London) UK trumpeter, bandleader, composer, arranger, author. Played with Bruce Turner's Jump Band '50s, led the Swing Kings '60s (backed visiting Americans, e.g. Charlie SHAVERS), led his Feetwarmers backing George MELLY from '70s: several albums with Melly, many successful appearances incl. TV. Not only a fine trumpet (and flugelhorn) player and bandleader, an important jazz journalist: he had operated a bookshop in London for jazz literature; published first book *Louis* '71 (with Max Jones), now superseded by James Lincoln Collier's biography of Louis ARMSTRONG, but still a good read; the *Who's Who Of Jazz* '72 (fifth edition '85), with more than 400 entries for jazz musicians and singers born before 1920, accurate and invaluable; *Billie's Blues* '75, still the best book on Billie HOLIDAY; *McKinney's Music* '78, a short, illustrated history/discography of McKINNEY'S COTTON PICKERS; *A Jazz Nursery* '80, an illustrated account of the Jenkins Orphanage Band (formed Charleston, S.C. by Rev. Daniel Jenkins, toured England 1895); *Stomp Off Let's Go!* '83, the definitive story of the Bob CROSBY band; and the definitive biography *Sidney Bechet: The Wizard of Jazz* '87.

CHINN & CHAPMAN (Michael Chapman, *b* 15 Apr. '47, Queensland, Australia; Nicky Chinn, *b* 16 May '45, London) Songwriting duo. Met in London '70 as struggling individuals; first collaborative hit 'Funny, Funny' for the SWEET (UK no. 13 '71). Working with Mickie MOST became most successful team in pre-punk '70s UK pop. No. 1 hit 'Blockbuster' for Sweet, three no. 2 hits and many top tens. Perhaps biggest success was with Mud; capitalising on singer Les Gray's penchant for imitating Elvis they had three no. 1 hits: 'Tiger Feet', 'Lonely This Christmas', *a cappella* version of Buddy HOLLY's 'Oh Boy' '74-5; other hits were 'Dyna-Mite', 'The Cat Crept In'. At the same time scored with Suzi QUATRO: two no. 1 hits with 'Can The Can', 'Devil Gate Drive'; other top tens 'Daytona Demon', '48 Crash', 'The Wild One' '73-5. Last fling with SMOKIE: five top 10 hits '75-8 incl. 'Living Right Next Door To Alice', 'If You Think You Know How To Love Me'. Teeny-pop audience waned as punk closed in; formed own Dreamland label, but it failed. Often silly bubblegum lyrics criticised, but none had a better grasp of the genre: by the end of success they were compared to LEIBER & STOLLER. Chapman moved to USA, prod. hit LPs for BLONDIE (*Parallel Lines* '78, incl. worldwide hit 'Heart Of Glass'; *Eat To The Beat* '79; *Autoamerican* '80); also prod. Pat BENATAR, Tanya Tucker, The KNACK ('My Sharona' '79); debut solo LP for ABBA's Agnetha

Faltskog '83; Patti SMITH, Divinyls, more Knack, etc.

CHISHOLM, George (*b* 29 Mar. '15, Glasgow) UK trombonist. Played in ballrooms, cafés in Scotland; first broadcast c.'32; to London '36; jammed in Kingly Street (then jazz centre) with visiting Americans Benny CARTER, Coleman HAWKINS; asked by Carter to join him on record dates in Holland. Played with UK bands incl. AMBROSE '37-9, recorded with Fats WALLER at Abbey Road EMI studios '39; then Squadronaires RAF dance band '39-50, BBC Showband '50-5; with Louis ARMSTRONG, UK bassist Lennie Bush (*b* 6 June '27, London) at Royal Festival Hall concert for Hungarian relief '58. With top brass bands (Yorkshire Imperial, Grimethorpe, album with Royal Doulton); attended several Dick Gibson annual jazz parties in Colorado since '80. Has toured, made album '81 as *George Chisholm/Keith Smith And Hefty Jazz*. One of the best UK jazz musicians, has made many radio, TV broadcasts, but lately more comedy than music.

CHITTISON, Herman (*b* '09, Flemingsburg, Kentucky; *d* 8 Mar. '67, Cleveland, Ohio) Jazz pianist. Infl. by Art TATUM; harmonically antecedent of Bill EVANS. Worked as accompanist; freelance records for Clarence WILLIAMS; to Europe '34; tracks recorded in Paris '39 issued on EMI anthology *Jazz Piano In Paris*; went to Egypt '38, worked there with Bill COLEMAN in Harlem Rhythmakers; back to USA '40, formed trio, popular in clubs. Played pianist for seven years on weekly CBS radio series *Casey, Crime Photographer*; own LPs '62,4 on Rivoli label; also with Jack TEAGARDEN on LP *Boning Up On Bones*.

CHOATES, Harry (*b* 26 Feb. '22, Rayne, La.; *d* 17 July '51, Austin, Texas) CAJUN multi-instrumentalist (mainly fiddle), vocalist, bandleader. Had the biggest-ever Cajun hit 'Jole Blon' '46: covered many times since, the song had its roots in Joe Falcon's 'Ma Blonde est Partie' and Leo SOILEAU's 'Jole Blonde'; so great was Choates' success that the Houston-based Gold Star label had to lease the record to Modern in L.A., but his rights to it reportedly went for $50 and a bottle of whiskey. He tried to repeat its success ('Jole Blon's Gone' a fairly transparent attempt), but his unprecedented musical synthesis far outweighed the hit that dogged his career: his jazzier style blended Cajun with Western swing and popular music, infl. musicians such as Doug KERSHAW and Dewey BALFA, who said, 'He had an upbeat, very uptempo drive that affected a lot of us fiddlers.' Alcoholism and a dissolute lifestyle took their toll; he died in jail awaiting a court hearing for 'contempt of court in a wife and child desertion case', as the *Austin American* reported, a sad end for a performer who did so much to popularise the genre. Ironically his French was weak. Recorded for Allied, Cajun Classics, D, De Luxe, Hummingbird, Macy's and O.T. LPs incl. *Jole Blon* on D, *The Fiddle King Of Cajun Swing* on Arhoolie.

CHOCOLATE WATCH BAND USA psychedelic band formed '65. Lineup: Dave Aguilar, vocals; Sean Tolby, Mark Loomis, Danny Phay, Gary Andrijasevich. Cult act whose records became collector's items late '70s-80s. Signed to Tower label '66; split '68. Rarely recorded original material; 'Let's Talk About Girls' written by Manny Freiser of Tongues of Truth, later incl. in *Nuggets* LP collection of psychedelia. Covered Bob DYLAN's 'Baby Blue'; several songs written by prod. Ed Cobb (former member of the FOUR PREPS); appeared with labelmates Standells in cult film *Riot On Sunset Strip* '66. Aguilar became professor of astronomy. Compilation LPs on Rhino (USA), Ace (UK).

CHORDETTES Barbershop-harmony female vocal quartet, formed '49 Sheboygan, Wisconsin; folk-oriented at first, turned sweet sound into string of hits: Dorothy Schwartz, Jinny Osborn, Janet Ertel, Carol Bushman; Schwartz replaced by Lynn Evans '52, Osborn by Margie Needham '53; Nancy Overton was a later member. Sang locally; won Arthur GODFREY Talent Scout show, became regulars on programme and signed to Archie BLEYER's Cadence label '54, first hit 'Mr Sandman', no. 1 for several weeks. Accurate harmony brought them 13 Hot 100 entries '54-61; other top 20s incl. 'Eddie My Love' (also hit for Fontane Sisters, Teen Queens), 'Born To Be With You', 'Lay Down Your Arms' (covered in UK by Anne

SHELTON), all '56; 'Just Between You And Me' '57, 'Lollipop' (by Mudlarks in UK) and 'Zorro' '58, 'Never On Sunday' '61. Compilation LP on Ace (UK), Barnaby (USA) '83.

CHORDS, The USA doo-wop vocal group formed c.'53 NYC. Lineup: Carl Feaster, Claude Feaster, James Keyes, Floyd McRae, James Edwards. One chart success started an era: 'Sh-Boom' recorded May '54 for Cat (subsidiary of Atlantic) was charming, typical product of genre, reached no. 3 R&B chart, no. 9 pop, but was covered by Canadians the CREW-CUTS, whose record made no. 1 pop and finished as one of the top 5 of the year, began long series of white covers of better black originals (*see* ROCK'N' ROLL). Chords never matched first success. Lead singer Carl died of cancer 23 Jan. '81.

CHRISTIAN, Charlie (*b* 29 July '16, Dallas, Texas; *d* 2 Mar. '42). Electric guitar pioneer; jazz giant before early death from TB. Father was blind guitarist, singer; began on trumpet, guitar from age 12, also bass and piano; toured with Alphonso Trent c.'38. Noticed by Teddy WILSON, Mary Lou WILLIAMS, others; 'discovered' by John HAMMOND; joined Benny GOODMAN Sep. '39, who was convinced when Christian was sneaked on to the stand at a gig; played mostly in sextet but also in big band. One of the first to realise the potential of amplified guitar as a different instrument: capable of sustained notes and being heard as solo instrument in a group (though Eddie DURHAM also made modern sounds, e.g. on Commodore, '38); playing was also BOP inflected: played at Minton's, where jazz was changing; relied overmuch on a few favourite riffing figures, but shared composer credit on Goodman's 'Solo Flight', 'Seven Come Eleven', 'Air Mail Special'; might have become even greater soloist had he lived longer. Almost all his recordings, mostly with Goodman sextets incl. Count BASIE, Lionel HAMPTON, Cootie WILLIAMS, Georgie AULD etc., on 2-disc CBS *Solo Flight: The Genius Of Charlie Christian*: incl. warm-up jams ('Blues In C', 'Waitin' For Benny') because NYC CBS studio recorded everything on 16″ acetates. An informal recording from Minton's also exists, and a '41 Blue Note date with The Edmond

HALL Quartet (incl. 'Profoundly Blue') on acoustic guitar.

CHRISTIE, Lou (*b* Lugee Sacco, 19 Feb. '43, Penn.) US pop singer. High-pitched style recalled Del SHANNON, Frankie Valli. Sang back-up sessions NYC; then had '63 (pre-BEATLE) hits 'The Gypsy Cried', 'Two Faces Have I'; then smash with falsetto 'Lightnin' Strikes' (no. 1 USA, no. 11 UK '66). Follow-ups (e.g. 'Rhapsody In The Rain') less successful until 'I'm Gonna Make You Mine' (no. 16 US, no. 2 UK '69) appeared on Buddah, by then premier USA bubblegum label. Worked revival and cabaret circuits singing hits compiled on LP *This Is Lou Christie*, '69.

CHRISTY, June (*b* Shirley Luster, 20 Nov. '25, Springfield, Ill.) Jazz singer, popular and infl. in '40s-50s. Worked as Sharon Leslie in early days. With local bands '38, then Chicago; joined Stan KENTON '45 replacing Anita O'DAY, who she sounded like until she developed more personal style; had hits with Kenton 'Tampico' (no. 4 '45), 'Shoo-Fly Pie' (no. 8 '46), 'How High The Moon' (no. 27 '48). Also known for 'Across The Alley From The Alamo', 'Lonely Woman', 'He Was A Good Man', etc. Won *Downbeat*, *Metronome* polls late '40s (LP later issued on CBS Harmony label: *Nat Meets June With Metronome All Stars*). Married Kenton's tenor soloist Bob COOPER '46; when Kenton disbanded '49 she went solo, stayed on Capitol label, often appeared with Kenton. Toured with Ted HEATH show, with Cooper; LPs incl. *Duet* with Kenton; own albums: *Fair And Warmer*, *The Misty Miss Christy*, *This Is June Christy* (last two digitally remastered and reissued by EMI UK '84-5), *The Song Is June*, *Those Kenton Days*, *Cool School*, *Off Beat*; also *Something Cool* with Pete Rugolo (*b* 25 Dec. '15, Sicily; Kenton arranger, later freelance, turned to TV scoring '60s e.g. *The Fugitive*). *The Best Thing For You* reissued '86 on Affinity UK. Semi-retired '60s but recorded with Kenton on his label; also *Impromptu* '77 on Discovery; *Best Of* compilation on Capitol USA.

CHUCK WAGON GANG Close harmony country gospel quartet. Original lineup was D. P. 'Dad' Carter, baritone (*b* 28 Sep. 1889, near Columbia, Ky.; *d* 28 Apr. '63); Ernest 'Jim' Carter, bass (*b* 10 Aug. '10, Sherman, Texas; *d* Feb. '71); Rose Carter, soprano (*b* 31 Dec., Altus, Okla.); Anna Carter, alto (*b* 15 Feb., Shannon, Texas). Dad and Carrie Carter met in a singing school, had nine children; the group was formed in Bledsoe, Texas to help make ends meet, made debut '35 on KFYO Lubbock as the Carter Quartet (no relation to the famous CARTER FAMILY of Virginia). Within a year they had switched to WBAP in Fort Worth, one of the most powerful in Texas, taking the name of a Western band which had left the station. They were heard five days a week for 15 years, with minor disruptions during WWII; Art SATHERLEY began recording them '36 on American Record Company Labels ARC, Okeh, Vocalion; then Columbia after ARC was taken over by CBS '38. Their earliest broadcasts and first two recording sessions incl. secular songs, but the gospel singing was so popular that it took over exclusively. They recorded 408 selections in 40 years; when their sponsor offered photos of the group in exchange for coupons from flour sacks, 100,000 were requested; in '55 they received a gold disc for 'I'll Shout And Shine' and were named the top USA gospel group by the National Disc Jockey Association. Dad played mandolin on early secular recordings; otherwise Jim's acoustic guitar was the only accompaniment until '54, when Jim was replaced by younger brother Roy Carter (*b* 1 Mar. '26, Calumet, Okla.) and a discreet electric guitar was played by Anna's husband, Howard Gordon (*b* 30 May '16, Denton, Texas; *d* 3 Oct. '67). Dad retired '56, replaced by yet another son, Eddie, who was not full-time after '57, replaced by the first non-family member, Pat McKeehan. Dad's last records were also the last made in Texas; all the rest were made in Nashville. They began playing concerts outside Texas late '40s, encouraged by Rev. J. Bazzal Mull, a blind Baptist minister and broadcaster who sold carloads of their records through the post; in later years Nashville session players such as Grady MARTIN and Harold BRADLEY were used on records; other singers incl. Haskell Mitchell, Jim Waits, Howard Welborn, Jim Wesson, Ronnie Crittendon. They appeared on TV in the '60s, sang over the years on the GRAND OLE OPRY and the Louisiana Hayride; in '66 at Carnegie Hall, Florida's

Gator Bowl and the Hollywood Bowl; they appeared in film *Sing A Song For Heaven's Sake* '67. Rose retired '66; Anna led a group '68 with her daughter Vickie, son Craig, Jim Black singing bass, but married Jimmie DAVIS late that year and subsequently sang in his trio. The group still occasionally appeared mid-'80s with Roy and the youngest Carter sisters Ruth Ellen and Betty, Ron Page singing bass. Their style never changed: pure Southern rural 'shape-note' singing (*see* GOSPEL MUSIC), with beautiful harmony found in the songs themselves; they were unusual in the genre in using female lead voices, and voices of rare liquid beauty at that. LPs on Columbia incl. *Greatest Hits, Looking Away To Heaven*; compilation *Chuck Wagon Gang* (Columbia Historical Series, available from Country Music Foundation) incl. tracks from '36-60: two secular songs from '36-7; 'He Set Me Free' '41 (written by Albert E. Brumley and said to have been the model for 'I Saw The Light', by Hank WILLIAMS); 'When I Thank Him For What He Has Done' '60, also by Brumley; favourites such as 'We Are Climbing', 'After The Sunrise' etc. and 'The Church In The Wildwood' '36, even more beautiful (and better recorded) than the other Carter Family's version made four years earlier.

CLANCY BROTHERS & TOMMY MAKEM Irish folksinging group: Tom, Pat and Liam (*b* '36) from Carrick-on-Suir, Eire; Makem *b* County Armagh, Northern Ireland. Brothers reared on trad. music in small rural community. Eldest, Pat and Tom, settled NYC late '40s, working in theatrical groups (prod. Sean O'Casey's *The Plough And The Stars*). After working with Elektra, Folkways labels Pat founded Tradition Records early '50s. Tommy was dance-band vocalist in Ireland, arrived NYC with Liam '56; four sang at parties. Blend of voices in 'Brennan On The Moor', 'The Irish Rover', 'The Leaving Of Liverpool' etc. struck chord with NYC Irish community. Greenwich Village club work coincided with folk revival; soon in forefront with Phil OCHS, Bob DYLAN, Richard FARINA, etc. First LP for Tradition late '50s *The Rising Of The Moon* made at home around tape recorder. Appeared at Newport Folk Festivals with Josh WHITE, Judy COLLINS, Pete SEEGER;

on Ed Sullivan show '61 at time of interest in all things Irish due to rise of Kennedys in USA politics. Signed to Columbia '61, label took over eponymous Tradition LP; made more than 40 altogether, bringing to worldwide audience 'The Jug Of Punch', 'Wild Mountain Thyme', 'Carrickfergus', etc. Split '69; Tommy sometimes replaced by Lou Killen, fourth Clancy Bobby. Many LPs on Tradition, Columbia, Vanguard still in print incl. *Fill Your Glass* '59, *In Person At Carnegie Hall* '63, etc. Tommy had always done solo work; reunited '70s with Liam (duet LPs on Blackbird); original lineup reunited '84 (LP *Reunion*); toured USA '85 for what they said was the last time.

CLANNAD Irish folk group, at first singing only in Gaelic, names spelled in Gaelic on LP sleeves: Marie Brennan, harp, vocals; Paul Brennan, flute, guitar, keyboards; Ciaran Brennan, bass, synth; Pat Duggan, mandola, guitar; Noel Duggan, guitar and vocals. Won praise from folkies both sides of Irish Sea for trad. approach; LPs *Clannad* '73, *Clannad II* '74, *Dulamen* '76, *Crannull, Fuain, Volume 2* issued on Irish labels; *Clannad In Concert* '79 brought wider appeal. *Crannull* reissued on Philips '82 along with *The Pretty Maid*; followed by *Magical Ring* on RCA '83, incl. wordless single 'Theme From Harry's Game', written for UK TV series, became chart hit (no. 5 UK '82); also English-language songs such as 'See Red', 'New Grange' (no. 65 '83). Surprise choice to record theme for hit UK TV series *Robin Of Sherwood*: 'Robin (The Hooded Man)' no. 42 '84; related LP *Legend* remained in UK album chart nearly a year; BAFTA award '85 for best TV music: won larger audience through TV while retaining early fans. Album *Macalla* '85 incl. vocal by U2's Bono; *Sirius* '87 prod. by Greg Ladanyi and Russ Kunkel. They never really claimed to be traditionalists; started out with Gaelic for its musical qualities (not a bad idea); by now they sound like a windswept FLEETWOOD MAC.

CLANTON, Jimmy (*b* Sep. '40, Baton Rouge, La.) Singer. Played in school group the Dixie Cats, met pianist Dick Holler (who later wrote 'Abraham, Martin & John': four top 40 versions '68-71), joined Holler's group (the Night Trainers, subsequently changed name to Rockets). Group went to New Orleans to make demos in Cosimo Matassa's studio. Lineup incl. Bobby Loveless, tenor sax; Grady Caldwell, bass; Junior Bergeron, drums. During demo session Matassa came by studio with Ace Records boss Johnny Vincent, who signed Clanton as solo with Matassa as manager. Debut single 'Just A Dream' with Mac REBENNACK, Allen TOUSSAINT in session incl. went gold, made USA top 5 '58. After several more top 40 hits, Clanton made film *Go, Jimmy, Go* (also starring Alan FREED, Chuck BERRY); title song made top 4 '59. Only UK hit 'Another Sleepless Night' no. 50 '60 (no. 22 USA). Drafted into US Army, then made top 10 with 'Venus In Blue Jeans' '62, then swamped by British Invasion. Lived in Pennsylvania in '80s, reportedly singing religious songs. Hits compilation released on Ace (UK) '84.

CLAPTON, Eric (*b* 30 Mar. '45, Ripley, Surrey, UK) Rock guitarist. Played in local R&B bands early '60s: Roosters, Casey Jones & The Engineers, then YARDBIRDS: LP *Five Live Yardbirds* '64; single 'For Your Love' UK no. 2/USA no. 6 '65; 15 months with John MAYALL and Bluesbreakers; mid-'60s London graffiti said 'CLAPTON IS GOD': unwanted deification completed in success of blues power-trio CREAM '66-8. With shortlived BLIND FAITH; sought anonymity (with George HARRISON) in Delaney & Bonnie (*see* BRAMLETT); further futile attempt to avoid limelight, 2-disc set *Derek And The Dominos* '70, with Duane ALLMAN, became rock classic incl. 'Layla', written for Harrison's wife Patti (*Derek And The Dominos In Concert* commercially issued '73). Unique warm sound from his Stratocaster guitar dubbed 'woman tone', instantly recognisable. Debut solo LP *Eric Clapton* '70 incl. J. J. CALE song 'After Midnight' (no. 18 USA hit), revealed mellow side and strong Cale infl. which would soon prevail. Meanwhile in demand as guest; new rock elite played when and where they pleased: contributed to BEATLES 'White Album' '68, LPs by Stephen STILLS, Aretha FRANKLIN, Frank ZAPPA (*We're Only In It For The Money* '67), many others; also John LENNON's Plastic Ono Band (*Live Peace In Toronto* '69), Harrison's '71

Bangla Desh charity concert. A shy man, denying superstardom; became heroin addict, retired to southern England; Pete Townshend talked him into comeback: *Eric Clapton's Rainbow Concert* '73 disappointing despite help from Townshend, Steve WINWOOD, Ronnie Lane, Ron Wood. Had acupuncture treatment in London, worked on farm in Wales, beat drugs. LP *461 Ocean Boulevard* '74 named after Miami house where he stayed while recording (in same studio where 'Layla' was made) revived laid-back style to which he's stuck since, incl. no. 1 hit with Bob MARLEY's 'I Shot The Sheriff'. Plays low-key guitar; relies on singing, good sidemen: allows guest guitars to compete (e.g. Albert Lee; Ry COODER on *Money & Cigarettes* '83); critics carp, wanting him to be someone else, while public rewards him with good sales. Appears in The BAND's film/3-disc set *Last Waltz* '76; played at Bob DYLAN's Blackbushe Aerodrome concert near London '78. Married Patti Harrison '79. Other LPs incl. *There's One In Every Crowd* '75 (incl. Jimmy Byfield's 'Little Rachel'), *No Reason To Cry* '76, *Slowhand* '77, *Backless* '78, *Just One Night* '80, *Another Ticket* '81, *Behind The Sun* '85; *E.C. Was Here* '75, *Another Ticket* '81 are live sets; *Best Of E.C.* '75, 2-disc *Timepieces* '82 are compilations. Played at George HARRISON's *Concert For Bangla Desh* '72; wrote and performed title music for *The Hit* '84, film with John Hurt. Other top 40 singles in USA incl. own songs 'Lay Down Sally', 'Wonderful Tonight', 'Promises', all '78; 2-sided hit 'Tulsa Time'/Cale's 'Cocaine' (which itself came from '68 Cream hit 'Sunshine Of Your Love'); 'I Can't Stand It' '81, 'I've Got A Rock'n'Roll Heart' '83. Has own Duck label; *August* '86 said to be his best in years, prod. by Phil COLLINS, incl. Robert CRAY's 'Bad Influence', with guests Collins, Tina TURNER, Gary Brooker, BRECKER Bros, etc. He guested onstage with Cray in London late '86 (soundpage flexi-disc incl. in May '87 *Guitar Player* magazine); well-filled *The Cream Of Eric Clapton* '87 incl. 'Layla', Cream tracks, much more.

CLARK, Buddy (*b* Samuel Goldberg, 26 July '12, Dorchester, Mass.; *d* 1 Oct. '49, L.A.) Superior singer with big bands. Attended law school, turned to music '32;

radio work and freelance recording began immediately, incl. Benny GOODMAN *Let's Dance* show '34-5, own 15-minute spots, *Hit Parade* '36-8, Wayne KING, Vincent Lopez, own show *Here's To Romance* early '40s, *The Contented Hour* '45; also film work: dubbed voice for Jack Haley in *Wake Up And Live* '37, for Mark Stevens in *I Wonder Who's Kissing Her Now* '47, also *Melody Time* '48, *Song Of Surrender* '49. CBS staff singer; recorded with Goodman, King, Eddy DUCHIN, others, often without label credit; under own name on Varsity '40 with septet incl. Pee Wee RUSSELL, Bud FREEMAN, Jess STACY; at last had hits '46-9 in Billboard top 10: 'South America, Take It Away!' '46, with Xavier CUGAT; delightful 'Linda' and 'I'll Dance At Your Wedding', both '47 with Ray NOBLE; under own name: 'Peg O' My Heart' '47, 'Ballerina' and 'You're Breaking My Heart' '48; duets with Doris DAY: 'Love Somebody', 'My Darling, My Darling', both '48. Passenger in private plane, crashed returning from football game. Excellent intonation, phrasing means work has not dated. Columbia compilation LPs out of print, incl. *Buddy Clark's Greatest Hits*.

CLARK, Buddy (*b* Walter Clark Jr, 10 July '29, Kenosha, Wis.) Bass, arranger. Worked in combos, toured and freelanced with many bands from '50; Monterey Jazz Festival '58; with Jimmy GIUFFRE (album *Lee Konitz Meets Jimmy Giuffre*, '59). Worked in TV and film studios; co-founder, arranger with SUPERSAX '72-5.

CLARK, Charles E. (*b* 11 Mar. '45, Chicago; *d* there 15 Apr. '69) Bass, cello. Pupil of Wilbur Ware; also studied classical and played on scholarship in Chicago Civic Orchestra. Played in Experimental Band of Muhal Richard ABRAMS; talented and popular founder member of AACM; records with Abrams and Joseph JARMAN '67-8; died of brain haemorrhage. ART ENSEMBLE OF CHICAGO dedicated *A Jackson In Your House* to him; LP incl. Roscoe MITCHELL's 'Song For Charles'.

CLARK, Dave Leader of Dave Clark Five: Clark (*b* 14 Dec. '42), drums; Mike Smith (*b* 12 Dec. '43) vocals, organ; Lenny Davidson (*b* 30 May '44) guitar; Dennis Payton (*b* 1 Aug. '43), sax; Rick Huxley (*b* 5 Aug. '42),

bass. Stuntman with over 40 film credits formed enormously popular local band in N. London suburb of Tottenham; hard to believe now that they were considered equal to BEATLES for a while: press talked about 'Tottenham Sound' as answer to 'Mersey Beat'. DC5 still hold record for number of appearances on Ed Sullivan TV show. First single was top 40 'Do You Love Me' '63, but Brian POOLE's Tremeloes had no. 1; by Oct. DC5 made it with 'Glad All Over', followed by no. 2 'Bits And Pieces' early '64 (both top 10 USA). Film *Catch Us If You Can* '65 was imitation of Beatles' *A Hard Day's Night* '65, though it marked debut of dir. John Boorman, who went on to better things (such as *Deliverance*, '72). Former drama student Clark prod., dir. UK TV spectacular *Hold On It's The Dave Clark Five*, a big hit at the time; wrote most of the band's hits and retained ownership of the records; bought exclusive rights to UK TV series *Ready Steady Go!* which presented all UK and USA stars of the '60s. As Beatles, ROLLING STONES went on to use of studio technology and psychedelia, DC5 had top 10 hits with syrupy 'Everybody Knows' '67, mawkish 'Red Balloon' '68, singalong 'Good Old Rock & Roll', 'Everybody Get Together' '69-70, but split '71. At height of '77 punk summer compilation LP *Thumping Great Hits* shot to no. 1 on UK LP chart. First video cassette from *Ready Steady Go!* '83 was no. 1 video '83, stayed in chart six months; two more vols., then compilations *Otis Redding Live*, *The Sounds of Motown*; *The Beatles Live* entered video chart at no. 2; Clark prod. TV series of *Ready* reruns that quadrupled viewing figures for UK's Channel 4 '85. Prod. futuristic London musical *Time* with Cliff RICHARD in first musical stage role: single 'She's So Beautiful' '85 by Richard with backing by Stevie WONDER, video dir. by Ken Russell; 2-disc LP of score '86 incl. Richard, contributions from Wonder, Julian LENNON; show opened Apr. '86: 'sets a new record in the gap between imaginative poverty and Babylonian material resources' (Irving Wardle in *The Times*). Clark always reckoned to be a better businessman than musician.

CLARK, Dee (*b* Delectus Clark, 7 Nov. '38, Blytheville, Ark.) Singer. To Chicago as a child; at 14 recording debut with the Hambone Kids (encouraged by his mother, Delecta, who sang spirituals). As member of the Goldentones (later known as the Kool Gents) won talent contest; local deejay Herb Kent took him to Vee Jay label subsidiary Falcon/Abner; several top 40 hits late '50s/early '60s: 'Just Keep It Up' no. 18 USA '58, also only UK hit of era at no. 26. Biggest USA hit was atmospheric 'Raindrops' '61 (with sound effects of heavy rain). After '65 no more hits in any Billboard chart; in '75 top 20 hit UK only with 'Ride A Wild Horse' on Chelsea label; then silence again.

CLARK, Dick (*b* Richard Augustus Clark, 30 Nov. '29, Mt Vernon, NY) DJ and TV host. Joined Philadelphia radio WFIL '51 as announcer, transferred to its TV channel '56; his pop show *Bandstand* became *American Bandstand* when networked on ABC from 5 Aug. '57. Format of lip-synched hit records, 'Record Revue' slot, dancing by local high school kids (who carried on soapy romances on screen) brought daily 90-minute show up to a million fan letters weekly. Success of show inspired glut of local labels (Cameo, Chancellor, etc.) which used show as path to national hits; youngsters elbowed Tony BENNETT, Al MARTINO etc. out of charts as Clark claimed to be monitoring national popularity, but Philly acts (Frankie AVALON, FABIAN, Bobby RYDELL) seemed to profit more than most. Spinoff *Dick Clark Show* ran concurrently from '58 for more than two years from NYC; Clark diversified into Jamie, Swan, Hunt labels, SRO Management, syndicated newspaper column, claimed to have made a million by age 30; Congressional investigation into payola '60 forced him to relinquish interests, losing estimated $8 million earnings, but network and sponsors continued support: squeaky-clean Clark got off lightly (*see* Alan FREED). British Invasion took shine off Clark's star, but USA's 'oldest living teenager', TV shows survived into '80s: spinoffs in '60s/70s incl. *Where The Action's At*, *In Concert*, *Soul Unlimited*; later anniversary programmes; he has TV production company, dinner theatre to his name; autobiography *Rock, Roll And Remember*. Nothing wrong with doing well, but infl. on music was negative: musical enthusiasms

inspired reaction, are now only of nostalgic interest.

CLARK, Gene (*b* 17 Nov. '41, Tipton, Mo.) Singer, songwriter, guitarist. Once a member of the NEW CHRISTY MINSTRELS; worked with the DILLARDS, Gram PARSONS, but best known as a member of the BYRDS, and widely regarded as the most interesting songwriter in that band. Collections incl. *Early L.A. Sessions* (released '72) and *Gene Clark With The Gosdin Brothers* '67 on CBS; *Fantastic Expedition* and *Through The Morning* '69, *White Light* '71 (aka *Gene Clark*) on A&M; *No Other* '74 on Asylum; *Two Sides To Every Story* '77 on RSO. *Kansas City Southern* '75 apparently appeared on Ariola in UK. *Roadmaster* is a set of scraps from as far back as '70 incl. fragments of aborted successor to *White Light*, with Clarence White, Byron Berline, Spooner Oldham etc., released on Edsel UK '87. *Collectors Classics* was on CBS '76; *Firebird* on Takoma; *So Rebellious A Lover* (with Carla Olson of the Textones) released '87 on Demon in UK.

CLARK, Guy (*b* 6 Nov. '41, Monihans, Texas) Country singer/songwriter. Worked as art director on TV station in Houston mid-'60s; to L.A., then Nashville '71 as songwriter. Wrote hits 'Desperados Waitin' For A Train' (Jerry Jeff WALKER, David Allan COE), 'The Last Gunfighter' (Johnny CASH), 'L.A. Freeway' (Walker), 'Heartbroke' (Ricky SKAGGS); Bobby BARE cover of 'New Cut Road' was a country hit; 'The Carpenter' covered by John CONLEE on LP *Harmony*, etc. Series of own LPs with likeable smoke-stained voice, laid-back style began on RCA: *Old No. 1* '75, *Texas Cookin'* '76, with Walker, Emmylou HARRIS, Waylon JENNINGS, Rodney CROWELL etc. in the cast; incl. own versions of 'Freeways', 'Desperados' (about old men waiting for death); plus 'Texas 1947', superb addition to American train-songs; 'Anyhow, I Love You' is both laconic and passionate; joyous celebrations of country fiddling, music in the park incl. 'A Nickel For The Fiddler', 'Virginia's Real' with Johnny Gimble on fiddle. Switched to WB for *Guy Clark* '78, *South Coast Of Texas* '81 (Clark rejected the LP after sleeves were printed and record mastered; switched to Crowell as producer and did it again), *Better Days* '83. Title track of *South Coast* is fine helping of nostalgic colour; WB tracks also incl. songs about lovers as fools/cynics: 'Who Do You Think You Are', 'Fool In The Mirror'; 'She's Crazy For Leavin' ' co-written by Crowell; 'Homegrown Tomatoes' is tribute to kitchen gardens. *Warner Brothers Music Show Live Album* '79, made on 2-track tape at the Cellar Door in Washington DC, is a collector's item; also *In Concert* on Dot. Singable, often funny songs about the real world ought to make him a household name, but he remains a cult artist; enthusiasm of fans at solo gig at the Half Moon in Putney, South London brought a grin: 'This beats the hell out of Wembley Stadium!' Wife Susanna writes too: 'Easy From Now On' co-written with Carlene CARTER, 'Come From The Heart' with Richard Leigh; 'Old Friends' and 'So Have I' were co-written by Guy and Susanna with Richard DOBSON.

CLARK, Petula (*b* 15 Nov. '32, Epsom, Surrey) Singer, actress. Made radio debut at 9; film *A Medal For The General* age 12. Other films incl. *London Town* '46, *Dance Hall* '50, *The Card* '52, *Finian's Rainbow* '68, *Goodbye Mr Chips* '69, *Never Never Land* '81. First UK hit: 'The Little Shoemaker' '54; became international star in '60s; with 'Downtown' the clear accuracy of her voice hit the USA charts like a blast of fresh air: it was no. 1 and 'I Know A Place' no.3 in '65; both won Grammies. 'My Love' was no. 1 '66; altogether 15 chart entries in USA '65-8, 27 in UK '54-72 not counting re-entries. 'Sailor' '61 and 'This Is My Song' '67 no. 1 in UK. One of her best-known fans was quirky Canadian classical pianist Glenn Gould, who wrote an essay about her. Ovation at '71 Academy Awards show singing 'All We Know'; scores of TV appearances; played Maria in London revival of *Sound Of Music*. Has lived in Switzerland for many years, married to record company executive Claude Wolff. Bestselling LPs: *I Couldn't Live Without Your Love* '66, *Colour My World* '67, *20 Greatest Hits* '77.

CLARK, Roy (*b* Roy Linwood Clark, 15 Apr. '33, Meherrin, Va.) Country guitarist, singer, comedian. Began as child prodigy in his father's country band; won USA country

music banjo championship twice '52-3. Tried out for St Louis baseball team; took up amateur boxing in Washington DC area where he lived. Played back-up guitar in various bands with Jimmy DEAN, Marvin RAINWATER, George HAMILTON IV, Wanda JACKSON (on her rock'n'roll records). Appeared on Dean's and Hamilton's TV series '58-61; recorded for Four Star, Debbie, Coral, Capitol '62-7: hits with 'Tips Of My Fingers' '63, 'Through The Eyes Of A Fool' '64. LPs showcased guitar as well as vocal talents: *Lightning Fingers* '65, *Happy To Be Unhappy* '67. Signed with Dot '68, hit jackpot with 'Yesterday When I Was Young': top 20 pop, top 10 country. Hits with 'I Never Picked Cotton' '70, 'Thank God And Greyhound' '71, but more success as concert act: highest paid country star '69-74. Named Entertainer of the Year '73 by CMA, Comedian of the Year '70-2; played Cousin Roy on *Beverly Hillbillies* TV series '62-71, co-host of *Hee-Haw* '69-75. More hits with 'Come And Live With Me' '73 (no. 1 country chart), 'Somewhere Between Love And Tomorrow' '74 (no. 2), 'Honeymoon Feeling' '74, 'Heart To Heart' '75. Albums with banjoist Buck Trent (*Pair Of Fives* '75), bluesman Gatemouth BROWN (*Makin' Music* '79); also his own: *The Incredible Roy Clark* '71, *Come Live With Me* '73, *Classic Clark* '75, *My Music And Me* '77, *Back To The Country* '81. Joined manager Jim Halsey's record label Churchill '82 with LPs *Live From Austin City Limits*, *Turned Loose*. Compilation *20 Golden Pieces* released in UK on Bulldog '84.

CLARK, Yodelling Slim (*b* Raymond Le Roy, 11 Dec. '17, Springfield, Mass.) Singer, yodeller in trad. country music. Worked as woodsman before taking up professional music; recorded for small labels '46-70 incl. Continental, Wheeling, Palace, Palomino. Named World's Champion Yodeller '47.

CLARK, Sonny (*b* Conrad Yeatis Clark, 21 July '31, Herminie, Pa.; *d* 13 Jan. '63, NYC) Piano. Highly rated young bop-infl. player died of heart attack. First of all-star series of LPs on Blue Note was quintet set *Dial S For Sonny* with Art FARMER, Curtis FULLER, Hank MOBLEY, Wilbur Ware, Louis Hayes, drums (*b* 31 May '37, Detroit; later with Cannonball ADDERLEY, Oscar

PETERSON trio, others; own quintets '70s; own LPs on VJ, *Breath Of Life* on Muse). Followed by *Sonny's Crib* '57 with John COLTRANE, *Sonny Clark Trio* with Paul CHAMBERS, Philly Joe JONES; *Cool Struttin' Volume 2*, quintet again with Chambers, Kenny BURRELL, Clifford JORDAN, was originally planned for earlier release; all '57. *Blues In The Night* c.'57-8 is by the trio; *Cool Struttin'* '58 is quintet again. Trio sessions of '58 released on several discs, incl. one in Japan, with Jymie Merritt, bass (*b* '26, Philadelphia; recorded with Art BLAKEY), Wes Landers, drums. *My Conception* '59 quintet set with Donald BYRD, Blakey, Mobley, Chambers; *Leapin' & Lopin'* '61 by sextet Sonny Clark All-Stars, with Charlie ROUSE, tenor; Ike QUEBEC on one track. Also trio sets: one in '60 on Time label and *Sonny Clark Memorial Album* on Xanadu, made '54 in Oslo. John ZORN plays alto sax in *Sonny Clark Memorial Quartet* on Black Saint.

CLARKE-BOLAND BIG BAND A Europe-based all-star international big band which made excellent LPs c.'60-71. Producer Gigi Campi operated a café in Cologne (Köln) Germany; a jazz lover, he accepted a dare, organised a band around co-leaders pianist/arranger François 'Francy' Boland (*b* 6 Nov. '29, Namur, Belgium) and drummer Kenny CLARKE: Europe was full of good jazzmen of all nationalities and Campi had the band in the studio within weeks. Most of the albums were made in Köln, most available on Hans-Georg Brunner-Schwer's MPS label, not well distributed outside Europe: it was the band of our dreams, the most exciting since the BIG BAND ERA, but most Americans never heard it. *Jazz Is Universal* '61 on Atlantic incl. Benny BAILEY on trumpet ('I didn't know I could play lead . . . all of us played above our level'), Aake Persson on trombone (*b* 25 Feb. '32, Hässleholm, Sweden; *d* 4 Feb. '75 in Stockholm), in the reed section Derek Humble (*b* '31, Durham, England; *d* 22 Feb. '71) and Sahib Shihab (*b* Edmund Gregory, 23 June '25, Savannah, Ga.: excellent, underrated reedman and teacher: LPs *All Star Sextets* '57 on Savoy, with Brew Moore on Fantasy, *Sentiments* '71 on Storyville), Jimmy Woode on bass, Boland and Clarke, others incl. guest Zoot SIMS. An Atlantic LP '63 as

Francy Boland Big Band added Idrees Sulieman on trumpet, Keg Johnson on trombone, Ronnie SCOTT; LP made next day was issued on Columbia in the USA; other LPs variously incl. Johnny GRIFFIN, Tony COE, Tootie Heath, Kenny WHEELER, many others; all good recordings by engineer Wolfgang Hirschmann. *Karl Drewo und die Clarke-Boland Big Band* '66 on Philips incl. Drewo and Sal Nistico on tenors. *Sax No End* also incl. Eddie 'Lockjaw' DAVIS, on Saba, later on Pausa, also on Prestige as *Fire, Soul, Heat & Guts*; *Out Of The Folk Bag* on German Columbia added second drummer Kenny Clare (*b* 8 June '29, UK; *d* 21 Dec. '84); *Open Door* on Muse was made in Prague; *17 Men And Their Music* was on Campi label in Italy; all '67. *Let's Face The Music* was also on Prestige; *More* on Campi; *Latin Kaleidoscope* on Campi, Polydor, Prestige; *Felini 712* on Polydor, all '68. *Volcano* and *Rue Chaptal* were made live at Ronnie Scott's, *All Blues* in Köln, *Francy Boland And His Orchestra* in Warsaw for Supraphon, *At Her Majesty's Pleasure* (aka *Doin' Time*) in Köln on Polydor, Black Lion, all '69. *Our Kind Of Sabi* '70 was on Polydor, *Change Of Scenes* '71 on German Verve incl. Stan GETZ. A proposed USA tour '70 scuppered partly by American red tape. *Blue Flame*, *Red Hot* and *White Heat* on MPS were all made the same day in '76 without Clarke, who was ill; there were other albums, incl. one backing Carmen McRAE; nearly all are out of print, but CD reissues are rumoured, a consummation devoutly to be wished. Clarke and Clare died within weeks of each other; on the last three albums Persson had been replaced by Frank Rosolino, who like him became a suicide. Boland and Campi worked together again with Sarah VAUGHAN, Gene LEES and the Pope '85; Boland also made small-group LPs with Shihab, Clarke etc. on various European labels: *Francy Boland Combo* '65, trio *Out Of The Background* '67, *Music For The Small Hours*, *Flirt And Dream* (with strings), all '67.

CLARKE, John Cooper Punk poet. First a Bob DYLAN clone, then fixture on Manchester punk scene, supporting local groups (the BUZZCOCKS, the FALL), reading his work at frantically high speed. Appeared at Poetry Olympics '80, held at Poet's Corner in Westminster Abbey. Poems on record had musical backing prod. by Martin Hannett and featuring 'The Invisible Girls' (incl. Buzzcocks' Pete Shelley, Bill Nelson from Be Bop Deluxe). First record was 'Psycle Sluts' '77 on local Rabid label (also LP *Où Est la Maison de Fromage* '80), then Epic contract; LPs *Disguise In Love* '78, *Walking Back To Happiness* '79 followed by *Snap Crackle And Bop* '80 (made top 30 UK album chart); *Me & My Big Mouth* '81 is good collection incl. 'Gimmix!'/'I Married A Monster From Outer Space' (sole hit single '79; 'Monster' is indictment of racism), 'Majorca' (package holidays), 'Beasley Street' (Thatcherism), 'Bronze Adonis', 'Kung Fu International', others. *Zip Style Method* '82 more serious, less punny. Toured with Linton Kwesi Johnson '83; tour film documentary *100 Years In An Open Neck Shirt* is also title of collection in book form.

CLARKE, Kenny (*b* Kenneth Spearman Clarke, 9 Jan. '14, Philadelphia; *d* 25 Jan. '85, Paris) Drummer; one of the most important innovators of post-war jazz. From musical family; played trombone, piano, vibes, studied theory in high school. Played with Roy ELDRIDGE, Jeter-Pillars band, Edgar HAYES (European tour '38), Teddy HILL '40-1 (got nickname 'Klook' from Hill, who complained about 'klook-mop' sound), then house band at Minton's (hired by Hill: *see* BOP). Gigs with Louis ARMSTRONG, Ella FITZGERALD, Benny CARTER, Red ALLEN in Chicago; US Army service; then with Dizzy GILLESPIE '46, again in '48, remaining some months in France after European tour. Toured USA with Billy ECKSTINE band; founder member of MODERN JAZZ QUARTET '52-5; moved to Europe '56. Attended Duke ELLINGTON fellowship programme at Yale U. '72; house drummer at Montreux Festival '73. He followed Jo JONES and others in keeping a 4/4 beat on the cymbals, but went further in liberating the rest of the drum kit to support the soloist or as an independent voice of its own. Said that he stopped beating 4/4 on bass drum because his foot got tired; in any case he began 'dropping bombs', bass drum accents becoming a witty addition to the language of jazz. Compositions incl. co-written 'Epistrophy' with Thelonious MONK and 'Salt Peanuts' with Dizzy, both classics having the sort of rhythmic iconoclasm that was part of bop. Sessions under his own name incl. Stockholm '38 (by 'Kenny Clark's Kvintett'); *Paris Bebop Sessions* on Prestige '50; on Savoy '54-6 incl. *Telefunken Blues, Bohemia After Dark, Kenny Clarke/Ernie Wilkins Septet*, all '55; *Klook's Clique, Meets the Detroit Jazzmen* with Pepper ADAMS, Paul CHAMBERS '56, more. With Bud POWELL and bassist Pierre Michelot (*b* 3 Mar. '28, Saint Denis, France) from '59 as the Three Bosses, ace Paris rhythm section, e.g. on Dexter GORDON Blue Note LP *Our Man In Paris* '63, others; Clarke and Michelot backed gypsy guitarist Elek Bacsik (*b* 22 May '26, Budapest) on a '62 LP. *Pieces Of Time* on Soul Note '83 also featured drummers Andrew CYRILLE, Milford Graves, Don Moye. Also co-led allstar CLARKE-BOLAND BIG BAND (*see above*).

CLARKE, Stanley (*b* 30 June '51, Philadelphia, Pa.) Bass, composer. Rock experience late '60s; then jazz with Horace SILVER '70, with Joe HENDERSON, Pharoah SANDERS, Stan GETZ, Chick COREA; member of Corea's Return To Forever. Played violin, cello; now both Fender electric and standup bass, and knows the difference. Own chart LPs, many with large groups and featuring own comps. incl. *Stanley Clarke* '74, *Journey To Love* '75, *School Days* '76, *Modern Man* '78 on Atlantic/Nemperor; on Epic: 2-disc *I Wanna Play For You* '77-8, half live and half studio recording; *Rocks Pebbles & Sand* c.'80, *Let Me Know You* '82, *Time Exposure*, all now on CBS labels; also *Fuse One* with Larry CORYELL, John McLAUGHLIN, Tony WILLIAMS, others, made for CTI '80; *Clarke/Duke Project, Project II* with George DUKE on Epic. Great infl. on jazz/rock bassists: played with Jeff BECK, New Barbarians (ROLLING STONES spin-off), made funk cover of Bruce SPRINGSTEEN's 'Born In The USA'.

CLARKE, Vince (*b* 3 July '61, Basildon, Essex) Synthesisers, composer. Founder member of DEPECHE MODE, for whom he wrote hits 'Just Can't Get Enough' (UK no. 8 '81), 'See You' (UK no. 6 '82); left them at height of their success, returned to home town to experiment. Recruited Alison ('Alf') MOYET through trade paper advert, duo formed Yazoo (Yaz in USA): combination of electronic whizz-kid with melodic talent (who named SIMON & GARFUNKEL as favourites) with fine girl singer steeped in jazz and blues: made hit LPs *Upstairs At Eric's* '82 (incl. 'Only You', UK no. 2 '82), *You And Me Both* '83. Other top 5 hits were 'Don't Go', 'Nobody's Diary' before they split '82. 'Only You' done *a cappella* by Flying Pickets, became UK no. 1 '83; covered by Judy COLLINS, Rita COOLIDGE, even Richard CLAYDERMAN. Hated live work, kept low profile; then surfaced with occasional group The Assembly, with Yazoo prod. E. C. (Eric) Radcliffe: single 'Never, Never' (UK no. 4 '83) incl. former Undertones singer Feargal SHARKEY. Projected album with 10 different singers incl. BLANCMANGE's Neil Arthur, The The's Matt JOHNSON, never happened; single 'One Day' mid-'85 with former Orange Juice vocalist Paul Quinn; prod. LP for London group Absolute; music for Volkswagen TV advert; has band Erasure with Andy Bell: debut LP *Wonderland*, UK no. 3 hit 'Sometimes' '86. Unique periodic output.

CLASH, The UK punk band formed '76: Joe Strummer (*b* John Mellors, 21 Aug. '52, Ankara, Turkey), guitar, vocals; Mick Jones (*b* 26 June '55, London), guitar, vocals; Paul Simonon (*b* '56, London), bass; Nicky 'Topper' Headon (*b* '56, Dover), drums. Figureheads of UK punk explosion, one of the few bands to capture punk's aggressive, vitriolic energy on record, outclassing and outlasting SEX PISTOLS and the rest. Strummer got name from playing ukelele as London busker; formed 101'ers with Don Kelleher (who later joined PUBLIC IMAGE LTD); band named after torture room in Orwell's *1984*, or perhaps after address of squat. Simonon and Jones were in seminal (and terrible) London SS. Enlisted Terry Chimes (renamed 'Tory Crimes' for street credibility) on drums, called band Clash after favourite word of writers of UK tabloid headlines. Supported Sex Pistols as quintet before Levene left; then on Pistols' ill-fated Anarchy tour; played one-day punk festival at 100 Club. Castigated everything with ruthless energy: first single '1977' declared 'No Elvis, no Beatles or Stones'; attacked commercial broadcasting ('Capital Radio'), un-

employment ('Career Opportunities'), US domination of Europe ('I'm So Bored With The USA'), racism (cover of Junior Murvin's 'Police And Thieves': from the beginning they could do savagely convincing white man's reggae). Strummer endorsed Baader-Meinhoff terrorist gang. Signed with CBS for six-figure advance, but refused to appear on TV's *Top Of The Pops*; first LP *The Clash* '77 captured frenzy of period, not issued in USA as too crude. 'Complete Control', prod. by Lee Perry, was band's response to unauthorised release of 'Remote Control' as single in UK. Chimes left, replaced by Headon; '78 single '(White Man) In Hammersmith Palais' another searing reggae track; played Rock Against Racism gigs. Accused of selling out when second LP *Give 'Em Enough Rope* prod. '78 at request of Columbia (CBS-USA) by American Sandy Pearlman, who had worked with very different BLUE OYSTER CULT; LP lacked energy of debut, but had high spots 'English Civil War', 'Stay Free'; made no. 2 on UK chart, but didn't make USA top 200 albums. 4-track EP *Cost Of Living* '79 incl. cover of Sonny Curtis's 'I Fought The Law'. 2-LP set *London Calling* '79 regarded by some as their best; prod. by cult figure Guy Stevens, incl. anthemic title cut, rockabilly 'Brand New Cadillac', florid 'Death Or Glory', reggae in 'Jimmy Jazz'. Extended USA tours left UK fans feeling as though watching Rolling Stones Mark II, but Clash went out of their way to introduce audiences to their own heroes: Bo DIDDLEY, Mikey Dread, renegade country star Joe ELY. Sporadic singles reinforced power (but 'Bankrobber' '80 badly produced); while album *Sandinista!* ('80; three discs for the price of one) is either a masterpiece or sprawling self-indulgence: great volume of dense material, incessant dub and reggae treatments. Despite being bored with USA, now went full out to crack market: Strummer reasoned that each time a Clash record was played on the air it kept FLEETWOOD MAC and their ilk off. UK edition of first LP set USA record for import sales; bowdlerised edition issued in USA didn't do as well. Mini-album 10″ *Black Market Clash* released only in USA '80. Amid rumours of estrangement between Strummer and Jones, who wrote songs together, LP *Combat Rock* overseen by establishment prod. Glyn JOHNS; diversified into Eastern, South American influences, drawing on rap, even ballads; featured guests Allen Ginsberg, Ely, Grandmaster Flash, Jones's girlfriend Ellen Foley; it divided fans: some saw it geared for US market; comparisons with Stones heightened by band playing at big festivals, backing The WHO at Shea Stadium. 'Rock The Casbah' big USA hit written by Headon, who had become heroin addict; Jones quit, Strummer reported, 'He said, "my accountant says I should check with him about writing songs", so I said go and write songs with your accountant.' After a hiatus, Nick Sheppard, Vince White replaced Jones, Pete Howard replaced Headon on drums (who made solo single 'Drummer Man', '85). Re-formed Clash played miners' benefits in UK '84, busked acoustically in Northern towns; LP *Cut The Crap* '85, then split, back to nucleus of Strummer and Simonon. Clash had 16 top 40 singles UK, one in USA – 'Train In Vain (Stand By Me)' '80; were subject of documentary film *Rude Boy* '80, following roadie Ray Gange on the road with band. Jones surfaced with LP *This Is Big Audio Dynamite* '85 with video maker Don Letts, single 'E=MC²', 'Medicine Man'; Strummer/Jones contributed to soundtrack of *Sid & Nancy: Love Kills* '86; collaborated on second B.A.D. LP *No. 10 Upping Street* '86, single 'C'Mon Every Beatbox' (tribute to Eddie COCHRAN). Headon was jailed for 15 months '87 for supplying heroin to a friend who died.

CLASSICS IV USA rock band formed '65 Jacksonville, Fla., credited by some with sparking '70s onslaught of 'Southern boogie'. Original lineup: James R. Cobb and Wally Eaton, guitars; Joe Wilson, bass; Kim Venable, drums. Cobb, from Birmingham, Ala., had been a studio musician; Veneble also from Ala.; Eaton was Jacksonville native. First hit 'Spooky' '67 arr. by Cobb; started on Louisville, Ky. radio to reach no. 3 USA/46 UK. Cinema usher Dennis Yost (from Jacksonville) added on vocals; 'Soul Train' co-written by Cobb and Buddy Buie was too obvious a follow-up, only minor hit; 'Stormy' '68 reached no.5 and 'Traces' '69 was third and last million-seller. 'Everyday With You Girl' made top 20 '69; subsequent outings billed as Dennis Yost & The Clas-

sics IV; switched from Imperial to MGM for 'What Am I Crying For?' '72, last top 40 entry; personnel changes were almost complete. Compilation album on United Artists '75; Cobb and Buie involved by then with ATLANTA RHYTHM SECTION, who revived 'Spooky'.

CLAYDERMAN, Richard (*b* Phillipe Pages, '54, Paris) Pianist; handsome blond does decorated versions of light classics, pop songs. Allegedly raised in one-room flat; learnt piano from father; given own piano at 6 by grandfather. Won talent contests; first prize Paris Conservatory of Music at 16; abandoned classical music to accompany Johnny HALLIDAY, Michael Sardou, Thierry Le Luron. Married at 18; day job as bank clerk; marriage over at 22; signed with Delphine label; first record 'Ballade Pour Adeline' written by producer Paul De Senneville for his daughter sold millions worldwide. Began international tours '78, promoted by Delphine boss Oliver Toussaint; sold huge quantities of records after concerts: 2,800,000 in France '80, making him biggest seller ever there; in Japan biggest seller in '80, '81; in South Africa four of five top LPs in May '81 were his. Broke into UK market late '82 via two LPs *Richard Clayderman*, *The Magic Of Richard Clayderman*, the latter heavily promoted on TV with handsome blond gazing soulfully at viewer: within months played major London date before sell-out audience. About 20 LPs listed in UK catalog '85, called *Dreaming*, *I Love You*, etc.

CLAYTON, Buck (*b* Wilbur Dorsey Clayton, 12 Nov. '11, Parsons, Kansas) Trumpet, arranger. Played in various bands; leading 14-piece unit '34, booked to Shanghai by Teddy WEATHERFORD; back in L.A. '36 leading own band; that Fall replaced Hot Lips PAGE with Count BASIE, stayed till US Army service '43. Arr. for Basie, Benny GOODMAN, Harry JAMES, others; worked for Norman GRANZ; led own sextet NYC '47; first European tour '49-50. Appeared in biopic *Benny Goodman Story* '55; with Goodman at Waldorf Astoria '57; led small group with Coleman HAWKINS, J. J. JOHNSON at Newport Jazz Festival '56; at Brussels World's Fair with Sidney BECHET '58; toured Europe with Newport Festival package '59; appeared in Newport film *Jazz On A Summer's Day* '60; etc. Lip and other health problems meant temporary absence from music '69; practising again '71. To France '78; taught at Hunter College '80s; toured Europe with The Countsmen '83. On records with Basie '37-9: solos on 'Good Morning Blues', 'Smarty', 'My Heart Belongs To Daddy', 'Don't You Miss Your Baby'; backed Jimmy RUSHING vocals on 'Boo Hoo', 'Exactly Like You'; many others. Lovely open and muted horn on Lester YOUNG small-group session of 27 Sep. '38 for Brunswick, esp. on 'Way Down Yonder In New Orleans'; also played on many Teddy WILSON and Billie HOLIDAY small-group records of the period. Copious freelance '50s work: *Jam Session* series on Columbia began '53 with LP side-length versions of 'Hucklebuck', 'Robbin's Nest'; also on that label with Frankie LAINE; backed Rushing on LPs *Jazz Odyssey*, *The Smith Girls*; on Vanguard: *Buckin' The Blues*, *Buck Meets Ruby* with Ruby BRAFF; on Prestige as *Basie Reunion* '58. Wrote as well as playing on Nat PIERCE album *Big Band At The Savoy Ballroom* recorded for RCA '57; wrote LP *Kansas City Woman* for Humphrey LYTTELTON, Buddy TATE on Black Lion '74; jam sessions on Chiaroscuro '74-5. One of the best-loved mainstream veterans, still teaching and arranging. Good autobiography with Nancy Miller-Elliot *Buck Clayton's Jazz World* '87

CLEFTONES, The USA doo wop group formed NYC '55. Lineup: Herbie Cox (*b* 6 May '39, lead), Charles James (*b* '40, first tenor), Berman Patterson (*b* '38, second tenor), William McClain (*b* '38, baritone), Warren Corbin (*b* '39, bass). Began at school in Jamaica, Queens as the Silvertones; signed with George Goldner's Rama Records, became first act on Gee Records (*see* the CROWS); then one of many doo wop groups signed to Roulette mid-'50s. Had five hits '56-62: 'You Baby You', 'Little Girl Of Mine' '56 failed to make top 50; Gene Pearson replaced McClain '59, then 'Heart And Soul' '61 beat rival JAN & DEAN version (white, West Coast) to top 20. 'For Sentimental Reasons' '61, 'Lover Come Back To Me' '62 again failed to make upper half of Billboard Hot 100. Second and third hits both top 10 R&B chart. Cox, James,

Pearson, Patterson still doing oldies shows mid-'70s.

CLEGG, Johnny (*b* 31 Oct. '53, Rochdale, UK) Singer, songwriter, guitarist; also plays umhuphe mouth bow, etc.; co-leader/leader of 'township jive' bands in South Africa. Spent early years in Zimbabwe, settled in S.A. at age 6; began to learn Zulu guitar at 14, also learned the language; became lecturer in anthropology at the U. of Witwatersrand. At 16 met Sipho Mchunu, whose background could not be more different: born in Natal where family was forcibly resettled; spent childhood as a goatherd, learned to play on homemade guitar, became migrant worker, street musician in Jo'burg. They played together in clubs, at parties, singing in Zulu and English, transcending cultural and racial barriers; made first single 'Woza Friday' '76, formed band Juluka (means 'sweat', also refers to the kinds of work which most people in S.A. have to do). First LP was *Universal Men*; hit 'Africa Kukhala Ambangcwele' made them stars, no. 1 before being banned. Bestselling LPs incl. *African Litany* '81, *Ubuhle Bemvelo* '82; *Scatterlings* on Safari UK, WB USA reached top 200 USA LPs '83 with folk-rock beat, Zulu harmonies, heartrending lyrics; *Stand Your Ground* also released in USA. Juluka struggled as an integrated band against officialdom and single-issue fanatics (touring North America and Europe '82-3 they were at first banned by UK musicians' union). Siphu had to give up full-time music to work on a farm, but Juluka said to be still a recording unit; Clegg formed Savuka (means 'we have awakened'). *Third World Child* '87 by Johnny Clegg & Savuka on EMI is a harder blend of Mbaqanga/township jive with international rock, all songs written or co-written by Clegg incl. remake of 'Scatterlings Of Africa', 'Asimnonanga' (Nelson Mandela tribute, banned in S.A.). Percussionist Dudu Zulu and drummer Derek DeBeer were also members of Juluka; band also incl. Steve Mabuso on keyboards, Jabu Mabuso on bass, Keith Hutchinson on keyboards and saxophone; in live act touring Europe '87 Clegg and Dudu demonstrated Zulu dancing as well. The LP deserves to sell as well as Paul SIMON's *Graceland*; Clegg's producer is

Hilton Rosenthal, who helped Simon set up those sessions.

CLEMENT, Jack (*b* Jack Henderson Clement, 5 Apr. '31, Whitehaven (suburb of Memphis), Tenn.) Country singer, songwriter, producer, publisher; aka 'Cowboy Jack'. Served in US Marines, settled in Washington DC, played banjo with Roy Clark, STONEMANS; formed bluegrass duo '53 with Buzz Busby; worked on radio WWVA. Took up steel guitar in Hawaiian band; returned to Memphis '54, worked as Arthur Murray dance instructor; recorded rockabilly singer Billy RILEY, leased tape for Fernwood to Sun records, which signed both Riley and Clement (as singer, prod. and songwriter). Prod. Jerry Lee LEWIS, Johnny CASH, Charlie RICH, Roy ORBISON; wrote hits 'Ballad Of A Teenage Queen', 'Guess Things Happen That Way' for Cash. Formed Summer Records '59 ('Summer hits, summer not, hope you like the ones we got'), lasted less than a year. Moved to Nashville '60, worked at RCA prod. Jim REEVES ('I Know One'), Ed BRUCE etc. To Beaumont, Texas '63; teamed with Bill Hall and ex-Sun employee Allen Reynolds working with old-time artists Moon MULLICAN, Cliff Bruner, younger people Dickey LEE, songwriting team FOSTER & RICE, George JONES, etc. Back to Nashville '64 to work with Cash; prod. 'Ring Of Fire'; wrote comedy numbers on *Everybody Loves A Nut* LP. Formed Jack Music, prod. Charley PRIDE hits, also Stonemans, Tompall & the GLASER BROTHERS, Mac WISEMAN, Louis ARMSTRONG, Doc WATSON, Waylon JENNINGS; wrote dozens of hits. Built Jack Clement Studio '70, formed JMI label '71 with Allen Reynolds (prod. of Crystal GAYLE), songwriter Bob McDill, Don WILLIAMS working for him (later became top singer, '70s): had design studio, construction company, etc.; prod. 13 gold albums incl. Pride's; lost money prod. horror film *Dear Dead Delilah* with Agnes Moorehead: JMI folded '74. Carried on singing, writing, prod. Cash, Jennings, Townes VAN ZANDT, etc. Has recorded for Sun, RCA, Hallway, Monument; Elektra LP *All I Want To Do In Life* '78. 'I've got a bunch of people who say I'm a genius . . . you've got to be pretty smart to get all them people to say that on cue' (quoted by Lola Scobey, Peter Guralnick).

Lives in Nashville because 'Nashville is where the fiddlers meet the violinist.'

CLEMENTS, Vassar (*b* Apr. '28, Kinard, S.C.) Bluegrass fiddler. With Bill MONROE on Grand Ole Opry '49, first recorded with him '50; played with JIM & JESSE, Faron YOUNG; sessioned with Emmylou HARRIS, Linda RONSTADT, Charlie DANIELS, Paul McCARTNEY, the Boston Pops; on NITTY GRITTY DIRT BAND set *Will The Circle Be Unbroken* '69; with Dickie Betts, Hot Tuna, Papa John Creach, GRATEFUL DEAD, MARSHALL TUCKER Band; active in '70s 'new grass' development: had own group mid-'70s, with not-quite-trad. Earl Scruggs Revue (*see* FLATT & SCRUGGS); some LPs on Chicago label Flying Fish: 2-disc set *Hillbilly Jazz* with David Bromberg, *Vassar*, *Bluegrass Session*, *Nashville Jam* with Doug Jernigan, Jesse McReynolds, Buddy Spicher; *Hillbilly Jazz Rides Again* '87; other LPs incl. *Crossing The Catskills* and improvised string band with *Vassar Clements, John Hartford & Dave Holland* on Rounder; *Vassar Clements* and *Superbow* on Mercury, *Southern Country Waltzes* on Rural Rhythm; also plays in group *Old And In The Way* on Sugar Hill with Jerry Garcia, David Grisman, others. Duet LP made in Nashville '85 with Stephane GRAPPELLI prod. by Tim Yaquinto released '87; should create jazzgrass genre.

CLEMENTS, Zeke (*b* 6 Sep. '11, Empire, Ala.) Veteran cowboy singer and country crooner. Began in vaudeville; joined National Barn Dance Chicago '28, Grand Ole Opry '30-50. Member of Otto Gray's Oklahoma Cowboys '32; also with brother fiddler Stanley (Curly) Clements as Bronco Busters. Most popular songs 'Smoke On The Water', 'Anytime', 'There's Poison In Your Heart'. Did voice of Bashful in Disney film *Snow White And The Seven Dwarfs* '37; popular in '40s for smooth vocal styling of cowboy songs.

CLEVELAND, Rev. James (*b* 23 Dec. '32, Chicago, Ill.) USA gospel singer, pianist; the Louis Armstrong of gospel: singing preacher with rough, rasping, righteous voice. Raised in poor family, sang at Pilgrim Baptist Church under Thomas A. DORSEY, studied piano infl. by Roberta

Martin. Joined Gospelaires '50 as pianist, third singer; then Martin's Singers; with the Caravans mid-'50s (hit 'The Solid Rock'), then the Meditation Singers (Detroit), Gospel All-Stars (Brooklyn), Gospel Chimes, gradually developing rocking style replete with dance steps. Recorded Soul Stirrers song 'The Love Of God' '60, became gospel classic with other Cleveland records 'Peace Be Still', 'Father I Stretch My Hands To Thee', 'Lord Remember Me'. Became West Coast based. Nominated for Grammy with Aretha FRANKLIN for her hit LP *Amazing Grace* '72; won own Grammy for *In The Ghetto* '74; worked with Quincy JONES in vocal arr. for TV series *Roots* '77; won Grammy for LP *Live At Carnegie Hall* '77, performed song from it on nationally televised Grammy Awards show, first gospel artist to do so. About 75 LPs available on Savoy, many with more than a dozen different choirs and gospel groups. Worked on such films as *The Idolmaker*, *Blues Brothers* (both '80). Pastor of L.A.'s Cornerstone Institutional Baptist Church.

CLIMAX BLUES BAND Blues band formed in UK '68 as Climax Chicago Blues Band, all from Stafford: Peter Haycock (*b* 4 Apr. '52), vocals, guitar; Colin Cooper (*b* 7 Oct. '39), vocals, sax; Derek Holt (*b* 26 Jan. '49), rhythm guitar, vocals; George Newsome (*b* 14 Aug. '47), drums; Arthur Wood, keyboards; Richard Jones, bass. Debut *Climax Chicago Blues Band* '69, then *Plays On* same year, both on Parlophone. Holt moved to bass as Jones left to attend University; band moved to 'progressive' Harvest label for *A Lot Of Bottle* '70. Successful USA tour '72 (NYC radio broadcast tape issued as *FM Live* '74), but stuck on college circuit at home. Wood and Newsome left after *Tightly Knit* '71, replaced by John Cuffley (drums) and (from '75) returned Jones, now on keyboards after stint with Principal Edwards Magic Theatre. LPs incl. *Rich Man* '72 still on Harvest, *Sense Of Direction* '74 on Polydor, *Stamp Album* '75 and *Gold Plated* '76 on BTM, all these on Sire in USA: latter appropriately titled LP broke through, with 'Couldn't Get It Right' (USA no. 3 hit, UK top 10). Band's sound had moved away from blues, though vocal blend (Cooper gruff and bassy, Holt falsetto) always apparent. *Shine On* '78 was on WB

UK; *Real To Reel* '79 on WB in both countries; steady roadwork paid off again with ballad 'I Love You' from *Flying The Flag* '80. *Lucky For Some* '81 was followed by switch to Virgin for *Sample & Hold* '83, only Cooper and Haycock left of original lineup; Cooper's departure after 14 LPs led to name change: Peter Haycock's Climax made *Total Climax* '85. Solid if often unexceptional, still a big live draw in USA; compilation *Loosen Up* on See For Miles label contains some of their best work.

CLINE, Patsy (*b* Virginia Petterson Hensley, 8 Sep. '32, Winchester, Va.; *d* 5 Mar. '63, Camden, Tenn.) Country/pop singer. Began in her teens; signed to Four Star Records '54; forced to record only songs published by record company. Appeared on Arthur GODFREY's Talent Scout TV show Jan. '57, sang 'Walkin' After Midnight', record went to top 5 country, top 20 pop. Signed to Decca, but restricted by old contract until '60. Divorced from Gerald Cline, married Charlie Dick '57. 'I Fall To Pieces' no. 1 country, top 10 pop '61, then she was badly injured in car crash; more hits followed: 'Crazy' no. 2 country, top 10 pop '61; 'She's Got You' no 1 country, pop hit in UK '62; 'When I Get Thru With You' '62, 'Leavin' On Your Mind' '63 both top 10 country; 'Sweet Dreams' top 5, 'Faded Love' top 10 country both '63. Died in plane crash 5 Mar. '63 that also killed Cowboy COPAS, Hawkshaw HAWKINS and Randy Hughes. First female country singer to cross over into pop and to rival Kitty WELLS as top female country star; posthumous popularity maintained with regular reissues. Elected to Country Music Hall of Fame '73; recordings dubbed with those of Jim REEVES to make ghoulish duet hits '81: 'Have You Ever Been Lonely', 'I Fall To Pieces'. LPs incl. *Country Hall Of Fame* '80, *Always* '82, *Golden Greats* '85, *The Patsy Cline Story* (2-disc set), all on MCA; *Greatest Hits With Jim Reeves* RCA '82, *The Legendary* MFP '81, *20 Golden Pieces* Bulldog UK '80. Loretta LYNN recorded LP of Cline songs; saw that Cline role was prominent in her own biopic *Coal Miner's Daughter*.

CLINE, Tammy (*b* 16 June '53, Hull, Yorkshire, England) Country singer. Worked in factory, sang in pub with local band the Falcons, married guitarist Rod Boulton; they formed duo Tammy and Dave Cline, joined band Uncle Sam to compete for spot at Wembley Festival, didn't make it. Solo appearances on radio, TV, then ITV's *Search For A Star*: formed own Southern Comfort Band, made several appearances at Wembley, named Best British Female Country Vocalist each year '80-4, represented UK at International Fan Fair Show in Nashville '80, International Country & Western Music Association Awards Gala in Galveston, Texas '84. Single 'Love Is A Puzzle'/'My Heart Strings Along' on CBS/UK '82; album *Tammy Cline & The Southern Comfort Band* on President '83, single 'I Wish I'd Wrote That Song'. Lives in Humberside since pointless government revision of local boundaries mid-'70s: insists she's still in Yorkshire.

CLINTON, Larry (*b* 17 Aug. '09, NYC; *d* '85) Bandleader. Played trumpet, wrote arrangements for Isham JONES, CASA LOMA, Tommy DORSEY, many others; had own bands '37-41, '48-50. Biggest composition was his own theme, 'The Dipsy Doodle', but did not record it then because Dorsey already had. Wrote jazz-oriented 'Satan Takes A Holiday', 'Tap Dancer's Nightmare', 'Dusk In Upper Sandusky' for Dorsey, 'A Study In Brown' for Casa Loma, many others; his own band mainly played sweet dance style: hits with 'Deep Purple', 'My Reverie', sung by popular vocalist Bea Wain (*b* 30 Apr. '17, NYC: went solo '39, had talk/record radio shows with husband late '40s NYC, Florida '70s). Made 214 sides in less than four years for RCA; later records on Decca incl. top 30 hits 'The Dickey-bird Song', 'On A Slow Boat To China', both '48.

CLOONEY, Rosemary (*b* 23 May '28, Maysville, Ky.) Singer. Moved to Cincinnati; while in high school, with sister Betty (*b* 12 Apr. c.'30) entered amateur events, etc.; worked on local radio mid-'40s; as vocal duo joined Tony PASTOR band for two years. Rosemary went solo, TV spot on *Songs For Sale*, Columbia contract, soon had hits: 'You're Just In Love' (duet with Guy MITCHELL) no. 29, 'Beautiful Brown Eyes' no. 11, then 'Come On-A My House'

no. 1 for six weeks (*see* David SEVILLE): bouncy arr. featured amplified harpsichord, Clooney's sexy, warm, very musical voice in semidialect; 'If Teardrops Were Pennies' no. 24, all '51. 13 top 40 hits '51-4 incl. 'Tenderly', Hank WILLIAMS's 'Half As Much', another dialect song 'Botch-A-Me', duet with Marlene Dietrich 'Too Old To Cut The Mustard', no. one hits with 'Hey There' (from Richard ADLER – Jerry Ross show *Pajama Game*), 'This Ole House' (revived '81 by Shakin' STEVENS in UK). Lesser hits incl. 'Pet Me, Poppa' from *Guys And Dolls*, then no. 10 'Mangos' '57; also made albums with Benny GOODMAN sextet, the HI-LO's vocal quartet: *Ring Around Rosie*, Duke ELLINGTON: *Blue Rose*. Own LPs incl. *While We're Young* (10″ LP), *Rosie's Greatest Hits*. Films incl. *The Stars Are Singing* and *Here Come The Girls* '53, *White Christmas* (with Bing CROSBY) and *Red Garters* '54 (latter soundtrack on 10″ LP), *Deep In My Heart* '54 (Sigmund ROMBERG biopic with José Ferrer, whom she married). Switched to RCA, had minor hit '60, made highly praised LP with Crosby *Fancy Meeting You Here*; also on RCA: *Clap Hands (Here Comes Rosie)*, *Rosie Solves The Swingin' Riddle*; on Coral: *Swing Around Rosie*, with Buddy Cole trio, now on Jasmine UK, and *Sweetest Sounds* with Les BROWN; on Reprise: *Love, Thanks For Nothing*; on Capitol with Crosby: *That Travellin' Two-Beat*. Semi-retired, raised five children, but fans still there: recent LPs on Concord (listed in jazz section of USA Schwann catalogue): *Everything's Coming Up Rosie, Rosie Sings Bing, Here's To My Lady* (2-disc set), *Sings Ira Gershwin, With Love; Sings Cole Porter, Harold Arlen, Irving Berlin, Jimmy Van Heusen*; shares album *Tribute To Duke Ellington* with Tony BENNETT, Crosby and Woody HERMAN. Backing on these by small groups, usually with Nat PIERCE, piano; Jake Hanna, drums (*b* 4 Apr. '31, Roxbury, Mass.), sometimes Cal TJADER, Ed Bickert, guitar (*b* 29 Nov. '32, Manitoba; has own LPs on Concord), Scott HAMILTON, etc. Also *My Buddy*, with Herman's big band.

CLOVERS, The USA black vocal group formed as quartet in Washington DC late '40s: John (Buddy) Bailey, lead tenor; Matthew McQuater, second tenor; Harold (Hal)

Lucas Jr, baritone; Harold Winley, bass: signed with Atlantic '50; Billy Mitchell replaced Bailey when he was drafted '52, stayed on when he came back: they had two lead tenors a decade before the TEMPTATIONS featured dual leads. Guitarist was Willie (Bill) Harris. They had 13 consecutive top 10 R&B hits '51-4 incl. 'Don't You Know I Love You' and 'Fool, Fool, Fool' (the first two, both written by Ahmet Ertegun, both at no. 1; the second covered by Kay STARR); 'Ting-A-Ling' (also no. 1), 'One Mint Julep', 'Your Cash Ain't Nothin' But Trash', 'Lovey Dovey', 'Devil Or Angel' (later a hit for Bobby VEE). Hits did not cross over to pop chart until '56 but white kids certainly bought them: they were much-loved as the first rock'n'roll vocal group. Top 30 pop hit '56 was 'Love, Love, Love'; switched to UA and had 'Love Potion No. 9' in top 30 of both charts '59. *Five Cool Cats* on Edsel UK has 16 of the Atlantic hits. They label-hopped, split up '61; Winley and Lucas led revival editions. Harris (*b* 14 Apr. '25, Nashville, Tenn.) had studied classical and jazz guitar; encouraged by Mickey Baker (*see* MICKEY & SYLVIA), who heard him practising in his dressing room, later became a prominent jazz guitarist, LPs on Mercury, Black & Blue, own Jazz Guitar label.

CLOWER, Jerry (*b* 28 Sep. '26, Liberty, Miss.) Worked for 18 years for chemical factory selling fertilizer; to help sales began spinning yarns. LP *Jerry Clower From Yazoo City, Mississippi Talkin'* on MCA '74 became country top seller; more of the same made him Country Comedian of the Year '74-82. Co-host of syndicated TV show *Nashville On The Road*; published book *Ain't God Good*.

COASTERS, The USA R&B vocal group, began in LA as the Robins, recorded with Johnny OTIS on Savoy, other labels (R&B no. 1 '50 with 'Double Crossing Blues'). Met writing/prod. team of LEIBER & STOLLER '53, became biggest act on their Spark label; 7 singles incl. 'Framed', 'Riot In Cell Block No. 9', 'Smokey Joe's Cafe': striking, humorous insights into ghetto life, all the more amazing that writers were white. Stylistic innovation was warm bass voice uttering witty or doleful comment.

Atlantic impressed by 'Smokey Joe', bought Robins' catalogue; lead singer Carl Gardner (*b* 29 Apr. '28, Texas), bass Bobby Nunn (*b* c.'25; *d* 5 Nov. '86) recruited Bill Guy (*b* 20 Jun. '36, L.A.) and Leon Hughes, changed name to the Coasters, after their West Coast origin (their former colleagues, whose management disapproved of Atlantic signing, continued briefly on Whippet). Coasters made R&B top 10 first time with 'Down In Mexico' '56; 2-sided 'Searchin'/'Young Blood' was no. 1 R&B, 3 and 8 respectively on pop chart '57, the latter with more suggestive lyrics and often revived since. Hughes, who was more dancer than singer, had been replaced by Young Jessie, then Cornel Gunter (ex-Flairs); Nunn gave way to Will 'Dub' Jones (ex-Cadets); this lineup made classics 'Yakety Yak' (no. 1 pop), 'Charlie Brown' (2), 'Along Came Jones' (9), 'Poison Ivy' (7): aural cartoons, with witty sax interjections by KING CURTIS, bass payoffs by Jones that entered the language of the era (from 'Charlie Brown': 'Why is ev'rybody always pickin' on me?'; from 'Yakety Yak': 'Don't talk back!'). Leiber & Stoller were foolishly accused of creating black stereotypes; they developed existing themes of obviously universal interest. Total of 19 Hot 100 entries incl. 'I'm A Hog For You', 'Run Red Run', 'Wait A Minute', 'Little Egypt' in top 40 took them to '64; Earl 'Speedoo' Carroll (ex-CADILLACS) replaced Gunter '61; had a few more hits incl. 'Let's Go Get Stoned' '65; by then Leiber & Stoller had split up and hits stopped. They were reunited with L&S '67 on CBS's Date label, but their songs had greater success with other artists, e.g. MONKEES with 'D.W. Washburn', ROLLING STONES 'Down Home Girl': the moment had gone, except for minor '71 hit with cover of CLOVERS' 'Love Potion No. 9' (salvaged when King bought the Date tracks). No less than Curtis MAYFIELD had dubbed them 'my biggest inspiration'; many versions of group worked revival shows, led by Nunn, Gardner, or Hughes, with Guy and Jones pairing; Nunn appeared in Phoenix a few days before his death. Compilations: *20 Great Originals* on Atlantic in UK; *Greatest Hits* on Atco USA.

COBB, Arnett (*b* Arnette Cleophus Cobbs, 10 Aug. '18, Houston, Texas) Tenor sax: Texas tenor in trad. that incl. Illinois

JACQUET, Herschel Evans, many more. Pro debut in Texas '33, replaced Jacquet in Lionel HAMPTON band '42, formed own band '47 and was leader through '50s except for bouts of illness, car crash; '59-60 had 16-piece group in Houston, managing El Dorado Club there; then Club Magnavox '70. Tours of Europe '70s, early '80s. LPs incl. *Arnett Cobb And His Mob* '52 with Jimmy COBB, Dinah WASHINGTON, in live performance on Phoenix label in UK; *The Complete Apollo Sessions* on French Vogue; *Very Saxy* and *Go Power!* (with Lockjaw DAVIS) on Prestige; *Jazz At Town Hall* with Jacquet '73; *Wild Man From Texas* '76 on Classic Jazz; 2 vols. of *Live At Sandy's* '78 on Muse; *Arnett Cobb Is Back* '78 and *Funky Butt* '80 on Progressive; *Keep On Pushin'* '84 on Beehive, with Junior MANCE, Panama Francis, George DUVIVIER (duet on 'Deep River'), plus Joe NEWMAN and Al Grey on 2 tracks. 'Stardust' shows 'the strong links between jazz balladry and R&B bawdy' (Brian Priestley in *The Wire*).

COBB, Jimmy (*b* Wilbur James Cobb, 20 Jan. '29, Washington DC) Drummer. Gigged locally with Billie HOLIDAY, Pearl BAILEY, others; toured with Earl BOSTIC '51; with Dinah WASHINGTON; gigged NYC; joined Cannonball ADDERLEY '57, Miles DAVIS '58-63; then with Paul CHAMBERS in Wynton KELLY Trio, touring Japan with J. J. JOHNSON '64, became quartet with Wes MONTGOMERY '65-6; trio again until Chambers died. Cobb joined Sarah VAUGHAN '71 and through '70s. Played on film soundtrack *Seven Days In May* with David AMRAM '64; PBS TV film with Vaughan at Wolf Trap Jazz Festival '70s. With Joe ALBANY trio NYC Apr. '80; Wolf Trap again same year. LPs with Davis, Chambers, Kelly, Vaughan.

COBHAM, Billy (*b* 16 May '44, Panama) Drummer, leader, composer. Sat in age 8 with pianist father NYC. While in US Army gigged with Billy TAYLOR, others '67; after discharge with Horace SILVER quintet '68 incl. European tour, Blue Note LPs *Serenade To A Soul Sister*, *You Got To Take A Little Love*. Also jingles, TV and film work (e.g. *Shaft* '71, music by Isaac HAYES). Formed fusion band Dreams '69-70; recorded with Miles DAVIS (*Jack Johnson,*

Bitches Brew, others); then with John McLAUGHLIN (*My Goal's Beyond* on Douglas), Mahavishnu Orchestra (*The Inner Mounting Flame, Birds Of Fire*) '71-3. Own bands incl. Spectrum '75; prod. LPs for AIRTO (*Virgin Land*), David Sancious (*Forest Of Feelings*). Own LPs on Atlantic: *Spectrum* c.'73 (quartet with Jan HAMMER, now ECM artist; later band named after LP); *Crosswinds, Total Eclipse, Shabazz* (live at Montreux) '74, *A Funky Thide Of Sings* '75, all 9 to 11 pieces with BRECKER brothers; *Live On Tour In Europe* (quartet co-led by George DUKE, who also played on *Crosswinds*); *Live And Times* '76. On CBS: *Magic* and *Alivemutherforya* '77, *Simplicity Of Expression* '77-8 (with large group). On Elektra by quartet Billy Cobham's Glass Menagerie: *Observations* '81, *Smokin'* '82 (live at Montreux), *Picture This* '87 on GRP with Grover WASHINGTON Jr. Impact on jazz/rock incl. Jack Bruce LP with Cobham, David Sancious *I've Always Wanted To Do This* '80. There also have been *Best Of* LPs on CBS, Atlantic. *Picture This* '88 on GRP, with guests Randy Brecker, Grover Washington Jr, etc., carries on in fusion mode.

COCHRAN, Eddie (*b* Cochrane, 3 Oct. '38, Oklahoma City, Okla.; *d* 17 Apr. '60, UK) Among best of original white rock'n'roll stars of '50s. Lived in Minn. until '49, family moved to Cal.; earliest work with Hank COCHRAN (no relation; Eddie dropped 'e', they worked as The Cochran Brothers); Hank left for career in country music; after two unsuccessful singles Eddie signed with Liberty; hits began in '57. Posthumous issue of early studio sessions was reminder that he was a better singer than most contemporaries, a good guitar player who co-wrote many songs (with Jerry Capehart), had an early grasp of studio technology and was at home with electric blues ('Milk Cow Blues'), anthemic rock'n'roll ('Summertime Blues'), or teen pop ('Teresa', 'Teenage Heaven', 'Sittin' In The Balcony'). Dynamic live performer; appeared in films '57, *The Girl Can't Help It* '56, *Untamed Youth* '57, *Go Johnny Go* '58. Hits mostly recorded in Hollywood with expert help (black L.A. session musicians such as drummer Earl Palmer had unsung role in period's pop). Best singles 'C'mon Everybody', 'Cut Across Shorty', 'Something Else', 'Summertime

Blues'; latter stands with some of Chuck BERRY's as definitive teenage comment: 'I called my congressman and he said, quote,/"I'd like to help you son, but you're too young to vote".' Broody James Dean-style good looks didn't hurt; like Gene VINCENT and Buddy HOLLY, more popular in UK (9 top 40 hits '58-63, plus two re-entries) than USA (3). Cochran had recorded version of 'Three Stars' '59, song about Buddy Holly, BIG BOPPER, Ritchie VALENS all killed in plane crash that year: himself killed in car crash near London following triumphant UK tour (Vincent badly injured): latest 'Three Steps To Heaven' swept to no. 1 UK. Covers of Cochran's hits incl. 'Cut Across Shorty' by Rod STEWART (on *Gasoline Alley* '70), 'Summertime Blues' by the WHO (*Live At Leeds* '70), 'C'mon Everybody' by the SEX PISTOLS ('79 film *The Great Rock'n'Roll Swindle*), '20 Flight Rock' by the ROLLING STONES (*Still Life* '82), etc.; STING played petrol pump attendant with Eddie Cochran fixation in '79 film *Radio On*. 4-disc *Complete Eddie Cochran* issued '80; 2-disc *25th Anniversary Album* '85 incl. unissued takes. Current LPs incl. *Singin' To My Baby* on Liberty/USA; many UK issues incl. latest *Best Of* on EMI/Liberty '85: 16 tracks incl. all USA/UK chart hits from short career.

COCHRAN, Hank (*b* 2 Aug. '35, Isola, Miss.) Country singer, songwriter. Raised in orphanage in Memphis, Tenn.; to Cal. and played clubs while still in teens. Formed country duo with future rock'n'roll legend Eddie COCHRAN (no relation), recorded for Ekko '53-5. Began writing songs, co-writing (with Harlan HOWARD) 'I Fall To Pieces' (hit for Patsy CLINE '61); wrote 'A Little Bitty Tear', 'Funny Way Of Laughin' ' for Burl IVES; 'Make The World Go Away', 'I Want To Go With You' for Eddy ARNOLD, 'Don't You Ever Get Tired Of Hurting Me?' for Ray PRICE, etc. Credited with discovering Willie NELSON (they also wrote songs together). Wrote songs in '70s for Nelson, Merle HAGGARD, Mel TILLIS, etc.; has won over 75 BMI songwriting awards. Married to country singer Jeannie SEELY. Recorded for Liberty '62, Gaylord '63, Monument '67; LPs incl. *With A Little Help From His Friends* (Capitol '78), *Make The World Go Away* (Elektra '80).

COCKBURN, Bruce (*b* '45, Ottawa) Canadian singer-songwriter. Folksy eponymous debut LP '70 on Epic, then more than a dozen low-key albums gradually edging to current electrified rock sound; lyrics evolved from fashionably mystical and ecological through religious (born-again Christian '74) to political. Worked through Europe as busker, studied at Boston's Berklee; first five LPs won Junos (Canadian equivalent of Grammy), but little impact outside. Lyrics and music seemed to find maturity in ninth LP *Dancing In The Dragon's Jaws* '79 (Millennium label): African, reggae, jazz infl. felt; first LP to chart in USA (no. 45), incl. first USA single hit 'Wondering Where The Lions Are' (no. 21 '80). *Humans* '80, *Bruce Cockburn/Resumé* '81 (hits compilation) charted in USA; meanwhile moved to city from rural retreat, recruited band (lineup in '85: Chi Sharp, percussion; Miche Pouliot, drums; Fergus Marsh, bass), prod. more aggressive, urban style: *Inner City Front* '82, *Trouble With Normal* '83; *Stealing Fire* '84 strongly infl. by tour of refugee camps in Central America, incl. sentiments overtly anti-USA foreign policy (e.g. 'If I Had A Rocket Launcher'). Music akin to DIRE STRAITS' lean yet muscular rock nevertheless found favour south of the border: reached top 50 LPs, incl. two singles in Hot 100, followed by *World Of Wonders* '85 on Canadian True North label, Revolver in UK.

COCKER, Joe (*b* John Robert Cocker, 20 May '44, Sheffield, England) UK singer with superbly rough white soul voice. Formed first band '59, recording and touring part-time '60s as Vance Arnold and the Avengers; signed by Decca '64, took leave of absence from job as gas fitter, but single flopped; formed Grease band, played in Northern pubs, moved to London, co-wrote 'Marjorine' with keyboardist Chris Stainton for a minor hit; then 'With A Little Help From My Friends' (LENNON and MCCARTNEY song, Jimmy Page and Stevie WINWOOD guesting on the record) was no. 1 UK '68 (both singles on Regal Zonophone), LP of that title on A&M went top 40 USA. He appeared at Woodstock '69; *Joe Cocker!* '69 with Leon RUSSELL and the Grease Band was no. 11 in USA '69; another BEATLE song 'She Came In Through The

Bathroom Window' was top 30 hit; 2-disc live *Mad Dogs & Englishmen* '70 incl. no. 7 hit USA 'The Letter': album was no. 2 USA, top 20 UK; souvenir of a tour of that name with Russell, Stainton and more than 40 others, critically successful but leaving Cocker broke and sick (from too much drink): Russell had put show together (also filmed) and just about stole it. *Joe Cocker* '72 and *I Can Stand A Little Rain* '74 were hit LPs, latter helped to no. 11 by no. 5 single 'You Are So Beautiful'; *Jamaica Say You Will* '76 was top 50, *Stingray* '76 no. 70; *Live In L.A.* '76 was tracks from a '72 tour with Stainton. Switched to Asylum (from A&M) for *Luxury You Can Afford* '78, still in top 80 LPs USA. By this time he was known for throwing up on stage. *Sheffield Steel* '82 on Island, *Civilised Man* '84 and *Unchain My Heart* '87 on Capitol charted in USA, though not in top 100; there will always be fans of that rough-edged voice. Recorded with CRUSADERS on their *Standing Tall* '81 (single 'I'm So Glad I'm Standing Here Today' was minor hit); no. 1 USA duet with Jennifer Warnes: 'Up Where We Belong' '82 (from film *An Officer & A Gentleman*). *Space Captain* '82 on Cube in UK compiled live tracks; there are other reissues and compilations.

COCKNEY REBEL UK pop band formed '73 by Steve Harley (*b* Steven Nice, 27 Feb. '51, London) Top 10 success with derivative 'Judy Teen', 'Mr Soft' '74; band split up, reformed with three new members, came back '75 with joyous no. 1 'Make Me Smile (Come Up And See Me)' (strongly reminiscent of Bob DYLAN's 'Absolutely Sweet Marie', '66), now billed as 'Steve Harley and Cockney Rebel'. Former journalist's large ego, smaller talent had led to feuding with pop music press; now it escalated: Cockney Rebels given constant critical drubbing. Caught between prevalent glam rock and desire to be seen as serious; albums were patchy, though *The Psychomodo* '75, *Best Years Of Our Lives* '76 had good points. Staccato version of BEATLES' 'Here Comes The Sun' made top 10 '76. With rise of punk the group split, embarrassed by Harley, who settled in USA for a while, made solo LPs *Hobo With A Grin* '78, *The Candidate* '79. DURAN DURAN covered 'Make Me Smile' on flip of UK no. 1 'The Reflex', '84;

Harley came back with a band '85, skirted charts with catchy 'Irresistible'; so far high point remains '75. Other LPs: *Human Menagerie* '74, *Loves A Rebel* and *Timeless Flight* '76, 2-disc *Face To Face* '77, *Best Of* '82. Harley sang on single from Andrew LLOYD WEBBER's *Phantom Of The Opera* '86, appeared in a musical based on Christopher Marlowe.

COE, David Allan (*b* 6 Sep. '39, Akron, Ohio) Flamboyant country singer: after almost 20 years in and out of reform schools and prisons, continuing iconoclasm made him part of 'outlaw' movement (*see* COUNTRY MUSIC). Released from Ohio State Correctional Facility '67 (allegedly a murderer), went to Nashville, signed with Shelby SINGLETON, recorded in heavy blues style (LPs *Penitentiary Blues*, *Texas Moon*); began career as *The Mysterious Rhinestone Cowboy* after signing with CBS '74; made breakthrough as writer: 'Would You Lay With Me In A Field Of Stone' (Tanya Tucker '75), 'Take This Job And Shove It' (Johnny PAYCHECK '77). Own LPs sold well, few hit singles: 'You Didn't Even Call Me By My Name' (top 10 country '75), 'Willie, Waylon & Me' (top 30 '76), 'The Ride' (about ghostly meeting with Hank WILLIAMS, no. 1 '83). Highly thought of by Willie NELSON, Waylon JENNINGS, Kris KRISTOFFERSON etc., his work is more rewarding for some fans than that of most hitmakers. *Outlaws* with Nelson issued on Charly UK '86; *I Love Country* '86 on CBS/UK is good hits compilation in schlock series; 17 LPs listed in USA '87 on CBS incl. *Once Upon A Rhyme* '75, *Tennessee Whiskey* '82, *Castles In The Sand* '83 (dedicated to Bob DYLAN), *Unchained* '85, *Son Of The South* '86 (with guests Willie, Waylon, Jessi COLTER, others), *A Matter Of Life And Death* '87. *For The Record (The First Ten Years)* is 2-disc compilation; *17 Greatest Hits 1974-85* on CD. Self-published autobiography *Just For The Record* is revealing.

COE, Tony (*b* 29 Nov. '34) UK reedman. Clarinet as a child, alto sax at 16, later tenor. Joined army, played in service band; then with Humphrey LYTTELTON on alto '57, toured USA. Formed own highly rated quintet '60, joined Count BASIE '65, Kenny CLARKE-Francy BOLAND Big Band for

European tours late '60s, working with Art FARMER, Johnny GRIFFIN, Stan GETZ; quintet Coe, Wheeler and Co. with Kenny WHEELER, other small groups called Martrix, Axel; recorded with Paul McCARTNEY '82; with Thad JONES big band at San Remo Festival same year. Heard in film scores *The Devils* '70, *The Boy Friend* '71, played Henry MANCINI main theme in *Pink Panther* movies (taking over from Plas JOHNSON). LPs with Clarke–Boland; own LPs on Nixa '58, '61; *Swingin' Till The Girls Come Home* '62; LP on EMI Columbia '67; *Pop Makes Progress* '69 with Robert FARNON; live at Ronnie SCOTT club '71 on 77 label (Dobel record shop used to be at 77 Charing Cross Road, London); *Zeitgeist*, Arts Council commission based on poems by Jill Robin, on EMI LP '76 with orchestra incl. Wheeler, vocalists Mary Thomas, Norma Winstone; quintet set *Coexistence* '79 on Lee Lambert label; *Tournée du Chat* '82 on French NATO was made at a jazz festival; *Sept Tableaux Phoniques/Erik Satie* '83 on NATO has two comps. by Coe, others by Dave HOLLAND, Lol COXHILL, etc.; *Nutty (on) Willisau* was made live at the Willisau Jazz Festival '84; *Le Chat se Retourne* '85 has duos, trios with clarinettist Alan Hacker and others. Coe's works have been played by several European bands; he teaches, contributes articles to books and periodicals. Recent work incl. session for Loudon WAINWRIGHT LP *I'm Alright*; own *Mainly Mancini* on Chabada '85 with bass (Chris Laurence), piano (Tony Hymas): reworks 'Panther', 'Days Of Wine And Roses', 'Mr Lucky', etc. on tenor, soprano, clarinet.

COGAN, Alma (*b* 19 May '32, London; *d* there 26 Oct. '66) Singer. Started in chorus of West End musical *High Button Shoes* with another young hopeful, Audrey Hepburn. First record 'To Be Worthy Of You' '52; featured in radio series *Take It From Here* '53-4; UK chart hits each year '59-61: 'Bell Bottom Blues', 'Little Things Mean A Lot' and 'I Can't Tell A Waltz From A Tango', all '54 followed by 'Dreamboat', no. 1, '55. Ed Sullivan TV show in USA '56 led to cabaret at Waldorf Astoria, minor US hit 'You, Me And Us'. First female singer to have her own major TV series in UK ('59-61, ITV). Wide popu-

larity: 'Just Couldn't Resist Her With Her Pocket Transistor' '60 no. 1 in Japan; 'Never Do A Tango With An Eskimo' was hit in Iceland. Best known for bright, uptempo numbers, but she also did ballads: LP *How About Love* '62 incl. 'If Love Were All', said to be Noel COWARD's favourite version of his song. Vivacious personality, 'the girl with the laugh in her voice', famous for large wardrobe of gowns. Hits compiled on *The Alma Cogan Collection* and *Second Collection*.

COHAN, George M. (*b* 3 July 1878, Providence, R.I.; *d* 5 Nov. '42, NYC) Singer, dancer, actor, composer, lyricist, director, producer. Broke away from European operetta-style shows to create dynamic, tubthumping American style, full of nostalgia and patriotism. Parents were in vaudeville; George and sister Josephine made top act The Four Cohans; he wrote 150 sketches by age 21. Josie semi-retired; three Cohans last appeared together '11. Wrote the most famous of war songs, 'Over There'; awarded Congressional Medal of Honor. Associated with more than 35 plays: musicals, straight drama, as writer and/or producer, incl. *Little Johnny Jones* ('The Yankee Doodle Boy', 'Give My Regards To Broadway') '04; *Forty-Five Minutes From Broadway* ('Mary's A Grand Old Name'), *George Washington Jr.* ('You're A Grand Old Flag'), both '06; *Fifty Miles From Boston* ('Harrigan') '08; *Little Nelly Kelly* '22 (revived '40 as film for Judy GARLAND); *Ah! Wilderness* (had long run, '33-4); last stage appearance *Return Of The Vagabond* '40. Appeared in films *The Phantom President* '32; *Gambling* '34. James Cagney won Oscar portraying Cohan in biopic *Yankee Doodle Dandy* '42; Joel Grey played him in '68 Broadway musical *George M!*. *Little Johnny Jones* revived '84 with Donny OSMOND; closed after one performance.

COHEN, Leonard (*b* 21 Sep. '34, Montreal, Canada) Gloomy poet became bard of bedsits. Member of Montreal country group The Buckskin Boys '54; then acquired considerable reputation as poet, novelist in Canada; early songs covered by Judy COLLINS, Tim HARDIN; appearance at Big Sur Festival '67 established him as performer. First LP *Songs Of Leonard Cohen* '68 still considered his best, incl. 'Suzanne', 'Hey, That's No Way To Say Goodbye', 'Stranger Song'. *Songs From A Room* '68 worked same formula of personal, often bitter experience steeped in religious symbolism. By '70 Cohen was touring with his group The Army, incl. prod. Bob Johnson, back-up singers; *Songs Of Love And Hate* that year incl. additions to canon 'Famous Blue Raincoat', 'Joan Of Arc', 'Avalanche' (covered by Nick Cave '84). Director Robert Altman used songs effectively in *McCabe & Mrs Miller* '71; Cohen filmed in concert and backstage '72 in *Bird On A Wire*, by Tony Palmer; album *Live Songs* '73. His style began to wear thin, though *New Skin For The Old Ceremony* '74 incl. memory of Janis JOPLIN in 'Chelsea Hotel No. 2'; audience was switching to better singer/songwriters (who owed debt to Cohen) e.g. James TAYLOR, Joni MITCHELL. *Death Of A Lady's Man* '78 was a strange, intriguing failure, with his funereal voice, backing incl. Bob DYLAN, Phil SPECTOR's 'wall of sound'. *Recent Songs* '79 drew on Cohen's European ancestry; *Various Positions* '84 revived affinity with country music; he was received ecstatically at European concerts that year, often playing generous sets of over three hours. His songs tapped a raw nerve, still stand up as austere chronicle; collection by Jennifer Warnes *Famous Blue Raincoat* '86 on Cypress USA/RCA UK was highly praised, then his new *I'm Your Man* '88, still on CBS.

COHN, Al (*b* Alvin Gilbert Cohn, 24 Nov. '25, Brooklyn, NY; *d* 15 Feb. '88) Tenor sax, arranger; also played other reeds. Exuberant, highly rated bop-infl. player, originally infl. by Lester YOUNG but tone acquired a darker colour over the years. Solos on Manny ALBAM-Ernie Wilkins RCA LP *Drum Suite* '56; LPs as leader incl. several on RCA mid-'50s; many with Zoot SIMS: on RCA '57, Epic '58, Coral '57, '59; Zim '61 (*Either Way*); Muse '73 (*Body And Soul*, with Jaki BYARD); Sonet '74 (made in Stockholm); also *Happy Over Hoagy* on Stash. Thanks to CD fine LPs are reappearing: *Natural Rhythm* with Freddie GREEN and *From A To Z* with Sims on Bluebird from mid-'50s. LPs on Concord Jazz since '81: quartet *Nonpareil* with Jake Hanna, drums; 2-disc *Tour de Force*, septet

with Hanna, piano, bass, guitar, three tenors: Cohn, Scott HAMILTON, Buddy TATE; quintet *Overtones* with Hank JONES, George DUVIVIER; *Standards Of Excellence*, quartet with Herb ELLIS; also two vols. of *Concord Jazz All Stars At The Northsea Festival*; *Tenor Gladness* '86 on Gemini with Totti Bergh on the other horn. Gigged '87 with Mose ALLISON.

COLE, Cozy (*b* William Randolph Cole, 17 Oct. '09, East Orange, N.J.; *d* 29 Jan. '81, Columbus, Ohio) Drummer. Family moved to NY '26; brothers Teddy and Donald played piano professionally; Cozy went pro '28; had own band, recorded with Jelly Roll MORTON '30; worked for Benny CARTER '33-4, Cab CALLOWAY '38-42, Benny GOODMAN, theatre work, own group at Onyx Club c.'43; also studied at Juilliard '40s. Own small groups late '40s, with Louis ARMSTRONG All Stars '49-53; started drum school with Gene KRUPA '54. Had pop hit '58: revived 'Topsy', BASIE arr. from late '30s by Edgar 'Puddinghead' Battle (1907-77) and Eddie DURHAM, as two-part drum vehicle; side 1 made no. 1 USA. Toured with own band; later joined quartet led by Jonah JONES, also swing era veteran who had big success in clubs of the '50s. Appeared in Goodman film *Make Mine Music* '44; *Glenn Miller Story* '54.

COLE, Lloyd (*b* 31 Jan. '61, Glasgow) Singer, songwriter. Formed the Commotions '82, with infl. deep in '60s: Bob DYLAN, Marc BOLAN, VELVET UNDERGROUND. First single 'Perfect Skin' top 30 UK hit; other enigmatic singles charted: 'Forest Fire', title cut of LP *Rattlesnakes* (all '84). LP incl. characteristic songs 'Four Flights Up', breathless 'Down On Mission Street'; band's sound reminiscent of '60s West Coast swirling guitars, organ, with obtuse, sometimes pretentious lyrics: 'She looks like Eva Marie Saint in "On The Waterfront"/She reads Simone de Beauvoir . . . ' from 'Rattlesnakes'. Brooding six-foot Cole with matinee-idol looks, vocal urgency, infectious tunes wins fans; played USA dates late '84 to some interest. *Easy Pieces* '85 justified fans, incl. hit singles 'Lost Weekend', 'Brand New Friend', imaginative 'Why I Love Country Music'.

COLE, Nat 'King' (*b* Nathaniel Adams Coles, 17 Mar. '17, Montgomery, Ala.; *d* 15 Feb. '65, Santa Monica, Cal.: some sources incl. ASCAP give '19 as year of birth) Jazz pianist, led trio, then leading ballad singer from late '40s until death from cancer. Raised in Chicago; father Baptist minister; brothers Eddie, Fred, Isaac all musicians; led own band '34; organised big band to tour with *Shuffle Along* revue, ending on West Coast, playing clubs as solo pianist. Formed King Cole Trio '39 with guitarist Oscar Moore (*b* 25 Dec. '12, Austin, Texas; *d* 8 Oct. '81, Las Vegas), whose electric guitar was still unusual then, and bassist Wesley Prince, replaced later by Johnny Miller: the drummer didn't show up first night at Hollywood's Swanee Inn; they decided they didn't need one. Tasteful jazz-oriented style with piano and guitar integrated, unison singing; Cole's vocals became more and more popular. Cole also wrote: best-known was trio's first hit 'Straighten Up And Fly Right' (no. 9 '42). Toured with Benny CARTER '44-5; made films *Here Comes Elmer* '43, *Stars On Parade* '44, *Breakfast In Hollywood* '46, *Make Believe Ballroom* '49; radio shows late '40s. Irving Ashby (later with Oscar PETERSON) and Joe Comfort replaced Moore, Miller; trio made records for Decca, Atlas, Excelsior, then Capitol; many compilations over the years (edition with unissued tracks planned by Mosaic USA). Cole's voice and phrasing were already exceptional; then three no. 1 hits with ballad/pop material: 'I Love You (For Sentimental Reasons)' '46, 'Nature Boy' '48 accompanied by Frank DeVol orchestra, 'Mona Lisa' arr. by Nelson RIDDLE '50. Trio was dissolved late '51; he became one of USA's best-loved artists, not a 'sepia Sinatra' but a star in his own right, with 78 hit singles in Billboard charts '44-64 (over three a year), 49 of them in top 40. Highlights: 'Too Young' (no. 1), 'Unforgettable' (14), both '51; biggest of 3 hit versions of 'Pretend' '53; 'Answer Me, My Love' '54; 'Ballerina' and 'Send For Me' '57. EP *Love Is The Thing* made no. 79 on singles chart '57 with 'Stardust', perhaps the best-loved American song: the beautiful introduction to the verse had not been heard for years when revived by Cole; composer Hoagy CARMICHAEL said it was his favourite version. Cole was beaten by members of White Citizens Council at a '56 concert in Birmingham, Ala.; next year a proposed TV series failed allegedly because of racist sponsors; this was at a time of reaction to rock'n'roll: nothing to do with Cole except that racists perceived it as 'nigger music'. Ironically, one-stop record dealers distributing to shops in black neighbourhoods reported that Elvis PRESLEY records sold better there than Cole's. Yet Brook BENTON, Sam COOKE, Otis REDDING, many others had heard Cole all their lives; his smoothness and lovely vocal colour had its effect on soul music; Chuck BERRY said 'If I had only one artist to listen to through eternity, it would be Nat Cole' (reported by Arnold Shaw). Cole made films *Blue Gardenia* and *Small Town Girl* '53, *Istanbul* and *China Gate* '57; *St Louis Blues* '58 (portrayed W. C. HANDY: soundtrack LP charted), *Night Of The Quarter Moon* '59, sang title song *Cat Ballou* '65. 24 LPs '56-66 in top 100 of Billboard LP chart incl. *Ballads Of The Day* '56 (reissued as *Close-Up* '69), *After Midnight* '57 (re-created trio with John Collins, guitar; Charlie Harris, bass, adding Lee Young, drums and with solos by Willie SMITH, Harry EDISON, Stuff SMITH, Juan Tizol), no. 1 LP '57 *Love Is The Thing* (with 'Stardust'), and *The Very Thought Of You* '58 with Gordon JENKINS, *To Whom It May Concern* '58 with Riddle, *Nat Cole Sings/George Shearing Plays* '62. *Welcome To The Club* '58 with big band pleased jazz fans: the band was Count BASIE's, with Gerald Wiggins on piano (*b* 12 May '22, NYC). *The Nat 'King' Cole Story* was a three-record set, now in USA in three separate LPs (re-created some trio selections in stereo, '61). *Meets The Master Saxes* on Spotlite UK from '42-3 with Lester YOUNG, Dexter GORDON, Illinois JACQUET; Red CALLENDER on some tracks. Countless 'Best Ofs', 'Golden Hits' LPs; EMI/UK reissued original Capitol LPs '85-6. His popularity as a vocalist obscured the influence of his jazz piano.

COLE, Natalie (*b* Feb. '50, L.A.) Singer; daughter of Nat 'King' COLE. Debut LP *Inseparable* '75, 10 years after Nat's death; incl. 'This Will Be' (no. 6 hit USA); title track also charted; seven top 40 hits '75-80 incl. 'I've Got Love On My Mind' (no. 5 '77), 'Our Love' (no. 10 '78). Other albums:

Natalie '76, *Unpredictable* '77 (no. 8 LP), *Thankful* '77, *Live* '78 (2-disc set), *I Love You So* '79, *We're The Best Of Friends* '79 (duet LP with Peabo BRYSON), *Don't Look Back* '80, *Happy Love* '81, all on Capitol, all made Billboard charts, but sales slipped: last Capitol LP, first Epic LP *I'm Ready* '83 did not make top 100 albums. *Unforgettable – A Tribute To Nat King Cole* (with Johnny MATHIS) '83 charted well in UK.

COLEMAN, Bill (*b* 4 August '04, near Paris, Ky.; *d* 24 Aug. '81, Toulouse, France) Trumpet. Family moved to Cincinnati, Ohio '09; debut in semi-pro bands of J. C. HIGGINBOTHAM, Edgar HAYES; to NYC '27. Worked for Luis RUSSELL '29, '31, '32; to Europe with Lucky MILLINDER '33; back in NY with Benny CARTER, Teddy HILL, Fats WALLER; to Europe again '35; worked in Bombay six months, back to Paris, to Egypt '38 co-leading Harlem Rhythmakers/Swing Stars; back to USA '40, with Carter, Waller, Andy KIRK, own trio, Ellis LARKINS trio incl. Carnegie Hall concert; USA tour '45 incl. Japan; with Sy OLIVER, Billy Kyle; then to France permanently '48. Played on some classic Russell records '29; Dicky WELLS Paris session '37 (scat vocal on 'Hangin' Around Boudin'); behind pop vocalist Eddy HOWARD on Columbia hits '40s; many jazz festivals, visits to UK, LPs *Mainstream At Montreux*; with Ben WEBSTER on Black Lion; *Nice 1974*, etc. Published *Trumpet Story* '81. Underrated, perhaps because he moved around so much; became pillar of Paris jazz community: Dan Morgenstern compared his 'skipping beat and light, pure tone' to earlier Jabbo SMITH, later Buck CLAYTON. Compilation LPs incl. *Bill Coleman: Paris '35-37* on Pathé Marconi (French EMI).

COLEMAN, Cy (*b* Seymour Kaufman, 14 June '29, NYC) Singer, pianist, composer. Recital at Steinway Hall age 6. Played supper clubs in Manhattan at 17; formed own trio '48 while still attending NY College of Music. Wrote 'Try To Change Me Now' and 'Witchcraft' (recorded by Frank SINATRA '52 and '58); 'Firefly' (hit for Tony BENNETT '58); musical *Wildcat* for Lucille Ball '60 with lyricist Carolyn Leigh (*b* 21 Aug. '26, NYC, *d* '83; also wrote 'Young At Heart' with Johnny Richards, etc.). Then followed shows *Little Me* '62 (with Leigh), *Sweet Charity* '66 (incl. 'Big Spender') and *Seesaw* '73 (with Dorothy Fields; *see* Jimmy McHUGH), *Barnum* '79, providing songs 'If My Friends Could See Me Now', 'Hey, Look Me Over', 'Real Live Girl' and 'I've Got Your Number'. Other songs incl. 'When In Rome', recorded by Barbra STREISAND among others; 'Pass Me By', written for film *Father Goose* '65; 'Sweet Talk'. Coleman's LPs incl. *Jamaica, If My Friends Could See Me Now, Age Of Rock. Songs of Dorothy Fields & Cy Coleman* '77 by Mark MURPHY on Audiophile.

COLEMAN, George (*b* 8 Mar. '35, Memphis, Tenn.) Tenor sax. Always pleasing modernist admired by other musicians for technique, good taste. Toured with R&B combos incl. B. B. KING, gigged in Chicago; to NYC mid-'50s: with Max ROACH '58-9, Slide HAMPTON '59-61, Wild Bill DAVIS '62, Miles DAVIS '63-4, Newport Jazz Festival '65; worked with his wife, bassist/vocalist/organist Gloria Bell Coleman (her LPs incl. quartet on Imperial '63, sextet *Sings And Swings Organ* '65 on Mainstream), played alto in soundtrack of Herbert Danska film *Sweet Love, Bitter* '66 (aka *It Won't Rub Off, Baby*) based on life of Charlie PARKER. Writes for groups of all sizes; had NEA grant, played many gigs at colleges. Records with Roach, Miles Davis, Hampton; five LPs with Chet BAKER quintet on Prestige '65; with Herbie HANCOCK on *Maiden Voyage* '65, other Blue Note LPs with Lee MORGAN, Horace SILVER, Elvin JONES, others; with Jones on Enja '73 (*Live At The Village Vanguard*); with Charles MINGUS on Atlantic '77 (*Three Or Four Shades Of Blues*); etc. Leads own quartet and octet: octet date at Camden Jazz Festival London '81 taped for UK TV, incl. Sal Nistico, second tenor; marvellous Bobby WATSON, alto (played on Art BLAKEY LPs on Concord label); Dannie Moore, trumpet, flugelhorn; Mario Rivera, baritone; Harold Mabern, piano; Clint Houston, bass; Billy HIGGINS, drums. Own albums incl. *Meditation* '77 on Timeless (duo with Tete MONTOLIU); *Big George* '77 on Affinity UK has octet with Maber, Rivera, Moore, Frank Strozier on alto (*b* 13 June '37, Memphis, Tenn.), Junior Cook on tenor (*b* 22 July '34, Pensacola, Fla.), Idris Muhammad, drums (*b* Leo Morris, '39, New Orleans), Lisle Atkinson, bass; *Amsterdam After Dark* '78 on Timeless has quartet with Hilton RUIZ, piano (*b* 29 May '52, NYC), Sam Jones, Higgins; *Live* '79 on Pye made at Ronnie SCOTT's Club London by quartet with Ray Drummond replacing Jones (another track from these sessions on 2-disc set from Debut records with booklet, celebrating Club's 25th anniversary). *Mama Roots* '81 on Muse has sextet co-led by Charles EARLAND; *Manhattan Panorama* '85 is a quartet with Mabern on Bob THIELE's Theresa label.

COLEMAN, Ornette (*b* 19 Mar. '30, Ft Worth, Texas) Alto sax; also tenor, trumpet, violin; composer. Began on alto age 14, took up tenor '46; gigged in Ft Worth till '49, played in R&B bands; settled in L.A. '50s, working as lift operator, studying theory and harmony; to New York '59 with quartet, playing plastic alto because he liked the sound, and Don CHERRY on pocket trumpet; these looked like toy instruments, giving critics something extra to complain about. Blazed trail for free jazz with original 'atonal' compositions. First LP *Something Else!!!* bravely recorded early '58 by Lester Koenig at Contemporary in L.A.; quintet incl. Cherry, Billy HIGGINS, Walter Norris, piano (*b* 27 Dec. '31, Little Rock, Ark.; own LP *Drifting* on Enja), early sympathiser Don Payne, bass. Live date at L.A. Hillcrest Club '59 had Charlie HADEN on bass, Paul BLEY on some tracks; two LPs resulted, one under Coleman's name (on Improvising Artists), Bley's (on America). Second Contemporary LP *Tomorrow Is The Question!* '59 had Cherry, Shelly MANNE, Red MITCHELL, who had introduced Coleman to Koenig, then to Percy HEATH and to John LEWIS, who arranged visit to summer jazz school at Lennox, Mass. Gig at NYC's Five Spot in Nov. '59, together with titles of Atlantic LPs that year *The Shape Of Jazz To Come*, *Change The Century* (with Coleman, Cherry, Haden, Higgins) put fat in the fire: new music had support of critics Nat Hentoff, Martin Williams, jazz academic and third stream composer Gunther Schuller; Lewis: 'Coleman is doing the only really new thing in jazz since the bop innovations of the mid-'40s'; others thought he was a fraud: Charles MINGUS said, 'Trouble

is, he can't play it straight,' but later thought better: 'I'm not saying everybody's going to have to play like Coleman. But they're going to have to stop playing Bird.' (Mingus, Coleman, Max ROACH, Kenny DORHAM played together as Newport Rebels mid-'60, not recorded.) Composer George Russell knew immediately what Coleman was doing: 'Ornette seems to depend mostly on the over-all tonality of the song as a point of departure for melody. By this I don't mean the key the music might be in . . . the melody and the chords of his compositions have an over-all sound which Ornette seems to use as a point of departure. This approach liberates the improviser to sing his own song, really, without having to meet the deadline of any particular chord.' LP *Free Jazz* '60 added Freddie HUBBARD, Eric DOLPHY, Scott LA FARO, Ed BLACKWELL to Coleman's group to make double quartet, with an atonal quartet on each stereo channel: probably a noble failure. *Ornette* '61 had Cherry, La Faro, Blackwell; *Ornette On Tenor* '61 (with Jimmy GARRISON replacing La Faro) showed Coleman at home on bigger horn. (Later Atlantic LPs *The Art Of Improvisation*, *Twins* had other tracks from these sessions.) After *Town Hall 1962* on ESP Coleman lay low to concentrate on composition; had also raised his price too high and could not get club work. *Chappaqua Suite* '65 is 2-disc set on CBS for quartet (incl. Pharoah SANDERS) and studio band dir. by Joseph Tekula. Other LPs incl. *Ornette Coleman In Europe Vols. 1 & 2* '65 from Fairfield Hall, Croydon, England; *At The Golden Circle, Stockholm* '65, two trio LPs on Blue Note; *Who's Crazy* '65, 2-disc film soundtrack made in Belgium, now on Affinity; *The Empty Foxhole* '66, trio LP on Blue Note, has son Ornette Denardo Coleman on drums, then 9 years old (*b* 19 Apr. '56); *Forms and Sounds(:) The Music Of Ornette Coleman* '67 on RCA is played by woodwinds and strings: Coleman plays trumpet on some selections, not at all on others. A session made at Royal Albert Hall in London Feb. '68 unissued except for one track on Plastic Ono Band LP with voice of Yoko ONO dubbed. *New York Is Now!* '68 has a quartet with Dewey REDMAN on Blue Note; *Ornette At 12* '68, *Crisis* '69 are on Impulse; *Friends And Neighbors* on Flying

Dutchman. *Science Fiction* and *Broken Shadows* '71 on CBS have Bobby BRADFORD on some tracks. *Skies Of America* '72 on CBS has quartet with Redman, Haden, Blackwell acc. by the London Symphony Orchestra cond. by David Measham: Coleman's work at rehearsals and recording earned him a standing ovation from the orchestra. To describe the composition in 21 segments he invented the word 'harmelodic', much used since and perhaps best defined (by Gary Giddins) as improvised coloration. The 'new thing' had combined revival of collective improvisation with harmonic freedom ('If I'm going to follow a preset chord sequence I may as well write out my solo') – the freedom that Coleman HAWKINS had found 30 years earlier improvising on chords instead of melody was extended by improvising on harmony itself. Coleman opened doors, but the early fuss about his music was overdone (especially for those who have listened to 'classical' music of this century), highlighting the essential conservatism of many critics. Other LPs on various labels incl. *J For Jazz Presents Ornette Coleman Broadcasts* '72; *Dancing In Your Head* '73 on A&M Horizon made in Joujouka, Morocco by sextet with two guitars plus local musicians (incl. repetitious treatment of a theme from *Skies*, delivering more than the usual hypnotic effect of such music). Childhood friend Prince LASHA said that he and Coleman were infl. by Red Conner, a Fort Worth tenor saxophonist who died in the '50s; it is arguable that Coleman's avantgardism arose directly from early R&B experience, a genre despised as tavern/sex music by some (just like early jazz); at any rate, harmelodics began to allow echoes of funk and rock, crossover appeal creating coalitions among listeners and musicians. He formed Prime Time, an electric group: *Body Meta* '76 had two guitars, electric bass; *Soapsuds* '77 a duo with Haden (both on Artist House), *Of Human Feelings* '79 two drummers incl. Denardo on Antilles. Denardo now looks after the business end as well as playing drums; on Caravan Of Dreams label *Opening The Caravan Of Dreams* and *Prime Design/Time Design* were followed by 2-disc *In All Languages* '87, one disc a reunion with Higgins, Haden, Cherry, the other by Prime Time. *Song X* '86 on

Geffen co-led by Coleman, guitarist Pat METHENY; demanding music played by quintet with Haden, Denardo and Jack DEJOHNETTE. Coleman has gone from *enfant terrible* to guru without much commercial success and without many albums; his loyal following does not generate the sales that big record companies want. Prime Time sidemen Charlie Ellerbee, Jamaaladeen Tacuma, drummer Ronald Shannon Jackson are now up-and-comers; Jackson (*b* 12 Jan. '40, Fort Worth, Texas) plays in Last Exit with Bill LASWELL, solo *Pulse* on Oao, and with his Decoding Society: *Decode Yourself* on Island; *Barbeque Dog, Mandance* on Antilles, *Nasty* and *Street Beat* on Moers Music, *Eye On You* on About Time, *When Colors Play* on Caravan Of Dreams; also *Power Tools* '87 on Antilles. Tacuma's *Music World* on Gramavision '87 is heavily electronic.

COLES, Johnny (*b* 3 July '26, Trenton, N.J.) Trumpet, flugelhorn. Began playing '39, mainly self-taught; with Philly Joe JONES '51, James MOODY '65-8, then Gil EVANS; with George COLEMAN at Newport '66; Herbie HANCOCK sextet '68; Ray CHARLES band '69-70; with Duke ELLINGTON; Charles again. LPs with Ellington, Hancock (*The Prisoner*, Blue Note), Kenny BURRELL (big band *Guitar Forms*) and Astrud Gilberto (*Look To The Rainbow*), both on Verve; *The Great Concert Of Charles Mingus* (Prestige), others. Own LPs incl. *The Warm Sound* '61, quartet on Epic; *Little Johnny C* '63, quintet on Blue Note; *Katumbo* '71, septet with Cedar WALTON on Mainstream; *New Morning* '82, quartet on Criss Cross with Horace PARLAN. Played mid-'80s with Count BASIE band led by Thad JONES.

COLLETTE, Buddy (*b* William Marcell Collette, 6 Aug. '21, L.A.) Reeds, piano, composer. One of the top flautists in jazz. Own band '40-1; with Les Hite '42; Benny CARTER '48-9; Gerald WILSON '49-50; gigged with everybody on West Coast; with Chico HAMILTON '56; own group '59 incl. Wilson, Red CALLENDER. Radio, TV work with Jerry Fielding mid-'50s, since then much studio work, film music, teaching. Many own LPs mostly on West Coast, since '54 incl. sets on Contemporary, Mercury,

Italian labels; Crown sessions '59-60 issued by label under names of Wardell GRAY, Stan GETZ, Erroll GARNER, none of whom were present. Helped start Legend label mid-'70s; LP *Now And Then* '73, septet with Leroy Vinnegar, Callender on both bass and tuba; *Blockbuster* '73, quintet set on RGB label.

COLLIER, Graham (*b* 21 Feb. '37, Tynemouth, England) Bass, composer. Trumpet from 11; band boy in British army at 16; while in army took up bass, composition; entered *Downbeat* competition while stationed in Hong Kong, won part of tuition at Berklee School of Music, Boston; gigged with Herb Pomeroy, Jimmy DORSEY; graduated '63. Formed own UK septet '64; much educational and studio work. First jazz composer to get funds from UK government Arts Council, '67: *Workpoints* for 12-piece band resulted. *Day Of The Dead* for Ilkley Literature Festival '77 (words from Malcolm Lowry novel *Under The Volcano* '47) led to BBC commission for TV version; toured India '79; gave up bass for full-time composition. LPs: *Deep Dark Blue Centre* '67, septet on Deram with Kenny WHEELER; sextet LP *Down Another Road* '69 and *Songs For My Father* '70, with seven songs played by 10-piece group, both on Fontana; *Mosaics* '70 on Philips with septet. Started own Mosaic label; 11 issues '74-8 incl. own records *Darius* '74, *Midnight Blue* '75; *New Conditions* and *Symphony Of Scorpions* '76, *The Day Of The Dead* '78 on two discs with 13 pieces plus narrator. Also educational recordings made '75 for Cambridge U. Press. Large composition *Hoarded Dreams* recorded at Bracknell Jazz Festival '83, broadcast on BBC radio; '85 performance from Camden (London) Jazz Festival shown on Channel 4 TV '85. Another recent comp. is called *Crystals Of Time And Place*. Infl. by Duke ELLINGTON, Gil EVANS; admires Mike Mantler, Carla BLEY 'when they are writing well'; also Vienna Art Orchestra's Mathias Rüegg. Has given up low-paid live work to stay at home and write, but tour of Greece with octet '83 was satisfying. Sextet album *Something British* released '88. With others in improvised music, wants to 'make the improvising part of the ebb and flow of the performance so that the piece changes all the while'.

COLLINS, Albert (*b* 1 Oct. '32, Leona, Texas) Blues guitarist, singer, songwriter. Born to sharecropping family, moved to Houston's black ghetto as a child; learned piano at school, but was also instructed on guitar by his cousin Lightnin' HOPKINS, who taught him to tune it in a minor key, which later became a Collins trademark. Played local blues club circuit with Clarence 'Gatemouth' BROWN at age 15; formed own group the Rhythm Rockers '49-51; joined Piney Brown's band for three years; became session player at 21, recording and/or performing with LITTLE RICHARD (replaced Jimi HENDRIX), Big Mama THORNTON, others. First record 'The Freeze' was a characteristic instrumental with heavily sustained single notes in a high register; billed as 'cold blues' player, 'like something cold in the ice box', according to an interview in CADENCE: the unique Texas blues never got enough exposure in an era dominated by Chicago, but Collins has been its foremost exponent. LP *Frosty* '62 collected singles, on small labels Kangaroo, Great Scott, and Hall in Houston sentenced to be regional hits only. In '68 he was recommended to Imperial by Bob Hite (member of CANNED HEAT and a noted blues collector; Imperial was then connected with Liberty/USA, Canned Heat's label); first of three Imperial LPs *Love Can Be Found Anywhere Even In A Guitar* was made that year: Collins sang on record for the first time, but on two of the three was backed by Nashville sidemen, in an attempt to widen his appeal. He also recorded for Blue Thumb, and for Bill SZYMCZYK's shortlived Tumbleweed label in Chicago '72, that prod. no doubt hoping to repeat his success with B. B. KING. Collins appeared at Newport and Fillmore West '69 (latter gig recorded by ex-FLEETWOOD MAC Jeremy Spencer, now on UK Red Lightnin' label as *Alive & Cool*); gigged in Seattle '72-5 and influenced the young Robert CRAY; at the Montreux Jazz Festival '75. Record success incl. four Grammy nominations was clinched at last on Alligator in Chicago, with a band incl. Larry Burton, guitar; Alan Batts, keyboards; Aron Burton, bass; Casey Jones, drums; A. C. Reed, tenor sax (related to Jimmy REED), Chuck Smith, baritone; billing as 'cold blues' player (actually red hot!) has been emphasised by album titles:

Ice Pickin' '78; *Frostbite* '80 (with Marvin Jackson, guitar; Johnny 'B.Goode' Gayden on bass; various horn players); *Frozen Alive!* '81 (live in Minneapolis incl. fresh version of 'Frosty'; Jackson, Reed, Batts, Gayden, Jones now called the Icebreakers); *Don't Lose Your Cool* '83 (with Larry Burton, Chris Forman on keyboards, extra hornmen); *Live In Japan* '84 (recorded late '82 with Collins, Reed, Gayden, Jones, Burton). On *Showdown!* '85, with Batts, Gayden, Jones, the Master of the Telecaster played host to protégés Cray and Johnny COPELAND: supersession went high in USA/UK charts. *Cold Snap* '86 incl. organist Jack McDUFF. Another great artist given his due by Bruce Iglauer; *see* ALLIGATOR.

COLLINS, Dolly (*b* Dorothy Ann Collins, 6 Mar. '33, Hastings, Sussex) English keyboardist, composer of folk revival. Studied under the composer Alan Bush (*b* 22 Dec. 1900, London; worked with Workers' Music Association) after recommendation from her uncle, author Fred Ball (*A Breath Of Fresh Air* '61); he told her 'to look at the material presented to you, like the tune of a folk song, find out what there was in it and use the material that's already there in the accompaniment, so that you don't actually bring any alien material into the work'. Came to fame through work with her sister (*see* Shirley COLLINS); worked with the INCREDIBLE STRING BAND on their hit LP *Hangman's Beautiful Daughter* '68, her portative pipe organ a hallmark of many fine albums; also with the YOUNG TRADITION on *Galleries* and the unreleased *The Holly Bears A Crown*, both '69; on Peter BELLAMY's *Transports* '77 her arrangements re-created the sound of an 18th-C. village band. She also worked on albums by Chris Darrow, Mark Ellington, Matthews Southern Comfort, Tony Rose. *Adieu To Old England* '74 is noteworthy for the simplicity and fidelity of the arrangements, yet *For As Many As Will* '78 (both with Shirley) was one of the first records to integrate a synthesiser into folk music. Illness prevented her playing for several years from late '70s, but she continued to write on commission, incl. advertising jingles and the music for clock chimes in Nottingham shopping centre. Her song suite *Anthems In Eden* (recorded with Shirley '69) was revived '86 for the Summerscope Festival in London.

COLLINS, Judy (*b* 1 May '39, Denver, Col.) Folksinger. Encouraged to study piano by blind father; switched to guitar with lure of folk music. Signed to Elektra: debut LP *A Maid Of Constant Sorrow* relied on trad. material; appeared on Chicago TV folk showcase Continental Café; by the time of *Judy Collins 3* '64 she drew on contemporary songs of Bob DYLAN, Phil OCHS, Tom PAXTON. *In My Life* '66 was orchestrated by Joshua RIFKIN, marking another milestone in '60s progress of genre; affair with Stephen STILLS (who wrote 'Suite: Judy Blue Eyes' for her), LP *Who Knows Where The Time Goes* '68 saw her embraced by hip Laurel Canyon superstar fraternity. With prescience (or just good taste) she was one of the first to cover songs by Joni MITCHELL: 'Both Sides Now' big hit UK and USA '70. Album *Whales & Nightingales* incl. trad. Scottish ballad 'Farewell To Tarwathie', backing vocal by humpbacked whales; also version of trad. 'Amazing Grace', became standard: hit in UK, USA '70, re-entered chart seven times in UK '71-2. Acted in prod. of *Peer Gynt* '69; dir. documentary about her former music teacher *Antonia: A Woman* '74 nominated for an Oscar. *Judith* '75 incl. hit version of Stephen SONDHEIM's 'Send In The Clowns'. Still rapturously received in concert; *Home Again* '84 saw her covering Vince CLARKE's 'Only You', Elton JOHN's 'Sweetheart On Parade'. Apart from her beautiful voice, she was infl. in recognising singer/songwriters such as Mitchell, Ian Tyson (*see* IAN & SYLVIA), Leonard COHEN, DONOVAN etc. Many LPs, all on Elektra, incl. *Concert* '64, *In My Life* '67, *Wildflowers* '68 (with 'Both Sides Now', no. 5 USA LP chart; LP titled *Both Sides Now* on budget label UK '82), *True Stories And Other Dreams* '73, *Running For My Life* '80, *Times Of Our Lives* '82, *Hard Times For Lovers* '83; compilations incl. *Colors Of The Day* '72, 2-disc *So Early In The Spring (The First 15 Years)* '77; *Love Songs* LP advertised on UK TV '85.

COLLINS KIDS Lorrie and Larry, vocal duo mid-'50s (Lawrencine May Collins, *b* 7 May '42, Tahlequah, Okla.; Lawrence Albert

Collins, *b* 4 Oct. '42, Tulsa). Sang and played guitar at school, on Cal. radio shows in early teens. Signed to Columbia '55, made classic rockabilly singles such as 'Rock Away Rock', 'In My Teens', 'Rock Boppin' Baby', 'Hop Skip & Jump' '56-9. Never made the charts, but featured on Town Hall Party TV show '53-60, Grand Ole Opry '59, Steve ALLEN show, etc. Split '65 when Lorrie married promoter Stew Carnall and settled in Reno. Larry continued behind the scenes: co-wrote 'Delta Dawn' ('72 pop-country hit), worked as prod., publisher. Albums incl. *Country Spectacular* '57, *Town Hall Party* '58, both Columbia; *Collins Kids* '83 on Bear Family label.

COLLINS, Phil (*b* Philip David Charles Collins, 31 Jan. '51, London) Drummer, singer, producer. Began as child actor; played Artful Dodger on stage in Lionel BART's *Oliver!* '64 (following SMALL FACES' Steve Marriott in role). Did film cameos in BEATLES' *A Hard Day's Night* '64, *Chitty Chitty Bang Bang* '69; auditioned unsuccessfully for lead in Zeffirelli's lavish '68 *Romeo And Juliet*. In art-rock band Flaming Youth; joined GENESIS as drummer; took over vocals '75 when Peter GABRIEL left, became group's central figure. Jazz infl. reflected in LPs by offshoot Brand X (*Unorthodox Behaviour* '75, *Moroccan Roll* '76). Debut solo LP *Face Value* '81 featured EARTH, WIND & FIRE horn section, incl. big hits 'In The Air Tonight', 'I Missed Again'. *Hello, I Must Be Going* '82 had UK no. 1 with revival of SUPREMES' 'You Can't Hurry Love'; live solo gigs proved viability, but still sticks to lumbering, anachronistic Genesis. Long wait for third album due to prod. commitments, incl. Adam ANT, ABBA's Frida, John MARTYN. Played drums on Band Aid record '84. *No Jacket Required* '85 incl. single 'Sussudio': criticised for resemblance to PRINCE's '1999' but made no. 1 spot in USA; also fine ballad 'One More Night'. Established as one of music's best all-rounders, becoming superstar: turned down for spot at Academy Awards singing own Oscar nominee, theme from *Against All Odds*, because committee had never heard of him. Contribution to Live Aid July '85 (*see* BAND AID) incl. playing drums for both Eric CLAPTON and re-formed LED

ZEPPELIN, solo sets at both Wembley and Philadelphia. Duet with Marilyn Martin 'Separate Lives' UK hit late '85; had UK/USA hit 'Easy Lover' '85 with Philip Bailey; contributed theme to *White Nights* '86; prod. LPs for Earth, Wind & Fire, Eric Clapton; prepared first full length acting role as Great Train Robber Buster Edwards '87.

COLLINS, Shirley Elizabeth (*b* 5 July '35, Hastings, Sussex) Singer, broadcaster with pivotal role in English folk revival. First tracks on HMV anthology *Folksong Today* '55; met Bob COPPER, then researching his '50s BBC broadcast *As I Rove Out*; this led to travel to USA, link with Alan LOMAX as editorial assistant on his *Folk Songs Of North America* and *Folk Songs Of Britain* (on Caedmon), also field researcher in USA South (encounters with racism and sexism curing her of any 'romantic notions'). Same year debut LP *Sweet England* '59 appeared on Argo, other tracks from the sessions on *False True Lovers* (Folkways): they were typical of the era but with strong American influence. Other now-rare folk-cum-skiffle anthologies incl. *A Jug Of Punch, A Pinch Of Salt, Rocket Along*; then charming *Heroes In Love* EP '63 on Topic, distillation of her style at the time; then ground-breaking *Folk Roots New Routes* '64 with Davey Graham, an important fusion of exotic and British folk with jazz and blues (reissued on Righteous '80), also EPs on Collector and Selection labels that year. *The Sweet Primeroses* '67 on Topic was transitional: with her sister Dolly COLLINS playing portative organ, it attracted a whole new audience and defined her singing style, which had become synonymous with Southern English (especially Sussex) tradition. Their *The Power Of The True Love Knot* '68 incl. Robin Williamson and Mike Heron (*see* INCREDIBLE STRING BAND); in August '68 the sisters premiered *Anthems In Eden* on BBC programme *My Kind Of Folk*; the '69 LP had an uncompromising suite on one side (with unlinked folk and contemporary songs on the other) about the aftermath of the Great War (WW1) which changed rural life forever: the fusion of folk and early music was unprecedented, the latter from David Munrow (1942-76) and his Early Music Consort, foremost band of its kind;

her then husband John Austin Marshall contributed the poignant 'Whitsun Dance', rounding off the suite (original LP on Harvest, now on See For Miles; Harvest reissued suite with side of new material on *Amaranth* '76). *Love, Death And The Lady* '70 was overshadowed by its predecessor, though 'Plains Of Waterloo' and 'Death And The Lady' showed remarkable powers. She helped found the first ALBION BAND, which then developed into one of the first important folk-rock bands (with FAIRPORT CONVENTION and STEELEYE SPAN), their debut LP *No Roses* among best of genre; she worked on *Morris On* '72, first of series of side-projects of husband Ashley Hutchings. *A Favourite Garland* '74 was sampler of new and old work, incl. (with *4. Folk Festival auf der Lenzburg*) the only commercially released tracks by Hutchings and Collins's Etchingham Steam Band, an acoustic dance band. Quiet charm of *Adieu To Old England* '74 and *For As Many As Will* '74 (sisters' swansong) should not be overlooked, though less innovatory than other work. She worked with various Albion permutations, guesting on LPs, appearing in National Theatre prod. incl. *The Passion* (became trilogy *The Mysteries*, an edited version recorded by HOME SERVICE '85). She gave up performing early '80s, though contributing to broadcast documentaries. *Anthems In Eden* was revived '86 for concert on London's South Bank with Dolly on flute organ, Catherine Bott of New London Consort taking Shirley's part.

COLLINS, Tommy (*b* Leonard Raymond Sipes, 28 Sep. '30, Bethany, Okla.) Country singer in '50s, became clergyman '58, re-entered music as songwriter '60s. Contract with Capitol '53 followed by uptempo novelties such as 'You Better Not Do That' '54, 'It Tickles' '55; also wrote hits for others: 'If You Ain't Lovin', You Ain't Livin' ' (Faron YOUNG), 'You Gotta Have A Licence' (Porter WAGONER). Infl. in West Coast country music, as later was Buck OWENS, member of Collins's band. Signed with Columbia '65, had hits 'If You Can't Bite, Don't Growl' '66, 'I Made The Prison Band' '68. Owens made LP *Sings Tommy Collins*; Merle HAGGARD recorded hits 'My Hands Are Tired', 'The Roots Of My Raising', 'Sam Hill', also wrote tribute to Collins

called 'Leonard'. LPs incl. *This Is Tommy Collins* '55, *Words & Music Country Style* '56, *Light Of The Lord* '59 (all Capitol); *Let's Live A Little* '66 (Tower), *The Dynamic* '67 (Columbia), *Country Souvenir* '81 (G&W). *This Is* reissued by Pathé Marconi in Europe '84

COLMAN, Stuart (*b* 19 Dec. '44, Harrogate) UK producer. Played bass guitar in local bands, joined Pinkerton's Assorted Colours: Samuel 'Pinkerton' Kemp, autoharp, vocals; Tony Newman and Tom Long, guitars; Dave Golland, drums; joining some time after their only big hit 'Mirrors, Mirrors' (no. 9 UK '66). Colman and Newman changed their name to Flying Machine and had no. 5 in USA with 'Smile A Little Smile With Me', but couldn't follow up; other members then were guitarist Steve Jones and drummer Paul Wilkinson (also an eponymous LP for Pye). Colman took his keen interest in '50s rock'n'roll to BBC Radio 1 as broadcaster '76 after the Teds marched on Parliament to protest at music's lack of airtime; took on electric blues/R&R/country show *Echoes* on Radio London '77 which continues to this day. First productions were for Radio 1, numerous owing to needletime restrictions of that era; he left contemporary pop to Bob Sargent (later prod. the BEAT etc.) and concentrated on revivalist fare: among acts was Shakin' STEVENS, who had his first UK top 20 with 'Marie Marie' '80, with Colman also playing bass, as he did on several later Shaky hits incl. three no. ones. Added ingredient along with Colman's crisp prod. was shrewd choice of songs, e.g. BLASTERS song for that first hit (Dave Alvin was unknown at the time). Received *Music Week* award for top producer '82 as well as BPI top prod. of year, all due to work with Shaky. Has since prod. Phil EVERLY, Cliff RICHARD ('She Means Nothing To Me'), Alvin STARDUST; rockabilly revivalists the Jets, the INMATES; and charity remake of 'Livin' Doll' by Richard and the Young Ones (no. 1 hit UK '86). Also prod. humour/music album *Comic Relief* from same stable (Kate BUSH, Howard JONES, etc.). Seal set on his mastery of authentic sound when he was asked to prod. LITTLE RICHARD comeback LP *Lifetime Friend* '86. With Dave EDMUNDS (who now produces

265

Shaky) an acknowledged master of aural nostalgia – and more.

COLON, Willie (*b* William Anthony Colón, 28 Apr. '50, Bronx, NYC) Trombonist, bandleader, singer, songwriter, producer, from Puerto Rican family. Played trumpet age 12, switched to trombone at 14, formed 14-piece Latin Jazz All Stars. First pro band had two trombones, imitating Eddie Palmieri's band. Signed to Fania at 17; debut LP *El Malo* '67, then *The Hustler* and *Guisando Doing A Job* established clichéd image as Hispanic street punk, maintained for some years; Puerto Rican lead singer Hector LAVOE was with Colon from first LP until '74. He introduced non-Cuban musical ideas incl. Panamanian rhythm, used Puerto Rican Yomo Toro on cuatro (10-stringed guitar, e.g. on hit 'La Murga' from Xmas LP *Asalto Navideño* '71). *Cosa Nuestra* '72 was first of several gold albums, incl. hit 'Che Che Colé', adapted Ghanaian children's song (later in Ntozake Shange's stage musical-poem 'for colored girls who have considered suicide when the rainbow is enuf'). *The Big Break* '73 incl. Panamanian and Brazilian songs, hit 'Ghana'e' (another West-African inspired song); *El Juicio* (The Trial) '72 mixed santeria (Cuban religious cult music) with Brazilian influences, jazz and Cuban rhythms; *Lo Mato* '73 incl. controversial hit song 'Calle Lune, Calle Sol' about street crime, also 'El Dia de Suerte' (a bomba about aspirations of an urban Latin), jazz-infl. 'Junio '73'. Another hit was 'La Banda' '73, from *Asalto Navideño Vol. 2*. In mid-'74 he handed the band over to Lavoe; for Lavoe debut solo LP *La Voz* '75 he expanded the horn section, combined Christian themes (in 'El Todopoderoso' – The Almighty) with Afro-Cuban cult references. *The Good, The Bad, The Ugly* '75 brought Rubén BLADES into band with Lavoe, incl. Brazilian, Cuban, Puerto Rican rhythms, Spanish pasodoble and rock, with SHA NA NA guitarist Elliott Randall on 'MC²'. Collaborated with veteran Puerto Rican singer/bandleader/composer/arranger Mon Rivera, a pioneer of the trombone front line, on *There Goes The Neighborhood* '75 on Vaya. Wrote, prod. Channel 13 TV salsa ballet *El Baquiné de Angelitos Negros* '77; moved further into prod. with Lavoe's *De Ti Depende* '76 with

Caribbean flavour, incl. violins. First collaboration with Celia CRUZ was *Only They Could Have Made This Album* '77, incl. samba/salsa hit 'Usted Abuso' and merengue 'Pun Pun Catalu'. Colon's first prod. with Rubén Blades was *Willie Colon Presents Rubén Blades: Matiendo Mano!* '77; their next joint LP *Siembra* '78 went gold with Blades' uncompromising lyrics. Voted Musician, Producer, Arranger, Trombonist of the Year by *Latin NY* readers '78. Prod. Lavoe album *Comedia* '78 with heavy violin bias, incl. hit biographical song 'El Cantante' (The Singer; written by Blades); own LP *Solo* '79 went gold, drawing on own NYC-Hispanic background, with female chorus, more electronics. Prod. Blades' 2-disc concept set *Maestra Vida* '80, which went gold; *Doble Energia* '80 with singer Ismael Miranda; solo *Fantasmas* '81 was *Latin NY* Album of the Year: Musician of the Year again. Prod. *El Sabio* (The Teacher) '80 for Lavoe; *Celia y Willie* '81 with Cruz brought her fresh young fans; *Canciones del Solar de los Aburridos* '82 (Songs from the Slums of Boredom) with Blades won Grammy. Formed new band '82, visited Continent for first time (BerlinFest); last albums with Lavoe (*Vigilante*) and Blades (*The Last Fight*) both '83. *Corazón Guerrero* (Warring Heart) incl. songs by Jacques BREL, Carole KING, Mark Knopfler as well as his own; also prod. 3-hour TV documentary *Latinoamericano una Sola Casa* (Latin Music: One House). *Tiempo Pa'Matar* '84 had large band incl. horns, flute, violin, percussion; to RCA for wider distribution with *Criollo* '84, Caribbean flavoured LP using horns, female voices, SOCA and CADENCE rhythms, song by Brazilians Caetano Veloso and Wally Salomão, as well as his own increasingly political, satirical lyrics. LP *Especial No. 5* '86 on Sonotone: he had visited London with FANIA ALL STARS '76, made first visit with his own band as 12" single 'Set Fire To Me' was club hit '86, then 'She Don't Know I'm Alive' '87 on A&M. Prod. Lavoe LP *Strikes Back*, Cruz's *The Winners* '87.

COLOSSEUM UK jazz-rock group formed '68; leader/drummer Jon Hiseman (*b* 21 June '44, London). Other founder members were Dick Heckstall-Smith (reeds; *b* 26 Sep. '34, Ludlow), Dave Greenslade, keyboards;

Tony Reeves, bass; guitarist Jim Roche, soon replaced by James Litherland. Hiseman and Heckstall-Smith had worked with pioneers Graham BOND and John MAYALL; Greenslade with Chris FARLOWE, others. First lineup (with Litherland) made LPs *Those Who Are About To Die* and *Valentyne Suite* '69; both reached UK top 20 albums. Litherland left to join Mogul Thrash, replaced by Dave 'Clem' Clempson (ex-Bakerloo, a Tamworth-based blues trio); this lineup promoted *Valentyne Suite*, but Reeves left mid-'70 (formed own shortlived label Greenwich Gramophone Co.), replaced by Mark Clarke, and Farlowe was enlisted, taking over vocal chores previously shared by Greenslade and Litherland or Clempson. The final lineup lasted another year and albums: *The Daughter Of Time Is Truth* '70, *Live* '71 (stayed longer in UK top 20 than any of the others) and *Collectors Colosseum* '71, released a month after they folded. Clempson joined HUMBLE PIE, replacing Peter FRAMPTON; Farlowe joined Atomic Rooster; Greenslade formed his own eponymous band. Hiseman formed Tempest with Clarke, singer Paul Williams (ex-Zoot MONEY), guitarist Allan Holdsworth (later SOFT MACHINE): LP *Jon Hiseman's Tempest* '74 followed by the departure of Williams and Holdsworth; guitarist Ollie Halsall joined and the trio made *Living In Fear* before splitting up in mid-'74. Hiseman then formed Colosseum II mid-'75 with completely new lineup: Don Airey, keyboards; guitarist Gary Moore (ex-THIN LIZZY), Neil Murray on bass (later National Health, Whitesnake), vocalist Mike Starrs (later Lucifer's Friend). This group made *Strange New Flesh* '76; Murray and Starrs left; Moore assumed vocal duties and bassist John Mole joined for albums *Electric Savage* and *Wardance*, both '77. In '78 Moore went back to Thin Lizzy (he had been moonlighting with them); Airey's guitarist brother Keith joined for the death throes late '78 but then Airey himself left to join Ritchie BLACKMORE's Rainbow. Well-liked by critics but with unstable lineups, Colosseum's jazz leanings probably kept them from greater commercial success. Hiseman met his wife, saxophonist/composer Barbara THOMPSON, in New Jazz Orchestra '65; she played on two Colosseum LPs; they were founder members of United Jazz & Rock

Ensemble '75 and he has worked in her fusion quartet Paraphernalia since '79.

COLTER, Jessi (*b* Miriam Johnson, 25 May '47, Phoenix, Ariz.) Country singer, songwriter. Played piano in church age 11; background singer with Duane EDDY, married him '61, separated '65; moved back to Phoenix and met Waylon JENNINGS, who encouraged her to concentrate on writing and singing. Wrote under the name Miriam Eddy; songs recorded by Eddy ARNOLD, Dottie WEST, Don GIBSON, etc. Changed name to Jessi Colter because her great great uncle was a member of Jesse James's gang. Signed to RCA '66, made LP *A Country Star Is Born* and several singles without much success. Married Jennings '69, recorded duets with him; 'Suspicious Minds' '70, 'Under Your Spell Again' '71 made charts. Signed with Capitol '74; with her own song 'I'm Not Lisa' made no. 1 country, top 5 pop. LP *I'm Jessi Colter* was hit, incl. 2-sided hit 'What's Happened To Blue Eyes', 'You Ain't Never Been Loved (Like I'm Goin' To Love You)'. Contributed to RCA LP *The Outlaws* '76, with Jennings, Willie NELSON, Tompall GLASER. Tours with Jennings, records sporadically, devotes much time to their children. Other LPs incl. *Jessi* '76, *Diamond In The Rough* '77, *Miriam* '77, *That's The Way A Cowboy Rocks 'n' Rolls* '78, *Ridin' Shotgun* '82 (all Capitol); *Leather & Lace* '81 (duets with Jennings on RCA). Recorded gospel LP '85 using her real name; planned to play with Robert Duval in film about Pentecostal evangelist and wife, score by Waylon.

COLTRANE, John (*b* John William Coltrane, 23 Sep. '26, Hamlet, N.C.; *d* 17 July '67, NYC) Tenor and soprano sax, composer. The most popular and influential jazz musician of the '60s; one of the most infl. of all time. Father was a tailor and amateur musician; pro debut in Philadelphia '45 with cocktail trio; US Navy band Hawaii '45-6; toured with Eddie VINSON R&B band '47-8; played alto, tenor and recorded with Dizzy GILLESPIE big band, sextet '49-51 (met Yusef LATEEF, who introduced him to Islamic literature, philosophy). Worked for Earl BOSTIC '52 (Art BLAKEY said later, 'If Coltrane played with Bostic . . . he learned a lot'). Worked for

Johnny HODGES '53-4; fired because he was a drug addict. First LP with Miles DAVIS quintet on Prestige '55 incl. Benny GOLSON tune 'Stablemates', became jazz standard. Then sessions led by Davis's bassist Paul CHAMBERS '55-6; *Two Tenors* with Hank MOBLEY; *Tenor Conclave* has four tenors: Coltrane, Mobley, Al COHN, Zoot SIMS; classic series of Davis LPs: *Cookin', Relaxin' Workin', Steamin'*, others incl. Davis's first Columbia sessions. Also *Tenor Madness* with Sonny Rollins, the other most infl. tenorist of the time; *Mating Call* with Tadd DAMERON quartet, all '56. Spring '57 Coltrane quit drugs and alcohol for good, putting his music first. Most of that year with Thelonious MONK, incl. long gig at NYC's Five Spot. Searched for means to harmonic richness, using strings of notes as though to play every note in a chord (technique later called 'sheets of sound' by Ira Gitler); Davis once asked him why he'd played such a long solo: reply was 'It took that long to get it all in.' He learned more harmonic background from Monk's complex music: recordings collected in 2-disc set on Milestone. Other LPs: *Blowing Session* (Mobley, Coltrane, Johnny GRIFFIN on tenor); *Mal Waldron Sextet*; *John Coltrane – Paul Quinichette Quintet* with WALDRON; *Sonny's Crib* with Sonny CLARK; *Art Blakey Big Band*; four LPs with Red GARLAND, Davis's pianist; *Wheelin' And Dealin'* (by 'Prestige All Stars'), others, all '57. LPs as leader '57-8 incl. *Blue Train* on Blue Note; also a dozen LPs on Prestige, most now reissued in 2-disc sets, incl. *Dakar* with Waldron, two baritones (Pepper ADAMS, Cecil PAYNE); *Coltrane Plays For Lovers* with Dameron, 2 discs with *Gene Ammons All Stars*, with AMMONS, Waldron, Quinichette, Adams, etc. Davis's style was changing from improvisation on standards to originals with fewer chords, longer melody lines, allowing more solo space; called Coltrane back although he also had Cannonball ADDERLEY (on alto). They recorded for Columbia and at Newport Jazz Festival '58; in Feb. '59 on Mercury without Davis as *Cannonball Adderley Quintet in Chicago*; in Mar. on Columbia full sextet made *Kind Of Blue* in 'modal' style, one of the most infl. albums of decade. Coltrane played high on tenor as though on alto, superimposing chords, exploring overtones:

a music teacher had recommended soprano sax some years earlier; Coltrane stopped at Selmer factory in Elkhart, Ind. early '59, picked up a soprano and began practising on it. *Giant Steps* and *Coltrane Jazz* '59 made for Atlantic on two dates '59: taste of things to come on quartet LPs with Chambers, Tommy FLANAGAN/Art Taylor (*b* 6 Apr. '29, NYC; later moved to France) on piano, drums at one date, Wynton KELLY/Jimmy COBB on the other; uptempo title 'Giant Steps' showed power, swing, joy and what some regarded then as quirky style fully under control. Formed own quartet Apr. '60 for eight week gig at Jazz Gallery NYC, with Steve Davis, bass; Steve Kuhn, piano (*b* 24 Mar. '38, Brooklyn); Pete La Roca, drums (*b* Peter Sims, 4 Apr. '38, NYC, had played with Sonny Rollins). Kuhn soon replaced by McCoy TYNER, La Roca by Billy HIGGINS, then by Elvin JONES: group widely regarded as the most infl. in jazz since Louis ARMSTRONG's Hot Five, with Coltrane's harmonic urgency, Jones' barely controlled, angry polyrhythms, Tyner pouring oil on troubled water. *Echoes Of An Era* made with Higgins for Roulette; then one-off *The Avant Garde* with Don CHERRY, Charlie HADEN, Ed BLACKWELL (Coltrane played soprano for first time on record); *My Favorite Things, Coltrane Plays The Blues, Coltrane's Sound* with own quartet, all on Atlantic '60. Some critics still puzzled by Coltrane; not the public: *My Favorite Things* soon sold 50,000 copies, compared to 5,000 for most jazz albums. Title song recorded again '65 in studio, '66 live at Village Vanguard: banal tune from *My Fair Lady* turned into exercise in mysticism by Coltrane soprano; chestnut 'Softly, As In A Morning Sunrise', folksong 'Greensleeves', Disney tune 'Chim Chim Cheree' used same way on other albums. Reggie Workman (*b* 26 June '37, Philadelphia), then Jimmy Garrison (*b* 3 Mar. '34, Miami) replaced Steve Davis on bass; Coltrane made another LP with Miles's sextet, *Someday My Prince Will Come* '61, with Mobley on second tenor; also *Olé Coltrane* '61, quartet plus Eric DOLPHY, Freddie HUBBARD, second bass Art Davis on Atlantic; but began association May '61 with Impulse label, most sessions prod. by Bob THIELE, which lasted rest of his life. Quartet often augmented, as on *Africa/Brass* '61, big band set; *Kulu se Mama* '65 with side-length Latin-infl. title track: Pharoah SANDERS, Donald Garrett on bass and bass clarinet, Frank Butler (*b* 18 Feb. '28, Kansas City), drums, Juno Lewis, percussion and vocal; Sanders, Rashied ALI, Coltrane's second wife Alice on piano, others featured '65-7. Ambitious LP-length work *Ascension* '65 used 11 pieces: Coltrane, Sanders, Hubbard, Tyner, Jones, Garrison, Art Davis, John Tchicai (*b* 28 Apr. '36, Copenhagen; also played with Archie SHEPP, Jazz Composers' Guild NYC) and Marion BROWN (alto saxes), Dewey Johnson (trumpet). LPs incl. *Impressions, Live At The Village Vanguard* '61; in '62 *Coltrane, Ballads, Duke Ellington And John Coltrane* (leaders duetting with each other's rhythm sections: Ellington assured Coltrane that first take of 'In A Sentimental Mood' was good enough: 'Why play it again? You can't duplicate that feeling. This is it.' Johnny HODGES later called it 'the most beautiful interpretation I've ever heard' of the song). Next *With Johnny Hartman* (ballads/vocals), *The Definitive Jazz Scene, Live At Birdland* '63; *Crescent, A Love Supreme* (four-part work central to canon, one of his best sellers), all '64; *Selflessness* (2 tracks from '63 with title from '65 *Kulu se Mama* session); *Transition, Sunship, Live In Seattle, Meditations,* '65; *Cosmic Music, Live At Village Vanguard Again, Concert In Japan,* all '66; *Expression, Interstellar Space* '67. Compilations incl. 2-disc *The Atlantic Years,* three 2-disc *Best Of* sets on Impulse. LPs issued posthumously incl. tapes controversially dubbed with her own harp playing by widow Alice; unreleased sets from vaults prod. for issue by Michael CUSCUNA (e.g. *First Meditations (for quartet),* earlier version of '65 *Meditations*); concert recordings continue to appear (e.g. *Bye Bye Blackbird* on Pablo: exciting live takes of title and 'Traneing In' made in Europe '62). Gentle, honest man loved by everyone who met him; expressed religious passion in music until death from liver cancer. With its transparent integrity, the music holds up well; it fulfilled the 'love and peace' era of '60s better than the flower-power brigade by addressing the hearts of listeners rather than the media. With soul and technique he has been more infl. than any other reedman since Coleman HAWKINS: voice is heard now

through contemporaries like Golson, younger men like George COLEMAN, Chico FREEMAN, now a new generation incl. Courtney PINE and Andy SHEPPARD: Coltrane is inescapable.

COLUMBIA The oldest currently active record label, the name now used separately by CBS in USA and by EMI in the rest of the world. Incorporated 1 Jan. 1889 by Edward E. Easton as the Maryland, Delaware and District of Columbia franchise of Jesse Lippincott's North American Phonograph Company, leasing and servicing graphophones (dictation machines based on Edison's phonograph); when this business failed, followed other franchises into entertainment business, but was the only one of Lippincott's 33 franchises that ever made money: provided records for coin-operated talking machines; first catalogue (1891) listed nearly 200 selections, all cylinders; by late 1890s was biggest record company in the world. Paris office opened 1889, became European headquarters 1897; London office opened 1900. Early machines used heavy batteries; reliable clockwork motors for home machines built 1894 by Eldridge Johnson. Columbia began pressing discs in USA in 1898, sold only in UK until '01, the year Johnson and Emile Berliner (inventor of the disc gramophone) formed the Victor Talking Machine Company. Ensuing patent war resolved '02 by labels sharing patent pool; Columbia made both discs and cylinders until '12; patents ran out, led to more competition; economic recession forced company to sell British subsidiary to its London manager Louis Sterling '22; USA Columbia failed '23. Sterling heard about new Western Electric electrical recording method (*see* RECORDED SOUND), available only to USA companies; bought USA Columbia from receivers, gaining access to Western Electric. British-based Columbia expanded worldwide; organised '25 under Columbia International in London: General Phonograph Co. Inc. (Okeh, USA), Columbia Nipponophone (Japan), Pathé Frère Pathéphone (France, subsidiaries in Europe and the Orient), Carl Lindstrom Organisation (Germany; Odeon and Parlophone labels had subsidiaries in Europe and South America), Transoceanic (Netherlands), Columbia labels in 19 countries. Also took over fledgling USA radio network United Independent Broadcasters, renamed Columbia Phonograph Broadcasting System; network lost money, Columbia pulled out; CBS dropped 'Phonograph' and later became profitable. Columbia had USA success with Paul WHITEMAN, Ted LEWIS, Bing CROSBY, etc.; then Depression: by '32 total sales of records in USA fell to 6% of '27 level. European industry not as badly hit, but rationalisation essential: in May '31 biggest UK record companies, Columbia and HMV, merged under Sir Louis Sterling to form Electrical and Musical Industries; for nearly 50 years EMI was the biggest record company in the world, with Columbia its flagship pop label. Radio Corporation of America (which now owned Victor: *see* RCA) had substantial stake in EMI; to avoid anti-trust problems EMI sold USA Columbia and Okeh subsidiaries to Grigsby-Grunow, makers of refrigerators, Majestic radios; Grigsby went to receivers '34. Meanwhile, American Record Company was formed '29 by merger of three companies incl. Romeo, Banner, Oriole and Perfect labels, became part of Consolidated Film Industries '30, who added BRUNSWICK, Vocalion, Melotone '31 and operated it as Brunswick Record Corporation, which now bought Columbia/Okeh from Grigsby's receivers for $70,000 (nine years earlier it had changed hands for $2.5 million). Meanwhile untapped markets for 'race' and 'hillbilly' records had been discovered; Frank Walker, Art SATHERLEY, Lester MELROSE, John HAMMOND had become talent scouts/field engineers; the new company had an enormous collection of American recordings. Edward Wallenstein, hired away from RCA to run it, made a deal with William S. Paley, president of CBS, which acquired control of ARC '38 for $700,000. CBS sold pre-'32 Brunswick and Vocalion material with label names to Decca USA, revived Columbia name (changing label colour from black to red) and had the most valuable vault in the record industry. For postwar Columbia, *see* CBS, EMI.

COLUMBO, Russ (*b* '08; *d* 2 Sep. '34) Singer, songwriter, also played violin, accordion. Joined Gus ARNHEIM band at L.A.'s Coconut Grove '29; Arnheim also signed The Rhythm Boys with Bing CROSBY; both crooners, Crosby and Columbo later became rivals. Columbo led own band '31, soon became sensation with silky ballad style: co-wrote theme 'You Call It Madness', 'Let's Pretend There's A Moon', others incl. 'Prisoner Of Love', recorded by Crosby, The INK SPOTS, Columbo, many others (no. 1 for Perry COMO '46). Toured USA, Europe; made short films, three features demanding more singing than acting: *Broadway Through A Keyhole* '33, *Moulin Rouge, Wake Up And Dream* '34 (latter incl. 'Too Beautiful For Words'). Killed in bizarre accident: a friend, using ancient pair of duelling pistols as paperweights, struck a match on one which turned out to be loaded: Columbo hit in head by ricochet.

COLYER, Ken (*b* 18 Apr. '28, Great Yarmouth, Norfolk, England; *d* 11 Mar. '88) UK trad. jazz trumpet, guitar, leader. Self-taught while at sea '39-45; formed own band '49, with Christie Bros Stompers '51; since '53 Ken Colyer's Jazzmen. Toured Europe, North America, etc. LPs incl. *The Rarest Ken Colyer* on Nola, *Sensation* ('55-9 Decca tracks reissued) on Lake; *Live At The Dancing Slipper 1969* on VJM, *Winging And Singing* '75 on German Happy Bird label. *The Great Revival* on Esquire has eight tracks by Colyer's band with the Christie brothers on one side (trumpeter Keith Christie later toured with Benny GOODMAN in Europe; clarinettist Ian left music for journalism); eight by Graeme BELL on the other. Colyer's band, with Lonnie DONEGAN on banjo, started the skiffle craze: *The Decca Skiffle Sessions 1954-57* on Lake features Donegan.

COMMANDER CODY AND HIS LOST PLANET AIRMEN Country rock band formed '67 in Ann Arbor, Mich., resurrected '69 in San Francisco by guitarist/vocalist Bill Kirchen (*b* 29 Jan. '48, Bridgeport, Conn.) who had scouted ahead. Lineup also incl. Commander Cody (*b* George Frayne IV, 19 July '44, Boise, Ida.) on keyboards, 'Buffalo' Bruce Barlow (*b* 3 Dec. '48, Oxnard, Cal.) on bass, guitarist John Teachy, Billy C. Farlow on harmonica (all also vocalists), plus drummer Lance Dickerson (*b* 15 Oct. '48, Detroit), Andy Stein (*b* 31 Aug. '48, NYC) on fiddle/saxophones and Steve Davis on pedal steel (aka The West Virginia

Creeper). Worked backing Gene VINCENT; then intended to become the first proficient hippie country band: Cody said they wanted to do for country music what Paul BUTTERFIELD had done for white blues. Infl. of rock'n'roll, boogie-woogie, Western swing, Cajun and novelties all mixed in with country, but subject matter of songs set them apart from country bands: 'Down To Stems And Seeds Again' mixed C&W mawkishness with marijuana metaphors; 'Lost In The Ozone' meant getting high ('ozone' became a catchphrase). They had a fluke top 10 hit with 'Hot Rod Lincoln' '72, starting one of the periodic fads for novelty songs; polished shambling bar band into a concert act, but had trouble capturing live quality on record. Debut LP *Lost In The Ozone* '71 encapsulated their range; *Hot Licks, Cold Steel And Truckers Favorites* incl. 'Semi Truck', 'Looking At The World Through A Windshield', Kevin 'Blackie' Farrell's tear jerking story song 'Mama Hated Diesels'. By then Davis had been replaced by Bobby Black (an exceptional steel player); through series *Country Casanova* '73, *Live From Deep In The Heart Of Texas* '74, *Commander Cody And His Lost Planet Airmen* and *Tales From The Ozone* '75 they were established as a crossover act, popular with both country and rock audiences. Tracks from the last two are compiled on *Commander Cody Returns From Outer Space* '87 on Edsel UK. They had switched from Paramount to WB with these albums, and dealings with Paramount at this time are captured in *Starmaking Machinery: Inside The Business Of Rock And Roll* '77 by Geoffrey Stokes, one of the best accounts of record industry machinations. Fatigue, disappointment at not breaking through to a larger audience caused split; swansong was live 2-disc *We've Got A Live One Here* '76, made in England with personnel changes, notably adding Norton Buffalo on harmonica, trombone, vocals. (*Sleazy Roadside Stones* '88 on Relix was made live '73 at Armadillo World Headquarters in Austin.) Cody made disappointing solo sets *Rock'n'Roll Again* and *Flying Dreams* '77-8 on Arista; *Lose It Tonight* '80 on Line/Peter Pan was stronger but still lacked Airmen's pizzazz, incl. 'Two Triple Cheese, Side Order Of Fries', the animated video for which was described as 'fastpaced,

fuming, ingenious' by *The Rolling Stone Book Of Rock Videos*, cost a mere $250 to make. Spin-off band the Moonlighters made *The Moonlighters* and *Rush Hour* '77-8 and were often used by Cody as backing group; this became official on his *Let's Rock* '86: lineup incl. Kirchen, Barlow, drummer Tony Johnson and Austin de Lone on guitar and keyboards; LP was a welcome return to Airmen-style eclecticism, incl. perhaps Cody's best truck-driving epic, 'Truckstop At The End Of The World'. De Lone had been a member of the infl. London pub-rock band Eggs Over Easy, whose LP *Good 'N' Cheap* '72 was reissued '86. Buffalo made underrated solo albums *Lovin' In The Valley Of The Moon* and *Desert Horizon* '77-8; he worked extensively in films and with people like Steve MILLER, David Soul, Bette MIDLER (introduced her to Johnson's 'Midnight In Memphis', one of the best songs in her film *The Rose*). Farlow released solo singles; Stein became well-known for work on *National Lampoon* films, made jazz LP *Goin' Places* '87 on Stomp Off; Dickerson worked with David BROMBERG, Mitch Woods & His Rockett 88s, etc.; others sessioned with Link WRAY, Hoyt AXTON, New Riders of the Purple Sage etc.

COMMODORES, The Soul group formed '68: became most successful Motown act of recent years after Stevie WONDER, with 20 hits in Billboard Hot 100 '74-82. Original lineup of school friends from Tuskegee (Ala.) Institute: Lionel RICHIE, vocals, tenor sax; Milan Williams (*b* 28 Mar. '49, Ms.), keyboards, guitar; William King (*b* 30 Jan. '49, Ala.), horns; Thomas McClary (*b* 6 Oct. '50, Fla.), guitar; added drummer Andre Callaghan, bass player 'Railroad', later Michael Gilbert on bass, Jimmy Johnson on sax in merger of groups called the Mystics and the Jays. Chose name from a dictionary; later joked that they were almost called the Commodes. To NYC '69, allegedly had early gig at Small's Paradise in Harlem (one of the last remaining legendary Harlem clubs from the '20s; *see* COTTON CLUB). Single on Atlantic prod. by Jerry Williams (*see* SWAMP DOGG) flopped; signed by Motown '71, supported the JACKSONS two years; by the time of first LP *Machine Gun* '74 sextet incl. first four named above plus

Ronald LaPread (*b* 4 Sep. '50, Ala.), bass, and Walter 'Clyde' Orange (*b* 10 Dec. '47, Fla.), drums: title track was first single hit (no. 22 USA); LP followed by *Caught In The Act* and *Movin' On* '75, instrumental hard funk was successful, but overtaken by ballads as Richie's songwriting emerged: 'Just To Be Close To You', 'Sweet Love', 'Easy', 'Sail On' were top 5 '75-9, while 'Three Times A Lady' '78 and 'Still' '79 were no. 1 hits. He pursued solo projects, left group c.'81 replaced by J. D. Nicholas (ex-Heatwave); they continued to chart (top 20 '84 with 'Nightshift'), left Motown. McClary also launched solo career. Other LPs incl. *Hot On The Tracks* '76, *Commodores* and 2-disc *Commodores Live!* '77, *Natural High* '78, *Midnight Magic* '79, *Heroes* '80, *In The Pocket* '81, plus compilation LPs; *Commodores 13* '83 was first album without Richie, followed by, *Nightshift* '85, a top 25 album.

COMO, Perry (*b* Pierino Como, 18 May '12, Canonsburg, Penn.) Singer. Had barber shop in home town; auditioned for Freddy Carlone band '33, toured state; joined Ted WEEMS '36; broadcasts, records on Decca until Weems broke up band, went to war '42; signed with Victor '43 and never looked back. First hit was Jerome KERN-Ira GERSHWIN song 'Long Ago And Far Away', from movie musical *Cover Girl* '44; Como had 42 top 10 hits in Billboard charts '44-'58; total USA chart entries '40-'55 second only to Bing CROSBY's. Films '44-6 (*Something For The Boys, Doll Face, If I'm Lucky*) noteworthy because Vivian Blaine, Carmen MIRANDA appeared in all three; big screen did not capture Como's personality, but face and voice a hit with fans. In '45 'Till The End Of Time' (from Chopin), 'If I Loved You'/'I'm Gonna Get That Gal', 'Temptation' (from Crosby film *Going Hollywood*), 'Dig You Later (A Hubba-Hubba-Hubba)' (from *Doll Face*) were all gold discs. In '46 'Prisoner Of Love' was no. 1, 'I'm Forever Chasing Rainbows' no. 7 (also Chopin), 'Surrender' another no. 1. 'Dig You Later', 'Chi-Baba Chi-Baba' (no. 1 '47) and a few others were novelties, establishing whimsical sense of humour. Revived 1898 song 'When You Were Sweet Sixteen'; old boss Weems provided background on 'I Wonder Who's Kissing Her Now' (both

'47). Fourth film *Words And Music* was '48 biopic of composers Richard RODGERS, Lorenz Hart; 'Blue Moon', 'With A Song In My Heart', 'Mountain Greenery' well sung. '49 hits incl. 'A You're Adorable', two songs from Rodgers' hit *South Pacific* (words by Oscar Hammerstein) 'Bali Hai' and 'Some Enchanted Evening' (no. 1). Duets with FONTANE SISTERS, Betty HUTTON ('A Bushel And A Peck'), Eddie FISHER made the charts '50-'52; Como took '34 song 'If' to no. 1 '51; in '52 'Don't Let The Stars Get In Your Eyes' was one of his biggest hits ever. Another Rodgers & Hammerstein song, 'No Other Love', one of three top 10 entries in '53; in '54 novelty 'Papa Loves Mambo', ballad 'Wanted' (no. 1) were his eleventh and twelfth gold discs. Then he became a bigger star than ever on TV, hosting weekly hour-long variety show '55-'63 of very high quality, with Mitchell Ayres as mus. dir. and Ray CHARLES contributing arrangements of Como/guest medleys. Another highlight was the request spot ('Letters'), with Como perched on a stool next to a music stand and a red rose, singing a few classy songs. His cardigan, relaxed informality became affectionate joke, charmed nearly every household; format has been emulated by Andy WILLIAMS in USA, Val DOONICAN in UK, but original is unique. Novelty 'Hot Diggity', ballad 'More' won gold discs in '56; 'Round And Round' '57, 'Catch A Falling Star' '58 were both rounds in form, both no. ones; 'Star' was written by Paul Vance and Lee Pockriss: lyricist Hal David had worked with Pockriss, now with new partner Burt BACHARACH provided lovely no. 4 flip side, 'Magic Moments' (a no. 1 in UK). 'Delaware' (no. 22 '60), novelty using names of American states, was Como's last gold disc for a decade. In June '70 Como appeared live for the first time in 25 years: it was a triumph, with Charles and mus. dir. Nick Perito's audience-teaser 'If I Could Read Your Mind' (album *Live At The International Hotel, Las Vegas*). Later that year 'It's Impossible' became Como's twentieth gold disc; he commenced world tours at nearly 60. 2-disc set *Perry Como's 40 Greatest Hits* was million-seller in UK '75; annual Christmas TV show was American institution. Had 26 top 40 entries in UK '53-'74; many compilation albums incl. two 2-disc sets in

USA *This Is Perry Como* Vols. 1&2; similar *Here Is* sets in UK.

CONCEPT ALBUM Material recorded for an LP intended to be integrated set on a theme. In 78 era there were not many 'albums' in popular music; buyer paid extra for the album itself, which held a few singles. In LP era jazz musicians were the first to take advantage of longer playing time (LP could resemble a live set) but others began to record LPs as opposed to singles; among first concept albums was Frank SINATRA's *In The Wee Small Hours* '55. A 'pop' LP usually incl. a couple of hits plus 'B' sides and failed singles; this began to change in the '60s: BEATLES *Sgt Pepper* '67 is best-known concept album of all. Idea of concept album began to induce yawns in '70s, acts such as CAMEL, DEEP PURPLE, PINK FLOYD, YES having worked it to death; nevertheless serious artists are now expected to produce enough material of musical value for album from which singles may be drawn, rather than the other way around. Album too obviously a concept probably fails; songs should be good enough to stand alone, as in Emmylou HARRIS's *The Ballad Of Sally Rose*, '85.

CONCORD JAZZ Label founded Concord, Cal. by car dealer/jazz fan Carl Jefferson. Turned local summer fete into music party '73; Joe PASS, Herb ELLIS complained about not being able to record: Jefferson saw that not much mainstream was recorded, so began doing it himself; 300 albums later, car dealership has long since been sold. Also instrumental in getting Concord Pavilion opened May '75; Concord Jazz Festival now annual institution. Concord Picante label started for Latin Jazz: first release *La Onda Va Bien* by Cal TJADER won Grammy '81; Concord Concerto for classical: *First Concerto For Guitar And Orchestra* (Laurindo ALMEIDA) nominated for Grammy same year. The George Wein Collection named after impresario incl. DIRTY DOZEN BRASS BAND (*My Feet Can't Fail Me Now*), Art BLAKEY LP *New York Scene* made live '84 in Manhattan club. In all 20 Concord albums nominated for Grammies, five won by '85. Label scorns too much multi-tracking technology, aims for natural live-set effect; many LPs recorded live at festivals, incl. Concord Jazz All Stars with Al COHN, Concord Super Band (without Cohn) in Tokyo: incl. fine young mainstream players like Scott HAMILTON, Warren Vaché, drummers Jake Hanna, Marvin 'Smitty' Smith; guitarists Charlie BYRD, Herb ELLIS, Barney KESSEL make own albums, play together in Great Guitars series; Almeida and Ray BROWN play in allstar quartet L.A. Four; neglected vocalists alone who have been served incl. Ernestine ANDERSON, Rosemary CLOONEY, Carmen McRAE, Mel TORMÉ, Joe WILLIAMS; highly rated CAPP-PIERCE big band (now called Juggernaut) has three LPs; new young stars making debuts incl. Blakey sidemen Donald HARRISON, Terence BLANCHARD; also established modernists Ron CARTER, Harold LAND, others. See also George SHEARING, Dave McKENNA, Ellis LARKINS, Jimmy ROWLES, Michel PETRUCCIANI, Bud SHANK, Buddy TATE, Red NORVO, Count Basie's two Franks (Wess and Foster on *Frankly Speaking*), etc. From Monty ALEXANDER to Snooky Young, jazz-oriented popular music forsaken by major labels yields market identity such that fans can buy records by label alone.

CONDON, Eddie (*b* Albert Edwin Condon, 16 Nov. '05, Goodland, Ind.; *d* 4 Aug. '73, NYC) Rhythm guitar. Competent musician in Chicago/dixieland style; sometime band leader, then club owner; indefatigable promoter, not to say sparkplug: organiser of gigs, recording sessions, author of many famed wisecracks: French critic Hugues Panassie (*Le Jazz Hot*, '34; *The Real Jazz*, '42) came to NYC to produce records; Condon said, 'Do I tell him how to jump on a grape?' On BOP: 'We don't flatten our fifths; we drink 'em.' Played banjo in Chicago; began fifty years of association with Bud FREEMAN, Gene KRUPA, Jimmy McPARTLAND, other Chicagoans; many records with them, Louis ARMSTRONG, Red McKENZIE, Bobby HACKETT, many others; own sessions on Commodore early '40s; LPs on Columbia '50s; all-star *Condon In Japan* '64 on Chiaroscuro. Gigged at Nick's NYC; from '42 promoted concerts at Town Hall; had own club Eddie Condon's '45-67. Autobiography *We Called It Music* '48; describes chore of getting Fats WALLER out of bed for historic records of 1 Mar. '29.

CONFREY, Zez (*b* Edward Elzear Confrey, 3 Apr. 1895, Peru, Ill.; *d* 22 Nov. '71, Lakewood, N.J.) Pianist, composer, bandleader. Formed band with brother Jim '15; made piano rolls; served in US Navy WWI; later played with violinist Benny Kabelski (became comedian Jack Benny); in Paul WHITEMAN band; led own band in '20s, often on radio; wrote hit song 'Sittin' On A Log' '34; best known for piano pieces called novelties, sometimes arr. for orchestra: 'Stumbling' '22, 'Dizzy Fingers' '23, 'Nickel In The Slot' '25, biggest hit 'Kitten On The Keys' '24, premiered at same concert as George GERSHWIN's *Rhapsody In Blue*.

CON FUNK SHUN USA soul-funk dance band, formed California '68 as Project Soul, to Memphis '72, changed name. Remarkably consistent lineup: Mike Cooper, lead vocals, guitar and Louis McCall, drums (high school friends who started group); Cedric Martin, bass; Danny Thomas, keyboards; Karl Fuller, Paul Harrell, Felton Pilate II, horns and various instruments (Pilate also does lead vocals). Backed Stax artists, recorded for Fretone, then Mercury from '76. Second LP *Secrets* '77 incl. 'Ffun', no. 1 soul single (no. 23 pop chart) same year. Third LP *Loveshine* '78 incl. 'Shake And Dance With Me', also no. 1 soul hit; other hits incl. 'Chase Me', 'Let Me Put Love On Your Mind', 'Lady's Wild', 'Too Tight' ('81, just made top 40 pop chart). LP *To The Max* UK '83.

CONJUNTO Spanish for 'combo' or 'band', synonymous with 'sonora' in Puerto Rico and Cuba for medium-sized band. Latin-American genre spilling over into country music. Cuban conjuntos were derived from carnival street bands; today's format of trumpets, piano, tres (six- or nine-stringed guitar), maracas (pair of shaken rattles), bass, bongo, conga, cowbell and voices was formed by Arsenio RODRIGUEZ in '30s, is now one of the basic units playing SALSA with larger brass sections, lineup generally incl. trumpets, piano, bass, timbales, bongos, congas; examples are Joe Quijano's Conjunto and Sonora Matancera, who for many years accompanied Celia CRUZ; also Sonora Ponceña and Conjunto Caché. Puerto Rican conjunto was a rural band

format: guitar, cuatro (small 10-stringed guitar-like instrument), güayo (a scraped hollow gourd); trumpets and clarinets became optional; some rural conjuntos are led by accordions. Mexican groups are accordion-led, with guitar, bass, bongos, more percussion; originally instrumental Mexican and Chicano conjuntos are now used to support popular political songs (corridos, rancheras) with bouncy beat to sweeten message. Accordion-led bands in Texas are often called conjunto bands; immigrant Germans working on railways are credited with bringing accordion to the area (and Bohemians with giving squeeze-box to CAJUN music); south-central Texas ethnic mix has strong German/Bohemian/Slavic element: the bands play polkas and waltzes as well as country. Freddy FENDER hit 'Wasted Days And Wasted Nights' is an example of country conjunto. *The Texas-American Conjunto: History Of A Working-Class Music* by Manuel Peña '86 published by U. of Texas at Austin. *See also* TEX-MEX.

CONLEE, John (*b* 11 Aug. '46, Versailles, Ky.) Soulful country singer. Raised on tobacco farm, played in folk trio in his teens, began work as a mortician. Became DJ in Fort Knox, to Nashville '71 playing rock records. Began recording for ABC '77, made country chart with 'Rose Colored Glasses' '78, hit no. 1 same year with 'Lady Lie Down'. Further top 5 hits incl. 'Backside Of 30' '79, 'Before My Time' '79, 'Friday Night Blues' '80, 'Miss Emily's Picture' '81, 'I Don't Remember Loving You' '82, 'Common Man' '83, 'As Long As I'm Rockin' With You' '84. LPs incl. *Rose Colored Glasses* ABC '78; *Forever* '79, *Friday Night Blues* '80, *With Love* '81, *Busted* '82, *In My Eyes* '83, *Blue Highway* '84, all on MCA. He had struck modern subject matter and ballad style for country music fans who now live mostly in suburbs, switched to CBS for *Harmony* '86, *American Faces* '87.

CONLEY, Arthur (*b* 4 Jan. '46) Soul singer. Demo of 'I'm A Lonely Stranger' picked up by Otis REDDING, released on his Jotis label; he took Conley to Muscle Shoals, rewrote with him Sam COOKE's 'Yeah Man'; retitled 'Sweet Soul Music' it hit no. 2 USA pop chart '67: gave name-checks to past and present soul stars a top typical brassy Stax backing, also underlined Conley's vocal similarity to sadly departed Cooke. Total of seven entries '67-70 in Billboard R&B chart (renamed 'soul' '69); 'Run On', 'God Bless' made Bubbling Under chart; soul cover of BEATLES' 'Ob-La-Di, Ob-La-Da' made no 51 pop chart '69. No more guidance from Redding, who died '67; label switch to Capricorn '71 didn't help; biggest hit remains classic black dance record, will keep his name alive.

CONLEY, Earl Thomas (*b* Portsmouth, Ohio). Country singer, songwriter who set a record '83: first artist (in any genre) with four no. 1 singles from the same album. One of eight children, his father a railway worker who lost his job during conversion from steam to diesel. Rejected scholarship to art school, travelled, served in US Army, joined gospel group with aunt and uncle; worked days in Huntsville, Ala. playing clubs at night. Songs attracted attention: Mel STREET had hit with 'Smokey Mountain Memories', Conway TWITTY took 'This Time I've Hurt Her More Than She Loves Me' to no. 1. He made singles for GRT, WB; hit no. 1 with 'Fire And Smoke' from LP *Blue Pearl* on Sunbird: RCA snapped up it and him; the LP went as high as no. 23 in the Billboard country album chart in '82. He had worked with co-producer Nelson Larkin since '71, felt the infl. of Merle HAGGARD, George JONES, but '. . . never could make those influences work until I started writing and singing for myself.' Beginning with songwriting as a craft he describes the process of interpreting the songs as painting pictures. First RCA LP *Somewhere Between Right And Wrong* '82 was a hit LP with title track in top 5; *Don't Make It Easy For Me* '83 was no. 4 with four no. 1 hits: title track, 'Your Love's On The Line', 'Angel In Disguise' and 'Holding Her And Loving You'; and a minor '75 hit, 'I Have Loved You, Girl (But Not Like This Before)' re-entered the chart to reach no. 2. *Treadin' Water* '84 was no. 2; most songs cowritten with his favourite partner Randy Scruggs (son of Earl Scruggs): 'Chance Of Lovin' You', 'Honor Bound', 'Love Don't Care Whose Heart It Breaks' were no. 1. *Greatest Hits* '85 was understandably a no. 1 album; *Too Many Times* '86 was no. 3, 'Nobody Falls Like A Fool', 'Once In A Blue Moon' at no. 1; duet 'Too Many Times' with Anita POINTER was no. 2; 'I Can't Win For Losin' You' reached no. 1 early '87.

CONNIFF, Ray (*b* 6 Nov. '16, Attleboro, Mass.) Trombone, arranger, bandleader. Worked for Bunny BERIGAN, Bob CROSBY, Artie SHAW '37-41; own octet '41; later Harry JAMES, Shaw again, freelance, studio work; on ABC staff NYC '54, to CBS '55. Gave up trombone; arr. pop records for Don CHERRY, Guy MITCHELL, Johnnie RAY, Johnny MATHIS, etc. Long series of successful easy-listening LPs, recycling standards with slick chorus for people who didn't like rock'n'roll: 37 albums in Billboard top 100 albums '57-73, 28 in top 40, 11 in top 10. (11 LPs charted UK '60-72.) Trumpeter Billy BUTTERFIELD featured on *Conniff Meets Butterfield* '59, *Just Kidding Around* '63. Still in USA catalogue: 2-disc set *Somewhere My Love* (no. 3 LP '66; theme from *Dr Zhivago* was no. 9 single) with *Bridge Over Troubled Water* (no. 47 LP '70); *Hawaiian Album* '67, *Greatest Hits. The Nashville Connection* ('82 UK) gives the treatment to country hits.

CONNOLLY, Billy (*b* 24 Nov. '42, Glasgow) Folksinger, songwriter, comedian. Apprentice welder in Scottish shipyards, then in Territorial Army; new career began in folk clubs mid-'60s. Made albums with Gerry RAFFERTY in The Humblebums; went solo, but shaggy dog stories between songs got longer until they took over. Moved south c. '71, eventually playing to Scottish expatriates in USA and Far East. In Scotland 'The Big Yin' was a superstar, but not until mid-'70s did other UK audiences appreciate (or understand!) him. Live LPs *Cop Yer Whack For This* '74, *Get Right Intae Him* '75 captured act: rambling, bawdy, scatological stories, often about inebriation: when this fails it is dismal; he's on form more often than not. His version of Tammy WYNETTE's 'D-I-V-O-R-C-E' was UK no. 1 '75; answer to Village People's 'In The Navy', 'In The Brownies', was minor '79 hit. His anthem was silly, endearing 'Welly Boot Song'. LP *Atlantic Bridge* '76 incl. his definitive C&W song, 'The Shitkicker's Waltz'. He diversified, appearing with Richard Burton in *Absolution*, Michael Caine in *Water* '84; on stage in straight dramatic role in *The Beastly*

Beatitudes Of Balthazar B early '80s; has appeared at AMNESTY INTERNATIONAL shows. Relationship with TV comedienne Pamela Stephenson is widely reported, much to his annoyance.

CONNOR, Chris (*b* 8 Nov. '27, Kansas City, Mo.) Singer. Father played violin; she studied clarinet for eight years, began singing with a band at U. of Missouri led by Bob BROOKMEYER. To NYC with Claude THORNHILL's vocal group the Snowflakes. Turned soloist; with Stan KENTON '52-3 she established a reputation in the line of Kenton singers Anita O'DAY and June CHRISTY as stylist in cool school. Went solo July '53; signed with Bethlehem: LPs incl. *This Is Chris, Lullabies Of Birdland, Chris.* Albums also issued with Carmen McRAE. Suspended by label '55 for refusing to record more than minimum required by contract. To Atlantic: first LP *Chris Connor* culled from sessions with backing bands led by Ralph BURNS, John LEWIS; one featuring Zoot SIMS. Others followed: *Chris Craft* '58, *Ballads Of The Sad Café* '59, *Chris In Person* '60, *Portrait Of Chris* '61, *Free Spirits* '62, *He Loves Me He Loves Me Not*, more; title track from *I Miss You So* was chart single (no. 34, '56), as was 'Trust In Me' (no. 95, '57). Changed to ABC-Paramount, *Sings Gentle Bossa Nova* '65; highly regarded appearance at Austin Jazz Festival '66. Comeback in mid-'70s; LPs with Kenton, Maynard FERGUSON; *Sweet & Swinging* made '78 NYC with small group on Progressive; *Love Being Here With You* '83 on Stash, *Classic* '86 on Contemporary: her voice is as good as ever, interpretations maybe even better.

CONTOURS, The Soul vocal quintet formed '58 in Detroit as quartet: Billy Gordon, Billy Hoggs, Joe Billingslea, Sylvester Potts. Hubert Johnson joined; his cousin Jackie WILSON got them audition with Berry GORDY (although not signed to Motown group, Wilson had big hits with songs written by Gordy); Contours made flop single, Wilson got them one more chance, this time joined by Huey Davis (guitar) on Gordy song 'Do You Love Me': no. 1 R&B, 3 pop '62; unfortunately for the group, covers by Brian POOLE and the Tremeloes, Dave CLARK Five were big hits in UK. Had seven top 40 hits in R&B chart '62-7 (minor classics 'First I Look At The Purse', 'Just A Little Misunderstanding'; latter became sole UK top 40 '70) but never made pop top 40 USA again. Continued to record in '70s with personnel changes: latterday Contours incl. Joe Stubbs (brother of FOUR TOPS' Levi Stubbs) and later TEMPTATION Dennis Edwards.

CONWAY, Russ (*b* Trevor H. Stanford, 2 Sep. '27, Bristol, England) Pop pianist. Self-taught; played in local accordion band age 10. Joined merchant navy as galley boy for two years age 15, then signalman in Royal Navy; during service lost part of a finger in a bread slicer. Re-enlisted RN (won DSM), then merchant navy again; back to civilian life as club pianist '55. Became audition pianist, then accompanist with Lita Rosa, Gracie FIELDS, Dorothy Squires, others; also touring. Signed with EMI and had own first hit 'Party Pops' '57. A score of hits followed, incl. 'Side Saddle' and 'Roulette', both no. 1 '59. A sell-out attraction at clubs and theatres, had own ITV series, made first appearance at London Palladium '66. He then slowed down because of ill health; recorded for Pye '71-2, but not with his former success. First UK entertainer to get a silver disc for LP sales, six of his LPs reaching top 10 albums chart '58-60. *Russ Conway Presents 24 Piano Greats* on Ronco '77 reached top 25.

COODER, Ry (*b* Ryland Peter Cooder, 15 Mar. '47, L.A.) Guitar; singer, leader; activist curator of American popular music. Played guitar at age 4; in teens with Jackie DESHANNON as duo performing locally; formed The Rising Sons with Taj MAHAL. Friendship with prod./arr. Jack NITZSCHE led to prolific session work: played on LPs by CAPTAIN BEEFHEART, Phil OCHS, Randy NEWMAN; also ROLLING STONES records *Let It Bleed* '69, chilling 'Sister Morphine' from *Sticky Fingers* '71; in soundtrack of Mick Jagger film *Performance* '70, on Nicky HOPKINS LP *Jamming With Edward* '72 (also with Stones). Own debut was *Ry Cooder* '70, then *Into The Purple Valley* '72: began exploration of Americana; songs about the Great Depression by Woody GUTHRIE, LEADBELLY, Sleepy John ESTES. Folk/blues set *Boomer's Story* '73 was about wanderers, with plenty of fine guitar playing; *Paradise & Lunch* '74 veered in rhythm & blues direction, was his first commercial success, with Jim Keltner on drums, Red CALLENDER, Plas JOHNSON; Oscar Brashear (*b* 18 Aug. '44, Chicago) on cornet; Bobby King among others on background vocals; duet with Earl HINES on 'Ditty Wah Ditty'. Infl. by unusual tunings used by Bahamian guitarist Joseph SPENCE, Hawaiian guitarist Gabby Pahinui, then by Tex-Mex accordionist Flaco JIMENEZ, next LP was *Chicken Skin Music* '76, incl. covers of 'He'll Have To Go', 'Goodnight Irene'; also live *Showtime* '77. *Jazz* '77 is Cooder's accurate, affectionate impression of that genre, Callender, Hines, Brashear in cast; songs by Bix BEIDERBECKE, Jelly Roll MORTON, others; trad. songs arr. by Spence: Cooder says the half-instrumental LP is his least favourite; it was trouble to make and not a good seller, but remains gorgeous. *Bop Till You Drop* '79 was first digitally recorded rock LP, incl. fine covers of Elvis PRESLEY's 'Little Sister', Arthur ALEXANDER's 'Go Home, Girl', others; Chaka KHAN and King among backing singers, with King taking lead on 'I Can't Win'. Began touring with John HIATT, Keltner, superb backing vocal team of King, Willie Greene, other first-class sidemen; they are all on *Borderline* '80: covers of Wilson PICKETT's '634-5789', Billy Emerson's '(Every Woman I Know Is) Crazy 'Bout An Automobile', Hiatt's 'The Way We Make A Broken Heart', Cooder's own 'Borderline', much else; *The Slide Area* '82 incl. rare Bob DYLAN song 'I Need A Woman', Curtis MAYFIELD's 'Gypsy Woman', Cooder's 'Mama, Don't Treat Your Daughter Mean', Cooder-Keltner's 'UFO Has Landed In The Ghetto' and 'I'm Drinking Again'. Cooder played on T-Bone BURNETT LP *Proof Through The Night*, Eric CLAPTON's *Money & Cigarettes*, both '83; concentrated on atmospheric film work: friendship with director Walter Hill led to composing and performing music for his *The Long Riders* '80, *Southern Comfort* '81, *Streets Of Fire* '84, *Brewster's Millions* '85, *Crossroads* '86; also Tony Richardson's *The Border* '81, Wim Wenders' *Paris, Texas* '84 and Louis Malle's *Alamo Bay* '85 (with contributions from Hiatt, Van Dyke PARKS, LOS LOBOS); also *Blue City* '86, directed by his friend

Michelle Manning. (Soundtrack from *Long Riders* was not issued because it's not enough to fill an album.) His playing and music also featured in *Candy* '68, *Blue Collar* '78 (wrote 'Hard-Workin' Man' for Beefheart), *Goin' South* '78 (title song over closing credits). His LPs haven't had expensive promotion because they don't fit in pigeonholes, while the whole point was that they take in everything; he supported lesser acts in concert, with loyal cult following and ecstatic critical praise, until his own success began to come late '70s: a master of bottleneck guitar with a deep understanding of popular music, seen now as a giant, he points out that in today's record business he would not get the contract he got in '70 as an untried artist. *Why Don't You Try Me Tonight* '86 was belated compilation; *Get Rhythm* '87 was a new slice of Americana, incl. the old Johnny CASH B side, other songs by Chuck BERRY, Otis BLACKWELL etc. served up Cooder style, cast incl. Parks on keyboards, Buell NEIDLINGER on acoustic bass, Keltner, King, Greene, Flaco, etc.

COOK, Barbara (*b* 25 Oct. '27, Atlanta, Ga.) Actress/singer, with joyful voice of light operatic range. Made professional debut at New York's Blue Angel, '50; Broadway debut in Yip HARBURG/Sammy FAIN show *Flahooley*, '51; ran for only 40 performances. Toured with *Oklahoma, Carousel*; won role in *Plain And Fancy* '55, with Arnold Horwitt/Albert Hague hit 'Young And Foolish'. Then originated Cunegonde in Leonard BERNSTEIN show *Candide*, '56; ran only 73 performances, became cult favourite and led to big chance for Cook: created role of Marion the librarian in Meredith WILLSON's *The Music Man*, '57, for 1375 performances and Antoinette Perry (Tony) award. In *The Gay Life*, for which Arthur SCHWARTZ, Howard Dietz reunited '61, ran only just over 100 performances; *She Loves Me* '63 more successful; ironically cast with Jack Cassidy, whose wife Shirley Jones got film role of Marion. In first straight part took over from Sandy Dennis in Muriel Resnick comedy *Any Wednesday*, '65. Toured late '60s, early '70s (*Funny Girl, The Gershwin Years*); returned to cabaret NYC. Successful debut *Barbara Cook At Carnegie Hall* recorded by CBS '75, incl. medley from *She Loves Me*; played hall again '80 (*It's Better With A Band* on MMG) incl. Bernstein medley, Irving BERLIN's 'I Love A Piano'; the stand-out track for fans was 'The Ingenue', written by her mus. dir. Wally Harper with David Zippel. Also guest shots on Perry COMO TV show, etc.; London club work late '70s. Other LPs incl. *As Of Today* from Columbia Special Products; new recording of RODGERS & Hammerstein's *Carousel* on MCA '87 prod. by Thomas Z. Shepard features her, with Samuel Ramey, Sarah Brightman, David Rendall, Maureen Forrester, Royal Phil. Orch. cond. by Paul Gemignani. Remains *the* ingenue for Broadway buffs, but a fine interpreter of songs in any context.

COOK, Will Marion (*b* 27 Jan. 1869, Washington DC; *d* 19 July '44, NYC) Composer, conductor, violinist. Studied at Oberlin, in Berlin, in NYC with Anton Dvořák. Wrote music for dancer Bert Williams, composed musicals incl. *In Darkeydom* ('14, with James Reese EUROPE). Toured USA and Europe with orchestra incl. Sidney BECHET ('18-9), command performance for King George V. Spent later years as choral and orchestral conductor. As a prominent black leader with formal musical training, he influenced the next generation; Duke ELLINGTON had long conversations with him about composition. His own works incl. early jazz classic 'I'm Coming Virginia'.

COOKE, Sam (*b* Sam Cook, 22 Jan. '35, Chicago; *d* 10-11 Dec. '64) Soul singer; enormously popular with both black and white audiences and a profound infl. on subsequent pop. Sang gospel music from age 9, with siblings as the Singing Children, later with the Highway QCs; then replaced retiring lead tenor Robert (R. H.) Harris in the Soul Stirrers '50: the group was an innovative one, allowing the lead tenor to shine and performing much contemporary material; it recorded for Specialty from '50 and Cooke acquired young female fans. In '56 Bumps BLACKWELL began recording him on secular songs as Dale Cook (the 'e' was added later), several ballads were released and Blackwell added white female backup singers to further sweeten the style on 'You Send Me'; label boss Art Rupe did not approve, fearing backlash from gospel fans; Blackwell and Cooke were released from

their contracts and took masters in lieu of back royalties to Bob Keene's Keen label: 'You Send Me' became one of the decade's biggest hits, no. 1 on both pop and R&B charts. His gospel feeling and uncanny control over pitch, timbre and melisma (the direction of the vocally improvised melody) were entirely new, and led to 29 top 40 hits '57-65. He formed his own Sar label, released gospel-flavoured R&B hits (giving Bobby WOMACK his start in the Valentinos); he took his own act to RCA '60; Alan Klein became his manager '62 and negotiated a new contract which gave him more control over his material than most artists had, let alone black ones. Blackwell may have seen him as a new Nat COLE, but RCA gave him weak material, slushy arrangements, prod. by Hugo (Peretti) and Luigi (Creatore); his talent won out and many good records were made. 'Bring It On Home To Me' featured Lou RAWLS as second voice; 'Little Red Rooster' had Ray CHARLES on piano and Billy PRESTON on organ. 10 LPs charted '58-65 incl. *Sam Cooke At The Copa* '64, recorded live; one account says that after appearing at the famous Copacabana night club in top hat and with a cane, he turned his back on white clubs; in any case his performances in black clubs, for people who knew who he was and where he was from, were different. His own song 'A Change Is Gonna Come' reached the top 10 '65 after he had been shot to death by a woman managing a motel; he may have taken a young woman to his room who then claimed that he forced her to take her clothes off; Klein believes that she may have intended to rob him. In any case USA's obsession with hand guns claimed another victim. An inquest ruled justifiable homicide but Klein did his own investigation and plans a film of Cooke's life. He also ended up controlling Cooke's recordings; 'Wonderful World' '60 (no. 12 USA; no. 27 UK) was used in a TV advert for blue jeans in UK '85, reissued and charted higher than the first time. Whether or not Cooke ever wore blue jeans, a retrospective listen to the architect of soul music began with *Feel It! Live At The Harlem Square Club* '85 on RCA, recorded '63 in a Miami club as black audiences knew him: voice soaring to be free. Other compilations incl. *Two Sides Of Sam Cooke* on Sonet

UK/Specialty USA, with some gospel material; 2-disc digitally remastered RCA set *Sam Cooke – The Man And His Music* '86, with three tracks from Specialty (two with Soul Stirrers), three from Keen, 22 from RCA superseded earlier 2-disc *This Is Sam Cooke*, partly in phoney stereo.

COOLEY, Spade (*b* Donnell Clyde Cooley, 17 Dec. '10, Pack Saddle Creek, Okla.; *d* Nov. '69, Oakland, Cal.) Singer, fiddler, leader. Got nickname from playing cards. Played with bands at Venice Pier Ballroom (Venice, Cal.); started own band and opened Santa Monica ballroom, keeping it filled during WWII when many ballrooms were losing money because of petrol rationing. No. 1 record on 'hillbilly' chart 'Shame On You', '45. Popular radio show; had 25-piece band with Tex WILLIAMS as vocalist, not recorded in studio at peak because of musician union's strike; made western films, had show on first commercial TV station in L.A. '47. Western swing genre began to fail; Cooley still a popular act, but drank heavily, had heart attacks; killed estranged second wife in July '61 and sentenced to life; allowed out to play benefit concert, had final heart attack. Club Of Spade label has made available eight albums: three vols. of *Best Of* radio transcriptions, three vols. of *Mr Music Himself*, two of Spade Cooley & Tex Williams: *As They Were*, *Oklahoma Stomp*; also *Swinging The Devil's Dream* on Charly UK.

COOLIDGE, Rita (*b* 1 May '45, Nashville, Tenn.) Sultry pop singer with hits in '70s, still drawing crowds on tour. Daughter of Baptist minister; sang regularly in church. Family moved to Florida; during college years formed group called R.C. & The Moon Pies. Worked in Memphis as backing vocalist then in L.A. singing with acts such as Delaney & Bonnie BRAMLETT. Toured with Joe COCKER and Leon RUSSELL, who wrote 'Delta Lady' about her ('69 hit for Cocker); she signed to A&M for pop/country hits: 'A Song I'd Like To Sing' '73, 'Mama Lou' '74, 'Higher & Higher' '77, 'We're All Alone' '77, 'The Way You Do The Things You Do' '78, 'I'd Rather Leave While I'm In Love' '79. 'Higher' was a cover of the Jackie WILSON hit and made all the charts; her real love was soul music. Married Kris KRISTOFFERSON '73, had hit duets with him ('A Song I'd Like To Sing', 'Loving Arms', etc.; 'From The Bottle To The Bottom' '73 and 'Lover Please' '75 won Grammies). Her LPs (all on A&M) incl. *Breakaway* '75, *It's Only Love* '76, *Anytime, Anywhere* '77, compilation *Very Best* '80; also *Full Moon* '74, *Natural Act* '78 with Kristofferson. They were divorced '80 but remain close, toured together '86. She has many fans, tours incessantly from straight-ahead rock shows to symphony pops; when she records again she will do an album without looking for a hit: the singles market requires a straitjacket which she refuses to wear.

COON-SANDERS Drummer Carlton Coon (*b* 5 Feb. 1894, Rochester, Minn.; *d* 3 May '32, Chicago), pianist Joe Sanders (*b* 15 Oct. 1896, Thayer, Kansas; *d* 14 May '65, Kansas City) led jazz-oriented dance band made famous by NBC radio broadcasts from Kansas City; both were vocalists. As Coon-Sanders' Novelty Orchestra, had hit 'Some Little Bird' on Columbia '21; then on Victor as Coon-Sanders Original Nighthawks Orchestra: hits incl. 'Night Hawk Blues' '24 (duet vocal), 'Yes Sir, That's My Baby' '25 (with vocal by Coon), 'Flamin' Mamie' '26 and 'I Got A Great Big Date With A Little Bitta Girl' '29 (vocals by Sanders), etc. They toured, had Chicago residencies mid-'20s, a happy band with few changes of personnel; after Coon's death Sanders (known as 'the old left-hander') carried on with residencies at Chicago's Blackhawk, but never regained former popularity. He also did Hollywood studio work '40s, was member of Kansas City Opera Company '50s.

COOPER, Bob (*b* 6 Dec. '25, Pittsburgh, Pa.) Reeds, especially tenor sax; almost the only oboe in jazz. With Stan KENTON '45-51, married June CHRISTY; with Howard RUMSEY's Lighthouse All Stars at famed West Coast club from '54; many records with Kenton on Capitol, Rumsey on Contemporary, tours with Christy (LP with her *Do-Re-Mi*); recorded with FOUR FRESHMEN, Shorty ROGERS, Buddy RICH, Laurindo ALMEIDA (*Viva Bossa Nova!*), many of the sidemen listed below. First own LPs: *Group Activity* '54, quintet with Shelly MANNE, Bud SHANK on baritone; *Shifting Winds* '55 octet with Cooper playing English horn and oboe as well as tenor, Shank on tenor and alto, Jimmy GIUFFRE playing three reeds: both recorded for Capitol, now on Affinity UK. Also *Coop!* '57 on Contemporary with Victor FELDMAN, Frank Rosolino, others (some tracks with CANDOLI bros); Capitol LP '61 with Shank, Rosolino, Conte Candoli, Buddy COLLETTE; *Tenor Sax Jazz Impressions* '79, quartet on Trend; *Plays Michel Legrand* '80, quartet on Discovery. Also a composer: film scores, worked on 12-tone octet for woodwinds, etc.

COOPER, Lindsay (*b* 3 Mar. '51, London) Reeds, piano, composer. Studied classical bassoon at Royal College of Music; entered rock and improvised music scene early '70s. Toured and recorded with Henry Cow '74-8, sessioned with Mike OLDFIELD, Steve Hillage; did occasional TV ads. Founder member mid-'70s of pool of female musicians and performance artists called FIG (Feminist Improvising Group), which toured Europe and released a cassette *FIG – Live*. Has worked in jazz with Mike WESTBROOK (*The Cortege* '82), the Maarten Altena Octet (*Tel* '83), in Europe with singer Maggie Nicols, bassist Joelle Leandre '83. Founder member of rock group David Thomas and the Pedestrians (*Variations On A Theme* and *Winter Comes Home* '83, *More Places Forever* '85). Own recordings reflect varied work, eclectic taste: *Rags* '80, *The Gold Diggers* '83 are film soundtracks; *Music For All Occasions* '86 is compilation of music recorded for TV, dance and theatre productions.

COOPER, Stoney & Wilma Lee Wilma Lee Leary (*b* 7 Feb. '21, Valley Head, W. Va.; *d* 22 Mar '77), Dale T. Cooper (*b* 16 Oct. '18, Harmon, W. Va.; *d* 22 Mar. '77). Leading performers of authentic mountain music. Wilma Lee in family gospel group The Leary Family; young fiddle player Stoney joined '39, they married '41, left group '47 as duo. Featured on WWVA Wheeling Jamboree '47-57; signed to Columbia, success with 'Tramp On The Street', 'Walking My Lord Up Calvary Hill', 'The Legend Of Dogwood Tree'. Signed to Hickory '55, joined Grand Ole Opry '57; had bigger hits 'Come Walk With Me' '58, 'Big Midnight Special', 'There's A Big Wheel' '59, cover of Roy ACUFF classic 'Wreck On The High-

way' '61. Joined Decca '65, remained popular act until Stoney's death. Wilma Lee carried on with daughter Carol Lee Snow (married to Hank SNOW's son Jimmie Rodgers Snow) and Clinch Mountain Clan performing old-time bluegrass and mountain songs. LPs incl. *There's A Big Wheel* '59 on Hickory, *Wilma Lee & Stoney Cooper* '77 on DJM, *A Daisy A Day* '80 on Leather, *Early Recordings* '82 on County, *Wilma Lee Cooper* '84 on Rounder.

COPAS, Cowboy (*b* Lloyd Estel Copas, 15 July '13, Muskogee, Okla.; *d* 5 Mar. '63, Camden, Tenn.) Top country singer of '40s, early '50s. Grew up on ranch, won talent contest at 16, teamed up with Natchee, American Indian who played fiddle. They split '40; Copas became regular on Cincinnati radio Boone County Jamboree show; signed to King, had honky-tonk hits through '40s: 'Tragic Romance', 'Filipino Baby', 'Signed, Sealed And Delivered', 'Gone And Left Me Blues'. With Pee Wee KING's Golden West Cowboys '46 as lead singer on hits 'Tennessee Waltz', 'Kentucky Waltz'; regular on Grand Ole Opry. Named Top Western Artist '48, '51; after 'Hangman's Boogie' '49, 'Strange Little Girl' '51, career slumped in '50s, but signed to Starday '59 and 'Alabam' no. 1 country chart '60. 'Flat Top', 'Sunny Tennessee', remake of 'Signed' hit in '61. Killed in plane crash with Patsy CLINE, Hawkshaw HAWKINS; 'Goodbye Kisses' made chart next month. LPs incl. *Beyond The Sunset* '70 on Ember, *Best Of* '73 on Starday.

COPELAND, Johnny (*b* '37, Homer, La.) Blues singer/guitarist. To Arkansas as an infant; to Houston, Texas '50; was a boxer as well as playing guitar. Led local bands backing visiting stars like Sonny Boy WILLIAMSON, Big Mama THORNTON; began recording '58 but no more than regional success. To NYC '75, became local star in Harlem; debut LP *Copeland Special* made '77 (featuring 'Black Arthur' BLYTHE), released on Rounder '81; since then *Make My Home Where I Hang My Hat* and *Texas Twister*, also on Rounder, all on Demon in UK; also *I'll Be Around* '84 on Mr R&B (Swedish label). Regarded as heir to blues chair of T-Bone WALKER and Freddie KING. *Showtime!* on Alligator/

Sonet '85 with Robert CRAY, Albert COLLINS made Billboard charts '86.

COPELAND, Keith (*b* 18 Apr. '46, NYC) Drums. Son of Ray COPELAND. High school in Brooklyn; USAF '63-7: wanted to play in Air Force band but was sent to communications school. Time in Germany allowed gigging in Frankfurt, Heidelberg, Cologne and Munich with Albert MANGELSDORFF, Benny BAILEY and many others; Paris '66-7: Johnny GRIFFIN, Dexter GORDON, Kenny CLARKE, Ted CURSON. With Stevie WONDER's Wonderlove band '71-2 incl. UK tour. To Boston's Berklee College of Music; gigged in R&B, with Jaki BYARD; invited to join faculty without degree '75-8, became good teacher. To NYC, joined Milt JACKSON at Village Vanguard, since then a rising star: excellent taste, technique, powerful and exultant swing, in demand for gigs, records. LP with Griffin *Return Of The Griffin* '78 on Galaxy; 15 months with HEATH bros. (Columbia LP *In Motion* Jan. '79; *The Bassist!* on Discovery with Sam Jones trio the same month). With Billy TAYLOR quartet '80-4, incl. LPs *Where Have You Been?* '80, with Joe Kennedy, violin (*b* 17 Nov. '23) on Concord Jazz, and *Once In Every Life* on Chicago's Beehive label, '83, with vocalist Johnny HARTMAN, Frank Wess. LPs with George RUSSELL: *Electronic Sonata For Souls Loved By Nature* on Soul Note, recorded in Milan '80; *African Game* made in Boston '83, issued on Blue Note '85. Quintet *Upper Manhattan Jazz Society* '81, on Enja '85: co-led by Charlie ROUSE and Benny BAILEY with Albert Dailey, piano, Buster Williams on bass (*b* Charles Anthony Williams Jr, 17 Apr. '42, Camden, N.J.; accompanied Nancy WILSON '64-8). Also *Live In Front Of The Silver Screen* '83 by Joe LOCKE – Phil Markowitz quartet with Eddie Gomez, made in Rochester for Little label; Rory STUART LPs on Sunnyside and Cadence; Billy Pierce's *William The Conqueror* '85 on Sunnyside (Pierce had jammed with Copeland in Boston, played for five years with Art BLAKEY); and guitarist Joshua BREAKSTONE's *Echoes* '86 on Contemporary. He played in Basle with Curson '83, toured Europe with Benny GOLSON '85, worked with Arnie Lawrence (reedman, *b* 10 July '38, Brooklyn), Dakota STATON '85;

UK tours with Russell '86-7. Has also taught at Long Island U. (Brooklyn), Eastman, Rutgers, Drummer's Collective NYC.

COPELAND, Ray (*b* 17 July '26, Norfolk, Va.; *d* 19 May '84, Sunderland, Mass.) Lead trumpet, arranger, composer, teacher. With Mercer ELLINGTON, SAVOY SULTANS, others late '40s; worked in paper factory '50-5, gigged in spare time with MACHITO, Lionel HAMPTON, Tito PUENTE, many others; also gigs NYC with own 14-piece band; led dates for Andy KIRK (wrote book of arr. for him), but turned down offer from Duke ELLINGTON to look after son Keith (*see entry above*). Played lead on Buck CLAYTON – Tony BENNETT record date '55; plays on *The Trumpet Album* '55-7 on Savoy, arr. by Ernie Wilkins, with Art FARMER, Charlie SHAVERS, Harold BAKER, etc. First black to play in band at Roxy Theatre '55 till it closed '60; one of those rare musicians who could play first-class lead as well as solos, he played too much lead at Roxy (and was not paid for it), lost his embouchure; gradually got it back but meanwhile turned down offer from Skitch HENDERSON '60 to join band on Johnny Carson's *Tonight* show: had too much integrity to take the job knowing that he couldn't play lead, recommended Clark TERRY. Copeland arr. '58 Roulette date for drummer Specs Powell (*b* Gordon Powell, 5 June '22, NYC; CBS staff musician for many years); with Pearl BAILEY – Louie BELLSON mid-'60s; Monterey Jazz Festival with Gil Fuller '65, etc. Recorded with Thelonious MONK '54 on Prestige (incl. 'Wee See'), on Riverside '57 (LP *Monk's Music*); Art BLAKEY big band '57; also with Johnny Richards orchestra; Randy WESTON Sextet '66, toured Africa with him for State Dept '67 (on his LPs *African Cookbook, Tanjah*) with Oliver NELSON's Jazz Interactions Orchestra (*Jazzhattan* on Verve '67). Toured Morocco with Weston '70; own comp. *Classical Jazz Suite In Six Movements* at Lincoln Center '70; played in Broadway pit bands '70-2; arr. and cond. *Attica Blues* for Archie SHEPP in France '81. Published book on jazz improvisation; taught in county school systems and high schools, at Amherst, Berklee; died of heart attack. Summoned to Europe by Monk, played easily witty solo on 'Wee See' Oct. '67 in Rotterdam: final legacy from a fine musician is mistitled 'Hackensack' on Unique Jazz aircheck LP *Thelonious Monk: Quartet & Octet In Europe.*

COPPER FAMILY UK unaccompanied singing family: registered in Rottingdean from 1593, can trace family singing trad. back several hundred years. Bob (*b* Robert James Copper, 6 Jan. '15, Rottingdean), daughter Jill Susan (*b* 24 Jan. '45), son John James (*b* 4 June '49), cousin Ron (*b* Ronald Walter; *d* 7 Jan. '78); also Jill's husband Jonathan Curtis Dudley, John's wife Lynne Margaret. Bob and his father James did BBC radio broadcast '51; Bob, uncle John, cousin Ron performed at international folk festival at Royal Albert Hall: semi-pro career began. Quartet until fathers died, then duo of Bob and Ron until late '60s when Jill and John joined; trio after Ron's death, then quartet or quintet incl. grandchildren. All permutations of group known for harmonic part-singing, rare in English trad. music; very influential on English folk revival (especially unaccompanied trio the YOUNG TRADITION, modelled on Coppers; also the WATERSONS, family quartet). Many groups covered their songs, associated with the family and collected in now-famous notebook by Bob's father and grandfather ('Hard Times Of Old England' recorded by STEELEYE SPAN, Dave Swarbrick, etc.). Bob has written three books on the family, all published by Heinemann: *A Song For Every Season* (won Robert Pitman literary prize '71), *Songs And Southern Breezes*, *Early To Rise*. Their few LPs incl. 4-disc set *A Song For Every Season* '71 on Leader; Bob and Ron did *English Shepherd And Farming Songs* (on Folk Legacy) and *Traditional Songs From Rottingdean* (EFDSS); Bob made *Sweet Rose In June* on Topic. Bob nursed ailing wife from '78 until her death '84; has returned to music, plans to update books. *Coppersongs: A Living Tradition* '88 on EFDSS incl. archive and contemporary material, first appearance on record of John and Lynne's children.

COQUE, Oliver de (*b* Oliver Sunday Akanite, Nigeria) Guitar, singer-composer. Emerged mid-'70s with unique brand of Ibo HIGHLIFE known as Ogene sound; his guitar lead established the Expo '76 Ogene Super Sounds with string of hits on Olumo label incl. *Ogene Super Sounds '76, Oje Mba Ewilo '77, I Salute Africa* and *Jomo Kenyatta '79, Identity '80, Udoka Social Club '81, Chief Emeka Odumegwu Ojukwu '82* (welcoming Chief back to Nigeria from exile in Ivory Coast). Colorful character known to fans as Oliver de Coke or Oliver de Fanta. Established own Ogene label '82, released five more hit LPs incl. *Ekueme Youth Club '82, Anyi Cholu '83, Ogene King Of Africa '84.* One of the top two or three highlife acts, keeps up hectic schedule playing for and praising social clubs in Eastern Nigeria.

COREA, Chick (*b* Armando Anthony Corea, 12 June '41, Chelsea, Mass.) Jazz/rock/fusion keyboards, composer. Puts tension into Romanticism; object of beauty often attained. Worked, recorded as sideman '60s with Herbie MANN, Hubert LAWS on Atlantic, Blue MITCHELL on Blue Note, Mongo SANTAMARIA on Riverside, others. Led own groups, made LPs *Tones For Joan's Bones '66* on Vortex, quartet with Joe Farrell (2-disc *Inner Space* later compiled on Atlantic by Michael CUSCUNA contains music from this period); *Now He Sings, Now He Sobs* on Solid State and *Circling In* on Blue Note '68 are by a trio with Roy HAYNES, Miroslav Vitous; *Is* '69 (on both Solid State, Blue Note) and *Sun Dance* on Groove Merchant are septet with Laws, Dave HOLLAND, Jack DeJOHNETTE. Joined Miles DAVIS '68, playing electric and acoustic piano on *In A Silent Way* and *Bitches Brew '69; Live/Evil, Black Beauty* and *Live At The Fillmore East '70; On The Corner '72.* Formed Circle with Holland, Barry ALTSCHUL: LPs *The Song of Singing*, adding Anthony BRAXTON on *Circling In* and *Circulus* (2 vols.), all '70 on Blue Note, plus *Live In German Concert* on CBS/Sony. Trio *A.R.C.* on ECM, adding Braxton for *Paris Concert* (ECM) and *Gathering* (CBS/Sony); two vols. of solo *Piano Improvisations* on ECM, a different *Chick Corea Quartet* on America, all '71. *Light As A Feather* on Polydor with Farrell, Stanley CLARKE, AIRTO, vocals by Flora PURIM, and *Return To Forever '72* on ECM; also *Crystal Silence* on ECM that year, duet with Gary BURTON. With varying personnel usually incl. Lenny

White on drums, Farrell, Clarke, Al DiMEOLA, band Return To Forever: *Hymn Of The Seventh Galaxy*, *Where Have I Known You Before*, *No Mystery*, *The Leprechaun*, *My Spanish Heart* (2 discs), *The Mad Hatter*, *Secret Agent* '73-8, all on Polydor; *Romantic Warrior* on CBS; *Return To Forever: Live* and *Musicmagic* are CBS compilations of NYC concert '77: six made USA pop LP chart, three in top 40, making the group among the most successful of such fusion bands. *Friends* is a quartet with Farrell, Eddie Gomez, Steve Gadd on drums; *C&H Homecoming* piano duos with Herbie HANCOCK; *Delphi 1* solo piano, all on Polydor '78. *In Concert, Zürich* '79 is duet with Burton on ECM. *Tap Step* '78-80, *Touchstone* '82 are collections with various personnel; *Three Quartets* '81 with Michael BRECKER, Gomez, Gadd; all on WB. *Trio Music* '81 on ECM with Haynes, Vitous; cut 'Time Remembered' for 2-disc *A Tribute to Bill EVANS* on Palo Alto label '82 with tracks by 14 others. Duo *On Two Pianos* with Nicolas Economou incl. pieces from Bartók's *Mikrokosmos* on DGG; *The Meeting* with classical/jazz pianist Friedrich Gulda on Philips; both '82. *Lyric Suite With Sextet* '82 with Burton, four strings incl. Fred Sherry on cello, solo *Children's Songs* '83 and *Septet* '85 (six strings incl. Sherry) all on ECM. *Bliss* on Muse made '70s with John Gilmore and Pete La Roca (originally *Turkish Women At The Bath* in La Roca's name on Douglas). LP *Live At Midem* '78, made at Paris and Cannes with Lionel HAMPTON, has been on several labels. Recorded Mozart's Concerto for two pianos and orchestra '84; own piano concerto premiered '86; formed trio Elektric Band with bassist John Patitucci, drummer Dave Weckl, using assortment of Yamaha, Synclavier electronics: LP *Elektric Band* '86 on GRP also has guitarist Carlos Rios on some tracks. He has also accompanied his wife, vocalist Gayle Moran.

CORNELL, Don (*b* '24, NYC) Singer, guitar. With Red NICHOLS, Lennie HAYTON, others late '30s, Sammy KAYE '42, rejoined Kaye '46. Big hit '50 'It Isn't Fair' on Victor; went solo on that label; switched to Coral, had more hits: 'I'll Walk Alone', 'I'm Yours' were top 10 '52; 'Heart Of My Heart' (no. 18 '53) was charming street-corner gang effort

with Johnny DESMOND, Alan Dale (*b* 9 July '26, Brooklyn); 'Hold My Hand' from film *Susan Slept Here* (no. 5 '54), 2-sided hits 'Most Of All'/'The Door Is Still Open To My Heart', 'The Bible Tells Me So'/'Love Is A Many-Splendored Thing' '55, six more top 100 entries to '57. Nice baritone voice went out of chart fashion, but popularity in clubs continued.

CORTEZ, Dave 'Baby' (*b* David Cortez Clowney, '39, Detroit, Mich.) USA R&B keyboard player. Father played piano, encouraged music studies; Cortez played piano 10 years, switched to organ. Singing with the Pearls; offered contract by Clock Records; his own 'The Happy Organ' was no. 1 '59. Had eight hits on four labels '59-66; only other big one was naggingly memorable 'Rinky Dink' on Chess, reached top 10 '62. Album of that title also charted. LP in late '60s with Willis JACKSON.

CORTIJO, Rafael (*b* Loiza Aldea, Puerto Rico; *d* '83 NYC) Bandleader, percussionist, composer. Obituary said he was as important in Latin-American music as Duke ELLINGTON was in jazz. Covers of Puerto Rican songs 'Caballero que Bomba', 'El Bombón de Elena' '57 (incl. in LP *Los Invita a Bailar* on Seeco) plus his own compositions, sung in powerful, husky voice of Ismael Rivera, incl. Puerto Rican-style female back-up chorus taken into dominant Cuban tradition. First band was the most important in Puerto Rico, appeared on TV show Del Mediodia; LPs on Tropical and Gema (some reissued on Rumba); *Baile con Cortijo y su Combo* was a compilation of original material. Rivera's vocal improvisations set a new standard of musicianship; other artists working with Cortijo y su Combo incl. pianist Rafael Ithier (later led EL GRAN COMBO), Roberto ROENA on bongos (leads own band, Apollo Sound), Colombian singer Nelson Pinedo (worked with Sonora Matancera, Tito RODRIGUEZ, Tommy OLIVENCIA, Sonido de Londres). When members of the band broke away to form El Gran Combo, Cortijo and Rivera went to NYC; Rivera albums with Cortijo incl. *Bienvenido!/Welcome!* and *Con Todos los Hierros* (*Everything But The Kitchen Sink!*) c.'66-7 on Tico; Cortijo's *Time Machine/Maquina de Tiempo* '74 described as one of the most avant-garde SALSA records ever (a flop at the time), blending plena, bomba, Cuban music, introducing Brazilian friction drum, early use of electric guitar. *Champions '75*, *Caballo de Hierro '78* incl. Cortijo's daughter Fé on lead vocals, latter with Mario BAUZA on trumpet and prod. by Charlie PALMIERI. Reunion of original combo remade early hits on '74 LP reissued '82 as *Ismael Rivera Sonero No. 1.*

CORYELL, Larry (*b* 2 Apr. '43, Galveston, Texas) Guitarist, mostly self-taught; described in '60s as 'perhaps the most original guitarist around' (*Downbeat*). Grew up in Washington; worked in Seattle; to NYC '65. Worked with Chico HAMILTON, fusion band Free Spirits, toured with Gary BURTON '67-8 (LPs *Duster*, *In Concert*), Herbie MANN (LP *Memphis Underground*). Own LPs on Vanguard with varying personnel incl. *Lady Coryell* with Jimmy GARRISON and *Basics* with Ron CARTER, both '68; *Spaces '70* with John McLAUGHLIN, Miroslav Vitous, Billy COBHAM; *At The Village Gate '71* (with one vocal by Julie Coryell); *The Real Great Escape, Offering, Introducing The Eleventh House '72*; *Larry Coryell And The Eleventh House* at Montreux and *The Restful Mind '74; Planet End '75. Barefoot Boy '71* on Flying Dutchman (now on RCA in USA) is a septet; *Fairyland* on Mega is a trio set from Montreux '71; *Level One '74* sextet on Arista. *Difference '75* is a collection on EGG from solo to septet; *Aspects* (11 pieces with BRECKER bros), *The Lion And The Ram* (quintet), *Two For The Road* (guitar duets with Steve Kahn), all '76, are on Arista. *Twinhouse '76* is duet with guitarist Philip CATHERINE, issued on both Elektra, Atlantic; *Live '77* with Catherine, pianist Joachim Kühn on Elektra; *Back Together Again '77* on Atlantic has Catherine, drummer Alphonse Mouzon, background vocals; *Splendid* made '78 with Catherine in Hamburg on Elektra has Kühn on one track. Recorded guitar lesson accompanied with 24-page booklet *Improvisation From Rock To Jazz '77. Standing Ovation '78* on Mood, *European Impressions '78* on Arista and *Bolero '81* on String are solo sets. *Return '79* on Vanguard is quintet with three BRUBECK bros and Ray Mantilla, percussion; *Tributaries '79* on Arista has three guitars (with Joe Beck,

John Scofield); *The Larry Coryell - Michal Urbaniak Duo '82* on Dutch Keystone label has Urbaniak on electric violin, two vocals by Urszula Dudziak; *Solos, Duos and Trios '82* on the Dutch Keytone label has a solo suite by Coryell, other tracks by other artists; *'Round Midnight '83* was made with Japanese trio; *Just Like Being Born '85* on Flying Fish has duets on electric and acoustic guitars with Brian Keane; *Together '85* on Concord Jazz duets with Emily Remler (warmly reviewed LP was followed quickly by Remler's own quartet date *Catwalk* on Concord, featuring Eddie Gomez). *Comin' Home '85* on Muse has a quartet with Albert Dailey, piano. Coryell played on Charles MINGUS LPs *Three Or Four Shades Of Blues '77* (as do Scofield and Catherine), *Me Myself An Eye '78. Scheherezade, The Firebird And Petrouchka* (Philips '84), like *Bolero*, are transcriptions of 'classical' music for guitar.

COSTA, Don (*b* 10 June '25, Boston, Mass.; *d* 19 Jan. '83) Conductor, composer, arranger, producer. No formal training. Started in local radio in '40s; arranged for Vic DAMONE, Sarah VAUGHAN, Vaughn MONROE, etc.; in '50s joined ABC Paramount A&R staff, later moved to United Artists. Arranged, conducted for Eydie GORME, Steve LAWRENCE; made Paul ANKA a star at 16. Record of the hit film theme by Manos Hadjidakis and Billy Towne 'Never On Sunday' '60 sold 10 million around the world, the first European song to win Oscar. Costa voted top orchestra leader by *Cashbox* magazine; formed own Don Costa Productions: soul group LITTLE ANTHONY AND THE IMPERIALS had two top 10 hits; Trini LOPEZ made no. 3 with Pete Seeger song 'If I Had A Hammer' on Frank SINATRA's Reprise label. Costa's work with Sinatra incl. hit singles 'Cycles', 'My Way', LP *Sinatra And Strings*. Helped Sinatra back from premature retirement '73, conducted TV special and album *Ol' Blue Eyes Is Back*. Arranged for Barbra STREISAND, Perry COMO, Dean MARTIN, The OSMONDS; scored films *Rough Night In Jericho '67*, Richard Widmark/Henry Fonda detective vehicle *Madigan '68*. Own LPs incl. *I'll Walk The Line, Never On Sunday; Out Here On My Own* with daughter Nikka: they were preparing another when he died.

COSTELLO, Elvis (*b* Declan Patrick McManus, 25 Aug. '55, Paddington, London) Singer/songwriter, easily most important to emerge from New Wave in UK. As with all good singer/songwriters, lyrics are worth listening to and fit tunes perfectly. Tried to keep early life a mystery, but he is the son of Ross McManus, big band singer with Joe LOSS, infl. by dad's record collection. First band was country-flavoured Flip City, some London gigs (no records, but later bootlegs); also played folk clubs as solo. Married young; was computer programmer for Elizabeth Arden ('vanity factory' in song 'I'm Not Angry'). Turned up with guitar to perform for baffled A&R men in legendary method of auditioning; once arrested for busking outside CBS convention. DJ Charlie Gillett (author of *Sound Of The City*) played early Costello tapes on *Honky Tonk* Radio London radio show. Signed with Stiff '77, early work prod. by Nick LOWE, overseen by maverick manager and Stiff boss Jake Riviera (Andrew Jakeman), singled out by critics for intensity and vitriol: 'Less Than Zero' indictment of English Fascism; 'Alison' later covered by Linda RONSTADT (to his well-publicised distaste); '(The Angels Wanna Wear My) Red Shoes' followed by first hit: 'Watching The Detectives', no. 15 UK '77, reggae track backed by the Rumour. Early interviews enhanced image: claimed that he understood only hatred and revenge, kept little black book with names of those who'd thwarted career. Debut LP *My Aim Is True* '77 recorded with Clover (lead singer went on to front Huey LEWIS And The News): hailed as instant classic, compared to work of Graham PARKER, Bruce SPRINGSTEEN, Van MORRISON. Backing group the Attractions formed with session bassist Bruce Thomas (Al STEWART, Sutherland Bros), drummer Pete Thomas (John STEWART, CHILLI WILLI), excellent keyboardist Steve Nieve (*b* Nason; attended Royal College of Music): revealed on Stiff tour (with Wreckless Eric, Ian DURY) to be tight, responsive unit (made own LP *Mad About The Wrong Boy* '81). *This Year's Model* '78 brought praise for striking songs '(I Don't Want To Go To) Chelsea', 'Pump It Up', 'No Action'; *Armed Forces* '79 best seller yet (original title: *Emotional Fascism*), incl. 'Oliver's Army', 'Accidents Will Happen', 'Green Shirt'. Promoting LP in USA

Mar. '79, had fist-fight with Steve STILLS in a bar in Columbus, Ohio (also punched by Bonnie BRAMLETT): allegedly racist remarks about Ray CHARLES hurt credibility with UK's Rock Against Racism as well as USA music press: incident probably due to drinking, typical rudeness; gave up touring in USA, but sales unaffected. *Get Happy* '80 infl. by soul music, incl. 20 tracks: 'Motel Matches', 'Clowntime Is Over', UK single hits 'I Can't Stand Up For Falling Down', 'High Fidelity', 'New Amsterdam', etc.; *Trust* '81 incl. hit 'Clubland', also 'New Lace Sleeves', 'Big Sister's Clothes'. Duetted with diverse artists George JONES, Yoko ONO, Tony BENNETT, John HIATT; fondness for country music already evident in own songs 'Radio Sweetheart', 'Stranger In The House'; then *Almost Blue* '81 was lavish set of favourite C&W songs, with sticker 'This album contains Country & Western music & may produce radical reaction in narrow minded people'. Documented on UK TV's *South Bank Show*, prod. in Nashville by Billy SHERRILL, LP incl. covers of hits by Don GIBSON, Gram PARSONS. New Wave treatment of Hank WILLIAMS classic 'Why Don't You Love Me' left it unrecognisable, but the rest was straight: incl. single hits 'A Good Year For The Roses', 'I'm Your Toy', 'Sweet Dreams'. *Imperial Bedroom* '82 co-prod., over-arranged by long-time George MARTIN associate Geoff Emerick; concept LP about pain of love and deceit incl. additions to canon 'Tears Before Bedtime', 'Town Crier', 'Beyond Belief', singles 'You Little Fool', 'Man Out Of Time'. Appeared in film *Americathon*, title song of film *Party, Party* was UK hit single '82; acted in UK TV series *Scully* '84; prod. records by the SPECIALS, SQUEEZE, BLUEBELLS, POGUES; he has also joined onstage acts like Ricky Scaggs, LOS LOBOS, Richard HELL, Delbert MCCLINTON; own songs covered by Robert WYATT, Dave EDMUNDS, George JONES etc. as well as Ronstadt. *I'm Your Toy* 12" EP '82 incl. alternate version of 'Toy' with orchestra, made at Royal Albert Hall, plus more tracks from Nashville. Generous 20-track collections *Taking Liberties* '81 (USA), *10 Bloody Marys & 10 How's Your Fathers* '84 (UK) yield insight into scope of work. *Punch The Clock* '83 also soul infl.; incl. 'Shipbuilding', Falklands lament among his finest (trumpet solo by Chet BAKER); also 'Everyday I Write The Book', first USA top 40 hit (but all LPs charted strongly in USA, *Armed Forces* at no. 10). Alter ego 'Imposter' prod. singles 'Pills & Soap' '83 (song incl. on *Punch The Clock*), 'Peace In Our Time' '84; LP *Goodby, Cruel World* '84 incl. hits 'I Wanna Be Loved', 'The Only Flame In Town', 'Turning The Town Red'. Late '84 toured USA and UK as solo supported by T-Bone BURNETT: went onstage together as Coward Brothers, doing unlikely songs: Scott McKENZIE's 'San Francisco', BEATLES' 'Baby's In Black'; released single 'The People's Limousine' '85. Burnett prod. LP *King Of America* '86, with all-star cast (David Hidalgo of Los Lobos, James BURTON, Jim Keltner, etc.), hailed as Costello's best since *Almost Blue*: credited to The Costello Show, songs to D. P. McManus, except cover of ANIMALS' '65 hit 'Don't Let Me Be Misunderstood'. *Blood And Chocolate* '86 on Imp prod. by Lowe; reunion with Attractions as strong as ever: his sweep of contemporary subject matter and absorption of popular culture is matched by lyrical talent, his work standing with that of any chronicler in popular music. He married the POGUES bassist Cait O'Riordan '86, contributed cover of Richard THOMPSON's 'The End Of The Rainbow' to Anti-Heroin Project LP *It's A Live-In World*; USA shows incl. guests the BANGLES, Tom PETTY, Tom WAITS, Huey LEWIS. *Out Of Our Idiot* '87 was another compilation of B-sides etc. incl. new track 'So Young' (from '79).

COTTEN, Elizabeth 'Libba' (*b* 1893, near Chapel Hill, N.C.; *d* 29 June '87, Syracuse, NY) Singer, songwriter, guitarist. Married at 15; moved to Washington DC after divorce and worked in department store; found lost Peggy SEEGER strayed from mother while Christmas shopping; hired by Seegers as a domestic, played at home for her own amusement. Mike SEEGER persuaded her to begin performing at age 60. Best known song is 'Freight Train', no. 5 hit UK '57, top 40 USA by Chas. McDevitt (*see* SKIFFLE); she had to go to court to establish ownership of song she wrote at age 12. Played guitar upside down and left-handed, with 2-finger picking style; with elements of ragtime and gospel, her picking style became standard in folk guitar playing. *Negro Folksongs* on Folkways followed by *Elizabeth Cotten Vol. 2: Shake Sugaree* '67, then *When I'm Gone*. She received Burl IVES Award '72 for contribution to folk music, Grammy '85 for *Elizabeth Cotten Live*; performed until a few months before her death.

COTTON, Billy (*b* 6 May 1899, London; *d* 25 Mar. '69, Wembley, Middlesex) UK bandleader, singer. Son of bandmaster; sang in church choir; joined army at 14 and became drummer boy; served in RFC WWI and led first band. Led band at Palais de Danse, Ealing, London; by '23 London Savannah Band at Southport, introducing USA dance fads like the Black Bottom; '24 at Wembley Exhibition, then dance halls in London, Liverpool, Brighton; London Astoria hotel '27, residency at Ciro's. Popular vocalist Alan Breeze present from '30; semi-hot band early '30s had Armstrong clone Nat Gonella on trumpet, black American trombonist Ellis Jackson (also fine dancer), did its best to help keep idea of jazz alive in Britain: 'I'm Just Wild About Harry', 'Super Tiger Rag', 'Somebody Stole My Gal' '32-3 (latter was band's theme), also covers of Duke ELLINGTON's 'Mood Indigo', 'Black And Tan Fantasy'. Increasingly became variety act during '30s, playing theatres rather than dance halls: cover of 'Begin The Beguine' late '30s a straight copy of Artie SHAW arrangement; by mid-'40s jazz had back seat to period pop songs and comedy. During WWII Cotton in charge of entertainment for Air Training Corps; after war, radio and music hall act started each show with catchphrase 'Wakey wakey!' In '50s band did 'I've Got A Lovely Bunch Of Coconuts' while pelting audience with cotton-wool balls; but musicianship always high, trumpet star retained: Grisha Farfel played Harry JAMES-styled solo spots '50s. After UK charts established '52, Cotton had top 20 hits 'In A Golden Coach' '53, 'I Saw Mommy Kissing Santa Claus' '53, 'Friends And Neighbours' '54; continued successful on TV and radio until his death. Compilations on many labels have incl. *The Golden Age Of Billy Cotton, Melody Maker, Rock Your Cares Away, Let's All Join In, That Rhythm Man*, etc. Autobiography *I Did It My Way* '70.

COTTON CLUB Built '18 as the Douglas Casino in Harlem (then becoming largest black community in the world, north end of Manhattan island) at corner of Lenox and 142nd street, with theatre on ground floor, dance hall upstairs; boxer Jack Johnson turned it into the Club Deluxe; then bootlegger Owney Madden into outlet for his beer, entertainment for white downtowners. Duke ELLINGTON residency '27-31 helped make it nationally famous with broadcasts, then Cab CALLOWAY. Cream of society visited, incl. Mayor Jimmy Walker, Lady Mountbatten (who dubbed it 'The Aristocrat of Harlem'). Revues written by Dorothy FIELDS and Jimmy McHUGH, Harold ARLEN, others as well as Ellington. Other important clubs in the area were Connie's Inn, owned by George and Connie Immerman, where Fats WALLER's *Keep Shufflin'* and *Hot Chocolates* were produced; Baron Wilkins' Exclusive Club, where Ellington played with Washingtonians '23 (on recommendation of Ada 'Bricktop' Smith); Smalls' Paradise, which admitted blacks (if they could afford it), where waiters danced the Charleston while balancing trays and owner Ed Smalls encouraged band to park their cars in front on slow nights to make the place look busy. Cotton Club moved downtown to Broadway and 48th '36; by then Harlem Renaissance was over, based as it had been on shaky foundation of white patronage, fuelled by Prohibition (ended '33). Book *Harlem: The Great Black Way 1900-1950* '82 by Jervis Anderson describes period; film *Cotton Club* '84 was slick disappointment.

COTTON, James (*b* 1 July '35, Tunica, Ms.) Harmonica, also drums, guitar. One of the giants of Chicago blues harp, following on from Walter HORTON, LITTLE WALTER. Inspired by Sonny Boy WILLIAMSON (Alex Miller); ran away from home to work with him; toured the south, recorded in Memphis for Sun '54; joined Muddy Waters in Memphis and worked with him off and on from '54, since then touring the world, based in Chicago. LPs incl. *Cut You Loose!* '69 on Vanguard; *High Energy* on Buddah; *High Compression* and *Live From Chicago* (rec. '86) on Alligator. *Take Me Back* '88 on Blind Pig incl. Sam Lay on drums, Pinetop Perkins on piano, other Waters alumni.

COUGHLAN, Mary (*b* c.'57) Irish singer. Grew up in Galway; was the first nude model in Limerick, the first female street sweeper in Ealing (London); went back home, got married, had three kids, sang in the bathtub. European guitarist and songwriter Eric Visser talked her into singing in pubs; they entered a talent contest, lost to a girl who sang 'Silver Threads And Golden Needles'. They made an album with Visser producing; adapted 'Tain't Nobody's Bizness If I Do' ('22) to a tango, also incl. sexy 'Seduced' and 'Mama Just Wants To Barrelhouse All Night Long', 'Meet Me Where They Play The Blues', 'Country Fair Dance', etc.; record companies laughed until *Tired And Emotional* '86 was issued on tiny Mystery label: her strong alto has a breathy edge like the sound of Ben WEBSTER's tenor; LP's personal mixture of folk, infl. of Billie HOLIDAY with accordions and synths became the best-selling record by an Irish artist for years and was picked up by WEA, who delayed *Under The Influence* '87 because the first one kept selling. Second album is slicker, beautifully arr./prod. by Visser, with solo saxophones, guitars, keyboards, tuba, real strings etc.; incl. Cole PORTER's 'Laziest Girl' ('27; sung by Marlene DIETRICH in film *Stage Fright* '50), Holiday's 'Good Morning Heartache' (the musicians play their chords backwards), Willard Robison's 'Don't Smoke In Bed' (hit for Peggy LEE '48), others co-written by Visser etc. and not a dud in the lot. She makes most pop music sound like bubblegum.

COUNCE, Curtis Lee (*b* 23 Jan. '26, Kansas City, Mo.; *d* 31 July '63, L.A.) Bass, leader. Prominent in West Coast jazz, which otherwise seemed to be dominated by whites in '50s: played with Wardell GRAY, Shorty ROGERS ('Martians Go Home' session '55); from '56 led own driving post-bop combos with excellent lineups; did film work, taught bass; died of heart attack. Fine LPs incl. *Landslide* '56-8, *Carl's Blues*, *Counciliation* '57-8 (aka *You Get More Bounce*), with Harold LAND, Carl PERKINS, Jack Sheldon on trumpet (*b* 30 Nov. '31, Jacksonville, Fla.; later worked as singer, actor, comedian; returned to music and toured UK '87), Frank Butler, drums (*b* 18 Feb. '28, K.C.; later worked as drug abuse counsellor; also on Miles DAVIS LP *Seven Steps To Heaven* '63, Teddy Edwards LP *Feelin'* '74, etc.); also *Exploring The Future* with Land, Butler, Elmo HOPE, Rolf Erickson on trumpet (*b* 29 Aug. '27, Stockholm). All have been reissued.

COUNTRY GAZETTE USA bluegrass group formed '71 by remaining members of Flying Burrito Brothers: Herb Pederson (*b* 27 Apr. '44, Berkeley, Cal.), banjo; Byron Berline, fiddle; Kenny Wertz, guitar; Roger Bush, bass. More popular in Europe, with successful tours, regular LPs. Berline was member of Bill MONROE's Bluegrass Boys '66-7; won National Fiddle Championship '64-65-70; formed own band Sundance '75. Pederson, key musician in Cal. country-rock scene, worked with (Lester) FLATT & (Earl) Scruggs '67, replaced Rodney Dillard in the DILLARDS '68-71, has worked with Linda RONSTADT, Emmylou HARRIS, John DENVER, Dan FOGELBERG, etc. Alan Munde (ex-Jimmy Martin's Sunny Mountain Boys) replaced Pederson '73. LPs incl. *Traitor In Our Midst* '73, *Don't Give Up Your Day Job* '74 (United Artists); *Live* '75, *Sunny Side Of The Mountain* '76, *What A Way To Make A Living* '77 (Transatlantic); *From The Beginning* '78 (Sunset), *All This And Money Too* '81 (Ridge Runner), *American Clean* '82 (Flying Fish). Berline LPs: *Dad's Favourite* '78 (Rounder), *L.A. Fiddle Band* '81 (Sugar Hill).

COUNTRY GENTLEMEN, The Progressive bluegrass group formed '57 by Charlie Waller (*b* 19 Jan. '35, Jointerville, Texas; moved to L.A. as a child) and John Duffey (*b* 4 Mar. '34, Washington DC) on guitars, who added Jim Cox on banjo and bass (*b* 3 Apr. '30, Vansant, Va.) and Eddie Adcock on mandolin (*b* 17 June '38, Scottsville, Va.). With accurate three-part harmony both instrumentally and vocally but also an eclectic choice of material, they offended some purists but weathered ups and downs of country/folk scene until they had helped inspire the 'newgrass' movement of more recent times. Four vols. of *Country Gentlemen* on Folkways from '60; *Bluegrass* '62 and *Country Gentlemen* '65 on Starday; also *Live At Roanoke* on Zap, others on Vanguard (now compiled as *Featuring Ricky Skaggs On Fiddle* '85 since Skaggs became a

big star). Many LPs through '70s on Rebel label, most still in print; Adcock had left to form Second Generation '71; Duffey formed Seldom Scene same year, recorded for Sugar Hill, which also issued LPs by the Gentlemen: *Sit Down Young Stranger* with Mike Auldridge, *Good As Gold* with Jimmy Gaudreau, *River Bottom*. Auldridge was a member of Seldom Scene and is one of the all-time great players of the dobro; own LP on Sugar Hill is *Eight String Swing*.

COUNTRY MUSIC Native American genre now popular around the world; variously known in the past as folk music, old-time music, hillbilly, C&W (Country & Western) etc. Fiddlers Uncle Eck Robertson and Henry Gilliand recorded for Victor in NYC June '22 (not issued until later); the Jenkins Family, a Georgia gospel group, first to broadcast in Atlanta same year. Ralph PEER recorded Fiddlin' John CARSON's 'old-time' music '23 as a favour to Atlanta furniture dealer who sold records: had surprise hit. Opera/parlour singer Vernon DALHART revived vaudeville career with 'Wreck Of The Old 97'/ 'The Prisoner's Song' (co-written by Nat SHILKRET) '25; recorded it for many labels, sold millions; also 'event' songs, cowboy songs, sentimental ballads, now nearly forgotten. Okeh issued the first country catalogue '24; record companies and mail-order catalogues advertised Old Southern Songs, Mountain Ballads, Familiar Tunes, Hill Country Music etc. Peer dubbed a four-piece band the Hill-Billies '25, the name stuck: northerners made profits but looked down at the music; term 'hillbilly' used for years though considered offensive (*Variety* wrote '26 that 'hillbillies' had 'intelligence of morons'). Blind guitarist Riley PUCKETT was first important country singing star, first to record a yodel (at first session '24), first influential guitarist; made over 80 trad. string band records from '26 with Gid Tanner's Skillet Lickers. Peer made first records by Jimmie RODGERS, CARTER FAMILY on 4 Aug. '27 in Bristol, Tenn.; two strains continued: trad. mountain music (Carters, also with Maybelle's infl. guitar style), and innovation (Rodgers combined 12-bar blues with yodels, used Hawaiian guitar, dixieland bands, etc.; regarded himself as all-round entertainer). Live country music was used on radio from

Miami to Milwaukee to sell goods (*see* Bob WILLS); first barn dance radio show Jan. '23, from Fort Worth, Texas; Chicago Barn Dance on WLS began Apr. '24, later called National Barn Dance (WLS owned by Sears & Roebuck, stood for World's Largest Store: rural audience kept its mail-order catalogue next to the Bible). George D. Hay was announcer, hired away by WSM Nashville; started WSM Barn Dance late '25; became GRAND OLE OPRY (*which see*). Other barn dances on WSB Atlanta, WWHA Wheeling, W.V. (Jamboree began '33), KWKH Shreveport (Louisiana Hayride '48). WWHA and WLS barn dances networked '33, Opry '39. Mexican border stations not allocated channels in USA-Canadian agreement, so ignored rules: WLS with 50,000 watts heard over midwest; Mexican radio with 100,000 and more heard in Canada, Hawaii late '30s. Meanwhile western movies had died with talking films, so singing cowboys invented: countless B-films '30s-40s with Tex RITTER, Jimmy WAKELY, others adopting 'Western' material; Gene AUTRY, Roy ROGERS easily the most successful: kids clamouring for cowboy songs were inoculated with country music. Films had streak of populism which appealed to rural audiences in Depression: bad guys often bankers or city-slickers with pencil-thin moustaches. Cowboy costumes became norm in country music (gaudiest made by Nudie of Hollywood), hillbilly music became Country & Western (term adopted by BILLBOARD chart '49 after long agitation, especially from West Coast country-music scene which Hollywood helped to create). Capitol had hits with Ritter, hired DJ Cliffie STONE as country expert; he signed Wakely, Tex WILLIAMS, Merle TRAVIS, Ernie FORD; Bakersfield, Cal. became regional country music centre early '60s with Buck OWENS empire. WESTERN SWING genre carried jazz infl. through WWII (especially in Cal.; *see* Wills, Spade COOLEY); pre-war popularity of Roy ACUFF made him G.I favourite (Armed Forces Network spread country music in Europe '50s; *see also* George HAMILTON IV). Bing CROSBY covered Ernest TUBB's 'Walking The Floor Over You', Autry's 'You Are My Sunshine', Wills' 'San Antonio Rose', LULU BELLE & SCOTTY's 'Have I Told You Lately That I Love You?' in '40s; but postwar death of big bands,

closure of ballrooms, rise of TV had same effect on country music as on jazz: entertainment industry treated them as minority interests (industry strikes also hurt; see BIG BAND ERA, ASCAP, BMI). Nashville became international centre of country music by default: southeast had loyal fans. Opry was conservative, but National Barn Dance even more so: lost infl. '40s (switched to WGN when WLS became Top 40 station '60, ended '70); Louisiana Hayride always popular but became stepping-stone to Opry. Bill MONROE's Blue Grass Boys were Opry regulars from '39, inventing BLUEGRASS genre from trad. materials; Opry stars toured USA in Camel Caravan during WWII: Opry's success lay in singing stars, beginning with Acuff, then Red FOLEY, Eddy ARNOLD, many others; Ernest Tubb joined '43 with electric guitars, honky-tonk style. West Coast had importance in establishing country music as big business early '50s, but also lost out: between '40-50 Nashville became centre of country music publishing, then in '50s of recording. Hank WILLIAMS went there to sell songs to Acuff-Rose (*see* Fred ROSE): his meteoric rise to stardom '49, big pop hits with his songs (e.g. by Tony BENNETT) established Nashville (and honky-tonk) for good. Opry's booking agency run by Jim DENNY obtained virtually all big stars in country music from early '50s, encouraging Nashville record industry: WSM studio made records beginning with Victor field trip late '20s; later there were transcription studios for hire, but record industry began in Nashville Dec. '45 when ex-announcer Jim Bulleit's Bullet label cut Sheb WOOLEY Dec. '45 (also first recorded Ray PRICE, B. B. KING; had hit 'Rag Mop' with Wills' brother Johnnie Lee '50, but biggest hit was pop: *see* Francis CRAIG). Owen BRADLEY prod. records in Nashville from '52; RCA rented studio time, then space, recording Elvis PRESLEY in Methodist Publishing Company rooms Jan. '56, built own studio '57: RCA A&R man Steve Sholes (responsible for buying Presley from Sun) hired Chet ATKINS as producer. Columbia bought a studio from Bradley '61; by late '60s city had dozens. Meanwhile songs had become realistic, still reflecting country values but also contemporary concerns: adultery allowed as subject matter with Floyd TILLMAN hit 'Slippin'

Around' (duet by Wakely and Margaret WHITING crossed over to pop chart '49), also 'Back Street Affair' by Webb PIERCE '52; alcoholism treated as something other than comedy in Cindy Walker lyric 'Bubbles In My Beer' (by Bob WILLS on MGM, '48), in Pierce's 'There Stands The Glass' '53 (and pedal steel became ubiquitous with Pierce's 'Slowly' '53). Hank SNOW and Kitty WELLS were giants in '50s, and crossovers to pop chart became common: Stonewall JACKSON, Don GIBSON, Jim REEVES, Patsy CLINE, Marty ROBBINS, etc. Country Music Disc Jockeys Association '54 became Country Music Association '58 to market and publicise country music: early morning record shows for rural listeners had almost disappeared, as had live music on radio; most country fans now lived in cities, were a market not being served: by '67 number of stations playing country music increased to over 2000; during '61-6 stations playing country exclusively went from 81 to 328. With Opry, CMA responsible for making Nashville music centre (also for making Nashville and Tenn. proud of it: many locals had tended to sneer at the business). Country Music Hall of Fame began '61 with election of Rodgers, Williams, Rose; next year Acuff added, abandoning intention to elect only dead entertainers; then executives like Sholes, Denny. Country Music Hall of Fame, Museum opened 31 March '67 in new, ultra-modern building; also houses CMA offices, Country Music Foundation Library and Media Center. Academy of Country Music formed Hollywood '64 for West Coast industry; both CMA, ACM give annual awards honouring musicians, songwriters as well as stars. By end of '50s producers led by Chet ATKINS had created the Nashville Sound: Bob DYLAN made *Blonde On Blonde* there '66, then *John Wesley Harding* '68, *Nashville Skyline* '69; Nashville made half the records in USA: best session players played on every label, so good they didn't need music, only chord sequences. Relaxed way to record had many good points but led to sameness: too-slick product was called 'countrypolitan', while the world changed. Folk boom had led to rediscovery of oldtime artists such as Doc WATSON, Lester FLATT; Monroe sold out bluegrass concerts in NYC; younger fans had to deal with rock 'n'roll, Vietnam,

Watergate, marijuana, etc.: as Denny and others updated country music scene c.'50 now it had to be done again. Impact of rock'n'roll mid-'50s, seen as a threat to country, ultimately added to it and strengthened it: Southern rock (e.g. ALLMAN Brothers) had some effect, as did maverick prod. such as Jack CLEMENT, GLASER Brothers; and honest image of Johnny CASH (frank attitude to problems with pills, minor brushes with the law), but Cash (like Dylan) was a giant who had control of his product: many younger artists were not allowed to decide how their work should be presented, so that the inherent strength of the genre was not being realised. Singer/songwriters David Allan COE, Kris KRISTOFFERSON, Tompall GLASER, Waylon JENNINGS, Billy Joe SHAVER, more experienced people like Willie NELSON became more independent. Many of them hung out at Glasers' studio: Jennings first became an 'outlaw' with co-operation of RCA publicity machine (*see below*) but the term was first applied more generally by Hazel Smith, writer who worked for Tompall. Young artists in Austin and Lubbock, Texas were also doing their own thing regardless of Nashville, and the result was the decentralisation of country music and the rise of 'redneck rock' (aka 'progressive country', partly the maturity of country rock, decade-old pop genre discovered by ex-folkies: *see* the BYRDS, Gram PARSONS). Nelson ran annual 4th of July country music picnics near Austin '72-6; a whole generation responded: local paper ran photo of Nelson, long-haired rocker Leon RUSSELL, U. of Texas football coach: 'first time the hippie and the redneck had gotten together,' said Nelson. Kerrville (Texas) Folk Festival (prod. by Rod Kennedy) has been going for 15 years: in '86 about 70 artists and groups appeared there incl. a great many of the contemporary Austin and Lubbock singer/songwriters, folkies Carolyn HESTER, ODETTA, Tom RUSH, etc. Ironically it was an RCA vice-president in Nashville who compiled tracks by Nelson, Tompall Glaser, Jennings, Jessi Colter (Jennings' wife): LP *Wanted: The Outlaws!* '76 with 'Good-Hearted Woman' (Waylon and Willie), 'Honky Tonk Heroes' (Waylon), 'Suspicious Minds' (Waylon and Jessi); also Glaser cover of biggest Jimmie Rodgers hit 'T For Texas'. With lean, spare sound like a roadhouse band, it became the first country LP to go platinum (a million copies for an LP in USA). Western Swing has been revived by ASLEEP AT THE WHEEL, others; 'They've moved the music back in the dance hall where it belongs,' said Floyd Tillman: at roadhouses and dance halls in Texas and other places, long-haired and straight musicians mixed; country was once again good-time music as well as big business. The Austin story is told in *The Rise Of Redneck Rock* by Jan Reid '77; in the mid-'80s the Austin scene had cooled down with economic recession, but new, smaller venues were springing up. The 'Lubbock mafia' incl. fiddler Tommy Hancock, his Supernatural Family Band and his daughters Traci and Conni (several albums on their own Akashic label), such fine singer/songwriters as Butch HANCOCK (no relation), Terry ALLEN, Joe ELY, Jimmy Gilmore; accordionist Ponty Bone and other fine sidemen (many of these contributed to *The Flatlanders* '72, released '80 on Charly UK). Others who sustain their performing, songwriting and recording careers without much help from the Nashville establishment incl. Guy CLARK, Richard DOBSON; some of these are still cult figures, some like Jerry Jeff WALKER have made pop charts; every album by Emmylou HARRIS does well in the pop charts, with songs by everybody from A. P. Carter to Rodney CROWELL as well as her own. Country rock, or new country, or whatever you want to call it, is among the strongest genres in music today; fine new singers and songwriters keep coming out of the woods and prairies: Reba McENTIRE, Nanci GRIFFITH, Lyle LOVETT, Robert Earl KEEN, Steve EARLE and Darden SMITH are a few of the recent discoveries being signed by major labels. The word 'hillbilly' even shows signs of coming back in reaction to the conservatism of Nashville while artists like George JONES and Bobby BARE, whose hard country was never polluted, are as popular as ever. Bluegrass is still transmuting (e.g. album *Hillbilly Jazz; see* Vassar CLEMENTS); related genres for anyone who wants to listen incl. TEX-MEX, CAJUN, CONJUNTO, ZYDECO. Dolly PARTON wrote first-class songs, now seems to have adopted a general-purpose show-business career; but country music is alive and well all over the place. Historical 2-disc anthologies of singing cowboys and bluegrass, and a 5-disc country music collection with a 16-page booklet are available from CMH Records; an 8-disc selection (143 tracks) with 56-page booklet from the Smithsonian Collection. Among the best books are *Country Music U.S.A.* by Bill C. Malone, classic text in new edition '86; *The Illustrated History Of Country Music* ed. by Patrick Carr '80.

COURTNEIDGE, Cicely (*b* Esmerelda Courtneidge, 1 Apr. 1893, Sydney, Australia; *d* 26 Apr. '80, Putney, London) Singer, dancer and actress. Father was prod. Robert Courtneidge; in his prod. *The Arcadians* '09 (809 performances in London); in musical *The Pearl Girl* '13 she first worked with actor/director Jack Hulbert, later her husband, called 'the perfect English gentleman'. Among many shows, she was teamed with him in nine incl. *By The Way* '25 in both London and NYC, *Under Your Hat* '38 (film version '40). Among shows: *Folly To Be Wise* '31 (introduced song 'The King's Horses'), *Full Swing* '42, *Something In The Air* '43 ('Home'), *Under The Counter* '45 (NYC '47), *Her Excellency* '49, *Gay's The Word* '51 ('Vitality', 'It's Bound To Be Right On The Night'), *Over The Moon* '53, *High Spirits* '64. Films (incl. film versions of shows) *The Ghost Train* and *Jack's The Boy* '32, *Soldiers Of The King* '33 ('The Moment I Saw You'), *Aunt Sally* '34 ('We'll Go Riding On A Rainbow', 'If I Had Napoleon's Hat'), *Me And Marlborough* '36, *The Imperfect Lady* '37 (USA), *Take My Tip* '38 ('I Was Anything But Sentimental'), *The L Shaped Room* '62, cameos in *Those Magnificent Men In Their Flying Machines* '65, *The Wrong Box* '66, *Not Now Darling* '72: made film of this West End farce at age 80, the same year becoming Dame of the British Empire. Compilation LPs have incl. *Cicely Courtneidge And Jack Hulbert* '68, *The Golden Age Of* '84, both on EMI labels. Autobiography *Cicely* '53.

COVAY, Don (*b* Mar. '38, Orangeburg, S.C.) USA soul singer, songwriter. Family moved to Washington DC; Don sang in family gospel group the Cherry Keys, then joined secular group the Rainbows, which allegedly incl. Marvin GAYE and Billy Stewart. He opened a live show for LITTLE RICHARD, who helped him make his first single 'Bip Bop Bip' under the name Pretty Boy, released on Atlantic '57. He recorded for a bewildering number of labels; as the Goodtimers for his first hit 'Pony Time' (no. 60 '61), under his own name for minor hits on Cameo ('62), and Rosemart ('64); but as Don Covay and the Goodtimers 'Mercy, Mercy' made the top 40 '64: Atlantic acquired Rosemart; four entries in the R&B chart followed '64-70 incl. 'See Saw' (no. 5 R&B, no. 44 pop), which he wrote. ('See Saw' was also a hit for Aretha FRANKLIN, and he also wrote her 'Chain Of Fools'.) His biggest hit came in '73 on Mercury: 'I Was Checkin' Out But She Was Checkin' In' was no. 29 pop; 'It's Better To Have (And Don't Need)' at no. 63 '74 was his last chart entry.

COVER Recording of a song already a hit by another artist; now more especially of a song already recorded by its composer. In earlier times any good song was widely covered; as records overtook sheet music sales term acquired modern meanings: when 'Open The Door Richard' swept USA '47 at least 14 versions hustled for sales (*see* Ralph BASS, Jack MCVEA); there were several versions of 'Pretend' '53 (instrumental by Ralph MARTERIE; vocals by Nat COLE, Eileen BARTON). COUNTRY songs were covered by Bing CROSBY, others '40s; Hank WILLIAMS songs were covered early '50s by Tony BENNETT, Rosemary CLOONEY, many others; KING label had both country and R&B rosters: blacks recorded country songs and vice versa. In mid-'50s 'cover' took on a special meaning as white artists covered R&B material, often with watered down lyrics (to say nothing of style): *see* ROCK for that story; composers made royalties but black acts lost record sales as Pat BOONE, Teresa BREWER, many others covered songs by Fats DOMINO, LITTLE RICHARD, Ray CHARLES, etc. Kids began to discover that black originals were more fun, passing judgement on each other according to who bought them instead of pale imitations. R&B star Domino first made pop chart '55; racism in the music business was forced to become less obvious as R&B, then rock'n'roll dominated charts. In early '60s UK pop stars covered Chuck BERRY, other black artists out of acknowledged admira-

tion; then BEATLES, ROLLING STONES etc. began writing their own songs, covered in turn: there are thousands of versions of Paul MCCARTNEY's 'Yesterday'. Nowadays a cover often revives a good song, makes more money for composer, like DURAN DURAN's '84 cover of COCKNEY REBEL's '75 'Make Me Smile', Eric CLAPTON's covers of J. J. CALE, Robert CRAY, Jimmy Byfield (*see* ROCKIN' JIMMY). The most dismal cover of '55 was 'I Hear You Knocking' by Gale STORM: the excellent Smiley LEWIS original did not even make pop chart; Dave EDMUNDS cover '70 in UK allowed a new audience to hear a good old song. Covers have always been rife in country music; Floyd TILLMAN had hit with his own 'Slippin' Around' '49, but duet by Jimmy WAKELY and Margaret WHITING made no. 1 on the pop chart; in today's country rock many artists are songwriters: Emmylou HARRIS and Rodney CROWELL perform on each other's version of his 'Leavin' Louisiana In The Broad Daylight'; *see also* Guy CLARK, Richard DOBSON, Terry ALLEN, Butch HANCOCK, many others; Willie NELSON can set a friend up for life by covering a song on an album.

COVINGTON, Julie UK singer/actress. At university late '60s Pete ATKIN urged her to pursue recording; led to late night TV music and satire programmes early '70s, *Rock Follies* '75, ambitious and successful drama series with co-stars Rula Lenska and Charlotte Cornwall, music by ROXY MUSIC's Andy Mackay. Chosen by Tim Rice and Andrew LLOYD WEBBER for title role of *Evita* album '76, with no. 1 UK hit 'Don't Cry For Me Argentina', but turned down stage role for political reasons, disapproved of releasing single out of context. Records on Virgin gave her hit with cover of ALICE COOPER's 'Only Women Bleed' (UK no. 12 '77). Debut LP *Julie Covington* '78 was strong package, with Richard THOMPSON, Steve WINWOOD, John CALE, UK folk-rock nucleus of Simon Nicol, Trevor Lucas, Ian MATTHEWS, John Kirkpatrick; incl. covers of Thompson's 'I Want To See The Bright Lights Tonight', Kate BUSH's 'Kick Inside', John LENNON's 'How'. Effective, unmannered, recognisably English style drew her towards FAIRPORT CONVENTION alumni; sang back-up on

Richard & Linda Thompson's *First Light*, ALBION BAND's *Rise Up Like The Sun* (both '78). Concentrated on acting: joined the National Theatre; appeared in David Hare's *Plenty* '80, highly praised *Guys & Dolls* revival '81. Fans hope she will resume recording one day.

COWARD, Sir Noel (*b* 16 Dec. 1899, Teddington, Middlesex, England; *d* 16 Mar. '73, Jamaica) Playwright, actor; talent spilled over into cinema, cabaret, revue, literature, criticism; and still the only English songwriter to approach the wit and wisdom of Cole PORTER. First hit 'Poor Little Rich Girl' from '23 revue *On With The Dance*; from then on standards flowed from his piano (he could play in only 3 keys); 'Room With A View' '28, 'I'll See You Again' '29, 'Someday I'll Find You' '30, 'Mad About The Boy' '32 typified the Jazz Age in England; disillusion during Depression was captured with double-edged wit in '20th Century Blues' '31: 'Whatever crimes the proletariat commits/It can't be beastly to the children of the Ritz'. 'The Stately Homes Of England' '38 put the upper classes in context: 'We know how Caesar conquered Gaul/And how to whack a cricket ball'. . . 'I've Been To A Marvellous Party' '39 caught the Bright Young Things: 'Poor Millicent wore a surrealist comb/Made of bits of mosaic from St Peter's in Rome'. . . 'Mad Dogs And Englishmen (Go Out In The Mid-Day Sun)' '32 remains definitive statement on the English abroad; the title of 'Don't Put Your Daughter On The Stage Mrs Worthington' '35 entered the language. Worked tirelessly for Allied propaganda during WWII: 'London Pride' was symbol of defiance during the Blitz; he played an important role in film *In Which We Serve* '42 (character obviously modelled on Mountbatten, most reckless of Admirals, idolised by his men); song 'Don't Let's Be Beastly To The Germans' '43 was unusually vitriolic yet some people took it literally (but Winston Churchill loved it). Post-war mood during years of austerity and rationing described in 'There Are Bad Times Just Around The Corner' ('There are black birds over/The white cliffs of Dover'). In mid-'50s his star seemed to wane as audiences turned to the 'kitchen sink' school of drama, but cabaret engagement in Las Vegas was

remarkable success '54, incl. rewrite of Porter's 'Let's Do It' ('Famous writers in swarms do it/Somerset and all the Maughams do it'). Album *Noel Coward Live In Las Vegas* '55 is superb souvenir. Plays were revived by UK's National Theatre in mid-'60s (first living playwright to be so honoured); he did cameo roles in films *Around The World In 80 Days* '56, *Our Man In Havana* '59, *Bunny Lake Is Missing* '65, *The Italian Job* '69, others; 70th birthday celebrations left no doubt who The Master was. He was knighted; Ned Sherrin mounted show *Cowardly Custard* '72 in London, a joyous occasion. Published autobiographies *Present Indicative* '33, *Future Indefinite* '49; biography *A Talent To Amuse* published '69 by Sheridan Morley, also the title of '73 compilation LP. His best plays were filmed: *Design For Living* '34 especially delightful, though brittle characterisation was lightened for the screen; *Brief Encounter* '46 is classic English weepy. Among albums, *Noel Coward: The Master*, with Gertrude Lawrence, is selection of recordings from '30-51 in bargain-priced 2-disc EMI set. He was dismissive of his own musical talent; 'How potent cheap music is,' he wrote in *Private Lives*: his was some of the most potent. Kenneth Tynan wrote of him: 'His triumph has been to unite two things ever disassociated in the English mind: hard work and wit.' While compiling this book we remember him saying, 'Work is more fun than fun.'

COX, Ida (*b* Ida Prather, 25 Feb. 1896, Toccoa, Ga.; *d* 10 Nov. '67, Knoxville, Tenn.) Blues singer. (Some sources indicate birthdate c. 1889.) Sang in church as a child, ran away from home, toured with minstrel shows; worked with Jelly Roll MORTON, King OLIVER in '20s, recorded from '23. A good businesswoman: toured with own revues from '29 into '40s, said to have been the best such shows on the road, her style infl. by vaudeville as well as rural blues. Recorded with Hot Lips PAGE, Fletcher HENDERSON '39-40, John HAMMOND's *Spirituals To Swing* concert '39; suffered stroke in '44, lived with daughter in Knoxville, but recorded with Coleman HAWKINS on Riverside '61. Compilations incl. *Blues Ain't Nothin' Else But . . .* on Milestone; two vols. of '23-4 Paramount tracks on Fountain; '39-40 tracks with Page on Queen-Disc album shared with Chippie Hill.

COXHILL, Lol (*b* Lowen Coxhill, 19 Sep. '32, Portsmouth, UK) Reeds, especially soprano sax; vocals; also actor. Worked with R&B groups incl. Alexis KORNER, visiting Americans like Otis SPANN; with pianist Steve Miller's Delivery blues band late '60s, Chris McGregor's Brotherhood of Breath mid-'70s, rock groups like avant-garde HENRY COW: eclectic, unique musical personality. Subject of British Arts Council documentary film *Frog Dance*: embellished soundtrack on Impetus '87 incl. solo sax, bagpipes, birds, seals etc. Other LPs: three with Miller incl. *C/M/M/C* '73 on Virgin/Island, *Story So Far* '74 on Caroline/Island, 2-disc live *Miller's Tale* '85 on Matchless. Own LPs: *Ear Of Beholder* '70 on Dandelion, *Toverbal Suite* '71 on Mushroom (both Dutch labels); *Fleas In Custard* '75 on Caroline with guitarist G. F. Fitzgerald (plus voices on some tracks), *Diverse* '76 and *The Joy Of Paranoia* '78 on Ogun, *Digswell Duets* '78 on Random Radar, solo *Lid* '78 on Italian Ictus, *Slow Music* '80 on Pipe, *The Johnny Rondo Duo Plus Mike Cooper* '80 on German FMP (Coxhill, Dave HOLLAND, guitarist Cooper). All on French Nato: *Chantenay 80*, *The Dunois Solos* '81, *Instant Replay* '81-2, track on *Sept Tableaux Phoniques/Erik Satie* '83 (others by Tony COE, Holland, etc.).

CRADDOCK, Billy 'Crash' (*b* 16 June '39, Greensboro, N.C.) Country-rock singer; nickname from hobby of stock-car racing. Began with brother Clarence in The Four Rebels '58; signed to Columbia, scored minor hit 'Don't Destroy Me' '59. Made more impression in Australia, leading some to believe he was Australian. Left Columbia (wanted to sing country, they wanted him for rock'n'roll-pop); returned to home town, married, worked day jobs and sang weekends. After 10 years signed for new Cartwheel label Nashville; first record 'Knock Three Times' made top 3 country '71. More hits: 'Dream Lover', 'You Better Move On', '71; 'I'm Gonna Knock On Your Door' '72. Switched to ABC for more than 30 hits incl. 'Rub It In', 'Ruby Baby' '74; joined Capitol '78 for hits 'I Cheated On A Good Wom-an's Love' '78, 'My Mama Never Heard Me Sing' '79, 'I Just Had You On My Mind', 'Sea Cruise' '80, 'Love Busted' '82. LPs incl. *Mr Country Rock* '73, *The First Time* '77 on ABC; *I Cheated On A Good Woman's Love* '78, *Changes* and *Laughing & Crying* '80, *The New Will Never Wear Off You* '82, *Greatest Hits* '83, all on Capitol.

CRAIG, Francis (*b* 10 Sep. 1900, Dickson, Tenn.; *d* 19 Nov. '66, Sewanee, Tenn.) Bandleader, pianist, songwriter. Wrote official football song 'Dynamite' for Vanderbilt U. Led band at Hermitage Hotel Nashville for more than 20 years; staff musician in local radio, also NBC network; helped introduce Kenny Sargent (later with CASA LOMA band), Phil HARRIS, Kitty KALLEN, Dinah SHORE, others. Went to Jim Bulleit, founder of new Bullet label, to record 'Red Rose', band's theme; hastily arranged own song 'Near You' with lilting piano, lyrics by Kermit Goell sung by Bob Lamm for other side of record: 'Near You' smash no. 1 hit '47, covered by ANDREWS SISTERS, Larry Green, Elliott Lawrence, Alvino REY; became standard, still comedian Milton Berle's theme. Disc also distributed on Decca, later remade for Dot; success contributed to set-up of first Nashville pressing plant. Follow-up also Craig's tune, 'Beg Your Pardon' no. 4 '48.

CRAMER, Floyd (*b* 27 Oct. '33, Shreveport, La.) Country piano. Toured as back-up, appeared on Louisiana Hayride, recorded for Abbott '53-4, then Nashville session man for RCA from '55. Played on hits with the BROWNS, Jim REEVES, Elvis PRESLEY ('Heartbreak Hotel', '56) etc. Describes distinctive piano style as 'whole-tone slur' or 'slip note'. Own hits include 'Last Date' '60, 'On the Rebound' '61, both own comps., went gold. More than 24 albums, incl. *Keyboard Kick Band* '77, on which he plays eight keyboards incl. synthesisers.

CRAMPS USA rockabilly revival band formed '75 NYC: Lux Interior, vocals; 'Poison' Ivy Rorschach, guitar (also songwriters), Bryan Gregory, guitar; Pam Gregory, drums (no bass). First gig was audition at CBGB's '76; didn't record until 'The Way I Walk' '78 on own Vengeance label, Pam replaced by Nick Knox on drums. Received TV coverage owing to bizarre appearance: Interior like crazed Elvis, Rorschach in lamé. 'Human Fly' was second single on Vengeance, then signed to IRS '79 after making demos with UK guitarist Chris Spedding (ex-Wombles, SEX PISTOLS sideman). *Gravest Hits* '79 reflected stage set of past years, incl. demented version of 'Surfer Bird' ('64 Trashmen hit), along with *Songs The Lord Taught Us* '80 prod. by ex-BOX TOP Alex Chilton. IRS (prop. Miles Copeland) got them valuable exposure supporting POLICE etc. and garnered intense cult following in Europe; featured in Copeland's video/LP extravaganza *Urgh! A Music War*. Kid Congo (Brian Tristan, ex-Gun Club; aka Kid Congo Powers, or just Congo Powers) replaced Bryan Gregory for *Psychedelic Jungle* '81, second or third LP depending whether five-song *Gravest Hits* is mini-LP or maxi-EP. *Off The Bone* '83 showcased the best of their output so far as they left IRS/Illegal: incl. three tracks from EP also issued that year, as well as 'Goo Goo Muck'. Continued on shock/rockabilly course (on Big Beat label UK) with live *Smell Of Female* '83 and *A Date With Elvis* '86, latter incl. indie hit 'Can Your Pussy Do The Dog'.

CRAWFORD, Hank (*b* 21 Dec. '34, Memphis, Tenn.) Saxes, piano, leader, composer. Joined Ray CHARLES band on baritone '58, switched to alto '59, became mus. dir.; left Charles '63 to start own small group. Atlantic LP *True Blue* made USA album chart '64; several others incl. *From The Heart, Soul Of The Ballad*: blues-drenched small-band soul music anticipated '70s jazz-funk. LPs on Kudu label *I Hear A Symphony* '76, *Hank Crawford's Back* '77 also charted; *Tico Rico* issued in UK '79; current LPs on Milestone in USA: *Midnight Ramble, Indigo Blue* '83, *Down On The Deuce* '84; *Roadhouse Symphony* '85 features Mac REBENNACK, David NEWMAN; *Mr Chips* '86 has Newman, Randy BRECKER, Bernard Purdie on drums.

CRAWFORD, Jesse (*b* 2 Dec. 1895, Woodland, Cal.; *d* 28 May '62, Sherman Oaks, Cal.) Organist: 'The Poet of the Organ'; 'Wizard of the Wurlitzer'. Toured as dance band pianist as teenager; played organ at Gem Theatre Spokane, Wash. '11, Grau-

mann Theatre L.A. '18; in Chicago early '20s; resident at NYC Paramount Theatre '26-33, often with wife on twin organs. Victor hit records in '20s incl. 'Remember' '25, 'At Dawning' '26, 'At Sundown' '27, etc. Much radio and concert work '30s; formed sweet dance band '37-8, often with his wife on twin electric organs. Recorded for Decca '40s-50s, with 20 LPs in '59 Schwann catalogue incl. *Lead Kindly Light, Enchanted Evening, Pops By The Poet, Popular Organ Favorites*; Deroy compilation *Cinema Organ Encores* '81.

CRAWFORD, Jimmy (*b* James Strickland Crawford, 14 Jan '10, Memphis, Tenn.; *d* 28 Jan. '80, NYC) Drummer. Jimmie LUNCEFORD was phys. ed. instructor at Crawford's Manassas High School; joined Lunceford's popular band '28-42: classy band had distinctive beat, Crawford was one of its stars. Worked in defence plant; in US Army '43-5; Ed HALL sextet late '40s; Fletcher HENDERSON's last group '50, on Henderson reunion album '57; became busy NYC freelance, playing in many Broadway shows, much studio work.

CRAWFORD, Johnny (*b* '46, L.A.) USA child TV star (co-star to Chuck Connors in '50s series *The Rifleman*). Signed to Del-Fi label as singer, minor hit 'Daydreams' '61; then with three in top 20 '62: 'Cindy's Birthday', 'Your Nose Is Gonna Grow', 'Rumors'. Lesser hits until washed away by British Invasion '64; became rodeo rider.

CRAWFORD, Randy (*b* Veronica Crawford, 18 Feb. '52, Macon, Ga.) USA soul singer, more popular in UK than USA, with 11 top 75 entries UK '79-84; incredibly, no solo showing in USA Hot 100 at all through '84; sang with CRUSADERS on their biggest hit 'Streetlife' '79 (no. 36 USA, 5 UK), duet with Rick SPRINGFIELD 'Taxi Dancing' '84 (from film *Hard To Hold*) was no. 59. Solos 'Imagine', 'Nightline' both made black singles chart USA '83, charted UK. One of five children; family to Cincinnati, Ohio '53; early musical infl. in church, but performed in clubs at 15 with father as chaperone. First engagement with band incl. William 'Bootsy' Collins, then joined jazz trio, where she learned some piano (useful when she paid her own way on holiday in St Tropez).

Appeared on TV, recommended to L.A. booking agent; performed with George BENSON NYC, during that residency met Cannonball ADDERLEY: later appeared on concept LP *Big Man* with his band, released after his death. Signed by WB after appearance at World Jazz Association gala concert in L.A. Subsequent output mainly jazz-based, but reached UK top 20 three times with 'One Day I'll Fly Away' (no. 3 '80), 'You Might Need Somebody', 'Rainy Night In Georgia' (both '81), six minor hits '82-3. Big break eludes fine singer, though enough hits in UK to make *Greatest Hits* compilation on K-Tel '84; albums have charted both UK/USA incl. *Now We May Begin* '80, *Secret Combination* '81 (highest USA entry at no. 72), *Windsong* '82 (all top 10 UK), *Nightline* '83. Earlier WB LPs incl. *Everything Must Change*, *Miss Randy Crawford*, *Raw Silk*.

CRAY, Robert (*b* 1 Aug. '53, Columbus, Ga.) USA blues guitarist, singer. Army family; spent time in Germany. Formed first band under infl. of BEATLES in Tacoma, Wash.; an Albert COLLINS concert helped decide musical direction; Chicago blues infl. loomed large (Buddy GUY, MAGIC SAM); father's fondness for Ray CHARLES played a part: early band incl. high school friend Bobby Murray on guitar; Robert Cray Band hit the road '74 with bassist Richard Cousins; the music was leavened with soulful vocals, but never far from blues roots. Toured hard; met John Belushi '77, whose love of blues exhibited in film/LPs *Blues Brothers*; Cray had non-playing part as member of Otis Day and the Knights in film *Animal House* '78. First LP *Who's Been Talkin'* '78 made at two sessions with horns, different rhythm sections, Curtis Salgado (harmonica; vocal on one track) and Cousins at one session; released '80 on indie Tomato label which went broke (reissued '86 on Charly UK). Second LP *Bad Influence* '83 on Hightone USA/Demon UK, where spot on TV's *Whistle Test* led to good sales, headline status at top venues: this time lineup was Cray, Cousins, Dave Olson on drums, Mike Vannice, tenor sax and keyboards; Warren Rand, alto sax; all tunes original except 'Got To Make A Comeback' (Eddie FLOYD), 'Don't Touch Me' (Johnny 'Guitar' WATSON). Mix of blues, soul revealed the most exciting new bluesman for a long time. Third LP *False Accusations* '85 more of the same, with personnel changes: lost Vannice and Rand, added Peter Boe on keyboards; toured UK, LP made UK indie charts. LP *Showdown!* '85 (Alligator/Sonet) began as Collins LP, became guitar showpiece for Collins, Cray, Johnny COPELAND: unusually successful all-star date. *Strong Persuader* '86 was first for major label (Mercury), 12″ single and CD had extra tracks. Collins has covered 'Phone Booth'; Albert KING made it title track on Fantasy LP; Eric CLAPTON covered 'Bad Influence' '86; Clapton jammed with Cray at London's Mean Fiddler Nov. '86: version of 'Phone Booth' was sound-page flexi-disc in May '87 *Guitar Player* magazine. Cray toured with Clapton '87, prepared for cameo part in Chuck BERRY biopic *Hail Hail Rock'n'Roll*. *All Night Long* on Japanese import P-Vine label incl. out-takes from *Who's Been Talkin'*, also tracks made with pianist Floyd Dixon. He named biggest influences as Jimi HENDRIX, Steve Cropper; admires Charlie Baty (Little Charlie & The Nightcats; *see* ALLIGATOR); he had won 11 W. C. Handy National Blues Awards and won six more Nov. '87 with his own incisive playing (eschews wah-wah pedals, other impurities), first-class singing of memorable songs that tell a story (cooperative songwriting, often with prod. Dennis Walker, Bruce Bromberg as 'D. Amy', results in 'Cray music'), backing trio integrated in all senses, the result is one of the biggest new acts of the '80s.

CRAZY OTTO Fritz Schulz-Reichel, Polydor pop artist who won a Golden Gramophone '57 for selling a million albums in knees-up pseudo-ragtime style. Johnny Maddox (*b* '29, Gallatin, Tenn.) played piano on staff at Dot label; recorded medley of old tunes: 'Crazy Otto Medley' no. 2 in USA '55, began fad for 'honkytonk' piano. Winifred ATWELL had similar hits in UK.

CREAM British rock trio formed '66, encouraged by producer/manager Robert Stigwood: Eric CLAPTON, guitar; Jack Bruce, bass; Ginger BAKER, drums. Played blues-based material, some trad. ('I'm So Glad', by Skip JAMES) but much written by

Bruce with lyrics by Pete BROWN; loud, passionate, sometimes self-indulgent; extensive improvisation in concert, unusual at the time: 'power trio' concept big infl. on heavy metal genre. Took USA by storm; sold 15 million records in three years. First three albums: *Fresh Cream* '66, *Disraeli Gears* '67, *Wheels Of Fire* '68. seven top 10 singles in UK incl. 'I Feel Free'; three in USA incl. 'Sunshine Of Your Love'. Trio format often augmented in studio but soon exhausted; group became restless, announced breakup '69 followed by farewell tour of USA, two concerts at Royal Albert Hall, London; one filmed as *Goodbye Cream*. Last LP *Goodbye* '69 incl. 'Badge', co-written by Clapton and George HARRISON. Compilation albums followed break-up.

CREEDENCE CLEARWATER REVIVAL USA rock band: John Cameron Fogerty (*b* 28 May '45), Tom Fogerty (*b* 9 Nov. '41), guitars and vocals, both *b* Berkeley, Cal.; Doug Clifford (*b* 24 Apr. '45, Palo Alto), drums; Stu Cook (*b* 25 Apr. '45, Oakland), bass. Had 13 classic top 60 singles in Billboard pop chart '68-72, seven of them 2-sided hits; another late hit '76, four years after they broke up. The greatest American singles band, they were to singles what the BAND were on albums: a summing up of an era's American popular music. Fogertys' collaboration with school friends Clifford and Cook began late '50s as the Blue Velvets; signed to Fantasy label '64, changed name to Golliwogs, emulating UK 'beat' groups of the period (seven flop singles later collected on '75 LP *The Golliwogs*). Tom had been centre of group; after name change to Creedence Clearwater Revival '67 John wrote and sang most of band's material: without visiting the bayou somehow invented 'swamp rock', with drive, lack of pretence, southern flavour: basic rock'n'-'roll not heard since '50s carved singular niche while other (especially West Coast) bands espoused radical politics or drugs; became favourite of Vietnam GIs. Concentrated on singles, sneered at then: quality of material also made classic albums, still sounds fresh as paint. First (eponymous) LP '68 displayed roots, with covers of 'I Put A Spell On You' (Screamin' Jay HAWKINS '56), 'Susie Q' (Dale HAWKINS '57, first top

40 hit for Creedence). *Bayou Country* '69 incl. 'Proud Mary', 'Keep On Chooglin' ' as J. Fogerty's writing developed; *Green River* incl. title song, 'Lodi', 'Bad Moon Rising' (perhaps rock's best-ever 'road' song; broke band worldwide), astutely titled 'Wrote A Song For Everyone' (Fogerty's songs have been covered by Elvis PRESLEY, Bo DIDDLEY, Dave EDMUNDS, Rick NELSON, The SEARCHERS, Jerry Lee LEWIS, Emmylou HARRIS, Solomon BURKE, Ike & Tina TURNER, etc.: distilled essence of rock'n'roll for grownups seemed to incl. everything). Overtly blue-collar *Willy & The Poorboys* '69 incl. trad. 'Midnight Special', LEADBELLY's 'Cotton Fields', Fogerty's skiffle-ish 'Down On The Corner', 2-sided hit with 'Fortunate Son'/'Poorboy Shuffle' (instrumental with washboard, harmonica). Album title was borrowed by Bill Wyman for *ad hoc* group '85. *Cosmo's Factory* '70 considered group's pinnacle; Forgerty called it 'the culmination of the whole thing': incl. marathon rework of 'I Heard It Through The Grapevine' (Marvin GAYE, '68), single charted '76; 'Up Around The Bend', country-flavoured 'Lookin' Out My Back Door'; 'Who'll Stop The Rain' later theme and title of Karl Reisz film '78 (called *Dog Soldiers* in UK); 'Run Through The Jungle', 'Travelin' Band' both featured by Bruce SPRINGSTEEN during '81-2 tour. After *Pendulum* '70 (incl. 'Have You Ever Seen The Rain?', 'Hey Tonight') Tom Fogerty left for unspectacular solo career, albums *Tom Fogerty, Excalibur, Zephyr National, Myopia* '72-4, then *Deal It Out* '81, all on Fantasy; with Ruby (Bobby Cochran, drums; Anthony Davis, bass; Randy Oda, guitar and keyboards, everybody on vocals) Tom also made *Ruby* and *Rock And Roll Madness* '77-8 on PBR International. Live concert at Royal Albert Hall, London, '71 is souvenir of original Creedence lineup at their peak; meanwhile the trio carried on with *Mardi Gras* '72, the band sharing the writing, resulting in a weaker album, though John's 'Sweet Hitch Hiker', 'Someday Never Comes' are as strong as ever. *Live In Europe* was issued '74, but group had finally stopped '72. Clifford released *Cosmo* that year on Fantasy. John's *Blue Ridge Rangers* '73 was album of trad. country covers which he prod. and arr., playing every note him-

297

self, but his name did not appear, intending illusion that group existed. *John Fogerty* '75 incl. wistful 'Dream/Song', rockers 'Almost Saturday Night', 'Rockin' All Over The World' (used on tour by Bruce Springsteen and by STATUS QUO to open '85 Live Aid show). *Hoodoo* '76 was issued a number (switching from Fantasy to Asylum) but was apparently scrapped or withdrawn: bootlegs or demos escaping; he was silent 10 years, destroying unsatisfactory work (to ensure against bootlegs); meanwhile Creedence played together at Tom's wedding late '70s, but John nixed reunion. An already high reputation became a legend: band's music praised by everyone, used in films incl. *An American Werewolf In London* '81, *The Twilight Zone* and *The Big Chill* '83, etc. *Centerfield* '85 was Fogerty's dramatic return with no. 1 LP USA; again played it all himself, so that layers of overdubbing resulted in stiffness that Creedence never had, but good songs incl. USA hits 'Old Man Down The Road', 'Rock'n'Roll Girls', also 'Big Train From Memphis', pensive 'I Saw It On TV'; potentially libellous dig at Fantasy boss 'Zaentz Can't Dance' had to be changed to 'Vance Can't Dance'. He did not tour to promote LP (didn't need to), but appeared at Sun session '85, with Edmunds, Carl PERKINS, Roy ORBISON, Johnny CASH on 'Big Train To Memphis' as a tribute to Presley. Album *Eye Of The Zombie* '86 again saw him arr./prod. and write it all, though he used Ry COODER sidemen; standout track was 'Sail Away'. Creedence compilations come and go; *20 Golden Greats* UK '78 did just that. Original LPs reissued, deleted at random in various countries. Clifford and Cook played on Doug SAHM LP *Groovers Paradise* '74; they made *The Don Henderson Band* '76 and *Red Hot* '77 on Atlantic (Henderson on keyboards and guitar, Russell Da Sheill on guitar, everybody singing) in the Creedence mould, but without success.

CRENSHAW, Marshall (*b* '54, Detroit) Singer/songwriter. Took up guitar at age 8, infl. by Buddy HOLLY and by guitar solo on the Kingsmen's 'Louie, Louie'. Played in bar bands, oldies band mid-'70s ('I couldn't stand . . . the current hits'), went to West Coast. Auditioned for *Beatlemania* with note-perfect rendition of 'I Should Have

Known Better', played John LENNON on tour. Moved to NYC, prod. Richard GOTTEHRER heard tape of his songs, resulted in first LP *Marshall Crenshaw* '82: 'Cynical Girl', 'Rockin' Around In NYC', 'She Can't Dance', nine others incl. cover of Arthur ALEXANDER's 'Soldier Of Love', also recorded by BEATLES '63 but not released. Songs and treatments, crisply produced, paid homage to 30 years of pop; Crenshaw hailed as new AOR talent. Second LP *Field Day* '83 disappointed; some say overproduced (by Steve Lillywhite), though 'Some Day, Some Way' was chart hit. Third LP *Downtown* late '85 saw him back on form, swampier prod. by T-Bone BURNETT incl. two members of NRBQ, Ben Vaughan song 'I'm Sorry, But So Is Brenda Lee'. His 'A Favourite Waste Of Time' was covered by Owen Paul for UK hit '86; appeared with band in soundtrack of *Peggy Sue Got Married* '86, played Holly in *La Bamba* '87; LP *Mary Jane & 9 Others* '87 confirmed eclecticism with four stars in *Downbeat*.

CREW-CUTS, The Canadian vocal group. Lineup: Rudi Maugeri (*b* 21 Jan. '31), Pat Barrett (*b* 15 Sep. '33), John Perkins (*b* 28 Aug. '31), Ray Perkins (*b* 28 Nov. '32). Formed '52 from Toronto Cathedral School Choir, inspired by the FOUR LADS, who came from same school. At first the Canadaires; changed name early '54 (haircut was not crew-cut but 'Chicago box': cropped on top, longer at sides). Vocal style of barbershop harmony infl. by R&B. First break was appearance on Gene Carroll TV show '54, Cleveland, Ohio; signed by Mercury, top 10 hit 'Crazy 'Bout You Baby', then started rash of covers of songs by black groups: 'Sh-Boom' '54 no. 1 hit, one of top 5 records of the year (original by the CHORDS was better music, reached no. 9 pop, no. 3 R&B: *see* entries for them and for ROCK). Crew-Cuts carried on with 'Earth Angel'/'Ko Ko Mo (I Love You So)' and 'Gum Drop', all top 10 pop hits '55 (PENGUINS' original 'Earth Angel' made no. 8 pop, no. 1 R&B); in all had 11 top 40 hits '54-7. To RCA '58, then several other labels; broke up '63 when Maugeri decided not to tour Japan. In '82 he was vice-president of Radio Arts Syndication on West Coast. LPs incl. *On The Campus*, *Rock'n'Roll Bash*, *High School Favorites*.

CRICKETS Group formed '55 to back Buddy HOLLY. Key fixtures were drummer Jerry Allison (*b* 31 Aug. '39, Hillsboro, Texas), singer/guitarist/songwriter Sonny Curtis (*b* 9 May '37, Meadow, Texas). As the Three Tunes with bassist Don Guess, they went to Nashville with Holly for Holly's second recording session '56. Sonny is Curtis's real name; no name was registered at birth, so when required to produce a birth certificate, he took the name by which he was best known. He had worked in and around Lubbock, Texas when Holly was making demos there; he had been playing mainly fiddle, but by all accounts a better guitarist than Holly, he played lead from time to time on demos and at Nashville session (also wrote 'Rock Around With Ollie Vee'). No hits resulted and Curtis joined Slim WHITMAN band for better wages, then Philip Morris Country Music Show in Nashville. Crickets on Holly's hits '57 were Allison, pianist Niki Sullivan, bassist Larry Welborn; Welborn was replaced by Joel B. Mauldin; Sullivan left late '57; group touring England '58 was trio of Holly, Allison, Mauldin; he recorded in NYC without Crickets, having split from them and prod. Norman Petty; the tour of Midwest USA which Holly undertook because he needed the money and which ended in his death incl. Tommy Allsup, guitar; Charlie Bunch, drums; Waylon JENNINGS, bass. Some of Holly's hits were credited to the Crickets for contractual reasons; when he went to NYC without them Curtis returned to join Mauldin and Allison, who also had solo single 'Real Wild Child' that year as 'Ivan', with Holly on guitar. They moved from Coral to Liberty label '61; changing lineup incl. Glen D. Hardin (*b* 18 Apr. '39, Wellington, Texas, keyboards; later in Emmylou HARRIS's Hot Band, etc.). More popular in UK than USA: toured UK with Bobby VEE, cut LP with him (*Bobby Vee Meets The Crickets* '62). Biggest UK hits with GOFFIN/KING song 'Please Don't Ever Change' (no. 5 '62), Curtis's 'My Little Girl' (no. 17 '63); they appeared in cheap pop movie *Just For Fun*, but BEATLES (whose name may have betrayed some infl. of original Crickets) washed them away '65. Curtis and Allison sessioned in USA; Curtis did single 'A Beatle I Want To Be', a curious solo LP *Beatle Hits – Flamenco Style*, also

solo *Sonny Curtis Style*; Curtis and Allison reunited to play on Eric CLAPTON debut solo LP '70 and re-formed Crickets, latterly with Englishmen Rick Grech (*b* 1 Nov. '46, Bordeaux, France), bass; Albert Lee, guitar. New Crickets made LPs *Rockin' '50s Rock-'n'Roll* (Barnaby/CBS '71, with Allison, Curtis, Hardin); *Bubblegum, Bop, Ballads And Boogies* '73 adding Grech, *A Long Way From Lubbock* '74 with Allison, Curtis, Grech and Lee, both on Mercury/Philips; and *Remnants* '74 on Vertigo/USA, with same lineup as *Lubbock*; these mostly prod. by Holly's former singing partner Bob Montgomery. By '77 were again trio of Allison, Curtis, Mauldin; toured with Jennings incl. Holly songs in act. Among songs Curtis wrote (or co-wrote, often with Allison): 'Walk Right Back' (hit for EVERLY Bros, for whom he played lead guitar '60s), 'More Than I Can Say' (hit for Bobby Vee, later for Leo SAYER), 'I Fought The Law' (hit for Bobby FULLER Four, later for the CLASH). He also made LPs *Sonny Curtis* '79, *Love Is All Around* '80 for Elektra; toured UK mid-'80s.

CRISS, Sonny (*b* William Criss, 23 Oct. '27, Memphis, Tenn.; *d* '77 L.A.) Alto, soprano sax, leader. Played in L.A.; in Europe '62-5; much work on community music projects '70-4, especially work with young people; visits to Europe '73, '74. Own records '47-56 on Savoy, Clef, Imperial with Wardell GRAY, Sonny CLARK, Buddy CLARK etc.; half of Impulse 2-disc set *The Bop Masters* '59; on Polydor in Paris '62-3; seven LPs on Prestige '66-9; small groups *Saturday Morning* on Xanadu, *Criss Craft* and *Out Of Nowhere* on Muse; big band with strings *Warm And Sonny* on Impulse, all '75.

CRITCHINSON, John (*b* 24 Dec. '34, London) UK jazz pianist. Self-taught after tuition from grandfather at age 3. Family moved to Bath; worked as farmer, served electrical apprenticeship, but meanwhile co-ran jazz club; turned pro, joined band in Bath which folded; to London '57, day job servicing organs for Boosey and Hawkes. Gave up on London, worked for Gas Board, tuned car engines, played in resort hotels. Break came May '79 with call to join house band at Ronnie SCOTT's club: still there, style infl. by Oscar PETERSON, full of joy.

Also played with Dick MORRISSEY – (Jim) MULLEN, then trio CDM with drummer Martin Drew, bassist Ron Mathewson from club; LPs (under Critchenson's name) incl. *Summer Afternoon* '82, *New Night* '84 on Coda.

CRITTERS, The USA '60s pop group. Line-up: Jim Ryan, guitar; Chris Darway, auto-harp; Kenny Corka, bass; Jeff Pelosi, drums; Bob Spinella, organ. Came from same jug-band trad. as Jim KWESKIN, LOVIN' SPOON-FUL etc.; cover of latter's 'Younger Girl' reached no. 42 '66. 'Mr Dieingly Sad' same year made no. 17, both on Kapp; Ryan arr. much of catchy, summery material. Made three albums: *Younger Girl* and *Touch And Go With The Critters* both '66 on Kapp; *The Critters* on Project 3 (label set up by prod. company responsible for first album); 'Don't Let The Rain Fall Down On Me' '67, second and last top 40 hit, also on Kapp. Only Critter who resurfaced after split was Ryan: added tasteful guitar to records by Carly SIMON, Kiki DEE, John Entwistle, Jim WEBB and others; also re-corded '68 with short-lived supergroup Millennium, whose *Begin* incl. Curt Boetcher, vocals; Michael Fennely, guitar, vocals; Red Rhodes, steel guitar, others.

CROCE, Jim (*b* 10 Jan. '43, Philadelphia, Pa.; *d* 20 Sep. '73, Natchitoches, La.) Sing-er, songwriter, guitarist. Played accordion at age 6; attended Villanova U., worked in bars and coffee-houses in duo from c.'63 with his wife Ingrid (also lyricist, composer; *b* 27 Apr. '47, Philadelphia). They made *Jim And Ingrid Croce* '69 on Capitol which flopped (*Another Day, Another Town* '76 on Pickwick probably a reissue); he went back to playing bars and driving a truck; met Maury Muehleisen (*b* '49, Trenton, N.J.; later Croce's lead guitarist), played on his *Gingerbread* '70 on Capitol; made demo tape for Terry Cashman and Tommy West, signed with ABC: first LP *You Don't Mess Around With Jim* '72 was no. 1, incl. top 10 title track, top 20 'Operator (That's Not The Way It Feels)'; *Life And Times* '73 was no. 7, with no. 1 single 'Bad, Bad Leroy Brown', *I Got A Name* went no. 1 a month after he and Muehleisen were killed in a plane crash. Posthumously, 'Time In A Bot-tle' from the first LP was a no. 1 hit, title

track from the second album was no. 10, from the last LP 'I'll Have To Say I Love You In A Song' no. 10 and 'Workin' At The Car Wash Blues' top 40. Compilation *Photo-graphs And Memories* '74 was on ABC; West and Cashman issued 2-disc *The Faces I've Been* '75 on their Lifesong label, in '77 reissued the other three, plus *Time In A Bottle: Jim Croce's Greatest Love Songs* '77 and *Bad Bad Leroy Brown: Jim Croce's Greatest Character Songs* '78. Songs and performances have not dated at all; his loss was a great one: *You Don't Mess With Jim* is now on high-tech Mobile Fidelity; *Photo-graphs And Memories, Time In A Bottle, Down The Highway* issued '85 on 21 Rec-ords.

CROSBY, Bing (*b* Harry Lillis Crosby, 2 May '03, Spokane, Wash.; *d* 14 Oct. '77, Madrid, Spain, on a golf course) Singer, actor. He got nickname from large ears, comic-strip character Bingo who had large, floppy ears. At local Gonzaga U. teamed with Alton (Al) Rinker (brother of Mildred BAILEY), hired by Paul WHITEMAN '26 in L.A., added Harry Barris to make trio The Rhythm Boys; Bing often solo: first record 'I've Got The Girl' '26. Trio booked at L.A. Coconut Grove '29 with Gus ARNHEIM band; began recording solo: 'I Surrender Dear' (with Arnheim) helped land first radio show '31; he commissioned theme 'Where The Blue Of The Night (Meets The Gold Of The Day)': *Pop Memories* (*see* CHARTS) calculates that he was easily the best-selling recording artist of the whole period 1890-1954, with well over 300 hits. German soldiers in WWII called him 'der Bingle'. Began steeped in minstrelsy, infl. by Al JOLSON, Louis ARMSTRONG, Bix BEIDERBECKE, Ethel WATERS; added own technique and virtually invented pop sing-ing: natural insouciance, cannily informal phrasing, husky voice as opposed to wimp-ish style of period (nodes on vocal chords prod. effect of 'singing into a rain barrel'); called himself 'The Groaner'. In fact he was one of the first to understand the microphone, then a recent invention, sing-ing to it as though to an individual listener. Broadcast for 20 years; about 2600 records, 120 LPs sold estimated 400 million by '75. Appeared in film *King Of Jazz* '30, fea-tured in *Big Broadcast of 1932*, first starring role in *College Humor* '33; over 60 films, many with first-class original songs written by Johnny Burke and Jimmy Van Heusen, Nacio Herb BROWN, others, incl. *Going Hollywood* '33, *Mississippi* '35 (score by RODGERS & HART), *Pennies From Heaven* '36, *Holiday Inn* '42 (Irving BERLIN score incl. 'White Christmas'), *Going My Way* '44 (won Oscar), *White Christmas* '54, *High Society* '56; series of comedy/musicals with close friend Bob Hope (maintained friendly feud until the end): *Road To Singapore* '40, *To Zanzibar* '41, *To Morocco* '42, *To Utopia* '45, *To Rio* '47, *To Bali* '52, *To Hong Kong* '62. Early records on Brunswick incl. 'Please', 'Learn To Croon', trail-blazing attempt to present all the songs from a show (*Scandals Of 1931*, by Henderson & Brown) on a 12″ 78 (shared chore with the BOSWELL Sisters). Signed with Decca; million-sellers began with 'Sweet Leilani' '37, Oscar-winning song from his film *Waikiki Wedding*; carried on with *San Antonio Rose* '40 (with brother Bob CROSBY's band: hit record of Bob WILLS song boost for WESTERN SWING genre; also recorded other COUNTRY songs), 'Swingin' On A Star' '44, Oscar winner by Burke and Van Heusen from *Going My Way* (Andy WILLIAMS sang in backing group; song was later incl. in songbook for schools); 'I Can't Begin To Tell You' '45; 'Alexander's Ragtime Band'/ 'The Spaniard That Blighted My Life' '47, duets with Al JOLSON, both songs written '11; 'Whiffenpoof Song' from c.1893, with Fred WARING, also made in '47; 'Galway Bay' '48. Had 46 top 10 hits '40-51, others with ANDREWS SISTERS. Other solo no. 1 hits incl. 'Only Forever' '40; 'Sunday, Monday or Always' '43; 'I Love You', 'I'll Be Seeing You' both '44; 'It's Been A Long Time' '45, with Les PAUL. And the Christmas songs: 'White Christmas' recorded '42; single said to have sold 30 million by '68, entering pop chart 18 years in a row. Duets with son Gary 'Play A Simple Melody'/'Sam's Song', made double-sided no. 3 hit '50; 'Moonlight Bay'/'When You And I Were Young, Maggie', also with Gary, charted '51; also made duets with Jane Wyman, first wife Dixie Lee (when she died he married actress Kathryn Grant, started new family), LP with Rosemary CLOONEY, etc. Last chart entry was no. 3 '56: duet with Grace Kelly from *High Soci-*

ety on 'True Love'. Decca issued *Bing's Hollywood* '62, 15-disc set of 189 film songs '34-56. Reissue of *The Chronological Bing Crosby* undertaken on Jonzo label by collector John McNicholas; first four vols. of enormous undertaking reach '28; Robert Parker's digitally remastered *Bing Crosby 1927 to 1934* on BBC Records UK incl. 'I Surrender, Dear', 'Blue Of The Night', tracks with Whiteman (and Beiderbecke), Anson WEEKS, Irving AARONSON, Lennie HAYTON, Duke ELLINGTON. Autobiography *Call Me Lucky* '53; Shepherd/Slatzer biography *Bing Crosby: The Hollow Man'* 81 is spoiled by its sneering tone.

CROSBY, Bob (*b* George Robert Crosby, 25 Aug. '13, Spokane, Wash.) Singer, bandleader; brother of Bing. Worked for Anson WEEKS, DORSEY brothers; hired to front band '35-42 assembled by Gil Rodin (arr., reeds; *b* 9 Dec. '06, Russia; *d* 10 June '74, Cal.). Sidemen mostly ex-Ben POLLACK; new band soon had hard core of fans: big swing-era size band unusual in having dixieland style; key members from New Orleans had grown up with jazz; band-within-a-band the Bob Cats played the real stuff. Original lineup incl. Yank Lawson on trumpet (*b* John Rhea Lawson, 25 Dec. '04, Round Rock, Texas), Bob Haggart on bass (*b* 13 May '14, NYC), Ray Bauduc on drums (*b* 18 June '09, New Orleans; *d* 8 Jan. '88), Nappy Lamare on guitar (*b* Hilton Napoleon Lamare, 14 June '07, N.O.; *d* 9 May '88), Deane Kincaide, Matty Matlock, Eddie MILLER; those passing through incl. Billy BUTTERFIELD, Buddy MORROW, Jess STACY, Muggsy SPANIER, Charlie SPIVAK, Joe SULLIVAN, Sterling 'Bozo' Bose on trumpet (*b* 23 Feb. '06, Florence, Ala.; *d* June '58, St Petersburg, Fla.), Irving Fazola on reeds (*b* Irving Henry Prestopnik, 10 Dec. '12, N.O.; *d* there 20 Mar. '49), Bob Zurke (*b* Robert Albert Zukowski, 17 Jan. '12, Detroit; *d* 16 Feb. '44, L.A.) on piano: many of the best white jazzmen of the time. Singers incl. Johnny DESMOND, Doris DAY, Kay STARR etc. as well as Crosby, who 'didn't know how to beat tempo' (Rodin said), 'but we didn't mind.' Of three front men proposed they made a good choice: he was even-tempered diplomat, not a bad singer and got better. Theme was 'Summertime', with GERSHWIN's permission. Most famous record is 'South Rampart Street Parade', backed with 'Dogtown Blues', both comp. and arr. by Haggart. On early record session band anonymously backed schoolgirl named Judy GARLAND (arr. by Glenn Osser). Recorded 'Martha' with old friend Connie BOSWELL in Nov. '37: it was a good seller, but same session also Bob Cats' first: Zez CONFREY's 'Stumblin' ' dixieland classic 'Fidgety Feet'; also 'Who's Sorry Now', 'Can't We Be Friends', 'Coquette', 'You're Driving Me Crazy'; the excellent small-group jazz of the Bob Cats has never lost public affection. Took part that month in first West Coast broadcast of CBS radio's *Saturday Night Swing Session*, introduced 'Rampart'. Bauduc and Haggart duo 'Big Noise From Winnetka' '38, novelty with Haggart whistling through his teeth while Bauduc used sticks on strings of Haggart's bass, is a famous period piece, though not one of the band's 41 hits '35-51: no. 1 hits incl. 'In A Little Gypsy Tea Room' '35 (vocal by Frank Tennille, father of Toni of CAPTAIN & TENNILLE), 'Whispers In The Dark' '37, 'Day In, Day Out' '39 (with vocalist Helen Ward); several records had vocals by Bing: novelty 'The Pussy Cat Song (Nyow! Nyot Nyow!)' was hit duet '49 with Bing and Patti Andrews. Band appeared in films (*Make Mine Music* '40); Bob made films (*Reveille With Beverly* '43, tongue-in-cheek *The Singing Sheriff, See Here, Private Hargrove*, both '44, Red NICHOLS biopic *The Five Pennies* '59). WWII put an end to the band's golden age, but Crosby occasionally led bands, organised reunions; he bore the burden of being Bing's brother with grace and was a popular entertainer in his own right. Many compilations on MCA, Aircheck, Ajax, Circle, Sunbeam, Hindsight, other labels; Bob Cats recorded for Capitol early '50s, Monmouth-Evergreen '70s; played at Nice Festival '81. Lawson/Haggart Jazz Band formed '50s, records on Decca; became World's Greatest Jazz Band '68 (*see* Bob WILBER). Haggart's studio work incl. arr. for 4-disc Louis ARMSTRONG set '56-7 re-creating New Orleans music; Lawson's LPs incl. *That's A Plenty* on Doctor Jazz, *Plays Mostly Blues* on Audiophile (recorded '86, with Haggart, Al Klink, Knocky PARKER, Nick Fatool, others). *Stomp Off, Let's Go!* '83 by John CHILTON tells story of the band.

CROSBY, STILLS, NASH & YOUNG USA vocal and instrumental supergroup formed '68 by ex-BYRD David Crosby (*b* David Van Cortland, 14 Aug. '41, L.A.), guitar, vocals; ex-HOLLIE Graham Nash (*b* 2 Feb. '42, Blackpool, England), harmony vocals; ex-BUFFALO SPRINGFIELD Stephen STILLS, guitar, vocals, at Laurel Canyon home of Joni MITCHELL. First two had chafed at restrictions in previous groups; teaming threatened to prod. milestones, did just that: acoustic-based trio debut *Crosby Stills And Nash* '69 (with Dallas Taylor, drums) blended breathtaking harmonies, also Stills' passionate love songs ('Suite: Judy Blue Eyes' about doomed romance with Judy COLLINS) with Nash's nursery-rhymish celebrations and Crosby's hippie politicking ('Wooden Ships'). Added another ex-Springfielder Neil YOUNG, multiplying musical options (both he and Stills played piano as well as guitar), adding another writer but also another ego. Second concert (with Young) at Woodstock Festival, where they admitted they were 'scared shitless'. Second LP (first with Young and ex-Motown bassist Gregg Reeves) was *Déjà Vu* '70, a more electric album with contrasts between writers more evident. Cover of Mitchell's 'Woodstock' was one of several songs of hippie ideals while Young's 'Ohio' (not on LP but released same year) lamented shooting of students at Kent State. Meticulous studio work combined with spontaneous, joyful stage act in 2-disc live *Four Way Street* '71, with former TURTLE John Barbata, drums, and Calvin 'Fuzzy' Samuels, bass, replacing Taylor and Reeves: by the time of its release the quartet had gone separate ways. Crosby made solo LP *If I Could Only Remember My Name* '71, then performed and recorded through '70s with Nash, whose solo LPs *Songs For Beginners* '71 and *Wild Tales* '73 lacked bones. With exception of Young (and Stills' first LP; *see* their entries) individuals paled beside the sum of their parts; re-formed '74 but no new records. Crosby and Nash had briefly toured with Young '73, threw in with Stills '77 to re-form original trio; Stills' partnership with Young resulted in LP *Long May You Run* '76 but Young walked out on tour. Trio made *CSN* '77 and *Daylight Again* '82 without relighting fire. Nash made *Earth & Sky* '80 but describes *Innocent Eyes* '86 as his first real solo LP, incl. shift towards high-tech (synths, etc.). 'It doesn't have David or Stephen on it, and it doesn't sound like anything they might have done.' Younger generation of punk era couldn't care less, but the old vocal mix could still thrill; the trio played Live Aid '85 despite Crosby's drug problem (which led to several months in jail '86). At their peak, their disparate yet complementary talents managed rare feat of combining commercial success with credibility: the best of L.A. and San Francisco all at once.

CROSS, Christopher (*b* Christopher Geppert, c.'51, San Antonio, Texas) USA singer/songwriter. Rise to stardom after fronting bar bands (e.g. Flash) in Texas began with signing to WB '78 on strength of writing. Tailored-for-radio sound hit with eponymous debut LP '80 incl. hits 'Ride Like The Wind' no. 2, 'Sailing' no. 1, 'Never Be The Same' no. 15, with glorious soaring backing vocals by labelmates Mike McDonald, Nicolette Larson, Valerie Carter. Single 'Say You'll Be Mine' was fourth hit (no. 20); '81 saw him sweep board at Grammy time with record-equalling five awards, but public exposure a two-edged sword: with keening, fragile voice, Cross is overweight and bearded, hence artist's flamingo logo on LP instead of photo. Hits continued with Oscar-winning song by Peter Allen, Burt BACHARACH and Carole Bayer SAGER 'Arthur's Theme (Best That You Can Do)' from Dudley Moore film, no. 1 '81. *Another Page* '83 brought more of the same: extrapolation of '70s USA soft rock (EAGLES, later DOOBIE Bros, etc.) without much character of its own; three more hits incl. 'Think Of Laura', promoted by use in TV soap opera *General Hospital* (again without any personal appearance). UK has resisted his charm; 'Arthur's Theme' at no. 7 '82 his only hit. Third LP *Every Turn Of The World* '85.

CROSSOVER A song or a record intended for one market that sells more widely, crossing over to another. As with COVERS, the most dramatic crossovers occurred in the '50s, when pop music was in flux; e.g. R&B hits by Fats DOMINO, LITTLE RICHARD, Chuck BERRY, many others crossed over to pop chart; during golden era of soul early '60s crossover became takeover. Country music crosses over regularly as a good song catches the public's fancy, from the songs of Hank WILLIAMS, duet hits of Jimmy WAKELY and Margaret WHITING, hits by Pee Wee KING, Ernie FORD etc. in late '40s-early '50s through Johnny HORTON and Marty ROBBINS late '50s, Jim REEVES in '60s, many more since.

CROUCH, Andrae Edward (*b* 1 July '42, Los Angeles) Gospel singer, songwriter, keyboards. Played piano and sang in church choirs at an early age. Formed band the COGICS (Church Of God In Christ Singers) early '60s, with twin sister Sandra, Blinky Williams, Billy Preston, Gloria Jones, Frankie Spring and Edna Wright; made one LP for Vee Jay and won numerous awards. New band Disciples formed '65; toured playing mixture of gospel, rock, soul; LP for Light *Take The Message Everywhere*, '69. Sandra had been singing back-up for Diana ROSS and others, rejoined brother '70. Continued touring; series of LPs featured guest shots by Stevie WONDER, the CRUSADERS and others; Crouch has also won Grammy awards '75-8-9, written songs recorded by Elvis PRESLEY, The Imperials, Pat BOONE. Autobiography is called *Through It All*.

CROUCH, Stanley (*b* 14 Dec. '45, L.A.) Drums; also poet, actor, teacher, writer, playwright. Cousin of Andrae CROUCH. Formed co-op group late '60s with Arthur BLYTHE, Bobby BRADFORD; later became Black Music Infinity, with Bradford, Charles TYLER on records. Book of poems *Ain't No Ambulances For No Nigguhs Tonight* '70.

CROWELL, Rodney (*b* 7 Aug. '50, Houston, Texas) Singer/songwriter, producer. Various bands in Texas; moved to Nashville early '70s. Early champion of his songs was Jerry REED. Back-up singer and guitar in Emmylou HARRIS's Hot Band, '75-8; she recorded more than a dozen of his songs. Beautiful voice of his own: solo LP *Ain't Livin' Long Like This* '78 showcased own writing, incl. guests Willie NELSON, James BURTON, Ry COODER. Other LPs: *What Will The Neighbors Think?* '80, *Rodney Crowell* '81. Married Rosanne Cash '79;

produced her successful crossover album *Seven Year Ache* '81. Many fine songs incl. 'Ashes By Now', 'Stars On The Water' (hit for Bob SEGER), 'Leaving Louisiana In The Broad Daylight' (incl. on first LP; more atmospheric Harris version '78 incl. Rick Danko on fiddle, Garth Hudson on accordion: Crowell and Harris also each performed on other's version). Songs have been recorded by Waylon JENNINGS and George JONES, as well as most of those above. Concentrated on production early '80s: *Survivors*, with Johnny CASH, Jerry Lee LEWIS, Carl PERKINS brought together remainder of Sun records' famous 'million dollar quartet' after Elvis PRESLEY's death; also LPs by Bobby BARE, Guy CLARK, Albert Lee, etc. Own albums *Street Language* '86, *Diamonds And Dirt* '88 on CBS.

CROWS, The USA doo-wop group formed NYC c.'48. Lineup: Daniel 'Sonny' Norton, lead; Harold Major, tenor; William Davis, baritone; Gerald Hamilton, bass. Served apprenticeship as street-corner symphony, entered talent contest at Apollo, spotted by Cliff Martinez, signed to George Goldner's Rama label; Davis's composition 'Gee' made top 4 R&B chart, top 20 pop: one of the first by a black group to be played on white radio stations. Gee label had hits by the CLEFTONES, Frankie LYMON; Goldner named it after Crows' hit. Guitarist/second tenor Mark Jackson joined, but Crows had no more hits; split up late '50s. Norton and Hamilton have since died.

CRUDUP, Arthur 'Big Boy' (*b* 24 Aug. '05, Forest, Miss.; *d* 28 Mar. '74, Nassawadox, Va.) Blues singer. Worked parties c.'39 in Clarksdale, Miss. area; recorded for Bluebird/Victor '41-2, '45-52, other labels in '50s (LP on Fire in Nashville '59 for which Elvis PRESLEY allegedly put up the money), Delmark '67, Liberty '70. Like others he was rediscovered, in his case because he was a direct infl. on Presley, who recorded three of his songs: 'That's All Right, Mama' on first release '54, 'So Glad You're Mine', 'My Baby Left Me' both '56. His songs were published by Hill and Range; Crudup never saw the royalties. At Ann Arbor Blues Festival '69, many others; toured England, on BBC TV '70-1; Australia '72; French film *Out Of The Blacks Into The Blues* '72; TV

film *Arthur Crudup: Born In The Blues* '73; toured with Bonnie RAITT '74. Fashionable to denigrate him now, but unfair to judge him by '71 RCA compilation subtitled *The Father Of Rock And Roll*: didn't incl. 'Goin' Back To Georgia', one of his best (c.'50, Judge Riley, Ransom Knowling on drums and bass), while his own 'My Baby Left Me' '51 is clumsy compared to Presley's: there was not much money for second takes in 'race music'. *I'm In The Mood* on Krazy Kat UK has '41-52 tracks.

CRUSADERS Group formed '50s by Stix Hooper (*b* 15 Aug. '38), called Modern Jazz Sextet in '50s, then Nite Hawks, Jazz Crusaders from '60, Crusaders from '72, adopting jazz-rock style and popularity. LPs incl. Wayne Henderson, trombone (*b* 24 Sep. '39, Houston), Joe Sample, keyboards (*b* 1 Feb. '39), Wilton Felder, saxes (*b* 31 Aug. '40), all born Houston, Texas; Larry Carlton, guitar (*b* 2 Mar. '48, Torrance, Cal.), using session bassists: *Chain Reaction* '75, *Scratch* '75; with guests but without Henderson: *Free As The Wind* '76; without Carlton and Henderson: *Street Life* '79 (vocal by Randy CRAWFORD on title track), *Rhapsody And Blues* '80 with Bill WITHERS on 'Soul Shadows', *Royal Jam* '81 (2-disc set with B. B. KING, Royal Phil. Orch., made at Royal Festival Hall, London). Others incl. *Standing Tall* '81 with guest Joe COCKER, *Live In Japan* '82, etc. 12 LPs in Billboard top 100 albums chart '71-84. Robert Christgau wrote of *Best Of The Crusaders* '76: 'Their basic project is soulful Muzak . . .' Henderson also prod. various artists, recorded with Roy AYERS. Felder also plays electric bass; he and Hooper are busy freelance session players. Sample played with L.A. Express, also Blue Note LP *San Francisco* with Harold LAND, Bobby HUTCHERSON; etc.

CRUZ, Celia (*b* 21 Oct., Havana) Afro-Cuban singer of operatic range: the 'Queen of Salsa' has made over 50 albums. Raised in Santos Saurez district; extended family incl. 14 children. Studied literature at teacher's training college; pushed into radio talent show by a cousin, which she won (in '35 or '45; sources conflict); sang on radio, switched to music full-time: studied ('solfage, theory – and piano. But I didn't like to cut my nails') at Havana Conservatory of Music. In early days she performed in AFRO-CUBAN religious context, continued to specialise in songs from that genre. To Mexico, Venezuela with revue Las Mulatas de Fuego '49; joined popular band La Sonora Matancera '50 for 15 years: string of LPs on Seeco; hit songs incl. 'Yerbero Moderno', 'La Danza del Cocoye', 'Caramelos', 'Burundanga'. Toured Latin America, USA, appeared in films. Left Cuba for the last time c.'59 with Sonora Matancera and settled in USA; married band's lead trumpeter Pedro Knight, who became her manager and mus. dir. when she left the band mid-'60s. Switched to Tico for 14 LPs incl. seven with Tito PUENTE; sang role of Gracia Divina in Larry HARLOW opera *Hommy* at Carnegie Hall '73, gained new generation of fans in NYC salsa style. Began recording with bandleader Johnny PACHECO on Vaya '74; first LP *Celia And Johnny* went gold, incl. Peruvian folk-bolero 'Vieja Luna' (Old Moon). Toured the world with Puente and FANIA ALL STARS; LPs incl. *Live At Yankee Stadium* with FAS (two vols.) and *Tremendo Caché* with Pacheco '75, *Recordando el Ayer* '76 (Remembering The Past) with Pacheco, Justo Betancourt and Papo LUCCA; collaboration with Willie COLON on *Only They Could Have Made This Album* '77, *'Brillante'* Best (hits compilation) and *Eternos* (with Pacheco) '78; appeared with singers Cheo FELICIANO, Santos Colon, Ismael Quintana, Adalberto Santiago, others on Puente tributes to the great Cuban singer/bandleader Beny MORÉ *Homenaje a Beny* '78-9; won *Latin NY* female vocalist poll each year '75-82, in '82 was honoured by tribute Madison Square Garden concert with La Sonora Matancera, Pacheco, Puente, Colon, Pete 'Conde' Rodriguez, Feliciano; also reunited with La Sonora Matancera on LP *Feliz Encuentro* on Barbaro; other albums incl. *Celia-Ray-Adalberto-Tremendo Trio!* '83 with Ray BARRETTO band, *Homenaje a Beny Moré Vol. III* and *De Nuevo* '85 with Pacheco, *The Winners* '87 on Vaya prod. by Colon. Continues to tour the world, international fame beginning to catch up with stature in Latin community.

CRYAN' SHAMES USA rock group formed c.'65, Chicago. Original lineup: Tom 'Toad'

Doody (*b* '45), vocals; Jim Fairs (*b* '48), lead guitar; Jerry 'Stonehenge' Stone (*b* '45), rhythm guitar; Jim 'J. C. Hooke' Pilster (*b* '47), percussion; Dave 'Grape' Purple (*b* '45), bass, keyboards; Dennis Conroy (*b* '48), drums. 'Sugar And Spice' '66 on Chicago-based Destination label was no. 49 hit; never equalled but led to CBS contract, three LPs: *Sugar And Spice*, *A Scratch In The Sky* and *Synthesis* '67-9; all made Billboard top 200 LPs, none higher than no. 156. For second album Stone and Purple had been replaced by Lenny Kerley and Isaac Guillory; by the last, Fairs and Conroy had also left. Fairs sessioned with Richie HAVENS, Pearls Before Swine; Kerley recorded with Dave Loggins; Guillory made two solo LPs in '70s (Fairs played on the first, released on Atlantic '74), relocated UK. 'Sugar And Spice' incl. in *Nuggets* '72, 2-disc compilation of mid-'60s psychedelic classics by so-called garage bands.

CRYSTALS, The USA vocal quartet. Lineup: Delores 'LaLa' Brooks, Dee Dee Kennibrew, others at various times incl. original lead singer Barbara Alston, Pat Wright, Mary Thomas, all from NYC, all *b* '45-6; also Frances Collins, Myrna Gerrard. 'Girl group' discovered by Phil SPECTOR; first record 'There's No Other (Like My Baby)' no. 5 R&B, no. 20 pop '61; then had hits with entire output on his Philles label (except 'He Hit Me (But It Felt Like A Kiss)', which was issued but withdrawn). 'Uptown' was no. 18 '62 pop chart; 'He's A Rebel' (written by Gene PITNEY) no. 2, 'He's Sure The Boy I Love' no. 18 '63 were in fact sung by Darlene LOVE, but classics 'Da-Do-Ron-Ron' (no. 5) and 'Then He Kissed Me' (no. 8), both '63, had punchy lead vocals of LaLa Brooks, marked beginning of 'wall of sound' prod. that made Spector famous. 'Little Boy' and 'All Grown Up' were minor hits '64. Many tracks remained unissued, like original versions of 'Chapel Of Love', 'It's My Party'; 'I Wonder' was only issued in UK and is much sought-after. Reissue 'Da-Do-Ron-Ron'/'Then He Kissed Me' was no. 15 hit UK '74; group tours oldies circuit with Dee Dee now leader.

CUBA, Joe (*b* José Calderón) Conga player, bandleader. Grew up in Spanish Harlem;

formed Joe Cuba Sextet '54, recorded for Mardi Gras, then Seeco for LPs *Steppin' Out, Diggin' The Most, Comin' At You, Breakin' Out, Para Enamorados Solamente/ José Cheo Feliciano* (incl. compilations); then to Tico as definitive '60s unit. Peak lineup: Cuba, congas; Tomas, vibes; Nick Jimenez, piano; Jimmy Sabater, timbales; Sabater and Cheo FELICIANO sharing lead vocals. First Tico LP was *Vagabundeando! Hangin' Out* c.'64 incl. Feliciano's classic 'El Raton', lyrics referring either to drugs or to Puerto Rican liberation (live version of the song on *Latin Soul Rock* '74 by FANIA ALL STARS was first big hit of '70s salsa boom). Other Tico LPs were *El Alma del Barrio/The Soul Of Spanish Harlem, Bailadores* and *Estamos Haciendo Algo Bien!/We Must Be Doing Something Right!* incl. hit 'El Pito (I'll Never Go Back To Georgia)' '66; Feliciano went solo and earlier lead vocalist Willie Torres returned; fifth Tico LP *Wanted Dead Or Alive* incl. crossover boogaloo 'Bang Bang', first boogaloo to sell a million (no. 63 on national USA pop chart '66) and 'Oh Yeah' (charted '67). *My Man Speedy!* and *Joe Cuba Sextet Presents The Velvet Voice Of Jimmy Sabater* (ballad LP) were further Tico LPs; *Lo Mejor de Joe Cuba/The Best Of Joe Cuba* incl. 'Bang Bang', 'El Pito' (both written by Sabater and Cuba), 'To Be With You', tracks from *Speedy*. They had peaked; Torres was replaced by Willie Garcia, then by Mike Guagenti. *Hecho y Derecho, Recuerdos de mi Querido Barrio/Memories Of My Beloved Spanish Harlem, Bustin' Out* were '70-3 LPs. *Tico-Alegre All Stars Live At Carnegie Hall* '75 incl. 'Boom Boom Lucumi' by Cuba Sextet; *Cocinando la Salsa* '76 ('Cooking The Sauce') featured Louie RAMIREZ but was not reckoned a success. The original Sextet reformed in Madison Square Garden '84 to celebrate 25 years of Feliciano's career.

CUBOP Genre of late '40s, blend of Afro Cuban-rhythms and Afro-American jazz in which (unusually) neither suffered dilution or loss. Musical traffic between Caribbean and USA always two-way and prolific, e.g. Jelly Roll MORTON's 'Spanish tinge'; Cuba especially important, even after Castro because of emigrants to NYC. USA swing bands of '40s were popularisers; e.g. J.

DORSEY's 'Green Eyes' and 'Maria Elena', Artie SHAW's 'Frenesi' were all songs by Latin composers with English lyrics. Infl. of Mario BAUZA in Cab CALLOWAY band on Dizzy GILLESPIE was important; pianist Noro MORALES was infl. by jazz; Stan KENTON, Woody HERMAN, Nat COLE, Gene KRUPA hired Cuban musicians, esp. percussionists. BOP resulted in close cooperation, more authentic music. 'The Peanut Vendor', recorded '30 by Louis ARMSTRONG ('39 by Raymond SCOTT, on flip side of 'The Businessman's Bounce'), revived late '40s by Kenton with percussionists from Machito band, incl. MACHITO himself; Kenton also arr. 'Machito' with Cuban-style horn section, inserted Latin elements into other pieces such as 'Fugue For Rhythm Section'. But Kenton was always derivative; best music was from Gillespie, Machito: they made a legitimate offshoot of bop, distinct from Latin jazz. Chano POZO was the most important of Latin percussionists in jazz; he first chanted and played rhythms in Afro-Cuban style with Gillespie at Carnegie Hall '47 (for records see his entry). Machito (with Bauza as mus. dir.) recorded Latin-jazz 'Tanga' '43, became his theme; later used guests Howard McGHEE, Dexter GORDON, Milt JACKSON, Flip PHILLIPS, Charlie PARKER, Brew Moore (tenor sax; *b* Milton Aubrey Moore, 26 Mar. '24, Indianola, Miss.; *d* 19 Aug. '73; recorded on West Coast, later emigrated to Denmark): 'No Noise' part I featured Phillips; part II, 'Mango Mangue', 'Okidokie' (aka 'Okiedoke Rhumba') Parker, all '48; 'Cubop City' '49 had solos by Moore, McGhee. These were recorded for Mercury, heard in broadcasts (compiled on Spotlite UK); Machito was regular guest at Bop City NYC where DJ Sid Torrin was MC. Also in '49 Cozy COLE led seven piece novelty act called Cuboppers, with horns infl. by Gillespie, Cuban beat: 'La Danza', 'Botao', 'Mosquito Bran'. See entry for Gillespie, who still recorded with Machito, others in '80s.

CUGAT, Xavier (*b* 1 Jan. 1900, Barcelona, Spain) Violinist, bandleader, composer. Moved to Cuba as a child, studied violin and played in Havana opera company, studied in Berlin, worked with Berlin S.O. To USA; worked at *L.A. Times* (also talented caricaturist); late '20s organised first Latin-

American dance band. Active in films from *In Gay Madrid* '30 through *The Phynx* '69 with Patti ANDREWS: probably had more footage in films than any other bandleader, the bulk of them '40s MGM musicals. One of three bands on National Biscuit Company's radio show *Let's Dance* '34-5 (*see* Benny GOODMAN); was populariser of Latin-American music: costumes, accents, Cuban sidemen looked authentic; rhythms often simplified for American dancers but always showed respect for Cuban songs. Own best-known composition was 'My Shawl'; *Pop Memories* lists 21 hits '35-49 incl. top 6 'The Lady In Red' '35, 'Perfidia' '41, 'Brazil' '43, 'Good, Good, Good (That's You – That's You)' '45, 'South America, Take It Away' '46 (vocal on latter by Buddy CLARK). He also recorded with Bing CROSBY. Residencies at Waldorf Astoria with Desi ARNAZ said to have inspired Cole PORTER to write 'Begin The Beguine' '35 (no. 13 Cugat hit that year) and Cab CALLOWAY to hire Mario BAUZA: if true, his popularising indirectly had significant impact. Cuban 'Babalu' was Cugat hit '44, later associated with Arnaz. Band's playing was always catchy and appealing, use of marimba lending a distinctive touch. Also famous for marrying glamorous women, e.g. singer Abbé Lane (photographed bathing in coffee when price of it was high in '50s), then guitarist-singer Charo. Compilation albums: *1933-40* on Sunbeam, *1944-45* on Circle, 2-disc *Best Of* on MCA; other LPs in '50s on Columbia, Mercury. Retired '70, turned band over to Tito PUENTE; returned to Spain '80; after strokes, heart attacks, hospitalised for lung problems '86, formed new 16-piece band, opened at resort in Salou, Spain in time for 87th birthday, still surrounded by lovely girls.

CULT, The UK new wave group, began '82 in Bradford, Yorks. as Southern Death Cult (name from newspaper headline): formed by vocalist Ian Astbury (*b* 14 May '62) after army service, with Barry, bass; Aky, drums; Buzz, guitar (apparently not even record companies know their real names). Single 'Fat Man' topped UK indie chart on basis of powerful live act, reached no. 43 on national chart, but group fell apart after tour late '83; they blamed media exposure. LP *Southern Death Cult* was compiled from live tracks/out-takes. Re-formed as Death Cult with Astbury, ex-Theatre of Hate guitarist Billy Duffy (*b* 12 May '61), ex-Ritual rhythm section of bassist Jamie Stewart, drummer Ray Mondo; after two singles became Cult '84, with ex-Sex Gang Children Nigel Preston on drums. Majestic 'Spiritwalker' (reminiscent of Banshees) topped indie chart mid-'84; then *Dreamtime* was no. 21 LP UK: Astbury's fascination with American Indian culture led to neo-hippie tag (he wore headband and long hair). 'Resurrection Joe' was near-hit late '84, but Cult's reputation was sealed with *Love*, chart LP '85: BIG COUNTRY's Mark Brzezicki replaced Preston, then drummer Les Warner (ex-Randy California, Julian LENNON etc.) joined permanently. Duffy's dominance of sound allied group with Big Country/U2 school of guitar-based rock, and 'She Sells Security' became band's first bona fide hit single. With echoes of Jimi HENDRIX, LED ZEPPELIN in Astbury/Duffy songs, they might have been transplanted from earlier times; most of their audience never heard originals. *Electric* '87 prod. by Rick Rubin, described by the *Observer* as 'a perfect (and amusing) Eighties *idea* of a late Sixties hard rock record'. They lack some originality, but stand out like an oasis in mid-'80s UK wasteland as popular post-punk attraction.

CURE, The UK pop/rock band formed '76 in Crawley, Sussex as Easy Cure. Then lineup: Robert Smith, guitar, songwriter (*b* 21 Apr. '57); Laurence Tolhurst, drums (switched to keyboards c.'82); Michael Dempsey, bass. Shortened name to Cure '78; guested on tour with SIOUXSIE & THE BANSHEES '79, leading to sporadic collaboration; played in Banshees mould of swirling, gothic UK pop music of late '70s. Albums *Three Imaginary Boys* '79, *17 Seconds* and *Boys Don't Cry* '80, *Faith* and *Happily Ever After* '81; minor chart entries 'A Forest', 'Charlotte Sometimes', 'Let's Go To Bed' '81-2. LP *Pornography* '82 well received; *Japanese Whispers* appeared '83, but band put on hold late '82 when Smith joined Banshees; resurfaced with 'Love Cats' (UK no. 7 '83), minor hit 'The Caterpillar' '84. Smith left Banshees mid-'84. *Concert: The Cure, Live* '84 is hits live; 'In-Between Days' '85 threatened further development. *The Head On The Door* '85 stayed in USA charts 38 weeks (they were a cult favourite there); *Standing On A Beach* '86 (greatest hits) also charted there; *Staring At The Sea – The Video* is full-length video incl. 17 hits. Tolhurst disclaims arty-rock label: 'I don't think we're a teeny-bop band yet. But I think people give too much importance to something that is entertainment, when all is said and done.' Friendships within band and lack of pretence keep them going; mid-'86 lineup incl. Smith, Tolhurst, Simon Gallup, Porl Thompson, Boris Williams. 2-disc *Kiss Me, Kiss Me, Kiss Me* '87 incl. music from film *The Cure In Orange*.

CURLESS, Dick (*b* 17 Mar. '32, Fort Fairfield, Maine) Deep-voiced truckdriving singer. Sang cowboy songs as the Tumbleweed Kid in teens; served in Korea '51-4, on Armed Forces Network as The Rice-Paddy Ranger. Worked in New England; won Arthur GODFREY Talent Scout TV competition '57, gigs in Las Vegas, Hollywood; records on small labels in Maine (Tiffany, Allagesh, etc.); truckdriving song 'A Tombstone Every Mile' picked up by Tower Records (Capitol subsidiary), made country top 5 '65 plus 'Six Times A Day' '65, 'All Of Me Belongs To You' '67, 'Big Wheel Cannonball' '70, 'Loser's Cocktail' '71, etc. With Buck OWENS' All American Show '69-71; preferred living/working in Northeast. LPs: *Hard Travelling Man* '71, *Last Blues Song* '72, *Keep On Truckin'* '75, all on Capitol; *End Of The Road* '74 on Hilltop; *The Great Race* '83; *Welcome To My World* '88 on Rocade.

CURSON, Ted (*b* 3 June '35, Philadelphia) Trumpet, flugelhorn. Worked in NYC with Mal WALDRON, Cecil TAYLOR, others; with Charles MINGUS '59-60. Quartet date of 20 Oct. '60 with Eric DOLPHY, Dannie RICHMOND incl. 'Folk Forms No. 1': Dolphy and Curson, both soon to leave Mingus, carry on impassioned conversation full of swinging tension while Mingus and Richmond lay out: one of the great moments in post-bop jazz. Has since worked mostly in Europe where he is a star of concerts, clubs, festivals, film and TV, also with visiting countrymen. The first foreign musician to be awarded grant by Finnish government.

'73. Many own LPs incl. *Tears For Dolphy* '64 on Arista; *The New Thing, The Blue Thing* '65 on Atlantic; *Ted Curson And Gustav Brom Orchestra* '65 on Supraphon (two arr. with big band, two quartet tracks with Miroslav Vitous); quartet session with Booker ERVIN '66 on Fontana; *Ode To Booker Ervin* '70 with Finnish sidemen on EMI/Columbia; *Ted Curson And Co.* '76 on India Navigation; *Jubilant Power* '76 on Inner City; three albums on Interplay: quintet *Blowin' Away* '78, *The Trio* '79, septet *I Heard Mingus* '80; octet *Snake Johnson* c.'80 on Chiaroscuro.

CURVED AIR UK art-school band: vocalist Sonja Kristina, violinist Darryl Way, Francis Monkman on keyboards and guitar, Florian Pilkington on drums (replaced mid-'70s by Stewart Copeland, later in POLICE). First album *Air Conditioning* '70 was top 10 UK; albums *Curved Air* '71 (aka *The Second Album*; incl. top 5 single 'Back Street Luv'), *Phantasmagoria* '72 were top 20; they continued to tour and record but had no more chart success as art-school rock passed from fashion. Way made instrumental single 'Little Plum' '82; Monkman became founder member of Sky with guitarist John WILLIAMS.

CUSCUNA, Michael (*b* 20 Sep. '48, Stamford, Conn.) Producer; also critic, broadcaster, writer. Countless sleeve notes, articles in periodicals; radio in Philadelphia, NYC; prod. *Jazz Alive* series, other syndicated programmes. Began prod. blues, pop records while in college '66-70, incl. Bonnie RAITT's second album *Give It Up* '72; on staff at Atlantic '72-3: prod. Garland JEFFREYS, Oscar BROWN, Ted CURSON, much else. Recorded '72 Ann Arbor Blues & Jazz Festival; ART ENSEMBLE live set issued on Atlantic, then *Fanfare For The Warriors* recorded with them in Chicago. Freelance from '73; prod. Larry CORYELL, Andrew HILL, Oliver LAKE, Lester BOWIE, Ran BLAKE, Cecil TAYLOR, many others. Coaxed Dexter GORDON, Anthony BRAXTON back from Europe; prod. Braxton on Arista '75-7, Gordon on CBS (releases '77-9). Prod. Wildflowers festival May '76, mixed and edited series of five LPs released '76 on Douglas, as well as Charles TYLER's *Saga Of The Outlaws*, eventually released on Nessa with sleeve note by Cuscuna. Prod. reissues and issues of unreleased material beginning with *Inner Space* '73, 2-disc set with Chick COREA and Hubert LAWS titles from '60s; did series of John COLTRANE unissued material on Impulse; got into Blue Note vault '75, discovering 130 LPs worth of unissued material as well as reissues; prod. Blue Note 2-disc compilations, but reissue programme had stop-and-start nature: after years of research formed Mosaic label with Charlie Lourie '82 for limited edition reissues; first release 4-disc *Complete Blue Note Recordings Of Thelonious Monk*, with unissued and alternate takes, discography, biographical booklet by Cuscuna. On A&R staff of revived Blue Note label at EMI NYC, in charge of reissues and release of unissued material.

CYRILLE, Andrew (*b* 10 Nov. '39, Brooklyn, NY) Drums, composer. Playing at age 11; considered chemistry as career; studied at Juilliard, with Philly Joe JONES; worked with Illinois JACQUET, OLATUNJI, others '50s; recorded with Coleman HAWKINS (*The Hawk Relaxes*), Walt Dickerson (*Relativity*) on Prestige; Bill Barron (*Hot Line*) on Savoy (Reedman Barron *b* 27 Mar. '27, Philadelphia; brother of pianist Kenny Barron; active in education). Worked with Roland KIRK, Cedar WALTON, with Cecil TAYLOR '65-75 (LP *Conquistador!* '65), incl. period as Artist in Residence at Antioch College, Ohio. Like Taylor he was an outcast, ideas far ahead of the time; Taylor recognised his uniqueness. Records with Jazz Composers Orchestra; with Jimmy LYONS (*Other Afternoons*), Grachan MONCUR (*New Africa*), own solo LP *What About* '69, all on BYG in France, now on Affinity in UK; with Marion BROWN on ECM (*Afternoon Of A Georgia Faun* '70). Formed trio of three percussionists with Milford Graves, Rashied ALI *Dialogue Of The Drums* (LP with Graves '74); *Celebration* '75 is by a septet with Ted Daniel (trumpet, flugelhorn), vocalist (Jennie Lee) and poet; *Junction* '76 has group with Daniel now called Maono, all three on IPS (Institute of Percussive Studies). Maono contributed 'Short Short' to Wildflowers festival May '76 NYC (*see* JAZZ). *Metamusicians' Stomp* '78, *Special People* '80, *The Navigator* '82 are all by Maono on Black Saint, all made in Italy. *The Loop* '78 on Ictus is solo set made in Italy; *Nuba* '79 is trio with Lyons and Lee; *Andrew Cyrille Meets Brötzmann In Berlin* '82 on FMP with reedman Peter Brötzmann (*b* 6 Mar. '41, Remscheid, W. Germany).

D

DAFFAN, Ted (*b* Theron Eugene Daffan, 21 Sep. '12, Beauregarde, La.) Honky-tonk country singer, songwriter, steel guitarist. Worked in electronics, took up steel, played in Hawaiian style; then country music with jazz flavour; joined Blue Ridge Playboys '34-5, Bar X Cowboys '36-40 in Houston, Texas. Wrote 'Truck Driver's Blues', perhaps the first truck driving song: hit for Moon MULLICAN, Cliff Bruner '39; led to contract with Columbia '39-51. Ted Daffan & His Texans had hits incl. 'Worried Mind' '40, 'Always Alone' '41, 'Born To Lose' '43, 'No Letter Today' '44, 'Headin' Down The Wrong Highway' '45, 'I've Got Five Dollars And It's Saturday Night' '50. Wrote most of his own hits, also 'I'm A Fool To Care' (pop hit for Joe Berry '61), hundreds of others. Gold disc for 'Born To Lose'. Owns publishing firm and record company in Houston.

DAILY, Pete (*b* 5 May '11, Portland, Ind.; *d* 23 Aug. '86) Cornet; bandleader. Began in Chicago; also played tuba in early years; to West Coast '42; with Ozzie NELSON band, others; formed dixieland combo Pete Daily's Chicagoans '46, popular in Hollywood nightclubs. Records on Capitol well into '50s incl. jolly vocal version of 'Minnie The Mermaid' (written by Buddy DESYLVA '30). Later took up valve trombone; disbanded late '50s, took up music again '75 until stroke forced him to quit.

DAIRO, I. K. (*b* Isaiah Kehinde Dairo, '30, Offa, Nigeria) Singer-composer, accordion; widely regarded as the father of JUJU music. Moved to his father's home town of Ijebu-Ijesha '37; unable to complete education, worked as apprentice barber, learning to make and play drums in spare time early '40s. Travelled widely in western Nigeria '42-6, working as cloth salesman, road builder, farm labourer, carpenter; settled in Ibadan, performing with early juju exponent Ojege Daniel. Served 10-year musical apprenticeship, developing and refining own ideas; formed 10-piece Morning Star Orchestra '57, changed name to Blue Spots '61; began recording with Decca, releasing huge number of records in 25 years; compilation of early sounds on *The Juju Music Of I. K. Dairo*. Soon famous in western Nigeria, but juju remained in the shadow of HIGHLIFE style; represented Nigeria at Negro Arts Festival in Dakar '65; as juju became main recreational music of Yoruba, Dairo was already the most popular artist. LPs from this period incl. *Taxi Driver*, *Ashiko Music Vols. 1 & 2*, *Iye Iye Iye* and *Iya Mi Iyo*. Singing mainly in Yoruban but also English, Hausa, Urohobo and Itsikerri, he modernised juju, introduced accordion and talking drum to it; fame spread throughout Nigeria, also to Benin. Visited UK several times; awarded MBE, the first African musician to be so honoured. Despite challenge from Ebenezer OBEY, Sunny ADE, retained popularity through '70s with string of hit LPs incl. *Kekere, Emi Oni Gbe Sajo, Talaka Nke Ebi*. Featured in TV documentary *Beats Of The Heart* '80. Recent LPs incl. *Iyo O Yemi* '83, *Mimo Mimo L'Olorun* '84. A devout Christian, also active in Aladura Church movement.

DALE, Jim (*b* James Smith, 15 Aug. '39, Rothwell, Northants., UK) Actor, comedian, singer. Studied judo and dance as a boy. Discovered by talent spotter Carroll Levis '52, toured with him as a comic who fell around a lot. Sang for a laugh while warming up BBC's rock'n'roll TV show *6.5 Special* '57; stayed for three years as singer/compère; four UK chart entries '57-58 incl. no. 2 'Be My Girl'; LP *Jim* '58. Wrote and recorded 'Piccadilly Line', parody of Lonnie DONEGAN hit 'Rock Island Line'. Turned to acting '60s; joined *Carry On* low comedy film team. Wrote lyric for Tom Springfield's music for film title *Georgy Girl* '66; single by SEEKERS sold a million. Legit. work incl. Shakespeare with

National Theatre Co. at Old Vic; toured USA with them '74; rave reviews in title role of Molière farce *Scapino*. Films incl. Disney's *Pete's Dragon* '77; career highspot and Tony award at age 45 with demanding title role of Phineas T. Barnum in Michael Stewart/Cy COLEMAN circus musical '80: back to his roots, falling over skilfully. Still in USA '85 in highly praised Broadway revival of Peter Nicholl's tragi-comic *Joe Egg*.

DALE, Kenny (*b* Artesia, N.M.) Country singer. Recorded for small label, Houston, Texas; Capitol picked up master of 'Bluest Heartache Of The Year', top 10 country hit '77. Further hits with 'Shame, Shame On Me' '77, 'Red Hot Memory' '78, 'Only Love Can Break A Heart' '79, 'When It's Just You And Me' '80, 'Moanin' The Blues' '82. Four Capitol albums named after hit title tracks '77-81.

DALHART, Vernon (*b* Marion T. Slaughter, 6 Apr. 1883, Jefferson, Texas; *d* 14 Sep. '48, Bridgeport, Conn.) Pioneer country singer. Began singing opera and in vaudeville; recorded 'The Wreck Of The Old 97'/'The Prisoner's Song' for Victor '24, first country record to sell in the millions. For a decade recorded songs like 'Kitty Wells', 'Molly Darling', 'Death Of Floyd Collins', 'New River Train' etc. under various names: Frank Evans, Bill Vernon, Guy Massey, Al Carver. Recording career ended '33: outsold everybody else in heyday, total estimated 75,000,000 records, but left little trace. Stopped selling during Depression, while even then people bought Jimmie RODGERS. Later worked as hotel clerk; elected to Country Music Hall of Fame '81.

DALTON, Lacy J. (*b* Jill Byrem, 13 Oct. '48, Bloomsbury, Penn.) Country/rock singer, songwriter. Began as folk/protest singer in Midwest late '60s; moved to Santa Cruz, Cal. early '70s; lead singer with psychedelic band Office using name Jill Corston; demo tape reached Billy Sherrill in Nashville Apr. '79, signed to Columbia in June. Gravelly, bluesy voice, self-penned songs won big following. Hit singles 'Crazy Blue Eyes' '79; 'Tennessee Waltz', 'Hard Times' '80, 'Takin' It Easy' '81, '16th Avenue' '83, 'Dream Baby' '83. Albums incl. *Lacy J. Dalton* '79, four others named after hit tracks,

as country LPs often are; she didn't record in '84 owing to disagreement with label over producer; came back with *Can't Run Away From Your Heart* '85. Jonathan Cain of JOURNEY had written 'Can't See Me Without You' for her but it was too close to rock to be incl. in that album; Cain then asked her to sing on a demo of a song he'd written for HEART and her agent took the demo to CBS in Nashville, who ordered an LP in the same vein: *Highway Diner* '86 is populist rock similar to that of Bruce SPRINGSTEEN, incl. 'Working Class Man' (no. 16 hit) and the earlier Cain song. On stage she sings Lyle LOVETT's 'God Will', about a lover who refuses to forgive repeated indignities ('God will, but I won't'), but the publisher refused permission to record it. Her honesty and vocal talent will get her to the top again.

DAMBA, Fanta (*b* Segou, Mali) Singer/composer, known as La Grande Vedette Malienne, born into 'a well-known family of wizards'. Began singing as a child; records in Bambara language early '60s; established herself with singles as leading interpreter of Mali's oral tradition; fame has spread throughout region outside Mali. Formed folk group '75 to accompany her; now often joined by daughters Nana and Aminata; also sings solo and accompanied by guitar and/or kora. LP *Hamet* '75 followed '76 by *Fanta Bamba And Batourou* and *Sekou Kouyate*, both featuring kora player Batourou Sekou Kouyate (who has solo LP *Keme Bounama* on American Mokossa label). More recent Fanta LPs incl. *Sekou Samega* and *Bahamadou Simogo*.

DAMERON, Tadd (*b* Tadley Ewing Dameron, 21 Feb. '17, Cleveland, Ohio; *d* 8 Mar. '65, NYC) Piano, composer/arranger. One of the most talented and important musicians in early-modern jazz, among the first to write bop for larger groups, finding beauty in modern harmonies uncommercial at the time. Comps. incl. 'Hot House', 'Good Bait', 'Lady Bird', 'Our Delight', many classics; ballad 'If You Could See Me Now' out of a phrase from a Dizzy GILLESPIE solo. Began writing for Harlan LEONARD in K.C.; Don REDMAN, Illinois JACQUET '40s, Dizzy's big band (tracks now on 2-disc Gillespie compilation on French

RCA); own quintet NYC '49 (collected under Fats NAVARRO's name on Blue Note; more Navarro with Dameron now on Milestone; he also recorded for Capitol, tracks now compiled on Affinity with Lennie TRISTANO session on the other side), Paris with Miles DAVIS '49 (Jazz Fair recordings were on CBS-Sony). Clifford BROWN *Memorial* now on Fantasy is a '53 Dameron group. Dameron's albums incl. lovely octet set *Fontainebleau* (with sound like a whole orchestra), quartet *Mating Call* with John COLTRANE, both '56 on Prestige; big band set *The Magic Touch* '61 (now on Fantasy) lacks tang compared to earlier work, but incl. Bill EVANS; nothing Dameron did was without some wit and beauty. Piano solos recorded by Chris Albertson '61 apparently not issued. Drug problems late '50s; later wrote record sessions for Milt JACKSON, Sonny STITT, Blue MITCHELL; for Benny GOODMAN's tour of USSR '62; suffered heart attacks, died of cancer. Said to have failed high school classes in theory and harmony; Gordon later described him as 'the romanticist of the whole period'. Recent LPs of his comps. by Barry Harris Trio on Xanadu '75 (Harris *b* 15 Dec. '29, Detroit; piano, composer; played and recorded with Coleman HAWKINS, many others; own LPs on several labels with trio, quintet, sextet); also by Dameronia, led by Philly Joe JONES: comps. of Dameron, others transcribed/arr. by Don Sickler, John Oddo; *Dameronia* '82 incl. Johnny COLES; *Look, Stop And Listen* '83 features Johnny GRIFFIN on 'If You Could See Me Now', Walter DAVIS Jr on 'Dial B for Beauty'; also incl. Benny GOLSON's 'Killer Joe'. Also quintet Continuum, with Jimmy HEATH, Slide HAMPTON, Kenny Barron, Ron CARTER, Art TAYLOR: album *Mad About Tadd* '83 on Palo Alto.

DAMNED, The UK punk band, formed July '76 by Dave Vanian, vocals; Brian James, guitar; Captain Sensible (*b* Ray Burns, 24 Apr. '54, Croydon), bass; Rat Scabies (Chris Millar), drums. Played legendary punk festival at London's 100 Club: first in genre to release LP, to have top 30 hit, to tour USA. First LP *Damned, Damned, Damned* early '77, prod. by Nick LOWE, captured energy of live act (treat for fans, with Captain Sensible cavorting in fancy dress, Vanian looking like Dracula's relative, Scabies in image

of Keith Moon). James was band's writer (classic punk single 'Neat, Neat, Neat'/ 'New Rose'). *Music For Pleasure* '78 prod. by PINK FLOYD's Nick Mason; James left '78 (formed short-lived Tanz Der Youth, then with Lords Of The New Church '82); Damned carried on (Culture Club's Jon Moss was drummer briefly '78). Increasingly disappointed die-hard punk fans with hit 'Love Song' (no. 20 '79 UK), LPs *Machine Gun Etiquette* '79, *The Black Album* '80; *Strawberries* '82 sold only to devoted fans. Sensible went solo with surprise no. 1 hit 'Happy Talk' '82 (Richard RODGERS & Hammerstein song from *South Pacific*); LP *Women And Captains First* (prod. by Tony Mansfield) also a surprise, mixing lightweight pop songs 'Wot' (also single hit), 'A Nice Cup Of Tea' with ballads: tribute to 'Croydon'; 'Brenda' co-written by ex-Soft Boy Robin Hitchcock. Left Damned '83; red beret, love of cricket kept him in the news; anti-nuclear 'Glad It's All Over' was a hit '84. Best-of *Sensible Songs* incl. tame cover of FRANKIE's 'Relax': a likeable punk who lives at home with Mum and Dad, could only happen in England. Meanwhile Damned's personnel even more various in '80s, with only Vanian, Scabies constants, but scored top 20 hits '85 with 'Grimly Fiendish', 'Shadow Of Love'; *Phatasmagoria* '85 was hit LP, reaching new mass audience: cover of Barry Ryan's 'Eloise' (no. 2 hit '68 UK) raced up the charts early '86, as if to emphasise change of direction; *Anywhere* '86 incl. cover of LOVE's 'Alone Again Or'. *Not The Captain's Birthday Party* '86 was live LP with original lineup. Never serious rivals to SEX PISTOLS or CLASH as punks, but still finding fans.

DAMONE, Vic (*b* Vito Rocco Farinola, 12 June '28, Brooklyn, NYC) Singer. Worked as usher at Paramount Theatre, won Arthur GODFREY Talent Scout show age 15, helped into cabaret NYC by Milton Berle. Own radio show on CBS '47-8, recorded for Mercury, first hit 'I Have But One Heart' '47, then million-sellers 'Again' and no. 1 'You're Breaking My Heart', both '49. Film debut in *Rich, Young And Pretty* with Jane Powell, FOUR FRESHMEN '51; same year sang 'Don't Blame Me' by Dorothy Fields/Jimmy McHUGH in *The Strip*, musical melodrama with Mickey Rooney, Louis

ARMSTRONG, Jack TEAGARDEN, Earl HINES, Barney BIGARD. Damone/Powell also together in *Athena* (he sang 'The Girl Next Door', first sung by Judy GARLAND in *Meet Me In St Louis* '44), duo guest shot in Sigmund ROMBERG biopic *Deep In My Heart* (both '54), bigger roles in *Hit The Deck* '55 (big song was Vincent YOUMANS' 'Sometimes I'm Happy'). Columbia records in '50s incl. his third gold disc, fine version of LERNER & LOEWE classic 'On The Street Where You Live', no. 4 USA '56: deliberately held back by producers of *My Fair Lady* film, then no. 1 UK '58. Title song from film *An Affair To Remember* hit in both USA/UK '57; LP *Closer Than A Kiss* with mus. dir. Frank DEVOL; then on Capitol (*Linger Awhile* '62), WB (*Country Love Songs* '65), RCA (*On The South Side Of Chicago* '67). Semi-retired into real estate business, then remarkable renaissance early '80s in UK, mainly due to persistent plays by BBC DJ David Jacobs, especially of '61 track 'The Pleasure Of Her Company' from Fred ASTAIRE comedy film, reissued on CBS UK '83. More than a dozen reissued LPs in UK incl. hits compilation *Sings The Great Songs* on CBS Cameo; *Strange Enchantment* on Capitol; *Make Someone Happy, Why Can't I Walk Away, Now And Forever, Stay With Me* etc. on RCA. Ballad voice described as 'the best set of pipes in the business' by Frank SINATRA. He is married to actress-singer Diahann Carroll.

DANA (*b* Rosemary Brown, '52, Londonderry) Pop singer. Convent girl auditioned for Irish entry, Eurovision song contest age 17 and won: 'All Kinds Of Everything' made no. 1 UK chart '70. Further hits until '76; own TV series '74; film debut '78 *The Flight Of Doves*. Plays summer seasons at seaside venues, pantomime in winter; also appears in family-oriented TV shows.

DANIELS, Billy (*b* 12 Sep. '15; *d* 7 Oct. '88) USA singer. Sang with Erskine HAWKINS '34-5 at Alabama State College; sang every day of '37 on radio for 12 different sponsors; claims as first film obscure *Sepia Cinderella* same year. Became well-known in clubs '40s. Many films; those with Frankie LAINE incl. *When You're Smiling* '50, *Sunny Side Of The Street* and *Rainbow Round My Shoulder* '51; in the first he sang

'That Ol' Black Magic' (song from '42): strong vocal and visual style made him a favourite of mimics in clubs, TV. Double act from '50 of comedy, vocalising with pianist Benny Payne (*b* 18 June '07, Philadelphia; with Cab CALLOWAY '31-43, recorded duets with Fats WALLER); they toured Europe (headlined at London Palladium '52,3), were one of the first black acts on USA TV. On stage with Sammy DAVIS Jr in *Golden Boy* '64, co-starred with Pearl BAILEY in all-black cast of *Hello Dolly* '75, starred in UK staging of *Bubbling Brown Sugar* '77 (more than 700 performances). Records on Mercury '40s; later LPs *Love Me Or Leave Me, Around That Time, Love Songs For A Fool*; *At Basin Street East* on Jubilee; *You Go To My Head* '57 with Benny CARTER; *The Magic Of Billy Daniels* '78 had disco version of 'That Ol' Black Magic'.

DANIELS, Charlie (*b* 28 Oct. '37, Wilmington, N.C.) Guitar, fiddler, singer, bandleader. Country-rock outfit incl. Charles Hayward, bass; Taz DiGregorio, keyboards; James Marshall, drums; Tom Crain, guitar. Daniels formed band the Jaguars working clubs, honky tonks in Southwest; '67 moved to Nashville, sessioned on Bob DYLAN's *Nashville Skyline*, Ringo STARR's *Beaucoups Of Blues*, also with Marty ROBBINS, Lester FLATT and Earl Scruggs, etc. Missed the road; formed Charlie Daniels Band '71, signed to Kama Sutra label for pop hits 'Uneasy Rider' '73, 'The South's Gonna Do It' '75. Started annual event The Volunteer Jam in Nashville Jan. '74 featuring top stars with CDB as headliners. LP *Fire On The Mountain* '74 went gold. Switched to Epic '76, made impression with 'Wichita Jail' '76, 'Heaven Can Be Anywhere' '77; no. 1 country chart with 'The Devil Went Down To Georgia' '79, also pop hit USA and UK: led to awards incl. Single of the Year, Instrumentalist of the Year, Instrumental Group of the Year CMA '79, Touring Band of the Year ACM '80. LP *Million Mile Reflections* '79 big hit; further singles: 'Behind Your Eyes' '80, 'In America' '81, 'Still In Saigon' '82. LPs also incl. *Uneasy Rider* '73 (reissued Epic '79), *Volunteer Jam VI* '80, *Full Moon* '81, *Windows* '82, *A Decade Of Hits* '83.

DANKWORTH, John (*b* 20 Sep. '27, London) UK alto sax, leader, composer. Studied at Royal Academy of Music; joined 'Geraldo's navy' (young musicians playing on Cunard liners got chance to visit NYC, hear BOP first hand). Guested with Ted HEATH; won Melody Maker poll '49; formed Johnny Dankworth Seven '50; vocalist Cleo LAINE joined '51 (they married '58); had Don RENDELL on tenor '53 (*b* 4 Mar. '26, Devon); bigger band from that year. Hits with novelty 'Experiments With Mice' '56 ('Three Blind Mice' in styles of various bandleaders), 'African Waltz' '61. Played Birdland NYC, Newport Jazz Festival '59; spent more time on composing, studio work '60S: many works incl. ballet *Lysistrata* for Bath Festival '62; *The Diamond And The Goose* for choir, soloists, orchestra, words by Benny Green; musicals *Boots With Strawberry Jam* '68 with Green (based on Shaw), *Colette* '79 for Cleo; film scores incl. *Saturday Night And Sunday Morning* '60, *The Servant* '63, *Darling* '65, *Morgan* '66 etc. Pieces for orchestra *What The Dickens, Zodiac Variations, A Million Dollar Collection* written and recorded '60s; he regarded them as a trilogy and once said that he would be pleased to be judged by them: *Dickens* was a hit, bumping Stan GETZ's *Jazz Samba* from the top of the UK jazz LP chart; received Ivor Novello awards '64 for *Dickens* and for *The Avengers* TV theme. He converted stables at Buckinghamshire home to music rooms, ran Wavenden Allmusic Plan there since '70: workshops for young musicians. Musical *Side By Side By Sondheim* premiered there, went on to become smash hit. Other LPs incl. *A Lover & His Lass* '76 with Cleo; *Fair Oak Fusions*, nine-part work for cello (Julian Lloyd Webber) and small group incl. five reeds; quintet *Gone Hitchin'*; *Metro* with Rod ARGENT, four others; *Octavious*, octet with Paul Hart; has also written string quartet, piano concerto. EMI compilation of '53-8 stuff incl. six vocals by Cleo.

DANNY AND THE JUNIORS USA vocal group formed '55 in Philadelphia: Danny Rapp, lead (*b* 10 May '41; suicide 8 Apr. '83), Joe Terranova (*b* 30 Jan. '41), Frank Maffei (*b* Nov. '40), Dave White (*b* Sep. '40); latter-day sideman was saxophonist Lennie Baker, who later co-founded SHA

NA NA. They signed with small local label as Juvenairs fresh out of high school; White and a friend (John Medora) wrote smash no. 1 (for seven weeks) 'At The Hop' '57-8 (originally called 'Do The Bop'; Leon Huff helped prod.); follow-up 'Rock And Roll Is Here To Stay' (top 20 '58) also written by White (who made solo LP on Bell '71 under real name David White Tricker). Featured on Dick CLARK show; toured with Alan FREED; had two more top 40 hits. 'At The Hop' was typical of the period's way of diluting rock'n'roll excitement into harmless dance music.

DANSE SOCIETY UK New Wave band formed Barnsley '79 by Steve Rawlings, vocals; Paul 'Gigi' Gilmartin, drums; Paul Nash, guitar; Tim Wright, bass; Lyndon Scarfe, keyboards. Emerged from local bands Y (Rawlings, Gilmartin) and Lipps (Nash, Wright). Cult status through sessions on John Peel BBC 1 radio show; then developed back in Yorkshire away from media. Doomladen songs allied them with (Southern Death) Cult, Sex Gang Children in '80s post-punk morass. Singles '81 on own Society label ('The Clock'), Pax ('There Is No Shame In Death'); rose from supporting act to headline; single 'Woman's Own'/'We're So Happy' showed musical improvement. Mini-LP 6-track *Seduction* achieved longest stay in indie chart to date '83 reaching no. 2 (single 'Somewhere' from LP did well; title cut was minor hit). Music moved towards electro dancefloor style; signed by Arista for single 'Wake Up' (minor hit); LP *Heaven Is Waiting* '84 incl. cover of ROLLING STONES' '2000 Light Years From Home', good sample of Rawlings' half-sung, half-spoken vocals, chilling guitar/keyboards over robotic rhythms. Despite diverse reference points (PINK FLOYD, JOY DIVISION, DOORS etc.), 'doom rockers' had yet to justify the fans. Final LP *Looking Through* '86 on own Society label, last single 'Hold On To What You've Got' before split. Rawlings retained name, others became Johnny and the Clouds.

DAOUDA (*b* Tou Kone Daouda, Abidjan, Ivory Coast) Singer-composer, from Burkinabe family. Began as TV technician; talented amateur singer and guitarist overheard in studio, offered TV spot and record contract; first single 'Les Gbakas d'Abidjan' '76 successful, turned to music full-time, second single 'Le Villageons' '77. Gifted lyricist introduced new mixture of local rhythms, SOUKOUS and MAKOSSA; first LPs *Mon Coeur Balance* and *Vive la Musique* '78-9 followed by two more; breakthrough hit came '83 with reworked first album retitled *Le Sentimental* '83: with Souzy Kasseya, guitar; Alhadji Toure, bass; Jimmy and Fredo (one of the hottest horn sections in Africa) and arranger Jimmy Hyacinthe, LP was huge hit in Francophone world, released on UK Stern label '85 in hopes of wider success. LP *La Femme de Mon Patron* '85 is makossa infl. LP with backing from Cameroonian sidemen.

DARBY & TARLTON Tom Darby and Jimmie Tarlton (*b* 8 May 1892, Chesterfield County, S.C.) Old Time duet singers, sound the basis for much country music. Tarlton was pioneer of steel guitar: began playing ordinary guitar with a chromed steel bar, learned much from Hawaiian guitarist Frank Ferera in Cal. '23; met Darby, duet became popular act in South. Records for Columbia '27-33 with Darby on guitar, Tarlton on steel, both singing: 'Birmingham Jail', 'Lonesome Railroad', 'Frankie Dean', 'Mexican Rag', etc. Forgotten until early '60s when Tarlton appeared at folk festivals, made solo LP *Steel Guitar Rag* '62 on Testament. Also *Darby & Tarlton* compilation on Arhoolie.

D'ARBY, Terence Trent (*b* 15 Mar. '62) Soul singer with remarkable gospel-trained voice, able to re-create any black style of the last 30 years. First LP *Introducing The Hard Line* '87 on CBS/UK was all his own songs except one and was too much of a showcase as well as being overproduced, like most debuts, resulting in a bunch of forgettable juke box singles. Perhaps he will survive his hype.

DARENSBOURG, Joe (*b* 9 July '06, Baton Rouge, La.; *d* June '85, L.A.) Clarinet. Played on Mississippi river boats, joined Kid ORY '44; with Louis ARMSTRONG in '56, again '61 through 'Hello Dolly!' sessions; other sessioning incl. John FAHEY LP *After The Ball* '73; led dixieland bands. One of the best low-register players around, as on

own hit 'Yellow Dog Blues' (no. 43 '58; the slap-tongue sound was not his usual style). Album *Barrelhousin' With Joe* on GHB label. He played with everybody and tells all in *Telling It Like It Is* '87, edited by Peter Vacher, a better-than-usual memoir.

DARIN, Bobby (*b* Walden Robert Cassotto, 14 May '36, Bronx, NYC; *d* 20 Dec. '73, L.A.) Singer. Studied drama in college; signed to Decca '56, Atco '57; first big hit with own song, amusing novelty 'Splish Splash', no. 3 '58 (hit by the Rinky Dinks, 'Early In The Morning' no. 24 '58, was also Darin); further top 10 entries 'Queen Of The Hop' '58, 'Dream Lover' '59, all on LP *The Bobby Darin Story* '61; followed by change from rock/pop to SINATRA style for no. 1 smash with Kurt WEILL's 'Mack The Knife' '59; no. 6 'Beyond The Sea' '60 (originally 'La Mer', by Charles TRENET), both on LP *That's All* '59. Other top 10 hits: 'You Must Have Been A Beautiful Baby' '61 (song from '38 by Johnny MERCER/Harry Warren adapted to cash in on Twist dance fad), 'Things' '62, 'You're The Reason I'm Living' '63, 'If I Were A Carpenter' '66. Film career incl. *Come September* '60 (also co-starred Sandra Dee; married her that year), *Captain Newman M.D.* '63 (Oscar nomination); divorced from Dee '67. Switched to Capitol '62, Atlantic '67; then career lost momentum. Always well-liked entertainer with fine voice; changed style again '71, became Bob Darin, singing anti-war songs. Had rheumatic fever as a child; heart valve operation '71; died in surgery. Among many LPs: *Darin Sings Ray Charles* '62, *From Hello Dolly To Goodbye Charlie* '64. *20 Golden Greats* compilation marketed on UK TV '85.

DARKO, George (*b* '51, Akropong, Ghana) Guitarist, composer. Played fontonfrom (a large drum) as a child; began on guitar while in high school in Okuapeman. Worked as printer on leaving school; first electric guitar was a bass; changed to rhythm guitar '70, joined local band the Reborn Avengers; then lead guitar with the Soul Believers '72, infl. by SANTANA, Jimi HENDRIX, BOOKER T; then with 4th Dimension made HIGHLIFE hit 'Ye De Nampa Aba'. While based in Kumasi with this group studied guitar with Konimo. Played in several bands in Ghana '70s, seeking to blend major infl. of Konimo and George BENSON. To West Berlin '79 in search of better studio facilities; linked with others in short-lived Fire Connection; band soon re-emerged as Bus Stop, with Lee Dodou, vocals; Bob Fiscian, keyboards; Stephan Mills, sax; Sometimer, bass; Jagger, drums. First LP *Friends* '83 incl. 'Akoe Te Brofo': fusion of HIGHLIFE and funk a massive hit in Ghana, also got international interest; that year band reworked it in English; result 'Highlife Time' became title track of second LP. Band toured Europe and USA '84, album and single also released on UK Oval label; three members left to form own group Kantata: their LP and single 'Asiko'/'Duke' also on Oval.

DARLING, Erik (*b* 25 Sep. '33, Baltimore, Md.) Folksinger; played guitar and banjo, specialising in 12-string guitar. Infl. by Burl IVES, Josh WHITE; early interest in CALYPSO. Formed the Tunetellers inspired by the WEAVERS; changed name to Tarriers, with Bob Carey and actor Alan Arkin (*b* '34; many films incl. *Catch 22* '70); had two top 10 hits '56: 'Cindy, Oh Cindy' (backing Vince Martin), 'Banana Boat Song' (aka 'Banana Boat (Day-O)' by Harry BELAFONTE). Arkin left, replaced by Alan Cooper; Darling left to replace Pete SEEGER in the Weavers '58-62, then formed the Rooftop Singers with Bill Svanoe and Lynne Taylor (had sung with Benny GOODMAN; *d* '82); they had no. 1 hit '63 with 'Walk Right In', which must have been Vanguard's biggest single. Mindy Stuart replaced Taylor; Patricia Street replaced Stuart, wrote songs with Darling: LP *The Possible Dream* '75 on Vanguard by Darling and Street. He made a solo LP on Elektra, *True Religion* and *Train Time* on Vanguard; accompanied Ed MCCURDY, Oscar BRAND, Judy COLLINS, Jack ELLIOTT etc.

DARRELL, Johnny (*b* 23 July '40, Cleburne County, Ala.) Holiday Inn manager Nashville got involved in country music, signed with United Artists, had hits 'As Long As The Wind Blows', 'Ruby Don't Take Your Love To Town', 'The Son Of Hickory Holler's Tramp', 'With Pen In Hand', 'Why You Been Gone So Long' '65-9. Often first to record songs which later became hits for

others ('Green, Green Grass Of Home', 'Ruby'). Duet with Anita Carter 'Coming Of The Roads' '69. Signed with Monument '73, Capricorn '74, Gusto '78 but did not repeat early success. LPs incl. *California Stop Over* on UA '70, *Waterglass Full Of Whisky* on Capricorn '74.

DARREN, James (*b* James Ercolani, 3 Oct. '36, Philadelphia, Pa.) Actor/singer. Singing, dancing skill of lesser teen idol won film contract with Columbia pictures; title song from film *Gidget* first hit '59; total of eight chart entries '59-'63 incl. top 10 'Goodbye Cruel World' '61 (deep-throated vocal pitched against gimmicky fairground organ), 'Her Royal Majesty' '62; several top 40 hits UK; also minor hits 'All' (from *Run For Your Wife*) '67, 'You Take My Heart Away' (from *Rocky*) '77. Has carved out second career as TV pop pundit, interviews with superstars widely syndicated '80s; own music was inconsequential.

DARTS UK doo-wop revivalists formed mid-'70s. Original lineup: Bob Fish (ex-Mickey Jupp band), Rita Ray, Griff Fender (Ian Collier), Den Hegarty, all vocals; Hammy Howell, piano; George Currie, guitar; Iain 'Thump' Thompson, bass; Horatio Hornblower (Nigel Trubridge), sax; John Dummer, drums (Thompson and Dummer from John Dummer Blues Band). Patronage of Radio London DJ Charlie Gillett secured deal with Magnet label; live act helped boost *Darts* LP to no. 9 late '77. Bass/leader Hegarty dominated colourful live act, cunning mix of revival covers and original tunes. Medley 'Daddy Cool/The Girl Can't Help It' no. 6 '77 then three successive no. 2 entries: covers of the Cardinals' 'Come Back My Love' and the AD LIBS' 'Boy From New York City' and 'It's Raining'. After dip with downtempo 'Don't Let It Fade Away', partied back to top 10 with 'Get It' and Gene CHANDLER's 'Duke Of Earl', both '79. By now Hegarty had departed, taking verve of live act with him despite vocal excellence of replacement Kenny Andrews; Howell quit to study, replaced by Mike Deacon (ex-Vinegar Joe), then rejoined; Dummer departed to form ribald True Life Confessions with wife Helen April; biggest post-'79 hit was cover for FOUR SEASONS' 'Let's Hang On' (no. 11

'80). First impact threatened to transcend nostalgia, but trod boards as revival act mid-'80s. TV-promoted *Amazing Darts* '78 first of a number of compilations, their most successful LP at no. 8 UK. Fender, Ray prod. *a cappella* girl group Mint Juleps' first LP for Stiff '85.

DASH, Julian (*b* 9 Apr. '16, Charleston, S.C.; *d* 24 Feb. '74, NYC) Tenor sax. Joined Erskine HAWKINS band after Alabama State College; stayed with it into '50s; featured solos incl. 'No Soap', 'Midnight Stroll', 'Double Shot', 'Gin Mill Special', 'Weddin' Blues', many others. Own records '50 prod. by Bob THIELE, reissued on *Classic Tenors Vol.2* '84: combo with Billy Kyle, echo chamber aimed 'My Silent Love', 'Long Moan', 'Creamin' ', 'Goin' Along' at R&B juke-boxes; still nice period pieces: too good a musician not to play pretty. Freelanced NYC; played on Buck CLAYTON *Jam Session* '54, etc.; last sessions on Master Jazz c.'70, incl. Jimmy RUSHING LP *Who Was It Sang That Song*.

DAVE & SUGAR Pop-country trio '75-82 with Dave Rowland, Vicki Hackeman, Jackie Franz; then Sue Powell, Melissa Dean, Jamie Kaye. Formed by Rowland, former pop singer and trumpeter, one-time member of The Stamps Quartet (toured with PRESLEY) and The Four Guys (Charley PRIDE's back-up vocal group). With Pride's encouragement recruited girls, signed with RCA; pop-styled harmony and slick stage work led to hits 'Queen Of The Silver Dollar' '75, 'The Door's Always Open' '76, 'I'm Knee Deep In Loving You' '77, 'Tear Time' '78, 'Golden Tears' '79, 'New York Wine And Tennessee Shine' '80, 'It's A Heartache' '81, 'Fool By Your Side' '81. LPs incl. *That's The Way Love Should Be* '77, *Stay With Me – Golden Tears* '79, *Greatest Hits* '81. Personnel changes led to Rowland going solo Mar. '82 with singles 'Natalie' (tribute to actress Natalie Wood), 'Lovin' Our Lives Away'.

DAVENPORT, Cow Cow (*b* Charles Davenport, 26 Apr. 1895, Anniston, Ala.; *d* 2 Dec. '56, Cleveland, Ohio) Pianist, singer, songwriter; pioneer of BOOGIE-WOOGIE style. Expelled from theological school for playing ragtime; joined carnival troupe c.'14, worked in vaudeville, with singers Dora Carr, Ivy Smith, etc.; recorded for seven different labels. Talent scout for Vocalion mid-'20s; spent time in prison after disastrous tour; tried operating music shop, then a café c.'35; had stroke '38 but recovered. Wrote or co-wrote 'Mama Don't Allow', 'You Rascal You', 'Do You Call That Religion?', many more; later with help of Art HODES received recognition from ASCAP. Big '42 hit 'Cow Cow Boogie' by Freddie SLACK and Ella Mae MORSE based on his 'Cow Cow Blues'. Compilation LP *Cow Cow Davenport 1925-30* on Magpie label UK '79.

DAVIES, Cyril (*b* '32, Buckinghamshire, England; *d* 7 Jan. '64 of leukaemia) Nickname 'Squirell'. With Alexis KORNER a pioneer of British blues. Played banjo early '50s in trad., then skiffle; late '50s played harmonica in burgeoning London blues scene with Korner, jamming with visiting black Americans; in early '60s they went electric, formed Blues Incorporated: future ROLLING STONES, CREAM passed through group; Davies left end '62 to form own All-Stars, taking over Screaming Lord SUTCH's Savages; employed Nicky HOPKINS, others. After his death vocalist Long John BALDRY took over most of All-Stars. Davies LPs incl. *The Legendary* '70 on UK Folklore label; 4-track 12" EP *Country Line Special* on PRT UK '84.

DAVIES, Gail (*b* 1 Sep. '48, Broken Bow, Okla.) Country music singer/songwriter. Father was musician on Louisiana Hayride. On the road with brother Ron (also songwriter: recorded by Helen REDDY, Hoyt AXTON), married jazz musician, separated; to West Coast, worked as session singer with Axton, Linda RONSTADT, etc. Writer's contract with Screen Gems, wrote 'Bucket To The South' (hit for Ava Barber '78). Signed to Lifesong label '78, made acclaimed album *Gail Davies* incl. country hits 'Poison Love', 'Someone Is Looking For Someone Like You', 'No Love Have I'. Label closed; went to Warner Bros '79, became first female in country music to prod. own records: hits 'Blue Heartache' '79, 'I'll Be There' '80, old Marty ROBBINS hit 'Singing The Blues' '81. To RCA '84; now one of the first in country to make videos: 'Jagged Edge Of

A Broken Heart', 'Break Away', 'Trouble With Love'. LPs incl. *The Game* '80, *I'll Be There* '81, *Givin' Herself Away* '82 all on WB; *Where Is A Woman To Go* (RCA '85).

DAVIS, Billie (*b* Carol Hedges, '45, Woking, Surrey, England) UK pop singer with a fine voice whose career probably suffered because her hits were all covers. Speaking role on Mike Sarne comedy record 'Will I What' '62; biggest hit 'Tell Him' '63 made no. 10, denied UK chart status to original by the Exciters; sound-alike follow-up 'He's The One' barely made top 40 same year. Had well-publicised relationship with ex-SHADOW Jet Harris that got in the way of both careers. Resumed recording after five years; superior version of much-recorded 'Angel Of The Morning' did not chart; next record 'I Want You To Be My Baby' no. 33 '68, her last hit.

DAVIS, Clive (*b* Brooklyn, NY) USA record company executive. Joined CBS as lawyer '60; became Vice President and General Manager '66. CBS's American Columbia label, long important USA major, was relying on original cast Broadway albums, film sound tracks, mainstream artists Tony BENNETT, Johnny MATHIS, Andy WILLIAMS etc. Davis's first signing was folk-rocker DONOVAN. Surprising himself with his acumen, Davis wrote later in autobiography *Clive: Inside The Record Business* '74 that 'It all began for me at the 1967 Monterey Pop Festival.' That year he signed Janis JOPLIN, SPIRIT, BLOOD, SWEAT & TEARS; in '68-9 Johnny WINTER, CHICAGO, SANTANA; then John McLAUGHLIN's Mahavishnu Orchestra; broke MOTT THE HOOPLE in USA, poached PINK FLOYD for USA; escalated SIMON & GARFUNKEL's *Bridge Over Troubled Water* '70 into best-selling CBS LP ever; signed Neil DIAMOND for $4m '73; ensured Bob DYLAN's staying with CBS with new contract (insisted on releasing 'Lay Lady Lay' as single: top 10 hit); helped sell a million of Walter CARLOS's *Switched-On Bach*. Not everything was perfect: during this period Columbia mishandled Thelonious MONK, etc. but Davis never claimed to be an expert on music; his instinct got CBS a corner on the most commercially successful pop of the era. Early Bruce SPRINGSTEEN excitement was mis-

handled after he left; in reaction to cultural/musical changes during '60s (which many resented) and because CBS suddenly was overextended as economic recession loomed, he was scapegoat in '73, dumped and charged with fiddling expenses (later cleared). To Bell '74; label soon changed to Arista, also owned Savoy; helped break Barry MANILOW in dawn of MOR, signed the KINKS, Aretha FRANKLIN, got co-writer's credit on songs for AIR SUPPLY: his acumen was still there.

DAVIS, Danny (*b* George Nowlan, 29 Apr. '25, Randolph, Mass.) Leader of Nashville Brass Band; trumpeter, singer, producer. Studied at New England Conservatory of Music; played with big bands of Bob CROSBY, Gene KRUPA, Art MOONEY late '40s-50s; became vocalist with Vincent Lopez at Astor Hotel NYC; then with Sammy KAYE, Freddy MARTIN. Became record prod. for Joy label '58, then on staff at MGM: prod. Johnny TILLOTSON, HERMAN'S HERMITS, Connie FRANCIS (six no. 1 hits). Moved to Nashville as prod. assistant to Chet ATKINS '65, worked with Waylon JENNINGS, Hank LOCKLIN, Eddy ARNOLD, etc. Formed Nashville Brass to create country version of Herb ALPERT sound; became steady album act. Not many hit singles, though 'I Saw The Light', 'Wabash Cannonball', 'Columbus Stockade Blues' did well '69-71; won Grammy '69 as Best Country Instrumental Performance, voted CMA Instrumental Group of the Year '69-74. LPs incl. *Nashville Brass* '72, *Travellin'* '73, *Bluegrass* '74, *Gold* '76, *Supersongs* '77, all RCA.

DAVIS, Eddie 'Lockjaw' (*b* 3 Mar. '21, NYC) Aka 'Jaws'. Tenor saxophone. Self-taught; muscular style in funky blues-jazz tradition, also good bakkad player. With Cootie WILLIAMS band '42-4 ('Sweet Lorraine', 'You Talk A Little Trash'), Lucky MILLINDER, Andy KIRK, Louis ARMSTRONG '44-5; freelanced '45-52 and led his own combo, often at Minton's, where his unique sense of harmony enabled him to fit in with young turks of bop. Own records prod. '46 by Bob THIELE reissued '84 on *Classic Tenors Vol. 2* incl. 'Afternoon In A Doghouse', 'Lockjaw' (hence nickname), 'Surgery', 'Athlete's Foot'; led to 'Spinal', 'Fracture', 'Calling Dr Jazz!' etc.

With Count BASIE '52-3: solos on 'Bread', 'Hobnail Boogie', 'Paradise Squat', etc.; then own groups, trio with Shirley SCOTT late '50s, freelance (played on *The Atomic Mr Basie* '57); rejoined Basie on tenor and as road manager '66-73; moved to Las Vegas. Has played many jazz festivals USA and Europe; often worked with Harry EDISON '70s-80s. Own albums incl. two vols. of *Cookbook* (one with Scott), now in 2-disc set; *Stolen Moments*, *Live At Minton's* '61 with Johnny GRIFFIN (2-disc set), all on Prestige; *Lock The Fox, The Fox And The Hounds, Love Calls* with Paul GONSALVES, all on RCA; more recently: *Tough Tenors Again'n'Again* '70 with Griffin on Pausa, *Montreux* '77 and *Straight Ahead* on Pablo, *Sweet And Lovely* '75 on Classic Jazz, *Heavy Hitter* '79 on Muse, *Jaws Blues* '81 on Enja; others on European Vogue, MPS.

DAVIS, Gary, Rev. (*b* 30 Apr. 1896, Laurens, S.C.; *d* 5 May '72, Hammonton, N.J.) Singer; guitar, banjo, harmonica, piano. Partly blind as an infant, totally blind by age 26. Taught himself music from age 6; worked as street singer, in string band, sang in church, often worked outside music. Baptist minister '33; toured as singing gospel preacher but also played ragtime, sang blues. First records for ARC group '35; later on Stinson, Riverside, Folkways, Bluesville (Prestige), others; made short films '64, '67, '72; TV documentaries '67, '70, film *Black Roots* '70; many festivals incl. Newport '68 on Vanguard label. Also wrote songs. Published collection of spirituals *The Holy Blues* '70; *Rev. Gary Davis/Blues Guitar* by Stefan Grossman '74. Infl. white generation of the '60s incl. Ry COODER, DONOVAN, Bob DYLAN. Compilation *1935-49* on Yazoo; *Children Of Zion* and *Ragtime Guitar* on Kicking Mule; 2-disc *When I Die* on Fantasy; others on Biograph, Prestige, Folkways, Adelphi.

DAVIS, Jimmie (*b* 11 Sep. '02, Beech Springs, LA.) Country and gospel singer, songwriter. Graduated Louisiana State U., professor of history at Dodd College, Shreveport; in vocal group The Tiger Four, appeared on Louisiana Hayride, worked days in Shreveport Courthouse. With Victor records '29, sang in blues style like Jimmie RODGERS, often sexual overtones: 'Pistol Packin' Papa', 'Organ Grinder's Blues', 'Pussy Blues'. To new Decca label '34, recorded many own comps. incl. classics 'Nobody's Darling But Mine' '35, 'It Makes No Difference Now' '38, 'You Are My Sunshine' '39; also made B movies such as *Strictly In The Groove* '42, *Frontier Fury* '43, *Louisiana* '47. Elected Governor of Louisiana '44-8, again '60-4, in between returning to show business, this time turning to gospel; named Best Musical Sacred Singer '57. Only success on modern country charts was 'Where The Old Red River Flows' '62; LPs incl. *Songs Of Consolation* '70 on Decca, *Greatest Hits* '75 on MCA, *Country Hits* '78 on Plantation, *Let Me Be There* '75 and *Soul Train To Glory* '79 on Canaan. Elected to Country Music Hall of Fame '72. Married to Anne Carter; *see* CHUCK WAGON GANG.

DAVIS, Mac (*b* 21 Jan. '42, Lubbock, Texas) One of the top country/pop singer/ songwriters of '70s. Moved to Atlanta '57, attended Emory U., worked as ditch digger, pump jockey, probation officer etc, wrote songs, played in a band evenings. Regional manager for Vee Jay records at the time they had the Beatles; made records for Vee Jay, Capitol. Wrote 'You're Good For Me' (Lou RAWLS, '67), then Elvis PRESLEY's 'In The Ghetto', 'Memories', 'Don't Cry Daddy'. Signed with Columbia '69, then made breakthrough as singer: 'Baby Don't Get Hooked On Me' '72 (no. 1 pop chart). Wrote 'Something's Burning' (Kenny ROGERS), 'I Believe In Music' (STATLER BROTHERS), 'Lonesomest Lonesome' (Ray PRICE), 'Everything A Man Could Ever Need' (Glen CAMPBELL), etc. Own further pop and country hits: 'Dream Me Home' '73, 'Stop And Smell The Roses', 'One Hell Of A Woman' '74, 'Rock'n'Roll, I Gave You The Best Years Of My Life' '75, 'Forever Lovers' '76. Became top TV and cabaret performer; slipped in record sales but came back on Casablanca label with 'It's Hard To Be Humble' '80, 'Texas In My Rear View Mirror' '81. LPs incl. *Baby Don't Get Hooked On Me* '72, *Mac Davis* '73, *Burnin' Thing* '75, *Forever Lovers* '76, *Thunder In The Afternoon* '77, all CBS; *Midnight Crazy* '81, *Soft Talk* '84 on Casablanca. Named Entertainer of the Year by ACM '75. Starred in film *North Texas Forty* '79.

DAVIS, Miles (*b* Miles Dewey Davis Jr, 25 May '26, Alton, Ill.) Trumpet, composer, leader; one of the most influential and popular jazz musicians of all time, also one of the most controversial, unusually willing to change direction and blaze new trails: yet it is the setting that changes, rather than the unique beauty of his own playing. Family moved to East St Louis when he was an infant; father was a dentist, gave him a trumpet for his 13th birthday. He was something of a prodigy, playing in local bands early '40s; he met and was infl. by Clark TERRY, then Charlie PARKER and Dizzy GILLESPIE as they passed through (the last two in Billy ECKSTINE band). Went to NYC to study at Juilliard '45 but soon worked on 52nd Street with Parker, Coleman HAWKINS, others; he never had the ability to play lightning-fast runs boppers liked, but his understatement on some of Parker's greatest records provided an alternative: he developed a lyrical style of great tonal beauty that did not depend on speed. Played in Eckstine and Benny CARTER bands, won *Esquire* magazine critics' poll as new star '47; recorded with Parker on Savoy and Dial, with Hawkins and Illinois JACQUET big band on Aladdin; with Tadd DAMERON (broadcasts); first session under his own name was Miles Davis All Stars on Savoy '47 (quintet with Parker; incl. 'Milestones'). In '48 his nine-piece group broadcast from the Royal Roost; at suggestion of arranger Pete Rugolo, Capitol recorded its library: 12 tracks on three dates '49-50, arr. by Gil EVANS, John LEWIS, Johnny Carisi and Gerry MULLIGAN, with Gunther SCHULLER, Sandy Siegelstein and Junior Collins playing French horn on various dates, John 'Bill' Barber on tuba, Lee KONITZ, J. J. JOHNSON (Mike Zwerin played trombone at the Royal Roost, still kicks himself for going back to college instead of on to the studio), Max ROACH or Kenny CLARKE on drums, others: modern jazz moved beyond bop, and the composer/arranger came to the foreground; when the sessions were issued almost complete '57 the LP was dubbed *Birth Of The Cool*, but the combo was commercial flop at the time. Made many other records on Blue Note, Prestige; his personal masterpieces 'Blue'n'Boogie' and 'Walkin' ' made '54 on Prestige with Clarke, Johnson, Lucky THOMPSON, Horace SILVER, Percy HEATH: Thompson had brought music to the date but it didn't work and the tunes were Miles's 'heads'. Early '54 he kicked heroin addiction which was destroying him; recorded Xmas Eve with Thelonious MONK and MODERN JAZZ QUARTET rhythm section; *The Musings Of Miles* June '55 quartet with Philly Joe JONES, Red GARLAND, Oscar PETTIFORD; recorded in July with quintet incl. Charles MINGUS, in Aug. with sextet incl. Jackie MCLEAN; *Miles* in Nov. had Garland, Jones, Paul CHAMBERS and John COLTRANE (*Musing* and *Miles* issued in 2-disc set *Green Haze*): the Miles Davis Quintet was born, made *Workin'*, *Steamin'*, *Cookin'*, *Relaxin'* '56, among the most enduring and influential classics of the decade, incl. Davis originals 'Tune Up', 'Blues By Five', gorgeous interpretations of standards 'If I Were A Bell', 'In Your Own Sweet Way', 'I Could Write A Book'; plus Carter's 'When Lights Are Low', Sonny ROLLINS's 'Oleo', Monk's 'Well, You Needn't'; more. He often used the distinctive timbre of the Harmon cup mute; his intimate lyricism was unsurpassed in feeling, alternately unrestrained and full of foreboding; he was criticised for playing so many standards, and because Coltrane played so much and Jones played so 'loud'; Prestige label-boss Bob Weinstock described the group as the Louis ARMSTRONG Hot Five of the modern era. Miles had left bosom of a middle-class family, experienced the hell of narcotics addiction; now he was not only an exceptional soloist but a fine composer and confident leader, his personal strength asserting itself: Gil Evans was among the first to point out that Miles is not afraid of what he likes. His style was ideal for the classic show tunes; he was the Bach of jazz summing it all up, but unlike Bach never became 'old-fashioned', continued to develop. His appearance at the Newport Jazz Festival '55 (after relative obscurity caused by the drugs) with an all-star group incl. Monk was a hit; he played with an all-star group in Paris '56, signed with Columbia Records (CBS), a relationship that lasted 30 years, with Teo MACERO prod. most of his albums (Prestige could not give him the money or the promotion that he deserved, and even allowed him to record for Columbia before his required four LPs for Prestige were delivered, as long as the Columbia work was not issued until later). Quintet LP *Round Midnight* '56 was made for Columbia, followed by the first of a series of collaborations with Gil Evans, who now emerged as a leading composer/arranger: *Miles Ahead* '57 was also the first time his horn was heard in what was obviously a setting for it, a propensity that would increase markedly in later years; he played flugelhorn on *Miles Ahead*, its mellow glow fitting Evans's music perfectly: soon lots of people took up flugelhorn, but Davis never again used it on an entire LP. Also in '57, while on the West Coast, Garland, Chambers and Jones made *Art Pepper Meets The Rhythm Section* for Contemporary, one of Pepper's greatest albums: the Davis quintet was so popular in jazz that everybody knew who 'the rhythm section' were. Davis was clean of drugs, but all the other members of the quintet were junkies at the time: Coltrane's habit was affecting his playing; Davis fired him, broadcast with replacement Sonny Rollins, and recorded film soundtrack *Ascenseur pour l'échafaud* in Paris with quintet incl. Kenny Clarke '57; guested on Cannonball ADDERLEY LP *Somethin' Else* on Blue Note '58. Coltrane cleaned up for good and came back for *Milestones* same year on Columbia, with Adderley on alto making a sextet. Garland was replaced by Bill EVANS, Jones by Jimmy COBB; tracks recorded by new sextet lineup were issued in Japan as *1958 Miles*, some in USA 2-disc compilation *Black Giants*. In '58 *Legrand Jazz* conducted by Michel LEGRAND incl. Davis, Chambers, Coltrane, Phil WOODS, six others; the sextet recorded at Newport; second LP with Gil Evans was *Porgy And Bess*, their versions of songs from GERSHWIN's opera. Years earlier Miles had remarked to George RUSSELL that he wanted to be able to choose from a much wider range of notes than that available in the jazz orthodoxy of the late '40s, still based on the chord changes of the best popular songs; this led to Russell's book on a modal theory of composition, and now to *Kind Of Blue* '59: sextet incl. Coltrane, Adderley, Chambers, Cobb, and Bill Evans, with Wynton KELLY instead of Evans on one track, taped five Davis originals which were not songs in the usual sense, but modal riffs, wisps on which to exercise emotional expression without the structural limitation of the classic Broadway song: thus composition itself became more fully a part of the jazz musician's pallet. Others incl. Russell had been doing this during the '50s with much less commercial success, but *Kind Of Blue* became the most widely influential LP since the '56 quintet LPs. In mid-'59 he was savagely beaten by a cop outside Birdland in NYC, charged with disorderly conduct and assault; the first charge was thrown out, the second dropped out by a judge who said 'It would be a travesty of justice to adjudge the victim of an illegal arrest guilty of the crime of assaulting the one who made the arrest.' He dropped his lawsuit against the city, not wanting to become a target for every cop looking for trouble. *Sketches Of Spain* '59-60 was Gil Evans's treatments of music by Joaquin Rodrigo, Manuel de Falla, three Evans tunes; ragged and droning ensembles as a setting for Miles's 'calling': iconoclastic beauty, jazz-tinged mood music or a striving towards a world ethnic music, it is still selling. *Someday My Prince Will Come* '61 incl. Cobb, Chambers, Kelly, Coltrane and/or Hank MOBLEY. Coltrane left finally to pursue his own path to greatness; with Mobley and Kelly the quintet recorded 2-disc *In Person At The Blackhawk* in San Francisco and *At Carnegie Hall* (with Evans orchestra on some tracks) '61; *Quiet Nights* '62-3 with Gil Evans; *Seven Steps To Heaven* incl. Ron CARTER, George COLEMAN on most tracks, Victor FELDMAN and Curtis COUNCE's drummer Frank Butler on some tracks, replaced by Herbie HANCOCK and the very young Tony WILLIAMS halfway through. Knowing he would have to replace Coltrane Davis broadcast in Sweden '60 with Sonny STITT; now Coleman was replaced by Sam RIVERS, then Wayne SHORTER, who since said that the reason he was hired was because he could play like Coltrane. Live work done in France, Berlin, Tokyo, San Francisco (the Hungry i), NYC '62-5 was issued; 2-disc *Live At The Plugged Nickel* '65 (issued '76) incl. Shorter, Hancock, Carter and Williams (who recorded '77 as *VSOP* with Freddie HUBBARD). This group played an increasingly intense style through the '60s, as witness furious version of 'So What' on *Plugged Nickel* (first recorded on the laid-back *Kind Of Blue*);

Hancock said that Davis seemed to be amalgamating all the infl. of jazz history: LPs incl. *Miles Smiles* '66, *Nefertiti* '67, *Miles In The Sky* '68; *Filles de Kilimanjaro* '68 announced an impending breakthrough in style: Carter was replaced by Dave HOLLAND on some tracks; Carter, Hancock and Chick COREA played electric instruments. *In A Silent Way* '69 added Joe ZAWINUL on organ and electric piano, John McLAUGHLIN on electric guitar, with Shorter playing soprano sax; a beautiful album, it merely puzzled some jazz fans, but 2-disc *Bitches Brew* in the same year put the fat in the fire: cast incl. Jack DeJOHNETTE replacing Williams, as well as Shorter, Zawinul, Corea, McLaughlin, Holland, and possibly Billy COBHAM, additional percussionists; its electronic jazz-rock fusion inspiring McLaughlin's Mahavishnu Orchestra, Shorter and Zawinul's WEATHER REPORT, Corea's Return To Forever, DeJohnette's Special Edition, others. Many jazz critics threw up their hands but Davis had merely announced that, as he and Duke ELLINGTON and many others had been saying for years, the word 'jazz' didn't mean anything much any more. He adopted the wahwah electronic trumpet device, eventually a portable microphone pinned to the horn, enabling him to wander about the stage as he pleased. His LPs reached Billboard's pop charts since '61; *Bitches Brew* made top 40, his biggest hit. Bennie Maupin on bass clarinet, Steve Grossman on soprano sax, AIRTO and Keith JARRETT, many others passed through as he carried on: 2-disc *Miles Davis At The Fillmore* '70 followed four nights at Bill GRAHAM's rock palaces, where audiences were puzzled at first, finally cheered; *Tribute To Jack Johnson* was film soundtrack, highly praised by critics as was 2-disc *Live-Evil*, both '71; *On The Corner* '73 followed by four 2-disc sets '74-6: *In Concert*, *Big Fun*, *Get Up With It* (a tribute to Ellington), *Agarta* '76, all charting in those years. Then he retired. He was physically tired, suffering pain from a car crash in which his legs had been crushed, tired of critics misunderstanding what he was doing and of the media concentrating on his life-style; he had been shot at by gangsters trying to extort money from him, arrested on various petty charges: he said c.'70 'It's just the whole attitude of the police force . . . It's

not so much the way black people are treated any more. It's the way they treat all the young people that think the same way, so no matter what color you are, you get the same shit. That's what the black people have been trying to say for years . . .' In '72 he attacked the record industry Grammy awards because they often went to white people who had made careers from copying black music, proposed to set up his own Mammy awards. Now he rested; compilations released '70s incl. *Basic Miles* '55-8, *Water Babies* '66-8 (previously unreleased quintet tracks on one side, tracks with electric instruments on the other); *Directions* '60-70. He came back with rock-oriented *The Man With The Horn* '81, 2-disc *We Want Miles* '82, *Star People* '83, *Decoy* '84, personnel variously incl. Bill Evans (no relation to other Evanses) and Bob Berg, saxes; Mike Stern, John SCOFIELD and Robben Ford, guitars; Adam Holtzman, keyboards; Steve Thornton, percussion; Felton Crewes, Marcus Miller and Darryl Jones, bass guitars; *You're Under Arrest* '85 used straight pop songs, Cyndi LAUPER hit 'Time After Time' issued on 12″ single. He left Columbia and went all the way with *Tutu* '86 on WEA to disco-style backing for his horn, synthesised mostly by Miller and said to be excellent stuff of its kind, but old fans don't care: it is merely dance music, sounding much the same whether it is slick or amateurish. He recorded with pop group Scritto Politti '88. He did not want to be seen as an entertainer, turning his back on the audience and disappearing offstage during performance; but of course he was always an entertainer, that category including the century's greatest musicians as well as the rest; he always sought audiences, in particular young black audiences, who never had the touchstone of the classic Broadway show-tune to relate to because they couldn't afford it, and he has yet to play a note that is not beautiful: through the loud, often pretentious rock he has fronted in recent years his hesitant sound still pierces, suggesting stealth as well as vulnerability. *Music From Siesta* '88 on WB was mostly synthesised by Miller for the film score, but is reminiscent of Gil Evans and the Miles of old; CBS issued 40 minutes more of the '61 Carnegie Hall concert, and there's still some left. Ian CARR's *Miles Davis: A Critical Biography* '82 is highly recommended; Jack Chambers' 2-vol. *Milestones* '85 is exhaustive without saying much about the music.

DAVIS, Sammy, Jr (*b* 8 Dec. '25, NYC) Singer, dancer, actor. Joined family vaudeville troupe led by adopted uncle Will Mastin, reduced to trio during Depression: Davises Sr, Jr and Mastin. Davis coached by legendary tapdancer Bill 'Bojangles' Robinson (*b* 25 May 1878, Richmond, Va.; *d* Nov. '49, NYC: called 'The Mayor of Harlem'; also coached Shirley Temple; tapping recorded on 'Doin' The New Low Down' '32 with Don REDMAN). Davis rejoined trio after US Army service '43-5; played support at Slapsie Maxie's in Hollywood '46: Davis triumphed with dancing, singing, impressions. Trio had club, theatre booking '47-50 with Bob Hope, Jack Benny, Frank SINATRA; Davis made solo tracks for Capitol '50 incl. 'The Way You Look Tonight', with impressions of the stars. Signed with Decca '54; car crash in Hollywood late that year caused loss of left eye; he turned misfortune into comedy: on subject of intolerance, he complained about being world's only 'one-eyed Jewish nigger'. Hit the big time: *Starring Sammy Davis Jr* no. 1, *Just For Lovers* no. 5, both '55; top 20 single hits '54-5 incl. 'Hey There', 'Something's Gotta Give' (from Fred ASTAIRE film *Daddy Long Legs*), 'Love Me Or Leave Me', 'That Old Black Magic'. Broadway debut '56 with trio in *Mr Wonderful*, by Jerry Bock, Larry Holofiener, George Weiss, over 400 performances incl. title song, 'Too Close For Comfort'. Played Sportin' Life in film of George GERSHWIN's *Porgy And Bess* '59 ('There's A Boat That's Leavin' Soon For New York'); also starred in German-English film of Kurt WEILL's *Threepenny Opera* '64. Member of Sinatra clan; LP *The Wham Of Sam* '60 was early release on Sinatra's Reprise label: then top 20 gold disc 'What Kind Of Fool Am I' '62 from *Stop The World I Want To Get Off* by Anthony NEWLEY, Leslie Bricusse; title track or no. 14 LP on Reprise. With Dean MARTIN, Bing CROSBY and Sinatra in spoof film *Robin And The Seven Hoods* '64; that year played boxer Joe Wellington in Charles Strouse/Lee Adams Broadway musical version of Clifford Odets' *Golden Boy* for over 500 performances; took it to London '68;

that year played hilarious hippy evangelist singing 'Rhythm Of Life' in film of Cy COLEMAN/Dorothy Fields show *Sweet Charity*. Mainly TV concerts, cabaret in '70s; first no. 1 and second gold disc with 'Candy Man' '72, another Newley/Bricusse song from *Willy Wonka And The Chocolate Factory*. Other Decca LPs incl. *At The Town Hall*, *Boy Meets Girl* with Carmen McRAE, *Here's Looking At You*, *I Gotta Right To Swing*, *That Old Black Magic*; *Best Of* on MCA/UK, 2-disc *At His Greatest* MCA/USA. Other LPs in Billboard top 200 incl. *At The Coconut Grove* '63, *As Long As She Needs Me* '63, *Salutes The Stars Of The London Palladium* '64, *The Shelter Of Your Arms* '64, all on Reprise; *Our Shining Hour* '65 on Verve with Count BASIE; *Sammy Davis Jr Now* and *Portrait Of Sammy Davis Jr*, both '72 on MGM. Other '70s LPs incl. *It's A Musical World* on MGM, *In Person* '77 on RCA, *The Song And Dance Man* on 20th Century Fox; latest incl. *Hello Detroit* on Motown, *Closest Of Friends* on compact disc from French Vogue. Had hip surgery early '85, soon danced again on Bob Hope TV special in May, but threatens to give up performing for directing and producing: 'I was brought up in the business that said there was room for everybody, for all tastes ... That's why they called it variety. There's no variety in show business anymore.' One of his own favourites is country singer Barbara MANDRELL, who shares his loathing for unprepared performers; whether Davis can stop giving everything he's got to audiences remains to be seen.

DAVIS, Skeeter (*b* Mary Frances Penick, 30 Dec. '31, Dry Ridge, Ky.) Country singer. Teamed with high school friend Betty Jack Davis (*b* 4 Mar. '32, Corbin, Ky.; *d* 2 Aug. '53) in Davis Sisters vocal duo: sang on radio incl. WWVA Jamboree (Wheeling, W. Va.), signed to Fortune label '49, RCA '50. No. 1 country hit 'I Forgot More Than You'll Ever Know' '53; then Betty Jack killed, Skeeter badly injured in car crash. Came back solo on RCA '58, joined Grand Ole Opry '59, had nearly 20 years of hits incl. 'Set Him Free' '59, '(I Can't Help You) I'm Falling Too' '60, 'My Last Date (With You)' '61, 'The End Of The World' '62 (pop hit as well), 'I'm Saving My Love' '63, 'Gonna Get Along Without You Now' '64,

'Fuel To The Flame' '67, 'What Does It Take' '67, 'I'm A Lover (Not A Fighter)' '69, 'Bus Fare To Kentucky' '71, 'I Can't Believe It's All Over' '73. Made duets with Bobby BARE ('A Dear John Letter' '65), Porter WAGONER, George HAMILTON IV. Signed with Mercury '76; no further single hits but remains popular stage act. Owns Crestmoor Music Publishing Co. LPs incl. *End Of The World* '62, *Singing In The Summer Sun* '63, *Bring It On Home* '72, *Skeeter Sings Dolly* '73, *Hillbilly Singer* '74, *I Can't Believe It's All Over* '75, *The Versatile* '76, *Tunes For Two* '76 and *More Tunes For Two* '81 (with Bare), *Sings Buddy Holly* (RCA reissue on Detour '83), *She Sings, They Play* '85 on Rounder/Sound Effects with NRBQ.

DAVIS, Spencer (*b* '39, Birmingham, England) Guitar, back-up vocals. Former teacher formed Spencer Davis Group playing R&B style in Birmingham '64; incl. Stevie WINWOOD and brother Muff Winwood on bass (Muff later became head of A&R at CBS UK, prod. DIRE STRAITS debut LP), Peter York on drums. Ten top 40 hits '64-8 incl. 'Keep On Runnin' ' '65, 'Somebody Help Me' '66, both no. 1; 'Gimme Some Loving' no. 2 '66, 'I'm A Man' no. 9 '67. LPs on Fontana incl. *Autumn* '66; Winwood's songs, keyboard, bluesy voice praised by critics: he left '67 to form TRAFFIC, replaced by Eddie Hardin. Others passing through incl. Ray Fenwick on guitars and vocals, Dee Murray on bass (later with Elton JOHN), Dave Hynes, drums. Minor hits '67-8; LPs on UA incl. *With Their New Face On* '68. Davis went to USA '70, formed acoustic duo '71, worked with blues legend Fred McDOWELL, tried reunion of SDG with York '73; worked with ROLLING STONES prod. Jimmy Miller early '80s. Other LPs: *Letters From Edith* '70 on CBS; *It's Been So Long* '71 with Peter Jameson, solo *Mousetrap* '72 on UA; *Giuggo* '73 and *Living In A Back Street* '74 on Vertigo.

DAVIS, Walter, Jr (*b* 2 Sep. '32, Richmond, Va.) Piano, composer. Played with Max ROACH, Dizzy GILLESPIE, Art BLAKEY in '50s; from '60 led own trio; also with Sonny ROLLINS, Blakey again in '70s. First records with Blakey on Debut; others with Rollins, Sonny CRISS, Archie SHEPP; own LPs incl. *Davis Cup* '59 on Blue Note with Donald

BYRD, Jackie McLEAN; *Abide With Me* '77 (solo, trio, quartet tracks), *Night Song* '78 (trio), both on Denon; *A Being Such As You* and *Uranus* (both solo), *Blues Walk* (trio), all made Nov. '79 in Italy; *400 Years Ago Tomorrow* '79 Paris (solo), *Live At Le Dreher* '81 (trio with Pierre Michelot, Kenny CLARKE) on French labels.

DAVIS, Wild Bill (*b* William Strethen Davis, 24 Nov. '18, Glasgow, Mo.) Organ, piano. Pianist, arr. with Louis JORDAN '45-8; began to play Hammond organ '49, started trend more popular in rhythm & blues than in jazz. Led trio with guitar, drums from '50s (annual summer appearance at Little Belmont in Atlantic City, N.J. for about 30 years); arr. of 'April In Paris' for Count BASIE '56 featured same muscular chordal drive as on Davis's organ playing, made no. 28 pop chart; records with Johnny HODGES in '60s; worked with Duke ELLINGTON '69-70, effective contribution on first movement of Duke's *New Orleans Suite* '70. Many earlier records with Arnett COBB, Illinois JACQUET, Buddy TATE etc. all out of print.

DAVISON, Wild Bill (*b* William Edward Davison, 5 Jan. '06, Defiance, Ohio) Cornet. Began on mandolin, guitar, banjo; became mainstay of Chicago style jazz '27-32; organised big band '31; after death of Frank TESCHEMACHER (Davison's car struck by taxi) worked in Milwaukee, Wisc. '33-41, also playing valve trombone. To Nick's in NYC '41: with spells in Boston, St Louis, regularly at Eddie CONDON's club NYC from '45, one of the best and most popular musicians in style loosely called Dixieland. Toured UK with Condon '57; moved to West Coast '60, often leading own bands. Newport Jazz Festival '78; solo tours of Europe continuing into '80s. Best records made for Commodore early '40s with Pee Wee RUSSELL, George Brunis; 'always a powerful and exciting player' (James Lincoln Collier).

DAWKINS, Jimmy 'Fast Fingers' (*b* James Henry Dawkins, 24 Oct. '36, Tchula, Ms.) Blues singer, guitarist. Self-taught in teens; to Chicago, working outside music '55-7, then in street for tips, formed own band for gigs, worked clubs, recorded as sideman;

worked with MAGIC SAM, others. Recorded for Delmark '68 and in '70s: LPs incl. *Fast Fingers, All For Business, Blisterstring.* Also acc. Luther ALLISON on that label '69; has played many blues festivals; toured Europe '70-1; won Grand Prix du Disque de Jazz of Hot Club of France '71 for *Fast Fingers.* Recorded in France that year; appeared at Ann Arbor Blues Festival with Otis RUSH '72, part of set issued on Atlantic; recorded in London '72; appeared in videotapes *Born In The Blues* '73, *Sincerely The Blues* '75, *Roots Of Country Music & Blues* '77. LP *Transatlantic 770* on Sonet UK. A modern bluesman with his own style, yet still in mainstream of tradition; very highly regarded as guitarist.

DAY, Bobby (*b* Robert Byrd, '32, Fort Worth, Texas) Singer, songwriter. Worked at Johnny OTIS's Barrelhouse Club; wrote 'Little Bitty Pretty One', but his own version beaten in charts by that of Thurston Harris '57 (*see* ALADDIN); his own six entries in Hot 100 '57-9 incl. 'Rock-In Robin' (no. 2), 'Over And Over' (no. 41). He also sang lead with the Hollywood Flames, who did beautiful ballads but had R&B hits with novelties: 'Buzz Buzz Buzz' no. 11 '57; met Earl Nelson in the Flames, formed act Bob & Earl, but Day was succeeded by Bob Relf (their biggest hit was 'Harlem Shuffle' '63). Day's songs were covered by Dave CLARK Five, JACKSON FIVE, etc.

DAY, Dennis (*b* Eugene Patrick McNulty, 21 May '17, NYC; *d* 22 May '88 of Lou Gehrig's disease) Singer. Worked in NYC radio '39, replaced Kenny Baker same year on Jack Benny show: also did comedy, stayed with Benny into TV series '50s and friends until Benny's death in '74; had own programmes. RCA hits in top 25 '47-51: biggest was 'Mam'selle', no. 8 '47; also 'Clancy Lowered The Boom' '49, 'Christmas In Killarney' '50; successful covers of hits: Bing CROSBY's 'Dear Hearts And Gentle People', Nat COLE's 'Mona Lisa', Patti PAGE's 'Mr And Mississippi', the WEAVERS' 'Goodnight, Irene' all charted higher, but Day's Irish tenor was well liked. Later records on Capitol. Films incl. *The Powers Girl* '43 with Benny GOODMAN, *I'll Get By* '50 with Harry JAMES, *Golden Girl* '51 with Mitzi Gaynor (Lotte Crabtree biopic).

DAY, Doris (*b* Doris Kappelhoff, 3 Apr. '22, Cincinnati, Ohio) USA singer, actress. Studied dancing in Hollywood; turned to singing after car crash, broken leg at age 14. On WLW in Cincinnati with Barney Rapp band; he changed her name to Day. With Bob CROSBY '40 in Chicago, late that year to Les BROWN band: sang on million-sellers 'My Dreams Are Getting Better' and 'Sentimental Journey', both no. 1 USA, last especially forever her song. Duetted with Buddy CLARK on another gold disc 'Confess'/'Love Somebody' '47. Date at Billy Reed's Little Club led to screen test '48; first film *Romance On The High Seas* '48 with Sammy CAHN/Jule Styne score gave her first big solo hit 'It's Magic'. Series of mostly backstage musicals for WB (co-stars Ronald Reagan, Gene Nelson, Jack Carson, Gordon MACRAE); co-starred with Kirk Douglas in *Young Man With A Horn* '50 (based loosely on Bix BEIDERBECKE); with comic Danny Thomas '52 in biopic of lyricist Gus Kahn. Big hits '52 with 'A Guy Is A Guy', duet with Frankie LAINE on '42 South African song 'Sugarbush'; duets with Johnnie RAY incl. 'Let's Walk Thata-way' (no. 4 UK). Big hit film *Calamity Jane* '53 in role similar to that of Betty HUTTON in *Annie Get Your Gun*: co-starred with Howard KEEL, sang exhilarating opener 'The Deadwood Stage', Oscar-winning ballad 'Secret Love' (her first no. 1, USA '54). Last WB film was *Young At Heart* '55 with Frank SINATRA (musical remake of *Four Daughters* '38, with Claude Rains/John Garfield); biopic of Ruth ETTING *Love Me Or Leave Me* '55, for MGM with Jimmy Cagney, gave her good dramatic as well as singing role, incl. chart hit 'I'll Never Stop Loving You'; soundtrack was no. 1 LP. 'Que Sera, Sera' ('Whatever Will Be, Will Be') won Oscar, from Hitchcock's *The Man Who Knew Too Much* (no. 2 hit). *The Pajama Game* '57 was probably her best musical film, big commercial hit; Billy ROSE's *Jumbo* '62, her last musical, did not do well at box office (last film Busby Berkeley worked on). In late '50s began series of light comedy films with Rock Hudson, Clark Gable, James Garner, Jack Lemmon; best-known was *Pillow Talk* '59 with Hudson (film considered sexy at the time). Minor hits with some title songs 'Tunnel Of Love' '58, 'Anyway The Wind Blows' '60 (from *Please Don't Eat The Dai-*

sies); last top 40 hit was 'Everybody Loves A Lover' '58 (no. 6). Eight 10″ LPs charted '49-55, all but 1 in top 5: *Young At Heart* with six songs by Day, two by Sinatra was no. 15. *Day By Day* '57 was no. 11. As films tapered off *The Doris Day Show* on TV '68-72; retired '70s except for occasional TV special; formed Pet Foundation in L.A.; back on TV '85 in *Doris Day's Best Friends* with executive prod. son Terry. 'Girl next door' image sent up by Oscar Levant: 'I knew her before she was a virgin.' But 39 films in 20 years made her top box office star, hid sometimes turbulent private life incl. marriages, first two to musicians, third to Marty Melcher ending in his death '68: he wasted $20m of her money on hare-brained investments, left her owing half a million (but she was loyal to him for 17 years). Apart from the usual *Greatest Hits* LPs, *Calamity Jane* and *Pajama Game* soundtracks back-to-back on CBS/UK; *Sentimental Journey* incl. lovely early stuff; also *Duet* with André Previn (trio) on Polydor '83. A. E. Hotchner's *Doris Day: Her Own Story* '75 is better than most such books; *see also* entry for Terry MELCHER.

DEAD BOYS USA Punk act formed Cleveland, Ohio '76 by Stiv (Steve) Bators, vocals; Cheetah Chrome (Gene Connor) and Jimmy Zero, guitars; Jeff Magnum, bass; Johnny Blitz, drums. Emerged from local bands to play CBGB's club NYC with more infl. bands (TALKING HEADS, TELEVISION), profiting from media spotlight and from being managed by venue owner Hilly Kristal. *Young, Loud And Snotty* '77 debut LP on Sire summed them up. CREAM prod. Felix Pappalardi recruited for *We Have Come For Your Children* '78, reinforcing suspicion that they were not far removed from incompetent heavy metal; Joey and Dee Dee Ramone added backing vocals. Band remembered best for 'Sonic Reducer' single, often anthologised. Bators recorded solo on Bomp label, which issued posthumous *Night Of The Living Dead Boys* '81, recorded live at CBGB's, but with re-recorded vocals (Bators may have been embarrassed by originals). Relocated to England, sang with the Wanderers, short-lived Punk 'supergroup' with Dave Parsons, guitar; Dave Treganna, bass; Rick Rock (Rick Goldstein), drums; LP *Only Lovers Left*

Alive '81. Joined ex-DAMNED guitarist Brian James in Lords Of The New Church with Treganna and Micky Turner (drums): peddling punk mid-'80s on Miles Copeland's IRS label with limited success.

DEAD KENNEDYS USA punk act formed San Francisco '78: USA equivalent of SEX PISTOLS undoubtedly infl. by their late '77 tour; like them adopted pseudonyms. Line-up: Jello Biafra, vocals; East Bay Ray (aka Ray Valium), guitar; Klaüs Flouride, bass; Ted, drums. Objective to shock rock mainstream, satirise West Coast lifestyle, as in first single 'California Über Alles'. Signed by Miles Copeland; milked outrage from titles like 'Too Drunk To Fuck' (no. 36 UK '81 despite airplay ban), 'Kill The Poor' (no. 49 '80). In USA name alone was enough to ensure commercial failure. Formed label Alternative Tentacles to promote similarly ostracised groups (compilation LP *Let Them Eat Jellybeans*); themselves appeared on compilations on various labels; first own LP *Fresh Fruit For Rotting Vegetables* '80 on Copeland's IRS label; *Plastic Surgery Disasters* '82 on own label. Occasionally intelligent lyrics amid musical mayhem: 'Nazi Punks Fuck Off' and 'Holiday In Cambodia' attacked both ends of political spectrum. Refusal to compromise, anachronistic punk thrash made them forerunners of USA 'hardcore' music movement of mid-'80s. Ted replaced by Bruce Slexinger, then by J. H. Pelligro. Biafra ran for mayor of San Francisco '79: platform required businessmen to wear clown suits, came fourth out of 10 in poll; also made solo EP *Witch Trial* '81 with UK keyboardist Morgan Fisher on New Rose label. LP *Frankenchrist* '85 led to lawsuit over obscenity of poster; *Bedtime For Democracy* '86 was followed by split. Flouride made *Cha Cha Cha With Mr Flouride* '86 incl. cover of 'Ghost Riders'; Kennedys compilation *Give Me Convenience Or Give Me Death* '87 saw approving press describe Biafra as a political performance artist.

DEAD OR ALIVE UK new wave band formed by gender-bender vocalist Pete Burns (*b* 5 Aug. '59); lineup '84 was Timothy Lever (*b* 21 May '61), keyboards; Michael Percy (*b* 11 Mar. '61), bass; Stephen McCoy (*b* 15 Mar. '62), drums. After first taste of fame fronting Mystery Girls (legendary gig at Eric's Club 4 Nov. '77 incl. Phil Hurst, drums; Julian Cope, bass, later of TEARDROP EXPLODES), Pete Wylie, guitar (later Wah!), Burns formed Nightmares in Wax '79: EP *Black Leather* on Inevitable label had Burns and Hurst with Mick Reid, guitar; Walter Ogden, bass: Burns said, 'We thought we'd form the worst band in history [playing] one note songs for ten minutes.' Had track on *Hicks From The Sticks* '80, compilation of provincial new wave. Changed name to Dead Or Alive '80; by then Burns had been through 30 musicians; now had Sue James, bass; Joe Musker, drums; Ming, guitar. Further flop singles on Inevitable; EP *Nowhere To Nowhere* on Rough Trade; then Burns spotted an opening in 'Hi-NRG' disco circuit, where his striking androgynous looks were an advantage: nearly signed by Virgin instead of Culture Club; considered much of same ilk. After false starts with singles laid cards on table with synthesiser/sequencer dominated cover of KC AND THE SUNSHINE BAND's 'That's The Way (I Like It)', no. 22 UK '84: chanted vocal counterpart 'Keep that body strong' in bizarre video featuring female body builders, establishing tacky image which Burns fostered in interviews. LP *Sophisticated Boom Boom* '84 recorded with German prod. Zeus B. Held, aimed squarely at dance-floor: big gay following as Burns aped Sylvester/Electro Soul sound, creating masterpieces of sheer synthetic tack. 'You Spin Me Around (Like A Record)' sleeper hit early '85, taking four months to reach no. 1; sound cloned to perfection with 'Lover Come Back To Me', 'In Too Deep', but shock value had worn off: music stood or fell by dance floor appeal. *Youthquake* entered UK LP chart at no. 9, then slipped. Burns found like Boy George that image is no substitute for consistent sound; given skill with media seemed likely to slip sideways into showbiz sphere. Auxiliary members for live shows '85 incl. Chris Payne, keyboards; Russell Bell, guitar (both ex-Gary NUMAN).

DEAN, Jimmy (*b* 10 Aug. '28, Plainview, Texas). Enormously popular country singer in '60s, also TV host, actor. With Tennessee Haymakers in USAF, then with Texan Wildcats in Washington DC area; first hit

'Bummin' Around' '53 on Four Star label. Pioneered country music on TV, hosting weekday, Saturday evening shows on WMAL (Virginia), then networked CBS show '60; signed with Columbia and had biggest hit 'Big Bad John' '61: no. 1 both country and pop, won Grammy as Best Country & Western Performance. Followed with 'Dear Ivan', 'P.T. 109' '62; 'The First Thing Ev'ry Morning (And The Last Thing Ev'ry Night)' '65. Switched to RCA for more hits 'Stand Beside Me' '66, 'A Thing Called Love' '68, 'Slowly' '71 (duet with Dottie WEST). Top line variety show on ABC-TV '63-6; appeared in series *Daniel Boone*, *Candid Camera*, etc. LPs incl. *Big Bad John* '62, *Jimmy Dean's Hour Of Prayer* '64 on Columbia; *Speaker Of The House* '67, *These Hands* '72 on RCA. Retired from music '70s as sausage business took over, but came back with LP and single *I.O.U.* on Casino '76.

DEARIE, Blossom (*b* 28 Apr. '26, East Durham, NY) Singer, pianist, songwriter. Played cocktail piano, accompanied vocal groups; worked with Woody HERMAN, Alvino REY; worked in Paris '52-6, with Annie ROSS, then formed vocal group Blue Stars (hit with 'Lullaby In Birdland' sung in French). Back in USA leading trio, has been a favourite of cabaret audiences since. LPs incl. *Blossom Dearie*, *Once Upon A Summertime* on Verve from '50s; *May I Come In* on Capitol; 2-disc *On Broadway* on DRG Archive; several on own Daffodil label: *Blossom Dearie Sings*, *Blossom Dearie 1975*, *Simply*, *Positively*, *Et Tu Bruce* '84, *Chez Wahlberg Part 1* '85.

DeBARGE USA soul family vocal group. Since JACKSONS grew up Motown had searched for suitably wholesome replacements; Jermaine Jackson discovered them. Family of 10 raised single-handed by music-loving mother in Detroit, then Grand Rapids, Mich.; she encouraged Bobby and Tommy to sing gospel on Detroit radio; they signed with Motown as members of disco group Switch. Mark DeBarge (vocals, trumpet) enlisted brothers Eldra and James (both vocals, keyboards), Randy (vocals, bass), sister Bunny in group to play around neighbourhood; chance visit to Motown led to meeting with Jackson, on-the-spot audition to personal interest of Berry Gordy. First single '78, four LPs since: *DeBarge* '81 (without James), *All This Love* '82, *In A Special Way* '83, *Rhythm Of The Night* '85, candyfloss pop-soul gaining in confidence, though still dispensable. Lead singer Eldra a Michael JACKSON figure, visually and vocally similar; James briefly married to Janet Jackson. Christian stance does not restrict choice of material, mostly from Motown writers performed with backing by Motown musicians. Crossed over to USA pop chart '83: 'I Like It' no. 31, 'All This Love' 17, 'Time Will Reveal' 18; 'Rhythm Of The Night' title track '85 kept from no. 1 only by USA for Africa charity record and MADONNA, made no. 4 UK: prod. by Richard PERRY with Jeff Lorber (synthesiser) and Paulinho Da Costa (percussion); jaunty Latin beat reminiscent of Lionel RICHIE also featured in Motown-backed film *The Last Dragon* '85. Though DeBarge, unlike Jacksons, probably lack depth of talent to write, perform, produce themselves to the top, shrewd guidance of Gordy may give them longevity which used to be associated with Motown acts. Brother Chico DeBarge signed with Motown as solo; El went solo '86.

De BURGH, Chris (*b* 15 Oct. '48, Argentina) UK singer/songwriter. While studying at Trinity College, Dublin, persuaded to tape some songs, which led to record deal; debut LP *Far Beyond These Castle Walls* '75 set style: sweeping songs of grandeur just when they were becoming quite unfashionable. *Spanish Train & Other Stories* '75 incl. 'A Spaceman Came Travelling', which became annual Christmas favourite; *At The End Of A Perfect Day* '77, *Crusader* '79 and *Eastern Wind* '80 continued to balance love songs with imaginative, epic themes, attracting critical hostility but firm cult following, especially in Europe and Canada. *Best Moves* '81 is collection of 'best loved' songs; *The Getaway* '82 incl. minor UK hit singles 'Ship To Shore' and 'Don't Pay The Ferryman' (latter also USA top 40 hit). *Man On The Line* '84 was his most assured and commercial album to date, prod. by Rupert Hine (in favour for work with Tina TURNER and Howard JONES, both of whom guested on it); incl. minor hits 'High On Emotion' and 'The Ecstasy Of Flight (I Love

The Night)', concluding with 'Transmission Ends', about destruction of planet Earth. *Very Best Of* '84 compiled hits; *Into The Light* '86 incl. 'The Lady In Red', no. 1 UK hit (Duke and Duchess of York named it a favourite).

DECCA International record label '29-80. Trademark first seen on portable gramophone made by Barnett Samuel & Son Ltd., popular with troops in WWI. Stockbroker Edward Lewis bought company '29, also failing Duophone label, formed Decca Records Ltd and dominated it for 50 years, making it second biggest record group in the world, then dragging it down. In '30s Decca had top bandleaders AMBROSE, Billy COTTON, Jack HYLTON; with purchase of British BRUNSWICK '32 had access to Bing CROSBY, Al JOLSON. Acquired Edison Bell Winner '33, Crystalate Co. (Imperial, Rex, Vocalion) '37; by '39 Decca was only record company in UK outside giant EMI combine. Decca offered Columbia USA for under $20,000 in '34, but ARC bought it first; determined to break into USA market, Lewis established American Decca same year under Jack Kapp, previously of Brunswick, who brought with him Crosby, the MILLS BROTHERS, Guy LOMBARDO, Louis ARMSTRONG. Kapp understood appeal of cheap records during Depression, sold top records for 35 cents, less than half then standard price; Decca soon became second biggest label in USA. In '42 Crosby recorded 'White Christmas', bestselling record of all time. Decca's WWII research into radar paid for by selling off American shares; by '45 financial ties cut: independent US Decca lasted just over 10 years as independent until taken over (for post-'45 US Decca see MCA). Lewis retained UK rights to US Decca recordings until '74, but dissatisfied with its handling of his UK product in USA he formed London Records '47 as his outlet in USA and Canada. Plenty of hits on UK Decca from MANTOVANI, David WHITFIELD, Dickie VALENTINE; on London label in USA Gracie FIELDS had no. 4 hit '48 ('Now Is The Hour'); early attempts to build American roster resulted in no. 1 hit for Teresa BREWER on London in USA ('Music, Music, Music' '50); Vera LYNN was first UK artist to reach no. 1 in USA ('Auf Wiederseh'n' '52), Mantovani's *Music Of* *ictor Herbert* '53 was first UK LP to be no. in USA; Whitfield's 'Cara Mia' was top 10 4 USA; Lonnie DONEGAN had then-rare K million seller with 'Rock Island Line' 6, also big USA hit; Tommy STEELE was K's most popular rock'n'roll singer until liff RICHARD; Billy FURY also had many K hits; 'Telstar' by the TORNADOS '62 was ird UK record to be no. 1 in USA. Decca came international: branches in Europe, her territories, but never matched EMI's obal reach. Built strong classical catague: first to issue long-playing records in K '50; wartime research paid off in justly mous technical quality ('ffrr' meant 'full equency range recording'); records by wiss conductor Ernest Ansermet still reowned 30 years later; part of success of antovani, Frank CHACKSFIELD ('Ebb ide'), Stanley BLACK etc. due to excellent und. Label made history '62 by turning own BEATLES in favour of Brian POOLE nd the Tremeloes; even so '60s was golden ecade: London USA was Decca's agent in asing best USA indie product: records om Dot, Sun, Liberty, Specialty, tlantic/Atco, others issued on London in K: was premier UK label for rock'n'roll, ith Pat BOONE, LITTLE RICHARD, EVERLY ROS, Bobby DARIN, Ricky NELSON, uane EDDY, the DRIFTERS, Eddie OCHRAN, Del SHANNON, Roy ORBISON; e CRYSTALS, the RONETTES, later Ike & ina TURNER from Phil SPECTOR's Philles bel, etc. ROLLING STONES, Tom JONES, ngelbert HUMPERDINCK sold around the orld; on classical side, Georg Solti made rst complete recording of Wagner's *Der ing des Nibelungen* on 19 LPs (prod. obert Culshaw understood potential of steo, wrote book *Ring Resounding* about projct). But following decade was a disaster: tones left Decca '70; others faded; London ded in UK as USA labels demanded own gos (pioneered by Pye in UK); RCA left ecca after 14 years to set up own UK ffice '71. During '70s worldwide receson, the MOODY BLUES (on new Threshold bel) were Decca's only international rock ct. Ailing Sir Edward Lewis hired Ken ast from EMI as Managing Director '74, e left '75: Lewis denied him power to do is job. POLYGRAM took over remains of ecca, London within days of Lewis's eath in Jan. '80: new pop material on Lon

don label worldwide for simplicity, as Polygram do not own Decca trademark in USA.

DEE, DOZY, BEAKY, MICK and TICH UK beat group '60s, originally Dave Dee and the Bostons. Lineup: Dave Dee (*b* '43, ex-policeman David Harmon), vocals; John 'Beaky' Dymond (rhythm guitar), Ian 'Tich' Amey (lead guitar), Trevor 'Dozy' Davies (bass), Mick Wilson (drums) (all *b* '44). To London from native Salisbury, Wiltshire to sign with managers/writers HOWARD & BLAIKLEY, who'd created the no. 1 hit 'Have I The Right' for the HONEYCOMBS '64. Concentrated exclusively on renamed DDDBM&T; scored second time out with 'You Make It Move' (no. 26 late '65), then with 'Hold Tight' (no. 4 '66), dance number adapted from the Routers' '62 instrumental hit 'Let's Go'. Catchy music, Carnaby Street chic gave group both radio and teen appeal; hits continued '66-8: 'Hideaway' uncharacteristically subdued/melodic no. 10, bouzouki-led 'Bend It' caused dancing on tables late '66 at no. 2, 'Save Me' no. 4, 'Touch Me Touch Me' no. 13, 'Okay!' no. 4, 'Zabadak!' no. 3, 'Legend Of Xanadu' no. 1, 'Last Night In Soho' no. 8, 'Wreck Of The Antoinette' no. 14. Last three story songs; though dramatic, new tack coincided with fall-off in popularity: in '69 had only two top 30 entries; Dee left to go solo (only hit 'My Woman's Man' at no. 42 '70), rest of group made 'Mr President' as DBM&T (no. 33 '70) before folding. After brief stab at acting Dee went into A&R with WEA, forming Double D label, then joining Magnet records as promotion boss. One-off reunions through '70s culminated in German tour '82: lack of success in USA almost total, but nonsense pop transcended language barrier in Europe.

DEE, Joey, and the Starliters House band at Peppermint Lounge NYC: Joey Dee, vocals (*b* Joseph Dinicola, 11 June '40, Passaic, N.J.); Carlton Latimore, keyboards; Willie Davis, drums; Larry Vernieri and David Brigati, vocalists, dancers. As Chubby CHECKER's 'The Twist' left top of chart late '61 Dee's 'Peppermint Twist' replaced it: socialites swarmed to Peppermint to do the dance that anybody could do. Only other top 10 was 'Shout – Part 1'; hit LP *Doin'*

The Twist At The Peppermint Lounge incl. both. nine top 100 singles '61-3 incl. 'Hot Pastrami With Mashed Potatoes', two dance fads for the price of one. Dee made two films *Hey Let's Twist, Vive Le Twist*. Band became nursery for fledglings: three of four original (Young) RASCALS were members (Eddie Brigati was David's brother); RONETTES were Dee's dancers/vocalists until rescued by Phil SPECTOR; in '66 Jimi HENDRIX was there.

DEE, Kiki (*b* Pauline Matthews, 6 Mar. '47, Bradford) UK pop singer. Sang with dance bands, changed name, cut '64 single 'Early Night' prod. by Mitch Murray; *I'm Kiki Dee* '68 debut LP on Fontana, but made headlines as first British girl to sign with Tamla/Motown. *Great Expectations* '70 proved hard title to live up to; she lacked distinctiveness of a Dusty SPRINGFIELD, though there was power in reserve. Signed by admirer Elton JOHN to his Rocket label '73 for *Loving And Free*; cover of Veronique Sanson's 'Amoureuse' made no. 13. Formed Kiki Dee Band with Roger Pope, drums; Phil Curtis, bass; Bias Boshell, keyboards; Jo Partridge, guitar; put muscle in music: title track of *I've Got The Music In Me* was Maggie BELL-style belter, no. 19 UK/12 USA '74. Live work followed but band broke up '75, ironically when Pope joined John's backing group. Reverted to type on Rocket records through '70s; greatest success in duet with John: 'Don't Go Breaking My Heart' was no. 1 both USA/UK '76, revived for Live Aid '85. Top 30 hits '75-7: '(You Don't Know) How Glad I Am', 'Amoureuse' (reissue with 'Loving And Free'), 'Chicago', 'First Thing In The Morning'. Left Rocket after two more albums; back in spotlight with no. 31 'Star' on Ariola label (LP *Perfect Timing* reissued '86 on Music For Pleasure). Did London show *Pump Boys And Dinettes* '84-5. Sessioned with Yvonne ELLIMAN, Elton John; singles prod. by EURYTHMICS' Dave Stewart: 'Another Day Comes (Another Day Goes)' '86, 'I Fall In Love Too Easily' '87. Promise of powerful voice not quite fulfilled by chart action.

DEEP PURPLE UK heavy metal pioneers. Originally formed '68 to showcase former SEARCHERS drummer Chris Curtis as vocalist. Backed by wealthy industrialist, first stable lineup (originally named Roundabout) was Ritchie BLACKMORE, guitar; Jon Lord (*b* 9 June '41, Leics.), keyboards; Ian Paice (*b* 29 June '48), drums; Rod Evans (*b* '45), vocals; Nick Simper (*b* '46), bass. Paice and Evans ex-Maze; Lord ex-Artwoods, Simper and Lord ex-Flowerpot Men. Lord said, 'We were going to be the English Vanilla Fudge.' First three LPs *Shades Of Deep Purple* '68, *The Book Of Taliesyn* and *Deep Purple* '69 sold well in USA, but Tetragrammaton record company went broke preventing group from capitalising on '68 USA hits: cover of Joe South's 'Hush' (no 4), Neil DIAMOND's 'Kentucky Woman' (38). LPs too reliant on obvious covers such as 'Hey Joe', 'We Can Work It Out', 'Help' etc. Restructuring brought greater identity with arrival of Ian Gillan (*b* 19 Aug. '45, Hounslow) on vocals and Roger Glover (*b* 30 Nov. '45) on bass, both ex-Episode Six Band moved from pop to heavier rock; after Lord-inspired *Concerto For Group And Orchestra* '70, recorded live at Royal Albert Hall with RPO, came arguably most infl UK hardrock album ever, *Deep Purple In Rock* '70: established formula of Gillan' wailing, high-register vocals, extended instrumental breaks, solid guitar riffs from Blackmore, wild organ from Lord; no. 4 in UK LP chart, incl. no. 2 single 'Black Night'. *Fireball* '71, *Machine Head* '72 no. 1 LPs UK but personnel problems (which lent tension to the music) exacerbated by heavy touring/recording schedule: *Made In Japan* '72 was live 2-disc set of band a performing peak, but after *Who Do We Think We Are* '73 Gillan and Glover left. By that time LPs were top 20 in USA too spawned single hits at home: 'Strange Kind Of Woman', 'Fireball' both '71. 'Smoke On The Water' from *Machine Head* became heavy metal anthem, made no. 4 USA and brought LP back to charts to sell 4 million Addition of unknown David Coverdale (*b* 22 Sept. '51, Saltburn) on vocals, Glenn Hughes (*b* Penkridge, ex-Trapeze) had little effect at first on popularity: *Burn* made top 10 USA/UK, *Stormbringer* top 10 UK, top 20 USA (both '74). But Blackmore left protesting at 'funky' new musical direction away from heavy metal: beginning of the end. American Tommy Bolin (ex-JAMES GANG) replaced Blackmore for R&B infl

Come Taste The Band, which just made top 20 UK, only 43 USA. Record company already bringing out compilations; band split July '76. Gillan bought studio with earnings from sessioning on *Jesus Christ Superstar* '72, started own group; Glover joined Blackmore's Rainbow; Paice and Lord formed short-lived Paice Ashton Lord; Coverdale formed Whitesnake, recruited Lord and Paice '78, became most successful Purple spinoff. Stories about Purple reforming rife in '70s; group agreed to sue Rod Evans for touring with group he called Deep Purple '80 but did not get together until late '83. *Perfect Strangers* '84, with Lord, Paice, Blackmore, Glover, Gillan, entered UK charts at no. 5 alongside IRON MAIDEN, scores of other young UK groups who had listened to Purple when spotty little kids. Big infl. on heavy metal worldwide; reunion risked shattering myth. *The House Of Blue Light* followed '87.

DEF LEPPARD UK heavy rock group formed Sheffield, England '77 by vocalist Joe Elliott (*b* 1 Aug. '60), Rick Savage, bass; Pete Willis, guitar. Originally called Atomic Mass, flew in face of punk movement, playing working men's clubs with covers of Bob SEGER, THIN LIZZY; added 15-year-old drummer Rick Allen, second guitar Steve Clark (who wrote original compositions); new name Elliott's idea, but others altered spelling. Self-financed EP *Getcha Rocks Off* on Bludgeon Riffola label brought contracts with AC/DC management and Phonogram label. Leaders with Samson, Angelwitch, IRON MAIDEN etc. in so-called New Wave of British Heavy Metal (term coined by *Sounds* mag) brought HM back to UK music scene as supergroups JUDAS PRIEST, LED ZEP, DEEP PURPLE etc. quit or went into tax exile; but when debut LP *On Through The Night* '80 made no. 51 in USA they decided to concentrate on that market, rapidly made headline status. UK fans reacted: *High'n'Dry* charted well short of first LP's UK no. 15 in spite of better prod. from AC/DC overseer Robert John 'Mutt' Lange; but improved dynamics, melodic muscle took it to top 40 USA, where video channel MTV constantly played the promo videos, keeping band in public eye during year-long wait for Lange to finish prior commitments, prod. third LP: founder member

Willis left during sessions for *Pyromania* '83, replaced by ex-Girl Phil Collen; made in 10 studios, LP incl. 3 USA hit singles (Marilyn Monroe-inspired 'Photograph' no. 12, 'Rock Of Ages' 16, 'Foolin' ' 28), which kept LP in top 5 most of the year: reached no. 18 UK and slipped. *High'n'Dry* sold 2 million, *Pyromania* 7 in USA alone. New Year's Eve '84 Allen lost use of arm in car crash in Sheffield; though parts for fourth album finished, release was delayed as his kit was adapted to enable him to accompany band onstage; others pledged to keep him in group. Delay prolonged by difficulties with new prod. Jim Steinman (*see* MEATLOAF), replaced by Nigel Green; to complicate matters unauthorised *First Strike* LP of demos from '79 on Flash label caused legal wrangles. Sense of rock tradition (cover of CREEDENCE's 'Travellin' Band' closes show) indicates staying power, along with stage act: Elliott's removal of Union Jack T-shirt to reveal Stars and Stripes shows he knows which side of bread is buttered. *Hysteria* '87 was finally prod. by Lange, with Green and others helping; the inner sleeve credits everybody down to the makers of Elliott's golf clubs. Book about the band *Animal Instinct* '87 by David Fricke.

DeFRANCO, Buddy (*b* Boniface Ferdinand Leonardo DeFranco, 17 Feb. '23, Camden, N.J.) Clarinet. Began studying at 12; with Gene KRUPA, Charlie BARNET, Tommy DORSEY, Boyd RAEBURN, Dorsey again '40s; Count BASIE septet '50; own big band, then quartet early '50s; settled in Cal. '55. Reluctant to tour, while clarinet had become unfashionable in any case: top 'modern jazz' musician won all the polls in '50s, has never had fame he deserved except among other musicians and diehard fans. Recorded with Art TATUM, Oscar PETERSON early '50s; played Nelson RIDDLE's *Cross-Country Suite* with composer at Hollywood Bowl and on Dot recording '59. Own first records on Capitol '49, MGM '51-3, GNP and Norgran '53-5; then many albums on Verve with big and small groups, top jazz co-stars from Norman GRANZ stable '57-9; big band on Advance Guard label '59 recorded in Albequerque, N.M.; four small-group LPs on Mercury '61-4; about 25 LPs by '64 incl. *Blues Bag* session on Vee Jay that year now on Affinity UK, with Lee

MORGAN, Curtis FULLER, Victor FELDMAN, Art BLAKEY, Victor Sproles on bass (*b* 18 Nov. '27, Chicago; has recorded with Ira SULLIVAN on Delmark, SUN RA on Saturn, many others), Freddy Hill on trumpet (*b* 18 Apr. '32, Jacksonville, Fla.; in same college band as Nat and Cannonball ADDERLEY). Then with big band at Glen Island Casino on RCA '67, quintet/quartet LPs on various small labels: *Free Sail* '74, *Boronquin* '75, *Like Someone In Love* and *Waterbed* '77; *Love Affair With A Clarinet* '77 is duets with guitarist Jim Gillis in set of 10 etudes; *Jazz Party/First Time Together* with Terry GIBBS quintet on Palo Alto '81. *The Liveliest* on Hep UK recorded with local musicians in Argentina '80; *Groovin'* on Hep is quintet that toured UK '85. Superb 5-disc box on Mosaic USA of '54-5 quartet with Sonny CLARK.

DeJOHNETTE, Jack (*b* 9 Aug. '42, Chicago, Ill.) Drummer; also piano, composer, sometime vocalist. Studied classical piano for 10 years, played drums in high school inspired by Max ROACH, studied at American Conservatory of Music; played R&B to free jazz, practising hours every day on both piano and drums. Went to NYC '66, gigged widely, with Charles LLOYD '66-9, making him famous; played on Miles DAVIS's *Bitches Brew* '69, joined Davis '70-1, incl. LP *Live-Evil*, demonstrating eclectic power: in '70s he became one of the most highly regarded drummers in the world. Led group Compost after leaving Davis (LP *Take Off Your Body* '72 on Columbia); recorded for ECM as leader since '76, from '79 with varying personnel as Jack DeJohnette's Special Edition. Records with Lloyd, Bill EVANS, Freddie HUBBARD, many others; own LPs: *The Jack DeJohnette Complex* '68 on Milestone, *Have You Heard?* '70 on Epic (made in Japan), *Sorcery* '74 on Prestige, all with Bennie Maupin on tenor sax, bass clarinet; *Cosmic Chicken* on Prestige '75, on ECM *Untitled* '76, *Pictures* '76, *New Rags* '77, *New Directions* '78, all with guitarist John Abercrombie; *Special Edition* '79 with David MURRAY, Arthur BLYTHE, Peter Warren on cello and bass; *New Directions In Europe* with Abercrombie, Lester BOWIE, Eddie Gomez; *Special Edition: Tin Can Alley* '80 and *Inflation Blues* '82 with Chico FREEMAN; *Album Album* on ECM, *The*

Piano Album '85 on Landmark, with Gomez, Fred Waits; *Irresistible Force* '87 on MCA/Impulse with Lonnie PLAXICO on electric and acoustic bass, Nana Vasconcelos on vocals and percussion, three others. Many LPs as sideman incl. Freeman's *Destiny's Dance*, *Song X* by Ornette COLEMAN, Pat METHENY.

DEKKER, Desmond Jamaican singer who had a string of successes for Leslie Kong's Beverlys label '69-70, and total of six UK chart hits '67-75. Debut was 'Honour Your Mother And Father' '63; formed own group the Aces and made more titles, scoring decisively with '007 (Shanty Town)' '67, picked up by the UK soul crowd for a no. 14 hit. He followed this with a series of similar songs incl. 'Rudie Got Soul', 'Rude Boy Train', 'Sabotage'; then 'Israelites' '69 hit no. 1 UK. Follow-ups 'It Mek' '69, 'Pickney Girl' and 'You Can Get It If You Really Want' '70 were also UK hits; the latter was written by Jimmy Cliff, reached no. 2; LP of that title was also released. Kong's death '70 ended the string of hits except for 'Sing A Little Song' '75 (top 20; 'Israelites' re-entered top 10 same year), though he continued to perform and record at intervals. During the 2-Tone phase he made albums *Black And Dekker* and *Compass Point* for Stiff, but most of the albums issued late '70s-'80s were retrospectives from the Beverlys catalogue: *This Is*, *Sweet 16 Hits*, *Double Dekker*, *Israelites*, most recently *The Original Reggae Hitsound* compilation '86.

DELANEY, Eric (*b* 22 May '24, London) Percussionist, bandleader. Studied drums privately '34, tympani at Guildhall School of Music '46-7; also recording and studio work. Played with GERALDO, developing 'Siamese twin drum kit' and revolving rostrum; formed own band '54 around tymps-at-the-front gimmick. Well-known record 'Oranges And Lemons' '57. Made many broadcasts incl. BBC Festival of Dance Music mid-'50s; Royal Variety Performance at London Palladium and USA tour '56; recorded with George MARTIN early '60s; leads small combo '80s.

DELMARK USA record label established '53 in St Louis by Bob Koester. Originally Delmar, named after Delmar Blvd which took in ethnic neighbourhoods, local jazz scene. Name changed for legal reasons; moved to Chicago '58, took over Seymour's Record Mart '59 (Jazz Record Mart now at 11 West Grand). Began with trad. jazz; still offers three vols. of George LEWIS, Earl HINES *At Home* LP, Art HODES, etc. but soon became best known for Chicago blues in 'Roots of Jazz' series: dozens of fine LPs by Junior WELLS, Jimmy DAWKINS, MAGIC SAM, Otis RUSH, Sleepy John ESTES, Roosevelt SYKES, Luther ALLISON, J. B. HUTTO, more. Modern jazz and R&B incl. Tab SMITH, Jimmy FORREST, Sonny STITT and first LPs by AACM artists: *Sound* by Roscoe MITCHELL '66 got five stars in *Downbeat*, was followed by albums by Joseph JARMAN, Anthony BRAXTON, Richard ABRAMS, others; SUN RA's first recordings '56 reissued on Delmark mid-'60s. Plans to reissue deleted LP by Bud POWELL, *Otis Rush In Japan*, *Magic Sam Live*, etc. Subsidiary label Pearl purchased mid-'70s, used for trad. jazz, blues reissues (no connection with UK classical label). One of the best small catalogues.

DELMORE BROTHERS Alton (*b* 25 Dec. '08, Elkmont, Ala.; *d* 8 June '64, Huntsville) and Rabon Delmore (*b* 3 Dec. '16, Elkmont; *d* 4 Jun. '52, Athens, Ala.) Country blues and boogie duo popular '30s-40s. Local fiddle champions in their teens, signed with Columbia '31, joined Grand Ole Opry '32, on various radio stations throughout South. Alton prolific songwriter with more than 1000 to his credit incl. 'Blues Stay Away From Me', 'Beautiful Brown Eyes', 'Freight Train Boogie', 'Brown's Ferry Blues', etc. Recorded for Victor, Bluebird, Decca, but biggest success on King '40-51. Moved to Houston, Texas, late '40s, but Rabon returned home '51, died of lung cancer. Alton moved to Huntsville, retired from music, worked on radio, teaching guitar, as door-to-door salesman; son Lionel successful songwriter in Nashville (hits by John ANDERSON). Delmores were infl. on J.&D. BURNETTE, Elvis PRESLEY, EVERLY BROS etc. Also worked with Arthur SMITH, Uncle Dave MACON, Brown's Ferry Four (gospel quartet at various times incl. Merle TRAVIS, Red FOLEY, Grandpa JONES). LPs incl. *16 All-Time Favorites* '63 on King, *The Delmore Brothers* '71 on County.

DENE, Terry (*b* Terence Williams, Dec. '38, London) Rock'n'roll singer inspired by Elvis PRESLEY; name 'Dene' from actor James Dean. Noticed singing between wrestling bouts by Jack Good, signed with Decca UK, appeared on *6.5 Special*, had first hit, all '57: cover of Marty ROBBINS's 'White Sport Coat' made UK top 20, as did 'Start Lovin' ' and 'Stairway of Love'. Army service '58, then marriage and psychiatric problems. Religious conversion early '60s followed by 20 years of active Evangelism. Book *I Thought Terry Dene Was Dead* '74 by Dan Wooding followed by album of same name. Recorded for gospel labels: *If That Isn't Love, Call To The Winds* (late '70s, Pilgrim); *Save The Last Dance For Me* ('82, Silvertown). Played UK pubs and clubs in rock'n'roll revival early '80s.

DENNY, Jim (*b* 28 Feb. '11, Buffalo Valley, Tenn.; *d* 27 Aug. '63) Vital behind-the-scenes person in country music. Moved to Nashville to live with an aunt '22, worked as messenger for National Life & Accident Insurance Co. which owned WSM Radio and Grand Ole Opry. Worked his way up to become booker for Opry Artists Bureau '51, with Jack Stapp took control of Opry from George D. Hay, turned it into star-studded show encouraging record companies to open Nashville studios. Formed Cedarwood Publishing with Webb PIERCE '54, Jim Denny Artists Bureau with Lucky Moeller. Having overcome own bitterness at poverty-stricken background, Denny tried to look after Hank WILLIAMS: 'I never knew anybody I liked better than Hank, but I don't think I ever really got close to him'; finally had to acquiesce in Hank's firing from Opry. Elected to Country Music Hall of Fame '66. Son William (*b* 25 Aug. '35) was Columbia studio manager '56, took over as president of Cedarwood '63, named Country Music Publisher of the Year '64, subsequently served with CMA. Younger son John E. (*b* 30 Dec. '40) president of JED Records '63-8, vice-president of Cedarwood.

DENNY, Martin (*b* 10 Apr. '21, NYC) Piano, composer. Toured with jazz band before WWII; settled in Hawaii late '50s; formed group with Julius Wechter, vibes and marimba (later started Baja Marimba Band), August Colon (bongos etc.), Harvey

Ragsdale (bass, marimbula): devised 'exotic' style with birdcalls, special effects, turning restaurants into tame jungles. Pleasant, tasteful stuff sold records on Liberty: *Exotica* '59 was no. 1 LP; version of Les BAXTER tune 'Quiet Village' no. 2 single same year. Other albums incl. *Martinique, The Enchanted Sea* '59, *A Taste Of Honey* '62. Arranger Arthur Lyman had same style on Hi-Fi label: LP *Taboo* no. 6 '58; single 'Yellow Bird' no. 4 '61; other LPs *Yellow Bird* '61, *I Wish You Love* '63. Success of genre helped by excellent recorded sound, widening availability of good record-playing equipment at the time.

DENNY, Sandy (*b* Alexandra Elene MacLean Denny, 6 Jan. '41, London; *d* there 21 Apr. '78) UK folk-rock singer, songwriter. Trained as nurse; attended same art college as Jimmy Page, Eric CLAPTON; sang to her own guitar accompaniment in London folkclubs mid-'60s. (*The Original Sandy Denny* recorded '67, released '78 has Tom PAXTON, trad. English songs.) Joined STRAWBS '67; LP *The Strawbs, Featuring Sandy Denny* incl. first version of her best-known song 'Who Knows Where The Time Goes', later covered by Judy COLLINS. Joined FAIRPORT CONVENTION '68; Simon Nicol said that at audition 'she stood out like a clean glass in a sinkful of dirty dishes.' Seminal LPs set scene for UK genre: *What We Did On Our Holidays* '68, *Unhalfbricking* '69 (sleeve photo featured her parents), *Liege & Lief* '69. Formed Fotheringay, named after Scottish castle, title of Sandy song on second Fairport album; band incl. Trevor Lucas (ex-Eclection), Jerry Donahue, both later of Fairport: highly praised eponymous LP was UK top 20 '70; *Nothing More – And Others* was compilation. Solo LP *North Star Grassman & The Ravens* '71 incl. Fairport, Fotheringay alumni, classic Sandy song 'John The Gun', covers of Bob DYLAN's 'Down In The Flood', Brenda LEE's 'Let's Jump The Broomstick'. Melody Maker's Top Female Vocalist '70, 71; appeared in all-star prod. of *Tommy*; sang on fourth LED ZEPPELIN LP. *Sandy* '72 was praised, had David Bailey sleeve photo, didn't sell well; *The Bunch* '72 again used Fairport members, was album of rock'n'roll covers incl. Buddy HOLLY's 'Learning The Game',

EVERLY BROS' 'When Will I Be Loved'. Best solo album *Like An Old Fashioned Waltz* '73 (title song covered by Emmylou HARRIS). Married Lucas, who joined Fairport; Sandy rejoined for *Fairport Convention Live* '74, *Rising For The Moon* '75. Worked at being wife and mother, except for *Rendezvous* '77 with stellar lineup incl. Stevie WINWOOD, Linda & Richard THOMPSON, Gallagher & Lyle. Died of brain haemorrhage following fall down stairs in a friend's home. Island Records issued a 4-disc boxed set *Who Knows Where The Times Goes* '86, covering career before, during and after Fairport, over a dozen previously unreleased songs incl. some from unfinished last Fotheringay LP.

DENVER, John (*b* John Henry Deutschendorf, 31 Dec. '43, Roswell, N.M.) Singer/songwriter with country flavour: clean-cut kid tapped massive MOR market '70s with delivery, material a notch above ordinary. Briefly in group with John STEWART, during which time each wrote best-known songs: Stewart's 'Daydream Believer', Denver's 'Leavin' On A Jet Plane' (worldwide hit for PETER, PAUL & MARY). With Chad MITCHELL trio for four years, went solo with albums *Rhymes & Reasons* '69, *Whose Garden Was This* and *Take Me To Tomorrow* '70; *Poems, Prayers & Promises* '71 was no. 15 LP USA, first gold LP incl. 'Take Me Home, Country Roads', no. 2 single (no. 50 country chart); 32 singles in Hot 100 USA '71-84 incl. four no. 1 hits '74-5 with 'Sunshine On My Shoulders', lugubrious 'Annie's Song' (also no. 1 UK), 'Thank God I'm A Country Boy' (flip side 'My Sweet Lady' charted on reissue '77), 'I'm Sorry'. 'Rocky Mountain High' was no. 9 '72; 'Back Home Again' no. 5 '74. Collaborations incl. *A Christmas Together* with Muppets (no. 26 LP '79, top 10 Billboard Xmas chart '83); also duets 'Perhaps Love' with opera star Placido Domingo (song Denver's; single charted under Domingo's name in UK and USA '81-2), 'Love Again' with Sylvie Vartan '84. LP sales are revealing; MOR artists sell lots of albums, which sell longer than singles: 21 LPs in top 200 Billboard LPs USA; *Arie* '71 reached only no. 75 but went gold; 15 LPs in top 40 '71-82; 11 went gold, 4 platinum (sold more than a million copies); *Greatest Hits* '73

(175 weeks in chart), *Back Home Again* '74, *Windsong* '75 were all no. 1; *Rocky Mountain High* '72 no. 4, *An Evening With John Denver* '75 no. 2, *Spirit* '76 no. 7, *Greatest Hits Vol. 2* '77 no. 6. *Arie* '71 reached only no. 75 but stayed 16 weeks in chart: it went gold. Denver sidemen '80s have incl. James BURTON, Glen D. Hardin (both ex-Elvis PRESLEY, ex-Emmylou HARRIS's Hot Band); *It's About Time* '83 (no. 61) incl. duet with Harris on 'Wild Montana Skies' (single made country chart), backing by the WAILERS on 'World Game'. *One World* '86 was another album for the fans.

DEODATO, Eumir De Almeida (*b* 22 June '42, Rio de Janeiro, Brazil) Piano, other instruments; composer. Debut with Astrud Gilberto; composition 'Spirit Of Summer', arranging won prizes at Rio song festival; first came to USA '67, arr. LPs for Frank SINATRA, Roberta FLACK, Aretha FRANKLIN, many others; worked on film scores *The Adventurers* '70, *Target Risk* '75, others. Jazz/rock arr. of main theme from Richard Strauss's *Also Sprach Zarathustra* (also theme from film *2001*) was no. 2 hit single USA '73; albums of mood music on CTI, MCA, Warner Brothers incl. *In Concert* '74, with AIRTO.

De PARIS, Sidney and Wilbur Brothers from Crawfordsville, Ind. Sidney (*b* 30 May '05; *d* 13 Sep. '67, NYC) played trumpet; Wilbur (*b* 11 Jan. 1900; *d* 3 Jan. '73 NYC) trombone. Father was music teacher, bandmaster. Reliable section man Wilbur worked with Louis ARMSTRONG, Jelly Roll MORTON, Noble SISSLE, Edgar HAYES, others; with Duke ELLINGTON '46-7. Sidney was much the better soloist, made fine records with McKINNEY'S COTTON PICKERS '29, Don REDMAN '32-6, Morton '39; Sidney BECHET '40 on Victor; with Bechet, Ed HALL '43 and James P. JOHNSON '44 on Blue Note, etc. Brothers worked together '27-8 and from '47, mainly at Jimmy Ryan's NYC '51-62 in a sort of modern Dixieland style which pleased tourists but disappointed many jazz fans: Wilbur was unimaginative leader, while Sidney suffered from ill health. Atlantic LPs late '50s incl. *The Wild Jazz Age, On The Riviera, Over And Over Again.*

De PAUL, Lynsey (*b* Lynsey Rubin, '51) UK singer/songwriter. Studied classical music, then art; turned to pop after graduation; first hit co-written with Barry Blue (Ron Roker) for vocal group the Fortunes: 'Storm In A Teacup' no. 7 '72; had first own hit same year with 'Sugar Me', no. 5, relying like all her hits on keyboard skills backing high, girlish voice and hammering home naggingly infectious hook. Turned to label-boss Gordon Mills for 'Getting A Drag' (no. 18) but scored better with own tunes; 'Won't Somebody Dance With Me' '73 reminiscent of MAM labelmate Gilbert O'SULLIVAN (in many ways her male counterpart) made no. 14 and won Ivor NOVELLO award following year, achievement repeated by TV theme 'No Honestly' (no. 7 '75). Other TV themes followed. Teamed with Blue for other songs; switched to Mike Moran for unsuccessful Eurovision entry 'Rock Bottom' '77, no. 19 UK. Concentrates on writing; makes news through friendship with actor James Coburn. Hits compilation on MAM *Lynsey Sings*; also *Tigers And Fireflies* on Polydor '79.

DEPECHE MODE UK synthesiser group formed in Basildon, Essex '80 by Andy Fletcher (*b* 8 July '61), Martin Gore (*b* 23 July '61), Vince CLARKE. First two ditched guitars '81 to be keyboard band; snapped up by young label-boss Stevo for his 'new romantic' Some Bizzare; appeared on label's eponymous sampler '81 with Soft Cell, BLANCMANGE etc. but escaped clutches and signed to Mute. Clarke gifted commercial songwriter; first single 'Dreaming Of Me' made no. 57, 'New Life' no. 11 '81, established Depeche Mode (French words could mean 'by telegraph') as teen heart-throbs. Clarke tired of pop lifestyle, left (later formed Yazoo, etc.) as 'Speak And Spell' reached no. 10 LP chart; crisis averted by emergence of Gore as songwriter, while ex-Hitmen keyboardist Alan Wilder (*b* 1 June '63) recruited '82. By end of '84 band had 10 top 10 hits and a no. 21; carried on '85 with 'Shake The Disease' at no. 18: percussive like many later hits, showing infl. of more avant-garde groups such as Test Department. *The Singles 81-85* displays progress from catchy if insubstantial early synth ditties to heavier European sound with accompanying leather look (Gore had relocated to

Berlin). Group is happy to remain with tiny indie label (whose boss Daniel Miller has prod. all records), thus able to mature at their own pace. Further LPs: *Black Celebration* '86, *Music For The Masses* '87.

DERRINGER, Rick (*b* Richard Zehringer, 5 Aug '47, Fort Recovery, Ohio) Guitarist/ producer. Formed first group at 13 in Union City, Ind. with Randy Hobbs on bass, Bobby Peterson keyboards, brother Randy on drums, calling group after VENTURES instrumental 'The McCoy'. Producer Bert BERNS took teenagers to NYC, cut 'Hang On, Sloopy' for his Bang label: 3-chord nursery-rhyme rocker shot to no. 1; then 'Fever' (no. 7, both '65), 'Come On, Let's Go' '66 before bubble burst ('Sloopy' and 'Fever' nos. 5 and 44 in UK on Immediate). After two LPs of pop on Bang to capitalise on hits, group signed to Mercury for psychedelic *Infinite McCoys* and *Human Ball* both '68, both prod. by Rick, and played at Steve Paul's Scene club NYC; Paul became manager, linked them with blues guitarist Johnny WINTER; *Johnny Winter And* '70, *Johnny Winter And: Live* '71 both prod. by Rick, sold well; changed name to Derringer from first of these. When Johnny stopped touring with drug problem, switched to brother Edgar WINTER, prod. breakthrough *They Only Come Out At Night* '73, incl. no. 1 USA instrumental 'Frankenstein', and playing with group; also prod. Johnny's comeback album *Still Alive And Well* '73; worked with both through '70s, on CBS labels, then on Paul's Blue Sky label, where meanwhile own first solo *All American Boy* '73 flattered to deceive: incl. no. 23 hit single 'Rock And Roll Hootchie Coo'; neither *Spring Fever* '75 nor any of four hard rock LPs by group called Derringer cut much ice. In demand behind desk and on sessions: played on albums by STEELY DAN, Todd RUNDGREN, Bette MIDLER, Donald Fagen, Joe Vitale, others; prod. off-the-wall *In 3-D* '84 by Weird Al Yankovic, selection of pop pastiches incl. Michael JACKSON's 'Beat It' retitled 'Eat It'.

DeSHANNON, Jackie (*b* 21 Aug. '44, Hazel, Ky.) USA singer/songwriter. Radio debut age 11; to West Coast via Chicago '60. Early success as songwriter as tunes were covered by the Kalin Twins, Brenda LEE ('Dum Dum'), others. Performed with Nighthawks (group later became CRUSADERS) and Nomads, but little personal success until 'What The World Needs Now Is Love' '65 (no. 7), ironically a Burt BACHARACH song. The SEARCHERS hit with her 'Needles And Pins' and 'When You Walk In The Room'; the BYRDS with 'Don't Doubt Yourself Babe'. Collaborated widely with other writers – Sharon Sheeley, Randy NEWMAN, Jimmy Page – and had fitful performing career; 'Put A Little Love In Your Heart' no. 4 USA '69, 'Love Will Find A Way' barely made top 40 same year, her last sizeable hit. She collaborated with Van MORRISON, singing background on his *Hard Nose The Highway* '73 and prod. by him, but as in brief collaboration with Ry COODER 10 years earlier, not much more resulted. More than 20 albums on several labels incl. country-flavoured *Jackie* '72 and *Your Baby Is A Lady* '74 on Atlantic; *New Arrangement* '75 incl. her 'Bette Davis Eyes', also no. 1 single for Kim CARNES. Success of songs has to compensate for lack of recognition as performer.

DESMOND, Johnny (*b* Giovanni Alfredo De Simone, 14 Nov. '20, Detroit, Mich.; *d* 6 Sep. '85, L.A.) Singer. Began in Detroit radio, clubs; formed vocal quartet the Downbeats which joined Bob CROSBY band as the Bob-O-Links; joined Gene KRUPA as solo '41; with Glenn MILLER AAF band (radio programme in England *A Soldier And A Song*) became known as 'the G.I. Sinatra'. Later at his peak called 'The Creamer'. Postwar radio work led to three-month gig on Don McNeill's *Breakfast Club* Chicago morning show: lasted six years. Records as solo on RCA, Coral, MGM, hits '50-57 incl. top tens 'Play Me Hearts And Flowers', 'Yellow Rose Of Texas' '55; LP on Columbia *Blue Smoke* late '50s. TV work '50s incl. *Hit Parade*, *Face The Music*; co-starred on Broadway with Vivian Blaine in *Say Darling* '58, later played Nicky Arnstein during run of *Funny Girl*; a few minor films incl. *China Doll* '58; continued working: on UK TV early '85 with a Miller band.

DESMOND, Paul (*b* Paul Breitenfeld, 25 Nov. '24, San Francisco, Cal.; *d* 30 May '77, NYC) Alto saxophone. His father played organ in silent cinema orchestras; he was a star in the Dave BRUBECK Quartet until it broke up '67; he wrote Brubeck's biggest hit, 'Take Five'. His lyrical style and light, airy tone was liked even by people who were not Brubeck fans; good jazz is seldom so pretty, and pretty jazz seldom has the foundation of musical integrity that he had: he was one of the most direct and valuable heirs of Lester YOUNG. His own albums began on Fantasy '54, 56; quartet set *Blues In Time* '57 with Gerry MULLIGAN recorded by Norman GRANZ; then *East Of The Sun* '59 on WB (also on Discovery): quartet with Jim HALL, Percy HEATH, Connie Kay; first LP on RCA '61 with strings, then *Two Of A Mind* '62 with Kay, Mulligan; quartet tracks with Hall '63-5 were on several RCA LPs; then big band albums on A&M with Ron CARTER, AIRTO: *Summertime* '68; *Crystal Illusions*, *Bridge Over Troubled Water* both '69, both added strings, *Water* also had Herbie HANCOCK. *Concert At Town Hall* '71 with MODERN JAZZ QUARTET on Finesse (now from PRT UK) followed by CTI LPs *Skylark* '73 (octet with two guitars, Carter, Jack DEJOHNETTE), *Pure Desmond* '74 (quartet with Carter and Kay). *Paul Desmond Quartet Live* recorded Toronto '75; tracks appeared on at least three labels. Desmond/Hall quartet tracks from WB and RCA compiled complete on 6-disc Mosaic set '87, one of the most beautiful compilations of the year. Died of lung cancer. Desmond was fond of scotch; when a spot was discovered on his lungs, he was amused that his liver was in perfect working order. He was a witty writer, but never finished his autobiography, to have been called *How Many Of You Are There In The Quartet?*.

DeSYLVA, BROWN & HENDERSON Legendary songwriting team: lyricists Buddy DeSylva (*b* George Gard DeSylva, 27 Jan. 1895, NYC; *d* 11 July '50, L.A.) and Lew Brown (*b* Louis Brownstein, 10 Dec. 1893, Odessa, Russia; *d* 5 Feb. '58, NYC); composer Ray Henderson (*b* 1 Dec. 1896, Buffalo, NY; *d* 31 Dec. '70, Greenwich, Conn.) Brown's first hit was 'Give Me The Moonlight, Give Me The Girl' '17, with Albert Von Tilzer; Henderson wrote 'That Old Gang Of Mine' '23 with Billy ROSE and Mort Dixon, 'Five Foot Two, Eyes Of Blue'

and 'I'm Sitting On Top Of The World' with Sam Lewis and Joe Young, 'Don't Bring Lulu' with Rose and Brown, 'Alabama Bound' '25 with DeSylva, whose first hit had been 'I'll Say She Does', written with Gus Kahn for Al JOLSON show *Sinbad* '18. DeSylva also co-wrote Jolson hits 'April Showers' '21, 'California, Here I Come' '24; collaborated with George GERSHWIN ('Nobody But You', 'Stairway To Paradise'), Jerome KERN ('Look For The Silver Lining'), Victor HERBERT ('A Kiss In The Dark'). Team finally came together writing *George White's Scandals Of 1925*; songs won them work on next year's edition: 'Birth Of The Blues' was smash hit, 'Black Bottom' became dance craze. Started own publishing firm '26; wrote shows incl. songs 'Varsity Drag', 'The Best Things In Life Are Free' (title of '56 biopic), 'You're The Cream In My Coffee', 'Button Up Your Overcoat', 'My Lucky Star', many more. Also films: story according to Eddie CANTOR (quoted by David Ewen) is that they wrote 'corniest song they could dream up' as a joke for Jolson; he loved it, used it in talkie *The Singing Fool* '29: 'Sonny Boy' one of his biggest; '29 record reissued '46 allegedly sold a million. Same year Charles Farrell/Janet Gaynor hit movie had title song, 'I'm A Dreamer', 'If I Had A Talking Picture'. DeSylva turned prod. '30; wrote music, words for 'Wishing', Vera LYNN hit '39; Henderson and Brown collaborated on several shows incl. *Scandals Of 1931* ('Life Is Just A Bowl Of Cherries' for Ethel MERMAN). Brown went to Hollywood; Henderson worked with others e.g. on *Curly Top*, '35 Shirley Temple film ('Animal Crackers'). DeSylva was a co-founder of Capitol Records.

DEVO USA rock band formed Akron, Ohio, '72 by Kent State graduates Jerry Casale, bass, vocals; Bob Casale and Mark Mothersbaugh, keyboards, guitar, vocals; Bob Mothersbaugh, lead guitar, vocals; Alan Myers, drums. Jerry and Mark main songwriters/frontmen. Took name from video *The Truth About De-Evolution*, prizewinner in '75 Ann Arbor Film Festival. Wacky visuals incl. overalls, flowerpot hats, jerky hypnotic sound (called 'robotic') brought attention, as did irreverent cover of ROLLING STONES 'Satisfaction': biggest hit at no. 41 UK followed 'Jocko Homo' as second single on band's Booji Boy label, marketed in UK by opportunist Stiff label. Greatest success in UK, where punk rendered lower charts vulnerable to quirkiness. Signed by Virgin, the band enlisted Brian ENO to prod. *Q: Are We Not Men? A: We Are Devo!* '78. *Duty Now For The Future* '79 had keyboards take greater role under prod. Ken Scott; *Freedom Of Choice* '80 embraced disco to their detriment, but relative conservatism allowed 'Whip It' to become their only USA hit at no. 14. By *New Traditionalists* '81 and *Oh No! It's Devo* '82, emotionless stance was wearing thin. Group contributed to soundtracks of *Heavy Metal* '81, *Doctor Detroit* '83, lent musical muscle to eponymous Toni Basil LP '81; Mothersbaughs sessioned on *Nosferatu* '79 by STRANGLERS guitarist Hugh Cornwell. Warner Brothers signed the band for USA, re-launched them with *Shout* '84, but reissue of old tracks to promote new single suggested that earlier stuff achieved more with less.

DeVOL, Frank (*b* 20 Sep. '11, Moundsville, W.Va.) Composer, arranger, conductor. Raised in Ohio; arr. and played lead alto sax for Horace HEIDT late '30s, then Alvino REY '39-40; from '43 studio work on radio, records, TV. Accompanied Nat COLE, many others at Capitol early '50s; then Robert GOULET, Doris DAY, Tony BENNETT, Vic DAMONE etc. on Columbia. Wrote themes, soundtrack music for TV (*My Three Sons* series), films incl. *The Big Knife* '55, *Pillow Talk* '59, *Whatever Happened To Baby Jane?* '62, *Hush, Hush Sweet Charlotte* and *Cat Ballou* '65, *The Dirty Dozen* '67, many more.

DEXTER, Al (*b* Albert Poindexter, 4 May '05, Jacksonville, Texas; *d* '84) Honky-tonk country singer popular in '40s. Worked as painter and decorator while playing in local groups '30s, formed own band The Texas Troopers '40. Signed to Brunswick '36-40, Columbia '40-9, scored with 'Pistol Packin' Mama' (sold 2 million '43), 'Honky Tonk Blues', 'Too Late To Worry, Too Blue To Cry', 'Rose Of Mexico', etc. for 12 gold discs '43-8. Also recorded for Decca '62-3, King '55, Dot '56, Capitol '62-4. Retired to run motel in Lufkin, Texas, nightclub in

Dallas. LPs incl. *Pistol Packin' Mama* '62 on Columbia.

DEXY'S MIDNIGHT RUNNERS UK rock band based in Birmingham, ever-changing lineup fronted by volatile Kevin Rowland (*b* 17 Aug. '53, Wolverhampton). Formed in post-punk period as powerful purveyors of dance music, drawing heavily on '60s soul, R&B; staunchly anti-fashion amid 'new Romantics' of early '80s. Arrived with no. 1 UK hit 'Geno', tribute to Geno WASHINGTON; 'There There My Dear' no. 7; debut LP *Searching For The Young Soul Rebels* '80 led to run-in with record company, leading to Dexy's hijacking tapes of own album, which revealed earnestly political Rowland (i.e. orthodox anti-Thatcher) whose abrasiveness also led to frequent run-ins with music press. 'Plan B' on Parlophone reached only no. 58; later records on Mercury/Phonogram. 'Celtic Soul Brothers' no. 45, then 'Come On Eileen' no. 1 both UK/USA '82-3, credited to 'Dexy's Midnight Runners with the Emerald Express' (instrumental group). LP *Too Rye-Ay* '82 rumoured to incl. collaboration with Van MORRISON: it didn't, but incl. his 'Jackie Wilson Said (I'm In Heaven When You Smile)' (UK no. 5) and stamped with his influence: fusion of black music sound with trad. Irish music, e.g. horns with violin of Helen O'Hara (*b* 5 Nov. '56); 'This One Last Mad Waltz', 'Until I Believe In My Soul' hybrids of Celtic soul. New version of 'The Celtic Soul Brothers' released: no. 20 UK '83, minor hit USA. *Don't Stand Me Down* '85 rumoured to be expensive production, ended long silence: band's image changed from dungarees and stubble to earnest business suits, but Rowland histrionics intact: new LP had six long tracks with snatches of dialogue. 'Because Of You' top 20 UK hit '86; seen as one of the more interesting UK bands of the era. Groups to come out of Dexy's incl. Bureau and TKO Horns.

DIAMOND, Jim (*b* 28 Sep. '53, Glasgow) UK vocalist. Decided on music after hearing Otis REDDING's 'My Girl' '67; became club singer at 16; played German air base circuit with Aberdeen band Gully Foyle early '70s. Formed Bandit '75 with James Litherland, guitar; Cliff Williams (later AC/DC), bass;

Graham Broad, drums: experienced musicians lent adequate setting for abrasive yet soulful vocals. Eponymous first LP '77 on Arista sunk in punk explosion; after further records with differing lineups he split to work with Alexis KORNER, veteran UK bluesman who helped him hone technique (appears on Korner's *Just Easy* '78). Formed heavy rock band in L.A. late '70s with Carmine Appice on drums, Earl Slick, ex-David BOWIE guitarist; money problems split group before recording; Diamond returned to UK to prod. Zoot MONEY. Teamed with former Jack Bruce/Jeff BECK keyboardist Tony Hymas as PhD, hit jackpot with 'I Won't Let You Down': classically simple ballad played off tortured vocal against synth wash, made UK no. 3 '82 and topped many charts worldwide, but Diamond contracted hepatitis, couldn't promote LP *Is It Safe?*. Finally embarked on solo career, scored with another ballad 'I Should Have Known Better' no. 1 UK '84, but uptempo followup 'I Sleep Alone' flopped; LP *Double Crossed* in trad. rock vein with talent incl. Simon Kirke, ex-BAD COMPANY. 'Hi-Ho Silver' top 10 '86 in POLICE's white reggae vein.

DIAMOND, Neil (*b* Neil Leslie Diamond, 24 Jan '41, Brooklyn) Singer/songwriter. Saw Pete SEEGER perform, learned guitar and began writing songs alongside pre-med study. Became part of Brill Building crowd after meeting with Ellie GREENWICH, Jeff BARRY. First hit for JAY AND THE AMERICANS ('Sunday & Me' no. 18 USA '65); joined Bert BERNS Bang label that year, wrote early hits for the MONKEES ('I'm A Believer', 'A Little Bit Me, A Little Bit You'); own first big hit 'Cherry, Cherry' no. 6 '66: 36 own top 40 hits USA '66-83 incl. first no. 1 '70 with 'Cracklin' Rosie' (also first UK hit at no. 3); had no. 1 'Song Sung Blue' '72, no. 2 'Love On The Rocks' '80; also no. 1 duet with Barbra STREISAND '78 'You Don't Bring Me Flowers'. Songs have been covered by the HOLLIES, Elvis PRESLEY, UB40 (no. 1 UK with 'Red Red Wine' '83), many others. 27 LPs charted in Billboard '66-84 incl. *Tap Root Manuscript* '70 (incl. 'Rosie', also 'African Trilogy', celebrating African contribution to popular music), live concert LPs *Neil Diamond/Gold* '70, *Hot August Night* '72,

Love At The Greek (Theatre) '76; soundtracks *Jonathan Livingston Seagull* '73 (first LP after signing with Columbia for seven-figure sum), *The Jazz Singer* '80 (remake co-starred Sir Laurence Olivier; LP yielded three hits but film heavily panned); hits compilations on Bang, MCA, CBS incl. *Classics – The Early Years* '83 (Bang stuff now on CBS); *Beautiful Noise* '76 prod. by Robbie Robertson, led to incongruous appearance in The BAND's *Last Waltz* '77 film, soundtrack. A pop superstar well-entrenched in lucrative MOR market: LPs *Heartlight* '82, *Primitive* '84, *Headed For The Future* '86 infrequent but selective.

DIAMONDS, The Canadian vocal quartet, late '50s: Dave Somerville, Mike Douglas, Ted Kowalski, Bill Reed. One of the best white groups performing covers of black R&B hits. Debut hit 'Why Do Fools Fall In Love' '56 less successful than original by Frankie LYMON and the Teenagers, but white domination of industry usually saw white cover do better in pop chart. Diamonds had 15 top 40 hits '56-61 incl. three top tens '57-8: good cover of the Gladiolas' 'Little Darlin' ' (written by their lead singer Maurice WILLIAMS), 'Silhouettes' (also millionseller for the Rays), 'The Stroll' (minor hit for Chuck WILLIS). By '61 Reed and Kowalski replaced by Californians John Felton and Evan Fisher; black groups coming into their own as golden era of soul dawned – Diamonds relegated to cabaret.

DIBANGO, Manu (*b* Emmanuel Dibango, '33, Douala, Cameroon) Singer-composer, arranger; plays reeds, piano. Sent to Paris at age 15 to prepare for professional career, persevered with music despite parental disapproval; studied classical piano, taking up saxophone '54. To Brussels '56, played sax and vibes in jazz bands; to newly independent Zaire '61 on visit, stayed five years, playing with Kabaselle And The African Jazz, running a night club and playing on over 100 singles. Back to Paris '65 with Kabaselle, made several LPs with him but determined to pursue own direction also made singles, incl. raunchy 'Tribute To King Curtis' '70. First solo LP *O Boso* '72, then *Soma Loba*; third *Soul Makossa* became worldwide dance-floor hit: album picked up by Atlantic, made no. 79 Billboard LP chart, title single top 40 in USA mid-'73; he became 'The Makossa Man', first African to have international hit. Success allowed band to expand to 14 pieces; to NYC where he played with top jazz musicians, Fania All Stars, etc. At peak of popularity returned to West Africa as mus. dir. of Orchestre RTI, house band of Ivorian TV. More LPs incl. *Super Kumba* '74, *Afradelic* '75, *Manu 76*, *African Rhythm Machine* and *Afrovision: Big Blow* '76; left Ivory Coast, spent rest of decade between Paris and Cameroon and touring Africa, releasing more LPs incl. *Waka Juju*, *A L'Olympia* and *Home Made*. To Jamaica '79; recorded *Gone Clear*, *Reggae Makossa*, *Ambassador* with legendary rhythm section Sly & Robbie (all on Island). Continued to tour in '80s, still finding time to help other musicians with their careers; LPs incl. live *Deliverance*, solo piano *Mélodies Africaines Vols. 1 & 2*, *Sweet And Soft*. Electro-pop experiments resulted in *Abele Dance* '84; eponymous hits compilation on Disques Festival. Has also written/performed film scores incl. *L'Herbe Sauvage*, *Ceddo*, *The Price Of Freedom*. LP *Electric Africa* on Celluloid '85 maintained pressure on competition for title of Africa's biggest star. Many albums available from Stern's African Record Centre in London.

DICKENS, Little Jimmy (*b* 19 Dec. '25, Bolt, W. Va.) Diminutive (4'10") country star of '50s, '60s. Began as Jimmy The Kid with Johnny Bailes and his Happy Valley Boys '42, went solo, signed with Grand Ole Opry '48, Columbia '49; initial hits with novelties: 'Country Boy', 'Take An Old Cold Tater And Wait' '49; 'A-Sleepin' At The Foot Of The Bed' '50, 'Out Behind The Barn' '52, 'I'm Little But I'm Loud' '53. His 'Hillbilly Fever' '50 is regarded as an early example of rockabilly; also one of the most effective singers of heart songs, with throbbing almost tear-filled vibrato on 'Take Me As I Am', 'My Heart's Bouquet'. Wore the showiest costumes of any country entertainer: 'He looked like Mighty Mouse in pyjamas,' said June Carter Cash. Made comeback '60s with 'The Violet And A Rose' '62, 'May The Bird Of Paradise Fly Up Your Nose' '65 (no. 1 country, no. 15 pop). Recorded for Decca '68-70, United Artists '71-3; always remained popular touring act. Elected to Country Music Hall of Fame '83.

LPs incl. *The Best Of Little Jimmy Dickens* '81 on Gusto.

DICKENSON, Vic (*b* 6 Aug. '06, Xenia, Ohio; *d* 16 Nov. '84, NYC) Trombone. Gigged around Midwest at 21; with Bennie MOTEN, then Claude HOPKINS '36-9; Benny CARTER '40; Count BASIE '40-1; Eddie HEYWOOD sextet '43-5; Blue Note records with Edmond HALL, James P. JOHNSON, Sidney DE PARIS '43-4, quartet session with Bill DOGGETT '52; freelanced on East Coast for many years. Appeared in CBS TV *The World Of Jazz* with Billie HOLIDAY, Lester YOUNG, Coleman HAWKINS, etc. '57; also PBS TV's *Just Jazz* '71. Played mostly dixieland style in postwar years with Eddie CONDON, Red ALLEN, Bobby HACKETT; but fluent and versatile veteran of the Swing Era, admired by young and old: master of trad. hot style and mellow ballad sound as well. Often with WORLD'S GREATEST JAZZ BAND; Newport and Colorado jazz festivals; LPs with Buck CLAYTON's jam sessions, Ruby BRAFF, many others. Complete Blue Note Edmond Hall/Dickenson/etc. sessions issued in box set on Mosaic '85.

DICKIE DOO & THE DON'TS Philadelphia novelty vocal group: Dicky Doo (*b* Gerry Granahan, 17 June '39) leader, tenor; Jerry Grant, lead voice; Harvey Davis, baritone; Al Ways, bass; Ray Gangi, tenor. Dick CLARK helped get contract with Swan label; two top 40 hits '58: 'Click Clack' written by Granahan and Grant; 'Nee Nee Na Na Na Na Nu Nu' inspired by Jonathan Winters comedy routine baby talk, recently revived by BAD MANNERS; three other minor hits '58-9. Granahan had biggest hit (no. 23) under his own name: 'No Chemise Please' '58 on Sunbeam.

DICKSON, Barbara (*b* 27 Sep. '47, Dunfermline, Scotland) UK vocalist, songwriter. Began in folk music; once sang in trio with Rab Noakes and Archie Fisher; solo LPs on Decca early '70s incl. *From The Beggar's Mantle, I Will Sing*. Sang Beatles songs in Willy Russell show *John, Paul, George, Ringo And Bert* '73, accompanying herself on piano; it opened in Liverpool, moved to London and her beautiful voice was the best thing in it. Signed with RSO label for

Answer Me '76 incl. top 10 title track, revival of '56 hit by David WHITFIELD, Frankie LAINE; top 20 hit early '77 with 'Another Suitcase, Another Hall' from the original LP of the Tim Rice/LLOYD WEBBER musical *Evita*, made before it opened: she was not in the show when it opened in the West End, but had already hit with its best song. *Morning Comes Quickly* '77 was made in Nashville, with excellent title song co-written by prod. Mentor Williams, guitarist Troy Seals, Barry Goldberg; other backup incl. Buddy Spicher on fiddle and mandolin, Janie FRICKE in the chorus. She switched to Epic for *The Barbara Dickson Album* '80 (no. 7 LP incl. no. 11 hit 'January February'), sold out the Albert Hall late that year with one-woman show; *You Know It's Me* (top 40 LP) and *Sweet Oasis* '81, *Here We Go* (live on tour) and *All For A Song* '82 (no. 3 LP incl. 'Caravan Song', earlier hits), *Heartbeats* '84. She took part in Russell's *Blood Brothers* on stage in London (mini-LP on Legacy) and had no. 1 hit duet with Elaine PAIGE early '85, 'I Know Him So Well' by Rice, Benny & Bjorn (ex-ABBA). *The Barbara Dickson Songbook* and *Gold* '85 on K-Tel were no. 5 and 11 in UK chart; *The Right Moment* '86 on K-Tel incl. Emmylou HARRIS's 'Boulder To Birmingham'. Gorgeous voice has not crossed over to USA charts, but gives much pleasure at home.

DIDDLEY, Bo (*b* Ellas McDaniel, 30 Dec. '28, McComb, Ms.) R&B singer, composer, guitarist; studied violin as a child. One of the most profoundly influential R&B artists of the mid-'50s, whose trademark 'hambone' or 'shave-and-a-haircut, six bits' beat has been imitated by countless lesser acts. His father's name was Bates; he was adopted. Moved to Chicago '34, self-taught on guitar; played in school band with Earl HOOKER; played trombone in a church band; led washboard trio '46-51. Recorded for Checker/Chess labels '55-74, had eight R&B hits '55-62, incl. two-sided 'Bo Diddley'/'I'm A Man' '55 at no. 2, also 'Diddley Daddy' (no. 11), 'Say Man' (no. 3, crossed to top 20 on pop chart), 'Road Runner', 'You Can't Judge A Book By The Cover', etc. 'Crackin' Up' '59 made the Hot 100 pop but not the R&B chart; he came back '67 with 'Ooh Baby' (top 20 R&B, Hot

100 pop). He appeared on the Ed Sullivan show and toured with a Dick CLARK show on the strength of his few hits but his powerfully rhythmic guitar and slightly menacing songs and delivery were more influential than chart entries would indicate, e.g. 'Diddey Wah Diddey', 'Who Do You Love', 'Bring It To Jerome', 'Dearest Darling', others on his classic *Bo Diddley* album ('55-8 tracks), just as important as the better known ones; the LP charted briefly '62 on Checker, reissued '87 on Chess, as well as *Go Bo Diddley* from the same period; also 2-disc set in *Chess Masters* series. Still tours and still thrills: *Toronto Rock'n'Roll Revival 1969 Vol. 5* on Accord; *Road Runner* on Black Lion UK was made at Joyous Lake, Woodstock late '70s.

DILLARDS, The USA bluegrass/country rock musicians: Douglas Flint Dillard (*b* 6 Mar. '37), Rodney Adean Dillard (*b* 18 May '42), both *b* East St Louis, Ill. Grew up across the river in Salem, Mo., playing guitar and banjo; took part in two revivals of BLUEGRASS, in '60s and later 'progressive' bluegrass. First single made in St Louis got local airplay '58; to L.A. and first Elektra LP *Backporch Bluegrass* '63, with Roy Dean Webb on mandolin (*b* 28 Mar. '37, Independence, Mo.), Mitchell Jane on bass (*b* 7 May '30, Hammond, Ind.), then *The Dillards Live – Almost* '64, *Pickin' And Fiddlin'* '65. Played dim-witted Darlin family on Andy Griffith TV show, also showcased music; upset purists with amplifiers at Newport Folk Festival '64, added drummer Paul York '68: Doug went solo that year, replaced by Herb Pederson for *Wheatstraw Suite* '68, *Copperfields* '69; Pederson left to form COUNTRY GAZETTE '71; *Roots And Branches* '72 appeared on Anthem/UA, *Tribute To The American Duck* '73 on Poppy; with personnel changes, carried on playing festivals, etc. Meanwhile Doug toured with the BYRDS, formed Dillard And Clark Expedition with Gene Clark (LP on RCA), sessioned (film soundtrack work incl. *Bonnie And Clyde* '67, *Vanishing Point* '71), acted; organised Doug Dillard Band Featuring Byron Berline for 'gospel-grass' LP *Heaven* '79 on Flying Fish, later *Jackrabbit* and *What's That?*. As interest in folk-roots grew the original band, still led by Rodney, turned up on Flying

Fish as well: *The Dillards vs. The Incredible L.A. Time Machine* '77, *Mountain Rock* '78 on Crystal Clear (direct-to-metal mastered), *Decade Waltz* '79 with Pederson back on Flying Fish. Both Dillards appeared in *The Rose* '79. Also Dillard-Hartford-Dillard (with John Hartford from St Louis days on fiddle) for *Glittergrass From The Nashwood Hollyville Strings* and *Permanent Wave*. Salem celebrated Dillard Day '79 with Homer Earl Dillard Sr on fiddle, his grandson Earl on banjo and everybody in between (*Homecoming And Family Reunion*); Rodney's *At Silver Dollar City* came out '86. Flying fingers, fine ballads and comedy never failed; they were sending up Joan BAEZ before it was fashionable.

DiMEOLA, Al (*b* 22 July '54, Jersey City, N.J.) Guitarist, leader, composer. Began on guitar at 9 inspired by the BEATLES, played steel guitar at 15, then heard Miles DAVIS with Chick COREA and converted to FUSION. Attended Berklee in Boston, joined Corea's Return To Forever '74, led own groups, toured and recorded in trio with John McLAUGHLIN, Paco DeLucia (*see* McLaughlin). He plays both acoustic and electric; his principal infl. are classical guitarists like Julian Bream, and Corea. LPs on CBS: *Land Of The Midnight Sun* '76, *Elegant Gypsy* '77, *Casino* '78 with keyboardist Barry Miles (*b* 28 Mar. '47, Newark, N.J.), 2-disc *Splendido Hotel* '80 with Corea, *Electric Rendezvous* '82, *Tour De Force 'Live'* '82, *Scenario* '83, all made top 200 LPs USA; then solo acoustic *Cielo e Terra* '85 on Manhattan. Formed Al DiMeola Project, with AIRTO, Phil Markowitz on keyboards (*see* Joe LOCKE), Danny Gottlieb on drums, bassist Chip Jackson: LP *Soaring Through A Dream* '85 on Manhattan.

DIO, Ronnie James (*b* Ronald Padavona, 10 July '49, Cortland, NY) USA heavy rock vocalist. Studied classical trumpet as a child in Portsmouth, N.H.; switched to electric bass, formed group Vegas Kings in school; changed name to Dio, group Ronnie and the Red Caps, later Ronnie Dio and the Prophets; seven singles '61-7. (This casts some doubt on birth date.) Left late '67 with guitarist Nick Pantas to form Electric Elves (later just Elves), cut two singles; car crash '70 killed Pantas, injured keyboardist Doug Thaler and drummer Gary Driscoll; guitarist Dave Feinstein unhurt. Mickey Lee Soule, keyboards and guitar, brought in; Thaler later rejoined as second guitar. Feinstein, Thaler left early '73; Craig Gruber joined on bass, Dio concentrating on songs. Group now called Elf made eponymous LP for Epic USA, but others in UK for DEEP PURPLE label Purple (*Carolina County Ball* '74, *Trying To Burn The Sun* '75) brought melodic heavy rock more attention. Purple's Ritchie BLACKMORE borrowed group (ousting new guitarist Steve Edwards) to record solo *Ritchie Blackmore's Rainbow* '75 while still with Purple; struck up songwriting partnership with Dio, group Rainbow became full-time concern (*see* BLACKMORE entry). Dio quit '79 to join BLACK SABBATH; lack of control/involvement in mixing live LP saw him leave to form own band '82; though departure was acrimonious (took drummer, fellow American Vinnie Appice with him), melodic approach had revitalised Sabbath. New group called Dio incl. ex-Wild Horses/Rainbow bassist Jimmy Bain, Irish guitarist Vivian Campbell (ex-Sweet Savage). With no need to compromise for the first time since Elf, Dio's insistence on writing songs rather than riffs brought band more radio play than most in genre; WB's initial 40,000 pressing of *Holy Diver* '83 turned into sales of half a million: made top 60 LPs in USA, no. 13 UK; *The Last In Line* '84 less well received by critics but made no. 23 USA LP chart, while three singles from it hovered below UK top 40, fourth 'Mystery' reached no. 34. Dio balanced penchant for anthemic pomp rock with reluctance to go over the top ('We Rock'); live shows with lasers, medieval imagery good value, with inclusion of old Sabbath and Rainbow crowd pleasers; *Sacred Heart* released '85. Same year Dio was prime mover in Hear'n'Aid, heavy metal charity-motivated supergroup with members of JUDAS PRIEST, Quiet Riot etc.; recorded Dio's 'Stars'. Dio describes favourite sound as 'big drum sounds, big guitar sounds, *no* ballads'; addition of keyboardist Claude Schnell plus his announced excursion into film music may broaden scope, while writing touch renders his end of heavy rock spectrum more accessible. Album *Dream Evil* made USA top 50 '87.

DION & THE BELMONTS USA vocal group formed '58 NYC by Dion DiMucci (*b* 18 July '39), lead; Fred Milano (*b* 22 Aug. '39), second tenor; Angelo D'Aleo (*b* 3 Feb. '40), first tenor; Carlo Mastangelo (*b* 5 Oct. '38), baritone, all from the Bronx. Dion started singing age 5, appeared on Paul WHITEMAN show 10 years later, cut first disc 'The Chosen Few' '57 backed by the Timberlanes on Mohawk label. Group named after local Belmont Avenue, hit with second single on Laurie 'I Wonder Why', no. 22; then 'No One Knows' (19), 'Don't Pity Me' (40) '58-9; polished image as besuited Italian-Americans hoping to equal best of black groups: then 'A Teenager In Love' epitomised their doo-wop-infl. sound, made no. 5 (covers by Craig DOUGLAS, Marty Wilde in UK); 'Where Or When' reached no. 3 '60. By then Dion had a drug problem; D'Aleo was drafted; only two more top 40 hits followed. Under management pressure Dion left (trio had two top 30s '61-2); rockaballad 'Lonely Teenager' made no. 12 '60, but return to earlier style (and uncredited Del-Satins as backup) took 'Runaround Sue' (dedicated to future wife, song by friend/mentor Ernie Maresca) to no. 1. Maresca encouraged use of Dion's high register and tape reverb effectively updated doo-wop. 'The Wanderer' '61 was no. 2, provided extra image as lovable rebel; total of 13 top 40 solo hits '60-3, 8 of them top 10 incl. remakes of DRIFTERS items 'Ruby Baby' and 'Drip Drop'; the advent of Beatlemania coincided with new drug problem: he dropped out until '68 return with 'Abraham, Martin And John', celebrating slain Lincoln, King and Kennedy at no. 4 (Dick Holler song later covered by Marvin GAYE, others). Recorded in folk-rock vein; had reunited with Belmonts for ABC LP '68, then for rock'n'roll revival gig at Madison Square Garden '73: live recording *Reunion* was a hit. Continued solo through '70s (with Phil SPECTOR on remake of 'Born To Be With You', CHORDETTES hit '58); 'Wanderer' reissue in UK made no. 16 '76 for third top 20 entry there. Had wider talent than most contemporaries; won personal battle with heroin and left classics of era that will never fade: remastered digitally on Ace '86, fresh as paint.

DIRE STRAITS UK rock band formed in Deptford, South London (same area as SQUEEZE) by former journalist and teacher turned guitarist, singer, songwriter Mark Knopfler, guitar (*b* 12 Aug. '49, London), brother David on rhythm guitar, with John Illsiey, bass (*b* 24 June '49, London), and Pick Withers, drums; named after perennial financial state. Early break came when band featured on Charlie Gillett radio show *Honky Tonk*; debut album *Dire Straits* '78 epitomised intimate sound, utterly unlike then-prevailing punk: laconic vocals infl. by J. J. CALE, Bob DYLAN; fluid guitar work made Knopfler most celebrated UK guitarist since Eric CLAPTON; incl. single 'Sultans Of Swing' (no. 8 UK/no. 4 USA '79) which some consider still to be their finest hour. *Communiqué* '79 was more of the same; rivalry led to sacking of brother Dave '80 (he's done solo LPs *Release* '83, *Behind The Lines* '85, *Cut The Wine* '87). *Making Movies* incl. Knopfler songs 'Romeo & Juliet', 'Tunnel Of Love', 'Skateaway', Hal Lindes for Dave and added Alan Clark, keyboards. Meanwhile Dylan recruited Knopfler and Withers for *Slow Train Coming* '79, panned for lyrics but hailed as his best sounding LP. *Love Over Gold* '83 incl. Tommy Mandel, keyboards, Terry Williams (ex-Rockpile) on drums, Dylan infl. title track, marathon 14-minute 'Telegraph Road', 7-minute single (no. 2 UK) 'Private Investigation'. In '83 *Twistin' By The Pool* EP took band back to good-time rock'n'roll roots; *Alchemy* '84 was live 2-disc souvenir; *Brothers In Arms* '85 no. 1 LP USA, incl. hits with Sting guest vocal on 'Money For Nothing' (USA no. 1), also rock'n'rolly 'Walk Of Life', folky 'The Man's Too Strong'; band embarked on 14-month world tour. Knopfler prod. Dylan's *Infidels* '84, also AZTEC CAMERA LP; has sessioned with Van MORRISON, STEELY DAN, McGARRIGLES, Bryan FERRY, Phil EVERLY, Chet ATKINS (*Stay Tuned* '85 on CBS); wrote music '83-4 to Bill Forsyth films *Local Hero* and *Comfort & Joy*, Pat O'Connor's *Cal*, all highly rated British films (first and third also soundtrack LPs); released singles from film music ('Goin' Home'/'Smooching' from *Local Hero* minor UK hit). Top guitarist's financial straits are no longer dire.

DIRTY DOZEN BRASS BAND New Orleans brass band playing hip arrangements, describing style as 'jazz gumbo'. Began with kazoos and drums '77; adopted traditional instrumentation '79. Current lineup: trumpets Gregory Davis (leader) (*b* 30 Jan. '57) and Efrem Pierre Towns (*b* 20 Dec. '62, Jamaica, NY: the only member not from New Orleans); Kevin Harris (*b* 26 July '55), tenor sax; Jennell Marshall (*b* 24 June '54), snare drum; Roger Hayward Lewis (*b* 5 Oct. '41), baritone sax (has worked 15 years with Fats DOMINO); trombonist Charles Lee Joseph (*b* 26 Oct. '54) and sousaphonist Kirk Matthew Joseph (*b* 16 Feb. '61; both sons of veteran N.O. trombonist Waldron 'Frog' Joseph); Lionel Paul Batiste (*b* 4 Dec. '51), bass drum. They've played street parades, at funerals, New Orleans club The Glass House, tours to Europe: 'Funerals you can't book ahead, although we've had requests from people who want us to play . . . when they do kick out,' says Davis. 'I just give them my booking agent's number.' First LP *My Feet Can't Fail Me Now* '84 on Concord Jazz (with Benny Jones replacing Batiste) incl. Duke ELLINGTON's 'Caravan', Jelly Roll MORTON's 'Bongo' (with his 'Spanish tinge'), infl. of Louis JORDAN, much else; second album *Mardi Gras In Montreux: Live* '85 on Rounder described as 'one of the best in-concert recordings I've heard' by Steve Lewis in *The Wire*.

DISCO Dance fad of the '70s, with profound and unfortunate influence on popular music. The word came from the French *discothèque* ('record library'), a club where the entertainment consisted of dancing to records; in the mid-'60s discos in the USA were taverns with a juke box and a scantily clad dancer in a cage, where a patron hoped that if he didn't blink he might see more flesh than the next fellow. But in larger cities the gay male subculture made discos into something more fancy, where a disc jockey searched in black pop for suitable dance music: late '60s hits of SLY AND THE FAMILY STONE were prototypical disco records; Manu DIBANGO's 'Soul Makossa' '74 and Shirley And Co.'s 'Shame, Shame, Shame' '75 were favourites (*see* SHIRLEY & LEE); in between came the Hues Corporation ('Rock The Boat') and George McCrae's 'Rock Your Baby', a no. 1 interna-

tional hit whose writers/producers went on to form KC AND THE SUNSHINE BAND. Among the first to be produced by Munich's studio wizard Giorgio Moroder (*b* '41) was Donna SUMMER, who became a disco favourite (later, she didn't particularly want to be a gay favourite, and anyway had more talent than most in the disco ghetto). Black young people patronised disco clubs too, perhaps because they could afford it: it is a cheap way to run a club compared to hiring live music. As the disco boom wore on, record companies began to cash in and records had bpm numbers (beats per minute) printed on the label to make it easier for the DJ to segue from one record to the next; but it remained a cult until the hit film *Saturday Night Fever* '77 made it palatable to the masses, also brought the BEE GEES back to the charts. The big-time fad lasted until c.'80, but by then it had had a disastrous effect on pop music for two related reasons the producers and the technology. Because the main thing was the thump-thump beat, other values could be ignored; producers, who already had too much power, used drum machines, synthesisers and other gimmicks at the expense of musical values, also co-writing 'songs' with the 'artists' in order to make more money out of it: hence the cluttered production of many pop records, the unswinging rhythm sections in pop groups and the second-rate songs foisted on a marvellous voice like that of Whitney HOUSTON. KC and CHIC were bands retaining the human element, but most disco hitmakers were virtually anonymous, and the anonymity has translated into the sameness of pop music in the '80s. It has always been hard to play dance music well; it is now too easy to make money doing it badly.

DISTEL, Sacha (*b* 29 Jan. '33, Paris) Guitarist, singer. Nephew of bandleader/prod. Ray Ventura. Studied piano at 5, guitar from 15; played dixieland while studying philosophy; switched to modern style inspired by Dizzy GILLESPIE. Won amateur contest '50; played in '50s with Stan GETZ, MODERN JAZZ QUARTET, Lionel HAMPTON, Gillespie, etc.; by end of '50s known as classy pop singer (minor hit 'Scoubidou' '59). Recorded in five languages; wrote theme for French film *The Seven Capital*

Sins, Jack Reardon added lyric, song became 'The Good Life': Grammy for Best Song '63, top 20 hit for Tony BENNETT. Own biggest hit was 'Raindrops Keep Falling On My Head' from film *Butch Cassidy And The Sundance Kid* '70. Won Golden Rose of Montreux for TV show *Happy End* '66. Good looks, Gallic charm sustain popularity on UK TV; UK LPs incl. *Love Is All* '76, *Forever And Ever* '78, *From Sacha With Love* '79, *The Sacha Distel Collection* (2-disc compilation) '80, *Move Closer* '85.

DIXIE CUPS, The USA female vocal group mid-'60s: Joan Marie Johnson (*b* '45), sisters Rosa Lee (*b* '44) and Barbara Ann Hawkins (*b* '43). Discovered at talent contest, auditioned for Red Bird label, rehearsed new song 'Chapel Of Love' by prod./writers Jeff BARRY, Ellie GREENWICH and Phil SPECTOR, who prod. own version with RONETTES (later on LP) and CRYSTALS (unissued). Spector's strange reluctance to do much with obvious hit prompted Barry/Greenwich to record Dixie Cups (originally called Little Miss and the Muffets); it was international smash hit, no. 1 USA '64. Other hits were 'People Say', 'You Should Have Seen The Way He Looked At Me'; then chanting of trad. New Orleans song during lull in recording session led to last hit 'Iko Iko' (no. 20 '65) with simple percussive backing, call-and-response vocal. Like many girl groups, success was brief but unforgettable.

DIXIELAND Jazz genre. Dixie was nickname for New Orleans, from 10-dollar bill issued there before 1860 with 'dix' (French for ten) on it: came to mean southern states; then used by white ORIGINAL DIXIELAND JAZZ BAND, which made first jazz records '17 (also King OLIVER's Dixie Syncopators, etc.). Then described imitation New Orleans style, played mostly by middle-aged white men beginning late '30s. Almost always had 'front line' of trumpet (or cornet), trombone, clarinet; ranged from sincere attempt to re-create original style ('revival' music) to noisy pseudo-jazz suitable for tourists (DUKES OF DIXIELAND, FIREHOUSE 5 + 2). West Coast, Hollywood studio musicians and SWING ERA veterans like trumpeter Dick Cathcart (*b* 6 Nov. '24, Michigan City, Ind.), drummer Nick Fatool (*b* 2 Jan.

'15, Milbury, Mass.), clarinettist Matty Matlock played dixieland as required (e.g. film *Pete Kelly's Blues* '55) but music was often latter-day Chicago Style (cf. Rampart Street Paraders; Columbia LPs mid-'50s sold to dixieland fans). Others (Pete DAILY, Bob SCOBEY) played enjoyable (probably inaccurate) turn-of-the-century cabaret, reeking with instant nostalgia but offering good playing, good old songs (or oldish-sounding new songs). Eddie CONDON, Muggsy SPANIER, many others found audiences in NYC for what was called 'pure' jazz as swing era began to decay, big bands lost their novelty late '30s; centre of movement was Greenwich Village club Nick's, later also Ryan's. Dixieland did not affect history of music, but gave pleasure and was introduction to jazz for many. Musicians like Bobby HACKETT were good enough to transcend category; older ones like Sidney BECHET, Louis ARMSTRONG, Kid ORY continued playing the style they'd invented to begin with. UK derivative trad. style began '40s, made charts in '50s (*see* JAZZ).

DIXON, Bill (*b* William Robert Dixon, 5 Oct. '25, Nantucket Island, Mass.) Trumpet, flugelhorn, composer. Originally inspired by Louis ARMSTRONG. Studied painting and music; freelance trumpet and arr. NYC '50s; met Cecil TAYLOR at the Sportsmen's Club in Harlem '51: important relationship lasted many years, incl. Dixon's playing on Taylor LP *Conquistador!* '65 on Blue Note: 'His specific lyricism . . . is unique: Cecil Taylor seldom again had the advantage of an ensemble member who resisted him this well' (J. Litweiler). Late '50s began to lead own groups, concentrating on playing own music from '61-2; became godfather of avant garde. Writing, painting, teaching art history and music as well as composing, helped many younger men (e.g. bassist Alan Silva, *b* 29 Jan. '39, Bermuda); formed United Nations Jazz Society '58, co-led Archie SHEPP – Bill Dixon Quartet (album on Savoy; played at Helsinki Youth Festival '62), formed New York Contemporary Five, initially writing all the music, with Shepp, John Tchicai, Don CHERRY, J. C. Moses (drums; *b* 18 Oct. '36, Philadelphia; less active in music since '70 owing to ill health), Don Moore (bass; *b* NYC '32); toured Europe with that group '63. Prod.

records for Savoy (e.g. 2-disc set *New Music: Second Wave* '62-8); with film-maker Peter Sabino organised October Revolution '64 with film-maker Peter Sabino, led to Jazz Composers' Guild '65 with Taylor's encouragement (*see* JAZZ). At Newport Jazz Festival with quartet, dancer/choreographer Judith Dunn '66. University of the Streets formed by young Puerto Ricans NYC '67; while teaching art history elsewhere Dixon formed Free Conservatory of the University of the Streets '68: he is modest about his role, but visit by people from Washington DC to drama class (run by actor/teacher Arnold Johnson) and orchestra rehearsal led by Dixon clinched Federal grant for one of the first such neighbourhood projects. (Milford Graves was another effective participant.) To music faculty Bennington College (Vt.) '68; visiting professor of music U. of Wisconsin/Madison '71-2; was offered permanent appointment, returned to Bennington to be near his small son; also taught at Ohio State, George Washington and Columbia Universities. Works in Bennington with student ensembles; has met opposition on the grounds that there is no such thing as 'black music', which misses the point: improvised music is now an international language, but blacks have taught it since Armstrong. Invited by French Ministry of Culture to Autumn Festival in Paris '76; specially wrote *Autumn Sequences From A Paris Diary*. Records have been few, partly because of disgust at the way art is controlled; beautiful LP *Intents And Purposes* '67 on RCA incl. *Metamorphosis: 1962-66* and *Voices* for ensemble with Jimmy GARRISON, Byard Lancaster, Jimmy CHEATHAM on bass trombone (has taught at Bennington, as did Garrison, Graves), plus English horn, cello etc.; also solo *Nightfall Pieces* with alto flute and flugelhorn overdubbed. Enterprise of small labels resulted in more issues: two vols. of *Considerations* with Silva, Steve Horenstein, others made '72-6 at Bennington issued by Fore in Italy; two vols. of *In Italy* and 2-disc *November 1981*, all on Soul Note; also limited editions: *For Franz* on Pipe label (Vienna '77); *Bill Dixon 1970-73* on Ferrari Edizione (Verona '83). *Bill Dixon Collection* on Cadence (NY '85) is 2-disc set of solos from Bennington '70-6. *Thoughts* '85 is a septet with three basses, released '87 on Soul Note. 'The man

who played through the wildest days of the free revolution with an unashamed lyricism is a non-conformist' (Barry McRae in *Jazz Journal* '81). Autobiography *The Fifth Of October* was in preparation.

DIXON, Willie (*b* 1 July '15, Vicksburg, Miss.) Bassist; also guitar, singer, songwriter; perhaps the single most important figure in classic era of urban Chicago blues. First moved to Chicago late '20s; in and out of music until '32; won Golden Gloves amateur heavyweight boxing title '36; turned pro, then to pro music instead '37: met guitarist/pianist Leonard Caston at the gym (aka 'Baby Doo'; *b* 2 June '17, Sumrall, Miss.); Dixon learned bass and worked with Caston in The Five Breezes, then The Big Three Trio mid-'40s. Backed up other bluesmen; worked as house bassist, composer, talent scout etc. for Chess label '52-6, other Chicago labels '56-60, played on and otherwise contributed to hits by Muddy WATERS, Bo DIDDLEY, Howlin' WOLF, Otis RUSH, many others; wrote 'Hoochie Coochie Man', 'I Just Want To Make Love To You', 'Little Red Rooster', 'Wang Wang Doodle', 'Seventh Son', scores more: Leonard Chess called him 'my right arm'. Formed own music publishing company, made film, TV, festival appearances (UK TV film *Chicago Blues* '70, *Out Of The Blacks And Into The Blues* '72, etc.). Not many LPs as leader: *Willie's Blues* '59 with MEMPHIS SLIM on Prestige Bluesville, also *I Am The Blues* on Columbia, *Mighty Earthquake & Hurricane* now on Pausa.

D'LEON, Oscar Venezuelan singer, bassist, bandleader, composer, arranger, whose LPs have been hits in Billboard salsa charts in the '80s. He was bassist and singer early '70s with Venezuela's top band Dimension Latina, a trombone-led outfit whose mus. dir. was trombonist/arr. César Monge; also incl. vocalist Wladimir Lozano. Albums on Top Hits (still D'Leon's label) incl. hits compiled on *Exitos de la Dimension Latina*. (Puerto Rican vocalist Andy Montañez joined Dimension Latina '77 from EL GRAN COMBO, worked with vocalists Lozano and Rodrigo Mendoza; Mendoza went on to sing with La Gran Banda de Venezuela, incl. LP *Sabrosito* on Faisan.) D'Leon formed own band Salsa Mayor '76 with two trombones (incl. William Puchi), two trumpets (incl. Cesar Pinto) and pianist/arr. Enrique 'Culebra' Iriarte; first LP by Oscar D'Leon y su Salsa Mayor was *Con Bajo y Todo* '76, with additional arr. by pianist Samuel Del Real (also played on singer Joe Ruiz's *Salsa* '84, recorded with his own band on Velvet). Alfredo Padilla on timbales and vocalist Leo Pacheco joined Salsa Mayor for live album *2 Sets con Oscar* '77; *El 'Oscar' de la Salsa* '77 incl. songs written by Cubans Ignacio Piñeiro (led Septeto Nacional) and Miguel Matamoros (Trio Matamoros). D'Leon parted with Salsa Mayor '78, releasing 2-disc set *Oscar D'Leon/Wladimir y su Salsa Mayor*, adding a third trumpet; reunion with Lozano incl. only Pinto and Iriarte from original Salsa Mayor lineup which continued with Padilla leading, Puchi as co-dir. (and playing violin, tres as well as trombone), and Pacheco with two other vocalists (*De Frente y Luchando . . . ! 'Nuestra Orquesta'* on Velvet). D'Leon's new band had three trumpets (incl. Pinto) and two trombones, incl. Iriarte, vocalist Edgar 'El Abuelo' Rodriguez; LPs incl. *El Mas Grande!* and *. . . Llegó . . . Actuó . . . y . . . Triunfó!. . .* '79 (latter made in NYC), *Al Frente de Todos* '80. *A mi si me gusta asi!* '81 was made in Puerto Rico with an extra trumpet, trombone and a saxophone; D'Leon became sole lead singer, Pinto was gone and first trumpet was Alfredo 'Pollo' Gil; Iriarte still shared arranging, joined by arr./pianists Enrico Enriquez (who played on the LP) and José 'Flaco' Bermudez (had worked with La Amistad, an offshoot of Dimension Latina, with vocalist Mendoza and keyboardist Jesus Chuito Narvaez: LP on Velvet). Bermudez and Gil shared arranging on *El Discobola* '82; *Oscar D'Leon . . . Con Dulzura* '83 featured a synthesiser; next three LPs '84-5 were arranged by Bermudez: *El Sabor de Oscar* had Daniel Silva sharing bass chores as D'Leon concentrated more on singing; Silva took over bass on *Con Cariño* and *Yo Soy*; each album incl. a song by young Cuban pianist/leader Adalberto Alvarez. D'Leon has also worked with La Critica, incl. their first LP *Oscar D'Leon Presenta . . . La Critica* '81, with trumpet front line; prod. their '85 Top Hits LP with trombone front line as co-mus. dir. with arr./trombonist

'Albóndiga' ('Meatball', nickname for César Monge), sang with Rodriguez. Stripped his own horns back to trombones '86, toured with band described as original 'La Dimension Latina'; *Oscar '86* arr. and co-prod. by Monge, *Riquiti . . . !* '87 by Monge and José 'Flaco' Bermudez, followed by more fresh material in *La Salsa Soy Yo* '87.

DOBSON, Richard (*b* 19 Mar. '42, Tyler, Texas) Country-rock singer, songwriter, guitarist. First LP *In Texas Last December* '76 on Buttermilk label, Houston incl. fine title song; 'Baby Ride Easy', covered by Billie Jo SPEARS & Del WOOD, Carlene CARTER & Dave EDMUNDS; and 'Piece Of Wood & Steel' covered by David Allan COE. *The Big Taste* '78 on Rinconada label, Galveston, followed by *Save The World* '82, on own RJD label: a superb set of songs, mostly about working for a living; 'Ballad Of Robin Wintersmith' covered by Nanci GRIFFITH; 'Lovin' Yolanda' by Don Sanders. Excellent band incl. David and Leland Waddell on bass, drums, Phillip Donnelly, lead guitar. *True West* '86 is another strong set, mostly love songs: 'You Ain't Gonna Do It To Me' would fit in Bob DYLAN's canon; 'Goosebumps' is excellent rockabilly/bar band fodder; 'So Have I' co-written with Susanna and Guy CLARK. Other songs have been covered by Clark, Rodney CROWELL, Linda Lowe. He has also published a novel, *Seasons And Companions*. *Save The World* was prod. by Jim Rooney, picker/poet who also plays on *True West*; his own LPs incl. *Ready For The Times To Get Better* '80, *Brand New Tennessee Waltz* '81; wrote books *Baby Let Me Follow You Down* (about USA folk revival '50s-60s), *Bossmen* (portraits of Bill MONROE, Muddy WATERS).

DR FEELGOOD UK R&B revival band formed '71 by guitarist Wilko Johnson (John Wilkinson), veteran of local Southend bands, vocalist Lee Brilleaux (*b* '48, London), bassist John B. 'Sparko' Sparks. Name from old Pirates B-side written by Willie Perryman (*see* PIANO RED); mixed new tunes with covers of Chuck BERRY, Elmore JAMES, Sonny Boy WILLIAMSON etc. Backed Heinz ('60s pop star, ex-Tornados) for a while; drummer 'Bandsman' Howarth, pianist John Potter replaced by drummer John

'The Big Figure' Martin; went to London circuit from native Southend, helped revive pub-rock scene with manic act, Johnson wielding Telecaster like machine gun as Brilleaux bawled and blew harmonica. Rough sound failed to translate to discs (*Down On The Jetty* in honest mono, *Malpractice* in stereo, both '75) until live *Stupidity* released '76, became surprise no. 1 LP UK as punk hovered in wings. Many early punk bands (Joe Strummer's 101ers, Eddie and the Hot Rods, BOOMTOWN RATS etc.) infl. by Feelgood's stripped-down sound, anti-fashion image, energetic act. After *Sneakin' Suspicion* '77 Johnson left after row during recording of *Be Seeing You* '77 (prod. by Nick LOWE): loss of talented writer and Brilleaux's onstage foil; John 'Gypie' Mayo (John Cawthra) replaced him with more mainstream style; *Private Practice* '78 incl. no. 9 hit, Nick Lowe's 'Milk And Alcohol'. *As It Happens* and *Let It Roll* '79; then into '80s with less commercial success but constant touring: live pull still strong. Mayo retired after *A Case Of The Shakes* '80, third live LP *On The Job* '81, replaced by ex-Count Bishop Johnny Guitar; *Casebook* '81 is compilation; *Fast Women & Slow Horses* '82 might have been the end, but they still clock up 250 gigs a year: Sparks and Martin left '82 because of road fatigue; *Doctor's Orders* '84 had gravel-voiced Brilleaux as only original member, with Gordon Russell, guitar; Phil Mitchell, bass; Kevin Morris, drums. Best in years was *Brilleaux* '86, incl. songs by Johnny CASH, John HIATT; saw them back on Stiff label, which Brilleaux had helped found with a loan in '76. First four LPs demonstrate pub-rock appeal; six charted in UK altogether.

DR HOOK AND THE MEDICINE SHOW USA rock/pop band formed New Jersey '68. Lineup: Ray Sawyer (*b* 1 Feb. '37), vocals; Dennis Locorriere (*b* 13 June '48), vocals, guitar; Bill Francis (*b* 16 Jan. '42), keyboards; George Cummings (*b* 28 July '38), pedal steel; John David (*b* 8 Aug. '42), drums: Locorriere and David from N.J., Sawyer and Francis from Ala., David from Cal.; later joined by Richard Elswit (*b* 6 July '45), guitar; Jance Garfat (*b* 3 Mar. '44), bass; John Walters, drums (replaced David '73); Bob 'Willard' Henke, guitar. Manager

got them appearance playing Shel Silverstein's 'Last Morning' in film *Who Is Harry Kellerman And Why Is He Saying All Those Terrible Things About Me?* '71; LP *Dr Hook And The Medicine Show* same year revealed satirists too subtle for pop charts: cartoonist Silverstein intended 'Sylvia's Mother' to be send-up of country music; listeners took it straight, made it hit (no. 5 USA/2 UK). Frontman Sawyer had lost an eye in a car crash, wore eye patch; stage act got zaniness across; Silverstein also wrote 'Roland The Roadie & Gertrude The Groupie', '(Freakin' At) The Freakers' Ball' etc.; also ballads: 'Queen Of The Silver Dollar' covered by Emmylou HARRIS; 'Ballad Of Lucy Jordan' by Marianne FAITHFULL. *Sloppy Seconds* '72 incl. Silverstein title track, also 'The Cover Of "Rolling Stone"' (no. 6 USA '72) got them cover of *Rolling Stone*; banned by BBC, regarded as advertising, so band made limited edition 'Cover Of The Radio Times'. *Belly Up* '73 followed by *Fried Face* '74; *Ballad Of Lucy Jordan* '75 was best-of, with Silverstein's best songs; filed bankruptcy and switched from Columbia to Capitol for *Bankrupt* '75; by now performing more of their own songs. *A Little Bit More* '76 incl. no. 11 hit title track, cover of Sam COOKE's 'Only Sixteen' no. 6: began transition from crazy rebels to smooth disco balladeers, but still loony on stage. Sawyer left '80; by then Silverstein had stopped writing for them. Other LPs incl. *Street People* and *Revisited*, both on Columbia '77; *Makin' Love And Music* '77, *Pleasure And Pain* '78, *Sometimes You Win* '79, *Greatest Hits* '80 on Capitol; *Rising* '80 and *Players In The Dark* '81 on Casablanca; hits 'When You're In Love With A Beautiful Woman' (no. 6 USA/1 UK), 'Sharing The Night Together' (6 USA/43 UK), 'Sexy Eyes' (5 USA/4 UK), 'Better Love Next Time' (12 USA/8 UK).

DODD, Ken (*b* 8 Nov. '29, Liverpool) UK comic, singer. Worked as travelling tinker; club work; first important appearance in variety in Nottingham '54. Zany, original stage act with wild hair, prominent teeth, rapid-fire gags, tickling stick; popular singer of romantic ballads for over 20 years: top 10 UK with first record 'Love Is Like A Violin' '60; more hits followed by no. 1 'Tears' '65, song by Frank Capano and Russian-born nightclub owner Billy Uhr. 'The River' (Le Colline sono in Fiore) no. 3 '65; 'Promises' no. 6 '66; hits thinned, but charted again '81 with 'Hold My Hand'. Much-loved on TV; also works hard with stage act, trying to keep theatres open all over UK. Compilation *20 Golden Greats Of Ken Dodd* on Warwick UK.

DODDS, Baby (*b* Warren Dodds, 24 Dec. 1898, New Orleans, La.; *d* 14 Feb. '59, Chicago, Ill.) Drummer; most famous in New Orleans JAZZ style. Youngest of six children, studied drums while working in sack factory. Marching band with Bunk JOHNSON; played cabaret; riverboats with Fate MARABLE; joined King OLIVER in Calif., to Chicago with him '22, played on classic Oliver records '23-4 with Louis ARMSTRONG and brother Johnny DODDS (used woodblocks on records because technology could not record full drum kit). In Chicago '20s with Honore Dutrey, Freddie KEPPARD, Lil ARMSTRONG, Johnny; freelance recording with Louis, Jelly Roll MORTON; in '30s with Johnny, also helped brother Bill run taxis; with Jimmie NOONE '40-1; with rediscovered Bunk Johnson '44-5, then back and forth to NYC, with Art HODES, on Rudi Blesh radio show *This Is Jazz* during revival era; to Europe '48 with Mezz MEZZROW; with Hodes again etc. Suffered strokes '49-50, began slowing down. *The Baby Dodds Story* as told to Larry Gara published '59.

DODDS, Johnny (*b* 12 Apr. 1892, Waverly, La.; *d* 8 Aug. '40, Chicago, Ill.) Clarinet, some alto sax. Worked off and on with Kid ORY c.'11-19, briefly with Fate MARABLE; with King OLIVER in Chicago, Calif., back to Chicago '19-23: demonstrated classic New Orleans clarinet style on famous Oliver records '23-4. With Honore Dutrey, Freddie KEPPARD at Kelly's Stables '24; took over residency there, often with brother Baby DODDS, Keppard returning for brief periods, until club suddenly closed for violating Prohibition '30. Prolific freelance records during this period with Louis ARMSTRONG (incl. Hot Fives and Hot Sevens), Jelly Roll MORTON (two Red Hot Pepper dates, June '27); Oliver (specially hired for solo on 'Someday Sweetheart' Sept. '26). Led own small bands Chicago through '30s; only visit to NYC for record session Jan.

'38; heart attack '39, teeth trouble; with new teeth played in Baby's quartet until March '40. Compilation *Johnny Dodds* '68 on RCA incl. small groups '28-9 with Dodds as leader plus Dutrey, Baby, Lil Armstrong, others; also Dixieland Jug Blowers '26. He was unsurpassed for tone, melodic ideas; helped point jazz away from clichés and novelty effects towards beauty. Along with Jimmy NOONE was biggest infl. on Benny GOODMAN, Pee Wee RUSSELL, many others.

DOGGETT, Bill (*b* William Ballard Doggett, 16 Feb. '16, Philadelphia, Pa.) Piano, organ, arranger. Formed own band '38, Lucky MILLINDER fronted it on tour; worked for Jimmy MUNDY, Millinder again; pianist, arr. for the INK SPOTS '42-4, worked for Lionel HAMPTON, Count BASIE, Louis ARMSTRONG, Louis JORDAN '40s; played Hammond organ from '51, made Blue Note session '52 with Vic DICKENSON, Jo JONES, John Collins on guitar (*b* 20 Sep. '13, Montgomery, Ala.; worked for Nat COLE from '51 until Cole's death); then R&B combo: huge 2-sided R&B hit 'Honky Tonk' '56 had Clifford Scott on tenor sax (*b* 21 June '28, San Antonio, Texas; guitar by Billy Butler linking choruses, Doggett playing BOOGIE WOOGIE-like slow shuffle on organ: no. 2 pop chart (in top 10 for 14 weeks), no. 1 R&B. Seven more top 100 hits '56-60 incl. 'Slow Walk' (no. 26 '56; Sil AUSTIN also had R&B hit). 'Honky Tonk' re-entered '61; success was marvellous tribute to infl. of R&B on pop beginning with 'jump bands' like Jordan's. Doggett won *Cashbox* award as top R&B act '57-9. Arr. and cond. LP for Ella FITZGERALD *Rhythm Is Our Business* '63 on Verve; with Della REESE '66. Touring into '80s, incl. Europe. Original hits on KING, *16 Bandstand Favorites* on Starday.

DOLBY, Thomas (*b* Thomas Morgan Dolby Robertson, 14 Oct. '58, Cairo, Egypt) UK keyboardist. Mixed love of music (piano, guitar) and passion for radio, electronics; led him early to synthesisers. Built own PA system, took it on the road with Fall, Members, etc. establishing him as electronics whiz-kid. Made *English Garden* '79, underrated first LP by Bruce Woolley and the Camera Club; left to back Lene Lovich, writing eccentric new wave chanteuse's minor '81 hit 'New Toy'; own first single

'Urges' for Armageddon label with help from XTC's Andy Partridge; worked in Fallout Club project with Trevor Herion, vocals; Matthew Seligman, bass; Paul Simon, drums. Three singles on Happy Birthday label incl. 'Wanderlust', confirmed melodic touch with synth layers, led to session work with Foreigner (4 '81), Joan ARMATRADING (*Walk Under Ladders* '81); signed by EMI same year, given own Venice In Peril label. First LP *The Golden Age Of Wireless* incl. two minor UK hits 'Europa And The Pirate Twins' no. 48 '81, 'Windpower' 31 '82; former colleagues Woolley, Partridge, Lovich helped impressively confident debut. Puts across image of English eccentric on videos; hired the real thing – TV scientist Magnus Pyke – for promo of 'She Blinded Me With Science' '83: made no. 5 in USA, where artists rated him too: Joe ELY went electronic after hearing 'One Of Our Submarines'; funk ace George Clinton recorded 'May The Cube Be With You' with him (as occasional Dolby's Cube); Joni MITCHELL sought him to co-prod. *Dog Eat Dog* '85 when he covered her 'Jungle Line'. Finally reached top 20 in UK with 'Hyperactive' from *The Flat Earth* '84, astonishingly varied LP that incl. cover of ex-CHARLATAN Dan Hicks's vintage 'I Scare Myself'. Dolby's one-man live shows (predating Howard JONES) used computers, videos, tapes, slide shows; latterly used band incl. Adele Bertei, co-vocalist on 'Hyperactive', video of which was typically inventive/manic. Has recorded with Ryuichi Sakamoto, Grace JONES; prod. Prefab Sprout's second LP *Steve McQueen* '85; backed David BOWIE on Live Aid; written script for Steven Spielberg. Arrived just in time to profit from early '80s move towards synth, but high standing among peers is evidence of talent that will last. Composed and played score for Ken Russell film *Gothic* '87. Album *Aliens Ate My Buick* '88.

DOLLAR, Johnny (*b* John Washington Dollar Jr, 3 Aug. '33, Kilgore, Texas; *d* Apr. '86) Country singer with many fans who never hit the really big time. Worked as truck driver, cattle rancher, DJ while singing evenings in Texas, New Mexico '53-61; led The Texas Sons '53-4, member of Martin McCullough's Light Crust Doughboys '55-7. Recorded for small Texas labels,

signed with Columbia '64; eight entries in country chart '66-70 incl. biggest hit 'Stop The Start (Of Tears In My Heart)' '66, others on Dot, Date, Chart labels. LPs incl. *Mr Personality* '66, *Johnny Dollar* '67, *Big Rollin Man* '73. Died of cancer.

DOLPHY, Eric Allan (*b* 20 June '28, L.A., Calif.; *d* 29 June '64, Berlin, Germany) Alto sax, clarinet, bass clarinet, flute, composer. Worked in L.A.; member of Chico HAMILTON quintet '58-9; to NYC '60 joining Charles MINGUS quartet with Ted CURSON, Dannie RICHMOND; own quintet at Five Spot with Booker LITTLE, Mal WALDRON, Ed BLACKWELL, Richard Davis on bass '61; often with John COLTRANE from '61; own group with Freddie HUBBARD '62; freelanced around NYC, recording as leader, sideman. With Mingus in Europe '64; concerts taped with Mingus and with Dutch, Scandinavian rhythm sections; died of complications of diabetes. Like John Coltrane a gentle, intelligent man, widely loved, one of the most infl. musicians of the decade, with a need to express himself spiritually that extended frontiers of the music – but paradoxically retaining elegance that Coltrane was more willing to risk: Dolphy was inspired by bird calls, marching bands, etc. as well as by deeper mysteries, and hard-won tonal purity in his playing remained a hallmark; for these reasons he may in the long run be greater infl. even than Coltrane. Mastered difficult bass clarinet (played now by Chico FREEMAN, David MURRAY, others) as Coltrane had explored soprano sax. LPs incl. *Looking Ahead* '60 by Ken McIntyre (*b* 7 Sep. '31, Boston; later became teacher, worked on Ph.D. in music), Waldron's *The Quest* '61 (with Ron CARTER, Booker ERVIN, Joe Benjamin, Charlie Persip on bass, drums); Carter's *Where?* '61 with Waldron; own LPs *Out There* with Carter, *Far Cry* with Carter, Waldron, Booker Little, Jaki BYARD '60 (latter incl. 'Tenderly', unaccompanied alto solo); also *Outward Bound* with Hubbard, three vols. of *Live At The Five Spot*, three of *Live In Europe*, all on Prestige, reissued in various formats (e.g. 2- or 3-disc sets). Also *Out To Lunch* with Hubbard on Blue Note, regarded as one of his best. With Mingus: *Mingus Presents Mingus* '60, quartet (*see* entry for Curson); *Mingus Mingus Mingus* '63 on Impulse; *Town Hall Concert* '64, Mingus's record dist. by Fantasy; 3-disc *The Great Concert Of Charles Mingus* '64 on Prestige, others. With Coltrane: *Ole Coltrane, Impressions, Africa/Brass* (Dolphy cond. large group) all '61 on Impulse. With Ornette COLEMAN: *Free Jazz* '60 (interestingly, recorded earlier same day as Dolphy's *Far Cry*). With Max ROACH: *Percussion Bitter Sweet* '61 on Impulse, with Little, Waldron, Abbey LINCOLN. European and informal dates incl. *Berlin Concerts, Stockholm Sessions* '61 on Enja; NYC sessions recorded mid-'63 by Alan Douglas have been on Douglas, Trip, FM labels, known as *Iron Man, Memorial Album*; four tracks now in *Music Matador* on Affinity UK; *Iron Man* and *Conversations* on OAO '87. *Last Date* recorded in Holland, June '64, on Limelight and Fontana labels. Dolphy's is one of the great unfinished careers in the history of art; work still coming to light sounds as fresh as the day of recording: tapes from Dolphy's private collection issued as *Other Aspects* '87 on Blue Note incl. beautiful 'Jim Crow', flute solos '60-2; *Vintage Dolphy* on GM incl. three compositions by Gunther SCHULLER from 20th Century Innovation series at Carnegie Hall.

DOMINO, Fats (*b* Antoine Domino, 26 Feb. '28, New Orleans, La.) Singer, pianist, bandleader; one of earliest, most popular of '50s rock'n'roll stars: 36 top 40 hits in eight years; 66 in all in Billboard's Hot 100 '55-68. First language was French; singing, playing in public age 10; heard by Dave BARTHOLOMEW, signed by Imperial: first recording session '49 incl. trad. 'Hey La Bas', indicating coming together of many decades of New Orleans history and musical influence: 'La Bas' was originally a voodoo god of luck, then identified in French/Catholic Louisiana with St Peter, finally became La Bas. First release was cleaned-up drug song 'The Fat Man': made R&B chart '50. Fifth release 'Every Night About This Time' used piano triplet for which he became famous, showing infl. of Little Willie Littlefield (*b* 16 Sep. '31, Houston, Texas; no. 3 R&B hit 'It's Midnight' on Modern '49). Fats's R&B hits incl. 'Goin' Home' '52; became crossover act '55 when Pat BOONE covered 'Ain't That A Shame', made no. 1 on pop chart, Fats's own record

made no. 10. Five pop chart entries '56 incl. 'I'm In Love Again', 'Bo Weevil'; 'Blue Monday' '57 featured in film *The Girl Can't Help It*, probably the best rock'n'roll movie. 'I'm Walkin'' was covered by Ricky NELSON that year, the beginning of Nelson's career in music. Most hits Domino-Bartholomew comps, though 'All By Myself' '55 essentially the same song recorded by Big Bill BROONZY many years earlier. Some standards: 'Blueberry Hill', 'What's The Reason I'm Not Pleasin' You' '56; 'Red Sails In The Sunset' '63; also Hank WILLIAMS's 'Jambalaya' '62, BEATLES' 'Lady Madonna' '68. Smoky, blues-tinged voice with trace of accent instantly likeable; party-music formula perfectly captured the innocent pleasure of early pop/rock with riffing saxes, rocking tenor solo (often by Lee ALLEN or Herb Hardesty), rolling BOOGIE WOOGIE infl. piano style with lots of triplets: band rocked hard with heavy backbeat but made it sound easy. Still played Las Vegas well into the '70s, London's Royal Festival Hall '80s; compilation albums still selling: any LP from Imperial masters (now owned by EMI) is authentic New Orleans stuff; *Domino* '65 on Mercury captured live act superbly.

DONAHUE, Sam (*b* 8 Mar. '18, Detroit, Mich.; *d* 22 Mar. '74, Reno, Nev.) Tenor sax, arranger, bandleader. Led own band late '30s; played for Gene KRUPA, Harry JAMES, Benny GOODMAN; own band early '40s (hit on Bluebird '41: 'Do You Care?' with vocal by Irene Day); took over Artie SHAW's US Navy band when Shaw was discharged, made good V-discs with it. Own band late '40s; worked for Tommy DORSEY; own band again; a dozen hits '46-8 incl. instrumentals 'My Melancholy Baby', 'Robbins Nest', 'Saxa-Boogie'; also vocals with Mynell Allen, Shirley Lloyd; Bill Lockwood ('Put That Kiss Back Where You Found It', 'I Never Knew'). He took over the Billy MAY band and led it for Ray ANTHONY organisation; led own band again, worked for Stan KENTON, then took over the Tommy Dorsey Orchestra five years after Dorsey died: it later became the Frank Sinatra Jr Show. Was still leading band in Reno when stricken with cancer. His bands and his booting tenor sax were always popular; his own LPs incl. *Young Moderns In*

351

Love and *Sam Donahue* on Capitol '50s; later *Sam Donahue And The Tommy Dorsey Orchestra* on RCA, recorded live at an NYC hotel.

DONALDSON, Lou (*b* 1 Nov. '26, Badin, N.C.) Alto sax. Mother a music teacher, took up clarinet at 15, studied music in US Navy; played with Charlie PARKER, Sonny STITT; to NYC, gigs at Five Spot, Half Note etc.; Golden Circle in Sweden '65. Funky, bluesy post-Parker style typical of BLUE NOTE in '50s-60s; good on ballads too. Dislikes the avant-garde. Combo from '61 usually incl. organ and guitar. First LPs on Blue Note with Horace SILVER; then *New Faces, New Sounds* '52-3 (2 vols. with Silver, no. 2 with Clifford BROWN, Elmo HOPE); many own combo LPs '50s, '60s incl. *The Time Is Right* '59, *Midnight Sun* '60 with Horace PARLAN, *Here 'Tis* '61 with Baby Face Willette, organ; *The Natural Soul* '62, *Good Gracious* '63 with John Patton, organ. Then on Argo for *Signifyin'* '63, *Possom Head* '64 with Patton; *Rough House Blues* '64 is nine-piece group arr. by Oliver NELSON. Back on Blue Note *Sweet Slumber* is nine-piece group incl. Ron CARTER, Freddie HUBBARD, Wayne SHORTER, Pepper ADAMS and McCoy TYNER; *Alligator Boogaloo* '67, *Midnight Creeper* '68 have George BENSON, Lonnie SMITH; *Say It Loud* '68, *Hot Dog* and *Everything I Play Is Funky* '69 feature Charles EARLAND. *Cosmos* '71 incl. girl vocal trio; *Sophisticated Lou* '72 strings. *Sweet Lou* '74 (Blue Note), *A Different Scene* '76, *Color As A Way Of Life* '77 (Cotillion) have big bands, vocalists. Combos again: *Forgotten Man* '81 (Timeless; sings on 'Whiskey Drinkin' Woman'), *Sweet Papa Lou* '81, *Back Street* '82 (Muse). *The Natural Soul*, albums with Benson, Earland, *Sweet Lou* plus *Sassy Soul Strut* '73 all made Billboard top 200 pop LPs.

DONEGAN, Dorothy (*b* 6 Apr. '24, Chicago) Pianist, jazz-oriented; also played organ. Became popular in Chicago clubs early '40s; intimate style was ideal for club work. Appeared in film *Sensations of 1945*; popular through '50s. LPs inc. *At The Embers* on Roulette, *Dorothy Donegan Live!* and *Donneybrook With Donegan* on Capitol. *Brown Gal* '87 on Krazy Kat UK compiles tracks from Gotham label by Camille

Howard (who played piano and sang with Roy MILTON), Lil ARMSTRONG, and two by Donegan.

DONEGAN, Lonnie (*b* Anthony Donegan, 29 Apr. '31, Glasgow) Singer, guitarist. Changed name in homage to bluesman Lonnie JOHNSON; sang, played in Chris BARBER, Ken COLYER trad. groups; launched SKIFFLE movement, playing onstage between sets: appeal of cheap Spanish guitar, tea-chest bass, washboard and 'anyone can do it' attitude launched untold numbers on pop road. Plundered USA country/folk heritage, used songs by Woody GUTHRIE, LEADBELLY etc.; had 31 top 30 UK hits '58-62 not incl. reentries but incl. one EP and one LP in singles chart; 'Gambling Man', 'Cumberland Gap', 'My Old Man's A Dustman' all no. 1. 'Rock Island Line' was no. 8 '56 in both USA, UK; Stan FREBERG recorded send-up in USA, Jim DALE ('Piccadilly Line') in UK. Other USA hits incl. 'Lost John' no. 58 '56, 'Does Your Chewing Gum Lose Its Flavour (On The Bedpost Overnight)' no. 5 '61. Favourite on pioneering UK pop TV shows *Oh Boy* and *6.5 Special*; banished suddenly to cabaret circuit in backwash of BEATLES, whom he had inspired. Dave Cousins (the STRAWBS) said that the three most important elements in UK pop had been Donegan, DJ John PEEL and the Beatles; roster of comeback LP *Puttin' On The Style* '77 admitted Donegan's influence: Elton JOHN, Ringo STARR, Brian May (QUEEN), Gary Brooker (PROCOL HARUM), Rory GALLAGHER, Albert Lee, Ron Wood; *Sundown* '78 didn't fare as well. Still working after heart attacks; new acts (e.g. the Shakin' Pyramids, Terry & Jerry) still turn up infl. by 30-year-old work. Donegan showed business acumen in buying copyright to MOODY BLUES 'Knights In White Satin' '60s.

DONNER, Ral (*b* Ralph Stuart Emanuel Donner, 10 Feb. '43, Chicago; *d* '84) Singer. Owed celebrity to sounding like Elvis PRESLEY, doing creditable imitations from age 15; worked on local TV; spotted by Sammy DAVIS Jr; tape of 'Girl Of My Best Friend' (song of obvious potential hit which Presley had not released on a single) sent to Gone Records, went top 20 USA '61. Biggest hits same year: 'You Don't Know What

You've Got (Until You Lose It)' no. 4, 'She's Everything (I Wanted You To Be)' no. 18; no chart action after mid-'62 despite work on bewildering variety of small labels. Made remarkable 2-disc album *1937-1977 I've Just Been Away For A While Now*, soundalike Presley tribute with his former sidemen Scotty Moore, D. J. Fontana, JORDANAIRES; narrator and Presley's voice in film *This Is Elvis* '81. Died of an incurable disease; hits stand test of time better than some.

DONOVAN (*b* Donovan Leitch, 10 May '46, Glasgow, Scotland) Singer/songwriter. Moved to London area age 10, first records at 18, on UK TV pop show *Ready, Steady, Go!* '65. Folkish first LP and hit single 'Catch The Wind' showed infl. of Woody GUTHRIE, incongruously but successfully produced by pop person Mickie MOST on Pye label UK, Hickory USA. His own 'Colours' and Buffy SAINTE-MARIE's 'Universal Soldiers' both hits; switched to Epic in USA; songs continued to be acoustic-based: 'Sunny Goodge Street' covered by Judy COLLINS, 'Season Of The Witch' by Julie Driscoll. Bob DYLAN's '65 film of UK tour *Don't Look Back* incl. digs at Donovan; he could not escape Dylan's shadow, though comparison was unfair to both. After appearance at '65 Newport Folk Festival and during burgeoning hippie scene Donovan tapped new audience with 'Sunshine Superman', 'Mellow Yellow'; both big hits in UK and USA, taken as encomia for soft drugs: 'Yellow' gave rise to silly fad for smoking dried banana skins. Further childlike hits: 'There Is A Mountain', 'Epistle To Dippy', 'Wear Your Love Like Heaven' (later used as jingle in cosmetic advert); embraced meditation philosophy, joined the BEATLES in India. 2-disc set *A Gift From A Flower To A Garden* '68 seemed innovatory at the time, with lavish cover art and lyric sheets; with hindsight was the apogee of English psychedelia. 'Jennifer Juniper' was a bit silly; 'Hurdy Gurdy Man' more imaginative; 'Goo Goo Barabajagal (Love Is Hot)' was rock outing with Jeff BECK '69. Adoption as darling of flower children turned to disaster; with reaction he was dismissed as twee. After 12 hits in USA top 40 '65-9, '71 tour was poorly attended. Published poems *Dry Songs And Scribbles*; starred in and scored

'72 German film *The Pied Piper*; scored others e.g. Zeffirelli's '72 *Brother Sun, Sister Moon*. Greatest hits compilation LP followed by concept LP *7-Tease* '74; *Slow Down World* supported by USA tour '76. His appearance at Amnesty International benefit show London '82 well received: no longer a world-beater, but affection still there.

DOOBIE BROTHERS USA rock band formed '70 in San José, Cal., where drummer John Hartman (*b* 18 Mar. '50, Falls Church, Va.) had gone to re-form MOBY GRAPE with Skip Spence, instead formed Pud with guitarist Tom Johnston (*b* Visalia, Cal.); bass Gregg Murphy replaced by Dave Shogren (*b* San Francisco). Guitarist Patrick Simmons (*b* 23 Jan. '50, Aberdeen, Wash.) added; changed name to Doobie Brothers from slang for marijuana cigarette. Established in Bay Area as hard driving band, but first LP for WB *The Doobie Brothers* '71, co-prod. by Ted Templeman and Larry Waronker, in acoustic vein of then-popular labelmates AMERICA. Added extra drummer Michael Hossack (*b* 18 Sep. '50, Paterson, NY), replaced Shogren with Tiran Porter (*b* L.A.) (had worked with Simmons in Scratch). Changes beefed up sound; with Templeman in complete control *Toulouse Street* '72 was a more accurate LP: with solid backbeat, interlocking guitars, everyone in on the harmonies, not unlike '70s version of Moby Grape. Johnston's more nasal voice and Simmons' softer one alternated vocals; opening track Johnston's 'Listen To The Music' no. 11 USA single. *The Captain And Me* '73 had USA hits in 'Long Train Runnin' ' and 'China Grove'; 'Music' from first LP made UK top 30 after tour there. Elements of country, folk, blues made this band's finest hour. *What Were Once Vices Are Now Habits* '74 cloned predecessor yet confounded critical charge of sameness with semi-*a cappella* USA no. 1 'Black Water'. Hossack had been replaced by Keith Knudson (*b* 18 Oct. '52, Ames, Iowa; ex-Bonaroo); then STEELY DAN refugees guitarist Jeff 'Skunk' Baxter (*b* 13 Dec.'48, Washington DC), keyboardist Michael McDonald (*b* St Louis); Johnston left because of ill-health; he'd been superseded as main writer; LP output '75-7 unmemorable but new lineup hit stride with *Minute*

By Minute '78, which yielded glorious USA no. 1 'What A Fool Believes'. Only tight harmonies remained of old Doobies' sound; LP rode on McDonald's electric keyboards, Ray CHARLES-inspired vocals: AOR but still classy. Success brought four Grammies for 'Fool'; it was now McDonald's band: Baxter and Hartman decided to get off gravy train, former to produce, latter to become a vet. *One Step Closer* '80 incl. no. 5 hit 'Real Love', repeated formula with recruits ex-Clover John McFee (*b* 18 Nov. '53, Santa Cruz, Cal.) on guitar, Chet McCracken (*b* 17 July '52, Seattle), drums and ex-Moby Grape Cornelius Bumpus (*b* 13 Jan. '52), sax and keyboards. Simmons's guitar-based songs now fitted in poorly; he went solo as band gave up. Meanwhile Johnston made defiantly old-fashioned solo LPs *Everything You've Heard Is True* '79, *Still Feels Good To Me* '81. McDonald's *If That's What It Takes* '82 was critically acclaimed, Simmons's *Arcade* less so; both had hit singles: McDonald's 'I Keep Forgettin' (Every Time You're Near)' no. 4 '82; Simmons's 'So Wrong' no. 30 '83. McDonald's second LP was *No Lookin' Back* '85. Began as folk-rockers, shifted gears and were successful each time; 'best of' LPs '77, '81 could be by different bands. Live 2-disc souvenir released '83; McDonald had duet hit 'On My Own' with Patti LaBELLE; Europe-only compilation *Sweet Freedom* '86 named after his second UK solo hit, incl. duet, tracks with Doobies and James Ingram. Both McDonald's albums are also on CD.

DOONICAN, Val (*b* Michael Valentine Doonican, 3 Feb. '28, Waterford, Eire) Singer, guitar. Worked in a factory; teamed with pianist/guitarist Bruce Clarke, first broadcasts Radio Eireann mid-'40s. Played drums in touring band for a while; joined The Four Ramblers, vocal group moved to London '52. After seven years went solo on advice of Anthony NEWLEY; own radio series *Dreamy Afternoon*, later called *A Date With Val*. Became family favourite: London Palladium TV dates '64; 14 singles in UK top 50 '64-73 incl. 5 top tens; several albums incl. *Val Doonican Rocks But Gently* (no. 1 '67; title refers to onstage gimmick of singing from a rocking chair). Though record sales have fallen away, easy-going style (derived from Perry COMO: he often hires

same prod. Ray CHARLES) has kept his TV music/variety show going for nine years.

DOORS, The USA rock band formed L.A. '65 by vocalist/poet Jim Morrison (*b* 8 Dec. '43, Melbourne, Fla.; *d* 3 July '71, Paris) and classically trained pianist Ray Manzarek (*b* 12 Feb. '35, Chicago), students at UCLA film school. Manzarek played in R&B band Rick and the Ravens with brothers Jim and Rick, met guitarist Robby Krieger (*b* 8 Jan. '46, L.A.), drummer John Densmore (*b* 1 Dec. '45, L.A.), both ex-Psychedelic Rangers. Morrison renamed band Doors after Aldous Huxley's book about drug experience *The Doors Of Perception* (Huxley borrowed it from poet William Blake). Controversial from the start, banned from Whiskey-A-Go-Go for performing Oedipal melodrama 'The End', in contrast to Krieger's pop song 'Light My Fire', driven by Manzarek's swirling organ and edited to make no. 11 USA single. First Elektra LP *The Doors* also incl. 11-minute version of 'The End'; they had emerged from underground: *Strange Days* '67 had epic in 'When The Music's Over', addressing Vietnam and social issues: made no. 3 LP chart, two singles top 30: 'People Are Strange', 'Love Me Two Times'. *Waiting For The Sun* '68 topped LP chart, but band were falling between teen audience, who lapped up KINKS infl. 'Hello I Love You' (USA no. 1/UK no. 15), and underground, who considered them trite now that they were popular. Songs like 'Five To One' (with line 'They got the guns but we got the numbers') convinced police and promoters that music mattered and a rock band could be a genuine threat; Morrison's drink/drugs problems had led to brushes with the law; allegedly exposed himself on stage in Miami March '69; live appearances dwindled. *Soft Parade* '69 unimpressive, though 'Touch Me' was no. 3 USA; *Morrison Hotel* '70 and *L.A. Woman* '71 gave up elaborate prod. for R&B earthiness; Morrison temporarily left band for sojourn in Paris to concentrate on poetry, found dead in bath, probably from drug-related heart attack, but few saw corpse except for his wife (who od'd '74) and an anonymous doctor, fuelling rock legend that he'd faked his own death. A month later 'Riders On The Storm' from last LP made no. 14 USA. Band made two uninspired LPs before quitting; Krieger and Densmore joined Jess Roden in Butts Band; Manzarek made self-indulgent LPs, turned prod. with L.A. punks X. Doors reunited to set Morrison's poetry to music; *An American Prayer* '78 was surprisingly successful. His refusal to conform and his demise made him hero for punk's new wave; unlike majority of contemporaries Doors' music actually increased in popularity: the STRANGLERS, ECHO AND THE BUNNYMEN, countless others offered retreads; sales of back catalogue soared. Live LP *Alive She Cried* exhumed '83 to stand with *Absolutely Live* '70: Doors remained obstinately open.

DOO-WOP *A cappella* style developed by vocal groups in NYC streets c.'45-55; also to some extent in other big USA cities, but most importantly in Harlem, Brooklyn and the Bronx, named after 'doo-waaah' device often used by backing singers. Teenagers sang on the corner for pleasure and to attract girls, influenced by the INK SPOTS, MILLS BROS, Delta Rhythm Boys, other 'race' stars; then they rehearsed on the corner, or in an alley or in a tenement hallway for the acoustics, hoping to get a chance to make a record. The typical group sang four-part ballad harmony, with a high tenor (often with a sweet falsetto), a mellower second tenor lead, a blending baritone and a bass. An uncountable number of records were made; few of them made much money at the time, but they are expensive collectors' items today. There were 'bird' groups: the CROWS, PENGUINS, Ravens, Wrens, Flamingos, Robins, Cardinals, Meadowlarks, many more (satirist Stan FREBERG wrote that 'Rankled record buyers complained that after a while these records molted'); others named after cars: the CADILLACS, Lincolns, Coupe De Villes, V-Eights; also the CHORDS and the CLEFTONES, the Valentines, Valentinos, Valtones, Velons, Velvets, Veneers, Versatiles, Vibraharps, Vibrations, Vocaleers and Vocaltones. Inevitably there was confusion over names: Velvetones in NYC and Chicago; Vibranairs in Baltimore and Vibranaires in Asbury Park, N.J. Among the best loved who don't have entries in this book were the Harptones: the Skylarks '52 became the Harps, then the Harptones '53, when they first recorded: Willie Winfield, lead tenor; Nicky Clark,

second lead and first tenor; Bill Dempsey, second tenor; Bill Galloway, baritone; Bill Brown, bass; Raoul J. Cita on piano (could double as tenor or baritone). They never had any hits big enough to reach the R&B chart. The CLOVERS had huge R&B hits '51-9, the PLATTERS were the first to have a no. 1 pop hit '55; the great groups of the late '50s-60s came out of the tradition: the DRIFTERS, FOUR TOPS, TEMPTATIONS and the rest. *See also* Hank BALLARD, Harvey FUQUA, Clyde McPHATTER, Frankie LYMON *et al.* Relic Records (*see* appendix) had more than 80 doo-wop compilations available mid-'87; *Street Corner Memories* '87 on Ace celebrates the Italian-Americans, with tracks by the Orients, Vito and the Salutations, etc. *They All Sang On The Corner* '83 by Philip Groia traces personnel changes in NYC groups with obvious affection, has several discographies and a good index.

DORHAM, Kenny (*b* Howard McKinley Dorham, 30 Aug. '24, Fairfield, Texas; *d* 5 Dec. '72, NYC) Trumpet; also tenor sax, piano, composer; highly rated modern soloist. From musical family; played trumpet Austin high school, college band with Wild Bill DAVIS; from '45 with Dizzy GILLESPIE, Billy ECKSTINE, Lionel HAMPTON, Mercer ELLINGTON, Charlie PARKER late '40s; freelanced NYC, joined Art BLAKEY Jazz Messengers '55, replaced Clifford BROWN in Max ROACH quintet '56; records on Prestige with Sonny ROLLINS, Hank MOBLEY, Tadd DAMERON, J. J. JOHNSON; Blue Note with Lou DONALDSON, Thelonious MONK, Horace SILVER; others; *Coltrane Time* '58 was quintet with John COLTRANE, Cecil TAYLOR; inc. Dorham tune 'Shifting Down'. Played in soundtrack of *A Star Is Born* '54; wrote French film scores *Witness In The City* and *Dangerous Liaisons* '59; also active in music education. Sides with Be Bop Boys '46 on Savoy; first own record as leader *Kenny Dorham Quintet* '53 on Charles MINGUS's Debut label, second *Afro-Cuban* '55 on Blue Note one of his finest, with Cecil PAYNE, Hank Mobley, Horace SILVER, etc. Led own band Jazz Prophets '56, two eponymous vols. on ABC-Paramount (one later in 2-disc set on Impulse with LP by Sonny CRISS); three vols. of *'Round About Midnight At The Café Bohe-*

mia on Blue Note (two in Japan). Others on Blue Note: *Whistle Stop* '61, *Una Mas* '63, *Trumpet Toccata* '64; on Prestige *Quiet Kenny* '59 with Tommy FLANAGAN, Paul CHAMBERS, Art TAYLOR; on Riverside (LPs, titles recycled on Milestone): *Jazz Contrasts* '56, *Two Horns, Two Rhythm* '57; *This Is The Moment* '58 (with Dorham vocals), *Blue Spring* '59; others on Jaro, Xanadu, Time, Pacific Jazz, United Artists, Steeplechase (Denmark): *Kenny Dorham Sextet* on Cadet '70 live in Chicago with Muhal Richard ABRAMS, Wilbur Campbell on drums.

DORSEY, Jimmy (*b* James Francis Dorsey, 29 Feb. '04, Shenandoah, Pa.; *d* 12 June '57, NYC) Alto sax, clarinet, bandleader; sometimes played trumpet or cornet '20s, '30s. Brother of Tommy DORSEY; their father was coal miner turned music teacher; both excellent musicians, led bands together (Novelty Six, Wild Canaries), were one of the first jazz groups to broadcast. Freelance and studio work through '20s with Jean GOLDKETTE, Paul WHITEMAN, Bix BEIDERBECKE, Red NICHOLS, Ted LEWIS, Rudy VALLEE, many others. Brothers organised bands for studio work, Broadway show *Everybody's Welcome* '31, made it full-time '34 with 11 pieces: drummer was Ray McKINLEY; one trumpet, three trombones (incl. T. Dorsey, Glenn MILLER!) got round, warm sound infl. by Bing CROSBY, whom Dorseys had often played for. On way to success when brothers had violent quarrel at Glen Island Casino gig '35; both then led very popular bands. Jimmy did a lot of radio work; arrs. incl. Fud Livingston at first, later Don REDMAN, Tutti CAMARATA, others; boy singer from the beginning was Bob Eberly; Helen O'Connell joined '39; they often sang duets. Jimmy had 23 top 10 hits '40-44, incl. no. ones 'Amapola', 'My Sister And I', 2-sided 'Green Eyes'/'Maria Elena', 'Blue Champagne', all '41, 'Tangerine' '42, all classics of the era. Eberly was extremely popular, beaten in '39 poll only by Crosby; Jimmy's band was sweeter than Tommy's, but still could swing. Brothers reunited '53 until Tommy's death; Jimmy carried on until cancer forced him to hand over to trumpeter Lee CASTLE. Band had hit 'So Rare' (no. 2 '57) four months before he died. Appeared in biopic *The Fabulous Dorseys* '47,

other films; *Tommy and Jimmy – The Dorsey Years* by Herb Sandford published '72. Greatest hits compilations on MCA in phoney stereo.

DORSEY, Lee (*b* 24 Dec. '24, New Orleans, La.; *d* 1 Dec. '86) R&B singer. Served in US Navy, had fairly successful career as light heavyweight boxer in Portland, Oregon; met local songwriter Allen TOUSSAINT at a party in New Orleans and signed to Fury label for '61 hits 'Ya Ya' (no. 7 USA; sanitised cover by Petula CLARK hit in UK), 'Do-Re-Mi' was no. 27 (covered by Georgie FAME in UK but didn't hit). Fury folded and Dorsey concentrated on his car repair business, but resumed working with Toussaint on Amy label for seven more Hot 100 entries '65-9: three top 40s incl. 'Working In The Coal Mine', top 10 both UK/USA; then classic statement of era's New Orleans sound from the two veterans in album *Yes We Can* '70; title track on Polydor (no. 46 in USA soul chart) was Dorsey's last chart entry. Guested on debut LP *I Don't Want To Go Home* '76 by SOUTHSIDE JOHNNY AND THE ASBURY JUKES (duet with Johnny on 'How Come You Treat Me So Bad'), led to ABC contract, LP *Night People* '78, issued just as label closed down.

DORSEY, Thomas A. (*b* 1 July 1899, Carrol Co., Ga.) Singer, pianist, guitarist, songwriter. His father was a revivalist Baptist minister, mother a church organist; his first composition was 'If I Don't Get There'. He studied music formally before and after moving to Chicago c.'16; began as Barrelhouse Tommy in Atlanta; in Chicago worked in clubs, acc. Ma RAINEY on tour, demonstrated music in shops, arranged for Chicago Music Publishing Company/Vocalion Records, began recording. Of his pseudonyms the best known was Georgia Tom; several record dates '28-32, most famously with the Hokum Boys: Tampa Red (*b* Hudson Whittaker, c.1900-01, Ga.; *d* '81) on guitar and Bob Robinson, lead vocal: 'Beedle Um Bum' and 'Sellin' That Stuff' recorded Dec. '28, were both popular enough to be covered next year by McKINNEY'S COTTON PICKERS; other Hokum Boys, Harum Scarums dates with Jane Lucas, Big Bill BROONZY. Then his religious background took over and he became the most important composer and publisher of GOSPEL MUSIC (*which see*).

DORSEY, Tommy (*b* Thomas Francis Dorsey, 19 Nov. '05, Shenandoah, Pa.; *d* 26 Nov. '56, Greenwich, Conn.) Trombone, bandleader: one of most successful of the BIG BAND ERA. Early details similar to those of brother Jimmy DORSEY. Formed own band '35 after split from Jimmy by taking over that of old friend Joe Haymes: among the first-rate sidemen who passed through were trumpeters Bunny BERIGAN, Yank Lawson, Charlie SHAVERS, Max KAMINSKY, Sterling Bose and Charlie Spivak (*see* Bob CROSBY), Pee Wee Erwin and Ziggy Elman (*see* Benny GOODMAN); also Buddy DE FRANCO, clarinet; Bud FREEMAN, tenor sax; Dave TOUGH, Buddy RICH and Louie BELLSON, drums; Carmen Mastren, guitar (*b* Carmen Nicholas Mastandrea, 6 Oct. '13, Cohoes, NY; *d* 31 Mar. '81, Valley Stream, Long Island); arrangers Paul WESTON, Axel Stordahl, Sy OLIVER, Deane Kincaide (*b* 18 Mar. '11, Houston, Texas; also with Bob Crosby, others; played tenor until '81); singers incl. Jack Leonard, Dick Haymes, Connie Haines (*b* Yvonne Marie Jamais, 20 Jan. '22, Savannah, Ga.; had solo hits '48-9; sang in gospel quartet with actress Jane Russell '54; new album *I Am What I Am* '85 on Bainbridge). At first Leonard, Stordahl, trumpeter Joe Bauer made up vocal group the Three Esquires; later the Pied Pipers incl. Jo STAFFORD and Frank SINATRA. Other bands were sweeter, still others could SWING more consistently; Glenn MILLER had more hits '40-3; but 'The Sentimental Gentleman of Swing' probably had the best dance band: as George T. Simon put it, he could do more things better. On ballads he was one of best trombonists in music, with seamless legato, beautiful tone, phrasing; Sinatra admitted learning about phrasing, dynamics from Dorsey. A good jazz musician too (but knew he was outgunned by Jack TEAGARDEN: story is that at '39 RCA Victor All-Stars session Tommy was asked to solo on 'The Blues', refused because Jack was there; beautiful solution had Dorsey's legato statement of the theme, counterpoint of Jack's improvisation). Band's theme 'I'm Getting Sentimental Over You' was first recorded '32 by a Dorsey brothers pickup

band. Nearly 200 hits '35-53 began at the top with no. 1 'Treasure Island', vocal by Edythe Wright (*b* Bayonne, N.J.; *d* 28 Oct. '65); other no. ones were 'The Music Goes Round And Round' '35 with Wright, 'Alone' '36 with Cliff Weston, 'You' '36 with Wright, 2-sided 'Marie'/'Song Of India' '37, both with solos by Berigan. 'India' was instrumental on Rimsky-Korsakov song, head arr. pinned down by trombonist Red Bone; 'Marie' was perhaps biggest hit of the era: Dorsey traded eight arr. for it during gig opposite Doc WHEELER's Sunset Royal Serenaders in Philadelphia. It used 'swing-choir' effect pioneered by Don REDMAN: Dorsey version recorded Jan. '37 had band chanting a paraphrase of the lyrics to countermelody while Leonard did straight vocal. 'Who' was similar follow-up. Further no. ones were 'Satan Takes A Holiday', 'The Big Apple' (by band-within-a-band the Clambake Seven), 'Once In A While' (with vocal quartet), all '37; 'Music Maestro, Please' '38 with Wright, 'Our Love' '39 (from Tchaikovsky), 'Indian Summer' and 'All The Things You Are' '39. Billboard chart hits '40-9 incl. no. ones 'I'll Never Smile Again' '40, 'There Are Such Things' '42, 'In The Blue Of Evening' '43, all with Sinatra, first two also with Pied Pipers, last two arr. Stordahl. Pine Top SMITH's 'Boogie Woogie' recorded '38 in Kincaide arrangement; sold a million by '41, made no. 5 '43 during ASCAP strike when bands couldn't record, re-entered at no. 4 '45, allegedly sold 4 million total. Oliver hired away from Jimmie LUNCEFORD, wrote 'Easy Does It', 'Quiet Please', 'Opus No. One', 'Well, Git It!', 'Yes, Indeed' (no. 4 '41); arr. 'Chicago', 'On The Sunny Side Of The Street'. Dorsey took over strings from Artie SHAW band when Shaw joined US Navy '42; then had 34 pieces counting singers. Became music publisher; started flop music paper *Bandstand* (only six issues), bought ballroom '44 (with partners Jimmy, Harry JAMES); was Dir. of Popular Music, Mutual Radio Network '45-6, but big band business going downhill: disbanded end '46 along with eight other big names, reformed two years later; with Jimmy again '53; they had CBS TV series '55-6 (summer replacement for Jackie GLEASON) where Connie FRANCIS, Elvis PRESLEY first appeared. Died of accidental combination of sleeping pills and liquor after big meal. Appears in biopic *The Fabulous Dorseys* '47, other films; *Tommy And Jimmy – The Dorsey Years* by Herb Sandford published '72. A 'Tommy Dorsey Orchestra starring Warren Covington' (trombonist, *b* '21, Philadelphia) had cha-cha hits '58. Original band portrayed in period opening scene of Martin Scorsese film *New York, New York* '77. Complete Dorsey, Dorsey-Sinatra collections reissued in 2-disc sets on RCA.

DOTTSY (*b* Dorothy Brodt, 6 Apr. '54, Seguin, Texas). Husky-voiced country singer with hits late '70s. Child star in Texas; big break came when signing with Texas impresario Happy Shahan led to contract with RCA '74. Hits: 'Storms Never Last' '75, '(After Sweet Memories) Play Born To Lose Again' '77, 'Here In Love' '78, 'Trying To Satisfy You' '79 (duet with Waylon JENNINGS). Dropped by RCA '80; since recorded for Tanglewood. LPs: *The Sweetest Thing* '76, *Trying To Satisfy You* '79.

DOUGLAS, Craig (*b* Terence Perkins, 13 Aug. '41, Newport, Isle of Wight) Singer. A twin (family had three sets). Won talent contest singing 'Mary's Boy Child' while others sang rock'n'roll. To mainland of Britain; appeared on BBC TV *6.5 Special* '58; recorded for Decca, then Top Rank; 'A Teenager In Love' (cover of DION USA hit) was no. 13, 'Only Sixteen' no. 1, both '59. (Latter song credited to Barbara Campbell, a pseudonym for Sam COOKE, Lou ADLER and Herb ALPERT.) 5 more top 40 hits before label went broke; 'Our Favourite Melodies' top 10 on Columbia; back to Decca for 'Oh Lonesome Me'; last hit 'Town Cryer' '63: washed away by BEATLES, who once backed him on a live date. Occasional records since incl. vocal version of theme from popular TV series *Tales Of The Unexpected*; hits collected with others on *Only Sixteen* '84 on See For Miles label.

DOWD, Tom USA producer who served with Atlantic records for 25 years from '48: began as staff engineer, working with the legends – Ray CHARLES, Aretha FRANKLIN, *et al.* – immediacy of sound was remarkable. As label brought in 8-track, stereo recording facilities, collaborated with prod. to make most of it – notably work

with LEIBER & STOLLER, black groups COASTERS, DRIFTERS, which could involve 30 takes per song and hours of editing – credited as co-prod. with Arif Mardin, Jerry Wexler on Franklin's records. Spell at Stax mid-'60s saw work on many more soul classics. Departed to freelance, prod. LPs with Eric CLAPTON from *461 Ocean Boulevard* '74, Rod STEWART from *Atlantic Crossing* '75, LYNYRD SKYNYRD from *Gimme Back My Bullets* '76; others as different as CHICAGO and MEATLOAF. Doubles on percussion and piano; sessioned with JAMES GANG on former '75.

DRAKE, Alfred (*b* Alfred Capurro, 7 Oct. '14, NYC) Singer/actor; Broadway star with stage presence, strong baritone voice. Debut '33 in GILBERT & SULLIVAN chorus; better roles (e.g. in *Straw Hat Revue* '39, showcase for new talent), straight acting (e.g. in *As You Like It* '41); was a smash hit in RODGERS & HAMMERSTEIN's *Oklahoma!* '43. Star of *Sing Out Sweet Land* '45 (with Burl IVES), *Beggar's Holiday* '47, *Kiss Me Kate* '49, *Kismet* '53; also musical film *Tars And Spars* '46; later more Shakespeare incl. *Othello, Hamlet*; TV plays incl. operettas; Broadway in *Kean* '61. Original cast albums: *Oklahoma!* on Decca/MCA; others on Columbia.

DRAKE, Nick (*b* 19 June '48, Burma; *d* 25 Nov. '74, Worcestershire) UK singer/ songwriter of UK folk revival. Family returned to England c. '55; he played reeds in school, switched to guitar at 16, soon began writing songs; was heard while attending Cambridge by Ashley Hutchings, then with FAIRPORT CONVENTION; recommended to Joe Boyd (manager of Fairport, John MARTYN, etc.) who signed him to Island. Debut LP *Five Leaves Left* '69 drew comparisons with Van MORRISON's *Astral Weeks* '68: dark, brooding, jazz-tinged introspection took on a bit more warmth in *Bryter Later* '70, incl. backing from John CALE, Fairport members Richard THOMPSON, Dave Pegg, Dave Mattacks; but his introversion/depression deepened: stopped performing live (which he always dreaded), underwent some psychiatric treatment; went to Paris to write songs for singer Françoise Hardy (allegedly recorded but unreleased); soon returned home. Last LP

Pink Moon '72 accompanied only by own guitar; tapes sent to Island by post. Quit songwriting and singing but started writing again; Boyd, Island boss Chris Blackwell, prod. John Wood tried to give support, but he died at parents' home of overdose of anti-depressant medication. His work is still influential; 'Life In A Northern Town' by Dream Academy '85 dedicated to him; renewed interest led to compilation *Heaven In A Wild Flower* '85; *Time Of No Reply* '86 incl. alternate takes, previously unreleased tracks, incl. in new edition of boxed set (now four discs) *Fruit Tree* '86.

DRAKE, Pete (*b* 8 Oct. '33, Augusta, Ga; *d* 29 July '88) Steel guitarist, publisher, producer, label boss. From musical family: older brothers Bill and Jack (*b* '24, Barnesville, Ga.) worked on Grand Ole Opry '44; many years members of Ernest TUBB's Texas Troubadors. Played with own band The Sons Of The South mid-'50s, joined Wilma Lee and Stoney COOPER '58, moved to Nashville '59, soon in demand on sessions with Jim REEVES, Roy DRUSKY, Don GIBSON, many others. Signed to Smash label '62, recorded unique talking guitar sound (incl. single and LP *Forever* '64, *Talking Steel Guitar* '65). Became top prod. (e.g. Ringo STARR's '69 Nashville album), co-owner of Stop label (signed Johnny Bush, George MORGAN, etc.); formed Window Music with Jack. Helped newcomers in Nashville; became disgusted with the way older artists treated by major labels, formed First Generation Records '77, signed Tubb and launched series of LPs by veterans *The Stars Of The Grand Ole Opry*. Prod. Tubb 2-disc album *The Legend & The Legacy* '79 with duets featuring Willie NELSON, Marty ROBBINS, etc.; became top seller. Own albums incl. *Steel Away* '74 on Canaan.

DRAPER, Rusty (*b* Farrell Draper, Kirksville, Mo.) Pop/country singer, actor. Worked night clubs, radio and TV early '50s; signed to Mercury '51, no. 15 pop hit 'No Help Wanted' '53: Hank THOMPSON, the CARLISLES had country hits with the song, but Draper had no. 6 country/no. 10 pop hit same year with 'Gambler's Guitar', further top 20 pop hits 'Seventeen', 'The Shifting, Whispering Sands' (no. 3), 'Are

You Satisfied?' all '55; 'In The Middle Of The House' '56, 'Freight Train' '57. 'Please Help Me, I'm Falling'/'Muleskinner Blues', 'Signed, Sealed And Delivered' were lesser pop hits '60-1. Switched to Monument '62; 'Night Life' was minor pop hit '63; 'My Elusive Dreams', 'California Sunshine', 'Buffalo Nickel', 'Two Little Boys' minor country hits '67-70. Appeared in productions of *Oklahoma*, *Annie Get Your Gun*, *Carousel*; as TV actor in *Rawhide*, *Laramie*, etc. LPs incl. *Country Classics*, *Hits That Sold A Million*, *Sing Along* on Mercury; *Plays Guitar*, *Something Old*, *Something New*, *Night Life* on Monument.

DREGS US rock band formed by guitarist Steve Morse (*b* Ohio; grew up in Michigan; moved to Georgia in early teens). First called Dixie Grits, the Dixie Dregs, since '81 Dregs. Lineup Morse, Rod Morganstein (drums), Andy West (bass), Allen Sloan (violin), Steve Davidowski (keyboards). First LP *Free Fall* '77 for local Capricorn label, home of ALLMAN BROS, MARSHALL TUCKER BAND; emphasis on instrumental skill rather than vocals much in Allman mould. *What If* '78 and *Night Of The Living Dregs* '79 with new keyboardist Mark Parrish, himself then replaced by T. Lavitz on *Dregs Of The Earth* '80, first album on Arista. Reduced name to Dregs and moved away from southern rock towards jazz rock for *Unsung Heroes* '81, *Industry Standard* '82, latter seeing inevitable departure of fiddler Sloan; balance redressed by guest spots from DOOBIE bro. Patrick Simmons on vocals, Alex Ligertwood from SANTANA, guitarist Steve Howe from YES. Howe especially highly rates Morse, who doubles on banjo and pedal steel and whose mastery of styles saw him nominated by readers of USA magazine *Guitar Player* as 'best overall guitarist' '82, *Industry Standard* as best guitar LP; dismissed by *Sounds* UK as 'the Mike OLDFIELD of the rodeo set'.

DRIFTERS, The USA classic R&B/soul vocal group with career spanning 30 years, at least that many members. Original lineup to back Clyde McPHATTER incl. Bill Pinkney (*b* 15 Aug. '25, Sumter, S.C.), bass; Gerhard and Andrew Thrasher, tenor and baritone (*b* Wetumpka, Ala.); all had gospel background. First six discs all top 10 R&B '53-5 incl. 'Money Honey', later covered by Elvis PRESLEY, 2-sided hit 'Such A Night'/'Lucille'. McPhatter's military conscription led to changes; Johnny Moore (*b* '34, Selma, Ala.) sang lead but group disbanded '58; manager (who owned name) selected NYC group the Crowns to be new Drifters: lineup Ben E. KING, lead baritone; Doc Green, baritone; Charles Thomas, tenor; Elsbery Hobbs, bass: with songs of LEIBER & STOLLER success was immediate: 'There Goes My Baby' no. 2 pop chart '59; King's plaintive lead with Latin rhythm, strings was profound infl. on '60s soul. String of smash hits followed: 'Dance With Me', 'This Magic Moment', 'Lonely Winds', no. 1 'Save The Last Dance For Me' before King left to go solo late '60: in hands of white songwriters they took sound from ghetto to universal world of romance, girls, parties. Lyricist Leiber augmented songs with Brill Building material, POMUS-SHUMAN compositions to continue trend with Rudy Lewis (ex-Clara Ward Singers) who sang lead on seven top '40 hits incl. 'Up On The Roof', 'On Broadway' (both top 10) before death from drugs '64. Moore had rejoined '63, now took lead: 'Under The Boardwalk' recorded day after Lewis's death was no. 4 '64, but same year's 'Saturday Night At The Movies' was last top 40 pop success: Motown took over black pop and Drifters drifted into supper-club circuit; Atlantic contract expired '72. Reissues showed in UK charts (e.g. 'At The Movies' was no. 3 UK '72); Moore took group to UK, signed with Bell, utilised best UK songwriters of era (Cook-Greenaway, Barry Mason, Tony Macauley) for top 10 hits 'Like Sister And Brother', 'Kissin' In The Back Row Of The Movies', 'Down On The Beach Tonight', five more top 30s '73-6 (though none hit in USA). Not as innovative as earlier lineups, Moore's Drifters had every right to profit from genre they'd helped to create; when he left '80 King returned as lead; lineup today could be any five from up to 50 past members. *Very Best Of* '86 on Telstar TV LP had both Atlantic and Bell hits.

DRIFTING COWBOYS, The Hank WILLIAMS's band, later re-formed. Don Helms (*b* 28 Feb. '27) had played steel guitar with Hank off and on since '43; guitarist Bob McNett (*b* 16 Oct. '25, Roaring Branch, Pa.) came to Nashville from Shreveport with Hank; in '49 fiddler Jerry Rivers (*b* 25 Aug. '28, Miami) and bassist Hillous Butram (*b* 21 Apr. '28, Lafayette, Tenn.) were added: toured with him and played on nearly all his records. After his death worked individually or as a group with Ray PRICE, Ferlin HUSKY, Carl SMITH, Marty ROBBINS, Hank SNOW; Rivers published a Williams biography *From Life To Legend* '64. Re-formed most successfully '77-84, with UK tours, Wembley appearance; LPs incl. *Jim Owen And The Drifting Cowboys – A Song For Us All* '79 on Epic, *A Tribute To Hank Williams* '80 on Standing Stone, *Live* '81 on Westwood.

DRIFTWOOD, Jimmy (*b* James Morris, 20 June '17, Mountainview, Ark.) Collector, author and performer of folksongs, playing guitar and mouth bow. LPs on RCA incl. 'Battle Of New Orleans', subsequently huge hit for Johnny HORTON; 'Tennessee Stud', hit for Eddy ARNOLD. Performed for teachers at National Education Association jamboree, on Pat BOONE TV show, at Carnegie Hall; won Grammies for best song ('Battle') and best folksong performance ('Wilderness Road'). *Songs Of Billy Yank And Johnny Reb* '61 spoiled by 'countrypolitan' production: the honesty of Driftwood's presentation sullied with an incessant snare drum (war songs, see?) and a slick Nashville chorus.

DRUSKY, Roy (*b* 22 June '30, Atlanta, Ga.) Country/pop singer/songwriter. Began to play guitar in US Navy '48-50, formed band The Southern Ranch Boys, signed to Starday '53 but no success; worked as DJ. Signed to Columbia on strength of songs, still no own hits but joined Grand Ole Opry '58 after writing no. 1 country hit for Faron YOUNG 'Alone With You'. Wrote hits 'Country Girl' '59 for Young, 'Anymore' '60 for Teresa BREWER. Joined Decca '59, finally had own hits: 'Another' '60, 'Three Hearts In A Tangle' '61 (country and pop), 'Second Hand Rose' '62. Hits on Mercury '63-6: 'Peel Me A Nanner', 'Strangers', 'Yes Mr Peters' (duet with Priscilla Mitchell, country no. 1), 'If The Whole World Stopped Loving'; 'Jody And The Kid' '68 (early Kris KRISTOFFERSON song), 'Such A Fool' '69, 'Long, Long Texas Road' '70,

'Satisfied Mind' '73. Signed to Capitol '74, then others; no more single hits, but highly praised LPs incl. *Peaceful Easy Feeling* '74 on Capitol, *Night Flying* '78 and *Roy* '81 on Big R in UK, *English Gold* '81 on Plantation. Many LPs on Decca and Mercury long out of print.

DUCHIN, Eddy (*b* 10 Apr. '10, Cambridge, Mass.; *d* 9 Feb. '51, NYC) Pianist, bandleader. Like Frankie CARLE, played sweet style, but without offending and not too elaborate: sometimes one-finger melody line. Studied pharmacy, turned to full-time music c.'29; good looks, style attracted fans; formed own band '31. Popularity reflected by many records on Victor, Brunswick, Columbia; radio work and films (incl. *The Hit Parade* '37, also with Duke ELLINGTON); theme was 'My Twilight Dream'. After military service '42-5 still popular with bigger, better band, but had passed peak; career shortened by leukemia. Biopic *The Eddy Duchin Story* '56 with Tyrone Power had Carmen CAVALLARO playing piano; LP of same name on Columbia collected reissues, while Decca soundtrack was no. 1 album in Billboard. Son Peter Duchin (*b* 28 July '37, NYC) also became popular bandleader, more advanced musically; was also member of boards of dir. of Harlem dance theatre, NY State Council on Arts, etc.

DUDLEY, Dave (*b* 3 May '28, Spencer, Wis.) Country singer famous for truck driving songs. Injury stopped pro baseball career '50; became DJ and singer in Wisconsin; formed Dave Dudley Trio '53, worked clubs and bars throughout Midwest for six years; formed larger band The Country Gentlemen '59, changed name to The Roadrunners '60, recorded for Vee '61, Jubilee '62; recorded 'Six Days On The Road' '61, but didn't get it released until '63: on Golden Wing label became top pop and country hit launching hundreds of truck driving songs. Signed to Mercury, had hits 'Mad' '64, 'Truck Drivin' Son Of A Gun' '65, 'Vietnam Blues' '66, 'There Ain't No Easy Run' '67, 'George (And The North Woods)' '69, 'The Pool Shark' '70, 'Comin' Down' '71. Faded from the charts, though recording for United Artists '75-6, Rice '77-9, Sun '80-2 incl. duet album with Charlie Douglas, DJ popular with truck drivers (named

DJ of the year three times by *Open Road* magazine). Several LPs on Mercury '64-70 with same titles as hit singles, plus *Will The Real Dave Dudley Please Sing* '72, *Original Traveling Man* '74; also *Special Delivery* '75, *1776* '76 on UA, *Interstate Gold* '81 on Sun.

DUKE, Doris (*b* Doris Curry, Sandersville, Ga.) Soul singer. Sang in gospel groups; sang back-up from c.'63 with Aretha FRANKLIN, Dusty SPRINGFIELD, Jackie WILSON, Frank SINATRA; own records '67 as Doris Willingham (married name); toured Europe '68 with Nina SIMONE, adopted name Doris Duke, LP *I'm A Loser* '69 prod. by Jerry Williams on short-lived Canyon label: album made top 20 in soul charts; singles 'To The Other Woman (I'm The Other Woman)' no. 7, 'Feet Start Walking' no. 36 (latter reached 109 in pop charts), all '70. Williams prod. highly rated *A Legend In Her Own Time* on Mankind; other albums incl. *B.C.* on CBS, *Flight Time* on Sandra, *Funky Fox* on Manhattan; still highly regarded, but lasting commercial success eluded her and all LPs went out of print.

DUKE, George (*b* 12 Jan. '46, San Rafael, Cal.) Keyboards, composer. Led trio from '65; toured with vocal group the Third Wave incl. Mexico '68, Duke writing most of the material; worked in San Francisco backing visitors Dizzy GILLESPIE, Kenny DORHAM, others; broke up '68. With Don ELLIS band, Frank ZAPPA '70; played on half a dozen Cannonball ADDERLEY albums incl. chart hits *The Black Messiah* '72, *Inside Straight* '73, *Phenix* '75; with Zappa again '73-5, co-led group with Billy COBHAM '75; since then various own groups, festivals, TV and film work, also prod. (no. 1 hit USA for Deniece Williams 'Let's Hear It For The Boy' '84; Angela Bofill LP *Tell Me Tomorrow* '85). Versatile success mainly in soft-fusion mode. LPs incl. *Jean-Luc Ponty Experience* with trio; *Crosswinds* and *Live On Tour In Europe* with Cobham on Atlantic, *Journey To Love* with Stanley CLARKE on Nemperor all charted in USA, as did *The Clarke – Duke Project* '81, *Clarke – Duke II* '83 on Epic. Own LPs began with *The George Duke Quartet* '56 on Saba, then *Save The Country* c.'70 on Pacific Jazz; *The Inner*

Source '71, *Feel* '74 with AIRTO and Flora PURIM, trio set *Faces In Reflections* '74, *I Love The Blues, She Heard My Cry* '75, *Liberated Fantasies* '76, *The Aura Will Prevail* '76, all on MPS (some on Verve or Pausa in USA). On Epic: *The 1976 Solo Keyboard Event* (aka *The Dream* on MPS), *From Me To You* and *Reach For It* '77, *Don't Let Go* '78, *Follow The Rainbow* and *Master Of The Game* '79, *A Brazilian Love Affair* '80, *Dream On* '82, *Guardian Of The Light* '83, *Secret Rendezvous* '84. Most LPs since *Feel* have charted, *Thief In The Night* '85 and *George Duke* '86 on Elektra.

DUKE, Vernon (*b* Vladimir Dukelsky, 10 Oct. '03, Parafianovo, Russia; *d* 16 Jan. '69, Santa Monica, Cal.) Songwriter. Studied at Kiev Conservatory at 13; family fled Revolution '20 to USA, Duke returned to Europe '23, wrote musicals in London; back to USA '29. Wrote many shows, also songs for others (also a string quartet, violin sonata, concertos for violin, cello, etc.); autobiography *Passport To Paris*. Excellent songs with originality and substance: best known incl. 'April In Paris' '32 (from *Walk A Little Faster*; lyrics by Yip HARBURG); 'I Like The Likes Of You' and 'What Is There To Say' (from *Ziegfeld Follies of 1934*; lyrics by Harburg); 'Autumn In New York' 35 (from *Thumbs Up*; own lyrics); 'I Can't Get Started' (from *Ziegfeld Follies of 1936*; lyrics by Ira GERSHWIN), 'Cabin In The Sky' and 'Taking A Chance On Love' (from *Cabin In The Sky* '40, filmed '43, lyrics by John Latouche).

DUKES OF DIXIELAND USA dixieland band led by brothers Fred (trombone; *b* 3 Dec. '29; *d* 21 Apr. '66, Las Vegas) and Frank Assunto (trumpet; *b* 29 Jan. '22; *d* 25 Feb. '74, New Orleans). Formed group '49 for Horace HEIDT talent show; played at Famous Door in New Orleans for four years; fame in '50s on TV, tours; records on Roulette, RCA, MCA, but mostly Audio Fidelity: sold especially well because among first stereo records. Both life-long musicians, born in New Orleans, taught by their father Jacob 'Papa Jac' Assunto (banjo, trombone; *b* 1 Nov. '05, Lake Charles, La.), prominent local player who toured with them after '55: all the more remarkable that work was suitable only for tourists. No credit to Louis

ARMSTRONG that he made LPs with them '59-60 (issued on both Audio Fidelity and Chiaroscuro). *Marching Along With The Dukes Of Dixieland Vol. 3* '57, *Best Of* '61 made LP charts, partly because of good early stereo sound.

DUNBAR, Aynsley (*b* '46) UK rock drummer. Played in John MAYALL's Bluesbreakers '66-7, formed Aynsley Dunbar's Retaliation '68-70, blues band with deep vocals of Richard Brox (also guitar, keyboards, cornet); Alex Dmochowski, bass; John Moorshead, guitar; Tommy Eyre, keyboards. *Aynsley Dunbar's Retaliation* '68, *Dr Dunbar's Prescription* '69, *To Mum From Aynsley And The Boys* '70 were less electric than other blues-based rock albums of the time. Dunbar left '70; last LP *Remains To Be Heard* that year had no drummer on one side. He joined Mothers of Invention '71-2 (*see* Frank ZAPPA), JOURNEY '75, JEFFERSON STARSHIP '79; had also sessioned with David BOWIE, Sammy HAGAR, Shuggie OTIS, Lou REED, Nils LOFGREN.

DUNCAN, Johnny (*b* 5 Oct. '38, Dublin, Texas) Country singer, successful songwriter. Played country dances with family band early '50s, incl. cousins Jimmy and Dan Seals (later of SEALS AND CROFTS and ENGLAND DAN AND JOHN FORD COLEY respectively). Moved to Clovis, N.M.; did some pop demos for Norman Petty (prod. Buddy HOLLY): DJ in Texas '61-4; landed DJ job in Franklin, Tenn. Appeared on Ralph Emery's WSM TV show as a singer '66, signed with Columbia, had several minor hits: 'Hard Luck Joe', 'To My Sorrow', 'You're Gonna Need Me', 'When She Touches Me', but did better as writer: 'Summer Sunday' (Chet ATKINS), 'I'd Rather Lose You' (Charley PRIDE), etc. Toured with Pride's roadshow '69-72, had top 20 hits 'There's Something About A Lady', 'Baby's Smile, Woman's Kiss' '71; top 10 'Sweet Country Woman' '73. '75 hits 'Jo And The Cowboy', 'Charley Is My Name' with voice of Janie FRICKE; then no. 1 hits with her: 'Stranger', 'Thinkin' Of A Rendezvous' '76, 'It Couldn't Have Been Any Better' '77; 'Come A Little Bit Closer' gave Fricke credit, and she soon had her own hits. Duncan continued with top 5 hits 'She Can Put Her Shoes Under My Bed

(Anytime)', 'Hello Mexico (And Adios Baby To You)', 'Slow Dancing', 'He's Out Of My Life'. LPs incl. *Johnny One Time* '68, *There's Something About A Lady* '71, *Sweet Country Woman* '73, *Best Of* '76, *Johnny Duncan* '77, *Come A Little Bit Closer* '77, *The Best Is Yet To Come* '78, *In My Dreams* '80, *You're On My Mind* '81.

DUPREE, Champion Jack (*b* William Thomas Dupree, 4 July '10, New Orleans) Blues singer, songwriter; played guitar, drums; but mainly described himself as the last of the barrelhouse piano players. Orphaned by fire, learned piano in same Coloured Waifs Home where Louis ARMSTRONG earlier learned cornet; nickname from days as a boxer (107 bouts; last in Indianapolis '40 where he remained some years). Had worked in New Orleans with Papa CELESTIN, others; hoboed, worked across USA as dancer, MC, singing pianist, etc. Began recording '40-1 on Okeh (first records on *Junker Blues*, Travelin' Man label), recorded almost every year thereafter, incl. Savoy with Brownie McGHEE '47, Apollo '49-50, King and others '51-5, Atlantic '58 (LP *Blues From The Gutter*); toured Europe '59, settled in Switzerland '60, Sweden '74. Worked with Chris BARBER band '64, recorded on UK labels as solo and with Keith Smith's Climax Jazz Band, John MAYALL, etc.; appearances at Marquee Club, Ronnie SCOTT's shown on BBC TV; recorded in France (with Mickey Baker '71) etc. Popular blues-based entertainer straddled country-urban blues traditions, said to have infl. Fats DOMINO. LPs in UK: *Blues For Everyone* (2 discs) on Gusto; *Champion Jack Dupree 1944-45* on Red Pepper, *Legacy Of The Blues Vol. 3* and *The Incredible* on Sonet; made in Copenhagen on Storyville: *This Is* '59, *Plays & Sings – Trouble, Trouble* and *Best Of The Blues* '61.

DURAN DURAN UK pop quintet formed Birmingham '78. Original lineup: Nick Rhodes (real name Nick Bates), keyboards; John Taylor, guitar; Steve Duffy (aka Tin Tin), vocals, bass; Simon Colley, bass, clarinet. Played first gig at Barbarella's (name of group comes from '67 sci-fi film *Barbarella*). Duffy and Colley left; J. Taylor moved to bass, Roger Taylor (drums) and

Alan Curtis (guitar) joined; Andy Wickett, Jeff Thomas passed through as vocalists; Andy Taylor recruited through advert in trade press, replaced Curtis (three Taylors not related). Group managed by owners of Rum Runner club and London art student Simon Le Bon recruited '80; signed by EMI after tour supporting Hazel O'CONNOR; debut single 'Planet Earth' reached UK top 20 (early '81); three more hit singles '81 plus eponymous LP (made top 3). All '82 releases made top 10 e.g. 'Hungry Like The Wolf', 'Save A Prayer' and 'Rio'; second LP *Rio* sealed group as teenybop sensation. Songs less tuneful, lyrically more obscure than in most such acts, but appearance of band and videos made in exotic locations (such as Sri Lanka) make up in marketplace for musical shortcomings. First '83 single 'Is There Something I Should Know' entered charts at no. 1; next 'Union Of The Snake' no. 3; 3rd LP *Seven And The Ragged Tiger* '83 big Xmas seller, but not as big as expected; *Arena* '84 was no. 4 LP USA (hit single 'Wild Boys'), *Notorious* released '86; they were apparently down to one Taylor '87 but it didn't seem to matter.

DURANTE, Jimmy (*b* 10 Feb. 1893, NYC; *d* 29 Jan. '80, Santa Monica, Cal.) Irrepressible comedian with big nose (aka 'Schnoz', 'Schnozzola'); played piano, half-sang in gravelly voice, mangled English as part of act, co-wrote many songs: became American institution. Organised dixieland band '16, formed trio Clayton, Jackson & Durante '23 (Lou Clayton *d* '50, Eddie Jackson), had Club Durant in Manhattan '23 (claimed 'e' was missing because they'd run out of signpainting money); became New York favourites of song, dance, comedy, starred in Broadway shows *Show Girl* '29, *The New Yorkers* '30, film *Roadhouse Nights* '30. Though he was star, Durante refused solo offers until Depression dealt death blow to vaudeville; then signed Hollywood contract with Clayton managing, Jackson contributing material. Films incl. *Cuban Love Song* '31, *The Passionate Plumber*, *Speak Easily* '32, *Broadway To Hollywood* '33, *George White's Scandals*, *Hollywood Party*, *Student Tour* '34: *Palooka* that year was first starring role, with James Cagney's brother William; featured 'Inka Dinka Doo', became trademark song. On

Broadway: *Strike Me Pink* '33, *Jumbo* '35 (songs by RODGERS & HART, cast of 90 humans plus animals), *Red Hot And Blue* '36 (with Bob Hope, Ethel MERMAN), *Stars In Your Eyes* '39, *Keep Off The Grass* '40. More films incl. *Music For Millions* '44 (incl. 'Toscanini, Iturbi and Me', 'Umbriago'), *This Time For Keeps* '47 (classic routine 'The Guy Who Found The Lost Chord'), *It Happened In Brooklyn* '47 ('The Song's Gotta Come From The Heart', with Frank SINATRA), *On An Island With You* '48 with Esther Williams; *The Milkman* '50 (with Donald O'Connor, song 'That's My Boy'). Much radio and TV work incl. own shows, co-star gigs with Garry Moore '43-6, Lennon Sisters '69-70; countless guest shots, often with Jackson. Re-created Club Durant on TV with Jackson; LP on theme with guests Bing CROSBY, Bob HOPE, Al JOLSON, Sophie TUCKER, Eddie CANTOR issued on Brunswick. Club, TV work through '60s, always closing act with 'Goodnight Mrs Calabash, wherever you are', never explained. Wrote or co-wrote songs incl. theme 'Inka Dinka Doo', 'Start Off Each Day With A Song', '(I Know Darn Well I Can Do Without Broadway, But) Can Broadway Do Without Me?'. Screen version of *Jumbo* '62 with Doris DAY incl. tender rendering of 'The Most Beautiful Girl In The World' to Martha Raye; then 70-year-old comic made touching LP of ballads *September Song* on WB: no. 30 hit LP '63. Last film role in Stanley Kramer's star-packed *It's A Mad, Mad, Mad, Mad World* '63: cameo had him literally kick the bucket. Had stroke '72, spent years in wheelchair. Goodnight Mr Durante, wherever you are.

DURHAM, Eddie (*b* 19 Aug. '06, San Marcos, Texas; *d* 6 Mar. '87) Trombone, guitar, arranger. Six brothers musicians. Toured with territory bands incl. Walter PAGE's Blue Devils, then with Bennie MOTEN '29-33, Cab CALLOWAY, Andy KIRK; with Count BASIE on tour of Arkansas '34; then Jimmie LUNCEFORD ('Pigeon Walk', 'Lunceford Special', 'Blues In The Groove'); back with Basie's historic band '37-8: Dicky WELLS wrote, 'Basie really began to get a book together when Ed Durham was in the band. Basie and Ed would lock up in a room with a little jug, and Basie

would play the ideas, Ed would voice them.' Wrote or co-wrote 'Out The Window', 'Time Out', 'John's Idea', 'Swinging The Blues'; 'Topsy' (with Edgar Battle; revived '58 for pop hit); 'Good Morning Blues', 'Sent For You Yesterday And Here You Come Today' co-written with Basie and vocalist Jimmy RUSHING; some say it was Durham and Buster SMITH who created 'One O'Clock Jump', one of the biggest hits of the whole era. He was an early master of electric guitar: beautiful work on Lester YOUNG session at Commodore '38. He arr. for Glenn MILLER ('Slip Horn Jive', 'Glen Island Special'), Jan SAVITT, Ina Ray HUTTON, Artie SHAW; own big band '40, then mus. dir. for Bon Bon and his Buddies: Bon Bon (George Tunnell) was black 'sweet' vocalist for white Savitt band, went solo; Durham co-wrote 'I Don't Want To Set The World On Fire' '41, recorded by Bon Bon; hit versions same year were by Horace HEIDT, INK SPOTS, Tommy Tucker. Mus. dir. of all-girl INTERNATIONAL SWEETHEARTS OF RHYTHM, later had own all-girl band; led touring band with Wynonie HARRIS early '50s; from '57 led small groups in East Coast residencies; working with Harlem Blues And Jazz Band early '80s. WKCR NYC broadcast marathon 69-hour round-the-clock celebration of Durham's 79th birthday, with lectures, interviews, music.

DURY, Ian (*b* 12 May '42, Upminster, Essex) UK singer, songwriter, bandleader. Attended Royal College of Art, became teacher, but rock'n'roll interest parallel to painting. First band Kilburn & the High Roads (after Kilburn High Road, important North London thoroughfare): stalwarts of London pub-rock scene had seven lineups in seven years; led by Dury, who was seriously affected by polio as a child, a wildly incongruous bunch during time of glam- and pomp-rock (LP *Wotabunch* released '77, after Dury's later success). Early Dury material ('Rough Kids', 'Billy Bentley', 'Upminster Kid') set scene for later work. Took a year off to write with Chaz Jankel; formed band the Blockheads, launched anthemic 'Sex & Drugs & Rock & Roll', then album *New Boots And Panties* '77: hailed as instant classic, also incl. tribute to 'Sweet Gene Vincent', London vignettes 'Billericay

Dickie', 'Plaistow Patricia'; outstanding writing, with poet's ear for unlikely rhymes and an endearing sense of humour. Band was streets ahead of punk competition: experienced musicians celebrating pop music instead of trying to kill it. On Stiff, Dave EDMUNDS prod. single of veteran English music hall comic Max Wall tackling Dury's 'England's Glory'; Dury and band integral part of first Stiff tour, with Elvis COSTELLO, Nick LOWE, Wreckless Eric; hit singles '78 saw Dury become household name: 'What A Waste' (no. 9 UK), 'Hit Me With Your Rhythm Stick' (Stiff's first no. 1). Follow-up LP *Do It Yourself* written on the road and showed it compared to *Panties*, but worthy additions to canon incl. 'Sink My Boats', 'This Is What We Find'. 'Reasons To Be Cheerful (Pt 3)' '79 was last top 10 hit; *Laughter* '80 was return to form, with Wilko Johnson replacing Jankel on guitar, songs such as 'Delusions Of Grandeur', 'Dance Of The Crackpots'. Changed labels to Polydor; debut was solo *Lord Upminster* '81, his 'party album', with Jankel back, ace rhythm section of Sly & Robbie. He maintained that couplet in 'The Body Song' – 'The leg, a source of much delight/Which carries weight and governs height' – was the best he ever wrote; album also incl. 'Spasticus Autisticus', Dury's anthem for the Year of the Disabled, which BBC foolishly banned as offensive: Dury wrote from personal experience. *4000 Weeks Holiday* '84 credited to Ian & The Music Students; incl. melancholy, jazzy 'Man With No Face', tribute to friend Peter Blake in 'Peter The Painter'. *Juke Box Dury* '81 was good compilation of Stiff stuff, reissued following year on budget label Music For Pleasure as *Greatest Hits*; incl. many of the above plus 'There Ain't Half Been Some Clever Bastards', 'Wake Up And Make Love With Me', 'In Betweenies', etc. Had found it hard to match success of late '70s but place in UK music secure; reformed original Blockheads '84, returned to charts with theme for TV adaptation of *The Secret Diary Of Adrian Mole*, 'Profoundly In Love With Pandora' '85, again united with Jankel. Made acting debut opposite Bob Geldof in film *No. 1*, had part in Roman Polanski film *Pirates*, BBC TV serial *King Of The Ghetto*, played title role in play touring the provinces *Talk Of The Devil* by

Mary O'Malley, jester in Channel 4 TV film *Rocinante*, all '85-6. Writing autobiography *It's All Lies*; co-starred with Bob DYLAN in *Hearts Of Fire* '87.

DUSTY, Slim (*b* David Gordon Kirkpatrick, '27, Kempsey, New South Wales) Australian singer, songwriter, guitarist; has sold more records there than anybody else, with some 70 gold and platinum records. Raised on farm, played guitar at 12; appeared on Kempsey radio. First records for Regal Zonophone '46; first big hit 'A Pub With No Beer' '57 was no. 3 in UK. MBE for services to entertainment '70; signed EMI Australia '76 for highest fee ever paid to Australian artist until then; had another Australian no. 1 '80 with 'Duncan'. *No. 50 – The Golden Anniversary Album* good seller '81. *Australia Is His Name* issued on Philo USA in '88.

DUVIVIER, George (*b* 17 Aug. '20, NYC; *d* there 11 July '85) Bass, arranger. Studied violin formally; played bass with Coleman HAWKINS, Lucky MILLINDER; sold first arr. to Jimmie LUNCEFORD '42. After WWII worked with Lunceford, Sy OLIVER, others incl. many singers: toured Europe with Nellie LUTCHER, Lena HORNE. Recorded with Count BASIE – Joe WILLIAMS, Frank SINATRA, Bud POWELL, Clark TERRY, Zoot SIMS – Joe VENUTI, many dozens of others; also much studio work. One of music's best-loved sidemen recorded as leader on a Coronet label in Paris '56 with quartet incl. Martial SOLAL on piano, Michel Hausser on vibes, Charles Saudrais on drums.

DYETT, Walter (1901-69) Musician, teacher; a Chicago institution. Began on violin; played banjo and guitar in Erskine Tate's Vendome Theatre Orchestra; conducted an all-black US Army band; became bandmaster at Wendell Phillips High School '31 (taught Nat COLE); according to Dempsey J. Travis the name of the school was changed to DuSable High School in '36. He directed five high school bands, annual spring *Hi-Jinks* show (for buying musical instruments; the Board of Education wouldn't pay for them), alumni jazz band in local clubs, annual summer entertainments for Shriners Conventions, etc. In a 150-piece concert band he could tell who had made a mistake; 'He could hear a mosquito urinate on a bale of cotton,' wrote Travis. Bassist Richard Davis said, 'Maybe you weren't afraid of the cops, but you were afraid of Captain Dyett.' His students incl. John Young, Dorothy DONEGAN, Joseph JARMAN, Johnny GRIFFIN, Bo DIDDLEY (on violin!), Gene AMMONS, Eddie HARRIS, Dinah WASHINGTON, comedian Redd Foxx, Fred Hopkins, Julian Priester, John Gilmore (star of SUN RA band for three decades), Wilbur Campbell, Von FREEMAN and his brothers, about 20,000 more, many of whom went straight into jobs with Lionel HAMPTON, Count BASIE, many others. One of the most important of the unsung heroes of 20th-century music: the teachers.

DYLAN, Bob (*b* Robert Allen Zimmerman, 24 May '41, Duluth, Minn.) USA singer/songwriter, the most important figure in white rock music: profound infl. on BEATLES, ROLLING STONES, Elvis COSTELLO, David BOWIE etc.; songs widely covered. From middle-class Jewish family; moved to iron-mining town of Hibbing at age 6, where father operated appliance store. Infl. by Johnnie RAY, Hank WIL-LIAMS, then rock'n'roll: like many growing up in '50s mid-west USA, heard R&B, country music, rock'n'roll while pop charts dominated by pap: ran away from home several times; formed groups in high school (ambition was 'To join LITTLE RICHARD!'). Tried to shroud early life in myth; once claimed to have been a member of Bobby VEE band; his various stories about origin of name 'Dylan' showed indifference to what interviewers think they want to know (name changed legally '62). Infl. by reading Woody GUTHRIE's *Bound For Glory*; began singing at coffee houses during brief stay at U. of Minn.; drifted across country to visit Guthrie in hospital; soon singing, playing guitar, harmonica in Greenwich Village folk clubs. Review by Robert Shelton in *NY Times* led to signing to CBS by John HAMMOND; first LP *Bob Dylan* '62 was standard blues, folk covers, giving little warning of what was to follow: voice seemed strange, album typically described by CBS record salesman as a 'piece of shit': yet his folksinging was already informed by rock'n'roll attitude. *The Freewheelin' Bob Dylan* '63 was very differ-

ent: 13 songs almost all his own incl. 'Blowin' In The Wind', 'Don't Think Twice, It's All Right' (top 10 hits by PETER, PAUL & MARY '63); 'A Hard Rain's A-Gonna Fall' became an anthem; 'Oxford Town' about Mississippi racism; 'Girl From The North Country' with 'Don't Think Twice' first of many realistic love songs; 'Talking World War III Blues' hard-edged surreal comedy with melting parking meters: Nat Hentoff notes observed, 'There's no place to hide in the talking blues . . . he is able to fill all the space . . . with unmistakeable originality'. Rockabilly 'Mixed-Up Confusion' left off LP to foster 'folk' authenticity, 'Talking John Birch Society Blues' because CBS lacked moral fibre (Ed Sullivan would have allowed song on prime-time TV, but network vetoed it); floodgates were opened anyway: 'Masters Of War', others announced the most important writer in genre since Guthrie himself. *The Times They Are A-Changin'* '63 had prod. Tom Wilson replacing Hammond; another anthem in title track (also hit single UK, but not USA), topical songs 'Lonesome Death Of Hattie Carroll', 'Only A Pawn In Their Game'; lyrics were swiftly seized, analysed. Star of Newport Folk Festivals '62-3-4 with Pete SEEGER, early champion Joan BAEZ. Transitional *Another Side Of Bob Dylan* '64 began to shed mantle of protest: his dislike of intense scrutiny manifest in disenfranchising songs 'My Back Pages', 'Chimes Of Freedom', 'It Ain't Me Babe'. Songs soon covered by diverse acts from Marlene DIETRICH to MANFRED MANN; he was publicly impressed by rock'n'roll sound and original material of BEATLES and by ANIMALS' version of 'House Of The Rising Sun' (which he had covered on first LP); acknowledged infl. of both on decision to use rock band (Wilson also encouraged it); this led to controversy comical now. Electric version by the BYRDS of 'Mr Tambourine Man' '65 no. 1 hit both USA, UK; Dylan's crossover *Bringing It All Back Home* '65 had brilliant acoustic side incl. 'Tambourine Man', 'Gates Of Eden', 'It's Alright, Ma (I'm Only Bleeding)', 'It's All Over Now, Baby Blue'; electric side of LP put him streets ahead of contemporaries: savage comedy in 'Maggie's Farm' and 'Subterranean Homesick Blues', ballads 'She Belongs To Me', 'Love Minus Zero', etc. Folk purists were outraged: he was booed at Newport '65. UK solo tour '65 filmed by Donn Pennebaker: *Don't Look Back* '67 is still one of the best rock films. *Highway 61 Revisited* '65 all electric, incl. 'Like A Rolling Stone', 'Ballad Of A Thin Man' (famous line 'Something is happening here, but you don't know what it is, do you Mr Jones?'), epic 11-minute 'Desolation Row'. Marriage '65 kept secret. Started trend by recording in Nashville: *Blonde On Blonde* '66 one of rock's first double LPs; Dylan said '78 'That's my sound. I haven't been able to succeed in getting it all the time'; incl. hit singles 'I Want You' and 'Rainy Day Women £12 & 35' (widely taken to be a drug song). 'Fans' booed and threw things at concerts on world tour '66, reacting violently to new music: guitarist Robbie Robertson thought, 'This is a strange way to make a buck', later said, 'We'd go back to the hotel room, listen to a tape of the show and think, shit, that's not so bad. Why is everybody so upset?'. Controversy about 'folk-rock' raged in *Sing Out* magazine; Dylan just called it music, said 'Folk music is a bunch of fat people.' In live performance typically did acoustic set then introduced the band; in English concerts '66 (widely bootlegged) he said, 'It used to be like that, now it goes like this': Dylan and The BAND poured energy, passion into reworkings of already classic songs against audience antipathy. He said that music was more important than boos, that those claiming to be oldest fans were not: his oldest fans were friends, knew what he was doing. In furious cycle of touring, recording, he wrote songs copiously in restaurants, hotel rooms; Richard FARIÑA said, 'He wasn't just burning the candle at both ends – he was taking a blowtorch to the middle!' Suffered neck injury, scars Aug. '66 in motorcycle crash: amid rumours that he was disfigured, dead, drying out from drugs, he rested in Woodstock, NY: tapes of songs made at The Band's house there bootlegged in 2-disc set *The Great White Wonder* (biggest-selling bootleg in history, commercially issued '75 as *The Basement Tapes*). First public gig in nearly two years at Woody Guthrie memorial concert; then LP *John Wesley Harding* '68 was a shock: laid-back while psychedelia was the rage; raw voice turned smoother, backing low-key and acoustic, lyrics deeper

than ever in 'Drifter's Escape', 'All Along The Watchtower' (covered by Jimi HENDRIX) etc.; also love song 'I'll Be Your Baby Tonight'. *Nashville Skyline* '69 incl. 'Lay Lady Lay', first top 10 single for three years and last to date (intended for film *Midnight Cowboy* but too late for inclusion), several other love songs, benign 'Country Pie', informal duet 'Girl From The North Country' with friend/fan Johnny CASH (other duets recorded, not released). Ace Nashville session men went on to form AREA CODE 615; CBS had not wanted to use word 'Nashville' in title, showing once again ignorance of its own marketplace: 'country rock' was getting under-way. 2-disc *Self Portrait* '70 was first Dylan set to receive overtly hostile criticism, should have been edited to one disc: incl. lacklustre covers of songs like SIMON & GARFUNKEL's 'The Boxer', RODGERS & HART's 'Blue Moon'; Dylan described it as 'my own bootleg record, so to speak': incl. live versions of 'Mighty Quinn', 'Like A Rolling Stone' from Isle of Wight Festival '69 (first scheduled public appearance in three years drew 250,000). *New Morning* '70 was much tighter, incl. widely covered 'If Not For You', also 'Three Angels', 'Father Of Night'. Long period of silence followed, broken only by cameos; received honorary doctorate from Princeton U. '70. 'George Jackson' '71 was one-off protest at death of black activist. Rapturously heard at George HARRISON's *Concert For Bangla Desh* '71: live triple album had a whole side of Dylan. Acting debut in Sam Peckinpah's *Pat Garrett & Billy The Kid* '73; also wrote atmospheric soundtrack incl. hit 'Knockin' On Heaven's Door'. CBS contract in doubt, LPs appeared on Asylum/Island, since reissued on CBS: first official LP with The Band *Planet Waves* '73 of very high quality, made in 72-hour blitz: incl. two takes of 'Forever Young', written with son in mind: as lovely ballad, then laden with humour; beautiful acoustic solo 'The Wedding Song'. First full tour in eight years sold out in hours '74; 2-disc *Before The Flood* was first official Dylan live album, incl. vigorous reworkings of 'Like A Rolling Stone', 'All Along The Watchtower'. Back on CBS, *Blood On The Tracks* '74 regarded by some as best LP: caustically examines love, marriage, relationships in 'Idiot Wind', 'Lily,

Rosemary & The Jack Of Hearts'. Low-key tour Rolling Thunder Review early '75, playing small local venues *ad hoc* affair incl. Baez, Joni MITCHELL, Ronnie HAWKINS, T-Bone BURNETT, Ramblin' Jack ELLIOTT, others, and filming of *Renaldo And Clara*: four-hour home movie released '78 starred Dylan and Baez, lost $2 million. *Desire* '75 is bestseller to date, featured Scarlet Rivera on violin; followed introspective mood of last LP with personal songs 'Sara', 'O Sister'; also 'Hurricane' (plea for release of jailed boxer Ruben Carter), 'Mozambique' (impishly jolly lyric about country with brutal dictatorship). *Hard Rain* '76 was disappointing souvenir of Rolling Thunder (concert film *Hard Rain* made by NBC in Colorado). His wife filed for divorce '77. Hiatus in studio recording ended with *Street Legal* '78: songs, band, arrangements of high quality incl. 'Changing Of The Guard', 'Señor', 'Where Are You Tonight?'. World tour '78 culminated at disused Blackbushe aerodrome south of London, supported by Joan ARMATRADING, Eric CLAPTON, 250,000 fans; *Bob Dylan At Budokan* '79 was souvenir of tour, issued in West as Japanese import sold well: prematurely recorded but incl. new versions of 'Tangled Up In Blue', 'I Want You', etc. He was Band's special guest at their *Last Waltz* finale '78, appears in 3-disc album and film. Announced that he'd become a born-again Christian: *Slow Train Coming* '79 hailed as best-*sounding* album, prod. by Jerry Wexler and Barry Beckett, with DIRE STRAITS' Mark Knopfler on guitar; low-key set also sold well, but many fans disappointed by religious emphasis (though songs had always been loaded with basically religious questions): 'Precious Angel' and 'When He Returns' merited attention. 'Gotta Serve Somebody' won his first Grammy. *Saved* '80 is poorest seller to date, victim of complete lack of sympathy with religious expression, though 'Solid Rock' e.g. is just that, while gospel music is one of the roots of rock. Dylan's remarks about snotty college-kid audiences in notes to *Biograph* (*see below*) are revealing; he generously concludes 'Maybe people need time to catch up with it.' Concerts of this period marked by heckling as he refused to perform pre-Christian material. Patchy *Shot Of Love* '81 attempted to balance religion and craft; title track co-prod. by Bumps

BLACKWELL; 'In The Summertime' and 'Every Grain Of Sand' were fine songs. *Infidels* '83 incl. Sly & Robbie rhythm section; 'comeback' album prod. by Knopfler (by now he had as many comebacks as Frank SINATRA); only 'Jokerman' seemed to recover power. World tour '84 followed by *Real Live* '84, another collection of updated versions: 'Tombstone Blues', 'It Ain't Me Babe', etc.; *Empire Burlesque* '85 prod. by Arthur BAKER, hailed by some critics as best since *Street Legal*. *Knocked Out Loaded* '86 continued to disappoint compared to earlier work, incl. 18-minute 'Brownsville Girl'; one-off single with Tom PETTY 'Band Of The Hand' was an undistinguished blues. He toured with the GRATEFUL DEAD for the first time '87. Compilation LPs incl. *Greatest Hits* '67 (incl. hit single 'Positively 4th Street'), *More Greatest Hits* '71 (2-disc set had side of unreleased songs incl. 'Tomorrow Is A Long Time', only Dylan song covered by Elvis PRESLEY, his own favourite among covers), *Dylan* '73 (embarrassing scrapings from '69-70, issued by CBS while he was between contracts). 5-disc set *Biograph* '85 has 52 tracks, 18 previously unreleased, digitally remastered and copiously documented mostly with his own words. Recommended Dylan books incl. first biography, Anthony Scaduto's valuable *Bob Dylan* '72; Michael Gray's *Song & Dance Man* '72, since revised, good on lyrics; *A Retrospective* '72 with major reviews, interviews ed. by Craig McGregor; densely critical *Darker Shade Of Pale* '85 by Wilfrid Mellers. *No Direction Home* '86, critical biography by Robert Shelton, was eagerly awaited after 20 years, panned by some critics as though they still want to examine Dylan's soul under a microscope; *All Across The Telegraph: A Bob Dylan Handbook* '87 ed. by Gray and John Bauldie is a collection from Bauldie's *Telegraph* fanzine. Dylan's 'novel' *Tarantula* '71 was received without much enthusiasm (contrary to ravings of grad students in '60s-70s he did not write great poetry but great songs); his *Writings & Drawings* '72 updated to *Complete Lyrics* '86, light on drawings. Long since a superstar, yet only 12 top 40 hits USA '65-79, while LPs make charts but peak quickly: few have sold a million. If he had written only love songs he would be famous, but other lyrics are steeped in literary and religious allusion, beautiful and sur-real imagery: he ignored role as spokesman, though words were scrutinised for secret significance and 'Dylanologists' picked through his garbage; white middle-class ter-rorists in '70s named themselves from a line in 'Subterranean Homesick Blues' ('You don't need a weatherman/to know which way the wind blows'): he had no intention of telling anybody what to think, but Weathermen/bombers, like some critics, missed point, became part of the problem.

E

EAGLES, The USA West Coast band formed '71 by Don Henley, drums (*b* 22 July '47, Texas) and Glenn Frey, guitar (*b* 6 Nov. '48, Detroit); with Bernie Leadon, guitar (*b* 19 July '47); Randy Meisner, bass (*b* Mar. '46, Nebraska). Founder members had impeccable credentials: worked with James TAYLOR, Linda RONSTADT, POCO; initially pursued country-rock style pioneered by Gram PARSONS, Flying Burrito Brothers. Debut *The Eagles* '72 recorded in London, prod. by Glyn JOHNS; made USA charts with 'Take It Easy' (no. 12 '72), co-written by Frey and Jackson BROWNE; became band's trademark: song about free-and-easy life on the road (parodied by Southside Johnny on *Reach Up And Touch The Sky* '81). *Desperado* '73 was well-received concept LP; guitarist Don Felder added for *On The Border* '74, incl. first no. 1 single 'Best Of My Love'; 'One Of These Nights' was no. 1 '75 and 'Lyin' Eyes' no. 2: LP *One Of These Nights* was Leadon's last with the band; replaced by highly rated guitarist Joe WALSH. By then they were unassailable as USA's top band, tapping massive AOR audience with effortless vocal and guitar harmonies, though vilified by some quarters in music press: success seemed too easy, while songs like 'Tequila Sunrise' ('73) not terribly relevant outside California; with the rise of country-rock acts like Emmylou HARRIS they seemed glossy, but commercially they could do no wrong. *Hotel California* '76 was biggest success: sold 11 million worldwide; both title track and 'New Kid In Town' were no. 1 '76-7, 'Life In The Fast Lane' no. 11. After such success they took three years to produce *The Long Run* '79; predictably not nearly as big, but with title track no. 8 hit, 'Heartache Tonight' their last no. 1. Internal friction and inability to better their own success led to split '81; 2-disc *Eagles Live* '80 was souvenir. They had 16 top 40 USA hits '72-80; nine albums charted (four at no. 1 incl. *Greatest Hits 1971-75* '76), *Greatest Hits*

Vol. 2 released '82. For all the carping in the UK music press they had eight chart singles there and seven chart LPs, three in top 5. Still sadly missed by a generation of bronzed West Coast Americans; along with hits they prod. memorable one-off 'James Dean'; 'Desperado' (hit for Ronstadt); 'Take It To The Limit' (brilliantly covered by Willie NELSON and Waylon JENNINGS). Walsh resumed solo career; Felder contributed a song to film *Heavy Metal*, made solo LP *Airborne* on Asylum; Frey's solo LPs are *No Fun Aloud* on Asylum, *The Allnighter* '85 on MCA; his 'Smuggler's Blues' was worldwide hit '85, featured in TV's *Miami Vice*, film *Beverly Hills Cop*. Henley's solo debut *I Can't Stand Still* '82 used L.A. sessionmen, former Eagles, Irish folk group the CHIEFTAINS, incl. 'Dirty Laundry', 'Johnny Can't Read'; second LP *Building The Perfect Beast* '84 incl. worldwide hit 'Boys Of Summer' '85.

EAGLIN, Snooks (*b* Fird (Ford) Eaglin, 21 Jan. '36, New Orleans) Guitarist, singer, songwriter. Blind since infancy. Played in band the Flamingoes c. age 16 with Allen TOUSSAINT; an all-round entertainer typed as bluesman, though Toussaint says he came up through the church rather than blues. He wrote 'Lucille', hit for LITTLE RICHARD. LP *Street Singer* on Folkways '58 (also on Storyville); recorded for folklorist Harry Oster's Folk-Lyric label '60; R&B singles on Imperial '60-1 (own inimitable covers of Fats DOMINO, Dave BARTHOLOMEW, Jesse BELVIN etc.; didn't sell); *Rural Blues* on Prestige/Bluesville '61 (now from Fantasy), *Portraits In Blues Vol. 1* '61-2 on Storyville. He preferred performing with a combo and was semi-retired for a while; talked back into concert hall, then studio by enthusiast Quint Davis for *Snooks Eaglin* '71 (vol. 2 of Legacy of the Blues series) on GNP/Sonet, incl. 'Lucille' (after 15 years of hearing Little Richard's version, solo was refreshing), also instrumental 'Funky

Malguena', other riches; also *Down Yonder* on GNP/Sonet; gigged with PROFESSOR LONGHAIR, recorded demos with him '71-2 (issued '87 on Rounder); *Possom Up A Simmon Tree* '71 on Arhoolie, *Baby You Can Get Your Gun* '87 on Demon UK. Like Longhair a unique talent.

EANES, Jim (*b* Robert Homer Eanes Jr, 6 Dec. '23, Mountain Valley, Va.) Bluegrass singer. Began on local radio early '40s; member of Roy Hall band '41-6, Bill MONROE's Blue Grass Boys '48; formed Blue Ridge Boys '50, changed name to Shenandoah Valley Boys '51; recorded for National '46, Capitol '51, Blue Ridge '51, Decca '52, later Mercury, Starday, others. Regulars on bluegrass circuit. LPs incl. *Oldies But Goodies* '63 (Smash), *Christmas Songs* '66 (King), *Your Old Standby* '68 (Zap).

EARLAND, Charles (*b* 24 May '41, Philadelphia, Pa.) Organ, composer; also soprano sax. Early start on alto sax; played tenor at 17 with organist Jimmy McGriff, switched to organ '63; has become today's most popular organist, with walking or rolling bass lines fitting either JAZZ or ROCK-ish settings. Played and recorded on Blue Note with Lou DONALDSON '68-9. First own LP c.'69 was quartet date on Choice label with George COLEMAN; same year sextet record *Black Talk* on Prestige was good seller, followed by series on that label with groups growing larger, some vocals added: *Black Drops* '70, *Living Black!* '70 (live at The Key Club, Newark), *Soul Story* '71 (Earland vocal), *Charles III* '72 (13 pieces plus Joe Lee Wilson, *b* 22 Dec. '35, Okla., vocals; Earland plays electric piano, soprano as well as organ), *Intensity* '72, *Live At The Lighthouse* '72, *The Dynamite Brothers* '73, *Leaving This Planet* '73, *Kharma* '74 (live at Montreux). To Mercury for *Odyssey* '75 with studio band; then to Muse for four LPs '77-8 (on first three reunited with Jimmy Ponder, *b* 10 May '46, Pittsburgh, who played guitar on first album): *Smokin'*, *Mama Roots*, *Infant Eyes*, *Pleasant Afternoon*. To Columbia with big studio bands for *Coming To You Live* c.'79-80 (with BRECKER brothers, girl group backing vocals), *Jam* '82. Recent quartet LPs on Muse '81-2 incl. *Mama Roots* '81 (co-led by

Coleman), *In The Pocket* '82. *Burners* on Prestige is issue of mid-'70s tapes; *Earland's Street Themes* is recent Columbia LP.

EARLE, Steve (*b* 17 Jan. '55, Fort Monroe, Va.) Singer, songwriter, guitarist; new country-rock star with first major label recordings. Songs had been covered by Carl PERKINS, Connie SMITH, others; Waylon JENNINGS incl. 'The Devil's Right Hand' on his first MCA LP. Earle's *Guitar Town* '86 on MCA, prod. by Tony Brown (Elvis PRESLEY), Emory Gordy Jr (Emmylou HARRIS) incl. songs with country values, *Rolling Stone* said his sound owed more to Keith Richards than Chet ATKINS: is that bad? Apart from guitar styles, *Guitar Town* was excellent rock with strong country flavour, or vice versa, with the virtue (more common in country than in other genres nowadays) of eschewing excess production, unlike the 'countrypolitan' style that Atkins perhaps regrets. *Exit O* '87 by Steve Earle and the Dukes was top 20 in Billboard country album chart mid-'87 while *Guitar Town* was still in the top 50.

EARTH, WIND AND FIRE USA soul dance band formed '69 by vocalist/drummer Maurice White (*b* 19 Dec. '41, Memphis, Tenn.) and his brother, bassist Verdine White (*b* 25 July '51). Despite its absurd name it is a musical outfit, slick in the best sense, incl. elements of Latin-funk beat, gospel, soul, rock etc. in infl. way. Their grandfather played piano in New Orleans, father was a doctor; Maurice studied at a Chicago conservatory, was a house drummer at Chess label, toured with Ramsey LEWIS '67-9, formed first band, recorded for Capitol as Salty Peppers, two LPs for WB as Earth, Wind & Fire: eponymous debut charted '71, *The Need Of Love* '72 made top 100 pop LPs; re-formed on Columbia, *The Last Days And Time* '72 continuing climb up the charts: *Head To The Sky* '73 in top 30 LPs, now with stable personnel incl. sweet soul singer Philip Bailey (*b* 8 May '51, Denver, Col.), Larry Dunn (*b* 19 June '53, Col.) on keyboards, Johnny Graham (*b* 3 Aug. '51, Ky.) and Al McKay (*b* 2 Feb. '48, La.) on guitars, Andre Woolfolk (*b* 11 Oct. '50, Texas) on reeds (augmented since late '70s by four-piece Phoenix Horns), Ralph Johnson (*b* 4 July '51, Cal.) on drums, joined c.'74 by a third brother Freddie White on drums (*b* 13 Jan. '55, Chicago). Equal and opposite to PARLIAMENT/Funkadelic lowdown boogie empire of George Clinton, uplifting rather than hedonistic. *Open Our Eyes* '74 was no. 15 LP USA; 2-disc *Another Time* '74 was reissue of first two WB LPs. *That's The Way Of The World* '75 was no. 1 LP incl. no. 1 single, Grammy-winning 'Shining Star' (LP also soundtrack to documentary film about the band); live/studio *Gratitude* same year also no. 1, with no. 5 hit 'Sing A Song'; *Spirit* '76 was no. 2, *All 'N All* '77 no. 3. Switched to own custom ARC label with *Best Of* '78, no. 6 LP with two top 10 hits incl. 'Got To Get You Into My Life', high point of otherwise panned Robert Stigwood movie *Sgt Pepper's Lonely Hearts Club Band*; won more Grammies. *I Am* '79 was no. 3 LP incl. no. 2 hit 'After The Love Has Gone', no. 6 'Boogie Wonderland' (latter with vocal group the Emotions); 2-disc *Faces* '80 was no. 10, *Raise!* '81 no. 5 (incl. no. 2 hit 'Let's Groove'); *Powerlight* '83 slipped out of top 10, *Electric Universe* '83 to no. 40. 2-disc *Beat It To Life* on Pair '86 is a reissue or compilation. Their '79 worldwide tour incl. special effects, dancers etc. was designed by magician Doug Henning; '79 tour featured Maurice duelling with a Darth Vador figure. He was infl. by his interest in Egyptology; had taken up kalimba (thumb piano) while with Lewis, it became band's trademark. He wrote Lewis's hit 'Sun Goddess' '75, prod. LP of that title; also prod. for Deniece Williams, Valerie Carter and Emotions (Jeanette, Wanda and Sheila Hutchinson), from Chicago, records on Stax/Volt (Theresa Davis depping for Jeanette), later Columbia (sister Pamela temporarily replacing Jeanette); biggest hit was no. 1 'Best Of My Love', written by Maurice and McKay, from no. 7 LP *Rejoice* '77.

EASTON, Sheena (*b* Sheena Orr, 27 Apr. '59, Glasgow) UK singer. Drama student opted for pop career; signed with EMI, received boost on *Big Time* TV show: she was subject of BBC programme describing process of manufacturing pop star. First single 'Modern Girl' made no. 56 early '80; first post TV-release '9 to 5' no. 3; 'Modern Girl' re-released reached no. 8; '9 to 5' was re-

titled 'Morning Train' to avoid confusion with title of Dolly PARTON film, was no. 1 USA. 'One Man Woman' made no. 14 to round off good first year, but mundanity of songs began to tell: cleverly switched to ballads, relying on prod. Chris Neil to pick them: 'When He Shines' and 'For Your Eyes Only' (James Bond theme) '81 were last big UK hits. To USA to promote first LP (*Take My Time* UK; *Sheena Easton* USA); decided to concentrate on that market: mellifluous cover of Bob SEGER's 'We Got Tonight' (duet with Kenny ROGERS) was no. 6 USA '83, no. 28 UK, confirming wisdom of decision. Having cultivated whiter-than-white image with no little success, she surprised everybody by enlisting disco king PRINCE to redirect career: 'Strut' no. 7 USA '84; his comp. 'Sugar Walls' went top 10 black chart (despite airplay restrictions due to supposed reference to female anatomy), bringing distinction as first singer to have singles in Billboard top 10 pop, black, disco, MOR and country charts. UK refused to buy changes in image, has abandoned her to USA. Borrowed MADONNA's street-urchin image and prod. Nile Rodgers for LP *Do You* '85. Seven albums in USA catalogue '88.

EASYBEATS, The Australian beat group formed '63 by émigré Europeans who met at youth hostel: George Young (*b* 6 Nov. '47, Scotland), rhythm guitar; Gordon 'Snowy' Fleet (*b* 16 Aug. '45, England), drums; Harry Vanda (*b* 22 March '47, Holland), lead guitar; Dick Diamonde (*b* 28 Dec. '47, Holland). Through Fleet met Englishman Stevie Wright (*b* 20 Dec. '48), won residency at Beatle Village club, Sydney. Second single 'She's So Fine' no. 1 Aussie chart followed by hits 'Wedding Ring', 'Sad And Lonely And Blue', 'Woman', 'Come And See Her', with Wright something of a teen heart-throb. Turned eyes to Europe/USA '66, recorded 'Friday On My Mind' in London with Shel Talmy (prod. KINKS, WHO): with an urgency rare in mellow sounds of the time, it made no. 16 USA, 6 UK, 1 Australia. Fleet left before USA tour, replaced by Tony Cahill (ex-Purple Hearts). Drug and management problems postponed follow-up; Talmy-prod. 'Who'll Be The One' eventually flopped. They changed style wildly to find audience: 'Hello How Are You', Tom JONES-styled ballad, was second and last UK hit (no. 20 '68) 18 months after 'Friday'. LP *Vigil* '68 equally confused with unlikely covers such as 'Can't Take My Eyes Off You', 'Hit The Road Jack'. Eventually prod. 'Friday'-style 'Good Times' (Steve Marriott on backing vocals) but it was too late; band split. Songwriters Vanda, Young stuck together, prod. debut solo LP for Stevie Wright (*Hard Road* '75), assisted Young's brothers Angus and Malcolm in starting AC/DC, Australia's most successful group; had mixed fortunes as Band of Hope, Marcus Hook, Paintbox, Flash and the Pan: as latter had no. 7 UK hit '83 'Waiting For A Train'.

ECHO & THE BUNNYMEN Post-punk UK band of Liverpool's 'second wave' late '70s. Ian McCulloch, vocals, guitar (*b* 5 May '59, Liverpool) began in prophetically named Crucial Three, with Pete Wylie (later Wah!), Julian Cope (TEARDROP EXPLODES); McCulloch and Cope also in A Shallow Madness '78. Echo first gigged at Eric's Club '78, period equivalent of the Cavern, where the BEATLES started; Echo was the name of their drum machine. Early records on Zoo label; initially criticised for doomy DOORS sound but moved from ghetto of critical approval of debut album *Crocodiles* '80 to mass popularity. Live act suggested by film *Apocalypse Now*: camouflage costumes, dry ice; LP *Heaven Up Here* '81, furthered reputation; short film *Shine So Hard* also released '81; A Crystal Day '83 was 24-hour Liverpool event culminating in Echo concert and other unusual gigs incl. tour of remote Scottish islands, first rock band to play at Royal Shakespeare Company theatre in Stratford. *Porcupine* '83 incl. first single hit 'The Cutter' (UK no. 8); more lavishly arr. *Ocean Rain* '84 incl. 'Silver', 'Seven Seas', 'Killing Moon' (no. 9). Frontman McCulloch gave good copy, rarely out of music press '85: opinionated, fiercely proud of group and Liverpool. Singles compilation *Songs To Learn & Sing* '85 incl. 'Rescue', 'Bring On The Dancing Horses' (featured in soundtrack of USA film *Pretty In Pink* '86). They slowly climb USA charts: *Echo & The Bunnymen* '87 almost made USA top 50 albums, best showing so far.

ECKSTINE, Billy (*b* William Clarence Eckstein, 8 July '14, Pittsburgh, Pa.) Singer; also plays trumpet, valve trombone, guitar. Singer/emcee in clubs, then sang with Earl HINES band '39-43: with tenor sax-arr. Budd JOHNSON infl. Hines to hire people like Charlie PARKER, Sarah VAUGHAN. Went solo, then with Johnson led big band '44-7 that was ahead of its time: those who passed through incl. Gene AMMONS, Art BLAKEY, Miles DAVIS, Kenny DORHAM, Dizzy GILLESPIE, Dexter GORDON, Fats NAVARRO, Lucky THOMPSON, Lena HORNE as well as Parker and Vaughan; arr. by Johnson, Tadd DAMERON, others. Fine outfit unsuccessful: few commercial recordings because of union disputes, big bands had become uneconomic (*see* BIG BAND ERA), modern jazz not commercial proposition (*see* BOP); records collected on 2-disc set *Mr B. & Band*, *Sings* (with band; etc. both on Savoy); *Together* '45 on Spotlight is Armed Forces Network broadcasts. Led octet briefly; took big, warm voice and jazz-infl. ballad style to market and had 12 top 30 hits on MGM '49-52, incl. top tens 'My Foolish Heart', 'I Apologize', 'I Wanna Be Loved'. Became much-loved American institution, playing clubs in Nevada, tours of Europe, Australia annually, Asia often, entertaining US troops. Gigs with bands incl. Maynard FERGUSON, Duke ELLINGTON '66. Albums on Mercury early '60s, Motown later; in UK from Mercury/Polydor: *Back To Back* (2-disc set with Vaughan), *Greatest Hits*; plus *Golden Hour* from Pye, *Something More* from Stax (RCA). *Everything I Have Is Yours* '85 is 2-disc compilation on Verve '49-57, incl. MGM hits, tracks with Sarah, others with Metronome All-Stars; sold well and generated profile of Mr B. on a CBS News programme. *Billy Eckstine Sings With Benny Carter* '87 on Emarcy with guest Helen MERRILL nominated for a Grammy '88.

ECM Jazz/fusion label formed by Manfred Eicher: first issue '70 was Mal WALDRON trio LP *Free At Last*. Established USA jazzmen, new avant-garde artists were available in Europe; major labels as usual doing very little. Often used Oslo studios; company offices now in Munich. More than 200 LPs in print incl. items by Sam RIVERS, Kenny WHEELER, AZIMUTH, Miroslav Vitous, John SURMAN, Dave HOLLAND,

Lester BOWIE, Paul BLEY, much more. 15th anniversary of label marked by 10 *Works* LPs, anthologies of ECM artists Pat METHENY, Keith JARRETT, Gary BURTON, Jack DEJOHNETTE, Chick COREA, tenor saxophonist Jan Garbarek (*b* 4 Mar. '47, Myson, Norway), bassist Eberhard Weber (*b* 22 Jan. '40, Stuttgart), multi-instrumentalists Ralph Towner (*b* 1 Mar. '40, Chehalis, Wash.), Terje Rypdal (*b* 23 Aug. '47, Oslo), Egberto Gismonti (*b* '47, Carmo, Brazil): virtually all label's artists are also composers, record for ECM without long-term contracts. Technical quality of records very high; many have won awards. Success has been so great that critics complain about slickness of product, and it is true that ECM has contributed a bit more than sleeve graphics to NEW AGE music, partly because young European musicians of very high technical accomplishment are playing fusion: Rypdal for example prefers the tone of some rock musicians to that of 'mellow type jazz guitarists', while David Darling (*b* 4 Mar. '41, Elkhart, Ind.) plays eight-string solid-bodied amplified cello of his own design. Some of the music lacks passion to the point of introversion, but much of the catalogue is hardly complacent: Old And New Dreams incl. ex-Ornette COLEMAN sidemen Charlie HADEN, Dewey REDMAN, Don CHERRY, Ed BLACKWELL (eponymous debut followed by *Playing* '82); five ECM sets by ART ENSEMBLE OF CHICAGO are among their best; Haden's *Ballad Of The Fallen* '84 was well received. Of Jarrett's many LPs, 2-disc *The Köln Concert* '75 has sold a million by now. ECM recorded free-form 'classical' composer Steve Reich, breaks new artists every year, e.g. USA quartet Everyman Band: eponymous debut LP followed by *Without Warning*, made '84 in Bearsville, NY. ECM also distribute the Carla BLEY-Mike Mantler Watt label.

EDDIE & THE HOT RODS UK band formed Southend mid-'70s, link between pub rock and punk. Lineup: Barrie Masters, vocals; Dave Higgs, guitar; Paul Gray, bass; Steve Nicol, drums. Followed DR FEELGOOD out of 'Canvey Delta' of Southend, playing loud, fast, aggressive music, at first augmented by harmonica player Lew Lewis, whose departure after playing on first single

'Writing On The Wall' and B-side of second was due to group's re-orientation towards punk; were not genuine punks but delighted to be adopted: even got good review in punk bible *Sniffin' Glue*. Early material was mostly covers: second single was SAM THE SHAM's 'Wooly Bully'; EP *Live At The Marquee* incl. ? AND THE MYSTERIANS' '96 Tears', Jim Morrison's 'Gloria', ROLLING STONES' 'Satisfaction'. Latter made no. 43 UK followed by 'Teenage Depression' at no. 35, both '76; by then Higgs, manager/lyricist Ed Hollis were writing most material, cf. LP *Teenage Depression* '76. Graeme Douglas from fellow Southenders KURSAAL FLYERS added on lead guitar '77; they backed MC5 singer Rob Tyner on 'Til The Night Is Gone'; made no. 9 themselves with amphetamined rocker 'Do Anything You Wanna Do', striking suitable rebellious stance in heyday of SEX PISTOLS. That was peak: 'Quit This Town' made only no. 36; second live EP *Live At The Sound Of Speed* followed by LP *Life On The Line* '77, their only top 30 album; *Thriller* '79, *Fish'n' Chips* (on EMI) failed to do as well: latter prod. by Al KOOPER, but Douglas had left (with much of verve). Masters (whose energetic stage act was unrivalled in acrobatic content) disbanded, sang with Inmates; Gray joined DAMNED, then UFO; Masters re-formed group with new members, sounding much like Lee Brilleaux and Feelgoods, their original inspiration: made live LP *One Story Town* '85 for local Waterfront label.

EDDY, Duane (*b* 26 Apr. '38, Corning, NY) Rock'n'roll guitarist. To Phoenix at 17, already playing; local DJ/promoter Lee HAZLEWOOD and guitarist Al Casey helped invent gimmick of 'twangy' sound: instrumental hits had simple melody lines played on bass strings, heavily amplified. Second single was 'Rebel Rouser', no. 6 hit USA '58 and still a nostalgic sound, followed by 14 top 40 hits USA '58-63: 'Forty Miles Of Bad Road' no. 9 '59; appeared in film and had hit with title 'Because They're Young' no. 4 '60; TV theme 'Peter Gunn' no. 27 '60: remake by Art of Noise big '86 hit; Eddy describes them as his modern equivalent. Group called the Rebels toured with Dick CLARK, incl. Casey, Steve Douglas on sax, Larry Knechtel on piano (later BREAD).

Switched from Clark's Jamie label to RCA '62, to Col-Pix '65. Plays in oldies shows more popular in UK than USA. Prod. LP by Phil EVERLY '73; had UK hit 'Play Me Like You Play Your Guitar' no. 9 '75; 'You Are My Sunshine' '77 on Asylum prod. by Hazlewood with vocals by Willie NELSON, Waylon JENNINGS (married to Eddy's ex-wife Jesse COLTER). Compilations in and out of print.

EDDY, Nelson, & Jeanette MacDonald Singers popular in films of '30s (Eddy *b* 29 June '01, Providence, R.I.; *d* 6 Mar. '67; soprano MacDonald *b* 18 June '01, Philadelphia, Pa.; *d* 14 Jan. '65). He taught himself singing by listening to opera records, then worked odd jobs to pay for lessons; he made opera debut in small role NYC '24, sang on radio, was signed to MGM by Louis B. Mayer early '30s, had minor roles in *Dancing Lady* and *Broadway To Hollywood* '33, *Student Tour* '34. She began in chorus of Broadway show *The Night Boat* '20, supporting roles in *Tip Toes* and *Bubbling Over* '26, starred in *Yes, Yes, Yvette* '27, *Sunny Days* '28, *Boom! Boom!* '29. Starred in early film musicals with Maurice CHEVALIER: *The Love Parade* '29, *Love Me Tonight* and *One Hour With You* '32, *The Merry Widow* '34. They starred together in Victor HERBERT's *Naughty Marietta* '35: instant stardom. Other films together were *Rose-Marie* '36, *Maytime* '37, *Girl Of The Golden West* and *Sweethearts* '38, *Bitter Sweet* and *New Moon* '40, *I Married An Angel* '42. She also made *San Francisco* '36, *The Firefly* '37 (made a star of Allan Jones; *see* Jack JONES), others; he made *The Chocolate Soldier* '41, *Phantom Of The Opera* '43, *Knickerbocker Holiday* '44, more. They were both active in radio; he starred '34-5 on *The Voice Of Firestone*, *Chase & Sanborn* show '37-9 with Don Ameche, Dorothy Lamour; had own shows in '40s.

EDISON, Harry (*b* 10 Oct. '15, Columbus, Ohio) Trumpet; aka 'Sweets'. With Alphonso Trent, Jeter-Pillars band, Lucky MILLINDER, then Count BASIE c.'37-50, often sitting in years later. Sang (sort of) on Basie's 'Open The Door, Richard' (no. 1 hit USA '47). Regular tours with JATP; worked with Buddy RICH; sought after for studio work (e.g. with Nelson RIDDLE on

Frank SINATRA LPs). Appeared in famous short film *Jammin' The Blues* with Lester YOUNG. Led own small groups; many tours, records: much-loved mainstream stalwart. With Louie BELLSON band '71, tours of Europe late '70s-80s, often with Eddie Lockjaw DAVIS, with The Countsmen '83. Countless records as sideman; own LPs incl. with Davis on Storyville '76, *Vol. 2: Opus Funk* on same label, also *Sonny, Sweets & Jaws* with Davis, Sonny STITT on Gateway. Own small group c.'58 with Jimmy FORREST: *Sweet Tracks* 2-disc set on French Vogue and *The Swinger* on Verve. Other LPs on Norman GRANZ's labels (dates are often those of UK release): *Blues For Basie* and *Simply Sweets* '77, *Just Friends* with Zoot SIMS, *Edison's Lights* '82, *Jazz At The Philharmonic 1983* with Davis and Al Grey (trombone, ex-Basie, *b* 6 June '25, Aldie, Va.). Many other LPs in and out of print, all of them rewarding.

EDMUNDS, Dave (*b* 15 Apr. '44, Cardiff, Wales) UK rock guitarist, singer, producer. Played in local bands '60s, then trio Love Sculpture, who had one-off no. 5 UK hit '68 with breakneck version of Khachaturian's 'Sabre Dance' (in compilation *The Love Sculpture Years* '87). Kept flame of '50s rock alive with cover of Smiley LEWIS's 'I Hear You Knockin'' (no. 1 UK '70; no. 4 USA '71), solo LP *Rockpile* '72, top 10 hits UK '73 'Baby I Love You', 'Born To Be With You'. Invested in studio Rockfield in Wales, prod. LPs early '70s by Del SHANNON, FLAMIN' GROOVIES, Man, BRINSLEY SCHWARZ, forming friendship with Brinsley bassist Nick LOWE. Edmunds was mus. dir., appeared with David ESSEX in film *Stardust* '73. Solo LP *Subtle As A Flying Mallet* '75 re-created basic rock sound: highly rated by contemporaries; one of few signings to LED ZEPPELIN label Swansong: album *Get It* '77 saw formation of fine band Rockpile, with Billy Bremner, guitar; Terry Williams, drums; and Lowe; Lowe and Edmunds were part of first Stiff tour '77. Edmunds' further LPs incl. *Tracks On Wax* '78, *Repeat When Necessary* '79 (cover of Elvis COSTELLO's 'Girls Talk' no. 4 UK; minor hit was Graham PARKER 'Crawling From The Wreckage'). Rockpile made LP *Seconds Of Pleasure* '80 before split (Bremner to PRETENDERS, released solo album *Bash* '83;

Williams worked with Paul Brady, then joined DIRE STRAITS). Edmunds' *Twangin'* '81 incl. cover of John Fogerty's 'Almost Saturday Night', duet with Stray Cats 'The Race Is On' (top 40 hit). *DE7th* incl. Bruce SPRINGSTEEN song personally passed on by composer, 'From Small Things . . . ' *Information* '83 and *Riff-Raff* '84 had Edmunds working with ELECTRIC LIGHT ORCHESTRA's Jeff Lynne. Always in demand as producer: albums by STRAY CATS, EVERLY Bros; Shakin' STEVENS, Jeff BECK, FABULOUS THUNDERBIRDS, DR FEELGOOD, etc.; appeared in Paul McCARTNEY's film *Give My Regards To Broad Street* '84; oversaw Carl PERKINS UK tour '85; worked with George HARRISON, Ringo STARR, Eric CLAPTON; supervised soundtrack for film *Porky's Revenge* '85. Own *Best Of* LP '81; live *I Hear You Rockin'* '87.

EDWARDS, Cliff (*b* 1895, Hannibal, Mo.; *d* '72, Hollywood) Singer, ukulele player, aka 'Ukulele Ike'. Very popular in vaudeville, appeared in Broadway shows and revues *Lady Be Good* '24, *Sunny* '25, *Ziegfeld Follies* '27, *George White's Scandals* '27, 70 films incl. *Hollywood Revue Of 1929* (sang 'Singin' In The Rain'). His records were popular, many with jazz sidemen like Miff Mole, Jimmy DORSEY etc.; his career was faltering when he did voice of Jiminy Cricket in Disney film *Pinocchio* '40: sang Oscar-winning 'When You Wish Upon A Star'. Kept going until TV, then faded. Reissues on Totem, Glendale, *A Bear In A Lady's Boudoir* on Yazoo.

EDWARDS, Stoney (*b* 24 Dec. '37, Okla.) Black country singer. Grew up listening to country music, worked as farm hand, truck driver, janitor etc. before singing in small Texas clubs, then in Oakland, Calif. where he signed with Capitol '70. Based on West Coast, has built cult following for honky-tonk sound which owes much to Lefty FRIZZELL. Hits incl. 'Poor Folks Stick Together' '71, 'She's My Rock' '72, 'Hank And Lefty Raised My Country Soul' '73, 'Mississippi You're On My Mind' '75, 'Blackbird (Hold Your Head High)' '76, 'If I Had To Do It Over Again' '78, 'No Way To Drown A Memory' '80. Deserves greater success, but helped to pave the way for similarly soulful singers, such as John CONLEE and

John ANDERSON. Albums incl. *A Country Singer* and *Down Home In The Country* '71, *She's My Rock* '72, *Mississippi You're On My Mind* '75, *Blackbird* '76, *No Way To Drown A Memory* '81 on Music America.

EDWARDS, Teddy (*b* Theodore Marcus Edwards, 26 Apr. '24, Jackson, Ms.) Tenor sax, composer, leader. To West Coast as a young man; there was always a lot more jazz being played there than the 'West Coast' or 'cool' school that was popular in the '50s; although prominent there since the '40s, like Curtis COUNCE, Wardell GRAY (who did not live long enough) and others, Edwards did not achieve as much national fame as he deserved, because unlike Charles MINGUS, Eric DOLPHY, Dexter GORDON, Howard McGHEE and others who began or worked there late '40s-early '50s, he kept California as his base. Almost all his recordings have been made there (except as noted). Worked many jazz concerts and festivals, wrote songs recorded by Jimmy WITHERSPOON, contributed to films *Any Wednesday* '66, *They Shoot Horses, Don't They?* '69. First own records '47-8 later issued on Onyx LPs *The Foremost!* and *Central Avenue Breakdown*, with Red CALLENDER, Hampton HAWES, Benny BAILEY, Addison Farmer, drummer Roy Porter among sidemen, incl. a track from a Dial date with Gordon. Recorded with Gerald WILSON, Witherspoon on Pacific Jazz; own LPs on that label '59 incl. Billy HIGGINS singing on 'Me And My Lover'. Then *Teddy's Ready* '60, *Together Again!* with McGhee and *Good Gravy* '61, *Heart And Soul* '62, all on Contemporary; *Nothin' But The Truth* '66 and *It's Alright* '67 on Prestige (made in NYC), *Feelin's* '74 on Muse, *The Inimitable* '76 on Xanadu (NYC), *Out Of This World* '80 on Steeplechase (Copenhagen). He also recorded with Benny GOODMAN on Capitol, Milt JACKSON on Impulse, Jimmy SMITH on Verve, Sarah VAUGHAN on Mainstream etc.

EDWARDS, Tommy (*b* 17 Feb. '22, Richmond, Va.; *d* 22-3 Oct. '69, Va.) Songwriter, singer. Entered show business age 9; played piano, sang in Richmond late '40s; wrote 'That Chick's Too Young To Fry' for Louis JORDAN. Signed by MGM on strength of demo record of his own song 'All Over

Again'; hit with 'The Morning Side Of The Mountain' (no. 24) and 'It's All In The Game' (no. 18) '51. Latter tune was written '12 as 'Melody In F major' by banker, amateur flautist Charles Gates Dawes, who was later USA Vice-President under Coolidge '25-9; words were added by Carl Sigman '51. MGM allegedly intended to drop him in '58, but suggested a remake of 'Game' in stereo at what would have been his last session: the backing was also updated; the rockaballad was no. 1 for six weeks in '58 and sold 3.5 million by '71. The song has reached the top 30 in both UK and USA in three different versions, incl. Cliff RICHARD '63-4, the FOUR TOPS '70. Edwards had five more top 40 hits '58-60 incl. remakes of 'Mountain', 'Please Mr Sun' ('52 hit by Johnnie RAY), 'I Really Don't Want To Know'.

ELDRIDGE, Roy (*b* David Roy Eldridge, 30 Jan. '11, Pittsburgh, Pa.) Trumpet; also plays piano, bass, drums, sings; nicknamed 'Little Jazz' by Otto Hardwicke. Lessons from elder brother Joe (*b* '08, Pittsburgh; *d* 5 Mar. '52, NYC), who played alto sax and violin; first gig a New Year's Eve job with Joe when almost 7 years old. With Horace HENDERSON, Elmer SNOWDEN, Teddy HILL, Fletcher HENDERSON, others during '30s; quit music to study radio engineering '38 but led own band late that year, by then famous among musicians for ideas, power and technique, his trumpet style influenced by saxophonists, in turn as influential as Louis ARMSTRONG's had been 10 years before, e.g. on young Dizzy GILLESPIE. More widespread fame as featured soloist with Gene KRUPA band '41-3: played drums occasionally while Krupa fronted; vocal duet with Anita O'DAY on 'Let Me Off Uptown' (no. 10 hit for Krupa '41). Had own band again '43, CBS staff work '44, with Artie SHAW '44-5, own big band '46, later small group. Rejoined Krupa '49, first JATP tour '49-50, Europe with Benny GOODMAN '50, then toured there solo. Own quintet at Birdland NYC '51; from then on led small groups, often co-leading with Coleman HAWKINS; freelanced solo, toured with JATP, many festivals. Also played flugelhorn from late '50s. With small group accompanying Ella FITZGERALD '63-5, appeared at President Carter's White House

jazz party '78. Played at Jimmy Ryan's club NYC regularly; had heart attack '80, appeared as vocalist '80s. Countless records incl. 2-disc *Dale's Wail* '53-4 with Oscar PETERSON on Verve; *The Trumpet Battle 1952* with Charlie SHAVERS and Lester YOUNG on Verve/Polydor, *Rockin' Chair* on Verve USA. *The Great English Concert 1958* with Hawkins, Stan GETZ is on Jazz Groove; two 2-disc sets on French Vogue called *Little Jazz* and *Paris Sessions*. *Never Too Old . . .* with Tiny GRIMES on Sonet UK. Recent LPs on Pablo incl. *Montreux '77*, *Happy*, *Little Jazz & Jimmy Ryan All-Stars*, *Jazz Maturity* '75 with Gillespie and Peterson, *What It's All About*, others. Compilations of influential early work incl. 2-disc *The Early Years* on Columbia USA ('35-49 tracks with Teddy Hill, Eldridge, Krupa, Teddy WILSON bands, vocals by Anita O'Day, Billie HOLIDAY); *The Krupa Years* on Phontastic ('40-2 broadcasts), *At Jerry Newman's* '40 and *Sweets, Lips And Lots Of Jazz* '41 from Minton's with Harry EDISON, Hot Lips PAGE, both on Xanadu; 2-disc *Tippin' Out* on Affinity UK has '43-6 Eldridge big band tracks from Decca USA.

ELECTRIC LIGHT ORCHESTRA UK pop band formed '71 by Jeff Lynne (*b* 30 Dec. '47), guitar, vocals; and Roy Wood (*b* 8 Nov. '46) from ashes of the MOVE, adding Bev Bevan (*b* 25 Nov. '46), drums; all from Birmingham. Originally tackled style of late BEATLE experiments fusing classical instruments to rock rhythm section; had some problems with sound balance in live act. LP *Electric Light Orchestra* late '71 (aka *Queen Of The Hours*) incl. top 10 UK hit '10538 Overture'. Wood quit '72; *ELO2* incl. cover of Chuck BERRY's 'Roll Over Beethoven' for second top 10 hit (of 13 '72-81, six in USA '75-81); *On The Third Day* '73 followed by *Eldorado* '74, *Face The Music* '75 with hit 'Evil Woman'; breakthrough was *A New World Record* '76: hit singles incl. 'Livin' Thing', 'Telephone Line'; no. 6 LP UK/5 USA. Kept banner of 'progressive rock' flying; LPs wildly unfashionable but commercially successful: *Ole ELO* '76 was a compilation; *Three Light Years* '78 a boxed set of three reissues; other LPs incl. *Out Of The Blue* '77, *Discovery* '79, *Time* '81; also compilations and reissues, *The Light Shines On* (2 vols.) etc. *Xanadu* '80 was abortive

377

soundtrack with Olivia NEWTON-JOHN and others. Rockabilly-styled 'Hold On Tight' was top 10 USA/UK '81, but repertoire of no real distinction (cumbersome concepts 'Wild West Hero', 'The Diary Of Horace Wimp') despite Lynne's ability to write catchy pop singles ('Mr Blue Sky', 'Last Train To London'); he regained some credibility working with Dave EDMUNDS '83-4. ELO came back '86 after long layoff with shows for Birmingham charities; new LP *Balance Of Power* had harder, stripped-down sound, incl. single 'Calling America'.

ELECTRIC PRUNES USA psychedelic rock group formed in Seattle c.'66, originally in the vein of contemporary groups such as Them, the Seeds, or the Music Machine. First lineup: Jim Lowe (*b* San Luis Obispo, Cal.), vocals, autoharp, harmonica, guitar; Weasel Spagnola (*b* Cleveland, Ohio), vocals, guitar; Ken Williams (*b* Long Beach, Cal.), lead guitar; Mark Tulin (*b* Philadelphia, Pa.), bass, flute; Preston Ritter (*b* Stockton, Cal.), drums. Signed with Reprise; initial single 'Ain't It Hard' flopped; next 'I Had Too Much To Dream Last Night' just missed top 10 USA '67, became classic of genre; 'Get Me To The World On Time' also made top 30 same year. First LP *The Electric Prunes* was their best-seller at no. 113 USA; by the time *Underground* (also '67) was released, Ritter had been replaced by someone called Quint; then, apparently, a completely new lineup took over name and contract: writer/arranger David Axelrod was allegedly involved with Mark Kincaid (*b* Topeka, Ks.), vocals, guitar; Ron Morgan, guitar; John Herren (*b* Elk City, Okla.), keyboards; Brett Wade (*b* Vancouver), bass, flute; Richard Whetstone (*b* Hutchinson, Ks.), vocals, drums; *Mass In F Minor*, an electric rock mass sung in Latin, was the new group's first and last chart entry in Jan. '68. *Release Of An Oath* and *The Kol Nidre* appeared that year, *Just Good Old Rock'n' Roll* in '69 (by which time Herren had left). No later LPs listed personnel. Best work of first lineup is reissued on *Long Day's Flight* '86 on Edsel UK.

ELGART, Les and Larry Led dance bands. Les (*b* 3 Aug. '18, New Haven, Conn.) played lead trumpet; brother Larry (*b* 20 Mar. '22, New London, Conn.) lead alto

sax, later lead soprano. Both had extensive Swing Era experience; Les led a band with Larry in it '45-6; led separate bands and freelanced; reunited '53 under Les until '58 when Larry took over, together again from '63 often billed as Les and Larry Elgart. A popular dance band with smooth sound; emphasis on ensemble, but sometimes featured jazz musicians. Records on Decca and MGM but mainly (mid-'50s and after '63) on Columbia; Les's *The Elgart Touch* '56, *For Dancers Also* '57 made top 15 in Billboard chart; Larry's LPs on MGM early '60s incl. *The City* and *Legends*, written by Bobby SCOTT; *Les & Larry Play The Great Dance Hits* charted '64; Larry Elgart & His Manhattan Swing Orchestra charted on RCA '82-3 with *Hooked On Swing* and *Hooked On Swing 2*.

EL GRAN COMBO (de Puerto Rico) Formed '62 by breakaway members of what was then Puerto Rico's no. 1 Rafael CORTIJO y su Combo. Led by pianist Rafael Ithier, lineup incl. Eddie Perez on sax, Martin Quiñones, congas, bongo player/dancer Roberto ROENA ('El Gran Bailarin', The Great Dancer); classically trained Kito Velez on trumpet; only Ithier and Perez remain in current lineup. Expressed aim was to become international commercial success; they became a Puerto Rican national institution: 13-piece lineup (piano, saxes, trumpets, trombone, singers, timbales, congas, bongos, bass) is considered by many the definitive and most spectacular salsa band, annual tours to Europe and Latin America testify to their success. Musically they differ from NYC salsa, identified with fusion and experimentation; Ithier has shaped them to a uniquely slick and precise outfit with a decidedly Puerto Rican 'downhome' flavour. First hit was 'La Muerte' (Death) '62 from LP *El Gran Combo . . . de Siempre* on Gema, then 'Acángana', from LP of that name; title track of *Ojos Chinos* (Chinese Eyes) '64, written by Velez, is still popular today in a more refined version, still sung with unison routines from the three singers that recall the great soul groups of the '60s (e.g. FOUR TOPS). Other hits incl. title track of *El Caballo Pelotero* '65, 'La Calle Dolor' (The Sad Street) from *El Swing del Gran Combo* '66, 'Falsaria' '68 (from *Smile It's el Gran*

Combo), title track of *Tu Querias Boogaloo* during the boogaloo era, 'Ponme el Alcolado Juana' from *Este Si Que el Gran Combo* '69; 30 '60s tracks were collected on *El Gran Combo Sus 15 Grandes Hits* and *15 Grandes Exitos Vol. 2*, both on Gema. Hits in '70s incl. love song 'Julia' '72 from *Por el Libro*, 'La Salsa de Hoy' '74 from *Disfrútelo Hasta el Cabo!*, 'Brujería' '79 from *Aqui No Se Sienta Nadie!*. In '73 they appeared with the FANIA ALL STARS at a historic concert in Yankee Stadium; in '76 in Jerry Masucci's film *Salsa* (and on soundtrack LP). Roena had left '69 (see his entry); vocalist Andy Montañez left '77 (last LP with them was *Mejor Que Nunca*), joined Dimension Latina (*see* Oscar D'LEON): first LP with them was *Los Generales de la Salsa* (aka *Presentanda: Andy Montañez*) on Top Hits; went solo; had smash hit eponymous LP '85 made in Puerto Rico. Velez had also left; he had composed and arranged for Cortijo, EGC and singer Ismael Rivera as well as playing trumpet; he led his own band in Puerto Rico with LPs on Ansonia, briefly worked in trumpet duo with Nelson Feliciano as Guanica Brass (LP on Coco); also played on *Combo Original* '74 on Coco, a Cortijo reunion which also incl. Ithier, Perez, Quiñones and Roena. 20 years of EGC hits were celebrated in 2-disc set *20 Años Exitos* '82 on Combo label, a mixture of remixes/new recordings, and concert at Madison Square Garden same year. In the '80s EGC personnel has been stable, with Ithier, piano, leader, arranger; vocalists Charlie Aponte, Jerry Rivas, Papo Rosario; Taty Maldonado and Victor E. Rodriguez, trumpets; Perez and Freddy Miranda, saxophones; Fanny Ceballos, trombone; Fernando Perez, bass; Edgardo Morales, timbales; Miguel Torres, conga; José Miguel Laboy, bongos. Baby Serrano played bongo on some of the LPs in the '80s, nearly all of which have rested high in the Billboard salsa chart, incl. (all on Combo label) *Happy Days* '81 (with hit 'El Menú', written by Perin Vazquez), *La Universidad de la Salsa* '83 (with 'Patria', by Vazquez), *In Alaska, Breaking The Ice* '84 (with two songs by Vazquez and dedicated to him), *Innovations* and *Nuestra Musica* '85, *Y Su Pueblo* '86. First UK appearance Oct. '86. 3-disc *25th Anniversary 1962-1987/Today, Tomorrow And Always* '87 on Combo.

ELLIMAN, Yvonne (*b* '51, Hawaii) Singer. Mary Magdalene in *Jesus Christ Superstar*, stage and screen '73: single of her big number 'I Don't Know How To Love Him' was no. 28 USA '71; first LP (of that name) on Polydor '72. Her *Superstar* co-star, DEEP PURPLE's Ian Gillan, signed her to Purple's label UK for *Food Of Love* '73; she sessioned for group's Jon Lord on *Gemini Suite* '71; on Eric CLAPTON's *461 Ocean Boulevard* '74 for Robert Stigwood's RSO label: stayed with Clapton's group through *Slowhand* '77 while releasing own stuff on RSO incl. *Rising Sun* '75. New labelmates BEE GEES wrote ballad 'Love Me' for her (no. 14 USA/6 UK '76), up-tempo 'If I Can't Have You' for *Saturday Night Fever* soundtrack '78 (single no. 1 USA/4 UK '78). Her other hits incl. 'Hello Stranger', 'Moment By Moment'; 'I Can't Get You Out Of My Mind' no. 17 UK '77; last was 'Love Pains' (no. 34 '79 USA). 'Your Precious Love', duet with Stephen Bishop, just missed Billboard Hot 100 '80. With her fine voice should never be short of session work.

ELLINGTON, Duke (*b* Edward Kennedy Ellington, 29 Apr. 1899, Washington DC; *d* 24 May '74, NYC) Pianist, bandleader, arranger, one of the century's finest composers. Father was butler at the White House, blueprint maker for US Navy. Acquired nickname as teenager from elegant dress, demeanour. Piano teacher was Miss Clinkscales; later in NYC had harmony lessons in back seats of taxis from Will Voderey and Will Marion COOK, tips from Willie 'The Lion' SMITH, but largely self-taught. Won NAACP poster-design contest, offered art scholarship, left high school to start sign-painting business, but piano playing attracted the girls. Gigged locally; went to NYC Mar. '23 but no work; returned Sep. with band The Washingtonians led by Elmer Snowden (*b* 9 Oct. 1900, Baltimore, Md.; *d* 14 May '73, Philadelphia, Pa.), incl. Arthur Whetsol, trumpet (*b* '05, Fla.; *d* 5 Jan. '40, NYC), Otto 'Toby' Hardwicke, saxophones (*b* 31 May '04, Washington; *d* there 5 Aug. '70), Sonny Greer, drums (*b* William Alexander Greer, 13 Dec. c.1895, N.J.; *d* 23 Mar. '82, NYC). Vocalist Ada Smith recommended them for a job at Barron's Exclusive Club, their first important gig (she went to Paris '24: known as

Bricktop for her red hair, she taught the Prince of Wales to do the black bottom, was one of the most famous club hostesses in the world). They went to the Hollywood Inn for four years, renamed the Kentucky Club after a fire. At the beginning of this period it was just another dance band; at the end it was Ellington's band playing his music; they broadcast from the club and began playing jazz, then just seeping into NYC. Duke became leader when Snowden left '25 (possibly because Greer didn't want to be leader). Whetsol left to study medicine, replaced by Bubber MILEY; Fred Guy joined on banjo (b 23 May 1897, Burkesville, Ga.; d 22 Nov. '71, Chicago); Charlie Irvis (1899-1939), who played a growling trombone, was replaced by Joe 'Tricky Sam' Nanton (b 1 Feb. '04, NYC; d 20 July '46, San Francisco) and they were joined for a brief period by the profoundly influential Sidney BECHET. Duke wrote music for revue *Chocolate Kiddies*, which toured Europe with Sam WOODING, but it is not clear whether Ellington's music was used. The band went to the COTTON CLUB when King OLIVER wasn't offered enough money: stayed from Dec. '27 to Feb. '31 except for tours; made short film *Black And Tan Fantasy* '29 NYC; broadcasts from Cotton Club made them famous. Ellington wrote music for club's floor shows (though much of it was written by Harold ARLEN, Jimmy McHUGH, Dorothy Fields) and discovered talent for tone colour, began to create unique body of composition: band could play 'hot' as any other black outfit, but from the beginning had sensual beauty in Ellington's music others lacked. First recordings Nov. '24; through Cotton Club period discs issued on many labels as Washingtonians, Ten Blackberries, Jungle Band, Harlem Footwarmers, Whoopee Makers, Duke Ellington And His Orchestra, His Cotton Club Orchestra, etc.; some issued on subsidiary labels under made-up names. Legend has it that European critics, especially Constant Lambert in the UK, first compared Ellington's tone colours to those of Delius and Debussy; in fact it was Robert Donaldson Darrell, later a distinguished classical critic, in *Disques* (USA magazine) for June '32: Darrell had reviewed 'East St Louis Toodle-Oo' in the *Phonograph Monthly Review* in June '27, and 'Black And

Tan Fantasy' in July, not realising it was the same band under another name: from Nov. '26 to Apr. '30 'East St Louis Toodle-Oo' was recorded eight times on six labels (not counting alternate takes) with eight different arrangements as the young composer experimented. Other classics of the era incl. 'Birmingham Breakdown', 'Jubilee Stomp', 'Flaming Youth'; 'Bandanna Baby' and 'Diga Diga Doo' (by McHugh and Fields) good examples of show music with amusing lyrics. Titles like 'Jungle Blues', 'Jungle Nights In Harlem', 'Jungle Jamboree' reveal flavour of club where musicians were black, patrons white; band turned necessity into gold: Nanton and trumpeter Bubber Miley used growling 'yow-yow' instrumental device which later had to be learned by Miley's replacements Cootie WILLIAMS, Ray Nance: thus a New Orleans trick learned by Miley from King Oliver was a permanent ingredient of the band's sound (Nanton stayed with Ellington '26 until his death; Miley's infl. '24-9 incl. co-writing 'East St Louis', 'Black And Tan Fantasy', others). 'Rockin' In Rhythm' '30 became band's theme (replacing 'East St Louis'); years later they still played 'The Mooche', 'Creole Love Call' ('27 recording featured Adelaide HALL's wordless vocal), 'Black Beauty' (for Florence Mills, first of many 'portraits'). 'Haunted Nights' '29 had reed section of Barney BIGARD, Harry CARNEY, Johnny HODGES, sounded bigger; on 'Mood Indigo' '30, the classic sound of melody played by blend of Nanton, Bigard and Whetsol (who'd returned) showed formidable skill of arranger. Also began writing for specific players, an infallible judge of what each could do. In '30 band incl. Whetsol, Cootie Williams, Freddy 'Posey' Jenkins (b 10 Oct. '06, NYC; d '78, Texas) on trumpets; Nanton on trombone, Juan Tizol on valve trombone (b Vincente Martinez, 22 Jan. 1900, San Juan, Puerto Rico; d 23 Apr. '84, Inglewood, Cal.); Hodges, Carney and Bigard on reeds; Guy on banjo, later guitar; Wellman BRAUD on bass; Greer on drums: all virtuosi, most of them with band off and on for decades. Irving MILLS managed band, published music, sometimes took co-composer credit; some records even issued as by Mills' Ten Black Berries. But Mills helped band get job at Cotton Club, landed first good record dates, work in film *Check And Double Check* '31 with radio comedy stars Amos'n'Andy, trip to Europe '33; having left Cotton Club '31 (replaced by Cab CALLOWAY) the band was provided by Mills with Pullman cars: alone among black bands on the road in the era, they never worried about where to sleep. First called Duke Ellington And His Famous Orchestra at record date for Brunswick 20 Jan. '31; session incl. 'Creole Rhapsody' on two sides of 10″ 78; in June for Victor same piece on both sides of 12″ 78: Ellington's first attempt to exceed limitation of medium. In Feb. '32 Lawrence BROWN, Ivie ANDERSON first recorded with band; session incl. 'It Don't Mean A Thing If It Ain't Got That Swing'; made Victor long-playing records same month (*see* RECORDED SOUND): two microphones were used to cut different masters of the same take, combined to make stereo tracks more than 50 years later (*Reflections In Ellington* '85, on Everymans label). Hardwicke came back '32, after working for Bricktop in Paris; Darrell tried to interview Ellington that year, hoping to write a book about him, but he was already evasive about himself and his work, also probably suspicious, not yet aware that serious critics would take him very seriously indeed until after Mills arranged the band's first trip to Europe '33. Best records of '30s incl. uptempo showpieces 'Stompy Jones', 'Jive Stomp', 'In A Jam', 'Merry-Go-Round', 'Showboat Shuffle' (with paddle-wheel effect in brass section), 2-part 'Diminuendo In Blue', 'Crescendo In Blue'; also smoochy ballads, mood tunes 'Prelude To A Kiss', 'Sophisticated Lady', 'Caravan' (written by Tizol), 'Clarinet Lament' featuring Bigard, '(There Is) No Greater Love'; controversial 'Reminiscin' In Tempo' (four 78 sides) written during tour after death of Ellington's mother '35; many fine vocals by Anderson. Treatments of others' tunes incl. version of '05 chestnut 'In The Shade Of The Old Apple Tree', with lovely muted solo by Jenkins; hit 'Rose Of The Rio Grande' '38 featuring Brown and Anderson. 'I Let A Song Go Out Of My Heart' '38, 'Pussy Willow', 'I'm Checkin' Out Goombye' '39 (jive vocal by Anderson and Greer) rounded out decade. Braud had left; '36-8 band had two bassists; late '39 Jimmy BLANTON joined on bass, and Ben WEB-

STER: Bigard had doubled on tenor sax, but star tenorist Webster now brought additional weight as well as solo voice to reeds. Mills connection ended '39, and Ellington amanuensis Billy STRAYHORN joined. From '35 Ellington had recorded for ARC labels; last Columbia session Feb. '40, first for Victor in Mar. had lineup with Ellington, piano, arranger, leader; Rex STEWART on cornet; Williams and Wallace Jones (*b* 16 Nov. '06, Baltimore, Md.; *d* 23 Mar. '83), trumpets; Nanton, Brown, Tizol on trombones; Bigard, Hodges, Carney, Webster, reeds; Guy, Blanton and Greer. Victor sessions '40 incl. 'Jack The Bear' (feature for Blanton), 'Ko-Ko' (opens with powerful foundation of Carney's baritone), 'Cotton Tail' (blazing Webster tenor), 'Harlem Air Shaft' (incl. enough ideas for several arrangements). Also 'Never No Lament' (aka 'Don't Get Around Much Any More' with words), 'Concerto For Cootie' (a genuine 3-minute concerto for Williams; with words became 'Do Nothin' Till You Hear From Me'); 'Bojangles' (portrait of dancer Bill Robinson), 'Me And You' with Anderson vocal, 'In A Mellotone', erotic 'Warm Valley', lovely 'Across The Track Blues', four duets by Ellington and Blanton, much else. First Strayhorn works were 'The Flaming Sword', hit 'Flamingo' (vocal by Herb Jeffries, *b* 24 Sep. c.'12, Detroit); transmuted '27 pop song 'Chloe' to Ellingtonia with elegant Nanton 'jungle' intro. This explosion in 20th-century music documented live 7 Nov. at Crystal Ballroom, Fargo, N.D.: fans brought disc-cutting equipment to dance date; result was available on Swedish Jazz Society label, now on three discs from Book of the Month Club: priceless survey incl. Webster essay on 'Stardust', never commercially recorded. (For small-group masterpieces of the period see entries for Hodges, Stewart, Bigard.) Cootie Williams left '40 to join Benny GOODMAN: music business was shocked; bandleader Raymond Scott wrote arrangement 'When Cootie Left The Duke': multi-talented replacement was Ray Nance (*b* 10 Dec. '13, Chicago; *d* 28 Jan. '76, NYC), who also sang, played violin. No letup in '41-2: Strayhorn's 'Take The "A" Train' became new theme; 'John Hardy's Wife', 'Blue Serge', 'Jumpin' Punkins' contributed by Mercer ELLINGTON, who had already written 'Things Ain't What They Used To Be'; Anderson sang 'I Got It Bad And That Ain't Good', from Ellington's *Jump For Joy*: hit show in L.A. but ahead of its time: not even L.A. could take 'I've Got A Passport From Georgia (And I'm Going To The USA)': it was taken out. Blanton was now dying of TB; replaced Dec. '41 by Alvin 'Junior' Raglin (*b* 16 Feb. '17, Omaha, Neb.; *d* 10 Nov. '55, Boston). Strayhorn did 'Rocks In My Bed' for Anderson, 'Chelsea Bridge', 'Johnny Come Lately' and 'Rain Check' for the band; Jeffries sang 'I Don't Know What Kind Of Blues I Got'; Tizol hit 'Perdido' became famous jazz anthem; Duke's works incl. 'C Jam Blues', 'Main Stem', 'Sherman Shuffle', 'I Don't Mind' (with Anderson), the beautiful 'I Didn't Know About You'. WWII had begun: Anderson's 'Hayfoot, Strawfoot', Nance's 'A Slip Of The Lip Can Sink A Ship' were for the forces: Nance sang 'It's so bodacious/to be loquacious' in July '42 as American Federation of Musicians recording ban broke run of masterpieces. Ellington played first Carnegie Hall Concert 23 Jan. '43: première of 50-minute composition *Black, Brown And Beige: Tone Parallel To The American Negro* (partly issued by Victor later, complete on Prestige after decades; '58 recording made with Mahalia JACKSON; complete version on Argo re-created by UK arranger Alan Cohen early '70s). Carnegie Hall became an annual event; new works incl. *Blutopia* '44; *New World A'Comin'* (based on Roi Ottley novel), *The Perfume Suite* (recorded by Victor; delightful duet for piano and bass 'Dancers In Love' also subject of semi-animated short film by George Pal), both '45. 'Deep South Suite' '46 had four parts; first was 'Magnolias Just Dripping With Molasses', last was train song 'Happy-Go-Lucky Local', with big tune later used without credit by Jimmy FORREST for early rock'n'roll classic 'Night Train'. Duke wrote show *Beggar's Holiday* (lyrics by John Latouche, *b* 13 Nov. '17, Richmond, Va.; *d* 7 Aug. '56, Calias, Vt.; also wrote lyrics for Vernon DUKE show *Cabin In The Sky* '40, George Moore opera *Ballad Of Baby Doe* '56, etc.): interracial cast chosen for acting ability; result had Alfred DRAKE falling in love with black police chief's daughter in '47. Same year *Liberian Suite* commissioned by Liberian government; incl. Al

HIBBLER vocal 'I Like The Sunrise', five dances. *The Tattooed Bride* '48 followed by *Harlem* '50, commissioned by NBC Symphony Orchestra. During recording ban 'Don't Get Around Much Any More' and 'Do Nothin' Till You Hear From Me' were top 10 hits; in '45 'I'm Beginning To See The Light' made no. 6, lyrics by Don George (*b* 27 Aug. '09, NYC); recording had resumed Dec. '44; RCA output through '46 incl. Hibbler vocals, series of remakes ('Black Beauty', 'Caravan', etc.); vocals by Nance incl. '(Otto Make That) Riff Staccato', 'Just Squeeze Me', revived '22 hit song 'My Honey's Loving Arms'; 'Long, Strong And Consecutive' and remake of 'I Let A Song Go Out Of My Heart' were sung by Joya Sherrill (*b* 20 Aug. '27, Bayonne, N.J.). One of the band's most poorly documented periods was the immediate post-war, when there were six trumpets and Oscar PETTIFORD on bass; but there are RCA tracks '46; more material has come to light: archivist Jerry Valburn is issuing 49 LPs on D.E.T.S. (Duke Ellington Treasury Series), broadcasts made '45-6 for the U.S. Treasury to sell bonds; another transcription series '46-7 issued e.g. on five London LPs UK '78 incl. soprano Kay Davis, Strayhorn works for Hodges' sensuous alto 'Violet Blue' and 'A Flower Is A Lovesome Thing' (later 'Passion'), 'Sono' with Carney, version of 'Happy-Go-Lucky Local' over six minutes long, much else. By now Webster, Hardwicke, Stewart, Ivie Anderson had left; Nanton died '46; Ellington signed new contract with Columbia '47-52. New decade's lineup varied with Nance, Harold BAKER, Cat ANDERSON, Clark TERRY, Willie Cook (*b* 11 Nov. '23, West Chicago, Ind.), others, trumpets; trombones Tizol, Brown, Wilbur DE PARIS, Claude Jones (*b* 11 Feb '01, Boley, Okla.; *d* 17 Jan. '62 aboard liner SS *United States*: had played with Don REDMAN, Fletcher HENDERSON, Chick WEBB); Quentin 'Butter' Jackson (*b* 13 Jan. '09, Springfield, Ohio; *d* 2 Oct. '76, NYC); Tyree Glenn (*b* 23 Nov. '12, Corsicana, Texas; *d* 18 May '74, Englewood, N.J.). Reeds incl. Hodges, Carney, Al Sears (*b* 22 Feb. '10, McComb, Ill.; joined band '44-9, star roles in Carnegie Hall concerts); Jimmy HAMILTON, Russell Procope (*b* 11 Aug. '08, NYC; *d* 21 Jan. '81, NYC; had played with Jelly Roll MORTON '28, with Webb,

Henderson, John KIRBY; with Ellington from '46 until Duke's death). Paul GONSALVES joined '50, but Hodges, Brown, Greer all left at once '51: Ellington looked around, pulled the Great James Robbery: took drummer Louie BELLSON, alto sax Willie Smith (*b* 25 Nov. '10, Charleston, S.C.; *d* 7 Mar. '67, L.A.; ex-Jimmie LUNCEFORD), old colleague Juan Tizol from Harry JAMES band. Rhythm section had Guy; Pettiford, sometimes Raglin, then Wendell Marshall on bass (*b* 24 Oct. '20, St Louie, Mo.). The quality of Ellington's work had slowly declined since '42; more personnel changes than at any other time in the band's history had been dispiriting; times were tough for bands anyway and from late '40s the band lost money, kept going by Ellington's royalties. The most die-hard Duke fans will admit that the longer works were less good, partly because he lacked formal training and their structure was always patchy: it is problematical whether jazz-based music can remain true to itself in lengthy works. More than 70 pop sides for CBS early '50s incl. junk like 'Cowboy Rhumba', but also 'Brown Penny', 'Maybe I Should Change My Ways' from *Beggar's Holiday*; 'You're Just An Old Antidisestablishmentarianismist' with George lyrics, hep vocal by Nance; 'Stomp, Look And Listen', 'Boogie Bop Blues', 'Lady Of The Lavender Mist', 'Fancy Dan', 'Air Conditioned Jungle', 'V.I.P.'s Boogie', famous remake of 'Do Nothin' Till You Hear From Me' by Hibbler; more; also contributions by Strayhorn, 'The Hawk Talks' by Bellson. *Masterpieces By Ellington* '50 incl. longer arr. of classics and *The Tattooed Bride*; *Ellington Uptown* '51 incl. *A Tone Parallel To Harlem*, became best-seller at hi-fi show with Bellson's 'Skin Deep', but six-minute version of 'The Mooche' was the highlight, with Bellson's rolling, inexorable beat, and clarinets: Procope on melody in low register, Hamilton obbligato in echo chamber. Other projects late '40s early '50s incl. sides on Mills' Variety label with small groups, a shortlived Sunrise label and Mercer Records, run by Mercer Ellington and Leonard Feather, which got caught in the squeeze between 78s and LPs; most of this has been reissued on various Prestige LPs, incl. Pettiford's 'Perdido' on the cello and Ellington-Strayhorn piano duets. Duke's

Capitol contract '53-5 was mostly a musical disappointment, yet incl. many interesting arrangements (compiled in a box by French EMI). Fans saw each appearance or album as an event, but after 70 pop hits '27-53 (according to *Pop Memories; see* CHARTS) Ellington did not astonish the public as in '40-2: most paid no attention to more ambitious work. Jazz had apparently moved on, but Ellington had done most of it already: as Miles DAVIS said, ' . . . all the musicians should get together one certain day and get down on their knees and thank Duke . . . ' Hodges returned by Feb. '56; band made two LPs for Bethlehem: *Historically Speaking – The Duke* opened with laconically witty version of 'East St Louie', in retrospect the great man hiding in the bushes, waiting for his moment, which came soon. The Newport Jazz Festival was inaugurated '54 by pianist/club-owner George Wein with wealthy Lorrilard family; Ellington played there July '56 with Cook, Nance, Terry, Anderson, trumpets; Jackson, John Sanders, Britt Woodman (played with Charles MINGUS), trombones; Carney, Hodges, Procope, Hamilton, Gonsalves, reeds; Jimmy Woode on bass (*b* 23 Sep. '29, Philadelphia; later emigrated to Sweden), Sam Woodyard, drums (*b* 7 Jan. '25, Elizabeth, N.J.). The band came on last, after people had started leaving; Duke grumbled, 'What are we, the animal act, the acrobats?' Ellington-Strayhorn had written fine three-part *Newport Jazz Festival Suite*; Ellington had revived 'Diminuendo And Crescendo In Blue': Woodyard set up rocking beat egged on by ringside fan Jo JONES, Gonsalves assigned to play bridge between two sections, did 27 choruses: audience was standing, cheering, dancing in the aisles; concert made headlines, CBS LP was no. 14 in charts; Duke made cover of *Time*, his status as elder statesman of American music never again in doubt. Band had made films incl. *Murder At The Vanities* and *Belle Of The '90s* '34, filmed play *Cabin In The Sky* '43; now Ellington scored and did cameos in *Anatomy Of A Murder* '59, *Paris Blues* '61; scored *Assault On A Queen* '66; wrote music for Canadian prod. of *Timon Of Athens*, show *My People* on centenary of Emancipation Proclamation '63, incl. sections called 'King Fit The Battle Of Alabam', 'What Color Is Virtue?'. Among best Ellington

383

LPs of later years: *Such Sweet Thunder* '57, good music having little to do with Shakespeare; lovely mood set *Ellington Indigos* '59, both for CBS; *The Queen's Suite* '59 for Elizabeth II (one copy made for her; no commercial issue until after Ellington's death); trio set *Money Jungle* (Ellington, Mingus, Max ROACH) plus small-groups *Duke Ellington Meets Coleman Hawkins, And John Coltrane*, all '62; world tours resulted in *The Far East Suite* '66, *Latin American Suite* '69; a moving tribute to Strayhorn's death . . . *And His Mother Called Him Bill* '67 incl. his last tune 'Blood Count'. Band accompanied Ella FITZGERALD's 2-disc sets of Ellington songs, then later on 2-disc *On The Côte d'Azur*; Reprise LPs incl. *Concert In The Virgin Islands* '65 (now on Discovery), *Francis A. & Edward K.* (with SINATRA); eight more Reprise LPs '62-4 were boxed in France '74 as 5-disc *Souvenirs*, incl. pop songs, songs from *Mary Poppins, Will Big Bands Ever Come Back?* (reworked Swing Era hits), *Greatest Hits* (reworked Duke's), *The Symphonic Ellington* recorded in Paris, Milan, Stockholm; *Afro-Bossa* was the best of the lot. *This One's For Blanton!* '72 on Pablo is duet with Ray BROWN, remakes of '40 duets; *Seventieth Birthday Concert* on Solid State opened with riotous version of 'Rockin' In Rhythm', once again band's theme. Late masterpiece *New Orleans Suite* '70 had five parts interleaved with portraits of Louie ARMSTRONG (with Cootie Williams), Wellman Braud (by Joe Benjamin on bass, *b* 4 Nov. '19, Atlantic City, N.J.; *d* 26 Jan. '74, Livingstone, N.J.), Sidney BECHET (by Gonsalves on tenor: Ellington had tried to persuade Hodges to polish his soprano, but he died days before session), Mahalia Jackson: suite's opening 'Blues For New Orleans' featured Wild Bill DAVIS on organ, but organ effect in the Jackson portrait created by three clarinets, tenor sax and flute, using tone-painter's palette of which André PREVIN said: 'Stan Kenton can stand in front of a thousand fiddles and a thousand brass and make a dramatic gesture, and every studio arranger can nod his head and say, "Oh yes, that's done like this." But Duke merely lifts his finger, three horns make a sound, and I don't know what it is.' With those named above plus Mercer Ellington, Cat Anderson, Carney and

Procope, LP incl. new boys Harold 'Money' Johnson (*b* 21 July '31, New Orleans), trumpet; Julian Priester (*b* 29 June '35; ex-SUN RA), Booty Wood (*b* c.'19; *d* 10 June '87, Dayton, Ohio) on trombones; Norris Turney (*b* 8 Sep. '21, Wilmington, Ohio), Harold Ashby (*b* 27 Apr. '25, Kansas City, Mo.), reeds; Rufus 'Speedy' Jones, drums (*b* '36, Charleston, S.C.; played with BASIE '64-6), others. In '65 Advisory Board of Pulitzer Prize Committee had rejected unanimous recommendation of music jury that Ellington should be awarded a special citation: jury members resigned amid murmurs of racial prejudice; more likely committee simply did not take his accomplishment very seriously. Duke said, 'Fate is being kind to me. Fate doesn't want me to be too famous too young.' It hurt, but other honours were heaped on him, incl. medals from LBJ, Nixon playing Happy Birthday on the piano, honorary degrees, etc. Sacred Concerts (not highly regarded by critics) began in San Francisco '65 (incl. 'Come Sunday' from *Black, Brown And Beige, New World's A'Comin'*, new 'In The Beginning God', singers Esther Merrill, dancer David Briggs). Second Sacred Concert NYC '68 (all new music, with singers Alice BABS, Tony Watkins, Devonne Gardner, Roscoe Gill), third at Westminster Abbey, London, Oct. '73, Duke already weak from final illness. Sacred Concert performed on 75th birthday in NYC, directed by Gill, pianist Brooks Kerr (*b* 26 Dec. '51, New Haven, Conn.); Ellington too weak to attend. He was one of the first to tire of the word 'jazz', saying that 'There are only two kinds of music: good and bad.' Among his innovations were amplifying Braud's bass in '28, using echo chamber in '38; he and Tizol were first to explore the idea of Latin jazz; but he never stopped innovating in tonal beauty. LPs named above more or less continuously available, often from France; many more still being issued, e.g. '62 recording of *Harlem* on Pablo '85, and more from Valburn's various labels: *Studio Sessions 1933-67* on Up-To-Date incl. scraps from Capitol better than some issued tracks and *Concerts In Canada* '56 is on Ellington '87; also two 2-disc sets of *All Star Road Band* on Bob THIELE's Doctor Jazz label from '57, '64; new LMR label in USA issued five generous CDs full of excellent recordings from the private stock, selected by Mercer and with notes by Stanley Dance, incl. such goodies as the *Degas Suite*, music for a film that didn't happen. Four Carnegie Hall Concerts '43-7 are on Prestige 2-disc sets. Since Depression-era record label mergers, early Ellington is all property of MCA, RCA, CBS: MCA material in and out of print in various editions; in France RCA and CBS compiled complete series incl. alternate takes. For most fans RCA series of 2-disc compilations (French or USA) plus two 3-disc sets *The Ellington Era 1927-1940* issued by Columbia USA '63 are adequate anthologies, together with French CBS 6-disc set *The Complete Duke Ellington 1947-1952* (without alternate takes, but with *Liberian Suite*). Digitally remastered *Duke Ellington: The Blanton-Webster Band (1939-42)* (3 CDs, 3 cassettes or 4 LPs) should have been the best reissue of the decade, but the transfers were badly done; the work was being done again '87 and will probably be excellent. Early biography was *Duke Ellington* by Barry Ulanov '46; books by Peter Gammond '58, G. E. Lambert '59 were useful; best are *The World Of Duke Ellington* by Stanley Dance '70; *Duke* by Derek Jewell '77, *Duke Ellington In Person* by Mercer Ellington with Dance '78; then *Duke Ellington* by James Lincoln Collier '87. Always urbane and witty, Ellington was also a private man, vain and superstitious: *Music Is My Mistress* '73 is not an autobiography, does not even mention Mercer's mother; he never wrote his music down, let alone his life, and did not even leave a will; but he left us the records. Collier examines the enigma of the band and its members as a composing machine: nobody can be sure who wrote what, except that Duke was always in charge; Collier compares him to a master chef, who 'plans the menus, trains the assistants, supervises them, tastes everything, adjusts the spices . . . and in the end we credit him with the result'.

ELLINGTON, Mercer (*b* 11 Mar. '19, Washington DC) Trumpet, composer, arranger, bandleader; son of Duke ELLINGTON. Studied formally at Columbia U., Juilliard, NYU; formed own band '39 with Dizzy GILLESPIE, Clark TERRY, arr. by Billy STRAYHORN; wrote 'Blue Serge', 'John Hardy's Wife', 'Things Ain't What They Used

To Be', 'Moon Mist' etc. recorded by Duke; after WWII military service led own band until '49; worked for Duke '50; own Mercer record label '50-2. With Cootie WILLIAMS '54, worked as assistant to Duke '55-9; resumed playing and had own band at Birdland '59. Own LPs *Stepping Into Society*, *Colors In Rhythm* on Coral (compilation *Black & Tan Fantasy* on MCA). DJ on WLIB NYC three years; rejoined Duke '65 managing band, playing trumpet. Took over leadership on Duke's death, hiring younger players incl. son Edward (daughter Mercedes had been first black girl to dance on network TV in mixed chorus line Oct. '63). Backed Diahann Carroll on *A Tribute To Ethel Waters* '78; played at Newport Jazz Festival '80; LPs *Continuum* on Fantasy, *Hot & Bothered* '86 on Dr Jazz, *Digital Duke* '87 on GRP (band incl. Branford MARSALIS, Louie BELLSON, Clark Terry). Led band for musical *Sophisticated Ladies* '80-1 based on Duke's music. *Duke Ellington In Person: An Intimate Memoir* with Stanley Dance '78.

ELLIOTT, Jack (*b* Elliott Charles Adnopoz, 1 Aug. '31, Brooklyn, NY) Singer, songwriter, guitarist, troubador: aka Ramblin' Jack, the singing cowboy from Brooklyn. Son of a doctor, like many another American child of his generation he was taken with Gene AUTRY, until discovering that singing cowboys were a creation of Hollywood. He changed his name to Buck Elliott and ran away from home ('a 45,000-acre ranch in the middle of Flatbush') to join the rodeo. He soon met Woody GUTHRIE, toured with him until Woody said 'Jack sounds more like me than I do'. Spent mid-'50s in Europe, acquiring a large following which had never been able to hear Guthrie; played with Derroll Adams (*b* Oregon '25; in Europe since late '50s) at London's Blue Angel, World's Fair in Brussels; back in USA on West Coast for a year, returned to UK '59, toured with the WEAVERS, came back to USA again just as folk boom was underway; played concerts and folk festivals. Like Arlo GUTHRIE he is major link between a bygone age and today's folk scene. He has recorded with Johnny CASH and Tom RUSH; his own records for Topic in England beginning c.'55 have been compiled on *Muleskinner*, *Roll On Buddy* (with

Adams), *Talkin' Woody Guthrie*; later LPs on many labels incl. 2-disc compilation *Essential* on Vanguard; 2-disc *Hard Travelin'* on Fantasy; *Sings Woody Guthrie, Ramblin'* and *Country Style* on Prestige; *Talkin' Woody Guthrie* on Delmark; others on Monitor, Archive of Folk; out of print items on Columbia and Reprise.

ELLIS, Don (*b* Donald Johnson Ellis, 25 July '34, L.A.; *d* 17 Dec. '78, North Hollywood) Trumpet, leader. Worked in dance bands, US Army bands '50s, Maynard FERGUSON '59; own trio and quartet early '60s, with George RUSSELL Sextet '61 (incl. Riverside LPs). Album *New Ideas* on Prestige was infl. by ideas of composer John Cage. Trumpet soloist with NY Philharmonic '63-4 in works by Larry Austin, Gunther Schuller; became prolific teacher, composer; after fine small group sets on Candid, Prestige, Pacific Jazz, led big band on albums for Pacific Jazz, then Columbia, restlessly innovating with time signatures, going farther than anyone else in this respect. Compositions such as 'New Nine' and '3-3-2-2-2-1-2-2-2' were derived from Indian music; he appeared at Monterey Jazz Festival '66 with custom-made trumpet that would play quartertones. In 'Tears Of Joy' he used an amplified string quartet and woodwind quintet, in 'Milo's Theme' electronically processed flutes, in 'Star Children' Indian drones and distant chorus. Most successful LPs on Columbia, quite successful during '60s psychedelic era: *Electric Bath, Shock Treatment, Don Ellis At Fillmore*; *Soaring* reissued on Pausa. Turned to film music and won Grammy for theme from *The French Connection* '73. Had a serious heart attack '75; was recovering and took up 'superbone' (slide/valve trombone), but had final attack.

ELLIS, Herb (*b* Mitchell Herbert Ellis, 4 Aug. '21, near Farmersville, Texas) Guitar. Began on banjo as small child, self-taught. With Russ MORGAN, CASA LOMA band '44, then J. DORSEY: left Dorsey with pianist Lou Carter, bassist John Frigo (3/4 of rhythm section leaving at once) to form trio Soft Winds '47-52, with Nat COLE format but all three singing, original arrangements in hip harmony, like mid-'50s groups FOUR FRESHMEN or HI-LOS but ahead of their

time: songs incl. 'I Told You I Love You, Now Get Out' (covered by Woody HERMAN), 'Detour Ahead', 'Ninety-Nine Guys', and Edgar Allan Poe's 'Annabel Lee'. (Carter later became Lou the Taxi Driver, made LPs and appeared on Perry COMO TV show with sentimental/novelty songs such as 'If I Had A Noseful Of Nickels I'd Sneeze 'Em Atchoo'; formed jingle company.) Ellis joined Ray BROWN in Oscar PETERSON trio '53-8, some say the greatest piano trio of all time; also accompanied Ella FITZGERALD, Julie LONDON; Steve ALLEN TV show band early '60s, other TV work with Della REESE, Merv Griffin, others; with Terry GIBBS; in '70s toured in guitar duo with Joe PASS, then Barney KESSEL. Tasteful, swinging, modern guitarist, many devoted fans; many LPs with Pass, Peterson, Brown, Kessel, Charlie BYRD, etc.; many own LPs incl. *Ellis In Wonderland* '56, *Nothing But The Blues* '57, *Meets Jimmy Giuffre* '59, *Thank You Charlie Christian* '60, *Softly, But With That Feeling* '61, all on Verve with all-star sidemen; *The Midnight Roll, Three Guitars In Bossa Nova Time, Herb Ellis And Stuff Smith, And Charlie Byrd* all '62-3 on CBS labels; *Man With A Guitar* '65 on Dot; *Hello Herbie* '69 on MPS; *Jazz/Concord, Seven Come Eleven, Soft Shoe* all on Concord Jazz '73-4; *Two For The Road* '74 with Pass on Pablo; *After You've Gone* '74, *Hot Tracks* '75. *Rhythm Willie* '75 (quintet with Freddie GREEN), *A Pair To Draw To* '76 (duet with Ross Tomkins on piano), *Wildflower* '77, *Soft And Mellow* '78, *Herb Ellis At Montreux* '79, *Herb Mix* '81, all on Concord. Also *Sweet And Lovely* (trio with Shelly MANNE), quartet set *When You're Smiling*, both '83 on Japanese label Atlas.

ELLIS, Shirley (*b* '41, Bronx, NYC) USA pop/soul singer. Began as a writer ('One, Two, I Love You' for the Heartbreakers on Vik in '50s). Sang with group the Metronomes, married Lincoln Chase who'd written 'Jim Dandy' (LaVern BAKER), 'Such A Night' (the DRIFTERS); he wrote 'The Nitty Gritty' for her, placed it with Congress label (subsidiary of Kapp) for no. 8 pop hit USA '63. Sequel '(That's) What The Nitty Gritty Is' very minor hit; then 'The Name Game' no. 3 '64, 'The Clapping Song' no. 8 '65, all nursery-rhyme-style chants with honking sax, percussion. 'The Puzzle Song' '65, 'Soul Time' '67 (on Columbia) were minor hits. 'Nitty Gritty' revived by Gladys KNIGHT and the Pips (no. 19 USA '69); 'The Clapping Song' many times: original was no. 6 in UK; Ellis EP charted UK '78 with three original hits, equally silly 'Ever See A Diver Kiss His Wife While The Bubbles Bounce Above The Water'; 'Clapping Song' no. 11 UK '82 by the Belle Stars.

ELLISON, Lorraine (*b* c.'43, Philadelphia, Pa.) Soul singer. Formed gospel group with sisters while in high school; the Ellison Singers performed at the Festival of Two Worlds in Italy '64. Lorraine's manager Sam Bell signed her to Mercury; 'I Dig You Baby' made R&B chart '65. The next year she was on Warner Bros, who released 'Stay With Me' (co-written, prod. by Jerry Ragavoy), which reached no. 11 R&B, Hot 100 pop; it is still regarded as a classic of the genre for its sheer intensity. 'Heart Be Still' on WB subsidiary Loma also made both charts in '69, but she never did it again, despite high regard of soul connoisseurs and good choice of material: 'You Really Got A Hold On Me', 'He Ain't Heavy, He's My Brother', 'Many Rivers To Cross', etc. All her work is out of print in USA; 'Stay With Me' was reissued by WB in UK '81.

ELY, Joe (*b* 9 Feb. '47, Amarillo, Texas) Country rock singer. Moved to Lubbock at 11. Worked clubs in Dallas-Fort Worth area, toured Europe with theatrical group, worked with a circus in southwest USA. Joined acoustic country band Flatlanders, with singer/songwriters Jimmy Dale Gilmore, Butch HANCOCK; described group as 'a kind of missing link' in West Texas music: LP made in Nashville *One Road More* '71, not released until '80 (on Charly UK). Ely formed own band, built reputation in Texas for mixture of Tex-Mex, honky tonk, blues, a rock'n'roll touch: Texas music. (Band incl. steel guitarist Lloyd Maines, later on Mercury in Maines Brothers Band.) Signed to MCA '77, made acclaimed LP *Joe Ely* incl. minor hit 'All My Love'. Highly regarded in Texas and Europe, but failed to make breakthrough in USA because music fits none of the categories which radio programmers rely on. Other LPs incl. *Honky Tonk Masquerade*

'78 (Ely title song; also incl. Gilmore's 'Tonight I Think I'm Gonna Go Downtown'); *Down On The Drag* '79 (prod. by Bob Johnson); discovered by the CLASH, who featured him as guest on UK tour; leaned to rock side with *Musta Notta Gotta Lotta* (incl. Gilmore's 'Dallas') '81, *Live Shots* (made in London) '81. Toured in Linda RONSTADT's backup; locked himself away in studio for three years, prod. *High Res* '84: synth technology harnessed to C&W roots. He made what would have been his seventh MCA LP, but chose to leave the label; his touring band mid-'86 incl. saxophonist Bobby Keyes and Austin guitarist David Grissom; Chicago critic Don McLeese wrote that whoever signed him next would get him at his peak: 'Just when you think you've got him pegged as a modern Buddy Holly, he dives deep into the mystic and comes up sounding like a Texas Van MORRISON.' *Lord Of The Highway* '87 came out on Hightone.

EMERSON, LAKE AND PALMER UK progressive/techno rock band formed '70 by Keith Emerson (*b* 1 Nov. '44, Todmorton), keyboardist who had made name with NICE, plans for band with Jimi HENDRIX, Mitch Mitchell having fallen through: recruited King Crimson bass Greg Lake (*b* 10 Nov. '48, Bournemouth), also accomplished vocalist; guitarless trio (in fashion of Nice) completed with ex-Atomic Rooster drummer Carl Palmer (*b* 20 Mar. '41, Birmingham). First gig Isle of Wight festival '70; eponymous debut LP accomplished if somewhat sterile, made no. 4 UK/18 USA helped by (USA only) single 'Lucky Man' (no. 48 '71). *Tarkus* '71 with cover art depicting ferocious half-tank, half-armadillo was more aggressive effort: no. 1 LP UK, 9 USA made them superstars. Live *Pictures At An Exhibition* (rocked-up Mussorgsky) no. 3 UK, 10 USA); live act featured portable stage with proscenium, Emerson's visuals (stabbing Hammond organ with knives, etc.). Fame grew with *Trilogy* '72, *Brain Salad Surgery* '73 (first on own Manticore label, supported by quad sound, tour with 36 tons of equipment). Singles incl. 'From The Beginning' (no. 39 USA '72) tended to be Lake's introspective compositions, while Emerson's flamboyant keyboard was band's trademark sound. Live triple LP *Welcome*

Back, My Friends, To The Show That Never Ends: Ladies And Gentlemen, Emerson Lake And Palmer '74 followed by break in tours, UK solo hits: Lake's 'I Believe In Father Christmas', Emerson's instrumental 'Honky Tonk Train Blues'. Band's comeback '77 was disappointment: albums featuring solo material *Works* (2-disc Vol. 1) made no. 9 UK/12 USA (worst seller so far UK), Vol. 2 (one record) did much less well; 70-piece orchestra recruited for tour was laid off except for biggest gigs because of poor ticket sales; Emerson's attempt to record own piano concerto with London Phil. during sabbatical failed. Meanwhile emergence of punk made them look like dinosaurs (as was intended). Soft-rock *Love Beach* '78 made no. 48 UK/55 USA; final *In Concert* set '79, then split. Emerson wrote film scores *The Inferno* '80, *Nighthawks* '81, etc.; Lake made solo *Greg Lake* '81, then replaced John Wetton in ASIA, supergroup Palmer joined when own group PM foundered; Emerson, Lake re-formed with Cozy Powell for LP *Emerson Lake & Powell* '86; Emerson, Palmer and Richard Berry made *To The Power Of Three* '88: more of the same.

EMI Electrical and Musical Industries Ltd, formed March '31 from merger of COLUMBIA and the Gramophone Company (*see* HMV); the biggest record company in the world for nearly fifty years. Columbia sold the Columbia and General Phonograph Companies of New York (incl. Okeh) because of poor trading conditions there and also to avoid anti-trust problems (HMV was linked to Victor there); the new company also incl. Pathé Frère in France, Carl Lindstrom and Electrola in Germany, Columbia Nipponophone in Japan, Pathé Orient and the China Record Co. in China, GramCo in India and the Odeon and Parlophone labels of the Transoceanic Trading Company (a Dutch company formed to look after interests of German labels overseas during WWI); also subsidiaries in Australia, Italy, Spain, Romania and South America: 50 factories in 19 countries. The only major labels not in the EMI empire were fledgling Decca in UK, Brunswick USA, former Gramophone subsidiary Deutsche Grammophon Gesellschaft (DGG) in Germany. With Sir Louie Ster-

ling as chairman, EMI opened the famous Abbey Road studios in north London Nov. '31; in Dec. Columbia's Alan Blumlein obtained the first patents for binaural (stereo) records (made as test pressings '33; *see* RECORDED SOUND). In the prewar period EMI had almost every major artist in the world on one or another of its labels: HMV house bandleader Ray NOBLE was not only a star in UK but (unusually for the time) also sold well in USA; EMI continued links with former USA partners Victor and CBS, so most of the major bandleaders of the BIG BAND ERA were on EMI in most of the world outside USA: Count BASIE, Duke ELLINGTON, Artie SHAW, Tommy DORSEY, Glenn MILLER, etc. During WWII EMI did war work; while Electrola was out of EMI's control the first German million-seller was Lale Anderson's 'Lille Marlene'. WWI had devastated HMV, which lost subsidiaries in Germany, Austria-Hungary and Russia; in '45 the company soon reasserted control over German and Italian companies, but Japan was lost (Nippon Columbia/Denon is still independent). EMI even won back control of HMV's dog trademark in Germany, lost when DGG was confiscated as enemy-owned property '17. In '45 Australian Sir Ernest Fisk became managing director, more interested in the electronics side than the music and failed at both. During the battle of the speeds in the late '40s, Fisk could see 'no future for the long playing record'; Decca issued LPs and some of EMI's top artists went over to Decca for that reason. Fisk also presided over the break-up of the worldwide cartel: historic rivalry between HMV and Columbia had continued since the merger; after WWII the company signed all the greatest classical artists and had the best of everything, incl. 45 conductors under contract and Walter Legge, one of the world's great classical producers, but with no coordination the company would sometimes record the same piece of music in different parts of Europe at the same time. RCA and CBS (USA Columbia) felt that they were not getting the best out of the deal, didn't understand the inefficient way EMI was competing with itself, and each felt that they could do better with a licensee that was not also handling its main rival: CBS switched to Philips '52, RCA to Decca '53. (In both cases there was a sell-off period of some years, allowing Elvis PRESLEY's early hits to go out on HMV '56.) Some EMI classical artists had gone to the USA to live, transferring to RCA or CBS; pop music was dominated by the USA labels: EMI lost it all, incl. e.g. Guy MITCHELL, bigger in the UK than at home. Fisk was forced out '51 but problems continued until Joseph Lockwood took over '54: his background was in flour milling engineering; he had run overseas subsidiaries of UK companies in Europe, South America, Australia; soon turned EMI into a profit-oriented modern international, so that pop mattered more than classical prestige; he expanded into TV and films and was knighted '60. Angel had been launched as a USA classical import label '53; in '55 EMI bought CAPITOL for £3 million: Lockwood was criticised for paying so much, but by '59 Capitol was worth £85 million. This brought Frank SINATRA back to EMI, and acquired Dean MARTIN, Nat King COLE, Tennessee Ernie FORD, etc. None of the big USA labels took to rock'n-'roll; Capitol signed Gene VINCENT and Wanda JACKSON, but continued to rely on the Sinatra/Martin roster, and later the KINGSTON TRIO. UK labels came up with pale imitations of USA rock'n'roll stars, each hailed as the UK answer to Presley until Cliff RICHARD '58, who racked up 100 chart entries in 30 years; his backing group the SHADOWS were also influential. Suddenly USA domination had ended: *Billboard* published an annual list of the world's best selling artists based on charts in 34 countries; in '63 the top four were Richard, Presley, the Shadows and Frank Ifield: all except Presley shared the same label (EMI/Columbia), as well as UK manager (Peter Gormley), agent (Frank Jarratt) and producer (Norrie PARAMOR). Number seven on the list was an up-and-coming Liverpool group, the BEATLES, who in '64 knocked Richard off the top. In the mid-'60s EMI had the Beatles, Cilla BLACK, the HOLLIES, Billy J. KRAMER (all on Parlophone); Richard, the Shadows, Ifield, GERRY & THE PACEMAKERS, the Dave CLARK Five, PETER & GORDON, the ANIMALS, HERMAN'S HERMITS, Georgie FAME, the YARDBIRDS, the SEEKERS (all on Columbia); MANFRED MANN (on HMV), Joe COCKER and the MOVE (on Regal-

Zonophone), and the BEACH BOYS on Capitol. In '63-4 EMI artists topped the UK charts for a total of 76 weeks, all but one of the artists being British, but this success was not repeated in the USA, where Capitol was allowed to pass on nearly all these artists (even the Beatles, whose first USA records came out on Vee Jay, later bought by EMI). In '63-5 15 major EMI acts charted in USA; only three were signed to Capitol for all of this period, three others for part of it. Of these acts (incl. Herman's Hermits, much bigger in the USA than in UK) seven had no. 1 hits, spending three months at the top. By '70 Capitol was losing money; in '71 the company's annual report stated that 'a total restructuring of the management was necessary'. EMI put in team headed by V. Bhaskar Menon, former head of EMI's Gramophone Company of India (another large country in which to distribute records), which succeeded in turning the company around. EMI's profits from the '60s were spent on diversification; but the '70s were a disaster: RCA, CBS and WEA established their own subsidiaries in many countries, no longer licensing product to others; they competed for sales and for local talent, while Britain's Labour government hampered EMI by restricting investment overseas; poor management and adverse trading in the music and medical electronics divisions brought the company to the edge of destruction. An attempt to sell half the music division to Paramount Pictures fell through; a takeover from Thorn Electrical Industries succeeded '79. Ironically, EMI's fortunes were changing for the better: just before its demise as an independent it took over United Artists Records, incl. LIBERTY, IMPERIAL and BLUE NOTE; the late '70s-80s roster incl. DURAN DURAN, Paul MCCARTNEY, QUEEN, PINK FLOYD, the KNACK, Kenny ROGERS, Sheena EASTON, Kate BUSH, Kim CARNES, the ROLLING STONES, David BOWIE, Bob SEGER, the J. GEILS Band, HEART and the Pet Shop Boys. The music division remains an autonomous part of Thorn/EMI; although Capitol was once again losing money in the '80s, much ground has been recaptured: Blue Note was revived '84 and Manhattan and EMI America labels formed in NYC; EMI bought Hispavox (Spain) and VDP (Portugal), giving EMI's Odeon in the potentially huge

Latin American market a repertoire boost; in Venezuela EMI established its first new subsidiary in South America since '27. When General Electric bought RCA, Thorn EMI managing director Colin Southgate tried to buy its record division to add to Capitol, but the German Bertelsmann company, who already owned some of it, acquired the rest. EMI are likely to make a substantial purchase in the USA if the opportunity arises; if their bid for the CBS record division had been successful the venerable Columbia name would once again have been under one ownership, but Sony won it '87.

EMMONS, Buddy (*b* 27 Jan. '37, Mishawaka, Ind.) Steel guitarist; Nashville session musician, designer of steel guitars and co-founder with Shot Jackson of Sho-Bud Guitar Company. Joined Little Jimmy DICKENS band '55; member of Ernest TUBB's Troubadors '57-62, Ray PRICE's Cherokee Cowboys '62-8. To L.A. '69 to play bass for Roger MILLER, sessioned with Judy COLLINS, Henry MANCINI, Linda RONSTADT, etc.; returned to Nashville '73, where he sessions, makes own albums, makes and promotes own guitars. Winner of *Guitar Player* magazine poll '78, ACM Steel Player five times. LPs incl. *Sings Bob Wills* '76 on Flying Fish; also *Buddies* '77 with Buddy Spicher and *Minors Aloud* '79 with Lenny BREAU, both on Sonet in UK.

ENGLAND DAN and JOHN FORD COLEY Songwriters; vocal, instrumental duo. Dan Seals (*b* 8 Feb. '50) and J. E. Colley (*b* 13 Oct. '51) both born in Texas, grew up in Dallas; Dan brother of Jim Seals of SEALS & CROFTS. Played in rock bands from '64 in high school, formed duo Southwest F.O.B. (LP *Smell Of Incense* '68 on Hip), flop LPs on A&M '71-2 (*Fables, I Hear The Music*); semi-retired, relaxed, mellowed; back with soft-country style on Atlantic subsidiary Big Tree, 'I'd Really Love To See You Tonight' (no. 2 USA '76), followed by five more top 40 entries '76-9 (some no. 1 on easy-listening chart). Toured Japan with THREE DOG NIGHT '78. LPs incl. *Nights Are Forever* (no. 17 '76), *Dowdy Ferry Road* '77, *Some Things Don't Come Easy* '78, *Dr Heckle And Mr Jive* '79, *Best Of* '80, all on Big Tree; *Just Tell Me You*

Love Me '80 on MCA. Seals went solo, emerged as big country star, prod. by Kyle Lehning: *Rebel Heart* '83 was top 40 in country chart, *San Antone* '84 top 25, *Won't Be Blue Anymore* reached no. 1, *On The Front Line* '86 no. 12 by end of year, all on EMI labels. Hit country singles '84-6 incl. 'My Baby's Got Good Timing' (no. 2); 'Meet Me In Montana' (duet with Marie OSMOND), 'Bop', 'Everything That Glitters Is Not Gold' and 'You Still Move Me', all no. 1. *The Best* '87 (on Capitol in UK) incl. all these; seven of 11 tracks written or co-written by Seals.

ENNIS, Skinnay (*b* Robert Ennis, 13 Aug. '09, Salisbury, N.C.; *d* 3 June '63, Beverly Hills, Calif.) Singer, bandleader. Founder-member of Hal KEMP band '25-38; formed band in Hollywood: Gil EVANS, Claude THORNHILL arr. early '40s. Sang and did comedy on top radio shows, incl. long residency with Bob Hope; appeared in many films; led service band WWII. Famous breathless singing style; best-known record with Kemp 'Got A Date With An Angel' became theme of own band, title of MGM LP mid-'50s. Residency at Statler-Hilton Hotel L.A. from '58. Choked to death on a bone in a restaurant.

ENO, Brian (*b* 15 May '48, Woodbridge, Suffolk) UK keyboardist, composer; founder member of ROXY MUSIC; one of the first to use the synthesiser, left Roxy after two LPs and became guru of pop avant-garde, like John CAGE as important for his example as for what he actually did, but also with pop success as producer/collaborator with others. His accessible *Here Come The Warm Jets* '74 was no. 26 LP UK. Work with King Crimson guitarist Robert Fripp began with *No Pussyfooting* and *Evening Star* '75-6 using Eno's tape-delay system, while Eno single 'Seven Deadly Finns' '74 foresaw punk rock. Recovering from road accident he invented 'ambient music' '75 to raise Muzak to a somewhat higher level, formed Obscure mail-order only label, associated with EG label, then licensed through Island; LPs which followed incl. *Taking Tiger Mountain (By Strategy), Discreet Music, Another Green World, Music For Airports, Music For Films, Apollo, Before And After Science, Ambient 4 On Land.* EG switched to

Polydor '77-8; Editions EG formed '81 and Obscure LPs became commercially available; 11-disc set of most of his work issued: *Working Backward 1983-1973* incl. *Music For Films Volume 2*, disc of *Rarities* incl. 'Finns'. Worked with Harold Budd on *The Pavilion Of Dreams* and *Plateaux Of Mirrors* '82, *The Pearl* '84. He kept his hand in high-class pop, teaming with David BOWIE for three albums '77-9, with TALKING HEADS '78-80 for three, plus co-writing Heads' hit single 'Once In A Lifetime' '81, also critically praised African-inspired LP *My Life In The Bush Of Ghosts* with Heads' David Byrne ('found' voices manipulated electronically) then co-prod. hit U2 LP *The Unforgettable Fire* '84. His own *More Blank Than Frank* and compact disc *Desert Island Selection* on EG/Polydor '86; early '87 saw EG switch to Virgin, LPs by Eno, Budd, Eno's old Roxy mate Bryan Ferry reissued on EG/Virgin.

EPSTEIN, Brian (*b* 19 Sep. '34, Liverpool; *d* 26-7 Aug. '67, London) Managed BEATLES, other Merseyside acts: Billy J. KRAMER, Cilla BLACK, GERRY AND THE PACE-MAKERS, etc. From prosperous family, little taste for pop music; managed record dept. of family furniture business. Asked by customers for early Beatle disc on Polydor, intrigued to find they were local group, heard them at Cavern Club 21 Aug. '61 and was fascinated. Smartened up their act, taught them reliability, sacked drummer Pete BEST for Ringo STARR, arranged Parlophone contract. Meticulous, good manager in early days; out of his depth in world of big money. Worst mistake was letting USA rights to Beatle merchandise go for almost nothing. Homosexual with unhappy love life, reportedly in love with John LENNON; losing control of Beatles (whose contract soon to expire); heavily into drugs, especially sleeping pills: died suddenly, probably of accidental cumulative overdose, though suicide mooted and enemies had threatened violence. Death shocked Beatles; Lennon said they would never have made it without him. Published autobiography *A Cellar Full Of Noise* '64.

ERVIN, Booker (*b* Booker Telleferro Ervin, 31 Oct. '30, Denison, Texas; *d* 31 July '70, NYC, of kidney disease). Tenor sax. Played

trombone as a boy; self-taught on tenor but later studied tenor and theory at Berklee in Boston. Played in USAF '51-2; toured with R&B band of Ernie Fields '54-8; then to NYC '58 and often with Charles MINGUS until '62. Most of '64-6 in Europe, again '68. Sinewy, virile Texas tenor style on both blues and ballads. Solos on Randy WESTON LP *African Cookbook*; Mingus albums *Blues & Roots*, *Oh Yeah*, *Mingus Ah Um*, *Mingus Dynasty*, others. Own albums incl. small group sets with excellent co-stars: *The Book Cooks* '60 on Bethlehem (now Affinity UK); *Cookin'* '60 on Savoy (also issued as *Down In The Dumps* with additional tracks from '61); *That's It!* '61 on Candid. On Prestige (many reissued in 2-disc sets): *Exultation* and *The Freedom Book* '63; *The Song Book, The Blues Book, The Space Book* '64; *Setting The Pace* (with Dexter GORDON) and *The Trance* '65; *Heavy!* '66. On Blue Note: *The 'In' Between* and *Booker Ervin* '68, the latter a 2-disc set incl. an LP originally under Horace PARLAN's name. Also a quartet LP with Ted CURSON '66 on Dutch Fontana; *Structurally Sound* '66 and *Booker And Brass* '67 on Pacific Jazz, the latter a big band set. Track 'Blues For You' from Berlin Jazz Festival '65 incl. on an Enja LP, the other side by Parlan.

ESCORTS, The UK pop band, one of the best 'second division' Merseybeat groups, formed '61. Lineup: Mike Gregory, bass; Terry Sylvester, rhythm guitar (both *b* '47); Pete Clark, drums; John Kinrade, guitar. Played usual round of Liverpool and Hamburg gigs; Brian EPSTEIN expressed interest in them, but nothing came of it; debut single, cover of Larry WILLIAMS's 'Dizzy Miss Lizzy', was regional USA hit, especially in Texas, but group could not travel to promote it. Strong songs were 'Mad World', 'Night Time'; 'From Head To Toe' (Smokey ROBINSON song) featured Paul McCARTNEY on tambourine and was covered by Elvis COSTELLO for minor hit '82, prompted by complete Escorts compilation *From The Blue Angel* '82. With better luck they might have become a major force. Split '66; Sylvester joined SWINGING BLUE JEANS, later the HOLLIES.

ESSEX, David (*b* David Cook, 23 July '47, London) UK singer/teen star. Grew up in tough East End, played drums in semi-pro Everons '63; 10 singles as singer '63-70 flopped; manager Derek Bowman encouraged sideways move to theatre: repertory, bit parts in forgotten films; then big break: cast from 600 to play Jesus in *Godspell* London late '71. Also starred in well-received film *That'll Be The Day* '73 as '50s rocker Jim MacLaine; film written by Ray Connolly, mus. dir. Neil Aspinall and Keith Moon. Essex wrote 'Rock On' for the film: first hit no. 3 UK/5 USA '73-4, followed by moody 'Lamplight' and 'America' both from debut LP *Rock On* ('Lamplight' minor last hit in USA). Second LP *David Essex* '74 had UK no. 1 'I'm Gonna Make You A Star', also 'Stardust' (no connection with Hoagy CARMICHAEL): no. 7 hit and title of film '75 co-starring Adam FAITH and Larry Hagman, which had MacLaine fall from grace through drugs. Much success on discs attributable to former jingle-writer Jeff Wayne, who prod. them; alternated between moody ('Rollin' Stone', no. 5 '75), brash ('Hold Me Close', no. 1 same year). Prod. himself from *Out On The Street* '76 onwards, with marginal negative effect on sales; returned to stage '78 to play Che Guevera in Tim Rice/Andrew LLOYD WEBBER's *Evita*: 'Oh What A Circus' from the show no. 3 '78; film *Silver Dream Racer* incl. 'Silver Dream Machine' (no. 4); non-singing role as Lord Byron in *Childe Byron* at Old Vic theatre. No. 2 hit '82 with plaintive 'A Winter's Tale', by Rice and Mike BATT; no. 8 '83 with 'Tahiti', presaging show *Mutiny*, based on *Mutiny On The Bounty*, panned by critics as insubstantial but successful with public when it finally opened '85, with sumptuous sets, imaginative design. Total to '84 of 17 top 40 UK singles, numerous gold albums, Grammy nomination (for 'Rock On'): unusual in combining pop with serious acting, but fans still predominantly young and female.

ESTES, Sleepy John (*b* 25 Jan. 1899, Ripley, Tenn.; *d* 5 June '77, Brownsville, Tenn.) Blues singer, guitarist, songwriter; blind in one eye from accident age 6, totally blind by about age 50. Nickname from tendency to doze due to low blood pressure. Often worked outside music; sang in street, at house-parties etc.; hoboed through south; with Rev. Gary DAVIS, Lightnin' HOPKINS,

John Lee HOOKER, Mance LIPSCOMB, Skip JAMES, very few others, lived long enough and still vigorous enough in black folk trad. to work festivals, tour Europe, make film/TV documentaries incl. *Citizen South-Citizen North* '62, *The Blues* '63 (by Sam Charters), *Thinking Out Loud* '72, *Born In The Blues* '73. First records on Victor '29; then Champion, Decca, Bluebird, Sun, Delmark, Vanguard (Newport '64), Fontana, Storyville, Adelphi and Albatross. Compilation LPs incl. *The Blues Of Sleepy John Estes* '34-40 (two vols. on Australian Swaggie label), *1929-40* (Folkways), *Down South Blues* (MCA); Delmark albums '62-70 incl. *Legend Of, Broke And Hungry, Brownsville Blues, Electric Sleep* (with Earl HOOKER, SUNNYLAND SLIM); *Portraits In Blues Vol. 10* on Storyville made in Europe '64.

ETTING, Ruth (*b* 23 Nov. c. '03, David City, Neb.; *d* 24 Sep. '78) Singer. No musical training; studied design in Chicago, did costume work in Chicago clubs, then sang in the clubs and in a theatre revue chorus. Married her manager, Chicago mobster Martin (Moe the Gimp) Snyder '22. Moved to NYC for big break in *Ziegfeld Follies Of 1927* with Eddie CANTOR, introduced Irving BERLIN's 'Shaking The Blues Away'. Given other good material: 'Love Me Or Leave Me' in *Whoopee* '28 (also sang her own song 'Maybe – Who Knows?'), 'Get Happy' in *9:15 Revue*, RODGERS & HART's 'Ten Cents A Dance' in *Simple Simon* '30 (from then on her song). In *Ziegfeld Follies Of 1931* she portrayed veteran contralto Nora Bayes, sang 'Shine On Harvest Moon', which Bayes introduced in *Follies Of 1908*. Guested on radio early '30s, own shows '35-6; meanwhile to Hollywood for films '33, incl. Cantor money-spinner *Roman Scandals*, then *Gift Of The Gab* and *Hips Hips Hooray*; on London stage '36 for Ray Henderson's *Transatlantic Rhythm*. Left Snyder, who responded by shooting her piano player, prospective second husband, who recovered. Had own radio show again '47-8. Queen of the Torch Singers; MGM made biopic *Love Me Or Leave Me* '55 with Doris DAY and James Cagney. Had more than 60 big hits '26-37, nearly all on Columbia, averaging ten a year '27-31; the biggest was *'Life Is A Song'* '35. Compilations: *Original Recordings* on Columbia issued '55, then *Hello, Baby* on Biograph, *Ten Cents A Dance* on ASV UK.

EUROPE, James Reese (*b* 22 Feb. 1881, Mobile Ala.; *d* 10 May '19, NYC) Active organiser of black concerts, musical clubs; to NYC '05; began association with Vernon and Irene CASTLE, popular white dance team, which made him famous, and signed Victor recording contract '14; led US Army band and took Paris by storm '18. Music was called Jazz; it was not, but he introduced features such as techniques of brass playing which he believed were racial/musical characteristics, and said that he had to rehearse his men to keep them adding more to the music than he wanted. Stabbed by crazy musician at concert in Boston.

EUROVISION SONG CONTEST International European pop contest, risible and outdated. Began '56, popular for several years, but during '60s became increasingly anachronistic, representing everything the BEATLES were sweeping away. UK first won '67 with Sandie SHAW's 'Puppet On A String' setting the seal on sure Eurovision success: pretty girl singing jaunty, martial-style pop ('Boom Bang-A-Bang' by LULU, 'Jack In A Box' by Clodagh Rogers, even Cliff RICHARD tried formula with 'Congratulations' '68). Has thrown up the odd mongrel hit: 'Love Is Blue' by Paul Mauriat was unsuccessful Luxembourg entry '67, no. 12 UK; Nicole's 'A Little Peace' (East Germany) was UK no. 1 '82. UK entrants mostly MOR stalwarts like Kathy Kirby, Ronnie Carroll, Alisons etc.; established songwriters like Les Reed, Norman Jewell, Bill Martin and Phil Coulter all had a try, as well as young Elton JOHN in '69 (unsuccessfully). Of winners, only DANA '70, Brotherhood Of Man '76, BUCKS FIZZ '81 and especially ABBA '73 went on to any real success. Appeal of annual TV show tongue-in-cheek; Monty Python comedy team parodied it mercilessly early '70s; news interest revived when Norway scored no points at all two years in a row. Tried to update '87 with heavy metal entry by Heavy Pettin' (they lost). Audience figures said to be falling, but generation of '50s has the sight of Katie Boyle intoning 'Luxembourg . . . deux points' seared on memory.

EURYTHMICS Pop duo: David Allan Stewart (*b* 9 Sep. '52, Sunderland), guitars, keyboards, composer, vocals; Annie Lennox (*b* 25 Dec. '54, Aberdeen), vocals. Stewart began as folkie mid-'60s, worked with folk group Amazing Blondel; formed Longdancer in LINDISFARNE mould, signed to Elton JOHN's Rocket label. Met Lennox '77 waitressing in Hampstead, formed the Tourists: band made three albums, had UK hits 'Loneliest Man In The World', cover of Dusty SPRINGFIELD's 'I Only Want To Be With You', 'So Good To Be Back Home Again'. Split '80 but Stewart, Lennox carried on together both personally, professionally. Debut LP *In The Garden* '81 made in Germany with guests Clem Burke (of BLONDIE), Holger Czukay, Marcus Stockhausen; blend of psychedelia, mildly avant-garde electronics incl. 'Belinda' and 'Never Gonna Cry Again'. Critics divided; Lennox and Stewart personal relationship over; *Sweet Dreams (Are Made Of This)* '82 was make-or-break album: established them with two big hits 'Love Is A Stranger' and title cut (no. 1 USA '83), aided by clever videos emphasising Lennox's androgynous appeal; *Touch* '83 even bigger, with UK/USA hits 'Who's That Girl', 'Right By Your Side', 'Here Comes The Rain Again'. RCA issued 4 tracks remixed from *Touch* in mini-album *Touch Dance* to critical hostility, adverse comments from duo. Landed plum job of scoring film *1984*; problems with producers led to music being shelved, shoved on soundtrack LP anyway by Virgin; incl. hit 'Sexcrime'. Stewart's expertise saw him in demand as prod.; worked '85 with Tom PETTY, Feargal SHARKEY, Bob DYLAN; Lennox's marriage to Hare Krishna devotee made news (it didn't last); she had cameo role in flop film *Revolution* '85. *Be Yourself Tonight* '85 was another hit LP, incl. guests Daryl HALL, Elvis COSTELLO, Aretha FRANKLIN duet with Lennox on 'Sisters (Are Doin' It For Themselves)'. Single 'It's Alright (Baby's Coming Back)' entered '86 another hit; LP *Revenge* '86 incl. 'When Tomorrow Comes'. Stewart prod. sessions for Bob Geldof, Mick Jagger, Daryl Hall, Bob Dylan late '85, '86; Eurythmics were still one of the best and brightest UK pop acts, thanks to Stewart's melodies and technique, Lennox's blue-eyed soul and looks; *Savage* '87 was reversion to hot-blooded synth-pop duo and was climbing the USA chart at year's end.

EVANS, Bill (*b* William John Evans, 16 Aug. '29, Plainfield, N.J.; *d* 17 Sep. '80, NYC) Piano, composer. Worked with Jerry Wald, Tony SCOTT; in Miles DAVIS combo '58. Played in film soundtrack *Odds Against Tomorrow* '59 (score by John LEWIS). LP debut as leader '56 with trio; early '60s began series of lyrical albums which found many fans in and outside jazz: often solo, usually with trio, created intimate moods of distinctive delicacy, harmonic approach. Lalo SCHIFRIN compared Oscar PETERSON and Evans to Liszt and Chopin: Peterson/Liszt conquered the piano, Evans/Chopin seduced it. He practised a kind of Zen on the piano, such as trying to draw vibrato out of it: impossible, 'but trying for it affects what comes before it in the phrase' (quoted by Gene LEES). Erratic career because of ill health was marked by loyal following among critics and public alike. Published several books of original comps. and transcribed solos; many jazz festival appearances, TV (especially in Europe); won innumerable polls as well as several Grammies, e.g. for *Conversations With Myself* '63 (accompanied himself by means of double- and triple-tracking), *Live At Montreux* '68 (both on Verve), *The Bill Evans Album* '71 on Columbia. Collaborator on bass '66-79 was Eddie Gomez (*b* 4 Oct. '44, Santurce, Puerto Rico; LP as leader on Denon with Chick COREA and Steve Gadd); they often performed duo (incl. *Intuition* '74, *Montreux III* '75, both on Fantasy). *Undercurrent* '59, duo LP with Jim HALL reissued on Fantasy '87 had one of the best-known sleeve photos of LP era: shot of woman floating in lake taken underwater by Toni Frissell. Records as sideman with Davis, Bobby BROOKMEYER (*Ivoryhunters*), Oliver NELSON (*Blues And The Abstract Truth*), Tony BENNETT (*The Tony Bennett/Bill Evans Album*, *Together Again* '75-6 are duet LPs, voice and piano). Also with Lee KONITZ and Jimmy GIUFFRE, George RUSSELL, others. Own LPs also incl. *Empathy* '62 with Shelly MANNE, *Trio* '64 with Gary PEACOCK, *The Bill Evans Trio Live* '64, *Trio* '65, *Bill Evans At Town Hall* '66, *Intermodulation* '66 with Hall, *A Simple Matter Of Conviction* '66 with Manne and

Gomez, *Further Conversations With Myself* '67, *Alone* '68, live *California Here I Come* '67 and *What's New* '69, all on Verve; *Montreux II* '70 on CTI; *Living Time* (big band arr. by Russell) and *Live In Tokyo* '72 on CBS, labels; *Symbiosis* '74 now on Pausa (big band with strings composed, arr. by Claus Ogerman). Also on Fantasy: *Since We Met* and *Re: Person I Knew*, both '74 at Village Vanguard; solos *Alone (Again)* and *Eloquence*, both '76; *Quintessence* '76, quintet set with Harold LAND, Ray BROWN, Kenny BURRELL, Philly Joe JONES; *Crosscurrents* '77, quintet with Konitz and Warne MARSH; *From The '70s* and *You Must Believe In Spring* '77, *I Will Say Goodbye* '79, all trio sets; LP *New Conversations* '78 (overdubbed himself for a third time), *Affinity* '78 (quintet with Toots THIELEMANS, nominated for Grammy, incl. Phil Markowitz tune 'Sno' Pea'), *We Will Meet Again* '79 (also quintet), all on WB. *The Paris Concert* '79 is two LPs on Elektra/Musician, recommended by Lees in his *Jazz letter*: ' . . . he had begun to evolve and grow again . . . on the clear evidence of these albums, was in his most fertile period when we lost him.' Lees wrote lyrics for Evans tunes, incl. 'Waltz For Debby'; some titles were anagrams: 'Re: Person I Knew' for Orrin Keepnews, the boss at Riverside; 'N.Y.C.'s No Lark' for Sonny CLARK, who Evans said was an influence. More than 40 LPs in print by this much loved-artist incl. the first, *New Jazz Conceptions* '56, also incl. in complete Riverside/Milestone recordings, issued '85 in 18-disc 2-box limited edition with 32-page booklet: solo to quintet sessions incl. some previously unissued; sidemen incl. Hall, Philly Joe, Zoot SIMS, Percy HEATH, Paul CHAMBERS, Freddie HUBBARD, Ron CARTER, Scott LA FARO, Cannonball ADDERLEY; 151 tracks incl. complete '61 Village Vanguard sessions. Trio with La Faro and Paul MOTIAN was legendary; other fine bassists were Gomez, Peacock; latest '78-80 was Marc Johnson (*b* '53, Nebraska) who now has LPs on ECM with John Abercrombie, own quartet Bass Desires with two guitars, drums; last drummer was Joe LaBarbera.

EVANS, Doc (*b* Paul Wesley Evans, 20 June '07, Spring Valley, Minn.; *d* 10 Jan. '77, Minneapolis) Cornet in dixieland style;

played other instruments until c.'31; also arr. in '30s. Also teacher, dog-breeder; ran own club and directed local symphony orchestra in Mendota, Minn. '60s. Often led own band. LPs on Audiophile label mid-'50s, often with Knocky PARKER on piano, among the prettiest, most affectionate and best recorded in revival genre. Compilation of '45-7 material on Jazzology.

EVANS, Gil (*b* Ian Ernest Gilmore Green, 13 May '12, Toronto, Canada; *d* 20 March '88, Mexico) Arranger, bandleader. Led band in Cal. '33-8; Skinnay Ennis took over and Evans stayed on as arr. for spots on Bob Hope radio show, played top hotels. With Claude THORNHILL '41-8 except for military service '43-5; began innovating: became a 'guru' (said George RUSSELL) whose basement flat in NYC was a meeting place for Russell, Charlie PARKER, Gerry MULLIGAN and others. Contributed to Miles DAVIS '49 *Birth Of The Cool* sessions; wrote for Peggy LEE, Tony BENNETT, Benny GOODMAN, etc.; arr. and cond. LPs *Look To The Rainbow* with Astrud Gilberto and *Guitar Forms* with Kenny BURRELL; best-known LPs with Davis: *Miles Ahead* '57, *Porgy And Bess* '58, *Sketches Of Spain* '59, *At Carnegie Hall* '61, *Quiet Nights* '64 (played piano on some sessions). Own LPs incl. *Big Stuff* on Prestige; *New Bottle, Old Wine* with Cannonball ADDERLEY and *Great Jazz Standards*, both on World Pacific, all '50s (later *Pacific Standard Time* on Blue Note: Brian Priestley points out in *The Wire* that on 'St Louie Blues', an Adderley solo is answered by a brass figure which turns out to be a favourite guitar fill of LEADBELLY's). Also *Out Of The Cool* and *Into The Hot* on Impulse early '60s (latter was Evans production of music by Cecil TAYLOR, Johnny Carisi); 2-disc packages incl. Tadd DAMERON LP Prestige, *Great Arrangers* with Gary McFARLAND on MCA. Other LPs incl. *The Individualism Of Gil Evans* on Verve, *Plays Jimi Hendrix* and *There Comes A Time* on RCA (he once wanted to do an album with Hendrix), *Priestess* on Antilles, *Svengali* on Atlantic, *Parabola* on Horo, *Little Wing* '78 on Inner City, *Blues In Orbit* '82 on Enja. Critical rapture on visits to UK: *Live At The Royal Festival Hall 1978* on RCA completed '81 by *The Rest Of Gil Evans Live At The R.F.H.* on Mole; *The British Orchestra* '83 on Mole is from Bradford Festival with UK jazzmen John Surman, Don Weller, etc.; also *Decoy* on CBS, *Absolute Beginners* (soundtrack) on Virgin, 2-disc *Live At Sweet Basil* '84 with the Monday Night Orchestra incl. George ADAMS on Gramavision/Electric Bird. 75th birthday concert in London.

EVERETT, Betty (*b* 23 Nov. '39, Greenwood, Ms.) Soul singer; one of the best. Played piano and sang in church from age 9; moved to Chicago '57, began recording on local labels Cobra, on C.J. '60, then One-Derful, where she had local hits 'I've Got A Claim On You' and 'I'll Be There'; then signed by Vee Jay: 'You're No Good' just missed top 50 late '63 (covered in UK by the SWINGING BLUE JEANS); biggest hit 'The Shoop Shoop Song (It's In His Kiss)' '64 was no. 10 (revived by Linda Lewis '75 for top 10 UK hit). 'I Can't Hear You' and 'Getting Mighty Crowded' did not reach top 50, but latter made no. 29 in UK '65. Duet hits with Jerry BUTLER made no. 5 ('Let It Be Me'), just missed top 40 ('Smile'); their LP *Delicious Together* charted '64 (no. 102) (*Still Delicious Together* on Charly UK). Vee Jay folded '67; Everett went to ABC for an unsuccessful year, bouncing back on Uni for her last top 40 hit 'There'll Come A Time' (no. 26 '69), also her first (no. 2) entry in national soul chart, where she had three more on Uni and two on Fantasy '69-71. Linda RONSTADT had no. 1 cover of 'You're No Good' '75. Hits compilation *Hot To Hold* on Charly UK.

EVERLY BROTHERS USA pop/C&W vocalists, guitarists: Don (*b* 1 Feb. '37), Phil (*b* 19 Jan. '39) both from Brownie, Ky. Parents Ike and Margaret Everly well-known in south and mid-west; Ike in particular as black-infl. guitarist in same mould as Sam McGEE, Merle TRAVIS, etc. Sons joined them on radio show in Iowa mid-'40s, went solo when they retired '50s: to Nashville writing songs for Acuff-Rose (Don's 'Thou Shalt Not Steal' was no. 14 country chart for Kitty WELLS '54); made country single for Columbia 'Keep On Lovin' Me', went to Archie BLEYER's Cadence label with Felice and Boudleaux BRYANT's 'Bye Bye Love' '57: sudden smash hit (no. 1 country, 2 pop,

6 in UK) put country harmony on pop chart, giving Nashville new lease of life as rock'n'roll was taking over, made brothers legends: 6 top 10 hits country chart '57-9; 25 top 40 pop hits '57-64 incl. 15 top 10, 4 at no. 1: 'Wake Up Little Susie' '57, 'All I Have To Do Is Dream' and 'Bird Dog' '58, 'Cathy's Clown' '60 (on WB: left Cadence in dispute over royalties; then to RCA '72). First LP *The Everly Brothers* '58 was no. 16 USA, had both 'Bye Bye Love' and 'Susie' on it; second *Songs Our Daddy Taught Us* did not chart: paid dues to roots with lovely versions of trad. songs before hectic stardom took over. *Fabulous Style Of The Everly Brothers* '60 was Cadence compilation; *It's Everly Time!* and *A Date With The Everly Brothers* on WB were both top 10 LPs '60; *Golden Hits* WB charted twice '62. Other LPs incl. *Sing Great Country Songs* '63, *Very Best Of*, *Gone, Gone, Gone* and *Beat & Soul* '65, *In Our Image* '66, *Hit Sound* and *The Everly Brothers Sing* '67, *Roots* '68 (incl. portion of childhood radio broadcast with parents), *Original Greatest Hits* '70 (2-disc compilation on Barnaby of Cadence hits): eight albums in all charted USA. Had summer TV series on CBS-TV, then *Stories We Could Tell* '72 and *Pass The Chicken And Listen* '73 on RCA; backup band incl. Warren Zevon on keyboards, Waddy Wachtel guitar. By then both had had personal problems, incl. addiction to speed, Don's nervous breakdown; violent split came when Phil smashed guitar on stage, walked out; Don announced 'The Everly Brothers died ten years ago.' Don wrote songs, made solo LPs *Don Everly* '71 and *Sunset Towers* '74 on Ode, *Brother Juke Box* '77 on Hickory; Phil hosted radio programme *In Session*; his song 'When Will I Be Loved' was a hit '75 for Linda RONSTADT; he made LPs *Star Spangled Springer* '73 on RCA, then *Nothing's Too Good For My Baby* and *Phil's Diner* '74, *Mystic Line* '75, *Living Alone* and *Phil Everly* '79 on various labels. Reformed '83, had chart albums '84: 2-disc live *Reunion Concert* on Passport just made it, *EB 84* on Mercury reached no. 38. Popular as ever in UK, they will not talk about split.

EVERYTHING BUT THE GIRL UK pop duo formed by vocalist Tracey Thorn (*b* 26 Sep. '62, Herts.) and guitarist Ben Watt (*b* 6 Dec. '62), students at Hull U. studying English

and drama. Thorn was in Marine Girls (LP *Lazy Ways* '83; *Beach Party* '80 reissued '87); Watt's father a pro jazz musician; they shared radical politics (Thorn writes for *Spare Rib*), liking for folk and jazz. Both signed to Cherry Red label; Thorn did solo *A Distant Shore* '82; Watt *North Marine Drive* '83, collaborated with Robert Wyatt on EP *Summer Into Winter* '82. Duo single 'Night And Day' intended to fuse jazz, folky harmonies, acoustic guitars; moved with label boss Nick Austin to his new Blanco y Negro label, scored no. 28 hit with 'Each And Everyone' '84 from LP *Eden*. Two more minor hits; they turned down *Top Of The Pops* TV appearance because of exam commitments. LP *Love Not Money* '85 in same gentle agit-pop/jazz/folk vein: prod. by Robin Millar, whose work with SADE it parallels; Simon Booth from pseudo-jazz pop group WORKING WEEK sessioned on LP, which incl. 'Sean', dedicated to Ulsterman Sean Downes, killed by rubber bullet (Watt's only lead vocal on LP), and song dedicated to Frances Farmer, actress with tragic life. They record with session players, tour with ever-changing back-up: lineup '85 incl. Rob Peters, drums; Mickey Harris, bass; Cara Tivey, keyboards. First Western group to play Moscow in six years '85; at home they confirmed ideological soundness by playing benefits during miners' strike. *Baby The Stars Shine Bright* '86 was smooth, lushly orchestrated LP, incl. single 'Come On Home'; cover of Patsy CLINE classic 'I Fall To Pieces' also '86; album *Idlewild* '88. Peculiar-looking duo claim to be antithesis of pop stardom; infl. by John MARTYN, Cole PORTER, Antonio Carlos Jobim, suggesting more substance to fragile music than detractors admit.

EWELL, Don (*b* 14 Nov. '16, Baltimore, Md.; *d* 9 Aug. '83, Deerfield, Fla.) Piano. Played revival music (*see* JAZZ) with Bunk JOHNSON, Kid ORY, Doc EVANS, etc.; with Jack TEAGARDEN '56-60; toured, freelanced; in Europe '71, early '80s. Not an innovative jazzman, but affectionate player in style of his favourites Fats WALLER, Jelly Roll MORTON. *Music To Listen To Don Ewell By* '56, *Man Here Plays Fine Piano!* '57 are delightful solo albums; also *Don Ewell Quartet* '57 with West Coast veterans Darnell Howard, clarinet (*b* 25 July c.1895,

Chicago; *d* 2 Sep. '66, San Francisco; also played with Ory, King OLIVER, Fletcher HENDERSON, Earl HINES), Minor 'Ram' Hall, drums (*b* 2 Mar. 1897, Sellers, La.; *d* 23 Oct. '59, Cal.; also played with Oliver, Ory) all on Good Time Jazz. Also *New Orleans Shuffle* '56 with Turk MURPHY on Columbia; *Jack Teagarden* '58 on Capitol; also with Teagarden at Newport Jazz Festivals '58-9, on Roulette and Verve '60-1. Other LPs incl. result of two-piano gig at Toronto's Golden Nugget '67: studio session *Grand Piano* now on Sackville with Willie 'The Lion' SMITH, fast company for any tickler. Several LPs on Chiaroscuro '70-4.

F

FABIAN (*b* Fabiano Forte, 6 Feb. '43, Philadelphia, Pa.) USA teen idol. Attended South Philly High, as did most of city's teen stars; introduced by Frankie AVALON to Chancellor label's Bob Marcucci, who agreed that he looked like a cross between Elvis PRESLEY and Ricky NELSON; singing ability was secondary. Flop singles with Chancellor act the Four Dates; then miming to 'I'm A Man' at a Dick CLARK record hop caused hormonal reaction in young females. He profited from Presley's absence in US Army service; 'I'm A Man' (Presley imitation from Doc POMUS and Mort Shuman) made no. 39, first of seven top 40 hits '59-60. Appeared on Clark's *American Bandstand*, toured with Caravan of Stars; 'Turn Me Loose', 'Tiger', 'Hound Dog Man' all top 10, latter title from first feature film. Admitted leaning on studio technology; was soft target for US House of Representatives investigating hyping of 'talentless' stars into charts through 'payola'. Film career incl. *High Time* with Bing CROSBY, *North To Alaska* with John Wayne, fizzled out; he appeared in TV sit-coms, posed nude in beefcake magazine '70s, took part in West Coast community project under Cal. governor Jerry Brown. Sued over portrait in film *The Idolmaker* '80 based on life of Marcucci; won out-of-court settlement early '86.

FABULOUS THUNDERBIRDS, The USA blues band formed Austin, Texas '75. Original lineup: Kim Wilson (*b* 6 Jan. '51, Detroit), vocals, harmonica; Keith Ferguson (*b* 23 July '46, Houston), bass; Jimmie Vaughan (*b* 20 Mar. '51, Dallas; Stevie Ray VAUGHAN's older brother), guitar ('arguably the finest and most authentic white blues guitarist of his time' – *Downbeat*); Mike Buck (*b* 17 June '52), drums. First LP *The Fabulous Thunderbirds* '79 on Takoma prod. by Denny Bruce; Fran Christina (*b* 1 Feb. '51, Westerly, R.I.; ex-ROOMFUL OF BLUES) joined during recording of *What's

The Word '80 on Chrysalis, replacing Buck; *Butt Rockin'* reached no. 176 Billboard LP chart '81: first LP with Christina as permanent member incl. session work from other Roomfuls, song 'One Too Many' co-written by Wilson, Nick LOWE, who replaced Bruce as prod. on *T-Bird Rhythm* '82. Loyal following after 10 years of touring, with covers of Bo DIDDLEY, Slim HARPO, Dave BARTHOLOMEW etc. interspersed with originals by Vaughan and Ferguson as well as Wilson ('Can't Tear It Up Enuff' on *T-Bird Rhythm*). Their mix of Chicago blues, Louisiana R&B infl. with dash of Tex-Mex gets little airplay on sanitised USA radio and LPs were not well promoted: last Chrysalis album sold 33,000 copies to tenacious fans in three weeks, then died. Ferguson left (now works in group Big Guitars From Texas with Buck), replaced by ex-Roomful Preston Hubbard (*b* 15 Mar. '53, Providence; also played some years in band with Scott HAMILTON). Without a label for three years, T-Birds recorded *Tuff Enuff* '85 in London, prod. by Dave EDMUNDS, released '86 on CBS, their most successful and slickest yet: no. 13 LP USA, title track top 10 single. Junior Brantley joined on keyboards '85, left '86 for up-and-coming Roomful: traffic in sidemen is now two-way. *Tuff Enuff* was followed by *Hot Number* '87.

FACES, The UK rock group formed from SMALL FACES after Steve Marriott left to form HUMBLE PIE. Bassist Ronnie Lane, drummer Kenny Jones and Ian McLagen on keyboards recruited Jeff BECK group outcasts vocalist Rod STEWART and guitarist Ron Wood. First LPs *First Step* '70 and *Long Player* '71 charted UK and USA, bolstered by covers (Eddie COCHRAN's 'Cut Across Shorty', Bob DYLAN's 'Winged Messenger'), but Stewart replaced Marriott as writer, partnership with Wood proving fruitful: *A Nod's As Good As A Wink To A Blind Horse* '72 had band in all its good-time glory, made no. 2 UK, 6 USA; Stewart's solo career had already begun and his hit 'Maggie May' (no. 1 both UK/USA) didn't hurt. Single 'Stay With Me' from *Nod* was no. 6 UK and their only USA single hit at no. 17: classic rocker with barrelhouse piano and unforgettable guitar riff from Wood was their finest hour. LP also incl. Lane's sensitive 'Debris', less well-known side of band. Often shambolic on stage, but remained big draw on USA stadium circuit with advantage of drawing from both Stewart's repertoire and their own. Patchy *Ooh La La* '73 failed to match success of *Nod* (no. 1 UK but peaked quickly; no. 21 USA); ex-FREE bassist Tetsu Yamauchi (*b* 21 Oct. '47, Fukuoka, Japan) joined on live *Coast To Coast: Overtures And Beginners* '73, preserving looseness of stage act. UK singles continued ('Cindy Incidentally' and 'Pool Hall Richard' each no. 2, 'You Can Make Me Dance Sing Or Anything' no. 12 '73-4), but they now came poor second to Stewart's solo career; Lane left to form folk-rock *Slim Chance* (LP '75); Wood made solo LPs *I've Got My Own Album To Do* '74 and *Now Look* '75, became temporary ROLLING STONE for tours '76, made solo *Gimme Some Neck* '79. With Stewart in tax exile, Jones and McLagen took part in brief Small Faces reunion, then Jones replaced Keith Moon in The WHO. Wood and Lane also collaborated on soundtrack *Mahoney's Last Chance* '76, Lane and Pete Townshend on LP *Rough Mix* '77; *Best Of Faces* was no. 24 UK '77. McLagen made solo *Troublemaker* '80, *Bump In The Night* '81. There was a reunion at finale of Stewart's Wembley gig in London '86. Lane's affliction with muscular sclerosis saw him active in ARMS, all-star musical fund-raising venture; disease was in remission in mid-'80s.

FAHEY, John (*b* 28 Feb. '39, Takoma Park, Md.) Giant of acoustic guitar, entirely self-taught; claims he can play as well as anybody except legendary Sam McGEE (of Grand Ole Opry). Rarely performs live, but prolific output of LPs has ensured devoted following. Early infl. mostly country music (especially McGee); discovered blues; wrote biography of bluesman Charley PATTON as thesis for Ph.D. at UCLA, in the process met and introduced record collector Bob Hite, guitarist Al Wilson, who later formed blues band CANNED HEAT. Borrowed $300 to form own Takoma label; early LP *The Transfiguration Of Blind Joe Death* c.'59 became cult item, with home-made sleeve and whimsical notes in calligraphy; he played banjo as well as guitar on it, incl. eclectic material: 'Bicycle Built For Two' (1892 hit first called 'Daisy Bell'), own compositions such as 'Beautiful Linda Getchell'; available on Sonet in UK/distributed by PRT, as are most of these: a different set called *Blind Joe Death*, *Death Chants*, *Fare Forward Voyagers*, *Old Fashioned Love*, best sellers: *Christmas Album* and *The Best Of John Fahey 1959-77*. This list is incomplete; Takoma began as a mail-order business and was not listed in Schwann catalogue USA; albums may have different titles in UK. Also Vanguard LPs *Requia* '67, *Yellow Princess* '69, once combined in *The Essential John Fahey*, *Requia* now on Terra in USA; Reprise LP *Of Rivers And Religions* '72 followed by *After The Ball* '73, charming LP drawing on '20s dance music with small band incl. clarinettist Joe DARENSBOURG; didn't sell. *Live In Tasmania* '81 was recorded there so Fahey could claim a first; *Let Go* '84, *Rain Forests, Oceans & Other Themes* '85 both on Varrick (division of Rounder) in USA. Fahey was first to record guitarist Leo KOTTKE; also rediscovered bluesmen Skip JAMES and Bukka WHITE, recording White on Takoma. Film work incl. song used in *Zabriskie Point* '70; was on A&R staff at Chrysalis label.

FAIN, Sammy (*b* 17 June '02, NYC) Composer, singer, pianist. Staff pianist for Jack Mills Publishers, also singer/pianist in radio, vaudeville. First published song 'Nobody Knows What A Red Headed Mama Can Do' '25, lyrics by Irving Mills and Al Dubin. Met main collaborator Irving Kahal '27 (*b* 5 Mar. '03, Houtzdale, Pa.; *d* 7 Feb. '42, NYC); their first hit 'Let A Smile Be Your Umbrella' '27 (in film *It's A Great Life* '30). 'Wedding Bells Are Breaking Up That Old Gang Of Mine' '29 was a hit for the FOUR ACES 25 years later. In film *The Big Pond* '30 Maurice CHEVALIER invented rum-flavoured chewing gum and sang 'You Brought A New Kind Of Love To Me'. Wrote 'When I Take My Sugar To Tea' '31: hit for the BOSWELL Sisters, featured in Marx Bros. film *Monkey Business*, in show

Everybody's Welcome (which also introduced classic 'As Time Goes By' by Herman Hupfield, *b* 1 Feb. 1894, Montclair, N.J.; *d* there 8 June '51). Fain appeared in show *Dames* '34 – as a songwriter. *Right This Way* '38 was Broadway debut of Joe E. Lewis, had two of their finest ('I'll Be Seeing You' and 'I Can Dream Can't I'); it ran for only two weeks. They wrote music for vaudeville-styled *Hellzapoppin*, biggest commercial hit of decade; also 'Are You Havin' Any Fun?' (sung by the Three Stooges) and 'Something I Dreamed Last Night' for *George White's Scandals of 1939*. Hit film *Anchors Aweigh* '45 had score by Sammy CAHN and Jule Styne, but Fain wrote 'The Worry Song' for famous sequence with Gene Kelly and cartoon mouse Jerry, with Ralph Freed (*b* 1 May '07, Vancouver, B.C.; *d* 13 Feb. '73, L.A.). Show *Flahooley* '51 with Yip HARBURG featured Yma SUMAC; scores for Disney features *Alice In Wonderland* '51, *Peter Pan* '53 with Cahn. '38 hit 'That Old Feeling' featured in biopic of singer Jane FROMAN *With A Song In My Heart* '52. With Paul Francis Webster (*b* 20 Dec. '07, NYC) wrote score for film *Calamity Jane* '53: Doris DAY had no. 1 hit with Oscar-winning 'Secret Love' (she also sang 'There's A Rising Moon' in *Young At Heart* '55); they won another Oscar '55 with title song from *Love Is A Many-Splendored Thing*; others nominated: 'April Love' '57 (title song of Pat BOONE film, no. 1 hit), 'A Certain Smile' '58 (no. 14 hit by Johnny MATHIS), 'A Very Precious Love' '58 (from film *Marjorie Morningstar*), 'Tender Is The Night' '61 (from film of F. Scott Fitzgerald novel), others. Kahal wrote almost solely with Fain, but did 'The Night Is Young And You're So Beautiful' '36 with Billy ROSE and Dana Suesse; Webster worked with Hoagy CARMICHAEL ('Memphis In June', others), Duke ELLINGTON ('I Got It Bad'), film composer Dmitri Tiomkin: 'Friendly Persuasion' '56, 'The Green Leaves Of Summer' (from *The Alamo* '60), others.

FAIRCHILD, Barbara (*b* 12 Nov. '50, Knobel, Ark.) Country singer, songwriter. Began pro career on local TV in Missouri '62; to Nashville '68 as writer, signed with MCA music and had songs recorded by Loretta LYNN, Liz ANDERSON, Conway TWITTY. Signed to Columbia '69, had own hits 'A Girl Who'll Satisfy Her Man' '70, 'Love's Old Song' '71, 'Teddy Bear Song' (no. 1 '72), 'Kid Stuff' '73, 'Baby Doll' '74, 'You've Lost That Lovin' Feelin'' '75, 'Cheatin' Is' '76, 'Let Me Love You Once Before You Go' '77. Faded somewhat from USA charts, has made many fans in UK since '79. LPs incl. *Someone Special* '69, *The Fairchild Way* '71, *Teddy Bear Song* '72, *Kid Stuff* '73, *Standing In Your Line* '75, *Free And Easy* '77, *Mississippi* '77, *This Is Me* '78, *The Answer Game* '82 with Billy WALKER, *The Biggest Hurt* '83.

FAIRPORT CONVENTION UK folk-rock band formed '66 in London, by Ashley Hutchings (*b* Jan. '45), Simon Nicol (*b* 13 Oct. '50) and Richard THOMPSON, guitars, vocals; Martin Lamble (*b* Aug. '49; *d* in road crash 12 May '69), drums; Judy Dyble (*b* '48), vocals; Ian Matthews (*b* 16 June '46, Scunthorpe) (rest all from London). Named after Nicol's home, band was mainstay of London 'underground' circuit late '60s alongside PINK FLOYD and SOFT MACHINE; debut LP *Fairport Convention* '67 was motley collection of original songs, covers of Joni MITCHELL material (prod. Joe BOYD being a friend of hers). *What We Did On Our Holidays* '68 introduced Sandy DENNY following Dyble's departure, emphasised Thompson's development as a writer (e.g. 'Meet On A Ledge'). Matthews left to pursue solo career, though playing on some tracks on third album: *Unhalfbricking* '69 was transitional LP; with substantial original work, imaginative Bob DYLAN covers, 11-minute workout on trad. 'A Sailor's Life' incl. fiddler Dave Swarbrick (*b* Apr. '41, London), who then became full-time member. Dave Mattacks (*b* Mar. '48, London) joined for seminal *Liege & Lief* '69: first full flowering of English folk-rock, trad. material performed at full throttle by rock band, but landmark caused schism in group; Hutchings, keen to pursue folk-rock, left to form STEELEYE SPAN; Denny formed short-lived Fotheringay; bassist Dave Pegg (*b* Nov. '47, Birmingham), colleague of Swarbrick's, ex-Ian Campbell, joined for *Full House* '70, which boasted impressive Thompson/Swarbrick compositions such as 'Walk Awhile' and 'Sloth' (which became mainstay of live act). Thompson left '71; four-man band persevered with patchy *Angel Delight* '71, impressive concept LP *Babbacombe Lee* '72. Return to form on *Rosie* '73 incl. guest appearances from Denny, Thompson, Ralph McTell; guitarists Trevor Lucas (*b* Dec. '43, Melbourne, Australia; ex-Eclection, Fotheringay; Denny's husband) and Jerry Donahue (*b* 24 Sep. '46, NYC) joined for *Fairport 9*, the most cohesive post-Thompson LP, featuring Swarbrick's growing skills; joined by Denny for *Fairport Live Convention* '74. *Rising For The Moon* '75 was fragmented, with impressive moments; Mattacks left halfway through recording, replaced by Bruce Rowland (ex-Joe COCKER, Ronnie Lane); Denny, Lucas and Donahue quit, leaving Pegg and Swarbrick to make limp *Gottle O'Geer* '76 with Nicol helping. *Live At The L.A. Troubador* was live LP made in '70 with *Full House* lineup (tapes of LED ZEPPELIN jamming with band at club are rumoured to exist). *Bonny Bunch Of Roses* '77 was return to form, with four-man line-up convincingly tackling their own and lengthy trad. material; by *Tipplers Tales* '78 the punch had gone for a while: Fairport seemed to split '77, with desultory live souvenir *Farewell, Farewell* '79. Pegg joined JETHRO TULL; Nicol and Swarbrick formed duo for folk-club work. Mattacks was busy session drummer, working with Elton JOHN, Paul McCARTNEY, George HARRISON and Nick HEYWARD; he came back with other ex-Fairports at annual reunions, high spot of UK folk calendar: *Moat On The Ledge* '82 was brilliant live record of '81 meeting. Fifth Swarbrick solo LP *Smiddy Burn* '81 reunited *Full House* lineup for the first time in 10 years; *Gladys' Leap* '85 was first Fairport studio LP in seven years: refreshing and experimental, with Nicol's vocals to the fore, and first Fairport record not to feature Swarbrick in 16 years, his place taken by Rick Sanders (ex-Soft Machine). Swarbrick formed acoustic quartet Whippersnapper with second fiddler Chris Leslie, Kevin Dempsey on guitar and Martin Jenkins, mandolin. *Expletive Delighted* '86 was the first all-instrumental Fairport LP, with Sanders, Martin Allcock (*b* 5 Jan. '57, Manchester; guitar, electric bouzouki), rhythm section of Mattacks/Nicol/Pegg, help from Thompson and Donahue; *House*

Full '86 reissued *Live At The Troubador*, remixed, with three more tracks. *Heyday* '87 on Hannibal is LP edition similar to previous cassette-only compilation of BBC broadcasts from '68-9. Fairport's infl. was profound, inventing folk-rock almost single-handed, paving the way for Steeleye Span, LINDISFARNE, infl. countless others by showing a way to avoid the domination of USA music at the end of '60s. 2-disc *History Of Fairport Convention* '72 is a good selection; rare tracks appear on Thompson LP *Guitar, Vocal* '77, Denny anthology *Who Knows Where The Time Goes* '86; book *Meet On The Ledge* '82 by Patrick Humphries provides full history. Donahue released solo debut *Telecasting* '86. See also ALBION BAND (with Hutchings), HOME SERVICE.

FAITH, Adam (*b* Terence Nelhams, 23 June '40, London) UK pop singer. Working in film laboratory, seen singing with skiffle group the Workingmen in Soho coffee bars by Jack GOOD. 'What Do You Want' was UK no. 1 late '59, 'Poor Me' two months later. Even by '50s UK pop standards Faith had a weak voice; lavish John Barry arr. and hiccough vocal style (which recalled Buddy HOLLY) made him a teen idol, second only to Cliff RICHARD in popularity. String of hits early '60s incl. 'Somebody Else's Baby', 'How About That', 'Lonely Pup In A Christmas Shop', 'The Time Has Come'. Interviewed on BBC-TV's *Face To Face*, revealed serious side; appeared in films *Beat Girl* and *Mix Me A Person* '60-1; spotted star potential of Sandie SHAW; own singing career declined with advent of BEATLES; two members of backing group Roulettes went on to become ARGENT. One of the few UK pop stars to successfully switch to acting: resurfaced as engaging small-time villain in TV's *Budgie* early '70s; outstanding performance in David ESSEX film *Stardust* '74. Since appeared in TV series *Minder*, West End play *Down An Alley Full Of Cats* '85, etc. Prod. Roger Daltrey solo LP '73; managed Leo SAYER; masterminded comeback of Lonnie DONEGAN mid-'70s. *Best Of Adam Faith* incl. hit singles. Known to friends as Tel; has made money dealing in property; used to be found in his 'office' – a table at Fortnum & Mason's restaurant in London – recalling the past and planning the future, until it was redecorated: he called it vandalism.

FAITH, Percy (*b* 7 Apr. '08, Toronto, Canada; *d* 9 Feb. '76, Encino, Cal.) Pianist, arranger, conductor, composer. Piano recital at Massey Hall age 15; played in silent cinemas; injured hands in a fire c.'26, ending prospect of concert career. Began arranging for hotel orchestras, then on radio '27. *Music By Faith* '38-40 on CBC (with Robert FARNON on trumpet) was carried in USA by MBS; his budget was cut and tired of feeling like the CBC's 'token Jew', he went to Chicago, '40, then NYC, naturalised '45; he arr./cond. *The Contented Hour*, Buddy CLARK and Coca-Cola radio shows etc.; recorded for Decca, RCA, then to Columbia A&R staff '50: wrote 'My Heart Cries For You' '50 (Guy MITCHELL hit based on folk song), was leader in 'popular instrumental' genre (called 'light music' in UK; see also MOOD MUSIC): own no. 1 hits '52-3 with Brazilian song 'Delicado' (amplified harpsichord played by Stan Freeman), 'Song From Moulin Rouge' (brilliant arr. with vocal by Felicia Sanders; flip side also charted: 'Swedish Rhapsody' was Faith's arr. of Hugo Alfven's 'Midsummer Vigil'). Faith LPs early '50s incl. 12" compilation *Soft Lights And Sweet Music* on RCA ('Oodles Of Noodles' was used for years as theme on late-night old movie showcase on Chicago TV); on Columbia: 10" *Carnival Rhythms*, *Fascinating Rhythms* (aka *Your Dance Date*), *American Waltzes*, *Carefree Rhythms*; 12" *Continental Music*, *Romantic Music* etc. Pioneered LPs of 'songs from' Broadway shows, first *Kismet* '54, then *House Of Flowers* '55 (Harold ARLEN score), *My Fair Lady*, *The Most Happy Fella*, *Lil' Abner*, into stereo era: *South Pacific*, *Porgy And Bess*, *The Sound Of Music*, *Camelot*, *Subways Are For Sleeping*, *Do I Hear A Waltz?*. He was among best studio arrangers, voicing for woodwinds especially notable, also predilection for Latin beat; chose clever material, e.g. Zez CONFREY's 'Kitten On The Keys', continental hit 'La Ronde', gorgeous arr. of Jerome KERN's 'Waltz In Swingtime'. Own tunes incl. 'Noche Caribe', 'Nervous Gavotte', 'Perpetual Notion' etc. Several film scores incl. *Love Me Or Leave Me* '55 (with Georgie Stoll; nominated for Oscar), *Tammy Tell Me True* '61,

I'd Rather Be Rich '64, *The Love Goddesses* '64, *The Third Day* '65, beautiful score for appalling film *The Oscar* '66 incl. melody 'Maybe September', recorded by Tony Bennett, also by Faith with vocalist Leslie Kendall. Arr./cond. albums and singles with Tony Bennett, Doris DAY, Sarah VAUGHAN, Johnny MATHIS, Wild Bill DAVISON (LP *Pretty Wild*), many others; of about 85 LPs of his own for Columbia, 33 charted '53-72 incl. *Kismet, My Fair Lady, Bouquet*, etc.; he was relegated by rock to schlock market. Third no. 1 hit was syrupy 'Theme From A Summer Place' '60, ironically with kling-kling-kling rock piano earlier satirised by Stan FREBERG, won Record of the Year Grammy; 'Love Theme From Romeo And Juliet' '69 won Grammy for Best Performance by a Chorus. There were tours of Japan, 2-disc sets: *The Columbia Album Of George Gershwin, Of Victor Herbert*, another for the Brazilian market; but he was mainly reduced to LPs of BEATLE songs, etc.: *Summer Place* '76 gave disco treatment to the hit. Stan Freeman (*b* 3 Apr. '20, Waterbury, Conn.) also played harpsichord on hit Faith arr. for Rosemary CLOONEY, made piano LPs on CBS labels, on MGM in piano duo with legendary cocktail pianist Cy Walter (*b* 16 Sep. '25, Minneapolis, Minn.; *d* 18 Aug. '68, NYC), who'd remember your favourite song even if he hadn't seen you for years.

FAITHFULL, Marianne (*b* 29 Dec. '46, Hampstead, London) Quintessential female '60s UK singer; blonde, ethereal beauty. Discovered at a party by ROLLING STONES manager Andrew Loog Oldham; Stones wrote 'As Tears Go By', debut hit at no. 9, released when she was 18; '65 hits 'Come And Stay With Me', 'This Little Bird', 'Summer Nights' epitomised ideal Swinging '60s female, well-publicised relationship with Mick Jagger not hurting. *Go Away From My World* '65 and *North Country Maid* were good LPs, frail voice supported by sympathetic prod. and apposite songs. Drug busts with Jagger kept her in headlines, as did controversial film debut *I'll Never Forget Whatsisname* '67, with first 4-letter word heard on British screen; film *Girl On A Motorcycle* '68 did not add to reputation, but appearances on stage in *Hamlet* and *Three Sisters* well-received.

Hapless suicide attempt in Australia while Jagger was working on film *Ned Kelly* (also a disaster) effectively ended relationship; she co-wrote 'Sister Morphine' on Stones' *Sticky Fingers* album; 'Wild Horses' on same LP widely taken to be his farewell to her. Throughout '70s drug problems and punctured romances kept name in news; LPs *Dreaming My Dreams* and *Faithless* '78 followed by real comeback, highly rated *Broken English* '79, with Stevie WINWOOD, songs by John LENNON, Shel SILVERSTEIN; incl. controversial 'Why D'Ya Do It'. Marriage to punk musician Ben Brierley led to *Dangerous Acquaintances* '81, *A Child's Adventure* '83. Fragile voice has turned to gravel with character, but fragility was not an act: deserves credit for survival, let alone successful London concert '81. *As Tears Go By* '81 was hits compilation; she said *Strange Weather* '87 on Island was first LP she's done without chemicals, with Mac REBENNACK, Bill Frisell on guitar, revisiting 'As Tears Go By'.

FAJARDO, José Antonio (*b* 18 Oct. '19, Cuba) Flautist, bandleader, arranger, composer, producer. Led Fajardo y sus Estrellas in Cuba (one track on *Charangas de Cuba y Nueva York* '76 on Tico, compilation of ten Cuban and NYC CHARANGAS from late '50s, early '60s); dance LPs on Panart '50s incl. *ChaChaCha In Havana*, *A Night At The Montmartre*, *Fajarda At The Havana Hilton*, *Ritmo de Pollos*, *Saludos From Fajardo, Vol. 6*, *Let's Dance With Fajardo*; then *Cuban Jam Session With Fajardo And His All Stars* incl. his own classic 'La Charanga' (LP reissued on French SonoDisc '76). Asked to perform '59 at Hotel Waldorf Astoria NYC for John Kennedy's presidential campaign, causing more uproar among Latin community than the Democrats: a gig at the Palladium NYC was quickly arranged; he settled in USA early '60s, forming own charanga (Columbia album *Mister Pachanga*, reissued on French Occidente '79). LPs on Coco incl. *Fajardo y sus Estrellas del 75* and *Fajardo '76 – La Raiz de la Charanga 'Charanga Roots'*, both made in Miami with bass, four violins, two singers, timbales, güiro, Alfredo Rodriguez on piano, Tany Gil on congas; *'Selecciones Clasicas' Recorded 1977*, new recordings of hits incl. 'La Charanga', made

in Miami and NYC with six violins incl. the young Cuban Alfredo de la Fé; *El Talento Total* '78, made in NYC and prod. by Ray BARRETTO. Switched to Fania for *Las Tres Flautas – Javier y su Charanga* '80 with Javier Vazquez's band, flutes of Fajardo, Pupi LEGARRETA, Johnny PACHECO; *Señor . . . Charanga!* '80, with lead vocalist Cali Aleman, prod. by Vazquez; *Pacheco y Fajardo* '82; *Hoy y Mañana* '84. Also appeared on *Alfredo Valdes Jr y su Charanga* '82 on Toboga, prod. by Roberto TORRES; Pepe Mora's . . . *Tributo al 'Beny'* '83 on Golden Notes; jam session *Maestro de Maestros Israel López 'Cachao' y su Descarga* '86 on Tania and FANIA ALL STARS *Viva la Charanga* '86. Appeared with Louie Ramirez and his Latin Jazz Ensemble on *Tribute To Cal Tjader* '87 on Caimán.

FALCO (*b* Johann Holzel, Feb. '57, Vienna) Austrian pop singer making international success. Called Hans or Hansi as a child; later known as John DiFalco, John Hudson. Performed with group Drahdiwaberl (Spinning Wheel) '80; first single 'All Vienna' was cult favourite after being banned because of line 'All Vienna is on heroin today'. First album *Einzelhaft* ('Incarcerated') '81 prod. by Robert Ponger, incl. international hit 'Der Kommisar'; *Junge Roemer* ('Young Romans') '84 written by Falco (lyrics), Ponger (music); *Falco 3* '85 prod. Written with Dutch brothers Robe and Ferdi Bolland, incl. hit 'Rock Me Amadeus'. Signed to WEA International '86, first single 'The Sound Of Musik'.

FALL UK new wave group formed '77 in Manchester by vocalist Mark E. Smith, only constant factor in lineup changes. Began with Tony Friel, bass; Karl Burns, drums; Martin Bramah, guitar. First releases on Step Forward label: 'Bingo Master's Breakout' and 'It's The New Thing' '78 showcase atonal vocals from Smith and uncompromising guitar-based backing that owed nothing to fashion. Burns left '79 to join Factory group Package, replaced by Mike Leigh, while guitarist Marc Riley, bassist Stephen Hanley (*b* '59, Dublin) joined; Bramah left to form short-lived Blue Orchids with keyboardist Una Baines; parent group cut first LPs *Live At The Witch Trials* and *Dragnet* '79. Group championed by Radio 1 DJ John Peel. Released LPs *Grotesque, Perverted By Language, Totale's Turns* on Rough Trade, but fans considered best work to be first LP and the Peel sessions; they confounded fans by rarely playing recorded material on stage, allowing Smith free rein to rant. Burns rejoined '81 after spell with Public Image Ltd, joining Smith, Riley, Steve Hanley and brother Paul Hanley (second drummer). Albums emerged arbitrarily on several labels, though most often on Kamera, then Beggars Banquet ('Draygo's Guilt', 'Creep'; compilation *Hip Priests And Kamerades* '85 is required listening for interested parties). Smith's USA-born wife Brix joined '84 (real name Laura Elise Smith; she has spinoff group the Adult Net: '60s covers on indie singles), added rhythm guitar, vocals and stability to lineup of Smith, Steve Hanley, Burns, Simon Rogers (bass, keyboards), Craig Scanlon, guitar. Always figuring high in UK indies charts and UK press readers' polls, continued with atonal brand of new wave with *This Nation's Saving Grace* '85, *Bend Sinister* '86. Burns left to form Thirst, replaced by John S. Woolstencroft; Smith wrote London stage show *Hey! Luciani*. First (many say best) material compiled on *Early Years 77-79* by Step Forward, but singles on Rough Trade 'How I Wrote Elastic Man', 'Totally Wired' come recommended. Little musical progression noticeable over nine years.

FAME, Georgie (*b* Clive Powell, 26 June '43, Leigh) UK R&B singer/pianist. Named by impresario Larry Parnes on joining Billy FURY backing group the Blue Flames and retaining both name and group when Fury quit rock'n'roll for ballads '62 (though Fury once fired Fame for refusing to stick to simple rock'n'roll piano). Other Flames – Colin Green, guitar; Tex Makins, bass; Red Reece, drums – got residency at London's Flamingo Club, where black USA servicemen were among the customers: 'GIs would come up and say, "Hey, man, have you heard Mose ALLISON? Eddie JEFFERSON? BOOKER T?" They even lent me their own records so I could hear it for myself.' Mick Eve was added on sax, John McLAUGHLIN replaced Green; in late '62 Fame acquired a Hammond organ: Jimmy SMITH as well as Booker T crept into syn-

thesis of R&B/soul/jazz. Regular personnel changes; Green returning, others going through such as drummers Jon Hiseman, Mitch Mitchell; first LP was infl. live *Rhythm And Blues At The Flamingo*, then *Fame At Last* (no. 15; both '64). Cover of Mongo SANTAMARIA's 'Yeh Yeh' (which Fame had heard by Jon Hendricks on Newport Festival LP) was surprise no. 1 UK late '64 (no. 21 USA '65); after three top 40 hits, top 10 LP *Sweet Things* '66 incl. another UK no. 1 with own 'Getaway' '66, then left the band. Ambition to sing with big jazz band fulfilled on *Sound Venture* '66, top 10 LP with Harry South; toured with Count BASIE later; more hits mixed covers with own song 'Because I Love You' in top 20; biggest hit of '67 was 'Ballad Of Bonnie And Clyde': novelty no. 1 UK/7 USA hit. CBS decided to make a British Andy WILLIAMS of him and LPs *Hall Of Fame, Two Faces Of Fame* charted in UK; it was his chance to work with strings and ballads. After more hit singles '69 he linked with former ANIMAL Alan Price on piano for duet 'Rosetta', easy-listening no. 11 '71: partnership lasted two years in TV, cabaret; he then worked on TV jingles, re-formed Flames for R&B-soaked *Georgie Fame* '74. He remained fashionable while horn sections, jazz-blues amalgams were popular; 'Yeh Yeh' revived by Matt Bianco for chart hit '85; vocal on Mondo Cane single 'New York Afternoon' got airplay '86 as he packed Ronnie SCOTT club in London for a week. Works with big bands in Scandinavia, Dutch Radio's Metropole Orchestra; tours with Flames and with Hoagy CARMICHAEL song-show *Stardust Road*; starred Nov. '86 in Swingin' On 10th Avenue, a celebration of George GERSHWIN's music with the London Symphony Orchestra at London's Royal Albert Hall. 'Really, what I've been doing is rehearsing for 25 years.' As a result he's never short of work (quotes from Dave Gelly in the *Observer*).

FAMILY UK progressive rock band evolved from Leicester R&B band called Farinas, then Roaring Sixties; became Family '66 at suggestion of USA prod. Kim Fowley, with whom they made demos. Lineup: Roger Chapman, vocals (*b* 8 Apr. '44, Leicester); John 'Charlie' Whitney, guitar (*b* 24 June '44); Jim King, sax, flute; Rick Grech, bass, violin (*b* 1 Nov. '46, Bordeaux, France); Harry Ovenall replaced on drums by Rob Townsend (*b* 7 July '47) before first album *Music In A Dolls House* '68 on Reprise. Spooky prod. effects, Chapman's natural vibrato made an outstanding 'underground' LP of the year, no. 29 UK. *Family Entertainment* '69 went to no. 6 UK with their best tracks 'Hung Up Down', 'The Weaver's Answer'. Supported ROLLING STONES at Hyde Park concert; then replacement of King by ex-Eclection John 'Poli' Palmer may have cost some appeal; Grech quit on eve of USA tour late '69 to join short-lived BLIND FAITH, replaced by John Weider (*b* 21 Apr. '47, ex-Eric BURDON); USA debut at Fillmore East allegedly ended with fist-fight between Chapman and Bill GRAHAM; Chapman lost voice, then visa: disastrous tour caused loss of momentum. 'No Mule's Fool' no. 29 UK late '69, presaged *A Song For Me* '70, no. 4 LP, first prod. by band. *Anybody* '70 was half live, half studio, reached no. 7; semi-compilation *Old Songs New Songs* '71 hurt momentum again. *Strange Band* (EP with 'Weaver's Answer'), single 'In My Own Time' were no. 11 and 4 UK. Arrival of John Wetton (*b* 12 July '49, Derby) added accomplished harmony to *Fearless* '71, probably best LP overall, first to chart in USA (no. 177 '72). *Bandstand* '72 (with no. 13 UK hit 'Burlesque') also charted low in USA but neither LP sold as well in UK as earlier albums: Wetton and Palmer quit (former to join King Crimson) replaced by Jim Cregan and Tony Ashton (*b* 1 Mar. '46, Blackburn) for *It's Only A Movie* '73; band split after farewell tour ending in home town. Chapman and Whitney maintained writing/performing partnership, forming Streetwalkers with shifting cast, made five LPs before split: Whitney left music, Chapman found success in Europe leading band the Shortlist. Townsend joined Medicine Head, then the Blues Band; Cregan went to Cockney Rebel, then Rod STEWART; Ashton sessioned. Their enthusiasm and inventiveness combined with bad luck to keep them from mega status. *Rise The Very Best Of Family* is hits package.

FAMOUS FLAMES, The Originally the Gospel Starlighters, led by singer/pianist Bobby Byrd (*b* 15 Aug. '34, Toccoa, Ga.). Became R&B group after recruiting James BROWN (summer '53) who soon became main lead singer and motivating force. First recorded in Feb. '56; lineup behind Brown was Byrd, vocal/piano; Johnny Terry, Sylvester Keels, Nashpendle Knox, vocals; Nafloyd Scott, guitar; Baroy Scott, bass. After they disbanded '57 Brown recruited most of The Dominions: Louis Madison, vocals and keyboards; Bill Hollings and J. W. Archer, vocals. In '59 this group also disbanded, became trio: Byrd and Terry (who had returned late '58) with Willie Johnson. A year later Terry and Johnson were replaced by Bobby Bennett and 'Baby' Lloyd Stallworth; this best-known edition recorded with Brown until '64, continued on stage with him until '66-7. Byrd had many releases of his own, remained important co-writer, backing singer and on keyboards with Brown until early '70s.

FANIA ALL STARS Superstar house lineup of Fania label (formed NYC '64 by lawyer Jerry Masucci, bandleader Johnny PACHECO) which filled gap left by demise of all-star groups of Alegre and Tico labels as Fania's catalogue became a unique record of the formative years of modern salsa. Personnel depended on availability; at its peak it incl. members of several bands, Pacheco, Willie COLON, Ray BARRETTO, Larry HARLOW; vocalists Celia CRUZ, Cheo FELICIANO, Hector LAVOE, Ismael Rivera, often guests from outside salsa. 2-disc *Live At The Red Garter* '68 was essentially a jam session (*descarga*); *Live At The Cheetah* Aug. '71 at NYC ballroom also issued on two LPs, portion on film incl. in documentary *Our Latin Thing (Nuestra Cosa)* prod. by Masucci, Harlow as mus. dir.: theme was Barretto's 'Cocinando' (cooking), from LP *Que Viva la Musica* '72. Throughout '70s FAS filled Madison Square Garden, other venues with ease. LPs incl. *Latin-Soul-Rock* '74, fusion set with guests Jan HAMMER, Billy COBHAM, Manu DIBANGO (doing crossover hit 'Soul Makossa'), Jorge 'Malo' Santana (guitar solo on live version of 'El Raton', with author Feliciano); 2-disc *Live At Yankee Stadium* '75 had Dibango on 'Congo Bongo', written by Harlow and Heny Alvarez; film footage in *Salsa* (soundtrack '76). Newcomer Rubén Blades debuted with FAS on *Tribute To Tito Rodriguez* '76, singing 'Los Muchachos de

Belen'. Crossover LPs '76-9 incl. *Delicate And Jumpy* with reduced band, guest Stevie WINWOOD; *Rhythm Machine*, with Eric Gale's guitar, standout track 'Juan Pachanga' (still a Blades classic); *Spanish Fever; Crossover* incl. disco-oriented tracks, Cruz's 'Isadora'. *Fania All Stars Live* from Madison Square Garden '78 had Cruz and Rivera singing 'Cucala'. *Habana Jam* '79 on Fania came from live concert in Cuba in March, incl. merengue star Wilfrido Vargas; *Havana Jam* on CBS was 2-disc live set from same series of concerts, with Kris KRISTOFFERSON, Rita COOLIDGE, Stephen Stills and WEATHER REPORT alongside Cuba's Orquesta Aragon, Irakere, and one track by FAS (Blades' composition 'Juan Pachanga'). (Fusion band Irakere formed c.'73, led by pianist Jesus 'Chucho' Valdez; two LPs on Milestone, one on CBS. With worldwide popularity it has toured USA only three times because of government paranoia about Cuba.) *Commitment* '80 was vocal feast incl. Lavoe on 'Ublabadu', Cruz duet with Pete 'El Conde' Rodriguez on 'Encantigo'. *California Jam* '80 moved to Latin jazz; *Social Change* '81 was seen as disappointing, with socially conscious lyrics, guests Gato BARBIERI, UK reggae band Steel Pulse. *Latin Connection* '81 incl. Rivera singing classic 'Bilongo'; *The Last Fight* '82 was soundtrack LP of film starring Colon and Blades. *Lo Que Pide la Gente* '84 saw Lavoe, Blades leave Fania for bigger labels; standout track: Lavoe's 'El Rey de la Puntualidad'. *Viva la Charanga* '86 featured José FAJARDO. Concert archive material released '86: *Live In Africa*, *Live In Japan* '76.

FANNY USA rock band formed '70 by Jean (bass, *b* '50) and June (lead guitar, *b* '49) Millington, *b* in Manila to US Navy family. In Cal. formed Sveltes, then Wild Honey; spotted by prod. Richard PERRY, changed name (courtesy George HARRISON) to Fanny. Band also had Alice de Buhr (*b* '50, Mason City, Iowa) on drums, Nickey Barclay (*b* 21 Apr. '51, Washington DC) on keyboards. LPs for Reprise '70-3: *Fanny* '70, *Charity Ball* '71, *Fanny Hill* '72 prod. by Perry, *Mother's Pride* '73 by Todd RUNDGREN. Mixtures of self-penned songs and covers (incl. Marvin GAYE's 'Ain't That Peculiar' ingeniously revamped around

slide guitar riff), but little success attended. Sole chart entry 'Charity Ball' single just made top 40. June left to join Isis; band continued heavier rock of last LP with *Rock And Roll Survivors* '75, first LP for Casablanca, first with replacement Patti Quatro and new drummer Brie Howard: incl. no. 29 USA single 'Butter Boy', but band close to splitting. Barclay emigrated to Europe, made solo *Diamonds In A Junk Yard* '76; Jean married guitarist Earl Slick, who'd sessioned on *Ladies On The Stage* '78, duet LP with June on UA; also continued as solo with Olivia label. Press willingly wrote them off as 'all girl band'; ability proven by wide sessioning: Jean with David BOWIE on *Young Americans*, Keith Moon; whole group with Barbra STREISAND; Barclay with Jesse Ed Davis, Joe COCKER.

FANTASY USA record label, now an independent conglomerate with one of the most valuable vaults in the business. Formed '49 in San Francisco; under Saul Zaentz became famous with Dave BRUBECK, also Cal TJADER, others; took over masters of Charles MINGUS/Max ROACH Debut label, later had bigger commercial success with CREEDENCE CLEARWATER. Changed hands c. '67; in early '70s new owners bought Prestige (formed '49 in N.J.) from Bob Weinstock, and Riverside (formed in NYC '53 by Orrin Keepnews and Bill Grauer) from ABC. Keepnews had worked as an editor for Simon & Schuster, began writing for Grauer's magazine *The Record Changer*, wrote the first-ever article about Thelonious MONK: later took on Monk when Prestige had dropped him as an eccentric and made some of his best LPs. Grauer died '63 of a heart attack; Riverside went broke '64; Keepnews formed Milestone: with his reputation for square dealing signed McCoy TYNER, others; came to Fantasy with Milestone and as Fantasy's V.P./dir. of jazz A&R, left to form Landmark label, now also distributed by Fantasy. Prestige/Riverside had both recorded Monk extensively; Prestige had Sonny STITT, Miles DAVIS, John COLTRANE, Eric DOLPHY, Mal WALDRON, Ron CARTER, much more; Riverside recorded Bill EVANS, Wes MONTGOMERY, Cannonball ADDERLEY, Johnny GRIFFIN, Mongo SANTAMARIA, and others; Sonny ROLLINS made great LPs for Prestige, Riverside, Milestone and Lester Koenig's Contemporary label (also Art PEPPER, Hampton HAWES, Curtis COUNCE, Shelly MANNE, many more), acquired by Fantasy '84 along with Good Time Jazz (Kid ORY, Don EWELL, Lu WATTERS, Bob SCOBEY, Jesse FULLER, Luckey ROBERTS etc.). Acquired Norman GRANZ's Pablo label early '87. Galaxy label formed for new LPs (*Return Of The Griffin*, Johnny's first LP on return to USA, with drummer Keith COPELAND); also Tommy FLANAGAN, etc. Meanwhile Fantasy began the first permanent well-designed reissue programme in jazz, 2-disc sets of Prestige, Riverside and Milestone dates incl. complete sessions for the first time; later OJC series (Original Jazz Classics), with the best LPs in the vaults in their original formats, sleeves, notes and all. The vaults also incl. blues and folk from Prestige, soul from Stax: the STAPLE SINGERS, Otis SPANN, Willie DIXON etc.; Creedence LPs are almost the only classic rock'n'roll continuously available in the original editions. Latest projects incl. sumptuous boxes of complete Monk and Evans sessions. With reissues from Mosaic, BLUE NOTE and KEYNOTE, and some of Bob THIELE's classic Signature sessions on his Dr Jazz label, jazz fans have never had it so good; Fantasy, now based in Berkeley, California, blazed the trail.

FARGO, Donna (*b* Yvonne Vaughn, 10 Nov. '49, Mount Airey, N.C.) Country singer. Daughter of tobacco farmer, sang in church as a child. Trained as teacher, taught high school in Covina, Cal.; sang in clubs in L.A. and met record prod. Stan Silver, who guided her career; they married '69 and she recorded for Ramco in Phoenix, Challenge in Hollywood. Signed to Dot '72 and with a song she wrote 'Happiest Girl In The Whole USA' was no. 1 in country chart, won a Grammy for Song of the Year, CMA Single of the Year, ACM Song, Album, Female Vocalist of the Year. Further hits incl. 'Funny Face' '72, 'Superman', 'You Were Always There' and 'Little Girl Gone' '73, 'You Can't Be A Beacon (If Your Light Don't Shine)' '74, 'It Do Feel Good' '75, 'Don't Be Angry' '76. Changed labels to Warner and had hits 'That Was Yesterday' '77, 'Do I Love You (Yes In Every Way)' '78, 'Somebody Special' '79. Stricken with

multiple sclerosis '79, but has fought against it and carried on; recent hits incl. 'Walk On By' '80, 'Lonestar Cowboy' '81, 'It's Hard To Be The Dreamer' '82 (on RCA), 'The Sign Of The Times' '83 (Cleveland International). LPs incl. *Happiest Girl In The Whole USA* '72, *My Second Album* '73, *All About A Feeling* '74, *Miss Donna Fargo* '75, *Whatever I Say Means I Love You* '76, all on Dot; *Country Sounds Of* on Music For Pleasure; *On The Move* '77, *Dark Eyed Lady* '78, *Just For You* '79, *Fargo* '81, all on Warners; *Brotherly Love* '81 on MCA Songbird.

FARINA, Richard (*b* '36, NYC; *d* 30 Apr. '66, Carmel, Cal.) Singer/songwriter, multi-instrumentalist,novelist. Born of Irish/Cuban parents, he ran guns to the IRA mid-'50s, when it looked like romantic rebel movement. His meeting with Mimi (Joan BAEZ's younger sister) was crucial: marriage drew him close to burgeoning folk revival. Their travels through Europe in the late '50s – early '60s were compared to Hemingway's a generation before; he recorded in London '63 with Ric Von Schmidt (and Bob DYLAN under alias 'Blind Boy Grunt'). Own songwriting came rapidly with Mimi as muse, incl. 'Pack Up Your Sorrows', 'Reno, Nevada', 'The Quiet Joys Of Brotherhood'. He played guitar, dulcimer, zither; they all but stole show at crucial '65 Newport Folk Festival, made LPs *Richard & Mimi Farina, Celebrations For A Gray Day, Reflections In A Crystal Wind*, all c.'65. His songs were covered by FAIRPORT CONVENTION, Sandy DENNY, Ian MATTHEWS, etc. Friend of enigmatic novelist Thomas Pynchon, who dedicated a novel to him; his song 'V' took title from Pynchon novel; after many re-writes his own *Been Down So Long, It Looks Like Up To Me* was published '66; he died in motorcycle crash on eve of publication party: friends and fans thought that his contribution had only just begun. *Memories* '68 and *The Best Of Mimi & Richard Farina* '71 were good collections. Mimi's *Solo* '86 on Philo also on CD on Rounder.

FARLOW, Tal (*b* Talmadge Holt Farlow, 7 June '21, Greensboro, S.C.) Modern jazz guitarist began playing '43 inspired by Charlie CHRISTIAN. Played with Marjorie

Hyams (ex-Woody HERMAN) '48, Red NORVO, Artie SHAW; mostly semi-retired from mid-'50s, teaching, playing for pleasure: more active recently, making fans happy. Made own shorter fingerboard for looser tuning, softer sound; also dividing device that allowed extra line while playing single notes; published instruction book *Tal Farlow Method*. Own LPs incl. *Autumn In New York* '54 and 2-disc compilation *Poppin' & Burnin'* '55-8 on Verve; *First Set, Second Set* '56 on Xanadu with Eddie Costa (piano, vibes; *b* 14 Aug. '30, Atlas, Pa.; *d* 28 July '62, NYC in car crash); made *Up Up And Away* with Sonny CRISS on Prestige '67; a 2-disc Prestige compilation called *Guitar Player*. *Trilogy* '76 is on Inner City and CBS/Sony in Japan; on Concord Jazz: *On Stage* '76 with Norvo, Hank JONES, Ray BROWN, Jake Hanna on drums; *A Sign Of The Times* '76 with Jones and Brown; further trio sets *Tal Farlow 78*, *Chromatic Palette* '81, quartet *Cookin' On All Burners* '82, *The Legendary Tal Farlow* '84. Toured UK May '85.

FARLOWE, Chris (*b* John Henry Deighton, 13 Oct. '40, Essex) UK singer-guitarist. With John Henry Skiffle Group, winners of all-England skiffle championship '57. Led semi-pro Thunderbirds beat group early '60s; records on Decca, Columbia incl. 'The Blue Beat' as the Beazers '64 (early reggae effort) but no commercial success. Solo 'Stormy Monday' on Sue label left deliberate impression that it was by an obscure American soul singer. Peaked on Andrew Loog Oldham's Immediate label: six UK chart hits '66-7 incl. no. 1 with cover of ROLLING STONES song prod. by Mick Jagger, 'Out Of Time' '66; LP *14 Things To Think About* (EMI/Columbia cashed in with compilation *Chris Farlowe And The Thunderbirds* incl. 'Stormy Monday'), further LPs *The Art Of Chris Farlowe*, *Farlowe In The Midnight Hour*, *Chris Farlowe Hits*, *The Last Goodbye*. Still sang well and grittily, but club scene that fostered Thunderbirds had gone by late '60s; he spent more time at his WWII memorabilia stall: LP *From Here To Mama Rosa* '70 leading band The Hill; sang with jazz-rock COLOSSEUM, left '71 to join Atomic Rooster; by '72 was full-time shopkeeper in Islington, North London. 'Out Of Time' reissue charted

again '75; formed new band incl. ex-Thunderbird guitarist Albert Lee for *Chris Farlowe And His Band – Live* on Polydor: didn't sell, left music again. Said in *Melody Maker* interview: 'I was once, may still be a great blues singer. And I could get up with Ray Charles and sing with 'im . . . Wouldn't show meself up neither!' Sang two songs on soundtrack of *Death Wish II* '82; having sold shop, moved to USA, returned to Britain late '83 to spend 30 days in jail, refusing to pay £300 rates on his shop in protest against left-wing policies of the Republic of Islington (as the borough in London has been called). New LP '85-6 with Thunderbirds.

FARMER, Art (*b* Arthur Stewart Farmer, 21 Aug. '28, Council Bluffs, Iowa) Trumpet, flugelhorn. Grew up in Southwest; to L.A. '45 with twin brother Addison Gerald Farmer (bassist; worked in Jazztet, then with Mose ALLISON; *d* 20 Feb. '63, NYC). Art played in Lionel HAMPTON band '52-3, settled in NYC; own quartet with Gigi GRYCE '54-6, with Horace SILVER, then Gerry MULLIGAN (incl. films *I Want To Live* '58, *The Subterraneans* '60); Jazztet with Benny GOLSON '59-62 (4 LPs on Argo '60-1, 1 on Mercury '62); quartet with Jim HALL '63-4 (*Interaction* and *Live At The Half Note* on Atlantic '63), then Steve Kuhn on piano (*Sing To Me Softly Of The Blues* on Atlantic '65). Worked in Europe, settled in Vienna '68 with frequent visits to USA. Has played mostly warmer-toned flugelhorn since mid-'60s on records. First recorded on West Coast '49; popular sideman on many LPs e.g. with Silver on Blue Note. Very prolific as leader: nearly 60 LPs beginning '53 with Quincy JONES (piano and arr.), then seven on Prestige through '56, with Gryce, Addison, Kenny CLARKE, Art TAYLOR, Sonny ROLLINS, other stars in various small groups. On ABC with Jones '57; quartet *Portrait Of Art Farmer* on Contemporary '58; quintet *Modern Art* '58, *Brass Shout* tentet and *Aztec Suite* big band '59, all on UA; quartets *Art* '60 and *Perception* '61 on Argo; big band on Mercury '62 with Oliver NELSON; *Baroque Sketches* arr. by Golson '66, *The Time And The Place* '67 live at NYC Museum of Modern Art, quintet *Plays Great Jazz Hits* '67 all on Columbia. LPs made in Rome, Vienna, Heidelberg etc. on Campi, MPS, Mainstream, Sonet, Pye; septet *Homecoming* '71 on Mainstream; quartet with Cedar WALTON, Sam JONES, Billy HIGGINS: *To Duke With Love, The Summer Knows* and live *At Boomers* (with Clifford JORDAN added) '75-6 all on Inner City; *On The Road* '77 on Contemporary has quintet with Art PEPPER; 5 LPs on CTI '77-9, others on Soul Note, Concord Jazz '80-2; LPs '83 with big band in NYC and string orchestra in Tokyo on Japanese labels. Like *Mirage* '82, *You Make Me Smile* on Soul Note '85 has quintet with Clifford Jordan; *Something To Live For* '87 on Contemporary features the music of Billy STRAYHORN.

FARNON, Robert (*b* 24 July '17, Toronto, Ontario) Composer, arranger, conductor; the most influential arranger of non-classical music, or what is called 'light music' in UK, since WWII. From musical family; played drums, then cornet, trumpet. Studied music with Louis Waizman (*b* Ludwig Waizmann, 6 Nov. 1863, Salzburg, allegedly in the same house where Mozart was born; *d* 24 Aug. '51, Toronto), composer who was staff arranger at CBC; another pupil was Percy FAITH, for whom Farnon played trumpet in CBC *Music By Faith* series (also wrote arr. for vocal group). Dizzy GILLESPIE said that Farnon was the best trumpet player in Toronto: 'He knew chords and played notes you just didn't hear other trumpet players play.' Sat in at Minton's, Eddie CONDON's in NYC; played in *The Happy Gang* on radio (records on RCA); had own CBC show plus work on commercial stations. First symphony '41 was played in Toronto, Philadelphia, New York; second '42 on CBC. Joined Canadian army '43; led Canadian Band of Allied Expeditionary Force (AEF): George MELACHRINO led UK band, Glenn MILLER the USA one; some thought Farnon's was best (though the best Canadian players in touring units) because of his writing (Farnon himself says Miller's was best). He listened to shortwave radio from America, copied songs off the air harmony and all, so that his band had the new songs before anybody else. Wrote film music in UK (settled in Guernsey '59): about 30 soundtracks incl. *Captain Horatio Hornblower* '51, *Where's Charley?* '52, *Gentlemen Marry Brunettes*

'55, Cliff RICHARD film *Expresso Bongo* '59, last CROSBY-Hope film *Road To Hong Kong* '62; also TV mini-series *A Man Called Intrepid* '80, etc. Wrote for UK bands GERALDO, Ted HEATH, AMBROSE; signed with Decca '46, arr./cond. for Gracie FIELDS, Anne SHELTON, Vera LYNN; also accompanied Frank SINATRA: rare *Great Songs From Great Britain* '62 on Reprise; Sarah VAUGHAN: *Vaughan With Voices* '63, aka *Blue Orchids*, made in Copenhagen; Tony BENNETT: *Snowfall – The Tony Bennett Christmas Album* '68, *Get Happy* '71 with L.P.O. in London's Royal Albert Hall, *With Love* and *The Good Things In Life* '72 (all charted in USA, the first three on CBS, last on MGM-Verve); Bennett said, 'I was the first singer . . . to have not just arrangements behind me but real orchestrated music'. Also with vocal group The Singers Unlimited (*see* The HI-LOS), *Lena – A New Album* '76 with Lena HORNE on RCA, *On Target* '82 with George SHEARING on MPS/Pausa; *Love Is . . .* '84 with tenor José Carreras '83 on Philips; with Pia Zadora: *Pia And Phil* '85 ('Phil' is London Philharmonic; the LP made Billboard pop chart early '86), *I Am What I Am* '86 on CBS, another planned (Zadora, *b* '56, got over terrible notices as an actress to get rave reviews as a singer, e.g. from Leonard FEATHER). Plus single '72 with underrated pop singer Tommy Leonetti (*d* 15 Sep. '79; biggest hit was 'Free' '56, top 30 USA on Capitol), albums with Tony COE, UK singer Ray Ellington, many more. He would have made LPs with Peterson and Gillespie in Berlin '62, but musicians' unions prevented it. Compositions incl. suites for Shearing, Oscar PETERSON; *Saxophone Triparti* '71 for three saxes and orchestra; arr. folk song 'Blow The Wind Southerly' for Gillespie and the American Wind Ensemble '78, *Canadian Impressions* (10-part suite, recorded '55), many more; short pieces incl. 'Jumping Bean'/'Portrait Of A Flirt' (his first 78 '48, the last later used as part of Peterson's suite), 'How Beautiful Is Night', 'Manhattan Playboy', 'Malaga', 'Melody Fair', 'Lazy Day', 'Country Girl' (based on Wordsworth poem 'The Solitary Reaper'; recorded by Bennett), many more. André PREVIN described Farnon to Johnny MERCER as 'the greatest arranger in the world'; arrangers admitting to his influence incl. Nelson RID-

DLE, Quincy JONES, Roger KELLAWAY, Neal HEFTI, Henry MANCINI, Johnny Mandel, John Williams, Pat Williams; Marion Evans (wrote for Bennett, Steve LAWRENCE, others) taught J. J. JOHNSON, Torrie Zito (also Bennett arranger), others; required them to study Farnon's series of LPs on Decca (London USA), now all out of print, incl. *Flirtation Walk* '54, *Two Cigarettes In The Dark* '55, *Something To Remember You By* '55 (music of Arthur Schwartz), *Together* '57 (music of DE SYLVA, BROWN & HENDERSON: USA title *Sunny Side Up*), *From The Highlands* '57, *From The Emerald Isle* '59, *Gateway To The West* '59 (American themes), *Symphonic Suite: Porgy And Bess* '66 (reissued by mail-order Musical Heritage Society in USA '84); compilations, reissues of 78s etc. on Decca's USA Richmond budget label incl. *Stardust* ('50-5 tracks), *Cocktails For Two* ('54), *By A Waterfall* ('54). *Hornblower* concert suite, *Rhapsody For Violin And Orchestra* recorded '59, on Delyse UK, Citadel USA; *The Music of Robert Farnon* '60 incl. 'Rhapsody', *Prelude And Dance For Harmonica And Orchestra* (with Tommy Reilly), other short pieces on Baby Grand in USA. Later instrumental LPs on Philips incl. *Sensuous Strings Of Robert Farnon* '62, *Conducts My Fair Lady And Other Musical Bouquets* '65, *A Portrait Of Johnny Mathis* and *Plays The Hits Of Sinatra* '65; also *Showcase For Soloists* '73 on Invicta, *In A Dream World* '74 on Rediffusion. Farnon reissues on CD have begun: Pye LPs from '74-6 now on PRT are *Sketches Of Tony Bennett And Frank Sinatra* '76 (incl. 'Country Girl'), *Robert Farnon And The London Philharmonic Orchestra At Royal Festival Hall* '74 ('My Fair Lady' medley, 'Porgy & Bess' suite, 'Farnon Fantasy' on his own tunes, plus 'Laura' and his own 'Colditz March', TV theme that won an Ivor Novello award). Current projects incl. arrangements for Marian MCPARTLAND and for George BENSON, instrumental *At The Movies With Robert Farnon* '86 on Horatio Nelson label (formed by his manager, producer Derek Boulton). He recorded many items for Chappell Music for use as background, theme music etc., some of these now compiled on UK Glasmere label; with incidental music for TV plays etc. the discography prepared by the Robert Farnon Appreciation Society

(formed '56 in UK) fills 86 A4 pages. Brother Dennis Farnon played trumpet and trombone at Chicago's Club DeLisa with Red Saunders band '49, wrote arr. for first Maynard FERGUSON band, TV/film music incl. Mr Magoo cartoons, serious works under the name Paul Gerard incl. a violin sonata; brother Brian was mus. dir. for Nat COLE, leads orchestra in Lake Tahoe, Nevada.

FEATHER, Leonard (*b* 13 Sep. '14, London) Composer, pianist, journalist, lecturer. Became jazz critic and concert promoter in England '30s; to NYC '39, to L.A. '60. An indefatigable spark-plug on behalf of jazz, he was instrumental in establishing *Esquire* magazine's annual awards '43 (the first to be made by critics); all-star poll-winners' recording date on Commodore late '43, concert early '44 (recorded on V-discs, later issued in Japan commercially) and *Esquire Jazz Book*; it all ended '47 when the book was co-opted by 'moldy figs' on behalf of (white) trad. jazz as opposed to the more important musicians of the day, who were mostly black. In the era's vicious war of words between modernists/traditionalists which seems quaint now, Feather did not coin the term 'moldy figs', but he later was the first to use 'Crow Jim' to describe discrimination in reverse among the black jazz fraternity. Prod. countless recording sessions, incl. MGM 10" LPs called *Hot vs. Cool*, *Dixieland vs. Birdland*, *Cats vs. Chicks*, commercially unsuccessful ideas but demonstrating that he had no axe to grind, wanting only to make good music. Especially active on behalf of women: first to record Una Mae CARLISLE '38, Hazel SCOTT '39; in mid-'40s Charlie CHRISTIAN-inspired guitarist Mary Osborne, all-girl dates led by Mary Lou WILLIAMS, pianist Beryl Brooker, bassist/vocalist Vivien Garry, INTERNATIONAL SWEETHEARTS OF RHYTHM; in mid-'50s German pianist Jutta Hipp. First to record Dinah WASHINGTON as solo artist '43; wrote 'Evil Gal Blues' and 'Salty Papa' for her (she continued to sing them the rest of her career); many other successful songs incl. 'Mighty Like The Blues' '38 (used by Woody HERMAN), 'Unlucky Woman' (aka 'Unlucky Blues') '44, sung by Helen Humes, Lena HORNE; his 'Baby Get Lost' was no. 1 R&B hit for Washington '49, also recorded by Billie HOLIDAY. As a writer he originated the famous 'blindfold test' in *Downbeat*, in which musicians pass judgement on records with no information about them; won Grammy '64 for album booklet in 3-disc CBS set *The Ellington Era*; his millions of words over 50 years incl. yearbooks of jazz which became unique *Encyclopedia Of Jazz* '60, then *Encyclopedia Of Jazz In The Sixties* '66, *Seventies* '76; it is hoped there will be another volume. Weekly column in *L.A. Times* syndicated to 350 papers. Almost continuously a broadcaster, beginning with *Platterbrains* radio show in NYC; *Leonard Feather Show* on KUSC L.A. won an award '78. Other books incl. *From Satchmo To Miles*, essays on jazz giants; memoir *The Jazz Years: Earwitness To An Era* '86.

FEATHERS, Charlie (*b* 12 June '32, Holly Springs, Miss.) Singer, guitarist, songwriter; legendary rockabilly who never made big time. Raised on farm, learned guitar from black sharecropper Junior Kimball, left home at 17 to work in oil fields with his father, playing in Texas clubs at night. To Memphis at 18; he hung around at Sun Records and claimed to have had a hand in arr. of 'Blue Moon Of Kentucky' (Elvis PRESLEY's first release). Own first record was on Flip '55; first Sun single 'Defrost Your Heart' same year. Recorded for Meteor, King, Kay, Walmay, Philips International '56-9, in country and rockabilly styles; gained legendary status but few sales. Carried on through '60s; LP for Barrelhouse '68; single 'That Certain Smile'/'She Set Me Free' on Rollin' Rock re-established legend and gained him date at London's Rainbow Theatre '77: event recorded by EMI's Harvest label. Formed own Feathers label, released *Charlie Feathers Vol. 1* and *Vol. 2*. Compilation of older material on Charly UK: *Rockabilly's Main Man*.

FELDMAN, Vic (*b* Victor Stanley Feldman, 7 Apr. '34, London; *d* 12 May '87, L.A.) Drums, piano, vibes. Self-taught prodigy, played with Glenn MILLER band at 10. To USA '55; played with Woody HERMAN, Lighthouse All Stars, Cannonball ADDERLEY '60-1, with Peggy LEE '61; with Benny GOODMAN to USSR '62; with June CHRISTY '65; gigged and recorded with

Miles DAVIS '63 in L.A.; wrote 'Seven Steps To Heaven', title track of Davis LP, and was offered a permanent job by Davis, but it went to Herbie HANCOCK because Feldman didn't want to leave his wife (Marylin, *d* '84). He was more and more successful in lucrative studio work: albums with STEELY DAN '75-80, many others. Records in UK '48-57 on Esquire, Tempo, with John DANKWORTH, Stan TRACEY, drummers Phil Seamen (*b* 28 Aug. '26, Staffordshire), Tony Crombie (*b* 27 Aug. '25, London), etc.; larger groups '55-7 with Ronnie SCOTT, Tubby HAYES, others. First USA recording by a quartet on Keynote '56, not issued; then sextet *Mallets A Fore Thought* '57 on Mode, trio *The Arrival Of Victor Feldman* '58, tentet *Latinville* '59 on Contemporary; nine more albums '60-73 on Riverside, World Pacific, etc.; trio sets *The Artful Dodger* '77 on Concord Jazz, *To Chopin With Love* '83 on Palo Alto.

FELICIANO, Cheo (*b* José Feliciano, Ponce, Puerto Rico) Baritone singer. Began as percussionist; moved to NYC, worked as valet for Tito PUENTE, Tito RODRIGUEZ; began singing professionally '57; MACHITO and Rodriguez recommended him to Joe CUBA, sang with his sextet until '67, hits incl. 'El Pito (I'll Never Go Back To Georgia)' and his own 'El Raton'. Idolised by Latin fans for sweet resonant style and romantic stage persona: went solo, appeared with Tico All Stars on *Descargas At The Village Gate* '66 (3 live discs), *The Alegre All Stars Vol. 3 'Lost And Found'*, *CESTA All Stars Live Jam Session* (all precursors of FANIA ALL STARS); sang boogaloo 'Ay Que Rico' and 'Busca lo Tuyo' on *Champagne* c. '68 by Eddie PALMIERI; also appeared on Orlando Marin's *Que Chevere Vol. II* on Alegre. *Cheo* '71 was first collaboration with talented black Puerto Rican composer Catalino 'Tite' Curet Alonso, who co-prod., wrote most of it: LP incl. hits 'Anacaona', 'Mi Triste Problema', 'Franqueza Cruel', Cheo's own 'Si Por Mi Llueve'. *La Voz Sensual de Cheo* '72 was lushly orchestrated, indulging his fondness for boleros. He appeared on classic FAS albums of the '70s incl. *Live At The Cheetah Vol. I* '71, 2-disc soundtrack *Our Latin Thing (Nuestra Cosa)* '72, *Latin-Soul-Rock* '74 (incl. new version of 'El Raton'), 2-disc *Salsa* (soundtrack of concert film '76), *Tribute To Tito Rodriguez* '76, *Fania All Stars Live* '78 (incl. Cheo on 'Felicitaciones'), *Latin Connection* '81 ('Nina'). Alonso contributed songs to all Cheo's LPs '73-82; *With A Little Help From My Friend* '73 (friend being Alonso) incl. 'Nabori', 'Salome', 'Hace Furo'. He played El Padrino (the Godfather) in *Hommy* at Carnegie Hall (Larry HARLOW's Latin version of 'Tommy'; album '73). Appeared on '73 debut LP by Puerto Rican band *Impacto Crea*, developed out of drug rehabilitation project; sang title track on same band's next LP *Cobarde* '74. LPs in '70s incl. *Felicidades* '73 (Xmas LP), *Buscando Amor* '74 (another bolero collection), *The Singer* '76 (with two songs by Rubén Blades). First self-prod. was *Mi Tierra y Yo* '77; from *Estampas* '79, *Sentimiento, tu . . .* '80 his LPs were made in Puerto Rico, where he now lived, as did Palmieri (whose eponymous LP '81 made in NYC featured three songs by Cheo). *Profundo* '82 had three songs by Alonso; *Cheo's Rainbow* '76 and *La Vida de Cheo Feliciano* '84 were compilations; he formed his own Coche label '84 in P.R., launched with live 25th anniversary set *25 Años de Sentimiento (En Vivo)*, mainly a greatest hits collection. *Regresa el Amor* '86 was another bolero collection; *Sabor y Sentimiento* '87 on Coche was full-blown salsa collection with two Alonso songs, co-prod. by Cheo and arr./mus. dir. Louis García, followed late '87 by *Te Regalo Mi Sabor Criollo*.

FELICIANO, José (*b* 10 Sep. '45, Lares, Puerto Rico) Singer, songwriter, guitarist. Born blind, second of 12 children; grew up in NYC's Spanish Harlem. Played accordion and guitar, dropped out of high school, played clubs in Greenwich Village 'not for coins but just for the hell of it'. First LP *The Voice And Guitar Of José Feliciano* the next year on RCA gained huge following in Central and South America; breakthrough in USA with *Feliciano!* '68, incl. single 'Light My Fire', cover of DOORS hit combining soul, Latin, folk-rock, made no. 4 in pop chart, won two Grammies incl. Best New Artist. Subsequent USA chart entries minor ('Hi-Heel Sneakers', controversial version of 'Star-Spangled Banner', both '68) but sell-out tours through '70s, more than 30 gold records in various countries. Emmy

nomination for TV theme *Chico And The Man* '74; acted in episodes of *McMillan And His Wife* '75, *Kung Fu*, *Lucas Tanner* as well as *Chico*. Sessioned with John LENNON mid-'70s, same day on Joni MITCHELL date which incl. hit 'Free Man In Paris'. Switched from RCA to ill-fated Private Stock label '76; with his wife Janna Merlyn Feliciano wrote score for film *Aaron Loves Angela* that year. After LP *Sweet Soul Music* '76, faded from record scene until comeback *José Feliciano* on Motown '80. Other RCA LPs incl. *A Bag Full Of Soul* '65; *Alive Alive-O* '69 (made at London Palladium concert); *Fireworks* '70 (incl. guitar arr. from Handel's *Royal Fireworks Music* alongside cover of ROLLING STONES' 'Satisfaction'); *That The Spirit Needs* '71; *Compartments* '74; *Just Wanna Rock'n'Roll* '75. Best-of compilation *Portrait* '85 promoted on UK TV. Other LPs on RCA International: *Como Tu Quieras*, *Grandes Exitos*, *Ya Soy Tuyo*.

FELLER, Dick (*b* 2 Jan. '43, Bronaugh, Mo.) Nashville-based songwriter, singer. Began performing with bands, writing songs late '50s; to Nashville '66, wrote songs without much success; worked in touring bands of Skeeter DAVIS, Warner MACK, Mel TILLIS, Stu Phillips. Johnny CASH gave him writer's contract, recorded 'Any Old Wind That Blows' (no. 1 country '72), others. Signed to United Artists, had own hits 'Biff, The Friendly Purple Bear' '73, 'Making The Best Of A Bad Situation' and 'The Credit Card Song' '74, 'Uncle Hiram And The Homemade Beer' '75 (on Asylum). Jerry REED got a no. 1 with Feller's 'Lord Mr Ford' '73, later signed him to writer's contract; Reed had hits with 'East Bound And Down', 'High Rollin' ', 'I'm Just A Redneck In A Rock And Roll Bar', 'I Love You (What Can I Say)', all Feller songs. Thanks to regular tours Feller is popular in Europe. Own LPs incl. *Wrote* '73 on UA, *No Word On Me* '75 and *Some Days Are Diamonds* '76 on Asylum, *Audiograph Live* '83 on Audiograph.

FELTS, Narvel (*b* 11 Jan. '38, Mo.; aka Narvel the Marvel) Singer; rock'n'roll, then country with unique dramatic falsetto vocal style. Had own Saturday morning radio show in Bernie, Mo. early '50s; later in bands with Harold Jenkins (who later became Conway TWITTY), Charlie RICH. Rock'n'roll hit with 'Honey Love' '59 on Pink label; made top 100 pop but banned owing to risqué lyrics. Recorded for small labels; to Nashville '72, signed to Cinnamon label, had country hits 'Drift Away' '73, 'When Your Good Love Was Mine' '74; signed to Dot when Cinnamon folded; biggest hit 'Reconsider Baby' '75, no. 1 both pop and country. Carried on with 'Somebody Hold Me' '75, 'Lonely Teardrops' and 'My Prayer' '76, 'The Feeling's Right' '77, 'One Run For The Roses' '78, 'Everlasting Love' '79. Records on small labels College '79, GMC '81, Lobo '82, Compleat '82-3, then Evergreen. LPs incl. *Drift Away* '74 on Cinnamon; *Reconsider Me* and *Greatest Hits* '75, *A Touch Of Felts* '77, *Inside Love* '78, all on ABC-Dot. He came back with country hits each year '83-7 on Evergreen

FENDER, Freddy (*b* Baldemar G. Huerta, 4 June '37, San Benito, Texas) Tex-Mex, country, rockabilly singer. From family of migrant workers; joined US Marines '53, began playing Texas honky tonks '56-9. Made records for many small labels with songs in Spanish and rockabilly titles popular in South incl. 'Wasted Days And Wasted Nights' and 'Crazy, Crazy Baby'. Arrested Baton Rouge, La. on drug charges, three years in Angola State Prison '60-3. Worked clubs in New Orleans '63-8, signed with Huey Meau's Cajun label without much success. Finally an update of 'Before The Next Teardrop Falls' performed partly in English and Spanish led to big pop and country hit '75: picked up by ABC-Dot, CMA Single of the Year, he was ACM Top New Male Vocalist. Further pop-country success with 'Wasted Days And Wasted Nights' and 'Secret Love' '75, 'You'll Lose A Good Thing' '76, 'Vaya Con Dios' '76; country hits with 'The Rains Came' '77, 'Talk To Me' '78, 'Walking Piece Of Heaven' '79. Joined Starflite label '79, then Warners '82, but unable to regain chart success. LPs incl. *Before The Next Teardrop Falls* '75, *Are You Ready For Freddie* and *Rockin' Country* '76, *Best Of* and *If You're Ever In Texas* '77, *Swamp Gold* '78, all on ABC-Dot; *The Texas Balladeer* '79 on Starflite. *El Major de Freddy Fender* '86 on MCA (from Dot).

FENDERMEN, The Jim Sundquist (*b* '37, Niagara, Wis.) and Phil Humphrey (*b* '37, Madison, Wis.) both played Fender guitars, each had own bands which they combined for 'Muleskinner Blues', first recorded '30 by its composer Jimmie RODGERS. Single made top 5 '60: raucous version of the 'blue yodel' was their only hit, but a good example of garage band music, a pre-echo of punk rock.

FERGUSON, Bob (*b* 30 Dec. '27, Willow Springs, Mo.) Country music producer, songwriter, performer. Worked as talent manager before becoming performer as Eli Possomtrot; led KWSC Ramblers '48-53; became film maker specialising in wildlife features such as *The Good Old Days* and *Tennessee Game And Fish* '59, won awards for best conservation TV series '58-9. Recorded for Sims label '61-2; best-known songs 'Eli's Blue' and 'My Past Is My Future'. Wrote 'Wings Of A Dove' (no. 1 for Ferlin HUSKY '60), 'Natividad' (George HAMILTON IV), 'Taos, New Mexico' (Waylon JENNINGS), 'Carroll County Accident' (Porter WAGONER); prod. for Dolly PARTON, Willie NELSON, Wagoner, Hamilton, many others '65-75. With Jesse Burt co-authored *So You Want To Be In Music*; retired from music, became preacher.

FERGUSON, Maynard (*b* 4 May '28, Montreal, Canada) Trumpet, other horns; leader. With Boyd RAEBURN '48 on reeds, then high-note specialist on trumpet with Stan KENTON '50-3; freelanced, formed own big band '57-65, alternately leading sextet towards end of that period. Don ELLIS, Jaki BYARD, others passed through; LPs on EmArcy, Roulette; he was respected by other musicians for technique, versatility (doubled on valve trombone, other horns); band was more popular with public than critics: it was well-recorded and any sort of big band was rare enough. Formed bigger band in England (LP *M.F. Horn* on Columbia '71, several more), toured Europe, USA; band shrank to 13 pieces again; more recently plays arr. of pop/rock, loud as ever. Columbia LPs in USA pop chart: *M.F. Horn/3* '73, *Primal Scream* '76, *Conquistador* (biggest hit at no. 22) and *New Vintage* '77, *Carnival* '78, *Hot* '79, *It's My Time* '80, *Hollywood* '82; *High Voltage* '87 on Intima has seven-piece electric combo described as 'MOR-ish' in *Downbeat*. 2-disc *The Birdland Dreamband* '88 on RCA/Bluebird reissues, five '56 tracks with all-star casts.

FERRANTE & TEICHER (*b* Arthur Ferrante, 7 Sep. '21, NYC; Louis Teicher, 24 Aug. '24, Wilkes-Barre, Pa.) Duo-pianists. Met while studying at Juilliard; majored in piano, took up teaching and performing, began as duo '47. Toured USA and Canada with leading orchestras playing RODGERS, KERN, GERSHWIN, etc. Modified pianos to produce effects such as gongs, drums, etc. Recorded duo-piano arr. of classics etc.; then signed with United Artists '60, added orchestral accompaniment for the first time on records and immediately had top 10 gold discs 'Theme From The Apartment' and 'Exodus' '60. 11 Hot 100 entries altogether '60-70 incl. 6 more film songs: 'Tonight' '61 (from *West Side Story*) and 'Midnight Cowboy' '69 were top 10. Last hit was arr. of Bob DYLAN's 'Lay Lady Lay': no. 99. 30 LPs charted in Billboard '61-72.

FIELDS, Gracie (*b* Grace Stansfield, 9 Jan. 1898, Rochdale, England; *d* 27 Sep. '79, Capri) UK singer, comedienne. Won singing contest age 7; pro debut at 12. Toured in revues; played Sally Perkins in West End hit *Mr Tower Of London* '18, ran for 7 years. First records '28; first of 15 films *Sally In Our Alley* '31 incl. 'Sally', most famous song. Said to be world's highest-paid entertainer '39 when she had surgery for cancer. Beloved by 'ordinary people' in dark pre-war days of Depression for broad Lancashire accent, quick informal humour; then married Italian comedian/film dir. Monty Banks '40 in USA; on return to UK he was threatened with wartime internment; they went to USA, taking money with them; UK public seemed to turn against her. Own USA radio shows '42-4; forgiven '46 by London Palladium audience; big hit '48 with 'Now Is The Hour' (no. 4 USA); USA radio show again early '50s; hit with film title song 'Around The World' '57, also 'Little Donkey' '59. Spent most of the rest of her life in semi-retirement in Capri; last London stage appearance at her 10th Royal Command Performance '78. Remembered for comedy specialities 'Walter, Walter', 'I Took My Harp To A Party', 'The Biggest

Aspidistra In The World'; inspirational 'Sing As We Go', 'Wish Me Luck'; sacred 'Ave Maria'. Compilations incl. *The Amazing Gracie Fields* on Monmouth (USA); in UK *Best Of BBC Broadcasts*, *Focus On Gracie Fields* and *Life Is A Song* on Decca; 2-disc *The Gracie Fields Story* on EMI.

FIFTH DIMENSION USA pop/soul vocal act first called the Versatiles, then Hi-Fis, new name '67. Lineup: Marilyn McCoo (*b* 30 Sep. '43, Jersey City), Florence LaRue (*b* 4 Feb. '44, Pa.), LaMont McLemore (*b* 17 Sep. '40), Ron Townson (*b* 20 Jan. '41), Billy Davis (*b* 26 Jun. '40); last 3 from St Louis. Earlier group incl. Floyd Butler and Harry Elston, later of Friends of Distinction. New group signed to Johnny RIVERS' Soul City label by manager Mark Gordon (who later married new recruit LaRue). Had no. 16 hit with cover of MAMAS & PAPAS' 'Go Where You Wanna Go', found stride with songs mostly written by Jim WEBB, prod. by Bones Howe: 'Up Up And Away' was no. 7, got four Grammies, became cabaret standard; LP with that title was no. 8 (McCoo and Davis married '69 in hot air balloon). *The Magic Garden* '68 didn't do as well, but *Stoned Soul Picnic* same year (no. 21 LP) still regarded as classic for exciting, original vocal arrangements: Laura NYRO title song was no.3 hit; 'Sweet Blindness' no. 15. Biggest triumph was *Hair* medley: 'Aquarius/Let The Sunshine In' from no. 2 LP *The Age Of Aquarius* was no. 1 USA/11 UK '69; LP incl. Nyro's 'Wedding Bell Blues' (no. 1 USA/16 UK in year of two marriages in group). Hits continued through '73; with group moving towards MOR biggest hits were 'One Less Bell To Answer' (no. 2 '70; no. 20 LP *Portrait*); '(Last Night) I Didn't Get To Sleep At All' (no. 8 '72, no. 58 LP *Individually & Collectively* also incl. no. 10 hit 'If I Could Reach You'). *Greatest Hits* '70 was no. 5, last big hit LP. Act became slick, lost soulful edge: appearance at Nixon's White House destroyed remaining credibility with black audience. Early exuberance not recaptured in reunion with Webb for *Earthbound* '75 on ABC (no. 136 LP); by then McCoo and Davis had left for own hits 'You Don't Have To Be A Star (To Be In My Show)' (saccharine no. 1 '76), 'Your Love' (no. 15 '77); later divorced. Other LPs incl. *The*

July 5th Album '70, *Love's Lines, Angles And Rhymes, Live!!* 2-disc set and *Reflections*, all '71, *Greatest Hits On Earth* '72 (compilation from both Soul City, Bell labels), *Living Together, Growing Together* '73.

FIOL, Henry (*b* 16 Jan. '47, NYC) Singer, composer, arranger, bandleader, producer, label boss; also painter. Father *b* Puerto Rico, mother Italian-American; converted to salsa instead of rock'n'roll c. age 13 after hearing Rafael CORTIJO y su Combo with singer Ismael Rivera on Puerto Rican visit. He says his conservatory was the street: played congas and sang in *rumbones* (social gatherings around rumba percussion and vocal jam sessions). Played and sang in chorus of various Latin bands '69-74, then formed NYC band Saoco: most members of Puerto Rican descent, played *tipico* (typical) Cuban music in progressive style with urban infl. but earthy feel, with CONJUNTO lineup of two trumpets, tres, piano, conga, bongo, timbales, maracas, güiro, bass, lead vocal and chorus; Fiol co-prod. and co-led with William Millan (tres, bass, mus. dir., co-arr.); first LP was *Siempre Seré Guajiro* '76 on Salsoul, incl. five Fiol songs in his effortless, hypnotic baritone (he gives legendary Cuban singer Abelardo Barroso as a major influence). On *Macho Mumba* '77 he shared lead vocals with Rafy Puente, though Puente was not credited on label or sleeve. Fiol left; band renamed William Millan y su Saoco Original had lead vocals by Ray Ramos and Luis Ayala on *Curare* '78; Fiol's first solo LP *fe, esperanza y caridad* (Faith, Hope and Charity) '80 was prod. by Roberto TORRES on his SAR label, with impressive band incl. Cubans Alfredo Valdés Jr on piano and Alfredo 'Chocolate' Armenteros on trumpet, plus Puerto Rican tres player Charlie Rodriguez; Fiol sang lead, Torres played maracas, güiro and clave, and sang in the chorus; bassist/arr. Russell 'Skee' Farnsworth arr. the extended tracks: he'd worked with Ricardo Ray in '60s and arr. Fiol's next LP, *El Secreto* '81, on which Fiol also played quinto (small conga drum), wrote three of six songs incl. standout title track. He sang Beny MORÉ'S classic 'Maracaibo Oriental' on LP SAR *All Stars Recorded Live In Club Ochentas Album 2* '81, lineup incl. violins, trumpets, trombone, tres and flute. First self-produced album *La Ley de la Jungla* (The Law Of The Jungle) '83 used a new front line, infl. by years of listening to jazz, replacing one trumpet with a tenor sax, adding another colour. He'd painted sleeve illustrations for the SAOCO LPs in which he appeared and all his own (also Cachao's *Dos* '77); *Corazón* '83 (first on his own label of that name) had a lugubrious self-portrait with Caribbean background, as well as Skee's bass and arrangements and the return of Ray Santiago (on piano) from Saoco; standout tracks were Fiol's 'La Ultima Rumba' and version of classic 'Caramelo a Kilo'. *Colorao y Negro* '85 had a raw, 'live' sound; *Juega Billar!* '86 continued his confident productions. As with many other artists (Duke ELLINGTON, Tony BENNETT, etc.), his feelings for art and tonal colour go together: he graduated from Hunter College, taught art in Catholic Schools of NY '68-73 and was an adviser to NYC public schools '73-82; similarly, 'I have always been deeply involved in my arrangements. Using my voice or one finger on the piano, I give the "arranger" the licks.'

FIREFALL USA country rock band formed '74 by Rick Roberts (*b* '50, Fla.), who had joined Flying Burrito Brothers for third LP '71; after they split that year he made LPs for A&M *Windmills* '72, *She Is A Song* '73 with superstar friends Don Henley, Jackson BROWNE, Joe WALSH, Chris Hillman, etc.; later anthologised in *Best Of*. Left L.A. for Boulder, Col.; formed group with ex-BYRD/Burrito Michael Clarke (first met when Roberts sessioned on Byrds' (*Untitled*) '70). Recruited guitarist Jock Bartley (*b* Kansas), formerly with Gram PARSONS' Fallen Angels, then Tommy Bolin's replacement in Zephyr; Mark Andes (ex-SPIRIT and JO JO GUNNE); Larry Burnette (*b* Washington DC) played guitar, wrote some material. Album *Firefall* '76 had bright harmony very much in West Coast EAGLES/POCO mould; David Muse provided keyboards on this and all other LPs, though not officially a member. First LP incl. 'You Are The Woman', no. 9 single; *Luna Sea* '77 incl. 'Cinderella', 'Just Remember I Love You'; *Elan* '78 'Strange Way'; LPs each sold a million. *Undertow* '80 had hit 'Headed For A Fall'; *Clouds Across The Sun*

'81 incl. 'Staying With It' with vocal by Lisa Nemzo (their last top 40 single at no. 37, also incl. in *Best Of* '81); *Mirror Of The World* '83 was prod. by Ron and Howard Albert. All undemanding stuff, perfect for USA radio; only first LP and *Best Of* still available in '86. Andes went to HEART.

FIREHOUSE FIVE PLUS 2 USA semi-pro dixieland band based in L.A.; 12 12″ LPs on Good Time Jazz label recorded '49-'69 (some material first on 10″ LPs), seven still in print '88. Trombonist Ward Kimball was animator at Disney studios; band wore firemen's outfits and had old-time fire wagon; played at Disneyland. Earliest lineup had Danny Alguire, cornet; Clarke Mallory, clarinet; Frank Thomas, piano; Harper Goff, banjo; Ed Penner, bass and bass sax; Monty Mountjoy, drums. Never worldbeaters, but had a good time. LP *Twenty Years Later* '69 had Kimball, Alguire, Don Kinch, trumpet; K. O. Eckland, piano; Bill Newman, banjo; George Bruns, tuba; Eddie Forrest, drums; George Arthur Probert Jr on soprano sax (*b* 5 Mar. '27, L.A.): played with Bob SCOBEY '52-3, Kid ORY '54; took job at Disney '55, moved to U.P.A. films '59 but played with Kimball and co. '55-71; formed own Once Or Twice Band '73, toured Europe mid-'70s.

FISHER, Eddie (*b* 10 Aug. '28, Philadelphia, Pa.) Singer. Excellent voice, he was especially effective with show tunes; one of the biggest stars of early '50s with 35 top 40 hits '50-6, 19 in top 10; continued hitting Hot 100 until '67. Did local amateur shows, sang on radio in high school, with Buddy MORROW, Charlie VENTURA bands '46; heard by Eddie CANTOR at Grossinger's resort in upstate New York, joined his radio show '49 and was instant hit. Pictures in uniform during military service '52-3 didn't hurt. No. 1 hits incl. 'I'm Walking Behind You', vocal version of international instrumental hit from Germany 'Oh! My Pa-Pa', 'I Need You Now' '53-4; 'Any Time', 'Wish You Were Here', 'Downhearted' also deserved it. 'Heart' from musical *Damn Yankees* was no. 6 '55; junky 'Dungaree Doll' no. 7 '55; other side also charted: 'Everybody's Got A Home But Me' from *Pipe Dream* was no. 20, one of his best. Last big hit: 'Cindy, Oh Cindy' at no. 10 '56, just

beaten with song by Vince Martin and the Tarriers at no. 9. On 'A Man Chases A Girl' (no. 16 '55) Debbie Reynolds sang refrain 'until she catches him' uncredited; they were married, friends with Elizabeth Taylor and her husband, larger-than-life producer Mike Todd; when Todd was killed in air crash Fisher left Reynolds for Taylor, big gossip story of era. He later married Connie Stevens; had no. 45 hit '66 with 'Games That Lovers Play'. Had four 10″ LPs in top 10 album chart '52-4, 12″ *I Love You* '55; other chart LPs incl. live 2-disc *At The Winter Garden* on Ramrod '63, *Eddie Fisher Today* on Dot '65; back with RCA *Games That Lovers Play* '66 charted, *People Like You* '67 just made it, *You Ain't Heard Nothin' Yet* didn't. Other '50s LPs on RCA incl. *May I Sing To You?* (reissue of 10″ LP as 12″ with more songs), *As Long As There's Music* (reissued '87 in UK); also *Young And Foolish* on Dot c.'66.

FITZGERALD, Ella (*b* 25 Apr. '18, Newport News, Va.) Singer. An orphan, lived in NYC with an aunt; won amateur contests, joined Chick WEBB band '34; immediate impact with jazz fans; hit record 'A-Tisket A-Tasket' '38 brought her to wider public (song co-adapted with Al Feldman from 1879 nursery rhyme; revived '44 in film *Two Girls And A Sailor*, with Van Johnson, June Allyson, Lena HORNE, Harry JAMES, Xavier CUGAT; Ella sang it in Abbott & Costello western *Ride 'em Cowboy* '42). Fronted band after Webb died '39; went solo '42. Records on Decca; toured with JATP from '46; became favourite female singer: she swings; her scat-singing is without equal; clear, accurate, flexible voice combined with warm vocal colour and sympathetic phrasing make nonpareil interpreter of American songs; the question of whether she's a 'jazz' singer is pointless: she transcends category. Hits in Billboard charts on Decca '40-'51 incl. three with the INK SPOTS, and one with Louis JORDAN; calypso-flavoured solo hit 'Stone Cold Dead In The Market' '46. Peerless musicianship in many compilations of Webb, Decca era on MCA, other labels. Made several films; best-known is *Pete Kelly's Blues* (Decca soundtrack LP shared with Peggy LEE, charted '55); greatest stardom began on Norman Granz's Verve label. Rare for 2-

disc sets to chart in '50s, but *Ella Fitzgerald Sings The Cole Porter Songbook* no. 15 '56, *Rodgers And Hart Songbook* no. 11 '57, both arr./cond. by Buddy Bregman (*b* 9 July '30, Chicago); *George And Ira Gershwin Song Books* recorded '58-9 (arr./cond. Nelson RIDDLE), charted '64 when issued in set; five LPs of Gershwin songs in all. Also made *Harold Arlen, Johnny Mercer, Jerome Kern* songbooks, latter with Riddle, all 2-disc sets; *Duke Ellington Songbook* with Duke in two 2-disc sets. Other Verve hit LPs: ballad set *Ella And Louis* with Louis ARMSTRONG '56, no. 12 (later combined with Vol. 2 in 2-disc set; also recorded 2-disc *Porgy And Bess* with Louis); live LPs *Mack The Knife, Ella In Berlin, Ella In Hollywood, Ella And Basie!, Hello, Dolly!* '60-4. Four singles on Verve in Hot 100 '56-63 incl. 'Mack The Knife' (also made no. 6 R&B chart '60). Other Verve LPs incl. *Like Someone In Love, Swings Brightly With Nelson* (Riddle), *Songs In A Mellow Mood* (with solo piano accompaniment by Ellis Larkins, *b* 15 May '23, Baltimore: fine pianist in any context; perennially valuable accompanist to many singers), *Rhythm Is My Business, In Hollywood* '61, *On The Sunny Side Of The Street* '63 with Basie, *Whisper Not* '65 with Marty Paich; with Ellington: *Ella At Duke's Place, Côte d'Azur*. On Capitol: *Brighten The Corner* '67 (sacred songs); on Reprise: *Ella* '69; on Columbia: 2-disc *Live At Carnegie Hall* '73. Eye surgery early '70s slowed her down a bit, but started all over again with Granz on Pablo: *Embraces Antonio Carlos Jobim* (yet another 2-disc songbook); *In London; Dream Dancing* with Riddle; *Ella Fitzgerald & Oscar Peterson* with Ray BROWN; *A Classy Pair* with Basie; *Fine And Mellow* '74; *Montreux '75; Montreux '76* with Tommy FLANAGAN; *Lady Time* '78; *Take Love Easy, Again, Speak Love* ('83), *Easy Living* (released '87), all with Joe PASS; *With The Tommy Flanagan Trio* '82; *Nice Work If You Can Get It* '83 (Gershwin duets with André Previn). With airchecks, reissues, compilations etc. her recordings over 50 years would fill pages. Among bits and pieces, 'Party Blues' '56 with Basie has Ella and Joe WILLIAMS scatting at each other; result is a lesson in exciting, joyful swing. Songbooks alone are proof of genius: each composer's work is distinctive, yet each gets its due from Ella.

FIVE SATINS, The Vocal quintet formed New Haven, Conn. '56. Original lineup: Fred Parris, lead (*b* 26 Mar. '36); Rich Freeman, tenor (*b* '40); West Forbes, second tenor (*b* '37); Lewis Peeples, harmony (*b* '37); Sy Hopkins, bass (*b* '38). Parris had led group called the Scarletts c.'54; then wrote song which became classic of doo-wop genre, suggested by US Army guard duty 'In The Still Of The Nite': Satins' '56 disc made top 40 that year, re-entered top 100 in '60, '61; other entries by three other acts. Bill Baker sang lead on '57 hit 'To The Aisle'. Had other hits on Ember label; split up early '60s as doo-wop went out of fashion; Parris re-formed group with new members '69 for revivals, re-created hit in movie *Let The Good Times Roll*, carried on with occasional appearances; had another chart entry '82 as Fred Parris & The Five Satins with medley 'Memories Of Days Gone By' on Elektra: incl. others' hits 'Earth Angel', 'Tears On My Pillow', 'Only You' etc. as well as 'In The Still Of The Nite'. His song should have earned him several hundred thousand dollars; grateful music business paid him less than $800.

FIXX UK new wave group formed by vocalist Cy Curnin (*b* 12 Dec. '57) and Adam Woods, who was at school in London with Curnin's sister. With Rupert Greenall (keyboards) and others made single 'Hazard In The Home' as the Portraits; then recruited Charlie Barrett, bass and Jamie West-Oram (ex-the Doll, Phil Rambow band), guitars; changed name to the Fix. Single on 101 label 'Lost Planes' '81 (now rare), plus live tracks on *101 Club – Live Letters* compilation. Sent single to prod./singer Rupert Hine, who took them on. For first single on major label (MCA) changed name to the Fixx (label rejected drug connotation, band refused more change); LP *Shuttered Room* '82 showcased lyricist Curnin's 'dry white whine' (as *Sounds* not-very-originally called it); musicianship (West-Oram quite experienced) and fashionable good looks assured 18-month chart stay in USA in spite of political content: anti-nuke etc. statements 'Stand Or Fall', 'Red Skies' made top 60 UK, 'Stand' reached no. 72 USA; but *Reach The Beach* '83 was USA breakthrough, no. 9 LP incl. hits 'Saved By Zero' (no. 17), 'One Thing Leads To Another' (no. 4) and 'The

Sign Of Fire' (no. 32), but none in UK. Toured incessantly (supported FLOCK OF SEAGULLS, POLICE, other 'name' British bands) while getting heavy MTV play (which ensured no. 2 'airplay' entry for 'Deeper And Deeper', track made for film *Streets Of Fire* not released as single). Barrett left '82, replaced by Alfie Agius (ex-TEARDROP EXPLODES), then by Danny K. Brown (regarded as semi-permanent member). Album *Phantoms* '84 went gold in two weeks: output all directed to USA in face of UK indifference, BEATLE-ish harmonies c. *Help* ('Lose Face') alternating with more modern elements. *Walkabout* '86 probably a USA hit; with Curnin's Bowie-esque mimes and 'meaningful' lyrics, they are archetypal new-wave-of-Second-British-Invasion, while UK looks for new thrills.

FLACK, Roberta (*b* 10 Feb. '39, Asheville, N.C.) Singer; a USA favourite since '70s. Played piano at 4; BA in music from Howard U. at 15; taught in Washington DC. Heard by Les McCANN at Mr Henry's pub, he took her to Atlantic label: 13 chart LPs '70-82 incl. no. 1 first LP *First Take*, which incl. 'The First Time Ever I Saw Your Face', written by Ewan MACCOLL; no. 1 single hit '72 for six weeks after being featured in Clint Eastwood film *Play Misty For Me* was first of her 11 top 40 singles, incl. duets with Donny HATHAWAY and Peabo BRYSON. LPs incl. *Chapter Two* '70, *Quiet Fire* '71, *Roberta Flack And Donny Hathaway* '72 (incl. no. 5 hit 'Where Is The Love'), *Killing Me Softly* '73 (incl. title song, her second solo no. 1, won three Grammies), *Feel Like Makin' Love* '74 (title song third no. 1 hit), *Blue Lights In The Basement* '78 (no. 2 hit with Hathaway, 'The Closer I Get To You'), *Roberta Flack* '78, *Featuring Donny Hathaway* '80. He died '79; *Live & More* '80 is live 2-disc set with Bryson. *Bustin' Loose* '81 is a soundtrack LP on MCA; *I'm The One* '82 is on Atlantic; *Born To Love* '83 is on Capitol with Bryson. (Duets with her and Natalie COLE also incl. in his LP *Collection* '84.) Flack and Bryson had no. 16 hit with Gerry GOFFIN ballad 'Tonight, I Celebrate My Love' '83.

FLAMINGOS, The Vocal group formed '52 Chicago; among best in doo-wop genre.

Original lineup: Sollie McElroy (sang lead until '54), Earl Lewis, Ezekiel and Jacob Carey, Johnny Carter, Paul Wilson. Sang on South Side, won talent show, dates at local Club DeLisa, Las Vegas. First single on Chance label 'If I Can't Have You' '53. Despite fine harmonies, smooth style, no success on Chance, Parrot '54, Checker '55, Decca '56, except third single for Checker, 'I'll Be Home', made no. 10 '56 on R&B chart (Pat BOONE had pop hit). But fame grew; releases on End label broke through in film *Rock, Rock, Rock* '57 with 'Lovers Never Say Goodbye' (no. 52 pop chart, 25 R&B). By this time a quintet led by Zeke Carey and Nate Nelson; classic version of evergreen 'I Only Have Eyes For You' was no. 11 pop, no. 3 R&B '59 (Art GARFUNKEL hit version '75 was very similar). Other hits '59-61 incl. 'Love Walked In', 'Nobody Loves Me Like You', 'Your Other Love', 'Time Was'; also minor hits 'Boogaloo Party' '66, 'Buffalo Soldier' '70. LPs on End incl. *Serenade, Requestfully Yours*.

FLAMIN' GROOVIES USA pop band formed in San Francisco '65. Original lineup: Cyril Jordan (*b* '48), Tim Lynch (*b* 18 July '46), Roy Loney (*b* 13 Apr. '46), guitars (all *b* San Francisco; Loney also vocalist); George Alexander (*b* 18 May '46, San Mateo, Cal.), bass. Formed at height of British Invasion; first called Chosen Few, then Lost And Found; soldiered on best part of 20 years staying true to 3-minute pop songs and Anglophiles to a man. Drummer Danny Mihm (ex-Whistling Shrimp) replaced Ron Greco when Jordan and Lynch returned from a visit to Holland; disinterest of record companies in guitar-based band kept them out of studios until they financed 10″ LP *Sneakers* themselves '69, sold 2000 copies on Snazz label; Epic signed them to record *Supersnazz* '70 (reissued on Edsel '86). More permanent contract with Kama Sutra; moved to NYC to record *Flamingo* and *Teenage Head* '71, garage classics later revered by punks and pub-rockers alike (latter's title track covered by Duck's Deluxe). But Lynch and Loney departed, former arrested for draft-dodging, latter to go solo, replaced by James Farrell, Chris Wilson (*b* 10 Sep. '52, Waltham, Mass.; ex-Loose Gravel). The next six years punctuated only by the odd single, a live EP on Skydog and

USA classic 'You Tore Me Down' on Bomp. Band relocated to UK to try to build on reputation there; Terry Rae, then David Wright replaced Mihm; at Rockfield studios in Wales renaissance took place under rock'n'roller Dave EDMUNDS, who prod. *Shake Some Action* '76, recaptured magic of yore: title track a hit in Europe. *Now* '78 was again on Sire, repeated formula to lesser effect, mixing covers (BYRDS' 'Feel A Whole Lot Better') with pre-worn originals. Buddah cashed in, reissued early material as *Still Shakin'* '76; Groovies revelled in adulation of new wave. *Jumpin' In The Night* '79 prod. by Roger Bechirian, Elvis COSTELLO's engineer; featured new guitarist Mike Wilhelm, who'd joined for *Now*. Wilson was sacked early '80s, joined short-lived London-based psychedelic popsters the Barracudas. Fun band who kept pop flag waving throughout, Groovies are now inactive.

FLANAGAN, Ralph (*b* 7 Apr. '19, Loranie, Ohio) Bandleader. Became pianist-arranger with Sammy KAYE '40; later wrote scores for Kaye, Charlie BARNET, Gene KRUPA, Tony PASTOR, others; worked with singers such as Mindy Carson, Perry COMO. Independent label exec. Herb Hendler asked Flanagan to do *Tribute To Glenn Miller* album (Rainbow Records); Hendler moved to RCA and Miller-style band was formed, sparking off dance-band mini-revival (Ray ANTHONY, Jerry Gray, others). Chart hits incl. 'Nevertheless', 'Rag Mop', 'Harbor Lights', all '50; 'Slow Poke' '52, 'Hot Toddy' '53; LPs incl. *Plays Rodgers & Hammerstein* '50, *Dance To The Top Pops* '52.

FLANAGAN, Tommy (*b* 16 Mar. '30, Detroit) Piano, also other instruments. Pro debut with Dexter GORDON, '45; to NYC '56, first accompanied Ella FITZGERALD that summer, many times since incl. tour of Japan '60s, also accompanied Tony BENNETT; often with Fitzgerald since '68. Has worked with all the best BOP musicians, worked in Greenwich Village duo with bassist Wilbur Little '73-4 (*b* 5 Mar. '28, Parmele, N.C.); recorded with J. J. JOHNSON, Milt JACKSON, Wes MONTGOMERY, Roy HAYNES, Art FARMER, John COLTRANE (*Giant Steps* '59), Coleman HAWKINS (*Today And Now* '63), Booker

ERVIN (*The Song Book* '64); with Ella: *In London, Live At Carnegie Hall, Montreux '75; Dizzy Gillespie Big 7 At Montreux* '75, many more. Own albums always yield tasty results, incl. *The Cats* '57 (Prestige sextet session with Coltrane, later reissued under his name), *Jazz . . . It's Magic* '57 quintet on Savoy; solo piano *Alone Too Long* '77 on Denon; duo-piano sets *Our Delights* '78 with Hank JONES on Galaxy, *Together* '78 with Kenny Barron on Denon; duos with bassists *Ballads And Blues* '78 on Enja (with George Mraz, *b* 9 Sep. '44, Czechoslovakia; to USA late '60s), *You're Me* '80 on Phontastic (with Red Mitchell, *b* 20 Sep. '27, NYC; settled in Stockholm); 2-disc Columbia albums *I Remember Bebop* and *They All Played Bebop* have several tracks by Flanagan with Keeter Betts on bass '77; several other pianists are also featured. Trio albums with Elvin JONES, Connie Kay, Jimmy SMITH, Haynes, Ron CARTER, Reg Workman, Richard Davis, Betts, many others: *Trio Overseas* '57 on Prestige; *Lonely Town* '59 on Blue Note; *Tommy Flanagan Trio* '60 on Moodsville; *Positive Intensity* '76 on Sony/CBS (same as *Trinity* on Inner City); *Plays The Music Of Harold Arlen* c.'80 on Inner City; *Tokyo Festival* '75 and *Montreux* '77 on Pablo; *Super Jazz Trio* '78 on RCA; *Something Borrowed, Something Blue* '78 on Galaxy; *Communication* '79 on Paddle Wheel; *The Magnificent* on Progressive; *Eclypso* '77, *Super Session* '80, *Giant Steps* and *Thelonica* '82, all on Enja; *The Master Trio* and *Blues In The Closet* '83 on Japanese label Baybridge.

FLATT & SCRUGGS Led bluegrass group '48-69: Lester Raymond Flatt (*b* 28 June '14, Overton County, Tenn.; *d* 11 May '79) and Earl Scruggs (*b* 6 Jan. '24, Flint Hill, N.C.). Flatt worked in textile mills, turned pro late '30s; played with Happy-Go-Lucky Boys '41-3; with wife Gladys joined Charlie Monroe and his Kentucky Pardners '43; then Bill MONROE's Bluegrass Boys '44 on guitar and as lead singer. Scruggs played banjo on radio at 15, during WWII worked in factory, joined Monroe '45: had evolved three-finger style and 'the same relationship to the five-string banjo that Paganini has to the violin. By sharply accentuating the melody line, Scruggs makes it stand out clearly in a shower of notes' (Bill C.

Malone). They left Monroe as a team '48, formed the Foggy Mountain Boys incl. the late Cedric Rainwater, later Jake Tullock (aka Cousin Jake) on bass, Jimmy Shumate, later Paul Warren on fiddle; Mac WISEMAN soon added. Group used steel dobro guitar (as opposed to Monroe's mandolin) played from '55 by Buck Graves (aka Uncle Josh). Signed to Mercury '48, recorded original version of 'Foggy Mountain Breakdown' (later re-made for film *Bonnie & Clyde* '68); also 'Pike County Breakdown', Scruggs comps. 'Earl's Breakdown', 'Flint Street Special', 'Randy Lynn Rag' (named after his son); Flatt's famous high-pitched vocals on 'Roll In My Sweet Baby's Arms', CARTER Family classic 'Jimmy Brown The Newsboy'. Switched to Columbia '51; became top bluegrass group, joining Grand Ole Opry '55, but unknown outside country music until late '50s: discovered at Newport Folk Festival by fans from every walk of life. Had country hit 'Cabin In The Hills' '59, but mainly worked outside mainstream of country; 'Ballad Of Jed Clampett' (for *Beverly Hillbillies* TV series) was huge hit (no. 1 country, top 40 pop) brought larger following. More country hits with 'Pearl, Pearl, Pearl' '63, 'You Are My Flower' and 'Petticoat Junction' (also TV theme) '64, 'Nashville Cats', 'California Uptight Band' '67, which had them moving away from pure bluegrass; Flatt was not happy with this and they split '69. Scruggs formed the Earl Scruggs Review with multi-instrumentalist sons Randy, Steve and Gary (who played electric bass, among other things); Flatt remained bluegrass stalwart with new group Nashville Grass. Columbia LPs by Flatt & Scruggs incl. *Carnegie Hall*, *Greatest Hits*; 2-disc *World Of*. Scruggs LPs on same label incl. *Kansas City State, Live! Austin, Today And Forever*, since '84 *Super Jammin'*, *Top Of The World*. Lester Flatt LPs '71-5 incl. *Flatt On Victor*, *Country Boy*, *Lester'N'Mac* and *On The Southbound* (last two with Wiseman), *Foggy Mountain Breakdown* and *Live*, all on RCA; also *Flatt Gospel* '76 on Canaan; collections on CMH (Country Music Heritage) incl. *Greatest Bluegrass Hits, Pickin' Time, Fantastic Pickin', Heaven's Bluegrass*, 2-disc *Living Legend*; also *Lester Raymond Flatt* on Flying Fish (Sonet UK). Historic Flatt & Scruggs tracks are already on CD.

FLEETWOOD MAC UK blues band '60s; AOR/rock band '70s. Took name from '67 unreleased instrumental track by John MAYALL's Bluesbreakers, whose lineup incl. John McVie (*b* 26 Nov. '45), bass; Peter Green (*b* 29 Oct. '46), guitar; Mick Fleetwood (*b* 24 June '42), drums. Green and Fleetwood had played together pre-Mayall in Peter B's Looners (with Peter Bardens), with Rod STEWART in Shotgun Express until '67; left Mayall together, recruiting Jeremy Spencer (*b* 4 July '48) and Bob Brunning, bass (soon replaced by McVie). Purist blues band for LPs *Peter Green's Fleetwood Mac* and *Mr Wonderful*, both '68; following top 30 singles ('Black Magic Woman', 'Need Your Love So Bad') scope was broadened, third guitarist Danny Kirwan (*b* 13 May '50) added: his guitar in style of B. B. KING, Spencer's bottleneck infl. by Elmore JAMES, Kirwan put in pop style. Surprise UK no. 1 late '68 with 'Albatross', haunting instrumental (no. 2 on re-issue '73); Green's sensitive, acoustic 'Man Of The World' no. 2 early '69; band established for blues feeling conveying commercial material. To Reprise label for *Then Play On* '69 (WB in USA, later in both countries); sales threat from Blue Horizon compilation *The Pious Bird Of Good Omen*: latter made no. 18, new LP no. 6. As power-chorded 'The Green Manalishi (With The Two-Pronged Crown)' made UK top 10 '70 and after recording *Kiln House* Green left, having got religion (made solo album *The End Of The Game* '70, quit business, came back '79; has made AOR LPs with group Kolors). Replaced by McVie's wife, Christine Perfect, ex-Chicken Shack (sang lead on their hit 'I'd Rather Go Blind' '69). Period of aimlessness ensued, momentum lost; Spencer joined religious cult, temporarily replaced for USA tour by Green; LPs *Future Games, Bare Trees* with California replacement Bob Welch (*b* 31 July '46) were flops in UK, though charted in USA; Kirwan was fired; lineup incl. Bob Weston on guitar, ex-SAVOY BROWN vocalist Dave Walker (first frontman in group's career) made *Penguin* '73; Walker left, then Weston after *Mystery To Me* '74. Welch contributed most of the songs to *Heroes Are Hard To Find* '74, departed to form hardrock band Paris. Having moved to the West Coast USA, band met Lindsay Buckingham (*b* 3

Oct. '47, Palo Alto) and Stephanie 'Stevie' Nicks (*b* 26 May '48, Phoenix), boy/girl guitar/vocal duo (made *Buckingham Nicks* for Polydor after meeting in group called Fritz): it was marriage made in heaven. LP *Fleetwood Mac* '75 melded sweet harmonies with Fleetwood's drums, McVie's solid bass; Christine contributed songs/vocals too; with Buckingham's distinctive acoustic and electric guitars new success was immediate. Three hit singles from USA 'debut' LP, but *Rumours* '76 eclipsed it with four top 10 hits (two entries in UK chart in heyday of punk) and by selling 25 million worldwide: both were no. 1 USA, latter for 31 weeks; 134 weeks in USA chart, 271 UK. Next LP *Tusk* '79 'only' sold 4 million: cost $1m in studio time, had none of the feel that made successful mix of three different singer/songwriters; title (with help of marching band) no. 8 USA, 6 UK; Nicks' 'Sara' no. 7 USA, but experiments by Buckingham as prod. in mixing and song structure lost fans and airplay. Live 2-disc set was stop-gap '80 until real follow-up *Mirage* '82 was no. 1 again (five weeks), with several hits; but members busy with solo projects, Nicks most successfully with *Bella Donna* '82, *The Wild Heart* '83, *Rock A Little* '85. Relationships in band failed (McVies, Buckingham/Nicks), fuelling rumours that would suit glossy West Coast soap opera; but various combinations of these wrote 12 songs for *Tango In The Night* '87 incl. single 'Big Love'; perhaps their best since *Rumours*. Buckingham left '87 (never liked touring), replaced by Rick Vito, Billy Burnette on guitars, vocals.

FLOCK OF SEAGULLS, A UK new wave group formed Liverpool '79 by brothers Mike (*b* 5 Nov. '57) and Ali Score, keyboards/vocals and drums. Lead guitar Paul Reynolds, Frank Maudsley on bass made up group with name inspired by Jonathan Livingston Seagull. Spotted by Bill Nelson, who prod. 'It's Not Me Talking' for his Cocteau label; signed with Jive for subsequent releases. Visually in fashionable post-punk 'Futurist' mould, with synth, electronic drum kit, etc.; ex-hairdresser Mike affected ever-stranger hair styles to get noticed; MTV boosted 'I Ran (So Far Away)' to no. 9 USA '82 with video's futuristic silver setting; UK had seen Gary NUMAN do it first and better; gave it only no. 43. 'Wishing (If I Had A Photograph Of You)' followed earlier 'Space Age Love Song' in having sci-fi-type movie footage; 'Wishing' was best stab at catchy melody, made no. 10 UK/26 USA, but status remained higher in USA: band headlined MTV '82 New Year's Eve Rock'n'Roll Ball. Eponymous first album followed by *Wishing* '83 with hit 'Nightmares', giving relief from space obsession with Hitchcockian setting, but peaked at no. 53 UK; despite two more top 40 hits UK '83-4, album *The Story Of A Young Heart* '84, *Dream Come True* '86, they were unlikely to match USA success without an MTV. Reynolds left '85; they split '86.

FLOYD, Eddie (*b* 25 June '35, Montgomery, Ala.) Soul singer. Joined legendary vocal group Falcons in Detroit (another member was Joe Stubbs, brother of FOUR TOPS frontman Levi Stubbs); they had five R&B hits '59-62, incl. pop top 20 hit 'You're So Fine' '59: Stubbs joined the Contours, replaced by Wilson PICKETT, whose lead vocal took 'I Found A Love' into Hot 100 '62. Eddie signed as a solo with Stax, where he had 12 Hot 100 entries '66-70 incl. 'Knock On Wood' '66 (no. 1 R&B chart, top 40 pop both USA/UK), 'I've Never Found A Girl (To Love Me Like You Do)' and 'Bring It On Home To Me' were top 5 R&B '68, no. 40 and 17 respectively in pop chart. Also notable as a songwriter ('634-5789' covered by Ry COODER); carried on having hits in black charts through '70s.

FOGELBERG, Dan (*b* 13 Aug. '51, Peoria, Ill.) USA singer/songwriter. Learned piano, acoustic slide guitar (gift from grandfather). Studied painting at U. of Ill. but spotted by EAGLES manager Irving Azoff; dropped out and moved to L.A. First LP *Home Free* prod. in Nashville by Norbert Putnam, typically polite country singer/songwriter debut; *Souvenirs* '74 more rock-oriented, more distinctively his own (though aided by prod./guitarist Joe WALSH; his electric guitar playing still shows infl. of Walsh). LP incl. first hit single 'Part Of The Plan' (no. 31); self-prod. *Captured Angel* had hit single; after hectic 18-month period during which he sessioned for Randy NEWMAN, Eric ANDERSEN, Roger McGuinn, Jackson

421

BROWNE, others, he parted company with live backing band Fool's Gold (lineup Tom Kelly, bass; Denny Henson, guitar; Doug Livingston, guitar and keyboards, didn't play on LPs), retreated to Colorado. *Nether Lands* '77 was followed by duo with flautist Tim Weisberg *Twin Sons Of Different Mothers* '78, incl. single 'The Power Of Gold'. Increasingly tight compositions broke through with *Phoenix* '79: sold over 2m and had two hits ('Longer' no. 2, 'Heart Hotels' no. 21, both '80). Song cycle *The Innocent Age* '81 with support incl. Emmylou HARRIS was most impressive work to date, swimming against musical tide for USA top 20 singles 'Run For The Roses' (no. 18), 'Same Old Lang Syne', 'Hard To Say', 'Leader Of The Band' (all top 10): hits spanned 18 months, kept 2-disc set in charts for 62 weeks. *Windows And Walls* '84 (hit 'The Language Of Love'), bluegrass-flavoured *High Country Snows* '85 and *Exiles* '87 maintained high standard of Epic LPs from near-recluse who once cancelled several important live dates: typed as a soft-rock balladeer by the hits, he has actually done a lot of different things, matured at his own pace.

FOLEY, Red (*b* Clyde Julian Foley, 17 June '10, Blue Lick, Ky.; *d* 19 Sep. '68, Fort Wayne, Ind.) Country singer, guitarist, harmonica player, songwriter, entertainer: smooth baritone and smooth personality won many fans outside C&W charts. Won amateur singing contest at age 17; started college but invited to appear on WLS National Barn Dance in Chicago (*see* COUNTRY MUSIC); with Cumberland Ridge Runners on that show '32, first records with them; headlined Renfro Valley Barn Dance on WHAS Louisville '37; also Boone County Jamboree on WLW Cincinnati; one of the first country singers to have network radio show (Avalon Time; co-star comic Red Skelton); with Hoosier Hotshots made trek to Hollywood '40s along with many others for B-movie westerns in heyday of singing cowboy genre. Early hit with wartime 'Smoke On The Water'. Joined Grand Ole Opry's network Prince Albert Show '45; said to be the first country star to record in Nashville, at WSM studio in Mar. that year. Later on Ozark Jubilee radio and TV show from Springfield, Mo. (many younger stars

got a break on show, networked for six years in '50s). TV co-star with Fess Parker in TV series *Mr Smith Goes To Washington* early '60s. Songwriting credits incl. 'Just A Closer Walk With Thee'; co-wrote own '49 top 10 hit 'Blues In My Heart' etc.; had own music publishing firm. Of his four daughters, Shirley Lee is married to Pat BOONE and Betty had a singing career of her own, incl. top 10 hit 'Old Moon' '59. He died of a heart attack while on a Grand Ole Opry tour a year after he was elected to the Country Music Hall of Fame. He was already well-known for 'Old Shep' in '40s (later covered by Elvis PRESLEY), highly regarded as a gospel singer ('Peace In The Valley', also covered by Presley); then 22 top 10 hits in country chart '48-54 of his own, plus 9 top 10 duets, made him one of the top sellers of all time. Own no. 1 hits incl. 'Birmingham Bounce' '50, 'Midnight' '52; but 'Chattanoogie Shoe Shine Boy' '50 was no. 1 both country and pop: jaunty novelty recorded in Owen BRADLEY's converted garage had drummer Ferris Coursey slapping his thigh to simulate snap of shoeshine boy's rag; the story goes that by the time the song was rehearsed he had to switch to left thigh because right was so sore. 'Sugarfoot Rag' on flip side was also well liked. Duets incl. 'A Satisfied Mind' with Betty '55; 'One By One' '54 and 'You And Me' '56 with Kitty WELLS (all top 5); 'Tennessee Border' no. 2 '47, 'Goodnight Irene' no. 1 '50 with Ernest TUBB. Also recorded with Evelyn Knight, Roberta Lee, ANDREWS SISTERS, Lawrence WELK. Compilations incl. 2-disc *Red Foley Story* with the JORDANAIRES, *Beyond The Sunset* and *Songs Of Devotion* on MCA; *I Believe* on Coral; in UK *Tennessee Saturday Night* on Charly has uptempo 'country boogie' '47-58.

FOLK MUSIC Originally music that ordinary people make in order to express themselves, using songs and techniques that they learn from families or neighbours, incl. ethnic music, such as the social and religious ceremonial music of Africans or American Indians, also handed down for generations. Folk music exists in every country and among every minority and occupation; in the USA Negro spirituals and BLUES were folk musics (it is arguable that JAZZ should be excluded, for jazzmen from the beginning were professional musicians who were always willing to obtain orthodox technical and academic expertise: an art form rather than a folk form). Work songs (sea shanties, cowboy songs etc.), political and protest songs (once called broadsides) and love songs are found everywhere. In this century it was still possible to find folk music in its pure state using a recording machine in the field, as Ralph PEER, John and Alan LOMAX and others did for decades; this is becoming difficult now that every mountain cabin sprouts a TV aerial. It is not too much to say that much of the popular music of the 20th century comes from the two strands of American folk: the black (ex-slave) and the white (see COUNTRY MUSIC, which used to be called 'folk', then 'hillbilly'), with the latter owing much to the UK and Ireland: as there are more regional accents per square mile in the UK than in North America, so there are many indigenous musics there, though none developed commercial success as blues and country music did in the USA. Francis James CHILD collected his *English And Scottish Ballads* in the 19th century; Cecil SHARP published *English Folk Songs: Some Conclusions* in UK '07, afraid that the folk song tradition in England was dying, also *English Folk Songs From The Southern Appalachians* '32: accents and songs of USA 'hillbillies' were traced back to Elizabethan England and Scotland. The English Folk Song & Dance Society in London (its building named after Sharp) and the Library of Congress archives in Washington DC (see LOMAX) are important collections. Folk music revival always seems to be happening; in fact folk music never goes away: it just requires a new definition every decade or so. The values of folk music do not change, but each generation brings a new bag of tricks to it, now that country people everywhere are no longer isolated from the mainstream of commercial music; it was always subject to outside influence, the importation of the accordion to the US Southwest by German labourers being a good example. Urban folk music began in the USA with Woody GUTHRIE, who came from the Dust Bowl to write songs in the folk idiom about poor people and politics, and his disciple Pete SEEGER, but suffered from political persecution for

years during the McCarthy era; Seeger's quartet the WEAVERS had huge hit records c.'50 but suddenly disappeared from the airwaves. It is a nasty paradox for those who love both music and freedom that while the USSR devoted resources to researching and preserving its multitude of folk styles before they disappeared, the Library of Congress's archive needed private donations and Seeger, collecting songs from around the world, was blacklisted. A. P. Carter (discovered by Peer; *see* the CARTER Family) thought nothing of copywriting songs he had collected; the more self-conscious Guthrie and Seeger were reluctant even to copyright their own work. Burl IVES, Oscar BRAND, Win Stracke ('Chicago's minstrel', *b* 20 Feb. '08, Lorraine, Kansas), many others kept the folk flame alive in the USA, with many children among fans; Jack ELLIOTT, a Guthrie acolyte, lived in England '55-61, recording there, influencing guitar playing and the emergent SKIFFLE music; when Seeger visited UK '61 he was impressed by the number of topical songs being written, leading to the founding of USA song outlet *Broadside*. Coffee houses in NYC's Greenwich Village were hothouses of folksingers and writers such as Elliott, Dave VAN RONK, Phil OCHS, Bob DYLAN, as well as outdoor hootenannies at Washington Square, but a USA revival began '58 with the KINGSTON trio on the West Coast, whose slickness and straight appearance offended no one. Joan BAEZ revived Child ballads at the first Newport Folk Festivals (but country people like Merle TRAVIS had never stopped performing them); she also introduced Bob Dylan to audiences. A generation disgusted by the paranoid politics of their elders practised the protest song and began writing their own, their talent and humour soon spilling over into any topic relevant to real life. Hank WILLIAMS had written scores of songs about the real lives of ordinary folk, laced with humour as well as sorrow; they are effectively folk songs because people all over the world identify with them without knowing or caring who wrote them. In the '60s jokes were made: 'Here's a folk song I wrote last week'; Bill BROONZY said when asked if he sang folk songs that he'd never heard a horse sing them. The singer/songwriters who wrote fine songs in the folk/country idiom since

'60 also incl. Tom PAXTON, Tom RUSH, Tim HARDIN, Arlo GUTHRIE, Buffy SAINTE-MARIE, IAN & SYLVIA, Loudon WAINWRIGHT, John PRINE, Steve GOODMAN, Dolly PARTON, Canada's McGARRIGLE Sisters, scores more; many of them were published in *Broadside* and in *Sing Out* (ed. by Irwin Silber '51-67). Folk-rock and country-rock were invented by those who were not afraid to adopt modern materials and techniques. The 'redneck rock' and 'outlaw' movements '70s (*see* COUNTRY MUSIC) were essentially moves back to folk values away from the slickness of Nashville: many of Guy CLARK's best songs are about time passing, Richard DOBSON's about working for a living, Butch HANCOCK's about West Texas; Terry ALLEN is a savagely funny urban cowboy who was also an art teacher; and they all write love songs. In the USA the Vanguard, Elektra and FOLKWAYS labels were the most important in the folk revival; in the UK Topic Records was formed by the British Marxist Party for political purposes (like KEYNOTE in the USA): first 78rpm single was 'The Man That Waters The Workers' Beer', by Paddy Ryan. It went independent mid-'50s, precarious history incl. connection with USA Folkways; it now has one of the most valuable UK folk music catalogues, while the Leader/Trailer labels were also important. The COPPER Family and the WATERSONS preserved British *a cappella* folk singing; A. L. LLOYD was an important traditionalist (and advisor to Topic); there were and are many fiddlers, drummers and pipers preserving traditional techniques, while Dolly and Shirley COLLINS and others innovated, wrote original music. UK folk-rock in the '60s differed from its USA counterpart, staying closer to the roots, alumni of FAIRPORT CONVENTION, STEELEYE SPAN etc. still doing fascinating work (*see* HOME SERVICE, the ALBION BAND, BRASS MONKEY, Richard THOMPSON, etc.); members of BYRDS, Burrito Bros. etc. in the USA continued to compose good songs, several ending up in neo-bluegrass units. British folkies (with their preoccupation with class) are as parochial in their politics in the '80s as the *Sing Out* gang of the '50s were, arguing about whether or not songs should be 'relevant' as the world changes around them, but their musical interests are wide: the name of

their forum, *Folk Roots* magazine (formerly *Southern Rag*; 50th issue mid-'87), reflects eclecticism also seen in the catalogues of labels such as Rounder and Flying Fish in the USA: roots music incl. anything that is not and will not be adulterated by commercial considerations, from Yiddish KLEZMER and the multi-part harmony of Eastern European choral singing through TEX-MEX, CAJUN, ZYDECO and early blues, to the above-mentioned singer/songwriters, as well as original chanteuses like Mary COUGHLAN, Michelle SHOCKED and Suzanne VEGA, thrash-folk bands like the POGUES and the Oyster Band, and political strummers like Billy BRAGG. As the term roots music continues to be more widely used, it will mean yet another injection of the values of folk into the mainstream of popular music, and not a moment too soon.

FOLKWAYS USA record label formed by Moses Asch with Marion Distler. Asch had formed Asch Records '39, recorded Burl IVES, Pete SEEGER; went broke; tried again with Disc Records; Folkways formed '48 and stayed the course. The new company recorded Cuban music, American Indians, square dancing, jazz but was dedicated primarily to folk music; early recordings by LEADBELLY made it nationally famous, and the 6-disc *Anthology Of American Folk Music* '53 kept tracks by the CARTER FAMILY, Mississippi John HURT, Blind Lemon JEFFERSON etc. in print while they were being ignored by the music mainstream. Asch kept costs down and prices high so he could experiment; over 200 songs by Woody GUTHRIE, 60 LPs by Pete Seeger, many folk and traditional country acts, reissues incl. the Almanac Singers' *Talking Union* tracks (from Keynote: see entries for Keynote, Seeger), with Asch, RBF and Broadside subsidiaries. Asch kept 1500-2000 LPs in print for decades, incl. language instruction, science, etc. Artists didn't get paid much, but knew that records would remain available; Verve/Folkways deal got wider distribution for many items late '60s. He was also co-founder of Oak Publications (with Irwin Silber, publisher of *Sing Out* magazine); Oak sold to Music Sales Ltd '67. Asch died '86; Folkways was taken over by the Smithsonian Institution, a fitting climax for an American institution.

FONTANA, Wayne (b Glyn Ellis, 28 Oct. '45, Manchester) UK singer, leader of beat group the Mindbenders. Began in skiffle, from school group the Velfins to semi-pro Jets. Legend had it that Fontana was auditioning/recording, his group didn't turn up and Mindbenders were formed on the spot; in any case they were Mancunians Bob Lang (b 10 Jan. '46), bass; Eric Stewart (b 20 Jan. '45), guitar; Ric Rothwell (b 11 Mar. '44), drums; name of group came from '63 Dirk Bogarde film The Mind Benders (they were originally the Jets). Minor hits '63-4; then cover of Major Lance's soul hit 'Um Um Um Um Um' brought no. 5 hit late '64. 'Game Of Love' (by American Clint Ballard, who wrote hits for HOLLIES, etc.) was no. 2 UK '65 but no. 1 USA, Canada, Australia; when other '65 releases went no higher than no. 20, singer and group blamed each other and split. Solo Fontana made singles and LP Wayne One '66, hit only with 'Come On Home' (no. 16 UK) and 'Pamela Pamela' (no. 11), sound lacking Mindbenders' edge. He retired; later played revival shows, especially in USA. Backing band had instant success with 'Groovy Kind Of Love', cover of Toni Wine/Carole Bayer SAGER song: no. 2 transatlantic '66; two more top 40s same year and two LPs, mostly R&B covers, followed before they quit. Stewart emerged in Hotlegs, then 10CC with Graham Gouldman, who'd been in later Mindbenders.

FONTANE SISTERS (b Bea, Geri and Marge Rosse, New Milford, N.J.) White vocal trio. Mother was local choir director and organist; joined all-girl troupe on tour, then family group with brother Frank on guitar; he was killed in WWII. Featured on Perry COMO programmes on radio, then TV; signed by RCA '49; minor hit '51 with 'Tennessee Waltz'. Switched to Dot '54 and had 18 Hot 100 entries '54-8, 10 in top 40; with backing by Billy Vaughn orchestra, had biggest hits with covers of rhythm & blues hits: no. 1 '54 with 'Hearts Of Stone' (Otis WILLIAMS AND THE CHARMS); others incl. 'Rollin' Stone' (the Marigolds) and 'Rock Love' '55, 'Eddie My Love' '56: original by the Teen Queens (Betty and Rosie Collins) was no. 3 R&B hit, did almost as well as Fontanes' version in pop chart as white kids began to buy black originals instead of white covers. Fontanes' odd one out was 'Seventeen' '55, white hit by Boyd Bennett (who wrote it), also covered by Rusty Draper. Last big hit was 'Chanson d'Amour' at no. 12, written by Wayne Shanklin (b 6 June '16, Joplin, Mo.; d 16 June '70, Santa Barbara, Cal.), who also wrote 'The Big Hurt' '59 and 'West Of The Wall' '62 for Miss Toni Fisher. Fontanes compilation Rock Love on Charly UK.

FORBERT, Steve (b '55, Meridian, Miss.) Singer/songwriter, new breed late '70. To NYC '76, landed record contract after many gigs; Alive On Arrival '78 saw him hailed as the new Dylan because of scratchy, distinctive vocals, acoustic guitar, harmonica playing: confident debut incl. 'Goin' Down To Laurel'. Jackrabbit Slim '79 was more of the same, with excellent 'Romeo's Tune' and 'Sadly Sorta Like An Opera', but did not achieve breakthrough; Little Stevie Orbit '80 won no new fans; Steve Forbert '82 should have done it, with songs such as 'Prisoner Of Stardom', effective cover of 'When You Walk In The Room', but did not break out of cult ghetto and has remained silent. Favourite with critics who retained fondness for '60s singer/songwriter genre; clearly had more to offer than most '70s contemporaries, but no room in prevailing musical climate.

FORD, Ernie (b Ernest Jennings Ford, 13 Feb. '19, Bristol, Tenn.) Country, pop and gospel singer; 'Tennessee Ernie'. Deep, warm voice, humour and easy country charm made him big star in '50s. Played trombone in school orchestra; worked as DJ, announcer in Atlanta, Knoxville; USAAF. After WWII in Pasadena, Cal. with bandleader Cliffie STONE on Hometown Jamboree radio show; led to Capitol contract '48, country hits 'Smokey Mountain Boogie', 'Anticipation Blues', 'Mule Train' '49; 'Cry Of The Wild Goose', 'Shotgun Boogie' '50: last three crossed over to pop chart; last is good example of fast-paced hillbilly boogie style which contributed to rock'n'roll. Enormous crossover hits '55: 'Ballad Of Davy Crockett' no. 6 country, no. 5 pop; 'Sixteen Tons' (by Merle TRAVIS) no. 1 on both charts; 'That's All' no. 12 country, no. 17 pop '56. Altogether 15 entries in hot 100 '49-59, 16 country chart '49-'71 incl.

'Hicktown' '65, 'Honey Eyed Girl' '69, 'Happy Songs Of Love' '71. Became national TV personality on *College Of Musical Knowledge* '53, *I Love Lucy* '54, *Daytime Show* '55; own variety show '56-61; also film *River Of No Return* '54. Turned to gospel '56 with *Hymns*, first country LP to sell a million. *Great Gospel Songs* '64 won a Grammy. Other LPs incl. *This Lusty Land* '55, *Spirituals* '68, *25th Anniversary* '74 (2-disc set later reissued as single LPs), *Ernie Sings, Glen Picks* '75 with Glen CAMPBELL, all on Capitol; *Very Best Of* '74 reissued '83 on Music For Pleasure UK. Also gospel released on Word from late '70s: *Swing Wide Your Gate Of Love* with the JORDANAIRES, *He Touched Me, Tell Me The Old, Old Story, There's A Song In My Heart. Ol' Rockin' Ern* reissued on Stetson '87 after 30 years restores the early boogie hits to the catalogue.

FORD, Frankie (*b* 4 Aug. '39, Gretna, La.) R&B singer. White teenager selected by New Orleans Ace label for Elvis PRESLEY/Ricky NELSON-type stardom; 'Sea Cruise' existing track by Huey 'Piano' SMITH and the Clowns: Smith's vocal removed, Ford's substituted, record made pop no. 14, R&B no. 11 '59, but success never repeated. Owns club in New Orleans; has toured Europe, USA in '80s pleasing enthusiasts of vintage R&B.

FOREIGNER UK/USA AOR supergroup formed NYC '76 by English expatriate guitarist Mick Jones (*b* 27 Dec. '47), who'd sessioned in Europe and played with UK heavy rockers SPOOKY TOOTH and Leslie West band. Joined by fellow Brit Ian McDonald, multi-instrumentalist late of King Crimson, completing lineup with Americans Al Greenwood, keyboards (ex-Storm), Ed Gagliardi on bass (*b* 13 Feb. '52, NYC), drummer Dennis Elliott (*b* 18 Aug. '50, London), also ex-Crimson. Lou Gramm (*b* 2 May '50, Rochester, NY; ex-Black Sheep) bestowed distinctive whiskey-soaked vocals, but debut *Foreigner* '77 basically workmanlike heavy rock in BAD COMPANY mould. USA hit singles attested to ready market: 'Feels Like The First Time' no. 4, 'Cold As Ice' no. 6, 'Long Long Way From Home' no. 20. *Double Vision* '78 more solid hard rock, offering three more hits:

top 5 title song and 'Hot Blooded', no. 15 'Blue Morning Blue Day'. By *Head Games* '80, despite two more top 20 singles, even leader/songwriter Jones thought things were becoming 'a little blasé and predictable': another Brit Rick Wills (ex-Peter FRAMPTON, ROXY MUSIC, SMALL FACES) had replaced Gagliardi for LP; Greenwood and McDonald departed soon after; *4* '81 showed wisdom of Jones's reshaping of band, now three-quarters foreign in USA eyes: co-prod. by Jones and AC/DC prod. Mutt Lange, mix of hard-edged rock with melodic songs got the best out of Gramm: 'Urgent', with sax solo from Junior WALKER, was USA no. 3, quite their best single for a while; UK new wave keyboardist Thomas DOLBY synthwashed 'Waiting For A Girl Like You' to no. 8 UK, their biggest hit there, and no. 2 USA, where LP topped chart. Compilation *Records* '82 preceded long wait for *Agent Provocateur* late '84, continuing in less overtly rockish mould of *4*: lush gospel-tinged choir-backed ballad 'I Want To Know What Love Is' the outstanding track (and transatlantic no. 1). But 'That Was Yesterday' becalmed at no. 15 USA; band may be uncomfortable in AOR vein that groups like REO SPEEDWAGON mine more convincingly; further, Gramm publicly expressed irritation at Jones's method of working (three years between LPs) and resurgence of interest in his former band Black Sheep: solo projects may fit in, but with multi-million-selling status Foreigners should not be rash: *Inside Information* early '88 was first prod. entirely by Jones, guests incl. synth wizard Tom Bailey of THOMPSON TWINS.

FORESTER SISTERS, The USA country-rock vocal quartet: Kathy, June, Kim, Christy from Lookout Mountain, Ga. Kathy and June sang in church as children, got college degrees, began gigging; Kim joined '80, soon youngest Christy left college to join: they formed their own band, began exploring songs, harmonies; toured 35 states with ALABAMA, Ronnie MILSAP, Ricky Scaggs, John ANDERSON, George JONES, others; made demos in Muscle Shoals, signed to WEA: debut single '(That's What You Do) When You're In Love' made no. 10 in country chart, 'I Fell In Love Again Last Night' no. 1 same year, *The Forrester*

Sisters no. 4 LP all '85; nominated for Grammy and by ACM as Vocal Group of the Year. LP *Perfume, Ribbons & Lace* '87 confirms promise of superb country rock with a heart: good songs incl. 'Blame It On The Moon' by producers J. L. Wallace and Terry Skinner, 'Back In My Arms Again' by HOLLAND-DOZIER-HOLLAND. Third LP *You Again* late '87 looked like another winner.

FORMBY, George (*b* George Hoy Booth, 26 May '04, Wigan; *d* 6 Mar. '61, Penwortham, England) Singing comedian. Son of famous Edwardian comedian, jockey at 15, first appearance on stage at 17. Played ukelele, sang saucy songs with toothy grin; made 20 comedy/musical films '34-46; usually played amiable dope who got the girl, incl. *Keep Your Seats Please* ('The Window Cleaner'), *Feather Your Nest* ('Leaning On A Lamp Post'), *Let George Do It* ('Mr Wu's A Window Cleaner Now', 'Grandad's Flannelette Nightshirt'), etc. UK's top male entertainer performed for troops worldwide '39-45, OBE '46. West End debut in *Zip Goes A Million* '51, musical version of G. B. McCutcheon's novel *Brewster's Millions*; left cast owing to illness, semi-retired. Alan Randall keeps memory and songs alive today; 'Lamp Post' was interpolated into West End revival of *Me And My Girl* '85. Compilations incl. 2-disc *Leaning On A Lamp Post* '83 on Music For Pleasure; also *A Chip Off The Old Block* '81 on ASV, with Formbys Sr and Jr.

FORREST, Helen (*b* 12 Apr. '18, Atlantic City, N.J.) Vocalist of big band era: a gifted singer, strong on lyric projection. Sang under various names in early career: Bonnie Blue, The Blue Lady, Marlene, etc. With brother's band in Washington DC, then Artie SHAW band '38 following Billie HOLI-DAY: first record with Shaw 'You're A Sweet Little Heartache' on Bluebird. After Shaw junked band, she joined Benny GOOD-MAN late '39, stayed till Aug. '41; cut lovely side with Lionel HAMPTON, Nat COLE trio July '40 'I Don't Stand A Ghost Of A Chance With You'. Hits with Harry JAMES as Billboard began printing charts: 'I Don't Want To Walk Without You' no. 2, 'He's My Guy' no. 9, 'I Had The Craziest Dream' no. 1, 'Mister Five By Five' no. 2 (all '42),

'I've Heard That Song Before' no. 1 '43: handed over to Kitty KALLEN, went solo. Made films *Springtime In The Rockies* '42, *Bathing Beauty* and *Two Girls And A Sailor* '44; sang 'Time Waits For No One' in *Shine On Harvest Moon* '44, had no. 2 hit with it. Teamed that year with Dick HAYMES on radio show, recorded duets incl. six top 10 hits: 'Long Ago And Far Away', 'It Had To Be You', 'Together', 'I'll Buy That Dream', 'Oh! What It Seemed To Be' all top 5 '44-6. Sang 'Out Of Nowhere' in film *You Came Along* '45. Less active in '50s; early '60s sang with Tommy DORSEY Orchestra (led by Sam Donahue); active on club circuit '70s. *Now And Forever* on Stash '83 has backing from Grady Tate, Frank Wess, Hank JONES, George DUVIVIER, others.

FORREST, Jimmy (*b* James Robert Forrest Jr, 24 Jan. '20, St Louis; *d* 26 Aug. '80, Grand Rapids, Mich.) Tenor sax, leader. Played with Fate MARABLE, Jeter-Pillars '30s; Jay McSHANN, Andy KIRK '40s; Duke ELLINGTON '49-50. Own R&B band, early '50s: scored hit with 'Night Train' (no. 1 R&B chart '52) taking composer credit for bluesy Ellington riff ('That's The Blues Old Man', credited to Johnny HODGES '40; 'Happy-Go-Lucky Local' to Duke and son Mercer c.'46). Duke took philosophical attitude, at least in public; Forrest took the money, having seen commercial value of tune: every high school band played 'Night Train'; few would have heard the beautiful originals. 'Hey Mrs Jones' also hit '52, both covered by Buddy MORROW for white market, 'Jones' without sly lyrics sung by Forrest's band. Recorded live with Miles DAVIS at Barrelhouse Club St Louis '52; single 'Night Train Mambo' '54 on Dot; out of music as guest of the authorities mid-'50s; played with BASIE mid-'70s; happily married and retired to Grand Rapids late '70s. R&B hits '51-3 compiled on Delmark LP *Night Train*. LPs as leader: *All The Gin Is Gone*, *Black Forrest* '59 are quintet sets with Gene Ramey, Elvin JONES, also on Delmark; more from these sessions may be issued. LPs on New Jazz or Prestige incl. *Forrest Fire!*, *Out Of The Forrest* (with Joe ZAWINUL), *Sit Down And Relax*, *Most Much* '60-1; *Soul Street* '62 incl. some 9-piece tracks dir. by Oliver NELSON. Live *Heart Of The Forrest* '78 on Palo Alto made in Alibi

Club, Grand Rapids, by a trio with Shirley SCOTT.

FOSTER & RICE Country music songwriters with more than 60 ASCAP awards for hit songs. Jerry Gaylon Foster (*b* 19 Nov. '35, Tallapoosa, Mo.) was rockabilly artist with records on small Texas labels; met aspiring singer Bill Rice; they formed partnership '59. First songs recorded by Dickey Lee (*b* Richard Lipscomb, 21 Sep. '41, Memphis; had pop top 40 hits '64-5, later country hits). Moved to Nashville '64, wrote hits for George JONES, Charley PRIDE ('The Easy Part's Over' '68), Johnny PAYCHECK ('Song And Dance Man' '73), Jerry Lee LEWIS ('39 And Holding' '80), many more. Split up '80. Rice now writes with his wife, Sharon; Foster concentrates on performing. Both have made solo records, Rice on Capitol '73, Foster on Cinnamon '73, Hitsville '76, Monument '78, Kari '80, neither with much success, though Foster has following in Europe for rockabilly style.

FOUNDATIONS UK pop/soul multi-racial group formed London early '67, discovered by record dealer Barry Class who heard them in basement Butterfly Club, recommended them to Pye label's Tony Macauley, who signed them to sing/play his songs. Lineup showed unusual range in age: Clem Curtis (*b* 28 Nov. '40, Trinidad), vocals; Alan Warner (*b* 21 Apr. '47, London), guitar, vocals; Peter Macbeth (*b* 2 Feb. '43, London), bass; Tim Harris (*b* 14 Jan. '48, London), drums; Tony Gomez (*b* 13 Dec. '48, Ceylon), organ; Mike Elliot (*b* 6 Aug. '29, Jamaica), sax; Pat Burke (*b* 9 Oct. '37, Jamaica), sax; Eric Allandale (*b* 4 Mar. '36, West Indies), trombone. First single Motown-infl. 'Baby Now That I've Found You' no. 1 UK, 11 USA; first of six UK hits late '67 to late '69, three in top 10. Elliot left; Curtis replaced as lead singer by Colin Young (*b* 12 Sep. '44, Barbados) for second millionseller 'Build Me Up, Buttercup' (no. 2 UK '68, second and last USA hit at no. 3 '69), written by Macauley and Mike D'Abo (ex-MANFRED MANN). 'In The Bad, Bad Old Days' no. 8 UK '69, but group displayed no songwriting ability of their own (or weren't encouraged to), disintegrated '70. Curtis has since led New Foundations lineups in UK clubs.

FOUR ACES, The USA vocal quartet. Al Alberts and Dave Mahoney met in US Navy, performed as duo '46; met Sol Vocarro (also trumpet) and Lou Silvestri (also drums); all from Pennsylvania. Paid for own first record '(It's No) Sin' on obscure Victoria label; peaked at no. 4 '51 but eventually sold a million. Signed to Decca; 'Tell Me Why' (co-written by Alberts and group's arr. Marty Gold) no. 2 (also a hit for Eddie FISHER). Became prototype '50s white male vocal group, sold 20 million records with accent on upper register; had 20 top 40 hits '51-6, though shuffle beat of ballads became monotonous. Hits incl. 'I'm Yours', 'Perfidia', 'Stranger In Paradise' (from *Kismet*, tune by Alexander Borodin). Some hits were typical street-corner-group fodder: 'The Gang That Sang "Heart Of My Heart" ', 'Wedding Bells Are Breaking Up That Old Gang Of Mine' (25-year-old song by Sammy FAIN); others were film themes, incl. their only no. 1 (for six weeks), Fain's film song 'Love Is A Many-Splendored Thing' '55. Minor hits '56-9 with advent of rock'n'roll; Alberts left to go solo mid-'50s, vanished from charts.

FOUR FRESHMEN, The USA vocal group formed '48 while attending music school in Indianapolis, Ind. as The Toppers. First lineup: lead singer Bob Flanigan (*b* 22 Aug. '26), second voice Don Barbour (*b* 19 Apr. '29), third Ross Barbour (*b* 31 Dec. '28), all from Indiana; bass Hal Kratzch, replaced '53 by Ken Errair (*b* 23 Jan. '30). Also played several instruments, making club work easier. Turned pro, discovered '50 in Dayton, Ohio by Stan KENTON, who helped get recording contract; they appeared in film *Rich, Young And Pretty* '51; Capitol about to drop them when 'It's A Blue World' was no. 30 hit '52. No more top 40 hits, but good singing, modern harmonies sold LPs: more than 30 on Capitol helped keep group together for years. Errair replaced by Ken Albers '56; Don Barbour replaced by Bill Comstock '60, who was replaced by Ray Brown '73. Chart LPs incl. *Voices In Modern* '54; *Freshmen Favourites*, *Four Freshmen And Five Trombones* '56; *And Five Trumpets, And Five Saxes* '57; *In Person, Voices In Love* '68; *And Five Guitars* '60. Their modern harmonies had their effect on pop through the BEACH BOYS.

FOUR LADS, The Canadian/USA vocal group formed in Toronto at Cathedral Choir School. Lineup: James Arnold, first tenor; Bernard Toorish, second tenor; Frank Busseri, baritone; Connie Codarini, bass. Got audition from gospel group Golden Gate Quartet during gig in Toronto; recommended to agent, played clubs, TV in NYC; signed to CBS as backing group; backed Johnnie RAY on 2-sided mega-hit 'Cry'/'The Little White Cloud That Cried' '51; own first hit on Okeh '52 'The Mocking Bird', then on Columbia: 'Istanbul' and 'Skokian' were novelties with a beat '53-4, then huge hits with ballads 'Moments To Remember' '55, 'No, Not Much!' '56, both no. 2, both written by Bob Allen (b 5 Feb. '27, Troy, NY; pianist, arr./cond./prod.) and Al Stillman (b 26 June '06, NYC; d 17 Feb. '79, NYC), who also wrote 'Who Needs You' '57, 'There's Only One Of You' and 'Enchanted Island' '58 for the Lads, 'Chances Are' and 'It's Not For Me To Say' for Johnny MATHIS. 'Moments To Remember' popular for years as sentimental end-of-term high school/college song. Only other top 5 hit: 'Standing On The Corner' '56 from musical *The Most Happy Fella*: made LP of Frank LOESSER songs '57; also *On The Sunny Side* with Claude THORNHILL (no. 14 LP '56), *Breezin' Along* with Ray Ellis. Unpretentious group's friendly sound had 15 top 40 hits '52-8, incl. remake of first hit '58 (original re-entered on Epic at no. 67 '56). *Greatest Hits* on Cameo UK.

FOURMOST, The UK Merseybeat group '60s: Brian O'Hara (b 12 Mar. '42), lead guitar; Mike Millward (b 9 May '42), rhythm guitar (ex-Kingsize Taylor and the Dominoes), Dave Lovelady (b 16 Oct. '42), drums; Billy Hatton (b 9 June '41), bass. Previously known as Four Jays, then Four Mosts; signed with Brian EPSTEIN, had three top 20 hits with first three singles '63-4: 'Hello Little Girl', 'I'm In Love', 'A Little Loving' (first two lesser LENNON/McCARTNEY songs); three more top 40 hits '65-5 incl. cover of FOUR TOPS' 'Baby I Need Your Loving', since anthologised on Merseybeat compilations. Millward temporarily replaced by Bill Parkinson, then left because of ill health '65; died subsequently of leukaemia. Less gutsy sound than contemporaries plus comic stage routines enabled

them to switch to cabaret when hits failed; suffered through George MARTIN's insistence on recording them as straight pop band, while BARRON KNIGHTS later found popularity with similar brand of humour. Recorded BEATLE songs as Format late '60s, but were spent chart force.

FOUR PENNIES UK pop group mid-'60s; quartet all from Lancashire: Lionel Morton, vocals, rhythm guitar; Fritz Fryer, guitar; Mike Wilsh, piano; Alan Buck, drums. Vocally strong group had no. 1 single 'Juliet' '64, written by Morton, once choir boy at Blackburn Cathedral; three top 20 hits followed: 'I Found Out The Hard Way', version of LEADBELLY's 'Black Girl', both '64; 'Until It's Time For You To Go' '65. Moved on to cabaret circuit, split '67. (Entirely different group called Four Pennies still singing 'Juliet' on club circuit, '80s.) Morton, married to actress Julia Foster, began solo career; Buck became producer Radio Luxembourg, then into other record/show-biz jobs; Fryer had group Fritz, Mike and Mo, then became highly regarded record producer, working with HORSLIPS, Stackbridge, CLANNAD, MOTORHEAD and Prelude, incl. latter's hit 'After The Goldrush'.

FOUR PREPS, The USA vocal group formed at Hollywood High School. Lineup: Bruce Belland, Glen Larson, Ed Cobb, Marv Ingraham. Clean-cut group were era's equivalent of today's California soft-rock (pretty harmonising may have been an infl. on the BEACH BOYS). Signed by Capitol, had 13 entries in Hot 100 '56-64, six top 40 incl. '26 Miles' (no. 2, written by Larson and Belland), 'Big Man' (no. 3), both '58.

FOUR SEASONS, The USA vocal group formed Newark, N.J. '56 by Frankie Valli (b Francis Castelluccio, 3 May '37, Newark), lead; vocalists Tommy DeVito (b 19 June '36, Bellville, N.J.) and Hank Majewski, replaced by Nick Massi (b 19 Sep. '35, NYC), Nick DeVito, guitar. Originally known as Four Lovers, scored no. 62 hit with Otis BLACKWELL's 'You're The Apple Of My Eye' '56. Ex-Royal Teen Bob Gaudio (b 17 Nov. '42, NYC) on piano replaced Nick DeVito, led to crucial elaboration of doo-wop based sound; other major factor was

Bob Crewe of Swan Records, who signed group '60, co-wrote with Gaudio (who'd written Royal Teens 'Short Shorts', big '58 hit): they highlighted Valli's 3-octave voice. Worked as session singers, under various names, chose Four Seasons (after NYC restaurant) as 'Sherry' stormed up charts: upbeat first single for black Vee Jay label with Valli's falsetto lead got airplay on black stations before appearance on *American Bandstand* revealed Italian-Americans. 'Sherry' and 'Big Girls Don't Cry' were no. 1 '62, 'Walk Like A Man' in '63, 'Rag Doll' '64: with Beach Boys were the only name group to stay popular during British Invasion led by BEATLES, even scored in UK with nine top 40 entries in '60s (biggest 'Rag Doll' no. 2). Business-oriented group formed publishing companies, became profit-sharing partnership; first LPs interspersed hit singles with covers of Moonglows, Sensations, Skyliners, etc. who'd inspired them: even cheekily covered own '56 Four Lovers hit. 26 USA top 40 hits in a decade are as well-known for covers as for originals, testifying to Gaudio-Crewe writing partnership: 'Bye Bye Baby (Baby Goodbye)' (BAY CITY ROLLERS), 'Walk Like A Man' (Divine), 'Working My Way Back To You' (Spinners), many more enjoyed second stab at chart. Songs varied; Valli's falsetto set off with precise, uplifting harmonies even charted under pseudonym of the Wonder Who '65 (with cover of Bob DYLAN's 'Don't Think Twice'). Hits tailed off as they went progressive after *Sgt Pepper*: *Genuine Imitation Life Gazette* '69 was expensive flop; prod. Crewe was dumped as they left Philips, bought rights to master tapes as they had when leaving Vee Jay, ensuring healthy future earnings. Massi left '65, replaced by Joey Long, bass; DeVito was bought out '70 by Gaudio and Valli. Flirted with Motown's new Mowest label (LP *Chameleon* '72; UK hit single 'The Night' '75), concentrated on cabaret and Valli's solo career: he had four hits '60s incl. '67 no. 2 with future MOR classic 'Can't Take My Eyes Off You', 4 more '74-6 incl. no. 1 'My Eyes Adored You' (only Motown-era cut they liked enough to buy back). Restructured group, new personnel, made comeback on disco boom: Valli joined by Gerry Polci, drums, joint lead vocals; Don Ciccone, bass (ex-Critters); John Paiva, guitar; Lee Shapiro,

keyboards: now on WB, LP *Who Loves You* '75 no. 38, biggest LP since '64 except hits compilations; incl. title track (no. 3 USA/6 UK), 'December '63 (Oh What A Night)', no. 1 both USA/UK; solo career continued in tandem with BEE GEE prod. 'Grease' (from film; no. 1 USA/3 UK '78): lucky to be singing at all, having overcome hearing problems mid-'70s via surgery. Anthologies continue (*Story* '75 was '62-8 stuff); new Seasons tour, record (*Helicon* '77, *Reunited Live* '81).

FOUR TOPS, The USA soul vocal quartet formed as the Four Aims '53 in Detroit, lineup then as now: Levi Stubbs, lead; Abdul 'Duke' Fakir, Renaldo 'Obie' Benson, Lawrence Payton. Perfected technique on chitterling circuit, but no record success despite spells on Chess, Red Top, Columbia, Riverside. Payton's cousin Billy Davis had written hits for Jackie WILSON (with whom Stubbs had sung in Royals before joining other Tops); he introduced them to co-writer Berry Gordy, who signed them up. First release *Breaking Through* on Motown's Workshop label was jazz LP in HI-LOS vein, but after a year on the road with Billy ECKSTINE Revue, spell as backing singers on Motown's first hits, teamed with Eddie and Brian Holland, Lamont Dozier, fast-rising Motown writing/prod. team: 'Baby I Need Your Loving' (no. 11 '64) was smash pop chart debut that set pattern with Stubbs' impassioned lead vocal; fourth single 'I Can't Help Myself' was no. 1 '65, reminiscent of H-D-H's other charges the SUPREMES, with orchestration, massed tambourines, etc. Seventh USA top 40 hit 'Reach Out I'll Be There' was their finest moment: no. 1 both USA/UK '66; 3 biggest '67 hits as big on UK dancefloors as USA: 'Standing In The Shadows Of Love' (no. 6 USA/6 UK), 'Seven Rooms Of Gloom' (14/12), 'Bernadette' (4/8). Popularity in UK lasted longer too, as psychedelic soul of SLY STONE and Isaac HAYES rendered straightforward emotionalism of Tops unfashionable at home; reissue of 'I Can't Help Myself' made no. 10 UK, while covers of Tommy EDWARDS' 'It's All In The Game' and MOODY BLUES' 'Simple Game' both went top 5. Tops split to ABC-Dunhill as Motown moved to West Coast, H-D-H formed own Invictus label; chopped and changed prod. and lost consistency. Team with Brian Potter, Dennis Lambert initially successful: USA hits with 'Keeper Of The Castle' and 'Ain't No Woman Like The One I've Got' '72-3, but *Shaft In Africa* soundtrack '74 less so. Group took break, played cabaret to keep in trim, pursued other projects: Benson and Payton wrote for Marvin GAYE, Aretha FRANKLIN respectively (Benson co-wrote 'What's Going On'). Surprise comeback on disco-oriented Casablanca label '81 with 'When She Was My Girl' (USA 11/UK 3), 'Don't Walk Away' (UK 16), LP *Tonight* '82 with West Coast prod. David Wolfert, white soul session players: listened hard and incorporated elements of contemporary black music without compromising glorious vocal blend. After *One More Mountain* with Casablanca, returned to Motown after sensational appearance with TEMPTATIONS on 25th anniversary TV special; still one of black music's most consistent and best-loved acts.

FOWLEY, Kim (*b* 21 July '42, Manila) Singer, songwriter, producer. His father played Doc on *Wyatt Earp* TV show; his grandfather was composer Rudolph FRIML. In late '50s he worked in L.A. with Sandy NELSON, Phil SPECTOR, sang in black vocal group the Jayhawks; as DJ in Boise, Idaho prod. first records by Paul REVERE and the Raiders '59, then West Coast novelties 'Alley Oop' by the Hollywood Argyles (no. 1 '60), 'Popsicles And Icicles' for the Murmaids (written by David Gates of BREAD; no. 3 '64), others. In UK mid-'60s he worked with P. J. PROBY, appeared on TV's *Ready Steady Go*, prod. sessions for SLADE, FAMILY, SOFT MACHINE, others; back in USA he sang on Frank ZAPPA's landmark *Freak Out* album, prod. Gene VINCENT and Warren ZEVON '69, co-prod. Jonathan RICHMAN with John CALE. His own first LP *Love Is Alive And Well* '67 on Capitol followed his organisation of love-ins during the West Coast's flower-power period; later he was active in punk, organising all-girl Runaways '76 with Joan Jett. Other records incl. *Born To Be Wild*, *Outrageous* and *Good Clean Fun* '68-9 on Imperial; *I'm Bad* and *International Heroes* '72-3 on Capitol; *Animal God Of The Streets* and *Snake Document Masquerade* '79 on Island; other LPs in UK: *Sunset Boulevard* on Illegal,

Living In The Streets on Sonet and *Visions Of The Future* on Capitol '78-9 (the last aka *Hollywood Confidential*). He released uncounted singles under various names, was also dancer, actor, published poetry, etc.

FRAMPTON, Peter (*b* 22 Apr. '50, Beckenham, Kent) UK guitarist. Formed pop band the Herd early '65, with Andy Bown, keyboards; Gary Taylor, bass; Andrew Steele, drums. After flop singles Parlophone dropped them; they signed to Fontana, where Ken HOWARD & (Alan) BLAIKLEY (team behind Dave DEE, DOZY, BEAKY, MICK & TICH) orchestrated blend of pop and flower power: second single 'From The Underworld' pushed to no. 6 with help from pirate radio, followed by similar 'Paradise Lost', no. 15 early '68. Frampton was dubbed 'The Face of '68' by teen mag *Rave*. Album named after second hit single incl. some of band's writing, but highest chart placing was formula pop of 'I Don't Want Our Loving To Die' (no. 5), written by Howard/Blaikley. Steele left, replaced by Henry Spinetti; Frampton, dissatisfied with teen idol status and disappointed with failure of 'Sunshine Cottage' (reversion to psychedelic style), left for HUMBLE PIE. (Bown and Spinetti made flop single 'The Game' without Frampton, then formed shortlived Judas Jump with Mike Smith and Allen Jones, saxists from Amen Corner, and Welsh vocalist Adrian Williams; Taylor and Steele reunited for one-off single 'You Got Me Hangin' From Your Lovin' Tree' '71; Taylor became DJ, later worked with Fox; Steele and Spinetti did session work; Bown joined folk group Storyteller, came back to Frampton later.) Humble Pie, with ex-SMALL FACES leader Steve Marriott, never lived up to sum of parts; Frampton left hard-rocker Marriott, his love of melody persisting from youthful infl. (e.g. Kenny BURRELL). First solo LP *Wind Of Change* demonstrated melodic pop with help from heavy friends Ringo STARR, Billy PRESTON, Klaus Voorman, etc. (entered BEATLE orbit sessioning on George HARRISON's *All Things Must Pass*, as well as Harry NILSSON's *Son Of Schmilsson*). Formed Camel (became Frampton's Camel, because of Peter Bardens' CAMEL) for live work, with Mike Kellie (ex-SPOOKY TOOTH), drums; Rick Wills (ex-Cochise), bass; keyboardist Mickey Gallagher: early music (cf. *Frampton's Camel* '73) high on melody, low on lyrical content. Band toured widely, laying basis of future success; Kellie replaced by ex-Mitch RYDER drummer John Siomos; by *Frampton* '75, bassist was Andy Bown (who later reverted to keyboards with STATUS QUO); LP contained trademark tracks: 'Baby I Love Your Way', 'Show Me The Way', voicebox-led 'Do You Feel Like We Do'; all USA top 20 hits '76 in different live takes on 2-disc *Frampton Comes Alive*, recorded at San Francisco's Winterland: it was one of decade's best sellers – no. 1 USA for 10 weeks, in chart for nearly two years, certainly biggest selling live pop album ever; rewarded for years of touring by worldwide audience. In retrospect, attractively acoustic songs with sinuous electric lead were inferior in live versions whacked out at stadium volume without nuance of delicacy; but at the time 15-million plus sales brought them following, especially girls (as Humble Pie's *Performance – Rockin' The Fillmore* '71 established just before Frampton left: manager Dee Anthony was behind both ventures). But *I'm In You* '77 was vapid studio followup, couldn't be rescued by superstar guests, although title track USA no. 2, LP no. 2 (in chart only 32 weeks). Starring role in Robert Stigwood/BEE GEES film *Sgt Pepper's Lonely Hearts Club Band* brought little lustre; with punk/new wave in full swing Frampton began to look like a dinosaur. Sabbatical dictated by near-fatal car crash '78 ended with *Where I Should Be* '79, no. 14 USA hit 'I Can't Stand It No More'; *Breaking All The Rules* '81 and *The Art Of Control* '82 saw locks shorn in new image, but fleeting moment of fame seemed past. *Premonition* '86 on Virgin updated sound with slabs of synth, but it didn't work.

FRANCIS, Connie (*b* Concetta Rosa Maria Franconero, 12 Dec. '38, Newark, N.J.) USA singer; said to have been the best selling female recording artist of late '50s – early '60s. Learned accordion at 3, local TV at 10, Arthur GODFREY TV talent scout show at 11; four years on *Startime* variety show; first single 'Freddy' on MGM May '55. 'Who's Sorry Now' (song from '23 recorded at suggestion of father) at no. 4; was first of 55 entries in Hot 100 '58-'69:

average of seven top 40 entries a year '58-64 incl. junky pop songs that stick in the mind whether we like it or not, slickly prod. with pseudo rock'n'roll beat and dominated by her big, strong, accurate voice ('Stupid Cupid' and 'Lipstick On Your Collar' are good examples) but also a large number of revivals of good old songs, e.g. 'My Happiness' (from '48; no. 2 '58), 'If I Didn't Care' ('39; no. 22 '59), 'Among My Souvenirs' ('27; no. 7 '59), 'Everybody's Somebody's Fool' ('50; her first no. 1 '60: second and last was 'My Heart Has A Mind Of Its Own' same year). Last top 40 hit was 'Be Anything (But Be Mine)' '64, of which there had been three hit versions in '52. Film debut in *Where The Boys Are* '61 (title song was no. 4 hit), then *Follow The Boys* '63 (no. 17 hit title), *Looking For Love* '64 (no. 45 title), *When The Boys Meet The Girls* '65. 25 top 50 hits UK '58-66 incl. no. 1 with 'Carolina Moon' '58 ('29 song on flip side of 'Stupid Cupid'). 60-odd LPs: 21 charted USA '60-6 incl. four compilations of hits, three soundtrack albums, live *Connie Francis At The Copa* '61, albums of country, Jewish and Italian songs. Did charity work for CARE, USO, UNICEF late '60s; sang for GIs in Vietnam; then victim of rape-robbery at knifepoint Nov. '74 after performing at Westbury (NY) Music Fair. Long hiatus in career; '77 hits compilation *20 Golden Greats* was no. 1 UK; warmly received comeback at Westbury '81, but dogged by problems since the crime.

FRANCO (*b* L'Okanga La Ndju Pene Luambo Makiadi, '38, Sona-Bata, Zaire) Singer-composer, guitarist, bandleader, probably Africa's most popular musician: legend in his lifetime, guitar virtuoso, leader for 30 years of one of the most infl. orchestras, TPOK Jazz, releasing more than 100 albums and uncounted singles. Began at age 12 with first master Ebengo Dewayon in the Watam Group; recorded with him '53, made first solo record later that year 'Bolingo na ngai na Beatrice' on Loningisa label; began to perform own live shows; in mid-'56 OK Jazz was born, 10-piece rumba band led by Franco, De La Lune and Essous. Band moved to Brazzaville '57, returned to Kinshasa '58, whereupon Franco was jailed for some months for a motoring offence, but soon recovered reputation as 'sorcerer of the guitar', so influential that at end of decade there were distinct schools: his and that of Dr NICO. Early works of OK Jazz on 6 vols. of *Authenticité* (through '62) and *L'Afrique Danse No. 6* (mid-'60s), all on Africaine label. Toured, recorded prolifically through '60s, keeping clear musical direction despite changes in personnel: list of graduates is Who's Who of Zairean music, incl. Vicky, Sam MANGWANA, Prince Youlou Mabiala, Wuta May, Mose Se Sengo (FanFan), Josky, Michelino and Dalienst. Mid-'70s LPs featuring many of these are *A.Z.D.A.* and *Mabele. 20ème Anniversaire* '76 celebrated decades; by this time Franco could fill dance halls anywhere, proved it with '78 tour, 2-disc *Live Recording*. Now a 23-piece outfit with 4 horns, 4 guitars, bass, singers and percussionists, captured on 2-disc *Le 24ème Anniveraire* '80. Social commentary sometimes got him into trouble; served 2 months '78 for songs 'Helene' and 'Jackie', but decorated later same year by President Mobutu, later dubbed 'Le Grand Maître' of Zairean music, second musician after Kabaselle to be so honoured. *Respect, Bimansha, Tailleur, Mandola* on Pop label '81, along with *Coup de Monde, À Paris, À Bruxelles*; shared *Co-operation* '82 with Mangwana '82, also 5 more LPs on Pop incl. 2-disc *Disque d'Or*; joined Tabu Ley on *Choc Choc Choc* and *L'Évènement*; '84 saw *Très Impoli, Candidat Mobutu, L'Ancienne Belgique* and *Chez Rhythmes*. Toured USA '83, made UK debut '84. Now spends much time in Brussels; established second band to back him in Europe early '80s; has night club/hotel and record label in Zaire; may still make breakthrough to international charts. Hit album *Mario* '85 shows no loss of power: described as the Balzac of African music, intends to keep playing until year 2000.

FRANK, Jackson C. (*b* '43, Buffalo, NY) USA singer/songwriter infl. in London during mid-'60s folk boom. Songs covered by Sandy DENNY, Bert Jansch, FAIRPORT CONVENTION; Frank himself made only LP *Jackson C. Frank* '65, reissued '78: cult classic prod. by Paul SIMON, second guitar played by young Al Stewart; incl. best-known song 'Blues Run The Game' (world-weary gem of genre), eight other originals. Regular feature on folkclub circuit; once

shared flat with Denny, Simon, Art GARFUNKEL; began work on second LP '68 but never completed it. Said to have been badly injured in fire at Woodstock home. Jansch called him 'as influential as Bob DYLAN' in mid-'60s; evidence of album suggests great ability unfulfilled.

FRANKIE GOES TO HOLLYWOOD UK pop band, controversial in early '80s. Lineup: Holly Johnson (*b* 9 Feb. '60) and Paul Rutherford (*b* 12 Dec. '59), vocals; Mark O'Toole, bass (*b* 16 Jan. '64); Peter Gill, drums (*b* 8 Mar. '60); Brian Nash, guitar (*b* 20 May '63). Only Holly had any experience, in Liverpool band Big In Japan '78. Came together there, taking name from old *Variety* headline about Frank SINATRA's film plans. Turned down by Arista, band made sado-masochistic video to accompany early version of 'Relax!', shown on infl. TV show *The Tube*, attracting attention of Trevor HORN; became first signing to his new ZTT label; marketed by former *New Musical Express* journalist Paul Morley, became the most talked-about band in the land. Early versions of notorious single incl. Ian DURY's Blockheads, though Frankies did play on released single. BBC Radio 1 DJ Mike Read banned it as obscene, ensuring no. 1 hit '83 for five weeks; next single 'Two Tribes' raced to top six months later; 'The Power Of Love' late '84: they matched 20-year-old record of GERRY AND THE PACEMAKERS by reaching no. 1 with first three singles (incl. 'Ferry Cross The Mersey' as B-side of 'Relax!'). Debut album *Welcome To The Pleasure Dome* '84 had record £1m in advance orders; contained versions of hits plus lively cover of Bruce SPRINGSTEEN's 'Born To Run'. Title track was group's fourth single, failed to set new record. Aside from moralists, FGTH have attracted adverse criticism for releasing dozens of different mixes, for being Horn's puppets, for being controversial for its own sake: synonymous with depravity, they appeared in Brian de Palma's film about sleaze *Body Double* '85. No group since the SEX PISTOLS made such headlines in such a short time, but second LP *Liverpool* '86 'betrays both a poverty of imagination and a fumbling lack of direction and momentum', wrote David Sinclair in *The Times*. In other words, they're just another band.

FRANKLIN, Aretha (*b* 25 Mar. '42, Memphis, Tenn.) Soul singer, aka 'Lady Soul', 'the Queen of Soul': she has had more million-selling singles than any other woman in the history of recorded sound, with 60 sides in Billboard's Hot 100 '61-82, 32 in top 40; 33 LPs in top 200 '62-83, 14 in top 20. Daughter of Rev. C. L. Franklin, nationally famous gospel singer; sang in father's Detroit Baptist church with sisters Erma and Carolyn; made first solo records at 14. Toured gospel circuit as teenager, began singing secular material and signed to CBS/Columbia '61-6: LPs incl. *Aretha, The Electrifying Aretha Franklin, The Tender, The Moving, The Swinging Aretha Franklin* (first and best of four CBS LPs to chart not incl. compilations, at no. 69 '62), *Laughing On The Outside, Unforgettable, Runnin' Out Of Fools* (no. 84 '64), *Yeah!!!, Soul Sister, Take It Like You Give It, Lee Cross* '67. CBS compilations incl. *Greatest Hits* and *Take A Look* '67, 2-disc *In The Beginning* '72. Eight CBS singles charted incl. 'Won't Be Long' '61 with Ray BRYANT Combo; only one top 40: 'Rock-A-Bye Your Baby With A Dixie Melody' (no. 37 '61), an Al JOLSON chestnut also revived by comedian Jerry Lewis (no. 10 '56). Won New Star award in a *Downbeat* international critics poll, but image remained unclear: then to Atlantic label where prod. Jerry Wexler, arr. Arif Mardin, engineer Tom DOWD found groove for her intensity, four octave range, breath control, gritty conviction: she stopped watering herself down, had five top 10 hits in '67 alone: 'I Never Loved A Man (The Way I Love You)', 'Respect' (no. 1), 'Baby I Love You', '(You Make Me Feel Like) A Natural Woman', 'Chain Of Fools'; in '68 '(Sweet Sweet Baby) Since You've Been Gone', 'Think', 2-sided hit 'The House That Jack Built'/'I Say A Little Prayer'. At the top after years of being mismanaged, with record shops not sure which bin to put her records in, she became 'controversial': i.e. difficult to interview. Fans didn't mind. Top 20 Atlantic LPs incl. *I Never Loved A Man The Way I Love You* and *Aretha Arrives* '67; *Lady Soul, Aretha Now, Aretha in Paris* (from Olympia Theatre), all '68; *Soul* '69 and *Aretha's Gold* '69; *This Girl's In Love With You* '70; *Live At The Fillmore West* and *Greatest Hits* '71; *Young, Gifted & Black* '72, *Let Me In Your Life* '74. But she was unhappy in her personal life; her friends waited for her in church: *Amazing Grace* was her triumphant return, recorded live in L.A. Jan. '72 with Rev. James CLEVELAND, Southern California Community Choir; LP won her eighth Grammy. 'If you wanna know the truth,' her father said, 'she's never left the church!' Old friend Mahalia JACKSON lived just long enough to know that Franklin had come home, if only for a visit; just a month later she sang at Jackson's funeral. Other LPs incl. *Spirit In The Dark* '70, *Hey Now Hey (The Other Side Of The Sky)* '73, *With Everything I Feel In Me* '74, *You* '75, *Sweet Passion* '77, *Almighty Fire* '78, *La Diva* '79; songs from film *Sparkle* '76, LP prod. by Percy MAYFIELD. When sales of singles tapered off she switched to Arista, worked at first with Mardin, hoping to recapture earlier success; also appeared in John Landis film *The Blues Brothers* '80 singing 'Respect' and 'Think'. Arista LPs *Aretha* '80, *Love All The Hurt Away* '81, *Jump To It* '82, disco-style *Get It Right* '83 charted, last three in top 30, but relations with label soured: Arista sought return of advances. Meanwhile, as she prepared to star in *Sing, Mahalia, Sing* in Detroit '84, her beloved father died. She bounced back, as usual: settlement with Arista out of court was followed by no. 13 LP *Who's Zoomin' Who?* '85, incl. first top 10 singles since '72 (title track; 'Freeway Of Love'); *Aretha* '86 featured duet with George Michael, cover of 'Jumpin' Jack Flash' with Keith Richard, '46 show tune 'Look The Rainbow'. The Queen of Soul has never exceeded the excitement of her Atlantic debut, but still reigns; mid-'87 she made 2-disc *One Lord, One Faith, One Baptism* in her father's Detroit church, with sisters, cousin Brenda Corbett, Joe Ligon from the Mighty Clouds Of Joy, Mavis STAPLES, 100-voice choir and Jesse Jackson preaching a moving sermon about drug use among black young people.

FRANKS, Michael (*b* 18 Sep. '44, La Jolla, Cal.) Singer-songwriter. Performed folk-rock material while in high school; studied contemporary lit. at UCLA, working at music in spare time; while at U. of Montreal gigged with Gordon LIGHTFOOT. Taught undergrad music courses early '70s, attending both UCLA and Berkeley; scored two films *Count Your Bullets* and *Zandy's Bride* '71. Wrote three songs for A&M LP by Sonny TERRY and Brownie McGHEE; recommended by them to new label Brut: first LP *Michael Franks* '73. Toured US playing support; did film work in UK; signed to Reprise for LP *The Art Of Tea*; then to Warners: LPs incl. *Sleeping Gypsy* '77, *Birchfield Nines* '78, *Tiger In The Rain* '79, *One Bad Habit* '80, *Objects Of Desire* '82, *Passion Fruit* '83, using such back-up as Flora PURIM, Kenny Rankin, Ron CARTER, The CRUSADERS, David SANBORN, Toots THIELEMANS, Eric Gale, Eddie Gomez, Astrud Gilberto and others. Songs have been covered by MANHATTAN TRANSFER ('Popsickle Toes'), Melissa MANCHESTER, Patti LaBELLE, Carmen McRAE, the CARPENTERS, others. Worked on projected musical *Noa Noa*, about Paul Gauguin's life in Tahiti.

FRAZIER, Dallas (*b* 27 Oct. '39, Spiro, Okla.) Child prodigy, country songwriter, singer. To Bakersfield, Calif. as a child; raised on farms. Won talent contest put on by Faron YOUNG '51, signed recording contract with Capitol '53, released a few singles and was regular on Cliffie STONE's *Hometown Jamboree*. Toured with Ferlin HUSKY '56-8; wrote 'Alley Oop', big pop hit for the Hollywood Argyles '60; moved to Nashville '63 to concentrate on writing and recording. With Capitol again, had hits ('Everybody Ought To Sing A Song', 'Sunshine Of My World' '68) but more successful as writer, e.g. 'There Goes My Everything' (Jack GREENE), 'Son Of Hickory Holler's Tramp' (O. C. SMITH), 'If My Heart Had Windows' (George JONES). With A.L. 'Doodle' Owens wrote several no. ones for Charley PRIDE ('All I Have To Offer You Is Me', 'I'm So Afraid Of Losing You Again', etc.). Signed to RCA '69, made good LPs, singles that didn't sell; returned to writing. Semi-retired since '76, though old songs since became hits (e.g. 'Elvira' for the OAK RIDGE BOYS, '81). LPs incl. *Elvira* '67 on Capitol; *Singing My Songs* '70, *My Baby Packed Up And Left Me* '71 on RCA.

FREBERG, Stan (*b* 7 Aug. '26, Pasadena, Cal.) USA satirist, shredding ridiculous aspects of pop music mid-'50s. Worked on stage with magician uncle at age 11; did funny voices on radio for Cliffie STONE in teens, then after WWII for WB, Disney, Lantz, Paramount animation studios, then with Daws Butler on kiddie TV show *Time For Beany*. Satire on records for Capitol began '50 with 'John And Marsha', send-up of radio soap operas; biggest hit was 'St George And The Dragonet' '53: queues at record shops for roast of radio/TV cop show *Dragnet*, using famous 'dummm-de-dumdum' theme by Walter Schumann, Sgt Friday's catchphrases ('Just the facts, m'am'), outrageous puns, impeccable comic timing, aided by Butler, June Foray, mus. dir. by Billy MAY. Sendups of pop were priceless: on 'The Great Pretender' a bop pianist refused to play 'that kling-kling-kling jazz'; in 'Banana Boat (Day O)' '57 Peter Leeds played wonderfully straight A&R man who wouldn't allow dialect. Lawrence WELK was sent up '57; 'The Old Payola Roll Blues' was topical in '60: created character 'Clyde Ankle' which captured era's hype of nontalents so effectively that there was no more to be done; in that pre-BEATLE era Freberg thought that pop music was so bad it could no longer be satirised and turned to advertising: instant coffee commercials, etc. were also funny. Concept LP *Stan Freberg Presents The United States Of America* charted '61 with music by May. Hits compilation *A Child's Garden Of Freberg* reissued '88 on Jasmine.

FRED, John (*b* 8 May '41, Baton Rouge, La.) Singer, bandleader. Cut first record late '58 with Fats DOMINO's band while still in high school: 'Shirley' by 'John Fred and the Playboys' reached no. 82 in pop chart. Other singles less successful, though using the JORDANAIRES and Mac REBENNACK on some sessions. Attended Southeastern U. '60-3; new Playboy Band gained regional following with singles on N-Joy, Jewel labels '63-5; switched to Paula; seventh Paula single 'Judy In Disguise (With Glasses)' became no. 1 in USA, no. 3 UK, a bubblegum piece owing much to the BEATLES' 'Lucy In The Sky'. A pop-soul band covering material by James BROWN, Wilson PICKETT, Otis REDDING, etc., Playboys toured Europe (with TRAFFIC in Hamburg); did psychedelic LP *Permanently Stated*; had one further hit 'Hey, Hey, Bunny' in '68 and broke up. Fred re-formed and made more singles '69-76 but no more hits. Later producing records as vice-president of RCS, Baton Rouge.

FREDDIE AND THE DREAMERS UK beat group formed in Manchester '59: former milkman Freddie Garrity (*b* 14 Nov. '40) with Derek Quinn (*b* 24 May '42), lead guitar; Roy Crewsdon (*b* 29 May '41), rhythm guitar; Bernie Dwyer (*b* 11 Sep. '40), drums; Pete Birrell (*b* 9 May '41), bass. Garrity had surfed on skiffle fad with brother Derek in the Red Sox, then Kingfishers who were renamed as Freddie's antics took over: an unlikely pop star, he played it for laughs while group sent up syncopated moves (*à la* SHADOWS) behind him. Auditioned for BBC children's TV; after an appearance EMI/Columbia signed them up. Top 5 UK hits '63-4: 'If You Gotta Make A Fool Of Somebody' (no. 3 first single), 'I'm Telling You Now' (written by Garrity and GERRY AND THE PACEMAKERS songsmith Mitch Murray; no. 1 USA two years later), 'You Were Made For Me' (by Murray), 'I Understand' (cover of 10-year-old Four Tunes song). Group made films *What A Crazy World*, *Every Day's A Holiday* '63-4; toured USA and profited from British Invasion with labels Tower, Mercury issuing stuff (sole USA-only hit was dance number 'Do The Freddie'). Hits ran out '65; group split early '70s. Garrity, Birrell starred in children's TV series *Little Big Time*; Garrity has worked cabaret circuits with new lineups.

FREE UK blues/rock group formed London '68: Paul Kossoff (*b* 14 Sep. '50, London; *d* 19 Mar. '76, USA), guitar; Paul Rodgers (*b* 17 Dec. '49, Middlesbrough), vocals; Andy Fraser (*b* 7 Aug. '52, London), bass; and Simon Kirke (*b* 28 July '48, Shropshire), drums. Ex-Black Cat Bones Kossoff and Kirke recruited Brown Sugar vocalist Rodgers; teenage prodigy Fraser had been with John MAYALL's Bluesbreakers; name Free suggested by Alexis KORNER. Neither *Tons Of Sobs* '68 nor *Free* '69 made impact on music scene waiting for new CREAM, so sudden success of single 'All Right Now' from *Fire And Water* '70 was unexpected: Rodgers/Fraser tune no. 4 USA/no. 2 UK; displayed Kossoff's wailing guitar, Rodgers' earthy vocal, Fraser's sinuous yet rock-solid bass upfront in mix. But *Highway* '70 did

not yield a follow-up: 'Stealer' flopped in UK, did not make top 40 USA; frictions in band left *Free Live* '71 as essential souvenir. Rodgers and Kossoff formed Peace and Toby respectively but failed; Kossoff and Kirke made easygoing instrumental rock LP *Kossoff Kirke Tetsu And Rabbit* '71 with Tetsu Yamauchi and Texan John 'Rabbit' Bundrick; after brief, stormy reunion with original lineup for *Free At Last* '72, Bundrick and Tetsu became members of new Free; had UK hits 'My Brother Jake' no. 4 '71, 'Little Bit Of Love' no. 13 '72, last LP *Heartbreaker* '73 yielded 'Wishing Well', no 15: final split after Kossoff collapsed onstage (Osibisa guitarist Wendell Richardson substituted). Rodgers and Kirke formed BAD COMPANY; Kossoff formed Back Street Crawler but died of heart attack; Tetsu joined FACES; Fraser formed Sharks with ace session guitarist Chris Spedding, later own Andy Fraser Band, but never fulfilled promise; Rabbit joined WHO as unofficial member. One of the best UK blues bands was impeded by problems of ego (various) and drugs (Kossoff), but 'All Right Now' remains anthem: no. 11 UK '78 on reissue. *Best Of Free* LP charted USA '75; 10th anniversary of Kossoff's death marked by 2-disc *Blue Soul*, live and previously unreleased Free tracks.

FREED, Alan (*b* 15 Dec. '22, Johnstown, Pa.; *d* 20 Jan. '65, Palm Springs, Fla.) USA DJ who gave rock'n'roll its name. Fronted jazz band Sultans of Swing in Ohio high school, became interested in radio at college. After WWII moved from WKST (New Castle, Pa.) through WKBN and WAKR in Akron, Ohio to WJW in Cleveland, where he started Moondog's Rock'n'Roll Party, playing rhythm and blues but rechristening it to avoid racial stigma. Surprise caused mini-riot when 25,000 fans tried to attend live Moondog Coronation Ball Mar. '52, but important fact was that majority were white. Moved to WINS NYC '54, carried on concert activities still breaking down racial barriers; syndicated shows in USA and to Europe (Radio Luxembourg); manic style and jive patter (lubricated with copious quantities of scotch) both irresistible and inimitable. Appeared in quickie films *Rock Around The Clock* and *Don't Knock The Rock* '56, *Rock, Rock, Rock* and *Mr Rock'n'Roll*

'57, others; also took favours from music sources (e.g. co-credit as writer of Chuck BERRY's 'Maybelline', which he helped to make hit); by refusing to play inferior white covers of black records he made enemies who later exploited his carelessness. Riot at Boston Arena led to charges of incitement, dropped 17 months later, but legal bills bankrupted him; fired from WABC late '59 for refusing to sign affidavit denying he'd accepted payola: honesty/naivety led to 26 counts of commercial bribery; escaped with fine, suspended sentence but career was broken. Others were luckier, but Freed was believed when he bragged that he'd never played a record he didn't like. Died while facing charges of income tax evasion; *Cashbox* wrote that 'he suffered the most . . . for alleged wrongs that had become a way of life for many others'.

FREEMAN, Bobby (*b* 13 June '40, San Francisco) USA R&B singer who played piano and sang with Romancers on Dootone label at age 14. Wrote classic 'Do You Wanna Dance' for no. 5 hit on Josie '58, followed with less successful 'Betty Lou Got A New Pair Of Shoes', 'Need Your Love', 'Shame On You Miss Johnson'. At his best live, with dancing skills and rousing act; persevered and returned to top 40 '60 with dance number '(I Do The) Shimmy Shimmy' on King. Signed by SLY STONE to DJ Tom Donahue's Autumn label which recorded Stone-prod. 'C'mon And Swim' as second release; second dance number and last big hit was no. 5 '64. Recorded soul for Double-Shot, Touch labels in the '70s, but revivals of 'Do You Wanna Dance' by the BEACH BOYS, Bette MIDLER, the RAMONES etc. keep him famous.

FREEMAN, Bud (*b* Lawrence Freeman, 13 Apr. '06, Chicago) Tenor sax in Chicago style, associated with Austin High Gang (*see* JAZZ). Played in Europe as early as '28: with tone similar to Lester YOUNG's but distinctive, swinging ideas, first great white player on the instrument and the only original tenor voice apart from Coleman HAWKINS until Young. Played with dance/jazz bands Roger Wolfe KAHN, Ben POLLACK, Paul WHITEMAN, Zez CONFREY, Red NICHOLS, Joe Haymes etc.; with Ray NOBLE '35, Tommy DORSEY, then Benny GOODMAN

'36-9. Records under own name late '28 Chicago with Red MCKENZIE, Gene KRUPA, six others; Windy City Five '35 NYC with Bunny BERIGAN, Claude THORNHILL, Eddie CONDON, Grachan Moncur (bass), Cozy COLE; with trio and octet on Commodore '38 (LP compilation *Three's No Crowd*); own small group Summa Cum Laude Orchestra '39-40 on several labels, notably Bluebird (Victor) July '39, with Condon, Pee Wee RUSSELL, Max KAMINSKY, four others: 'China Boy', 'Easy To Get', 'I've Found A New Baby' and 'The Eel' (latter tour-de-force also cut '33 at a Condon date). Bud Freeman and his Chicagoans session '40 with Jack TEAGARDEN has been reissued many times as classic of Chicago style. Played in US Army '43-5, since then freelance, often with trio (Dot LP as Summa Cum Laude Trio); many jazz festivals. Published *You Don't Look Like A Musician*. Founder member of WORLD'S GREATEST JAZZ BAND; lived in London from '74. Own LPs on Monmouth-Evergreen c.'70 incl. *The Compleat Bud Freeman* (with delightful tune 'Mr Toad'), *Music Of Hoagy Carmichael* and another with Lee WILEY; on Chiaroscuro: *The Joy Of Sax* '74 with Jess STACY; *Swinging Tenors* on Affinity had Freeman trio on one side, Eddie MILLER on reverse; also *Stop, Look And Listen To Bud Freeman* on Affinity; *Last Night When We Were Young* c.'62 on Black Lion UK; Cambridge City Jassband on Plant Life Jazz UK; with Bob Barnard Jazz Band '76 on Swaggie; with Jimmy McPARTLAND on Circle, Teagarden on Verve etc. Returned to Chicago; *The Real Bud Freeman* '84 on Principally Jazz label is quintet set with mixture of standards, witty Freeman originals; compact disc edition has three more tunes.

FREEMAN, Chico (*b* 17 July '49, Chicago, Ill.) Saxophones, bass clarinet, composer. Father is Von FREEMAN (*see below*). Played with the FOUR TOPS, ISLEY BROS, EARTH, WIND & FIRE; was member of AACM '72. Won awards at the Notre Dame Jazz Festival '73, *Downbeat* polls. Played in Jack DEJOHNETTE's Music Machine, as well as in Special Edition (quartet *Tin Can Alley* on ECM); on Don PULLEN album *Warriors* '78; mostly own groups since late '70s. On half of *Fathers And Sons* '81 with Von,

Cecil McBee, DeJohnette (Columbia LP; MARSALIS family on the other side). First own LP *Streetdancer Rising* '75 on Dharma, then *Morning Prayer* '76 with Henry THREADGILL, Muhal Richard ABRAMS, Cecil McBee, others, now on India Navigation; others on that label incl. *Chico* '77 (one side a duo suite with McBee), *Kings Of Mali* '77, *The Outside Within* '78, ballad set *Spirit Sensitive* '79, *The Search* '82 with vocalist Val Ely. On Contemporary: *Beyond The Rain* '77, *Peaceful Heart, Gentle Spirit* '80, *Destiny's Dance* '81 with Bobby HUTCHERSON, Wynton MARSALIS, McBee; also *No Time Left* '79 on Black Saint. On Elektra Musician: *Tradition In Transition* '82 with McBee, DeJohnette, drummer Billy Hart (*b* 29 Nov. '40, Washington DC), Clyde Criner, piano; Wallace Roney, trumpet: LP incl. 'Free Association', 'Each One Teach One', 'Mys-story', MONK's 'Jackie-ing' etc.; *Tangents* '84 features Bobby MCFERRIN on some tracks. Toured '85 with quartet incl. McBee, drummer Fred Waits (*b* 27 Apr. '43, Jackson, Ms.), Mark Thompson (from NYC) on piano; played many of the tunes on *Transition*, playing incl. bits of Pharoah SANDERS and John COLTRANE, R&B etc. all absorbed and under control; plays difficult bass clarinet beautifully. His conservative compositions fall into 'new traditionalist' category; in person his playing seems to have power and technique in reserve; he is also a personable leader on the stand. *The Pied Piper* '86 on Blackhawk incl. John Purcell on woodwinds, Thompson, McBee, Elvin JONES, Kenny Kirkland. Also played on McBee's *Alternate Spaces* on India Navigation with Don PULLEN, etc.; toured with quintet incl. Branford MARSALIS, and with The Leaders: lineup incl. Arthur BLYTHE, Lester BOWIE, McBee, Don Moye, pianist Kirk Lightsey. *Tales Of Ellington* '87 incl. Ellington tunes and Duke-inspired originals. Quintet tour '88 incl. father Von, Lightsey, Moye, Lonnie PLAXICO.

FREEMAN, Von (*b* Earl Lavon Freeman, 3 Oct. '22, Chicago) Tenor sax. Attended Du Sable High School with Bennie GREEN, Gene AMMONS; studied there under legendary Capt. Walter DYETT. Brothers also musicians: George (guitar), Bruz (drums). Played with Horace HENDERSON, SUN RA;

recorded with Charlie PARKER on Savoy, but work mostly confined to Chicago. Had band with brothers, David Shipp on bass (*d* '82), Andrew HILL '51; recorded with Hill '52 in Chicago: two cuts on obscure Ping label with Hill on organ, Pat Patrick on baritone, Malachi Favors on bass (later with ART ENSEMBLE), Wilbur Campbell on drums; played with Dexter GORDON in Chicago '70, etc. Plays on George Freeman LPs *Birth Sign* '69 on Delmark, *New Improved Funk* c.'76 on People (George also made *Man & Woman* c.'74 on Groove Merchant). Own LPs incl. 4 quartet sets: *Doin' It Right Now* on Atlantic '72 with Sam JONES, Jimmy COBB, John Young (*b* 16 Mar. '22, Little Rock, Ark.) on piano (incl. own tunes 'Portrait Of Johnny Young', 'Brother George'); *Have No Fear* and *Serenade & Blues* on Nessa, both recorded mid-'75 with Chicagoans Young, Campbell, Shipp: incl. Freeman tunes 'After Dark', 'Von Freeman's Blues', 'Have No Fear, Soul Is Here'. Wonderfully relaxed Nessa session sounds 'Just the way I'd play at the Enterprise Lounge': excellent rhythm section provides jaunty lope even at slow tempos, bold humour and Freeman's unique tone the keynote throughout. *Young And Foolish* '77 with Shipp, Young, drummer Charles Walton on obscure Dutch Daybreak label made at festival in Laren; return to Laren '78 resulted in *Lockin' Horns* with Willis JACKSON quartet on Muse; one side of *Fathers And Sons* '81 on Columbia with son Chico FREEMAN completes discography of underrated master. *Young And Foolish* reissued on Affinity '88 at time of first visit to UK, in two-tenor quintet with Chico.

FRICKE, Janie (*b* 19 Dec. '52, South Whitney, Ind.) Nashville session singer, now country star in her own right. Sang in church, later did jingle singing to pay fees while attending U. of Indiana. Moved to L.A. '73 to work as session singer; not enough work so moved to Nashville, where she has sung on over 1600 records: work on records by Dolly PARTON, Elvis PRESLEY, Loretta LYNN, Crystal GAYLE, Johnny DUNCAN, Vern Gosdin unmistakable; with Johnny CASH on 'The Cowboy And The Lady'; work with Duncan on no. 1 country hit 'Stranger' '76 led to Columbia contract '77, first hit 'What're You Doing Tonight';

update of 'Please Help Me I'm Falling' '78 gave her top 10 hit, then a string of top country hits: 'Down To My Last Broken Heart' '80, 'I'll Need Someone To Hold Me' '81, 'Don't Worry About Me Baby' '82, 'He's A Heartache (Looking For A Place To Happen)' and 'Tell Me A Lie' '83, 'Let's Stop Talking About It' and 'Your Heart's Not In It' '84. Having toured with ALABAMA and with prod. Bob Montgomery, moved from ballads into country-rock sound. Named best new female vocalist '78-9, top female vocalist '82-4. LPs incl. *Singer Of Songs* '78, *Love Notes* '79, *From The Heart* '80, *I'll Need Someone To Hold Me* '81, *Nice'n'Easy* '81 (with Duncan), *Sleeping With Your Memory* '82, *It Ain't Easy* '82 (hit title track 'It Ain't Easy Bein' Easy'), *Love Lines* '83, *Somebody Else's Fire* '85. Duets on Merle HAGGARD LP *It's All In The Game* '84.

FRIEDHOFER, Hugo Wilhelm (*b* 3 May '01, San Francisco; *d* 17 May '81, L.A., Cal.) Film composer. Played cello in cinema orchestra, wrote music for silent films, orchestrated scores for early talkies beginning with *Keep Your Sunny Side Up* c.'30. Assigned to work with Erich Wolfgang Korngold (*b* 29 May 1897, Brünn, Czechoslovakia; *d* 29 Nov. '57, Hollywood) and Max Steiner (*b* 10 May 1888, Vienna; *d* 28 Dec. '71, Beverly Hills) because he could speak German; they became more famous, but he had probably the greater skill; one of the first to understand that music for talkies was not the same as music for silent pictures. For many years he orchestrated others' work, incl. all of Errol Flynn's best-known films for Korngold, who would allow no one else to do it; for Steiner he actually ghost-wrote part of *Gone With The Wind* '39. One of his best was *One Eyed Jacks* '61, dir. by its star Marlon Brando; both film and score were butchered by the studio; soundtrack LP on UA is now a valuable collector's item. He said 'I have seen two authentic geniuses in this industry, Orson Welles and Marlon Brando. And this town, not knowing what to do with genius, destroys it.' It did not destroy Friedhofer, but kept him a secret, except among musicians. Won Oscar for his own *The Best Years Of Our Lives* '46 (LP on Entr'acte by LPO cond. by Collura); was nominated many times: said that nomination was the greater honour, because musicians voted on the nominees, final winner chosen by the less knowledgeable.

FRIEDMAN, Kinky (*b* Richard Friedman, 31 Oct. '44, Palatine, Texas) Country singer, bandleader. Psychology degree from U. of Texas; served in Peace Corps in Borneo; formed band the Texas Jewboys in Austin, playing outrageous country-flavoured stuff. First LP on Vanguard, *Sold American* '73 incl. 'Let Saigons Be Bygones', 'We Reserve The Right To Refuse Service To You'. One Friedman tune is called 'They Ain't Making Jews Like Jesus Anymore'. Black humour and four-letter words toned down for appearance on Grand Ole Opry; toured with part of Bob DYLAN Rolling Thunder Review '76; LP *Lasso From El Paso* '77 on Epic: title song was actually 'Asshole From El Paso'. The act was a good example of the freedom in country genre demanded by 'redneck rock'.

FRIML, Rudolph (*b* 7 Dec. 1879, Prague; *d* 12 Nov. '72, L.A.) Czech-born composer whose operetta style, like that of Sigmund ROMBERG, was superseded by American songwriters of the 20th century (Jerome KERN, Irving BERLIN, Cole PORTER, George GERSHWIN etc.) but whose work survived, especially on film, as late as the '50s. *Rose Marie* was written by Otto HARBACH and Oscar HAMMERSTEIN II '24 to ais music: filmed '36 (with Allan Jones, Nelson EDDY and Jeanette MacDonald) and '54 (with Howard KEEL); incl. title song and 'Indian Love Call', country hits for Slim WHITMAN '52-4. *Naughty Marietta* '35 established the popular team of Eddy-MacDonald, *The Firefly* '37 had Jones and MacDonald; *The Vagabond King* '56 incl. Kathryn Grayson, Rita Moreno.

FRIPP, Robert (*b* May '46, Dorset, England) Guitarist, composer, bandleader, teacher. With drummer Michael Giles (*b* '42, Bournemouth) and brother Pete Giles on bass made pop LP *The Cheerful Insanity Of Giles, Giles And Fripp* '68 on Deram, then split; Fripp and Michael Giles with Ian McDonald (*b* '46) on keyboards, sax, flute, vocals, Greg Lake on bass and vocals formed art-rock band King Crimson '69, made *In The Court Of The Crimson King* for Island (later on Polydor; Atlantic in USA) with lyricist Pete Sinfield also handling the light show for the live act; they also played at the ROLLING STONES free concert in Hyde Park in July; the LP went gold in the USA and the band carried on through many changes of personnel with Fripp as the only constant factor. McDonald and Giles left to make eponymous LP '71 on Cotillion; Lake left to form EMERSON, LAKE & PALMER but worked on *In The Wake Of Poseidon* '70, with Fripp on mellotron, Giles brothers sitting in, Mel Collins on reeds and Gordon Haskell on vocals and bass. *Lizard* '71 was finished with drummer Andy McCulloch, but Haskell left during its making (made *It Is And It Isn't* '71 on Atco in USA); *Island* '72 had Boz Burrell on bass and Ian Wallace on drums (Burrell and Haskell both vocalists, taught by Fripp to play bass). All the LPs charted well in the USA but tours were not particularly successful; disbanded '72 (live *Earthbound* issued in UK). Collins, Wallace and Burrell joined Alexis KORNER; Sinfield made *Still* '73 on Manticore; Fripp re-formed with Jamie Muir on percussion, David Cross on violin and mellotron, John Wetton (ex-FAMILY, later ASIA) on bass and vocals, drummer Bill BRUFORD (who left successful YES to join): this lineup did *Lark's Tongue In Aspic* '73; Muir dropped out and quartet made *Starless And Bible Black* '74; last studio LP *Red* '74 was made with help of Collins, McDonald; final USA tour resulted in live *USA* '75. Fripp combines electronics with classical technique, often playing while seated; whether music is portentous or pretentious is up to its fans, of whom there are many. In Oct. '74 he said 'King Crimson is completely over'; he made LPs *No Pussyfooting* and *Evening Star* '75-6 on Island/Antilles with Brian ENO and his tape-delay system, which developed into 'Frippertronics' for USA tour, LPs *Exposure* '79, *God Save The Queen* and *Under Heavy Manners* '80, *The League Of Gentlemen* and *Frippertronics/Let The Power Fall* '81, also *Network*, *God Save The King*, all on Polydor USA, EG UK. *I Advance Masked* '82 and *Bewitched* '84 on A&M. Re-formed King Crimson (intending to call it Discipline) '81 with Bruford, Tony Levin on bass, Adrian Belew on guitar (ex-Frank ZAPPA, David BOWIE, TALKING HEADS) for LPs *Discipline*

'81, *Beat* '82, *Three Of A Perfect Pair* on WB. He also sessioned with Bowie, Peter GABRIEL (with Levin), Talking Hheads, BLONDIE; prod. Daryl Hall LP *Sacred Songs* '80 on RCA. Wetton joined URIAH HEEP, Bruford GENESIS; they formed UK (*see* Bruford's entry). *A Young Person's Guide To King Crimson* first issued '75, now a 2-disc set with 20-page booklet from Polydor; *Robert Fripp And The League Of Crafty Guitarists: Live!* '86 from Fripp's master classes at Claymont Court, W.V. on Editions EG, also on video.

FRISHBERG, Dave (*b* 23 Mar. '33, St Paul, Minn.) Songwriter, pianist, singer. Began on piano as a child; intended to be a journalist, but inspired by Jimmy ROWLES on '46 Woody HERMAN small-group records to be a professional pianist. Studied journalism at college, elected music courses; served in USAF '55-6, started jingle company and worked at WNEW radio NYC; toured with Kai WINDING, played with Al COHN and Zoot SIMS, Ben WEBSTER; recorded with Jimmy RUSHING on ABC-Paramount and RCA; accompanied Carmen McRAE, Blossom DEARIE, Johnny TILLOTSON, ODETTA; met and learned from Johnny MERCER and Frank LOESSER. Wrote 'Peel Me A Grape' for Dick HAYMES and Fran Jeffries '62, funny songs to order for TV show *The Funny Side* '71 with Gene KELLY; worked with Herb ALPERT, made unreleased album with Anita O'DAY '75; began writing for himself and performing his own work with trio, opening Bing CROSBY show in Concord, Cal. '77. His are good American songs, marriages of music and words meant to be understood: witty, satirical, often nostalgic, some are love songs in disguise, as Whitney Balliett described them. He told Balliett that Mercer and Loesser 'knew that good lyrics should be literate speech that says something in a lyrical way. They knew that good lyrics come up to the edge of poetry and turn left.' Frishberg's voice is what Woody Allen might sound like if he were a cabaret singer, but he swings, and the slightly wimpish aspect helps the songs to complete success. Songs have been recorded by Dearie, Cleo LAINE, etc.; his own albums incl. octet set '68 on CTI, *Solo And Trio* '75 on Seeds; *Getting Some Fun Out Of Life* and *You're A Lucky Guy* on Concord

Jazz with small groups, two vols. of *Songbook* on Omnisound, *Live At Vine Street* '84, *Can't Take You Nowhere* '87 on Fantasy (made live in San Francisco).

FRIZZELL, David (*b* 26 Sep. '41, Texas) Country singer. Began late '50s touring with brother Lefty (*see below*). Signed to Columbia '64, recorded country and rockabilly without much success; became part of Buck OWENS empire in Bakersfield, Calif. working in TV, touring with Owens. Country hits 'L.A. International Airport' and 'I Just Can't Help Believing' '70 on Columbia; joined Cartwheel label ('Goodbye' minor hit '71), ABC-Dot, then Capitol '73 (minor hit 'Words Don't Come Easy'). Made demo with Shelley West (*b* 23 May '58, Nashville), daughter of Dottie WEST, of 'You're The Reason God Made Oklahoma'; turned down by all the record companies, then used in Clint Eastwood film *Every Which Way You Can* '80, became no. 1 country hit. More duet hits incl. 'Texas State Of Mind' '81; solo hits for David incl. 'I'm Gonna Hire A Wino To Decorate Our Home' '82. Albums incl. *Carryin' On The Family Names* '81, *Family Album* '82, *The Family's Fine, But This One's All Mine* '82, *On My Own Again* '83, all on Warner/Viva; *David Sings Lefty* '87 on Playback.

FRIZZELL, Lefty (*b* William Orville Frizzell, 31 Mar. '28, Corsicana, Texas; *d* 19 July '75) One of the great honky tonk singers. Radio work in El Dorado '38-9; worked in South Texas and New Mexico '44-50; boxing was another interest: left hook led to nickname. Demo of 'If You've Got The Money, I've Got The Time' led to Columbia contract '50, became no. 2 hit; continued with 'I Love You A Thousand Ways', 'Look What Thoughts Will Do', 'I Want To Be With You Always', 'Always Late', 'Mom And Dad's Waltz', 'Travelin' Blues', 'Give Me More, More, More', 'Don't Stay Away', 'Forever', 'I'm An Old, Old Man', all top 10 country hits '51-2. Joined Grand Ole Opry '52, but next year to West Coast, became regular on *Town Hall Party*, *Country America*. Hits tailed off, but incl. 'I Love You Mostly' '55, 'Cigarettes And Coffee Blues' '58, 'Long Black Veil' '59. Move back to Nashville '62 followed by biggest hit 'Saginaw, Michigan' (no. 1 '64) and 'She's

Gone, Gone, Gone' (top 10 '65). Deeply infl. by Jimmie RODGERS, distinctive, drawling vocal style in turn infl. Johnny Rodriguez, John ANDERSON, Willie NELSON, Merle HAGGARD; partly owing to Haggard's idolisation had new lease of chart life '70s: signed with ABC-Dot, for hits 'I Never Go Around Mirrors' and 'Lucky Arms' '74, 'Life's Like Poetry' '75. LPs incl. *Songs Of Jimmie Rodgers* '52 (reissued '73), *Saginaw, Michigan* '64, *Remembering Greatest Hits* '76, *Lefty Frizzell* '82, *The Legend Lives On* '83, all on CBS labels; *The Legendary* '73, *The Classic Style* '75 on ABC; *20 Golden Hits* '82 on CSP/Gusto; *Lefty Frizzell Boxed Set* '84 on Bear Family. Elected to Country Music Hall of Fame '82. Brother David (*see above*) also had hits.

FROEBA, Frankie (*b* Aug. '07, New Orleans, La.; *d* 18 Feb. '81, Miami, Fla.) Piano. Father played piano; worked age 15 solo, in groups, as theatre pianist. To NYC '24; led own bands Atlantic City, N.J. With various bands late '20s-early '30s incl. Enoch LIGHT, Irving AARONSON; part of early Benny GOODMAN lineup on *Let's Dance* radio show '34-5. Recorded on Columbia records '35-6, sidemen incl. Bunny BERIGAN, Joe Marsala, Cozy COLE, etc. Residency New York 18 Club '35-44; also led swing band dates for Decca with Bobby HACKETT, Buddy MORROW, etc. Played clubs '40s, mainly solo; also on radio, especially WNEW '41 through early '50s. Made pseudo-ragtime 'honky-tonk' fad records mid-'50s (*see* CRAZY OTTO); after '55 mostly solo in Miami area. Compositions incl. 'It All Begins And Ends With You' '36, 'The Jumpin' Jive' '39.

FROMAN, Jane (*b* 10 Nov. '07, St Louis, Mo.) Broadway singer. Had formal training; sang on WLW radio Cincinnati, with Paul WHITEMAN in Chicago; to NYC and success on radio, on stage (*Ziegfeld Follies Of 1934* etc.), musical films (*Stars Over Broadway* '35, *Radio City Revels* '38). Hit record '34 with 'I Only Have Eyes For You' (song by Al Dubin and Harry Warren from film *Dames*). Badly injured early '43 in plane crash in Portugal while on tour entertaining troops; recovered, opened in *Artists And Models* late '43 (folded after 28 performances); injuries gave trouble, career waned; made comeback early '50s with TV show *USA Canteen* and a few more hits incl. 'I'll Walk Alone', by Sammy CAHN and Jule Styne from '44 film *Follow The Boys*, revived in Froman biopic *With A Song In My Heart* '52 (Susan Hayward played Froman, who sang in soundtrack), and 'I Believe', inspirational hit introduced on her TV show (biggest version was by Frankie LAINE).

FROMHOLZ, Steve (*b* 8 June '45, Temple, Texas) Country-rock singer; cult following since mid-'70s. Joined Dallas County Jug Band in his teens; later teamed with Dan McCrimmon in duo Frummox: made LP *From Here To There* '69 on ABC-Probe. Toured with Stephen STILLS' Manassas, but left before they made the big time; went to work with Michael NESMITH on West Coast. Made LP *How Long Is The Road To Kentucky* for Nesmith's Countryside label, not released. Moved back to Texas '74, based in Austin; Willie NELSON recorded his 'I'd Have To Be Crazy' (country top 10 '76), helped out on Fromholz LP *A Rumor In My Own Time* '77 on Capitol; next LP *Frolicking In The Myth* '78 didn't sell; dropped by Capitol and signed with Nelson's Lone Star label: excellent album *Just Playin' Along* '79. Had three songs on film soundtrack *Outlaw Blues*; works Texas country-rock circuit.

FUGS, The Mid-'60s USA rock theatre phenomenon. Poets ('vocalists') Ed Sanders (marched on Pentagon; published literary journal *Fuck You*), Tuli Kupferberg (jumped off the Brooklyn Bridge and survived in Allen Ginsberg's *Howl*) were almost old enough to be Beatniks; became hippie-era satirists with drummer Ken Weaver, varying personnel incl. Peter Stampfel and Steve Weber of HOLY MODAL ROUNDERS; ran off-off-Broadway NYC for over 900 performances. LPs *The Village Fugs* on Broadside reissued as *First Album* '65 on pioneering ESP label, followed by *Virgin Fugs* '65 and *Indian War Hoop* '66 (with playwright Sam Shepard on drums); ESP out-takes on *Fugs 4, Rounders Score* '75. Switched to Reprise for *Tenderness Junction* and *It Crawled Into My Hand, Honest* '68, *The Belle Of Avenue A* '69, *Golden Filth* '70 (recorded at one of their last

shows in '68: 'best tune was written by William Blake under the romantic sway of a lesbian troll'). Sanders made solo LPs on Reprise *Sanders' Truckstop* '72 (whether parody of or departure from country rock depends on listener) and *Beer Cans On The Moon* (incl. song about a robot in love with Dolly PARTON). His are 'dirty jokes at their most divine' (quotes from Robert Christgau) while other rockers were merely pointlessly dirty. Sanders also wrote bestselling *The Family* about crimes/trial of Charles Manson; Kupferberg became cartoonist, dir. of Revolting Theatre company. Music was reminiscent of early VELVET UNDERGROUND, comedy of Lenny Bruce, both of Frank ZAPPA's early Mothers of Invention.

FUJI African style featuring vocals and percussion emerging in Lagos, Nigeria, mid-'70s. During the 19th century Islam took strong hold on the Yoruban people, being more tolerant than Christianity towards trad. religion and arts; by early 20th century trad. music was synonymous with Islamic music. Styles emerged, used to mark religious occasions, other festivities; among them Waka (female vocals and percussion), Sakara (dun-dun drums and one-string fiddle) and Apala (*see* Haruna ISHOLA); these in turn acquired recreational uses. Repertoire of various ensembles flourishing in '40s-50s incl. praise singing; professional drum ensembles emerged, recording prolifically and finding ready audiences in urban centres; out of all this fuji finally emerged to become most popular recreational music in Western Nigeria. Fuji ensemble usually features 10 to 12 vocalists and percussionists, with amplification, western-style drum kit adding commercial appeal. Fuji is now most closely associated with BARRISTER and KOLLINGTON.

FULLER, Blind Boy (*b* Fulton Allen, '08, Wadesboro, N.C.; *d* 13 Feb. '41, Durham, N.C.) Blues singer, guitarist. One of 10 children, went blind late '20s, but meanwhile had learned guitar; became foremost exponent of Piedmont blues style: more eclectic than that of Mississippi delta and with strong folk element. Worked streets, parties; teamed with Sonny TERRY, Gary DAVIS, etc. Recorded '35-40 for ARC labels, Decca,

Vocalion, Okeh. Compilation LPs: *Truckin' My Blues Away* on Yazoo, *Blue And Worried Man* on Travelin' Man; *Shakedown Shimmy* '35-8 and *On Down* '37-40 on Magpie.

FULLER, Bobby (*b* 22 Oct. '43, Baytown, Texas; *d* 18 July '66, L.A.) Singer, songwriter. Formed Bobby Fuller Four in El Paso with ·brother Randy, DeWayne Quirico, Jim Reese; played local dates for three years, moved to L.A., got recording contract. Surviving evidence discloses infl. of Buddy HOLLY with admix of Tex-Mex, country rock; biggest hit 'I Fought The Law' ironically written by Sonny Curtis of the CRICKETS (USA no. 9 '66); follow-up was cover of Holly's 'Love's Made A Fool Of You'. Death (in freak car crash, say some sources) was mysterious, officially suicide; friends suspected murder. Randy kept group going unsuccessfully, soon split. *Bobby Fuller Memorial Album* '66 on President incl. 'I Fought The Law', distinctive Fuller tunes 'Another Sad And Lonely Night', 'Saturday Night', 'Little Annie Lou', which suggest much talent lost. The CLASH exuberantly covered 'I Fought The Law' '80; further legacy in music of LOS LOBOS, the BLASTERS. Other compilations are *Best Of The Bobby Fuller Four* '81 on Rhino, *Memories Of Buddy Holly* '84 on Rockhouse.

FULLER, Curtis (*b* 15 Dec. '34, Detroit) Trombone. Studied music in high school, played in US Army band with Cannonball ADDERLEY, Junior MANCE; gigged in Detroit with Kenny BURRELL and others; to NYC '57 and has been leading modern jazz trombonist ever since: infl. by J. J. JOHNSON, style has by now entered 'mainstream', if it must have a label. With Benny GOLSON's Jazztet, in and out of Art BLAKEY's Jazz Messengers, to Europe with Dizzy GILLESPIE big band '68, with Jimmy HEATH (LP *Love And Understanding* on Muse), Count BASIE band '75, etc. Many LPs with Golson, Bud POWELL, Sonny CLARK, John COLTRANE, Philly Joe JONES, Paul QUINICHETTE, Art FARMER, Gil EVANS, others. Own LPs began with obscure Transition session in Chicago '55, then many fine quintet/sextet LPs with all-star lineups: *New Trombone*, *With Red Garland*, *With Hampton Hawes And French*

Horns (David AMRAM and Julius Watkins) on Prestige '57; *The Opener*, *Bone And Bari* (with Houston Tate on baritone), *Curtis Fuller Vol. 3* on Blue Note '57; *Sliding Easy* on UA '59; *Blues-ette*, *Arabia*, *Imagination*, *Images* on Savoy '59-60 (a 2-disc compilation is now called *All-Star Sextets*); LPs on Warwick, Smash (Trip), Epic, '60-1; *Soul Trombone And Jazz Clan* '61 and *Cabin In The Sky* '62 with strings and French horns on Impulse; *Crankin'* and *Smokin'* on Mainstream '73-4; *Four On The Outside* on Timeless, *Fire And Filigree* on Bee Hive label (Evanston, Ill.) '78.

FULLER, Gil (*b* Walter Gilbert Fuller, 14 Apr. '20, L.A.) Composer. Wrote for Les Hite, Jimmie LUNCEFORD, Tiny BRADSHAW, etc. Went to NYC after WWII service, wrote for all of the big bands incl. Afro-Cuban MACHITO, Tito PUENTE; one of the first (with Tadd DAMERON, Gil EVANS, George RUSSELL) to write in bop idiom for big band, writing for Billy ECKSTINE; for Dizzy GILLESPIE composed and/or arr. 'Manteca', 'Swedish Suite', 'One Bass Hit', 'Ray's Idea', 'Things To Come' etc., many premiered at Carnegie Hall '48; 'Fuller Bop Man', 'Tropicana' for James MOODY. Had own music publishing companies, wrote book about his arr. methods; made big band LP *The Scene Changes*; worked outside music early '50s; wrote for Stan KENTON c.'55, again '65, writing music for Gillespie's appearances with Kenton's 'neophonic orchestra'; led Monterey Jazz Festival band '65, LP with it on World Pacific; later *Night Flight* on same label. He also wrote for Ray CHARLES c.'62, did film work, stock arrangements, etc. An all-round musician, typed by important early work as a be-bopper. Contributed valuable pages of reminiscence to Dizzy's autobiography *To Be Or Not To Bop*. George Russell: 'I always had great respect for Gil Fuller . . . a brilliant man, as his *Things To Come* indicated.'

FULLER, Jesse (*b* 12 Mar. 1896, Jonesboro, Ga.; *d* 29 Jan. '76, Oakland, Cal.) Singer songwriter, guitarist; aka 'Lone Cat'; work tinged with folk-blues, country music, but essentially 'last of the Negro minstrels'. Seriously mistreated at home, ran away aged 10; worked as singer, tap-dancer but mostly

443

outside music until '51: cow-herding, broom-making, car-washing etc. Worked as shoeshine boy outside Universal studios early '20s; was extra in *Thief Of Bagdad* and *East Of Suez* '24, other films. Broadcast on Oakland radio KNX late '30s. During '50s worked radio, TV, clubs, concerts, by then virtually a one-man band, playing guitar, harmonica, kazoo, fotdella (piano-string bass operated by foot pedal, sometimes spelled 'footdella'). Recorded for Cavalier '55, Good Time Jazz (*Folk Songs, Spirituals And Blues*; *The Lone Cat* both '58; *San Francisco Bay Blues* '60); toured Europe with Chris BARBER '60-1; more recording for Folk-Lyric '62, then Bluesville (Prestige) *San Francisco Bay Blues* '63: incl. 'Everybody Works At Home But My Old Man', 'I Want A Girl Just Like The Girl Who Married Dear Old Dad'; but own title song much covered by latter-day folkies. Played Newport Folk Festivals '64, '69; toured Europe and USA; recorded for Fontana, Oakland, Rhythm, Hollywood, Flair, Money labels. Confined to a wheelchair after breaking his hip '75.

FULSON, Lowell (*b* 31 Mar. '21, Tulsa, Okla.) Rhythm and blues singer, guitarist: linking figure between classic blues and R&B. Father was Cherokee Indian; family was musical, incl. three uncles who were ministers. Worked as field hand, tap-dancer; with Texas ALEXANDER '39; entertained in USO shows US Navy '43-5; first records on Cal. R&B labels '46-52, Aladdin beginning '49; worked with Ivory Joe HUNTER, Hot Lips PAGE band, Clifton CHENIER, many others '50s; has carried on in clubs, festivals, TV appearances etc. He gave early breaks to Ray CHARLES, Stanley TURRENTINE; ability to adapt style while remaining true to roots indicated by six hits in R&B chart '49-54, four more '65-7. Top 5 incl. 'Everyday I Have The Blues' no. 5 and 'Blue Shadows' no. 1, both '50 on Swing Time, 'Reconsider Baby' no. 3 '54 on Checker (became standard in genre), 'Tramp' no. 5 '66 on Kent. Collections incl. *In A Heavy Bag* and *I've Got The Blues* on Jewel, *Lowell Fulson & His Guitar* on Arhoolie, *The Ol' Blues Singer* on Grand Prix USA, *Man Of Motion* on Charly UK, *Lowell Fulson* in Chess/PRT series in UK, 2-disc *Baby Won't You Jump With Me* on Swedish Crown Prince label (collects

'46-51 tracks incl. earliest sides, guitar duets with brother Martin).

FUNK A term originally applied to bad smells or body odour, particularly sexual; recorded in dialect '06, used by novelist Thomas Wolfe '29. It was used to mean 'low down' or 'gutbucket' in the musical sense, then in early '50s to describe a genre of post-bop modern jazz which, while using modern harmonies, also concentrated on swing and a re-injection of what would later be called soul; hence Milt JACKSON's 'Opus De Funk' '54. Horace SILVER, later Lee MORGAN and Herbie HANCOCK on Blue Note established hard bop's more general popularity, e.g. with tunes 'Señor Blues', 'Sidewinder', 'Maiden Voyage' respectively. The word was widely used in R&B and soul music, e.g. James BROWN's 'Ain't It Funky Now?' '69, acquired new importance during the DISCO era: disco was a phenomenon of urban black males as well as gays, relying on black pop, but it became fashionable, slick and over-produced (Brown, regarding himself with much justification as the original disco man, recorded 'It's Too Funky In Here' c.'79, which may have had any of several meanings). Black artists once again had to take their music back, retaining an iconoclastic attitude and their R&B roots to describe a music with rough edges, its energy inspired by something more than dollar signs. George Clinton and his PARLIAMENT/ FUNKADELIC empire was the best example. Since then the word has acquired too many meanings, describing white acts trying to play black dance music or in phrases such as 'jazz-funk' (neither jazz nor funk, but one of many sub-genres in an increasingly empty pop scene).

FUQUA, Harvey (*b* 27 July '29, Louisville, Ky.) Vocalist, writer, producer, etc. Mover and shaker in black vocal groups formed Moonglows in Cleveland '51 with Bobby Lester (*b* 13 Jan. '30), Alexander Graves (*b* 17 Apr. '30), Prentis Barnes (*b* '21), and Billy Johnson (*b* '24) on guitar. Sang bass on R&B hits '54-7 on Chess incl. no. 2 'Sincerely' (covered by McGUIRE Sisters for pop market), 'See-Saw', 'Please Send Me Someone To Love'; also recorded as Bobby Lester and the Moonlighters on Checker; as Harvey and the Moonglows had '58 hit 'Ten

Commandments Of Love' with Harvey's bass lead; all those named also made pop charts. Recruited Marquees (incl. Marvin GAYE) for new edition, then became A&R man at Chess '60 (hits with Etta JAMES as Etta & Harvey), took Gay along to Detroit, forming own Harvey, Tri-Phi labels: signed Johnny BRISTOL, Spinners, Junior WALKER; soon swallowed by Tamla/Motown, there as writer/prod. through rest of '60s (both Fuqua and Gaye married sisters of Motown boss Berry Gordy). Started own prod. company, had 10 hits in pop Hot 100 '71-5 through RCA, two in top 40 ('I Can Understand It' '73 by New Birth, 'K-Jee' '71 by instrumental Nite-Liters). New Moonglows on RCA '72.

FURY, Billy (*b* Ronald Wycherly, 17 Apr. '41, Liverpool; *d* 28 Jan. '83, London) UK singer. Sacked from jobs in teens because of punch-ups. Sang for anybody who would listen; bundled on stage at Birkenhead Essoldo at short notice, impressed paying customers and impresario Larry Parnes, who became manager, signed him for tour. First hit on Decca 'Maybe Tomorrow' '59; called 'greasiest, sexiest, most angst-ridden Brit-rocker of them all', became one of the biggest names in UK pop '60-5: 'Halfway To Paradise', 'Jealousy', 'I'd Never Find Another You', 'Last Night Was Made For Love', 'Like I've Never Been Gone', 'When Will You Say I Love You', 'In Summer' were his top 5 hits alone. An animal lover, made film *I've Gotta Horse* '65, about racehorse-loving pop star. Surgery for heart trouble caused by childhood rheumatic fever '67; bought a farm in Sussex, moved to Wales; played a few dates; played pop star Rocky Tempest in film *That'll Be The Day* '73; more surgery '75. Spent more time on farm; planned comeback late '82, working on TV show *Unforgettable*, made LP for Polydor, planned tour; heart attack after recording session. LP *The Only One* released Mar. '83; K-Tel compilation *Memories* in June.

FUSION Term sometimes used to describe 'third stream' classical-jazz work by John LEWIS, Gunther SCHULLER in '50-60s; now usually applied to jazz-rock, usually incl. electronic instruments. Soft-rockers SOFT MACHINE experimented with 'jazz'; CHICA-GO introduced horns to a large rock group, but turned out to be less than innovative. *Switched-On Bach* '69 by Walter CARLOS first demonstrated the possibilities of synthesisers; Miles DAVIS LPs *In A Silent Way*, 2-disc *Bitches Brew* '69 were seminal and controversial, fusing jazz, rock drums, electric guitars and pianos: participants John McLAUGHLIN formed Mahavishnu Orchestra, Chick COREA Return To Forever, Joe ZAWINUL and Wayne SHORTER WEATHER REPORT, the music often pretentious but a commercial success, like 'progressive rock' of yore; critics were divided: Weather Report's most diehard fans admit that some of their albums were much better than others. A true fusion cannot be forced, but these musicians are doing what they want to do, and they did not choose the label; many like Al DIMEOLA from Return To Forever have gone on to form new groups. The music at its best is about textures: with few rules or roots, if it relies too heavily on science the result is noodling. Advertising and reviews in *Downbeat* magazine are revealing: a lot of rock is reviewed in what used to be a jazz magazine; glossy ads for digital samplers, synths, electronic drums seem to outnumber those for trad. musical tools; young musicians are evidently deeply interested in fusion, probably a hopeful sign after 30 years of rock's domination, while highly rated jazz sideman Michael BRECKER plays an electronic saxophone on his debut solo LP '87, along with his usual instruments. Art-rock bands like King Crimson were coming at fusion from the direction of rock; some recent fusion is harder, more aggressive and more demanding music infl. by 'free jazz', and consequently will have a smaller audience, e.g. LPs by Bill LASWELL's Last Exit, *Album* by PUBLIC IMAGE LTD (prod. by Laswell; more rock than jazz, but at least J. Lydon's awful singing is only one of the instruments. Bill BRUFORD's Earthworks may be more accessible, with Django Bates on keyboards (*see* LOOSE TUBES). Human Chain (duo Bates, Steve Argüelles on percussion) use electronic noisemakers with tongues-in-cheek, giving musical value with delightful little pieces that reveal most pop as junk; yet TALKING HEADS and Matt JOHNSON, each in their own way, make fusions of electronics and pop/rock which is more interesting than that which uses electronically generated sound merely to fill up the spaces. The impact of synthesisers etc. has happened coincidentally at a time when popular music as a whole has been in a trough so long that many don't know what they want to play and have to try to invent something new; this will take years to shake down. Whether fusion will be of lasting value or not, it is probably permanently with us. *See also* NEW AGE, SPACE MUSIC: fusions of rock, folk, science with MOOD MUSIC. In late '80s separate charts for Fusion and Jazz records emerged, as well as new word 'fuzak'.

G

G, Johnny (*b* John Gotting, 11 Feb. '49, London) One-man band, popular on London and Continental pub-rock circuit late '70s-80s. In band the Louts with John Spencer (*The Last LP* '78); has continued often working with him. Solo debut *G-Sharp, G-Natural* '79 followed by *G-Beat* '80, incl. '(I Don't Wanna Go To) The Hippies Graveyard', Spencer's car anthem 'Everybody Goes Cruising On A Saturday Night'; *Water Into Wine* '81 was finest hour, with trad. 'Skye Boat Song' done reggae style, King Crimson's '21st Century Schizoid Man' handled as Delta blues: album incl. help from the Rumour's Bob Andrews and Bob Goulding, Medicine Head's Peter Hope-Evans. Acute observer of London life in the style of Ian DURY, notably on 'Suzie Was A Girl From Greenford' and 'Carving Up The Concrete'. Joint LP with Spencer *Out With A Bang* '85 made in Holland.

GABRIEL, Peter (*b* 13 May '50, UK) Pop singer, songwriter. Co-founded and starred in art-rock group GENESIS through their first seven LPs, went solo; released four LPs all called *Peter Gabriel*, all top 10 on Charisma in UK: the third was rejected by Atlantic, issued on Mercury USA: no. 1 UK, no. 22 (his biggest hit) in USA, incl. 'Biko', inspiring Steve VAN ZANDT's Sun City anti-apartheid project; fourth was subtitled *Security* on Geffen in USA, incl. 'Shock The Monkey', his first top 40 single USA, Gabriel being a natural for MTV music video channel. 2-disc live set '83 did well on Geffen, followed by instrumental *Birdy* '85, incl. music from the film, and *So* '86, incl. duet 'Don't Give Up' with Kate BUSH. Like Bush, he is disliked by some critics because his work is imaginative without leaving his audience behind: quirky pulses informed by African music, an intelligent eclecticism and a gorgeous voice all help. He was also a prime mover in WOMAD, annual international World of Music, Arts and Dance Festival, first financed partly by reunion concert with Genesis. (Vols. of *WOMAD Talking Book* cassettes (various artists) in UK.)

GADD, Steve (*b* '45, Rochester, NY) Drummer. Studied at Eastman in Rochester, playing in clubs evenings (had sat in with Dizzy GILLESPIE at 11); served in US Army, played with big band in Rochester, formed trio and went to NYC '72, soon the ultimate session drummer, solos transcribed and published. Recorded with Chick COREA, Al DiMEOLA, Carla BLEY, George BENSON, Aretha FRANKLIN, Barbra STREISAND, Stevie WONDER, STEELY DAN, Paul SIMON, David SANBORN, countless more. With keyboardist Richard Tee, Cornell Dupree on guitar, three others in Stuff, jazz/R&B group with LPs on WB (sold well in Japan but not at home); had worked with bassist Eddie Gomez in Corea's groups; with these three plus Ronnie Cuber on reeds formed The Gadd Gang (*Downbeat* headline: 'not just the same old Stuff'), a more friendly group in which everybody solos: eponymous LP '87 prod. in NYC by Kiyoshi Itoh, with material by Bob DYLAN ('Watching The River Flow'), Wilton Felder, ballads by Gomez and Tee (who also sings), remake of rock'n-'roll classic 'Honky Tonk' (Bill DOGGETT), etc. Also *Gaddabout* '86 on Projazz with Tee, Cuber, four others.

GAILLARD, Slim (*b* Bulee Gaillard, 4 Jan. '16, Detroit) Singer, songwriter; plays piano, guitar, vibes. Duo Slim & Slam with Slam STEWART on bass had several hits '38-9, biggest was 'Flat Foot Floogie', a huge novelty hit on Vocalion, covered by Fats WALLER, Benny GOODMAN, MILLS Bros, many others. Formed own combo '39; on West Coast '45-6 after military service (Slim says an early fan was movie star Ronald Reagan), to NYC '47; other hits (co-written with Lee Ricks) were 'Cement Mixer (Put-ti Put-ti)' (Alvino REY had biggest of several hit versions '46), 'Down By The Station'

(Tommy DORSEY, Guy LOMBARDO in top 20 '49). He invented jive language '40s; good example is 'Vout Oreenie' c.'46, an expression of approval. Not a jazzman, but part of the scene; recorded with Charlie PARKER, Dizzy GILLESPIE, Jack MCVEA '45 (*see* McVea's entry: four tracks are on Savoy's *Complete Charlie Parker*, also *Chicken Rhythm* '45-6 compilation on Storyville). When BOP was attacked as degenerate (e.g. by L.A. 'disc jerkey' Ted Steele), Gaillard's 'Yep Roc Heresay' quoted as example of lyrics 'full of bawdiness, references to narcotics' etc.: this was a recitation of a menu from restaurant serving Middle Eastern food. Lives in UK, amusing (and amused) raconteur on UK TV '80s. Compilation *Opera In Vout* '46-52 on Verve; also Dot LP *Slim Gaillard Rides Again* '50s (now *Dot Sessions* on MCA), *Cement Mixer* on Folk-Lyric, *Roots Of Vouty* on Putti Putti; *The Voutest, At Birdland* and *Anytime, Anyplace, Anywhere* on Hep, the last recorded in London '82 with Buddy TATE and Jay MCSHANN.

GALLAGHER, Rory (*b* 2 Mar. '49, Ballyshannon, Co. Donegal) Blues guitarist. Raised in Cork; left school to play with Fontana Showband, purveyors of chart covers at village dances, later called the Impact; Gallagher formed trio called Taste with Norman Damery, Eric Kittrington; toured UK and Continent for two years, signed by Polydor with Richard McCracken (*b* 26 June '48) on bass, John Wilson (*b* 3 Dec. '47), drums. Band was vehicle for Gallagher's high-octane blues guitar and raw, adequate vocals; LPs *Taste* '69, *On The Boards* '70, *Live* '71 and *Live At The Isle Of Wight* '72 indicated that he was more at home on the stage. Trio split '71 (other two signed up guitarist Jim Cregan forming Stud; then Cregan joined FAMILY). Gallagher continued as solo act, beginning with *Rory Gallagher* on Polydor '71, on Chrysalis from '75: purveyed basic blues, using few effects (regarded as crutches of lazy guitarists); own lack of pretension marked by ubiquitous plaid shirt. Used more original material as solo, though 'Bullfrog Blues' etc. still staples. Most popular chart period '72-3 when *Live In Europe* was no. 9 LP, *Blueprint* no. 12 UK. Used Gerry McAvoy, bass, Wilgar Campbell,

drums on first three; then De'Ath replaced Campbell and Lou Martin added on keyboards, marking first divergence from trio format. Both newcomers ex-Killing Floor, both quit after *Calling Card* '76, Ted McKenna on drums restored trio lineup. 10 solo LPs charted UK '71-82; nine in USA '72-9: LPs apart from those above incl. *Deuce* '71, *Tattoo* '73, 2-disc *Irish Tour* '74, *Sinner . . . And Saint* '75, all on Polydor; *Against The Grain* '75, *Photo-Finish* '78, *Top Priority* '79, *Stage Struck* '80, *Jinx* '82. He sessioned on Mike Vernon's *Bring It Back Home* '71, Muddy WATERS' *London Sessions* '72, Jerry Lee LEWIS' *London Sessions* '73, Lonnie DONEGAN's *Puttin' On The Style* '77, Mike BATT's *Tarot Suite* '79. Uncompromising approach won him strong but inevitably diminishing following: love of bluesmen Freddie, Albert and B. B. KING, penchant for acoustic and bottleneck made him look like anachronism to '80s listeners looking for new fads, but you feel that he'd be happy playing in pubs somewhere for those who appreciate him.

GAMBLE & HUFF Kenny Gamble and Phil Huff, producers active in Philadelphia, Pa. since early '60s, had huge success '70s with Philadelphia International label and the 'Philly' sound, a sort of crisp big band dance beat with black flavour. Kenny Gamble and the Romeos early '60s incl. Thom BELL on keyboards, Roland Chambers on guitar, both later in P.I.'s house band MFSB; Bell became a protégé, then a competitor as producer. Huff played piano on rock'n'roll sessions in NYC for LEIBER & STOLLER, also helped prod. DANNY & THE JUNIORS' 'Let's Go To The Hop', etc. Back in Philadelphia he began working with Gamble, joined Romeos; they prod. freelance incl. Archie BELL & the Drells, Dusty SPRINGFIELD, Wilson PICKETT, Jerry BUTLER, others; formed Excel, then Neptune labels, latter distributed by Chess, then Philadelphia International, whose distribution brought CBS a market in the black community it otherwise lacked. Hit acts incl. the O'JAYS, Harold Melvin and the Bluenotes, THREE DEGREES. Mid-'70s they fell foul of one of the industry's bouts of moral fervour, Gamble fined for payola; they carried on with O'Jays, Teddy PENDERGRASS, others, sometimes co-writing hits.

GANELIN TRIO Soviet jazz trio combining Russian soul with infl. of Sunny MURRAY, Albert AYLER, ART ENSEMBLE etc. formed in Vilnius, Soviet Lithuania c.'71 by Vyacheslav Ganelin (*b* '44, Kraskov), piano, composer; also percussion, electric guitar etc. Vladimir Chekasin (*b* '47, Sverdlovsk) on reeds, drummer Vladimir Tarasov (*b* '47, Archangelsk), all multi-instrumentalists. USSR jazz was (understandably) derivative until the '70s, when avant-garde movement began; the artists invent the structures, are not required to belong to a category, which is partly why jazz (or better, improvised music) has at last become an international language, as opposed to being completely dominated by Americans. Western audiences and critics often miss the point as far as the Ganelin Trio are concerned, but their music cannot be ignored. Russian, then Soviet artists (in any genre) have always related their art to other areas of contemporary art: hence Ganelin is a composer, Tarasov is a student of painting, sculpture, architecture and plays in symphony orchestras; all of them are familiar with ethnic ('third world') musical forms, etc. They composed a large suite each year: 'We borrow some elements not only from jazz but from chamber music, folk music and other genres,' says Chekasin. Ganelin: '. . . The chief quality of our work is the absence of purely rational, "dry" elements. Our music is always organic and natural; audiences sense the absence of pretence.' First LP *Con Anima* '75 on Melodiya '76, followed by *Concerto Grosso, Poi Segue. Non Troppo* (said to be uninspired performance) is on Enja; a different 2-disc version is on Hat Art; there were fragments on samplers (*Poco a Poco* on Muza; *Katalog* on Amiga) and *Vyacheslav Ganelin Trio* on Poljazz; all other records are on the indefatigable Leo label of London, the most important source of contemporary Soviet jazz: *Catalogue* '79 (aka *Live In East Germany*; a résumé of 10 years together), *Con Fuoco, Ancora da Capo* parts 1 & 2 (part 1 was poorly recorded at the source: tapes come to Leo by diverse methods), *New Wine, Vide, Strictly For Our Friends, Baltic Triangle. Opus a 2* was issued on Melodiya without Chekasin, who was involved in other projects; Leo has released Chekasin's solo *Exercises*, quartet *Nostalgia* (said to be spoiled by rock/disco straitjacket),

big band *New Vitality*. Of the trio's *Con Affetto* (recorded '83 in Moscow, released '86 on Leo), Kevin Whitehead wrote in *Cadence*: 'Free exchanges are draped over and shaped by skeletal thematic material, to form a loose suite that's laced with zany humour . . . Chekasin shows that comic but polished blowing of two saxes at once is no joke . . . a "Mack The Knife" painstakingly reconstructed from the unrecognisable fragments they began with.' *Inverso* '84 on Leo has Ganelin programming drum machines, with Pyatras Vyshniauskas on alto and soprano sax and Grigory Talas on electric bass, all three then cheerfully ignore the drum machines. Books incl. Frederick Starr's *Red & Hot: The Fate Of Jazz In The Soviet Union* '83, which brings the story up to the '70s, and *Russian Jazz: New Identity* '85, edited by émigré label boss Leo Feigin, with the latest news incl. contribution from Starr, translated Russian reviews and a chapter on being dedicated enough to start your own record label with totally unfamiliar music.

GANG OF FOUR UK punk/new wave band formed in Leeds '77 by students Jon King, vocals; Hugo Burnham, drums; Andy Gill, guitar; Dave Allen, bass. Seminal debut EP *Damaged Goods* '78 on Fast Product label; title cut, 'Armalite Rifle', 'Love Like Anthrax' showed jerky, staccato, ultimately unsettling basic style. Signed to EMI '79; no compromises for label that rejected SEX PISTOLS: single 'At Home He's A Tourist' banned from TV's *Top Of The Pops* because they would not change reference to contraceptives. LP *Entertainment* '79 was well received as thinking man's punk. *Solid Gold* '81 was prod. by NYC's Jimmy Douglass and reflected live work there; press claimed music had lost edge, band claimed they had developed. David Allen quit in middle of another USA tour '81; Busta Cherry Jones (ex-Sharks, TALKING HEADS) depped but Sara Lee (ex-Robert Fripp's League Of Gentlemen) was permanent replacement later. *Songs Of The Free* '82 prod. by Mike HOWLETT; merged approaches of first two LPs, with female backing vocal on excellent near-hit 'I Love A Man In A Uniform' (anti-military stance lost airplay as Falklands War loomed). Lee played only on some tracks of *Hard* (Jon Alstrop on oth-

449

ers), her 'session' status destabilised band, a situation exacerbated when Burnham sacked, Steve Goulding (ex-Graham PARKER) depping; band was now effectively a gang of two. Final *Live At The Palace* '84 made for Polygram just before split. EP and first LP are examples of politically-motivated new-wave music at its best: Lee, Gill and King were like a new wave DR FEELGOOD. Allen formed moderately successful Shriekback; Burnham formed short-lived Illustrated Man.

GANT, Cecil (*b* 4 Apr. '13, Nashville; *d* there 4 Feb. '51) Blues singer, pianist. Worked local clubs mid-'30s until induction into US Army. Though his piano was blues-based, vocally he was crooner of considerable crossover appeal: sang at War Bond rally in L.A., signed with Gilt Edge label; cut ballad 'I Wonder' late '44 billed as 'Pvt. Cecil Grant'; made no. 1 on 'Harlem Hit Parade' (as 'race' chart was called then); sold impressively nationwide. Toured as 'The G.I. Sing-sation' dressed in Army khaki, breaking attendance records at major venues, attracting both black and white audiences, but was unlucky, perhaps too early: it was left to Nat COLE and Billy ECKSTINE to find the lucrative 'sepia Sinatra' market. Other releases on King '47, Bullet '48-9, Downbeat/Swingtime '49, Imperial '50; but moment of juke box glory was gone. Died of pneumonia. Compilation LPs in UK late '70s; *Rock This Boogie* '83 on Krazy Kat.

GAP BAND. The USA funk band formed early '70s by Wilson brothers Ronnie, trumpet, keyboards; Charles, lead vocals, keyboards; Robert, bass. Sang in father's church in Tulsa, Oklahoma; named band after initials of three local streets. Became Leon RUSSELL's back-up band (own LP *Magician's Holiday* '74 for his Shelter label); single 'This Place Called Heaven' on A&M; then three Mercury LPs all charted '79-80, four more '82-5 on Total Experience incl. *Gold Gap* compilation '85. String of top 10 hits in black chart incl. no. ones 'Burn Rubber On Me' '81 from *Gap Band III*, 'Early In The Morning' and 'You Dropped A Bomb On Me' '82, both on biggest-selling (no. 14) LP *Gap Band IV*; last two hits also made pop top 40. *Gap Band V* was subtitled *Jammin'*, reached no. 28.

GARBER, Jan (*b* 5 Nov. 1897, Morristown, Pa.; *d* 5 Oct. '77, Shreveport, La.) Bandleader who alternated between sweet and hot. Attended U. of North Carolina, became violinist in Philadelphia S.O., formed Garber-Davis Orchestra with pianist Milt Davis, then jazz-oriented band early '20s. With success of Guy LOMBARDO's Royal Canadians, Garber took over sweet Canadian band of Freddy Large, became popular attraction with spot on Burns and Allen comedy radio series. Switched back to swing policy '42, hired younger staff incl. Liz Tilton, sister of Benny GOODMAN singer Martha; this band appeared in film *Here Comes Elmer* ('43, also with Nat COLE). Resuscitated 'Mickey Mouse' style; film (*Make Believe Ballroom*), two hit records ('You're Breaking My Heart', 'Jealous Heart'), all '49. 'The Idol Of The Air Lanes' continued playing West Coast for years.

GARDEL, Carlos (*b* 24 Dec. 1890, Toulouse, France; *d* 24 June '35, Colombia) Singer who became the major exponent of the tango, nicknamed 'La Voz Azul' ('The Blue Voice') and 'Zorzal' ('Thrush'). In 1893 his mother (Berthe Gardes) moved to Buenos Aires; he later changed the spelling of his name and was elusive about his origins; registered as Uruguayan national '20, became Argentine citizen '23. First sang in bars and at parties after leaving school; formed duet with José Razzano '13, made first recording '17: 'Mi Noche Triste' used urban slang (Lunfardo) to describe a lover's misery; the introduction of lyrics into the tango set a trend and launched him as the most important singer in the new genre. The duo prospered, toured Europe; Gardel went solo '25, performed for the Prince of Wales in Buenos Aires that year. Peak success was '25-9: he sold 70,000 records in first three months of a visit to Paris. A superb singer with 'a tear in his throat', ideally suited to the melancholy and yearning of tango songs; worked hard at superstar image with pomaded hair and sharp suits matching wealthy lifestyle; performed in 10 films '31-5 incl. *Tango On Broadway* '34. Died in airplane crash en route to Cali,

Colombia; when his remains reached Buenos Aires Feb. '36 his funeral attracted the biggest crowds in the nation's history. He is still synonymous with the tango; compilations incl. *Los Grandes Exitos de Carlos Gardel.*

GARFUNKEL, Art Pop singer, actor. International fame with Paul SIMON in SIMON & GARFUNKEL '60s (*which see*); split caused partly by Garfunkel's decision to pursue acting career, making debut in *Catch 22* '70. He appeared to considerable acclaim in *Carnal Knowledge* '71; spent six-figure sum and two years on debut solo LP *Angel Clare* '73 (title from character in Thomas Hardy's *Tess*), incl. USA hits 'All I Know' (top 10 '73), 'I Shall Sing' (top 40 '74). *Breakaway* '75 incl. Simon's song 'My Little Town'; *Watermark* '77 had hit cover of Sam COOKE's 'Wonderful World' (singing with Simon and James TAYLOR); *Fate For Breakfast* '79 and *Scissors Cut* '81 were characterised by lush over-production, songs by Jim WEBB, Andrew GOLD, Stephen BISHOP. Evergreen 'I Only Have Eyes For You' was top 20 hit USA, no. 1 UK '75; 'Bright Eyes' '79 (theme of film *Watership Down*) was another UK no. 1. For reunions with Simon see their entry; proposed studio duo LP was scrapped '82. He was praised for film *Bad Timing* '79, played guilty white liberal in hip-hop cop film *Good To Go* '86 (film was panned); album *The Animals' Christmas* '86 with Amy Grant, written by Webb, tells the story of the Nativity from the animals' point of view. He has one of the purest voices in pop, is one of the few singers to make a successful transition to acting, but chooses projects only sporadically.

GARLAND, Judy (*b* Frances Gumm, 10 June '22, Grand Rapids, Mich.; *d* 22 Jan. '69, London) USA singer, actress. Parents in show business; started singing act with sisters; George Jessel named her Garland. First short film '35 with Deanna Durbin; first feature was musical *Pigskin Parade* '36; sang 'You Made Me Love You' to picture of Clark Gable in *Broadway Melody* '38, became star. Andy Hardy series co-starred Mickey Rooney late '30s-40s, but most famous role was Dorothy in *Wizard Of Oz* '39, singing 'Over The Rainbow'. More than 30 films altogether incl. *Easter Parade*

'48 with Fred ASTAIRE, *Summer Stock* '50 with Gene KELLY. Records began on Decca late '30s, hits when Billboard began printing charts '40 with 'I'm Nobody's Baby' (song from '21; used in '40 film *Andy Hardy Meets Debutante*); title duet with Gene Kelly from nostalgic musical *For Me And My Gal* '42 was no. 3 hit Jan. '43; 'The Trolley Song' from *Meet Me In St Louis* '44 also no. 3; 'On The Atchison, Topeka And The Sante Fe' with the Merry Macs no. 10 '45 (from Garland film *The Harvey Girls* '46; other hit versions by Tommy DORSEY, Bing CROSBY, lyricist Johnny MERCER). From then on she sold albums: set of '78s from *Meet Me In St Louis* was no. 2 album USA '45; soundtrack from *A Star Is Born* '54 on Columbia was no. 5 LP: making of film with James Mason was plagued with problems but a triumph, one of her best: incl. 'The Man That Got Away'. LP *Miss Show Business* '55 on Capitol was no. 5 LP; other '50s LPs incl. *Judy* and *Alone* (Capitol), *Greatest Performances* (Decca compilation). Show-business legend in her teens, never had a childhood; nervous energy, insecurity led to problems with alcohol, pills (weight problem already obvious in *Summer Stock*). Unreliability made '50s patchy years, but Carnegie Hall concert '61 was triumphant comeback: 2-disc live Capitol set topped LP chart for 13 weeks. *The Garland Touch* '62, soundtrack from *I Could Go On Singing* '63 were both hits (film with Dirk Bogarde was first singing/acting role since *A Star Is Born*, and last). Decca compiled 2-disc *The Best Of Judy Garland* '64 (abridged to one LP *Greatest Hits* '69); 2-disc *Live At The London Palladium* '65 with daughter Liza MINNELLI reached no. 41 (abridged to one disc '73); New York show issued on live *At Home At The Palace – Opening Night* '67 on ABC. Despite well-known health problems, sudden death shocked public; legend is that when she died a tornado touched down in Kansas. More albums issued: compilations, airchecks etc. incl. *Born In A Trunk (1935-40), Vol. 2 (1940-45), Vol. 3: Superstar 1945-50*, all on A.E.I. (USA); *Garland At The Grove* with Freddy MARTIN issued on EMI/UK '83.

GARLAND, Red (*b* William Garland, 13 May '23, Dallas, Texas; *d* 23 Apr. '84) Piano. Started on reeds as a child; discovered in home town by Hot Lips PAGE; played with all the big names from '45: influential from period with classic Miles DAVIS Quintet on Prestige '56-8; also recorded with John COLTRANE, Art PEPPER, others; toured with own trio, retired to Dallas '65 when his mother died except for trips to NYC to record, club dates in L.A. etc. Own albums incl. about 30 trio LPs on Prestige, Moodsville, Jazzland labels '56-62; MPS/BASF '71, Galaxy and Muse '77-9, Japanese Trio '80, Baystate/Timeless '82: Moodsville LP '59 added Eddie DAVIS; *The Quota* '71 on MPS had Jimmy HEATH on two tracks; earlier sets on Prestige added Kenny BURRELL or Ray BARRETTO. Quintet sessions on Prestige '57 with Coltrane, Donald BYRD variously issued as *Saying Something*, *All Morning Long*, *Soul Junction*, *High Pressure*, *Dig It*. *Red's Good Groove* on Jazzland '62 incl. Blue MITCHELL, Pepper ADAMS; *Strike Up The Band* '79 on Galaxy had Julian Priester, George COLEMAN; sextet *Red Alert* '77 on Galaxy had Harold LAND, Nat ADDERLEY, multi-instrumentalist Ira Sullivan (*b* 1 May '31, Washington; based in Chicago, then Fla. early '60s; LPs incl. *Nicky's Tune* on Delmark). Solo piano sets on Moodsville '60 issued as *Red Alone*, *Alone With The Blues*.

GARNER, Erroll (*b* Erroll Louis Garner, 15 June '21, Pittsburgh, Pa.; *d* 2 Jan. '77, L.A.) Piano. Self-taught, never learned to read music; irrepressible humour, swing and gift for melody made him one of the most popular of jazz artists. Toured and/or recorded with Charlie PARKER, Slam STEWART, others; first own records now on compilation *Classic Pianos* on Doctor Jazz with Earl HINES, James P. JOHNSON, Art HODES; also *The Dial Masters* '47 on Spotlite; *Yesterdays* '45-9 and 2-disc *Elf* '49 on Savoy USA; complete Savoy sessions on three discs in UK. He won many polls starting with Esquire New Star '46, appeared in Paris '48, toured Europe '57-8, was first jazz musician to be booked by classical impresario Sol Hurok '58. Wrote 'Misty' '54, words added by Johnny Burke: beautiful early recordings by Dakota STATON, then Sarah VAUGHAN; it has been a pop hit five times so far: no. 14 '59 by Johnny MATHIS, no. 21 '63 by Lloyd PRICE, no. 63 '65 by the Vibrations, no. 44 '66 by Richard 'Groove'

HOLMES, no. 14 '75 by Ray STEVENS: ASCAP has repeatedly honoured it as one of the most-played standards of past decades. He recorded it for the soundtrack of Clint Eastwood film *Play Misty For Me* '71; he wrote themes for film *A New Kind Of Love* '63; famous songs incl. 'Dreamy', 'That's My Kick', 'Moment's Delight', 'Solitaire', 'Passing Through', many more. The House of Representatives wished him a happy birthday on 15 June '76; the Dayton Ballet Company toured with a ballet set to his music early '80s; *The Erroll Garner Songbook* arr. by Sy Johnson published by Cherry Lane Music (another vol. in preparation). Garner LPs to make Billboard top pop albums incl. *Other Voices* no. 16 '57 (incl. 'Misty'), *Concert By The Sea* no.12 '58 (recorded live in Carmel, Cal. '56 outdoor concert; one of the best-selling jazz LPs of the decade), both on Columbia; also *Dreamstreet* '61 on ABC, *One World Concert* '63 on Reprise (live at Seattle World's fair); many more were hits in jazz charts. Other LPs from the '50s: *Plays Misty*, *Solitaire* and *Afternoon Of An Elf* on Mercury; *Soliloquy*, *Dreamy*, *Play It Again*, *Erroll* and 2-disc *Paris Impressions* on Columbia; *Greatest Garner* on Atlantic. He began prod. his own LPs c.'60; many of his best on various labels were later available on his own Octave label, now on RCA in France, Bulldog in UK incl. some of those above plus *Closeup* '61 from ABC-Paramount, *Amsterdam Concert* '64 from Philips; *Campus Concert* '62, *A Night At The Movies* '64 from MGM (all these with bassist Eddie Calhoun, drummer Kelly Martin); also *A New Kind Of Love* '63 from Mercury (with 35-piece orchestra); *That's My Kick* '67 from MGM (with Milt HINTON, guitarist Artie Ryerson, drummer George Jenkins, Johnny PACHECO); *Gemini* (plays harpsichord as well as piano), *Feeling Is Believing* '69 (title track had words added by Sammy CAHN, became 'Something Happens'), *Up In Erroll's Room* and *Magician*, all from MPS; *Plays Gershwin And Kern* from EmArcy. There is also a 3-disc set (2 cassettes) from the Book-Of-The-Month Club in USA: 30 tracks '61-70. Beware of cheap CBS compilations; some have slushy studio orchestra, perhaps dubbed.

GARRETT, Snuff (*b* Thomas Garrett, '39, Dallas, Texas) USA A&R man and producer at Liberty Records '58-66. Nickname probably from Garrett brand of tobacco product. Worked for a record distributor in Dallas at 15; became DJ in Lubbock at 17, met Buddy HOLLY; had TV show, teen-age nightclub in Wichita Falls; to Hollywood and Liberty '58: prod. hits by Johnny BURNETTE, Bobby VEE, Gene McDANIELS. Using songs from Brill Building stable and making sure that words could be heard, had great infl. on white pop of period: became head of A&R at 22; hired Phil SPECTOR to work for Liberty NYC; with arr. by Leon RUSSELL prod. hits by Gary LEWIS and the Playboys '65-6; prod. MOR albums *50 Guitars Of Tommy Garrett*, six of which charted '61-9 (with solos by Tommy Tedesco). Left Liberty, formed own Viva label with Jimmy Bowen, had no hits and sold out, semi-retired. Prod. comeback hits on Kapp for SONNY & CHER '72-3.

GARRISON, Jimmy (*b* James Emory Garrison, 3 Mar. '34, Miami, Fla.; *d* 7 Apr. '76) Bass. Grew up in Philadelphia; played with Bobby TIMMONS, Al HEATH; drove a truck '55-8, then to NYC and full-time music: became urgent, fundamental force in the great John COLTRANE quartet of '61-6 (LPs on Impulse). Worked with Hampton HAWES, Archie SHEPP, Elvin JONES; taught at Bennington College (*see* Bill DIXON) and Wesleyan '70-1; with Jones '73-4; died of lung cancer. Co-led Impulse sextet session with Jones *Illumination*; recorded with leaders Jones (*Puttin' It Together*, *The Ultimate* on Blue Note), with Shepp on Impulse and Arista (*There's A Trumpet In My Soul*), others as well as Coltrane.

GATLIN, Larry, and Gatlin Brothers Band Larry (*b* 2 May '48), Steve (*b* 4 Apr. '51) and Rudy Gatlin (*b* 20 Aug. '52), country music harmony vocal group; family from Seminole, Texas; Larry also solo singer and songwriter. Brothers sang at family and church functions; had weekly TV show in Abilene with younger sister Donna making quartet. Larry left to go to U. of Houston; joined The Imperials gospel group '69, embarked on writing career when Dottie WEST recorded his songs, signed him to contract. Move to Nashville '71 led to writing songs for Johnny CASH film *The Gospel Road*, contract with Monument '73: first hit

'Sweet Becky Walker', LP *The Pilgrim* got rave reviews. Further hits with 'The Bigger They Are, The Harder They Fall', 'Delta Dirt', 'Broken Lady', 'Statues Without Hearts' '74-6 established major star; 'Broken Lady' won Grammy. Joined brothers for LP *With Family And Friends* '76, had three top 3 solo hits 'I Don't Wanna Cry' (another Grammy), 'Love Is Just A Game', 'I Just Wish You Were Someone I Love'; became Larry Gatlin and the Gatlin Brothers '78 with 'Night Time Magic', 'I've Done Enough Dyin' Today' and 'All The Gold In California' all big hits. Latter named ACM Single of the Year, Gatlin top male singer, LP *Straight Ahead* Album of the Year. Further hits incl. 'Take Me To Your Lovin' Place' '80, 'It Don't Get No Better Than This' '81, 'Sure Feels Like Love' '82, 'Houston (Means I'm One Day Closer To You)' '83, 'Denver' '84. Continues to write own songs; also writes with BEE GEES. Other LPs incl. *Rain-Rainbow* '74, *Broken Lady* '76, *High Time* '76, *Love Is Just A Game* '77, *Straight Ahead* '79, *Help Yourself* '80, *Not Guilty* '81, *Houston To Denver* '84; Gatlin Brothers' *Partners* '86.

GAUGHAN, Dick (*b* Richard Peter Gaughan, 17 May '48, Glasgow, Scotland) Singer, guitarist and songwriter. Family had long history of working-class folk song, to which had been added Fenian and trade union songs. Guested on other people's sessions, then own debut *No More Forever* '72 on Trailer. Worked with trad. folk band Boys of the Lough and folk-rock band Five Hand Reel in '70s, concurrent with solo LPs. *Kist O' Gold* '77 on Trailer confirmed status as singular interpreter; *Coppers & Brass* '77 (Scots and Irish dance music played on guitar) and *Gaughan* '78, both on Topic, further enhanced reputation; *Handful Of Earth* '81 on Topic remains a pinnacle of contemporary UK folk, its versions of Leon ROSSELSON's 'World Turned Upside Down', Burns' 'Now Westlin Winds' and the trad. 'Erin-Go-Bragh' epitomising his skills. *Parallel Lines* '82 on FolkFreak was a collaboration with Andy Irvine; then *A Different Kind Of Love Song* '83 on that label was return to solo form, incl. potent 'Think Again' (covered by Billy BRAGG). Illness took him away from performing; then he returned '84, a concert captured on *Live In*

Edinburgh on Celtic Music. During the miners' strike of '84-5 he campaigned on behalf of miners, but never confused politics with bad art; *True And Bold* '86 on STUC was a magnificent collection of songs of Scottish miners. In the political climate it was overlooked that he had always sung mining and industrial songs, with Harry Boardman contributed to the High Level Ranters' pioneering anthology *The Bonnie Pit Laddie* '75 on Topic, subtitled 'a Miner's Life in Music and Song'. Also contributed to the Woody Guthrie tribute anthology *Woody Lives* '87 on Black Crow. He argues the case for 'a consistent and workable aesthetic based on a class view of folk music', as when reviewing Ian Watson's book *Song And Democratic Culture* '84.

GAYE, Marvin (*b* Marvin Pentz Gaye, 2 Apr. '39, Washington DC; *d* 1 Apr. '84) Singer, star of black pop and one of the greatest crossover acts of his generation. Father was clergyman; he sang in church, then doowop group the Rainbows (incl. Don COVAY) at 15; won talent contest with Harvey FUQUA'S 'The Ten Commandments Of Love' (Fuqua was the judge), joined USAF at father's behest; one source says he was invalided out for psychological reasons. The Rainbows became the Marquees, recorded for Okeh; he renewed friendship with Fuqua, whose Moonglows were still recording for Chess; Gaye joined the group, then went to Detroit with Fuqua; both ended up with Tamla/Motown, married sisters of Berry Gordy. Gaye was session drummer on early hits by Smokey ROBINSON and the Miracles; pop/R&B hits began with prophetic 'Stubborn Kind Of Fellow' '62 (backup by Martha and the Vandellas). He was versatile from the start: hits incl. dance craze 'Hitch Hike' '63, 12-bar blues 'Can I Get A Witness' '63, rocker 'Baby Don't You Do It' '64, romantic and sensual ballads: 'How Sweet It Is To Be Loved By You' '65; biggest of '60s were 'I Heard It Through The Grapevine' (no. 1), 'Too Busy Thinking About My Baby' (no. 4) '68-9. First LP was *Soulful Mood* '61; others: *That Stubborn Kinda Fellow* '63, *How Sweet It Is To Be Loved By You* '65, *Moods Of Marvin Gaye* '66, *In The Groove* '68, *M.P.G.* and *That's The Way Love Is* '69. Also had top 20 duet hits with Mary Wells '64 (LP *Together* '64),

Kim Weston '67, but both left Motown; then nine top 50 hits with lovely Tammi Terrell '67-70 incl. 'Your Precious Love', 'Ain't Nothing Like The Real Thing', 'You're All I Need To Get By'; LPs with her *United* and *You're All I Need* '67, *Easy* '69: Terrell, *b* '46, Philadelphia, made own LP *Irresistible* '69, *d* 16 Mar. '70 of a brain tumour. Of Gaye's three pop chart entries in '70 only 'The End Of Our Road' barely made the top 40. Apart from being devastated by Terrell's death, he was better at starting trends than being told what to do, understood that an LP should be more than two hits and 10 bits of filler: had trouble with Motown management (it is thanks partly to his efforts that other artists like Stevie WONDER got latitude for their projects); he avoided TV, rarely performed live and sometimes didn't show up; used drugs; had trouble with tax authorities. Meanwhile he came back '71 with song cycle/concept album *What's Going On*: no. 6 LP incl. no. 2 title track, 'Mercy Mercy Me (The Ecology)' and 'Inner City Blues (Make Me Wanna Holler)', both top 10. No. 14 LP *Trouble Man* '72 had 10 instrumental tracks, three vocals incl. top 10 title single; *Let's Get It On* '73 was no. 2 LP with no. 1 hit title track; duet LP with Diana ROSS *Diana & Marvin* was no. 26 with three single hits; 2-disc *Marvin Gaye Live At The London Palladium* '77 was no. 3 hit album with no. 1 single 'Got To Give It Up'. After stormy 14-year marriage to Anna Gordy he was ordered by a judge to give her royalties on an album; he filed bankruptcy, made uneven 2-disc *Here, My Dear* '79; she considered lawsuit for invasion of privacy. He had married second wife Janice '77; she left him for Teddy PENDERGRASS. *In Our Lifetime* '81 was no. 32 LP; he switched to Columbia; *Midnight Love* '82 incl. 'Sexual Healing': after many nominations he won a Grammy for 'Best R&B Performance, Male' with no. 3 pop hit, pursued by categories to the end: he was shot to death by his father during a quarrel. *Dream Of A Lifetime* '85, *Romantically Yours* '86 issued by Columbia. A troubled, greatly talented man who created a lasting body of work. LPs now on Motown incl. *Tribute To Nat King Cole*, 3-disc *Anthology*, many more compilations: *Marvin Gaye And His Girls* incl. Wells, Weston, Terrell; *And His Women* on Tamla

CD incl. tracks with Ross; CD *Compact Command Performance* has 15 hits.

GAYLE, Crystal (*b* Brenda Gail Webb, 9 Jan. '51, Paintsville, Ky.) Country-pop crossover singer, younger sister of Loretta LYNN. Family moved to Indiana '55; she listened to both country and pop; joined sister's road show '70, recorded for Decca '70-2 with minor hits 'I've Cried (The Blue Right Out Of My Eyes)' and 'I Hope You're Havin' Better Luck Than Me'. Signed with United Artists '74; under guidance of prod. Allen Reynolds soon hit charts with 'Wrong Road Again' '74, 'Somebody Loves You' '75, 'I'll Get Over You' (first crossover to pop hot 100) and 'You Never Miss A Real Good Thing' '76, 'I'll Do It All Over Again' and 'Don't It Make My Brown Eyes Blue' (pop no. 2) '77. Named ACM's Female Vocalist of the Year '76-7-9, CMA's '77-8; won Grammy for 'Brown Eyes'. Albums reflected pop success, incl. such songs as 'It's Alright With Me', 'Cry Me A River'. 'Ready For The Times To Get Better', 'Why Have You Left The Ones You Left Me For', 'Talking In Your Sleep' all country no. 1 hits '78; 'Sleep' made top 20. Switched to Columbia '79, now country music's highest paid female star; 'Half The Way' was pop no. 18 '79. Switched to Elektra/Warners '82, duet country hit with Eddie Rabbitt 'You And I' '82; with nine hot 100 entries '76-81, too many country hits to list here. Albums incl. *Crystal* '75, *Somebody Loves You* '76, *We Must Believe In Magic* '77, *When I Dream* '78, *We Should Be Together* '79, *Classic* '79, *The Singles Album* '80, *A Woman's Heart* '81, *Love Songs* '82, all on UA; *Miss The Mississippi* '79, *These Days* '80, *Hollywood, Tennessee* '81, *A Crystal Gayle Collection* '83, all on CBS; *Love Songs* '83 on Pickwick; *Cage The Songbird* '83, *Nobody Wants To Be Alone* '85, *Country Pure* and *Straight To The Heart* '86 plus *A Crystal Christmas* on WB, followed by *What If We Fall In Love*, a 'makeout' duet LP with Gary Morris, who co-wrote 'Making Up For Lost Time' with Dave Loggins.

GAYTEN, Paul (*b* 29 Jan. '20, Kentwood, La.) R&B pianist, vocalist, bandleader '50s. His uncle was Little Brother MONTGOMERY. He played in touring Don Dunbar band '30s, based in Jackson, Ms., probably in local Southland Troubadours '40; led various combos in clubs from mid-'40s; vocalist Annie Laurie (admired by Dinah WASHINGTON) shared credit on no. 8 R&B hit 'I'll Never Be Free' '50; he wrote 'For You My Love', no. 1 R&B hit for Paul Darnel, no. 12 for Nat COLE '49-50. Among many records, backed Boston quintet the Tune Weavers (with lead singer Margo Sylvia) on ballad 'Happy, Happy Birthday Baby', no. 3 R&B, 5 pop '57; Clarence 'Frogman' HENRY on 'Ain't Got No Home' (no. 3 R&B, no. 20 pop hit '56) (co-writing credit for 'Troubles, Troubles' on flip side); backed R&B singer Oscar Wills (*b* 10 Feb. '16, Houston, Texas; *d* in car crash 21 Oct. '69, Kingman, Ariz.) on his 'Flatfoot Sam' '57, humorous slice of life in ghetto. 'Nervous Boogie' on flip was instrumental cut using leftover studio time: made Billboard Hot 100 as did similar 'Windy', 'The Hunch' '58-9, Gayten's only pop hits, with riffing saxes, rolling New Orleans piano, rocking solos by tenor saxophonist Lee ALLEN (who wrote and recorded 'Walkin' With Mr Lee' while he was a Gayten sideman): like Dave BARTHOLOMEW, Gayten had infl. through New Orleans studio scene to the mainstream as A&R man for Chess. Moved to West Coast and had own Pzazz label.

GEFFEN, David (*b* '44, L.A.) Label boss. Worked at William Morris booking agency; formed Asylum label mid-'60s with Elliott Roberts 'because I couldn't find a record company doing what I wanted to do'. Geffen and Roberts had been early managers of CROSBY, STILLS & NASH; now they captured era's West Coast scene: had hits with singles (e.g. JO JO GUNNE) but album sales began '72-3 with LP chart entries by Joni MITCHELL, Jackson BROWNE, Linda RONSTADT and the EAGLES, all soon superstars. He scored a coup '74 by coaxing Bob DYLAN away from CBS for two LPs; signed Andrew GOLD and Tom WAITS, re-formed the BYRDS; then AOR began to lose its appeal for Geffen: he started his own Geffen label and brought John LENNON out of five-year seclusion for *Double Fantasy* '80. Geffen handled Elton JOHN, Peter GABRIEL in USA; incl. Mitchell, ASIA, Don Henley, Neil YOUNG on roster, new acts such as WAS (NOT WAS), Greg Copeland,

LONE JUSTICE. Lately Geffen has widened his interests to incl. film production.

GEILS, J., BAND USA white R&B band formed by folk guitarist Jerome Geils (*b* 20 Feb. '46, NYC), who met harmonica player Magic Dick (*b* Richard Salwitz, 13 May '45, New London, Conn.), bassist Danny Klein (*b* 13 May '46, Worcester, Mass.) while studying engineering. In '67 added vocalist Peter Wolf (*b* Peter Blankfield, 7 Mar. '46, NYC), and drummer Stephen Jo Bladd (*b* 13 July '42, Boston); Wolf, whose taste for doo-wop, '50s rock'n'roll fitted neatly, was former DJ at WBCN Boston and striking frontman: tall, spindly, dynamic. Keyboardist Seth Justman (*b* 27 Jan. '51, Washington DC) completed lineup '67 (by '80s Justman was composing nearly all band's music). *J. Geils Band* '71 first of nine for Atlantic. R&B covers, e.g. Smokey RO-BINSON's 'First I Look At The Purse', Bobby WOMACK's 'Looking For A Love' (their first top 40 USA, no. 39 '72) interspersed with originals like reggae-tinged 'Give It To Me' (no. 30 '73), 'Must Have Got Lost' (biggest '70s single at no. 12 '74). Albums lost fire in '70s, but live show always recommended; Wolf's marriage to film star Faye Dunaway may have cost credibility with fans. Other Atlantic LPs were *The Morning After*, live *Full House* '72; *Bloodshot* (no. 10 LP USA), *Ladies Invited* '73; *Nightmares* '74; *Hotline* '75; *Blow Your Face Out* '76; *Monkey Island* '77. Signing to EMI/America '78 rejuvenated them: *Sanctuary* had no. 35 single 'One Last Kiss', while *Love Stinks* '80 no. 18 LP USA, had two more top 40 entries; *Freeze-Frame* '81 no. 1 LP for four weeks: title track no. 4 USA/27 UK, while swaggering, macho 'Centerfold' was no. 1 USA/3 UK, less typical balladic 'Angel In Blue' no. 40 USA. Toured widely in '80s, Europe with ROLL-ING STONES '82; live *Showtime!* '82 no. 23 LP USA, incl. recent hits: rousing 'Land Of 1000 Dances' marred only by Wolf's self-indulgent stage rap. He went solo '83, working with writer/prod. Michael Jonzun; title track of his *Lights Out* no. 12 USA single '84; Justman found vocal mantle hard to shoulder with other chores: post-split LP *You're Gettin' Even While I'm Gettin' Odd* '84 no. 80, single 'Concealed Weapons' no. 63. Took a while to hit the top: 'It was a

great sense of accomplishment after all we'd been through,' said Wolf, who rejected accusations of selling out with Justman's commercial material: 'We never said we were a blues band.' Like Stones, continued despite detractors; success will be hard to maintain without Wolf.

GENESIS UK art-rock band, became stadium/pop biggies. Began at Charterhouse school as songwriters calling themselves Garden Wall: Tony Banks (*b* 27 Mar. '50), keyboards; Michael Rutherford (*b* 2 Oct. '50), guitar, bass and vocals; Peter GABRIEL, vocals; Anthony Phillips, guitar. Jonathan KING re-named them, godfathered pop LP *From Genesis To Revelation* '69 on Decca (London in USA); they practised for months, developed a theatrical stage show; *Trespass* '70 was on Buddah in USA as they gained cult following. Chris Stewart, John Silver, John Mayhew had passed through on drums, succeeded by Phil COLLINS; Phillips left, replaced by Steve Hackett (*b* 12 Feb. '50), they switched to Charisma for *Nursery Cryme* '71, *Foxtrot* '72 (first UK chart entry), *Selling England By The Pound* and *Genesis Live* '73 (first USA chart hits). Charisma leased LPs to Atco, then Atlantic beginning with 2-disc *The Lamb Lies Down On Broadway* '74, concept starring Gabriel, who then left for solo career; they auditioned many singers, decided that Collins would do, hired second drummer for tours (incl. Bill BRUFORD '76); switched from costumes etc. to laser/stadium shows. *A Trick Of The Trail, Wind And Wuthering, Seconds Out, And Then There Were Three* '76-8 were followed by *Duke* '80 (also the name of their custom label), *Abacab* '81, *Three Sides Live* '82 (one studio), *Genesis* '83: three of these were no. 1 in UK, three top ten USA. Collins has became a much-loved superstar; see entries for Collins, Gabriel.

GENTLE GIANT UK progressive group formed '70. Shulman brothers Ray (bass and guitar; *b* 8 Dec. '49, Portsmouth), Derek (sax, vocals; *b* 2 Feb. '47, Glasgow), Phil (sax, trumpet; *b* 27 Aug. '37, Glasgow) began in R&B band the Howlin' Wolves on UK south coast; changed name to Simon Dupree and the Big Sound at manager's request; first releases on Parlophone were

R&B covers but no. 9 hit 'Kites' was fashionably ethereal, with 'oriental' talkover by
actress Jackie Chan: switch to beads and
caftans backfired and band were shunted
into cabaret to trade on one hit. Shulmans
split from drummer Tony Randall, bassist
Pete O'Flaherty; recruited Royal Academy
of Music grad Kerry Minnear on keyboards
(b 2 Apr. '48, Salisbury) and guitarist/blues
enthusiast Gary Green (b 20 Nov. '50,
Stroud Green); drummer Malcolm Mor-
imore replaced after debut LP *Gentle Giant*
70 showed off brothers' instrumental virtuosity in some wilfully obscure and experimental music that ran contrary to previous
leanings, but fitted very well with other
blues bands turned progressive' of the time,
e.g. MOODY BLUES, JETHRO TULL, etc.;
time changes, multi-layered sounds and almost medieval vocal harmonies the norm.
Arrival of Welsh drummer John Weathers
(b Carmarthen; ex-Eyes of Blue, the Grease
Band) solidified sound for *Three Friends*
'71. Phil Shulman then left; remaining
brothers stabilised after poor *In A Glass-
house* '73; conceptual *The Power And The
Glory* '74 consolidated their USA success
(though switching labels twice in USA
didn't help). Band carried on through '70s
as most early contemporaries (King Crimson, etc.) went to the wall. Concentrated on
USA market, where seven LPs charted '72-
7: *Octopus, The Power And The Glory, Free
Hand* (best showing at no. 48), *Interview,*
live 2-disc *Playing The Fool, The Missing
Piece* (no UK LP entries, even pre-punk).
Broke up '80 after *Civilian* LP, less complex than its predecessors; Ray Shulman
described it as 'a disaster'.

GENTRY, Bobbie (b Roberta Streeter, 27
July '44, Chickasaw Co.) Singer. Studied
philosophy, music in L.A.; worked as secretary, Las Vegas dancer, then stormed pop
chart with 'Ode To Billie Jo' (no. 1 USA/13
UK '67). Beautifully produced story song
(arr. by Jimmy Haskell, engineer Kelly Gordon) about indifference to teenage tragedy
won several Grammies; Gentry won CMA
award as most promising female vocalist;
film of song made '76 with additional music
by Michel LEGRAND: reissue of original and
theme music from film both made Hot 100
'76. Other minor hits incl. duet with Glen
CAMPBELL 'All I Have To Do Is Dream' '70

(no. 27 USA/3 UK), second no. 1 in UK
with 'I'll Never Fall In Love Again' '70.
Gentry TV series in UK, radio show on
Armed Forces Network, work in Las Vegas
clubs. LPs *Ode To Billie Jo* '67, duet album
with Campbell, others on Capitol and Ode.

GERALDO (b Gerald Bright) UK dance
band leader; adopted Latinised name opening at the Savoy Hotel '30 with his Gaucho
Tango Orchestra, suitably dressed in someone's idea of native costume; soon added
conventional sweet fare, sounding like Jan
GARBER or Guy LOMBARDO in the USA:
one of the few UK dance bands of the era
that never played hot at all. Compilations
still available on EMI, Polygram, other labels. After WWII he organised bands for
transatlantic P&O liners and hired young
boppers like Ronnie SCOTT, who were willing to play sweet for the free trip to NYC
and back so they could hear modern jazz on
52nd Street: the gig was known as Geraldo's
Navy, necessity of playing 'strict tempo'
perhaps giving rise to composition 'P&O
Blues' by Mike CARR.

GERRY AND THE PACEMAKERS UK
Merseybeat group. Lineup: Gerry Marsden
(b 24 Sep. '42), vocals; Les Maguire (b 27
Dec. '41), piano; Les Chadwick (b 11 May
'43), bass; Freddie Marsden (b 23 Nov. '40),
drums: all b Liverpool except Maguire,
from nearby Wallasey. Gerry and Freddie
passed through skiffle groups (e.g. Mars
Bars), gigged in Hamburg with Chadwick,
added Maguire on return: second group
after BEATLES signed by Brian EPSTEIN.
Rock'n'roll background evident in albums
(e.g. first, *How Do You Like It?* '63); singles
focused on Gerry's ever-sunny disposition.
Made history as first act to have no. 1 sin-
gles with first three releases: 'How Do You
Do It?' and 'I Like It' (both written by
Mitch Murray), syrupy and untypical
RODGERS & HAMMERSTEIN ballad 'You'll
Never Walk Alone', now a soccer anthem
(all '63, all prod. by George MARTIN). 'I'm
The One' no. 2, 'Don't Let The Sun Catch
You Crying' no. 6 '64; last first and biggest
USA hit at no. 4 '65 (seven top 40 singles
USA altogether, nine in UK). First USA
chart album called *Don't Let The Sun Catch
You Crying; Second Album* less successful;
Ferry Cross The Mersey soundtrack of film

'65, with 9 of 12 songs written by group; title song was no. 8 UK/6 USA, last top 10 entry. Gerry went solo '67; starred with Anna Neagle in *Charlie Girl* on West End stage, went on children's TV; re-formed Pacemakers occasionally for revival shows, recorded LP of LENNON-McCARTNEY songs (ironically: 'How Do You Do It?' was first recorded, then rejected, by Beatles as follow-up to first hit 'Love Me Do'). Marsden regarded himself as all round entertainer, but some LP tracks plus only known live records (EP *Gerry In California* '65) hint at raunchy rocker behind toothsome exterior. Still works cabaret, panto; back in news '83 when another Liverpool group FRANKIE GOES TO HOLLYWOOD equalled record of three consecutive charttoppers (first, 'Relax', had cover of 'Ferry Cross The Mersey' on flip); then re-cut 'You'll Never Walk Alone' '85 with showbiz friends as the Crowd to raise money for families of victims of horrific fire at Bradford City Football Club: made no. 1.

GERSHWIN, George (*b* Jacob Gershvin, 26 Sep. 1898, NYC; *d* 11 July '37, Beverly Hills) USA composer, songwriter, pianist. Influenced by ragtime and jazz, with great melodic gift; early death from brain-tumour was the single greatest loss to USA music this century. No interest in music as a child until family acquired piano when he was 12; first hit was 'Swanee' '19 (lyrics by Irving Caesar): incl. in show *Sinbad* with Al JOLSON, sold a million in sheet music, 2 million records (various artists). Wrote songs for *George White's Scandals* '20-24, collaborating with lyricist brother Ira (*b* Israel Gershvin, 6 Dec. 1896, NYC; *d* 17 Aug. '85, Cal.), who until he proved himself had used name Arthur Francis. First complete musical together was *Lady Be Good* '24, incl. besides title song 'The Man I Love' (dropped from three shows, still became a classic), 'Fascinatin' Rhythm'. Other works incl. *Tip-Toes* '25 ('That Certain Feeling'), *Oh Kay* '26 ('Someone To Watch Over Me'), *Funny Face* '27 (' S'Wonderful'), *Rosalie* '28 (with Sigmund ROMBERG; Gershwin songs incl. 'How Long Has This Been Going On?'), *Show Girl* '29 ('Liza'), *Girl Crazy* '30 ('Bidin' My Time', 'But Not For Me', 'Embraceable You', 'I Got Rhythm'), *Strike Up The Band* '30 ('I've Got

A Crush On You'). Films incl. *A Damsel In Distress* '37 ('A Foggy Day', 'Nice Work If You Can Get It'), *Shall We Dance?* '37 (title song, 'They Can't Take That Away From Me', 'Let's Call The Whole Thing Off'), *Goldwyn Follies* '38 ('Love Walked In', 'Love Is Here To Stay'). More ambitious works incl. *Rhapsody In Blue* '24, commissioned by Paul WHITEMAN, orchestrated by Ferde Grofe (*b* 27 Mar. 1892, NYC; *d* 3 Apr. '72, Santa Monica, Cal.). Grofe is best known for his *Grand Canyon Suite* with donkeys clopping in 'On The Trail' used as cigarette commercial for many years; song 'Daybreak' (lyrics by Harold Adamson) from Grofe's *Mississippi Suite* was hit '42; also wrote 'Count Your Blessings' '33; in fact he was an innovator c.'15 while playing piano for Art Hickman in San Francisco, helping to invent the big dance band. But his orchestration was wrong for Gershwin's *Rhapsody*: recording early '50s by Hugo WINTERHALTER (Byron Janis, piano) touched it up, tried to make it swing; revelation came much later using original arr. on CBS LP, Michael Tilson Thomas conducting jazz band accompanying Gershwin's solo piano roll: tempi quicker, piece brighter, surely what he intended. Gershwin's *Concerto In F* for piano and orchestra '25 commissioned by Walter Damrosch; good tunes incl. bluesy flugelhorn solo in slow movement. Tone poem *An American In Paris* '28 used as ballet for Gene Kelly in Oscar-winning film of same name '51. Also wrote preludes for piano, *Cuban Rhapsody*, *Variations On I Got Rhythm*, etc. masterpiece is opera *Porgy And Bess*, based on novel by DuBose Heyward; with libretto by Heyward, words by Ira, incl. 'I Love You, Porgy', 'Summertime', 'I Got Plenty O' Nothin', 'Bess, You Is My Woman Now', 'It Ain't Necessarily So'; it flopped '35-6 but revival '42 ran longer than any revival in history of USA musical theatre; black American company toured world with it '52-6, incl. USSR; first American opera ever seen at La Scala in Milan; filmed '59 with Sammy DAVIS Jr, Pearl BAILEY, Dorothy Dandridge, etc. original version with complete score, recitatives instead of spoken interludes in '75 concert version (cond. Lorin Maazel), '76 staging at Houston, Texas (cond. John DeMain), both issued on record: Edward Greenfield wrote in *Gramo-*

phone that it ranked with Berg's *Wozzeck* and Britten's *Peter Grimes* as 20th-century operatic portrait of human nature. Glyndebourne Festival production '86 in UK was extravagantly praised by critics. Celebration of his music on records, radio, TV goes on; he is easily most popular American composer: he did not quite fuse popular and 'classical' idioms, but was not yet 39 when he died. Ira carried on as one of the great lyricists; collaborated with Jerome KERN ('Long Ago And Far Away'), Harold ARLEN ('The Man That Got Away'), Vernon DUKE ('I Can't Get Started'), etc.

GETZ, Stan (*b* 2 Feb. '27, Philadelphia, Pa.) Tenor sax. Played with Jack TEAGARDEN, Tommy DORSEY, Benny GOODMAN, Stan KENTON, several other bands while still a teenager, then with Woody HERMAN '47-9, member of the 'Four Brothers' reed section that gave band its sound, most exciting of any white band of era; solo on 'Early Autumn' brought more fame: with Zoot SIMS, Lee KONITZ, Gerry MULLIGAN, Art PEPPER, Pepper ADAMS, a few others, led a new generation of first-class white jazz reedmen popular around the world: Getz's tone, gift for beauty making him particularly fine ballad player. First own records on Savoy '46 with quartet The Be Bop Boys; led small groups, appeared in film *The Benny Goodman Story* '56; *The Hanged Man* '65, etc. Early records '48-53 on variety of labels; long association with Norman GRANZ began '52: many LPs incl. *West Coast Jazz* '55, *The Steamer* '56, others with Oscar PETERSON trio, Mulligan, J. J. JOHNSON, etc. Toured with JATP, lived in Europe '58-61, recorded in Paris, Stockholm, Copenhagen, Stuttgart, Baden-Baden, Warsaw; LP *Focus* '61 on return, with orchestra led by Hershey Kay (*b* 17 Nov. '19, Philadelphia; also wrote ballet/opera scores), arr. with strings by Eddie SAUTER announced return. *Jazz Samba* '62 with Charlie BYRD introduced bossa nova, reached no. 1 on Billboard's top pop albums chart; *Big Band Bossa Nova* '62 with Gary MCFARLAND band made no. 13; *Jazz Samba Encore!* '63 with Luiz Bonfa, guitar, vocalist Maria Toledo on some tracks was no. 88; *Reflections* '64 no. 122; then *Getz/Gilberto* '64 with Joao Gilberto and his wife Astrud reached no. 2, with no. 5 hit single 'The Girl From

Ipenema'; *Getz Au Go Go* '64 with Astrud no. 24: six pop hit LPs in two years made him one of the era's most popular jazz musicians; when the bossa nova fad was played out the beauty of his treatment was still fresh as paint; also won Grammies '62, 64. Sessioned on *Bob Brookmeyer And Friends* on Columbia '64; back on Verve, *Sweet Rain* '67 with Chick COREA made top 200 LPs. Played on film soundtrack *Mickey One* '65, composed, arr. by Sauter; recorded with Boston Pops on RCA; with orchestras, big bands arr. by Claus Ogerman, Richard Evans, Johnny Pate; quartet in Paris with Gary BURTON, Steve SWALLOW, and Roy HAYNES, in NYC with Corea, Ron CARTER, Grady Tate (*b* 14 Jan. '32, Durham, N.C.: drums, also sings; worked with Peggy LEE), all '66-7. 2-disc *Dynasty* '71 on Verve recorded in London, partly at Ronnie SCOTT's; quartet had organ, guitar, drums. *Communications* '71 in Paris with SWINGLE Singers, Michel LEGRAND; he also recorded with the Kenny CLARKE – BOLAND big band. Met Corea in London, asked him to write for new group; *Captain Marvel* recorded '72 with Corea, Stanley CLARKE, Tony WILLIAMS, AIRTO; issued '75 on Columbia, made top 200 LPs (same LP now on Verve in UK). Meanwhile band without Airto recorded live *At Montreux* (Polydor), *Portrait* (Lotus/Joker) July '72. Many LPs feature Lou Levy on piano; Getz recorded '74 in Milan, Warsaw for the first time with pianist Albert Dailey (*b* 16 June, Baltimore, Md.; *d* '84). *The Best Of Two Worlds* has Joao Gilberto, Dailey, others; *This Is My Love* vocalist Kimiko Kassei; *The Master* a quartet with Dailey, *The Peacocks* Jimmy ROWLES (incl. some vocals, duos for tenor and piano), all on CBS '75. *Live At Montmartre* '77 has Joanne BRACKEEN on piano (2 vols. on Steeplechase; also 2-discs on Inner City called *Stan Getz Gold*). *Another World* '77 on Columbia has quartet at Montreux with Andy Laverne on piano; *Mort d'un Pourri* on Philips, *Children Of The World* and *Forest Eyes* on CBS '77-8 all with orchestras; *The Great Jazz Gala '80*, *Midem Live '80* recorded at Cannes with up to 11 pieces incl. Laverne, Joe Farrell, second tenor, plus vocalist Gayle Moran; various tracks on Personal Choice, Bellaphone, Jazz Gate, Rare Bird, RCA. *The Dolphin* '81 had quartet with Levy,

Pure Getz '82 with Jim McNeely, piano, both Concord Jazz. *Poetry* '83 on Elektra is beautiful duet LP with Dailey: two solos by him; they toured West Coast USA early '84. *Line For Lyons* '83 has Chet BAKER, McNeely, *Let There Be Love* on Concord Jazz has vocalist Dee Bell, 11 pieces incl. Willie COLON. Also available in USA: *Best Of Stan Getz* on Columbia; *Getz Meets Mulligan In Hi-Fi* '57 on Verve.

GIBBONS, Carroll (*b* '03, Clinton, Mass.; *d* May '54) Piano, bandleader. Went to England '24, played piano in the Boston Orchestra, a relief band at the Savoy Hotel for the Savoy Orpheans; it incl. Americans Howard Jacobs on alto sax (worked with Gibbons for many years), Joe Brannelly on banjo (later with AMBROSE for 10 years). He took over the Orpheans '27, they toured in Germany, disbanded '28 as Gibbons went to HMV as Director of Light Music: led New Mayfair Dance Orchestra on records, with various small groups accompanied Noel COWARD, Paul ROBESON, Gracie FIELDS, many others incl. George Metaxa, a Romanian-born musical-comedy star (a hit in Coward's *Bitter Sweet*, '29). Assistant Ray NOBLE took over when Gibby went to the USA to work in films; he returned to England '31, re-formed the Orpheans and led them for the rest of his life. Band-within-a-band was 'Carroll Gibbons and his Boy Friends'. Records and broadcasts were extremely popular and his drawling sign-off 'G'night, everybody' was very familiar. EMI reissues incl. 2-disc *The Carroll Gibbons Story*, with 32 tracks from '25-46, incl. '37 original version of 'So Rare', a big hit for Jimmy DORSEY '57; he also recorded solo piano medleys of pop songs, of which 20 are incl. on *Carroll Re-Calls The Tunes*.

GIBBONS, Steve UK singer/songwriter. Began in the Dominettes, local Birmingham group '58; became Uglys '62; continued through '60s with various lineups (one incl. Dave Pegg, later FAIRPORT CONVENTION, JETHRO TULL), several flop singles. Final lineup with Trevor Burton (ex-MOVE), guitar; Richard Tandy, keyboards; Dave Morgan, bass; Keith Smart, drums became Balls, equally unsuccessful. Gibbons was ousted by Jackie LOMAX '70, came back; final Balls lineup Gibbons, Burton,

Denny Laine (later Wings), guitar; Alan White (later YES), drums. Gibbons joined Idle Race when Balls folded, only to find that group folding. First LP *Short Stories* '71 after 13 years in the business, assisted by Burton, Albert Lee on guitars, SPOOKY TOOTH's Gary Wright on keyboards. Steve Gibbons Band formed Feb. '72: Bob Lamb (ex-Locomotive), drums; Dave Carroll and Bob Wilson, guitars (both ex-Tea and Sympathy); Bob Griffin, bass (replaced '75 by Burton). At Pete Townshend's suggestion signed by Polydor, cut promising ranchy guitar-rock LP *Any Road Up* '76; *Rolling On* '77 incl. cover of Chuck BERRY's 'Tulane', no. 12 hit; *Caught In The Act* '77 attempted to capture live act. Gibbons shaved beard as concession to punk, but *Down In The Bunker* '78 fell between two stools. Lamb prod. acclaimed UB40 LP *Signing Off* '80, left to become full-time producer. Gibbons LPs *Street Parade* '80 and *Saints And Sinners* '81 veered towards rockabilly – by latter, lineup was Burton, P. J. Wright, guitar and keyboards; Alan Wickett, drums. Burton replaced '86 by Roger Iniss; group made 'Personal Problem' on Aura label with Bob Seger hit 'Old Time Rock'n'Roll' as B-side: if Gibbons is answer to Seger from UK's industrial heartland, he must be due for another hit soon: came back with *On The Loose* '86, live in London.

GIBBS, Georgia (*b* 17 Aug. '20, Worcester, Mass.) USA pop singer; biggest successes were in mid-'50s. Other birth dates also found; real name Fredda Lipson or Gibson. Worked in radio on *Hit Parade*, *Camel Caravan*, own singing show; sang with bands from age 15; as Fredda Gibson with Hudson-DeLange band '38 ('If We Never Meet Again') (Will Hudson, *b* 8 Mar. '08, Barstow, Cal.; Edgar DeLange, *b* 12 Jan. '04, Long Island City, NY; *d* 13 July '49, L.A. were arr./songwriters who led band together briefly; Hudson wrote arr. for many fine bands; they co-wrote 'Moonglow', 'Organ Grinder's Swing', etc.). Gibbs worked with Frankie TRUMBAUER '40 ('Laziest Gal In Town'), Artie SHAW '42 ('Not Mine'/'Absent Minded Moon'); about then took name Georgia Gibbs; later a regular on popular Jimmy DURANTE-Garry Moore radio show, dubbed 'Her Nibs' by Moore.

Strong, accurate voice and showmanship brought her 15 top 40 hits '50-9, from cover of inane novelty 'If I Knew You Were Comin' I'd've Baked A Cake' '50 on Coral. Signed to Mercury '51; apart from 'Kiss Of Fire' (no. 2 '52), 'Seven Lonely Days' (no. 11 '53), her biggest hits were covers of R&B material: 'Tweedle Dee' (no. 2 '55; LaVern BAKER original no. 4 R&B, only 14 pop), 'Dance With Me Henry' (no. 1 '55, with watered-down lyrics based on 'Work With Me Annie' by Hank BALLARD and overtly sexual 'Roll With Me Henry' by Ballard, Johnny OTIS and Etta JAMES). By the time Gibbs covered 'Jim Dandy' '56, white kids had caught on: Baker made no. 3 R&B, 17 pop; Gibbs didn't chart. Began label-hopping to RCA, last chart hit 'The Hula-Hoop Song' on Roulette (no. 35 '58). LPs incl. *Swingin' With Her Nibs* on Mercury; *Georgia Gibbs* on Epic '63; *Something's Gotta Give* on Imperial '64. Semi-retired to Italy.

GIBBS, Terri (*b* 15 June '54, Augusta, Ga.) Blind country singer. Child prodigy on piano, sang gospel in early teens, formed band in high school; landed five-year residency at Augusta Steak House '75 with band Sound Dimension; demo tapes led to contract with MCA '80. Debut single 'Somebody's Knockin' ' became big pop-country hit '81. Some success on country charts, but perhaps too soulful for the market at first; she may yet make breakthrough. Albums incl. *Somebody's Knockin'* '81, *I'm A Lady* '81, *Some Days It Rains All Night* '82, *Over Easy* '83, all on MCA; then *Old Friends* on WB.

GIBBS, Terry (*b* Julius Gubenko, 13 Oct. '24, Brooklyn, N.J.) Vibes, also drums; won Major Bowes amateur contest at 12, turned pro on drums, served in WWII, worked for Tommy DORSEY, Chubby Jackson, Buddy RICH, Woody HERMAN late '40s, with Charlie SHAVERS-Louie BELLSON, then Benny GOODMAN small groups; formed own groups. He was seen as the only vibist in bop (with Milt JACKSON), succeeding Lionel HAMPTON on the instrument; in fact he was closer in style to Hampton than Jackson: with roots in the swing era he was a popular mainstream artist. First records as leader on Prestige '49, on Savoy '51, Bruns-

wick '52-4, adding brass and reeds '54 (one of these reissued as *Terry* on Jasmine UK), five reeds on Emarcy '55 arr. by Manny ALBAM, on EmArcy '58 arr. by Pete Rugolo; continued with small groups but also led highly rated big bands, with 19 pieces on EmArcy '56, on Mercury '59, plus *Live At The Summit* '61 and another LP from the Summit Club '62 on Verve. The band had a West Coast Kenton flavour but was closer to Herman in its devotion to swing: excellent previously unreleased two vols. of *Dream Band* '59 on Contemporary '87 with Conte CANDOLI, Bill PERKINS, Mel LEWIS, others; arr. by Bill Holman, Al COHN, Manny Albam, Lennie NIEHAUS, Med Flory (later formed SUPERSAX). Later small-group LPs incl. quartets *The Family Album*, now called *February 19th 1963* on Jazz Vault UK, *Take It From Me* '64 (latter with Kenny BURRELL, Sam JONES, Louis Hayes) now on MCA USA, Jasmine UK; LPs on Limelight '63, on Dot '65-6; he became more involved with studio work as mus. dir. on TV shows (e.g. Steve ALLEN), did not record for more than 10 years. Few LPs on obscure or Japanese labels since '78, then *Jazz Party – First Time Together* on Palo Alto with Buddy DEFRANCO, *The Latin Connection* '86 on Contemporary.

GIBSON, Bob (*b* 16 Nov. '31, NYC) Folksinger, songwriter. Father was a singer, as Gibby Gibson had radio show after WWI. Heard Burl IVES, Woody GUTHRIE, LEADBELLY on radio; learned guitar and five-string banjo. He worked outside music; went to visit Pete SEEGER, helped to build chimney; first appeared on TV '54, was winner on the Arthur GODFREY talent show; began touring, ended up in Greenwich Village, where he had lived as a child: helped get folk music into club The Bitter End, then a coffee bar with bongo players, poets (owned by Fred Weintraub, who later became film producer). Manager Albert Grossman intended to set up group like PETER, PAUL & MARY with Gibson, Bobby Camp and a girl who was taller than either. Worked at Village Vanguard, Blue Angel in NYC, Gate Of Horn in Chicago: 'That first job there turned out to be eleven months long. That's how it used to be. You worked places two weeks minimum. Now it's one nighters . . . If you don't have an audience, it's almost impossible to build one.' Later on TV's *Hootenanny*; sang at Newport Folk Festivals, Carnegie Hall, recently at Kerrville Folk Festival in Texas. Four LPs on Riverside began with *Offbeat Folksongs*, whereupon Stinson issued audition tape (still available as *Folksongs Of Ohio*) for which 'I've never gotten a penny.' LPs on Elektra began with *Ski Songs* '59 (Gibson hung out in Denver, wrote songs with locals for a musical about skiing that never happened). Live LP *The Gate Of Horn* '60; *Where I'm Bound* '64 incl. his own songs; left music, returned with *Bob Gibson* on Capitol c.'71 incl. John PRINE's 'Sam Stone', Jerry Wexler of Atlantic (Prine's label) enjoined the Gibson LP in court. Live *Funky In The Country* on his own Legend label, now on Mountain Railroad; *A Perfect High* and *Uptown Saturday Night* on Hogeye (label formed for Gibson and Tom PAXTON LPs); *Homemade Music* '78 with Hamilton Camp on Mountain Railroad. He has co-written songs with Shel SILVERSTEIN, Camp, Paxton (prod. several Paxton LPs); he wrote/acted in play with music *The Courtship Of Carl Sandburg* c.'84, ran 14 weeks in Chicago; wrote for children, planned new LP with Camp. Quotes from interview by Arthur Wood in Peter O'Brien's *Omaha Rainbow*.

GIBSON, Don (*b* 3 Apr. '28, Shelby, N.C.) Country-pop singer and songwriter. Turned pro age 14 on local radio; to Knoxville '52, became regular on radio *Barn Dance*. Songwriting led to contract with Acuff-Rose, record contract with RCA '54; moved to MGM without success, back on RCA '57 on strength of writing hits 'I Can't Stop Loving You' (for Kitty WELLS), 'Sweet Dreams' (for Faron YOUNG); prod. by Chet ATKINS, own first smash hit was 'Oh Lonesome Me'/'I Can't Stop Loving You' (2-sided hit no. 1 country, 7 pop), followed by 'Blue Blue Day' (no. 1 country, 20 pop), both '58. 14 entries in pop hot 100 '58-61; 37 top 40 hits in country chart '58-71; other duet country hits with Dottie WEST '69-70, Sue Thompson '71. Other soulful country top 10 hits were 'Give Myself A Party'/'Look Who's Coming' '58; 'Who Cares', 'Don't Tell Me Your Troubles' '59; 'Just One Time', 'Sweet Dreams' '60; 'Sea Of Heartbreak', 'Lonesome Number One'

'61; 'I Can Mend Your Broken Heart' '62, '(Yes) I'm Hurting', 'Funny, Familiar, Forgotten Feelings' '66; moved to Hickory label '70; 'Country Green' made no. 5. Most successful songs are 'I Can't Stop Loving You' (major pop hit for Ray CHARLES '62) and 'Sweet Dreams' (hit for Reba McENTIRE, Emmylou HARRIS, Patsy CLINE; title of Cline biopic '85). Gibson's LPs incl. *That Gibson Boy* '59, *No One Stands Alone* '60, *Girls, Guitars & Gibson* '61, *King Of Country Soul* '66, *All Time Country Gold* '70, *20 Of The Best* '82 (UK), all on RCA; *Rockin', Rollin' Gibson* on Bear Family (two vols. of reissues of RCA material); *A Legend In His Own Time* '83 on Cambra.

GILBERT & SULLIVAN Successful songwriting team working in English, marrying music and words to make seamless masterpieces, are a relatively recent phenomenon: in the 20th century RODGERS & HART were perhaps the greatest of many, but *The Beggar's Opera* was unique in the 18th century (music by J. Pepusch, libretto by John Gay; ballad opera first prod. 1728; shares same plot as Bertolt Brecht-Kurt WEILL's 20th-century *Dreigroschenoper*, or 'Three-Penny Opera'); in the 19th Sir Arthur Seymour Sullivan (*b* 13 May 1842; *d* 22 Nov. 1900), Sir William Schwenck Gilbert (*b* 18 Nov. 1836; *d* 29 Mar. '11) were likewise unique. Sullivan was a composer, Gilbert a successful humorist and playwright; their comic operettas full of good tunes and patter routines are still popular today. Impresario Richard D'Oyly Carte brought them together for *Trial By Jury* in 1875; Gilbert read the script to Sullivan; increasingly dissatisfied with it, he closed the book violently, but 'he had achieved his object . . . I was screaming with laughter the whole time', wrote Sullivan. Yet Sullivan soon felt he prostituted his talent: his songs often have an effortless grace, nobody setting English lyrics better than he did; but Queen Victoria told him he was wasting his time. He quarrelled constantly with Gilbert. *The Sorcerer* 1877 was followed by *H.M.S. Pinafore* '79, *The Pirates Of Penzance* '79, *Patience* '81, *Iolanthe* '82, *Princess Ida* '84, *The Mikado* '85; *Ruddigore* '87 was controversial, with a supernatural aspect: characters stepping down from ancestral portraits; they weren't allowed to call it 'Ruddy Gore', 'ruddy' being a euphemism for sacrilegious oath 'bloody'. It was followed by *The Yeomen Of The Guard* '88, *The Gondoliers* '89, *Utopia Limited* '93, *The Grand Duke* '96. Both got very rich. They poked fun at conventions, sending up Parliament and the legal system; *Pinafore* scored off the Admiralty and was a direct hit on cheap romantic novels, where high-class young ladies can fall in love with sailors; Poo-Bah in *The Mikado* bore closer resemblance to a British bureaucrat than a Japanese one, and the portrait still rings true 100 years later. All the shows have been recorded; *Mikado* film '50s with soprano Valerie Masterson is a delight, and a new production '86 was a hit in London, set in '20s England instead of Japan; Linda RONSTADT was a hit as Mabel in *Pirates* '80, also filmed; D'Oyly Carte opera company went broke '82 but was back home in its Sadler's Wells theatre early '87 with a new *Ruddigore*, faithful to all the tradition.

GILKYSON, Terry (*b* Hamilton Henry Gilkyson, c.'19, Phoenixville, Pa.) Songwriter, singer. During WWII did weekly folk music programme for Armed Forces Radio Service; recorded his 'Cry Of The Wild Goose' for Decca, covered by Frankie LAINE for '50 hit; sang on WEAVERS hit '51; formed Easy Riders trio with Frank Miller and Richard Dehr, had million-seller 'Marianne' '57 based on Bahamian folk tune; wrote 'The Bear Necessities' for Disney film of Kipling's *Jungle Book*, etc. Daughter Eliza is folk-rocker: album *Love From The Heart* on Helios (as Lisa Gilkyson) followed by *Pilgrims* '88 on Gold Coast.

GILLESPIE, Dizzy (*b* John Birks Gillespie, 21 Oct. '17, Cheraw, S.C.) Trumpet, composer, leader, singer: with Charlie PARKER one of the most important innovators in jazz. Father was amateur musician; began on trombone at 14, trumpet at 15, studied harmony and theory; reputation for pranks, zany humour eventually led to nickname, but always a hard worker, understanding importance of technical ability. Famous for upturned trumpet which resulted from an accident; he liked the better sound dispersal and has been playing a bent horn ever since. Infl. by Roy ELDRIDGE, followed him into

Teddy HILL band '37, first tour of Europe; recorded with Lionel HAMPTON '39, featured soloist with Cab CALLOWAY '39-41, already with harmonic/rhythmic innovations leading to BOP ('Pickin' The Cabbage' '40); fired by Cab in famous spitball incident (not guilty). Worked for Benny CARTER (first played 'Night In Tunisia' '42), Lucky MILLINDER ('Little John Special' '42 incl. trumpet riff which became 'Salt Peanuts'), Earl HINES; subbed for four weeks in the Duke ELLINGTON band; wrote 'Woody'n'You' '44 for Coleman HAWKINS record date. Mus. dir. for famous Billy ECKSTINE band '44, formed own big band '45, more successfully '46-50; toured Scandinavia '48; Europe '52-3 with combo. *Jazz At Massey Hall* '53 is famous concert recorded in Toronto with Charlie PARKER, Bud POWELL, Charles MINGUS, Max ROACH. Big band organised by Quincy JONES '56-8 toured Europe, Latin America '56 for US State Dept: popular around the world, an excellent advertisement for USA but money was cut off partly because of complaints about using taxpayers' money to support a 'jazz band'. Led combos since except for one-off events. Many festivals, JATP tours, world tours, awards, polls won; one of the half-dozen most influential musicians in history of jazz. Compositions incl. 'Cubana Be, Cubana Bop' co-written with George RUSSELL, Chano POZO; 'Manteca' with Pozo and Gil FULLER, both '47; also 'Birks Works', 'Con Alma', 'Kush', many more; also famous for standard 'Tin Tin Deo', written by Pozo and Fuller. Dizzy wrote that 'Manteca' '47 was probably his best-selling record, but *Pop Memories* lists 'Salt Peanuts' (on Guild '45, with Parker) as pop hit in the novelty category. Tadd DAMERON's ballad 'If You Could See Me Now' is from a Dizzy solo: even more than most jazzmen he composes every time he plays. Latin infl. strong: polyrhythms important in bop; Pozo in big band late '40s had profound effect (see CUBOP); Latin link has been maintained: made Latin-jazz LP '54 on Norgran/Verve, recorded '56 in Argentina with tango band; in Cuba '77 with Arturo Sandoval, others; on Pablo label with MACHITO (*Afro-Cuban Jazz Moods* '75), with Mongo SANTAMARIA '80, with Sandoval (*To A Finland Station* '82), sat in with Sandoval at Ronnie SCOTT's in London '85. Singing, clowning, showmanship made him popular, always with wit, hint of the put-on. First vocal on record was 'Oop-Pop-A-Da' '47, then 'Salt Peanuts', 'Swing Low Sweet Cadillac', 'Umbrella Man', 'In The Land Of Ooo Blah Dee', etc. Played at White House for four Presidents; ran for President '63 (write-in vote almost got him on California ballot). *Dizzy Gillespie: The Development Of An American Artist 1940-46* is a 2-disc anthology from the Smithsonian Institution; late '40s big band recordings on 2-disc RCA set; many compilations, airchecks, concert recordings on various labels incl. '48 big band and '53 sextet dates at Salle Pleyel on 2-disc French Vogue set. Dizzy formed own label in Detroit, went broke; excellent 2-disc Savoy set *DeeGee Days* collects '51-2 tracks incl. early John COLTRANE date, vocals with Joe 'Bebop' Carroll (*b* 25 Nov. '19, Philadelphia; *d* 1 Feb. '81, Brooklyn; with Woody HERMAN '60s). Recorded in Hollywood '50 with strings arr. by Johnny Richards (*b* John Cascales, 2 Nov. '11, Schenectady, NY; *d* 7 Oct. '68, NYC; wrote for Stan KENTON); with Richards again on Verve '54; *One Night In Washington* '55 at Club Kavakos on Elektra incl. 'Afro Suite' with 'Manteca'. Many LPs with small groups, big bands on Norman GRANZ's Verve label '53-61; reissues incl. *Greatest Trumpet Of Them All* '57, 2-disc sets *Dizzy Gillespie With Stan Getz* '53,6; *With Roy Eldridge* (and Harry EDISON) '54-5, Sonny ROLLINS and Sonny STITT '57. *The New Continent* '62 on Limelight was big band concept set cond. by Benny Carter. Quintet LP '62 on Philips with Charlie VENTURA, Lalo SCHIFRIN was the first studio BOSSA NOVA album made in USA. *Something Old, Something New* '63 on Philips had quintet with James MOODY, Kenny Barron, Chris White on bass (*b* 6 July '36, NYC), Rudy Collins on drums (*b* 24 July '34, NYC; recorded with Ray COPELAND on Randy WESTON LP *Tanjah*; also with Junior MANCE, Gene AMMONS, etc.). *Dizzy Gillespie et les Double Six* made in Paris '63 with Kenny CLARKE, Bud POWELL, Pierre Michelot; vocal group dubbed later. *Reunion Big Band* '68 on Verve/MPS recorded live at Berlin Philharmonic Hall, with arr. by Gil Fuller. Other albums on Solid State, Gateway, Perception etc. followed by new era with Granz on

Pablo: *Dizzy Gillespie's Big 4* '74 has Joe PASS, Ray BROWN, Mickey Roker; *Jazz Maturity* '75 adds Roy Eldridge; *The Trumpet Kings Meet Joe Turner* '74 has Eldridge, Edison, Clark TERRY, vocals by Turner; three Pablo LPs incl. three Gillespie groups at Montreux '75, with Johnny GRIFFIN, Eddie DAVIS, etc. *Bahiana* '75 is Latin holiday, *Dizzy's Party* '76 a quintet; *Free Ride* '77 has Schifrin orchestra; *Dizzy Gillespie Jam* sextet at Montreux; *Digital At Montreux 1980* trio with Toots THIELEMANS on guitar, drummer Bernard 'Pretty' Purdie (*b* 11 June '39, Elkton, Md.: first black to graduate from Elkton High School, led white C&W band; later much teaching, studio work: played with MICKEY & SYLVIA '61, later mus. dir. for Aretha FRANKLIN). *Plays And Raps In His Greatest Concert* live at Montreux '81 with Moody, Milt JACKSON; too many Gillespie LPs to list them all: proof of enduring popularity with the general public as well as jazz fans, and they are still coming: *Groovin' High* and *One Bass Hit* on Musicraft (reissues of '45-6 small groups); new LPs mid-'80s incl. *New Faces* with Branford MARSALIS; *Closer To The Source* with guests Marsalis, Marcus Miller, Stevie WONDER is easy-going summertime listening. In '87 America was celebrating his 70th birthday and he once again fronted a big band on tour; in June '88 he led all-star big band at Playboy Festival then took 'United Nations Band' to Europe, with Moody, Sam RIVERS and Paquito D'Rivera on reeds, plus AIRTO, Flora PURIM, Monty ALEXANDER, Cuban drummer Ignacio Berroa etc. *To Be Or Not To Bop* '79 with Al Fraser is one of the best music autobiographies, full of anecdotes and interviews.

GILLEY, Mickey (*b* 9 Mar. '37, Ferriday, La.) Rockabilly, later honky-tonk singer with string of hits from '74. Piano-playing cousin of Jerry Lee LEWIS; for many years in his shadow. Moved to Houston '55, worked in construction; played clubs evenings, recorded rock'n'roll for many small labels; formed own label Astra '64, joined 20th Century Fox '65, Paula '66; had country hit 'Now I Can Live Again' '66 but had to wait for bigger breaks: on Playboy label '73, had no. 1 country hits 'Room Full Of Roses' (pop no. 50), 'I Overlooked An Orchid', 'City Lights' '74, 'Window Up Above' '75, 'Don't

The Girls All Get Prettier At Closing Time', 'Bring It On Home To Me' '76 (last made no. 101 on Billboard Bubbling Under chart, narrowly missing Hot 100). Hits led to ACM awards as Entertainer of the Year, Male Vocalist of the Year, Single of the Year '76. Hits continued; switched to Epic label for more hits incl. 'Stand By Me' (no. 22 pop crossover) from soundtrack of film *Urban Cowboy* '80, made at thriving Gilley's Club in Houston, 'largest honky tonk in the world'; also 'Paradise Tonight' '83, duet hit with Charley McLain; 'That's All That Matters' made 101 pop again; 'True Love Ways' '80, 'You Don't Know Me' '81 made pop Hot 100. LPs incl. *Down The Line With Mickey Gilley* '68 on Paula; *Welcome To Gilley's* '75 on Pye UK; *Overnight Sensation* '75 on Playboy; *Mickey At Gilley's* '78 on Checkmate; *The Songs We Made Love To* '79, *That's All That Matters To Me* '80, *Christmas At Gilleys's* '81, *Put Your Dreams Away* '82, *Fool For Your Love* '83, *You've Really Got A Hold On Me* '84, all on Epic.

GIMBLE, Johnny (*b* '26, near Tyler, Texas) Country fiddle, among best and busiest. Raised on a farm, gigged locally at 12; with brothers formed Rose City Swingsters, played on Tyler radio. To Shreveport, La. c.'43, played in Jimmie DAVIS band, with Bob WILLS off and on (also played electric mandolin). Left music for a while, western swing being out of fashion; returned, since '68 has recorded and toured with scores of artists incl. Merle HAGGARD, Loretta LYNN, Johnny Rodriguez, ASLEEP AT THE WHEEL, Guy CLARK, etc. CMA instrumentalist of the Year '74, nominated for a Grammy that year for 'Fiddlin' Around'. LPs incl. *Texas Dance Party* on Columbia, recorded live '75; 2-disc sets *Texas Fiddle Collection* and *Still Swingin'* with Texas Swing Pioneers on CMH.

GIRLSCHOOL UK heavy metal group formed '78: Kim McAuliffe, rhythm guitar, vocals; Kelly Johnson, lead guitar; Enid Williams, bass; Denise Dufort, drums. McAuliffe and Williams ex-Painted Lady; recruited others and released 'Take It All Away' on South London independent label City. Supported MOTORHEAD on '80 tour, gaining exposure, no. 28 chart entry for *Demolition* '80: no-frills heavy metal LP of

Johnson/McAuliffe compositions with cover of Gun's 'Race With The Devil' minor hit single. *Hit'N'Run* '81 no. 5 LP, incl. cover of ZZ TOP's 'Tush'; title track was their best chart placing with solo single at no. 35; EP *St Valentine's Day Massacre* made no. 5 on singles chart under name Headgirl (Girlschool and Motorhead together); lead track was cover of Johnny KIDD's 'Please Don't Touch'. EP *Wildlife* no. 58 with lead track 'Don't Call It Love'; LP *Screaming Blue Murder* '82, prod. by SLADE's Noddy Holder/Jim Lea team, showed touches of that band's tongue-in-cheek approach; incl. obligatory cover (Marc BOLAN's '20th Century Boy'); made no. 27 LP chart. By *Play Dirty* '83, Williams had left (formed shortlived group with Sham 69's Dave Parsons), replaced by ex-Killjoys bassist Gil Weston; by *Running Wild* '85 band had left Bronze label for Polygram, boasted new members Chris Bonacci and Jacki Bodimead. Image change saw glitzy clothes replace denim'n'leather, nearer to style of Runaways. Girlschool big in Japan, where they released *Live And More* LP: genuinely strong enough musically to transcend 'girl group' novelty tag. Hit single with Gary GLITTER '86, LP *Nightmare At Maple Cross* on new GWR label, group slimmed to Bonacci, Dufort, Weston, McAuliffe.

GIRLS OF THE GOLDEN WEST Hillbilly duo of '30s-40s, made comeback '60s. Millie (*b* Mildred Fern Good, 11 Apr. '13) and Dolly (*b* Dorothy Laverne Good, 11 Dec. '15), both from Muleshoe, Texas, among earliest female country singers, starting radio career in St Louis '30, regulars on WLS *National Barn Dance* '33-7, then in Cincinnati on *Boone County Jamboree* and *Midwestern Hayride* '37-42. Records on Victor, Columbia, Conqueror; most popular songs 'Tumbled Down Shack Of My Dreams', 'Home Sweet Home In Texas', 'When The Bees Are In The Hive', 'Little Old Rag Doll'. Appeared on *50-50 Club* in Cincinnati early '60s, recorded for Blue Bonnet label '63-7: six albums of *Girls Of The Golden West*.

GIUFFRE, Jimmy (*b* James Peter Giuffre, 26 Apr. '21, Dallas, Texas) Reeds, leader, composer, teacher. U. degree '42, with Army Air Force Orchestra '44; played with

Boyd RAEBURN, Jimmy DORSEY, Buddy RICH, Woody HERMAN late '40s; wrote 'Four Brothers' for Herman, much else. Gigged with Spade COOLEY '50, then back to jazz with Lighthouse All Stars (house band at Hermosa Beach Cal. club), Shorty ROGERS, etc. Many record dates, compositions; larger works *Pharoah, Suspensions* recorded by Gunther Schuller on Columbia; led own trio, performed his popular 'The Train And The River' on TV special *The Sound Of Jazz* '57 and Newport Jazz Festival '58 (film *Jazz On A Summer's Day* '60). Plays baritone sax, contributes arr. and tunes to uniquely beautiful LP *Lee Konitz Meets Jimmy Giuffre* '59 on Verve, with KONITZ and Hal McKusick on altos, Ted Brown (*b* 1 Dec. '27, Rochester, NY) and Warne MARSH on tenors (Marsh and Konitz take most of the solos), Bill EVANS, Buddy CLARK, drummer Ronnie Free (*b* 15 Jan. '36, Charleston, S.C.). Having won polls on clarinet late '50s gave up other reeds, but returned to them c.'65; has been active as music educator as well as keeping up own studies; many compositions incl. chamber music, larger pieces, ballet music. Taken for granted by public for many years, if not by critics; hindsight reveals career marked by much tonal beauty. Has recorded with Bob BROOKMEYER, Herb ELLIS, Shelly MANNE, many others; albums *Tenors West* and *West Coast Scene* with composer/arr. Marty Paich (*b* 23 Jan. '25, Oakland, Cal.; highly regarded in West Coast jazz scene '50s, then in Hollywood studios). Wrote arr. for Sonny STITT, Anita O'DAY on Verve. Own LPs began with '54-5 Capitol sessions now on Affinity as *Four Brothers* and *Tangents In Jazz*; LP on Atlantic '56 with six to nine pieces, then trio sets '56-8 incl. *Western Suite*; many albums on Verve incl. quartet *Ad Lib* '59, *In Person* '60; *Jimmy Giuffre With Strings* '60 recorded in Baden-Baden, cond. by Wolfran Röhrig; trio sets *Seven Pieces* and *The Easy Way* '59 incl. Jim HALL; *Fusion* and *Thesis* on Verve, *In Concert* on Italian Unique Jazz label have trio with Paul BLEY and Steve SWALLOW (all '61); *Free Fall* '62 on Columbia incl. that trio, also Giuffre clarinet solos. On later LPs he plays soprano, alto, tenor saxophones, clarinet and flute, incl. *Quiet Song* '74, trio with Bley and guitarist Bill Connors (*b* 24 Sep. '49, L.A.; has recorded

with Chick COREA, solo album *Hymn Of The Seventh Galaxy* on ECM). 2-disc trio set *Mosquito Dance* on DJM is also two LPs on Choice: *Music For People, Birds, Butterflies And Mosquitos* '72, *River Chant* '75; *IAI Festival* '78 on Improvising Artists label has quartet with Bley, Connors, Konitz; *Dragonfly* '83 another quartet on Soul Note.

GLASER BROTHERS Tompall (*b* Thomas Paul Glaser, 3 Sep. '33), Chuck (*b* Charles Vernon Glaser, 27 Feb. '36), Jim (*b* James William Glaser, 16 Dec. '37), all from Spaulding, Neb.; popular country harmony trio Tompall and the Glaser Brothers, also with solo careers. Performed on local radio and TV, county fairs, Arthur GODFREY Talent Scout programme; moved to Nashville '57, signed by Marty ROBBINS as singers, songwriters, recording on Robbins label (backed Robbins on huge country-pop hit 'El Paso' '59); moved to Decca '58, made singles with folksy sound, no great success; to MGM '66, first hits incl. 'Gone On The Other Hand', 'Through The Eyes Of Love', 'One Of These Days', 'California Girl', 'Gone Girl', 'Rings', 'Ain't It All Worth Living' '66-72. Glaser Sound Studios '69 designed by Chuck, also business manager, talent scout; prod., recorded their own and others' hits there: became hangout for future Outlaws (Willie NELSON, Waylon JENNINGS, Steve YOUNG, others). Voted Vocal Group of the Decade by *Record World* '72. Meanwhile lead singer Tompall had written for Robbins ('Running Gun'), also hits for Jimmy DEAN ('Stand Beside Me'), Bobby BARE ('Streets Of Baltimore'), others; Jim had recorded solo on Starday '60-3, Monument '65-7, RCA '68-9 (chart entries incl. 'God Help You Woman'); wrote hits for Skeeter DAVIS ('What Does It Take'), Warner MACK ('Sittin' In An All Nite Cafe'), Gary PUCKETT ('Woman, Woman', pop no. 4 '67), others, often writing with Jimmy Payne. Chuck credited with discovering John HARTFORD (co-prod. Hartford's classic 'Gentle On My Mind'), later Kinky FRIEDMAN, Dick FELLER; prod. many acts; wrote hits such as 'Where Has All The Love Gone' for Hank SNOW, set up Glaser publishing companies (for each of the three performance rights societies; *see* ASCAP). With all this hectic activity, group split '73. Chuck formed Nova Booking

Agency, handling Hartford, Jennings, Jerry REED; suffered massive stroke '75 which paralysed entire left side, incl. vocal chords; wasn't supposed to walk or talk again, refused to believe it. Jim recorded for MGM and MCA '73-8, had minor hits 'I See His Love All Over You', 'Forgettin' About You', 'Woman, Woman', 'She's Free, But She's Not Easy'; was always in demand as session singer. Tompall became part of Outlaw movement, with Jennings, Nelson; featured with them and Jessi COLTER on hit LP *Wanted: The Outlaws*; own records blended trad. and contemporary infl.; hits incl. 'Musical Chairs' '74, 'It'll Be Her' '77. Chuck regained voice; brothers reunited '80, scored no. 1 hit with 'Lovin' Her Was Easier' '81, further hits 'Just One Time', 'I Still Love You'. Jim left (replaced by Shaun Neilson, who had worked in gospel music); had hits on Noble Vision label with 'The Man In The Mirror', 'If I Could Only Dance With You', 'I'll Be Your Fool Tonight'; LPs *The Man In The Mirror* '83, *Past The Point Of No Return* '85, *Everybody Knows I'm Yours* '86. Tompall's solo albums incl. *Charlie* '73, *Take The Singer With The Song* '74 on Polydor; *Songs Of Shel Silverstein* '74, *The Great Tompall* '76 on MGM; *Tompall & His Outlaw Band* '77, *The Wonder Of It All* '78 on ABC. Group's LPs incl. *This Land* '62 on Decca, *Nights On The Borderline* '86 on Dot. *Tompall & The Glaser Brothers* '67, *Now Country* '70, *Award Winners* '72, *Hits From Two Decades* '73, *Vocal Group Of The Decade* '75, all on MGM; *Lovin' Her Was Easier* '81, *After All These Years* '82 on Elektra.

GLASS, Philip (*b* 31 Jan. '37, Baltimore, Md.) Composer. Studied violin at 6, then flute; entered Juilliard '58 and by the mid-'60s had composed many pieces in various contemporary idioms, won BMI and other awards, but wasn't satisfied: 'I just didn't believe in my music anymore.' He met Indian sitar virtuoso Ravi Shankar in Paris '65, was hired to notate Eastern music for Western musicians, adopted the modular style and repetitive structures of Eastern music, slowly adding simplified harmony and modulation, inventing a style sometimes called solid-state music, or minimalism. He later said, 'In Western music, we take time and divide it – whole notes into half notes into quarter notes – but in Eastern music they take very small units and add them together … Then you join cycles of different beats, like wheels within wheels, everything going at the same time and always changing.' He formed the 7-piece Philip Glass Ensemble '68 (three saxophones doubling on flutes, three electric organists and a sound engineer). He formed Chatham Records '71; first release was *Music With Changing Parts*; the first two parts of *Music In Twelve Parts* '71-4 (more than four hours) were recorded by Virgin Records '74. Formed Tomato Records '78; then became the first living composer since Aaron Copland and Igor Stravinsky signed to an exclusive contract by CBS Masterworks. *Glassworks* '82 on CBS is a suite of six pieces averaging about six minutes each, played by the septet incl. two French horns, viola section; four pieces are lyrical, soothing, repetitive mood music, saved from being typical NEW AGE music by the others, which are rhythmically and cyclically busy with the help of a bass synthesiser, similar to his score for Francis Ford Coppola's motion-picture montage *Koyaanisqatsi* '83 (on Island): they achieve their effect of relief by stopping suddenly. By early '79 he had ovations in art colleges, the Metropolitan Opera House, Carnegie Hall and The Bottom Line, an NYC rock club: he had become world famous as a result of *Einstein On The Beach* '76 (4-disc set on CBS was no. 33 on Billboard's classical chart '84), a 4.5-hour multimedia pageant devised with avant-garde designer Robert Wilson, who said 'Listen to the pictures.' *Einstein* had no real libretto and was sung/chanted by a chorus, with no soloists; the more conventional *Satyagraha* '80 was mythic ritual based on the life of Gandhi, with text in Sanskrit from the *Bhagavad Gita*. Other operas incl. *Akhnaten* '84, *The Juniper Tree* '85 (for children, a collaboration with composer Robert Moran), *The Making Of The Representative For Planet 8* '86 (his first full-length opera in English, based on a novel by Doris Lessing). Other works on records incl. *The Photographer* '83 on CBS (no. 10 '83), about Eadweard Muybridge (1830-1904: *b* Edward James Muggeridge in Kingston-Upon-Thames; changed name to make it more Anglo-Saxon, moved to California and became photographic pioneer; killed his wife's lover but was acquitted of murder); other film scores: documentary *North Star* '75 (about sculptor Mark de Suvero, on Virgin); Paul Schrader's *Mishima* '86 (Nonesuch). *Songs From Liquid Days* '86 (CBS) has lyrics by David Byrne, Laurie ANDERSON, Paul SIMON and Suzanne VEGA sung by Linda RONSTADT and others, played by the Glass Ensemble and the Kronos String Quartet. His style, use of electronics and crisp production have been an infl. on high-tech pop; other composers who have infl. popular music (and been infl. by it) are Terry Riley (*b* '35: *In C, Rainbow In Curved Air*) and Steve Reich (*b* 3 Oct. '36, NYC); they began with 'phase' or 'pulse' music created on tape, involving listeners by guiding their expectations. Reich's *Music For 18 Musicians* '76 on ECM sold 25,000 copies the first year, unusual for new music; *The Desert Music* '86 on Nonesuch may do as well.

GLEASON, Jackie (*b* Herbert John Gleason, 26 Feb. '16, Brooklyn, NY; *d* 24 June '87) USA comedian in movies, TV; also character actor, composer. Early films incl. Glenn MILLER vehicle *Orchestra Wives* '42; on Broadway in *Artists And Models* '43, *Follow The Girls* '44, *Along Fifth Avenue* '49, *Take Me Along* '59. Part in early TV series *The Life Of Riley* led to '50s stardom: began with *Cavalcade Of Stars* '49; created priceless sketches, many with Art Carney, incl. characters the Sad Sack, the Loudmouth, Reggie Van Gleason; the Honeymooners became a series '55, preceded by a Gleason self-indulgence: *Stageshow* was a variety show fronted by Tommy and Jimmy DORSEY, usually eclipsed by Perry COMO on another channel, but on which Elvis PRESLEY made his first TV appearance early '56. Biography *The Golden Ham* '56 by Jim Bishop. His best film roles were *The Hustler* '61 with Paul Newman (nominated for Oscar as supporting actor); Chaplinesque *Gigot, Requiem For A Heavyweight* (written by Rod Serling; co-star Anthony Quinn), both '62. Played comic lawman Buford T. Ford in Burt Reynolds films (*Smokey And The Bandit* '77). He wrote both script and music for *Gigot*, wrote his own TV theme 'Melancholy Serenade': he could not read music, others wrote it down for him; of mood music LPs on Capi-

tol, some featured solos by Bobby HACKETT (*Music To Make You Misty*, '54). Four 10" LPs, six 12" were top 10 USA '53-6, nine more charted '57-69. He also wrote a ballet, designed clothes, jewellery, children's games, etc.; lived a full life and enjoyed every minute.

GLITTER, Gary (*b* Paul Gadd, 8 May '44, Banbury, Oxfordshire) UK pop singer. King of glam-rock in mid-'70s, the LIBERACE of UK pop, giving it some much-needed humour. Birthdate is in some dispute. Aliases in '60s incl. Paul Raven, Paul Monday (as Monday made flop cover of BEATLES' 'Here Comes The Sun'). He was prod. assistant on TV pop show *Ready, Steady, Go* '65; appeared on original *Jesus Christ Superstar* LP with Murray HEAD, Yvonne ELLIMAN; breakthrough came from meeting with Mike Leander: co-written single 'Rock & Roll (Parts I & II)' intended as one-off, but reached no. 2 UK mid-'72. Glitter Band music was basic rock'n'roll with heavy drumbeat, Gary cavorting in outrageous costumes: similar to T. Rex, MUD, SWEET but with even less subtlety. No. 1 hits 'I'm The Leader Of The Gang (I Am)', 'I Love You Love Me Love'; seven more top tens incl. 'Hello, Hello, I'm Back Again', 'Do You Wanna Touch?' followed '72-5; then glam-rock era was over, though Glitter retained affection of audience (SEX PISTOL John Lydon was longstanding fan). From late '70s comebacks as frequent as farewells: went to Australia and New Zealand, appeared on stage in *Rocky Horror Show*, launched UK tour Gary Glitter's Rock'n'Roll Circus early '80s (an expensive flop). 'Another Rock'n'Roll Christmas' gave him top 10 hit Dec. '84; LP *Boys Will Be Boys* same year reunited him with Leander; appeared in soup advert '85 parodying himself, LP *Alive & Kicking* same year; remade 'I'm The Leader' '86 with GIRLSCHOOL. Compilation *Golden Greats* '78.

GODFREY, Arthur (*b* 31 Aug. '03; *d* 16 Mar. '83) Entertainer and talent scout. Ukulele, banjo in vaudeville; later sang in homespun baritone. Announcer/DJ on Baltimore radio '30; Arthur Godfrey and all the Little Godfreys in Washington DC '35, etc. Networked morning show postwar; then Talent Scout show and Arthur Godfrey and his

Friends were broadcast simultaneously on radio/TV; theme was 'Seems Like Old Times'; mus. dir. was Archie BLEYER. He was a very big star on the airwaves, with a special CBS vice-president at his beck and call, popular enough to get away with kidding sponsors, rare then; on one occasion a fan sent him a device with a magnifying glass and tweezers for finding the chicken in Lipton's chicken soup: he displayed it on TV. Countless pop people of era were contestants on talent show or regulars on other shows: EVERLY Bros, Pat BOONE, McGUIRE sisters etc. His folksiness was for the public; he became a tyrant, made news by firing Julius LaROSA on the air (with a million-selling hit, LaRosa had hired an agent). Godfrey recorded novelties, sentimental songs on Bluebird, Decca, Columbia: duets with Mary MARTIN, Janette Davis (a regular on programme from '46); six top 20 hits '47-51 incl. millionseller 'Too Fat Polka'/'For Me And My Gal' (no. 2 '47, 16 weeks in chart); last hit was two-sided 'Dance Me Loose'/'Slow Poke'. Recovered from surgery for lung cancer after years of advising people not to smoke, but if they did to smoke Chesterfields; had radio show through '60s, made commercials.

GOFFIN, Gerry (b 11 Feb. '39, Queens, NYC) Lyricist, producer. With over 30 top 20 hits, one of the most successful non-performing songwriters of era. Began writing lyrics over 'inane melodies' as a child; reluctantly qualified as chemist at Queens College of the City of NY, where he met and married composer Carole KING. Working for Don Kirshner, team had worldwide hit '61 ('Will You Love Me Tomorrow', SHIRELLES); became pop's most prolific, celebrated partnership until eclipsed by their fans LENNON and McCARTNEY (see entry for King). Goffin's versatile lyrics ranged from preteen angst ('Girls Grow Up Faster Than Boys', Cookies '63) to breathtaking sensuality ('(You Make Me Feel Like) A Natural Woman', Aretha FRANKLIN '67); also had successful collaborations with Barry MANN ('Who Put The Bomp' '61), Jack Keller (b 11 Nov. '36, Brooklyn; 'Run To Him' '61, by Bobby VEE; 'How Can I Meet Her' '62 by the EVERLY Bros), Russ Titelman ('Yes I Will' '65, the HOLLIES). After divorce from King '68 output

slowed down from frustration with music business, also depression, ill health; while King's subsequent songs sometimes criticised for wide-eyed optimism, Goffin's post-'60s lyrics were often pessimistic. Teamed with keyboardist Barry Goldberg (ex-Electric Flag, etc.) and Muscle Shoals musicians for 2-disc album *It Ain't Exactly Entertainment* on Adelphi label: biting lyrics about politics, lost identity bravely sung in voice that made Bob DYLAN sound like Pavarotti. Also with Goldberg: 'I've Got To Use My Imagination' (Gladys KNIGHT and the Pips), 'It's Not The Spotlight' (Rod STEWART), both '73; less bluesy and more sentimental collaborations with composer/prod. Michael Masser (b 24 Mar. '41, Chicago) incl. 'Theme From Mahogany' '75 (Diana ROSS), 'Tonight I Celebrate My Love' '82 (Roberta FLACK/Peabo BRYSON), 'Saving All My Love For You' '85 (Whitney HOUSTON). Still occasionally writes with King and eldest daughter Louise (based in London, signed to Stiff label). Ambivalent about success, due to relative neglect: broad appeal of hits hides deeply personal lyrics, addressing adult emotions with understated simplicity. Most ambitious work ('Audience For My Pain') too intense for pop market; would do better in theatrical setting.

GO-GO's, The USA all-girl new-wave quintet formed '78 by fashion designer Jane Wiedlin (b 20 May '58, Oconomowoc, Wis.), guitar, and former cheerleader, lead singer Belinda Carlisle (b 17 Aug. '58, Hollywood; ex-Black Randy and the Metro Squad). Group originally called Misfits was expanded by expert guitarist Charlotte Caffey (b 21 Oct. '53, Santa Monica) to help out novice Wiedlin, whose attraction to new wave had been via fashion. First drummer Elissa Bello replaced by seasoned Gina Schock (b 31 Aug. '57, Baltimore) in '79; band now called Go-Go's took bright pop to UK after signing with Stiff. Songs mixed girl-group harmonies with fashionable energy in much the same way as BLONDIE; 'We Got The Beat' unaccountably overlooked when released on Stiff (despite tour with MADNESS), but became second (and biggest) hit after group signed by USA-based IRS label: made no. 2 late '81 after 'Our Lips Are Sealed' was no. 20. LP they both came from, *Beauty And The Beast*, no. 1 USA for six weeks:

prod. by Richard GOTTEHRER, who had also prod. Blondie, reinforcing comparison. Original bassist Margot Olavera had been replaced '80 by Kathy Valentine (*b* 7 Jan. '59, Austin, Texas); second LP *Vacation* '82 no. 2, had no. 8 hit in title cut (with hilarious formation-waterskiing video: group never afraid to mix humour with music). More hits '84 with 'Head Over Heels' no. 11, 'Turn To You' no. 32, but no hits at all in UK, though 'Our Lips Are Sealed', cowritten by Wiedlin and Terry Hall of Fun Boys Three, was no. 7 '83 when covered by that group. Difficulty in finishing *Talk Show* '84 suggested problems, confirmed by split after release of no. 18 LP. Leader Wiedlin had left during recording; had already recorded with Sparks; released solo *Jane Wiedlin* '85, *Fur* '88; Carlisle's *Belinda* '86 did well in USA. Valentine and Schock intended to carry on, but Go-Go's moment was past.

GOLD, Andrew (*b* 2 Aug. '51, Burbank, Cal.) USA singer/songwriter. Father Ernest (*b* 13 July '21, Vienna; to USA before WWII) scored films incl. *On The Beach* '59, *Exodus* '60, others; mother Marni Nixon was screen voice of Natalie Wood in *West Side Story* '61, Audrey Hepburn in *My Fair Lady* '64, etc. Multi-instrumentalist Andrew studied piano from '50s, later guitar, bass, drums. Met Wendy Waldman '68, through her Kenny Edwards, bass; with Karla BONOFF they formed group Bryndle (unreleased A&M LP). Made solo single in London late '60s with friend Charlie Villiers; played bass for Maria MULDAUR. Met Linda RONSTADT through Edwards, with whom he still collaborated occasionally as the Rangers; she signed both for backing band. Gold's presence on her LPs from *Heart Like A Wheel* onwards was crucial to her new success after '78. He broadened scope from guitarist to arranger, often overdubbing instruments, employing this technique on *Andrew Gold* '75, superb solo LP of finely crafted pop ('Endless Flight' later covered by Leo SAYER). Second LP *What's Wrong With This Picture* '77 brought no. 7 single (no. 11 UK) 'Lonely Boy', used Ronstadt's band: paid pop dues with cover of 'Do Wah Diddy Diddy' and Buddy HOLLY's 'Learning The Game'. Had sessioned widely for the L.A. soft-rock fraternity (Muldaur, Carly SIMON, J. D. SOUTHER, Art GARFUNKEL, etc.), so took few risks in leaving Ronstadt (continued to play on her albums). More single hits in UK ('Never Let Her Slip Away' no. 55, 'How Can This Be Love' no. 19, 'Thank You For Being A Friend' no. 42 UK, 25 USA, all '78) from *All This And Heaven Too. Whirlwind* '80 continued in easygoing USA pop vein but single hits dried up and he turned once more to session work. Teamed in '85 with 10CC stalwart/UK songsmith Graham Gouldman as Wax: LP *Magnetic Heaven* '86 on RAC.

GOLDKETTE, Jean (*b* 18 Mar. 1899, Valenciennes, France; *d* 24 Mar. '62, Santa Barbara, Cal.) Pianist, leader. Lived in Russia and Greece; family came to USA '11. Played piano in Chicago, Detroit; formed own band '24, signed with Victor, hired first-class talent: arrangers Russ MORGAN, Bill Challis (*b* '04, Wilkes Barre, Pa.; later worked for Paul WHITEMAN, DORSEY Bros); also sidemen Tommy, Jimmy DORSEY, Bix BEIDERBECKE, Eddie LANG, Joe VENUTI, Frankie TRUMBAUER, etc. Took over important venue Greystone Ballroom in Detroit when owners could not meet his payroll. Smaller, more flexible band than that of Paul Whiteman, soon became legendary: allegedly 'cut' the fledgling Fletcher HENDERSON band in performance, but business was not good enough despite hits on Victor '24-9 listed in *Pop Memories*: disbanded '27; farewell appearance at NYC's Roseland Ballroom. Many of the men went over to Whiteman. The business had been built up to incl. several bands (hired Don REDMAN to run McKINNEY'S COTTON PICKERS, best of the lot); Jean Goldkette Inc. controlled the The Graystone Company but both were controlled by the National Amusement Corporation, of which Charles Horvath was president; by the early '30s Goldkette and Horvath did not get along: Horvath was no doubt the better businessman and Goldkette wanted to be a concert pianist while still receiving an income from the agency. Played with Detroit Symphony Orchestra c.'30; continued booking bands, led own bands occasionally, but the band of the '20s with its great sidemen remained his greatest hour and there have been few reissues even of that.

GOLDMARK, Dr Peter Carl (*b* '06 Budapest; *d* '77 N.J.) President CBS labs; invented modern long-playing record. Physics degree U. of Vienna; built receiver there for John Logie Baird's historic BBC TV transmission from London, '26; worked on TV for Pye in Cambridge; went to new CBS TV lab NYC, soon became president. Built first successful colour TV system '40, worked better than RCA's but failed because incompatible with monochrome transmission: by the time FCC approved colour broadcasting there were already millions of black-and-white sets in use. An enthusiastic amateur musician, did not own a record player; irritated by clicking and thumping of record changer while listening to music at friend's house '45, designed entirely new system of disc-cutting and playback, thinking only of classical music: had no idea of revolutionising record business (*see* RECORDED SOUND). Goldmark retired '72 holding more than 160 patents.

GOLDSBORO, Bobby (*b* 18 Jan. '41, Marianna, Fla.) Pop-country singer with tear-jerking vocal style; successful writer of own hits and for others as well. Raised on country music, but switched to rock'n'roll; studied music at Auburn U., auditioned for Roy ORBISON and toured world as lead guitarist of his band The Candy Men '62-4. Signed to Laurie '63, had first pop hit with own 'Molly'; to UA, had 25 pop hits '64-73, only two in top 10: 'See The Funny Little Clown' no. 9 '64; sentimental 'Honey' '68 no. 1 both country and pop (no. 2 in UK, where some earlier songs covered by UK artists). From then on hits charted both pop and country until '73: his own 'With Pen In Hand' '72 just made Billboard pop chart at no. 94 (but royalties account did well: versions by Billy Vera and Vikki CARR went much higher; Johnny Darrell had country hit with it). 'A Butterfly For Bucky' '76 just missed Hot 100; then on Epic from '77, Curb from '80 continued with country hits: 'The Cowboy And The Lady' '77, 'Goodbye Marie' '80, 'The Round-Up Saloon' '81. LPs on UA that reached Billboard LP chart: *Solid Goldsboro* '67, *Honey* '68 (no. 5 LP USA) and *Word Pictures* (with hit 'Autumn Of My Life') '68, *Today* '69, *Muddy Mississippi Line* and *Greatest Hits* '70, *We Gotta Start Lovin'*, *Come Back*

Home '71; *Summer (The First Time)* '73, 2-disc *10th Anniversary Album* '74 (now on Liberty). On Epic: *Goldsboro* '77, on Curb: *Roundup Saloon* '82.

GOLSON, Benny (*b* 25 Jan. '29, Philadelphia, Pa.) Tenor sax, arr./composer, leader. Studied piano as a child, sax from age 14; studied at Howard U. in Washington DC, gigged in Philadelphia. Friends with John COLTRANE from an early age, as well as the HEATH brothers, other locals; nicknamed 'Professor'. Left Philadelphia '51 in Bull Moose Jackson band, where he met Tadd DAMERON, who encouraged interest in composing, arranging; played in Dameron's group, then with Lionel HAMPTON '53, Johnny HODGES '54 (with Coltrane), Earl BOSTIC (after Coltrane). Coltrane took Golson tune 'Stablemates' to Miles DAVIS recording session '55, Mal WALDRON '56, both on Prestige: became modern jazz classic, along with 'Whisper Not', 'I Remember Clifford', others. With Dizzy GILLESPIE big band '56-8 that toured for the US State Dept; Art BLAKEY's Jazz Messengers several months; own quintet mid-'59, then formed Jazztet with Art FARMER late '59 until '62. More and more active as a writer, virtually gave up performing for a while: did studio work, wrote for Peggy LEE, Lou RAWLS, Nancy WILSON, Sammy DAVIS Jr, many others. Entire concert of his compositions at NYC's Town Hall '75; by then well-known tunes incl. 'Along Came Betty', 'Blues March', 'Just By Myself', 'Little Karin', 'Five Spot After Dark'. Many fine albums under his own name all with superb cast incl. *Benny Golson's New York Scene* '57 on Contemporary; *The Modern Touch* and *Benny Golson's Philadelphians* '57-8, both on Riverside (later Milestone 2-disc *Blues On Down*); *Gone With Golson, Groovin' With Golson, Gettin' With It* all on New Jazz (Prestige) '59; *Take A Number From 1 To 10* '60 on Argo; *Just Jazz!* sessions '62 on Audio Fidelity issued on various LPs with and without dubbed strings and woodwinds arr./cond. by Golson. Quartet LPs *Turning Point* on Mercury (Wynton KELLY, Paul CHAMBERS, Jimmy COBB), *Free* on Argo, with Tommy FLANAGAN, Ron CARTER, Art Taylor, both '62, described by Golson late '60s as own favourites (quoted by Leonard Feather). Arr./cond. large international orchestra on *Stockholm Sojourn* '64 on Prestige. Long hiatus as leader broken by quintet *Are You Real* '77, unissued; then *Killer Joe* '77 on Columbia: large orchestra with strings arr. by Golson, Bobby Martin; with vocalist Mortonette Jenkins and female back-up vocal group. *California Message* '80, *One More Mem'ry* '81, *Time Speaks* '82, *This Is For You, John* '83 all small-group LPs on Timeless. Appeared at Ronnie SCOTT's in London '85 with excellent quartet incl. Mickey TUCKER, Phil BOWLER, Keith COPELAND, played 'Voices All' (mysteriously suggestive riff), 'Jam The Avenue' (tonepoem reminiscence of teen-aged jam sessions in Philadelphia), 'Blue Heart' ('blues ballad'), as well as early classics ('Are You Real?') and tunes by Tucker. Golson's tenor is easily authoritative, originally influenced by Lucky THOMPSON, to a lesser extent by Don BYAS, then by a touch of Coltrane.

GONG Avant-garde rock band formed by Daevid Allen (*b* Melbourne, Australia). In Paris early '60s he published poetry, collaborated with beat poets Ferlinghetti, Ginsberg and novelist William Burroughs, etc. Then to Canterbury UK and Majorca; met Mike Ratledge, Robert Wyatt, Kevin Ayers; formed SOFT MACHINE, left band '68 when refused permission to re-enter UK. Returned to Paris, improvised with other musicians, Gong being formed as a result of sessions incl. those for his LPs *Magick Brother, Mystick Sister* '69, *Banana Moon* '71. First Gong LP was *Camembert Electrique* '71 on Byg; same year band did film soundtrack *Continental Circus*. Appeared at Glastonbury Fayre '72 and on Revelation LP of festival bands. Lineup was Allen (guitar, vocals), Gilli Smyth (space whisper), Tim Blake (synthesisers); Steve Hillage (guitar); Mike Howlett (bass); Didier Malherbe (sax); Pierre Moerlen (drums). Music was mixture of rock, jazz, hippy mythology, not without charm; members hid at times behind whimsical pseudonyms, Allen being Bert Camembert, the Alien Australian, etc. Malherbe Bloomdidio Bad De Grasse and so on. Signed to Virgin: trilogy of LPs on tales of Planet Gong, pot head pixies etc. *Radio Gnome Invisible Part 1 (Flying Teapot), Angel's Egg* and *You* '73-4, music becoming funkier as tale went on. Allen quit group '75, went to Majorca to

work on *Planet Gong* book, also recording with local band Euterpe on *Good Morning*. Gong continued with new members such as Allan Holdsworth on guitar, Moerlen taking over leadership; Virgin LPs *Shamal* and *Gazeuse* '76-7 followed by disagreement with label: Virgin released album of concert clips with varying personnel *Gong Live* '77; band retaliated with *Gong Is Dead* '77 on Tapioca with classic lineup incl. Allen under pseudonyms, members still under contract to Virgin appearing on sleeve with faces blanked out on sleeve. Last Virgin LP *Expresso II* '78; signed with Arista, by now much changed in style and personnel, made LPs *Downwind, Time Is The Key, Pierre Moerlen's Gong Live*, split early '80s. Allen meanwhile moved to NYC, made LPs *Now Is The Happiest Time Of Your Life* '77, *Daevid Allen N'Existe Pas* '78, *New York Gong - About Time* '79, *Playbax* '80, others, incl. EPs, now mainly on Charly in UK, which also issued *Fairy Tale* '80 by Mother Gong, band formed by Gilli Smyth and guitarist/vocalist Harry Williamson to re-create original Gong aura (Malherbe also played on it); also *Robot Woman* '81 during and immediately after Glastonbury Festival, and *Robot Woman 2* '82 on Butt.

GONSALVES, Paul (*b* 12 July '20, Boston, Mass.; *d* 14 May '74, London) Tenor saxophone, also guitar; aka 'Mex'. Listened to Jimmie LUNCEFORD, especially Duke ELLINGTON records as a boy; played guitar at 16; gigged in Boston on tenor, infl. by Don BYAS; with Count BASIE '46, Dizzy GILLESPIE '49-50; joined Duke ELLINGTON '50 and stayed the rest of his life except for a short stay with Tommy DORSEY '53: ' . . . Tommy was a wonderful guy but . . . musically it was atrocious' (quoted by Stanley Dance). Regarded at first as an imitator of Ben WEBSTER, but became famous for lovely ballad playing, despite *tour de force* at Newport '56 (*see* Ellington entry). Very few own LPs incl. *Gettin' Together!* '60 with Nat ADDERLEY, *Mexican Bandit Meets Pittsburgh Pirate* '73 with Roy ELDRIDGE, both now on Fantasy; *Cleopatra Feelin' Crazy, Salt & Pepper* with Sonny STITT, *Tell It The Way It Is* now all on Jasmine UK; *Rare Paul Gonsalves Sextet In Europe 1963* on Jazz Connoisseur label; *Buenos Aires* '68 on Catalyst. Sessioned with Clark TERRY, Dinah

WASHINGTON, Ray CHARLES, Billy TAYLOR etc. and with other Ellington sidemen: *Inspired Abandon* (with Lawrence BROWN on Impulse), *Just A-Sittin' And A-Rockin'* (Ray Nance, Black Lion). Solos with Ellington incl. 'Days Of Wine And Roses', 'Chelsea Bridge', 'So Little Time' in mid-'60s; recorded versions of tunes associated with Johnny HODGES: 'Warm Valley', 'Day Dream'; did 'Portrait Of Sidney Bechet' on Duke's *New Orleans Suite* LP '70 in sad circumstances: Hodges was to play it, but died two days earlier. He was often unreliable (drugs and drink); in a '73 incident, having missed a concert the night before, he sheepishly entered the room during an Ellington master class at U. of Wisconsin: they played a duet; Duke forgave him yet again. Died 10 days before Ellington; Duke wasn't told.

GONZALES, Babs (*b* Lee Brown, 27 Oct. '19, Newark, N.J.; *d* 23 Jan. '80) Vocalist. He and his brothers were all called Babs; he sang in clubs; wore turban in Hollywood late '40s, calling himself Ram Singh; worked as chauffeur for Errol Flynn; called himself Ricardo Gonzales (Mexican rather than 'Negro') so as to get a room in a good hotel. Organised vocal group Three Bips And A Bop with Tadd DAMERON on piano '46-8, wrote and recorded 'Oop-Pop-A-Da' for Blue Note (covered by Dizzy GILLESPIE); recorded for Capitol c.'50 when that label was flirting with bop; vocalist and road manager with James MOODY from '51; recorded with Jimmy SMITH, Johnny GRIFFIN, Bennie GREEN (*Soul Stirrin'* '58 on Blue Note); performed at Ronnie SCOTT club in London as early as '62, one of the first Americans to play there. A hard-working promoter of jazz, he also published his own autobiographies *I Paid My Dues . . . Good Times, No Bread* '67, *Movin' On Down De Line* '75.

GOOD, Jack (*b* '31, London) Innovative producer of pop TV. After Oxford U. joined BBC as trainee mid-'50s. Pop music on UK TV pop was at best secondhand; Good presented it with its natural vitality, beginning on *6.5 Special* Feb. '57: total breakaway from BBC's usual procedure was broadcast live, sometimes from basement of coffee bar in Soho; visual sweep of camera work, apparent spontaneity were unique (Good warmed teenage audience to fever pitch beforehand). Show was such a success with home-grown talent (Adam FAITH, Joe BROWN, Lonnie DONEGAN, Cliff RICHARD, Tommy STEELE) that film of same name was also a hit. Good and BBC were wary of each other; he left for commercial TV and show *Oh Boy*, introducing live legends Gene VINCENT, Eddie COCHRAN (contributed to a malevolent, leather-clad image of Vincent, seeing him as 'a rock'n'roll Richard III'). *Boy Meets Girl* and *Wham!* were less successful; he left for USA '64, prod. MONKEES TV special, episodes of *Shindig*. Returned to UK '64 for imaginative *Around The Beatles* '73 to prod. 'rock Othello' film *Catch My Soul*. Made desultory TV series *Let's Rock* '80, unsuccessfully revived *Oh Boy*. His infl. on *Ready, Steady, Go*, best-known UK pop show of '60s, was evident; nowadays *The Tube* has more technology available, but Good was the first to do it well.

GOODMAN, Al (*b* 12 Aug. 1890, Nikopol, Russia; *d* 10 Jan. '72, NYC) Pianist, arranger, composer, conductor. Studied at Peabody Conservatory in Baltimore, played in vaudeville, cinemas; conducted for Al JOLSON, the Shubert theatre's musicals, many Broadway shows; on soundtrack of *The Jazz Singer* '29 with Jolson, the first talking picture. Songs were effective in shows but were not hits outside theatre; best-known was 'When Hearts Are Young' with Sigmund ROMBERG. Worked on many radio shows '30s-40s, incl. own shows with orchestra, guest singers, his orchestral arrangements of pop songs, standards always elegant in craftsmanship. Many records over the years, into the '50s on obscure labels, all long out of print.

GOODMAN, Benny (*b* Benjamin David Goodman, 30 May '09, Chicago; *d* 13 June '86) Clarinet, leader. From poor family: studied music at Hull House, imitated Ted LEWIS in public at age 12. Infl. by Jimmie NOONE, Frank TESCHEMACHER, New Orleans Rhythm Kings' Leon Rappolo. A prodigy, playing first gigs still in short trousers, joining musicians' union at age 13. First recorded solo with Ben POLLACK band '26; played other reeds, even trumpet on records late '20s. John HAMMOND was an early fan; Goodman later married Hammond's sister. Busy freelance career and many records: formed band mid-'32 to accompany Russ COLUMBO; among early records, he played on Bessie SMITH's last recording session and Billie HOLIDAY's first (both prod. by Hammond) in '33: led studio band for Holiday and for another session with solos and vocals by Jack TEAGARDEN; both bands incl. Teagarden, Dick McDonough, guitar (b '04; d 25 May '38, NYC); Frankie Froeba, piano (b Aug. '07, New Orleans; d 18 Feb. '81, Miami) and Gene KRUPA. Also the beautiful 'Blues of Israel' session under Krupa's name Sep. '35, with Israel Crosby on bass, also Jess STACY, others by this time playing in Goodman's big band: chance to form band came '34 with gig at Billy ROSE's Music Hall (unsuccessful), then *Let's Dance* radio show from Dec. '34 to May '35 (also with sweet bands Xavier CUGAT, Kel Murray); USA tour began in May, flopped at first; in Oakland, Cal. in August there was a crowd waiting and Goodman thought they must have arrived in the wrong place. There and at Palomar Ballroom they finally found college-age audience who'd tuned in *Let's Dance* in the evening, looking for dance music on the radio: the big band jazz style invented by black leaders Don REDMAN and Fletcher HENDERSON was a hit, the SWING ERA began, Goodman became world-famous and remained at the top of the music business for decades. Theme was 'Let's Dance', adapted from tone poem by Carl Maria von Weber; he had 164 hits '31-53, 75 of them on Victor with the classic band '35-9, before Billboard began printing charts (it was the increase in record sales during the Swing Era that demanded charts): they incl. 'Blue Moon', 'It's Been So Long' and 'Goody Goody', 'You Turned The Tables On Me', 'The Glory of Love' and 'These Foolish Things', all with vocals by Helen Ward; 'I Let A Song Go Out Of My Heart', 'And The Angels Sing' with Martha Tilton; others with guest vocalists Jimmy RUSHING, Mildred BAILEY; and the instrumentals: Henderson's arr. of 'Sugar Foot Stomp' (from King OLIVER's 'Dipper Mouth Blues'), 'Sometimes I'm Happy' (by Vincent YOUMANS), 'Blue Skies' (by Irving BERLIN), 'King Porter Stomp' (by Jelly Roll

MORTON); Henderson's own 'Down South Camp Meeting', 'Stealin' Apples', 'Big John's Special', etc. 'Don't Be That Way' and 'Stomping At The Savoy' (originally written by Edgar SAMPSON for Chick WEBB); Count BASIE's 'Jumpin' At The Woodside', 'One O'Clock Jump'; 'Swingtime In The Rockies' by Jimmy Mundy (b 28 June '07, Cincinnati, Ohio; d 24 Apr. '83, NYC; also played trumpet; mus. dir. for French Barclay '60s). 'Sing Sing Sing' was hit 'killer diller' (term applied especially to Mundy's work), interpolating 'Christopher Columbus' (Henderson hit) with 'Sing Sing Sing' (by Louis PRIMA), issued in two parts on a 12″ 78, unusual then. 'Bei Mir Bist Du Schön' came from Yiddish musical by Sholom Secunda; became hit for the ANDREWS SISTERS; arr. for Goodman by Mundy with vocal by Martha Tilton was enlivened by trumpeter Ziggy Elman (b 26 May '14, Philadelphia; d 26 June '68, Van Nuys, Cal.), who inserted 'frahlich' passage in 6/8 time, based on dance trad. at Jewish parties, also used in 'And The Angels Sing' (words by Johnny MERCER). Goodman played tenor sax lead on Bill Miller arr. 'Riffin' At The Ritz'. All this was high-class pop music of the day, still loved by millions, reissued on 8 *Complete* 2-disc Bluebird (RCA) sets, many other compilations. Goodman played Carnegie Hall in Jan. '38 (asked how long an intermission he wanted, Goodman replied, 'I dunno. How much does Toscanini get?'); Stacy's impromptu solo on 'Sing Sing Sing' still astonishes today: acetates of concert were discovered and issued early '50s on Columbia; 2-disc set of period's air checks also issued early '50s was one of the first such sets. Excitement at Paramount Theatre gig NYC Mar. '37 presaged later frenzy over Frank SINATRA, Johnny RAY, Elvis PRESLEY, the BEATLES. Like many bands, Goodman's was better live than in the studio: it always played well; the reed sound was pretty and precise; good soloists incl. Bunny BERIGAN, Harry JAMES as well as Ellman on trumpets; Irving 'Babe' Russin (b 18 June '11, Philadelphia; d 4 Aug. '84, Panorama City, Cal.) and Arthur Rollini (b 13 Feb. '12, NYC; brother of Adrian) on tenors, but the band didn't swing like black ones (especially without stimulus of dancers): Krupa was not that good a drummer (he got better, but never was as good as any number of black ones), while white musicians in general were still learning to play the big band style which Henderson spent years learning to write. Meanwhile, Goodman was called 'King of Swing', but was one of the first white bandleaders to hire the inventors of the music: Henderson, Sampson, Mundy to write; later Henderson to play piano; Benny Goodman Trio recorded as early as mid-'35 with Krupa and Teddy WILSON; quartet added Lionel HAMPTON '36 and was the first integrated group to play in public; stars of Duke ELLINGTON and Basie bands were guests at Carnegie Hall (incl. Basie; Ellington waited for his own concerts). Krupa left '38 to form own band, replaced by Dave TOUGH; James left late that year; Goodman switched to Columbia '39; the small group became a sextet with Charlie CHRISTIAN, Cootie WILLIAMS (lured from Ellington), Georgie AULD on tenor, Artie Bernstein on bass (*b* 3 Feb. '09, Brooklyn; *d* 4 Jan. '64, L.A.); Nick Fatool or Harry Jaeger, then Tough on drums; sometimes guests Hampton, Basie (on one unissued session, Basie and his rhythm section plus Lester YOUNG); sextet records '39-41 were probably Goodman's finest achievement: 'Six Appeal', 'Seven Come Eleven', 'Wholly Cats', 'Breakfast Feud', etc. had up-to-date, almost boppish sound, very high level of quality in solos (issued in 2-disc *Solo Flight: Charlie Christian* anthology). Goodman was a hard worker (and demanding boss), a fine musician and always a great soloist: some fans preferred the warmer, woodier tone of Artie SHAW as a clarinettist, but Goodman's invention never flagged. He was best (most free) in a small-group context, but he always swung, having conversational quality essential in jazz: he shaped notes as well as lines. Disbanded '40, had surgery for back pain, re-formed for a few more years; big band fared well on Columbia with arr. by Eddie SAUTER and others; Mel POWELL arr. and played piano '41, Peggy LEE sang. Band had 11 top 10 hits '41-8, incl. 'Jersey Bounce' no. 2, 'Why Don't You Do Right' no. 4 (Lee's first big hit), both '42. Goodman himself 'sang' very occasionally ('Oh Babe!'). The Swing Era was almost over: popular music was moving away from jazz, which itself was changing; Goodman re-

corded for Capitol with a boppish band incl. Stan Hasselgard, the only clarinettist Goodman ever featured alongside himself, but he disliked bop, perhaps partly because his knowledge of harmony wasn't good enough to deal with the modern idiom. Became elder statesman/cultural ambassador; at London Palladium mid-'49 with pianist Buddy GRECO, clubs '54 with Powell; formed bands for tours: Far East '56-7, Brussels World Fair '58, USSR '62; many tours of Europe incl. three early '70s with band using mainly British musicians, own band '81-2. Visited Chicago '85 for Hull House tribute. LPs incl. compilation *Benny Goodman Combos* '51 (CL 500 was first 12" Columbia pop LP); *B.G. In Hi-Fi* '55 on Capitol (no. 7 chart LP, reissued '85 by EMI/UK); 2-disc soundtrack *The Benny Goodman Story* '56 on Decca (no. 4 album; film is accurate in outline, but detail and script poor: typical of genre); *Benny Goodman In Moscow* '62 and *Together Again!* '63 (reunion of '36 quartet), both on RCA; *Benny Goodman Today* '71 (two discs, live in Stockholm), *Live At Carnegie Hall* '78, both on London; others. He appeared Feb. '85 at Kool Jazz Festival tribute to his brother-in-law, in Oct. taped a special for PBS called *Let's Dance*. Acerbic to the last, in an interview '86 he described Wynton MARSALIS as an 'undernourished' trumpet player; on one late occasion, playing at the sort of huge venue where swing bands never played, he insisted on no amplification at all, so that the sound was inadequate. He was in fact widely disliked, often appallingly rude to sidemen (and women: Helen Forrest described him as 'the rudest man I have ever met'). 'He put together some wonderful bands, but he had a reputation for spoiling the fun,' wrote NYC bassist Bill Crow in a series of articles in Gene LEES' *Jazzletter*; a correspondent wrote 'The good news is he's dead; the bad news is he didn't suffer.' But his place in history is secure; the amount of early work in print is astonishing: 37 LPs in the Schwann catalogue on the Sunbeam label alone, incl. *Hotsy-Totsy Gang* and *Whoopee Makers* '28-9, *Accompanies Girls 1931-33*, two LPs of *Camel Caravan 1937* (radio show), three LPs of wartime V-discs, *Broadcasts From Hollywood 1946-7*, etc. First band appeared in films *The Big Broadcast Of 1937*, *Hollywood*

Hotel, Stage Door Canteen, etc. He recorded classical music beginning '37 incl. Mozart and Weber, commissioned works from Béla Bartók, Aaron Copland, others. Autobiography *The Kingdom Of Swing* with Irving Kolodin published '39; biodiscography *B.G. On The Record* by Connor and Hicks '69, both updated since.

GOODMAN, Steve (*b* 25 July '48, Chicago; *d* 20 Sep. '84) Singer/songwriter, guitarist in folk-country vein. Played in NYC '67, returned to U. of Illinois but gave up studies '69 for full-time music. *Steve Goodman* '71 was auspicious debut on Buddah, incl. help from ace Nashville sidemen, fiddler Vassar CLEMENTS, etc. also best-known song 'City Of New Orleans' (covered by Arlo GUTHRIE for no. 18 hit '72, also by Willie NELSON and Judy COLLINS). *Somebody Else's Troubles* '73 assured him of fame when Bob DYLAN guested on it (as 'Robert Milkwood Thomas'). *Words We Can Dance To* '76 was followed by *Say It In Private* '78, which featured John PRINE and Pete SEEGER on 'The 20th Century Is Almost Over', later covered by Johnny CASH. Growing following pleased with *Jessie's Jig & Other Favorites* '76, *High And Outside* '79, *Hot Spot* '80; all LPs except first on Asylum but the last prod. for own Red Pajamas Productions; the rest on Red Pajamas label: *Artistic Hair* '83, *Affordable Art* '84 (incl. 'A Dying Cub Fan's Last Request', amusing story-song from life-long baseball fan), *Santa Anna Winds*. Fine songs, wit and high spirits stilled when battle with leukaemia lost. 2-disc *A Tribute To Steve Goodman* '85 made live in Chicago: his albums incl. help from David AMRAM, long-time touring partner Jethro Burns (of HOMER & JETHRO), David BROMBERG, old friend Prine and many others; all those named plus Guthrie, NITTY GRITTY DIRT BAND, Richie HAVENS, John HARTFORD, Bonnie RAITT, others came to the party, performing mostly Goodman's songs incl. lovely version of 'I Can't Sleep' by Bonnie Koloc. In '85, at the first Newport Folk Festival since '69, Guthrie did 'City Of New Orleans' as a duet with Joan BAEZ, dedicated to Goodman: he is sorely missed, but he left the world a happier place. Singer/songwriter Koloc made several albums in '70s, then *With You On My Side* '88 on Flying Fish.

GORDON, Dexter (*b* 27 Feb. '23, L.A.) Tenor sax. Father was a doctor. Studied clarinet and music theory at 13, then alto; quit school and took up tenor '40. With Lionel HAMPTON late '40 through to '43, Louis ARMSTRONG '44, Billy ECKSTINE '45; played with Charlie PARKER NYC; recorded for Dial in L.A. '47: 'The Chase' (with Wardell GRAY) and 'The Duel' (with Teddy EDWARDS) among the most exciting records of the era and among Dial's best sellers. Freelanced and led own various combos through '50s, e.g. with sextet backing Helen HUMES on Discovery label '50, with Red CALLENDER, pianist Ernie Freeman: timeless R&B, jazz, rock'n'roll: in fact beyond category. Acting/playing role in prod. of *The Connection* '60. First overseas gig at Ronnie SCOTT's in London; moved to Copenhagen '62 and did not return to USA until '65. Infl. by Coleman HAWKINS, Lester YOUNG and Parker, one of the first to play bop tenor, developing beautiful modern ballad style with subtle experiments in tonality. A profound infl. on Sonny ROLLINS, John COLTRANE, etc. but remained relatively unsung until resurgence began in '60s, continued in '70s: active overseas, visiting USA '69, '72 to record; also appeared at Newport Jazz Festival NYC '72, finally returned '76 to deserved attention in USA studios due partly to work of fans like Michael CUSCUNA, who prod. three Columbia LPs '77-8. At Carnegie Hall '78, Blues Alley in Washington DC '80, etc. Own records began '43 on Mercury/Clef with Harry EDISON, Nat COLE, etc. '47 sessions with Callender, Jimmy ROWLES, others reissued on Xanadu, Storyville; Dial stuff on Spotlite, also 2-disc collections on Savoy *Long Tall Dexter* and *Hunt* (with Gray). '52 sessions with Gray on Fontana, Swingtime, Trio; then small group sets, always superbly backed: *Daddy Plays The Horn* on Bethlehem, *Dexter Plays Hot And Cool* on Dootone/Savoy, both '55; *Pulsation* '60 on Jazzland (later as *The Resurgence Of Dexter Gordon*); then series of Blue Note albums: *Doin' Alright*, *Dexter Calling* '61; *Landslide*, *Go* and *A Swinging Affair* all '62; *Our Man In Paris* '63, with rhythm section of Bud POWELL, Kenny CLARKE, Pierre Michelot, and *One Flight Up* '64 recorded in France; *Clubhouse* and *Gettin' Around* '65 made in three sessions in

New Jersey and Paris. Storyville LP *Cry Me A River* '64 preceded gigs at Montmartre/Copenhagen same year with quartet (Tete MONTOLIU, piano; usually Niels-Henning Ørsted Pedersen on bass and Alex Riel, drums) issued on six Steeplechase LPs. *The Montmartre Collection* '67 in three discs, two on Black Lion, one on Trio; *Live At The Amsterdam Paradisio* '69 now on Affinity UK; *A Day In Copenhagen* '69 with Slide HAMPTON on MPS, Pausa and Prestige. The Prestige series incl. *The Tower Of Power* and *More Power* '69 with James MOODY (reissued '78 in 2-disc *Power*); *The Panther* with Tommy FLANAGAN, *The Chase* with Gene AMMONS, *The Jumpin' Blues* with Wynton KELLY all '70; quintets *Tangerine*, *Ca' Purange'* and *Generation* all '72. 15 more LPs '72-6 on Steeplechase, Dexterity, Futura; *Blues à la Suisse* at Montreux '73 on Prestige. Then Columbia LPs with 4 to 11 piece combos: *Home Coming* '76 (live at Village Vanguard), *Sophisticated Giant* '77, *Manhattan Symphonie* '78, *Great Encounter* '78 (live at Carnegie Hall), *Gotham City* '81 (with George BENSON, Art BLAKEY). *Jive Fernando* '81 with George DUKE is on Chiaroscuro; *American Classic* '82 on Elektra. *At Montreux* '70 issued on Prestige '85. Rave reviews for acting in excellent Bertrand Tavernier film *'Round Midnight* '86: character based on Powell/Lester YOUNG, but he played himself, as Gary Cooper and John Wayne did: another great American actor. Soundtrack album on Blue Note prod. by Herbie HANCOCK (on whose first album as leader Gordon played), with Ron CARTER, Wayne SHORTER, others incl. guest vocalists Chet BAKER, Bobby MCFERRIN, Lonette McKee; also out takes in *The Other Side Of 'Round Midnight*. It was Gordon who insisted that Michelot play in some scenes, because that is the way it was, and who rejected one of Hancock's arrangements as too complicated: the music in the film is timeless, like the rest of Gordon's work. Actress/singer McKee also appeared in film *Cotton Club*, on TV's *The Enforcer*, on stage in *Lady Day At Emerson's Bar And Grill* in NYC '87.

GORDON, Robert (*b* '47, Washington DC) USA rock singer. After teenage work as guitarist/singer with the Maryland groups Newports, Confidentials, moved to NYC,

witnessed PUNK happening while working outside music to support family. Separated from wife, joined Tuff Darts, sang on their tracks on new wave compilation LP *Live At CBGBs*. Later disclaimed this work, but had met Richard GOTTEHRER, who became his prod./manager, got record deal with Private Stock. First LP collaboration with guitar legend Link WRAY; they toured with joint band; single 'Red Hot' '77 made top 100. *Fresh Fish Special* '78 incl. 'Fire', allegedly written for Gordon by Bruce SPRINGSTEEN (later hit for POINTER SISTERS). Switched to RCA, had another minor hit 'Someday, Someway' '81.

GORE, Lesley (*b* 2 May '46, Tenafly, N.J.) Singer. Discovered by Quincy JONES while still in high school; first release on Mercury 'It's My Party' hit no. 1 USA '63, top 10 UK; 'Judy's Turn To Cry', 'She's A Fool', 'You Don't Own Me' followed, all top 5 '63. 15 more Hot 100 entries '64-7, four in top 20: 'That's The Way Boys Are', 'Maybe I Know' '64; 'Sunshine, Lollipops And Rainbows' '65, 'California Nights' '67. Left Mercury, Jones and charts; signed with Bob Crewe, then Mowest (Motown) '71, began writing own material, carried on as writer: with brother Michael wrote songs for *Fame* '80. *Golden Hits* compilation on Mercury. Often toured with Lou CHRISTIE '80s; duet single medley of '50s hits 'Since I Don't Have You'/'It's Only Make Believe' mid-'86.

GORME, Eydie (*b* 16 Aug. '31, Bronx, NY) Singer. Sang on radio at age 3; worked as Spanish interpreter after high school, turned to music: Coral record contract '53, began appearing on Steve ALLEN TV show, met Steve LAWRENCE there (married '57): they became and remain a popular club act. Her bright, clear voice, swinging style were a godsend to writers of good songs like 'Too Close For Comfort' (from musical *Mr Wonderful*), first of 14 Hot 100 entries '56-69, most on ABC-Paramount, arr./cond. by Don COSTA (but talent unfashionable: only five reached top 40, one top 10). LP now called *Guess Who I Saw Today* (on MCA in UK) incl. fine selection of standards, third chart hit 'I'll Take Romance', '37 song with words by Ben Oakland (*b* 24 Sep. '07, NYC; *d* 26 Aug. '79, Beverly Hills), music by Oscar Hammerstein II. Biggest hit at no. 7

'63 with 'Blame It On The Bossa Nova', song by Barry MANN, Cynthia Weil. Broadway debut with Lawrence in *Golden Rainbow* '67; Emmy awards for TV specials featuring songs of George GERSHWIN, Cole PORTER, Irving BERLIN; Grammy for best female vocalist '67. 12 chart LPs incl. *Eydie Gorme, Swings The Blues, Vamps The Roaring 20's* and *In Love*, all '57-8, all top 20 LPs, all on ABC-Paramount, none in print in USA according to Schwann catalogue. To Columbia for LPs *Blame It On The Bossa Nova* '63, *Gorme Country Style* '64, *Amor* and *More Amor* '64-5 (songs in Spanish, with Trio Los Panchos), *Don't Go To Strangers* '66, *Softly, As I Leave You* '67, *Greatest Hits* '67 (*Amor* and *Greatest Hits* still in print USA); to RCA: *Tonight I'll Say A Prayer* '70. *Vamps The Roaring 20's* is on Memoir in UK. Steve and Eydie had TV show '59, two top 40 duet hits '63 on Columbia: 'I Want To Stay Here' and 'I Can't Stop Talking About You'. Duo LPs incl. *We Got Us* (now on Jasmine UK), *At The Movies, Together Forever; Together On Broadway* on Columbia charted in USA '67; *What It Was, Was Love* and *Real True Lovin'* '69 on RCA; *Our Love Is Here To Stay* is Gershwin LP now on UA/EMI. *See also* Steve's entry.

GOSPEL MUSIC Thriving genre with its own charts in BILLBOARD. The Protestant revival at the beginning of the 19th century prod. the spiritual, mainly for rural meetings; black slaves adapted/invented their now-familiar spirituals. During this period the 'shape-note' and 'brush arbor' school of singing was profoundly influential in rural areas: as a means of improving singing in church, the rudiments of sight-reading were taught using notes on the page whose shape denoted their pitch, rather than their position on the stave; 'brush arbor' refers to the practice of clearing a small area and building an arbor for outdoor singing meetings. The tradition has survived in country music to the present day (*see* the CHUCK WAGON GANG). 'Hillbilly hymns' have always been popular, e.g. 'The Old Rugged Cross', 'Just A Closer Walk With Thee'; 'I Saw The Light' and others by Hank WILLIAMS; also songs by Thomas A. Dorsey *(see below);* many if not most country artists have made successful LPs of gospel ma-

terial. The City-Revival movement c.1850 was an urban phenomenon which resulted in white gospel hymnody, borrowing forms and melodies from Tin Pan Alley and remaining musically conservative; George Beverly Shea (*b* '09, Winchester, Ontario, Canada) was king of traditional gospel music: his bass-baritone was on ABC radio and the Armed Forces Network for eight years from '44 and he was associated with the Billy Graham Crusades. Contemporary white urban gospel music is of little musical importance: the poppish crooning of Amy Grant has won awards and an appearance on the Johnny Carson show; Leslie Phillips is called 'Queen of Christian Rock'; the Chicago band Rez plays music described by Glenn Kaiser, vocalist/songwriter/guitarist and senior pastor with Jesus People USA, as '*intense* hard rock, something just short of heavy metal', while a band called Stryper goes the distance, looking and playing like heavy metal people but mentioning Jesus in the lyrics. There are Grammy awards in the gospel category; the Gospel Music Association has bestowed annual Dove Awards since '69, with separate traditional and contemporary awards for white and black gospel artists; but it is black gospel music which has profoundly influenced the rest of popular music. Blues singers often used religious imagery; Gary DAVIS was a Baptist minister, much of whose repertoire was religious; Blind Willie JOHNSON's records for Columbia '27-30 are entirely religious but highly prized by blues collectors. For decades black choirs imitated the Fisk Jubilee Singers (formed at Fisk University 1867 by a white teacher) who invented their own tradition, were a smash hit at the World Peace Jubilee in Boston 1872 (the first time a black group of any kind was incl. in a big musical programme in the USA), eventually performed for crowned heads in Europe. Black churches before the Civil War (1860-65) took their starting point from white hymnody, but moved in a different direction: the black pentecostal churches encouraged the use of musical (especially rhythm) instruments among the congregation, expecting everybody to join in. Among those prominent in black gospel music was W. Herbert Brewster Sr (*b* 1899; wrote 'Move On Up A Little Higher'); he innovated musically with tempo changes and melismatic cadenzas (allowing singer to use his/her voice wordlessly, as a musical instrument), and many others; but Dorsey was the most important of his generation. His father was a revivalist Baptist minister, mother a church organist; his first composition was 'If I Don't Get There'. He studied music formally before and after moving to Chicago c.'16; as a pianist, guitarist, singer and songwriter had a secular career (as Georgia Tom; *see* DORSEY, Thomas A.); then his religious background took over: he coined the term 'gospel song'; sold them on sheets of paper called 'ballets' for pennies (songs were called 'Dorseys' for 20 years). He was the first to accompany religious songs on piano outside church, hiring singers to demonstrate them; he founded the first female gospel quartet (earlier gospel groups were mostly male, sang *a cappella*); he achieved fame at National Baptist Convention '30 with 'If You See My Saviour' and formed Thomas A. Dorsey Gospel Songs Publishing Company '30; he was associated with Sallie Martin from '32 (*b* 1896; she wrote 'Nearer My God To Thee'), discovered Clara Ward and Mahalia JACKSON. He toured internationally with the Gospel Choral Union '32-44; formed National Convention of Gospel Choirs and Choruses '33 and served it until '70s; was assistant pastor of Chicago's Pilgrim Baptist Church, toured as lecturer '60s-70s; was seen in *The Devil's Music: A History Of The Blues* BBC TV '76. He wrote about 1000 songs and published half of them, incl. 'Peace In The Valley' (for Jackson, '37), 'Take My Hand Precious Lord' (both recorded by Elvis PRESLEY '57), 'Sweet Bye And Bye', etc. One of his most important deeds: promoting a singing contest between Sallie and Roberta Martin (1907-69) (not related) at DuSable High School (Chicago '36), one of the first examples of charging admission for a gospel music performance. Sister Rosetta THARPE sang gospel songs in a Cab CALLOWAY show at the COTTON CLUB '38; that year black gospel groups were incl. in John HAMMOND's *Spirituals To Swing* concert, incl. Tharpe. Black gospel had its own radio shows from '40s; dean of gospel disc jockeys was Joe Bostic (*b* '09), who prod. the first Negro Gospel and Religious Music Festival at Carnegie Hall '50, with Jackson; '51 show featured James CLEVELAND;

moved to Madison Square Garden '59 becoming the First Annual Gospel, Spiritual and Folk Music Festival. Gospel moved to TV '50s; Jackson appeared on Ed Sullivan Show and was fast becoming a national institution. The Ward Singers were the first gospel group to appear at Newport Jazz Festival '57; Bessie Griffin (*b* '27) took gospel to cabaret in *Portraits In Bronze*, prod. by Bumps BLACKWELL in New Orleans '59; the Wards went into nightclubs and Jackson sang at John Kennedy's inauguration, '61; the Wards went to Radio City Music Hall and Clara starred in one of the first gospel musicals (Langston Hughes's *Tambourines To Glory*, '63). Rock'n'roll had happened; white artists like Elvis Presley and Jerry Lee LEWIS were infl. by the uninhibited style of black (and white) Southern churches; Ray CHARLES stopped imitating Nat COLE and took his Baptist background to rhythm & blues, even borrowing gospel tunes. But the wildest black rhythm & blues artists (e.g. LITTLE RICHARD and Screamin' Jay HAWKINS) crossed over to the pop charts, singing about sex in the ecstatic, devil-destroying 'sanctified' style, and religious blacks thought it scandalous. Meanwhile the infl. of gospel groups was also felt, principally male quartets, still *a cappella*. Gospel records had become big business from '45, with rhythm & blues labels Apollo, Specialty, Peacock, King, Savoy, others issuing gospel records by the Dixie Hummingbirds (estab. '28), the Soul Stirrers ('35; first to add a fifth voice, allowing 4-part harmony support for the lead singer, first to use guitar accompaniment), the Swan Silvertones ('38, with Claude Jeter's falsetto, and shouting lead singers), the Golden Gate Jubilee Quartet (began recording '39; their 'Stalin Wasn't Stallin' ' is a fascinating wartime period piece), the STAPLE SINGERS, many others. Girl groups incl. the Southern Harps Spiritual Singers, where Griffin came from, and the Original Gospel Harmonettes with singer/songwriter Dorothy Love Coates. These groups had long been an infl. on rhythm & blues, doo-wop etc. but explosion of black SOUL music '60s came directly from them: Ward infl. Aretha FRANKLIN, whose first records were made in her father's church; the great Sam COOKE came out of the Soul Stirrers: he was the idol of black teenage girls before he turned to pop;

his velvet melisma on 'You Send Me' '57 sent it to the top of the charts, the first soul classic. James BROWN was infl. by the ecstasy of Archie Brownlee (the Five Blind Boys); Silvertones infl. the TEMPTATIONS, etc. the soulful honesty of black gospel entered the mainstream of popular culture for good. The Edwin HAWKINS Singers had a huge international hit with 'Oh Happy Day' '69; Cleveland, Alex BRADFORD, others still nurture talent in the churches. Most of the artists mentioned here have albums listed in the 'Religious, Hymns, Sacred' section of the USA Schwann LP catalogue. *Jesus Is The Answer* on Charly UK collects Silvertones, Staples, Highway QCs, Caravans, Greater Harvest Choir, Argo Singers, Harmonising Four, Five Blind Boys Of Alabama (not the Brownlee group, who were from Mississippi); subsidiary New Cross has inaugurated series of black gospel: first reissues from '50s-60s incl. *Get Your Soul Right* (Silvertones), *Pray On* (Staples). *Black Gospel* by Viv Broughton '85 is an illustrated survey; 2-disc *Black Gospel* on MCA has 28 tracks by the Mighty Clouds Of Joy, Sensational Nightingales, Dixie Hummingbirds etc. issued at the same time as the book. Tony Heilbut's *The Gospel Sound: Good News And Bad Times* '71 was a seminal study.

GOTTEHRER, Richard USA producer, songwriter. Long part of writing team with Bob Feldman and Jerry Goldstein, initially under contract to a publisher but soon on their own. An interchangeable group of girl singers used for session work on demos provided their first and biggest hit, 'My Boyfriend's Back' by the Angels (no. 1 USA '63), followed by lesser entries by the Powder-Puffs, Baby Dolls, Pin-Ups, Patti Lace and the Petticoats, etc. They also created labels for their own output, but had less success with established artists such as Little Eva and Mary Wells. Turning performers, they had three top 40 hits '64-5 as the Strangeloves ('I Want Candy', no. 11), made records as the Sheep, then split up. Gottehrer became a successful producer, first with the CLIMAX (Chicago) BLUES BAND in the early '70s, later with the first two BLONDIE LPs (incl. smash hit 'Denis'), rock singer Robert GORDON, Richard HELL and the Voidoids, then with Joan ARMATRADING and the GO-GO'S.

GOULD, Morton (*b* 10 Dec. '13, Long Island, NY) Pianist, composer, arranger, conductor. Of Russian and Austrian extraction; first composition published age 6; about 1000 incl. symphonies, TV soundtracks, flute concerto (for Georg Solti, Chicago S.O., flautist Donald Peck), ballets *Interplay*, *Fall River Legend*, *I'm Old Fashioned* for Jerome Robbins, *Audubon* (aka *Birds Of America*) for George Balanchine (never staged; conducts suite *Apple Waltzes* from it). On Broadway: *Billion Dollar Baby* '46 with Betty Comden, Adolph Green; *Arms And The Girl* '50 with Dorothy Fields; film scores incl. *Delightfully Dangerous* '45 (also appeared with orchestra). Records of pop material in light classical treatment on Decca, Columbia (LPs *Symphonic Serenade*, *Starlight Serenade* etc. '50s); on RCA: LPs of songs from Broadway shows etc.; music of Ives, Rimsky-Korsakov, Nielsen (clarinet concerto with Benny GOODMAN) with C.S.O., also Miaskovsky's Symphony No. 21 '68, commissioned by that orchestra '40.

GOULET, Robert (*b* 26 Nov. '33, Lawrence, Mass.) Singer. First pro job as teenager in Summer Pops concert in Canada; doing TV variety show in Toronto, auditioned for new LERNER & Loewe musical *Camelot*, landed plum role as Lancelot in show with Richard Burton, Julie ANDREWS '60. Did Ed Sullivan show on TV at that time; became popular handsome singer. Married Carol Lawrence '63, later divorced. *Camelot* original cast LP was no. 1 several weeks; Goulet went on to sell a lot of albums: 17 chart LPs incl. *Always You* and *Two Of Us* '62; *Sincerely Yours* (no. 9 LP), *The Wonderful World Of Love, In Person* (live at Chicago Opera House) all '63; *Manhattan Tower/The Man Who Loves Manhattan* '64 (written and cond. by Gordon JENKINS), *Without You* and *My Love Forgive Me*, all '64. Last incl. biggest hit single in title track (no. 16); after that sales slowly slipped. *I Wish You Love* '70 was compilation album.

GRACIE, Charlie (*b* Charles Anthony Graci, 14 May '36, Philadelphia) Singer, guitarist; an original talent treated poorly by Philly star-making machine. Youthful guitar prodigy played Paul WHITEMAN TV show age 14; won prizes incl. family's first fridge.

Recorded for Cadillac and 20th Century labels in variety of styles: mixture of jump blues, country boogie with infl. of Roy ACUFF, Joe TURNER, B. B. KING was near enough to rockabilly. Signed to Cameo, recorded 'Butterfly', written by Cameo owners Bernie Lowe and Kal Mann, credited to 'Anthony September', pseudonym of *American Bandstand* prod. Tony Mammarella, later implicated in payola scandal (*see* Dick CLARK). No. 1 hit USA gave Gracie name to live up to; unfortunately little of his gritty guitar work was allowed on record, label dealing in teen idols, not rockabilly heroes. Pushed into mould he didn't fit, Gracie's chart life predictably shortlived; followup 'Fabulous' made no. 16, but was too close to 'Don't Be Cruel' for comfort: Elvis PRESLEY's publishers sued for publication rights, and won. Gracie turned to Otis BLACKWELL for 'Cool Baby', sung in film *Disc Jockey Jamboree* '57; ironically, Blackwell had written 'Don't Be Cruel' as well as Presley's 'All Shook Up'. No more top 40 hits in USA, but scored in UK with four top 20 hits: 'Butterfly', 'Fabulous', 'I Love You So Much It Hurts', 'Wanderin' Eyes', plus 'Cool Baby' at no. 26. Live act appreciated in UK, too; continued touring there into '80s. USA fortunes not helped by out-of-court settlement of suit alleging non-payment of royalties: little promotion followed. Banished from *Bandstand*, recorded for Coral, Roulette, Felsted, President Diamond, Sock'n'Soul labels, playing more of the black music he preferred. LPs incl. pre-fame material *Charlie Gracie's Early Recordings* on Revival, *Cameo/Parkway Sessions* on London. Small in stature (5'4"), bigger in talent, underrated by history.

GRAHAM, Bill (*b* Wolfgang Grajonca, '31, Berlin) Promoter. Identified with '60s West Coast scene, one of rock's greatest entrepreneurs. Born of Russian parents, made way via European orphanages to Bronx, NY; fought in Korea, financed business studies by driving taxi. Moved into concert promotion 6 Nov. '65 as manager of San Francisco Mime Troupe: hired skating rink for benefit concert, JEFFERSON AIRPLANE headlining. Renamed venue (in black ghetto) Fillmore; success of local San Francisco bands made hall's popularity, eventual legend: first to turn hippie music into cash.

Renamed Carousel Ballroom Fillmore West '67, simultaneously former cinema Village Theatre in NYC became Fillmore East (and short-lived record label concurrently). When he closed both venues '71 claiming that subculture had become commercialised, critics claimed he had hastened the process. Continued in promoting tours by Bob DYLAN, etc. managing bands like Airplane, later SANTANA; organised Watkins Glen pop festival 28 July '73 (with GRATEFUL DEAD, The Band etc. at more than 500,000 people the biggest yet); also CROSBY, STILLS, NASH & YOUNG reunion tour '74, The Band's *Last Waltz* '76, ROLLING STONES tour '82, etc. He was clearly in it for more than the money: witness '75 effort SNACK (Students Need Athletics, Culture and Kicks), involvement in Live Aid '85, etc. But his power was such that bands crossed him at their peril. Devil or angel, many shared feelings at closure of Fillmores: 'When we began the original Fillmore, I associated with the employed musicians. Now, more often than not, it's with officers and stockholders in large corporations – only they happen to have long hair and play guitars. Woodstock was the beginning of the end.' Nevertheless as the concert business picked up '87 he was still at it, incl. July 4th gig in Moscow with Santana, James TAYLOR, Bonnie RAITT.

GRAHAM, Larry (*b* 14 Aug. '46, Beaumont, Texas) As bassist with SLY AND THE FAMILY STONE one of the most influential bassists in history of rock, undulating yet hardedged patterns practically inventing much of the dance music of the '70s; then he formed funk band Graham Central Station; then emerged as ballad singer. Family moved to Oakland, Cal. when he was 2; by teens he could play guitar, bass, drums, harmonica; had three-octave vocal range; played in mother's trio, later in back-up bands for Jackie WILSON, Jimmy REED, the DRIFTERS etc. while attending college. Recruited by area DJ Sylvester Stewart (Sly Stone) for Sly '67-72; smooth voice was good foil for Stone's. Formed Graham Central Station from USA band Hot Chocolate (no connection with UK band of same name): Hershall Kennedy, keyboards; David Vega, guitar; Willie Sparks, drums; Patrice Banks, percussion; added ex-Billy PRESTON keyboardist Robert Sam. Dance music earned Grammy for Best New Group, top 40 pop hit ('Your Love' '75), seven LPs in pop album chart '74-9, incl. *Ain't No 'Bout-A-Doubt It* '75 (best showing at no. 22), *Mirror* '76 (entirely written by Graham), *Now Do U Wanna Dance* '78; last two credited as 'Larry Graham and Grand Central Station': *My Radio Sure Sounds Good To Me* '78 (with wife Tina added vocalist), *Star Walk*. Turned solo balladeer: four LPs charted incl. first solo LP *One In A Million You* '80 made no. 26 album chart with top 10 pop title track, but *Just Be My Lady* (no. 46), *Sooner Or Later*, *Victory* did less well. Sales in black charts always good: 'I Never Forgot Your Eyes' made no. 34 on black singles chart '83; multi-talented Graham has made a lot of fans happy.

GRAMMER, Billy (*b* William Wayne Grammer, 28 Aug. '25, Benton, Ill.) Country singer, and one of the first great Nashville session guitarists. Worked as toolmaker in naval gun factory, served in US Army; on radio, TV in Washington DC '49-59, to Nashville after hit 'Gotta Travel On', first record on new Monument label, top 5 hit both pop and country '59. Other hits: 'Bonaparte's Retreat', and 'The Kissing Tree' '59, 'I Wanna Go Home' '63, 'Bottles' and 'The Real Thing' '66. Played in Jimmy DEAN, Hawkshaw HAWKINS, Grandpa JONES bands; own albums incl. *Travelin' On* '61 on Monument; *Country Guitar* '64, *Gospel Guitar* '65 on Decca; *Sunday Guitar* '67 on Epic; also recorded for Rice, Mercury.

GRAND FUNK (RAILROAD) USA heavy metal band of '70s originally formed as Terry Knight and the Pack. Garage-band one-hit wonders ('I Who Have Nothing') (no. 46 '66) incl. Detroit DJ-turned-singer Knight (*b* 9 Apr. '43) and Don Brewer on drums (*b* 3 Sep. '48, Flint, Mich.); Mark Farner (*b* 29 Sep. '48, Flint) was temporarily bass player. By Feb. '69, Knight-less band the Fabulous Pack had Mel Schacher on bass (*b* Apr. '51, Owosso, Mich.; ex-? AND THE MYSTERIANS); Farner moved to guitar. Knight, now entrepreneur, prevented split by demanding complete control, incl. name change to Grand Funk Railroad. *On Time* '69, first LP for Capitol, was basic

blues/rock on which image was built: like STATUS QUO in '70s UK, they stripped music to basics and found youth identification factor with heavy metal/macho mix: went from unpaid opening slot at '69 Atlanta pop festival (released as 2-disc *Live Album* '70) to showcase Shea Stadium gig '71 (sold out in 72 hours, better than the BEATLES). Knight masterminded rise (rented Times Square billboard, etc.). LPs almost secondary, but sold well: *Grand Funk* and *Closer To Home* '70, *Survival* and *E Pluribus Funk* '71, 2-disc compilation *Mark, Don And Mel 1969-71* '72 were all brash, basic three-chord metal, mostly written by Farner; went gold, spawned three top 30 singles. They sued Knight for independence; lawsuits followed as *Phoenix* '73 proved they could do it without him and threatened degree of subtlety: introduced keyboardist Craig Frost (*b* 20 Apr. '48, Flint). Name shortened to Grand Funk; Todd RUNDGREN prod. *We're An American Band* '73, title track written by Brewer no. 1 hit, became heavy metal anthem; 'Walk Like A Man' no. 19. *Shinin' On* '74 incl. no. 11 title hit, another no. 1 with heavy version of 'The Locomotion'. Dropped more heavy metal edge when pop prod. Jimmy Ienner (Raspberries, etc.) took over: 'Some Kind Of Wonderful', 'Bad Time' from *All The Girls Of The World Beware!!!* '74 were top 5 hits '74-5, but harmony etc. alienated fans who wanted sweaty, shirtless, long-haired image/sound: no. 10 LP was poorest seller since second release. Changed name back to Grand Funk Railroad for live 2-disc *Caught In The Act* and *Born To Die* '75, but band had peaked. Switched labels; Frank ZAPPA prod. *Good Singin', Good Playin'* '76 on MCA; they split. Farner made brace of solo LPs: *Mark Farner, No Frills* '77-8; Brewer, Schacher, Frost and guitarist Billy Elworthy formed Flint (eponymous LP on Epic '79); Frost then joined Bob SEGER. Re-formed without Frost, with new bassist Dennis Bellinger (yet another musician from Flint) for *Grand Funk Lives* '81 on Full Moon; *What's Funk?* '83 did not make top 200 LPs. Brewer later joined Frost in Seger's Silver Bullet Band. They had flown in face of fashion and alarmed the Woodstock generation with their loud music and neanderthal appearance, but the shock value had worn off.

GRAND OLE OPRY USA country music programme; one of the first radio Barn Dance shows, began late '25 and still going strong. George Dewey Hay (*b* 9 Nov. 1895, Attica, Indiana; *d* 9 May '68, Virginia Beach, Va.) was journalist on *Memphis Courier*, then announcer on paper's station WMC, where he scooped the fledgling industry with first announcement of death of President Harding; to WLS Chicago, '24 where he was announcer for new Chicago Barn Dance (later National Barn Dance); voted nation's most popular announcer by *Radio Digest* magazine; hired by National Life and Accident Insurance Company as dir. of new station WSM Nashville, Tenn. Broadcast an hour of 85-year-old fiddler Uncle Jimmy Thompson Nov. '25; audience response justified first WSM Barn Dance 27 Dec. '25 with Hay as MC: dubbed self as 'The Solemn Old Judge' though he was just 30. Offhand remark '27 dubbed show Grand Ole Opry (*see* DeFord BAILEY). Hay allowed only string bands for many years (no drums or horns; Bob WILLS guest shot '44 had snare drum hidden behind curtain); first string band was Dr Humphrey Bate and his Possum Hunters (Bate *d* '36; actually was a physician; also enjoyed classical music; played harmonica). Band's repertoire incl. ragtime, SOUSA marches; daughter Alcyone Bate played piano age 13 on first programmes; was still at Opry 50 years later. Other early Opry stars were Uncle Dave MACON; influential guitarist Sam MCGEE (c.1895-'75), fiddler brother Kirk. Bands incl. Crook Brothers, Gully Jumpers, Fruit Jar Drinkers, Binkley Brothers Dixie Clodhoppers, etc. with singing incidental; but Roy ACUFF from '38, although leading trad. band, became huge singing star, soon joined by Eddy ARNOLD, Red FOLEY, many others: important trend as singers were soon biggest stars of genre. Bill MONROE's Blue Grass Boys represented trad. string band (as well as Acuff's Smoky Mountain Boys); BLUEGRASS genre kept going by Opry until explosion of interest in '60s-70s. Ernest TUBB brought electric guitars '43; his popularity could not be denied, though Opry remained suspicious of honky-tonk genre: Hay was adamant about basic country values, posing Bate and the others in pastures wearing overalls for publicity photos, while many had little rural connection.

Sensational guest shot by Hank WILLIAMS '49 led to contract although he was known to be unreliable; had to be fired '52. Meanwhile WSM allowed studio audience, which soon outgrew progressively larger rooms; show first networked on NBC '39, sponsored by Prince Albert tobacco, with Hay, Acuff, Macon, Little Rachel, the Weaver Brothers and Elviry; same crew made first Opry film '40; Opry stars toured USA in Camel Caravan during WWII, helped keep up wartime morale. Opry took over local Ryman Auditorium '43, country music shrine for 30 years. Records made in WSM studio late '20s for Victor field trips (Victor came back '44 to record Arnold); WSM engineers operated Castle Studios from '47, Nashville's first transcription studio; ex-Opry announcer Jim Bulleit started Bullet, first Nashville record label '45; Owen BRADLEY, true father of Music Row's recording industry, began as WSM music director; Chet ATKINS first came to Nashville to play on Opry with CARTER FAMILY. Snooky Lanson, Kitty KALLEN, Dinah SHORE, Phil HARRIS, many others not solely identified with country music had links with WSM, which was one of the last radio stations in USA still maintaining studio staff orchestra; also operated first USA FM station '41 (a brave venture: few bought new receivers to get WNV47; WSMFM opened '68 when interest revived); also first Nashville TV station '50, etc. Hay finally left Opry '53: Jim DENNY ran Opry's booking agency, encouraging growth of Nashville music business by making it home base for so many stars. 369-acre Opryland USA park opened 16 March '74, with new 4400-seat auditorium at centre: Opry looks like going on forever.

GRANT, David (*b* 8 Aug. '56, Hackney, London) UK soul/pop singer. Rose to fame in duo Linx with bassist Sketch (Peter Martin, *b* 29 June '54, London); released single 'You're Lying' on own label '80; picked up by Chrysalis in replay of SPECIALS signing, leading to press speculation about Linx as leaders of home-grown soul movement: blacks paralleling ska revival of 2-tone? Answer was no, though duo aided by keyboardist/ prod. Bob Carter created soul-flavoured hits with refreshing lightness of touch, Grant's Michael JACKSON-like vocals set in inventive background: 'Intuition' (no. 7), 'Throw Away The Key' (21), 'So This Is Romance' (15). Linx split amicably '82 (hits LP *Last Linx* '83; Sketch resurfaced with white funksters 23 Skidoo); Grant revamped image, changing contact lenses for spectacles, donning headband and sweat-suit trousers, turned to faceless funk ideal for aerobics classes: *David Grant* '84 prod. by Steve Levine played on Jackson sound/lookalike qualities, giving him little chance to shine in own right: 'Stop And Go', 'Watching You Watching Me', 'Love Will Find A Way' all top 25 '83. Duet hit with Jaki Graham 'Could It Be I'm Falling In Love' '85 rejuvenated career as cover of Spinners '73 hit encouraged him to drop disco blinkers: *Hopes And Dreams* '85 creditably varied (prod. by Derek Bramble, ex-Heatwave), incl. hit plus contributions from reggae band Aswad (on Grant-written title track), Sketch (on 'Cool September'), members of Go West. Shimmering version of Todd RUNDGREN's 'Mated' another duet hit with Graham '85. Given room to breathe he will be a lasting singing/writing talent.

GRANT, Earl (*b* '31 Oklahoma City; *d* 11 June '70, Lordsburg, New Mexico) Pop singer, organist, other instruments. Organ at age 4, played in father's Baptist church, studied at K.C. Conservatory, New Rochelle NY, DePaul U. Chicago, etc. Taught music, joined army, became pop entertainer while serving at Fort Bliss, Texas; returned to U. of Southern Cal. as grad student, played local clubs; began recording for Decca '57, top 10 hit 'The End' '58. Other minor hits: 'Evening Rain' '59, 'House Of Bamboo' '60, 'Swingin' Gently', 'Sweet Sixteen Bars' '62, 'Stand By Me' '65. Voice similar to that of Nat COLE, with more husky strength; rumour that he was Cole's brother untrue. 'Ol' Man River' big on juke boxes c.'60; easy treatment spoiled somewhat by stiff pop drumming. Consistent LP seller; made more than 50, incl. *Nothing But The Blues* '59, *Ebb Tide* '61 (LP said to have sold 500,000; title single said to have sold a million), *At Basin Street East* '62, *Fly Me To The Moon* '64, *Just One More Time* '65. Regular in clubs; appeared in films *Imitation Of Life* '59, *Tender Is The Night* '62. Died in crash of Rolls-Royce returning from gig in Juarez, Mexico.

GRANT, Eddy (*b* 5 Mar. '48, Guyana, West Indies) Singer, songwriter, producer, studio boss. Began as mainstay of UK pop group the Equals in '60s, often seen as forerunner of 2-Tone movement of late '70s: wrote their hits 'Baby Come Back', 'Black Skin Blue Eyed Boys' '68-70; was outrageous frontman with hair dyed white; compilation *Best Of The Equals* '69 is an exuberant collection. On their split he opened Coach House Studios in North London '73, intended to control every facet of production, forming own label Ice '74 and overseeing pressing and distribution. Prod. records by the Gladiators. Among his own *Eddy Grant* '75, *Message Man* '77, *Walkin' On Sunshine* '79, latter was a critical favourite, Grant using his synthesisers to create music with almost steel drum as well as orchestral effects (title track covered by Rockers' Revenge '82 for no. 2 UK hit). Own first hit was 'Living On The Front Line', no. 11 '79: it won him a whole new audience with its 'street cred' (street in Brixton where young blacks hang out is the 'front line'). Subsequent ballad 'Do You Feel My Love' was no. 8 '80; LP *Love In Exile* '80 satisfied, *Can't Get Enough* '81 was a bigger success: top 40 UK album followed by hits 'I Don't Wanna Dance' (no. 1 '81), 'Electric Avenue' (no. 2 '83, also about a street in Brixton, seen as comment on riots there). Wrote and performed theme song 'Romancing The Stone', which then wasn't used in the '84 film; LP *Going For Broke* '84 had ingenious mixture of pop and politics; *Live At The Notting Hill Carnival* and compilation *All The Hits* also '84. Grant remains a larger-than-life figure: performed in Poland and Cuba '85 and maintains a studio in Barbados. Album *File Under Rock* '88 was on Blue Wave Label.

GRANT, Gogi (*b* Audrey Brown, 20 Sep. '24, Philadelphia, Pa.) Pop singer. Moved to L.A. at age 12. Infl. by Russ COLUMBO, Ruth ETTING; won statewide contest for teen singers, also TV talent shows; had several hits '55-6 on Era incl. top 10 'Suddenly There's A Valley', no. 1 'Wayward Wind'; switched to RCA and just made Hot 100 with 'Strange Are The Ways Of Love' '58, backed throughout by Buddy Bregman band. RCA LP *Granted . . . It's Gogi* reissued '87 in UK. She also dubbed vocals or Ann Blyth in film biography of Helen MORGAN '57.

GRANZ, Norman (*b* 6 Aug. '18, L.A.) Entrepreneur, promoter, producer, label boss. Attended UCLA; after WWII service worked as film editor; began series of jazz concerts at L.A. Philharmonic Auditorium '44: took jazz At The Philharmonic (JATP) on tour which ended in Canada. Innovated from the start by recording concerts; record sales enabled more tours; also prod. film short, classic *Jammin' The Blues* with Lester YOUNG, photographed by Gjon Mili, nominated for Oscar '44. Leased records to small labels, then to Mercury '48-51; started Clef, Norgran, Verve; consolidated on Verve '57. Toured the world with JATP, booked other tours as well; shrewd but fair, he maintained relationships for many years with Ella FITZGERALD, Count BASIE, Stan GETZ, scores of others who would have had considerably less work in the lean years for jazz of '50s and '60s without him: people who couldn't get along with Granz probably had bigger egos than he had. Retained rights to as many recordings as possible; sold Verve to MGM (thence to Polygram) and Fitzgerald Songbook series is still on Verve; but unable to stay away) started Pablo label in 70s: his wonderful '50s recordings of Art TATUM (for example) are now on that label. Helped make a star of Joe PASS; nabbed Duke ELLINGTON's *The Queen's Suite* for its first commercial release; carried on making live recordings (many at Montreux); fine issues on Pablo soon rivalled classic Verve list. Slower output in '80s reflected health problems; Pablo sold to FANTASY late '86.

GRAPPELLI, Stephane (*b* 26 Jan. '08, Paris, France) Violinist. One of the very few non-American jazz musicians to become world-famous; with Joe VENUTI, Stuff SMITH, Jean-Luc PONTY, Svend ASMUSSEN, Eddie SOUTH, Ray Nance and Joe Kennedy one of the few jazz violinists (not all of these have made a living primarily on the violin). Used to spell name 'Grappelly'. Most famous as principal member with Django REINHARDT of the Quintet of the Hot Club of France '34-9; also an accomplished pianist, playing piano on 28 Apr. '37 Paris session with Django and Coleman HAWKINS. Spent

WWII in England, made records with Reinhardt again there '46; later worked mostly in France, also toured the world. Unabashed romanticism balanced by ability to swing, logic in improvisation. Long taken for granted; then duets on UK TV early '70s with Yehudi Menuhin were a delightful novelty: they made LPs on EMI incl. *Tea For Two, Strictly For The Birds, Jealousy, Fascinatin' Rhythm*, etc. Other LPs: *Skol* and *Tivoli* with Oscar PETERSON on Pablo; *Reunion* with George SHEARING on Verve; *Homage To Django* '72 (2 discs, with British musicians) and '73 LP with Bill COLEMAN, now on Classic Jazz in USA; *A Two-fer* with Hank JONES on Muse; *Giants* with Ponty; *Happy Reunion* with Martial Solal; live LP with virtuoso mandolinist David Grisman on WB '81 made Billboard pop LP chart. Others: *I Remember Django* and *Limehouse Blues* (both with Barney KESSEL), *I Got Rhythm* and *Just One Of Those Things*, all on Black Lion; *I Hear Music* on RCA; *Violinspiration* (with Diz Disley Trio), *Afternoon In Paris* and *Violin Summit* (with Smith, Ponty, Asmussen) all on BASF/MPS (other labels in USA); *Venupelli Blues* with Venuti on Byg; *Feeling + Finesse = Jazz* '62 (with Pierre Cavalli, guitar), *Duke Ellington's Jazz Violin Session* with Asmussen and Nance, *Paris Encounter* with Gary BURTON, all on Atlantic; *Live At Carnegie Hall, On The Road Again* (with Teresa BREWER) on Doctor Jazz; *At The Winery* '80, *Vintage* '81 and *Stephanova* '83 on Concord Jazz; *Plays Jerome Kern* '86 on GRP with strings; *Uptown Dance* on Columbia; others on EMI and French labels, plus many compilations of 78s with Reinhardt.

GRATEFUL DEAD USA rock band, almost sole survivor of San Francisco hippy era: began in psychedelic/acid rock, have absorbed country rock and even disco, but mainly one of the most improvisatory of all rock bands. No top 40 singles; only three of their many LPs reached higher than no. 25 on LP chart; indisputably a live act: tour six months every year. Jerry Garcia (*b* Jerome John Garcia, 1 Aug. '42) began on guitar at 15; added banjo and played in folk groups early '60s, drifting through the Wildwood Boys and Hart Valley Drifters, meeting Robert Hunter along the way (later Dead's lyricist; among most successful in terms of number of songs written and/or recorded, yet least famous of rock writers). By '64 called Mother McCree's Uptown Jug Champions incl. Ron 'Pigpen' McKernan (*b* 8 Sep. '45, San Bruno, Cal.; *d* 8 Mar. '73), keyboards, harmonica, vocals; Bob Weir (*b* Robert Hall, 16 Oct. '47), John 'Marmaduke' Dawson (*b* '45), guitars, vocals, both from San Francisco, as was Garcia, who later added pedal steel to his bag: one of the secrets of the band's longevity has been its willingness to experiment. They became the Warlocks '65, without Dawson but adding Phil Lesh (*b* Philip Chapman, 15 Mar. '40, Berkeley), bass, vocals; Bill Kreutzmann (*b* 7 Apr. '46, Palo Alto), drums; adopted electric instruments and took part in public LSD parties before drug was outlawed, later chronicled in Ken Kersey's *Electric Kool-Aid Acid Test*. Garcia found name Grateful Dead in Egyptian prayer book; signed with WB '67. *Grateful Dead* '67 was conventional rock album with energy-laden R&B style; Mickey Hart joined on percussion, stayed through '70, came back again '75. *Anthem Of The Sun* '68 and *Aoxomoxoa* '69 were experimental, patched together; 'St Stephen', 'China Cat Sunflower' best cuts. Expensive studio time left them in debt to label. 2-disc *Live Dead* '70 was better: 'Dark Star' regarded as rock classic. Next LPs were acoustic country-rock style, with Hunter's songs and Garcia one of the first rock artists to take up pedal steel: *Workingman's Dead* incl. first minor hit 'Uncle John's Band' (also 'New Speedway Boogie', their reaction to Altamont disaster; *see* ROLLING STONES). *American Beauty* incl. 'Truckin' ', 'Box Of Rain': good sellers made label happy; still their best albums for non-aficionados. *Vintage Dead* (live from S.F. Avalon Ballroom), *Historic Dead* both recorded '66, released '70-1 on Sunflower, deservedly poor sellers; 2-disc *Grateful Dead* '71, 3-disc *Europe* '72 both live, among biggest hits. Heavy drinker Pigpen had been ill and out of action '71, rejoined for tour of Europe but died of liver disease. Keith Godchaux (*b* 14 July '48, S.F.) joined on keyboards, wife Donna on backing vocals; they stayed until '79, replaced by Brent Mydland (*b* '53); Keith died after car crash 23 July '80. *History Of The Grateful Dead Vol. 1* (live at Fillmore East early '70) and

best-of albums *Skeletons From The Closet, What A Long Strange Trip It's Been* were released on WB, but loyal following (called Deadheads) enabled them to finance their own Grateful Dead label, with subsidiary Round Records for solo projects; began with studio LPs *Wake Of The Flood* '73, *Grateful Dead From The Mars Hotel* '74 and *Blues For Allah* '75, their best sellers at no. 18, 16, 12 in LP chart respectively. 2-disc live set *Steal Your Face* '76 made at S.F. Winterland '74 (concerts were filmed: *The Grateful Dead Movie* released '77). These LPs seen as self-indulgent floundering by many critics, but fans, like the band, regard the concert as important, not the record, which is a souvenir, an artifact: unlike many contemporaries they retained hippy ideals. Nevertheless LPs on Arista improved by outside producers: Keith Olsen (FLEETWOOD MAC) for *Terrapin Station* '77 (with horns, strings and chorus arr. by Paul Buckmaster) and Lowell George (LITTLE FEAT) for *Shakedown Street* '78. *Go To Heaven* '80 had minor hit single 'Alabama Getaway', last of 5 Hot 100 entries; 2-disc sets *Reckoning* and *Dead Set* recorded live '80, released '82. Still touring, stirring musical pot with disco beat; infl. of Lesh (experienced composer of electronic music) results in atonal aspects of jazzish improvisations. Band has kept busy and innovative in many areas: had 23 tons of equipment, large entourage from the beginning; in '74 used state-of-the-art sound system allowing them to play as loud as wanted but with excellent sound. Always had well-deserved reputation for playing benefits: spent $500,000 shipping equipment to the Great Pyramids in Egypt on best-known occasion '78, benefit for Egyptian Department of Antiquities. Splinter group New Riders of the Purple Sage surfaced '70 at country rock stage, with Garcia, Dawson, Hart, Lesh, Dave Nelson; when they began to record for Columbia (later MCA) Lesh and Hart dropped out, Spencer Dryden (*b* 7 Apr. '43, NYC) added on drums; Dave Torbert, later Skip Battin (*see* BYRDS), then Stephen Love, bass; Garcia played on their debut LP '71, replaced by Buddy Cage (from Toronto) on pedal steel for albums *Powerglide* '72, *Gypsy Cowboy* and *Adventures Of Panama Red* '73, *Home, Home On The Road* '74, *Brujo* and *Oh What A Mighty Time* '75, *New Riders*

'76, *Who Are These Guys* '77, *Marin County Line* '78; *Before Time Began* '87 on Relix by the New Riders had one side of '68-9 stuff with Garcia; the other of 'backwards tapes' playing around for the category of Deadish exotica. Meanwhile Weir's solo debut was thinly disguised Dead LP *Ace*, on Garcia's solo *Garcia* he played everything except drums, and Hart made *Rolling Thunder* with Garcia, Grace Slick, Steve Stills and a horn section, all '72 on WB. Garcia made *Hooteroll?* with Howard Wales on Douglas '71, *Live At The Keystone* late '73 with Merle Saunders, solos *Compliments Of Garcia* '74 and *Reflections* '76 on Round. Hunter made *Tales Of The Great Rum Runners* '74, *Tiger Rose* '75 on Round; *Jack O'Roses* '81 on Relix. Other Round LPs/groups incl. *Old And In The Way* with Garcia, David Grisman, *Keith And Donna* (Godchaux) and *Seastones* with Lesh, all '75; *Kingfish* with Weir and *The Diga Rhythm Band* with Hart '76. Dead's labels wound up because of distribution problems; further projects: Garcia's *Cats Under The Stars* (written by Hunter), Weir's *Heaven Help The Fool* with Mydland, Bobby Cochran on guitar, both '78, and *Bobby And The Midnights* '80 with Weir, Cochran, Mydland and Billy COBHAM, all on Arista. Hart scored part of film *Apocalypse Now* '79; leftover bits using his collection of percussion instruments issued on *The Rhythm Devils Play River Music* '80 on Passport. With all this activity the band still keeps Deadheads happy and remains the largest-grossing live act in USA. *In The Dark* '87 on Arista was their first studio LP for seven years. Garcia collapsed July '86 from exhaustion, effects of weight problem and abscessed tooth, all combined to reveal unsuspected diabetes: he was grateful that he was not dead, had to rest for a while whether he liked it or not. Lesh's songwriting collaborator Bobby Peterson *d* early '87.

GRAY, Claude (*b* 26 Jan. '32, Henderson, Texas) Deep-voiced country singer, 'The Tall Texan'. Worked as radio announcer in Meridian, Miss.; had hit on D label with Willie NELSON's 'Family Bible' (no. 10 country chart '60), then chart career of 18 more country hits '61-71. On Mercury 'I'll Just Have Another Cup Of Coffee', 'My Ears Should Burn' (both top 5 '61; on Col-

umbia 'Mean Old Woman' '66; string on Decca incl. 'I Never Had The One I Wanted' '66, 'How Fast Them Trucks Can Go' '67, LPs incl. *Songs Of Broken Love Affairs* '62, *Country Goes To Town* '63 on Mercury; *Sings* '67, *The Easy Way* '68 on Decca; *Presenting Claude Gray* '75 on Million.

GRAY, Dobie (*b* Leonard Victor Ainsworth, 26 July c.'43, Brookshire, Texas) Singer. From large sharecropping family; grew up in Houston, then to West Coast seeking fortune as singer: had minor hit 'Look At Me' '63, then 'The In Crowd' (which he co-wrote) reached no. 13 USA, 25 UK: beaten in charts by Ramsey LEWIS USA, Bryan Ferry UK, but Gray sold a million; song seemed to sum up the era. He tried acting in NYC and West Coast prod. of *Hair*; joined L.A. septet Pollution (LP '71). Total of eight Hot 100 entries on five labels '63-78: 'Drift Away' was no. 5 USA '73, his only top 10 entry; 'Loving Arms' same year sold 600,000 copies but only reached no. 61; 'Out On The Floor' made charts in UK '75; 'You Can Do It' made top 40 '78. LPs incl. *Drift Away* and *Loving Arms* '73, *Hey Dixie* '74 on MCA; *New Ray Of Sunshine* '75 on Capricorn; *Midnight Diamond* '78 on Infinity was doing well when label went broke: this respected artist has suffered from that kind of luck.

GRAY, Dolores (*b* 7 June '24, Chicago) Singer, dancer, actress. Sang on Rudy VALLEE radio shows, then Wayne KING '45; starred in musical *Sweet Bye And Bye* '46 (music by Vernon DUKE, lyrics by Ogden Nash, book by S. J. Perelman and Al Hirschfield): it opened, closed during a printers' strike against NYC newspapers; no reviews appeared and good word-of-mouth couldn't save it. She starred in *Annie Get Your Gun* in London; on Broadway in *Two On The Aisle* '51, *Carnival In Flanders* '53, *Destry Rides Again* '59; films *It's Always Fair Weather*, *Kismet* '55; *The Opposite Sex* '56, *Designing Woman* '57; London revival of SONDHEIM's *Follies* '87. Own TV show early '50s; Decca singles incl. covers of hits: Jo STAFFORD's 'Shrimp Boats', Hank WILLIAMS's 'Kawliga'; LPs incl. original cast and soundtrack albums, *Warm Brandy* on Capitol. Strong voice, good showmanship always please.

GRAY, Wardell (*b* '21, Oklahoma City, Okla.; *d* 25 May '55, Las Vegas) Tenor sax. Played with Earl HINES '43-5, many others; settled on West Coast; played in NYC '48 with Benny GOODMAN, then with Count BASIE, but mostly freelanced. Began infl. by Lester YOUNG, then by bop; highly regarded and headed for stardom when found with a broken neck: drug violence suspected. Almost all recordings on West Coast, always with good sidemen; '46-50 on various labels incl. Dial (tracks with Charlie PARKER), Spotlite, Savoy; solo on 'Twisted' '49 later vocalised by Annie Ross. *Live In Hollywood* on Xanadu and *Out Of Nowhere* on Straight Ahead both made live on same date at the Haig '52; Top Rank session in Chicago '55 later on Onyx, Polydor. 2-disc compilation on Prestige, now *Memorial* in two vols. on Fantasy: *1949-53* and *1950-1*. *The Chase And The Steeple Chase* is on MCA with Dexter GORDON and Paul QUINICHETTE; in UK: 2-disc sets *Central Avenue* on RCA, *The Hunt* on Savoy with Gordon.

GRECH, Rick (*b* 1 Nov. '45, Bordeaux, France) UK bassist/violinist. Family moved to Leicester early '50s; played violin in city's youth symphony orchestra. Joined the Farinas, R&B-based band who evolved into the Roaring Sixties, then FAMILY, after singles for Fontana incl. acclaimed version of Chris Kenner's 'I Like It Like That' '65. After LPs *Music In A Doll's House* and *Family Entertainment* with Family '68-9, left on eve of group's USA tour; became least famous quarter of 'supergroup' Blind Faith, with Eric CLAPTON, Ginger BAKER, Stevie WINWOOD, name of group suggesting a certain self-doubt, justified when they split after one LP. With Baker in Air Force for unsuccessful LPs; Winwood re-formed TRAFFIC with Jim Capaldi, drums and Chris Wood, sax, who'd left Airforce with him after first LP to cut folky *John Barleycorn Must Die* '70 as trio, with Winwood doubling on bass: enticed Grech to join (with USA drummer Jim Gordon, freeing Capaldi to sing lead); sound of band, now touring proposition, captured on *Welcome To The Canteen* '71; Grech left after playing on *Low Spark Of High Heeled Boys* late '71, their move towards funky rock away from his folkish roots displeasing him; he was now an in-demand session player. Joined CRICKETS, shifting activities to USA; co-prod. *GP* '73, debut solo LP of Gram PARSONS: connection was Glen D. Hardin, ex-Cricket keyboardist who led session musicians; played on following year's *Grievous Angel*; also with all-star band for Clapton's comeback Rainbow Concert '73 (live LP issued); *The Last Five Years* '73 was a collection of his songs by previous groups. Remained in USA, in another supergroup with Mike BLOOMFIELD, Carmine APPICE, vocalist Ray Kennedy, Barry Goldberg on keyboards; bailed out with Bloomfield after '76 LP *KGB* (sold 500,000) to concentrate on 'pure country in the Gram Parsons style'; this venture called SDM (Square Dance Machine), but no success/contract forthcoming as punk took hold: not much heard since. A subtly understated player, Ric(k) (his Christian name listed both ways on countless sleeves) racked up credits from Rod STEWART to Viv Stanshall, Muddy WATERS to the BEE GEES; respected by musicians, he might have made more public impression if he had stuck to anything for more than a couple of years.

GRECO, Buddy (*b* Armando Greco, 14 Aug. '26, Philadelphia, Pa.) Pianist, arranger, composer, singer. From musical family, his father a music critic who had a radio show. Led a trio '44-9, joined Benny GOODMAN '49-52, formed own trio and became best-known to the public as a very good cabaret singer who accompanied himself. Many TV spots, own summer series; recorded with Goodman on Capitol, as solo for London, Coral (top 30 hit '51 'I Ran All The Way Home'), Kapp (LP *Broadway Melodies: Songs From The Hit Shows*); best-known work on Epic (albums *Buddy's Back In Town*, *I Like It Swinging*, *Buddy's Greatest Hits*, *Sings For Intimate Moments*) and Reprise (*With Big Bands And Ballads*, *In A Brand New Bag*, *Away We Go*). Engaging hipness and sheer talent sold albums and had cult following, but no chart action. Had minor hit with Bobby VINTON's 'Mr Lonely' '62; when Vinton did it himself '64 it made no. 1.

GREEN, Al (*b* 13 Apr. '46, Forrest City, Ark.) Soul singer, songwriter. Grew up in Grand Rapids, Mich.; sang in family gospel roup the Green Brothers all over Midwest. oined local group the Creations, some of vhom later joined Junior WALKER's All tars; others formed Hot Line Music Journal label in Detroit and signed Green as a olo. Had minor hit with 'Back Up Train' i8; 'Lovers' Hideaway' and 'Don't Hurt Me Vo More' did well on soul chart, while Guilty' and 'Hot Wire' made Hot 100 when iter reissued on Bell. Green switched to Hi ibel (distributed by Bell) for cover of EMPTATIONS' 'I Can't Get Next To You' from LP *Get Next To You* '70; single made o. 60). Wrote own million-seller 'Tired Of 8eing Alone' '71; meanwhile began writing vith Hi prod. Willie Mitchell, drummer Al ackson (*see* BOOKER T): they wrote hits Let's Stay Together' (no. 1 '71), 'Look Vhat You Done For Me', 'I'm Still In Love Vith You', 'You Ought To Be With Me', all 72; and 'Call Me' '73; Green wrote 'Here I \m' '73 with Mabon Hodges; 'Sha La La Makes Me Happy)' '75 was written by Aitchell. 14 albums also charted '71-7, incl. op 10 LPs *Let's Stay Together* and *I'm Still n Love With You*, both '72, and *Call Me* 73; first LP on Hi *Green Is Blues* charted iter, in '73; *Al Green* '72 is compilation on 8ell of '67-8 recordings. 13 top 40 singles 71-6 incl. eight gold discs adds up to nagic: Green's beautiful sweet-soul voice vas compared to that of Otis REDDING. He •ecame a clergyman, and now sings only ospel music; appeared with Patti LaBELLE 82 on Broadway in *Your Arms Too Short To 3ox With God*; LPs incl. *Higher Plane* and *Precious Lord*; *I'll Rise Again* '83 and *Trust n God* '84 on Myrrh; *He Is The Light* late 85 on A&M. 14 LPs reissued in Hi Series rom Demon in UK incl. three gospel al•ums.

GREEN, Bennie (*b* 16 Apr. '23, Chicago; *d* 23 Mar. '77) Trombone. From musical amily; brother Elbert played tenor sax with Roy ELDRIDGE. With Earl HINES '42-7 except for two years in US Army band; played vith Gene AMMONS, Charlie VENTURA, Hines combo; gigged in NYC with quintet 53-7, then less active in music for a while. Played with another quintet '68, several nonths with Duke ELLINGTON '69 incl. *Sacred Concert*, Newport Jazz Festival '69, hen played in Las Vegas show bands; Newport/NYC '72. Very highly regarded

bop-infl. musician on an instrument which became unfashionable in modern jazz; never really had his due. Played on Sep. '53 Charles MINGUS *Jazz Workshop* with Mingus, John LEWIS, Art Taylor, three other trombones: J. J. JOHNSON, Kai WINDING, Willie Dennis; on Vanguard LP *Jo Jones Special* c.'56. Own LPs incl. Prestige 2-disc compilation of sessions from '51 with Eddie DAVIS, Art BLAKEY etc. and part of '55 sessions also issued as *Bennie Green Blows His Horn*; also on Prestige: *Bennie Green With Strings* '52, *Bennie Green And Art Farmer* and *Walkin' Down*, both '56. On Blue Note: *Back On The Scene* and *Soul Stirrin'* '58, *Walkin' And Talkin'* '59. Chicago sessions '58 for Vee Jay with Sonny CLARK, Paul CHAMBERS etc. (and a vocal by Babs GONZALES) are now on Affinity UK; '59-60 sessions for several labels incl. Bethlehem; *Gliding Along* '61 on Jazzland; LP '64 for Argo/Cadet also appeared on Chess. Played on *The George Benson Cookbook*.

GREEN, Freddie (*b* Frederick William Green, 31 Mar. '11, Charleston, S.C.; *d* 1 Mar. '87, Las Vegas) Rhythm guitar. Nicknamed 'Esquire' by Buck CLAYTON; 'Pepper' by Lester YOUNG (short for 'Pepperhead', then shortened to 'Pep'); also 'Quiet Fire'. The rise of the electric guitar began with Charlie CHRISTIAN; since it has become a solo instrument, guitarists have not learned the art of keeping time as it was practised during the Big Band Era. Green was discovered at the Black Cat in Greenwich Village by John HAMMOND; auditioned for Count BASIE in his dressing room at Roseland Ballroom '37, joined that band and never left it: the last and the greatest of 4-to-the-bar rhythm guitarists; the anchor of one of the greatest rhythm sections in history (Basie, Green, Walter PAGE on bass, Jo JONES on drums). Played on virtually all Basie's records in his long career, plus many sessions with Clayton, Benny GOODMAN, Teddy WILSON, Lionel HAMPTON, Al COHN, Joe NEWMAN; on *The Jo Jones Special* '56, many more; own LP on RCA '50s. Sang 'Them There Eyes' on Young session at Commodore '38. Almost never played solo notes; never played amplified guitar, yet can be heard on most of the records: 'Basie never did play much with his left hand, so Freddie substituted for it,' said

Clayton. He played with Basie band led by Thad JONES, then Frank Foster after Basie's death; last recordings on *Diane Schuur & The Count Basie Orchestra* '87 on GRP; they dedicated the LP to 'Father Time'. Trombonist Dennis Wilson said, 'It's as if in the Bible they said, "Let there be time," and Freddie started playing.' (Quotations from an article by Eric Levin.)

GREEN, Johnny (*b* 10 Oct. '08, NYC) Composer, conductor, pianist; led own band '33-41. Collaborated with Ira GERSHWIN, Yip HARBURG, Johnny MERCER, Billy ROSE, Paul Francis Webster, others; most famous for first hit 'Coquette' '28, 'Body And Soul' and 'I'm Yours' '30 (latter a hit for Eddie FISHER '52), '(You Came Along From) Out Of Nowhere' '31, 'I Cover The Waterfront' and 'You're Mine, You' '33, 'Easy Come, Easy Go' '34 (featured in film about dance marathons *They Shoot Horses, Don't They?* '70). Much radio work, on staff at CBS '30s; settled in Hollywood '42: important role at MGM brought five Oscars; worked on films *Easter Parade* '48, *Summer Stock* '50, *An American In Paris* and *The Great Caruso* '51, *Brigadoon* '54, *High Society* '55, *Raintree County* '57, *West Side Story* '61, *Bye Bye Birdie* '63, many more. Also guest conductor of symphony orchestras.

GREEN, Lloyd (*b* 4 Oct. '37, Mobile, Ala.) Steel guitarist, one of Nashville's busiest session musicians. Began on Hawaiian guitar at 7; in teens played in bars, honky tonks in Ala. To Nashville '57, joined Faron YOUNG; next decade was on the road with George JONES, Roger MILLER, Roy DRUSKY etc. Since '64 has sessioned with Young, Elvis PRESLEY, Don WILLIAMS, Paul McCARTNEY, Charley PRIDE, the BYRDS, many others. Own records on Chart, Little Darlin', Monument, Epic etc. incl. LPs *Cool Steel Man* '67, *Mr Nashville Sound, Bar Hoppin'* and *Day For Decision* '68, *Hit Sounds* '69, *Steel Rides* '75, *Ten Shades Of Green* '76, *Stainless Steel* '77, *Steelin' Feelings* '78, *Sweets Cheeks* and *Lloyds Of Nashville* '80, *Green Velvet* '83.

GREENBAUM, Norman (*b* 20 Nov. '42, Malden, Mass.) Singer/guitarist. Began singing folk at Boston U.; moved to L.A. and formed jug band Dr West's Medicine Show

and Junk Band with Evan Engber, percussion; Bonnie Walach guitar and vocals; Jack Carrington, guitar, vocals, percussion. LP with title track 'The Eggplant That Ate Chicago' (minor hit, no. 52 '66), lightshows and makeup in live act could not resist tide of psychedelia: split '67. Solo *Spirit In The Sky* '69 on Reprise prod. by Eric Jacobsen, no. 23 LP USA; third single was title track, driven by fuzz guitar and with fashionable quasi-spiritual lyrics, was no. 3 USA, no. 1 UK (where it stayed in charts for 20 weeks), his first and last top 40 hit: remains classic of era. Follow-up single 'Canned Ham' flopped; LP *Back Home* '70 was patchy despite help from ex-CHARLATAN Dan Hicks; third and last LP *Petaluma* '72 named after area of California where he retired, became goat breeder. Doctor & The Medics covered 'Spirit In The Sky' for no. 1 hit UK '86.

GREENE, Jack (*b* Jack Henry Greene, 7 Jan. '30, Maryville, Tenn.) Country singer. The Green Giant worked in construction etc. and sang in local clubs at weekends; on radio in Knoxville, Atlanta, with Cecil Griffith & the Young 'Uns '48-9, Rhythm Ranch Boys '50, Peach Tree Cowboys '51, Harold Lee & the River Ranch Boys '52-5. Joined Ernest TUBB band on drums '62, signed to Decca '65, had long string of hits incl. five at no. 1 in country chart '66-9: 'There Goes My Everything', 'All The Time', 'You Are My Treasure', 'Until My Dreams Come True', 'Statue Of A Fool'. CMA Male Vocalist, Album, Single and Song of the Year '67 for 'There Goes My Everything'. Duets with Jeannie SEELY incl. no. 2 hit 'Wish I Didn't Have To Miss You' '69, LP same name, also *Two For The Show*. Toured extensively, visited Wembley '73, '76. Left Decca/MCA '75 when hits slowed down, remained popular touring act, came back on 2-disc set *Live At The Grand Ole Opry*, single 'The Rock I'm Leaning On' '80 on Frontline label; later on EMH Records '83-4. LPs incl. *All The Time* and *What Locks The Door* '67, *Statue Of A Fool* '69, *Lord Is That Me* '70, *There's A Whole Lot About A Woman* '71, *Greene Country* '72, *Best Of* '76, *Yours For The Taking* '80.

GREENWICH, Ellie (*b* 23 Oct. '40, Brooklyn) Composer, producer, performer: the only rival to Carole KING as the most infl. female in '60s pop. She recorded her own songs as Ellie Gay, Ellie Gee and the Jets; then became part of the BRILL BUILDING fraternity: she had success with various collaborators (hits for the Exciters, Darlene LOVE, BOBB B SOXX etc.) but teamed professionally and personally with Jeff BARRY; they had a conveyor belt of hits, mostly for Phil SPECTOR's Philles label: for the CRYSTALS ('Da Do Ron Ron', 'Then He Kissed Me'), the RONETTES ('Be My Baby', 'Baby I Love You', 'I Can Hear Music'), the CHIFFONS, the SHIRELLES, Ike & Tina TURNER ('River Deep, Mountain High'), etc. Manfred MANN's 'Do Wah Diddy Diddy' was the hit version of a song they'd planned to record themselves as the Raindrops; their duo of '63-4 named after the Dee CLARK hit used overdubbing techniques to sound like a choir: five Hot 100 entries on Jubilee began with a demo of 'What A Guy', which cost $150 to make, reached top 50; the biggest was the second ('The Kind Of Boy You Can't Forget', no. 17), the third encountered consumer resistance, 'That Boy John' being released at about the time JFK was shot. Barry did not like appearing in public; he was replaced by Bobby Bosco when the Raindrops briefly toured, the lineup completed by Greenwich, her sister and another girl, though their only LP showed only three people on the cover. The Red Bird label (see LEIBER & STOLLER) turned out to be mainly an outlet for Greenwich/Barry hits, the first being the smash 'Chapel Of Love' by the DIXIE CUPS, followed by others by the Jelly Beans, the SHANGRI LAS and the Butterflys. They divorced '65 but continued working together, taking young Neil DIAMOND under their wing: his early hits on Bang were written and/or produced by them. Ellie resisted transfer to the West Coast when Jeff was offered a lucrative deal there and they subsequently worked together less. She concentrated on jingles in the '70s, also sessioned as a singer on other people's records (BLONDIE, Dusty SPRINGFIELD, Cyndi LAUPER etc.). She also released solo LPs of her material: *Ellie Greenwich Composes, Produces And Sings* (UA '67) and *Let It Be Written, Let It Be Sung* (MGM '73, now on Verve/Polydor). She re-emerged as a songwriter in the '80s with new partners (Ellen Foley incl. her songs in *Another Breath* '83, prod. by Vini Poncia);

she played herself in an off-Broadway musical *Leader Of The Pack* (after '64 Shangri Las hit); when it transferred to Broadway, the theatre was just around the corner from the Brill Building.

GREGORY, Johnny (*b* John Gregori, 12 Oct. c.'28) UK violinist, arranger, bandleader. Father was Frank Gregori, who led the band at the posh London restaurant Quaglino's for 10 years. Worked in father's band at London Normandy Hotel in teens, then arranger as well as freelance in clubs. As arranger on records e.g. on Russ Hamilton singles 'We Will Make Love' (no. 2 UK), 'Rainbow' (no. 4 USA), both '57; also with Connie FRANCIS, Matt MONRO, Cleo LAINE, Anthony NEWLEY, Nana Mouskouri and others. Her own LPs using pseudonyms (e.g. 'Nino Rico'); spectacular success leading Latin-American style big band as Chaquito: more than 20 LPs '60 to mid-'70s. Also '60 first Cascading Strings LP under own name, massive seller in Japan. Also film, TV music; broadcasting; own series with BBC Radio Orchestra '84. Many LPs incl. *The Chaquito Story, Contrasts, Golden Memories*, etc. *This Is Chaquito* '68, *TV Thrillers* '72 entered UK charts.

GREGSON, Clive (*b* 4 Jan. '55) UK singer, songwriter, guitarist. Balding former civil servant (once worked in same government department as Ian Curtis of JOY DIVISION), diehard FAIRPORT CONVENTION/Richard THOMPSON fan; formed band Any Trouble '75 in Manchester, signed to Stiff label with Phil Barnes, bass; Chris Parks, guitar; Mal Harley, drums; happy to get former Fairport and SQUEEZE producer John Wood to oversee debut LP *Where Are All The Nice Girls?* '80. Over-the-top *Melody Maker* front-page spread that year hurt band until second LP *Wheels In Motion* '81 delivered on promise, incl. clutch of folk-rockish Gregson songs, e.g. 'Trouble With Love', 'Open Fire', 'To Be A King'; good cover of Thompson's 'Dimming Of The Day'. 'Official bootleg' *Live At The Venue* '82 incl. another good cover in Bruce SPRINGSTEEN's 'Growin' Up'. To the surprise of everyone, EMI America, which had just landed David BOWIE, signed the band; *Any Trouble* '83 had personnel changes, was lacklustre despite Gregson original 'Northern Soul'; 2-disc set *Wrong End Of The Race* was better with Gregson title track and 'Coming Of Age'; good covers of 'Learning The Game', 'Baby, Now I've Found You'; reworkings of earlier Stiff stuff. Despite some success in USA band didn't hit. Gregson did solo Demon LP *Strange Persuasions* '85, sang back-up on Thompson LPs *Hand Of Kindness* '83, *Across A Crowded Room* '85; works folk clubs with singer Christine Collister: *Home And Away* '86 was concert cassette available by post with 15 songs, some previously unrecorded, 'justifying all the praise' wrote Nick Beale in *Folk Roots* when it was released on Cooking Vinyl '87 with cleaned-up balance. They gigged as Clive Gregson and Christine Collister Band '87; *Mischief* '87 on Special Delivery was an improvement technically. Gregson was also responsible for producing *Step Outside* '86 for the Oyster Band (three LPs on Pukka; second on Cooking Vinyl *Wide Blue Yonder* '87 incl. guest Collister).

GRIFF, Ray (*b* 22 Apr. '40, Vancouver, B.C., Canada) Singer, pianist, songwriter, publisher. Grew up in Winfield, Alberta; played drums in local band the Winfield Amateurs; formed own band the Blue Echoes, playing high school hops, weekend gigs, local TV; sent demos to Nashville. Johnny HORTON recorded his 'Mr Moonlight'; Jim REEVES recorded his religious song 'Where Do I Go From Here', encouraged him to come to Nashville '64; he worked in a piano factory, formed Blue Echo Music Company; Marty ROBBINS recorded 'She Means Nothing To Me Now' and Ray signed contract with RCA/Groove '65; first hit on MGM 'Your Lily White Hands' '67, biggest hit on Royal American 'The Mornin' After Baby Let Me Down' '71. Records on several labels without achieving major chart success, but he won several BMI songwriting awards; among his successes were 'Canadian Pacific' (George HAMILTON IV), 'Baby' (Wilma BURGESS), 'Step Aside' (Faron YOUNG), 'Who's Gonna Play This Old Piano' (Jerry Lee LEWIS), 'It Couldn't Have Been Any Better' (Johnny DUNCAN), and 'Where Love Begins' (Gene WATSON). Bluesy piano style; his own LPs incl. *A Ray Of Sunshine* '68, *Expressions* '75, and *Songs For Everyone*

'76, all on Dot; *The Last Of The Winfield Amateurs* '77 on Capitol; *Canada* '79 on Boot.

GRIFFIN, Johnny (*b* John Arnold Griffin III, 24 Apr. '28, Chicago) Tenor sax. Attended Du Sable High School, played with Lionel HAMPTON '45-7, others; Art BLAKEY, then Thelonious MONK '57-8; own quintet with Eddie DAVIS '60-2. Driving hard-bop player visited Europe '63, following year joined many USA jazzmen who have relocated there. Albums with Blakey incl. one on Bethlehem, *Selections From Lerner & Loewe* and *A Night In Tunisia* on RCA, *Jazz Connection* on Atlantic, all '57; also *Full House* with Wes MONTGOMERY on Riverside, *Bud In Paris* with Powell on Xanadu, many others. Single on Okeh '53 as Little Johnny Griffin and his Orchestra: 'Chicago Riffin'' and 'Flying Home' (vocal by Babs GONZALES). Own LPs began on Argo/Chess c.'56, then Blue Note: *Introducing Johnny Griffin* '56, *The Congregation* and *Blowing Session* '57, all quartet LPs except the last (with John COLTRANE and Hank MOBLEY). On Riverside/Milestone: *The Johnny Griffin Sextet* and quartet *Way Out!* '58, sextet *The Little Giant* '59, *Big Soul Band* '60 with 11 pieces, quintets *Studio Jazz Party* '60 and *Change Of Pace* '61, big band *White Gardenia* '61, small group *The Kerry Dancers* '61-2, *Grab This* '62, *Do Nothin' Till You Hear From Me* '63. Atlantic sessions with fine bop trombonist Matthew Gee (*b* 25 Nov. '25, Houston, Texas; own *Jazz By Gee* on Riverside '56) followed by 13 LPs on European and Japanese labels, all with excellent support: *Live In Tokyo* '76 with Horace PARLAN also on 2-disc Inner City set, *The Jamfs Are Coming* '77 with Art TAYLOR on Timeless, etc. Also plays on Pablo LPs made live at Montreux '75 incl. *Count Basie Jam Session* and *Dizzy Gillespie's Big 7*. Galaxy LPs began with *Return Of The Griffin* '78 with Keith COPELAND, first USA LP in 15 years; *Bush Dance* '78, *To The Ladies* '79 (incl. 'Soft And Furry', 'Honeybucket'), *Call It Whachawana* '83 with Mulgrew MILLER all made at Berkeley; *NYC Underground* '79 at Village Vanguard. *Paris Reunion Band* '86 on Sonet with Woody SHAW, others from expatriate period.

GRIFFITH, Nanci (*b* 6 July '53, Seguin, Texas, near Austin) Singer, songwriter, guitarist; one of the more exciting 'new country' artists, described in newspaper article as a 'folkabilly poet' writing 'walking novels', with an ear for dialogue and real people's lives. Her song 'Love At The Five And Dime' was no. 3 country hit by Kathy Mattea '86 on Mercury; Lynn ANDERSON covered 'Fly By Night' and 'Daddy Said'. Griffith was a schoolteacher, worked nights in bars and roadhouses until music won out; moved to Nashville. Also writes short stories and novels (*Two Of A Kind Heart* to be published '88; *Love Wore A Halo Back Before The War* to follow). LPs: *There's A Light Beyond These Woods* recorded live '77-8, *Once In A Very Blue Moon* '84 (incl. Richard DOBSON's 'Ballad Of Robin Wintersmith'; title song like others in her repertoire written by Pat Alger and Fred Koller), *The Last Of The True Believers* '85 with Nashville sidemen like Bela Fleck on banjo, Mark O'Conner on fiddle, and *Poet In My Window* '86, all on Philo; major label debut *Lone Star State Of Mind* '87 on MCA incl. title song by Alger/Koller, Christine Lavin's beautiful 'From A Distance', Paul Kennerley's 'Let It Shine on Me', her own 'Ford Econoline' (covered by Anderson '88), remake of 'There's A Light Beyond These Trees', song from first album about growing up. Toured Eire and UK '88; new album *Little Love Affairs* '88 has duet with John STEWART: she is one of those sensible artists who will record strong songs by others as well as her own, instead of feeling obliged to fill a set with half-cooked originals, so that each album is a strong set indeed.

GRIMES, Tiny (*b* Lloyd Grimes, 7 July '16, Newport News, Va.) Guitar. Began on piano '35 in Washington; pianist/dancer in NYC '38, switched to electric guitar in group Cats And A Fiddle '40-1; with Art TATUM and Slam STEWART on West Coast '41-4, group the Rocking Highlanders in NYC '44-7, touring into '50s, settled in Philadelphia, back in NYC '60. Tiny Grimes Quintet '44 with Charlie PARKER incl. 4 tracks, vocals by Grimes on 'Romance Without Finance', 'I'll Always Love You Just The Same'. Town Hall concert with other guitarists '71 on *The Guitar Album* on Columbia; own quartet LP *Pro-*

foundly Blue '73 on Muse; also *One Is Never Too Old To Swing* with Roy ELDRIDGE on Sonet UK; *Some Groovy Fours* '74 on Classic Jazz with blues pianist Lloyd Glenn (*b* 21 Nov. '09, San Antonio, Texas; *d* 23 May '85, A&R man, leader; had R&B hits on Swingtime '50-1, worked with Lowell Fulson, others).

GRISMAN, David (*b* '45, Hackensack, N.J.) Mandolinist; also other instruments, composer, leader. Played in Even Dozen Jug Band with Maria MULDAUR, John SEBASTIAN; met Jerry Garcia in San Francisco scene mid-'60s; to Boston to form rock band with Peter Rowan, who had bluegrass background (on fiddle and vocals with Bill MONROE); Earth Opera '67-9 was a noble, unsuccessful attempt at fashionable rock band (Grisman played sax). Records on Elektra incl. minor hits 'Home To You', LP *The Great American Eagle Tragedy*, both '69. They split, both sessioned, came together again '73 with Garcia in Old And In The Way (*see* GRATEFUL DEAD); Garcia's *ad hoc* group also incl. Vassar CLEMENTS. Grisman and Rowan formed Muleskinner with fiddler Richard Greene; Grisman and Greene formed The Great American Music Band (Taj MAHAL played bass); Grisman did film work; formed stringband David Grisman Quintet '77: debut LP on Kaleidoscope represents 'newgrass', but Grisman is tired of labels, calls it 'dawg music'. *Hot Dawg* '79 on Horizon label (distributed by WB) incl. Grisman compositions, Stephane GRAPPELLI tune 'Minor Swing' from his Django REINHARDT days. *David Grisman Quintet* '80 and *Mondo Mando* '81 both made Billboard LP chart, as did *Live* '81, Grisman/Grappelli duet LP. He published *Mandolin World News*, with group members contributing. Later albums: *Rounder Album*, *Mandolin Abstractions* (with Andy Statman), *Acoustic Christmas* '84, all on Rounder; *Swingin' with Svend*, *Acousticity* '86, (ASMUSSEN) '88 on MCA.

GROSSMAN, Stefan (*b* 16 Apr. '45, Brooklyn, NY) Virtuoso revivalist guitarist. Became student, champion and biographer of Rev. Gary DAVIS; also studied with Mississippi John HURT, Skip JAMES, Son HOUSE, Mance LIPSCOMB, Fred McDOWELL: studied their techniques as all-round entertainers rather than pure bluesmen, playing rag-time as much as anything, and has dedicated himself to keeping that music alive. Played in Even Dozen Jug band with Peter Siegel, with the FUGS '66, Mitch RYDER '67; worked in UK and lived in Rome, recording and publishing books on ragtime guitar, records on Transatlantic, instruction tapes on Happy Traum's Homespun Tapes. Formed Kicking Mule label with Ed Denson, recording acoustic fingerpickers incl. himself: LPs on Kicking Mule incl. *Acoustic Music, Bottleneck Serenade, Memphis Jellyroll, Hot Dogs, Yazoo Basin Boogie, Country Blues Guitar Festival; Under The Volcano* with John Renbourn (*see* PENTANGLE).

GROUNDHOGS UK blues band formed c.'63 by guitarist Tony 'T.S.' McPhee (*b* 22 Mar. '44, Lincolnshire), with Pete Cruikshank (*b* 2 July '45), bass; John Cruikshank, vocals, harmonica; Bob Hall, piano; David Boorman, drums. Backed visiting USA bluesmen, made LP with John Lee HOOKER for Xtra label (had taken name from a Hooker song), disbanded. McPhee, J. Cruikshank made two singles as Herbal Mixture with Mick Meekham, drums; McPhee played briefly with John Dummer Blues Band, then legendary Hapsash and the Coloured Coat (with Mike BATT); re-formed Groundhogs '68 with P. Cruikshank, Steve Rye, harmonica; Ken Pustelnik, drums. Blues LPs for Liberty *Scratching The Surface* '68 (prod. by Batt), *Blues Obituary* '69 (without Rye) preceded entry into progressive arena with socio-political lyrics: balding McPhee was unlikely guitar hero, but *Thank Christ For The Bomb* '70 was pushed to no. 9 in UK LP chart by appearance at that year's Isle of Wight festival; *Split* '71 made no. 5, *Who Will Save The World* '72 no. 8. Clive Brooks (ex-Egg) replaced Pustelnik for *Hogwash* '72 and *Solid* '74; *Hogging The Stage* is a live album from '70s, incl. tracks from *Live At Leeds* '71, one of those LPs which may or may not have existed: in fact it was a promo for radio stations. McPhee had also collaborated with acoustic blues singer Jo Ann Kelly late '60s, made less aggressive, more electronic album *The Two Sides Of Tony (T.S.) McPhee* '73; now he tired of Hogs' format, disbanded again to work from

home, own studio; surprised everyone by re-forming '76, with Dave Wellbeloved and Rick Adams, guitars, Martin Kent, bass; Mick Cook on drums for *Crosscut Saw* and *Black Diamond* (without Adams) '76; but rise of punk put paid to hopes. McPhee formed unsuccessful Terraplane, retired; re-formed yet again for *Razor's Edge* '84, with Alan Fish on bass, Mick Kirton on drums; incarnations threaten to make it the longest-running band since CHICKEN SHACK. Sound of Hogs not unlike BLACK SABBATH with bluesier musical base; McPhee an excellent technician but lacking wider vision. Compilation of non-vintage stuff was *Running Fast – Standing Still* '86.

GRUPO NICHE Young salsa band originating in Cali, Colombia. Leader, mus. dir. and arr. Jairo Varela also shares lead vocals, sings in chorus, plays güiro (scraper) and writes most of the songs, some referring to Cali. He shared arr. chores with Alexis Lozano early '80s, then band's sole trombonist; later LPs arr. entirely by Varela. Lineup '86 incl. pairs of trumpets, trombones, sax/flute, tres, piano, bass, timbales, congas, bongos, güiro, maracas, two lead singers and three-strong chorus. Their highly distinctive and exciting brand of salsa sometimes incl. infl. of soca; on record they are pleasingly under-produced, giving LPs the feel of live performance. LPs incl. *Querer Es Poder* '81, *Preparate . . . Grupo Niche Vol. 2* '82 on Codiscos, made in Colombia (the first incl. Varela's hit tune 'Buenaventura y Caney'; three lead singers on LP incl. black woman vocalist La Coco Lozano, who does not appear on subsequent Niche LPs). After *Niche* '83 on Niche, made in NYC, lead singer Alvaro del Castillo left to record with his own band, Orquesta la Calentura, e.g. LPs *Llegamos!* '86, *Bueno y más!* '87 on Zeida Codiscos; Lozano also left, forming Orquesta Guayacan in Bogotá, prod. their first LP *Llego la Hora de la Verdad* '86 on Latin Sound, arr. all tracks except one by Niche's pianist Nicolas Cristancho. Niche's *No Hay Quinto Malo* '84 on Codiscos, made in Colombia, regarded by some as their best; *Se Pasó!* '85 (*Triunfo* on Codiscos) made in NYC; *Me Huele a Matrimonio* '86 on Zeida Codiscos in Colombia. *15 Exitos 15* '86 on Mexican Musart label incl. shortened versions of hits from LPs. *Grupo Niche con Cuerdas* '86 on Faisan departed as title 'with strings' indicates into more production and orchestration; it works very well, incl. two new tracks and new versions (perhaps re-mixes) of songs from *Matrimonio*, done in Puerto Rico, augmented by leading P.R. trumpeters/arrangers Tommy Villariny and Edgar Nevarez.

GRYCE, Gigi (*b* 28 Nov. '27, Pensacola, Fla.; *d* 17 Mar. '83) Alto sax; also flute, piano, etc.; composer, arranger, leader. Studied composition in Boston, gigging in local groups from '46; mounted concert in Hartford with 23 pieces incl. Horace SIL-VER. Scholarship to Paris '52; worked with Max ROACH, Tadd DAMERON in USA, toured Europe with Lionel HAMPTON '53, wrote and played for Oscar PETTIFORD and led own groups incl. co-led Jazz Lab Quintet '55-8 with Donald BYRD; arr. record sessions for others incl. Clifford BROWN, Art FARMER, etc. Own records '53 on five Paris concert dates with various groups collected on Vogue, Blue Note, Prestige, etc. One side of *Jordu* '55 on Savoy by Gryce (the other by Phil WOODS) with trio tracks by Duke JORDAN, Oscar PETTIFORD, Kenny CLARKE: Gryce dubbed in later. Other LPs: tracks from three '55 dates by quartet with Percy HEATH, Art BLAKEY, Thelonious MONK and by nine-piece band (two vocals by Ernestine ANDERSON) issued on Byg, Signal, Savoy; Jazz Lab Quintet LP '57 issued on several labels; he played on *Monk's Music* '57, one of Monk's best; *Gigi Gryce Quartet* '58 on Metrojazz; quintet sets *Sayin' Something*, *The Hap'nin's*, *Rat Race Blues* '60 on Prestige; *Reminiscin'* '61 on Mercury and Trip. Best-known tune was 'Nico's Tempo'.

GUARNIERI, Johnny (*b* John Albert Guarnieri, 23 Mar. '17, NYC; *d* 7 Jan. '85, NYC) Piano, composer. Allegedly descended from famous family of violin makers; studied classical music and turned to jazz '37; played with Benny GOODMAN '39-40 (with sextet played 'A Smo-o-o-oth One', 'Air Mail Special', etc.) and Artie SHAW '40-1, playing harpsichord on Shaw's Gramercy Five sessions ('Summit Ridge Drive', 'Special Delivery Stomp', etc.). With other bandleaders; later staff work with NBC;

from '43-7 made hundreds of records with various groups (originally infl. by Earl HINES, Fats WALLER, Teddy WILSON, etc. but became versatile craftsman who could play in many styles); then with own groups on various labels through '50s; relocated to L.A. '62 and had various residencies incl. Hollywood Plaza Hotel '63-5, nearly a decade at the Tail O' The Cock in North Hollywood up until '81. Later specialised in playing in 5/4 time, performing his own piano concerto in this style '70. Toured Europe '74, '5. LPs incl. *Plays Harry Warren* on Jim Taylor Presents label; *Piano Dimensions* on Dot; *Plays Walter Donaldson* on Dobre, *Stealin' Apples* and solo *Superstride* on Taz (*Plays Fats Waller* in UK) and *Gliss Me Again* on Classic Jazz, all from mid-'70s; solo *Echoes Of Ellington* on Sounds Great (early '80s).

GUESS WHO, The Canadian rock group. Original lineup: Randy Bachman (*b* 27 Sep. '43), guitar; Garry Peterson (*b* 26 May '45), drums; Bob Ashley, bass; Chad Allan, vocal; all *b* Winnipeg. Formed early '60s as Allan and the Silvertones; later Reflections, then Expressions; sometimes with singer Carol West on stage but not on records on various Canadian labels. Changed name to Guess Who because Quality label hoped to pass them off as British; top 40 hit with cover of Johnny KIDD's 'Shakin' All Over' on Scepter label USA '65. Toured with Dick CLARK that year; Allan left to continue studies, replaced early '66 by Burton Cummings (*b* 31 Dec. '47, Winnipeg). CBC-TV show *Where It's At* from '67, Allan as host on initial series. Recorded NYC '68 with producer Jack Richardson: USA hits on RCA 'These Eyes', 'Laughing', LP *Wheatfield Soul*, all million-sellers '69. Lineup on LP: Bachman, Cummings, Peterson, Jim Kale (*b* 11 Aug. '43, Winnipeg), bass. Top 10 single 'No' Time' followed by 2-sided no. 1 'American Woman'/'No Sugar Tonight' all '70; also played White House that year. Bachman quit, formed Brave Belt with Allan (later BACHMAN-TURNER OVER-DRIVE). '71 lineup: Kale, Peterson, Cummings (vocals, sax, piano), guitarists Greg Leskiw, Kurt Winter. Further personnel changes, top 40 hits followed: 'Hand Me Down World', 'Share The Land' '70; 'Albert Flasher', 'Rain Dance' '71; gap till '74:

495

'Star Baby', 'Clap For The Wolfman', 'Dancin' Fool'. Other RCA LPs incl. *Canned Wheat Packed By The Guess Who* '69; *American Woman, Share The Land* '70; *So Long, Bannatyne* '71; *Rockin', Live At The Paramount* '72; *Artificial Paradise* (package incl. sham giveaway competition), *Road Food* '74; recruited ex-JAMES GANG guitarist Domenic Troiano; *Flavours* '74; *Power In The Music, Born In Canada* '75. Also compilation albums. Continued on club circuit North America; LP *All This For A Song* on Hilltak label '79. Songwriter Cummings had fairly successful solo career: top 40 singles 'Stand Tall' '76, 'You Saved My Soul' '81, LPs on labels incl. Hilltak.

GUITAR, Bonnie (*b* Bonnie Buckingham, 25 Mar. early '30s, Seattle, Wash.) Country singer, songwriter; also session guitarist, hence the name. Started own label Dolphin, later called Dolton, to make records for fans; signed local high school the Fleetwoods (Gary Troxel, Barbara Ellis, Gretchen Christopher, all *b* '39-40) who had national hits incl. no. 1 entries 'Come Softly To Me', 'Mr Blue', both '59; also the VENTURES, even bigger act. She sold out when her own career got under way (label ended up with Liberty, now EMI). Own song 'Dark Moon' no. 6 Billboard pop chart '57 on Dot label (beaten by Gale STORM at no. 4 on same label: Storm's last hit, Guitar's first). Had two more minor pop hits on Dot, one on Dolton; more country charts: eight top 40 country hits '66-9 incl. top tens 'I'm Living In Two Worlds' '66, 'A Woman In Love' '67, 'I Believe In Love' '68. LPs incl. *Whispering Hope* and *Moonlight* '59, *Dark Moon* '60, *Two Worlds Of Bonnie Guitar* and *Miss Bonnie Guitar* '66, *Award Winner* '67, *Affair!* '69 (all on Dot), *Allegheny* on ABC-Paramount, others on minor labels. Later country chart entries incl. 'Happy Everything' '72 on Columbia; 'Honey On The Moon' '80 on 4-Star. Others recorded her songs, incl. Eddy ARNOLD, with whom she toured in the '60s.

GUITAR SLIM (*b* Eddie Jones, 10 Dec. '26, Greenwood, Miss.; *d* 7 Feb. '59, NYC) Blues singer, guitarist. Best known of several bluesmen who used the name; 'The Things That I Used To Do' was no. 1 R&B hit '54 on Specialty: arr. by Ray CHARLES

who also played piano, remains classic blues track. He sang with conviction and was an influential pioneer on electric guitar, with a gritty tone and a flamboyant stage act: one of the first to move around the stage to limit of long lead on instrument. Died of pneumonia. Compilation LP on Ace UK.

GUN CLUB USA new wave band formed in L.A. '80 by vocalist and *Slash* (fanzine) writer Jeffrey Lee Pierce, writer Don Snowden (who left before recording) and guitarist Kid Congo (Brian Tristan). Name changed from Creeping Ritual at suggestion of Circle Jerks' Keith Morris. Congo left to join CRAMPS (but rejoined at intervals later), replaced by ex-Der Stab guitarist Ward Dotson; ex-Bags drummer Terry Graham and bassist Bob Ritter added for *Fire Of Love* '81 (on Slash's label): sound was a sort of punk/blues fusion, notably Pierce's arr. of Robert JOHNSON's 'Preaching The Blues' and 'Cool Drink Of Water'; his guitar style infl. by Television's Richard Lloyd. They were still primarily enthusiasts; Pierce had headed BLONDIE fan club, Congo the RAMONES L.A. club; but signing to Blondie guitarist Chris Stein's Animal Records for *Miami* '82 forced a more serious approach, incl. cover of CREEDENCE's 'Run Through The Jungle'. *Death Party* EP '83 also co-prod. by Stein, with new lineup of Pierce, Jim Duckworth on lead guitar, Dee Popp, drums. Pierce also played solo NYC gigs. Second LP *The Las Vegas Story* '84 on Animal had guest appearance from BLASTERS' Dave Alvin, but further personnel changes destabilised band, which broke up Dec. '84. Other members formed Fur Bible; Pierce went solo, cut *Wildweed* '85, eccentric as ever: prod. by Craig Leon (Ramones, Suicide, Blondie), backed by ex-CURE Andy Anderson, drums; ex-Man John McKenzie, bass; Murray Mitchell, sax, guitar. 5-track EP *Flamingo* same year had this band on one side, new touring group the other. New sessions in '86 prod. by Cocteau Twins prod. Robin Guthrie. Gun Club widely anthologised: posthumous issues incl. *Sex Beat* '81 on Lolita with first LP lineup, *Love Supreme* '82 on Offence, 'official' *Dance Kalimba Boom* '85 on Megadisc with *Las Vegas* lineup of Pierce, Congo, Graham, Patricia Morrison on bass; also live/studio compilations *The Birth The Death And The*

Ghost '83 on ABC, *Two Sides Of The Beast* '85 on Dojo.

GUTHRIE, Arlo (*b* 10 July '47, Coney Island, NY) Singer, guitarist, songwriter; eldest child of Woody (*see below*). Sang Woody's songs in public age 13 at Gerde's Folk City. Grew up among visitors like Jack ELLIOTT, Cisco HOUSTON, Pete SEEGER and Bob DYLAN; attended college briefly in Montana but found that he couldn't really do anything but sing: had first coffeehouse gig in Cambridge, Mass.; soon appeared at WNYC's annual Folk Song Festival (Carnegie Hall '67) hosted by Oscar BRAND: told that he had 25 minutes, he filled it up with 'Alice's Restaurant Masacree', hilarious story-song about his arrest for littering in Stockbridge, Mass. on Thanksgiving Day '65 (the offence made him ineligible for the draft). Title track of his debut LP on Reprise became an anthem of the era, once played on WBAI continuously as fundraising gimmick; turned into a film '69 by Arthur Penn (soundtrack charted, two cuts by Arlo; single 'Alice's Rock'n'Roll Restaurant' made Hot 100 same year on Reprise, with Doug KERSHAW on violin). Songbook *This Is The Arlo Guthrie Book* published '69 incl. memorabilia of Guthrie family. Other LPs on Reprise: *Arlo* '68, *Running Down The Road* '69 (incl. 'Coming Into Los Angeles', sung at Woodstock Festival), *Washington County* '70, *Hobo's Lullabye* '72 (incl. his only top 20 hit, Steve GOODMAN's 'City Of New Orleans'), *Last Of The Brooklyn Cowboys* '73 (incl. Irish jigs, reels with fiddler Kevin Burke, country songs backed by Buck OWENS band), *Arlo Guthrie* '74 (incl. 'Presidential Rag'), 2-disc *Together In Concert* (with Seeger) '75, *Amigo* '76. All these charted in Billboard. Toured with band Shenandoah '77; *Best Of* issued that year; *Arlo Guthrie With Shenandoah* '78 incl. 18-minute track 'The Story Of Reuben Clamzo & His Strange Daughter In The Key Of A'. *Outlasting The Blues* '79 also featured the band; in '79 dir. Peter Starr incl. his 'The Motorcycle Song' in animated film *No No Pickle* and other Guthrie material in award-winning semi-documentary about professional motorcycle racing *Take It To The Limit*. *Power Of Love* '81 on WB was a welcome return to the charts; 2-disc *Pre-*

cious Friend '81 with Seeger also on WB. Band now incl. son Abe on synthesiser; he also works solo or in combination with Seeger, David Blomberg, John Sebastian, Roger McGuinn, Joan BAEZ. One of his newer songs, 'Oh Mom', is about a teenager who has no use for his mother's old-fashioned (liberal) values: she is a '60s person. His biggest influences were the EVERLY Bros and the BEATLES: they each 'had a very simple-sounding musical style that's actually quite complex . . . They are deviously simple.' He rarely plays 'Alice' now, but opened with it for nostalgia at '85 revival of Newport Folk Festival; he was joined by Baez on 'City Of New Orleans' as a tribute to Goodman. Formed own label Rising Son to reissue LPs as well as soundtrack to PBS documentary *Woody Guthrie/ Hard Travelin'*. He is one of the most likeable people in music and one of the most important keepers of the folk flame, his material reflecting optimism and humour rather than gloomy protest.

GUTHRIE, Woody (*b* Woodrow Wilson Guthrie, 14 July '12, Okemah, Okla.; *d* 3 Oct. '67, Queens, NY) Singer, songwriter, guitarist; dean of American folk artists, already a legend when struck down with Huntington's chorea, an inherited, progressive wasting disease which finally killed him. Born into a pioneer family; sister killed in coal oil stove explosion, father failed in property business, mother committed to mental institution. Woody quit high school at 16 and hit the road with harmonica in his pocket. Played and sang in pool halls, on street corners, etc.; learned guitar, worked in with cousin Jack Guthrie (well-known C&W singer) in uncle Jeff Guthrie's magic shows. To West Coast '35; already writing songs which would total about 1000, incl. folk classics 'Pastures Of Plenty', 'This Land Is Your Land', 'So Long, It's Been Good To Know Ya' (later no. 6 hit '51 by Gordon JENKINS and the WEAVERS), 'This Train Is Bound For Glory', 'Roll On, Columbia', 'Reuben James' (about the sinking of a ship), etc. He often put new words to old tunes, but as a true folk artist opposed restrictions of copyright laws on his own songs as well as others. Sang on radio in L.A., Mexico; to NYC on radio's *Cavalcade Of America*, *Pipe Smoking Time*, others; recorded series of 'Dust Bowl Ballads' for Alan LOMAX's Library of Congress archive. His sympathy for the underdog led him to entertain migrant workers, union members; he wrote for Communist papers *Daily Worker* NYC, *People's World* on West Coast; his guitar carried a sign saying 'This machine kills fascists.' Back to West Coast '38, singing with Will Geer and Cisco HOUSTON on radio, in migrant camps. Mimeographed songbook *On A Slow Train Through California* discovered by Pete SEEGER. Back to NYC '40, met Seeger at concert for migrant workers; back West and commissioned to write songs for the Bonneville Power Administration: 17 recordings from May '41 rediscovered '87 to be issued on LP. Almanac Singers formed '41 NYC with Millard Lampell, Lee Hays, Seeger, others: they sang across the country, then settled in cooperative apartment house in Greenwich Village '41. Worked briefly with Headline Singers (LEADBELLY, Sonny TERRY, Brownie MCGHEE). Wrote article 'Ear Music' for magazine *Common Ground*; response led to autobiography *Bound For Glory* '43; joined Merchant Marine with Houston '43: they collected musical instruments, sang in North Africa, Sicily, UK; survived torpedo attacks. After WWII recorded hundreds of songs for Folkways label. Seriously ill from mid-'50s and bedridden in '60s; his son Arlo began performing his songs; his constant visitors incl. young Bob DYLAN. Prose/poem collection *Born To Win* published '65; *Woody Sez* '74 (from daily column for *People's World* '39-40). *Bound For Glory* filmed '77 with David Carradine as Guthrie. *Tribute To Woody Guthrie* concerts recorded at Carnegie Hall Jan. '68, Hollywood Bowl Sep. '70; incl. Dylan, Arlo, Seeger, Judy COLLINS, Richie HAVENS, Jack ELLIOTT, many others; script by Lampell from Woody's writings, actors Peter Fonda, Will Geer, Robert Ryan: 2-disc sets issued '72, one on Columbia, another on WB. Woody's own LPs: *Legendary Performer* on RCA (out of print mid-'80s); *Early Years* on Tradition; two with Houston on Stinson; *Poor Boy*, *Dust Bowl Ballads*, *This Land Is Your Land* and 2-disc *Folk Songs* on Folkways.

GUY, Buddy (*b* George Guy, 30 July '36, Lettsworth, La.) Blues singer, guitarist. Began on home-made guitar at age 13; worked in Baton Rouge area, to Chicago '57; worked outside music, then increasingly highly regarded as sideman, then in own right in modern generation of Chicago bluesmen, both as singer and guitarist; also a showman: won 'Battle of the Blues' at Blue Flame Club, 58; recorded that year with MAGIC SAM on Cobra and under own name on Artistic; house musician at Chess label from '60 (own single on Chess 'Stone Crazy' was no. 12 R&B hit '62); recorded for Argo, Arhoolie, Fontana, Atco, etc. with Junior WELLS and Otis RUSH gigs issued on Vanguard; as 'Friendly Chap' on Wells' Delmark LP *Hoodoo Man* '66, with him again on Atlantic '68, etc. Appeared in films *The Blues Is Alive And Well In Chicago* '70, BBC TV *Supershow* and *Chicago Blues* '70, French film *Out Of The Blacks And Into The Blues* '72, etc. LP with Wells *Drinkin' TNT 'n' Smokin' Dynamite* on Blind Pig label, Sonet in UK (has ROLLING STONE Bill Wyman on bass), also *Original Blues Brothers – Live* on Blue Moon UK, made in Checkerboard club, Chicago. Own LPs incl. debut *A Man And His Blues* '68, *This Is Buddy Guy*, *Hold That Plane*, *Hot And Cool* (in UK), all on Vanguard; *Buddy And The Juniors* on Blue Thumb (incl. Wells, Junior MANCE); *Stone Crazy!* on Alligator; in UK: *Breaking Out*, *DJ Play My Blues*, *The Dollar Done Fell*, all on JSP; *Buddy Guy* on Chess; *Got To Use Your House* on Blues ball; '58-64 compilation with Chicago bands incl. Rush, Otis SPANN, Sonny Boy WILLIAMSON, etc.: *In The Beginning* on Red Lightning.

H

HACKETT, Bobby (*b* Robert Leo Hackett, 31 Jan. '15, Providence, R.I.; *d* 7 June '76, Chatham, Mass.) Cornet. From large family, father was a blacksmith; first pro jobs at 14 on stringed instruments in restaurants, ballrooms; worked in Boston-area clubs with other white jazzmen of his generation such as Pee Wee RUSSELL, Eddie CONDON, Brad Gowans (trombone, clarinet, arr.; *b* 3 Dec. '03, Billerica, Mass.; *d* 8 Sep. '54, L.A.), all of whom played on his first records '38 and with Bud FREEMAN's Summa Cum Laude Orchestra '39. To NYC '37; guested at Benny GOODMAN Carnegie Hall concert '38; led own big band '39; played guitar, occasionally trumpet or cornet with Horace HEIDT '39-40, Glenn MILLER '41-2, CASA LOMA band '44-6, also staff work in network radio, revues, clubs; became better-known in '50s playing cornet solos on albums of mood music by comedian Jackie GLEASON, also making TV appearances; led own hotel sextet late '50s with arr. by Dick Cary (*b* 10 July '16, Hartford, Conn.; trumpeter was also first pianist in Louis ARMSTRONG's All-Stars '47-8). Identified as a dixieland player, a modern Bix BEIDERBECKE, but his skill transcended category: beautiful tone, good taste and lyrical ideas allowed him to play with anybody, endeared him to critics, public and musicians alike. Worked with Tony BENNETT mid-'60s; appeared on TV film *Just Jazz* '71 with Vic DICKENSON, etc.; guested with World's Greatest Jazz Band. Albums incl. *The Hackett Horn*, compilation of '38-40 from Columbia Special Products USA; *Live At The Rustic Lodge* '49 on Jass is a jam session with reedman Tony Parenti (*b* 6 Aug. 1900, New Orleans; *d* 17 Apr. '72, NYC; worked with Eddie Condon, Muggsy SPANIER, Miff Mole, etc.; recorded for Riverside); *Coast Concert* '55 (particularly fine octet set) and *Jazz Ultimate* '57, both on Capitol with Teagarden (*see* his entry); *Bixieland* with Condon on Columbia; *Live From The Voyager Room* on Shoestring (two

vols., '56-8 airchecks of sextet); *Sextet Recordings* from '62 and '70 on Storyville; four vols. of quintet *Live At The Roosevelt Grill* '70 on Chiaroscuro and *Live From Mannasas* on Jazzology, all with Dickenson; others.

HADEN, Charlie (*b* 6 Aug. '37, Shenandoah, Iowa) Bass, composer. From musically active family; emerged as modern player and composer with trad. strengths. With Art PEPPER, Paul BLEY, etc.; then several LPs with Ornette COLEMAN from '59: continued to play with him while active with Jazz Composers Orchestra and activities as diverse as *College Concert* LP on Impulse with great traditionalists Henry ALLEN and Pee Wee RUSSELL. Film work incl. *Last Tango In Paris* '72 with Gato BARBIERI. Albums with Don CHERRY, Carla BLEY (*Escalator Over The Hill*), many others. With Cherry, Ed BLACKWELL, Dewey REDMAN on ECM as Old And New Dreams. Own LPs began with *Liberation Music Orchestra* '69 on Impulse: committed music about oppression, particularly of Spanish-speaking peoples, by generals and politicians; 13-piece group incl. Roswell RUDD, Andrew CYRILLE, Cherry, Bley, Barbieri, etc. Sessions on Artists House, Horizon labels with Hampton HAWES, Keith JARRETT, Paul MOTIAN, Archie SHEPP, Cherry, Coleman; duet *Gitane* '78 on All Life with guitarist Christian Escoudé; then on ECM: *Magico* and *Folk Songs* '79, followed by more Liberation Music: *The Ballad Of The Fallen* '82, with Cherry, Bley, Redman, Motian, etc. *Quartet West* '86 on Verve, with Billy HIGGINS, Ernie Watts on sax (*b* '45, Norfolk, Va.), Alan Broadbent on piano (*b* '47, N.Z.) presents scope of diversity.

HAGAR, Sammy (*b* 13 Oct. '47, Monterey, Cal.) Heavy metal singer/guitarist. Persuaded by Elvis PRESLEY against following in father's footsteps as pro boxer; played in semi-pro bar band the Justice Brothers;

joined Montrose, band formed '73 by Ronnie Montrose, who had played with Van MORRISON, Boz SCAGGS, Edgar WINTER, turned to heavy metal: *Montrose* '73 good example of energetic USA HM of period, incl. anthemic cut 'Bad Motor Scooter'. *Paper Money* '74 not as upfront, but incl. interesting cover of ROLLING STONES' 'Connection'. Other members of group were Bill Church, bass; Denny Carmassi, drums. Hagar left after disagreements with leader, soon proved to have been underrated guitarist (not allowed to shine by Montrose): formed own band with Church, Alan Fitzgerald on keyboards; *Nine On A Ten Scale* '76 incl. 'Keep On Rockin' ', covered by Bette MIDLER in *The Rose*; after *Sammy Hagar* '77 Carmassi joined. *Musical Chairs* '78 followed by live *All Night Long* same year, incl. fine version of 'Scooter'. Good value support act for KISS, BOSTON, KANSAS, etc. *Street Machine* '79 regarded as classic of genre, but *Danger Zone* same year failed to match it; by this time band incl. Chuck Ruff on drums, Gary Pihl on guitar, Geoff Workman, keyboards: 'I've Done Everything For You' no. 36 UK '80; cover by Rick SPRINGFIELD no. 8 USA '81; also wrote title track for *Heavy Metal* animated film. Compilation *Loud And Clear* was apt description of HM singer's voice; switch from Capitol to Geffen for *Standing Hampton* '82 marked leap to headlining status; *Three Lock Box* '83 first USA top 20 LP, incl. 'Your Love Is Driving Me Crazy', no. 13 USA. Again demonstrated independence, taking time out for tour with Journey guitarist Neal Schon, recording live *Through The Fire* '84; band HGAS took initials of Hagar, Schon, Kenny Aaronson (bass) and ex-SANTANA Mike Shrieve (drums); cover of 17-year-old PROCOL HARUM hit 'Whiter Shade Of Pale' made Hot 100. Returned to studio for *Voice Of America* '84, incl. no. 38 hit 'Two Sides Of Love', 'I Can't Drive 55' best so far at no. 6. Turned back on hard-won fame '85 by joining VAN HALEN, replacing David Lee Roth: now in shadow of another major-league guitarist (Eddie Van Halen), he will probably not become bozo clone of bare-chested Roth; solo career may continue. Despite archetype HM-singer looks (mane of curls, rugged physique) Hagar is one of the few who can really sing.

HAGGARD, Merle (*b* 6 Apr. '37, Bakersfield, Cal.) Country singer, songwriter; also plays guitar and fiddle; 'the poet of the ordinary man'. Family had migrated from Oklahoma '34, like Okies in John Steinbeck novel *Grapes Of Wrath*, memorably filmed by John Ford '40, with Henry Fonda playing character who might have been Haggard's father, who died '46. Merle ran away from home '51, drifted until sent to San Quentin '58 for burglary. Paroled '60, having practised music inside; to Bakersfield, met manager Fuzzy Owen, Bonnie Campbell Owens (*b* 1 Oct. '32, Blanchard, Okla.; ex-wife of Buck OWENS), played bass in Wynn STEWART band, hits on Owens' Tally label with Stewart's 'Sing A Sad Song', Liz ANDERSON's '(From Now On All My Friends Are Gonna Be) Strangers'. Own style heavily infl. by Lefty FRIZZELL at first; had duet hit with Bonnie singing harmony 'Just Between The Two Of Us' '64; married '65, Capitol signed both of them same year. Formed band the Strangers, named after first top 10 hit. Marriage over '75, but they still sang duets for fans late '70s; meanwhile Leona Williams (*b* Leona Belle Helton, 7 Jan. '43, Vienna, Mo.) joined act, married Merle '78 (split up five years later). Recorded duet albums with both wives, but himself one of the most successful country artists of the last 20 years with over 60 hits in country chart, more than half at no. 1, his own songs among the best, incl. 'The Fugitive' (aka 'I'm A Lonesome Fugitive'); 'Branded Man', 'Mama Tried', 'Hungry Eyes', 'Workin' Man Blues', 'Okie From Muskogee' '66-9. 'Okie' also no. 41 on pop chart: thoughtful commentary on what was happening in USA at the time co-written with band on a bus in Oklahoma; soon another song ('The Fightin' Side Of Me') said about America 'If you don't love it, leave it', but did not mean that America was perfect. Several more singles crossed over to Hot 100 '70-7; 'If We Make It Through December' reached top 30; CMA named him Entertainer and Male Vocalist of the Year '70, *Okie From Muskogee* was Album of the Year; ACM named him Male Vocalist five times '66-74. 'Here Comes The Freedom Train' (not his own song) no. 10 country chart '76, bicentennial of USA. Switched to MCA '77, continued with hits 'If We're Not Back In Love By Monday' '77, 'I'm Always

On A Mountain When I Fall' '78, 'The Way I Am' '80; to Epic '82 for duet LPs with George JONES (*A Taste Of Yesterday's Wine* '82) and Willie NELSON (*Poncho & Lefty* CMA album of the year '83), solo hits 'Big City', 'That's The Way Love Goes', 'Natural High', 'Kern River' '82-5. Singles aimed at radio and juke box play: neither arrangements nor band's playing could be called adventurous, but fans listen to the words. Unusually for mainstream country artist Haggard made impact with concept LPs: *Same Train, A Different Time* '69 is tribute to Jimmie Rodgers; *A Tribute To The Best Damn Fiddle Player In The World – Bob Wills* '70 drew attention of country fans to Wills near the end of his long career; *A Land Of Many Churches* '73, *I Love Dixie Blues – New Orleans Jazz* '74, *My Love Affair With Trains* '76, *My Farewell To Elvis* '77. Over 50 albums altogether also incl. *Hag* '71, *Let Me Tell You About A Song* '73, *Keep Movin' On* '75, *Songs I'll Always Sing* '77 (two discs), *Roots Of My Raising* '77, *Way It Was In '51* '78, all on Capitol; *Serving 190 Proof* '79, *Rainbow Stew* '82 on MCA; *Songs For The Mama That Tried* '81 on MCA/Songbird; *That's The Way Love Goes* '83, *The Epic Collection* '84 (recorded live), *Kern River* '85, all on Epic. *It's All In The Game* '84 on Epic incl. 'Let's Chase Each Other Round The Room', also duets with Janie FRICKE; *Just Between The Two Of Us* '66 is duet album on Capitol with Bonnie; *Heart To Heart* with Leona on Mercury '83 in UK. Among many compilations is *Branded Man* '85 (Capitol UK) with 20 top 10 hits '65-76. *Amber Waves Of Grain* '86 on Epic recorded live in Nebraska and Indiana during USA farming crisis, 'a surefooted blend of nostalgia and righteousness' (Simon Frith); *Walking The Line* '87 a compilation of various duet and solo tracks by Haggard, Nelson and Jones; *Seashores Of Old Mexico* '87 was second full duet LP with Nelson; *Chill Factor* '87 had nine of 11 songs written by Hag, Bonnie among background singers.

HAIG, Al (*b* 22 July '24, Newark, N.J.; *d* 16 Nov. '82) Piano. Played with Charlie BARNET on West Coast '45, already one of the first bop pianists, ubiquitous sideman with Charlie PARKER, Dizzy GILLESPIE, Fats NAVARRO in '40s (to France with Parker '49); then fell victim to syndrome of white musician in black music: he was accepted initially by black musicians but they felt pressure on them to hire other blacks when there were not enough jobs to go round. Haig played with Stan GETZ, Wardell GRAY, Chet BAKER in '50s, but cocktail piano gigs and periods of obscurity took over. Own small-group records '48-54 on various labels (compilations *Trio & Quintet* on Prestige; two vols. of *Meets The Master Saxes* on Spotlite, '48 tracks with Getz, Gray, Coleman HAWKINS, John HARDEE, Zoot SIMS, Allen Eager, etc.); mysterious '65 LP on obscure Mint label; then the inevitable question 'Whatever happened to Al Haig?' led to comeback: trio date *Invitation* in London with Kenny CLARKE, quartet *Special Brew* in London with old associate Jimmy Raney on guitar (*b* 20 Aug. '27, Louisville, Ky.), Haig on electric piano on some tracks, both '74, issued on Spotlite. Solo sessions *Piano Interpretations*, *Piano Time*, and *Duke 'n' Bird*, duets with bass *Interplay*, all '76, issued on Trio (Japan), Seabreeze (USA) (some solos on Spotlite LP *Solitaire*); duo, trio, quartet and quintet LPs *Serendipity*, *A Portrait Of Bud Powell*, *Manhattan Memories*, *Reminiscence*, *Plays Jerome Kern* '76-8 also variously on Trio, Seabreeze, Inner City, Interplay; *Strings Attached* '75 on Choice with Raney; '77 tracks on Columbia 2-disc collections *Bebop Piano*, *They All Played Bebop*; *Al In Paris* and *Parisian Thoroughfare* both duos with Pierre Michelot '77 on Musica; *Stablemates* '77 with UK trumpeter Jon Eardley, tenor Art Themen; *Expressly Ellington* '78 with Themen, *Quintet Of The Year Revisited* all on Spotlite. Most records since '75 feature bassist Jamil Nasser (*b* 21 June '32, Memphis), who had played with Ahmad JAMAL Trio for more than a decade from '62.

HALEY, Bill (*b* William John Clifton Haley, 6 July '25, Highland Park, Mich.; *d* 9 Feb. '81, Harlingen, Texas) Singer, guitarist, bandleader, pioneer of rock'n'roll. Toured with C&W bands, worked as DJ '49, led bands called the Four Aces of Western Swing, Down Homers, Saddlemen; signed with Philadelphia label Essex '50; recorded country songs, then covered R&B hits 'Rocket 88' (no. 1 '51 by Jackie BRENSTON), 'Rock The Joint' (no. 11 '49 by Jimmy Preston), decided that R&B-influenced dance music was the way to go. Changed name of group to Bill Haley And His Comets; his 'Crazy Man Crazy' was no. 15 hit '53 and was covered by bandleader Ralph MARTERIE, who got some juke box play and lent legitimacy to the style, regarded as a fad. Haley switched to Decca, where he was prod. by Milt Gabler, who had prod. hits by Louis JORDAN in 'jump band' style and later claimed to have pushed Haley in that direction, though it is clear he was already going there. He covered Joe TURNER's no. 2 R&B hit 'Shake Rattle And Roll' '54: no. 7 hit (with lyrics whitewashed) became his first gold disc, followed by top 20 hits 'Dim Dim The Lights', 'Mambo Rock'; 'Rock Around The Clock', recorded Apr. '54, seemed to flop, but used in film soundtrack *Blackboard Jungle* it became his only no. 1 hit '55 (no. 4 in R&B chart; his only no. 1 in UK as well), eventually sold 22 million. Next biggest was 'See You Later, Alligator' (no. 6 '56); he had 14 top 40 hits '53-8, was washed off charts by younger stars, though party music continued selling for years. Best record was uptempo instrumental 'Rudy's Rock' (no. 34 '56), with tenor sax Rudy Pompilli (*b* c.'28; *d* 5 Feb. '76); it was more exciting than the rest, which was teen-age dance fodder: anyone who already listened to country music and R&B was not impressed by R&B songs played with slapped bass and chunky country rhythm with loud backbeat. Of two LPs that charted in '56, *Rock Around The Clock* was a compilation, while *Rock'n'-Roll Stage Show* was titled as though live, but wasn't; in UK, where BBC fuelled mania for rock'n'roll by refusing to play it, the latter sold so well it made no. 30 on singles chart. Compilations still sell: several in print in USA; more in UK, where issues incl. 5-disc box on MCA and *Hillbilly Haley* on Rollercoaster label: '48-51 material 'from before it all began'. Unlikely hero was a chubby, unpretentious man with a famous 'kiss curl' on his forehead; he enjoyed his success and it was an irony that he was associated in the public mind with hoodlums (*Blackboard Jungle*) and teenagers ripping up seats in cinemas. Band appeared in films *Rock Around The Clock* and *Don't Knock The Rock*; remained more popular in UK than in USA, ultimately less influential than truer rockabillies.

HALL, Adelaide (*b* 20 Oct. c.'04, NYC) Singer. Father was music teacher at Pratt Institute; she appeared in *Shuffle Along* '21; to Europe in *Chocolate Kiddies* revue '25 ('with Josephine BAKER at one end of the line and me at the other'); *Desires Of 1927* in NYC. On the same bill with Duke ELLINGTON in NYC she was humming backstage, picked up by an open mike; Duke asked her to record: 'Blues I Love To Sing' and 'Creole Love Call' '28 with wordless vocals were landmarks in Duke's output, by then she had given up dancing to concentrate on singing. Recorded 'I Can't Give You Anything But Love' from *Blackbirds Of 1928*, thereafter associated with her. Back to Europe with *Blackbirds*; toured USA, starred in *Cotton Club Review* etc.; to Europe for the fourth time '38. Her husband Bert Hicks (*d* '63) opened clubs La Grosse Pomme in Paris, The Old Florida in London (latter bombed in the Blitz); she had radio show with Joe LOSS, lived in London ever since: re-established cabaret at posh hotels in '80s, still gigging in '88. Films incl. appearance on screen singing in Korda's *Thief Of Bagdad* '42. Recorded in London '70: *That Wonderful Adelaide Hall* on Monmouth; also compilation *There Goes That Song Again* on Decca.

HALL & OATES (*b* Daryl Hohl, 11 Oct. '48, Pottsdown, Pa.; John Oates, 7 Apr. '49, NYC) USA AOR vocal duo. Pianist Hall was Philadelphia session musician; guitarist Oates a journalism student when they met at Battle of the Bands '67 between Temptones and Masters. Group Gulliver with Hall, Tim Moore (guitar, later solo artist), Jim Helmer (drums), Tom Sellers (keyboards, bass) made eponymous LP for Elektra '69 before Oates joined; they signed as duo to Atlantic for *Whole Oates* '72, ill-conceived folkish LP largely forgotten. Prod. Arif Mardin then let Oates have his head: years of sessions in black-dominated scene had left him with love of soul music; *Abandoned Luncheonette* '73 was indistinguishable from the real thing: black group Tavares covered 'She's Gone'; 'When The Morning Comes' also outstanding. *War Babies* '74 was sci-fi concept LP using Utopia as backing group; lyrical concerns of urban life and deprivation sat uneasily with overblown prod. by Todd RUNDGREN; live act with jazz-rock backup (bassist Rick Laird, ex-Mahavishnu) was a disaster. Switch to RCA, link with prod. Chris Bond saw them combine soul vocal blend (regarded as the new RIGHTEOUS BROS by some) with pop sensibility; hits came at last: seven top 40 entries '76-9 with light, glossy pop/soul incl. delayed no. 7 with reissued 'She's Gone'; also 'Sara Smile' (no. 4), 'Rich Girl' (subject Hall's girl friend/writing partner). Yet another hiccup in direction was unsuccessful *Beauty In A Back Street* and *Along The Ledge* '77-8, leading to break with Bond; Hall made solo *Sacred Songs* with King Crimson's Robert Fripp; RCA said it was too left field but released it '80; same year duo decided to prod. themselves; *Voices* '80 was not stunning but *Private Eyes* '81 found a new consistency, helped by regular band: in Bond era they used session players, inferior people on tour; now they had Tom 'T-Bone' Wolk, on bass; Charlie DeChant, sax, keyboards; Mickey Curry, drums; G. E. Smith (ex-Scratch Band) on guitar. Most successful USA pop singles act of early '80s: 14 top 40 hits by late '84, incl. five at no. 1: 'Kiss On My List', 'Private Eyes', 'I Can't Go For That (No Can Do)', all '81; 'Maneater' '82, 'Out Of Touch' '84; singles collection *Rock'n'Soul Part 1* recommended. They crossed over frequently to black chart; enlarged credibility with *Live At The Apollo* '85, using ex-TEMPTATIONS David Ruffin and Eddie Kendricks on backing vocals, incl. Temptations medley in act. Meanwhile, Paul YOUNG had UK no. 4/USA no. 1 with Hall's 'Every Time You Go Away' (from *Voices*), raising credibility still further (but not consistent themselves in UK, where only 'I Can't Go For That', 'Maneater' have reached top 10). Hall moonlighted with Elvis COSTELLO ('The Only Flame In Town', minor USA/UK hit), prod. Diana ROSS; their *Bigbamboom* '85 was a hit; following tour of the same name they announced they would split. Hall solo *Three Hearts In The Happy Ending Machine* '86 co-prod. by EURYTHMICS' Dave Stewart, incl. UK hit 'Dreamtime'.

HALL, Edmond (*b* 15 May '01, Reserve, La.; *d* 11 Feb. '67, Boston, Mass.) Baritone sax, then mainly clarinet. Father was member of Onward Brass Band; of 3 brothers, also musicians, most prominent was Herbert (*b* 28

Mar. '07, also played reeds, still touring early '80s). Toured with territory bands to Fla., then to NYC in a band with Cootie WILLIAMS; with Claude HOPKINS '29-35, Lucky MILLINDER '36, again '37; with small groups incl. Zutty Singleton, Joe SULLIVAN, Henry ALLEN, Teddy WILSON; turned down offer from Duke ELLINGTON '42; own groups for long residencies until joining Louis ARMSTRONG's All-Stars '55-8; continued gigging, touring Europe '60s. Work with Armstrong incl. European concert LP *Ambassador Satch* '55; Blue Note records incl. Edmond Hall Celeste Quartet '41 with Meade Lux LEWIS playing celeste, Charlie CHRISTIAN, Israel Crosby on bass: 'Profoundly Blue' was one of Blue Note's first hits; his All Star Quintet '44 incl. Red NORVO, Teddy Wilson; played on Blue Note Jazzmen sessions led by himself '43, Sidney DE PARIS and James P. JOHNSON '44: all collected in Mosaic 6-disc set of *Complete Edmond Hall/James P. Johnson/Sidney De Paris/Vic Dickenson Blue Note Sessions*. Other albums: compilation *Take It Edmond Hall With Your Clarinet* '41-7 on Queen Disc; *At The Club Hangover 1954* on Storyville with Ralph Sutton Quartet.

HALL, Jim (*b* James Stanley Hall, 12 Dec. '30, Buffalo, NY) Guitarist, one of the most highly regarded in modern jazz for harmonic and rhythmic subtlety, yielding to no one in technique and swing. Played with local groups, moved to L.A. '55, played with Chico HAMILTON quintet '55-6, Jimmy GIUFFRE Trio '56-9; duo on Bill EVANS' *Undercurrents* '59 is one of his best-known LPs; backed Ella FITZGERALD '60-1, then with Sonny ROLLINS: famous quartet tracks with Rollins '62-4 reissued in 2-disc set on RCA '87; quartet tracks with Paul DESMOND '59-65 on WB and RCA compiled complete on Mosaic 6-disc set '86. Co-led quartet with Art FARMER; led own trios and did much studio work, toured the world, since '70s often appeared with Ron CARTER in duo, also played solo. First own LPs were trio sets *Jazz Guitar* '57 (with piano and bass, drums dubbed later), *Good Friday* '60 on Pacific Jazz; *Guitar Workshop* '67 (made at Berlin Jazz Festival) and *In A Sentimental Mood* '69 on Pausa (aka *It's Nice To Be With You* on MPS); quartet

Where Would I Be? '71 and duo with Carter *Alone Together* '72 on Milestone; *Concierto* '75 on CTI with Desmond, Chet BAKER, Roland Hanna on piano, Steve GADD on drums, and Carter; trio *Live!* '75 made in Toronto with Terry Clarke on drums, Don Thompson on piano, duo *Commitment* '76 with Thompson on Horizon; same trio made *Live In Tokyo* and *Jazz Impressions Of Japan* '76 on Japanese A&M; duo *Jim Hall And Red Mitchell* '78 live at Sweet Basil on Artist House; *Circles* '81 with Clarke, Thompson (bassist Rufus Reid on one track), duos *First Edition* with George SHEARING, *Live At Village West* and *Telephone* '82 with Carter, then new trio *Jim Hall's Three* '86 with Steve LaSpina on bass, Akira Tana on drums (on 'Bottlenose Blues' Hall plays 12-string guitar), all on Concord Jazz. Other LPs with Evans, etc.

HALL, Tom T. (*b* 25 May '36, Olive Hill, Ky.) Country singer, songwriter, author, TV personality. Known as The Nashville Storyteller, or the Mark Twain of Country Music: he writes about his own experiences of places, people. First band was bluegrass-styled Kentucky Travellers '52-4; worked as DJ in Roanoke, Va.; served in US Army in Europe, began writing songs and performing. Returned to work as DJ; went to Nashville '62 with songs: wrote hit 'D.J. For A Day' for Jimmy C. NEWMAN '63, then 'Mad' and 'What Are We Fighting For' for Dave DUDLEY, 'Artificial Rose' and 'Back Pocket Money' for Newman, others for Roy DRUSKY, Burl IVES, etc. Married Dixie Dean '64, who had emigrated from England '62. Signed to Mercury '67, own first hit 'I Washed My Face In The Morning Dew'; breakthrough with 'Harper Valley PTA' for Jeannie C. RILEY '68 (no. 1 pop and country hit). Own top 5 country hits with 'Ballad Of Forty Dollars' and 'Homecoming', no. 1 with 'A Week In A Country Jail' '68-9; plus 'Margie's At The Lincoln Park Inn' for Bobby BARE, 'George And The North Woods' for Dudley, 'Uptight Band' for FLATT & SCRUGGS; own hits continued with songs about ordinary people and their lives: 'The Year That Clayton Delaney Died', 'Old Dogs, Children And Watermelon Wine', 'Ravishing Ruby'. Albums on Mercury charted in Billboard's top pop LPs '71-5: *In Search Of A Song, The Rhymer And*

Other Five And Dimers, For The People In The Last Hard Town, Songs Of Fox Hollow; several singles crossed over to pop Hot 100 '71-5: 'I Love' reached no. 20 '74; 'Watergate Blues' just missed Hot 100 '73. To RCA '77 and had fewer hits, though making fine LPs, singles such as 'The Old Side Of Town' and 'Soldier Of Fortune' ('79-80). He wrote books which incl. *Why I Write Songs . . . Why You Can*, best-seller *The Story Teller's Nashville* ('79). Host of syndicated TV show *Pop Goes The Country*. Returned to Mercury and chart career took off again with hit 'Everything From Jesus To Jack Daniels', highly praised LP *The Storyteller And The Banjoman*, with Earl Scruggs. Recent hits incl. 'Famous In Missouri' and 'P.S. I Love You' '84. Other LPs incl. *Homecoming* '70, *I Witness Life* '70, *100 Children* '71, *The Storyteller* '72, *The Magnificent Music Machine* '77, *Natural Dreams* '84, *Songs In A Seashell* '85, *Best Of* sets, all on Mercury; *New Rider, Same Train* '78, *Places I've Done Time* '79, *Ol' T's In Town* '80 on RCA; *World Class Country* from period between RCA and Mercury issued on UK Range label '83.

HALLIDAY, Johnny (*b* Jean-Philippe Smet, '43, Paris) Invented French rock'n'roll '60. French mother, Belgian father; brought up by an aunt, grew up in the music hall, touring with cousin and her husband, American dancer Lee Halliday; appeared on stage at 5, made films, then inspired by Elvis PRESLEY film *Loving You* '57. Second record was a hit '60. He represents France (to the French) the same way Maurice CHEVALIER did, but he decided to be tops in France and ignore the rest of the world; he is not a rock singer at all, but with music-hall skill makes the French think he is: 'a mixture of Cliff RICHARD, LIBERACE and Tom JONES', said Jean-Bernard Hebey (DJ, now TV-radio producer). Married Sylvie Vartan, singer of Yé-Yé (mindless pop genre); they were magazine fodder until splitting '74. He has 60 gold records (100,000 copies in France); his adroit changes of style have incl. album *Hamlet – Halliday* '76, a bizarre musical version of Shakespeare, also a hit; he has filled 6500-seat Zenith concert hall in Paris for series of concerts lasting three months; the Johnny Halliday Boutique on the Left

Bank sells T-shirts, photos, jogging outfits, etc. (marketing logo is a red heart pierced with a fist). Almost no discs ever released outside France. Won praise for acting in Jean-Luc Godard film *Detective* '85; planned film about a safecracker with Costa Gavras (dir. of *Z* '68).

HAMBLEN, Stuart (*b* Carl Stuart Hamblen, 20 Oct. '08, Kellyville, Texas) Songwriter, country singer, actor, later gospel singer. Graduated from McMurray College, Abilene; moved to Southern Cal. '28, formed group to sing Western songs on radio at beginning of singing cowboy era (*see* COUNTRY MUSIC). Signed to Victor '29, joined BEVERLY HILLBILLIES '30; became top Western singer-songwriter with 'My Brown-Eyed Texas Rose', 'Out On The Texas Plains', 'Golden River', 'My Mary', etc. Appeared in cowboy films, usually as a bad guy. Had reputation as hell-raiser, but converted early '50s by a Billy Graham Revival Crusade, became gospel singer. Following hits such as 'I Won't Go Hunting With You Jake (But I'll Go Chasin' Wimmin)' and 'Remember Me (I'm The One Who Loves You)' '49-50, had lasting success with 'It Is No Secret' (incl. by Elvis PRESLEY on his *Peace In The Valley* EP '57, many other recordings), 'Open Up Your Heart (And Let The Sun Shine In)', 'This Ole House' (pop hit by Rosemary CLOONEY '54; revived UK by Shakin' STEVENS '81). Ran for President on Prohibition ticket '52, lost by 27 million votes. Had long-running syndicated radio programme *The Country Church*; LPs incl. *It Is No Secret* '54, *In The Garden* '58 on RCA; *I Believe* '60 on Columbia, *This Old House Has Got To Go* '65 on Kapp, *Cowboy Church* '74 on Word, *A Man And His Music* '75 on Lamb & Lion.

HAMILTON, Chico (*b* Foreststorn Hamilton, 21 Sep. '21, L.A.) Drums. Started on clarinet; played with schoolmates Charles MINGUS, Illinois JACQUET, Ernie Royal (*b* 2 June '21, L.A.; played trumpet with many bands incl. Count BASIE, Woody HERMAN; studio and freelance work). Worked with Lionel HAMPTON, Lester YOUNG; studied drums during WWII with Jo JONES; worked as house drummer at Billy Berg's club in Hollywood. First recorded with Slim and Slam '41; worked with Lena HORNE for

years from '48 incl. European tour; studio work incl. drumming in soundtrack of Bing CROSBY – Bob Hope *Road To Bali* '52; but meanwhile prominent in West Coast 'cool jazz' movement: with original piano-less Gerry MULLIGAN quartet '52, then own quintet '56 with Buddy COLLETTE, Jim HALL and Fred Katz on cello, featured in film *Sweet Smell Of Success* '57; other groups with Charles LLOYD, Gabor SZABO; first to employ Eric DOLPHY '58. Recorded drums solos 'Drums West' '55, 'Mr Jo Jones' '56 on World Pacific; 'Happy Little Dance', 'Trinkets', 'No Speaks No English Man' on WB '59. Music for French film *Repulsion* '65; toured with Horne again that year; by now based in NYC, successful jingle company and studio work occupied him, but began playing and touring again '70s incl. Montreux, *Reunion* TV special '75 with Collette and Katz, much other TV, film work. LPs on Pacific Jazz/World Pacific '53-8 incl. 4 trio sets, 5 quintets. With Dolphy: 2 tracks for Pacific Jazz, 2 from Newport Jazz Festival issued on Italian label, 2 LPs on WB (one with strings), all '58. Sextet on World Pacific featured Katz, Hall, Carson Smith on bass, Collette and Paul HORN, reeds; quintet sets on WB (*Gongs East* now on Discovery) and *That Hamilton Man* on Sesac (LP called *The 1959 Quintet* on Jazz Legacy and Jazz Vault) incl. Dolphy. Columbia albums '60-1 incl. Lloyd, Szabo; a Reprise album '63 was also issued on WB; 7 Impulse LPs '62-6 began with quintet with Lloyd and Szabo (*Passin' Thru* and *Man From Two Worlds* now on MCA), also incl. *The Further Adventures Of El Chico* (quintet with Charlie MARIANO and Ron CARTER plus Latin percussion), *The Dealer* (quartet with Larry CORYELL), both '66. *The Gamut* on Solid State '67 had 9-piece group incl. 4 trombones, plus vocals by Jackie Arnold; 2 more on that label '74-5 incl. *El Exigente*, also issued on Flying Dutchman. *Peregrinations* and *Chico Hamilton And The Players* on Blue Note '75-6 both incl. Arthur BLYTHE; *Reaching For The Top* '78 is on Nautilus and *Nomad* on Electra.

HAMILTON, George IV (*b* 19 July '37, Winston-Salem, N.C.) Singer; the 'International Ambassador of Country Music'. Began with hit written by John D. LOUDERMILK, fellow North Carolinian: 'A

Rose And A Baby Ruth' no. 6 pop hit while Hamilton still at University, followed by top 40 hits 'Only One Love', 'Why Don't They Understand', 'Now And For Always' '57-8 plus 'The Teen Commandments' with Paul ANKA, Johnny NASH, all on pop label ABC-Paramount; toured with EVERLY Bros, DION & THE BELMONTS, Sam COOKE, etc.; made album of Hank WILLIAMS songs *Sing Me A Sad Song*, joined Grand Ole Opry '59; 'Before This Day Ends' '60 was no. 4 in country chart. Signed to RCA by Chet AT-KINS '61, became successful pop-country singer worldwide: 'Abilene' no. 1 '63 (no. 15 pop chart); such hits as 'Fort Worth, Dallas Or Houston', 'Early Morning Rain', 'Break My Mind', 'She's A Little Bit Country' '64-70 placed him at forefront for folk-country movement with Bobby BARE, Waylon JENNINGS. Recorded more of Loudermilk's songs ('Break My Mind', 'Bad News', 'Blue Train'); chose material by writers from outside country music, such as Gordon LIGHTFOOT, Joni MITCHELL, Bob DYLAN; became immensely popular in Canada, with own TV series and several LPs recorded in North Country; popular in UK since debut there '67: first country star to have own summer season at British seaside resort. First USA country star to appear in USSR, Czechoslovakia (recorded with Czech group), host of first country festivals in Sweden, Finland, Norway, Germany, Holland; had own TV series in South Africa, New Zealand, Hong Kong. International tours sold out; albums had large worldwide sales, but popularity in USA suffered: absent from USA charts entirely after '75. Changed labels '77 to ABC-Dot; records prod. by Allen Reynolds: albums such as *Fine Lace And Homespun Cloth* '77, *Forever Young* '79 were critically praised but didn't sell well; then without a label for a while. Managed by Mervyn Conn; recordings geared to UK market where he spends much time, though still a member of Grand Ole Opry. LPs incl. *Steel Rail Blues* '66, *Folksy* '67, *In The Fourth Dimension* '68, *Canadian Pacific* '69, *Back Where It's At* '70, *West Texas Highway* '71, *Country Music In My Soul* '72, *Famous Country Music Makers* '73, *Trendsetter* '75, *George Hamilton IV Story* '76, *Back Home At The Opry* '77, *Cuttin' Across The Country* '81, all on RCA; *Feel Like A Million* '78 on Anchor; *Reflec-*

tions '79 on Lotus; *One Day At A Time* '82 on Word; *Songs For A Winter's Night* '82 on Ronco; *Music Man's Dream* '84 on Range.

HAMILTON, Jimmy (*b* 25 May '17, Dillon, S.C.) Clarinet. Studied piano, trumpet, trombone; settled on reeds. Worked for Lucky MILLINDER, Teddy WILSON, etc. then Duke ELLINGTON '43-68. Led own group, moved to the Virgin Islands; continued playing and teaching, working with Mercer ELLINGTON early '80s. Highly valued soloist with Ellington, also played tenor sax; 'Artie Shaw's rival for the loveliest clarinet sound in big band music' (G. Giddins). Featured with Ellington on '52 recording of 'The Mooche'; also on 'Air-Conditioned Jungle', 'V.I.P.'s Boogie', 'Smada', 'Flippant Flurry', introduction to 'Newport Suite' at Newport Jazz Festival '58, many more. Own LP *It's About Time* on Prestige '61; quartet *Rediscovered At The Buccaneer* '85 on Who's Who; with Alvin Batiste, John CARTER, David Murray in *Clarinet Summit* on India Navigation: live LPs '82, *Southern Belles* '88.

HAMILTON, Roy (*b* 16 Apr. '29, Leesburg, Ga.; *d* 20 July '69) Singer. Big, beautiful baritone in mould of Billy ECKSTINE, Al HIBBLER had ballad success in pop market, big infl. on following decade's soul music. With Searchlight Gospel Singers in Jersey City '48; local DJ Bill Cook became his manager and obtained contract with Epic; 'You'll Never Walk Alone' was no. 1 R&B hit '54; 'If I Loved You' and 'Ebb Tide' were top 5 same year. There were four hit versions of 'Unchained Melody' in '55 alone, written by Alex North for prison drama *Unchained* '55 (North *b* 4 Dec. '10, Chester, Pa.; film work incl. *Viva Zapata!* '52, *The Rose Tattoo* '55, *The Long Hot Summer* '58, many more; *Revue For Clarinet And Orchestra* commissioned by Benny GOODMAN); Les BAXTER instrumental was no. 1 on pop chart but Roy's (with lyrics by Hy Zaret, *b* 21 Aug. '07, NYC) was no. 4 pop and the biggest R&B record of the year. He had nine more Hot 100 entries '55-61, faded from charts; recorded for MGM, RCA, etc. Died of heart attack.

HAMILTON, Scott (*b* 12 Sept. '54, Providence, R.I.) Tenor sax. Influenced by father's record collection; played harmonica professionally at 14, took up tenor at 16, formed quartet at 18 with Chuck Riggs (drums), Chris Flory (guitar), Phil Flanigan (bass); Hamilton went to NYC '76, soon found lots of work (with Benny GOODMAN '77, again in '82); group re-formed with Norman Simmons, Mike Ledonne or usually John Bunch on piano. (Schoolmate Preston Hubbard, bassist with the FABULOUS THUNDERBIRDS, had earlier played with Hamilton for several years.) Record debut '78 as sideman on *A Tribute To Duke*, Concord Jazz LP with Bing CROSBY, Rosemary CLOONEY, Tony BENNETT, Woody HERMAN; own debut as leader *Scott Hamilton Is A Good Wind Who Is Blowing Us No Ill*: has now played on about 30 LPs on Concord. Never learned to sight-read, so 'I'm forced to do what I really like'; plays a Selmer saxophone older than he is; has become a star in today's climate of reappraisal and renewal of jazz styles, playing swing-era tenor as though nothing had happened since. Big tone, breathy on ballads like Ben WEBSTER and Paul GONSALVES (other infl. incl. Illinois JACQUET, Eddie DAVIS). Swinging good taste heard on albums by Herman, Clooney, guitarist Ed Bickert (*b* 29 Nov. '32, Manitoba), pianist Dave McKenna (*b* 30 May '30, Woonsocket, R.I.), Concord All-Stars; other LPs incl. *Scott's Buddy* and *Back To Back* with Buddy TATE, *Tour de Force* with Tate and Al COHN, *Skyscrapers* and *In New York City* with trumpeter Warren Vaché; own sets as leader: *Two, Tenorshoes, The Shining Sea, Apples And Oranges* with various artists; most recent *Close Up, In Concert, The Second Set, Scott Hamilton Quintet* '87. Label boss Carl Jefferson says 'I wish I had 50 more like him.' On other labels *Grand Appearance* and *All-Star Tenor Spectacular* on Progressive; *Bob Wilber With The Scott Hamilton Quartet* on Bodeswell; *The Swinging Young Scott Hamilton* '77 on Famous Door, with Vaché, Bunch, Butch Miles on drums, Michael Moore on bass; Bunch's Famous Door LPs as leader incl. *John's Other Bunch* '77, with Hamilton, Vaché, Connie Kay, Moore. LP with Bunch, Flory, Flanigan, Riggs plus Ruby BRAFF '86: *A Sailboat In The Moonlight* on Concord; *Mr Braff To You* on Phontastic '86 with Braff but no drums. Clarinettist Allan Vaché, younger brother

of Warren, leads quintet LP *High Speed Swing* '86 on Audiophile: the Swing Era is alive and well. *See also* Flip PHILLIPS.

HAMMER, Jan (*b* 17 Apr. '48, Prague, Czechoslovakia) Keyboards, drums, composer in fusion/AOR mode. Played with Miroslav Vitous in high school; won competition in Vienna '66, scholarship to Berklee; to USA as Russians invaded. With Mahavishnu, then Billy COBHAM's Spectrum '70-5; records with Stanley CLARKE, SANTANA (on drums), with guitarist John Abercrombie on ECM, Jeremy Steig on Capitol, Elvin JONES on Blue Note, etc. Own LPs incl. *Make Love* '68 on MPS; *The First Seven Days* '75, *Oh Yeah* '76, *Melodies* '77 on Nemperor/Atlantic; *Time Is Free* '76 on Vanguard; *Black Sheep* '78 on Asylum; *Live* with Jeff BECK '77; *Untold Passion* '82 and *Here To Stay* '83 on CBS with Neal Schon (*see* JOURNEY). Virtuosity and rare ability to make sense of rock-jazz fusion asymmetry had already established his influence when his *Miami Vice* TV theme was a no. 1 hit '85 in USA. *The Early Years* on Nemperor is compilation of '74-9 work.

HAMMOND, John (*b* John Henry Hammond, 10 Dec. '10, NYC; *d* 10 July '87, NYC) Legendary producer, mostly for labels that ended under umbrella of CBS. From wealthy family; spent pocket money on blues/jazz records as schoolboy; personal wealth was enough to allow him to freelance as producer during the Depression: first prod. was pianist Garland WILSON (12" 78s, unusual then); recorded Fletcher HENDERSON for then-independent Columbia '32; prod. Bessie SMITH's last session and Billie HOLIDAY's first '33; an early champion of Benny GOODMAN, then Count BASIE; prod. classic 'Shoe Shine Boy' small-group date in Chicago '36 with first recorded solos of Lester YOUNG: 'The studio was so small we couldn't use a bass drum because we only had one mike and I wanted Walter PAGE's bass to have its proper authority. It didn't really matter because [drummer] Jo JONES kept such perfect time . . . We cut them at 10 a.m. and it was one of the most perfect sessions I ever had.' Jones said, 'They'd never heard of anybody recording like that before. It took them hours to make four sides. We did it in an hour straight, then out, finish!' Prod. *From Spirituals To Swing* '38-9, Carnegie Hall festivals of jazz and blues stars incl. boogie-woogie pianists (Alfred Lion was inspired to form Blue Note label); concert later issued on Vanguard LPs (he'd tried to find Robert JOHNSON for the concerts, but was too late). He joined Columbia Records '39, persuaded Goodman away from Victor and Basie away from Decca; recorded Mildred BAILEY, Ray McKINLEY; shoehorned Charlie CHRISTIAN into Goodman's sextet, against Goodman's initial scepticism. Responsible for casting all-black opera *Carmen Jones*, Billy ROSE – Oscar Hammerstein prod. '43. Officer of NAACP; supported causes with left-wing political figures (Scottsboro case '31; black boys accused of rape in Tennessee); saved from harm during post-war witch-hunts by social standing, but also because he supported causes, not politics, was never a dupe; he fought even in the segregated US Army for work for black musicians. After WWII president of Keynote, then recording dir. at Majestic; went to Mercury along with these labels; successful late '40s getting Czech classical records for Mercury, but Soviet 'revolution' spoiled that. Became vice-president at Mercury, made Mitch MILLER head of A&R there; dir. of popular music at Vanguard '53-9; having attended recording session for CBS TV's *The Sound Of Jazz* '57 prod. 3-disc Mildred Bailey memorial set for Columbia, then brought back on staff there as executive producer by Goddard Lieberson, signed Ray BRYANT, Pete SEEGER, Aretha FRANKLIN, Carolyn HESTER, Bob DYLAN, George BENSON, Leonard COHEN, found Bruce SPRINGSTEEN: Dylan was called 'Hammond's folly', Aretha had to go elsewhere for sympathetic studio producers, Springsteen suffered for years from hype that had nothing to do with Hammond; but the subsequent success of all three capped his career. Ubiquitous story in London is that when he visited CBS/UK in Soho Square, reception there had never heard of him; if it isn't true it may as well be. Autobiography *John Hammond On Record* with Irving Townsend '77; awards, honours incl. special Grammy '71, two 90-minute specials *The World Of John Hammond* '75 on PBS (Dylan's first TV appearance in years).

HAMMOND, John (*b* John Paul Hammond, 13 Nov. '42, NYC) Blues guitarist, singer. Took up slide guitar mid-'50s; had scholarship to art college; switched to music, entirely self-taught. Began working solo, slavishly imitating trad. black singers of country blues; turned to electric band but has remained the most faithful of white musicians to pure blues, despite lack of financial success: he is probably the first of generations of revivalists who will play the original styles out of sheer love. Sang at Newport Folk Festival '63 while waiting for release of debut LP *John Hammond* on Vanguard; others on that label incl. *Big City Blues* '64, *So Many Roads* '65, *Country Blues* '66, *Mirrors* '67. Began playing electric blues with sidemen incl. later members of The BAND (it was while working with Hammond that they met Bob DYLAN), also briefly Jimi HENDRIX. Earliest electric work not released until switch to Atlantic for *I Can Tell* '68, *Sooner Or Later* '69, *Southern Fried* '70 (with Duane ALLMAN on some tracks). Contributed to soundtrack of Dustin Hoffman film *Little Big Man* '70, a Columbia picture: Clive DAVIS laid down rule that in order to do film score Hammond had to become Columbia artist; switched to Columbia with cooperation of Jerry Wexler at Atlantic: his father (producer John HAMMOND; see above) didn't particularly want him there, but chance to do the picture was too good to pass up. Columbia (CBS) LPs incl. *Source Point* ('71, but recorded during late Vanguard period), *I'm Satisfied* '72, *When I Need* '73. Album by short-lived *Triumvirate* with Michael BLOOMFIELD, Dr John (Mac REBENNACK); *Spirituals To Swing* '73 on Vanguard echoed father's '38 project. Other LPs on various labels incl. *Can't Beat The Kid* and *My Spanish Album* '75, *Factwork* and *Hot Tracks* '78; *Mileage* '80, *Frogs For Snakes* '82, *Live* on Rounder; 2-disc *Best Of* on Vanguard in UK *Spoonful* on Edsel, *Live* on Spindrift, *Nobody But You* '87 on Demon/Fiend. *Nobody But You* '87 has solo and combo tracks incl. Gene Taylor from the BLASTERS.

HAMPTON, Lionel (*b* 12 Apr. '13, Louisville, Ky.) Vibes, drums, piano, singer, leader. Father killed in WW1; lived in Alabama, grew up mostly in Chicago, but sent to a Catholic boys school in Kenosha, Wisconsin, where a nun taught him to play snare drum (school drum-and-bugle corps came in second in a competition at Racine, Wisconsin). Back in Chicago became newsboy because newsboy band of *Chicago Defender* marched in parades; learned marimba. Left town playing drums with any band that would have him; made first records on drums and piano '29 with Paul Howard's Quality Serenaders (band also incl. Les Hite and Lawrence BROWN). Hite formed a band soon fronted by Louis ARMSTRONG; Hampton first played vibraphone, an amplified xylophone with vibrato and sustaining capability, on 'Memories Of You' '30 with Louis. Leading own band in L.A., recorded with Benny GOODMAN, Gene KRUPA and Teddy WILSON '36; gave up band to go with Goodman: became famous, first to demonstrate use of vibes in jazz; recorded with Goodman's small groups '36-40, but also contracted by Victor subsidiary Bluebird to lead small-group pick-up sessions '37-41, intended to compete on juke-boxes with Teddy WILSON records on CBS labels: at 23 recording sessions, made nearly 100 sides of extremely high quality, using whichever musicians from Goodman, Count BASIE, Duke ELLINGTON and other bands happened to be available: among many masterpieces were 'On The Sunny Side Of The Street' with Johnny HODGES and Hampton vocal, 'I Know That You Know' from same session, 'I'm Confessin'' with Hampton vocal, all '37; '39 date with Benny CARTER yielded Carter's 'When Lights Are Low', Hampton's 'Hot Mallets', incl. tenors Chu BERRY, Coleman HAWKINS, Ben WEBSTER all on same session, plus one of Dizzy GILLESPIE's first recorded solos; 'Twelfth Street Rag' featured unique Hampton percussive two-finger piano style at furious tempo, also '39; at Hollywood date '40 with Nat COLE, Hampton played piano on 'Central Avenue Breakdown', drums on 'Jack The Bellboy'. Meanwhile organised own big band '40: had co-written 'Flying Home', recorded it for Bluebird with 10 pieces as well as with Goodman, made it into screamer with big band recording May '42 that stayed in print for many years. Album *The Mess Is Here* on Magic reissues '44-5 stuff which was probably the low point of his career, but the band was a crowd-pleaser maintained until '65 with emphasis on showmanship

and loud, exciting entertainment; jazz stars who passed through incl. Illinois JACQUET, many others. Recorded for Decca (top 10 singles 'Hey! Ba-Ba-Re-Bop' '46, 'Rag Mop' '50), for MGM, then Norman GRANZ's labels from '53; played many festivals and world tours. Reunions with Goodman incl. film *The Benny Goodman Story* '55, LP *Together Again* '63 on RCA with original quartet, with quartet again at Newport Jazz Festival '73. Led own small groups since '65 except for events such as festivals; led all-star big band at London's Capitol Jazz Festival taped for TV, made LP with it in NYC '82. Among best-loved of all jazz musicians, showmanship not obscuring percussive but pretty improvisation on ballads and never-failing swing; in '80s he was playing as well as ever. Bluebird sessions reissued complete in USA and France; other LPs incl. several on own label Glad-Hamp; Decca compilations on MCA/USA incl. 2-disc *Best Of*, *Steppin' Out*, *Hamp's Boogie-Woogie* etc.; *Leapin' With Lionel* on Affinity UK incl. hits; of many LPs on Verve only 2-disc compilation *The Blues Ain't News To Me* in USA; Polydor imports incl. *Hamptologia* (2 vols. from '51), 5-disc set on Mercury *Flying Home* '51-5; many other compilations, concerts on Timeless, Joker, Vogue, other labels demonstrate worldwide popularity; series *Lionel Hampton Presents* on Who's Who In Jazz label demonstrates versatility: incl. LPs of music by Dexter GORDON, Gerry MULLIGAN, Earl HINES, Charles MINGUS etc.; Hampton prod. and plays on all of them.

HAMPTON, Slide (*b* Locksley Wellington Hampton, 21 Apr. '32, Jeannette, Pa.) Trombone, composer. Grew up in Indianapolis; played with Lionel HAMPTON, Maynard FERGUSON; formed octet for LP on Strand late '59 with Freddie HUBBARD, Booker LITTLE, George COLEMAN; four LPs on Atlantic, one on Epic '60-2, varying personnel; worked as mus. dir. for Lloyd PRICE band; to Europe '68, toured UK with Woody HERMAN, settled in radio work in Berlin. Like Benny BAILEY, others, found more work and appreciation in Europe. Recorded with octet incl. Coleman in Paris '62; with Sacha DISTEL '68; *The Fabulous Slide Hampton Quartet* '69 on Pathé-Marconi (album *1969* issued '84 in UK).

International big bands with Bailey, John Surman, Johnny GRIFFIN, Czech bandleader Vaclav Zahradnik, etc. in Prague on Supraphon '71-2, Italy on Carosello and Horo '72, Munich on MPS '74; *World Of Trombones* '79 in NYC incl. rhythm section with Albert Dailey, nine trombones incl. Curtis FULLER. Very popular in Europe; many festivals, records as sideman (*A Day In Copenhagen* with Dexter GORDON, etc.); no records at all as leader now listed in USA Schwann catalogue.

HANCOCK, Butch (*b* George Hancock, 12 July '45, Lubbock, Texas) Singer/songwriter; guitar, harmonica. Began playing as a child; later on he dropped out of architectural school and worked for his farmer father (also named George: published *Go-Devils, Flies And Blackeyed Peas* '85, memoir of growing up on West Texas plains). Butch's muse was activated while driving tractors; infl. by rock'n'roll in the '50s, then by folk music, wrote first songs after hearing PETER, PAUL & MARY; performed locally, by '70 forming the Flatlanders in Lubbock with Joe ELY and songwriter Jimmy Gilmore; they signed with Shelby Singleton's Plantation label, made *One More Road*, unreleased until '80 on Charly UK, after Ely had become well-known. Hancock lived in an abandoned jailhouse in Clarendon, Texas '73-5, wrote innumerable songs, then relocated to Austin where he is still based. LPs on own Rainlight label began with solo set *West Texas Waltzes & Dust-Blown Tractor Tunes* '78, followed by 2-disc *The Winds Dominion* '79, backed by Ely, Gilmore, Ponty Bone (accordion), various Maines brothers, etc. Most of these helped out on *Diamond Hill* '80; then two LPs recorded on same day in '81 at the Alamo Lounge, Austin: solo set *1981: A Spare Odyssey* and *Firewater (Seeks Its Own Level)* with a band. Recording hiatus ended '85 with *Yella Rose*, with back-up vocalist Marce Lacouture, probably his most commercial (rockish) offering to date; *Split And Slide II (Apocalypse Now, Pay Later)* '86 is a solo set. (The original story of Split and Slide is on *The Winds Dominion*; they are the Gog and Magog of country rock.) Influenced by Bob DYLAN ('Who isn't?' he says cheerfully), Hancock's lyrics combine humour, carefully considered West Texas attitudes and a journalist's

perception: 'Words are visual, like architecture. You can do anything you want with 'em: you can paint with 'em, go bowlin' with 'em . . . ' (His paintings have been exhibited in Austin.) 'Standin' At The Big Hotel' covered by Jerry Jeff WALKER, 'She Never Spoke Spanish To Me' by Ely, others by Alvin Crow, Doug SAHM. In Texas Hancock's performing style has usually been folkish; gigs in London in Apr. '86, some shared with Wes McGHEE, some with a pick-up band, proved that his songs and delivery make excellent down-home rock'n'roll. Like many others nowadays, has fans all over the world who don't care about major labels or chart success.

HANCOCK, Herbie (*b* Herbert Jeffrey Hancock, 12 Apr. '40, Chicago; aka Mwandishi, Swahili name meaning 'composer') Keyboards, composer. From musical family; to NYC with Donald BYRD early '61; worked with Phil WOODS, Oliver NELSON, Eric DOLPHY; with Miles DAVIS '63-8 but also freelanced; immediately began to infl. all of pop music with Blue Note LPs: quintet LP *Takin' Off* '62 with Dexter GORDON, and Freddie HUBBARD (incl. 'Watermelon Man', no. 10 pop hit by Mongo SANTAMARIA '63) followed by all-star septet *My Point Of View* and *Inventions And Dimensions*, trio with Paul CHAMBERS and Latin percussion incl. Willie BOBO both '63 (*Dimensions* now a Pausa LP called *Succatash*). *Empyrean Isles* '64 (incl. 'Cantaloupe Island'), with Hubbard, Ron CARTER, Tony WILLIAMS, and *Maiden Voyage* '65 (added George COLEMAN to personnel, incl. title track, 'Dolphin Dance') were big sellers by jazz standards. Scored M. Antonioni film *Blow-Up* '66 (famous trendy film period-piece): arr. and cond. soundtrack LP on MGM (charted in Billboard), incl. many fine sidemen, one vocal track by the YARDBIRDS. Continued Blue Note series with *Speak Like A Child* '68 incl. 'Riot', 'The Sorcerer', pieces also performed with Davis; left Davis and began playing both electric and acoustic piano on his own records with *The Prisoner* '69. Switched to WB for *Fat Albert Rotunda* (incl. music written for Bill Cosby TV special), *Mwandishi* '70, *Crossings* '71: last two increasingly used electric instruments (mellotron, synthesiser, electric bass, etc.); featured Bennie Maupin on reeds (*b* 29 Aug. '46, Detroit; played on Davis's *Bitches Brew*, LPs on ECM, Hancock LPs up to '82). Switched to Columbia for *Sextant* '72, first pop chart entry since *Blow-Up*: with *Head Hunters* '73 (incl. no. 42 hit single 'Chameleon') and *Thrust* '74 (both at no. 13), 2-disc *Treasure Chest* (WB compilation of '69-70 material) Hancock had three albums in Billboard Top Pop LP chart '74: having helped to invent funk he reaped reward with 17 chart LPs altogether '73-84. *Dedication* '74 is a solo keyboard Japanese concert issued only on CBS/Sony in Japan. *Death Wish* '74 with big band was soundtrack for violent Charles Bronson/Michael Winner film. *V.S.O.P.* '76 made live at Newport Jazz Festival by quintet with Wayne SHORTER, Hubbard, Carter, Williams, other personnel incl. Maupin on some tracks; in '77 all-star quintet made 2-disc set at concerts in California (on Columbia); *Tempest In The Colosseum* made in Tokyo and trio set with Carter and Williams made live in San Francisco issued on CBS/Sony; studio album *Sunlight* with large orchestra incl. Hancock's synthesised vocals. Duo-piano concerts *An Evening With Herbie Hancock And Chick Corea* '78 made live in several locations; two 2-disc sets charted, one on Columbia and one on Polydor under Corea's name. *Feet Don't Fail Me Now* '78 has lots of background vocals, septet *Direct Step*, solo piano *The Piano* (both '78) and *Five Stars* '79 (by V.S.O.P. quintet) all made in Tokyo, issued on CBS/Sony, as was another trio set with Carter and Williams '81; 2-disc quartet set same year adding Wynton MARSALIS also made in Tokyo but issued more widely. *Monster, Mr Hands, Magic Windows, Lite Me Up, Future Shock, Sound System* '80-4 are more or less disco records; a clever video of 'Rockit' from *Future Shock* prod. by Godley & Creme (*see* 10CC) was extensively played on MTV cable channel (despite MTV's apparent policy of not covering black music), won awards; six chart singles in UK '78-84 incl. 'Rockit' at no. 8 '83. LP *Village Life* with Foday Suso issued '85. Some jazz fans profess to be disgusted with Hancock, but the fan can take his/her choice of many LPs, classic Blue Notes recently reissued, others (like Japanese concerts) not more widely distributed since better music simply doesn't sell as well: meanwhile it's hard to

blame Hancock for making money. He also recorded solo piano version of 'Dolphin's Dance' '82 for 2-disc Palo Alto album *A Tribute* to Bill EVANS, with 14 other pianists; also as sideman over the years with Shorter, Hubbard, Bobby HUTCHERSON, Wes MONTGOMERY, Paul DESMOND, Joe Farrell, Milt JACKSON, George BENSON, the POINTER SISTERS, Johnny NASH, Stevie WONDER, etc.; other work has incl. scores for films *Round Midnight* '86 (won an Oscar, played on soundtrack), forthcoming *Back To The Beach* with Frankie AVALON and ANNETTE Funicello (that's what it says here); also PBS TV series *Rockschool*, *Showtime Coast To Coast* TV show '87 with Joni MITCHELL, David SANBORN, Bobby MCFERRIN.

HANDY, John (*b* John Richard Handy III, 3 Feb. '33, Dallas, Texas). Alto and tenor saxophones, other instruments; also composer, educator. Not related to Captain John Handy (1900-71), well-known New Orleans musician. Played clarinet at 13, won amateur featherweight boxing championship '47, took up alto '49, studied formally. To NYC '59, recorded with Charles MINGUS '58-9 on Columbia (*Mingus Ah Um*), Atlantic, UA; worked with Randy WESTON '59, led own group, toured Europe; with Mingus at Monterey Jazz Festival '64, own quintet there '65 with violinist Michael White (incl. Handy comp. 'Spanish Lady', recorded on Columbia): from tough, hard-edged bop-infl. solos with Mingus (incl. duets with Booker ERVIN), his music became more adventurous, while he also did film, TV work, appeared with symphony orchestras, etc. as well as much teaching in various capacities since late '40s. Own LPs on Roulette '57, '59, '61; on Columbia: quintet LP with Monterey personnel '66, varying personnel '67, '68; *Hard Work* '76, *Carnival* '77 on ABC/Impulse; *Karuna Supreme* '75 and *Rainbow* '80 on MPS with Indian musicians.

HANDY, W. C. (*b* William Christopher Handy, 16 Nov. 1873, Florence, Ala.; *d* 28 Mar. '58, NYC) Songwriter and publisher; also played cornet. Was bandmaster of a minstrel show at age 22; subsequently led his own bands, founded music publishing company in Memphis c.'08 with Harry

Pace; they moved it to NYC '18. He gradually lost his sight during '30s but continued active until his death. First hit song, 'Memphis Blues' '12, was written '09 as 'Mr Crump', a mayoral campaign song for E. H. 'Boss' Crump in Memphis; other world-famous Handy songs are 'St Louis Blues' '14, 'Yellow Dog Blues' (two hit versions in USA '58), 'Beal Street Blues' '16, 'Loveless Love' '21 (better known as 'Careless Love', hit by Ray CHARLES '60-2), 'Aunt Hagar's Blues' '22; plus 'Hesitating Blues', 'Long Gone', 'Chantez-Les Bas', 'Atlanta Blues', many others. Bessie SMITH made a famous version of 'St Louis Blues' '25, with young Louis ARMSTRONG accompanying her; Fats WALLER recorded beautiful versions of 'St Louis' '26 and 'Beale Street Blues' '27 on the pipe organ, with a vocal by Alberta HUNTER on one take of Beale Street; but there are countless recordings of all these songs. Handy was delighted with Armstrong's LP *Plays W. C. Handy* '54. It used to be said that Handy's songs were not really blues, but we are less pedantic now; the middle 'tango' section of 'St Louis' is a good example of what Jelly Roll MORTON called 'the Spanish tinge': Handy used the idioms, both musical and lyrical, of black folk music, and was one of the first songwriters to use 'blue' notes (flatted thirds and sevenths). Handy published *Blues: An Anthology* '26, *Book Of Negro Spirituals* and pamphlet *Negro Authors And Composers Of The United States* '38, autobiography *Father Of The Blues* '41. Biopic *St Louis Blues* '57 with Nat 'King' COLE is regarded as dire. Blues awards in USA are named after Handy; Robert CRAY has won several recently.

HANOI ROCKS Finnish glam-rock group formed '80-1. Lineup: Gyp Casino, drums; Sam Yaffa on bass; Nasty Suicide and Andy McCoy, guitars; Mike Monroe, vocals. Styled on NEW YORK DOLLS/ALICE COOPER decadent school, music edging from ROLLING STONES-ish R&B to hard rock. Debut *Bangkok Shocks, Saigon Shakes* on Swedish Johanna label followed by *Oriental Beat*; they moved to UK, recruited new drummer Razzle (Nicholas Dingley, *b* England); *Self Destruction Blues* '82, *Back To Mystery City* '83 also available only on import outside Scandinavia, where they

topped chart with 'Love's An Injection'; third LP's collection of B-sides, singles and out-takes symptomatic of sloppy approach despite quality of best work (e.g. 'Malibu Beach Nightmare' from *Mystery City*). Gigs in UK led to CBS contract; *Two Steps From The Move* '84 (with help on lyrics from ex-MOTT THE HOOPLE frontman Ian Hunter) most polished LP yet, yielded UK near-hit cover of CREEDENCE CLEARWATER's 'Up Around The Bend', but with typical two-steps-forward-one-step-back approach, rawer live LP *All Those Wasted Years* available on another label, ironically prod. by another ex-Mott, Overend Watts. Main songwriter McCoy left '85 after death of Razzle in USA motor crash (MOTLEY CRUE's Vince Neil convicted as a result); frontman Monroe's bleached-blond good looks were band's trademark: he went solo, while McCoy took Suicide to form Cherry Bombz with ex-Toto Coelo vocalist Anita. McCoy had songs, Monroe style; title *All Those Wasted Years* sums up band tipped for superstardom more than once. *Best Of Hanoi Rocks* on Lick '85.

HARBACH, Otto (*b* 18 Aug. 1873, Salt Lake City, Utah; *d* 24 Jan. '63, NYC) Lyricist. Parents were Danish immigrants. Worked as journalist, in advertising; but chief love was Broadway since '01. Worked with Karl Hoschna (*b* 16 Aug. 1877, Bohemia; *d* 22 Dec. '11, NYC) on *Madame Sherry* '10; wrote *The Firefly* '23, *Rose-Marie* '24 with Rudolph FRIML, *The Desert Song* '26 with Sigmund ROMBERG, *Wildflower* '23 with Oscar Hammerstein II, music by Herbert Stothart (*b* 11 Sept. 1885, Milwaukee, Wis.; *d* 1 Feb '49, L.A.; mus. dir. of many shows, later at MGM; also wrote 'I Wanna Be Loved By You', 'Cuban Love Song', etc.) and Vincent YOUMANS; then with Jerome KERN: *Sunny* '25, *Criss-Cross* '26, *The Cat And The Fiddle* '31, *Roberta* '33; libretto of *Lucky* '27. Also worked with George GERSHWIN, etc.

HARBURG, Yip (*b* E. Y. Harburg, 8 Apr. 1896, NYC; *d* 5 Mar. '81, Hollywood, in car crash) Lyricist. 'Yip' was a contraction of 'yipsel', which means 'squirrel'; ASCAP gives birth date of 1896, other sources say 1898. College with Ira GERSHWIN; worked as journalist, wrote verse on the side; ran electrical business during '20s until crash in '29. Wrote 'Brother Can You Spare A Dime' with Jay Gorney (b Daniel Jayson, 12 Dec. 1896, Bialystok, Russia), 'April In Paris' with Vernon DUKE, 'It's Only A Paper Moon' with Harold ARLEN, all '32. Biggest successes were with Arlen ('Happiness Is Just A Thing Called Joe', etc.; songs for *Wizard Of Oz* film incl. 'Over The Rainbow'); worked with Jerome KERN, Sammy FAIN, others incl. Burton Lane: *Finian's Rainbow* '47 incl. 'How Are Things In Glocca Morra?'.

HARDCASTLE, Paul (b 10 Dec. '57, London) Studio genius; a back-room boy who scored with one of the '80s most insistent and unlikely hits. Began dabbling with tape recorders and synthesisers as a teenager; joined Direct Drive (signed to DJ Charlie Gillett's Oval label), then funk band First Light '82; formed own Total Control label '84; his 'Rainforest' was used as theme to a hip-hop film. He made no. 1 UK early '85 with '19', which went on to no. 1 in 13 countries: moved by TV documentary on Vietnam veterans, he used part of soundtrack on hypnotic 'scratch' single whose success coincided with tenth anniversary of war's end; set to nagging 'N-n-n-nineteen' riff (19 was the average age of soldiers in Vietnam; court case with USA broadcaster prevented the hit's release in USA, but vets took it up). Inspired cricket parody, Rory Bremner's 'Nineteen Not Out'. Then in uncomfortable position of having to follow up something unique; LP *Paul Hardcastle* '86 inevitably disappointed, merely demonstrating mastery of studio techniques. He also remixed songs for Ian DURY and Belle Stars; single 'Just For The Money' employed actors Bob Hoskins, Lord Olivier (amply covering lack of musical originality), reached an ironic no. 19 UK. 'Don't Waste My Time' was an engaging funk single featuring session singer Carol Kenyon. Also wrote new theme for UK TV's *Top Of The Pops* 'The Wizard'. He doesn't sing, will always be happier in the back room.

HARDEE, John (b 20 Dec. '18, Corsicana County, Texas; d 18 May '84, Houston) Tenor sax, infl. by Chu BERRY, Coleman HAWKINS. From musical family; began on piano at an early age, then trumpet, other instruments; picked up his uncle's C-melody sax at age 13. Wrote music for college band; toured with territory bands; finished college, worked as school bandmaster, got married and drafted, all in '41. Sat in at Duke ELLINGTON concert at Army Air Force Base in New Jersey; jammed in NYC in uniform. First recorded on Signature label '46; three dates on Blue Note during 'swingtet' era (see Ike QUEBEC), one led by Tiny GRIMES; recorded with Earl Bostic on Gotham; in '47 backed Helen HUMES on Mercury, recorded with Grimes on new Atlantic label; in '49 with Billy TAYLOR on Regal (later Savoy), but c.'48-52 were perhaps the leanest years for jazz since the Depression: Hardee went back to Texas, taught in high schools, retired '76. Gigged in Dallas all the while; played Nice Jazz Festival '75, made quartet album for Black and Blue in France, not issued. First session at Blue Note had yielded regional hit 'Tired' (instrumental version of Pearl BAILEY's first hit) backed with 'Blue Skies' on 78 issue; one of the few 78 albums issued by Blue Note was Hardee's, never forgotten by tenor fans. Savoy sides in 2-disc *The Tenor Sax Album;* Blue Note sessions reissued in 4-disc limited edition on Mosaic '84: *Complete Blue Note Forties Recordings Of Ike Quebec And John Hardee*, a fine tribute to a man who enjoyed teaching music to young people for 25 years.

HARDEN, Arlene (b 11 Mar. '45, England, Ark.) Pop-country vocalist. Member of Harden Trio with brother and sister Bobby and Robbie; trio had hit with country-rock novelty 'Tippy Toeing' '66 (no. 3 country, top 50 pop); LPs *Tippy Toeing* '66, *Sing Me Back Home* '67 on Columbia. Arlene went solo; minor hits 'He's A Good Ole Boy' '68, 'Lovin' Man' '70, 'Married To A Memory' '71, 'Would You Walk With Me, Jimmy' '73. Also recorded on Capitol, Elektra; has been regular on syndicated TV show *American Swingaround*, Porter WAGONER and Ralph Emery shows. Solo LPs incl. *Sings Roy Orbison* '70 on Columbia, *I Could Almost Say Goodbye* '75 on Capitol. Bobby Harden also recorded solo for Columbia and United Artists without much success.

HARDIN, Tim (b 23 Dec. '41, Eugene, Oregon; d 29 Dec. '80, L.A.) Singer/songwriter whose commercial success came from other artists' recordings of his songs. Following late '50s service in US Marines he drifted onto folk circuit; appearance at Newport Folk Festival '66 was well received; album *Tim Hardin* '66 demonstrated world-weary style of smoky folk. He is best-known for 'If I Were A Carpenter' (hit by the FOUR TOPS, Bobby DARIN, Johnny CASH and June Carter), 'Reason To Believe' (PETER, PAUL & MARY, Rod STEWART), 'Black Sheep Boy' (Scott WALKER), 'Hang On To A Dream' (the NICE), 'Misty Roses' (Johnny MATHIS). He moved to Woodstock late '60s; Bob DYLAN LP *John Wesley Harding* '68 widely rumoured to have been infl. by Hardin, even to have been named after an outlaw ancestor. He made an album in the early '60s released in '67 on Atco called *This Is Tim Hardin*; four eponymous numbered LPs on Verve/Forecast (no. 3 was *Live In Concert*) plus a *Best Of* '70; LPs on Columbia: ambitious *Suite For Susan Moore And Damian* '70, *Bird On A Wire* '70, *Painted Head* '73; *Archetypes* '73 on MGM; excellent *Nine* '73 on Island/Antilles. Lived in UK '70s, playing in clubs and wine bars; was considered for the role of Woody GUTHRIE in *Bound For Glory* '76; returned to USA and died of drug overdose just as a new record deal was under way with Polygram. CBS and Polygram issued memorial LPs '81-2. His own live performance of 'If I Were A Carpenter' (e.g. on an Elektra LP *Neil Bleecker & MacDougal* '65 in UK) was a hypnotic folk-blues; any comparison with hit recordings of it are almost coincidental, yet his own sales were not great.

HARDY, Françoise (*b* 17 Jan. '44, Paris) French singer, actress, model. Signed by Vogue '60; 'Tous les Garçons et les Filles' ('All The Boys And Girls'; Italian title 'Quella della mia età') was international hit '62; by '66 she was the biggest-selling French singer. She also wrote songs, played guitar, spoke several languages and was a trendsetter in Continental fashion, one of the first stars to wear her hair long and straight; she appeared in several of Roger Vadim's films; her first US production was *Grand Prix* '66. *Greatest Hits* CD on Vogue. Other UK hits 'Et Même' and 'All Over The World', no. 16 '65 her biggest.

HARGROVE, Linda (*b* 3 Feb. '50, Tallahassee, Fla.) Country singer-songwriter whose LPs failed to achieve success critics said they deserved. Played piano and French horn in her teens; joined local rock band on organ. To L.A. '70, began writing; Sandy Posey was first to record one of her songs. Contract with Pete Drake's Window Music led to more of her songs being recorded by Jan Howard, Olivia NEWTON-JOHN, etc. With Michael NESMITH wrote 'Winonah', 'I Never Loved Anyone More' etc. (latter recorded more than 40 times). Recording contract with Elektra; album *Music Is Your Mistress* '73 incl. such stunning songs as 'New York City Song', 'Don't Let It Bother You'. Continued writing good songs, made country top 40 with 'Love Was (Once Around The Dance Floor)' '75; made albums *Blue Jean Country Queen* '74 on Elektra; *Love You're The Teacher* '75, *Just Like You* '76, *Impressions* '78, all on Capitol; signed with RCA '78, made a couple of singles, became a born-again Christian and no longer sings her secular material.

HARLOW, Larry (*b* 20 Mar. '39) Jewish American bandleader who began in rock and jazz, developed passion for Cuban music after a prolonged visit in the early '60s. Third generation musician; multi-instrumentalist, playing piano, vibes, bass, reeds. Took eight months to form Orchestra Harlow; first album *Heavy Smokin'* '66 on then-new Fania label prod. by label boss/bandleader Johnny PACHECO incl. five Harlow songs in various Cuban rhythms, incl. Cuban veteran trumpeter Alfredo 'Chocolate' ARMENTEROS in horn section of two trumpets/two trombones. Next came *Bajandote – Gettin' Off* '67; in July that year began partnership with 17-year-old Puerto Rican singer Ismael Miranda (who had sung with Harlow's brother Andy's band; Larry also prod. Andy's LPs *Sorpresa la Flauta*, *La Musica Brava*, *Latin Fever* on Vaya). *El Exigente* had boogaloo hits in title track (written by Harlow and Miranda) and 'Freak Off' (by M. & J. Weinstein), era's flower-power imagery on sleeve. *Orchestra Harlow Presenta a Ismael Miranda* incl. 'La Contraria', cover of Hugh MASEKELA's hit 'Grazin' In The Grass', R&B infl. 'Horsin' Up' (a 'new' dance). First FANIA ALL STARS albums, 2-disc *Live At The Red Garter* '68, had Harlow on piano; following LPs incl. *Me And My Monkey* – *'Mi Mono y Yo'* with BEATLE cover title track and Cuban-style Latin hits like 'El Malecon'; *Electric Harlow* had Harlow on electric piano. Beginning '70s he contributed to the process of modernising the Cuban sound, leading to salsa boom: title track of *Abran Paso! Ismael Miranda con Orchestra Harlow* was 'new wave salsa' hit written by Miranda. *Tribute To Arsenio Rodriguez* '71 (celebrated Cuban *son* composer, master tres player) featured four songs by him and hit 'Arsenio' written by Harlow-Miranda in his style: album incl. Puerto Rican virtuoso guitarist Yomo Toro on tres (but his main instrument is cuarto, small 10-stringed guitar; both increasingly came to be used in salsa). *La Oportunidad – Ismael Miranda con Orchestra Harlow* '72 incl. hits 'Confidencia', 'Las Mujeres Son' and 'Señor Sereno'. Miranda went on to front Orquesta Revelacion; Harlow retired to work on *Hommy – A Latin Opera* (version of WHO's *Tommy*), premiered at Carnegie Hall March '73, co-written with Jenaro 'Heny' Alvarez; Marty Sheller shared arr. chore with Harlow and three others, shared conducting with Harlow and composed interlude music (he became infl. exposed experimental studio prod. of salsa). Harlow prod. album; show starred Celia CRUZ, Cheo FELICIANO, Justo Betancourt. *Salsa* '74 with lead vocalist Junior González was Harlow's most important and successful LP: epitome of new electric salsa sound, recognition of his arrival and Cuban infl. throughout (four Arsenio tracks incl. 'La Cartera'); it marked return to charanga sound with electric violin of Lewis Khan on 'La Cartera' and 'El Paso de Encarnacion'. *El Judio Maravilloso* '74 (The Marvellous Jew) incl. Rubén BLADES in the chorus, also violinist Pupi LEGARRETA. Reunion with Miranda for *Con Mi Viejo Amigo* '76 marked beginning of relatively static period, but good LPs incl. *La Raza Latina* '77 (attempted history of salsa), *El Albino Divino* '78 (The Divine Albino) with Nestor Sanchez singing lead role, and *Rumbambola* '79 with Harlow on full array of keyboards, updating classic Noro MORALES title tune. *Our Latin Feeling* '80 saw Harlow joined on 'Nada, Nada' by exhilarating 5-string electric violin of Alfredo de la Fé. Harlow appeared as soloist in '84 and

'86 at the Third World Music Festival of the Caribbean in Cartagena, Colombia; he met soca/calypso singer Arrow there and played on 'Colombia Rock' on his *Soca Savage* '85. Harlow's orchestra joined by new lead vocalist Ray Perez on *Señor Salsa* '85 on Tropical Budda.

HARMONICATS Harmonica trio. Jerry Murad (lead) and Al Fiore (chording) left Borrah Minevich's Harmonica Rascals (popular variety group appearing on TV well into '50s) to form Harmonicats in Chicago '44 with Don Les (bass). 'Peg O' My Heart' on obscure Vitacoustic label was surprise no. 1 hit '47 (during musicians' union strike: harmonica was not considered a musical instrument); next year they reached no. 22 with 'Hair Of Gold' on Universal; got Mercury contract: no more big hits, but singles sold well over the years: 'Malaguena', 'The Harmonica Player', 'Just One More Chance', 'Hora Staccata', etc.; also duets with Jan AUGUST. Murad published *Jerry Murad's Harmonica Technique For The Super-Chromatic*; played solo on hit record 'The Story Of Three Loves' (no. 14 '53), film theme by Miklos Rozsa: orchestra cond. by Mercury house conductor Richard Hayman (*b* 27 Mar. '20, Cambridge, Mass.) who'd spent three years with Minevich c.'40, did arranging in film studios, played own harmonica on hit 'Ruby', another '53 film theme; later cond. strings on Cannonball ADDERLEY LP. Harmonicats carried on, made LPs on Columbia; *Cherry Pink And Apple Blossom White* no. 17 LP '61; single made Hot 100 '60. Later LP was *The Love Songs Of Tom Jones*.

HARPER, Roy (*b* 12 June '41, Manchester) UK Singer/songwriter: praises sung by many contemporaries, but he has not escaped from '60s folkish image. Infl. by blues and skiffle; after a spell in RAF escaped to London, was a busker for a year. *The Sophisticated Beggar* '66 and *Come Out Fighting Ghengis Smith* '67 were quirky chronicles of the time; *Flat Baroque & Berserk* '70 was more interesting, incl. astringent 'I Hate The White Man' and 'Hell's Angels' (backed by the NICE). He was a staple of London underground and free concerts; life-long friend Jimmy Page incl. 'Hats Off To Harper' on *Led Zeppelin III* '70, has

515

guested on Harper's albums. He enjoyed fruitful collaboration with arr. David Bedford which began with *Stormcock* '71 and reached zenith with 'When An Old Cricketer Leaves The Crease' from *HQ* '75; he appeared in belated 'Swinging '60s' film *Made* '72. LP *Bullinamingvase* '77 incl. delightful 'One Of These Days In England', which had Paul and Linda McCARTNEY on backing vocals. At his disciplined best, songs contain poetic insight as well as vitriol, but he tends towards self-indulgence and has remained a cult figure. Pink Floyd incl. him as a vocalist on *Wish You Were Here* '75 and musicians such as Chris Spedding and Bill Bruford have been only too keen to play with him. *Harper 1970–1975* '75 is a valuable retrospective; *Flashes From The Archives Of Oblivion* '75 featured JETHRO TULL's Ian Anderson. Harper suffered from ill health; *The Unknown Soldier* '80 and *Work Of Heart* disappointed. Awareness Records intend making his early work available again, reissues of *Stormcock* and *Folkjokeopus* '69; *Born In Captivity* '85 showed little loss of powers; *Whatever Happened To Jugula* '85 credited Harper and Page; live *In Between Every Line* '86 followed by . . . *Descendants Of Smith* '88.

HARPERS BIZARRE USA harmony vocal/instrumental group formed San Francisco '63. First lineup: Theodore 'Ted' Templeman (*b* 24 Oct. '44), lead vocals, trumpet, drums; Dick Scoppettone (*b* 5 July '45), vocals, guitar; Dick Yount (*b* 9 Jan. '45), vocals, guitar, bass, drums; Eddie James, vocals, guitar, bass; all from Santa Cruz, Cal. First called the Tikis, were signed to Autumn label: described on the sleeve of a mid-'80s sampler of Autumn output (*The Autumn Records Story* on Edsel UK; *Nuggets Vol. 7: Early San Francisco* on Rhino USA) as 'a whitebread quartet who performed Beatle songs in bermuda shorts and madras jackets'. After mid-'60s singles e.g. 'Pay Attention To Me', 'I Must Be Dreaming', switched to Warner Bros and changed name, gaining new member, drummer John Petersen (ex-BEAU BRUMMELS, also from Autumn). First LP *Feelin' Groovy* '67 was prod. by Larry Waronker; title song (by SIMON & GARFUNKEL, aka '59th Bridge Street Song') was their only top 20 single hit. Album incl. three songs by

the then unknown Randy NEWMAN ('Simon Smith And The Amazing Dancing Bear'), 'Come To The Sunshine' by Van Dyke PARKS (with Newman and Parks playing piano here and there), 'Happy Talk' (from RODGERS & HAMMERSTEIN's *South Pacific*), etc. *Anything Goes* same year followed same formula, with more Newman and Parks, Edith PIAF's 'Milord', Doug KERSHAW's 'Louisiana Man'; title track was Cole PORTER standard, made top 50 as a single, as did follow-up cover of Glenn MILLER's 'Chattanooga Choo-Choo'. James apparently left the group; third LP *The Secret Life Of Harpers Bizarre* incl. a Newman song, oldie 'Sentimental Journey', Jimmy DRIFTWOOD's 'Battle Of New Orleans'; last LP *4* '68 incl. several originals, but also covers (BEATLES' 'Blackbird'; 'I'm Leavin' On A Jet Plane'), an Indian peyote chant and the theme song from the Peter Sellers – hash cookie movie *I Love You, Alice B. Toklas*. They were clearly trying to touch all the bases of sophistication and drug culture chic, but the LPs were not strong sellers and the last did not spawn a single: by '70 they had broken up. Templeman became a successful producer at WB (CAPTAIN BEEFHEART, LITTLE FEAT, Van MORRISON, then the DOOBIE Bros and VAN HALEN). The group re-formed for an LP '76 without Templeman and with Scoppettone on lead vocals; *As Time Goes By* appeared on The Forest Bay Co. label, where manager James Scoppettone was connected.

HARPO, Slim (*b* James Moore, 11 Jan. '24, Baton Rouge, La.; *d* there 31 Jan. '70) Harmonica, also guitar; blues singer; aka Harmonica Slim in early years. Self-taught; like others in genre worked in and out of music; in juke joints, at parties etc. Excello label had been formed '53 as subsidiary of gospel label Nashboro; first Nashville blues label didn't have many big hits, but recorded 'Baby Let's Play House' by Arthur Gunter (*b* 23 May '26, Nashville; *d* 16 Mar. '76, Port Huron, Mich.), soon covered by Elvis PRESLEY; 'Lil' Darlin'' by the Gladiolas usurped by the DIAMONDS; Excello recorded important artists in 'swamp blues', who played a traditional rural style with urban power and wrote many songs: Lonesome Sundown (singer, guitarist, pianist; *b* Cornelius Green, 12

Dec. '28, La.), Harpo, Lightnin' Slim. Harpo recorded mid-'50s with singer/ guitarist Lightnin' Slim (his brother-in-law, *b* Otis Hicks, 13 Mar. '13, St Louis, Mo.; *d* 27 July '74, Detroit); Lightnin' had R&B hit 'Rooster Blues' '59 on Excello; Harpo's best-known was 'I'm A King Bee' '57, also 'Rainin' In My Heart' '61; no. 1 on R&B chart with 'Baby Scratch My Back' '66. Harpo's wife Lovell often co-wrote songs. Compilations in USA on Excello: *Best Of Slim Harpo*, 2-disc *Knew The Blues*; also *Best Of* on Rhino; collections by both Harpo and Lightnin' Slim on Flyright, Sonet UK: Flyright's *Shake Your Hips* has 'My Little Queen Bee', 'Baby Scratch My Back'; *Knew The Blues* (one-disc edition on Sonet UK) has unique cover of Johnny CASH's 'Folsom Prison Blues'.

HARRIOTT, Joe (*b* Arthurlin Harriott, 15 July '28, Jamaica; *d* 2 Jan. '73, Southampton, England) Alto sax. Studied clarinet at boys' school, played in dance band, to UK '51; played in various jazz combos, toured UK with MJQ late '59. While in hospital '60 decided that jazz was stagnating, became determined to innovate at same time as Ornette COLEMAN was blazing new trails, but probably not infl. by him: sought in particular to invent fusion of jazz and Indian music. Records incl. quartet tracks on MGM, Melodisc, Polygon, Columbia (EMI) '53-5, all with Phil Seamen on drums; quintet sessions '59-60 issued on Columbia and Jazzland with Bobby Orr; *Freeform* '60 on Jazzland with Seamen apparently also issued on Capitol (USA) as *Abstract*. More Columbia LPs: three quintet albums '61-4; Joe Harriott/John Mayer Double Quintet sessions '65-7 with Mayer on violin, harpsichord, three Indian musicians issued on three different albums with Kenny WHEELER on some tracks, incl. 2-disc *Indo-Jazz Fusions* on EMI: there is not enough of Harriott but what there is is intriguing; he had obviously heard Eric DOLPHY. Nonet session '67 with Stan TRACEY and trumpeter Kenny Baker (*b* 1 Mar. '21, Yorkshire; played lead for Ted HEATH '46-9) issued on LP with '67 quintet date plus Lansdowne String Quartet and duet 'Abstract Doodle' with pianist Pat Smythe. Last *Hum Dono* '69 had duo, trio, quartet tracks, one with Ian CARR, one Norma Winstone vocal. All

records long out of print; he won praise from white UK jazz establishment that was then too small to support many players, let alone black innovators; was reduced to scuffling: his spiritual successor Courtney PINE looks like having more luck.

HARRIS, Barry (*b* 15 Dec. '29, Detroit, Mich.) Piano, composer. Influenced himself by Charlie PARKER, Bud POWELL, later Thelonious MONK, his crisp playing is itself an underrated infl. on his own and younger generations. Worked for Max ROACH, Cannonball ADDERLEY; moved to NYC c.'60; accompanied Coleman HAWKINS '60s; played and taught in NYC, forming club/school Jazz Cultural Center '82. Albums incl. trio *Breakin' It Up* '58 on Argo/Cadet, trios *At The Jazz Workshop* and *Preminado* '60-1 on Riverside; solo *Listen To Barry Harris* '61, quintet *Newer Than New* '61 on Riverside, sextet *Luminescence!* and *Bull's Eye* '67-8 on Prestige; eight more trio sets on Riverside, Prestige and Xanadu. *Live In Tokyo* '76 on Xanadu has Charles MCPHERSON and Jimmy Raney added on some tracks; *Plays Barry Harris* '78 is all his own tunes, incl. 'Father Flanagan', no doubt with fellow Detroiter Tommy FLANAGAN in mind. *Stay Right With It* on Milestone contains tracks from the solo LP and *Preminado*. He also contributed trio tracks to CBS 2-disc sets *I Remember Bebop* and *They All Played Bebop*.

HARRIS, Eddie (*b* 20 Oct. '36, Chicago) Tenor sax; also keyboards, reed trumpet; singer, composer. Played vibes in high school, then reeds and piano. Began recording on Vee Jay; had top 40 hit '61 with theme from film *Exodus*; Vee Jay LPs incl. *Exodus To Jazz*, *Breakfast At Tiffany's* '61; more Vee Jay records up until '63; then on Columbia: LPs with orchestra '64, quartets with Cedar WALTON, Kenny BURRELL, Ron CARTER etc. '64-5 (playing lots of film themes); then several Atlantic LPs incl. probably his best-known album: co-led Les McCANN and Eddie Harris Quintet live at Montreux '69 *Swiss Movement*; also his own *The Electrifying Eddie Harris* '67, *Live At Newport* and *Free Speech* '70, *Come On Down!* '71; *Eddie Harris In The UK* '72 with Zoot MONEY, Stevie WINWOOD, Jeff BECK, Rick Grech, Albert

517

Lee etc.; *Instant Death* '72 with Richard
ABRAMS, guitarist Ronald Muldrow; *Bad
Luck Is All I Have* '74, with Muldrow playing guitorgan, a cross between a guitar and
a Hammond organ. By this time Harris
used electronics imaginatively, incl. Var-
itone attachment to his tenor; the music
remained rock/pop oriented with jazz flavour. *That Is Why You're Overweight* '75
had large groups, back-up singers; *The Versatile Eddie Harris* '77 was smaller groups;
Playing With Myself '79 was solo LP on
RCA with Harris playing several instruments, followed by quartet sets *Exploration*
'80 on Chiaroscuro, *Sounds Incredible* on
Angelaco, both '80; *Steps Up* '81 on Danish
Steeplechase label with Tete MONTOLIU;
Eddie Who? '86 and *People Get Funny* '87 on
Timeless.

HARRIS, Emmylou (*b* 12 Apr. '49, Birmingham, Ala.) Singer, bandleader; the queen of
country rock. Began as folksinger covering
Joni MITCHELL songs in NYC '67; first LP
Gliding Bird '69 on Jubilee didn't sell (with
arr. by Ray Ellis); anyway label soon folded.
She was singing in clubs when she was
rediscovered by Gram PARSONS and Chris
Hillman; she sang with Parsons on *GP* '73
and *Grievous Angel* '74; the symmetry of
their work together is best demonstrated on
*Gram Parsons & The Fallen Angels Live
1973* (issued '82), notably on 'Love Hurts'.
After Parsons' death in '73 she emerged
virtually singlehandedly blazing the way for
a whole genre: her enchanting proper debut
Pieces Of The Sky '75 incl. tribute to him
'From Boulder To Birmingham', covers of
the BEATLES' 'For No One', Shel
Silverstein's 'Queen Of The Silver Dollar',
Dolly PARTON's 'Coat Of Many Colors';
also songs by C&W stars Merle HAGGARD
and the LOUVIN Brothers. She has continued pulling her material from wherever
she likes and making it her own, also guesting on countless fine LPs incl. Bob
DYLAN's *Desire* '75. Her *Elite Hotel* '76
incl. songs by Hank WILLIAMS, Don GIB-
SON, Buck OWENS, LENNON/McCARTNEY,
Parsons/Hillman, Rodney CROWELL; she
was also co-writing songs with Crowell and
others; the band incl. James BURTON,
Glen D. Hardin on keyboards, fiddler/ mandolinist Byron Berline, other first-class talent. By the time of *Luxury Liner* she was

fronting the aptly named Hot Band, with
Crowell, Albert Lee, Ricky Scaggs; album
incl. 'Poncho & Lefty' by Townes VAN
ZANDT, 'C'est la Vie' by Chuck BERRY.
Quarter Moon In A Ten Cent Town '78 incl.
guests Willie NELSON, The BAND's Rick
Danko and Garth Hudson, exemplary set
incl. 'Leaving Louisiana In The Broad Daylight' by Crowell and Donivan Cowart (she
guested on Crowell's sessions). Strong rumours at the time of a joint album by Harris, Linda RONSTADT and Parton were
stalled by their guest appearances on *Blue
Kentucky Girl* '79. By the end of the decade
she was obviously one of those artists whose
work will be celebrated for decades to come.
Vocally she used all of the trad. techniques
in country music with consummate
skill – the catch in the voice, the sob in the
bending of a note – yet every album
reached high in the pop LP chart (*Luxury
Liner* is the best so far at no. 21). *Roses In
The Snow* '80 incl. cover of SIMON &
GARFUNKEL's 'The Boxer'; *Light In The
Stable* '80 was Xmas album; *Evangeline* '81
was predictably charming, but her performance of Robbie Robertson's title song with
the BAND in a sequence specially shot for
The Last Waltz '78 (film and 3-disc set) was
even better. *Cimarron* '81 was inspired, incl.
Bruce SPRINGSTEEN's 'The Price You Pay';
LP also incl. work by Paul Kennerley, on
whose concept album *The Legend Of Jesse
James* '80 she guested. Live LP *Last Dance*
was a nice souvenir. In '75-6 had two entries in Hot 100 singles chart (cover of old
CHORDETTES hit 'Mr Sandman' from
Evangeline made top 40 '81), but greater
success achieved more recently in country
chart; duet with John DENVER 'Wild Montana Skies' no. 14 '83; in '84 three hits in top
30 incl. cover of Johnny ACE '55 hit 'Pledging My Love', Kennerley's beautiful 'In My
Dreams', both no. 9, both from LP *White
Shoes* '83: the usual stellar cast incl. T-Bone
BURNETT and Bonnie Bramlett; other
standout tracks incl. title song by Jack
Tempchin, Donna SUMMER's 'On The
Radio', fascinating rework of 'Diamonds
Are A Girl's Best Friend': old Jule Styne
chestnut slowed down into erotic cynicism,
effectively creating a new song (reminiscent
of Bonnie RAITT's '79 rework of 'The Boy
Can't Help It'). Concept album *The Ballad
Of Sally Rose* '85 co-written/prod. with her

by Kennerley; incl. help from Waylon JENNINGS, Parton, Ronstadt, ace session drummer Russ Kunkel, many others. *13* '86 incl. cover of Bruce Springsteen's 'My Father's House', carried on the most successful series of albums in American white popular music since those of Bob DYLAN. Long-awaited set with Parton and Ronstadt was worth waiting for: they joked about calling it *The Queenston Trio*, then *Twisted Sisters*; the beautiful *Trio* '87 was a top 5 country album in mid-'87, hit single 'Telling Me Lies' (co-written by Linda THOMPSON and Betsy Cook) was top 20 and climbing. Harris also trio'd with the JUDDS on lovely track 'The Sweetest Gift'. With the domination of 'countrypolitan' at an end (*see* COUNTRY MUSIC), Harris has been the most successful of many artists to bring country values and sounds to good songs from every genre, raising country out of the ghetto of minority musics.

HARRIS, Gene (*b* 1 Sep. '33, Benton Harbor, Mich.) Pianist, overlooked and underrated. Formed quartet the Four Sounds '57, became the Three Sounds '58; recorded for Blue Note from late '50s (albums *Black Orchids*, *Feelin' Good*, *Moods*), then on Verve c.'63 (*Anita O'Day And The Three Sounds*), Limelight '65 (*Three Moods*, *Beautiful Friendship*); back on Blue Note for seven albums '72-7 incl. *Yesterday*, *Today And Tomorrow* and *Astral Signal* with just the trio, but others were augmented; the last two *In A Special Way* and *Tone Tantrum* incl. strings, background singers, etc. Some of the albums sold well and the trio was always popular in clubs, but critics did not pay enough attention to Harris's keyboard: he may yet emerge to the fame he deserves. He had also recorded with Nat ADDERLEY on Riverside, on Blue Note with Lou DONALDSON and Stanley TURRENTINE (whose *Blue Hour* '61 with the trio was reissued '86 as a classic); Harris sets '81-2 on obscure Jazzizz and Jam labels with bassist John Heard and Jimmy Smith on drums got lost in the shuffle; played in Benny CARTER septet *A Gentleman And His Music* '85 on Concord with Smith, Scott HAMILTON, Joe WILDER; *Gene Harris Trio Plus One* '86 on Concord incl. Ray BROWN, Mickey Roker, and reunites him with Turrentine for blistering live set from NYC club. Brown,

Roker and Harris got raves at Ronnie SCOTT's Club in London Nov. '86.

HARRIS, Phil (*b* 16 Jan. '04; *d* Linton, Ind.) Bandleader, singer, actor. Grew up in Nashville, played drums with Francis CRAIG; had own bands from mid-'30s, popular with novelty vocals but also hired good musicians; used 'Rose Room' as theme. First film '33 (starring role in *Wabash Avenue* '50; later played more or less straight roles in *The High And The Mighty* '54, *The Wheeler Dealers* '63, etc.). Own radio show '34 *Let's Listen To Harris*; joined Jack Benny show '36-46: band played on each programme, and Harris had comedy role as stereotyped musician; own show '47-54 with wife Alice Faye (*b* Alice Jeanne Leppert, 5 May '12, NYC; very popular singer became famous with Rudy VALLEE in *George White's Scandals* on stage and film '30s; over 30 films incl. title role in *Lillian Russell* '40, remake of *State Fair* '62; albums incl. *In Hollywood* reissues '34-7 on Columbia, *Sings Her Famous Movie Hits* on Reprise c.'62). Harris was a natural on early TV, continuing through '60s; later did C&W material. Best-known for novelty songs on RCA in '40s: 'That's What I Like About The South', 'Woodman, Spare That Tree', 'The Preacher And The Bear'; had hits with 'Smoke! Smoke! Smoke! (That Cigarette)' '47, 'The Old Master Painter' '49, no. 1 novelty 'The Thing' '50 (jaunty mystery about what was in the box: 'You'll never get rid of the [boom-ba-boom] no matter what 'cha do'; words and music by Charles Randolph Green, based probably on a rude song). LP in USA *Coconut Grove 1932* on Sunbeam; *Best Of* on RCA International has all the novelties. Harris's comedy carried on an old tradition: 'The Preacher And The Bear' was the first record to sell two million copies and the biggest hit of the entire pre-1920 period, by Arthur Collins (*b* 7 Feb. 1864, Philadelphia; *d* 3 Aug. '33): this comedy/dialect artist had nearly 50 huge hits 1898-1920, about 90 more in duet with Bryan Harlan; he also sang with the Peerless and Big Four Quartets.

HARRIS, Richard (*b* '32) Irish actor had success on records during hippie era. Album *A Tramp Shining* was no. 4 '68, written by Jim WEBB incl. 'MacArthur Park', no. 2 hit USA (no. 4 UK). Harris half sang, half talked through arty but sincere sentimentality, lushly orchestrated. LPs '68-74 incl. *The Yard Went On Forever*, *My Boy*, *Slides*, readings from *Jonathan Livingston Seagull* with music, all on Dunhill; reading of *The Prophet By Kahlil Gibran* on Atlantic. He played King Arthur in film version of *Camelot* '67; among many other films were *Shake Hands With The Devil* '59, *The Guns Of Navarone* '61, *Mutiny On The Bounty* '63, *A Man Called Horse* '69, title role in *Cromwell* '70, *Robin And Marion* '75.

HARRIS, Wynonie (*b* 24 Aug. '15, Omaha, Neb.; *d* 14 June '69, Oakland, Cal.) R&B vocalist in shouting style, billed as 'Mr Blues'. A farm boy; sang in church; given tap shoes at age 12, became song-and-dance man in vaudeville; worked in Chicago clubs '30s. Appeared in film *Hit Parade Of 1943*, then joined Lucky MILLINDER band as singer; recorded 'Hurry Hurry' and 'Who Threw The Whiskey In The Well' for Decca '44. Went solo '45, recorded for Aladdin, Hamp-tone, Bullet etc. Own band '47 incl. Dexter GORDON, Hot Lips PAGE, Tab SMITH; 'Wynonie's Blues' featured Illinois JACQUET. First hit record on King 'Drinkin' Wine, Spo-Dee-O-Dee', cover of Stick McGhee hit (Atlantic), 'Good Rockin' Tonight' '47 subsequently widely covered incl. by Elvis PRESLEY. Records usually dynamic, raucous; hoarse vocals against booting sax, often risqué titles such as 'Sittin' On It All The Time', 'I Like My Baby's Pudding'. R&B hits on King incl. 'Good Morning Judge' '50, 'Lovin' Machine', 'All She Wants To Do Is Rock', 'Bloodshot Eyes' all '51. Sales fell off with advent of rock'n'roll; opened café in Brooklyn mid-'50s, another on West Coast '63, re-making hits on Reprise '63; played Harlem Apollo date '67; was working as bartender at time of death. USA LPs on Aladdin, King long out of print; UK compilation *Rock Mr Blues* on Charly.

HARRISON, Donald (*b* 23 June '60, New Orleans, La.) Alto sax. Joined Art BLAKEY's Jazz Messengers Mar. '82: LPs with Blakey *Oh, By The Way* '82 on Timeless, *New York Scene* '84 on Concord Jazz (incl. own tune, straight-ahead delight 'Controversy'). Coleads group with Terence BLANCHARD on

LPs *New York Second Line* '84; *Discernment* '86, both also on Concord; *Nascence* '86 and *Crystal Stair* '87 on Columbia. Also played in Don PULLEN quintet '85 (*Sixth Sense* on Black Saint). A rising star to watch.

HARRISON, George Singer, guitarist, songwriter (*see* BEATLES). Wrote several memorable songs as a Beatle ('If I Needed Someone', etc.), often piqued at not being allowed to shine more on LPs; his interest in Eastern religion, study of the sitar was an infl. on pop in late '60s. He released first solo LP by a Beatle, *Wonderwall* '68, followed by similar *Electronic Sounds* '69, both on their experimental Zapple label. Proper solo debut was *All Things Must Pass* '70: 3-disc set prod. by Phil SPECTOR incl. Bob DYLAN songs, guests Eric CLAPTON, Gary Brooker, Ginger BAKER, strong selection of Harrison material incl. 'My Sweet Lord', no. 1 UK/USA: inspired by hit 'Oh Happy Day' '69, by gospel group Edwin HAWKINS Singers, but similarity to '63 no. 1 'He's So Fine' by the CHIFFONS (written by Ronald Mack) caused lawsuit (case settled '76; cost Harrison $.5m). He oversaw Bangla Desh benefit concert and film '71, appears in fine form on 3-disc *Concert For Bangla Desh* '72 (prod. by Spector) with Dylan, Clapton, Ringo STARR, Leon RUSSELL (tax bureaucracies tied up money for years, providing lessons for future benefits). *Living In The Material World* '73 incl. strong Harrison songs 'Give Me Love' and 'Try Some, Buy Some' (latter originally written for Ronnie Spector); limp *Dark Horse* '74 was also the name of his label; *Extra Texture* '75, *33 1/3* '76 (incl. 'This Song', about 'Sweet Lord' fiasco), *George Harrison* '79 seemed to indicate decline of imagination. *Best Of* '76 collected best work, solo and with the Beatles. Sessioned on LPs by John LENNON, Starr, NILSSON, Peter Skellern; *Somewhere In England* '81 incl. 'All Those Years Ago', tribute to murdered Lennon. *Gone Troppo* '82 was widely regarded as his last solo album, but *Cloud Nine* '87 prod. by ELO's Jeff Lynne, with guests Eric Clapton, Ringo, Elton JOHN, incl. transatlantic no. 1 'Got My Mind Set On You'; single 'When We Was Fab' is about the Beatles making records: with Clapton, whose *August* '87 was hailed as his best, Harrison (the 'mysterious' Beatle) may be among the few of that generation to keep the flame alive. He also worked with the Monty Python crowd: seen in Eric Idle's parody Beatle documentary *The Rutles* '77, helped finance Python film *The Life Of Brian* '79, leading to formation of his HandMade Films (*A Private Function* '85, etc.; prod. MADONNA film *Shanghai Surprise* '86 for first flop). Appeared on Mike BATT's *The Hunting Of The Snark* '86.

HARRISON, Jimmy (*b* 17 Oct. 1900, Louisville, Ky.; *d* 23 July '31, NYC) Trombonist, also vocalist. Played in carnival bands, developing comedy routines; to NYC '23, at Small's Sugarcane Club with his friend June Clark on trumpet (*b* Algeria Junius Clark, 24 Mar. 1900, Long Beach, N.J.; *d* 23 Feb. '63, NYC; quit full-time music c.'37, suffered from TB), Bill BASIE on piano; worked with other bands but best known with Fletcher HENDERSON from '27: fired for a short period because he was a poor reader, but became the band's trombone star, playing fast and high under the infl. of Louis ARMSTRONG. Close pals with Coleman HAWKINS and especially Jack TEAGARDEN, the greatest black and white trombonists of the late '20s; the three often stayed up all night jamming together. Died of cancer; a continuing influence for years.

HART, Freddie (*b* 21 Dec. '28, Lochapoka, Ala.) Country singer with sentimental ballad style. One of 15 children from very poor family; joined US Marines, after discharge worked in a band NYC; to Arizona '51 and joined Lefty FRIZZELL's band, began writing songs. Signed with Capitol, made little impression as recording artist but was regular on *Home Town Jamboree* TV series in Hollywood. Signed to Columbia '57, had first hits with 'The Wall', 'The Key's In The Mailbox', 'What A Laugh!' '59-61. To Kapp label '65 and cult record 'Hank Williams' Guitar'; minor hits 'Togetherness', 'Born A Fool' '67-8. Re-joined Capitol and was about to be dropped after 15 hits in country chart '59-70, 9 in top 40, when he had biggest hit: 'Easy Loving' '71, no. 1 country and top 20 pop, only song to win CMA Song of the Year two years running ('71-2). More hits '72-7 incl. 'My Hang-Up Is You', 'Bless Your Heart', 'Trip To Heaven', 'Hang In There Girl', 'The First Time',

'Why Lovers Turn Strangers'. Fewer hits in recent years, but had business interests; joined Sunbird label '80. LPs incl. *Best Of* '64 on Harmony; *The World Of Freddie Hart* '72 on Columbia; *Hart Of Country Music* '66, *Neon And Rain* '67, *Straight From The Hart* '68, all on Kapp; *New Sounds* '70, *Easy Loving* '71, *If You Can't Feel It* '73, *The First Time* '75, *The Pleasure's Been All Mine* '77, *Only You* '78, *My Lady* '79, all on Capitol.

HARTFORD, John (*b* 30 Dec. '37, NY) Multi-instrumentalist, singer, songwriter. Raised in St Louis, Mo. where he played folk and country music in bars. Worked as DJ, sign painter, deckhand on Mississippi river boat; went to Nashville as session musician '66; signed as writer with GLASER Bros, made big breakthrough with 'Gentle On My Mind', recorded by over 300 artists: John's record on RCA made country chart; Glen CAMPBELL had pop hit. Won Grammy for Best Country Song '66. Working solo, accompanying his singing with banjo, fiddle, guitar and percussion effects from an electrified board on which he dances, uses own songs and those drawn from trad., country music. Often performs at bluegrass festivals, records with bluegrass musicians; was regular guest on TV shows *Hee-Haw, Today, Dinah Shore, Merv Griffin* etc. LPs incl. *Looks At Life* '66, *Housing Project* '68, *The Love Album* '69 on RCA; *Mark Twang* '76, *Dillard – Hartford – Dillard* '77, *All In The Name Of Love* '78 and *Slumbering On The Cumberland* '80 on Flying Fish.

HARTLEY, Keef (*b* '44, Preston, Lancs) UK drummer whose first pro engagement was replacing Ringo STARR in Rory Storm and the Hurricanes '62. Hopped off the Merseybeat bandwagon (via Freddie Starr's Midnighters) into London R&B boom; joined Artwoods '64 for three years, then replaced Aynsley Dunbar in John MAYALL's Bluesbreakers: first played on *Blues Alone* '67, on which Mayall played everything but drums, then *Crusade* and *Diary Of A Band* '67-8 before leaving to form his own group. Keef Hartley Band incl. bassist Gary Thain (*b* New Zealand, *d* 19 Mar. '76), guitarist/writer Miller Anderson: both played on LPs *Halfbreed* '69, *The*

Battle Of NW6 and *The Time Is Near* both '70 (latter no. 41 LP UK, only chart placing), *Overdog* and *Little Big Band* both '71 (latter recorded live at Marquee Club with brass augmentation). Mick Weaver joined on keyboards from second LP; otherwise session musicians added as needed. Material split between blues standards and Miller originals; unusually for a leader, Hartley neither wrote nor sang. Continued as live attraction until '73, though *Seventy Second Brave* and *Lancashire Hustler* '72-3 were essentially solo LPs (without Anderson). Hartley returned to the road, backing folksinger Michael Chapman; he formed shortlived Dog Soldier with Anderson and bassist Paul Bliss, Mel Simpson on keyboards (one LP '75); he sessioned for Chapman until '78, then faded from sight.

HARTMAN, Dan (*b* Harrisburg, Pa.) USA producer/performer. Joined Edgar WINTER Group as bassist '72; played on hit LP *They Only Come Out At Night* '73 and successors, donning integral bass/jump suit for stage act's futuristic image. Sessioned with Edgar's brother Johnny, his guitarist Rick DERRINGER, Todd RUNDGREN (*Initiation* '75). Wrote Edgar's no. 14 hit 'Free Ride' '73. Went solo '76; in family spirit, Edgar contributed horns and Derringer guitar to *Images* '76, released on manager Steve Paul's Blue Sky label. Did well in disco boom with infectious 'Instant Replay' (USA no. 29/UK no. 8 '78), LP of same name; 'This Is It' was UK no. 17 '79; LP *Relight My Fire* came out as disco fad spluttered. Retired to concentrate on prod. at Connecticut studio the Schoolhouse: output ranged from raw Southern rock of .38 Special (LPs *.38 Special, Special Delivery* '77-8), his own *It Hurts To Be In Love* '79, AVERAGE WHITE BAND's *Cupid's In Fashion* '82, to Neil SEDAKA's *Come See About Me* '84. Hartman doubles on guitar and keyboards, often adding these as well as backing vocals to LPs he produces. Contributed 'I Can Dream About You' to film *Streets Of Fire* (USA no. 6 '84, UK hit '85); had ditched disco for smooth white soul sound not unlike that of HALL & OATES, showing off enviable high-register voice. USA follow-up 'We Are The Young' no. 25 late '84; prod. James BROWN comeback single 'Living For America', '86 hit; multi-

talented Hartman can pick trends, remains top prod. of black/dance music.

HARTMAN, Johnny (*b* John Maurice Hartman, 3 July '23, Chicago; *d* 15 Sep. '83, NYC) Singer. Sang and played piano from age 8; scholarship to study voice '39; sang with Earl HINES, then Dizzy GILLESPIE '47-9, went solo. Dark baritone infl. by Billy ECKSTINE, Frank SINATRA; TV with Sammy DAVIS, *Tonight*, *Today* shows; toured the world; Newport Jazz Festival '75; recorded with John COLTRANE on Impulse. Own LPs incl. *First, Lasting & Always* on Savoy ('47 material), Impulse recordings now on MCA: *I Just Dropped By To Say, Voice That Is* '65; last LPs '80: *This One's For Tedi* with Tony Monte Quartet on Audiophile; *Once In Every Life* on Chicago's Bee Hive label, with Billy TAYLOR, Joe WILDER, Keith COPELAND, Frank Wess, Al Gafa. Fine voice deserved more fame.

HARVEY, Alex (*b* 5 Feb. '35, Glasgow; *d* 4 Feb. '82, Belgium) UK rock singer, leader. Began as guitarist in skiffle; then voted 'The Tommy STEELE of Scotland' in newspaper competition: persevered nevertheless; Alex Harvey Big Soul Band formed '59, became live draw with mix of brash R&B, Harvey's Scots humour; backed visiting Americans Eddie COCHRAN, Gene VINCENT etc.; lineup captured live in Germany on *Big Soul Band* '64, often incl. Bobby Thompson, bass; Gibson Kemp, drums. Split group, recorded *The Blues* '64 with brother Les, returned to Glasgow with him '66 to form Blues Council with Bobby Patrick, then went solo. Spotted playing guitar in London's 100 Club by mus. dir. of *Hair*, played in that for five years (recorded *Roman Wall Blues* '69). Took plunge back into rock, recruited Scots band Tear Gas (had poorly received LPs *Piggy Go Getter, Tear Gas*, ready to split), new lease of life as Sensational Alex Harvey Band: Zal Cleminson (*b* 4 May '49), Chris Glen on bass (*b* 6 Nov. '50), Hugh McKenna on piano (*b* 28 Nov. '49), Ted McKenna on drums (*b* 10 Mar. '50) were visually arresting, with Harvey in striped T-shirt wielding can of spray paint, Cleminson in clown make-up: put musical muscle into Harvey's narrative epics. *Framed* '72 well received; title track (LEIBER & STOLLER chestnut meat and drink for Harvey's melodrama); empathy with teen-age audience achieved with mixture of country, heavy metal, cabaret ('There's No Lights On The Christmas Tree, Mother; They're Burning Big Louie Tonight'). Supporting SLADE, MOTT THE HOOPLE etc. brought headline status; LPs edged into charts: *Next* '73 (with title track by Jacques BREL, stage act favourite 'Faith Healer') didn't chart until *The Impossible Dream* '74 made no. 16, *Tomorrow Belongs To Me* '75 no. 9; *Next* then reached no. 37. *Live* '75 caught band in element, made no. 14; first hit single same year: no. 7 UK with cover of '68 Tom JONES hit 'Delilah', followed by lesser hits 'Gambling Bar Room Blues', 'The Boston Tea Party'. Band reached peak during sellout Christmas shows at Hammersmith Odeon '76, with Harvey spray-painting 'brick wall' backdrop to dramatic musical accompaniment; *Penthouse Tapes* and *SAHB Stories* top 15 LPs '76; but diverse LPs sold by live appeal, in turn maintained by punishing workload, and break proved fatal: group recorded *Fourplay* without leader, who compiled LP of interviews about Loch Ness monster. Band split after *Rock Drill* '77: punk rock was breaking new, younger heroes and Harvey's health suffered from living rock'n'roll life style to the full. Formed short-lived New Band for *The Mafia Stole My Guitar* '79, with Simon Chatterton, drums; Matthew Cang, guitar; Don Weller, sax; Gordon Sellars, bass; Tommy Eyre, keyboards; toured until death from heart attack. Cleminson joined fellow Scots Nazareth; Ted McKenna Rory GALLAGHER, later Michael Schenker Group, which Glen had helped form two years previously. Harvey's song characters Vambo, the Tomahawk Kid, Sergeant Fury were the nearest rock equivalent to comic book heroes; these and his colourful stage presence lent title to overdue hits compilation *The Legend* in '85.

HAT ART Swiss avant-garde jazz label founded mid-'70s by Werner X. Uehlinger to record saxophonist Joe McPhee; Hat Hut records first appeared in the USA '75 (parent company is called Hat Hut Records Ltd); Hat Art was formed to record the Vienna Art Orchestra; Hat Music was also formed but rationalisation ensued and only Hat Art survives, with about 40 issues by McPhee, Steve LACY (incl. one LP with Mal WALDRON), Albert AYLER (from '66), Anthony BRAXTON, SUN RA, the GANELIN Trio, David MURRAY, Tony COE (Coe, Oxley & Co.), Max ROACH, Cecil TAYLOR, Jimmy Lyons and Sunny Murray, sets by the Vienna Art Orchestra and various European artists. Some of these have been reissued from Hat Hut and items by Taylor, Braxton, Lacy, McPhee, Phillip Wilson may return in the future. Quality is extremely high and packaging unique. Issued 2-disc *Cobra* '87 by John ZORN.

HATCH, Tony (*b* '39, Pinner, Middlesex) UK composer, arranger, leader, singer. Attended London Choir School, Bexley, Kent; began as tea boy for music publisher, became song-plugger, writing songs in spare time; joined Top Rank Records '59 in A&R. Wrote 'Look For A Star', used in film *Circus Of Horrors* '60: Garry Mills record went top 10 UK '60, four versions top 30 in USA: Mills, Garry Miles (Buzz Cason), Dean Hawley, Billy Vaughn. Worked with the Coldstream Guards Band for three years, also as recording manager Pye Records, supplying hits for Emile Ford, Lonnie DONEGAN, the SEARCHERS, Petula CLARK: wrote 'Downtown' for her, sold 3m copies '64-5. Second UK no. 1 with 'Where Are You Now (My Love)' by wife-to-be Jackie Trent. Often co-writing with her, published 'I Know A Place', 'Who Am I?', 'Colour My World', 'I Couldn't Live Without Your Love', 'My Love', 'Don't Sleep In The Subway', 'The Other Man's Grass', 'Joanna', 'Call Me', etc. gaining several songwriting awards. Made LPs *Beautiful In The Rain* (as bandleader), *Showcase* (as Tony Hatch Singers and Swingers); as vocal duo with Trent had hit 'The Two Of Us', toured as cabaret act, played London Palladium and made TV special *Mr And Mrs Music* '69 (LP of that name on Pye). Prod. show *Nell* '70 starring Trent; formed music publishing company M&M Music. Wrote TV themes for *Crossroads*, *Emmerdale Farm*, *Man Alive*, etc.; at one point had seven themes a week on TV. Notorious for sharp criticism as panellist on long-running TV talent show *New Faces* mid-'70s; mastermind behind vocal group Sweet Sensation, writing UK no. 1 'Sad Sweet Dreamer' for them '74. Wrote book *So You Want To Be In Show*

Business '76, carried on in TV to '80s; single 'Airline' on Tube label '82.

HATHAWAY, Donny (*b* 1 Oct. '45, Chicago; *d* 13 Jan. '79, NYC) Multi-talented sweet-soul singer with beautiful voice. Raised in St Louis; grandmother Martha Crumwell was gospel singer; billed at age 3 as Donny Pitts, Nation's Youngest Gospel Singer, accompanying himself on ukelele. Attended Howard U., Washington on scholarship; classmate was Roberta FLACK; joined cocktail jazz trio to pay for education; session work with Carla THOMAS, Jerry BUTLER, the STAPLE SINGERS, Flack etc. Work for Percy MAYFIELD at Curtom label in Chicago incl. 'June and Donnie' duets with June Conquest; did prod. work for Chess; met King Curtis, got Atlantic contract as writer/prod., performer. First LP *Everything Is Everything* '70 incl. minor hit 'The Ghetto', charted '71 after second *Donny Hathaway*; *Live* album '72, *Extension Of A Man* '73 also charted. No top 40 pop singles except duets with Flack: 'You've Got A Friend' '71 no. 29; 'Where Is The Love' '72, 'The Closer I Get To You' '78 both top 5; LP *Roberta Flack And Donny Hathaway* no. 3 '72; *Roberta Flack Featuring Donny Hathaway* no. 25 '80. Others incl. *Best Of* '78, *In Performance* '80. Fell 15 floors to his death, listed as suicide; friends couldn't believe it, but career had slumped mid-'70s because of personal problems.

HAVENS, Richie (*b* 21 Jan. '41, Brooklyn) Black folk singer; brought soul feeling to folk-rock genre: 11 albums charted USA, one re-entered; long a popular live act. From large family in Bedford-Stuyvesant ghetto; left school to pursue music; two LPs on Douglas, switched to Verve; played Newport Folk Festival '66, then Monterey '67, Miami '68, Isle of Wight and Woodstock '69. Verve LP *Something Else Again* just made top 200 LPs '68, whereupon earlier Verve *Mixed Bag*, Douglas *Electric Havens* also made it. 2-disc set *Richard P. Havens 1983* no. 80 '69; six albums on Stormy Forest label '70-4 charted incl. 2-disc *On Stage* '72 at no. 55, biggest hit *Alarm Clock* '71 at no. 29 (incl. his only hit single, cover of George HARRISON's 'Here Comes The Sun', no. 16 '71). Style went out of fashion; *The End Of The Beginning* '76 on A&M

made bottom of LP chart; *Mirage* '77 on A&M, *Connections* '79 on Asylum sold to loyal fans; only *Special* on Polydor now listed in catalogues. Single 'Death At An Early Age'/'Moonlight Rain' issued UK '83. New album '87 distributed by Moss Music.

HAWES, Hampton (*b* 13 Nov. '28, L.A.; *d* there 22 May '77) Piano, composer. Pro debut while in high school, active on West Coast with Big Jay MCNEELY, Dexter GORDON, others; led own trios after US Army service '52-4, mostly with bassist Red Mitchell (*b* Keith Moore Mitchell, 20 Sep. '27, NYC; settled in Scandinavia after '68). A modern stylist infl. by Bud POWELL; an underrated composer. Recorded as sideman with Wardell GRAY (*Live In Hollywood* on Xanadu); *Piano East/West* '53 (now on Fantasy) had Hawes on one side, East Coast pianist Freddie Redd on the other, with commercial constraint typical of era's self-conscious arrangements; three vols. of *The Trio* '55 and three of *All Night Session* '56 are mature genius, the latter recorded in one unedited session with Mitchell, Jim HALL, drummer Chuck Thompson, all on Contemporary label. Trio LP by Charles MINGUS with Dannie RICHMOND '57 is often reissued; back to Contemporary for *Four!* (quartet with Barney KESSEL), *For Real!* (with Scott LA FARO, Frank Butler on drums, Harold LAND), *Sonny Rollins & The Contemporary Leaders*, all '58; sentenced to ten years in prison hospital for possession of heroin: released '64 after writing to President Kennedy. Further Contemporary LPs '64-6 incl. *The Green Leaves Of Summer*; under-appreciated at home, he toured the world '67-9: albums *Hampton Hawes In Europe* on MPS with bassist Eberhard Weber, trio *Spanish Steps* '68 on Black Lion, solo *The Challenge* '68 on Storyville, *Key For Two* '69 now on Affinity with second piano Martial Solal, bassist Pierre Michelot, Kenny CLARKE. Back home he was prevented by cabaret card law from performing in NYC. Albums incl. *The Two Sides Of Hampton Hawes* (2-disc set, one with strings added) and *Memory Lane* (two vocals by Joe TURNER), both '70, now on Jasmine; *A Little Copenhagen Night Music* '71 on Arista; infl. during that decade by modal music (*see* George RUSSELL), played electric piano, synthesiser; further albums: *Live At The*

Jazz Showcase In Chicago '73 with Cecil McBee and Roy HAYNES on Enja; quintet/nonet sets *Universe* (with Land), *Blues For Walls, Northern Windows* (with Carol Kaye on electric bass) on Prestige '72-4; *Live At The Great American Music Hall* '75 on Concord Jazz has duos with bassist Mario Suraci, solo piano suite 'The Status Of Maceo'; *Killing Me Softly With His Song* '76 with Ray BROWN and Shelly MANNE was the last of the great series on Contemporary. He died of a stroke. *As Long As There's Music* on Artists House (duets with Charlie HADEN) and *Hampton Hawes At The Piano* on Contemporary were released after his death; he also played on Haden's *The Golden Number* on A&M, dedicated to him; performed/recorded with Joan BAEZ mid-'70s. Autobiography *Raise Up Off Me* with Don Asher.

HAWKINS, Coleman (*b* 21 Nov. '04, St Joseph, Mo.; *d* 19 May '69, NYC) Aka 'Hawk', 'Bean'. Tenor saxophone, also played other reeds in early years. Studied music Topeka, Kans., made first recordings with Mamie SMITH's Jazz Hounds '23; also played with Bessie SMITH, Ma RAINEY; then Fletcher HENDERSON '23-34. With Henderson (infl. by Louis ARMSTRONG) overcame tubby, moaning sound of tenor; lost trad. staccato, slap-tongue technique; playing loud and with stiff reed to be heard solo over the band, developed large, deep, rich tone; c.'26 (possibly under infl. of Art TATUM) began to improvise on chord structure of tune rather than melody: established the tenor sax as important voice in jazz, remained its foremost authority for 40 years. Among dozens of solos with Henderson: 'The Stampede' '26, 'St Louis Shuffle' '27, 'Queer Notions' (own comp., adventurous harmony) '33, 'Hocus Pocus' '34. Also recorded with Mound City Blue Blowers, McKINNEY'S COTTON PICKERS '29, Chocolate Dandies dates '29-30, small groups with Henry 'Red' ALLEN (compiled on Smithsonian Institution LP), big-band date with Spike HUGHES '33. To Europe '34; recorded with Jack HYLTON, Django REINHARDT, many others; back in USA '39 formed band and recorded 'Body And Soul'. Virtually a solo with rhythm section on a technically interesting song, the record was a summary of his style: harmonic commentary on

chords became lovely strings of arpeggios, with controlled passion from the urgency of getting it all in, and from dividing the beat into unequal parts: most jazz musicians did this, but Hawk imparted further forward motion by 'swallowing' the second part of the beat until it almost disappeared. 'Body And Soul' was good for romantic dancing, a big hit, an enduring jazz milestone. Always lyrical rather than bluesman; best records are ballads: 'I Can't Believe That You're in Love With Me', 'I Surrender Dear' (from a Dandies date with Roy ELDRIDGE, '40); 'The Man I Love', 'My Ideal' (from separate '43 sessions); 'I Only Have Eyes For You' ('44 with Eldridge, Teddy WILSON). Encouraged the bop pioneers, hired them for record dates (*Bean And The Boys*, '46); sextet tracks made in Hollywood '45 have strong bop flavour (with Howard McGHEE, Denzil BEST, etc.), now on *Hollywood Stampede* LP from French EMI. Fewer records late '40s-early '50s as jazz fell on hard times, but first to record an unaccompanied saxophone solo: his own comp. 'Picasso' '48 displayed the result of his studies; he never stopped listening to everything. At the centre of mainstream '50s, '60s: toured with JATP several times '46-68; played on 'all-star' dates with Buck CLAYTON. On Thelonious MONK's *Monk's Music*, reunions with Allen *Warhorses* (dixieland chestnuts) and *High Standards* (now on Jass), *Coleman Hawkins Encounters Ben Webster* (acolyte WEBSTER, who was four years younger, called Hawk 'the old man'), joyous big-band reunion of Henderson men, all '57-8; Benny CARTER's *Further Definitions* '61; *Duke Ellington Meets Coleman Hawkins* '62 (one of the more beautiful LPs of the decade); own Impulse set *Today And Now* '63, with Tommy FLANAGAN, piano; also *Sonny Meets Hawk* '63 with ROLLINS, two tenor giants 25 years apart in age. One of the most important musicians in the history of jazz, or indeed of 20th-century popular music. Early work available on Henderson compilations, others on CBS, RCA, Commodore, etc.; *Classic Tenors* (two vols.) on Bob THIELE's Dr Jazz label; *The Complete Coleman Hawkins On Keynote* on four CDs contains 61 tracks of 144; *The Essential Coleman Hawkins* on Verve '48-57 incl. 'Picasso'.

HAWKINS, Dale (*b* Delmar Allen Hawkins, 22 Aug. '38, Goldmine, La.) Rockabilly singer, one of the first to have hits. 'Suzie-Q' (no. 27 USA '57) was an anomaly at the time: on Checker label, primarily black R&B outlet, with R&B beat using cowbell, classic rockabilly guitar solo by James BURTON (covered by CREEDENCE CLEARWATER '68). Hawkins had only one other top 40 hit ('La-Do-Dada' '58), but live act was popular; many subsequent records had Roy BUCHANAN on guitar. Hawkins label-hopped, late '60s prod. records by Bruce Channel (*b* 28 Nov. '40, Jacksonville, Texas), another white blues singer: 'Hey Baby', no. 1 '62 with harmony vocal by Delbert McClinton, was said to have infl. the BEATLES; Hawkins prod. minor, later hits; also hits by the Five Americans (Dallas quintet; top 40 hits incl. no. 5 'Western Union' '67).

HAWKINS, Edwin, Singers Black San Francisco gospel group formed '67 by pianist/ choir dir. Hawkins (*b* c.'43) and soprano Betty Watson: 46 young people recorded eight trad. songs in church, arr. by Hawkins; had 1000 LPs made, sold about 600 to raise money for the choir, called Northern California State Youth Choir. Early '69 local DJ began playing album heavily, especially 'Oh Happy Day' (song from 1755, revised 1855 and found in standard Baptist hymnal); distributed by Buddah, who changed the name of the group, the single sold a million by June, made no. 2 in USA and UK, and won a Grammy: real emotion was a novelty in pop music at the time; it resulted in 'a rush to make gospel records by the labels who were responsible for the removal of gospel and religious music from the black stations' (J. Murrells) and inspired George HARRISON's 'My Sweet Lord'. Soloist Dorothy Coombs Morrison was credited on the record.

HAWKINS, Erskine (*b* Erskine Ramsey Hawkins, 26 July '14, Birmingham, Ala.) Trumpet; bandleader. Father killed in WWI. Played drums age 7, then trombone, then trumpet at 13. At Montgomery State Teachers College led 'Bama State Collegians; band visited NYC '34 led by J. B. Sims, '36 by Hawkins. Bookings incl. success at Harlem's Savoy Ballroom; recorded for Vocalion but switched to Victor '38,

stayed till '50. Arrangers in heyday incl. pianist Avery Parrish (wrote classic blues 'After Hours', recorded by band in '40; *b* 24 Jan. '17, Birmingham; injured in bar in L.A. '42 and never played again; *d* Dec. '59, NYC), alto sax Bill Johnson (*b* 30 Sep. '12, Jacksonville, Fla.; *d* 5 July '60, NYC), trumpeter Sam Lowe (*b* 14 May '18, Birmingham; later mus. dir. for rock'n'roll bands; excellent chapter on his work in Stanley Dance's *The World Of Swing*). Hawkins was high-note specialist on trumpet, billed as 'The 20th Century Gabriel'; other soloists incl. Dud BASCOMB, Julian DASH, Paul Bascomb (Dud's brother; absent from '38-40 leading own group). Band made about 140 sides for Bluebird or Victor, evolved from swing band to R&B-ish 'jump band' style, always at home with the blues. Novelty swing version of Gilbert & Sullivan's 'Let The Punishment Fit The Crime' '38 had vocal by alto saxist Jimmy Mitchelle; biggest hit was 'Tuxedo Junction' '39 written by Hawkins, Dash and Johnson; covered by Glenn MILLER, became classic of era; 'Dolemite' was top 10 pop hit '40; 'No Soap' (by Lowe), 'Swingin' On Lenox Avenue', 'Gin Mill Special', 'Uptown Shuffle' '38-9, 'Tippin' In' '45 all highly valued. Hawkins received honorary Doctorate in Music from Alabama State '47. Changed to Coral label '50-2 (R&B hit 'Tennessee Waltz' '50), then King. By '60s leading smaller combo except for special engagements; guested with Sy OLIVER at Carnegie Hall '74, played Nice Festival '79 backed by the NY Jazz Repertory Orchestra. French RCA has issued complete '38-50 material on 2-disc sets, all excellent entertainment; compilations of airchecks etc. incl. *One Night Stand 1946* on Joyce, *Sneaking Out* and *Tuxedo Junction* on First Heard in UK; nothing at all listed in USA catalogues.

HAWKINS, Hawkshaw (*b* Harold F. Hawkins, 22 Dec. '21, Huntingdon, W. Va.; *d* 5 Mar. '63, Camden, Tenn.; aka 'the Hawk') Country singer, songwriter; tall man with deep voice, 'Western'-based vocal style; popular for many years, especially in Canada, without big record success. Began on local radio '36; became regular on WWVA Wheeling Jamboree '46-54; signed with King '45 and had hits with 'I Wasted A Nickel' '49, 'Slow Poke' '51. Joined Grand

Ole Opry '55, signed with Columbia '59 (hit 'Soldier's Joy'), RCA '60-3, rejoined King and had biggest hit 'Lonesome 7-7203' (no. 1 country chart '63). Married to country star Jean SHEPARD; died in plane crash with Cowboy COPAS and Patsy CLINE.

HAWKINS, Ronnie (*b* 10 Jan. '35, Ark.) Rockabilly singer: much-loved pioneer. Led first lineup of Hawks while a student at U. of Arkansas, recorded for a local label. Backed Carl PERKINS, Conway TWITTY (claims to have turned down chance to record 'It's Only Make Believe' in favour of Twitty) before moving to Memphis and auditioning unsuccessfully for Sun. Made 'Bo Diddley' for Quality label, sometimes reckoned first rockabilly record; went to Toronto, Canada (where he now has bar the Hawk's Nest to fall back on); 'Mary Lou' was USA no. 26 '59, while others ('Forty Days' etc.) lesser hits. Recruited new Hawks lineup of four Canadians and Levon Helm (from Arkansas); played Canadian clubs and Eastern seaboard, his wailing style countered perfectly by Robbie Robertson's stabbing guitar: purveyed mixture of Chuck BERRY, Bo DIDDLEY, Larry WILLIAMS, version of Diddley's 'Who Do You Love' featuring Robertson's almost psychedelic guitar. Continued recording for Roulette; Helm emerged as backing band's featured vocalist during sessions for *Mojo Man* '64 and led them off on their own; they met Bob DYLAN the next year and became The BAND. Hawkins recorded for own Hawk label, Atlantic (*Ronnie Hawkins* '70 made at Muscle Shoals, probably his best, incl. minor hit 'Down In The Alley'), Monument. Reunion with The Band in their *Last Waltz* film incl. performance of 'Who Do You Love'. Also appeared in *Heaven's Gate* '81.

HAWKINS, Screamin' Jay (*b* Jalacy Hawkins, '29, Cleveland, Ohio) R&B singer, rock'n'roll pioneer with stage act on 'surrealistic borderline' (Arnold Shaw). Was Golden Gloves middleweight boxing champion '47; sang and played piano with Tiny GRIMES, others; went solo c.'55 with talent for humorous lyrics; has recorded for a dozen labels, refusing to imitate Fats DOMINO for Atlantic. 'I Put A Spell On You' '56 on Okeh was biggest hit (with some of the moans and groans edited out so that DJs would play it); did not make any charts, but later covered by Alan Price, CREEDENCE CLEARWATER. He was carried onstage in a flaming coffin; props incl. skull on a stick, rubber snake, black satin bat-wing cape, smoke-box built many years ago by an electrician at the Apollo theatre. His manic drive and black humour were copied by Arthur BROWN, infl. countless others; his act is still imitated by BLACK SABBATH etc. whose fans never heard of Hawkins. But for all the props his vocal style was the basis, and it was too strong: by the time Hawkins was scaring teenagers (while LITTLE RICHARD by comparison merely entertained them) the music business was already putting the brakes on rock'n'roll by making it pretty. Other well-known songs (all his own) incl. 'I Hear Voices', 'Alligator Wine', 'Feast Of The Mau Mau' (all recorded '60s). He opened for ROLLING STONES at Madison Square Garden '80; Keith Richard played on 'Armpit No. 6' and remake of 'Spell' issued '80 in UK on Polydor. Compilations: *Frenzy* on Edsel (Okeh stuff), *Screamin' The Blues* on Red Lightnin' (c.'53 to mid-'60s).

HAWKINS, Ted (*b* 28 Oct. '36, Biloxi, Ms.) Singer, guitarist, songwriter. Defies category, singing gospel/soul infl. material, originals, songs like 'Blowin' In The Wind', 'Green Green Grass Of Home', Johnny HORTON's 'North To Alaska' so that they become his own, like hearing them for the first time. Self-taught on guitar from age 9; inspired at age 12 by Red FOLEY's 'Peace In The Valley' and by Sam COOKE with the Soul Stirrers; his mother was an alcoholic prostitute and he ate out of garbage cans. He first performed at 13 in a reform school. Intended to go East after a spell in a Mississippi prison, but drifted to Florida, Chicago; to West Coast '66, became a busker on Venice Beach at L.A.'s Thornton Avenue. Recorded for Dolphins of Hollywood, heard single on the radio but never saw any money. First album *Watch Your Step* '71 on Rounder (it came out while he was in jail); then *On The Boardwalk* '85 on Windows On The World, with a tougher, more world-weary delivery and some backing musicians (though production never distracts); *Happy Hour* '86 on Rounder. He was championed by UK DJ Andy Kershaw (presenter of TV's *Whistle Test*), emigrated to UK Oct. '86 and found more appreciation than in the USA.

HAYES, Clancy (*b* Clarence Leonard Hayes, *b* 14 Nov. '08, near Parsons, Kansas; *d* 13 Mar. '72, San Francisco) Banjo, singer, songwriter. Began on drums, then guitar, banjo; sang on Cal. radio late '20s; with Lu WATTERS '38-50 (often on drums), Bob SCOBEY '50s; later a regular at Earthquake McGoon's (Turk MURPHY's) Club; guested with WORLD'S GREATEST JAZZ BAND. Unpretentious folksy style and strong baritone made a natural vocalist in imitation turn-of-the-century style of California revival music; Scobey single on Good Time Jazz label '53 'Silver Dollar'/'Ace In The Hole' got air play; same year recorded his own 'Huggin' And Chalkin' ' with Scobey, which had been a no. 1 hit '46 for Hoagy CARMICHAEL; a few years later Ma RAINEY's 'C.C. Rider' backed with 'Travellin' Shoes' (co-written by Hayes) on California label. Charming vocals on Scobey LPs mid-'50s incl. 'Parsons Kansas City Blues', 'I Want To Go Back To Michigan', 'Careless Love', 'Angry', many more, mixing DIXIELAND chestnuts, vaudeville, nostalgia. Own albums incl. *Swingin' Minstrel* '63 on Good Time Jazz and *Oh By Jingo* on Delmark.

HAYES, Edgar (*b* 23 May '04, Lexington, Kentucky; *d* 28 June '79, San Bernardino, Cal.) Pianist, bandleader. Attended Fisk, Wilberforce Universities; from early '20s worked as sideman, led pit band at Harlem's Alhambra theatre; with Lucky MILLINDER, then formed own band '37, initially with Kenny CLARKE, Dizzy GILLESPIE, Earl BOSTIC, reedman/arr. Joe Garland (*b* 15 Aug. '03, Norfolk, Va.; *d* 21 Apr. '77, Teaneck, N.J.); recorded for Decca '37, '38 band incl. Clarke, Garland, veterans trombonist Clyde Bernhardt (*b* 11 July '05, Goldhill, N.C.; also played with Fats WALLER, Jay McSHANN, Claude HOPKINS, Dud BASCOMB; recorded as Ed Barron, led own band '50s, still playing '80s), reedman Rudy Powell (*b* 28 Oct. '07, NYC; *d* 30 Oct. '76; with Waller '34-7, many others). Last recording session '38 incl. hit with corny arr. of 'Stardust'; flip side was Garland arr.

of time-honoured riff which he called 'In The Mood': British writer C. H. Rolph heard it played '19 by cinema orchestras in London; it appeared on record as Wingy MANONE's 'Tar Paper Stomp' '30 (aka 'Wingy's Stomp'), then Horace HENDERSON's 'Hot And Anxious', recorded by Fletcher HENDERSON '31, Don REDMAN '32; Garland's version was covered '39 by Glenn MILLER and became the biggest hit of the Swing Era, but Hayes' disc had more soul. He toured Europe '38, led band till '41, moved to West Coast '42, worked solo, led combos; co-led band at Billy Berg's L.A. with guitarist Teddy Bunn '46. Active into '70s, playing mainly solo dates at clubs, restaurants.

HAYES, Isaac (*b* 20 Aug. '42, Covington, Tenn.) Singer, songwriter, producer, actor. From sharecropping family; moved to Memphis as teenager; played sax and piano, made record on local label, '62; worked at Stax (*see* ATLANTIC), playing with Mar-Keys and on Otis REDDING sessions '64. Wrote songs with David Porter incl. hits for Carla THOMAS, SAM & DAVE, others; own records for Stax subsidiary Enterprise '67 (*Presenting Isaac Hayes*), but made no. 8 pop LP chart with *Hot Buttered Soul* '69: long, lavish arrangements seemed to cap soul era. Even bigger triumph with score for film *Shaft* '71: won Oscar, 'Theme From Shaft' no. 1 hit, won Grammy. Other hits in pop and soul charts with songs by Burt BACHARACH, Jimmy WEBB; distinctive live act with shaven head, dark glasses, cape and tights, large orchestra (captured in film *Wattstax* '73); he scored and acted in films *Tough Guys*, *Truck Turner* '74; switched to ABC label, but soon ignored by disco market he'd helped to create: went broke but came back; co-wrote '79 hit 'Déjà Vu' for Dionne WARWICK, made 2-disc set *A Man And A Woman* with her; soon had hits in soul chart with 'Zeke The Freak', 'Don't Let Go', 'Do You Wanna Make Love', duet LP with Millie JACKSON *Royal Rappin's*, all '78-9. Appeared in John Carpenter film *Escape From New York*, episode of TV's *A-Team*. Other LPs on various labels incl. *The Isaac Hayes Movement* '70, *Black Moses* '71, *Joy* and *Live At The Sahara Tahoe* '73, *Disco Connection* '75, *Juicy Fruit (Disco Freak)* '76, *New Horizon* '77, *Hotbed* '78,

Don't Let Go '79, *And Once Again* '80. Stax stuff now reissued, incl. hits compilations.

HAYES, Tubby (*b* Edward Brian Hayes, 30 Jan. '35, London; *d* there 8 June '73 during heart surgery) Tenor sax, other reeds; also vibes. The best-known, best-loved British jazzman of his generation, still greatly missed. Father played on BBC; Tubby turned pro age 15. Led own groups incl. Jazz Couriers '57-9 with Ronnie SCOTT; first played in USA '61; played with Duke ELLINGTON at Royal Festival Hall '64; appeared in films incl. *Dr Terror's House Of Horrors* '65 with quintet. USA LPs incl. *Tubby The Tenor* '61 on Epic, made in NYC with Horace PARLAN, George DUVIVIER, Dave Bailey on drums, Clark TERRY and Eddie Costa (vibes) on some tracks (additional track from this session on Columbia compilation *Almost Forgotten*); also *Tubby's Back In Town* '62 on Smash with Roland KIRK, James MOODY, three others. UK LPs on Tempo, Fontana, others began '55: quintet *After Lights Out* '56 appeared on Tempo, Imperial, Savoy, Jasmine (aka *Changing The Jazz At Birmingham Palace*); quintet with Scott made four LPs on Tempo '57-8, also *Message From Britain* '59 on London and Jazzland; quartet *Tubby's Groove* '59 now on Jasmine; quintet *A Tribute: Tubbs* '63 on Spotlite made live at the Golden Slipper in Nottingham; big band *Tubb's Tours* '64 and quartet *Mexican Green* '67 both now on Mole.

HAYMES, Dick (*b* 13 Sep. '16, Buenos Aires, Argentina; *d* 30 Mar. '80) Singer, star of '40s movie musicals. Mother was concert singer; family settled in NYC, then West Coast; during '30s Haymes wrote songs, sang on radio, had bit parts in movies. Tried to sell songs to Harry JAMES, who hired him to sing instead: rich, warm baritone with good phrasing made him a rival to Bing CROSBY, Frank SINATRA. With James '40-1, Benny GOODMAN '42, with Tommy DORSEY during recording ban '43. No. 1 hit with 'I'll Get By' '44 with James; more than 40 big hits as solo on Decca '43-51 incl. no. ones 'It Can't Be Wrong', 'You'll Never Know'; 'Till The End Of Time', 'Little White Lies', 'Mam'selle', all top 5; duets with Crosby and ANDREWS SISTERS, Judy GARLAND, Ethel MERMAN; accompaniment incl. Gordon

JENKINS, Artie SHAW, Victor YOUNG. Radio show mid-'40s *Everything For The Boys* with Helen FORREST led to duet hits '44-6. Portrayed songwriter Ernest R. Ball (*b* 22 July 1878, Cleveland, Ohio; *d* 3 May '27, Santa Ana, Cal.) in '44 film *Irish Eyes Are Smiling*; also starred in *Four Jills In A Jeep* '44, *State Fair* '45, *One Touch Of Venus* '48, *Cruisin' Down The River* '53, several more. Other radio shows incl. *Lucky Strike Hit Parade*, own nightly series '49-50; later TV work; Capitol LP *Moondreams* c.'55. Had financial worries, deportation threats; when a European tour was planned with Billie HOLIDAY '52, he was ordered by the Internal Revenue to stay at home: the tour fell through. His mus. dir. was Bobby SCOTT early '60s; worked overseas that decade, returned to USA '71 for TV, club work. Several compilations available attest to his enduring popularity: *Best Of, You'll Never Know* on MCA; *As Time Goes By, For You, Me, Evermore,* and *Imagination* on Audiophile.

HAYNES, Roy (*b* 13 Mar. '26, Roxbury, Mass.) Drummer, one of the most versatile and tasteful in modern jazz. Gigged, recorded with practically everybody, from Lester YOUNG and Thelonious MONK to Gary BURTON, Larry CORYELL, Chick COREA; worked with Sarah VAUGHAN '53-8; led own groups; worked a lot with Stan GETZ in '50s, again '65; led own Hip Ensemble from '70. Own LPs began in Stockholm and Paris '54 with Joe Benjamin on bass; then *We Three* '58 on New Jazz (Prestige) with Phineas NEWBORN, Paul CHAMBERS, *Just Us* '60 with different trio; then quartet LPs *Out Of The Afternoon* '62 on Impulse with Roland KIRK and Tommy FLANAGAN, *Cracklin'* with Booker ERVIN and *Cymbaliam*, both '63 on New Jazz, *People* '64 on Pacific Jazz. Septet incl. George ADAMS, Marvin Peterson on trumpet: *Hip Ensemble* '71, *Senyah* '73 on Mainstream (also a track on compilation *Booty*). Others incl. quartet *Togyu* '73 on RCA/Japan; *Jazz a confronto 29* '75 on Horo; various groups recorded at Berkeley *Thank You, Thank You* and *Vistalite* '77-8 on Galaxy; quartet *Live At The Riverbop*, Paris '79 on French Blue Marge label; quartet *True Or False* '86 on Freelance made live in Paris. *Out Of The Afternoon* reissued '85 on MCA.

HAYTON, Lennie (*b* Leonard George Hayton, 13 Feb. '08, NYC; *d* 24 Apr. '71, Palm Springs, Cal.) Pianist, bandleader, arranger, composer. Gigged with Bix BEIDERBECKE, etc.; worked for Paul WHITEMAN '28-30, appeared with him in film *King Of Jazz* '30; radio work incl. Bing CROSBY shows early '30s; led band on first *Lucky Strike Hit Parade* '35 (early USA 'Top of the Pops' continued on TV for many years); own dance band '38-40; mus. dir. for MGM '40-53; married Lena HORNE '47. Film work in various capacities incl. all-star *Ziegfeld Follies* '44, *On The Town* '49 (Hayton's score won Oscar; ballet sequence 'Slaughter On 10th Avenue' was top 20 hit), *Singin' In The Rain* '52, many others; later worked on *Star!* '68 (with Julie ANDREWS playing Gertrude Lawrence), *Hello, Dolly!* '69 with Barbra STREISAND.

HAZLEWOOD, Lee (*b* 9 July '29, Mannford, Okla.) Singer, songwriter, producer. Son of an oilman, attended Southern Methodist U.; drafted during Korean war, became country DJ in Phoenix '53; began experimenting with session guitarist Al Casey, putting echo on country sounds, etc. Wrote and prod. 'The Fool', with vocal by Sanford Clark, backing by Casey; placed it on Dot, became top 10 hit USA '56. Electronic gimmickry, prod. tricks were infl. on Phil SPECTOR. Co-founded Jamie Records '57 in Philadelphia with Lester Sill and Dick CLARK, using it (and Clark's TV show) to sell hits by minimalist guitar player Duane EDDY; formed Gregmark with Sill, hired Spector, had hits with the Paris Sisters ('61-2; trio from San Francisco); threatened to quit business when swamped by British Invasion, instead at request of Jimmy Bowen prod. hits by film-star offspring Dino, Desi and Billy on Reprise '65; then reached top with 'These Boots Are Made For Walkin' ', no. 1 for Nancy SINATRA, also 'Sugar Town' no. 5, both on Reprise '66. Made duets with her: 'Jackson' no. 14 '67, other minor hits; LPs *Nancy And Lee, Nancy And Lee Again*; own blues-tinged LP *Love And Other Crimes* on Reprise incl. good sidemen such as James BURTON; duet with Sinatra 'Did You Ever' was no. 2 UK '71; solo LP *Poet, Fool Or Bum* received one-word verdict 'Bum' in UK's *New Musical Express*. Not much heard since.

HEAD, Murray (*b* '46) UK singer, actor. Intended studying fine art in London, but sang with rock band playing debutante parties; thrown out of band, won Radio Luxembourg talent contest, signed with EMI. Parts in TV, films incl. *The Family Way* '66, film with Paul McCARTNEY score; in London cast of musical *Hair*; sang Judas on LP of *Jesus Christ Superstar*, leading to USA top 20 with single of title track '71. Same year had major role in John Schlesinger film *Sunday, Bloody Sunday*, won UK Variety Club's Most Promising Newcomer award. Recorded for Immediate, then CBS (concept album *Nigel Lived*); more film roles; LP *Say It Ain't So* on Island '75; then musical career hampered by legal problems. His songs were covered by Tina TURNER, Roger Daltrey, Cliff RICHARD, Gary Brooker, Colin BLUNSTONE; gave up films following *Madam Claude* '78, returned to music; albums *Between Us* '79 on French Philips, *How Many Ways* in UK '81 did little and Head was written off until appearing at London's Barbican theatre late '84 in one-off first performance of *Chess*, musical by Tim Rice and boys from ABBA; single from it 'One Night In Bangkok' on RCA was worldwide hit '85. Albums *Restless* '84 and *Sooner Or Later* '87 on Virgin.

HEAD, Roy (*b* 9 Jan. '43, Three Rivers, Texas) Rock'n'roll-based country singer. Began early '60s as pop singer with own band the Traits. Signed with Sceptor '64, then smaller label Back Beat: R&B flavoured 'Treat Her Right' made top 3 on USA pop chart '65. Earlier records reissued; 'Just A Little Bit', 'Apple Of My Eye' made top 40 '65, three more minor hits '66, all on two different labels. Made Hot 100 once more '71 with '(The World's Going Up In A) Puff Of Smoke' '71, then stuck with country market. Minor hit with Mickey NEWBURY's 'Baby's Not Home' '74 on Mega, changed to Shannon for biggest country hit 'The Most Wanted Woman In Town', top 20 '75. Signed to ABC-Dot for 'The Door I Used To Close', 'Come To Me' '76-7; has since recorded for Elektra, several smaller labels. LPs incl. *Head First* '76, *Ahead Of His Time* '77, *Tonight's The Night* '78, all on ABC-Dot; *In Our Room* '79, *The Many Sides* '80 on Elektra. Always has many fans, but fell between stools: rock-based style has not always appealed to country charts.

HEART USA rock group fronted by sisters Ann (*b* 19 June '51, San Diego, Cal.) and Nancy Wilson, lead vocalist and guitarist respectively. After navy service family settled in Seattle, girls worked in local music scene, Nancy solo folksinger and Ann member of hard rockers White Heart (Steve Fossen, bass; Roger Fisher (*b* '50), guitar; Mike Fisher; group previously known as Army, played LED ZEP covers). Ann Wilson joined sister and band (incl. Michael Derosier, drums; Howard Leese, keyboards), relocated to British Columbia (Roger Fisher had draft problems); released *Dreamboat Annie* '76 on local Mushroom label, sold out initial pressing on West Coast concert circuit alone: contained mixture of heavy metal-ish rock and ballads, on each of which Ann excelled; incl. singles 'Crazy On You' (top 40) and 'Magic Man' (top 10). Album sold 2.5m and made no. 7 on Billboard LP chart, but band felt small label held them back; made mid-contract switch to CBS/Portrait which caused problems: sub-demo quality *Magazine* (recorded '76, released '78) competed with *Little Queen* '78; courtroom battle gave Mushroom the right to release *Magazine*, so remixing and new vocals were done to limit damage. *Little Queen* (with hit single 'Barracuda') was no. 9, *Magazine* 17 despite confusion; *Dog & Butterfly* (also '78, on Portrait, incl. single 'Straight On') also made 17. Wilson sisters had relationships with Fisher brothers (Mike was now soundman); Ann's split with Roger led to his departure and *Bebe Le Strange* '80 was best-seller so far at no. 5, despite Leese having to double on instruments. *Greatest Hits Live* was another confusing issue: 2-disc set had six of 18 tracks live; made no. 13 in USA, slimmed to one LP for UK release '81, where it made little impact. Long-serving rhythm section of Leese/Fossen replaced by seasoned Mark Andes (bass; ex-SPIRIT, JO JO GUNNE, FIREFALL) and drummer Denny Carmassi (ex-Montrose, Sammy Hagar). *Private Audition* '82, *Passionworks* '83 (collaboration with lyricist Holly Knight), *Heart* '85 (no. 1 LP USA) confirmed ability to turn out accomplished, glossy AOR; hit singles continued, but excitement of yore was missing.

Nancy became part-time actress in *Fast Times At Ridgemount High* and *The Wild Life*.

HEATH BROTHERS Bassist Percy (*b* 30 Apr. '23, Wilmington, N.C.), reedman James Edward (*b* 25 Oct. '26, Philadelphia), drummer Albert (*b* 31 May '35, Philadelphia, aka 'Tootie'). Two younger brothers were at centre of Philadelphia jazz scene early '50s with Benny GOLSON, John COLTRANE, many others; Percy had already recorded with Miles DAVIS, Thelonious MONK, many others when he became founder member of MODERN JAZZ QUARTET '54. As the Heath Brothers they made LPs *Marchin' On* '75 in Oslo, with Stanley Cowell on piano, adding six pieces for *Passin' Thru* on Columbia '78; then Percy and Jimmy carried on without Al: *Live At The Public Theatre* with Akira Tana on drums, *In Motion* '79 with Keith COPELAND, *Expressions Of Life* '80 with Tana (all on Columbia); *Brotherly Love* '81 on Antilles with Tana. Al's LPs as leader incl. *Kawaida* '69 on Trip (octet incl. Don CHERRY, Herbie HANCOCK, Ed BLACKWELL), *Kwanza (The First)* '73 on Muse with Kenny Barron, Curtis FULLER (also on an Italian label as *Oops!*). Tenorist Jimmy led various all-star groups on Riverside (Milestone) beginning with *The Thumper* '59 with Al (called *Fast Company* on Milestone); *Really Big* '60, *The Quota* '61, *Triple Threat* '62, *Swamp Seed* '63 with Al and Percy (*Seed* has Connie Kay drumming on some tracks); quintet *On The Trail* '64 with Al and Paul CHAMBERS. *The Gap Sealer* '72 on Cobblestone has Al, Bob Cranshaw playing electric bass, Jimmy playing soprano, flute and tenor; *Love And Understanding* '73 on Muse has Fuller, Cranshaw, Cowell playing electric piano, Bernard Fennell on cello and Billy HIGGINS on drums; *Picture Of Health* '75 on Xanadu is quartet with Barry HARRIS, piano; Sam JONES, bass; and Higgins; *Peer Pleasure* '87 on Landmark is just that. Percy also made LPs with Paul DESMOND and Jim HALL on RCA; many others: cumulatively the brothers have made a great many albums by now, all marked by good tone, good taste.

HEATH, Ted (*b* 30 Mar. 1900, Wandsworth, London; *d* 18 Nov. '69, Surrey) Trombone, bandleader. Played for Jack HYLTON, AMBROSE; left GERALDO '44 to form own band for BBC series, led it until illness in '64 (carried on in his name for five years; many reunions later). Well-recorded by Decca, with good arrangements (Tadd DAMERON was on staff mid-'50s) and many UK jazz luminaries passing through, it was among the best big bands of the post-war years (in any country): Sunday concerts at the Palladium became an institution from '45; records sold well in USA, enabling many tours there. Among many compilations listed in UK catalogues: *Big Band Favourites* (28 Swing Era classics on double-play Decca cassette); Jasmine LPs: *Strike Up The Band* incl. 'Vanessa' and 'Hot Toddy' (single hits '53), 'On The Bridge', 'La Mer', etc.; *Fats Waller Album* incl. arr. of Waller's 'London Suite'; also *At The London Palladium, Hits I Missed, Kern For Moderns, Rodgers For Moderns, Shall We Dance, Spotlight On Sidemen, Olde Englyshe, Swing Session, Swings In Stereo.*

HEAVEN 17 UK synth pop band formed '80 by Martyn Ware (*b* 19 May '56) and Ian Craig-Marsh (*b* 11 Nov. '56) after departure from HUMAN LEAGUE (according to rumour, leaving group the name for £20,000 payoff), adding vocalist, former photographer Glenn Gregory (*b* 16 May '58). Released minor hit 'We Don't Need This Fascist Groove Thang', striking syntho-protest in UK pop's orthodox anti-Thatcher political mood. Innovative, successful electro-funk album *Penthouse & Pavement* '81 saw rock band as business corporation: *Music Of Quality And Distinction* '82 marketed as B.E.F. (British Electric Foundation); collection of classic songs incl. guest vocalists Gary GLITTER, Sandie SHAW, Tina TURNER, TV person Paula Yates (mother of Bob Geldof's children); Turner's 'Ball Of Confusion' hailed as stand-out track and was beginning of her return to stardom: the band prod. her cover of Al GREEN's 'Let's Stay Together', her first real success in a decade, which led to her hit LP *Private Dancer* '84. As B.E.F. they released innovative cassette-only *Music For Stowaways* (Sony Walkman then being called Stowaway). Heaven 17's own electro-soul 'Temptation' was UK no. 2; more political commentary 'Crushed By The Wheels Of

Industry' no. 17 (vocal by Carol Kenyon), both from LP *The Luxury Gap* '83, which featured EARTH, WIND & FIRE horn section, was critically panned. *How Men Are* '84 followed by a hiatus: Gregory dueted with Propaganda's Claudia Brucken on soundtrack of film *Insignificance* '85; *Endless* '85 was cassette and CD-only *Best Of*; band met Jimmy Ruffin recording Paul Weller's 'Soul Deep' for striking coal miners in '85, teamed with him for '86 hit single 'The Foolish Thing To Do'; *Pleasure One* '86 was sterile new album. Single 'Steel City' '86 as the Hillsboro Crew was tribute to Sheffield Wednesday Football Club.

HEAVY METAL Genre developed from late '60s blues progressions by 'power trios' like CREAM and the Jimi HENDRIX Experience: guitar-based rock with amplified guitar and bass reinforcing each other to create, thick, brutal wall of sound. Term was popularised by STEPPENWOLF, whose '68 hit 'Born To Be Wild' contained the phrase 'heavy metal thunder' from William Burroughs' novel *Naked Lunch*. USA's VANILLA FUDGE used the Hammond organ, then associated with SOUL music; they provided model for DEEP PURPLE, arguably the most important UK HM group of '70s, who aimed to be Fudge's UK equivalent and whose album *In Rock* '70 was seminal: like most HM, had long tracks rarely capable of release on singles. USA groups GRAND FUNK and MOUNTAIN were major practitioners of '70s, while BLACK SABBATH in UK demonstrated obsession with occult, sword-and-sorcery imagery later adopted by BLUE OYSTER CULT. New Wave of British Heavy Metal (DEF LEPPARD, IRON MAIDEN, SAXON etc.) sprang up because legendary groups named above had disbanded or gone into tax exile: HM relies on live concerts, where devotees (known as 'headbangers') can interact; fans are often long-haired, with badges of allegiance on jackets; Masters of Rock Festival held annually at Donington, East Midlands, is best example of this. America's US Festival is usually dominated by HM. Fans tend to be working class, and surprisingly well-behaved; tremendously loyal, regenerating audience is 90% male owing to phallic imagery of guitars and rampant sexism, especially in macho lyrics of bands like WHITESNAKE, AC/DC. Groups like LED ZEP-

PELIN (more trad. blues-based) eschewed HM label, but to outsiders the sheer loudness of many acts puts them in the same category: volume that endangers hearing of fans is unnecessary in strictly musical terms, but HM is at the centre of the rock-concert-as-ritual, incl. loudness which has unfortunately affected popular music in general. 'Heavy metal is the basic rock and roll message,' said John Swenson, *Rock World* editor. 'It accepts everybody. The least sophisticated kid can get as much out of it as its dedicated followers.' There was a boom in USA heavy metal early '80s, then a backlash; MTV reduced the number of metal videos broadcast; Dee Snider, TWISTED SISTER vocalist, blamed it on record companies: 'They oversigned metal bands, just like they did with disco and new wave bands.' Affinity with simple, loud, three-chord PUNK was expressed from late '70s by Def Leppard, MOTORHEAD etc.; HM magazine *Kerrang!* is spinoff from punk-oriented UK music paper *Sounds*.

HEFTI, Neal (*b* 29 Oct. '22, Hastings, Neb.) Trumpet, piano, composer, arranger. Wrote first arr. in high school; later worked for Charlie BARNET, Earl HINES, Charlie SPIVAK, Horace HEIDT, then joined Woody HERMAN '44: arr. incl. 'Jones Beachead' (aka 'Half-Past Jumpin' Time'), 'The Good Earth', 'Wildroot', 'Everywhere'; contributed to 'Caldonia', 'Northwest Passage', updated band's theme 'Woodchopper's Ball', etc. Wrote for Charlie VENTURA '46, Harry JAMES '48-9. Wrote dozens of arr. for Count BASIE '50-60 for octet, then big band, which recorded over 40 of them beginning with 'Little Pony' '51, incl. album *The Atomic Mr Basie* '57 ('Lil' Darlin', 'The Kid From Red Bank', 'Splanky', nine others same session: band of that period was excellent ensemble rather than soloist's outfit; Hefti's charts are extremely well-judged and still selling records). He led his own groups now and then (LPs incl. *The Band With Young Ideas*, now on Jasmine UK); mus. dir. for his wife Frances Wayne (the former Herman vocalist; LPs on Epic, Brunswick); studio work incl. Reprise label ('62 Frank SINATRA sessions incl. some with Basie); scored many films incl. Neil Simon's *Barefoot In The Park* and *The Odd Couple*, both also TV series; other TV work incl. *Batman* (clever

title theme of tongue-in-cheek series was top 40 hit '66). Concert tours, lectures mid-'70s.

HEIDT, Horace (*b* 21 May '01, Alameda, Cal.; *d* 1 Dec. '86, L.A.) Pianist, bandleader. Played football; took up piano seriously after injury in U. of Cal. game; turned pro '23. Successful, corny show/vaudeville band Horace Heidt And His Californians (once featured trained dog Lobo) had long stay at NY Palace Theatre '30; from mid-'30s known as Horace Heidt And His Musical Knights (or as Brigadiers), began to become famous (and more musical) on radio and records. Heidt himself had no talent, was shrewd manager, always finding new ways to entertain: hired blind whistler Fred Lowery (*b* Palatine, Texas; whistled on film theme hit 'The High And The Mighty', no. 9 '54); actor Art Carney was singing comedian, member of vocal group the Don Juans; Frank DeVol played tenor sax; Alvino REY played electric guitar, unusual then; Frankie CARLE, Bobby HACKETT, Jess STACY, Irving Fazola on clarinet, trombonist Warren Covington and Shorty Sherrock on trumpet (*b* Clarence Francis Cherock, 17 Nov. '15, Minneapolis; *d* 19 Feb. '80, North Ridge, Cal.; also played with Bob CROSBY, J. DORSEY, Gene KRUPA, own band), Joe Rushton on bass sax (*b* 7 Nov. '07, Evanston, Ill.; *d* 2 Mar. '64, Cal.), arr. Bill Finegan, vocalist Gordon MacRAE all worked for Heidt. Big fame giving away money '38-41 on radio show *Pot O' Gold*: callers chosen at random from national phone directories would receive $1000 just for answering the phone; show forced off the air by the FCC as an illegal lottery; films called *Pot O' Gold*, *Treasure Chest* '41-2; out of music for most of '46 during dispute with MCA; '48-53 talent show *Youth Opportunity* broadcast from different town each week (accordionist Dick Contino was a winner who became popular in Midwest), moved to TV; he retired on investments. His son Horace Jr also led a band.

HELL, Richard (*b* Richard Myers, 2 Oct. '49, Lexington, Ky.) USA punk rocker. Grew up in Wilmington, Del.; to NYC to work in bookshop, write poetry, take drugs. Schoolfriend Tom Miller moved in '68; they formed Neon Boys '71 with another schoolmate Billy Ficca on drums; bassist Myers changed name to Hell, guitarist Miller to Verlaine. Recorded early Hell & Verlaine compositions 'Love Comes In Spurts'/'That's All I Know Right Now' (released '80 on Shake label as retrospective single). Formed Television late '73 with Ficca, Richard Lloyd on guitar; by mid-'75 he was ousted, anarchistic vision and rudimentary playing no longer suiting; spent a year in the Heartbreakers, spinoff from the NEW YORK DOLLS formed with Johnny Thunders; then formed own Voidoids. Defiantly ripped and torn clothes in glamrock era may have been Malcolm McLaren's model for the SEX PISTOLS (McLaren being the Dolls' last manager). Finally his own boss with Voidoids: lineup Ivan Julian (*b* 26 June '55, Washington), Robert Quine (*b* 30 Dec. '42, Akron, Ohio), guitars; Marc Bell (ex-Wayne County), drums. *Blank Generation* '76 EP recorded for Ork label, also 7th release on Stiff, UK being first to recognise punk philosophy: featured remake of 'Love Comes In Spurts'; LP of same title on Sire '77; toured with CLASH '77, returned to tour with Elvis COSTELLO, whose manager, Stiff boss Jake Riviera, signed him to Radar: 'Kid With The Replaceable Head' single resulted, prod. by Nick LOWE and featuring expanded band: Bell had left to join RAMONES, replaced by Frank Mauro; Jerry Antonius played bass/keyboards. Hell wrote column for *East Village Eye*; drugs and depression caused some lost time; he returned in some style on Red Star label for *Destiny Street* '82 for which Fred Maher replaced Mauro and Naux (*b* 29 July '51, San José, Cal.) replaced Quine, now with Lou REED. Proto-punk role recorded in films *Smithereens* '82 and *Blank Generation*: song and title are reminder of how far ahead of field he was.

HELMS, Bobby (*b* Bobby Lee Helms, 15 Aug. '33, Bloomington, Ind.) Country-pop star of late '50s. Teenage star on Bloomington TV; appeared on Grand Ole Opry at 17; signed to Decca '56 and had biggest hit: 'Fraulein': no. 1 country, stayed a year in the chart; also top 40 pop; 'My Special Angel' also no. 1 country, top 10 pop. Novelty 'Jingle Bell Rock' also made pop top 10, all '57; 'Jingle' re-charted each December '58, 60, 61, 62. Other hits incl. 'Borrowed

Dreams', 'Jacqueline' '58, 'New River Train' '59, 'Lonely River Rhine' '60. Appeared on Ed Sullivan, Dick Clark, *Country America*, *Jubilee USA* TV shows. Comeback '67 with minor hits on Little Darlin' ('He Thought He'd Die Laughing' '67), Certron ('Mary Goes 'Round' '70). LPs incl. *My Special Angel* '57, *Country Christmas* '58 on Decca; *Fraulein* '62 on Harmony; *I'm The Man* '66, *Sorry My Name Isn't Fred* '67 on Kapp; *All New, Just For You* '68 on Little Darlin'; *My Special Angel* '80 on President.

HEMPHILL, Julius (*b* c.'40, Fort Worth, Texas) Alto sax, other reeds; composer. Studied clarinet with John CARTER; played in US Army band '64; moved to St Louis '68, was member of Black Artists Group (BAG) with Oliver Lake, Lester BOWIE. His works have been presented on stage in NYC, Washington; *The Orientation Of Sweet Willie Rollbar* was filmed '72. Played and recorded with Anthony BRAXTON (*New York, Fall 1974* on Arista), Bowie (*Fast Last* on Muse), KOOL AND THE GANG (*Hustler's Convention*), etc. Own LPs began with *Dogon A.D.* '72, made in St Louis for Mbari label (later issued on Arista) with Phillip Wilson, Abdul Wadud on cello, Baikida E. J. Carroll on trumpet; side-long 'The Hard Blues' added Hamiet BLUIETT. *Coon Bid'ness* '75 was first to come out on Arista, with Wadud, Bluiett, Arthur BLYTHE, Barry ALTSCHUL, Daniel Ben Zebulon on conga; these LPs established him as an excellent musician and important composer. Contributed 'Pensive' to Wildflowers series on Douglas May '76, with Wadud, Wilson, Don Moye, Bern Nix on guitar; duet *Live In New York* later the same month with Wadud on Red Record (Italian label) incl. another version of 'Pensive'. *Blues Boyé* on Mbari and 2-disc *Roi Boyé And The Gotham Minstrels* on Canadian Sackville '77 are solo sets with alto, soprano and flute. *Raw Materials And Residuals* '77 on Black Saint has Wadud and Moye; *Buster Bee* '78 has solos by Hemphill and Lake and two duets; *Flat-Out Jump Suite* '80 made in Milan with quartet incl. Wadud, on Black Saint; *Georgia Blue* '84 on Minor Music was recorded at Willisau Jazz Festival. Composing *Long Tongues*, a sort of opera with saxophones as characters; also co-founder of WORLD SAXOPHONE QUARTET (*which see*).

HENDERSON, Fletcher (*b* James Fletcher Henderson, 18 Dec. 1897, Cuthbert, Ga.; *d* 28 Dec '52, NYC) Pianist, arranger, bandleader; aka 'Smack', said to be from a smacking sound he made with his lips. One of the great innovators in popular music; from middle-class background but apparently a lackadaisical, unbusinesslike man who got worse under pressure. Played piano from age 6; moved to NYC '20 for postgraduate work in chemistry, instead played for black-owned Pace-Handy music company, became recording dir. for its Black Swan label, led band on tour with Ethel WATERS, etc.; elected leader of a band resident at Club Alabam '23, Roseland Ballroom '24, incl. Coleman HAWKINS, Joe SMITH, Don REDMAN, Jimmy HARRISON. The band played pop tunes, novelties, simulated blues, but jazz was in the air. Louis ARMSTRONG hired '24; stayed only a year but his infl. very important; Buster Bailey kept coming back. Redman wrote virtually all the arrangements until '27: he divided brass and reed sections (saxes doubled on clarinets; trombones could play against trumpets), played voices against each other in call-and-response, riffs under soloists, etc.; variations for sections as though improvised in unison was beginning of big band jazz: meanwhile they began to swing under Armstrong's influence. The list of players who passed through is a list of the best: Tommy LADNIER, Bobby Stark, Benny MORTON, Buster Bailey, Kaiser Marshall, Fats WALLER, many more. Despite lack of firm leadership, musicians stayed because the music was so good: 'St Louis Shuffle', 'The Stampede', 'Tozo', 'Henderson Stomp', 'Whiteman Stomp', 'Hop Off', scores more. Redman left '27; Henderson suffered head injuries in '28 car crash, allegedly becoming even lazier; the band broke up in '29, following a date to play a show prod. by Vincent YOUMANS, when a white conductor began firing his men, Henderson doing nothing about it. He re-formed with Hawkins, Harrison, sometimes Morton; talent parade continued with Henry ALLEN, Claude Jones, J. C. HIGGINBOTHAM, Sandy WILLIAMS, Rex STEWART, Benny CARTER. He lost the Roseland gig to more reliable Claude HOPKINS; Hawk left '34, partly because the band was going nowhere, succeeded briefly by Lester YOUNG, then Ben

WEBSTER, Chu BERRY: thus Henderson had hired all the greatest tenor players in pre-war jazz. Now he did his own writing, with contributions from brother Horace (*see below*), Carter and others: he refined the style, perfecting a smoother music specifically for dancing, but still jazz-oriented and with plenty of space for soloists: 'Sugar Foot Stomp' (from King OLIVER's 'Dipper Mouth Blues'), and Jelly Roll MORTON's 'King Porter Stomp' had been recorded several times since early days; Horace's 'Big John's Special', 'Down South Camp Meetin'', 'Wrappin' It Up' (all '34), as well as plenty of pop tunes of the day. Went broke, disbanded, sold bundle of charts to Benny GOODMAN, who touched off Swing Era (*see* BIG BAND ERA) '35 and had hits with all of them. Henderson's style dominated pop music for the next 15 years; he re-formed and made some of his best records: as Dicky WELLS wrote, 'You just had to play the notes and the arrangement was swinging.' Waller's 'Stealin' Apples', Horace's arr. of Edgar SAMPSON's 'Blue Lou', 'Christopher Columbus' (a hit, based on riffs by Chu Berry and others) and Louis PRIMA's 'Sing, Sing, Sing (With A Swing)' all recorded '36 (Goodman interpolated the last two for the most successful 'killerdiller' of the era). Henderson admired the back-to-basics approach of the Count BASIE band, lending Basie his charts when Basie came to NYC; continued to write for Goodman (e.g. 'Sometimes I'm Happy', though Goodman said Henderson had to be convinced he could do lovely ballad charts). Joined Goodman as sextet pianist '39, formed another band '41 with Goodman's help, was a hit again at Roseland but it was his last spark as a leader. Rejoined Goodman '47, Ethel Waters '48-9, led sextet '50, had stroke late that year and never played again. Also wrote for Teddy HILL, Jack HYLTON, many others; his infl. can still be heard in any big band (e.g. *see* SUN RA). *Tribute To Fletcher Henderson* '57 was joyous, swinging alumni success, unlike most all-star dates. Best Henderson set is badly titled 4-disc *A Study In Frustration* on CBS: '23-38 compilation incl. almost all those mentioned above; there is nothing frustrating about the music. Others on MCA, Biograph, Swing; *Wild Party* on Hep UK has excellent transfers of seminal '34 tracks; '36-41 tracks compiled on *The End Of An Era* on Contact Records, Milan.

HENDERSON, Horace (*b* 22 Nov. '04, Cuthbert, Ga.) Pianist, arranger, bandleader; brother of Fletcher (*see above*). Attended Wilburforce U., formed band the Collegians, led it during summer holidays, incl. Benny CARTER, Rex STEWART; Horace's band was still called the Collegians when Don REDMAN took it over '31: Redman had management and record contract, but valued Horace's services as pianist/arr. '31-2. For a week Horace worked for Duke ELLINGTON band Nov. '32. He wrote arrangements for Charlie BARNET, Tommy DORSEY, Earl HINES, Jimmie LUNCEFORD and others; was thought perhaps a better pianist than Fletcher but not as good an arranger: nevertheless, from a recording session of 19 Mar. '31 up until '39, of about 120 arrangements recorded by the Fletcher Henderson band, many are uncredited and others were written by Edgar SAMPSON, Russ MORGAN, Will Hudson, Nat Leslie, trumpeter Dick Vance (*b* 28 Nov. '15, Mayfield, Ky.) etc., but discographies can credit almost as many to Horace as to Fletcher: about 28-30 for each, and Horace played piano on others. Horace's incl. some of the most interesting: his own 'Hot And Anxious' '31 (also recorded by Redman '32; later reduced to 'In The Mood': *see* Edgar HAYES), 'Nagasaki' (both Fletcher and Redman '32-3), 'Queer Notions' '33 (modern-sounding tune by Coleman HAWKINS), Horace's own 'Big John's Special' '34 (later a hit by Benny GOODMAN), 'Christopher Columbus' '36 (composition credited to Chu BERRY, probably Fletcher's biggest hit). Horace's recording dates as leader incl. '33 session with Fletcher's band; he made 21 titles in '40, but one of those five dates was credited as 'Fletcher Henderson conducts Horace Henderson and his Orchestra': a very talented man, always in the shadow of his older and more famous brother. Led own bands early '35, '37-40; US Army service; accompanied Lena HORNE; own band again '45-9; small groups from '49. Worked in Chicago c.'50, records on Decca but no success; led band on Catalina Island '60s; settled in Colorado, cond. band at Broadmore Hotel, Colorado Springs; took part in History of American Music project for Smithsonian Institution; lived in Denver, still playing organ in clubs there c.'80. Also wrote 'Love For Scale', 'Rug Cutter's Swing', 'Kitty On Toast', 'Comin' And Goin' ', 'Jamaica Shout', etc.

HENDERSON, Skitch (*b* Lyle Cedric Henderson, 27 Jan. '18, Halstad, Minn.) Bandleader, pianist, composer. Attended U. of Cal.; Juilliard; studied with Arnold Schönberg, conductor Fritz Reiner, others; then switched to pop: played piano in dance bands, theatre orchestras etc.; accompanied Judy GARLAND on tour; mus. dir. of Bing CROSBY radio show; led own dance band '47-9 which incl. French horns, recorded for Capitol. NBC music staff '51: mus. dir. of Steve ALLEN show '55-6; led band on *Tonight* show during summer '62 after host Jack Paar suddenly left, stayed on when Johnny Carson took over that fall: band rarely allowed to shine, but book incl. arr. by Neal HEFTI, Ernie Wilkins, etc.; sidemen incl. trumpets Clark TERRY, Doc SEVERINSEN, Snooky Young (*b* 3 Feb. '19, Dayton, Ohio; played with LUNCEFORD, BASIE, CLARKE-BOLAND BIG BAND, Thad JONES/Mel LEWIS, etc.). Left NBC '66; conductor of Tulsa Symphony Orchestra '71-2, guest conductor of many others; mus. dir. for New York City Opera revival of Kurt WEILL's *Street Scene*, etc. Albums: *Sketches By Skitch* on RCA; on Columbia: *Skitch . . . Tonight!* (charted '65), *Eyes Of Love, A Tribute To Irving Berlin*.

HENDRICKS, Jon (*b* 16 Sep. '21, Newark, Ohio) Singer, songwriter. One of 17 children; sang on radio after family moved to Toledo, Ohio, '32, sometimes accompanied by Art TATUM. Toured Europe, led own vocal quartet; to NYC '52; wrote vocal version of 'Four Brothers' (*see* Woody HERMAN), other songs; lyrics for George RUSSELL album *New York, New York* '59 ('The city so nice/They had to name it twice'); meanwhile co-founder of vocal trio Lambert, Hendricks & Ross '57-64 with Annie Ross and Dave Lambert. David Alden Lambert (*b* 19 June '17, Boston, Mass.; *d* 3 Oct. '66, Westport, Conn.) was an organiser and mus. dir. of vocal groups; collaborated on new version of 'Four Brothers'; they recruited Ross (*b* Annabelle Short,

25 July '30, Mitcham, Surrey, England). She had written 'Twisted' '52, composing words to fit a solo by Wardell GRAY; she became ill '62 during a tour of Europe and left the group, replaced by Yolande Bavan; then freelanced in UK. She was a partner in legendary jazz club Annie's Room in London '65-6; is also a fine actress (e.g. *Kennedy's Children* in London '75). Hendricks wrote lyrics to Count BASIE arrangements, for solos as well as ensemble passages; the trio made multi-track recording so that they sounded like a whole band; Roulette LP *Sing A Song Of Basie* early '58 was a sensation among jazz fans: they went on the road full-time, made other successful LPs on Columbia, World Pacific, ABC/Impulse, with Bavan on RCA. Hendricks gave up trio when Lambert left '64, in demand since as lyricist and performer: his wit and swing are unique in vocal jazz. Hendricks also wrote musical presentation *Evolution Of The Blues*, given at Monterey Jazz Festival '60 (Columbia LP; revived in San Francisco '75); lived in London late '60s; was jazz critic on *San Francisco Chronicle* '73-4; occasionally revived trio format with wife Judith and daughter Michelle. Own LP on World Pacific in '50s; King Pleasure (who deserves some credit for starting the whole thing with his version of James MOODY's version of 'I'm In The Mood For Love') made LP with Hendricks on Prestige; other Hendricks LPs incl. *Fast Livin' Blues* on Columbia, *Salute To Joao Gilberto* on Reprise, *In Person At The Trident* on Smash, *Blues For Pablo* on Arista, *Cloudburst* '72 on Enja, *Love* '81-2 on Muse.

HENDRIX, Jimi (*b* 27 Nov. '42, Seattle, Wash.; *d* 18 Sep. '70, London) Guitarist, singer; without doubt the most prodigiously original, inventive and influential guitarist of the rock era. Left-handed, he played right-handed instrument upside down rather than a left-handed one. One story had him born Johnny Allen Hendrix, his name changed by his father to James Marshall Hendrix. Self-taught on guitar as schoolboy, infl. by Robert JOHNSON, B. B. KING. Enlisted in US Army paratroopers '61, invalided out late '62; with Army friend, bassist Billy Cox, moved to Nashville; formed trio called the Casuals, played in numerous bands incl. Bobby Taylor & the Vancouvers

(who later took three singles into Hot 100 '68, with lead guitarist Tommy Chong, later famous as half of the comedy duo Cheech & Chong). Hendrix left to play lead guitar in LITTLE RICHARD's road band '63-5, learning from one of the great rock'n'roll showmen; also played on stage with the ISLEY BROS, Solomon BURKE, Wilson PICKETT, Joey DEE & the Starliters and allegedly a singing wrestler called Gorgeous George. Records made in this era are not of interest (although later scraped up and issued) except an obscure single with L.A.-based singer/guitarist Arthur Lee (later leader of Love), who used Hendrix on 'My Diary' c.'63-4, credited to singer Rosa Lee Brooks: first record known to feature Hendrix's guitar. He left Richard after a dispute over wages; went to NYC '65, worked for singer Curtis Knight in his band called the Squires, signed usurious three-year record contract with local company that would haunt him the rest of his life: few records were made, but they were endlessly recycled later in more than a dozen LPs, mostly duplicating one another. He also recorded with saxist Lennie Youngblood (incl. Hendrix song 'Red House'); new friends/influences incl. Bob DYLAN, John HAMMOND; began to use drugs intemperately, first trying LSD; led own band called Jimmy James & the Blue Flames (after legendary Junior PARKER group; incl. Randy Craig Wolfe, later RANDY California of SPIRIT). Bryan 'Chas' Chandler, bassist with the ANIMALS, went to hear Hendrix at Café Wha in Greenwich Village: he wanted to move into the business side of pop and convinced Hendrix to come to the UK, where Chandler would manage him and find a record deal. The 'Swinging London' phenomenon was then at its height, pop's royalty overwhelmingly English after the complete success of the British Invasion; Hendrix's technical skill was now completely developed and allowed him to become a dazzling showman: he played the guitar behind his head and with his teeth, stroked the neck along microphone stand, used feedback and dynamics to new effect, sometimes used lighter fuel on his guitar to set it alight, setting London on its ear. He changed his name from Jimmy to Jimi; trio the Jimi Hendrix Experience was formed with Noel Redding on bass (who had contacted Chandler because he heard the Animals needed a guitarist) and John 'Mitch' Mitchell on drums (had been child actor, then worked with Georgie FAME and his Blue Flames, coincidental similarity with Hendrix's NYC group). Debut single was 'Hey Joe', cover of USA hit by L.A. group the Leaves; several record companies turned it down before Polydor took it and it was in the UK top 10 within days in early '67. 'Purple Haze' reached top 3 (became first USA chart entry, on Reprise); 'The Wind Cries Mary' was top 10, 'Burning Of The Midnight Lamp' top 20; first LP *Are You Experienced?* was no. 3 LP UK, no. 5 USA (along with hastily scraped-up Curtis Knight LP *Get That Feeling* on Capitol, no. 75 LP USA). Trio appeared at the Monterey Pop Festival and film (live LP released '70 had one side by the Experience, the other by Otis REDDING, equally revelatory to white audiences); the Experience toured USA supporting MONKEES: no one admits to having put together that unlikely package. All this was '67; in '68 *Axis: Bold As Love* was no. 3 LP USA, 5 UK; 2-disc *Electric Ladyland* (sensational gatefold sleeve photo of Hendrix and large group of unclothed women) was no. 1 LP USA, top 10 UK (where it competed with *Smash Hits* LP, also top 10; top 10 USA '69). In late '68 his legendary cover of Bob DYLAN's 'All Along The Watchtower' was top 5 UK; as biggest USA single it reached top 20 (his greatness coincided with switch to emphasis on LPs instead of singles in USA charts). At its peak success began to crumble: Hendrix and Redding grew apart; he was fuddled by self-indulgence in drugs and groupies, believed management was cheating him: this is unlikely, as Chandler remained Hendrix's champion long after he died; but his erstwhile business partner Mike Jeffrey first eased Hendrix out of their joint management firm, then began dubious business dealings which emerged later (full truth will never be known, as Jeffrey was killed in an aviation accident '70s). In '69 the Experience broke up; Redding departed to front such bands as Fat Mattress ('69-70), later a Noel Redding Band (mid-'70s); Mitch stayed with Hendrix, Billy Cox rejoining his old friend on bass; this lineup played the Woodstock Festival '69, with its legendary version of 'The Star-Spangled

Banner': Hendrix imitates the 'rockets' red glare, the bombs bursting in air' on his guitar, landing back on the melody in exactly the right place like the most agile of jazzmen. For an LP '70 he formed Band Of Gypsies, with Cox and Buddy Miles on drums; but chemistry was not right and it broke up. He tried to create his dream studio in NYC; the Electric Lady continued to function after he died, but building it was a nightmare, mainly because his contract problems multiplied almost daily, with record royalties being frozen while lawyers made money. Mitchell came back; with Cox the trio made a film in Hawaii called *Rainbow Bridge* and appeared at the massive Isle of Wight festival in '70: it was the last time a UK audience saw either Hendrix or Jim Morrison of the DOORS alive. After a short continental tour he resumed nightclubbing in London with his girlfriend Monika Danneman; he died in her flat choking on his own vomit in his sleep (surprisingly common accident resulting from mixing drink and drugs; Swing Era leader Tommy DORSEY died the same way). He was mourned by Eric CLAPTON, Jeff BECK and Jimmy Page, English friends and guitarists who knew he was the master of them all. *The Cry Of Love* '71 was the last LP Hendrix himself approved; there was a documentary film *Jimi Hendrix* (2-disc soundtrack with interviews charted '73 in USA), and a flood of compilations and outright trash: as well as pre-fame barrel-scrapings engineer Alan Douglas grafted backings onto incomplete Hendrix tracks from the Electric Lady, in some cases using musicians who never met Hendrix (*Midnight Lightning, Crash Landing, Nine To The Universe* etc. all on Polydor). Polydor, to whom all of Hendrix's best work had reverted, compiled a complete 13-disc *Tenth Anniversary Box* '80 (incl. *Electric Ladyland*, also available separately or on two single LPs); these are a starting place for a serious student of modern popular music. Hendrix's technique and reinjection of the values of black music into rock'n'roll was an achievement as complete as that of Charlie PARKER in jazz and had a similar effect in that imitators and acolytes were less talented; in Hendrix's case his power trio format led to the excesses of heavy metal and loudness for its own sake. 2-disc *Live At*

Winterland '87 was made in San Francisco '68, incl. exciting live versions of 'Manic Depression' and 'Spanish Castle Magic', also some tedium: perhaps rock ultimately could not have contained his penchant for free jamming; if he had lived he might have widened his musical base and become even more influential.

HENRY, Clarence (*b* 19 Mar. '37, New Orleans) R&B singer, songwriter. Studied piano and trombone as a child; played in local bands at age 18, became famous overnight when his 'Ain't Got No Home', leased to Chicago's Argo label, made no. 3 R&B/no. 20 pop late '56: he could 'sing like a girl' (falsetto) and 'sing like a frog' in a funny voice: nearly perfect R&B novelty gave him the nickname 'Frogman'; flip side just as good, 'Trouble, Trouble' sharing writer credit with bandleader Paul GAYTEN, an uptempo romp which belied its title. He returned to charts '61-2 with records prod. by Gayten and Allen TOUSSAINT: '(I Don't Know Why I Love You) But I Do', 'You Always Hurt The One You Love' (both top 20 R&B and pop), and minor hits 'Lonely Street', 'On Bended Knees'/'Standing In The Need Of Love' etc.; switched labels to Parrot for near miss 'Have You Ever Been Lonely'. He remained a favourite in New Orleans clubs for years.

HENRY COW Avant-garde rock band formed '68; founder members Tim Hodgkinson (organs and reeds), Fred Frith (guitar; also violin and viola, piano, xylophone). The name had some connection with American composer Henry Cowell (1897-1965), but everybody's forgotten exactly what. Chris Cutler joined on drums '72; they played at the Edinburgh Festival and used name Cabaret Voltaire in London (another group of that name formed a year later in Manchester). Appeared at Bath International Music Festival '73, helped play Mike OLDFIELD's 'Tubular Bells' in London. Ran the Explorer's Club with Derek BAILEY, Lol COXHILL, Cornelius Cardew's Scratch Orchestra, others; recorded *Leg End* (aka *Legend*) for Virgin with John Greaves on bass, also one side of *Live At Dingwall's Dance Hall* as the Greasy Truckers. Lindsay Cooper joined '74 on

reeds, piano etc.; they recorded *Unrest* for Virgin; toured Europe with CAPTAIN BEEFHEART, UK with German band Faust; Frith made *Guitar Solos I* on Caroline; band made *Desperate Straights* '74 on Virgin with Slapp Happy: Peter Blegvad, Anthony Moore, vocalist Dagmar Krause had made LP *Sort Of* on Polydor '72; *Slapp Happy* '73 unreleased, re-recorded for Virgin '74, original version and reissued *Sort Of* on Recommended '81. Henry Cow/Slapp Happy merged, made *In Praise Of Learning* '75 on Virgin, unmerged. Cow toured Europe incl. gigs with Robert WYATT; 2-disc *Concerts* '76 on Caroline; Frith's *Guitar Solos II* '76 with Bailey, Hans Reichel and G. F. Fitzgerald. They played at the Roundhouse in London '77 with Mike WESTBROOK Brass Band, Frankie Armstrong as the Occasional Orchestra. Next LP was *Western Culture* '79 on Broadcast (own label); they have all kept busy: Frith, Cutler, Krause formed Art Bears, made *Hopes And Fears* '78, *Winter Songs* '79, *The World As It Is Today* '81 ('frankly political and bitter'); Cooper made *Rags* '81 (song cycle based on Victorian sweat shops) with Frith, Cutler, Georgie Born on cello and bass, others; Frith's *Guitar Solos III* on Rift (own label) with several other guitarists; also five LPs on USA Ralph label, solo *Live In Japan* on Recommended Japan, *Voice Of America* on Rift, *French Gigs* with Coxhill, *Live In Prague And Washington* with Cutler, all since '80; Hodgkinson has done many things on his own Woof label; all have sessioned widely. Frith's work incl. *Live, Love, Larf & Loaf* on Rhino, with guitarists John French, Henry Kaiser, Richard THOMPSON.

HENSKE, Judy (*b* Chippewa Falls, Wis.) Folk singer. To West Coast c.'60; joined the Whiskeyhill singers organised by Dave Guard (ex-KINGSTON TRIO), sang on their '62 LP; in '63 her solo albums were released on Elektra, incl. *Judy Henske* and *High Flying Bird*. She married Jerry Yester (ex-ASSOCIATION, LOVIN' SPOONFUL; they formed a duo and made LPs for Frank ZAPPA's Straight label: *Farewell Aldebaran* '69 and *Rosebud* '71 with Craig Doerge, John Seiter and David Vaught). Almost a household name during the urban folk boom of the early '60s for her striking appearance (she is very tall) and her dynamic vocal style; she was critically praised but not commercially successful.

HERBERT, Victor (*b* 1 Feb. 1859, Dublin, Ireland; *d* 24 May '24, NYC) Composer. Played cello in symphony orchestras; was conductor in USA, wrote first original music for a silent film (*The Fall Of A Nation*); founder-member of ASCAP; recorded for Victor. Wrote about 40 operetta-style musical shows which continued to be revived and filmed after his death. Among the best-known shows and songs: *Babes In Toyland* '03 (filmed '34 with Laurel & Hardy), *Mlle Modiste* '06 ('Kiss Me Again'; filmed '30), *Naughty Marietta* '10 ('Ah! Sweet Mystery Of Life'; film '35 made stars of duo Nelson EDDY/Jeanette MacDonald), *Sweethearts* '13 (film '38 with Eddy/-MacDonald), *Orange Blossoms* '22 ('A Kiss In The Dark'). Piano piece 'Indian Summer' from *The Velvet Lady* '19 became hit '39 with lyrics by Al Dubin, whose better-known collaboration was that with Harry WARREN.

HERMAN, Woody (*b* Woodrow Charles Herman, 16 May '13, Milwaukee, Wis.; *d* 28 Oct. '87, L.A.) Clarinet, also alto sax; leader, singer. Sang/danced from age 6; travelled from '30 with band that incl. Tony MARTIN in reed section; started own band '33 but failed; worked for Gus ARNHEIM, Isham JONES etc.; took over Jones's band '36 and led dixielandish 'Band That Plays The Blues', with the small group Woodchoppers as band-within-a-band: among first hits on Decca was 'Woodchopper's Ball' '39 (written by flugelhorn player Joe Bishop, *b* 27 Nov. '07, Monticello, Ark.; *d* 12 May '76, Houston, Texas; charted again '43); more than 50 hits '37-52 also incl. band's theme 'Blue Flame' (named after notorious locker room trick), no. 1 'Blues In The Night' '42, latter from film of same name, with vocal by Woody, Carolyn Grey. The band had begun as a cooperative; as men were drafted Herman bought their shares, modernised the band, infl. by Duke ELLINGTON, others; Dizzy GILLESPIE wrote 'Down Under', 'Swing Shift', 'Woody'n'You'; the band's evolution seemed revolutionary because it did not record during the musicians' strike of '42-3; Decca was one of the first labels to settle with James C. PETRILLO's union, but issued only four of 24 titles recorded '44; the band that switched to Columbia had become the best white band of the BIG BAND ERA (disbanding and re-forming '47 and '49), Herman proving to be one of the all-time best recruiters of new talent in the music business, also with the rare ability (like Count BASIE) to perfect an arrangement by editing it after the band worked it out. 'One unmistakable quality of big-band jazz at its best is *joie de vivre*: that is Woody's quality' (Barry Ulanov). Bassist Chubby Jackson (*b* Greig Stewart Jackson, 25 Dec. '18, NYC) and pianist/arr. Ralph BURNS joined late '43, both from Charlie BARNET band; Jackson helped to recruit the rest: trumpet/arr. Neal HEFTI; also Dave TOUGH, Flip PHILLIPS; Bill Harris on trombone (*b* Willard Palmer Harris, 28 Oct. '16, Philadelphia; *d* 21 Aug. '73, Fla.; with Benny GOODMAN '43-4): his solo on Burns' 'Bijou (*Rhumba à la Jazz*)' '45 is one of the most famous of trombone solos; he also wrote the beautiful 'Everywhere' (arr. by Hefti). Guitarist Billy Bauer (*b* 14 Nov. '15, NYC; later played with Lennie TRISTANO) replaced last remaining member of old band: '44-6 band was called Herman's Herd (later the First Herd): vitality, swing high spirits still sound fresh as if the records were made yesterday. Both CANDOLI brothers in trumpet section mid-'44 (16-year-old Conte played on weekly radio series for Old Gold cigarettes while on summer holiday from high school), Burns on piano, Margie Hyams on vibes (*b* '23, NYC; later married George SHEARING and retired); band appeared in film *Sensations Of 1945*, *Earl Carroll's Vanities*, others; was sponsored on network radio by Wildroot hair oil (after which a Hefti arr. was named); played Carnegie Hall concert 25 March '46 with Pete Candoli, Shorty ROGERS and Sonny BERMAN in trumpet section, John LA PORTA among reeds, Red NORVO on vibes (his joining in Jan. '46 precipitated new edition of Woodchoppers), drummer Don Lamond (*b* 18 Aug. '20, Oklahoma City): incl. premier of *Ebony Concerto*: nothing to do with jazz, but written for the band by Igor Stravinsky. The band won polls, sold records: top 10 hits '45-6 incl. Ellington's 'Do Nothing Till You Hear From Me', film theme 'Laura', Louis JORDAN's 'Caldonia' (with Herman vocal, trumpet passage transcribed from a Dizzy solo), Sammy CAHN-Jule Styne song 'Let It Snow! Let It Snow! Let It Snow!'; singer Frances Wayne (*b* Chiarina Francesca Bertocci, 26 Aug. '24, Boston) had hit on flip side of 'Caldonia', 'Happiness Is Just A Thing Called Joe', also 'Saturday Night Is The Loneliest Night Of The Week' (on Decca), 'Gee, It's Good To Hold You' (she married Hefti, later sang with his band on Coral label). (For other Herman classics of the era, see entries for Burns and Hefti.) He toured Cuba with small group '47, re-formed band: Second Herd known as 'Four Brothers' band after composition by Jimmy GIUFFRE, with blend of reeds Zoot SIMS, Stan GETZ, Serge CHALOFF, Herbie Steward (*b* 7 May '26, L.A.): writing and reed sound left no doubt about infl. of Lester YOUNG, Charlie PARKER, set the tone for the West Coast 'cool' style of '50s; also played 'Early Autumn' (adapted fourth part of Burns's 'Summer Sequence', with ethereal solo by Stan GETZ), 'Lemon Drop', 'That's Right', etc. The Second Herd unfortunately incl. many sleepy heads (junkies); Herman led small group late '49-early '50, formed Third Herd; recorded on Capitol, then on own Mars label '52-3 (re-recording of 'Early Autumn' was last chart hit single), toured Europe '54; continued re-forming for tours etc. Musicians passing through incl. Nat PIERCE, Al COHN, Bill CHASE, drummer Jake Hanna; after playing in first two Herds Harris returned '56-8 (also played with JATP; own LPs incl. *And Friends* on Fantasy, *Memorial Album* on Xanadu, both '57); trombonists also incl. Carl Fontana (*b* 18 July '28, Monroe, La.) and Urbie Green (*b* 8 Aug. '26, Mobile, Ala.; worked for Frankie CARLE, Gene KRUPA, Herman '50-2, Benny GOODMAN '56-7, appeared in film *The Benny Goodman Story*; fine sideman on many LPs); reeds: Richie Kamuca (*b* 23 July '30, Philadelphia; *d* 22 July '77, L.A.), Sal Nistico, Arno Marsh (*b* 28 May '28, Grand Rapids, Mich.), vocalist Joe Carroll (best known for work with Dizzy GILLESPIE), Albert Dailey, Cecil PAYNE, keyboardist Lyle Mays, many others. The number of herds is uncounted: Herman led more good bands than anyone else, loved not only by the public but by musicians. Pierce said to George T. Simon, 'We never feel we're actually working *for* the man. It's

more like working *with* him.' His witty clarinet accents added much to the late '40s classics; some members of the Second Herd looked down at his 'old-fashioned' playing, but Gerry MULLIGAN said of one arrangement that Herman's solo was the only one that had anything to do with the tune. He played more alto sax than before in mid-'50s; first sang with Jones, showing humour and mellow personality in blues-inflected phrasing on ballads and blues (such as 'Panacea' from the Carnegie Hall concert). Compilations from '36-44 on MCA, Affinity, Sunbeam, Hindsight; essential anthology is 3-disc CBS set *The Thundering Herds* (or *The Three Herds*); '48-50 stuff on Capitol's *Classics In Jazz* (also *Early Autumn*); Old Gold broadcasts, V-discs etc. on London, Hep, Fanfare, other labels; countless LPs since incl. *Live At Monterey* '59 on Atlantic; Phillips LPs early '60s incl. unusual version of 'A Taste Of Honey', made a few hours after JFK was shot: recording session had to be abandoned, but track is cited as an example of how deeply jazz playing can be affected by the moment. *Concerto For Herd* '67 live at Monterey on Verve (written by Bill Holman, *b* 21 May '27, Olive, Cal.); six LPs on Fantasy incl. *Giant Steps* '73 (one of several Grammy winners), *Herd At Monterey* '74. On Concord Jazz: *And Friends At Monterey* '79 with Getz, Dizzy GILLESPIE, Woody SHAW, Slide HAMPTON; *Live At Concord Jazz Festival* '81 with Cohn and Getz; *World Class* '82, made in Japan with 16-piece band plus Nistico, Pierce, Cohn, Flip Phillips; *Presents A Great American Evening* '83 with small group; *My Buddy* with Rosemary CLOONEY. '46 Carnegie Hall concert has been in and out of print on MGM. In the late '60s Herman's manager gambled away the band's income tax money; he told Artie SHAW, 'I'm going to be on the road for the rest of my life.' The taxman persecuted him to the point of selling his home, but he never complained, never held a grudge.

HERMAN'S HERMITS UK pop group formed '63. Lineup: Peter 'Herman' Noone (*b* 5 Nov. '47) on vocals, piano, guitar; Karl Green (*b* 31 July '47), guitar, harmonica; Keith Hopwood (*b* 26 Oct. '46), guitar; Derek 'Lek' Leckenby (*b* 14 May '45), guitar; Barry Whithman (*b* 21 July '46), drums:

Lek was from Leeds, Green from Salford, rest from Manchester where group was formed. Noone had studied acting, singing; appeared in plays, TV; joined group then called the Heartbeats. Spotted by Mickie MOST, first single 'I'm Into Something Good' was no. 1 UK/13 USA: they had total of 20 top 40 hits in UK '64-70 on EMI/Columbia, 18 in USA '64-8 (11 in top 10) on MGM, their sunny good-time music an alternative to R&B imitators in the British Invasion. Biggest hits incl. 'Mrs Brown, You've Got A Lovely Daughter', 'I'm Henry VIII, I Am' (music hall song written '11), both no. 1 in USA; cover of the Rays' 'Silhouettes'; 'Listen People' (from film *When The Boys Meet The Girls*), 'A Must To Avoid' and 'Leaning On The Lamp Post' (from film *Hold On!*). They also made film called *Mrs Brown, You've Got A Lovely Daughter*; had 10 LPs in USA album chart incl. 2 film soundtracks: their first 3 LPs made top 5, incl. first of 3 *Best Of* LPs, which stayed in USA LP chart 105 weeks. Noone went solo, had no. 12 UK hit 'Oh You Pretty Thing' '71 (cover of David BOWIE); rejoined others '73 for revivals, lived in France, hosted UK TV show; Hermits recorded without him unsuccessfully on Buddah. He tried comeback late '70s with group called the Tremblers in L.A. (LP *Twice Nightly*); made LP *One Of The Glory Boys* '82, appeared on Broadway in *Pirates Of Penzance* '82, then in London.

HESTER, Carolyn (*b* Texas) Folksinger. To NYC '56 to study theatre, having appeared on TV at 13 in Texas; toured with New Lost City Ramblers and made an obscure first LP before the urban folk boom was well underway. She married Richard FARINA; made her second LP for Tradition '61 (still available in USA), and her third for Columbia '62, on which Bob DYLAN played harmonica. She and Farina were popular in the UK, among the first of the new folkies to appear there (at the Edinburgh Folk Festival and on TV); they separated in '62. Her debut at NYC's Town Hall resulted in live recordings; she formed a folk-rock band the Carolyn Hester Coalition which also recorded, but her folk roots were perhaps stronger than her need for commercial success (she had been among those protesting against ABC-TV's decision to ban Pete

SEEGER from *Hootenanny*). In the '70s she continued gigging at colleges and festivals, made an LP for RCA and was on the board of directors of the annual Kerrville (Texas) Folk Festival, where she still appeared in the mid-'80s.

HEYWARD, Nick (*b* 20 May '61, London) UK pop person, moving force behind Haircut 100, who appealed during early '80s infantile pop era. Single hits incl. 'Favourite Shirts (Boy Meets Girl)' (no. 4 '81), 'Love Plus One', 'Fantastic Day'; concerts were hysterical, similar to those of BAY CITY ROLLERS. Haircut's only LP with Heyward, *Pelican West* '82, incl. all hit tracks, all written by him. He left '82; group carried on with new deal, LP *Paint On Paint* '83, then split (drummer Blair Cunningham joined PRETENDERS '86). Heyward made confident, diverting solo LP *North Of A Miracle* '83, relying on session people (Tim Renwick, Dave Mattacks) instead of contemporaries, incl. 'The Day It Rained Forever', 'Whistle Down The Wind', blue-eyed soul 'Take That Situation'; belated follow-up *Postcards From Home* '86 was less substantial. Supported WHAM! at their final show '86, joined onstage by Haircut alumni.

HEYWOOD, Eddie (*b* 4 Dec. '15, Atlanta, Ga.) Pianist, composer, arranger. Father Eddie Sr was well-known bandleader, as was uncle LeRoy Smith. Played with Wayman CARVER, Benny CARTER, Don REDMAN, others; formed own sextet '41 in NYC, later worked in California, appeared in a couple of films incl. good thriller *The Dark Corner* '46: soundtrack incl. 'Heywood Blues'; group was also well-known for his arr. of 'Begin The Beguine'. Stopped playing because of partial paralysis of hands; resumed '50, continued veering towards pop and away from jazz: composed 'Canadian Sunset' and played on huge hit record by Hugo WINTERHALTER '56. Had to quit playing again late '60s but resumed '72; received awards from hometown radio station and from BMI incl. one for a million broadcast performances of 'Sunset'; prod. Swing Era revival LPs for Time-Life. Compilation *The Biggest Little Band Of The Forties* on Commodore.

HIATT, John (*b* '52, Indianapolis, Ind.) Singer/songwriter. First musical job as staff songwriter at Nashville publishing house at $25 a week; songs covered by THREE DOG NIGHT, Conway TWITTY (whose version of 'Heavy Tears' topped country chart). Worked with Nashville prod. Norbert Putnam; made break with two LPs of demo quality *Hangin' Around The Observatory* '74 and *Overcoats* '75, which he now disowns. Built up repertoire, toured solo extensively, signed with MCA in L.A. '78: LPs *Slug Line* '79, *Two Bit Monsters* '80 critically acclaimed; songs covered by Dave EDMUNDS, Maria MULDAUR, Rick NELSON, many others; film soundtracks *American Gigolo*, *Cruising* used Hiatt material. Joined Ry COODER band on tours, records: contributed to *Borderline* '80, *The Slide Area* '82 on vocals, guitar, wrote with Cooder for film soundtrack *The Border* '82 and sang two songs. LP *All Of A Sudden* '82 on Geffen made in London with David BOWIE, prod. by Tony Visconti; toured in Buffy SAINTE-MARIE band '82; then *Riding With The King* '84, best LP to date, with one solo and one band side, latter made in London with Nick LOWE: standout cut 'She Loves The Jerk'. *Warming Up To The Ice Age* '85 continued anglophile connection with Elvis COSTELLO (arguably his English equivalent) duetting on cover of Spinners' 'Living A Little, Laughing A Little'; album prod. by Putnam described as 'like Parliament/Funkadelic meets ZZ Top at Big Pink'. Songs were stronger than ever on *Bring The Family* '87 with Lowe and Cooder, *Slow Turning* '88 with David LINDLEY.

HIBBLER, Al (*b* Albert Hibbler, 16 Aug. '15, Little Rock, Ark.) Singer with deep baritone voice. With Jay MCSHANN ('Get Me On Your Mind'), then Duke ELLINGTON '43-51: 'Don't You Know I Care?', 'I'm Just A Lucky So And So', 'I Ain't Got Nothin' But The Blues', 'Pretty Woman', 'Strange Feeling' (from the *Perfume Suite* '45), all on Victor; on Columbia: 'I Like The Sunrise' from *Liberian Suite*, 'Don't Be So Mean Baby' ('Cause Baby's So Good To You)' (song by Peggy LEE and Dave Barbour), classic versions of 'Don't Get Around Much Any More' and 'Do Nothin' Till You Hear From Me', all '47; 'Good Woman Blues'

'49, etc. The most popular male singer Ellington ever had; he worked out a method of bringing Hibbler to the microphone, their shoulders touching, and leaving him in just the right place so that it was not obvious that the singer had been born blind. He recorded 'Solitude' with Billy STRAYHORN; went solo, recorded with Count BASIE and Johnny HODGES on Mercury, solo on Aladdin ('S'posin' '), Mercury ('It Must Be True'/'No Greater Love') and Decca: vocal version of Alex North film theme 'Unchained Melody' was no. 5 '55. An unforgettable voice.

HICKS, Dan (*b* 9 Dec. '41, Little Rock, Ark.) Vocalist, songwriter; played guitar and drums. Moved to Santa Rosa, Cal. in his teens, infl. by big band jazz during high school years; joined the CHARLATANS, one of the first of the San Francisco rock groups. Under the infl. of Django REINHARDT he formed the Hot Licks, signed to Epic as Dan Hicks and his Hot Licks, with female vocal backing group the Lickettes. *Original Recordings* '70 was followed by unreleased LP; he switched to Blue Thumb for live *Where's The Money* '71, *Striking It Rich* '72 and *Last Train To Hicksville* '73. The first two of these incl. sparkling versions of 'Canned Music' and 'I Scare Myself', the latter a *tour de force* for violinist 'Symphony' Sid Page, who was also featured on the Epic LP. These albums explored swing and vocal jazz in a rock context similar to later work by MANHATTAN TRANSFER and the POINTER SISTERS, but in a gutsier way; 'Walkin' One And Only' from *Striking It Rich* had been covered by Maria MULDAUR on her hit eponymous LP on Reprise '70. Lacklustre *It Happened One Bite* '78 on WB was an intended soundtrack for a film never released. He worked as a cartoonist (e.g. on California's *B.A.M.* magazine). First and last LPs reissued on Edsel UK '86.

HIGGINBOTHAM, J. C. (*b* 11 May '06, Atlanta, Ga.; *d* 26 May '73, NYC) Trombonist; aka 'Jay C.' or 'Jack'. Underrated by many critics, but not by jazz fans or musicians: extrovert 'gut bucket' style brought into Swing Era; always forceful, swinging, with superb attack, admired by Tommy DORSEY, Louis ARMSTRONG, many others. From musical family; studied tailoring, worked as mechanic, but music won: sat in with Chick WEBB at Savoy Ballroom NYC '28, went with Luis RUSSELL '28-31, Fletcher HENDERSON '32-3, Benny CARTER '33, early Lucky MILLINDER band '34-6, Henderson '37, Armstrong '37-40. Worked with Henry ALLEN in combos '40s, worked in Boston, Cleveland, NYC; played in stellar trombone section on Henderson reunion LP '57 with Benny MORTON, Dicky WELLS; led own bands '60s (Newport Jazz Festival '63), toured Scandinavia. Also recorded with Sidney BECHET, Coleman HAWKINS, Chocolate Dandies, Jelly Roll MORTON, others; countless solos as sideman. LPs incl. Tiny GRIMES album on Prestige *Callin' The Blues*; albums *Higgy Comes Home* on Cable, *Comin' Home!* on Jazzology are the same.

HIGGINS, Billy (*b* 11 Oct. '36, L.A.) Drummer. Played in R&B combos at 19. Member of original Ornette COLEMAN quartet at the Five Spot '59, recorded on Atlantic; also LPs with Sonny ROLLINS (RCA), on Blue Note LPs by Sonny CLARK, Dexter GORDON, Herbie HANCOCK, Jackie McLEAN, Hank MOBLEY; since played, recorded, toured with Gordon, Clifford JORDAN, Cedar WALTON, Jimmy HEATH, Curtis FULLER, many others. Has played on rock and funk LPs, his technique and versatility being a crossover influence (*see* his entries in index) but LPs as leader have been few: quartet with Walton, Bob Berg on tenor, Tony Dumas on bass recorded *Soweto* in Milan '79, *Once More* in Bologna '80 (both on Italian Red label); in NYC *The Soldier* late '79 with Walton, Walter Booker on bass (*b* 17 Dec. '33, Prairie View, Texas), Monty Waters on alto (*b* 14 Apr. '38, Modesto, Cal.) (vocal on 'Sugar And Spice' by Roberta Davis).

HIGHLIFE African style of popular music emerging in Ghana and Sierra Leone by '20, subsequently having dominating infl. for decades. Fusion of indigenous dance rhythms and melodies with Western sounds began in coastal towns of Ghana, incl. regimental brass bands, sea shanties, hymns; instrumentation incl. African drums, harmonicas, guitars, accordions; early styles called Osibibisaba, Ashiko, Dagomba, but

by '20 known collectively as highlife. During '30s distinct styles emerged: ballroom dance style for coastal elite, village brass band style, and rural guitar bands playing less westernised style for less westernised audience. By this time bands were springing up all along the coast of West Africa, incl. Nigeria; during '30s-40s thousands of records were issued for the West African market and the music began to establish an international reputation. During WWII big band jazz became an infl. and in '47 the most important post-war band emerged: E. T. MENSAH and the Tempos Band, touring widely with enormous impact and spawning hundreds of imitators. The '50s and '60s were a golden age, with bands like Tempos, Black Beats, Uhurus and Broadway in Ghana; Bobby BENSON, Rex Lawson, Roy Chicago and Victor OLAIYA in Nigeria; and the rural guitar bands had also flourished, in early '50s evolving a fusion of highlife and comic theatre: the concert party. Leaders in this style were E. K. NYAME, Onyina, Kakaiku, and (in '60s) Nana Ampadu's AFRICAN BROTHERS International Band. By the '70s highlife was perhaps past its peak; JUJU began to take over in western Nigeria, though highlife was maintained in eastern Nigeria by Celestine UKWU, Osita OSADEBE, Prince Nico, the Ikengas, the ORIENTAL BROTHERS INTERNATIONAL BAND. Even in Ghana highlife was affected by the disco invasion, though styles continued to be developed by C. K. Mann, the Sweet Talks and Alex Konadu. Not just an Anglophone African phenomenon, highlife infl. for example the modern Congolese sound; and the single most infl. African style to have emerged remains open to innovation.

HI-LIFE INTERNATIONAL African 6-7 piece band playing refined blend of highlife, soukous and kwela styles, formed in London '82 by Ghanaian guitarist Kwabena Oduru-Kwarteng (ex-Ranchis), with Kofi Adu on drums (ex-Boombaya, Ojah Band, Alpha Waves, Pigbag), Sam Asley on congas (ex-Sonkofa and Aklowa cultural troupes), Herman Asafo-Agyei on bass (ex-Bassa-Bassa), Stu Hamer on trumpet (ex-Dizzy GILLESPIE), South African Frank Williams on saxophone. First LP *Travel And See* '83 on Sterns captured band already exciting dance fans in UK before living up to its name with European tours. *Music To Wake The Dead* '84 in USA on Rounder; *Nawa For You* '85 on Sterns incl. single 'Come To Africa'. Played several festivals '85 incl. International Youth Year celebrations in Greece; also underwent personnel changes, Williams leaving to form Kintone, a more jazz-oriented outfit (debut LP *Going Home* '85 on Sterns). The band is often joined onstage by Alfred Bannerman, guitar virtuoso from OSIBISA.

HILL, Andrew (*b* 30 June '37, Port au Prince, Haiti) Piano; composer. Family came to USA '41, settled in Chicago; he began playing piano '50, baritone sax as well; worked in R&B at 15; recorded on obscure Ping label in Chicago '55 with Von FREEMAN, baritone Pat Patrick, drummer Wilbur Campbell, others. Album *So In Love With The Sound Of Andrew Hill* '55 with Malachi Favors, drummer James Slaughter issued on Warwick; also played with Gene AMMONS, Johnny GRIFFIN, others in Chicago; to NYC accompanying Dinah WASHINGTON; worked in L.A. '62 with Roland KIRK; back to NYC '63 and made record debut with Blue Note, no self-conscious avant-gardist but a composer to be reckoned with: LPs with all-star small groups, original compositions incl. *Black Fire* and *Smoke Stack* '63, *Judgement, Point Of Departure* (with Eric DOLPHY) and *Andrew!* '64; *Compulsion* '65; *Involution* '66 (half of 2-disc set, the other album by Sam RIVERS); *Grass Roots* and *Dance With Death* '68; *Lift Every Voice* (with vocal septet) and *One For One* '69-70 (2-disc set has quartet and sextet, latter featuring old mate Patrick, now playing alto and flute as well as baritone). Then *Invitation* '74 on Steeplechase; *Spiral* '74-5 on Arista is quintet with Ted CURSON and Lee KONITZ, Robin Kenyatta on alto on one cut; quartet set *Divine Revelation* '75 on Steeplechase; trios *Nefertiti* '76 on East Wind, *Strange Serenade* '80 on Soul Note; quartet *Shades* '86 on Soul Note with Clifford JORDAN, Rufus Reid on bass, Ben Riley on drums. Also solo sets: *Homage* on East Wind, *Live At Montreux* on Arista ('Come Sunday'), both '75; *From California With Love* '78 on Artists House, *Faces Of Hope* '80 and *Shades* '87 on Soul Note. Active in TV and theatre, educational work;

works with wife, organist Laverne Gillette; publishes own music and uses proceeds to help music and musicians.

HILL, Bertha (*b* 15 Mar. '05, Charleston, S.C.; *d* 7 May '50, NYC, after hit-and-run car accident) Blues singer. One of 16 children; had 7 of her own. Sang in church age 9; left home as dancer with Ethel WATERS bill at LeRoy's NYC '19, nicknamed 'Chippie' there because of her youth; worked with Rabbit Foot Minstrels as singer/dancer, as single on TOBA circuit of black theatres; first records: four sides with Louis ARMSTRONG, Richard M. Jones on piano in Chicago '25-6. She made 29 sides in '20s, all in Chicago, often with Jones; other accompaniment such as Scrapper Blackwell ('Non-Skid Tread'), Lonnie JOHNSON, Georgia Tom (*see* Thomas A. DORSEY), etc.: 'One of the best accompanied, biggest toned, most swinging blues singers of the twenties' (Barry Ulanov). No records in Depression; worked outside music mid-'40s; returned to music in Chicago when discovered by jazz scholar Rudi Blesh working in a bakery '46. Residencies in NYC late '40s, recorded '46-7 on Circle label incl. radio show *This Is Jazz*, broadcast to Europe by State Dept; appeared at jazz festival in France '48 with pianist Claude Bolling. Compilation on Biograph no longer listed in Schwann catalogue.

HILL, Teddy (*b* 7 Dec. '09, Birmingham, Ala.; *d* 19 May '78, Cleveland, Ohio) Reeds, leader. Played drums and trumpet in school, switched to reeds; played with Luis RUSSELL late '20s, led own bands from '32: compilation *Teddy Hill & Cab Calloway* on Queen Disc has eight tracks from '35-6 with Roy ELDRIDGE, Dicky WELLS, Bill COLEMAN, Chu BERRY, Russell Procope, Frankie Newton; he later hired Dizzy GILLESPIE. Toured Europe '37. May have had his doubts about BOP at first, but gave up touring after '40, ran famous club Minton's in NYC: house band was incubator, giving young turks opportunity to jam: pick-up recordings from there have Charlie CHRISTIAN, Thelonious MONK, Gillespie, others stretching their wings.

HILL, Tiny (*b* 19 July '06, Sullivan, Ill.; *d* '72) Drummer, vocalist, leader. Weighed more than 350 pounds, led band described as 'swinging cornball', especially popular in Midwest. Hired good jazz-oriented trumpet players such as Sterling Bose. Best-known record 'Angry', used as theme; hit version of 'Slow Poke' on Mercury (no. 30 '52). Carried on working well into '60s; made dancers happy, offended no one. '30s-40s compilations on Circle, Hindsight labels.

HILLMAN, Chris (*b* 4 Dec. '42, L.A.) Guitar, bass, mandolin. While still at school played mandolin in bluegrass quintet the Scottsville Squirrel Barkers with Bernie Leadon (later an EAGLE) and Kenny Wertz (later with Country Gentlemen); they made LP in five hours (*Bluegrass Favorites*) for budget Crown label; he then joined the Golden State Boys '62, incl. Vern and Rex Gosdin (who later made LP with Gene CLARK before achieving fame in country music), and Don Parmley. Offered opportunity to make LP by country-rock godfather Jim Dickson; changed name to the Hillmen; eponymous LP came out on L.A. label Together; nothing happened. After 16 months as the Hillmen, group split mid-'63; Hillman joined Green Grass Group (apparently a second-division NEW CHRISTY MINSTRELS) for two months; joined Roger McGuinn, David Crosby and Gene Clark (then calling themselves the Beefeaters) in first incarnation of the BYRDS (completed by Michael Clarke). Left the Byrds late '68 to form Flying Burrito Bros with Gram PARSONS and others; stayed with that band through best period, leaving late '71 to become founder member of Manassas with Stephen Stills and fellow Burrito Al Perkins; meanwhile also made Byrds reunion LP which disappointed everyone; after two years Hillman, Perkins, keyboardist Paul Harris left Manassas for Souther-Hillman-Furay band with J. D. SOUTHER, Richie Furay, which failed partly because principals didn't get along. Hillman flopped with solo *Slippin' Away* '76, *Clear Sailin'* '77 on Asylum; joined ex-Byrds in ill-fated McGuinn, Clark & Hillman, which cut two LPs (another without Clark) '79-80. Diehard Byrd-freaks were beginning to despair when Hillman reappeared on Sugar Hill label as *The Hillman* with Vern and Rex Gosdin, then neo-bluegrass *Morning Sky* '82 with Herb Pederson, Byron Berline,

etc., *Desert Rose* '84 with Pederson, James BURTON, etc., bringing smiles to faces of the faithful as major if unsung character in country-rock found niche. Low-profile tours of Europe were applauded; his continuing presence will be cherished. As born-again Christian, devotional LP *Ever Call Ready* on Word reunited him with Leadon.

HILLTOPPERS Vocal group formed by lead singer Jimmy Sacca at Western Kentucky College with Seymour Speigelman, tenor; Don McGuire, bass; Billy Vaughn, baritone. 'Trying' was sent by local DJ to new Dot label formed by Randy Wood in Gallatin, Tenn.; it made top 10. College sweaters, beanies worn on Ed Sullivan show became trademark; big act had 18 hits '52-7: biggest was 'P.S. I Love You' (song by Gordon JENKINS, Johnny MERCER). Vaughan (*b* 12 Apr. '19, Glasgow, Ky.) became mus. dir. at Dot, had 28 hits '54-68 as MOR bandleader (first was 'Melody Of Love' at no. 2). They all worked for Dot, Sacca as distributor in NYC; he re-formed for clubwork '67. Dot moved to Hollywood '56; Wood sold it '65, formed Ranwood.

HI-LO's, The USA pop vocal group; probably the most technically accomplished of all. Original lineup: Eugene Thomas Puerling (*b* 31 Mar. '29, Milwaukee, Wis.); Clark Burroughs (*b* 3 Mar. '30, L.A.); Robert Morse (*b* 27 July '27, Pasadena); Robert Strasen (*b* 1 Apr. '28, Strasbourg, France). Organised by Puerling; took name from the fact that Strasen and Morse were well over 6' tall, towering over the others; shared a house to save money, worked as salesmen, soda jerks, parking cars etc. singing weekends and evenings. Heard by bandleader Jerry Fielding, signed to Trend label, then Starlite. Puerling provided intricate arr., Burroughs' voice (reaching high G over middle C without difficulty) adding distinctive touch; flood of bookings incl. Red Skelton TV show, tour with Judy GARLAND, spot at Las Vegas hotel; LPs for Columbia: *Suddenly It's The Hi-Lo's* '57, *Love Nest* and *Now Hear This* '58. Strasen replaced '59 by Don Shelton (*b* 28 Aug. '34, also plays reed instruments), then highpoint: *The Hi-lo's And All That Jazz* with Marty Paich Dektette, band featuring trumpeter Jack Sheldon (*b* 30 Nov. '31), Bill

Perkins (*b* 22 July '24, San Francisco), Herb Geller (*b* 2 Nov. '28, L.A.) and Bud SHANK on reeds. After *Ring Around Rosie* with Rosemary CLOONEY and *All Over The Place* '60, more LPs for Columbia, then Kapp, signed with Reprise: *The Hi-Lo's Happen To Folk* '62, *To Bossa Nova* '63; split up '64. Puerling and Shelton moved into ad jingles, formed Singers Unlimited '66 with Len Dressler and Bonnie Herman (also jingle singers); this group based in Chicago, heard by Oscar PETERSON, recorded for German BASF/MPS: several LPs incl. *Sentimental Journey* '76, *Eventide* '78 with Robert FARNON. Puerling, Morse, Shelton and Burroughs reunited '78 for *The Hi-Lo's! Back Again* on MPS.

HINES, Earl (*b* Earl Kenneth Hines, 28 Dec. '03, Duquesne, Pa.; *d* 22 Apr. '83, Oakland, Cal.) Pianist, bandleader, songwriter, occasional singer; aka 'Fatha'. Had four careers: became world famous with Louis ARMSTRONG, Jimmie NOONE and as soloist in Chicago in '20s; led excellent big bands '28-47; slowly reduced to playing dixieland in West Coast clubs; then rediscovered as soloist late '50s and astonished the world with his joyous, swinging technique until a week before he died: finest piano stylist of the century, with the possible exception of Art TATUM. Began playing with bands in Pittsburgh '18 (Duquesne is a suburb or district of Pittsburgh); spotted by singer Lois Deppe, toured with her '23; with Armstrong's Chicago Stompers at Sunset Café in Chicago '27: recorded 'Chicago Breakdown' with 10-piece group in May '27; then 19 sides with Armstrong and his Hot Five, Savoy Ballroom Five, etc. all in '28, all now available in Armstrong collections, incl. classic duet 'Weather Bird', just trumpet, piano; about 17 sides (some now lost) with 5-6 piece Jimmy NOONE's Apex Club Orchestra May-Aug. '28 (Jimmie Noone & Earl Hines *At The Apex Club* on MCA). First records under own name Dec. '28: 8 piano solos for QRS (a piano roll company, but these were records, not rolls), incl. own compositions 'Blues In Thirds' (aka 'Caution Blues'), 'A Monday Date', etc. now available on Milestone. (Four other solos '28-9 incl. '57 Varieties'.) Like Armstrong, he invented a style which was more revolutionary than we can now appre-

ciate: he played rhythmic patterns in his left hand which were an advance over those in RAGTIME or Stride piano; in the right hand he played melody lines high in the treble, perhaps to carry over the sound of a band: this was called 'trumpet style'. Extrovert technique helped make excellent bandleader: he recorded with 10-piece band (also '28) which grew into a full-size 'swing band' before the term was used; broadcasts through the '30s from the Grand Terrace ballroom in Chicago of what was called 'western swing' (as opposed to NYC styles) had their impact on the jazz incubator that was KANSAS CITY at the time; got nickname 'Fatha' from radio announcer. 'At the Grand Terrace, I couldn't afford to buy stars, so I had to find them,' he said: he hired first-class men like trumpeters Shirley Clay (*b* '02, Charleston, Mo.; *d* 7 Feb. '51, NYC), Freddie Webster (*b* '16, Cleveland, Ohio; *d* 1 Apr. '47, Chicago), Walter Fuller (*b* 15 Feb. '10, Dyersburg, Tenn.; also sang); Trummy Young on trombone (*b* James Osborne Young, 12 Jan. '12, Savannah, Ga.; *d* 10 Sep. '84, San José, Cal.; also sang; later in Armstrong's All-Stars), also Budd JOHNSON, Darnell Howard, Omer SIMEON, Ray Nance, Truck Parham, Marshall Royal, singer Herb Jeffries; bought arr. from Horace HENDERSON, Jimmy MUNDY, Eddie DURHAM, Edgar Battle, Johnson, others; disbanded '40, re-formed same year on West Coast; hiring the best, he inevitably had an incubator of BOP in mid-'40s with men like Bennie GREEN, Dizzy GILLESPIE, Charlie PARKER, Billy ECKSTINE, Willie Cook, Wardell GRAY. Compilations incl. *South Side Swing* '34-5 on MCA; *The Father Jumps* '39-45 on RCA has good notes by Stanley Dance (also published *The World Of Earl Hines* '77); three 2-disc French RCA sets *The Indispensable Earl Hines* '39-66 also incl. hits 'Boogie Woogie On St Louis Blues', 'Jelly, Jelly' (Eckstine vocal), 'Stormy Monday Blues', also Hines's favourites 'Second Balcony Jump', 'The Earl'. He disbanded '47, joined Armstrong's All-Stars '48-51; led own small groups at Hangover Club in San Francisco; toured Europe with a group co-led by Jack TEAGARDEN '57; ran own club in Oakland '63; engagements at The Little Theatre NYC '64 resulted in rediscovery: he toured with trio or quartet often incl. Johnson, made scores of

LPs in last 25 years incl. priceless solo sets: his style hadn't changed; he could metaphorically walk a tightrope without falling off, like Tatum, but wit and beauty always triumphed over technique for its own sake. Small group sets incl. *Once Upon A Time* '66 (now on Jasmine); on Chiaroscuro: *At The Overseas Press Club* '70 with Maxine SULLIVAN; *Back On The Street* '73 with Jonah JONES; 2-disc *An Evening With Earl Hines* quartet '73, with vocalist Marva Josie; *A Buck Clayton Jam Session* '74; solo LPs on same label: *Quintessential Recording Session* '70, duplicating '28 selections; *Live At The New School* '73; *Quintessential Continued* '73; *Quintessential* '74; other solo sets: *Tea For Two* '65 on Black Lion, prod. by Alan Bates (title cut is daring masterpiece); *I've Got The World On A String* '66 on Italian Joker label; *Dinah* '66 on RCA made in Paris; *Earl Hines At Home* c.'70 on Delmark, taped in Earl's home by Wayne Farlow, charming vocal on 'It Happens To Be Me', notes by Dance; *Solo Walk In Tokyo* '72 on Biograph; on Audiophile: *My Tribute To Louis Armstrong*, *Hines Come In Handy* (songs by W. C. HANDY), *Hines Does Hoagy* (CARMICHAEL) all made in two days July '71, a few days after Armstrong died. Now on Australian Swaggie label: four LPs of Duke ELLINGTON songs recorded '71-5 ('C-Jam Blues' is another exhilarating high-wire act), *Plays Cole Porter* and two vols. of *Plays George Gershwin* (also on Classic Jazz in USA, Festival in France). Scores more LPs, every one a joy; through it all a lovable man whose spirit shines in the music. Also contributed to Ry COODER LP *Jazz*, etc.; his many fine compositions incl. best-known, often recorded 'Rosetta', written c.'32.

HINTON, Milt (*b* Milton John Hinton, 23 June '10, Vicksburg, Ms.) Bass. Mother was music teacher; started on violin, switched to bass in Chicago high school; played with Eddie SOUTH there, with Cab CALLOWAY '36-51; Louis ARMSTRONG '53-4, Benny GOODMAN at Basin Street Mar. '55. Recorded with George RUSSELL/Hal McKusick sextet on RCA LP '56, with many other bassists on 3-disc Impulse set *The Bass*, with Red NORVO quintet on Famous Door LP *Second Time Around* '75; also Milt Hinton Sextet on same label: *Here Swings The*

Judge with Jon Faddis on trumpet (*b* 24 July '53, Oakland), John Bunch, Frank Wess, Budd JOHNSON, Jo JONES, also duets with Hinton and Ben WEBSTER. Duet LP with Art HODES on Muse *Just The Two Of Us*; *The Judge's Decision* '85 on Exposure is a quintet set. Hinton has probably played on more jazz records than any other musician in history, his excellent tone and taste making him one of the busiest freelances in the business. House bassist at Michael's Pub NYC '70s; also active in community, church work; TV and music education; has accompanied singers, playing at White House with Pearl BAILEY several times, also there on Duke ELLINGTON's 70th birthday: a very popular man.

HIRT, Al (*b* Alois Maxwell Hirt, 7 Nov. '22, New Orleans, La.) Trumpet, combo leader. Father a policeman; played in Junior Police band; studied formally; served in US Army, worked in DORSEY Bros band, with Ray McKINLEY, Horace HEIDT; eight years on staff at N.O. radio station; then formed combo with fine clarinettist Pete Fountain (*b* 3 July '30, N.O.; with Lawrence WELK on TV '57-9; 12 chart LPs on Coral '60-9 incl. no. 8 *Pete Fountain's New Orleans* '60, *Bourbon Street* '62 with Hirt; also *For The First Time* with Brenda LEE on Decca '68). Hirt's first LPs on Coral incl. Fountain; then he became a household name on TV and as tourist attraction: 17 chart LPs on RCA '61-8 incl. *Honey In The Horn* (with Anita KERR Singers on some tracks), *Cotton Candy* and *Sugar Lips* '63-4, all top 10; also *Beauty And The Beard* with ANN-MARGRET '64, *Pops Goes The Trumpet* with Boston Pops Orchestra '65, etc. Hirt's combo tantalised music lovers because it was obviously capable of even more; even Miles DAVIS had kind words about Hirt's skill in a blindfold test, but he settled for a comfortable niche and made plenty of fans happy. Fountain has 11 albums in print on MCA, two on Capitol, *New Orleans Jazz* with Eddie MILLER on First American label; Hirt has several on Monument incl. 2-disc set with Fountain; others on Accord, GHB; *Best Of* on RCA, *Solid Gold Brass* on RCA International.

HMV His Master's Voice, UK record label. Emile Berliner sold the rights to his disc gramophone (*see* RECORDED SOUND) in Europe and most of the world to a group of English investors in 1898 for £5000; they formed the Gramophone Company and built a factory in Hanover (now the site of Polygram's compact disc factory). In the late 1890s English painter Francis Barraud painted 'His Master's Voice', a picture of his dog Nipper listening to an Edison cylinder phonograph (in Kingston-upon-Thames, southwest London); he offered it to the Edison Bell Company, whose chairman James Hough turned it down, saying 'Dogs don't listen to phonographs.' The Gramophone Company paid £50 for the picture and £50 for the copyright, on condition that he painted a gramophone over the phonograph; it hangs in the EMI London office today and has become one of the most famous trademarks in the world. Gramophone set up branches all over Europe, Africa, Asia and the Pacific; just after the turn of the century, with patent wars raging in USA, it was the biggest record company in the world, and the leading British company until merger with COLUMBIA to form EMI '31. Artist roster incl. Harry LAUDER, John McCormack, speeches by Winston Churchill (on budget of '09, aftermath of war '18), and opera stars Adelina Patti, Dame Nellie Melba, Enrico Caruso. The company had sent recording engineer Fred Gaisberg to Italy '02; he heard Caruso and negotiated £100 for 10 records, cabling London for approval; the directors cabled back FEE EXORBITANT FORBID YOU TO RECORD; Gaisberg went ahead anyway and recorded the world's first million sellers. Links with Victor in USA assured flow of USA product, with stars like Caruso being leased to Victor in return. Though using HMV logo (and picture of Nipper) as early as 1900, Gramophone used recording Angel as label logo until 1909 (revived Angel '53 as EMI classical label in USA). In Russia, Egypt, India, Muslim countries, adoption of the trademark took longer, as the dog was considered unclean; in India a variation had a cobra listening to the gramophone; Nipper was also slow to be adopted in Italy, where a bad singer was said to sing like a dog. Berliner saw the picture on a visit to London and asked permission to use the trademark in USA; Berliner, then Victor and RCA have used it to this day. Victor were also allowed to use it in Japan, sold out Japanese interest before WWII; independent Japanese Victor Company (JVC) still uses it. After '31 merger HMV remained premier EMI label until Columbia took lead in '50s pop; HMV still had no. 1 hits (MANFRED MANN's 'Do Wah Diddy Diddy' '64, Louis ARMSTRONG's 'What A Wonderful World' '68), but on 1 Apr. '68 it became a classical-only label, remaining EMI's premier classical label today, though as Andrew LLOYD WEBBER's *Requiem* showed, it can still reach a mass audience.

HODES, Art (*b* 14 Nov. '04, Nikoliev, Russia) Pianist in trad. jazz style, specialising in blues. Emigrated to USA age 6 months; grew up in Chicago, played dances at Hull House, worked in midwest, mainly Chicago, until '38; East Coast, mainly NYC, until back to Chicago '50 (meanwhile edited magazine *Jazz Record* '43-7; *Selections From The Gutter* '77, profiles from the magazine, ed. Hodes and Chadwick Hansen). Overlooked and patronised by some as a white man sticking to trad. style; in fact he does it with genuine feeling and always did. Record debut with Wingy MANONE '28, worked with Mezz MEZZROW, many others; LPs (many solo) incl. *Art Of Hodes*, *When Music Was Music* and *I Remember Bessie* on Euphonic; five LPs on Jazzology incl. *Home Cookin'* '74, *Echoes Of Chicago* '78, also earlier stuff from '43-4; two LPs on Delmark label with Pops Foster, George Brunis, Barney BIGARD; *Just The Two Of Us* (duet with Milt HINTON) and *Someone To Watch Over Me* both '81 on Muse; two vols. with Magnolia Jazz Band on GHB made in San Francisco '84; several more incl. solos *South Side Memories* '83 and *Blues In The Night* '85 on Sackville.

HODGES, Johnny (*b* Cornelius Hodge, 25 July '05, Cambridge, Mass.; *d* 11 May '70, NYC) Alto sax, also soprano in early years. Nicknames 'Rabbit', 'Jeep'. Brother-in-law of Don Kirkpatrick, pianist/arr. for Don REDMAN. Played drums and piano, switched to sax at 14, had lessons from Sidney BECHET, followed Bechet into quartet led by Willie 'The Lion' SMITH in NYC c.'24; played with Chick WEBB, Luckey ROBERTS; joined Duke ELLINGTON '28 and stayed for life, except '51-5 when he led his own septet. With Benny CARTER the most infl. alto player until Charlie PARKER; if few musicians infl. others as much as Parker, Hodges did something just as remarkable: he continued to set a standard with his tone and his lyricism long after Parker was gone. Hodges and Harry CARNEY on baritone were easily the most important colours in the Ellington tonal palette, and Rabbit remains one of the most beautiful voices of the century. He could play hot as anybody (on 'Bandana Babies', Nov. '28), but strongest suit was lyricism: he set the tone on gorgeous '38 recording of 'I Let A Song Go Out Of My Heart' (no. 1 hit); prolific freelance work incl. famous version of 'Sunny Side Of The Street' with Lionel HAMPTON '37. 'Johnny Hodges And His Orchestra' was an Ellington small-group unit; '38-9 sides incl. 'Jeep's Blues', 'The Jeep Is Jumpin' ','Empty Ballroom Blues' etc. are on CBS *Hodge Podge* LP; but eight tracks recorded '40-1 (available on various RCA compilations) have Jimmy BLANTON on bass, and are among the finest small-group sides ever recorded by anybody: 'Things Ain't What They Used To Be' was an instant classic; 'Squaty Roo' was another Hodges nickname, and propelled by Blanton is a straight-ahead swinger; Hodges wrote 'Good Queen Bess' and named it for his mother; 'That's The Blues Old Man' marked the last time Hodges recorded on soprano saxophone and the first appearance of the riff which later became 'Happy-Go Lucky Local', still later the '52 hit 'Night Train' by Jimmy FORREST. Ellington wrote 'Warm Valley' for Hodges, recorded it with the full band '40, but his amanuensis Billy STRAYHORN now mastered the romantic, sensual side of Hodges, beginning with 'Day Dream' and 'Passion Flower' for the '40-1 small-group dates. Later, Hodges' own group '51-5 often sounded like an Ellington unit, using ducal songs and sidemen (but Hodges was also one of the first to employ John COLTRANE, '54). Strayhorn had written 'A Flower Is A Lovesome Thing', recorded as 'Passion' on Verve '55 (actually after return to Ellington) with Strayhorn on piano; it is a plea of almost unbearable eroticism. Fine Hodges on *Ellington Indigos* '57; album *And His Mother Called Him Bill* '67, made after Strayhorn's death, contained several features for the voice that

Strayhorn loved so much: new version of 'Day Dream', 'After All' from '41, 'Blood Count' (Strayhorn's last composition). 'Blues For New Orleans' from the *New Orleans Suite* '70 was Hodges's last recording, and a fine one; Ellington was trying to get him to play soprano on 'Portrait Of Sidney Bechet', but he died before the session. Other Hodges LPs (all small groups) incl. *The Johnny Hodges All-Stars* '47 (incl. Strayhorn's 'A Flower Is A Lovesome Thing', 'Lotus Blossom', 'Violet Blues'), half of a Prestige 2-disc set with other Ellington/Strayhorn stuff; *The Big Sound* '57, *Back To Back* and *Side By Side* with Ellington, *The Jeep Is Jumpin'* '51-5, *The Smooth One* '59-60 all on Verve; *Sportpalast, Berlin* '61 on Pablo; *Everybody Knows* '64 on Impulse/Jasmine, albums on RCA '60s incl. *Triple Play*.

HOGG, Smokey (*b* Andrew Hogg, 27 Jan. '14, Texas; *d* there 1 May '60) Blues singer, guitarist; best-known of three Smokey Hoggs, all cousins (John Hogg *b* '12; Willie Anderson Hogg *b* '08). Born on a farm, learned guitar as a child, worked at picnics, country dances, etc. First records for Decca in Chicago '37; after WWII for Exclusive, Modern, others. Had no. 9 R&B hit '49 'Little School Girl' on Modern. He was one of those fascinating bluesmen of the period who retained trad. down-home appeal while also getting attention from modern listeners during the rise of R&B; in mid-'50s his records were still found on juke boxes in black taverns. Compilation LPs *You Better Watch That Jive* '74 on Pye (UK), *Goin' Back Home* '84 on Krazy Kat.

HOLIDAY, Billie (*b* Eleanora Fagan, 7 Apr. '15, Baltimore, Md.; *d* 17 July '59, NYC) Singer. She heard records by Bessie SMITH as a child and always admired Louis ARMSTRONG, but she owed little to earlier artists: she was the first and is perhaps still the greatest of jazz singers, if the essence of jazz singing is to make the familiar sound fresh, and to make any lyric come alive with personal meaning for the listener. Her father, Clarence, played banjo and guitar for Fletcher HENDERSON; he was proud of her success but had little infl. on her: she wrote in *Lady Sings The Blues* ('56, with William Dufty): 'Mom and Pop were just a couple of kids when they got married. He was eighteen, she was sixteen and I was three.' (Probably not accurate, but tells a story, like her way with a song.) She had a traumatic childhood (scrubbed floors in a brothel, was raped as a child) though her own book is unreliable, because fuzzy on details. Her parents were married, divorced; mother Sadie married a dockworker named Gough who was a kind stepfather but soon died; they went to NYC '29. She was entertaining in Harlem clubs as a teenager, where the girls were required to pick up tips from tables using their labia; her disdain for this stuff earned her the nickname 'Lady' (she had innate dignity, as well as physical beauty, which never left her in spite of everything). She began singing; John HAMMOND heard her and prod. her first record '33 with a nine-piece Benny GOODMAN band; she said John Bubbles played piano (see BUCK AND BUBBLES) but the discographies say Joe SULLIVAN and that trumpeter Shirley Clay (b '02, Charleston, Mo.; d 7 Feb. '51, NYC) was the only black musician on the session. Deane Kincaide wrote the arrangements; guitarist Dick McDonough commissioned Johnny MERCER to write lyrics for 'Riffin' The Scotch', but that and 'Your Mother's Son-In-Law' were over-arranged for her. She appeared in a short film *Rhapsody In Black* early '35 with Duke ELLINGTON, then made sensational debut in Apr. at the APOLLO; MC Ralph Cooper advised Frank Schiffman to book her with a famous description: 'It ain't the blues – I don't know what it is, but you got to hear her.' Cooper bought her gown and slippers, rehearsed the house band for 'Them There Eyes' and 'If The Moon Turns Green'; comic Pigmeat Markham shoved her out on stage; she did 'The Man I Love' for an encore: the Apollo's discerning audience bestowed its approval. She had been calling herself Halliday, not wanting to use her father's name; but she returned to the Apollo in Aug. as Holiday, meanwhile in July making the first of about 100 records ('35-42), nearly all with small groups led by Teddy WILSON, on which her fame mainly still rests: they were made quickly and cheaply for juke boxes, using head arrangements played by whichever sidemen happened to be in town (the greatest jazzmen of the era); their average sale then was about 3000 copies; at early sessions she received $25 a side (or $50 dollars a session, for four sides; accounts differ): records are still selling 50 years later. The songs were often second-rate and even silly (black artists got songpluggers' leftovers that other artists didn't want); she transmuted them into gold, sometimes turning a melody line inside out. She sang behind the beat, endowing lyrics with languor, irony, resignation or sexuality, depending on requirements. Her vocal texture was coarse, but profoundly affecting; her timbre and her time were unique. At the first session she met life-long soulmate Lester YOUNG, who named her Lady Day; reasoning that a Lady's mother must be a Duchess, he called Sadie that; Billie named him Prez (for President); the nicknames stuck as long as they lived. She liked the songs of Irene Wilson (then Teddy's wife), named the first chapter of her book after 'Some Other Spring'. Mildred BAILEY heard her and said, 'That girl's got it'; Frank SINATRA, Carmen McRAE, Lena HORNE, Helen Oakley (later Mrs Stanley Dance) were early fans; jazz fans, critics and musicians recognised her greatness, but she never broke through to the public at large in her lifetime, and her self-confidence was never great. She sang with Count BASIE '37 (no studio recordings; airchecks later issued of 'Swing, Brother, Swing' and 'They Can't Take That Away From Me'), Artie SHAW '38 (only 'Any Old Time' recorded by Victor); but she didn't like life on the road and would not tolerate the racism. Her record company had objected to her record with Shaw, but the former American Record Company (by then owned by CBS) allowed sessions at Commodore '39 because they didn't want to record 'Strange Fruit', a setting of a powerful anti-lynching poem by Lewis Allen; this first Commodore record (with Frankie Newton) was backed with her own song 'Fine And Mellow'. In '42 she made a record with Paul WHITEMAN; after the musicians' union recording ban she began working '44 with Milt Gabler (who had run Commodore) at US Decca (now MCA) where she asked for and got backing with strings: an early Decca record was 'Lover Man', one of her most famous, but although her lyrical interpretations are always fine, the banal arrangements and too-slow tempi of the Decca series have an overall slushy effect. First solo concert was NYC Town Hall, early '46; made film *New Orleans* that year (dire Hollywood version of the history of jazz is saved only by musical content, Holiday and Armstrong playing a maid and a butler). She had been introduced to opium by her first husband James Monroe and to heroin by him or by Joe Guy; she kicked the habit 'cold turkey' in a NYC clinic, successful only as long as she was away from the music scene: she was sentenced '47 to a year in the Federal Reformatory for Women at Alderson, W.V.; her cabaret card was revoked, NYC law not allowing anyone convicted of a felony to work in a place where liquor was served (a law revoked in Sep. '67 by Mayor John Lindsay). A benefit concert organised by Norman GRANZ for Nov. '47 was spoiled by her manager Joe Glaser; it netted $514. At a Carnegie Hall concert Mar. '48 she sang her own 'Don't Explain', written with Andy RAZAF; her excellent accompanist in that period was Bobby Tucker (*b* 8 Jan. '23, Morristown, N.J.); the concert was sold out, and the audience got six encores. She was unlucky with the men in her life, or had a self-destructive streak: with Guy occurred the arrest that led to prison; John Levy somehow got her NYC club work without a card, but he regarded her as a business investment and kept her short of money, and she may have been used as bait by narcotics police. On the West Coast with Levy '49 she was arrested for possession of opium, but Dr Herbert Henderson testified that she was not using hard drugs at the time and took her into his home, since hotels turned her out; tests at a Belmont Cal. sanitorium pronounced her clean. A tour of northern Cal. with Red NORVO and Charles MINGUS was a flop. In mid-'50 she toured with a Gerald WILSON band and Levy walked out leaving them with no money; that year she made a short film with the Basie sextet. In '49-50 she was often accompanied by Horace HENDERSON; in '51 she shared a bill with Stan GETZ at Storyville in Boston (airchecks later issued on LP); she made records for Aladdin '52 and signed with Granz '53, subsequently recording for Mercury and Verve. Toured Europe '54, played the first Newport Jazz Festival that year (Young made a surprise appearance). By the mid-'50s her range had narrowed, her voice

deteriorated; her unique timbre was still there and when she was in the mood she was still a great interpreter, but years of alcohol and drugs were taking their toll. With long-time companion Louis McKay she was arrested early '56 in Philadelphia for possession of drugs; they got married but the stormy relationship got worse; she took treatment with substitute drugs; in '57 trial was postponed indefinitely and she separated from McKay. Accompanists in this period incl. Carl Drinkard and the excellent Jimmy ROWLES, who had first played for her in '42; and finally Mal WALDRON, with whom she appeared at the '57 Newport Festival. She played concerts in Central Park that year; made a poignant appearance on the CBS TV programme *Sound Of Jazz* with Young and many others (the best treatment jazz had received on TV until then); began recording for Columbia: she wanted a string orchestra cond. by Ray Ellis; *Lady In Satin* '58 is a sad document. Her health began to fail; talk of filming her autobiography came to nothing (until the disastrous '71 version: Diana ROSS did her best with a dire script). A European tour fell through at the last moment (*see* Dick HAYMES); she began to spend lonely weeks in her NYC flat. Dr Henderson visited her at a San Francisco club Sep. '58 and saw signs of cirrhosis: she was off drugs but drinking heavily to compensate. At the first Monterey Jazz Festival she received an ovation but was not singing well; nevertheless, Dan Morgenstern wrote of a '58 TV appearance, 'Some say that what Billie does now is no longer singing; whatever it is, it sure as hell communicates.' In late '58-early '59 she visited Europe, was booed in France and Italy, appeared on TV in UK; back home she resumed lonely nights at home. In Mar. she attended Young's funeral; in Apr. played a successful Storyville date in Boston, but at the end of May went into a coma and to hospital with liver trouble and cardiac arrest. The evidence was that she was not on drugs at the time; she began to recover but as a kidney infection took over she was arrested for possession and fingerprinted on her deathbed. She (and Sadie) had always been generous with food, money and places to sleep, especially for musicians; during her lifetime both the black and the white press were chiefly interested in her personal problems; when she died there was 70 cents in her bank account. Sinatra said in '58, 'Lady Day is unquestionably the most important influence on American popular singing in the last 20 years.' She was not a blues singer, but everything she sang had a blues feeling; she was one of the completely original giants of jazz. John CHILTON's *Billie's Blues* '75 is a good biography (named after another of her own songs), with a bibliography and a chapter about the records. The '33-42 sides have been issued in two 3-disc boxes (*The Golden Years* Vols. 1 and 2) or three 2-disc sets (*The Billie Holiday Story*), plus the single LP *Lady Day* (incl. 5 tracks with Young), all on Columbia (CBS); *Fine And Mellow* and *I'll Be Seeing You* are Commodore collections; *The Complete Billie Holiday On Verve 1946-1959* is a 10-disc set made in Japan; there are smaller Verve sets, compilations on MCA and other labels; e.g. *At Storyville* on Black Lion features Getz, Drinkard, others from '51-3.

HOLLAND, Dave (*b* 1 Oct. '46, Wolverhampton, England) Bass, other instruments. Studied at Guildhall School of Music; played with Ronnie SCOTT, Tubby HAYES, John SURMAN, Humphrey LYTTELTON, Kenny WHEELER etc. and was hired by Miles DAVIS at age 20. One of the brighter stars of today, his technique impeccable, semi-abstract contemporary jazz always highly praised. LPs with Davis '68-71; with Circle (Chick COREA, Anthony BRAXTON, Barry ALTSCHUL) '71-2, Stan GETZ '73-4, Sam RIVERS; also began playing cello. LPs incl. *Town Hall* '72 with Braxton on Trio; on ECM with Corea, Rivers, Kenny WHEELER etc.; trio *Gateway 2* with John Abercrombie, Jack DEJOHNETTE; his own LPs on ECM: *Improvisations For Guitar And Cello* with Derek BAILEY '71, *Conference Of The Birds* '72 with Braxton, Rivers, Altschul (*Downbeat*: 'If you've found new music lacking in swing, cohesion and variety . . . don't miss this one'), *Emerald Tears* '77 (solo bass), *Life Cycle* '82 (solo cello), formed quintet: *Jumpin' In* '83 with Wheeler, Julian Priester on trombone, Steve Coleman on alto sax, Steve Ellington on drums; *Seeds Of Time* '85 with Marvin Smith replacing Ellington, *The Razor's Edge* '87 with Robin Eubanks replacing

Priester. Steve Coleman & Five Elements' *World Expansion* '87 on JMT combines jazz-funk with hip-hop.

HOLLAND-DOZIER-HOLLAND Songwriting team, one of the most successful of the '60s: brothers Eddie (*b* 30 Oct. '39) and Brian Holland (*b* 15 Feb. '41) and Lamont Dozier (*b* 16 June '41), all from Detroit. Eddie worked for Berry Gordy's publishing company and sang on demos, then had hits on Motown sounding like Jackie WILSON: his first, 'Jamie', made the R&B chart and top 30 pop; three others made the pop Hot 100. Brian was a Motown producer ('Please Mr Postman' for the MARVELETTES, with Robert Bateman); Lamont had first recorded at 15 with the Romeos, went to NYC and worked outside music; back in Detroit '58 he recorded for Motown empire labels as Lamont Anthony without much success. From '62-8 the legend 'Holland-Dozier-Holland' became familiar to pop fans, appearing under the title on hit records written and/or produced by them: 'Where Did Our Love Go', 'Baby Love', 'Stop! In The Name Of Love', 'I Hear A Symphony', 'You Keep Me Hangin' On', others for the SUPREMES; 'Baby, I Need Your Loving', 'I Can't Help Myself', 'Reach Out, I'll Be There', others for the FOUR TOPS; also Marvin GAYE, Martha & the Vandellas, the ISLEY Bros etc.: they created the sound of an era, but fought with Gordy for their royalties, parted acrimoniously, formed own labels Invictus and Hot Wax; in '69 Motown alleged breach of contract, settled out of court. The new labels had hits with CHAIRMEN OF THE BOARD, Freda PAYNE and Honey Cone: latter experienced backing singers Edna Wright (*b* '44, L.A.), Shellie Clark (*b* '43, Brooklyn), Carolyn Willis (*b* '47, L.A.) backed Burt BACHARACH on an Andy WILLIAMS TV show; Eddie signed them to Hot Wax and they had seven Hot 100 entries '69-72 incl. no. 1 'Want Ads' '71. (Willis was replaced by Denise Mills, later turned up as a featured vocalist with SEALS & CROFTS.) Lamont had a hit '72 with 'Why Can't We Be Lovers', Brian '73 with 'Don't Leave Me Starvin' For Your Love', both on Invictus; Lamont left to go solo on the advice of the Four Tops; had hits '73-5 on ABC incl. no. 15 'Trying To Hold On To My Woman'; also prod. Aretha

FRANKLIN's *Sweet Passion* '77, etc. Made it up with Motown, returning with Four Tops to prod. them there again. Their songs are classics, covered countless times.

HOLLIDAY, Jennifer (*b* Houston, Texas) USA soul singer. Grew up in choir of Rev. C. L. Jackson's Pleasant Grove Baptist Church, nationally renowned gospel group appearing regularly on TV. Got Broadway break when spotted by dancer Jamie Patterson in Houston with *A Chorus Line*; sent Holliday an air ticket and arranged audition for *Your Arm's Too Short To Box With God*; she got a part and stayed for 18 months, moving to *Dreamgirls*, another musical: she lived the part of Effie Melody White of female vocal trio the Dreamettes, based on SUPREMES. Tom Eyen/Harry Krieger (lyrics/composer) wrote much material especially for her; result ran for two years from Dec. '81, earned her rave reviews, Tony for best actress in a musical, Grammy for best R&B female vocalist ('And I'm Telling You I'm Not Going'). Long-awaited solo LP *Feel My Soul* '83 prod. by Maurice White (EARTH, WIND & FIRE) no. 31 USA LP chart. Returned to the stage with title role of *Sing, Mahalia, Sing*, based on life of Mahalia JACKSON; second LP *Say You Love Me* released late '85; various prod. incl. Arthur BAKER, Michael JACKSON (wrote 'You're The One'). Despite finding fame as surrogate Supreme, she owes more to gospel infl. and her idol Aretha FRANKLIN; seems determined not to do too much too soon. Effie was all but edged out of Dreamettes because she did not fit the slim, glamorous Diana ROSS stereotype (the parallel with Florence Ballard); Holliday matches her large frame with an even larger voice.

HOLLIES, The UK beat group of the '60s, formed in Manchester '62, named after Buddy HOLLY (as BEATLES named after CRICKETS). Original lineup: Allan Clarke (*b* 15 Apr. '42, Salford), vocals; Graham Nash (*b* 2 Feb. '42, Blackpool), rhythm guitar, harmony vocals; Tony Hicks (*b* 16 Dec. '43, Nelson), lead guitar; Eric Haydock (*b* Feb. '43, Stockport), bass; Don Rathbone, drums. Hicks and Haydock ex-Dolphins; Clarke and Nash ex-Two Teens, Deltas; Rathbone soon replaced by Bobby Elliott (*b* 8 Dec. '43,

Burnley), from Shane Fenton & the Fentones. Signed by EMI in post-Merseyside search for more Beatles; recorded for Parlophone under house prod. Ron Richards. They began by covering COASTERS hits; 'Ain't That Just Like Me' failed, but 'Searchin' ' made no. 12 UK. 'Stay' (cover of Maurice Williams and the Zodiacs) showed evidence of vocal harmonies that would set them apart; 'Just One Look' (also '74) refined this further, with Nash permitted solo vocal: cover of Doris Troy USA hit made no. 2 behind Beatles: Hollies had arrived. Escaped cover dead-end by evolving writing team of Clarke/Hicks/Nash, credited on B sides as 'L. Ransford'; mixed with transatlantic pedigree pop (Gerry GOFFIN, Graham Gouldman), original input ensured longevity: 'Here I Go Again' (no. 2), 'We're Through' (7), 'Yes I Will' (9), 'I'm Alive' (1), 'Look Through Any Window' (4) were hits '64-5, while cover of George HARRISON's 'If I Needed Someone' made no. 20. By '66 hits appeared in USA top 20 too, while Hicks's catchy, repetitive figures, unusual instrumentation added to appeal. Continued bright, harmony-laden pop: 'I Can't Let Go' (2), 'Bus Stop' (5), 'Stop Stop Stop' (2, with Hicks's banjo) were hits '66, year in which ex-Dolphin Bernie Calvert (*b* 16 Sep. '43, Burnley) replaced Haydock. LPs *Evolution* and *Butterfly* '67 showed infl. of progressive rock but fans wouldn't wear it; Nash left end '68 to 'make records that say something' with CROSBY, STILLS & NASH, replaced by ex-SWINGING BLUE JEANS Terry Sylvester (*b* 8 Jan. '45, Liverpool); his keening, vibrant vocal edge was sorely missed. Eight UK top 10 hits '67-70, continued USA success, yet projects like *The Hollies Sing Dylan* '69 betrayed lack of direction. Maudlin ballad 'He Ain't Heavy, He's My Brother' was a hit '69-70 (no. 7 USA); Clarke went solo '71 and some thought the end was near, but writing not affected much since it had been subcontracted to the likes of Roger Cook, Roger Greenaway, Tony Macauley. Replacement singer Mikael Rickfors (*b* Sweden) brought only 'The Baby' (no. 26 '72), but USA no. 2 '72 with old CREEDENCE-infl. Clarke-sung record 'Long Cool Woman In A Black Dress' brought him back to group. Hit 'The Air That I Breathe' (UK no. 2/USA 6 on Polydor) was last of decade. Clarke continued to record solo without much success, though he was first to cover Bruce SPRINGSTEEN when he was still unknown; Hollies continued in cabaret until major surprise when Nash rejoined them after 'Holliedaze' hit medley (no. 28 UK) '81; LP *What Goes Around* '82 was result, promoted worldwide (cover of 'Stop In The Name Of Love' was USA no. 29 hit). Group continued mid-'80s without Nash again and back on EMI; lineup: Clarke, Hicks, Elliott, Alan Coates and Steve Stroud (ex-BUCKS FIZZ), Dennis Haines (ex-Gary NUMAN) on keyboards. A pop institution with sound among most distinctive of era; 28 UK/12 USA top 40 hits attests ability to do a simple thing well.

HOLLOWAY, Brenda (*b* 21 June '46, Atascadero, Cal.) Soul singer: one of the first successful Motown artists, unusual in that stable in being from the West Coast. Studied classical violin as a child but got bitten by the pop bug; signed by Motown while a teenager: three top 40 hits incl. classic, funereally slow deep soul ballad 'Every Little Bit Hurts' '64 (covered in UK by the Spencer DAVIS group, an introduction to the soulful voice of the young Stevie Winwood); second was 'When I'm Gone' '65; third 'You've Made Me So Very Happy' '67, covered '69 by BLOOD, SWEAT & TEARS. 'Just Look What You've Done', 'Operator' made R&B chart; 'You Can Cry On My Shoulder' and 'Together Till The End Of Time' were minor pop hits. Paradoxically, although a West Coast artist she did not get the back-up and promotion she deserved at Motown while label boss Berry Gordy was contemplating a move to the West Coast, and allowing others to take over day-to-day decision making. She sang back-up on Joe COCKER's debut LP *With A Little Help From My Friends* '68, then apparently retired, her biggest hits quite unforgettable.

HOLLY, Buddy (*b* Charles Hardin Holley, 7 Sep. '36, Lubbock, Texas; *d* 3 Feb. '59) Singer, songwriter; a richly talented and distinctive pioneer of rock'n'roll who took a keen interest in production techniques, so that his hits of 30 years ago still sound fresh. Infl. by music of Hank WILLIAMS and by seeing Elvis PRESLEY at early gig in Lubbock, Holly formed C&W duo with school friend Bob Montgomery; they played on Texas radio, made demo-quality records later issued on LP *Holly In The Hills*. Holly signed to Decca, went to Nashville three times to record with prod. Owen BRADLEY in '56, later sessions with The Three Tunes: Sonny Curtis, Jerry Allison (*see* CRICKETS), bassist Don Guess; sides incl. early version of 'That'll Be The Day' but none made charts (later released as *That'll Be The Day* and *The Great Buddy Holly* on various MCA labels; also *The Nashville Sessions* in UK). Back in Texas he formed the Crickets and crossed the border to work at studio in Clovis, New Mexico, run by Norman PETTY (*which see*). Petty and Holly developed their recording techniques together (while Lee HAZLEWOOD and Al Casey were doing the same thing in Phoenix, Arizona): Petty learned to record rock'n'roll drums, while Holly was the first from a C&W background not only to use drums, but to apply heavy backbeat of black R&B; the first to experiment with double-tracking and overdubbing (e.g. own vocal on 'Words Of Love'). Petty was also manager, taking credit as co-composer on some songs. Tapes were offered to Roulette, who turned them down; then to Bob THIELE, prod. at Coral/Brunswick (ironically then a division of Decca), who signed them up; new version of 'That'll Be The Day' released on Brunswick as by the Crickets: it was no. 1 both UK and USA, followed by 'Oh Boy' (backed with 'Not Fade Away'): no. 3 UK/10 USA; on Coral under Holly's name 'Peggy Sue'/'Every Day' was no. 6 UK/3 USA, all in '57. All the records were Coral in UK, where Brunswick still functioned as an independent. On 'Peggy Sue' Allison played only tom-toms and Holly recorded his guitar so closely the plectrum could be heard on the strings; his uniqueness lay in his hiccoughing vocal style and portrayal of teen-age angst as well as his writing and production; like Gene VINCENT, Eddie COCHRAN and others, he was more popular in UK (where groups named themselves BEATLES and HOLLIES after Buddy and his Crickets). They toured Australia and England early '58, had hits with 'Think It Over', 'Rave On'; Holly recorded 'Early In The Morning' (song by Bobby DARIN) without Crickets but with chorus and tenor sax (played by Sam 'The Man' Taylor); 'It's So

Easy' (astonishingly, in retrospect) failed to chart in USA, 'Heartbeat' made only 82 (both with Tommy Allsup on guitar); by Oct. Holly and Crickets had split and all had split from Petty. Holly undertook heavy touring because he needed the money; having chartered a plane in Iowa to get to the next gig he was killed in a crash along with the BIG BOPPER and Ritchie VALENS (his bassist Waylon JENNINGS narrowly missed being on the same plane). Holly was only 22; with Elvis PRESLEY in the army, no one was better placed to assume the mantle; it is arguable that he had more talent, and he might have survived the pressures with his personality intact; he would certainly not have allowed the sort of interference with his career that Presley invited from 'Col.' Tom Parker. His last big hit was 'It Doesn't Matter Any More' (no. 13 '59), a Paul ANKA song recorded with orchestra; his biggest success, as a legend and the first rock'n'roll martyr, came after his death. Petty released demo tracks with dubbed backings; throughout the '60s 'new' Holly records continued to crop up; as late as '83 a collection of alternate takes, etc. was issued as *For The First Time Anywhere*. Today the compilations and Best-Ofs incl. a 6-disc *Complete Buddy Holly* on MCA/USA; 2-disc *Legend* in UK; *The Real Buddy Holly* '86 was lavish audio/video package, incl. interviews with Crickets, Everlys, Keith Richards, etc. His '58 UK tour was seen by teenaged Paul McCARTNEY, who later bought the Holly song catalogue and has sponsored Buddy Holly Week in London each Sep. since '76. Acts emulating Holly were successful, such as Bobby VEE and Adam FAITH; Don McLEAN's 'American Pie' '71 took Holly's death as its cue ('the day the music died'); the artists covering the songs are a potted history of rock'n'roll itself. Film *Buddy Holly Story* '78 with Gary Busey was better than the Hollywood biopics of 20 years earlier, but that's not saying much; Francis Ford Coppola film *Peggy Sue Got Married* '86 featured Holly's song.

HOLMES, Richard 'Groove' (*b* Richard Arnold Holmes, 2 May '31, Camden, N.J.) Organist. Left-handed, also plays bass, has the strongest bass lines of any jazz organist. Single 'Misty' (Erroll GARNER song) almost reached top 40 '66 on Prestige; three LPs

on that label made the Billboard pop LP chart '66: *Soul Message* (incl. 'Misty'), *Living Soul* (live at Count BASIE's club in Harlem) and *Misty*. He was discovered by Les McCANN; his first records '61 (on Pacific Jazz) featured McCann and Ben WEBSTER; *Groovin' With Jug* on that label features Gene AMMONS. Among many LPs on Prestige '66-8 is *That Healin' Feelin'* with Rusty Bryant on tenor: *b* 25 Nov. '29, Huntington, W.V., Bryant had a juke-box hit early '50s on Dot with honking rock'n'roll style 'Night Train' (*see* Jimmy FORREST), made a comeback in the '60s on Prestige. Holmes also recorded '68-76 on Groove Merchant, Flying Dutchman, World Pacific; a Blue Note LP was called *Comin' On Home* '74; latest LPs are on Muse: *Shippin' Out* '77 with Dave Schnitter on tenor (*b* 19 Mar. '48, Newark, N.J.), *Good Vibrations* '77 and *Broadway* '80, both with Houston Person on tenor (*b* 10 Nov. '34, Florence, S.C.).

HOLMES, Rupert (*b* Northwich, Cheshire) Singer/songwriter born to Anglo-American parents, father US Infantry bandleader serving in UK. Holmes studied clarinet and composition at Manhattan School of Music, played bass in rock band; by age 20 was sessioning (sang on the Cufflinks' 'Tracy', no. 9 hit '69); arr. for Gene PITNEY, the DRIFTERS, PLATTERS etc.; wrote songs for the Partridge Family and the Buoys. 'I made around 300 singles and numerous jingles, yet there was not one that I was proud of.' Also scored films *Five Savage Men* (western about gang of rapists), soft-porn *Memories Within Miss Aggie*. Spent 10 weeks in UK doing nothing; returned to USA and signed to Epic for first album *Widescreen* '74, impressive debut incl. 'Second Saxophone', full of references to Swing Era classics. Barbra STREISAND liked it, asked him to arr. and prod. her *Lazy Afternoon* LP, using four of his songs; also used his songs in remake of *A Star Is Born* and LP *Superman*. Meanwhile came further Holmes LPs *Rupert Holmes* '75, *Singles* '77, *Pursuit Of Happiness* '78, last for ill-fated Private Stock label. Other '70s chores incl. prod. LPs for STRAWBS, SAILOR, Sparks, John Miles; while MANHATTAN TRANSFER, Dionne WARWICK, Barry MANILOW, Mac DAVIS, others covered Holmes's songs. Next LP *Partners In Crime* '79, again for ill-fated label (Infinity) incl. hits 'Escape (The Pina Colada Song)' (no. 1), 'Him' (6), 'Answering Machine' (36). MCA picked up Infinity, released *Adventure* '80, which was relative flop; he switched to Elektra for seventh LP *Full Circle* '81. All are now out of print in USA; compilation *Songwriters For The Stars* on Polydor in UK by Jimmy WEBB and Holmes.

HOLY MODAL ROUNDERS, The Folk/ country band formed in the early '60s in NYC by vocalists Peter Stampfel (*b* 29 Oct. '38, Wauwautosa, Wis.) on banjo and fiddle, guitarist Steve Weber (*b* 22 June '44, Philadelphia). Weber was the better musician, but famously reluctant to rehearse (or even, allegedly, to get out of bed), while Stampfel knew an uncountable number of songs: their 'progressive old-timey' or 'acid folk' found an audience that never goes away. ('Rounder' was USA slang for an idler, probably dissolute, but perhaps of considerable experience.) First LPs were *The Holy Modal Rounders* and *II* '64 on Prestige (now 2-disc *Stampfel & Weber*); they collaborated with the FUGS on ESP LPs, made their own *Indian War Hoop* '67 on that label, with budding playwright/actor Sam Shepard on drums; went further in acid direction with *The Moray Eels Eat The Holy Modal Rounders* '68 on Elektra, adding Dave Levy on electric guitar, Richard Tyler on bass and keyboards (Stampfel had run a band called the Moray Eels in which he played bass), floundered on with *Good Taste Is Timeless* '71 on Metromedia, with Michael McCarty and John Wesley Annis replacing Shepard and Levy, adding Robin Remaily on guitar, mandolin, fiddle and vocals. ('Living Off The Land'/'Boobs A Lot' on Metromedia was probably their only single.) Meanwhile they recorded original cast LP of Sam Shepard play *Operation Sidewinder* for Columbia c.'68 but play flopped and LP was not issued; more Elektra material remains unreleased. Stampfel's girlfriend Antonia's 'Bird Song' was the song from soundtrack of film *Easy Rider* '69 that nobody remembers: despite a loyal following, the unevenness of these albums and the impossibility of categorising their music kept them in left field; the '72 band incl. saxophonist Ted Deane was said to be the best ever, but did not record. Found a home on new Rounder label (named after them) with *Alleged In Their Own Time* '75 incl. Stampfel, Weber, Remaily, Tyler, the excellent Karen Dalton on vocals, plus Luke Faust (from INSECT TRUST) on vocals, guitar and banjo, Hunt Middleton on guitar, Dave Reisch on bass: this was succeeded (and exceeded) by joyful *Have Moicy!* '75, with the Unholy Modal Rounders (without Weber) and the Clamtones, incl. Stampfel, Paul Presty on guitar and vocals, Remaily, Jeff & Jill Frederick, Antonia, Michael Hurley (as 'Snock'), Dick Nickson (aka Frog) on drums: rated a record of the year by *Village Voice*, *Rolling Stone* (see also *Spiders In The Moonlight* by Jeff Frederick and the Clamtones). Reunions of post-'71 HMR incl. *Last Round* (came out '78 on Adelphi), *Going Nowhere Fast* ('81 on Rounder); live '81 Stampfel-Weber reunion to be released as 2-disc *Cruel And Unusual, The Punishment Brothers*. Meanwhile Stampfel teamed unsuccessfully with Mark Bingham (guitarist who contributed to Kurt WEILL tribute *Lost In The Stars* on A&M), singer/songwriter John Parrot; formed Bottle Caps '81 (referring to his bottlecap collection, featured on earlier album sleeves): *Peter Stampfel & The Bottle Caps* '86 on Rounder won NY Music Award for best independent record, with John Scherman, lead guitar; W. T. (Tom) Overgard, rhythm guitar; Jonathan (Jabe) Best, keyboards; all vocalists except Peter Moser on drums, Allan Greller on bass. The Unholy Modal Rounders (without Weber) made a privately released album of 'songs' by Buckminster Fuller ('Roam Home To The Dome' to the tune of 'Home On The Range', etc.). Weber contributed to *The East Village Other* on ESP, also to Hurley's LPs: Hurley drew distinctive LP covers, made LPs on Rounder, also *Armchair Boogie* '71 on Raccoon. Dalton made *It's So Hard To Tell Who's Going To Love You The Best* '69 on Capitol, *In My Own Time* '71 on Just Sunshine/Paramount.

HOME SERVICE, The UK folk-rock band formed '80 out of ALBION BAND as the First Eleven (incl. John Kirkpatrick), changing to nostalgic name of the original domestic BBC network. Lineup: Bill Caddick (*b* June '44, Wolverhampton), vocals, guitar; Graeme Taylor (*b* 2 Feb. '54, London); Michael Gregory (*b* 16 Nov. '49, Gower,

Wales); Roger Williams and John Tams, various instruments and vocals; Howard Evans, trumpet; Jonathan Davie, bass. Threatens to become the most infl. band of its kind since FAIRPORT CONVENTION, integrating English brass sound with electric rock, a sound described as SOUTHSIDE JOHNNY meets the Salvation Army; but commitments to theatre, TV and film work mean that live work and recordings are limited. Caddick's solo LPs had incl. *Rough Music* '74, *Sunny Memories* '77 and *Reasons Briefly Set Down By The Author To Perswade Every One To Sing* '79; also collaborated with Tim Laycock and Peter Bond on *A Duck On His Head* '80. He and Tams, another folk scene regular, now became songwriters in style of Richard THOMPSON. Taylor, Davie had been in Gryphon; brass section was classically trained (Evans and Williams also concurrently members with Kirkpatrick of BRASS MONKEY). One-off single 'Doing The Inglish' '82 was gratefully received; long-overdue debut album *The Home Service* '84 disappointed fans, perhaps because so much was expected, though live favourites 'Don't Let Them Grind You Down', 'Walk My Way' transferred well. National Theatre work peaked with music for cycle of York Mystery Plays: resulting LP *The Mysteries* '85 was rich English folk-rock, drawing on trad. sources and original material, augmented by Linda THOMPSON. Third LP *Alright Jack* '86 on Making Waves soon reissued on Hobson's Choice, as UK label/distributor failed '87: finally captured band's personality on record, justified their already substantial reputation; but Caddick had left '85, disappointed at lack of concert work, one of the reasons for the split from the Albion Band to begin with; his leaving ended projected splinter group the Rough Band, which had planned an album. Caddick's solo LP *The Wild West Show* was described in *Folk Roots* magazine as his best yet, with June TABOR guesting on one track. In '86 Home Service lineup incl. Andy Findon on sax, Steve King on keyboards.

HOMER & JETHRO (Homer *b* Henry D. Haynes, 27 July '18, Knoxville, Tenn.; *d* 7 Aug. '71; Jethro *b* Kenneth C. Burns, 10 Mar. '23, Knoxville) Country comedy team and noted Nashville session musicians.

Began in early teens on local radio; to Renfro Valley Barn Dance (Tenn.) '38. Split up during WWII, Homer serving in Europe, Jethro in Pacific ('I was the unsung hero. They wouldn't let me sing'). Regrouped upon discharge; joined Spike JONES touring show briefly, then Chicago's National Barn Dance through '50s; also regulars on popular *Don McNeil Breakfast Club* morning radio show: made Chicago area home base. Recorded for King '46-8, then signed by Steve Sholes (*see* COUNTRY MUSIC) to RCA from '48. Dead-pan send-ups of country, pop songs backed up by solid musicianship (Homer on rhythm guitar, Jethro excellent mandolin, banjo). First hit was 'Baby It's Cold Outside' with June Carter (*see* CARTER FAMILY) '49; '(How Much Is) That Hound Dog In The Winder' no. 2 country chart '53; other entries incl. 'Hernando's Hideaway' '54, 'The Battle Of Kookamonga' '59 (no. 14 pop chart; parody of Johnny HORTON hit 'The Battle Of New Orleans'), BEATLE take-off 'I Want To Hold Your Hand'; other discs got juke-box and airplay even when they didn't chart: 'Don't Let The Stars Get In Your Eyeballs', 'The Ballad Of Davy Crew-Cut'. Many TV spots incl. *Tonight* show; when Johnny Carson asked Homer why he chewed chewing gum he replied, 'What the hell else you gonna do with it?' Did popular adverts for Kellogg's Corn Flakes on radio, TV '60s. Nominees to Country Music Hall of Fame '85; asked what the irreverent Homer would have said about that, Jethro speculated: 'It's about time . . . It couldn't happen to nicer people. We certainly deserve it.' Album *Ooh! That's Corny* '63 after gag catch-phrase used with really bad jokes. Others incl. *Musical Madness* '56, *Barefoot Ballads* '58, *The Worst Of Homer & Jethro* '58, *Songs My Mother Never Sang* '61, *Songs For The 'Out' Crowd* '67, *Nothing Like An Old Hippie* '68, many others. Latest compilation was *Country Comedy* '75. Jethro still plays sessions, clubs, festivals all over North America; toured for 11 years with Steve GOODMAN and played at Goodman's memorial concert in Chicago.

HONEYCOMBS UK beat group formed as Sherabos '63. Lineup: Denis D'ELL (Dalziel), vocals, harmonica; Martin Murray, lead guitar; Alan Ward, rhythm guitar; John Lantree, bass; Honey Lantree, drums.

Took new name from female drummer, main selling point of group. Songs written by HOWARD & BLAIKLEY, who discovered them in London pub; first single 'Have I The Right', strident pop that sounded like cross between 'Telstar' hitmakers the Tornados and Dave CLARK Five: not surprisingly, since it was prod. by Joe Meek, Tornados mentor: his last no. 1 before he committed suicide; also no. 5 in USA. Since Honey didn't sing, promotion live and on TV was vital; group scuppered changes by departing on lengthy Australian tour so that inferior follow-ups 'Is It Because' and 'Something Better Beginning' barely made top 40 UK. On returning they replaced Murray with Peter Pye after recording LP to follow eponymous first, *All Systems Go* '65; 'That's The Way' reached no. 12 mid-'65, but further singles flopped and they faded. D'Ell tried solo career '70s with little success.

HONEYS, The Vocal trio formed c.'66: Marilyn Wilson, Diane Rovell, Ginger Blake. Marilyn Rovell engaged to BEACH BOYS leader Brian Wilson; he produced several singles for sisters and their cousin Blake. First two released '63; then gap until next in '69. Switched from Capitol to UA for new attempt in '72; excellent LP under name of *American Spring* resulted. Trio chose name of 'Spring', but in UK (where far more interest shown in LP than in USA) there was already a contemporary group with that name, so prefix was added. Brian co-prod. this time with Stephen Desper and/or David Sandler. Also cut one single for CBS early '70s as Spring, but lack of success led to another long hiatus until '82-3, when trio regrouped as The Honeys, made superb album *Ecstacy* for Rhino label. Marilyn and Brian by then estranged; LP produced by session musician Louie Maxfield (under alias of Lou Natkin) and engineer Mark Avnet. Despite quality, missed chart again.

HOOKER, Earl (*b* Earl Zebedee Hooker, 15 Jan. '30, Clarksdale, Ms.; *d* 21 Apr. '71, Chicago) Blues singer, songwriter, guitarist, multi-instrumentalist; cousin of John Lee HOOKER. Brought modern feeling to roots music, becoming king of the electric slide. Wrote 'Hold On, I'm Comin', 'Two Bugs

And A Roach', many more. To Chicago as a child; attended Lyon & Healy music school; worked the streets with Bo DIDDLEY, played small gigs; toured with Ike TURNER '49-50, infl. Ike, Elvin BISHOP, Jimi HENDRIX. Appeared on *Ready Steady Go* (UK TV) with the BEATLES '65. Records on many labels incl. Checker, Blue Thumb, Blues Way, etc. Died of TB. Collections now available on Arhoolie: *First And Last Recordings*, *Hooker & Steve* with MILLER, *Two Bugs And A Roach*; also *Earl Hooker* on Antilles; on Red Lightnin' in UK: *There's A Fungus Among Us* (also said to be last recordings, instrumentals with Jimmy DAWKINS), *The Leading Brand* with Jody Williams (*b* Joseph Leon Williams, 3 Feb. '35, Mobile, Ala.), also singer, guitarist.

HOOKER, John Lee (*b* 22 Aug. '17, Clarksdale, Ms.) Blues singer, guitarist; with Lightnin' HOPKINS and his cousin Earl HOOKER, one of the most influential and successful of trad. bluesmen with the white revivalists of the '60s: not a shouter, but with a laid-back, laconic vocal style that conveyed humour as well as the blues. First played electric guitar '48, returned to acoustic early '60s. Among many songs: 'I Don't Want To Go To Vietnam', 'Boogie With The Hook', 'House Rent Boogie', 'It Serves Me Right To Suffer', 'Boogie Chillen' (W. C. Handy Hall of Fame Award), 'One Scotch, One Bourbon, One Beer' (hit for Amos MILBURN). Won French Académie du Jazz Record Prix '68, many other polls and awards; appeared at many festivals, blues tours, TV films and shows incl. Dick Cavett talk show '69; influenced Johnny WINTER, John MAYALL, Buddy GUY, CANNED HEAT (with whom he made LP *Hooker 'n' Heat*, released '71). Own LPs incl. *Alone* and *Goin' Down Highway 51* on Specialty; *Black Snake* and *Boogie Chillun* on Fantasy; *No Friend Around, This Is Hip, Everybody Rockin', Moanin' The Blues, Solid Sender*, all on Charly; 2-disc set in the Chess masters series; *Do The Boogie*, '48-52 tracks on Happy Bird (from Germany); *It Serves You Right* on Jasmine; *Tantalisin' With The Blues* on MCA ('65-71 tracks); also *Sittin' Here Thinkin'* on both Muse and Happy Bird from the late '50s; many more. *Jealous* '86 on Pausa was first LP in years; another was planned.

HOPE, Elmo (*b* 27 June '23, NYC; *d* 19 May '67) Bop-era pianist, infl. by Bud POWELL (his childhood friend); his personal use of harmony combined with sure technique made him unique. Recorded with Sonny ROLLINS, Clifford BROWN, Lou DONALDSON '53-4; Jackie McLEAN '56; to West Coast, contributing compositions and piano to *Exploring The Future* (Curtis COUNCE '58), *The Fox* (Harold LAND '59), also played with Lionel HAMPTON in L.A. Own records incl. trio and quintet dates on Blue Note '53-4; on Prestige: *Meditations* and *Wail, Frank, Wail* (with Frank Foster) '55, *Informal Jazz* '56 (with John COLTRANE and Hank MOBLEY, later issued as *Two Tenors*); also *Art Blakey/Elmo Hope* '57 on Pacific Jazz with Land, *Elmo Hope Trio* on HiFi Jazz (later on Contemporary), *Homecoming* '61 on Riverside (also *The All Star Sessions* on Milestone), *Hope-Full* '61 on Riverside (solo set with Bertha Hope, additional piano on some tracks), *Here's Hope, High Hope* trios '61 on VSOP, *Hope From Riker's Island* '63 on Chiaroscuro, trio *Last Sessions* '66 on Inner City.

HOPKIN, Mary (*b* 3 May '50, Pontardawe, Wales) UK singer; had a fairy-tale rise to the top: model and '60s icon Twiggy saw Welsh folk-singer on TV, recommended her to Paul McCARTNEY, who signed her to Apple; first single 'Those Were The Days' zoomed to the top '68 (no. 2 USA), followed by 'Goodbye', 'Temma Harbour' and 'Knock, Knock, Who's There', all top 10. LP *Postcard* '69 emphasised charming voice; more successful folk LP *Earth Song* '71 featured Dave Cousins (from folk-rock STRAWBS), Ralph McTell; was prod. by Tony VISCONTI: they married '71. On tour she was said to lack stage presence; anyway she retired to raise a family; returned with 'If You Love Me' '76 (top 40 UK); sang back-up on David BOWIE's *Low* '77; *The Welsh World Of Mary Hopkin* '79 on Decca was sung in Welsh; group/album *Oasis* '84, with Peter Skellern, Julian Lloyd Webber.

HOPKINS, Claude (*b* 24 Aug. '03, Alexandria, Va.; *d* 19 Feb. '84, NYC) Pianist, arranger, bandleader. Led excellent bands in the Swing Era that employed such people as Jabbo SMITH, Vic DICKENSON, Edmond HALL. Obtained degree at Howard U.; joined Wilbur Sweatman as pianist mid-'20s, led band accompanying Josephine BAKER in Europe '25; led bands in Asbury Park N.J., NYC, Washington DC; took over Charlie Skeet band '30 and had long runs at Savoy and Roseland ballrooms, Cotton Club. Band appeared in films *Dance Team* '31, *Wayward* '32, *Barber Shop Blues* '33, *Broadway Highlights* '35. Abundant airtime ensured success; record of 'Trees' sung by Orlando Robertson was big seller '35. Disbanded '40, went to West Coast, sometimes leading, sometimes arr. for others. Mid-'40s formed band to play Zanzibar club NYC; led combo in Boston and NYC, Zanzibar again '50-1. Worked as sideman from mid-'50s, with groups led by Henry ALLEN, Wild Bill DAVISON, others. Active into '70s. LP *Harlem 1934* on Swing Classics; another compilation '32-3 on Jazz Archives incl. own composition, 'Anything For You'. Excellent musician never attained the fame he deserved, but made solo piano LPs *Crazy Fingers* on Chiaroscuro and *Soliloquy* on Sackville early '70s.

HOPKINS, Nicky (*b* 24 Feb. '44, London) UK session keyboardist. Joined Screamin' Lord SUTCH's Savages after leaving school; then Cyril DAVIES' All-Stars late '62: electric piano on 'Country Line Special' '63 marked him out as player of promise. After rest in hospital due to exhaustion and emotional problems, session career saw him play with the cream of UK pop: the WHO, several LPs with the ROLLING STONES, the KINKS and the EASYBEATS (through association with USA prod. Shel Talmy), others. Solo album *The Revolutionary Piano Of Nicky Hopkins* '66; Talmy-prod. single 'Mr Pleasant' '67 written by Kinks' Ray Davies; tried life on the road again with Jeff BECK Group '68-9 (incl. LP *Truth*); formed supergroup/LP *Sweet Thursday* '69, with Jon Mark and Alun Davies, guitars; Harvey Burns, drums; Brian Odgers, bass; reportedly turned down offer to become full-time Stone: session career suits him. Had sessioned with JEFFERSON AIRPLANE during a Beck tour; decided to become USA resident, settled in Mill Valley, Cal.; played with QUICKSILVER MESSENGER SERVICE and Steve MILLER Band (on three LPs each) but returned to UK '74. The BEATLES were the era's only major group never to request his services, but he sessioned for John Lennon (*Imagine*) and George Harrison in '70s; Harrison, Mick Taylor from the Stones and Beatle acolyte Klaus Voorman all sessioned on Hopkins' second solo LP *The Tin Man Was A Dreamer* '73, where he proved that his writing and singing could not match his piano playing; third solo was *No More Changes* '75. Tempted back on stage by Graham PARKER '80 to dep for Bob Andrews in Rumour.

HOPKINS, Sam 'Lightnin' ' (*b* 15 Mar. '12, Centerville, Texas) Blues singer, guitarist; but more than a blues singer: a minstrel, the last of the street singers. Many of the large number of songs credited to him were musical stories made up on the spot. Raised in Leona, Texas; to Houston late '20s and never left it for long, though he toured the world, recording prolifically. Played and sang on city buses with Alger ALEXANDER '45-50s; played Carnegie Hall '60. Adopted nickname working with pianist Wilson 'Thunder' Smith, with whom he recorded on Aladdin '46-7; recorded with his brother Joel (*b* 3 Jan. '04; *d* 15 Feb. '75, Galveston) in Houston '47-9. Made singles for several labels through '54, then LPs from '59 on Transition, Folkways, Candid, Heritage (UK), Prestige; with his brother John Henry (*b* 3 Feb.'01) on Arhoolie '64. Apart from many radio and festival appearances, TV and films incl. *The Blues* '62, *The Sun's Gonna Shine* '67, *The Blues According To Lightnin' Hopkins* '68, *Blues Like Showers Of Rain* '70 (UK), *Sam Lightnin' Hopkins* (Artists In America series) and *Boboquivari* (both '71 for PBS-TV), soundtrack for film *Sounder* '72 (with Taj MAHAL). Tracks with brothers and Barbara Dane (*b* 12 May '27, Detroit) on Arhoolie, also *Early Recordings Vols. 1&2, In Berkeley, Lightnin' Sam Hopkins, Texas Blues Man*; on Prestige: *Hootin' The Blues, Soul Blues, Gotta Move Your Baby* (with Sonny TERRY); Fantasy 2-disc sets *Double Blues, How Many More Years I Got*; on Rhino: *Los Angeles Blues*; in UK: *Lightnin' Strikes Back* on Charly; *Blues In My Bottle* on Prestige; *Electric Lightnin'* on JSP; *Live At The Bird Lounge* (Houston) on Bulldog, etc.

HORN, Paul (*b* 17 Mar. '30, NYC) Reeds. Mother was pianist for Irving BERLIN; at-tended Oberlin, Manhattan School of Music; played in SAUTER-FINEGAN band '56, with Chico HAMILTON quintet '56-8, joined NBC staff '59, began leading own quartets/quintets. Made TV documentary *The Story Of A Jazz Musician*, appeared on other TV shows; accompanied Tony BENNETT '65-6; became particularly well-known for flute work and as an early student of the modal style of composition of George RUSSELL and Miles DAVIS. To India '67-8, studied transcendental meditation and became a teacher of it; moved to Canada '70, scored films for National Film Board of Canada, *Island Eden* for government of British Columbia etc. Toured schools as clinician, published flute solos *Paul Horn/Inside*. Albums for Dot (and Imperial) '57-8; Calliope, World Pacific, HiFi Jazz '58-60; three on Columbia '61-3; *Jazz Suite On The Mass Texts* '64 with quintet, chorus, orchestra cond. by composer Lalo SCHIFRIN, and three other LPs for RCA incl. a BOSSA NOVA set with Oliver NELSON band; then his best-known work, *Inside* '68 on Epic, recorded in the Taj Mahal in India. Single 'Green Jelly Beans' and 'Dancing Children' '69 on Epic. LP on Ovation '70 and *Gassy Jack's Place* '73 on Pacific North (Canadian label) followed by another Epic LP and *Special Edition* on Mushroom (Canadian; also on Island), both '74; then *Paul Horn + Nexus* and *Altura do Sol*, both '75 on Epic; *Paul Horn In India* '76 on Blue Note with Indian musicians; *Dream Machine* '78 on Mushroom, made in Hollywood with Schifrin, Oscar Brashear on trumpet, Jim Keltner on drums, nine others with Israel Baker, concert-master; quartet LP *Live At Palm Beach Casino, Cannes 1980* on Rare Bid; *Traveler* '87 on Global Pacific has boys' chorus, Christopher Hedge (co-composer, multi-instrumentalist). *China* with Mingyue Liang on trad. instruments was on Golden Flute, re-issued '87 on Kukuck with different tracks; recorded '76-86.

HORN, Shirley (*b* 1 May '34, Washington DC) Jazz/cabaret singer, fine pianist. Studied at Howard U. and privately; helped by Miles DAVIS, Quincy JONES, others; led trio from '54. First LP *Live At The Village Vanguard* '61 now on Can-Am Int'l; also recorded for Mercury. Acclaimed LPs on

Steeplechase incl. *Garden Of The Blues, A Lazy Afternoon, All Night Long* '81, then *Violets For Your Furs*, the last three with drummer Billy Hart (*b* 29 Nov. '40, Washington DC; plays with Joanne BRACKEEN, many others; own album *Oshumare* on Gramavision '86). She taped a live LP May '87 at Vine Street Bar & Grill, her first West Coast gig for 23 years; *How I Thought About You* came out on Verve. If singers of intimate quality were more highly regarded nowadays, Horn would be a household name.

HORN, Trevor (*b* 15 July '49, Newcastle) Internationally known record producer. First surfaced with Buggles, whose prophetic 'Video Killed The Radio Stars' was a UK no. 1 '79. *The Age Of Plastic* '79 was effervescent collection of techno-pop in conjunction with partner Geoffrey Downes; subsequent Buggles singles ('Elstree') showed them ingenious purveyors of tongue-in-cheek pop in style of 10CC. UK music scene astounded when they joined supergroup YES, but they stayed only for LP *Drama* '80; Downs went to ASIA, Horn prod. Yes after leaving the group, notably *90125*; grandiose prod. style enhanced records by Dollar, ABC; Malcolm McLaren's *Duck Rock* '83 was masterly LP marking pop switch to a rootish sound. Horn formed ZTT label '83, made big splash with seismographic prod. for FRANKIE GOES TO HOLLYWOOD, so successful that group was berated for being little more than his puppets. Other ZTT acts such as Propaganda and Art Of Noise have benefited from his handling.

HORNE, Lena (*b* 30 June '17, Brooklyn, NY) Singer, actress. First appeared on stage at 6; turned pro as singer/dancer at the COTTON CLUB '34, toured and recorded with Noble SISSLE '35-6, appeared on stage in Lew Leslie's *Blackbirds* of '39, '40; toured with Charlie BARNET late '40-early '41, became a great favourite in clubs. Like Billie HOLIDAY and Ella FITZGERALD, she recorded ('Out Of Nowhere', 'Prisoner Of Love', etc.) with Teddy WILSON small groups in the '30s (though Holiday made most of the records: *Ella, Lena And Billie* on CBS is a selection). She also recorded with Barnet and Artie SHAW. When she sang 'Fine And Mellow' in a show at Carnegie Hall '41, Holiday was upset; Horne did exactly the right thing: she called at the club where Billie was working and asked permission to sing it, which was granted. She made films *Panama Hattie* '42; *Cabin In The Sky, Stormy Weather, Thousands Cheer, I Dood It* and *Swing Fever*, all in '43; *Broadway Rhythm* and *Two Girls And A Sailor* '44, *Ziegfeld Follies* and *Till The Clouds Roll By* '46, *Words And Music* '48, *Duchess Of Idaho* '50, *Meet Me In Las Vegas* '56. Accompanists have incl. Horace HENDERSON and Lennie HAYTON (she married Hayton in Paris '47). European tours incl. successful show at the London Palladium; she appeared on Broadway in *Jamaica* '57-9; played a straight dramatic role in the film *Death Of A Gunfighter* '69, but had not got a starring role in Broadway show *Destry Rides Again* '59 because Andy Griffith, already signed as Destry, would not play opposite a black. At first she and Hayton suffered a certain amount of inconvenience from neighbours etc. as an interracial couple in Hollywood, but for the most part she has been able to rise above racism: her combination of sheer class and obvious sincerity has kept her at the top of the supper club circuit, and her one-woman Broadway show *The Lady And Her Music* was a triumph in '81 (2-disc album on Qwest): on the eve of her 65th birthday she remained one of the most glamorous women and best-loved entertainers in the world. She published autobiographies *In Person: Lena Horne* '50, *Lena* '66. Her distinguished family entered the black bourgeoisie in the decade 1867-77, when America was almost colour-blind, until Congress sold out to racist elements in the South: *The Hornes An American Family* by Gail Lumet Buckley published '86. LPs incl. *At The Waldorf-Astoria* '57, *Give The Lady What She Wants* '58, *Porgy And Bess* (with Harry BELAFONTE) '59, *Lena On The Blue Side* '62, *Lena . . . Lovely And Alive* '63 (reissued '87 in UK), all chart hits; also *It's Love, Lena: A New Album* ('76; arr. by Robert FARNON), all on RCA; *Lena And Gabor* '70 (with Gabor SZABO) on Skye; *I Feel So Smoochie* on Lion; *Here's Lena Now!* on 20th Century Fox; *Lena Goes Latin* '63 on DRG; *The One And Only* on Polydor; *Standing Room Only* on Accord; *Stormy*

Weather on Stanyan; *Lena In Hollywood* on Liberty; 2-disc *Lena* with Hayton and Marty Gold bands on Pair; *A Date With Fletcher Henderson* ('44 tracks) on Sunbeam; many more.

HORSLIPS Irish folk-rock group formed '70; turned pro '72 on St Patrick's Day. Lineup: Barry Devlin, bass and vocals; Charles O'Connor, mandolin, fiddle and vocals; Jim Lockhart, keyboards; Eamon Carr, drums; Declan Sinnott, guitar (replaced by Gus Gueist, then John Fean; Sinnott later with Moving Hearts). Had hits in Ireland '72 ('Johnny's Wedding', 'Green Gravel'), then formed own label Oats, licensed through others outside Eire; LP *Happy To Meet . . . Sorry To Part* '73 made on ROLLING STONES mobile studio, featured self-indulgent (but then fascinating) 'concertina' sleeve: best-selling LP of all time in Eire, with mix of trad., original folk tunes incl. outstanding 'Furniture'. Cranked up rock content for *The Tain* '74, concept LP built around a Celtic legend, performed in its entirety on tour in UK as support for STEELEYE SPAN, breaking them to mainland audience. *Dancehall Sweethearts* '74 failed to match *Tain*, though continued policy of merging trad. tunes into contemporary-sounding original material; *The Unfortunate Cup Of Tea* '75 was too poppy for folk fans on whom they still relied, so reverted to pure unamplified folk for *Drive The Cold Winter Away* '76 before starting folk-rock synthesis anew. *The Book Of Invasions – A Celtic Symphony* '77 was first UK top 40 LP and best since *Tain*, which it paralleled as another mythic concept album: showed off members' multi-instrumental skills (all except lead vocalist Devlin doubled on trad. Irish instruments, a regular feature of stage act). But growing acceptance in USA led to increasingly rock-oriented productions; studio LPs – *Aliens* '77, *The Men Who Built America* '79 (concept LP on Irish immigration to USA), and *Short Stories/Tall Tales* '80 – lacked band's original freshness: they sensed this too and split up, leaving *The Belfast Gigs* '80 as second live offering, flawed by Fean's sub-heavy metal guitar. They played UK, USA, north and south of Ireland without fear or favour and were much-loved in home country. All records still available from Horslips

Records, incl. compilations of early singles and folkier material. Lure of USA megabucks caused decline; spinoff group Host with the group's diehard folkies Fean, O'Connor and Carr, plus Chris Page, bass, Peter Keen, keyboards, made concept LP *Tryal* on Aura '84, based on 19th-century witch trial.

HORTON, Johnny (*b* 3 Apr. '29, Tyler, Texas; *d* 5 Nov. '60, Milano, Texas). Country singer, becoming the biggest star of a new decade when he was killed in a car crash: wife Billie Jean Jones was then widowed twice; had been married to Hank WILLIAMS. The Singing Fisherman, worked in Alaska, Cal. fishing industries; attended U. of Seattle; worked on local radio East Texas, Hometown Jamboree in Cal.; recorded for Abbott, Dot, Mercury without much success; moved to Shreveport and became regular on Louisiana Hayride. Signed to Columbia, had hits 'Honky Tonk Man', top 10 'I'm A One-Woman Man' '56; 'Coming Home' '57; top 10 'All Grown Up' '58; 'When It's Springtime In Alaska' was no. 1 country '59, first of series of saga songs: 'The Battle Of New Orleans' (*see* Jimmy DRIFTWOOD) was no. 1 country and pop '59; 'Sink The Bismark' no. 6 country, no. 3 pop (suggested by the film), 'North To Alaska' no. 1 country, no. 4 pop (from a John Wayne movie), both '60. Early hits recharted after his death; LPs still selling. Albums incl. *Honky Tonk Man* '58, *Makes History* '59, *Spectacular* '60, *On Stage* '67, *The World Of* '71, *On The Road* '73, all on Columbia; *The Unforgettable* '68 on Harmony; CBS compilations *Rock'n'Rollin'* '81 on Bear Family and *America Remembers* '82 on CSP/Gusto. Biography *Your Singing Fisherman* '83.

HORTON, Walter 'Shakey' (*b* 6 Apr. '17, Horn Lake, Ms.; *d* '81) Harmonica. Self-taught at age 5, recorded with Memphis Jug Band '27, toured south with various groups, settled in Chicago from c.'40, working Maxwell Street for tips: became the father of the modern Chicago blues harp, infl. on the younger LITTLE WALTER and James COTTON. Recorded in Memphis for Modern/RPM '51, Chess and Sun '52; worked and recorded in Chicago on Chess, Cobra, States with Muddy WATERS, Johnny

SHINES, Otis RUSH, his own combo, etc.; made UK film *American Folk Blues Festival '68*, *Good Mornin' Blues* '78 for PBS-TV. Still worked Maxwell Street for tips '74. Records as a sideman are uncountable; in the early '50s he alternated with Little Walter on Muddy Waters classics; on a few they both played. Horton's own albums incl. *Can't Keep Loving You* and *Fine Cuts* on Blind Pig; *Big Walter Horton/Carey Bell* (*b* 14 Nov. '36, Macon, Ms., another fine harp player) on Alligator USA, Sonet UK; *The Deep Blues Harmonica Of Walter Horton* on JSP UK; *An Offer You Can't Refuse* with Paul BUTTERFIELD on Red Lightnin' UK. *Harmonica Blues Kings: Big Walter/Alfred Harris* '86 on Delmark-Pearl incl. six sides made for United '54 with Willie DIXON, MEMPHIS SLIM. Among his last recordings, *Little Boy Blue* '88 on JSP was made '80.

HOT CHOCOLATE UK pop group formed in London '69 by Jamaican-born vocalist Errol Brown and bassist Tony Wilson, from Trinidad. First break as songwriters for Apple; wrote 'Think About Your Children' for Mary HOPKIN, 'Bet Your Life I Do' for HERMAN'S HERMITS; Apple secretary suggested name for them and first single was reggae-tinged version of LENNON's 'Give Peace A Chance'. Left Apple (then disintegrating fast) for RAK, where Mickie MOST took them under prod. wing: dynamic ballad 'Love Is Life' '70 was no. 6 and set pattern for numerous hits: Brown's velvety voice allied to percussive pop with sparkle was Most's golden touch. Concentrated on singles released sparingly; refused to be rushed into live performance or album. First seven issues alternated big and small hits; 'I Believe In Love' '71 and 'Brother Louie' '73 were top 10: latter poignant tale of mixed-race romance akin to TEMPTATIONS/Marvin GAYE social consciousness; went to no. 1 USA when covered by the Stories, paving way for Chocolate's own six USA top 40 hits '75-8. UK tour '73 saw interracial lineup: Patrick Olive (*b* Grenada), congas; Larry Ferguson (*b* Nassau), keyboards; Harvey Hinsley (*b* Mitcham, south London; ex-Outlaws, Cliff Bennett's Rebel Rousers), guitar; Tony Connor (*b* Romford; ex-Audience; replaced original drummer Ian King). First LP *Cicero Park* '74 broadened scope of lyrics in

title track to incl. ecology. Single hits incl. 'Emma' '74, 'Disco Queen' and 'You Sexy Thing' '75: all dance-floor smashes with radio appeal, Brown's unmistakeable vocals topping off pop confection. With shaved head for striking visual effect, Brown became Hot Chocolate; co-writer Wilson left for solo career (without much luck, on Bearsville label; Curtis MAYFIELD-infl. LPs *I Like Your Style* '76, *Catch One* '79); Patrick Olive took over on bass. Shortfall of originals that followed helped by astute selection from outside: Russ Ballard's 'So You Win Again' was first no. 1 (USA no. 31) '77, while 'I'll Put You Back Together Again' (from mawkish musical *Dear Anyone*) made no. 13 '78. Final USA hit with 'Every 1's A Winner' '78 (UK no. 12; later adapted as radio jingle). Hits faltered '79-81, four of six missing top 40; Brown moved to L.A. to recharge batteries, result was return to top 10 with 'Girl Crazy' (7) and 'Chances' (32), both '82. Chocolate bucked fashion by ignoring it: 25 UK top 40 hits '70-84 proving that good songs sell with classy voice against classy production.

HOUSE, Son (*b* Eddie James House Jr, 21 Mar. '02, Riverton, Ms.) Blues singer, guitarist. Born on a plantation; he was a Baptist pastor early '20s; turned to music c.'27. Served time at Parchman State Farm in Ms. '28-9; worked with Charley PATTON '29; recorded for Paramount '30; test pressings were made for ARC '33 but the company chose Charley Patton's; he was recorded for the Library of Congress '41-2 (on Arhoolie now); often worked outside music and was inactive in music '48-64 when he was rediscovered, his vitality unimpaired: having had one career in music playing and singing solely for blacks, he had another performing solely for whites at colleges and festivals, perhaps the greatest surviving delta bluesman. He played at Newport Folk Festivals '64 and '69 (released on Vanguard), recorded for Blue Goose (*Real Delta Blues* '64), played Carnegie Hall '65, recorded for Columbia '65, at Café A-Go-Go NYC '65-6 (portion released on Verve), made short film *Son House* '69, recorded for the Roots label '69; other records were available on Liberty (at London's 100 Club), Transatlantic (with Stefan Grossman) (both '70). Compilations have been available on Yazoo and

Biograph. He was mostly inactive in the '70s because of poor health.

HOUSTON, Cisco (*b* Gilbert Vandine Houston, 18 Aug. '18, Wilmington, Del.; *d* 29 Apr. '61, San Bernardino, Cal.) Folksinger, guitarist. Raised on West Coast, learned guitar in high school, became itinerant during the Depression; travelled and sang with Woody GUTHRIE. Served in the Merchant Marine; then was active in the Almanac Singers (see the WEAVERS, Pete SEEGER) and at the first Folkways recording sessions. Had one of several hit recordings of 'Rose, Rose, I Love You' '51, on Decca with Gordon JENKINS. During the '50s he performed at colleges and folk clubs, toured India with Sonny TERRY and Brownie MCGHEE for the State Department, performed in the UK and at the '60 Newport Folk Festival. He was one of those, like Guthrie and Seeger, who kept the flame of populist music burning when it was worth nothing commercially, living long enough before dying of cancer to see urban folk music make a new contribution to American popular culture, and to be admired by Bob DYLAN, who met him while visiting Guthrie in New Jersey. LPs incl. *American Folk Songs* and *Songs Of The Open Road* on Folkways, *Sings Woody Guthrie* and *The Legendary Cisco Houston* on Vanguard, *Cisco Houston* on Archive of Folk. Collected songs *900 Miles: The Ballads, Blues And Folksongs Of Cisco Houston* published '65.

HOUSTON, Cissy (*b* c.'32, Newark, N.J.) Soul singer. Began singing with family gospel group the Drinkard Singers, which recorded for RCA, Savoy; at various times incl. Judy Clay (soul hit 'Greatest Love' on Atlantic, '70; also duets with William BELL), Cissy's nieces Dee Dee and Dionne WARWICK. Became lead singer of the Sweet Inspirations, who sang back-up with Solomon BURKE, Wilson PICKETT, Aretha FRANKLIN etc.; appeared with Elvis PRESLEY in Las Vegas '68; had nine of their own soul hits '67-71, five crossing over to pop: biggest was 'Sweet Inspiration' (no. 5 soul, no. 18 pop '68). Cissy went solo, had hits 'I'll Be There', 'Be My Baby' '70-1, album *Cissy Houston* on Janus; also recorded 'Midnight Train To Georgia', later a hit for Gladys KNIGHT. Retired to raise her family, incl. daughter Whitney (*see below*); came back with *Cissy Houston* '77 on Private Stock; sang backup on LPs by Chaka KHAN, Aretha, Luther VANDROSS; own LPs *Warning – Danger* and *Step Aside For A Lady* on Columbia '79-80; worked club gigs with daughter Whitney. All the while she never left the church, served as mus. dir. at the New Hope Baptist Church in Newark, directing the choir, hosting its weekly radio show. At George's in Chicago '86 her eclectic material incl. Willie NELSON's 'Always On My Mind', Neil SEDAKA's 'Breaking Up Is Hard To Do'; local critic Rick Kogan wrote that with her 'emotional punctuation' singing Cole PORTER's 'After You' 'she was able to touch anyone who had loved and lost.' It is an indictment of the music industry that she has not recorded more often.

HOUSTON, David (*b* 9 Dec. '38, Bossier City, La.) Country singer; big star of '60s with 17 top 10 hits '63-71, six at no. 1 (not counting duets). Descended from both Sam Houston and Robert E. Lee; advised on early career by godfather Gene AUSTIN. Appeared on Louisiana Hayride at age 12; signed to Sun Records briefly '57; to Nashville '62, signed to Epic for hits 'Mountain Of Love' (no. 2 '63), 'Livin' In A House Full Of Love' (no. 3 '65), several other top 40 entries; then with prod. Billy SHERRILL for 'Almost Persuaded' '66, first country no. 1 for each of them, also pop no. 24 and Grammy for Best Male Country Performance; followed by 'With One Exception', 'You Mean The World To Me' '67, 'Have A Little Faith', 'Already It's Heaven' '68, 'Baby Baby (I Know You're A Lady)' '69, all no. 1 country, nearly all reached one or another pop chart. Also did duets with Barbara MANDRELL ('After Closing Time', no. 6 '70) and Tammy WYNETTE ('My Elusive Dreams', no. 1 country '67, made Hot 100 pop). Continued to make country chart '70s in a less spectacular manner; to Starday/Gusto label '77 with hit 'So Many Ways', then label-hopped. LPs incl. *Wonders Of The Wine* '70, *The Day Love Walked In* '72, *A Perfect Match* '73 (with Mandrell), *Good Things* '73, *A Man Needs Love* '75, *Greatest Hits* '76, all on Epic; *David Houston* '77 on Starday/Gusto, *From The Heart Of Houston* '79 on Derrick, *From Houston To You* '81 on Excelsior.

HOUSTON, Thelma (*b* Leland, Ms.) Gospel-based singer who has made otherwise routine disco records palatable. Sang in local Baptist church; moved to L.A. and sang after high school with gospel group the Art Reynolds Singers. Married at 17, had two children; worked for social services; performed in L.A. clubs and was discovered '68 by Steve Gordon, manager of FIFTH DImension: debut LP *Sunshower*, prod. by Jim WEBB, incl. classic version of ROLLING STONES 'Jumping Jack Flash'. In three years on Dunhill only mild hit 'Save The Country' (no. 74, '70); she moved to Motown/Mowest and '74 Grammy nomination for 'You've Been Doing Wrong For So Long'. Recorded themes for films '76 *The Bingo Long Travelling All-Stars And Motor Kings*, *Norman . . . Is That You?*. Breakthrough with Gamble-Huff disco success 'Don't Leave Me This Way', no. 1 USA '77; incl. on Tamla LP *Any Way You Like It*, no. 11 chart LP USA '77; *The Devil In Me* also charted '77. Duet LP with Jerry BUTLER *Thelma And Jerry* on Motown did well in charts '77, so it was followed by *Two To One* '78. Also made direct-to-disc album for Sheffield Labs label *I've Got The Music In Me* with session band Pressure Cooker. To RCA for *Never Gonna Be Another One* '81; MCA for *Thelma Houston* '83; got executive prod. credit for MCA *Qualifying Heat* late '84, hoped to become headliner at last, but the RCA LP was the last to chart.

HOUSTON, Whitney (*b* 9 Aug. '63, Newark, N.J.) Daughter of Cissy HOUSTON, cousin of Dee Dee and Dionne WARWICK, calls Aretha FRANKLIN Aunty Ree: has both family talent and beauty. Made solo debut at 11 with 'Guide Me, O Thou Great Jehovah' in Baptist church; played NYC club dates with her mother early '80s, also worked as model, acted on TV. Clive DAVIS at Arista signed her with 'key man' clause: if he leaves the company she can go with him. Debuted with eponymous hit LP '85 with four producers incl. Jermaine Jackson; won a Grammy and sold 14 million copies: unusually, of 10 songs eight were ballads, hit singles 'You Give Good Love', 'Saving All My Love For You', 'How Will I Know' and 'Greatest Love' accompanied by classy videos, latter making MTV, unusual for a black artist. She was the first female artist in history of Billboard charts to have an album enter at no. 1; did it again with second LP *Whitney* '87, with hit 'I Wanna Dance With Somebody (Who Loves Me)'. Definitely a huge new star, she will succeed Diana ROSS for sheer class: in '88 'Where Do Broken Hearts Go' became 7th consecutive no.1 USA hit, breaking Beatles' record.

HOWARD & BLAIKLEY UK songwriting team whose success was rivalled only by LENNON & McCARTNEY: Ken Howard (*b* 26 Dec. '39), Alan Blaikley (*b* 23 Mar. '40), both from Hampstead, London. Wrote 10 top 10 hits for Dave DEE, Dozy, Beaky, Mick & Tich '65-8, no. 1 for the HONEYCOMBS ('Have I The Right?' ' 64), hits for the Herd (*see* Peter FRAMPTON), LULU; first in UK to write a hit for Elvis PRESLEY. Wrote concept LP *Ark II* '69 for Flaming Youth (Phil COLLINS' first group). Background as BBC TV trainees stood them well when expanding into stage musicals; first one *Mardi Gras* '76 ran for six months in London's West End. Kept writing hits through '70s for BAY CITY ROLLERS, Pet CLARK, Engelbert HUMPERDINCK, others; music for TV shows *Flame Trees Of Thika* '81, *By The Sword Divided* '83, *Miss Marple* '85; on anniversary of John Lennon's murder Dec. '85 Howard was responsible for controversial TV biographical documentary.

HOWARD, Don (*b* Donald Howard Koplow, 11 May '35, Cleveland, Ohio) A 17-year-old in high school who had a fluke hit, a million-selling no. 4 USA '52-3. He heard 'Oh Happy Day' sung by a girl friend and copyrighted it; a demo was played on the air locally, then leased to the Essex label: a happy tune given a treatment by Howard which can only be described as sepulchral, the record was a runaway novelty. Nancy Binns Reed came forward to claim authorship; she had written the song while a counsellor at a girls' camp where Howard's friend heard it, and the royalties were shared.

HOWARD, Eddy (*b* 12 Sep. '14, Woodland, Cal.; *d* 23 May '63, Palm Desert, Cal.) Singer, bandleader, songwriter. Attended medical school, then began singing on L.A. radio; worked with several bands, then with

Dick JURGENS '34-40: hits on Vocalion incl. 'Careless' and 'My Last Goodbye', his own compositions. Formed own band '41, a popular 'sweet' band for many years, still active in the studios into the '60s; he led a vocal trio and sang solo in a pleasant, unpretentious style, still redolent of nostalgia. 10 top 20 hits '46-52 began on Majestic (later on Mercury) with 'To Each His Own' (no. 1), written for a film of that name (but not used) by Ray Evans and Jay Livingston, who also wrote 'Mona Lisa', 'Tammy' (nominated for an Oscar, from the '57 Debbie Reynolds movie), many others. The record was backed by a new recording of 'Careless', which was the band's theme; other hits incl. 'My Adobe Hacienda', 'I Wonder, I Wonder, I Wonder', and 'Sin (It's No Sin)' (his second no. 1, '51; also a hit by the FOUR ACES). Howard's single of 'Happy Birthday' and 'The Anniversary Waltz' was a juke box staple for years.

HOWARD, Harlan (b 8 Sep. '29, Lexington, Ky.) Country singer; one of the most successful songwriters in the history of country music. Grew up in Detroit, became paratrooper based in Georgia; later moved to L.A. and worked as bookbinder while trying to get songs published. Johnny BOND and Tex RITTER took an interest, published first hit 'Pick Me Up On Your Way Down' (Charlie Walker no. 2) '58; then 'Heartaches By The Number' (Ray PRICE, no. 2 country; Guy MITCHELL no. 1 pop), 'Mommie For A Day' (Kitty WELLS no. 5), all '59, 'Excuse Me (I Think I've Got A Heartache)' (Buck OWENS no. 2) '60, many more. Married Jan HOWARD '60, then to Nashville; she sang on his demo records, had hits of her own. Harlan won a record 10 BMI songwriting awards '61; among other notable songs: 'Too Many Rivers', by Brenda LEE; 'I Fall To Pieces', by Patsy CLINE, 'Tiger By The Tail', by Owens; 'No Charge', by Tammy WYNETTE, 'Busted', by Ray CHARLES; he's said to have had 60 no.1 country hits. He wrote 'Never Mind' 'specially for Nanci Griffith (on *Little Love Affairs*). He recorded for Capitol; later albums incl. *All Time Favorite Country Songwriter* '65 on Monument, *Mr Songwriter* '67 and *Down To Earth* '68 on RCA, *To The Silent Majority, With Love* '71 on Nugget: 'Sunday Morning Christian' was his own top 40 hit '71.

HOWARD, Jan (b 13 Mar. '32, West Plains, Mo.) Country singer. Married Harlan Howard, '60, divorced late '60s. Sang on his demo records; string of own hits (13 in country top 40, '60s) began with 'The One You Slip Around With' '60 on Challenge, 'Evil On Your Mind' and 'Bed Seeds', both '66, 'My Son' '68, all on Decca. Toured and recorded with the Carter sisters '64 (see CARTER FAMILY); big duet hits with Bill ANDERSON: popular member of his touring, TV show late '60s-early '70s; with Johnny CASH '73-7, Tammy WYNETTE '79-81. LPs incl. *Rock Me Back To Little Rock, Count Your Blessings, Woman* c.'68 on Decca, *Bad Seeds* on Coral '72, *Sincerely* '78 on GRT.

HOWELL, Peg Leg (b 5 Mar. 1888, Eatonton, Ga.; d 11 Aug. '66, Atlanta) Blues singer, guitarist. Raised on a farm; self-taught on guitar c. age 20; worked as a farmer but lost a leg from a gunshot wound '16. Worked streets and parks for tips with a group '23-34, subsequently mostly outside music. Served time for bootlegging '25; lost the other leg from diabetes '52. One of the first blues singers to record, for Columbia '26-9; then for Testament '63. LPs: *1928-9* on Matchbox, *The Legendary* on Testament.

HOWLETT, Mike UK-based musician/prod. (b Fiji) who learned euphonium and guitar in youth. Emigrated to Australia by age 18; played Sydney's Whiskey A Go Go in three-piece group the Affair with girl vocalist; won talent contest in UK and decided to stay. After playing bass with shortlived group early '70s (Quadrille and Highway, with Bernie Holland), joined European hippie-rock band Gong '73-6, also prod. their posthumous *Live, Etc* '77 (Gong alias Mr T. Being). At onset of punk, cut hair and formed new wave group Strontium 90 with Sting and Stewart Copeland; gigged with this group in Paris '77 at Gong reunion show, having added Andy Summers, whereupon they left him to become POLICE. Early Virgin ventures as house producer were paying off; gave up playing except for odd sessions (with Nik Turner '78, Duffo '79): like many prod. of period, used knowledge of studio technique to help raw punks get onto vinyl with minimum loss of impact. Earliest assignments were with Penetration (*Race Against Time* '78), Punishment of Luxury (*Laughing Academy* '79), Fischer Z (*Word Salad* '79); described his studio *modus operandi* as 'getting a guy to play within his limitations and to make the best of what he can do', skilfully overdubbing to achieve desired effects but maintaining a clear sound: worked with Martha and the Muffins, Any Trouble, synthesiser bands Orchestral Manoeuvres and BLANCMANGE, new wave pop incl. TEARDROP EXPLODES, THOMPSON TWINS, China Crisis, FLOCK OF SEAGULLS. Recent sessions with Joan ARMATRADING.

HUBBARD, Freddie (*b* Frederick Dewayne Hubbard, 7 Apr. '38, Indianapolis, Ind.) Trumpet, flugelhorn, piano, composer. Studied French horn in high school, won music scholarship; Wes MONTGOMERY was a fellow student; played with the Montgomery bros, Sonny ROLLINS, Max ROACH; LP with Curtis FULLER *Gettin' It Together* '60; joined Art BLAKEY '61 and became one of the brightest stars of the decade with his own series of quintet/sextet LPs, mostly on Blue Note, with fine sidemen: *Open Sesame* (with Tina BROOKS), *Goin' Up* (with Hank MOBLEY) '60; *Hub Cap*, *Ready For Freddie* '61; *Hub-Tones*, *Here To Stay* (not issued at the time) '62; *Breaking Point* '64; *Blue Spirits* and 2-vol. live *The Night Of The Cookers* '65. There were also an LP on Fontana and two on Impulse (sextet set and another with up to 12 pieces plus strings, arr. and cond. by Wayne SHORTER). *Backlash* '66, *High Blues Pressure* '67, *Soul Experiment* '69 (two guitars and electric bass) were all on Atlantic; quintet *The Hub Of Hubbard* on MPS was followed by *Red Clay* (with Herbie HANCOCK's electric piano) and *Straight Life* (with George BENSON), both '70 on CTI; *Sing Me A Song Of Songmy* '71 on Atlantic with choir and strings followed same year by *First Light* on CTI with strings; then Hubbard's first pop chart entries: *Sky Dive* '72 with Keith JARRETT, Benson etc. and *Keep Your Soul Together* '73, both on CTI. As he felt the commercial pull of fusion/electric music he also regularly came back to his jazz roots, e.g. *In Concert* '73 on CTI, two vols. made live at the Chicago Opera House with a conventional sextet: this music does not make the Billboard pop LP chart, whether we like it or not; Hubbard's accountant no doubt pre-

fers the fusion. His first Columbia LP *High Energy* '74 made the chart, as did his last CTI LPs *Polar AC* and a compilation, *The Baddest Hubbard*. *Gleam* '75 on CBS/Sony was made live in Japan; *Liquid Love*, *Windjammer*, *Bundle Of Joy* and *Super Blue* '75-8 on Columbia were his last pop chart entries though *The Love Connection* and *Skagly* '79 were aimed at the same audience. In '80 a septet set *Back To Birdland* on Real Time, quintet 2-disc *Live At The Northsea Jazz Festival* on Pablo were for the jazz fans; nonets *Jazz Of The '80s* (live In Japan) and *Mistral* (in a Hollywood studio) are both on East Wind. '81 was a busy year: *Rollin'* on MPS was made at the Villingen Jazz Festival with the same group (except for the drummer) as *Northsea*; *Outpost* on Enja is by a quartet, his most intimate outing so far; *Anthology* on Black Shell was made live in Italy by a quintet; *Ride Like The Wind* on Elektra/Musician has 14 pieces plus strings; *Splash* on Fantasy has a different lineup on each of seven tracks; *Keystone Bop*, *Classics* and *A Little Night Music*, all on Fantasy, were made live at San Francisco's Keystone Korner by a sextet which had Bobby HUTCHERSON and Joe Henderson on tenor (*b* 24 Apr. '37, Lima, Ohio; many LPs on Timeless, Blue Note, Enja, Milestone, Contemporary; also worked with BLOOD, SWEAT & TEARS). *Born To Be Blue* on Pablo was made at the end of the year by a sextet with Harold LAND; *Face To Face* '82 with Pablo regulars Oscar PETERSON, Joe PASS, Niels-Henning Ørsted Pedersen and on drums Martin Drew, from the house band at Ronnie SCOTT's in London. *Sweet Return* to Atlantic '83 has Joanne BRACKEEN, Roy HAYNES, Eddie Gomez, Lew Tabackin on reeds and extra percussion on some tracks. Hubbard seemed to rest for a while after '83 and no wonder, having done something for everyone. Attended Blue Note relaunch party '85; *Life Flight* '87 on that label is an easy ride, with his fat tone throughout: one side with guests George Benson, Stanley TURRENTINE, fine R&B beat laid down by Idris Muhammad; the other with his current working band incl. Larry Willis on keyboards, Ralph Moore on tenor, Carl Allen on drums, others.

HUGHES, Spike (*b* Patrick Cairnes Hughes, 19 Oct. '08, London; *d* 2 Feb. '87) Bassist, composer, bandleader, critic. Recorded with British jazz groups, then came to NYC '33 and fulfilled Decca recording contract by hiring Chu BERRY, Coleman HAWKINS, Benny CARTER, Henry ALLEN, Wayman CARVER, Sid CATLETT, others to record his compositions, 'Firebird', 'Pastoral', 'Arabesque', etc., and his own arrangements of 'Bugle Call Rag', 'Someone Stole Gabriel's Horn', etc. (*Spike Hughes And His All American Orchestra*, now on Jasmine). 'No one in the outfit had the idea that he had so much hell in that valise until we started rehearsing,' Dicky WELLS told Stanley Dance in '71. 'It was a good thing he had a gang like he had . . . these were cats who could see around a corner.' His scores were ahead of their time and still make a uniquely lovely album. When 'Donegal Cradle Song' was later published, Hughes transcribed Hawkins's solos and incl. them in the orchestration. He gave up performing, became a critic (pseudonym 'Mike' in *Melody Maker*), and later wrote a book about Toscanini, volumes of memoirs etc.

HUMAN LEAGUE Synth-pop band first formed in Sheffield '77. Original lineup featured Ian Craig Marsh and Martyn Ware, who left '80 to form HEAVEN 17. Early Human League shows were multi-media events incorporating slide shows against relentless barrage of synthesisers, too left field for commercial success. LP *Reproduction* '79 was example of this period. Following departure of Ware and Marsh vocalist Philip Oakey (*b* 2 Oct. '55) persevered with Susanne Sulley (*b* 26 Mar. '63) and Joanne Catherall (*b* 18 Sep. '62), vocals; Ian Burden (*b* 24 Dec. '57), bass; Jo Callis (*b* 2 May '51), guitar; Adrian Wright, synths. He recruited Callis from the Rezillos, spotted Sulley and Catherall in a local disco. *Travelogue* '80 did little; breakthrough came as self-confessed non-musicians began working with producer Martin Rushent, their perfect foil, who had enjoyed success with STRANGLERS, BUZZCOCKS, ALTERED IMAGES; resultant *Dare* '81 was their finest hour: UK synth-rock at its best incl. 'Don't You Want Me' (UK no. 1 '81, USA no. 1 '82). But it became a millstone for the band because they couldn't equal it; *Love & Dancing* '82 was panned as an instrumental re-dubbed version of *Dare*. '(Keep Feeling) Fascination'

was UK no. 2/USA no. 8 hit '83, while 'Mirror Man' (UK no. 2/USA no. 30) recaptured charm of 'Don't You Want Me'. Long silence broken by *Hysteria* '84, incl. hits 'The Lebanon' (uncharacteristically political), 'Life On Your Own', beguiling 'Louise'; but the LP showed little progression from *Dare*. Oakey collaborated with Giorgio Moroder on soundtrack of film *Electric Dreams* '84, incl. hit title track; then LP *Philip Oakey & Giorgio Moroder* '86; League returned with highly praised album *Crash* '86.

HUMBLE PIE UK rock band formed '69 by refugees Peter FRAMPTON and Steve Marriott, from the Herd and SMALL FACES respectively, singer/songwriters, guitarists, bandleaders looking for credibility instead of pop idol status. Recruited Greg Ridley (*b* 23 Oct. '47) on bass, drummer Jerry Shirley (*b* 4 Feb. '52) to complete supergroup. First single 'Natural Born Bugie' augured well (no. 4 UK '69), but neither *As Safe As Yesterday Is* nor *Town And Country* (both '69) pulled up any trees: contrast between hard rockin' Marriott and acoustic-based Frampton pulled band in two directions, while liquidation of Immediate label nearly broke them up. Resurfaced on A&M and with Dee Anthony as manager laid down foundation of USA success with much road work (Anthony later did the same for Frampton solo, mid-70s). After *Humble Pie* '70 and *Rock On* '71, *Performance – Rockin' The Fillmore* '71 showed a band now dominated by Marriott; Frampton left soon after to be replaced by COLOSSEUM's Dave 'Clem' Clempson. Move in heavy metal direction with *Smokin'* '72 brought few rewards, so Marriott moved towards soul, with black female vocal trio: Clydie King, Venetta Fields, Billie Barnum, collectively the Blackberries, showcased on live/studio 2-disc *Eat It* '73. But his own attempts to 'sing black' were embarrassing; band folded after *Thunderbox* '74, *Street Rats* '75. Clempson sessioned before forming Strange Brew with Ridley and drummer Cozy Powell (ex-Jeff BECK). Shirley formed Natural Gas with BADFINGER guitarist Joey Molland; Marriott cut appalling eponymous LP full of cliché-ridden heavy metal. Reformed Pie with Shirley and Bobby Tench (ex-Beck, Streetwalkers), vocals and guitar;

bassist Anthony Jones; but neither *On To Victory* '80 nor *Go For The Throat* '81 went for the throat. Marriott reverted to pub-rock mid-80s, playing R&B with crudely named Packet Of Three – a great waste of a pop talent that worked better sparking off an equal talent (Ron Lane in Small Faces; Frampton in early Pie).

HUMES, Helen (*b* 23 June '13, Louisville, Ky.; *d* Sep. '81, Santa Monica, Cal.) Singer. Only child of attorney father, schoolteacher mother. Played piano, organ in church; sang, played in band at Booker T. Washington Community Center with Jonah JONES, Dicky WELLS; recorded 'Black Cat Blues'/'Worried Woman's Blues' for Okeh '27 while still at school. Later worked in a bank; sang with Al Sears band on trip to Buffalo NY, joined full-time '37, worked at Cincinnati Cotton Club, where Count BASIE heard her. Recorded with mixed group led by Harry JAMES '37-8; joined Basie '38 at $35 a week. Sides with Basie incl. 'Thursday', 'Dark Rapture' '38; 'My Heart Belongs To Daddy', 'Sing For Your Supper', 'Blame It On My Last Affair', 'If I Could Be With You One Hour Tonight', 'Bolero At The Savoy', 'Between The Devil And The Deep Blue Sea' all '39; 'All Or Nothing At All', 'It's Square But It Rocks' '40. Quit owing to hardship of the road, began solo career in NYC clubs '41-3; toured with Clarence Love band '43-4; settled in Cal.; joined Norman GRANZ for JATP tours; also worked solo. R&B hit with Bill DOGGETT 'Be-Baba-Leba' '45 on Philo label, similar sides for Aladdin, Modern, Mercury, Decca, other labels into early '50s. Live record from L.A. Shrine concert 'Million Dollar Secret' had risqué lyric, made no. 6 R&B chart '50. Contributed to film soundtracks *Panic In The Streets*, *My Blue Heaven* '50; toured Hawaii '51 and '52; syndicated TV film with Basie *Showtime At The Apollo* '55; to Australia with Red NORVO '56: popular there, she returned three times, staying 10 months '64. Appeared in show *It's Great To Be Alive* L.A. '57; Newport Jazz Festival '59; toured the world '59-67. Retired on death of her mother '67 until persuaded to sing at Basie concert '73; then flood of dates: Montreux Jazz Festival (live LP *On The Sunny Side Of The Street* for Black Lion '74, reissued '83); NY

Cookery New Year's Eve show, etc. Keys to the City of Louisville '75; Nice jazz Festival that year, again '78. A singer of quality ballads, she said, 'The blues never did interest me very much'; *Downbeat* ranked her with Ella FITZGERALD and Mildred BAILEY as one of the best singers of the BIG BAND ERA. Other LPs incl. *Helen, And The Muse All Stars*, both on Muse '79-80 with Buddy TATE, others; *Swingin' With Helen* with Wynton KELLY on Contemporary (recorded '61, reissued '83); two others on that label.

HUMPERDINCK, Engelbert (*b* Arnold George Dorsey, 2 May '36, Madras, India) Singer. His father was an engineer; the family came home to Leicester '47. Dorsey apprenticed as an engineer for a while, but was singing in clubs before doing his national service, after which he resumed singing in '56, recorded for Decca '58 but did poorly until '65, when former flatmate Gordon Mills, who was then managing Tom JONES, borrowed the name of a 19th-century German opera composer (*Hansel And Gretel*) for Dorsey: he got a second chance with Decca; 'Release Me' was no. 1 UK, no. 4 USA '67 (one of the most often-recorded country music songs of all since original hit by Ray PRICE '54). 'There Goes My Everything' was no. 2 UK/20 USA, 'The Last Waltz' no. 1 UK/25 USA the same year. He had 22 Hot 100 entries in the USA '67-80 (never a no. 1), 14 chart hits in the UK '67-73; 16 chart LPs in the USA '67-79, nine in the UK '67-74: *Greatest Hits* '74 was no. 1; then *Getting Sentimental* on Telstar no. 35 (sold on TV). Record sales have cooled off considerably, but a big voice is always a cabaret attraction, even without much style. He's no longer hungry.

HUNLEY, Con (*b* Conrad Logan Hunley, 9 Apr. '45, Luttrell, Tenn.) The blue-eyed soul singer of country music. Worked the Corner Lounge in Knoxville for 10 years before going to Nashville '75, where businessman Sam Kirkpatrick set up Prairie Dust label for him '76. Had minor hits 'I'll Always Remember That Song' and 'Breaking Up Is Hard To Do' '77; signed with WB and had unbroken string of hits: 'Week-end Friend' '78, 'I've Been Waiting For You All My Life' '79, 'They Never Lost You' '80, 'She's Stepping Out' '81, 'Oh Girl' '82.

Joined MCA '83, then back to Prairie Dust '84. Soulful style made him one of the most popular country acts of the early '80s. WB LPs incl. *Con Hunley* '79, *I Don't Want To Love You* '80, *Don't It Break Your Heart* '80, *Ask Any Woman* '81, *Oh Girl* '82.

HUNT, Pee Wee (*b* Walter Hunt, 10 May '07, Mt Healthy, Ohio; *d* 22 June '79, Plymouth, Mass.) Trombone, vocalist, bandleader. Took up banjo in college; was with Jean GOLDKETTE late '27-early '28; in a theatre orchestra, then became founder member of the CASA LOMA Orchestra '29-43, featured on vocals incl. recorded duet with Louis ARMSTRONG '38. Became a disc jockey, joined the Merchant Marine, formed own small band on West Coast '46 and had a novelty no. 1 hit '48 with a purposely corny version of the dixieland chestnut from '14, '12th Street Rag'. A nicer record, a danceable revival of a '19 pop song 'Oh!', was a surprise hit in '53 at no. 3 and 23 weeks in the charts.

HUNTER, Alberta (*b* 1 April 1895, Memphis, Tenn.; *d* 18 Oct. '84, NYC) Singer. Also worked under names May Alix, Helen Roberts, Josephine Beatty. Daughter of railway porter and bordello chambermaid. Sang in school as a child; to Chicago '07; worked in and out of music, then got more club dates with Tony Jackson, King OLIVER, Sidney BECHET, Louis ARMSTRONG, etc. Began recording on Black Swan in NYC with Fletcher HENDERSON's Novelty Orchestra '23, replaced Bessie SMITH in NYC show *How Come* same year. Paramount records '23-4 all with Henderson; was with Louis Armstrong's Jazz Babies (as Beatty) on Gennett '24, also with Armstrong on Okeh '26; with Perry BRADFORD, Original Memphis 5, Fats WALLER '27 ('Beale Street Blues', 'Sugar', 'I'm Goin' To See My Ma' with Waller on pipe organ are among the most charming records of the era, now on a French RCA LP). Played London, Nice '27, London Palladium '28, with Paul ROBESON in *Showboat* at Drury Lane Theatre in London '28-9. After Paris dates '29 returned to NYC; in shows *Change Your Luck*, *Cherry Lane Follies*, *Thanksgiving Revels* '30, *Four Star Revue* '32, *Struttin' Time* '33. Back in Europe replaced Josephine BAKER at Casino de Paris '34-5;

in UK film *Radio Parade Of 1935*. Records in London '34 incl. 'Miss Otis Regrets', 'Stars Fell On Alabama', 'Two Cigarettes In The Dark', four more reissued on EMI LP *Jack Johnson And His Orchestra* '85. With Armstrong at Connie's Inn NYC '36; toured Greece, Turkey, Middle East '36-8; own radio show NYC '38-40; with Ethel WATERS in *Mamba's Daughters* '39, then toured with it. Recorded with Charlie SHAVERS on Decca '39, Eddie HEYWOOD on Bluebird '40; entertained troops with USO during WWII; understudy to Eartha KITT in *Mrs Patterson* '54-5; own show *Debut* '56; then quit music, became nurse, telling hospital colleagues nothing about her showbusiness background. Returned to music: LPs with Buster Bailey's Blues Busters for Prestige/Bluesville, *Alberta Hunter With Lovie Austin & Her Blues Serenaders* on Riverside, both '61, with Jimmy Archey on Folkways '62. Club and TV work through '70s incl. commercials for Clairol '78; Newport Jazz Festival '78; remarkable recordings for soundtrack of Geraldine Chaplin film *Remember My Name* '78. Compilations *Young Alberta Hunter* ('21-9) and *Classic: The Thirties* on Stash; *The Glory Of Alberta Hunter*, *Amtrack Blues*, *Look For The Silver Lining* all on Columbia. She was a letter writer and saved some of the letters, put to good use in biography *Alberta Hunter: A Celebration In Blues* '87 by Frank C. Taylor with Gerald Cook (accompanist).

HUNTER, Ivory Joe (*b* 10 Oct. '14, Kirbyville, Texas; *d* 8 Nov. '74, Memphis, Tenn.) R&B singer, songwriter, pianist. Son of guitarist Dave Hunter; mother sang gospel. Became programme dir. at Beaumont, Texas radio station; first records for Library of Congress '33. First commercial recordings with Johnny Moore's Three Blazers: started own Ivory label and had regional hit with own 'Blues At Sunrise'. To West Coast '42, there helped start Pacific records; recorded for 4 Star '47, went to King that year and had R&B hits 'Landlord Blues', 'Guess Who', and 'I Quit My Pretty Mama', all '49, the last two featuring members of Duke ELLINGTON band in backing. Next signed with MGM; 'I Almost Lost My Mind' was R&B chart no. 1 '50, 'I Need You So' no. 2 same year. By now his smooth style appealed to country music fans as well, paving way for later success of Ray CHARLES in this area. He had recorded more than 100 tunes when he went to Atlantic in '54; first pop chart success with 'Since I Met You Baby' (no. 12 '56), 'Empty Arms' (no. 43 '57), 'Yes, I Want You' (no. 94 '58). Meanwhile Pat BOONE covered 'I Almost Lost My Mind', made no. 1 USA pop chart, no. 14 UK. After 'City Lights' on Dot label (no. 92 '59) sales of records fell off; he turned to country, becoming regular on Grand Ole Opry late '60s. In '70 Sonny JAMES had country chart no. 1 with cover of 'Since I Met You Baby', Hunter made Epic LP *The Return Of Ivory Joe Hunter*, appeared at Monterey Jazz Festival; said to have written between seven and 8000 songs, incl. 'My Wish Come True' and 'Ain't That Lovin' You Baby', top 20 hits for Elvis PRESLEY in '59 and '64. Died of cancer. Albums on Archive of Folk in USA, Route 66 (*7th Street Boogie*) and Bulldog (*Artistry Of*) in UK.

HUNTER, Tab (*b* Arthur Gelien, 11 July '31, NYC) Actor, sometime singer. He was a champion ice-skater, joined the Coast Guard and became an established teen heart-throb before he had seven Hot 100 entries '57-9; by far the biggest was the first: 'Young Love' on Dot was no. 1 in UK and USA. It was a truly awful record, but he later redeemed himself, well-cast in the film version of the Richard Adler – Jerry Ross musical *Damn Yankees* '58, though Gwen Verdon and Ray Walsh stole many scenes. He had a TV series '60, made mostly B pictures since, except for *Judge Roy Bean* '72 with Paul Newman.

HURT, Mississippi John (*b* 8 March 1892, Carroll County, Ms.; *d* 2 Nov. '66, Grenada, Ms.) Country blues/folk singer, guitarist. Discovered by Tommy Rockwell (Okeh label), searching in the field for talent; sent to Memphis to record '28; the record sold well and he went all the way to NYC to make some more at the end of the year, but then the Depression happened. The recording artist went back to work herding cows for 35 years, until Tom Hoskins, remembering the name of one of the '28 songs, asked for him in Avalon, near Greenwood, and found him. His excellent guitar playing and

his gentle, home-spun folk style, full of good humour and unlike that of any other Delta bluesman, brought him three years of stardom at the end of his life. *Mississippi John Hurt: Folk Songs And Blues* '63 was made by a label variously called Piedmont, Gryphon, or Chesapeake, which also recorded *Worried Blues* Mar. '64 at the Ontario Place Café (Washington DC); he did remakes of 'Avalon Blues', 'Spike Driver Blues' etc. from '28; the delightfully raunchy 'Candy Man Blues'; 'My Creole Belle', a sweet love song with a beat, based on part of a rag published in 1900; many more. Vanguard recorded him at the Newport Folk Festivals '63-4 and also released *Today*, *The Immortal* (with delightful anecdotes about Hurt on the sleeve by Dick Waterman) and *Last Sessions*, all prod. by Patrick Sky; then a *Best Of* compilation. He was a gentle man with a sly wit; his swan song represented some of the prettiest music of the decade. Biograph and Yazzoo reissued the '28 sessions.

HUSKY, Ferlin (*b* 3 Dec. '27, Flat River, Mo.) Pop-country singer, comedy star, highly regarded entertainer. Name sometimes spelled Huskey; began as DJ '48 using name Terry Preston; recorded for Four Star '51, then Capitol from '53 still as Preston. First hit 'Hank's Song'; duets same year with Jean SHEPARD: 'A Dear John Letter' no. 1 country chart, 'Forgive Me, John' no. 4, all '53. Reverted to real name for subsequent recording, then confused matters further by inventing hayseed comic Simon Crum, at first for stage shows, later for no. 2 hit 'Country Music Is Here To Stay' '58. Meanwhile crossed over to pop chart: '(Since You're) Gone' (no. 1 country, no. 4 pop), 'A Fallen Star' (no. 8/47) '57; 'Wings Of A Dove' (no. 1/12) '60; 'The Waltz You Saved For Me' (no. 13/94) '62; 29 top 40 hits in country chart '55-71 (not counting Simon Crum). Appeared in several films, co-starring with Zsa Zsa Gabor in *Country Music Holiday* '58. Hasn't recorded for some years, but still a popular concert artist. LPs incl. *Walkin' And A Hummin'* '61, reissued on Stetson '87; *White Fences And Evergreen Trees* '68, *One More Time* '71, *Your Love Is Heavenly Sunshine* '72, *Just Plain Lonely* '73, all on Capitol; *True, True Loving* '74 on Probe, *Freckles And Polliwog*

Days '75 and *Foster And Rice Songbook* '77 on ABC, *Live* '83 on Audiograph.

HUTCHERSON, Bobby (*b* 27 Jan. '41, L.A.) Vibraphone, marimba. Inspired by Milt Jackson at age 15; studied with Dave Pike (*b* 23 Mar. '38, Detroit); before long sounded less like Jackson than most vibes; won *Downbeat* poll '64 and began making own albums on Blue Note '65, playing marimba as well. Has a fresh, personal, swinging style, often using four mallets; his many records as a sideman alone would have made him well-known and popular; played on *Out To Lunch* (Eric DOLPHY), *Idle Moments* (Grant Green), *Life Time* (Tony WILLIAMS), all on Blue Note; own LPs (mostly quintets) incl. *Dialogue* '65 with Sam RIVERS, Andrew HILL; *Components, Happenings* and *Stick Up!* '66; *Total Eclipse* '67 with Harold LAND and Chick COREA were all made on the East Coast; then an LP on Cadet made in Hollywood late '67-early '68 with Land was followed by *Patterns* '68; then Land and Hutcherson co-led a group until '71: *Spiral* '68, *Now* and *Medina* '69, *San Francisco* and *Head On* '71 were all by this group, plus a track from the Ljubljana Jazz Festival '70 which appeared on Enja. Hutcherson continued on Blue Note with *Natural Illusions* '72 (quintet plus flutes and strings), *Live At Montreux* '73, *Cirrus* '74 with Land, six others; *Linger Lane* '74 (with back-up vocals), *Montara* '75 (with extra percussion), *Waiting* and *The View From Inside* '76, *Knucklebean* '77, *For Bobby Hutcherson/Blue Note Meets The L.A. Philharmonic*, made at the Hollywood Bowl '77. By this time Blue Note had ceased to be the label we all knew and loved (*see* BLUE NOTE) and Hutcherson switched to Columbia: *Highway One* '78, big-band *Concretion: The Gift Of Love* and quintet *Un Poco Loco* '79 all featured George Cables on keyboards (*b* 14 Nov. '44, Brooklyn; also recorded with Freddie HUBBARD on CTI, with Woody SHAW on Columbia, Joe Henderson on Milestone, etc.). *Dance Of The Sun* '77 (with drummer Eddie Marshall, Cables, two others) and the later *Four Seasons* are on Timeless. Hutcherson's *Solo/Quartet* '81-2 appeared on Contemporary; *Good Bait* '84 (with Branford MARSALIS, Cables, Philly Joe JONES and Ray Drummond), *Colour Schemes* '86 (quin-

tet with Mulgrew MILLER, AIRTO, Billy HIGGINS, John Heard on bass), *In The Vanguard* '87 are on Fantasy's Landmark label.

HUTCHINSON, Leslie 'Hutch' (*b* 1900, Grenada; *d* 18 Aug. '69, Hampstead, London) Pianist, singer; velvet voice and polished piano style made him UK's favourite cabaret artist for decades. To NYC to study law '16 but music took over; to Paris to study piano c.'24; formed dance band, specialised in Cole PORTER's songs, with the composer's blessing and help. Worked at Bricktop's famous cabarets in Paris; opened in RODGERS & HART revue *One Damn Thing After Another* '27 in London; also *This Year Of Grace* (Noel COWARD), *Good News*, Porter's *Wake Up And Dream*, Cochran's *1930 Revue*; meanwhile broadcasting, recording for Parlophone and appearing in the top restaurants, hotels. Recorded '38 with West Indian bandleader Ken 'Snakehips' Johnson as Leslie 'Jiver' Hutchinson. Entertained troops during WWII; appeared in revue again: *Happidrome* '42 was an adaptation of a BBC radio show; *Seventy Years Of Song* '43 at the Royal Albert Hall was for War Relief Fund. Retired late '40s, came back '53 and remained popular in clubs, TV. Appeared in Kenya '67 as his health worsened. His name was in the news early '80s as books were published about Lord and Lady Mountbatten, end of Empire etc. (perennially popular subject in UK): he may have been one of her lovers. EMI reissues incl. *Moonlight Cocktail*, 2-disc *Hutch At The Piano*; on Decca: *With A Song In My Heart*; on Joy: *The Magic Of Hutch*.

HUTTO, J. B. (*b* Joseph Benjamin Hutto, 26 Apr. '26, Blackville, S.C.; *d* '85) Blues singer; guitarist, also drums, piano. Raised in Augusta, Ga.; sang in family gospel group. To Chicago mid-'40s; worked outside music while learning guitar; worked occasional gigs, formed J. B. Hutto and the Hawks late '40s. Recorded on Chance label '54 (fine bottleneck guitar on 'Dim Lights'), worked outside music, recorded for Vanguard '65, etc. At age c.43 voted rock/pop/blues act deserving wider recognition by *Downbeat* '69. More records, festivals, TV spots etc. incl. UK film *Chicago Blues* '70. One of the tougher exponents of the urban Chicago blues style; described as 'almost violently strong' by Bob Koester (see DELMARK). LPs incl. eponymous Testament album in Masters of Modern Blues Series, with Walter HORTON, Johnny Young, guitar (*b* 1 Jan. '18, Vicksburg, Ms.; *d* 18 Apr. '74, Chicago), Lee Jackson, bass; Fred Below, drums; *Hawk Squat* '68 with SUNNYLAND SLIM and *Slidewinder* '72 on Delmark, *Blues For Fonessa* '76 on Amigo (Sweden), *Live At Sandy's Jazz Revival* as J. B. and the Housebreakers on Baron; last works: *Slideslinger* and *Slippin' And Slidin'* on Varrick as J. B. Hutto and the New Hawks (on Demon in UK). His nephews incl. Ed Williams and James 'Pookie' Young in Lil' Ed and the Blues Imperials: *see* ALLIGATOR label.

HUTTON, Betty (*b* Elizabeth June Thornburg, 26 Feb. '21, Battle Creek, Mich.) Vocalist; blonde bombshell of movie musicals. With sister Marion (*b* 10 Mar. '19, Little Rock, Ark.; *d* Jan. '87) worked for Vincent Lopez '38; Marion left to go with Glenn MILLER; Betty remained a star in the Lopez band, landed spot in *Two For The Show* on Broadway '40, then *Panama Hattie*; lead in first film *The Fleet's In* '42; played speakeasy queen Texas Guinnan in *Incendiary Blonde* '45; *Annie Get Your Gun* '50; *The Greatest Show On Earth* '52; others. Five top 10 hits on Capitol '44-9 incl. no. 1 '45 'Doctor, Lawyer, Indian Chief'. Later had TV series, appeared in London, etc. A much-loved star of the period for her personality as well as her voice and looks.

HUTTON, Ina Ray (*b* Odessa Cowan, 13 Mar. '14, Chicago; *d* 19 Feb. '84, Ventura, Cal.) Pianist, vocalist, bandleader. Daughter of pianist Marvel Ray; half-sister of singer June Hutton (*b* 11 Aug. c.'20, Chicago; *d* 2 May '73, Encino, Cal.; with Charlie SPIVAK, replaced Jo STAFFORD in the Pied Pipers with Tommy DORSEY; married arr. Axel Stordahl). Ina Ray began as tap dancer in a Gus Edwards revue; later on Broadway in *George White's Melody* '34 and *Ziegfeld Follies of 1934*, forming all-girl band that year. A slim blonde in clinging gowns, billed as 'The Blonde Bombshell of Rhythm', her main contribution was her baton-waving style, with some dance steps and a fair amount of wiggling. Band played all the important venues, did European tour, film

shorts; she formed all-male band on eve of WWII, with arrangements by tenorman George Paxton (who later led own band from '44, with strings at first; later became music publisher). She disbanded after the war, married bandleader Randy BROOKS '49; formed new band early '50s; divorced '57; band did not last either. Her film appearances incl. *Big Broadcast Of '36* '35, *Ever Since Venus* '44; sang 'Every Man A King' in *Brother Can You Spare A Dime* '74, compilation of Depression-era film clips and newsreels.

HYLAND, Brian (*b* 12 Nov. '43, NYC) USA pop singer. Scored still in teens with novelty 'Itsy Bitsy Teeny Weeny Polka Dot Bikini', an early example of bubblegum written by Paul Vance/Lee Pockriss (no. 1 USA '60); follow-up 'Lopsided, Overloaded, And It Wiggles When I Rode It' failed to match success: Hyland switched from Leader to ABC and made no. 20 with better 'Let Me Belong To You' (top 20 '61). 'Ginny Come Lately' '62 continued in the sub-ANKA adolescent-angst vein (no. 21 '62) but major success of period was 'Sealed With A Kiss', teenie weepie that made no. 3 both UK/USA. Final hit of early '60s was 'Warmed Over Kisses (Left Over Love)', top 30 UK/USA and since revived by Dave EDMUNDS. Came again mid-60s with 'The Joker Went Wild' and 'Run, Run Look And See' (top 25 USA, prod. by Snuff GARRETT); then had one-off no. 3 in '73 with 'Gypsy Woman', cover of Curtis MAYFIELD '61 hit for the Impressions, prod. by Del SHANNON, who'd wanted to prod. Hyland in '68 but got sidetracked. Made eponymous album for UNI with Shannon, revived another soul hit (Jackie WILSON's '59 'Lonely Teardrop'), but never made change from teen heart-throb to serious artist, ironically a change Shannon made with more success. 'Sealed With A Kiss' made no. 7 UK on reissue '75; like it or not he's remembered for timeless kitsch.

HYLTON, Jack (*b* 1892, Lancashire, England; *d* 29 Jan. '65) Piano, bandleader. Began as cinema organist; led small 'jazz' group in the Queen's Hall Roof Ballroom; he led a top UK dance band late '20s, '30s, with sidemen such as Ted HEATH ('25). Played in Paris and Berlin late '20s. Often played hot; hired Coleman HAWKINS '34-5, '39. Went to the USA himself and led a band there '35-6. Later became a theatrical producer. Albums of reissues by EMI: incl. *Hits From Berlin 1927-31, The Golden Age Of Jack Hylton, Plays DeSylva, Brown & Henderson,* etc. Also *Jacks's Back* on ASV, *Jack Hylton* on Jasmine, etc.

HYMAN, Dick (*b* Richard Roven Hyman, 8 Mar. '27, NYC) Piano, organ, composer. Studied with Teddy WILSON, served in US Navy '45-6, played with Red NORVO '49-50, toured Europe with Benny GOODMAN '50, recorded for MGM '54-8 (trio record of 'Moritat' was no. 8 hit '56); on staff at NBC; mus. dir. for Arthur GODFREY at CBS '58-61; studio work as composer/arranger. His settings of Shakespeare were recorded by Earl Wrightson (*Shakespeare's Greatest Hits* '64); he scored TV programmes of Sir John Gielgud's recitations of Shakespeare '66. He wrote arr. for Enoch LIGHT's band; interesting himself in electronics, he recorded *The Electric Eclectics Of Dick Hyman* and *Pieces For Moog* for Light's Command label; mus. dir. for David Frost TV specials; his many compositions and publications incl. *Duets In Odd Meters And Far-Out Rhythms* '65, a piano concerto, works for Moog, solos for organ, *Songs From The Plays Of Shakespeare,* editions or arrangements of piano solos by Leonard FEATHER, Jelly Roll MORTON, etc. Along with his studio and commercial work (in the early '70s he played the organ for the TV game show *Beat The Clock*) he has always played jazz: at Eddie CONDON's club (with Condon at '72 Newport Festival), Dick Gibson's Colorado Jazz Parties annually from '67 (LP on MPS), LP *Cleopatra* with Paul GONSALVES on Impulse; most of his own records have been made for labels which now are defunct: *Traditional Jazz Piano* and *Solo Piano Fantomfingers* (Project 3); *Genius At Play* and *Shakespeare, Sullivan And Hyman* (with Maxine SULLIVAN) (Monmouth-Evergreen); *Theme & Variations On 'A Child Is Born'* (Chiaroscuro: 12 variations in the style of 12 different jazz pianists, incl. Hyman; also recorded with Ruby BRAFF on that label); also *Let It Happen* on RCA by the Jazz Piano Quartet with Hank JONES, Marian MCPARTLAND and Roland Hanna (*b* 10 Feb. '32, Detroit; played with Charles MINGUS, Carmen MCRAE, etc.); *Jelly Roll Morton Orchestral Transcriptions* on Columbia; *Satchmo Remembered* on Atlantic (live at Carnegie Hall); *Waltz Dressed As Blue* on Grapevine. He has become a master of jazz repertory: he was a highlight at the Sacramento Dixieland Jubilee '85, playing with Peanuts Hucko's Pied Piper Quintet (with Bob Haggart, Canadian vibraphonist Peter Appleyard, drummer Gene Estes) as well as playing superb solo sets of the music of Willie 'The Lion' SMITH, James P. JOHNSON, Fats WALLER, etc.

IAN & SYLVIA Folk/country duo. Ian Tyson (*b* 25 Sep. '33, British Columbia) worked as lumberjack, rodeo performer, attended Vancouver art school; worked as commercial artist in Toronto, played guitar and sang with friends in folk clubs. Sylvia Fricker (*b* 19 Sep. '40, Chatham, Ontario) worked in home town, travelled to Toronto weekends to sing; they began performing together '59, married in '64. To NYC; managed by Albert Grossman (Bob DYLAN, The BAND, PETER, PAUL & MARY, Gordon LIGHTFOOT); first LP on Vanguard *Ian & Sylvia* made fans happy, but *Four Strong Winds* '63 (Neil YOUNG covered Ian's title song), *Northern Journey* '64 (with Sylvia's 'You Were On My Mind', no. 3 hit USA '65 by We Five) attracted international attention, made Billboard LP chart. More Vanguard LPs incl. *Early Morning Rain, Play One More, So Much For Dreaming* '65-7 all charted; *Nashville* was recorded there with top-notch sidemen, fully acknowledged their debt to country music, putting off a few folkie fans. *Lovin' Sound* '67 on MGM charted; they formed band Great Speckled Bird, after two LPs for Columbia they separated: Ian prod. Syvia's solo LP *Woman's World* on Capitol, had his own Canadian TV series; his first solo LP *Ol' Eon* on A&M/Canada '75, later *Old Corrals & Sagebrush* and *Ian Tyson* on Columbia, *Cowboyography* '87 on his own Eastern Slope Label: LP and 'Navajo Rug' (co-written with Tom Russell) won country album and single of the year in Canada and he was top country artist in Canadian musical awards. He is a busy rancher in Alberta, but still writes songs that communicate with the listener 'like two horses nickering to each other in the dark' (*Swing 51*). Sylvia continued writing songs, had radio and TV work in Canada.

IAN, Janis (*b* Janis Fink, 7 Apr. '51, NYC) Singer, songwriter. Father was a music teacher; she studied piano at 3, guitar at 11, began writing and performing at 12. Made 'Society's Child (Baby I've Been Thinking)', about an interracial love affair; at first no one would play it, but then she was featured on a Leonard BERNSTEIN TV special, and had a no. 14 hit '67 at age 16. Eponymous debut LP followed by *For All The Seasons Of Your Mind* and *The Secret Life Of J. Eddy Fink* '68, one more on Verve and an LP on Capitol, then quit at 19. She could not stop writing: comeback *Stars* '74 on Columbia saw her in LP chart again, but *Between The Lines* '75 was no. 1 LP in USA, helped by Grammy-winning no. 3 single 'At Seventeen', anthem of teen-age angst by the now mature 24-year-old. *Aftertones* '76, *Miracle Row* '77, *Janis Ian* '78 all charted; *Night Rain* '79, an experiment with disco producer Giorgio Moroder, did not; *Restless Eyes* '81 again reached top 200 LPs. *Best Of* on CBS/UK. Collaborating with Nashville writer Rhonda Kye Fleming '86; new songs to be recorded by Kenny ROGERS, ALABAMA.

IBRAHIM, Abdullah (*b* Adolph Johannes Brand, 9 Oct. '34, Capetown) Piano, composer; his style the most successful synthesis of jazz with African feeling. Piano lessons at age 7; converted to Islam '68 but records may be listed in catalogues as Dollar Brand. Played with Tuxedo Slickers, Streamline Brothers, Willie Max big band; first album as leader with sextet *Jazz Epistles* incl. Hugh MASEKELA; at least five more, mostly trio sets, in S.A. '60-2; went to Europe; Duke ELLINGTON heard trio in Zurich, got them deal for *Duke Ellington Presents The Dollar Brand Trio* on Reprise '63, made in Paris; *Anatomy Of A South African Village* on Fontana and *The Dream* on Black Lion (both also on Freedom) made '65 in Copenhagen, all with Johnny Gertze on bass, Makaya Ntshoko on drums. Married singer Bea Benjamin '65; he was soon internationally famous, touring the world, often solo; played more instruments from '60s: recorded on African flutes, soprano sax. Solo piano LPs (with occasional vocals and flute) incl. *African Sketchbook* '63 on Enja, *This Is Dollar Brand* '65 on Black Lion, *African Piano* '68 on Spectator (Denmark); *African Portraits* and *Sangoma* '73 on Sackville (made in Toronto), *Ode To Duke Ellington* on Inner City and *Memories* on Jap. Philips made in Ludwigsburg, all '73; *African Breeze* '74 on East Wind and *Anthem For The New Nations* '78 on Denon, both made in Japan; *Nisa* '78 on African Violets made in Stuttgart; *Matsidiso* (named after baby daughter) and *South African Sunshine* '80 both on German Pläne label; *African Dawn* '82 on Enja. Duo sets incl. *Ancient Africa* '72, made in Copenhagen with an unknown drummer; *Streams Of Consciousness* '77 on Baystate with Max ROACH, and *Good News From Africa* '73, *Echoes From Africa* '79, both on Enja with Johnny Dyani on bass, vocals, bells (*see* Dudu PUKWANA about Dyani). *The Children Of Africa* '76 on Enja has Cecil MCBEE on bass, Roy Brooks, drums (*b* 2 Sep. '38, Detroit); other LPs reveal formidable talent as composer/ arranger: *African Space Program* '73 on Enja has 12-piece group incl. Cecil Bridgewater, Hamiet BLUIETT, McBee, Brooks. Discographies are confused, but apparently he made more LPs for S.A. Gallo, Koh-i-Noor, Sun labels: some say *Soweto* and *Black Lightning* were made early '60s, *Capetown Fringe* in '70s, latter aka *Mannenberg* on an African issue; but all were also issued on Chiaroscuro USA and all were sextet sets with Basil 'Mannenberg' Coetzee on tenor (Mannenberg also a town in S.A.). To confuse things further, a septet LP made for Gallo '75 (in S.A. according to one source) also incl. Mannenberg (as well as Blue MITCHELL and Harold LAND) and also may be the legendary *Mannenberg* LP. *Journey* '77 has nonet with Bluiett, Dyani, Don CHERRY in NYC, also on Chiaroscuro. Quartet set *Africa: Tears And Laughter* '79 on Enja was made in Stuttgart, *African Marketplace* '79 on Elektra in NYC by 12-piece band incl. McBee, *Dollar Brand At Montreux* '80 on Enja is a quintet, *Duke's Memories* '81 on String and *Zimbabwe* '83 on Enja are quartets; *Ekaya* '83 on Ekapa a septet made in N.J. with Ricky Ford and McBee. Living in NYC, now calling the group Ekaya; gig at Sweet Basil was filmed

for TV documentary with Ford, Ben Riley on drums; released beautiful *Water From An Ancient Well* on Blackhawk '86. The emotional wellspring of his music is still South African: the regime there has bulldozed and tried to obliterate the neighbourhood where he grew up, but it won't go away. Like Ellington, he mistrusts the label 'jazz': 'We simply call it the music of the people.'

ICICLE WORKS UK new wave trio formed '80 in Liverpool, by Ian McNabb, guitars, keyboards, vocals; Chris Layhe, bass, keyboards, violin; Chris Sharrock, drums. First release was 6-track EP cassette, attracted attention of BBC DJ John Peel, a patron of new bands: works combined wordiness of Julian Cope (TEARDROP EXPLODES) with grandiose guitar sound of Wah!, also emulating both with dollops of '60s influences. Album *Icicle Works* '84 prod. by Hugh Jones (ECHO AND THE BUNNYMEN); single from it 'Birds Fly (Whisper To A Scream)' made no. 37 in USA after they toured there with PRETENDERS and Dave Gilmour (ability to support new wave band *and* PINK FLOYD guitarist may have worked against them). 'Nirvana', UK-only release on own Troll kitchen label, had reached no. 15 on indie chart, but only proper top 40 success in UK came with Arthur Lee-infl. 'Love Is A Wonderful Colour' from the debut LP, also at no. 15. 'Birds Fly' made only no. 53 on UK re-release; LP no. 25 UK LP chart (top 40 USA); second LP *The Small Price Of A Bicycle* '85 with Jacques Loussier guesting on keyboards was ignored by music press; several singles in wildly varying styles sold poorly; release of greatest non-hits *Seven Singles Deep* (on Beggars Banquet in UK, Arista in USA) smacked of desperation to some. They had just graduated from guitar-based USA styles when UK audience fell for the likes of Rain Parade, Long Ryders etc. McNabb, like Cope, threatened to produce more than just nostalgia, but UK pop audience won't pay attention to a band which remains defiantly uncategorisable. New LP was *Understanding Jane* '86.

IDOL, Billy (*b* William Broad, 30 Nov. '55, Stanmore, Middlesex) UK new wave singer. Began as guitarist in Chelsea; left with bassist Tony James to become Generation X, recruiting Bob 'Derwood' Andrews on guitar and John Towe on drums (later replaced by ex-Subway Sect Mark Laff). Idol dropped guitar to concentrate on vocals; band played preview night at London's Roxy club Dec. '76 but were never hardline punks, preferring to change with the fashions, rather too much perhaps. *Generation X* '78 prod. by Martin Rushent was disappointing, the more so as they had held out for a good record deal longer than some; but 'Your Generation' (feeble rewrite of Pete Townshend's sentiments) made UK top 40, and 'King Rocker' from *Valley Of The Dolls* '79 (prod. by ex-MOTT Ian Hunter) made no. 11 despite sounding strangely rockabilly. James and Idol sacked Andrews and Laff, changed name to Gen X, chose European-based Brit Keith Forsey to prod. last LP *Kiss Me Deadly* '81, made with ex-CLASH drummer Terry Chimes, guest guitars John McGeoch (Magazine), Steve Jones (SEX PISTOLS), James Stephenson (Chelsea, eventually added full-time). But reception was still poor, so Idol (who had lived in USA as a child) relocated to NYC, where 'Dancing With Myself' was a dance-floor hit; he incl. recut track on mini-LP with cover of 'Mony Mony', own 'Hot In The City', recruiting USA's Steve Stevens (guitar), Phil Feit (bass), Steve Missal (drums) to back him; album made no. 23. Rode MTV video channel to success, bleached locks and Presleyesque sneer delighting teenies. Combination of Idol-Stevens tunes and Forsey prod. made lively pop in *Billy Idol* '82; *Rebel Yell* '84 was seasoned by a trace of pantomime menace; three single hits '83-4 ('Eyes Without A Face' no. 4) backed up by good videos; on release of remixed mini-LP *Vital Idol* '85, 'White Wedding' (top 40) went top 10 in UK, with 'Rebel Yell' following suit; *Whiplash Smile* '86 did well, with hit 'To Be A Lover' (BOOKER T cover): a decade on from punk he was flourishing. James went on from Gen X mid-'80s to form Sigue Sigue Sputnik: textbook example of pure hype flopped.

IF UK jazz-rock group formed late '60s by Dick Morrissey, saxophones, flute; Terry Smith, guitar. Morrissey had played with Ginger BAKER and Phil Seamen in Harry South band (*Sound Venture* collaboration '66; sessioned on Georgie FAME's *Two Faces Of Fame* '67). First LPs *If* and *If 2* (both

'70) incl. Dennis Elliott, drums; John Mealing, keyboards; Dave Quincy, sax; Jim Richardson, bass; J. W. Hodgkinson, vocals. Never made commercial breakthrough in UK due to absence touring in USA, where market for jazz-rock was stronger. After *If 3* and *4* '71-2 Morrissey was the only one left; lineup with Dave Wintour on bass, Dave Greenslade on keyboards rehearsed but came to nothing when they left to form rock band Greenslade; Morrissey formed new lineup with Cliff Davis, drums; Walt Monaghan, bass; Geoff Whitehorn, guitar; Gabriel Magno, keyboards; this group made *Not Just A Bunch Of Pretty Faces* '74 and *Tea Break Over, Back On Your Heads* '75, then split. Smith and Quincy formed Afro-rockers Zzebra (two LPs '74-5); Mealing went into production (STRAWBS, others); Davis backed Ted NUGENT; Elliott joined King Crimson. Morrissey teamed with guitarist Jim Mullen; they likewise did not make big time despite adding a dash of funk to suit changing fashion: they co-led *Cape Wrath* and *Lovely Day* '79 on Harvest (EMI), renamed the group MORRISSEY-MULLEN (*which see*).

IFIELD, Frank (*b* 30 Nov. '37, Coventry, England) UK pop singer with 15 chart hits '60-6. Parents Australian; grew up there and first worked in tent shows and circuses as a 'spruker' age 13, pulling in crowds by 'spieling' and making first record same year ('Did You See My Daddy Over There'): he was soon the biggest recording star in the Antipodes. To UK '59; broadened C&W-style repertoire to country/pop with help of Norrie PARAMOR; 'I Remember You' '62 was no. 1 UK, first record to sell a million in UK alone; also made no. 5 in USA (words written by Johnny MERCER for '42 film *The Fleet's In*, dir. by Victor Schertzinger, who got credit for tune). Next release same year, 'Lovesick Blues', was also no. 1 UK (no. 44 USA), also on Columbia/EMI UK and on Vee Jay in USA: in a preview of its business acumen with the BEATLES two years later, EMI's USA label Capitol did not bother to pick up its right to Ifield's hits until after the Chicago indie label had sold a great many of them. (Vee Jay later issued LP called *Jolly What!* four tracks by the Beatles, eight by Ifield). By the time Capitol caught up there were only two more minor Ifield hits in the USA, but he carried on in the UK with two no. ones, 'Wayward Wind' and 'Confessin' ', both '64. 'Nobody's Darlin' But Mine' was no. 4 '63, 'Don't Blame Me' no. 8 '64: all his hits were oldies, and there's nothing wrong with that. UK compilations: *A Portrait* on PRT, *20 Golden Greats* on K-Tel.

IGGY POP (*b* James Newell Osterburg, 21 Apr. '47, Ypsilanti, Mich.) USA singer, self-styled godfather of punk rock whose seminal work with the Stooges kept popping up in New Wave repertoire. He was drummer and lead singer with first band, the Iguanas, in Detroit; then joined Prime Movers, also played blues with ex-Paul BUTTERFIELD drummer Sam Lay. Formed Psychedelic Stooges '67 with Ron Asheton, guitar, Scott Asheton, drums; Dave Alexander, bass. Outrageous gigging followed, taking Jim Morrison's stage persona to extemes: tales of self-mutilation with beer bottles, vomiting, walking on fans' outstretched hands, worse. Competent hard rock captured on *The Stooges* '69 on Elektra, DOORS label: incl. anthems to frustration '1969' and 'No Fun' (later covered by SEX PISTOLS), animal lust in 'I Wanna Be Your Dog'. Disbanded after *Fun House* '70, which like predecessor sold poorly: Iggy cleaned up drug habit, met newly famous European disciple David BOWIE, who persuaded him to re-form for *Raw Power* '73, co-writing all songs with lead guitarist James Williamson, with Ron Asheton now on bass: his best yet, but disbanded again '74, his lifestyle too extreme for Bowie's MainMen organisation to keep together. Anarchic live set *Metallic KO* '76 and *Kill City* '78 surfaced later, fuelling myth. Iggy had two more good tracks in him: *The Idiot* '76 and *Lust For Life* '77 each contained stand-out track in 'Nightclubbing' and 'The Passenger' respectively, assisted by co-writer/producer Bowie. Ironically these were electronic rock, as punk was rerunning his earlier stuff. Further LPs were mixed: *New Values* '79 (with Williamson and multi-instrumentalist Scott Thurston, a latter-day Stooge), *Soldier* '80, *Party* '81, *Zombie Birdhouse* '82. Autobiography *I Need More* '82. He was a link between the Doors and punk, but needed collaborator (Bowie, Williamson) for his best work, still being covered: 'China Girl' by co-writer Bowie,

'Nightclubbing' by Grace JONES. He came back with *Blah Blah Blah* '86 on A & M (first hit single 'Real Wild Child'), *Instinct* '88 with Steve Jones.

IGLESIAS, Julio (*b* 23 Sep. '43, Madrid) Singer. Croons love songs; sales of more than 100 million copies of about 60 LPs in five languages got him in the *Guinness Book Of Records*: sometimes called the 'Spanish Sinatra', though his style is pedestrian compared to Sinatra's best. *1100 Bel Air Place* '84 sold a million copies in the USA in its first five days, incl. duet with Willie NELSON on 'To All The Girls I've Loved Before'; meanwhile Columbia rushed out *Hey!, Moments, From A Child To A Woman*, 2-disc *In Concert*.

IMPERIAL USA label. There have been at least five Imperial record labels. An obscure Imperial existed in the USA c.'05; the Crystalate Gramophone Manufacturing Company Ltd prod. Imperial records in UK '20-34: at first the indifferent light classics, music hall songs etc. were only British, but then Imperial leased masters from Banner in USA (later ARC, finally CBS property), hence first solo by Louis ARMSTRONG released in UK was on Imperial (on Fletcher HENDERSON's 'Alabamy Bound', '25). UK Decca bought Crystalate '37; long defunct trademark passed to Polygram '80. The other Imperials all now belong to EMI: a longstanding domestic label for EMI-Brazil, the former main domestic label of EMI Bovema-Negram in Holland (whose biggest act was the Cats, whose '70 hit 'Marian' was no. 1 as far afield as Lebanon and Malaysia), and the best-known Imperial of all, that formed by Lew Chudd in L.A. in '47. Its only national hit in its early years was Slim WHITMAN's C&W classic 'Indian Love Call' '52 (no. 10 pop chart); the label concentrated on R&B, where Fats DOMINO had hits '50-4, but then he broke through to the pop top 10 '55 with 'Ain't That A Shame', racked up 59 hits before moving to ABC '63. Imperial's base as an indie was extremely narrow: the label signed Phil SPECTOR's Teddy Bears, but only after their big hit 'To Know Him Is To Love Him' '58; the only big artist after Domino was Ricky NELSON, with 36 chart entries '57-65, incl. Imperial's only no. 1 hits: 'Poor Little Fool' and

'Travelin' Man'. Another big hit was 'Let There Be Drums' '61 by Sandy NELSON, but there were many minor classics ('I Hear You Knockin' ' by Smiley LEWIS '55), 21 C&W hits by Whitman '52-70, etc. Chudd sold out to Liberty '63; Imperial became a general pop label with Johnny RIVERS, CHER, Jackie DeSHANNON, etc. Liberty/Imperial were taken over by United Artists '69 and Imperial was phased out (Whitman went on UA); EMI absorbed Liberty/UA '79. In Japan King and EMI/Toshiba reissued rare Imperial stuff, incl. the Teddy Bears' only album.

INCREDIBLE STRING BAND UK folk duo who inspired cult following late '60s. Mike Heron (*b* 12 Dec. '42) and Robin Williamson (*b* 24 Nov. '43), both from Glasgow, could play over 30 instruments between them; first LP *Incredible String Band* '66 also incl. Clive Palmer; second *5000 Spirits, Or The Layers Of The Onion* '67 was enchanting collection of wistful mysticism, child-like innocence: had the same incandescent effect on UK folk scene as BEATLES *Sergeant Pepper* had same year on the larger world; incl. 'First Girl I Loved', covered by Judy COLLINS, helping USA fame cemented by their appearance at Newport Folk Festival '67. *Hangman's Beautiful Daughter* '68 carried on, balancing 13-minute 'A Very Cellular Song' with mock-Gilbert & Sullivan 'The Minotaur's Song'. They inhabited their own world, and concerts were communal events; they were increasingly self-indulgent with 2-disc *Wee Tam & The Big Huge* '68, *Changing Horses* '69, *I Looked Up* and 2-disc *U* '70, inspired by dabblings with stage and film presentations, lineup expanding and contracting as required: ancillary members incl. Licorice McKechnie, Rose Simpson (girlfriends: didn't get along, disruptive factor) and Malcolm LeMaistre. 2-disc best-of *Relics* '71 accompanied by *Be Glad, For The Song Has No Ending*; title was an irony: by then tweeness was becoming embarrassing, move towards electric rock unsuccessful. Heron's solo LP *Smiling Men With Bad Reputations* '71 redressed balance somewhat incl. guests The WHO, John CALE, Richard THOMPSON. Duo carried on: *Liquid Acrobat As Regards The Air* '71, *Earthspan* '72, *No Ruinous Feud* '73, *Hard Rope & Silken Twine* '74; split was followed

by compilation *Seasons They Change* '76. Early albums on Elektra, then Reprise USA, Island UK. Solo LPs recovered integrity: Heron made eponymous LP '79 on Casablanca; Williamson is now a highly regarded folk-roots veteran, with *Journey's Edge* '77, *American Stonehenge* '78, *A Glint At The Kindling* '79, *Songs Of Love And Parting* '81, also *Music For The Mabinogi* and two vols. of *Legacy Of The Scottish Harpers* (plays Celtic harp), *Winter's Turning* '87 all on Flying Fish; *Songs For Children* '88 on Claddagh.

INK SPOTS, The Black USA vocal quartet; enormously popular (though MILLS Bros were more influential). Original lineup: Jerry Daniels, guitar and lead tenor; Orville 'Hoppy' Jones, bass (*b* 17 Feb. '05, Chicago; *d* there 18 Oct. '44); Ivory 'Deek' Watson, Charlie Fuqua (also played guitar). They formed while working as porters at Paramount Theatre NYC; sang hot numbers, recorded for Victor, played in England with Jack HYLTON band mid-'30s; switched to Decca. Daniels was replaced by Bill Kenny (*b* '15; *d* 23 Mar. '78); they hit the big time '39 with Kenny's high tenor lead, talking choruses by Jones on slow ballads, beginning with 'If I Didn't Care'. First no. 1 hits were 'Address Unknown' '39, 'We Three (My Echo, My Shadow, And Me)' '40. Jones died '44, replaced by Kenny's brother Herb; Watson later replaced by Billy Bowen. Discs on Decca incl. nearly 50 hits '39-51, 11 top 10s '40-9; 'The Gypsy' and 'To Each His Own' both no. 1 '46; 'Maybe' '40, Duke ELLINGTON's 'Don't Get Around Much Anymore' '43 were no. 2; hits with Ella FITZGERALD '44-5 incl. 2-sided no. 1 hit 'I'm Making Believe'/'Into Each Life Some Rain Must Fall', Ellington's 'I'm Beginning To See The Light'. They appeared in films *Great American Broadcast* '41, *Pardon My Sarong* '42. Kenny recorded solo incl. gospel songs 'It Is No Secret' (with the Song Spinners, top 20 hit '51). In '52 there were two groups of Ink Spots, Fuqua and Kenny each owning 50% of the name (Fuqua's Ink Spots recorded for King with Watson, Harold Jackson, tenor Jimmy Holmes). A set of their Decca 78s made Billboard's album chart '46; their hits compilations on Decca/MCA are always in print; also *18 Hits* on King.

INMATES, The UK rock quintet whose R&B sound was highly regarded but out of its time: Peter Gunn, guitar and vocals; Bill Hurley, vocals; Ben Donnelly, bass; Tony Oliver, guitar; Jim Russell, drums and vocals. They came from same pub rock genre as DR FEELGOOD; if they had been a few years earlier they might have done better: album *First Offence* '79 on Radar UK incl. singles 'Dirty Water' (remake of the Standells' '66 hit made Hot 100 in USA, though words were altered for London) and 'The Walk' (their only UK chart entry, in top 40); the LP made top 50 in USA on Polydor. *Shot In The Dark* and *Heatwave In Alaska* did less well despite some prod. from successful Shakin' STEVENS prod. Stuart Coleman. *Five* '84 issued on Lolita UK.

INSECT TRUST NYC pop group of late '60s. Lineup: Nancy Jeffries, piano and vocals; Bill Barth, guitar; Luke Faust, guitar, banjo, fiddle, harmonica; Trevor Koehler and Robert Palmer, reeds. Far too eclectic for chart action, they took in blues, psychedelia, jazz, jug band, other influences, made LPs *The Insect Trust* on Capitol late '60s, *Hoboken Saturday Night* '70 on Atco, now highly prized collectors' items. Faust, Koehler, Barth also recorded with Octopus and Holy Modal Rounders; Palmer (not to be confused with UK singer, same name) became highly regarded music journalist: published books *Deep Blues*, biographies of Jerry Lee LEWIS, LEIBER & STOLLER, countless features in periodicals.

INTERNATIONAL SWEETHEARTS OF RHYTHM Female swing band formed '37 at Piney Wood Ms. Country Life School for poor and black children. Lineup mostly black women but some white, oriental, Mexican (hence 'International'). Toured to raise money for the school, appeared at Howard Theatre in Washington, then at the APOLLO in Harlem; went off on their own '40, fleeing in the school bus chased by police when they found that some girls would not graduate because they'd been touring with band. Set up house in Arlington, Va., rehearsing under Eddie DURHAM: band incl. leader Edna Williams (Armstread) (trumpet, arranger); Pauline Braddy (tutored on drums by Sid CATLETT, Jo JONES), Willie May Wong (sax), 14 others. Booked into Apollo theatre, Savoy Ballroom NYC, won high praise: musicians in the audience demanded to know what male band was playing backstage, assuming girls were pantomiming. They were paid half union scale; Durham was disgusted with their backers and left to form his own all-girl band; vocalist-guitarist Anna Mae Winburn (*b* Tenn.) was appointed leader: she'd led a male band (once incl. Charlie CHRISTIAN) until stranded when the band was raided by Fletcher HENDERSON; the new mus. dir. was Jesse Stone (*b* Atchison, Kansas, '01; composed 'Idaho' '42 for a Roy ROGERS movie). New members incl. trumpeter-vocalist Ernestine 'Tiny' Davis, saxist Vi Burnside in Lester YOUNG mould. White members of the band tried to pass for black when touring south, suffering strange double indignity of being women and white. Stone left after two years, replaced by Maurice King (later arr. for Gladys KNIGHT, Detroit Spinners). Their best year was '45: they played for sell-out crowds at Chicago Rhumboogie club, played black army camps, made film shorts (incl. *That Man Of Mine*, with vocalist Ruby Dee), sailed for Europe in July to play service depots on Continent. Lineup changes from '47 led to band folding '49; Winburn reformed Sweethearts of Rhythm '50, kept it going five years while having four kids: band down to octet, finally folded '55. Compilation *International Sweethearts Of Rhythm* on Rosetta label. Other all-girl bands were led by Phil Spitalny (1890-1970); *see* Ina Ray HUTTON (Ivy Benson in the UK); talent scouts knew of talented women all over the USA who never even got a chance to leave town.

INXS Australian rock band headed by singer Michael Hutchence (*b* 12 Jan. '60, Sydney, NSW), son of salesman. Family lived in Hong Kong; returned to NSW at 13, met Andrew Farriss (keyboards) at school. Family split up, mother took Hutchence to L.A., but he returned to Sydney '79, formed band called Farriss Brothers with Andrew, Jon (drums), Tim (guitar), plus Kirk Pengilly (guitar, sax), Garry Beers (bass). Changed base to Perth, name to Inxs (pron. 'In Excess'); back to Sydney, recorded for Deluxe label; second single 'Just Keep Walking' '80 made Down Under top 40; first LP *Inxs* '80, next two singles and LP *Underneath The Colours* also successful '81 (USA debut *The Inxs*; 12" EP *Dekadance*, all releases on Atco/Atlantic in USA). Top 5 LP *Shabooh Shoobah*, single 'The One Thing' hits, all '82. 'Thing' also made USA top 30. Toured USA twice; producer Nile Rodgers (ex-CHIC) heard them, shaped hit 'Original Sin' '83 (no. 58 USA, hit in France, Australia). It was written in Florida, as was 'Melting In The Sun', both on LP *The Swing* '84. 'We walked down the beach and got tar on our feet [from oil slicks]. Walked back and we got ripped off on drink prices. It's like Manhattan on the beach.' Later they decided they liked Florida after all; toured there late '85 for LP *Listen Like Thieves*, single 'This Time', followed by *Kick* '87. Seen as Aussie DURAN clones by some; support on tour was Boston guitarist Jon Butcher, who got good reviews.

IRON BUTTERFLY USA heavy rock band formed '66. Original lineup: Doug Ingle, keyboards (b 9 Sep. '46, Omaha, Neb.); Ron Bushy, drums (b 23 Sep. '45, Wash. DC); bassist Jerry Penrod, vocalist Darryl DeLoach, guitarist Danny Weiss, all b San Diego. Spotted playing in bars on Sunset Strip; signed to Atlantic's Atco subsidiary; first LP *Heavy* '68 charted in Billboard, helped by band's touring with DOORS etc. Last three named above left (Weiss later joined Rhinoceros), replaced by bassist Lee Dorman (b 15 Sep. '45, St Louis), Erik Keith Braunn (b 11 Aug. '50, Boston), guitar and vocals. Second LP *In-A-Gadda-Da-Vida* '69 had Ingle's 17-minute title track on second side, sold 3 million, stayed in USA charts over two years; edited version of title made top 30 as single. Heavy organ-based music with classical overtones was taken very seriously at the time. Follow-up *Ball* '69 was no. 3 LP, but it was downhill from then on. Braunn was replaced '69 by Mike Pinera (b 29 Sep. '48, Tampa, Fla.; ex-Blues Image) and Larry Reinhardt (b 7 July '48, Fla.); he formed Flintwhistle with Penrod and DeLoach. Band broke up after *Live*, *Metamorphosis*, compilation *Evolution*, all '70-1. Braunn and Bushy re-formed '75 with Howard Reitzes and Phil Kramer for *Scorching Beauty* and *Sun And Steel*, but moment was long gone. Like VANILLA FUDGE, Butterfly were heavy metal pioneers but foundered on overblown concepts compared to sex appeal of DEEP PURPLE, LED ZEPPELIN.

IRON MAIDEN UK heavy metal group formed in midst of punk '76 by bassist Steve Harris (b 12 Mar. '57, Leytonstone, London); kept on in face of fashion with changing lineup until settling on nucleus of guitarist Dave Murray (b 23 Dec. '58, Clapham, London) from local group Urchin, vocalist Paul Di'anno (b 17 May '59, Chingford, Essex), drummer Doug Sampson. Group profited from New Wave of British Heavy Metal movement peddled by *Sounds*, encouraging new young bands replacing tax exiles DEEP PURPLE, JUDAS PRIEST etc. to supply live music to HM fans. Tracks made as demos incl. anthem 'Iron Maiden' (after medieval torture instrument giving group name) released by the popular demand created by plays at North London's Soundhouse disco; EP sold out in a few days and led to EMI contract. Sampson replaced for first album sessions by ex-Samson drummer Clive Burr (b 8 Mar. '57, East Ham, London); ex-Remus Down Boulevard guitarist Dennis Stratton (b 9 Nov. '54, Canning Town, London) beefed up sound: LP standard HM, incl. recut 'Iron Maiden', but Derek Riggs's artwork of grotesque 'Eddie the Head' gave them an unforgettable logo. LP reached no. 4 after tour supporting Judas Priest; Stratton's departure due to 'musical differences', replaced by another ex-Urchin Adrian Smith (b 27 Feb. '57, London), saw temporary decline; half-live *Killers* '81 had only four new tracks, Di'anno below par: it entered charts at no. 10 and declined; Di'anno was replaced by ex-Samson Bruce Dickenson (b 7 Aug. '58, Sheffield), longer-haired and less punky; also took some writing load from Harris. *Number Of The Beast* introduced BLACK SABBATH-like occult overtones, hit no. 1, but by *Piece Of Mind* '83, made in Bahamas, they were tax exiles themselves. Burr replaced for LP by ex-Pat Travers/Trust drummer Nicko McBain (b 5 June '54, London); it made no. 3 UK, breached top 20 USA, vindicating decision to quit UK; *Power Slave* '84 promoted in 11-month tour of 26 countries, went in at no. 2 UK; tour captured in 2-disc/video *Live After Death* '85 with lavish pseudo-Egyptian set, Eddie the Head in action (12-foot mummy operated by member of security staff). Stage show always value for money; video incl. alternate takes of live LP tracks. Maiden have happy knack of scoring hit singles, with 12 top 40 entries in UK: highest was 'Run To The Hills' (no. 7 '82), while popular stage tune 'Running Free' made charts in both studio ('80) and live ('85) versions. They provide nothing new but have fun doing it, taking their sword-and-sorcery HM with an unusual sense of humour; having world-wide following (incl. Poland) they will keep going until road-weary. Album *Somewhere In Time* '86.

ISHOLA, Haruna (*b* '18, Abadan, Nigeria; *d* '83) Singer-composer, studio owner. Helped popularise Apala style and dominated it for decades. Neo-traditional Apala began among Muslim Yoruba; characterised by Iyalu talking drums accompanying one or more vocalists, it emerged as a distinct form around '25, usually performed by amateurs during period of fasting; professionals enlarged instrumental base with drums of DunDun family and the agidigbo (a large hand piano); by '40s it had lost religious aspect and become a music of entertainment. By the '50s Haruna Ishola and his Apala Group had emerged as leading exponents, releasing countless singles and 26 LPs on Decca's West Africa label. Success led to opening his own 24-track studio at IjebuIgbo, near Abadan; on his death many top Nigerian musicians recorded songs in his memory. Three of his last albums can still be found outside Nigeria: *Egbe Oredegbe*, *Oluma Nikan Lobe*, and *Onise Nsise*. Another major Apala star of '60s-70s was Alhaji Ayinla Omowura; equally prolific were Kasumu Adio and Fatayi Ayilara.

ISLEY BROTHERS Black USA family group from Cincinnati, Ohio: began late '50s in R&B, had crossover success in pop, went disco in late '70s: had 36 Hot 100 entries '59-81 and second generation is still going strong. Brothers O'Kelly (*b* 25 Dec. '37; *d* '86; later dropped the 'O'), Rudolph (*b* 1 Apr. '39), Ronald (*b* 21 May '41) and Vernon, killed in an accident in '50s, were encouraged by their father, a professional singer, went to NYC as a vocal group, tenor Ronnie singing lead. They were unsuccess-

ful '57-9 (album *The Isley Brothers And Marvin And Johnny* later issued on Crown); signed by RCA that year, prod. by Hugo & Luigi: in Sep. 'Shout' in gospel call-and-response style made top 50 and became R&B classic, since covered many times (LP *Shout* '59), re-entered chart '62, same year as next hit, 'Twist And Shout' on Wand (covered by BEATLES on their first album). LP *Twist And Shout* on Wand '62; with money from 'Shout' they had moved entire family to Teaneck, N.J.; toured R&B circuit with band incl. Jimi HENDRIX '64; signed to Tamla/Motown: worked with HOLLAND-DOZIER-HOLLAND, but only the first single 'This Old Heart Of Mine (Is Weak For You)' made top 40 (at no. 12 '66), re-entered UK chart at no. 3 '68: they continued popular in UK, 15 chart entries there '63-83. Other LPs incl. *Take Some Time Out* on Sceptor, *Twisting And Shouting* '64 on UA, *This Old Heart Of Mine* '66 and *Soul On The Rocks* '68 on Tamla. Back in USA '69 they revived their own T-Neck label, which they'd started earlier in the decade; first release 'It's Your Thing' made no. 2 and won a Grammy. That year they added new generation of young brothers Ernie and Marvin on various instruments, brother-in-law Chris Jasper on keyboards, non-related Everett Collins on drums. 20 T-Neck LPs charted '69-83 beginning with *It's Our Thing* '68, *Brothers Isley* '69. 2-disc *Live At Yankee Stadium* incl. one side each by the Isleys, the Edwin HAWKINS Singers, Brooklyn Bridge, various artists. *Get Into Something*, *In The Beginning* (reissues with Hendrix) and *Givin' It Back* all issued '71; first two are the only Isley/T-Neck LPs *not* to chart. Other hit LPs incl. *Brother, Brother, Brother* '72; 2-disc *The Isleys Live*, *Greatest Hits*, *3 + 3* (helped to no. 8 by no. 6 hit single 'That Lady'), all '73; *Live It Up* '74, *The Heat Is On* '75 (no. 1 LP with no. 4 single 'Fight The Power'), *Harvest For The World* '76, *Go For Your Guns* '77, compilation *Forever Gold* '77, *Showdown* '78, 2-disc *Winner Takes All* '79, *Go All The Way* '80, *Grand Slam* and *Inside You* '81, *The Real Deal* '82, *Between The Sheets* '83: phenomenal list of hits incl. six top 10 LPs, and isn't over yet: *Masterpiece* on WB charted '85, as did younger generation as Isley, Jasper, Isley on CBS with *Broadway's Closer To Sunset Blvd* and *Caravan Of Love*. Other compilations have been issued on Pickwick, Camden, Motown in USA, Bulldog in UK (where T-Neck LPs were on Epic). They covered white rock (Neil YOUNG, Bob DYLAN) for important soul/rock synthesis, infl. Lionel RICHIE, Michael JACKSON, others.

ITCHY FINGERS UK saxophone quartet: Mike Mower (*b* 9 June '58, Bath), composer, tenor sax and flute; Howard Turner (*b* 9 Nov. '57, Amersham), baritone sax and bass clarinet; Martin Speake (*b* 3 Apr. '58, Barnet), alto sax; John Graham (*b* 6 Mar. '61, Birmingham) on soprano, alto, tenor, clarinet. Mower's compositions have been commissioned by the BBC Big Band, BBC Radio Orchestra and the Arts Council; also played with Tina TURNER, STYLE COUNCIL, etc. asked to take 12-piece group Hiatus to Zurich '85, financial constraints meant taking only reeds; success was immediate: at first British Jazz Festival Joe ZAWINUL described them as 'world class in every respect'. Graham and Turner failed music college; Speake works at Ray's Jazz Shop in London, played with Style Council. First LP *Quark* '87 on Virgin co-prod. by Mower, Richard Cottle (keyboardist on David BOWIE world tour '87): lots of beautiful sound in spite of Cottle's ubiquitous synthesiser, rock rhythm section (bassist Lawrence Cottle, drummer Jeremy Stacey), Danny McCintosh on guitar, Stanley Unwin on reads (reads droll comedy, as he did on SMALL FACES *Ogden's Nut Gone Flake* '68); also McCoy TYNER and eight brass on 'It's Lovely Once You're In'. It is disingenuous of Virgin to compare them to the WORLD SAXOPHONE QUARTET, who don't need all this production; but neither do Itchy Fingers: you can tell on stripped down 'Hiatus', lovely 'Dakhut'.

IVES, Burl (*b* Charles Icle Ivanhoe Ives, 14 June '09, Jaspar County, Ill.) Folksinger, actor; played guitar, banjo. Tried teachers college, quit and went on the road during the Depression; arrived in NYC '33, fell in with Woody GUTHRIE, LEADBELLY, Josh WHITE, etc. By WWII a Renaissance man: singer, broadcaster, actor, researcher, author of several books incl. song collections: as radio's Wayfaring Stranger he arr. and popularised 'Blue Tail Fly', 'Foggy

Dew', 'Big Rock Candy Mountain' etc. On Broadway from late '30s incl. *Sing Out Sweet Land* '44, revival of *Showboat* '54, *Cat On A Hot Tin Roof* '55; cinema debut in *Smoky* '46; unforgettable cameo as small-town sheriff in *East Of Eden* with James Dean '55, took role of Big Daddy into film version of *Cat On A Hot Tin Roof* '57, won Oscar for *The Big Country* '58; also *The Day Of The Outlaw* '58, *Our Man In Havana* '59, etc. Records on Columbia post-WWII incl. 'The Doughnut Song': 'As you go through life/Make this your goal:/Watch the doughnut/Not the hole'. Only chart entry in this period was no. 21 hit '49 with one of several recordings of '(Ghost) Riders In The Sky' (from Gene AUTRY film); during this period he was, with the WEAVERS, almost the only nationally known performer keeping the flame of folk music burning. He testified to House Unamerican Activities Committee on the American Communist Party's use of folk music to its own ends. Switched to Decca and had nine Hot 100 hits '57-64, seven in C&W chart '52-72; biggest hits: 'Wild Side Of Life' '52, 'A Little Bitty Tear', 'Funny Way Of Laughin' ', 'Call Me Mr In-Between' all '62. LPs on Columbia incl. collection *The Wayfaring Stranger* c.'55, then *The Times They Are A'Changin'* late '60s; greatest hits compilations on MCA of Decca reissues. Always a hit with children: *Junior Choice* (on EMI/UK '79) incl. 'Aunt Rhody', 'I Know An Old Lady', 'Ballad Of Davy Crockett', etc. He recorded songs by Roger MILLER, Shel SILVERSTEIN, Tom T. HALL as well as Bob DYLAN; inspirational albums on Word: *Stepping In The Light*, *Bright And Beautiful*, *How Great Thou Art*; C&W LP *Payin' My Dues Again* c.'76.

IVY LEAGUE UK vocal harmony group of '60s, formed by songwriters John Carter (John Shakespeare) and Ken Lewis (James Hawker) (both *b* '42, Birmingham). Carter-Lewis and the Southerners made BBC radio appearances, had near-hit 'Your Momma's Out Of Town' '63, once incl. guitarist Jimmy Page; then linked with another pseudonymous singer-songwriter, Perry Ford (*b* Bryan Pugh, '40, Lincoln), specialised in vocal backings to order (e.g. on the WHO's 'Can't Explain') before making own discs on Piccadilly label. Scored three UK hits '65 in close-harmony style reminiscent of FOUR SEASONS: 'Funny How Love Can Be', 'That's Why I'm Crying', 'Tossing And Turning'. LP *This Is The Ivy League* '65 revealed hopeless lack of direction, incl. trad. 'Floral Dance', DYLAN's 'Don't Think Twice It's All Right', own originals. Carter left early '66, replaced by Tony Burrows; Lewis replaced by Neil Landon; both continued association; 'Willow Tree' no. 50 for one week mid-'66; group became the Flowerpot Men, scored one-off with vogueish Carter-Lewis song 'Let's Go To San Francisco' (UK no. 4), then became Friends, quit. Carter-Lewis continued to write/perform together: as First Class (with Burrows) had no. 4 USA/13 UK hit 'Beach Baby', BEACH BOYS pastiche with Carter singing lead.

J

JACKIE & ROY Jackie Cain, Roy Kral, vocal duo (*b* Jacqueline Ruth Cain, 22 May '28, Milwaukee, Wisc.; Roy Joseph Kral, 10 Oct. '21, Chicago, Ill.) Kral also pianist, composer, arranger; radio work in Detroit after WWII service, then teamed with Cain as bop duo in Charlie VENTURA band '48-9; unusual arr. sometimes had them in unison with band's instrumentalists. Records with Ventura lineup incl. two live LPs *In Concert* with 'Flamingo' arr. by Pete Rugolo, plus Cain solo on 'Over The Rainbow' (she is also a fine ballad singer); also *A Charlie Ventura Concert* made two weeks before band split, incl. Kral-Ventura comp. 'Euphoria', 'I'm Forever Blowing Bubbles' ('84 reissue: *Bop For The People* on Affinity UK). Married '49, formed own bop sextet (three boys, three girls); disbanded, worked on Chicago TV, rejoined Ventura most of '53. Most LPs throughout career now out of print incl. *Bits And Pieces* on ABC, with some arr. by Quincy JONES, sidemen Phil WOODS, Clark TERRY, etc.; *Grass* in '60s on Capitol with songs by Paul SIMON, BEE GEES, DONOVAN, Kral colleague Fran Landesman. *Like Sing* (Columbia) has songs by André PREVIN; *By Jupiter* and *Girl Crazy* were on Roulette; LP of BEATLE songs on Atlantic; *Changes* and *Lovesick* on Verve; *Time And Love* and *A Wilder Alias* on CTI (latter featured Kral comps.). Also TV commercials, notably for Plymouth '60; many tours, jazz festivals, TV spots. Available in USA: MCA reissues on 2-disc *Jackie & Roy, By The Sea* '76 on Studio 7, and new series of LPs on Concord with three to five sidemen: *Star Sounds* '79, *East Of Suez* '80, *High Standards* '82; then *We've Got It: The Music Of Cy Coleman* '84 on Discovery, *Bogie* '86 on Fantasy (songs associated with Humphrey Bogart) and *One More Rose* '87 on Audiophile (songs of Alan Jay LERNER; said to be one of their best). Roy's sister Irene Kral was also a fine singer (*b* 18 Jan. '32, Chicago; *d* 15 Aug. '78); she worked with Woody HERMAN, Maynard

FERGUSON, Laurindo ALMEIDA (Grammy-winning *Guitar From Ipanema* '64), *Better Than Anything* with Junior Mance trio, *Wonderful Life* on Mainstream, others: beautiful duo with pianist Alan Broadbent *Where Is Love* c.'76 on Choice was a Grammy nominee.

JACKSON, Janet (*b* 16 May '66, Gary, Ind.) Singer; youngest of nine children (*see* the JACKSONS) and the eighth to make records. She began at 6, appearing with her brothers doing impersonations (Mae West, CHER, etc.); before she was 10 she was spotted on TV with her brothers by producer Norman Lear, leading to more TV work, notably on *Fame*. She sang on demos for her sister LaToya; own eponymous debut LP '82 on A&M reached no. 64 on USA pop album chart; *Dream Street* '84 did less well, despite help from her brothers and Cliff RICHARD (duet on 'Two To The Power Of Love'); *Control* '86 was prod. by Jimmy Jam and Terry Lewis at their Flyte Time studio in Minneapolis, with Janet co-writing and co-producing: four UK/USA hit singles incl. title track, all top 5 in USA with 'When I Think Of You' at no. 1.

JACKSON, Jermaine (*b* Jermaine LaJaune Jackson, 11 Dec. '54) Singer, bassist, producer; originally the middle member of Jackson Five (*see* the JACKSONS). Followed his brother Michael in embarking on a solo career '72: LP *Jermaine* was top 30 in USA LP chart, single 'That's How Love Goes' top 50, 'Daddy's Home' '73 top 10. Albums *Come Into My Life* '73, *My Name Is Jermaine* '76, *Feel The Fire* '77 sold respectably but did not make top 100 LPs. Meanwhile he married the boss's daughter (Hazel Gordy): when the Jackson Five left Motown he left the group (replaced by brother Randy). *Let's Get Serious* '80 was top 10 LP, helped by title track (written by Stevie WONDER), a top 10 single both USA/UK; he had other top 40 hits that year, LPs

Jermaine '80, *I Like Your Style* '81, *Let Me Tickle Your Fancy* '82 (top 20 hit with title single, backed by DEVO). He also produced at Motown (acts Switch, Michael Lovesmith). Was reunited with his brothers for Motown 25th Anniversary TV special '83; later that year switched to Arista label; *Jermaine Jackson* '84 titled *Dynamite* in UK after hit single (top 20 USA); 'Do What You Do' from the LP was a hit in both countries; other tracks incl. duets with Michael, with Whitney HOUSTON; he duetted with Houston on her eponymous debut hit album '85, followed by his own *Precious Moments* that year. He has also worked in film soundtracks: 'When The Rain Begins To Fall' with Pia Zadora for *Voyage Of The Rock Alien,* solo title song to Jamie Curtis body-building movie *Perfect.*

JACKSON, Joe (*b* 11 Aug. '55, Burton on Trent) UK singer. Studied piano and violin as teenager, attended Royal Academy of Music. Early band Arms & Legs made three flop singles. Break came with early days of punk, though his vocal style was compared unfavourably with Elvis COSTELLO, Graham PARKER. *Look Sharp* '79 incl. scathing 'Sunday Papers' and gave him no. 21 USA/13 UK hit with 'Is She Really Going Out With Him?' (He was a sharp dresser and the press dubbed it 'spiv rock'.) *I'm The Man* '79 incl. 'It's Different For Girls' (UK no. 5 '80) and impressive 'On The Radio'. *Beat Crazy* '80 was reggae; his cover of Jimmy Cliff's 'The Harder They Come' was praised. *Jumpin' Jive* '81 was a delightful surprise: a homage to the music of Cab CALLOWAY and Louis JORDAN that contributed to revival of UK interest in jazz roots of pop. *Night & Day* '82 was his biggest hit: incorporated jazz flavour, but recorded in NYC also featured Jackson experimenting with R&B, salsa and funk; no. 4 album USA, 6 UK incl. transatlantic no. 6 with 'Steppin' Out', two other USA top 20 hits. He contributed music to soundtrack of film *Mike's Murder* '83; *Body & Soul* '84 was impressive, incl. 'Happy Ending' and 'Be My Number Two': living in NYC, continued soaking up musical styles. 3-sided *Big World* '86 attempted to convey concert atmosphere; *Will Power* '87 was instrumental from solo piano 'Nocturne' to 50-piece treatments. He also sessioned for Suzanne VEGA.

JACKSON, Mahalia (*b* 26 Oct. '11, New Orleans, La.; *d* 27 Jan. '72, Chicago) Gospel singer, probably the greatest of all: her rhythmic feeling and big, powerful and beautiful contralto could only be (and was) compared to that of Bessie SMITH, but she refused to be associated with blues or jazz; later sang secular/inspirational material such as 'You'll Never Walk Alone'. Her father was a lay preacher; she secretly listened to Bessie's records. Moved to Chicago aged 16 with her family; worked as a maid, nurse, laundress; turned down offer from Earl HINES, joined Greater Salem Baptist Church Choir: quintet was formed featuring her which toured churches. (*See also* GOSPEL MUSIC.) She continued to work, opening a beauty salon, flower shop, eventually going into property business, but her fame as a gospel singer was worldwide. First records for Decca '37, accompanied by Estelle Allen on piano and organ incl. 'God's Gonna Separate The Wheat From The Tares'; later records for Apollo incl. her own 'Move On Up A Little Higher', said to have sold a million. Signed with Columbia '54; recorded with Percy FAITH etc.; sang at Newport Jazz Festival '57-8 ('The Lord's Prayer' at the end of *Jazz On A Summer's Day,* film of '58 Festival); sang in both studio and Newport performances '58 of Duke ELLINGTON's *Black, Brown And Beige* (saying that she regarded Ellington's band as a 'sacred institution' rather than a jazz band). She appeared in film *St Louis Blues* '58 (biopic of W. C. HANDY starring Nat COLE). Toured the world; often on TV '50-60s, incl. Ed Sullivan Show; sang at inauguration of John Kennedy '61. LP on Apollo: *No Matter How You Pray*; Columbia albums: *The World's Greatest Gospel Singer, In Concert, My Faith, Mighty Fortress, Best-Loved Hymns Of Doctor King, Right Out Of The Church,* and *Bless This House,* 2-disc compilations *The Great Mahalia Jackson,* and *America's Greatest Hymns*; also *Amazing Grace* and *Newport '58* from Columbia Special Products, *I Sing Because I'm Happy* (2 vols.) on Folkways. She worried about her close friend Aretha FRANKLIN, who sang 'Precious Lord' at Jackson's funeral as Jackson had at the funeral of Martin Luther King. Her biography *Just Mahalia, Baby* by Laurraine Goreau published '75 by World books.

JACKSON, Michael (*b* Michael Joe Jackson, 29 Aug. '58, Gary, Ind.) Singer, stardom from age 11 as lead singer on four consecutive no. 1 hits with brothers (*see* the JACKSONS). Six solo singles on Motown were top 25 hits '72-5 incl. three top 5, 'Ben' at no. 1 (song from a film about a rat). His voice was breaking during the mid-'70s; he played the scarecrow in *The Wiz* '78, black remake of *Wizard Of Oz* starring Diana ROSS; their duet 'Ease On Down The Road' from the film just missed the top 40. Albums *Got To Be There* and *Ben* '72 top 15 USA; *Music & Me* '73, *Forever, Michael* '75 did less well; he switched to Epic and worked with producer Quincy JONES on *Off The Wall* '79: no. 3 LP USA with four top 10 hits sold several million copies. Motown recycled old tracks, some previously unreleased, some solo and some with brothers as *One Day In Your Life* '81; reissued title track was his first no. 1 hit in UK. *Thriller* '82 (with Jones) incl. seven top 10 hits ('Billie Jean' was no. 1 both USA/UK, 'Beat It' no. 1 USA, 3 UK, with guitar solo by Eddie VAN HALEN): the album sold about 40 million at last count; a video playing nearly half an hour was also a hit. *Farewell My Summer Love* '84 on Motown reissued tracks more than 10 years old, made top 50 USA LP chart. Duets with Paul MCCARTNEY on 'The Girl Is Mine' and 'Say Say Say' were also top 10 UK '82-3. He made adverts for Pepsi Cola; his hair caught fire from a stage light, but he recovered, signed new deal with Pepsi. He also recorded with his brothers, toured with them '85-6, but ticket prices were so high promoters are said to have lost money. Michael is portrayed by the media as a sad introvert, but having been a star for more than half his life and easily one of the biggest superstars of the '80s it is hard to see how he could lead a normal life. *Bad* '87 was more slick dance music, with single 'I Can't Stop Loving You', duet with Siedah Garrett; he is especially big in Japan now, where he is seen as the sort of beautiful young idol who should die young and tragically, but he's already too old to die young.

JACKSON, Millie (*b* '44, Thompson, Ga.) Singer. One of the best soul singers of her era; records, stage act marked by four-letter words, attempt at ultra-raunchy image. Lived with preacher grandfather, attended church six times a week, ran away to NYC age 14. Worked as model in Brooklyn '61, mainly in confession mags; on a bet jumped onstage at Harlem's Palm Café '64 to sing. Then worked as singer, made single '69 for MGM, signed with Spring Records '71, had first hit in soul chart 'A Child Of God', LPs *Millie Jackson, It Hurts So Good* (title track no. 3 on soul chart); top 30 pop hit 'Ask Me What You Want', all '72; named most promising female vocalist by NATRA. 'It Hurts So Good' featured in movie *Cleopatra Jones*; went pop top 30 '73. LP *Millie* '73 followed by breakthrough *Caught Up* '74: concept LP had Jackson portraying betrayed wife on one side, the other woman on reverse; incl. hit single 'If Loving You Is Wrong (I Don't Want To Be Right)', earning gold disc and Grammy nomination. Since then most LPs have charted; albums incl. *Still Caught Up* '75, *Free And In Love* '76 (completing trilogy prod. by Brad Shapiro); *Lovingly Yours* '76, *Feelin' Bitchy* '77, *Get It Outcha System* '78, *Royal Rappin's* '79 (duet LP with Isaac HAYES), *A Moment's Pleasure* '79, *Live And Uncensored* '79, *For Men Only* '80, *I Had To Say It* '80, *Just A Lil Bit Country* '81, *Live And Outrageous (Rated XXX)* '82 (incl. notorious 'Fuck U. Symphony'); *ESP (Extra Sexual Persuasion)* '84, incl. such tracks as 'Slow Tongue (Working Your Way Down)', 'Sexercise'. No major pop singles '73-85 partly owing to radio ban on her work, but 'Act Of War' top 40 UK '85 (duet with Elton JOHN on his Rocket label). Picketed by anti-apartheid groups after appearing in South Africa; announced '85 that she had visited United Nations as guest of Organisation for African Unity, would not return to S.A. and supported benefit concerts for S.A. blacks.

JACKSON, Milt (*b* 1 Jan. '23, Detroit) Vibes, piano. Aka 'Bags'. Studied music at Mich. U.; discovered by Dizzy GILLESPIE '45, came to NYC; played with Gillespie, others; Woody HERMAN '49-50, Gillespie again '50-2, then founder member of MODERN JAZZ QUARTET. The first vibist in modern jazz and far and away the most popular and influential, he uses a unique slow vibrato, swings with a bluesy, even gospel feeling, while keeping it under control for decades in the context of the MJQ's delicacy. Led own groups during MJQ's summer vacations, often co-leading with Ray BROWN. Many of his earliest records '47-52, on Galaxy in Detroit, Savoy and Gillespie's DeeGee label in NYC, then on Blue Note, featured Percy HEATH, John Lewis and Kenny CLARKE, the first MJQ lineup; his earliest well-known LP was probably *Opus de Funk* on Prestige '54, with Heath, Clarke, Horace SILVER and Henry Boozier on trumpet (a pseudonym?); *Milt Jackson Quartet* '55 had Silver, Heath and Connie Kay, the MJQ's perennial drummer after Clarke went to France. LPs on Savoy '56 followed by *Ballads And Blues* '56, *Plenty, Plenty Soul* '57, *Bags And Flutes* '57, *Soul Brothers* with Ray CHARLES, *Bean Bags* '58, *Bags And Trane* '59 with John COLTRANE, *Ballad Artistry Of Milt Jackson* '59 with strings arr. by Quincy JONES, *Vibrations* '60, all on Atlantic; also *Paris Session* on Philips and *Bags Opus* on UA '58. *Statements* '62 on Impulse had quartet with Kay, Paul CHAMBERS, Hank JONES; *Bags Meets Wes* '61 with Wes MONTGOMERY was debut on Riverside/Milestone, followed by sextet *Invitation* '62, big band LPs *Big Bags* '62 and *For Someone I Love* '63, quintet *Live At The Village Gate* '63. Quintet *Jazz'n'Samba* '64 (Impulse) followed by Mercury/Limelight LPs incl. quartet *In A New Setting* '64, quintets *Live At The Museum Of Modern Art* '65, *Born Free* '67. A Verve LP with strings '68 followed by Impulse LPs *That's The Way It Is* and *Just The Way It Had To Be* '69, both made live at Shelly's Manne-Hole in Hollywood by a quintet with Brown, and *Memphis Jackson* (made in L.A.) with big band led by Brown. *Sunflower* '72 with strings, quintet/sextet *Goodbye* '73 and *Olinga* '74 (the last plus strings) were on CTI. Jackson's desire to lead own groups coincided with split of MJQ mid-'74 (but reunions continue); records on Norman GRANZ's Pablo label began at Montreux '75, then *The Big Three* '75 with Joe PASS, *At The Kosei Nenkin* '76 (quintet in Japan), *Feelings* '76 (strings), *Milt Jackson–Ray Brown Jam* '77 at Montreux, *Soul Believer* '78, *Bag's Bag* '79, *Night Mist* '80, *Ain't But*

A Few Of Us Left '81, *Memories Of Thelonious Sphere Monk* '82, *Jackson, Johnson, Brown & Co.* '83, all with Brown; plus *Soul Fusion* '77 with Monty ALEXANDER Trio, two LPs with Count BASIE '78, *Big Mouth* '81 (septet with three percussionists, female vocal quartet), *Two Of The Few* '83 (duet with Oscar PETERSON); also *Loose Walk* '79 on Italian Palcoscenico label, made in Milan (quintet with Sonny STITT).

JACKSON, Stonewall (*b* 6 Nov. '32, Tabor City, N.C.) One of the more genuine country singers of '50s-60s. His real name, after great-great-grandfather, General in Confederate Army. Entertainer in US Navy; from '54 worked as farmer, carpenter, logger while saving for a trip to Nashville: had log-trucking company in Moultrie, Ga., drove to Nashville '56, signed songwriting contract with Wesley Rose, auditioned for Grand Ole Opry and was the only unknown in modern times (with no records at all) to get Opry contract. With Columbia '57, first hit 'Life To Go' '58, then 'Waterloo' '59, no. 1 country, top 10 pop '59. Distinctive rural voice that 'Nashville Sound' could not diminish. Had impressive string of hits '60s incl. 'Why I'm Walkin' ' '60, 'A Wound Time Can't Erase' '62, 'B.J. The D.J.' '63, 'Don't Be Angry' '64, 'Help Stamp Out Loneliness' '67, 'Me And You And A Dog Named Boo' '71. Faded from charts mid-'70s; still popular with trad. country fans. LPs incl. *Dynamic* '59, *Sadness In A Song* '61, *Trouble And Me* '65, *All's Fair In Love And War* '67, *The Real Thing* '70, *Live At The Grand Ole Opry* '71, all on Columbia; *Greatest Hits* '81 on Lakeshore, *Solid Stonewall* '82 on Phonorama.

JACKSON, Wanda (*b* Wanda Lavonne Jackson, 20 Oct. '37, Maud, Okla.) Country/rock'n'roll singer of the late '50s and '60s. Family moved to Bakersfield; father taught her guitar and piano; they returned to Oklahoma where she had her own radio show at 13; after high school she joined Hank THOMPSON and his Brazos Valley Boys, toured with them and with Elvis PRESLEY '55. Signed to Decca as country singer and had duet hit with 'You Can't Have My Love' (no. 8 C&W chart '54); switched to Capitol '56, left Thompson and was one of the few female rockers of the '50s: 'Let's

Have A Party' made top 40 both USA/UK '60; 'Mean Mean Man' scored in UK '61; other USA top 40s were 'Right Or Wrong', 'In The Middle Of A Heartache' '61. She was also popular in Holland, Germany and Japan, cutting versions of hits in these languages (e.g. 'Fujiyama Mama'). As the original country-flavoured rock'n'roll (rockabilly) style seemed to fade, she went back to country music and stayed there, helped by her husband Wendell Goodman and with her own tight-knit band The Party Timers; she racked up 26 country hits '61-71 in a female honky-tonk style: 'If I Cried Every Time You Hurt Me' also made pop Hot 100 '62; other country hits were 'Tears Will Be A Chaser For Your Wine', 'My Heart Gets All The Breaks', 'A Girl Don't Have To Drink To Have Fun', etc. She wrote some of her own songs as well as '(Let's Stop) Kickin' Our Hearts Around' for Buck OWENS (no. 8 '62), others. She turned to gospel music in '70s, although still performing old hits on tours. LPs incl. *Rockin' With Wanda* '60, *Two Sides Of Wanda* '64, *Reckless Love Affair* '65, *You'll Always Have My Love* '67, *Many Moods Of Wanda* '69, *Portrait* '70, *A Woman Lives For Love* '70, *Praise The Lord* '73, all on Capitol; *Country Gospel* '74 and *Closer To Jesus* '78 on Word; *When It's Time To Fall In Love, Now I Have Everything, Make Me Like A Child Again* on Myrrh '75-6; *I'll Still Love You* '77 on DJM and *Greatest Hits* '79 on Gusto. 2-disc *Let's Have A Party* '86 on Charly UK has 32 tracks '56-63, incl. covers of Chuck BERRY, Jerry Lee LEWIS, Presley etc. with sidemen incl. Owens, Merle TRAVIS, Roy CLARK, Joe Maphis (*b* c.'21, *d* 27 June '86; well-known picker, singer, songwriter wrote 'Dim Lights, Thick Smoke (And Loud Loud Music)', played guitar on TV theme *Bonanza* etc.).

JACKSON, Willis (*b* 25 Apr. '32, Miami; *d* 25 Oct. '87) Tenor sax, composer; aka 'Gator', 'Gatortail'. Like Jimmy FORREST and Hank CRAWFORD, a link between R&B and jazz; invented gator horn, a long saxophone with a ball-shaped bell with small opening, that sounds between alto and soprano. Pro at 14; studied music in Fla. college; with Cootie WILLIAMS '50-5, recording own 'Gator Tail', hence his nickname. Single on Apollo '50 'Chuck's Chuckles',

'Dance Of The Lady Bug' incl. Booty Wood, trombone (later with Duke ELLINGTON), Bill DOGGETT, Panama Francis; others on Atlantic, Deluxe, Atco labels '52-7 ('Back Door' and 'Later Gator' on Atco arr. by Quincy JONES, incl. Al CAIOLA, Kenny BURRELL); was married to Ruth BROWN and accompanied her. Series of crowd-pleasers on Prestige: tracks issued on various LPs '59-60 with organist Jack McDUFF; '61 tracks on both Prestige and Moodsville; then *Together Again, Again* '61 with McDuff, *Thunderbird* '62 with Freddie Roach on organ (*b* 11 May '31, Bronx, NY), *Shuckin'* '62 with Burrell, Tommy FLANAGAN, Roy HAYNES, Latin percussion; *Neapolitan Nights, Loose, Grease And Gravy, The Good Life, More Gravy, Boss Shoutin'* '62-3; *Jackson's Action, Live Action, Soul Night, Tell It* all made live at The Allegro NYC '64; *Soul Grabber, Star Bag, Swivel Hips, Gator's Groove, Gatorade* '67-71. On other labels, *Gator Tails* '64 on Verve had large orchestra accompaniment; *Smokin' With Willis* '65 was a sextet LP on Cadet; a sextet LP on Upfront late '60s incl. George BENSON and Dave 'Baby' CORTEZ. *The Way We Were* '75 on Atlantic and an LP on Cotillion '76 had vocalists and large orchestra. Later LPs on Muse: *West Africa* '73, *Headed And Gutted* '74, *In The Alley* '76, *The Gator Horn* '77, *Bar Wars* '77 with Charles EARLAND on organ, *Single Action* '78, *Lockin' Horns* '78 (live at Laren Jazz Festival with Von FREEMAN), *Nothing Butt* with Earland and *Ya Understand Me?* with Richard 'Groove' HOLMES '80. Also *In Chateauneuf du Pape 1980* on Black & Blue with Holmes.

JACKSONS, The (Jackson Five) USA pop vocal/instrumental group formed c.'65: Jackie (*b* Sigmund Esco Jackson, 4 May '51), Tito (*b* Toriano Adryll Jackson, 15 Oct. '53), Marlon (*b* Marlon David Jackson, 12 Mar. '57), Jermaine and Michael (who have their own entries), all born in Gary, Indiana. The other children of Joe and Catherine Jackson are Rebbie (*b* Maureen; first LP *Centipede* '84 on CBS made no. 63 in Billboard, followed by *Reactions* '86), LaToya (*b* '55; her LPs '80-4 reached top 200 USA on Polydor and Private I), Randy (*b* Steven Randall Jackson, 29 Oct. '61), and Janet (also has her own entry). Joe was a part-time musician, played in local R&B group the Falcons (not the same group that once incl. Wilson PICKETT); when the children began to play dad's guitar and mother's piano he allowed five oldest boys to enter talent competitions, which they inevitably won, with Michael singing lead, Tito on guitar, Jermaine on bass, cousins Johnny Jackson, keyboards, Ronnie Rancifer on drums. Early showcases for Michael's talent incl. covers of the TEMPTATIONS' 'My Girl', Joe TEX's 'Skinny Legs And All' (for the latter he would lift the skirts of female members of the audience looking for skinny legs, leading to rumour that he was a 30-year-old midget). Billed as the Jackson Five, they first recorded for Steeltown (tracks later issued on *The Bumper Funk Book* in UK on Pye (PRT) early '70s). They supported black acts in Eastern USA though Michael was only 10, learning stagecraft from James BROWN, the CHI-LITES, Temptations, Gladys KNIGHT & the Pips; various stories credit either Gladys or Joe Taylor, leader of the Vancouvers, with recommending them to Motown; their first four singles on that label all topped USA pop chart '69-70, a feat that has never been equalled: 'I Want You Back', 'ABC', 'The Love You Save', 'I'll Be There' were also top 10 in UK '70; the next two were no. 2 '71. Michael began recording solo that year and his success was immediate, but he continued singing with the group; they had 16 top 40 singles altogether on Motown '69-75; best-selling LPs incl. *Diana Ross Presents The Jackson Five, ABC, Third Album,* all top 5 LPs '70; also *Maybe Tomorrow, Goin' Back To Indiana* (soundtrack of TV special), *Lookin' Through The Windows, Skywriter, Get It Together, Dancin' Machine, Moving Violation*; 3-disc *Anthology* '76 incl. Michael's and Jermaine's solo hits. As their Motown contract drew to an end other labels closed in; they moved to Epic, but Jermaine stayed with Motown, replaced by Randy; Motown wouldn't allow them to be called Jackson Five so they became the Jacksons. Bestselling USA LPs incl. *The Jacksons* '76, *Goin' Places* '77, *Destiny* '78 (no. 11 LP USA), *Triumph* '80, 2-disc *Jacksons Live* '81, *Victory* '84 (no. 4 LP USA); of seven top 40 singles on Epic 'Enjoy Yourself' '76, 'Shake Your Body' '79 and 'State Of Shock' '84 were top 10 (the latter no. 3, from LP *Triumph*; lead vocal shared by

Mick Jagger); 'Torture' '84 (no. 17) had Jermaine sharing lead. Michael finally left the group '86 after his phenomenal success raised their price so high that '86 tour was criticised and may have lost money. They were also featured in a TV cartoon series and commended by Congress for their 'contributions to American youth': altogether a remarkable bundle of talent; the most recommendable albums remain the various anthologies and Greatest Hits packages.

JACQUET, Illinois (*b* Battiste Illinois Jacquet, 31 Oct. '22, Broussard, La.) Tenor sax. Grew up in Texas; father was a bassist. To West Coast '41; joined Lionel HAMPTON and played famous solo on 'Flyin' Home'; with Cab CALLOWAY '43-4, Count BASIE, '45-6; had own bands and toured with JATP. Appeared in famous short film *Jammin' The Blues* '44 with Lester YOUNG. Had early reputation as honker: the extrovert, crowd-pleasing style, using freak high notes and other gimmicks, was what the crowds wanted, but he always knew how to play ballads: a solid Texas tenor infl. by Herschel Evans. Surprised NYC audiences playing bassoon mid-'60s; toured Europe '70s with Milt BUCKNER and Jo JONES; with a Buddy RICH combo NYC '74, etc. Appeared at London club The Canteen early '80s with Slam STEWART, played lovely version of Duke ELLINGTON's 'I Didn't Know About You'; formed big band: album due '88 on Atlantic. Others incl. Verve 2-disc anthology *The Cool Rage* '51-8, with Basie, Kenny BURRELL, Ben WEBSTER, etc.; 2-disc Argo reissues *Illinois Jacquet* from '63 (plays bassoon); *With Wild Bill Davis* '73, *Jacquet's Street* '76 on Classic Jazz; on Prestige: 2-disc collection *How High The Moon, Bottoms Up* '68, *King!* '69, big band *Soul Explosion, Blues: That's Me*. Continental imports on Verve incl. *Groovin'* '51-3, *The Kid & The Brute* with Webster, *Swing's The Thing* with Roy ELDRIDGE, etc; also in UK: *Blues From Louisiana* (Town Hall Concert NYC '73 with Buckner, Arnett Cobb, Panama Francis), *Birthday Party* with Gerry MULLIGAN, James MOODY etc. both on JRC.

JAM, The UK new wave trio '74-82. Lineup: Paul Weller (*b* 25 May '58, Woking, Surrey), vocals, guitar; began performing in Woking '72, teamed with bassist Bruce

591

Foxton (*b* 1 Sep. '55, Woking), drummer Rick Butler (*b* 6 Dec. '55), heavily infl. by Mod sounds of SMALL FACES, The WHO, Tamla/Motown and R&B. Seen as neo-conservatives at early gigs, performing against Union Jack; disabused any notions of extreme right affiliation, but Weller said 'Vote Tory'. Early albums *In The City* and *This Is The Modern World* (both '77) were bracing, strident, timely, displayed little of the subtlety that would later characterise Weller's work. Every LP till '80 incl. covers revealing Weller's penchant for Wilson PICKETT, the KINKS, Martha and the Vandellas, etc. They earned grudging punk credibility, but also broke through commercially: 'All Around The World', 'Strange Town', 'When You're Young' were all top 20 in UK. *All Mod Cons* '78 was best work to date, incl. chilling 'Down In The Tube Station At Midnight', hit cover of Ray Davies' 'David Watts'. *Setting Sons* '79 was transitional, emphasising Weller's growing writing skill with acerbic 'Eton Rifles', 'Little Boy Soldiers', sympathetic 'Saturday's Kids'. Band's stature confirmed when 'Going Underground' '80 was first single in seven years to enter chart at no. 1: all three of their number ones did it, among 19 UK chart hits (not counting many re-entries); other chart toppers were 'Town Called Malice' and 'Beat Surrender' in '82. *Sound Affects* '80 incl. perhaps Weller's best song, the bitter, acoustic 'That's Entertainment' (apparently not considered hit material: its first chart entry at no. 21 was as an import), as well as 'Man In The Corner Shop', 'Set The House Ablaze', BEATLE-infl. 'Start'. *The Gift* '82 incl. 'Town Called Malice', 'The Planner's Dream Gone Wrong': that year Weller thought they should quit while they were ahead before they got stale, folding the most important band in the country. *Dig The New Breed* '82 was exemplary live LP, tracks culled from shows '77-82; *Snap* '83 is definitive 2-disc compilation (edited version *Compact Snap* on CD); *The Jam: A Beat Concerto* '83 by Paolo Hewitt is definitive book. Weller formed STYLE COUNCIL, Buckler went to Time UK, Foxton solo'd, formed band 100 Men '86.

JAMAL, Ahmad (*b* 2 July '30, Pittsburgh) Pianist, leader. Pro debut in high school, toured as accompanist; adopted Islamic name (from Fritz Jones). Formed trio, had debut at Chicago's Blue Note '51-2, recording as Ahmad Jamal's Three Strings with guitarist Ray Crawford, bassist Eddie Calhoun. From the beginning his piano style attracted attention, spare and deceptively light like that of Count BASIE, uniquely swinging like Erroll GARNER; influential and widely praised: 'All my inspiration today,' said Miles DAVIS c.'57, 'comes from Ahmad Jamal, the Chicago pianist', adding later, 'Listen to the way Jamal uses space. He lets it go so that you can feel the rhythm section and the rhythm section can feel you.' Calhoun was replaced by Richard Davis, then the wonderful Israel Crosby (*b* 19 Jan. '19, Chicago; *d* there 11 Aug. '62); they made two LPs for Epic and its first for Argo '55, subsidiary of Chicago's Chess R&B label: *Chamber Music Of The New Jazz. Count 'Em* '56 had Crosby, Walter Perkins on drums; *But Not For Me* '58 made at Pershing Hotel in Jan. with Crosby, Vernell Fournier on drums: many Jamal LPs made jazz charts, but this one unexpectedly and deservedly made no. 3 on the national Billboard pop LP chart, first of five to cross over. Vol. 2 from the Pershing issued sometime later; studio LP was made in June with Perkins; Fournier was back for date in September at Spotlight Club in Washington DC, where Jamal's first tracks made outside Chicago filled LPs incl. *Poinciana* and *Ahmad Jamal, Volume IV* (second pop chart entry, no. 11); third hit (no. 32) *Jamal At The Penthouse* '59 had trio back in Chicago with string section dir. by Joe Kennedy. *Happy Moods* by the trio and *Listen To The Ahmad Jamal Quintet* with Crawford on guitar and Kennedy on violin, both '60; *Ahmad Jamal's Alhambra* '61 made at that Chicago venue, tracks on two Argo LPs; tracks made *At The Blackhawk* same year in San Francisco turned up on several Argo, Cadet and Chess LPs. *Macanudo* '62 had Jamal with Richard Evans orchestra in NY; by *Naked City Theme* '63-4 the great Crosby was gone and the trio incl. Jamil Sulieman on bass, Chuck Lampkin on drums. *The Roar Of The Greasepaint* '65 on Argo was followed by *Extensions* '65 on Cadet with Fournier back on drums. More Cadet LPs incl. *Heat Wave* '66, with Fournier replaced by Frank Gant, *Cry Young* '67 (third pop chart entry at no. 168), *The Bright, The Blue And The Beautiful* '68, the last two with the Howard Roberts Chorale. Switched to ABC/Impulse for *Tranquility* '68, *Jamal At The Top* '69 (recorded at the Village Gate; reissued on Affinity as *Poinciana*); *The Awakening* '70 followed by the last Impulse LPs: *Free Flight* and *Outertimeinnerspace* from Montreux '71 saw Jamal playing some electric piano. *Live At Oil Can Harry's* on Catalyst was made in Vancouver with Gant, John Hurd on bass, Calvin Keys on guitar; '77-80 LPs on 20th Century incl. *Steppin' Out With A Dream*, adding Seldon Newton's percussion; *Genetic Walk* with Hurd, Gant, Keys, several others incl. a horn section (last pop chart entry at no. 173), and *Intervals*. *Live At Bubba's* '80 from Fort Lauderdale, Fla. on Kingdom Gate label had Sabu Adeyola on bass, Payton Crossley on drums; *Night Song* '80 on Motown had Oscar Brashear on trumpet with Keys and many others incl. strings and choir; *In Concert* and *Live In Concert* '81 from Cannes had Adeyola, Crossley and Gary BURTON; these were on Chiaroscuro, other labels. *American Classical Music* '82 on Shubra was made with Adeyola, Crossley, Newton. Latest LPs are 2-disc sets *Digital Works* and *Live At Montreal Jazz Festival 1985*, LP *Rossiter Road* '86 on Atlantic. Some Impulse LPs have been reissued on MCA.

JAMES, Dick (*b* '21, London; *d* there 1 Feb. '86) Singer, music publisher. Sang with North London dance band in early teens; regular vocalist at Cricklewood Palais at 17. Joined Henry HALL band and made first broadcast '40. Joined army '42, after WWII singing with top bands incl. GERALDO; member of vocal group Stargazers, gave up full-time singing '53 ('I couldn't see much future for a fat bald-headed singer'). Entered publishing with Sydney Bron's company, found 28 hits incl. five no. ones. Continued own recording career: theme from TV's *Robin Hood* was a top 20 hit '56; also charted with 'Garden Of Eden' '57. Formed own Dick James Music (DJM) '61; through Parlophone Records connection met Brian EPSTEIN, arranged BEATLES' first TV appearance, formed Northern Music to publish Lennon-McCartney songs, became millionaire. During '60s also handled Billy J. KRAMER, GERRY AND THE PACEMAKERS;

signed Elton JOHN and his lyricist Bernie Taupin as untried unknowns '67; formed DJM records '69 for John's hits; label carried Jasper Carrott, Rah Band, John Inman after Elton John formed Rocket label '76. Wealthy John sued James '85 for more royalties, collected more than £1m.

JAMES, Elmore (*b* 27 Jan. '18, Richland, Ms.; *d* 24 May '63, Chicago) Blues singer, guitarist; taught himself on home-made lard can instrument; influenced by Robert JOHNSON and Kokomo ARNOLD, he modernised the Delta blues for all time, influencing in turn J. B. HUTTO, B. B. KING, Jimi HENDRIX, many others. Worked in jukes, sawmills, etc.; served in US Navy '43-5; on radio's *King Biscuit Time* '47; often outside music; did not record until '51-2 on Trumpet in Jackson, Ms., Meteor in Chicago (had R&B hits 'Dust My Broom' '52 on Trumpet, 'I Believe' '53 on Meteor), then with own Broomdusters on Checker, Flair, etc. from '53. Further chart entries 'The Sky Is Crying' '60 on Fire, 'It Hurts Me Too' '65 on Enjoy. LPs incl. *Street Talkin'* with Eddie Taylor on Muse; in UK: *The Original Meteor And Flair Sides*, *King Of The Slide Guitar* and *Best Of* on Ace; *Red Hot Blues* on Blue Moon, *To Know A Man* on Line (West Germany), *One Way Out* and *Got To Move* on Charly.

JAMES, Etta (*b* '38, L.A.) R&B singer, one of the greatest. Discovered by Johnny OTIS in San Francisco; they wrote 'Roll With Me, Henry', an answer to Hank BALLARD's 'Work With Me, Annie'; released as 'Wallflower' it was no. 2 R&B hit '55, followed closely by 'Good Rockin' Daddy' (no. 12) on Modern. It was 'Wallflower' that inspired Georgia GIBBS' million-selling rip-off; division of royalties on that was very complicated, with the Bihari Bros (Modern), Otis, Etta, Ballard etc. all getting a piece. No more hits until '60: broke in Chicago, signed by Chess (who paid her hotel bills and bought the Modern contract) on recommendation of Harvey Fuqua of the Midnighters; 10 R&B hits followed on Argo '60-3, eight in top 10; six more on Cadet '67-70; 24 hits crossed over to Hot 100 pop chart '60-70. Also had hits with Fuqua as Etta & Harvey ('If I Can't Have You' and 'Spoonful' '60) and with Sugar Pie DeSanto

'65-6; had no hits of her own '65-6 partly because of battle with drug addiction; among young European rockers she was as big a star in the early '60s as Chuck BERRY, Bo DIDDLEY and the rest; her searing ballads ('All I Could Do Was Cry') had forecast the age of soul music to come. Beginning '67 ('Tell Me Mama') the records were made in the Muscle Shoals soul hit factory. Albums in pop LP chart incl. *At Last!* '61, *Etta James Top Ten* '63, live *Rocks The House* '64 on Argo; *Tell Mama* '68 and *Etta James* '73 on Cadet (some proceeds went to drug rehabilitation programmes). In '72 she returned to the R&B singles charts with 'I've Found A Love'; further LPs incl. *Etta James* '73, *Come A Little Closer* '74, *Etta Is Better Than Evah!* '75, *Deep In The Night* '78 on WB. Astonishingly, no LPs at all were listed in USA Schwann catalogue mid-'80s; then *Late Show* '86 on Fantasy made live in L.A. club with Eddie 'Cleanhead' VINSON, Shuggie OTIS etc. In UK: 2-disc *Chess Masters*, *Tuff Lover* and 10" *Good Rockin' Mama* on Ace/Cadet. She was scathing about Leonard Chess's musical judgement (quoted by Arnold Shaw), but the music will never die.

JAMES GANG USA rock trio formed '66 by drummer Jimmy Fox, who recruited bassist Tom Kriss and guitarist Glenn Schwartz to play BEATLE, YARDBIRD, ROLLING STONES songs at school dances. Schwartz quit '69 to join Pacific Gas and Electric, replaced by Joe WALSH. *Yer Album* '69 betrayed continued UK infl. and the fact that they continued as trio (having ditched a few keyboardists) says much for versatility of vocalist/guitarist Walsh: LP incl. originals, covers of Yardbirds ('Lost Woman'), BUFFALO SPRINGFIELD ('Bluebird') all in hard rock style and was surprise hit on BluesWay, making top 100 USA albums. Kriss was replaced by Dale Peters; *Rides Again*, *Thirds* and *Live In Concert* '70-1 followed; all made top 30 LPs on parent ABC label, but even European tour supporting WHO failed to bring superstardom: first of these contained Walsh classic 'The Bomber'; live set eschewed acoustic progression of *Thirds* in favour of heavy metal greatest hits treatment made in Carnegie Hall. Departure of Walsh in late '71 necessitated recruits, Canadian-based guitarist Dom Troiano (*b*

Modugno, Italy) and vocalist Roy Kenner, also Canadian. *Straight Shooter* and *Passin' Thru* '72 were regarded as poor; Troiano left to join Guess Who, was replaced at Walsh's suggestion by Tommy BOLIN, but band's days were numbered despite newcomer's skills: Bolin co-wrote all but one song on *Bang* '73 but this and *Miami* '74 sold poorly (on Atco). Group split when Bolin left to join DEEP PURPLE; a later lineup (rhythm section with guitarists Bubba Keith and Richard Shack) tried again but *Newborn* '75 did not make top 100. Walsh-era Gang could have become major force, but his departure at time of polarisation of music into pop/rock left them nowhere. *Best Of* on ABC recommended.

JAMES, Harry (*b* Harry Hagg James, 15 Mar. '16, Albany, Ga.; *d* 5 July '83, Las Vegas) Trumpet, leader. Father was bandmaster in circus. Played drums at 7, trumpet lessons from father at 10, became one of the most popular trumpet players of the century. With Ben POLLACK '35-6 he wrote 'Peckin' ', which became a dance fad; then a star in the Benny GOODMAN band '37-8, leaving Goodman with his help and blessing to start own band: early hits incl. 'One O'Clock Jump', Count BASIE head arrangement which Goodman had also recorded; theme 'Chiribiribin', written in Italy in 1898 (recorded twice in '39, once with a Frank SINATRA vocal); 'Two O'Clock Jump'; employed good vocalists Sinatra, Dick HAYMES, Helen FORREST, Kitty KALLEN. Not too successful as a hot bandleader, he added strings, eschewed jazz-based Goodman style for good dance music, flashy stuff like trumpet showcase coupling 'Flight Of The Bumble Bee'/'Carnival Of Venice'. 23 top 10 hits '41-7 incl. 'You Made Me Love You', 'Music Makers' (billed as Harry James and his Music Makers), 'Strictly Instrumental', 'I'll Get By' with Haymes, several vocals by Kallen '45. First married to vocalist Louise Tobin, then to glamour queen Betty Grable '43 (broke the hearts of many GIs); they did a vaudeville act together '53, divorced '65. He appeared in films with Goodman, then several in '40s with his own band; finally *The Benny Goodman Story* '56. Ray CONNIFF arranged for him late '40s; jazzmen Willie Smith on alto, trombonist Juan Tizol joined mid-'40s,

Louie BELLSON '50; they all left to join Duke ELLINGTON '51, known as The Great James Raid (Tizol and Smith came back '54). From mid-'50s he did not always have a band but organised for tours, long engagements; hired good people (often featured Buddy RICH), more jazz oriented, sounding like Basie, with arrangers like Ernie Wilkins, Neal HEFTI. He played in soundtrack for actor Kirk Douglas in film *Young Man With A Horn* '50. LPs available incl. broadcast airchecks on Hindsight and Sunbeam; *All Time Favorites*, *Greatest Hits* (with Sinatra) and *Man With The Horn* from Columbia Special Products, *Harry James & Dick Haymes* on Circle (from '40); later work on Capitol from '50s: *Hits Of Harry James* and *More Harry James In Hi-Fi* (now on Pausa); 2-disc Verve set *Crazy Rhythm*, '60s re-creation of 23 Swing Era hits; Sheffield Labs direct-cut discs from the '70s *Comin' From A Good Place, Still Harry After All These Years, The King James Version*: always a good musician, among the best things he did were on small-group records with Lionel HAMPTON, Teddy WILSON, others: especially beautiful was 2-sided 78 'Just A Mood' '37, with just Wilson, John Simmons on bass, Red NORVO on vibes; but he lived long enough to enjoy much more advanced technology.

JAMES, Joni (*b* Joan Carmello Babbo, 22 Sep. '30, Chicago) Singer. Worked as a dancer after high school; in chorus at Edgewater Beach Hotel in Chicago; switched to singing, signed by MGM. Paid for and prod. recording of 'Why Don't You Believe Me' herself: her third release, it was a million-selling no. 1 hit '52, reaching no. 11 UK. Having written that money-spinner, Lew Douglas, Frank Lavere and Ray Rodde did it again same year with 'Have You Heard?', her second gold disc at no. 5. In '53 'Wishing Ring' made no. 20 and her cover of 'Your Cheatin' Heart' by Hank WILLIAMS was a third gold disc; 'Is It Any Wonder' and 'Almost Always' (with a Latin beat) made the top 20, 'My Love, My Love' the top 10. No hits in '54; 'How Important Can It Be?' was no. 2 and 'You Are My Love' no. 6 '55, and she never made the top 10 again, though she had 13 more Hot 100 entries up to '60 ('There Must Be A Way', no. 33 '59, was her second and last hit in UK at no. 24).

Her voice was not strong and her phrasing was unexceptional, but her Prom-queen style lent an intimate wistfulness to the '52-3 hits that reeks nostalgia for anyone who was young then.

JAMES, Skip (*b* Nehemiah Curtis James, 9 June '02, Bentonia, Ms.; *d* 3 Oct. '69, Philadelphia) Blues singer, guitarist with unique style, 'pinching' to get octaves; played piano almost as well: among the most infl. of all the original bluesmen. Raised on plantation; father abandoned family (later became Baptist minister); childhood nickname was 'Skippy'. Studied guitar from age 8, learned basic piano in high school, played piano and organ in church. Hobo'd through south, working jukes, road houses etc.; studied at divinity school in Yazoo City mid-'20s; recorded for Paramount '31 (26 sides for $40; they're still selling). Formed gospel group, toured churches '31-5; ordained Baptist minister '32, Methodist minister '46, worked outside music '50s, returned '64 in coffee-houses, Newport Folk Festival '64; toured with Mississippi John HURT '64; Newport gig on Vanguard, '66 gig on Verve. Good profile in Peter Guralnick's *Feel Like Goin' Home* '71. Said to have infl. Robert JOHNSON; Samuel B. Charters described 'intense lyricism'; 'I'm So Glad' covered by CREAM, 'I'd Rather Be The Devil' by John MARTYN, etc.; his originals easily outshone them. LPs: *Vol. 1* on Melodeon, *Early Recordings* and *Tribute* on Biograph, *1931* on Matchbox, 2-disc *I'm So Glad* on Vanguard; *Skip James–The Greatest Of The Delta Blues Singers* on Storyville made '64 in Falls Church, Va.

JAMES, Sonny (*b* James Loden, 1 May '29, Hackleburg, Ala.) Pop/country singer, the Southern Gentleman, with no fewer than 23 country no. ones. Made stage debut at 4; toured with Loden Family act playing fiddle and guitar. Served in Korea, signed with Capitol '55 and was renamed Sonny James by prod. Ken Nelson. 'For Rent' '56 made country charts; first country singer to get pop no. 1 with 'Young Love' '57: Tab HUNTER cover was no. 1 longer, but it was a much better song the way Sonny sang it (also no. 1 country). 'First Date, First Kiss, First Love' made no. 25 pop (9 country) same year; he never made the pop top 40 again despite 16 more Hot 100 entries '57-71; he recorded for NRC '60, RCA '61, went back to Capitol and scored 27 country hits '63-71. Cliff RICHARD covered 'The Minute You're Gone' (no. 9 '63); no. 1 hits incl. 'You're The Only World I Know' '64, 'Behind The Tear' '65, 'Take Good Care Of Her' '66, then 16 *consecutive* no. ones '67-71, one of the most remarkable feats in the history of charts. Appeared in low-budget films incl. *Second Fiddle To A Steel Guitar* and *Nashville Rebel* '66, *Las Vegas Hillbillies* and *Hillbilly In A Haunted House* '68. Switched to Columbia '72, continued with hits incl. 'When The Snow Is On The Roses', 'Is It Wrong (For Loving You)', 'Little Band Of Gold', 'Come On In' '72-6. Recorded for Monument '79, Dimension '82, and still at it. LPs incl. *The Minute You're Gone* '63, *My Xmas Dream* '65, *Till The Last Leaf Shall Fall* '66, *Need You* '68, *In Person* '69, *The Sensational* '71, all on Capitol; *When The Snow Is On The Roses* '72, *The Guitars Of Sonny James* '75, *200 Years Of Country Music* '76, *In Person, In Prison* '77, *This Is The Love* '78, all on CBS/Columbia; *I'm Lookin' Over The Rainbow* '82 on Dimension.

JAMES, Tommy, and the Shondells USA pop group originally formed '60 in Niles, Michigan by Tommy James (*b* Thomas Jackson, 29 Apr. '47, Dayton, Ohio). Began as high school hobby; made cover of Raindrops' 'Hanky Panky' (written by BARRY/GREENWICH) for local Snap label, then split up. Pittsburgh DJ turned up a copy '66; his plays created local demand; licensed to Roulette it went to no. 1. James formed new lineup with Ronnie Rosman (*b* 28 Feb. '45, keyboards), Mike Vale (*b* 17 July '49, bass), Joseph Kessler on guitar, Vince Pietropaoli on drums, George Magura on sax; last three soon left replaced by Eddie Gray (*b* 27 Feb. '48) on guitar, Peter Lucia (*b* 2 Feb. '47) on drums. Safe follow-up to 'Hanky Panky' was similarly R&B-inflected 'Say I Am (What I Am)'; it made only no. 21, so Roulette put them in hands of songwriters/producers Bo Gentry and Richie Cordell: result was brilliant bubblegum, banal but successful hook-laden pop aimed at the feet. 14 top 40 hits (incl. first two) '66-70 incl. 'I Think We're Alone Now' (no. 4), 'Mirage' (10), 'Mony

Mony' (3), 'Crimson And Clover' (1), 'Sweet Cherry Wine' (7), 'Crystal Blue Persuasion' (2). 'Hanky Panky' had scraped in at no. 38 in UK; only 'Mony Mony' of other hits scored there, but at No. 1, perhaps because it was heavier, more R&B than other later hits. 'Mony Mony' co-written by James, Gentry, Cordell and Bobby 'Montego Bay' Bloom; at that point group wrested control from Gentry and Cordell; 'Crimson And Clover' epitomised effective later vocal and instrumental layering: single was edited down from LP track over five minutes long. James was ill '70; Shondells split to become unsuccessful Hog Heaven; he worked solo through '70s; 13 Hot 100 entries '70-81 but only three in top 40: 'Draggin' The Line' (no. 7), 'I'm Comin' Home' (40; both '71), 'Three Times In Love' (no. 19 '81, on Millennium label). He covered Gary GLITTER songs (Glitter being his UK heir) while own hits were covered by a variety of styles: Joan Jett had USA no. 7 with 'Crimson And Clover' '82 (followed it with a Glitter song); others covered by Lene Lovich, Rubinoos, Billy IDOL, reggae vocal group the Heptones. Chance discovery by Philadelphia DJ still made waves 20 years later. Shondells *Best Of* on Roulette; James solo LP *Easy To Love* on Millennium.

JAN & DEAN USA pop vocal duo: Jan Berry (*b* 3 Apr. '41), Dean Torrence (*b* 10 Mar. '40), both from L.A. High school friends on sun-kissed West Coast invented surf music along with the BEACH BOYS; had 24 Hot 100 entries '59-66. They attended high school with Nancy SINATRA, Phil SPECTOR, Sandy NELSON, Bruce Johnson (future Beach Boy), Arnie Ginsberg, others; played and sang with some of these; played with recording equipment: Jan, Dean and Arnie made demo of Arnie's song 'Jennie Lee'; Dean went into US Army for six months and the record came out on the Arwin label as by Jan & Arnie: went to no. 8 '58. When Dean came out, Arnie was going into the Navy; Jan and Dean carried on, had hits but also continued with college just in case, Jan studying art, Dean pre-med. 'Baby Talk' was no. 10 '59 on Dore, 'Heart And Soul' no. 25 on Challenge; they were signed by Liberty; 'Linda' was no. 28 '63. Beach Boy Brian Wilson helped them with first LP *Jan & Dean Take Linda Surfin'* and co-wrote

'Surf City' with Jan: after nine mostly minor hits on three labels, 'Surf City' was no. 1 for two weeks '63. Jan did most of Jan & Dean's writing; 10 LPs charted, incl. hits compilation and soundtrack from a FABIAN beach movie *Ride The Wild Surf* '64, written by Jan. 'Drag City' was no. 10, 'Dead Man's Curve' no. 8, 'The Little Old Lady From Pasadena' no. 3 '63-4; they never made the top 10 again. Dean said to have sung lead on the Beach Boys' no. 2 hit 'Barbara Ann' '66. Lifelong friendship was becoming strained when Jan hit a parked truck at 65 mph Apr. '66: three passengers died, he suffered brain damage; it was years before he could remember an entire song lyric. He made demos for Lou ADLER as therapy. Dean made solo LP *Save For A Rainy Day*, formed Kittyhawk graphics studio which designed a great many LP covers. They made abortive comeback '73, occasionally gigged more successfully from '78. TV movie *Dead Man's Curve* '78 is not a bad treatment of the story. Compilations have been on various EMI labels, incl. 2-disc *Legendary Masters No. 3* on Liberty; live *One Summer Night* on Rhino '82, 2-disc *California Gold* on Pair '86.

JAPAN UK 'new romantic' group formed early '70s by brothers David (*b* 23 Feb. '58) and Steve Batt (*b* 1 Dec. '59), both from Beckenham, Kent; adopted names David Sylvian and Steve Jansen. Recruited bassist Mick Karn (*b* 24 July '58), drummer Richard Barbieri (*b* 30 Nov. '57); began performing in earnest '77 with lead guitar Rob Dean. Combined heavy metal flash, infl. of Motown; mixed US covers with David's originals; classically trained Karn was the only real musician in the group, whose make-up, 'glam' image led to resistance in heyday of punk. Signed by Euro label Ariola: album *Adolescent Sex* '79 was rushed LP of wildly varying styles, incl. cover of Barbra STREISAND's 'Don't Rain On My Parade'. Tour with BLUE OYSTER CULT was incongruous but interest in Japan, where single 'The Unconventional' was a hit, was encouraging. *Obscure Alternatives* '79 revealed fascination with trad. Eastern music and music of Erik Satie: instrumental 'The Tenant' stood out. Link with ROXY MUSIC producer John Punter led to *Quiet Life*, criticised for Roxy influence, but it was best

yet, with Karn doubling on sax, incl. cover of VELVET UNDERGROUND's 'All Tomorrow's Parties'. Ex-YARDBIRDS manager Simon Napier-Bell then signed band, moved them to Virgin as live following in UK, Germany, Japan threatened to sell records; *Gentlemen Take Polaroids* '80 seemed not to suffer from band not touring owing to legal wrangling, standout 'Taking Islands In Africa' written by David and Yellow Magic Orchestra keyboardist Ryuichi Sakamoto. Dean left, their synth-oriented sound giving him little scope; later backed Gary NUMAN. Ariola began compilations, cashing in on popularity: *Assemblage* '81 made no. 26 in UK charts and five retrospective singles notched top 40 places '81-3 (biggest was cover of Smokey ROBINSON's 'I Second That Emotion', no. 9 '82). *Ghosts* '81 went gold; most cohesive LP to date had no. 5 hit UK in title track; oriental motif followed in tracks like 'Cantonese Boy' (no. 24 single) and Mao-inspired cover artwork. But individual projects and antipathy between Sylvian and Karn caused split. Karn also a sculptor; channelled energy into this, also sessioning for Numan, Robert PALMER, releasing solo LP *Titles* '82; Sylvian teamed with Sakamoto, for no. 30 hit 'Bamboo Houses' '82, adding vocals to 'Forbidden Colours' from Japanese soundtrack to *Merry Christmas Mr Lawrence* for no. 16 hit '83. Barbieri, unsung hero of band's synth sound, prod. LP for Swedish group Lakejer, composed for Ballet Rambert. Japan ended with live LP/video *Oil On Canvas* '83; Karn has recorded with ULTRAVOX's Midge Ure (single 'After A Fashion' UK no. 39 '83); collaborated with Peter Murphy (Bauhaus) in duo Dali's Car (LP *The Waking Hour*). Barbieri and Jansen worked together: LP *Worlds In A Small Room* '85 released in Japan only; Sylvian issued well-received solo LP *Brilliant Trees* '84, video *Steel Cathedrals*, cassette *Alchemy–An Index Of Possibilities*, 2-disc *Gone To Earth* '86 with Jansen, Barbieri, Robert Fripp, Bill Nelson; *Secrets Of The Beehive* '87 was arr. by Sakamoto. Karn's *Dreams Of Reason Produce Monsters* '87 had Sylvian on 'Buoy', Jansen on drums and co-producing. Japan music was often insubstantial; Sylvian's NEW-AGE style has substantial cult following, *Brilliant Trees* a top 5 album, but no USA chart hits for Japan or Sylvian.

JARMAN, Joseph (*b* 14 Sep. '37, Pine Bluff, Ark.) Reeds, many other instruments; composer. Founder member of the ART ENSEMBLE OF CHICAGO. To Chicago as a child; studied drums under Walter DYETT, reeds in US Army. Founder member of AACM '65. 'Imperfections In A Given Space' '65 performed with John Cage, theatre pieces incl. 'Tribute To The Hard Core' '66, 'Indifferent Piece For Six' '67. Plays on all Art Ensemble records; compositions for that group on record incl. 'Ericka', 'Fanfare For The Warriors', 'Old Time Southside Street Dance', 'Ohnedaruth', many others. Also heard on Lester BOWIE LP *Numbers 1 & 2* '67 (effectively Art Ensemble album), Roscoe MITCHELL LPs *Nonaah* '77, *The Maze* '78, all on Nessa; *Together Alone* '71 on Delmark (duo with Anthony BRAXTON). Own LPs incl. *Song For* '67, *As If It Were The Seasons* '68 on Delmark (among earliest and still exciting work from AACM musicians); solo set *Sunbound* '76 on AECO; 2-disc *Egwu-Anwu (Sunsong)* on India Navigation with Don Moye; *The Magic Triangle* '79 with Moye and Don PULLEN, *Black Paladins* and *Earth Passage* with Moye and others, all on Black Saint; *Inheritance* '83 with Moye, bassist Fred Hopkins, Geri Allen on keyboards, on Japanese Baybridge.

JARREAU, Al (*b* 12 Mar. '40, Milwaukee, Wis.) Singer. Sang at parties, etc. infl. by Johnny MATHIS; became rehabilitation counsellor with master's degree in psychology but kept singing; gigs at clubs in San Francisco led to signing with Reprise and international stardom with versatile voice, style infl. by Nat COLE, Billy ECKSTINE etc. First LP *We Got By* '75 followed by *Glow* '76 (made Billboard top 200); switch to WB for 2-disc live set *Look To The Rainbow* '77 (leaped to top 50), *All Fly Home* '78, *This Time* '80, *Breakin' Away* '81 (no. 9 LP incl. hits with title track and 'We're In This Love Together'), *Jarreau* '83, *High Crime* '84, *Live In London* '85, *L Is For Lover* '86 (prod. by Nile Rodgers). Other LPs: *1965* on Bainbridge, *Jarreau Does Withers* on Allegiance.

JARRETT, Keith (*b* 8 May '45, Allentown, Pa.) Piano, other instruments; composer. From large, musical family; played concert of his own compositions at 16. Worked with Roland KIRK, Art BLAKEY, Charles LLOYD '65-6, Miles DAVIS '70-1. Told Leonard Feather that he had no favourites but admired anyone who was sincere. After working with Davis he turned away from electronic fusion; he recorded with Jack DEJOHNETTE, Gary BURTON, others; until '77 he made his own small-group LPs for Atlantic, Columbia, Impulse, with a remarkably consistent lineup incl. Paul MOTIAN, Charlie HADEN, often Dewey REDMAN; from '71 he made orchestral and solo LPs on ECM. Andy Hamilton in *The Wire* (June '86) wrote that he and Chick COREA 'inherited the Romantic tradition of Bill EVANS and diluted and spent it'. Jarrett seems to need strong collaborators to keep him from a whimsical pretentiousness, and much of his ECM output appeals to fans of new age and space music, but it is hard to speculate that he makes too many records as long as they keep selling. He vocalises as he plays, which irritates some listeners. LPs on Atlantic and its subsidiary, Vortex: *Life Between Exit Signs* '67, *Restoration Ruin* '68 (Jarrett playing several instruments and vocalising, with string quartet dubbed on some tracks), *Somewhere Before* '68 (recorded at Shelly's Manne-Hole, L.A.), *The Mourning Of A Star*, *Birth* and *El Juicio* '71 ('The Judgement' was first of eight Jarrett albums to make Top 200 LPs in USA). Much from '68 remains unissued, incl. an album with vocals and guitar by Scott Jarrett; there were also singles on Vortex, e.g. 'You're Fortunate'/'Sioux City Sue New'; Bob DYLAN songs 'Lay Lady Lay'/'My Back Pages' '68-9. On Impulse: *Fort Yawuh* '73 (at Village Vanguard); *Treasure Island*, *Death And The Flower* and *Backhand* '74; *Mysteries*, *Shades*, *Byablue* charted '76-7; *Bop-Be* '77 did not. Also *Expectations* '72, adding guitarist Sam Brown, AIRTO, horns, strings on Columbia; trio set *NDR Jazz Workshop* '72 on Norddeutscher Rundfunk. Small group sets on ECM: *Ruta + Daytya* '72 (duo album with DeJohnette), *The Survivors Suite* and *Eyes Of The Heart* '76, both with the quartet of Motian, Haden, Redman; *My Song* '77 (charted) and *Nude Ants* '79 with quartet of Garbarek, Palle Danielsson on bass, Jon Christensen, drums; *Standards* (3 vols.) and *Changes* '83-5 with Gary PEACOCK and DeJohnette. With strings on ECM: 2-disc *In The Light*

'73, *Arbour Zena* '75 (with Garbarek, Haden) both charted; *The Celestial Hawk* with the Syracuse Symphony led by Christopher Keene. Composition *Ritual* is played by two pianos (with Dennis Russell Davies). Solo keyboards: 3-disc *Solo Concerts* '73, 2-disc *The Köln Concert* '75 (a steady seller), 2-disc *Staircase/Hourglass/ Sundial/Sand* '76 (charted), 2-disc *Hymns/Spheres* '76 (organ at Ottobeuren Abbey), *Sun Bear Concerts* '76 (a 10-disc set made at concerts in Japan), 2-disc *Invocations/The Moth And The Flame* '79 (plays organ, piano, soprano sax), *G.I. Gurdjieff Sacred Hymns* '80, *Concerts Bregenz* '81 (three discs in all); *Book Of Ways* '87 on ECM is solo clavichord.

JASON AND THE SCORCHERS USA country/rock band formed '81 by Jason Ringenberg (*b* 22 Nov. '59), vocals, guitar; Warner Hodges (*b* 4 June '59), guitar (father was guitarist with Johnny CASH); Perry Baggs (*b* 22 Mar. '62), drums. Ringenberg grew up next to the Rock Island Line; spent formative years in Illinois C&W and bluegrass bands. Signed by EMI America; debut EP *Reckless Country Soul* '82 followed by mini-LP *Fervor* '83, with breakneck cover of Bob DYLAN's 'Absolutely Sweet Marie', Ringenberg's own 'Pray For Me Mama (I'm A Gypsy Now)' and 'Hot Nights In Georgia'. *Lost & Found* '85 was more of the same: frantic reworking of Hank WILLIAMS's 'Lost Highway', Jason's rebel rock on 'Shop It Around', 'Broken Whiskey Glass' etc.; *Still Standing* '86 incl. ROLLING STONES' '19th Nervous Breakdown' with originals such as 'Golden Ball & Chain'. In vanguard of guitar-based '80s USA rock.

JAXON, Frankie (*b* 3 Feb. 1895, Montgomery, Ala.) Blues-styled singer, played piano and sax. Orphaned as a small child; to Kansas City at 10 to go to grammar school; began working in vaudeville there. Aka 'Half-Pint' Jaxon because he was only 5'2" tall. First records in Chicago '27, with Georgia Tom, Tampa Red (*see* Thomas A. DORSEY) '28, others; had own radio show from Chicago World's Fair '33, recorded with his Hot Shots '33; his eclectic blues/jazz/show-biz hokum made him very popular on radio in '30s, performing on several stations in Chicago, other midwestern towns with band as Frankie 'Half-Pint'

Jaxon and his Quarts of Joy. With Harlem Hamfats on Decca '37; then to NYC on Decca with excellent jazz support: Lil ARMSTRONG, Henry 'Red' ALLEN, etc. Wrote several songs, incl. 'Fan It', later recorded by Woody HERMAN. Left music for a government job '41. Sides with Tampa Red on Collectors Item LP *Saturday Night Scrontch*; Decca reissues out of print.

JAY AND THE AMERICANS USA harmony vocal group formed NYC '61. Lead singer John 'Jay' Traynor, ex-Mystics, formed the group with Kenny Vance (*b* 9 Dec. '43), Sandy Deane (*b* Sandy Yaguda, 31 Jan. '40), Marty Sanders (*b* 28 Feb. '41), added ex-mortician Howie Kane (*b* 6 June '42). First of 18 Hot 100 entries on UA was 'She Cried', no. 5 '62, prod. by LEIBER & STOLLER; Traynor left and was replaced by David 'Jay' Black (*b* 2 Nov. '38), who sang lead on subsequent hits: Leiber & Stoller's 'Only In America' made top 40 '63; 'Come A Little Bit Closer' was the biggest hit at no. 3 '64: written by BOYCE & HART, extremely well recorded, prod. by Artie Ripp for Leiber & Stoller with a driving Latin/rock version of the 'baion' beat which was a thread in the pop music of the period (Bobby FREEMAN's 'Do You Wanna Dance' '58, Ritchie VALENS's 'La Bamba' '59, the McCoys 'Hang On Sloopy' '64, others by Marty ROBBINS, the DRIFTERS, etc.), it was one of the year's delightful records. They never did as well again, but carried on through the '60s psychedelic tidal wave with a sort of superior cabaret style: 'Let's Lock The Door', 'Cara, Mia', 'Some Enchanted Evening', 'Sunday And Me', 'Crying' were all top 30 hits '65-6. They organised their own company JATA and scored no. 6 hit with revivals of 'This Magic Moment', certified gold (originally a hit by the Drifters '60) and 'Walkin' In The Rain' (Phil SPECTOR hit by the RONETTES '64). LPs *Come A Little Bit Closer*, *Blockbusters* ('Cara, Mia'), *Greatest Hits*, *Sunday And Me* all charted '64-6; then JATA-prod. *Sands Of Time* and *Wax Museum* '69-70. Walter Becker and Donald Fagen of STEELY DAN were members of their backup group for a while; Black and Vance made solo LPs in the '70s; Black just made the Hot 100 '80 with 'The Part Of Me That Needs You Most' on a Midsong label.

JAZZ Native American art form originated c.1900-05 by black musicians, chiefly in New Orleans, La., characterised by improvisation and self-expression through the music: the performer is a composer and a troubador. It was also spelled 'jass'; some think the word came from the French *jaser* (to talk, perhaps indiscreetly); attempts to trace the word back to Africa have been inconclusive. It was used in print as early as '09 in reference to dancing, in '13 about US Army musicians 'trained on ragtime and "jazz" ' (Oxford English Dictionary Supplement). Clarence WILLIAMS claimed to be first to use the word on sheet music c.'15, describing 'Brown Skin, Who You For?' as 'Jazz Song': 'I don't exactly remember where the words came from, but I heard a lady say it to me when we were playin' some music. "Oh, jazz me, Baby," she said.' It certainly had sexual connotation: USA slang for male seminal emission is 'jism' or 'jizz'; song titles such as 'Jazz Me Blues', 'Jazzin' Babies Blues' were common. Jazz conquered the world and remains at the root of 20th-century popular music; it has evolved, as any art form will, encountering resistance every step of the way, but it is not true that it was not taken seriously in the USA: James Lincoln Collier has uncovered hundreds of serious articles on the subject published there in the '20s. Great black jazzmen did not get the recognition or the money they deserved because of racism, but jazz was never suppressed commercially: white businessmen hired the great black practitioners to play for enthusiastic white audiences from the beginning, while theories to the contrary were cooked up by the American left, which tried to co-opt jazz (as it did folk music) as a music of the oppressed for political reasons; more recently, broadcasting in the USA was turned over entirely to accountants who are interested only in easy money: the pop charts and radio 'play lists' stimulate each other, many Americans never hear any jazz, yet it remains popular around the world. The word has been used to describe any jazz-infl. popular music, from Paul WHITEMAN as the 'King of Jazz' to the 'jazz rock' or 'jazz funk' of recent times, and now has so many derogatory connotations that many young musicians today will not use it. There have been countless fine white jazz musicians,

particularly among Italians and Jews, but the great innovators (advancing the music's stylistic frontier) have all been black. Jazz was quickly played all over America, but New Orleans was the most important incubator because of its location; Afro-Americans retained an astonishing degree of African heritage for 300 years (because slaves could not take part in American culture), while Louisiana slave-owners were French-speaking Catholics rather than Anglo-Saxon Protestants, and didn't forbid slaves to play music and dance as strictly as others did. The early development of jazz was probably similar to that of the BLUES, incl. the call-and-response patterns of work songs, and 'blue' notes (not found in the diatonic scale, but replacing the third and the seventh notes of that scale); these and other elements such as improvisation, polyphony, and an attitude towards making music as a social activity are still ubiquitous in African traditional music. As a seaport New Orleans was host to musical influences from all over the Caribbean, incl. Irish and Spanish 'tinges'; blacks entertained whites, so that Tin Pan Alley's popular songs of the day were thrown into the stew; RAGTIME, a formal music but emphasising syncopation, was a final ingredient. At the end of the Spanish-American war army units from Cuba were demobbed in New Orleans; second-hand brass instruments could be had at prices even poor people could afford: every town in the USA had a local brass band, but New Orleans had them in every neighbourhood. Influence was two-way: the self-taught wanted to learn to play 'straight', while musicians in marching and concert bands were proud of their ability to read and to play either straight or 'ragtime', using crying tones, slurred notes, etc. (the early 'Fidgety Feet' was a syncopated march). Pre-WWI New Orleans was relatively easy-going; whites, mixed-race peoples and blacks got along (though there was hierarchy of colour, mulattoes having pretensions and blacks always the poorest); alderman Joseph Story set aside a neighbourhood for brothels and gambling in 1897, hence the District, or Storyville; during WWI Storyville was closed by order of the US Navy. Though chiefly pianists had worked there, while bands played mostly at picnics, funerals, in the street etc., musicians had worked on riverboats and closure accelerated emigration to the West Coast and especially up the Mississippi to Chicago, thence to NYC. Pianist/vocalist Tony Jackson (*b* 5 June 1876; *d* 20 Apr. '21, Chicago; wrote 'Pretty Baby') and cornettists Buddy BOLDEN, who never recorded, and Freddie KEPPARD, who recorded very little, were among the first players of jazz; Jelly Roll MORTON claimed to have invented it in 1902. Alan Philip Jaffe (*b* '36, *d* 9 Mar. '87) established Preservation Hall early '60s as venue for New Orleans old-timers; Kid Thomas Valentine (*d* 16 June '87 aged 91) was one of the last. Early jazz history was confused by the fact that first jazz records (made Feb. '17 in NYC) were by the ORIGINAL DIXIELAND JAZZ BAND, white men from New Orleans who had adopted the style. Spikes' Seven Pods Of Pepper, with Kid ORY, cornettist Thomas 'Papa Mutt' Carey (*b* 1891, Hahnville, La.; *d* 3 Sep. '48, Elsinore, Cal.), recorded in L.A. '22, but the New Orleans style was captured by King OLIVER and his Creole Jazz Band '23-4: 24 sides and two alternate takes were made in Chicago and Richmond, Ind. by classic New Orleans lineup with lead cornet (Louis ARMSTRONG on second cornet), clarinet, trombone, piano, banjo, drums: the 'front line' played a collective improvisation, with everybody listening to everybody else: an improvised counterpoint. The acoustic recording process restricted Baby DODDS to woodblocks instead of his drum kit and the records sound dim now, but they preserved the style in the nick of time. Morton made piano solos '23; the Red Onion Jazz Babies recorded '24: quintet with Armstrong, reedmen William 'Buster' Bailey (*b* 19 July '02, Memphis, Tenn.; *d* 12 Apr. '67, Brooklyn) and Sidney BECHET (with Armstrong, Oliver and Morton one of the greatest of all New Orleans musicians), with vocals by Alberta HUNTER, probably the best example we have of how the bands played in the bars and dance halls of New Orleans; Clarence Williams' Blue Five '23 made similar classics with his wife Eva Taylor singing, Armstrong, Bechet, Charlie Irvis on trombone, Williams instead of Lil ARMSTRONG on piano. Louis began his series of Hot Fives and Hot Sevens with electrical recording process '25, instantly setting soloists free from the strictures of the classic style, be-

coming the first and still one of the greatest soloists in recording history: music was permanently changed as musicians all over the country heard these records. Young white players imitated black heroes Jimmie NOONE, Oliver, Armstrong, invented free-wheeling small group 'Chicago style', solos between ensemble passages; they incl. the Austin High Gang, so-called because some attended Austin High School (Frank TESCHEMACHER, Jimmy and Dick McPARTLAND, Bud FREEMAN); also Eddie CONDON, Red McKENZIE, Joe SULLIVAN, Gene KRUPA, Benny GOODMAN, etc.; the style was documented on records as early as '27 by McKenzie And Condon's Chicagoans, others; the Friar's Society Orchestra became the New Orleans Rhythm Kings, began recording '22; this white group incl. at various times Wingy MANONE, Muggsy SPANIER, clarinettists Leon Ropollo (*b* 16 Mar. '02, La.; *d* there 14 Oct. '43), Eddie Miller (later with Bob CROSBY); George Brunis on trombone (later with Spanier's Ragtimers); drummer Ben POLLACK; Morton recorded with them '23, making it perhaps the earliest interracial group. Armstrong was a Chicago cabaret star in the late '20s; Morton recorded there with his Red Hot Peppers; the black popular culture scene, then close to the Loop, is affectionately described in Dempsey J. Travis's *An Autobiography Of Black Jazz* '83. Bix BEIDERBECKE first recorded '24; his pure, beautiful tone had almost as great an infl. as Armstrong. Morton and Oliver went to NYC in the late '20s and made beautiful records, but their style was already considered old-fashioned; the move was the beginning of their decline. Williams was one of the first New Orleans musicians to infl. music in NYC, where Luckey ROBERTS, James P. JOHNSON, Fats WALLER, Willie 'The Lion' SMITH played 'stride' piano, a two-fisted style built on ragtime emphasising tenths in the bass, while Fletcher HENDERSON with Don REDMAN (inspired by Armstrong's brief stay in the band) and Duke ELLINGTON (similarly inspired by gigs with Bechet, later by the Oliver-inspired trumpet of Bubber MILEY) began to invent jazz composition for larger groups leading to the BIG BAND ERA, touched off in '35 by the sudden success of Goodman playing Henderson's arrangements: for 15 years a jazz-based style dominated big-time popular music for the only period in the history of jazz. Meanwhile, territory bands played all over the country: Troy Floyd's 11-piece band played the Plaza Hotel in San Antonio, Texas, incl. Herschel Evans (*see* Count BASIE), one of dozens of fine tenors to come from Texas; Roy Johnson and his Happy Pals incl. Jack TEAGARDEN at one time, as did Peck's Bad Boys in Texas (*see* Peck KELLEY); the band of Alphonso Trent (*b* 24 Aug. '05, Arkansas; *d* there 14 Oct. '59) incl. Jeter-Pillars (later bandleaders), Stuff SMITH, Harry EDISON, etc.; Jimmy BLANTON, Charlie CHRISTIAN scuffled in the provinces; McKINNEY'S COTTON PICKERS out of Detroit (led by Redman) made many fine records; the Blue Devils, led by Walter PAGE, melded into the most prolific of territory bands, that of Bennie MOTEN, whose 'Western swing' was admired in the East (while jazz also infl. a style of big band country music, also called WESTERN SWING). At the height of the Swing Era (as the Big Band Era was also called) the hothouse of KANSAS CITY JAZZ exploded: Basie inherited the Moten band, came East with a looser, powerfully swinging blues-based big-band style re-injecting some basic values, its rhythm section completing the smoothing out of New Orleans 2/4 into 4/4, paving the way for later developments. Blues piano (BOOGIE WOOGIE) was a fad '40s. Coleman HAWKINS in Henderson's band had invented the tenor saxophone as a jazz instrument, with Ben WEBSTER his principal acolyte; Basie's Lester YOUNG presented an alternative, playing a higher, lighter, 'cooler' sound, as though on alto; Billie HOLIDAY was Young's vocal partner, lyrical, deceptively laconic, the greatest of all jazz singers. The K.C. band of Jay McSHANN incl. Charlie PARKER; he gathered with Dizzy GILLESPIE, Thelonious MONK, Kenny CLARKE, Max ROACH, Bud POWELL and others in NYC and as the Swing Era began to decay a new generation of black artists created BOP '40-5, the most controversial development of all. The big band style passed into repertory, along with the New Orleans style, as latter was being re-created by the revival movement in the early '40s, most prominently on the West Coast by Lu WATTERS, Bob SCOBEY, etc. The legendary Bunk JOHNSON was redis-

covered and recorded, past his prime; through the '50s middle-aged white men (and remnants of the Chicago school incl. many fine players) played neo-New Orleans DIXIELAND; the DUKES OF DIXIELAND, a second-rate band in New Orleans, sold a lot of records. There were many 'moldy figs' who never accepted big band music as jazz; bop gave them apoplexy: it was a commercial disaster (despite the personal popularity of Gillespie) and jazz had a lower profile in the '50s than at any other time in its history, but bop was an exciting and necessary step towards freedom for a new generation of artists. It cooled off into 'modern' or 'progressive' jazz; the 'cool' progressive school was largely West Coast and white: reedman Dave Pell (*b* 26 Feb. '25, Brooklyn) formed an octet '55 out of the Les BROWN band; Pell's music was so cool and white it was washed out, but he was frank about playing 'mortgage-paying music'; Dave BRUBECK was considerably more interesting at the time, the most commercially successful jazzman of the '50s by a long way. Great records were made by Gerry MULLIGAN, Chet BAKER, Lee KONITZ, Art PEPPER and others, who stayed the course to become giants in their own right, while the underrated West Coast black scene incl. Elmo HOPE, Carl PERKINS, Curtis COUNCE, Hampton HAWES, many others (*Jazz West Coast* '86 by Robert Gordon is good on this era). Among other white musicians of '50s, Lennie TRISTANO, Red RODNEY, Stan GETZ, Zoot SIMS, Warne MARSH, many others have been consistently admired. The Blue Note and Prestige labels carried the can '50s, recorded many 'blowing sessions': the tenor sax was king as Sonny ROLLINS, Johnny GRIFFIN, Hank MOBLEY, Sonny STITT, Tina BROOKS, John COLTRANE, Gene AMMONS and Dexter GORDON held sway, taking up where John HARDEE and Ike QUEBEC had left off in the late '40s (though Quebec came back with a series of beautiful LPs '60s). The arranger/composer again came to the fore, Ellington still the godfather; Monk was shamefully neglected; Tadd DAMERON, Gil FULLER, Gil EVANS, George RUSSELL, Mal WALDRON contributed beauty. The distinctive, volatile genius of Charles MINGUS shaped many fine musicians, incl. Eric DOLPHY; Art BLAKEY's Jazz Messengers turned out scores of stars, set the pace for Blue Note, whose output became more and more funky (giving rise to modern terms jazz-funk, disco-funk etc.; *see* FUNK). Miles Davis's Quintet '54-6 incl. Coltrane and followed modal trail blazed by Russell's textbook; Coltrane's quartet formed '60 became the infl. group of the new decade, while Ornette COLEMAN led the way to 'free jazz': the new avant-garde in black music incl. Albert AYLER, Charles LLOYD, Pharoah SANDERS, Archie SHEPP, Bill DIXON, Cecil TAYLOR, SUN RA: despite the dominance of rock in the '60s, it was once again hip to buy jazz records. ESP Disc in NYC, formed by lawyer Bernard Stollman, recorded some of the newest music from '64. The 'October Revolution' was a series of concerts at NYC's Cellar Café '64; Dixon formed the Jazz Composers Guild with Carla and Paul BLEY, others; it failed, but led to JCOA (Jazz Composers Orchestra Association), formed by Carla and Mike Mantler for publishing and recording, beginning with 2-disc *JCOA* '68 of Mantler's music played by a large orchestra with Taylor, Sanders, Don CHERRY, Roswell RUDD, Steve LACY, many others; continuing with albums by Bley, Cherry, Charlie HADEN, etc. Chicago again became a hive of seminal activity: local tenors Fred ANDERSON and Von FREEMAN had remained faithful to themselves for little commercial reward, but AACM was formed '66 and guru Richard ABRAMS inspired the ART ENSEMBLE OF CHICAGO, many others: musicians took charge of their music, found their own venues, put out their own records and took the music back to the community whence it came. Frank LOWE, Charles TYLER, Leo SMITH, Julius HEMPHILL, Bobby BRADFORD, Anthony BRAXTON are a few of the composer/leaders coming to the fore in the '70s. The Jazz & People's Movement interrupted taping of the Merv Griffin, Dick Cavett and Johnny Carson talk shows in NYC late '70 (thus hitting all three networks) to ask why more black music was not heard on TV; an all-star group led by Roland KIRK appeared on the Ed Sullivan show partly as a result (Kirk asked Sullivan why he never had Coltrane on his show; Sullivan asked, 'Does John Coltrane have any records out?'). The new music was often called 'free jazz', but it is of course not 'free' at all; experiments of the

'60s that tried to do away entirely with form fell by the wayside and structure became another tool in the composer's kit: bop had changed the rhythmic nature of jazz, but still tied players to a number of beats in a measure; classic New Orleans jazz hadn't subscribed to European harmony, but the boppers tied themselves to chord structures; now free jazz (or 'improvised music' or just 'the music') liberated harmony and rhythm and recovered collective improvisation. The celebratory Wildflowers Festival NYC '76 resulted in five albums on Douglas prod. by Michael CUSCUNA, with contributions from Leo Smith, Braxton, Hemphill, Hamiet BLUIETT, Randy WESTON, Sam RIVERS, Jimmy LYONS, Andrew CYRILLE, AIR, Sunny MURRAY, several others. Many younger players today could be described as revivalists, in the same way that Brahms was technically a 'classical' composer: because they are not extending the forms; after the furious innovation of the '60s-70s, jazz is more a repertory music than ever, as musicians concentrate on writing and playing their best, refusing to follow trends or accept labels: Sun Ra's Arkestra is apt to break out with Henderson's 'Big John Special' in concert; the Art Ensemble act incl. elements of New Orleans street bands, much else; the DIRTY DOZEN BRASS BAND updates the style of the New Orleans front line; Scott HAMILTON plays tenor in the style of the soloists of the Swing Era; Bobby WATSON, Wynton and Branford MARSALIS, Terence BLANCHARD and Donald HARRISON are among the latest grads of Blakey's academy; drummer Keith COPELAND, leader, reedman and composer Chico FREEMAN (Von's son), guitarist Rory STUART are among the younger musicians who can play 'inside' or 'outside'. On the frontier, Chicago's venerable Hal RUSSELL and his young white NRG Ensemble play sharp, biting and witty music; reedmen David MURRAY, John CARTER, Henry THREADGILL lead exciting ensembles. Ironically, as the word falls into disuse among musicians jazz is more an international music than it was in earlier decades, when eclecticism was too self-conscious: in the UK Courtney PINE, Philip Bent, Steve Williamson and Andy Sheppard are talented new players, while the big white band LOOSE TUBES are first-class musicians, entertaining themselves as well as listeners; Bill Ashton's National Youth Jazz Orchestra finds young players of amazing virtuosity; the Vienna Art Orchestra of Mathias RÜEGG, the Willem Breuker Kollektief in Amsterdam and the USSR's GANELIN Trio blaze their own trails. Veterans still swing: Bud Freeman, Illinois JACQUET, Doc CHEATHAM, Eddie JOHNSON, many others. The studied Romanticism of NEW AGE music is sometimes jazz-influenced; neither this nor jazz-rock FUSION is accepted by diehard critics and fans of the real thing, despite commercial success of scores of LPs by Keith JARRETT, Larry CORYELL, Chick COREA (especially Return To Forever), WEATHER REPORT etc.; others taking it up incl. Barbara THOMPSON, Bill BRUFORD and Bill LASWELL. Something may come of fusion yet if it learns to rely on musical values instead of electronics and leftover pop licks, but *Billboard* decided '88 to have separate albums chart for fusion and the real stuff. Commercial jazz 'revivals' come and go; the music of Spyro Gyra, Chuck MANGIONE, Lee RITENOUR, Grover WASHINGTON Jr etc. is easy-listening music, alcohol-free beer compared to Czech Pilsner, and there's nothing wrong with that, but there are more real jazz records available now than ever (new and reissued), new jazz labels emerging in each decade (Nessa, ECM, Concord Jazz, Hep, Cadence, Blackhawk, Finesse, Discovery, Criss Cross, etc.) while major labels chase elusive customers in the rock arena. The jazz bibliography is huge: the Belgian Hugues Panassié wrote *Le Jazz Hot* '34, devoting too much space to white jazzmen; in *The Real Jazz* '42 he corrected himself, but with the advent of bop he split with long-time collaborator Charles Delaunay and stayed in the New Orleans camp: Europe had its mouldy figs, too. In the USA R. D. Darrell was reviewing jazz records in the '20s; *New Yorker* critic Winthrop Sargeant's *Jazz: Hot And Hybrid*, journalist Wilder Hobson's *American Jazz Music* were the first American books in the late '30s; Otis Ferguson wrote in *The New Republic* '36-41; the floodgates have been open ever since. Gunther Schuller's *Early Jazz* '68 is scholarly, unsurpassed; James Lincoln Collier's *The Making Of Jazz* '78 is a solid readable history, succeeding work by Marshall Stearns,

Barry Ulanov; Joachim Berendt's *The Jazz Book* '84 (latest edition) has a musician's understanding of the music; *Hear Me Talkin' To Ya* '55 is 'The story of jazz as told by the men who made it', compiled by Nat Hentoff, Nat Shapiro; Ira Gitler's similar oral history *Swing To Bop* '85 and *Jazz Masters Of The 40s* '66 are excellent on that era; *The World Of Duke Ellington* '70, *The World Of Swing* '74, *The World Of Earl Hines* '77, *The World Of Count Basie* '80 are oral histories compiled by Stanley Dance. Ross Russell's *Jazz Style In Kansas City And The Southwest* '71 is unique and valuable. A. B. Spellman's *Black Music: Four Lives* '66 is an early classic on the avant-garde; Valerie Wilmer's *As Serious As Your Life* '77 is full of detail and John Litweiler's *The Freedom Principle* '84 is full of love, sending the reader to the record shelf. Books, articles, sleeve notes by Martin Williams, Gary Giddins or Chicago journalist J. B. Figi will repay study. *New Yorker* critic Whitney Balliett defined jazz as 'the sound of surprise'; his *American Musicians: 56 Portraits In Jazz* '86 collects valuable profiles, most incl. interviews and anecdotes. CADENCE magazine carries long interviews with contemporary musicians; *Jazzletter* published by lyricist/journalist Gene LEES is more mainstream, relating jazz to the wider popular music of which it is the backbone. *See also* BOP, BIG BAND ERA, KANSAS CITY JAZZ, SWING IN MUSIC.

JEFFERSON AIRPLANE, STARSHIP Rock band formed '65 in San Francisco by vocalist Marty Balin (b Martyn Buchwald, 30 Jan. '43, Cincinnati, Ohio), who took over a club, renamed it the Matrix with Airplane as house band, lineup incl. lead guitarist/vocalist Jorma Kaukonen (b 23 Dec. '40, Washington), guitarist/vocalist Paul Kantner (b 12 Mar. '42, S.F.), vocalist Signe Toly Anderson, Jerry Peloquin on drums, Bob Harvey on upright bass, last two replaced by Skip Spence and Jack Casady (b 13 Apr. '44, Washington) before first records were produced: single 'It's No Secret'/'Runnin' Round This World', lacklustre LP *Jefferson Airplane Takes Off*. An early champion was Ralph J. Gleason, *San Francisco Chronicle* critic who later wrote *Jefferson Airplane And The San Francisco Sound*; the band was heavily infl. by folk and blues at first but became with the GRATEFUL DEAD and the QUICKSILVER MESSENGER SERVICE (after the earlier CHARLATANS), part of the city's musical triumvirate of acid rock, also sparking off an explosion of new bands, partly due to RCA's then-unprecedented advance of $20,000 on signing them. Meanwhile the Great Society was also formed, inspired by the Airplane and performing at the Matrix, with vocalist Grace Slick (*b* Grace Wing, 30 Oct. '39, Chicago), her then-husband Jerry Slick on drums, brother-in-law Darby Slick on lead guitar, rhythm guitarist David Minor and drummer Peter Vandergilder; they made single 'Somebody To Love'/'Free Advice' (latter written by John Philips) for North Beach label owned by KSAN DJ Tom Donahue, both sides incl. in compilations *The Autumn Records Story* '85 and *Nuggets Volume Seven: The San Francisco Story* '86 on Rhino. Producer Sylvester STEWART (aka SLY STONE) allegedly stormed out of the studio after they required 50 takes for the A side; LPs later on Columbia *Conspicuous Only In Its Absence* and *How It Was* were taped at the Matrix. In late '66 Spence left Airplane, joined MOBY GRAPE and released solo *Oar* on Columbia, replaced in the Airplane by Spencer Dryden (*b* 7 Apr. '43, NYC); Anderson left on maternity leave which turned out to be permanent, replaced by Slick, who was and is one of the best singers in the genre, bringing 'Somebody To Love' and 'White Rabbit' from Great Society repertoire: versions by the Airplane both made top 10 '67, helping LP *Surrealistic Pillow* to no. 3: UK edition foolishly mixed tracks from first two albums; proper USA edition incl. several good songs by Balin, whose infl. was less pronounced on *After Bathing At Baxter's* '67, following criticism of his lyrics within the group; *Baxter* did less well and they took more care over *Crown Of Creation* '68, which reached no. 6 in Billboard LP chart without any hit: they had no more top 40 hits; they were a delicately poised act which easily went off kilter, but sold albums and were rivalled only by the Dead as a USA live attraction among S.F. acts (many of which never broke through). They sparred with RCA over lyrics ('fantastic trips' in 'White Rabbit' was thought to refer to drugs; the word 'shit' was deleted from

Baxter's lyric sheet) but *Crown* incl. David Crosby's song 'Triad', a tail of troilism (rejected by the BYRDS but later incl. in CSN&Y's *Four Way Street*), also Slick's acerbic 'Greasy Heart' and surreal 'Lather'; title track was Kantner's first science fiction epic, quoting from John Wyndham's *The Chrysalids*. (They felt free to quote: Slick's 'Rejoice' harked back to James Joyce's *Ulysses*; Dryden's 'A Small Packet Of Value Will Come To You Shortly' quoted Thelonious MONK's 'Blue Monk'.) They appeared in D. A. Pennebaker film *Monterey Pop* (inept editing had Slick on camera during Balin's lead vocal on 'Today'); they toured Europe '68, played at Woodstock and Altamont '69; Beat poet Lawrence Ferlinghetti referred to them in ode to Richard Nixon *Tyrannus Nix* and they appeared in Jean-Luc Godard's unfinished film *One AM (One American Movie)* '69. *Bless Its Pointed Little Head* '69 was a live LP; *Volunteers* '69 incl. the pastoral 'Meadowlands', 'Wooden Ships' (written by Kantner, Crosby and Stephen Stills, later incl. in *Crosby, Stills & Nash*), also 'We Can Be Together' with line 'Up against the wall, motherfuckers' (lyric sheet emasculated). *The Worst Of Jefferson Airplane* compiled on RCA '70; they formed own Grunt label, personnel changes began: Dryden left '70 to join Riders of the Purple Sage, replaced by Joe E. Covington, later by ex-TURTLE John Barbata; Balin left '71, prod. band Grootna, sang with bar band Bodacious D.F. (RCA LP '73), went solo (LPs on EMI-America '80-1 incl. his stage show *Rock Justice*). Casady and Kaukonen performed separately as Hot Tuna, often opened at Airplane gigs; electric violinist Papa John Creach (*b* 28 May '17, Beaver Falls, Pa.) began playing with both Airplane and Tuna. Airplane's *Bark* '71 was followed by last studio album *Long John Silver* '72, with more lyrical problems and a sleeve that folded out to make a stash box. Ex-Quicksilver vocalist/bassist David Freiberg joined mid-'72, but Casady and Kaukonen left to make Hot Tuna full time: after eight top 20 LPs, live *Thirty Seconds Over Winterland* '73 reached only no. 52; *Early Flight* '74 compiled obscure tracks, did not make top 100 LPs; *Flight Log* was 2-disc anthology. Grunt also issued Hot Tuna LPs, solo sets: Kantner's *Blows Against The*

605

Empire '70, Slick and Kantner's *Sunfighter* '71, Kaukonen's *Black Kangaroo* '72, Slick, Kantner & Freiberg's *Baron Von Tollbooth And The Chrome Nun* '73, *Your Heart Is My Heart* by Joe E. Covington's Fat Fandango '73, Slick's *Manhole* '74. *2400 Fulton Street* '87 was a good compilation, the CD edition with 11 extra tracks incl. such ephemera as their radio advert for Levi jeans; that year also saw 'White Rabbit' used in soundtrack of Vietnam war film *Platoon*. Meanwhile Airplane survivors formed Jefferson Starship '74, abbreviated to Starship '85: first lineup incl. Slick, Kantner, Kaukonen, Barbata, Creach, Freiberg, Craig Chaquico on lead guitar (from Steelwind, also a Grunt band); Kaukonen soon replaced by multi-instrumentalist Peter Sears. Seeds had been sown in Kantner's *Blows Against The Empire*, coeval side-projects with Hot Tuna; first Starship LP *Dragonfly* '74 went gold, by which time Balin had joined; his 'Miracles' helped *Red Octopus* '75 to reach no. 1 on four separate occasions, staying in charts 50 weeks; *Spitfire* '76 also reached the top; *Earth* '78 was top 10, the year Slick left after a riot at Lorelei Festival in Germany did over $1m worth of damage, sparked by their refusal to go on stage. *Gold* was a best-of followed by *Freedom At Point Zero* '79, *Modern Times* '80, *Winds Of Change* '82 and *Nuclear Furniture* '84; these marked recruitment of vocalist Mickey Thomas (solo LP *Alive Alone* on Elektra); Aynsley DUNBAR joined on drums (singled out for his 'nice hot licks' in playwright Sam Shepard's *The Tooth Of Crime* '74); Kantner released solo *Planet Earth Rock And Roll Orchestra* '83, an ill-starred attempt to recapture SF spirit of *Blows Against The Empire*. Songs from band's earlier incarnations were carried over; *Jefferson Starship* video '83 incl. 'Somebody To Love' and 'White Rabbit'. They became more commercial and personnel changes occurred over the years incl. Kantner's departure and Slick's rejoining; Kantner formed KBC Band with Balin and Casady (*KBC Band* '86 on Arista); Starship contributed to soundtrack of film *Youngblood* '85. *Knee Deep In Hoopla* '86 was made by Slick, Thomas, Sears, Chaquico and Donny Baldwin on drums, incl. chart hits 'We Built This City' and 'Sara', made effective use of MTV-type video; *Video Hoopla* '86 incl.

these hits and 'Tomorrow Doesn't Matter Tonight'. Sears left before major international success of *No Protection* '87 on BMG Records, with UK no. 1 single 'Nothing's Gonna Stop Us Now' (from film *Mannequin*) helped by a video. Alone with the Grateful Dead they have survived 20 years, but last original member, Slick, left '88.

JEFFERSON, Blind Lemon (*b* July 1897, Couchman, Texas; *d* probably Dec. '29) Blues singer, songwriter, guitarist. Born blind and worked as singing beggar, teamed at one time with LEADBELLY. He was one of the first and finest to codify the blues by recording it, and was probably the biggest selling artist in the genre in his lifetime, thought to have infl. everyone who subsequently sang the blues, incl. Louis ARMSTRONG. Thought to have died in Chicago of exposure in a snowstorm, possibly after suffering a heart attack; buried in Texas; a grave marker was dedicated in '67. First records late '25 or early '26, religious songs under the name of Deacon L. J. Bates; made about 100 sides, nearly all for Paramount. Wrote many songs: best known 'Black Snake Blues', 'Pneumonia Blues', 'See That My Grave Is Kept Clean'. Compilations incl. 2-disc sets *Blind Lemon Jefferson* and *Immortal*, single LP *Black Snake Moan* on Milestone; *1926-29* and *Master Of Blues* on Biograph.

JEFFERSON, Eddie (*b* Edgar Jefferson, 3 Aug. '18, Pittsburgh; *d* 9 May '79, Detroit) Singer, lyricist. Originated the technique of writing lyrics to jazz solos, later a commercial success for John Lambert, Hendricks & Ross. Jefferson recorded for Hi-Lo '51; with James MOODY '53 as vocalist/manager, wrote lyrics for Moody's solo on 'I'm In The Mood For Love', but King Pleasure had written his own (*b* Clarence Beeks, 24 Mar. '22, Oakdale, Tenn.; won amateur night at the Apollo '51, had no. 5 R&B hit with 'Moody's Mood For Love' '52, no. 3 hit 'Red Top' '53, faded from charts). Jefferson was a tap dancer '67-8, rejoined Moody '68-73, formed group Artistic Truth with Roy Brooks '74-5. He was shotgunned to death in the street outside a club after an opening engagement. Recorded with Moody; own LPs *Body And Soul*, *Come Along With Me* on Prestige, *Charlie Parker Memorial* on Chess;

Things Are Getting Better, then *Still On The Planet* '76 with Richie Cole, both on Muse; *Jazz Singer* (tracks from '59-61) and *Main Man* '77 on Inner City.

JEFFREYS, Garland (*b* '44, NYC) Singer with black, white, Hispanic ancestry. Grew up in Brooklyn, studied art in Europe before deciding on music as career. Had sung solo in Brooklyn clubs since '64, later with small-time bands: LP *Grinder's Switch With Garland Jeffreys* '69 after linking with band called Ravens from Buffalo, changing their name. Signed as solo for Atlantic, released eponymous debut LP '73, same year recorded 'Wild In The Streets', applauded by critics as US equivalent of ROLLING STONES' 'Street Fighting Man', but no commercial success. Briefly signed with Arista who saw him as a disco artist, soon left. LPs on A&M failed to sell in sufficient quantities, all mixing romance with social issues, featuring cream of USA session players incl. Dr John (Mac REBENNACK): *Ghost Writer* '77 (with 'Why-O', about bussing in Boston), *One-Eyed Jack* '78, *American Boy And Girl* '79 (with 'ethnic' couple on sleeve). Toured in a truck with band, no record deal; also in Europe, where sales were better, audiences were less blinkered. Single 'Matador' top 10 in many countries. *Escape Artist* '81 on Epic incl. 'Miami Beach' on racial strife, reggae tracks made with Dennis 'Blackbeard' Bovell in London and featuring Linton Kwesi Johnson and Big Youth. Chose the Rumour, Graham Parker's backing band, as being the one best able to carry off rock/R&B/soul/reggae mix live, toured with them and recorded *Rock'n'Roll Adult* '82. *Guts For Love* '83 was sixth LP to chart in USA, but only two in top 100 LPs, none higher than no. 59 (*Escape Artist*); he is a neglected writer/performer because he does not fit into any convenient pigeonholes in American music.

JENKINS, Gordon (*b* 12 May '10, Webster Groves, Mo.; *d* 1 May '84) Composer, arranger, conductor. Worked in radio as a multi-instrumentalist, then wrote arr. for Isham JONES, Benny GOODMAN, Vincent Lopez, Lennie HAYTON, Andre KOSTELANETZ, many others; wrote 'P.S. I Love You', 'When A Woman Loves A Man' '34, Goodman's closing theme 'Goodbye' '35,

many more. Conducted *The Show Is On* '35 on Broadway; worked for Paramount Pictures, then NBC network in Hollywood '38-44, for Dick HAYMES on radio '44-8, signed with Decca '45 and eventually became managing director. 9 top 10 hits '48-51 incl. 'Maybe You'll Be There' with vocalist Charles La Vere, 'Don't Cry Joe (Let Her Go, Let Her Go, Let Her Go)', 'Bewitched'. He spotted the WEAVERS in the Village Vanguard early '50; then-boss Dave Kapp didn't like them because a folk quartet didn't fit into any of his categories, but Jenkins got them a recording session, made one of the biggest singles Decca had: 'Goodnight Irene'/'Tzena, Tzena, Tzena' as 'Gordon Jenkins and the Weavers', his arr. for orchestra sympathetic, not as unlikely as it might have been. He accompanied many other artists on big hits, incl. Haymes, Louis ARMSTRONG, the ANDREWS SISTERS. Chart LPs were *Seven Dreams* '54 on Decca, *Manhattan Tower* '56 on Capitol: written '45, this was an ambitious attempt at a kind of high-class mood music suite. He conducted for Judy GARLAND in London '57; arr./conducted for Nat COLE on Capitol, 'Stardust' and 'When I Fall In Love' among his finest work; for Frank Sinatra on Reprise incl. *All Alone* '62, *September Of My Years* '67 (won Grammy), many tracks on others.

JENNINGS, Frank (*b* 12 Feb. '44, Hammersmith, London) UK country singer with pronounced American style, with his band Syndicate one of the most popular acts on the UK country scene. Formed first group Country Syndicate in Reading '68, turned full-time pro '72, won TV's *Opportunity Knocks* and signed to EMI '75, recorded in Nashville '76-7. Of Anglo-Irish background, he successfully blended Faron YOUNG-Mel TILLIS sounds with his own, featuring steel guitarist Barry Smith (with him since '68), fiddle, keyboards and guitar. Hits incl. 'Heaven Is My Woman's Love', 'Me And My Guitar', 'Woman In The Back Of My Mind'. Own TV series *Ponderosa Country* '79-80 on BBC South; appeared regularly on *Pebble Mill At One*, *Crackerjack*, BBC radio. LPs incl. *Heaven Is My Woman's Love* '76, *Ponderosa Country* '78, *Me And My Guitar* '79, *Country Collection* '80 (on Champ).

JENNINGS, Waylon (*b* 15 June '37, Littlefield, Texas) Country-rock singer, songwriter. With well over 50 albums and having changed the nature of the country music business in the outlaw movement of the '70s, he is a living legend. Began as DJ in Lubbock, Texas, where he met Buddy HOLLY, joining his group on bass '58; was nearly on Holly's last flight, but had taken the bus. Back to DJ work; met Herb ALPERT, signed with him as solo act; early years in Nashville incl. work with Bobby BARE, Chet ATKINS, Johnny CASH. Appeared in film *Nashville Rebel* '66, had minor hit cover of Jim WEBB's 'MacArthur Park' with the Kimberleys '69, contributed song to Mick Jagger film *Ned Kelly* '70. Best of '60s work collected on 2-disc *Waylon Music* '80, which incl. covers of BEATLES' 'Norwegian Wood', 'You've Got To Hide Your Love Away'. He chafed at restrictions imposed by Nashville star system; encouraged by country-rock fusion of Bob DYLAN, Gram PARSONS, Kris KRISTOFFERSON and pioneered the outlaw movement alongside Willie NELSON, who prod. his *This Time* '74. Seminal LP of movement was *Honky Tonk Heroes* '73, which displayed him at his full-throated best; compilation *Wanted! The Outlaws* '76 said to have been the first country LP to sell a million, with Waylon, his wife Jessi COLTER, Nelson and Tompall GLASER: it highlighted the authenticity of the so-called outlaws, incl. Waylon's classic 'My Heroes Have Always Been Cowboys'. Tribute to Hank WILLIAMS 'Are You Sure Hank Done It This Way?' was minor pop hit '74; same year CMA named him Male Singer of the Year. With outlaw movement well under way he made 'Don't You Think This Outlaw Bit's Done Got Out Of Hand?'. With the ability to dictate his own musical destiny he entered fruitful period with *Ol' Waylon* '77, incl. classic 'Luchenbach, Texas', 'Belle Of The Ball', Rodney CROWELL's 'Till I Gain Control Again'. Collaboration *Waylon & Willie* '78 (on CBS) incl. his 'Red Headed Stranger', continued with *Waylon & Willie II* '82 and *Take It To The Limit* '83, with fine version of EAGLES' title song, Paul SIMON's 'Homeward Bound'. *I've Always Been Crazy* '78 incl. medley of Holly hits with the CRICKETS; *Music Man* '80 incl. theme from *The Dukes Of Hazzard* TV show; *Greatest Hits*

'79 was well chosen, from poignant 'Amanda' to gutsy 'Lonesome, Orn'ry & Mean'. *It's Only Rock'n'Roll* '83 was flawed, though incl. 'Living Legends (A Dying Breed)'; *Waylon & Company* '83 was interesting if patchy collection of duets with Emmylou HARRIS, Hank WILLIAMS Jr, Ernest TUBB; *Never Could Toe The Mark* '84 was less inspired, *Turn The Page* '85 a marginal improvement. All these are on RCA; he switched to MCA for renaissance *Will The Wolf Survive* '85, with LOS LOBOS title song: by his own admission the first LP he'd made in some time without the aid of drugs. It did not incl. his long-time steel guitar player Ralph Mooney, restored on *Hangin' Tough* '87, with cover of Gerry RAFFERTY's 'Baker Street'. *A Man Called Hoss* '87 is concept: musical autobiography instead of the book he doesn't want to write. He guested on Neil YOUNG LP *Old Ways* '85, appeared with him at Farm Aid; made well-received *The Highwayman* '85 with Cash, Nelson, Kristofferson. His ear for the best songs for his distinctive voice, writing talent and choice of sidemen and producers, single-minded devotion to C&W as means of self-expression have made him a giant. It was rumoured that he'd return to acting, playing John Wayne in remakes of *Stagecoach* and *The Alamo*. Book *Waylon & Willie* by Bob Allen published '79. 19 albums have made the pop chart, best entry at no. 12 *Waylon & Willie*. Other chart top 50 LPs incl. *Dreaming My Dreams* '75, *Are You Ready For The Country* '76, *Waylon Live* '76 (recorded in Austin '74), *What Goes Around Comes Around* '79, *Black On Black* '82, *Leather And Lace* '81 with Jessi.

JETHRO TULL UK rock band formed '68 in Blackpool from various local bands, named after 18th-century inventor of the seed drill, later tending towards folk-rock. Original lineup: Ian Anderson (*b* 10 Aug. '47, Edinburgh), vocals, flute; Mick Abrahams (*b* 7 Apr. '43, Luton), guitar; Glenn Cornick (*b* 24 Apr. '47, Barrow-in-Furness), bass; Clive Bunker (*b* 12 Dec. '46), drums. From the start, Dickensian figure Anderson was the focal point, pirouetting as he piped; Abrahams was also important as Tull accrued underground following: *This Was* '68 was a strong debut, fluidity of Abrahams' playing, Anderson's dexterity highlighted on Roland KIRK's 'Serenade To A Cuckoo'. Abrahams left, formed much-loved Blodwyn Pig, which recorded *Ahead Rings Out* '69, *Getting To This* '70, then solo *Mick Abrahams* '71, *At Last* '72, tutor LP *Learning To Play With* '75. From *Stand Up* '69 he was replaced by Martin Barre (*b* 17 Nov. '46); Tull went from strength to strength, with 'Living In The Past', 'Sweet Dream' and 'Witch's Promise' all top 10 '69-70. *Benefit* '70 assured Tull's standing with 'progressive' fans, broke band in USA, marked debut of Jeffrey Hammond-Hammond on bass, longtime friend and infl. on Anderson who'd inspired 'Song For Jeffrey' on the first album. Cornick had left to form Wild Turkey (*Battle Hymn* '71, *Turkey* '72). Tull's *Aqualung* '71 still regarded by many as their finest hour: an ambitious semi-concept dominated by Anderson's fascination with tramps, it seemed seamless (no. 7 LP in USA, where 19 LPs charted altogether). *Thick As A Brick* '72 was lavishly packaged, balanced set of songs (no. 1 USA); 2-disc *Living In The Past* '72 was 2-disc compilation of singles etc., side 3 live from Carnegie Hall (no. 3 USA); then *Passion Play* '73, another concept, was heavily panned (but no. 1 in USA): Anderson was so annoyed by reviews that he announced Tull would cease touring; kept promise for a year, and *War Child* '74 was more coherent work (no. 2 USA). *MU: The Best Of Jethro Tull* '75 kept fans happy; *Minstrel In The Gallery* '75 was first step towards English folk-rock (no. 7 LP USA): Anderson had been working with STEELEYE SPAN, and infl. was two-way. He pursued that direction to great effect on *Songs From The Wood* '77 (last top 10 entry USA at no. 8) and *Heavy Horses* '78; *Too Old To Rock-'n'Roll, Too Young To Die* '76 was harder; *Repeat* '77 was another best-of (*MU/Repeat* '82 was double-play cassette-only of the compilations). 2-disc *Bursting Out* '78 was obligatory live set. *Stormwatch* '79 introduced former FAIRPORT CONVENTION bassist Dave Pegg (replaced ex-Gods John Glascock, who died following surgery), good foil for Anderson's fascination with folk tunes; *A* '80 was harshly received; *Broadsword & The Beast* '82 and *Under Wraps* '84 seemed aimed solely at long-term fans (the cassette edition of latter incl. extra tracks); Anderson's long-awaited solo album

Walk Into Light '83 showed little of the originality that had made Tull such an important band in the late '60s; neither did Tull LP *Crest Of A Knave* '87: he has become sole frontman, Tull little more than his backing group; notwithstanding, they retain a worldwide following after nearly 20 years. Anderson played on LSO album *A Classic Case* '85.

JIM & JESSE USA bluegrass duo. Jim (guitar; *b* 13 Feb. '27) and Jesse McReynolds (mandolin; *b* 9 July '29) both vocalists, both *b* Coeburn, Va. From musical family; fiddler grandfather had recorded for Victor. Raised on Clinch Mountain farm, began playing as teenagers, on radio from '47, recorded for Kentucky label early '50s, then Capitol. Jesse in armed forces '52-4, entertained troops with Charlie LOUVIN; reformed with Jim '54; led band the Virginia Boys. Folk boom of early '60s led to discovery by new young audience; signed to Epic, had string of country hits incl. 'Cotton Mill Man' and 'Better Times A'Coming' '64, 'Diesel On My Tail' and 'Ballad Of Thunder Road' '67, 'Greenwich Village Folksong Salesman', 'Yonder Comes A Freight Train' and 'Golden Rocket' '68. Meanwhile moved to Nashville, regulars on Grand Ole Opry from '66; back on Capitol early '70s, had mild success with 'Freight Train' '71, but as folk boom faded hits died off. High-flying harmonies and immaculate picking still a popular act; have played at London's Wembley Country Music Festival many times. LPs incl. *We Like Trains/Diesel On My Tail* on Epic.

JIMENEZ, Flaco (*b* Leonardo Jimenez, 11 Mar. '39, San Antonio, Texas) Tex-Mex accordionist, songwriter; best known from his crossover work with Ry COODER, Freddy FENDER, Willie NELSON, Doug SAHM, Carlos SANTANA, Peter Rowan. Nickname 'Skinny'. His father was Santiago JIMENEZ Sr; younger brother Santiago Jr is also a prominent accordionist. Played bajo sexto with his father, debuting on disc early '50s on 'Los Tecolotes'. Virtually all his early work appeared on locally released singles, often made to cash in on local crazes or recent events, though he avoided much of the political subject matter found in corridos (song-stories) recorded by

Mexican-American musicians (but later made *Corridos Famosos* on Dina with Los Caparales). Greater fame came through work with Doug Sahm on *Doug Sahm & Band* '73 on Atlantic, sales of which were boosted by other luminaries such as Mac REBENNACK and Bob DYLAN. Cooder found Flaco's work, allegedly by chance, and determined to work with him (*Chicken Skin Music* '76, *Showtime* '77, soundtrack for *The Border* '82, *Get Rhythm* '87). Flaco recorded prolifically, having regional hits with his own songs such as 'El Pantalon Blue Jean' (*El Gran Flaco Jimenez* on Dina, *Tex-Mex Breakdown* on Sonet), and 'El Bingo' (*El Internacional Flaco Jimenez* on Dina), which dealt with the game's effect on family life. *Flaco Jimenez & His Conjunto* on Arhoolie proved a turning point; regular tours of Europe (at first with Rowan, *b* 4 July '42 in Boston, Mass.; guitarist, saxophonist, vocalist, writer; played in Earth Opera, Seatrain, with Bill MONROE, Old And In The Way) helped establish reputation abroad. *Tex-Mex Breakdown* '83 saw him take suspect path according to purists, tailored to a European audience and unfavourably compared to his earlier work. Other albums incl. *El Principe del Acordeon* '77 on DLB, *El Sonido de San Antonio* '80 on Arhoolie (with his father), *Viva Seguin* '83 on Rogue (UK reissue of earlier *Mis Polkas Favoritas* on DLB), *On The Move* '84 on Dina, *San Antonio Sound* '85 on Waterfront, *Augie Meyers Presents San Antonio Saturday Night* '86 on Sonet (with Los Paisanos, Los Hnos Barron and Los Formales), *Peter Rowan* '78 on Flying Fish (on Special Delivery '87 in UK). *See also* entry for Santiago, below.

JIMENEZ, Santiago Sr (*b* '13 June, San Antonio, Texas; *d* there 22 June '84) Tex-Mex accordionist and songwriter; with other accordionists, especially Narciso MARTINEZ, one of the pioneers of musica norteña, the music of the Mexican-Texas border; latterly better-known as father of Flaco (*see above*) and Santiago Jr. Encouraged by his own father, Patricio, a dance musician from Eagle Pass, Texas. First record, 'Dices Pescao'/'Dispensa el Arrempujon' '36 on Decca, made innovative use of tololoche, a tejano contrabass which began to be used in the CONJUNTO music of the '40s. Recorded

for Globe, Imperial, Mexican Victor; scored regional hits with 'La Piedrera' and 'Viva Seguin', both incl. on *Texas-Mexican Border Music Vol. 12: Norteño Acordeon Part 2: San Antonio In The 1940s And 50s* on Folkyric; he is also heard on *Vol. 4 Part 1*. Retained trad. approach, also preserved in the work of Santiago Jr on *El Mero Mero* '82 and *Santiago Strikes Back!* '84 on Arhoolie, unlike Flaco's more modern style; this was largely due to his preference for the two-row button accordion which he never abandoned despite advances in accordion technology and his instrument's increasingly old-fashioned status. Appeared in *Chulas Fronteras* '76 (Brazos Films) with Flaco, Martinez, others. *Santiago Jimenez con Flaco Jimenez y Juan Viesca* '80 on Arhoolie has original material written after his string of hits from '30s to '50s, which epitomised the roots of this danceable music; Flaco's *Homenaje a Don Santiago Jimenez* '85 on Dina incl. material co-written by father and son.

JIVE FIVE, The Doo-wop vocal group. Leader Eugene Pitt (*b* 6 Nov. '37) formed first group The Genies with school friends from Brooklyn ('54); later had chart hit 'Who's That Knockin'' (no. 71 '59). They split up; Roland Trone and Claude Johnson formed Don & Juan, had big hit 'What's Your Name?' (no. 2 '62). Pitt formed Jive Five with Billy Prophet, Jerome Hanna, Richard Harris and Billy Johnson; had own big hit with 'My True Story' (no. 3 '61), based on story of sweetheart's marriage to his best friend. Group toured with Dick Clark, had further hits 'Never Never' (no. 74 '61), 'What Time Is It?' (no. 67 '62), 'I'm A Happy Man' (no. 36 '65). With fading fame the name of the group changed with alacrity: The Shadow became Showdown, Jyve Fyve, etc. Then Pitt headed a Jive Five lineup incl. original second tenor Prophet, brothers Herbert and Frank Pitt, Beatrice Best, Charles Mitchell: album for Ambient Sounds label *Here We Go!* ('82) showed his soaring, vibrant vocal lead still in business.

JOEL, Billy (*b* 9 May '49, Long Island, NY) Singer, songwriter, pianist. Piano lessons as a child; formed first group Echoes at 14 (later renamed Lost Souls), left to join Hassles '68: unsuccessful LPs *Hassles* and *Hour*

Of The Wolf on UA with John Dizek, vocals; Howard Blauvelt, bass; Jonathan Small, drums; Richard McKenner, guitar; hard-rock spin-off *Attila* '70 made by Joel and Small under that name incl. amusingly pompous 'Amplifier Fire – Part I: Godzilla Part II: March Of The Huns'. Signed to Family label '71: sombre LP of own compositions *Cold Spring Harbor* '72 was marred by speeding up of tape at mastering process (later remixed, reissued on Columbia '84); legal problems extricating himself from label/managerial contracts saw him playing bars as 'Bill Martin', where he was spotted by Columbia/CBS; *Piano Man* '74 described the experience: LP, title single made top 30 '74. *Streetlife Serenade* '74 incl. no. 34 hit 'The Entertainer'; he was compared to Elton JOHN, coy lyrics married to catchy tunes, but like John could and did dig deeper (e.g. on 'Say Goodbye To Hollywood' on *Turnstiles* '76). *The Stranger* '77 incl. four USA hit singles: title song, one of his best, was not one of them; mawkish love song 'Just The Way You Are' was USA no. 2/UK 19, won two Grammies '79 (hit later for soul star Barry WHITE). Another banal yet boppy number 'My Life' helped *52nd Street* '78 to become no. 1 LP; *Glass Houses* '80 was also no. 1 (incl. 'You May Be Right', no. 7 USA, and 'It's Still Rock'n'Roll To Me', his first no. 1 single), but neither topped *Stranger*: although only no. 2 LP it became biggest selling Columbia LP ever at 5 million (eclipsing SIMON & GARFUNKEL's *Bridge Over Troubled Water*). No. 8 LP *Songs In The Attic* '81 featured pre-*Stranger* songs recorded in concert; no. 7 *The Nylon Curtain* '82 saw him portray Vietnam Vet and unemployed steelworker in 'Allentown' and 'Goodnight Saigon'; *An Innocent Man* '83 made no. 4, with five top 30 singles UK *and* USA, incl. 'Tell Her About It' (no. 1 USA): LP paid homage to groups/styles that infl. him, incl. DRIFTERS, James BROWN, Otis REDDING, LITTLE ANTHONY AND THE IMPERIALS, FOUR SEASONS. Pastiche of latter 'Uptown Girl' was no. 3 USA/1 UK; video featured soon-to-be wife, model Christie Brinkley. 2-disc *Greatest Hits* '85 incl. 'You're Only Human (Second Wind)', dedicated to would-be youthful suicides, of which he nearly was one in '60s: he devotes much time to a charity in the field. Carried on with LP *The Bridge* '86; played in Lenin-grad and Moscow mid-'87, concerts taped as 2-disc *Kohuept* ('In Concert'; one disc on CD).

JOHN, Elton (*b* Reginald Kenneth Dwight, 25 Mar '47, Pinner, Middlesex) UK singer, songwriter, pianist. Unprepossessing and soon balding, an unlikely superstar; one of the few megastars of the '70s, a dismal decade for pop. Began as Bluesology pianist mid-'60s; took name from Bluesology singer Long John BALDRY, saxophonist Elton Dean (later with SOFT MACHINE). Auditioned for publisher Dick JAMES, began writing with lyricist Bernie Taupin (*b* 22 May '50, Lincolnshire); they didn't meet for months, writing songs by post. James set up DJM label for John; he later started own Rocket label (records on Uni, then MCA in USA; after '81 on Geffen). (The relationship with James ended in court '85.) *Empty Sky* '69 was pleasant if undistinguished debut; *Elton John* '70 incl. first single hit 'Your Song', made top 5 USA LP chart, as did *Tumbleweed Connection* '70, also year of triumphant USA debut. Hiatus occurred with lamentable soundtrack *Friends* '71, patchy live LP *17-11-70* '71; *Madman Across The Water* returned to top 10 USA LPs, though it was already clear that his prolific talent easily filled a less exciting era than the '60s had been. Backed by trio of Nigel Olsson, drums; Dee Murray, bass; Davey Johnstone, guitar; six albums all no. 1 USA: *Honky Chateau* '72 incl. top 10 hits 'Rocket Man', 'Honky Cat'; *Don't Shoot Me I'm Only The Piano Player* '73 incl. 'Crocodile Rock' (no. 1 single USA), 'Daniel' (no. 2); 2-disc *Goodbye Yellow Brick Road* '73 incl. no. 2 title track, 'Bennie And The Jets' (no. 1); *Caribou* '74 incl. 'The Bitch Is Back' (no. 4), 'Don't Let The Sun Go Down On Me' (no. 2); *Captain Fantastic And The Brown Dirt Cowboy* '75 incl. 'Someone Saved My Life Tonight' (no. 4); *Rock Of The Westies* '75 incl. 'Island Girl' (no. 1). *Greatest Hits* '74 also made no. 1 LP slot; reissue of first LP in '75 made no. 6. It was said that 2% of all records sold were his. *Here And There* '76 reached no. 4, recorded '74 live, one side in London, one in NYC; 2-disc *Blue Moves* '76 incl. 'Sorry Seems To Be The Hardest Word'; at no. 3 his last top 10 LP USA. As commitment to heavy recording schedule required by the James contract began to tell, he was already the biggest of stars, courted by the showbiz establishment; live shows were colourful (he was dubbed rock's LIBERACE, famous for his collection of outrageous spectacle frames). Cover of the BEATLES' 'Lucy In The Sky With Diamonds' '74 had guitar by John LENNON as 'Dr Winston O'Boogie'; appeared with Lennon at Madison Square Garden '75 in what turned out to be Lennon's last concert ('I Saw Her Standing There' was '81 hit; John is godfather to Sean Ono Lennon). Played Pinball Wizard in film of The WHO's *Tommy* '75. *Greatest Hits Vol. II* '77 incl. 'Lucy', 'Philadelphia Freedom', 'Don't Go Breakin' My Heart' (duet with Kiki DEE), all no. ones USA. Latter was his only no. 1 hit in UK: Dee was an old friend, early signing to Rocket; signed Neil SEDAKA and Cliff RICHARD for USA only. As the most visible member of rock aristocracy he was pilloried by the punk movement though he wrote songs with Tom ROBINSON. He was no longer working with Taupin, who published a book of his lyrics for Elton, prod. album *American Gothic* '72 by David ACKLES; made solo LPs *Taupin* '71, *He Who Rides The Tiger* '80; co-wrote '85 hit 'We Built This City (On Rock'n'Roll)' for Starship. Elton's *A Single Man* '79 saw him working with lyricist Gary Osbourne, but biggest hit was instrumental 'Song For Guy' (no. 4 UK '80). *The Thom Bell Sessions* '79 was a mini-LP made in '77 incl. 'Mama Can't Buy You Love'; *Victim Of Love* '79 made no. 35 USA; *21 At 33* '80 and *The Fox* '81 did better, incl. work with Taupin, but were not up to old standard; *Jump Up* '82 incl. 'Blue Eyes', tribute to Lennon 'Empty Garden'. *Too Low For Zero* was only no. 25 in USA, but pleased fans: had him reunited with Taupin, Olsson, Murray and Johnstone, guest Stevie WONDER; incl. 'Cold As Christmas', 'I Guess That's Why They Call It The Blues' (no. 4), energetic 'I'm Still Standing'. *Breaking Hearts* '84 incl. no. 5 'Sad Songs (Say So Much)'; *Ice On Fire* '85 continued renaissance, incl. duet with George Michael on 'Wrap Her Up', 'Nikita' just missing the elusive no. 1 UK solo hit. He appeared with Wonder, Dionne WARWICK, Gladys KNIGHT on '85 charity disc 'That's What Friends Are For', became the first rock star since the Beatles to have a wax effigy of

himself at Madame Tussaud's, was the first Western rock star to play Moscow (documented in film *From Elton With Love* '79). Critics were always ready to count Elton out, but after 30 top 40 hits '70-82 in USA, 16 in top 10, plus 24 chart LPs '70-84 with an incredible six in a row at no. 1, they almost learned to live with him. He was also famous for owning Watford Football Club near London; he announced '84 that he would tour no more, changed his mind; released *Leather Jackets* LP '86 (incl. duet with Richard). At an '86 concert he wore spangled jumpsuits, a huge turban with an ostrich plume, etc., used a LITTLE RICHARD tape instead of opening act; Chicago critic Daniel Brogan speculated that John wanted the audience to make a connection (Little Richard/John both piano players, bisexual, given to wild costumes), commented that a Liberace tape would have been closer to the mark. Throat operation early '87 was supposed to keep him out of action, but *Elton John Live In Australia With The Melbourne Symphony Orchestra* was on the way on MCA.

JOHNNIE AND JACK Vocal duo with country hits in '50s. Johnny Wright (*b* 13 May '14, Mt Juliet, Tenn.) and Jack Anglin (*b* 13 May '16, Columbia, Tenn.; *d* 8 Mar. '63). Wright went to Nashville '33, married Kitty WELLS, began working with Jack (who also played guitar) '38. They toured with a band '40s; all three were on the Grand Ole Opry c.'47, Johnnie & Jack were stars on *Louisiana Hayride*, returned to the Opry with Wells '52. The duo recorded for Apollo ('Jole Blon', 'Paper Boy'), then RCA: first big hit 'Poison Love' '51 (no. 5 in country chart). 'Crying Heart Blues' was a hit same year; four more chart entries '54, two '58 and one '59 were followed by a last hit on Decca '62. More than half their hits were in the top 10 and they were favourite regulars on the Opry. Jack was killed in a car crash on his way to Patsy CLINE's funeral. Johnny had 11 solo hits '64-9 incl. no. 1 'Hello Vietnam' '65; his son Bobby (*b* 30 Mar. '42, Charleston, West Va.) appeared on *Hayride* at age 8, had hits beginning '67 with 'Lay A Little Happiness On Me', top 20 'Here I Go Again' '71; also acted in TV's *McHale's Navy*, other shows. Johnny formed *Kitty Wells – Johnny Wright Family Show* for TV

'69; Bobby and Johnny did an album of Johnnie & Jack material for Starday '77.

JOHNNY AND THE HURRICANES USA instrumental combo of late '50s-60s led by saxophonist Johnny Paris (*b* John Pocisk, '40, Walbridge, Ohio); incl. Paul Tesluk, organ; Lionel 'Butch' Mattice, bass; Tony Kaye, drums; Dave Yorko, guitar. First known as the Orbits; recorded with rockabilly Mack Vickery; to Detroit backing hopeful singers but local entrepreneurs Harry Balk and Irving Micahnik (later Del SHANNON's manager) signed band instead. First disc 'Crossfire' for managers' Twirl label was reverb-laden dance number which seemed exciting at the time, written by pianist T. J. Fowler; leased to Warwick it reached no. 23 USA '59. Drummer Don Staczek replaced Kaye for 'Red River Rock', an adaptation of trad. 'Red River Valley' (no. 5 USA, 3 UK); it was Tesluk's rinky-dink Hammond organ rather than Paris's rasping, imitation R&B sax that made it distinctive. Formula of rocking old tunes accounted for most of nine chart entries '59-61 in USA, except for another Fowler original 'Rockin' Goose', on which Paris honked. 'Beatnik Fly' was Burl IVES' 'Blue Tail Fly', 'Revival' was 'When The Saints Go Marching In', 'Reveille' was the army bugle call, etc. Micahnik and Balk handled leasing arrangements and claimed composer credit for out-of-copyright material (as Ira Mack and Tom King). Band split late '61 because of tour fatigue, alleged dissatisfaction with management; hits had dried up anyway. Paris went to Europe, settled in Hamburg; played in BEATLE era there, later made *Live At The Star Club* '65 for his own Attila label, toured with new Hurricanes '70s, into '80s.

JOHN'S CHILDREN UK hippy/progressive rock band formed '64 as R&B band the Few (later renamed Silence). Discovered by pop impresario/YARDBIRDS manager Simon Napier-Bell, they recorded 'The Love I Thought I'd Found'/'Just What You Want, Just What You Get' for Columbia/EMI with lineup of Andy Ellison, vocals; Geoff McLelland, guitar; Chris Townson, drums; John Hewlett, bass. McLelland was replaced by Marc BOLAN, a Napier-Bell protégé who'd not been launched as a star

yet; EMI rejected 'Not The Sort of Girl (You'd Take To Bed)' and album *Orgasm* '67, though latter was issued in USA on White Whale, finally by UK indie Cherry Red '82 as historical artifact with extra tracks. (Phoney 'live' album had audience from BEATLE film soundtrack added.) They signed to WHO management's Track label and released 'Desdemona', a Bolan tune banned for mildly suggestive lyric. Live shows were legendary, especially Fourteen Hour Technicolour Dream on 29/30 Apr. '67 at London's Alexandra Palace, where Bolan caused ear-splitting feedback; shows elsewhere featured destruction, fighting and violence that caused a riot in Germany; they were thrown off tour supporting Who. Bolan left to form Tyrannosaurus Rex after arguments about follow-up 'A Midsummer Night's Scene'; another Bolan song 'Go Go Girl' released after his departure later turned up in Rex repertoire as 'Mustang Ford'; to milk the last of his departed talent, B-side of 'Desdemona' ('Remember Thomas A Becket') was reworked as 'Come And Play With Me In The Garden'. They split after poor record sales and another disastrous tour of Germany. Ellison made handful of solo singles for CBS, then linked with Townson to form Jet with ex-Sparks bassist Martin Gordon, Peter Oxendale on keyboards, ex-Nice guitar David O'List: eponymous LP for CBS flopped '75; Ellison and Gordon formed pseudo-new wavers Radio Stars with Ian McLeod on guitar, Steve Perry, drums (3 LPs for Chiswick). Ellison's energy as frontman lent some entertainment value to John's Children; their reputation has grown out of proportion owing to Bolan's involvement and because of lack of recorded output to prove/disprove claims of greatness.

JOHNS, Glyn (*b* 15 Feb. '42, Epsom, Surrey) UK record producer. Interest in music began in skiffle boom; for a time he combined trainee engineering job at IBC studios with singing career; left to concentrate on the latter under Jack GOOD, but demand from former clients led to freelance engineering (unheard of then), his brother Andy Johns following his example. Early sessions with ROLLING STONES led to relationship with Andrew Oldham; he engineered most of the acts on Oldham's Immediate label, incl. Chris FARLOWE and SMALL FACES (phasing effect on 'Itchycoo Park' was the work of Johns and his assistant George Chkiantz). Moved into production with Steve MILLER Band, taking over Miller's abortive self-production of *Children Of The Future* '68: sound effects (only a year after BEATLES' *Sgt Pepper*) were considered revolutionary at the time. Continued to produce Miller; also *Led Zeppelin* '69, FAMILY's *Family Entertainment* '69, the WHO's *Who's Next* '71 (all co-produced), Stones' *Get Yer Ya-Yas Out* '70, Beatles' *Let It Be* '70, etc. During '70s became associated with West Coast USA soft rock, dating from production of the EAGLES' first three LPs '72-4: credited with turning them from bad rock-'n'roll band into the layered-harmony soft-rockers they became, creating one of the most popular and imitated sounds of the decade. Carried on with UK songwriters/performers Gallagher & Lyle and Andy Fairweather-Low, both on A&M: prod. many acts for that label, incl. Ozark Mountain Daredevils, Joan ARMATRADING, Paul Kennerley, Live Wire; played leading role in Kennerley's all-star C&W concept LPs, *White Mansions* '78, *The Legend Of Jesse James* '80, helping to 'cast' them. His insistence on involvement in every aspect of arranging, recording process put him in forefront of 'creative' producers of the '70s, who swung pendulum back from '60s vogue for self-production; it also caused riffs with several clients (e.g. the Stones) but helped many more. Worked with cream of British rock and even New Wave (*Combat Rock* '82 by the CLASH), but he will always be associated with soft rock.

JOHNSON, Blind Willie (*b* '02, Marlin, Texas; *d* '49, Beaumont, Texas) Gospel singer and guitarist in country blues style. Blinded at age 7 by his stepmother during a fight with his father, became a street musician; married Angeline '27, who sang on some of the records, taught him many songs from 19th-century hymn-books. He recorded 30 sides for Columbia '27-30; he may also have recorded a couple of secular songs under the name Blind Texas Marlin which are now lost. Best-known sides incl. the first, 'Jesus Make Up My Dying Bed', also 'Let Your Light Shine On Me', 'You're Gonna Need Somebody On Your Bond'.

His powerful style and integration of voice and guitar made him a legend in the '40s among blues collectors, but he continued to live in poverty. After Angeline put out a fire in their home they lay down on a wet bed; a few days later a hospital refused to admit him because he was blind: died of pneumonia. Compilations on Folkways; also *Praise God I'm Satisfied* on Yazoo.

JOHNSON, Budd (*b* Albert J. Johnson, 14 Dec. '10, Dallas, Texas; *d* 20 Oct. '84, K.C.) Tenor sax, other reeds; arranger, sometime vocalist. Prolific and popular freelance musician best-known for associations with Earl HINES, but also a prime mover behind modern jazz. Brother Frederick 'Keg' (*b* 19 Nov. '08, Dallas; *d* 8 Nov. '67, Chicago) played trombone and guitar; worked with Louis ARMSTRONG '33, Benny CARTER, Fletcher HENDERSON '33-4, Cab CALLOWAY '34-48, Lucky MILLINDER '49-50, many others; with Ray CHARLES '61 until his death. They were taught music by Portia Pittman, a daughter of Booker T. Washington; her son Booker Pittman (*b* 3 Oct. '09, Fairmont Heights, Maryland; *d* 13 Oct. '69, Brazil) was also a reedman who played with Lucky Millinder, first went to Brazil '36. Budd played piano and turned pro on drums '24, tenor '26; played in various Texas and territory bands, joined Louis Armstrong '33, first worked for Hines '34 depping for Cecil Irwin (*b* 7 Dec. '02, Evanston, Ill.; *d* 3 May '35 near De Moines, Iowa), joining full-time when Irwin was killed in a crash of the Hines band's bus. Left to arrange for Gus ARNHEIM, returned to Hines as lead alto '37, worked for both Fletcher and Horace HENDERSON '38, back with Hines on tenor and as mus. dir. '38 through '42. Briefly with Don REDMAN '43, Al Sears (USO tour), Georgie AULD (as staff arranger); with Dizzy GILLESPIE and Oscar PETTIFORD at the Onyx Club NYC early '44 (and often with Gillespie for several years), mus. dir. for Billy ECKSTINE band, wrote arrangements for Woody HERMAN, Buddy RICH's first band, Boyd RAEBURN: thus at a crucial time in the evolution of jazz he had written for Hines, Gillespie, Eckstine, Herman and Raeburn, the bands that employed all the young bop musicians, and played with all these bands except Raeburn's. In addition he helped organise the Coleman HAWKINS record date incl. Gillespie in early '44 that is often called the first bop session. He rarely led his own groups and made few records of his own, hence remained underrated outside the business. In late '40s-early '50s he worked for Sy OLIVER, MACHITO, Bennie GREEN, Cab CALLOWAY, etc.; was mus. dir. for Atlantic Records, had his own publishing company; wrote for and played with Benny GOODMAN '56-7 incl. tour of Asia; with Quincy JONES '60, Count BASIE '61-2; with Hines '65, Gerald WILSON big band early '66, toured USSR with Hines small group mid-'66, also South America; etc. At a Hines solo recital in London mid-'70s he turned up unannounced for some delightful duets. Prolific freelance recording with Frankie LAINE – Buck CLAYTON, Jimmy RUSHING, Sarah VAUGHAN, all on Columbia; with Rushing on RCA; 4 LPs of Buck Clayton Jam Sessions on Chiaroscuro '74; on Master Jazz with Roy ELDRIDGE Sextet LP *The Nifty Cat* '70; *Blues And Things* '67 by the Earl Hines Quartet with Rushing (Johnson also plays soprano; date also issued on World Record Club). On Famous Door: sextet *Here Swings The Judge* '64 by Milt HINTON & Friends. He was mus. dir. of JPJ Quartet with bassist Bill Pemberton (*b* 5 Mar. '18, Brooklyn), pianist Dill Jones (*b* Dillwyn Owen Jones, 19 Aug. '23, Wales), drummer Oliver Jackson (*b* 28 Apr. '34, Detroit); LP *Montreux '71* on Master Jazz. Records under his own name incl. sessions with Pittman on Columbia; others on Swingville, Cadet; on Master Jazz: septet LP *Blues A La Mode* '58, *Budd Johnson and the Four Brass Giants* on Riverside, *Colorado Jazz Party* on MPS.

JOHNSON, Bunk (*b* William Geary Johnson, 27 Dec. 1889, New Orleans; *d* 7 July '49, New Iberia, La.) Trumpet, cornet. He gave birth date of 1879, but later research disproved this. A New Orleans legend who had played second cornet with Buddy BOLDEN; then with various bands until Evan Thomas's Black Eagle Band '32: Thomas was murdered on the bandstand, Johnson lost his horn in a fight and was having trouble with his teeth; he soon gave up music. He was rediscovered by jazz fans '37 and worked as a music teacher in a WPA programme; made his first records

June '42 with Lu WATTERS at the time of the New Orleans revival (*see* JAZZ), also for Commodore '42, with Kid ORY '44, continued to record occasionally until Dec. '48; unfortunately he was past his prime. He claimed to have taught and influenced Louis ARMSTRONG, but Armstrong denied it. Sidney BECHET's brother, a dentist, made some teeth for him; he worked with Bechet in Boston '45. He was also said to be hard to get along with, perhaps understandably: Armstrong generously paid tribute to the purity of tone he had once had, but the success he had no doubt once deserved had passed him by.

JOHNSON, Eddie (*b* 11 Dec. '20, Napoleonville, La.) Tenor saxophone. To Chicago age 2; sang on radio age 12 with 2 other boys: 15-minute daily spot sponsored by Hoover vacuum cleaners. The Harmony Hounds sang at Chicago World's Fair '34, then their voices broke. Took his brother's sax from the closet, had lessons from uncle Joe Poston (see Jimmie NOONE). Played with local Danny Williams band; entire band offered music scholarship to Kentucky State College, which had decided to imitate Alabama's 'Bama State Collegians. Played with Johnny Long, then Horace HENDERSON, and Moral Young (local bandleader, later musical director of *I Love Lucy* TV show). Chicago colleagues during this era incl. singer Joe WILLIAMS, pianist Jimmy Jones (*b* 30 Dec. '18, Memphis; *d* 29 Apr. '82, Burbank; longtime accompanist for Sarah VAUGHAN, and later Ella FITZGERALD; led own trio, also prolific freelance arranger). Was infl. by both Coleman HAWKINS and Lester YOUNG; played in Hawkins octet in Chicago '41; Rhumboogie Club house band '42; offers from Duke ELLINGTON and Louis JORDAN '46: went with Jordan because money was better. Left full-time music '48; sat in on Ellington's *Mary Poppins* session mid-'60s; retired as computer engineer, made first LP as leader: lovely *Indian Summer* '81 on Nessa label, with excellent Chicago combo incl. Paul Serrano, trumpet; John Young, piano; Eddie de Haas, bass; George Hughes, drums.

JOHNSON, J. J. (*b* James Louis Johnson, 22 Jan. '24, Indianapolis, Ind.) Trombone, composer. Played with Benny CARTER '42-5, Count BASIE '45-6, played in bop combos NYC, toured with Illinois JACQUET '47-9, made USO tour of Korea and Japan with Oscar PETTIFORD '51. His technique became almost unbelievable: the trombone was a rhythm instrument in early jazz; Fred Beckett (*b* 23 Jan. '17, Nettleton, Mo.; *d* 30 Jan. '46, St Louis, of TB contracted in US Army) was an infl. on J.J., playing without the slurs and rasps of older trombone styles (with Andy KIRK, Harlan LEONARD, briefly Lionel HAMPTON). With roots in the swing era, J.J. was one of the first to develop the exceptional fluency necessary to play bop on an instrument that was not designed for it. By the time he recorded as a leader for Savoy and Prestige '46-9, first-time listeners thought that he must be playing a valve trombone. However, the trombone was an unfashionable instrument in modern jazz (dominated by trumpet and saxophones partly because few could play the trombone well enough), and those were lean years for jazz anyway; he worked in a Sperry factory as an inspector for nearly two years '52-4, but continued to gig. *Four Trombones* '53 was a Charles MINGUS workshop with Kai WINDING, Bennie GREEN, Willie Dennis (*b* 10 Jan. '26, Philadelphia; *d* 8 July '65 in a car crash). J.J. formed a quintet with Winding as 'Jay and Kai' '54-6, with a reunion in '58: '54 LPs on Savoy (with Mingus), Prestige and RCA (*Live At Birdland*), on Bethlehem '55, five on Columbia '55-6 (incl. *Jay & Kai Octet*, six trombones incl. Urbie Green, Jimmy Cleveland; *Jay And Kai At Newport*) proved that public had not tired of the trombone; combination of two of them despite initial poor reaction from club owners was almost as popular as Dave BRUBECK for a while. He was established as the model on the instrument as Charlie PARKER and Dizzy GILLESPIE were on theirs, not only for technique but for beautiful, personal tone. Jay and Kai reunited on an Impulse LP '60, on three A&M LPs '68 with strings (one released only in Japan), and on *All-Star Jam* '82 on Aurex (Japanese label), with Dexter GORDON, Clark TERRY, Roy HAYNES, Tommy FLANAGAN, Kenny BURRELL, Richard Davis on bass. J.J.'s own LPs incl. *The Eminent J. J. Johnson* on Blue Note (2 vols. from '53, '55, the first with Clifford BROWN); *J Is For Jazz*, Dial *J.J.* 5,

First Place, J.J. In Person, J.J. Johnson And Voices (with choir, Frank DeVOL orchestra), *Blue Trombone, A Touch Of Satin* on Columbia '56-60; also *J.J. Inc.*, excellent quintet with three horns inc. Clifford JORDAN, Freddie HUBBARD (LP also first to incl. entirely J.J.'s tunes). *Perceptions* '61 on Verve is 6-part J.J. composition played by 21-piece Gillespie band cond. by Gunther Schuller. Then came *J.J.'s Broadway* '63 on Verve, *Proof Positive* '64 on Impulse. Compositions incl. 'Rondeau For Quartet And Orchestra', written for the MJQ; 'Sketch For Trombone And Orchestra' and 'El Camino Real' were commissioned for '59 Monterey Jazz Festival (John LEWIS, mus. dir.); 'Camino' incl. on first of four LPs on RCA '64-6 with big bands incl. *The Dynamic Sound Of J.J. With Big Band* '64, *Goodies* '65. He spent much of the '70s in studio work, composing film and TV music; then *Pinnacles* '79 on Milestone; *The Yokohama Concert* '77 with Nat ADDERLEY, *Concepts In Blue* '80 with Terry, Count BASIE LP *The Bosses*, all on Pablo. Formed new quintet '87 (with Cedar WALTON, alumnus of '59-60 group), relocated from L.A. back to Indianapolis.

JOHNSON, James P. (*b* James Price Johnson, 1 Feb. 1894, New Brunswick, N.J.; *d* 17 Nov. '55, NYC) Piano, composer. A link between RAGTIME and JAZZ, the East Coast equivalent of Jelly Roll MORTON; master and indeed virtual inventor of the NYC STRIDE style of piano; inspiration of Duke ELLINGTON and teacher of Fats WALLER. To NYC at 14; played at rent parties at 17. Infl. by a Harlem community of black seamen and longshoremen originally from the southern coast ports, incl. Gullahs (from Sea Islands of Carolina and Georgia, who spoke a dialect that had African words in it): their 'ring shouts', cakewalks etc. became an element of stride piano. Luckey ROBERTS was also an influence; Johnson was also associated with Perry BRADFORD, Clarence WILLIAMS. Played club dates, Southern vaudeville circuit, also theatre work (toured England '22 with *Plantation Days*, starring Florence Mills). First recordings '21; accompanied singers Bessie SMITH, Ethel WATERS, etc.; wrote hits 'Old Fashioned Love' (with Cecil Mack), 'Charleston' (both in revue *Runnin' Wild* '23; latter became national dance craze), 'If I Could Be With You (One Hour Tonight)' (introduced by Ruth ETTING; Henry Creamer wrote lyrics: *b* 21 June 1879, Richmond, Va.; *d* 14 Oct. '30, NYC; also wrote 'Way Down Yonder In New Orleans', etc.), 'A Porter's Love Song To A Chambermaid' (with Andy RAZAF); stride showpieces 'Carolina Shout', 'Mule Walk', 'Keep Off The Grass' etc. Wrote *Yamekraw: A Negro Rhapsody* for orchestra, chorus, jazz band and solo piano (Carnegie Hall '28), named after a settlement near Savannah, Ga.; made into 9-minute screen drama '30 (music played for film by Hugo Marianni and his Mediterraneans; no musicians on screen). Worked in Waller's show *Keep Shufflin'* '28; led the band in *St Louis Blues* '29, 16-minute film with Bessie Smith, members of Fletcher HENDERSON band; he appears briefly, but the piano introduction to the cabaret scene could only be his. Wrote *Symphony Harlem* '32, short opera *De Organiser* with poet Langston Hughes; appeared in John HAMMOND's *Spirituals To Swing* concert '38 at Carnegie Hall. The next day he was recorded by folklorist Alan LOMAX for the Library of Congress, who apparently did not know who he was, asked him to play and sing the blues: the records were catalogued by the Library as 'by a blues singer from Kansas City'. He led his own band; played with Wild Bill DAVISON '43 in Boston, led own band '44, Carnegie Hall solo concert '45, played Town Hall concerts NYC with Eddie CONDON, at Condon's club '46; worked in Cal. prod. of his revue *Sugar Hill* '49 (songs recorded by Nat COLE, Billie HOLIDAY, Louis ARMSTRONG), worked with the clarinettist Albert Nicholas (*b* 27 May 1900, New Orleans; *d* 3 Sep. '73, Switzerland). Severe stroke '50 left him disabled. He spent most of the '30s composing, able to live on royalties from hits; he was more fortunate than Scott JOPLIN in getting his more ambitious work performed; on the other hand, he wrote to Mrs Sprague Coolidge, patroness of chamber music, trying to get his string quartet *Spirit Of America* played: apparently she did not bother to answer; it is now lost, with much else. He was equalled only by Earl HINES and Art TATUM in technical skill at the keyboard, admired the boppers (e.g. Dizzy GILLESPIE), was ahead of his time in foreseeing the day

when 'jazz musicians of the future will have to be able to play all different kinds . . . just like the classical musician.' *Father Of The Stride Piano* on Columbia incl. five solos from '20s, duet with Williams from '30, 10 sides recorded by Hammond '39 (five solos, five with small band). *Yamekraw* is on Folkways, as well as *The Original James P. Johnson* ('43-5 solos). *James P. Johnson* on Australian Swaggie has '44 piano tracks with drums and solos on Waller songs. Complete Blue Note recordings '43-4 incl. in *The Complete Edmond Hall/James P. Johnson/Sidney De Paris/Vic Dickenson Blue Note Sessions*, limited edition 6-disc set on Mosaic, incl. eight solos, 13 tracks by Johnson's Blue Note Jazzmen, others with Hall and De Paris.

JOHNSON, Lonnie (*b* Alonzo Johnson, 8 Feb. 1899(?), New Orleans; *d* 16 June '70, Toronto) Guitarist, vocalist; also played violin and piano. Gigged locally with his brother, James 'Steady Roll' Johnson; went to Europe c.'17, thought to have toured with Will Marion COOK; returned to USA to find that flu epidemic '18-19 had killed most of his family. Worked outside music early '20s, but still gigging; c.'25 won talent contest organised by Okeh Records, joined staff until '32: in this capacity recorded with Louis ARMSTRONG's Hot Seven '27, several records with Duke ELLINGTON '28, the Chocolate Dandies '28 (led by Don REDMAN; Johnson plays a lovely solo on one of the first recordings of 'Stardust'); Armstrong with Luis RUSSELL band '29; also recorded duets with Eddie LANG '28-9 (Lang sometimes called 'Blind Willie Dunn'). Johnson's own records on Okeh (also Gennett '27, Columbia '31-2) began '25 with Charles Creath's Jazz-O-Maniacs, continued with nearly 100 sides, incl. blues and hokum, many accompanied by just his guitar, others with accompaniment or vocal duet by Spencer WILLIAMS, Clarence WILLIAMS, James P. JOHNSON, J. C. Johnson (*b* 14 Sep. 1896, Chicago; *d* 27 Feb. '81, NYC; later a civic leader in Harlem); Lonnie Johnson also used pseudonyms Jimmy Jordan, George Jefferson, Bud Wilson; also recorded duets with Clara SMITH and Victoria SPIVEY. Moved to Cleveland '32, worked in factories by day; to Chicago and recorded on Decca '37-8 (16 sides, some with

Roosevelt SYKES; also with Jimmie NOONE, Johnny and Baby DODDS '40), on Bluebird (Victor) '39-42 with piano and bass; etc. He worked club dates, released many singles late '40s, finally made R&B chart '50 with 'Confused' on King. He played a concert in London '52, worked as chef in Philadelphia c.'60, made *Blues By Lonnie Johnson* on Prestige/Bluesway '60; appeared in NYC with Ellington, toured Europe with blues package, made album *Tomorrow Night* in Copenhagen on Storyville (incl. 'Swingin' With Lonnie'), all '63. Worked in Toronto late '60s. Other LPs incl. *Blues And Ballads* (with Elmer SNOWDEN on Prestige); *It Feels So Good* on Queen Disc incl. Okeh sides '27-30; some Bluebird sides were incl. in *Bluebird Blues* (RCA); also *Mr Johnson's Blues* on Miami; *Tears Don't Fall No More* and *Mr Trouble* on Folkways. Complete recordings from '20s in series on Matchbox UK.

JOHNSON, Marv (*b* 15 Oct. '38, Detroit) Soul/R&B vocalist. The artist on the first ever Motown record. After a teenage career in local vocal group The Serenaders, he was spotted by Berry Gordy singing on a float in a carnival. First release (on UA, as Motown was initially only a production company) was his first hit, 'Come To Me' (no. 30 '59). Of eight more USA Hot 100 entries '59-61, the most significant were 'I Love The Way You Love' and 'You Got What It Takes' (both top 10) and '(You've Got To) Move Two Mountains' (no. 20). 'You Got What It Takes' at no. 5 was his biggest hit in the UK. Although his hits previewed the Motown sound he faded from the charts, except for 'I Miss You Baby (How I Miss You)', which made top 40 on the soul chart '66 on the Gordy label; in '69 'I'll Pick A Rose For My Rose' was no. 10 in UK on Tamla Motown in UK, but did not chart at all in USA, whereupon 'I Miss You' was released in the UK and reached the top 30. Compilation *Early Classics* on EMI/UK '79.

JOHNSON, Matt (*b* '61, London) UK new wave singer/songwriter; works as The The. Tea boy in a recording studio at age 15 after working in schoolboy groups; began experimenting with studio techniques, cultivating carefully atmospheric style. Formed the Gadgets with Tom Johnson, Michael

O'Shea, former members of Plain Characters; made two LPs on Vinyl Solution label, *Gadgetree* '79 and *Love, Curiosity, Freckles And Doubt* '80 (a third remained unreleased); went solo to concentrate on parallel project The The, the name a send-up of punk's obsession with definite article names. Early influences of VELVET UNDERGROUND, Tim BUCKLEY, Throbbing Gristle led to individual if introspective music. Supported groups like DAF, Scritti Politti, Wire with backing tapes, synth player Keith Laws '79. Wire's Graham Lewis and Bruce Clifford Gilbert helped with single 'Controversial Subject' '80 for 4AD label, released to critical praise. He contributed 'Untitled' to *Some Bizzare Album* '81, signed to that label; contributed to Cherry Red sampler *Perspectives And Distortions*, temporarily backtracked to 4AD for his first solo LP (as Matt Johnson) *Burning Blue Soul* '81 (since reissued): made single-handed except for help of Lewis and Gilbert, masterpiece of new psychedelia largely ignored at the time. Some Bizzare boss Stevo signed him to CBS, negotiating with MD Maurice Oberstein from the back of a lion in Trafalgar Square after persuading Decca to fund LP sessions. 'Cold Spell Ahead' '81 was second Some Bizzare single, followed by reworked version 'Uncertain Smile' '82. *Soul Mining* '83 was amazingly varied LP, incl. single 'Perfect' with ex-NEW YORK DOLL David Johansen on harmonica, fragile accordion-laced 'This Is The Day', African beat of 'Giant'. Cassette version incl. extra tracks; album featured 13 musicians, number of members The The has had since '79. Johnson performed live with a shifting cast, sessioned with Marc ALMOND in Marc and the Mambas, made LP *The Pornography Of Despair*, not released. Long awaited *Infected* '86 on Epic/Some Bizzare did not disappoint critics: a brilliant achievement, delivering on the implicit promise that studio technology and electronic sounds can be marshalled to resemble music; densely full of his ideas and energy yet not overproduced, his vocal delivery (unlike that of many ex-new wavers) not irritating, but suited to his lyrics about pessimistic politics and dark view of love. Sleeve illustration of copulating demon was censored by CBS; lyrics and videos (one for each track) also caused controversy; incl. 'Heartland' hit single, but title single banned by BBC. Compared in his time to Soft Cell, TEARS FOR FEARS and Lou REED, he is a gifted writer who will emerge from his cult status.

JOHNSON, Pete (*b* 24 Mar. '04, Kansas City, Mo.; *d* 23 Mar. '67, Buffalo, NY) Pianist. Worked on drums with other pianists '22-6; played piano from '26 to '38 in K.C. clubs. To NYC '38 with Joe TURNER to do a spot on Benny GOODMAN radio show; appeared at Apollo theatre; returned to K.C. but back in NYC Dec. in John HAMMOND's *Spirituals To Swing* concert. Long residence at Café Society with Meade Lux LEWIS and Albert AMMONS, the three great boogie-woogie pianists at the height of the fad. Worked there and in Cal. '47-8 in duo with Ammons; also occasionally in duo with Lewis. Lived in Buffalo from '50; toured USA with Piano Parade package '52, worked with Lewis again that year; with Turner, then Jimmy RUSHING '55; JATP tour of Europe '58 (tour also incl. Turner), Newport Jazz Festival '58; suffered from ill health but worked occasionally. *The Pete Johnson Story* '65 edited by Hans J. Mauerer. LPs: *Pete's Blues* on Savoy; *Boogie Woogie Mood* on MCA '40-4 (reissues); *Joe Turner And Pete Johnson* on EmArcy; with Turner on Atlantic, Rushing on Columbia; tracks on various albums incl. *Spirituals To Swing* on Vanguard, *Boogie Woogie Classics* on Blue Note with Ammons.

JOHNSON, Plas (*b* Plas John Johnson Jr, 21 July '31, New Orleans) Tenor and alto saxes, flute; studied soprano with his father. Ubiquitous sideman on West Coast rock'n'roll, R&B records in '50s made him a legend among teenagers conscious of who was playing on the records, but soon revealed to all as a well-rounded, underrated musician. Studio work in '60s, incl. originating Henry MANCINI's *Pink Panther* music on film and LP '66; played in studio band for Merv Griffin on TV '70. Continued to gravitate towards jazz in '70s, working with Ray BROWN, Herb ELLIS, own group, etc. Records (apart from countless studio sessions, e.g. with Harry BELAFONTE, Shorty ROGERS '58) incl. Capitol LP '60 with Red CALLENDER, drummer Earl Palmer, Ernie Freeman on organ plus strings; *The Blues* '75 with Brown, Ellis, Bobbie Hall on con-

gas, Jake Hanna on drums, Mike Melvoin on keyboards and *Positively* '76 adding drummer Jimmie Smith (*b* James Howard Smith, 27 Jan. '38, Newark, N.J.; also recorded with Jimmy FORREST, Erroll GARNER, etc.), both on Concord Jazz.

JOHNSON, Robert (*b* 8 May '11 (?), Hazlehurst, Ms.; *d* 16 Aug. '38, Greenwood, Ms.) Blues singer, songwriter, guitarist. Raised and worked on farm; ran away from home to work with Son HOUSE c.'30; also worked with Johnny SHINES, Howlin' WOLF, Sonny Boy WILLIAMSON, Elmore JAMES. He recorded in a San Antonio hotel room '36 and in a back room of a Dallas office building '37 a total of 45 sides for ARC labels, incl. alternate takes (but some were probably remasterings of existing takes). Only 'Terraplane Blues' was anything like a hit in the restricted 'race' market of the time; 'I Believe I'll Dust My Broom' was adapted by James and became a post-war anthem of electric blues. When John HAMMOND tried to locate Johnson for his *Spirituals To Swing* concert of Dec. '38, he was dead. Son House heard three versions of his death: that he had been stabbed by a jealous husband, stabbed by a woman, and poisoned; and Shines said, 'I heard that it was something to do with the black arts.' None of the details of his life can be ascertained with certainty, but perhaps 'Hellhound On My Trail' and 'Me And The Devil Blues' are his most revealing titles: House also recalled that Johnson was not a good guitar player when he was younger, but that he disappeared for a time and suddenly turned up greatly improved. In a genre depending on the guitar not so much supporting the voice as simultaneously singing with equal intensity, he had become the greatest of all; Julio Finn (who has played harmonica with Muddy WATERS, and on ART ENSEMBLE LP *Certain Blacks*) develops the theme in his book *The Bluesman* '86: not all blacks in the USA accepted the religion of white men who kept them enslaved long after slavery was supposed to be abolished; the elements of African religions that added up to Voodoo survived until well after Johnson's time, and perhaps survive still; Finn believes that Johnson went 'to the crossroads' and made a deal with the devil in order to be able to express himself as a helpless Negro in the Mississippi of the '30s. Whether or not the white blues revivalists of the '60s who covered his songs believed in such things, Johnson may have done; as Finn points out, 'magic looks exactly like reality – only its effect is different.' 'Terraplane' was covered by CAPTAIN BEEFHEART, 'Crossroads' by CREAM, 'Love In Vain' and 'Stop Breakin' Down' by the ROLLING STONES. 32 Johnson tracks were issued on Columbia/CBS on two LPs '61 and '70; they have been continuously available ever since as *Robert Johnson: King Of The Delta Blues Singers*. Books: *Robert Johnson* '69 by Bob Groom; *Robert Johnson* '73 by Samuel B. Charters. Film *Crossroads* '86, with music by Ry COODER and Sonny TERRY, is based loosely on what is known of his life.

JOHNSON, Tommy (*b* c.1896, Terry, Ms.; *d* 1 Nov. '56, Crystal Springs, Ms.) Blues singer, guitarist: made only a handful of records, but was among the most influential of all. His brothers were musicians; he learned some guitar from brother Ledell (who said years later that Tommy acquired his final polish by selling himself to the devil: the interview in *Living Blues* is quoted by Julio Finn; *see* Robert JOHNSON). He often worked outside music as a farmer; hoboed through the south, worked jukes, parties, picnics, the streets, often with Ishman Bracey (*b* 9 Jan. '01, Byram, Ms.; *d* 12 Feb. '70, Jackson, Ms.). Recorded for Victor in Memphis '28, Paramount in Grafton, Wisc. '30, 15 sides altogether, solo except for fine second guitar by Charlie McCoy (*b* 26 May '09, Raymond, Ms.; *d* 28 Jan. '50, Chicago) on the first four sides, a kazoo on one Paramount side, New Orleans Nehi Boys (clarinet and piano) on the last. Bracey recorded almost exactly the same dates, times and places. Johnson's Victor sides have been reissued on Roots (*The Famous 1928 Tommy Johnson/Ishman Bracey Session*) and Historical LPs: 'Canned Heat Blues' gave the '60s blues band their name; his 'Cool Drink Of Water Blues' begins with the famous line 'I asked her for water/She gave me gasoline'. With those of Robert Johnson, his are among the most spine-tingling of Mississippi Delta blues. Good study *Tommy Johnson* by David Evans published '71 Studio Vista series edited by Paul Oliver.

JOHNSTONS, The Irish folk group of late '60s, early '70s formed around nucleus of Paul BRADY, Adrienne and Luci Johnston and Mick Moloney. Served a similar role in UK to that of Judy COLLINS in USA, popularising good songs by Leonard COHEN ('Seems So Long Ago, Nancy', 'Story Of Isaac'), Gordon LIGHTFOOT ('If I Could'), Ralph McTell ('Streets Of London'), Joni MITCHELL ('Both Sides Now' was a no. 1 hit in Eire), while their series of LPs on Transatlantic '67-71 incl. *The Johnstons, Give A Damn, The Barleycorn* and *Bitter Green* culminating in *Colours Of The Dawn*, by which time '60% of the material on the LP' was original. Moloney left '71; Brady and Adrienne prod. *If I Sang My Song* before they too called it a day. Among compilations *Streets Of London* on Sonas is perhaps most representative, while *Ye Jacobites By Name* on Contour incl. mainly trad. material, incl. 'Paddy's Green Shamrock Shore'. Brady went on to become a successful solo act; Adrienne made an RCA LP '75; Moloney released two fine LPs *Mick Moloney With Eugene O'Donnell* and *Strings Attached*, as well as guesting on LPs by O'Donnell, James Keane and Martin Mulvihill; he prod. albums by the Irish Tradition and Paddy Tunney, Irish-American anthology *Cherish The Ladies*.

JO JO GUNNE USA rock band formed in L.A. by ex-SPIRIT members vocalist Jay Ferguson, bassist Mark Andes; they left Randy California's ever more way-out musical ideas to form straight-ahead good-time band, recruiting Matthew Andes on guitar (Mark's brother) and Curly Smith on drums (*b* 31 Jan. '52, Wolf Point, Montana). Among first signings to David GEFFEN's Asylum label: named after Chuck BERRY song, photogenic appearance with catchy songs from Mark and Ferguson led to quick success (perhaps too quick): boogie rocker 'Run Run Run', with rolling piano from Ferguson, made no. 27 USA/6 UK '72; with entertaining LP *Jo Jo Gunne* that year was a promising start, but things went downhill fast: Mark went solo, replaced by Jimmie Randell (*b* 14 Feb. '49, Dallas) for *Bite Down Hard* and *Jumpin' The Gunne* '73, and sales slumped. Matt followed his brother, replaced by Stan Donaldson, then John Staehely (*b* 25 Jan. '52, Austin; yet another ex-Spirit), but band self-destructed after *So . . . Where's The Show?* '74. Andes brothers returned to Spirit; Ferguson cut several solo LPs (with help from Joe WALSH): second *Thunder Island* '78 charted, helped by title track (top 10 single); *Real Life Ain't This Way* '79 also made top 100 LPs; 'Shakedown Cruise' made no. 31 singles chart; switched to Capitol from Asylum for *White Noise* '82, last LP chart entry at no. 178. Mark Andes found success with FIREFALL, later Heart.

JO JO ZEP AND THE FALCONS Australian rock band headed by Malta-born sax-player, singer Joe Camilleri. Worked in '60s bands King Bees, Adderly Smith Blues Band, Lipp and the Double Decker Brothers, then Pelaco Brothers; formed Melbourne-based Jo Jo Zep and the Falcons '76, at first R&B sextet with Wayne Burt (ex-Alvin STARDUST, guitar), Gary Young (ex-Daddy Cool, drums), Wilbur Wilde (sax), others. Signed to EMI-Oz same year; early singles incl. covers of Chuck BERRY's 'Run Rudolph Run', Joe Liggins's 'The Honeydripper', etc. First hit EP *Loud And Clear* '78; this band incl. Young, Wilde, Jeff Burstin, Tony Faehse (guitars), Camilleri sharing vocals with Faehse. Switched to Mushroom label early '79, had major hit with 'Hit And Run', chart LP *Screaming Targets*. R&B style by then discarded; infl. by Elvis COSTELLO, Graham PARKER; chart LP *Hats Off, Step Lively* produced by keyboardist Pete Solley. More line-up changes followed; by '82 Camilleri performing under name Jo Jo Zep with almost anonymous backup; hit single 'Taxi Mary' '82; LP *Cha* on A&M USA; early '85 formed own Spirit label, mounted tour Balling Up In Zydeco with signings Jane Clifton, Nick Smith, Billy Baxter, Steve Hoy.

JOLSON, Al (*b* Asa Yoelson, 26 Mar. 1886, Russia; *d* 23 Oct. '50, San Francisco) Singer, songwriter. Billed himself as The World's Greatest Entertainer, not without justification: an inspiration for Bing CROSBY, many others, for his dedication to pleasing his audience, not for his style. To USA as a child; broke into vaudeville before his voice broke, then turned to whistling; had act with brother Hirsch (Harry) as 'The Hebrew and the Cadet'. His brother was the first of the two to perform in blackface ('02); later Al became famous for it and Harry was accused of doing it to cash in. His first recording was for Victor '11 ('That Haunting Melody', song by George M. COHAN); allegedly had trouble standing still in order to sing into acoustic horn. Invented catch-phrase 'You ain't heard nothin' yet!' around '06; allegedly used it '18 at a benefit when he followed Caruso. Appeared in 10 Broadway shows '11-31 incl. *Sinbad* '18; starred in the first talking picture *The Jazz Singer* '27 (though not a jazz singer by any definition); his second film *The Singing Fool* '28 was the first talkie in many cinemas hastily re-wired for sound. Married third wife actress Ruby Keeler '28; he had broken into vaudeville by singing from the audience, then in '29 sang 'Liza' to her from the audience at Broadway premiere of *Show Girl*. He was successful on radio (with Paul WHITEMAN '33-4, *The Shell Chateau* '35-6, etc.). They separated '39; he was devastated and his career was faltering; he talked her into co-starring in *Hold On To Your Hats* '40 but she left before Broadway opening; the show was a hit, but his voice failed and he had to close it after 158 performances. He made 10 more films '29-45; entertained troops from North Africa to Alaska during WWII; to Hollywood '44 as a producer and considered playing himself in biopic, but looked at himself in the mirror: Larry Parks played Jolson in *The Jolson Story* '46, *Jolson Sings Again* '49, but Jolson sang in the soundtracks and his voice was never better. Teenagers bought his records because they thought he looked like Parks (who later appeared before the House Unamerican Activities Committee: his career was ruined). Jolson entertained troops in Japan and Korea '50 a month before he died, by then a show-biz legend. He was most famous for 'My Mammy', 'Sonny Boy', George GERSHWIN's 'Swanee', delivered in blackface with white gloves and on one knee, using emotional declaration at the expense of melody; his style died with him, but he also co-wrote songs (or bought an interest in them by performing them: he may never have written anything, but could make a song a hit by performing it) incl. 'Avalon', 'California, Here I Come', 'Me And My Shadow', 'Back In Your Own Back Yard', 'All My Love', 'There's A Rainbow

'Round My Shoulder', 'The Anniversary Song', others; collaborators incl. Billy ROSE, Ray Henderson (*see* DeSYLVA, BROWN & HENDERSON), Sheldon Brooks (*see* Sophie TUCKER) and Harry Akst, also his accompanist for many years (*b* 15 Aug. 1894, NYC; *d* 31 Mar. '63, Hollywood). He was also famous for 'April Showers', 'Toot, Toot, Tootsie, Goo'Bye', 'Rockabye Your Baby With A Dixie Melody' (revived by Jerry Lewis '56, Aretha FRANKLIN '61). Four sets of 78s topped the album charts '46-9; *The Best Of Jolson* '62 was no. 40 LP chart. Compilations incl. 2-disc *Best Of, Rainbow Round My Shoulder, Rock-A-Bye Your Baby, You Made Me Love You* on MCA; five vols. of *On The Air* on Totem; *California, Here I Come* and *Steppin' Out* on Sunbeam.

JONES, Elvin (*b* Elvin Ray Jones, 9 Sep. '27, Pontiac, Mich.) Drummer. Younger brother of Hank and Thad JONES. Worked with them in Detroit; then to NYC '56, working with Pepper ADAMS – Donald BYRD quintet, others; then with John COLTRANE quartet '60-5, probably the perfect drummer for the most influential combo of that decade, joining the line of Jo JONES with Count BASIE in the late '30s, Max ROACH during the bop era and Philly Joe JONES with Miles DAVIS in the '50s in advancing the frontier of the possible in the rhythm sections of mainstream black music. His hands and feet appear to be four separate entities, often doing the unpredictable, yet the overall dynamic is a 'circle of sound': intensely rhythmic, supporting soloists, yet yearning towards more freedom, as Coltrane did. Such a strong musical personality did not like playing with another drummer when Coltrane added Rashied ALI (although his first LP as leader, *Together* '61 on Atlantic, incl. Philly Joe); anyway the era of the Coltrane quartet seemed to be over as its leader pursued experiments. Jones joined Duke ELLINGTON in Europe early '66 but left him after a few days; he has led various iconoclastic lineups ever since, usually without brass and often without keyboards, well documented on records, as well as doing clinics, free concerts in prisons, etc. Other LPs: *Elvin!* '61-2 on Riverside, *And Then Again* '65 on Atlantic incl. brothers; *Illumination* '63 on Impulse was co-led by Jimmy GARRISON and incl. McCoy TYNER,

three others; *Dear John C* early '65 on Impulse was a quartet with Charlie Mariano on alto (*b* 12 Nov. '23, Boston), Richard Davis on bass, Hank or Roland Hanna on piano. Sextet *Midnight Walk* on Atlantic featured Thad, Hank MOBLEY, Dollar Brand; *Heavy Sounds* on Impulse is a quartet with Davis, Frank Foster and Billy Greene on piano, while trios *Puttin' It Together* and *The Ultimate* on Blue Note initiate his pianoless era, with Garrison on bass and Joe Farrell on tenor, soprano and flutes, all '68. On Blue Note: quintet *The Prime Element* '69 has Farrell, George COLEMAN, Lee MORGAN, Wilbur Little on bass (*b* 5 Mar. '28, Parmele, N.C., a valuable sideman on many records), plus extra percussion; *Poly-Currents* '69 has Farrell (English horn on one track), Pepper Adams, Coleman, Little, Fred Tomkins on flute on two tracks (composed 'Concerto for two flutes'); *Mr Jones* same month has same cast without Tomkins; *Coalition* '70 is without Adams. *Genesis* '71 has three reeds: Foster, Farrell and Dave Liebman (*b* 4 Sep. '46, Brooklyn; worked with Miles Davis '73-4; own LPs on PM, ECM, Horizon), Gene Perla on bass (*b* 1 Mar. '40, N.J.); *Merry-Go-Round* '71 had 11 pieces, restoring the keyboard with both Chick COREA, Jan HAMMER, and on reeds Farrell, Liebman, Foster, Adams and Steve Grossman (*b* 18 Jan. '51, Brooklyn); *Live At The Lighthouse* same year was a quartet with Grossman, Liebman and Perla; *The Prime Element* '73 had 11 pieces again, incl. extra percussion, Hammer on mini-Moog as well as pianos. Meanwhile, four LPs called *Sky Scrapers* c.'70 on a Honeydew label are by a trio (Coleman and Little), adding trumpeter Marvin 'Hannibal' Peterson on the last; *Live At The Town Hall* '71 on PM has Corea, Perla, Farrell, Foster. *Live At The Village Vanguard* '73 on Enja with Coleman and Little has Peterson on one track; quintet *Mr Thunder* was made in Warsaw, available on Polish and French labels; *Elvin Jones Is On The Mountain* '75 on PM has Perla and Hammer (adding synth to the keyboards). On Vanguard: *New Agenda* '75, *The Main Force* '76, *Time Capsule* '77 and *Summit Meeting* '76 have eight or nine pieces (the last with James MOODY, Al Dailey, Clark TERRY); quartet LP *Very R.A.R.E.* '79 has Art PEPPER, Hanna, Davis. *Remembrance*

'78 on MPS/Pausa was made in Stuttgart; quintet *Soul Trane* with Andrew WHITE and piano trio *Heart To Heart* with Davis, Tommy FLANAGAN '80 are on Japanese Denon; *Earth Jones* and *Brother John* '82 are on Palo Alto; also LPs on Enja with Flanagan as leader. *Reunited* '86 on Blackhawk is co-led with Tyner, incl. Pharoah SANDERS, Richard Davis on bass, Jean-Paul Bourelly on guitar.

JONES, George (*b* 12 Sep. '31, Saratoga, Texas) Country singer, with more than 250 albums to his credit, regarded by many as the greatest country singer of all time and admired outside country music by people as diverse as Linda RONSTADT, Elvis COSTELLO, Emmylou HARRIS and Dave EDMUNDS. From a religious family background; began playing guitar with duo Eddie & Pearl '47; served in US Marines. Worked honky tonks in East Texas with a style heavily infl. by Hank WILLIAMS and Roy ACUFF. Signed to Pappy Daily's Starday label '52, embarking on one of the most rewarding artist/producer relationships in the history of country music, lasting 16 years through Starday, Mercury, UA and Musicor. 'Why Baby Why' was a top 5 country hit '55; he tried country weepers and rock'n'roll under the name Thumper Jones; according to one source recording 'Heartbreak Hotel' as 'Hank Smith and the Nashville Playboys'; then had more hits on Mercury with 'Treasure Of Love' '58, 'White Lightning' '59 (his first no. 1), 'The Window Up Above' '60, 'Tender Years' '61 (second no. 1); also had hit duets with Melba MONTGOMERY, Margie Singleton, Brenda Carter and Gene PITNEY. Topped country chart '62 with 'She Thinks I Still Care' on UA, followed by 'You Comb Her Hair' '63, 'The Race Is On' '64. Named no. 1 country male vocalist by Cashbox '62, Billboard '63; switched to Musicor '65 and carried on with 'Love Bug' '65, 'Walk Through This World With Me' '67 (no. 1), 'When The Grass Grows Over Me' '68 etc.: 59 country-chart entries '55-71, 31 in top 10. Married Tammy WYNETTE 16 Feb. '69, though for publicity reasons it was maintained that they'd married 22 Aug. '68: it was a stormy marriage between two strong personalities; Jones was a heavy drinker by then. On one occasion, she hid his car keys

and he was said to have driven 10 miles to Nashville on a lawn mower for a bottle. They toured all over the USA together; when his contract with Musicor ran out he signed with Epic (her label), was prod. by Billy Sherrill, whose lush pop/country arrangements could not disguise his pure country voice: he had such hits as 'Loving You Could Never Be Better' '72, 'Once You've Had The Best' '73, 'The Grand Tour' '74 and 'These Days I Hardly Get By' '75; also duets with Tammy incl. no. 1 'We're Gonna Hold On' '73, 'Golden Ring' '76. Their duets are regarded as perhaps the best of all in a genre which has always liked male-female duets. The king and queen of country were divorced 13 Mar. '75; several of her hits were aimed pointedly at his life style. He continued to have hits but his personal life was a shambles; he filed bankruptcy late '79 and volunteered for treatment for alcoholism; friends rallied round and he made his first gold album *I Am What I Am* '80 incl. multi-award winning single 'He Stopped Loving Her Today'. He was named CMA vocalist '80, long after he was obviously one of the all-time greats. In recent years he has recorded duets with Johnny PAYCHECK, Merle HAGGARD, Willie NELSON, Costello, Harris, LP with Wynette. LPs incl. *Long Live King George* '58 on Starday; *Novelty Side* '60, *No. 1 Male Singer* '61 on Mercury; *My Favorites Of Hank Williams* '62, *What's In Our Hearts* '63 (with Montgomery), *King Of Broken Hearts* '64 on UA; *Old Brush Arbors* '66, *Songs Of Dallas Frazier* '68, *My Country* '69 on Musicor; *In A Gospel Way* '72, *Memories Of Us* '74, *Alone Again* '76, *Bartender's Blues* '78, *My Very Special Guests* '79 (duets), *Still The Same Ol' Me* '81, *Jones Country* '83, *Who's Gonna Fill Their Shoes* '85 on Epic; also *Rockin' The Country* '85 on Mercury (Starday, Mercury reissues from '50s); *Burn The Honky Tonk Down, Heartaches And Hangovers* on Rounder; *Golden Ring, Greatest Hits, Encore, Together Again* on Epic (all duets with Wynette), *Blue Moon Of Kentucky* on EMI UK (compiles 20 fine tracks from UA '62-5), many more. *Too Wild Too Long* '88 is up to his highest standard.

JONES, Grace (*b* 19 May '52, Jamaica) West Indian soul singer. Statuesque 6-foot exotic beauty was raised in NYC, became successful model on European circuit before broadening career into music at height of disco boom '77. Early records prod. by Tom Moulton were fairly tame: *Portfolio* '77, *Fame* '78, *Muse* '79 featuring disco-diva crooning over standard dance-track backing, but went down well. Wild fashion taste and stunning looks won support of the hip set and the gay crowd. Stage act masterminded by French designer/artist and current beau Jean-Paul Goude raised eyebrows everywhere (captured on *One Man Show* video); this was combined with a new musical approach: she went to native West Indies for the cream of reggae musicians (e.g. Sly Dunbar and Robbie Shakespeare) for sinuous reggae/funk backgrounds for half-spoken half-sung delivery: unlike her previous disco hits, these were distinctive, still danceable and very hip. *Warm Leatherette* '80 had title track cover of the Normal's depiction of car accident; also cover of the PRETENDERS' 'Private Life', ROXY MUSIC's 'Love Is The Drug'. Island Records boss Chris Blackwell produced it personally. *Nightclubbing* '81 repeated the prescription, covering David BOWIE/IGGY POP title track, introducing Jones as writer in 'Pull Up To The Bumper' (co-credited Kookoo Baya), top 5 USA soul hit (and UK hit on '86 re-release). *Living My Life* '82 was much more relaxed and reggae-inspired, all but one song with Jones's lyrics: first top 100 USA LP. She diversified into the James Bond film *A View To A Kill*, visually arresting TV advert for Renault; returned to recording with ZTT label-boss/prod. Trevor HORN. 'Slave To The Rhythm', written for FRANKIE GOES TO HOLLYWOOD, was UK hit '85 and extended (in true ZTT fashion) to an LP in various versions incl. interview with Jones, a willing accomplice. This led to more accusations of being a puppet (cf. Goude), but she maintained that she was always in control. Compilation *Island Life* '85 testified to eight eventful years; left Island for new Manhattan label, *Inside Story* '86 was improvement on recent work. $250,000 was spent on video of 'I'm Not Perfect (But I'm Perfect For You)'. She will be remembered for brutal, androgynous image as well as lugubrious vocals.

JONES, Grandpa (*b* Louis Marshall Jones, 20 Oct. '13, Niagra, Ky.) Country singer,

comedian, banjo player. Began on guitar, won talent contest at 16; put on old man disguise at 22 because he sounded older on radio, working with Bradley KINCAID band; also switched to banjo in Uncle Dave MACON style, told stories and tall tales about mountain folk. Formed Grandpa Jones and his Grandchildren '37, disbanded during WWII; became regular on Grand Ole Opry, later on TV's *Hee-Haw*. Recorded for King (LPs incl. *16 Sacred Gospel Songs* (with Merle TRAVIS and the Delmore Bros as the Brown's Ferry 4), *The Other Side Of Grandpa Jones*, *24 Great Country Songs*). His only C&W chart hits were 'The All-American Boy' '59 on Decca, 'T For Texas' '62 (Jimmie RODGERS song) on Monument; but famous for up-tempo 'Old Rattler' and 'Mountain Dew', extremely well-recorded on Decca '50s with fine banjo picking and hilarious lyrics. More LPs: *Sixteen Greatest Hits* on Starday, *Gospel According To Grandpa Jones* on Skylite, *The Man From Kentucky* on Bulldog, *20 Of The Best* on RCA International, three 2-disc sets on CMH: *The Grandpa Jones Story*, *Old Time Country Music*, *Family Album*. Elected to Country Music Hall of Fame '78.

JONES, Hank (*b* 31 July '18, Pontiac, Mich.) Piano. Brother of Thad and Elvin JONES. Infl. by Art TATUM, Teddy WILSON; to NYC '44 and infl. by Bud POWELL, Al HAIG; toured with JATP, accompanied Billy ECKSTINE, later Ella FITZGERALD ('48-53); worked with Benny GOODMAN '56-8; much freelancing and studio work. A valuable sideman on innumerable records; own records (solo and trio), '47-'53 on Norman GRANZ's labels; then on Savoy: *The Trio* '55 with Kenny CLARKE, bassist Wendell Marshall; other tracks with Joe WILDER, Donald BYRD, Herbie MANN, others on various LPs called *Hank Jones Quartet/Quintet*, *Night People*, *The Many Faces Of The Blues* etc., all '55; solo set *Have You Met Hank Jones* '56. *Hank Jones Quartet* '56 on Epic with drummer Osie Johnson (*b* 11 Jan. 23, Washington; *d* 10 Feb. '66, NYC), guitarist Barry Galbraith (*b* 18 Dec. '19, Pittsburgh) and Milt HINTON on bass: this quartet was a highly rated NYC rhythm section, in early '60s often making three recording sessions a day. They also made *The Talented Touch* '58 on Capitol; *Hank*

Jones Trio '58 on ABC without Galbraith has interpretations of rags by Scott JOPLIN, others. Songs from *Porgy And Bess* '60 on Capitol and *Here's Love* 63 on Argo have Elvin, Hinton, Kenny BURRELL; an Impulse LP '66 has the Oliver NELSON band. Solo LPs: *Satin Doll* '76 on Trio and *Tiptoe Tapdance* '77-8 on Galaxy; trio sets with bassists Eddie Gomez, Richard Davis, Ray BROWN, Ron CARTER, George DUVIVIER, drummers Alan Dawson, Jimmy Smith, Shelly MANNE, Tony WILLIAMS etc. on Japanese labels Trio, Interface, Progressive, East Wind, etc. incl. *Hanky Panky* '75, *Love For Sale* and *Arigato* '76, *The Great Jazz Trio At The Village Vanguard* '77 (also on Inner City), *Direct From L.A.* '77, *Milestones* '78, *Easy Love* '79, *Live In Japan* '79, *Chapter II* '80, *Re-Visited* (at the Vanguard, 2 vols.) '80, *Threesome* '82, *The Club New Yorker* '83, *Monk's Moods* '84; on French Black & Blue: *I Remember You* '77, *Compassion* '78, *Bluesette* '79. Also *Jones-Brown-Smith* '76 on Concord Jazz; *Bop Redux* '77 and *Groovin' High* '78 on Muse; *Just For Fun* '77, *Ain't Misbehavin'* '78 (with guitar and reeds on one track) on Galaxy; *Have You Met This Jones* '77 on MPS/Pausa; *The Trio* '77 on Chiaroscuro with Bobby Rosengarden (*b* 23 Apr. '24, Elgin, Ill.) on drums, Hinton on bass; *Kindness, Joy, Love & Happiness* '77 on Inner City (also on East Wind), *The Great Jazz Trio* '80 on Phonogram. 'The Great Jazz Trio and Friends' at *Aurex Jazz Festival* '81 incl. Gomez, Benny GOLSON, Art FARMER, Nancy WILSON, drummer Buddy Williams. Piano duets with Tommy FLANAGAN: *I'm All Smiles* on Verve, *Our Delights* and *More Delights* '78 on Galaxy.

JONES, Howard (*b* 23 Feb. '55, Southampton, England) Singer, synthesisers. Joined first band age 15 in Canada after family's emigration; returned to UK to study at Manchester U., where he acquired his first synthesiser. Began playing pubs and clubs around High Wycombe with mime artist Jed Hoile. His brand of 'one-man band' music found success with debut single 'New Song' (UK no. 3 '83); three more top 10 hits his inoffensive synth-pop was in tune with pop blandness of the early '80s; *Human's Lib* '84 entered UK LP chart at no. 1, incl. all the hit singles and displaying limi-

tations of the style. *Dream Into Action* '85 was a marginal improvement with funky 'Look Mama'. 'No One Is To Blame' featured guest Phil COLLINS; LP *One To One* '86 prod. by Arif Mardin (Culture Club, Chaka KHAN, Scritti Politti).

JONES, Isham (*b* 31 Jan. 1894, Coalton, Ohio; *d* 19 Oct. '56, Hollywood) Bandleader; he also played piano, tenor sax; arranger, composer. Had more than 70 big hits '20-38, most of them in the top 10 until '32 when he switched from Brunswick to Victor. Led Chicago trio on tenor '15, then larger groups, had no. 1 hits 'Wabash Blues', 'On The Alamo', 'Swingin' Down The Lane', 'Spain', 'I'll See You In My Dreams' '21-5; 'Stardust' had been recorded in uptempo versions by the Chocolate Dandies, others, but in '30 Jones established the Hoagy CARMICHAEL classic as a romantic ballad and one of the all time great American popular songs. The band reached its peak '30-5, with Pee Wee Erwin on trumpet (*b* George Erwin, 30 May '13, Falls City, Neb.; *d* 20 June '81, Teaneck, N.J.), Jack Jenney on trombone (*b* Truman Elliot Jenney, 12 May '10, Mason City, Iowa; *d* 16 Dec. '45, L.A.), Woody HERMAN on vocals and clarinet, Gordon JENKINS as arranger, others incl. popular vocalist Eddie Stone. Jones's own composition 'You're Just A Beautiful Dream Come True' '31 became the band's theme; other songs he co-wrote incl. 'I'll See You In My Dreams', 'On The Alamo', 'Swingin' Down The Lane', 'It Had To Be You', etc. Collaborators incl. Charles Newman (*b* 22 Feb. '01, Chicago; *d* 9 Jan. '78, Beverly Hills, Cal.), Gus Kahn. He disbanded '36; members under Herman organised cooperative band; he re-formed '37-42, thereafter led bands occasionally, based on West Coast mostly composing. He also recorded with Al JOLSON for Brunswick; late '30s recorded for Decca and Vocalion. Reissues incl. *The Great Isham Jones & His Orchestra* in RCA LPV series, *Swingin' Down The Lane* on Ace Of Hearts (from Brunswick), two vols. on Sunbeam ('29-30 and '36). There was also a 10″ LP on Capitol early '50s, all his own tunes sung by Curt Massey.

JONES, Jack (*b* 14 Jan. '38, L.A.) Singer. Mother was actress Irene Hervey; father

Allan Jones was popular light classical singer '30s; had acting/singing role in Marx Bros films *A Night At The Opera* '35, *A Day At The Races* '37; biggest hit with operetta *The Firefly* '37 (with Jeanette MacDonald; *see* Nelson EDDY); sang Rudolph FRIML's 'Donkey Serenade'. Jack's mainstream SINATRA-style was surprisingly successful in the '60s, when everyone had gone rock mad, perhaps owing to very good choice of material as well as his engaging style and pleasant light baritone. He had 20 Hot 100 entries '62-8 (on Kapp until late '67, then on RCA); first was 'Lollipops And Roses' and he also had success with 'Call Me Irresponsible' (by Sammy CAHN and Jimmy VAN HEUSEN, who also wrote many songs for Sinatra; this was featured in the Jackie GLEASON film *Papa's Delicate Condition* and won an Oscar '63). Few singles reached the top 40; the biggest were 'Wives And Lovers' '63 and 'The Race Is On' '65, both top 15. Of 17 LPs reaching Billboard's Top 200 albums chart the biggest hits were *Dear Heart* and *The Impossible Dream* '65-6, both reissued '85 on MCA; also 2-disc *Best Of* on MCA. RCA LPs incl. *If You Ever Leave Me, Where Is Love?, A Time For Us* '68-9. He remained popular in clubs after record sales slowed.

JONES, Jo (*b* Jonathan Jones, 7 Oct. '11, Chicago; *d* 3 Sep. '85, NYC) Drummer; one of the most important in history. He studied music for years, also played piano, reeds and trumpet; went to Kansas City '33, worked with Count BASIE '35-6, rejoined shortly and stayed until '48 except while in the US Army. He minimised the use of the bass drum and kept time on the top cymbal, freeing the drum kit to do more than simply mark time: Kenny CLARKE, Max ROACH and others developed this in the bop era of the '40s. He was not the only swing era drummer to practise the new, lighter concentration on the cymbal, and in later years constant beating of the cymbal by other drummers was often irritating (sometimes because badly recorded); but he did it with such finesse, humour and good taste (rarely taking solos) that he was the most influential of his generation: the rhythm section of the Basie band in its classic years swung like a light, well-oiled machine, and he lifted every session he played on. He made record dates with Teddy WILSON, Lionel Hampton, many others '37-8, with the Benny GOODMAN sextet '41, later on LPs with Buck CLAYTON, Sonny STITT, Ruby BRAFF, Paul QUINICHETTE, Coleman HAWKINS, Jimmy RUSHING, Illinois JACQUET, Nat PIERCE, many others. Toured Europe with Ella FITZGERALD, Oscar PETERSON '57; with JATP that year; led own trios in NYC '57-60, taught and ran a music shop. LPs as leader incl. *Jo Jones Special* on Vanguard '55, an absolute delight, reissued with another Vanguard LP as *The Essential Jo Jones* on French Vogue; 2-disc set *The Drums* on Jazz Odyssey, on which he played, talked about his life and music; session with Harry EDISON '60 on Archive Of Folk; *The Main Man* on Pablo; *Our Man Papa Jo* on Denon c.'82, perhaps his last session, with Hank JONES, Major Holley on bass (*b* Major Quincy Holley Jr, 10 July '24, Detroit; aka 'Mule'), Jimmy Oliver, sax.

JONES, Jonah (*b* Robert Elliott Jones, 31 Dec. '08, Louisville, Ky.) Trumpet, vocals. Played in riverboat bands etc.; with Horace HENDERSON '28, Jimmie LUNCEFORD '31, often with Stuff SMITH '30s (shared comedy vocals), McKINNEY'S COTTON PICKERS '35, Fletcher HENDERSON '40, Benny CARTER '40-1, Cab CALLOWAY '41-52. (With Calloway, it was Jonah who threw the spitball that got Dizzy GILLESPIE fired.) Also frequent sideman on record sessions with Teddy WILSON / Billie HOLIDAY etc. Tracks from this period on Commodore LP *Swing Street Showcase*, with Hot Lips PAGE. With Earl HINES sextet '52-3, Broadway pit band in *Porgy And Bess* '53; toured Europe as solo, etc. Formed combo for night-club work and became unexpected commercial success, singing and playing mostly muted horn: Capitol LPs *Muted Jazz, Swingin' On Broadway, Jumpin' With Jonah* were all top 15 albums '58: it should have happened to a lot more of the experienced stalwarts of mainstream jazz, but fans were happy that at least it happened to the ebullient Jones. He was still popular and still touring in the '80s. Other quartet LPs on Decca and Motown; also co-led LP *Back On The Street* '73 on Chiaroscuro with Hines, Buddy TATE, Cozy COLE, two others.

JONES, Nic (*b* Nicholas Paul Jones, 9 Jan. '47, Orpington, Kent) Folk singer, instrumentalist; one of the UK folk revival's most accomplished interpreters, held in great esteem for fiddle and guitar playing. Infl. by Chet ATKINS, Martin CARTHY, Bert Jansch, Davey Graham; his playing is percussive similarly to Carthy's, rather more restrained and ornamented. Member of group Halliad; first solo album *Ballads And Songs* '70 on Trailer incl. 'Sir Patrick Spens', 'Little Musgrave', 'The Outlandish Knight'; *Nic Jones* '71 incl. 'further version' of the latter: LPs revealed highly ornamented style which later became more economic. Played on *The Silly Sisters* '76 (Maddy Prior and June TABOR), also toured with them; accompanied Tabor on her *Ashes And Diamonds, The Noah's Ark Trap, From The Devil To A Stranger*, demonstrating growing mastery; made *Bandoggs* '78 on Transatlantic (short-lived band of that name incl. Pete & Chris Coe and Tony Rose). His *Penguin Eggs* '80 on Topic raised him to the ranks of the best, *Melody Maker* folk album of the year described as 'truly essential'; standout tracks were Paul Metser's 'Farewell To The Gold' and Harry Roberts' 'The Humpback Whale' (widely and mistakenly believed to be trad. song when the album was released). With star in the ascendant, was critically injured in a car crash '82, had not fully recovered '87.

JONES, Philly Joe (*b* Joseph Rudolph Jones, 15 July '23, Philadelphia, Pa.; *d* there 30 Aug. '85) Drums; other instruments. One of the most important modern jazz drummers preceding Elvin JONES (no relation). Played in local combos backing Dexter GORDON, other visiting musicians; to NYC gigging widely, with Miles DAVIS off and on from '52; in '56-8 a member of the Davis sextet for albums on Prestige such as *Workin'*, *Steamin'*. Davis once said, 'I wouldn't care if he came up on the stand in his BVDs and with one arm, just so long as he was there. He's got the fire I want.' The fire was a kind of controlled explosion, always in good taste but with the feeling that there was plenty of power and emotion in reserve; some were afraid that Jones's energy would overpower a Miles Davis sextet, but they also didn't like John COLTRANE (recommended to Miles by Philly Joe): Davis knew what he wanted; the combo was perhaps the greatest of the era. Jones's solos

were never over the top either, but full of listenable and musical surprise. He rejoined Davis briefly '62, freelanced on the West Coast, visited Japan '65, taught in London and Paris '67-9, spent time in Europe early '70s. His own LPs, always with good sidemen such as Johnny GRIFFIN, Mickey TUCKER, Tommy FLANAGAN, Paul CHAMBERS, Jimmy Garrison, many others, began with sextet *Time For Dracula* '58, big band *Drums Around The World* '59, sextet/septet *Showcase* '59 on Riverside; *Philly Joe's Beat* '60 (also *Together* '61 led by Elvin Jones) on Atlantic. *Trailways Express* '68 on Black Lion was made in London, with Kenny WHEELER; *Round Midnight* '69 on Lotus in Italy with Dizzy Reese on trumpet (*b* 5 Jan. '31, Jamaica); *Mean What You Say* '77 in NYC for Swedish Sonet label (with Tucker). *Philly Mignon* '77 (with Gordon, Nat ADDERLEY), *Drum Song* and *Advance!* '78 on Galaxy. Led Dameronia, 9 or 10-piece combo that played compositions of Tadd DAMERON, others: *To Tadd With Love* '82, *Look Stop Listen* '83 on Uptown with Cecil PAYNE, Larry Ridley on bass (*b* 3 Sep. '37, Indianapolis), Walter Davis Jr on piano, Donald Sickler on trumpet, various others.

JONES, Quincy (*b* Quincy Delight Jones Jr, 14 Mar. '33, Chicago) Trumpet, keyboards, bandleader, composer, arranger, producer, record industry executive: one of the most successful skilled craftsmen in music, who can and does turn his hand to anything. Had a vocal quartet in church in Seattle at age 10; started on trumpet '47 (lessons from Clark TERRY). Played with Lionel HAMPTON '51-3 (first recorded composition: 'Kingfish' on MGM; played trumpet solo); wrote arrangements for Ray ANTHONY, others; mus. dir., member of Dizzy GILLESPIE band that toured the world '56. Octet arrangements *'Scuse These Bloos* '53 recorded in Stockholm with Art FARMER, Clifford BROWN or Jimmy Cleveland on some tracks, excellent Swedish sidemen, while on tour with Lionel Hampton; reissued '87 on resurrected UK Esquire label: his roots were deep in the swing era; by the time of *This Is How I Feel About Jazz* '56 his jazz chops seemed conservative, but his musical smarts had many facets. Worked for Barclay Records in Paris '57-8; wrote an LP for Count BASIE; mus. dir. of Harold

ARLEN show *Free And Easy* '59, toured Europe with it '59-60. He played less trumpet but often fronted big bands; worked for Mercury Records '61-8, became vice-president '64, prod. big hits for Lesley GORE; LPs as leader, also as mus. dir. for Peggy LEE (on Capitol), Sarah VAUGHAN (on Mercury), Billy ECKSTINE, Frank SINATRA etc.: wrote arrangements and led the band on Sinatra's LPs with Basie: studio LP *It Might As Well Be Swing* '64 and Sinatra's first released concert set, 2-disc *Sinatra At The Sands* '66. Began writing film scores, incl. *The Pawnbroker* '65; *In Cold Blood* '67; *Cactus Flower, In The Heat Of The Night* and *Bob And Carol And Ted And Alice* '69; *The Anderson Tapes* '71; *The Getaway* and *The New Centurions* '72, *The Wiz* '78 (all-black adaptation of *Wizard Of Oz*), many others, several nominated for Oscars; he was mus. dir. for Academy Awards show '71. TV music incl. *Sanford And Son*, Bill Cosby shows, *Duke Ellington . . . We Love You Madly!* on CBS '73, series *Roots* '77, *Rebop* on PBS, etc. *Black Requiem* written '71 for Houston Symphony Orchestra, choir and Ray CHARLES, a friend since Seattle. Soul and R&B figured larger in his work with Roberta FLACK, Aretha FRANKLIN (*Hey Now Hey* '73), Michael JACKSON (prod. *Off The Wall*, then *Thriller*, biggest selling LP of all time), also Al JARREAU, others; prod. American Band Aid record 'We Are The World' '85. President of Qwest Records: prod. for his own label Patti AUSTIN LPs, also *L.A. Is My Lady* '84 with Sinatra (both album and title track single were chart entries). His own 8 Hot 100 chart singles '70-81 incl. 'Killer Joe' '70 (both pop and soul charts), 'Stuff Like That' '78 (vocals by ASHFORD & SIMPSON, Chaka KHAN); both 'Just Once' and 'One Hundred Ways' with vocals by James Ingrams made top 20 '81. 'Summer In The City' won a Grammy '73 for best instrumental. Own LPs incl. *Live At Newport 1961* on Trip; *Great Wide World Of Quincy Jones* '59 on several labels; *Great Wide World Live!* '61, *Birth Of A Band* '59 (2-disc set with Terry, Zoot SIMS, Phil WOODS, Lee MORGAN etc.), *Birth* Vol. 2 '59-63, all on EmArcy; *Mode* (ABC) and *Quintessence* (Impulse) now 2-disc *Quintessential Charts* on MCA; *We Had A Ball* on Polydor; also hits in pop LP chart: *Big Band Bossa Nova* '62, 2-disc compilation

Ndeda '72 on Mercury; *Walking In Space* '69 (won Grammy), *Gula Matari* '70, *Smackwater Jack* '71 (Grammy), *You've Got It Bad Girl* '73 (incl. 'Summer'; LP reissued on high-tech Mobile Fidelity label), *Body Heat* '74, *Mellow Madness* '75 (introduced BROTHERS JOHNSON), 2-disc compilation *I Heard That!* '76, *Roots* (TV score) '77, *The Dude* '81 (with hit Ingrams vocals), all on A&M, plus *Best Of* sets. Book-length profile *Quincy Jones* by Raymond Horricks '85.

JONES, Rickie Lee (*b* 8 Nov. '54, Chicago) USA singer/songwriter. 'Easy Money', a lowlife tale of good-time girls, was recorded by Lowell George (of LITTLE FEAT) on solo LP *Thanks I'll Eat It Here* '79, brought her to WB's attention; she was unfairly categorised as West Coast soft rock when her first (eponymous) LP '79 was prod. by Larry Waronker (Randy NEWMAN, Maria MULDAUR); that she had roots wide and deep in '40s pop, folk, jazz etc. soon became obvious. LP incl. 'Chuck E's In Love' (USA no. 4 hit, UK no. 18), also unsuspected depth in songs like 'On Saturday Afternoons In 1963'. Yet relative commercial failure of LPs conspired with widely spaced output to reduce public profile. After disappointment of *Pirates* '81 she filled part-live *Girl At Her Volcano* '83 with covers: Left Banke's 'Walk Away Rene', DRIFTERS' 'Under The Boardwalk'; also RODGERS & HART's 'My Funny Valentine'. Her between-songs monologues show the infl. of Beat poets, which she shares with former boyfriend Tom WAITS (cover of whose *Blue Valentine* '78 she adorned); ability to move from jazzy croon to scat to energetic pop brings comparison with Joni MITCHELL, who also spurns the obvious commercial route to go her own way. *The Magazine* '85 got mixed reviews, par for the course for an artist like her.

JONES, Sam (*b* 12 Nov. '24, Jacksonville, Fla; *d* 15 Dec. '81) Bassist, also cello; composer. Infl. by LUNCEFORD, Count BASIE, the Billy ECKSTINE band and early boppers on records. To NYC; with Illinois JACQUET, Cannonball ADDERLEY, many others; Dizzy GILLESPIE '58-9, Thelonious MONK '59; Adderley's famous and popular quintet '59-65; Oscar PETERSON Trio '66-9. With Cedar WALTON '71; many LPs with Adderley,

Peterson, Walton, Clifford JORDAN, Sonny STITT, Red GARLAND, Lucky THOMPSON, others. Powerful, big-toned player on both instruments. Own LPs on Riverside: *The Soul Society* '60 (by 'Sam Jones' Soul Society') with Bobby TIMMONS, Nat ADDERLEY featured Jones on cello on half the tracks, with Keeter Betts on bass (*b* William Thomas Betts, 22 July '28, NYC); *The Chant* '61 ('Sam Jones Plus 10') was similar but with both Adderleys; *Down Home* '62 had Ron CARTER on bass. *Seven Minds* '74 with Walton, Billy HIGGINS, string quartet on Japanese East Wind followed by quintet *Cello Again* '76 with Higgins, sextet *Changes And Things* '77 (with Louis Hayes on drums: *b* 31 May '37, Detroit) on Xanadu. Sextet *Something In Common* '77 on Muse had Walton and Higgins; quintet *Visitation* '78 on Steeplechase was recorded in Copenhagen; *The Bassist!* '79 on Interplay/Discovery is a trio set with Kenny Barron, Keith COPELAND; *Something New* '79 on Inner City/Sea Breeze has a 12-piece group.

JONES, Spike (*b* Lindley Armstrong Jones, 14 Dec. '11, Long Beach, Cal.; *d* 1 May '65, L.A.) Drummer, bandleader. Played in orchestras on radio (Al JOLSON, *Kraft Music Hall* etc.), formed own band Spike Jones and his City Slickers with accent on comedy, funny noises using bells, whistles, pistols etc. but quality of musicianship always high. Signed to Victor, on Bluebird at first; instant success with own 'Der Fuehrer's Face', first of seven top 10 hits '42-9, incl. sendups 'Cocktails For Two', 'Chloe', 'Hawaiian War Chant', 'William Tell Overture' and no. 1 2-sided hit 'All I Want For Christmas Is My Two Front Teeth'/'Happy New Year' '48. 'Dance Of The Hours' '49 was followed by re-entry into charts of the big hit, several more lesser hits '50-3. On radio late '40s; began featuring his wife, vocalist Helen Grayco; had TV show *Spiketaculars*, appeared in several films '43-54; played Las Vegas '60s. Key elements in heyday were vocalists Doodles Weaver, Red Ingle, vocalist/trumpeter George Rock; after murdering a pop tune or a classic he would acknowledge applause with a straight face: 'Thank you, music lovers.' LPs on Verve early '50s: *A Christmas Spectacular*, *Dinner Music For People Who Aren't Very Hungry*;

later with a dixieland band on Liberty. Reissues incl. two vols. of *Best Of* and *Murdering The Classics* on RCA, *King Of Corn* ('43-4 material) on a Corn label, *On The Air* '43-4 on Sandy Hook, '46 tracks with Grayco on Hindsight, other compilations on RCA International.

JONES, Thad (*b* Thaddeus Joseph Jones, 28 Mar. '23, Pontiac, Mich.; *d* 20 Aug. '86, Copenhagen) Trumpet, cornet, flugelhorn, composer. Brother of Hank and Elvin JONES; worked with them in Detroit late '30s. Served in US Army WWII; on the road after the war with revues, etc.; own LP on Charles MINGUS's Debut label '54 with brother Hank, Frank Wess, Mingus, Kenny CLARKE and other Mingus workshop sessions on Debut and Period (*Thad Jones – Charles Mingus* reissue on Prestige); a Metronome All-Star track on Clef with Mingus '55, etc. Meanwhile he joined Count BASIE '54-63 and was a major contributor to that band along with Ernie Wilkins, Frank Foster, Frank Wess and Neal HEFTI. Wrote an album for Harry JAMES mid-63; worked with George RUSSELL sextet, played with Thelonious MONK at Carnegie Hall, worked with Gerry MULLIGAN, carried on writing for Basie, joined music staff at CBS network, all '64. Co-led quintet with Pepper ADAMS '65 (LP *Mean What You Say* on Milestone) incl. Mel LEWIS; same year formed 18-piece band with Lewis: Jones wrote most of the arrangements (with contributions from Bob BROOKMEYER, and others); the Thad Jones – Mel Lewis Orchestra LPs incl. *Suite For Pops* and *Live In Munich* on Horizon; *Consummation* on Blue Note; *Central Park North*, *Monday Night*, *Live At The Village Vanguard* and *Presenting* on Solid State; 2-disc *Thad Jones – Mel Lewis* was a compilation on Blue Note drawn from many of these. Jones and Lewis also recorded with the Swedish Radio Jazz Group (*Greetings And Salutations* '75 on Biograph); Jones left '78, went to live in Denmark, worked with Danish Radio Big Band (Lewis still led the band Monday nights at the Village Vanguard after 20 years). Combo called the Thad Jones Eclipse with Horace PARLAN, others has LPs on the Danish Metronome label; *Three And One* on Steeplechase is a quartet LP.

Played on highly rated Joe WILLIAMS LP on Delos '85; led Count Basie Orchestra on tour '85, left because of ill health. His writing and flugelhorn playing with the Jones – Lewis band for many years proved, if it needed proving, that beautiful big band music will never die. Best-known composition 'A Child Is Born' has become standard.

JONES, Tom (*b* Thomas Jones Woodward, 7 June '40, Pontypridd, Wales) Pop singer. Began singing as a child; worked in construction, but sang nights in working-men's clubs billed as 'Tiger Tom'; later as Tommy Scott and the Senators, making a fair living with the type of big, rich voice favoured by the Welsh. Discovered by another Welshman, Gordon Mills (*d* 29 July '86 in L.A. age 51), who changed his name to Tom Jones, which was indubitably Welsh and had the advantage of free publicity from the hit '63 film of the Henry Fielding novel. First hit was 'It's Not Unusual' '64, written by Mills and Les Reed: Jones made a demo and they took the song to Sandie SHAW's agent, who said 'That'll never be a hit.' Jones sang it on a Decca record; it won an Ivor Novello award, sold 3 million copies, was no. 1 UK/10 USA '65. Jones had 29 Hot 100 entries in USA '65-77 but no chart toppers, only three in top 5 ('What's New Pussycat?' '65, written by Hal David and Burt BACHARACH for soundtrack of zany '65 film; 'Without Love (There Is Nothing)' '69; 'She's A Lady' '71); 28 hits in UK incl. two at no. 1: the first and 'Green Green Grass Of Home' '66 (no. 11 USA); several at no. 2 incl. 'I'll Never Fall In Love Again' '67 (no. 49 USA; re-entered '69 at no. 6) and 'Delilah' '68 (no. 15 USA). He was a good album seller, with 18 in the USA LP chart '65-81, 4 in top 10 '69-70; 18 hit LPs in UK incl. 9 in top 10 '67-71: *Fever Zone* '68 (on Parrot USA; similar *13 Greatest Hits* on Decca in UK) sold a million; *20 Greatest Hits* '75 was no. 1 UK. Live LPs did well, e.g. *Tom Jones Live In Las Vegas* and 2-disc *Live At Caesar's Palace* both USA/UK, plus *Live At The Talk Of The Town* as early as '67 in UK (*Tom Jones Live* in USA '69). Mills had noticed that the most adoring fans were often middle-aged matrons (their daughters were swooning at the time over weeds with beards, not brawny Welshman). USA TV special *This Is Tom Jones* '69 was

an enormous success; on the USA tour that followed, women threw their underwear at him. Mills made him a huge club attraction; did the same later with Engelbert HUMPERDINCK, Gilbert O'SULLIVAN. Jones moved to West Coast mid-'70s (lower taxes, closer to Las Vegas); received a tumultuous welcome in Cardiff '83 on his first visit to Wales for 10 years. His son became his manager when Mills died; he hadn't bothered to release a single for some years, but 'The Boy From Nowhere' '87 came from proposed musical *Matador* based on the life of '60s bullfighter El Cordobes; Jones contributed several songs to album. *Things That Matter Most To Me* '87 on Mercury is a compilation of country-ish tracks; 'I've Been Rained On Too' was a top 20 hit in that chart.

JOPLIN, Janis (*b* 19 Jan. '43, Port Arthur, Texas; *d* 4 Oct. '70, Hollywood) Singer: the most successful white blues singer of the '60s. From a middle-class background, she was a loner as a teenager, taking refuge in poetry and painting; apart from becoming a good singer she was a '60s icon for the way she kicked over the traces after growing up in the '50s, but vulnerability was never far beneath her racy image. She left home '60, sang in bars and clubs in Houston, Austin; by '65 on West Coast; back in Austin '66 (she is remembered in Jan Reid's *The Improbable Rise Of Redneck Rock* '77 for connection with gas-station-turned beer-bar run by Kenneth THREADGILL, a hangout for country music 'outlaws'); back to San Francisco to sing with Big Brother And The Holding Company: lineup Sam Andrew, guitar (*b* 18 Dec. '41, Taft, Cal.); Peter Albin, bass, guitar, vocals (*b* 6 June '44, San Francisco); guitarist James Gurley and David Getz on drums, piano, vocals. They became a Bay Area sensation; eponymous Big Brother LP on Mainstream was minimally produced, but with appearance at Monterey Pop Festival '67 led to switch to Columbia: *Cheap Thrills* '68 was a poorly recorded live set, but a no. 1 LP with no. 12 hit (cover of Erma Franklin's top 10 R&B hit '67, 'Piece Of My Heart'); with its cover art by Robert Crumb it is still a potent '60s souvenir. As a band, precision was not Big Brother's strong point; she took Andrew with her and formed the Kozmic Blues

Band for *I Got Dem Ol' Kozmic Blues Again, Mama* '69 (no. 5 LP with top 50 single 'Kozmic Blues'), formed a new Full Tilt Boogie Band for *Pearl* '71, which was issued unfinished: she killed herself with heroin, no doubt accidentally. Both LP and fine cover of Kris KRISTOFFERSON's 'Me And Bobby McGee' were no. 1. As a blues singer she did not go over big with blacks (flopped in Memphis late '68 at Stax Records Review concert), but there was no gainsaying her inspired use of her voice: she was warned that her full tilt style meant that her voice would not last long, but took the attitude that she didn't want to be an inferior performer so that she could be inferior longer. With changing lineups Big Brother issued *Be A Brother* '70 (incl. some uncredited Joplin vocals), *How Hard It Is* '71, split '72. *In Concert* '72 had her with Big Brother on one side, Full Tilt on the other; soundtrack from '74 TV documentary was issued as 2-disc *Janis*; compilations: *Anthology* '80, *Farewell Song* '82. Biography *Buried Alive* '73 by Myra Friedman was praised; film *The Rose* '79 with Bette MIDLER based loosely on her life.

JOPLIN, Scott (*b* 24 Nov. 1868, Texarkana, Texas; *d* 11 Apr. '17, NYC) Pianist and composer; the greatest of all composers of ragtime. Played cornet in the Queen City Negro Band of Sedalia, Mo. 1890s; played at Chicago World's Fair 1893; sold first compositions 'Please Say You Will', 'Picture Of Her Face' 1895, first rags in 1899: 'Original Rags' was sold outright to a publisher in Kansas City, but 'Maple Leaf Rag' was published in Sedalia by John Stark, who gave Joplin a royalty agreement, unusual then in business between a white man and a Negro. It was easily the biggest ragtime hit of all, and Stark moved his business to St Louis in 1900. Joplin intended to create a body of serious American music in the ragtime style, but even if the form could have borne the weight of Joplin's ambition for it, the music business of the time would not allow the necessary development, for racist and other reasons (*see* RAGTIME). 'The Ragtime Dance' '02 was a 20-minute ballet; Stark published it but sales were poor. An opera, *The Guest Of Honor*, was to have been published '03 but never appeared and is now lost. He also wrote songs for a musical comedy called *If*. He and Stark tried to establish the 'classic rag' in the teeth of a national obsession with ragtime as rinkytink party music; it became the fashion in Joplin's lifetime to play rags at breakneck speed, partly because of coin-operated player pianos in penny arcades, and despite the fact that some of them were printed with the instruction 'Do not play fast'. He went to NYC '10; his opera *Treemonisha* was performed in Harlem '11 at his expense, and he was depressed at its failure; he died in a mental hospital. He wrote about 50 piano rags, as well as collaborations (such as 'Sunflower Slow Drag', with Scott Hayden). They were revived properly c.'70, along with rags by other composers, by Joshua RIFKIN and William BOLCOM, who played them as the stylish, often subtle miniatures they are; they recorded collections on several labels, especially Nonesuch. Joplin's rags have also been recorded by Max MORATH on Vanguard, James Levine on RCA, Dick HYMAN on RCA (incl. 5-disc complete set), André PREVIN and violinist Itzhak Perlman on EMI/Angel, Gunther SCHULLER with the New England Conservatory Ragtime Ensemble, many others. Film/Broadway composer Marvin Hamlisch (*b* 4 Dec. '44, NYC) used 'The Entertainer' in the soundtrack of *The Sting* '74; the hit film brought Joplin's music to a much wider audience than any records. *Treemonisha* was revived by the Houston Grand Opera '76 with Schuller conducting (2-disc album on DGG). Joplin made piano rolls in '16, available on Biograph; but ordinary piano rolls (also made by James P. JOHNSON, Fats WALLER, many others) provide only a one-dimensional idea of the musician's skill, with no dynamics at all.

JORDAN, Clifford (*b* 2 Sep. '31, Chicago) Tenor sax. Began on piano, switched to tenor at 14. Played R&B and with visiting jazzmen in Chicago; went on the road with Max ROACH, then Horace SILVER. Led quartet with Chicagoan Andrew HILL '62, toured with Roach '63, Charles MINGUS '64 (passionate playing on Mingus LP *Live At The Jazz Workshop* '64), Roach again '65. Spent much time in Europe from '69; has done lecture concerts etc.; designed record sleeves; does portrait photographs of musicians. Own albums began with *Blowing In*

From Chicago with John Gilmore (see SUN RA), reissued in *Blowin' Sessions* with a Johnny GRIFFIN LP: all three tenors were classmates at Du Sable High School; septet *Clifford Jordan All Stars*, quartet *Cliff Craft*, all on Blue Note '57. Other LPs: *Spellbound* '60 on Riverside; *A Story Tale*, *Starting Time*, *Bearcat* '61-2 on Jazzland; *These Are My Roots* '65 on Atlantic (LEADBELLY songs arranged by Jordan); a Vortex LP in '66; *In The World* '69 and *Glass Bead Game* '73 on Strata-East; *Night Of The Mark VII* '75 on Muse. Quartet The Magic Triangle with Cedar WALTON, Billy HIGGINS, Sam JONES recorded three vols. of *On Stage* plus *Firm Roots* and *The Highest Mountain*, all '75 on Steeplechase; also *Half Note* with Albert HEATH replacing Higgins. With various lineups: *Remembering Me* '76, *Inward Fire* '77, *The Adventurer* '78 on Muse; *Hello Hank Jones* '78 on Eastworld; *Repetition* '84 on Soul Note; quartet *Royal Ballads* '86 on Criss Cross, *Dr Chicago* '87 on Beehive with Jaki BYARD.

JORDAN, Duke (*b* Irving Sidney Jordan, 1 Apr. '22, Brooklyn) Pianist, composer. Played with a sextet that won an amateur contest at NY World's Fair '39; later with Charlie PARKER, Stan GETZ, Roy ELDRIDGE, Oscar PETTIFORD, others in the bop era. He held his own as an individual stylist at a time when modern jazz piano was dominated by Bud POWELL. He played in many duo gigs NYC '50s, spent much time in Europe from '59, when he wrote music for French film *Les Liaisons Dangereuses* under the name Jack Marray. Soundtrack incl. Thelonious MONK quartet (recorded in NYC), but Jordan wrote music played by Art BLAKEY's Jazz Messengers, with Jordan on piano; he also appeared on screen. Compositions also incl. early modern jazz classic 'Jordu', incl. on his own early recording sessions '54-5, trio dates that appeared on Prestige and Savoy. Other LPs: quintets *Flight To Jordan* '60 on Blue Note, *East And West Of Jazz* '62 on Charlie Parker Records; *Brooklyn Brothers* '73 on Muse (quartet co-led by Cecil PAYNE, with Sam JONES), *The Murray Hill Caper* '73 on Spotlite also with Payne. Small-group LPs on Danish Steeplechase label, several with Jones: *Flight To Denmark* '73; *Truth, Misty Thursday*, *Duke's Delight* and *Lover Man*

'75; *Live In Japan* and *Flight To Japan* '76; *Duke's Artistry* and *The Great Session* '78; *Thinking Of You* and *Change A Pace* '79. Also solo set *Midnight Moonlight* '79 on Steeplechase, solo contributions to anthologies *The Piano Players* '75 on Xanadu, *I Remember Bebop* and *They All Played Bebop* on Columbia; trio set *Blue Duke* '83 on Japanese Baystate label.

JORDAN, Louis (*b* 8 July '08, Brinkley, Ark.; *d* 4 Feb. '75, L.A.) Alto sax, singer, leader. Worked with Chick WEBB '36-8; recorded for Decca from '39 as Louis Jordan and his Tympany Five, though group was in fact larger. Enormously popular jump band genre was influential on rhythm & blues, hence rock'n'roll; crossed over to pop chart with 19 hits '44-9: 'G.I. Jive'/'Is You Is Or Is You Ain't My Baby' sold a million '44 as did 'Choo Choo Ch'boogie' '46; other hits incl. 'My Baby Said Yes' '45 with Bing CROSBY, 'Baby, It's Cold Outside' '49 with Ella FITZGERALD, 'Ain't Nobody Here But Us Chickens' and one of several covers of Jack MCVEA's 'Open The Door, Richard' '47. Self-penned material often covered, from 'Caldonia' (Woody HERMAN, '45) and 'Saturday Night Fish Fry' (Pearl Bailey and Moms Mabley, '49) to 'Inflation Blues' (B.B. KING, '83). Style of 'Reet, Petite And Gone', 'That Chick's Too Young To Fry' etc. being revived today by young artists like Joe JACKSON and Rent Party. Prod. by Milt Gabler, Jordan left Decca just before Gabler prod. Bill HALEY's 'Rock Around The Clock'; Haley's simple party records reaped rewards that perhaps should have been Jordan's. He recorded for Ray CHARLES's Tangerine label in the mid-'60s and continued pleasing crowds until '74 heart attack. *Best Of Louis Jordan* on MCA; *Look Out!*, 2-disc *Jivin' With Jordan* on Charly UK cover '39-53.

JORDAN, Sheila (*b* Sheila Dawson, 18 Nov. '28, Detroit) Jazz singer, one of the best: but the number of jazz singers who have achieved wide public fame is small; she has won *Downbeat* critics' poll for Talent Deserving of Wider Recognition eight times '63-86, but jazz singers don't become household names. Studied piano at age 11, later harmony and theory with Lennie TRISTANO; was married '50s to Duke JOR-

DAN. Sang on one track of Peter Ind LP '60 (bassist Ind *b* 20 July '28, Uxbridge, Middlesex, UK; also studied with Tristano, recorded with him, also on *The Real Lee Konitz* '57 on Atlantic; formed UK Wave label, now runs London club the Bass Clef). Remarkable, famous version of 'You Are My Sunshine' on George RUSSELL's *The Outer View* '63, now on Milestone compilation *Outer Thoughts*; sang in chorus on Carla BLEY's *Escalator Over The Hill* '71; recorded soundtrack of CBS TV show *Look Up And Live* '72, with Don Heckman (reeds, composer, bandleader, critic etc.; *b* 18 Dec. '35, Reading, Pa.); with Roswell RUDD '72-5 (one track on *Numatik Swing Band* '73 on JCOA, then *Flexible Flyer* '74 on Arista); formed quartet with Steve Kuhn (keyboards, composer; *b* 24 Mar. '38, Brooklyn, NYC): *Playground* '79 on ECM; she also sang on Steve SWALLOW's *Home* '79 (*Music To Poems By Robert Creeley*) and Kuhn's *Last Year's Waltz* '81, *Theatre* '83 by the George Grunz Concert Jazz Band, all on ECM; also Aki Takase's *ABC* '82 on East Wind. Own LPs incl. *Portrait Of Sheila* on Blue Note '62, *Sheila* '77 on Steeplechase (in Oslo with Arild ANDERSEN), *Old Time Feeling* '82 on Palo Alto (duo with bassist/composer Harvie Swartz, *b* 6 Dec. '48, Chelsea, Mass.), *The Crossing* '84 on Blackhawk.

JORDAN, Stanley (*b* '59) Guitarist. Began on classical piano age 6, changed to guitar at 11 infl. by Jimi HENDRIX and Carlos SANTANA, later Wes MONTGOMERY; from musical frustration, developed system of playing guitar like a keyboard, with special tuning and both hands playing melody lines by tapping the strings. Self-produced first album *Touch Sensitive* '83 on Tangent; played at concert celebrating relaunch of Blue Note label Feb. '85 (album *One Night With Blue Note: Preserved*); his own LP *Magic Touch* on Blue Note '85 (prod. by Al DiMEOLA) was no. 1 jazz LP USA for 30 weeks; *A New Set Of Standards* early '87 was not an advance. Some guitarists always said the instrument should be approached like a keyboard; Jordan has developed a remarkable way to do it, also thinks it might be possible to do it on an acoustic guitar by redesigning it, to avoid being tied to electronics; has degree from Princeton in music

and electronics. Production values of the Blue Note LPs are not high; material like BEATLE songs, Paul SIMON's 'The Sound of Silence' and 'Silent Night' are hardly an adequate showcase. He's still young, has good sense: 'I think that as a technician I'm pretty significant, but I can't claim to be a significant musician – not yet.'

JORDAN, Steve (*b* Estaban Jordan) Tex-Mex accordionist, songwriter, one of the best of the new generation, coming to prominence appearing in David Byrne's film *True Stories* '86 (soundtrack on EMI). Like Flaco JIMENEZ he has borrowed from other genres to create an idiosyncratic style; unlike Flaco he uses synths, phase shifters etc. Also renowned for showmanship. Nevertheless his repertoire is firmly rooted in polkas, rancheras and corridos (songstories) of Tex-Mex music. Began recording '60s; worked with his brothers Bonnie and Silver on McAllen-based Falcón label, later recorded for Fama, Freddie, Hacienda, California-based Aguila, his own El Parche label (named after his 'trademark' eye patch), then RCA: *Turn Me Loose* '86 on RCA was nominated for a Grammy. Recorded soundtrack for *Born In East L.A.* same year as *True Stories*. Other albums: *Mirada Que Facina* on Freddie, *My Toot Toot* on RCA International, both '85; *Steve Jordan* '87 on Arhoolie (reissue of *Las Coronelas* on RyN).

JORDANAIRES, The Vocal quartet formed '48 in Springfield, Mo. by Gordon Stoker, who has remained the only constant member. They appeared on the Grand Ole Opry '49 and were well-known throughout the South, especially for gospel material; they backed Red FOLEY on his million-selling 'Just A Closer Walk With Thee' '50 and became nationally famous when they backed Elvis PRESLEY on many records beginning '56. Lead tenor Stoker sang in a trio with Ben and Brock Speer on Presley's first RCA recording session in early '56; the 'Hound Dog' date in July incl. Stoker, Neal Matthews, Hoyt Hawkins, Hugh Jarrett as the Jordanaires (*see* entry for Presley). From then on they sessioned on countless country records, often making several a day. They won a Grammy '65 for the best religious album; combined with the Imperial quartet on Elvis's 'Indescribably Blue' ('67, his 54th gold disc), etc. LPs incl. *Church In The Wildwood* on Vocalion (MCA), *The Jordanaires* on Columbia.

JOURNEY USA AOR band formed San Francisco '73 by Neal Schon (*b* '55, San Mateo, Cal.), guitarist infl. by CREAM-era Eric CLAPTON and Jimi HENDRIX, who allegedly turned down an offer from Clapton at 16 to spend two years with SANTANA '71-3. Original lineup incl. Ross Valory on bass (ex-Frumious Bandersnatch, *b* '50, S.F.), Prairie Prince (*b* 7 May '50, Charlotte, S.C.) on drums, George Tickner, guitar; Prince left to play with Tubes, Tickner left rock; replaced by much-travelled UK drummer Aynsley DUNBAR, ex-Santana Gregg Rolie (*b* '48), keyboards; Rolie's singing/songwriting crucial, but neither he nor Schon great vocal shakes, as LP *Journey* '75 proved with emphasis on instrumentals. *Look Into The Future* and *Next* '76-7 broached top 100 USA LPs, but band still needed frontman: first choice Robert Fleischmann was ditched for Steve Perry (*b* '49, Hanford, Cal.) who, together with ace prod. Roy Thomas Baker (QUEEN etc.), propelled *Infinity* '78 to no. 21. Once-progressive band went overtly commercial, peddling competent, uninspired AOR that Americans lapped up; Dunbar fled to JEFFERSON STARSHIP, crying sellout; band with new drummer Steve Smith (graduate of Berklee) cried all the way to the bank with more platinum LPs: *Evolution* '79, *Departure* '80, live 2-disc *Captured* '81. Road-weary Rolie quit, replaced by ex-BABYS keyboardist Jonathan Cain, from Chicago; *Escape* '81 was no. 1 LP USA, spawned video game *Journey-Escape*, mega-hit singles incl. top 5 'Who's Crying Now', 'Open Arms'. *Frontiers* '83 had four top 40 singles; Perry, Smith and Schon also pursued separate projects: Schon made LPs with Jan HAMMER, Sammy HAGAR; Perry did best with solo *Street Talk* '84, three single hits incl. no. 3 'Oh Sherrie'. Wringing out every dollar, Columbia anthologised less successful early LPs as *In The Beginning* '79. Polished, harmonious, guitar-based, squeaky-clean with just a touch of macho, Journey epitomises everything about radio AOR that fans love, opponents detest; it is hard to disagree with Pete Frame (*Rock Family Trees*), who observed that 'A single record like "Louie Louie" . . . probably had more influence on the development of rock than Journey's entire output.' After *Raised On Radio* '86 Smith left.

JOY DIVISION UK rock band who began as Warzawa '77 (taking that name from track on David BOWIE's *Low* '77). Their leaden, eerie music was infl. by Bowie, VELVET UNDERGROUND. Vocalist Ian Curtis (*b* '57, Macclesfield; *d* 17 May '80) was gaunt, isolated focal point; with Bernard Sumner (aka Albrecht; *b* 4 Jan. '56) on guitar and vocals, bassist Peter Hook (*b* 13 Feb. '56), drummer Stephen Morris (*b* 28 Nov. '57), Joy Division were the mainstay of Manchester's Factory Records, formed by TV journalist Tony Wilson, whose short-lived series had given SEX PISTOLS their TV debut. *Unknown Pleasures* '79 was a chilling and effective debut LP in the aftermath of punk rock; single 'Transmission', championed by DJ John PEEL, highlighted hypnotic rhythms and saw them at centre of a cult following (*Peel Sessions* issued '86 as 12" single); during recording of second LP Curtis committed suicide. 'Love Will Tear Us Apart' was a no. 13 UK hit '80, later covered by Paul Young, P. J. PROBY; *Closer* was Curtis's memorial with *Still* '81 was posthumous 2-disc compilation. An unhealthy cult grew up around Curtis; remaining trio recruited keyboardist Gillian Gilbert (*b* 27 Jan. '61) to form New Order, attracting more hostile press for alleged Nazi-derived connotations ('joy division' was military brothel, 'new order' Hitler's plan for the world). New band's first LP was *Movement* '81. 'Blue Monday' was the best-selling 12" single in UK chart history (in chart three times '83-4); that and 'Confusion' '83 were made in NYC with Arthur BAKER. *Power, Corruption & Lies* '83 maintained image, with Hook's threatening bass, Sumner's distant vocals; similar *Low Life* '85 incl. hit 'Shellshock'; followed by *Brotherhood* '86. Book *An Ideal For Living* by Mark Johnson is a history of both groups.

JOY OF COOKING Group formed '67 in Berkeley, Cal. by vocalists Toni Brown (*b* 16 Nov. '38, Madison, Wis.; also piano), Terry Garthwaite (*b* 11 July '38, Berkeley; also guitar). Backed by Fritz Kasten (*b* 19 Oct.,

Des Moines, Iowa) on drums and sax, Ron Wilson (*b* 5 Feb. '33, San Diego) on percussion and harmonica, brother David Garthwaite on bass. First LP *Joy Of Cooking* emphasised percussive backing; second *Closer To The Ground* '71 replaced David with Jeff Neighbor (*b* 19 Mar. '42, Grand Coulee, Wash.) on bass and trombone, also saw songwriter Brown introducing country element. After disappointing *Castles* '72, girls went to Nashville to record duo *Cross Country* '73. Though 'Mockingbird' from first LP was minor hit, little commercial success accrued; Brown went solo (LPs *Good For You Too* '74, *Angel Of Love* '80); Terry kept Joy Of Cooking alive with Glan Frandel, guitar; Steve Roseman, piano; but LP by this lineup not released because of contractual problems. *Terry* '75 was solo debut, followed by reunion with Brown for critically acclaimed *The Joy* '77; Terry went solo again with *Hand In Glove* '78, others; also had partnership with Rosemary Sorrels. They are often cited as an early example of women as bandleaders in rock, rare then; but their folk-tinged West Coast music and thoughtful lyrics are worthy of greater note than that.

JUDAS PRIEST UK heavy metal band formed '73 in Birmingham by Rob Halford, vocals (*b* 25 Aug. '51); Glenn Tipton (*b* 25 Oct. '48) and K. K. (Kenneth) Downing, guitars: front line has remained unchanged. With rhythm section of drummer John Hinch and bassist Ian Hill, they caused a stir on the small Gull label with *Rocka Rolla* '74, LP of promising songs but tinny production (by Rodger Bain). *Sad Wings Of Destiny* '75, with new drummer Alan Moore, was prod. by the group, Max West and Geoffrey Calvert: fulfilled promise with standout tracks 'Tyrant', 'Victim Of Changes', 'Ripper', etc.; twin guitar attack of Tipton, Downing was perfectly complementary, with Halford's shrill vocals the icing on the cake. Left Gull for CBS, who gave necessary push to career, but *Sin After Sin* '77 disappointed, despite presence of ace session drummer Simon Phillips, prod. by ex-DEEP PURPLE Roger Glover: their former aggression and beefy sound were lacking. Tour with new drummer Les Binks supporting LED ZEPPELIN in USA spread live reputation; New Wave of British Heavy Metal (SAXON, DEF LEPPARD, IRON MAIDEN etc.) threatened UK position, but *Stained Class* and *Killing Machine* (aka *Hell Bent For Leather* in USA), both '78, rectified things, with anthems like 'Beyond The Realms Of Death' and 'Take On The World' respectively, latter in football-chant style they soon copyrighted (no. 14 hit UK). *Unleashed In The East* '79, live LP from Japan, was first USA hit LP, united them with best prod. to date in Tom Allom. Ex-Trapeze drummer Dave Holland replaced Binks for *British Steel* '80, *Screaming For Vengeance* '82, *Defenders Of The Faith* '84; first of these was highest-ever UK LP at no. 4, helped by hit singles 'Living After Midnight' and 'Breaking The Law' (both no. 12 UK); all LPs beginning with *Unleashed* were top 20 in UK; *Vengeance* first gold LP in USA. They have undergone changes in musical tack (now heavier, more considered) and image-wise (Halford has shorter hair than most punks); they also show good taste in covering others' songs on stage (e.g. Joan BAEZ's 'Diamonds And Rust', FLEETWOOD MAC's 'Green Manalishi'); *Turbo* released '86. Their 'thinking man's metal' (if that is not a contradiction in terms) makes them all but equal to the other famous Birmingham HM groups, Led Zep and BLACK SABBATH.

JUDDS, The USA mother and daughter country duo: Naomi (*b* '48), Wynonna (*b* '66). Naomi left Kentucky for West Coast '68; marriage failed; she brought two daughters (Ashley *b* '70) home to Ashland, Ky., sang around the house with Wynonna; as registered nurse, cared for daughter of Nashville prod. Brent Maher; he heard tapes made on $30 cassette player from K-Mart, they made demo with guitarist Don Potter, signed to RCA, won Grammy '85 with lovely harmony, good songs by Mickey JUPP, Harlan HOWARD, others; insipid arrangements typical of Nashville/RCA. Five no. 1 country singles '84-5. Albums: *The Judds* '84 (top 10 country LP), chart; *Why Not Me* '84 (no. 1 LP and title single), *Rockin' With The Rhythm* no. 1 '85 (incl. Paul Kennerley's 'Have Mercy'), *Heartland* '87. *Give A Little Love* '87 in UK has 15 tracks from *Heartland* and a mini-LP from '84; *Heartland* was still in top 30 of USA country chart after 70 weeks.

JUJU An African genre from Yoruba-speaking Western Nigeria, a guitar-based music which developed in the '30s from older 'palm-wine' styles: Gombe, Ashiko, Konkoma. The term itself originated then and is usually associated with Tunde King. Further development occurred in the '40s as leaders like Ojoge Daniel, Ayinde Bakare played at major ceremonies and various functions, often honouring notable people in their songs. Instrumentation was added, varying from accordion and mandolin to percussion. I. K. DAIRO added elements of HIGHLIFE in '50-60s but gradually electric guitars took over; from mid-'60s 'Miliki system' of Ebenezer OBEY, the pioneer of modern juju, grew in popularity. Nigerian Civil War boosted the style, causing the return to Eastern Nigeria of leading high-life musicians, so that by the early '70s juju had completely eclipsed highlife in the West. Leading exponents in the '70-80s have been King Sunny ADE, Segun ADEWALE, Dele ABIODUN and Idowu Animahsaun. Today juju groups range in style from traditional to modern, always with two or three guitars in harmony, bass, percussion, and the omnipresent talking drum, a steady dance beat allowing improvisation on all instruments; juju has always absorbed new ideas, and over the years keyboards, Hawaiian guitars and synthesisers have been used. Juju also has a stong religious and moral bias. Following the successful showcasing of Sunny Ade in the early '80s, the light and spacey feel of juju has become the first African style to acquire an international following; with an endless capacity to adapt and a talented new generation waiting in the wings, it will continue to be popular.

JUPP, Mickey UK R&B singer from Southend who began in that town's burgeoning R&B scene '63 with the Orioles, second most popular local group after the Paramounts (who later went progressive and became PROCOL HARUM). Jupp on piano and vocals with Dougie Shedrake (guitar), Ada Baggerley (bass), Tony Diamond (drums) had repertoire of standards like 'Money' and 'Wrong Yo-Yo'. By '65 a new lineup of Bob Clouter (drums), John Bobin (bass), Mo Witham (guitar) was equally unsuccessful at finding a record

deal despite local fame, and soon split. Off scene for three years (allegedly because of marital problems), he returned to Southend and formed Legend with Steve Geare, bass; Chris East, guitar; Nigel Dunbar, drums; made three LPs of easy-going R&B, mostly self-composed: acoustic/bluesy *Legend* '69, *Red Boot Album* '71, *Moonshine* '72; best of last two albums plus singles compiled in *Mickey Jupp's Legend* '78 on Stiff, for which lineup had reverted to Bobin, Witham and (on last LP) Clouter. Success of Southend groups DR FEELGOOD (who later covered his 'Down At The Doctors' for a UK hit) and KURSAAL FLYERS (likewise 'Cross Country', but no hit), he returned '75 to live work on London pub circuit, record deal with Stiff: *Juppanese* '78 had Dave EDMUNDS' Rockpile on one side, session players under ex-Paramount Gary Brooker on the other. He's since struggled to find consistency on a variety of labels with little reward (though popular in Europe), with different producers: Godley & Creme for *Long Distance Romancer* '79, Sutherland Bros for *Oxford* '80, Francis Rossi (STATUS QUO) for *Shampoo Haircut & Shave* '83; *Some People Can't Dance* '82 yielded 'Joggin' ' used as theme for London Marathon and apt description of easy-going career. Other songs covered by SEARCHERS, Nick LOWE, others; those who passed through bands incl. Bill Fifield, once Legend drummer (c. *Red Boot*) who adopted name Bill Legend in joining T. Rex, Bob Fish (later DARTS) in '75 band, girl singer Joy Sarney (hit with 'Naughty Naughty Naughty' UK '77).

JURGENS, Dick (*b* 8 Jan. '10, Sacramento, Cal.) Trumpet, composer, bandleader. Formed first band '28; played highly regarded sweet dance music in hotels and on the radio. Introduced with 'Here's That Band Again!', featured vocalists Eddy HOWARD, Ronnie Kemper on novelties. Jurgens co-wrote his theme 'Day Dreams Come True At Night', hits 'Careless' '39, 'Elmer's Tune' (Glenn MILLER had no. 1 version '41; Jurgens' own was no. 8), 'One Dozen Roses' '42. *Pop Memories* credits the band with 25 hits '39-47, 12 in top 10. He entertained troops during WWII, formed another band post-war, worked into '70s. LPs on Hindsight incl. '36-9 material; badly titled *Big Band Swing* on Seagull: the band always played well, with rich ensemble sound rather than slurping saxophones, but was not known for its swing.

JUSTIS, Bill (*b* 14 Oct. '26, Birmingham, Ala.; *d* 15 July '82) Alto sax, arranger, producer. Arranged campus music at Tulane (New Orleans), Arizona U.; went to work at Sun Records in Memphis '57 as staff musician and producer; hit with his 'Raunchy' (first called 'Backwoods'), with co-author Sid Manker on guitar: leased to Philips, it made no. 2 USA/11 UK '57-8, paving the way for other rock'n'roll instrumentals. He arranged for Johnny CASH, Charlie RICH, Jerry Lee LEWIS at Sun; there were hits but the more free-wheeling era of off-the-wall genius like that of 'Cowboy Jack' CLEMENT was over as Sun tried to hang onto national pop audience. Justis formed own label Play Me (failed); worked for RCA/Groove (with Rich again), to Nashville on Monument, ABC (prod. Fats DOMINO '63), Sound Stage (hits for the Dixiebelles '63-4).

K

KACHAMBA BROTHERS BAND African kwela band formed in Malawi '61. Brothers Daniel (guitarist; eldest) and Donald (flute; *b* '55) Kachamba lived in Salisbury, Rhodesia with their Ngoni parents '57-61, began playing at parties in and near Blantyre, the capital of Malawi; kwela had spread from South Africa and they soon became the most accomplished interpreters of it in Malawi. Donald left '70 to pursue a solo career touring East Africa and Europe, but made LP *The Kachamba Brothers Band* in Malawi in '72; continued to tour widely and made live LP *Donald Kachamba's Kwela Band* '78 in Austria, faithfully recreating the flute-guitar Kwela style of '50s-60s which was already no longer played in Malawi. Also *Donald Kachamba's Band* on Kenyan AIT label.

KAHN, Roger Wolfe (*b* 19 Oct. '07, Morristown, N.J.; *d* 12 July '62, NYC) Saxophonist, bandleader, songwriter. Son of millionaire Otto Kahn; once formed a band, paid members for several weeks, disbanded without playing a gig. Band known as the Million Dollar Band '20s had Victor contract, residencies at NY Biltmore; semi-hot style '25-32 had 18 big hits, featured variously such people as Joe VENUTI, Miff Mole, Eddie LANG, Artie SHAW, Jack TEAGARDEN, J. DORSEY; turned sweet later. Lost interest in music, turned to aviation, was test pilot during WWII.

KALAHARI SURFERS A studio group playing music of Warrick Swinney (*b* 12 Sep. '58, Port Elizabeth, South Africa), who began at U. of Capetown, continued in Durban; now creates his tapes at Shifty Studios in Johannesburg. Early collaborators incl. Hamish 'McDub' Davidson and drummer Brian Rath; he also worked with Ian Herman on drums. First release was double single 'Burning Tractors Keeps Us Warm' on West German Pure Freud label; then cassette *Gross National Products* on Shifty.

First LP *Own Affairs* '84 on UK's Recommended label incl. 'Prayer For Civilisation', incl. in Recommended's quarterly magazine/sampler LP (which is recommended): tapes of chaplains and politicians asking divine help (e.g. as the *Enola Gay* took off in August '45) are backed by an inexorable (not overbearing) rock beat, interspersed with vocal chorus 'In the name of God we kill' which sounds like something from Kurt WEILL: fine saxophone is provided by Rick Van Heerdon, whose friend Ann helps in the chorus; it is very well made, bears repeated listening. Still on Recommended, this lineup made *Living In The Heart Of The Beast* '85; on *Sleep Armed* '86, concerned with life in S.A. suburbia, Rath and McDub rejoined Swinney, who toured Europe '87 using tapes and local backing musicians. Rounder in USA issued LP by Fosatu (Workers Choirs) from Shifty; plans CD compilation of Surfers' last two albums.

KALLE, Le Grand (*b* Joseph Kabaselle Tshamala, '30, Matadi, Zaire; *d* '82) Singer and composer, the acknowledged father of the modern Congo sound, infl. Tabu Ley, FRANCO and leading African jazz for over a decade. Was a chorister in a Catholic school; made debut at 19 with L'Orchestre de Tendance Congolaise; earliest recordings on the first Congolese labels Editions Ngoma, Editions Essego. Joined Surboum Jazz early '50s, playing fusion of jazz, folklore and Afro-Cuban; then formed legendary African Jazz outfit '53, going against fashion by abandoning the popular polkas and mazurkas and playing rumbas and sambas instead. With an acoustic lineup and playing new fusions of black music, the band flourished during the years leading to Independence in '60, marking the transition from trad. to modern in Zairean music. Members during this era incl. famous musicians Manu DIBANGO, Dr NICO, Essous, Malapet, Rossignol, Dechaud, Rochereau. Most records were 78s; *Joseph Kabaselle et*

L'African Jazz on Africain is good 2-disc compilation incl. 'Independence Cha-Cha'; shortly afterwards Kalle recorded 'Okuka Lokole', celebrating '60 visit of Louis ARMSTRONG to Zaire. Extensive West African tour '61 infl. development of music in Francophone countries, e.g. BEMBEYA JAZZ in Guinea. The band's fame had also spread across the Atlantic, with 'Para Fifi' and 'Kalle Kato' becoming crossover hits late '50s. Having released hundreds of singles the band dominated musical Kinshasa with its unique blend of vocals, guitars and percussion; sounds from the mid-'60s can be found on *Authenticitie Vol. 5* on Africain. In '63 Dr Nico and Taby Ley left to form African Fiesta; after a successful tour in '65, Kabaselle stepped down to take stock; despite the proliferation of bands and wider dissemination of music on radio and 45 singles, he made a grand comeback in Brazzaville '66. He went to Paris '70 to make several LPs with Dibango and Cuban musicians; the mature sound of this band, collectively known as *L'African Team*, still available on the Africain LP of that name. His career dipped in the '70s but such was his abiding infl. that he was named the first 'Grand Maître' by the national union of musicians '80. On his death many notable songs were composed in his memory, incl. 'Homage à Grand Kalle' on the Franco/Tabu Ley LP *L'Événement*.

KALLEN, Kitty (*b* 25 May '23, Philadelphia, Pa.) (Some sources give other dates.) Singer. Began on local children's radio show; sang on radio with Jan SAVITT at 14; with Jack TEAGARDEN, Jimmy DORSEY, Harry JAMES, others '39-45; on radio with Danny KAYE, David ROSE, etc. Sang duet with Bob Eberly on no. 1 Dorsey hit 'Besame Mucho' ('Kiss Me') '44; top 10 hits with James band: '45: 'I'm Beginning To See The Light' (Duke ELLINGTON-Don George song; James and Johnny HODGES also got credit), '11:60 P.M.', 'I'll Buy That Dream', 'It's Been A Long, Long Time' (no. 1), 'Waitin' For The Train To Come In'. Recorded with Artie SHAW on Musicraft ('My Heart Belongs To Daddy'); along with many other band singers she carried on as a single when the Swing Era was over, on Musicraft, Signature, Mercury, then Decca. She had three hits in '54; 'Little Things Mean A Lot' was one of the biggest of the year: the lovely song suited her perfectly, written by Carlton Franklin Stutz (*b* 19 Dec. '15, Richmond, Va.; was accountant, teacher, then DJ as well as songwriter) and Edith Lindeman Calisch (*b* 21 Mar. 1898, Pittsburgh; wrote children's books, worked on *Richmond Times Dispatch* '33-64). This revived her career; 'In The Chapel In The Moonlight' was top 5, 'I Want You All To Myself' top 30. She recorded on Decca, retired '57 but came back '59 and had top 40 hits 'If I Give My Heart To You' '59 on Columbia, 'My Coloring Book' '62 on RCA. Albums incl. a 10″ Mercury LP, *It's A Lonesome Old Town* on Decca, *If I Give My Heart To You* on Columbia, *My Coloring Book* on RCA, *Delightfully* on Movietone.

KALTHUM, Om (*b* '10 in Tammay, a village in the Egyptian delta; *d* '75) Singer in classical Islamic style. Grew up in trad. family with religious background; early on her father recognised her powerful voice and took her with him to sing at religious festivities; growing fame brought increased wealth to the family, but embarrassed at daughter singing religious songs in public her father dressed her as a boy. She was much praised by singer Shaykkh Abu al-'lla for her singing of Maqam, the classical Islamic singing tradition; he took her and her father to Cairo and taught her in the '20s. She gradually broadened her repertory but still sang classical poetry and the songs of Mohammed, resisting pressure to sing popular songs (musica sharbeya). She made her first record with Victor in Cairo c.'25, followed by many more; she gradually changed from singing only with male vocal quartet to the use of a small orchestra '26. Her fame spread as a classical singer for the next fifty years throughout the Arab world, but with very wide appeal among ordinary people; for many years she sang in the same theatre on the first Thursday every month in Cairo, and it was an honour for a foreign dignitary to be taken to hear her. She was famous for her stamina (a concert lasted over four hours) as well as vitality, power and range of expression. She was married to Dr Hisnan Hifnami, but had no children. Last concert in Cairo '73 preceded serious illness; on her death Radio Cairo chanted the Koran following the announcement, a mark of status normally reserved for heads of state. Her records and cassettes (e.g. from EMI/Greece) still sell up to 75,000 a year.

KAMINSKY, Max (*b* 7 Sep. '08, Brockton, Mass.) Trumpet. Began at age 12 in Boston; played in a few big bands (Tommy DORSEY, Artie SHAW) but never for long: he associated with the white Chicago-style small groups (*see* JAZZ) and was most popular in NYC clubs in the late '40s, when he also made his best records, on Commodore with Pee Wee RUSSELL and George Brunis, of what were considered Dixieland classics ('That's A-Plenty', 'Panama', 'Royal Garden Blues', etc.). But he was not a revivalist: along with trumpeters Wild Bill DAVISON and Bobby HACKETT he was one of the best of a generation that played the music it had always played, paying no mind to critics (some thought it was old-fashioned; for purists it wasn't old-fashioned enough). He toured Europe with a Jack TEA-GARDEN – Earl HINES All Star combo '57, the Orient with Teagarden '58, played in London '70, etc. but was most at home in NYC: played at Jimmy Ryan's until '83. Published *My Life In Jazz* '63. Prolific freelance recording (famous Bud FREEMAN session on Victor '39 with Russell) but very little as leader: LPs on Jazztone (*Chicago Style*), Westminster (*Ambassador Of Jazz*), UA long out of print.

KANDA BONGO MAN (*b* Kanda Bongo, '55, Inongo, Zaire) Singer-composer. Born into the third generation of modern Zaire music, he left school at 18 to play in a local Kinshasa band; joined Orchestre Bella Mambo '76 as vocalist and had string of hit singles; went to Paris '79, working to perfect his own high-speed soukous, jumping straight into the music without the slow introduction favoured by the older generation, also abandoning the horn section, preferring to run a smaller, tighter band for both touring and recording. First solo LP *Iyole* on Afro-Rythmes label, followed by *Djessy* '83, his best-seller *Amour Fou* '84. Still based in Paris, he stole the show at the WOMAD festival '83 and returned to the UK several times in '84, toured Canada '85, sessioned on other LPs while preparing his own fourth solo set.

KANE, Eden (*b* Robin Sarstedt, 29 Mar. '42, Delhi, India) UK pop singer, after short film career (*Drinks All Round* '60). Lucky with management and musical team: writer Johnny Worth (who wrote as Les Vandyke) and arranger Johnny Keating set his unmemorable voice to produce acceptable pre-beat pop. After dubious first record 'Hot Chocolate Crazy' (intended by management to double as Radio Luxembourg advert jingle), hits by Worth/Keating were 'Well I Ask You' (no. 1), 'Get Lost' (10), 'Forget Me Not' (3), 'I Don't Know Why' (7) '61-2. Subsequent flops led to change of label from Decca to Fontana for one more hit ('Boys Cry', no. 8 '64, was not a Worth song). He was often bracketed with Adam FAITH, who also used the Worth/Keating team, but like him, Frank IFIELD, Helen SHAPIRO and others, Kane was washed away by the Merseybeat. Brother Peter Sarstedt had two top 10 hits '69 incl. no. 1 'Where Do You Go To My Lovely'; under his real name Robin had no. 3 hit 'My Resistance Is Low' '76; link with Peter and Clive (another brother) for '70s comeback was unsuccessful.

KANSAS USA AOR band formed '70 in Kansas, by Topeka schoolmates Kerry Livgren (*b* 18 Sep. '49), guitar, keyboards; David Hope, bass; Phil Ehart, drums. After a period as White Clover (augmented by classically trained Robbie Steinhardt on violin), they split when Ehart left to tour Europe '72; on return he re-formed, guitarist Richard Williams and Steve Walsh on keyboards replacing Livgren, but it was Livgren's rejoining that kicked band into gear. They were signed by ex-MONKEES mastermind Don Kirshner after re-adopting the name Kansas; built upon a hard-won live following. LPs *Kansas* '74-5, *Masque* '75, *Song For America* '76 sold steadily if not spectacularly; *Leftoverture* '76 bolstered by no. 11 single (USA) 'Carry On Wayward Son' (at no. 51 UK came closest to denting UK indifference); group's pomp-rock was very much derived from UK sources: high harmonies of YES, dual guitars of WISH-BONE ASH, etc. USA fans bought in quantity (2m plus) to put band up with other faceless AOR supergroups like REO SPEEDWAGON, JOURNEY, etc. Platinum *Point Of Know Return* '77 incl. no. 6 single in philosophical 'Dust In The Wind', no. 28 title track; followed by live *Two For The Show* '78; then self-produced *Monolith* '79, *Audio Visions* '80, *Vinyl Confessions* '82. Walsh had made solo *Schemer-Dreamer* '80 and sung with ex-GENESIS Steve Hackett; he left '81, replaced by John Elefante (*b* '58, NYC). Principal songwriter Livgren made Kansas soundalike *Seeds Of Change* '80. *Drastic Measures* '83 and *Best Of* '84 were further Kansas releases; they reorganised with Walsh, Ehart, Williams, bassist Billy Greer (ex-Streets), highly rated guitarist Steve Morse (ex-Dixie Dregs): this lineup made album *Power* '87.

KANSAS CITY JAZZ Regional centres and territory bands have always revitalised American popular music and introduced new strains; the BIG BAND ERA began in '35 with Benny GOODMAN playing a style that had already been developed by black bandleaders Fletcher HENDERSON and Don REDMAN to a high degree of smooth sophistication: they wrote arrangements for dancers which had to swing if they were well played. In '37 Count BASIE came East from Kansas City and upset the applecart, playing a looser, blues-based style that had enough sophistication, but also retained more basic jazz values: the band was packed with great soloists and did not depend so much on arrangers; it could not only make up 'head' arrangements on the bandstand or at a rehearsal, but as Basie put it in his autobiography, the amazing thing was that they could play it the same way the next night. Jimmy BLANTON, Charlie CHRISTIAN, many other musicians of great importance came from the midwest or the southwest, for which K.C. was the most important regional centre because of its political corruption: Tom Pendergast (*b* 1872) ran the town from the '20s until '38 when he was indicted for income tax fraud; neither prohibition of alcohol nor its repeal made any difference to K.C., nor indeed did the Depression: 20 or 30 night clubs operated all the way through (while Pendergast went to bed at 9 each night). Musicians were not highly paid but they could work around the clock, and the town was a hot-house for jazz talent. COON-SANDERS' Nighthawks were a popular white band who became famous broadcasting from K.C. in the early years;

the band of Bennie MOTEN was from '23-32 the most prolifically recorded of all territory bands; Harlan LEONARD worked for Moten, later emerged with his Rockets; Basie took over remnants of Moten's band. Vocalists from K.C. incl. Julia LEE, Walter BROWN, Basie's Jimmy RUSHING; other important bands were Andy KIRK's Clouds of Joy, incl. fine pianist/composer Mary Lou WILLIAMS, and that of Jay McSHANN, whose band incl. Brown and Charlie PARKER: the spirit of the K.C. style, with its blues blues content and the infl. of Parker, Basie sidemen Lester YOUNG, Jo JONES, took elements of Kansas City jazz into BOP, thence into 'modern' jazz down to today. Ross Russell's *Jazz Style In Kansas City And The Southwest* '71 is a valuable survey.

KARAS, Anton (*b* 7 July '06, Vienna; *d* there 9 Jan. '85) Zither, composer. Trained as a locksmith, found a zither in the attic and became a virtuoso. Playing in a tavern '49 when film director Carol Reed asked him to compose score for *The Third Man*; he agreed, with no experience of composition; 'The Third Man Theme' made him rich, and his music will forever be inseparable from a great film. Both his own recording and that of Guy LOMBARDO (with Don Rodney playing the zither part on guitar) were in the USA charts for 11 weeks '50, both reaching no. 1; his album on Decca UK (London USA) also did well. He bought his own tavern and lived happily almost ever after.

KASSEYA, Souzy (*b* '49, Shaba, Zaire) Singer, composer, guitarist. Began playing at an early age, with many bands incl. Vox Afrique with Sam MANGWANA; also became producer, working with Tshala MUANA, Bebe MANGA, François Lougah. Moved to Paris '77, became sought-after session guitarist; made first solo LP *Le Retour de l'As* '84, with the pick of Paris' African session players incl. Ringo Starr on guitar, Salsero on drums. LP incl. 'Le Téléphone Sonne' which in remixed version became dance-floor hit in several countries (on Earthworks in UK). He appeared in UK '84 playing with Sam Mangwana and the African All Stars; second LP *The Phenomenal Souzy*

Kasseya '85 was also on Earthworks; next issue was 12″ single 'La Vie Continue'.

KATZ, Steve (*b* 9 May '45, NYC) USA guitarist, producer. Folk boom drew him from Brooklyn to Greenwich Village at 15, where Dave VAN RONK tutored him for 18 months. Joined Even Dozen Jug Band '63 (*see* Maria MULDAUR). Joined Blues Project, replacing Artie Traum; followed Al KOOPER to BLOOD, SWEAT & TEARS, outlasted him there (through *New Blood* '72). Played on Blues Project *Reunion In Central Park* '73, then with American Flyer, softrock supergroup with Eric Kaz (ex-BLUES MAGOOS), Doug Yule (ex-VELVET UNDERGROUND), Craig Fuller (ex-Pure Prairie League); split after disappointingly undistinguished albums *American Flyer* '76, *Spirit Of A Woman* '77. Turned to production, incl. three mid-'70s LPs by Lou REED, three by Irish folk-rockers HORSLIPS late '70s, others for Rory Block, Graf, Elliott Murphey. Also sessioned on harmonica for Reed, LYNYRD SKYNYRD, Duke Jupiter.

KAYE, Danny (*b* David Kuminsky, 18 Jan. '13, Brooklyn, NY; *d* 3 Mar. '87, L.A.) Comedian, actor, singer. Adept at novelty songs and tongue-twisters, but also affecting on ballads. A camp counsellor and entertainer in the Catskills; played in *Straw Hat Revue* '39, Broadway vehicle for newcomers; successful on Broadway in *Lady In The Dark* (music by Kurt WEILL) and *Let's Face It* (Cole PORTER) '41; first film *Up In Arms* '44: more than 20 films incl. *A Song Is Born* '48, *White Christmas* '54, title roles in *The Secret Life Of Walter Mitty* '47, *Hans Christian Andersen* '52 (score by Frank LOESSER), *The Court Jester* '56, as Red NICHOLS in *The Five Pennies* '59. His wife Sylvia Fine wrote special material for him, incl. songs for *Let's Face It* (also title songs for films *The Moon Is Blue* '53, *Man With The Golden Arm* '56). He recorded for Columbia, then Decca; Decca novelties incl. delightful 'Handout On Panhandle Hill' (in trad. American 'Big Rock Candy Mountain' genre); his only chart entry was 'I've Got A Lovely Bunch Of Coconuts', top 30 '50. Album of 78s on Columbia '45, LP soundtrack of *Hans Christian Andersen* on Decca '53 also charted (latter at no. 1). Renowned for his humanitarianism, he was perhaps at

his best entertaining children, when his love shone transparently through. Other albums: 10″ LPs on Columbia, 10″ Decca soundtrack of *Knock On Wood* '54; *Danny At The Palace* on Decca; compilations on Decca, Harmony; all out of print.

KAYE, Sammy (*b* 13 Mar. '10, Rocky River, Ohio; *d* 2 June '87, Ridgeway, N.J.) Reeds, composer, leader of sweet dance band. Like Kay KYSER, used gimmick of singing song titles; slogan 'swing and sway with Sammy Kaye'. Began at Ohio U., Cleveland after graduation, then on Cincinnati radio, long run in Pittsburgh; finally one of the most successful dance bands well into '60s. Radio show *Sunday Serenade* late '40s-50s; Kaye was a good front man and his excellent stage show featured 'So you want to lead a band', in which fans volunteered to wave the baton; it transferred to TV '50s. He wrote his own theme, 'Kaye's Melody', also hits 'Until Tomorrow' '41, 'Remember Pearl Harbor' '42, 'Wanderin' ' '50 (vocal by Tony Alamo); *Pop Memories* credits the band with more than 100 '37-53, mostly in top 10, incl. no. ones 'Rosalie' '37, 'Love Walked In' '38, 'Dream Valley' '40, 'Daddy' '41 (written by Bobby TROUP), 'Chickery Chick' '45 (novelty by Sidney Lippman, *b* 1 Mar. '14, Minneapolis, and Sylvia Dee, *b* Josephine Proffitt Faison, 22 Oct. '14, Little Rock, Ark.; *d* 12 June '67, NYC; wrote ' "A" – You're Adorable', hit for Perry COMO '49; together wrote 'My Sugar Is So Refined'; 'Too Young', hit for Nat COLE '51; Broadway show *Barefoot Boy With Cheek* '47, based on comic novel Max Shulman). Other Kaye no. ones: 'I'm A Big Girl Now' and 'The Old Lamplighter' '46, 'Harbor Lights' '50. 'It Isn't Fair' no. 3 '50, written '33 by Richard Himber (*b* 20 Feb. '07, Newark, N.J.; *d* 11 Dec. '66, NYC; conducted for Sophie TUCKER, own dance band, etc.) and Frank Warshauer (*b* 4 Sep. 1893, Brooklyn; *d* 28 Nov. '53, NYC: played drums for Victor HERBERT, Arthur Pryor, John Philip SOUSA): fine arrangement of big romantic ballad left space for Kaye after band's intro: 'Here, to sing this beautiful song, is Don CORNELL'. Band's other vocalists incl. Jimmy Brown, Tommy Ryan (who took over Blue BARRON band '44). Two more hits on Decca '62 and '64 (instrumental 'Charade' reached top 40). Arranger

Charlie Albertine, who created Les ELGART sound '60s, worked for Kaye late '60s. Albums of RCA 78s on early Billboard album chart: Stephen FOSTER songs '45, *Dusty Manuscripts* '48, *Plays Irving Berlin* '50; switched to Columbia '50, early Columbia 12″ LPs *Swing And Sway With Sammy Kaye, Music, Maestro, Please!, Midnight Serenade*; on Harmony: *Dancing With Sammy Kaye In HiFi*, songs from *My Fair Lady*; on Decca, *Come Dance To The Hits* '64 made top 100 LPs USA, while *Swing And Sway, Dance To My Favorites* '61, *The '30s Are Here To Stay* '69, 2-disc *Best Of* are still in print on MCA. Compilations: five LPs on Hindsight of '40-6 stuff have vocals by Ryan, Cornell, Nancy Norman, Betty Barclay, Billy Williams and the Three Kaydets; LP on Ranwood label is shared with Blue Barron. Records are listed in jazz section of the USA Schwann catalogue, which seems strange; George T. Simon on Kaye's NY debut at the Commodore Hotel '38: 'The "swing" of Sammy Kaye can truthfully be described as follows:' followed by inches of blank space. Today's pop music doesn't swing either, but Kaye's was never meretricious.

KC AND THE SUNSHINE BAND Dance band formed '73 in Florida, had explosive success in disco. Harry Wayne Casey (*b* 31 Jan. '51, Hialeah, Fla.) worked for a record distributor; struck up songwriting partnership with bassist Richard Finch (*b* 25 Jan. '54, Indianapolis), who was an engineer at TK Studios in Hialeah; with KC on vocals and keyboards they made 'Blow Your Whistle' as KC and the Sunshine Junkanoo Band (junkanoo being Bahamian pop music); it and the next release were R&B hits; 'Do It Good' and 'Queen Of Hearts' were hits in Europe; they wrote, produced and recorded 'Rock Your Baby' with veteran R&B vocalist George McCrae, who'd sung on 'Do It Good': it was no. 1 on both R&B and pop charts in the USA and many other countries. Casey and Finch are white; the rest of the band was black as they embarked on a remarkable series of loose-limbed, funky hits that characterised the 'Miami sound': lineup incl. Jerome Smith (*b* 18 June '53), guitar; Robert Johnson (*b* 21 Mar. '53), drums; Ronnie Smith (*b* '52), trumpet, all from Florida; Fermin Goytisolo, congas (*b*

31 Dec. '51, Havana); Charles Williams, trombone (*b* 18 Nov. '54, Rockingham, N.C.); James Weaver, trumpet; Denvil Liptrot, sax. 'Get Down Tonight', 'That's The Way (I Like It)', '(Shake, Shake, Shake) Shake Your Booty' '75-6 were all no. 1 both R&B and pop (they were the first act since the BEATLES '64 to have three no. 1 hits in 12-month period); 'I'm You're Boogie Man' was no. 1 pop, 2 R&B, while 'Keep It Comin' Love' was no. 2 pop, 1 R&B, both '77. As well as a handful of lesser Hot 100 entries, their other top 40 hits were 'I Like To Do It' (no. 37), 'Boogie Shoes' and 'It's The Same Old Song' (both no. 35), and they finished off with 'Please Don't Go', another no. 1 '79. KC and/or Finch wrote and/or prod. records for Teri DeSario ('Yes, I'm Ready', no. 2 '79), Betty Wright (back-up singer: 'Where Is The Love' won a Grammy; she had earlier hits of her own, notably 'Clean Up Woman', no. 6 '71); Fire (female back-up group) and Leif Garrett (*b* 8 Nov. '61, Hollywood), whose 3 top 20 hits '77-8 incl. 'I Was Made For Dancin' '. Albums incl. *KC And The Sunshine Band* (no. 4 LP '75), *Part 3* (no. 13 '76), four more on TK incl. *Greatest Hits*; *KC Ten* on Meca; *The Painter* '81 and *All In A Night's Work* '82 on Epic. Only the last of these is still in print; dance music goes out of fashion quickly these days, but they had set their record.

K-DOE, Ernie (*b* Ernest Kador Jr, 22 Feb. '36, New Orleans) R&B singer. Sang with gospel groups, then the Moonglows, the Flamingos, then back in New Orleans with the Blue Diamonds, which became a popular local act and recorded for Savoy. He made solo records on Specialty, Herald, then Minit; 'Hello My Lover' was a regional hit '59, then 'Mother-in-Law', prod. by Allen TOUSSAINT, was no. 1 '61 on both R&B and pop charts. It was an amusing novelty, with Benny Spellman's bass refrain, Toussaint's piano, but it was also more than that: an example of good-humoured, laid-back New Orleans R&B. K-Doe had become a first-class entertainer, serving his apprenticeship in the Dew Drop Inn, the Club Tijana and the Sho-Bar; after a handful of lesser hits he remained popular in local clubs. Spellman had a Hot 100 entry at no. 80 with 'Lipstick Traces' in '62.

KEEL, Howard (*b* Harold Clifford Keel, 13 Apr. '19, Gillespie, Ill.) Singer, actor. One of several leads to follow Alfred DRAKE in long run of RODGERS & HAMMERSTEIN's *Oklahoma!*; broke into films with big voice and good looks: starred with Betty HUTTON in Irving BERLIN's *Annie Get Your Gun* '50, then many others with Kathryn Grayson, Esther Williams, Jane Powell, Doris DAY, etc. incl. Jerome KERN's *Show Boat* '51; *Lovely To Look At* '52 (remake of Kern's *Roberta*); Cole PORTER's *Kiss Me Kate!* and *Calamity Jane* '53 with Sammy FAIN songs; remake of Rudolph FRIML's *Rose-Marie*, *Seven Brides For Seven Brothers* (Johnny MERCER songs), Sigmund ROMBERG biopic *Deep In My Heart*, all '54; *Kismet* '55 (music adapted for film by Herbert Stothart; originally from Russian composer A. Borodin for the stage version, which starred Drake). Keel was back on Broadway in *Saratoga* '59; toured in *No Strings* '63. Also played straight dramatic film roles, leading to fat part in TV's *Dallas* mid-'80s: he probably finds it child's play.

KEEN, Robert Earl (*b* 11 Jan. '56, Houston, Texas) Country singer-songwriter on his way up. Began writing and playing bluegrass in college in Texas; switched to folk/country rock; first LP *No Kinda Dancer* on Workshop picked up by Rounder. Co-wrote 'This Old Porch' with Lyle LOVETT, which they've both recorded.

KEÏTA, Salif (*b* '49, Djoliba, Mali) Vocalist, composer; educated in Bamako; an albino, descended from ancient kings who formed Malian empire in the 13th century. Began with the Rail Band, a highly rated Malian group formed '70 with government sponsorship (album on German Bärenreiter-Musicaphon label); left '73 to join big band Les Ambassadeurs, its leader Kante Manfila a legendary acoustic guitarist and composer; he extended its repertoire by adding local rhythms and music to existing Congo/Cuban sound: albums from Safari Ambiance label '77 incl. *Les Ambassadeurs du Motel de Bamako* (also on Sono-disc/Sonafric in France). He received an award from President Sékou Touré of Guinea in recognition of musical achievements '77; wrote 'Mandjou' (later title track of an album on Celluloid, telling history of Mali and paying tribute to Sékou Touré. Single 'Primpin' was big hit throughout West Africa, available on compilation *Best Of The Ambassadeurs* '83 on Celluloid) (aka *Dance Music From West Africa* on Rounder; live version of 'Primpin' also on Dutch album *Africa Roots Vol. 1* on Stemra). The band left Mali for Abidjan, capital of the Ivory Coast and musical capital of Francophone Africa, in effort to crack international market, changing name of band to Les Ambassadeurs Internationaux; albums reflecting mature sound of band with stunning sax and guitar solos and unmistakeably Islamic vocals incl. *Djougouya* and *Tounkan* in '80s. After a decade together tension between Keïta and Manfila caused split; Keïta formed Super Ambassadeurs, toured Europe to appreciative audiences: his album *Soro* '87 on Stern's was impeccably produced at the 48-track Harry Son studio in Paris, but retained African values and deserved to be the biggest African hit of the year.

KELLAWAY, Roger (*b* 1 Nov. '39, Waban, Mass.) Pianist, composer, arranger, conductor, producer; very highly regarded by other musicians. Studied piano from age 7; played bass, a little percussion, began composing in high school; studied at New England Conservatory, played bass with Jimmy McPARTLAND, Ralph MARTERIE; piano with Kai WINDING '62, singer Mark MURPHY '63; with Al COHN/Zoot SIMS, Bobby BROOKMEYER/Clark TERRY; formed own trio. Worked in Don ELLIS band '66, mus. dir. for Bobby DARIN '67-9, toured '74 with Joni MITCHELL and Tom Scott's L.A. Express (reedman Scott *b* 19 May '48, L.A.; played with Ellis, Oliver NELSON; LPs on CBS, Atlantic, Ode, Elektra, MCA). Studio work incl. arr. for SUPERSAX, Carmen McRAE (on Blue Note '75), LPs for MELANIE, Maria MULDAUR; recorded with Nelson, Sonny ROLLINS, Gerry MULLIGAN, Baja Marimba Band, George HARRISON, etc.; also TV, film music; classical compositions recorded since '73 incl. *Esque* for trombone and bass; music for cello quartet also recorded on A&M. LPs as arr./cond. incl. *Center Of The Circle*, *Cello Quartet*, *Come To The Meadow* on A&M, all out of print; jazz work incl. trio *A Jazz Portrait* '63 on Regina, *Trio* '65 on Prestige, *Spirit Feel*

'67 on Pacific Jazz, *The Nostalgia Suite* '78 on Discwasher with trio plus cello/percussion. Solo LP called *Stride* c.'66, then *Ain't Misbehavin'* '86 on Choice/Bainbridge; he sang and played on *Say That Again* c.'70 on Dobre; made duo album *Leaves On The Water* '85 on Choice with lyricist/vocalist Gene LEES, mostly songs they co-wrote; *Fifty-Fifty* on Stash is duo with bassist Red Mitchell. Re-formed Brookmeyer/Terry Quintet with Kellaway was rumoured for '88.

KELLEY, Peck (*b* John Dickson Kelley, 1898, Houston, Texas; *d* 26 Dec. '80, Houston) Pianist, leader. Legendary musician who led Peck's Bad Boys in '20s; musicians who passed through incl. Jack TEAGARDEN, Pee Wee RUSSELL, Louis PRIMA; legendary because he refused offers from other bandleaders, rarely left Houston, playing long residencies there through mid-'50s. Teagarden's brother Charlie said that he 'was very advanced, more like Art TATUM than a stride pianist'. 2-disc *Peck Kelley Jam* with Dick Shannon Quartet on Commodore recorded '57, issued much later; 2-disc *Out Of Obscurity* on Arcadia has solo home tapings plus interview from '50s (fourth side by Lynn 'Son' Harrell, now resident pianist at Dallas County Club aged 85).

KELLY, Gene (*b* 23 Aug. '12, Pittsburgh, Pa.) Dancer, actor, singer; also choreographer, later film director. Like Fred ASTAIRE, he was underrated as a (soft-voiced) singer because of his excellent dancing. On Broadway in *Leave It To Me* '38, *One For The Money* '39, starred in *Pal Joey* '41; first film *For Me And My Gal* '42 with Judy GARLAND. More than 30 films, mostly musicals, incl. *Cover Girl* '44 (songs by Jerome KERN, Ira GERSHWIN), *Anchors Away* '45 (with Frank SINATRA), *On The Town* '49 (film version of Leonard BERNSTEIN show, with Sinatra), *Summer Stock* '50 (with Garland), then two of the best musical films ever made: *An American In Paris* '51 (written by Alan Jay LERNER, music by the Gershwins), *Singin' In The Rain* '52 (with contributions from Adolph Green, Betty Comden, Lennie HAYTON, Nacio Herb BROWN), topped off with *Brigadoon* '54 (music by Lerner & Loewe) and *It's Always Fair Weather* '55 (Comden

& Green, cast incl. Dolores GRAY and the wonderful Dan Dailey), which are also first class. Good straight actor in *Marjorie Morningstar* '58 (did the best he could in a dreadful film), *Inherit The Wind* '60.

KELLY, Wynton (*b* 2 Dec. '31, Jamaica; *d* 12 Apr. '71, Toronto) Piano. To USA c. age 4; played R&B from '43, late '40s with Eddie DAVIS, then accompanied Dinah WASHINGTON. With Dizzy GILLESPIE before and after military service '52-4; own trio '58, with Miles DAVIS '59-63. Played with natural clarity and exuberance; during and after the period with Miles he contributed to the tendency towards funk, but his own playing retained more integrity than that. Riverside (Milestone) LPs with Ernie Henry (alto sax; *b* 3 Sep. '26, Brooklyn; *d* 29 Dec. '57, NYC; played with Tadd DAMERON '47, later Dizzy GILLESPIE, Thelonious MONK), Blue MITCHELL (LP *Big Six*), Clark TERRY (*Serenade To A Bus Seat*), Nat ADDERLEY (*That's Right*), etc. Own albums began with 10″ Blue Note trio set *New Faces, New Sounds* '51; complete Blue Note sessions issued in Japan as *Piano Interpretations By Wynton Kelly*. *Wynton Kelly* '58 on Riverside (later *Keep It Moving* on Milestone) has Kenny BURRELL, Paul CHAMBERS; Philly Joe JONES added on some tracks; during time with Miles he regularly worked with Chambers and Jimmy COBB, on *Kelly Blue* '59 adding Benny GOLSON and Adderley on some tracks. Vee Jay LPs *Kelly Great!*, *Kelly At Midnight* '59-60 had Philly Joe instead of Cobb; *Wynton Kelly* '61 on Vee Jay had Cobb, Chambers, Sam JONES on additional bass (some tracks were reissued with dubbed strings). After he left Miles he led a trio with Paul Chambers and Jimmy Cobb; Verve LPs '63-5 incl. *Undiluted, Smokin' At The Half Note* (with Wes MONTGOMERY) again had some tracks reissued with large group dir. by Claus Ogerman dubbed. *Blues On Purpose* '65 on Xanadu, *Full View* '66 on Milestone were followed by *In Concert* '68 issued on Affinity, with Ron McLure replacing Chambers.

KEMAYO, Elvis (*b* '49, Cameroon) Singer, composer, producer, arranger. Joined first band Negro Fiesta as vocalist and guitarist at 18; left for Paris '72, stayed five years, studying music and touring Europe; performed with Manu DIBANGO at Paris Olympia '77. Released singles and first LP *Africa l'An 2000* on Fiesta label. Moved to Gabon late '70s, became art director at Gabon TV, also following up first LP with *Paradise Noir* '81. A distinguished and sought-after producer and arranger, he helped 15-piece soukous band Les Diablotins become one of Africa's top outfits, producing seven albums for them '81-3 incl. *Weekend à Libreville* and *Africa No. 1*, a tribute to Gabon's infl. radio station. His own *10ième Anniversaire* '84 was a best-selling dance album, a collection of the year's most popular Makossa tunes featuring such session musicians as Toto Guillaume and Alhadji Toure. Reunited with Diablotins for their 2-disc *Diablotins '85*.

KEMP, Hal (*b* James Harold Kemp, 27 Mar. '05, Marion, Ala.; *d* 21 Dec. '40, Cal. of pneumonia following severe injuries in car crash) Reeds, bandleader; led one of the most popular dance bands of the '30s, with more than 60 hits. Began at U. of North Carolina '24-6; Carolina Club Orchestra recorded on Okeh; toured Europe '30 with Bunny BERIGAN. Key men were with him from the start: pianist-arranger John Scott Trotter (*b* 14 June '08, Charlotte, N.C.), tenor sax/vocalist Saxie Dowell (*b* 29 May '04, N.C.), vocalist/drummer Skinnay ENNIS. Band played semi-hot at first, turned sweet but could still swing; Kemp composed pretty theme 'When Summer Is Gone'; Trotter created distinctive style, muted trumpets playing clipped notes (often triplets) against reeds (often low-register clarinets) sometimes through megaphones for effect. Bob Allen sang ballads; Ennis's breathless style had biggest hits: 'Got A Date With An Angel' recorded twice. No. 1 hits were 'There's A Small Hotel' and 'When I'm With You' '37, 'This Year's Kisses' and 'Where Or When' '37. Girl singers incl. Maxine Gray, Deane Janis, Nan Wynn, Janet Blair. Trotter left '35, had long career with Bing CROSBY, also arranged for Al JOLSON, many others; Art Mooney joined as arranger. Vocal trio the Smoothies created; radio work incl. *Music From Hollywood* '37 with Alice Faye; own show *Time To Shine* '38-9; film *Radio City Revels* '38. Ennis left '38 to form own band;

Dowell left early '39 on the strength of hit novelty 'Three Little Fishies' which he wrote and sang; wrote 'Playmates' '40; became song plugger '48, likeable DJ on Chicago radio '50s. There were more personnel changes and '40 was a bad year, but things were looking up when the accident happened. Compilation of '34 tracks on Insight. Mooney had hits on MGM in corny/nostalgia style with unison singing, banjos: 'I'm Looking Over A Four Leaf Clover' no. 1 '48.

KENDALLS, The Country music vocal duo, one of the most successful of recent years, unusually a father and daughter: Royce (*b* 25 Sep. '34) and Jeannie (*b* 13 Nov. '54), both *b* St Louis, Mo. Royce performed on Arkansas radio stations with his brother Floyce early '50s. Following army service he settled down operating a barber shop in St Louis; sang with Jeannie and they decided to try their luck in Nashville. They made demos '69, signed to Pete Drake's Stop Records; first hit with 'Leavin' On A Jet Plane' '70; less luck on Dot '72 and UA '76; rediscovered and signed to new Ovation label, their second release 'Heaven's Just A Sin Away' was no. 1 country, crossed over to pop chart '77, won a Grammy and CMA Record of the Year. Their unique harmony gives them a contemporary sound with enough trad. flavour to keep them in country charts, hits incl. 'Pittsburgh Stealers' '78, 'You'd Make An Angel Wanna Cheat' '79, 'I'm Already Blue' '80, 'Teach Me To Cheat' '81. Switched to Mercury and carried on with 'Cheater's Prayer', 'Thank God For The Radio' etc. Albums incl. *Two Divided By Love* '72 on Dot, *Old Fashioned Love* and *Just Like Real People* '78-9 on Ovation, *Stickin' Together*, *Movin' Train* and *Two Heart Harmony* on Mercury.

KENTON, Stan (*b* Stanley Newcomb Kenton, 19 Feb. '12, Wichita, Kansas; *d* 25 Aug. '79, L.A.) Pianist, bandleader, composer. Wrote his first arrangement '28. Played with Gus ARNHEIM, Vido Musso (reedman; *b* 17 Jan. '13, Sicily; *d* 2 June '29, Cal.; played with Benny GOODMAN, others; own bands); debuted with own band Memorial Day '41 at Balboa Beach, Cal. and recorded for Decca '41-2. Early arrangements were by Kenton and Ralph Yaw (*b* 22 Oct.

1898, Enosburg Falls, Vermont; wrote 40 fine arrangements for the early band, gave up arranging '47, worked in Bakersfield in C&W; wrote 'No Longer A Prisoner' for Hank SNOW). Kenton band recorded theme 'Artistry in Rhythm' at its first Capitol date '43, then 'Eager Beaver'; soon became famous. George T. Simon praised the band in '41, calling it 'one of the greatest combinations of rhythm, harmony and melody that's ever been assembled by one leader', but also wrote of its 'continual blasting'; others wrcte of an inability to swing. From '44 Kenton hired people like Musso, Stan GETZ, Shelly MANNE, Kai WINDING, Bob COOPER, Art PEPPER, Maynard FERGUSON, bassist Eddie Safranski (*b* 25 Dec. '18, Pittsburgh; *d* 9 Jan. '74, L.A.), arranger Pete Rugolo (*b* 25 Dec. '15, Sicily; scored TV's *The Fugitive* '60s), vocalists Anita O'DAY, June CHRISTY, Chris CONNOR. In the late '40s Kenton's band was the most important and innovative white band, along with that of Woody HERMAN: six top 10 hits '44-6 incl. 'And Her Tears Flowed Like Wine' (with O'Day), 'Tampico' and 'Shoo-Fly Pie' (with Christy), 'How High The Moon' '48 with Christy was no. 27. Kenton was a hard worker, a good businessman, a bundle of nerves who often suffered from ill health and once threatened to quit music to become a psychiatrist. He was good to his employees, who were fiercely loyal. He disbanded, rested in '49; assembled 40-piece group with strings '50, calling act 'Innovations In Modern Music', thereafter organising and disbanding once a year; in '56 he was the first USA band to play the UK since '37, helping to break down UK musicians' union restrictions. 'September Song' and 'Laura' were top 20 hits '51, lovely arrangements with chorus, modern harmony, autumnal colours; 'Delicado' '52 reached no. 25, a noisy cover of the year's hit instrumental (no. 1 by Percy FAITH). No further pop hits, except for spoken-word novelty 'Mama Sang A Song', top 40 '62. Kenton's later music consisted of commercial arrangements ('September Song'), jazz pieces by Rugolo, Gerry MULLIGAN, Shorty ROGERS, Bill Holman (tenor sax, *b* 21 May '27, Olive, Cal.), and (increasingly) a sort of semi-classical stuff for big band composed by Bill Russo (*b* 25 June '28, Chicago) and Bob Graettinger (*City Of*

Glass), which appealed mostly to high-school bandmasters. This could be a back-handed compliment in that the music may be fun or challenging to play, but the difference between Herman and Kenton was that Herman always entertained (and swung), while Kenton was often loud, pretentious and 'progressive', an adjective usually denoting music that will date quickly. He sold albums of the lighter stuff: pop chart entries incl. albums of 78s, then 10″ LPs '46-53, then *Stan Kenton In Hi-Fi* '56 (hits remakes), *Cuban Fire!* '56, music from *West Side Story* '61 (won Grammy), 2-disc *Stan Kenton Today* '72 (made in London for high-tech Phase Four label). He led summertime Stan Kenton Clinics '59-63, led 27-piece group '61 with four specially made mellophoniums; launched the Los Angeles Neophonic Orchestra '65 for 'third stream' music by various composers with guests Mulligan, Dizzy GILLESPIE, Buddy DeFRANCO, European crossover concert pianist Friedrich Gulda, etc. He testified before the US Senate '67, working for revision of music copyright law. He was opinionated, describing the BEATLES as 'children's music' and country music as 'a national disgrace' (so much for his old comrade Yaw). LPs incl. *The Formative Years* on Decca/MCA; *Greatest Hits* on Capitol (original '40s masters); *The Kenton Era*, an elaborate 4-disc set with a booklet on Capitol: the first of the discs incl. interesting early stuff from Balboa years. Others on Capitol in '50s incl. *Duet* with Christy, *City Of Glass & This Modern World* (from 10″ LPs '51-3), *Sketches On Standards* '53-4, *Kenton With Voices*, *Rendezvous* '57, *Back To Balboa*, *Ballad Style*, *Lush Interlude* and *The Stage Door Swings* '58, *Standards In Silhouette* and *Viva Kenton* '59, *Road Show* (live set with Christy and FOUR FRESHMEN); in '60s: *Adventures In Standards* and *Adventures In Blues* '61, *Adventures In Jazz* '62 (won Grammy), *Artistry In Bossa Nova* '63, *Kenton/Wagner* (!) '64, many more. Left Capitol c.'70, made a deal for old master tapes and reissued early work as well as new albums on Creative World label: reissues incl. most of the above, masters from earliest years, e.g. *Some Women I've Known* '44-63 with singers O'Day, Christy, Connor, Jeri Winter, Ann Richards (his wife), Jean Turner; new releases incl. *Solo: Stan Kenton*

Without The Orchestra '73; more than 60 LPs on Creative World listed. Also 2-disc *The Comprehensive Kenton* on Capitol, several discs of early work on Hindsight, Sunbeam. *Kenton Straight Ahead* '73 by Carol Easton gives details of all the bands as well as a portrait of Kenton, a complicated man and a ferocious idealist.

KEPPARD, Freddie (*b* 27 Feb. 1890, New Orleans; *d* 15 July '33, Chicago) Cornet, bandleader. A New Orleans veteran who took his Original Creole Orchestra to California c.'14 and caused a sensation. Jazz was still a new ragtime music called 'jass'; the band did a 'white-tie, all-musical act, with neither blackface minstrel clowning, nor even verbal comedy', according to Rudi Blesh, incl. Creole violinist Jimmy Palao (1885-1925), George Baquet on reeds (*b* 1883; *d* 14 Jan. '49, Philadelphia, Pa.; from famous N.O. family of clarinettists; also played with Buddy BOLDEN), Oliver 'Dink' Johnson on drums (*b* 28 Oct. 1892, Biloxi, Ms.; *d* 29 Nov. '54, Portland, Oregon), bassist/manager Bill Johnson (*b* William Manuel Johnson, 10 Aug. 1872, New Orleans; moved to Mexico '60s, *d* '72), Norwood Williams on guitar, Eddie Vinson on trombone. They played an arrangement of the Sextet from *Lucia di Lammermoor*, 'Carnival Of Venice' was a cornet speciality, and 'Livery Stable Blues' had the front line instruments imitating barnyard animals. Keppard was allegedly offered a chance to record by Victor late '16, turned it down fearing that other bands would steal his stuff; in '17 the ORIGINAL DIXIELAND JAZZ BAND stole it anyway: young white men from New Orleans were the first to record jazz, had a smash hit with 'Livery Stable Blues'. It is a fairly safe bet that Keppard's band did it with somewhat more class. The band toured the Orpheum vaudeville circuit to Chicago, NYC; Keppard worked with King OLIVER briefly '20, settled in Chicago. He made only one record date as a leader, in Chicago '26: the quintet incl. Johnny DODDS and a trombonist whose name was Eddie Vincent, according to Brian Rust's *Jazz Records*; 'Stock Yards Strut' was issued on Paramount, vocal 'Salty Dog' on the other side by Papa Charlie Jackson. He also recorded as a sideman with Doc Cook's Dreamland Orchestra and with Erskine Tate. He died after some years of obscurity caused by TB.

KERN, Jerome (*b* 27 Jan. 1885, NYC; *d* 11 Nov. '45, NYC). Songwriter; one of the greatest in USA history. Learned piano at early age; studied at NY College of Music; went to England: early song 'Mr Chamberlain' had lyric by P. G. Wodehouse. Back in NYC wrote c.100 songs for interpolation into various Broadway shows; own first show *The Red Petticoat* '12; 'They Didn't Believe Me' '14 with lyric by Herbert Reynolds, for imported UK show *The Girl From Utah*, was perhaps Kern's first masterpiece, incl. a change of key and several innovations in construction, resulting in an unforgettable song that was still singable: the craft of the Tin Pan Alley hack was raised to the level of art song, and the American musical show broke away from the European operetta style. George GERSHWIN claimed to imitate Kern; young Richard RODGERS spent all his pocket money seeing Kern's shows over and over; Kern's songs may be almost as important as the emergence of JAZZ in the 20th-century success of American music. He wrote or contributed substantially to 37 Broadway shows, incl. landmark *Show Boat* '28: with lyrics by Oscar Hammerstein II, hits 'Bill', 'Make Believe', 'Why Do I Love You?', 'Ol' Man River', 'Can't Help Lovin' Dat Man'; *Show Boat* also had a plot (based on Edna Ferber novel): earlier musicals had been empty vehicles for songs. Other shows (with some of the songs) incl. *Sally* '20 (lyrics by Buddy DESYLVA: 'Look For The Silver Lining'); *Sunny* '25 (lyrics by Hammerstein, Otto Harbach, incl. 'Who?'); *Roberta* '33 (with Harbach: 'Smoke Gets In Your Eyes', 'The Touch Of Your Hand'; film '35 added 'Lovely To Look At', 'I Won't Dance'; also filmed as *Lovely To Look At* '52); *Very Warm For May* '39 (Hammerstein: 'All The Things You Are'). Apart from films of shows, original films incl. *Swing Time* '35 (Fred ASTAIRE/Ginger Rogers; incl. instrumental 'Waltz In Swingtime'; with Dorothy Fields' lyrics: 'The Way You Look Tonight', 'Pick Yourself Up', 'Never Gonna Dance', 'A Fine Romance', 'Bojangles Of Harlem'); *High, Wide And Handsome* and *When You're In Love* '37; *Joy Of Living* '38, *One Night In The Tropics* '40; *Lady Be Good*

('The Last Time I Saw Paris', lyrics by Hammerstein), *You Were Never Lovelier* '42, *Song Of Russia* '43 (instrumental music), *Cover Girl* '44 ('Long Ago And Far Away', etc.; lyrics by Ira GERSHWIN), *Can't Help Singing* '44, *Centennial Summer* '46. Books incl. *Jerome Kern: His Life And Music* '80 by Gerald Bordman.

KERR, Anita (*b* 31 Oct. '27, Memphis, Tenn.) Singer, pianist, record producer, leader of Anita Kerr Singers, other vocal groups. Began as a child on her mother's Memphis radio show, later led trio in high school. Formed Singers '49, began with radio and session work, signed to Decca '51 and made singles and albums, no chart hits. Appeared on Arthur GODFREY Talent Scouts (CBS-TV '56), Jubilee USA (ABC '60). Important contribution to Nashville sound, appearing on records by Jim REEVES, the BROWNS, Red FOLEY, etc. Anita Kerr Quartet with Gil Wright (tenor), Dottie Dillard (alto), Louis Nunley (baritone) was the one of the busiest vocal groups in Nashville. As Anita & Th' So-And-So's had minor pop hit 'Joey Baby' on RCA '62. Began doing orchestral arrangements for RCA and became one of the first women to produce country records (Skeeter DAVIS LP *The End Of The World*). Moved to California '67, had minor chart LPs on Dot '69: *The Anita Kerr Singers Reflect On The Music Of Burt Bacharach & Hal David* and *Velvet Voices And Bold Brass*. Signed to WB, wrote instrumental music as the Sebastian Strings for the maudlin narration of 'poet' Rod McKuen. Worked on TV and film music and formed the Mexicali Singers. Other LPs incl. *Voices In Hi-Fi* '58 on Decca, *Georgia On My Mind* '65 on RCA Camden, etc.

KERSHAW, Doug (*b* 24 Jan. '36, Tiel Ridge, La.) Plays 20 instruments, best known for Cajun fiddle, songwriting. Poor family, spoke French; learned English at school in Lake Arthur from age 7; studied mathematics in college, but wrote songs from age 18. Formed group with two brothers, then just Rusty & Doug; performed on radio incl. *Louisiana Hayride, World's Original Jamboree* in Wheeling, West Va.; *Grand Ole Opry* '57; also Ed Sullivan, Dick Clark shows, etc. Rusty & Doug had hit 'Hello Sheriff' in

country chart '58 on Roy ACUFF's Hickory label; Doug spent three years in US Army (volunteer): back in Nashville, autobiographical 'Louisiana Man' became no. 10 country hit '61, now covered hundreds of times. Third hit 'Diggy Liggy Lo' '61; split with brother '64, signed with WB, appeared on first Johnny CASH TV show with Bob DYLAN. Played at Nixon inaugural; minor single hit again with 'Diggy Liggy Lo' '69. LPs on WB incl. *The Cajun Way* '69, *Spanish Moss* '70, *Doug Kershaw* and *Devil's Elbow* '71, *Douglas James Kershaw* '73, *Mama Kershaw's Boy* '74, live *Alive And Pickin'* '75, *The Ragin' Cajun* '76, *Flip Flop Fly* '77, *Louisiana Man* '78; *Louisiana Cajun Country* '79 on Starflite; also *Instant Hero* on Scotti Brothers.

KERSHAW, Nik (*b* 1 Mar. '58, Bristol, England) Vocalist, songwriter. Early work in local HM band Half Pint Hogg led him to apply to join DEEP PURPLE in '74: he was rejected, moved to jazz-funk group Fusion, then landed solo deal. *Human Racing* '84 appealed both to critics, pre-pubescent UK pop audience, with hit singles 'Wouldn't It Be Good', 'I Won't Let The Sun Go Down On Me', 'Dancing Girls', title track; also Kershaw's 'Bogart' (recalled ROXY MUSIC's tribute '2HB' 10 years before). *The Riddle* '85 contained imaginative 'Don Quixote'; title track was also a hit. He appeared at Live Aid '85, at Royal Albert Hall benefit for Greenpeace early '86; toured USA with Paul YOUNG; Eric CLAPTON incl. a Kershaw song in *Behind The Sun* '85. He has more to offer than most teen idols, but sales of his album *Radio Musicola* '86 were disappointing.

KESSEL, Barney (*b* 17 Oct. '23, Muskogee, Okla.) Guitar. Worked for Ben POLLACK in Chico Marx Orchestra '43; appeared in Lester YOUNG film short *Jammin' The Blues* '44; toured with JATP with Oscar PETERSON '52-3; much studio work, pop A&R at Verve '57-8; TV and film work incl. Elvis PRESLEY films. Has published instruction books. Own records began with singles on Atomic '45; sextet incl. Dodo Marmarosa; Verve quartet LP '53; 10 LPs on Contemporary '53-61 incl. reissue of tracks on 10″ releases; *Let's Cook!* '57 reissued on Boplicity '86 has Ben WEBSTER on two tracks. LPs on Reprise '62-3 incl. sextet with Paul HORN, Bud SHANK, Victor FELDMAN, two big band sets; quartet LP *On Fire* '65 on Emerald aka *Slow Burn* on Phil Spector label; *Guitar Workshop* '67 on Saba live from Berlin Festival is shared, with tracks by Jim HALL; trio sets *Swinging Easy* and *Blue Soul* '67 on Black Lion, quintet *Hair Is Beautiful* '68 on Polydor have some tracks on both labels (latter has second guitar by Ike Isaacs, *b* 28 Mar. '23, Akron, Ohio). Back on Contemporary for *Feeling Free* '69 with Bobby HUTCHERSON, Elvin JONES, Chuck Domanico on bass. Trio LP *Reflections In Rome* '69 on Italian RCA has Kessel playing 12-string and electric as well as his regular guitar. *What's New* on Mercury and *Limehouse Blues* on Black Lion both made in Paris, Barney Kessell Group LP on Black Lion in London, all '69. *Two Way Conversation* '73 is duo on Swedish Sonet label with bassist Red Mitchell (*b* 20 Sep. '27, NYC); *Summertime In Montreux* '73 on Black Lion has solo, trio, quartet and quintet tracks. *Barney Plays Kessel* '75, *Soaring* and *Poor Butterfly* '76, *Jelly Beans* '81 are all on Concord Jazz; quartet *Spontaneous Combustion* '87 with Monty ALEXANDER is on Contemporary.

KEYNOTE USA record label formed '40 by music shop owner Eric Bernay, recording mostly folk music, etc. appealing to the left: Paul ROBESON, Almanac Singers (*see* Pete SEEGER). Harry Lim (*b* 23 Feb '19, Djakarta, Indonesia, then called Batavia) came to USA '39, began recording jazz for Keynote '43, financing sessions; quickly became known for good music, good pressings (made by Capitol): began to have problems getting good pressings '46 (Capitol too busy), bought West Coast pressing plant but pressings were poor; Lim left '47, label taken over by Mercury '48; Lim lost all rights. Most famous sessions with Lester YOUNG, one each with Count BASIE and Johnny GUARNIERI on piano; several Coleman HAWKINS dates incl. All American Four with Teddy WILSON, John KIRBY, Sid CATLETT; his Sax Ensemble with Tab SMITH, Don BYAS and Harry CARNEY plus Guarnieri, Catlett, Al Lucas on bass; many of these were 12″ 78s, unusual at the time, allowing extra blowing room. Lim recorded sidemen from Woody HERMAN band, Red NORVO, trumpeter Joe Thomas (*b* 24 July '09, Webster Grove, Mo.; *d* 6 Aug. '84, NYC), guitarist George Barnes (*b* 17 July '21, Chicago Heights, Ill.; *d* '77), Milt HINTON, many more who rarely got chance to record as leaders; also Lennie TRISTANO's first sessions, Neal HEFTI, ex-Fats WALLER sideman Gene Sedric, Benny CARTER, Juan Tizol, Bud FREEMAN, Willie SMITH, many more. A few Keynote sessions were reissued but most were effectively lost until '86: Polygram issued sumptuous box of 21 LPs plus 7″ disc with newly discovered Tristano 'Untitled Blues', all pressed in Japan; 334 tracks, 115 previously unissued; excellent booklets with notes by Lim, Bob Porter, Don Morgenstern, indexes, rare photographs. Most Keynote tracks are first rate; others are still very good and fascinating period stuff. Lim recorded Al HAIG '49 for his own short-lived HL label, prod. sessions for Seeco incl. one with Wardell GRAY, worked at Sam Goody NYC record shop '56-73, formed Famous Door label: recorded Norvo, Barnes, Hinton, Paul QUINICHETTE, Scott HAMILTON, Mundell LOWE, trombonists Carl Fontana and Bill Watrous, tenor saxist Eddie Barefield, others; still gets good sound.

KHAN, Chaka (*b* Yvette Marie Stevens, 23 Mar. '53, Great Lakes, Ill.) Singer. Grew up on Chicago's South Side; formed group the Crystalettes at age 11, took name Chaka (Fire) when working with the Black Panthers in a breakfast programme. Quit school and worked with group Lyfe and the Babysitters '69, then formed Rufus with Kevin Murphy and Andre Fisher, both ex-AMERICAN BREED: new soul/dance group had 9 top 40 single hits '74-9 incl. 'Tell Me Something Good' (no. 3 '74), 'Sweet Thing' (no. 5 '76); also 11 chart LPs incl. no. 4 *Rags To Rufus* '74, *Rufusized* and *Rufus Featuring Chaka Khan* '75, both at no.7. After two more top 15 LPs she went solo while still obligated for two more Rufus LPs; when she made them, *Masterjam* '79 was again a top 15 LP but *Camouflage* '81 barely made the top 100. Rufus were on ABC, then MCA; Rufus fans followed her to solo work on WB, but the eclectic use she made of her gorgeous voice confused them: first LP *Chaka* '78 incl. no. 21 USA single 'I'm Every Woman', duet with George BENSON

'We Got The Love', reached no. 12 in LP chart; *Naughty* '80 made only no. 43; *What Cha' Gonna Do For Me* '81 was no. 17, with no. 53 title single, all prod. by Arif Mardin with West Coast WB session players. In '82 she released *Chaka Khan* (no. 52 LP) and *Echoes Of An Era* on Elektra/Musician, with Chick COREA, Freddie HUBBARD, Stanley CLARKE, Joe Henderson, an affectionate tribute to '50s jazz; and reunited with Rufus in Feb. to record *Live: Stompin' At The Savoy* '83 on WB: 2-disc set with one side recorded in studio incl. top 10 hit 'Ain't Nobody', reached no. 50. Solo *I Feel For You* '84 was a no. 14 LP, helped by no. 3 title hit written by PRINCE, then *Destiny* '86 reached no. 67, single 'Love Of A Lifetime' only no. 53.

KID CREOLE & THE COCONUTS Disco band formed by Kid Creole (aka Argyl Knepf, August Darnell; *b* Thomas August Darnell Browder, '51, Montreal). With brother Stoney Browder (*b* '49 NYC), 'Sugar-Coated' Ray Hernandez (aka Coati Mundi; *b* '50 NYC), others formed Dr Savannah's Original Buzzard Band playing eclectic 'mulatto music' NYC mid-'70s; cult dance-floor success had one top 40 hit USA '76. Darnell signed to Ze label, prod. others' records (incl. Coati Mundi); formed Kid Creole and the Coconuts '79 without brother but with Hernandez as co-composer, lovely dancing/singing Coconuts trio incl. Darnell's wife. LPs incl. *Off The Coast Of Me* '80, *Fresh Fruit In Foreign Places* '81, *Wise Guy* '82. No pop chart entries in USA but Spanish rap 'Me No Pop I' no. 32 UK '81 (also a hit in Argentina, elsewhere); 'I'm A Wonderful Thing Baby' no. 4 UK '82, 'Stool Pigeon', 'Annie, I'm Not Your Daddy' also UK hits '82 owing to UK interest in style rather than content, though Darnell had more to offer than most in genre: his own flamboyant wit, ebullient frontman Hernandez, talented trio (all made solo LPs), costumes and nonsense made sensational live act (e.g. '83 tour 'The Lifeboat Party'). LP *Tropical Gangsters* '82 incl. the hits; *Doppelganger* '83 incl. 'Lifeboat Party', 'Seven Year Itch'. UK's Granada TV commissioned film *Something Wrong In Paradise*, seen late '84 to wide praise. Darnell split up with wife, took stock and came back with single 'Endicott' mid-'85;

played at Montreux Jazz Festival '85; *In Praise Of Older Women And Other Crimes* '86 on Sire retained flamboyance, also addressed social issues; *Best Of* '84 collected hits; *I, Too, Have Seen The Woods* '87 incl. single 'Dancin' At The Bains Douches'. Coati Mundi took part in MADONNA film *Who's That Girl*; Coconuts had jumped ship, formed their own group Boomerang; leader's showmanship suggests flash in the pan with durability.

KIDD, Johnny (*b* Frederick Heath, Willesden, London, 23 Dec. '39; *d* 6-7 Oct. '66, Bury, Lancs.) Singer, songwriter; led seminal UK rock'n'roll band. Played guitar, banjo during SKIFFLE era, formed group Freddie and the Nutters for local gigs. Wore eyepatch over defective eye; changed style to rock'n'roll, name of group to Captain Kidd and the Pirates; by '59 Johnny Kidd and the Pirates. Lineup: Clem Cattini (drums), Alan Caddy (guitar), Brian Gregg (bass). Played on *Saturday Club* radio show, signed to HMV label; first single 'Please Don't Touch' written by Kidd with manager Guy Robinson, reached top 30 '59 (recorded without the Pirates). Next year 'You've Got What It Takes', cover of Marv JOHNSON hit, did well but 'Shakin' All Over' no. 1 smash, beaten (maybe) only by Cliff RICHARD's 'Move It' for title of the classic early Brit-rock single. Further hits incl. Kidd original 'Restless' (also '60), 'Linda Lu' ('61, cover of Ray Sharpe single); band left, Cattini, Caddy and Gregg retaining nautical gear to back Tommy STEELE's brother as the Cabinboys before joining The Tornados. Kidd replaced them from Cuddly Duddly's backup group (John Patto, Frank Farley, Johnny Spence; Patto shortly replaced by guitarist Mick Green); hits continued with minor success 'A Shot Of Rhythm And Blues', then abandoned mix of covers with original R&B to jump on Merseybeat train, probably a mistake despite top 5 hit 'I'll Never Get Over You', top 20 'Hungry For Love', all '63; toured with visitors Jerry Lee LEWIS and Gene VINCENT. Last hit '64 with 'Always And Ever'; Green left, replaced by John Weider; band continued to please crowds but records didn't sell. Band split again '66, Weider joining Eric Burdon; Kidd brought in Buddy Britten's Regents as new Pirates, incl. Nick

Simper (bass), later of DEEP PURPLE; then was killed in car crash. Posthumous cult status among UK rockers; HM bands Motorhead & Girlschool combined for hit revival of 'Please Don't Touch' '81. Compilations: *Best Of* on Nut/EMI, *Rarities* on See For Miles. Green's ability to play simultaneous lead/rhythm made him premier UK axe-man before Eric CLAPTON; he played with Billy KRAMER's Dakotas, Engelbert HUMPERDINCK, Cliff BENNETT; re-formed Pirates with Green and Farley during mid-'70s R&B revival sparked by DR FEELGOOD (with Green-infl. guitarist Wilko Johnson): *Out Of Their Skulls* '77 was recorded half live, half in the studio and showed Green had lost none of his touch; *Skull Rock* and *Happy Rock 'n' Roll* '78-9 were less impressive, but still marked a happy reunion, even if the backdrop of the lighted galleon was no longer there.

KIHN, Greg (*b* '52, Baltimore) USA singer-songwriter. Began as folksinger; moved to San Francisco at behest of fellow Baltimorean Matthew King Kaufman, manager of hard-rockers Earth Quake and founder of Berserkley label. First recordings on label sampler *Berserkley Chartbusters*: backed by Earth Quake, also on Jonathan Richman's 'Roadrunner', later a single hit. Formed band playing rhythm guitar, with Larry Lynch, drums; Steve Wright, bass; Earth Quake's Robbie Dunbar on lead guitar for *Greg Kihn* '76, replaced by Dave Carpender for *Greg Kihn Again* '77, which moved towards harder sounds with rocky covers of Bruce SPRINGSTEEN's 'For You' and Buddy HOLLY's 'Love's Made A Fool Of You'. *Next Of Kihn* '78 made top 200 LPs USA, as did *With The Naked Eye* '79 incl. another Springsteen cover 'Rendezvous'; three singles almost made Hot 100 '78-81, band remained cult favourite. After *Glass House Rock* '80 slipped in LP chart, ex-Earth Quake keyboardist Gary Phillips was recruited and fortunes changed: single 'The Breakup Song (They Don't Write 'Em)' made no. 15, from LP *Rockihnroll* '81, which made top 40 LPs; concert taped for infant MTV brought solid live act to wider audience (clips still used years later); Carpender replaced after *Kihntinued* '82 by Greg Douglass, former Steve MILLER band acolyte. Disco-styled 'Jeopardy' (from LP

Kihnspiracy '83) reached no. 2 USA, only 63 UK despite popularity in the rest of Europe (shared UK-only live LP with Rubinoos '78 when Berserkley bands toured, also *Powerlines* '80). Continued punning ways with *Kihntagious* '84 (slipped badly in USA LP charts), solo album *Citizen Kihn* '85 on EMI/America (no. 51).

KILGORE, Merle (*b* Merle Wyatt Kilgore, 9 Aug. '34, Chickasha, Okla.) Country singer, songwriter who has had better luck with his songs recorded by others. Worked as DJ in Shreveport while still in school; formed hillbilly band and appeared on Louisiana Hayride '51, local radio in Louisiana and Texas; signed to Imperial '54 and recorded rockabilly without much success. Wrote 'More And More', country no. 1 for Webb PIERCE '54. Recorded for 'D', Starday '50s-early '60s, had small hits 'Dear Mama', 'Love Has Made You Beautiful'. Wrote hits 'Johnny Reb' for Johnny HORTON '59, 'Wolverton Mountain' for Claude KING '62, 'Ring Of Fire' for Johnny CASH '63. Recorded for Ashley, Columbia, WB etc.; appeared in films *Five Card Stud* '68, *Nevada Smith* '66; toured for years with Hank WILLIAMS Jr Show, played himself in *Living Proof*. LPs incl. *Tall Texan* '63 on Mercury, *Ring Of Fire* '65 on Hilltop.

KINCAID, Bradley (*b* 13 July 1895, Granard County, Ky.) The Kentucky Mountain Boy with his Houn' Dog guitar was the most popular American folk singer of the '30s. Learned folk songs from his family; became regular on Chicago's WLS National Barn Dance while still in college; he published 13 songbooks (*My Favorite Ballads And Old-Time Songs*) which all sold 100,000 copies or more '28-36. Recorded throughout '30s for Bluebird, Decca, Capitol, Polk; appeared all over USA teaching old songs to audiences. Joined Grand Ole Opry '44-9; bought radio station in Springfield, Ohio '49; semi-retired '54 but came back '60s for several LPs of the old songs. LPs incl. five *Bradley Kincaid* albums on Bluebonnet '63-8, *Bradley Kincaid The Kentucky Mountain Boy* '73 on McMonigle, anthology *Mountain Ballads and Old-Time Songs* on Old Homestead; *Radio's 'Kentucky Mountain Boy' Bradley Kincaid* by Loyal Jones published '80 by Appalachian Center, Berea College.

KING Country and R&B record label complex incl. Queen, Federal, De Luxe; established '45 in Cincinnati, Ohio by Syd Nathan, who left department store business, built a music factory in disused icehouse that did everything from recording and pressing to printing sleeves for LPs. The *Boone County Jamboree* on local WLW radio became *Midwestern Hayride* '45; the town was a regional centre for country music, also a gateway to the steel mills of the north, with a black population and a local Cotton Club that booked big-name black bands. Nathan signed Lucky MILLINDER vocalist Bull Moose Jackson (*b* Benjamin Clarence Jackson, '19, Cleveland, Ohio), hired Millinder's arranger Henry Glover as producer/writer. Jackson had R&B hits (on Queen initially, to keep R&B and C&W separate) with 'I Love You, Yes I Do' (re-made on Seven Arts '61, top 10 again), 'All My Love Belongs To You', 'I Can't Go On Without You' '47-8, written by Glover with Nathan grabbing credit (as 'Sally Nix' or 'Lois Mann', his wife's maiden name); 'Little Girl, Don't Cry' '49, co-written by Millinder. Jackson was a crooner; the King R&B sound was different from the West Coast style (though Jackson also recorded 'Ten-Inch Record', 'I Want A Bow-Legged Woman', etc.). Country acts incl. DELMORE Bros (recorded 'Blues, Stay Away From Me' during 'hillbilly boogie' craze), Grandpa JONES, Bradley KINCAID, later Moon MULLICAN, Cowboy COPAS, Hawkshaw HAWKINS; no. 1 C&W hit '49 'Why Don't You Haul Off And Love Me' was co-written and sung by Wayne Raney: long before Sun Records combined black and country music, Nathan gave country songs to black artists and vice-versa; he owned the songs (published by Lois Music) and sold them twice: blacks did not buy country records, but bought (e.g.) Raney's hit covered by Jackson '49 for no. 2 R&B hit. Wynonie HARRIS, Lonnie JOHNSON, Ivory Joe HUNTER, LITTLE WILLIE JOHN were King R&B artists (Harris recorded C&W tune 'Bloodshot Eyes'); Glover brought Millinder and Tiny BRADSHAW to the label, jump bands did even better than solo singers: Earl BOSTIC had R&B no. 1 '50 with 'Flamingo'; milestone was 'Honky Tonk' by Bill DOGGETT, no. 1 R&B, 2 pop '56. Ralph BASS joined '51 with his Federal label, incl.

Billy Ward & his Dominoes (lead singer Clyde MCPHATTER): no. 1 hits 'Sixty-Minute Man', 'Have Mercy, Baby'. Nathan bought De Luxe label from New Jersey; the Charms ('Hearts Of Stone' no. 1 '54) became Otis Williams and the Charms for more hits. The Five Royales (*Roots Of Soul* on Charly), Hank BALLARD's Midnighters (*What You Get When The Gettin' Gets Good*) recorded for King; Joe TEX, the PLATTERS, Otis REDDING started there. Music changed; Nathan's judgement was not always good: he refused to record James BROWN's 'Do The Mashed Potatoes', it came out on Dade (Fla.) label as by Nat Kendrick (drummer) & The Swans, no. 8 R&B hit, but Nathan still didn't know who he was dealing with: Brown went on strike '64 when he was the hottest black artist in the country; his live act set audiences on fire but he did nothing for Nathan until he got his own way '65: from then on he chose his own material and published his own music. Glover went to Roulette '56, recorded Joey DEE's 'Peppermint Twist'; Gene Redd was R&B A&R at King, recorded early James Brown hits; Glover came back to King and went with it to Starday after Nathan died. Columbia issued King compilations *18 King Size Rhythm & Blues Hits* and *Anthology Of Rhythm & Blues Vol. 1* with notes by Seymour Stein; now out of print; many reissues and compilations are available on several labels.

KING, Albert (*b* Albert Nelson, 25 Apr. '23, Indianola, Ms.) Blues singer, influential guitarist. One of 13 children; sang in church, moved to Arkansas c.'31, sang in gospel groups, worked day jobs and taught himself guitar on home-made instrument; gigged locally. To Gary, Ind. and Chicago early '50s, recorded for Parrot '53, Bobbin '59 in St Louis, then King: no. 14 R&B hit '61 with 'Don't Throw Your Love On Me So Strong'. First LP *The Big Blues* '62 on King; early records compiled on *Travelin' To California* (King/Polydor). Top 40 R&B hits '66-71 incl. 'Think Twice Before You Speak' on Sahara, the rest on Stax; '66-8 hits incl. 'Born Under A Bad Sign', 'Cold Feet' etc. with BOOKER T AND THE MGs and the Memphis Horns, compiled on *Laundromat Blues* on Edsel UK '84. LP *King Of The Blues Guitar* on Atlantic '68; others on Stax,

Milestone, Fantasy, many now available from Fantasy group: *Born Under A Bad Sign* '67, *Jammed Together* '69 with Steve Cropper and Pop STAPLES, *The Lost Session* from '71, *I'll Play The Blues For You* '72, *Live Wire/Blues Power* live at the Fillmore; *Albert King Does The King's Thing* (tribute to Elvis, probably the same LP aka *Blues For Elvis*), *The Pinch, Lovejoy* (after tiny Illinois township where King lived), *Years Gone By, Albert King/Little Milton Chronicle, I Wanna Get Funky, San Francisco '83* and *I'm In A Phone Booth, Baby* on Fantasy. Also *Truckload of Lovin'* '75, 2-disc *Albert Live* '76, on Utopia, *Chronicle* and *New Orleans Heat* '79 on Tomato. Fusion of Delta blues, touch of psychedelia made style similar to that of B. B. KING but with smokier voice like no other; also infl. by Lonnie JOHNSON, T-Bone WALKER, thence an influence himself to a generation.

KING, B. B. (*b* Riley B. King, 16 Sep. '25, near Indianola, Ms.) Guitarist, blues singer. From poor plantation family; his parents separated when he was 4, mother died when he was 9. Sang in church, began to learn guitar at 15, formed gospel group; turned to the blues after US Army service; played local gigs; moved to Memphis '47, shared flat with cousin Bukka WHITE; worked on WDIA singing commercials, then own DJ show as Riley King, the Blues Boy from Beale Street (soon shortened to B.B.). Worked with Bobby Blue BLAND, Johnny ACE, etc., also solo; at a gig in Twist, Arkansas '49 men fighting over a girl named Lucille knocked over a kerosene heater, setting the room on fire; King fled with everyone else, but ran back inside to get his guitar: he called his guitar Lucille, and a monologue/song based on the incident became staple of stage act. Record deal with Modern Music (RPM, Kent, Crow, Modern Oldies labels) led to 31 hits in R&B chart '51-68, 15 in top 10: first two, '3 O'Clock In The Morning' and 'You Know I Love You' at no. 1. His style was not pure enough for blues purists but too pure to cross over to the pop charts; he worked the chitlin circuit (from '55 with his own 13-piece band: he survived 18 car crashes, did 342 one-night stands in '56 alone), the personal integrity evident in his music meaning that he would rather lose money than miss a gig. Switched

to a new booking agent late '50s, supported popular acts like Lloyd PRICE and made more money, but was often booed by black as well as white kids. Influenced by T-Bone WALKER and Django REINHARDT, his combination of Delta blues, R&B beat, guitar style (as a second voice, with 'bent' notes emphasising a note by sliding to it) and his warm, honest vocal styling made him the greatest blues artist of his generation; he invented and was the greatest practitioner of the style that infl. Eric CLAPTON in UK, Mike BLOOMFIELD in USA, many others; in '64 he had the first of six top 40 pop hits ('Rock Me Baby'). But in '66 his bus was stolen, his wife divorced him, tax authorities hassled him; his career was stymied: he had switched to ABC (and Bluesway, now MCA); they released *Live At The Regal* '65, one of his best albums, but then put him in front of an orchestra (*Confessin' The Blues* '66). He had never lost the black audience that had supported him for many years; the R&B hits continued, but now the long overdue breakthrough occurred: at San Francisco's Fillmore West '66 he received a standing ovation from a white audience that had discovered the blues behind rock'n'roll, as years earlier some of their parents discovered the black jazz behind the swing bands. In '68 he toured Europe, played at NYC's Village Voice; in '69 appeared at the Newport Jazz Festival and on the *Tonight* show (comedian Flip Wilson depping for Johnny Carson), and toured with the ROLLING STONES; toured Europe and Australia '70, appeared on the *Ed Sullivan Show* '71, went to Africa '72. Meanwhile his records were released on ABC's new Bluesway subsidiary: *Blues Is King* '67 (live in a Chicago club) was said to capture his guitar sound best of all his LPs; *Blues On Top Of Blues, Lucille* (first to make pop LP chart), *His Best – The Electric B. B. King* (incl. no. 10 pop hit 'Paying The Cost To Be The Boss'), all '68 were followed by *Live And Well* (top 60 pop LP), *Completely Well* (no. 38, both '69): latter incl. 'So Excited', new treatment of Walter BROWN's 'Confessin' The Blues', no. 15 pop hit single 'The Thrill Is Gone': band was Hugh McCracken, second guitar; Paul Harris, keyboards; Gerald 'Fingers' Jemmott, bass; Herbie Lovelle, drums. On *Indianola Mississippi Seeds* '70 (no. 26 LP), 1.5 minutes of 'Nobody Loves Me But My

Mother (And She Might Be Jivin' Too)' sets the tone, with just B.B.'s voice and piano, for tracks from *Completely Well* sessions, others with sympathetic young team: Russ Kunkel, drums; Bryan Garofalo, bass; Carole KING, piano on four tracks, Leon RUSSELL on piano and Joe WALSH, rhythm guitar on three incl. top 40 hit 'Ask Me No Questions', Russell's 'Hummingbird' (last two LPs prod. Bill SZYMCZYK, strings and horns added discreetly). *Live In Cook County Jail* '71 was milestone, with septet incl. horns, his biggest hit LP at no. 25. *Live At The Regal* was reissued; *B. B. King In London* '71, *L.A. Midnight* '72, *Guess Who* '72 (reissued in UK on Music For Pleasure as *King Of The Blues*) followed by *To Know You Is To Love You* '73 incl. top 40 title track. More: 2-disc *Together For The First Time . . . Live* '74, *Together Again . . . Live* '76, both with Bobby Bland; *Lucille Talks Back* '75, *King Size* '77, *Midnight Believer* '78, 2-disc *Now Appearing At Ole Miss* '80, *There Must Be A Better World Somewhere* '81 (won a Grammy), *Love Me Tender* '82, *Blues'n'Jazz* '83, *Why I Sing The Blues* and *Six Silver Strings* '85. He was the first bluesman to tour the USSR, late '70s. A concert at London's Hammersmith Odeon Oct. '78 was typical of his long-overdue success: the UK audience forgot its usual reserve, flooded down to the stage after a superb evening's music to pay homage. *B. B. King: The Authorised Biography* '80 by Charles Sawyer tells the whole story.

KING, Ben E. (*b* Benjamin Earl Nelson, 23 Sep. '38, Henderson, N.C.) Soul singer. Grew up singing in his father's diner; went pro with vocal group the Crowns '56 and was still there when DRIFTERS manager George Treadwell sacked his own group, replaced them with talented youngsters he'd spotted further down the bill. He sang lead on Drifters' 'There Goes My Baby' (also co-wrote it), 'Save The Last Dance For Me' etc.; went solo at suggestion of Atlantic: SPECTOR-LEIBER song 'Spanish Harlem' was no. 10 pop chart, self-penned 'Stand By Me' no. 4 '61, later covered with nearly equal success by Aretha FRANKLIN and John LENNON respectively. 'Amor' no. 18 '61, 'Don't Play That Song' no. 11 '62 (also later covered by Franklin), 'I (Who Have Nothing)' no. 29 '63 (covered by everybody

from Tom JONES to transvestite disco king Sylvester). Hits continued in soul chart: 'Tell Daddy', 'Seven Letters', 'It's All Over', 'What Is Soul?' (provided title of legendary black music series on Atlantic '60s). Many of these were prod. by Bert BERNS. Left Atlantic end of decade but returned after unsuccessful spells with Maxwell/Crewe and Mandala; 'Supernatural Thing Part 1' blazed into pop chart at no. 5 '75, following similarly titled LP that was subtitled *The Ben E. King Story* (song later bizarrely covered by SIOUXSIE & THE BANSHEES). Collaborated with AVERAGE WHITE BAND for *Benny And Us* '77, gigged with them; rejoined Drifters '82 when Johnny Moore quit. He and Clyde MCPHATTER were the most distinctive and successful of Drifters who went solo; the fact that he wrote or co-wrote many songs is often overlooked.

KING, Carole (*b* Carole Klein, 9 Feb. '42, Brooklyn) USA singer/songwriter, producer. Subject of Neil SEDAKA hit 'Oh Carole' '59; wrote flop sequel 'Oh Neil'. Teamed with husband Gerry GOFFIN, introduced by Sedaka to Brill Building industry NYC, cranked out dozens of classic pop songs of era: 'Will You Love Me Tomorrow' no. 1 by SHIRELLES '60, 'Take Good Care Of My Baby' by Bobby VEE '61; formed own label Dimension, had no. 1 dance hit 'Do The Loco-Motion' by their babysitter LITTLE EVA (babysat with Louise Goffin, whose LP *This Is The Place* was released '88). King had own hit with 'It Might As Well Rain Until September' '62; other songs on demos so good that artists usually just copied them: 'Chains' by the Cookies, 'Up On The Roof' and 'When My Little Girl Is Smiling' by the DRIFTERS, 'One Fine Day' by the CHIFFONS, 'I'm Into Something Good' by HERMAN'S HERMITS and by Earl-Jean (McCree, lead singer of Cookies; group also backed Little Eva), many others. Style matured, became more streetwise but still wistful, e.g. 'Some Of Your Lovin' ', 'Goin' Back', among Dusty SPRINGFIELD's best. Shortlived Tomorrow label formed late '65 with releases by King and by a band called Myddle Class, incl. second husband Charlie Larkey (continued writing with Goffin); King/Larkey formed band The City, made one LP (she disliked touring). She carried audience that had grown up with her on

LPs on Ode label: *Now That Everything's Been Said* '69, *Carole King: Writer* '70, then *Tapestry* '71: LP of its time with no. 1 hit 'It's Too Late' sold 14 million, helping to make singer/songwriter genre one of the most important of '70s (though too much emphasis on it became a problem: not every singer could write such good songs). Albums exploring changes of style, content incl. *Music* '71, *Rhymes And Reasons* '72, *Fantasy* '73, *Wrap Around Joy* '74, *Really Rosie* '75, *Thoroughbred* '76; switched to Capitol for *Simple Things* '77, *Touch The Sky* '79 and *Pearls* '80 (re-makes of classic Goffin/King songs). 10 more top 40 singles '71-80 incl. 'Jazzman' (no. 2 '74); other LPs incl. *Welcome Home* '78 on Avatar. Death of third husband Rick Evers '78 caused pause in output; then *One To One* '82 on Atlantic: for second Atlantic LP *Speeding Time* '83 returned to prod. Lou ADLER, synthesiser played by son-in-law Robbie Kondon.

KING, Claude (*b* 5 Feb. '33, Shreveport, La.) Country singer with rich voice, also had pop success. Began in teens at local functions; worked on construction; radio debut on Louisiana Hayride '58 as protégé of Johnny HORTON; managed by Horton's manager Tillman Franks, signed to Columbia '61, had country/pop hits with 'Big River, Big Man', 'The Comancheros', then no. 1 country/top 10 pop 'Wolverton Mountain' '62 (written by Merle KILGORE). Last pop Hot 100 entry was 'The Burning Of Atlanta' '62; further country hits with 'Sam Hill' '64, 'Tiger Woman' '65; began to fade from chart, made comeback with Horton tribute album and single 'All For The Love Of A Girl' '69. 27 entries in country chart '61-71; less luck on Cinnamon '74, True '77-81. LPs incl. *Meet Claude King* '62, *Tiger Woman* '65, *I Remember Johnny* '69, *Chip'n'Dale's Place* '71, all on Columbia; *Greatest Hits* '77 on True, *Best Of* '80 on Gusto.

KING CURTIS (*b* Curtis Ousley, 7 Feb. '34, Fort Worth, Texas; *d* 13 Aug. '71, NYC) Tenor saxophone; one of the best ever to play on rock'n'roll hits whose work crossed over to soul and jazz. Began working in home town late '40s, with Lionel HAMPTON '52, returned to NYC '53 (where he had played with Hampton), worked with Buck

CLAYTON, etc.; began sessioning: worked with Nat COLE, Joe TURNER, Chuck WILLIS ('What Am I Living For'), COASTERS: brilliantly idiomatic solos on hits like 'Yakety Yak' '58 made him famous. Cut 'Reminiscing' that year with Buddy HOLLY, worked with LaVern BAKER, Bobby DARIN, Brook BENTON, Neil SEDAKA, the DRIFTERS. In '62 began making records under his own name (King Curtis & The Noble Knights, & the Kingpins) which appealed to wide market: 15 top 100 entries '62-71 incl. versions of pop, R&B hits 'Spanish Harlem', 'Ode To Billy Joe', 'I Heard It Through The Grapevine', 'Sittin' On The Dock Of The Bay'; instrumentals did not do well on charts in this era: classic 'Memphis Soul Stew' '67 was one of only two of his hits to make top 40. In early '60s sessioned with Sam COOKE, ISLEY BROS, Solomon BURKE, the SHIRELLES, Nina SIMONE etc. Toured USA with Cooke, with BEATLES; mid-'60s worked with Aretha FRANKLIN, Herbie MANN, Wilson PICKETT; then Duane ALLMAN, Eric CLAPTON, John LENNON; then was murdered outside his apartment. LPs on Prestige incl. *Soul Meeting, King Soul* with Nat ADDERLEY, *Best – One More Time*, 2-disc *Soul Groove*; on Atlantic: *Blues Montreux* '70 with Champion Jack Dupree (*b* 4 July '10, New Orleans); in UK *20 Golden Pieces* on Bulldog is compilation of early singles incl. 'Soul Twist' (no. 13 USA '62); *King Curtis* on Red Lightnin' label is collection of '62 stuff from Fantasy (Prestige); Red Lightnin' (in Norfolk, England) also planned to compile unissued tracks from Atlantic/Atco.

KING, Earl (*b* Solomon Johnson, 7 Feb. '34, New Orleans, La.) Guitarist, blues singer in infl. N.O. R&B scene; also plays piano. Made R&B chart with 'Don't Take It So Hard' '55 on King, 'Always A First Time' '62 on Imperial; recorded with PROFESSOR LONGHAIR '63-4; venerable local hits compiled on *Let The Good Times Roll* on Ace, *Street Parade* on Charly, *New Orleans Rock-'n'Roll* on Sonet, *Trick Bag* on French EMI. *Glazed* '86 on Black Top (Rounder)/Demon backed by ROOMFUL OF BLUES, licks traded with Roomful's guitarist Ronnie Earl: will reach wider audience for 'engaging vocalist with an off-hand manner' playing 'incisive, less-is-more guitar . . . coming up with wild, unpredictable lyrics' (Jim Roberts in *Downbeat*). LP's title and sleeve photo refer to Earl's office/hangout, a Tastee Doughnuts shop. His songs have been covered by others incl. Jimi HENDRIX, whose 'Let The Good Times Roll' was a version of King's 'Come On'.

KING, Freddie (*b* 3 Sep. '34, Gilmer, Texas; *d* 28 Dec. '76, Dallas) Influential blues guitarist, singer. Grew up in Texas; family moved to Chicago when he was 16; sneaked into clubs, jammed with Muddy WATERS, played with Willie DIXON, LaVern BAKER, MEMPHIS SLIM; made own first record '56; signed with Federal (King) '60: had top 10 R&B hits 'Hide Away' (for Chicago lounge); prod. 'Lonesome Whistle Blues', 'San-HoZay', 'I'm Tore Down', lesser hits 'See See Baby', 'Christmas Tears', all '61. Released more than 70 sides, about 30 instrumentals, but no more hits; by '66 he was back in Texas with no record deal. Meanwhile songs were covered in UK by Eric CLAPTON, Mick Taylor and Pete Green with John MAYALL, by Stan Webb with CHICKEN SHACK; Clapton also later covered 'Have You Ever Loved A Woman' on *Layla*. Recognised as extremely influential, King toured UK with blues shows, signed with Atlantic's Cotillion label '68, made LPs prod. by KING CURTIS (*see above*) incl. *My Feeling For The Blues* '70; then with Leon RUSSELL's Shelter label: *Getting Ready ...* '71, *Texas Cannonball* '72, *Woman Across The River* '73; on RSO: *Burglar* '74 with Clapton, Gonzales, prod. in UK by Mike Vernon; also *Larger Than Life* '75. Died of ulcers, heart trouble. Other LPs: *17 Hits* and *Sings* on King; in UK *Rockin' The Blues Live*, *Gives You A Bonanza Of Instrumentals* on Crosscut. *Takin' Care Of Business* on Charly UK is Federal compilation, spelling name 'Freddy'.

KING, Jonathan (*b* 6 Dec. '44, London) Maverick UK pop entrepreneur. First fame while at Cambridge U. with coy protest song 'Everyone's Gone To The Moon' (no. 4 '65); then wrote, produced 'Good News Week' (no. 5) as Hedgehoppers Anonymous; later hosted TV show, was assistant to Sir Edward Lewis at Decca Records, where he was embroiled in controversy over sleeve of ROLLING STONES *Beggars Banquet* LP and discovered GENESIS, producing lamentable debut *From Genesis To Revelation* '69; enjoyed own top 30 hit 'Let It All Hang Out' '70. Predicted teenypop phenomenon of early '70s, producing early BAY CITY ROLLERS hits, contributed his own increasingly awful stuff under a variety of pseudonyms: 'Johnny Reggae' as the Piglets, 'Loop Di Love' as Shag, 'Jump Up And Down And Wave Your Knickers In The Air' as St Cecilia, 'Una Paloma Blanca' under his own name, etc. Even he could not suppress his own skill with good material: his own cover of the Stones' 'Satisfaction', the FOUR TOPS' 'It's The Same Old Song' (as Weathermen), Tavares' 'It Only Takes A Minute' (as One Hundred Ton And A Feather) were well done. Formed own label UK, gave early breaks to 10CC, KURSAAL FLYERS; also Australian Kevin Johnson's only UK hit 'Rock'n'Roll (I Gave You The Best Years Of My Life)' '75. He predictably claimed to have foreseen punk rock, but by '80 his impetus was gone; he was DJ in London and NYC; in '80s hosted engaging UK TV show *Entertainment USA*, combining travelogue and music (managed to report on KANSAS CITY without touching on that town's enormous contribution to popular music, perhaps because it began before he was born). He persistently and loudly criticised Live Aid '85, but his carping vanity could be taken for granted. *Jonathan King's Entertainment USA* '86 was chart LP; *King Size Hits: The Hits Of Jonathan King* '82 compiled his less objectionable work. Prod. TV show *No Limits* '86.

KING, Morgana (*b* 4 June '30, Pleasantville, NY) Singer, actress. Jazz-based pop singer. Worked NYC clubs '56-60; albums for EmArcy, United Artists, chart LP on Mainstream *A Taste Of Honey* '64, with own technically interesting dramatic style owing less to jazz; other albums on Reprise, Trip; *New Beginnings* '73 on Paramount also charted; made films *The Godfather* '71, *Godfather II* '74; now on Muse with combo: *Stretchin' Out* '77, *Everything Must Change* '78, *Higher Ground* '79, *Looking Through The Eyes Of Love* '81, *Portraits* '83.

KING, Pee Wee (*b* Frank King, 14 Feb. '14, Abrams, Wis.) Bandleader. Of Polish origin; his father led a polka band; he grew up in

Milwaukee, played fiddle and accordion, led own band while still in teens. He was heard on local radio in Racine, Green Bay, Milwaukee; moved to Chicago and the WLS Barn Dance '34-6, joining Gene AUTRY show. When Autry went to Hollywood '36 King took over his band, renamed it The Golden West Cowboys and made it one of the most popular bands in country music in the WESTERN SWING style, appearing regularly on the Grand Ole Opry and on a daily radio show in Knoxville. He brought the western style to the Opry, both in dress and music, was one of the first to use electric instruments, and featured such vocalists as Ernest TUBB, Eddy ARNOLD, Cowboy COPAS and Redd Stewart (b 27 May '21, Ashland City, Tenn.; co-wrote with King such enormous country hits as 'Slow Poke', 'Tennessee Waltz', 'Bonaparte's Retreat'). The band recorded for Bullet '45, King '45-6, RCA '46-61, Briar '62-4, Starday '64-6. The Billboard C&W chart began '49; band's hits were 'Tennessee Tears' '49, 'Slow Poke' '50 (no. 1 country and pop; sold a million), 'Silver And Gold' '52, 'Bimbo' '54. King was elected to the Country Music Hall of Fame '74. LPs incl. *Anytime Hits* '50, *Swing West* '55, *Country Barn Dance* '59 all on RCA; *Together Again* '64 on Starday, *Tennessee Waltz* '67 on Nashville, *Best Of* '75 on Starday, *Ballroom King* '83 on Detour.

KING SISTERS, The Vocal group, usually as the Four King Sisters: Alyce, Donna, Louise and Yvonne Driggs, from Salt Lake City; father William King Driggs was a vocal teacher. At first they were a sextet, with another sister and a friend; the quartet joined Horace HEIDT '36-8 with no experience, then with Alvino REY (Louise's husband) '39-43. Biggest of a dozen own hits on Bluebird '41-5 were 'The Hut-Hut Song (A Swedish Serenade)' and 'It's Love-Love-Love' (from film *Stars Over Broadway*). Had TV show *The King Family* '60s. Alyce could sing unusually low for a woman, which gave them a fuller sound, made them one of the most interesting of '30s-40s girl groups.

KING, Wayne (b 16 Feb. '01, Savannah, Ill.; d 16 July '85) Midwestern bandleader known as 'The Waltz King'. Worked as mechanic and for an insurance company in Chicago, also in a theatre pit band (alto sax), with bandleader Del Lampe at Trianon Ballroom: Lampe opened the Aragon '27, hired King to lead band there. He made the Aragon his home base, playing four-square dance music; wrote his own theme 'The Waltz You Saved For Me'. Hired '31-8 by fledgling cosmetic company for weekly radio spot: old people used more cosmetics than the young in those days, King's music became more and more embalmed (though musicianship always high), the *Lady Esther Serenade* became a top-rated show, the company prospered and King earned $15,000 a week on the radio alone. His own smooth sax was featured, along with poetry readings by Phil Stewart, then Franklyn McCormack. Best-known vocalist in early years was Ernie Burchill. King had other radio shows, with vocalist Buddy CLARK '40-1; military service in Chicago area WWII; new band mid-'45; more radio, then TV '49-52; continued with special engagements, played the Aragon on its last night in '64. He invested wisely and became very rich. About 35 hit records '30-41 incl. 'Goofus' (own composition), 'Wabash Moon', 'Dream A Little Dream Of Me', 'Good Night, Sweetheart', 'I Don't Know Why (I Just Do)', all '31, all on Brunswick; 'Josephine' '37, 'Maria Elena' '41 on Victor. Some numbers had vocal trio. He sang himself in a thin mournful voice on 'Adorable' '33. Later albums on Decca/MCA.

KINGSMEN, The Rock'n'roll band formed in Portland, Oregon '60, whose one big hit became a classic. Original lineup incl. Jack Ely, lead singer; Bob Norby, bass; Lynn Easton, drums; probably Mike Mitchell, lead guitar, Don Gallucci, organ; Norman Sundholm, guitar and bass: details are unsure because confusion ensued after recording of 'Louie, Louie' in '63. Song was written '55 by Richard Berry; Louie was a bartender, a customer saying that he intended going to Jamaica to find his true love. It was covered by Rockin' Robin Roberts and the Wailers for a regional hit in the Northwest c.'60; the Kingsmen recorded it in two hours for $50 dollars as a demo for a job audition (they didn't get the job): Ely taught the song to the rest of the band, inadvertently changing the structure and making it more intense; the studio was so primitive that he had to scream the lyrics at a microphone over his head; the result was a basic 3-chord rock'n'roll record: a beat with an emotional vocal ejaculation. The words were thought to be obscene, but the Federal Communications Commission said 'We found the record to be unintelligible at any speed we played it.' Another local band, Paul REVERE and the Raiders, recorded it a few days later; the preferred local version remained the Wailers', but the Kingsmen's began to climb the national charts. At a time when Elvis PRESLEY had sold out and the BEATLES hadn't happened yet, rock' n'roll was in danger of being prettified; mysterious and sexy, powerful yet laid back, 'Louie, Louie' was a good party record: it reached no. 2 on Wand (no. 26 UK '64 on Pye). Easton and his mother had registered the name of the group, and he wanted to front it; Ely and Norby quit, Dick Peterson joined on drums and Easton became the lead singer, with the pressing difficulty that he couldn't sing 'Louie, Louie'. Attendance at gigs dropped off, Easton lip-synced the record wherever he could, Ely had formed his own Kingsmen; all went to court: Ely was prevented from using the name, Easton from lip-syncing; the band shared vocal chores and Peterson took over 'Louie'. Their only other top 40 hits were 'Money', fluke 'Jolly Green Giant' (made in five minutes) '64-5. They disbanded '69. John Belushi insisted on using 'Louie, Louie' in soundtrack of *Animal House* '78, allegedly because he lost his virginity while it was playing; Peterson re-formed with Mitchell, Barry Curtis (bassist/guitarist; played on 'Green Giant'), permission to use the name; they did a video of the song for MTV at the original Animal House location in Eugene, Ore. ('We had a big toga party and supplied all the beer the kids could drink,' said Peterson), gigged weekends at oldies shows; in '84 the state of Washington talked about making 'Louie' the state song; California Cooler used it in a national advertising campaign; it refuses to lie down: there is an album of 10 different versions. In '86 the band incl. Curtis, Peterson, Mitchell, Marc Willett and Kim Nicklaus. (Quotations from Daniel Brogan in the *Chicago Tribune*.)

KINGSTON TRIO, The Commercial folk trio formed '57; with short hair, matching shirts they avoided left-wing taint usually applied to folk groups: Bob Shane (*b* 1 Feb. '34, Hilo, Hawaii), Nick Reynolds (*b* 27 July '33, San Diego, Cal.), Dave Guard (*b* 19 Nov. '34, San Francisco) all played guitars, banjos and sang. Their no. 1 hit with 'Tom Dooley' '58 was something of a coup, the nearest thing to American folk music in the top 10 since the WEAVERS in '50-1 (from 'Tom Dula', 1866, about an innocent man hanged for murder; collected and performed by Frank Proffitt: *b* '13, Laurel Bloomery, Tenn.; *d* 24 Nov. '65; LPs on Folkways, Folk-Legacy, Topic; the song was also recorded '52 for Elektra by Frank Warner). They had 17 Hot 100 entries '58-63; 'M.T.A.' '59 was about a man who must 'ride forever 'neath the streets of Boston' because he doesn't have a ticket to get off the subway; but the only other top 10 was 'Reverend Mr Black' '63; both big hits also did well in the R&B chart. Guard wrote 'Scotch And Soda' '62, reached only no. 82 as a single, but became a cabaret standard. Guard left to go solo '61 (his Whiskey Hill Singers released an LP '62), replaced by John STEWART. The trio had 23 chart LPs, of which four stayed in the charts two years, indicating a hunger for folk music that was not being met by the music industry until PETER, PAUL and MARY, Joan BAEZ, Bob DYLAN, others soon came along. 20 LPs were on Capitol of which 14 were in the top 10; switched to Decca '65; last chart entry '69 was a 2-disc set on Tetragrammaton, made live '66 in Las Vegas. They split '67 as Reynolds quit, Stewart returned to a solo career; he has many fans worldwide. A New Kingston Trio '73 incl. Shane, Roger Gambill, George Grove; all six were together on a PBS TV special '82.

KINKS, The UK pop group, the most durable and idiosyncratic of the era (with the ROLLING STONES its longest survivor), due to the songwriting of Ray Davies (*b* 21 June '44). Lineup incl. brother Dave Davies (*b* 3 Feb. '47), both on vocals and guitar, both from Muswell Hill, North London; Mike Avory on drums (*b* 15 Feb. '44, Hampton, Middlesex), bassist Peter Quaife (*b* 31 Dec. '43, Tavistock, Devon). Began after Ray's stint at art college with Ray and Dave as

The Ravens. Signed to Pye (Reprise in USA, later Arista in both countries); third single 'You Really Got Me' was no. 1 UK/7 USA, guitar sound pioneering heavy metal and garage band sound, first of 23 chart hits in UK, 22 Hot 100 entries in USA '63-83. 'All Day & All Of The Night' was more of the same, another big hit, but 'Tired Of Waiting' '65 was first to characterise Davies' caustic, world-weary Englishness. Subsequent hits 'Dedicated Follower Of Fashion', 'A Well Respected Man', 'Sunny Afternoon', 'Dead End Street' '65-7 were unique contributions to popular culture, utterly English while virtually every other group was aping USA counterparts (except the BEATLES, whose music also owed as much to music hall as to rock'n'roll). Troublesome USA tour '65 ensured that the Kinks did not tour there again for four years, adding to cult reputation. *The Kinks* '64 and *Kinda Kinks* '65 were above-average pop LPs, but *Well Respected Kinks* and *Face To Face* '66 were transitional, with Davies' writing growing in confidence. 'Waterloo Sunset' '66 was a remarkably mature vignette, often regarded as apogee of '60s singles. *Something Else By The Kinks* '67 was an incongruous album for the time: while the Beatles (*Sgt Pepper*)and the Stones (*Their Satanic Majesties Request*) wallowed in psychedelia, *Something Else* represented the kitchen-sink school of rock: jaunty 'Harry Rag', caustic 'David Watts' (later a hit for the JAM), satirical 'Death Of A Clown', wry 'Two Sisters'. *Live At Kelvin Hall* '67 was endearingly shambolic, capturing band's peak as a pop group. Superb singles continued '67-8 with 'Autumn Almanac', 'Wonderboy', 'Days'; *Village Green Preservation Society* '68 is arguably their best-ever set, a lament for a disappearing England captured on the title track, 'Last Of The Steam-Powered Trains' and 'Do You Remember Walter?', making it one of the few concept albums of the '60s that worked. Quaife left '68, replaced by John Dalton (*b* 21 May '43), replaced in turn '76 by Jim Rodford (ex-ARGENT). *Arthur, Or The Decline And Fall Of The British Empire* '69 continued the concept theme, dealing with English 'little men', written for a Julian Mitchell TV play which was never written; incl. title track, 'She Bought A Hat Like Princess Marina', 'Some Mother's

Son', 'Victoria'. *The Kinks* '70 was an authoritative 2-disc compilation of Davies' songs: touching yet forthright, uncompromising, parochial and poetic, sharp but never harsh. That changed with *Lola vs Powerman & The Moneygoround Pt 1* '70, a bitter denunciation of the music industry yielding 'Lola', which became the band's anthem. Davies scored films *The Virgin Soldiers* '69 (with David BOWIE in a minor role), lamentable *Percy* '71; appeared in TV play *The Loneliness Of The Long Distance Piano Player* '70. *Muswell Hillbillies* '71 was return to superb form; *Everybody's In Showbiz . . . Everybody's A Star* '72 was cumbersome half live set, but standout track 'Celluloid Heroes', a tribute to the Golden Age of Hollywood, is contender for Davies' best song ever. He was fascinated by the possibility of adapting an album for the stage: *Village Green*, *Arthur* were early efforts; *Preservation* '73, *Preservation Act II* '74, *Soap Opera* '75 and *Schoolboys In Disgrace* '76 were largely unsuccessful concept sets. Davies brothers opened their own studio mid-'70s, formed own Konk label with acts such as Claire Hamill (album *Stage Door Johnnies*), Café Society (with Tom ROBINSON). The Kinks were one of the few '60s acts not always vilified by punk rockers; while '70s achievements were mostly disposable, the earlier work still venerated: Davies' infl. was heard in Ian DURY, Paul Weller's JAM, Elvis COSTELLO; the PRETENDERS covered the obscure Davies song 'Stop Your Sobbing' on their first single. At the end of the '70s the Kinks came back: *Low Budget* '79 stopped the decline; *One For The Road* was dreary 2-disc live set for USA market; *Give The People What They Want* '81 was well-titled but incl. good Davies in 'Art Lover' and 'Predictable'; *State Of Confusion* '83 saw them back in form, with 'Come Dancing', 'Don't Forget To Dance', scathing 'Young Conservatives'. It seemed too good to be true that after 20 years Davies hadn't lost his touch and *Word Of Mouth* '84 indicated that perhaps he had. Dave Davies had solo hits '60s with 'Death Of A Clown', 'Susannah's Still Alive' but waited until *AFL1-3603* '80 and *Glamour* '81 for solo LPs, moderately successful. Ray scored TV film *Return To Waterloo* '84, and appeared in *Absolute Beginners* '86, which featured his 'A Quiet Life' in its soundtrack. Later compilations have incl. *Celluloid Heroes* '76, *A Compleat Collection* '84; Kinks songs were covered by Peggy LEE, HERMAN'S HERMITS, Bowie, VAN HALEN, others as well as those mentioned above. Jon Savage's *The Kinks: The Official Biography* '84 is a good history.

KIRBY, John (*b* 31 Dec. '08, Baltimore, Md.; *d* 14 June '52, Hollywood) Bass, leader. Played trombone, then tuba; with Fletcher HENDERSON '30-3, bass with Chick WEBB '33-5, Henderson again, Lucky MILLINDER, then formed own sextet '37, at first incl. Pete Brown on reeds, trumpeter Frankie Newton, but the most famous lineup had Charlie SHAVERS, Buster Bailey and Russell Procope on reeds, Billy Kyle on piano and O'Neill Spencer on drums (*b* 25 Nov. '09, Springfield, Ohio; *d* 24 July '44, NYC; played with Millinder '31-6); Benny CARTER and Zutty Singleton on some records. Kirby was one of the most important combo leaders of the period: the bright, swinging finesse of the group (with many arrangements as well as muted trumpet by Shavers, vocals by Maxine SULLIVAN, Kirby's then wife) was so popular that it crossed over to gigs at white hotels and a network radio show '40, *Flow Gently Sweet Rhythm*. Sullivan left to go solo, Shavers to Tommy DORSEY, Kyle to the US Army; popularity slowly declined: the magic moment was over. Reunion at Carnegie Hall with Sid CATLETT replacing Spencer flopped; Kirby died in obscurity of diabetes. *The Complete Charlie Shavers With Maxine Sullivan* '55 on Bethlehem was effectively a reunion. Hits incl. 'Pastel Blue' (with Spencer vocal), 'Undecided' (written by Shavers); also swing arrangements of classics, folk songs. 2-disc *John Kirby: The Biggest Little Band 1937-41* from Smithsonian Collection/Columbia Special Products is good compilation incl. titles above, but no Sullivan vocals; others on Circle, Classic Jazz.

KIRK, Andy (*b* Andrew Dewey Kirk, 28 May 1898, Newport, Ky.) Reeds, tuba, leader. Raised in Denver, Col.; among teachers was Paul WHITEMAN's father. Worked 10 years as a postman, toured and recorded with 11-piece local band led by violinist George Morrison; joined Terrence Holder band in Dallas (later known as the Dark Clouds of Joy); took over '29; fronted by Blanche Calloway in Philadelphia briefly '31, then by vocalist Pha Terrell (*b* 25 May '10, Kansas City; *d* 14 Oct. '45, L.A.) '33-41. Slowly became famous as Andy Kirk and his 12 Clouds of Joy, mostly in Midwest out of Kansas City; then international stardom '36 with easy, flowing swing and Terrell's ballads. Disbanded '48. Kirk played bass sax at first, later mainly conducted; the band's most important assets were pianist/arr. Mary Lou WILLIAMS, later Kirk's wife, as well as Terrell, Dick Wilson on tenor (*b* 11 Nov. '11, Mount Vernon, Ill.; *d* of TB 24 Nov. '41, NYC), Henry Wells (*b* '06, Dallas; later also vocalist) and Ted 'Muttonleg' Donnelly (*b* 13 Nov. '12, Oklahoma City; *d* 8 May '58, NYC) on trombones; in later years Fats NAVARRO, Don BYAS, Howard McGHEE. He formed a band on the West Coast, managed a hotel in NYC, occasionally formed band for special gigs from '55, toured Europe '60s; worked for musicians' union NYC. Big hits incl. 'Christopher Columbus' (instrumental), 'Until The Real Thing Comes Along' (theme, with 'Cloudy'), 'Dedicated To You', 'Skies Are Blue', 'What Will I Tell My Heart?', 'I Won't Tell A Soul (I Love You)' '36-8, 'Now I Lay Me Down To Dream' '40, all with Terrell vocals and 'I Know' '46 with the Jubilaires. Compilations incl. *Cloudy* on Hep UK (probably the beginning of a chronological series), *Instrumentally Speaking* and 2-disc *Best Of* on MCA/USA, *Walkin' And Swingin'* on Affinity UK (good single-disc best-of).

KIRK, Rahsaan Roland (*b* Ronald T. Kirk, 7 Aug. '36, Columbus, Ohio; *d* 5 Dec. '77, Bloomington, Ind.) Reeds, composer. Began with a garden hose at age 6. Educated at Ohio State School for the blind; studied trumpet at 9 but switched to reeds; played in school band from '48, soon a part-time pro with local groups. The idea of playing three instruments at once came to him in a dream at age 16; discovered the manzello (resembling an alto sax but with soprano sound) and the stritch (a straight alto); played three-part harmony with tenor sax using trick fingering; also played flutes, whistles, siren, bagpipes, etc.; more than 40 instruments altogether: he breathed and spoke through flutes, one of the few to overcome their antipathy for jazz. He was received by critics with suspicion at first, but achieved wide, affectionate acceptance by everyone: no self-conscious avant-gardist, he did everything for good musical reasons, incl. experiments, classical adaptations, pop tunes: a complete original. Worked with Charles MINGUS '61, first trip to Europe same year; also recorded with Jaki BYARD. His new name also came to him in a dream. Suffered stroke '75 but came back. Own LPs, mostly with small groups: *Early Roots* '56 on King, Bethlehem, now on Charly UK; *Introducing Roland Kirk* '60 on Argo/Cadet, with Ira SULLIVAN; *Kirk's Work* and *Funk Underneath* '61 on Prestige with Jack MCDUFF (also as 2-disc set *Pre-Rahsaan*); then on Mercury, Trip, Limelight, some tracks found on more than one album: *We Free Kings* '61, *Domino* '62, *Reeds And Deeds* '63, *Roland Kirk Meets The Benny Golson Orchestra* '63, *Kirk In Copenhagen* '63, *Gifts And Messages* '64, *I Talk To The Spirits* '64 (Kirk on flutes only; two tracks are vocals by Ms C. J. Albert; two are duets with Kirk, Horace PARLAN or vibist Bobby Moses), *Rip, Rig And Panic* and *Slightly Latin* '65. Soundtrack *In The Heat Of The Night* '67 has large band dir. by Quincy JONES. *Now Please Don't You Cry, Beautiful Edith* '67 was on Verve; series on Atlantic incl. *Here Comes The Whistleman* c.'66, *The Inflated Tear* '67 (aka *That's Jazz No. 3*), *Left And Right* with large orchestra incl. strings and *Expansions* '68, *Volunteered Slavery* '68 partly made at Newport Jazz Festival, *Rahsaan/Rahsaan* '70 partly at Village Vanguard, *Natural Black Inventions* and *Blacknuss* '71, *Prepare Thyself To Deal With A Miracle* '72, *A Meeting Of The Times* '72 (with three vocals by Al HIBBLER, one by Leon Thomas), *Bright Moments* '73 (live at the Keystone Korner), *The Case Of The Three-Sided Dream In Audio Color* '75, *Other Folks Music* '76. On WB: *The Return of the 5000 lb. Man* '76, *Kirkatron* '76, *Boogie Woogie String Along For Real* '77 with string orchestra on title track. 2-disc *Kirk's Works* on EmArcy is compilation from '62-5; 2-disc *The Vibration Continues* issued on Atlantic/WEA '78.

KISS USA HM band formed late '72 by Paul Stanley (*b* Paul Stanley Eisen, 20 Jan.

'52, NYC), guitar; Gene Simmons (*b* Gene Klein, 25 Aug. 49, Haifa, Israel), bass. Drummer Peter Criss (*b* Peter Crisscoula, 20 Dec. '47, NYC) advertised in *Rolling Stone*; Ace (Paul) Frehley (*b* 27 Apr. '51, NYC) auditioned. They experimented and rehearsed with makeup, costumes in a Manhattan loft for three months, played hard rock with macho pose in clubs for a year; spotted and signed by TV's *Flipside* prod. Bill Aucoin, within weeks on fledgling Casablanca label run by Aucoin's chum Neil Bogart. Hype was backed up by a year's hard touring: on 31 Dec. '74 they supported BLUE OYSTER CULT in NYC; a year later the bill was reversed. *Kiss* and *Hotter Than Hell* '74 were undistinguished hard rock shorn of the panstick; *Dressed To Kill* '75 was an improvement, incl. stage favourite 'Rock And Roll All Nite', but vinyl couldn't capture the act, where group became cartoon characters: Simmons as blood-drooling Phantom of the Opera, Criss the cat, Frehley the spaceman and Stanley the clown combined glitter costumes with sets, flash bombs etc.; not surprisingly it took 2-disc live set *Kiss Alive* to break them: it sold a million; live version of 'Rock And Roll All Nite' was no. 12 hit. *Destroyer* '76 followed up well, prod. by metal master (ALICE COOPER) Bob Ezrin, incl. untypical hit single (no. 7) in Criss's slushy ballad 'Beth'. Marvel Comics paid them the ultimate tribute of publishing a Kiss comic book; Kiss Army fan club swelled to six figures; each member did a solo LP '78 (remaining in character on cover artwork): Frehley sold best but all were undistinguished. 2-disc *Alive II* '78 punctuated studio LPs *Rock And Roll Over* '76, *Love Gun* '77 (their best seller at no. 4), 2-disc *Double Platinum* '78 and betrayed lack of confidence in studio work, but fans made up to imitate favourites packed the venues, so all seemed well. Criss left '80, replaced on *Kiss Unmasked* '80 by session player Anton Fig, then more permanently by Brooklynite Eric Carr, who became a fox to replace the cat. As that title indicated they modified their image: music remained thunderously unsubtle, especially after initial attempt to soften sound *Music From The Elder* '81 (incl. some Lou REED songs) was worst-seller since '74. Frehley left to form Frehley's Comet after *Creatures Of The Night* '82, replaced by Vinnie Vincent, then Mark Norton; for *Lick It Up* '83 they switched to Mercury label and discarded makeup; on *Animalize* '84 Mark St John was in Frehley's seat, Bruce Kulick on *Asylum* '85. Average-to-good HM band were trapped by their image, but the last two LPs were still top 20 USA; *Crazy Nights* '87 will probably find customers. Other albums incl. *The Originals* (3-disc reissue of first three LPs; made no. 36 in Billboard).

KITCHENER, Lord (*b* Aldwyn Roberts, c.'21, Arima, Trinidad) CALYPSO/SOCA singer and composer, one of the all-time greatest, aka 'Kitch'. Left his father's blacksmith trade to sing in the Young Brigade calypso tent early '40s, soon becoming a star; went to ATILLA's Old Brigade tent '46, had success with 'Tie Tongue Mopsy' and 'Double Ten', leading a postwar drive towards new melodic emphasis. To UK with Lord Beginner (Egbert Moore: 1904-80), arriving on the *Empire Windrush* 21 June '48, a ship that came to symbolise postwar West Indian emigration to the UK; a Pathé newsreel captured Kitch singing 'London Is The Place For Me'. First records in UK on Parlophone, Jan. '50 with Cyril Blake's Calypso Serenaders, session directed by Denis Preston, jazz enthusiast and pioneer of calypso recording in UK. 'Nora' was released a month later and was a hit not only in the Caribbean but selling tens of thousands in West Africa. He toured Ghana (then Gold Coast) and is considered to have been an infl. on HIGHLIFE. 'Nora' and next release 'The Underground Train' now on compilations *Port Of Spain Shuffle Vol. 1* and *Caribbean Connections Vol. 2* (on Charly's new New Cross subsidiary UK '87). Early performances in UK pubs led to the Sunset, a West Indian club in Soho, where 'Kitch Come Go To Bed' was a favourite of Princess Margaret, who was said to have bought 100 copies of the lyrics. It was incl. along with 'Trouble In Arima' '54 in Melodisc collections *King Of Calypso* Vols. 1 & 2; during the '50s he kept a stream of records going back to Trinidad, returning there late '62 and winning the Road March '63 with 'The Road': he has won 10 times (rivalled only by Mighty SPARROW, who has won eight times), earning the title 'Road March King of the World'. He makes use of call-and-response patterns in his Road March compositions, allowing the chorus to carry a fair share. The National Panorama Competition began '63; the winning band has played a Kitch song no fewer than 15 times to '85, leading to criticism that he benefited by getting records out early and giving music sheets to the bands. He has criticised what he saw as falling standards (in England in '50s he said that Sparrow's were not true calypsos, called them 'calypsongs'; his 'No More Calypsongs' was incl. in *Kitch '67* on RCA International). He released an annual LP '71-5 on his own Trinidad Records label; 'Rainorama' was an international hit (incl. in *We Walk 100 Miles With Kitch* '73); he named his home in Diego Martin 'Rainorama Palace'. 'Tribute To "Spree" Simon' was an all-time record-breaker: it won Panorama, Brassorama (brass band) and Calypso Monarch competitions (together with 'Fever'; both incl. in *Carnival Fever In Kitch* '75), as well as the Road March. Having won the Calypso Monarchy for the first time he withdrew from competition. *Home For Carnival* '76 on KH, incl. Road March winner 'Flag Woman'; he joined NYC-based Charlies, owned by Trinidadian Rawlston Charles; LPs continued with *Hot And Sweet* '77. He had been critical of the new soca style, but adopted it and had the first international soca hit 'Sugar Bum Bum', issued as a 12″ single and in the Charlies LP *Melody Of The 21st Century* '78. Other albums incl. *Spirit Of Carnival* '79, *Shooting With Kitch* '80, *Soca Jean* '81, *Authenticity* '82, *200 Years Of Mas* '83, *The Roots Of Soca* '84 (incl. big hit 'Gee Me The Ting'); then *The Master At Work* '85 on Kalico (incl. crossover 'Breakdance') and *Kitch On The Equator* '86 on Ben Mac; 12″ single '86 on Ben Mac soca-ized versions of old hits 'Trouble In Arima' '54, 'Love In The Cemetary' '63. Claims to have composed more than 1000 calypsos. His Calypso Revue tent over the years featured stars Mighty SHADOW, Black STALIN, Merchant, Scruncher, Lord Melody, Crazy, Singing Diane. *The Grand Master* '87 incl. hits 'Kaka Roach' and brilliant 'Pan In A Minor', latter adapted by many steel orchestras for the National Panorama Contest.

KITT, Eartha (*b* 26 January '28, Columbia, S.C.) Singer; sexy night-club star with throaty voice. Began entertaining as a child; joined Katherine Dunham's dance troupe, toured the world, headlined in top clubs in Europe; appeared as Helen of Troy on stage in Orson Welles prod. of *Faust*, made successful French films; came home to Broadway's *New Faces Of 1952*, NYC clubs, broke records at the Mocambo on the West Coast. Hit records '53-4 incl. 'Uska Dara' (sung partly in Turkish), 'C'est Si Bon' (It's So Good), 'I Want To Be Evil', 'Santa Baby', 'Somebody Bad Stole De Wedding Bell', 'Lovin' Spree'. 'Under The Bridges Of Paris' '55 was UK hit. Continued success in cabaret; complains on TV talk shows that there are few places for beginners to practise an art like hers: rock clubs aren't the same thing. LPs: with Doc CHEATHAM trio on Swing (from Europe; also tracks on new Disques Swing series '87), *Love For Sale* and *The Romantic Eartha Kitt* on Capitol; *Best Of* on MCA; *At The Plaza* '65 on GNP Crescendo; *C'est Si Bon* '83 on Polydor (live club performance); *I Love Men* on Record Shack '84 incl. UK hits with discoish title single and 'Where Is My Man'; *My Way* '87 is a tribute to Martin Luther King, made live with 100-voice choir at the Caravan Of Dreams for that label.

KLAATU Canadian rock group '76-81. Eponymous debut LP of pleasant, layered pop by unknown session players Gary Draper, David Lang, Dino Tome and John Waloschuk was leased by Capitol to Daffodil in UK with no biographical info. A rock writer in the *Providence Journal* speculated in '77 about re-formation of the BEATLES, citing Klaatu as involving Beatle members (there was a similar rumour in the '60s about a group called the Futs). Capitol (Fab Four's USA label) compounded the rumour by circulating the article; sales of the LP (with self-consciously psychedelic reference points to *Sergeant Pepper*, PINK FLOYD, etc.) soared as radio got into the act. When the secret got out, media and public interest in the group quickly waned, though they produced further LPs *Hope* '77, *Sir Army Suit* '78, *Endangered Species* '80, *Magentalane* '81, and compilation *Klassic Klaatu* '82.

KLEZMER Yiddish genre from Eastern Europe, especially Odessa; a Jewish dance/folk music with lineup similar to early jazz bands, unorthodox tonality, interlocking rhythms (Odessa has been called the New Orleans of the Russian Empire). Exported to USA by early '20s, almost died out but records were made; revival now underway by groups incl. Klezmer Conservatory Band on Vanguard (three LPs incl. *A Touch of Klez!* '85), group called simply Klezmorim (plural for klezmer musicians, bands) with two brass, two reeds, tuba, percussion; Arhoolie LPs incl. *East Side Wedding* (said to be more authentically Yiddish); on Flying Fish *Metropolis* and *Notes From Underground* (more jazzish). Also on Shanachie: *Jewish Klezmer Music* by Zev Feldman and Andy Statman and *The Andy Statman Klesmer Orchestra* '83. Echoes of Kurt WEILL, Prokofiev, Gypsy music, early silent film music may help to explain why so many good jazz musicians are Jewish.

KLUGH, Earl (*b* c.'54, Detroit) Guitar. Self-taught, infl. by Chet ATKINS as a child, teaching and recording with Yusef LATEEF at 15, later joining George BENSON, then replacing Billy Connors in Chick COREA's Return To Forever, where he gained experience with electronics, but continued playing acoustic nylon-stringed guitar. His music is a blend of pop, R&B, jazz becoming easy-listening which can be enjoyed for his guitar playing alone. Nearly all his LPs reached Billboard pop LP chart, all on EMI labels (Blue Note, Liberty, UA, Capitol) except as noted: *Earl Klugh* and *Living Inside Your Love* '76, *Finger Paintings* '77, *Magic In Your Eyes* '78, *Heart String* '79 and *One On One* (on Tappan Zee '79, duo with pianist/composer Bob James), *Dream Come True* '80, *Late Night Guitar* '80, *Crazy For You* '81, *Two Of A Kind* (with James) '82, *Low Ride* '83, *Wishful Thinking* '83, *Nightsongs* '84, *Soda Fountain Shuffle* '85 on WB. Soundtrack albums incl. *How To Beat The High Cost Of Living* '80 (with Hubert LAWS) on Columbia, collaborations with composer Pat Williams on *Marvin & Tige* c.'83 on Capitol, *Just Between Friends* '86 on WB.

KNACK, The USA pop quartet formed in L.A. '78 by Doug Fieger (*b* 20 Aug., Detroit), vocals and guitar; Berton Averre (*b* 13 Dec., Van Nuys), guitar; Prescott Niles (*b* 2

May, NYC), bass; Bruce Gary (*b* 7 Apr. '52, Burbank), drums. Fieger and Averre were long-time collaborators; former had played bass in Sky, a Detroit group which made *Don't Hold Back* '71 before moving to the West Coast and splitting. Gary had extensive session credits with Jack Bruce, the DOORS' Robby Krieger, Lonnie DONEGAN, etc. Experienced players combined to ride new wave bandwagon with groups like Tom Petty and the Heartbreakers, Dwight TWILLEY, etc. Launched themselves from L.A.'s Troubador Club, where BUFFALO SPRINGFIELD had been spotted '67; they peddled power pop of *Hard Day's Night*-era BEATLES, and as a record company always looking for the next Big Thing, Capitol signed them and brought in expatriate UK bubblegum expert Mike Chapman to shine them up, as he'd done BLONDIE. *Get The Knack* '79 was instant pop, instant success: undeniably catchy 'My Sharona' was USA no. 1/UK no. 6 single, helped sell over 5m copies of LP; 'Good Girls Don't' also made top 20 later in '79. Backlash soon set in, as critics pounced on plastic sound, moronic and sexist lyrics; *But The Little Girls Understand* '80 incl. 'Baby Talks Dirty' which just made top 40; LP sold disappointingly as novelty faded. Switched producers for belated third LP *Round Trip* '82; band split. Fieger had prod. Rubber City Rebels '80, formed Taking Chances, guested effectively on *Born To Laugh At Tornados* '83 by fellow Detroiters Was (Not Was); the others continued for a short time as the Game. 'My Sharona' briefly brought rock dancing back, and was actually played at Xenon and Studio 54, but when the Knack fell they plummeted.

KNEPPER, Jimmy (*b* 22 Nov. '27, L.A.) Trombone; also bass trombone, baritone horn; arranger, composer. Began on alto horn at 5, trombone at 9; worked with many white big bands late '40s-early '50s, also combos with Charlie PARKER, etc.; joined Charles MINGUS Jazz Workshop '57; worked with Tony SCOTT, Stan KENTON; rejoined Mingus '59; toured Africa with Herbie MANN '60, USSR with Benny GOODMAN '62; played in *Funny Girl* Broadway pit band '64-6, others; with Thad JONES-Mel LEWIS band on world tours; Lee KONITZ Nonet '75, etc. He played on most

of Mingus's records '57-62 on half a dozen labels (e.g. *Tiajuana Moods* '57 on RCA) (Mingus severed the relationship by punching Knepper in the mouth; see entry for Mingus). Knepper was established as one of the very best on his instrument: at home with the blues, always swinging, always musical. Recorded with Pepper ADAMS '58: *Pepper-Knepper Quintet* on Metrojazz (MGM) with Elvin JONES, Doug Watkins, Wynton KELLY; also with Gil EVANS, others; own LPs incl. quintet LPs '57 with Mingus on his Debut label and on Bethlehem, both with Dannie RICHMOND (latter now called *Idol Of The Flies* on Affinity); next record under his own name was nearly 20 years later, again a quintet with Richmond: *Cunningbird* '76 on Steeplechase also incl. Al COHN. More quintets: *Jimmy Knepper In L.A.* '77 on Inner City; *Just Friends* '78 on Hep. Sextet LP *Tell Me . . .* '79 made in Holland on Daybreak followed by return to quintet for *Primrose Path* '80 on Hep, made in London. *I Dream Too Much* '84 is on Soul Note.

KNIGHT, Gladys, and the Pips Soul vocal group formed '52 in Atlanta, Ga.: lead singer Gladys Knight (*b* 28 May '44), Merald 'Bubba' Knight (*b* 4 Sep. '42), William Guest (*b* 2 June '41), Brenda Knight, Elenor Guest. An incredibly longlived family act (the Guests are cousins) began on Merald's 10th birthday, when Gladys, who had been singing in a touring church group before she was 5, had won talent competitions and appeared several times on TV, organised an impromptu group. They opened for acts such as Sam COOKE and Jackie WILSON in '56, but an abortive record contract resulted in Brenda and Elenor being replaced by Edward Patten (another cousin, *b* 2 Aug. '39) and Langston George. George stayed until just before the first top 10 hit 'Every Beat Of My Heart', though he may have been involved in it: the situation is confused because two versions charted the same week in May '61, by 'The Pips' on Vee Jay and 'Gladys Knight & The Pips' on Fury (though only the Fury record made the R&B chart). Total of 39 Hot 100 entries '61-83 (20 in UK) and 24 albums '67-85 was carried on with top 20 'Letter Full Of Tears' on Fury '62, then mostly minor hits while Gladys became a mother (only top 40 was 'Giving Up' '64 on Maxx) until they signed with Motown subsidiary Soul: 'Everybody Needs Love' made the top 40 July '67, but 'I Heard It Through The Grapevine' was no. 3 USA Oct. '67: Marvin GAYE's '68 no. 1 version said to have been cut earlier and held up by a dispute with Motown, but those who heard Gladys's voice riding over a beat that rocked and floated at the same time will never forget the first one. The Motown era lasted into '73, incl. hits 'If I Were Your Woman' (no. 9 '70), 'Neither One Of Us (Wants To Be The First To Say Goodbye)' (no. 2 '73), and a fine cover of Kris KRISTOFFERSON's 'Help Me Make It Through The Night'. Sooner or later many artists quarrelled with Motown; the Pips went to Buddah Records '73 immediately having their biggest success: no. 9 LP USA *Imagination* '73 had half the songs written by white singer/songwriter Jim Weatherly incl. three single hits: 'Where Peaceful Waters Flow' (top 30), 'Midnight Train To Georgia' (no. 1; 'Midnight Plane To Houston' in Weatherly's original version), and 'Best Thing That Ever Happened To Me' (no. 3); LP also incl. Gerry GOFFIN/Barry Goldberg's 'I've Got To Use My Imagination' (no. 3). 'On And On' from '74 film *Claudine* was no. 5 for 5 top 5 million-sellers in a row. Medley 'The Way We Were/Try To Remember' '75 was no. 11 USA (and their biggest in UK along with 'Baby Don't Change Your Mind' '77, both at no. 4). Gladys made her acting debut in *Pipe Dreams* '76; there was a split with Buddah and a brief split with the Pips as Gladys was prevented from working with them because of a dispute with Buddah (they were on Casablanca; Gladys on CBS/Columbia) before an inevitable reunion. There have been no more big hits, but four chart albums, and faithful fans will always give a listen to see what's going on. Other albums incl. *Everybody Needs Love* '67, *Feelin' Bluesy* '68, *Silk'n'Soul* and *Nitty Gritty* '69, *If I Were Your Woman* '71, *Standing Ovation* '72, *All I Need Is Time* '73, compilations 2-disc *Anthology* '74 and *A Little Knight Music* '75, all on Motown/Soul; *I Feel A Song* and *2nd Anniversary* (of signing with Buddah) '75, *Still Together* '77, *The One And Only* '78, all on Buddah; *The Touch Of Love* '80 on K-Tel. On Columbia/CBS: *About Love* '80 (top 50

LP), *Touch* '81, *Visions* '83 (no. 34 LP), *Life* '85, *Greatest Hits* '86.

KNOX, Buddy (*b* Wayne Knox, 14 Apr. '33, Happy, Texas) Rockabilly singer, career paralleling that of Buddy HOLLY, beginning at same studio (*see* Norman PETTY). Knox had written 'Party Doll' early as '48, formed the Rhythm Orchids '55 with Jimmy Bowen on bass, Don Lanier on lead guitar. Petty cut 'Party Doll' and Bowen's 'I'm Stickin' With You' in '56 (using a cardboard box instead of a drum kit because he didn't know how to record rock'n'roll drums); released them on local Triple-D label: the record was a runaway 2-sided hit, picked up by then-new Roulette label NYC, split up with different B sides and each sold a million. 'Party Doll' made no. 1, Bowen (as 'with the Rhythm Orchids') no. 11. Knox discovered the style when teenager Don Mills had sat in on drums on a Rhythm Orchids date, later added drummer Dave Alldred (who had worked with Petty's trio) to the group. Total of eight chart placings on Roulette incl. 'Rock Your Little Baby To Sleep' (17), 'Hula Love' (9), ''Somebody Touched Me' (22) '57-8. He promoted them on Alan FREED's package tours, film *Jamboree*; last Hot 100 entry was often-banned 'I Think I'm Going To Kill Myself' '59. Sound had developed by then to incl. session guitarists, Bobby DARIN on piano; Bowen rarely played bass in the studio, members of CRICKETS often appearing and (on 'All For You') Holly himself. Bowen had four Hot 100 entries, later became a prominent producer, first at Chancellor, then Reprise, now at MCA. Lanier recorded less successfully. Knox moved into straight pop, then into country: Holly's old partner Bob Montgomery produced his minor country hit 'Gipsy Man' '68 on UA. He moved to Canada, toured in '70s. Knox's USA hits equalled Holly's in the latter's lifetime; compilations LPs *Greatest Hits* and *Libert Takes* on Charly UK.

KOERNER, 'Spider' John (*b* 31 Aug. '38, Rochester, NY) Folksinger, guitarist, also plays harmonica. Attended U. of Minnesota, began as folksinger on West Coast, appeared at Newport Folk Festivals '64 (released on Vanguard, filmed as *Festival*), '65, '69. First specialised in blues, recorded in trio with Dave Ray and Tony Glover: *Blues, Rags & Hollers, More Blues, Rags & Hollers, The Return Of Koerner, Ray & Glover* '63-5, also solo *Spider Blues* '65, duo *Running Jumping, Standing Still* '69 with Willie Murphy, all on Elektra. With Ray & Glover on *Live At St Olaf Festival* on Mill; also *Some American Folk Songs Like They Used To Be* '74, solo set *Music Is Just A Bunch Of Notes* '72 on Sweet Jane; *Nobody Knows The Trouble I've Seen* '86 on Red House.

KOLLINGTON, Ayinya (*b* '53, Ibadan, Nigeria) Singer-composer in Yoruban, second only to BARRISTER in popularity in FUJI. Initially he appeared to be in no hurry, releasing unspectacular LPs mid-'70s on EMI (e.g. *Ayanga Baba Yin*). But then he changed his approach, adding a bata drum as the focal point of his music and rechristening his band The Fuji '78. With a new distinctive sound he emerged from Barrister's shadow, and several years of bitter rivalry ensued; with a slightly faster rhythm and a sharper attack on social injustice in his lyrics he soon had a devoted following, issuing more albums on the Olumo label incl. *Ajodun Ominira Nigeria 1981*, before establishing his own label in '82, releasing *Mo Tun De Pelu Ara, Asiko Lo To* (attacking politicians and praising teachers), *Nigeria Elections 1983, Nigeria Kole Ku* (again condemning waste and profligacy of politicians), and *Ijoba Ti Tun* (welcoming the military government). *Itelorun* ('Satisfaction') and *Knock-Out Special* came out in '84. The rivalry has died down; the popularity of fuji and the size of the market guarantee a bright future for both.

KONIMO (*b* Daniel Amponsah, '34, Fause, Asante Region, Ghana) Singer, composer, guitarist. Began on church organ at age 5; sent by his uncle to the Presbyterian School in Kumasi, where he was introduced to European classical music. Transferred to Adisadel College in Cape Coast; formed a school band and began to learn guitar. Worked briefly as teacher and music master in his village school, becoming acquainted with various brass instruments through the village band; but soon moved to Accra's Medical Research Institute, also making his first record: HIGHLIFE song 'Go Inside'. He returned to Kumasi '55, formed the Antobre group, playing pop and highlife, performing regularly on radio, but also maintaining a professional career, joining the chemistry department at the U. of Kumasi '60, also was studying Spanish guitar. Studied in UK on scholarship; returned mid-'60s to record several songs with Dr K. Gyasi; translated Asante ballads into English (LP *Ashanti Ballads* '68). Back to UK '69 to the U. of Salford, also preparing programmes of music for the BBC External Service. Recorded again with Gyasi on the Essiebons label on return to Ghana. In the '70s he decided to work in the 'palm wine' style of guitar-band highlife and led a seven-piece acoustic ensemble with Spanish guitar, talking drum (atumpan), hand pianos, gyama drum and gong; made classic LP *Odonson Nkoao* mid-'70s; began to receive international recognition for varied, valuable contributions to African music: he performed for Commonwealth Institute Music Village '84, also in Channel 4 TV series *Repercussions*.

KONITZ, Lee (*b* 13 Oct. '27, Chicago) Alto sax. Gigged locally, toured with Claude THORNHILL '47-8, worked with Miles DAVIS '48-50. He visited Scandinavia, worked for Stan KENTON for year, led his own groups; but became close to Lennie TRISTANO and turned down work with name groups to stay in what was (in retrospect) the avant-garde of the white school of 'cool jazz' of the '50s: with Stan GETZ, Zoot SIMS, Gerry MULLIGAN, Jimmy GIUFFRE, Warne MARSH and a handful of others one of the greatest and best-known of this school, but also perhaps 'cooler' than any of them: his musical intelligence, his languid style and the harmonic infl. of Tristano make a unique voice with tonal beauty at its centre, infl. by Charlie PARKER but not dominated by him, unlike many other altos. Recorded with Tristano '49; own early sessions '49-53 (some made in Paris) on Prestige incl. *Young Lee*, compilation reissue *Ezz-thetic*; also with Mulligan quartet on World-Pacific '53; own quartet in Boston '54-5 on Storyville. Recorded in Köln '56 playing alto, tenor and baritone saxes, with reedmen Hans Koller (*b* 12 Feb. '21, Vienna, also infl. by Tristano), Lars Gullin (*b* 4 May '28, Sweden; *d* there 17 May '76), others; tracks issued on Carish (Italian

667

Parlophone). On Atlantic: LP with Marsh '55, *Inside Hi-Fi* '56, *Worthwhile Konitz* '56 (Japan only), *The Real Lee Konitz* '57. On Verve: *Lee Konitz Quintet*, quartet *Tranquility* '57, *An Image* '58 with strings arr. by Bill Russo, *You And Lee* '59 with brass section, *Lee Konitz Meets Jimmy Giuffre* '59: with reed section incl. Hal McKusick on alto, Giuffre on baritone, Marsh and Ted Brown on tenor, solos by Konitz and Marsh, this LP with its rich reed sounds was one of the most beautiful of the decade. NYC quartet recordings '60-1 issued on Wave UK; trio set *Motion* '61 on Verve. He concentrated on teaching on West Coast '62-4, toured Europe as solo '65-6. Solo 'Blues For Bird' at *Charlie Parker 10th Memorial Concert* on Limelight '65 followed by *Modern Jazz Compositions From Haiti* '66: compositions of Gerald Merceron played by a quartet on a GM label. An ingenious teacher, he often used tapes by mail for lessons; in '65 made a Music Minus One LP of alto duets, overdubbing himself on some tracks and leaving others open for the student. *The Lee Konitz Duets* '67 on Milestone used overdubbing on one track, with Konitz playing alto, baritone; on sets of variations on 'Alone Together' he played tenor and electric alto in some places. *Zo-Ko-Ma* '68 on MPS incl. guitarist Attila Zoller (*b* 13 June '27, Hungary) and Albert MANGELSDORFF. Many other LPs incl. *Altissimo* '73 on Japanese Philips with four altos: Konitz, Gary BARTZ, Charlie MARIANO, Jackie MCLEAN; solo *Lone-Lee* '74, *I Concentrate On You* '74 (duo with bassist Red Mitchell), *Windows* '75 (duo with pianist Hal Garper) all on Steeplechase; other duos with piano: *Spirits* '71 on Milestone with Sal Mosca (*b* 27 Apr. '27, NY), *Duplicity* '77 on Horo with Martial Solal. Other LPs on European labels: *European Episode* '68, *Stereokonitz* '68, *Lee Konitz à Juan* '74, *Oleo* '75, *Jazz Confronto 32* '76, *London Concert* '76, *Yes, Yes, Nonet* '79 with Jimmy KNEPPER, two LPs on MPS '79-80, *High Jingo* '82 on Japanese Atlas, *Toot Sweet* '82 on Owl with Michel PETRUCCIANI. Also *Peacemeal* '69, *Satori* '74 on Milestone; *Meets Warne Marsh Again* '76 on Pausa; *Tenorlee* on Choice, *Pyramid* on Improvising Artists, *Lee Konitz Nonet* and *Quintet* on Chiaroscuro, all '77; *Live At Laren* '79 and *Ideal Scene* '86 on Soul Note; *Art Of The Duo* '83 on Enja with Mangelsdorff. Popular around the world, he cannot make an uninteresting record.

KONTE, Lamine (*b* Kolda, Senegal) Singer-composer, guitarist, kora player. From musical family; studied kora with his father Dialy Keba Konte, then with Souldiou Cissoko, a kora player of international repute. Studied at the School of Arts in Dakar, practising every day to create his own style; by '60 had formed his own group with friends and had established a national reputation as a contemporary artist, introducing new infl. while also maintaining trad. of Senegalese music. He represented Senegal at the Black Arts Festival in Dakar '65; moved to Paris '72 but the group broke up, leaving him to pursue a solo career. Of his two LPs '75, *La Kora du Senegal: les Rythmes, les Percussions et la Voix de Lamine Konte* features solo kora tracks with trad. arr. and a few Afrocuban tunes, *Les Rythmes, les Percussions et la Voix de Lamine Konte* has more adventurous arr. of kora, balaphon, bass, tam-tam and vocals. Eclectic *Tinque Rinque* '77 is a pot-pourri of kora, rock'n'roll, folk music with both acoustic and electric lineups, demonstrates both virtuosity and breadth of vision. After LP *Baara* '79 he worked with Bozambo on soundtrack of film *Bako L'Autre Rime*. Not as commercial as his fellow Senegalese Toure Kunda and Youssou N'DOUR, but a musician of outstanding technical ability.

KOOL AND THE GANG Disco-funk band, began mid-'60s: 19 top 40 pop singles '73-85. Robert 'Kool' Bell (*b* 8 Oct. '50) on bass and vocals, Ronald Bell (*b* 1 Nov. '51, both from Youngstown, Ohio) on tenor sax began with Dennis Thomas on sax, Robert Mickens on trumpet as Jazziacs in high school in Jersey City, N.J.; lead guitarist Claydes Smith (*b* 6 Sep. '48), George 'Funky' Brown on drums (*b* 5 Jan. '49, both from N.J.) have been long-time members of 7-10 piece group. As Jazziacs played at Café Wha in Greenwich Village on same bill with Richie HAVENS; first single 'Kool And The Gang' made top 20 R&B '69: dance hits derived from SLY STONE style, live LPs *Live At The Sex Machine* '71, *Live At P.J.'s* '72, *Good Times* '73 preceded breakthrough no. 33 LP *Wild And Peaceful* '74 incl. three hits. *Kool Jazz* '74 was a compilation; *Light*

Of Worlds '74, *Spirit Of The Boogie* '75, *Love & Understanding* were all top 100 LPs, but *Open Sesame* '76 and *The Force* '77 were not: they slipped as disco boom they had anticipated got underway. They added lead vocalist James 'JT' Taylor (*b* 16 Aug. '53, S.C.) and came back with *Ladies Night* '79 (prod. by DEODATO), no. 13 LP with title single no. 1 R&B, top 10 pop; *Celebrate!* '80, no. 10 LP with single 'Celebration' at no. 1 pop (adopted as theme of hostages returning from Iran); *Something Special* '81, *As One* '82, *In The Heart* '83, *Emergency* '84 all top 30 LPs; *Victory* incl. 'I.B.M.C.' ('Itty Bitty Midi Committee') celebrating Ronald's prod. of LPs since '83 in studio at home; Robert and Taylor bought land '87 on Bouley Island, off the Ivory Coast of Africa, planning to build a studio. They long had their own De-Lite label, but *Forever* '87 appeared on Mercury. Best compilation is 2-disc *Twice As Kool* '83 on De-Lite.

KOOPER, AL (*b* 5 Feb. '44, Brooklyn, NY) Singer, songwriter, guitarist, keyboards. Major rock figure of '60s, '70s. Joined Royal Teens at 15 after their novelty no. 3 hit 'Short Shorts' '58; became session musician; dropped out of U. of Bridgeport (Conn.); back in NYC on odd jobs at Adelphi studios, sessions; co-wrote 'This Diamond Ring', no. 1 for Gary LEWIS and the Playboys '65, but garnered more attention that year playing organ on Bob DYLAN's 'Like A Rolling Stone', LP *Highway 61 Revisited*, appearing with him at Newport Folk Festival (later worked on *Blonde On Blonde*, *New Morning*); formed Blues Project with Steve KATZ: LPs *Live At Café Au Go-Go* '66, *Projections* '67, *Blues Project At Town Hall* '67. Formed group BLOOD, SWEAT AND TEARS with Katz; prod. first LP *Child Is Father To The Man* '68, left as they achieved commercial stardom. Staff prod. at CBS; worked with Don ELLIS, Appaloosa etc.; prod. and played on enormously successful *Super Session* LP '68 with Stephen STILLS, Mike BLOOMFIELD, so laid back that it's hard to see now what the fuss was about. Also *Live Adventures Of Mike Bloomfield And Al Kooper*, solo sets *I Stand Alone*, *You Never Know Who Your Friends Are*, all '69; also guested on *Let It Bleed* (ROLLING STONES), *Electric Ladyland* (Jimi HENDRIX). *Kooper*

Session incl. 15-year-old Shuggie OTIS '70; *Easy Does It* '70 was 2-disc set; *The Landlord* was film soundtrack; *New York City* '71 recorded partly in London; *A Possible Projection Of The Future* '72, *Naked Songs* '72, *Unclaimed Freight* '75; all except *Landlord* (United Artists) on CBS. In '73 played on revived Blues Project's *Reunion In Central Park* on MCA; *Act Like Nothing's Wrong* '76 on UA was his first new solo LP in three years; he appeared nude on sleeve. From mid-'70s concentrated more on production; helped with LYNYRD SKYNYRD's first three LPs '74-5; The Tubes debut LP '75; Nils LOFGREN's *Cry Tough* '76; EDDIE AND THE HOT RODS' *Fish And Chips*, released by EMI '80 but recorded much earlier. Took part in Blues Project reunion NYC St Patrick's Day '81; later that year toured with Dylan. On some records used pseudonym Roosevelt Gook. Autobiography *Backstage Pass* '76.

KORA West African musical instrument played exclusively by a hereditary caste of male professional musicians, a double harp made from a large calabash covered in cowhide, with 21 strings originally made of leather but now more usually of nylon. It is played by Mandinka musicians, who share a common heritage with other groups of the ancient Mali empire, and is today mostly found in Senegal and Gambia. The musician is known as a jali (plural jaliya), plays for entertainment; he praises notable individuals, while the repertoire also incl. historical epics and family lineages. (The musician story-teller is also called a griot.) Singing and playing are strictly organised with a fixed refrain and a fixed melody, but room is still found for improvisation. In earlier times the players survived by patronage, but today, like many musicians, most have alternative ways of making a living. Best known contemporary kora players are perhaps the Konte family; Alhaji Bai Konte (*b* '20s, Jambur), one of Gambia's leading players, was taught by his father, developed his own style; he is heard on *Alhaji Bai Konte: Kora Melodies From The Republic Of The Gambia* '74 on Rounder. He trained his son Dembo Konte (*b* '48), who performs more modern material and plays with the Gambia National Troupe. Father and son formed a trio late '70s with Malamini

Jobarteh (b '42), who was brought up in Konte household and has toured North Africa, France, USSR, UK as a soloist; Jobarteh and Dembo play together on *Jaliya* '85 on Sterns. Other notable kora records incl. *Senegal: La Musique des Griots*, Babou Diebate's *Folklore du Senegal (Casamnace) Vol. 1*, Amadu Bansang Jobarteh's *Master Of The Kora*. More recently, some kora masters have attracted wider audiences by amplifying the sound, supporting it with non-trad. instruments, etc.; these incl. Lamine KONTE, Nory Konte, Foday Musa Suso.

KORGIS UK pop group formed '79 by James Warren (b 25 Aug. '51, Bristol, Somerset), guitar, vocals; Andy Creswell-Davis (b 10 Aug. 49, Yatton, Somerset), vocals, keyboards etc. Warren grew up in Bristol, joined group Dawn '68; Davis at Weston-Super-Mare Technical College, worked with groups Blue Crew, Strange Fruit, The Kynd; they joined in Stackridge (LPs *Stackridge* '71, *Friendliness* '72, *Man In The Bowler Hat* '73, *Extravaganza* '74, *Mr Mick* '76), a band remembered fondly as a cross between BEATLES and Wurzels; provided such material as 'Dora The Female Explorer', 'Slark', 'Do The Stanley', 'Let There Be Lids'; boasted fan club called The Rhubarb Thrashing Society; split '76. Warren and Davis formed Korgis with various friends incl. multi-instrumentalist Stuart Gordon, keyboardist Phil Harrison, both of Bath-based Short Wave Band. Single 'If I Had You' no. 13 UK '79, followed by LP *The Korgis* '79 and melodic hit 'Everybody's Got To Learn Sometime', no. 5 UK, no. 18 USA '80; by this time Davis had left. Second LP on Rialto *Dumb Waiters* featured four Davis songs, minor UK hit 'If It's Alright With You Baby'; band fell apart. Warren concentrated on writing and studio work; Davis worked with TEARS FOR FEARS, developed own material; with Warren as Korgis again '84, duo's first single for Warren's Marvellous Music label 'True Life Confessions' '85.

KORNER, Alexis (b 19 Apr. '28, Paris; d 1 Jan. '84) Guitar, vocals; force behind UK R&B boom '60s. Educated in Europe; played in jazz and skiffle bands; opened London Blues and Barrelhouse Club '55

with Cyril DAVIES, jammed with visiting USA bluesmen; formed Blues Incorporated '61, with future ROLLING STONE Charlie Watts; others who played with or passed through groups incl. Graham BOND, Ginger BAKER, Jack Bruce, Long John BALDRY, Mick Jagger, future members of PENTANGLE, FREE, LED ZEPPELIN, etc. Worked '60s in TV with a rhythm section, formed trio Free At Last, went solo; formed New Church '69 (LP *The New Church*); large group CCS (Collective Consciousness Society) promoted by Mickie MOST: hits incl. 'Whole Lotta Love' (both USA/UK). Formed Snape '72 with Mel Collins, Ian Wallace, and others from King Crimson (*Accidentally Born In New Orleans* '72 on WB; *Snape Live On Tour* on Brain). *R&B From The Marquee* '63 reissued '84; an *Alexis Korner's All Star Blues Incorporated* LP was issued on Transatlantic '69; Korner compilation *Bootleg Him* early '70s in USA; other issues incl. *Get Off My Cloud* '75 on Columbia/USA, *Just Easy* '78 on Intercord, *Me* '79 on Jeton, *Profile* '81 from Polygram/Germany, *Juvenile Delinquent* '84 on Charisma.

KOSTELANETZ, Andre (b 23 Dec. '01, St Petersburg, Russia; d 14 Jan. '80, USA) Arranger, conductor of high-class pop and light classical music. Popular on radio from '30s to '50s; accompanied soprano Lily Pons on Columbia/USA, later Perry COMO on RCA incl. no. 1 hit 'Prisoner Of Love' '46; soprano Beverly Sills in *Music Of Victor Herbert* (EMI/Angel/USA '76). Best records were lovely arrangements of Broadway show tunes by George GERSHWIN, Jerome KERN, Cole PORTER, Vincent YOUMANS on Columbia 78s, reissued on LP in the '50s; also *Lure Of The Tropics* incl. items like 'Malagueña' (written '30 by Ernesto LECUONA) in far-off days of what was called 'light music' in UK. *Meet Andre Kostelanetz* was a no. 4 compilation LP '55; mood music in '60s: *New York Wonderland*, *Sounds Of Love* etc.

KOTTKE, Leo (b 11 Sep. '45, Athens, Ga.) Guitarist, songwriter, singer; excellent acoustic guitar playing, ironic and often humorous lyrics ensured long-term cult following. Began on guitar at 11; lived in 12 different states. First LP *Twelve String*

Blues '69 on Oblivion made in Minneapolis coffee-house; *Circle 'Round The Sun* on Symposium; instrumental *Six And 12-String Guitar* on Takoma (*see* John FAHEY) sold several hundred thousand copies. Signed with Capitol for *Mudlark* '71, *Greenhouse* '72, live instrumental *My Feet Are Smiling* '73, *Ice Water* '73, instrumental *Dreams And All That Stuff* '74 (best chart showing at no. 45) and *Chewing Pine* '74, with bass and drums. On Chrysalis: instrumental *Leo Kottke* '76, *Burnt Lips* '78, *Balance* '79, *Live In Europe* '80, *Guitar Music* '82, *Time Step* '83; then *A Shout Towards Noon* '86, *Regards From Church Pink* '88 on Private Music.

KRAFTWERK European electric/techno/art rock group formed '70 in Düsseldorf by Ralf Hutter and Florian Schneider, vocals and electronics. They started a studio, made two LPs incl. *Tone Float* by a group called Organisation infl. by PINK FLOYD, TANGERINE DREAM; left and chose German word meaning 'power plant' for their own work, in turn soon infl. synthesiser pop bands. First LPs *Kraftwerk 1* and *Kraftwerk 2* on Philips; *Kraftwerk* and *Ralf and Florian* on Vertigo '71-3 (titles as imaginative as the repetitious, 'minimalist' sound); added Klaus Roeder on violin and guitar, Wolgang Flur with more electronics for *Autobahn* '74, which was a no. 5 LP; side-long title track edited for no. 25 hit USA (11 UK). *Exceller 8* was compilation ('Accelerate', pun on 'Autobahn') they appeared in the USA on Capitol for *Radio-Activity* '75 (with Karl Bartos replacing Roeder), *Trans-Europe Express* '77, *The Man-Machine* '78; *Computer World* '81 was on WB (incl. 'Computer Love'; single with 'The Model' on reverse was a UK no. 1). 'Tune' from *Express* was used by rap artist Afrika Bambaataa. *Techno Pop* '83 was on EMI UK. They toured USA late '70s with their machines, talked about a tour by electronic dummies while they stayed at home; after *Electric Café* '86 the synthesisers spent their royalties on one-night stands with digital switchboards. Studio wizardry infl. New Order (*see* JOY DIVISION), HUMAN LEAGUE, ULTRAVOX etc. but whether humans can interface is not known. It remains to be seen whether worthwhile music can be made in anything more than a peripheral way.

KRAMER, Billy J., and the Dakotas UK beat group of '60s. Kramer (*b* William Ashton, 19 Aug. '43, Liverpool) was lead singer with a local group the Coasters; story has him stepping up to the mike when his guitar was stolen: anyway he was spotted and signed by Brian EPSTEIN, who moved him to Manchester band the Dakota, signed them to Parlophone. George MARTIN thought Kramer's voice too weak, but suggested covering LENNON-MCCARTNEY song to get a hit: 'Do You Want To Know A Secret' reached no. 2, with help from judicious double-tracking, Martin's piano; 'Bad To Me' with same formula was no. 1, 'I'll Keep You Satisfied' no. 4, all '63. Dakotas lineup was Mike Maxfield, lead guitar; Robin McDonald, rhythm guitar; Ray Jones, bass (Maxfield's SHADOWS-styled instrumental 'The Cruel Sea' was no. 18 '63). Lennon-McCartney's 'From A Window' (no. 10 '64) was flanked by songs from USA writers: Mort Shuman's 'Little Children' (no. 1 '64), Burt BACHARACH's 'Trains And Boats And Planes' (no. 12 '65), but they inevitably slipped, despite USA hit on Imperial with 'Bad To Me'/'Little Children' (both sides in top 10), top 30 entries for other Beatle songs: they clearly basked in reflected glory. They split '66; Kramer was dropped by Parlophone '67; 'Sorry' and 'The Town Of Tuxley Toymaker' flopped on Reaction and he went on club circuit.

KRISTOFFERSON, Kris (*b* 22 June '36, Brownsville, Texas) Singer/songwriter, actor with gravelly voice. Had colourful early career as Rhodes Scholar, pop singer, soldier, helicopter pilot; studying in UK mid-'50s he fell in with Tommy STEELE's manager, who changed his name to Kris Carson; singles flopped. He was a janitor at CBS studios in Nashville mid-'60s: said to have cleaned ashtrays while Bob DYLAN made *Blonde On Blonde*. He was encouraged by Johnny CASH, who later recorded 'Me & Bobby McGee': covered by Janis JOPLIN, Roger MILLER, became a standard. Cash wrote sleeve note for debut LP *Me & Bobby McGee* '71, which also incl. 'Help Me Make It Through The Night', 'Sunday Morning Comin' Down'. *The Silver-Tongued Devil & I* '71 confirmed major stature as a writer; he made well-received acting debut in *Cisco Pike* '72 with Gene

Hackman; but marriage to Rita COOLIDGE accompanied a decline in his writing: *Jesus Was A Capricorn* '72, *Full Moon* '73 and *Spooky Lady's Sideshow* '74 were lacklustre. His acting career boomed however, in *Cisco Pike* '72, Sam Peckinpah's *Pat Garrett & Billy The Kid* (with Dylan) and *Bring Me The Head Of Alfredo Garcia* '74, Martin Scorsese's *Alice Doesn't Live Here Anymore* '75, *A Star Is Born* '76 with Barbra STREISAND, others. *Easter Island* '78 was a better LP; *Songs Of Kristofferson* '77 and *Help Me Make It Through The Night* '80 are good compilations. Acting career was hurt by unfair flop of Western *Heaven's Gate* '80, guaranteed by critical savagery before it was even released; though he was well received in the Willie NELSON film *Songwriter* '85. Songs have been covered by Perry COMO, Gladys KNIGHT, Nelson, others; he appeared with Waylon JENNINGS, Nelson, Cash on hit LP *The Highwayman* and with Nelson at Farm Aid '85. At his best he is a genuinely perceptive writer whose work will continue to be covered; *Repossessed* '86 was highly rated, his first collection of new songs in five years.

KRONOS QUARTET USA string quartet formed in Seattle '74 by violinist David Harrington (*b* 9 Sep. '49, Portland, Ore.). Established themselves playing at Mills College in Berkeley, Cal.; Hank Dutt joined '77 on viola (*b* 4 Nov. '52, Muscatine, Iowa), violinist John Sherba (*b* 10 Dec. '54, Milwaukee, Wis.) and cellist Joan Jeanrenaud (*b* 25 Jan. '56, Memphis, Tenn.) in '78. They worked on or contributed to recordings by Warren Benson and Dane Rudhyar (on CRI), David GRISMAN (on WEA); first own recording was cassette-only *Kronos Quartet* '82 on Sounds Wonderful, incl. the Quartet No 8 by Australian composer Peter Sculthorpe (*b* 29 Apr. '29, Launceton, Tasmania). *In Formation* '82 on Reference Recordings flaunted their unorthodox stance with titles such as Alan Dorsey's 'Whatever Happened To The Hoodoo Meat Bucket' and John Whitney's 'The Junk Food Blues'. *Monk Suite* '85 (with Ron CARTER) and *Music Of Bill Evans* '86 (with Eddie Gomez and Jim HALL) were produced for Landmark by Orrin Keepnews. 2-disc *Cadenza On the Night Plain* '85 on Gramavision compiled the quartet music of Terry RILEY, incl. his 'G Song', expanded from his work on film *Le Secret de la Vie* '73. They signed to Nonesuch: *Kronos Quartet* '86 reprised the Sculthorpe quartet, plus works by Philip GLASS, Aulis Sallinen (*b* 9 Apr. '35, Salmi, Finland), Colin Nancarrow (*b* 27 Oct. '12, Texarcana, Ark.) and Jimi HENDRIX ('Purple Haze'). *White Man Sleeps* '87 was followed by *Tonggeret* by Idjah Hadidjah (which draws on Indonesian music, as does the Sculthorpe). They also contributed to Glass's *Songs From Liquid Days* and soundtrack *Mishima*, soundtracks *True Stories* (David Byrne) and *The Plague Dogs* (Patrick Gleeson), John ZORN album *Spillane* and GRATEFUL DEAD lyricist Robert Hunter's music for *Twilight Zone* TV episode 'The Devil's Alphabet', all '86-7. They have championed the music of Béla Bartók, Anton Webern, Ornette COLEMAN, James BROWN ('Sex Machine' with robot), Steve Reich, Kevin Volans, Ken Benshoof, Tom Constanten (former Dead keyboardist), others; their *Kronos Hour* was a syndicated radio series combining performance and interviews. Not the least of their services to music has been garnering a much wider audience than string quartets usually get, as well as opening audiences' ears with acoustic instruments.

KRUPA, Gene (*b* 15 Jan. '09, Chicago; *d* 16 Oct. '73, Yonkers, N.Y.) Drummer, bandleader. Active in Chicago with the Benson Orchestra, others (Edgar A. Benson's dance band had hits '21-5; also employed Frankie TRUMBAUER); first recorded late '27 with McKENZIE-CONDON's Chicagoans, said to be first recording with full drum kit; to NYC '29, worked with Red NICHOLS, Irving AARONSON, others; first records under own name made in Chicago Nov. '35 as 'Gene Krupa And His Chicagoans' with octet: Benny GOODMAN, Jess STACY, guitarist Allan Reuss (*b* 15 June '15, NYC), trumpeter Nate Kazebier (*b* 13 Aug. '12, Lawrence, Kansas; *d* 22 Oct. '69, Reno, Nevada), two others from the Goodman band plus Israel Crosby on bass; incl. beautiful 'Blues Of Israel'. By that time Goodman had sparked off the Swing Era; Krupa soon became a pop hero: the original model of the hair-tossing, gum-chewing, stick-flying flashy drummer. He featured in the Goodman small groups, was the star of hit 'Sing Sing Sing' (2-sided 12″ 78 interpolated 'Christopher Columbus'), played at Goodman's historic Carnegie Hall concert Jan. '38 and left a few weeks later to form his own band. Critics are divided about how good a drummer he was at this time; he certainly possessed little subtlety and the Goodman band often sounded leaden compared to its black models, at least on record, a fact for which Krupa must take some blame. But he was the one who took the drums out of their timekeeping role at the back of the band so that they could become a solo instrument; if a great many drum solos have been bad ones, that is hardly his fault. He himself improved; his own extrovert outfit '38-43 was popular, had about 20 hits (best known are 'Let Me Off Uptown' with vocal by Anita O'DAY and Roy ELDRIDGE, 'Knock Me A Kiss' (Eldridge)); other vocalists were Irene Daye, Johnny DESMOND. The band appeared in films *Some Like It Hot* '39, *Ball Of Fire* '41; in '43 he was framed on a marijuana charge (refused to pay off crooked cops) and served time in prison. He returned to Goodman that year, with Tommy DORSEY '44, formed band with strings which did not record because of musicians' union strike; led another band until '51 with Charlie VENTURA, arr. by Gerry MULLIGAN, others; appeared in films *George White's Scandals* '45, *Meet The Band* '47, *Make Believe Ballroom* '49; hits 'Chickery Chick', 'Boogie Blues' with O'Day; Ventura left to form a combo; other vocalists were Buddy Stewart, Bobby Scots (on hit 'Bonaparte's Retreat' '50). He toured with JATP early '50s, again '59; ran drum school NYC with Cozy COLE from '54; occasionally led combos, often with Ventura; reunions with Goodman incl. quartet LP '63, film *The Benny Goodman Story* and soundtrack LP '56; also appeared in *The Glenn Miller Story* '54; *The Gene Krupa Story* '59 with Sal Mineo is a Hollywood low point, one of the worst biopics ever made. He died of leukaemia. LPs on Verve with JATP; *Drummin' Man, Plays Gerry Mulligan Arrangements, Percussion King, Original Drum Battle* with Buddy RICH etc.; compilations by big band from Columbia Special Products, on Aircheck ('44-6); *World's Greatest Drummer* on Sunbeam ('52-61).

KURSAAL FLYERS UK pop group named after ride in Southend amusement park, formed '74 by Paul Shuttleworth (*b* 24 Dec. '47, London), vocals; Richie Bull (*b* 23 Oct. '48, Corringham, Essex), banjo; Will Birch (*b* 12 Sep. '48, London), drums; Vic Collins (*b* 10 Sep. '50, Rochford, Essex), pedal steel; Graeme Douglas (*b* 22 Jan. '50, Rochford), lead guitar; Dave Hatfield, bass. Spotted on London circuit by Jonathan KING, signed to his UL label. Each had pedigrees in semi-pro local bands (the Thomahawks, Surly Bird, etc); Bull had toured with USA C&W artists. By *Chocs Away* '75 Hatfield had left and Bull moved to bass. Songs by Birch (lyrics) and Douglas or Bull (music) were clever enough, but band couldn't make break to big halls; dry prod. of LP didn't help. *The Great Artiste* '76 fared not much better despite hit potential of 'Cruisin' For Love' and 'Hit Records'. Moved to CBS '76, teamed with prod. Mike BATT and hit with epic 'Little Does She Know' (no. 14 '76): when the balance had been found, trouble struck as Douglas departed for EDDIE AND THE HOT RODS (replaced by Barry Martin), forcing Birch to turn exclusively to Bull for music and losing several degrees of subtlety. Fine LP *Golden Mile* '76 remained. They switched to prod. Muff Winwood attempting to get a harder sound, but he was too busy to cut the whole album and the unnecessary *Five Live Kursaals* '77 came out instead. Collins quit to reform Thomahawk '77, replaced by John Wicks; Shuttleworth quit to go solo; Wicks and Birch formed Records, with limited success in USA; Martin formed label Making Waves. Band re-formed '85 to push compilation *In For A Spin*, compiled by Birch '83, issued by Edsel: the evidence (incl. unreleased Winwood-prod. tracks) shows classic '60s group born a decade too late. As motley a crew as ever seen on stage, with infl. from rock to folk, country and bluegrass, they were a delight live and a critical success, but didn't sell records. Birch is a house prod. for Stiff/Demon (Long Ryders '85).

KUTI, Fela Anikolapu (*b* Fela Ransome Kuti, 15 Oct. '38, Abeokuta, Nigeria) Singer, composer, bandleader, plays saxophone, trumpet, keyboards; a controversial politician in Nigeria who says he wants to run for president, probably the most successful dissident musician working today. Has fought for basic rights of ordinary people despite vilification and even imprisonment by the government; a hero to many Africans, he has became an international star, with over 50 politically pointed LPs. Strongly infl. in opposite directions by his Yoruban parents: father was Protestant missionary, son of Rev. J. J. Ransome Kuti; mother Funmilayo active in Nigerian nationalist movement. First musical venture came after being introduced by J. K. Braimah to Victor OLAIYA, whose brand of HIGHLIFE was fast becoming dominant: Kuti joined Olaiya's Cool Cats as a singer but carried on with studies, obtained a school certificate, worked in a government office for six months, persuaded his mother that music could be a full-time career, went to London's Trinity College of Music '58, studied theory and the trumpet for four years and formed his first band, Koola Lobitos with Braimah (in London to study law). Returned to Nigeria, worked briefly for Nigeria Broadcasting and played with reformed band music described as highlife jazz, releasing singles incl. 'Yeshe Yeshe', 'Mr Who Are You'. The Sierra Leonean soul singer Geraldo Pino arrived in Lagos '66-7 and created a big stir: Kuti flitted between Nigeria and Ghana for two years trying to define the direction of his music, finally announcing the launch of afro-beat in Lagos '68. Departing for the USA '69, where he spent 10 months, made single 'Keep Nigeria One' out of financial necessity more than sympathy with Federal government. The band played shows in L.A. but for Kuti it was a period of education; he read widely in black history, returned to Lagos to shake things up with a politicised afro-beat; formed co-operative compound in the Surulere suburb, later called the Kalakuta Republic; opened a club called the Shrine, changed the name of the band to Africa '70 and embarked on a series of albums, cautiously at first with *Fela's London Scene* '70; *Jeunko'ku, Open And Close, Live With Ginger Baker* '71; afro-beat classics *Shakara* and *Roforofo Fight* '72, *Gentleman* and *Afrodisiac* '73, *Alagbon Close* '74 followed by a purple patch of political music-making, 17 LPs in three years incl. *Expensive Shit, Noise For Vendor Mouth, Confu-*

sion, *Unnecessary Begging, Zombie, Yellow Fever, Kalakuta Show, Colonial Mentality* and *Opposite People*. His constant attacks on military corruption and social injustice .combined with the tight afro-beat of the band made him a hero throughout West Africa, but brought down the wrath of the government, who burned the Kalakuta Republic to the ground '77, destroying master tapes, throwing his mother out of a window, breaking her leg. He continued with albums *Shuffering And Shmiling* '78, then *Unknown Soldier, V.I.P. (Vagrants In Power), I.T.T. (International Thief Thief)*, all '79, the year of the return of civilian rule. He started his own political party, M.O.P. (Movement of the People), and continued attacking waste, greed and corruption, carrying the message abroad to Europe and the USA. By now he was an international celebrity and a mature musician, as well as a thorn in the side of successive Nigerian regimes, themselves doomed by endemic corruption in the Nigerian marketplace and successive traumas of international economics. Africa '70 grew to a troupe of 80 and recorded prolifically, incl. *Authority Stealing, Coffin For Head Of State* (when his mother died, her coffin was carried past soldiers' quarters), *Black President, Original Sufferhead, Live In Amsterdam, Perambulator, Army Arrangement*. The return of military government in Jan. '83 did not bode well; in Sep. '84 Kula was arrested on eve of USA tour, sentenced to five years' jail for alleged currency violations, but paroled in 18 months, partly owing to Amnesty International. Is highly regarded on the Continent but only a cult figure in UK, where his band, now called Egypt 80, a travelling troupe of 30 dancers and musicians (9-piece brass section) plus technicians, children etc., cannot afford to tour outside London. His long, carefully crafted songs make good use of musical dynamics, knit together with polyrhythmic percussion and guitars. First USA tour '86 (finally) incl. Amnesty benefit; he was given the Key to the City in Austin and Detroit; the mayor of Berkeley named 14 Nov. after him; at the end of the month he appeared in London and taped a studio segment for TV's *The Tube*. He said the government having passed a law forbidding anyone to use the word 'republic' to describe his home, he had built another house and threatened to call it 'Empire'. The album *Teacher Don't Teach Me Nonsense* was issued '87 on Mercury with Egypt 80.

KWELA African pop style emerging in South Africa c.'40, spreading to Malawi, Zambia and Zimbabwe '50s. Term may have been used in connection with a new Zulu vocal style called 'bombing', but by the early '50s was closely associated with penny-whistle street music, a simulated mixture of marabi and jazz. One source says it was named after police vans that looked for street gamblers; the penny-whistle players were used as covers for small gatherings where gambling was going on. Following mbaqanga and other styles its free exuberance won converts to jive, the term for easy fusions of Western and African pop in Johannesburg, which was popularised by Lemmy 'Special' Mabaso, who performed on streets and at local functions (discovered by promoters at age 10). The standard line-up was two penny-whistles, a home-made guitar and tea-chest bass. After 'Tom Hark' was written by Aaron Lerole, the term came to be used indiscriminately to describe any black township music; another leading exponent was saxist Spokes Mashiyane. Early examples can be heard in the soundtrack of the film *Come Back Africa* '58. It was soon exploited commercially but the music heard on records often bore little resemblance to the home-grown variety.

KWESKIN, Jim (*b* 18 July '40) Guitarist, singer, leader of Jim Kweskin Jug Band '60s. Raised in New England, worked in Cambridge, Mass. area; formed band '63 with Geoff Muldaur, Bill Keith (formerly banjo with Bill MONROE), others; later Maria D'Amato (married Muldaur, later solo star), Richard Greene (formerly with Monroe, later Blues Project, Muldaur, etc.), others. Played ragtime, bluesy goodtimey music which was an important component of the folk boom of the '60s. LPs on Vanguard incl. eponymous '63 debut, *Jug Band Music* '65, *Relax Your Mind* '66, *See Reverse Side For Title* '67; others on Reprise. Kweskin's later solo albums on Reprise; also *Lives Again, Side By Side* on Mountain Railroad.

KYSER, Kay (*b* James King Kern Kyser, 18 June '06, Rocky Mount, N.C.; *d* 23 Jul. '85, Chapel Hill, N.C.) Bandleader. Couldn't play or read a note of music. Fronted first band at U. of N.C. mid-'20s; led jazzish bands '20s, early '30s; switched to sweet style. Good summer spot at a Santa Monica hotel '34; recommended by Hal KEMP for residency at Chicago's Black Hawk restaurant '34-5; became popular through broadcasts. Began audience participation music quiz for slow Monday nights, at first Kay Kyser's Kampus Klass, eventually popular on radio as Kollege of Musical Knowledge. Comic singer Ish Kabibble (Merwyn Bogue) also played section trumpet, had novelty hits ('Three Little Fishies'), funny haircut like BEATLE 20 years early: he went solo late '40s, led big band L.A. '49, combo The Shy Guys '50s; sold real estate, retired to Hawaii. Kyser had singing song title gimmick: vocalist sang one line, band vamped while Kyser introduced number. Arranger George Duning later became film music composer (*Picnic* '56, *Star Trek* episodes on TV, much more). Band featured in films *That's Right, You're Wrong* '39, several more: *Swing Fever, Thousands Cheer, Stage Door Canteen*, all '43. Kyser volunteered for military but was rejected; played many hospitals, camps, defence plants, etc. Van Alexander (*b* 2 May '15, NYC) joined Duning on staff c.'42; had arranged Chick WEBB/Ella FITZGERALD hit 'A-Tisket, A-Tasket' '39, later led own band; sax section improved with addition of Herbie Haymer (*b* 24 July '15, Jersey City; *d* 11 Apr. '49, Santa Monica, in car crash), others; band's music improved, sometimes said to swing. From beginning of Billboard charts band had 20 top 10 hits '40-8, incl. 'Praise The Lord And Pass The Ammunition!', no. 2 '42; 'Jingle, Jangle, Jingle', no. 1 '42; also 'There Goes That Song Again', '45; Hoagy CARMICHAEL songs 'Ole Buttermilk Sky', 'The Old Lamplighter', both '46; 'Managua, Nicaragua', '47; 'Woody Woodpecker' (no. 1), Frank LOESSER's 'On A Slow Boat To China', both '48. Vocalists passing through incl. Jane Russell, later film star; Mike Douglas, later TV talk show host; Ginny Simms, others. Kyser was personable, popular front man; he and band wore academic robes while asking quaint questions in Kollege caper: if contestant didn't know the answer (especially a serviceman during WWII) Kyser would provide it. He allegedly once out-grossed Glenn MILLER, made $1 million in 1940. Band and quiz on TV '49-50; he then retired to home state, worked for Christian Science church.

L

LaBEEF, Sleepy (*b* Thomas Paulsley LaBeff, 20 July '35, Smackover, Ark.) Rockabilly guitarist and deep-voiced singer, probably the only rockabilly basso profundo. Family name originally LaBoeuf; he was the last of 10 children in farming family, got nickname at school because of droopy eyelid. Sang in church, heard hillbilly music and R&B on the radio, traded a rifle for a guitar at 14, and was one of those not astonished by Elvis PRESLEY: '. . . I knew exactly where he was coming from.' Went to Houston, later Nashville, working as a surveyor, singing informally in gospel groups; made records of current hits for Pappy Daily, who sold them over the radio; recorded for Daily's Starday label '56-8, Columbia '59, smaller labels. Made lower reaches of Billboard country chart with 'Every Day' '68 on Columbia, 'Black Land Farmer' '71 on Shelby Singleton's Plantation label; he was the only performer left on Sun when Singleton bought it from Sam Phillips. A seasoned performer who can throw anything from Muddy WATERS to straight country into a set and never leaves the audience dissatisfied, he never got much promotion or luck but is widely appreciated in Europe. Good profile in Peter Guralnick's *Lost Highway* '79. Albums: *Bull's Night Out, Rockabilly* '77, *Downhome Rockabilly* and *Western Gold* on Sun, then excellent *Electricity* and *It Ain't What You Eat It's The Way How You Chew It* on Rounder c.'80, latter with old friends like drummer D. J. Fontana, pianist Earl Poole Ball on some tracks (these two also worked with Elvis Presley and Johnny CASH). Some albums named and other compilations on Charly, Sonet, Ace, Rockhouse in UK. He was an impressive guest on Hank Wangford's *A To Z Of Country Music* on UK Channel 4 TV '87, followed by first live LP *Nothin' But The Truth* (recorded '85) on Rounder/Demon, made at his regular venue, Harpers Ferry, Allston, Mass.: flawed like many live albums by too many similar tempos, voice too far back in the mix.

LaBELLE, Patti (*b* Patricia Holt, 24 May '44, Philadelphia) Singer. Formed quartet Patti LaBelle and the Blue Belles from earlier groups, with Nona Hendryx (*b* 18 Aug. '45), Sarah Dash (*b* 24 May '42; both from Trenton, N.J.) and Cindy Birdsong; hits incl. top 20 'I Sold My Heart To The Junkman' '62; became trio when Birdsong left to go to the SUPREMES and had LP *Dreamer* '67 on Atlantic; managed by Vicki Wickham (who had prod. UK TV show *Ready Steady Go* on which they appeared), who changed their name to LaBelle, direction to more contemporary rock with Hendryx contributing more original songs. They backed Laura NYRO on *Gonna Take A Miracle* on Columbia; their own LPs incl. LPs *LaBelle* and *Moonshadow* '71-2 on WB, *Pressure Cookin'* on RCA; *Nightbirds* '74 went top 10 on Epic helped by no. 1 single 'Lady Marmalade'. *Phoenix* and *Chameleon* both charted '75-6; LaBelle went solo for *Patti LaBelle, Tasty, It's All Right With Me* and *Released* on Epic '77-80; switched to Philadelphia International for *The Spirit's In It* '81; *I'm In Love Again* '84 was a top 40 LP in the USA, her best solo showing; *Patti* '85 on Columbia made no. 72. She was a major contributor to hit *Beverly Hills Cop* soundtrack '84 (incl. dance hits '85 'Stir It Up', 'New Attitude'; (latter 2-sided hit, with instrumental 'Axel F' by Harold Faltermeyer). Appearance at Live Aid '85 was a high point of the show; her pilot variety show was broadcast on NBC '85. She made Home Box Office special '86; singles 'On My Own' (duet with ex-DOOBIE Michael McDonald) and 'Oh People' on MCA charted, as well as LP *The Winner In You*: it's about time this fine singer hit the big time.

LA COSTA (*b* La Costa Tucker, 12 Dec. '49, Snyder, Texas) Country singer, elder sister of Tanya Tucker. Worked in band Country Westerners with Tanya '68-70; worked as medical records technician; following Tanya's success signed with Capitol and had top 3 country hit with second release 'Get On My Love Train' '74. Further hits through '78; faded from the charts for a while but came back '82 with 'Love Take It Easy On Me' on Elektra. Her pleasant pop/country style was always overshadowed by Tanya. LPs incl. *With All My Love* '75 and *La Costa* '77 on Capitol.

LACY, Steve (*b* Steven Lackritz, 23 July '34, NYC) Soprano sax, composer. Began on clarinet, heard Sidney BECHET's '41 record of Duke ELLINGTON's 'The Mooche' and took up soprano, the only modern jazzman to concentrate entirely on the instrument and developing his own rough-edged tone; he probably infl. John COLTRANE to take it up. Began with dixieland groups: mysterious and legendary *The Complete Jaguar Sessions* on Fresco Jazz '86 reissues two 10" LPs from '54 by trumpeter Dick Sutton's Sextet with Lacy; *Cadence* says it illustrates close tie between trad. and avant-garde, especially in overall sound of the group and Frank Caputo's baritone sax. Lacy gave up other work to study and play with Cecil TAYLOR '56-7; then with Gil EVANS; with Thelonious MONK '60; played on Taylor's *In Transition* '55 with Buell NEIDLINGER, drummer Dennis Charles (on Transition, later on Blue Note); own first LP on Prestige '57 with Wynton KELLY, Neidlinger, Charles: *Soprano Today* (aka *Steve Lacy With Wynton Kelly* on other labels) incl. Thelonious MONK's 'Work', and Lacy's interest in Monk's music continued: he played it and returned to it out of love and just to see what happened (finding a similarity with the visual rhythm and proportion of artist Paul Klee); each Lacy visit to Monk was a new listening reward: LPs incl. *Steve Lacy Plays The Music Of Thelonious Monk* '58 on Prestige New Jazz, with Neidlinger, Elvin JONES, Mal WALDRON (reissue *Reflections* on Fantasy); with Roswell RUDD played Monk exclusively in NYC '62-5, album *Schooldays* '63 on Emanem; *Epistrophy* '69 on Byg with French sidemen (aka *Steve Lacy Plays Monk* on Affinity) and *Eronel* '79 on Italian Horo label (solo soprano); also unissued trio

takes '61 for Atlantic and 'Ask Me Now', a duet with Charlie ROUSE for 2-disc Monk tribute *That's The Way I Feel Now* '84 on A&M, version of 'Pannonica' on trio set *Disposability* '65 on Italian Vik label; came back with *Only Monk* '87 on Soul Note. Other early Lacy albums incl. *The Straight Horn Of Steve Lacy* '60 on Candid, *Evidence* '61 with Don CHERRY on Prestige. He played mostly in Europe from '65, with his own increasingly 'free' compositions becoming an artist brave enough to stand on the edge of music in total improvisation, like UK guitarist Derek BAILEY, Dutch drummer Han Bennink; recording prolifically on many labels, his labour of love always rewarding musically and resulting in increasing fame. Reunited with Rudd on *Trickles* '76 on Black Saint. Solo LPs incl. *Lapis* '71 on French Saravah label; *Solo* '72 on Emanem; *Stabs/Solo In Berlin* on Free Music, *Solo At Mandara*, *Torments (Solo In Kyoto)* all '75, last two made in Japan, on Japanese and French labels respectively; *Axieme* '75 (2 vols.) on Italian Red; *Steve Lacy* and *Chops* '76 on Quark, both made in Montreal; *Straws* '77 on Italian Cramps; *Clinkers* '77 and *Ballets* '80 on Hat labels; *Only Monk* '85 on Soul Note and *The Kiss* '86 on Lunatic (made in Japan, also incl. Monk tunes). Often worked with reedman Steve Potts: *Estilhaços – Live In Lisbon*, *The Gap* (in Paris), *Chops* (Zurich), *The Crust* (100 Club in London), *Scraps* (Paris) and *Flakes* (Rome), all '72-4; *Saxophone Special* '74 on Emanem made in London's Wigmore Hall with Bailey, Evan Parker, Trevor Watts and Potts on reeds; on 'Sops' they all played soprano (Watts *b* '39, Yorkshire; with John STEVENS a founder member of the Spontaneous Music Ensemble: LPs on Tangent, Emanem; *see* Bobby BRADFORD). Other LPs on HAT ART labels: *Stamps* '77, *The Way* (two discs by pianoless quartet with Irène Aebi on violin, like Mahler's *Das Lied* inspired by Chinese texts) and *Tips* '79, *Songs* '81, 4-part composition 'The 4 Edges' by the Steve Lacy Sextet '81, *Prospectus* '82, all with Potts; trio set *Capers* '79, duets *Herbe de l'Oubli*, *Snake-Out* and *Let's Call This* '81 with Waldron. Others with Potts: *Steve Lacy's Dreams* '75, *The Owl* '79, both on Saravah; *Raps* '77 on Adelphi, *Follies Live In Berlin* '77 on Free Music, *Points* '78 on Le Chant du Monde and *Troubles* '79 on Black Saint. Other LPs on various small European labels; contributed 'Roma' to *Amarcord Nino Rota* LP '81 on Hannibal; played with Bailey's group Company, on LPs *Company 4* '76 (duo), *5* '77 (with septet), both on Ictus. Also *Chirps* '85 on SAJ (duo with Evan Parker), sextet *The Condor* '85 on Soul Note, overdubbed *Outings* '86 on Izmez, *Hocus Pocus* '86 on Himalaya; duos *Deadline* '85 on Sound Aspects with Gumpert on piano, *Sempre Amore* '86 on Soul Note with Waldron (a revealing set of tunes by Ellington and Billy STRAYHORN), *One Fell Swoop* (quartet with Charles TYLER) and sextet *The Gleam* '86 on Silkheart. *Momentum* '87 on RCA's Novus label was his major-label debut, with his more-or-less regular sextet of Potts, Aebi (who vocalises and plays cello as well as violin), pianist Bobby Few, bassist Jean-Jacques Avinel, drummer Oliver Johnson. The wonder is not that he releases so many records but that they are of such a consistently high standard.

LADNIER, Tommy (*b* 28 May 1900, Florenceville, La.; *d* 4 June '39, NYC) Trumpet; one of the finest of his generation after Louis ARMSTRONG: it was Ladnier, not Louis, who had tuition from Bunk JOHNSON. Great solos on Fletcher HENDERSON sides '26-7; visited Europe several times with Sam WOODING, Noble SISSLE, etc.; backed singers Lovie AUSTIN, Alberta HUNTER; with Sidney BECHET in his Feetwarmers early '30s, then times were so bad that Becher and Ladnier operated a tailor shop together. He was 'rediscovered'; made only one session under his own name, on Bluebird (about a dozen titles made late '38 with Mezz MEZZROW; four by sextet incl. Bechet were issued as 'Tommy Ladnier and his Orchestra'). Played with Bechet at John HAMMOND's Spirituals To Swing concert Dec. '38; had heart attack in Mezzrow's flat: four days later Bechet invented 'Blues For Tommy' at Port of Harlem Jazzmen session for Blue Note.

LADYSMITH BLACK MAMBAZO African choral group formed on an amateur basis '65 in Ladysmith, S.A. Originally from Swaziland, now based in Durban, the members were at first drawn from the Shabalala and Mazibuko families, led by Joseph Shabalala.

His first group won prizes in *ngomabusuki* choir competitions, but he was not satisfied with the sound; the phrasing that made the group famous came to him in a dream: both freeflowing and strict, incredibly precise. He picked name meaning black axe of Ladysmith '73; they soon won so many prizes they were banned from competitions. Twelve members, eight or 10 on stage at a time; sung mostly in Zulu, also in English or Sotho, lyrics reflect everyday concerns and religious themes; style of unaccompanied harmony is called Mbube. First recorded on Mavuthela label (part of the Gallo company); 13 LPs have made them S.A.'s best selling group with sales over four million, incl. LPs *Ukusindiswa, Amabutho, Amaghawe* and *Indlela Yasezulwini*. First international album was *Induku Zethu* '83 on London-based Earthworks label; they toured Germany twice '85; late that year made lovely 'Homeless' with Paul SIMON for his transatlantic smash *Graceland* LP; *Ulwanule Oluncgwele* '86 on Shanachie in USA, others; Simon prod. their *Shaka Zulu* '87 on WB. All farm boys, their popularity at home is partly nostalgia for tribal simplicity; the sheer beauty of their music has brought international stardom: true simplicity as high art.

La FARO, Scott (*b* 3 Apr. '36, Newark, N.J.; *d* 6 July '61 in car crash near Geneva, N.Y.) Bassist. He was only 23 when he won a New Star Award in *Downbeat* critics survey; infl. Steve SWALLOW, Gary PEACOCK, other modernists. Recorded with Bill EVANS (*Portrait In Jazz* '59, *Explorations* '61, *Sunday At The Village Vanguard, Waltz For Debby*, all on Riverside; *More From The Vanguard* on Mainstream, last three all from same '61 session). Also recorded with Victor FELDMAN on Contemporary, Pat Moran (pianist, *b* Helen Mudgett, 10 Dec. '34, Enid, Okla.) on Audio Fidelity, Booker LITTLE '60 on Time/Bainbridge/Island (*The Legendary Quartet Album*).

LAGRENE, Bireli (*b* c.'66, France) Guitarist of enormous talent; a Gypsy and inevitably compared to Django REINHARDT. LPs *Routes To Django* and *15* '82, *Down In Town* '83 on Antilles; *Bireli Swing 81* released '83 on German Austrophon Diepholz. First LP already issued on CD by the Japanese; he concentrated on playing rather than records for a while, then broke out at the ripe old age of 21, and away from the Django groove, on West German Jazzpoint label '86: on *Bireli Lagrene* he plays six- and 12-string guitars with guests Larry CORYELL, bassist Miroslav Vitous; on *Stuttgart Aria* he plays electric guitar, with Jaco PASTORIUS, four others incl. synths. First Blue Note album *Inferno* '88. He can explore everything with his prodigious technique; he will be around for a long time.

LAINE, Cleo (*b* Clementina Dinah Campbell, 28 Oct. '27, Southall, Middlesex) UK singer; also actress. Her father came to England with West Indian Expeditionary Force during WWI, married English girl. She was an extra in film *Thief Of Bagdad* '40 (which also featured Alberta HUNTER); first pro job '51, joined John DANKWORTH combo '52, then with his big band '53; married him '58 and left the band to branch out, though they continued to work together, from '72 in USA and to increasing acclaim. Her remarkable range was extended by Dankworth's arrangements, coaxing up the top end; some tried to type her as a jazz singer, which she probably is not, but the beauty of her voice and the flawlessness of her ear has often left critics gasping for superlatives. She has performed '20th-century lieder', settings of Shakespeare, and Schoenberg's *Pierrot Lunaire* in her own interpretive way; the latter event left some purists outraged (but Schoenberg, after all, was in part commenting on the cabaret tradition). She recorded Walton's *Façade* (with Annie Ross); 2-disc *Cleo Laine Live At Carnegie Hall* '73 on RCA and *Smilin' Through* '82 (prod. by Dankworth, Dudley Moore on piano) on CBS were nominated for Grammies; *Best Friends* '78 with guitarist John Williams, *Sometimes When We Touch* '80 with flautist James Galway (both on RCA) were hits. Other LPs: *A Lover And His Lass* '76 with Dankworth on Esquire, *Cleo* '78 on Arcade; *Day By Day* '74 on Buddah; *A Beautiful Thing* '74, *Born On A Friday* '76, 2-disc *Porgy & Bess* with Ray CHARLES '76, *Gonna Get Through* '80, all on RCA; *Feel The Warm* '76 on EMI; Dankworth's *Collette* '80 on RCA/Evolution; *The Incomparable Cleo Laine* '80 on Black Lion; *This Is Cleo Laine* '81 on EMI; *Let The Music Take You* '83 on CBS with Williams; also recitals, compilations etc.: *Word Songs* '78 on RCA, *Platinum Collection* '81 on Cube/PRT, *Off The Record* '84 on Sierra/WEA, all 2-disc sets; plus *Shakespeare And All That Jazz* and *Woman Talk* on Fontana, *Day By Day* on Stanyan, *I Am A Song* on RCA, *In Retrospect* with Dankworth on Polydor, tracks on *John Dankworth 1953-9* (EMI reissue), etc. Projects in '87 incl. *Cleo Sings Sondheim* on RCA, then songs of the unique American composer Charles Ives. A versatile entertainer, she played the lead in the Sandy Wilson musical *Valmouth* '58, sang in Brecht-WEILL *Seven Deadly Sins* at Edinburgh Festival '61, appeared in film *The Roman Spring Of Mrs Stone* '61, played in London revival of Jerome KERN's *Showboat* '71-3, in '77 *Cleo On Broadway* and Jubilee Royal Variety Show at the London Palladium, etc.

LAINE, Denny (*b* Brian Hines, 29 Oct. '44, Jersey) UK singer/songwriter. Fronted Denny and the Diplomats, Midlands group formed '62 which incl. Roy Wood, Bev Bevan (later MOVE); left to join MOODY BLUES, which incl. members of Diplomats' rivals Gary Levene and the Avengers, El Riot and the Rebels. First single flopped (Laine/Mike Pinder co-written 'Lose Your Money'); Laine's reading of US blues singer Bessie Banks' 'Go Now' was no. 1 UK '65, top 10 USA and charted worldwide. Followup proved problematical; Laine left '66, formed Denny Laine's Electric String Band with Andy Leigh, bass; Viv Prince, drums; violinists Angus Anderson, John Stein; cellists Haflidr Halynisson and Clive Gillinson: Deram singles flopped despite support from DJ John Peel on his *Top Gear* show; Colin BLUNSTONE covered 'Say You Don't Mind' for '70s hit; use of amplified strings undoubtedly infl. ELECTRIC LIGHT ORCHESTRA. Laine joined Move renegade Trevor Burton to form Balls, changing lineup incl. Steve Gibbons, vocals; Alan White (later YES), drums; Richard Tandy (later ELO), keyboard; Jackie LOMAX, guitar, vocals; Mike Kellie (ex-SPOOKY TOOTH): promising group lasted only '69-early '71, made no albums. He concurrently worked in Ginger BAKER's ill-fated Air Force, appearing on both that group's LPs. Paul

McCARTNEY had admired Laine since 'Go Now'; snapped him up as right-hand man, rhythm guitarist, harmony vocalist in Wings. He served in that group through '70s, soloing on stage with 'Go Now' or 'Say You Don't Mind', co-writing mega-hit 'Mull Of Kintyre' with boss. McCartney's drug bust in Japan and John LENNON's murder '80 combined to make touring unlikely; Laine left Apr. '81; assisted (now ex-) wife Jo Jo in her singing career. Solo LPs remarkable few: *Aah Laine* '73, *Holly Days* '76 (collection of Buddy HOLLY songs, of which McCartney owns copyright), *Japanese Tears* '80; two LPs on President label '85: *Hometown Girls* and retrospective *Weep For Love* with Wings on title track. Having sold his share of 'Mull Of Kintyre' to McCartney he declared bankruptcy '86.

LAINE, Frankie (*b* Frank Paul LoVecchio, 30 Mar. '13, Chicago) Pop singer with lots of style, big baritone voice able to fill halls without a microphone: one of the most popular of late '40s-early '50s. Worked dance marathons during Depression; replaced Perry COMO in Freddy Carlone band in Cleveland '37; to West Coast mid-'40s, also working at songwriting. Some fame on Al Jarvis radio show '45 (Jarvis was an important West Coast DJ: invented 'Make Believe Ballroom' concept early '30s, helped touch off Swing Era by plugging Benny GOODMAN records). Successful gig at Billy Berg's club L.A. '46 led to Mercury contract; around 70 hits '47-69 began with 'That's My Desire' (with Manny Klein combo): 'That Lucky Old Sun', 'Mule Train', 'The Cry Of The Wild Goose' (song by Terry Gilkyson) were all no. 1; went to Columbia '51 and 'Jezebel'/'Rose, Rose, I Love You' with Mitch MILLER saw both sides in top 3. Duets with Jo STAFFORD incl. Hank WILLIAMS' 'Hey Good Lookin' ' (top 10 '51), 'Way Down Yonder In New Orleans'; with Doris DAY 'Sugarbush' (top 10 '52); with the FOUR LADS 'Rain, Rain, Rain'; with Jimmy Boyd 'Tell Me A Story'. 'Jealousy' was no. 2 hit '51; Oscar-winning 'High Noon' ('Do Not Forsake Me') film theme was no. 5 '52 (Tex RITTER sang in soundtrack); inspirational 'I Believe' was no. 2 '53, another 2-sided hit with Williams's 'Your Cheatin' Heart'; he also reached no. 21 with Hank's 'Tonight We're Settin' The

Woods On Fire' '52. 'Hey Joe!' '53 was no. 6 hit. He was usually accompanied by Paul WESTON on records, often with his own accompanist Carl Fisher on piano. 'Moonlight Gambler' '56, was no. 3, 'Love Is A Golden Ring' (with the Easy Riders) at no. 10 '57 was his last hit until no. 51 entry '63 with 'Don't Make My Baby Blue'; switched to ABC Paramount for several more incl. three in top 40. Remained popular in TV, clubs. He always had good taste in accompaniment: Klein had played trumpet with Goodman, was described by Joe WILDER as 'one of the great trumpet players of all time'; Laine's LP *Jazz Spectacular* incl. Buck CLAYTON (still available from Columbia Special Products, as is *Too Marvelous For Words*). Fisher (*b* 9 Apr. '12, L.A.; *d* 28 Mar. '54, Sherman Oaks, Cal.) worked with Pee Wee HUNT '46; wrote 'We'll Be Together Again' with Laine '45 (Laine's excellent lyric incl. line 'Don't let the blues make you bad'), others; helped Laine break his act and stayed with him through success. Boyd (*b* '39) was a child star who had no. 1 hit 'I Saw Mommy Kissing Santa Claus' '52; also no. 25 duet '53 with Rosemary CLOONEY on 'Dennis The Menace'. Laine's other LPs for Columbia incl. *Command Performance*, *Rockin'*, *You Are My Love*; *Frankie Laine on MCA/USA has ABC stuff*; LP on Hindsight has '47 tracks with Fisher orchestra; *Greatest Hits* compilations always in print.

LAKE, Oliver (*b* '44, Marianna, Ark.) Alto, tenor, soprano saxes, flute, also synthesiser. Grew up in St Louis; founder member of BAG (Black Artists Group). Member of WORLD SAXOPHONE QUARTET, has led own Jump Up funk-reggae combo since '80: *Oliver Lake & Jump Up* and *Plug It* on Gramavision, then *Dancevision* '86 on Blue Heron; also his own uncompromising post-DOLPHY jazz albums: *Heavy Spirits* on Arista; *Holding Together, Prophet, Clevont Fitzhubert* and *Expandable Language* '84 on Black Saint; *Gallery* '87 on Gramavision, with bassist Fred Hopkins, pianist Geri Allen, drummer Pheeron akLaff, trumpeter Rasul Sidik on one track; then *Impala* '88.

LAMBERT, Donald (*b* '04, Princeton, N.J.; *d* 8 May '62, Newark) Fine left-handed pianist in East Coast stride style (with strong beat emphasising tenths in the bass; *see*

James P. JOHNSON, Fats WALLER). Infl. by Paul Seminole (*b* '04, *d* Asbury Park, N.J., '32) with whom he did a double act. Lambert was not ambitious, disliked New York, preferring neighbourhood bars in New Jersey where he could play as and what he pleased; but Eubie BLAKE described him as one of the greatest and even Art TATUM was alleged to be unwilling to follow him. Made four sides on Bluebird '41, jazzing the classics; albums (all '59-62 material, some privately made at Wallace's Tavern): *Giant Stride* on Jazzology, *Harlem Stride Classics 1960-62* on Pumpkin, *Meet The Lamb* on IAJRC (International Association Of Jazz Record Collectors, Islington, Ontario).

LANCE, Major (*b* 4 Apr. '42, Chicago) Soul/R&B singer, a contemporary of Percy MAYFIELD and Otis Leavill, who helped to found a Chicago soul sound with 11 Hot 100 entries '63-5 on Okeh, of which the biggest were 'The Monkey Time' and 'Um, Um, Um, Um, Um, Um' '63-4 (both top 10 USA); Wayne FONTANA and the Mindbenders had UK hit with the latter and their cover was also a USA hit later in the same year. He had several more hits in the soul chart '66-71; left CBS '68 and recorded for Dakar, Curtom, Volt, WB, Playboy, others; 'Stay Away From Me (I Love You Too Much)' on Curtom '70 was no. 13 soul, 67 pop. His delightfully deft approach is out of fashion; hits are collected on *Monkey Time* (Edsel UK).

LAND, Harold (*b* Harold De Vance Land, 18 Feb. '28, Houston, Texas) Tenor sax. Grew up on West Coast; self-taught; gigged at Creole Palace with Froebel Brigham on trumpet, drummer Leon Petties; with others they made four tracks as 'Harold Land All Stars' session '49 issued on Savoy. He played with Max ROACH-Clifford BROWN Quintet '54-5 (LPs on EmArcy or Trip), Curtis COUNCE '57-8 on Contemporary and Dootoo (*Exploring The Future* now on Boplicity); also played on a never-issued session '59 with trombonist Frank Rosolino, rediscovered and issued on Specialty '86; also with Gerald WILSON. The period's West Coast black jazz scene was undervalued because of the prominence of the white 'cool jazz' genre, but Carl PERKINS, Hampton HAWES, Counce, Land, others (to say

nothing of Charles MINGUS, Ornette COLEMAN and Eric DOLPHY, though they made their reputations elsewhere) are evidence that hotter stuff was going on. Quintet set on Contemporary '58 (now *Harold In The Land Of Jazz* in Fantasy's Original Jazz Classics series) was his next LP under his own name; then his most famous: *The Fox*, made '59 in L.A. with Elmo HOPE, Dupree BOLTON, Herbie Lewis on bass, Frank Butler, drums; originally on Hifijazz and long out of print, reissued on Contemporary '69 it lived up to legendary reputation: bop with lyricism, crystalline heat. More LPs: *West Coast Blues!* with Wes MONTGOMERY and *Eastward Ho! Harold Land In New York* with Kenny DORHAM, both '60 and originally on Jazzland; *Take Aim* '60 on Blue Note (quintet with Petties); Atlantic LP '61 with Red MITCHELL, Petties, Carmell Jones (trumpet; *b* '36, Kansas City; moved to Europe '65); *Jazz Impressions Of Folk Music* '63 on Imperial with Jones. Land also played on Jones's *Business Meetin'* '62 on Pacific Jazz (nonet tracks with Bud SHANK, Leroy Vinnegar, arr. by Wilson; quintet items with Gary PEACOCK). A Cadet LP '68 with Bobby HUTCHERSON was followed by *Choma* with Hutcherson on Mainstream early '70s, incl. son Harold C. Land on keyboards (*b* 25 Apr. '50, San Diego; has recorded with Wayne Henderson on Atlantic, etc.; Lands father and son play with Wilson orchestra); *Mapenzi* '77 on Concord Jazz (co-led with Blue MITCHELL: Land played on Mitchell LPs on RCA c.'75, Impulse '77); *Live At Junk* '80 made in Tokyo; *Xocia's Dance* '81 on Muse with Hutcherson, Oscar Brashear, Billy HIGGINS etc. Land also plays on Hutcherson LPs on Blue Note, etc. A fine musician who has not achieved the fame he deserves.

LANE, Christy (*b* Eleanor Johnstone, Peoria, Ill.) Country singer. Sang in her teens in local clubs; married Lee Stoller '59 and raised children. Urged on by her husband, she took up music when the children were older; worked in clubs, state fairs, radio; he formed LS label in Madison, Tenn. and she eventually made country charts with 'Tryin' To Forget About You' and 'Let Me Down Easy' '77. Named best new female artist by ACM '78; signed with UA '79; made breakthrough with TV-advertised inspirational album *One Day At A Time* '82 (title track was '81 hit). Albums incl. *Christy . . . Is The Name* '77, *Love Lies* '78 on LS; *Simple Little Words* '79, *Ask Me To Dance* '80, *Fragile – Handle With Care* '82; also *Amazing Grace*, *At Her Best* and *Footprints In The Sand* on EMI labels.

LANG, Eddie (*b* Salvatore Massaro, 25 Oct. '02, Philadelphia; *d* 26 Mar. '33, NYC) Guitarist; one of the best and a legend of early jazz. His father made fretted instruments; violinist Joe VENUTI was a school friend; Lang began on violin as a child. Worked in restaurants and variety from '18; joined Mound City Blue Blowers and went to Europe with them '24; already famous, prolifically recording from '25. With Venuti '26, then they both went to Roger Wolfe KAHN's band, Adrian ROLLINI's big band '27, Paul WHITEMAN '29-30 incl. film *King Of Jazz*. Again with Kahn '32, worked as accompanist for Bing CROSBY; died of complications following tonsillectomy. He played on virtually all of Venuti's small-group sides; as Ed Lang and his Orchestra he made septet sides with Tommy and Jimmy DORSEY and big band sides with Hoagy CARMICHAEL on piano, one with vocal by Mildred BAILEY, all '29; with J. C. Johnson on piano, King OLIVER, Lonnie JOHNSON and Carmichael on percussion as Blind Will Dunn's Gin Bottle Four. His most intimate recordings were among the most sought-after of collector's items until reissued in the LP era: duets with Venuti (accompanied on piano by Frank Signorelli), guitar solos (usually accompanied by Arthur Schutt, Rube Bloom or Signorelli), guitar duets: two sides with Carl Kress and (as Blind Willie Dunn) 10 with Lonnie Johnson. *Virtuoso* and *Violin Jazz* on Yazoo have the solos and duets with Venuti, Kress and Johnson; two volumes of Lang and Johnson, one of Lang and Venuti on Australian Swaggie label are the best compilations. Kress (*b* 20 Oct. '07, Newark, N.J.; *d* 10 June '65, Reno, Nevada) also duetted with Dick McDonough, George Barnes; played banjo in trio '60 with Clarence Hutchenrider (*see* CASA LOMA ORCHESTRA).

LANIN, Lester (*b* 26 Aug. '11) Society bandleader and band contractor; brothers Sam and Howard in the same business; Lester became more famous in '50s because of LPs on Epic, Mercury etc. now long out of print. Provided strict tempo dance music at every presidential inaugural ball since Eisenhower, also in Europe incl. UK Royal weddings; Elizabeth II once allegedly changed the date of a party because Lanin was already booked. Benny GOODMAN, T. & J. DORSEY, Ralph FLANAGAN, Carmen CAVALLARO, many others played Lanin gigs years ago; he was still active mid-'80s.

LANZA, Mario (*b* Alfred Arnold Cocozza, 31 Jan. '21, Philadelphia, Pa.; *d* 7 Oct. '59). Singer; a tenor of operatic quality who never appeared on the stage: he got a late start and probably lacked self-discipline, but was extremely popular in the '50s. Studied while working as a piano mover; sang in service shows while in the military; worked his way up to the Hollywood Bowl and was a hit in film *That Midnight Kiss* with Kathryn Grayson. Other films: *Toast Of New Orleans* '50 (soundtrack single 'Be My Love' was no. 1 '50), *The Great Caruso* '51 ('Vesta La Giubba' from *Pagliacci*, an international best-seller for Caruso in '04 and '07, was a no. 21 hit for Lanza; 'The Loveliest Night Of The Year' was a no. 3 hit: adapted from 'Over The Waves', an 1888 waltz by Juventino P. Rosa, words by Paul Francis Webster and arr. by Irving AARONSON), *Because You're Mine* '52 (title song was top 10 hit), *Serenade* '56, *The Seven Hills Of Rome* '58, *For The First Time* '59. His voice was dubbed for actor Edmund Purdom in '54 film of *The Student Prince* ('24 show by Sigmund ROMBERG and Dorothy Donnelly ran for 608 performances); the soundtrack LP was a lovely album, but a casualty of hi-fi: it was remade in stereo by Lanza when he was eating himself to death and the perfectly good original was withdrawn. Other hits were 'Because' '51, Rimsky-Korsakov's 'Song Of India' '53, 'Drink, Drink, Drink' from *Student Prince*. All the soundtrack LPs were best-sellers, several incl. *Student Prince* at no. 1; also Xmas LP '59 and *Lanza Sings Caruso Favorites* '60; *I'll Walk With God* '62 also charted. Some are still in print, plus compilations such as 5-disc *The Collection* on RCA/UK. 'Be My Love' was written by Nicholas Brodsky, with words by Sammy CAHN, and nominated for an Academy award.

LA PORTA, John (*b* 1 Apr. '20, Philadelphia, Pa.) Reeds, composer, teacher. Played with Woody HERMAN, Charles MINGUS ('54 sides with Mingus on Savoy, Period have been widely reissued, bootlegged); contemporary classical with Leonard BERNSTEIN, Igor Stravinsky. Albums incl. appearances in *Anthropology* on Spotlight, *Rare Broadcast Performances* on Jazz Anthology (both airchecks from late '40s with Lennie TRISTANO, others); quintet LPs '54 on Mingus's Debut label; an LP made in Venezuela '56 with local musicians and *The Clarinet Artistry Of John La Porta* '57, with trio tracks on one side, a Brahms sonata on the other, both on Fantasy; and a quartet LP with Ron CARTER on Everest '58. He joined Bostons's Berklee School (later College) of Music, from '62 in charge of instrumental performance of students. Has published books through Berklee as well as album *Berklee Saxophone Quartet*.

LARKINS, Ellis (*b* 15 May '23, Baltimore, Md.) Pianist; highly regarded especially as an accompanist: a favourite of every singer he has worked with, his excellent ear allowing him to offer unusual sympathy to an interpretation. His father was a janitor who played violin in a local orchestra; he studied at Juilliard '40, played in NYC clubs '40s-50s; accompanied Mildred BAILEY on Majestic, played with Coleman HAWKINS and Dicky WELLS on Signature in the '40s; in the '50s he accompanied Larry ADLER, Joe WILLIAMS; with Ella FITZGERALD (*Ella Sings Gershwin* on Decca), Chris CONNOR (*Sings Lullabies Of Birdland* on Bethlehem); with Ruby BRAFF on Bethlehem and Vanguard (*Two By Two: Ruby And Ellis Play Rodgers & Hart*); own albums on Decca: *Manhattan At Midnight Blue & Sentimental, Soft Touch*. Left performing for studio work, came back in '70s: *The Grand Reunion* '72 with Braff on Chiaroscuro, *Ellis Larkins* on Antilles, *Smooth One* '77 on Classic Jazz (made in Paris), *Swingin' For Hamp* '79 on Concord Jazz (with bass, drums, singer Tony Middleton). Also with Sylvia Sims and own LP *Plays The Bacharach And McKuen Songbook* on Stan KENTON's Stanyan label; 2-disc *Ella Fitzgerald Live At Carnegie Hall* '73 on Columbia; *Stardust* with Sonny STITT on Prestige, etc.

LaROSA, Julius (*b* 2 Jan. '30, Brooklyn, NY) Singer. Joined US Navy '47; sang in Navy clubs to get out of boring jobs. Arthur GODFREY heard him in Pensacola, Fla. '50; he joined Godfrey's radio show Nov. '51, then the TV show; he got thousands of fan letters a week, his light baritone and boyish charm part of 'all the little Godfreys'; he had hits on Archie BLEYER's Cadence label '53-5, of which the biggest were 'Anywhere I Wander' (no. 4 early '53, from film *Hans Christian Andersen*) and 'Eh Cumpari', a Sicilian song similar to 'Old MacDonald Had A Farm' with instruments instead of animals: charted in September, reached no. 2, sold a million helped by Bleyer's charming arr. and good recorded sound. Since his star was rising he hired himself an agent and was fired on the air by Godfrey, who was a tyrant ('That was Julie's swan song. . .') The press criticised Godfrey, 'and what did I do but go and apologise to him for what was happening – guilty because I had done what Daddy didn't want me to do! I now understand that he was an imperfect man . . .' Had a few more hits on Cadence, then RCA '56-8; film *Let's Rock* (aka *Keep It Cool*) '58 with Paul ANKA, DANNY & THE JUNIORS was a misguided attempt to make him into a teen idol. He continued learning his trade in clubs and is a highly regarded vocalist, described by Gene LEES as 'the most brilliant member of the SINATRA school', with excellent intonation and regard for the lyrics. A success in Las Vegas '68, then a popular DJ at WNEW radio in NYC until '77 when the station changed hands; on tour he does a big commercial show and a smaller, hipper show for other clubs. LP *It's A Wrap!* '84 on Audiophile with Loonis McGlohon Group (pianist/ accompanist); LaRosa also admires pianist Dave MCKENNA.

LASHA, Prince (*b* William B. Lasha, 10 Sep. '29, Fort Worth, Texas) Flute, composer; also reeds. Surname pron. La*shay*. Childhood friend of Ornette COLEMAN; they worked together '40s; he went to West Coast, worked with alto saxophonist Sonny Simmons: they recorded *The Cry* '62, *Firebirds* '67, both on Contemporary; *Firebirds Vol. 3* '77 on Birdseye (live at Monterey Jazz Festival), 'Journey To Zoar' c.'80 on Enja, last three with Bobby HUTCHERSON,

Buster Williams on bass (*b* 17 Apr. '42, Camden, N.J.), Charles Moffett. *Search For Tomorrow: Firebirds Vol. 2* '74 (live at Berkeley Jazz Festival) was made with different band incl. Ron CARTER: Enja 'Zoar' LP is also called *Search For Tomorrow* in USA Schwann catalogue. *Firebirds Live At Berkeley Jazz Festival* '77 on Birdseye with the regular group, except Simmons replaced by Hadley Caliman (*b* 12 Jan. '32, Idabel, Okla.; own LPs on Mainstream); *Firebirds Featuring Webster Armstrong* '83 on Daagnim, a different group again featuring the vocalist. Lasha also made a CBS LP in London '66 with octet incl. Stan TRACEY; quartet LP *Inside Story* '65 on Enja with Herbie HANCOCK, Cecil McBEE and drummer Jimmy Lovelace. Simmons (*b* Huey Simmons, 4 Aug. '33, Sicily Island, La.) grew up in Oakland; also recorded with Elvin JONES, Eric DOLPHY; own LPs on Contemporary, ESP, Arhoolie. Drummer Moffett (*b* 11 Sep. '29, Fort Worth) worked with Coleman, Sonny ROLLINS; his sons are also musicians; own LPs: *The Gift* '69 on Savoy, self-prod. *The Charles Moffett Family* c.'74 on LRS Records. Charnett Moffett (*b* c. '67) is an up-and-coming bassist: recorded with Wynton MARSALIS, Tony WILLIAMS, Frank LOWE, Mulgrew MILLER etc., first album as leader *Nett Mann* '87 on Blue Note.

LAST, James (*b* 17 Apr. '29, Bremen, Germany) Leader of big cabaret/show band, supplying posh middle-of-the-road dance music for a huge audience. Studied piano '39, bass at music school '43; voted best bassist in German jazz poll '50, '51, '52; joined Northwest German Radio Orchestra '55, began arranging for radio '56, first LP *Non-Stop Dancing* '65 discovered 26 hit songs in 90-second bits for continuous dancing. Wrote hit 'Games That Lovers Play' ('Eine Ganze Nacht' in German; English words by Larry Kusick and Eddie Snyder recorded' by Eddie FISHER and Wayne NEWTON). Only three LPs (on Polydor) have reached top 200 in USA, but Continental popularity is phenomenal; he had four LPs in UK charts simultaneously '67: 52 hit albums in UK '67-86 (second only to Elvis PRESLEY) incl. *James Last Goes Pop, Polka Party, Golden Memories, Violins In Love,* many volumes of *Non-Stop Danc-*

ing, Classics Up To Date, etc. Made an LP with Astrud Gilberto '86 in Florida. Touring personnel of 60 people (17 nationalities) incl. 46 musicians (all American vocalists); shows sell out with no advertising. As with Lawrence WELK band on USA TV in '50s, slickness should not be undervalued; good musicians can play anything: a German *Show Express* programme seen on Anglia TV UK early '87 incl. Kris KRISTOFFERSON's 'Me And Bobby McGee': excellent small vocal group, good brass writing and playing, first-class rock drumming would be an improvement on most of today's pop.

LASWELL, Bill Bassist, producer. Gigged in Detroit mid-'70s, plays with idiosyncratic improvising groups like Material, Massacre, Curlew, etc. on various labels. Not into showing off dexterity as a performer, but the bass itself: infl. by reggae. Own LPs: *Baselines* '82 on Rough Trade UK/Elektra USA, with drummers Ronald Shannon Jackson, Phillip Wilson plus many other sounds *Praxis* on Celluloid; *Hear No Evil* 88 on Venture/Virgin with international cast. Toured Japan, Germany with Last Exit, quartet with Jackson, Peter Brötzmann on sax, Sonny Sharrock on guitar (*b* 27 Aug. '40, Ossining, NY; Sharrock is one of the only jazzmen using steel guitar, since his days with Herbie MANN '67-73; also recorded with Wayne SHORTER '69, Miles DAVIS '70; own LPs incl. *Black Woman* on Vortex, *Paradise* '74 on Atco with his wife Linda). Last Exit's eponymous LP of furious fusion on Enemy '86 followed by *The Noise Of Trouble/Live In Tokyo* '87 with Akira Sakata added on reeds; both got five stars in *Downbeat*; also live fragments in *Cassette Recordings 87* on Enemy. Sharrock's *Seize The Rainbow* on Enemy incl. two bassists (Laswell and Melvyn Gibbs), two drummers (Abe Speller and Pheeroan akLaff). Laswell also made duo with Brötzmann *Low Life* on Celluloid; hit the big time as producer with Herbie HANCOCK's *Future Shock* '83 incl. hit 'Rockit'; also *Sound System* '84. Recording sessions are well planned, but the music is not written down: 'The people who write it out *sound* like they wrote it out, and sound like they're reading it when they play.' He erased Fela KUTI's sax from *Army Arrange-*

ments, substituting organ parts ('The fact is, Fela can't play sax') but works for the artist rather than the record label: the sound on radio is the sound of money; 'I've never actually done a record for money,' etc. but perhaps his studio sound is only in advance of the noise on radio: '. . . I never need songs. I think it's a primitive, old-fashioned format. The only interesting thing in the last 50 years is noise – the sound of technology.' Other prod. incl. *She's The Boss* (Mick Jagger) *Mr Heartbreak* (Laurie ANDERSON), *Electric Africa* (Manu DIBANGO), *Starpeace* (Yoko Ono), Nona Hendryx on RCA; played on and co-prod. James Blood ULMER's *America – Do You Remember The Love?* '86 on Blue Note. Having acquired reputation as drum machine expert, used star flesh and blood on *Album* '86 by PUBLIC IMAGE LTD, but sleeve lists no personnel; he'd like the question to be whether it's any good, not who plays on it. (Quotes from interviews with Bill Milkowski in *Downbeat*, Vivien Goldman in *The Observer*.)

LATEEF, Yusef (*b* William Evans, '21, Chattanooga, Tenn.) Reeds; also composer, teacher. Began on alto sax in high school in Detroit, then tenor, later exploring oboe, various flutes, making some himself. With Lucky MILLINDER in NYC '46, others; Dizzy GILLESPIE '49; formed a combo in Detroit '55; back to NYC with quartet '60; with Charles MINGUS '60-1, OLATUNJI '61-2, then Cannonball ADDERLEY for two years. Also a painter; published *Yusef Lateef's Flute Book Of The Blues* (2 vols.), other books of arrangements and improvisations. Strong Middle-Eastern infl. almost from the beginning; he was soon one of the first to object to being categorised as jazz artist, preferring to consider music as a whole. Prolific records began on Savoy '57: LPs *Jazz And The Sounds Of Nature* and *Prayer To The East*, two other sets in various issues as *Jazz For Thinkers, Stablemates, Morning, Jazz Moods*; Prestige/New Jazz session same year issued as *The Sounds Of Yusef* and *Other Sounds* (reissued as *Expressions*). *Yusef Lateef At Cranbrook* (Academy of Art in Detroit) '58 on Argo followed by *The Fabric Of Jazz* and *The Dreamer* on Savoy, *Cry! Tender* on Prestige/New Jazz, all '59. Quintets *Contemplation* on Vee Jay with Nat ADDERLEY and Sam JONES; *Lost*

In Sound on Charlie Parker, Reactivation, several other labels; *Three Faces Of Yusef Lateef* and larger group *The Centaur And The Phoenix* on Mainstream/Riverside, all '60. Quartets *Eastern Sounds* and *Into Something* '61 on Prestige labels followed by Impulse LPs incl. *The Live Sessions, Live At Pep's* (Lounge, Philadelphia), *The Golden Flute*, others '63-6, then on Atlantic for four LPs '67-9, *The Gentle Giant* '74, 2-disc *10 Years Hence* '75, *The Doctor Is In . . . And Out* '76; *Autophysiophysic* '77 on CTI, *In Nigeria* '83 on Landmark. Many reissues on Prestige, Savoy, Mainstream, MCA (*Live Session* from Impulse) incl. 2-disc sets as well as original formats.

LATTIMORE, Harlan (*b* '08, Cincinnati, Ohio) Singer. Mother was an operatic soprano; worked at WLW radio Cincinnati, had residency in a Chicago theatre, returned to WLW, worked with Don REDMAN from '32. Columbia records that year issued as Harlan Lattimore and his Connie's Inn Orchestra; subsequent sides (mostly on Brunswick) as Don Redman and his Orchestra. His pleasant, gently swinging light baritone was used as a foil against Redman's patter on 'I Heard', the band's furious swinging on 'Tea For Two'; he also sang on 'Got The South In My Soul', 'That Blue-Eyed Baby From Memphis', etc. Left music after military service in WWII.

LATTISAW, Stacy (*b* 25 Nov. '66, Washington DC) Singer in contemporary dance music. First break at age 11 supporting Ramsey LEWIS, singing five-song set to 30,000 people. Turned down offer from TK Records, whose boss Frederick Knight (former Stax singer) had written 'Ring My Bell' for her; he gave it to Anita Ward for transatlantic no. 1. She signed with Cotillion, already home of other youthful soul prodigies in SISTER SLEDGE; Van McCoy prod. flop debut LP *Young And In Love* '79; she teamed with ex-Mahavishnu drummer turned disco producer Narada Michael Walden: title track of *Let Me Be Your Angel* '80 made no. 21 USA pop chart, 'Jump To The Beat', infectiously percussive track written by Walden and lyricist Bunny Hill was no. 3 UK. Her vocal exuberance, youthful delight in singing was reminiscent of pre-pubescent Michael JACKSON (she later supported him on tour). *With You* '81 incl. no. 26 pop hit 'Love On A Two-Way Street' (cover of no. 3 hit '70 by the Moments); *Sneakin' Out* '82 had R&B hit 'Attack Of The Name Game'; *Sixteen* '83 incl. top 40 hit 'Miracles'; *Perfect Combination* '84 (duet album with Johnny Gill) followed by *I'm Not The Same Girl* '85, switch to Motown for *Take Me All The Way* '86.

LAUPER, Cyndi (*b* 20 June '54, NYC) Singer. Distinctive 'Minnie Mouse' vocals irritate some, enchant others; first heard in group Blue Angel, who released highly rated eponymous album '80, prod. by SIMON & GARFUNKEL veteran Roy Halee. Band split '82; she surfaced with *She's So Unusual* '83, no. 4 LP with four top 5 singles: 'Time After Time' (no. 1), exuberant 'Girls Just Want To Have Fun' (also used as film title), hymnal 'All Through The Night', nagging 'She Bop' (controversial, dealing with masturbation). Sang theme in soundtrack of Steven Spielberg's *Goonies* '85, sang on USA For Africa's 'We Are The World'. If she had worked harder she might have stolen some of MADONNA's glory in '85. Scatty image was modified for *True Colours* '86; title track was hit, guests incl. BANGLES, Billy JOEL.

LAVOE, Hector (*b* Hector Perez, 30 Sep. '46, Ponce, Puerto Rico) Singer, composer, bandleader. To NYC age 6; took up trombone and singing at 10; professional debut at 14; worked with Orchestra New Yorkers in chorus singing voguish Cuban songs of the day; joined Johnny PACHECO band in its pachanga heyday; then became lead singer in newly formed Willie COLON band '66: combination of Lavoe's fresh, young voice and Colon's radical approach, with spontaneity and exuberance ahead of precision, became a new ideal for young Latin musicians, a backlash against what was seen as routine virtuosity of older groups. Contract with Fania began series of hit LPs and singles with *El Malo* (The Bad Guy) '67 (also set image; *see* Colon's entry). In '74 Lavoe took over the band and continued to perform old hits with more emphasis on horns; Colon prod. many of his albums, incl. first solo LP *La Voz* '75, with band expanded to incl. two trumpets and two trombones (Colon had used only trombones). First hit

was surprising 'El Todopoderoso', strongly religious and Christian as opposed to emphasis on Afro-Cuban religions in much of salsa. Lavoe's style was beloved for familiarity, an extension of aggressive and irreverent street-talk; as a solo artist he seemed even freer and more expressive. He sang with FANIA ALL STARS on *Live At Yankee Stadium* Vol. 1 '75, doing 'Mi Gente' (My People), a Pacheco composition from *La Voz*, which became an anthem of pride among Latin audiences (film footage from this concert was incl. in Fania's film *Salsa* and 2-disc soundtrack album '76); another hit from *La Voz* was 'Rompe Saraguey', an old Cuban *son* which referred to the santeria religion and featured a brilliant piano solo by Mark Dimond. He also sang with Rubén BLADES on Colon's *The Good, The Bad, The Ugly* '75; his *De Ti Depende, It's Up To You* '76 had pianist Joe 'Professor' Torres from the original Colon band replacing Dimond, incl. hit 'Periodico de Ayer' (Yesterday's Newspaper), written by C. Curet Alonso and arr. by Colon. Lavoe was *the* salsa singer by '77, star of countless TV spots, Caribbean shows. Recurrent drug problems limited his output; then *Comedia* late '78 was a mature and mellow record, yet Lavoe's voice was even more cutting and effective, especially on Blades' biographical song 'El Cantante', about an unstable singer; arr. by Colon it became an emotive confessional in Lavoe's stage act and his biggest hit. *Recordando A Filipe Pirela* '79 was prod. by Colon; Xmas LP *Feliz Navidad* '79 was dir. by Pacheco, incl. Yomo Toro on cuatro and featured veteran singer Daniel Santos. Further LPs incl. *El Sabio* '80 (prod. by Colon), *Que Sentimiento!* '81 (by Lavoe), *Vigilante* '83 with Colon and *Revento* '85, which saw horns down to two trombones and three tracks by top NYC arranger Isidro Infante, who also shared piano chores with Torres: standout tracks incl. 'La Fama' (Lavoe composition) and cover of Joe JACKSON's 'Cancer' with Richie Ray guesting on piano. He appeared with Celia CRUZ on *Homenaje a Beny Moré Vol. III* '85 in series of Tito PUENTE LPs; he has sung on more than a dozen Fania All Stars sets altogether, incl. 2-disc film soundtrack *Our Latin Thing* '72, *Tribute To Tito Rodriguez* '76, *Habana Jam* '79 ('Mi Gente' again), *Commitment* '80 ('Ublabadu'), *Lo*

Que Pide la Gente '84 ('El Rey de la Punctualidad'), *Viva la Charanga* '86. He appeared in London in '75 with his band, with FAS '76, '84 with his own band again; recently members of Angel CANALES' band have been gigging with him, adding harder, rawer edge to repertoire. *Strikes Back* '87 on Fania was reunion with producer Colon.

LAWAL, Gaspar (*b* Ijebu-Ode, Nigeria) Drummer and percussionist, singer/composer. He came to the UK in the early '70s; made international reputation as session musician, working with Ginger BAKER's Air Force, Stephen Stills, ROLLING STONES, Funkadelic, Barbra STREISAND, countryman Sonny OKOSUN, etc. Joined quintet Clancy for LPs *Seriously Speaking* and *Everyday* on WB '75. Returned to Nigeria '77; back in UK to record first solo LP *Ajomase* '80 on Cap; formed own outfit African Oro Band (single 'Kita Kita' '81). Second LP *Abiosunni* '85 yielded theme music for a BBC World Service programme. Highly regarded and still much in demand for sessions, live work.

LAWRENCE, Steve (*b* Steven Leibowitz, 8 July '35, Brooklyn, NY) Singer. On Steve ALLEN's *Tonight* show on TV from '54; met Eydie GORME there (married '57); they became and remain a popular club act. He also writes ('Two On The Aisle' his best-known song); appeared on Broadway in *What Makes Sammy Run?* '64; has not done badly battling the rockers in charts: 21 Hot 100 entries '57-64 incl. pop covers on Coral (version of Buddy KNOX's 'Party Doll' made no. 5), top,10 hits '59-61: 'Pretty Blue Eyes' and 'Footsteps' on ABC, 'Portrait Of My Love' on UA, 'Go Away Little Girl' was no. 1 for two weeks '62. His chart LPs incl. cleverly conceived *Academy Award Losers* '64 (great songs that didn't win) with Billy MAY, *Everybody Knows* and *The Steve Lawrence Show* '67, all on Columbia. Steve and Eydie had TV show '59, he had his own show '65. For their duo work see Eydie's entry.

LAWS, Hubert (*b* 10 Nov. '39, Houston, Texas) Flute, also other instruments; composer. Studied saxes in junior high school; later inspired by Julius Baker of the N.Y. Philharmonic. First job with Jazz Crusaders

'54-60 (records on Pacific Jazz; later became CRUSADERS); played, recorded with Mongo SANTAMARIA on Columbia '63, Sergio MENDES on Atlantic '65, also with James MOODY on Cadet, with Lena HORNE, Benny GOLSON, hit Quincy JONES LPs *Body Heat*, *Walking In Space* on A&M, many others; also Metropolitan Opera and N.Y. Phil. orchestras '68-74, own Carnegie Hall concerts in '70s. Published *Flute Improvisation* (Hulaws Music). Own albums began on Atlantic with *The Laws Of Jazz* '64, quartet set with Chick COREA; *Flute By-Laws* '65 was a larger combo, still with Corea; then *Afro-Classic* '70 on CTI with AIRTO, Gene BERTONCINI, Ron CARTER, Fred Waits, others. *The Rite Of Spring* '71-2 with much the same gang incl. music of Bach, Ravel, Debussy, also on CTI; back to Atlantic for *Wild Flower* '72 with Airto, Corea, Santamaria, Carter, Gary BURTON, others. Then *Morning Star* '72 had large orchestra dir. by Don Sobesky; *Carnegie Hall* '73 had combo similar to *Afro-Classic*; *Then There Was Light* '74 (aka *In The Beginning*) had 13-piece group incl. brother Ronnie (*b* 3 Oct. '50) on tenor; *The Chicago Theme* '75, *The San Francisco Concert* '75 had large groups with strings, all on CTI. To Columbia for *Say It With Silence* '78, *Family* and *How To Beat The High Cost Of Living* '80, *Make It Last* and *Romeo And Juliet*, plus '85 LP with music by Telemann, Harold Blanchard, arr. of 'Amazing Grace' by Laws and Sobesky, synthesiser, strings etc. cond. by Jones. *Fusion Super Jam* '81 had septet plus vocals by sister Eloise Laws made live at Aurex Jazz Festival for Japanese label. Ronnie Laws also sings; has played and recorded with Walter Bishop Jr, EARTH, WIND & FIRE; own album *Pressure Sensitive* originally on Blue Note now joined by six others on EMI labels incl. *Solid Ground* '81, which he wrote and produced, featuring Hubert and Eloise.

LAWSON, Rex (*b* '30s, Kalabari, Nigeria; *d* '69) Singer/composer, trumpeter and bandleader. Born of a Kalabari father and an Igbo mother, he became one of the great bandleaders in the HIGHLIFE style; he sang in all the major Nigerian languages, but 'Sawale' (in Yoruban) captured the hearts of all Nigerians. Already playing trumpet at age 12, he began as a bandboy for Lord Eddyson, leader of the Starlight Melody Orchestra in Port Harcourt; Eddyson turned him over to Sammy Obot (later leader of the Ghanaian highlife band the Uhurus); Lawson's talent flourished and he left the band in Lagos to continue his apprenticeship with the great highlife musicians of the era, incl. 'Pa Bobby' BENSON, Victor OLAIYA, Roy Chicago and Chris Ajiko. During the golden era of highlife he formed his own band '60, initially the Nigeraphone Studio Orchestra of Onitsha, soon better known as the Mayors Dance Band; he adopted the title 'Pastor' and set out on an illustrious recording career: a good compilation of early tracks was *Dancing Time No. 3* on Philips/Fontana; the 11-piece band cranked out hit after hit: 'Jolly Papa', 'Oko', 'Yellow Sisi', 'Gowon Special'; many compiled on *Cardinal Rex Lawson – Greatest Hits* and *Rex Lawson's Victories* (incl. 'Sawale') on Nigerian Polygram. He died at the peak of his fame; the band carried on as the Professional Seagulls, but Lawson's music was still in demand: the Akpolla label (Lagos) issued LPs *The Highlife King In London*, *Love M'Adure Special* and *Victories Vol. 2* in '80.

LEADBELLY (*b* Huddie William Ledbetter, 20 Jan. c.1889, Mooringsport, La.; *d* 6 Dec. '49, NYC) Blues/folk singer, songwriter, guitarist, other instruments. Born on plantation, raised in Texas; learned Cajun accordion as a child, later guitar, harmonica. He was a father at 15, married '16, again '35. 'Leadbelly' may have been a corruption of his name or a reference to physical strength, a buckshot wound or sexual prowess. He was jailed for assault in Texas c.'16, escaped; jailed for 30 years for murder in Apr. '16, pardoned after 6.5 years; worked outside music, was jailed again Feb. '30 in Louisiana (10 years for 'assault to kill with intent to murder'). He was discovered by folklorists John and Alan LOMAX; they recorded him for the Library of Congress; he sang his way out of prison for the second time '34. Worked as chauffeur and folksinger for Lomaxes, appeared with John in a *March Of Time* newsreel '35, recorded for the LoC and ARC labels, performed on college circuit, in theatres; moved to NYC from '37 to work clubs, political rallies, etc.

The modern era of folk music in the USA began with the meeting in NYC of Leadbelly's country folk-blues, Woody GUTHRIE's itinerant dust-bowl troubador and Pete SEEGER's incipient urban folk style. Leadbelly was taken up by NYC left-wing intellectuals in an early example of radical chic, but this did not lead to financial security; he served a term for assault NY '39-40 and often worked outside music. He recorded for Victor, Stinson, Capitol, Folkways (Moe Asch recorded about 900 songs), worked with Guthrie, Seeger, Josh WHITE and Burl IVES at a benefit for migrant workers '40, later with Guthrie, Sonny TERRY, Brownie MCGHEE as the Headline Singers, and for People's Music (see Seeger entry), sang on the radio. To Hollywood '44, short film *Three Songs By Leadbelly* '45; toured France '49; died of amyotrophic lateral sclerosis, disease that killed baseball star Lou Gehrig. Film biography *Leadbelly* released '76 dir. by Gordon Parks. Among the many songs he wrote or collected are 'Alberta', 'The Boll Weevil', 'Cotton Fields', 'The Midnight Special', 'Pick A Bale Of Cotton', 'Rock Island Line' (top 10 USA/UK '56 by Lonnie DONEGAN), 'Goodnight Irene' (no. 1 USA '50 by the WEAVERS). His story-telling was part of his fame; he specialised in 12-string guitar; style was midway between that of country blues singers such as Blind Lemon JEFFERSON (with whom he worked c.'17) and the nightclub style of White. He taught Seeger the importance of rhythm, and was capable of generating tremendous rhythmical excitement (e.g. on Victor recording '40 with Golden Gate Quartet of 'Pick A Bale Of Cotton'). Early '34-40 material on Biograph; one LP each on Tradition, Columbia, Capitol (EMI in Europe); many LPs on Folkways, Stinson. RCA LP out of print.

LECUONA, Ernesto (*b* 1896) Cuban pianist, bandleader; probably the most successful composer Cuba has produced. Began composing dance music at 11, played recital in NYC at 17. His Palau Brothers Cuban Orchestra was featured in movie musical *Cuban Love Song* '31, starring Jimmy DURANTE, opera star Lawrence Tibbett, Cuban/Hollywood star Lupe Velez; title song and score by Jimmy McHugh/ Dorothy Fields, but also 'El Manicero'

('The Peanut Vendor'), a national hit that year (written by Moises Simons) recorded by Don Azpiazú, Louis ARMSTRONG, others. The Lecuona Cuban Boys recorded for Columbia, toured Europe '30s, mounting Latin revues. He wrote cantatas, musical shows etc. but is best known for songs covered hundreds of times, incl. 'Siboney' ('31 hit by Alfredo Brito; recorded '53 by quartet with Dizzy GILLESPIE and Stan GETZ, etc.). 'Para Vigo Me Voy' ('Say "Si Si" ') (recorded '33 by Xavier CUGAT; a hit with English lyrics by Al Stillman for Glenn MILLER, the ANDREWS Sisters '40, later for the MILLS Bros, etc.), 'Canto Karabali' ('Jungle Drums'), 'La Comparsa', 'Malagueña' etc. Some were intended as light classical pieces; darkly dramatic orchestral arr. of 'Malagueña' was lead track on Andre KOSTELANETZ LP *Lure Of The Tropics* early '50s, while 'Andaluzia' '30 became no. 1 hit by Jimmy DORSEY '40 with vocal by Bob Eberly as 'The Breeze And I' (lyrics by Stillman). Lecuona's daughter Ernestina sang with his band; his niece, mezzo-soprano Margarita, made records incl. an album on Montilla, but had her name on others as the writer of songs, particularly 'Tabu' and 'Babalu': Ernesto's Lecuona Cuban Boys made the first recording of the former; Miguelito Valdez and Desi ARNAZ were famous for 'Babalu' (though Arnaz's version was not considered very authentic); both songs were covered almost as often as any of Ernesto's.

LED ZEPPELIN UK heavy metal band, one of the biggest acts of the '70s. Lineup: Jimmy Page, guitar (*b* 9 Jan. '44, Heston, London); Robert Plant, vocals (*b* 20 Aug. '48, Bromwich); John Paul Jones, bass (*b* John Baldwin, 3 Jan. '46, Sidcup); John Bonham, drums (*b* 31 May '48, Redditch; *d* 25 Sep. '80). Name allegedly suggested by Keith Moon; first came together for session with P. J. PROBY on *Three Week Hero* '69; Page's credits incl. the WHO, KINKS, Them, DONOVAN as well as YARDBIRDS; met Jones sessioning; his original choices incl. drummer B. J. Wilson (later PROCOL HARUM), vocalist Terry Reid; Reid declined but recommended Plant, who urged Bonham for drum chair (both had been in Midlands group Band of Joy). With demise of CREAM and YARDBIRDS (early gigs billed as 'The

New Yardbirds': descended from them and fulfilled their gigs), Jeff BECK's inability to form a steady group, Led Zep plugged a gap in the rock arena and took the USA by storm (initially resenting lack of UK success). Their rise was due in part to manager Peter Grant, aggressive music business figure since '50s. Eponymous debut LP '69 made in 30 hours, set tone: bone-crunching rock'n'roll with guitar hero Page, passionate singer Plant, solid rhythm section; *Led Zeppelin II* '69 incl. anthem 'Whole Lotta Love', drum marathon 'Moby Dick', rock mysticism in 'Ramble On'. To some they seemed over the top, but the era of rock as ritual was underway and they soon broke BEATLES' box-office records; in any case they had more going for them than later imitators: *III* '70 was a hybrid LP, with hallmark riffing on 'Immigrant Song', slow blues 'Since I've Been Loving You', largely acoustic side 2 indicating folk direction they were often tempted to take: both Page and Plant were fans of Bert Jansch, INCREDIBLE STRING BAND; long-term champions of folk-poet Roy HARPER (tribute on 'Hats Off To Harper'). *IV* '71 known as the Runes LP: their name appeared nowhere on sleeve; incl. stage favourites 'Black Dog', 'Rock & Roll'; folk direction pursued with 'The Battle Of Evermore' (Plant's duet with Sandy DENNY), anthemic 'Stairway To Heaven' at first stately and acoustic, climaxing in orgiastic trademark mêlée their best-known song, still heard on USA radio. *Houses Of The Holy* '73 was still more diverse, putting off some fans with eclecticism but finally fuelling their reputation. They took '74 off, started their own Swan Song label for BAD COMPANY, Dave EDMUNDS, Maggie Bell as well as their own albums, but doing little in the way of discovering new acts. *Physical Graffiti* '75 was an awesome 2-disc set for fans, while *Presence* '76 was regarded as disappointing; 2-disc *The Song Remains The Same* was live soundtrack of self-indulgent, mystical film (Page obsessed with the occult); only eight tracks incl. marathon workouts of stage favourites. In punk era they continued to fly above fluctuations; *In Through The Out Door* '79 was reassuringly loose collection of blues and rock'n'roll which delighted fans. They played big shows at Knebworth, UK, first for four years at home; Plant appeared with Edmunds at Kampuchea benefit in London '79, singing 'Little Sister'; Bonham was a member of Paul MCCARTNEY's 'Rockestra': when he died it was rumoured that the band would continue with a new drummer, but a terse statement announced that Zep could not continue without him. *Coda* '82 incl. previously unreleased tracks '69-79. Page and Plant joined FOREIGNER onstage May '82 in Germany; there was talk of a supergroup with them and members of YES, but nothing happened. Jones retired to his studio, surfaced in McCartney's soundtrack to *Give My Regards To Broad Street* '84, scored tacky horror film *Scream For Help* '85 (soundtrack incl. Page). Plant undertook low-key UK gigs with scratch band the Honeydrippers, revelling in anonymity to perform R&B and rock standards; *Pictures At Eleven* '82 with help from Phil COLLINS had his vocal histrionics notably subdued from Zep peak; *The Principle Of Moments* '83 incl. hit 'Big Log'; *The Honeydrippers Vol I.* '84 incl. guests Page and Beck, Plant on entertaining selection of R&B standards incl. 'Sea Of Love', 'Rockin' At Midnight'; his *Shaken'n'Stirred* '85 showed continued willingness to experiment. Page emerged with soundtrack for risible film *Death Wish II* '82, appeared with Beck, Bill Wyman, Charlie Watts, Ron Wood and Eric CLAPTON at ARMS benefit show for MS victim Ronnie Lane in UK/USA '83, surprising everybody with an instrumental version of 'Stairway'; finally unveiled new band *The Firm* '85, incl. former FREE and Bad Company vocalist Paul Rodgers, likeable single 'Radioactive' but *The Firm Means Business* '86 was loudly panned. He kept commitment to acoustic side appearing with Harper at '84 Cambridge Folk Festival and on his LP *Whatever Happened To Jugula* '85. Page, Plant and Jones were reunited with Collins on drums at Live Aid '85; strong rumours that Power Station drummer Tony Thompson would join trio in re-formed Zep again came to nothing. Halfway through the '80s their reputation was in the ascendant; vilified by punks, their full-throated stuff is back in favour, having influenced SAXON, VAN HALEN etc. Plant solo album *Now And Zen* '88; rumours of Zep reunion were stronger than ever. *Power & Glory* '85 by Chris Welch is a good history; *Hammer Of The*

Gods '85 by Stephen Davis is an insider's view of their rise, with occult links explained (deaths of Bonham, Plant's son, etc.).

LEE, Brenda (*b* Brenda Mae Tarpley, 11 Dec. '44, Lithonia, Ga.) Singer; one of the most successful of the '60s, with 50 Hot 100 entries USA '57-73, pop hits in UK, Japan, Germany etc., then on country chart well into the '80s. Began as child prodigy on the radio in Congers, Ga. '49; on *Jubilee USA* with Red FOLEY '55-8, with Steve ALLEN, Perry COMO on TV USA, Jack GOOD's *Oh Boy* in UK '58-9, etc. Signed with Decca USA '55, had minor hits 'One Step At A Time' (no. 15 in C&W chart), 'Dynamite'; then high in both pop and R&B charts with 'Sweet Nothin's' '59, 'I'm Sorry' (no. 1 pop), 'That's All You Gotta Do', 'I Want To Be Wanted' (no. 1 pop), several more, all '60. She married childhood sweetheart Ronnie Shacklett '64, settled in Nashville with daughters Julie and Jolie. She also had 15 LPs in the album charts '60-9, now all out of print. She was essentially the most successful crossover artist of the decade: one of the few female rockers (as 'Little Miss Dynamite', with 'Dum Dum', 'Sweet Impossible You', etc.); but 'I'm Sorry' was a classic smoocher and in jukebox terms the end of an era: 'rock' soon eclipsed rock'n'roll, while her transparent sincerity and her use of melisma (with far less self-consciousness than e.g. Buddy HOLLY) revealed a basically country singer. She never had another no. 1 pop hit after '60 but with lots of top 40 entries the diminutive girl with the big voice was named Most Programmed Female Vocalist '61-5 in USA. When she faded from the pop charts she turned up in the country again, with hits almost every year right up to the present. LPs all on MCA: USA compilations *Greatest Country Hits*, 2-disc *Brenda Lee Story*; also *Only When I Laugh* '81, *Feels So Right* '85; in UK *The Early Years*, *Love Songs Just For You*, 2-disc *25th Anniversary Album*. Also in all-star 2-disc *The Winning Hand* '83 on Monument, with Dolly PARTON, Willie NELSON, Kris KRISTOFFERSON.

LEE, Dickey (*b* Dickey Lipscomb, 21 Sep. '41, Memphis, Tenn.) Country/pop singer, songwriter. Boxed and played football in high school, also led band the Collegiates, country at first but switching to rock'n'roll; landed radio series in Santa Barbara, Cal. Signed with Sun Records, teamed with Jack CLEMENT and Allen Reynolds to prod. lightweight rock'n'roll. Completed major in commercial art at Memphis State U., moved to Beaumont, Texas and wrote 'She Thinks I Still Care', no. 1 country hit for George JONES '62, became a standard. Lee had pop hits 'Patches' (a million-seller on Smash, written by Barry Mann and Larry Kobler, prod. by Clementin Beaumont), 'I Saw Linda Yesterday', 'Laurie (Strange Things Happen)' '62-5; but had a great love for country music and moved to Nashville '70, signed with RCA and producer Allen Reynolds; second single 'Never Ending Song Of Love' went top 10 country '71, followed by 'Ashes Of Love', 'The Busiest Memory In Town', 'Rocky' (no. 1), '9,999,999 Tears' and 'If You Gotta Make A Fool Of Somebody' all '72-7. Moved to Mercury '79, but good albums *Dickey Lee* '79, *Again* '80, *Everybody Loves A Winner* '81 had less chart success; he devoted more time to writing: he laid foundation of the Don WILLIAMS style, wrote hits for Brenda LEE, Glen CAMPBELL, Tammy WYNETTE.

LEE, Johnny (*b* 3 July '45, Texas City, Texas) Honky-tonk country singer who struck gold with film *Urban Cowboy* '80. Led rock'n'roll band Johnny Lee and the Road-Runners in high school; worked throughout '60s playing top 40 hits across Texas; met Mickey GILLEY '68 and worked as his front man for more than 10 years. Scored minor country hits on small labels '75-8 with 'Sometimes', 'Red Sails In The Sunset', 'Country Party', 'This Time'; his 'Lookin' For Love' was lifted from the *Urban Cowboy* soundtrack: after nine years as house singer at Gilley's club in Pasadena, he had a no. 1 country, no. 5 pop hit. Further hits followed with 'One In A Million', 'Bet Your Heart On Me'. He married Charlene Tilton (Lucy in TV's *Dallas*, dubbed 'the poison dwarf' by UK TV critic Clive James) in Feb. '82; the stormy marriage lasted less than three years. Albums on Asylum, then WB incl. *Lookin' For Love, Sounds Like Love, Hey Bartender, Till The Bars Burn Down, Workin' for A Livin', Keep Me Hangin' On.*

LEE, Julia (*b* 13 Oct. '02, Boonesville, Mo.; *d* 8 Dec. '58, Kansas City, Mo.) R&B singer, pianist. Piano lessons at 10; four years later joined Walter PAGE's Kansas City band as vocalist. In brother George E. Lee's band, then solo residency at Milton's Tap Room K.C. until early '40s. Recorded with Jay McSHANN for Capitol '44; soon signed as solo artist, recording blues and boogie items until '52, often a risqué nature. At Harry Truman's inaugural party (he of course was a son of Missouri); gigs on West Coast '48-50; worked in K.C. the rest of her life. Best-known singles 'King Size Papa', 'Snatch And Grab It', 'My Man Stands Out', 'I Didn't Like It The First Time' incl. in Charly UK LP *Tonight's The Night*; *Ugly Papa* and *A Porter's Love Song* are on Jukebox: latter has poignant 'I'll Get Along Somehow', Benny CARTER and Vic DICKENSON on 'Christmas Spirits'.

LEE, Laura (*b* Laura Lee Rundless, '45, Chicago) Soul and gospel vocalist. Family moved to Detroit mid-'50s; Lee joined The Meditation Singers and worked on *Amen* LP for Jubilee label, others for Hob and Gospel. Began soul career '66; first hit single 'Dirty Man' on Chess, entering Hot 100 chart late '67. Two more minor hits; switched to Cotillion, then to Dozier-Holland-Dozier label Hot Wax: 'Women's Love Rights', title cut of '71 LP, reached no. 36, followed in '72 by 'Since I Fell For You', 'Rip Off', 'If You Can Beat Me Rockin' '. Despite new LP *Two Sides Of Laura Lee* and further singles (for Invictus '73-5, Ariola '76, Fantasy '79), sales fell away; she resumed gospel career in '83 with series of LPs with the Rev. Al GREEN on Myrrh label. A fine soul singer with appeal to early '70s women's lib movement; compilation LP expected on HDH-Demon (UK).

LEE, Peggy (*b* Norma Delores Egstrom, 26 May '20, Jamestown, N.D.) Singer; one of the most perennially popular of her generation; also songwriter and actress. Beaten by a stepmother for eleven years, instead of becoming a child-abuser herself she became non-violent. Sang in North Dakota, on West Coast; joined Benny GOODMAN '41 after gig with vocal trio at Chicago hotel: hits with Goodman began with 'I Got It Bad And That Ain't Good' '42, from Duke

ELLINGTON show *Jump For Joy*, followed by 'Blues In The Night' (with sextet), 'Somebody Else Is Taking My Place' (no. 1), 'The Way You Look Tonight', all '42; no. 4 '43 with 'Why Don't You Do Right?' (they performed it in film *Stage Door Canteen* '43). Left Goodman, married Dave BARBOUR '43 (divorced '52). She retired but could not stay away: inveigled by Capitol's Dave Dexter to sing two sides in a jazz album (unusual then) it was clear that she was a great interpreter; she played a character as she sang and made you believe it. With Capitol '45-51, Decca '52-6, back to Capitol; had more than 40 hits through '59 and came back to the top 40 '69. She and Barbour wrote 'It's A Good Day' (no. 16 '47) and 'Mañana' (no. 1 '48), others; he led the orchestra on the latter and many others. Top 10 hits: 'Waitin' For The Train To Come In' '45, 'I Don't Know Enough About You' '46, 'Golden Earrings' '47, 'The Old Master Painter' '50 (duet with Mel TORMÉ), 'Lover' '52, 'Fever' '58. She was reunited with Goodman on 'For Every Man There's A Woman' '48, duetted with Bing CROSBY on 'Watermelon Weather' '52. Her smokey, laid-back sexuality had something teasingly neurotic about it, vulnerable but also untouchable in the end; a comparison of her 'Fever' with the original by LITTLE WILLIE JOHN is revealing. Her portrayal of a complete breakdown in film *Pete Kelly's Blues* '55 was nominated for an Oscar; she appeared in *The Jazz Singer* '53 (remake of '27 Al JOLSON film), *Mr Music* '50 (with Crosby); she was heard in soundtrack of Disney cartoon feature *The Lady And The Tramp* '55 and contributed to the score. She continued to write, with Quincy JONES ('New York City Blues'), Cy COLEMAN ('Then Was Then'), Ellington ('I'm Gonna Go Fishin' '), others. Decca 10″ LP *Black Coffee* regarded as a classic (now with tracks added on MCA/USA, Jasmine/UK); also (on Capitol) *The Beauty And The Beat*, with George SHEARING; *Blues Cross Country*, with Jones (early '60s, now on Pathé Marconi); *Sugar'n'Spice* '62 with Benny CARTER (top 40 LP, now on Pausa USA). Many of the Capitol LPs are being digitally remastered and reissued by EMI, incl. the Shearing, *The Man I Love* '57 (top 20 LP, cond. by Frank SINATRA), *Things Are Swingin'* '56 (top 20), *If You Go, All Aglow Again* and *Pretty Eyes*. There are compilations on MCA in both USA and UK (incl. 'Sugar' from *Pete Kelly*), CBS/UK reissue of hits with Goodman. Her top 40 hit '69 was 'Is That All There Is', which might be a depressing song about the onset of disappointment, or might not: her classy ambivalence could be interpreted as saying 'Yes that's all, but it maybe it hasn't been so bad.' She has suffered from ill health; her last chart LPs were in '70 but she could still fill any club, any time.

LEER, Thomas (*b* Thomas Wishart, Glasgow) New wave singer, keyboardist. First band in Scotland played Motown covers; changed name to 'good aggressive punk-type name'. Moved to London, joined group Pressure who split '78; abandoned punk for European-infl. keyboard sounds (CAN, KRAFTWERK, etc.); issued 'Private Plane' on own Oblique label – home recording with bass, drum machine, stylophone – to critical acclaim. First LP *The Bridge* with Robert Rental (also an avant-garde keyboardist) on Industrial label: one side of quirky electropop, second of ambient mood music with 'found sound' (TV, etc.) and tape loops. '4 Movements' '81 was 12″ single on Cherry Red, successfully mixed both styles, predating soul obsession of hip-hop with its cutting techniques, but 'Contradictions' '82 (2×12″ set) regarded as disappointing; after a further single he bought a Fairlight and made *The Scale Of Ten* '85 on Arista, an album showing that restrictions can have their advantages; incl. classic single, insidious 'International', tale of heroin smuggling (lyric updated B side of first single with same title); elsewhere however was much seamless pop. Leer had sessioned on The The's *Soul Mining* '83 (*see* Matt JOHNSON), employed several of the same musicians on his own album. He formed duo Act '87 with former Propaganda singer Claudia Brücken; he worked on jazz-influenced *Plastic And Physical,* she on solo *Prima Donna;* Act's first album is *Laughter, Tears and Rage,* all on Trevor HORN'S ZTT label.

LEES, Gene (*b* 8 Feb. '28, Hamilton, Ontario, Canada) Lyricist, songwriter, vocalist, journalist. Grew up in St Catharines, Ontario (with Kenny WHEELER); worked as journalist for Canadian newspapers, music and drama editor at *Louisville Times* (Ky.), editor of *Downbeat* magazine '59-61, contributing editor of *Stereo Review* '62-5, columnist and contributing editor for *High Fidelity* '65; contributed to many publications, wrote sleevenotes, broadcast on radio/TV in USA/Canada, etc. Songs '62-85 recorded by Frank SINATRA, Tony BENNETT, Peggy LEE, Sarah VAUGHAN, Carmen McRAE, etc.; lectured in Latin America on jazz, first to translate bossa nova songs, incl. Antonio Carlos Jobim's 'Corcovado' (named for mountain near Rio) as 'Quiet Nights Of Quiet Stars', 'Samba do Aviao' ('Song Of The Jet'); also 'Waltz For Debby' (tune by Bill EVANS), all recorded by Tony Bennett, others; also from French: Charles AZNAVOUR's 'Que C'est Triste Venise' became 'Venice Blue', sung by Aznavour in both languages. First LP *Sings The Gene Lees Songbook: Quiet Nights And Quiet Stars* '70 made in Toronto, orchestra with strings, Ed Bickert on guitar, Mike Renzi on piano, reissued '87 on Stash with new vocal tracks (the old master tape was lost): appealing combination of intimacy and wide vocal range well-suited to his romantic ballads with memorable lyrics, especially the bossa nova songs. Duo *Leaves On The Water* '85 on Choice with pianist Roger KELLAWAY presents mostly their co-written songs, also 'Waltz For Debby' (again), two by Dave FRISHBERG. Translated poems of Pope John Paul II for LP *The Planet Is Alive: Let It Live* '85 on own Jazzletter label with Sarah Vaughan (*see* her entry). Also published short stories, novel *And Sleep Till Noon*, *The Modern Rhyming Dictionary: How To Write Lyrics* '82, biography of Oscar PETERSON to be published '88, work on Henry MANCINI underway. With *High Fidelity* again late '70s, awarded ASCAP/Deems Taylor award '79 for columns; with international following among critics and academics, started own influential *Jazzletter* '81, monthly with no advertising, full of good writing on all aspects of high-class popular music, from Edith PIAF to film composers, mostly jazz oriented; taking in aspects of language, popular culture, independent attitude of eloquent disgust with music business. Bylines apart from Lees incl. Mike Zwerin (*b* 11 May '30; trombonist, played with Miles DAVIS, Claude THORNHILL, Maynard FERGUSON; books

incl. hilarious autobiography *Close Enough For Jazz* '83), also Dick Sudhalter, Grover Sales, NYC bassist Bill Crow on USSR tour with Benny GOODMAN (Zoot SIMS: 'Any gig with Benny was like working in Russia'). *The Singers And The Song* '87, *Meet Me At Jim And Andy's* '88 are collections of *Jazzletter* essays. His son Philip Lees is highly-regarded jazz pianist (*b* Kentucky; lives in Paris).

LEFT BANKE USA pop group formed '66 in NYC by keyboardist/writer Michael Brown (*b* 25 Apr. '49, NYC; real name Lookofsky, son of session violinist Slash Brown); others were Rick Brand, guitar; Tom Finn, bass; George Cameron, drums; Steve Martin, vocals. First single 'Walk Away Renee' on Smash featured Brown's prominent harpsichord against strings, was no. 5 USA '66 (no. 14 USA/3 UK two years later covered by the FOUR TOPS). Track's feel (akin to YARDBIRDS' 'For Your Love') pursued by 'Pretty Ballerina', no. 15 early '67. LP named after hit was Brown's swansong; as followups ('Desiree', others) failed to hit he left, replaced by Jeff Winfield; shorn of principal writer, they struggled to record *Too* '69 before fading away. Brown recorded with shortlived Montage (eponymous LP '69 on Laurie, *Hot Parts* on Kama Sutra) before forming Stories with Ian Lloyd on bass, guitarist Steve Love, Bryan Madey on drums; he played on *Stories* '72, *About Us* '73 with that lineup and left again, moving into A&R as the group had its only top 40 hit with cover of Hot Chocolate's 'Brother Louie'. He then made *The Beckies* '76 for Sire with Mayo McAllister, Gary Hodgden before continuing to session. Other Left Bankers meanwhile regrouped for a single 'Queen Of Paradise' '80 on Camerica. Brown was considered a pop genius by some, overrated and unpredictable by others; his reputation rests on one hit he wrote as teenager.

LEGARRETA, Felix 'Pupi' Cuban violinist, flautist, singer, bandleader, arranger, composer. Fled Castro's Cuba c.'60; worked with Mongo SANTAMARIA. Own debut was *Salsa Nova* (New Spice) '62 on Tico, combining jazz with typical Cuban charanga format, Carlos 'Patato' Valdez on congas, lead vocalist Totico. Played mid-'60s on studio-recorded *Pacheco, His Flute And Latin Jam* on Fania; switched to Fania/Vaya '70s: own LPs incl. *Pupi y su Charanga* '75, with three violins and cello, Gonzalo Fernandez on flute, Oscar Hernandez on piano; *Toda la Verdad* '76 was reissue of *Salsa Nova*; *(Pupi Pa' Bailer)* '80 prod. by Ray BARRETTO, arr. by Pupi. Played on Larry HARLOW's *El Judio Maravilloso* '74 and *El 'Albino Divino'* '78; *Pupi & Pacheco: Los Dos Mosqueteros – The Two Musketeers* '77 (arr. by Pupi, with two cellos and five violins incl. Pupi; Pacheco prod., played flute and guiro); *Habana Jam* (*see* FANIA ALL STARS) and *El Fugitivo* '79, latter co-prod. with Pacheco; *Las Tres Flautas* '80 with Javier (Vazquez) y su Charanga (the other two flutes were Pacheco and José FAJARDO). He played violin on *Cachao y su Descarga* '77 Vol. 1 and Cachao's *Dos* on Salsoul, arr. *Roberto Torres Presenta: Ritmo de Estrellas* '80 on Guajiro label (prod. by TORRES, incl. Ruddy and Kelvin Zervigon from Orquesta Broadway (*see* CHARANGA). Contributed to *Rica Charanga* '86 by Rudy Calzado, *Charanga – Tradición Cubana en Nueva York* '87 by new charanga Orquesta Son Primero, led by Charlie Santiago.

LEGRAND, Michel (*b* 24 Feb. '32, Paris) Pianist, composer. Father Raymond led a variety band; he accompanied singers, arr. strings for Dizzy GILLESPIE '52; to USA and recorded with Frankie LAINE, other pop and jazz artists. Columbia LPs incl. *I Love Paris, Bonjour Paris*, chart LPs *Holiday In Rome, Vienna Holiday, Castles In Spain* '55-6; *Legrand Jazz* '58 (10-piece group with Miles DAVIS, John COLTRANE, Miles's last work as a sideman). Also *Brian's Song* on Bell, *Sarah Vaughan/Michel Legrand* on Mainstream, both '72; over 100 LPs altogether. Many film scores incl. *The Thomas Crown Affair* '68 (theme 'Windmills Of Your Mind' won Oscar for best song), *The Go-Between* '70, *Summer Of '42* '72 (Oscar for best score). *The Umbrellas Of Cherbourg* '64 featured the voice of his sister Christiane (*b* 21 Aug. '30; also sang with the Blue Stars '55-7, the Double Six Of Paris '58-60, was soloist with the Swingle Singers). *Cherbourg* soundtrack was on Philips; new 2-disc version of complete score on Polydor '85; also a symphonic suite on Columbia/USA (backed with suite from *The Go-Between*).

LEHRER, Tom (*b* Thomas Andrew Lehrer, 9 Apr. '28, NYC) Pianist, singer, satirist. Studied piano as a child; degrees from Harvard and taught mathematics there. His songs were performed for friends in private at first, then on own 10″ LPs *Songs By Tom Lehrer, More Of Tom Lehrer*, later *That Was The Year That Was* '65, *An Evening Wasted With Tom Lehrer* '66 on Reprise: his total output. The earlier work was reissued on Reprise; the 10″ LPs in their original formats on Decca UK '81. He entertained in clubs '53-60, '65-7; on TV with David Frost mid-'60s. He was bracketed with iconoclasts Lenny Bruce and Mort Sahl in the cosy years of Eisenhower, but his best work is timeless: he seemed to anticipate Bob DYLAN in implying that nothing could or would be done, so that examining our own attitudes is all we can do; in his case he did it with laughter. 'National Brotherhood Week' and 'I Wanna Go Back To Dixie' attacked racism but also weak-minded, patronising liberal attitudes to it ('I wanna go back to my dear old mammy/Her cooking's lousy and her hands are clammy/but what the hell, it's home'). 'We Will All Go Together When We Go' is as true now as during the Cold War; 'Vatican Rag', 'Werner Von Braun', 'The Old Dope Pedlar' are still caustically funny; 'Be Prepared' sent up the Scouts; 'Lobachevsky' is about plagiarism in mathematics; 'The Masochism Tango' had something for everyone. Stopped writing in the late '60s because even he could not laugh at Vietnam; he said he saw nothing funny in Watergate either. He wrote two songs for children's TV show *The Electric Company* '72; *Tomfoolery* '80 was a London musical revue based on his work; *Too Many Songs By Tom Lehrer* '81 was complete published collection of words and music.

LEIBER & STOLLER USA songwriters, producers: Jerry Leiber (*b* 25 Apr. '33, Baltimore), Mike Stoller (*b* 13 May '33, Belle Harbor, NY). Met in L.A. '50, where their families had moved postwar; both black-music fans living in a white neighbourhood. Early songs recorded by Amos MILBURN, Jimmy WITHERSPOON, Floyd Dixon (pia-

695

nist, singer; aka 'Skeet'; *b* 8 Feb. '29, Marshall, Texas). First national R&B hit was 'Hard Times' by Charles BROWN; they were still in their teens. Patronage of Johnny OTIS was important (though he later lost court case when he claimed credit for 'Hound Dog', written for his singer Big Mama THORNTON). They formed Spark label '53 with Lester Sill and chose the Robins (backed Little Esther on big Otis hits '50) as protégés for their 'playlets' (Leiber's term for songs whose humorous lyrics read like stories): 'Riot In Cell Block No. 9', 'Smokey Joe's Cafe', 'Framed' led to Atlantic buying the label, renaming Robins the COASTERS and hiring Leiber & Stoller as independent producers (among the first in the business) to work with Ruth BROWN, Joe TURNER, LaVern BAKER, etc. Moved to East Coast, worked Robins/Coasters trick with DRIFTERS, who'd already recorded some of their songs for Atlantic; every record was carefully pre-planned with up to 60 takes and much editing to achieve the desired effect, but they sounded spontaneous (their assistant Phil SPECTOR later took the method to its limit). They said, 'We don't write songs, we write records.' After hits 'Save The Last Dance For Me', 'Up On The Roof', 'On Broadway' with the Drifters, they relied on BRILL BUILDING songwriters, concentrating on production; the introduction of strings and Latin rhythms was an innovation, taken over wholesale by black groups. Meanwhile Elvis PRESLEY's hit with 'Hound Dog' '56 led to more work: 'Love Me', score for *Jailhouse Rock* '57, etc. and the wheel had come full circle with Jewish boys who wrote black writing songs for a white boy who sang black. The only competition in their field were Doc POMUS & Mort Shuman, with whom they occasionally collaborated. Left Atlantic, formed Red Bird label '64: DIXIE CUPS' 'Chapel Of Love' sold a million, setting precedent for girl groups with whom label was identified; sold out to partner George Goldner '66 and linked once more with Coasters on CBS, with little success (*The Red Bird Story* '87 on Charly collects rare SHANGRI-LAS tracks, etc.). Continued freelance producing '70s with artists like Elkie BROOKS, PROCOL HARUM, Peggy LEE, T-Bone WALKER, Stealer's Wheel; writing was pushed to the background but their songs continue to be covered. They took R&B from the ghetto into mainstream, created pop classics transcending musical and racial categories.

LENNON, John UK singer/songwriter who rose to fame as one-quarter of the BEATLES and half the songwriting team of Lennon-McCARTNEY, one of the most successful of the century. Was instrumental in forming the group, having begun with the Quarrymen while still in school, but contemplated solo career from the time Beatles stopped touring '66. Collaborations with lover Yoko Ono incl. *Unfinished Music Number 1: Two Virgins, Number 2: Life With The Lions* and *Wedding Album* '68-9, avant-garde improvised works reflecting her arty pretensions. *Live Peace In Toronto* '69 was a stroll through mixed Beatles and rock'n'roll set with Eric CLAPTON, others; one of his first gestures for world peace (he returned his MBE '69 in protest at British involvement in Nigerian Civil War). Carried on with single 'Give Peace A Chance' (no. 2 USA/UK '69) and bed-in for peace at Amsterdam Hilton following marriage (to Ono); singles continued with jagged, frightening 'Cold Turkey' infl. by Janov's 'primal scream' therapy, sugared philosophical pill 'Instant Karma' (prod. by Phil SPECTOR); unpredictable scattershot approach '69-70 informed his '70s music. First solo LP *John Lennon/Plastic Ono Band* '70 flashed back to unhappy childhood with songs like 'Mother'; notable track was acerbic 'Working Class Hero' (later covered by Marianne FAITHFULL); stripped-down instrumentation with only Ringo STARR, bassist Klaus Voorman underlined personal, often brutal nature of the work. *Imagine* '71 continued introspective mood with songs like 'Jealous Guy' and 'Crippled Inside', but Spector's prod./arr. softened edges. The title track became his best-known work, a hymn to non-materialism extrapolated from Ono's *Grapefruit* book: the LP was no. 1 both USA/UK, also contained thinly veiled attack on McCartney 'How Do You Sleep'. The Lennons decamped to NYC where he spent the rest of his life, though anti-establishment stance provoked a four-year wrangle for 'green card' enabling him to live and work there. Although it successfully alienated the authorities, *Sometime In New York City* '72 crammed too many causes into one album, one side backed by Elephant's Memory, the other a 'live jam' with members of the Mothers of Invention. 'It became journalism and not poetry,' he later said. He hadn't learned lessons of hit '71 singles 'Power To The People' and 'Happy Xmas (War Is Over)': you need a good tune even if you're an ex-Beatle. *Mind Games* '73, *Walls And Bridges* '74 went easier on the politics, but lacked bite; the former continued his obsession with his own childhood, with his drawings as an 11-year-old on the cover; the LPs book-ended a period of separation from Ono: they reunited after he celebrated his first solo USA no. 1 hit with backing vocal by Elton JOHN by appearing at Madison Square Garden with John Nov. '74: he sang the hit, 'Whatever Gets You Through The Night', and Beatle standards 'I Saw Her Standing There' and 'Lucy In The Sky With Diamonds'. *Rock 'n'Roll* '75 paid homage to Hamburg era, cover saw him lounging under a neon sign wearing a leather jacket; incl. minor hit cover of Ben E. KING's 'Stand By Me'; compilation *Shaved Fish* same year was his last release for five years as he retired to bring up his son Sean. He took out a newspaper advert '79 to explain decision to become a recluse in NYC's Dakota apartment building; emerged the following year with Ono to sign with newly formed Geffen label, releasing no. 1 LP *Double Fantasy*: they had released simultaneous albums both called *Plastic Ono Band* '70; now they alternated 14 songs on one LP: instead of reliving his own childhood he celebrated Sean's happier one with 'Beautiful Boy', her role with 'Woman'; as the optimistic 'Just Like Starting Over' reached top 10 USA he was shot to death 8 Dec. on the steps of the Dakota by schizophrenic fan Mark Chapman. An international outpouring of grief astonished many, yet in spite of his uneven solo output, his mind often cluttered by bitterness, his aspirations were those of a generation: Chapman's undiagnosed mental illness prevented the possible fruits of a more stable life, as well as ending constant rumours of Beatles re-formation. Posthumous tributes incl. Ono's *Seasons Of Glass* '81, compilation *The John Lennon Collection* '82 incl. '70s hits with best of *Double Fantasy*, *Heart Play* '84 (an unfinished interview), *Milk And Honey* '84 (out-takes, six each by John

and Ono); *Menlove Avenue* '86 had Warhol cover, out-takes from *Walls And Bridges*, *Rock'n'Roll*. More compilations of his bits and pieces were to be issued '88 by Ono.

LENNON, Julian (*b* John Charles Julian Lennon, 8 Apr. '63, Liverpool) Son of BEATLE John, the second Beatle progeny to play professionally (after Zak Starkey), born three weeks after 'Please Please Me' became no. 1 in UK, touching off Beatlemania; he was raised by his mother Cynthia away from media spotlight after John left her for Yoko Ono. Signed with Charisma '83, issued *Valotte* '84: light pop/rock with session musicians, Julian on keyboards and guitar, showed remarkable vocal similarity to his father; critics looked unfairly for similar depth of songwriting in beginner: named after French studio where it was made, it did better in USA than UK, sold two million worldwide, incl. catchy hit 'Too Late For Goodbyes' (harmonica solo by Toots THIELEMANS). *The Secret Value Of Daydreaming* '86 (like the first prod. by Phil Ramone) was similarly unprepossessing. He plays Lennon/McCartney's 'Day Tripper' in stage act; has inevitably revived rumour of Beatles reunion by providing lookalike/soundalike substitute for John. Unlike Paul McCartney's brother (late of Scaffold), who changed his name to Mike McGear to escape similar comparisons, Julian seems prepared to live with it. His relations with Ono make headlines; if music becomes a little more challenging, it will too. Sang on 'original cast' LP of London show *Time* '86.

LENOIR, J. B. (*b* 5 Mar. '29, Monticello, Ms.; *d* 29 Apr. '67, Urbana, Ill.) Blues singer, also guitar, harmonica. Given names were initials only; sometimes aka J. B. Lenore. Parents both played guitar; worked on his father's farm, then through south from early '40s, to Chicago by '49; worked outside music but club gigs with Muddy WATERS, others. Recorded for Chess from '51, Checker '55-8, other labels incl. Decca, Blue Horizon '60, Columbia '65; toured Europe '65-6 (concert tracks on Fontana), recorded for Polydor in Illinois '66. His legend and influence were not matched by commercial success; he died of a heart attack following injury in a car crash. 2-disc *Chess Masters* '84 in UK compiles 28 tracks from '51-8 incl. 'Don't Dog Your Woman', 'Eisenhower Blues', 'Korea Blues', etc.

LEONARD, Harlan (*b* Harlan Quentin Leonard, 2 July '05, Butler, Mo.) Reeds, leader; aka 'Mike'. Attended Lincoln High School in Kansas City; studied clarinet under Major N. Clark Smith, the ex-military bandleader who also taught Walter PAGE, Charlie PARKER, many others; studied saxophones with Paul Tremaine, who later led society dance bands in NYC. Turned pro at 17, joined Bennie MOTEN '23, led reed section until band split '31; Leonard and trombonist Thamon Hayes were among those who left, formed 12-piece Kansas City Skyrockets with trumpeter Ed Lewis (later lead with Count BASIE), Vic DICKENSON, Jesse Stone on piano: the band was very successful, went to Chicago '34 but got kicked out of town by James C. PETRILLO'S local musicians' union: Stone went to work for Earl HINES, Hayes quit performing in disgust and worked in a K.C. music store. Leonard re-formed Harlan Leonard and his Rockets, which recorded for Bluebird '40 (16 sides once available in RCA LPV series): 14-piece band had Ernie Williams, Myra Taylor as vocalists, with Efferge Ware on electric guitar, Jesse Price (Basie's original drummer), good soloists in Henry Bridges on tenor and Fred Beckett on trombone; excellent swing band was a link between the Swing and Bop eras, with arr. by Stone, Buster SMITH, Eddie DURHAM, Tadd DAMERON, trumpeter James Ross, others. (Charlie Parker should have played on the records but had lasted only five weeks; Leonard was a disciplinarian.) Bridges received an offer from Benny GOODMAN and was about to leave when he was drafted: the war wrecked the band, Leonard quit music, worked for the IRS on West Coast. Bridges (*b* c.'08, Okla.) had played with Charlie CHRISTIAN, later with him in Alphonso Trent band; left full-time music after WWII; Beckett (*b* 23 Jan. '17, Nellerton, Ms.; *d* 30 Jan. '46, St Louis) was among the most advanced of K.C. trombonists: worked with Smith, Andy KIRK '37, Lionel HAMPTON '40-4, was drafted and caught TB in the army.

LERNER, Alan Jay (*b* 31 Aug. '18, NYC; *d* 14 June '86, NYC) Lyricist. Wrote radio

sketches for Celeste Holm and Alfred DRAKE, also wrote for Victor Borge, Hildegarde (*b* Hildegarde Loretta Sell, c.'06, Adell, Wis.; popular singer-pianist in clubs and on radio '40s); pageants for radio's *Cavalcade Of America*; Broadway show *Love Life* '48 with Kurt WEILL. Composer Frederick Loewe (*b* 10 June '01, Berlin, Germany *d* 14 Feb. '88) had written European hit 'Katrina' at 15; in USA played piano, worked as unsuccessful bantamweight boxer, ranch hand; with Earle Crooker wrote 'A Waltz Was Born In Vienna' '36, musical *Great Lady* '38, also musical for St Louis Opera; then with Lerner. After *What's Up?* '43, *The Day Before Spring* '45, they wrote some of the most popular shows of all time: *Brigadoon* '47, filmed '54: 'Heather On The Hill', 'Almost Like Being In Love'; *Paint Your Wagon* '51, filmed '69: 'I Talk To The Trees', 'They Call The Wind Maria'; *Camelot* '60, filmed '67; *My Fair Lady* '56, filmed '64: 'On The Street Where You Live', 'Get Me To The Church On Time', 'I've Grown Accustomed To Her Face', 'I Could Have Danced All Night'. They won Oscars '58 for score and title song of *Gigi* (also incl. 'Thank Heaven For Little Girls'), made 2-disc set on RCA *An Evening With Lerner & Leowe*. Lerner also won an Oscar '51 for his screenplay of *An American In Paris*; he collaborated with Burton Lane (*On A Clear Day You Can See Forever* '65, filmed '69; title song won Grammy), André Previn (*Coco* '69), Leonard Bernsten (*1600 Pennsylvania Avenue* '76), etc. *A Hymn To Him* '87 compiles his lyrics, edited by Benny Green.

LETTERMEN, The Pop vocal trio of '60s: Tony Butala (*b* 20 Nov. '40, Sharon, Pa.), Jim Pike (*b* 6 Nov. '38, St Louis), Bob Engemann (*b* 19 Feb. '36, Highland Park, Mich.) Began in L.A. '60, recorded for WB, switched to Capitol and had 20 Hot 100 entries '61-71, smooth harmony, shrewd choice of songs kept them afloat during British Invasion. Only top tens were 'When I Fall In Love' '61, medley 'Goin' Out Of My Head'/'Can't Take My Eyes Off You' '67, both no. 7. Jim's brother Gary replaced Bob '68; Butala kept trio going with further changes. Surprising 32 LPs charted '62-74, incl. compilations; biggest were *A Song For Young Love* '62, *Best Of* '66, *Live* '67 (incl.

medley), *Goin' Out Of My Head* '68, *Hurt So Bad* '69.

LEVEL 42 UK disco-pop group formed '80: Mark King, bass and lead vocals (*b* 20 Oct. '58); Phil Gould, drums (*b* 28 Feb. '57); Boon Gould, guitar (*b* 4 Mar. '55), Mike Lindup, keyboards (*b* 17 Mar. '59). Began as mainly instrumental jazz-funk band playing for London fans; multi-instrumentalist King had contributed to debut LP by M of 'Pop Muzik' fame '79 with Phil Gould and Grace JONES sideman Wally Badarou on keyboards; now concentrated on bass with solid driving style infl. by Stanley CLARKE (he endorses own Jaydee bass). First LPs *The Early Tapes* ('82), *Level 42* '81 showed pop sensibilities creeping in as singles flirted with lower end of UK pop chart; *The Pursuit Of Accidents* '82 yielded 'The Chinese Way' (no. 24, sounding EARTH, WIND & FIREish), *Standing In The Light* '83 brought KOOL-style chanter 'The Sun Goes Down (Living It Up)', first top 10 hit. King's solo LP *Influences* '84 was panned as self-indulgent but showed off many skills, '60s grounding in cover of CREAM's 'I Feel Free'. *True Colours* '84 had hard funk of 'Hot Water' (no. 18); live *A Physical Presence* followed by *World Machine* '85, showing marked swing towards pop, with Badarou arranging, co-writing and co-producing much chart material for commercial sheen, high chart placings of 'Something About You' and balladic 'Leaving Me Now'. Faceless in the tradition of jazz-funk bands Freeez, Incognito, Beggar and Co. etc. they have raised profile somewhat, use video well; like labelmates Shakatak (on Polydor), current form will keep them darlings of compact disc fans. *Running In The Family* '87 was more of the same.

LEWIS, Bobby (*b* 17 Feb. '33, Indianapolis) R&B singer, pianist. Grew up in orphanage, learning piano from age 5, moved with adoptive family to Detroit, became popular performer in Midwest. Recorded for many labels, incl. UA later, but his only hits were on Beltone '61: 'Tossing And Turnin' ' was no. 1, then 'One Track Mind' no. 8 for a total of 20 weeks in the R&B chart.

LEWIS, Bobby (*b* 9 May '46, Hodgensville, Ky.) Country singer, the only one to play a lute; popular in '60s. Appeared on local TV *Hi-Varieties* show '64, the *Old Kentucky Barn Dance* '57-9, CBS's *Saturday Night Country Style* '58; signed to Sabre, Fraternity labels '63-4 without success, UA '64: country top 10 with 'How Long Has It Been' '66, his best showing though he continued to chart, label-hopping in '70s through 'She's Been Keeping Me Up Nights' '79 on Capricorn. LPs on UA '65-9 incl. *Little Man With A Big Heart*, *How Long Has It Been*, *A World Of Love*, *An Ordinary Miracle*, *Things For You And I*.

LEWIS, Furry (*b* Walter Lewis, 6 Mar. 1893, Greenwood, Ms.; *d* 14 Sep. '81, Memphis) Blues singer, guitarist; also harmonica. Like Jesse FULLER, Mance LIPSCOMB, Mississippi John HURT, others, he played ragtime, ballads etc., as well as blues. Raised on a farm, taught himself on a home-made guitar from age 6, ran away from home c.'06 to chase medicine shows. Worked with W. C. HANDY and solo in Memphis area '08-16, also hoboed through the South and lost a leg in a train accident '16. He may have been the first to play slide guitar with a bottleneck rather than a knife-blade. Supported himself for more than 40 years as a streetcleaner despite wooden leg; rediscovered in late '50s he never earned enough to give up the day job. He appeared in films/videotapes *The Blues* '63, *Homewood Show* '70 on PBS, *Roots of American Music* '71; *Blues Under The Skin*, *Out Of The Blacks Into The Blues* (French), *Thinking Out Loud*, all '72, *Good Morning Blues* '78 on PBS, others. Joni MITCHELL wrote 'Furry Sings The Blues' after meeting him. Records on Vocalion, Victor '27-9 (LP *In His Prime* on Yazoo); also *Furry Lewis Blues* '59 on Folkways, *Back On My Feet Again* '61 on Prestige/Bluesway; recorded for Rounder '63, '67-8; also *In Memphis* on Matchbox '70, with Fred McDOWELL on Biograph '71, with Bukka WHITE '68-9 on Asp, Adelphi; other LPs: *Presenting The Country Blues* '69 on Blue Horizon, *Furry Lewis* '71 on Xtra; *The Fabulous Furry Lewis* on Southland and 2-disc *Shake 'Em On Down* on Fantasy; portions of concerts were issued on Sire, Ampex, Elektra.

LEWIS, Gary, and the Playboys USA pop group formed '64, L.A.; lineup: Gary

Lewis, drums, vocals (*b* Gary Levitch, 31 July '46); guitarists Al Ramsey and John West, David Walker on keyboards, bassist David Costell. Son of Jerry LEWIS was given a set of drums on 14th birthday, formed group which appeared at Disneyland '66; signed to Liberty by Snuff GARRETT they had five top 5 hits in their first 18 months incl. 'This Diamond Ring' (no. 1), all arranged by Leon RUSSELL; next four made the top 20, but Lewis was drafted in late '66; previously recorded issues raised their Hot 100 entries to 15 by mid-'69, but the group except for Walker scattered (the others replaced by Jimmy Karstein, Tom Tripplehorn and Carl Radle, all from Tulsa, Okla.). Lewis was swamped by the tide of psychedelia which drowned party pop in the late '60s; he did well during the BEATLE era, better than other 'children of the stars' (Dino, Desi & Billy, sons of Dean MARTIN and Desi ARNAZ with Billy Hinsche, had two top 25 hits '65). Greatest hits compilations on Rhino USA, UA/EMI UK.

LEWIS, George (*b* George Lewis Francis Zeno, 13 July 1900, New Orleans; *d* there 31 Dec. '68) Clarinet; also alto sax. Given a toy fife at age 6, saved his money and bought a clarinet at 16, from the next year playing with local bandleaders incl. Kid ORY, also in brass marching bands. Played in Evan Thomas's band with Bunk JOHNSON when Thomas was murdered on the bandstand '32; was rediscovered a few years later with Johnson and played on his records. Some said he was no better than Johnson, who was certainly long past his prime; but his warm vibrato was much loved around the world: he worked mostly in New Orleans but at Hangover Club in San Francisco with Lizzie Miles '52 etc., also toured Europe and Japan, working until '68 despite ill health. He appeared in a scene for *New Orleans* '46 but it was cut from the finished film. *Call Him George* by Jay Allison Stuart published '61, *George Lewis* by Tom Bethell '77. LPs and compilations on Storyville incl. '44-5 tracks, '53 items made in L.A., broadcasts from the Hangover '53, '58-9 in Copenhagen, material from Delmark label, 2-disc '54 concert from Ohio State U. originally on Disc Jockey label. Several volumes of *George Lewis In Europe/The Pied Piper*

'59 on Rarities; *On Parade, Doctor Jazz, Memorial* on Delmark; *Jazz At Preservation Hall* '63 on Atlantic; *The Perennial George Lewis* '59 on Verve; others on Jazzology, Storyville, GHB; lists in record catalogues muddle this George Lewis with the other one, below.

LEWIS, George (*b* '52, Chicago) Trombonist, composer. Took up trombone at age 9, later studied philosophy at Yale, attended AACM school in Chicago, had theory lessons from Richard ABRAMS, became virtuoso. *The George Lewis Solo Trombone Record* '76 on Sackville incl. 'Piece For Three Trombones Simultaneously' by means of overdubbing; quartet *Chicago Slow Dance* '77 on Lovely Music is a single composition played by a quartet incl. synthesiser. Sextet *Shadowgraph* '77 (aka *Monads*) incl. Roscoe MITCHELL, Abrams; *Jila* '78 (aka *The Imaginary Suite*) is duet with reedman Douglas Ewart, who plays on most of these; *Homage To Charlie Parker* '79 is a quartet with electronics, all these on Black Saint. Also *From Saxophone & Trombone* '81 on Incus with Evan Parker.

LEWIS, Huey, and the News USA pop/rock band formed '79 in San Francisco by singer Lewis (Hugh Anthony Cregg III), keyboardist Sean Hopper when Clover disbanded. Clover was formed '68 by guitarist Alex Call and John McFee, bassist John Ciambotti, others; they made legendary LPs *Clover* '70 and *Forty-Niner* '71 on Fantasy (repackaged as *Chronicle* '79); with Lewis and Hopper they worked in London, recorded for Vertigo UK/Mercury USA '77: *Clover* on Mercury, *Unavailable* on Vertigo may be similar; *Love On The Wire* on both labels. Without Lewis they also backed Elvis COSTELLO on his debut *My Aim Is True* '77, disbanded '79 after their good-time country rock had kept them together more than 10 years. McFee joined DOOBIE Bros; Ciambotti turned songwriter (wrote Tommy Tutone hit '8675309/Jenny'); Lewis and Hopper jammed in S.F. bars, calling themselves American Express; did a disco version of 'Exodus' for laughs; 'Exodisco' was heard by Phonogram in London, where Lewis had gone to session with Dave EDMUNDS, Nick LOWE; he returned to S.F. with a cash advance and recruited new lineup with Hopper, guitarist Chris Hayes, three members of San Francisco band Soundhole: Johnny Colla, guitar and sax; Billy Gibson, drums; bassist Mario Cipollina (brother of Quicksilver Messenger Service's John). LPs for Chrysalis: *Huey Lewis And The News* '80 did little; *Picture This* '82 incl. top 40 hits incl. 'Do You Believe In Love', top 10 USA; self-produced albums purveyed a more rockish, hook-laden sound than Clover but with characteristic Lewis good humour; then came *Sports* '83 and years of hard live work paid off: no. 1 LP eventually yielded six top 10 hits in 'Heart And Soul', 'I Want A New Drug', 'The Heart Of Rock & Roll', 'Walking On A Thin Line', 'Bad Is Bad' and 'If This Is It', the latter also their first UK hit at no. 7. 'Power Of Love' written by Lewis/Hopper/Colla, used in soundtrack of hit Spielberg film *Back To The Future*: no. 1 hit USA '85, entered UK charts twice (first released two months before film); a lawsuit caused by similarity of title theme from *Ghostbusters* (no. 1 hit '84 by Ray Parker Jr, former session guitarist for Marvin GAYE, Stevie WONDER, etc.) settled out of court (Parker was the 'guilty' party). They also contributed 'Trouble In Paradise' to *USA For Africa* LP. Lewis deserves credit for long-serving commitment to live music, retaining sense of humour in 20 years on the road; he is also a nifty harmonica player: learned it hitching around Europe as a teenager, plays it on sessions with Edmunds, others. *Fore* '86 incl. no. 1 USA hit USA 'Stuck With You'.

LEWIS, Hugh X. (*b* 7 Dec. '32, Yeaddiss, Ky.) Country singer, songwriter. Worked in coal mines; moved to Nashville '63; initial success as a writer: 'B.J. The D.J.' for Stonewall JACKSON, 'Take My Ring Off Your Finger' for Carl SMITH; signed with Kapp and had own hits 'What I Need Most' '64, 'I'd Better Call The Law On Me' '65, 'You're So Cold' '67. Continued as writer; made minor chart comeback '78 with 'Love Don't Hide From Me' on Little Darlin'. Also appeared in low-budget films *Forty-Acre Feud* '66, *Gold Guitar* '67, etc. LPs incl. *Just Before Dawn* '65, *My Kind Of Country* '66, *Just A Prayer Away* '67, *Country Fever* '68, all on Kapp; *Goodwill Ambassador* '80 on President.

LEWIS, Jerry (*b* Joseph Levitch, 16 Mar. '25, Irvington, N.J.) Comedian, TV host, film director; also singer. Partnership with Dean MARTIN until '56 for very popular comedy films; they had novelty hit 'That Certain Party' '48 on Capitol; making a radio advert for a film in the mid-'50s, they made a shambles of the session by swearing at each other and the tape, with studio technicians laughing helplessly in the background, disappeared and was bootlegged. Lewis has a deep affection for popular music (used Count BASIE in *Cinderfella* soundtrack '60); had hits on Decca: 'Rock-A-Bye Your Baby With A Dixie Melody' reached the top 10 '56 in a latter-day Al JOLSON style; 'It All depends On You' '57 did less well.

LEWIS, Jerry Lee (*b* 29 Sep. '35, Ferriday, La.) Rockabilly/country singer, pianist; nicknamed 'the Killer' in school. Went to bible school at 15, was expelled; first married at 16. With his vocal style (manic yet precise, predictable yet improvised each time) and his 'pumping piano', replete with finger-stabbing boogie and pointless yet exciting glissandos, no one except Elvis PRESLEY defined rock'n'roll more clearly; but like Presley before him he did not at first reveal his personality in the studio: made audition tape for Jack CLEMENT at Sun Records in Memphis '56, invited back by Sam Philips, first single was cover of Ray PRICE C&W hit 'Crazy Arms' that did well regionally. On tour with Johnny CASH and Carl PERKINS, Perkins recalled later, Lewis suffered shyness; they told him to 'make a fuss. So the next night he carried on, stood up, kicked the stool back, and a new Jerry Lee was born.' 'Whole Lotta Shakin' Goin' On', made at the end of his second session, was no. 1 in national C&W, R&B charts, no. 3 pop; 'Great Balls Of Fire', 'Breathless' and 'High School Confidential' (title song of his film) all huge hits on all three charts, all '57-8; also in UK. On an Alan Freed tour, according to writer John Grissim, he insisted on closing the show; when Chuck BERRY also had a big hit in the charts, Freed insisted that Lewis open, so he did a blistering 3-minute set, poured lighter petrol on the piano and set fire to it, saying 'I'd like to see *any* son of a bitch follow that!' He married his third wife '58 without bothering to divorce the second: Myra was 13 or 14 years old and his second, third, fourth cousin, depending which source is consulted. He brought her along on a UK tour, where the press decided to apply its own standards to the American South; he was booed off the stage, the tour cancelled. His only top 40 pop hit through the '60s was a cover of Ray CHARLES's 'What'd I Say', no. 30 '61. He switched to Smash/Mercury '64, touring hard and giving good value, but developing problems with alcohol and pills, his always-threatening persona contributing to an effective blacklisting: he could not get on TV or big tours and radio stations would not give his records the exposure they needed. In '68 he played Iago in a rock'n'roll version of *Othello* called *Catch My Soul* in L.A. He switched to country songs and had 12 top 5 hits in that chart '68-71, incl. reissues of country songs from the Sun period; 'To Make Love Sweeter For You', 'There Must Be More To Love Than This', 'Would You Take Another Chance On Me' were no. 1, as was 'Chantilly Lace' in '72. Cover of Kris KRISTOFFERSON's 'Me And Bobby McGee' crossed over to no. 40 '72, his last top 40 entry in pop chart. He always played a wide range of material on stage and came back to rock'n'roll '70s; *The Session* '73 made in London with Peter FRAMPTON, Rory GALLAGHER, etc., incl. remakes of hits and 'Drinkin' Wine Spo-Dee-O-Dee', a '49 R&B hit which he had played that year in his first public performance, sitting in with a C&W band in a Ford dealer's lot. Signed with Elektra '78; he was hospitalised mid-'82 with perforated ulcers and given a 50-50 chance of survival: before the end of the year he was back on the road. In '82 he appeared with his cousin Mickey GILLEY on the Grammy Awards TV show. A gun nut like Presley, in '76 he shot his bass player in the chest; he once tried to drive through the gates at Presley's Graceland house, waving a pistol. It was the same Dr George Nichopoulos who dispensed too many pills to both Presley and Lewis. Both Lewis's sons were killed in accidents; the marriage to Myra lasted 13 years, but it wasn't easy (she published book *Great Balls Of Fire* '82). Of five ex-wives two are dead, the fourth found at the bottom of a swimming pool '82 as a divorce settlement was about to be made, the fifth

of a drug overdose '83 after 77 days of marriage, after she had told her family she intended to leave him. He said to a Chicago audience in '86, 'Elvis? He's dead. We got rid of his ass.' *Sun-Times* critic Don McLeese said that Lewis's was the most exciting set in a revival weekend that incl. the EVERLY Bros and Fats DOMINO. More albums incl. *Live At The Star Club Hamburg* '64, *I'm On Fire* from the same period, *Another Time, Another Place* '68 (title song no. 2 C&W hit), *Memphis Country* '70, *Best Of The Country Music Hall Of Fame Hits* '81 in UK, all on various Polygram labels; *Jerry Lee Lewis* '79 (incl. 'Rockin' My Life Away') on Elektra; *Monsters* '83 and *I Am What I Am* '84 on MCA. Compilations and reissues of Smash/Mercury material are numerous; Sun tracks are reissued on Sun, Rhino and Power in the USA, on Charly UK incl. 12-disc set *Jerry Lee Lewis: The Sun Years* complete and *Million Dollar Quartet*, a studio tape of Lewis, Cash, Perkins and Presley singing gospel songs, formerly widely bootlegged; *Keep Your Hands Off It* '87 on Zu-Zazz UK incl. unissued Sun tracks from '59-60.

LEWIS, John (*b* John Aaron Lewis, 3 May '20, La Grange, Ill.) Pianist, composer, leader. Grew up in New Mexico. Studied piano from '27; attended U. of N.M.; met Kenny CLARKE in US Army '42-5; attended Manhattan School of Music (MA '53, joined Board of Trustees '66); played and arr. for Dizzy GILLESPIE big band ('Two Bass Hit', 'Emanon', 'Minor Walk', 'Stay On It'); 'Toccata For Trumpet And Orchestra' for Gillespie at Carnegie Hall '47; with Miles DAVIS Birth of the Cool combo '49 ('Move', 'Budo', 'Rouge'). Founder member and mentor of MODERN JAZZ QUARTET from '52. His music is confident, uncluttered, elegant and swings. Wrote soundtrack for French film *No Sun In Venice* '57, recorded by quartet; mus. dir. of Monterey Jazz Festival from '58; music for Harry BELAFONTE TV special *New York 19*, William Inge play *Natural Affection* '63, TV film *Cities For People* '75, much more; TV and festivals overseas. Played solo at Newport Jazz Festival '75. Has taught at Harvard, City College NYC, etc. *See* MODERN JAZZ QUARTET. Own albums: trio set *2 Degrees East, 3 Degrees West* '56 on Pacific Jazz (now on

Pausa); *European Windows* '58 on RCA with Stuttgart Symphony Orchestra; *Odds Against Tomorrow* '59 on UA (score for Belafonte film); on Atlantic label: small group sets incl. *The John Lewis Piano* '56 with Connie Kay, Percy Heath, Barry Galbraith on guitar; *Afternoon In Paris* '56 with Sacha DISTEL *Improvised Meditations And Excursions* '59, *The Wonderful World Of Jazz* '60, *European Encounter* '62 with Svend ASMUSSEN; with large groups: *The Golden Striker* '60 with Joe WILDER, Gunther SCHULLER, others (title track theme from film *One Never Knows*), *Jazz Abstractions – John Lewis Presents Contemporary Music* '60 ('Abstraction' comp. & cond. by Schuller, with Ornette COLEMAN, etc.), *Original Sin* '61 (score for San Francisco Ballet), *A Milanese Story* '62, *Essence* '62 with Gary MCFARLAND. Discovered and helped European artists such as Albert MANGELSDORFF (quartet LP on Atlantic made in Baden-Baden '62). Other LPs: with singer Helen MERRILL '76 (*b* 21 July '30, NYC; active in Europe and Japan until '72; own LPs *The Feeling Is Mutual, A Shade Of Difference* on Mainstream; Japanese LPs with Teddy WILSON, Gary PEACOCK, others); album on Mercury with Helen Merrill '76, *John Lewis Solo/Duo with Hank Jones* '76, *An Evening With Two Grand Pianos* in NYC and *Piano Play House* in Tokyo with Jones '79; solo tracks on 2-disc Columbia compilations *I Remember Bebop, They All Played Bebop* '77; solo *Piano, Paris 1979*, 'I'll Remember April' on Palo Alto LP *A Tribute* (to Bill EVANS) '82; *Mirjana* '78, quartet made in France; trio *The John Lewis Album With Putte Wickman And Red Mitchell* '81 (clarinet and bass) on Stockholm radio; sextet *Kansas City Breaks* '82 on Finesse with Joe Kennedy, violin; quartet *Slavic Smile* '82 on French RCA with Bobby HUTCHERSON; quintet versions of *J. S. Bach Preludes And Fugues* '84 on Japanese Philips made in NYC.

LEWIS, Meade Lux (*b* 4 Sep. '05, Chicago; *b* 7 June '64, Minneapolis, Minn.) Pianist in BOOGIE-WOOGIE blues piano genre. Nickname from 'The Duke of Luxemburg' as a child. Infl. by Jimmy YANCEY; recorded 'Honky Tonk Train Blues' for Paramount '29; wielded a shovel for Works Progress Administration, drove taxi, washed cars; re-

discovered by John HAMMOND '35, played in his *Spirituals To Swing* concert with Albert AMMONS and Pete JOHNSON, was key figure with them in boogie-woogie fad of '40s which resulted in over-exposure of it, touring with them in piano trio. Re-recorded 'Train' for EMI '35, Victor and Decca '36, Blue Note '40, Clef '44; died in car crash. Albums incl. 10″ LP *Boogie Woogie Interpretations* on Atlantic, *Cat House Piano* and *Meade Lux* on Verve, *Out Of The Roaring Twenties* on ABC-Paramount, *Blues Boogie Woogie* on Stinson; 3-disc limited edition *The Complete Blue Note Recordings of Albert Ammons and Meade Lux Lewis* on Mosaic '83 incl. duets with Ammons, two versions of 'Honky Tonk Train Blues' and 21 other solos by Lewis '39-44, incl. four 'Variations On a Theme' played on the harpsichord.

LEWIS, Mel (*b* Melvin Sokoloff, 10 May '29, Buffalo, NY.) Drummer, leader. Father was drummer; made pro debut at 15; highly rated West Coast studio/session player recorded with Art PEPPER, Pepper ADAMS, Gerry MULLIGAN, many others. Member of Mulligan's concert band '60, toured Europe; to Europe with Dizzy GILLESPIE '61, USSR with Benny GOODMAN '62, house drummer at Monterey Jazz Festival '59-62. Moved to NYC '63, did TV work etc.; co-formed Thad JONES – Mel Lewis Orchestra '66: it has played Monday nights at the Village Vanguard ever since. Lewis's albums incl. septet LPs on San Francisco Jazz Records '56, Mode '57; jazz versions of tunes from GILBERT & SULLIVAN's *Mikado* on Andex '58; sextet *Mel Lewis And Friends* '76 on A&M with Michael BRECKER, Ron CARTER, Hank JONES, Freddie HUBBARD, Gregory Herbert on reeds (*b* 19 May '47, Philadelphia; LPs with Woody HERMAN, Johnny COLES); *The New Mel Lewis Quintet Live* '79, made in Germany; quintet *Mellofluous* '81 on Gatemouth. For co-led big band LPs see Jones's entry; he left '78, the band was getting younger and someone joked 'Thad and Mel got divorced and Mel got the kids.' Albums by the Mel Lewis Orchestra: *Naturally* '79 on Telarc, live LP from the Vanguard on Gryphon '80 (with Clark TERRY, Bob BROOKMEYER etc.), *Plays Herbie Hancock Live At Montreux* '80 on MPS or Pausa, *Make Me Smile And Other*

New Works By Bob Brookmeyer '82 on Finesse, made at the Vanguard; studio album *The Mel Lewis Orchestra: 20 Years At The Village Vanguard* '85 on Atlantic has no big names but lots of future stars, playing Duke ELLINGTON's 'C-Jam Blues' arr. by Bill Finegan, more standards and originals arr. by Jones, Brookmeyer, Jerry Dodgion, Jim McNeely, others: recorded at MediaSound Studios, mixed directly onto two-track master tape with no editing and sounds great.

LEWIS, Ramsey, Jr (*b* 27 May '35, Chicago) Piano, leader, composer. Studied piano from age 6, later Chicago Music College and De Paul U.; formed a trio '56 with Eldee Young on bass, occasionally cello (*b* 7 Jan. '36, Chicago), Isaac 'Red' Holt on drums (*b* 16 May '32, Rosedale, Ms.); they had played together in teenage band; stayed together until '66 when Young and Holt were replaced by Cleveland Eaton and Maurice White, who was replaced by Maurice Jennings '70. *Ramsey Lewis And His Gentlemen Of Jazz* was the first of more than 30 albums '56-71, nearly all made in Chicago, released on Cadet or Argo, sometimes with added orchestra and/or voices: popular among jazz fans from the beginning; commercial formula breaking through to nationwide audience with a kind of polite soul music, not unfaithful to roots: broke club records and sold out Carnegie Hall. A Christmas LP '62, *Bach To The Blues* and *Live At The Bohemian Caverns* '64 reached Billboard top 200 pop LPs; *The In Crowd* '65 was no. 2 LP incl. no. 5 title single, an instrumental cover of song by Dobie GRAY. 30 Lewis LPs charted altogether '62-84, incl. *Hang On Ramsey!*, *Wade In The Water* '66 (top 20); 13 Hot 100 singles '64-9 were nearly all instrumental covers of pop hits: 'Hi-Heel Sneakers', 'Hang On Sloopy', 'Wade In The Water', BEATLE songs. Lewis also played on a Max ROACH session for Argo, later on Chess UK in 2-disc compilation *Percussion Discussion*. He switched to Columbia '72, in top 20 LPs with *Sun Goddess* '74 incl. tracks with EARTH, WIND & FIRE; charted with *Don't It Feel Good* '75, *Salongo* '76, *Love Notes* '77, *Tequila Mockingbird* '77, *Legacy* '78, *Routes* '80, *Three Piece Suite* '81, *The Two Of Us* '84 with Nancy WILSON. Also *Blues For The Night Owl* on Odyssey (CBS budget label),

Reunion with Holt and Young '82, *Fantasy* '85, *Keys To The City* '87 etc.

LEWIS, Smiley (*b* Amos Overton Lemmon, 5 July '20, La.; *d* Oct. '66) R&B singer. Contemporary of Fats DOMINO, with same label (Imperial) and prod. (Dave BARTHOLOMEW). Best known for original version of 'I Hear You Knocking' with Huey 'Piano' SMITH at the keyboard (Bartholomew composer credit; no. 2 R&B chart '55; awful cover by TV actress Gale STORM made no. 2 pop chart; Dave EDMUNDS took song to no. 2 USA/no. 1 UK '70). 'One Night Of Sin' with cleaned up lyric became 'One Night', one of Elvis PRESLEY's better efforts '57. Also recorded with Allen TOUSSAINT for lesser labels; died of stomach cancer. Wonderful voice in R&B context, but lacked warm colour of Domino's; back-room feeling on 'Knocking' perhaps too tough, not pretty enough for pop chart then. Enthusiasm of Londoner Bill Baker resulted in compilation *Shame Shame Shame* '70; two vols. of *Smiley Lewis Story* released on United Artists '77.

LEWIS, Ted (*b* Theodore Leopold Friedman, 6 June 1892, Circleville, Ohio; *d* 25 Aug. '71, NYC) Clarinettist, singer, bandleader, songwriter, master showman. Became popular entertainer after long years in vaudeville; had more than 100 hits '20-'33, all on Columbia; also accompanied Ruth ETTING, Sophie TUCKER; his own playing was not very good, deliberately corny; he used sidemen Fats WALLER, Benny GOODMAN, Jimmy DORSEY, Jack TEAGARDEN; Muggsy SPANIER was featured on almost half the hits, but the music got sweeter after '33. He wrote his theme 'When My Baby Smiles At Me' (big hit '20; remade on Decca '38 it made top 20); his trademark phrase (in battered top hat) was 'Is everybody happy?'; accent and languid movements somewhat reminiscent of W. C. Fields. He appeared in many revues; films incl. early talkie *Is Everybody Happy?* '29, biopic of same title '43. Among biggest hits: 'All By Myself' '21, 'O! Katherina' '25, 'Just A Gigolo' '31, 'In A Shanty In Old Shanty Town' '32, 'Lazybones' '33. Albums: *A Jazz Holiday* on ASV/UK; other compilations on Sunbeam, Biograph, MCA in USA.

LIBERACE (*b* Wladziu Valentino Liberace, 16 May '19, West Allis, Wis.; *d* 4 Feb. '87, Palm Springs, Cal.) Pianist, also sometime singer, composer ('Rhapsody By Candlelight' etc.). Praised by Ignace Paderewski at 7, concert debut at 11, played as teenager with Chicago Symphony; his fate was sealed when he impulsively played novelties 'Three Little Fishes', 'Mairzy Doats' as encores, dressing them with arpeggios like classical pieces: audiences loved it. To NYC '40, played cocktail piano; toured in USO shows; became famous in '50s on TV, with shmaltzy style appealing to a certain age group. His trademarks were incredible vulgarity in sequinned jackets, ermine capes etc. and candelabra on the piano; he tried to give it up late '50s for a buttoned-down look, but fans wouldn't let him. Singles, 10" LPs on Columbia sold well '52-4: albums such as *Liberace By Candlelight, Concertos For You, An Evening With Liberace* etc.; singles incl. 'September Song', 'Story Of Three Loves' (movie theme borrowed from Rachmaninov's 18th variation on a theme of Paganini; there were several hit versions); on some of these he was accompanied by his brother George (*b* 31 July '11; violinist, conductor; later administrator of the Liberace Museum). Played lead in film *Sincerely Yours* '55 ('Absurd' – Leslie Halliwell); a camp part in *The Loved One* '65 did him more credit. He sued the UK newspaper *Daily Mirror* '59 after columnist Cassandra implied homosexuality, and won; he was sued '82 for palimony by a chauffeur/bodyguard (former Las Vegas dancer). 30 years after his first fame he could still fill Radio City Music Hall; each concert brought busloads of fans from all over the country; income was said to be millions of dollars a year; he had five homes filled with gaudy fixtures and costumes; he was savaged by critics, but said that after reading the reviews he cried all the way to the bank. Columbia *Greatest Hits* LP '69; LPs from '60s on MCA.

LIBERTY USA record label formed '55 in Hollywood by West Coast businessmen with Al Bennett as Vice President and head of A&R. The new label bought Richard Bock's Pacific Jazz label '57, changed its name to World Pacific; also had hits of its own with Julie LONDON, Timi YURO and the Chip-

munks (*see* David SEVILLE). Eddie COCHRAN was signed in '56; he became one of the most influential of all rock'n'roll singers, but his chart success at the time was not great, with only one top 10 hit. In the '60s Liberty's Snuff GARRETT was one of the hottest producers in the USA, making hits with Rocky Burnette, Bobby VEE, Gene MCDANIELS, Gary LEWIS and the Playboys; he hired Phil SPECTOR and Leon RUSSELL to assist. The label also had CANNED HEAT and distributed CREEDENCE CLEARWATER outside North America by agreement with Fantasy. Liberty had a deal with Decca UK, who released product in UK on London, but switched to EMI and their own logo. In '63 Liberty bought IMPERIAL, in '66 BLUE NOTE; in '69 the company was itself taken over by United Artists, who had started their record company in NYC '57. Apart from film soundtracks, UA's roster incl. JAY AND THE AMERICANS, Bobby GOLDSBORO, Don McLEAN, the CRYSTALS (from '65); UA also distributed Art Talmadge's Musicor label, with Gene PITNEY. In the '70s Kenny ROGERS, Paul ANKA and Gerry RAFFERTY sold well, but Liberty-UA fell into debt to its distributor, CAPITOL, and was absorbed into the UK-based international EMI early '79 and merged into EMI America, which had been launched 1 Jan. '78 as an additional outlet for UK product (but two of the new label's first three no. 1 hits were by Americans Robert John and Kim CARNES), had hits with Sheena EASTON, Cliff RICHARD, David BOWIE. Blue Note had been mismanaged and was phased out '81, but re-issues by EMI's Toshiba and Pathé-Marconi in Japan and France kept turning up in the USA, so Blue Note was re-launched Feb. '85, dir. by Bruce Lundvall, who also headed a new East Coast label Manhattan, formed by EMI in '84. *See* BLUE NOTE, EMI.

LIBRE (CONJUNTO LIBRE) Influential experimental band co-founded NYC '74 by Manny Oquendo (*b* '31, Brooklyn), Andy Gonzalez (*b* '51 NYC) after working together in Eddie PALMIERI orchestra. Concept was music based on Latin roots, not merely imitating them, with jazzier, street-real sound; they perpetuated Palmieri's trombanga (trombones and flute) lineup, were characterised by rugged and aggressive sound, attempted to get away from the 'cold, unemotional and mechanical sound' of studio salsa sessions (quoted on their first LP sleeve). Bassist Gonzalez had worked with Dizzy GILLESPIE, Kenny DORHAM, Monguito Santamaria, Ray BARRETTO, others; sessioned with Justo Betancourt, Johnny PACHECO, MACHITO, Willie COLON, Tito RODRIGUEZ, Chico O'FARRILL, Charlie PALMIERI. Oquendo as a child lived upstairs from Almacenas Hernandez, leading Latin record shop; played timbales '47 with Chano POZO, '48 with José Curbelo; early '50s with Tito PUENTE, Tito Rodriguez; sessioned with Pacheco, Larry HARLOW and others; helped establish trombanga sound '62-7 with Eddie Palmieri's Conjunto La Perfecta. Both Gonzalez and Oquendo were in Grupo Folklorico y Experimental Nuevayorquino, whose LPs *Concepts In Unity* '75 and *Lo Dice Todo* '77 on Salsoul incl. the backbone of Libre, who then signed with that label. Other Libre founder-members incl. Andy's brother Jerry on trumpet, flugelhorn, congas; brothers had been members of Latin Jazz Quintet co-founded by Jerry, who'd worked with Dorham, Gillespie, Tony WILLIAMS' Lifetime, George BENSON, toured with the BEACH BOYS etc.; made LP *Ya Yo Me Cure* '80 on American Clave with Andy; led his own Fort Apache Band on *The River Is Deep* on Enja, recorded at '82 Berlin Jazz Festival (where Libre also played); worked on Kip Hanrahan fusion LP *Desire Develops An Edge* '85 on American Clave (vocals by Jack Bruce). Former La Perfecta trombonists Barry Rogers, José Rodrigues played on Libre's first three LPs; flautist Dave Valentin (on all but one) was founder member of Ricardo Marrero and the Group while he and Marrero attended NYC Music & Art High School late '60s (LPs incl. *Time* '77 on Vaya), has pursued solo career playing fusion since late '70s. Pianist Oscar Hernandez was infl. by Herbie HANCOCK, McCoy TYNER; worked with Barretto, many others. Libre's lineup with trombanga section (3-4 trombones with flute) incl. piano, bass, timbales, bongos, congas, güiro, lead vocals and chorus, sometimes added strings or string synthesiser, tres, baritone sax, flugelhorn, more percussion. Ed Byrne played trombone on Libre's first LP *Con Salsa . . .*

Con Ritmo Vol. 1 '76, incl. treatment of Rafael Hernandez's 'Lamento Borincano (El Jibarito)'; for *Tiene Calidad – 'Con Salsa . . . Con Ritmo' Vol. 2* '78 Byrne arr. the Cuban bolero 'Duerme' in COLTRANE-style chord changes, also Miles DAVIS's 'Tune Up'; LP incl. 'Suavecito', composed '28 by Cuban Ignacio Piñeiro (led Cuban Septeto Nacional); 'Imagines Latinas', co-written by Andy and Colombian poet Bernardo Palombo for a TV series of that name. *Los Lideres de la Salsa* '79 was compilation of 'El Jibarito', 'Imagines Latina', one track by Folklorico and three new tracks. Band then became Manny Oquendo y su Conjunto Libre, with Andy as mus. dir.; *Increible* '81 celebrated their sixth anniversary; *Sonido, Estilo y Ritmo* '83 incl. Freddie HUBBARD's 'Little Sunflower', with Jerry on flugelhorn and Steven Turre on conch shell; also a plena, 'Elena, Elena', arr. by Andy. They have toured in Europe, South America, Africa; outside work has kept their output low: Oscar now plays with Rubén Blades' Seis del Solar, played on only one track of last LP. Libre appeared in Leon Ichaso's film *Crossover Dreams* '85 starring Blades.

LIGHT, Enoch (*b* 18 Aug. '07, Canton, Ohio; *d* 31 July '78, NYC). Bandleader, record entrepreneur. Led band the Enoch Light and the Light Brigade in theatres, hotels, radio etc.; toured Europe; biggest hit was 'Summer Night' '37 with vocal by Johnny Muldowney, on Vocalion. Later did studio work on violin, incl. *Hit Parade* on radio; recorded versions of current hits for sale in dime stores; made charts on Grand Award '57 with dixielandish 'Roaring Twenties' albums by the 'Charleston City All-Stars'. Started Command label: always interested in the technical side, he struck it rich with advent of stereo; several vols. of *Persuasive Percussion, Provocative Percussion* etc. were top 5 LPs, also bongo records by 'Los Admiradores', etc.: the original pingpong stereo, with first-class engineering. He went on to be one of the first to record on 35mm movie film instead of tape, an advance at the time; Command recorded fine sets of Beethoven, Brahms symphonies by William Steinberg and the Pittsburgh S.O. He was man. dir. of Command until '65, recording big band sets, movie themes etc. Command was taken over by ABC, then MCA; large quantities of Command records were badly pressed, finally dumped c.'70 at bargain prices (the Pittsburgh's records disappeared and the orchestra could do nothing). Light started again with Project 3 label, finally responsible for more than 30 chart LPs '57-70, under names Terry Snyder All-Stars, Command All-Stars as well as the Light Brigade, Enoch Light and the Brass Menagerie, etc.; Project 3 LPs still available incl. guitarist Tony Mottola's (*b* 18 Apr. '18, Kearney, N.J.; worked with Raymond SCOTT, Perry COMO; scored and played for films and TV, etc.).

LIGHTFOOT, Gordon (*b* 17 Nov. '38, Orillia, Ontario) Singer/songwriter. Worked as pianist and arr. of commercial jingles; infl. by Tom PAXTON, IAN & SYLVIA, Bob DYLAN, he began writing his own personal and poignant songs: 'For Lovin' Me' was a top 30 hit for PETER, PAUL & MARY, who reached only no. 91 with 'Early Morning Rain' (it has since become a standard), and Marty ROBBINS had a no. 1 country hit with 'Ribbon Of Darkness', all '65. Lightfoot's first LPs were on UA, now Liberty: *Lightfoot* '66 was followed by *Did She Mention My Name* and *The Way I Feel*; *Sunday Concert* '69, made live at Massey Hall in Toronto, was first to make Billboard's top 200 LPs. Switched to Reprise and *Sit Down Young Stranger* '70 leaped to no. 12, helped by no. 5 hit single 'If You Could Read My Mind'. *Summer Side Of Life* '71, *Don Quixote* and *Old Dan's Records* '72 were followed by *Sundown* '74, no. 1 LP USA incl. no. 1 hit title single, also no. 10 hit 'Carefree Highway'. *Cold On The Shoulder* '75 was a top 10 LP; 2-disc compilation *Gord's Gold* incl. an LP of new versions of older songs. *Summertime Dream* '76 incl. no. 2 hit 'The Wreck Of The Edmund Fitzgerald'. Switched to WB for *Endless Wire* '78, *Dream Street Rose* '80, *Shadows* '82, *Salute* '83; *East Of Midnight* '86 was his 23rd LP, prod. and co-written by David Foster in a modernising effort, Lightfoot's style being singularly out of fashion in these days of gaudy trash; whether or not the results were successful is for fans to judge. Other sets incl. *Back Here On Earth* on Liberty, 2-disc *Songbook* on Pair '86. Songs were covered by Dylan, Johnny CASH, Elvis PRESLEY,

Jerry Lee LEWIS, Barbra STREISAND, Waylon JENNINGS, Glen CAMPBELL, etc.

LIJADU SISTERS Singers-composers Kehinde and Taiwo Lijadu (*b* Nigeria) began as session singers, achieving international status with a unique blend of trad. influences, funk, disco, afro-beat, singing mostly in Yoruba, sometimes in English and Ibo. First LP *Iya Mi Jowo* '69 was on Decca; series of innovatory LPs in '70s incl. *Danger, Mother Africa, Sunshine, Horizon Unlimited* ('79); also *Lijadu Sisters* on EMI. They appeared in the TV documentary *Konkomba* '81. Compilation *Double Trouble* appeared in USA '84 on Shanachie.

LIMELITERS, The USA folk trio formed '59: Glenn Yarbrough, tenor, guitar (*b* 12 Jan. '30, Milwaukee, Wis.); Alex Hassilev, baritone, guitar and banjo (*b* 11 July '32, Paris); Lou Gottlieb, bass, string bass (*b* '23, L.A.). Gottlieb was witty front man, had doctorate in musicology from UCLA; Hassilev was an actor who also had several languages; Hassilev and Yarbrough had run a club in Aspen, Col. called The Limelite. They were more literate than the KINGSTON TRIO, for whom Gottlieb wrote some arrangements; toured with Chris CONNOR, George SHEARING, comics Mort Sahl, Shelley Berman; did a Hollywood Bowl show with Eartha KITT. Single 'A Dollar Down' was minor hit '61; they did better in clubs and on albums: 10 charted '61-4; bestsellers were live concerts *Tonight: In Person* at the Ash Grove, Hollywood (no. 5 RCA LP helped their first LP on Elektra to the top 40), *The Slightly Fabulous Limeliters* was no. 8, all '61. They slowly slipped until washed away by the British Invasion. Yarbrough's voice was particularly good; he wrote 'Lass From The Low Country', 'All My Sorrows', etc.; went solo '63 (replaced by Ernie Sheldon) and continued selling records on RCA: 10 solo LPs charted '64-9, only one in top 40 (*Baby The Rain Must Fall* '65; title track was no. 12 single hit); made albums of songs by California 'poet' Rod McKuen, one on WB; also recorded for Tradition incl. *Looking Back* '70.

LINCOLN, Abbey (*b* Anna Marie Woolfridge, 6 Aug. '30, Chicago) Jazz singer, actress. Worked in dance bands as teenager, went to West Coast '51, sang in Hawaii as Gaby Lee; back on mainland changed name to Abbey Lincoln, worked in clubs, recorded for Liberty, appeared in film *The Girl Can't Help It* '57. Recorded for Candid '60 and with then-husband Max ROACH: *Freedom Now Suite* '60 now on Amigo UK, *It's Time* on MCA (compilation from Impulse), *Sounds As A Roach* '68 (live recording from Oslo now on Lotus). Albums incl. *That's Him!* (with Sonny ROLLINS), *It's Magic, Abbey Lincoln Is Blue*, all late '50s, now from Fantasy; *Affair* with Roach from Liberty, reissued by EMI France; *Talking To The Sun* on German Enja. She was also active in community affairs, taught drama at Cal. State U., appeared on TV (sang on Flip Wilson show, acted in *Mission Impossible*, etc.), in film *Nothing But A Man*; changed name to Aminata Moseka '75.

LIND, Bob (*b* 24 Nov. '44, Baltimore, Md.) Singer/songwriter. Moved to Chicago as a child, became a Bob DYLAN fan; attended University in Colorado and won first prize in a hootenanny contest; sang in Denver club The Analyst; signed by World Pacific, had transatlantic top 5 hit with 'Elusive Butterfly' '66, minor 2-sided hit in USA in the same year with 'Remember The Rain'/'Truly Julie's Blues'. Debut LP *Don't Be Concerned* '66 also charted (titled after hook line of 'Butterfly' lyric), incl. another minor masterpiece in 'Cheryl's Goin' Home'. *Photograph Of Feeling* was prod. by Jack NITZSCHE; *The Elusive Bob Lind* '68 came out on Verve/Folkways, *Since There Were Circles* '71 on Capitol. The gentle minstrel gave up on show business, retired to New Mexico.

LINDISFARNE UK folk-rock band formed in Newcastle late '60s, named after the island off Northumberland. Lineup: Alan Hull (*b* 20 Feb. '45), vocals and guitar; Rod Clements (*b* 17 Nov. '47), bass; Ray Jackson (*b* 12 Dec. '48), harp and mandolin; Simon Cowe (*b* 1 Apr. '48), guitar; Ray Laidlaw (*b* 28 May '48), drums. Hull had been solo folksinger, worked in groups the Chosen Few, Brethren; contributed most of Lindisfarne's material. *Nicely Out Of Tune* '70 characterised their good-time folk-rock incl. anthemic 'We Can Swing Together'. Bob

Johnston prod. *Fog On The Tyne* '71: no. 1 LP UK, still regarded as their best: title song remained concert favourite, while Johnston's work with Bob DYLAN evident in 'Meet Me On The Corner' and 'Passing Ghosts'. *Dingley Dell* '72 disappointed, but *Lindisfarne Live* '73 showed why they were a favourite live act. Hull's solo *Pipe Dream* '73 was good collection of songs; he fronted a reconstituted Lindisfarne on *Happy Daze* '74 without a lot of success: Clements, Cowe and Laidlaw had left to form Jack The Lad, recorded *Jack The Lad* and *Old Straight Track* '74 before Clement went on to session with Bert Jansch, Ralph McTell, etc. Hull's *Squire* '75 was a worthy successor to *Pipe Dream*. Jackson was in demand for sessions with Rod STEWART, Long John BALDRY, Peter Hammill, etc. *Finest Hour* '75 was a good compilation of the band's work on Charisma. Retained a fanatical following in northeast England; reunions beginning Christmas '76 became an annual Newcastle ritual: *Back And Fourth* was an energetic reunion mid-'78 ('Run For Home' was UK top 10 hit on Mercury, their biggest hit in USA at no. 33 on Atco); *Magic In The Air* late '78, *The News* '79, *Sleepless Night* '82, *Lindisfarntastic* Vols. 1 & II '84, *Dance Your Life Away* '86 kept fans happy. Multi-instrumentalist Steve Dogget was new member.

LINDLEY, David (*b* '44, Marino, Cal.) Multi-instrumentalist and songwriter, best known as one of the most accomplished, innovative USA session players in '70-80s; solo career '80s notable for eclecticism, good music and little commercial success. In '60s he played with West Coast old-timey and string bands incl. Mad Mountain Ramblers and the Dry City Scat Band; in '66 he had turned up in Kaleidoscope, perhaps the most eclectic of so-called West Coast groups: initial lineups coalesced into Lindley on lead guitar, banjo, fiddle and vocals; Charles Chester Crill on keyboards, harmonica, fiddle and vocals; Chris Darrow on guitar, vocals; Soloman Feldthouse on guitar, vocals and various exotic instruments; John Vidican, drums. The archivist is not helped by Crill's delight in assuming various names: Connie Crill, Fenrus Epp, Max Buda, Templeton Parceley. They played at the Newport Folk Festival '68; their act fused American and ethnic elements and sometimes incl. flamenco and belly dancing; albums *Side Trips* '67, *Beacon From Mars* '68 on Epic did not do much; Vidican and Darrow were replaced by Paul Lagos and Stuart Brotman on *Incredible Kaleidoscope* '69 on Epic, which reached no. 139 on the Billboard LP chart, and *Bernice* '70 on CBS, which didn't. All were soon sought-after collectors' items. A reunion album *When Scopes Collide* '76 on Pacific Arts/Island may have incl. Lindley under pseudonym De Paris Letante; another LP on Polydor was called *Brother Mary* (aka *Zabriskie Point*). Compilations *Bacon From Mars* and *Rampé Rampé* '83-4 on Edsel anthologised their best and most obscure material, incl. work with Larry WILLIAMS. Lindley moved to UK, worked with Terry Reid early '70s; demand as session player led him to work with AMERICA, David BLUE, LITTLE FEAT, Maria MULDAUR, Graham Nash, Linda RONSTADT, Leo SAYER, Rod STEWART, Warren ZEVON; he was best known for work with Jackson BROWNE (falsetto singing on 'Stay' from *Running On Empty* '78) and with Ry COODER, with whom he worked on record, as a live duo in Asia and Australia early '80s, on *The Long Riders* soundtrack '80. Solo career began with *El Rayo-X* '81 and *Win This Record!* '82 on Asylum; live recordings (e.g. 'Mercury Blues'/'I'm A Hog For You Baby' on Electra in France) testified to the power of El Rayo-X, as his band was known. Dropped by the label in USA, but *Mr Dave* '85 was on Asylum in Europe, where he had a loyal following and the kudos of having him on the label outweighed his lack of commercial appeal in sales terms.

LINDSEY, LaWanda (*b* 12 Jan. '53, Tampa, Fla.) Country singer. Her father, Lefty Lindsey, led the Dixie Showboys on local radio in Savannah, Ga.; she sang with the band age 5 and was a regular member in her teens. With help from Conway TWITTY she moved to Nashville '67, signed to Chart label and made country chart debut with 'Party Bill'; had other hits through '70s incl. duets with Kenny Vernon. Recorded for Capitol '72-5, Mercury '76-9. LPs incl. *Pickin' Wild Mountain Berries* '71 with Vernon, *Greatest Hits* '72 on Chart, *This Is LaWanda Lindsey* '73 on Capitol.

LIPSCOMB, Mance (*b* 9 Apr. 1895, Navasota, Texas; *d* 30 Jan. '76) Blues guitarist, singer. Like Furry LEWIS, Mississippi John HURT and others, he played ballads, spirituals, ragtimey and children's songs as well as blues; when they were rediscovered and began recording again, Lipscomb made his first record: he had played for friends and neighbours as a tenant farmer for 50 years when Chris Strachwitz of Arhoolie Records went to Texas to record him. When he performed at the Berkeley Folk Festival in '61 it was the first time he'd left Texas; his roots in dance music and the ethnic music of Texas made him an all-rounder; and with his fine slide guitar he became one of the best-loved of the country blues genre. He was featured in film *A Well Spent Life*, by Les Blank. LPs on Arhoolie: six vols. of *Texas Sharecropper & Songster* (no. 5 incl. 'Texas Blues'), *You'll Never Find Another Man Like Mance* '64.

LITTLE ANTHONY AND THE IMPERIALS USA doowop group formed by Anthony Gourdine (*b* 8 Jan. '40, NYC) after the Duponts (which he joined '55) folded. First called the Chesters, they cut one single at the Apollo before joining End label and having name changed by DJ Alan FREED. Group incl. Clarence Collins (*b* 17 Mar. '41, NYC), Ernest Wright (*b* 24 Aug. '41, NYC), Tracy Lord, Nat Rogers. First single for End was 'Tears On My Pillow', their biggest hit at no. 4 '58; one more top 40 entry 'Shimmy, Shimmy, Ko-Ko-Bop' '60 before splitting up. Re-formed '64 with Anthony, Collins, Wright and Sammy Strain (*b* 9 Dec. '41), had further hits on DCP label incl. top tens 'Goin' Out Of My Head' and 'Hurt So Bad' '64-5; continued on a variety of labels for a total of 10 Hot 100 entries '58-74 USA. 'Better Use Your Head' was no. 54 '66 on Veep, no. 42 '76 in UK on UA for their only UK hit. Strain joined the O'Jays '75, was replaced by Kenny Seymour; Anthony went solo, became born-again Christian and came back with inspirational LP *Daylight* '80, prod. by B. J. Thomas. Imperials without Anthony scored no. 17 hit in UK '77 with percussively danceable 'Who's Gonna Love Me' on Power Exchange label. Compilations incl. *Outside Lookin In* in UK, *Best Of* in USA, both on Liberty.

LITTLE, Booker (*b* 2 Apr. '38, Memphis, Tenn.; *d* 5 Oct. '61, NYC of uraemia) Trumpet; one of the most promising young players on the instrument, moving beyond the powerful infl. of Clifford BROWN etc. and becoming a new voice. Toured with Max ROACH '58, played on Roach LPs *Max Roach Plus Four* on EmArcy, live at Newport Jazz Festival (both on EmArcy, now on Japanese Fontana), *Deeds, Not Words* on Riverside and *Sessions, Live* on Calliope, compilation *Conversations* on Milestone, all '58; *The Many Sides Of Max Roach* on Trip/Mercury and *Award-Winning Drummer* on Bainbridge '59; *Freedom Now Suite* '60 on Candid, *Percussion Bitter Sweet* '61 on Impulse. Appeared with Mal WALDRON, John COLTRANE, Eric DOLPHY '59-61, notably on Dolphy's *Live At The Five Spot* and *Far Cry* on Prestige. Own LPs: on UA '58 (later on Blue Note) with Roach, George COLEMAN, Tommy FLANAGAN, Art Davis on bass; quartet LP '60 now on Bainbridge with Scott LA FARO; sextet on Candid '61 with Roach, Dolphy; *Victory And Sorrow* '61 on Bethlehem, now on Affinity UK with Coleman, Julian Priester, Don Friedman, Reggie Workman and Pete La Roca.

LITTLE EVA (*b* Eva Narcissus Boyd, 29 June '45, Belhaven, N.C.) Singer. Relocated to NYC to complete her education; sessioned at 16 on Ben E. KING hit 'Don't Play That Song' with Earl-Jean McRea, Dorothy Jones and Margaret Ross, aka the Cookies. Babysat for BRILL BUILDING husband/wife team Gerry GOFFIN and Carole KING; impromptu steps as King played piano inspired Goffin's dance-craze lyrics: 'The Loco-Motion' was a smash no. 1 USA/2 UK '62, with Cookies backing while saxes honked; this at height of dance-craze fashion which saw hits by Chubby CHECKER, Sam COOKE, the ISLEY Bros etc.; inspired 'answer' record 'Little Eva' by the Locomotions (Leon Huff and Philadelphia musicians out for a novelty hit). Goffin and King steered away from dance mania with 'Keep Your Hands Off My Baby', no. 12 hit for Eva same year, but Dimension label milked her talent: LP *Lllloco-Motion* '62 incl. the hit, plus covers and other things outside her range (i.e. 'I Have A Love' from *West Side Story*). Back to the dance floor for lesser hits 'Let's Turkey Trot' and 'Old

Smokey Locomotion' '63, as well as anonymous appearance on big Dee Irwin transatlantic hit 'Swingin' On A Star' same year; Cookies hit with 'Chains' (later covered by the BEATLES), several others, later backed Eydie GORME; sister Idalia Boyd, also on Dimension, had minor hit with another fad, 'Hula Hooping'. Eva recorded for Spring and Amy but faded; affection for the big one remained: 'Locomotion' reached no. 11 UK '72 on reissue.

LITTLE FEAT USA blues/rock band formed '69 in L.A. by ex-Mothers of Invention guitarist Lowell George (*b* 13 Apr. '45; *d* 29 June '79, Arlington, Va.), who'd also played with Standells. Former boss Frank ZAPPA supplied both name of group (from George's shoe size) and bassist Roy Estrada; lineup incl. Ritchie Hayward, drums (ex-Fraternity of Man) and Bill Payne on keyboards (*b* 12 Mar. '49, Waco, Texas), who played together in Factory. *Little Feat* '71 was low-budget impressive debut, combining blues (covers of Howlin' WOLF) with George's unique compositions fusing blues, country and not a little of Zappa's humour. Truckdrivers' anthem 'Willin' ' was standout track, with Ry COODER guesting on guitar. Eight of 11 songs on *Sailin' Shoes* '72 were George's, incl. 'Cold Cold Cold' and 'Tripe Face Boogie'; LP sleeves designed by Neon Parks still famous; lack of commercial success caused split: members worked with Robert PALMER, DOOBIE Bros, Bonnie RAITT before re-forming without Estrada (who joined CAPTAIN BEEFHEART) but with Kenny Gradney (*b* New Orleans) on bass and Sam Clayton on congas (both ex-Delaney & Bonnie BRAMLETT), and second guitarist Paul Barrere (*b* 3 July '48, Burbank, Cal.) (who'd failed audition for bass!). *Dixie Chicken* '73 and *Feats Don't Fail Me Now* '74 were best commercial Feats, retaining second-line New Orleans influences: Allen TOUSSAINT's 'On Your Way Down' on *Chicken* was great moment. George's soulful vocals and slide guitar were rarely captured fully in the studio; he is said to have prod. bootlegs *Electrif Lycanthrope* and *Aurora Backseat* which showed group in best form. Tour with Doobies '75 confirmed popularity in Europe, but Payne and Barrere were moving band away from roots towards imitation jazz; this was first apparent on *The Last Record Album* '76 and flawed *Time Loves A Hero* '77 badly. By the time of the first official live LP *Waiting For Columbus* '78, made in front of adoring London fans, split was inevitable: George left the stage during meandering instrumental 'Day At The Dog Races'. He cut underrated solo album *Thanks I'll Eat It Here* '79, concentrating on singing rather than guitar (to critics' disgust); incl. cover of 'Easy Money' by then-unknown Rickie Lee JONES. He died of heart attack on tour with session band. Last Feat LP *Down On The Farm* was completed and released, also reverential *Hoy Hoy* '81 (collection of alternates/out-takes). George had sessioned widely on slide guitar, with Etta JAMES, John CALE, John Sebastian, others; prod. GRATEFUL DEAD; was one of the '70s more endearing figures: the band could not survive without him. Barrere cut solo *On My Own Two Feet* '83; Hayward sessioned, joined Robert Plant band; Payne sessioned, wrote with his wife, Fran Tate. Feat's synthesis of USA styles never broke out of cult following, but George's songs were covered by Palmer, NAZARETH, Linda RONSTADT, others; all the albums are still in print; best-of compilation *As Time Goes By* '86. Terry ALLEN dedicated 'Heart Of California' to George Payne, Hayward, Gradney, Barrere re-formed with Craig Fuller (ex-Pure Prairie League) and Fred Tackett (played with Bob DYLAN, and Randy NEWMAN for New Orleans Jazz and Heritage Festival '88, album *Let It Roll*).

LITTLE MILTON (*b* Milton Campbell, 7 Sep. '34, Inverness, Ms.) Guitarist, blues singer. Sang in church, began on guitar at about 10, played in public at age 14; infl. by T-Bone WALKER, B. B. KING; led trio in Memphis '50, recorded for Sun with Ike TURNER band, recorded on Meteor, Bobbin, Checker: no. 14 R&B hit 'So Mean To Me' '61, then 15 more '65-71 incl. no. 1 'We're Gonna Make It'; went to Stax for more hits. Appeared in film *Wattstax*. Remains important pop/soul figure close to blues roots. Eight early tracks in 9-disc set from Sun vaults *The Blues Years* from Charly UK; *Raise A Little Sand* on Red Lightnin' UK from Bobbin (St Louis) years has backing from Fontella BASS, bandleader Oliver Sain; other LPs: *Grits Ain't Groceries*,

Blues'n' Soul, Waiting For Little Milton, Walking The Back Streets on Stax; *Age Ain't Nothin' But A Number* on MCA; *Annie Mae's Cafe* '86 on Malaco.

LITTLE RICHARD (*b* Richard Wayne Penniman, 5 Dec. '35, Macon, Ga.) R&B singer, pianist and bandleader who became one of the kings of rock'n'roll. One of 12 children; born slightly deformed, with one short leg and arm. Family were active in Pentecostal churches, but father sold bootleg whiskey. He sang and learned some piano in church; sang on stage with Sister Rosetta THARPE at Macon City Auditorium; left home at 14 because of homosexual activities and to join medicine show; became well-known in whistle-stop black Southern vaudeville. Infl. in Atlanta by Billy Wright, a blues singer who wore makeup and had wild dress sense. First recorded for RCA '51 at WGST Atlanta through white R&B DJ Zenas Sears; 'Every Hour' was small local hit. He was inspired to play more piano by obscure, legendary Esquerita (Eskew Reeder; recorded R&B in New Orleans mid-'60s). Second RCA session early '52 was less successful. His father was shot to death that year; the killer was let off and Richard became the family's support; he washed dishes at Macon's bus station, formed band the Tempo Toppers, recorded for Peacock '53 incl. sides with Johnny OTIS, formed Little Richard and the Upsetters; sent demo tape to Specialty, label formed on West Coast '44 by Art Rupe to make R&B, gospel records: Specialty had hits with Roy MILTON, others; then million-selling 'Lawdy Miss Clawdy' with Lloyd PRICE; Bumps BLACKWELL joined '55 and heard Little Richard's tape as he was looking for a blues singer with gospel quality. First recording session in Cosimo Matassa's New Orleans studio with house band incl. Earl Palmer on drums, Alvin 'Red' Tyler on baritone sax (*see* Dave BARTHOLOMEW), Lee ALLEN on tenor; Huey 'Piano' SMITH was probably there; Richard clowned on piano with tavern novelty 'Tutti Frutti': Blackwell had lyric cleaned up by Dorothy La Bostrie and the result made no. 2 R&B chart late '55, no. 17 pop early '56, its opening 'a-wop-bom-aloo-mop-a-lop-bam-boom' also opening an era in popular music. Absurdly, it was a no. 12 pop hit by Pat BOONE same month (B-side of ballad 'I'll Be Home'), also less absurdly covered by Elvis PRESLEY; along with Jerry Lee LEWIS, Presley himself, Richard defined the essentially anarchic, hedonistic nature of the rock'n'roll phenomenon, in his case with outrageous sexuality, costumes, makeup and pompadour, gospel-infl. screaming; he appeared in film *Don't Knock The Rock* '56. Many later hits were 2-sided: 'Slippin' And Slidin'/'Long Tall Sally' (another dirty song), 'Rip It Up'/'Ready Teddy' '56 (both covered by Elvis), 'The Girl Can't Help It' (title song from the best rock'n'roll movie ever made), 'Lucille'/'Send Me Some Lovin', 'Jenny, Jenny'/'Miss Ann', 'Keep A Knockin' '57; 'Good Golly Miss Molly' '58 (last top 10 hit). He had formed a new Upsetters for touring, but quit on tour in Australia '57 to turn to the church, and partly because he was working very hard and wasn't seeing enough of the money; in a famous incident he threw a valuable ring into the sea to prove that he meant what he said. Recorded gospel for George Goldner in NYC '59 with limited backing, other instruments dubbed on various issues on several labels (now on Bulldog in UK). He accepted a tour in the UK with Billy PRESTON in his backing group, ROLLING STONES on their first big tour and Sam COOKE; intended to sing gospel songs, which would have hurt ticket sales, but Cooke's hits were so successful ('Twistin' The Night Away') that Richard couldn't turn down the challenge: sang rock'n'roll after all and 'wrecked the place', according to Cooke's manager, J. W. Alexander. Upsetters had worked backing LITTLE WILLIE JOHN; Richard made an uncredited session with them under their name, prod. by H. B. BARNUM c.'60; two singles were issued but the rest was lost. Reunited with Blackwell, whose former protégé Quincy JONES prod. his best gospel album, *The King Of Gospel Singers* '62 on Mercury with Howard Roberts Chorale, now long out of print: it was a fine album but completely different; few bought it and those who did felt cheated. He recorded religious songs for Atlantic '62-3, came back to Specialty '63-4 with Palmer, Don 'Sugarcane' Harris on bass, others: 'Bama Lama Bama Loo' was up to standard, but only no. 82 in pop chart: the music business had recovered from the on-

slaught of crossover acts in the '50s and pop had been made smoother and less exciting again; many were probably angry with Richard (his behaviour in '57 cost a lot in cancelled gigs); he had always been unpredictable: Blackwell told the story of a recording session on a Sunday with 40 people waiting on double time from 10 a.m. to 8 p.m., when Richard announced that 'The Lord does not want me to record today.' He recorded for Vee Jay, Modern, Okeh, Brunswick mid-'60s; many were mediocre records, all of them mishandled by the record companies; e.g. the Brunswick issues incl. demos and studio warm-ups. The Vee Jay and perhaps some Modern sessions incl. Jimi HENDRIX, known to Richard as Maurice James, and who learned a lot from a great showman (Hendrix was not stranded in the UK by Richard as legend had it but sacked in NYC). Reprise LPs represented a real comeback and made fans happy: *The Rill Thing* '70 (incl. 'Freedom Blues'; almost made top 40), *The King Of Rock'n'Roll* '71, *The Second Coming* '72. His gay image and patter kept him off TV (except talk shows), while the tension and guilt between his spiritual and secular feelings dogged him, but the live act rarely failed, not that the real fans ever gave up on him: he had inspired the BEATLES, Mick Jagger, David BOWIE, countless others; on stage he cut Ike and Tina TURNER, Janis JOPLIN, Jerry Lee LEWIS, etc. and could pack any room in Las Vegas. He appeared in films *Catalina Caper* (*Never Steal Anything Wet*) '67, *Sweet Toronto* (from '69 Toronto Pop Festival; retitled *Keep On Rockin'* with John LENNON segment removed), *Let The Good Times Roll* '73, *The London Rock'n'Roll Show* '72 (at Wembley); he sessioned '71-2 on albums *To Delaney From Bonnie* on Atco, *Sunfighter* by JEFFERSON STARSHIP, and on soundtrack of caper movie *$* ('Dollars'; titled *The Heist* in UK) '71 (score by Quincy Jones). Other LPs incl. *Right Now!* on United and *Talking 'bout Soul* on Dynasty '73, *Head On* '75 on Mercury, *Little Richard Live* '76 on K-Tel (remakes of 20 Specialty hits), *God's Beautiful City* '79 on World. Specialty LPs have all the original hits; *Little Richard: His Greatest Recordings* on Ace UK has 16 of them digitally remastered. *The Life And Times Of Little Richard* by Charles White '84 is very good. He drove his sports car into a telephone pole on Santa Monica Blvd '85, survived with 36 pins in his right leg; new LP *Lifetime Friend* on WEA '86.

LITTLE RIVER BAND Australian AOR group formed '75 from international pool: singer Glenn Shorrock (ex-Esperanto) and drummer Derek Pellicci were from UK; guitarists were Beeb Birtles from Holland, Australian Graham Goble and Italian Rick Formosa (had been resident in Canada); bassist was New Zealander Roger McLachlan (ex-*Godspell* tour band). Birtles had played with future teen star Rick SPRINGFIELD in Zoot, also with Goble and Pellicci in Mississippi, whose West Coast-influenced sound was apparent in the new band's eponymous '75 debut album: single 'It's A Long Way There' was no. 28 hit in USA, reminiscent of CSN&Y, EAGLES at their most melodic. Formosa and McLachlan replaced before *After Hours* '76 by George McArdle and David Briggs respectively; *Diamantina Cocktail* '77 was compiled from Australian LPs and went gold in USA, incl. no. 14 USA single 'Help Is On Its Way'; from then on big success was easy with top 10 singles made for USA radio: *Sleeper Catcher* '78 incl. 'Reminiscing', 'Lady'; *First Under The Wire* '79 incl. 'Lonesome Loser', 'Cool Change'; Briggs was replaced by Steve Housden and Wayne Nelson joined on bass but sound remained harmonious soft rock. Live 2-disc *Backstage Pass* '80 was followed by *Time Exposure* '81 incl. 'The Night Owls', 'Take It Easy On Me'. Shorrock went solo '82, replaced by John Farnham; they fell out of the top 20 for the first time since '77; prod. John Boylan went with Shorrock and like fellow CSN&Y imitators AMERICA, they enlisted George MARTIN. More LPs: *The Net* '83, *Playing To Win* '85, *No Reins* '86, latter with Farnham, Goble, Housden, Nelson, newer members. Success inspired AIR SUPPLY etc. to imitate *them*, but infl. will ultimately be slight.

LITTLE WALTER (*b* Marion Walter Jacobs, 1 May '30, Marksville, La.; *d* 15 Feb. '68, Chicago) Blues harmonica, probably the greatest of all. Studied harmonica from age 8; later ran away from home, played clubs, radio (King Biscuit Time, Mother's Best Flour Hour '44-6), to Chicago '47. Played in Maxwell Street for tips, his jazz-infl.

phrasing soon bringing work as sideman with Tampa Red, Big Bill BROONZY, Memphis Slim; recorded for small labels '47-50; on many Muddy WATERS hits: 'Baby Please Don't Go' '52, 'Got My Mojo Working' '57, many more. Own hits on Checker incl. 10 entries in R&B chart, all but two in top 10; instrumental 'Juke' '52 and 'My Babe' '55 were no. 1. He also recorded with Otis RUSH '57, toured with group the Jukes, toured Europe with R&B package '62, with ROLLING STONES '64, many other tours, festivals. Died of blood clot following a fight in the street. LPs in UK: 2-disc compilations *Chess Masters* on Chess; *Quarter To Twelve*, *Thunderbird*, *We Three Kings* (with Waters, Howlin' WOLF), all on Red Lightnin' label.

LITTLE WILLIE JOHN (*b* John Davenport, 15 Nov. '37, Camden, Ark.; *d* 26 May '68 in Washington State Penitentiary) R&B singer who had a huge infl. in the soul era. Moved to Detroit, sang with Paul Williams band (some sources say also with Duke ELLINGTON, Count BASIE); recorded for Savoy by the time he was 16. Signed with King and had 14 R&B chart hits '56-61, the same number of hits crossing over to the pop Hot 100 incl. 'Fever' '56, 'Talk To Me, Talk To Me' '58, 'Sleep' '60, all prod. by Henry Glover and all top 40 pop. 'Fever' was later covered by Peggy LEE for a big hit, so remains John's best-known record; some sources say Otis BLACKWELL wrote it, others that John and Eddie Cooley co-wrote it. His records were also covered by Elvis PRESLEY, Sunny and the Sunglows, Johnny Preston, others; his sister Mabel recorded for Stax and joined Ray CHARLES's Raelettes. He was a master of the blues ballad, with more passion than many another who sang with more frenzy; unfortunately he was unstable, perhaps unable to handle his own charisma: he carried a gun while a big attraction at the Apollo theatre, killed a man with a knife in a bar in Seattle and was jailed May '66 for manslaughter; died of pneumonia. Compilations: *15 Hits* on King USA; *Grits And Soul* on Charly UK has 16.

LLOYD, A. L. (*b* Albert Lancaster 'Bert' Lloyd, '08; *d* 29 Sep. '82) British author, musicologist, singer; the most infl. and revered figure in post-war folk revival. Apart from records, two books have been pivotal: *The Penguin Book Of English Folk Songs* '59 was co-edited by Ralph Vaughan Williams (*b* 12 Oct. 1872, Gloucestershire; *d* 26 Aug. '58, London), had sold 50,000 copies by mid-'80s, making it best-seller in the genre; *Folk Song In England* '67 is standard infl. on revival artists. *Der Grosse Steinitz: Deutsche Volkslieder demokratischen Charakters aus sechs Jahrhunderten* '55 and '62 in East Germany was a similar treatment of German folksong. He was a mentor for countless acts incl. Anne BRIGGS, Martin CARTHY, FAIRPORT CONVENTION, the WATERSONS and the YOUNG TRADITION. He lived in Australia in his mid-teens, 'sheepminding' as he called it; collected 'bush ballads' for nine years; returned to UK during Depression, went to sea in whaling industry; chanced to hear BBC programme about unemployment in USA, approached BBC about similar venture on UK from the point of view of the working man; *The Singing Englishman: An Introduction To Folk Song* '44, published by the Workers' Music Association led to *Folksong In England* when it needed revision and updating. Worked as broadcaster, journalist (also wrote about Spanish Civil War), was involved in radio series *Ballads And Blues* '53 (also inspired an early folk club formed by Ewan MACCOLL), with performances by Big Bill BROONZY, Alan LOMAX, Lloyd, MacColl, Jean RITCHIE etc. (This was still the heyday of radio in UK, TV still in infancy, beyond most people's pockets.) Later worked on MacColl/Parker *Radio Ballads*; one programme, 'Singing The Fishing' '60, had extract on *The Electric Muse* '75 on Island/Transatlantic, Lloyd singing 'Shoals Of Herring' intercut with Sam Larner reminiscing about life as a fisherman typical of MacColl's programming. 'The Banks Of The Condamine'/'Bold Jack Donahue' was a 78 on Topic with Al Jeffrey; most of his work was on microgroove: in '50s EPs *The Banks Of The Condamine, Convicts & Currency Lads* on Australian Wattle label; *Row Bullies Row, The Blackball Line* and *Bold Sportsmen All* all with MacColl on Topic. They also recorded with Harry H. Corbett, later famous in BBC TV comedy *Steptoe & Son*. Work appeared on Riverside in USA; thematic albums incl. *A Selection From The Penguin Book Of English Folk Songs* '60 on Collector/Folklyric; *The Iron Muse* '63 examined industrial folk songs, with Briggs, Bob Davenport, Ray Fisher, Louis Killen, Matt McGinn, the Celebrated Workingmen's Band; *The Bird In The Bush* '66 was erotic songs, with Frankie ARMSTRONG, Briggs, Alf Edwards, Dave Swarbrick; *Leviathan!* '67, about whaling, ironically found a new market in Japan '80s (all on Topic). Other albums incl. *First Person* on Topic, *The Best Of A. L. Lloyd* on Transatlantic/Prestige; *Haul On The Bowlin* and *Off To Sea Once More* on Stinson with MacColl; *English And Scottish Ballads Vols. 1-5, The Whaler Out Of New Bedford, The Unfortunate Rake* all on Folkways; *Sea Shanties, The Great Australian Legend, The Valiant Sailor* all on Topic; and his field recordings incl. *Rumanian Folk Music* (10″ LP '50s), *Folk Music Of Bulgaria* '64, *Of Albania* '66, all on Topic. Another *Selection From The Penguin Book Of English Folk Songs* '85 on Fellside incl. Carthy, John Bowden, Jez Lowe, Linda Adams, Roy Harris. Ian Watson's book *Song And Democratic Culture In Britain* acknowledged its debt to Lloyd; his legacy is enormous.

LLOYD, Charles (*b* 15 Mar. '38, Memphis, Tenn.) Tenor sax, flute, composer, leader. From middle-class black family; took up sax '48; classmates incl. Booker LITTLE, George COLEMAN. Played alto with R&B bands incl. B. B. KING, Bobby BLAND; to West Coast '56, took up flute '58; studied dentistry but switched to music. Played alto with Gerald WILSON; joined Chico HAMILTON '61-4, switched to tenor '62 (LPs with Hamilton on Columbia, Reprise, Impulse). Toured with Cannonball ADDERLEY, formed own quartet '65 and signed with Columbia: LPs '64-5 began with *Discovery* with bassist Richard Davis, pianist Don Friedman (*b* 4 May '35, San Francisco), drummer John Curtis Moses (*b* 18 Oct. '36, Philadelphia; also played with Eric DOLPHY, Cedar WALTON, many others; to Europe with New York Contemporary 5 '63 etc.; less active in '70s owing to illness); *Of Course, Of Course* with Gabor SZABO, Ron CARTER, Tony WILLIAMS; he switched to Atlantic: new quartet with Keith JARRETT, Cecil McBEE, Jack DeJOHNETTE made

Dream Weaver, Live At Antibes, Forest Flower, Charles Lloyd In Europe, all '66. Ron McClure replaced McBee; in '67 *Love-In* was made live at the Fillmore; *Live In The Soviet Union* saw some tracks from the tour issued on Melodia, Muza, Supraphon. Documentary film *Charles Lloyd – Journey Within* '69 made by Eric Sherman. LPs on Kapp/MCA (*Moonman, Warm Waters*) and A&M (*Geeta, Waves*) followed c.'71-2; he also played electric piano and organ. His most popular music was rooted in the '60s; he semi-retired to teaching music and transcendental meditation on the West Coast. *Weavings* '78 incl. horns, strings and rhythm, Lloyd on soprano, tenor and flute; *Big Sur Tapestry* '79 was duet with harpist Georgia Kelly on title track, plus 'Homage To The Universe', Lloyd playing oboe, recorder, flutes, both on Pacific Arts. French pianist Michel PETRUCCIANI looked up Lloyd; a new quartet made *Montreux '82* on Elektra Musician (incl. new version of 'Forest Flower') and *A Night In Copenhagen* '83 for Blue Note, with Lloyd on tenor and flute, Petrucciani, drummer Son Ship Theus, Palle Danielsson on bass; also vocalist Bobby MCFERRIN on the Blue Note.

LLOYD WEBBER, Andrew (*b* 22 Mar '48 London) Composer. Son of composer William Lloyd Webber, dir. of London College of Music (*d* '82). Studied at Royal Academy of Music but largely self-taught; determined to create successful UK musical theatre. Met lyricist Tim Rice '65; they wrote songs, unproduced musical *The Likes Of Us*; pop oratorio *Joseph And His Amazing Technicolor Dreamcoat*, at first about 15 minutes long: staged '68 at a school and well reviewed by Derek Jewell (*d* '85), pop critic on London newspaper; it evolved '72-3, full-length version staged five times in London, four in USA. *Come Back Richard, Your Country Needs You* unproduced; *Jesus Christ Superstar* recorded '70, first staged NYC '71, filmed '73; ran in London eight years. Wrote film scores *Gumshoe* '71, *Odessa File* '74. Musical *Jeeves* based on P. G. Wodehouse '75; Rice had dropped out, playwright Alan Ayckbourne wrote lyrics; show flopped. Rice proposed show based on life of Eva Peron; *Evita* recorded '76 with Julie COVINGTON. Single 'Don't Cry For Me, Argentina' no. 1 in UK '76 and re-

entered charts '78 as show staged in London with Elaine PAIGE and David ESSEX; ran four years NYC. ('Another Suitcase In Another Hall', recorded by Barbara DICKSON, also charted in UK '77.) Rice and Webber have not worked together since. Started Really Useful Company '78 to retain control of all his work. *Cats*, based on T. S. Eliot, began as a song cycle; another smash hit when staged in '81, grossing $400,000 a week in both NYC and Boston. Song 'Memory' has words by director Trevor Nunn, based on Eliot's 'Rhapsody On A Windy Night'. Wrote *Variations* for cello and rock band for brother Julian Lloyd Webber and 'Tell Me On A Sunday' for Marti Webb; combined them in review *Song And Dance* '82. At one time had four shows running in London; bought Palace Theatre for $1.3m to restore it, closing *Song and Dance*. With three shows each in NYC and London (*Cats* booking a year ahead) *Starlight Express* opened in London '84, based on train motif, lyrics by Richard Stilgoe: with the Victoria Apollo theatre completely rebuilt for it and cast on roller skates, *Starlight* was most expensive musical ever mounted; another hit, despite mixed reviews: 'A millionaire's folly, which happens to be open to the public' said a London critic: passed break-even point late '85. Invested in Howard Goodall/Melvin Bragg musical *The Hired Man*, lost money. *Requiem* (for his father) was recorded Dec. '84, premiered (except for early draft) Feb. '85, with second wife Sarah Brightman, tenor Placido Domingo, boy treble Paul Miles-Kingston: score has lower strings but no violins (they would conflict with boy choir's range): NYC premiere was televised; LP leapt to top of USA classical chart; single from it sold 40,000 copies in a week in UK. Reviews mixed: religious mystery not explored, but popular appeal of one or two good tunes mixed with musical trademarks cannot be denied. *Phantom Of The Opera* starred Brightman, with Michael Crawford in the title role, novice Charles Hart writing lyrics: music premiered late '85, staged early '86, prod. as a video by Ken Russell; NYC premiere early '88 set record for advance ticket sales; film by Steven Spielberg talked about. Next project to be *Aspects Of Love*, based on novel by David Garnett '55. Really Useful Company went public '86. Lloyd Webber's work is evolving from imitation rock (*Superstar*) to opera, with no spoken dialogue at all; he is an inspired businessman and productions have to be praised for technical perfection: the Victorian gloss on *Phantom* is achieved by micro-circuitry, with 102 tiny trap doors for candles in the Phantom's lair. Rice carried on writing with others, in '85 celebrated 99 weeks of his work in singles chart; show *Chess* '86 with score by Benny Andersson and Bjorn Ulvaeus (ex-ABBA) 'shows the dinosaur mega-musical evolving into an intelligent form of life' (Irving Wardle in *The Times*, probably by comparison with the Dave CLARK show *Time*). Rice was also 'rock brain of the year' on BBC radio '86.

LOBO USA singer/songwriter Kent Lavoie (*b* 31 July '43, Tallahassee, Fla.); scored 16 Hot 100 entries in USA '71-9, 8 in top 30. With group called the Rumors at university in Florida; then the Sugar Beats, who had a local hit with help of prod. Phil Gerhard; after US Army service Lavoie worked with Me & The Other Guys, then was rescued from obscurity by Gerhard, who signed him to Big Tree Records; took name Lobo (Spanish for wolf) so he could start over again if he flopped, but did well with his likeable songs: 'Me And You And A Dog Named Boo' was top 5 both USA and UK '71; 'I'd Love You To Want Me' was his biggest hit, no. 2 USA '72/top 5 UK '74 on Jonathan KING's UK label. LPs incl. *Introducing Lobo* '71 (incl. 'Dog Named Boo'), *Of A Simple Man* '72 (top 40 LP incl. the other two top 10 singles), *Calumet* '73, *Just A Singer* '74, *A Cowboy Afraid Of Horses* '75. With Gerhard and using his real name he also produced LPs for Jim Stafford, which incl. top 10 novelties 'Spiders And Snakes', 'Wildwood Weed' '73-4. He was silent '76-8, then back in the top 30 '79 on MCA/Curb with 'Where Were You When I Was Falling In Love', also an eponymous LP prod. by Bob Montgomery. He writes TV/radio jingles, making tapes in home-based studio.

LOCKE, Joe (*b* 18 Mar. '59, Palo Alto, Cal.) Vibes, composer. Instructor at Hochstein School of Music in Rochester NY '77, toured and recorded with Spider Martin Quintet '76-8, backing guests Dizzy GILLESPIE, Pepper ADAMS, others; led own quintet in upstate NY '79-81; guest lecturer/clinician at Eastman School of Music (Rochester), several others from '83, same year composed and performed the score for the documentary film *El Salvador – Another Vietnam* (won prize at Paris Film Festival). The Joe Locke – Phil Markowitz Quartet (with Eddie Gomez, Keith COPELAND) played at Carnegie Hall '84 *Live In Front Of The Silver Screen* on Little label in Rochester (aka *Restless Dreams* on chief CD in UK). Pianist Markowitz (*b* 6 Sep. '52) also composer, teaches at Eastman; wrote 'Sno Pea', recorded by Bill EVANS; played with Art PEPPER, Miroslav Vitous, Mel LEWIS Orch. at Village Vanguard, many others; toured Europe with Chet BAKER, recorded with Baker, BRECKER Bros.; toured with Al DIMEOLA, played on his LP *Soaring Through A Dream* '85. Locke's *Scenario* '85 on Cadence prod. by bassist Fred Stone, with Jerry Bergonzi, tenor sax (worked with Dave BRUBECK; own LP with quartet Con Brio on Plug label '85); Andy Laverne, piano (five years with Stan GETZ); Adam Nussbaum, drums (with Getz, Gil EVANS, Gary BURTON).

LOCKLIN, Hank (*b* Lawrence Hankins Locklin, 15 Feb. '18, McLellan, Fla.) Veteran USA country singer with distinctive nasal tenor voice who specialises in heart songs. Especially popular in Ireland, where he was voted most popular country singer five years in a row. Did farm work, road construction, singing in clubs evenings and weekends across the South; signed with 4-Star label '49 (no. 2 hit 'Let Me Be The One' '54), Decca '54; to RCA '57 and string of big hits incl. 'Geisha Girl' '57, 'Send Me The Pillow You Dream On' '58 (which he wrote, also recorded for 4-star; covered by Dean MARTIN '65 for top 25 pop hit); no. 1 country hit 'Please Help Me I'm Falling' '60: song by Don ROBERTSON was an international hit, top 10 in USA/UK pop charts; inspired 'answer' discs; re-recorded '70 with Danny Davis & The Nashville Brass it charted again. Locklin never had another that big, but carried on with country hits every year into the '70s. He bought a ranch called the Singing L near McLellan in mid-'60s and was made honorary mayor. Recorded for MGM '74-6, Plantation '77; remains popular in Europe because of frequent touring. LPs incl. *Foreign Love* '58, *Happy Journey* '62, *My Love Song For You* '67, *Lookin' Back* '68, *Bless Her Heart, I Love Her* '70, *Irish Songs, Country Style* '71, *Mayor Of McLellan, Florida* '73, *Famous Country Music Maker* '76, all on RCA; *Golden Hits* '77 on Ember, *All Kinds Of Everything* '79 on Top Spin, *Mr Country* '83 on Pickwick.

LOESSER, Frank (*b* 29 June '10, NYC; *d* there 28 July '69) Songwriter. Never interested in anything but songwriting, after a long slow start he became one of the best. Wrote words for 'I Wish I Were Twins' '34 (record by Fats WALLER), 'Moon Of Manakoora' (music by Alfred Newman, from film *The Hurricane* '37), 'Two Sleepy People' and 'Small Fry' with Hoagy CARMICHAEL, 'I Don't Want To Walk Without You' with Jule Styne (for film *Sweater Girl* '42, hit record by Harry JAMES & Helen Forrest), others. He wrote dummy tunes for his own lyrics for demos; 'Praise The Lord And Pass The Ammunition' was one of the biggest hits of WWII with his demo tune; from then on he wrote his own music, incl. 'Spring Will Be A Little Late This Year' '44 for film *Christmas Holiday*, 'Baby, It's Cold Outside' for *Neptune's Daughter* '49 (with Red Skelton and Esther Williams; hit records by Johnny MERCER & Margaret WHITING, Dinah SHORE & Buddy CLARK, Ella FITZGERALD & Louis JORDAN, others), 'On A Slow Boat To China' (Kay KYSER, Eddy HOWARD, Freddy MARTIN, others), then shows: *Where's Charley?* '48 with Ray Bolger (adapted from English play *Charley's Aunt*, 1892), songs incl. 'My Darling, My Darling', 'Once In Love With Amy'; then masterpiece *Guys And Dolls* '50: 'A Bushel And A Peck', 'If I Were A Bell', 'I've Never Been In Love Before', 'Luck Be A Lady', more; also film *Hans Christian Andersen* '52 with Danny KAYE ('The Inch Worm', 'Thumbelina', 'No Two People' etc.), shows *The Most Happy Fella* '56, *How To Succeed In Business Without Really Trying* '61, other shows and films. A workaholic and a heavy smoker, he died of cancer.

LOFGREN, Nils (*b* c.'52, Chicago) USA singer/songwriter/guitarist. Brought up in Maryland by Swedish/Italian parents, gravitated to nearby Washington DC club scene. Formed Grin '69 with ex-Reekers drummer Bob Berberich (*b* '49, Md.), bassist Bob Gordon (*b* '51, Okla.); live act impressed Neil YOUNG, who hired him to play piano on *After The Goldrush* '70 and recommended him to sometime backing band Crazy Horse, whose eponymous debut LP he graced the same year, writing two songs. Fame helped Grin get a contract with Spindizzy/Columbia: *Grin* and *1+1* '71 were praised by critics; *All Out* '72 was strengthened by presence of elder brother Tom on guitar; all three made Billboard's top 200 LPs without setting sales records. He guested with Young on Tonight's The Night tour, LP of that name; after Grin's disappointing *Gone Crazy* '73 they split. Speculation of Lofgren link with ROLLING STONES (he idolised Keith Richard) ended by *Nils Lofgren* '75 on A&M, first and best solo LP, incl. spunky rockers 'Back It Up' and 'Keith Don't Go (Ode To The Glimmer Twin)'; piano-based cover of Gerry GOFFIN/Carole KING's 'Goin' Back' proved him more than just another guitar hero. *Back It Up* '76 was KSAN radio broadcast released on A&M, confirming promise with gritty live version of 'Beggars Day', one of the songs written for Crazy Horse. But *Cry Tough* '76 set a patchy pattern, prod. by Al KOOPER; soul-flavoured *I Came To Dance* and tired 2-disc live set *Night After Night* '77 in comparison with first live disc showed that undoubted talent was spread too thin; *Nils* '79 was more reflective: three songs with lyrics by Lou REED, fine cover of Randy NEWMAN's 'Baltimore', improved quality of his own (fewer) songs (incl. 'No Mercy', story of a reluctant boxer) confirmed that he needed input from other writers to sustain an entire album. He yielded street-punk image to Tom PETTY et al. new stance as reflective singer/songwriter found fewer takers: *Night Fades Away* '81 barely made top 100 LPs in USA, and *Wonderland* '83 did not chart at all (both on new Backstreet label, MCA in UK). He returned to Young for *Trans* '82 LP and tour; signed by UK indie Towerbell but put solo career on hold '84 to join Bruce SPRINGSTEEN's E Street Band on departure of Steve VAN ZANDT, touring '84-5; belated release of *Flip* '85 saw modest return to form, with rocker 'Secrets In The Street', ballad 'Delivery Night' all too reminiscent of former glory. Stage presence is remarkable: does back flip on trampoline (hence LP title), plays guitar hero convincingly. *Best Of Grin* on Epic/UK; *Best Of A&M/USA*, similar *A Rhythm Romance* in UK; first solo set or hard-to-find (much bootlegged) *Back It Up* recommended; new live 2-disc set *Code Of The Road* '86 was much better *Night After Night*.

LOFTON, Cripple Clarence (*b* 28 Mar. 1887, Kingsport, Tenn.; *d* 9 Jan. '57, Chicago) Blues singer, pianist; also drummer, whistler, tap dancer, despite probably being partly disabled from birth. A classic rent party entertainer, particularly well-liked for his piano. To Chicago '17; owned a tavern there late '30s. Recorded for Vocalion/ARC group '35, Yazoo c.'37, Solo Art/Riverside '39, Pax/Session '43 tracks reissued on Storyville, coupled with Jimmy YANCEY tracks from same dates. Other compilations: *1935-6 Recordings* on Magpie, with Walter Davis on Yazoo (*b* 1 Mar. '12, Grenada, Ms.; *d* probably 22 Oct. '63, St Louis; also pianist/singer).

LOGAN, Ella (*b* Ella Allan, 6 Mar. '13, Glasgow; *d* 1 May '69, Burlingame, Cal.) Singer, actress. Aunt and foster-mother of singer Annie Ross (*see* Jon HENDRICKS). Born into theatrical family; toured European music halls; to USA '32; with Abe Lyman band '33-4. Broadway musical *Calling All Stars* '34, then films *Flying Hostess* '36; *Top Of The Town, Woman Chases Man, 42nd Street* all '37; *Goldwyn Follies* '38. Began recording '30, often as band singer with Lyman, AMBROSE, Adrian ROLLINI, etc.; also on radio. Known for swinging trad. tunes: Brunswick records late '30s incl. versions of 'I Was Doing All Right', 'Bluebells Of Scotland', 'The Old Kent Road' etc. with jazz backing; also duet with Hoagy CARMICHAEL on his 'Two Sleepy People'/'New Orleans'. On Broadway in George White's *Scandals Of 1939, Sons O' Fun* '41-2; vaudeville revue *Show Time* '42; records with Spirits Of Rhythm '41. Entertained troops overseas WWII; club circuit postwar, then lead role in *Finian's Rainbow* '47, introducing Yip HARBURG-Burton Lane songs 'How Are Things In Glocca Mora', 'Old Devil Moon', 'If This Isn't Love', etc. Later years with touring musicals, solo club dates, occasional TV.

LOGGINS & MESSINA USA soft-rock duo of '70s, formed by Kenny Loggins (*b* 7 Jan. '48, Everett, Wash.) and Jim Messina (*b* 5 Dec. '47, Maywood, Cal.) Messina was a veteran of BUFFALO SPRINGFIELD and POCO whose first project for Columbia as prod. was Loggins, whose experience as performer with little-known bands Gator Creek and Second Helping, fading psychedelics the ELECTRIC PRUNES was less impressive than his writing for publishers ABC Wingate, incl. 'House At Pooh Corner', '71 hit for NITTY GRITTY DIRT BAND (later co-wrote no. 1 hit for DOOBIE Bros. '79, 'What A Fool Believes' with Michael McDonald). First LP *Kenny Loggins With Jim Messina Sittin' In* '71 went gold, incl. 'Danny's Song' (covered by Anne MURRAY, top 10 hit '73). Essentially an MOR act despite 'hip' image, fitting on radio with AMERICA, similar acts. *Loggins And Messina* '72 incl. lightly rocking 'Your Mama Don't Dance'; no. 4 hit; 'Thinking Of You' and 'My Music' were both top 20 '73, completing top 40 score (10 Hot 100 entries altogether). *Full Sail*, live 2-disc *On Stage, Mother Lode* '73-4 were all top 10 albums; *So Fine* '75 featured '50s covers (like the CARPENTERS' *Yesterday Once More*), dropped to no. 21; *Native Sons* '76 made top 20; compilation *The Best Of Friends*, live 2-disc *Finale* '77 completed tally. Messina released solo sets *Oasis* '79, *Messina* '81, but Loggins's success incl. *Celebrate Me Home* '77, *Nightwatch* '78 (top 10 LP incl. hit duet with Stevie Nicks 'Whenever I Call You Friend'); *Keep The Fire* '79, live 2-disc *Kenny Loggins Alive* '80, *High Adventure* '82 all went top 10; *Vox Humana* '85 did less well. He also had one side of soundtrack LP *Caddyshack* '80 incl. top 10 hit 'I'm Alright'; total of 11 top 40 hits '78-85 incl. duet 'Don't Fight It' with Steve Perry of JOURNEY (no. 17 '82), 'Welcome To Heartlight' (inspired by writings of schoolchildren, no. 24 '83) and 'Footloose', theme from film of that name, co-written with Dean Pritchard (no. 1 '84), followed by 'Danger Zone' from *Top Gun* '86.

LOMAX, Alan and John Folklorists, song collectors, archivists, authors: John Avery

Lomax (*b* 23 Sep. 1875, Goodman, Ms.; *d* 26 Jan. '48, Greenville), his son Alan (*b* 31 Jan. '15, Austin, Texas). John collected songs as a child; obtained degrees from U. of Texas, where an English teacher told him that his collection was of no value, and at Harvard, where he was encouraged by George Lyman Kittredge (1860-1941; published books on English and Scottish ballads; *see also* Francis James CHILD). Using Edison cylinder equipment and subsidised by a publisher he collected songs for three years, published *Cowboy Songs And Other Frontier Ballads* '10 (122 songs, 18 with music; revised '37), *Songs Of The Cattle Trail And Cow Camp* '17. He held various academic posts, was also in banking; when the bank failed he became full-time folklorist, with teen-aged Alan helping; Library of Congress provided portable recording equipment '33 and *American Ballads And Folk Songs* was published '34, the year he became honorary consultant and head of the LoC's Archive of Folk Music (founded '28, supported by donations until '37, now has collection of more than 26,000 recordings from cylinders to tape, 3000 78s made by John and Alan in '30s alone; also commercial recordings, books, periodicals, dissertations, etc.). With and without Alan, John recorded LEADBELLY in Louisiana prison '33, Bukka WHITE at Parchman Farm '40 and Muddy WATERS at Stovall '41-2, both in Mississippi; many others. Alan attended U. of Texas, Harvard, Columbia (began broadcasting on Columbia's School of the Air '39); as assistant archivist at LoC '37-42 made one of the most valuable recordings of all: playing, singing and reminiscence of Jelly Roll MORTON '38 (*see* Morton's entry). Alan subsequently studied on field trips and wrote about Haitian, Bahamian, English, Scottish, Irish, Italian and Spanish folk music; he worked for Decca Records '47-9, prod. 19-vol. set of traditional material for Columbia mid-'50s, co-edited '60-1 a 10-disc one for Caedmon in Britain; a 7-disc set of Southern Folk Music Heritage on Atlantic resulted from perhaps the last such field trip to take place in the USA. Work in broadcasting incl. collaboration with Ewan MACCOLL on UK radio's *Ballads And Blues*. He prod. concert/recitals and was a consultant for folk festivals, incl. Newport Folk Festival, where he temporarily forgot '65 that he dealt with living art forms, disapproving along with many others of electric blues, long thriving on the south side of Chicago and elsewhere. His publications incl. *Mister Jelly Roll* '49, *The Rainbow Sign* '50, *The Penguin Book Of American Folk Songs* '61, *Folk Song Style And Culture* '68, etc. He was engaged for many years in attempts systematically to classify traditional songs and dances.

LOMAX, Jackie (*b* 10 May '44, near Liverpool) UK singer, songwriter. Fronted local bands (the Undertakers played Hamburg); unsuccessful Lomax Alliance was managed by Brian EPSTEIN; signed as solo with Apple '68 for highly rated *Is This What You Want?*, prod. by George HARRISON, with Eric CLAPTON, Paul McCARTNEY and Ringo STARR in backing group: it charted briefly in the USA, but nobody knows how well it really did because the BEATLES' label was such a mess. With Denny LAINE in Balls '69; went to USA and switched to WB for critically praised *Home Is In My Head* '70, *Three* '71; then joined progressive group Badger in UK for *White Lady* '74 on Epic, prod. by Allen TOUSSAINT, regarded as disappointing. New contract with Capitol brought *Livin' For Lovin'* '75, *Did You Ever Have That Feeling?* '77, but though critics and fans had high hopes he never succeeded commercially.

LOMBARDO, Guy (*b* 19 June '02, London, Ontario; *d* 5 Nov. '77) Bandleader. Formed band early '20s in Canada (first records '24 on Gennett, made in Richmond, Indiana) with brothers Lebert (lead trumpet), Victor (baritone sax), Carmen (*b* 16 July '03; *d* 17 Apr. '71, Miami, Fla.; led reed section and vocal trio, sang solo, wrote songs). Guy was a violinist turned front man, never played with the band; 'the sweetest music this side of heaven' by Guy Lombardo And His Royal Canadians was established by '30 as America's most popular dance music by a successful residency at NYC's Roosevelt Grill: sweet trumpets (usually muted), vibrato-laden reeds, later a twin-piano gimmick was not usually said to swing, yet the band's playing seemed to float over the beat: a dozen titles are listed in Brian Rust's *Jazz Records 1897-1942* as evidence that the band could play hot any time it wanted; in any case musicianship was so high that Louis ARMSTRONG named it his favourite band. Carmen's vibrato was that of the flute player he trained to be; he played the tenor sax like an alto. It was not a corny band, but a hip '20s dance band that never changed. Skip Nelson, Don Rodney and sister Rose Marie Lombardo were among vocalists mid-'40s; from late '40s nearly all vocals were by Kenny Gardner. Victor led his own band '47-51, came back. Guy was a well-known speed-boat racer, good enough to win trophies. The band did a lot of radio work, also films *Many Happy Returns* '34, *Stage Door Canteen* '43, *No Leave, No Love* '46; annual New Year's Eve broadcast always closed with band's theme 'Auld Lang Syne'. Carmen co-wrote some of the biggest hits: 'Coquette', 'Sweethearts On Parade' '28 (latter covered by Armstrong), 'Boo Hoo' and 'A Sailboat In The Moonlight' '37 (the first covered by Count BASIE with Jimmy RUSHING, 'Sailboat' by Teddy WILSON and Billie HOLIDAY), 'It's Easier Said Than Done' '38, 'Seems Like Old Times' '46, 'Our Little Ranch House' '50 and 'Get Out Those Old Records' '51 (vocal duet by Carmen and Kenny); 'Powder Your Face With Sunshine' '49 was a hit for several artists. Carmen also wrote scores for shows, summer entertainments at Jones Beach NY late '50s and '60s. The band sold more than 100 million records, with over 200 hit sides '27-54, on Columbia '27-31, Brunswick '32-4, Decca '34-5, Victor '36-8, then back on Decca; recorded with Kate SMITH '32, on Decca with Hildegarde, Bing CROSBY, ANDREWS SISTERS. 26 no. 1 hits began with 'Charmaine' '27, ended with 'The Third Man Theme' '50 (*see* Anton KARAS), incl. (apart from some of Carmen's) 'You're Driving Me Crazy' '30, 'Stars Fell On Alabama' '34, 'What's The Reason I'm Not Pleasin' You' '35 (also a hit for Fats WALLER), 'Red Sails In The Sunset' '35, 'So Rare' '37 (revived by Jimmy DORSEY for no. 2 hit '57), 'Penny Serenade' '39, 'The Band Played On' and 'Intermezzo' '41, 'Managua, Nicaragua' '47. 10 compilations on MCA incl. mono hits in phoney stereo; similar RCA set *A Legendary Performer*; 2-disc compilation in honest mono on Pair; airchecks on Sunbeam from '35, Hindsight from '50; on Capitol: *Guy Lombardo In Hi-Fi* c.'55 remade hits in good sound; medley LPs were top 20 '57-8

with 40 songs on each, incl. *Berlin By Lombardo*.

LONDON, Julie (*b* 26 Sep. '26, Santa Rosa, Cal.) Singer, actress. Sang as a teenager with a band on West Coast; sultry looks won film contract, roles in low-budget epics from '44; married to Jack Webb (star of *Dragnet* cop show on radio and TV, star and prod. of *Pete Kelly's Blues* '55); then to pianist-songwriter-actor Bobby Troup (*b* 18 Oct. '18, Harrisburg, Pa.), who got her contract with new Liberty label: LPs were successful '55 into '60s; first *Julie Is Her Name* had laid-back delivery of romantic songs accompanied only by bass of Ray Leatherwood (*b* 24 Apr. '14, Itasca, Texas), guitar of Barney KESSEL: no. 2 LP incl. top 10 single 'Cry Me A River', used in an amusing scene in *The Girl Can't Help It* '56, the best rock-'n'roll movie ever made. The LP's reissue decades later, with the original, conventionally sexist sleeve pic featuring the bare shoulders of a maturely attractive woman, was refreshing at a time when pop music seemed to be dominated by anorexic or barely pubescent teenagers. Troupe also starred in TV series *Emergency*. *Lonely Girl* and *Calendar Girl* (all songs with names of the months in them: 'I'll Remember April', 'Memphis In June', etc.) were top 20 '56, have been reissued in Europe along with *About The Blues*, *Julie*, *London By Night*, *Make Love To Me*, *Swing Me An Old Song*, *Your Number Please*.

LONE JUSTICE USA rock group formed '84: Maria McKee (*b* 17 Aug. '64, L.A.), songwriter, vocalist, guitarist, performed at 16 in L.A. clubs with half-brother Bryan MacLean (ex-LOVE); formed band, supported U2 and the ALARM on USA tours; interest from Bob DYLAN led to signing with Geffen label. First LP *Lone Justice* '85 was a strong debut; songs written or co-written by bassist Marvin Etzioni (two), MacLean (one), Tom PETTY ('Ways To Be Wicked') and the rest by McKee, incl. 'Sweet, Sweet Baby (I'm Falling)'; the two songs named were Hot 100 singles and the LP was no.56. Ryan Hedgecock on guitar, Don Heffington, drums, and keyboardist Benmont Tench from Petty's Heartbreakers played on the LP. She wrote 'A Good Heart', no. 1 UK hit for Feargal SHARKEY;

duetted with on Dwight YOAKUM on 'Bury Me' (his debut LP *Guitars Cadillacs etc etc*); next Lone Justice album *Shelter* '87 incl. 'I Found Love', minor USA hit but no. 1 UK: band incl. Gregg Sutton, bass; Rudy Richman, drums; Shayne Fontayne, guitar (had gigged with Steve Forbert), Bruce Brody, keyboards (had worked with John CALE, Patti SMITH). McKee looks like a talent to watch.

LONG, Johnny (*b* c.'16, Newell, N.C.; *d* 31 Oct. '72, Parkersburg, W. Va.) Violinist, bandleader. Raised on farm; led band at Duke U. '32, competing with rival college band Blue Devils led by Les BROWN. Pro from '37; played for dancers yet steered clear of purely mickey-mouse sound. Hit record '40 'A Shanty In Old Shanty Town', with 'hip' vocal by band. Generally regarded as Mr Nice Guy in big band business; popular on radio, made some films but failed to break into TV. Occasionally played Las Vegas late '50s. Returned to Marshall U. early '70s intending to teach.

LOOSE TUBES 21-piece UK cooperative band playing original music. Rehearsal band '83, played its first London gig '84, released a debut LP on their own label and played a now-legendary gig at Ronnie SCOTT's '85, at the end of which they marched out into the streets of Soho at 3 a.m., still playing, with the audience following. A conventional big-band lineup is augmented by flutes, synthesiser, tuba (played by Dave Powell, *b* 13 Feb. '56, London, 'like a foghorn on amphetamines'), etc.; they have no leader, perform in V-formation or circle so that everyone can see cues; a different member of the group chooses tunes and their order each gig. If they had tried to set up such an outfit it wouldn't have worked, but it happened by accident; clarinettist Dai Pritchard (*b* 28 Feb. '57, Pontypridd) said, 'What we do isn't new stuff. It's fairly old stuff, old stuff and very old stuff. But put into strange new combinations' (quoted in *The Wire*). Unique, spontaneous precision incl. elements of the whole history of jazz, plus African, other nuances; they poach fans from every musical genre, their own music full of joy and sparkling improvisation, individual and collective. Django Bates (keyboards; *b* 2 Oct. '60,

Beckenham) and bassist Steve Berry (*b* 24 Aug. '57, Gosport) wrote most of the music at the start; others joining in incl. trumpeters Dave DeFries (*b* 24 May '52, London), John Eacott (*b* 19 Dec. '60, Reading), Chris Batchelor (*b* 9 Apr. '62, Beckenham); flautist Eddie Parker (*b* 28 May '59, Liverpool); trombonist John Harborne (*b* 27 Dec. '60, London); the band is actively working on the idea of collective composition. Ashley Slater (*b* 20 Apr. '61, Schefferville, Quebec) is bass trombonist, announcer and resident clown; Bates and Slater toured UK with an international George RUSSELL band early '86. Bates also plays trumpet, tenor horn; once attended Royal College of Music for two weeks, worked with Tim Whitehead's Borderline (LP *English People* '82 on Spotlite), Dudu PUKWANA's Zila; quartet First House with Ken Stubbs (*Eréndira* on ECM '84); also plays in Bill BRUFORD's quartet Earthworks (LP '87) with Iain Ballamy (*b* 20 Feb. '64, Guildford), duo Human Chain with Steve Argüelles (*b* 16 Nov. '63, Crowborough); Ballamy, Whitehead (*b* 12 Dec. '50, Liverpool) play reeds in Loose Tubes; Argüelles drums and percussion. Members have played with George COLEMAN, STYLE COUNCIL, Bryan Ferry, Elton JOHN, Thomas DOLBY, Toots THIELEMANS, Bobby WATSON, Maria MULDAUR, London Symphony Orchestra etc. etc. The others are Steve Buckley (*b* 6 Jan. '59, Orpington), Mark Lockheart (*b* 31 Mar. '61, Lymington), Julian Argüelles (*b* 28 Jan. '66, Lichfield) on reeds; Lance Kelly (*b* 13 June '64, Reading) on trumpet; Steve Day (*b* 9 Apr. '63, Walsall), Richard Pywell (*b* 29 Mar. '59, Farnborough), trombones; John Parracelli, guitar. Many double on various instruments; LPs also have Nic France on drums, who left because of conflicting commitments: anyone's leaving this close-knit outfit is traumatic. Colin Lazzerini plays typewriter and bass telephone, runs Loose Tubes label. They were criticised by single-issue fanatics because none of them were black or female; by late '86 Thebe Lipere (*b* 2 July '52, Pretoria, S.A.) played percussion ('They asked me to join when they first started . . . I've worked with a lot of bands but I've never known a personal harmony like this one: it's like one big family'). Debut LP was nice souvenir; direct-to-metal mastered *Delightful Precipice* '86 captures better their sound, spirit and excellent playing: slapstick humour, eclectic music with real substance. Third album *Open Letter* '88 is first from new deal with EG Records, first on CD; first single also released. Became the first jazz orchestra to play at the Proms '87, BBC's annual classical music festival. Label also has LPs by Human Chain, quartet The Iains led by Ballamy, quintet led by Whitehead, duo with Stan Sulzmann (reeds, *b* 30 Nov. '48, London) and John Taylor playing the music of Kenny WHEELER.

LOPEZ, Israel 'Cachao' (*b* c.'18, Cuba) Bassist, pianist, arranger, composer, bandleader; also plays trumpet and bongos. One of the most infl. of all Latin musicians, credited by some with introducing the mambo to dance halls. From musical family, said to incl. 35 bassists. Played with Havana Symphony Orchestra from age 13 to 44, but had played bongos in dance band at 9: joined danzónera '37 which soon became Orquesta Arcaño y sus Maravillas, named after legendary flautist Antonio Arcaño Betancourt (*b* 29 Dec. '11). Danzóneras played danzónes, ballroom dance evolved in 1870s from 17th-18th century French contradanza; Cachao added swing with elements of mambo, derived from Congolese religious music: he and brother (cellist/ pianist Orestes Lopez) composed most of Arcaño's repertoire of danzónes (up to 25 a week!) and the swing element took it from high society to sweep the country's dance halls. Cachao retired '49 from the exhausting Arcaño routine to work in revue, opera, etc. In '59 he re-formed disbanded Orquesta Arcaño to make danzónera LPs *El Gran Cachao* and *Con El Ritmo de Cachao* on Kubaney label, when other danzóneras had become charangas, playing CHACHACHA and other rhythms; also worked with José FAJARDO '57-60. Meanwhile Panart organized series of jam sessions (descargas) from '56 with Cuba's best musicians, mixing Cuban idioms with extended soloing in an unprecedented loose format: *Cuban Jam Sessions* in two vols. followed by Vol. 3 dir. by tres player Niño Rivera; Cachao did 'short jam sessions' as singles, then album *Cuban Jam Sessions In Miniature 'Descargas'* – *Cachao y su Ritmo Caliente*

Vol. 4. With Vol. 5 by Fajardo and his All Stars, these had a profound effect on the Latin scene in New York, which Cachao soon joined, working with various bands, then with Tito RODRIGUEZ incl. LPs *Tito, Tito, Tito* on UA, *Big Band Latino* on Musicor. With Tico All Stars on *Descargas At The Village Gate – Live* '66 (three vols.); moved to West Coast, also worked in Las Vegas. Back to NYC and *Tico-Alegre All-Stars Live At Carnegie Hall* '74; then own LPs '77: *Cachao y su Descarga Vol. I* and *Dos* (Vol. 2) (Cuban street scene painted by Henry FIOL on the cover) were co-prod. by musicologist Rene Lopez to re-create Havana descargas; lineup incl. five violins, incl. veteran Pupi LEGARRETA and younger Cuban Alfredo de la Fé, with Charlie PALMIERI on piano, Manny Oquendo on timbales, Alfredo 'Chocolate' ARMENTEROS on trumpet, Mario Muñoz 'Papaito' Salazar, Carlos 'Patato' Valdez on percussion: LPs incl. danzónes (recalled days with Arcaño), also descargas prod. with no commercial restraint; second incl. haunting descarga 'Trombon Melancolico' written by Cachao; the LPs received little airplay/promotion at the time, but have acquired cult fame since. He appeared on flautist Lou Perez's *Nuestra Herencia* '77 with CANDIDO, singer Adalberto Santiago; moved to Miami: session work there incl. *Recuerdan a Chappottin* by El Chano Montes y su Conjunto '82, . . . *Tributo al 'Beny'* by Pepe Mora '83, *Con Sacrificio* by Hernan Gutierrez y su Orquesta '84, *La Reina de la Guajira* '85 by La India de Oriente (real name Luisa Maria Hernández), Roberto TORRES album *Elegantemente Criollo* '86. Also played in backing band for vocal duo Hansel & Raúl (*see* CHARANGA), e.g. Orquesta Calle 8 on their hit LP *Tropical* '86 on RCA International. Headed Miami-based descarga band on *Maestro de Maestros: Israel Lopez 'Cachao' y su Descarga* '86 incl. Francisco 'Paquito' Hechavarria on piano, conga player Tany Gil co-writing, co-arr., co-dir.; Fajardo was also there.

LOPEZ, Trini (*b* Trinidad Lopez III, 15 May '37, Dallas, Texas) Pop singer. Played guitar at 15 in Dallas clubs; formed combo to tour Southwest; Don COSTA discovered him at PJ's Hollywood club, prod. hits on Reprise which were likeable and refreshing, especially on jukeboxes. PETER, PAUL & MARY had top 10 hit with Pete SEEGER's 'If I Had A Hammer' '62; Lopez/Costa version (from no. 2 LP *Trini Lopez At PJ's*) went to no. 2 '63, getting more out of a good song than PPM's soporific harmonies. Three others made top 40 ('Kansas City', 'Lemon Tree', 'I'm Comin' Home, Cindy'); 14 LPs charted '63-7, nine in top 50. Good party music then; later *Transformed By Time* on Roulette still in print '87, plus hits compilation on K-Tel '84 in UK. He also appeared in film *The Dirty Dozen* '67, allegedly more briefly than originally planned.

LOS LOBOS Rock/Tex-Mex fusion band formed '74 in East L.A.: David Hidalgo, guitar, accordion; Cesar Rosas, vocals, bajo sexto guitar; Conrad Lozano, bass; Louie Perez, drums. As Ry COODER LP *Chicken Skin Music* '76 gave wider exposure to Tex-Mex, the Lobos' own wide influences incl. Clifton CHENIER, Flaco JIMENEZ, Ritchie VALENS, Doug SAHM, Albert COLLINS, FAIRPORT CONVENTION. They built up a strong L.A. following, in '70s contributed to *Si Se Puede* ('It Can Be Done') for the United Farm Workers and released their own *Just Another Band From East L.A.* Steve Berlin of the BLASTERS was an early fan and joined full-time after guesting on their official debut mini-LP *. . . and a time to dance . . .* '83, prod. by Berlin and T-Bone BURNETT, with cover of Ritchie Valens's '58 hit 'C'mon Let's Go'. They received considerable attention after winning *Rolling Stone* poll award; *Will The Wolf Survive* '85 was confident full-length LP, title song covered by Waylon JENNINGS in his *How Will The Wolf Survive* same year. Rosas and Hidalgo sessioned on Cooder's soundtrack music for *Alamo Bay* '85, Hidalgo on Elvis COSTELLO's *King Of America* '86. They backed Paul SIMON on 'All Around The World' on his LP *Graceland* '86; toured UK early '87; album *By The Light Of The Moon* '87 again prod. by Burnett. Band supervised soundtrack to film *La Bamba* '87, based on life of Ritchie Valens, which also featured Marshall CRENSHAW, Carlos SANTANA, STRAY CATS' Brian Setzer: soundtrack LP and title single were no. 1 hits. Next project was to be an acoustic album of traditional Mexican songs, recording beginning '88.

LOSS, Joe (*b* Joshua Alexander Loss, '10, London) UK bandleader. Violinist debuted with first band '30 at Astoria Ballroom in Charing Cross Road, then at Kit-Kat club '32-4, successful ever since with strict tempo dance music. Popular vocalist '34-42 was Chick Henderson (*d* '44 in Royal Navy); 'Begin The Beguine' was a Henderson hit (while Billy COTTON borrowed the famous Artie SHAW version, Loss had his own). 'A Tree In The Meadow' reached top 20 in USA '48 on RCA with vocal by Howard Jones. Loss's music was still in demand in the '80s for society affairs and was reputed to be among the favourites of the British Royal Family.

LOUDERMILK, John D. (*b* 31 Mar. '34, Durham, N.C.) Songwriter, singer. First musical experience was banging a drum for the Salvation Army; he also learned guitar, ukelele, trumpet, saxophone; made TV debut at 12 with Tex RITTER; as Johnny Dee had radio show at 13; attended U. of N.C., on music staff at WTVD in Durham, where he sang 'A Rose And A Baby Ruth': recorded by George HAMILTON IV for no. 6 hit USA '56. As Dee recorded his own 'Sittin' In The Balcony' on Colonial label; Eddie COCHRAN had the bigger hit but both went top 40 '57. Went to Nashville for a year, ready to go to work in his father-in-law's hardware store if music didn't work out, but it worked out in spades, first with Jim DENNY's Cedarwood Music, then with ACUFF-Rose. His best-known song is 'Abilene', popularised by Hamilton but now a country standard; others: 'Waterloo' (Stonewall JACKSON), 'Bad News' (Johnny CASH), 'Ebony Eyes' (EVERLY Bros), 'Stayin' In' (Bobby VEE), 'Talk Back Trembling Lips' (no. 1 country hit for Ernie Ashworth '63 on Hickory, Acuff's label), 'Tobacco Road' (NASHVILLE TEENS and about 40 others), 'Break My Mind' (Gram PARSONS, Richard THOMPSON), 'Indian Reservation' (by Paul REVERE in USA, Don Fardon in UK), 'Language Of Love' (Loudermilk's only top 40 pop hit under his own name, '61). Own country hits '63-7 incl. 'Bad News', 'Blue Train (Of The Heartbreak Line)', 'Th' Wife', 'That Ain't All', 'It's My Time'. Artists covering his songs also incl. Kitty WELLS, Anne MURRAY, Lonnie DONEGAN, BOXCAR WILLIE, Chet ATKINS (once his boss), many more. A large and engaging figure and a popular performer, appearing with no frills, just a guitar; especially popular in UK, where he appeared at Wembley '72; but dislikes touring. LPs incl. *Language Of Love, Twelve Sides Of Loudermilk, A Bizarre Collection Of The Most Unusual Songs* '66, *Suburban Attitudes In Country Verse* '67, *The Open Mind Of John D. Loudermilk* '69, *Best Of* '73, all on RCA; *Elloree* '71 on Warner Brothers, *Encores* '75 and *Just Passin' Through* on MIM.

LOUVIN BROTHERS C&W vocal duo, playing guitar and mandolin: Charlie (*b* 7 July '27, Rainesville, Ala.) and Ira (*b* 21 Apr. '24, Rainesville; *d* 20 June '65 in car crash). Their arrangements were very simple; their beautifully pure harmony owed more to the 'high lonesome' Appalachian sound than to Nashville. They had country chart hits on Capitol '55-62 ('I Don't Believe You've Met My Baby', 'Hoping That You're Hoping', 'You're Running Wild'/'Cash On The Barrel Head', 'My Baby's Gone' all top 10); were also famous for heartfelt gospel singing (LP *The Great Gospel Singing Of The Louvin Brothers*). They wrote songs, incl. 'Love Thy Neighbour As Thyself', now a staple of bluegrass revivalists. Charlie carried on as a single, having country hits every year until well into the '70s, as well as duet hits with Melba MONTGOMERY '70-1. LPs incl. *The Best Of The Early Louvin Brothers* '55-8 on Rebel; *The Louvin Brothers, Songs That Tell A Story, Tragic Songs Of Life* ('56) on Rounder USA, Stetson UK; Charlie's solo *Country Souvenirs* on Accord.

LOVE, Darlene (*b* Darlene Wright, '38, L.A.) USA pop/soul singer. First group was the Blossoms, who recorded unremarkably as a quartet on Capitol '58-60, then as a trio on Challenge and Okeh '60-2; sessioned with James DARREN, Bobby DARIN, Nino Tempo, April Stevens etc. When Phil SPECTOR moved to the West Coast he recruited Love to sing lead on 'He's A Rebel', written by Gene PITNEY: as by the CRYSTALS it was no. 1 USA, top 20 UK, followed up with 'He's Sure The Boy I Love'. He gave her another name for 'Zip-A-Dee-Doo-Dah', unusual treatment of Oscar-winning song from '47 Walt Disney film *Song Of The South* (long unseen because of Uncle Tom-ish treatment of Joel Chandler Harris's *Uncle Remus* stories, film was re-released in USA mid-'80s): as by BOB B SOXX & THE BLUE JEANS, the song went top 10 '62. Then he allowed her six singles of her own, of which '(Today I Met) The Boy I'm Gonna Marry' and 'Wait Til' My Bobby Gets Home' were top 40. She remained with the Blossoms as they sessioned through '60s, regulars on TV's *Shindig* and toured with Elvis early '70s. She made a live comeback LP on Rhino in mid-'80s.

LOVE, M'Pongo (*b* M'Pongo Landu, '56, Kinshasa, Zaire) African female singer-composer, known as 'La Voix du Zaire'. Crippled with polio at age four, nevertheless determined to pursue music as a career; worked as a secretary after high school but soon turned pro. Toured East Africa '77; on return performed at World Festival of Black Arts (FESTAC) in Lagos; first LP *L'Afrique Danse* '77 followed by *La Voix du Zaire* on Safari Ambience label, backed by excellent session musicians Eko Roosevelt, Jules Kamga, Vicky Edimo, Alhadji Toure; by the '80s she was established as one of the best of Zaire's talented crop of female singers. *Femme Commerçante* '83 incl. Sammy Massamba and Dino Vangu; *Basonguer* '84 is considered by many to be her best album, with Bopol on bass, Wuta May helping with vocals. She toured Scandinavia '84 to mark the Year of the Disabled; *M'Pongo Love Chant Alexandre Sambat* was released '85 on Invido.

LOVERBOY Canadian rock group formed in Vancouver '79 by songwriting partners Mike Reno (vocals, ex-Streetheart) and guitarist Paul Dean (ex-Moxy), recruiting session drummer Matt Frenette and locals Scott Smith on bass, Doug Johnson on keyboards. Eponymous debut LP '80 an immediate success in Canada, reached no. 13 USA LP chart; minor hits were 'The Kid Is Hot Tonight', 'Turn Me Loose' (top 40 in USA): MTV soon put their glossy, lightweight hard rock across: *Get Lucky* '81 incl. 'Working For The Weekend'; video helped single to top 30, followed by 'When It's Over', also top 30, with backing vocal by Nancy Nash; *Keep It Up* '83 emphasised reliance on tried and tested rock'n'roll clichés of fast women and even faster cars:

'Hot Girls In Love' (no. 11) made the point. MTV followed the band into the Mohave Desert to make video for no. 34 hit 'Queen Of The Broken Hearts'; a lucky viewer won a competition and came along; the band won more airtime. Second and third albums went top 10; *Lovin' Every Minute Of It* '85 did not.

LOVETT, Lyle (*b* 1 Nov. '57, nr Houston, Texas) Country singer, songwriter. Grew up 25 miles north of Houston in the Klein Community, named after an ancestor who helped found it in 1840s. Degrees in journalism and German from Texas A&M, began writing songs, began performing '79; wrote a song for and sang in TV movie *Bill On His Own* with Mickey Rooney '83, played in Europe that year; made demo tracks with Billy Williams, from Phoenix band J. David Sloan: result was writing contract with Criterion Music, record deal with MCA/Curb. *Lyle Lovett* '86 has WESTERN SWING, band infl. by ten songs, nine written by Lovett, one ('This Old Porch') co-written with Robert Earl KEEN, another up-and-coming talent; the album and several singles charted: 'You Can't Resist It' has Rosanne CASH singing backup, 'Closing Time' was covered by Lacy J. DALTON. Appearance at Texas songwriters concert saw *Washington Post* describe him as 'the real find' of the show, 'a Lone Star Tom Waits'. Guy CLARK invited him to sing at Austin Opera House gig; strong songs with sharp observation have him opening shows for Emmylou HARRIS and Randy NEWMAN. He guested on Nanci GRIFFITH album. His album *Pontiac* '87 shot to top 20 in USA country chart, incl. new version of 'If I Had A Boat', which had appeared in NYC *Fast Folk* audio magazine '85.

LOVIN' SPOONFUL USA folk/rock quartet of '60s: John Sebastian (*b* 17 Mar. '44, NYC), lead singer, co-founder with Zal Yanovsky (*b* 19 Dec. '44, Toronto), plus rhythm guitarist Steve Boone (*b* 23 Sep. '43, N.C.), drummer Joe Butler (*b* 19 Jan. '43, Long Island). Founders had been members of Mugwumps with future MAMAS & PAPAS; new group had seven top 10 singles in row '65-6 on Kama Sutra in a feckless, almost sentimental electric jug-band style, mostly written by Sebastian and still redolent of the period's optimism: 'Do You Believe In Magic', 'You Didn't Have To Be So Nice', 'Daydream', 'Did You Ever Have To Make Up Your Mind?' (both no. 2), 'Summer In The City' (no. 1), 'Rain On The Roof', 'Nashville Cats'. Like the '60s optimism, it ended in tears: members of the group were arrested for possession of marijuana and allegedly incriminated others; there were more hits '67-9 but only three in top 40. Sebastian's 'Darling Be Home Soon' was no. 15 '67, from score of *You're A Big Boy Now* (Francis Ford Coppola's first film); Yanovsky left the group, replaced by Jerry Yester (former prod. of the ASSOCIATION). LPs in '60s: *Do You Believe In Magic, Daydream, What's Up, Tiger Lily?* (soundtrack of Woody Allen film), *Hums Of The Lovin' Spoonful, Best Of* (no. 3 LP '67), *You're A Big Boy Now* (soundtrack), *Everything Playing* (first album without Yanovsky; Sebastian left to go solo), *Best Of Vol. 2*. 2-disc compilation '76 superseded by *Best Of* on Buddah, *Vol. 2* on Rhino, *Distant Echoes* on Accord. Sebastian's LPs '70-1 incl. *John B. Sebastian* on MGM and Reprise (no. 20, his best), *Live* on MGM, *cheapo-cheapo productions presents Real Live John Sebastian* and *The Four Of Us* (re-formed group) on Reprise (the magic was gone); *Tarzana Kid* '74 (collab. with Lowell George), *Welcome Back* '76 on Reprise; fluke no. 1 single with latter's title track, from a TV show.

LOWE, Frank (*b* 2 May '41, Memphis, Tenn.) Tenor sax, also other reeds; composer. Formal study at U. of Kansas, San Francisco Conservatory; worked for Stax Records '59; infl. by Ornette COLEMAN, John COLTRANE, Cecil TAYLOR; also by Sonny Simmons and Donald Garrett (bass, reeds, percussion; attended Du Sable High School in Chicago; co-founder with Richard ABRAMS of Experimental Band); has never stopped developing, playing inside as well as out; as Bob Rusch points out in *Cadence* magazine interview, Lowe is one of the few of his generation who never sounded like a Coltrane clone. Worked with SUN RA '66, Alice Coltrane '70-3. LPs *Live At The Village Vanguard* with Noah Howard (*b* 6 Apr. '43, New Orleans; LPs with Archie SHEPP, Don Ayler; own LPs on ESP, Byg, etc.), *Relativity Suite* with Don CHERRY, *Duo Exchange* with Rashied ALI on Ali's Survival label. Lowe's LPs: quintet *Black Beings* '73 on Base/ESP with Joseph JARMAN; classic *Fresh* '74-5 on Arista, incl. 'Chu's Blues' with Memphis Four, whoever they are: fine down-home R&B wail sounds as if it was recorded in a basement, the rest of the LP a sextet with Joseph and Lester BOWIE incl. two MONK tunes; quintet *The Flam* '75 on Black Saint with Leo SMITH; quartet *Tricks Of The Trade* and *The Other Side* '76 on French labels, recorded in Paris; quintet *Doctor Too-Much* '77 on Kharma with Smith, Phillip Wilson; *Lowe & Behold* '77 on Musicworks, 11 pieces in concert; *Don't Punk Out* '77 on QED, duet with guitarist Eugene Chadbourne; *Skizoke* '81 on Cadence, with working sextet incl. Butch Morris, cornet; Damon Choice, vibraphone; Larry Simon, guitar; Wilbur Morris, bass; Tim Pleasant, drums: straight ahead and mellow; 'skizoke' means touchdown, home run, the max. *Exotic Heartbreak* '81 on Soul Note without Simon, Amina Claudine Myers replacing Choice; *Decision In Paradise* '84 on Soul Note is a different group with Charles and Charnett Moffett, Geri Allen on piano, Grachan MONCUR III and Cherry.

LOWE, Mundell (*b* 21 Apr. '22, Laurel, Ms.) Jazz guitarist. Worked with Ray McKINLEY, Ellis LARKINS, Red NORVO late '40s, SAUTER-FINEGAN band, on NBC staff NYC '50-8; made nine albums '54-60, mostly on Riverside, doing his own composing/arranging: quartet used Glenn MILLER veterans Trigger Alpert and Al Klink, Ed Shaughnessy on drums (*b* 29 Jan. '29, Jersey City; played with Benny GOODMAN, Charlie VENTURA, Tommy DORSEY); 11-piece *New Music Of Alec Wilder* had Joe WILDER leading brass section with two flugelhorns (both on Riverside '56); also sets of *Porgy & Bess*, TV themes on Camden (RCA budget label) with all-star big band. Lowe retired to West Coast studios, emerged from lucrative TV work (*I Dream Of Jeannie, Hawaii Five-O* etc.) for small-group albums *California Guitar* '74 on Famous Door, *Guitar Player* and *Incomparable* on Dobre, *Transit West* '83 on Pausa.

LOWE, Nick (*b* '49, Woodbridge, Suffolk, England) Singer/songwriter, bass guitar, producer. Formed first band with Brinsley

Schwarz while still in school, Sound 4 Plus 1 ('63); reunited in Schwarz group Kipington Lodge late '60s, cut flop singles; relaunched as BRINSLEY SCHWARZ '69, folded '75 after six albums. Produced Graham PARKER & the Rumour; new manager Andrew Jakeman (aka Jake Riviera) formed Stiff label with ex-Brinsley manager Dave Robinson; Stiff's first solo release was Lowe single 'So It Goes'. Much early Stiff stuff produced by Lowe, incl. the DAMNED, Wreckless Eric, etc.; produced Elvis COSTELLO hit albums '77-80; also more Parker and DR FEELGOOD. Left Stiff with Riviera and Costello end of '77; scored own UK top 10 hit 'I Love The Sound Of Breaking Glass' '78; 'Cruel To Be Kind' '79 also charted in USA. Own debut LP *Jesus Of Cool* did well '78 (titled *Pure Pop For Now People* in USA). Formed Rockpile with Dave EDMUNDS; could not record as such for contractual reasons but LPs by either effectively Rockpile; group folded after one imperfect album under its own name '80. Married Carlene CARTER; produced her as well as PRETENDERS debut single; produced album by Paul Carrack, formed band Noise To Go with him; also produced John HIATT and the FABULOUS THUNDERBIRDS. Own album *Nick The Knife* barely made bottom of UK chart '82; lack of more commercial success for himself possibly due to too much diversification. Fun compilations: *16 All Time Lowes, Nick's Knacks*.

LUCCA, Papo (*b* Enrique Lucas Jr, Ponce, Puerto Rico) Pianist, arranger, composer, producer, mus. dir. of Sonora Ponceña, band formed mid-'50s in Puerto Rico, led by his father Enrique (Quique) Lucca. Papo also plays vibes, tres, synthesiser, flugelhorn, percussion; one of salsa's most ingenious arrangers and producers, pianism described by Isabell Leymarie: 'Deeply anchored in a strong clavé rhythm [the basis of Cuban music], his style reveals acute harmonic and rhythmic intuition, and his subtle use of arpeggios, patterns, block chords and other devices . . . sets him off from other Latin pianists.' The band is something of an institution in Puerto Rico, but has never ossified. Albums (all on Inca label) incl. *Hachero Pa' un Palo, Fuego en el 23* (title track by Arsenio Rodriguez), *Algo de Locura* c.'68-70. From *Desde Puerto Rico* a Nueva York '72 their '70s LPs were made in NYC, several prod. by Larry HARLOW; lead singers were Luigi Texidor and Humberto Luis (Tito) Gomez through *Sonora Ponceña* '72; Miguelito Ortiz replaced Gomez on *Sabor Suren* '74; '75 saw best-of album *Lo Mejor de Sonora Ponceña*, incl. big hit 'Acere Ko', title tracks and other hits from several albums, and *Tiene Pimienta* (with another hit title track) arr. by Papo, who played synth on 'Mayeya'. On *Musical Conquest* '76 Papo arr. and cond., co-prod. with Louie RAMIREZ, with Luis 'Perico' ORTIZ as mus. dir. (incl. big hit 'El Pio Pio'); on *El Gigante del Sur* '77 their current style began to crystallise: crisp, lucid, restrained yet swinging, with Ramirez as prod., Papo as assistant prod. and arr. (except disco-oriented 'Noctural', arr. by Perico, who also played trumpet on it); on this LP the band was joined by lead singer Yolanda Rivera, and it was Texidor's last: he went solo (LP *El Negrito del Sabor* '79, also appeared on Tito PUENTE albums *Homenaje a Beny* '78-9). Sonora Ponceña marked 20th anniversary with 'Jubileo 20', one of the hit tracks on *Explorando* '78, regarded as one of their best albums, all arr. by Papo, who now took over as producer with trumpets increased from three to four; another hit was 'Moreno Soy'. Gomez came back to sing lead, replacing Texidor on this album only; but he sang in the chorus on next LP *La Orquesta de Mi Tierra* '78. Earlier Xmas LP *Navidad Criolla* arr. by Papo was reissued '78; the band joined Celia CRUZ on her *Le Ceiba* on Vaya and performed with her in TV film *Salsa* '79, released his compilation *Energised*; from '80 returned to Puerto Rico to record: *New Heights* '80 incl. Dizzy GILLESPIE's 'Night In Tunisia' and Toñito Ledeé joined Yolanda and Ortiz as a lead singer, Papo co-arr. with Elias Lopés. *Unchained Force* '80 was dedicated to long-serving band members, trumpeters Ramon A. Rodriguez 'El Cordobes' (Tony), Delfin Perez, bassist Antonio Santaella (Tato). Papo arr. *Night Raider* '81, incl. cover of 'Cuestiones de Amor' by Adalberto Alvarez, young Cuban pianist who then led Son 14; his 'Soledad' was incl. on *Determination* '82 (both songs from Son 14's *Son Como Son* '81 on Areito), which also incl. 'Aungue Te Quiero' by Cuban Joseito González, leader of Orquesta

Rumbavana, from their eponymous LP on Areito. Yolanda was replaced by Pichy Perez on *Future* '84, incl. two Alvarez tunes, and Papo played flugelhorn on Woody SHAW's 'Woody's Blue'. They reworked, updated hits incl. 'Jubileo 20' to 'Jubileo 30' on *Jubilee* '85, on which Ortiz was replaced by Manuel 'Mannix' Martinez; the same year two compilations were also issued to mark 30th anniversary. Papo also played and/or arr. on LPs with Cruz, Johnny PACHECO, Ismael Quintana, Cheo FELICIANO, Justo Betancourt (*Presencia!* '76), *Afecto y Cariño* '76 by Ernie Agosto, *Calidad* '82 by Adalberto Santiago, *Feliz y Contento* '84 by Nelson Gonzalez y su Orquesta Revelacion, others. Papo replaced Harlow '78 as pianist with FANIA ALL STARS, played on many of their LPs incl. *Habana Jam* (with live version of 'Moreno Soy' sung by Texidor), as well as *Puerto Rica All Stars* '76, with singers Andy Montañez, Marvin Santiago, Paquito Guzman, trumpeter/bandleader Mario Ortiz. He gigged with Sonora Ponceña early '87 in NYC incl. album *Back To Work*.

LULU (*b* Marie McDonald McLaughlin Lawrie, 3 Nov. '48, Glasgow) Scottish pop singer. Led band the Glen Eagles in clubs at 15; changed name to Lulu and the Luvvers; the first Scottish hit of the 'beat' era was their cover of the ISLEY Bros 'Shout', no. 7 in May '64. 'Leave A Little Love' was no. 8 the following year; she might have become a significant singer but went solo early '66 to become a popular if mediocre entertainer instead; four more top 10 hits '67-9 incl. 'Boom Bang-A-Bang' at no. 2 '69; was a TV personality in the '70s and was mostly absent from the charts; only top 10 was David BOWIE song 'The Man Who Sold The World', no. 3 '74. In the USA she went straight to no. 1 '67 with title song from film *To Sir With Love*, which she sang in the soundtrack and which did not chart at home. Her only other top 40 items in the USA were 'Best Of Both Worlds' '67, which also did not chart in UK; 'Oh Me Oh My (I'm A Fool For You Baby)' '69 from LP *New Routes* on Atco, made in Muscle Shoals, prod. by all of Atlantic's talent: Jerry Wexler, Tom DOWD, Arif Mardin. It reached no. 88 USA but did not chart in UK, where the single did not reach the top

40. She was married '69-73 to BEE GEE Maurice Gibb. She made LPs *Don't Take Love For Granted* on Rocket '79, *Lulu* on Alfa '81. 'Shout' re-charted in both old and new versions '86; she has also DJ'd occasionally for Capitol Radio.

LULU BELLE AND SCOTTY Husband/wife duo of '30s-40s. Lulu Belle (*b* Myrtle Eleanor Cooper, 24 Dec. '13, Boone, N.C.), Scotty (*b* 8 Nov. '09, Spruce Pine, N.C.; *d* 1 Feb. '81, Gainesville, Fla.) were known as the Sweethearts of Country Music. They were regulars on the National Barn Dance for 24 years, with records on Conqueror, Vocalion, Columbia, Bluebird, Mercury and Starday. Scotty studied to be a teacher and performed as Skyline Scotty on West Virginia radio '28-30, joining WLS in Chicago '33 and teaming with Lulu Belle, who had joined a year earlier and had been singing with Red FOLEY, then playing bass with the Cumberland Ridge Runners. They married 13 Dec. '34 and became famous with songs like 'Whippoorwill Time', 'Remember Me', 'Have I Told You Lately That I Love You?' (covered by Bing CROSBY with the ANDREWS SISTERS '50), 'Empty Christmas Stocking', many, like 'Mountain Dew' (also a hit for Grandpa JONES), written by Scotty. They appeared in films such as *Shine On Harvest Moon* '38, *County Fair* '41, *National Barn Dance* '44; had their own daily TV show on WNBQ '49. Retired from performing '58; Scotty finally became a teacher. LPs incl. *Sweethearts Of Country Music*, *Sweethearts Still*, *Down Memory Lane* '62-5 on Starday, *Have I Told You Lately That I Love You* '69 on Old Homestead.

LUMAN, Bob (*b* Robert Glynn Luman, 15 Apr. '37, Nacogdoches, Texas; *d* 27 Dec. '78, Nashville) Country and rockabilly singer who made transition back to country music. Performed in small clubs and bars in Texas, Louisiana; a promising baseball player, chose music instead. First break replacing Johnny CASH on Louisiana Hayride '56; moved to California's Town Hall Party '57-8, recorded rock'n'roll for Imperial; worked at Showboat Hotel in Las Vegas '58-60, signed with new WB label and made pop top 10 with 'Let's Think About Living'. Unable to follow that up; went into US Army, on discharge moving to Nashville

and Hickory label for minor country hits '64-6, more success on Epic with 'Ain't Got Time To Be Unhappy' '68, 'Every Day I Have To Cry Some' '69, 'Honky Tonk Man' '70, 'When You Say Love' and 'Lonely Women Make Good Lovers' '72, 'Still Loving You' '73, 'Proud Of You Baby' '75. Switched to Polydor '77, in country top 10 with 'The Pay Phone'. Lung problems hospitalised him '76; *Alive And Well* '77 prod. by Cash; he died of pneumonia. LPs incl. *Let's Think About Living* '60 on WB, *Livin' Lovin' Sounds* '65 on Hickory, *Come On Home And Sing The Blues To Daddy* '69, *Is It Any Wonder That I Love You* '71, *Neither One Of Us* '73, all on Epic; *Bob Luman Rocks* '77 on DJM.

LUNCEFORD, Jimmie (*b* James Melvin Lunceford, 6 June '02, Fulton, Mo.; *d* 13 July '47, Seaside, Oregon) Bandleader. He studied music with Paul WHITEMAN's father, Wilburforce J. Whiteman, obtained degree from Fisk and was proficient on all the reeds; worked for Elmer Snowden, Wilbur Sweatman in the '20s, formed his own band '27 but fronted it only and did not play (except flute on 'Liza'). It was a well-drilled, sharply dressed, sophisticated show band with arrangements mostly by Sy OLIVER (who also played trumpet); stars incl. Willie SMITH on alto sax and drummer Jimmy CRAWFORD. Trummy Young joined on trombone and vocals '37. Joe Thomas (*b* 19 June '09, Uniontown, Pa.) played reeds and sang '33-47; Eddie DURHAM played trombone and solo guitar '35-7. Tommy Stevenson was trumpet stylist '33-5 (*b* c.'14; *d* Oct. '44 NYC of pneumonia; later worked for Blanche Calloway, Don REDMAN, Coleman HAWKINS, Lucky MILLINDER, Cootie WILLIAMS); then Paul Webster '35-44 (*b* 24 Aug. '09, Kansas City; *d* 6 May '66, NYC; had worked for Lunceford '31, also territory bands, rejoined Lunceford; he later worked for Cab CALLOWAY, BARNET etc.). Reedman Dan Grissom also sang on ballads, he was called Gruesome by jazz fans, but his singing was commercial and popular. Oliver's writing was unique; his oddly loping 2-beat style was unforgettable and always swung: the most famous is ' 'Tain't What You Do (It's The Way That You Do It' ('39, vocal by Young and band), also 'Organ Grinder's Swing', 'For Dancers

Only'. He was poached by Tommy DORSEY '39, replaced by Gerald WILSON, Billy Moore (*b* 7 Dec. '17, Parkersburg, W.V.; worked for Berlin Radio '60-3, lived in Denmark); Oliver said pianist Eddie Wilcox was also a fine arranger (*b* 27 Dec. '07, Method, N.C.; *d* 29 Sep. '68, NYC). *Pop Memories* credits Lunceford with 22 hit records '34-46, more than any other black jazz-oriented band of those years except Duke ELLINGTON and Cab Calloway (Count BASIE's hits only began '38); hits incl. 'Rhythm Is Our Business' '35 and 'Blues In The Night' '42 (vocals by Smith), 'The Merry-Go-Round Broke Down' '37 with Oliver singing, 'I'm Gonna Move To The Outskirts Of Town' and 'I Dream A Lot About You' '42-4 with vocals by Grissom, 'The Honeydripper' with the Delta Rhythm Boys (vocal quartet, recorded for Decca; also with Ella FITZGERALD, Mildred BAILEY, Charlie Barnet; Moore toured Europe with them '64), novelty 'Cement Mixer (Put-Ti, Put-Ti)' '46 on Majestic label, with vocal by Thomas. 'Honeydripper' was written by bandleader Joe Liggins (1915-87), whose own recording was no. 1 on R&B chart for 17 weeks (also had huge hits 'Got A Right To Cry' '46, 'Rag Mop' and 'Pink Champagne' '50, the latter being no. 1 R&B for 11 weeks). Lunceford recorded for Decca until '45 except for c.'39-40 on CBS labels; popular and infl. hits were Oliver's 'Cheatin' On Me' and 'Ain't She Sweet' (both sung by Young and vocal trio, latter with interjection 'Solitoodie!') as well as 'Margie', 'My Blue Heaven', 'Four Or Five Times', 'By The River St Marie', 'I Wanna Hear Swing Songs' (credited to Oliver and Moore), 'What's Your Story Morning Glory' (by Moore, a hit according to Geo. T. Simon). 'Baby Won't You Please Come Home' had a vocal by Thomas; 'White Heat' and 'Jazznocracy' were written by Will Hudson (white arranger who worked for Irving MILLS, co-led Hudson-DeLange band). Lunceford did some broadcasting, but never as much as many white bands; despite the band's popularity the lucrative hotel gigs were mostly out of reach for blacks. It was a hard life; he died suddenly on the road; the rumour persists that he was poisoned by a bigoted restaurant owner after successfully insisting that the band be fed. The band kept going for a while under

Wilcox and Thomas, but lived on in the hearts of jazz fans and dancers of all races. Compilations: six LPs on MCA/USA, Decca stuff also on Jasmine, Affinity in UK; boxed set from CBS/France; airchecks etc. on Sunbeam, Aircheck, First Heard, etc. There was a reunion 'Jimmie Lunceford In Hi-Fi' album mid-'50s on Capitol which was very well done.

LUND, Art (*b* 1 Apr. '15, Salt Lake City, Utah) Singer, actor. Taught high school in Kentucky, sang in local bands in spare time. Toured with Jimmy Joy '39-41; with Benny GOODMAN until military service, still using name Art London ('Winter Weather', duet with Peggy LEE); rejoined him '46, success with 'Blue Skies', 'On The Alamo', then went solo to MGM label: 'Mamselle' hit no. 1; further top 20 hits with 'Peg 'O My Heart', 'And Mimi' (all '47), 'On A Slow Boat To China' ('48), 'Mona Lisa' ('50). To Broadway, appearing in *The Most Happy Fella* ('56), *Donnybrook* ('61). Has appeared in many films, on TV in minor roles.

LUTCHER, Nellie (*b* 15 Oct. '15, Lake Charles, La.) Singer, piano. Played in big bands with bass-playing father; joined band The Southern Rhythm Boys, becoming main attraction before moving to West Coast as solo in mid-'30s. Played March of Dimes (polio) benefit '47, sang 'The One I Love Belongs To Somebody Else' and was signed to Capitol by Dave Dexter: first single 'Hurry On Down' sold a million that year. Further big hits: 'Real Gone Guy' and 'Fine Brown Frame' ('47-8). Also popular in UK, touring major venues early '50s; made four sides in London. As success waned during rock'n'roll era, made successful career in real estate, also serving as officer of L. A. Musicians' Union Local 47 for many years. Continued to gig occasionally (New York's Cookery, '73); KCET-TV special *Nellie* '82; Nellie Lutcher Day celebration in Lake Charles '83; compilation LP *Real Gone Gal* on Capitol/UK '84, with sleeve note by Fred Dellar; also *My Papa's Got To Have Everything* on Juke Box Lil from Norway.

LYMON, Frankie (*b* 30 Sep. '42, NYC; *d* 28 Feb. '68, NYC) Singer. Formed vocal group The Premiers at Edward W. Stitt High school with Sherman Garnes (*b* 8 June '40; *d* '78), Joe Negroni (*b* 9 Sep. '40; *d* '77), Herman Santiago (*b* 18 Feb. '41), Jimmy Merchant (*b* 10 Feb. '40); heard singing on stairs of 165th street tenement by Richard Barrett, leader of The Valentines, talent scout for George Goldner's Rama and Gee labels; under new name of The Teenagers with Frankie Lymon made 'Why Do Fools Fall In Love?' late '55; with Lymon's brilliant soprano lead became a best-loved hit of the era: top 10 in USA, remained in charts 21 weeks; no. 1 UK. Other minor hits that year: 'I Want You To Be My Girl', 'I Promise To Remember', 'The ABCs Of Love'; also in film *Rock, Rock, Rock* with 'I'm Not A Juvenile Delinquent', flop single in USA but top 20 hit UK '57. 'Baby, Baby' top 5 UK Apr. '57 but USA sales dwindled; during UK tour '57 Goldner began producing Lymon as solo act: 'Goody Goody' no. 22 USA, no. 24 UK '57; group appeared in film *Mr Rock And Roll* '57; Lymon signed solo on Roulette, group tried various replacements. Lymon's version of Bobby DAY's 'Little Bitty Pretty One' made no. 58 USA '60, but he had a drug problem: his option was not picked up by Roulette. Forced to undergo cure at Manhattan General Hospital '61; attempted comeback learning to dance, play drums, but convicted on narcotics charge '64; found dead on grandmother's bathroom floor. His brother Lewis, lead singer with The Teenchords (recorded for Fury, Juanita, End), did one-off gig with Teenagers in Philadelphia '73; group re-emerged '80, still with Santiago, Merchant. Diana ROSS had world-wide hit '81 with 'Why Do Fools Fall In Love'; she had earlier sponsored The JACKSON FIVE (with Lymon soundalike Michael) who had all the success the Teenagers missed. Royalties on the song 'Why Do Fools Fall In Love' have reached a million dollars; in '86 three women claiming to be Lymon's widows (incl. Zola Taylor, who once sang with the PLATTERS) were fighting with Roulette Records over it. Compilation on Gee: *The Teenagers With Frankie Lymon*.

LYNN, Judy (*b* 12 Apr. '36, Boise, Idaho) Country showgirl who enjoyed more success in Las Vegas than on records. Daughter of former bandleader Joe Voiten; named Queen of the Snake Valley Jamboree '52, America's Champion Yodeler '53, Miss Idaho and finalist in Miss America competition '55. Signed to ABC-Paramount '56, co-hosted first national telecast of the Grand Ole Opry; married Nashville booking agent John Kelly, formed 8-piece band and dressed in flamboyant Western costumes; the Judy Lynn Show was top touring attraction early '60s, on TV's Jimmy DEAN show, etc. and breaking records in Vegas. Records on several labels but only minor single hits, 'Footsteps Of A Fool' '62 the only country top 10. LPs incl. *Full House* '63, *Here Is Our Gal Judy Lynn* '64, *Best Of* '64 on UA; *Honey Stuff* '66, *Golden Nuggets* '67 on Musicor; *At Caesar's Palace* '69 on Columbia.

LYNN, Loretta (*b* Loretta Webb, 14 Apr. '35, Butcher Hollow, Ky.) One of the most successful female singers in modern country music: an unmistakable voice with echoes of earlier trad. country singers, also a songwriter incl. autobiographical 'Coal Miner's Daughter'. Married Oliver V. 'Mooney' Lynn before her 14th birthday; they moved to Washington state, had four children before she was out of her teens (a grandmother at 32, six children in all; eldest son died in farm accident '85). Urged and supported by Mooney she took up singing, formed band the Trailblazers, worked local clubs; made '60 top 20 country hit 'Honky Tonk Girl' for Zero label, handling promotion herself. Moved to Nashville, became a regular on the WILBURN Bros syndicated weekly TV show; turned down by Capitol, Columbia, signed with Decca for many hits: 22 in country top 10 '62-71 incl. 'Before I'm Over You', 'Blue Kentucky Girl', 'You Ain't Woman Enough', 'Don't Come Home A'Drinkin' ', 'Your Squaw Is On The Warpath', 'Coal Miner's Daughter' and 'You're Looking At Country', carried on with 'Rated X', 'Love Is The Foundation', 'Trouble In Paradise', 'The Pill' (controversial '75 hit which some radio stations refused to play), 'She's Got You' and 'Why Can't He Be You' '77. Also teamed with Ernest TUBB for LPs and single hits incl. 'Mr & Mrs Used To Be' '64, 'Who's Gonna Take The Garbage Out' '69. She split from the Wilburns late '60s; they sued her for breach of contract; when that was settled she formed United Talent booking agency with

Conway TWITTY, also recording duets; named vocal duo of the year four times by CMA: LP *United Talent*; hits such as 'Lead Me On', 'Louisiana Woman, Mississippi Man', 'As Soon As I Hang Up The Phone' '71-4. She was the first woman to be CMA's entertainer of the year '72; named artist of the decade '79 by the ACM; own chain of Western wear shops, music publishing company, travelling rodeo show; first woman in country music to become a millionaire, first to be on cover of *Newsweek* ('73); became TV celebrity with frank talk on chat shows. Autobiography *Coalminer's Daughter* '76 was nine weeks on *NY Times*' best-seller list, filmed '80 with Sissy Spacek in title role (won Oscar). *I Remember Patsy* '77 was tribute LP to Patsy CLINE, who helped her in the early days; other LPs (all on Decca/MCA) incl. *Songs From My Heart* '64, *First City* '66, *Who Says God Is Dead* '67, *Wings Upon Your Horns* '69, *Writes 'em And Sings 'em* '70, *I Wanna Be Free* '71, *Here I Am Again* '72, *Back To The Country* '76, *United Talent* (with Twitty) '76, *Out Of My Head And Into My Bed* '78, *Loretta* '80, *Lookin' Good* '80, *Makin' Love From Memory* '82, *Lyin', Cheatin', Woman Chasin', Honky Tonkin', Whiskey Drinkin' You* '83, *Just A Woman*, '85.

LYNN, Vera (*b* Vera Welch, 20 Mar. '19, London) The most durable of UK vocalists. Joined dancing troupe age 11, formed own troupe at 15. Became band singer, making first broadcast with Joe LOSS '35. With Charlie Kunz 18 months, then AMBROSE; went solo '41. Appeared in *Apple Sauce* revue at London Palladium; radio series *Sincerely Yours* aimed at servicemen; toured war zones singing hits like 'White Cliffs Of Dover' and 'We'll Meet Again', became known as The Forces' Sweetheart. Retired temporarily late '45 to early '47; first USA hits 'You Can't Be True, Dear' and 'Again' ('47-8). Starred in *London Laughs* at Adelphi theatre for two years, then became first UK female singer to have a USA no. 1 with 'Auf Wiederseh'n, Sweetheart', 'Yours' making USA top 10 same year ('52). Had own USA radio series, plus many TV spots. No. 1 UK single 'My Son, My Son' '54; last top 20 entry 'Travellin' Home' '57. Radio, TV popularity continued; OBE '69, CBE '75: she is now Dame Vera. LPs have always sold well; *20 Family Favourites* was in UK top 30 in '81 and again in June '84 (40th anniversary of D-Day landings). Autobiography *Vocal Refrain* '75.

LYNYRD SKYNYRD Blues/boogie band formed '66 in Jacksonville, Fla.: Ronnie Van Zant (*b* 15 Jan. '49; *d* 20 Oct. '77, McCombe, Ms.), vocals; Gary Rossington and Allen Collins, guitars; Billy Powell, keyboards; Leon Wilkeson, bass; Bob Burns, drums, all from the same neighbourhood. Previous names the Noble Five, the Wild Things, 1%; then named after Leonard Skinner, a teacher who'd suspended them for long hair. Added Ed King (ex-Strawberry Alarm Clock) as third guitar; *Pronounced Leh-nerd Skin-nerd* '73 was phonetically titled debut prod. by Al KOOPER, who'd spotted them in Atlanta bar; incl. classic 10-minute 'Freebird', tribute to Duane ALLMAN that became their anthem and FM staple: its bluesy vocals and weaving 3-guitar battling as track rose to a climax summarised their music there and then. *Second Helping* '74, also prod. by Kooper, considered their best by many; incl. 'Sweet Home Alabama', top 10 answer to Neil YOUNG's 'Southern Man', '74 single attacking Gov. George Wallace. Burns and King left '75, replaced by Artimus Pyle and (in '76) Steve Gaines, ex-Smokehouse and Detroit (with Mitch RYDER). WHO manager Peter Rudge took over band after support on Who's *Quadrophenia* tour '73, made them into a main USA live attraction. *Nuthin Fancy* and *Gimme Back My Bullets* '75-6 were solid but unimpressive; spark was rekindled by 2-disc live *One More From The Road* '76 made at Fox theatre in Atlanta: Gaines's vinyl debut saw them in fine form on home territory, band augmented by Gaines's sister Cassie, other girl backing singers trading off against Van Zant's bourbon-soaked voice. But days after release of *Street Survivors* '77, with ironic fiery cover art, band's chartered plane crashed en route to a gig, killing Van Zant, Steve and Cassie and road manager; others injured. Band could not carry on without splendid macho frontman; pre-Kooper tapes were released as *First . . . And Last* '78; 2-disc *Gold And Platinum* '79, *Best Of The Rest* '82 were compilations. The Rossington Collins band kept Southern flag flying, incl. Wilkeson and Powell (LPs *Anytime, Anyplace, Anywhere* '80, *This Is The Way* '81 charted strongly); younger brother Donnie Van Zant formed .38 SPECIAL (seven LPs on A&M incl. *Strength In Numbers* '86); Pyle formed own band. Skynyrd added guts and fire to ALLMAN Bros southern guitar rock blueprint; live version of 'Freebird' made no. 21 in UK '82 and fellow confederates Molly Hatchet still play it. They clocked up almost 2000 gigs; it's said that touring stunted creativity: first two LPs regarded as their best. It is ironic that their hard-drinking lifestyles were ended prematurely by an accident, but 10 years on they had not been replaced in USA rock firmament; in mid-'87 RIAA certified five of their LPs as multi-platinum; they re-formed '87 for sentimental tour with brother Johnny replacing Ronnie (Johnny Van Zant band had LPs *No More Dirty Deals* '80, *Van Zant* '85 on Geffen, another due soon).

LYONS, Jimmy (*b* 1 Dec. '32, Jersey City; *d* 19 May '86, NYC) Alto sax, flute. Close association with Cecil TAYLOR: record debut with him in Copenhagen '62; played on his great Blue Note LPs *Unit Structures* and *Conquistador!*; also on Taylor's 3-disc *One Too Many Salty Swift And Not Goodby* '78 on Hat Art, *Winged Serpent* '84 on Soul Note etc.; also *Into The Hot* with Gil EVANS on Impulse, etc. Own LPs: *Other Afternoons* '69 on Byg/Affinity with Lester Bowie, Andrew CYRILLE, Alan Silva on bass; 'Push Pull' on *Wildflowers 4* (*see* JAZZ) with his wife Karen Borca on bassoon; *Jump Up/What To Do About* '80 on Hat Hut with Sunny Murray Trio; 3-disc set *Push Pull* '78, *Riffs* '80 on Hat labels and *Wee Sneezawee* '83 on Black Saint, all with

Borca; *Give It Up* '85 on Black Saint. Collaborated on projects with Cyrille, Lester Bowie, Joseph JARMAN, David MURRAY, others. He was compared to Jackie McLEAN, Ornette COLEMAN in forging a breakthrough to post-Charlie PARKER style.

LYTTELTON, Humphrey (*b* 23 May '21, Windsor, Berks., England) Trumpet, leader, composer, broadcaster, author; also cartoonist; aka 'Humph'. School at Eton, where his father was a well-known house master. Formed small dixieland band '48, accompanied Sidney BECHET; expanded to octet during '50s-60s, modernised sound inspired by love of Duke ELLINGTON's music. Toured USA '59; backed Buck CLAYTON on his visits to Europe '60s; has also played with Louis ARMSTRONG, Bud FREEMAN, Eddie CONDON. Hosted jazz shows on BBC TV '50s-60s; own weekly radio show *Best Of Jazz* featured classic repertoire on record. Publications incl. *I Play As I Please* '54, *Second Chorus* '58, self-illustrated; later *Take It From The Top* '75, *Why No Beethoven?* '84; embarked on series with *Best Of Jazz* '78 followed by *Enter The Giants* '81. His perceptions from a musician's point of view about the innovations of the greatest jazz musicians are unique: full of love and of great value to the non-musical listener. Many LPs incl. *Bad Penny Blues* on Cube, compilation of '49-56 tracks (title tune was top 20 UK hit '56); *Sir Humph's Delight, Spreading Joy, Kansas City Woman* (with Buddy TATE, compositions by Clayton), *Echoes Of Harlem* (recorded '81), others on Black Lion; *It Seems Like Yesterday* released on Calligraph '84 with Wally Fawkes, clarinet (*b* 21 June '24, Vancouver; also draws Flook, popular UK comic strip).

M

MABON, Willie (*b* 24 Oct. '25, Memphis) R&B singer, pianist, also harmonica. To Chicago with family age 16; recorded for Apollo (as Big Willie), Aristocrat, then Chess: had top 10 R&B hits '52-4 with his own compositions 'I Don't Know' (covered by Buddy MORROW), 'I'm Mad', 'Poison Ivy'. He subsequently recorded for Federal, Mad, Formal, USA; worked outside music late '60s; recorded for Antilles in Chicago and Black & Blue in France '72; appeared at Montreux Jazz Festival, recorded on America in France and on Big Bear in England with Mickey Baker, all in '73; many other festivals and club dates. LPs incl. *I Don't Know And Other Chicago Blues Hits* on Antilles, *I'm The Fixer* on Flyright, *The Comeback* '79 on Big Bear. A modern R&B performer using horns almost from the beginning; his hits were among those revived by early white R&B fans/performers such as Georgie FAME, thus influencing later pop music.

McBEE, Cecil (*b* 19 May '35, Tulsa, Okla.) Bassist, composer. Began on clarinet, took up bass at 17, studied at Wilberforce (Ohio), conducted US Army band at Fort Knox. By the mid-'60s was working with Grachan MONCUR, Jackie McLEAN, Miles DAVIS, etc.; made significant contribution to the great popularity of Pharoah SANDERS and Charles LLOYD groups. Too many fine records as a sideman to mention, except that some of the latest are with Chico FREEMAN; his own works incl. solo 'Love' on Sanders album *Thembi* '70; *Mutima* '74 on Strata-East, 13-piece group incl. George ADAMS, Cecil McBee Jr, vocalist Dee Dee Bridgewater; sextet sets *Music From The Source* and *Compassion* '77 on Enja, both with Freeman, Don Moye and Steve McCall on percussion; and *Alternate Spaces* '79 on India Navigation, with Freeman, Moye, Don PULLEN; quintet *Flying Out* '82 on India Navigation. Toured with Freeman '85-6; also worked with Joanne BRACKEEN

(who only hires the best); in mainstream with Harry EDISON and Buddy TATE at Kool Jazz Festival '85.

McCALL, C. W. (*b* William Fries, 15 Nov. '28, Audobon, Iowa) Talking country vocalist who turned advertising character into country star mid-'70s. Played in school orchestra as a child, but studied commercial art at Iowa U. and worked in advertising; created trick driver C. W. McCall for advertising campaign '73 and did voice-overs for TV adverts; the persona caught on and the result was C&W hit 'The Old Home Filler-up And Keep On Truckin' Cafe' '74. Signed to MGM; 'Wolf Creek Pass' and 'Classified' did well, then 'Convoy' '75-6 used language of CB radio and became world-wide smash: a film was based on it dir. by Sam Peckinpah, starring Ali MacGraw, Kris KRISTOFFERSON. McCall scored a few more hits ('There Won't Be No Country Music', 'Roses For Mama'). LPs incl. *Wolf Creek Pass* '75, *Black Bear Road* '76 on MGM; *Wilderness* '76, *Rubber Duck* '77, *C. W. McCall & Co.* '78, *Roses For Mama* '78 on Polydor.

McCANN, Les (*b* Leslie Coleman McCann, 23 Sep. '35, Lexington, Ky.) Pianist, singer. Accompanied Gene McDANIELS '59, formed trio and has mined R&B/funk groove. LPs on Pacific Jazz '59-64; began singing '61: *Les McCann Sings* incl. Ben WEBSTER, George Freeman on guitar, Richard 'Groove' HOLMES on some instrumental tracks, big band with Harold LAND, Charles LLOYD, arr./cond. Gerald WILSON on others, vocal tracks with trio; *The Gospel Truth* and *Soul Hit* '63 incl. Joe PASS, Paul CHAMBERS on some tracks; *Jazz Waltz* '63 incl. members of CRUSADERS. Switched to Limelight '64-7: 'Plays The Hits' albums '66 incl. covers of Ike & Tina TURNER, DONOVAN, McDaniels ('Compared To What'), 'Bang! Bang!' boogaloo hit, Plas JOHNSON in band on some tracks. Greatest success with 10 albums on Atlantic '68-76: *Much Les* '68 reached Billboard top 200 LPs early '69; *Swiss Movement* '69 (live at Montreux, quintet featuring Eddie HARRIS, Benny BAILEY, Leroy Vinnegar, Donald Dean on drums) was no. 29 LP incl. single hit 'Compared To What'/'Cold Duck'; *Second Movement* '71 with Harris, *Invitation To Openness* '72, *Talk To The People* '72, *Another Beginning* '75, *Hustle To Survive* '75 all charted. Quartet *Live At Montreux* (2-disc set) '72 incl. Roland KIRK on two tracks, another 'What'. *Les McCann The Man* '78 on A&M incl. big band with strings; *The Longer You Wait* '83 is on Jam.

McCARTNEY, Paul Guitarist, singer, songwriter, bandleader; he was world-famous as a BEATLE and with John LENNON half of the most successful songwriting team of the century; then pursued solo career. Film of final Beatle album *Let It Be* '70 saw him trying in vain to hold the band together; he was unhappy with what Phil SPECTOR did to the music and quit amid acrimony, though it is obvious in retrospect that the group was finished, as much by John's choice as Paul's. George HARRISON's electronic experiments were released first, but McCartney's eponymous '70 LP was first real solo LP by a Beatle, exacerbating feelings by its release a fortnight before *Let It Be*: he wrote, sang, played, produced it all; 'Hot As Sun', 'Teddy Boy' had been intended for the group; 'Maybe I'm Amazed' was covered by Rod STEWART, 'Every Night' by Phoebe Snow: critics were loudly disappointed, but hindsight reveals homegrown charm. One-off single 'Another Day' was a ballad in the style of 'Eleanor Rigby'. *Ram* '71 was recorded with wife Linda, incl. several good songs. They formed band Wings with Denny LAINE and drummer Denny Siewell: debut LP *Wild Life* '71 was regarded as a disaster, McCartney's charm dissipated to the vanishing point. The dichotomy of his post-Beatles career and willingness/ability to turn his hand to anything were captured by singles in Feb./Mar. '72: 'Give Ireland Back To The Irish' was an uncharacteristic political polemic, 'Mary Had A Little Lamb' a nursery rhyme. He had always insisted that the Beatles could just turn up and play: he realised the dream with a scratch tour of UK universities '72;

by then Wings incl. former Joe COCKER guitarist Henry McCulloch, who also played on effective reggae single 'C Moon'. Wings contributed theme of James Bond film *Live & Let Die* '73; reduced to Linda, Paul and Laine, they released *Band On The Run* same year, which was a renaissance of McCartney's all-round skills: the best Wings album incl. rousing title track and 'Jet', fine ballads 'Bluebird' and 'Picasso's Last Words'. *Venus & Mars* '75 was patchy, with memorable 'Listen To What The Man Said' and 'Magneto & Titanium Man' as well as TV soap opera theme 'Crossroads'; *Wings At The Speed Of Sound* '76 an improvement, jaunty 'Let 'Em In' covered by Billy Paul in USA, 'Silly Love Songs' interpreted as a message to fans. Folksong single 'Mull Of Kintyre' '77 was biggest selling UK single ever until BAND AID, at 2.5m copies. *London Town* was weak, *Wings Best* a good compilation, both '78. *Back To The Egg* '79 was lavish 3-disc set, debut of Rockestra, with members of PINK FLOYD, LED ZEPPELIN, the WHO, the SHADOWS and PROCOL HARUM. Plea from United Nations for charity concert for Kampuchean refugees aroused strongest-ever Beatle reunion hopes but it was Wings who played at Hammersmith Odeon Dec. '79 (incl. in album *Concert For The People Of Kampuchea* '81). 'Wonderful Christmastime' was McCartney solo single '79; LP *McCartney II* '80 also completely solo, revelling in freedom offered by synthesisers and studio technology in 'Coming Up' and 'Temporary Secretary', beguiling (if baffling) 'Waterfalls'. *Tug Of War* '82 saw McCartney reunited with Beatle prod. George MARTIN; result was the best album since *Band On The Run*, with 10CC's Eric Stewart (who would work with McCartney often in future), duets with Stevie WONDER (on 'Ebony & Ivory', no. 1 USA/UK) and with Carl PERKINS; the idiosyncratic 'Ballroom Dancing' and one of his best, 'Wanderlust'. *Pipes Of Peace* '83 also with Martin, not as cohesive but displayed great pop charm, incl. duets with Michael JACKSON. For years McCartney had worked in secret on film debut: *Give My Regards To Broad Street* '84 was critically panned, but soundtrack LP was well received, with good reworkings of Beatle songs and a McCartney ballad of vintage quality, 'No More Lonely Nights'; cast of guests incl.

Dave EDMUNDS, Ringo STARR, Chris Spedding and John Paul Jones. McCartney kept a low profile for a while, appearing at Live Aid '85 to sing 'Let It Be'; then *Press To Play* '86 had guests Pete Townshend and Phil COLLINS. While his post-Beatles work has been variable, some of it is as good as anything he ever did; his unique contribution to pop was recognised in '79 with a unique rhodium disc, for selling over 200m albums.

McCLAIN, Charly (*b* Charlotte Denise McClain, 25 Mar. '56, Jackson, Tenn.) Former model made it to the top as country singer early '80s. Began age 9 in a band with her brother called Charlotte and the Volunteers; they worked local dates and had TV spots '64-70; she worked as a model, then changed her named to Charly and became regular singer with the Mid-South Jamboree; she teamed with Memphis prod. Larry Rogers and signed to Epic '76, had hits 'Lay Down' '76, 'Make The World Go Away' '77, 'That's What You Do To Me' '78, 'When A Love Ain't Right' '79, duet with Johnny Rodriguez 'I Hate The Way I Love It' '79, finally hit no. 1 on country charts with 'Surround Me With Love' and 'Men' '80, both prod. by Norro Wilson. Voted Most Promising Female Vocalist by *Music City News* readers '80, dubbed 'Princess of Country Music'. Top 3 hits with 'Who's Cheatin' Who' '81, 'Sleepin' With The Radio On' '82, duet 'Paradise Tonight' '83 with Mickey GILLEY. Married band member Wayne Massey '83; they had duet hit 'You Are My Music, You Are My Song' '85; he has guested on her albums, which incl. *Here's Charly McClain* '77, *Let Me Be Your Baby* '78, *Alone Too Long* '79, *Women Get Lonely* '80, *Surround Me With Love* '81, *Too Good To Hurry* '82, *Paradise* '83, *Radio Heart* '85, all on Epic.

McCLINTON, Delbert (*b* 4 Nov. '40, Lubbock, Texas) Singer, songwriter, guitarist, harmonica player; a behind-the-scenes infl. for 20 years who finally saw the charts in the '80s. Deeply infl. by the blues, picked up tips from black blues harp players, played in clubs from age 15 in many obscure bands; early records were among the first by white artists to be played on local black stations, such as cover of Sonny Boy

WILLIAMSON's 'Wake Up Baby' on Le Cam. Played harp on Bruce Channel's no. 1 hit 'Hey! Baby' '62, toured as far as Europe with him: in UK taught harp to a young northern group, subsequently heard the fruits on the BEATLES' first single, 'Love Me Do'. Led Ron-Dels for Hot 100 entry 'If You Really Want Me To, I'll Go' '65 on Smash; did it again '72 with Glen Clark as Delbert & Glen on Clean with 'I Received A Letter', a McClinton composition which was covered for a country hit by Waylon JENNINGS. Albums on ABC '75-7 incl. *Victim Of Life's Circumstances, Genuine Cowhide, Love Rustler* incl. nearly all his own songs, but sank without a trace. Emmylou HARRIS had no. 1 country hit '78 with his 'Two More Bottles Of Wine'; comedians John Belushi and Dan Aykroyd used his 'B Movie Boxcar Blues' in hit film *Blues Brothers*. He signed with Capricorn '78; LP *Keeper Of The Flame* reached no. 146 on Billboard's LP chart, but Capricorn went broke. Switched to Capitol and *The Jealous Kind* '80 reached no. 34, with no McClinton songs but incl. top 10 single 'Giving It Up For Your Love'. *Plain From The Heart* '81 also charted, incl. 'Shotgun Rider' and 'Sandy Beaches' (his own song), both minor hits. He'll be back again and again; the musicians all know who he is: sang on Roy BUCHANAN LP *Dancing On The Edge* '86.

McCLINTON, O. B. (*b* Obie Burnett McClinton, 25 Apr. '42, Senatobia, Ms.; *d* 23 Sep. '87, Nashville) Singer, songwriter, guitarist with hits in country chart '70s. Wrote a song early '70s called 'The Other One' (Charley PRIDE being a much better known black country singer); he also called himself 'The Chocolate Cowboy'. Father was clergyman and a farmer (owned his own spread, unusual in Mississippi then). Infl. by Hank WILLIAMS as a child; disliked farm work, ran away from home, got as far as Memphis, spent all his money on a guitar. Won scholarship to college to sing in choir; worked as DJ in Memphis (met Al Bell); began writing songs while in US Air Force; wrote R&B for Fame Publishing in Muscle Shoals (songs recorded by Clarence Carter, Otis REDDING, others); signed by Bell (then Stax executive) to new Enterprise subsidiary as country singer: first country chart single was 'Don't Let The Green Grass Fool You'. Dissatisfied with debut LP *O. B. McClinton Country* '72, prod. his own *Live At Randy's Rodeo* '73, also prod. other artists. Hits incl. 'Six Pack Of Trouble' '72, 'Yours And Mine' '75; switched to Epic for 'Hello, This Is Anna' and 'Natural Love' '78; on Sunbird early '80s with 'Not Exactly Free'. He died of cancer.

MacCOLL, Ewan (*b* 25 Jan. '15, Perthshire, Scotland) Folksinger, songwriter. Left school at 14, among other things was a street singer; with actress Joan Littlewood formed Theatre Workshop in London '45, wrote eight plays, many translated into several languages. Turned to traditional music '50 and played important role in its revival, recognising the important of folk clubs for disseminating it. He married Peggy SEEGER; with Charles Parker they embarked '57 on series of eight 'radio-ballads' (documentaries about folk music), several issued on Argo. Along with studio work and teaching of younger musicians, he formed the London Critics Group with Seeger and Frankie Armstrong, others to study the problems of presenting traditional music; they wrote songs and made LPs; he also collected and published anthologies of songs. He was Chairman of the Pete SEEGER Committee in London '61 when Seeger was being persecuted for his politics. UK folk music owes him an enormous debt. He was one of those who was disappointed when Bob DYLAN turned out not to be a pure folkie; his song 'Dirty Old Town' was covered by Rod STEWART. His best-known song is 'The First Time Ever I Saw Your Face'; a hit for Roberta FLACK '71, won Grammies '72, became cabaret standard. Many LPs issued/reissued on many labels incl. *English And Scottish Folk Ballads* (with A. L. LLOYD), *Bundook Ballads*, *The Jacobite Rebellions*, *Steamwhistle Ballads*, *The Manchester Angel*, all on Topic; volumes of *Blood And Roses*, *Cold Snap*, *Kilroy Was Here*, *Different Therefore Equal*, *Hot Blast*, *Saturday Night At The Bull & Mouth* all with Peggy on Blackthorne, some on Folkways in USA with her name first, plus *Freeborn Man* and *At The Present Moment* on Rounder. Other members of the family recorded: Kirsty MacColl made LPs *Desperate Character* '81, *Kirsty MacColl* '85, UK hits

'There's A Guy Works Down The Chip Shop Swears He's Elvis' '81, 'A New England' '85, sang on POGUES' hit single early '88.

McCOY, Charlie (*b* 28 Mar. '41, Oak Hill, Va.) Multi-instrumentalist, famed Nashville sideman, best known for harmonica. Began playing harmonica and guitar in rock'n'roll bands in Miami; worked with Stonewall JACKSON's touring band '59-60; signed to Cadence '61 and scored minor pop hit with 'Cherry Berry Wine', sessioned for Archie BLEYER with Andy WILLIAMS, Johnny TILLOTSON ('It Keeps Right On A'Hurtin'' and 'Out Of My Mind', '62-3). Sessioned through the '60s on records by Bob DYLAN, Perry COMO, Joan BAEZ, many country artists; signed with Monument, recorded R&B-styled material without much success: *The Real McCoy* '69 didn't do much, but two years later his version of 'Today I Started Loving You Again' gained air play and became a chart hit. Further singles success with 'I Really Don't Want To Know' '72, 'Orange Blossom Special' '73, 'Boogie Woogie' '74 led to Grammy '72, CMA Instrumentalist of the Year '72-3, ACM Best Specialty Instrumentalist '77-8-9. Member of Nashville country-rock group AREA CODE 615, worked with Barefoot Jerry; more recently as a prod. with new artists like Laney Smallwood. LPs incl. *Charlie McCoy* '72, *Goodtime Charlie* '73, *Fastest Harp In The South* '73, *The Nashville Hit Man* '74, *Charlie My Boy* '75, *Harpin' The Blues* '76, *Country Cookin'* '77, *Appalachian Fever* '79, all on Monument. LP *Stone Fox Chase* in UK '77 incl. 'Today I Started Loving You Again'; title track was theme tune for UK TV music show *Old Grey Whistle Test*.

McCOY, Clyde (*b* 29 Dec. '03, Ashfield, Ky.) Trumpet, bandleader. Member of family that had famous Appalachian feud with Hatfields (according to publicity). Played on riverboats, Louisville venues as teenager; first band at 19; various jobs and gigs, then had hit on Columbia '31 with Clarence WILLIAMS tune 'Sugar Blues'; remake on Decca '36 said to have sold a million: emphasis on wah-wah sound of the trumpet gave it a novelty impact. seven hits in '30s incl. 'Tear It Down'. Followed legendary Benny GOODMAN Paramount theatre engagement that year; led successful band until '42, took it into US Navy with him. Took up where he left off after WWII; ran Denver night-club mid-'50s; at NYC's Round Table with combo '60; always forced to reprise 'Sugar Blues'. LP of that title on Capitol, also '36 tracks on Hindsight and '51 re-makes on Circle.

McCRACKLIN, Jimmy (*b* 13 Aug. '21, St Louis, Mo.) R&B singer, playing piano and harmonica. Recorded for Excelsior in L.A. '45, others incl. Peacock, RPM/Modern; at height of R&B infl. on Checker in Chicago '57: he went commercial and scored with dance hit 'The Walk', top 10 '58 both pop and R&B charts. Further, lesser hits on Art-Tone '61-2, Imperial '65-6; recorded for Stax c.'71 (incl. LP *Yesterday Is Gone* with the Memphis Horns), Vanguard '75. LPs in UK: '50s tracks on *Blast 'Em Dead!*, also *Jimmy McCracklin & His Bluesblasters*, both on Ace; *Blasting The Blues* on JSP.

McCURDY, Ed (*b* 11 Jan. 19, Willow Hill, Pa.) Folk singer, songwriter, guitarist. First sang on WKY radio, Oklahoma City '37; in Canada late '40s, made first album for Canadian label Whitehall. Much writing and performing for children in Canada, moved to NYC '54, made album of ballads for Riverside and with Oscar BRAND was one of the most prolific folk artists of the period before the folk boom really got underway: when it did he performed at Newport Folk Festival '59, '60, '63. He was an emcee at the Bitter End in Greenwich Village, helping new talent; recorded for Elektra, Prestige, other labels; often worked with Erik Darling. He suffered from ill health late '60s but toured Europe '76. His best-known song is 'Last Night I Had The Strangest Dream'. LPs still in print on Tradition incl. *Ballad Singer's Choice*, *Songs Of The West* and a best-of compilation.

McDANIEL, Hattie (*b* 10 June 1895, Wichita, Kansas; *d* 26 Oct. '52, Hollywood) Singer, actress; aka 'Hi-Hat Hattie', 'The Colored Sophie Tucker', 'The Female Bert Williams'. A great actress who made about 80 films, mostly features but incl. Our Gang shorts. She worked with Mae West, Al JOLSON, many others, usually playing a maid; had musical role in '36 version of Jerome KERN's *Show Boat* (in which she had toured on stage) and *Thank Your Lucky Stars* '43; among best-known non-singing work: *Gone With The Wind* '39 (Academy Award as Best Supporting Actress, the first black to win an Oscar), Disney's *Song Of The South* '46, *Amos & Andy* radio show '45-7, title role in radio sitcom *Beulah* '47-50, then replaced Ethel WATERS as TV's *Beulah* '51-2. But the show business world knew her as a truly fine singer with a big, powerful and expressive voice, though she made comparatively few records (began on Merritt '26 in Kansas City; on Okeh '26-7, some with Lovie AUSTIN; on Paramount '29); early discs incl. some of her own songs, such as 'Boo Hoo Blues' and 'Any Kind Of A Man Would Be Better Than You'. She worked with Harry JAMES band '40, Count BASIE '41, toured with Waters entertaining troops '42, but money in films was better than in music.

McDANIELS, Gene (*b* Eugene McDaniels. Kansas City, Mo.) Singer. Classically trained with gospel background, graduated from Omaha U., attended Conservatory of Music; had pop success on Liberty with songs written by pop teams Goffin/King, Pomus/Shuman, Bacharach/David etc., prod. by Tommy Garrett: quasi-spiritual 'A Hundred Pounds Of Clay' was top 3 hit '61; five more top 40 entries '61-2 incl. 'Tower Of Strength', 'Chip Chip' (both top 10). Appearance in UK film *It's Trad Dad* '62 (an early Richard Lester epic aka *Ring-A-Ding Rhythm*, with Kenny BALL, Chris BARBER, Acker BILK, etc.) added to brief fame. When black consciousness was required he reverted to Eugene, recorded soulish social commentary for Atlantic early '70s, incl. LPs *Headless Horseman Of The Apocalypse* and *Outlaw* (which acerbic Robert Christgau thought should have been called *A Hundred Pounds Of Horseshit*). Big voice deserved better use.

McDONALD, Country Joe (*b* 1 Jan. '42, El Monte, Cal.) Singer, songwriter, guitarist, bandleader: urban folkie whose band Country Joe and the Fish established him in protest but who wrote mostly non-protest songs. Formed rock band in high school as vocalist, began playing guitar and harmonica; joined US Navy; attended college in L.A. but moved to San Francisco, formed Fish with guitarist/vocalist Barry Melton (*b* '47, Brooklyn), David Cohen on keyboards and guitar, Bruce Barthol on bass and harmonica, Chicken Hirsch on drums; appeared in coffee-houses etc. First record was stage opener 'I Feel Like I'm Fixing To Die Rag' '65, incl. in music magazine *Rag Baby* published by McDonald and Ed Denson, a former *Sing Out!* editor who managed the group, landed Vanguard record deal '66: sometimes savage, often hilarious pro-nonsense anti-war act was preserved on LPs *Electric Music For The Mind And Body* '67 (incl. 'Not So Sweet Lorraine'), *I-Feel-Like-I'm-Fixin'-To-Die* and *Together* '68, *Here We Are Again* '69 (rock critics griped because eclectic LP incl. members of Big Brother and the Holding Company, JEFFERSON AIRPLANE, Count BASIE band and Oakland Symphony Orchestra). They played at the Monterey Pop Festival, became famous for F-U-C-K cheer ('Give me an F! Give me a U! . . . , later changed to F-I-S-H), and for savage anti-war lines like 'Be the first family on your block to have your boy come home in a box!' They toured Europe late '67, were scheduled to play in Chicago during Democratic convention '68, but he cancelled because he could smell violence and could not accept responsibility for anyone getting hurt: not really a protester but a conservative who cares, his famous quote is 'the most revolutionary thing you can do in this country is change your mind.' Played at Woodstock Festival '69 and toured Europe again; *Greatest Hits* and *C. J. Fish* (live from tour) issued '69-70. He wrote and performed music for Danish film *Quiet Days In Clichy* based on Henry Miller and began to make solo LPs: *Thinking Of Woody, Tonight I'm Singing Just For You* (a country album made in Nashville), *Hold On – It's Coming, Incredible! Live!*, *Paris Sessions* and *War, War, War*, (based on WWI poems of Robert W. Service, *Rhymes Of A Red Cross Man*) were all issued early '70s. The Fish broke up '70; Melton and McDonald formed a lineup to appear in film *Zacharia* '71 (satirical rock western written by avant-garde comedy outfit Firesign theatre, whose script was garbled in the filming). McDonald appeared in Chilean political film *Què Hacer*; toured with group All Stars '73 incl. women, performed anti-sexism songs; wrote 'Save The Whales' mid-'70s, performed on behalf of veterans' rights '82. Other LPs incl. *Paradise With An Ocean View* '75 (incl. 'Breakfast For Two'), *Love Is A Fire* '76, *Goodbye Blues* '77, *Rock And Roll Music From The Planet Earth* '78 (incl. 'Bring Back The Sixties, Man'), *Leisure Suite* '80, *Reunion* '77 (with Fish), all on Fantasy. Melton made solo albums on Vanguard, Columbia, Music Is Medicine.

McDOWELL, Fred 'Mississippi' (*b* 12 Jan. '04, Rossville, Tenn.; *d* 3 July '72, Memphis) Blues singer and one of the great bottleneck guitar players. Travelled as itinerant musician late '20s-30s; settled in Mississippi as farmer '40; first records made by Alan LOMAX '59, whereupon he toured the world and received the fame he deserved until he died of cancer. Concert segments and studio sessions were made for many labels, incl. *Amazing Grace* and *My Home Is The Delta* on Testament; *Delta Blues, Keep Your Lamp Trimmed, With The Blues Boys* on Arhoolie; *Long Way From Home* on Milestone; *Somebody Keeps Callin' Me* on Antilles; *With Furry Lewis* on Biograph; *Standing At The Burying Ground* on UK Red Lightnin', recorded live in London '69 (duet with Jo Ann Kelly on one track).

McDUFF, Jack (*b* Eugene McDuffy, 17 Sep. '26, Champaign, Ill.) Organist, composer. The most popular jazz organist after Jimmy SMITH, 'Brother' Jack McDuff was self-taught, later studied more formally; led own group in Midwest early '50s, formed another '59 and has toured the world ever since, some of his albums crossing over from jazz to Billboard's pop charts. He worked with Willis JACKSON '57-8 and has been reunited with him on records; has also recorded with Roland KIRK, Sonny STITT, Gene AMMONS. Own first LP was *Brother Jack* '60 on Prestige; about 20 LPs on that label through '66 incl. *Tough Duff* and *The Honeydripper* '60-1 with Jimmy FORREST, *Mellow Gravy* '62 with Ammons, *Screamin'* '62 (top 200 LPs '63), *Live!* '63 with George BENSON on guitar (top 100 LPs same year), *Prelude* '63 with Benny GOLSON's big band, *Hot Barbeque* '65 with Benson, *Together Again!* with Jackson made top 200 LPs '66.

Switched to Atlantic '66-7 for four LPs, two with big band arr. by J. J. Jackson; three Cadet/Chess LPs '68-9 incl. *Gettin' Our Thing Together* with big band arr. by Richard Evans; four Blue Note LPs '69-70 incl. *Down Home Style* (charted '69; two tracks issued on a Libery single incl. title and 'Theme From 'Electric Surfboard', Hot 100 entry). Back on Cadet/Chess '71-6 for five more, incl. '73-4 big band set with McDuff playing several keyboards incl. Moog; then *Having A Good Time* c.'80 on Sugar Hill. Eight Prestige sets including a 2-disc compilation *Rock Candy* are still selling.

McENTIRE, Reba (*b* 28 Mar. '55, McAlester, Okla.) Country singer and big new star of the '80s. The 'outlaw' movement (*see* Willie NELSON, Waylon JENNINGS, COUNTRY MUSIC etc.) reacted against the slick 'countrypolitan' studio style; McEntire, along with Ricky Scaggs, Dwight YOAKUM, the JUDDS, George STRAIT, etc. is one of the artists now completing a renaissance of traditional country musical values, many crossing over with choice of good songs. Red STEAGALL helped her get a Mercury contract '75 and she first reached the country charts '76; she fought free of stylistic influences and found her own excellent voice: Mercury LPs incl. *Unlimited, Feel The Fire, Best Of, Behind The Scene*; switched to MCA: *Just A Little Love* and *My Kind Of Country* on MCA were all chart LPs in '84, the latter incl. two no. 1 country singles ('How Blue' and 'Somebody Should Leave'); *Have I Got A Deal For You* charted '85 on MCA; in '86 *Reba Nell McEntire* on Mercury did well, but *Whoever's In New England* and *What Am I Gonna Do About You* on MCA were both no. 1 country LPs, both with no. 1 title-tracks and 'One Promise Too Late' from the latter also topping the chart. *The Last One To Know* had reached no. 4 early '88, its title track already no. 1. Evidence of her wide appeal was reviews of her albums in *Rolling Stone* and the *Village Voice*, as well as a feature article in the *Wall Street Journal*; she has won every award the country music industry has and in '87 she was the first to be named CMA's Female Vocalist of the Year four years in a row. Her *So So So Long* '88 was said to be a more pop-country effort.

Younger bother Pake McEntire has two albums on RCA.

MACERO, Teo (*b* Attilio Joseph Macero, 30 Oct. '25, Glens Falls, NY) Saxophonist, composer, producer. Studied at Juilliard '48-53, also ran a dance band; composer of jazz-influenced 'classical' music, had Guggenheim grants: *Fusion* was performed by NYPO with Leonard BERNSTEIN '58. Worked with Charles MINGUS off and on '53-7, in Jazz Workshop, records on Debut, Savoy, Period; led own quintet session with Mingus on Debut '53 (multi-tracked himself playing two tenors and two altos on 'Explorations', unusual then). Own LPs also incl. two nonet sets on Columbia '55 and '59, quintet album '57 on Prestige; ballet suite *Time Plus Seven* with chamber orchestra was recorded '65, and issued on Swedish Finnadar. He joined staff at Columbia (CBS/NYC) '57 as a music editor; turned producer and helped make some of the best records of the following 20 years: he prod. Mingus's masterpieces *Mingus Ah-Um* and *Mingus Dynasty* '59-60, Thelonious MONK LPs (Monk wrote 'Teo', recorded '64), took over from George Avakian to prod. almost all Miles DAVIS albums from *Kind Of Blue* onwards, obtaining with confidence of boss Goddard Leiberson extra time for *Sketches Of Spain* '59, which was a technical as well as musical breakthrough. A fine musician and technical wizard who 'always understood the duality: music as music, and music as product' (Ian CARR), Macero's ability to work with the difficult Davis has doubtless resulted in a large unmeasurable influence on popular music, to say nothing of all the rest of his work. With CBS's decline as an innovating label, Davis has left and Macero has made recent records of his own, incl. *Teo* '80 on American Clavé, *Impressions Of Charles Mingus* '83 on Palo Alto. Prod. *Open Letter* '87 for LOOSE TUBES.

McFARLAND, Gary (*b* 23 Oct. '33, L.A.; *d* 3 Nov. '71, NYC) Vibes, composer. From musical family but did not read music until late '50s, then became one of the most successful writers of big band arrangements of the '60s, only to die prematurely of a 'heart attack' (allegedly, a prankster put liquid methodone in his drink). Studied at

Berkeley '59, went to NYC; *Concert In Jazz* '61 by Gerry MULLIGAN on Verve incl. two McFarland compositions, *Essence* '64 by John LEWIS on Atlantic incl. six. On Verve he wrote album *All The Sad Young Men* for Anita O'DAY and his own *How To Succeed In Business Without Really Trying* (jazz version of Broadway score) '61, LPs with Bill EVANS, Stan GETZ (*Big Band Bossa Nova*, no. 13 LP in Billboard pop album chart '64); he made *Soft Samba* '64 and began a series of LPs on Impulse with *Point Of Departure*, followed by *Profiles, Simpatico, Tijuana Jazz*. He toured with a quintet mid-'60s and led house band at *Downbeat Jazz Festival* in Chicago '65; he was co-founder of the Skye label, on which his *America The Beautiful* ('a jazz lament for America') reached the top 200 LPs in Billboard '69.

McFERRIN, Bobby (*b* 11 Mar. '50, NYC) Jazz singer. The term is used advisedly: his voice is beautiful, from bass lines to falsetto; he is steeped in the whole history of black music and never fails to swing. From a family of singers (his father sang on soundtrack of film *Porgy And Bess* '59 for Sidney Poitier; his mother is a judge for the Metropolitan Opera); played piano professionally until '77, when he heard a voice telling him to sing in public as he had sung to himself: toured '80 with scat master Jon HENDRICKS; own debut with solo act '82: he improvises entirely solo, playing all the parts; he can sound like an entire doo-wop group, tapping his body percussively and using even the sound of his breathing as music. First album *Bobby McFerrin* '82; then *The Voice* '84 recorded at live German concerts, both on Elektra Musician; he copes with surprise guests on stage, such as Wayne SHORTER and comic Robin Williams on *Spontaneous Improvisation* '86 on Blue Note (also on video), live in L.A. (except for 'Turtle Shoes' with Herbie HANCOCK and 'Another Night In Tunisia' with Hendricks and MANHATTAN TRANSFER: latter won a Grammy and is also available on MT's Atlantic LP). *Simple Pleasures* '88 celebrates '60s pop classics as well as originals. Sessioned on LPs by WEATHER REPORT (*Sportin' Life*) and Chico FREEMAN (*Tangents*) '84, Joe ZAWINUL (*Dialects*) '86, Dexter GORDON (*A Night In Copenhagen*) and

in film *Round Midnight* '86 starring Gordon, where he sounds uncannily like a muted trumpet; out-takes from film incl. lovely straight version of 'What Is This Thing Called Love?' (on LP *The Other Side Of Round Midnight*). A delightful live act, making up songs on people's names etc., involved in mutual affection with audience: 'I go out with a blank slate, and whatever happens, happens.'

McGARRIGLE, Kate and Anna (Kate *b* '46, Anna '44, both in Quebec). Canadian folksinging/songwriting sisters, grew up in French-speaking family surrounded by traditional music. They sang with their parents and briefly with sister Jane as the McGarrigle Sisters; also played several instruments. Family moved to Montreal by '58; Kate and Anna performed with Michele Forest as a trio in coffee-houses and on TV; as the Mountain City Four with Peter Weldon and Jack Nissenson, they were commissioned by the National Film Board '67 to provide a song for *Helicopter Canada*, a Canadian centennial film which was nominated for an Oscar. Anna's 'Heart Like A Wheel' was recorded by McKendree Spring '72, later was title track of hit LP by Linda RONSTADT; Anna's 'Cool River' and Kate's 'Work Song' were recorded by Maria MULDAUR; they had split up for a while as Kate lived in New York State and married Loudon WAINWRIGHT, but began performing together again '74-5: debut LP *Kate & Anna McGarrigle* '76 on WB was prod. by Joe BOYD with excellent sidemen incl. Steve Gadd, Lowell George, Tony Levin: one of the delightful debuts of the decade, wistful and poignant but never twee or self-indulgent, with Kate's jaunty 'Kiss And Say Goodbye', yearning '(Talk To Me Of) Mendicino'; Anna's 'Heart Like a Wheel' and 'Jigsaw Puzzle Of Life'. It is one of those albums that retains its unique charm a decade later; perhaps inevitably, *Dancer With Bruised Knees* '77 was regarded as a disappointment, but *Pronto Monto* '78 redressed the balance, and *The French Album* '81 displayed their bilingual abilities in the chanson style, self-produced on local Hannibal label. *Love Over And Over* '83 on Polydor was a return to the charm of the debut, with guest guitarist Mark Knopfler on the title track, their tribute to the Brontë novelists; also 'Move Over Moon', 'On My Way To Town', etc. They retain a strong cult following, especially in the UK, where Kate sessioned '78 on the ALBION BAND's *Rise Up Like The Sun*, Richard & Linda THOMPSON's *Sunnyvista*. She wrote the heart-rending 'I've Had Enough', covered by Ronstadt (singing lead), Dolly PARTON and Emmylou HARRIS on *Trio* '87.

McGEE, Sam and Kirk Veteran country music duo: Sam (*b* 1 May 1894, Franklin, Tenn.; *d* 21 Aug. '75 in tractor accident), brother Kirk (*b* 4 Nov. 1899, Franklin). Father was a fiddler; bought Sam a banjo when he was 12; Kirk listened for a few years and soon began playing too. They were influenced by local black musicians in their teens; Sam became one of the first whites to play instrumental breaks and runs in the black style, and became one of the best guitar players who ever picked up the instrument. They heard Uncle Dave MACON on tour '23, soon joined his Fruit Jar Drinkers, Sam on banjo and Kirk on guitar, on the WSM radio show that soon became the GRAND OLE OPRY. Began recording '28, incl. Sam's solo 'Railroad Blues' on guitar (early tracks later issued on County label: *Mountain Blues* and *Old-Time Mountain Guitar*; also tracks on *Uncle Dave Macon: Early Recordings*). Formed trio the Dixieliners '30 with Fiddlin' Arthur Smith, popular on radio; they split before WWII, reunited on records late '50s on Folkways (*The McGee Brothers And Arthur Smith*; *Milk 'Em In The Evening Blues*). Meanwhile they recorded with Macon (Smith with the DELMORE Brothers); McGees joined comedy act with Sara and Sally which toured with Bill MONROE; they played with Monroe '44-6; also had outside interests, Kirk in property and Sam in farming. All this time they were still regulars on the Opry; they won disagreements with newer Opry stars in mid-'50s, continued playing in their traditional style and were soon rediscovered by a new younger audience. Sam made *Grandad Of Country Guitar* on Arhoolie; they both appeared on a Starday LP with the Crook Brothers, also on *Opry Old Timers* on that label and *Whoop 'Em Up Cindy* on Guest Star; *Pillars Of The Grand Ole Opry* and *Flat-Top Pickin' Sam McGee* were issued on their own MBA label.

McGHEE, Brownie (*b* Walter Brown McGhee, 30 Nov. '15, Knoxville, Tenn.) Blues singer, guitarist; also piano, kazoo, etc. Polio as a child left him with one short leg. Father taught him guitar c.'22; he attended high school but dropped out to hobo as an itinerant musician: met Sonny TERRY '39 in W.Va. and they worked together almost continuously thereafter (*see* Terry's entry). Often worked with his brother late '40s: Granville H. 'Stick' McGhee (*b* 23 Mar. '18, Knoxville; *d* of cancer 15 Aug. '61, NYC), so nicknamed because he used a stick to push his brother around on a cart as a child. They recorded together on Decca '47, worked in trio as the Three B's in Harlem clubs. Stick's 'Drinkin' Wine, Spo-Dee-O-Dee, Drinkin' Wine' '49 was the first big hit on the Atlantic label, no. 3 R&B (a top 30 national hit according to *Pop Memories*; *see* CHARTS), followed up with no. 2 R&B hit 'Tennessee Waltz Blues' '51. Stick recorded for King, Savoy, Prestige '50s; but Sonny Terry and Brownie McGhee were a world-famous duo.

McGHEE, Howard (*b* 6 Feb. '18, Tulsa, Okla.; *d* 17 July '87, NYC) Trumpet; also piano, reeds. Aka 'Maggie'. One of the great trumpeters of the BOP era, he recorded prolifically as a sideman, yet subsequently passed through periods of obscurity; but then jazz has often not been the best way to make a living: his personal musical integrity always transcended eras. Played clarinet as a child, switching to trumpet infl. by Louis ARMSTRONG. Played with Lionel HAMPTON '41, Andy KIRK '41-2 (Kirk band recorded 'McGhee Special' '42), with Charlie BARNET, Georgie AULD etc. then mostly small groups: first own record '45 for Modern in L.A. was sextet incl. Charles MINGUS; Dial date '46 became McGhee session when Charlie PARKER was too messed up to play. Some '46-7 Dial sides also reissued on Spotlite; '48-52 sides on Savoy, some with Milt JACKSON, HEATH Brothers compiled in 2-disc *Maggie*; on Blue Note '49-53 with small groups incl. '48 dates with Fats NAVARRO; LPs on Bethlehem incl. quintet '55, 10-piece group '56 with arr. by Frank Hunter, septet '60 with Pepper ADAMS, Bennie GREEN, Ron CARTER, Tommy FLANAGAN, arr. by Hunter. Quintet on Felsted '60 with Tina BROOKS, Milt

HINTON, drummer Osie Johnson, Freddie Redd on piano; quartet *Maggie's Back In Town* '61 on Contemporary; tracks '61-2 on Fontana, Argo, UA; *Cookin' Time* '66 on Hep/Zim featured big band he was leading then. Came back with sextet sets *Here Comes Freddy* '76 on Sonet with Illinois JACQUET, *Jazzbrothers* '77 on Jazz-craft/Storyville with Charlie ROUSE, *Live At Emerson's* '78 on Zim with Rouse and Frank Wess, *Home Run* '78 on Jazzcraft with Benny BAILEY, *Young At Heart* '79 on Storyville with Teddy EDWARDS, also *Together* on Contemporary with Edwards.

McGHEE, Wes (*b* 26 Oct. '48, Lutterworth, Leicestershire) Country singer/songwriter, guitarist with cult following in UK, fills halls in Austin, Texas: he may become the first UK performer in the country style to attain international stardom. Worked in Hamburg in '60s, led own band in UK early '70s; after years of college/pub gigs was enchanted by what is now broadly called country rock: ignored by record companies he decided to do it himself. With bassist Arthur Anderson (played with Ritchie BLACKMORE, Screamin' Lord SUTCH) he built studio at home in Golders Green, North London, released *Long Nights And Banjo Music* '78 on own Terrapin label (backing incl. Rick Lloyd, later with Flying Pickets): though eclipsed by later LPs, it demonstrated that authentic Tex-Mex can be produced well outside Texas if the artist believes in what he is doing and has talent. Inspired by a lengthy visit to Austin they made *Airmail*, with B. J. Cole (pedal steel), drummer Terry Stannard, backing vocalist Hank Wangford; returned to Texas to make *Landing Lights* with Texas sidemen Ponty Bone on accordion, Lloyd Maines on steel, Fred Krc on drums (pron. Kirsch; *b* Alfred Edward Krc, 17 Apr. '54, Houston; played/recorded with Jerry Jeff WALKER, also led the Explosives: LP *Restless Natives* '81 on Ready Go label, with Kim Wilson from FABULOUS THUNDERBIRDS; backed vocalist/pianist/guitarist R. C. Banks '87 on Amazing, with McGhee, Bone, others; also *Freddie 'Steady' Krc & Wild Country* '87, also on Amazing). Guitarist/mandolinist Dermot O'Conner had also joined (*b* 3 Dec. '47, London); by the time the LP was issued '83 on McGhee's TRP label Anderson had

left the partnership. By now there was public movement towards what is being called roots music, and signs of commercial progress at last: 2-disc set *Thanks For The Chicken* '85 made live in Austin with Krc, Bone, fine picking from O'Conner and McGhee; they were already well-known for 'Texas Fever'; further first-class songs incl. 'Neon And Dust', 'How Do We Get There From Here'. *Zacatexas* '86 made in UK with Bone, Krc, O'Conner; 'Monterrey' stands out. Stardom for the band seems guaranteed sooner or later; UK pub gigs early '86 were enlivened by visits onstage from Terry ALLEN, Butch HANCOCK.

McGOVERN, Maureen (*b* 27 July '49, Youngstown, Ohio) Singer, queen of screen songs in '70s. Secretary became part-time folksinger; 20th Century label boss Russ Regan was looking for someone to record 'The Morning After' (theme from disaster movie *The Poseidon Adventure*, written by Al Kasha and Joel Hirschorn); her record was USA no. 1 mid-'73 and the song won an Oscar that year. In '75 the theme from *The Towering Inferno* (by the same writers) won another Oscar, but her single did not go as far; she reached top 20 with 'Different Worlds' '79, theme from TV's *Angie*. LPs incl. *Academy Award Performances* on 20th Century, *Maureen McGovern* on WB.

McGRIFF, Jimmy (*b* 3 Apr. '36, Philadelphia, Pa.) Organist. Played bass locally, studied organ with Jimmy SMITH; formed a trio and has been popular in clubs ever since. Modestly declares that he doesn't play jazz, though 'his uncannily voicelike, propulsive organ is one of the great things in black music' (*Wire* '88). Began recording with a bang: first LP on Sue *I've Got A Woman* '62 was no. 22 LP in Billboard, top 20 hit title single (he also played piano); of seven LPs on that label '62-5 (incl. Xmas album and live set made at the Apollo) *Topkapi* (movie themes) and *Blues For Mr Jimmy* also made the top 200 LPs, as did *The Worm* on Solid State '68. There were over 25 more albums on Solid State, UA, Groove Merchant, Capitol and Blue Note, some with orchestra, all out of print in mid-'80s; *City Lights* and *Movin' Upside The Blues* '80-1 on JAM, *Countdown* and *Skywalk* '82-3 and *The Starting Five* '86 on

Milestone (latter with Rusty Bryant, David NEWMAN) with 5-10 pieces are still selling.

McGUINNESS FLINT UK country-rock band formed '69 by ex-MANFRED MANN guitarist Tom McGuinness (*b* 2 Dec. '41), ex-John MAYALL drummer Hughie Flint (*b* 15 Mar. '42), added Scottish songwriting multi-instrumentalists Benny Gallagher and Graham Lyle, who'd been employed by Apple writing songs for Mary HOPKIN, others; vocalist Dennis Coulson. Goodtime musical policy saw mandolin-heavy hit stompers 'When I'm Dead And Gone', 'Malt And Barley Blues' (UK top 5 '70-1). Gallagher and Lyle left, became successful soft-rock duo (LPs on A&M incl. UK chart entries *Breakaway* '76, *Love On The Airways* '77); band added Dixie Dean on bass, had little more success, though *Lo And Behold* '74 is a collector's item, a set of lesser Dylan songs prod. by Mann. Coulson made eponymous solo LP for Elektra '73 with Gallagher and Lyle and left band, replaced by Lou Stonebridge on keyboards and vocals, Jim Evans on pedal steel and fiddle. After LP of originals *C'Est La Vie* '74 they split, though McGuinnness and Flint worked together in Blues Band. Stonebridge later fronted the Dance Band.

McGUIRE, Barry (*b* 15 Oct. '37) USA folkrock vocalist, famous for one world-wide hit. Lead voice with NEW CHRISTY MINSTRELS, e.g. on their biggest hit 'Green, Green' (top 20 '62); left to go solo on Dunhill, involved with prod. Lou ADLER and singer/songwriter P. F. Sloan: hit big with Sloan's powerful protest song 'Eve Of Destruction' '65, no. 1 USA, 3 UK. LP of same name was top 40 USA; minor hit singles 'Cloudy Summer Afternoon' and 'Child Of Our Times', LP *This Precious Time* did not equal the big one. Circle of friends incl. MAMAS & PAPAS, mentioned in their celebrated historical 'Creeque Alley'. Following LPs *The World's Last Private Citizen* '70 and *Barry McGuire & The Doctor* '71 (with guitarist/songwriter Dr Eric Hord) he turned to Christianity, became major religious artist on labels such as Word and Sparrow.

McGUIRE SISTERS USA close-harmony pop trio popular in the '50s. Chris (*b* 30 July '29), Dotty (*b* 13 Feb. '30), Phyllis (*b* 14 Feb. '31) were from Middletown, Ohio; they were a hit and a winner on Arthur GODFREY talent show '54, signed with Coral had 17 top 40 hits '54-61, incl. two at no. 1: 'Sincerely' '55, 'Sugartime' '57. Their sweet style, similar to that of the CHORDETTES, is redolent of early '50s pop and has disappeared without trace, except for periodic revivals of the Beverly Sisters in England.

MACHITO (*b* Frank Raul Grillo, 16 Feb. '12, Tampa, Fla.; *d* 15 Apr. '84, London) Bandleader. Raised in Cuba, son of cigar manufacturer; as a child sang and danced with father's employees. Met group El Sexteto Rendicion; they split to form Jovenes de Rendicion, asked him to join on maracas and singing. Worked with several bands '28-37; to USA singing with La Estrella Habanera; recorded '37-9 with Alfredito Valdez, El Quarteto Caney, El Conjunto Moderno, La Orchestra Hatuey; appeared with others incl. Noro MORALES. Formed band with Mario BAUZA, split up; Machito joined Orchestra Siboney, recorded with Xavier CUGAT; formed own Afro-Cubans late '40, Decca records '41 with Bauza as mus. dir.; sister Graciela led band while he was in US Army '43; after discharge due to injury, band became key outfit in CUBOP movement, recording for Clef, Coda etc. '40s. Played NYC Town Hall concert '47, sharing the bill with Stan KENTON; band linked with Charlie PARKER on records such as 'No Noise', 'Mango Mangue', 'Okidoke' '48-9; 10″ LP *Afro-Cuban Suite* also featured Flip PHILLIPS, Buddy RICH, Harry EDISON; compilations of this material incl. 2-disc sets *Afro-Cuban Jazz/Machito – Chico O'Farrill – Charlie Parker – Dizzy Gillespie* '77 on Verve, *'Mucho Macho' Machito* '78 on Pablo. LPs on Roulette '57-8 incl. Doc CHEATHAM, Joe NEWMAN, Cannonball ADDERLEY, Herbie MANN, Johnny GRIFFIN, Eddie Bert (trombone; *b* 16 May '22, Yonkers, NY; later played with Elliot Lawrence, Thad JONES, MINGUS, etc.); reissues incl. *Machito And His Jazz Orchestra* as *Super Mann* on Trip, *Kenya* as *Latin Soul Plus Jazz* on Tico. Though much of the band's work not so jazz-oriented, there were fine dance LPs on Tico, Seeco, Forum, Coral labels. *Machito*

At The Crescendo and *The World's Greatest Latin Band* made in Hollywood c.'60 on GNP; an RCA LP was made '67; on Mericana '71 the band incl. Chocolate ARMENTEROS, arr. by O'FARRILL; band appeared at last public appearance of Tito RODRIGUEZ '72. When the salsa boom began, it was pretty much the style he had been playing all along. *Afro-Cuban Jazz Moods* '75 on Pablo made with Dizzy GILLESPIE; split with Bauza '76; on *Fire Works* '77 mus. dir. was son Mario Grillo; *Machito And His Salsa Big Band 1982* (won Grammy), *Live At North Sea* '82 and *Machito!!!* '83 all incl. Armenteros, on Dutch Timeless label. At Ronnie SCOTT's club when fatal stroke occurred.

McHUGH, Jimmy (*b* 10 July 1894, Boston, Mass.; *d* 23 May '69, Beverly Hills, Cal.) Songwriter. Worked as office boy at Boston Opera House, then rehearsal pianist, then for publishers in NYC. Co-wrote 'When My Sugar Walks Down The Street' '24 with Gene AUSTIN (and the omnipresent Irving MILLS, who published it), recorded by Austin, also associated with Phil HARRIS; then 'I Can't Believe That You're In Love With Me' '26 (words by Clarence Gaskill). He worked as a manager for Mills and collaborated with Dorothy Fields (*b* 15 July '05, Allenhurst, N.J.; *d* 28 Mar. '74; daughter of comedian Lew Fields): they wrote revues for the COTTON CLUB; *Lew Leslie's Blackbirds Of 1928* with Adelaide HALL, Bill 'Bojangles' Robinson, incl. 'Diga Diga Doo' and 'Doin' The New Low Down' (both recorded by Duke ELLINGTON and Don REDMAN, one of Redman's takes having Bojangles tap-dancing on it), also 'I Must Have That Man', 'I Can't Give You Anything But Love'; *Hello Daddy* '28; *The International Revue* '30 ('On The Sunny Side Of The Street', 'Exactly Like You'). Fats WALLER was said by the prod. of *Blackbirds* to have sold melodies of 'I Can't Give You Anything But Love' and 'Sunny Side Of The Street' to McHugh: they sound like Waller's, especially the former, and this would fit with his profligacy: he could write songs almost as fast as he could spend the money. McHugh and Fields went to Hollywood and wrote songs for films incl. *Cuban Love Song* '30, *Dinner At Eight* '33 ('Don't Blame Me'), *Every Night At Eight* '35 ('I'm

In The Mood For Love'), *Roberta* '35 (collaborated with Jerome KERN), others. She also worked with Kern, Cole PORTER, Arthur Schwartz, had an important partnership with Cy COLEMAN (*Sweet Charity* '66 incl. 'Big Spender'; others). McHugh worked with Frank LOESSER, Johnny MERCER, Ted Koehler, others; most important after Fields was Harold Adamson (*b* 10 Dec. '06, Greenville, N.J.): they wrote songs for *Calendar Girl* '47 ('Have I Told You Lately That I Love You'), *A Date With Judy* '48 ('It's A Most Unusual Day'), many more. Adamson also worked with Hoagy CARMICHAEL, Vincent YOUMANS, Burton Lane, Victor YOUNG.

McINTYRE, Hal (*b* Harold McIntyre, 14 Nov. '14, Cromwell, Conn.; *d* 5 May '59, L.A.) Alto sax, clarinet, arranger, bandleader. He had band in Connecticut '35-6; joined Glenn MILLER '37, soon played lead alto. Helped by Miller to form own band '41 with Ellington flavour, arr. often written by tenorist Dave Matthews; had good singers incl. Helen Ward (ex-Benny GOODMAN) and played top venues incl. President Roosevelt's birthday party at Statler Hotel in Washington DC early '45. Same year had no. 3 hit 'Sentimental Journey' on Victor, went on USO tour: had to use stand-in musicians but enhanced popularity in the end; recorded for other labels incl. MGM; carried on well into '50s when other bands had quit; planned comeback but died in fire caused by cigarette. Compilation LP *Ecstasy* on Golden Era.

MACK, Bunny (*b* Cecil Bunting MacCormack, '40s, Freetown, Sierra Leone) African singer/composer. Took up harmonica and penny-whistle at 6, made first public appearance at 8. Moved on to banjo, sang in church choirs, took up guitar; played with friends in band called the Daverns incl. broadcasts, but kept his name off the air because of parental displeasure. Took stage name Kenny Marson, joined Soundcasters '66; band went to UK and released first single '67; in '69 'Oh How I Miss Her' was minor UK hit but problems with Home Office forced them to leave for Germany; they performed in Europe for a year but then split up. He joined a series of groups, finally in late '70s teamed with Akie

Dean, also from Sierra Leone, prod. of the Afronationals and a man with definite ideas about crossover music: second single with Dean 'Funny Lady'/'Discolypso' on Rokel/Discolypso label brought commercial breakthrough; 12″ single 'Let Me Love You'/'Love You Forever' confirmed success. First LP *Let Me Love You* '81 became disco hit, sold 100,000 in Nigeria alone. Using the best session players such as Alfred Bannerman, George Lee, Jake Sollo and Papa Mensah, his disco/funk/calypso fusion featured English lyrics and a thumping dance beat; voted musician of the year by *Africa Music* magazine and gold disc for *Let Me Love You*; *Supafrico* '81 continued in successful discolypso direction.

MACK, Lonnie (*b* '41, Harrison, Ind.) Blues/rock guitarist, singer, songwriter. Born in log cabin, learning guitar from age 5; he played at local functions with his brothers, played country music in bars at 13, turned to rock'n'roll, already a seasoned performer in a music dominated by amateurs: he was always too early and too good. Worked as sideman in Troy Seals band early '60s; used up recording session for Fraternity label cutting instrumentals 'Memphis' (cover of Chuck BERRY classic) and 'Wham'; forgot about it. The band went on tour backing Chubby CHECKER (one of the amateurs) while the single was released: 'Memphis' was no. 5 hit '63, followed by lesser hits same year; album *The Wham Of That Memphis Man* almost reached top 100 LPs, was soon forgotten but rediscovered and given a rave review in *Rolling Stone* '68: Mack was tracked down playing in a Florida dance hall, Elektra bought the Fraternity masters (reissued as *For Collectors Only* '70, again as *The Wham* '73) and signed Mack; albums *Glad I'm In The Band* '69 and *Whoever's Right* '70 resulted, but in '71 Mack announced his retirement: after nearly 20 years on the road he probably wanted more than a cult following, but he didn't stay away. *The Hills Of Indiana* '72 was on Elektra; *Home At Last* '77 and *Lonnie Mack With Pismo* '78 on Capitol (latter country-styled album incl. David LINDLEY in backing); *Strike Like Lightning* '85 on Alligator was made in Texas with Stevie Ray VAUGHAN, followed by *Second Sight* '86. Seals had LPs on Atlantic '73, CBS '77.

MACK, Warner (*b* Warner McPherson, 2 Apr. '38, Nashville, Tenn.) Country singer, songwriter who had 14 consecutive top 10 hits in '60s. Grew up in Vicksburg, Ms.; worked for a tyre company and as radio announcer on WVIM Vicksburg before landing regular spot on Louisiana Hayride and contract with Decca '57: 'Is It Wrong' went top 10 country and stayed in chart for 36 weeks. Further chart success eluded him for the time being, though he wrote hits for others; then '64-70 had his own hits with 'Sittin' In An All Nite Cafe', 'The Bridge Washed Out', 'Talking To The Wall', 'Drifting Apart', 'Leave My Dreams Alone', 'Love Hungry', etc. Faded from charts in '70s, concentrated on writing and running his Country Store in Madison. Continued recording for MCA, then Pageboy; toured UK early '80s. LPs incl. *Drifting Apart* '67, *Many Moods* '67, *Country Beat* '68, *I'll Still Be Missing You* '69, *Love Hungry* '70, *You Make Me Feel Like A Man* '71 etc.; *Prince Of Country Blues* '83 on Pageboy.

McKENNA, Dave (*b* 30 May '30, Woonsocket, R.I.) Pianist. Worked with Charlie Ventura '49, Woody HERMAN '50-1, served in US Army in Korea; worked with Ventura again, Gene KRUPA, many others; in '60s with Eddie CONDON, Bobby HACKETT (incl. Hackett album *Blues With A Kick* on Capitol). Moved to Cape Cod '67 and has mostly worked there, in'70s sometimes alternating sets with Teddy WILSON; often seen on festival scene since late '70s and on Concord Jazz records. Whitney Balliett wrote in the *New Yorker* (and in collection *American Musicians: 56 Portraits In Jazz* '86) that McKenna practises 'pure improvisation'. McKenna says there's no such thing, and is not even sure he's a jazz musician, but with an especially strong left hand and excellent time, fans (who incl. many musicians) say he can sound like a whole ensemble. Own albums mostly solo incl. *By Myself* '76 on Shiah; *No Holds Barred* '77 on Famous Door with Scott HAMILTON, Al COHN etc.; *Cookin' At Michael's Pub* on Marian McPARTLAND's Halcyon label; *No Bass Hit* and *Major League* with Hamilton, *Plays The Music Of Harry Warren* with Jake Hanna and Bob Maize, also *Giant Strides* '79, *Left Handed Compliment, Celebration Of Hoagy Carmichael* '83,

The Key Man! '84, *Dancing In The Dark (And Other Music Of Arthur Schwartz)* '85, *My Friend The Piano* '86 all on Concord Jazz.

MacKENZIE, Gisele (*b* Gisele Lefleche, 10 Jan. '27, Winnipeg, Canada) Pop singer with unusually good voice. Played piano with Bob Shuttleworth Band in Canada, he became her manager; had daily radio show in Canada, moved to USA, became regular on *Your Hit Parade* '53-7; recorded for X and Vik (RCA subsidiaries), had one big hit: 'Hard To Get' (no. 4 '55), backed by Richard Maltby band. Eponymous RCA LP reissued '87 in UK.

McKENZIE, Red (*b* William McKenzie, 14 Oct. 1899, St Louis, Mo.; *b* 7 Feb. '48, NYC) Played comb-with-tissue-paper with a kazoo-like sound. Led Mound City Blue Blowers from '23, visited London '25 and made some trio records '24-5 (adding Frankie TRUMBAUER on two sides); he resumed recording (and began singing) '29, using interesting sidemen: various sessions '29-35 incl. Eddie CONDON, Jack TEAGARDEN, Bunny BERIGAN, Muggsy SPANIER, etc.; a '35 session incl. quintet from the Bob CROSBY band. Best-known record is '(If I Could Be With You) One Hour', from Nov. '29: instrumental track is mostly a lovely solo by Coleman HAWKINS. One more recording session '47.

McKENZIE, Scott (*b* 1 Oct. '44, Arlington, Va.) Pop singer. Linked with future MAMAS & PAPAS leader John Phillips in the Journeymen '64; when Phillips found success in West Coast folk-rock boom '67 McKenzie junked career as solo balladeer in NYC (on Capitol) to follow him. Single on Epic 'No, No, No, No, No' preceded signing to Lou ADLER's hippie-ish Ode label (logo was a daffodil); the Phillips-composed song 'San Francisco (Be Sure To Wear Flowers In Your Hair)' incl. the best of hippie good vibes and drew thousands to SF for the 'summer of love', a 'new generation with a new explanation'. The record was no. 3 USA '67, prod. by Phillips, who also played guitar, with Mama Cass on bells. The dream may have failed but the idealism was of the highest quality, approved by the rest of the West: the disc was no. 1 in UK,

Germany, Belgium, Denmark, Norway, a huge hit in many other countries: total sales over 7m. Profiled by *Time* magazine, McKenzie had to cope with being appointed spokeman for a generation. His only other single hit was 'Like An Old-Time Movie' (no. 24 USA '67); LPs incl. *Voice Of Scott McKenzie* '67 and (after 3-year 'retirement') folk-rock *Stained Glass Morning* '70.

McKINLEY, Ray (*b* 18 June '10, Fort Worth, Texas) Drummer, singer, leader. Worked with Smith BALLEW '32, DORSEY Brothers '34, staying with Jimmy until '39. Partners with Will BRADLEY in popular big band '39-43, formed own band, with a tuba playing along with the brass for a rich sound; also 17-year-old trumpeter Dick Cathcart, who later played in soundtrack for Jack Webb in film *Pete Kelly's Blues* '55, also heard in subsequent TV series. Recorded for Capitol; popular arr. incl. 'Big Boy' (vocal by Imogene Lynn), 'Hard Hearted Hannah' (McKinley vocal). Joined USAAF and worked with Glenn MILLER, leading or coleading the band (with Jerry Gray) after Miller's death until late '45; led own band '46-50 with arr. by Eddie SAUTER, Deane Kincaide; hits on Majestic incl. 'Red Silk Stockings And Green Perfume' with McKinley vocal; on RCA 'You Came A Long Way (From St Louis)', with small group and ensemble vocal. Worked as solo vocalist, occasionally forming bands for engagements; led Glenn Miller band '56-66 for the estate, succeeded by Buddy DE FRANCO. Continued occasionally leading into the '70s. Compilations incl. *Class Of '49* on Hep, *Ray McKinley And His Musicians* '46-9 on First Heard.

McKINNEY'S COTTON PICKERS Popular jazz-oriented black dance band '26-c.'39. Bill McKinney (*b* 17 Sep. 1895, Cynthiana, Ky.; *d* there 14 Oct. '69) was a circus drummer after WWI, joined The Synco Jazz band in Springfield, Ohio; turned drum chair over to Cuba Austin (*b* c.'06, Charleston, West Va.; *d* unknown date) to become front man. They were signed by Jean GOLDKETTE organisation, changed name and had a residency at Greystone Ballroom in Detroit, toured as far as NYC; Goldkette hired Don REDMAN '27 as mus. dir., ensuring fame: Redman had got Fletcher

HENDERSON band off to a flying start, and Henderson would later refine its style to make it the basic style of the BIG BAND ERA, while Paul WHITEMAN led a band which was the second-greatest hit-maker of the whole first half of the century (after Bing CROSBY), but under Redman the Cotton Pickers became the first modern 'big band': of all the dance bands of the late '20s, its records have dated least. Discographies were confused for years because a few early records under McKinney's name were actually Goldkette sides, because Goldkette paid Redman to rehearse some of his white bands as well, and because on the occasion of some '29 record dates in New York, the band's business in Detroit was so good that they were not allowed to go, so Redman recorded with a pick-up group of men from other bands; to confuse matters further, a Redman Chocolate Dandies date '28 was essentially the Cotton Pickers. Many fine records on Victor incl. hits 'Milenberg Joys' '28, 'If I Could Be With You One Hour Tonight' '30, called no. 1 by *Pop Memories* (*see* CHARTS), with Carter solo, vocal by George Thomas (*b* Charleston; *d* '30 in car crash; aka 'Fathead', also played saxes; recorded with Duke ELLINGTON '26). They left Detroit and Goldkette '30 (they were never paid enough), split mid-'31: some left to go with Redman's new band; Benny CARTER was mus. dir. for a year; they continued touring but well-publicised dissension and above all the Depression hurt: they split finally '34. Other bands used Cotton Pickers name; McKinney re-formed '35, ran a café in Detroit '37, continued fronting bands until '40, worked in Ford factory. All the McKinney sides reissued on five LPs on French RCA, incl. sidemen such as Joe Smith, Langston Curl, John Nesbitt on trumpets; Claude Jones and Ed Cuffee on trombones, reedmen incl. Prince Robinson; later Rex STEWART, Carter, Ralph Escudero on tuba etc. Monograph *McKinney's Music* '78 by John CHILTON tells the story of popular, legendary band. *See also* Redman's entry.

McLAUGHLIN, John (*b* 4 Jan '42, Yorkshire) Electric guitarist who is not a great soloist, but whose sound, textures, ideas made him a pioneer in FUSION. Played with Mike CARR, Graham BOND, Brian AUGER; first solo LP *Extrapolation* '69 with English musicians on Polydor charted in USA '72; went to USA and played on *Shhh/Peaceful* and *Bitches Brew* with Miles DAVIS '69, also in Tony WILLIAMS group Lifetime; made solo albums '71-2 *Devotion* on Douglas with rock drummer Buddy Miles, *My Goal's Beyond* on Polydor (since on other labels) with Jerry Goodman on violin (ex-Flock), Alla Rakha on tabla, drummer Billy COBHAM; then added bassist Rick Laird, Jan HAMMER on keyboards to form Mahavishnu Orchestra (named under infl. of guru) for jazz/rock/Indian fusion LPs *The Inner Mounting Flame, Birds Of Fire* (no. 15 LP USA) and live *Between Nothingness And Eternity* '72-3 on Columbia (CBS) to public and critical acclaim, but group split up because of internal dissension. He made duet LP *Love, Devotion, Surrender* '73 with Carlos SANTANA, used Mahavishnu name for himself and various lineups: *Apocalypse* '74 (with prod. George MARTIN, LSO cond. by Michael Tilson Thomas), *Visions Of The Emerald Beyond* '75, *Inner Worlds* '76; also formed and recorded with groups Shakti (*Shakti With John McLaughlin* '76, *A Handful Of Beauty* and *Natural Elements* '77) and The One Truth Band (*Electric Dreams* '79). Other LPs: *Electric Guitarist* '78 with Santana, Williams, Goodman, Cobham, Jack Bruce, Stanley CLARKE, Chick COREA; *Friday Night In San Francisco* '81 and *Passion, Grace & Fire* '83 in trio with Al DiMEOLA and Paco DeLucia, all on CBS. *Belo Horizonte* '81 and *Music Spoken Here* '82 were on WB. Plays one track in soundtrack LP *Round Midnight* '86.

McLEAN, Don (*b* 2 Oct. '45, New Rochelle, NY) Talented singer/songwriter whose big hit almost became an albatross. He began in folk music, performing free on behalf of Pete SEEGER's efforts to clean up the Hudson River; his first album *Tapestry* '70 had been turned down many times because of the song 'And I Love You So': the LP was issued on Media Arts, soon taken over by UA; the song was later covered by Perry COMO for a top 30 hit '73. Second album *American Pie* '71 incl. irresistibly catchy title track, said to have been inspired by the death of Buddy HOLLY, but also a sentimental song about America that could be embraced by everybody as the USA reeled from Vietnam and Watergate: the 8.5 minute track as a two-sided single was no. 1 for four weeks (no. 2 UK), kept the album no. 1 for seven weeks and even pulled the first LP into the charts. 'Vincent'/'Castles In The Air' from the same LP was a no. 12 hit and 'Vincent' (no. 1 UK) was being played daily in the entrance to Van Gogh museum in Amsterdam; third album *Don McLean* '72 was no. 23 LP, incl. top 30 'Dreidel'; *Playin' Favorites* '73 got back to folk/country roots and did not chart in USA, but incl. 'Everyday', top 40 single in UK; *Homeless Brother* '74 was no. 120 LP, incl. 'The Legend Of Andrew McCrew', a true story about a black hobo who died '13, was exhibited in carnivals as a 'petrified man', not buried until '73. He had to stop performing 'American Pie' to make it go away. 2-disc *Solo* '76 incl. all the hits, followed by switch to Arista label for *Prime Time* '77; with the coast clear he had hits again on Millennium label: top 30 LP *Chain Lightning* '81 incl. no. 5 cover of old Roy ORBISON hit 'Crying' (no. 1 in UK), also top 30 hit 'Since I Don't Have You'; *Believers* '82 made top 200 LPs, incl. new top 30 version of 'Castles In The Air' (also minor hit in UK). *Dominion* '83 on EMI/UK was 2-disc set made in concert at London's Dominion Theatre: he was playing 'American Pie' again at last.

McLEAN, Jackie (*b* John Lenwood McLean, 17 May '32, NYC) Alto sax, composer. Father was a guitarist with Tiny BRADSHAW. Played with Sonny ROLLINS and studied music with Bud POWELL after school; recorded with Miles DAVIS on Blue Note '52; on classic Charles MINGUS albums on Atlantic *Pithecanthropus Erectus* '56, *Blues & Roots* '58; played with Paul BLEY, others; acted and played off-Broadway in Jack Gelber's *The Connection* '69-70. Already a sensation as a teenager, he is one of those who were infl. but not dominated by Charlie PARKER, his own more linear intensity making a powerful contribution to hard bop in the era of classic records on Blue Note and Prestige; in the '60s-70s he took up flute, developed as a teacher, composer and playwright, also did anti-drug counselling. First recording session as leader '55 incl. Mal WALDRON, later reissued in sets on Trip and French Rou-

lette with '57 session which was originally on Jubilee. Prestige/Status/New Jazz LPs '56-7 with excellent personnel variously incl. Waldron, Elmo HOPE, Red GARLAND, Paul CHAMBERS, Doug Watkins, Art Taylor, many others (some now on Fantasy), incl. *Lights Out, Jackie's Pal, McLean's Scene, Alto Madness, Makin' The Changes, Strange Blues*, several more incl. *Contour*, a 2-disc compilation with '56 tracks incl. Donald BYRD. About 20 LPs on Blue Note '59-'67, nearly all quintets with support of similar high quality, incl. *Jackie's Bag* (USA LP culled from two session '59-60; Japanese edition *Street Singer* has all '60 tracks with Tina BROOKS), 2-disc albums *Jacknife* '65-6, *Hipnosis* '62-7; *New Soil* and *Swing, Swang, Swingin'* '59; *Capuchin Swing* '60; *Bluesnick* and *A Fickle Sonance* '61, *Let Freedom Ring* and *Tippin' The Scales* '62; *Vertigo, One Step Beyond* and *Destination Out* '63; *It's Time* and *Action* '64 (both with Cecil McBEE); *Right Now!* and *Consequence* '65; *New And Old Gospel* '67 with Ornette COLEMAN on trumpet. *Dr Jackle* '66 on Danish Steeplechase joined by six more LPs on that label '72-4 incl. *The Meeting* and *The Source* with Dexter GORDON; duet LP *Antiquity* with Michael Garvin features temple blocks, bells, bamboo flutes, etc.; and *New York Calling* by Jackie McLean and the Cosmic Brotherhood, with Jackie playing tenor his son Rene McLean (*b* 16 Dec. '46) playing alto, soprano and tenor (Rene's sextet LP on Steeplechase is called *Watch Out!*). *Altissimo* '74 on Japanese Philips is a Lee KONITZ LP with four altos (McLean, Konitz, Gary Bartz, Charlie Mariano) plus piano trio. *New Wine, Old Bottles* on East Wind/Inner City has quartet of McLean, Hank JONES, Ron CARTER, Tony WILLIAMS; *Moments* '79 on RCA a larger group. Teaching post since '72 at U. of Hartford, Connecticut.

McNEELY, Big Jay (*b* Cecil McNeely, 29 Apr. '28, Los Angeles, Cal.) Tenor sax, bandleader. Legendary showman in R&B, playing a coarse, exciting horn while rocking on the floor on his back, etc. had an infl. on early white rock'n'rollers. Recorded for Exclusive '46, Savoy '49 ('Deacon's Hop'), Aladdin, Federal, WB; paradoxically his biggest hit was a ballad, self-written oft revived 'There Is Something On Your

Mind', no. 5 R&B, top 50 pop '59 on Swingin' label, with vocal by Sonny Warner. Later worked for the post office, but could draw crowds in L.A. clubs any time. Compilations on Ace UK '84: *Meets The Penguins*, *From Harlem To Camden*; also Imperial reissues *Deacon Rides Again* on Pathé Marconi with vocalists Mercy Dee, Jesse BELVIN.

MACON, Uncle Dave (*b* David Harrison Macon, 7 Oct. 1870, Smart Station, Tenn.; *d* 22 Mar. '52, Murfreesboro) First singing star of the Grand Ole Opry, billed as the Dixie Dewdrop; humour and banjo playing over 40 years of appearances made him 'King of the Hillbillies'. Grew up in Nashville, where his parents ran the Broadway Hotel, a home for travelling entertainers. He married Mathilda Richardson (1889), bought a farm near Murfreesboro and set up a Macon Midway Mule And Wagon Transportation Company (later immortalised in a song, 'From Here To Heaven'). Until '18 he enjoyed local affection as a comic and a banjo player; a pompous farmer asked him to play at a party and he demanded $15: he was accepted. An agent from a theatre chain was there and he began touring in the South; when he joined the Opry (with band The Fruit Jar Drinkers, name probably chosen by George Hay), he was 56 years old, a repository of banjo styles, songs full of social commentary: Macon recorded America changing, beginning in '24 with fiddler Sid Harkreader (*d* 19 Mar. '88) and tunes like 'Hillbilly Blues' (the first title using the word 'hillbilly') and 'Keep My Skillet Good And Greasy'. He popularised classics like 'Arkansas Traveller' and 'Soldier's Joy', carried on until '38 with songs about political corruption, economic depression, trains, the coming of the automobile and much else, accompanied by Sam and Kirk McGEE, the DELMORE Brothers, fiddler Mazy Todd, his son Dorris, incl. solo sides and duets with Sam. He toured with Opry stars late '20s-30s; was featured in film *The Grand Ole Opry* '40, toured as a comedian with Bill MONROE's tent show '46-50 and remained a regular on the Opry until not long before his death at 83. His joy at performing was captured in his whoops and hollers on the records; he was elected to the Country Music Hall of Fame '66. Compilations incl. *Wait Till The Clouds Roll By* ('26-39) on Historical, *Uncle Dave Macon: Early Recordings* on County, *First Featured Star Of Grand Ole Opry* on Decca, *The Dixie Dewdrop* on Vetco, *Original Masters* on Folkways, *Laugh Your Blues Away* on Rounder, *First Row, Second Left* on Bear Family.

McPARTLAND, Jimmy (*b* James Duigald McPartland, 15 Mar. '07, Chicago) Trumpet in Chicago style (*see* JAZZ); his brother Dick (*b* Richard George McPartland, 18 May '05, Chicago; *d* 30 Nov. '57, Elmhurst, Ill.) was a well-known guitarist in the genre, who replaced Eddie LANG in the Mound City Blue Blowers (*see* Red McKENZIE), but had to retire from music late '30s because of ill health. Jimmy replaced his idol Bix BEIDERBECKE in the Wolverines, continued playing Bix-inspired horn with Ben POLLACK, Roger Wolfe KAHN, Russ COLUMBO, Smith BALLEW; joined his brother's Embassy Four in Chicago '34, formed own band late '30s; took part in Normandy invasion '44, met and married Marian McPARTLAND '45 (*see below*). Led own bands in Midwest late '40s, '50s; worked long spells at Nick's etc. in NYC from late '50s; acted in TV play *The Magic Horn*; in '65 played at 75th anniversary party for Chicago's Austin High School, where it all began. Played in '60s with Bud FREEMAN, reedmen Peanuts Hucko (*b* 17 Apr. '18, Syracuse, NY), Tony Parenti (*b* 6 Aug. 1900, New Orleans; *d* 17 Apr. '72, NYC); at Newport Jazz Festival with Marian '78, still working in the '80s. Albums incl. *On Stage* '67 on Jazzocracy, with Bobby HACKETT on 2-disc *Shades Of Bix* on MCA.

McPARTLAND, Marian (*b* Marian Margaret Turner, 20 Mar. '20, Windsor, England) Pianist, songwriter. From musical family; studied at Guildhall School of Music, played in piano duo (stage name was Marian Page); entertained troops in WWII, met Jimmy McPARTLAND in Belgium '44 (m. '45, div. c.'65); they played for Eisenhower in Paris. To USA '46, played in combo with Jimmy, formed own trio '51 and soon became highly rated in her own right, maturing from derivative stylist to fine ballad player with her own harmonic ideas. She has written soundtrack music, songs

('There'll Be Other Times' recorded by Sarah VAUGHAN; 'Twilight World' played by Doc SEVERINSEN on TV, recorded by Tony BENNETT; 'Ambiance' recorded by Thad JONES-Mel LEWIS band, nominated for a Grammy); she toured with Benny GOODMAN sextet '63; also broadcaster and journalist: her award-winning *Marian McPartland's Piano Jazz* show on NPR has been running since '79, featured interviews and duets with Bobby SHORT, Bill EVANS, Tommy FLANAGAN, Mary Lou WILLIAMS, many more. Formed Halcyon label '69 (not to be confused with UK label of the same name, using same numbering system); played at Newport with Jimmy '78. LPs incl. *Let It Happen* on RCA by Jazz Piano Quartet, with Dick HYMAN, Hank JONES, Roland Hanna; 2-disc *At The Hickory House* on Savoy (NYC club '52-3); several albums on Halcyon with Jimmy, incl. tracks compiled from '48-9 as well as more recent material; other sets on Halcyon: music written for her by the composer on *Plays Alec Wilder, Solo Concert At Haverford* '74, *The Maestro And Friend* '74 (duos with Joe VENUTI made in Nice), *Now's The Time* '77, *Live At The Carlyle* '79, several more; on Concord Jazz: *At The Festival, Portrait Of Marian McPartland* '79, *Personal Choice* '82, all with small groups, solo piano *Willow Creek & Other Ballads* '85; *Plays The Music Of Billy Strayhorn* '87. Book *All In Good Time* '87 collects her essays on musicians.

McPHATTER, Clyde (*b* 15 Nov. '33, Durham, N.C.; *d* 13 June '72, Tea Neck, N.J.) One of the great lead singers of the '50s, with a powerful infl. on the following soul era. Father was clergyman; sang in church and turned pro at 14 with a gospel group; met Billy WARD and joined his Dominoes '50, had first top 10 hit 'Do Something For Me', then smash R&B no. 1 'Sixty Minute Man', top 10 'I Am With You', all '51; 'That's What You're Doing To Me' and no. 1 'Have Mercy Baby' followed '52; McPhatter trained his successor Jackie WILSON and left to form the DRIFTERS, recording for Atlantic: instant classic no. 1 'Money Honey' '53 followed by two-sided top 10 'Such A Night'/'Lucille', 'Honey Love' (no. 1), 'Bip Bam', 'What'cha Gonna Do' '54-5. Another hit was lovely arr. of 'White Christmas' with lead vocals by both

McPhatter and bass Bill Pinkney. McPhatter was drafted; while on leave he recorded solo 'Seven Days' for R&B hit '56, also first pop chart entry at no. 44: on leaving the service he became a pop star in his own right as big R&B hits crossed over: 'Treasure Of Love' and 'Without Love (There Is Nothing)' reached pop top 20; other big ones incl. 'Just To Hold My Hand', 'Long Lonely Nights', 'Come What May'; 'A Lover's Question' was no. 1 R&B, no. 6 pop '58. Switched to MGM (with less appropriate songs and arrangements), then Mercury; last big crossovers were 'Ta Ta' and 'I Never Knew'; 'Lover Please' '62 was second and last pop top 10 entry but did not make R&B chart; 'Crying Won't Help You Now' '65 made R&B chart but not pop. His classics were the sort of records which caused young people to discover black pop music, contributing to the explosion of rock'n'roll; he should have been a star of '60s soul music but his too-poppish career on Mercury left him relegated to the oldies circuit.

McPHERSON, Charles (*b* 24 July '39, Joplin, Mo.) Alto sax, infl. by both Johnny HODGES and Charlie PARKER. Worked with Charles MINGUS on records and tours c.64-70 incl. music for Monterey '64-5, LPs *Blue Bird* and *Pithecanthropus Erectus* '70, etc. Own LPs with many fine sidemen, incl. Barry HARRIS, Sam JONES, many others. On Prestige: *Be-Bop Revisited* '64, *Con Alma* '65, *The Quintet Live!* '66 at the Five Spot incl. Mingus alumnus Lonnie Hillyer on trumpet (*b* 25 Mar. '40, Monroe, Ga.). Also *From This Moment On, Horizons, McPherson's Mood* '68-9; then on Mainstream for three LPs '72-3, some tracks with those named above, some with Gene BERTONCINI on guitar, others with strings arr. by Ernie Wilkins; then *Beautiful, Live In Tokyo, New Horizons* and *Free Bop!* '75-8 on Xanadu, *The Prophet* '83 on Discovery.

McRAE, Carmen (*b* 8 Apr. '22, NYC) Singer: one of the most highly regarded of all jazz singers, but like all the best true jazz singers, her interpretations of good songs cannot be used as radio fodder, so does not receive the wider commercial exposure she deserves; also, as Gary Giddins has pointed out, as with many fine female singers her interpretations have an intelligent female sensibility: males and less interesting pop crooners get a better chance in the marketplace. Discovered by songwriter Irene Kitchings (once married to Teddy WILSON); worked with Benny CARTER, Count BASIE '44; then married to Kenny CLARKE, made first records with Mercer ELLINGTON '46-7 as Carmen Clarke. Worked as singer and intermission pianist in clubs during lean years early '50s but began to become critical favourite, recording for obscure labels, then Decca '54; she had singles in Hot 100 '56-7 with 'The Next Time It Happens' (from musical show *Pipe Dream*) and 'Skyliner' (2-disc *Greatest Of* on MCA); has toured the world (especially Japan), played Monterey and Newport Jazz Festivals, TV appearances etc. She recorded with Dave BRUBECK '60-1; had accompanists such as Dave FRISHBERG, but continued to play piano in her act, made solo LP *As Time Goes By* '73. Other albums incl. *I Am Music* on Blue Note; *Sound Of Silence* (now on Bainbridge), *Just A Little Lovin'*, *Portrait Of Carmen*, *For Once In My Life*, 2-disc *Great American Songbook*, all on Atlantic; *It Takes A Whole Lot Of Human Feelings* and *Ms Jazz* on Groove Merchant; *Carmen McRae*, *Carmen's Gold*, *Live And Doin' It*, *Alive!*, *In Person*, *I Want You*, all on Mainstream; *You Can't Hide Love* '76 on Pausa, *Two For The Road* (with George SHEARING) and *You're Lookin' At Me* (songs associated with Nat King COLE) on Concord Jazz; *Fine And Mellow* recorded live at Birdland West on Concord '88. *Velvet Soul* and *Any Old Time* issued on Denon '86-7; *Ms Magic* on a Dunhill CD with strings, guest soloists reissues tracks from Buddah and Trio.

MacRAE, Gordon (*b* 12 Mar. '31, East Orange, N.J.; *d* 24 Jan. '86) Singer, actor, with pleasant baritone. Began as a child in revue with singer/dancer Ray Bolger. Musical films incl. *The Desert Song* '53, *Oklahoma!* '55 (led to album *Cowboys Lament* '57, with orchestra dir. by Van Alexander), *Carousel* '56; also on Broadway in *I Do, I Do!* '67. 18 top 30 hits on Capitol '47-54 listed by *Pop Memories* (*see* BILLBOARD) incl. 'I Still Get Jealous' (from *High Button Shoes*, by Sammy CAHN and Jule Styne) and top 10 film songs 'It's Magic', 'Hair Of Gold, Eyes Of Blue' '47-8, 'C'est Magnifique' '53 (from

Can-Can), etc. Also had duet hits with Jo STAFFORD '48-50.

McSHANN, Jay (*b* James Columbus McShann, 12 Jan. '09, Muskogee, Okla.) Pianist, bandleader, songwriter, aka 'Hootie'. A popular musician for more than half a century, leader of one of the best KANSAS CITY bands after Count BASIE, Charlie PARKER among the sidemen; hits incl. 'Confessin' The Blues' '41 (co-written with vocalist Walter BROWN), 'Get Me On Your Mind' '43 with Al HIBBLER vocal (Decca tracks compiled on MCA/USA, Affinity/UK); also no. 1 R&B hit 'Hands Off' '55 with vocalist Priscilla Bowman on Vee Jay. Rediscovered every few years, boogie-woogie flavoured piano never failing to please; toured the world almost annually since late '60s. LPs incl. *Early Bird* ('40-3 airchecks with Parker on Spotlite and French RCA), *McShann's Piano* on Capitol, *The Big Apple Bash* on Atlantic, *Confessin' The Blues* '71 on Classic Jazz; *Goin' To Kansas City* '72 on Master Jazz and Swaggie has quintet with Buddy TATE, Julian DASH, KC rhythm section: Gene Ramey on bass, drummer Gus Johnson from '38-43 band later worked for Basie. There are also solo piano tracks on 'Master Jazz Piano' compilations on both labels. *After Hours* '77 is on Storyville, *Blues And Boogie* '78 on Philips, *The Band That Jumps The Blues* reissued '83 on Black Lion. Canadian Sackville label offers *Man From Muskogee* '72 (quartet with Claude Williams, violin), duets with Tate *Crazy Legs & Friday Strut* '76, solo *Tribute To Fats Waller* and *Kansas City Hustle* '78, *Tuxedo Junction* '80.

McTELL, Blind Willie (*b* 5 May '01, Thomson, Ga.; *d* 19 Aug. '59, Midgeville, Ga.) Blues singer, 12-string guitarist, also played accordion, harmonica, kazoo, violin. Born blind; hoboed around the South; worked as a singing carhop at a drive-in restaurant in Atlanta late '40s; active as a preacher in his last years. First recorded for Victor '27-9, many other labels incl. Atlantic '49-50, Prestige-Bluesville '56 (LP *Last Session*). A great folk poet, closer to the more delicate Piedmont mould than harsher, more familiar Delta style. Collections: *Early Years* '27-33, *Doing That Atlanta Strut* on Yazoo; *Library Of Congress Record-*

ings on Melodeon; *Love Changin' Blues, 1929-33* and *Trying To Get Home* on Biograph.

McTELL, Ralph (*b* 3 Dec. '44, Farnborough, UK) Singer, songwriter and guitarist in folk vein. A strong and accomplished guitarist, infl. by blues artists (hence stage name). Debut *Eight Frames A Second* '68 on Transatlantic followed by *Spiral Staircase* '69, incl. best-known song 'Streets Of London'; other records on EMI and Famous labels; *Not Till Tomorrow* '72 was debut on Reprise. Re-recorded 'Streets' 74 for top 10 UK hit; 'Dreams Of You' was top 40 '75. *Streets* '75, *Right Side Up* '76 (aka *Weather The Storm* '82 on Mays), live *Ralph Albert & Sydney* '77 (reissued '82) and *Slide Away The Screen* (reissued with additional material as *Love Grows* '82 on Mays) were all from WB. He appeared on children's TV series *Alphabet Zoo* and *Tickle On The Tum*; *Water Of Dreams* and *Songs From Alphabet Zoo* '82 were proof of an ability, like that of Woody GUTHRIE, to entertain on different levels. Member of short-lived touring band the GPs '81 with Richard Thompson, Dave Mattacks and Dave Pegg (live recording being prepared for issue on Woodworm '88). *Bridge Of Sighs* on Mays and *Blue Skies Black Heroes* on Leola '88 typifed his later work, with mature songs and strong arrangements; former incl. 'The Hiring Fair', co-written with Simon Nicol of FAIRPORT CONVENTION and also incl. on their *Gladys' Leap*. *Best Of Tickle On The Tum* that year incl. guest Billy CONNOLLY as Billy Bins. Also presented TV series *Ralph McTell's Streets Of London*.

McVEA, Jack (*b* 5 Nov. '14, L.A., Cal.) Tenor sax, leader. Played in his father's dance band; went on his own '32, played in various L.A. bands; joined the original Lionel HAMPTON big band '40-3, playing alto and baritone; formed own L.A. combo '43, played on first JATP concert records '44. Taught Art PEPPER how to read music in Lee Young band. Gradually followed public taste from swing through 'jump band' era to rhythm & blues; recorded in Hollywood '45 with Slim GAILLARD, unusual lineup: Charlie PARKER, Dizzy GILLESPIE, Bam Brown on bass, New Orleans veteran Zutty Singleton on drums

(now Savoy *Complete Charlie Parker Sessions*); Gaillard wanted a re-make of his '38 novelty hit 'Flat Foot Floogie', Parker and Gillespie made up 'Dizzy Boogie', while Gaillard's 'Popity Pop' was about a motorcycle, and laid-back novelty 'Slim's Jam' incl. solos for the horns and plenty of Gaillard's jive: as he introduces McVea, the latter knocks and says 'Open the Door, Richard!', reference to a routine by black vaudeville comic Dusty Fletcher in which the comic has come home late and wants to get in while Richard is occupied in something he is loath to interrupt. McVea began performing a riff based on the routine with his combo; Ralph BASS recorded it for L.A. Black And White label; McVea also performed it in film *Sarge Goes To College* '47: by then it had taken the country by storm, the biggest hit of the year, until the riff was so familiar that WOR in NYC banned it, along with Richard jokes. Count BASIE on RCA, the Three Flames on Columbia had no. 1 hits with 'Richard' (Basie's so uncharacteristic of the band that it is not incl. in 'complete' French RCA compilation); McVea and Fletcher on National tied at no. 3, Louis JORDAN on Decca, Charioteers (also on Columbia) at no. 6; Pied Pipers on Capitol were no. 8 (according to *Pop Memories* '86); the also-rans incl. Hank Penny on King, Hot Lips PAGE on Apollo, Sid CATLETT on Manor, and others. McVea and Fletcher shared composer credit with John Mason, from whom Fletcher had learned it, and Don Howell, who didn't exist (the publisher got an extra slice); McVea made flop followup 'The Key's In The Mailbox', by Jack McVea and his Door Openers; Tiger Haynes' Three Flames got an NYC TV show out of it '49. McVea also played on T-Bone WALKER's classic 'Stormy Monday Blues' on Black And White (a hit '42 by Earl HINES and Billy ECKSTINE), helping Walker to find himself as a big infl. on electric guitar; backed Gatemouth BROWN on the first sides recorded by Don Robey's Peacock label in Houston '49; recorded for Exclusive; drove a bus and played for all-girl touring R&B band the Sepia Flames (Clora Bryant on trumpet, Jackie Glenn on piano). Switched to clarinet '66 to play in dixieland combo at Disneyland, deservedly comfortable berth for a hard-working entertainer. Interview by Bob Rusch in *Cadence* magazine. Compilations: *Come Blow Your Horn* on Ace, *Open The Door Richard* on Juke Box Lil, *1944-1947* on Solid Sender.

MADDOX, Rose (*b* Roseea Arbana Brogdon, 15 Dec. '26, Boaz, Ala.) Country singer. Began with family band, The Maddox Brothers and Rose, with Cal on guitar and harmonica, Fred on bass, Henry on mandolin and Don providing comedy, established a reputation on West Coast for traditional emotional style with spangly 'western' costumes: 'the most colourful hillbilly band in the land'; gained resident spot on Louisiana Hayride, later appearances on Grand Ole Opry; they recorded for King, Columbia, Capitol, disbanded. Rose went solo on Capitol, had 10 hits in Billboard's country chart '59-64 incl. 'Sing A Little Song Of Heartache' (no. 3 '62); also duets with Buck OWENS incl. two double-sided hits: 'Mental Cruelty'/'Loose Talk' '61 and 'We're The Talk Of The Town'/'Sweethearts In Heaven' '63. LPs on Capitol incl. *Bluegrass*, with Bill MONROE, Don Reno and Red Smiley among sidemen. Semi-retired; then made comeback in California/Nevada clubs, also flourishing folk festival circuit; she recorded for UNI but became seriously ill: the Vern Williams band, with whom she'd performed in many shows, played a series of benefits to help with the bills. In '82 they appeared with her at San Francisco's Regional Folk Festival and at her son's funeral; also made gospel LP together, *A Beautiful Bouquet* on Arhoolie, which also released volumes of airchecks by the family band from '40s. Other LPs incl. *The Maddox Brothers And Rose* (1952-8) on Columbia Historic Edition; Rose's solos *Queen Of The West* on Varrick and *Reckless Love And Bold Adventure* on John FAHEY's Takoma label. Sang rockabilly in London '87; like many veterans of the genre, she deserves to be better known outside country music.

MADNESS UK ska/pop group formed late '76 as North London Invaders by Mike Barson, keyboards (*b* 21 Apr. '58) and Lee Thompson, sax (*b* 5 Oct. '57); personnel fluctuated around a core of Chris Foreman (*b* 8 Aug. '58; took up guitar, yielding drum chair to Gary Dovey), Chas Smash (*b* Carl Smyth, 14 Jan. '59; played bass briefly, replaced by Mark Bedford, *b* 24 Aug. '61).

John Hasler drummed, then Daniel 'Woody' Woodgate (*b* 19 Oct. '60); Graham 'Suggs' McPherson (*b* 13 Jan. '61, Hastings) recruited by Barson, who heard him singing on a bus. First gig in '78 saw return of Smash, who jumped onstage to dance and remained as second vocalist. Music was bluebeat/reggae infl. like Coventry's SPECIALS, but with more humour, in style of Ian DURY. Changed name to Morris and the Minors, then Madness (after title of Prince Buster hit); invited to record for Specials' 2-Tone label '79 they cut Buster tribute 'The Prince': no. 16 hit after a year of being ignored by punk generation. Played at wedding of Stiff boss Dave Robinson late '79, signed to Stiff (not wanting to be taken for second-rate Specials, and partly filling gap left by departure from Stiff of Elvis COSTELLO and Nick LOWE): it was an inspired match, Robinson's skill with video giving them an important tool expressing visuals (e.g. the 'Train' dance on cover of first LP, *One Step Beyond* '79). Tour with Specials marred by right-wing extremist fans disowned by the band (song 'Don't Quote Me On That' from *Work Rest And Play* EP '80). They quit the tour for the USA, but did not break there until '83 with no. 7 single 'Our House'. Amazing run of 15 top 10 UK hits '79-83 helped by zany humour and distinctive slapstick on video, incl. 'My Girl', 'Baggy Trousers', 'Embarrassment', 'Return Of The Los Palmos Seven', others; run broken early '82 by 'Cardiac Arrest', denied airplay because of its title, but followed by 'House Of Fun' at no. 1. *Absolutely* '80 also in goodtime mood; *Seven* '81 (numbering band, not albums) showed introverted side to Barson that led to his departure after *The Rise And Fall* '82 and *Keep Moving* '84. By this time they were producing quality pop no longer restricted to youth market (they had played matinee gigs for under 16s in early years): 'House Of Fun' '82 proved it; *The Rise And Fall* incl. 'Tomorrow's Just Another Day' (top 10 UK, one of their best-crafted tracks) and 'Our House' (top 10 both UK/USA). On Barson's departure the rest of the band got in on songwriting; Smash took up trumpet, while backing vocals by Afrodisiak (ex-Costello) broadened sound still further. They left Stiff to form own label Zarjazz (through Virgin); famine aid disc 'Starvation' '85 incl. various reggae/2-Tone musicians; they backed Feargal SHARKEY on 'Listen To Your Father'. Long-awaited sixth LP *Mad Not Mad* '85 added to hits tally, incl. cover of Scritti Politti's 'The Sweetest Girl'. They were increasingly involved in politics, playing benefits opposing nuclear power and arms; five members took part in Red Wedge tour for Labour Party '86; they split up '86: farewell single was 'Ghost Train'. Their development from skinhead ska to maturity while humour remained intact was one of the rewarding developments in UK pop of the era; with SQUEEZE they kept alive the tradition of the BEATLES and the KINKS. Video/vinyl compilation *Complete Madness* '82 was no. 1 UK, followed by *Utter Madness* '86; band and Robinson clashed when he did TV ads in pastiche of their style.

MADONNA (*b* Madonna Louise Ciccone, 16 Aug. '58, Rochester, Mich.) Pop singer, actress. Brought up on Motown soul; trained as dancer at U. of Michigan; took interest in music through infl. of boyfriend, drummer Steve Bray. Moved to NYC, then to Paris as backup singer for French disco star Patrick 'Born To Be Alive' Hernandez; soon back to NYC with a succession of New Wave groups, graduating from drummer in Breakfast Club to lead singer in Emmy, which took her name when Bray came East to join. Demo tape got her contract with Sire, aided by exposure from new boyfriend DJ Mark Kamins, who prod. first single 'Everybody'; meanwhile vaultingly ambitious Madonna hired Michael JACKSON's manager to push her. Ex-Miles DAVIS sideman Reggie Lucas prod. most tracks for *Madonna* '83 (later retitled *The First Album*, with classier sleeve photo), added some distinction to otherwise routine disco tracks enlivened only by her voice, described as Minnie Mouse on helium. LP incl. no fewer than five single hits incl. 'Holiday', prod. by a new boyfriend, John 'Jellybean' Benitez (ace dance music expert also worked with Billy JOEL, POINTER Sisters, others; signed prod. deal with WB '85). 'Holiday' made top 20 UK as well, but UK breakthrough came with 'Like A Virgin', title track of second LP '84 prod. by Nile Rogers: single was no. 3 UK, both LP and single no. 1 USA. New and old discs turned

to gold; in UK she was the first female to have three hits in top 15 since Ruby Murray 30 years earlier. First film (now disowned) was non-musical blood and guts skinflick *A Certain Sacrifice*; hits from second *Vision Quest* incl. 'Crazy For You', 'The Gambler'; *Like A Virgin* became no. 1 LP UK nearly a year after its release. Her secret was good promotion, clever timing and stage persona, with distinctive layered clothing (showing the famous belly button), cut-off tights, 'boy toy' belt, exaggerated makeup: boys lusted while girls (incl. pre-teens) became clones. Picture discs in UK helped. Film *Desperately Seeking Susan* '85, debut of dir. Susan Seidelman, was surprise smash hit: hers was not a leading role but her acting received critical raves compared to her singing; featured song 'Into The Groove' benefited. Her marriage to movie brat Sean Penn turned into a media event as publicity seekers suddenly didn't want any for the moment. She worked with Nick Kamen, widely regarded as sexy after fame for Levi TV advert, co-writing and prod. his UK hit 'Each Time You Break My Heart'; her film *The Missionary* '86 was retitled *Shanghai Surprise*, co-starred Penn and was widely panned: the role, far removed from pre-teen sexuality, suggested a change in image, but album *True Blue* '86 was more of the same. Film/LP *Who Was That Girl?* '87 marked by tour in which she unashamedly aped Marilyn Monroe; *You Can Dance* '87 had seven dance tracks remixed. She is an ideal icon, her skilful stage act, image, music combining to make an oddly innocent pop phenomenon, harking back to the flirtatious glamour of earlier times: it was an illusion then, more so now; but she seems likely to endure one way or another.

MADRIGUERA, Enric (*b* 17 Feb. '04, Barcelona, Spain; *d* 7 Sep. '73, Danbury, Conn.) Violinist, composer, bandleader. Child prodigy on violin, played concerts as a child; mus. dir. for Columbia Records in Colombia; formed dance band in Cuba, USA debut '29: played Latin-American style watered down somewhat for USA, like Xavier CUGAT; also straight sweet dance music. Vocalists incl. his wife, Patricia Gilmore. Recorded for Columbia, Victor, Brunswick, Majestic, Decca; biggest hits '32-44 incl. 'The Carioca'/'Orchids In The

Moonlight' '34 (no. 1), both by Vincent YOUMANS for '33 film *Flying Down To Rio*; 'True' '34; 'Here's To Romance' '35 (film title song); 'I Love You' '44, from Broadway show/film *Mexican Hayride*. co-wrote 'Adios' (band's theme) '31, big hit for Glenn MILLER '41; 'The Minute Samba', covered by Percy FAITH; ballet *Follies Of Spain*, others.

MAGIC SAM (*b* Samuel Maghett, 14 Feb. '37, Grenada, Miss.; *d* 1 Dec. '69, Chicago) Superb blues singer, with high, soaring voice, exciting lyrical guitar style. Grew up on farm, learned to play at 10 on homemade instrument; to Chicago high school '50; played in gospel group, then Homesick James band, formed own band to play 708 Club '55, known as Good Rockin' Sam. With Shakey Jake band '57; same year cut first single for Cobra, 'All Your Love', noted for eerie chord progression and dramatic vocal. More records for Cobra, Chief; club, college dates in Chicago area early '60s, two LPs for Delmark, led to booking at '69 Ann Arbor Blues festival: *Blues Unlimited* wrote that 'The music alone moved the people who weren't expecting it from someone they'd never heard of, and they screamed for him the rest of the evening.' Died of heart attack that year. 2-disc *Magic Sam Live* (Delmark, '80) incl. Ann Arbor set plus material from Chicago Alex Club gigs '63-4.

MAHAL, Taj (*b* Henry St Claire Fredericks, 17 May '40, NYC) Singer, songwriter, multi-instrumentalist, laid-back urban folk-blues style. Father was West Indian jazz musician, mother gospel singer from N.C.; lived in Brooklyn, then Springfield, Mass.; took up guitar as teenager, got degree in animal husbandry from U. of Mass., began playing in coffee-houses '64, to West Coast '65, worked with Ry COODER in group Rising Sons (they were supposed to record for Columbia but it fell through), then with CANNED HEAT; won banjo-playing contest at a fiddlers' convention '67; first LP *Taj Mahal: The Natch'l Blues* on Columbia '68: it reached top 200 LPs but his music was too original with its underlying sardonic humour to make an immediate impact. 2-disc sets *Giant Step/De Ole Folks At Home* '69, *The Real Thing* '71 did better, reaching

the top 100 with a ragtime flavour; meanwhile he had toured Europe to acclaim. He wrote a song for the soundtrack of *Sounder* '71 and appeared in the film; albums *Happy To Be Just Like I Am* and *Recycling The Blues & Other Related Stuff* '72 (with the POINTER Sisters on two tracks of the latter, *Oooh So Good 'N Blues* '73, *Mo' Roots* '74, *Music Keeps Me Together* '75 charted low in the top 200 as the market for eclecticism of the late '60s-early '70s dried up. Switched to WB for *Satisfied'n'Tickled Too* and *Music Fuh Ya'* (*Musica Para Tu*) '77, his last LP to chart, but his audience is loyal and he has continued to tour (often solo) and record steadily: LPs incl. *Brothers* '77, *Evolution (The Most Recent)* '78 on WB; *Taj Mahal And International Rhythm Band Live* '79 on Crystal Clear; *Taj Mahal And International Rhythm Band* on Magnet and *Going Home* on Columbia '80, *Live* '81 on Magnet. The Crystal Clear LP is a high-tech direct-to-disc album and the Columbia records are all still in print in the USA: presumably they sell steadily, proving (if proof were needed) that charts don't tell the whole story. Lived in Hawaii for some years, adding the South Pacific to his art, re-emerged on record to challenge 'chocolate-covered-granola-bars music' with *Taj* '87 on Gramavision, incl. Wayne Henderson on keyboards, drummer Babatunde OLATUNJI, others.

MAHOGANY RUSH USA/Canadian heavy metal group formed '70 in Montreal by guitarist Frank Marino (*b* 22 Aug. '54, Del Rio, Texas) who began jamming with locally-based rhythm section of Paul Harwood (*b* 30 Feb. '39, Quebec) on bass, drummer Jimmy Ayoub (*b* 7 Dec. '41, Honolulu). Concert in Montreal Expo grounds '71 won them contract with Katai label; gained notoriety when Marino, undoubtedly infl. by Jimi HENDRIX in his playing, said he was visited by Hendrix's spirit while in a coma after car crash, reinforcing this by playing with his teeth and incl. 'Purple Haze' and 'Star Spangled Banner' in stage act. After *Child Of The Novelty* '73 and *Strange Universe* '75 saw him moving away from pyrotechnics to songs, the band signed to CBS: when the latter was issued in USA on 20th Century, the label also reissued the first two (incl. *Maxoom*), enabling Marino to claim that they were marketed as new product. *IV*

'76 saw them hit the road; *World Anthem* '77 and *Live* '78 fared well in HM circles; Marino liked live sound so much he persevered with half-studio, half-live *Tales Of The Unexpected* '79. *What's Next* '80 added Marino's brother Frank on rhythm guitar, altering formula slightly, but even bigger change was variety of covers on that LP: DOORS' 'Roadhouse Blues', Bo DIDDLEY's 'Mona', B. B. KING's 'Rock Me Baby'. *Power Of Rock'n'Roll* '81 continued in heavy rock vein; *Juggernaut* '82, *Full Circle* '86 were billed as by Frank Marino. Never claimed to be original; like many another second-rank HM band are ploughing a profitable furrow.

MAHOTELLA QUEENS Vocal group formed '64, South Africa, by Robert Bopape (earlier involved with the Dark City Sisters) as a vehicle for his songwriting. With the help of well-established vocalists incl. Mahlathini (called 'The Lion of Soweto'), the group became one of the most prolific and popular vocal 'jive' acts in S.A., touring widely, often supported by Abafana (another top vocal group with gold albums). The Queens and Mahlathini released hundreds of singles, scores of LPs, mostly not available outside S.A., incl. *Meet The Mahotella Queens*, with their simanje-manje beat. *Phezulu Eqhudeni* '83 issued in UK on Earthworks, with the Queens, Mahlathini and the Mthunzini Girls. They broke up, re-formed and made *Thokozile* '88 on Earthworks with Mahlathini; their music is called mgqashiyo, a tougher brand of MBAQANGA (*which see*). They have been influential, with many imitators incl. Malcolm McLaren, e.g. 'Jive, Baby, Jive' on his *Duck Rock* LP.

MAINES BROTHERS BAND Country-rock sextet of musical brothers, most of whom have the same last name: an integral part of the Lubbock, Texas scene (*see also* COUNTRY MUSIC). Band began '50s with father and uncle James and Sonny Maines; legend has it that another uncle, Wayne, taught Buddy HOLLY his first guitar chords. Brothers are all from tiny Acuff, outside Lubbock: Lloyd is a full-time producer at Don Caldwell's local studio; described by Terry ALLEN as 'the only mountain in Lubbock', he prod. Allen's 2-disc masterpiece *Lubbock*

With Everything, proved to Allen (a refugee from the Flatlands) that he couldn't stay away after all. Lloyd also prod. Butch HANCOCK, many others; played in Joe ELY band, joined his brothers on guitar, dobro, steel guitar and harmony vocals; Steve on rhythm guitar; Kenny on guitar and harmonics; all sing except Donnie on drums and percussion, who recently took leave to do some ranching, replaced by Louisiana's Mark Gillespie. Richard Bowden (from North Carolina) plays fiddle, mandolin, trumpet and sings. Jerry Brownlow plays bass, sings; older brother Randy played keyboards and guitar (both from White Face, near Lubbock): Randy left '82 replaced by Big Spring's Cary Banks, also vocalist and songwriter. Albums on Texas Soul: *The Maines Brothers And Friends* '78, *RT. 1. Acuff* '80, *Hub City Moans* '81, *Panhandle Dancer* '82; *High Rollin'* '84 and *The Boys Are Back In Town* '85 on Mercury-Polygram incl. chart singles; *Red, Hot And Blue* back on Texas Soul incl. rockin', boppin' version of Allen's 'Pink And Black Song', Jerry's 'Dark Hearts', Blind Blake's 'Diddy Wa Diddy', 'You Can't Get The Hell Out Of Texas' by John Hadley/Jim Stafford.

MAKEBA, Miriam (*b* Zenzile Makeba, 4 Mar. '32, Johannesburg, S.A.) Singer, called the Empress of African Song. Her full name in Xhosa would take four lines. Father was a schoolteacher; she became the first black South African to attain international stardom. She attended Methodist Training School in Pretoria, sang in school choir and also helped her mother clean white people's homes. From '54 she toured with the Black Manhattan Brothers vocal group for three years; then in musical reviews that incl. all the leading South African musicians; with the Skylarks (group also launched Letta Mbulu, Mary Rabotapa and Abigail Kubheka). She made anti-apartheid film *Come Back Africa* '58; musical show *King Kong* '59 about a boxer (incl. 'Back Of The Moon') toured S.A., ran for a year in London. Hugh MASEKELA played in the show's orchestra; as the political situation worsened they left S.A. for good, or until its racial policies change. She appeared on BBC-TV '59, moved on to the USA, where she was introduced by Trevor Huddleston to Harry BELAFONTE, who landed her a spot on the Steve ALLEN TV show, followed by gigs at the Village Vanguard, other top clubs; also appeared with him on records (live *Returns To Carnegie Hall* '60, *An Evening With Belafonte/Makeba* '65, etc.), own album *Miriam Makeba* '60 on RCA, etc. Best-known for 'Westwinds', 'Pata Pata' and 'Qogothwane' or 'The Click Song', using the percussive sounds in the Xhosa language. Other albums incl. *Forbidden Games*, *The Voice Of Africa*, *The World Of Miriam Makeba* on RCA, *The Click Song* on various labels. She was married to Masekela, toured widely; her delightful personality and mixture of trad. Xhosa songs and jazz-infl. pop always pleased audiences. Second husband was USA black activist Stokeley Carmichael; neither this nor her own political emphasis helped bookings, but she was not seduced by limousines and the bright life: continued on her own way, moved to Guinea '69 with Carmichael; from base in Conakry continued to tour, perform before heads of state (she had sung at President Kennedy's birthday party at Madison Square Garden); received countless awards and was a living symbol of liberation: opposition to apartheid incl. memorable address to UN General Assembly '64. She survived cancer in the USA, 11 car crashes; has been married five times; she was deeply moved when young white South Africans told her that they will be glad when she can come home. Albums on Disque Espérance label prod. by Caiphus Semenya incl. *A Promise* '74, *Pata Pata* '77, *Country Girl* '78; more recently *Appel à l'Afrique* and *Miriam Makeba And Bongi* on Syliphone (Guinea); her daughter Bongi's solo LP *Blow On Wind* is on the German Pläne label. Makeba's *Sangoma* '88 from WEA has 19 trad. tribal songs, prod. by Russ Titelman. She can fill the largest venues anywhere in the world except South Africa, where even her records are banned. Autobiography *Makeba: My Story* '88 with James Hall.

MAKOSSA African dance rhythm originating in Cameroon, establishing itself as one of the most popular, spreading to Nigeria, Gabon, the Central African Republic and to Europe, where it has combined with cadence in a series of dance floor hits: as one of a variety of local beats (bikutsi, ashiko,

magambeu) it went from strength to strength after the international Manu DIBANGO hit 'Soul Makossa' '73. It has been described as a Cameroonian fusion of highlife, Congo and local traditions, with fast and bouncy melodies against a steady bass/drum rhythm. Leading exponents now incl. guitarists Toto Guillaume (*b* '55, Douala), who made his name with the Black Styles in the '70s, Eboa Lottin (*b* '42, Douala) and the innovative Misse Ngoh (*b* '49, Mbonjo); also singer/composer Moni Bile and omnipresent session bassist and arranger Alhadji Toure.

MALTBY, Richard (*b* 26 June '14, Chicago, Ill.) Trumpet; arr. and bandleader. Worked on staff at WBBM radio; wrote 'Six Flats Unfurnished', '42 hit for Benny GOODMAN; on NYC staff in network radio from mid-'40s; working for RCA subsidiary labels, had no. 21 hit with 'St Louis Blues Mambo' '54 on X; toured with jazz-oriented dance band from '55, hiring excellent sidemen such as Al COHN; second hit no. 14 '56 with catchy theme from controversial movie about drug addiction *Man With The Golden Arm*, brassy arr. extremely well recorded on Vik.

MAMAS & THE PAPAS, The Folk-rock vocal group formed '65 in NYC: John Phillips (*b* 30 Aug. '35, Parris Island, S.C.); Dennis Doherty (*b* 29 Nov. '41, Halifax, Nova Scotia), Michelle Phillips (*b* Holly Michelle Gilliam, 6 Apr. '44, Long Beach, Cal.), Cass Elliot (*b* 19 Sep. '43, Baltimore, Md.; *d* 29 July '74, London). Phillips had attended US Naval Academy briefly; married model Gilliam '62 and she joined his group the Journeymen; Doherty had been a member with Zal Yanovsky of the Halifax Three, which made two LPs for Epic, before they joined Elliot and her first husband John Hendricks in Cass Elliot and the Big Three, who changed name to the Mugwumps (from American history: a fence sitting politician has his mug on one side, wump on the other). Added drummer Art Stokes, John Sebastian on harmonica, made an LP and split up: Yanovsky and Sebastian formed the LOVIN' SPOONFUL, Doherty joined John and Michelle Phillips in their group, Elliot (whose big, warm voice resembled that of Alison MOYET) fronted another group briefly but joined the others on the

West Coast, where they sang backgrounds on Lou ADLER's Dunhill label and began recording as the Mamas and the Papas. They were the right group at the right time, still redolent of nostalgia for the flower-power era, the last time pop music could be commercial and still appear to be innocent: good songs, good singing, slick production (incl. excellent sound) made nine top 40 hits '66-7 incl. six in top 5: 'California Dreamin' ', 'Monday, Monday' (no. 1 for three weeks), 'I Saw Her Again', two-sided 'Words Of Love'/'Dancin' In The Street', 'Dedicated To The One I Love' and auto-biographical 'Creeque Alley' (about all the groups they'd been in). Some of these were revivals of songs that were already classics (the Golden Age of pop had been quick to arrive, and would be over even quicker), while Phillips wrote others: not only wrote the anthemic 'California' but 'San Francisco (Be Sure To Wear Flowers In Your Hair)', a no. 4 hit for Scott MCKENZIE (ex-Journeymen). First LP *If You Can Believe Your Eyes And Ears* was no. 1, *The Mamas & The Papas* no. 4 and *Deliver* no. 2 for seven weeks; compiled hits *Farewell To The First Golden Era* was no. 5, but it was also the last golden era for them: Phillips' marriage was failing and the group split up after *The Papas & The Mamas* '68 (no. 15 LP) and a few more Hot 100 singles, except for a reunion *People Like Us* '71, which everyone agreed wasn't very good. Dunhill and the group (except for Elliot) squabbled over royalties; Elliot carried on as a single with no. 12 hit 'Dream A Little Dream Of Me' '68 (backed by the others), some lesser hits '68-70, LPs *Dream A Little Dream, Bubblegum, Lemonade & Something For Mama* (*Make Your Own Kind Of Music* '69 was a reissue of the second LP with title track added; *Dave Mason & Cass Elliot* was a duet '71 on Blue Thumb). She was always badly overweight and her much-loved voice was stilled by a heart attack at the age of 30. Doherty made flop solo LPs, became popular TV host in Nova Scotia; Phillips made LP *John The Wolfking Of L.A.* '70; with Adler co-produced Robert Altman film *Brewster McCloud* '70; joined the jet set. Michelle made films *The Last Movie* '71 (briefly married to co-star Dennis Hopper), *Dillinger* '73 with Warren Oates, Ken Russell's *Valentino* '77; LP *Victim Of Romance*

'77 on A&M. Phillips was arrested on drugs charge '80: stiff sentence reduced, he and actress daughter Mackenzie Phillips toured with anti-drug lecture, then re-formed the group, touring '82 with Doherty, Elaine McFarlane (*see* SPANKY AND OUR GANG).

MAMBO An Afro-Cuban rhythm, originally developed in Afro-Cuban religions, themselves derived from Congolese religious cults. The word is probably of Congo/Angolan origin. Some credit the blind tres player/bandleader Arsenio Rodriguez, some Israel 'Cachao' LOPEZ with introducing the rhythm to Cuban dance halls; Lopez was arr./bassist with Antonio Arcaño y sus Maravillas; brass and sax riffs began to be used in the manner of the North American big jazz bands, but backed by powerful Cuban rhythm sections; the result was a sort of hot jazz-oriented rumba with a heavier, more solid beat. It became a dance fad in the USA '50s until supplanted by the chachacha, which was easier for white musicians to adapt and for Americans to dance to, but the mambo had more infl. on Latin music in the long run. The most successful mambo bands were those of Tito RODRIGUEZ, Tito PUENTE, MACHITO, Beny MORÉ and Perez PRADO, who became famous with his international hit 'Cherry Pink And Apple Blossom White'.

MANCE, Junior (*b* Julian Clifford Mance Jr, 10 Oct. '28, Chicago) Pianist, leader, composer. Worked with Gene AMMONS, Lester YOUNG; after Army service '51-3 led own combo in Chicago, then toured, recorded with Dinah WASHINGTON '54-5, Cannonball ADDERLEY '56-7, Dizzy GILLESPIE '58-9, Johnny GRIFFIN '60-1; formed own trio, toured with Joe WILLIAMS '62-4. Recorded with Aretha FRANKLIN (LP *Soul* '69 on Atlantic). Live act is popular, often in commercially bluesy way like Ray BRYANT, Les MCCANN; but a more accomplished musican and composer than that. Eight trio LPs '60-2 on Verve, Jazzland, Ozone and Riverside incl. *Trio Live At The Village Vanguard* (reissued '85 on Fantasy) followed by two big band sets with arr. by Dave Cavanaugh, trio album *That's Where It Is*, all '64 on Capitol; after a layoff due to an obscure disease of the middle ear, Atlantic LPs '66-70 incl. *I Believe To My Soul,*

Live At The Top Of The Gate (with David 'Fathead' NEWMAN on some tracks). Other albums: *That Lovin' Feelin'* c.'68 on Milestone, *The Junior Mance Touch* '73 with strings on Polydor, *Holy Mama* '76 on East Wind/Inner City, *Live At Sweet Basil* '77 on Japanese Flying Disc label, *Deep* '80 on JSP, duo LPs with Martin Rivera on bass on Nilva and Sackville (*For Dancers Only*) '83. *Truckin' And Trakin'* '83 on Beehive with Rivera, Newman, drummer Walt Bolden incl. 'Mean Old Amtrak'.

MANCHESTER, Melissa (*b* 15 Feb. '51, NYC) Singer, songwriter. Daughter of bassoonist with NY Metropolitan Opera Orchestra. High School of Performing Arts; writing songs for publisher, recording commercial jingles age 15. Studied with Paul SIMON; became member of Harlettes, Bette MIDLER back-up group '71, then solo act in clubs. LPs for Bell *Home To Myself* '73, *Bright Eyes* '75 well-received; then on sister label Arista, with producer Vin Poncia; third LP *Melissa* incl. hit 'Midnight Blue' (no. 6 USA '75). Further top 10 singles 'Don't Cry Out Loud' '79 (written by Peter Allen-Carole Bayer SAGER); 'You Should Hear How She Talks About You' '82; LPs for Arista: *Better Days & Happy Endings*, *Don't Cry Out Loud*, *Emergency*, *Hey Ricky* (incl. '83 title single), *Greatest Hits*. First performer to have two recorded film themes nominated for Oscars same year ('80; *Ice Castles*, *The Promise*). Following mid-'70s ABC-TV show *Good Vibrations From Central Park*, with TEMPTATIONS, SLY AND THE FAMILY STONE, *NY Times* reported 'the cool Miss Manchester completely steals the show.'

MANCINI, Henry (*b* 16 Apr. '24, Cleveland, Ohio) Composer, conductor. Studied at Juilliard, went to West Coast as studio musician and first came to public attention scoring hit TV series *Peter Gunn*, incl. no. 8 hit '59 for Ray ANTHONY with title theme, followed by Mancini's own no. 21 theme from *Mr Lucky* '60, for which he got a Grammy. These were hailed as the first modern jazz TV scores, but they were actually pretty Hollywood: Mancini however went on to greater things, incl. 19 more Grammies, and Oscars '61 for both best score (*Breakfast At Tiffany's*) and best song: 'Moon River',

with words by Johnny MERCER, a no. 11 hit single, won three Grammies: surely one of the best-loved songs of the decade. About 30 other film scores incl. Orson Welles' masterpiece *Touch Of Evil* '58; scores with hit singles incl. *The Great Imposter* '61, *Hatari!* '62 ('Baby Elephant Walk' provided hits for others as well), *Days Of Wine And Roses* and *Charade* '63, *A Shot In The Dark* '64 and best of all *The Pink Panther* '64, played on the top 40 hit single by Plas JOHNSON, and still going strong in cartoons; but his biggest hit was not his own composition: love theme from Nino Rota's score for Zeffirelli's *Romeo And Juliet* was no. 1 for two weeks '69. He conducted top symphony orchestras around the world; more ambitious work incl. concert suite *Beaver Valley '37*. A phenomenal 38 Mancini LPs charted '59-77 incl. 18 in top 40; biggest hits were TV or film albums incl. *Breakfast* (no. 1 LP for 12 weeks '61); many are still in print incl. duets with Doc SEVERINSEN, all from RCA originals except *The Long Hot Summer* '58, reissued '85 on MCA (Alex North's music cond. by Mancini). *Premier Pops* '88 on Denon is an hour of his most popular stuff, with the Royal Philharmonic Pops Orchestra recorded in London. Biography by Gene LEES in preparation.

MANDEL, Harvey (*b* 11 Mar. '45, Detroit) USA guitarist. Raised on Chicago blues, played in Charlie MUSSELWHITE's Southside band; own albums on various labels incl. *Christo Redentor* '68, *Righteous* '69, *Games Guitars Play* '70 (all on Philips), *Electronic Progress* '71, *Get Off In Chicago* and *The Snake* '72 (Charles LLOYD guesting on flute on the latter), *Shangrenade* '73, *Feel The Sound Of Harvey Mandel* '74; the first of these, with Musselwhite, Pete Drake on steel guitar, Hargus 'Pig' Robbins and Graham BOND on keyboards, etc. was regarded as his best solo work, showcasing extended soloing and mastery of feedback technique. He also played with blues band CANNED HEAT for a year, then with John MAYALL's Bluesbreakers for three LPs (*USA Union*, *Back To The Roots*, *Beyond The Turning Point* '70-1). Formed instrumental group Pure Food And Drug Act but *Choice Cuts* '72 failed to sell, perhaps because '60s heyday of such groups was past: lineup was Don 'Sugarcane' Harris on violin, Coleman

Head and Randy Resnick on guitars, bassist Victor Conte and drummer Paul Lagos. He toured USA/UK '74 supporting Canned Heat with a new band, retaining some earlier personnel and adding vocalists; sessioned with ROLLING STONES '75 for *Black And Blue* and was tipped to replace Mick Taylor, but didn't. Lengthy session credits inc. work with Bond, Ron CARTER, Jimmy WITHERSPOON, violinist Dewey Terry on duo LP *Chief* '73, soft-rockers Love on *Reel To Real* '74. *Best Of* on Janus '75 compiled later solo work. He sang on only one track in his career: decision to remain instrumentalist perhaps hurt commercially but probably indicated integrity.

MANDINGO GRIOT SOCIETY Afro-American kora-based band formed in Chicago '77 around the playing of Foday Musa Suso, *b* in Gambia to musical family, descended from the first kora player, Jalimadi Woleng Suso. He was a fully-fledged griot at 18 (a professional musician who praises and tells stories), went to U. of Ghana, taught kora there at Institute of African Studies, met drummer Adam Rudolph; in Chicago they formed the group with Joe Thomas on bass, Hamid Drake on drums, John Markiss on guitar: carved unique niche in African music with mixture of modern and trad. instruments, blending Mandingo music with infl. of R&B, reggae, Latin and jazz. LPs on Flying Fish incl. *Mighty Rhythm* '78 (with guest Don CHERRY). *Mandingo Griot Society* '81. They remained in Chicago, playing locally, doing African music workshops; *Watto Sitto* '85 with guest Herbie HANCOCK was issued on international Celluloid label. Suso also released trad. *Kora Music From The Gambia* on Folkways. *See also* KORA.

MANDRELL, Barbara (*b* 25 Dec. '48, Houston, Texas) Country singer, bandleader, multi-instrumentalist and TV star. From musical family, by her teens she could play sax, steel guitar, banjo and bass. Joined The Mandrells, with parents and two unrelated boys; they appeared on TV shows, Town Hall Party '59, Hometown Jamboree; she then toured with Johnny CASH '62, entertained troops in Vietnam '66-7; married drummer Ken Dudney '67: persuaded by him, managed by her father she moved to

Nashville and signed with Columbia '69, immediately hit country chart with covers of soul hits 'I've Been Loving You Too Long', 'Do Right Man – Do Right Woman', 'Treat Him Right', 'Show Me' '69-72, also duet with David Houston on 'Closing Time'. Guided by Billy SHERRILL she was doing well but records did not make the top 5: she switched to ABC-Dot '75 (later MCA); first single 'Standing Room Only' made country top 5; several hits later 'Sleeping Single In A Double Bed' '77 was no. 1. Much success on record credited to prod. Tom Collins, who fed her the best songs from his publishing company, many by the young team of Kye Fleming and Dennis Morgan. LPs *Moods* and *Just For The Record* were acclaimed by critics and public; following no. 1 hits like '(If Loving You Is Wrong) I Don't Want To Be Right' and 'Years', she was named CMA Female Vocalist of the Year '79; moved to TV with own NBC series '81-2; continued to dominate charts with 'Crackers' and 'The Best Of Strangers' '80, 'I Was Country When Country Wasn't Cool' '81, 'Operator, Long Distance Please' '82, 'In Times Like These' '83, 'Happy Birthday Dear Heartache' '84. The first female artist to be CMA's Entertainer of the Year two years running ('80-1), she is one of the most successful country stars of the last decade. Seriously injured in a car crash Oct. '84 near home in Henderson, Tenn. she was unable to work in '85. Albums incl. *Treat Him Right* '71 and *I Almost Made It* '74 on Columbia; *This Is Barbara Mandrell, Lovers, Friends And Strangers, Love's Ups And Downs* '76-8 on ABC; *Love Is Fair* '80, *Live* '81, *He Set My Life To Music* '82, *Spun Gold* '83, all on MCA. *Sure Feels Good* '87 appeared on EMI America.

MANDRELL, Louise (*b* 13 July '55, Corpus Christi, Texas) Country singer who usually performs in duet with husband R. C. BANNON. Began playing guitar, banjo and fiddle as a child and played bass in sister's band '71 (*see* Barbara MANDRELL, above). A regular on Stu Phillips TV show '73-4; joined Merle HAGGARD as background vocalist and featured singer '76-7; signed to Epic '78 and scored hits with 'Put It On Me' '78, 'Everlasting Love' '79; 'Reunited' (duet with Bannon) made top 10 '79.

Switched to RCA '81, had further hits '81-4 with 'You Sure Know Your Way Around My Heart', 'Some Of My Best Friends Are Old Songs', 'Runaway Heart', 'Save Me' and 'I'm Not Through Loving You Yet'. She was a regular on sister's TV show '81-2. RCA albums incl. *Close-Up* '82, *Too Hot To Sleep* '83, *Maybe My Baby* '85.

MANFRED MANN UK R&B/pop group formed '62 as Mann-Hugg Blues Brothers by Manfred Mann (*b* Mike Lubowitz, 21 Oct. '40, Johannesburg, S.A.) on keyboards, Mike Hugg (*b* 11 Aug. '42, Andover, Hants.) on drums. Signed to HMV as Manfred Mann with Dave Richmond, bass (soon replaced by Tom McGuinness), Mike Vickers, guitar and reeds; ex-Oxford undergrad Paul Jones (*b* Paul Pond, 24 Feb. '42, Portsmouth) on vocals and harmonica. Flop single 'Why Should We Not' was instrumental, betraying jazz roots; moved towards pop with 'Cock-A-Hoop', found hit groove with '5-4-3-2-1', no. 5 hit '64 adopted as theme tune by *Ready Steady Go* pop TV show. Searched diligently for material to cover: USA R&B provided Bo DIDDLEY's 'Do Wah Diddy Diddy' (no. 1 UK/USA '64) and 'Oh No Not My Baby' (11 UK); Bob DYLAN 'If You Gotta Go, Go Now' (2 UK '65), 'Just Like A Woman' (10 UK '66), 'The Mighty Quinn' (1 UK/10 USA '68) (Dylan said that of covers he liked Mann's best). 'Pretty Flamingo' was no. 1 '66 UK; 'Semi-Detached Suburban Mr James' no. 2. *Five Faces Of Manfred Mann* '64 displayed versatility; they played R&B with jazz flavour on albums, chafed at being pop stars (cf. song 'The One In The Middle'); Jones quit '66, replaced by Mike D'Abo (ex-Band of Angels); Vickers left, McGuinness switched to guitar, Jack Bruce played bass briefly, then Klaus Voorman (*b* 29 Apr. '42, Berlin; had been member of Brian EPSTEIN's Paddy, Klaus & Gibson; designed sleeve of BEATLE album *Revolver* '66). Jazz roots shone in *Up The Junction* '68 (soundtrack of an attempt at fictionalised social commentary; it had Dennis Waterman in cast, later TV's *Minder*). They had switched to Fontana '66 but after 12 UK top 10 hits '64-9 (6 in USA Hot 100) the split personality ended: Mann and Hugg disbanded and formed brass-heavy Chapter Three with Craig Collinge on drums, bassist Steve York, Bernie Living,

Derek Coxhill, Sonny Corbett and Harry Beckett on horns for LPs *Manfred Mann Chapter Three, Chapter Three Volume Two* '69-70; Mann disbanded again and formed progressive Earth Band: five UK hits '73-9 incl. 'Joybringer' '73, based on 'Jupiter' from Gustav Holst's *The Planets*; Mann's pop judgement made him early champion of Bruce SPRINGSTEEN: cover of 'Blinded By The Light' was no. 1 USA '76 (no. 6 UK; also recorded his 'For You'); returned to Dylan for minor UK/USA hit 'You Angel You'. Earth Band LPs incl. *Manfred Mann's Earth Band* '72, *Glorified, Magnified* '73, *The Good Earth* '74, *Nightingales & Bombers* '75, *Roaring Silence* '76; *Criminal Tango* '86 incl. incongruous cover of The JAM's 'Going Underground'. Jones had been part of Alexis KORNER's Blues Nights at Ealing, played with Brian Jones pre-ROLLING STONES; after Manfred Mann pursued sporadic career as actor, DJ and singer: had hits 'High Time' and 'I've Been A Bad, Bad Boy' '67, LPs *My Way* and *Privilege* '67, the last a soundtrack; sang on the original *Evita* LP '76; was keen to get back to singing the blues: McGuinness had formed McGUINNESS FLINT post-Mann, later got together with Jones in the Blues Band, formed to play London pubs, recorded *The Official Blues Band Bootleg Album, Ready* and *Itchy Feet* '80-1. The original Manfred Mann is fondly remembered; *Best Of* '77 and *Semi-Detached Suburban* '79 were compilations, *The R&B Years* '86 of early '60s. Jones' *Blues On 2* '86 was culled from sessions for BBC Radio 2 show.

MANGA, Bebe (*b* Elizabeth Prudence Manga Bessem, '48, Mante, Cameroon) African singer-composer and pianist. Self-taught; began pro singing in clubs in Douala, moved to Libreville in Gabon, where she sang mixture of European ballads and Douala folksongs. Moved to Abidjan, then Paris '80 to make first LP *Amie*, with mokossa, Congolese and Western pop tunes; title track brought her fame two years later: written by Ebanda Alfred and backed by Nelle Eyoum (both ex-Los Camaroes, leading Cameroonian band), it sold more than a million and spawned numerous covers. She toured Caribbean and Japan '83, was awarded French Marracas d'Or '83; moved to NYC to try to break out of African pigeon-hole but was unsuccessful; now plays occasionally with Haitian outfit Tabou Combo. Some of her tracks, such as 'Bele Sambo', 'A Loba' and 'Soir au Village', incl. in 3-disc compilation of Cameroonian music *Fleurs Musicales du Cameroon* '83 on Afro-Vision.

MANGELSDORFF, Albert (*b* 5 Sep. '28, Frankfurt, Germany) Trombonist, composer, leader. From musical family; elder brother was a saxophonist; attended Hot Club meetings (illegal as Nazis had banned jazz, although Louis ARMSTRONG records continued to be sold there). He studied violin, then guitar; took up trombone at age 20 and immediately began playing bop, infl. by Lennie TRISTANO early '50s; played in international band at Newport Jazz Festival '58, appeared several times at Newport '60s. John LEWIS praised him highly and made LP *Animal Dance* with him '62; after tour of Asia mid-'60s his music began to turn avant-garde; he has often toured playing solo, developing radical new ways of playing the trombone incl. more than one note at a time, and has long been one of the best-known and highly regarded European jazz musicians. Played guitar on albums by his brother made in Poland '57, Berlin '61 (Emil continued to record with small groups on CBS '66, Electrola '67, Europa '69, Telefunken '75-7, etc.). First recordings '54 as leader/trombonist incl. David AMRAM (on unreleased acetates); many LPs on various labels incl. Emil, bassist Peter Trunk, Klaus Doldinger on tenor (*b* 12 May '36, Berlin; formed jazz-rock group Passport '71), Hans Koller (reeds; *b* 12 Feb. '21, Vienna; played jazz all through the war, formed first important combo after the war incl. Albert; made short film *Jazz Yesterday And Today* for J. E. Berendt; also well-known as painter), others. Among later albums: quintet set *Tension* '63 on CBS; *And His Friends* '67 on MPS has duets with Don CHERRY, Lee KONITZ, Elvin JONES, Karl Berger on vibes (*b* 30 Mar. '35, Heidelberg), pianist Wolfgang Dauner (see below); nine-piece Jazz Ensemble of Hession Radio made *Wild Goose* '69 on MPS, *Live In Tokyo* '71 on Enja; small-group sets incl. *Spontaneous* '71 on Enja; *Birds Of Underground* '72 and *The Wide Point* '75 (trio with Jones, Palle Danielsson on bass), both on BASF; *Trilogue* '76 with Jaco PASTORIUS, *A Matter*

Of Taste '77 with John SURMAN, *A Jazz Tune I Hope* '78 with Dauner, Jones, Eddie Gomez; also *Albert Live In Montreux* '80 with Ronald Shannon Jackson, *Triple Entente* '82, all on MPS. Solo LPs incl. *Trombirds* '72, *Solo Now* and *Tromboneliness* '76, all on MPS. He also plays with the Globe Unity Orchestra (ECM LPs *Intergalactic Blow* and *Compositions*, with Kenny WHEELER, Evan Parker, Steve LACY, many others). *Two's Company* '82 on Mood is a duet LP with Dauner (*b* 30 Dec. '35, Stuttgart), an avant-garde composer of electronic music, also theatrical events, workshops and TV for children, etc.: LPs incl. *Sunday Walk* '68 on CBS with Jean-Luc PONTY. United Jazz & Rock Ensemble formed '75; Dauner, Mangelsdorff, others formed Mood label for UJRE, among the most popular bands in Germany: 6-disc boxed compilation was best-seller. LPs by Ian CARR's Nucleus, Barbara THOMPSON etc. also on Mood.

MANGIONE, Chuck (*b* Charles Frank Mangione, 29 Nov. '40, Rochester, NY) Trumpet, flugelhorn, piano, composer. Father introduced him to jazz and to stars like Dizzy GILLESPIE; studied at Eastman, co-led combo with pianist brother Gap (*b* Gaspare Charles Mangione, 31 July '38, Rochester) incl. LPs *The Jazz Brothers* and *Spring Fever* '61 on Riverside/Milestone incl. Sal Nistico (now 2-disc set on Milestone). Gap teaches and composes in Rochester; Chuck went to NYC, played with Maynard FERGUSON, Woody HERMAN, Art BLAKEY ('65-7), dir. Jazz Ensemble '68-72 at Eastman, formed own quartet '68. *Friends & Love* '71 was PBS broadcast with Rochester Philharmonic, 2-disc set on Mercury, incl. Hot 100 single 'The Hill Where The Lord Hides'; his easy-listening jazz-flavoured LPs have been selling well ever since, incl. 2-disc *Together* (also with RPO), *Quartet*, live *Land Of Make Believe* with orchestra, '71-3. Switched to A&M label: *Chase The Clouds Away* '75 made top 50 LPs with title Hot 100 hit; *Belavia* '75 (his mother's maiden name) did well; *Main Squeeze* '76 slipped to no. 86 but *Feels So Good* '77 was no. 2 LP with no. 4 title hit. *Children Of Sanchez* '78 was no. 14; 2-disc *An Evening Of Magic* '79 was made live at the Hollywood Bowl; *Fun And Games* was top 10 LP incl. 'Give It All You Got', top 20 hit for Winter Olympics. *Tarantella* was benefit for Italian earthquake victims, with guests Gillespie, Chick COREA, Gap; *Love Notes, Journey To A Rainbow, Disguise, Save Tonight For Me* '82-6 and *Eyes Of The Veiled Temptress* '88 are on CBS. Other albums incl. *70 Miles Young* on A&M, compilations on Mercury; other singles incl. 'Land Of Make Believe' with vocal by Esther Satterfield.

MANGWANA, Sam (*b* '45, Kinshasa, Zaire) African singer-composer, bandleader. Began at 18 with Rochereau's African Fiesta as singer and arranger; stayed with them for many years, occasionally also performing with Los Batitchas, the Negro Band, L'Orchestra Tembo, others; invited '72 to join the other giant of Zairean music, Franco and the TPOK Jazz, staying three years. By now well-known and acquainted with the cream of the country's musicians, he went solo '76, formed the African All Stars, touring widely '76-82, visiting almost every country in Africa as well as the West Indies and Europe, establishing a truly pan-African popularity with relaxed and lilting style reflected on *Georgette Eckins* and *Matinda* on Disques Sonics. Formed own label Sam '79; continued to lease records to other companies such as Star Musique and Celluloid, e.g. albums *Affaire Disco, Est Ce Que Tu Moyens, Affaire Video, N'Simba Eli, Les Champions*. Milestone came with big hit 'Maria Tebbo' '82 on LP of the same name; also made *Cooperation* that year with Franco. Album *Canta Mocambique* '84 and hit single 'Furaha Ya Bibi' '85 were further successes. Now based in Paris.

MANHATTANS, The Sweet soul vocal group formed '64 in Jersey City, doing well for 20 years with traditional good singing based on doo-wop. Original lineup: George 'Smitty' Smith, lead vocals (*d* '70); Winfred 'Blue' Lovett, bass and recitations (*b* 16 Nov. '43); Edward 'Sonny' Bivins, tenor (*b* 15 Jan. '42); Kenneth Kelly, tenor (*b* 9 Jan. '43); Richard Taylor, baritone. Lovett, Bivins and Taylor also write songs; Lovett wrote their first hit, 'I Wanna Be (Your Everything)' '65 (top 20 R&B chart, also reached pop Hot 100); they continued with more top 30 R&B hits on the Newark-based Carnival label; they re-corded for King subsidiary Deluxe and 'If My Heart Could Speak' '70 was top 30 soul, as the black chart was called by then, and Hot 100 pop; Smith died of spinal meningitis, was replaced by Gerald Alston (*b* 8 Nov. '42) and they signed with Columbia '72. Their first top 40 pop crossover was 'Don't Take Your Love' '75, but by then their albums were reaching the national top 200 (*There's No Me Without You* '73, *That's How Much I Love You* '75); 'Kiss And Say Goodbye' '76 was no. 1 both soul and pop charts, pulling LP *The Manhattans* into the top 20 of the album chart. *It Feels So Good, There's No Good In Goodbye* and *Love Talk* '77-9 were successful albums; 'Shining Star' '80 was their third big pop hit at no. 5 and LP *After Midnight* reached no. 24. *Black Tie* '81, *Forever By Your Side* '83, *Too Hot To Stop It* '85 continued to please fans; revival of Sam COOKE's 'You Send Me' '85 was top 20 black hit, Hot 100 pop.

MANHATTAN TRANSFER Vocal quartet treating popular music as repertory music, with four-part harmony treatments of material from '20s onwards, incl. Swing Era, doo-wop etc. First formed '69 as good-time jug-band sort of group; by '72 lineup incl. Tim Hauser (*b* c.'40), the only surviving original member, plus Alan Paul (*b* c.'49), Janis Siegel (*b* c.'53), Laurel Masse (*b* c.'54). All were experienced; Hauser had been working in groups since '58 and Siegel had been a member of the Young Generation, a group groomed by LEIBER & STOLLER which didn't do much. MT did what they did very well, becoming popular in cabaret and with a wide audience, perhaps anticipating a time when more musicians and singers will feel free to borrow more freely from their musical roots (those at any rate who know that they have roots); they've kept on doing it, moved on to more modern material and their jazz vocalisings just keep getting better, following on from Lambert, HENDRICKS (Jon) & Ross and others, in fact singing many of Hendricks' lyrics. *Jukin'* came out on Capitol '75, recorded earlier, with Gene Pistilli in lineup (he co-wrote hit 'Sunday Will Never Be The Same', top 10 hit for SPANKY AND OUR GANG '69). Lineup as above began on Atlantic with *The Manhattan Transfer* '75 and all have done well. After *Comin' Out* and *Pastiche* '76-8 Masse left, replaced by Cheryl Bentyne; *Extensions* '79 was followed by *Mecca For Moderns* '81 (no. 22 LP incl. no. 7 single 'Boy From New York City'), *Bodies And Souls* '83, *Bop Doo-Wop* and *Vocalese* '85; *Live* '87 (made in Tokyo) was essentially a live version of *Vocalese*, backing group of Don Roberts on reeds, Wayne Johnson on guitars, Yaron Gershovsky on keyboards, Alex Blake on basses, Buddy Williams, drums; followed by *Brazil* '88. Siegel did solo album *Experiment In White* '82.

MANILOW, Barry (*b* 17 June '46, Brooklyn, NYC) Arranger, songwriter, singer became massive MOR act from '74: slum kid from broken home, beaten up at school for being ugly, ended with knack of communicating directly to the lonely. Accordion at age 7, piano at 13; studied at Juilliard but left to work at CBS as mail clerk; later studied at New York College of Music, got into arranging for TV shows; arr. (and re-wrote) off-Broadway musical *The Drunkard* '67, later ran for eight years, also arr. and played piano in 3-piece band for show *Now*; arr. for weekly TV talent show *Callback*, others. Meanwhile married, divorced; accompanied singers in clubs, auditions; from '69 wrote, arr., sometimes sang jingles for soft drinks, McDonald's hamburgers, State Farm Insurance, Chevrolet, toilet cleaner, etc. (later arr. jingles into song 'Very Strange Melody' on no. 1 album). Half of flop night club duo Jeanie (Lucas) and Barry '70-1, also made first single for Bell: co-written 'Could It Be Magic' by group Featherbed (Manilow double tracked). Accompanist at gay bathhouse '72, met Bette MIDLER, also on her way up: became mus. dir. through her first two albums. Second flop single for Bell also '72: 'Sweetwater Jones' under real name. Went solo with Midler's back-up group when she took a year off '74, got spot in Dionne WARWICK show in Central Park (became friends; later prod. her hit LP *Dionne* '79). Soon hired own back-up trio: Debra Byrd, Reparata (Lorraine Mazzola), Ramona Brooks, called Flash Ladies; Brooks replaced by Monica Burruss, name changed to Lady Flash. Meanwhile Clive DAVIS took over at Bell, now changed to Arista; first two LPs on Bell reissued on Arista, several tracks on first (*Barry Manilow I*) remade:

LP incl. track 'Sing It', made in Times Square booth '48 with voice of grandfather urging small boy to 'Sing it – sing "Happy Birthday". Don't you want to make a record?' Album no. 9 in Billboard chart; also incl. four-year-old song 'Brandy', retitled 'Mandy': single was no. 11 UK, no. 1 USA. 16 chart singles in UK '75-83; 25 top 40 hits '74-83 incl. two more no. ones 'I Write The Songs', 'Looks Like We Made It'. Five albums in top 10 of UK album charts since '79 incl. *I Wanna Do It With You* (title cut also top 10 single); 13 albums in top 40 of LP chart USA '74-84 incl. two hits compilations, no. 1 *Barry Manilow Live* '77; first of several annual TV specials that year: *Variety* wrote 'Fortunately, his big hits have been reasonably literate and musically sophisticated songs.' His feat of five LPs in charts at once was previously accomplished by Frank SINATRA and Johnny MATHIS; in '78 became first artist to have three triple platinum LPs in 18 months (sales of 3m each): *This One's For You*, *Barry Manilow Live*, *Even Now*. Critics can joke about his nose, but not about his success; he sold out five nights at Royal Albert Hall in London '82, Richard Williams writing in *The Times*: 'His vocal equipment may be limited but he has the gift of singing to a single member of the audience without excluding the other 5,999 . . . [a skill] which should not necessarily be scorned.' Manilow says, 'I'm just a musician who sings a little.' He regrets that 'sometimes when I open my mouth, what comes out sounds like Pat BOONE . . . I get angry at myself because I can't do what Tom WAITS does. His voice comes from his kishkas when he sings. I could try to sing like that for the rest of my life and I could never sing as good as him.' He moved away from sweet ballads with '40s-sounding *2:00 AM Paradise Cafe* '84 with guests Sarah VAUGHAN, Gerry MULLIGAN, Mel TORMÉ; *Swing Street!* '87 with Mulligan, KID CREOLE, Stan GETZ, duet 'Summertime' with Diane Schurr. Autobiography *Sweet Life: Adventures On The Way To Paradise* '87.

MANN, Barry, and Cynthia Weil Longest surviving (creatively thriving) songwriting team to graduate from the BRILL BUILDING, today publishing their own work as Dyad Music. Mann (*b* 9 Feb. '39, Brooklyn) and Weil (*b* '42, Manhattan) have written in very style of pop individually, with each other and in pairs with others; over 150 million copies of their recorded songs have been sold. Mann began composing at 12 as a hobby, dropped out of Pratt Institute after a year of studying architecture, began writing and recording songs and playing piano on demos. His first hit was 'She Say (Oom Dooby Doom)' '59 by the DIAMONDS (top 20 '59); signed to Aldon Music a year later and co-wrote hits for Steve LAWRENCE ('Footsteps'), Bobby RYDELL ('I'll Never Dance Again'), the LETTERMEN ('Come Back Silly Girl'), the Paris Sisters ('I Love How You Love Me'), Teddy Randazzo ('Way Of A Clown'). 'B' side of Randazzo's record was co-written by lyricist Weil; trained as an actress and dancer, she began writing for Frank LOESSER, switched to Aldon; they married '61. Under contract they wrote for timely teen idols such as Paul Peterson, Shelley Fabares, Dickey Lee, as well as for Don Kirshner's personal friend Eydie GORME ('Blame It On The Bossa Nova', 'I Want You To Be My Baby'). They hit their stride in the '60s with street-wise 'urban protest' songs, writing with deep sympathy about young people's struggle in the harsh city, finding salvation in love: classics incl. 'He's Sure The Boy I Love', 'Uptown' by the CRYSTALS; 'On Broadway' by the DRIFTERS and its 'answer' song 'Magic Town' by the Vogues; 'Only In America' by JAY AND THE AMERICANS; 'We Gotta Get Out Of This Place' by the ANIMALS; 'Kicks' by Paul REVERE and the Raiders and 'Looking Through The Eyes Of Love' by Gene PITNEY. They grew with their audience, leaving new young groups to write their own anthems; the last 20 years have seen 'I'm Gonna Be Strong' (Pitney), 'You've Lost That Lovin' Feeling' and 'Soul And Inspiration' (the RIGHTEOUS BROTHERS), 'I Just Can't Help Believin'' (B. J. Thomas), 'Here You Come Again' (Dolly PARTON), 'Just Once' (Quincy JONES with James Ingram, discovered by Mann/Weil). Mann's efforts without Weil incl. 'Sometimes When We Touch' (co-written, recorded by Dan Hill) and 'How Much Love' (likewise with Leo SAYER); film work incl. co-writing score for *I Never Sang For My Father* '69. Weil co-wrote 'He's So Shy' with Tom Snow for the POINTER SISTERS, worked with Lionel

RICHIE on his 'Running With The Night'. They also worked with Snow, Ingrams, others for lengthy list of '80s AOR album tracks. Mann teamed with prod. Steve Tyrell to provide music for film and TV, incl. Bonnie RAITT's 'Stand Up To The Night' for film *Extremities*. Their unfulfilled ambition was to write a Broadway show; the only disappointment has been Mann's failure as a recording artist: he began '59 with 'Dix-A-Billy' under the pseudonym Buddy Brooks, peaked '61 with classic novelty 'Who Put The Bomp (In The Bomp Bomp Bomp)' (no. 7 USA), co-written with a reluctant Gerry GOFFIN. Teen-fodder followed ('Teenage Has-Been', 'Johnny Surfboard', 'Talk To Me Baby', etc.) progressing to amusing parody 'The Young Electric Psychedelic Hippie Flippy Folk And Funky Philosophic Turned-on Groovy 12-string Band' '68. He turned album artist with *Lay It All Out* '71 on New Design/CBS, *Survivor* '75 on RCA, *Barry Mann* '80 on Casablanca; all critically well-received but tending to provide hits for everyone except Mann.

MANN, C. K. (*b* Charles Kofi Amankwaa Mann, '30s, Ghana) African singer-composer, guitarist, bandleader; star of highlife in the '70s, credited with keeping it going during the rock/disco invasion. Formerly a seaman, he joined Kakaiku's Guitar Band in the '60s, establishing his own band the Carousel Seven '69 with hit single 'Edina Brenya'; when highlife was under threat from other influences, a declining record industry etc. he rejuvenated it with the osode beat, a trad. Ghanaian recreational dance, teaming with vocalist Kofi Yankson in series of hits dominating the scene in the first half of the '70s. *Party Time With CeeKay* '73 was one of the biggest-selling LPs ever in Ghana, followed by *Funky Highlife* '75, *With Love From C.K.* '76; others were *Menu Me*, *Womma Yengor* and *Osode* (with Bob Cole). Still active, he was featured in compilation *Roots To Fruits* '82.

MANN, Herbie (*b* Herbert Jay Solomon, 16 Apr. '30, Brooklyn, NY) Flautist. Played with Mat Mathews Quintet '53-4 (accordionist Mathews *b* 18 June '24, Holland; to USA '52; records on Brunswick and Dawn with Mann, *Four French Horns* '57 on Savoy with David AMRAM, etc). Mann recorded for Bethlehem '55-6, Prestige, Riverside, Epic, Verve, Savoy '56-8 (Savoy tracks with Phil WOODS reissued as *Be-Bop Synthesis*); wrote TV music, toured Europe, etc.; formed AfroJazz sextet '59, toured Africa for State Dept '60; visited Brazil '61, has toured the world ever since: he began recording for Atlantic '60, often using Latin sidemen such as Patato Valdez, Willie Bobo, Johnny PACHECO, etc. and albums began to reach the pop chart with *Live At The Village Gate* '62: with bassists Ahmed ABDUL-MALIK and Ben Tucker (*b* 13 Dec. '30, Nashville, Tenn.), Hagood Hardy on vibes (*b* '26 Feb. '37, Angola, Ind.; later with Martin DENNY, George SHEARING), Rudy Collins on drums (*b* 24 July '34, NYC), Ray Mantilla and Chief Bey on additional percussion, LP incl. an early piece of jazz-funk, Tucker's 'Comin' Home Baby', and was a top 30 pop LP: Mann became the most popular jazzman ever to take up the flute. 25 LPs reached top 200 pop albums '62-79 incl. bossa nova LP made in Rio '63, with Sergio MENDES, Antonio Carlos Jobim; two live sets from Newport '63-5; *Memphis Underground* '69, with Roy AYERS and Larry CORYELL; *Stone Flute, Memphis Two-Step* and *Push Push* '70-1 (latter with guest guitars John Abercrombie and Duane ALLMAN) were on Mann's Embryo label, distributed by Atlantic. From about '72 he often called his various groups Family of Mann, often featured ex-Ray CHARLES sideman David 'Fathead' Newman. *London Underground* '73 and *Reggae* '74 were back on Atlantic, made in London, former with Mick Taylor, Albert Lee, Stephane GRAPPELLI, others; latter with Tommy McCook, leader of Jimmy Cliff's band. *Discotheque* '75 was top 30 LP incl. dance hit 'Hi-Jack'; *Waterbed* same year with Newman was no. 75, with remake of 'Comin' Home Baby', covers of Ray CHARLES 'I Got A Woman' and boogaloo hit 'Bang! Bang!', vocal by Cissy HOUSTON on 'Violets Don't Be Blue'; *Surprises* '76 was big band set, also with Newman and Houston; *Super Mann* '79 again reached top 100 LPs. Among many other albums: *Nirvana* '61-2 on Atlantic with Bill EVANS Trio, *Glory Of Love* '67 on A&M, *Concerto Grosso In D Blues* '68 on Atlantic with or-

chestra, big band *Big Boss Mann* '65 on Columbia (aka *Latin Mann*), *Gagaku & Beyond* '76 on Finnadar with Japanese musicians, tone poems *All Blues/Rain Forest* '80 on Herbie Mann Music, with flute, bass, tabla and percussion.

MANNE, Shelly (*b* Sheldon Manne, 11 June '20, NYC; *d* 26 Sep. '84, L.A.) Drummer. Father and two uncles were also drummers; worked on transatlantic liners; with bandleaders Raymond SCOTT, Les BROWN; then Stan KENTON, Woody HERMAN '46-52, toured with JATP, settled on West Coast and became the most in-demand drummer in movies and TV in the '50s, as well as appearing on about half the jazz records made on the West Coast. He appeared in the film *Man With The Golden Arm* '56 and played in hit Henry MANCINI score for TV's *Peter Gunn* '59; operated club Shelly's Manne Hole '60-74 in L.A. Long association with Contemporary label as leader '53-62 (as well as countless albums as sideman) began with appropriately titled *West Coast Sound*, with Art PEPPER, Bob COOPER, Jimmy GIUFFRE, Bud SHANK, Curtis COUNCE, Shorty ROGERS. Trio set *Shelly Manne And His Friends* '56 had André PREVIN and Leroy Vinnegar; the same year they made *My Fair Lady*, a hit LP that started vogue for jazz treatments of Broadway scores, incl. *L'il Abner* and *Pal Joey* '57, *Gigi* and *The Bells Are Ringing* '58, *West Side Story* '59, some with Previn as nominal leader, some with Red Mitchell on bass instead of Vinnegar. Often worked with Victor FELDMAN, Russ Freeman on piano (*b* 28 May '26, Chicago), Monty Budwig on bass (*b* 26 Dec. '29, Pender, Neb.), incl. *Shelly Manne And His Men Play Peter Gunn* and *Son Of Gunn* '59, *The Proper Time* '60; with Feldman in four vols. of *At The Black Hawk* '59, with Freeman, Conte CANDOLI, Richie Kamuca *At The Manne Hole* and *Checkmate* '61, etc. *Sounds Unheard Of* '62 was duet with guitarist Jack Marshall. Other albums: *Two, Three, Four* '62 on Impulse with Coleman HAWKINS, Hank JONES; with Bill EVANS and Budwig on Verve '62; big band *Manne – That's Gershwin!* '65 on Capitol; quintet *Perk Up* '67 on Concord Jazz; quintet *Outside* '69 and sextet *Alive In London* '70 from Ronnie SCOTT club, both on Contemporary; *Mannekind* '72 on Mainstream;

Rex '76 on Discovery (songs by Richard RODGERS), *Essence* and *French Concert* '77 on Galaxy; *Jazz Crystallizations* '78 on Pausa, *The Manne We Love* '78 on East Wind; *Interpretations* (of Bach and Mozart) and *Double Piano Jazz Quartet Live At Carmello's* (two vols.) '80 on Trend; *Hollywood Jam* (sextet with Budwig, Cooper, Pepper) and *Fingering* (trio with Monty ALEXANDER, Ray BROWN) '81 on Atlas; *Remember* '84 on Jazzizz (trio with Budwig and pianist Frank Collett). Manne was also founder member of L.A. Four, with Brown, Shank and Laurindo ALMEIDA (eight LPs on Concord Jazz c.'67-82).

MANONE, Wingy (*b* Joseph Matthews Manone, 13 Feb. 1900, New Orleans; *d* 9 July '82, Las Vegas) Trumpet, vocalist, bandleader. Lost his right arm in a streetcar accident as a child; took up trumpet and was playing on riverboats at 17. Occasional record gigs from '25 incl. 'Tar Paper Stomp' '30 (by 'Barbecue Joe and his Hot Dogs'), aka 'Wingy's Stomp', marking the first recorded appearance of the riff that soon became 'Hot And Anxious' by Horace HENDERSON, then 'In The Mood' by Edgar HAYES and Glenn MILLER, the biggest hit of the Swing Era. Led own band '34-41 with such sidemen as future Bob CROSBY alumni Ray Bauduc, Eddie MILLER, etc.; also Bud FREEMAN, Jack TEAGARDEN, George Brunis, many others came and went: hits on Okeh/Vocalion '35-6 incl. 'Nickel In The Slot', with vocal by Manone and guitarist Nappy Lamare; on Bluebird '36-8 one of several recordings of Slim GAILLARD's 'Flat Foot Floogie'. 'Annie Laurie' '38 had affecting Manone vocal: garbled words, sweet and swinging at the same time, also a solo by Chu BERRY; in '39 the band incl. Berry, Buster Bailey and Cozy COLE, with wonderful solos, e.g. on 'Limehouse Blues'. In the '50s he did radio work with Bing CROSBY, settled in Vegas '54, worked occasionally well into '70s.

MANTOVANI (*b* Annunzio Paolo Mantovani, 15 Nov. '05, Venice; *d* 30 Mar. '80, Tunbridge Wells, England) Violinist, composer, conductor. Father was violinist under Toscanini at La Scala, Milan. Worked in London at 16, led Hotel Metropole orchestra '25, began broadcasting, recording; conducted for many stars such as Noel COWARD. *The Young Mantovani 1935-39* (EMI/UK) recaptures the dated charm of his hotel playing, with bass, drums, accordion and half a dozen strings, some doubling on guitar, mandolin, accordion etc.; vocals by George Barclay, Stella Roberts and Al BOWLLY. Hits in the USA as early as '35-6 with instrumentals 'Red Sails In The Sunset', 'Serenade In The Night'; he also composed amusing little instrumental novelties, such as 'Bull Frog' late '40s. 'Charmaine' '50 was lifted from an album and sold a million copies; his treatment of the '13 song introduced the 'cascading strings' gimmick, and he became the king of mood music, helped by excellent post-war Decca/UK sound quality; 10″ LPs of Strauss waltzes, etc. sold a million; he was the first recording artist to sell a million stereo albums. 'Song From Moulin Rouge' was no. 1 UK '53 but competed with Percy FAITH in USA. Above all he was an album seller: dozens are still listed in UK catalogues; 51 were hit LPs in the USA '53-72, most in the top 50, all instrumental except *Kismet* '64, the Broadway score with music by Borodin, sung by Robert Merrill, Regina Resnik and chorus. Some said that *Film Encores* '57, *Gems Forever* '58, *Songs To Remember* '60 etc. all sounded the same.

MAPFUMO, Thomas (*b* '45, Marondera, Zimbabwe) African singer-composer, bandleader. As a Shona speaker growing up under white minority rule, he began via trad. drumming and mbira music, but soon played Western music: songs of the BEATLES, Wilson PICKETT, Otis REDDING, occasionally during mid-'60s on the radio. He recorded his first song in Shona as the civil war was getting under way, but little was being heard of indigenous music; he formed the Hallelujah Chicken Run Band '73, which played mainly copyright music but experimented in Shona, and in '74 was approached by Teal Records: a series of Shona singles in chimurenga style ('music of struggle') made use of innuendo and trad. proverbs and earned eight gold discs in a row, also attracting government investigation. He formed the Acid Band '76 as lead singer and writer, also worked with the Pied Pipers, another top band; *Hokoya* '77 ('watch out') by the Acid Band was banned by the Smith government and Mapfumo was detained for 90 days; the government tried to discredit him with the liberation movement, allegedly forcing him to perform at a fund-raising event for Bishop Muzorewa, but he remained unbowed and popular; he formed the Blacks Unlimited '78, made LP *Gwindingi Rine Shuma* in Harare '80 (issued by Earthworks UK '86); after Zimbabwe's independence he was undoubtedly leader of the country's most popular band and signing with Earthworks enabled international breakthrough: *The Chimurenga Singles 1976-1980* were compiled '84 and followed by new albums *Ndangariro* and *Mabasa*. He toured the UK '84-5, *Mr Music* '85 confirmed his stardom; LP and single *Chimurenga For Justice* were made in London; mellow single 'Hupenyu Wanyu' '86 on Rough Trade reappropriated the Bo DIDDLEY beat.

MAPHIS, Joe, and Rose Lee (Otis W. Maphis, *b* 12 May '21, Suffolk, Va. and Rose Lee, *b* 29 Dec. '22, Baltimore, Md.) Husband and wife team called Mr and Mrs Country Music, his guitar style one of the most innovative in '50s and still echoing in contemporary styles. His family moved to Maryland; he played piano in the Railsplitters, his father's square dance band; took up guitar, banjo and fiddle and worked with Blackie and his Lazy K Ranch Boys on WRVA Richmond, Va. '39, moved to WLW Minneapolis as Cousin Joe '42, fronted US Army Special Services group called the Swingbilly Revue '44; after discharge back to WRVA on the Old Dominion Dance Show '48 and met Rose Lee. She began on radio '37 as singer/guitarist Rose of the Mountains; they married, moved to L.A. '51, appearing on Cliffie STONE's Hometown Jamboree, then Town Hall Party for 10 years. He sessioned with Johnny BOND, Tex RITTER etc., worked in TV music (*The Virginians, FBI Story* etc), films (*Thunder Road, God's Little Acre*, both '58); they signed to Columbia '52, recorded for other labels but had no hit singles. He wrote 'Dim Lights, Thick Smoke And Loud, Loud Music' (became country standard); played on many West Coast rock'n'roll records incl. Ricky NELSON's first sessions, introduced Nelson to James BURTON and James Kirkland, who became the backbone of his band. Joe and Rose moved to Nashville '68 and are still active, appearing regularly on TV's *Hee-Haw* '81-5. Son Jody was part of the impressive Earl Scruggs Revue '72-9 and is a session musician in Nashville. LPs incl. *Hi-Fi Holiday For Banjo* '58 on Columbia, *Joe Maphis & Merle Travis* '63 on Capitol, *King Of The Strings* '65 on Starday, *Gospel Guitar* '69 on Word, *Dim Lights, Thick Smoke* '75 and *Boogie Woogie Flat Top Guitar Pickin' Man* '78 on CMH.

MARABLE, Fate (*b* 2 Dec. 1890, Paducah, Ky.; *d* 16 Jan. '47, St Louis, Mo.) Piano, calliope, bandleader. Left home at 17 and played on a riverboat out of Little Rock, Ark., played in duo with white violinist Emil Flindt (who wrote 'The Waltz You Saved For Me'), formed own band c.'17; left Streckfus Line '40 because of infected finger causing layoff. Led band in St Louis mid-'40s, died of pneumonia. Made only one record: 'Frankie And Johnny'/'Pianoflage' '24 on Okeh (10-piece band incl. drummer Zutty Singleton), but no bandleader has ever employed more talent: the list of sidemen who played for Marable on their way up north begins with Henry ALLEN, Louis ARMSTRONG, Jimmy BLANTON, Earl BOSTIC, and continues through the alphabet, a role call of USA music that infl. even more who heard it, incl. Bix BEIDERBECKE, Jess STACY, etc.

MARIACHI One of Mexico's regional styles, originating in states of Colima, Jalisco, Michoacan, Nayarit and Sinaloa (i.e. mainly on the Western seaboard). Brass arrangements have come to epitomise Mexico for tourists and filmgoers (and thanks partly to the 'Ameriachi' style of Herb ALPERT). Etymology of the term is uncertain; often said to come from French for 'marriage' but was in use decades before the French intervention of 1861-7: it may be a corruption from Virgin Mary celebrations. Earliest ensembles on record at turn of the century incl. bass guitarron, violins and vihuela; later trumpet, trombone, flute or clarinet added. Cirilo Marmolejo has been credited with possibly the first use of trumpet c.'25. USA recording engineers recorded the music before the Mexican Revolution (1910-20); post-revolution governments fostered it as an ideological tool. Anthologies on

Folklyric are the best and most readily available of the music's roots, incl. Mariachi Vargas (aka 'El Mejor Mariachi del Mundo' – 'the best mariachi in the world'), Cuarteto Coculense and Mariachi Coculense 'Rodriguez' de Cirilo Marmolejo. Albums incl. *The Earliest Mariachi Recordings 1908-1938* and *Mariachi Coculense de Cirilo Marmolejo 1933-36*.

MARIANO, Charlie (*b* Carmine Ugo Mariano, *b* 12 Nov. '23, Boston, Mass.) Saxes, flute, nadaswaram (a South Indian double-reed instrument), also teacher. Began on sax at 17, played in US Army, attended Berklee, played and recorded around Boston (on Motif label; *see* Nat PIERCE), worked with Stan KENTON '53-5; to L.A., working with Frank Rosolino, Shelly MANNE, others. LPs '51-7 on Imperial, Prestige, Fantasy, Bethlehem (now on Affinity), World Pacific with Herb Pomeroy, Jaki BYARD, Rosolino, Manne, others. (Highly rated trombonist Rosolino *b* 20 Aug. '26, Detroit; tracks on Savoy's *The Trombone Album* from '52; LPs on Capitol and Bethlehem '54-6, some now on Affinity; LPs on Reprise '61, Horo, MPS, Sackville, Vantage '73-8; suicide 26 Nov. '78). Mariano was married to Toshiko AKIYOSHI; quartet LPs with her on Candid '60 and in Tokyo '63. He played on Charles MINGUS LPs on Impulse '63, taught at Berklee c.'65-71, worked with Radio Malaysia orchestra for several months, discovering the nadaswaram; lived mostly in Europe from '71, making trips to India to study music. He was obviously infl. by Charlie PARKER but always open to new ideas, preferring Europe because experimentation there was less subject to commercial pressures. He was a member of the United Jazz And Rock Ensemble (on six LPs), Eberhard Weber's Colours (several LPs on ECM). Other LPs incl. three with Japanese musicians in Tokyo '67-8, incl. reedman Sadao Watanabe (*b* 1 Feb. '33; LPs on Inner City, Columbia; *Parkers Mood* on Elektra and *Good Time For Love* on WEA, both '86); octet *Cascade* and *Solos And Duos* with Philip CATHERINE on Keytone '74; *Reflektions* '74 on Finnish RCA with Finnish musicians (and Sabu Martinez); *The Door Is Open* '75 by group Pork Pie with Catherine, Jaspar van't Hof, others, and

Helen Twelvetrees '76 with Jack Bruce, Jan HAMMER, others, both on MPS; sextet *October* on CMP/Inner City; *Crystal Bells* '79 on CMP, *Tea For Four* '80 on Finnish Leo, *Some Kind Of Changes* '82 on German Calig, *Jyothi* '83 on ECM with The Karnataki College Of Percussion, *The Charlie Mariano Group* '85 on Mood.

MARILLION UK rock band formed '79 as Silmarillion, based in Aylesbury: name from Tolkien novel was shortened when vocalist Fish joined '80 (*b* Derek Dick, 25 Apr. '58, Dalkeith, Scotland). Founder member and sole remaining original is guitarist Steve Rothery (*b* 25 Nov. '59, Brompton, Yorks); Mark Kelly (*b* 9 Apr. '61, Dublin) joined on keyboards '81, bassist Pete Trewavas '82 (*b* 15 Jan. '59, Middlesbrough), Mick Pointer on drums. Interest engendered by session for BBC Radio 1's Tommy Vance led to tour and contract with EMI, though they were being compared to Peter GABRIEL-era GENESIS owing to Fish's vocal resemblance and use of stage makeup and costumes. But after the self-effacing pop of the early '80s a progressive revival seemed to be at hand and their live appeal led to headlining gigs at Hammersmith Odeon after one single, 'Market Square Heroes' reaching only no. 60 (17-minute 'Grendel' on B side was staple of stage act). *Script For A Jester's Tear* '83 entered chart at no. 7, elaborate sleeve artwork (also a Genesis trademark) enclosing '70s-style rock. Pointer replaced by session veteran Ian Mosley (*b* 16 June '53, Paddington, London; played in *Hair* and *Jesus Christ Superstar* shows and in ex-Genesis guitarist Steve Hackett's band), who joined during recording of *Fugazi* (no. 5 LP UK '84). They scored top 40 singles but live act was still forte; release of live *Real To Reel* late '84 was risky after only two studio albums, but necessary to counter bootlegs: it reached no. 8. They threw off spectre of Genesis with no. 1 LP *Misplaced Childhood* as Fish dropped makeup and they reached new heights of confidence; a concept LP beloved of '70s progressives, yet was still commercial enough to yield three hit singles incl. 'Lavender' (based on nursery rhyme) and 'Heart Of Lothian': yet lyricist Fish had made few concessions, spinning web of Celtic intrigue. Loyal following continued

769

despite new commercial status – again, like Genesis fans.

MAR-KEYS, The Studio session players who had instrumental hits: guitarist Steve Cropper (*b* 21 Oct. '41, Willow Springs, Mo.), bassist Donald 'Duck' Dunn (*b* 24 Nov. '41, Memphis), drummer Terry Johnson, Jerry Lee Smith on keyboards, Wayne Jackson on trumpet, Don Nix on baritone sax, Charles 'Packy' Axton on tenor. Axton's mother and uncle had formed Satellite label (renamed Stax); white youngsters who loved black music began by backing Rufus and Carla THOMAS (*see* SOUL MUSIC). Their own hit was 'Last Night', written and arranged by Chips Moman (no. 3 USA pop chart '61, when label was still Satellite); they continued with 'Morning After', 'Pop-Eye Stroll', 'Philly Dog' etc. but never reached top 40 again. Mar-Keys name was soon retired as Cropper became a founder member of BOOKER T AND THE MGs, took Dunn with him; but MGs and Mar-Keys played together on stage, backing all the label's stars in now-legendary Stax soul revues. Eventually saxist Andrew Love and Jackson added Floyd Newman on baritone and became the Memphis Horns, remaining ace session group; Axton formed the Packers, had R&B hit with Mar-Keys soundalike 'Hole In The Wall' '65; Nix had solo career, wrote 'Goin' Down' (much covered by J. J. CALE, Jeff BECK etc.), then turned producer, working with Beck, John MAYALL, Freddie KING, Delaney and Bonnie BRAMLETT, etc.

MARLEY, Bob (*b* Nesta Robert Marley, 6 Feb. '45, St Ann's Parish, Jamaica; *d* 11 May '81, Miami, Fla.) Singer, songwriter, guitarist in the Jamaican national idiom of reggae; greatness as a musician combining with his transparent honesty and hatred of violence to make him the only world-wide superstar the genre has had. His mother was Jamaican, father English; he read palms as a child, but began singing after spending a year in Kingston at age 6; moved there permanently '57, growing up in the tough slum of Trench Town, where youths became street anarchists, jobless in Eden because of the island's primitive economy after more than 400 years of colonial rule. He was an ordinary mischievous child, mad

about football, but unusually sensitive and possessing an innate ability to lead others which he used only unconsciously. Began playing/singing '60 with Bunny Livingston (*b* Neville O'Riley Livingston, 23 Apr. '47) and Peter McIntosh (aka 'Tosh'; *b* Winston Hubert McIntosh, 19 Oct. '44; *d* 11 Sept. '87); both had begun playing on homemade instruments. Marley had a smoky tenor, Bunny a higher, keening voice and Tosh a powerful baritone; they were infl. by Sam COOKE, Brook BENTON, the DRIFTERS and the Impressions (with Curtis MAYFIELD); Marley also later cited the infl. of Fats DOMINO, Elvis PRESLEY, country singer Jim REEVES, plus indigenous music developing at the time (*see* REGGAE). They took lessons from Joe Higgs (of duo Higgs & Wilson); he was an infl. not only because he insisted on correct harmonies but because he already wrote songs about ganja (marijuana) and Rastafarianism before it was fashionable; he also gave Marley tuition on guitar and songwriting. Marley was at first turned away from Leslie Kong's recording studio, just one of a gaggle of youths hanging around, but was taken back by Jimmy Cliff and Desmond DEKKER, made his first record '62 ('Judge Not', written with Higgs' help). The Teenagers, aka Wailing Rudeboys, was a group incl. the trio, Junior Braithwaite (lead singer, though Marley led the group), Beverly Kelso and Cherry Smith; Alvin Patterson played traditional Afro-Jamaican burru drums, aka 'Willie', 'Pep', 'Franceesco', later famous as Seeco, the Wailers' percussionist; he was an important infl. from the beginning, but was also acquainted with Clement 'Sir Coxsone' Dodd: first track for Dodd was 'Simmer Down' '63, written by Bunny, backed by the Skatalites; Coxsone dubbed them the Wailing Wailers on the instant nationwide hit. The ska beat was slowed down and became 'rude boy' music (*see* REGGAE); though Braithwaite was the best singer his infl. waned; some of the songs were bitter and loaded with politics, but there were also fascinating covers (e.g. the BEATLES' 'And I Love Her', Tom JONES' 'What's New Pussycat') and adapted versions of songs by the Contours, Junior WALKER, Bob DYLAN, others as Marley studied songwriting and the new worldwide politics of youth at a time when Jamaica itself was a political maelstrom. Despite sometimes having several hits in the Jamaican top 10, the group was paid practically nothing by Coxsone; in early '66 Marley married Rita Anderson, then went to Wilmington, Delaware to stay with his mother, his name changed to Robert Nesta on his passport; returned to Kingston the same year, now under the spell of Rastafarianism. Bunny's 'Rude Boy', Rita's 'Pied Piper' and other records had been hits; ska had evolved further into 'rock steady', relaxed and sensual, often with 'protest' lyrics as the Jamaican political scene heated still more. The Wailers had made more than 50 tracks for Coxsone; formed own Wailin' Soul label which failed; recorded more than 80 demos for JAD (label operated by Danny Sims and Johnny NASH), then ten tracks for Kong '69 released as *Best Of The Wailers* (Bunny didn't like the title, told Kong that he would die; a year later he dropped dead at age 38). Marley worked in the USA for a few months '69, returned again; the group recorded for Lee Perry late '69-early '70, some sides issued on their own Tuff Gong label (Marley's street nickname). Perry's label Upsetter had the Upsetters as the house band, led by bassist Aston Francis Barrett (*b* '46, aka 'Family Man' or 'Fams') and his brother, drummer Carlton Lloyd 'Carly' Barrett (*b* '50), eventually merging with the Wailers as rock-steady became reggae, still slower, steeped in Rasta and ganja, its hypnotic beat and powerful politics appealing around the world. Many fans felt that records made with Perry were the best of all: Tyrone Downie (*b* '56) played keyboards on 'Trench Town Rock', no. 1 for five months '71. Meanwhile in '70 Marley went to Sweden with Nash to work on a soundtrack (film/record never released), then to London, joined by the Wailers, to play backup on Nash LP *I Can See Clearly Now*, with four songs by Bob. The LP did well but Marley's single 'Reggae On Broadway' flopped. At the end of '71 the trio was broke, depressed, cold, homesick and in trouble with the government over work permits; Marley went to Chris Blackwell at Island Records and offered to make an album: he gave them £8000. Even then, Blackwell later recalled, it was not a lot of money for an album, but it was all gambled: he had no idea whether they could do it or not, but he knew who Marley was, having released his first UK single, 'One Cup Of Coffee', leased from Kong. The band went home and made *Catch A Fire*, released late '72 UK, early '73 in USA (by Capitol, who did not promote it). Marley reserved Jamaican distribution for his own Tuff Gong label. Released as Michael Manley became Prime Minister of Jamaica by a landslide (despite censorship of true Jamaican music on the radio, all the artists supporting Manley), and as produced by Blackwell, it changed the direction of reggae, giving rock fans something new to dance to and a new kind of lyrical consciousness. Earl Lindo (*b* '53; aka 'Wire', pron. 'Wya') replaced Downie on keyboards; sextet incl. trio and the Barretts. Next LP *Burnin'* '73 (originally called *Reincarnated Souls*, but Bunny's title track was dropped) incl. 'I Shot The Sheriff', covered by Eric CLAPTON (no. 1 USA, 9 UK '74; other Marley songs covered incl. Taj Mahal's 'Slave Driver', Barbra STREISAND's 'Guava Jelly'). *African Herbsman* '73 collected Perry tracks incl. 'Trench Town Rock' on Trojan, label formed by Blackwell with Lee Goptal and retained by Goptal when they split up. Wailers toured UK, appeared on TV's *Old Grey Whistle Test*; on returning to Jamaica, Bunny left: a strict Rasta, he lost weight, was terribly homesick on tour, never toured with the Wailers again. They toured USA '73, Higgs subbing for Bunny, opening at Max's Kansas City in NYC for a new talent called Bruce SPRINGSTEEN; they worked hard but met much lack of understanding and made no money; they were sacked while opening for SLY AND THE FAMILY STONE. Toured UK '73 without Higgs; Marley and Tosh quarrelled and Wire left to join Taj MAHAL: the first edition of the Wailers was almost finished. LP *Natty Dread* '74 was minimalist, powerful, full of moral authority; it incl. Marley, Carly, Fam, Bernard 'Touter' Harvey on organ (too young to tour), harmonies by Rita, Marcia Griffiths and Judy Mowatt, and Lee Jaffe on harmonica, a fast friend of Marley who had taken 'Sheriff' to Clapton's bassist Carl Radle and who was the only white person ever to play as a Wailer. Girl trio was called the I Threes by Marley; Griffiths had single/LP *Young, Gifted and Black* on Harry J with husband Bob ANDY, a hit in Europe.

Early versions of Marley's 'Road Block' and 'Knotty Dread' were issued on Tuff Gong in Jamaica and huge hits but not played on Jamaican radio, historically operated by foreigners totally out of touch with the island's music. Blues/rock guitar lines were dubbed in UK by Al Anderson (*b* '53, N.J.), who had worked with Island artist John MARTYN, first heard reggae played for him by Paul Kossoff of FREE: played lead for Afro-rock band Shakatu, left to join new Wailers. Original trio performed together May '74 in Kingston, opening for Marvin GAYE, with Downie on keyboards, his first appearance with the band outside the studio; he joined the new edition. Marley prod. *Escape From Babylon* '75 by Martha Valez on Sire. A Tuff Gong series of spots was a landmark in Jamaican radio. USA tour in June incl. Anderson, Downie, Jaffe and the Barretts plus Rita and Judy (as the I Twos: pregnant Marcia stayed home). Their popularity was growing. First reggae on USA network TV was 'Kinky Reggae' on a MANHATTAN TRANSFER TV show. They were asked to open for a ROLLING STONES tour, but refused; in London in July Lyceum concerts were sold out, recorded as fiery *Bob Marley And The Wailers Live!*. Bunny, Tosh and Marley last played together at Stevie WONDER benefit for blind Jamaican children Oct. '75; gentle Bunny changed his name to Bunny Wailer and went his own way: albums incl. *Blackheart Man* '76, *Protest* '77, *Sings The Wailers* '81 on Mango; the more volatile Tosh's output incl. ganja anthem 'Legalise It', title track of LP '76, then *Equal Rights* '77 on CBS, who then dropped him; he toured opening for the Stones, released *Bush Doctor* '78, *Mystic Man* '79 on their label, then *Wanted: Dread And Alive* '81 on EMI. He was murdered by robbers in his home in Kingston as last LP *No Nuclear War* '87 was released on Parlophone. Marley became a superstar '76, in constant demand for concerts, endlessly interviewed by journalists flooding into Kingston. Anderson and Jaffe defected to Tosh, whose *Legalise It* LP also incl. Sly & Robbie. *Rastaman Vibrations* '76 incl. Earl 'Chinna' Smith on rhythm guitar, a session player with his own Kingston band the Soul Syndicate; Don Kinsey replaced Anderson: *b* in Indiana, had toured with Albert KING, recorded on Island in trio White Lightning

with brother Woody on drums, Busta Cherry Jones on bass. The new album disappointed hard-core reggae fans but was his biggest hit ever; his only top 10 LP in the USA (incl. 'Roots, Rock, Reggae', his only USA Hot 100 hit). He had got out of a contract with Sims when signing with Island by yielding his publishing to Sims' Cayman Music; now he did not take credit for all his songs, but spread them among band and friends to keep money from Cayman. Asked if the Manley government would try to use him he'd said that only Rasta had the truth; now 'Rat Race' from the LP sent up the politicians and was a hit on Tuff Gong. A date of 5 Dec. '76 was set for a free concert in Kingston: Tosh, Bunny, BURNING SPEAR were asked to join the bill; the Manley government, whose socialism was floundering as the island continued to heat up, announced an election for Dec. hoping to cash in. Manley's People's National Party was opposed by the Jamaica Labour Party, led by anthropologist, folklorist, former record producer Edward Seaga. On 3 Dec. gunmen shot up Marley's home, wounding several people incl. Bob, Rita and Kinsey, manager Don Taylor most seriously; miraculously no one was killed. Reasons mooted for the attack were political jealousy, one of sidekick Skill Cole's scams gone wrong, Taylor's gambling or Marley's scandalous affair with the light-skinned Miss World, Cindy Breakspeare; but the incident was never explained. Marley, Rita and Kinsey appeared in concert as scheduled two days later, with Downie, Carly, Cat Coore from Third World on bass, horns, and drummers from Ras Michael and the Sons of Negus. Marley went to London to record; Blackwell had recruited Anderson and Kinsey, now found Julian 'Junior' Marvin (*b* Jamaica, raised in UK and USA; aka Junior Kerr, Junior Hanson), who had played with T-Bone WALKER, Billy PRESTON, Ike & Tina TURNER and Wonder, and made two LPs with his own band, Hanson. *Exodus* '77 and *Kaya* '78 were recorded, the former incl. four-to-the-bar 'rockers' drumming (militant style the rage then in Jamaica) and three songs about the attempted murder; *Kaya* more mellow, with dance and love songs. On a European tour '77 the Wailers played football with French journalists; Marley injured his foot, the toenail came off and cancerous cells were found: urged to have the toe amputated, he refused, had minor surgery and seemed to recover. Despite increasing violence he returned to Kingston early '78; a peace concert had been organised, possibly by racketeers to calm down the slum youths so that they could get back to business. Tosh was backed by World Sound and Power, with Sly & Robbie; Ras Michael performed; Marley got Manley and Seaga to shake hands on stage, but they were uncomfortable. He then went on the most strenuous tour so far: the USA (filled Madison Square Garden), Europe, Canada and West Coast USA, with Marvin, rehired Wire and Anderson, Downie, Seeco and the Barretts; Tosh guested in L.A.; tour album was 2-disc *Babylon By Bus*; he toured Asia, returned to Jamaica to record new songs. He visited Ethiopia late '78, began working on song 'Zimbabwe'; played Boston benefit '79 for Amandla (amandla ngawetu, 'freedom for the people') for African freedom fighters; his masterpiece *Survival* '79 incl. 'Zimbabwe', widely covered in Africa. His health began to fail; he caught cold in NYC, felt better on West Coast; visited Africa early '80, the trip marred by the discovery that Taylor was a thief: Marley had never made a profit on tour because Taylor skimmed it to finance his gambling. Last LP *Uprising* '80 gave up horns and rock sound in favour of an African flavour; before its release the Wailers played for Zimbabwe's independence celebrations in April, perhaps the high point of his life. He was warned not to return to Jamaica, where civil war seemed imminent, because he was still seen as a Manley supporter and the CIA was supporting Seaga; he toured Germany, but his health worsened: he died of cancer without seeing his home again. Like Bob Dylan, he never sold that many records, though five LPs were top 10 in UK incl. posthumous *Confrontation* '83 (tracks not previously released outside Jamaica, released on second anniversary of his death) and *Legend* '84, the last at no. 1; compilations and reissues of early work have appeared on CBS, WEA labels, others; *Chances Are* incl. 'Reggae On Broadway'. He made millions, but a lot was stolen and he gave a lot away. He was criticised for driving an expensive car, but he could park it in any slum in Kingston without even rolling the windows up, and no one would touch it. The records are still selling and he is still loved by millions; he preached, among other things, that the only way black people could be superior to whites was by refusing to practise their racism. With no father and separated from his mother as a child, he had suffered loneliness as well as poverty, but he wore no mantle later: 'I and I don't have to suffer to be aware of suffering. So is not anger and alla dat, but is just truth, and truth haffa bust out of man like a river' (quote from *Bob Marley* by Stephen Davis '83, a good biography). Marley's son Ziggy and his Melody Makers released album *Conscious Party* '88 on Virgin to good reviews, toured USA.

MARMALADE Scottish pop group formed '66 from the ashes of the Gaylords, who had performed north of the border since '61, attracted attention of Cliff RICHARD's svengali Norrie PARAMOR and made several flop singles '64-5 ('Little Egypt', 'The Name Game'). Lineup: Junior Campbell (*b* 31 May '47), keyboards and guitars; Pat Fairlie (*b* 14 Apr. '46), guitar; Dean Ford (*b* Thomas McAleese, 5 Sep. '46), lead vocals; Graham Knight (*b* 8 Dec. '46), bass; Ray Duffy, drums. Marmalade signed with CBS '66, replaced Duffy with Englishman Alan Whitehead; their first hit was 'Lovin' Things', no. 6 '68. After hiccup with HOWARD/BLAIKLEY's 'Wait For Me Marianne' (no. 30) their biggest hit and only no. 1 was cover of BEATLES 'Ob-La-Di, Ob-La-Da' (from the White Album, '68) which the Fab Four did not release as a single (rival cover by the Bedrocks made the top 20). Tony Macauley song 'Baby Make It Soon' reached no. 10 '69; they switched to Decca for more control over their material and the Campbell/Ford writing team proved equal to the challenge with top 3 hits 'Rainbow' and 'Reflections Of My Life' (latter also top 10 USA). Campbell left to study at Royal College of Music (came back '72-3 with top 15 solo hits 'Hallelujah Freedom' and 'Sweet Illusion', later prod. and wrote jingles, film music). His replacement, ex-Poets guitarist/keyboardist Hughie Nicholson, took up the writing reins incl. two no. 6 entries 'Cousin Norman' and 'Radancer'; another ex-Poet Dougie Henderson replaced Whitehead; Fairlie left

'72; then Nicholson left to form Blue (intended to be more credible, less commercial); a *News Of The World* exposé of Marmalade's sex life on the road split them, with Ford the only remaining original member in '74. But Knight returned as Ford left to go solo, picked up top 10 hit '76 with aptly titled 'Falling Apart At The Seams', a Macauley song. A much-changed Marmalade are still a fixture on the club circuit, a '60s pop band that refuses to lie down.

MARSALIS, Branford (*b* '60, New Orleans, La.) Saxophones. Father is pianist/teacher Ellis Marsalis; brother is trumpeter Wynton (*see below*); played with them on one side of *Fathers And Sons* '82 on CBS (Chico and Von FREEMAN on the other side). He followed Wynton into Art BLAKEY's Jazz Messengers '81, replacing Bobby WATSON on alto (LPs *Killer Joe* '81 on Japanese Union Jazz label and *Keystone 3* '82 on Concord Jazz). He joined Wynton's band '82 playing tenor and soprano, touring the world; played on Miles DAVIS LP *Decoy* '84, toured '85-6 with Sting (*see* POLICE) incl. LP *The Dream Of The Blue Turtles* (with pianist Kenny Kirkland, *b* '57, Brooklyn, NY), also film *Bring On The Night* (about making of *Turtles*), soundtrack LP; 2-disc *Nothing Like The Sun* '87. Own LPs incl. *Scenes In The City* '83, with bassists Charnett Moffett, Ron CARTER, Phil BOWLER, pianists Kirkland, Mulgrew MILLER, drummer Marvin Smith and others on various tracks; *Royal Garden Blues* '86, *Renaissance* '87; also 'classical' LP *Romances For Saxophone* '86, all CBS; also recorded with Bobby HUTCHERSON, Tina TURNER, others incl. Dizzy GILLESPIE (*Closer To The Source* and *New Faces*), subbed for David MURRAY in World Saxophone Quartet gig, etc.; was set to act in *School Daze*, about college life, with Vanessa Williams.

MARSALIS, Wynton (*b* 18 Oct. '61, New Orleans, La.) Trumpet, bandleader; already a superstar when barely out of his teens. Charlie PARKER dominated jazz in the '40s, Miles DAVIS in '50s, John COLTRANE in '60s: Marsalis has come along after a long gap as jazz styles and furious experimentation were assimilated; he is not a style-setter to compare with these others, but there may

never be another domination of the scene on that scale. Father is pianist/teacher Ellis Marsalis (whose quartet LP *Syndrome* '84 is on Elm), brother is saxophonist Branford (*above*): all three played on *Fathers And Sons* '82 on CBS, with James Black on drums, Charles Fambrough on bass (Chico and Von FREEMAN on the other side). He was given his first trumpet at age 6 by Al HIRT, began studying both classical and jazz at 12, played through teens in local marching bands, etc., first trumpet in local civic orchestra; went to high school with Terence BLANCHARD and Donald HARRISON. He attended Juilliard in NYC and played in pit band for SONDHEIM musical *Sweeney Todd*; joined Art BLAKEY's Jazz Messengers at 18, playing on Blakey LPs *Live At Montreux And Northsea* on Timeless '80; *Recorded Live At Bubba's*, *The All American Hero* and *Wynton Marsalis' First Recordings* (with Ellis on one track) all made at Bubba's Jazz Restaurant in Fort Lauderdale, Fla. '80, on Who's Who, Toledo and Kingdom Jazz Gate labels; also *Album Of The Year* on Timeless and *Straight Ahead* on Concord Jazz '81; *Keystone 3* '82 is the only Blakey LP with both Wynton/Branford. Wynton also plays on one track of Blakey's *Aurex Jazz Festival '83* made in Tokyo. Toured with Herbie HANCOCK '81, incl. 2-disc *Herbie Hancock Quartet* on CBS, made in Japan with Tony WILLIAMS and Ron CARTER. He made *The Young Lions* '82 on Elektra at the Kool Jazz Festival with James Newton's flute on one track, Chico FREEMAN on the other; meanwhile signed with CBS as leader of band incl. Branford: debut *Father Time* '81 incl. tracks from Hancock tour with Branford added, was nominated for a Grammy; *Think Of One* '83 won a Grammy, with Kenny Kirkland on piano, Jeffrey Watts on drums, Ray Drummond and Phil BOWLER on basses. *Hot House Flowers* '84 had standards (strings arr. by Robert Freedman, because he grew up listening to *Clifford Brown With Strings*); *Black Codes (From The Underground)* '85 incl. Kirkland, Watts, Charnett Moffett on bass (Carter on one track), followed by *J Mood* '86, lovely *Standard Time* '87 with two originals, eight standards incl. Marcus Roberts' piano solo 'Memories Of You', Watts on drums, Bob Hurst on bass. In '84 he became first to win Grammies as both best jazz and classical soloist; he made a speech accepting the jazz award on behalf of Louis ARMSTRONG, Parker, Thelonious MONK, others 'who gave an art form to the American people that cannot be limited by enforced trends or bad taste'. Won again in both categories '85. Infl. by Miles DAVIS as well as others, derides Davis's recent work; when he walked on stage during a Davis gig as if to play, Davis stopped the music. His technique is astonishing and secure; huge success at such an early age brought barbs from some critics, and he has a big mouth: in a TV interview with Billy TAYLOR he gave Herb ALPERT as an example of a white jazz musician; this must have been news to Alpert. But he may be learning that a big mouth is not enough; he admitted in *Downbeat* (Nov. '87, interview with Stanley CROUCH) that when he was with Blakey 'I was just playing scales in whatever key my tune was in . . . that was enough to be considered musical in my era.' As Branford was quoted in *The Wire*, 'Wynton is good for jazz. End of conversation.' Which only means that he sells records and that a lot of people are tired of rock. His classical LPs incl. an LP of concerti by Mozart, Haydn and Hummel with the National Philharmonic, another with two mid-20th-century pieces by Tomasi and Jolivet with the Philharmonia, scraping the bottom of the trumpet-concerto barrel, and *Carnaval* with the Eastman Wind Ensemble (fastest-ever 'Flight Of The Bumblebee'). On *Baroque Music For Trumpets* '88 with the English Chamber Orchestra he was multi-tracked. He has quit playing classical music, having discovered that he can't do everything: there is a lot of jazz to learn and only so much time. To the extent that jazz today is repertory music, many young musicians will sound like revivalists, but Wynton has time on his side: he may invent something yet. In any case we may never hear the end of the Marsalises: brother Delfeayo (*b* c.'65) plays trombone (also prod. Branford's '86 LP, Courtney PINE's second album); Jason (*b* c.'77) plays drums.

MARSH, Warne (*b* 26 Oct. '27, L.A.; *d* there 18 Dec. '87) Tenor sax, composer. An underrated musician who made relatively few records. Met Lennie TRISTANO in US Army '47, often worked and studied with him through '60s, developed similarly personal approach to harmony and time. To West Coast '66, began teaching '68; joined SUPERSAX '72 and wrote some arr. for it. Recorded with Joe ALBANY '57 on Riverside, on Art PEPPER LP *The Way It Was* on Contemporary, etc. *Live In Hollywood* '52 with Hampton HAWES and Shelly MANNE is on Xanadu; other LPs on Imperial, Kapp, Mode Atlantic '56-7; shares solos with Lee KONITZ on *Lee Konitz Meets Jimmy Giuffre* '59 on Verve (Konitz also studied with Tristano; see his entry for other LPs with Marsh); on Revelation: *The Art Of Improvising* '59, two vols. *Live At The Half Note* with Konitz, Bill EVANS, Paul MOTIAN, Peter Ind (bassist, *b* 20 July '28, Uxbridge, England); *Ne Plus Ultra* '69 with Gary Foster on alto (*b* 25 May '36, Leavenworth, Kansas); *First Symposium* '72 with Foster, Clare Fischer. Three vols. of *Live At Montmartre* '75 with Konitz (made in Copenhagen) and duo *Big Two* with Red Mitchell (in Oslo) on Storyville. *All Music* '76 on Nessa made in Chicago during Supersax tour, with drummer Jake Hanna, bassist Fred Atwood, Lou Levy on piano (*b* 5 Mar. '28, Chicago; recorded with Frank SINATRA, Peggy LEE, Nancy WILSON): incl. tunes by Marsh, Konitz, Tristano, Levy. *How Deep/How High* on Interplay or Discovery incl. '77 quartet tracks with Roy HAYNES, Sam JONES, Sal Mosca on piano; '79 duos with Mosca. *Warne Out* '77 on Interplay is a trio set; quartet sets *Star Highs* '79 with Hank JONES, Mel LEWIS, bassist George Mraz, and *A Ballad Album* '83 with Levy are on Dutch Criss Cross; sextet *In Norway/Sax Of A Kind* '83 on Hot Club; duo *Warne Marsh & Susan Chen* '86 on Interplay (pianist Chen also studied with Tristano); *Back Home* '86 is quartet on Criss Cross, Jimmy Halperin playing second tenor on 'Two, Not One'. He collapsed on stage at Donte's Jazz Club while playing 'Out Of Nowhere'.

MARSHALL TUCKER BAND Country-rock band formed '71 in South Carolina around Tommy Caldwell (*b* '50, Spartenburg, S.C;. *d* 28 Apr. '80) and brother Toy (*b* '48), bass and lead guitars. Father was semi-pro country musician; Toy had accompanied him. Toy led the Rants '62-5, then did four years in US Marines, joined brother's band '71, bringing vocalist/keyboardist Doug Gray and multi-instrumentalist Jerry Eubanks with him from previous group the Toy Factory; with drummer Paul Riddle and George McCorkle (ex-Rants) on rhythm guitar, group was renamed after the owner of a rehearsal room they used. Toy's guitar style was often compared to that of Dickie Betts (*see* ALLMAN BROS), with whom they toured on support '73 to promote eponymous debut LP; every album has gone gold: *A New Life* '74, *Searchin' For A Rainbow* and 2-disc (one live) *Where We All Belong* '75, *Long Hard Ride* '76, *Carolina Dreams* '77; latter made platinum with top 15 single 'Heard It In A Love Song'. With other Capricorn label bands, they campaigned for Jimmy Carter and played at the White House '77 after he won. After *Together Forever* and *Greatest Hits* '78 they switched to WB, but success of *Running Like The Wind* '79 and *Tenth* '80 was marred by Tommy's death in a car crash. Succeeded by ex-Toy Factory worker Franklin Wilkie; they continued to score with *Dedicated* '81, *Tuckerized* '82 and *Just Us* '83. Very much in mould of Allmans, Wet Willie, LYNYRD SKYNYRD, but a little more laid back and tasteful; country crossover potential illustrated by Waylon JENNINGS' '76 country hit with cover of their first single, 'Can't You See', written by Toy, also in demand on guitar/steel guitar for sessions, appearing on LPs by Elvin BISHOP, Charlie DANIELS, Hank WILLIAMS Jr.

MARTERIE, Ralph (*b* 24 Dec. '14, Accera, Italy; *d* 10 Oct. '78, Dayton, Ohio) Trumpet, bandleader. Father musician with Chicago Civic Opera; family name Martiri. At 17 played theatre jobs, then with local bands; on NBC radio staff, played with Percy FAITH, Paul WHITEMAN; served in USN, had own show on ABC; joined Mercury records staff '49, toured as dance band leader from '51, billed as 'Caruso of the trumpet'. First hit instrumental version of ballad 'Pretend' with electric guitar lead, no. 16 USA '53: Nat COLE, Eileen BARTON had hit versions with words. 'Caravan' no. 11 same year; up-tempo treatment with guitar introduced new generation to ELLINGTON classic. 'Skokiaan' no. 3 '54, biggest of several covers; other lesser hits through '57. Less fame in rock'n'roll era but kept working; died following gig at

county fair. LPs incl. *Marvellous Marterie* '59, *Dancer's Choice* '63, *Dance Party* '64.

MARTIN, Benny (*b* 8 May '28, Sparta, Tenn.) Country singer and fiddler who never quite made the big time. Appeared on local radio '40s, debut on Grand Ole Opry '47; was a member of Roy ACUFF's Smoky Mountain Boys and Lester FLATT and Earl Scruggs' Foggy Mountain Boys; recorded solo for Mercury, RCA, Decca, had minor hit 'Rosebuds And You' '63 on Starday. Albums incl. *Old Time Fiddlin' And Singin'* '58 on Mercury, *With Bobby Sykes* '66 on Hilltop, *Tennessee Jubilee* '77 on Sonet.

MARTIN, Dean (*b* Dino Crocetti, 7 June '17, Steubenville, Ohio) Singer, actor, TV host. Worked as coal miner, boxer, etc; decided to sing instead; in Atlantic City '46 teamed with comic Jerry LEWIS, and the pair made 16 films '49-56, showed affection for earlier comedy by recycling gags such as the Marx Brothers peanut vendor scene on TV's *Colgate Comedy Hour*. When they split up many thought that Martin would disappear while Lewis remained a star: Lewis's films turned self-indulgent, while Martin's laid-back flair for spoofing himself made him a hit on TV '65-74. Over 30 more films incl. some with Frank SINATRA's 'rat pack', of which he was a charter member; straight dramatic roles incl. *The Young Lions* '58; films with John Wayne were *Rio Bravo* '59 and *Sons Of Katie Elder* '65; he also walked through spoof Matt Helm private eye films in the '60s. Of 34 Hot 100 entries '50-'69 in the pop charts, more than half made top 40; from '49 engagement with Lewis at Ciro's in Hollywood he was often backed through '50s by alto-saxist/bandleader Dick Stabile (*b* 29 May '09, Newark, N.J.) incl. such hits as top 5 'That's Amore' '53, from film *The Caddy*, and one of his most charming, two-sided hit 'Sway'/'Money Burns A Hole In My Pocket' '54, the former a Mexican song ('Quien Sera'), the latter written by Bob Hilliard/Jule Styne for film *Living It Up*. 'Memories Are Made Of This' '55 was written by the Easy Riders (Terry GILKYSON, Richard Dehr and Frank Miller), who backed him on the record. 'Return To Me' '58 (co-written by Carmen Lombardo) was no. 4; he moved to Sinatra's Reprise label from Capitol and had no. 1 hit with treacly

'Everybody Loves Somebody' '64: revival of '48 hit by Sinatra became his theme. 'The Door Is Still Open To My Heart' '64 and 'I Will' '65 were top 10; he had 24 chart LPs '62-72, later recorded for WB; of his chart LPs only *Dino – Italian Love Songs* '62 on Capitol remains in print in USA; EMI/Pathé have reissued *A Winter Romance* with Gus Levene orchestra (late '50s) and *Cha Cha de Amor* (early '60s) with Nelson RIDDLE. 2-disc compilation *Dreams And Memories* issued on Pair '86; EMI/UK reissued ballad set *Pretty Baby* '84.

MARTIN, Freddy (*b* 9 Dec. '06, Cleveland, Ohio; *d* 1 Oct. '83) Tenor sax, bandleader. Grew up in orphanage, playing drums in band there; played sax at Ohio State U. with student group booked as off-night replacement for Guy LOMBARDO; played with various bands and formed own band '31-2; gigs at Brooklyn's Hotel Bossert and Manhattan's Roosevelt Grill; recorded as 'Hotel Bossert Orchestra' on Columbia '33, other records under several names incl. Bunny BERIGAN; Martin hits began on Brunswick '33-6, then Bluebird and Victor: the band became one of the most popular sweet dance bands, not far behind Lombardo's, with more than 80 hit records until well into the '50s, Martin's playing earning him designation 'Mr Silvertone'. Vocalists incl. trombonist/arranger Russ MORGAN in early days, Merv Griffin '48-52 (*b* 6 July '25, San Mateo, Cal.; later built empire as TV host), many more in between. 'I Saw Stars'/'Then I'll Be Tired Of You' was big 2-sided hit '34, also 'Isle Of Capri' '35, 'The Hut-Sut Song' '41 (vocal by Eddie Stone), then huge no. 1 hit '41: 'Piano Concerto In B Flat' on Tchaikovsky's most famous tune featuring pianist Jack Fina (13 Aug. '13, Passaic, N.J.; *d* 14 May '70, Cal.; formed own band '46, recorded for Mercury, MGM; also composer). Same year Martin also reached top 10 with 'Tonight We Love', same tune with words by Bobby Worth. Further mining of 'classical' tunes incl. 'Grieg Piano Concerto' '42, 'Bumble Boogie' '46 with Fina (from Rimsky-Korsakov's 'Flight of the Bumblebee'), 'Sabre Dance Boogie' '48 (by Khachaturian); also 'Warsaw Concerto' '43, by Richard Addinsell (1904-77) for UK film *Dangerous Moonlight* (USA title: *Suicide Squadron*), a 2-sided hit with 'From Twi-light 'Til Dawn' (vocal by Bob Haymes). Other big hits: 'Rose O'Day'/'Miss You' '42 (former with vocal by Stone, not listed in Billboard but a no. 1 hit according to *Pop Memories*); Billboard no. 1 hits incl. 'Symphony' '45 (lovely European song of that year, vocal by Clyde Rogers), 'To Each His Own' '46 (a big song of the year: also a hit for Eddy HOWARD, the INK SPOTS, Tony MARTIN, the Modernaires) and 'Managua, Nicaragua' '47. Martin's version of the novelty 'I've Got A Lovely Bunch Of Coconuts' made the top 10 '48, eventually sold a million. The band appeared in films *The Mayor Of 42nd Street* '42; *Hit Parade Of 1943*, *Seven Days Leave*, *Stage Door Canteen*, *What's Buzzin' Cousin?*, all '43; *Melody Time* '48. Last hits '53-4 with 'April In Portugal' and 'Lonesome Polecat' (from film *Seven Brides For Seven Brothers*). Remained a popular leader, with gigs at L.A. Coconut Grove from '38 until venue changed hands '60s; semi-retired '70s, still occasionally at Las Vegas hotels etc.; fronted Lombardo's band '77 when Guy was hospitalised. LPs on Capitol in '50s incl. *Concerto!*, *Salute To The Smooth Bands*, *C'mon Let's Dance*, *As Time Goes By*; also compilations incl. *Shall We Dance* on RCA, *Greatest Hits* on Decca, LP on California's Ranwood label shared with Russ Morgan.

MARTIN, George (*b* 3 Jan. '26, London) Producer. WWII service in Fleet Air Arm, three years at Guildhall School of Music, worked in BBC music library, then as assistant to Oscar Preuss at EMI's Parlophone label. Saw a gap for comedy records and filled it with Peter Ustinov, Peter Sellers and Bernard Cribbins (top 30 hits '62 with 'Hole In The Ground', 'Right Said Fred', 'Gossip Calypso'); also prod. Scots dance band leader Jimmy Shand, leading UK jazzman John DANKWORTH, no. 1 hit 'You're Driving Me Crazy' for trad. band Temperance Seven; dabbled in skiffle with the Vipers whom he spotted in a coffee bar (three hits '57) but turned down Tommy STEELE. When the BEATLES approached him '62 they'd been turned down by majors; he recognised raw talent, encouraged them to change drummers and the rest is history. He prod. other Brian EPSTEIN acts who needed more, not less, from him: he double-tracked Billy J. KRAMER to get hits from his thin voice and found success for Cilla BLACK in spite of an unremarkable voice; he made 3 no. 1 hits in a row for GERRY AND THE PACEMAKERS: from Apr. '63 Martin productions were no. 1 UK 39 out of 52 weeks. His early role was arranger, keyboard player for the Beatles but he soon became a sounding-board for Lennon and McCartney's ideas; his classical training was valuable as they played with strings on 'Yesterday', 'Eleanor Rigby', 'Tomorrow Never Knows' on to 'Strawberry Fields Forever'; he reached an acknowledged apogee of 4-track recording technique with *Sgt Pepper's Lonely Hearts Club Band* '67, using three soon-antiquated machines: he created such sound effects as that at the end of 'For The Benefit Of Mr Kite', for which a tape recording of a steam organ was cut into many small pieces and reassembled. He daringly broke free of EMI's corporate clutches '65, forming Associated Independent Recordings, retaining the Beatles (but receiving only 1% royalty); until then he had not even got credit on LP sleeves, and his move significantly raised the status of producers in pop. Ron Richards (prod. the HOLLIES) and two other young producers joined him in AIR, whose studios in London and (later) Monserrat were and are among the best in the business. He continued to prod. McCartney post-Beatles, also working with AMERICA, Jeff BECK, UFO, Kenny ROGERS, many others, also retaining a foot in the middle-of-the-road with Ella FITZGERALD and Neil SEDAKA. He tends (as with America) to work with an artist over a span of albums, building rapport; inevitably none of these have equalled the Beatles' spectacular fame, but Martin nevertheless remains in the forefront of his trade.

MARTIN, Grady (*b* 17 Jan. '29, Marshall County, Tenn.) Guitarist. One of the most flexible of Nashville session musicians, who adapted to any style and played on countless hits in the '50s-60s, helping to create 'the Nashville Sound'. He started out in the late '40s, sharing with Jabbo Arrington some electrifying twin-lead guitar work on early records by Little Jimmy DICKENS; soon in demand on sessions with Webb PIERCE, Red FOLEY, Carl SMITH, Buddy HOLLY, Bobby HELMS, Marty ROBBINS, Johnny HORTON, etc., also led session group the Slewfoot

Five on Decca in '50s; sessioned in '60s-70s with Joan BAEZ, J. J. CALE, Steve GOODMAN, and Leon RUSSELL; recently toured with Willie NELSON and was teaching Merle HAGGARD to play electric lead. LPs incl. *The Roaring '20s* '57, *Big City Lights* '59, *Touch Of Country* '64, all on Decca; also *Cowboy* on Monument; Slewfoot Five tracks on *Guitar Genius: Hank Garland, Grady Martin & Les Paul* on Charly UK.

MARTIN, Jimmy (*b* James Henry Martin, 10 Aug. '27, Sneedville, Tenn.) Bluegrass singer and bandleader. Worked as housepainter and sang on radio in Morristown, Tenn. '48-9; then lead singer with Bill MONROE '49-53, his strong, reedy voice sliding to and from sustained notes a perfect foil for Monroe's high tenor harmony on many classic records. He recorded with the Osborne Brothers on RCA '54-5, then formed his own Sunny Mountain Boys, working on WJR Barn Dance in Detroit '55. WRVA Richmond '56, Louisiana Hayride '57; signed with Decca '56 and made some outstanding bluegrass LPs in the next 20 years, though shunned by purists for the use of drums. He worked extensively on the Wheeling Jamboree and the Grand Ole Opry, made country charts with hits such as 'Rock Hearts' '56, 'Widow Maker' '64. LPs incl. *Good'n'Country* '58, *Widow Maker* '64, *Big Instrumentals* '66, *Free Born Man* '68, *Singing All Day And Dinner On The Ground* '70, *Fly Me To 'Frisco* '74, all on Decca/MCA; *Me And Ole Pete* and *Will The Circle Be Unbroken* '80 on Gusto.

MARTIN, Mary (*b* 1 Dec. '13, Weatherford, Texas) One of the all-time great ladies of the Broadway theatre. Sang in night clubs, signed to secondary role in *Leave It To Me* '38, brought down the house with 'My Heart Belongs To Daddy', had top 10 hit with it early '39 backed by Eddy DUCHIN. She sang on radio and in films; work with Bing CROSBY incl. duets on Decca, also 'The Waiter And The Porter And The Upstairs Maid', a hit '41 with Crosby and Jack TEAGARDEN (song from film *Birth Of The Blues*). Top 10 hit 'I'll Walk Alone' '44; records with Guy LOMBARDO incl. hit 'Almost Like Being In Love' (from show *Brigadoon*) '47; she starred on Broadway in *One Touch Of Venus* '43, *Lute Song* '46, toured in road show of *Annie Get Your Gun*; became immortal in role of Nellie in *South Pacific* '49, one of the biggest Broadway hits (and one of the first and biggest-selling original cast albums) of all time. Legendary TV special with Ethel MERMAN '53; on stage in *Peter Pan* '54, on TV '55; starred in *Sound Of Music* '59; *Jenny* '63 flopped. Co-starred with Robert Preston in *I Do, I Do* '66; lived in Brazil c.60. She also recorded duets with Arthur GODFREY (top 10 'Go To Sleep' '50) and with her son Larry ('Get Out Those Old Records' c.'51) who grew up to become J. R. Ewing in TV's *Dallas*.

MARTIN, Tony (*b* Alvin Morris, 22 Dec. '12, Oakland, Cal.) Singer. Played sax in dance bands, turned singer, sang on Ray NOBLE hits '38 incl. 'I Hadn't Anyone Till You' '38, had 35 hits of his own '38-54: 'It's A Blue World' '40 (no. 2), 'To Each His Own' '46 (no. 4), but most of his best-known records were adaptations: 'Tonight We Love' '40 from Tchaikovsky, 'There's No Tomorrow' '49 from Italian 'O Sole Mio' (later also Elvis PRESLEY's 'It's Now Or Never'), 'I Get Ideas' '51 from Argentine tango 'Adios Muchachos' '32 (Martin's hit was thought salacious at the time, as though most pop songs did not have genteel sexual innuendo in them), 'Kiss Of Fire' '52 from A. G. Villoldo's tango 'El Choclo' '13, 'Stranger In Paradise' '54 from show *Kismet* (tune from Borodin opera *Prince Igor*), 'Here' '54 from Verdi's *Rigoletto* were all top 10. Of many films the best-known were *The Big Store* '41 with the Marx Brothers, *Casbah* '48, *Deep In My Heart* '54. He was also famous for being married to dancer Cyd Charisse, but his big voice did credit to the hits. RCA LP *Tenement Symphony* reissued '87 in UK.

MARTINEZ, Narcisco (*b* 29 Oct. '11, Tamaulipas, Mexico) Musica norteña accordionist and songwriter (the 'music of the north', heard on the Mexican-Texan border). Grew up in rural Texas, but never naturalised. Began playing one-row instrument c.'27, moved on to two-row; teamed with Santiago Almeida (on bajo sexto) in about '35 and struck it lucky with 'La Chicharronera'/'El Troncónal' on Bluebird (both in *Texas-Mexican Border Music Vol. 10: Narcisco Martinez 'El Huracan del*

Valle' on Folklyric). Recorded many sides, mostly instrumentals, in many dance styles for Bluebird until '40, virtuosity and style earning him the nickname 'the hurricane of the valley'; probably the most-recorded in the genre and among first to tour outside Texas, as far as California. Recorded postwar for Ideal and Falcón, other labels, under his own name or backing acts e.g. Carmen y Laura. Appeared in *Chulas Fronteras* (Brazos Films) '76 with Santiago JIMENEZ Snr, Los Alegres de Teran, others. With Jimenez, whom he greatly influenced, the father of CONJUNTO. Also in LPs *Texas-Mexican Border Music Vol. 4: Norteno Acordeon Part 1*, *Vol. 12 Part 3* on Folklyric; *Chulas Fronteras* and *The Texas-Mexican Conjunto* on Arhoolie.

MARTINO, Al (*b* Alfred Cini, 7 Oct. '27, Philadelphia, Pa.) Singer in nice Italian ballad style *à la* Vic DAMONE, countless others. 'Here In My Heart' was no. 1 '52 with Monty Kelly orchestra (Kelly *b* '19, Oakland, Cal.) on obscure B.B.S. label; he was signed by Capitol, had more hits incl. 'Take My Heart' with Kelly, 'When You're Mine' with Les BAXTER '52-3, disappeared. Came back thanks to TV exposure (America's answer to Val DOONICAN) on 20th Century Fox label '59, switched back to Capitol and had 34 Hot 100 entries '59-77, of which only 'I Love You Because' and 'I Love You More And More Each Day' '63-4 were top 10. He sold albums: 24 in top 200 '62-75, incl. top 10 *I Love You Because* and *Painted, Tainted Rose* '63, *Spanish Eyes* '65. Title single 'Spanish Eyes' was no. 15, aka 'Moon Over Naples', instrumental written by German bandleader Bert Kaemfert (*b* c.'24, Hamburg; *d* 21 June '80), who also had no. 1 hit LP/single *Wonderland By Night* '60, 19 more hit LPs in USA '61-71; also prod. BEATLES' earliest records.

MARTYN, John (*b* '48, Glasgow, Scotland) Guitarist, singer, songwriter. Learned guitar from Scottish folksinger Hamish Imlach and was a sensation on UK folk circuit while still in his teens, his debut album *London Conversation* reflecting roots while *The Tumbler* (also '68) incl. flautist Harold McNair, who had earlier worked with DONOVAN. *Stormbringer* '70 was made in Woodstock, NY with his then-wife Beverly and members of the BAND; *Road To Ruin* was first collaboration with PENTANGLE double bassist Danny Thompson. *Bless The Weather* '71 incl. touching title track, impressive 16-minute instrumental 'Glistening Glyndebourne'; *Solid Air* '73 found him involved with electric guitar and vocal phrasing infl. by veteran bluesmen, with Skip JAMES's 'I'd Rather Go Blind', title track written about his friend Nick DRAKE, his best-known song 'May You Never' and exuberant 'Over The Hill'. *Inside Out* '73 and *Sunday's Child* '75 continued to display eclecticism, the latter incl. version of trad. 'Spencer The Rover'; *One World* '77 was made in Jamaica with reggae dubmaster Lee Perry; *So Far So Good* '77 was a useful compilation of '70s work. *Grace & Danger* '80 marked his collaboration with Phil COLLINS, which continued on *Glorious Fool* '81, which also incl. Eric CLAPTON; *Well Kept Secret* '82 carried on unique musical fusions and *Piece By Piece* '86 celebrated 20 years as a performer, incl. guest, long-time fan Robert PALMER. Live *Philentropy* was made at UK concerts '82-3; *Foundation* '88 was a new studio album. Like Roy HARPER, Martyn has many fans among folk, rock and pop stars, but has yet to receive the wider fame he deserves.

MARVELETTES USA female vocal group formed '61 at Inkster (Mich.) High School as the Marvels to enter a talent contest: founder members (all *b* '44): Gladys Horton (lead), Katherine Anderson, Wanda Young, Juanita Cowart, and Georgeanna Tillman Dobbins (*d* 6 Jan. '80 of sickle cell anaemia). A teacher introduced them to Berry Gordy, they were signed to Tamla, renamed Marvelettes and had 23 hits in the USA Hot 100 '61-9, most notably the first: 'Please Mr Postman' was co-written by Dobbins, who left the group (along with Cowart) very early on; it was no. 1 USA and later covered by the BEATLES. Many of the later hits were written by Smokey ROBINSON. 'Playboy' '62 and 'Don't Mess With Bill' '66 were top 10; 'Beechwood 4-5789' was top 20 '62, later covered by the CARPENTERS; 'When You're Young And In Love' was top 30 USA and their only UK hit (top 20) '67, later covered by the Flying Pickets; the sublime 'My Baby Must Be A Magician' was top 20 USA '68. At the end of the decade the only remain-ing original member was Anderson and the lineups had become virtually anonymous, but their place in pop had been assured.

MASEKELA, Hugh (*b* '39, Witbank, Johannesburg, S.A.) Trumpet, bandleader, composer, singer. Father was a sculptor; raised by a grandmother; began singing and playing piano at an early age, infl. by film *Young Man With A Horn* at 13, obtained a trumpet at 14; along with African musics he was influenced early on by mainstream jazz of the Swing Era, then bop. Played in Huddleston Jazz Band, encouraged by veteran anti-apartheid campaigner Trevor Huddleston; when Huddleston was deported Masekela and Jonas Gwangwa formed the Merry Makers of Springs, experimenting with a fusion of bop and mbaqanga; at 19 he joined the pool of African jazz musicians backing popular singers, touring S.A. and playing in the orchestra for show *King Kong* (*see* Miriam MAKEBA). Finding revue formats restricting, he joined the Jazz Epistles '59 with Dollar Brand (*see* Abdullah IBRAHIM), playing on their eponymous album; apartheid was also heating up and Masekela joined the best talent in the country, along with his then-wife Makeba, Brand and many others, in leaving the country to avoid its stupid cruelty. He was helped by John DANKWORTH, Harry BELAFONTE and Dizzy GILLESPIE; he studied at the Royal Academy of Music in London and the Manhattan School of Music in the USA, and embarked on a career as a jazz musician. Tracks '62-6 on various Mercury and MGM LPs incl. *Trumpet African, The Africanisation Of Oooga Booga, The Lasting Impression Of Hugh Masekela*, 2-disc *24 Karat Hits* on Verve, etc. alternating between original compositions with African titles and covers of contemporary Western pop. He moved to the West Coast and formed Chisa Records, leased material to Uni at first; basically quartet albums sometimes augmented incl. *The Emancipation Of Hugh Masekela, Hugh Masekela's Latest, Alive And Well At The Whiskey a Go-Go, The Promise Of The Future* (incl. 'Grazing In The Grass', written by Philemon Hou: no. 1 USA '68, sold 4m worldwide) and *Masekela*, all '67-9; he sold out Carnegie Hall '68. LPs on Chisa label '70-1 were *Reconstruction*, made in L.A., incl. Monk Montgomery,

Wilton Felder, Wayne Henderson, Joe Sample in 11-piece band, and *Hugh Masekela And The Union Of South Africa*, incl. Gwangwa. The direct inspiration of Africa had been missing; meanwhile he went to Lagos to play with Fela KUTI in Africa '70, made *Home Is Where The Music Is* '72 in London with Eddie Gomez, Dudu PUKWANA, and two others on Blue Thumb, followed by LPs with African group Hedzoleh Sounds: variously titled albums '73-6 on Blue Thumb/Casablanca/Chisa *Introducing Hedzoleh Sounds* (made in Nigeria), *I Am Not Afraid* (adding Sample, Stix Hooper), *The Boy's Doin' It*, *Colonial Man* (Patti AUSTIN among background singers), *The African Connection, Melody Maker*. Returned to USA, made *Herb Alpert/Hugh Masekela* '77 on Horizon; back to Africa, this time nearer home, in Zimbabwe '80, Botswana '82: he persuaded the Jive Africa label to park a mobile sound studio just across the border from S.A.; having established himself as an international star, he is probably making the best music of his career, rejuvenated by mbaqanga, foot-tapping music of freedom once frowned upon by blacks with aspirations. Recent LPs incl. *Home, Dollar Bill, Technobush* '82-4, *Waiting For The Rain* '86; *Tomorrow* '87 is a dance album on WEA.

MASON, Dave (*b* 10 May '46, Worcester, England) UK singer, songwriter, guitarist. First group Jaguars, modelled on Shadows early '60s; then formed Hellions with Jim Capaldi, drums; Luther Grosvenor, guitar; John 'Poli' Palmer, keyboards; later of TRAFFIC, SPOOKY TOOTH, FAMILY respectively: name of group changed to Deep Feeling after Kim-Fowley prod. 'Daydreaming of You'. Mason was a roady for the Spencer DAVIS Group; friendship with Stevie WINWOOD led to Traffic '67, an instant success: he wrote single 'Hole In My Shoe' (no. 2 UK) but left late '67 after first LP *Mr Fantasy*; released solo single 'Just For You', prod. Family LP *Music In A Doll's House*, sessioned on Jimi HENDRIX's *Electric Ladyland* '68, rejoined Traffic for second eponymous LP (one of his four songs, 'Feelin' Alright', much covered e.g. by Joe COCKER, THREE DOG NIGHT, GRAND FUNK, etc.). Joined Traffic splinter group Mason, Capaldi, Wood and Frog; guested with Delaney & Bonnie BRAMLETT,

who played on his first solo LP *Alone Together* with Leon RUSSELL, Capaldi, Rita COOLIDGE: no. 22 LP '70 in USA. In '70 he released *Dave Mason & Cass Elliot* (top 50 LP), played with Derek and the Dominos (having played with Eric CLAPTON in Delaney & Bonnie), rejoined Traffic yet again for live *Welcome To The Canteen*. Projected mostly live 2-disc set released as two single LPs *Headkeeper* '72 and *Dave Mason Is Alive!* '73; he switched from Blue Thumb/MCA to CBS for solid, unspectacular singer/songwriter LPs *It's Like You Never Left* '73 (with Graham Nash, Stevie WONDER), *Dave Mason* '74, *Split Coconut* '75 (with Nash, David CROSBY, MANHATTAN TRANSFER), *Let It Flow* '77, *Mariposa de Oro* '78, all top 50 LPs USA, but ignored in home country. Other LPs incl. 2-disc *Certified Live* '76, compilations on MCA and CBS; *Old Crest On A New Wave* '80 reached no. 74 USA, title summed it up. His fluid, melodic guitar playing is often overlooked; it took Duane ALLMAN to replace him in Derek and the Dominos. *Alone Together* is still thought to be his best.

MATHIS, Country Johnny (*b* 28 Sep. '33, Maud, Texas) Country singer popular in '50s-60s. Began at *Big D Jamboree*, Dallas '52-4; teamed with Jimmy Lee for duets on Chess, Talent and D Records: Jimmy & Johnny made C&W top 10 with 'If You Don't Somebody Else Will' '54 on Chess. Recorded solo for Decca, UA and Little Darlin', made chart with 'Please Talk To My Heart' '63 on UA. A fairly prolific songwriter, his work recorded by Johnny PAYCHECK, George JONES, Webb PIERCE, etc. LPs incl. *Great Country Hits* '64 on UA, *In The House Of The Lord* '67 on Hilltop, *He Keeps Me Singing* '69 on Little Darlin', *Heartfelt* '81 on President.

MATHIS, Johnny (*b* John Royce Mathis, 30 Sep. '35, San Francisco, Cal.) Singer, son of a vaudeville singer. Sang in church choir but initially made his name in athletics as hurdles champion, basketball player and world-class high jumper. Sang at Black Hawk club, signed by manager Helen Noga (co-owner of club), impressed by his range and extraordinary breath control; contract with CBS followed; for a while he tried to maintain athletics and singing concurrently but had to choose between Olympic trials and recording sessions '56: 'Wonderful Wonderful' went top 15 '57; first chart LP same year had same title, but the hit wasn't on it. 'It's Not For Me To Say' was no. 5, 'Chances Are' no. 1 and its other side 'The Twelfth Of Never' top 10, all '57: no one who was a teenager then will ever forget those hits, with his light baritone and unusual, fast vibrato lending a wistful, bittersweet quality to love songs. He had 40 Billboard Hot 100 entries '57-73; cover of Erroll GARNER's 'Misty' was no. 12 '59, 'Gina' and 'What Will Mary Say' made top 10 '62-3; duet hit 'Too Much, Too Little, Too Late' with Deniece Williams was no. 1 '78; another with Dionne WARWICK 'Friends In Love' was top 40 '82 (they each had a chart LP of that title '82-3). He never equalled '57 in singles charts, but remained extremely popular in concert and a phenomenal album seller, with 64 albums in top 200 '57-84. Top 10 LPs (not counting annual appearance of *Merry Christmas* five years in a row) incl. his first 11 LPs '57-60: *Johnny's Greatest Hits* '58 (stayed in the charts for 10 years) and *Heavenly* '59 (incl. 'Misty') were no. 1; 2-disc *Rhythms And Ballads Of Broadway* '60 reached no. 6. Other best-selling LPs were *Portrait Of Johnny* '61 (no. 2), *Johnny's Newest Hits* '63. After a court case he parted with Noga '64, switched to Mercury (*Tender Is The Night* '64 was no. 13; *The Shadow Of Your Smile* '66 went top 10); he had a problem with pills but kicked it; he returned to Columbia '68 where he's been ever since. 2-disc *Johnny Mathis' All-Time Greatest Hits* '72 reached only no. 172 in Billboard, but kept selling and went gold; duet albums with Williams *You Light Up My Life* (incl. no. 1 hit) and *That's What Friends Are For* reached top 10 and top 20 respectively in '78. 31 sets currently available incl. 2-disc package of *Warm* ('57, with Percy FAITH) and *Open Fire, Two Guitars* ('59, with Al CAIOLA and Tony Mottola); also 2-disc *Silver Anniversary Album: The First 25 Years*. He continued selling singles in the UK incl. disco-flavoured 'I'm Coming Home' and 'I'm Stone In Love With You' '73-5, both prod. by Thom Bell; Xmas song 'When A Child Is Born' '76 was his first UK no. 1. He has now had albums in the charts nearly every year for nearly 30 years, a record not

many will match; eight of his albums and compilations are already out on CD.

MATTHEWS, Ian (*b* Ian Macdonald, June '46, Lincolnshire) Vocalist, guitarist. He was a teenage footballer, moved to London and formed band Pyramid, then joined FAIRPORT CONVENTION, playing on *Fairport Convention* '67, *What We Did On Our Holidays* '68 (incl. 'Book Song', his best known with the band) and *Unhalfbricking* '69, though by then he'd left to form Matthews Southern Comfort, a C&W band with Gordon Huntly, one of the UK's best pedal steel players. They had UK no. 1 '70 with Joni MITCHELL's 'Woodstock'; LPs *Matthews Southern Comfort*, *Second Spring* and *Later That Same Year* all c.'70 were pleasant. He left; the band struggled on for a while as Southern Comfort ('Best Of' compilation '75 was unsatisfactory, issued despite his public disapproval). His solo albums began with *If You Saw Through My Eyes* '71, with Fairport alumni; *Tigers Will Survive* '72 was a strong album; great things were expected from his new band Plainsong (incl. guitarist Andy Roberts), but they split after promising start with *In Search Of Amelia Earhart* '72. *Valley Hi* '73 was prod. by Mike NESMITH, an admirer of Matthews' work; *Some Days You Eat The Bear* '73 and *Journeys From Gospel Oak* '74 pleased the fans; *Go For Broke* '76 had him working with celebrated Nashville session player Norbert Putnam. *Hit And Run* '77 was lacklustre, *Stealin' Home* '78 was stronger, and his best effort in the USA, where it was his third chart entry and reached no. 80 in Billboard. *Siamese Friends* '79 did not do well; *Spot Of Interference* was a strong rock album with ARGENT's Robert Henrit, incl. Matthews' 'I Survived The 70s'. *Discreet Repeat* '80 was a good 2-disc compilation, showing his style on songs by Tim HARDIN, Tom WAITS, John MARTYN and Robert PALMER. He appeared at Fairport's '86 reunion concert, first time he'd sung with them in nearly 20 years.

MAY, Billy (*b* 10 Nov. '16, Pittsburgh, Pa.) Trumpet; arranger and bandleader. Wrote hit arr. 'Cherokee', 'Pompton Turnpike' etc. for Charlie BARNET '38-40; with Glenn MILLER played trumpet solos on classics 'Song Of The Volga Boatmen', 'American

Patrol', arr. 'Ida', 'At Last', 'Serenade In Blue' (last two with Bill Finegan), many others: resented Miller, who did not always give credit where credit was due. Played, arranged, conducted on radio '40s; mus. dir. and played trumpet on septet session for ex-Jimmie LUNCEFORD star Willie SMITH at Keynote '45. Formed own popular band '50 in Lunceford mould: his writing for unison reeds became instantly recognisable; sold the band to Ray ANTHONY '54; on staff at Capitol records he made LPs with Peggy LEE (*Pretty Eyes*), George SHEARING (*Burnished Brass*), Jeri SOUTHERN (*Meets Cole Porter*); worked with Nat King COLE (hit singles 'Walkin' My Baby Back Home' '52, 'Can't I?' '53, more), Frank SINATRA (*Come Fly With Me, Come Dance With Me, Come Swing With Me*). As one of the best-known in the field he branched out: works incl. Bing CROSBY – Rosemary CLOONEY LP *Fancy Meeting You Here* on RCA, Ella FITZGERALD's *Sings The Harold Arlen Songbook* and two albums with Anita O'DAY on Verve, *Sinatra Swings* and *Francis A. And Edward K.* (with Duke ELLINGTON) on Reprise. TV and film work incl. theme for hit TV show *Naked City*. Also mus. dir. on some of Stan FREBERG's comedy records at Capitol; wearing Hawaiian shirt at sessions, he was described affectionately by Freberg as looking like a porpoise at a luau. His infl. has entered the mainstream of American music. Capitol LPs '50s incl. *Big Band Bash, A Band Is Born, Bacchanalia, Sorta-May, The Great Jimmie Lunceford, Fancy Dancing, Naughty Operetta*, some now digitally remastered and reissued by EMI.

MAYALL, John (*b* 29 Nov. '33, Macclesfield, Cheshire) UK R&B bandleader; also vocalist, guitarist, writer producer; also harmonica and keyboards, but mainly a leader who was largely responsible for shaping '60s rock: many of its biggest stars passed through his hands. His interest in blues grew as a teenager; after national service he formed Powerhouse Four while at college '55, built reputation backing visiting USA bluesmen. Came to London '62-3 at behest of blues godfather Alexis KORNER; formed first Bluesbreakers with bassist John McVie, drummer Peter Ward, Bernie Watson on guitar, replaced by Hughie Flint (*b* 15 Mar.

'42) and Roger Dean before recording *John Mayall Plays John Mayall* '65. Adding Eric CLAPTON on lead guitar made classic Bluesbreakers lineup: Clapton had made his name in the YARDBIRDS, but left in protest at their pop direction; he revelled in trad. blues format and *Bluesbreakers – John Mayall With Eric Clapton* '65 was no. 6 LP in UK, served as a rock guitar primer for Gary MOORE and for uncounted others: 'Steppin' Out' was a standout track. Jack Bruce replaced McVie; he and Clapton left '66 to form CREAM; Mayall rebuilt the band, replacing Flint with Aynsley DUNBAR and Clapton with Peter Green, re-hiring McVie. *A Hard Road* showed Green to be as impressive as Clapton in his own way, while Mayall's sleeve note promised no horns. But history repeated itself: Green and McVie left to form FLEETWOOD MAC; tired of virtuoso guitarists, Mayall hired Dick Heckstall-Smith on sax, ex-Artwoods drummer Keef Hartley and unknown guitarist Mick Taylor for *Crusade* '67, 2-disc live set *Diary Of A Band*; while Mayall himself recorded *The Blues Alone* with Hartley. He introduced a new set of musicians for *Bare Wires* '68: Taylor and Heckstall-Smith were joined by Henry Lowther, trumpet, bassist Tony Reeves and drummer Jon Hiseman; this last Bluesbreakers lineup left to form COLOSSEUM, Taylor later replacing Brian Jones in the ROLLING STONES. Mayall's albums were henceforth credited to him alone, ever-changing personnel incl. bassist Steve Thompson, drummer Colin Allen (later with Stone The Crows), guitarist Jon Mark and Johnny Almond on sax and flute (later a jazz duo Mark-Almond). The former pair with Taylor and Mayall made *Blues From Laurel Canyon* '69, suggesting an alignment with USA musics; the latter two joined Mayall and Thompson in daring drummerless quartet for *The Turning Point* '70. *Back To The Roots* '71 reunited Mayall, Clapton, Hartley and Taylor for a nostalgic LP. Mayall relocated to the USA, continued to work there and declined in influence as his blues was tempered with soul; *Notice To Appear* '76 on Polydor was made with Allen TOUSSAINT; *Lots Of People* in the same year on ABC was made live in L.A. He recruited McVie and Taylor for a reunion tour '82, but had all but retired from music. His son Gary DJs in London ('Gaz's Rockin'

Blues'), a walking encyclopedia of Jamaican music.

MAYFIELD, Curtis (*b* 3 June '42, Chicago, Ill.) Singer, writer, producer, label boss; a significant force in black pop since he was a teenager. Sang in gospel groups; formed the Impressions '57 with Jerry BUTLER; 'For Your Precious Love' '58 was top 10 R&B hit, no. 11 pop on Vee Jay's Abner label; Butler went solo and Mayfield wrote and played guitar on his no. 1 R&B hit 'He Will Break Your Heart' '60 (no. 7 pop) on Vee Jay; kept the Impressions going on ABC with 'Gypsy Woman' (later covered by Ry COODER), 'It's All Right', 'I'm So Proud', many more, singing lead, often writing and producing for 38 Hot 100 hits '61-75, most of them huge hits in the soul chart. Meanwhile he also worked on staff for Okeh and formed his own labels, created hits for Major Lance, Gene CHANDLER, others; he formed Curtom label c.'68 and left the Impressions to go solo, but he continued to direct them (2-disc compilation *Curtis Mayfield/His Early Years With The Impressions* '73 on ABC reached top 200 LPs). Chandler and the Impressions were on Curtom and his solo albums hit the pop charts from the start: *Curtis* '71, 2-disc *Curtis/Live!* and *Roots* '72; then the hip, danceable *Superfly* '72, soundtrack from blaxploitation film, was no. 1 LP USA for four weeks. *Back To The World* '73 was top 20 LP; live *Curtis In Chicago* '73 with guests Butler, Chandler, the Impressions surprisingly only reached no. 135; *Sweet Exorcist* and *Got To Find A Way* '74 did better; *There's No Place Like America Today, Give, Get, Take And Have, Never Say You Can't Survive* '75-7 hovered below top 100 LPs. Curtom was distributed by Buddah, WB, then RSO; *Heartbeat* '79 on RSO was top 50 LP, followed by duet LP *The Right Combination* with Linda Clifford and *Something To Believe In* '80, which didn't do as well. Others incl. *Do It All Night* '78, *Love Is The Place* '81 on Boardwalk; *We Come In Peace With A Message Of Love* '85 on CRC keeps the faith: talent and optimism have earned permanent stardom.

MAYFIELD, Percy (*b* 12 Aug. '20, Minden, La.; *d* 11 Aug. '84, L.A.) Singer, songwriter, pianist. Son of dancer father, singer mother; settled in Houston, Texas mid-'30s; to West Coast late '40s, records for Specialty with Amos MILBURN, Cecil GANT, Jesse BELVIN, etc., helped pioneer modern urban R&B that soon had crossover appeal. With Chess in Chicago '55; wrote standard 'Please Send Me Someone To Love', featured by Joe WILLIAMS with Count BASIE, also a hit for the Moonglows '57. Recorded for Imperial '59, Cash '60; wrote for Ray CHARLES ('Hit The Road, Jack' no. 1 '61; 'Hide Nor Hair' no. 20 '62). Soft-voiced singer never had deserved personal success. Recorded for RCA (*Blues – And Then Some* '71), Atlantic, TRC (*Bought Blues*); often at Chantilly Lace Club L.A. mid-'70s. Compilations incl. *The Incredible Percy Mayfield* on Sonet UK; *My Heart Is Always Singing Sad Songs* on Ace (Specialty sides incl. eight previously unreleased); *Greatest Hits* on Specialty USA.

MBALAX The national pop style of Senegal, emerging there in the '70s. Senegalese music was heavily infl. first by Calypso and then by Latin, especially Cuban music; elements of soul and funk were introduced in the '60s, with imported Congolese music equally popular; in '70s a specifically Senegalese brew began to emerge, a return to roots also being encouraged by Senghor's philosophy of Negritude. Drawing on the kora tradition and other local elements as well as Cuban influences, and making use of Western instruments, mbalax slowly defined itself: essentially percussion-based, featuring the tama (a small talking drum) as a lead instrument, it also uses congas, timbales, electric guitars and horns; characterised by complex rhythms, it is usually sung in Wolof, with distinct Islamic inflections. Of many Mbalax bands in Senegal, the most popular is that led by Youssou N'DOUR. Other leading groups are Super Jamono (albums incl. *Le Ventilateur, Geedy Dayaan*), Orchestra Boabab (*Coumba* on MCA) and Guelewar (*Sama Yaye Demna N'Darr*). Many top bands feature on a good compilation, *Panorama du Sénégal Vol. 1* on MCA.

MBAQANGA The dance music of the black townships of South Africa, emerging in the '30s and still popular 50 years later. A stomping music with a powerful bass part underpinning the guitars, it drew on a number of earlier forms to emerge as a new pop style. The South African music industry remains the most highly developed in Africa; the first Bantu recordings were made '12, with the first recording studio established '31 by Eric Gallo. Most of the music is derived from the collision of Zulu/Sotho music with Afro-American styles; out of this has grown township jazz, pennywhistle kwela and shebeen-inspired marabi. Mbaqanga drew on all of these, and when the record companies recorded the bands and gave them airplay, the music grew rapidly in popularity. The term itself is derived from the word for a quickly made steamed mealie bread, and was apparently first used in connection with music by Mike Xaba to mean quick money; it is also used today to mean something like 'jive', for all the township musics. Mbaqanga bands today usually have a modern electric lineup with drums, bass, vocals, guitars, perhaps brass; they are characterised by guitars, vocals and brass entering at different points, providing a unique dance rhythm. Good compilations incl. two vols. of *Zulu Jive* on Earthworks, *Rhythms Of Resistance* on Shan, *Soweto Street Music: The Definitive Collection* on Zensor.

MBARGA, Prince Nico (*b* Nicholas Mbarga, '50, Abakaliki, Nigeria) Singer, composer, guitarist, bandleader. Born of Cameroonian father and Nigerian mother; grew up in Cross River State among the Etura people. He first mastered the traditional wooden xylophone, then began his musical career in high school bands; in '69 the family fled to Cameroon during the Nigerian civil war; he played in a hotel band called the Melody Orchestra, starting on congas, moving through trap drums, bass and rhythm guitar before settling on lead guitar. He returned to Nigeria '72 with other musicians and played panko – a combination of highlife, Congo and makossa – at the Plaza Hotel in Onitsha, having a hit single 'I No Go Marry Me Papa' '73; a series of singles failed to score until Prince Nico and his Rockafil Jazz released 'Sweet Mother' '76, from an LP of the same name: sung in pidgin English to enhance its appeal, it remained a best seller for more than two years, made him a household name and is still perhaps the best-known African pop song ever. He

never equalled it, but a series of albums of dance music have maintained a high standard and have been successful enough so that he owns a hotel/night club in Onitsha and the Sweet Mother hotel in Calabar. LPs, each better than the last, all on the Rogers All Stars label, incl. *Music Line, Free Education* and *Good Father* '77; *No Die No Rest* and *Happy Birthday* '78; *Family Movement* and *Cool Money* '79; *Polygamy* '80 and *Lucky Marriage* '81. Hits compilations incl. *Best Of* and *Akie Special; Let Them Say* '82 came out on Polydor. In '83 four of the members of his band were expelled from Nigeria as Cameroonians, under a government policy of expulsion of aliens; this put a stop to the series for a while as he rebuilt the band.

MBULU, Letta (*b* Orlando, South Africa) Singer, composer. Like so many of S.A.'s top musicians, she now lives in exile, with her husband Caiphus Semenya (singer, composer, arranger, producer). She performed with African Jazz and Variety, with Hugh MASEKELA, Semenya and Miriam MAKEBA (with whom she later worked as the Skylarks). Still in her teens she appeared in London with the hit S.A. musical *King Kong*; later a three-week NYC engagement '64 confirmed international stardom. In '74 she was named best performer at Onda Nueva World Music Festival in Venezuela. Toured with Harry BELAFONTE '77-81. Albums *Music In The Air* and *Sacred Drums* appeared '77, *Letta* '78; also *Naturally* on Fantasy USA; her most recent LP is *Sound Of A Rainbow*. She has now been at the top of African music for a quarter of a century.

MCA Record label. Began as Music Corporation of America, a booking agency formed by Jules Stein before WWII; moved into management, films (Universal Studios), music publishing; entered record business early '60s, buying Decca USA, which had begun '34 as a subsidiary of DECCA UK: Sir Edward Lewis hired Jack Kapp to run it; Kapp made USA Decca the second biggest USA label for a time, selling records cheaply during the Depression (which had worked for Lewis in the UK), roster incl. Louis ARMSTRONG, Bing CROSBY (the best-selling recording artist of the first half of the century by a wide margin), the AN-

DREWS SISTERS, Count BASIE, Jimmy DORSEY, Guy LOMBARDO, Art TATUM etc. Historic Brunswick and Vocalion label names and recordings incl. titles by Duke ELLINGTON, Fletcher HENDERSON etc. were purchased from CBS late '30s. Jack Kapp and his brother Dave (1904-76) had operated a music store in Chicago '21-31; Dave was a vice-president at Decca '35-52, worked for RCA '52-3, formed own Kapp label '54-67, sold it to MCA. (Another brother, Paul, was a pianist songwriter, producer; had worked in MCA's radio dept '30-3.) Jack Kapp initially signed Basie to a contract that would not have paid any royalties; at the height of the BOOGIE WOOGIE craze he tried to copyright those words, so that any song title using them would have earned him money. But by the time he died '49 his legacy was a more open-minded attitude to genres than the other majors had; he made many records that deserve reissue, to say nothing of infl. hits by Louis JORDAN; Decca's traditional interest in country music was marked by big Ernest TUBB hit 'I'm Walking The Floor Over You' '43. Acts in the '50s incl. the WEAVERS, Bill HALEY (prod. by Milt Gabler, who had prod. Jordan, before that founded Commodore, one of the best-loved jazz labels of late '30s), with Buddy HOLLY on subsidiary Coral, CRICKETS on Brunswick; country music remained important: Brenda LEE and Patsy CLINE (both big crossover successes), Webb PIERCE, Kitty WELLS, Tubb, many more. Rick NELSON and Loretta LYNN were added '60s, from the UK the WHO; later Neil DIAMOND (on Uni), POINTER SISTERS were big. Labels acquired by MCA over the years incl. ABC, ABC-Paramount, Bluesway, Chess, Impulse, Dot, Dunhill, Enoch LIGHT's Command and the venerable USA classical indie Westminster. In '74 all the labels were grouped together as MCA; in the UK product was switched to EMI, breaking last link with UK Decca; later MCA tried to establish overseas subsidiaries but failed; operated in the USA, UK and Canada, with product licensed to WB for the rest of the world. MCA seemed to flounder: the first-class technology lavished by Command on records by the Pittsburgh S.O. cond. by William Steinberg went out of print c.'72 and the orchestra had no redress; in an interview Steinberg

exploded, 'Gangsters! That's what they are! Gangsters!' MCA was apparently unaware of the riches it owned; valuable historical tracks went in and out of print in various countries, often in awful phoney stereo, while the contemporary catalogue wasn't up to much; gossip was that the country music had carried the label for a long time. But the winds of change were blowing in the record industry: the press office of MCA UK was useless to the editor of this book, unable to answer questions about its own artists, but there was a shakeup '87 and things seemed to improve. Meanwhile producer/exec. Jimmy Bowen in the USA helped Reba MCENTIRE to win every award country music can bestow; MCA's new Master series made albums by UK-born guitarist Albert Lee, dobro genius Jerry Douglas and others, immaculately recorded instrumental music with country-rock flavour (a bit NEW AGE, but more fun than most of that genre); and MCA signed Steve EARLE, Lyle LOVETT and Nanci GRIFFITH, among best 'new country' talents, Tony Brown often co-producing with the artists; if the quality of much of today's country music breaks through to the success it deserves, MCA will be well placed for international success after all.

MC5 Raucous rock band formed '67, Detroit; name probably stood for Motor City Five. Lineup: Rob Tyner, vocals; Wayne Kramer (b 30 Apr. '48, Detroit), guitar; Fred 'Sonic' Smith, guitar; Rob Tyner, vocals; Michael Davis, bass; Dennis Thompson, drums. Shouting revolution and profanity, they were commercially unsuccessful but an infl. on later punk. They played for riots in Chicago '68; debut LP *Kick Out The Jams* '69 on Elektra (recorded live '68) incl. lyric with 'motherfucker' in it; it was top 30 LP but some shops would not stock it. Manager (John Sinclair of the White Panther Party) was jailed for marijuana; Elektra dropped them; Atlantic signed them and rock critic Jon Landau prod. *Back In The USA* '70, hailed by rock critics but reached only no. 137 in Billboard; *High Time* '71 did not chart. They struggled solo in various capacities; Kramer was jailed for dealing in cocaine, returned to music and played on Was – Not Was single 'Wheel Me Out'.

MEATLOAF (*b* Marvin Lee Aday, 27 Sep. '47, Dallas, Texas) Rock singer, actor. Early work with local R&B and rock bands followed by move to West Coast, role in touring prod. of *Hair*; moved to Detroit, recorded *Stoney & Meat Loaf* '71 (reissued '79 with names reversed). Met playwright/songwriter/keyboardist/arranger Jim Steinman '73, auditioning for a play; played rocker Eddie in film *Rocky Horror Picture Show* '75 and was album highlight with 'Whatever Happened To Saturday Night': Steinman and backing singer Ellen Foley were also involved in *Rocky*; they made Wagnerian rock'n'roll LP *Bat Out Of Hell* '77, prod. by Todd RUNDGREN, with Meatloaf's songs drawing unashamedly on sweeping rock styles of Bob SEGER and Bruce SPRINGSTEEN; it reached no. 14 USA and went platinum, stayed in the UK charts five years: lengthy soap-opera tracks 'You Took The Words Right Out Of My Mouth' and 'Paradise By The Dashboard Light' appealed to those still keen on overblown 'progressive' rock; critics are still trying to figure it out, but Meatloaf's exuberance rewarded. Predictably, a follow-up was difficult: *Dead Ringer* '81 was more of the same but not as successful, though CHER and Springsteen's E-Street Band appeared; epics incl. title track and 'Read 'Em And Weep'. Steinman made solo album *Bad For Good* '81 and successful collaboration with Bonnie TYLER; Meatloaf acted in film *Americathon* '79 and engagingly with BLONDIE's Debbie Harry in *Roadie* '80. Overblown rock was definitely out of style in LP *Midnight At The Lost & Found* '83; *Bad Company* was more disciplined, with Roger Daltrey as guest vocalist on title track, gloriously overproduced 'Modern Girl' (no. 17 UK hit '84). *Hits Out Of Hell* '85 was virtually a *Bat* reissue, *Blind Before I Stop* '86 returned to epic style incl. duet with John Parr on 'Rock'n'Roll Mercenaries'. His hard-rocking power appeals, and tongue-in-cheek attitude to larger-than-life image.

MEEK, Joe (*b* Robert Meek, '29, Newent, Glos.; *d* 3 Feb. '67) UK producer. Emerged from national service as radar technician; went into TV as engineer, thence to records as 'balance engineer' at IBC studios, one of only two independent studios in London mid-'50s. Engineered artists for Pye and Philips; transferred to the other indie Landsdowne, worked on early Lonnie DONEGAN hits. Began writing songs, e.g. 'Put A Ring On Her Finger' for Tommy STEELE; designed new studio for Lansdowne; went freelance, building own studio above a North London shop; formed own Triumph label, which was ahead of its time despite no. 7 hit '60 with Michael Cox's 'Angela Jones'; thenceforth leased work to majors through RGM Sound. Robert Stigwood actor protégé John Leyton scored no. 1 with 'Johnny Remember Me' '61; team of Meek, arr. Charles Blackwell, writer Geoff Goddard followed up with no. 2 'Wild Wind': dated now, they were remarkable for being made in converted bathroom, toilet and living room on secondhand equipment. 'Tribute To Buddy Holly' '61 by Mike Berry and the Outlaws (no. 24) was followed by other hits by the Outlaws and the TORNADOS, house bands on other Meek records, characterised by 'overdriven' sound; 'Telstar' by the Tornados was USA/UK no. 1 (though writers of a similar French song sued for breach of copyright). Beatlemania sounded warning knell for Meek; with rivals more in touch with trends (Shel Talmy, Andrew Oldham, Mickie MOST) and despite Tornados follow-ups and no. 5 for their former bass player Heinz with 'Just Like Eddie', his hits faded after his last no. 1, the Honeycombs' 'Have I The Right' '64; he hadn't moved from his studio and it had become inadequate; the introverted innovator committed suicide on the eighth anniversary of Buddy Holly's death. The records acquired value in the hands of collectors (e.g. RGM Appreciation Society); 'Tornado' and its like arguably predated synth pop by 20 years, while use of backward tape effects and treated domestic noises (like flushing toilet) made him one of a kind.

MELACHRINO, George (*b* '09, London; *d* June '65) Vocalist, composer, arranger, conductor; played viola, reeds incl. oboe, piano. From musical family; began composing at age 4; played solo violin in public at 13; formed jazz band at Trinity College; broadcast on BBC from '27, star billing by '38; played in Savoy Orpheans. Led the British Band of the Allied Expeditionary Force

(AEF): Glenn MILLER led the USA one, Robert FARNON the Canadian; Melachrino sang with all three. Post-war formed Melachrino Music Organisation, generating concerts, broadcasts, recordings, film music etc., incl. the Melachrino Orchestra, Melachrino Strings, the Blue Rockets, Masqueraders, Jack Cole's Music Masters, etc. He wrote music for revue *Starlight Roof*; about 15 film scores incl. *No Orchids For Miss Blandish* '48, said to be one of the worst films ever made. He made about 100 78s, mostly on HMV; more than 50 LPs '50s (mostly on RCA in USA) incl. mood music series *Music For Dining, Music For Relaxation, Music For Two People Alone, Music To Help You Sleep, Music For Faith And Inner Calm*, etc.; later stereo LPs on ABC Paramount *Light Classics In Hi-Fi, Melachrino's Magic Strings*. His writing for a chamber-music-sized string orchestra was better than average in this genre, his harmonic touch distinguishable from the rest.

MELANIE (*b* Melanie Safka, 3 Feb. '47, Queens, NYC) Singer/songwriter. Single 'Beautiful People' on Columbia flopped c.'67; came back on Buddah with album *Born To Be* '69, incl. 'What Have They Done To My Song, Ma', a hit in France and covered by the New Seekers for top 15 USA hit. *Melanie* '69 was followed by top 20 LP *Candles In The Rain* '70, incl. 'Lay Down (Candles In The Rain)', no. 6 title hit written after her appearance at Woodstock: it was her fans who started the fad for holding aloft candles, matches at concerts. Top 40 'Peace Will Come (According To Plan)' was a typically optimistic prediction of the period; live *Leftover Wine*, studio LP *The Good Book* '70-1 on Buddah were followed by top 15 LP *Gather Me* '71 on Neighborhood, own label with manager/husband Peter Schekeryk, incl. no. 1 hit 'Brand New Key'. From then on it was downhill as her childlike voice and demeanour no longer enchanted: *Garden In The City* and 2-disc compilation *Four Sides Of Melanie* '71-2 didn't do as well; *Stoneground Words* '72 on Neighborhood was no. 70 LP; 2-disc live *Melanie At Carnegie Hall* and studio LP *Madrugada* were the last to chart. Other albums incl. *As I See It Now* and *Sunset And Other Beginnings* '74-5, *Photograph* '76 on Atlantic; *Phonogenic/Not Just Another Pret-*

ty Face '78 on Midsong/RCA boasted BRECKER Brothers and David SANBORN among backing musicians, plus mus. dir. Hugh McCracken on guitar, had four Safka songs, covers of BEATLES, MAMAS & PAPAS, but didn't make it. *Ballroom Streets* '79 on RCA was followed by single 'One More Try' '81 on Portrait, which almost made Hot 100.

MELCHER, Terry (*b* 8 Feb '42, NYC) Producer, vocalist. Son of Doris DAY and trombonist Al Jorden, who later committed suicide; took surname of Day's later husband Marty Melcher. He initially recorded with little success as Terry Day, then with Bruce Johnson as Bruce & Terry and as the Rip Chords; he also prod. his mother's last chart LP *Love Him!* '64, single 'Move Over Darling' same year (top 10 UK, did not chart USA). He prod. the BYRDS first LPs, *Mr Tambourine Man* and *Turn! Turn! Turn!*, each incl. hits; then Paul REVERE and the Raiders on four LPs '65-7; obscure duo Gentle Soul, with Ry COODER and Van Dyke PARKS among backing; also prod. Pat BOONE, Wayne NEWTON; co-wrote songs with Bobby DARIN, etc.; and was a director of the original Monterey Pop Festival, member of the board of Monterey Pop Foundation. Marty Melcher failed at everything he did, resented his stepson's obvious success; when he died mid-'68 his poor financial investments had lost Day and her son enormous sums; Terry's position as executor meant months of arduous dealing with lawyers. During this period he went to a commune to audition a hippy songwriter named Charles Manson, but turned him down; in mid-'69 Manson and his tribe of spaced-out acolytes went to a rented house owned by Melcher and committed five bizarre and brutal murders, the crime of the decade: Melcher hired bodyguards for himself and his mother until the trial was over, but suffered a breakdown and was badly injured in a motorcycle accident to boot. He prod. three more LPs by the Byrds '70-1 (incl. their last hit 'Chestnut Mare'), but real comeback was own solo LP *Terry Melcher* '74 on Reprise, overlooked and underrated but incl. fine cover of Jackson BROWNE's 'These Days'. Formed prod. company with Johnson mid-'70s: Equinox prod. David CASSIDY, Barry MANN's *Survi-*

vor (another underrated album), Melcher's disappointing *Royal Flush* (RCA/Equinox). Came to UK late '70s to prod. eponymous LP for group Freeway; prod. TV's *Doris Day's Best Friends* '85. Successful producer had career blighted by horror, but some of his work is still selling; he gave his stepfather credit for ambition to achieve: 'It doesn't matter where you get your ass kicked, Versailles or a six-floor walk-up, the motivation is the same.' (Quote from A. E. Hotchner's *Doris Day: Her Own Story* '75.)

MELLENCAMP, John Cougar (*b* 7 Oct. '51, Seymour, Ind.) USA rock singer. Working-class kid of Dutch extraction learned his music from black Detroit and Chicago radio stations; sidetracked by failed marriage at 18; wrote first song at 23. Took demo of Paul REVERE and the Raiders' 'Kicks' to NYC, where David BOWIE manager Tony DeFries christened him Johnny Cougar, prod. LP of covers *Chestnut Street Incident* '76 (on MCA). Demo-quality material not up to scratch; label, artist, manager parted company. Better luck on Riva label with another superstar manager, Billy Gaff (Rod STEWART): *A Biography* '78 not released in USA; but Australian hit 'I Need A Lover' incl. on eponymous '79 LP: no. 64 album, no. 28 single USA. Two more top 40 hits in similar AOR mode from *Nothing Matters And What If It Did* '80 (no. 37 album), prod. by Steve Cropper: 'This Time' and 'Ain't Even Done With The Night'. Though music often cliché-ridden, sub-James-Dean act won him substantial cult status; *American Fool* '82 had better songwriting; was no. 1 LP (best-seller of '82) with no. 2 single 'Hurts So Good', no. 1 'Jack And Diane' (articulating working-class life: 'Life goes on/Long after the thrill is gone'). Toured with band (Larry Crane, Mike Wanchic, guitars; Toby Meyers; bass; Kenny Arnoff, drums); prod. comeback album for boyhood hero Mitch RYDER (*Never Kick A Sleeping Dog* '83). Attached real surname to unsolicited stage name DeFries saddled him with ('I'm stuck with it . . . I just laugh about it now'), returned to top 10 with 'Crumblin' Down', 'Pink Houses' '83-4, both from LP *Uh-Huh* (no. 9); *Scarecrow* '85 made USA no. 2. Pat BENATAR had covered 'I Need A Lover'; he wrote 'Colored Lights' for the BLASTERS.

Billboard said he was the first living male artist in a decade with an LP and two singles in the top 10 at once; another single from *Scarecrow* made it early '86. Regarded as lightweight in UK, where only hit was no. 25 'Jack And Diane': he began by suiting the American predilection for well-manicured rebels, but he seemed to be growing: blues-tinged *The Lonesome Jubilee* '87 incl. dobro, fiddle, accordion, moving towards what might be called the new classic USA mainstream, and he still lives in Seymour.

MELLY, George (*b* 17 Aug. '26) UK singer. Sang with Mick Mulligan jazz band '51-62; drew popular Flook comic strip '56-71; worked as journalist. Scandalous/hilarious book *Owning Up* about jazz career attracted attention; the spirit of his music had not been washed away by rock'n'roll after all: he returned to singing with John CHILTON '73; had BBC TV show *Good Time George*. A great admirer of Bessie SMITH; a popular and likeable raconteur on TV shows about jazz, wearing outrageous clothes (one of the few Brits who looks like an American tourist). Views on music are a bit mouldy fig: jazz should be 'good time music', as though Smith's art came from starring on Broadway. LPs with Chilton's Feetwarmers incl. *Nuts* (he was famous for cover of Eva Taylor's 'Hot Nuts'), followed *Son Of Nuts* '73 on WEA, *Melly Is At It Again* '76 on Reprise; *Sings Hoagy* '78 (from Ronnie SCOTT's Club), *Sings Fats Waller* '79, *Let's Do It* '80, *Like Sherry Wine* '81, *Makin' Whoopee* '83, all on Pye/PRT. Other books incl. *I Flook* '62, *Revolt Into Style* (rock criticism), more autobiography *Rum, Bum And Concertina* '77, *Mellymobile* '83.

MELROSE, Lester (*b* 1891, Olney, Ill.) Music publisher, talent scout, record producer. Involved with brothers, associated with King OLIVER, Jelly Roll Morton '20s; with Gennett record label, later with ARC; when the worst of the Depression was over and juke boxes were being placed in taverns all over the country, he wrote to Victor and Columbia offering to provide 'race' records and later claimed to have recorded 90% of the genre released by the major labels '34-51. The number of great black artists he was associated with is astonishing: Bukka

WHITE, Lonnie JOHNSON, Leroy CARR, Victoria SPIVEY, Roosevelt SYKES, Sonny Boy WILLIAMSON, many more: he made Big Bill BROONZY house guitarist and assembler of backing groups at Vocalion and Bluebird; he managed Big Boy CRUDUP's recording dates and Crudup was supposed to get 35% of the money from them, but said he never did; Crudup's songs were published through Hill and Range by Melrose; three of them were covered by Elvis PRESLEY and must have been worth a lot of money, but Melrose and his heirs kept it; a lawsuit wasn't settled at the time of Crudup's death. Brother Walter Melrose (*b* 26 Oct. 1889, Sumner, Ill.) was also a music publisher, managed to get co-credits for 'High Society' (first published c.'01), 'Tin Roof Blues' (aka '54 pop hit 'Make Love To Me'), 'Milenberg Joys' (often credited to Jelly Roll Morton), 'Sugarfoot Stomp' (Swing Era hit from King Oliver's 'Dipper Mouth Blues'), etc., some of these copyrighted by the ORIGINAL DIXIELAND JAZZ BAND; perhaps Melrose wrote the words. Another brother Franklyn Taft Melrose (*b* 26 Nov. '07, Sumner; *d* Sep. '41, murdered near Hammond, Ind.) was jazz pianist, worked with Wingy MANONE, Bud FREEMAN, Johnny and Baby DODDS '28-9, recorded solos '29.

MEMPHIS SLIM (*b* Peter Chatman, 3 Sep. '15, Memphis, Tenn.; *d* 24 Feb '88, Paris). Blues singer, pianist, songwriter: stands astride trad. and urban blues, at home in either. Hoboed through the South like many other bluesmen in '30s, but settled in Chicago '37, often working with Big Bill BROONZY; made many records and was one of the first to take his art to Europe, c.'60, living in Paris from '63. Among his dozens of songs, 'Alberta' became one of Broonzy's specialities, and 'Every Day (I Have The Blues)' was a no. 2 R&B hit '55, sung by Joe WILLIAMS, from the album *Count Basie Swings/Joe Williams Sings*, which also incl. 'The Comeback'. Recorded '40-1 for Okeh with Washboard Sam (*b* Robert Brown, 15 July '10, Walnut Ridge, Ark.; *d* 13 Nov. '66, Chicago; also a vocalist, also recorded with his half-brother Broonzy, etc.), for Bluebird with Broonzy; also recorded for 10 more labels '46-59; *The Real Folk Blues* series on Chess which included '50-2 tracks on Prestige/Bluesville: played on *Willie's Blues*

'59 with Willie DIXON, played and sang solo on *All Kinds Of Blues* '60. Instrumental *Boogie Woogie Piano* '61 made in Paris, now on CBS/UK. Other albums: *Rockin' The Blues* on Charly, *Legacy Of The Blues 7* on Sonet, *The Blues Every Which Way* on Verve with Dixon, 2-disc *Raining The Blues* on Fantasy; plus *U.S.A.* '54 on Pearl, *Travelling With The Blues, This Is A Good Time To Write A Song* (aka *I'm So Alone*), *Live At Bayonne* '60-1 on Storyville; *With Guests* Lowell FULSON, Carey BELL etc. on Inner City; *I'll Just Keep Singing The Blues* '61 with small group incl. Sam Chatman, now on Muse; many others. He is not to be confused with pianist Cow Cow DAVENPORT, who also used name Memphis Slim, nor with the famous Chatmon family, whose surname is often spelled Chatman (*see* Charley PATTON).

MEN AT WORK Australian pop group formed in Melbourne '79 by Colin Hay (*b* 29 June '53, Scotland), rhythm guitar, vocals; Ron Strykert (*b* 18 Aug. '57, Aus.), guitar; multi-instrumentalist Greg Ham (*b* 27 Sep. '53, Aus.); John Rees, bass and vocals; Jerry Speiser, drums. Played Melbourne and Sydney pub circuits, signed by Aus. CBS. 'Who Can It Be Now' had Ham's sax trading lines with Hay's high-pitched voice over understated backing, reached no. 2; 'Down Under' (tale of Australians abroad) was no. 1; LP *Business As Usual* '82 was also no. 1, staying there for 10 weeks and beating N.Z. band Split Enz's record. USA support tour with FLEETWOOD MAC helped 'Who Can It Be Now' to no. 1 USA '82; 'Down Under' did it again, both from *Business As Usual*, no. 1 LP USA for 15 weeks, a staggeringly fast conquering of USA; UK capitulated to self-mocking humour of 'Down Under' (and witty video): no. 1 there '83; *Business As Usual/*'Down Under' topped USA/UK charts simultaneously for the first time since Rod STEWART's 'Maggie May'/*Every Picture Tells A Story* '72, and beat the MONKEES' 12-week chart-topping feat for a debut LP. But UK popularity faded fast: lesser songs sounded plagiarised to UK listeners because of reggae rhythms, while Hay's vocal resemblance to Sting allowed POLICE's return to chart to sweep Men away '83. In USA *Cargo* '83 joined *Business* in top 10; single hits in USA

'83 incl. two in top 10. Founders and main songwriters Hay, Ham and Strykert ditched the others late '84 before release of *Two Hearts*; Peter McIan, prod. of hit LPs, had been replaced by Hay/Ham partnership; Strykert left before *Hearts* released, followed by Ham, leaving Hay sole man at work: new LP flopped. *Looking For Jack* '87 was solo by Hay, now calling himself Colin James Hay, prod. by Robin Miller (SADE), with Herbie HANCOCK, Wayne SHORTER guesting.

MENDES, Sergio (*b* 11 Feb. '41, Niteroi, Brazil) Piano, composer. Early participant in bossa nova movement, touring South America, settling in USA mid-'60s. An Atlantic LP '63 was arr. by Antonio Carlos Jobim; *The Swinger From Rio* '64 incl. Jobim on guitar, Art FARMER; he formed group Brazil '65 (then Brazil '66, etc.), toured and recorded with it on Atlantic '65, A&M thereafter (*Fool On The Hill* '66, etc.) *Vintage 74* on Bell incl. Jobim; *The New Brazil '77* on Elektra, *Alegria* '80 on WEA, *Sergio Mendes* '83 and *Confetti* '84 carried on series of easy listening albums.

MENDOZA, Lydia (*b* 31 May '16, Houston, Texas) Tex-Mex vocalist, guitarist, songwriter; greatest female artist in the genre, earning nickname 'La Alondra de la Frontera' ('The Lark Of The Border') with astonishing voice and wide repertoire, from standard Tex-Mex love songs and corridos (song-stories) to art songs, accompaniment from the 12-string guitar to accordion conjuntos, mariachi bands and orchestras. Began performing with her family, who played popular songs of the day wherever they could (restaurants, barbershops), recorded in '20s: early family records as Cuarteto Carta Blanca; first session in San Antonio they cut 20 songs for $140. Began to sing solo with her own guitar, recorded solo '34; 'Mal Hombre' allegedly learned from chewing-gum wrapper, a local hit and something of a theme for her. Strong regional following helped '30s-80s by records on Arhoolie, Azteca, Columbia, Falcón, Gaviota, Globe, Ideal, Victor, others. Appeared in documentary film *Chulas Fronteras* '76, singing in a club in Galveston, Texas; talking and cooking at home in Houston. Performed at Jimmy Carter inaugura-

tion '77; further nicknamed 'La Gloria de Texas' ('The Glory of Texas') late '70s. Many tracks in series *Texas-Mexican Border Music* on Folklyric, incl. *Vol. 15: Lydia Mendoza Part 1: First Recordings 1928-38*, *Vol. 16 Part 2: First Recordings From The 1930s*; also *Lydia Mendoza con Su Guitarra* and *Una Voz y una Guitarra* on Azteca, *La Gloria de Texas* on Arhoolie.

MENSAH, E. T. (*b* Emmanuel Tettah Mensah, '19, Ussher Town, Accra, Ghana) African singer, composer, trumpeter and bandleader; 'the King of Highlife', without doubt the single most important leader in the genre. Father was amateur guitarist; he played in an elementary school fife band, studied organ and saxophone in high school, on leaving school formed the Accra Rhythmic Orchestra with his brother Yebuah. By this time he had picked up trumpet; when WWII came to Africa, with arrival of thousands of Allied troops, he joined with Scottish saxophonist Jack Leopard in the Black And White Spots, playing army camps and clubs. Another result of the war was the infl. of swing on African music (*see* BIG BAND ERA); after the war, following spells with the Kumasi Philharmonic Orchestra etc. he joined the Tempos, then incl. drummer Guy Warren, Joe Kelly on trumpet. The band entered a period of reorganisation and was relaunched as the first fully professional highlife dance band; with trumpet, trombone, reeds, double bass, drums, congas, bongos/clips and maracas, the 12-piece outfit began recording for Decca c.'50: hit singles and early albums established E. T. Mensah and the Tempos as the top band in Ghana. They sang in several West African languages as well as English and Spanish; they played calypso, charanga, merengue, chachacha etc. but it was in highlife in the golden age of African dance music that they made a permanent reputation, touring West Africa and particularly in Nigeria. He also toured with Nkrumah, acting as Ghana's musical ambassador. The band's albums incl. *Tempos On The Beat*, *A Saturday Night* (incl. classic 'Yaa Amponsah'), *Tempos Melodies*, *King Of Highlifes*; they also featured on Decca highlife compilations in the '60s. As with all the best African bands, there were spin-offs from the Tempos as musicians graduated from the ranks, incl. the Red Spots and the Rhythm Aces; new recruits brought in elements of R&B and the Twist as the decade wore on. LP *The King Of African Highlife Rhythm* '69 marked an era drawing to a close; the bigger bands disappeared (having lasted much longer than they did in the West) and Mensah gave up music, turning to government work as a pharmacist; he came back in the mid-'70s, with a roots revival underway, making six albums of which only *E. T. Mensah: The King Of Highlife Music* '77 and *E. T. Mensah Is Back Again* '78 were released, on Afrodisia; he went to Lagos '83 to record *Highlife Giants* with Victor OLAIYA, the 'evil genius' of highlife. *All For You* '86 on London's RetroAfric label is a generous compilation of '50s hits: sweet music with an African lilt.

MENUDO Pop group formed '77 in Puerto Rico; ultimate in throw-away bubblegum: quintet of kids who retire when they become 16. In '84 there had been 13 members in nine combinations:, giving each generation of Hispanic pubescent girls their own heart-throbs. Once sold out Madison Square Garden NYC for four shows in two days. Record piracy costs them a fortune in Latin America; merchandise recoups it: T-shirts, badges, posters, stationery, dolls, etc.

MEN WITHOUT HATS Canadian new wave pop group formed in Montreal early '80 by brothers Ivan and Jeremie Arrobas, respectively vocals/composition and drums. Both played synths, aligning group to electro-pop style just reaching Canada. *Folk Of The '80s* EP picked up by Stiff '81 created cult following outside Canada; lead track 'Antarctica' edited for UK single release on Statik; Stiff also released 12" single 'Nationale 7' in the USA. Jeremie left before recording of LP *Rhythm Of Youth* '82, replaced by two brothers Stefan (guitar, violin) and Colin (keyboards), the former adding folk infl. to quirky pop. Allan McCarthy (keyboards/percussion) completed the new lineup. LP prod. by manager Marc Durand was boosted by surprise international hit 'Safety Dance', an electro-folkdance that put across anti-nuclear message on video amid riot of maypoles, costumes, medieval jollity (parodied by Al YANKOVIC as 'The Brady Bunch'); LP was no. 13 USA, single no. 3. *Folk Of The '80s Part III* '84 did not reach top 100 USA LPs despite following two years of heavy touring; *Pop Goes The World* '87 was debut on Mercury label.

MERCER, Johnny (*b* 18 Nov. '09, Savannah, Ga.; *d* 25 June '76, L.A.) Composer, lyricist, singer, co-founder of CAPITOL Records. Hit duets on Decca '38-40 with Bing CROSBY; 25 more on Capitol '42-52 incl. no. 1 hits '45-6 with Mack David's 'Candy' (duet with Jo STAFFORD), also his own 'Ac-Cent-Tchu-Ate The Positive' (from film *Here Come The Waves*) and Oscar-winning 'On The Atchison, Topeka And The Santa Fe' (with Harry WARREN, from *The Harvey Girls*); he also shared Oscars for 'In The Cool Cool Cool Of The Evening' '51 (with Hoagy CARMICHAEL), 'Moon River' '61 and 'Days Of Wine And Roses' '62 (with Henry MANCINI). He was a director of ASCAP '40-1; wrote or co-wrote more than 1000 songs, one of the best-loved, most admired figures in USA music, nearly every lyric intelligent, optimistic, memorable; and his singing had the same qualities. He wrote words/music for 'I'm An Old Cowhand' '36, 'Dream (When You're Feeling Blue)' '45, others; hits/collaborators incl. 'Blues In The Night', 'That Old Black Magic', 'One For My Baby', 'Come Rain Or Come Shine' (with Harold ARLEN); 'Lazy Bones', 'How Little We Know', 'Skylark' (Carmichael); 'Tangerine' and 'I Remember You' (Victor Schertzinger; the latter a no. 1 hit '42 by J. DORSEY); 'Jeepers Creepers' and 'You Must Have Been A Beautiful Baby' (Warren); also 'Satin Doll' (Billy STRAYHORN/Duke ELLINGTON), 'Early Autumn' (Ralph BURNS), 'You Were Never Lovelier' (Jerome KERN), 'P.S. I Love You' (Gordon JENKINS; written in '34, a big hit for the HILLTOPPERS '53), 'When A Woman Loves A Man' (with Jenkins, Bernard Hanighan; classic record by Billie HOLIDAY), 'Laura' (David Raskin), 'Too Marvelous For Words' (Richard A. Whiting: *b* 12 Nov. 1891, Peoria, Ill.; *d* 10 Feb. '38, Beverly Hills; also wrote 'She's Funny That Way', 'Miss Brown To You', 'You're An Old Smoothie', many others), 'Day In – Day Out' (Rube Bloom, *b* 24 Apr. '02, NYC; *d* there 30 Mar. '76, also wrote 'Fools Rush In', 'Spring Fever', etc.), many more. Sang with Benny GOODMAN on radio; own shows incl. *Johnny Mercer's Music Shop* '43-4 with Paul WHITEMAN as mus. dir., sidemen ex-Bob CROSBY band. Broadway shows incl. *St Louis Woman* '46, *Top Banana*, *Li'l Abner* and *Saratoga* in '50s; contributed to musical films incl. *Hollywood Hotel* '37, *The Fleet's In* '42, about 30 more; wrote songs for *Seven Brides For Seven Brothers* '54 (with enricVincent de Paul, *b* 17 June '19 NYC; *d* 27-8 Feb. '88, L. A.). Albums incl. duet with Bobby DARIN *Two a Kind* on Atco; compilations: *Ac-Cent-Tchu-Ate The Positive* on Capitol; *Audio Scrapbook* on Magic/Submarine, *Johnny Mercer's Music Shop* (with Stafford, Paul WESTON, Jack TEAGARDEN) on Artistic.

MERCER, Mabel (*b* 1900, Staffordshire, England; *d* 20 Apr. '84, Pittsfield, Mass.) Cabaret singer; an enormous infl. with loyal cult following, though she made few records. Father was USA jazz musician, mother British variety actress; joined Bricktop in Paris '31, worked there until '38; then to USA. Admirers incl. Frank SINATRA, Lena HORNE, Nat King COLE; songs written for her incl. 'The End Of A Love Affair' (by pianist Edward Carolan 'Bud' Redding: *b* 17 Aug. '15, Louisville, Ky.), 'While We're Young' (co-written by Alec WILDER), 'Fly Me To The Moon' (aka. 'In Other Words'; by pianist Bart Howard: *b* Howard Joseph Gustafson, 1 June '15, Burlington, Iowa; her accompanist for four years, emcee and mus. dir. at Blue Angel for eight years). Her delivery was described by Wilder as 'graceful *parlando*'; she concentrated on neglected songs of value, bringing interpretive quality of narrative. Albums incl. *Mabel Mercer* on Decca/MCA; on Atlantic: *Sings Cole Porter* '55 (reissued '85), with Cy Walter and Russ Freeman, pianos, Frank Carroll, bass; also *Midnight At Mabel Mercer's*, *Once In A Blue Moon* (revived Xmas carol 'The Twelve Days Of Christmas'), *Merely Marvelous*, then (in stereo) 2-disc sets *The Art Of Mabel Mercer* and *At Town Hall* (with Bobby SHORT).

MERENGUE A crisp, jaunty 2/4 dance rhythm originating in the Dominican Republic c. 1840s. Rural instrumentation incl. the accordion, which swept the country late 19th century; the barrel-shaped, double headed tambora drum, played with a stick at one end and muted by hand at the other; and the metal güiro or scraper, played with a kind of wire fork to give a hard hissing sound. The alto saxophone was adopted, in a style reminiscent of New Orleans Creole clarinettists. *Merengues From The Dominican Republic* '77 on Lyrichord incl. examples of country merengue recorded by Verna Gillis. Urban brass-led bands retained the tambora, güiro and sax; some of the earliest bands to record incl. Damiron and Chapuseaux, who played an Americanised version '40s; more authentic merengue introduced to NYC '50s can be heard on the accordion/sax-led *Angel Viloria And His Conjunto Tipico Cibaeño* on Ansonia. Viloria's singer Dioris Valladares also worked with Xavier CUGAT, Noro MORALES, José Curbelo, Enric MADRIGUERA, led his own band and was an original member of the Alegre All Stars, made LPs on Ansonia, Alegre, Musicor and took part in historic jazz-oriented Latin jam session (descarga) recordings of the Alegre All Stars '60s (*see* Charlie PALMIERI). In the early '80s merengue became a major force, significant Dominican immigration in NYC; the pace of the style became more frantic and the concerts and LPs became more popular than salsa; the merengue boom was slowing down somewhat in '86. Wilfrido Vargas, D.R. trumpeter, singer, bandleader, composer, producer, was in the vanguard, starting from pure merengue but incorporating traces of SOCA, CADENCE, funk, rap, etc.; *Punto y Aparte!* '78 on Karen marked a watershed, track 'El Barbarazo' in particular seen as 'new merengue'. Hit albums incl. *. . . ahora* '81, *Abusadora!* . . . (with singer Sandy Reyes), *Wilfrido Vargas & Sandy Reyes* '82 and *El Funcionario* '83 on Karen, the latter no. 1 on Latin charts; *El Africano* '84 from Mexican Melody label was hits compilation from '81-3 LPs. (Ariola in Spain issued *El Funcionario* as *El Africano*, just to make things confusing, as well as other Vargas LPs.) Hit LP *El Jardinero* '84 on Karen was made in D.R., introduced synthesiser, electric guitar, incl. track 'Lo Ajeno Se Deja Quieto', performed by Vargas y Los Beduinos on BBC2 Arena TV show *Latin Sound* '86. *Wilfrido 86 – La Medicina* '85 on Karen, made in D.R. and Venezuela, another hit LP, took fusion further. He prod. LPs for others incl. *The New*

York Band on Karen and *Pegando Fuego* on Sonotone (both '86; all women except male pianist), switched to Sonotone for his *La Música* '87; appeared on *Johnny Ventura vs Wilfrido Vargas por el Campeonato Mundial!* on Discolor mid-'70s; veteran D.R. bandleader, singer, composer, arranger and producer Ventura also made *12 Aniversario* '76 on Discolor, *Lo Que Te Gusta* '81, *Flying High (Volando Alto)* '83 and *Carpullo & Sorullo* '86 on Combo; he moved to CBS for hit *El Señor del Merengue* '86 (synth work on 'Olvida Tus Penas' reminiscent of '60s pop/TV themes). D.R. composer, singer, leader Cuco Valoy has tended to incl. a variety of Latin rhythms in LPs on Discolor and Kubaney '70s-80s; switched to Team with a new lineup for *Cuco Valoy y su Nueva Tribu – Mejor Que Nunca* '85 and *Con Sabor del Tropico* '86. Other leading bands and artists in merengue have been Conjunto Quisqueya, Jossie Esteban y La Patrulla 15 (hit *Acariciame* '87), Millie y Los Vecinos (with vocalists Millie and Jocelyn Quesada; *Dinastia* '85, *Special Delivery* '86 on RCA International); Alex Bueno y La Liberacion, Fausto Rey and Freddy Kenton. The album *El Monje y El Rebelde* '85 on CBS combined the Colombian superstar vallenata accordionist Alfredo Gutiérrez with the modern D.R. band of July Mateo 'Rasputin', for a fusion of downhome rural merengue with the urban brass sound. Dominican accordionist Francisco Ulloa's *Merengue!* on Kubaney '85 issued on UK GlobeStyle label '87. The *méringue* played in Haiti is very different, a much gentler music originating in the early 19th century: there the term covers styles from a polite piano music, often with violins, to an urban combo style; *Méringues And Folk Ballads Of Haiti* on Lyrichord focuses on guitar and banjo folk méringues.

MERMAN, Ethel (*b* Ethel Zimmerman, 16 Jan. '09, Astoria, NY; *d* 15 Feb. '84) Singer, actress; one of the great ladies of the USA musical stage. *Merman: An Autobiography* '78 (with George Eells) tells the story of the native New Yorker who lived at home with her parents, worked days as a secretary while singing in clubs at night, skipped vaudeville and went straight to Broadway. Big break in *Girl Crazy* '30; always associated with big song: George GERSHWIN's 'I Got

Rhythm'. Other hit shows incl. Cole PORTER's *Anything Goes* '34 (film '36), Irving BERLIN's *Annie Get Your Gun* '46 (song 'There's No Business Like Show Business' became her trademark), Berlin's *Call Me Madam* '50 (film '53), *Gypsy* '59 (Jule Styne/Stephen SONDHEIM; Merman should have got the film role '62 instead of Rosalind Russell), several others. Teamed with Mary MARTIN in legendary Ford TV show '53; appearances on TV variety shows in the '50s were overpowering because her big voice and personality was meant for the stage: she could fill any theatre without a microphone, the last of the greats. Hilarious non-singing role as Milton Berle's mother-in-law in Stanley Kramer film *It's A Mad Mad Mad Mad World* '63. A dozen hit records '32-51 naturally incl. show songs: 'You're The Top'/'I Get A Kick Out Of You' '34 from *Anything Goes*, duet with Ray Middleton 'They Say It's Wonderful' '46 and with Dick HAYMES 'You're Just In Love' '51, both from *Madam*, three duet hits (incl. 'Dearie', from *Copacabana Show of 1950*) with dancer/singer/actor Ray Bolger (*b* 10 Jan. '04, Dorchester, Mass.; *d* 15 Jan. '87; he played scarecrow in film *Wizard Of Oz* '39; his many Broadway shows incl. smash hit *Where's Charley?* '48, film version '52: his top 20 hit 'Once In Love With Amy' '49 from that show was one of the few 12″ 78s ever to sell that well).

MERRILL, Helen (*b* Helen Milcetic, 21 July '30, NYC) Jazz singer. Turned pro c.'45; inactive late '40s but sang with Earl HINES Sextet '52; recorded for EmArcy '54-8, incl. an LP with Clifford BROWN arr. by Quincy JONES; 62 tracks incl. alternate takes now compiled on 4-disc *The Complete Helen Merrill On Mercury*. Recorded for Atlantic '59; went to UK '59, stayed in Europe and found more success in Italy, then Japan, than she had at home. Japanese LPs incl. *Helen Merrill In Tokyo* on King; relocated in Japan '67, LPs for JVC not released in USA incl. items with Teddy WILSON, Gary PEACOCK. *The Artistry Of Helen Merrill* '68 on Mainstream was made in USA, followed by *The Feeling Is Mutual* and *A Shade Of Difference*; returned to USA '72, lived in Chicago. More LPs incl. *Music Makers* '86 with Steve LACY, Stephane GRAPPELLI on

Owl, made in Paris; *Rodgers & Hammerstein Album* '82 on DRG. *Collaboration* made in '50s with Gil EVANS, remade not long before his death, on EmArcy.

MERSEYBEATS, The UK pop group '60s formed by Tony Crane, lead guitar and vocals, and Billy Kinsley, bass; both ex-Mavericks. Other members were Aaron Williams on rhythm guitar and drummer John Banks. One of the few Mersey groups to make as much impact on record as live, thanks to prod. Jack Baverstock; opened their account with cover of SHIRELLES' 'It's Love That Really Counts' (no. 24 '63) and Peter Lee Stirling's 'I Think Of You', at no. 5 their biggest hit '64, plus two at no. 13 incl. Jackie DESHANNON's 'Wishin' And Hopin' '. Hits were romantic ballads, but other tracks on albums show that they rock-'n'rolled with the best. Kinsley left during '64, replaced by Bob Garner; hits diminished as Mersey beat boom faded (with their name they couldn't escape association). Three more top 40 hits '64-6 were the end: Kinsley returned but group folded early '66. Kinsley and Crane carried on as the Merseys, recruiting the Fruit Eating Bears as backing group, scored no. 4 '66 with haunting 'Sorrow', went into cabaret as psychedelia raged. Banks teamed with Big Three's Johnny Gustavson as John and Johnny for 'Bumper To Bumper'; Crane formed self-named group '70s; Kinsley formed poppy Liverpool Express with Tony Coates, guitar; Derek Cashin, drums; Roger Craig, keyboards for three top 40 singles '76-7. Reflected glory for original groups accrued when David BOWIE covered 'Sorrow' on *Pin Ups* '73, Elvis COSTELLO did 'I Stand Accused' on *Get Happy!!* '80.

METHENY, Pat (*b* 12 Aug. '54, Lees's Summit, Kansas City, Mo.) Guitarist, composer. Played French horn in school, took up guitar at 13 and was teaching while still in his teens: infl. at first by Wes MONTGOMERY, soon became superstar, his lyricism admired by other musicians as well as the public: it finds favour with New Age audience, though it has more guts than that suggests. Played with Gary BURTON '74-7 (three LPs on ECM), then formed group with keyboardist Lyle Mays (*b* 27 Nov. '53, Wausaukee, Wis.); played and/or recorded

with Paul BLEY, Sonny ROLLINS, Julius HEMPHILL, many more; film score work incl. John Schlesinger's *The Falcon And The Snowman* '85 (performed theme 'This Is Not America' with David BOWIE), also episodes of Steven Spielberg's *Amazing Stories*. Own albums incl. *Bright Size Life* '76, *Watercolors* '77, *Pat Metheny Group* '78, *New Chautauqua* '79, *American Garage* '80, *As Falls Wichita, So Falls Wichita Falls* '81, *Offramp* '82, *Travels* '83, *Rejoicing* '83, *First Circle* '84, all on ECM; *Song X* '86 on Geffen with Ornette COLEMAN is challenging music, much of it co-written by Metheny. *Still Life (Talking)* '87 on Geffen is back in more accessible groove, no. 1 '87 in Billboard jazz chart, with Mays, five others incl. two vocalists. Mays' eponymous solo LP '86 on Geffen will please New Age fans.

MEZZROW, Mezz (*b* Milton Mesirow, 9 Nov. 1899, Chicago; *d* 5 Aug. '72, Paris) Reeds, especially clarinet. Began on sax while in jail '17, turned pro c.'23. He was not a great musician, but an indefatigable sparkplug and organiser, like Eddie CONDON, with whom he often worked; also famous for supplying marijuana, always carrying a shoebox full with him (a marijuana cigarette was a meziroll, or a 'mighty mezz'; cf. 'The Reefer Song' '43, by Fats WALLER). He played in Ben POLLACK band '28, recorded on C-melody sax with Condon '29; organised recording bands '33 with Teddy WILSON, Benny CARTER, Max KAMINSKY; '34 with Carter, Kaminsky, Bud FREEMAN, Willie 'The Lion' SMITH, John KIRBY, Chick WEBB; '36 with Freeman, Smith, Frankie Newton; '37 with Sy OLIVER, J. C. HIGGINBOTHAM; Mezzrow-Ladnier Quintet '38 with Tommy LADNIER. Took part in '38 sessions organised by Hugues Panassié. Formed own record label King Jazz c.'45, recorded himself with Sidney BECHET, Hot Lips PAGE, Sammy Price on piano; visited France '48, '51; spent more and more time there. Published book *Really The Blues* with Bernard Wolfe '46. Albums incl. *Paris* '55 on Swing, with visiting Americans; two vols. of *The King Jazz Story* with Bechet on Storyville.

MICKEY & SYLVIA Guitarists, songwriters McHouston 'Mickey' Baker (*b* 15 Oct. '25,

Lexington, Ky.), Sylvia Vanderpool (*b* 6 Mar. '36, NYC). He was among highly-rated session players in black music: played on 'Losing Hand' by Ray CHARLES and Ruth BROWN's '(Mama) He Treats Your Daughter Mean', both '53; with Henry Van Walls on piano, bassist Lloyd Trotman and Connie Kay on drums he was part of Atlantic's house rhythm section, playing on hits with the COASTERS, many others; also recorded for Savoy, King, Okeh, etc. accompanying LITTLE WILLIE JOHN, Screamin' Jay HAWKINS, etc. often playing slide guitar style; with Sil AUSTIN '56, etc.; published infl. music books such as *Jazz Guitar*. Sylvia replaced Little Esther at Savoy, on Savoy label, sang with Hot Lips PAGE billed as Little Sylvia; became Mickey's guitar student '55; they married, formed duo and their fifth record 'Love Is Strange' was no. 2 R&B/11 pop hit '56 on RCA labels Vik and Groove: extremely well recorded, a sort of wistful calypso, with Mickey's blues guitar breaks, Sylvia's sexy lead vocal, it was uniquely influential and one of the best records of the era; the song (written by Baker with Ethel Smith) was subject of unsuccessful lawsuit claiming it to be similar to 'Billy Blues', unusual for such a suit in being tried with a jury. They had other R&B/pop crossovers incl. 'There Oughta Be A Law' '57, split up '61 after playing on Ike & Tina TURNER's 'It's Gonna Work Out Fine', last hit 'Baby You're So Fine' on their own Willow label. He duetted with Kitty Noble as Mickey and Kitty, later moved to France. Sylvia had no. 3 pop hit 'Pillow Talk' '70 on Vibration label; with new husband Jim Robinson became label boss: beginning '68 All Platinum label had success with soul, vocal groups, then disco music and one of the first rap hits, on Sugar Hill. Baker's albums incl. *Blues & Jazz Guitar*, *Jazz Rock Guitar* on Kicking Mule/Sonet, *Take A Look Inside* on Big Bear UK.

MIDLER, Bette (*b* 1 Dec. '45, Paterson, N.J.) Singer, actress; the only authentic cabaret star to emerge in rock-oriented '70s. Father was a house painter for the US Navy; mother '. . . sewed beautifully. She made all our clothes for years, until my parents discovered the Salvation Army.' Began as extra in film *Hawaii* '66, also played in *Fiddler On The Roof* and *Tommy*; performing at gay venues in NYC early '70s, her pianist/mus. dir. was Barry MANILOW. *The Divine Miss M* '72 won her a Grammy and made her a star, perfectly capturing her image as 'trash with flash'; enthusiastic cover of old ANDREWS SISTERS hit 'Boogie Woogie Bugle Boy' was no. 8 hit '72; *Bette Midler* '73 was less inspired follow-up, but excellent *Songs For The New Depression* '76 incl. duet with Bob DYLAN on his 'Buckets Of Rain'. *Broken Blossom* and *Live At Last* '77 kept cult happy; she found likely companion in duet with Tom WAITS on his LP *Foreign Affairs* same year. Played Janis JOPLIN character in film *The Rose* '79, was nominated for an Oscar; soundtrack LP sold a million and title track was no. 3 hit '80. *Divine Madness* was film and live LP '80, incl. unique interpretations of songs by Bruce SPRINGSTEEN, Bob SEGER and ROLLING STONES. Film *Jinxed* '82 was unsuccessful; album *No Frills* '83 was not; film *Down And Out In Beverly Hills* '86 (with LITTLE RICHARD) was 10th biggest grosser of the year; *Ruthless People* '86 was eighth; *Outrageous Fortune* '87 looked to do as well. She published best-selling children's book *The Saga Of Baby Divine* '83; *Mud Will Be Flung Tonight* '85 was first comedy LP, in Joan Rivers mould: another facet of rich talent.

MIDNITE FOLLIES ORCHESTRA UK band playing classic arr. of Sam WOODING, Duke ELLINGTON, Cab CALLOWAY, Fletcher HENDERSON etc. as well as originals; formed '78 by multi-instrumentalists Keith Nichols (*b* 13 Feb. '45, Ilford, Essex), arranger Alan Cohen (*b* 24 Nov. '34, London). Albums on EMI '78, ASV '80. Lineup incl. cornettist Digby Fairweather (*b* 25 Apr. '46), drummer Laurie Chescoe (*b* 18 Apr. '33, London; worked with Monty Sunshine, Bruce Turner). Nichols was a child actor and accordion champion, then specialised in ragtime: led scholarly Ragtime Orchestra mid-'70s, New Sedalia and other groups; wrote for Dick HYMAN's New York Jazz Repertory Company, Pasadena Roof Orchestra, etc.; both worked with New Paul Whiteman Orchestra (LPs '74 on Argo, '75 on Wave), led by multi-instrumentalist/journalist Dick Sudhalter (*b* 28 Dec. '38, Boston, Mass.), author of one of the first classic jazz biographies (*see* Bix BEIDER-BECKE). Cohen leads a quintet on soprano sax; he recorded Ellington's *Black, Brown And Beige* '72 on Argo, was mus. dir./arr. for Bing CROSBY Decca LP *Feels Good, Feels Right* '76, TV show *Cotton Club At The Ritz* '85 (*see* Cab CALLOWAY), Charlie Watts Big Band (video and LP '86), much else.

MIKKELBORG, Palle (*b* 6 Mar. '41, Copenhagen, Denmark) Trumpet, flugelhorn, keyboards, composer, leader. Self-taught: began on trumpet '56, turned pro '60. Led Danish Radio Jazz Group late '60s, also played in Radio Big Band; formed quintet with drummer Alex Riel (*b* 13 Sep. '40, Copenhagen) '66, played at Montreux and Newport '68; own groups V8 early '70s (with Riel), later Entrance; has worked with Philip CATHERINE, Don CHERRY, Bill EVANS, Gil EVANS, Abdullah IBRAHIM, Charlie MARIANO, George RUSSELL, vocalist Karin Krog (*b* 15 May '37, Oslo, Norway), many others; arr./cond. orchestra on Dexter GORDON album *More Than You Know* '75. Composed for groups incl. symphony orchestra, gamelan ensemble; works incl. *Aura* '84 for Miles DAVIS, his great influence. He has mastered the electric trumpet; on a UK tour with Russell early in '86 he found thrilling beauty in the new timbres, without Davis's need for rock backing tapes. Plays on ECM LPs *Densere* '77 in Jan Garbarek/Bobo Stenson Quartet, *Waves* '78 and *Descendre* '79 with guitarist Terje Rypdal, L. SHANKAR's *Vision* with Garbarek, *Theatre* '83 by keyboardist/leader George Grunz (*b* 24 June '32, Basle, Switzerland), with Julian Priester, Sheila JORDAN, etc.; also *Guamba* '87 with Gary PEACOCK quartet. Own albums incl. *Ashoka Suite* '70, *Entrance* '77 on Danish Metronome label, live at Montreux '78 on Atlantic, trio *Heart To Heart* '86 on Storyville.

MILBURN, Amos (*b* 1 Apr. '27, Houston, Texas (some sources say '24); *d* there 3 Jan. '80) Singer, pianist, songwriter. Began in down-home style, developed smooth tavern-ballad style; worked Houston clubs, went to West Coast '46, toured in Texas/Louisiana '47-9, back to Coast. Recorded for Aladdin label '49-53 with group Aladdin Chicken Shackers; 11 top 10 R&B hits began with his own song 'Hold Me Baby', incl. two-sided 'Rooming House Boogie'/'Empty Arms Blues', 'Let's Rock A While'/'Tears, Tears Tears'; 'Bad, Bad Whiskey' '50 was no. 1 R&B (written by tenor saxist Maxwell Davis *b* 14 Jan. '16, Independence, Kansas, *d* '67; played with Fletcher HENDERSON etc.; house bandleader for Aladdin, Federal, Modern '48-54 on many R&B hits, also with Ray ANTHONY, Ella Mae MORSE, etc.); it led to series of drinking songs of which 'Let Me Go Home, Whiskey' (no. 3 '53) was one of the best: medium tempo, bass and drums slightly behind the beat, subtle guitar commentary on each phrase, smooth vocal made believable lonesome bar-room song, R&B classic (composer credit was 'Shifte Henri': bassist credited by singer Earl Coleman in Ira Gitler's *Swing To Bop* with writing 'Dark Shadows' and 'Jailhouse Rock'). He toured with Johnny OTIS, Charles BROWN; recorded for King '61, Motown late '60s but had no more hits, sometimes worked outside music, suffered stroke '70. Apollo theatre gigs early '50s were filmed, seen in films '55-6 incl. *Showtime At The Apollo*. Compilation LPs incl. *Chicken Shack Boogie* on UA (title track said to have been hit, appears on no charts), *Just One More Drink* on Cadillac, *Let's Have A Party* (biggest hits) and *13 Unreleased Masters* on Pathé-Marconi.

MILEY, Bubber (*b* James Wesley Miley, 3 Apr. '03, Aiken, S.C.; *d* 20 May '32, Welfare Island, NY) Trumpet. From musical family; sisters were known as the South Carolina Trio. Worked with Mamie SMITH, etc.; with Elmer Snowden's Washingtonians in NYC '23, stayed on with Duke ELLINGTON '24-9, inventing one of the most resonant sounds in 20th-century music, the growling, vocalised plunger-muted trumpet that was a cornerstone of Ellington's classic 'Jungle Band' of the Cotton Club era, subsequently had to be imitated by Cootie WILLIAMS, others. Played on Ellington's 'Flaming Youth', 'Creole Love Call', 'East St Louis Toodle-oo', many others; Ellington said, 'Our band changed character when Bubber came in. That's when we forgot all about the sweet music.' He drank too much, became unreliable; went to France with Noble SISSLE '29, recorded with Jelly Roll MORTON, King OLIVER, Leo REISMAN; formed band '30 subsidised by Irving

MILLS: Bubber Miley and his Mileage Makers cut eight sides for Victor '30, all with period vocals; he was forced to quit music by TB.

MILLER, Eddie (*b* Edward Raymond Miller, 23 June '11, New Orleans) Tenor sax, also clarinet, occasional vocals. New Orleans infl. made his tenor a unique voice in the Swing Era, sweet yet swinging: played alto sax, joined Ben POLLACK '30 and switched to tenor; gigged with DORSEY Bros. pick-up band, was star of Bob CROSBY band '34-42, many reunions since. Often worked with Crosby guitarist Nappy Lamare; occasionally led own band (as in film *You Can't Ration Love* '43 with Donald O'Connor); on Red NICHOLS' last gig in Las Vegas '65; played many jazz festivals, with Pete Fountain in New Orleans '67-76; toured with World's Greatest Jazz Band. Lovely solos on Crosby records; few records under his own name incl. Capitol sides early '50s, *With A Little Help From My Friend Pete Fountain* on Coral; quintet *It's Miller Time* on Famous Door and *Lazy Mood For Two* with Lou Stein on 77, both from '70s.

MILLER, Frankie UK R&B singer, *b* Glasgow. To London with Stoics; discovered playing pubs by Robin Trower, who'd just left PROCOL HARUM. Duo formed Jude with bassist Jim Dewar (ex-Stone The Crows) and drummer Clive Bunker (ex-JETHRO TULL), but never recorded. Miller cut *Once In A Blue Moon* '73 with BRINSLEY SCHWARZ backing for Chrysalis; attempt to form own band failed; went to New Orleans and made best LP *High Life* '74, with Allen TOUSSAINT (title from Miller beer): songwriting was split 50:50, standout tracks incl. Toussaint's 'Brickyard Blues', Miller's 'Devil Gun'. He persuaded Henry McCullock (ex-Grease Band) to stay in a band with Chrissie Stewart, bass; Mick Weaver, keyboards; Stu Perry, drums. Returned to USA to make *The Rock* '75 with country prod. Elliott Mazer: great single 'A Fool In Love', but again poor sales. Formed Full House with Ray Minhinnit, guitar; Charlie Harrison, bass; James Hall, keyboards; Graham Deacon, drums; band only survived to make LP *Full House* '77 incl. biggest hit at no. 6 UK: maudlin singsong 'Darlin' '. Other LPs incl. *Double Trouble*

'78, *Perfect Fit* '79, *Easy Money* '80 on Chrysalis, *Standing On The Edge* '82 on Capitol, of which three made lower reaches on USA LP chart. Signed with Phonogram '86; recorded with fellow Scot, ex-THIN LIZZY guitarist Brian Robertson: *Dancing In The Rain* '86 was disappointing hard rock aimed at USA market, co-writing by Jeff BARRY. Other songs covered by Delbert MCCLINTON, Ray CHARLES, Betty Wright, others.

MILLER, Glenn (*b* Alton Glenn Miller, 1 Mar. '04, Clarinda, Iowa; *d* 15 Dec. '44 in English Channel) Trombone, arranger, leader. Sideman on freelance recordings; arr. for Ben POLLACK '26-8; played in pit bands on Broadway while studying music; toured with Smith BALLEW, worked for DORSEY brothers, Ray NOBLE, Glen Gray, Ozzie NELSON; formed own band, failed '37, re-formed '38; 3-month gig at Glen Island Casino (Long Island) began May '39, a famous venue because of broadcasts from bandstand. Began tradition of ending broadcasts with medleys – 'something old, something new'; gig at Meadowbrook (roadhouse on New Jersey's Pompton Turnpike), broadcasts for Chesterfield cigarettes followed; Miller's became the most popular dance band in the world. Joined US Army '42, formed all-star service personnel band and was posted to England '44; did not get along with the BBC: he had wangled Army commission to play for US troops, broadcast on US Armed Forces Network. Band was posted to France; Miller's plane never arrived. A hard-driving leader, he took a fatherly but possessive attitude towards his personnel, was also a tough businessman: perhaps an uptight individual who was just beginning to loosen up when he died. The band had little jazz content; among the singers, Ray Eberle was not as good as his brother Bob Eberly (with Jimmy Dorsey); similarly, Marion Hutton's sister Betty was a bigger star: the businessman in Miller thought that talent ran in families. Vocal combo the Modernaires were typical of the period. Other bands were more exciting, but Miller's won polls (in sweet category); had more than 40 top 10 records in three years after Billboard began keeping charts '40, phenomenal score for the time. Success was due to band's reliable section playing, pretty trademark sound of clarinet lead over reed section, good arrangements and Miller's choice of material, a summary of USA pop music: '39 hits incl. 'Little Brown Jug', jive version of 70-year-old tavern/glee-club song (arr. Bill Finegan); the band's theme 'Moonlight Serenade' (Miller comp.), b/w 'Sunrise Serenade' (by Frankie CARLE) (2-sided hit eventually sold 2 million); 'In the Mood', a riff played by black bands for years ('Hot and Anxious' credited to Horace HENDERSON): new arr. by Joe Garland was first played by Edgar HAYES and became Miller hit during Glen Island gig. 'Tuxedo Junction' came from Erskine HAWKINS band '40. Romantic 'Moonlight Cocktail' was slowed down piano rag by Luckey ROBERTS; among the best arr. were Gray's 'A String Of Pearls' and Finegan's 'Song Of The Volga Boatmen', all '41. 'Chattanooga Choo Choo' featured in band's first film (*Sun Valley Serenade*, also '41); '(I've Got a Gal in) Kalamazoo' in second (*Orchestra Wives*, '42). 'American Patrol' '42 was Gray arr. of a march written in 1891. Many of these, plus 'Don't Sit Under the Apple Tree (With Anyone Else But Me)', are still redolent of wartime nostalgia, when goodbyes took place in railway stations all over the USA. Add good period pop tunes – 'Adios', 'Perfidia', 'My Prayer', 'Elmer's Tune', etc. – this is the formula still regarded as the essence of '40s pop music. Original recordings are still selling; Miller had broadcasts recorded, and many of these have been issued; total number of LP reissues is enormous: 40 currently available in UK alone. Among countless compilations, the original Bluebird 78s have been compiled in a series of 2-disc albums; 2-disc set *Glenn Miller – A Memorial 1944-1969* was good value with 30 selections, but original 78s were always badly transferred to master tape for some reason: RCA's first digital transfer, a single CD selection, was a failure, but the work was done again and a 3-CD set '87 was an unqualified success (another good transfer is 'American Patrol' in the soundtrack of Woody Allen's *Radio Days*; see RECORDED SOUND). Miller bands authorised by his estate have been led by Tex BENEKE, Ray MCKINLEY, Buddy DEFRANCO, Peanuts Hucko, others; a band led by Dick Gerhardt played at Glen Island Casino in April '84 (first time since '40); another led by Glenn's

brother Herb played in UK '84. A ghost band made *In A Digital Mood* '84 on GRP, with Julius LAROSA, Mel TORMÉ, Marlene VerPlanck re-creating the Modernaires. George T. Simon's *Glenn Miller And His Orchestra* is a good book; biopic *The Glenn Miller Story* '54 has good soundtrack but the usual poor script values, writers putting 'Little Brown Jug' in '44 instead of '39 in order to jerk tears.

MILLER, Jody (*b* 29 Oct. '41, Phoenix, Ariz.) The complete crossover country-pop singer. Father played country fiddle; four sisters all amateur vocalists; she led folk trio the Melodies in school, worked as secretary, moved to West Coast '63 to pursue singing; actor Dale Robertson introduced her to Capitol label and she began as folk singer with LP *Wednesday's Child*. Mary Taylor wrote 'Queen Of The House' (sequel to Roger MILLER hit 'King Of The Road'); big pop and country hit '65 won Jody a Grammy for Best Female Country Performance. LPs *The Nashville Sound Of Jody Miller* and *Sings The Hits Of Buck Owens* didn't do so well; she retired to Oklahoma '68 to raise her daughter; lured back to music by offer to record for Billy Sherrill on Epic in Nashville '70, immediately hit country top 10 with 'Look At Mine', followed by 'He's So Fine', 'Baby I'm Yours', 'Be My Baby', updates of '60s pop hits. Success with Sherrill continued for years but no attempt was made to change with the times; in early '80s she retired again to breed quarter horses in Blanchard, Oklahoma. LPs incl. *Look At Mine* '72, *There's A Party Goin' On* '72, *Good News* '73, *County Girl* '75, *Here's Jody Miller* '77.

MILLER, Mitch (*b* Mitchell William Miller, 4 July '11, Rochester, NY) Producer, arranger. Studied at Eastman, played oboe in touring orchestra '34 conducted by Leo REISMAN and Charles Previn (André's father), with George GERSHWIN on piano; with Budapest String Quartet etc.; on A&R staff at Mercury late '40s, then pop chief at Columbia with Percy FAITH, Paul WESTON '50s. Recorded his own slightly eccentric popular instrumentals ('Oriental Polka', etc.), had hits of which biggest was cover of the WEAVERS' 'Tzena, Tzena, Tzena', strangest a vocal adaptation of Tchaikovsky's

1812 Overture: 'Napoleon' '54. Played oboe and English horn on Alec WILDER album (conducted by Frank SINATRA) '45, later on Faith LPs *It's So Peaceful In The Country*, *Music Until Midnight* (incl. single 'Elaine'). As an A&R man he was enormously infl. in the period, overseeing careers of Guy MITCHELL, others, also in buying in Hank WILLIAMS songs and recording them with Tony BENNETT, Rosemary CLOONEY, Jo STAFFORD, Frankie LAINE. He took 'Let Me Go, Devil', a dreary anti-alcohol waltz, had new lyrics written, made a record with his discovery, 18-year-old Joan Weber (who sang with her husband's band in Paulsboro, N.J.), had it plugged in TV play about a DJ accused of murder: 'Let Me Go, Lover' was no. 1 hit '54, in charts 15 weeks; Hank SNOW had a country hit with it (he sang it 'Let me go, woman', and his band didn't seem to know what to do with it); it wasn't much of a song and Weber never had another hit, but that was the kind of thing Miller could pull off. He passed on Buddy HOLLY, bid for Elvis PRESLEY '55 but would not meet Col. Parker's price; he did not quite join the ignorant chorus who wanted to censor rock'n'roll, saying on one occasion 'You can't call any music immoral.' But he disliked it and effectively abdicated to conduct singalongs on TV: album *Sing Along With Mitch* '58 with male chorus was no. 1 for eight weeks, followed by 20 more in four years, nearly all top 10 LPs; this was all very well, but had no influence on anything, while singles charts were taken over by the trashy likes of FABIAN and Frankie AVALON, selling as many records for cynical independents as Miller had done in his prime. Columbia's market share slipped until the Clive DAVIS era of the late '60s. Conducted LSO in Gershwin '88 on Arabesque, with David Golub on piano.

MILLER, Mulgrew (*b* 13 Aug. '55, Greenwood, Ms.) Piano. One of the new stars in recent edition of Art BLAKEY's Jazz Messengers. Blakey's *New York Scene* '84 on Concord Jazz features Miller on lovely ballad medley ('My One And Only Love', 'Who Cares', 'It's Easy To Remember'), also Middle-Eastern flavoured Miller comp. 'Falafel'. Also worked with Johnny GRIFFIN, Woody SHAW, etc.; with Mercer ELLINGTON '77-80, Betty CARTER '80; two

albums on Blue Note with Tony WILLIAMS mid-'80s; on Terence BLANCHARD-Donald HARRISON set *New York Second Line* '84, also on Concord; own LPs: *Keys To The City* '85 on Landmark, with Ira Coleman on bass; Marvin 'Smitty' Smith on drums; *Work!* '87 with Charnett Moffett and Terri Lyne Carrington; *Wingspan* '88 is quintet with Moffett.

MILLER, Ned (*b* Henry Ned Miller, 12 Apr. '25, Raines, Utah) Country singer, songwriter who wrote dozens of hits (mostly with his wife, Sue). Worked as pipe-fitter, moved into music full-time, signing with Fabor (subsidiary of Abbot in Cal.) '56 and recorded without much success. Wrote songs such as 'Dark Moon', 'Snowflake', 'Behind The Tear', recorded by Bonnie GUITAR, Jim REEVES, Sonny JAMES etc. In '62 'From A Jack To A King', a song written five years earlier, was an international pop/country hit: his own recording of it made no. 2 country/no. 6 pop USA, no. 2 UK; for the next eight years he scored with 'Invisible Tears', 'Do What You Do Do Well', 'Teardrop Lane', etc. Recorded for Capitol '65, Gene AUTRY's Republic label '70; now based in Prescott, Arizona. LPs incl. *From A Jack To A King* on Fabor/London, *Teardrop Lane* on Capitol.

MILLER, Roger (*b* 2 Jan. '36, Fort Worth, Texas) Laid-back genius whose skill at composing catchy tunes with clever lyrics made him the most popular country-pop singer of the '60s. He was raised by an aunt and uncle in Erick, Oklahoma, a town so small 'that the city limit signs are back to back'. He learned guitar, banjo and fiddle; joined US Army and served in Korea; he auditioned for Chet ATKINS in Nashville, playing guitar in one key and singing in another: he worked as a bellboy in the Andrew Jackson Hotel (now demolished) but wrote songs: his 'Invitation To The Blues' was a top 20 country hit '58 by Ray PRICE (Patti PAGE also covered it); got full-time writing contract and songs were covered by Jim REEVES, George JONES, Ernest TUBB; he played fiddle for Minnie Pearl, drums for Faron YOUNG, bass for Price; recorded for Starday '58-60, had country hits on RCA '60-3: 'You Don't Want My Love' was no. 16 (Andy WILLIAMS covered it for minor pop hit); 'When Two Walls Collide' (co-written with Bill ANDERSON) was no. 6 country hit, 'Lock Stock And Teardrops' made top 30. Signed with Smash (Mercury subsidary), suddenly hit big with charming, singable humour: 'Dang Me' '64 and 'King Of The Road' '65 were no. 1 country ('King' was covered hundreds of times), 'Chug-A-Lug', 'Engine Engine No. 9' and 'England Swings' were top 10; all were top 10 pop: he collected 11 Grammies '64-5, a record that will probably never be broken. 'One Dyin' And A Buryin' ', 'Kansas City Star', 'Husbands And Wives', 'Walkin' In The Sunshine' were all top 10 country, top 40 pop '65-7; droll humour was evident in 'You Can't Roller Skate In A Buffalo Herd' and 'My Uncle Used To Love Me But She Died'. He helped to discover other song-writers such as Bobby Russell ('Little Green Apples'), Kris KRISTOFFERSON ('Me And Bobby McGee'); he appeared on Johnny Carson, Andy Williams, Steve ALLEN TV shows; had his own NBC series '66; worked on film soundtracks *Waterhole 3* '67 and Disney's cartoon *Robin Hood* '73. He never equalled his mid-'60s success, but pleased fans with albums on Columbia (*Sorry I Haven't Written Lately* '74, *Supersongs* '75, *Old Friends* '82 with Willie NELSON), RCA/Windsong (*Off The Wall* '78); other LPs incl. *Painted Poetry* on Starday, *Dang Me* on Smash, *Golden Hits* on Mercury, 2-disc compilation *Spotlight On Roger Miller* on Philips '67, etc. Back in the spotlight after writing hit musical show *Big River* '85 based on Mark Twain.

MILLER, Steve (*b* 5 Oct. '43, Milwaukee, Wis.) USA guitarist, bandleader. Mother was a singer, Les PAUL a family friend; played in Marksmen Combo with brother Jimmy and another teenager, William 'Boz' SCAGGS. Continued with Scaggs in other groups, but after high school graduation split to play Chicago blues. Miller-Goldberg Blues Band (with guitarist Barry Goldberg) made single 'Mother Song'; Miller retired owing to management problems to become janitor at a recording studio. Went to West Coast at height of San Francisco's burgeoning scene '66: first Steve Miller Blues band incl. Tim Davis, drums; Lonnie Turner, bass; James 'Curley' Cooke, guitar; recorded backing Chuck BERRY at Fillmore; Scaggs

returned from India to replace Cooke; Jim Peterman was added on organ; they played at Monterey, recorded three songs for *Revolution* soundtrack, signed for record-breaking advance and promise of artistic freedom with Capitol and recorded *Children Of The Future* '68 with prod. Glyn JOHNS in London, dropping 'blues' from band's name but incl. blues classics like 'Key To The Highway'. The adventurous format of the first side of the LP, with five segued Miller tunes, was reminiscent of *Sgt Pepper*, which Johns had engineered; title track was notable for sound effects, later a Miller trademark. *Sailor* '68 was a classic of the era, incl. psychedelic 'Song For Our Ancestors', while 'Living In The USA' featured driving harmonica and was their first Hot 100 entry (re-entering top 50 '74). *Grave New World* and *Your Saving Grace* '69 featured Ben SIDRAN as keyboardist (and producer), Scaggs and Peterman having left; latter also had Nicky HOPKINS on keyboards and standout tracks were gentle country pop of title track and atmospheric 'Motherless Children', trad. song given new treatment. *Number Five* '70 exaggerated country content, being recorded in Nashville; Turner and Davis quit and *Rock Love* '71 was a half live/half studio mess, with bassist Ross Vallory, Jack King on drums. *Recall The Beginner* '72 introduced ex-Van MORRISON drummer Gary Mallaber, Sweet Inspirations bassist Gerald Johnson; featured Miller's trademark high/low octave harmonies. *The Joker* '73 rewarded Capitol's investment with no. 2 LP USA, no. 1 hit title track with jokey piece of country picking, showcased personae (Space Cowboy, Gangster of Love, Maurice, etc.) he'd used in past songs. He retired to country life, became a farmer; came back to music with *Fly Like An Eagle* '76, *Book Of Dreams* '77, made at same sessions and featuring synth-linked tracks in style of updated *Children Of The Future*. He now scored consistent hit singles: 'Take The Money And Run' no. 11, 'Rock'n Me' no. 1 USA/11 UK, 'Fly Like An Eagle' and 'Jet Airliner' both top 10 USA. *Circle Of Love* '81 was off the boil: confused country-rock title track with 18-minute disco track 'Macho City'. But Mallaber's band Kid Lightning supplied guitarists/songwriters John Massaro and Kenny Lee Lewis, revival with *Abracadabra*

'82 and danceable title track as no. 1 USA/2 UK. *Live* '83 was followed by disappointing *Italian X-Rays* '84, *Living In The 20th Century* '86 (return to blues roots, partly a tribute to Jimmy REED). Miller is never predictable; still plays Buddy GUY blues live, paddles in MOR mainstream for periods, needing outside stimuli from personnel to keep him honest. Parallels with JEFFERSON Starship, the only other S.F. survivors of the '60s.

MILLINDER, Lucky (*b* Lucius Millinder, 8 Aug. 1900, Anniston, Ala.; *d* 28 Sep. '66, NYC) Bandleader. Did not play, but was a popular frontman from '30 into the '50s; he toured Europe '33, took over the Mills Blue Rhythm Band '34 (*see* Irving MILLS); sidemen were among the best: Henry ALLEN, Harry EDISON, Buster Bailey, Tab SMITH, John KIRBY, J. C. HIGGINBOTHAM, etc.; hits on Columbia '35-7 incl. 'Truckin' ' (vocal by Allen), 'Ride, Red, Ride' (Millinder vocal); in '40s the band was the most popular in Harlem: among those passing through were Freddie Webster, Dizzy GILLESPIE, Lucky THOMPSON, Eddie 'Lockjaw' DAVIS, Bill DOGGETT, Panama Francis, vocalists Wynonie HARRIS, Bull Moose Jackson, Sister Rosetta THARPE (who also played electric guitar). The band was reduced in size and had R&B hits '49-51: 'D'Natural Blues', 'I'll Never Be Free' on RCA; 'I'm Waiting Just For You' '51 with vocal by Annisteen Allen on King. The story of the band is a history of the evolution of Swing Era big-band jazz into R&B 'jump bands', with infl. on rock'n'roll. *Apollo Jump* on Affinity UK has '42-5 hits incl. 'I Want A Tall, Skinny Papa' with Tharpe, 'Who Threw The Whiskey In The Well' with Harris (*Let It Roll* on MCA/USA is similar); earlier and later hits also deserve compiling.

MILLS BROTHERS The most popular vocal group of all time, with 70 hit records '31-68. Brothers from Piqua, Ohio, Herbert (*b* 2 Apr. '12), Harry (*b* 19 Aug. '13; *d* 28 June '82), Donald (*b* 29 Apr. '15), accompanied on bass notes and guitar by John (*b* 11 Feb. 1889; *d* '35), who was replaced by father John Sr (retired '56; *d* '67). Sweet close-harmony style was perfected late '20s; in early days they imitated instrumental

sounds with their voices: sang on WLW radio Cincinnati; to NYC '30, network radio; many hits were two-sided incl. first: no. 1 'Tiger Rag'/'Nobody's Sweetheart' (no. 4); 'Dinah' '32 was also no. 1 backed with no. 10 'Can't We Talk It Over?', both with Bing CROSBY; other big hits: 'St Louis Blues', 'Bugle Call Rag' '32; 'Swing It, Sister', 'Sleepy Head' '34, all no. 2, all on Brunswick; switched to Decca label and recovered from the Depression on cut-price records, some with Ella FITZGERALD, Louis ARMSTRONG. Biggest hit of all was 'Paper Doll' '43, no. 1 for 12 weeks, selling several million copies, phenomenal for the era; 'You Always Hurt The One You Love' was no. 1 '44, both songs always associated with them, as well as 'I Love You So Much It Hurts'/'I've Got My Love To Keep Me Warm' and 'Someday (You'll Want Me To Want You)' '49, all top 10. 'Be My Life's Companion' '52 was first hit on which they were accompanied (by Sy OLIVER band) by anything other than their guitar; 'The Glow-Worm' same year with Hal McIntyre band was their last no. 1, song adapted from '08 hit originally from a German operetta. They switched to Dot label '58; top 40s entries: cover of Silhouettes' R&B hit 'Get A Job' '58, 'Cab Driver' '68. Many compilation LPs on MCA, Dot, Ranwood.

MILLS, Irving (*b* 16 Jan. 1894, NYC; *d* Apr. '85) Music publisher, lyricist, manager, sometime vocalist; fronted jazz bands. He was an early champion of Duke ELLINGTON, got the band more lucrative gigs and record contracts, published Duke's music and saw to it that the band travelled in style; had lyrics written for 'Solitude', 'It Don't Mean A Thing', 'I Let A Song Go Out Of My Heart', etc. Also managed other lucrative acts incl. Cab CALLOWAY; assembled pick-up bands for recording sessions and to promote music he published: hits by Irving Mills and his Hotsy-Totsy Gang incl. 'Ain't Misbehavin' ' '29 with Bill 'Bojangles' Robinson, first chart hit with 'Stardust' '30 with composer Hoagy CARMICHAEL on piano, J. DORSEY on reeds. Mills backed Bubber MILEY band c.'30; The Mills Blue Rhythm Band '31-7 (aka Harlem Hot Shots, Chocolate Dandies, Earl Jackson and his Musical Champions, Duke Wilson and his Ten Black Berries, etc.) was also his brainchild, with vocalists incl. Chick BULLOCK, Billy BANKS ('and his Blue Rhythm Boys') etc.; excellent sidemen incl. Sheldon Hemphill on trumpet (*b* 16 Mar. '06, Birmingham, Ala.; *d* Dec. '59, NYC), bassist Hayes Alvis (*b* 1 May '07, Chicago; *d* 29 Dec. '72, NYC) (both later with Ellington), Edgar HAYES, Joe Garland (later wrote classic arr. of 'In The Mood'; *see* HAYES); arr. was Benny CARTER on a '32 date; Lucky MILLINDER took over mid-'30s (*see his entry*). Mills is most famous for his association with Ellington, which ended '39: Mills' Variety and Master labels went broke; anyway Ellington didn't need him any more. He made a lot of money out of Ellington, but in the context of the mid-'20s Ellington might have found the going harder without Mills' acumen and connections.

MILSAP, Ronnie (*b* 16 Jan. '46, Robbinsville, N.C.) One of the most popular of country-pop entertainers. Blind from birth, went to State School for the Blind '52, learned to play piano, violin and cello, organised rock band the Apparitions with other students. Attended junior college in Atlanta studying law, working evenings in clubs singing R&B; signed with Sceptor '65, toured with soul acts the Miracles, Bobby BLAND etc.; first single written by Nik Ashford and Valerie Simpson: 'Let's Go Get Stoned'/'Never Had It So Good', latter a top 20 R&B hit; also 'Denver', written by Dan Penn and Spooner Oldham, Jim WEBB's 'Old Lady At The Fair'. Recorded for small labels; Sceptor compilation on *Mr Mailman* on DJM and Phoenix, other tracks from the period on *Vocalist Of The Year* on Crazy Cajun, *Plain And Simple* on Pickwick. To Memphis '68 as session singer and musician, still working clubs; met Elvis PRESLEY on New Year's Eve '69, sang harmony on his hits 'Don't Cry Daddy', 'Kentucky Rain'; signed with Chips Moman's Chips label and had Hot 100 entry with 'Loving You Is A Natural Thing' '70. LP *Ronnie Milsap* '70 on WB prod. by Penn; incl. Kris KRISTOFFERSON's 'Please Don't Tell Me How The Story Ends': new version later on RCA was a hit; WB later recycled tracks on another album. He moved to Nashville and sang for a year with the house band at Roger MILLER's King Of The Road Motel '72, signing with Charley PRIDE's manager Jack D. Johnson and with RCA. First coun-

try hit was 'I Hate You' '73, with clever Penn lyric; third single 'Pure Love' topped country chart and he has never looked back: other chart-toppers have been '(I'd Be) A Legend In My Time' '74, 'Daydreams About Night Things' '75, 'Stand By My Woman Man' '76 (won Grammy), 'It Was Almost Like A Song' '77, 'Only One Love In My Life' '78, 'Nobody Likes Sad Songs' '79. Ten RCA singles also reached the pop Hot 100 '74-82, incl. 'Smoky Mountain Rain' '80, '(There's No) Gettin' Over Me' '81 (no. 5), 'I Wouldn't Have Missed It For The World' '81, 'Any Day Now' '82, all top 40. He takes a positive approach, trying to create a happy mood; grateful for excellent education, he has also done much charitable work on behalf of the blind. Interest in electronics led to building his own Ground Star Laboratory studio in Nashville, one of the best in the business. In '74-76-77 he was CMA Male Vocalist of the Year, also Entertainer of the Year '77. First RCA LP was *Where The Heart Is* '73, also *Pure Love* '74, *20-20 Vision* '76; 2-disc *In Concert* '75 was made on tour with Glen CAMPBELL, incl. duets with Dolly PARTON, much else; *Ronnie Milsap Live* was recorded at the Grand Ole Opry and was CMA Album of the Year '77; albums that have crossed over to the top 200 pop LPs are *A Legend In My Time* (CMA Album of the Year) and *Night Things* '75, *It Was Almost Like A Song* '77, *Only One Love In My Life* '78, *Images* '79, *Milsap Magic* and *Greatest Hits* '80, *Out Where The Bright Lights Are Glowing* (a Jim REEVES tribute album) and *There's No Getting Over Me* '80, *Inside Ronnie Milsap* '82, *Keyed Up* '83, *One More Try For Love* '84, *Greatest Hits Vol. 2* '85. *Lost In The Fifties Tonight* '86 has hit title track, also 'Happy Happy Birthday Baby'; *Collector's Series* compiles tracks from '75-83; two 2-disc sets '86 on Pair label are *Believe It!* and *Back On My Mind Again*. Hit duet '87 with Kenny ROGERS on 'Make No Mistake, She's Mine'.

MILTON, Roy (*b* 31 July '07, Wynnewood, Okla.) R&B singer, drummer, bandleader. Infl. by gospel music, formed combos from late '20s to play for dances, etc.; to West Coast mid-'30s; formed Roy Milton and his Solid Senders, appeared in 'soundie' film shorts for juke boxes; first records '45 on own label, then on Hamp-Tone; 'R.M.

Blues' was top 20 hit on Juke Box label '49; on Specialty '47-54: top 10 R&B hits '49-52 incl. one of several versions of dance riff 'The Hucklebuck' '49, 'Information Blue' '50, no. 2 'Best Wishes' '51. He also recorded for Dootone, King, Warwick; top 30 hit on Warwick '61 saw reissue of an old Specialty side 'Baby You Don't Know' also make top 30. He often worked outside music; with Johnny OTIS on Kent label and at Monterey Jazz Festival '70. His 'jump band' style rivalled that of Louis JORDAN in popularity; his combination of backbeat and gospel feeling made him one of the fathers of rock'n'roll. *Roy Milton And His Solid Senders* on Specialty/Sonet has all the hits; *Instant Groove* on Classic Jazz was recorded much later.

MIMMS, Garnet (*b* 26 Nov. '33, Ashland, W. Va.) Soul singer in NYC 'symphonic' or 'uptown' style. Grew up in Philadelphia; made first record with gospel group the Norfolk Four on Savoy '53; after military service formed doo-wop group the Gainors, recorded for Red Top; Mimms and Sam Bell split to form Garnet Mimms and the Enchanters with two others. Tired of competing with the likes of Chubby CHECKER and Bobby RYDELL they went to NYC: Bert BERNS signed them, called in Jerry Ragavoy to help with writing 'Cry Baby': no. 1 R&B/4 pop '63 on UA was one of the most intense of pop hits, some time before Aretha FRANKLIN and others redefined soul music. Next was revival of Jerry BUTLER hit 'For Your Precious Love'; Enchanters split and Mimms carried on solo for several more hits incl. another Berns-Ragavoy song 'I'll Take Good Care Of You' '66, top 30 pop and his second soul chart entry at no. 15. He supported Jimi HENDRIX in UK '67, recorded for Verve and MGM but had no more hits, despite the success of the soul era which he had helped to inaugurate, except for a frantic dance track: 'What It Is' (as Garnet Mimms and Truckin' Co.) was created by the producers behind the funk band Brass Construction, charting in UK '77 for one week. Excellent compilation of '63-6 hits *Warm & Soulful* on Liberty UK.

MINGUS, Charles (*b* 22 Apr. '22, Nogales, Arizona; *d* 5 Jan. '79, Cuernavaca, Mexico)

Bassist, bandleader, composer; also piano and vocals: with Jelly Roll MORTON, Duke ELLINGTON and Thelonious MONK, one of the most important composers in 20th-century black music, thence infl. other musics profoundly; also a great talent scout, hiring scores of the best musicians, many of whom never played better than when they were with him. Ancestry incl. Swedish, American Indian, Afro-American, possibly Scottish ('Mingus' is an old spelling of 'Menzies'). His light-skinned father was a staff sergeant in the US Army; mother died soon after birth, family moved to L.A.; sisters studied classical violin and piano; stepmother would allow only religious music at home, but took him to Holiness Church, where 'moaning and riffs . . . between the audience and the preacher' made an early impression. Studied trombone in school, helped by Britt Woodman (*b* 4 June '20, L.A.), classmate who later played with Ellington '51-60, also with Mingus; then cello, switching to bass as Buddy COLLETTE pointed out that Jordan High School band needed a bassist (band also incl. Chico HAMILTON, Dexter GORDON, Ernie Royal). His excellent pitch sense and poor teachers made him a slow reader of music, but better teachers incl. Joe Comfort (Lionel HAMPTON, Nat COLE trio), Red CALLENDER, later H. Reinschagen (of the NY Philharmonic). He replaced Callender in Lee Young band, led own Strings and Keys trio; first records were transcription sessions for broadcast with Louis ARMSTRONG band '43. Played and recorded on West Coast with Howard McGHEE, Illinois JACQUET, Dinah WASHINGTON, Ivie ANDERSON, others incl. own groups; with Hampton '47-8; he was working for the Post Office when asked to join Red NORVO Trio '50-1 with Tal FARLOW: the successful trio helped usher in West Coast 'cool jazz'; Mingus placed in bass category in a *Downbeat* poll, but racism combined with union rules to cause his replacement by a white bassist for a TV broadcast and he left the trio, having intended to relocate in NYC anyway: innovators such as Lennie TRISTANO were in NYC; Mingus was already composing and had decided to identify with black music (though he would hire whites, saying 'All the good ones are colorless'). He was soon highly rated as teacher as well as bassist:

infl. by pianists (like Tristano) as well as Charlie PARKER, he took the bass beyond the Jimmy BLANTON/Oscar PETTIFORD concept of playing melodic solos and played it like a guitar. Joined his idol Ellington early '53 (broadcasts recorded) but strong personality led to violent scene with Juan Tizol: Mingus was one of the few Ellington ever fired. Formed Jazz Composers Workshop and Debut label '53-7 with Max ROACH, an early attempt to control artistic output (some records later reissued on Fantasy); Debut recorded first dates under their own names by Teo MACERO, Kenny DORHAM, Paul BLEY, John LA PORTA, Sam Most (*b* 16 Dec. '30, Atlantic City, N.J.; reedman and one of the first jazz flautists: became L.A. studio musician); first issue was famous concert at Toronto's Massey Hall '53 with Mingus, Roach, Parker, Dizzy GILLESPIE, Bud POWELL (badly recorded; new bass part later overdubbed). Debut jam session *Four Trombones* led to Mingus playing on Savoy LP by J. J. JOHNSON and Kai WINDING (incl. his 'Reflections', different from anything else they recorded). Sextet tracks '54 with La Porta and Macero reissued many times: on Savoy, 'Eulogy for Rudy Williams' (swing era reedman *b* '09, Newark, N.J.; drowned Sep. '54) was his first tribute to a fellow musician, while other tracks were loaded with interpolations (he always recomposed his own and others' material: thus 'Weird Nightmare', '46 and '60 with vocals, 'Pipe Dream' '46, 'Smooch' '53 recorded by Miles DAVIS, and 'Vassarlean' '60 are all the same tune). *Abstractions* (prod. by Leonard Feather; now on Affinity) added Thad JONES on 'Minor Intrusion', 'Stormy Weather', etc. The mature composer began to emerge on two LPs which were made live at Café Bohemia late '55: with Mal WALDRON, Eddie Bert on trombone (*b* 16 May '22, Yonkers, NY), George Barrow on tenor, drummer Willie Jones (*b* 20 Oct. '29, Brooklyn), Roach on some of the tracks; the records incl. interpretations/interpolations of standards e.g. 'A Foggy Day', 'Septemberly'; 'All The Things You C Sharp' combined Jerome KERN, Rachmaninov; plus originals 'Haitian Fight Song', 'Jump Monk', etc. *Pithecanthropus Erectus* '56 on Atlantic incl. Jones, Jackie MCLEAN, Waldron, J. R. Monteroes, announced arrival of volatile

genius: title tone poem incorporated swinging roots in blues and gospel with modern harmonies, unmistakable Mingus sound. '57 yielded Jazz Workshop session *The Clown* on Atlantic, with Shafi Hadi on reeds (*b* Curtis Porter, 21 Sep. '29, Philadelphia), first appearance of long-term sidemen Jimmy KNEPPER on trombone, Dannie RICHMOND on drums; trio date with Hampton HAWES and Richmond on Jubilee; Workshop sextets *East Coasting* and *Scenes In The City* (both now on Affinity). *The Clown* and *Scenes In The City* are among his less well-known albums, possibly because each has a long track flirting with the jazz-poetry movement, while spoken words do not bear repeated listenings. The fiery masterpiece *Tijuana Moods* on RCA has no such drawback: with Knepper, Richmond, Hadi, others incl. brilliant trumpeter Clarence Shaw (*b* 16 June '26, Detroit; subsequently dropped from view), Mingus said 'This is the best record I ever made' when it was finally issued '62. He tried psychoanalysis, went to NYC's Bellevue hospital for help '58, bureaucrats there locked him up: friends incl. Nat Hentoff had to get him out. Same year saw fine collection *Blues & Roots* on Atlantic with four reeds, two trombones, no trumpet: he was now in his stride as composer/leader, teaching the best young musicians to play his music as they felt it, but demanding that they give it everything they had: the tonal colours in his powerful work, like those of Monk and Ellington, are instantly recognisable and will never date, but also incl. his own uniquely urgent swing. Live quintet LP *Wonderland* '59 on UA incl. John HANDY, Booker ERVIN; CBS dates same year with 8-10 pieces (prod. by Macero) resulted in classic versions of 'Pussy Cat Dues', 'Boogie Stop Shuffle', 'Jelly Roll', 'Goodbye Pork Pie Hat', 'Fables Of Faubus', many more: LPs *Mingus Ah-Um* and *Mingus Dynasty* bristled with brilliant solos, vital swing; later reissued in 2-disc *Better Git It In Your Soul*, unedited/additional tracks in confusingly titled 2-disc *Nostalgia In Times Square* '79 (title tune not recorded for CBS, but on *Wonderland*). Sessions for short-lived Archie BLEYER Candid label '60 (prod. by Hentoff) reissued complete in 4-disc limited-edition Mosaic box '86 incl. incandescent quartet tracks with Richmond, Ted

CURSON, Eric DOLPHY incl. 'Folk Forms', 'All The Things You Could Be By Now If Sigmund Freud's Wife Was Your Mother', 'Original Faubus Fables' (incl. savage lyrics CBS wouldn't allow, skewering racist governor of Georgia); octet tracks incl. 'Lock 'Em Up' (aka 'Hellview of Bellevue'); other tracks with Dolphy, Knepper, Roy ELDRIDGE, Tommy FLANAGAN, Jo JONES represent short-lived Newport Rebels/Jazz Artists Guild: elder statesman Eldridge told Mingus 'I wanted to find out what bag you were in. Now I know you're in the right bag.' He priced himself out of the Newport Jazz Festival '60, formed Newport Rebel Festival incl. gig with Roach, Dorham, Ornette COLEMAN, not recorded. Same year saw *Charlie Mingus Live* (now on Affinity) from Antibes Jazz Festival, with Dolphy, Curson, Ervin, Richmond; and big band *Pre-Bird* on Mercury, early compositions incl. 'Half-Mast Inhibition' (cond. by Gunther SCHULLER). *Oh Yeah* and *Tonight At Noon* '61 on Atlantic incl. Roland KIRK in sextet; Mingus played piano, with excellent Doug Watkins on bass (latter LP incl. tracks left over from '57 *Clown* sessions). *Money Jungle* '61 was trio set with Roach and Ellington on UA: a tense, exciting LP incl. tunes by both Duke and Mingus, unlike anything else either of them ever did: reissued '86 on Blue Note with previously unissued tracks. To make the Ellington date he took time from preparing music for a Town Hall big band gig: it was meant to be a public rehearsal, but he forgot to tell the public; the date was moved up five weeks and he quarrelled with Knepper, who was helping to copy the music, punching him in the mouth; the event was a disaster, but poorly recorded shards were issued on UA. A deal with Impulse '63 led to collection *Mingus Mingus Mingus Mingus Mingus*, six-piece suite *The Black Saint And The Sinner Lady* (both with 10-11 pieces, the latter regarded as one of his best), and solo *Mingus Plays Piano*, all prod. by Bob THIELE. He toured with small groups, always incl. the faithful Richmond: 3-disc *The Great Concert Of Charles Mingus* '64 on Prestige is especially fine, with Dolphy, Clifford JORDAN, Jaki BYARD; a Town Hall concert '64 with the same sextet redeemed him in that venue (sleeve of Fantasy LP wrongly stated venue as Tyrone Guthrie theatre in Minne-

apolis: *My Favorite Quintet* '65 was made there); *Live At The Jazz Work-Shop* '64 with Jane Getz on piano incl. side-long 'Meditations (For A Pair Of Wire Cutters)' with exciting work by Jordan, and 'New Fables' adding Handy (on Fantasy, French American). 2-disc *Mingus At Monterey* '64 incl. an Ellington medley and another version of 'Meditations', 11-piece band incl. Callender on tuba. He walked out of Monterey Festival '65 for his own obscure reasons; 2-disc *Music Written For (And Not Heard At) Monterey, 1965* played at UCLA a week later, issued '66 by Charles Mingus Enterprises, which soon ran out of money; master tapes were wiped by Capitol while in storage (limited edition set dubbed from LPs was issued '84 on East Coasting label, prod. by his widow Susan with Fred Cohen: it contains material unavailable elsewhere and is a revealing document of Mingus at work). The late '60s were lean years: he always worked hard, often changing his mind as he went, making things difficult for sidemen; his pride often got in the way, but the music had always come first. In '66 he was evicted by city marshals from a flat in NYC; much of his music was lost; his instruments were only rescued from the Welfare Dept flames by friends: the event made a coda to a grainy documentary film underway at the time, *Mingus* (by Thomas Reichman), capturing the nervous intensity in which he lived and worked. Period of semi-retirement followed; Fantasy provided some money in exchange for rights to Debut material. No new records for four years; *Blue Bird* and a revived *Pithecanthropus* on America were made in Paris '70 by a sextet which included Richmond, Byard, Charles MCPHERSON and Bobby Jones (*b* 30 Oct. '28, Louisville, Ky.) on reeds. Autobiography (with Nel King) *Beneath The Underdog* '71 was stream-of-consciousness fantasy, unreliable as biography but incl. reminiscences of Fats NAVARRO, others, and hilarious imaginary party attended by the major jazz critics: the book was allegedly edited from trunkful of probably libellous stuff, now lost. He was acknowledged '70s as living legend and musical cornerstone, if never adequately rewarded; big band set *Let My Children Hear Music* '71 on CBS was prod. by Macero, incl. 'Don't Be Afraid, The Clown's Afraid Too'; *Charles Mingus*

And Friends '72 was sold-out celebratory concert in Avery Fisher Hall NYC: 22 pieces incl. Gerry MULLIGAN, Gene AMMONS, drummer Joe Chambers (*b* 25 June '42, Stoneacre, Va.; own LP *The Almoravid* on Muse), cond. and prod. by Macero for CBS: Bill Cosby emcee'd (and sang Scat with Gillespie on 'E's Flat, Ah's Flat Too'): 2-disc set on CBS. All the rest of his LPs as leader on Atlantic: *Mingus Moves, Mingus At Carnegie Hall, Changes One* and *Changes Two* '73-4 all incl. Richmond, George ADAMS, Don PULLEN: nine pieces at Carnegie Hall incl. Handy, Kirk, Hamiet BLUIETT; among trumpet players, Jon Faddis (*b* 24 July '53, Oakland, Cal.; toured mid-'87 with Gillespie big band) had depped for ailing Eldridge at '72 concert while Jack Walrath (*b* 5 May '46, Stuart, Fla.) was steady member of the last sextet with Adams and Pullen, which recorded the *Changes* LPs, among the best of his late career, with good notes by the faithful Hentoff. *Cumbia & Jazz Fusion* '77 is an exciting big-band film score (*Music For 'Todo Modo'* on the other side), typically scathing, swinging Mingus vocal: 'Who says mama's little baby loves shortnin' bread?/That's some lie some white man upped and said!/Mama's little baby loves truffles! caviar! . . .' *Three Or Four Shades Of Blues* '77 is an uneven LP with Philip CATHERINE and Larry CORYELL on electric guitars, George Mraz (*b* 9 Sep. '44, Pisek, Czechoslovakia) helping on bass: Mingus suffered from amyotrophic lateral sclerosis, fatal wasting disease (aka Lou Gehrig's disease, from baseball star who died of it '41). He last recorded on Hampton LP of Mingus tunes late '77 in Who's Who In Jazz series/label; band incl. Hampton, Richmond, Mulligan, Walrath, recent Mingus discovery Ricky Ford on tenor (*b* 4 Mar. '54, Boston); *Me Myself An Eye* early '78 on Atlantic had Mingus dir. from a wheelchair, Eddie Gomez on bass; 20+ pieces also incl. George COLEMAN, Ford, Knepper, Pepper ADAMS, both Chambers and Richmond on drums, with ace session player Steve GADD added on side-long 'Three Worlds Of Drums'. He went to his beloved Mexico, hoping for a cure, but the volcano was silenced, the passion living on in the music. Concert LPs are still issued, especially from Europe in the '60s, some of them bootlegs: *Sextet In Berlin,*

Mingus In Stuttgart etc. Excellent critical biography *Mingus* '82 by Brian Priestley.

MINK DeVILLE (*b* Willy DeVille, '53, NYC) An early New York punk vocalist/guitarist, he formed a band mid-'70s and appeared on compilation *Live From CBGBs* '76, leading to authentic debut *Mink DeVille* '77 (aka *Cabretta*) creating a white R&B style on originals such as 'Venus Of Avenue D' and 'Mixed Up, Shook Up Girl'; 'Spanish Stroll' (infl. by Lou REED) was top 20 UK hit. *Return To Magenta* '78 was more of the same, while *La Chat Bleu* '80 was made in Paris, said by some to be his best to date (though Capitol didn't like it), incl. songs co-written with Doc POMUS as well as originals e.g. zydeco-style 'Mazurka'. Switched to Atlantic: *Coup de Grâce* '81 was prod. by Jack NITZSCHE; *Where Angels Fear To Tread* incl. 'Each Word's A Beat Of My Heart'. *Sportin' Life* '86 was recorded at Muscle Shoals, but was still unlikely to break him in the mainstream. Reportedly working with Mark Knopfler in Studio. Four LPs reached top 200 USA, cult status endures; Capitol LP cailed *Savoir Faire* is probably recycled material. He contributed three songs to controversial Al Pacino movie *Cruising* '80.

MINNELLI, Liza (*b* '46) Singer, dancer, actress; daughter of Judy GARLAND and film director Vincente Minnelli (1910-86; his masterpiece was *An American In Paris* '51). A cabaret artist and musical show singer in the same mould as her mother, with the same star quality. Her films (not all musicals) incl. *Charlie Bubbles* '67, *The Sterile Cuckoo* '69 (she won Oscar nomination), *Tell Me That You Love Me Junie Moon* '70, *Cabaret* '72 (she was nominated and won), *Lucky Lady* '76, *A Matter Of Time* '76, *New York, New York* '77 (*see* Georgie AULD). *Cabaret* was adapted by Jay Presson Allen from *Goodbye To Berlin* by Christopher Isherwood, dir. and choreographed by Bob Fosse; original cast LP of '66 stage show charted on CBS label with Jack Gifford, Jill Hayworth, Bert Convy, Lotte Lenya; film starred Joel Gray and Michael York as well as Minnelli and soundtrack LP charted on ABC '72: one of the most nearly perfect screen musicals since WWII has music by John Kander (*b* 18 Mar. '27, Kansas City, Mo.), lyrics by Fred Ebb (*b* 8 Apr. '32,

NYC). Minnelli appeared on Broadway in *Flora, The Red Menace* '65 (LP on RCA) and *The Act* '77 (on DRG), both written by Kander and Ebb; she won Tony awards for these and for *Liza At The Winter Garden* '73 (on CBS), was nominated for a Tony while starring in *The Rink* with Chita Rivera, but dropped out '84 for successful cure for drug problem of 15 years' standing (began with Valium, taken at first for muscles). Her other albums incl. *Liza! Liza!* '64 on Capitol, 2-disc *Live At The London Palladium* '65 with Garland on Capitol (edited to one disc, charted again '73), *New Feelin'* '73 on A&M, *Liza With A 'Z'* (TV soundtrack) and *The Singer* '72-3 on CBS; other sets incl. 2-disc *Foursider* on A&M, *Maybe This Time* on Capitol.

MINSTRELSY An American musical entertainment popular around the world, which began in the 1820s, reached its stride c. 1850 and still had its effects well into the 20th century. It was the first massive input of black culture into the mainstream. In the 18th century there were occasional setpieces requiring the performer to 'black up' with burnt cork; the *New York Journal* referred to a 'Negro dance, in character' on stage in 1767. There were black minstrels, such as William Henry Lane (c.1825-52, aka Master Juba, one of the few to tour with a white company), but the majority were white until after the Civil War; blacks as well as whites were required to 'black up'. The phenomenon of popular black culture was widely discussed, for instance in the *Knickerbocker Magazine* (1845) on Negro poets: 'Let one of them, in the swamps of Carolina, compose a new song, and it no sooner reaches the ear of a white amateur, than it is written down, amended (that is, almost spoilt), printed, and then put upon a course of rapid dissemination, to cease only with the utmost bounds of Anglo-Saxondom, perhaps with the world. Meanwhile, the poor author digs away with his hoe, utterly ignorant of his greatness.' (Quoted by Eileen Southern in *The Music Of Black Americans*, by Gene LEES in his *Jazzletter*, etc.) Patterns still extant today were established: minstrelsy was essentially black music, while the most successful acts were white; songs/dances of black origin were watered down by white performers, then

taken up by the blacks, who ended up imitating their own styles; and the affectionate, patronising vision of plantation life was similar to the unrealistic depiction of reality on TV sitcoms of today. In 1829 Thomas Dartmouth Rice became famous with the 'Jim Crow' song and dance, copied from a stable-hand: 'Jim Crow' was a plantation slave, while 'Zip Coon' (song by George Washington Dixon) was a city dandy. Much material was copied from songs and dances of slavery, but much was original: Stephen FOSTER was the most successful songwriter of the 19th century. The first full-length minstrel shows were organised by quartets: the Virginia Minstrels (1843) incl. Daniel Decatur Emmett (1815-1904), who wrote 'I Wish I Was In Dixie's Land' for Bryant's Minstrels in 1859; the Christy Minstrels (formed 1844), incl. Edwin P. Christy (aka Christie, 1815-62), who wrote 'Goodnight Ladies' and other songs, toured Europe, committed suicide by jumping out of a hotel window in NYC. Shows were in three parts: songs and jokes, speciality acts and novelties (called the 'olio', probably from the Spanish *olla*, or 'potpourri') and a walk-around finale. (A late invention was the cakewalk, in which members of the audience were invited to invent the most ridiculous strutting march, for which the prize was a cake.) Many songs were sympathetic: 'The Negro Boy' (aka 'I Sold A Guiltless Negro Boy'), 'A Negro Song' (aka 'The Negro's Humanity'), but minstrelsy became more overtly racist after the Civil War: the image of the 'darky' as a comic buffoon insulated whites from having to deal with the reality of free black Americans, and survived in films and TV until well into the 1950s. But minstrel shows were popular among ordinary blacks; although conditions were terrible for black performers, and a full-time first-class black minstrel troupe was not organised until 1865 (Brooker and Clayton's Georgia Minstrels), by the 1880s black talent was in demand and a great many performers obtained valuable experience. The dances (breakdowns, double-shuffles, heel-and-toe, etc.) and the 'Ethiopian' instrumentation (especially the banjo) were authentic and profoundly influential, the rhythms leading to ragtime and beyond: many ragtime songs were 'coon songs' (*see* RAGTIME), directly descended from minstrelsy. Lew Dockstader's Minstrels still performed, and George M. COHAN was a partner in a minstrel show, as late as the year 1908; a white blacked-up minstrel show was popular on UK television in the 1960s. Black and white performers still 'blacked up' in 20th-century vaudeville; Bert Williams (b 1874, Antigua; d '22, NYC), a black dancer described by W. C. Fields as 'the funniest man I ever saw and the saddest man I ever knew', had to black up all his career. Sophie TUCKER gave it up as soon as she could, but Al JOLSON milked blackface for sentimentality until the end.

MIRANDA, Carmen (b Maria do Carmo Miranda da Cunha, 9 Feb. '09, near Lisbon, Portugal; d 5 Aug. '55, Cal.) Singer, dancer. To Brazil as a child; sang on radio '20s; recorded, made four films '34-8, becoming well known as exponent of carnival rhythms such as marcha, samba; to USA '39 for Broadway revue *The Streets Of Paris* with Abbott & Costello: her first-act finale with 'South American Way', wearing six-inch heels and her trademark headgear made of fruit, made her an instant star, billed as 'Brazilian Bombshell'. Spoke little English at first, made comic accent a plus; strong personality, cosmetics, costumes made big hit with press. First hit was 'Mama Eu Quero' '41, with Banda do Lua, incl. singer/guitarist José Carioca, from film *Down Argentine Way*, with Betty Grable and Don Ameche; *Springtime In The Rockies* '42 incl. a bizarre version of 'Chattanooga Choo Choo'; *The Gang's All Here* '43 incl. Busby Berkeley choreography in 'The Lady With The Tutti Frutti Hat' and Ary Barroso's hit song 'Brazil'. Other Miranda hits on Decca incl. 'Cuanto la Gusta' '48 (samba written by Barroso, from film *A Date With Judy*, with Xavier CUGAT), 'The Wedding Samba' '50, both with the ANDREWS Sisters. On Broadway in Olsen & Johnson's *Sons O' Fun* '41; other films incl. *That Night In Rio* '41, several more. She continued in clubs, topped the bill for a season at the London Palladium '48, toured Cuba '55; she died of a heart attack while preparing a TV spot with Jimmy DURANTE. She was caricatured affectionately in a Bugs Bunny cartoon, by Jerry LEWIS singing 'Mama Eu Quero' in film *Scared Stiff* '53 and in countless night club acts. Compilation LP *South American Way* on MCA.

MISUNDERSTOOD Rock band formed in California '65 by Glenn Ross Campbell, steel guitar, with Greg Treadway, guitar; Steve Whiting, bass; Rick Moe, drums; vocalist Rick Brown. Made single 'You Don't Have To Go' for local Blues Sound label; recorded other (unreleased) material prod. by expat DJ John PEEL, who suggested they go to London, where they replaced Treadway '66 with UK guitarist Tony Hill. Singles incl. 'I Can Take You To The Sun'/'Who Do You Love' (the Bo DIDDLEY number) before split caused by Brown's being drafted. Campbell re-formed '69 with mainly UK members: vocalist Steve Hoard, Neil Hubbard on guitar, Chris Mercer (ex-John MAYALL) on sax, two others; two singles flopped and he re-formed again as Juicy Lucy with Hubbard, Mercer. Lucy made four LPs (two charted in UK '70) and had two chart singles in UK incl. another version of 'Who Do You Love' (no. 14), split '72. Campbell's steel was the only thing in common with Misunderstood, who remained legendary because there was not much released material, made up by Cherry Red's compilation *Before The Dream Fades* '82. Campbell was still active in The Influence early '80s; Hubbard played with ROXY MUSIC, Kokomo.

MITCHELL, Blue (b Richard Allen Mitchell, 13 Mar. '30, Miami, Fla.; d 21 May '79 of cancer) R&B and jazz trumpeter. Worked with Earl BOSTIC, others early '50s; with Horace SILVER '58-64, took group over as Blue Mitchell Quintet '64-9 with Chick COREA; worked with Ray CHARLES, John MAYALL. Apart from prolific freelance work as a sideman, with seven LPs as leader on Riverside/Milestone '58-63 incl. *Blue's Moods* '60 (with Wynton KELLY, Sam JONES, Roy Brooks on drums); compilation of '58-62 tracks now on 2-disc *A Blue Time*. Eight Blue Note LPs '63-9 incl. *The Thing To Do* and *Down With It* '64-5 with Corea; *Heads Up!*, *Collision In Black* and *Bantu Village* '67-9 featured larger groups. Five Mainstream LPs '71-4 were followed by big band *Stratosonic Nuances* and *Booty* '75-6 on RCA, *African Violet* and *Summer Soft*

'77 on Impulse/MCA with various smaller lineups.

MITCHELL, Chad, Trio Folk/pop vocal group of early '60s: Chad Mitchell, Mike Kobluk, Joe Frazier were all from Spokane, Wash., *b* '39; had minor hits on Kapp: novelties and comedy incl. 'Lizzie Borden'. Switched to Mercury; Chad left; group renamed Mitchell Trio replaced him with young unknown John DENVER, but had no more hits.

MITCHELL, Guy (*b* Al Cernick, 27 Feb. '27) Enormously popular, likeable pop singer of early '50s. Born in Yugoslavia, grew up in Detroit, joined US Navy '45, signed with Columbia '50: 22 top 40 hits '50-9 were mostly jolly novelties and adaptations prod. by Mitch MILLER, began with 'My Heart Cries For You' (adapted from 18th-century French tune by Percy FAITH), 'The Roving Kind' (from an English folk song; also recorded by the WEAVERS), 'You're Just In Love' (duet with Rosemary CLOONEY on song from Broadway's *Call Me Madam*), 'Sparrow In The Tree Top', 'My Truly, Truly Fair', Hank WILLIAMS's 'I Can't Help It', 'Pittsburgh, Pennsylvania', duets with Mindy Carson (*b* 16 July '27, NYC; sang with Paul WHITEMAN on radio, had hits on RCA early '50s), many more, all '50-3. Just when his era seemed to be over, he had his biggest hit and first no. 1 with cover of Marty ROBBINS's country hit 'Singing The Blues' '56, did it again with Ray PRICE's 'Heartaches By The Number' '59. He is still popular in UK, where he can tour clubs any time he wants.

MITCHELL, Joni (*b* Roberta Joan Anderson, 7 Nov.'43, McLeod, Alberta, Canada) Singer/songwriter and guitarist. After two decades, with Bob DYLAN and Van MORRISON, she is one of the most enduring of the troubadors who began in the '60s, showing pop music how to become an art form. Her songs have been covered by Dylan, FAIRPORT CONVENTION, Judy COLLINS, Tom RUSH, NAZARETH, Gordon LIGHTFOOT, Johnny CASH, CROSBY, STILLS & NASH, many others. She studied art in Calgary, began singing in local folk clubs, moved to Toronto, married folksinger Chuck Mitchell; they moved to Detroit '65

and the marriage ended '66; she moved to NYC and signed with Reprise. *Song To A Seagull* '67 and *Joni Mitchell* '68 were above average folk fodder for the time; her songs began to be widely noticed and *Clouds* '69 (with just guitar accompaniment) incl. 'Songs To Aging Children Come' (heard in film *Alice's Restaurant*) and 'Both Sides Now', covered by Collins for a top 10 hit '68; Rush had covered 'The Circle Game'; the lyrical maturity of her work was obvious. Her romantic attachments were as widely reported as her music; she wrote 'Willy' for Graham Nash. *Ladies Of The Canyon* '70 incl. 'Big Yellow Taxi', her first chart single; those who liked the song could not understand why it rose no higher than no. 67, but album sales were already far more important than singles in musical terms; *Canyon* also incl. 'Woodstock': Mitchell had not attended the famous festival, but wrote the song moved by CSNY's description of it: there were three hit versions in USA; (Ian) MATTHEWS Southern Comfort took it to no. 1 UK. *Blue* '71 featured James TAYLOR, incl. 'My Old Man', a long song-poem on which she accompanied herself at the piano: years later she thought that 'the *Blue* album, for the most part, holds up.' Critics and public alike made it one of the top albums of the year. *For The Roses* '72 incl. 'You Turn Me On, I'm A Radio'; she moved to Asylum label and her next two albums both reached no. 2 USA '74: *Court & Spark* incl. 'Help Me', her only top 10 single, also Annie Ross's jiving 'Twisted', her first cover marking an increasing eclecticism; on live 2-disc *Miles Of Aisles* featured Tom Scott's highly rated band L.A. Express. *The Hissing Of Summer Lawns* '75 was as radical and experimental as its evocative title, yet it reached no. 4; *Hejira* '76 and 2-disc *Don Juan's Reckless Daughter* '78 were also examples of her disregard for commercial considerations ('Paprika Plains' occupied an entire side on the latter). *Mingus* '79 was a noble failure, intended collaboration with the jazz giant foiled by his death in Jan. that year, yet her treatments of his themes still made a top 20 album. 2-disc live *Shadows Of Light* '80 featured backing by Pat METHENY, Jaco PASTORIUS, Michael BRECKER; incl. timeless 24-year-old Frankie LYMON hit 'Why Do Fools Fall In Love', chart hit 'In France

They Kiss On Main Street' and the luminous, sardonic 'Coyote' (which she also did in The BAND's concert/film/album *Last Waltz*). Marriage to bassist Larry Klein accompanied change of label to Geffen for *Wild Things Run Fast* '82, another accessible album, with guests Taylor, Lionel RICHIE, and a cover of '(You're So Square) Baby, I Don't Care', the LEIBER & STOLLER hit for Elvis PRESLEY, along with elegant originals. *Dog Eat Dog* '86 was prod. by Thomas DOLBY, incl. guests Don Henley and Michael McDonald; the album and the video took full advantage of studio technology, but never at the expense of wit and musical imagination. She painted her own sleeve illustration, as she has often done; a successful one-woman show of her work had taken up much of her time and she was undecided whether to concentrate on painting or on music. In spite of an occasional selfindulgence and an unhealthy '70s obsession with the strains of stardom, she has transcended the narcissism of the '60s to become firmly established as one of the giants of an era: *Chalk Mark In A Rain Storm* '88 was perhaps her most relaxed album.

MITCHELL, Red (*b* 20 Sep. '27, NYC) Bass, also piano and vocals. Played piano with Chubby Jackson, bass with Charlie VENTURA, Woody HERMAN, Red NORVO, Gerry MULLIGAN, all '49-55; with Hampton HAWES '55-7, co-led quintet with Harold LAND, worked with Hawes again, relocated to Europe. His horn-like projection and adoption of tuning an octave lower than standard on the bass were influential. Albums as leader on Bethlehem '55, Pacific Jazz '60 with Jim HALL, Atlantic '61 with Land, also *Presenting Red Mitchell* '57 on Contemporary, now on Fantasy. Several European LPs incl. *Meets Guido Manusardi* '74 (Italian pianist; now on Pausa in USA), *Chocolate Cadillac* '76 on Steeplechase, with Idrees Sulieman, Horace PARLAN, others on Swedish Sonet, Caprice, Phontastic labels, etc.; *Empathy* '80 on Gryphon with guitarist Joe Beck and solo *When I'm Singing* '82 on Enja were made in NYC; *Holiday For Monica* '83 on Phontastic with Parlan, Nisse Sandström on tenor, vocals by Monica Zetterland. His brother Whitey (*b* Gordon B. Mitchell, 22 Feb. '32) also

played bass, made LP on ABC '56 with sextet incl. Steve LACY.

MITCHELL, Roscoe (*b* 3 Aug. '40, Chicago, Ill.) Reeds, composer. Played in high school, then US Army; with Henry THREADGILL in conventional post-bop small group, then joined Richard ABRAMS's Experimental Band and later became co-founder of the ART ENSEMBLE OF CHICAGO. He has continued to pursue parallel solo projects as one of the most interesting and important composers in contemporary black music, exploring sound and space, playing all the reed instruments as well as percussion. Early LPs as leader were leading up to the Art Ensemble: *Sound* '66 on Delmark incl. Lester BOWIE, Malachi Favors, three others; *Old/Quartet* '67 and *Congliptious* '68 on Nessa are quartet LPs, the latter as Roscoe Mitchell Art Ensemble. On Sackville, *The Roscoe Mitchell Solo Saxophone Concerts* '73-4 has nine tracks using four saxophones, opening and closing with short versions of 'Nonaah'; *Quartet* '75 incl. Abrams, George Lewis on trombone, Spencer Barefield on guitar; also *Duets With Anthony Braxton* '76. On Nessa, the monumental, beautiful 2-disc *Nonaah* '76-7 incl. side-long solo development of title composition and a quartet version for four altos (Mitchell, Threadgill, Joseph JARMAN, Wallace McMillan), also other solos, duos, trio 'Tahquemenon' with Abrams and Lewis: Mitchell describes his warming up before a concert until the alto says, 'OK, you can play me now': Terry Martin's notes speak of the solo work as 'the diverse images a single mind and instrument can be made to reveal', the rest as 'an enlargement of the circle'. *LRG/The Maze/S II Examples*, is also two LPs, squeezed onto one CD (on Chief in UK): 'LRG' is a trio with Lewis on low and Leo SMITH on high brass instruments; 'Examples' is a soprano solo; 'The Maze' is a masterpiece played by percussionists Don Moye, Douglas Ewart, Thurman BARKER, Jarman, Braxton, Threadgill, Favors and Mitchell, shot through with space and light, in the recording as well as the playing: gatefold photograph by Ann Nessa on the LP edition gives some idea of what was involved; the engineers at CBS studios in NYC were astonished at efficiency with which the recording was made.

Sketches From Bamboo '79 on Moers Music is by the Creative Orchestra, incl. Kenny WHEELER, Smith, Lewis, Ewart, Braxton, Hugh Ragin, McMillan, 11 others; quintet Sound Ensemble incl. Barefield, bassist Jaribu Shahid, Ragin on brass instruments, Tani Tabbal on percussion: they sound like a larger group on marching, stomping good-time *Snurdy McGurdy And Her Dancin' Shoes* '80 on Nessa; *3 × 4 Eye* '81 on Black Saint incl. 'Variations On A Folk Song Written In The Sixties'; *More Cutouts* '81 incl. Ragin, Tabbal; *New Music For Woodwinds And Voice* '81 and *Space Improvisations* on Arch have Gerald Oshita on wind instruments, Tom Buckner's voice; *The Flow Of Things* '86 on Black Saint with Favors, Jodie Christian on piano, Steve McCall on drums is intense: three versions of title are high-energy roller-coasters. Solo album *Live At The Mükle Hungiken* '87 on Cecma adds bass sax to his repertoire; a 'classical album' is on Lovely Music label.

MITCHELL-RUFF DUO Pianist Dwike Mitchell (*b* 14 Feb. '30, Jacksonville, Fla.) and Willie Ruff (*b* 1 Sep. '31, Sheffield, Ala.) on bass and French horn. Ruff is also a professor of music at Yale. They left the Lionel HAMPTON band '55 and have been touring the world ever since, celebrating the basics of American music in schools and colleges, on TV, at Rotary Club lunches, to the Russians (at Moscow's Tchaikovsky Conservatory '59) and the Chinese ('81). Ruff calls it 'the oldest continuous group in jazz without personnel changes'; they demonstrate improvisation using interaction with audiences (especially kids) in small towns all over the USA, inspiring pride: 'Nobody else in the world invented jazz but Americans. It's one of the riches you should be proud of. If you ever travel you'll find that people in other lands know this part of your culture because they enjoy it.' LPs incl. two on Epic, three on Roulette '55-60; Atlantic LPs '61 with Charlie Smith on drums, '65 with Helcio Milito; Brazilian songs '66 with added sidemen on Epic, set of Billy STRAYHORN songs '69 on Mainstream; aptly titled *Virtuoso Elegance In Jazz* '83 on Kepler. They recorded with Dizzy GILLESPIE '70 (album *Enduring Magic* now on Blackhawk), at Dartmouth College '71 (on Mainstream). Book *Willie*

And Dwike: An American Profile by William Zinnser published c.'84.

MIZE, Billy (*b* 29 Apr. '29, Kansas City) Country bandleader, songwriter and TV host. Began late '40s on KERO-TV, Bakersfield, Cal.; then a regular on many country shows originating in L.A., host of Gene AUTRY's Melody Ranch show and a member of Tommy Duncan's band. Led own group the Tennesseans early '60s, winning Band of the Year (non-touring) award from ACM '68. Recorded for Columbia, Imperial, UA late '60s-70s, scoring minor country hits; wrote songs for Merle HAGGARD, Marty ROBBINS, Charlie Walker, many others. Heads Billy Mize Productions, responsible for several syndicated series, specials such as *Merle Haggard And His Friends* '81. Still plays the odd club date with the Tennesseans.

MOBLEY, Hank (*b* 7 July '30, Eastman, Ga.; *d* 30 May '86, Philadelphia) Tenor sax. Grew up in New Jersey; began in R&B with Paul GAYTEN '50; worked with Max ROACH, Dizzy GILLESPIE, then Horace SILVER '54, group which became the Jazz Messengers, led by Art BLAKEY, leaving with Silver '56 but returning to Blakey '59, then to Miles DAVIS early '60s. His unspectacular but subtle, solid, and swinging post-bop tenor was a favourite with many jazz fans, yet curiously underrated by critics and the general public, until lung problems forced him to slow down in the '70s. First LP as leader was *Hank Mobley Quartet* '55 on Blue Note, with Blakey, Silver and Doug Watkins on bass; the three on Savoy '55-6; Prestige sessions '56 reissued as 2-disc *Messages*. Seven LPs worth of material on Blue Note '56-8 incl. two unissued sessions; he also made *Blowing Session* '57 on Blue Note with John COLTRANE and Johnny GRIFFIN, *Tenor Conclave* on Prestige, etc.; live *Monday Night At Birdland* '58 was septet gig on Roulette; the rest were all on Blue Note: *Peckin' Time* '58, *Soul Station* and *Roll Call* '60 (both with Blakey), *Workout* and *Another Workout* '61 (the latter not issued until '85) all incl. Wynton KELLY and Paul CHAMBERS, stablemates in the Davis band, and are among his finest. Twelve more on Blue Note '63-70, all with fine sidemen, incl. *High Voltage* with Blue MITCHELL, Jackie

MCLEAN, others, and *Far Away Lands*, with Cedar WALTON, Donald BYRD, Ron CARTER and Billy HIGGINS, both '67; many of the other albums will no doubt be reissued in due course: Mobley was one of those who defined the mainstream jazz of the era.

MOBY GRAPE Rock band formed '66 in San Francisco, named for punch line of absurd joke ('What's blue, large, round and lives in the sea?'). Nucleus of group formerly the Frantics: Bob Mosley (*b* 4 Dec. '42, Paradise Valley, Cal.), bass; Jerry Miller (*b* 10 July '43, Tacoma, Wash.), guitar; Don Stevenson (*b* 15 Oct. '42, Seattle), drums; adding second guitar Peter Lewis (*b* 15 July '45, L.A.; ex-Peter and the Wolves) and Alexander 'Skip' Spence (*b* 18 Apr. '46, Windsor, Ontario, Canada; ex-drummer with JEFFERSON AIRPLANE) on rhythm guitar. Guided by ex-Airplane manager Matthew Katz, they all sang, established reputation for tight harmonies, 3-guitar weaving. Columbia won the race to sign them, but spoiled debut *Moby Grape* '67 as fine West Coast rock with simultaneous release of five singles. There were foreshadows of CROSBY, STILLS & NASH ('8:05'), the DOOBIE Bros. ('Omaha') etc. with Miller playing lead, Spence rhythm and Lewis finger-picking. *Wow* '68 was also marred by gimmicks, incl. a track that could be played at 78 rpm and indulgent bonus *Grape Jam* with Al KOOPER and Mike BLOOMFIELD. Spence left to go solo (LP *Oar* '69); remaining quartet made *Moby Grape '69*, but Mosley quit before release (joined Marines), band folded, trio re-formed plus Bob Moore to make *Truly Fine Citizen* '70 in Nashville, which was universally panned. Meanwhile a fake Grape played at Altamont, manager Katz claiming to own the name. Spence helped John Hartman to form Doobie Bros., though not a member; *20 Granite Creek* '71 was first of several reunions but a shadow of the first album; Miller, Lewis and Mosley worked as Maby Grope '74; *Grape Live* '79 featured future Doobie Cornelius Bumpus on keyboards and sax with Spence, Lewis, Miller and drummer John Oxendine, Christian Powell on bass. Like BRINSLEY SCHWARZ in UK, their career was unfairly blighted by hype; reissue of first LP on Edsel '84 showed that (for the time, anyway) there was some substance.

MODERN JAZZ QUARTET Combo formed '51 by composer-pianist John LEWIS, bassist Percy Heath (*see* HEATH Brothers), Milt JACKSON on vibes, drummer Kenny CLARKE, who all played in Dizzy GILLESPIE big bands '45-50. The great bop pioneer Clarke was succeeded '55 by Connie Kay (*b* Conrad Henry Kirnon, 27 Apr. '27, Tuckahoe, NY). Kay was a key member of the Atlantic house band early to mid-'50s, playing on many R&B hits; he later played on several early Van MORRISON LPs; his delicacy and precision in the MJQ confirmed him as a first-class all-rounder. The group's instrumentation allowed chamber music of wit and elegance, the additional element of swing making it one of the most popular groups of the post-war years. Lewis met Clarke in US Army; his *Toccata For Trumpet And Orchestra* was played by Gillespie at Carnegie Hall '47; he played/arr. with Miles DAVIS 'birth of the cool' combo '49. Lewis, Jackson and Clarke recorded with Ray BROWN as Milt Jackson Quartet on Gillespie's Dee-Gee label mid-'51, with Heath and Lou DONALDSON as Milt Jackson Quintet on Blue Note early '52 (incl. early version of Jackson's 'Bags' Groove'), then as the MJQ: reissued Prestige tracks '52-5 incl. LPs *Django* with Clarke, *Concorde* with Kay on Fantasy. They recorded almost exclusively for Atlantic '56-74, incl. *Fontessa* '56, *Live At Music Inn* '56 (incl. clarinet by Jimmy GIUFFRE on some tracks), songs from Lewis's score for Roger Vadim's film *No Sun In Venice* '57 (aka *One Never Knows*, *When The Devil Drives*, *Sait-on Jamais?*) incl. 'The Golden Striker', and one of their best studio LPs, *The Modern Jazz Quartet* '57, incl. a ballad medley, Gillespie's 'Night In Tunisia', one of several versions of Lewis's 'La Ronde' (this one featuring Kay; the tune first written for Gillespie as 'Two Bass Hit'), and wonderful version of 'Bags' Groove', an exercise in dynamics, hard swing with subtlety. Other LPs: with Sonny ROLLINS at Music Inn '58, *Pyramid* '59 (compilation of tracks from various sessions), *Third Stream Music* '59 (with Beaux Arts String Quartet, Gunther Schuller cond.), 2-disc *European Concert* '60 (originally on single LPs), LP with large orchestra '60 cond. by Schuller, *The Comedy* '61 (Lewis's impressions of *commedia dell'arte*, vocal on 'La Cantatrice' by actress Diahann Carroll), *Lonely Woman* '62, *The Sheriff* '63, *Collaboration* '64 (with Laurindo ALMEIDA), *Blues At Carnegie Hall* '66, *Plastic Dreams* '71 (additional instruments, Lewis playing harpsichord on some tracks), *The Legendary Profile* '72, *Blues On Bach* '73, 2-disc *The Last Concert* '74. They reunited on *Together Again!* '82 at Montreux and *Together Again 1984*, both on Pablo; *Three Windows* '87 with NY Chamber Symphony (prod. by Nesuhi Ertegun) found them back on Atlantic. Other LPs incl. *Longing For The Continent* '58 on Denon, with SWINGLE Singers on Philips '66, *Under The Jasmin Tree* '67, *Space* '69 on BEATLES' Apple label; an album on UA '58. Some complained that the MJQ's music wasn't jazz, perhaps because it wasn't loud enough; this is incredible, given some of the stuff that has been described as jazz in the past, but Lewis's various projects tried to break down the barriers between genres *(see his entry).*

MOJOS Blues-based UK pop band formed in Liverpool '60 as the Nomads, then followed the BEATLES playing at the Cavern, other local venues: vocalist Stu James (*b* 14 July '45), bassist Keith Alcock (*b* 3 Oct. '44), guitarist Nicky Crouch (*b* 9 Feb. '43), Terry O'Toole on keyboards (*b* 20 Dec. '41), drummer Bob Conrad (*b* 14 Aug. '44). Signed during Merseybeat boom, enjoyed biggest hit 'Everything's Alright' in top 10 '64, minor hits incl. 'Seven Daffodils', written by Lee Hays of the WEAVERS. Toured with Dave CLARK, ROLLING STONES; like many lesser groups faded when the fad burst. Appeared in pop film *Every Day's A Holiday* '65 with FREDDIE AND THE DREAMERS, persevered until '67; personnel briefly incl. Aynsley DUNBAR on drums, bassist Lewis Collins (*b* '46), who switched to acting and found fame in TV's *The Professionals* '70s. *Working* '82 on Edsel is definitive compilation; David BOWIE covered their hit in *Pin-Ups* '73.

MOLLY HATCHET Southern rock band formed '71 in Jacksonville, Fla. by guitarists Dave Hlubeck (*b* '52, Jacksonville) and Steve Holland (*b* '54, Dothan, Ala.; ex-Ice). Jacksonville bassist Banner Thomas was the only other constant member in early years. Drummer Bruce Crump and ex-Rum

Creek vocalist Danny Joe Brown (*b* '51, Jacksonville) added '75; guitarist Duane Roland (*b* 3 Dec. '52, Jeffersonville, Ind.) '76; band signed to Epic '77. Chose name from 17th-century Salem prostitute who despatched clients with cleaver. Lineup, hell-raising Southern lifestyle made them natural successors to LYNYRD SKYNYRD, whose crown was up for grabs after tragic plane crash '77. *Molly Hatchet* '78 prod. by Tom Werman (CHEAP TRICK, Ted NUGENT, etc.), sold nearly a million; *Flirtin' With Disaster* '80 made top 20 LPs; *Beatin' The Odds* '80 sold over two million. Popular, gruff-voiced Brown departed to rest (he's a diabetic), cut eponymous solo LP '81; replaced by Jimmy Farrar on *Take No Prisoners* '81 but rejoined, bringing John Galvin on keyboards for *No Guts . . . No Glory* '83; Crump and Thomas had left, but Crump rejoined on Brown's return (new bassist Riff West, *b* 3 Apr. '50, Orlando, Fla.). With settled lineup they embarked on *The Deed Is Done* '84, forsaking Werman for Terry Manning, the engineer behind the rise of ZZ TOP: closing acoustic 'Song For The Children' showed another facet to band known for raw rock. Live 2-disc *Double Trouble – Live* '85 shows band on stage and in element: they tour heavily (200+ gigs a year); live set made top 50 LPs in UK, incl. cover of Skynyrd's anthem 'Freebird', underlining the fact that they've come as close as anybody to replacing them.

MONCUR, Grachan III (*b* '37, NYC) Trombonist, composer. His father Grachan Moncur II (*b* 2 Sep. '15, Miami, Fla.) played bass with SAVOY SULTANS, was half-brother of Al Cooper, that band's leader; also recorded with Teddy WILSON, incl. vocal sides with Billie HOLIDAY, Mildred BAILEY. Grachan III was raised in Newark, N.J., studied at Juilliard; his style became wholly contemporary, but based on classic smoothness of mainstream jazz trombone. He worked with Ray CHARLES, then Art FARMER-Benny GOLSON band early '60s, Jackie MCLEAN, Sonny ROLLINS, Archie SHEPP. Own LPs incl. *Evolution* '63 (sextet with McLean) and *Some Other Stuff* '64 (quintet with Wayne SHORTER) on Blue Note; quartet tracks from Village Vanguard on 2-disc Impulse set '65 with drummer Beaver Harris (*b* William Godvin Harris, 20

Apr. '36, Pittsburgh, Pa.; they later co-led 360 Degree Music Experience, with Dave BURRELL) (other tracks in set by Cecil TAYLOR, etc.). Two LPs on French Byg label '69 incl. *New Africa* with Shepp, Burrell, bassist Alan Silva, Roscoe MITCHELL, Andrew CYRILLE: now *African Concepts* on Affinity. He wrote and recorded *Echoes Of Prayer* '74 with Jazz Composers Orchestra Association on JCOA (*see* Carla BLEY); then returned to Newark as teacher and drug counsellor. He plays there with organist Big John Patton (*b* '36, Kansas City, Mo.), who made nine albums on Blue Note '63-8, most of them with Grant Green on guitar (*b* 6 June '31, St Louis; *d* 31 Jan. '79; LPs on Blue Note, Verve); the last, *Accent On The Blues*, featured James ULMER. Moncur and Patton made quintet LP *Soul Connection* '83 on a Nilva label.

MONEY, Zoot UK keyboardist/vocalist (*b* George Bruno Money). Began musical career in Bournemouth; joined early blues boom in London with Alexis KORNER (Blues Incorporated); formed own Big Roll Band '64 with Andy Somers, guitar; Paul Williams, bass and vocals; Nick Newell, tenor sax; Clive Burrows, baritone; Colin Allen on drums: made singles on Decca and Columbia; finally charted with 'Big Time Operator' (no. 25 '66), but meanwhile popular act succeeded Georgie FAME at the Flamingo. LPs *It Should Have Been Me* '65 and *Zoot* '66 later became collectors' items when Somers became Andy Summers in POLICE. R&B gave way to psychedelia and Money followed '67, renaming band Dantalion's Chariot, with Somers, Allen and Pat Donaldson on bass; they were regulars at Middle Earth club, cut infamous 'The Madmen Running Through The Fields' before Money cut losses and took his kaftan to the USA in Eric BURDON's New Animals, Somers following after a spell with SOFT MACHINE. Money returned to join vocalist Steve Ellis (ex-Love Affair) in group Ellis: LPs *Riding On The Crest Of A Slump* '72 and *Why Not* '73 before group split; Money spent a couple of years with Grimms, an ever-changing mix of poets and musicians; moved to Kevin Coyne band, once again meeting Somers, the pair moving to Kevin AYERS' employ mid-'70s before Somers/Summers turned punk. Money's

solo LPs incl. *Transition* '68, *Welcome To My Head* '69, *Zoot Money* '70; *Mr Money* '80 on Magic Moon, *Big Roll Band* '84 on RSO/Polydor; toured '83 with re-formed Animals.

MONK, Thelonious Sphere (*b* Thellous Junior Monk, 11 Oct. '17, Rocky Mount, N.C.; *d* 17 Feb. '82, NYC) Pianist, composer, leader. With Jelly Roll MORTON, Duke ELLINGTON and Charles MINGUS he is one of the greatest of composers in jazz. To NYC as an infant; began on piano at 11, accompanied mother's singing in church; began gigging '39, was house pianist at Minton's (*see* BOP), also worked with Kenny CLARKE, Lucky MILLINDER, etc.; was among the young boppers hired by Coleman HAWKINS '44 for some of the first bop records. His piano technique was unorthodox; some thought he lacked technical skill, but he had all the technique needed to be Monk: his angular, idiosyncratic compositions were so difficult to play properly that they frightened many musicians, to say nothing of the public, yet he always had a cult following, had no trouble hiring the best sidemen, and tunes became standards: 'Round Midnight', 'Misterioso', 'Straight No Chaser', 'Blue Monk', 'Epistrophy' (recorded as early as '42 by the Cootie WILLIAMS band), etc. His NYC career was hampered because he ran foul of the 'cabaret card' law then in effect, and could not work in a place where liquor was served '51-7; he did not have a contract with a major label until '62, and then CBS did not appreciate him: at one point they tried to get him to record BEATLE songs, but released excellent live recordings only after his death. He toured the world with Giants of Jazz '71-2 (incl. Dizzy GILLESPIE, Art BLAKEY, etc.), suffered from ill health late '70s, was honoured at President Carter's White House Jazz Party '78. He occasionally led big bands after '59, but studio records were almost all small-group dates. When Blue Note began recording what was then avant-garde music, Ike QUEBEC and others urged them to record Monk: he made six recordings sessions for the label '47-52 with trios to sextets, returning in '57 to contribute two tracks on *Sonny Rollins Volume 1*, all collected in 4-disc box *The Complete Blue Note Recordings Of Thelonious Monk* on Mosaic.

He recorded with Charlie PARKER and Gillespie on Clef (Verve) '50, made seven sessions for Prestige '52-4 with sidemen incl. Blakey, Rollins, Miles DAVIS, Ray COPELAND, others. Piano solos made in Paris '54 were issued complete on PRT UK '85; four tracks with Gigi GRYCE quartet '55 on Savoy incl. Blakey and Percy HEATH were reissued '86 in UK; LP with Blakey's Jazz Messengers on Atlantic '58 is still available in USA; otherwise he recorded exclusively on Riverside '55-61: 19 dates began with trio incl. Clarke, Oscar PETTIFORD, incl. quartet date led by Clark TERRY '58, also many piano solos; ended with live sextet date from San Francisco's Blackhawk '60 and quartet dates '61 all with Charlie ROUSE, a regular member of his group from then on. Riverside material was reissued in various 2-disc sets on Milestone, incl. the priceless *Pure Monk* '73, which compiles all the solos; some of it is being reissued in Fantasy OJC (Original Jazz Classics) series with original sleeve artwork, incl. *Monk's Music* '57, one of his best: septet incl. Blakey, Copeland, Hawkins, Gryce, John COLTRANE and bassist Wilbur Ware (*b* 8 Sep. '23, Chicago; *d* '73); the LP begins with short invocation, 'Abide With Me' played by horns only (written 1861 by William Henry Monk, no relation), incl. blowing sessions on 'Epistrophy' and 'Well, You Needn't', also 'Off Minor', 'Ruby, My Dear', 'Crepscule With Nellie' (twilight with Mrs Monk). CBS albums were mostly quartet sets with Rouse, John Ore on bass and Frankie Dunlop on drums succeeded '64 by Butch Warren, then Larry Gales on bass, Ben Riley on drums: *Monk's Dream, Criss-Cross, Monk, Straight, No Chaser, Underground* '62-7 all incl. one or two piano solos, except the last, which incl. vocal by Jon HENDRICKS on 'In Walked Bud'; *Solo Monk* '64 opened with 'Dinah': affectionate, humorous spoof of '25 song 'bristles with Monkian melodic ideas and Monkian rhythmic delays' (Martin Milliams's sleeve note), giving the lie to talk of technical shortcomings. *Monk's Blues* '68 had 15 pieces cond. by Oliver NELSON; 2-disc live sets incl. *Tokyo Concerts, Live At The It Club, Live At The Jazz Workshop* '63-4; Lincoln Center concert '63 incl. quartet, tentet tracks arr. by Hall Overton issued on various albums. The Giants of Jazz tour recorded live in London '71; the next day Monk made studio recordings solo and with trio incl. Blakey and bassist Al McKibbon for Black Lion, prod. by Alan Bates; these were issued complete for the first time in 4-disc *The Complete Black Lion And Vogue Recordings Of Thelonious Monk* '86 on Mosaic (with '54 Paris tracks). One of the greatest of all American artists was not recorded again in the last decade of his life. Various European tours have been bootlegged; '67 broadcast recording from Rotterdam incl. quartet, quintet with Terry, octet with Copeland, Phil WOODS, Johnny GRIFFIN, trombonist Jimmy Cleveland. Steve LACY, who played with Monk '60 and at Lincoln Center concert, played Monk's music exclusively for some time; the group Sphere (LPs on Elektra) specialises in it, as does a new group formed by bassist Buell NEIDLINGER. Son Thelonious Jr is a drummer. 2-disc tribute *That's The Way I Feel Now* '84 on A&M incl. some poppish silliness (opening track spoiled by absurdly loud rock drumming) but also fine work by Lacy, Griffin, Rouse, Bobby MCFERRIN, Carla BLEY, others.

MONKEES, The Pop group formed '66 when NBC-TV observed success of British Invasion, especially BEATLES' films *A Hard Day's Night* and *Help*, decided to create homegrown heroes, after auditioning LOVIN' SPOONFUL and deciding that manufactured group would be less trouble. Musical talent was an asset (though Steve Stills was rejected: bad teeth) but members would not have to play on records. Lineup turned out to be vocalist Davy Jones (*b* 30 Dec. '46, Manchester, England), Mickey Dolenz (*b* 8 Mar. '45, L.A.) on drums, bassist Peter Tork (*b* Torkelson, 13 Feb. '44, Washington DC), guitarist Mike NESMITH. Dolenz, Jones had been child actors, Nesmith the only real musician; music was engineered by bubblegum king Don Kirshner of Screen-Gems Music, who relied on tested writers to come up with the goods; pleasant pop got prime time exposure to teens and sub-teens around the world: predictably, hits resulted. First single 'Last Train To Clarksville' (by BOYCE & HART) was no. 1 USA/23 UK; second 'I'm A Believer' (by Neil DIAMOND) a transatlantic no. 1. Other hits incl. 'A Little Bit Me A Little Bit You' (Diamond),

'Pleasant Valley Sunday', 'Alternate Title' (no. 2 UK), 'Daydream Believer' (by John STEWART, no. 1 USA/5 UK), 'Valleri' (Boyce & Hart), all '66-8. There were flops interspersed, and anyway it couldn't last as they fought to control their own careers: they wanted to play on the records. Tork left after disastrous reception of film *Head* (since hailed as cult classic); the others split '69 when Nesmith formed First National Band. Jones and Dolenz re-formed '75 with Boyce and Hart, but split after release of *Jones, Dolenz, Boyce And Hart* '76; Jones turned actor (London cast of *Godspell* '86 etc); as London-based TV producer Dolenz had hit with charming *Metal Mickey*, a sitcom for kids with a robot; Nesmith pursued country rock career (see his entry). They reformed without Nesmith for a tour '86 (he joined them onstage in L.A.); full-blown reunion dogged by contractual problems; *Pool It* '87 on Rhino without Nesmith. Meanwhile their creators said to be recruiting new group from today's kids: there may be a fight over the name. Compilations on Rhino and Arista; nostalgia for them has a firm base: though reviled at the time by critics their close-harmony hits hold up well compared to other '60s stuff and to much that has happened since. More important was audience they found for pop on TV, from Kirshner's cartoon Archies (did not exist, yet had massive '69 hit 'Sugar Sugar') to JACKSON FIVE (with real talent), OSMONDS, Partridge Family (*see* David CASSIDY), etc.

MONRO, Matt (*b* Terry Parson, 1 Dec. '30, Shoreditch, London; *d* 7 Feb. '85, Ealing, Middlesex) UK cabaret singer popular around the world. Took part in amateur talent contests while doing national service, later drove buses, etc.; encouraged by Winifred ATWELL to turn pro, changed his name, sang on radio and in dance halls late '50s with Cyril Stapleton and BBC show bands. George MARTIN hired him to imitate Frank SINATRA (as 'Fred Flange') on Peter Sellers hit comedy LP *Songs For Swinging Sellers* '59; he later received compliments from Sinatra on diction and phrasing in handling ballads, from others incl. Bing CROSBY, who thought that his recording of 'I Get Along Without You Very Well' was one of the most beautiful records he'd

ever heard. UK hits incl. 'Portrait Of My Love', 'My Kind Of Girl' (also his only top 40 hit in USA), 'Softly As I Leave You', 'Walk Away', 'Yesterday', all top 10 '60-5. He had two LPs in top 100 in USA; hit LPs in UK incl. *I Have Dreamed, This Is The Life, Invitation To The Movies* '65-7; then *Heartbreakers* '80 on EMI (TV promoted) reached top 10 albums. You don't have to make the charts when you can top the bill at the Sands in Las Vegas, as he did in '83.

MONROE, Bill (*b* 13 Sep. '11, Rosine, Ky.) Singer, mandolinist, bandleader in traditional style: with Jimmie RODGERS, the CARTER Family, Roy ACUFF and a few others one of the giants of country music; father of the BLUEGRASS genre which in fact was named after his band, the Bluegrass Boys. Began playing mandolin as a child because nobody else in the family played it; after his father died lived with his uncle, fiddler Pendleton Vandiver, who was later immortalised in 'Uncle Pen'; infl. by guitarist/fiddler Arnold Shultz, who played square dances, other black musicians: the best bluegrass, like jazz, has plenty of room in it for individual self-expression. Played in band with brothers Birch (on fiddle) and Charlie (guitarist, *b* 4 July '03; *d* '75) on radio '29-34; Birch quit, Bill and Charlie as duo made about 60 sides for Victor, split up '38, Charlie forming own successful band, the Kentucky Pardners. Bill had started writing ('Kentucky Waltz' '34), sang only harmony until now, formed Kentuckians, then Bluegrass Boys, played on Grand Ole Opry from '39 (opened with 'Mule Skinner Blues'). At various times the group incl. David 'Stringbean' Akeman on banjo (as rhythm only), Sally Ann Forrester on accordion, but classic band had fiddler Chubby Wise, Howard Watts (better known as Cedric Rainwater) on bass, Lester FLATT on guitar and Earl Scruggs playing a five-string banjo in three-fingered Appalachian style, until Flatt & Scruggs left '48 to form their own band. This lineup recorded for Columbia from '45; Monroe and Flatt co-wrote 'My Rose Of Old Kentucky', 'Will You Love Another Man?', 'Blue Moon Of Kentucky' (later covered by Elvis PRESLEY), etc. He switched to Decca '50, as Jimmy Martin joined on lead vocals and guitar, his highpitched voice fitting the style perfectly;

Monroe wrote what he called 'true' songs: 'Uncle Pen', 'A Letter From My Darling', 'When The Golden Leaves Begin To Fall', etc.; instrumentals such as 'Pike County Breakdown' and 'Scotland' (tribute to the jigs and reels that formed part of the basis of trad. country music); religious songs such as 'Walking To Jerusalem'. Just as the country music business thought that bluegrass was pretty old-fashioned, the rest of the country realised its value as heritage; Monroe played the Newport Folk Festival '63, then for crowds in NYC, e.g. at New York University's Law School Auditorium: 'There's people from Japan, Europe, country people, tarheels, rednecks, college graduates . . . It's honest music, bluegrass is. It feels good to play it.' (Monroe quoted by Melvin Shestack.) Other alumni of Monroe's groups incl. Mac WISEMAN, Don Reno, daughter Melissa (b '36) and son James (b '40), who also led his own band, the Midnight Ramblers. The style has long since entered the repertoire of folk music, nowadays called roots music. More than 20 albums in print in USA on MCA; historical reissues incl. 2-disc *Feast Here Tonight* on Bluebird (RCA, duets with Charlie) and a Columbia Historic Edition of the Bluegrass Boys; seven others incl. three by Charlie available from the Country Music Hall Of Fame, Nashville.

MONROE, Vaughn (b 7 Oct. '11, Akron, Ohio; d 21 May '73, Stuart, Fla.) Trombone, leader; mainly singer with big distinctive baritone. Started as trumpet player with dance bands; also studied opera at Carnegie Tech. To Boston mid-'30s fronting society band; began handling vocals, still studying voice at New England Conservatory. Formed big band (theme 'Racing With The Moon' became famous); opened '40 at Seilers Ten Acres, Wayland, Mass. First hit on Bluebird 'There I Go' '40 followed by transfer to parent Victor label, top 10 hits 'My Devotion', 'When The Lights Go On Again' '42, 'Let's Get Lost' '43, 'The Trolley Song' '44, 'Rum And Coca Cola', lovely romantic ballad 'There! I've Said It Again' '45. First no. 1 Xmas '45 with jaunty Johnny MERCER tune 'Let It Snow! Let It Snow! Let It Snow!', followed by top 10 hits incl. 'I Wish I Didn't Love You So', 'You Do', 'How Soon', no. 1 'Ballerina' (all '47); peri-od infl. of country (folkish-cowboy) songs incl. 'Cool Water' '48, 'Red Roses For A Blue Lady', no. 1 'Riders In The Sky', 'That Lucky Old Sun', 'Mule Train' all '49, 'On Top Of Old Smoky' '51; also ballad 'Someday' '49, novelties 'Sound Off', 'Old Soldiers Never Die' '51; final top 20 hit 'They Were Doing The Mambo' '54. Films incl. *Meet The People* '44, *Carnegie Hall* '47, acting role in *Singing Guns* '50. RCA publicity man from '55, singing on radio and TV ads. Led occasional bands mid-'60s, nostalgia lineups. USA LPs incl. *Best Of*, 2-disc *This Is Vaughn Monroe*.

MONTANA, Patsy (b Rubye Blevins, 30 Oct. '14, Hot Springs, Ark.) The yodelling cowgirl, still one of the best yodellers in country music, and also the first female in country music to sell a million records, with 'I Wanna Be A Cowboy's Sweetheart' '36 on Vocalion. She began professionally in her mid-teens, recorded for ARC '33, joined WLS National Barn Dance '34, teamed with the Prairie Ramblers '34-52, incl. Charles Hurt, Jack Taylor, Shelby Atchison and Floyd 'Salty' Holmes, had repertoire incl. mountain tunes, cowboy ballads, gospel and pop; used piano and reeds as well as the usual country instruments. Hits incl. 'I'm An Old Cowhand', 'Singing In The Saddle', 'Goodnight Soldier', 'Little Old Rag Doll', etc. She recorded for Decca '42-9, RCA '49-51; retired '59, came back late '60s recording for Starday, Surf and Melotone, touring regularly, often with her daughter, Judy Rose. She won fans in UK and Europe with tours in '70s. LPs incl. *Cowboy's Sweetheart* '65 on Starday, *Patsy Montana & Judy Rose – Mum & Me* '77 on Lock; compilations *Original Hits From The West, Cowboy's Sweetheart* and *Very Early on Cattle*; also *Patsy Montana And The Prairie Ramblers* in Columbia Historical Series.

MONTEZ, Chris (b 17 Jan. '43, L.A.) Singer, schoolmate of the BEACH BOYS who cut first single at 17: 'She's My Rockin' Baby'. Chicano sound mixed pop with infl. from south of the border. Became protégé of Jim Lee, record producer who formed Monogram label for him; second single on Monogram 'Let's Dance' was as insubstantial as most dance-craze hits, but was international hit (no. 16 USA/3 UK). Relative flop followup (no. 43) 'Some Kinda Fun', co-written with Lee, still sold a million, reached top 10 UK where he toured in a package incl. BEATLES. After these '62-3 hits his nasal delivery with rinky-dink organ backing was tiresome; he re-emerged on A&M '66 as a crooner with six top 40 hits USA that year with old standards. But 'Let's Dance' won't lie down; on reissue it made top 10 UK '72, just missed top 40 '79; its infectious Chicano sound and one-finger keyboard make it (along with Ritchie VALENS' 'La Bamba') a cabaret staple still.

MONTGOMERY, Little Brother (*b* Eurreal Wilford Montgomery, 18 Apr. '06, Kentwood, La.; *d* 6 Sep. '85, Chicago, Ill.) Blues singer, composer, one of the great pianists in 'barrelhouse' style, bridging the gap between jazz and blues. Father owned a honkytonk; began on piano at age 5, moved to Chicago '28, worked rent parties etc. with others incl. Pine Top SMITH; toured the South through '30s but Chicago was home base from '42: he played clubs, festivals, toured Europe several times '60s-70s. First records were two solo sides for Paramount '30: 'No Special Rider Blues' and 'Vicksburg Blues' remained among his best-known tunes; 22 sides for Bluebird '35-6 made in New Orleans were mostly solo, incl. more versions of 'Vicksburg', also piano showpiece 'Farish Street Jive'. Worked with Edith Wilson '70s; appeared in *The Devil's Music – A History Of The Blues* (BBC TV '76). Recorded for small Chicago labels '50s, with Otis RUSH on Cobra '58, for Folkways and Prestige '60, EMI/Columbia in London '60, Riverside '61; Blackbird/Adelphi, Matchbox, Delmark in Chicago '70s. Albums incl. *Blues, Church Songs, Farro Street Jive* on Folkways, *Tasty Blues* on Prestige, *Bajes Copper Station* on Blues Beacon (live at Amsterdam Bejaz Club '72), *Tishomingo Blues* on JSP UK.

MONTGOMERY, Melba (*b* 14 Oct. '38, Iron City, Tenn.) Singer whose country phrasing has kept her popular with fans in that genre for 25 years, although she has never hit the really big time. Grew up in Florence, Ala. in musical family; sang in church and played guitar and fiddle; in a group with her brothers made finals of a talent contest '57. Family moved to Nashville '58 and she

was featured girl vocalist with Roy ACUFF '58-62. Went solo, signed with Nugget '62, UA '63; had first chart entries that year with 'Hall Of Shame' and 'The Greatest One Of All'. She had duet hits with George JONES '63-4, 'We Must Have Been Out Of Our Minds' and 'Let's Invite Them Over' being superb examples of cheatin' songs; teamed with Gene PITNEY for a while, recorded for Musicor '66-70, then Capitol, where she had duet hits with Charlie LOUVIN '70-1. Moved to Elektra '73 and with producer Pete Drake had no. 1 country hit 'No Charge', a semi-narrated tear-jerker which also went top 40 pop. Back on UA '77-9 she had top 20 hit 'Angel Of The Morning' '77; recorded for Kari '80-1; often did background vocals at Nashville sessions. LPs incl. *Bluegrass Hootenanny* '65 on UA with Jones, *Melba Toast* '68 on Musicor, *Melba* '73 and *Don't Let The Good Times Fool You* '75 on Elektra, *Melba Montgomery* '78 on UA.

MONTGOMERY, Wes (*b* John Leslie Montgomery, 6 Mar. '25, Indianapolis, Indiana; *d* 15 June '68 of heart attack) One of the most influential guitarists of all time. Self-taught as a teenager; worked with Lionel HAMPTON '48-50, worked day jobs and played in Indianapolis clubs, recorded from '57 with brothers Monk (William, bassist; *b* 10 Oct. '21; *d* 20 May '82), Buddy (Charles, on vibes; *b* 30 Jan. '30), first as Mastersounds, then as Montgomery Brothers. Worked with organ trio '58-9, with John COLTRANE Sextet at Monterey Festival '60, recorded and played with Wynton KELLY Trio '62-6, made commercial big band albums mid-'60s, signed with A&M, appeared with Herb ALPERT on TV. He began influenced by the rhythmic style of Charlie CHRISTIAN, added unison chords, etc., had unusually mellow sound due partly to picking with his thumb rather than a plectrum. Jazz fans and critics professed displeasure with his commercial work, but by then he was so influential, and like Charlie PARKER had so many imitators, that jazz guitar had begun to sound hackneyed anyway, which as in Parker's case was not the originator's fault. Best LPs are from Fantasy/Riverside/Milestone group: 2-disc compilations *Movin'*, *The Alternative*, *While We're Young*, *Pretty Blue*, *Groove Brothers* (with brothers); single LPs *Trio*, *Yesterdays*,

Portrait Of Wes, The Incredible Jazz Guitar, Encores, Full House (with Kelly, Johnny GRIFFIN, Paul CHAMBERS, Jimmy COBB), all c.'59-63. Verve sets incl. *Movin' Wes, California Dreaming*, 2-disc *Small Group Recordings, Tequila* '66 (arr. by Claus Ogerman), others; A&M LPs incl. *A Day In The Life, Down Here On The Ground, Road Song*.

MONTOLIU, Tete (*b* Vincente Montoliu, 28 Mar. '33, Barcelona, Spain) Pianist. Born blind; became interested in jazz listening to Duke ELLINGTON records; began slowly in Spain's meagre jazz scene, accompanying visiting stars like Don BYAS; as an excellent, unpretentious soloist and perennial accompanist has become a top European star. On Spanish Ensayo label with Eric Peter on bass, Peer Wyboris on drums, he backed Lucky THOMPSON '70 and played on Ben WEBSTER's last studio session '72 (now on Nessa as *Body & Soul* and *Did You Call?* respectively); also *Ben Webster Meets Don Byas* '68 on MPS (with Al HEATH on drums, Peter Trunk on bass); recorded with Lionel HAMPTON '56, Roland KIRK '63, Anthony BRAXTON '74, etc. With these and other bassists and drummers incl. Billy HIGGINS, George Mraz, Sam JONES, Niels-Henning Ørsted Pedersen etc. he made a score of trio albums on Timeless, Steeplechase, other labels. Solo piano albums incl. *Interpreta a Serrat* '69 on Discophon; *Songs For Love* '71 on Enja; *That's All* '71, *Music For Perla* '74, *Words Of Love* '76, *Boston Concert* '80, all on Steeplechase; *Yellow Dolphin Street* and *Catalonian Folksongs* '77 on Timeless; *Lunch In L.A.* '79 on Contemporary adds Chick COREA on one track for a piano duo. *Temi Latino Americani* and *Temi Brasiliani* '73, *Boleros* '77 on Ensayo add Latin percussion to trio; he also recorded in Latin style with Tete Montoliu y su Conjunto Tropical.

MOOD MUSIC Term loosely meaning background music, applied in '50s to what is called light music in UK, probably due to series of MELACHRINO LPs: *Music For Dining, Music For Relaxation, Music To Dream By* etc. led to ribald suggestions for the next title in the sequence. Light music ran aground in the rock era, but still has fierce devotees in UK (a smaller music market than the USA but apparently with more room for variety); mood music lived on in the USA in the form of insipid piped-in music in pretentious restaurants. It used mostly strings but the best had what amounted to a symphony orchestra playing original arrangements of good songs, sometimes original tunes; MANTOVANI was the most commercially successful artist in the genre by a long way, but not the best by an equally wide margin. The best practitioners of light music also did film and studio work and backed vocalists on LPs and singles, incl. Gordon JENKINS, Nelson RIDDLE, and Paul WESTON in the USA, Frank CHACKSFIELD, Stanley BLACK etc. in UK. Two Canadians were among the best: Robert FARNON is probably the most influential studio arranger in the business, and Percy FAITH did beautiful work in the early '50s, until reduced by Columbia USA to attempting lush albums of BEATLE and disco material. *See* NEW AGE and SPACE MUSIC for the mood music of today: more pretence and less talent.

MOODY BLUES Progressive rock band formed '64 in Birmingham, England. Original lineup incl. Denny LAINE, vocals and guitar (later with Paul McCARTNEY in Wings); Mike Pindar, keyboards; Clint Warwick, bass; Graeme Edge, drums; Ray Thomas on flute, sax and vocals. R&B-based group hit with second single, cover of Bessie Banks' USA soul ballad 'Go Now', but follow-ups and album *The Magnificent Moodies* '65 did less well. Laine and Warwick left; recruits Justin Hayward (guitar) and John Lodge (bass) marked new policy of pseudo-philosophical music to get stoned by. *Days Of Future Passed* '67 was a concept album with full orchestration; their most famous song 'Nights In White Satin' was top 20 single, re-entered UK charts '72, '79, no. 2 USA '72. Hayward and Thomas's vocal blend sat prettily atop a wash of strings, abetted by Pindar's Mellotron, a new synthesiser which enabled them to tour without the orchestra. Producer Tony Clarke, arr. Peter Knight played major roles in six gold LPs, from '69 on their Threshold label: *In Search Of The Lost Chord* '68, *On The Threshold Of A Dream* '69, *To Our Children's Children's Children* '69, *A Question Of Balance* '70, *Every Good Boy De-*

serves *Favor* '71, *Seventh Sojourn* '72, with occasional hit singles; all mood music for the permissive generation's lazy ears. Splinter projects incl. Lodge and Hayward's Blue Jays duo (LP '75 and no. 8 single 'Blue Guitar'), Hayward's *Songwriter* and Lodge's *Natural Avenue* LPs; Edge recruited guitarist Adrian Gurvitz for more rockish *Kick Off Your Muddy Boots* '74; Pindar made *Thomas From Mighty Oaks*, *The Promise* and *Hopes Dreams And Wishes* '75-6; none were commercially successful except the Blue Jays and despite rumours of strife they returned with *Octave* '78. Ex-YES keyboardist Patrick Moraz replaced Pindar and *Long Distance Voyager* '81 proved that formula still worked by topping USA album chart. Their music is the reason nobody uses the word 'progressive' any more. Compilations incl. 2-disc *This Is The Moody Blues* '74, *Out Of This World* '79, *Voices In The Sky* '85; 2-disc *Caught Live +5* '77 incl. three sides recorded live at the Albert Hall, one of studio tracks. Hayward has continued solo work; 'Forever Autumn' from Jeff Wayne's *War Of The Worlds* project '78 was no. 5 UK; LPs continued with *Moving Mountains* '85, *Other Side Of Life* '86, *Sur la Mer* '88.

MOODY, Clyde (*b* '15, Cherokee, N.C.) Country singer, guitarist and songwriter known as The Woodchopper and later as The Hillbilly Waltz King. He began as a member of the Happy-Go-Lucky Boys '38-40 with Lester FLATT. Then with Mainer's Mountaineers, then Bill MONROE's Bluegrass Boys as guitarist and lead singer (most notable number: 'Six White Horses'), also singing duets with Monroe. One of the first to be signed as a songwriter with new ACUFF-Rose publishing company in Nashville '44. Formed own band the Woodchoppers, signed with King '46, scored hits like 'Shenandoah Waltz', 'Carolina Waltz', 'Cherokee Waltz' and 'Waltz Of The Wind'. Moved to Washington DC late '40s to appear in new TV show, then to Durham, N.C. for long-running series. Joined New Dominion Barn Dance in Richmond, Va. late '50s; appeared at Bluegrass festivals and toured with Ramblin' Tommy Scott's show. Albums incl. *All Time Country And Western Waltzes* '69 on King, *Moody's Blues* '67 on Old Homestead.

MOODY, James (*b* 26 Mar. '25, Savannah, Ga.) Tenor and alto sax, flute; bandleader. Father played trumpet with Tiny BRADSHAW; James played in US Air Force '43-6, joined Dizzy Gillespie '46-8 incl. European tour, along with Dexter GORDON was one of the first bop tenors. First session as leader for Blue Note '48 with Modernists (octet incl. Cecil PAYNE, also Art BLAKEY and Chano POZO on some tracks). Based in Paris '48-51; on a Swedish date '49 he recorded 'I'm In The Mood For Bop' (aka 'I'm In The Mood For Groovin' ') on tenor and recorded on alto for the first time on 'I'm In The Mood For Love'; released on Prestige in the USA the latter was a juke box hit; King Pleasure wrote words to fit Moody's solo and 'Moody's Mood For Love' was a top 5 R&B hit '52, also on Prestige (LP *Moody's Mood For Love* '56 on Argo had vocal by Eddie JEFFERSON). He led a septet in USA '51-62, playing flute from mid-'50s; played in group with three tenors '62 (with Sonny STITT, Gene AMMONS), with Dizzy GILLESPIE '63-8, worked in Las Vegas late '70s and has re-emerged as touring jazzman '80s, occasionally sings a chorus or two: never one of those who doesn't like the audience, engaging personality makes him a delightful club act. The septet incl. at various times Jefferson, Payne, Babs GONZALES, Bennie GREEN, recorded for Mercury, Prestige '54-6 (LPs *Workshop*, *Wail, Moody, Wail*, *Moody's Moods* etc.), Argo/Chess '56-64. Other LPs incl. *Group Therapy* '64 on DJM with Art FARMER, Tommy FLANAGAN; quartet sets *Don't Look Away Now* '69 on Prestige, *Too Heavy For Words* '71 on MPS/Pausa (latter with Al COHN, second tenor); *Never Again* with Mickey TUCKER on organ, *Feelin' It Together* with Kenny Barron, both '72 on Muse; two sextet LPs on Vanguard '75-7 incl. *Beyond This World*; intelligently mellow *Something Special* '87 on Novus has Idris Muhammad on drums, Todd Coolman on bass, Kirk Lightsey on piano, incl. update of 'Moodys's Mood'; *Moving Forward* '88 celebrates jazz standards.

MOONDOG (*b* Louis Thomas Hardin, 26 May '16, Marysville, Kansas) A blind street personality in NYC, self-taught in music, who played original music on various percussion and original reed instruments called oo, utsu, uni, samisen, etc. Albums on Prestige '56-7 incl. *Caribea* (additional percussion by Sam Ulano and Ray Malone, who also tap-danced), *More Moondog* (with Malone; incl. 'Conversation And Music At 51st Street And 6th Avenue'), *The Story Of Moondog*. Possession of these LPs guaranteed a certain *cachet* among young people in the golden age of the Beat movement, especially outside NYC. He also recorded for Brunswick and Columbia incl. an orchestral album '69, joined ASCAP '70, played concert on German radio '74.

MOONEY, Art (*b* 4 Feb. '11, Brooklyn, NY; *d* 21 May '73, Fla.) Bandleader, arranger. Led band in Detroit area '30s; after WWII military service formed new band, opened NYC '45 with Neal HEFTI arr.; went corny for 'I'm Looking Over A Four-Leaf Clover' on MGM '47: featuring banjo by ex-Paul WHITEMAN sideman Mike Pingatore, sold over a million. Stuck with formula of vocal choruses, banjo strumming; by late '50s divided time between music and running The Meadows, restaurant in Framlingham, Mass. LPs incl. *Art Mooney And His Orchestra In HiFi* (MGM), *The Best Of Art Mooney* (RCA).

MOORE, Christy (*b* Christopher Andrew Moore, 7 May '45, Dublin, Eire) Singer, guitarist, songwriter. Played in various groups in Eire (incl. trio the Rakes of Kildare with Donal Lunny); moved to UK '66 and played in folk clubs; record debut was *Paddy On The Road* '69, a collaboration with Dominic Behan which he later more or less disowned. Continued to build following; on return to Eire he made *Prosperous* '71 on Tara, which established him and led to foundation of Irish folk band PLANXTY, on whose first two LPs he played (*Planxty* '72 and *Cold Blow And A Rainy Night* '74 on Polydor). Made series of LPs playing both trad. and contemporary material: *Whatever Tickles Your Fancy* '75 and *Christy Moore* '76 on Polydor, *The Iron Behind The Velvet* and *Live In Dublin* '78 on Tara, the latter with Lunny and Jimmy Faulkner. Helped re-form Planxty '79, their *Words And Music* '82 on WEA Eire perhaps their most rounded album. Moore and Lunny formed MOVING HEARTS, a band which melded trad. Uillean pipes with saxophones

and a rock rhythm section, songs reflecting their abiding interest in political issues. *The Spirit Of Freedom* '83 was Moore's next solo album, incl. 'Plane Crash At Los Gatos' by Woody GUTHRIE, Bobby Sands' 'Back Home In Derry'; *The Time Has Come* same year (both on WEA) reprised earlier material ('Faithful Departed', 'The Lakes Of Pontchartrain', 'All I Remember') alongside his own title track and 'The Wicklow Boy'. *Ordinary Man* '85 on Demon and *Unfinished Revolution* '86 on WEA continued with uncompromising Republican and sexual political stances, despite which he was criticised for not tackling other available issues, such as abortion and divorce law in Eire. He remains Eire's foremost political musician. He contributed to *Dublin Songs – The Official Millennium Album* '88 on K-Tel, along with Paul BRADY, the Dubliners and Paddy Moloney of the CHIEFTAINS.

MOORE, Gary (*b* Belfast) UK heavy metal guitarist. Began at age 11, using *Bluesbreakers* LP with Eric CLAPTON as model. Joined Skid Row by age 16 (LPs *Skid Row* '70, *Thirty Four Hours* '71); another member briefly was rhythm guitarist Phil Lynott, who left, formed THIN LIZZY, playing bass. Formed three-piece Gary Moore Band with bassist Frank Boylan, drummer Pearce Kelly; made unexceptional *Grinding Stone* '73, disbanded to join Lynott, but stayed only a few months owing to personality clashes; played on standout track 'Still In Love With You' on *Nightlife* '74. Turned to jazz-rock with COLOSSEUM II, played with them on *Strange New Flesh*, *Electric Savage*, *War Dance* '76-7, but like bassist Bill Murray (who was later with WHITESNAKE) and keyboardist Don Airey (joined Rainbow) felt the strong pull of heavy metal. Depped for Lizzy's Brian Robertson when he'd injured his hand '77; rejoined full-time replacing the Scotsman when he left to form Wild Horses, this time making a whole album with the band (*Black Rose* '79) as well as borrowing Lynott and drummer Brian Downey for his own solo *Back On The Streets* '78: single 'Parisienne Walkways' (top 10 UK) featured Lynott's vocal, Moore being unsure of his own voice; album and single (lyrical guitar playing reminiscent of SANTANA) showcased many styles. Formed G-Force with Mark

Nauseef, drums; Willie Dee, bass and keyboards; Tony Newton, vocals; eponymous '80 LP sold badly (but was recycled later, along with live G-Force material). Returned to sideman role with bassist Greg Lake; went solo again '82 with Murray and Airey from Colosseum II plus drummer Ian Paice (ex-DEEP PURPLE): *Corridors Of Power* '82 incl. cover of FREE's 'Wishing Well', reached no. 30 UK LP chart, with Moore taking all vocals; Airey left replaced by ex-UFO Neil Carter; Murray rejoined Whitesnake, replaced by ex-Rainbow Craig Gruber; *Victims Of The Future* '84 revealed unsuspected mature rock voice and reached no. 12. Paice was replaced by Bobby Chouinard (ex-Billy Squier drummer) for live 2-disc *We Want Moore* '84; *Run For Cover* '85 was no. 12 again, his most accomplished album to date, preceded by a one-off hit single with Lynott, powerful antiwar anthem, 'Out In The Fields', with both trading vocals; he followed up with another chart hit, re-make of 'Empty Rooms' from *Victims Of The Future*. Undoubted ability on guitar now reinforced by vocals and songwriting, he has hard core of fans worldwide (especially in Japan), and will remain a respected figure in heavy metal, while appealing as pop singles act with lyrical side of his talent, a gift he shared with the late Lynott. *Anthology* on Raw Power accompanied by new live LP *Rockin' Every Night* '86, hit single 'Over The Hills And Far Away' '87 seen by critics as rip-off of BIG COUNTRY, was in fact rediscovery of Thin Lizzy's folk beginnings.

MOR 'Middle of the road' music, a fuzzy marketing term for mainstream pop that is not rock. *See also* AOR.

MORALES, Orquesta Hermanos Family band whose Puerto Rican orquesta was prolific on records in '30s. When Papa Morales died, several brothers went to the USA: Paco was a composer; Humberto published a tutor on playing Latin percussion instruments; Esy was a flautist, bandleader, composer, recorded for Brunswick, Rainbow: Esy's 'Jungle Fantasy' has been covered by Charlie PALMIERI, Yusef LATEEF, Herbie MANN, many others. Pianist/bandleader/composer Noro Morales (*b* 4 Jan. '11, San Juan, PR; *d* there 4 Jan. '64)

was the most successful: to USA '35, formed own band '39, recorded for MGM, other labels; his 'Bim Bam Bum' was played by Xavier CUGAT in '42 Jerome KERN movie musical *You Were Never Lovelier*; 'Oye Negra' covered by Percy FAITH, others; he wrote 'Walter Winchell Rumba', many more. Over the years Tito RODRIGUEZ and MACHITO sang with him; Esy played flute; Doc SEVERINSEN was a sideman '50-1. He was popular in white hotels but also among Latins, winning a *La Prensa* poll '47; he led a big band early '40s, but was best known in a genre which 'peaked during the 1940s, and has totally vanished since then, the quintet for piano and percussion' (wrote John Storm Roberts). The authenticity of his Latin music was often weakened by the demands of 'downtown' supper club gigs, but his playing always had logical and rhythmic integrity. Another brother settled in Cuba: Obdulio Morales recorded for Panart and Montilla; compositions incl. 'Enlloro', covered by Faith among others; he was mus. dir. of Antobal's Cuban All Stars, succeeded by Chico O'FARRILL when he died; Mario Antobal's brother was Don Azpiazú, who introduced 'El Manisero' ('The Peanut Vendor') to the USA with hit record '31.

MORATH, Max (*b* 1 Oct. '26, Colorado Springs, Colo.) Pianist; ragtime revivalist already at it long before a Scott JOPLIN rag was used in the film *The Sting* '73. His mother played piano in silent cinemas; he studied piano and composition, worked in radio and TV as announcer etc., in summer stock theatre; wrote/performed National Educational Television series *The Ragtime Era* '59-60, *Turn Of The Century* '61-2; toured USA with shows *Ragtime Revisited* '64-7, *Max Morath At The Turn Of The Century* (after four-month off-Broadway run), etc.; latest touring show is *Living A Ragtime Life*, 'the nearest thing to a high-class vaudeville show that exists in this country', according to UPI. Morath has edited six collections of ragtime music for publication; recorded for Epic, New World Records; on Vanguard: *The Great American Piano Bench*, 2-disc sets *Plays Ragtime*, *Best Of Scott Joplin & Others*. On RCA with *These Charming People* and with William BOLCOM and Joan Morris in *More Rodgers*

& Hart, with Morris on *Till The Clouds Roll By*, songs with words by P. G. Wodehouse.

MORÉ, Beny (*b* Bartolome Moré, 24 Aug. '19, Santa Isabel de las Lajas, Cienfuegos, Cuba; *d* 19 Feb. '63) Singer, composer, arranger, bandleader; nicknamed 'El Barbaro del Ritmo' ('The Barbarian of Rhythm'); still revered for the versatility of his voice and his unrivalled capacity to stir audiences. Began playing the guitar at parties; to Havana '40, sang and played in cafés and parks, joined Miguel Matamoros' band in Mexico and there met Perez PRADO, just beginning his rise to popularity with the mambo: he sang on many records with Prado, who greatly infl. Moré's own work back in Havana. He also sang with the bands of Mariano Merceron, Ernesto Duarte and Rafael de Paz, with whom he recorded the great Afro-Cuban song 'Yiri Yiri Bon' still associated with him. Formed own Banda Gigante in Havana '53 with classic big band jazz lineup but with traditional Cuban rhythm section at its heart, adding fire and soul. Seven vols. of *Beny Moré: Sonero Mayor* on Cuban Areito demonstrate range and powers of interpretation: Vol. 1 incl. classics 'Maracaibo Oriental', 'Francisco Guayabal', song painting 'Cienfuegos'; Vol. 2 mixes danceable son montunos ('Mi Saoco') and boleros; Vol. 3 incl. 'Yiri Yiri Bon', 'Rumberos de Ayer' (dedicated to Chano POZO), and a chachacha about his hometown 'Santa Isabel de las Lajas'; Vol. 4 has rollicking mambos, boleros 'Oh! Vida' ('Oh Life') and 'Corazón Rebelde' ('Rebel Heart') and bolero-cha combination 'El Barbaro del Ritmo'; Vol. 5 is the most danceable, incl. the son montuno 'Soy del Monte', guaracha 'El Conde Negro', and 'Ensalada del Mambo', leading to thematic Vol. 6, incl. eight tracks with Prado; Vol. 7 incl. classic montuno 'Babarabatiri'. A tradition of tributes incl. Pepe Mora's . . . *Tributo al 'Beny'* and two vols. of Charanga De La 4's *Recuerda a Beny Moré*, early '80s, Tito PUENTE's three vols. of *Homenaje a Beny* '78, '79, '85. On the '78 album Celia CRUZ sings 'Yiri Yiri Bon'; in '79 Cruz and Puente filled Carnegie Hall with their tribute show; that year she sang the song with Puerto Rican band Sonora Ponceña in Jeremy Marre's TV film *Salsa*. In the '80s tourists visiting Cuba could see *The Beny Moré Show*, a spectacular run-through of his material, in cabaret at the Hotel Rivera. He sang 'Mi Saoco' with Banda Gigante in film clip shown on BBC2 Arena programmes *What's Cuba Playing At?* '84, *Latin Sound* '86.

MORGAN, George (*b* George Thomas Morgan, 28 June '25, Waverley, Tenn.; *d* July '75, Madison, Tenn. of a heart attack) Smooth-voiced country crooner whose peak success was late '40s-early '50s, but remained a major star until his death. The family moved to Ohio early '30s; he worked as a truck driver, salesman; made radio debut in teens while attending Akron U. Served in US Army '44-7; worked in a bakery in Wooster, Ohio and sang on local radio WWST; went to WWVA Jamboree, Wheeling, W. Va., then to WSM Nashville as DJ/singer '48-9, signed to Columbia '48; his first record, his own song 'Candy Kisses', was a no. 1 country hit '49 and was covered by Red FOLEY and Elton BRITT. 'Room Full Of Roses' was no. 4, 'Rainbow In My Heart' and 2-sided hit 'Cry-Baby Heart'/'I Love Everything About You', all '49, made an auspicious start to a career. 20 hits in 20 years also incl. 'Almost' '52, 'I'm In Love Again' '59, 'You're The Only Good Thing' '60 in top 10. His romantic style should have been a crossover success; he never made it to the pop chart officially, but Tim Spencer's hit song 'Room Full Of Roses' was covered in the pop chart by Sammy KAYE, Eddy HOWARD and Dick HAYMES: *Pop Memories* '86 is a new tabulation (*see* CHARTS) that gives both Morgan and the SONS OF THE PIONEERS (incl. Spencer) credit for a pop hit as well. Morgan joined WSM's Grand Ole Opry '49; switched to Starday label '67-8 for more hits, made it back to the country top 20 on Pete Drake's Stop label with 'Lilacs And Fire' '70, did it once more on Decca/Four Star '74 with 'Red Rose From The Blue Side Of Town', reunited with steel guitar player Little Roy Wiggins, who had played on the early hits. His daughter, Lorrie Morgan, also started to make a name for herself as a singer and songwriter, recording for Hickory and MCA late '70s, signing as a writer with ACUFF-Rose. LPs incl. *Red Roses For A Blue Lady* '62 and *Remembering*

The Greatest Hits '75 on Columbia, *Barbara* '68 on Starday (title track top 60 country), *Candy Mountain Melody* '74 on MCA.

MORGAN, Helen (*b* 1900, Danville, Ill.; *d* 8 Oct. '41, Chicago) Singer; with Ruth ETTING the biggest of the 'torch' singers of the late '20s-early '30s, popularising gimmick of sitting on piano while singing. Starred on Broadway in Jerome KERN's *Show Boat* (song 'Bill') and *Sweet Adoline* ('Why Was I Born?'), sang in soundtrack of film *Show Boat*, all '28-9; hit records on Victor. TV biopic *The Helen Morgan Story* starred Polly Bergen (who made excellent LP of torch songs on Columbia/CBS, incl. 'The Party's Over'), then film '57 with actress Ann Blyth, Gogi GRANT singing on soundtrack. Morgan once had eight tracks reissued on an RCA LP in Vintage series, the other side by Fanny BRICE.

MORGAN, Jane (*b* Jane Currier, Boston, Mass.) Singer. Studied at Juilliard as lyric soprano, sang in clubs; offered contract in France, became hit in Continental clubs, later billed as 'the American girl from France'. Hits on Kapp '56-9 incl. 'Two Different Worlds' (duet with pianist Roger WILLIAMS), million-seller 'Fascination' (adapted from 'Valse Tzigane', '04). Voice successfully shovelled syrup against the rock'n'roll tide; *Greatest Hits* LP on MCA.

MORGAN, Jaye P. (*b* Mary Morgan, '32, Mancos, Col.) Singer. Born in log cabin; toured with family variety troupe, sang with Frank DeVol orchestra at 18, also with Hank PENNY on RCA, two years on Robert Q. Lewis radio show, also *Stop The Music.* 17 Hot 100 entries '54-60 on RCA, of which 'That's All I Want From You', 'The Longest Walk' were top 10 '54-5. Also recorded with Eddy ARNOLD, Perry COMO. LP *What Are You Doing The Rest Of Your Life* on Bainbridge.

MORGAN, Lee (*b* 10 July '38, Philadelphia, Pa.; *d* 19 Feb. '72, NYC) Trumpet, composer. With Dizzy GILLESPIE big band '56-8 (solo on 'Night In Tunisia' on Verve), with Art BLAKEY's Jazz Messengers '58-61, '64-5 (LPs on Blue Note, others); recorded as sideman with John COLTRANE (*Blue Train* on Blue Note), others; own quintet. Highly

rated post-bop modernist infl. by Clifford BROWN had commercial hit with title track of Blue Note LP *The Sidewinder* '63, one of the few masterpieces of early funk, used in TV advert '70s, reissued as promotional 12" single by EMI-UK '85, often incl. in Blue Note anthologies. Album *A-1* '56 on Savoy co-led with Hank MOBLEY; own LPs as leader on Vee Jay/Trip '60, Prestige '62 (*Take Twelve*), six on Blue Note '56-8 with fine support from Horace SILVER, Gigi GRYCE, Benny GOLSON, George COLEMAN, and others; about 20 more on Blue Note '63-71 variously incl. Clifford JORDAN, Wayne SHORTER, Jackie McLEAN, Joe Henderson, Mobley, Ron CARTER, Paul CHAMBERS, Billy HIGGINS, Cedar WALTON, most of the best from the Blue Note stable. *The Sidewinder* was no. 25 pop LP '64; *Search For The New Land* '66 and *Caramba!* '69 made top 200. *Live At The Lighthouse* '70 was recorded at that Hermosa Beach club, more tracks from same session issued on Trip. One of the most popular leaders of his era was shot to death by his girl friend at a club gig.

MORGAN, Russ (*b* 29 Apr. '04, Scranton, Pa.; *d* 8 Aug. '69, Las Vegas) Bandleader, trombonist, singer, songwriter, arranger. Coalminer, then cinema pianist, played in local groups; to NYC early '20s: arr. for Victor HERBERT, John Philip SOUSA; Jean GOLDKETTE in Detroit '26, mus. dir. on Detroit radio; arr. for Fletcher HENDERSON, Chick WEBB, Louis ARMSTRONG, DORSEY Bros, BOSWELL Sisters; conducted orchestra on Broadway, wrote for Cotton Club reviews, mus. dir. for Brunswick. Henderson recorded Morgan compositions for two labels '34, probably hoping to sign with Brunswick, but it didn't work. Morgan wrote 'Phantom Phantasie' (on Bluebird); discographies are undecided about whether Morgan or Will Hudson wrote 'Tidal Wave' (both Bluebird and Decca). Morgan played with Freddy MARTIN '34, formed own band from '36 with smooth pop style: good front man, pleasant singing, 'wah-wah' style trombone used sparingly, good radio exposure all made for success of 'Music In The Morgan Manner'. Co-wrote songs 'Somebody Else Is Taking My Place' '37, 'Sweet Eloise' '42, 'You're Nobody Till Somebody Loves You' '44, 'So Tired' '48, etc. 14 top 25 hits '42-51 incl. several of the above; five in '49 alone incl. 'Forever And Ever' (introduced vocal quartet soon famous as the AMES Brothers), 'Sunflower', smash no. 1 'Cruising Down The River' (British song had won amateur song contest at Hammersmith Palais). Two brothers joined band, also sons Jack and David; film *Disc Jockey* '51, TV show mid-'50s, straight acting role in *The Great Man* '56. Settled Las Vegas for nine months a year from '65. Jack (also trombonist) still booking band in '85. Compilations incl. *Golden Favorites* (Decca), *There Goes That Song Again* (Pickwick; title no. 5 hit '44), *One Night Stand 1944-6* (Joyce), others.

MORRISON, Van (*b* George Ivan Morrison, 31 Aug. '45, Belfast, N. Ireland) Singer/ songwriter, multi-instrumentalist. A great troubador who has married lyrics, tunes, and arrangements infl. by folk, soul and R&B into a style that is not a hybrid but unique and his own, its most compelling component an almost unbearable nostalgia, transmuted into art by talent. He is one of the few artists of the rock era to whom critics can accurately ascribe genius. He is scornful of the music press and the record business, rarely grants interviews; like Dylan, he knows that the important thing is the music, and that fans who want revelation are missing the point. Grew up infl. by father's record collection (incl. LEADBELLY, Hank WILLIAMS) when the BEATLES were listening to Buddy HOLLY; he left school at 15, joined the Monarchs, played rigorous gigs in Germany; returned to Belfast and formed Them. He disbanded '66 because the music business would not allow the band simply to be what it was, and he had also learned the necessity for complete control over the recording process (the profusion/confusion of Them LPs on several labels is a good example of what the record business will do to you if you don't watch out). Bert BERNS had been impressed by Morrison's handling of Berns's 'Here Comes The Night', sent him a one-way ticket to NYC; they worked on Morrison's first LP *Blowin' Your Mind* '67, reissued under many titles; Morrison was scornful about the finished product, though it incl. top 10 hit with engaging 'Brown Eyed Girl' and offers insight into his early creative

process (tracks from this period too have been subject to recycling in various forms). Following Berns's sudden death he was stranded in NYC, signed solo deal and taped *Astral Weeks* in 48 hours, one of the decade's most haunting, enigmatic albums, regularly featuring in critics' list of the all-time best; Celtic mysticism played against largely string-based instrumentation, with 'Madame George' and 'Cyprus Avenue' regarded as classics. *Moondance* '70 is overall more integrated, with a harder, brass-based lineup; the title track has Morrison a first-rate jazz singer, followed by beautiful, gently rocking, richly lyrical 'Into The Mystic', famous 'Caravan'. *Van Morrison, His Band And Street Choir* '70 was lighter and optimistic, incl. hit 'Domino'; *Tupelo Honey* '71 mellower still, with celebratory 'I Wanna Roo You' and 'Moonshine Whiskey'. He guested on The BAND's *Cahoots* '71 (later appeared in their valedictory *Last Waltz* film/concert/album '76 singing 'Caravan'). *Saint Dominic's Preview* '72 returned to brooding mysticism of *Astral Weeks*, incl. marathon 'Almost Independence Day', exuberant 'Jackie Wilson Said (I'm In Heaven When You Smile)' (covered by DEXY'S MIDNIGHT RUNNERS for '83 hit). *Hardnose The Highway* '73 was patchy, though version of trad. 'Purple Heather' was definitive, 'Warm Love' a minor hit. *It's Too Late To Stop Now* '74 was 2-disc live set: he insisted that every note be live, not tinkered with in the studio; the result is regarded as one of rock's best live albums. *Veedon Fleece* same year was a result of his first visit to Belfast in eight years, and as beguiling as *Astral Weeks*, though some fans were baffled by inscrutable lyrics. A hiatus was filled with rumours: an album's worth of material with the CRUSADERS was scrapped; he tried various combinations of musicians, settled on Mac REBENNACK for *A Period Of Transition* '77, flawed by some uncertainty, but incl. notable 'The Eternal Kansas City' and 'Flamingos Fly'. *Wavelength* '78 was altogether more successful and *Into The Music* '79 a serene and contemplative work, as was the beautiful *Common One* '80, incl. marathon 15-minute 'Summertime In England', benign 'Haunts Of Ancient Peace'. With the new decade he seemed to enter artistic rebirth: *Beautiful Vision* '82 again revelled in Celtic background and featured swinging, cheerful autobiographic 'Cleaning Windows', also 'She Gives Me Religion', 'Dweller On The Threshold'. *Inarticulate Speech Of The Heart* '83 incl. inscrutable 'Rave On, John Donne', wistful 'Cry For Home'. *Live At The Royal Opera House, Belfast* '84 drew on recent material; immaculately executed concert recording was regarded as disappointing by critics who wanted new stuff. *A Sense Of Wonder* '85 was impeccable, notably the title track and 'Tore Down A La Rimbaud'; *No Guru, No Method, No Teacher* '86 was return to Celtic feeling, with 'Tir Na Nog' and 'One Irish Rover'; by *Poetics Champion Compose* '87 he was beginning to repeat himself, but never becoming tiresome. An honest working man whose work happens to transcend category, he is described as enigmatic, because the work can speak for itself: if he could explicate the songs he wouldn't have to write them, and he is not required to talk about himself with anyone who knocks on the door. *Irish Heartbeat* '88 with the CHIEFTAINS made fans of both happy. Books: Ritchie Yorke's *Van Morrison: Into The Music* '75 is outdated, overwritten, but not as bad as some say; Johnny Rogan's *Van Morrison* '84 is more recent.

MORRISSEY-MULLEN UK jazz-inspired band co-led by reedman Dick Morrissey (*b* 9 May '40, Surrey) and guitarist Jim Mullen (*b* 26 Nov. '45, Glasgow). Morrissey led a quartet '60s, formed jazz-rock band If with Terry Smith; own LPs incl. *Storm Warning* '67, with *Jimmy Witherspoon At The Bull's Head* '68, both on Fontana; *After Dark* '83 on Beggars Banquet. Mullen led groups in Glasgow; to London, worked with Pete Brown '69-71, Brian Auger '71-3; they have both worked with AVERAGE WHITE BAND, Herbie MANN; formed Morrissey-Mullen '77. Albums incl. *Cape Wrath* and *Lovely Day* '79-80 on EMI/Harvest, *Badness* '82, *Life On The Wire* '83, *It's About Time* '84 on Beggars Banquet, *This Must Be The Place* '85 on Coda.

MORROW, Buddy (*b* Muni 'Moe' Zudekoff, 8 Feb. '19, New Haven, Conn.) Trombone, bandleader. Joined Yale Collegians; attended Juilliard '34, played with Paul WHITEMAN, Eddy DUCHIN, Artie SHAW, Vincent Lopez, Bunny BERIGAN, Tommy DORSEY in mid-to-late '30s. Did studio work; with Bob CROSBY '41-2, then US Navy Band. With Jimmy DORSEY '45; then several years of studio work before forming his own band in '51 (surprisingly, the Big Band Era being all but over): it was a very good band indeed, having minor hits with good arrangements of R&B covers on RCA: biggest was 'Night Train', also 'Hey Mrs Jones' (*see* Jimmy FORREST), 'Re-enlistment Blues' (co-written by Robert Wells; sung in film *From Here To Eternity* by Merle TRAVIS), Willie Mabon's 'I Don't Know' (good vocalist in Frankie Lester on the last two). Morrow was well recorded: RCA did a better job with him early '50s than with Elvis PRESLEY in '56. Band made charts '56 on Mercury's Wing label with film theme 'Man With The Golden Arm'; he later led Glenn MILLER and Tommy DORSEY ghost bands between bouts of studio work.

MORSE, Ella Mae (*b* 12 Sep. '24, Mansfield, Texas) Singer, jazz oriented; technically one of the best of her era: she could swing anything, but fell into a crevasse between pure jazz and pop pap. She was too good for the radio in the trough of the early '50s; even so she had more than a dozen hits '42-53, several in the top 10. She sang with Jimmy DORSEY '39; hits began with Freddie SLACK band: 'Cow Cow Boogie' '42 helped establish Capitol label; 'House Of Blue Lights' '46 was no. 8; she also went solo: 'Shoo Shoo Baby'/'No Love, No Nothin' ' saw both sides in top 5 '43; she retired for a few years, came back with no. 3 hit 'The Blacksmith Blues', then top 25 'Oakie Boogie', both '52, both directed by Nelson RIDDLE; '40 Cups Of Coffee' '53 with 'Dave Cavanaugh's Music' also did well. Capitol producer Cavanaugh did well by her; album *Barrelhouse, Boogie And The Blues* incl. all Cavanaugh material; in general the later A&R men were less imaginative, though 'I'm Gone' '56 was written by Quincy JONES and King Pleasure, based on a saxophone solo. She retired again *c.* '57. Other LPs incl. *The Hits Of Ella Mae Morse* and *Sensational* (mostly later stuff except '52 Cavanaugh single 'Jump Back Honey'/'Greyhound'), all from EMI/Pathé in France. 'Cow Cow Boogie', 'Blacksmith Blues' (written by Jack Holmes as 'Happy Payoff Day') were million-sellers.

MORTON, Benny (*b* Henry Sterling Morton, 31 Jan. '07, NYC; *d* 28 Dec. '85) Trombone; with J. C. HIGGINBOTHAM, Dicky WELLS, Sandy WILLIAMS and a few others, one of the best on the instrument in the big bands of the Swing Era. Turned professional c.'24, played with Fletcher HENDERSON '26-8, again '31; with Chick WEBB '31, Don REDMAN '32-7 (recorded four sides '34 as leader of nonet drawn from Redman band incl. Red Allen, Don Kirkpatrick, etc. with vocals by sidemen); with Count BASIE '37-40, then small groups with Teddy WILSON, Ed Hall; own band '44-6; made 12″ 78s for Blue Note '45 with 'All Stars' incl. Barney BIGARD, Ben WEBSTER, Israel Crosby (reissued by Mosaic '86), also on Keynote with Trombone Choir. Played in about 20 Broadway show pit bands '44-59, also studio work, freelance gigging until joining World's Greatest Jazz Band '70s.

MORTON, George 'Shadow' (*b* '42, Richmond, Va.) Producer, songwriter. Lived in Hicksville, Long Island at age 16; had a vague connection with the Young RASCALS; made two obscure singles on RCA himself as The Marquis ('I Feel Majestic') and The Gems ('Hot Rod'); acquainted with Ellie GREENWICH (attended same high school), he linked with her and Jeff BARRY, hoping to work as a songwriter (at which he claimed he had no previous experience). Discovered the SHANGRI LAS and became their svengali; when their course was run he worked with teenager Janis IAN, making top 20 single 'Society's Child' and two LPs '67; helped launch VANILLA FUDGE '67-8, prod. their first three LPs incl. hit with psychedelic version of 'You Keep Me Hangin' On'. He acquired his nickname by disappearing for spells. He worked briefly with MOTT THE HOOPLE, re-emerged '74 as prod. of prophetically titled NEW YORK DOLLS second LP *Too Much Too Soon*; submerged again until two LPs on RCA '76 for the little-known Tom Pacheco. Charisma remains from the '60s.

MORTON, Jelly Roll (*b* Ferdinand Joseph Lemott, 20 Oct. 1890, New Orleans, La.; *d* 10 July '41, L.A., Cal.) Pianist, composer, arranger, bandleader; the first great composer in jazz. Details of his birth came to light '86, published by Laurie Wright in *Storyville* magazine: a baptismal certificate was found for which earlier scholars had looked in the wrong parish, perhaps purposely misled by the family. Morton gave his year of birth as 1885; he made himself older perhaps to give more weight to his claim to have invented jazz: he was one of the most flamboyant characters in the history of the music. Lemott is the name on the certificate; his father's (free Creole) family's name seems to have been Lamothe; he adapted stepfather's surname of Mouton; much of his ancestry was Haitian. He heard Buddy BOLDEN and Freddie KEPPARD (*see* JAZZ), began playing piano in brothels and was kicked out of his godmother's house '05-7, acquired an immediate taste for the money and for show business: soon experienced in black vaudeville, 'He thought he was a funny man, and my God, he was as funny as a sick baby. He never made nobody laugh' (Benjamin F. 'Reb' Spikes, 1888-1982, was interviewed many times incl. for Rutgers U. Institute of Jazz '80 by Patricia Willard, quoted by Wright). Morton was apparently at various times a pimp, gambler and pool shark, but always had his greatest success in music. Gigged in New Orleans and other Louisiana/Mississippi towns, made it to NYC by '11 but worked in Texas '12-14, Chicago '14-17, on West Coast '17-22, then back to Chicago: first recordings '23-4 with small groups incl. New Orleans Rhythm Kings; two duets with King OLIVER '24 were failures, but may have inspired later duets by Louis ARMSTRONG/Earl HINES, which were not. 19 piano solos made in Richmond, Indiana for Gennett '23-4 (on Fountain label UK '72) are invaluable: all his own compositions, incl. several with 'Spanish tinge' (habañera infl. became a permanent part of jazz repertoire). Two sides for Gennett early '26 by 'Jelly-Roll Morton's Incomparables' were by a trio, the only ones by a touring group as opposed to studio pick-up bands; four more solos were made for Vocalion Feb. '26, then about 89 sides (incl. alternate takes) by 'Jelly-Roll Morton and his Red Hot Peppers' for Victor between Sep. '26 and Oct. '30 made him famous forever. '26-7 sides made in Chicago incl. 'Dead Man Blues', 'Sidewalk Blues', 'Hyena Stomp' with comedy (bad jokes, klaxons, etc.) but the rest were mostly pure music. Others in

NYC (or Camden, N.J.) incl. trio sides with Barney BIGARD and Zutty Singleton (and six more piano solos); one of the most successful dates, first NYC session June '28, incl. trio 'Shreveport Stomp' with Tommy BENFORD and Omer SIMEON, beautiful quartet 'Mournful Serenade' (paying tribute to Oliver's 'Chimes Blues') added Julius 'Geechie' Fields (b c.'03, Georgia) on trombone; septet sides adding Ward Pinkett, trumpet (b 29 Apr. '06, Newport News, Va.; d 15 Mar. '37, NYC), Bill Benford on tuba, Lee Blair on banjo incl. fine 'Georgia Stomp', 'Boogaloo', others. In the studio Morton's genius arranged tunes, decided voicings, harmonies etc. on the spot to make classically beautiful recordings of the genre, and it followed that his composing/arranging/leading from the piano were all of a piece, like that of Duke ELLINGTON. Ironically, Ellington despised him for his bragging and vulgarity; but despite social handicaps Morton, like Ellington, knew his own worth and had an innate dignity which could not be taken away. 'Black Bottom Stomp', 'Original Jelly Roll Blues' and 'Grandpa's Spells' (all '27, with Kid ORY on trombone) were national hits, as was 'Wolverine Blues' '29 with Johnny DODDS; by the early '30s, though, he was seen as old-fashioned and record sales were falling: he did not record again until '38 for the Library of Congress (see Alan LOMAX), except for a Wingy MANONE session '34; the priceless LoC documentaries, incl. reminiscence as well as pianism, have never been properly transferred and issued complete. Morton scuffled without much reward, lost money in an ill-fated cosmetics company; Victor recorded him again '39 (on Bluebird) with band incl. Singleton, Sidney DE PARIS, Albert Nicholas on clarinet (b 27 May 1900, New Orleans; d 3 Sep. '73, Basle, Switzerland), others incl. Sidney BECHET on some tracks, 'Winin' Boy Blues' and 'I Thought I Heard Buddy Bolden Say' also with Morton vocals; sides for Commodore same year incl. band with Red ALLEN, Nicholas, Singleton, Wellman BRAUD; and ten gorgeous piano solos (plus alternate takes) incl. 'King Porter Stomp' (first recorded '23 in Richmond, later by the Peppers; was a hit throughout the Swing Era by Fletcher HENDERSON, Benny GOODMAN), 'The Naked Dance', several vocals incl. 'Winin'

Boy', 'Mamie's Blues'; and his version of Scott JOPLIN's 'Original Rags': compared with a straight performance of Joplin's published work, Morton's makes it clear that his claim to have invented jazz was not so farfetched: he was a living link between ragtime and jazz. Four solos made privately in Washington DC '38 (incl. an organ track) have been issued on French Vogue; duo, trio and solo recordings made in Baltimore '38 and air checks from guest appearance '40 on NBC radio's CHAMBER MUSIC SOCIETY OF LOWER BASIN STREET have been issued on Australian Swaggie. He suffered from ill health, died just as the revival was gathering steam (see JAZZ); if he had lived a little longer he would have been a star all over again. Lomax's book *Mr Jelly Roll* '50 was easily superseded by Wright's *Mr Jelly Lord* '80.

MOST, Mickie (b Michael Hayes, 20 June '38, Aldershot, Hants.) Producer and pop svengali, changing name late '50s searching for success with Alex Murray as The Most Brothers, whose backing band incl. future SHADOWS Hank Marvin and Bruce Welch on guitars, bassist Jet Harris, drummer Pete Chester. Abandoned light-harmony rock when he met South African-born wife, emigrated to S.A. where he formed Mickie Most and the Playboys and exploited the non-availability of USA music with 11 consecutive no. 1 records with covers (Chuck BERRY's 'Johnny B. Goode', etc.). Returned to UK '62, did package tour circuit and reached no. 45 '63 with 'Mister Porter', but wisely decided to retire and use studio expertise picked up abroad. First worked with the ANIMALS, a raw R&B band he spotted in a Newcastle club: single 'House Of The Rising Sun' exceeded three minutes, unheard of then, but was no. 1 both USA and UK; though Alan Price quit band over rows with dictator Most, his down-to-earth approach turned a rowdy live band into studio winners. He polished HERMAN'S HERMITS, whose run of hits began with UK no. 1 '64 'I'm Into Something Good'; also prod. DONOVAN from '66, LULU and Jeff BECK from '67; he played major role in shaping Donovan's career, while Beck later disowned hits like 'Hi Ho Silver Lining' and 'Love Is Blue'. Most formed own RAK label '70, turned to bubblegum acts like Mud,

Suzi QUATRO, Racey; but also signed classy, long-lived pop thoroughbreds HOT CHOCOLATE, soft-rockers Smokie. His commercial judgement rarely failed; he even signed up his main rivals in bubblegum production, (Nicky) CHINN & (Mike) CHAPMAN, whose songs were published by RAK's publishing arm. Was panellist on TV talent show *New Faces*; also prod. pop show *Revolver* '70s; continues to run RAK profitably, though at a smaller output (Kim Wilde a major '80s star). Motto 'Find good songs, go in the studio, make good records and then go home' led to turning down 'troublesome' acts like the WHO, ROLLING STONES.

MOTELS New wave group formed '72 in L.A. by vocalist Martha Davis (*b* San Francisco), who originally named band Warfield Foxes: lineup incl. Dean Chamberlain, guitar; Richard D'Andrea, bass. Track 'Counting' on WB demo tape did not get contract (later on Rhino label sampler *Saturday Night Pogo* '78). Co-frontperson Chamberlain left to form Code Blue, D'Andrea to ex-BLONDIE Gary Valentine's band the Know; from then on Davis, a single parent (married c. age 15) who has successfully fought cancer, was in sole charge, her haunting, restrained yet menacing vocal style the trademark. She recruited guitarist Jeff Jourard as collaborator, with his brother Martin on saxophone, bassist Michael Goodroe and UK session drummer Brian Glascock (credits with BEE GEES, Joan ARMATRADING, IGGY POP etc.); formed for a gig at Hollywood's Whisky A Go Go, the band jelled well and made *Motels* '79 for Capitol, incl. classic single 'Total Control' (later covered by Tina TURNER) showcasing Davis's understated yet effective vocal style with taut backing from band: a world away from BLONDIE, not only in hair colour. Jourard was ousted; former session drummer Tim McGovern (ex-The Pop) replaced him for *Careful* '80, again prod. by label staff man John Carter; first LP had sold well in Australia, but the new one made USA top 50. McGovern was replaced (resurfaced later with the Burning Sensations) by Guy Perry (ex-Elephant's Memory) on *All Four One* '82, cut twice, once with McGovern which label rejected, again with Davis, Goodroe and session men: band now became live-only act and records (under

Kim CARNES producer Val Garay) a solo act in all but name. *All Four One* reached top 20, incl. no. 9 single 'Only The Lonely' (not the Roy ORBISON song). Two more hit singles (from *Little Robbers* '83) proved strategy successful; all were backed up by inventive videos: 'Only The Lonely' parodied Kubrick film *The Shining*; 'Take The L (Out Of Lover)' was presented in comicbook form. Davis and Garay split after abortive LP sessions '85, and she brought band back to studio for *Shock* '85, prod. by Richie Zito with new keyboardist Scott Thurston.

MOTEN, Bennie (*b* 13 Nov. 1894, Kansas City, Mo.; *d* there 2 Apr. '35) Pianist, composer, leader of the most prolific and successful of territory bands (*see* JAZZ). Began with five pieces early '20s, grew to classic big band size by late '20s: sextet recorded for Okeh '23 incl. Thamon Hayes on trombone; octet incl. Harlan LEONARD made first recordings of 'South' and 'Vine Street Blues' '24; 'South' was a nationwide hit '25, the band switched to Victor and 'Kansas City Shuffle' was a hit '27, 'Moten Stomp' '28, new electric recording of 'South' '29 (charted again '44, reissued during musicians-union's strike). Ed Lewis played trumpet from '27; Eddie DURHAM and Count BASIE joined '29, Basie taking over the piano while Moten directed; Lewis left early '32 to join Hayes's Kansas City Skyrockets (later taken over by Leonard), but the depression hit record sales and Moten's last recording session was late '32, incl. Ben WEBSTER, Hot Lips PAGE, Jack Washington, Dan Minor, Walter PAGE, Jimmy RUSHING; Moten died while having tonsils out (now regarded as an unnecessary operation) just as the Big Band Era was about to explode: after a struggle with Walter Page, Basie took over the nucleus of the band, soon made even more history, paid fine tribute to his old boss with lovely, lilting treatment of 'South' '47. Two Benny Motens, incl. Clarence Lemont Moten (*b* 30 Nov. '16, NYC; *d* 27 Mar. '77, New Orleans), a bassist who played with Hot Lips Page, Henry ALLEN, Dakota STATON, many others, were not related.

MOTIAN, Paul (*b* Stephen Paul Motian, 25 Mar. '31, Philadelphia, Pa. of Armenian descent) Drummer, composer; also pianist. An exceptionally talented and tasteful contemporary musician whose name ought to be a household word. Listened to Turkish music as a child; tried guitar under the infl. of cowboy movies but switched to drums age 12; served in US Navy; first recorded mid-'55 on Progressive label with pianist/singer Bob Dorough (*b* 12 Dec. '23, Cherry Hill, Ark.; recorded with Miles DAVIS on *Sorcerer*). Played and recorded with Bill EVANS trio '59-63 incl. Scott LA FARO; when he suddenly left he and Evans did not speak for 15 years, but were reconciled and would have played together again but for Evans's death. Motian was curious, had to investigate everything that was going on: first played with Paul BLEY '64 (LP *Turning Point*), then with Mose ALLISON, Arlo GUTHRIE (incl. Woodstock Festival), Charles LLOYD (incl. tour of Asia); also played/recorded with Lennie TRISTANO; with Keith JARRETT '66-9, again '71-5 during one of Jarrett's most creative periods: quartet with Charlie HADEN, Dewey REDMAN was not well documented on records; *Eyes Of The Heart* on ECM, meant to be a live concert recording, is heavily edited. Motian was active in JCOA group, incl. Carla BLEY albums *Escalator Over The Hill*, *Tropic Appetites*; Haden's Liberation Orchestra on Impulse, A&M, ECM; first LP as leader was *Conception Vessel* '72 with Haden, Sam Brown on guitar, duets with Jarrett; then quintet *Tribute* '74, trio *Dance* '76, with Charles Brackeen on reeds, bassist David Izenson; *Le Voyage* '79 with Jean-François Jenny-Clark instead of Izenson; quintet on *Psalm* '81 incl. Bill Frisell (*b* 18 Mar. '51, Baltimore, Md., raised in Colorado; studied at Berklee, with Jim HALL and others; now one of the most sought-after guitarists both in USA and Europe). Motian switched to Soul Note for quintet albums *The Story Of Maryam* '83 and *Jack Of Clubs* '84, both made in Milan with Frisell, bassist Ed Schuller (son of musicologist Gunther), Jim Pepper and Joe Lovano on reeds; also *Misterioso* '86. Trio *It Should've Happened A Long Time Ago* '84 with Lovano and Frisell was back on ECM. Reunited with Bley on lovely Bley album *Fragments* '86 on ECM, then *The Paul Bley Quartet* '88, also with Frisell and John SURMAN, the poetry in Motian making an equal part in thoughtful, evocative tone poems.

MOTLEY CRUE USA heavy metal band formed '81 by Nikki Sixx, bass, and Tommy Lee, drums; recruiting guitarist Mick Mars and vocalist Vince Neil (*b* Vincent Neil Wharton). Image owed a lot to the NEW YORK DOLLS, but with WASP and Ratt they flew in the face of prevailing fashion by offering HM with all the trimmings. Album of demos *Too Fast For Love* '82 released on own Leathur (sic) label, sold 20,000 in four months in L.A. alone; when they opened for KISS '83 they began to conquer country-wide following, returned to sell out three nights at Santa Monica Civic. *Shout At The Devil* '83 made USA top 50 albums; *Theatre Of Pain* '85 made top 10, incl. single cover of Brownsville Station's 'Smokin' In The Boys' Room'. Neil was convicted of manslaughter '85 after death of passenger Nicholas 'Razzle' Dingley (drummer with HANOI ROCKS) in car crash Dec. '84; repentant, he was allowed to finish tour before doing time; Crue have since exhorted audiences not to drink and drive; sleeve of album carried warning.

MOTORHEAD UK heavy metal band formed '75 by bassist Ian 'Lemmy' Kilminster (*b* '45, Blackpool) after being sacked from Hawkwind because of drug bust on Canadian tour which threatened to jeopardise it. Originally named band Bastard, took new name from Hawkwind B-side titled after USA slang for speed freak. Introduced to ex-Pink Fairies guitarist Larry Wallis and drummer Lucas Fox; determined on power trio format, with bass almost as lead instrument against wall of crashing guitar; rookie drummer Phil 'Philthy Animal' Taylor replaced Fox for LP that was shelved (later issued on UA as *On Parole* '80). Wallis ousted as unreliable by ex-Blue Goose, Curtis Knight guitarist 'Fast' Eddie Clarke, originally mooted as second guitarist; made single 'White Line Fever'/'Leavin' Here' for Stiff only to have UA block release. Attracted live punk following due to stage act of volume with breakneck speed; *Motorhead* '77 recorded for Chiswick after UA gave them up, represented sledgehammer act. Signed to Bronze, *Overkill* (prod. by Jimmy Miller, ex-ROLLING STONES, TRAFFIC) and *Bomber*, both '79, both made UK top 30 LPs (latter peaking at 12), title tracks first top 40 hits.

831

Ace Of Spades '80 and live *No Sleep Till Hammersmith* '81 (latter entered UK chart at no. 1) proved to be their peak; EP *The Golden Years* '80, a live EP and duet single 'Please Don't Touch' with labelmates Girlschool '81 all made top 10, but band split with *Spades* prod. halfway through *Iron Fist* '82, lost Clarke following Lemmy's plan to duet with punk Plasmatics' Wendy O. Williams on Tammy WYNETTE country classic 'Stand By Your Man'. From then on magic fast and furious formula was diluted. Ex-THIN LIZZY guitarist Brian Robertson stayed through *This Perfect Day* '83 but was too good; Taylor left early '84 and Lemmy revamped band entirely, bringing in twin guitars, ex-Persian Risk Phil Campbell and unknown Wurzel, replacing Taylor with ex-Saxon drummer Pete Gill. New lineup made four tracks for compilation *No Remorse* '84; then problems with label kept them quiet until *Orgasmatron* '86 on GWR, prod. by Bill LASWELL. Band's live act good value (on *Bomber* tour, replica Heinkel swooped over audience); no musical progress in 10 years but fans love it. Clarke turned up in Fastway with vocalist Dave King.

MOTOWN The most successful black-owned record company, one of the most successful black-owned corporations in USA history, output fundamental to the sound of the '60s. Formed by Berry Gordy III (*b* 28 Nov. '29, Detroit); family had been prominent Georgia farmers (so prominent that they left '22 at a time when lynchings of blacks had reached an all-time high). He was a boxer (had worked out with a Golden Gloves champion named Jackie WILSON; later won at least nine of 15 fights); served in US Army; worked for his father days, haunted jazz clubs nights; ran jazz record shop '53-5 (potential customers were into R&B); worked in Ford factory, began writing songs: wrote for Wilson for three years incl. big hits 'Reet Petite', 'That Is Why (I Love You So)', 'I'll Be Satisfied', 'Lonely Teardrops'. Formed prod. company with second wife Raynoma Liles, recorded and leased hits by Marv JOHNSON; meanwhile met Smokey ROBINSON '57, changed name of Matadors to Miracles, leased their records. Writing partner Billy Davis, sisters Gwen and Anna Gordy formed Anna label,

distributed by Chess, had hit with 'Money (That's What I Want)', sung by Barrett Strong, written and recorded by Berry: Gordy had only wanted to be a successful songwriter, but was convinced by Smokey that the only way to reap the rewards meant starting a record company: Jobete Music Publishing, Hitsville USA, ITM (International Talent Management), Motown Record Corporation (short for Motortown) etc. established secretiveness and cross-collateral royalty accounts, so that many Motown million-sellers were not certified gold by the RIAA (Record Industry Association of America) because no outsiders saw the books, and artists were paid salaries until they had hits, but were tied to the company and subject to Gordy's whims. First release mid-'59 was 'Way Over There' by Smokey and the Miracles on Tamla label, also Smokey's first solo production; blues singers Amos MILBURN, Mabel John (sister of LITTLE WILLIE JOHN), Singing Sammy Ward generated local cash; then Miracles' 'Shop Around' was no. 1 R&B, no. 2 pop early '61. Gwen and Anna married Harvey FUQUA and Marvin GAYE respectively; Davis left and Anna Records died; Fuqua's undercapitalised TriPhi/Harvey labels suffered the problems of all small labels, especially black ones, and he joined the staff: Motown became a family operation tightly controlled by Gordy, and soon dominated the decade's black pop, seriously challenged by only the southern sound of Stax and Muscle Shoals (*see* SOUL). Motown developed, looked after Mary WELLS, the SUPREMES, the JACKSON 5, Martha REEVES and the Vandellas, Gladys KNIGHT and the Pips, the TEMPTATIONS, the MARVELETTES, the FOUR TOPS, Stevie WONDER, Junior WALKER, many more; tight in-house staff incl. the songwriting/production teams HOLLAND-DOZIER-HOLLAND, ASHFORD & SIMPSON; A&R director William 'Mickey' Stevenson lured local jazz musicians into studio band by the chance to record on Jazz Workshop label which mostly didn't materialise: pianist Joe Hunter, Dave Hamilton on vibes and guitar, Benny Benjamin on drums, the all-important James Jamerson on bass. Barney Ales was v.p. in charge of distribution, the only white person in the company for years: if distributors thought Ales owned the company, that was good for business. Maxine Powell (had local finishing and modelling school) and experienced choreographer Cholly Atkins were brought in to teach acts deportment and stage movements; touring Motown shows were also tightly chaperoned. Not everyone submitted to Gordy's autocratic style and tight purse strings: Wells, Reeves, H-D-H and the Four Tops eventually jumped ship; Florence Ballard, the Supremes' original leader, died on welfare after Gordy decided that Diana Ross could be a sepia Barbra STREISAND; Gaye was the first to get his own way, making innovatory LPs instead of pop singles; Wonder wrote his own ticket when he turned 21, already a star. But the proof of Gordy's genius in the studio and deciding who should do what was in the hits: at least 110 singles in Billboard pop top 10 '61-71, and still selling today in countless compilations and anthologies, the sound as tight and compelling as that of Phil SPECTOR, yet less claustrophobic; the hits of the Motown decade are perhaps the ultimate party music, and more than that, thanks to Robinson's songwriting. Gradually Gordy gave up the hands-on control in the studio, yet still controlled the company absolutely; he moved it to L.A. '71 as if to signify that the golden era was over, his dabbling in films proving less than completely successful. Motown grossed $40 million in '73 and employed 135 people, but by then it had had become just another record company. Berry sold it to MCA mid-'88. *Where Did Our Love Go?* '85 by Nelson George tells the whole story, one of the best books of its kind; *see also* entries for individual Motown acts.

MOTT THE HOOPLE Rock band formed in Hereford, England '68. First vocalist Stan Tippens replaced by vocalist/guitarist Ian Hunter (*b* 3 June '46, Shrewsbury), who soon became cynosure; others were guitarist Mick Ralphs (*b* 31 Mar. '44, Hereford), bassist Overend (Peter) Watts (*b* 13 May '47, Birmingham); Verden Allen on keyboards (*b* 26 May '44, Hereford), drummer Dale 'Buffin' Griffin (*b* 24 Oct. '48, Ross-on-Wye). Moved to London '69, met DJ Guy Stevens, who suggested name-change from Silence to Mott The Hoople, after obscure novel by Willard Manus. *Mott The Hoople* '69 was very much an album of its time,

guitar balance infl. by The BAND: striking Escher cover, Hunter's Dylanesque delivery, driving rock'n'roll established them on London club circuit; *Mad Shadows* '70, *Wildlife* and *Brain Capers* '71 along with rigorous touring made them favourites, but real mainstream success eluded them until David BOWIE chanced upon them at a gig, prod. *All The Young Dudes* '72 just as Mott were on verge of split: title track (Bowie song) gave them no. 3 hit '72, established a major draw. Hunter published *Diary Of A Rock Star* '73; LP *Mott* '73 incl. 'Ballad Of Mott', exuberant 'All The Way To Memphis' (UK no. 10 '74). When his 'Can't Get Enough' wasn't accepted by the band, Ralphs left to form BAD COMPANY and had transatlantic top 20 with it; he was replaced by ex-SPOOKY TOOTH Luther Grosvenor; ex-Love Affair Morgan Fisher replaced Allen. 'The Golden Age Of Rock'n'Roll' was top 20 hit, but *The Hoople* was patchy; poignant single 'Saturday Gigs' sounded like epitaph, but they persevered with excellent souvenir *Mott The Hoople Live*, all '74. Former Bowie guitarist Mick Ronson joined for *Drive On* '75 and *Shouting & Pointing* '76, but original charm was now dissipating. Hunter and Ronson went off to work together on split '76; *Greatest Hits* issued that year.

MOUNK'A, Pamelo (*b* Bembo Pamelo Mounk'a, Congo) Singer, composer; acknowledged the most popular in Congo-Brazzaville. Made debut '63 with his friend and 'master' Tabu Ley in Afrisa; moved on to the Bantous, with Kosmos and Samba Mascott; released over 70 singles made in makeshift Brazzaville studios; by the '70s he had carved out his niche, singing of love and its victims and refusing to be infl. by newer sounds from abroad. Fast maturing talent can be heard on *Les Grands Succès Africains Vol. 9* on Pathé Marconi, but big breakthrough came when he was invited by Eddy'son Records to record in Paris: result *L'Argent Appelle l'Argent* '81 on Sonics was smash hit with the best of the Congo's musicians: Master Mwana, Pablo, Salsero, Eddy Gustav. More LPs incl. *Samantha, Ça ne se Prête Pas, Propulsion, Camitana* and *Selimandja*; reunion with Ley celebrated 20 years in music with *20 Ans de Carrière* '83. *Metamorphose* '85 incl. backing by Redoubtables D'Abeti, followed by *En Pleine Maturité*.

MOUNTAIN USA heavy rock group formed '69 by bassist Felix Pappalardi (*b* '39, Bronx, NYC; *d* 17 Apr. '83, NYC) and guitarist Leslie West (*b* Leslie Weinstein, 22 Oct. '45, NYC). Pappalardi had graduated from Michigan Conservatory of Music and drifted into folk, playing bass for Tim HARDIN in Greenwich Village before making reputation as session player, arranger and producer. Prod. YOUNGBLOODS debut '67, then CREAM albums *Disraeli Gears*, *Wheels Of Fire* and *Goodbye* '67-9, co-writing '67 hit 'Strange Brew' with Eric CLAPTON and wife, lyricist Gail Collins. While prod. single for NYC group the Vagrants, he was impressed by lead guitarist West; prod. solo LP *Leslie West – Mountain* '69 (Vagrants disintegrated after two singles); duo added keyboardist Steve Knight (ex-Devil's Anvil) and drummer Norman Smart, formed group taking name of LP. Heavy rock in Cream, GRAND FUNK mould right for the times: fourth gig was Woodstock festival, ensuring immortality. Album *Mountain Climbing* '70 incl. no. 21 single 'Mississippi Queen'; *Nantucket Sleighride* '71 was high point, Smart replaced by Corky Laing (*b* 28 Jan. '48, Montreal): hard-driving wide-screen rock of title track contrasted West's lyrical guitar with his roaring vocal style; Pappalardi shared vocals with a thinner, nasal voice, still co-writing with Collins. *Flowers Of Evil* '71 followed by *Mountain Live (The Road Goes Ever On)* '72; the latter and 2-disc *Twin Peaks* '74 both featured epic versions of 'Sleighride', taking Cream-inspired improvisations to extremes. Band split '72; Pappalardi (whose impaired hearing couldn't have been helped by massive onstage volume) concentrated on solo work while West and Laing recruited ex-Cream Jack Bruce to form West, Bruce and Laing, who made *Why Don'cha* and *Whatever Turns You On* '72-3 before Bruce left; posthumous *Live And Kickin'* '74 appeared just as Mountain reformed with rhythm guitar David Perry instead of keyboardist Knight: *Avalanche* '74 followed by split again '75. Laing appeared on West's *The Great Fatsby* and *Leslie West Band* '75 before West's career sputtered amid financial and drug problems; Laing

made his own *Makin' It On The Street* '77. Pappalardi went to Japan, prod. *Felix Pappalardi And Creation* '76; prod. punks DEAD BOYS '78; was found dead at home: Collins was charged with murder. Though far from being innovators, as a live band whose studio work has not worn well, Mountain were in the forefront of '70s rockers. They also provided theme for UK/ITV magazine programme *Weekend World*.

MOUSKOURI, Nana (*b* 10 Oct. '36, Athens, Greece) Pop singer with 'the voice of longing'. Met husband Manos Hadjidakis (who wrote 'Never On Sunday') '58, made first record '59 and became a hit in Greece, went to Germany to record, had million-selling Continental hit with 'Weisse Rosen Aus Athen' '62 ('The White Rose Of Athens'), written/arranged by Hadjidakis for film *Traumland der Sehnsucht* ('Dreamland Of Desire'), based on Greek tune aka 'The Water And The Wine'. She had eight hit LPs in UK '69-76, appeared on *An Evening With Harry Belafonte/Mouskouri* '66, remains a popular MOR artist. *Nana* '84 on Philips incl. songs by Neil SEDAKA, Allen TOUSSAINT.

MOVE, The UK pop group formed '66 by members of Birmingham groups: guitarist/vocalist Roy Wood from Mike Sheridan and the Nightriders; lead guitarist Trevor Burton (*b* 9 Mar. '49, Birmingham), vocalist Carl Wayne (*b* 18 Aug. '44, Birmingham), Christopher 'Ace' Kefford on bass (*b* 10 Dec. '46) and drummer Bev Bevan. Manager Tony Secunda steered them from soul covers to West Coast sound based on strong songwriting of Wood. 'Night Of Fear' was no. 2 hit early '67, promoted by TV-smashing set at London's Marquee that made headlines: band dressed in gangster suits, psychedelic threads, anything Secunda came up with, Wood writing to suit. 'I Can Hear The Grass Grow' and 'Flowers In The Rain' (on EMI's newly revived Regal Zonophone label) were suitable top 5 hits for the 'Summer of Love' '67; Wood's interest in classical music, rock'n-'roll, country and even hymns made amusing musical melange. Secunda's use of Prime Minister Harold Wilson naked in his bath as an advertising image backfired and the image was toned down. 'Fire Brigade' was no. 3 but 'Wild Tiger Woman' flopped; BEATLE-infl. 'Blackberry Way' used harpsichord, cello and strings for no. 1 hit '68, but underscored the fact that they had no identity of their own. Lineup changes were thick and fast: Kefford replaced mid-'68 by Burton, switched to bass; Burton left '69 to join the Uglys, replaced by Rick Price (*b* 10 June '44); Wayne left to pursue cabaret career '69; Idle Race mastermind guitarist Jeff Lynne was recruited, lured by promise of new group pursuing pseudo-classical direction in newly-important album market. As Wood, Lynne and Bevan prepared ELEC-TRIC LIGHT ORCHESTRA, Move remained vehicle for catchy single hits until fizzling out '72, Price jumping ship '71 to join Mongrel.

MOVING HEARTS Irish rock group formed '81, often categorised as folk band because of members' backgrounds. Original lineup: Brian Calnan, drums, percussion; Keith Donald, saxes; Donal Lunny, synthesiser, bouzouki, vocals; Christy MOORE, vocals, guitar, bodhrán; Eoghan O'Neill, bass, vocals; Davy Spillane, whistles, Uilleann pipes. *Moving Hearts* '81 regarded as exciting event in Irish music, blend of pipes and saxes a masterstroke, with songs like Philip Chevron's 'Faithful Departed' (before he went to the POGUES), 'Hiroshima, Nagasaki, Russian Roulette'. Additional tracks same year joined by Mick Hanly on single incl. 'On The Blanket', about 'dirty protests' of IRA prisoners in Northern Ireland jails. *Dark End Of The Street* '82 followed, by which time Matt Kelleghan had become drummer; Moore left, replaced by Hanly for concert album *Live Hearts* '83 and single tracks 'Oil Sheiks' and 'Promises'; Flo McSweeney replaced Hanly '84, a single with her and other singles incl. in *The Irish Folk Connection* '85 on Tara. It was difficult to keep band together; they went out with a flourish with The Last Reel, a celebratory concert in Dublin's National Stadium in Nov. '84, but instrumental suite *The Storm* '85 on Tara was so well received that they have reassembled for some dates: May '86 Self-Aid benefit concert was 2-disc live album in Eire, track 'The Lark' on *Live For Ireland* '87 on MCA. Members also sessioned; Lunny with PLANXTY, O'Neill in

Chris Rea band; Lunny's eponymous debut solo album '87 was on Gael-Linn, Hanly's *Still Not Cured* on WEA Ireland (with Rusty Old Halo), Spillane's *Atlantic Bridge* '88 on Cooking Vinyl.

MOYET, Alison (*b* 18 June '61, Basildon, England) Singer, aka 'Alf'. Served apprenticeship with R&B bands in Southend, steeped in Billie HOLIDAY as well as Muddy WATERS and Howlin' WOLF. Strived to emulate DR FEELGOOD, but joined Basildon studio wizard Vince CLARKE in forming duo Yazoo: the combination of his synthesiser tunes and her voice was a surprise hit (*see* his entry); her big beautiful bluesy voice was the only thing on TV's *Top Of The Pops* to make a music lover sit up and listen. She gigged with Alexis KORNER and fans hoped she would pursue her love of the blues, but it was a one-off event. A year's work went into disco-ish *Alf* '84 on CBS, a success on release, among the decade's coffee-table LPs, incl. hits 'Love Resurrection', 'All Cried Out', 'Invisible' (latter written for her by Lamont Dozier). Hit single '85 with cabaretish treatment of the old Holiday song 'That Old Devil Called Love' (reedman John Altman formed mainstream/bop big band to back her during this period; the band was still struggling '87); she also worked with the National Youth Jazz Orchestra; marriage and motherhood saw performing/recording slow down; second solo LP *Chasing Rain* '87 more straightforwardly rockish, incl. hits 'Is This Love?', 'Weak In The Presence Of Beauty'. Considered as albums, her material and production have not matched the promise of the voice.

MUANA, Tshala (*b* '50s, Lubumbashi, Zaire) Singer, composer, dancer. Born into a family of singers and dancers, active from an early age in cultural troupes, first made her mark adapting trad. dance Mutuashi to the modern scene. Turned to singing, performing with several bands in Kinshasa, after a few years of apprenticeship making her first singles. She left Zaire for the Ivory Coast in late '70s, determined to pursue an international career; had hits endearing her to the notoriously difficult Ivorian public. Toured Africa extensively '81-4; she was voted second best African female singer '82 and '83, but first LP *Tshala Muana* '84 on Safari Ambience label, made in Paris, brought her no. 1 vote '84. Visited USA '85; made second album *M'Pokolo* with Alhadji Toure and Prosper N'Kouri; also *Amina*, on USA African Record Center label. With Mbilia BEL and M'Pongo LOVE among the most popular Zairean female artists.

MULDAUR, Maria (*b* Maria Grazia Rosa Domenica D'Amato, 12 Sep. '43, NYC) Singer, also plays guitar and fiddle. Listened to rock'n'roll, blues, jazz; organised vocal groups in high school and could have signed a contract at 16, but stayed in school instead; by the time she graduated from high school she had been captivated by oldtime fiddling (of Gaither Carlton, Doc WATSON's father-in-law) and became involved in Greenwich Village folk scene. Worked in Even Dozen Jug Band, with John Sebastian, Stefan GROSSMAN, Steve KATZ, David GRISMAN, Joshua RIFKIN, guitarist Peter Siegel (later A&R exec. at Elektra, Polydor, ATV): organised by Victoria SPIVEY to record on her label, they made an LP for Elektra '64 instead. Then she joined the Jim KWESKIN Jug Band, where she met and married Geoff Muldaur (*b* '45). They made duo LPs *Pottery Pie* '69 on Reprise and *Sweet Potatoes* '72 on WB, then separated both personally and professionally; she made solo LP *Mud Acres* '72 on Rounder, then *Maria Muldaur* '73 on Reprise, with a wide range of material and sidemen incl. Dr John (Mac REBENNACK), Ry COODER, guitarist Amos Garrett; LP went top 20 and single 'Midnight At The Oasis' to no. 6 (with Garrett solo break). *Waitress In The Donut Shop* '74 incl. horn arrangements by Benny CARTER, followed by *Sweet Harmony* '76, *Southern Winds* '78, *Open Your Eyes* '79; all but the last charted, but sold less and less well and WEA dropped her. She gigged with bands as diverse as Jerry Garcia and Carter: 'I imagined that an audience would be just as tired of the older material as I would be . . . I suppose there are some hippies wearing bedspread dresses living in Sonoma County in a treehouse who wish I'd never gone electric.' Recording for small labels means fewer problems, still keeps her many fans happy. Further LPs incl. *Gospel Night* on Takoma, *There Is A Love* '82 on Myrrh,

Sweet & Low '84 on Spindrift. Her phrasing and light timbre has been compared to that of Mildred BAILEY; with Carter she performed Duke ELLINGTON's 'Transblucency (a blue fog you can almost see through)', a wordless vocal first sung by Kay Davis with Duke '46; it became title track of '85 LP on Uptown. She also contributed to film soundtrack *Steelyard Blues* '72 with Paul BUTTERFIELD, Mike BLOOMFIELD. *Live In London* came out '87 on Making Waves UK, whereupon that distributor/label folded. Geoff made solo folk/blues LPs for Prestige '64-5, more elaborate productions on Reprise '75-6, back to roots on Flying Fish with *Geoff Muldaur And Amos Garrett* '78, *Blues Boy* '79.

MULLICAN, Moon (*b* Aubrey Wilson Mullican, 29 Mar. '09, Corrigan, Texas; *d* 1 Jan. '67, Beaumont, Texas) King of the Hillbilly Piano Players, getting his name playing in houses of ill repute in Houston. Pioneered country boogie, having an infl. on rock'n'roll. Learned to play a pump organ at 8 years old and soon took to piano; moved to Houston '30 and formed a band, toured Louisiana and Texas honky tonks; worked with Ted DAFFAN and Floyd TILLMAN, he joined Leon Selph's Blue Ridge Playboys '40. Signed to King '45 and saw peak popularity late '40s-early '50s with 'New Jole Blon', 'I'll Sail My Ship Alone', 'Cherokee Boogie' and 'Sweeter Than The Flowers', a tribute to mothers. As well as leading his own band he worked for Ernie FORD, Red FOLEY and was a member of band and staff of Governor Jimmie DAVIS '60-3. Troubled by ill-health and was semi-retired, having infl. Jerry Lee LEWIS and many others. LPs incl. *Moon Over Mullican* '57 on Coral, *Mr Honky Tonk Man* '67 on Spar, *Unforgettable* '67 on Starday, King compilations *Sweet Rockin' Music* on Charly, *Seven Nights To Rock* on Western Swing.

MULLIGAN, Gerry (*b* Gerald Joseph Mulligan, 6 Apr. '27, NYC) Baritone sax, composer, bandleader. Worked with Gene KRUPA '46-7 (wrote 'Disc Jockey Jump'); Miles DAVIS '48-50 on records: wrote 'Jeru' (his nickname), 'Boplicity', 'Venus De Milo', 'Godchild' for famous Birth of the Cool sessions. Wrote and played for Elliot

Lawrence, Claude THORNHILL; first album as leader was *Mulligan Plays Mulligan* '51 on Prestige (now from Fantasy); moved to West Coast; jam sessions made at tiny L.A. club the Haig early '52 have been issued. Trio tracks with Red MITCHELL, Chico HAMILTON, and quartet tracks with Chet BAKER, Joe Mondragon on bass and Jimmy ROWLES were issued on Pacific Jazz, label formed '52 by Richard Bock (*b* '27; *d* 6 Feb. '88). Then a pianoless quartet opened at the Haig (perhaps because club was being renovated and didn't have a piano) with Chet Baker, Chico Hamilton, Bob Whitlock on bass, which was so popular that it put Pacific Jazz on the map and allowed the media to launch 'West Coast jazz', a non-genre which did not include many blacks: this was not Mulligan's fault, and the music holds up very well indeed. A larger group with Mondragon, Hamilton, Baker, Pete CANDOLI, and Bud SHANK recorded for Capitol; various small-group sidemen incl. Larry Bunker, then Frank Isola replacing Hamilton, Mondragon and Carson Smith for Whitlock; Lee KONITZ was added at the Haig June '53. They also recorded for Fantasy (now on 2-disc *Gerry Mulligan & Chet Baker* on Prestige); all '52-3 tracks except the Fantasy incl. in *The Complete Pacific Jazz And Capitol Recordings Of The Original Gerry Mulligan Quartet And Tentette With Chet Baker* on Mosaic: 5-disc box incl. unedited, previously unissued tracks, etc. Trombonist Bob BROOKMEYER replaced Baker; quartet went to Paris '54 with Mitchell and Isola; then Jon Eardley (*b* 30 Sep. '28, Altoona, Pa.) replaced Brookmeyer; Mulligan formed sextet '55-8 which toured Europe (LPs *Mainstream Jazz* '55 on EmArcy incl. Eardley, Brookmeyer and Zoot SIMS); he made *Gerry Mulligan, The Arranger* on CBS '57 with 15 pieces, appeared as single with all-star lineups on classic CBS-TV *The Sound Of Jazz*; appeared at Newport Jazz Festival regularly from first one in '54, incl. film *Jazz On A Summer's Day* '58; recorded with Stan GETZ, Paul DESMOND, Thelonious MONK, Baker again, all '57; new group with Art FARMER '58 appeared on CBS-TV *Timex Jazz Show*, recorded soundtrack music for *I Want To Live* on UA (Susan Hayward played prostitute Barbara Graham, executed in gas chamber on slim evidence).

Mulligan/Farmer recorded at Newport '58 and Mulligan also played and recorded with Duke ELLINGTON there; recorded with Ben WEBSTER '59; appeared with McRae, Farmer, Hamilton, Buddy CLARK etc. in film *The Subterraneans* '60 (adapted from Jack Kerouac, with music by André PREVIN): Mulligan, who played a clergyman, was by then addicted to heroin. He had avoided it as a young man in NYC when everyone around him was dabbling, succumbed later ('I think I managed to not be an adult in just about every imaginable area' – interview with Ira Gitler in *Swing To Bop* '86). He kicked the habit c. '65; meanwhile had formed big band '60-6, also variety of small groups; toured with Dave BRUBECK '68-72, formed large ensemble The Age Of Steam '72 (album on A&M), reunited with Baker (*Carnegie Hall Concert* '74 on CTI), etc. He has toured the world, won all the polls, popular not only with fans but critics and other musicians: he is a musical sparkplug, likely to make something happen wherever he goes. Brubeck said that with Mulligan 'you feel as if you're listening to the past, present and future of jazz all at one time' (quoted by Leonard Feather). Small-group LPs incl. *What Is There To Say?* '59 with Farmer and *Jeru* '62 with Tommy FLANAGAN on CBS, *Meets Johnny Hodges* '60 on Verve, *Night Lights* '63 on Philips with Farmer, *Idle Gossip* '76 on Chiaroscuro, *Lionel Hampton Presents* '77 on Who's Who with Hampton, Hank JONES; big-band LPs incl. *Presents A Concert In Jazz* '61 on Verve, *Holiday With Mulligan* '61 (vocals by actress Judy Holliday, a close friend who died of cancer '65) and *Walk On The Water* '80, both on DRG (latter won a Grammy). His album with Annie Ross from the Pacific Jazz years was reissued '88 by EMI. Other albums incl. *La Menace* '82 on DRG (incl. themes from '72 French Canadian action film), *Little Big Horn* '83 on GRP; many more big-band and small-group LPs on Verve, Mercury, Limelight etc. '60-74. He also recorded with pianist Pete Jolly (*b* Peter A. Cragioli, 5 June '32, New Haven, Conn.), Acker BILK, etc. *Symphonic Dreams* '87 on PAR (Pro Acoustic Recordings) made with Houston S.O., cond. Erich Kunzel. Led a big band once again mid-'88, making many fans happy.

MUNDY, Jimmy (*b* 28 June '07, Cincinnati, Ohio; *d* 24 Apr. '83, NYC) Violinist, tenor sax; arranger and composer. One of the best arrangers of the Swing Era: sold some charts to Earl HINES ('Cavernism', 'Copenhagen'), worked for him until '36; for Benny GOODMAN from '35 ('Swingtime In The Rockies', 'Jumpin' At The Woodside', 'Solo Flight', 'Air Mail Special', others), led own big band briefly '39, freelanced for Count BASIE ('Super Chief', 'Queer Street', 'Blue Skies'), many others. Worked as mus. dir. for Barclay label in France from '59; later went back to NYC, did more freelance work.

MUNGO JERRY UK pop group led by Ray Dorset (*b* 21 Mar. '46, Ashford, Kent) on lead vocals, guitar. Began as skiffle band Good Earth, with Colin Earl (*b* 6 May '42, Hampton Court) on piano, Paul King (*b* 9 Jan. '48, Dagenham), guitar, banjo; changed name and had rapturous reception '70 at Newcastle Under Lyme's Hollywood Music Festival, blowing GRATEFUL DEAD, FAMILY etc. off the stage: goodtime music was just right for summer outdoors, proved when first release, Dorset composition 'In The Summertime' with washboard and jug rhythm and infectiously catchy chorus, was UK no. 1/USA 3. 'Baby Jump' '71 invaded Marc BOLAN's teeny territory, but repeated no. 1 UK; following singles reverted to acoustic skiffle sound with Dorset's cheerful, highpitched Bolanesque sound a distinctive factor. Three LPs had original lineup before King and Earl quit to form King-Earl Boogie Band; Jerry's hits continued: six more top 40 singles '71-4 incl. gentle 'Lady Rose', strident 'Alright Alright Alright' in top 5; but Dorset and his everchanging band had lost original freshness (he released solo *Cold Blue Excursion* '72, deliberately veering from formula: it was panned). Last hit was no. 13 'Longlegged Woman Dressed In Black', a Continental hit with new English lyrics. Dorset soldiered on, still popular in clubs; 'Summertime' is still an all-time seasonal anthem (like Young RASCALS' 'Feelin' Groovy'), still sounds fresh. Compilations on Pye/PRT.

MURPHY, Mark (*b* 14 Mar. '32, Syracuse, N.Y.) Jazz singer. Singing jazz is no way to get rich, and male singers are even rarer than female ones, but Murphy has been doing it for 30 years. '. . . It's a harmonic thing with me. Harmonics and time . . . Some nights I sing ballads and I love the melodies because they go and they sit right on top of the harmonies. Then someone will write, "Gee, he wasn't singing jazz that night." Then I come here and sing a tune and the reviewer says, "Yeah, but he wasn't singing the lyric." ' He also scats, and has loyal fans around the world and in three generations. First LPs on Decca *Meet Mark Murphy* and *Let Yourself Go* c.'57, then three on Capitol (arr. by Bill Holman) incl. *This Could Be The Start Of Something* (Steve ALLEN title track; LP now on Pausa) and *Playing The Field* (half big band tracks); then *Rah* '61 and *That's How I Love The Blues* on Riverside (now from Fantasy). He started by singing jazz versions of top 40 songs and saw rock drive jazz vocalists out of the marketplace; worked in Europe '65-75; recorded in England; *Midnight Mood* '67 made in Germany, now on Pausa; except for *Sings Dorothy Fields & Cy Coleman* '77 on Audiophile he recorded for Muse, for a fee rather than royalties, but with artistic freedom: *Bridging A Gap, Mark II, Mark Murphy Sings* '75, *Stolen Moments, Satisfaction Guaranteed* '79, *Bop For Kerouac* '81, *Brazil Song* with Viva Brazil '83, *Living Room* '84 with Ted CURSON and Grady Tate, *Sings Nat's Choice (The Nat Cole Songbook Vol. 1), Nat Cole Songbook Vol. 2. September Ballads* with Art FARMER, Larry CORYELL etc. issued on Milestone CD '88. (Quote from interview in *Cadence* by Bob Rusch.)

MURPHY, Turk (*b* Melvin E. Murphy, 16 Dec. '15, Palermo, Cal.; *d* 30 May '87) Trombonist, bandleader; active in revival (*see* JAZZ) from earliest days. Studied music in high school, but Depression prevented any higher education; worked for popular New England bandleader Mal Hallett (*b* 1896, Roxbury, Mass.; *d* 20 Nov. '52, Boston) who also hired trombonists Jack TEAGARDEN and Jack Jenny. Murphy was founder member of Lu WATTERS band late '30s, then led own small groups. One of the most faithful of the revivalists, using banjo, no drums; he admired more modern music, reserved scorn for 'neo-Dixie'. Co-owned

Earthquake McGoon's in San Francisco with pianist Pete Clute. Best-known LP was live CBS album made at a jazz festival in New Orleans '55; another CBS LP of same era was *Music Of Jelly Roll Morton* with pianist Wally Rose (*b* 2 Oct. '13, Oakland, Cal.). Other LPs incl. two vols. of *San Francisco Jazz* '49-51 on Good Time Jazz with Bob SCOBEY, Rose, clarinettist Bob Helm (*b* 18 July '14, Fairmead, Cal.) on some tracks. Also three of *Live On East Street* '58 on Dawn Club, three on GHB '74; *Natural High* '79 on Sonic, also *Ragtime* on Atlantic, other albums on Merry Makers label. Though a traditionalist, he was on the lookout for new material; he was the first to play 'Mack The Knife' in jazz, later a hit for Louis ARMSTRONG.

MURRAY, Anne (*b* 20 June '47, Springhill, Nova Scotia) Singer; international success in country and pop. Born and raised in small coal-mining community; studied at U. of New Brunswick, taught physical education at Prince Edward Island, auditioned for Halifax TV show *Sing Along Jubilee* but appeared on *Let's Go*, prod. by William Langstroth, mus. dir. Brian Ahern: the show was a success; guided by Ahern she signed with Apex, made LP *What About Me* '68, turned full-time pro, signed with Capitol for *This Is My Way* '69 incl. 'Snowbird': single was top 10 country and pop USA, top 10 UK, etc. She was a regular on Glen CAMPBELL TV show; they made duet LP '71 and toured together. 25 solo Hot 100 entries '70-82 incl. 'Danny's Song' '73, 'You Won't See Me' '74 in top 10; topped country chart with remake of George JONES classic 'He Thinks I Still Care' '74; other country hits incl. 'Son Of A Rotten Gambler' '74, 'The Call' '76, etc. Married Langstroth '75 and settled down to raise a family, but returned '78 with producer Jim Ed Norman on LP *Let's Keep It That Way*, topped both pop and country charts with 'You Needed Me' '79 (one of several Grammy awards, also ACM's Song of the Year); further country no. 1 hits same year with 'I Just Fall In Love Again', 'Shadows In The Moonlight', 'Broken Hearted Me'. 'Nobody Loves Me Like You Do' was hit duet with Kenny LOGGINS '85. Among many LPs: *Talk It Over In The Morning* '71, *Danny's Song* '73, *Highly Prized Possession*

'74, *Keeping In Touch* '76, *New Kind Of Feeling* '79, *A Country Collection* '80, *The Hottest Night Of The Year* '82, *Heart Over Mind* '84. *Harmony* was no. 12 LP on USA country LP chart mid-'87 and climbing.

MURRAY, David (*b* 19 Feb. '55, Berkeley, Cal.) Reeds. Father played guitar, mother piano in church; he played in church, led R&B groups as a teenager, met people like Stanley CROUCH, Bobby BRADFORD, Arthur BLYTHE; studied formally on West Coast, went to NYC '75, played with Cecil TAYLOR, Don CHERRY, Anthony BRAXTON. Contributed to Wildflowers Festival '74 (*see* JAZZ); first-class musician has recorded prolifically, mostly on tenor sax, also soprano. *Low Class Conspiracy* '76 on Adelphi incl. Fred Hopkins, Phillip Wilson; two vols. of Low Class Conspiracy live in Amsterdam '77 called *Penthouse Jazz* and *Holy Siege On Intrigue* on Circle label added Crouch, Don PULLEN, Butch Morris on cornet. *Solomon's Sons* '77 on Circle had solo tenor track, duets with flautist James Newton and a Newton solo track. Quartet sets *Last Of The Hipman* on Italian Red label, *Let The Music Take You* on French Marge both recorded in Rouen the same day; quintet *The London Concert* on Cadillac and trio *3D Family* on Hat Hut at Willisau, all '78. On India Navigation: *Flowers For Albert* '76 with Wilson, Hopkins, Olu Dara on trumpet; *Live At The Lower Manhattan Ocean Club* '74 (two vols.) with Hopkins, Wilson, Lester BOWIE; *New Music/New Poetry* with Amira Baraka and Steve McCall; on Black Saint: quartet *Interboogieology* '78, trio *Sweet Lovely* '79; octets *Ming* '80, *Home* '81, *Murray's Steps* '82, *New Song* '86, *New Life* '87; quartet *Morning Song* '83, big band *Live At Sweet Basil* '84, *Children* '84 with James Blood ULMER, Lonnie PLAXICO, Marvin 'Smitty' Smith on drums; also *In Our Style* '86 on DIW, a duo with Jack DEJOHNETTE with Hopkins on two tracks, and *The Healers* '87 on Black Saint, a duo with Randy WESTON. Played bass clarinet in NYC concert '83 with Jimmy HAMILTON, John CARTER, Alvin Batiste: two beautiful vols. of *Clarinet Summit* released '85 on India Navigation incl. his solo 'Sweet Lovely'; the Summit's *Southern Bells* '88. His solo albums incl. *Surreal Saxophone* on Horo, *Organic Saxophone* on Palm, *Concep-*

tual Saxophone on Cadillac, all '78; *David Murray Solo Live* '80 in two vols. on Cecma. Played in WORLD SAXOPHONE QUARTET until '86.

MURRAY, Sunny (*b* James Marcellus Arthur Murray, 21 Sep. '37, Idabel, Okla.) Drummer. Self-taught from age 9; went to NYC '56, played with Henry ALLEN, Willie 'The Lion' SMITH, then Jackie MCLEAN, Ted CURSON; met Cecil TAYLOR '59 and became a leading light of the avant garde. Went to Europe with Taylor and Jimmy LYONS '63; joined trio with Albert AYLER and Gary PEACOCK; played with Don CHERRY, John COLTRANE, Ornette COLEMAN, etc. Returned to France '68 for several months, played with Archie SHEPP, Grachan MONCUR III, etc. An album was recorded privately by LeRoi Jones '65 with quintet incl. Cherry, Ayler, Jones speaking on one track; it was released in Jihad under Murray's name. *Sunny Murray Quintet* '66 was on ESP; a sextet recorded for CBS '68 but session wasn't released; Sunny Murray's Untouchable Factor played at the Wildflowers Festival '76 (with David MURRAY; *see* JAZZ), made *Apple Cores* '78 on Philly Jazz (latter with Don PULLEN, Cecil McBEE, Frank Foster); the rest of his LPs were made in Europe: *Big Chief* '68-9 on French labels with French sidemen; *Homage To Africa* '69 (with Shepp, Roscoe MITCHELL, Lester BOWIE, nine others), *Sunshine* and *An Even Break (Never Give A Sucker)* with similar, smaller groups all '69 on Byg, the latter also on Affinity; quartet *Live At Moers Festival* on Moers, trio *African Magic 'Great African Encounter'* made in Cologne on Circle, both '79.

MUSIC HALL genre The British variety circuit. Pub entertainment became national institution when Charles Morton converted his Lambeth pub into a music hall, invested £35,000 (a fortune then) in the Oxford Music Hall in London's Oxford Street (now one of the busiest shopping streets in Europe), which opened in 1861. Morton was known as the 'father of the halls'; before long there were chains all over the UK. The music hall inspired American sentimental ballads and American vaudeville, was itself infl. by ragtime c.'12 (an American Invasion 50 years before the BRITISH INVASION). In a

nation which still clings to its class distinctions, the music hall was curiously classless: the upper class were fans, as well as artists, literati and politicians: music hall songs are thought to have infl. the poetry of Rudyard Kipling. A few music hall artists became well-known in the USA: Vesta Victoria sang 'There I Was Waiting At The Church'; Scottish singer Harry Lauder was an international star; but the greatest stars of all were Marie LLOYD, Gracie FIELDS and George FORMBY Jr, who meant nothing overseas. An important difference between British and American popular music has been that rural and ethnic Americans preserved their own music until it entered the mainstream, whereas the British left their folk music behind when they flocked to the cities; as Ian Whitcomb put it in *After The Ball* '72, 'There was no Welsh hillbilly, no Cornish ragtime, no Highland jazz.' Also, songs in music hall were sold to individual artists, rather than being common property as in vaudeville; thus Charles Coburn (1852-1945; no relation to the American actor) was famous for 'The Man Who Broke The Bank At Monte Carlo', but the result was that British songs could not attempt to appeal universally in the way that Tin Pan Alley's did (though in the ragtime era 'It's A Long Way To Tipperary', 'Pack Up Your Troubles In Your Old Kit Bag', 'Roses Of Picardy', 'McNamara's band' etc. (all '14-17) crossed over and probably infl. American songwriters like Irving BERLIN). A difference in entertainment generally was the attitude to sex, which in music hall songs and comedy was funny; Americans took it too seriously and created a distinction between vaudeville (more or less family entertainment) and burlesque (definitely not). The golden age of the halls ended with WWI, but it survives in British working men's clubs (especially in Northern England), on TV variety shows and in pop music: the cheekiness of the early BEATLES smacked of British variety, and was a large part of their appeal.

MUSSELWHITE, Charlie (*b* Charles Douglas Musselwhite III, 31 Jan. '44, Kosciusko, Ms.) Probably the best living white blues harmonica player. Choctaw Indian ancestry; father played mandolin; raised in Memphis, Tenn.; began on harmonica age 13.

Worked outside music, moved to Chicago '62, sat in at black blues clubs; worked with J. B. HUTTO, Mike BLOOMFIELD – Barry Goldberg Blues Band; accompanied Big Joe WILLIAMS, John Lee HOOKER on records; own LPs for Vanguard from '66 incl. *Tennessee Woman, Stand Back! Here Comes Charlie Musselwhite, Stone Blues*; more recently *Goin' Back Down* and *Takin' My Time* on Arhoolie, *Harmonica According To Musselwhite* on Kicking Mule. Tours North America, summers in Europe; live *Cambridge Blues* on Blue Horizon from Cambridge Folk Festival.

N

NASH, Johnny (*b* 19 Aug. '40, Houston, Texas) USA pop/soul/reggae singer, songwriter. Breakthrough on Texas TV's *KPRC Matinee* led to rejection of university place and signing by ABC Paramount; only top 40 hit was 'A Very Special Love' '57 (also 'The Teen Commandments' '58 in trio with labelmates Paul ANKA and George HAMILTON IV); with roles in films such as *Key Witness* he seemed set for MOR career. Then 'Let's Move And Grove Together' '65 was no. 4 in soul chart; having visited the Caribbean while filming racial melodrama *Take A Giant Step* '58, he returned there to work with prod. Byron Lee, making an abrupt about-turn to reggae: his own 'Hold Me Tight' was no. 5 UK and USA, also made USA soul chart; 'You Got Soul' and cover of Sam COOKE's 'Cupid' did well (his vocal debt to Cooke, hitherto unremarkable, was now acknowledged). He patronised then-unknown songwriter Bob MARLEY, recording his 'Guava Jelly' and reaching top 15 both UK/USA with his 'Stir It Up'; Nash's own 'I Can See Clearly Now' was no. 1 USA, no. 5 UK '72; LP of that title was no. 23 USA, top 40 UK, with four songs by Marley (and backing by the Wailers), Marley's first important royalties. He carried on in soulful/reggae style with 'Tears On My Pillow' (no. 1 UK '75), Cooke's 'What A Wonderful World' (no. 25 UK '76). In the end he had done better in UK (six top 10 entries '68-75) than in USA. He ran own JAD and Joda labels with partner Danny Sims in '60s, writing Joey Dee hit 'What Kind Of Love Is This' and prod. Sam and Bill's 'For Your Love' '65 (his own later hits were on Epic); he built his own studio in Jamaica and continued sporadic career in films during spells of residence in Sweden (i.e. *Love Is Not A Game*).

NASHVILLE TEENS UK beat/pop group formed '62 in Weybridge, Surrey. Lineup: Arthur Sharp, vocals; Pete Shannon and John Allen, guitars; Ray Phillips, bass and vocals; John Hawken, keyboards; Barry Jenkins, drums. Played Hamburg clubs '63-4; backed Jerry Lee LEWIS at Star Club (a poorly recorded live LP exists). Tour backing Bo DIDDLEY brought them back to UK; Mickey MOST spotted them, prod. cover of John D. LOUDERMILK's 'Tobacco Road' propelled by Hawken's pounding piano, with vocals of Sharp and Phillips prominent, for no. 6 UK/14 USA hit, followed by Loudermilk's 'Google Eye' (top 10 UK). They were a noted live attraction, two genuine vocalists making them an original band despite mining overworked R&B lode. But they failed to win good backing from their label, Decca; 'Find My Way Back Home' and 'This Little Bird' '65 were their final top 40 entries. They continued to gig, reverted to backing USA visitors; Jenkins left '66 to join ANIMALS while Hawken joined Renaissance, then STRAWBS; another future Renaissance man, guitarist Mick Dunford, passed through. They split '73, re-formed early '80s and reissued 'Tobacco Road'; *Nashville Teens* on New World label '74 contained hits and outakes; *Live At The Red House* '82 on Shanghai had Phillips as only original member, with drummer Adrian Metcalf, Len Surtes on bass, Peter Agate on guitar. Decca EP versions from '64 with 'I Need You Baby' and 'Parchman Farm' are worth seeking out as evidence of underrated band.

NATIONAL BARN DANCE Variety show aimed at rural audience ('24-70). Started on WLS in Chicago by George D. Hay, who later organised Grand Ole Opry. Among many who passed through Barn Dance were Red FOLEY, Gene AUTRY, Pee Wee KING, LULU BELLE AND SCOTTY, Bob ATCHER, Rex ALLEN. WLS is one of the most powerful stations in the Midwest; call letters stood for 'world's largest store': originally owned by Sears & Roebuck, from whose mail-order catalogue rural America shopped. Midwestern kids looking for 'cowboy' music tuned in '40s-50s. WLS went top 40 late '50s; when the station changed hands '60 the Barn Dance moved to WGN.

NAVARRO, Fats (*b* Theodore Navarro, 24 Sep. '23, Key West, Fla.; *d* 7 July '50, NYC) Trumpet; one of the most tragic losses to heroin of the period (he also had TB). Nickname was 'Fat Girl'. His beautiful tone and quicksilver lightning technique can be compared only to that of Dizzy GILLESPIE; he was one of the founders of modern jazz on the instrument. Began on piano at 6, trumpet at 13, mostly self-taught; he also played tenor sax in Florida; with Andy KIRK '43-4, recommended by Dizzy to replace him in Billy ECKSTINE band '45-6, played with Illinois JACQUET, Lionel HAMPTON, recorded with Tadd DAMERON, Bud POWELL small groups, others; tracks compiled on LPs *Memorial Album* and 2-disc *Fat Girl* on Savoy, two vols. of *The Fabulous Fats Navarro* on Blue Note, featured with Dameron on 2-disc Milestone set. Also 'Stealin' Apples' with Benny GOODMAN sextet on Capitol, Metronome All Stars date on RCA.

NAYLOR, Jerry (*b* 6 Mar. '39, Stephenville, Texas) Country singer and DJ. Formed band early '50s, appeared on Louisiana Hayride '54, worked shows with Elvis PRESLEY, Johnny CASH, Johnny HORTON. He did some DJ work, studied electronics, joined US Army '57 and was stationed in Germany; recorded for some small Texas labels and met Glen CAMPBELL, heading for West Coast with him; more DJ work '60. Joined CRICKETS '61, replacing Joel B. Mauldin, worked with them off and on for four years, often taking lead vocals. Went solo mid-'60s, recording for Tower, Columbia, MGM; had minor pop hit 'But For Love' on Columbia '70; moved into country '74 on Melodyland label and hosted *Continental Country Show* on KLAC in L.A., named Best Syndicated Country Music Show by Billboard '73 and '74. Made country charts with 'Is This All There Is To A Honky Tonk?', 'The Last Time You Love Me', 'If You Don't Want To Love Her' '75-8; recorded for WB '79, Jeremiah '80-2.

NAZARETH Rock group formed in Scotland '69. Lineup: Dan McCafferty, vocals;

Manny Charlton, guitar; Darrel Sweet, drums; Pete Agnew, bass, all *b* Scotland; chose their name from lyrics to The BAND's 'The Weight'. They play quasi-heavy metal and specialise in hard-rock versions of songs by people who don't write hard rock, such as Joni MITCHELL and Bob DYLAN. Scottish guitarist Zal Cleminson joined '78, left '80; in '81 they added keyboardist John Locke, guitarist Billy Rankin. The stable lineup and the fact that nearly all of their LPs charted and were still available mid-'86 (on A&M in the USA) testifies to audience loyalty for this kind of music. Best seller was *Hair Of The Dog* '75, helped by their only USA single hit, top 10 'Love Hurts' (by Boudleaux BRYANT); other albums are *Sound Elixir* on MCA in USA and *The Catch* '84 on Vertigo in UK. McCafferty did a solo album in '75.

N'DOUR, Youssou (*b* '59, Dakar, Senegal) African singer-composer, leading exponent of mbalax. From musical family, singing in public at 12, soon acquiring nickname *Le Petit Prince de Dakar*; performed regular spot at Dakar's Miami nightclub by '76 with the Star Band de Dakar (formed '60 and the most established band in the country). He recorded for the first time with them '78, left '79 with some others to form his own outfit, Étoile de Dakar, soon had first hit, 'Xalis Money'. After LPs *Toulou Badou Ndiaye*, *Absa Gueye* and *Thiapathioly*, they went to record in Paris '81, reorganising as Super Étoile; new albums incl. *Diongoma*, *Mouride*, live *À Abidjan*, *Ndiadiane Ndiaye* and an international African hit, *Immigrés*. By this time 14 strong, incl. sax, guitars, percussion, vocalists singing in Wolof with emphasis on trad. Wolof rhythms, the band performed regularly at N'Dour's Dakar club Thiosanne, became a noted draw in Western Europe with solid dance music and a good stage show. Contributed to Paul SIMON's *Graceland* album '86; toured with Peter GABRIEL; he is one of those who will take African music onto a larger world stage. *Inédits 84-85* on Celluloid '87 is souvenir of collision of African funk, rock, jazz; *Nelson Mandela* on Polydor '87 is one of the first African albums on CD.

NEAR, Holly (*b* 6 June '49, Ukiah, Cal.) Singer, songwriter, actress. Sang in public from childhood, worked in films and TV as a teenager, had a leading role in rock musical *Hair*. With an excellent voice and inspired by seeing Ronnie Gilbert with the WEAVERS as a child, she took up an independent stance with mostly original material, refused to bother with major labels and all that that entails, forming her own Redwood label and recording *Hang In There* '73, *Live Album* '74, *You Can Know All I Am* '76 and *Imagine My Surprise* '79, with vocal and instrumental help from Jeff Langley, also from Ukiah. These sold respectably by word-of-mouth, winning awards and respect from independent label industry, followed by *Fire In The Rain*, *Speed Of Light*, *Journeys* and *Watch Out!*, *Lifeline* (with Gilbert), *Harp* (with Gilbert, Arlo GUTHRIE, Pete SEEGER), *Don't Hold Back* '87. Gilbert sang one of Near's songs at the last Weavers concert. Near tours, preferring smaller venues; does benefits (e.g. for WAVAW, Women Against Violence Against Women), contributed to 'survival' album *Out Of The Darkness* on Fire On The Mountain label, as did SWEET HONEY IN THE ROCK, whose album on Redwood won an award (see their entry).

NEIDLINGER, Buell (*b* 2 Mar. '36, Westport, Conn.) Bassist, composer. Turned on to jazz by Louis ARMSTRONG records; studied piano, trumpet, cello as a child; served apprenticeship in NYC playing dixieland and mainstream jazz with Rex STEWART, Vic DICKENSON, Eddie CONDON, others; first teacher was Walter PAGE. First played contemporary music '55-60 with Cecil TAYLOR: *New York City R&B* c.'60 on Candid, not released for 11 years and now listed under Taylor's name, was a Neidlinger date. Also made *Soprano Today* '57 with Steve LACY on Prestige; played Fender bass on R&B sessions; played in Houston Symphony '60-2 (and with Arnett COBB in local clubs), with Taylor for the last time at '62 concert. Sessioned with Frank ZAPPA and Jean-Luc PONTY, Van Dyke PARKS, Andrew WHITE, Robert Ceely on the Beep label; formed K2B2 label (pron. K squared B squared) with tenor saxophonist Marty Krystall in L.A.: *Ready For The 90's* '80 is a quartet LP, *One Night Together* '81 by Krystall Klear and the Buells a quintet, Gene Cipriano added on reeds; these two are among

Neidlinger's personal favourites, probably because of having control on one's own label. *Swingrass* on Antilles and *Buellgrass* on K2B2 also had Peter Ivers on harmonica, since murdered. *Marty's Garage* on K2B2 has quartet tracks from '71-3 with Krystall and two tracks from '60-1, one with Taylor, one with Archie SHEPP; *Buellgrass* has mostly standards (by ELLINGTON, MONK) with a few originals. New group Thelonious on K2B2 plays Monk's music, with Krystall, John Beasley on piano, Billy Osbourne on drums. *See also* Taylor's entry.

NEIL, Fred (*b* '37, St Petersburg, Fla.) Singer-songwriter whose songs have had much success for other artists. He performed on the Grand Ole Opry as a teenager and Buddy HOLLY recorded some of his songs; he was active in the Greenwich Village folk scene of the early '60s and recorded on the FM label, then *Bleecker And MacDougal* '67 and *Little Bit Of Rain* '70 on Elektra, *Fred Neil* '66, *Everybody's Talkin'* '69, *Other Side Of This Life* '70 and *Sessions* '71 on Capitol. None sold well, although his 12 string guitar playing was especially well regarded; the nearest he came to personal fame was when Harry NILSSON covered 'Everybody's Talkin'' (used in soundtrack of *Midnight Cowboy*, the producer allegedly preferring it to Bob DYLAN's 'Lay Lady Lay') and had a top 10 hit with it. He retired to Florida, but his songs have been covered by Frank SINATRA, Linda RONSTADT, Roy ORBISON, Tim BUCKLEY ('Dolphins'), José FELICIANO, JEFFERSON AIRPLANE, others. He allegedly inspired the Airplane's 'Ballad Of You And Me And Pooneil'.

NELSON, Oliver (*b* 4 June '32, St Louie, Mo.; *d* 28 Oct. '75, L.A., Cal.) Saxophones, flute, arranger, composer. From musical family; began on piano and already played in public as a child; worked with Jeter-Pillars as a teenager, Louis JORDAN early '50s, served in US Marines, then with Wild Bill DAVIS, Louie BELLSON, others; prolific as a straight-ahead swinger and recording artist in jazz, also became highly regarded in classical and studio work. He wanted to play more and do less TV work, but died suddenly of a heart attack. He wrote a woodwind quartet and a song cycle '60-1, pieces for orchestra incl. commissions from the American Wind Orchestra, the Berliner Jazztage Festival and Mayor Carl Stokes of Cleveland, Ohio; studio work incl. TV's *Million Dollar Man*, etc. published *Patterns For Saxophone*. Small-group LPs on Prestige: *Meet Oliver Nelson* '59; *Takin' Care Of Business* (with Johnny Smith), *Nocturne*, *Soul Battle* (with Jimmy FORREST and KING CURTIS) '60; *Screamin' The Blues* '60 and *Straight Ahead* '61 with Eric DOLPHY (later in 2-disc set *Images*), *Main Stem* '61 with Hank JONES. Switched to Impulse for one of his best: *Blues And The Abstract Truth* '61, with Freddie HUBBARD, Dolphy, Bill EVANS, followed by *More Blues And The Abstract Truth* '64 with Phil WOODS, Pepper ADAMS; then *With Oily Rags* (CHAS & DAVE) on Flying Dutchman '74, *Stolen Moments* on Inner City '75. Big band sets: *Afro-American Sketches* '61 on Prestige; *Fantabulous* '64 on Argo; *Sound Pieces For Jazz Orchestra* and *Michelle* '66, *Live From Los Angeles* and *Musical Tribute To JFK* '67 on Impulse; *Black, Brown And Beautiful* '69, *Berlin Dialogue For Orchestra* '70, *Swiss Suite* '71 and an album with Johnny HODGES and Leon Thomas on Flying Dutchman; several more on Verve, etc. The Impulse LPs (some now on MCA) were prod. by Bob THIELE as were the Flying Dutchmans, some of which were also on RCA.

NELSON, Ozzie (*b* Oswald George Nelson, 20 Mar. '06, Jersey City, N.J.; *d* 3 June '75) Bandleader, songwriter, vocalist, multi-instrumentalist, later TV star. Studied law and was active athlete in college, also led dance band, turning pro after graduation '30. Vocalist Harriet Hilliard (*b* Peggy Lou Snyder, c.'12, Des Moines, Iowa) joined band '32, they were married '35; successful band with good arrangements had nearly 40 hit records ('30-6 on Brunswick, '37-40 on Bluebird), incl. no. 1 *And Then Some* '35, mostly with Ozzie's vocals; style resembled Rudy VALLEE. Charlie Spivak played trumpet in early band, then Harry Johnson, with Abe Lincoln on trombone, Charles Bubeck on baritone sax (obbligato baritone with last chorus was a trademark sound). Theme was college song 'Loyal Sons Of Rutgers'; he wrote songs such as 'And Then Your Lips Met Mine' '30 and 'I'm Looking For A Guy

Who Plays Alto And Baritone, Doubles On Clarinet And Wears A Size 37 Suit' '40. Among many radio shows were comics Joe Penner '33-5 and Red Skelton '41 (Hilliard played Skelton's mother in 'mean little kid' skit). He made several films as single or with band; Harriet had been a ballet dancer in vaudeville, appeared on Broadway in *The Blonde Sinner* '26, played second lead in film *Follow The Fleet* '36 with Fred ASTAIRE and Ginger Rogers. They began archetypal family sitcom *The Adventures Of Ozzie And Harriet* on radio '44, made film *Here Come The Nelsons* '51, transferred to TV '52-68; sons David and Ricky took part; even their TV home was modelled after their real home in Hollywood. Ricky became a pop star (*see* Rick NELSON, below). Ozzie and Harriet made an LP on Imperial, Ricky's label, with semi-rock'n'roll backing; toured with road shows '60s-70s, back to TV with *Ozzie's Girls* '73-4; autobiography *Ozzie* '73.

NELSON, Rick (*b* Eric Hilliard Nelson, 8 May '40, Teaneck, N.J.; *d* 31 Dec. '85, De Kalb, Texas) Pop singer switched to country rock. Began on parents' radio sitcom (*see* Ozzie NELSON, above), appeared in film *Here Come The Nelsons* '51, to TV with show '52; appeared in film *Story Of Three Loves* '53. In '56 a girlfriend told him she was in love with Elvis PRESLEY, so he became a recording star: performed an awful version of Fats DOMINO's 'I'm Walkin'' on the show; released on Verve it was a top 20 hit, was outsold by 'A Teenager's Romance' on the other side. He went to Imperial, ironically Domino's label; had a total of 53 Hot 100 hits '57-73; 18 singles were two-sided hits, with 17 titles in top 10 '57-62. He progressed as a singer; many of the rockabilly-flavoured songs were written by Dorsey and/or Johnny BURNETTE and his backing band incl. guitarist James BURTON, later with Presley. 'Poor Little Fool' '58 and 'Travelin' Man' '61 were no. 1 (latter with no. 9 'Hello Mary Lou' on the other side); other top fives were 'Be-Bop Baby' and 'Stood Up' '57, 'Believe What You Say' '58, 'Never Be Anyone Else But You' '59, 'Young World' and 'Teen Age Idol' '62. He dropped the 'y' from 'Ricky' '60, signed a 20-year contract with Decca '63 (now MCA) but like many others was swamped by the

British Invasion spearheaded by the BEATLES '64: he changed his style to country-rock fusion; *Country Fever* '67 was a representative album; cover of Bob DYLAN's 'She Belongs To Me' was top 40 '69. 11 LPs charted '57-64, but no more until he formed Stone Canyon Band '69, which at various times incl. members of POCO, EAGLES, LITTLE FEAT; *Rick Nelson In Concert* '70 (live at the Troubador in L.A.) was no. 54 LP; *Rick Sings Nelson* made top 200 albums same year; in '71 old fans booed his new image at Madison Square Garden rock'n'roll revival show and he wrote 'Garden Party' about how you can't please others unless you're pleased with yourself first: it was his first top 10 hit for almost ten years; album *Garden Party* '72 was no. 32, LP; *Windfall* '74 just made top 200. The 20-year contract must have been rationalised; *Intakes* '77 was on CBS/Epic; *Playing To Win* '81 on Capitol made no. 153 with songs by Graham PARKER, John Fogerty, John HIATT. Several compilations on Liberty of the Imperial hits incl. *The Singles Album 1958-1963*; Decca stuff on *The Rick Nelson Singles Album 1963-1976* compiled by Tim Rice; *String Along With Rick* on Charly UK has minor Decca hits. He also appeared in films *Rio Bravo* '58 with John Wayne and Dean MARTIN, *The Wackiest Ship In The Navy* '60, *Love And Kisses* '65; his daughter Tracy became an actress (no relation to Tracy NELSON, below). He and six others incl. his fiancée were killed in the crash of a private DC-3 en route to a gig in Dallas, which was said to have been caused by a drug-related fire on board; two people survived.

NELSON, Sandy (*b* Sander Nelson, 1 Dec. '38, Santa Monica, Cal.) Rock'n'roll drummer who had some of the few instrumental hits of the rock'n'roll era. He went to high school with JAN & DEAN, Phil SPECTOR, etc.; first group Kip Tyler and the Flips had future BEACH BOY Bruce Johnston on piano, recorded for Ebb and Challenge. He played on Spector's Teddy Bears' big hit 'To Know Him Is To Love Him' '58, sessioned for Gene VINCENT on *Crazy Times* '59, then struck out as solo: fifth release on Original Sound label 'Teen Beat' reached top 5 '59; he was signed by Imperial, lost his left foot in a car crash, had one more top 10

hit 'Let There Be Drums' '61. He had more minor hits '62, updated 'Teen Beat 65', then faded. Compilations on Liberty USA.

NELSON, Tracy (*b* 27 Dec. '47, Madison, Wis.) Country-blues singer, a cult figure who hasn't achieved commercial success she deserves. She began in folk clubs in Wisconsin, early '60s, graduated to blues, joining the Fabulous Imitations '65, later forming White Trash Blues Band. Moved to San Francisco '67 and joined Mother Earth as lead singer; they recorded and built up a reputation on the West Coast; made a highly praised LP *Mother Earth Presents Tracy Nelson Country* '70 in Nashville, with Scotty Moore and other Nashville session men; Mother Earth split '72 and she moved to Nashville permanently, recording for Atlantic (*Tracy Nelson* '74), Columbia, MCA (*Time Is On My Side* and *Sweet Soul Music*), sang back-up for Willie NELSON (no relation), others.

NELSON, Willie (*b* 30 Apr. '33, Abbott, Texas) Country singer, guitarist and songwriter who achieved superstar status in late '70s. Raised by grandparents after parents were divorced; began on guitar as a child and played in local honky tonk bands as a teenager, also in polka bands favoured by local Czech community. Served in USAF in Korea, worked in Waco as a farm labourer, vacuum cleaner salesman, then as DJ on local radio station. Next he had a daytime country show in Fort Worth, played in honky-tonk evenings; he'd begun writing songs and sold his early efforts 'Family Bible' and 'Night Life' for less than $200 (the former was a top 10 country hit by Claude GRAY '60; 'Night Life' reached top 30 by Ray PRICE '64, no. 31 by Gray '68). He moved to Nashville '60, joined Ray Price's Cherokee Cowboys on bass, had more writing success: 'Funny (How Time Slips Away)' (top 15 pop hit '64 and Joe Hinton's biggest; he died 13 Aug. '68), 'Hello Walls' (no. 1 country hit '61 by Faron YOUNG), 'Crazy' (no. 2 country hit by Patsy CLINE '61), more. He had recorded in Texas, mainly demos; signed with Liberty '62, made two LPs incl. *And Then I Wrote* '63, top 10 hit 'Touch Me' same year; recorded for Monument Oct. '64 but nothing was released; appeared on Grand Ole Opry that year, joined RCA in Dec. and made some 18 albums in eight years, incl. *Country Music Concert '66* (reissued '76 as *Willie Nelson Live*), *Texas In My Soul '68*, *Laying My Burdens Down '70*, *Yesterday's Wine '71*, *The Words Don't Fit The Picture '73*; also had minor hit singles 'The Party's Over' '67, 'Little Things' '68, 'Bring Me Sunshine' '69. His songs tended to be more complex technically than the usual country tune; he sang in a highly personal, yet lackadaisical and almost conversational way. He grew tired of the increasing slickness of Nashville; when his house in Ridgetop, Tenn. burned to the ground he took advantage of the opportunity to move back to Texas '71. He organised the first 4th of July Festival '72 in Dripping Springs, near Austin; it was a financial disaster, but subsequent events were more and more successful until '80, when they were so successful they were too big to be what they were intended to be, and were abandoned. Meanwhile he had changed his image: growing long hair and a beard and wearing jeans, he signed with Atlantic, made LPs *Shotgun Willie* and *Phases And Stages*, which brought recognition from the rock press (the latter LP made the pop album chart when reissued '76); he had hit country singles 'Stay All Night', 'Bloody Mary Morning', duet with Tracy NELSON (no relation) 'After The Fire Is Gone', all '73-4. When Atlantic closed their Nashville office he signed with Columbia (CBS) and made concept LP *Redheaded Stranger '75*: it was the first (of 33 '75-85) to make the pop album chart; first single 'Blue Eyes Cryin' In The Rain' was no. 1 country hit, also made pop top 20; his old labels began scrabbling in their vaults and he had eight singles in the country charts on three labels '76, with 'If You've Got The Money, I've Got The Time' (on Columbia) hitting no. 1. He had achieved success by refusing to be limited by commercial considerations, and carried on: he made a gospel set *The Troublemaker '76*, tribute to Lefty FRIZZELL *To Lefty From Willie '77*, *Willie And Family Live '78* recorded in Lake Tahoe, 2-disc *One For The Road '79* with Leon RUSSELL. The new mood in country music was already being called the 'Outlaw' movement; RCA released *Wanted: The Outlaws '76* with tracks by Nelson, Waylon JENNINGS, Tompall

GLASER and Jessi Colter: it was the first country LP to sell a million copies. The same year 'Good Hearted Woman', a duet by Waylon and Willie, was no. 1 country, made the pop top 30 and was named CMA single of the year. *Stardust '78* on CBS was his first set of standards, prod. by BOOKER T Jones; it stayed in the pop album chart 117 weeks, sold millions, incl. no. 1 country hits with Hoagy CARMICHAEL's 'Georgia On My Mind' and Irving BERLIN's 'Blue Skies'. The first *Waylon And Willie* album on Jennings' label RCA incl. no. 1 hit with Ed BRUCE song 'Mammas Don't Let Your Boys Grow Up To Be Cowboys', which also won a Grammy '78; they toured together and outgrossed every other country act, released further duet LPs *WWII '82* on RCA, *Take It To The Limit '83* on CBS. Nelson moved into films: *Electric Horseman '79* (soundtrack LP had one side by Willie, the other instrumental), *Honeysuckle Rose '80* (soundtrack LP no. 11, with hit single 'On The Road Again'), *Thief '81*, *Barbarosa '82*, *Song-Writer '85* (with Kris KRISTOFFERSON; LP charted), film of *Redheaded Stranger '87*. He made duet LPs *Angel Eyes '84* with guitarist Jackie King, *San Antonio Rose '80* with his old boss Price, *Brand On My Heart* with Hank SNOW, *Old Friends* with Roger MILLER, *In The Jailhouse Now* with Webb PIERCE, *Funny How Time Slips Away* with Faron YOUNG; *Half Nelson '85* is a selection of duets, but the most successful duet set apart from those with Jennings was *Poncho & Lefty* with Merle HAGGARD '83, a top 40 pop LP and CMA album of the year, title track no. 1 country hit. Among many RCA recyclings of Nelson material was *Before His Time '77*, remixed by Jennings; other Columbia LPs incl. *The Sound In Your Mind '76*, *Somewhere Over The Rainbow '81*, *Always On My Mind '82* (pop hit LP for 99 weeks, reaching no. 2; title single a top 5 hit), *Tougher Than Leather* and *Without A Song '83*. Nelson could make a songwriter a lot of money by including a song on an album: 'Poncho & Lefty' was written by his friend Townes VAN ZANDT; *City Of New Orleans '84* incl. title song by Steve GOODMAN when that much-loved singer/songwriter was dying of leukaemia. *Me And Paul '85* had title song about his drummer, Paul English; *The Promiseland '86*, *Island In The Sea '87* followed, the latter half written by Nelson, Jennings co-writing some of the rest. *Seashores Of Old Mexico* '87 is another duet LP with Haggard. Now that he is a superstar it is clear that on early recordings his songs and vocal delivery were confined by straight country contexts, yet still repay attention: reissues and compilations on many labels incl. *Once More With Feeling* and *Good Hearted Woman*, 2-disc sets on Pair '86; *One Step Beyond* '87 on Starburst/Magnum incl. 20 tracks from RCA, all his own songs; *Touch Me* '85 and *Country Willie* '87 on EMI each have 20 from the Liberty era. Columbia USA issued a limited edition 10-disc set, a tribute to an artist who not only crosses over but flattens the fence: *Master Of Suspense* '87 on Blue Note by ex-Charles MINGUS trumpet player Jack Walrath has Nelson on Hank WILLIAMS's 'I'm So Lonesome I Could Cry' backed by Walrath septet, 'I'm Sending You A Big Bouquet Of Roses' (hit by Eddy ARNOLD '48, Dick HAYMES '49) backed by trumpet, piano, his own guitar. Daughter Susie published family memoir *Heartworn Memories* '87.

NERO, Peter (*b* Peter Bernard Nierow, 22 May '34, NYC) Pianist. Played with Paul WHITEMAN, symphony orchestras; gigged in Manhattan late '50s until discovered by RCA, whose promotion machine at that time could still make a star. His piano was infl. by the likes of Oscar PETERSON, but in the end he could not escape a cocktail-bar image. 20 chart LPs '61-72 incl. *Hail The Conquering Nero* '63 (his biggest at no. 5); others were called *Songs You Won't Forget*, *Career Girls*, *The Screen Scene*, *Nero Goes 'Pops'* (with Arthur Fiedler and the Boston Pops Orchestra), etc.; he changed labels to Columbia and came out with *I've Gotta Be Me*. *Summer Of '42* '71 was one of his best sellers: movie theme title track was his only hit single at no. 21. He gave up on the pop world and made trio set *Peter Nero Now* mid-'70s for Concord Jazz.

NESMITH, Mike (*b* 30 Dec. '42, Houston, Texas) USA singer/songwriter, guitarist. First fame as a MONKEE; as the group's only real musician, he was the first to rebel against their manipulation. He had worked in folkish ensembles and (allegedly) as a session guitarist at Stax Records in Memphis; outside projects while still a Monkee incl. writing Linda RONSTADT's first hit (with Stone Poneys) 'Different Drum' '67, and instrumental LP *When The Wichita Train Whistle Sings* '68. He organised the First National Band '70 with Orville 'Red' Rhodes (*b* 30 Dec. '30, Alston, Ill.) on steel guitar and dobro, John London (*b* John Kuehne, 6 Feb. '42, Bryan, Texas) on bass, John Ware (*b* 2 May '44, Tulsa, Okla.), drums; they made albums *Magnetic South* '70 (incl. no. 21 single 'Joanne'), *Loose Salute* '70, *Nevada Fighter* '71. Only the first two made Billboard's Top 200 LPs; single 'Silver Moon' was no. 42 late '70 and title track of third album made the Hot 100. The group folded; Nesmith and Rhodes recruited bassist Johnny Meeks (formerly one of Gene VINCENT's Blue Caps), Michael Cohen on keyboards and drummer Jack Rinelli for Second National Band, which made only *Tantamount To Treason* '71; Nesmith and Rhodes forged on with ironically titled *And The Hits Just Keep On Comin'* '72. The RCA contract was concluded with *Pretty Much Your Standard Ranch Stash* '73; offer of his own Countryside label by Elektra fell through when David GEFFEN replaced Jac Holzman at that label; Nesmith's gentle country-rock ended up on Pacific Arts, which released periodic albums from concept LP *The Prison* '75 through *Infinite Rider On The Big Dogma* '79 (a Top 200 LP) to *Elephant Parts* '81, a mixed-media package of music and dance. He had already moved into production (LPs by Rhodes, Ian MATTHEWS, Bert Jansch, Garland Frady), increasingly into directing videos: *Elephant Parts* won the first ever Grammy for a video.

NESSA US jazz label formed '67 in Chicago; now at Whitehall, Michigan. Small output of very high quality; issues only LPs which deserve to stay in print, then keeps them there. Packaging, technology always first class; most records produced with economy and skill by Chuck Nessa. About 30 issues to date incl. sets by AIR, members of ART ENSEMBLE OF CHICAGO, Bobby BRADFORD, and John STEVENS, Leo SMITH, Hal RUSSELL, Charles TYLER; tenor men Von FREEMAN, Warne MARSH, Eddie JOHNSON, Fred ANDERSON, Lucky THOMPSON, Ben WEBSTER; choice Roscoe MITCHELL items incl. two 2-disc sets. To issue CDs '88, on Chief label in Europe.

NEVILLE Brothers, The New Orleans-based R&B clan, stirring together many elements of black music: Arthur Lanon Neville (*b* 17 Dec '37), keyboards, vocals, percussion; Charles (*b* 28 Dec. '38), sax, flute, percussion; Aaron (*b* 24 Jan. '41), keyboards, vocals; Cyril (*b* 10 Jan. '48), vocals, percussion. Their sister Athelga sang with the DIXIE CUPS; Aaron's son Ivan is a composer, keyboardist and vocalist. In New Orleans the 'second line' referred to the mourners or keeners who followed funeral ceremonies; the marching band played funereal music on its way to the cemetery, but purged the sorrow on the way back: the second line sang, danced, played along and was associated with the joy of homecoming: this spirit is at the centre of the music of Lee DORSEY, Allen TOUSSAINT, PROFESSOR LONGHAIR, Mac REBENNACK, the Nevilles, many others. Between '54 and 67 various combinations achieved some success: Art's Hawkettes made 'Mardi Gras Mambo' quickly and cheaply at WWEZ radio studio; it became staple of the Mardi Gras 'Indian' celebrations, annually reissued, but they never saw much money from it. Teamed with local reedman/arranger Harold Battiste on Specialty '56, prod. infl. New Orleans sides such as 'Cha Booky Doo', 'Zing Zing', 'Oooh-Whee Baby' (compilation *Mardi Gras Rock'n'Roll* on Ace); Art and Aaron worked with Larry WILLIAMS on big hits 'Short Fat Fanny', 'Bony Moronie' '57; Art was replaced by Aaron in Hawkettes '58-60 while he served in US Navy. Aaron made singles such as 'Over You' (cover of Sam COOKE song reached national R&B chart '60), 'Every Day' (written while in jail); they worked with Toussaint, recorded his songs (written under nom-de-plume 'Naomi Neville') such as 'Let's Live', 'Waiting At The Station', 'Wrong Number (I Am Sorry, Goodbye)', all on 2-disc Rhino anthology *Treacherous* and Aaron collection *Humdinger* on EMI Stateside. When Specialty moved to West Coast '60 Joe Banashak bought their contracts for his Instant and Minit labels, but cash was still elusive. Aaron had no. 1 R&B hit (no. 2 pop) 'Tell It Like It Is' '66, title track of Par-lo LP '68, staple of anthologies like *Treachery*, Rhino's 3 disc

History Of New Orleans Rock'n'Roll. Art formed the Neville Sound c.'67 which became the Funky Meters, then the Meters, with Cyril, guitarist Leo Nocentelli (*b* 15 June '46), Joseph 'Zigaboo' Modeliste on drums (*b* 28 Dec. '48), George Parker Jr on bass: they acted as a local version of BOOKER T AND THE MGs, backing Dorsey on national hits 'Ride Your Pony', 'Get Out Of My Life, Woman', 'Working In The Coal Mine' as well as Rebennack (as Dr John, on 'Right Place, Wrong Time'), LaBELLE (on 'Lady Marmalade'), Robert PALMER (alongside LITTLE FEAT on *Sneaking Sally Through The Alley*), Paul McCARTNEY; also led their own commercial career: six national pop hits '69-70 all prod. by Toussaint and Marshall Sehorn, incl. 'Sophisticated Cissy' and 'Cissy Strut' in top 30; LPs incl. *The Meters, Look-Ka Py Py, Struttin'* '69-70 on Josie, *Best Of* on Virgo, *Cissy Strut* on Island; plus Charly compilations from this era *Here Come The Metermen* and *Second Line Strut*. Critical acclaim, signing to Reprise still did not bring bigger success, attempt to break into wider market incl. cover of Neil YOUNG's 'Birds' on *Cabbage Alley* '72; *Rejuvenation* '74 incl. 'Hey Pocky A-Way'; *Fire On The Bayou* '75 incl. title track and new version of Hawkettes hit; *Trick Bag* '76 incl. cover of 'Honky Tonk Woman': ROLLING STONES had hired them as opening act for a tour, but that didn't help, nor did attempt at psychedelic soul (with Tower of Power horns) on *New Directions* '77 on WB (though 'Be My Lady' made Hot 100). They returned to roots as *The Wild Tchoupitoulas* '76 on Island: the Mardi Gras had begun as revelry permitted by French slave-owners; slaves banded together to form mock Indian tribes, forerunners of today's Golden Eagles, Yellow Pocahantas etc.; historically violent celebrations became taunting song contests: Tchoupitoulas were captured in Les Blank film *Always For Pleasure* (Flower Films) and on one spell-binding album, using eidetic, often supernatural imagery: 'I walked through fire and I swam through mud/Snatched feathers from an eagle/Drank panther's blood' (from 'Meet De Boys On The Battlefront'); songs covered by David LINDLEY in the USA, the London Apaches in UK. 'Iko Iko' was derived from Sugar Boy Crawford's 'Jock-A-Mo' (itself

covered by Dixie Cups, Dr John, GRATE-
FUL DEAD); 'Brother John' was dedicated to
John Williams, chief of the Apache Warriors tribe and former singer with Huey
SMITH and the Clowns. This lineup had
added Aaron, Teddy Royal on guitar; was
also heard in film *The Big Easy* '87. Meanwhile they became the Neville Brothers,
with all four brothers plus Ivan, Bryan Stolz
on guitar, Daryyl Johnson on bass, Willie
Green on drums: eponymous LP on Capitol
'78 prod. by Jack NITZSCHE did not do
them justice, was poorly promoted; *FiYo On
The Bayou* '81 on A&M (on Demon in UK
'86) was better, with Jimmy Cliff's 'Sitting
In Limbo', reworking of Art's 'Iko
Iko'/'Brother John', Nat COLE hit 'Mona
Lisa' (dedicated to Bette MIDLER), Aaron's
version of 'The Ten Commandments Of
Love' (later incl. in his *Orchid In The Storm*
'86 on Passport USA, Demon UK). Legal
problems delayed release of *Nevilleization*
'84 on Black Top USA, Demon UK; made
in the Tipitina club '82, it captures them
better than any other, incl. Duke
ELLINGTON's 'Caravan', remake of 'Tell It
Like It Is', much else. Coeval *Nevilleization
II* on Spindletop '87 was a disaster, adulterated with overdubs; the brothers disowned
it. The anthology *Treacherous* '86 paid them
proper tribute, incl. such rare material as
Aaron's contribution 'I Love Her Too' from
Heart Beat, flawed biopic of Jack Kerouac
and Neal Cassady. *Uptown* '87 on EMI
America was consciously commercial, with
guests such as Jerry Garcia, Carlos
SANTANA, a wan and voguish impersonation of themselves; symptomatic was release
of 'Whatever It Takes' on a 12" single with
four alternative mixes. Their heart lies in
their muscular live act, where they are peerless; like the Grateful Dead, with whom
they performed in the '80s, they are a formidable improvising band. They signed
with Atlantic '88.

NEW AGE Genre emerging in mid-'80s, a
blend of acoustic music, soft rock, white jazz
and some electronics; difficult to define except as MOOD MUSIC: inevitably the
babyboom generation has demanded its
own aural wallpaper to succeed the Percy
FAITH – MANTOVANI – MELACHRINO output of earlier decades. The new mood
music like the old is technically slick, musi-

cally inoffensive; new elements are
minimalism, improvisation, and somewhat
pretentious presentation: the cascading
strings of earlier times promised only soothing sounds for tired businessmen; new age
music wants to be more substantial. It is also
a reaction against the vocalism and sheer
loudness of pop/rock, which does not make
good background music. Albums by guitarists Leo KOTTKE and John FAHEY might
have filled the bill starting in the '60s (new
age is often called 'new acoustic'). Many
great jazz records over the years by Bill
EVANS, Stan GETZ, Paul BLEY and many
others have worked as dinner-party music;
other artists such as Chick COREA, Keith
JARRETT and Larry CORYELL have made so
many records that some inevitably seemed
to be time-fillers; the ECM label has been
criticised for the laid-back ambience of records by these and others: guitarist John
Abercrombie made nine ECM LPs '74-81;
the *Los Angeles Free Press* wrote of *Timeless*
'74 (with Jan HAMMER and Jack
DEJOHNETTE): 'You lie back, close your
eyes and journey-soft . . .' But jazz (or near-
jazz) suffers from its avant-garde image for
the Pepsi generation and others who cannot
listen closely. Brian ENO's white noise and
Mike OLDFIELD's *Tubular Bells* are antecedents of New Age, as is the meditative
sound of *Spectrum Suite* '74 by Stephen
Halpern (long an apostle of serious relaxation, he wrote a book called *Sound Health*
'85). The Windham Hill label was formed
'76 by guitarist Will Ackerman (named after
his California construction company) to distribute his own first record *In Search Of
The Turtle's Navel* to a few fans; in '84
it had sales of $20 million, copying ECM's
artwork style, with several artists incl.
pianist/composer George Winston, Mark
Isham on keyboards, others. The product is
flawlessly recorded (important to yuppies,
proud of their state-of-the-art record players); the label's success was largely by word-
of-mouth, with records sold in bookshops
and health-food shops, showing again how
poorly audiences are served by major labels,
which spend most of their money promoting pop-rock despite the fact that the people
who created that market are now older, and
today's 15-year-olds themselves a minority.
If some people's ears need a rest after decades of listening to amplifiers, no one

should be surprised; but the sampler *An Evening With Windham Hill* sounds like a soundtrack to a soft-focus love story, earning the rubric 'sonic laxative'. The term 'new age' was first widely applied to Windham Hill product, although an outfit called Vital Body Marketing in NYC were already producing a New Age Music Catalogue listing hundreds of LPs of 'music that touches the spirit'. Ackerman disapproves of the term because it doesn't mean anything, but then some say that most of the music on his label doesn't mean much either. His subsidiary labels Magenta, Duke Street and Hip Pocket are intended to be jazz-oriented; excellent Anthony BRAXTON sets *Seven Standards 1985* were issued on Magenta, but other issues were described by Peter Vacher in London's *Jazz Express* as 'manufactured in a wholly calculated way', 'solos by synthesiser, music by machines, rhythm by piledriver'. The UK Coda label Landscape series intends to be adventurous: Simon Frith wrote about Claire Hamill's *Voices* '86 that 'her composition of a lush orchestral score with just the sound of her voice may be technically interesting, but the result is still Yuppie Muzak.' It is hard to say to what extent a critic's ears are conditioned by years of listening to pop, but Landscape's sampler *Standing Stones* has almost an entire side given to an electronic version of a Bach Brandenburg Concerto: this sort of thing was done two decades ago by Walter Carlos, and is no longer interesting. Eno's EG label has released chirpy items by Bill BRUFORD, Robert FRIPP's League Of Crafty Guitarists (some of the New Age stuff seems to be rising from the ashes of art rock). The MMC label, formed '81 in UK by drummer Peter Van Hooke, had a list of LPs by Rod ARGENT, trumpeter Dave DeFries (who also plays on quartet LP *Sunwind*), vocalist Herbie Armstrong (backed by a quartet with Van Hooke and Isham), etc.; a 2-disc MMC sampler *The First Frames* incl. tracks from the first 10 releases. Other labels on the bandwagon are Global Pacific, Rosewood, Pan East (from Japan; Frith says Masahide Sakuma's *Lisa* '86 is 'interesting and intelligent noise'). See also SPACE MUSIC. Meanwhile other artists turn out thoughtful, beautiful, listenable chamber music just as they've always done: *see* Bobby SCOTT, Kenny WHEELER, AZI-

MUTH, Joe LOCKE, etc.; many new age fans are probably looking for chamber jazz, if they only knew it.

NEWBORN, Phineas, Jr (*b* 14 Dec. '31, Whiteville, Tenn.) Jazz pianist; also played other instruments. Father led popular R&B band in Memphis on drums; brother Edwin Calvin Newman (*b* 27 Apr. '33) is guitarist, also played other instruments; brothers played with their father, recorded for Peacock; Phineas formed quartet and took it to NYC '56, made *Here Is Phineas* '56 on Atlantic, *Phineas Rainbow* and *Fabulous Phineas* on RCA (latter reissued in France '83), *Downhome Reunion* on UA, all '56-8 with Calvin on guitar. Highly praised for technique by Count BASIE and others. Other LPs (without Calvin) incl. two on RCA with larger groups '57, trio albums: *We Three* '58 on Prestige with Roy HAYNES, Paul CHAMBERS; two LPs on Roulette '59 (now in set on Vogue) with Haynes, John Simmons (bassist *b* '18, Haskell, Okla.; *d* 19 Sep. '79, L.A.; worked with Roy ELDRIDGE, Benny GOODMAN, Cootie WILLIAMS, Louis ARMSTRONG, Eddie HEYWOOD, Erroll GARNER, etc. appeared in short film *Jammin' The Blues* with Lester YOUNG); further trio sets, all with first-rate bass and drums: four on Contemporary '61-9 (some now reissued by Fantasy), *Look Out . . . Phineas Is Back!* '76 on Pablo, *Phineas Is Genius* '77 on Japanese Philips; also trio *Phineas Newborn Plays Again* '59 made in Rome on Italian label, *Solo Piano* '74 on Atlantic. He worked in a duo with Charles MINGUS early '58 incl. soundtrack of John Cassavetes' first film *Shadows*. Highly regarded by critics for technique, but some questioned a lack of warmth or soul: perhaps it depends how you listen; in '87 he was recording sonatas by Alexander Scriabin (1872-1915) for VSOP Records.

NEWBURY, Mickey (*b* Milton S. Newbury Jr, 19 May '40, Houston, Texas) Singer/songwriter who wrote many hits for others. Began writing songs in high school, also singing tenor in a harmony quartet; joined USAF '58 and was stationed in England; returned to Galveston '63 and worked on shrimp boats. Moved to Nashville '65 as he took his writing seriously; got a contract with Acuff-Rose (Wesley Rose was listed in his ASCAP biography as chief collaborator). He slept in the back of his car for a few months; eventually had songs recorded by Eddy ARNOLD ('Here Comes The Rain Baby'), Don GIBSON ('Funny, Familiar, Forgotten Feelings', later a pop hit by Tom JONES), Carl SMITH ('How I Do Love Them Old Songs'). Signed to RCA for two LPs '67-8: *Harlequin Melodies* and *Sings His Own* incl. songs that defy categorisation but often ended up in the pop charts (e.g. 'Just Dropped In' by Kenny ROGERS and the First Edition). He went to Mercury, made highly praised *Looks Like Rain* '69, incl. classics 'She Even Woke Me Up To Say Goodbye', 'San Francisco Mabel Joy' and 'I Don't Think Much About Her No More'. Moved to Elektra for series of albums that again generated large praise, small sales, incl. *Frisco Mabel Joy* '71, *I Came To Hear The Music* '72, *Heaven Help The Child* '73, *Live At Montezuma/Looks Like Rain* '74. He had a top 30 pop hit with his 'An American Trilogy' '71, based on three Civil War songs, also recorded by Elvis PRESLEY live in Las Vegas '72; his 'Sunshine' made the Hot 100 '73. He provided hits for Johnny Rodriguez, Tompall and the GLASER Brothers, Roger MILLER, Waylon JENNINGS, Marie OSMOND and others, but big stardom eluded him. Further LPs incl. *Rusty Tracks*, *Eye On The Sparrow* and *The Sailor* '77-9 on ABC-Hickory (now MCA), *After All These Years* '81 on Mercury.

NEW CHRISTY MINSTRELS Big commercial folk group formed '61 NYC by Randy Sparks (*b* 29 July '33, Leavenworth, Kansas), named after the mid-19th-century Christy Minstrels (*see* MINSTRELSY). They were successful because their big sound was refreshing at the time and because members contributed original material, such as their biggest hit 'Green Green' (no. 14 '63), by Sparks and Barry MCGUIRE. Their only other top 40 hits were 'Saturday Night' and 'Today' '63-4 (the latter from the comedy western *Advance To The Rear* '64 for which Sparks wrote the music) but they had nine hit LPs '62-5, of which *Ramblin'* (incl. 'Green Green') and *Today* '63-4 were the biggest. They played at the White House and had a TV show mid-'64; Sparks sold them to a management group and continued as manager for a while; they continued touring and recording for some years. Mike Settle was mus. dir. in mid-'60s until he left, taking others incl. Kenny ROGERS, to form the First Edition. Sparks also formed The Back Porch Majority, did studio work, wrote special material for Burl IVES, John DENVER, etc.; in '70s became a rancher in Cal. and toured as Randy Sparks and the Patch Family.

NEWLEY, Anthony (*b* 24 Sep. '31, Hackney, London) UK actor, singer, songwriter. Played the Artful Dodger in David Lean film of *Oliver Twist* '48, other films; made London debut in revue *Cranks* '55; wrote lyrics for four songs in UK film called *Idle On Parade* (EP was a UK hit '59; music by Joe Henderson), had seven hits in UK top 10 '59-61 incl. Peter de Angelis song 'Why?', Lionel BART's 'Do You Mind' (both no. 1); crossovers to Hot 100 in USA incl. novelty 'Pop Goes The Weasel' '61. Meanwhile, he met Leslie Bricusse (*b* 29 Jan. '31, London), who had written 'My Kind Of Girl' for a Eurovision song contest, a hit for Matt MONRO '61 and adopted by Frank SINATRA. They collaborated, with Newley also directing and starring, in show *Stop The World, I Want To Get Off!* '61, songs incl. 'Gonna Build A Mountain', 'Once In A Lifetime', and 'What Kind Of Fool Am I?', an international hit which won a Grammy '62. In '64 they wrote (with John Barry) the James Bond theme 'Goldfinger' (sung in the soundtrack by Shirley BASSEY), and another show *The Roar Of The Greasepaint, The Smell Of The Crowd* incl. 'Who Can I Turn To?' Newley concentrated on acting, directing and producing until '74, when they got together again for the film *Willie Wonka And The Chocolate Factory* '70 incl. 'The Candy Man', a no. 1 hit '72 for Sammy DAVIS Jr. They also wrote scores for *The Good Old Bad Old Days* '71 and for a TV version of *Peter Pan*. Newley toured in cabaret, appeared on TV, made LP of his songs for UA (*The Singer And His Songs* '78).

NEWMAN, David (*b* 24 Feb. '33, Dallas, Texas) Saxophones, flute. Called 'Fathead' by a music teacher as a child; nickname stuck. Began with local groups, toured in R&B with Lowell FULSON, T-Bone WALKER, then was a star in Ray CHARLES band

'54-64, rejoined '70-1; worked with KING CURTIS c.'66, with Herbie MANN '72-4, throughout brought R&B feeling to his own jazz albums. He made three for Atlantic '58-61, then *House Of David* '67, all with small groups; two more '68 with larger forces, voices, arrangements etc. *Captain Buckles* '70 was a quintet set with Blue MITCHELL on Cotillion/Atlantic; *Lonely Avenue* '71 a septet with Roy AYERS. Mac REBENNACK played on Atlantic LP '72 with added strings and brass on some tracks; Ayers and Ron CARTER played in sextet *Newmanism* '74. *Mr Fathead* '76 on WB had a different large group on every track; *Keep The Dream Alive* '77 was smaller group, *Concrete Jungle* had strings/horns dubbed, both on Prestige '77; *Resurgence!* '80 (sextet with Cedar WALTON), *Still Hard Times* '82 (with Hank CRAWFORD) are on Muse; *Heads Up* '87 is a quintet on Atlantic. Plays on Jimmy McGRIFF's *The Starting Five* and Crawford's *Mr Chips* '86 on Milestone.

NEWMAN, Jimmy C. (*b* 27 Aug. '27, High Point, La.) Cajun/country singer who combines Cajun fiddle and accordion with straight country in band Cajun Country; the 'C' in his name stands for Cajun. He formed his style in the Lake Charles area of Louisiana where he regularly appeared on radio late '40s. He moved to the *Louisiana Hayride*, signed with Dot, had first country hit 'Cry, Cry Darling', all in '54. Moved to Grand Ole Opry '56, scored his biggest hit '57 with smooth ballad 'A Fallen Star', top 5 country and top 30 pop. He went to MGM '58, had hits such as 'You're Making A Fool Out Of Me' and 'A Lovely Work Of Art' '60, but his Cajun roots were in danger of disappearing, so he switched labels again to Decca, had hits 'Alligator Man' '61, 'Bayou Talk' '62. One of the first to record songs by Tom T. HALL, he was a country chart regular through the '60s with 'DJ For A Day' '63, 'Artificial Rose' '65, 'Back Pocket Money' '66, 'Blue Lonely Winter' '67. He has continued to make an impact, keeping the Cajun sound alive in country music, becoming a big draw in Europe and especially the UK. LPs incl. *Folk Songs Of The Bayou Country* '65 and *Country Time* '69 on Decca, *Cajun Country* '82 on RCA; also reissues *Early Recordings* (with Al Terry) on Flynight; *The Happy Cajun, Cajun Country*

Classics and *Alligator Man*, all on Charly UK.

NEWMAN, Joe (*b* Joseph Dwight Newman, 7 Sep. '22, New Orleans, La.) Trumpet, leader, composer; also vocalist. Took Alabama State College band on the road; joined Lionel HAMPTON '42-3, Count BASIE '43-7; co-led touring groups with Illinois JACQUET, with drummer J. C. Heard; then with Basie '52-61, established among the most highly regarded of mainstream jazzmen, deeply infl. by Louis ARMSTRONG, but up-to-date personal style full of musical pleasure. Involved with Jazz Interaction since '60s, promoting awareness and education, writing music for its orchestra (e.g. *Suite For Pops*); played with New York Jazz Repertory Orchestra. A dozen small-group LPs under his own name for Vanguard, RCA, Savoy etc. '54-6 had tasty all-star casts; *Salute To Satch* '56 on RCA was big band LP; sextet *The Happy Cats* '57 on Coral now on Jasmine UK; co-led quintet with Zoot SIMS on Roulette '57, 11-piece band '58 on Roulette, combined in 2-disc set *Similar Souls* on Vogue; others on Danish Met label, Mercury, Honeydew, Black & Blue. *Jive At Five* '60, *Good'n'Groovy* '61 both on Prestige with Tommy FLANAGAN; *In A Mellow Mood* '62 on Stash with rhythm trio; *Swing Lightly* on Hall of Fame Jazz with Ruby BRAFF; duets with Jimmy ROWLES '79 on Cymbol made in London; *Hangin' Out* '84 on Concord Jazz co-led with Joe WILDER, with Hank JONES, Rufus Reid on bass, Marvin Smith on drums.

NEWMAN, Randy (*b* 28 Nov. '44, L.A.) Singer/songwriter, pianist with devoted cult following for his wry, ironic lyrics and deceptively gentle humour. From musical family; began with a writing contract at age 17; arranged sessions at WB leading to solo contract. Alan Price had two-sided hit in UK '67 with Newman songs 'Tickle Me'/'Simon Smith & His Dancing Bear'; his songs have been covered by Ray CHARLES, Ringo STARR, Nina SIMONE, Peggy LEE ('Love Story') and THREE DOG NIGHT, whose version of 'Mother Told Me (Not To Come)' was no. 1 USA '70. His debut LP *Randy Newman* '68 was stylishly orchestrated by Van Dyke PARKS; *12 Songs* '70 featured sideman Ry COODER and consolidated Newman's fame as a writer. He contributed a chilling performance of 'Gone Dead Train' to soundtrack of Mick Jagger film *Performance* '70. Harry NILSSON paid tribute with an entire album of *Nilsson Sings Newman* '70, with Newman on piano. *Randy Newman Live* '71 displayed him at his acerbic best in concert, accompanied only by his piano; the poignant 'I Think It's Going To Rain Today' (covered by Judy COLLINS), caustic 'Davy The Fat Boy', 'Old Kentucky Home'. *Sail Away* '72 is one of his best, with Cooder, drummer Jim Keltner, bassist Wilton Felder, sax solo by Abe Most on ironic 'Lonely At The Top'; also incl. 'Simon', 'Sail Away' (beautifully orchestrated for a yearning nostalgia, eulogising the slave trade; less intelligent listeners took it literally), also sexy, slow rock'n'roll 'You Can Leave Your Hat On', 'Political Science' (American provincialism), much else. He played devil's advocate to some of the simpering, denim-clad bards of the era whose simplicity was not much to the point, demonstrated again with 'Dayton, Ohio – 1903' on *Sail Away*, and next LP *Good Old Boys* '74 (with background vocals by members of the EAGLES): if Newman had real sympathy for American myths or Southern rednecks, perhaps the real world is too complicated for single-issue fanatics and comfortable middle-class liberals. After a sabbatical, *Little Criminals* '77 again incl. some Eagles, song 'In Germany Before The War' and hit single 'Short People', in which those of less than average height stood for all victims of bigotry ('They don't deserve to live'); despite the ridiculousness, foolish listeners of various heights fuelled a controversy which took one of his lesser songs to no. 2. *Born Again* '79 took on KISS fans and other targets, had harmony vocals by Stephen BISHOP; *Trouble In Paradise* '83 was star-studded, with Christine McVie, Linda RONSTADT, Bob SEGER, others taking part: duet with Paul SIMON on 'The Blues' reached Billboard chart, album also incl. 'Christmas In Capetown', 'I Love L.A.' (used in soundtrack of *Down And Out In Beverly Hills* '86, became international hit single). Of his uncles, Emil Newman conducted orchestra on tour and on some of Randy's album tracks; Lionel and Alfred scored and/or wrote film music: Alfred Newman (*b* 17 Mar. '01, New Haven,

Conn.; *d* 17 Feb. '70, L.A.) won nine Oscars for *Mother Wore Tights* '47, *The King And I* '56, *Camelot* '67, etc. Randy was nominated for his *Ragtime* '81 score, also did music for *The Natural* '84, looked like following his uncles (and Cooder, another artist who deserved more than cult fame) into more film work.

NEW ROMANTICS, The Pop movement in UK c.'80 created round London club scene of the era: cues from black music and synthesiser pop combined with new fashion image to stress exclusivity after iconoclasm of punk. Steve Strange and ex-Rich Kids drummer Rusty Egan set musical agenda at clubs like Billy's in Soho and the Blitz in Covent Garden, where SPANDAU BALLET played one of its first gigs. Euro-popsters like KRAFTWERK were *de rigueur*; fashion flamboyance – even kilts – and makeup (introduced by Culture Club, Hazi Fantaysee) took androgyny in pop to new heights. Some Bizzare label run by Stevo showcased new bands on *Some Bizzare Album* '81; Soft Cell scored with synthesised cover of Northern soul hit 'Tainted Love' same year, Strange and Egan hired the Rainbow Theatre as 'The People's Palace' for St Valentine's Day Ball: a debs ball for a new élite. By the time they opened the Camden Palace (formerly the Music Machine) Apr. '82 the movement was fading: no more than an orgy of conspicuous consumption, it celebrated the importance of image, rather than pretending it didn't exist, as punk did; but soon only Culture Club was left, and not for long.

NEWTON, Wayne (*b* 3 Apr. '42, Roanoke, Va.) Cabaret singer, dependable on ballads. Inspired by a childhood visit to Grand Ole Opry touring show; regular TV appearances began with Jackie GLEASON TV show early '60s; first top 40 hit was Bert Kaempfert song 'Danke Schoen' '63 (prod. by Bobby DARIN, reached no. 13 USA), then late '40s ballad 'Red Roses For A Blue Lady' (no. 23 '65), English hit by Peter Callendar and Geoff Stephens 'Daddy Don't You Walk So Fast' was biggest (no. 4 '72, on Chelsea). He returned to the top 40 with country song 'Years' (no. 35 '80 on Aries II). He had many minor hit singles and ten LPs in the charts '63-72, all long out of print. He is a big attraction in Las Vegas and has done very well investing in hotels; when it was proposed that the BEACH BOYS play at USA Centennial celebrations, a Secretary of the Interior named Watt objected, proposing Newton instead; the whole nation laughed, and Newton probably laughed with it.

NEWTON-JOHN, Olivia (*b* 26 Sep. '48, Cambridge, England) MOR singer. Grandfather was Nobel prize-winning scientist; grew up in Australia, formed schoolgirl vocal quartet; solo, she won talent contest sponsored by Johnny O'Keefe (the 'Australian Elvis') with return to UK as prize. Worked there with Australian Pat Carroll (who later married Olivia's producer, John Farrar) as Pat and Olivia before Carroll's work permit ran out, then joined Tomorrow, MONKEE creator Don Kirshner's manufactured two-boy/two-girl vocal group, went solo when planned TV series fell through. Sugary version of Bob DYLAN's 'If Not For You' reached no. 7 UK/25 USA; country-flavoured pop hits in UK helped by connection with prod./fiancé SHADOWS guitarist Bruce Welch, which led to showcase on Cliff RICHARD TV spots: 'Banks Of The Ohio', George HARRISON's 'What Is Life', John DENVER's 'Take Me Home Country Roads' all hits '71-3. Surprise breakthrough in USA with 'Let Me Be There' '73, MCA LP of same title (which incl. six tracks from two-year-old LP on Universal), coming after Eurovision flop with strident 'Long Live Love', led to swift relocation westward; when the hit won a Grammy for Best Country Vocalist success seemed assured (though '76 CMA award as Best Female Vocalist led to resignations). Split with Welch personally/professionally led to his former associate (in Marvin Welch and Farrar) taking over as producer. Of four top 5 hits in USA '74-5 (two at no. 1) only one charted in UK; big hit USA albums incl. *If You Love Me, Let Me Know, Have You Never Been Mellow, Clearly Love, Come On Over, Don't Stop Believin', Making A Good Thing Better, Greatest Hits* set all '75-7 on MCA. She raunched-up her image playing leather clad role in *Grease* '78 and scored big hits both solo and with John Travolta, singles plus soundtrack LP; *Totally Hot* '78 was another hit album; soundtrack *Xanadu* '80 with then-fashionable ELECTRIC LIGHT

ORCHESTRA was a hit LP with three hit singles (incl. duet 'Suddenly' with Richard), although the film flopped; then she slid further into raunch, pushing aerobic sex in *Physical* '81 (no. 1 title single; no. 5 with 'Make A Move On Me'). 'Heart Attack' was a no. 3 single '82, incl. in *Greatest Hits Vol. II*; soundtrack *Two Of A Kind* incl. four tracks by her ('Twist Of Fate' a top 5 hit). By '85 she had posed half-topless with riding crop in Helmut Newton photo for sleeve of *Soul Kiss*: title track reached top 20, album top 30 LP chart placing in USA since '77: time for another change of image for the charismatic warbler with the unremarkable voice.

NEW WAVE Movement in pop, began c.'77 in the wake of punk (seen especially in USA as too unpleasant for mass consumption). New breed of young rockers emerged with energy of punk but with more finesse and ability; the majority were American (BLONDIE, Tom PETTY AND THE HEART-BREAKERS, MINK DEVILLE, Modern Lovers, TALKING HEADS, etc.) though UK close behind with power-pop movement (Rich Kids, The Records, etc.). Punk failed to displace the established stars; more tuneful, less outrageous New Wave gradually eclipsed artists of early '70s until few acts more than 10 years old were still on top. The term fell into disuse because it was too general, taking in any new acts in the early '80s except Heavy Metal, though New Wave of British Heavy Metal claimed to replace self-satisfied ageing superstars with hungry young variety.

NEW YORK DOLLS Rock group formed '71 by Johnny Thunders (*b* John Genzale) and Rick Rivets, guitars; Arthur Kane, bass; Billy Murcia (*b* '51; *d* 6 Nov. '72, London), drums. Added singer David Johansen (*b* 9 Jan. '50, Staten Island, NY). Murcia died of drink/drugs on an early tour of UK, where they impressed with trash-rock stance combining ROLLING STONES raunch (Johansen visually like Jagger) and repertoire swiped freely from USA rock (MC5), girl groups (the SHANGRI LAS), etc. Murcia was replaced with Jerry Nolan and Rivets with Sylvain Sylvain before eponymous debut LP '73, but of the glam-rock image only amateurishness transferred to vinyl; even

855

prod. Todd RUNDGREN couldn't save it (he later described them as a 'novelty act'). But critical excitement (in the heyday of ALICE COOPER, the Sweet) kept them going through *Too Much Too Soon* '74, prod. by Shadow MORTON; by then their fan club had melted away. Mercury dropped them; Malcolm McLaren briefly managed them and, enchanted by their posing and defiance of musical criteria, returned to London to create the SEX PISTOLS after the Dolls failed to adopt his 'red leather and Soviet flag' image. Thunders and Nolan formed the Heartbreakers (no relation to Tom PETTY band), aligned themselves with UK punk in LP *LAMF* '77, continued chronicling Thunders' love affair with drugs; further LP: *Live At Max's Kansas City* '79. Johansen and Sylvain worked together until '79 under Dolls' name or Johansen's; Johansen went commercial with LPs on Steve Paul's Blue Sky label, of which *In Style* '79, *Here Comes The Night* '81, *Live It Up* '82 reached Billboard's Top 200 LPs; *Sweet Revenge* came out on Passport. Sylvain released two flop LPs on RCA. The Dolls obtained posthumous fame when cited by New Wave (see above) as one of the first punk acts, by which was meant their couldn't-care-less attitude: their LPs were reissued and a '72-vintage cassette-only album *Lipstick Killers* on ROIR. In their day just another glam-rock act; ten years on, groups like HANOI ROCKS were imitating them. Johansen came back with *Buster Poindexter* '87 on RCA: new persona mining songs from standards to soca developed from affectionately tacky cabaret act in NYC clubs, with Joe Delia on piano, Tony Machine on drums, Soozy (Tyrell Kirschner) singing duets; he appeared on TV's *Saturday Night Live*, played a crooked record promoter in a *Miami Vice* episode, had cameo in film *Married To The Mob*.

NICE, The UK progressive rock trio of '68-71. Keith Emerson, keyboards; Lee Jackson, bass (*b* 8 Jan. '43, Newcastle); Brian Davidson, drums (*b* 25 May '42, Leicester). They served in various R&B bands, came together backing P. P. ARNOLD, originally with David O'List on guitar. Emerson's flamboyant keyboard attracted attention and they left Arnold; debut LP *The Thoughts Of Emerlist Davjack* '68 displayed Emerson's

interest in 'fusion' of rock and classical, incl. manic 'Rondo' (rocked-up Mozart). O'List quit, later went to ROXY MUSIC. *Ars Longa Vita Brevis* '68 had entire side taken up with title track; reverse incl. 'Intermezzo' from Sibelius's *Karelia Suite*. Version of Leonard BERNSTEIN's 'America' (from *West Side Story*) brought them minor single hit in USA '68 as well as Bernstein's ire, saw them banned from London's Royal Albert Hall for burning an American flag on stage. *Nice* '69 was a stopgap as they toured heavily; half was recorded live at New York's Fillmore and incl. Bob DYLAN's 'She Belongs To Me'. *Five Bridges* '70 was another lavish concept: Jackson wrote a suite about the bridges in his home town, recorded with full orchestra. By the time of live *Elegy* '71 they had split; later packages incl. *Autumn '67*, *Through Spring* '72, *Ameomi Rodivivi* '76. Emerson found greater fame and flamboyance in EMERSON, LAKE & PALMER; Davidson became a session drummer, with brief spell in GONG, worked in Refugee with Jackson, who made five LPs with his Jackson Heights, but never caught on.

NICHOLS, Herbie (*b* Herbert Horatio Nichols, 3 Jan. '19, NYC; *d* 12 Apr. '63, NYC) Pianist, composer. He studied classical piano as a child, turned to jazz with fresh compositions and a unique harmonic sense. He served in the US Army '41-3, later played at Minton's, was an associate of Thelonious MONK, but was treated even worse by the musical climate than Monk was: in those days many musicians had to make a living playing dixieland for tourists, and Nichols never escaped, commercially unsuccessful with his own music, then dying of leukaemia. Six recording sessions are his entire legacy: quartet sides made for Savoy '52 incl. two vocals by bassist Chocolate Williams, with Shadow Wilson on drums and a guitarist, probably New Orleans veteran Danny Barker (*b* 13 Jan. '09), were reissued '86, with almost equally elusive tracks by Monk on the other side of the album. 22 trio tracks on Blue Note '55 originally issued as two 10″ and one 12″ LP, later in 2-disc compilation *The Third World*, with drummers Art BLAKEY, Max ROACH, bassists Al McKibbon, Teddy Kotick on various tracks. 5-disc limited edition *Complete Blue Note Recordings On Mosaic* '87 with many unissued tracks was the compilation of the year, making it clear what an exceptional composer he was, to say nothing of his first-class pianism. *Out Of The Shadow* '57 on Bethlehem incl. George DUVIVIER and Dannie RICHMOND, once reissued on Affinity. A. B. Spellman's *Four Lives* '66 incl. good biographical essay.

NICHOLS, Red (*b* Ernest Loring Nichols, 8 May '05, Ogden, Utah; *d* 28 June '65, Las Vegas) Trumpet, bandleader. He was famous for a long series of records by mostly small groups beginning with Red And Miff's Stompers on Edison '26, then on Brunswick and allied labels from late '26 with about 150 sides (not counting alternate takes), usually as Red Nichols and his Five Pennies (usually 7-8 pieces), on Bluebird (Victor) as Red Nichols and his World Famous Pennies '34, then fewer records incl. big band sessions '39-40 as Red Nichols and his Orchestra on Bluebird and Okeh. The band had already got larger (11 pieces plus vocal trio incl. Connie BOSWELL at one '32 session); the best sides were the earliest, until '29 featuring Miff Mole on trombone (*b* Irving Milfred Mole, 11 Mar. 1898, Roosevelt, Long Island, NY; *d* 29 Apr. '61, NYC). Mole was one of the first to conceive of the jazz trombone as something more than a sort of bass accompaniment to the New Orleans-style front line (*see* JAZZ); he was highly regarded by musicians and fans alike, though soon put in the shade by Jack TEAGARDEN as a soloist. He worked as an NBC staff musician '29-38, his duties incl. playing for Toscanini and dir. Bessie SMITH broadcasts. In the '40s he played in dixieland combos at clubs like Nick's, was later reduced by ill health to work as a street vendor. Nichols's trumpet was derivative (after Bix BEIDERBECKE) but his sidemen incl. at various times in the early years, in addition to Mole, Jack and Charlie TEAGARDEN, Jimmy DORSEY, Glenn MILLER, Will BRADLEY, Benny GOODMAN, Gene KRUPA, Pee Wee RUSSELL, Adrian ROLLINI, Eddie LANG, Lennie HAYTON, Ray McKINLEY, Joe VENUTI, Wingy MANONE, indeed every good white musician of the era except Beiderbecke himself. Many of the Brunswicks were good sellers, especially 'Ida, Sweet As Apple Cider' '27 and two-sided hit 'Embraceable You'/'I Got

Rhythm' '30. Nichols's career was rejuvenated by *The Five Pennies* '59, a typically sentimental biopic with Danny KAYE playing Nichols, who played his own solos in the soundtrack; but it was generally agreed that whatever jazz feeling he had once possessed was gone, and he remained the favourite of the sort of listeners who usually preferred the businessman's bounce.

NICO (*b* c.'40, Berlin; *d* 18 July '88) Singer, actress; German model best-known for connection with the VELVET UNDERGROUND. In Fellini's *La Dolce Vita* '59; moved to London mid-'60s, was involved with ROLLING STONE Brian Jones, leading to single for Andrew Loog Oldhams's Immediate label 'The Last Mile' '65, prod. by Jimmy Page. Went to NYC '66, appeared in Andy Warhol film *Chelsea Girls*, joined Velvets: *Velvet Underground & Nico* '67 displayed haunting drone on 'All Tomorrow's Parties' and 'I'll Be Your Mirror'; debut solo LP *Chelsea Girl* '68 featured Bob DYLAN's 'I'll Keep It With Mine', rumoured to have been written for her but actually intended for Judy COLLINS. She gigged regularly in NYC, Jackson BROWNE and Tim BUCKLEY opening shows for her; *The Marble Index* '69 prod. by John CALE, *Desert Shore* '71 by Joe BOYD, featured her gloomy gothic harmonium. She attended one-off Velvets reunion in Paris '72 with Cale and Lou REED; *The End* '74 incl. her version of the DOORS' oedipal title song, and featured ROXY MUSIC's Phil Manzanera. Concert appearance with Cale, Brian ENO and Kevin AYERS released as *June 1, 1974*; regular live appearances kept her legend alive and she released *Drama Of Exile* '81; by mid-'80s she was back in vogue with resurgence of interest in the Velvets; *Do Or Die* '83 and *Behind The Iron Curtain* '86 were live sets, with her interpretation of such European songs as David BOWIE's 'Heroes', the latter with her permanent new group The Faction.

NICO, Dr (*b* Nicholas, Kasanda Wa Mikalay, '39, Luluaborg, Zaire; *d* '85) Guitarist, composer. He graduated '57 as a technical teacher, but inspired by his musical family (father an amateur accordionist, brother Mwamba Dechaud an excellent rhythm guitarist), he took up the guitar and in time became a virtuoso soloist. A founder member of the seminal group African Jazz, led by Joseph Kabaselle, he became the most infl. guitarist in modern Congo sound, acquiring nickname 'Dr Nico' following his performances with the band during independence celebrations '60. Best of the band's many singles issued on 2-disc *Joseph Kabaselle et L'African Jazz* on Africain; it split up '63 when Dr Nico and singer Rochereau left to form their L'Orchestra African Fiesta, which became one of the most popular in Africa, spawning many imitators and making dozens of singles, the best compiled in Africain's *L'Afrique Danse* series (vols. 5, 8, 10). More LPs incl. material from late '60s-early '70s appeared on Safari Ambiance incl. *Toute l'Afrique Danse*, *Sanzo Zomi Na Mibale*, *Bunga* and *Afrique Tayokana*. He withdrew from the music scene mid-'70s following collapse of his Belgian record label, feeling that he'd been cheated; he played the odd show and made a few singles but waited for a better deal, which came '83 with Africa New Sound, based in Lome, Togo: accompanied by his brother he made LPs backed by Les Redoubtables d'Abeti, incl. *Mikalay*, *Dieu de la Guitare*, *Aux USA* and *Homage au Grand Kalle*; more material remained unreleased. He made two more LPs in Paris '84-5 and arranged for his first American release on African Music Gallery label when his death robbed Africa of one of its best musicians.

NIEHAUS, Lennie (*b* 11 June '29, St Louis, Mo.) Alto sax, composer. Moved to West Coast as a child; worked with Jerry Wald, '51, joined Stan KENTON; served in US Army '52-4, then with Kenton again until '59. With Bud SHANK and Art PEPPER he was one of the most prominent in the West Coast alto sax school of the period, which seemed to combine the infl. of Charlie PARKER with the style of Benny CARTER. His primary infl. was Lee KONITZ. He retired to commercial work in films and TV. Arr. for night club acts etc.; has now been off the scene for so long that all his LPs have long been out of print: there were five on Contemporary '54-6 and one on EmArcy '57, all small group sets with good sidemen. As a soundtrack composer he works often with Clint Eastwood; incl. masterful Parker biopic *Bird* '88

NILES, JOHN JACOB (*b* 28 Apr. 1892, Louisville, Ky.; *d* 1 May '80, near Lexington) Singer, songwriter, folklorist, multi-instrumentalist: played piano, lute etc.; preserved the trad. dulcimer and home-made folk instruments. He sang in a high tenor, as befitting a man who collected songs in the mountains; like Richard Dyer-Bennett he kept the folk flame alive by presenting it formally rather than as hillbilly music. His father was a folk-singer and a square-dance caller; his mother played organ in church. He worked as a surveyor in the mountains, performed from c.'10; served in WWI and was badly injured in a plane crash; worked as gardener, horse groom, chauffeur (for photographer Doris Ulmann), collecting songs the while; collaborated with Marion Kerby on touring folk music programmes. His published collections incl. *Singing Soldiers* '24, *Songs My Mother Never Taught Me* '27, *One Man's War* and *Seven Kentucky Mountain Songs* '29, *Songs Of The Hill Folk* '36, *Ballads, Carols And Tragic Legends From The Southern Appalachian Mountains* '37, *The Anglo-American Study Book* '45, *Shape-Note Study Book* '50, major compilation *Ballad Book Of John Jacob Niles* '61 (with songs arranged in groups as Francis James CHILD had collected the words). *Folk Ballads For Young Actors* and *Folk Carols For Young Actors* were published '62; music publishers G. Schirmer celebrated their bicentenary with *The Songs Of John Jacob Niles*. *The Niles-Merton Song Cycles* '72 were his settings of the poems of best-selling author and Trappist monk Thomas Merton. He made albums of 78s for Victor incl. *American Ballads* '39, *Early American Carols And Folk Songs* '40, *American Folk Lore* '41; there were later microgroove reissues and collections on RCA incl. *50th Anniversary Album* '57 (on Camden), *John Jacob Niles: Folk Balladeer* '65; he formed his own Boone-Tolliver label (*American Folk Songs And Ballads*), also recorded for Folkways (*Folk Songs* incl. 'I'm So Glad Trouble Doesn't Last Forever') and Tradition, incl. 2-disc *Ballads, I Wonder As I Wander* '57 (he wrote music for title song), *An Evening With John Jacob Niles* '60, *Best Of* '67. Longer works incl. *Lamentations*, an oratorio inspired by Hitler in '41 but not completed until '51; by then he also hated the similar tyranny of communism. He concertised well into his '80s, received five honorary degrees and lived long enough to see the rebirth of interest in folk music which he had done much to preserve.

NILSSON, Harry (*b* Harry Nelson, 15 June '41, NYC) Singer, songwriter. Grew up on West Coast. Combined work in a bank with attempted commercial songwriting; limited success with songs for Ronettes, others; also wrote jingles, sang on demos. Signed with RCA; debut LP *Pandemonium Shadow Show* '67 provided hits for MONKEES ('Cuddly Toy') and THREE DOG NIGHT ('One') but sold badly; wacky sense of humour resulted in close relationship with John LENNON. *Aerial Ballet* '68 shared its predecessor's whimsy, incl. Randy NEWMAN's 'Simon Smith And His Amazing Dancing Bear', also a hit single in Fred NEIL's 'Everybody's Talkin' ', used in *Midnight Cowboy* soundtrack and no. 6 hit USA/23 UK (his own projected theme for the film, 'I Guess The Lord Must Be In New York City', also made top 40 USA). Meanwhile his songs were being covered, 'Ten Little Indians' by the YARDBIRDS, '1941' by Tom Northcott, etc. After soundtracks *Skidoo* and *The Point!*, the latter an animated TV film, LPs *Harry* and *Nilsson Sings Newman* and *Aerial Pandemonium Ballet* (compilation of the first two LPs), all '69-71, he hit the jackpot with 'Without You', written by BADFINGER's Tom Evans and Pete Ham and acquired through the Apple connection: no. 1 hit boosted LP *Nilsson Schmilsson* to no. 3, but the album was his most coherent and deserved to do well; it also incl. third and last top 10 hit 'Coconut' in his whimsical style, but now the wit that Lennon had liked was replaced by breathy ballad style of the big hit. *Son Of Schmilsson* '72 also did well but was too clever; *A Little Touch Of Schmilsson In The Night* '73 was a set of standards with Gordon JENKINS which made top 50 LPs; *Son Of Dracula* '74 was a soundtrack with Ringo STARR (for whom he'd sessioned on *Ringo* '73) and a relative flop; no. 60 LP *Pussycats* '74 was a set of rock covers prod. by Lennon; the rest of his LPs did not reach the top 200 LPs and lacked the individual touches of earlier work: *Duit On Mon Dei*, *Sandman*, . . . *That's The Way It Is* and *Knnillsson* '75-7, plus *The World's Greatest Lover* (did not

chart at all) and *Greatest Hits* '76 (incl. 'Kojak Columbo', not a hit but a throwback to the old humour). A talent who never took himself too seriously.

NIRVANA Psychedelic rock band formed in UK '67, led by Patrick Campbell-Lyons (*b* Waterford, Eire) and Alex Spyropoulos (*b* Greece). Songwriter Campbell-Lyons had moved to England to attend university, instead joined Second Thoughts, among whom was Chris THOMAS (later producer). They supported the High Numbers (later better known as the WHO) at the Star Club in Hamburg; Campbell-Lyons and Thomas wrote 'I'm Finding It Rough', recorded by the EVERLY Bros; when they split '67, Campbell-Lyons enrolled at art school on a filmmaking course, but met Spyropoulos and Ray Singer (later connected with Elton JOHN); they formed Nirvana, intended to be rock-oriented but with classical leanings (incl. French horn, cello). Signed to Island '67 and made three classic psychedelic singles, 'Rainbow Chase' (their only hit, top 40 UK '68), 'Pentecost Hotel' and 'Tiny Goddess', as well as LPs (now rare collectors' items) *The Story Of Simon Simopath* and *All Of Us*. At this point they fell out with Island boss Chris Blackwell, a story apparently documented on 'Christopher Lucifer', on their third LP *Nirvana – To Marcos III*, due to appear on Island but finally on Pye '70, incl. session work by SPOOKY TOOTH, Billy Bremner on guitar and backing vocalist Lesley Duncan. Campbell-Lyons took over the name Nirvana '71, released bizarre *Local Anaesthetic* on Vertigo, assisted by Jade Warrior and Mel Collins; a similar lineup made *Songs Of Love And Praise* on Philips '72, incl. inferior remake of '68 hit. *Me And My Friend* '73 came out on Sovereign under his own name, while he also worked as a producer for Vertigo with Mickey Jupp, Gracious, Clear Blue Sky; in '76 he worked for Electric Records with Arthur and Aliki (BROWN and Ashman) and the Cisco Kid (himself). His song 'Waterfall' represented Jamaica at the Rio Song Festival that year, sung by Jimmy Cliff; he released a single '77 on Chrysalis under the name of P.C. Lyons, also cut 'The Hero' as Erehwon for Harvest and launched his own Public Records late '70s, making concept LP *The Electric Plough* '81 which incl. an

859

updated version of 'All Of Us' with lyrics in Latin under the title 'Habemus De Loca'; plus a synthesised single 'The Picture Of Dorian Gray' as Nirvana on the Zilch label. A unique if bizarre talent.

NITTY GRITTY DIRT BAND USA band formed early '66 with deeper roots in folk and country music than most country-rock or folk-rock bands of the period. Bruce Kunkel (*b* c.'48, Long Beach, Cal.) and Jeff Hanna (*b* 11 Aug. '47, Detroit) began playing and singing together on West Coast, recruited Jimmie Fadden (*b* 9 Mar. '48), John McEuen (*b* 19 Dec. '45), Leslie Thompson and Ralph Barr, all from Long Beach except Barr, originally from Boston. All six played guitars and sang; Thompson also played bass, Kunkel and McEuen played violin, Fadden harmonica. Jackson BROWNE was also an early member. They called themselves the Illegitimate Jug Band because they didn't have a jug player; after high school they changed their name and turned pro; signed with Liberty and released *Nitty Gritty Dirt Band* and *Ricochet* '67. Chris Darrow joined in time for *Rare Junk* and *Pure Dirt* '68; between *Alive* and *Dead And Alive* '69 Darrow, Kunkel and Barr left; Jim Ibbotson (*b* 21 Jan. '47, Philadelphia) joined on drums and keyboards. They appeared in films incl. trashy *For Singles Only*; they should have been better suited to LERNER & Loewe musical *Paint Your Wagon* '69 but most of their footage was cut. Up to this point only the first LP had charted briefly (incl. Hot 100 single 'Buy For Me The Rain'), but they remained faithful to their audience and were rewarded with success of *Uncle Charlie & His Dog Teddy* '70, no. 66 LP incl. their only top 10 hit, Jerry Jeff WALKER's 'Mr Bojangles' (prologue on single was the title idea of the LP). The label complex switched them to UA for partly live *All The Good Times* '72 (incl. Hank WILLIAMS's 'Jambalaya'); then their masterpiece, organised by manager Bill McEuen, John's brother: they recruited Roy ACUFF, Doc WATSON, Merle TRAVIS, Maybelle CARTER, Earl Scruggs and Jimmy Martin (of Bill MONROE band) for a celebratory 3-disc C&W set *Will The Circle Be Unbroken* '72, pulled off without sentimentality or folkiness; Acuff was suspicious of what

looked to him like long-haired hippie types, but was won over in the end; Martin reportedly liked them so much he wanted to hire them. *Stars And Stripes Forever* '74 was a 2-disc live set by Hanna, McEuen, Ibbotson and Fadden; studio set *Dream* '75 incl. Linda RONSTADT on vocals; 3-disc set *Dirt, Silver & Gold* '76 was a compilation of hits, unreleased tracks etc. Shortened name beginning with *The Dirt Band* '78, with Ibbotson gone, and newcomers Richard Hathaway, Al Garth and Merle Bregante added (latter two from LOGGINS & MESSINA), as well as strings and horns; *An American Dream* '80 (title track was no. 13 hit) was followed by *Make A Little Magic* same year (title track at no. 25 was their third and last top 40 entry) and *Jealousy* '81, back on Liberty. Then they apparently changed their name back to Nitty Gritty Dirt Band and have made it big in the country charts: 'Dance Little Jean' was no. 9 country hit '83; 'Long Hard Road (The Sharecropper's Dream)', 'Modern Day Romance' both no. 1, 'High Horse' no. 2, 'I Love Only You' no. 3, all '84-5. *Let's Go* on Liberty was no. 26 country LP '83, *Plain Dirt Fashion* and *Partners, Brothers And Friends* both top 10 country albums on WB '84-5, as was compilation *Twenty Years Of Dirt* '86; *Hold On* '87 also did well. *Circle* was reissued on Capitol '86.

NITZSCHE, Jack (*b* Bernard Nitzsche, 22 Apr. '37, Chicago, Ill.) Producer, songwriter, arranger. Went to high school in Michigan, music college in Hollywood; began copying music, writing lead sheets etc. '57; worked with Sonny Bono at Specialty, with Original Sound label '59 (author credit on instrumental hit 'Bongo Bongo Bongo' '60 by Preston Epps), worked with Lee HAZLEWOOD, then was recommended to Phil SPECTOR when he wanted to relocate to the West Coast from NYC: collaborated with him on most of his biggest hits from no. it 'He's A Rebel' '63 until the inexplicable failure in USA of 'River Deep, Mountain High' '66. He also released his own instrumental 'The Lonely Surfer' on Reprise (briefly in top 40 '63), an album of the same title and two other obscure solo LPs. Other early credits incl. co-writing SEARCHERS' hit 'Needles And Pins' with Bono, also work with Doris DAY, Terry

MELCHER, Frankie LAINE, the MONKEES, Tim BUCKLEY, Bobby DARIN, Marianne FAITHFULL, mainly as arranger; he prod. Jackie DeSHANNON LP *Me About You* '68 on Liberty, Ron Nagle's *Bad Rice* '70 on WB. He played piano with the ROLLING STONES c.'68, wrote some arrangements for them; he had arranged Neil YOUNG's epic 'Expecting To Fly' for BUFFALO SPRING-FIELD, later played piano in Young's backing group Crazy Horse, wrote string arrangements on *Harvest* LP and toured with them once, his only work on the road. He worked on Mick Jagger film *Performance* '70 with Randy NEWMAN (incl. co-writing 'Gone Dead Train'). Album *St Giles Cripplegate* on Warner/Reprise '72 incl. six pieces, numbered rather than titled, played by London Symphony Orchestra (though never a commercial success, it was reissued '81 on UK indie label Initial). He continued to work in films, incl. *The Exorcist* '73, *One Flew Over The Cuckoo's Nest* '75 (score nominated for an Oscar), *Blue Collar* '78 (co-wrote 'Hard Workin' Man' with Ry COODER and Paul Shrader, performed by CAPTAIN BEEFHEART in soundtrack), several more. More album production work incl. three early LPs by MINK DeVILLE (incl. highly praised debut), Graham PARKER LP *Squeezing Out Sparks* '79. One of the most versatile of the backroom boys.

NOBLE, Ray (*b* 17 Nov. '03, nr London, England; *d* 3 Apr. '78, London) Pianist, bandleader, arranger, songwriter: elegant sweet/swing style was popular on both sides of the Atlantic, and some of his songs became standards. Mus. dir. at HMV Records '29-34; early records as New Mayfair Orchestra used now-forgotten show and novelty tunes, but Al BOWLLY began recording with the band late '30; Noble's arr. and songwriting developed until it was one of the best dance bands around, with soloists such as Louis ARMSTRONG-inspired trumpeter Nat Gonella (*b* 7 Mar. '08, London). Noble wrote both words and music for lovely songs incl. 'Love Is The Sweetest Thing' '33, 'The Very Thought Of You' '34, 'The Touch Of Your Lips' '36, 'I Hadn't Anyone Till You' '38, many more; instrumentals incl. 'Cherokee' '38, a hit in USA by Charlie BARNET and harmonically interesting enough to be used as a vehicle by modern jazzmen (it was improvising on 'Cherokee', Charlie PARKER said, that he first played the music he'd been hearing in his head). Noble's records were issued in the USA on Victor; 'Love Is The Sweetest Thing' and 'The Old Spinning Wheel' (words and music by Billy Hill; radio theme of child singer Mary Small) were no. 1 hits '33, 'The Very Thought Of You' and 'Isle Of Capri' '34; he came to the USA late '34 bringing Bowlly, drummer/manager Bill Harty with him, led a band assembled for him by Glenn MILLER, incl. Bud FREEMAN, Claude THORNHILL, Will BRADLEY, Charlie SPIVAK, Sterling Bose, other top sidemen; 'Paris In The Spring' and 'Let's Swing It' were top hits '35. Bowlly returned to England '36, was later killed by a bomb; Noble accompanied Fred ASTAIRE on huge hits 'Nice Work If You Can Get It', 'A Foggy Day', 'Change Partners' '37-8 on Brunswick, switched to that label himself, then to Columbia '40; the hits carried on until there were about 60 altogether in the USA '31-48 incl. the Astaire sides. 'By The Light Of The Silv'ry Moon' (written for Ziegfeld Follies in '09 by Edward Madden and Gus Edwards, later heard in many films; also recorded '42 by Fats WALLER and the Deep River Boys) sold a million copies after moving in and out of regional bestseller lists for over a year; charted at no. 23 '41, again in '44 (reissued during musicians' strike) with a vocal by Roy 'Snooky' Lanson, later famous on radio/TV show *Your Hit Parade*. Noble's last no. 1 was delightful 'Linda' '47 (words and music by Jack Lawrence) with vocal by Buddy CLARK, who also sang on 'I'll Dance At Your Wedding', no. 3 same year. Compilations in UK incl. *Ray Noble Plays Ray Noble* on EMI ('31-6 sides with Bowlly), *We Danced All Night* on RCA, others; in the USA broadcasts from '39-40 on Sunbeam and others from '35 on LP shared with Joe Haymes band on Aircheck; there were six LPs on Monmouth Evergreen, one in RCA Vintage Series.

NOONE, Jimmie (*b* 23 Apr. 1895, nr New Orleans; *d* 19 Apr. '44, L.A.) Clarinet. With Leon Rappolo of the New Orleans Rhythm Kings, he was the greatest infl. on Benny GOODMAN and other clarinettists of the Swing Era, with his beautiful tone and flowing style, but he made few records and has been badly served by reissues. Played with New Orleans giants (Freddie KEPPARD, etc.), in Chicago '18-43, went to West Coast, died of heart attack. First records as leader at Apex Club '28, with unusual instrumentation of four rhythm, two reeds: with Earl HINES on piano, Joe Poston on alto sax (*b* c.1895; *d* May '42), Bud Scott on banjo (*b* 11 Jan. c.1890; *d* 2 July '49, L.A.; also worked with King OLIVER and Jelly Roll MORTON), Johnny Wells on drums (*b* c.'05, Ky.; *d* 25 Nov. '65, NYC: first a singer/comedian/dancer, switched to drums at the Apex, later played with Joe SULLIVAN), Lawson Buford on tuba; delightful tracks such as 'Apex Blues', 'I Know That You Know' have been almost continuously in print on Decca/MCA, in poor transfers with echo or phoney stereo added; tracks from '29 with other pianists, '30 with vocals by May ALIX and Mildred BAILEY, four more sides '31 with Hines, and from mid-'30s with slightly larger groups incl. Charlie SHAVERS, Israel Crosby etc. are almost never reissued. There are also four trio tracks '40 accompanying singer Ed Thompson on Bluebird, and quartet tracks recorded at the Yes Yes Club as demos for proposed recording session, these last available on Swaggie (Australia), Folkways (USA). Complete Apex Club tracks on four Swaggie LPs from Australia is an excellent edition; also compilation in honest mono on Affinity. His widow married territory bandleader Troy Floyd (*see* JAZZ); his son Jimmie Jr (*b* 21 Apr. '38, Chicago) plays in his father's style, has recorded with Jeannie and Jimmy CHEATHAM, with Hal Smith's Creole Sunshine Orchestra, in UK under his own name with John R. T. Davies Rhythmic Five & Six on Stomp Off label.

NORMA JEAN (*b* Norma Jean Beasler, 30 Jan. '38, Wellston, Okla.) Modern-styled straight country singer, popular in '60s. Began on radio, TV in Oklahoma City '56, joined Ozark Jubilee '58-60, sang with Billy Gray, Merle Linsley, Leon McAuliffe bands. To Nashville '60, joined Porter WAGONER show, signed to Columbia, then RCA '63: country top 10 with 'Let's Go All The Way' '64. Other hits: 'Go Cat Go' '64, 'I Wouldn't Buy A Used Car From Him' '65, 'Heaven Help The Poor Working Girl' '67.

She semi-retired '65 to spend more time with her family, replaced on Wagoner show by Dolly PARTON. LPs incl. *Let's Go All The Way* '64, *Pretty Miss Norma Jean* '65, *Jackson Ain't A Very Big Town* '67, *Love's A Woman's Job* '68, *I Guess That Comes From Being Poor* '70, *Norma Jean* '71, *Thank You For Lovin' Me* '72, all RCA.

NORVO, Red (*b* Kenneth Norville, 31 Mar. '08, Beardstown, Ill.) Xylophone, vibraphone, bandleader. Studied piano as a child; went to Chicago at 17 and soon led a marimba band; later had solo vaudeville act incl. tap-dancing; led band '29, became staff musician at NBC with Victor YOUNG, then Paul WHITEMAN, met Mildred BAILEY: they were married, went to NYC with Whiteman. Two solos recorded for Brunswick '29 never issued; small-group records '33-5 incl. variously Teddy WILSON, Benny GOODMAN, Jimmy DORSEY, Artie SHAW, Charlie BARNET, Gene KRUPA, Bunny BERIGAN, Chu BERRY, Jack Jenny (*b* 12 May '10, Mason City, Iowa; *d* 16 Dec. '45, L.A.; trombonist legendary for silky style, manic behaviour): compilation *Red Norvo & His All Stars* '33-8 on Columbia Special Products USA. He led octet '36 with Dave BARBOUR, Eddie SAUTER, recorded for Decca; then larger band same year with Bailey singing, Sauter arr. on Brunswick until '39: on radio Norvo and Bailey were known as 'Mr and Mrs Swing'. Among his freelance activities was quartet session '37 in L.A. with Wilson, Harry JAMES, John Simmons, no drums incl. lovely two-sided 'Just A Mood'. He continued with band until '44, switching from xylophone to vibes '43, Bailey working separately; they divorced but remained close. Joined Goodman '45, Woody HERMAN '46, settled on West Coast '47; recorded for Capitol '48 with Stan Hasselgard (*b* Ake Hasselgard, 4 Oct. '22, Sweden; *d* 23 Nov. '48 in car crash; the only clarinettist ever featured by Goodman alongside himself). Norvo returned East '49 to lead sextet with Tony SCOTT, Dick HYMAN, Mundell LOWE; formed trio '50 with Tal FARLOW and Charles MINGUS, later Jimmy Raney and Red MITCHELL, highly regarded for subtle beauty of chamber-music style. First tour overseas '54; guested with Goodman on TV '58; his quintet joined Goodman and four others for

10-piece tour '59, gig at Basin Street. Worked in Las Vegas for much of '60s; on TV with Frank SINATRA, Dinah SHORE etc.; played jazz festivals, Dick Gibson's Colorado Jazz Parties. Records with Goodman and Herman; many sides with Bailey (as 'Mildred Bailey And Her Orchestra') in her 3-disc compilation. Other albums: *And His Orchestra* '38 on Circle, *Time In His Hands* '45 with Slam STEWART on Xanadu, *Red Norvo's Fabulous Jam Session* '45 on Spotlite UK (Dial dates with Wilson, Stewart, Charlie PARKER, Dizzy GILLESPIE, Flip PHILLIPS, others), *All Star Sessions* '47 on Pausa, 2-disc trio compilations '50-1 on Savoy, '53-5 on Prestige. Later albums incl. *The Forward Look* '57 on Reference; *Vibes à la Red, Second Time Around* and *In New York* '77 with Scott HAMILTON, all on Famous Door; with Ross Tompkins on Concord '79, *Just Friends* '83 on Stash with guitarist Bucky Pizzarelli's trio.

NRBQ Eclectic American band playing nearly everything, formed '67 in Miami, Fla. as New Rhythm and Blues Quintet: without a single hit, still have a loyal cult following 20 years later. Original lineup: Terry Adams on keyboards and harmonica, guitarist Steve Ferguson, both from Louisville, Ky.; Joey Stampinato on bass and vocalist Frank Gadler, both from NYC; Tom Staley on drums, from Ft Lauderdale, Fla. They all sang except Staley. Encouraged by Slim HARPO, they played a club in NYC and were signed to Columbia (CBS/USA) who mismanaged their potential: albums *NRBQ* '69 and *Boppin' The Blues* '70 with Carl PERKINS didn't do much at the time. Guitarist Al Anderson (*b* 26 July '47, Windsor, Conn.; led local country-rock band Wildweeds) joined '71; *Scraps* '72 and *Workshop* '74 came out on Kama Sutra; Ferguson and Gadler left, Tom Ardolino joined on drums and the Whole Wheat Horns became a more or less permanent fixture (saxes Gary Windo and Keith Spring, Adams's brother Donn on trombone); they formed own Red Rooster label, released *All Hopped Up* '77 followed by *At Yankee Stadium* '78 on Mercury, *Kick Me Hard* '79 on Red Rooster (distributed by Rounder), *Tiddlywinks* '80 on Rounder, *Grooves In Orbit* '83 on Bearsville; *Tapdancin' Bats* c.'84, *She Sings, They Play*

'86 with Skeeter DAVIS and EP *Christmas Wish* '86 on Rounder. The Kama Sutra LPs were reissued on an obscure label, *Scraps* on Rounder; the first Columbia LP and the Mercury are still in print: incessant touring, insouciant stage presence keeps the fans loyal. They perform covers, originals, sometimes anything the audience asks for; Adams has written songs covered by Dave EDMUNDS, Bonnie RAITT; Windo and Adams toured with Carla BLEY '77, played on her Watt LPs *European Tour 1977* and *Musique Méchanique* '78, Windo playing bass clarinet on the latter as well as tenor sax. Al Anderson made eponymous LP for Vanguard '72, backed by Terry Adams and Tom Staley, others.

NUGENT, Ted (*b* 13 Dec. '48) Rock guitarist. Worked with Lourds (French for 'heavy'); then formed band Amboy Dukes in Detroit '65, with original lineup of John Drake, vocals; Steve Palmer, guitar; Bill White, bass; Rick Lober, keyboards; T. T. Palmer, drums: played pseudo-psychedelic music with heavy metal overtones. Eponymous first LP '67 (the year Nugent graduated from high school) made Billboard chart early '68 on Mainstream label; Andy Solomon and Greg Arama replaced Lober and White; *Journey To The Center Of Your Mind* '68 had title track in top 20, helping LP to no. 74. *Marriage On The Rocks/Rock Bottom* '69 marked switch to Polydor, Rusty Day replacing Drake; slimmed to quartet of Nugent, Solomon, K. J. Knight (drums) and Rob Ruzga (bass), first three sharing vocals. Live *Survival Of The Fittest* '70 marked by new billing: Ted Nugent & the Amboy Dukes, followed by next label switch; group reduced to trio with Rob Grange (bass), Vic Mastrianni (drums) for *Call Of The Wild* '73, *Tooth, Fang & Claw* '74: did not make charts but still in print in '86. Nugent dropped Amboy Dukes tag, embarked on solo billing. Long-haired heavy-rock guitarist is clean-living family man, hard worker; has had remarkable run of chart LPs on only two labels. On Epic: *Ted Nugent* '75, *Free-For-All* '76 (vocals by MEATLOAF), *Cat Scratch Fever* '77, 2-disc *Double Live Gonzo!* and *Weekend Warriors* '78, *State Of Shock* '79, *Scream Dream* '80 (tied with Gonzo for best chart showing at no. 13), *Intensities In 10 Cities* and *Great Gonzos!*

best-of '81; then on Atlantic: *Nugent* '82, *Penetrator* '84, *Little Miss Dangerous* '86 with new guitarist/vocalist David Amato (title track used in *Miami Vice* TV episode *Definitely Miami* '86, in which Nugent played a baddy). Played in heavy metal charity project 'Hear'N'Aid' '85; worked on soundtrack of *Nomads* '86, album *If You Can't Lick 'Em . . . 'Lick 'Em* '88 from WEA has nine Nugent Songs plus one co-written with Jon Bon Jovi.

NUMAN, Gary (*b* Gary Webb, 8 Mar. '58, London) UK singer, synthesiser player. Joined The Lasers at 16, changed name to Tubeway Army '77: lineup Numan, vocals and guitar; Paul Gardiner, bass; Numan's uncle Jess Lidyard, drums; made two singles 'That's Not It' and 'Bombers', recruited second guitar Sean Burke, replaced Lidyard with Barry Benn, disbanded mid-'78. Reformed Army to cut demos (issued as *Tubeway Army* '79 on Beggars Banquet). He'd doubled on keyboards before, but interest in synth was timely (inspired by Eurorock groups CAN, KRAFTWERK): stream of keyboard bands followed him into charts as punk faded. LP *Replicas* '79 developed ideas further, though singing was suitable punk monotone. Single 'Are "Friends" Electric' with insidious synth hook over relentless rhythm was surprise no. 1, abetted by picture-disc format; album followed suit; 'Cars' also no. 1 and with album *The Pleasure Principle* credited to Numan solely, now backed by Gardiner, Ced Sharpley (ex-Druid) on drums, Chris Payne on keyboards and viola. 'Cars' also made top 10 USA. He added guitarist Russell Bell, keyboardist Billy Currie (the latter from ULTRAVOX, another influence); '79 stage shows incl. robots, fluorescent tubes and other novelties, but sound was somewhat two-dimensional. Collaborated with Robert PALMER on his *Clues* '79, writing 'I Dream Of Wires'. His own *Telekon* '80 was no. 1 LP, single 'I Die You Die' no. 6, but signs that interest was flagging and music press criticism led to retirement from live performance: *Living Ornaments 1979-80* made no. 2 in album chart by being available for one month, then deleted. The new decade was littered with synth bands; backing group now called Dramatis, with Dennis Haines replacing Currie, failed to carve

own niche despite Numan fronting them for top 40 single 'Love Needs No Disguise'; he summed up his career on *Newman Numan*, came back with albums *Dance* '81, *I Assassin* '82, *Warriors* '83; number of guests on these LPs incl. guitarist Bill Nelson, drummer Roger Taylor from QUEEN, Jim Morrissey on sax, Pino Palladino on bass, etc. suggests that he was held in esteem by fellow musicians. Hard core of fans remained to give him top 20 hits with 'We Take Mystery To Bed' (top 10), 'Music For Chameleons' and 'White Boys And Heroes' '82, 'Warriors' and 'Sister Surprise' '83; top 40 'Berserker' '84 was first release on own Numa label, also LPs *White Noise Live* and *The Fury* '85. Videos and stage shows always impresssive, place as synth pioneer assured; if it seems he has wrung maximum mileage from his ideas, refreshing duet single 'Change Your Mind' '85 with Shakatak keyboardist Bill Sharpe showed possible willingness to adapt. He is also well known for interest in flying, owns several vintage planes.

NYAME, E. K. (*b* '27, Kwahu, Ghana; *d* '77) Composer, singer, guitarist; the most popular guitar-band leader in Ghana. Self-taught; first played with amateur groups, day job as a clerk. Wanted to modernise highlife, the national style, introducing notation, training of musicians; formed his own group '50, incl. guitars, clips, bongos, drums and string bass; formed Akan Trio '52 for concert parties (African comic theatre) with the band entertaining the audience before and after performances with highlifes, ragtimes, calypsos. Toured Liberia with Prime Minister Nkrumah, playing at state functions; success of tour and the trio's growing popularity at home enabled him to turn pro full-time. The concert parties were initially in English, but Twi became the standard during the '50s. He had begun recording in '51 after success with his song 'Small Boy Nye Me Bra', in the course of next two decades made a phenomenal 400 singles on Decca, Queenophone, HMV, Skanaphone. His biggest hits incl. 'Menia Agya Meni Na' and 'Maye Maye Meni Aye'; he continued to innovate in the guitar-band context and develop highlife. He remade some of his most popular tunes mid-'70s on LP *Sankofa* ('go back and retrieve'). On his sudden death he was given a state funeral for which over 10,000 turned out. His long time associate and friend Kobina Okine (1924-85) composed memorable highlifes incl. classic 'Tetteh Quashie'.

NYRO, Laura (*b* 18 Oct. '47, Bronx, NYC) Singer/songwriter, pianist. One of the best and brightest of the singer/songwriter genre of the late '60s, still going strong with gospel/R&B infl. songs and performance though the genre no longer captures charts or headlines. She had only one minor hit single, ironically not her own song (cover of DRIFTERS' 'Up On The Roof' reached Hot 100 '70); her albums never sold all that well, but her own unique performance had and still has a cult following, while her songs were smash hits for others. Father was a piano tuner who also played trumpet; she wrote songs as a child, attended High School of Music and Art; music publisher Paul Barry helped get contract with Verve/ Forecast: debut *More Than A New Discovery* '66 preceded appearance at Monterey Pop Festival '67, where she was jeered by Janis JOPLIN fans. Of the songs from the first LP, 'Wedding Bell Blues' got some airplay; the FIFTH DIMENSION had no. 1 hit with it and took 'Blowin' Away' to no. 21, BLOOD, SWEAT & TEARS reached no. 2 with 'And When I Die', all '69; Barbra STREISAND had no. 6 with 'Stoney End' '70, minor hit with 'Flim Flam Man' '71. Manager David GEFFEN meanwhile took her to Columbia (CBS/USA); *Eli And The Thirteenth Confession* '68 made top 200 LPs incl. 'Stoned Soul Picnic' and 'Sweet Blindness' (no. 3 and 13 respectively for Fifth Dimension), 'Eli's Coming' (no. 10 for THREE DOG NIGHT), all '69. *New York Tendaberry* '69 at no. 32 was her bestselling LP, incl. 'Time And Love', another hit for Streisand '71; *Christmas And The Beads Of Sweat* '70, *Gonna Take A Miracle* '71 (with backing vocals by LABELLE). She retired to a fishing village in Massachusetts; meanwhile the confessional art lost ground to MOR fodder; Columbia reissued the first LP as *The First Songs* '73; she came back with the power of her urban blues somewhat diminished: *Smile* '76 made top 100 LPs; live *Season Of Lights* '77 did less well; *Nested* '78 didn't chart. *Impressions* '80 was a best-of set (incl. '68 song 'Save The Country', top 30 '70 for Fifth Dimension, Hot 100 entry for Thelma HOUSTON). She came back to the top 200 LPs with *Mother's Spiritual* '84. Her songs were also covered by Aretha FRANKLIN, Frank SINATRA, Linda RONSTADT, several others.

O

OAK RIDGE BOYS Originally a country gospel vocal quartet formed '57 in Oak Ridge, Tenn. by Smitty Gatlin, turned full-time pro '61, broadened appeal by turning to country music. Lineup '80s incl. William Lee Golden (*b* 12 Jan. '39, Brewton, Ala.), Richard Sterban (*b* 24 Apr. '43, Camden, N.J.), Duane Allen (*b* 29 Apr. '43, Taylortown, Texas), Joe Bonsall (*b* 18 May '48, Philadelphia, Pa.); band incl. Mark Ellerbee, Harold Mitchell, Garland Craft, Don Breland. They won Gospel Music Association Dove award several times, Grammy awards '71 for 'Talk About The Good Times', '76 for 'Where The Soul Never Dies', CMA awards '78; chart hits incl. no. 1 'Cryin' Again' '78. Heavy touring, TV appearances keep them on top: no. 1 country hits '83-5 incl. 'American Made', 'Love Song', 'I Guess It Never Hurts To Cry Sometimes', 'Everyday', 'Make My Life With You', 'Little Things', 'Touch A Hand, Make A Friend'. LPs incl. *Old Fashioned Gospel Quartet Music, All Our Favourite Songs, Smokey Mountain Gospel* on Columbia (CBS/USA), three vols. of *Spiritual Jubilee* on Accord, *Sensational* on Starday; albums on ABC-Dot (now on MCA) incl. *Room Service, Oak Ridge Boys Have Arrived, Y'all Come Back Saloon* '77, *Together* '78; string of hits on parent MCA label incl. *Fancy Free, Bobbie Sue, American Made* (no. 2 country LP) and *Deliver* (no. 6, both '83), *Step On Out* '85 (no. 3). Golden issued solo *American Vagabond* '86, was voted out of group '87 with 'continuing musical and personal differences', replaced by band member Steve Sanders.

OBEY, Ebenezer (*b* '42, Idogo, Nigeria) Singer, composer, guitarist, bandleader. The most popular and influential juju bandleader in Nigeria. Infl. by I. K. DAIRO, the father of moden juju, he began '54 with the Royal Mambo Orchestra, moved to the Guinea Mambo Orchestra '58, also played with the Fatai Rolling Dollar and Federal Rhythm Brothers, formed own International Brothers '64: soon released first single 'Ewa Wowun Ojumi Ri', with a unique blend of talking drums, guitars, vocals and percussion. By the time of first visit to London '69, they were releasing four LPs a year, incl. hits *In London, Board Members, Christmas Special, The Horse, The Man And His Son*. He renamed the band Inter-Reformers '70 and made dozens more LPs incl. *Around The World* '74, *Edumare Dari* '75, *Murtala Muhammed* '76, *Adam And Eve* '77; by this time he had christened his music the Miliki System, opened nightclub the Miliki in Lagos as a permanent base. A devout Christian, he is concerned in many songs with morality and honesty, others maintaining the traditional praise-singing of Yoruba music. As each new release chalked up advance sales of 100,000 or more, he began to look at the international market, licensing records to the Oti label in London '80: *Current Affairs, Eli Yato, What God Has Joined Together*, also hits compilations. Emulating his great rival Sunny ADE, he released *Je Ka Jo* and *Miliki Plus* '83 on Virgin, the latter a compilation incl. 'What God Has Joined Together' (double cassette incl. both albums), then *Solution* '84 on London-based Sterns label, all the while maintaining phenomenal popularity at home and making successful tours with the 18-strong Inter-Reformers of UK and USA.

OCEAN, Billy (*b* '50, Trinidad) UK pop/R&B vocalist. Emigrated to UK late '50s with family, already joining in family singsongs on ukelele. In the East End of London he discovered soul singers Sam COOKE, local heroes the BEATLES and the ROLLING STONES; he was apprenticed to a tailor and cutter after leaving school, who lent him money to buy a piano, leading to playing and singing with obscure local groups. He completed a college course in tailoring, worked in a Savile Row shop; released flop single under the name of

Scorched Earth '74 and lost his job; went to work in the giant Ford factory in East London, combining shift work with musical life: long hours ended with deal with GTO Records. First single under his own name was 'Whose Little Girl Are You'; second 'Love Really Hurts Without You' made top 3 UK/top 30 USA early '76. His USA outlet ran into problems, but hits continued in UK with 'L.O.D. (Love On Delivery)' and 'Stop Me (If You've Heard It All Before)' top 20 '76, 'Red Light Spells Danger' top 3 '77. Then GTO refused to release 'Who's Gonna Rock You': cover by the Nolan Sisters made top 20 '80, first of a stream of Ocean covers by the Dells, Lenny Williams, Latoya Jackson, as his own career stagnated: 'American Hearts' and 'Are You Ready' were minor hits '79-80; GTO were bought by clumsy giant CBS, who could not make hits of Ocean albums *Nights (Feel Like Getting Down)* and *Inner Feeling* (though title track of *Nights* was incl. in hugely successful *Jane Fonda's Workout Record*). Completing obligations to CBS, Ocean signed with London-based Jive label, worked with NYC prod. Keith Diamond on *Suddenly* '84, a smash hit incl. singles 'Caribbean Queen (No More Love On The Run)' (no. 1 USA/top 10 UK, won Grammy), 'Loverboy' (top 5 USA/UK). He made his first-ever live tour, appeared on Live Aid, was chosen to sing theme from hit film *Jewel On The Nile*: 'When The Going Gets Tough, The Tough Get Going' co-prod. by Wayne Braithwaite (plays with Herbie HANCOCK) and Barry Eastmond, who co-wrote it with Ocean and Mutt Lange, incl. with next hit 'There'll Be Sad Songs (To Make You Cry)' in new LP *Love Zone* '86 also a hit in both USA/UK. Few artists have persevered in the face of so much adversity and struck so big. He also prod. Ruby Turner (another Jive artist, whose 'If You're Ready, Come Go With Me' charted in UK '86); his *Tear Down These Walls* '88 came out on Arista.

OCHS, Phil (*b* 19 Dec. '40, El Paso, Texas; *d* 9 Apr. '76, NYC) Singer/songwriter, still one of the most fondly remembered of the '60s. He attended a military academy, studied journalism, moved to NYC '61 and plunged into folk-protest movement. *All The News That's Fit To Sing* '64 was a typical album of the era; *I Ain't Marchin' Any-*more '65 was an improvement, incl. caustic 'Here's To The State Of Mississippi'; title song became an anthem of the period. *In Concert* '66 remains one of the best live albums of the era, incl. his version of his best-known song, 'There But For Fortune', a world-wide hit for Joan BAEZ '65. Ochs was compared to Bob DYLAN, but while Dylan found new audiences with innovative music, Ochs stuck to folk-protest, saying at one point that he wanted to be 'the first leftwing star'; Dylan (under tremendous pressure himself) treated Ochs cruelly, but Ochs leapt to Dylan's defence '64: 'It is as if the entire folk community was a huge biology class and Bob was a rare, prize frog ... hopping in all different directions while they're trying to dissect him ... To cater to an audience's taste is not to respect them, and if the audience doesn't understand that, they don't deserve respect.' *Pleasures Of The Harbor* '67 was Ochs' most assured LP to date, incl. beautiful 'Flower Lady', witty 'Outside Of A Small Circle Of Friends' and epic 'Crucifixion', about JFK murder. *Tape From California* '68 was seen as an unsuccessful attempt to emulate Dylan, though title track was outstanding and 'The War Is Over' an excellent anti-Vietnam song (he claimed that John LENNON stole its title for his Bed-Ins '69). *Rehearsals For Retirement* '69 was a bitter album after the riots at the Democratic convention in Chicago '68, incl. 'Doesn't Lenny Live Here Any More?' about Lenny Bruce. *Phil Ochs' Greatest Hits* '69 was ironically titled set, mocking an Elvis PRESLEY album with sleeve note '50 Phil Ochs fans can't be wrong!', incl. top session players Ry COODER, James BURTON, Tom Scott, members of the BYRDS, songs such as 'Chords Of Fame', 'No More Songs', 'Jim Dean Of Indiana'. Live *Gunfight At Carnegie Hall* '71 was contentious, recorded complete with audience antipathy, cry of 'Phil Ochs is dead!' as he rocked out on hits of Presley, Buddy HOLLY, Merle HAGGARD's 'Okie From Muskogee'. Ochs quit the USA, wandered around Europe, wrote for London's *Time Out* magazine; he was mysteriously assaulted in Africa, narrowly escaping death, suffering severely damaged vocal chords. He appeared with Dylan at the Benefit For Chile concert '74, released single 'Here's To The State Of Richard

Nixon' in the wake of Watergate; he suffered from manic depression, refused to answer to his name, rechristened himself 'John Butler Train'. He committed suicide at his sister's house. *Chords Of Fame* '76 is an excellent 2-disc collection lovingly compiled by his brother Michael, the title also used for '84 TV documentary; *A Toast To Those Who Are Gone* '86 is compilation of previously unreleased material.

O'CONNOR, Hazel (*b* 16 May '55, Coventry, England) UK new wave singer. After turbulent youth spent travelling as singer, English teacher, nude model, she signed with tiny Albion label '78; the strident style she adopted was well-suited to punk era, but songwriting was often gentler. After series of flop singles she gained exposure in film *Breaking Glass* '80, from which came no. 5 single 'Eighth Day'; though film has not worn well, soundtrack LP was no. 5 UK and she won a Variety award for her performance. By the time of *Sons And Lovers* '80 she had zero credibility with the pop press, having had 'unfair' exposure in film. The LP did not chart, but catchy 'D-Days' was top 10 in less flighty singles market; best single 'Will You' (also from LP) made no. 8 with classic sax break. *Cover Plus* '81 was no. 32 LP, but her moment had gone. Backing group Megahype split up: Ed Case, drums (ex-999), Andy Quinta, keyboards (went to Icehouse), Wesley Magoogan, sax (went to The Beat), Steve Kinch on bass, her brother Neil O'Connor (ex-Flys). She came back in mellower mood on RCA with *Smile* '84, singles: for Greenpeace with MANFRED MANN's Earthbound vocalist Chris Thompson '85, 'Life Could Be So Good' '86 on Red Bus. Her autobiography *Uncovered Plus* created little interest; management and record company problems are described in book *Expensive Habits* ('The dark side of the music industry') '86 by Simon Garfield. She should have been a bigger star with proper post-film push, but the fact that the soundtrack LP was on A&M, other records on tiny not-terribly-competent label didn't help; she appeared in TV series *Jangles*; played a leading role in Howard Goodall musical *Girlfriends* '87.

O'DANIEL, Pappy (*b* Wilbert Lee O'Daniel, 11 Mar. 1890, Malta, Ohio) Western swing bandleader, songwriter and governor of Texas. Grew up in Kansas, moved to Texas to work as flour salesman with Burrus Mills, became sales director; Bob WILLS, leader of the Wills Fiddle Band, suggested a radio programme to advertise the flour: the group was called the Light Crust Doughboys with O'Daniel as MC, had programme on KFJZ Fort Worth '31-2, recorded for Victor; switched to Vocalion and WBAP '33; Wills quit and formed his Texas Playboys: O'Daniel became Doughboys' frontman and sued Wills, trying to prevent him from getting his own radio work, hoping to make him come back, but without success, the case creating a precedent in Texas law. O'Daniel then left Burrus himself and set up his own Hillbilly Flour '35; new band the Hillbilly Boys with vocalist Leon Huff played vital role in successful campaign for Governor '38, disbanded '40. He made his mark on Western swing, also got co-writing credit for songs such as 'Put Me In Your Pocket' and 'Beautiful Texas'.

O'DAY, Anita (*b* 18 Dec. '19, Chicago, Ill.) Singer; one of the few true jazz vocalists, her unique and up-to-date phrasing infl. many imitators and winning approval of both white and black jazz fraternities. She participated in dance marathons as a teenager, sang with Max Miller combo '39 in Chicago; fame with Gene KRUPA '41-3 began with no. 4 hit 'Just A Little Bit South Of North Carolina', top 20 'Georgia On My Mind', top 10 'Let Me Off Uptown' (duet with Roy ELDRIDGE), also 'Thanks For The Boogie Ride' and 'The Walls Keep Talking' with Eldridge, 'Two In Love' with Johnny DESMOND, 'Bolero At The Savoy' etc. Went to Stan KENTON, sang on that band's first big hit 'And Her Tears Flowed Like Wine', no. 4 '44; recommended her replacement Shirley Luster when she left and Kenton changed her name to June CHRISTY: Christy and Chris CONNOR were O'Day's principal acolytes. Back with Krupa for top 10 'Chickery Chick', 'Boogie Blues' '45. She worked solo, did guest spots with Duke ELLINGTON, Benny GOODMAN, recorded for Bob THIELE's Signature label with Will BRADLEY, Ralph BURNS, Benny CARTER, Alvy West and the Little Band (small group with accordion, hip sound, briefly successful on radio), these now compiled on Doctor Jazz incl. title track *Hi Ho Trailus Boot Whip*, top 30 hit '47. 'Tennessee Waltz' was a top 30 hit '51 on London; then began long association with Norman GRANZ from '52: LPs (mostly on Verve) incl. *Sings Jazz* '52 with Burns, Roy Kral combo, etc. (reissue *The Lady Is A Tramp* '57), *Songs By Anita O'Day* '54-5 with her own combos (reissue *An Evening With Anita O'Day* '57); *Anita* (aka *This Is Anita*) and *Pick Yourself Up* '55-6 with Buddy Bregman; *Drummer Man* '56 (reunion with Krupa and Eldridge); *Anita Sings The Most* '57 with Oscar PETERSON (aka *Sings For Oscar*); *At Mr Kelly's* with combo and *Sings The Winners* with Russ Garcia and Marty Paich bands '58, *Swings Cole Porter With Billy May* and *Cool Heat* with Jimmy GIUFFRE '59, *Anita O'Day And Billy May Swing Rodgers And Hart, Waiter, Make Mine Blues* with Garcia, *Incomparable!* '60 with Bill Holman, all '60; *Trav'lin' Light* with Johnny Mandel and *All The Sad Young Men* with Gary McFARLAND '61, *Time For Two* with Cal TJADER, *Anita O'Day & The Three Sounds* (see Gene HARRIS) '62. Despite all this recording her career was slipping: she was inactive for much of the '60s; for a long time she had drunk too much, then drank very little while she was on heroin for eight years (autobiography *High Times Hard Times* '81 with George Eells pulls no punches); came back still swinging to find fans still waiting: she put out *Anita O'Day* and *Once Upon A Summertime* on her own AOD label (now on Glendale), she recorded live at the Berlin Festival '70 (*In Berlin* on Pausa); made unissued album with Dave FRISHBERG '75; there were first-class tours of Japan, six LPs issued there mid-'70s, incl. *Live In Tokyo, My Ship, Live At Mingos, Angel Eyes* '75-8 which also came out on her own Emily label, named after her dog. *There's Only One* '78 on Dobre was followed by *Mello'Day* '79 on GNP/Crescendo, with septet incl. Lou Levy on piano and Laurindo ALMEIDA, her best-planned album for years. *Live At The City* and *Second Set* '79 came out on Emily, as well as *The Night Has A Thousand Eyes*, then *S'Wonderful* '85, big band with Hank JONES, others. Compilations incl. 2-disc big bands set on Verve. She made soundies and short films with Krupa and Kenton '41-56, appeared in *The Gene Krupa Story* '59 as her-

self, also in *Jazz On A Summer's Day* '60 (film of '58 Newport Festival), played singers in *Zigzag* (aka *False Witness*) '70, *The Outfit* '74.

O'DELL, Kenny (*b* 31 May '16, Roanoke, Ala.) Country gospel singer, known as the Old Country Boy. Began on local radio in New Orleans mid-'30s, moved to Nashville and had gospel show on WLAC for many years. Recorded for Mercury '51-6 and Audio Lab '56-62 without much commercial success, though songs like 'Banking With My Lord' and 'Thirty Pieces Of Silver' gave him a considerable following. LPs incl. *Hymns For The Country Folks* '63 on Audio Lab.

ODETTA (Odetta Holmes Felious Gorden, *b* 31 Dec. '30, Birmingham, Ala.) Folk-blues singer, songwriter, actress, teacher. Grew up in L.A., studied music at City College there, joined chorus of tour company of Yip HARBURG-Burton Lane show *Finian's Rainbow* '49, finished studies and decided to stick with folk music, making pro debut in San Francisco '52, at the Blue Angel NYC '53; helped in early days by Pete SEEGER and Harry BELAFONTE, appearing with Belafonte on TV special '59, on one of his biggest-selling albums (2-disc *Returns To Carnegie Hall* '60). Her own first LPs were *Odetta Sings Ballads And Blues* '56, *Odetta At The Gate Of Horn* '57 on Tradition, then *Odetta And The Blues* '62 on Riverside, with Buck CLAYTON, Vic DICKENSON, Herb Hall (Edmond HALL's brother), piano and arr. by Dick WELLSTOOD, young Ahmed ABDUL-MALIK on bass, drummer Berisford 'Shep' Shepherd (*b* '17; also played on Bill DOGGETT's 'Honky Tonk'). *Odetta* on Fantasy, *Odetta Sings Folk Songs* on RCA '63 (latter made top 75 LPs USA). On Vanguard: *At Town Hall* '62, *One Grain Of Sand* '64, *At Carnegie Hall* '67, *Sings Ballads And Blues*; also compilations on Vanguard, Tradition. Nearly all of these are still in print or recently reissued, testifying to long-term popularity; her classical training also led to concerts with Symphony of the Air, acting-singing in Gian Carlo Menotti's opera *The Medium*. She wrote songs 'Music', 'Give Me Your Hand', 'Got To Be Me'; acted in Arthur Miller's *The Crucible* in Stratford, Ontario; she appeared in films

Sanctuary '60, *The Effects Of Gamma Rays On Man-In-The-Moon Marigolds* '72. LP *It's Impossible* on Fourleaf Clover label in UK '78. First album in 12 years was live concert *Movin' It On* '86 on Rose Quartz label.

O'FARRILL, Chico (*b* Arturo O'Farrill, 28 Oct. '21, Havana, Cuba) Composer-arranger. Father Irish, mother German; studied composition, then law; studied in USA '36-40 at Gainesville, Ga. Played trumpet in Cuban bands, infl. by Bunny BERIGAN, Harry JAMES, Bobby HACKETT; he described in Ira Gitler's *Swing To Bop* '85 how he first heard modern jazz on records brought back from NYC in '45: new harmonic changes, asymmetrical phrasing; he thought, 'If this is the shape of things to come, how in the hell am I going to cut it?' But he began arranging '46, came to USA '48, immediately worked with Gil FULLER for Dizzy GILLESPIE, was recommended by Stan Hasselgard to Benny GOODMAN when Goodman was leading his only bop band '48. Wrote 'Undercurrent Blues', 'Shishka-bop' for Goodman, 'Carambola' and 'Manteca' ('54) for Gillespie, 'Cuban Suite' for Stan KENTON; also arr. for MACHITO, others. Led own band mid-'50s, moved to Mexico late '50s, worked on a symphony (premiered in Mexico '72), returned to the USA '65 and wrote for Count BASIE, Glenn MILLER band led by Buddy DeFRANCO, Kenton, CANDIDO (LP '73), Gato BARBIERI, Frank Wess; also studio work. Worked with Gillespie, Machito on Verve, later with Gillespie on Pablo; own LPs incl. *Married Well* on Verve, *Spanish Rice* co-led with Clark TERRY, *Nine Flags* on Impulse.

O'JAYS, The Black vocal group formed '59 in Canton, Ohio as the Mascots, still popular decades later. Eddie Levert (*b* 16 June '42) and Walter Williams (*b* 25 Aug. '42) recruited William Powell (*d* 26 May '77), William Isles and Robert Massey; became locally popular and recorded for King in Cincinnati; championed by Cleveland DJ Eddie O'Jay, changed their names; record for Dayco leased to Apollo, but nothing happened. H. B. BARNUM took them to L.A. and they ended up on Imperial, where the hits began: 'Lonely Drifter', 'Lipstick Traces (On A Cigarette)', 'Stand In For Love', 'Let It All Out' all made pop and/or R&B charts, compiled on *Working On Your Case* '85 on EMI Liberty UK. For some reason the purchase of Imperial by Liberty broke their run of luck and they label-hopped; more hits on Thom BELL and Gamble & Huff's Neptune label '67-70; their biggest success came on moving to Gamble & Huff's new Philadelphia International '72 as trio (Isles left '66 complaining that Barnum worked them too hard; Massey left '72 but remained as a consultant, later formed own Devaki label). Powell left '76, died of cancer; replaced by Sam Strain (*b* 9 Dec. '41, ex-LITTLE ANTHONY & THE IMPERIALS). 27 Hot 100 hits '72-80 incl. four in top 5: 'Back Stabbers' '72, no. 1 pop hit 'Love Train' '73, 'I Love Music' '75, 'Use Ta Be My Girl' '78. They sold albums, incl. compilation of Neptune hits *The O'Jays In Philadelphia* '73; 14 chart LPs '72-83 incl. top 20 LPs *Back Stabbers* '72 (incl. 'Love Train'), *Ship Ahoy* '73 (incl. top 10 'Put Your Hands Together', 'For The Love Of Money'); *Live In London, Survival, Family Reunion, Message In The Music, So Full Of Love* and *Identify Yourself* '74-9. *The Year 2000* '80 charted on TSOP, *When Will I See You Again* on Epic; *My Favorite Person* '82 on Phil. Int. saw Williams and Levert doing more writing and production; *Love And More* '84 and *Love Fever* '85 on Phil. Int. made black LP charts; *Let Me Touch You* '87 on EMI made with Gamble/Huff/Bell.

O'KANES, The An acoustic country band whose eponymous debut album on Columbia '87 was in the top 40 early '88. Kieran Kane and Jamie O'Hara were successful Nashville songwriters: O'Hara wrote hit 'Grandpa (Tell Me 'Bout The Good Old Days)' for the JUDDS; they formed a band to play their own work, playing guitar, acoustic bass and drums, with Richard Kane on fiddle and Jay Spells on accordion. Vocal harmony in the style of the EVERLY BROTHERS, minimalist arrangements and excellent songs, with intelligent lyrics celebrating the usual down-to-earth concerns of country music, add up to a front-porch sound infl. by blues, folk, swing and bluegrass which typifies some of the best popular music being made today. Second album *Tired Of The Runnin'* '88 was in top 30 of Billboard's country chart mid-'88.

OKOSUN, Sonny (*b* '47, Benin City, Nigeria) Singer, composer, guitarist. From musical family, inspired by Elvis PRESLEY and Cliff RICHARD, but became an actor first, with Eastern Nigeria Theatre, taking up guitar only in '64, forming first band the Postmen '66, playing pure pop. Joined Sir Victor Uwaifo as second guitarist '69-71, learning his trade on tours of Europe and Japan; developing his own style, a mixture of Bendel highlife and SANTANA-style rock which he called Ozzidi after a traditional Ijaw god, he formed Paperback Ltd '72, later changing the name to Ozzidi. The rock infl. was still strong and he began to fuse rock and reggae with Ozzidi; his first three LPs *Ozzidi, Living Music* and *Ozzidi For Sale* '76-7 each sold over 100,000, but the next, *Fire In Soweto,* became a huge hit throughout West Africa and was licensed to Oti in London. Further hits incl. *Papa's Land* '77, *Holy Wars* '78, *Third World* and *The Gospel According To Ozzidi* '80. He was the first African star to perform in the newly independent Zimbabwe; his popularity widened with his penchant for protest songs, overseas touring and hit LPs *Mother And Child* '82, *Togetherness* and *Which Way Nigeria* '83. He toured Europe, Cuba, and throughout Africa, but his rock/reggae fusion and trenchant lyrics also appealed in the USA, where he made a successful tour '84 and released compilation *Liberation* on Shanachie. *Revolution II* '85 is on EMI.

OKUKUSEKU The Okukuseku International Band of Ghana, formed '69 in Accra by Kofi Sammy and Water Proof. Singer-composer Sammy began with Kakaiku's guitar band in the palm-wine style of highlife, had moved on to K. Gyasi and his Noble Kings; Proof had been an actor, served an apprenticeship with E. K. NYAME's No. 1 band. Though neither could play the guitar they came together to form Okukuseku's No. 2 Guitar Band, recording single 'Osona Ba' '69 at Ghana Films Studio; failing to acquire instruments or equipment they left for Kumasi '70, where they borrowed instruments from Ambassador Studios and made several more singles, popular enough to persuade the chairman of Ambassador, A. Kwasi Badu, to lend them equipment: in the '70s they became one of the country's top bands, releasing

two LPs, *Agyanka Due* and *Bosoe Special.* They left for Nigeria '79 because of economic depression, lack of recording facilities; they made LPs *Okponku Special* and *Original Kekako* in Lagos, moved to the highlife stronghold of Eastern Nigeria, landed a contract with Rogers All Stars of Onitsha. They continued to play Asante highlife, singing in Twi but in time adding songs in Pidgin and Ibo, adopting Nigerian highlife inflections without losing their fans back home. LPs incl. *Yebre Ama Owou* '80, *Suffer Suffer* '81, *Take Time* and *Black Beauty* '83, *Odo Ye De* '84. Internationally popular, they returned to Ghana '85, settled in Koforidua.

OLAIYA, Victor (*b* Victor Abimbola Olaiya, '20s, Ijebuu, Nigeria) Singer, composer, trumpeter. Known to his fans as the 'Evil Genius' of highlife, he began with Bobby BENSON, playing a mixture of waltzes, quicksteps, boleros, chachachas, highlifes, but following E. T. MENSAH's infl. tour on Nigeria in the early '50s left and formed his own Cool Cats, concentrating on highlife. His fame grew with a succession of hits and he was asked to play at Nigeria's independence celebrations '60; by this time the band had been renamed the All Stars, Victor UWAIFO and Fela KUTI passing through in early '60s, the period reflected in compilation *In The Sixties.* During the decline in highlife late '60s, Olaiya, a Yoruban, was one of the few Nigerians who continued to make a living from it. By the '70s he had his own night club in Lagos, the Papingo, and also active in the various musicians' unions in Nigeria. By the '80s he was fronting the ten-piece International Stars Band, maintaining popularity with live act, LPs such as compilation *Highlife Reincarnation, Country Hard-O* and *Highlife Giants,* the latter with Mensah.

OLATUNJI, Babatunde (*b* Ajidi, Nigeria) Virtuoso drummer, able to sound like a whole band with a few drums; one of the best-known African musicians, with LPs on Columbia '50s but few since. First in many years: *The Beat Of My Drum* '87 on Blue Heron, with 17 musicians. Carlos SANTANA (who covered his 'Jingo' on his first LP), ten drummers incl. AIRTO, five-strong chorus, 12-minute version of

'Akiwowo' (from '59 LP *Drums Of Passion*) with solo by Santana. Proceeds to go to establishing Centre of African Performing Arts in Ajido; the record should be sent to 'all the electronic drum manufacturers and players, as a reminder of where the drum originated and what it really sounds like' (Diane Patrick in *Wire*).

OLDFIELD, Mike (*b* 15 May '53, Reading, England) Composer, multi-instrumentalist. A precocious guitarist at 14, he made folk album *Sallyangie* '68 with sister Sally; he worked with Kevin AYERS on his *Shooting At The Moon*, *Whatevershebringswesing*, *Confessions Of Dr Dream* '71-4, meeting composer David Bedford (*b* 4 Aug. '37, London), who had studied at the Royal Academy of Music. Oldfield wrote, arranged, produced and recorded his own *Tubular Bells* '73, which inaugurated the Virgin label and made Oldfield's fortune. He played a large number of stringed instruments and keyboards, the 49-minute solo instrumental requiring more than 1000 overdubs; it was a no. 1 LP UK, no. 3 USA; its global success was assured when it was used as the theme of film *The Exorcist* '73; an undeniably impressive achievement, it is now thought to have been an antecedent of new age music and was the apogee of progressive rock, also signalling its dead end. Following it was predictably a problem; *Hergest Ridge* '74 was similar, also no. 1 UK, top 100 USA; *Ommadawn* '75 was no. 4 UK, 176 USA; *The Orchestral Tubular Bells* '75 was made with Bedford conducting Royal Philharmonic Orchestra: top 20 UK, did not chart in USA. *Boxed* '76 had his first three albums, with the first two remixed, and a fourth LP, *Collaborations*, of new material, some of it involving Bedford. He played guitar when Bedford's *Star's End* '74 was played by the RPO, who commissioned it. EP *Take Four* '78 incl. top 4 UK singles 'Portsmouth', 'In Dulce Jubilo'; among other singles was theme from UK kiddie TV show 'Blue Peter' (top 20). He broke further from long thematic concepts on *Incantations* '78, *QE2* '80 (featured Phil COLLINS) and *Five Miles Out* '82. *Exposed* '79 was 2-disc live set made on European tour; *Crises* '83 was a commercial album, helped by UK no. 4 'Moonlight Shadow', with vocalist Maggie Reilly; *Islands* '87 incl.

vocal on title track by Bonnie TYLER. Highly praised score for film *Killing Fields* '84 denoted possible future direction; *The Complete Mike Oldfield* '86 was a compilation. Sally made LPs *Water Bearer* '78, *Easy* '79, *Celebration* '80, *Strange Day In Berlin* '83; Bedford's LPs incl. *Nurses Song With Elephants* '72 (with Ayers and Oldfield), *The Rime Of The Ancient Mariner* '75, *The Odyssey* '76.

OLIVENCIA, Tommy (*b* Santurce, Puerto Rico) Bandleader, trumpeter, musical director, producer. As well as leading one of P.R.'s best bands, he was a distributor for Alegre Records and a promoter, and is noted for bringing along many fine soneros (Latin singers) who have shared his repertoire and gone out on their own, incl. Lalo Rodriguez (*see* Eddie PALMIERI), Paquito Guzman, Chamaco Ramirez, Simon Perez, Sammy Gonzales, Gilberto Santa Rosa, Frankie Ruiz. Olivencia's first records were on his own Tioly label; he signed with Inca '72, notable LPs incl. *Tommy Olivencia 1977*, prod. by the young innovative Luis 'Perico' ORTIZ, with singers Perez and Guzman. Guzman's LPs on Inca incl. *Paquito Guzman* '72 (album of boleros prod. by Ray BARRETTO) and the excellent *Mintiendo Se Gana Mas* '77; he switched to Top Hits (TH) and *Champán y Ron* '86 was a big hit. Olivencia's *Fiesta de Sonoros* '78 was a hits compilation with a feast of lead singers; he moved to TH and released *Sweat Trumpet ... Hot Salsa* '78 and *Tommy Olivencia y su Orquesta* '79, lead singers on latter Guzman with Santa Rosa, who went on to work with Willie ROSARIO, then made his own hit LP *Good Vibrations* '86 on Combo. Ruiz and Carlos Alexis sang lead on *Un Triangulo de Triunfo!* '81 and *Tommy Olivencia* '83, Alexis replaced by Hector Tricoche on *Celebrando Otro Aniversario* '84, Ruiz's last with Olivencia. Olivencia and band backed veteran Colombian singer Nelson Pinedo (*see* Rafael CORTIJO, Tito RODRIGUEZ) on his LP *... Desde Puerto Rico* '84 on Audiorama; Olivencia also prod. and Guzman singing in the chorus. Ruiz debuted with his own band on *Solista ... Pero No Solo* '85 on TH; album of dance covers of Latin pop ballads topped Billboard's salsa chart for months '86 and *... Voy Pa' Encíma!* '87 was another no. 1 LP, young sensation Eddie Santiago in the chorus, whose *TH Presenta a Eddie Santiago 'Atrevido y Diferente'* '86 was another chart-topper. Meanwhile Paquito Acosta replaced Ruiz on Olivencia's *Ayer, Hoy, Mañana y Siempre . . . !* '85, *30 Aniversario* '87.

OLIVER, King (*b* Joseph Oliver, 11 May 1885, Louisiana; *d* 10 Apr. '38, Savannah, Ga.) Cornettist, composer, bandleader: perhaps the greatest artist of all in the classic style of New Orleans jazz. Said to have been born on a plantation, where his mother was a cook; began on trombone; lost sight in one eye in childhood accident; learned some cornet from Bunk JOHNSON, played in various bands, with Kid ORY and led own bands '12-17, rejoined Ory, left N.O. '19, worked in Chicago, California, returned to Chicago and led Creole Jazz Band at Lincoln Gardens from Apr. '22, sending for Louis ARMSTRONG to play second cornet mid-year; toured, visited NYC solo '24, returned to Winter Gardens. Jazz was already a nationwide fad when Oliver began recording; the white ORIGINAL DIXIELAND JAZZ BAND made the first jazz records '17, but Oliver was already the King before he left N.O., the nickname allegedly bestowed by Ory. The recordings of the Creole Jazz Band were the best examples of the N.O. style to be captured, despite the limitations of the acoustically-made 78 sides (the drummer had to play woodblocks instead of his usual kit), with Oliver and Armstrong, cornets; Honoré Dutrey, trombone; Johnny DODDS, clarinet, Lil Hardin ARMSTRONG, piano; Baby DODDS, drums; Arthur 'Bud' Scott or Johnny St Cyr, banjo; Charlie Jackson on bass sax (on five tracks), Paul Anderson 'Stump' Evans (*b* 18 Oct. '04, Lawrence, Kansas; *d* 29 Aug. '28, Douglas, Kansas) on C-melody sax (on four). Four sides made by Columbia have (probably) Ed Atkins on trombone and Jimmie NOONE on clarinet. 41 tracks were recorded (incl. three alternate takes) on four different labels, all in '23; four were rejected and are lost; two Paramount sides have survived on only one copy of the original 10″ 78. 18 Paramount/Gennett sides have been available on Milestone USA, and 15 Okeh sides in EMI's World Records Retrospect series UK; the Smithsonian Institution's 2-disc set incl. 29 tracks; another collection is available from

Australian Swaggie. Excellent Swaggie anthology *Chicago Jazz 1923-29* has the Columbias, plus tracks by Lil's Hot Shots, Erskine Tate's Vendome Orchestra etc., all with Louis and/or Dodds. Oliver was the complete jazz musician, never playing anything the same way twice: the rich honesty of his style and the human warmth of his muted crying tones made him one of the founding fathers of American music; Louis Armstrong made it clear that Papa Joe was his primary infl. and the only one he ever needed. Oliver recorded with Jelly Roll MORTON, Clarence WILLIAMS, BUTTER-BEANS & SUSIE, accompanying singers Katherine Henderson, Eva Taylor, Victoria SPIVEY, Hazel Smith, Elizabeth Johnson, Lizzie Miles, Sippie Wallace, Texas Alexander; his regular band recorded '26-8 as the Savannah Syncopators, Aurora Aristocrats, Dallas Dandies etc. but the records are compiled as by King Oliver and his Dixie Syncopators. This was a somewhat larger band, electrically recorded and already a step away from the classic N.O. format; its 'Farewell Blues', 'Willie The Weeper', 'Every Tub', 'Someday Sweetheart', many others are breathtakingly beautiful. The band incl. variously Bigard, Evans, Ory, Scott, Omer SIMEON, Johnny Dodds, Luis RUSSELL, Albert Nicholas on clarinet (*b* 27 May 1900, N.O.; *d* 3 Sep. '73, Switzerland), Jimmy Archey on trombone (*b* 12 Oct. '02, Norfolk, Va.; *d* 16 Nov. '67, Amityville, NY), drummer Paul Barbarin (*b* 5 May 1899, N.O.; *d* there 10 Feb. '69), Lawson Buford on tuba, others; the band made nearly 50 sides for Vocalion and Brunswick (incl. alternate takes), recording in NYC from mid-'27. 24 tracks were once collected on two Ace Of Hearts LPs in the UK; there is a one-disc selection on MCA/USA; the most complete collection is on the Italian Joker label in not-very-good transfers. (Engineer Robert Parker has made a gorgeous digital transfer of 'Someday Sweetheart' for CD; he should do them all.) Oliver recorded for Victor '29-30 (2-disc set from French RCA); his last records were made for Brunswick/Vocalion '31, mostly as King Oliver and his Orchestra, the last two (Vocalion) sides as the Chocolate Dandies. By this time he was suffering from serious dental trouble; finally pyorrhoea forced him to have most of his teeth removed and his gums were usually bleeding. Beginning with the Victor records he did not always play and rarely took solos; although his music was considered old fashioned he was still a strong bandleader; the sidemen incl. his nephew Dave Nelson (*b* '05, Donaldson, La.; *d* 7 Apr. '46, NYC), sometimes Red ALLEN and Bubber MILEY on trumpets; Archey, Hilton Jefferson on alto sax, James P. Johnson on piano; he also played on two delightful sides by Jimmie Johnson and his Orchestra '29 with Nelson, Archey, James P., Fats WALLER, others incl. male vocal trio: 'You've Got To Be Modernistic' and the lovely 'You Don't Understand', both written by Johnson, the latter also recorded by Bessie SMITH. Lester YOUNG worked for Oliver '32; there was a disastrous tour of the South '35; he died destitute and broken-hearted, working as a janitor in a pool hall, unable to get medical treatment because of welfare dept red tape. The unique reference book *Pop Memories* lists several big hits: 'Dipper Mouth Blues' and 'High Society' '24, 'Someday Sweetheart' and 'Willie The Weeper' '27, 'Four Or Five Times' '28 and 'St James Infirmary' '30 (with Miley). He copyrighted 'High Society', a N.O. classic; among the many new classics he wrote or co-wrote were 'Dipper Mouth' (as 'Sugar Foot Stomp', it remained a hit throughout the Swing Era), 'West End Blues', 'The Chimes', 'Snag It', many more. Soon after his death collectors were paying higher and higher prices for his out-of-print records. Classic biodiscography *King Joe Oliver* by Brian Rust and Walter C. Allen published '55; new edition '87 edited by Laurie Wright is a massive update.

OLIVER, Sy (*b* Melvin James Oliver, 17 Dec. '10, Battle Creek, Mich.; *d* May '88, NYC) Trumpeter, vocalist, composer, arranger. Raised in Ohio, both parents music teachers. Worked with Jimmie LUNCEFORD '33-9 and largely responsible for that popular band's style, incl. easy two-beat lope with humour, vocal chorus on 'My Blue Heaven' '36, 'Tain't Whatcha Do' and 'Ain't She Sweet' '39; also 'Organ Grinder's Swing', 'By The River St Marie', 'For Dancers Only', 'Posin' ', all big hits. Lured away by Tommy DORSEY's ability to pay more, he wrote originals 'Easy Does It', 'Swing High', 'Well, Git It!', 'Opus No. 1' for him,

the last two top 20 hits '42 and '45. Led own band '46, worked for record companies incl. Decca for a decade, arranged freelance, occasionally formed bands for record dates; led band in NYC mid-'70, again late '70s-early '80s. Own LPs incl. *Jimmie Lunceford Arrangements In Hi-Fi* on Decca, others on Decca and Dot; with Chris CONNOR on Bethlehem '56.

OLYMPICS, The USA doo-wop group formed '57 by lead singer Walter Ward (*b* '40, Jackson, Ms.), tenors Eddie Lewis (*b* '37, Houston, Texas) and Charles Fizer (*b* '40, Shreveport, La.), bass Melvin King (*b* '40, Shreveport). All were in L.A. high school except Lewis; they signed with Demon and were assigned songwriters Fred Smith and Cliff Goldsmith: first and biggest hit was classic novelty 'Western Movies' '58 (top 10 USA, top 20 UK), complete with gunshots and ricochet effect. '(I Wanna) Dance With The Teacher' '59 was a minor hit; they went to the Arvee label and had minor hits, only 'Shimmy Like Kate' reaching the UK chart; they went to Chess subsidiary Argo, but their first Argo record 'Peanut Butter' (top 20 USA '61) had to come out on Arvee for legal reasons. 'The Bounce' on Tri-Disc '63 went top 40; minor hit 'Good Lovin' ' on Loma later covered by the Young RASCALS for a million-seller. More minor hits on Mirwood were the last '66; they also recorded for All-American, California Gold; were still together on the rock'n'roll revival circuit many years later. Rhino Records in L.A. compiled hits on *The Official Record Album Of The Olympics* '84 as the 1984 Olympic Games were taking place there; one hopes that the title helped sales: the album is good nostalgia.

OMOGE, Madam Comfort (*b* '29, Ilititun, Ondo State, Nigeria) African singer/composer whose Asiko Ikale Group occupy a unique place. She began performing at the age of 17 but she remained an amateur, spending most of her time looking after her husband, the Oba of Igbodigo, and their seven children; then she formed the 17-piece percussion group '72, playing an updated version of traditional Ere Aboba Asiko music using only trad. instruments, with no electric or studio effects. First LP on Decca '76 was *Biri*; others incl. *Ore Mi*,

Agbala Woma, Olorun Mi Iwo, Munene Munene. With revival in '80s of trad. styles such as Apala, Fuji and Waka, she confirmed her national reputation with *Ona Orun Jin* and *Nigeria Settle* '83, *Adeleke Special* '84.

ONLY ONES, The UK new wave group formed by Peter Perrett, singer-guitarist (ex-England's Glory) who'd been active solo/frontman since late '60s, with bassist Alan Mair (ex-SPOOKY TOOTH); Peter FRAMPTON drummer Mike Kellie; guitarist John Perry, who had worked with Ratbites From Hell, also with GRATEFUL DEAD lyricist Robert Hunter: altogether a strange set of credentials for a new wave group. First single 'Lovers Of Today' on own Vengeance label as Peter and the Pets led to CBS contract: 'Another Girl Another Planet' was a cult hit. LPs *The Only Ones* '78 and *Even Serpents Shine* '79 showcased Perrett's tortured, Lou REED-style vocals; never punks, they derived much from USA glam-rock. *Special View* compilation issued in USA, failed to accrue more than limited following. *Baby's Got A Gun* '80 was their most successful album, making top 40 LP chart, but writing was on the wall with last-chance single 'Fools', Perrett duet with Penetration vocalist Pauline Murray on untypical C&W-flavoured tune. Split early '81 after filling London's Lyceum for farewell gig; splinter group Decline And Fall didn't last long. *Alone In The Night* compilation '86.

ONO, Yoko (*b* 18 Feb. '33, Tokyo) Japanese vocalist. Moved to NYC at 14, in early '60s made some reputation with poems, films, events. Jazz fans were mystified when her voice was dubbed onto an Ornette COLEMAN track. She met John LENNON at art exhibition, married him early '69; she was omnipresent in the last days of the BEATLES and was unfairly blamed for their split by fans. She contributed limited vocal talent to his Plastic Ono Band projects, appeared on his LP sleeves (naked on *Two Virgins*), participated in Bed-In for Peace, etc. *Yoko Ono/Plastic Ono Band* '70 presented her less-than-outstanding music; she was reckoned to have introduced John to electronic music and free jazz, and her book *Grapefruit* '70 was said to have inspired his song 'Imagine'. Her *Approximately Infinite*

Universe '73 was regarded as an improvement, though she remained anything but a serious artist in critical eyes, her up-and-down vocal style regarded as mannered rather than exotic or profound. Split from Lennon '74 but they were reunited '75, had son Sean (each had a child from previous marriages). Continued in media spotlight after his death, *Seasons Of Glass* '81 and unsettling single 'Walking On Thin Ice' her reaction to his loss; she also masterminded posthumous *Milk And Honey* '82; her *Every Man Has A Woman* '84 was an unusual package: her songs performed by artists such as Harry NILSSON, Elvis COSTELLO, Roberta FLACK, etc. Though seemingly inept in the beginning, she was never accorded credit she deserves for influence, her pre-new wave vocal style heard in Lene Lovich, Patti Smith, etc. She was preparing albums of Lennon's scraps '88 to forestall bootlegs.

ORBISON, Roy (*b* 23 Apr. '36, Vernon, Texas; *d* Dec. '88) Country-pop singer, songwriter. Formed band the Wink Westerners at school, playing popular dance-band style; with rise of rockabilly '54-6, changed repertoire and name to Teen Kings. Cut first records at Norman PETTY studio in Clovis, then recut 'Ooby Dooby' for Sun in Memphis (Clovis record released only in limited quantity), had surprise no. 59 hit '56, credited to Roy Orbison and the Teen Kings; band split owing to lack of follow-up success on Sun. He bought back Sun contract, hit with song 'Claudette' (recorded by EVERLY Bros. for top 30 hit '57), became house writer at Acuff-Rose in Nashville '58. Made flop single for RCA, signed with Monument, two rockabilly singles flopped; then his ballad 'Only The Lonely' married R&B and country in classic style, set off by keening but strong high-register vocal, reached no. 2 USA/1 UK, very much setting the style, songs co-written with Joe Melson, Bill Dees: despairing, emotional vocals (though never over the top), often with JORDANAIRE-style backing, made ballads pure gold: 'Blue Angel', 'Running Scared', 'Crying', 'Dream Baby', 'In Dreams' '60-3 almost all top 10 both USA/UK; 'It's Over' no. 1 UK, ballad with a beat 'Oh, Pretty Woman' '64 no. 1 both countries. By the end of '65 he'd made UK top 40 17 times, USA top 40 20 times; he was the only USA vocalist except for Elvis PRESLEY to ride out the British Invasion (the BEATLES were big fans; their early slow-tempo version of 'Please Please Me' was a tribute to him). Switch to MGM '65 was the end of the big hits, though 'Ride Away' that year was no. 25 USA; made acting debut in film *The Fastest Guitar Alive*. His wife Claudette was killed in a motorcycle accident '66; sympathy buying took cover of Don GIBSON's 'It's Too Soon To Know' to no. 4 UK. He made an album of Gibson songs '66, regarding him as a mentor. He had reached a low point in his career, reduced to touring clubs, when two sons were killed in a fire at home '68. He turned to country music '70, recorded for various labels, remained a big draw; soon recognised as an infl. master: others covered his songs, 'Crying' a UK no. 1 '80 by Don MCLEAN, 'Blue Bayou' a USA no. 3 '77 by Linda RONSTADT; he came back to USA Hot 100 '80 with 'That Lovin' You Feelin' Again', a duet with Emmylou HARRIS from film *Roadie*; signed with infamous UK ZTT label for 'When Hearts Run Out Of Time' (from film *Insignificance*). Honest tear-jerkers are classics and he has fanatical following, especially in UK. LPs incl. *Big O Country* '83 on Decca UK (covers of Hank WILLIAMS, Gibson), Sun compilations *The Big O* and 2-disc *The Sun Years* on Charly, 2-disc *All-Time Greatest Hits* and other compilations on Monument; *In Dreams: The Greatest Hits* '87 is 2-disc set on Virgin of new recordings, faithful to the originals.

ORCHESTRAL MANOEUVRES IN THE DARK UK pop duo: Andy McCluskey, bass and vocals (*b* '60), Paul Humphreys, synths (*b* '61), both from West Kirby, Merseyside. They met at school, grew up in '70s listening to KRAFTWERK and CAN; formed group Equinox, later pretentiously named The Id '77, then OMD '78, played first gig at legendary Liverpool Eric's during burgeoning 'second wave of Merseybeat'. Their contemporaries were TEARDROP EXPLODES, ECHO & THE BUNNYMEN, Wah!. First OMD single 'Electricity' on JOY DIVISION's Factory label; subsequent singles 'Red Frame, White Light' and 'Messages' '80 were minor UK hits, incl. on LP *Orchestral Manoeuvres In The Dark* '80. Breakthrough came with hypnotic 'Enola Gay' (named after the B-29 that dropped the first atomic bomb '45): no. 8 UK '80, subsequently no. 1 in several countries in Europe. *Organisation* '80 featured unlikely cover of Chris Montez's 'The More I See You'. Top 10 hits 'Souvenir' and 'Joan Of Arc' '81 established them as a top concert draw, though hypnotic rhythms with backing tapes led to criticism of remote austerity. *Architecture & Morality* '81 saw them firmly in pop mainstream, though musical infl. still came from largely uncommercial direction; *Dazzle Ships* '83 incl. ambitious 'Genetic Engineering', while *Junk Culture* '84 was more overtly pop, with hits 'Talking Loud & Clear', infectious 'Tesla Girls'. *Crush* '85 was disappointment; they were heard in soundtrack of hit USA film *Pretty In Pink* '86; album *The Pacific Age* '86 incl. hit 'Forever (Love & Die)'.

ORIENTAL BROTHERS INTERNATIONAL BAND Highlife band from Eastern Nigeria, split into three. The original Orientals, led by Opara brothers Dan Satch, Warrior and Godwin Kabaka, was formed early '70s, toured and released outstanding dance tracks on over 20 albums incl. *Orientals Special* '74, *Nwa Ada Di Nma* '75, *Murtala Mohammed* '77, *Best Of The Orientals* '82: they were among the most popular highlife bands of the '70s, but always beset by leadership problems; the first to split was guitarist Godwin Kabaka Opara, who formed Kabaka International Guitar Band '77, making a dozen albums of his own blend of highlife, called Ikpokrikpo, still with typically Ibo lyrics reflecting lessons to be learned from traditional wisdom and culture. Kabaka's best-sellers incl. *Onye Mere Ihe Akaya* '78, *Egbula Nwa Onya* and *Nwanne Di Namba* '82. Then vocalist Warrior left '80 to form Dr Sir Warrior and the (Original) Oriental Brothers, like Godwin before him a solo success, with a dozen albums in five years, incl. *Onye Oma Nmanu* '80, *Onye Obula* '81, *Ugo Chinyere* '83. Despite confusion of names, the original Orientals under Dan Satch Opara carried on, e.g. with albums *Onye Ije* '82, *Onye Nwe Ala* '83, and there seem to be enough dance fans for all three bands.

ORIGINAL DIXIELAND JAZZ BAND The group that recorded the first jazz records.

Original lineup: cornettist Dominic James 'Nick' LaRocca (*b* 11 Apr. 1889; *d* 22 Feb. '61, New Orleans), clarinettist Larry Shields (*b* 13 Sep. 1893; *d* 21 Nov. '53, L.A.), trombonist Edwin Branford 'Eddie' Edwards (*b* 22 May 1891; *d* 9 Apr. '63, NYC), drummer Tony Spargo (*b* Antonio Sbarbaro, 27 June 1897; *d* 30 Oct. '69, Forest Hills, NY), pianist Henry Ragas (*b* 1890; *d* '19, NYC). The young white enthusiasts from New Orleans were a sensation in New York and beat their black betters such as Freddie KEPPARD, King OLIVER etc. to the studio. They recorded two sides for Columbia Jan. '17, but the label was not enthusiastic; 'Livery Stable Blues' was made Feb. for Victor and a huge hit by June, soon exceeded in sales by 'Darktown Strutters' Ball' on Columbia. They recorded for Aeolian Vocalion the same year, but the records were of the obsolescent vertical-cut type (*see* RECORDED SOUND) and their big hits were all on Victor except for the one Columbia; the biggest was 'Tiger Rag', an estimated no. 1 hit '18. LaRocca copyrighted 'Tiger Rag', 'Fidgety Feet', other New Orleans classics; the acoustically-made records were regarded by many as novelties, and did much to establish jazz as a noisy party music in the public mind. With a changing lineup they carried on through '22, switching to Okeh that year; Sbarbaro used the name on Vocalion '35 with a sextet incl. Russ MORGAN on trombone; LaRocca, Shields and Sbarbaro were reunited in a 14-piece band and with Edwards as the Original Dixieland Five on Victor '36: at this time LaRocca was interviewed by Leonard Feather and professed to believe that it was white musicians who had made the worthwhile music, and black musicians who learned from them, rather than the other way around (described by Feather in his *The Jazz Years* '86). The last gasp was a septet led by Edwards with Shields and Sbarbaro, backing vocalist Lola Bard on Bluebird '38. By then appeal was limited to old fans nostalgic for the 'jazz age': jazz itself had long since passed them by.

ORLANDO, Tony (& Dawn) (*b* Michael Cassevitis, 3 Apr. '44, NYC) R&B/pop singer. Born of Greek/Spanish parents; began in doo-wop with Four Gents and the Milos before being hired by Don Kirshner and Al Nevins as demo singer for BRILL BUILDING songwriting teams: was the first to sing 'Will You Love Me Tomorrow', 'Take Good Care Of My Baby', etc. His demo of Gerry GOFFIN and Carole KING's 'Halfway To Paradise' was top 40 hit '61 on Epic; Barry MANN and Cynthia WEIL's 'Bless You' was no. 15 same year. When Kirshner sold Aldon Music to Screen Gems Orlando departed to record with sporadic success through '60s with no further hits except top 30 'Make Believe' '69 with session group Wind. He gave black vocal treatment to white pop (voice similar to Ben E. KING) but seldom got credit, eventually settling into music publishing executive role. Approached by ex-Token Hank Medress with song 'Candida' he recut the vocal as a favour, specifying anonymous release, choosing name Dawn from a daughter of a Bell Records promo man; smash no. 3 USA/9 UK resulted. Telma Hopkins (*b* '48, Louisville, Ky.) and Joyce Vincent (*b* '46, Detroit), both ex-Stax/Motown session vocalists, recruited as Orlando was tempted out from behind his desk; follow-up 'Knock Three Times' was no. 1 USA/UK. Twelve USA top 40 hits followed, often soul covers (Sam COOKE's 'Cupid', etc.), also appalling schmaltz ('Tie A Yellow Ribbon Round The Ole Oak Tree', US/UK no. 1 '73). From late '73 label credit was Tony Orlando & Dawn; another USA no. 1 was revival of Jerry BUTLER '60 hit 'He Will Break Your Heart', retitled 'He Don't Love You (Like I Love You)' '75. His career with Dawn had little street credibility, but there was much poetic justice in 20 Hot 100 entries '70-7, a late success for one of the better white soul vocalists.

ORLEANS USA soft rock/harmony group formed '72 by session guitarist/songwriter John Hall (worked with Taj MAHAL, Loudon WAINWRIGHT III, Al KOOPER etc.), Larry Hoppen guitar, Wells Kelly on drums and keyboards (*d* 29 Oct. '84, London), both ex-Boffalongo. Made reputation in bars from Ithaca to Woodstock in NY state; LP *Orleans* '73 incl. all John/Joanna Hall songs laid out style of harmony pop with class. Switched from ABC to emergent Asylum label for *Let There Be Music* '75, with Lance Hoppen added on bass. Single 'Dance With Me', attractive acoustic (and almost *a cap-*

pella), was no. 6 hit '75. 'Still The One' made top 5 '76, from *Waking And Dreaming* LP which added drummer Jerry Marotta, Hall and Hoppen now reinforcing added musical muscle with dual lead guitars in almost Allmanesque style. After *Before The Dance* '77 Marotta and Hall left together; third Boffalonga alumnus Bob Leinbach on keyboards, R. A. Martin on horns joined; *Forever* '79 had no. 11 single 'Love Takes Time', but that was the last hit. *One Of A Kind* '82 saw Marotta return. Hall carried on with John Hall band, featured in film *No Nukes* '80, had minor hit with its theme 'Power'. Hall and wife Joanna have written for Janis JOPLIN ('Half Moon'), Tymes ('Ms Grace'), others; made solo LPs through early '80s. On demise of Orleans Kelly joined MEATLOAF, but died of drug OD.

ORLONS, The Vocal group formed in Philadelphia c.'59. Originally a girl quintet in junior high school; lead singer Shirley Brickley (*b* 9 Dec. '44) re-formed with Steve Caldwell (*b* 22 Nov. '42), Rosetta Hightower (*b* 23 June '44), Marlena Davis (*b* 4 Oct. '44), gigged with the Cashmeres, which became the Dovells; that group's lead singer Len Barry (*b* Leonard Borisoff, 6 Dec. '42) recommended them to their label Cameo-Parkway; they began recording '60, hit the USA top 20 five times '62-3 with 'The Wah Watusi', 'Don't Hang Up', 'South Street' (all top 4), 'Not Me' and 'Cross Fire!'. They sang on records by labelmates Dee Dee Sharp, Bobby RYDELL; had more minor hits '63-4. Caldwell left to manage a group; Brickley led the girl trio with less success until Hightower left to marry an English musician, re-formed again later and was gigging in Philadelphia '80s with Jimmy Lewis and Ella Webster. The Dovells were a male doo-wop quintet whose biggest hits were 'Bristol Stomp' and 'You Can't Sit Down' '61-2; Barry had solo top 40 hits on Decca '65-6 incl. '1-2-3'.

ORTIZ, Luis 'Perico' (*b* 26 Dec. '49, Santurce, Puerto Rico) Virtuoso trumpeter; multi-instrumentalist, arranger, producer, composer, bandleader, label boss; one of salsa's key figures since '70s, his style blending tipico Latin music with modern urban jazz-inflected salsa, other elements. Studied at Puerto Rico Music Conservatory, pro

debut at 17 playing trumpet with Mario Ortiz; also played in backing bands for Engelbert HUMPERDINCK, Sammy DAVIS Jr, Trini LOPEZ, etc.; to NYC '72, worked for Tito PUENTE, Mongo SANTAMARIA (arranged, played flute and timbales). He arr. tracks on Ismael Miranda's first solo album and *Roberto Roena y su Apollo Sound 6* '74; played trumpet on LPs by FANIA ALL STARS, Ismael Quintana, Celia CRUZ and Johnny PACHECO '74-5; subsequently arr. and/or played for FAS, Roena, Sonora Ponceña, Hector LAVOE, Cheo FELICIANO, Willie COLON and Rubén BLADES, Tipica 73, Pacheco, Tommy OLIVENCIA, etc.; in '78 he contributed to albums by Lavoe, Pete 'El Conde' Rodriguez, Larry HARLOW; arr. hits from Colon-Blades *Siembra* in '78, the biggest-selling salsa album ever, and prod. *Fuera del Mundo/Out Of This World* for charanga Tipica Ideal; made debut as bandleader at NYC's Corso Club and was named Best Trumpeter of the Year by *Latin NY* magazine, but his own first LP *My Own Image* on Turnstyle that year disappointed, made with 27 NYC session players (incl. Blades on acoustic guitar). Crisp, polished salsa LPs *Super Salsa* '78 and *One Of A Kind* '79 on New Generation with lead singer Rafael De Jesus were an improvement: he was named Best Trumpeter, Best Arranger, Best New Band and Best Musician in Latin NY critics awards '79; these were followed by *Lo Mejor* and *El Astro* '81. He prod. and played on the charanga LP *Inspiraciones* by Gene Hernandez y Novedades on Alegre, arr. Colon's 'Nueva York' (Fania LP *Solo*), worked with Justo Betancourt, Ernie Agosto, Conjunto Clasico. He prod., played, sang in the chorus, wrote some of the arr. on successful LPs by smoky-voiced singer Santiago Ceron (*b* Dominican Republic, to NYC '63, three LPs with Arsenio Rodriguez): debut *Tumbando Puertas*, then *Navegando en Sabor, Canta si va' Cantar* '80-1, all on Salsa International. He played and co-arr. (with Alfredo Valdes Jr) on *Charlie Rodriguez y su Conjunto – Canta: Ray Reyes* '80, others. Own LPs on new Perico label, playing, producing, writing, arranging, singing in chorus, occasional lead; horns incl. two trumpets doubling on flugelhorn, two trombones: *Sabroso!* '82, *Sabor Tropical* '83 (Perico also played flute), *El Isleño* '84 (three trombones added) incl. lead singer Roberto Lugo. Perico prod. and dir. *Entre Amigos* '84 on Collectors Series with Lugo, Blades, Rafael Ithier and members of Dominican merengue band Conjunto Quisqueya; Perico's *La Vida en Broma* '85 incl. Lugo, introduced new lead singer Domingo Quiñones, from Ceiba, Puerto Rico (Lugo made solo debut *Este Es . . . Roberto Lugo* '86 on Sonotone). Perico's *In Tradition* '86 incl. Quiñones and incorporated fusion elements such as synths played by Oscar Hernandez (from Blades' band; Blades wrote sleeve note); *Breaking The Rules* '87 continued in that vein, the first 48-track recording in the Latin music industry.

ORY, Kid (*b* Edward Ory, 25 Dec. 1886, La Prince, La.; *d* 23 Jan. '73, Hawaii) Trombone, bandleader. Multi-instrumentalist who began on banjo at 10, organised a band playing home-made instruments; he played with Buddy BOLDEN, took his own band to New Orleans c.'11, variously employed Mutt Carey, Louis ARMSTRONG, King OLIVER, Johnny DODDS, Jimmie NOONE, Sidney BECHET, George LEWIS in one of the most successful bands in the city. To West Coast '19 on doctor's advice; formed band there and was the first black jazz band to record '22 (*see* JAZZ). Gave the group to Carey and went to Chicago '25 to record with Louis Armstrong on Hot Five sides incl. his own composition 'Muskrat Ramble', later a dixieland staple; played '25-7 with Oliver (on alto sax at first), many other bands, returned to West Coast '30, played with Carey, spent most of the decade running a chicken farm with his brother. He was a master of the New Orleans 'tailgate' trombone style (so called because the trombonist aimed his slide over the tailgate of the wagon in N.O. streets, so as not to knock anybody's hat off), playing rhythmic bass part in the 'front line', but also soloing in a gruff, hearty way. As the revival period got underway he came back to music with a Barney BIGARD band mid-'42, played string bass, alto sax, cornet but went back to trombone after exposure on Orson Welles' radio programmes about jazz '44. He led successful bands through the '50s, mostly in Cal., often at Disneyland, but also overseas tours, jazz festivals; he retired and moved to Hawaii '66. He played in New Orleans at a festival '71. He appeared in films *New Orleans* '46 (reunited with Armstrong, also recorded with him again), also as bandleader in *Crossfire* '47, *Mahogany Magic* '50, *The Benny Goodman Story* '56. Albums on Good Time Jazz also feature him on occasional vocals: *Kid Ory's Creole Jazz Band 1944-45* incl. Carey, Omer SIMEON, Bud Scott on guitar, drummer Minor Hall and clarinettist Darnell Howard on some tracks; *1954* incl. Hall, Don EWELL, Alvin Alcorn on trumpet, George Probert on clarinet, Ed Garland on bass, Bill Newman on guitar; *1955* has Newman replaced by Barney KESSEL; *The Legendary Kid* '55 has Alcorn, Hall, Wellman BRAUD on bass, three others. A much-loved veteran: during the revival, Ory didn't have to revive anything; he'd been there when it all happened.

OSADEBE, Osita (*b* Stephen Osita Osadebe, '36, Atani, near Onitsha, Nigeria) Singer, composer, guitarist, bandleader; one of Nigeria's most popular highlife musicians, with more than 20 albums to his credit. Joined Stephen Amache's band '59, later played with the Central Dance Band; formed own Soundmakers International '64. Strongly infl. by the traditional Ibo highlife of the '50s-60s, he innovates within that tradition, refusing to adulterate his music with other styles and sounds; he has recorded for the Philips/Phonogram/Polydor record labels for over 20 years. *Osadebe* '75 was followed by two vols. of *Osadebe* '76, two of *Osadebe* '77; a series of albums were dedicated to the various social clubs that flourish among the Ibo, e.g. *People's Club Special*. *Onu Kwulonjo* '81 went gold; *Onye Ije Anatago* '82 celebrated the return from exile of Emeka Ijukwu; Governor Jim Nwobodo of Anambra State was honoured by *Jim's Special*; other hits of the '80s: *Igakam Ogongo, Onye Kwusia Olie Onliya, Onyeiwe Ewetaro; Osondi Owendi* '84 sold 750,000 copies, earned special award from Polygram.

OSBORNE BROTHERS Bobby Osborne, mandolin and tenor vocals (*b* 7 Dec. '31, Hyden, Ky.), and Sonny Osborne, 5-string banjo and baritone vocals (*b* 29 Oct. '37, Hyden) have led the bluegrass act which over the years has attracted the larger country music audience. The family moved to Dayton, Ohio '42; Bobby made his pro debut on WPFB in Middletown, Ohio '49, moved to West Va. and joined the Lonesome Pine Fiddlers; while he served in US Marines '51-3, Sonny appeared on the Grand Ole Opry '50, joined Bill MONROE '52, worked with Jimmy MARTIN '53; the Osborne Brothers were formed '53, recording for King '53, RCA '54-5, MGM '56-63. They were regulars on WWVA Wheeling Jamboree '56-64, were one of the first bluegrass groups appearing on college dates '59. A distinctive three-part harmony sound was perfected when Bennie Birchfield joined '59, later replaced by Ronnie Reno, then Dale Sledd, in late '70s by Jim Brock, then Bobby Osborne Jr. Bluegrass fans were shocked when they adopted a progressive image, using electric instruments, steel guitar and drums, but this led to TV spots, folk festivals, contract with Decca '63 and Grand Ole Opry spot '64. Chart breakthrough with 'Up This Hill And Down' '66 followed by further hits 'Rocky Top' '68, 'Tennessee Hound Dog' '69, 'Georgia Pinewoods' '71. They appeared in films *Music City USA* and *Road To Nashville* '66, guested on WILBURN Bros TV show, Porter WAGONER show, Midwestern Hayride. They switched to CMH label mid-70s. Albums incl. *Country Pickin' and Hillside Singing* '60 And *Cuttin' Grass* '61 on MGM; *Voices In Bluegrass* '65, *Modern Sound Of Bluegrass* '67, *Rube-eeee* '70, *Country Roads* '73, *Pickin' Grass And Singin' Country* '74, all on Decca/MCA; *From Rocky Top To Muddy Bottom* '76, *Essential Bluegrass* (with Mac WISEMAN) '78, *Bobby Osborne & His Mandolin* '82 on CMH.

OSIBISA African pop/Afro rock fusion band, formed London '69, still one of the most commercially successful African bands of all time, with their 'criss-cross rhythms which explode with happiness'. Teddy Osei (sax, flute, drums; singer) was born in Kumasi, Ghana; qualified as a building inspector, turned to music and formed his first band The Comets '58: big hit 'Pete Pete' '59 from LP *Afro-Rhythm Parade 1*. To London '62; after some hardship was awarded scholarship to study music by government of Ghana, formed band Cat's Paws and developed his plan of breaking black music down to its constituents and starting from there. In '69 his brother Mac Tontoh (trumpet, flugelhorn; ex-Comets, Uhurus) and old friend Sol Amarfio (drums, bongos; ex-StarGazers, Rhythm Aces) came to London and Osibisa was formed (named after osibisaba, the Fanti word for highlife). They were joined by Nigerian Lasisi Amoa on congas/sax, West Indians Spartacus R on bass, Wendell Richardson on guitar and vocals, Robert Bailey on keyboards. First hit was 'Music For Gong Gong' '70; they made albums *Osibisa* '71, *Woyaya* and *Heads* '72 on MCA, *Happy Children* '73 and *Osibirock* '74 on WB, *Welcome Home* on Island; also soundtrack to blaxploitation film *Superfly TNT* '73 on Buddah. All charted in USA, where records sold better than in UK; other albums incl. *Black Magic Night*, *Ojah Awake*; they made UK singles chart twice '76 with 'Sunshine Day' and 'Dance The Body Music'. There are few countries they haven't visited, highlights incl. tours of Australia, Japan, Africa, USA, Nigerian FESTAC '77, Zimbabwe independence celebrations '80. Many changes in personnel but the three Ghanaians have remained constant, Kiki Gyan and Alfred Bannerman among those who've passed through. Recent offerings incl. *Mystic Nights* '80, *Mystic Energy* '81, *Osibisa Unleashed* '82, *Live At The Marquee* '83. Art Garfunkel covered Amarfio's song 'Woyaya' '76; Osei and Tontoh collaborated with other Ghanaian stars on album *Pete Pete*.

OSMONDS, The Mormon children taught music by their parents: Alan (*b* 22 June '49), Wayne (*b* 28 Aug. '51), Merrill (*b* 30 Apr. '53), Jay (*b* 2 Mar. '55), Donny (*b* Donald Clark Osmond, 9 Dec. '57), Marie (*b* 13 Oct. '59), all from Ogden, Utah, and Jimmy (*b* 16 Apr. '63, Canoga Park, Cal.). The four oldest visited Disneyland '62 wearing identical suits and sang barbershop harmony; recommended to Andy WILLIAMS by his father, they were regulars on his TV show for four years; also appeared on the Jerry LEWIS TV show, toured with Pat BOONE, etc. The five oldest had 11 hit singles and 12 hit LPs '71-8 in USA, joined towards the end by the two youngest. Donny was the darling of the teenyboppers, with 15 hit singles, 10 LPs; Donny and Marie had their own TV show '76-8, had seven hit duet singles, six chart LPs; Jimmy had a successful solo career for about a year when he was 9 (particularly popular in Japan). Their live act caused hysteria among teenyboppers; they were said to have sold more pictures of themselves than records; when they were too old for that they disappeared from the pop charts, but the brothers were still working mid-'80s, had minor country hit 'Any Time' '85. 'Merrill and Jessica' (Boucher) cut country duet 'You're Here To Remember, I'm Here To Forget' '87. Donny and Marie did TV adverts for Hawaiian Punch early '80s; he starred in revival of George M. COHAN show *Little Johnny Jones* '82 (ran for one night); he was making an album '87 with African prod. George Acogny, his first for nearly 10 years. Marie made debut at age 3 on Andy Williams show, published *Marie Osmond's Guide To Beauty And Dating* late '70s, wed basketball star Steve Craig '82, divorced '85; remains successful in country charts: had no. 1 country hit '73 (top 5 pop) with 'Paper Roses' (first published '60, hit by Anita BRYANT; nominated for Grammy as Best Country Song '74); of her four solo chart LPs '73-7 three were prod. by Sonny JAMES; duet with Dan Seals '85 'Meet Me In Montana' was no. 1; LPs *There's No Stopping Your Heart* '85, *I Only Wanted You* '86 both charted well, both had hit title singles.

O'SULLIVAN, Gilbert (*b* Raymond O'Sullivan, 1 Dec. '46, Waterford, Ireland) MOR singer/songwriter. He attended art school in Swindon; sent tapes to record companies, landed deal with CBS and moved to London. Two flop singles on CBS, one on Major Minor; worked as postal clerk. Signed with Management Agency And Music early '70 and became family pet of Gordon Mills, manager of Tom JONES and Engelbert HUMPERDINCK. 'Nothing Rhymed' was top 10 hit UK late '70; of 14 hits on MAM label '70-5, seven were top 10, 'Alone Again (Naturally)' was no. 1 USA/3 UK, 'Clare' (after Mills' child) and 'Get Down' were no. 1 UK, top 10 USA; top 10 LPs UK '71-4 incl. *Himself*, no. 1 *Back To Front, I'm A Writer Not A Fighter, Stranger In My Own Back Yard*; but O'Sullivan lived on an allowance, royalties from songs and records tied up, unable even to gig live

without Mills' permission; Mills moved to USA to look after Jones as O'Sullivan's hits slowed down: *Back To Front* had grossed £1,700,000, O'Sullivan received £60,000. After legal action he recovered title to his songs (some now MOR evergreens), back royalties of nearly £2,000,000 early '85, a music business horror story described in *Expensive Habits* '86 by Simon Garfield. In face of injunction threat from MAM, he made LPs *Off Centre* '80 (top 20 UK hit 'What's In A Kiss?'), *Life And Rhymes* '82 on CBS.

OTIS, Johnny (*b* '21, Vallejo, Cal.) Drums, vibes, leader, composer, music publisher, etc. Greek parents named Veliotes ran a grocery store in a neighbourhood that became a ghetto; he grew up black and remained black. Took up drums '39, worked with many bands incl. Harlan LEONARD, recorded with Lester YOUNG on Aladdin. Own big band in L.A. Club '45; hit with 'Harlem Nocturne' on Excelsior label from first recording session; smaller group from '47 as Big Band Era ended; became one of the inventors of rhythm & blues; co-owned Barrel House club '48-50; masterminded hits by Mel Walker, Little Esther, own group for Savoy: 11 R&B hits '50-2 incl. two at no. 1, but he did not see much money. Wrote 'Every Beat Of My Heart' for Jackie WILSON and the Royals '51, but nothing happened: smash hit ten years later for Gladys KNIGHT and the Pips. Recorded with Ben WEBSTER on Mercury '53. Recorded for Peacock '54, prod. Johnny ACE, Big Mama THORNTON: she recorded 'Hound Dog', Otis helping LEIBER & STOLLER to write it. He later said they cut him out when the money from the Elvis PRESLEY version '56 started coming. Discovered Etta JAMES '55, wrote 'Roll With Me, Henry', an answer to Hank BALLARD's 'Work With Me, Annie'; James recorded it, Georgia GIBBS covered it as 'Dance With Me, Henry', one of the biggest hits of the year, royalties split among Otis, James, Ballard. He had a daily DJ radio show and a weekly TV show for live music in L.A. '50s, touring R&B revue The Johnny Otis Show. He learned the 'shave-and-a-haircut, six-bits' rhythm mid-'40s from pianist/leader Count Otis Matthews, who had come to Berkeley, Cal. mid-'30s from Mississippi; it was popularised by Bo DIDDLEY, but Otis cashed in with 'Willie And The Hand Jive' '58, top 10 R&B and pop hit: The Johnny Otis Show had further Hot 100 entries 'Crazy Country Hop', 'Castin' My Spell' (vocal by Marci Lee), 'Mumblin' Mosie' '58-60, UK hits 'Ma He's Making Eyes At Me' and 'Bye Bye Baby' (vocals by Marie Adams) '57-8, all on Capitol. Formed Dig label '50s to promote new talent, but no luck; formed Blues Spectrum label mid-'70s for compilations of Louis JORDAN, Charles BROWN, Johnny Otis, etc.; published book *Listen To The Lambs* after Watts riot '65. Album *Cold Shot* '68 on Kent was debut of 13-year-old Shuggie Otis (*see below*), incl. R&B hit 'Country Girl'. Compilations incl. 2-disc sets *The Original Johnny Otis Show* in Savoy Roots of Rock'n'Roll series, *Great Rhythm And Blues Vol. 3* on Bulldog, *Rock'n' Roll Revue* on Charly, *The Johnny Otis Show* on Capitol (from France), *The New Johnny Otis Show* on Alligator/Sonet '82.

OTIS, Johnny Jr 'Shuggie' (*b* 30 Nov. '53, L.A.) Blues-rock guitarist, son of Johnny OTIS (above). Played bass professionally at 12, sessioned on bass, guitar, harmonica, keyboards at 13, incl. guitar on Johnny's album *Cold Shot* on Kent; sought out by Al KOOPER for *Kooper Session* '68 on Columbia; own LPs *Here Comes Shuggie Otis* '70, *Freedom Flight* '71, *Inspiration Information* and *Omaha Bar-B-Que* '75 on Epic. Sessioned on bass on Frank ZAPPA LP *Hot Rats*, played on LP by violinist Sugarcane Harris; has been mostly retired for personal reasons, except for session work on Johnny's Blues Spectrum label, appearance with The New Johnny Otis Show '81.

OTWAY, John (*b* 2 Oct. '52, Princes Risborough, UK) Punk-era singer specialising in bizarre humour. Early partnership with guitarist Wild Willy Barrett. Cut flop tracks prod. by Pete Townshend '74, worked as dustman until punk explosion and endearing anarchy of '(Cor Baby That's) Really Free' (top 30 UK '77). Debut album *John Otway & Wild Willy Barrett* '77 incl. much mania, but also charming 'Geneve'; live act was sensation, with Otway hurling himself around stage. *Deep & Meaningless* '78 incl. 'Beware Of The Flow-

ers (Cos I'm Sure They're Gonna Get You, Yeah)'; *Way & Bar* '80 had minor hit with electro-funk 'DK50/80'; *Gone With The Bin: The Best Of Otway & Barrett* was compilation as they split; disappointing solo *Where Did I Go Right?* '79 was prod. by Neil Innes; *All Balls & No Willy* '82 was an improvement, with crazy cover of Roy ORBISON's 'In Dreams'. *Deep Thought* '80 was a USA release, compiled from three LPs and incl. two Townshend tracks from '74; a Stiff EP *I Did It Otway* incl. sendup of 'Green Green Grass Of Homes', also incl. on *John Otway's Greatest Hits* '86, cleverly done up like an expensive Japanese import. He undertook TV adverts, fringe theatre; Barrett still gigs with own band, released *Organic Bondage* '86. They provided fun during the selfconscious earnestness of the punk era.

OUEDRAOGO, Hamidon (*b* '40, Dori, Burkina Fasso) Singer, composer, guitarist, known throughout Sahel region of West Africa as 'La Vedette Voltaïque' and 'Le Chanteur de Sahel'. Inspired by his guitarist father; worked as a pharmacist in the capital, Ouagadougou, but returened to his village and worked in a garage '57-60, teaching himself harmonica, then accordion. Singing in French, Peulh and More, won first prize in national cultural festival '70, now sings with and composes for L'Orchestra Rythme de Yalenga. LPs incl. *Pozo Zaiga* '76, *Kodol* '77.

OUTLAWS, The Southern rock band formed in Tampa, Fla. late '60s; became one of the last in genre to make national mark on signing to new Arista label. Like LYNYRD SKYNYRD, MOLLY HATCHET, possessed multi-guitar front line: Hughie Thomasson and Billy Jones, leads, Henry Paul, rhythm; other members were Monte Yoho, drums, Frank O'Keefe, bass. More vocal-based than contemporaries though, allying EAGLES-style harmonies to hard-driving guitars. *Outlaws* '75 was refreshingly uptempo debut, prod. by Paul Rothchild (DOORS, etc.), incl. top 30 hit 'There Goes Another Love Song'. Opened for STONES, WHO, etc. but failed to improve on promising vinyl debut: after similar *Lady In Waiting* '76, *Hurry Sundown* '77 (O'Keefe replaced by Harvey Arnold, Paul by Freddy

Salem; Paul had some success as Henry Paul Band: *Grey Ghost* '79, *Feel The Heat* '80). *Bring It Back Alive* '78 packaged the live act, with second drummer David Dix added, playing on alone as Yoho left. *Playing To Win* '78, *In The Eye Of The Storm* '79, *Ghost Riders In The Sky* '80 (title track second and last top 40 single) followed by *Los Hombres Malo*, by which time Thomasson was the only original member left. The sound remained the same, however; as with STATUS QUO in the UK, this was at once their strength and weakness. *High Tides Forever* '82 was a compilation; re-formed '86 for *Soldiers Of Fortune* with Paul, Thomasson.

OVERSTREET, Tommy (*b* 10 Sep. '37, Oklahoma City, Okla.) Country singer with smooth baritone, easy-listening feel, as befits a cousin of popular '20s crooner Gene AUSTIN. Began as Tommy Dean on Saturday morning TV show in Houston, Texas; attended U. of Texas '56-7, served in US Army, toured with Austin '61-2, worked clubs around Texas, moved to Nashville '67, was office manager at Dot's Nashville office, began recording for Dot. Made country top 5 with 'Gwen (Congratulations)' '71, followed by top 10 hits through '76, building up reputation as top class entertainer with five-piece band the Nashville Express. Last top 5 was 'Don't Go City Girl On Me' '77. Joined Tina label '79, Elektra '79-81, AMI and Gervasi without chart success. LPs incl. *This Is Tommy Overstreet* '71 on Dot, *Welcome To My World Of Love* and *Sings Of Love* '74-5 on Ember, *'I'm A Believer* and *Live From The Silver Slipper* '76 on ABC-Dot, *I'll Never Let You Down* '79 on Elektra, *Dream Maker* '83 on Intercord.

OWENS, Bonnie (*b* Bonnie Campbell, 1 May '32, Blanchard, Okla.) Country singer; a farm girl who married two country superstars and became one of the best-known back-up singers in the business. Married Buck OWENS and one of their two sons is singer Buddy Alan (*b* 22 May '48, Tempe, Arizona); a talented yodeller, she teamed with Buck on *The Buck And Britt Show* on radio KTYL, Mesa, Arizona '48-50. They moved to Bakersfield, Cal. '51 where Bonnie took a back seat, raising the boys; they divorced '55 and she appeared occa-

sionally on *The Trading Post* on KERO TV Bakersfield '55-62. Teamed with Merle HAGGARD, recorded with him on Tally '63-5; she had solo hits 'Why Daddy Don't Live Here Anymore' and 'Don't Take Advantage Of Me', duet hit with Haggard 'Just Between The Two Of Us' '64; they married '65, signed with Capitol. She sang back-up and toured with his band the Strangers for ten years; they were named Most Promising Duet '66 by Billboard, Best Vocal Group '65 and '67 by ACM; acted in film *Killers Three* '68. They divorced '76; she continued to work handling Haggard's business affairs, occasionally singing back-up. LPs incl. *Just Between The Two Of Us* '65 (duet), *Don't Take Advantage Of Me* '65, *Lead Me On* '66, *Mother's Favourite Hymns* '68, all on Capitol.

OWENS, Buck (*b* Alvis Roger Owens, 12 Aug. '29, Sherman, Texas) Country singer, guitarist, bandleader; one of the most successful of the post-war decades. Family moved to Arizona '36; he worked as farm labourer, married '48: son Buddy Alan is a country singer; *see* Bonnie OWENS, above. Buck and Bonnie appeared on KTYL radio, Mesa, Arizona as part of *The Buck and Britt Show*; he formed Mac's Skillet Lickers, playing Arizona clubs. Working as a truck driver between Arizona and the San Joaquin Valley '50-1, decided to move to the West Coast, became lead guitarist with the Bill Woods band '51-5, leading to session work with Sonny JAMES, Wanda JACKSON and Tommy COLLINS; he toured in Collins's band, made early recordings (album *Blue Love* now on Sundown in UK), signed with Capitol '57: first country chart hit was 'Second Fiddle' '59, then top 10 hits 'Under Your Spell Again' '59, 'Above And Beyond' '60, 'Foolin' Around' '61, 'Under The Influence Of Love' '62. Duet hits with Rose MADDOX incl. 'Mental Cruelty', 'Loose Talk' '61. Throughout the '60s he enjoyed 39 chart hits, 19 at no. 1, incl. 'Act Naturally' '63 (covered by the BEATLES), 'Together Again' '64, 'I've Got A Tiger By The Tail' '65, 'Open Up Your Heart' '66. With a fast-tempo, heavily accented brand of instrumentation from his band, the Buckaroos, his clear, ringing tenor and an earnest, almost pleading style, he had the most distinctive country sound of the '60s.

The Buckaroos, formed '60, incl. Don Rich (*b* 15 Aug. '41, Olympia, Wash.; *d* 17 July '74, Morro Bay, Cal. in motorcycle accident), guitarist and fiddler with a high-piercing vocal style who qualified as music teacher before joining Owens '60, wrote songs incl. 'Waiting In Your Welfare Line', no. 1 hit for Owens '66. Rich teamed with Buddy Alan for top 20 hit 'Cowboy Convention', duet LP *We're Real Good Friends* '70-1; had his own hits as leader of the Buckaroos; CMA named him Instrumentalist of the Year '74. Doyle Holly (*b* 30 June '30, Perkins, Okla.) was a Buckaroo '63-71, following a spell with Johnny BURNETTE band '61-3; a bass player and comedian, he formed his own band the Vanishing Breed '71, later signed with Barnaby, had hits 'Queen Of The Silver Dollar' and 'Lila' '73, album *Doyle Holly* '74 prod. by Waylon JENNINGS, Ray STEVENS and Tompall GLASER. Steel guitarist Tom Brumley (*b* 11 Dec. '35, Powell, Mo.) is the son of Albert Brumley, author of 'Turn Your Radio On' and 'I'll Fly Away'; joined Buckaroos '63, went to Rick NELSON's Stone Canyon Band '63-76, now does session work. The Buckaroos were CMA Instrumental Group of the Year '67-8, along with Owens were innovators of the West Coast, California or Bakersfield sound; Owens formed Blue Book Music, Omac Artists, Buck Owens Studios: the town was called Buckersfield. He owned several radio stations, had syndicated TV show *Buck Owens Ranch House* '66-72, co-hosted TV's *Hee-Haw* with Roy CLARK, still appears on the show. He had duet hit with Buddy 'Let The World Go On A-Turnin' ' '68; Buddy had hits 'Lodi' and 'Big Mama's Medicine Show' '69-70; Owens's hits slipped in '70s; duets with Susan Raye incl. 'The Great White Horse' '70, 'Looking Back To See' '72; solo hits incl. 'Ruby (Are You Mad)' '71, no. 1 'Made In Japan' '72, 'On The Cover Of Music City News' '74. Signed with WB '75, had minor hits, returned to top 10 with 'Play Together Again, Again' '79, duet with Emmylou HARRIS. His classic hits are kept alive with updated versions by younger stars, but Owens himself still has many fans. Albums incl. *Carnegie Hall Concert* '66, *Dust On Mother's Bible* '66, *It Takes People Like You To Make People Like Me* '68, *Tall Dark Stranger* '69, *Bridge Over Troubled Water* '72, *Too Old To Cut The Mustard* '72 (with Buddy), all on Capitol; *Buck 'Em* '76 and *Our Old Mansion* '79 on WB.

OWOH, Orlando (*b* early '40s, Owo, Oyo State, Nigeria) Singer, composer, guitarist. Playing a form of Yoruba 'palm wine' highlife known as Toye music, Owoh is one of the few who stuck with highlife despite the rise of juju. His music and lyrics are very down to earth and are preferred by an older generation. He began '60 playing bongos with the Fakunle Major Band in Oshogbo, then with Keninde Adex; then moved to Lagos, where he was taught guitar by Fatai Rolling Dollar. He fought on the Federal side in the Nigerian Civil War '67-70, returned to music, forming his Omimah Band (hit single 'Oriki Ilu Oke'); constant tours of Nigeria were combined with albums on Decca such as *Labalaba Fara W'Eiye*, *In Great Britain*, *Ire Loni*, *Ajanaku Daraba*. After a dispute with Decca over royalties he recorded for Electromat, returned to Decca on the new Afrodisia label, left again '81 to record with Shanu Olu; in a new series of LPs his saucy and provocative lyrics endeared him to the public, incl. *Money For Hand, Back For Ground*, *Ileya Special*, *Apartheid* and *Ganja*. In '83 Decca released compilations, incl. *In The Sixties*.

OXFORD, Vernon (*b* 8 June '41, Benton County, Arkansas) Country singer, fiddler; with vocal style similar to Hank WILLIAMS. Father was a prize-winning fiddler; family moved to Wichita, Kansas; Vernon entered the Cowtown fiddle contest, Kansas State Championship. Led own band, worked clubs in Midwest; married '62, moved to Nashville; meeting songwriter Harlan HOWARD led to RCA contract: good records failed to make the charts and he was dropped. Unknown to him, however, he had a cult following in Europe; a club tour early '70s revealed that he was quite a star: RCA/UK issued a 2-disc album and he was re-signed to RCA in Nashville, this time making the charts with 'Shadows Of My Mind', top 20 'Redneck' '76. He was still too traditional for contemporary Nashville, and despite more minor hits he never made the big time in the USA. In Europe it was a different story, with tours '75-85 incl. visits to the UK's annual country jamboree at

Wembley. He left RCA '78 and records for Rounder. LPs incl. *Woman Let Me Sing You A Song* '66, *By Public Demand* '75, *I Just Want To Be A Country Singer* '77 on RCA; *Tribute To Hank Williams* '78 on Meteor and *Nobody's Child* '79 on Release; *His And Hers* '80 on Rounder, followed by *A Better Way Of Life, Keepin' It Country, If I Had My Wife To Love Over*. Second of these reissued on Sundown in UK '87, with all-star Nashville cast: Buddy Spicher, Lloyd GREEN, Hargus 'Pig' Robbins, Pete DRAKE, Charlie McCOY.

OYSTER BAND UK rock group. Grew out of earlier folk band Fiddler's Dram, whose 'Day Trip To Bangor' was a sizeable hit, and concurrent Oyster Ceilidh Band, who shortened the name after *Jack's Alive* '80 on Dingle's. Lead singer Cathy LeSurf went solo, recorded with ALBION BAND, FAIRPORT CONVENTION, others. They gradually mixed rock and new wave elements with a sound appreciation of UK folk over series of albums *English Rock'n'-Roll - The Early Years 1800-1850, Lie Back And Think Of England*, dance tune album *20 Golden Tie-Slackeners* and *Liberty Hall*, and '82-5 on their own Pukka label, personnel settling as John Longley Jones (*b* 19 Oct. '49, Aberystwyth, Wales), vocals and melodeon; Ian David Francis Kearey (*b* 14 Oct. '54, London), vocals, bass, guitar, banjo; Alan Prosser (*b* 17 Apr. '51, Wolverhampton), vocals and guitar; Russell Andrew Lax (*b* 14 Feb. '59, Chatham, Kent), percussion; Ian Telfer (*b.* 28 May '48, Falkirk), vocals, fiddle, winds, concertina; Alan Victor Greenwood (23 Sep. '51, Liskeard), sound. *Liberty Hall* and *Step Outside* '86 on Cooking Vinyl typified their later style; *Wide Blue Yonder* '87 on Cooking Vinyl confirmed their status, with trad. 'Molly Bond', cover of Nick LOWE's 'The Rose Of England', and strong writing: 'The Day The Ship Goes Down' and 'The Early Days Of A Better Nation' by Telfer/Jones, 'The Generals Are Born Again' by Telfer/Prosser. They toured extensively, won awards from folk voters, and had tracks on anthologies on Cooking Vinyl and Folk Roots; they backed Billy BRAGG and Leon ROSSELSON on 'Ballad Of A Spycatcher' '88.

P

PABLO, Lubadika Porthos (*b* '50s, Zaire) African singer-composer, bassist, guitarist. Played with bands in the '70s incl. Kin Bantous, Lovy du Zaire, Groupe Celibithou, and Orchestre Kara; went to Paris to play with Sam MANGWANA and the African All-Stars on classic 'Georgette Eckins', joined talented session musicians on Salsa Musique label, playing on albums by Pamelo MOUNK'A, Master Mwana Congo, Assi Kapela, pursued solo career with albums of fast, sweet soukous: *Concentration, Idie, Revient En Force, En Action.* Tracks 'Bo Mbanda' and 'Madeleina' on Island label's African compilation '81 brought wider fame; played with Les Quatre Étoiles in London '84, released first UK LP *Pablo Pablo Pablo* '85 on Globestyle. Still much sought after for sessions, while solo career goes from strength to strength.

PACHECO, Johnny (*b* 25 Mar. '35, Santiago de los Caballeros, Dominican Republic) Flautist, singer, composer, arranger, label boss, producer etc.; also sax, percussion. Played native merengues on the sinfonia de mano (a small accordion) as a child, heard charangas on Cuban radio; to NYC at age 11, grew up in the Bronx. Played tambora (a double-headed Dominican drum, basic to merengue) in bands while still at school, incl. a group with Dominican singer Dioris Valladares, who previously sang with accordion and sax-led group of Angel Viloria, who had introduced authentic merengue to NY Latin scene early '50s. Took up sax, played in school band with trombonist Barry Rogers (who went to work with Eddie PALMIERI, LIBRE, others); turned pro as percussionist with Tito Prado, Stan KENTON, George BENSON; played flute and sang with Xavier CUGAT; joined Charlie PALMIERI's Charanga Duboney '59, after Palmieri heard him practising flute in night club kitchens, had musical differences: Palmieri wanted to emphasise melody and orchestration, Pacheco wanted to emphasise

rhythmic figures with less orchestration; left to form Pacheco y su Charanga with a younger, brasher sound (meanwhile made LP with MACHITO band and its pianist/arranger Rene Herendez '60 reissued under Pacheco's name '81 as *Early Rhythms*). Pacheco y su Charanga played clubs, hotels, ballrooms and became the most popular charanga during the charanga/pachanga craze of '60-4. Recorded as leader on Alegre: *Pacheco y su Charanga Vol. I* '60 incl. Elliot Romero among singers, ex-Sonora Matancera, *Vol. II* c.'61 incl. Manny Oquendo (*see* LIBRE) and Afro-Cuban Jose 'Chombo' Silva on violin. Silva had toured Europe '50 with James MOODY, recorded with Cal TJADER on legendary Cuban Jam Session LPs (*see* LOPEZ, Israel 'Cachao'), also with Machito, Mongo SANTAMARIA, Ray BARRETTO, Charlie Palmieri, Alegre All Stars, etc. *Pacheco y su Charanga Vol. III – Que Suene la Flauta* '62 was reissued '78 during Charanga revival that happened as alternative to mainstream salsa; *Vol. IV – Suav'ito* c.'63 incl. black Puerto Rican lead singer Pete 'El Conde' Rodriguez: noble-looking El Conde ('The Count') became a leading salsa singer with his distinctive smoky voice, was Pacheco's main lead singer until '73. Pacheco also contributed tracks to LP *Las Charangas – Palmieri, Fajardo, Pacheco* and played on first Alegre All Stars jam session LP c.'60; *Habia una Vez/Once Upon A Time* was a Pacheco compilation on Alegre. With Jerry Masucci he formed Fania label '64, which dominated the Latin record scene for two decades by bringing along promising young artists rather that poaching acts from other labels: Larry HARLOW, Bobby VALENTIN, Joe BATAAN, many others became stars on Fania, with Pacheco as recording director on early releases. In '64 he was one of the first NY bandleaders to drop the violins/flute charanga format and adopt the pure Afro-Cuban conjunto of vocals, trumpets, piano and percussion; some said his purist sound was imitative, but it certainly reflected the joy of Cuban roots. Conjunto LPs began on Fania with *Canoñazo*, Pacheco At The New World's Fair and *Pacheco te Invita a Bailar*; the last had lead singers Monguito 'El Unico' (Ramon Quian) and Chivirico Davila instead of El Conde; they took part in *Viva Africa* c.'66, celebrating Pacheco's popularity in West Africa. Afro-Cuban Monguito, with distinctive nasal voice, had worked with Orquesta Broadway, then Arsenio Rodriguez; went on to make solo Fania LPs *Pacheco Presents Monguito, El Unico y su Conjunto, De Todo un Poco, Escuchame/Listen To Me*; worked with Larry Harlow, Herbie MANN in the late '60s, with the Fania All Stars '68 (*Live At The Red Garter*), toured Africa '80 and recorded for Abidjan-based Sacodis label, for Roberto TORRES' Toboga label '80s and released *Yo Soy la Meta* '85 on the NYC Caiman label. Monguito and Pacheco (on flute) appeared on the Tico All Stars LPs *Descargas At The Village Gate – Live* '66. *Pacheco His Flute And Latin Jam* on Fania was studio charanga jazz jam session incl. Silva on sax, Felix 'Pupi' LEGARRETA, Rogers, Valentin, singer Carlos 'Caito' Diaz from Sonora Matancera, Orestes Vilato on timbales. After *Viva Africa* Pacheco returned to his charanga sound for *Pacheco y su Charanga – By Popular Demand*, with Romero and El Conde on vocals, then back to conjunto for *Sabor Tipico, Volando Bajito* and *La Perfecta Combinacion* c.'70, the 'perfect combination' being Pacheco and El Conde: this LP introduced the tres (9-string Cuban guitar) into his conjunto, incl. 'La Esencia del Guaguanco' (written by C. Curet Alonso and one of Pacheco's all-time best tracks). *Los Compadres* (Pacheco and El Conde) was followed by *Pacheco/Betancourt – Los Dinamicos* which featured rising salsa star vocalist Justo BETANCOURT; *10 Great Years* was a Pacheco compilation; after *Tres de Cafe y Dos de Azucar* '73 El Conde left to go solo: albums *El Conde* '74, *Este Negro Si Es Sabroso* '76 incl. Alonson's 'Pueblo Latino' ('Latin People'), *A Touch Of Class* '78, *Soy la Ley* '79, *Fiesta Con 'El Conde'* '82, all on Fania, retaining the conjunto format; he also performed and recorded with the Fania All Stars from their inception, and also with Harlow, Celia CRUZ, Puente, others. His *El Maestro* '75

and *The Artists* '77 featured Afro-Cuban lead singer Hector Casanova; *Pacheco y Melon: Llego Melon* '77 incl. Mexican singer Angel Luis Silva 'Melon'; *Los Amigos* '79 had Casanova again then he too went solo with tipico trumpets and tres conjunto: albums *Casanova* '80 and *Montuno y las Muchachas* '83 on Fania, and *Casanova y Montuno: Solido* '86 on Curramba, Pacheco as mus. dir. and playing guiro; Casanova also recorded with Puente, Cruz, etc. Pacheco went on with *Johnny & Daniel: Los Distinguidos* '79 (with veteran former heart-throb Daniel Santos, vocals); *Pacheco y Monquito – La Crema, Sabrosura* and *The Champ* (all '80) were compilations; *El Zorro de Plata Presenta al Flaco de Oro* '81 featured Celio Gonzales, vocals; *Pacheco y Fajardo* '82 had both Pacheco and Jose Fajardo on flutes with a large charanga; *De Pelicula* '82 with veteran Afro-Cuban singer Roland La Serie; *De Nuevo los Compadres* '83 was a reunion with El Conde, *Flying High* '84 with Melon, *Jicamo* '85 with Conde again. He was mus. dir. of the Fania All Stars since their inception and appeared with them in London '76. The Fania empire has declined, losing the leading artists it had created, such as Colon and Rubén Blades; Pacheco has been working on albums on other labels: *Santiago Ceron – E Fenomeno* on Sabroso and *Israel Sardifias – La Verdad!* on Bacan '84, *Los Guaracheros de Oriente – Con Tumbao* '85 on Caiman, Casanova's Curramba LP. Pacheco had also collaborated with Celia Cruz on Vaya (from the Fania stable): successful albums *Celia & Johnny* '74, *Tremendo Cache* '75, *Celia, Johnny, Justo & Papo: Recordando El Ayer* '78, *Celia, Johnny And Pete* '80 (with El Conde), *De Nuevo* '85.

PAGE, Oran 'Hot Lips' (*b* Oran Thaddeus Page, 27 Jan. '08, Dallas, Texas; *d* 5 Nov. '54, NYC) Trumpet, bandleader, vocalist. Began on reeds, switched to trumpet at age 12; worked in oil fields in Texas; in band accompanying Bessie SMITH, Ida COX on black vaudeville circuit, worked with Troy Floyd, other territory bands; joined Walter PAGE's Blue Devils, then Bennie MOTEN; led own quintet in Kansas City '35, with Count BASIE at the Reno Club just before Basie went to NYC and became famous, but manager Joe Glaser took over, hoping to make another star like Louis ARMSTRONG out of him. Led own big band and recorded for Decca and Bluebird '38-40. Instrumental version of 'I Let A Song Go Out Of My Heart' was a hit '38 (Bluebird tracks once compiled on an RCA LPV album '60s); worked for Artie SHAW '41-2 (sang and played on hit 'Blues In The Night') later led big band for special arrangements, often led small groups. Successful duet with Pearl BAILEY 'The Hucklebuck'/'Baby It's Cold Outside' '49. He might have been better off staying with Basie, did not add a fortune to Glaser's bank account, but he was a fine musician and a much-loved entertainer. Tracks on *Swing Street Showcase* compilation on Commodore, LP shared with Jonah JONES; also *Trumpet Battle At Minton's* '41 on Xanadu with Joe Guy.

PAGE, Patti (*b* Clara Ann Fowler, 8 Nov. '27, Oklahoma) Pop singer with 78 hits '48-62 on Mercury, a great many top tens '50-4: her distinctive vocal colour and good diction made her a natural star of the era. Sang on Chicago radio '47 with Jimmy Joy band; Joy's road manager Jack Rael became her manager, sometimes led band on her records; she appeared on then-important *Breakfast Club* on Chicago radio, sang with Benny GOODMAN Septet spring '48; first hit 'Confess' mid-'48, first top 10 'I Don't Care If The Sun Don't Shine' '50, first no. ones 'All My Love' (adapted Ravel's 'Bolero' by Mitchell Parrish), 'Tennessee Waltz' (by Redd Stewart and Pee Wee KING), both '50, then 'I Went To Your Wedding' '52: the last two were no. 1 for 13 and 10 weeks respectively, but the unrewarding nursery rhyme 'Doggie In The Window', no. 1 for only 8 weeks in '53, seemed to go on forever in music-starved era: written by Bob Merrill (*b* 17 May '21, Atlantic City, N.J.), who also wrote 'If I Knew You Were Comin' I'd've Baked A Cake', another song that drove some people crazy (*see* Eileen BARTON), and hits for Guy MITCHELL such as 'Pittsburgh, Pennsylvania', but was also capable of better work, such as *Funny Girl* (with Jule Styne; *see* Barbra STREISAND). Page had more hits, but no more chart-toppers. It was a time when song pluggers were still at work, and a new song would get more than one recording: Jo STAFFORD did 'You Belong To Me',

Joni JAMES 'Why Don't You Believe Me', Les PAUL & Mary Ford 'Mockin Bird Hill', SAUTER-FINEGAN 'Now That I'm In Love', Joan Weber 'Let Me Go, Lover!' (*see* Mitch MILLER); Page had hits with all of them, as well as 'Steam Heat' (from *The Pajama Game*), many more. Hank SNOW had a country hit with 'Wedding'; many of Page's hits had a country flavour, incl. 'Detour' and 'Mister and Mississippi' '51, 'Changing Partners' and 'Cross Over The Bridge' '53-4; along with a few more hits on Columbia (her last top 40 was film theme 'Hush, Hush, Sweet Charlotte' '65 at no. 8). She made country LPs incl. *Country Hits* on Mercury, *Gentle on my Mind* on Columbia. Along with Stafford, Kay STARR and Rosemary CLOONEY, one of the best-loved of the era; hits compilations still available include two CDs, one each on Mercury, Columbia.

PAGE, Walter (*b* 9 Feb 1900, Gellatin, Mo.; *d* 20 Dec. '57, NYC) Bassist, bandleader; one-quarter of one of the most famous rhythm sections in history: aka 'Big 4' because he was one of the first to play four beats to the bar during transition from 2/4 New Orleans heritage to smoother 4/4 of the Big Band Era. Joined Bennie MOTEN '18-23; left to tour with road show which folded, took over band which became Walter Page's Blue Devils, based in Oklahoma City '25-31: legendary outfit recorded only two sides '29 on Vocalion, with Hot Lips PAGE, Buster SMITH, Jimmy RUSHING. Handed it over to trumpeter James Simpson, went back to Kansas City, rejoined Moten '31-4, freelanced, joined Count BASIE '35-42, with Freddie GREEN on guitar, Jo JONES on drums and helped re-invent swing. With Basie again '46-8; with Hot Lips Page '49, freelanced in NYC. He made small-group recordings with Teddy WILSON, Billie HOLIDAY; *Jo Jones Special* LP on Vanguard, etc. last record date was Basie reunion group on Prestige. Died of pneumonia. 'He started that "Strolling" or "Walking" bass, going way up and then coming right on down. He did it on four strings, but other bass players couldn't get that high so they started making a five-string bass. That rhythm section would send chills up me every night' (Harry EDISON, quoted by Stanley Dance in *The World Of Count Basie*).

PAIGE, Elaine (*b* Elaine Bickerstaff, 5 Mar. '51, Barnet, Hertfordshire) UK singer, actress. Played in Anthony NEWLEY show *The Roar Of The Greasepaint*, London prod. of *Hair*, *Rock Carmen* at the Roundhouse, *Jesus Christ Superstar* '73, first leading role in *Grease*, then 18 months in *Billy*; quit to look for non-musical work and got nowhere; landed lead in LLOYD WEBBER's *Evita* '78 and became a star, both star and show showered with awards. Left after 20 months to be pop singer; LP *Sitting Pretty* (now on Music For Pleasure) incl. single 'Don't Walk Away Till I Touch You', which didn't do much. Concert hall debut '81 at Royal Festival Hall; starred that year in Lloyd Webber's *Cats* (incl. no. 5 chart hit 'Memory'); LP *Elaine Paige* '82 reached top 60 UK LPs, not bad for an artist whose fans were mostly showgoers. Had her own BBC TV special, joined Royal Gala opening of new venue the Barbican Centre; *Stages* '83 (show songs) on K-Tel in deal with WEA was no. 2 album, *Cinema* '84 no. 12. *Love Hurts* '85 on WEA again went top 10. Working with Rice on new show *Chess*, she recorded duet with Barbara DICKSON 'I Know Him So Well' for no. 1 single; *Christmas* LP '86, new singles '86 on WEA, RCA.

PALMER, Robert (*b* 19 Jan. '49, Batley, West Yorkshire, England) White soul singer. Joined first band Mandrakes at age 15; came to London as lead singer of the Alan Bown Set '68, left to join experimental jamrockers Dada '69 (LP '70 on Atco), which evolved from 12-piece lineup into Vinegar Joe (Palmer and Elkie BROOKS, vocals; Pete Gage, guitar; Pete Gavin, drums; Steve York, bass; Mike Deacon, keyboards); hard nosed R&B sound brought gigs on college/club circuit, LPs *Vinegar Joe* and *Rock'n'Roll Gypsies* '72, *Six Star General* '73 before split. Palmer made solo *Sneakin' Sally Through The Alley* '74 in New Orleans, New York with Meters, LITTLE FEAT backing, still his most cohesive work: title track (by Allen TOUSSAINT), medley of Palmer's 'Hey Julia' and Lowell George's 'Sailing Shoes' were classic white soul. *Pressure Drop* '75 incl. reggae infl. (cover of Toots Hibbert's title track); *Some People Can Do What They Like* '76 made USA top 10 LPs, coincided with move to Bahamas. *Double Fun* '78 recorded there, most com-mercial yet: still recording his own plus other people's songs, had first top 20 USA single hits with Andy Fraser's 'Every Kinda People'; second Moon Martin's 'Bad Case Of Loving You (Doctor Doctor)' from *Secrets* '79. *Clues* '80 saw partially successful venture into electro-pop: disastrous collaboration with then-hot Gary NUMAN on 'I Dream Of Wires', 'Found You Now'; first UK top 40 hit with more convincing 'Looking For Clues'. *Maybe It's Live* '82 was hodge-podge of live/studio with top 20 UK 'Some Guys Have All The Luck', cover of '73 Persuaders hit. After uneven *Pride* '83, threw in with Andy and John Taylor (not related; ex-DURAN DURAN) to form hard-rock Power Station, commercially successful but artistically questionable project for eponymous LP '85; Palmer split before Live Aid appearance (replaced by Michael Des Barres, ex-Silverhead, Chequered Past). Solo *Riptide* '85 tainted by widescreen hard-rock excess. He has flirted with electronic music, electrodisco, ballads, hard rock without fully applying himself to any of it; had loyal fans, more in Europe than in USA. 'Addicted To Love' '86 from *Riptide* was transatlantic hit, tongue in-cheek video with miming band of sexy girls; *Kick Me Out* '69 (original title *The Alan Bown Set*) reissued on See For Miles. On *Heavy Noon* '88 his eclecticism extended to '44 Johnny Burke/Jimmy Van Heusen song 'It could Happen to You'.

PALMIERI, Charlie (*b* '27, NYC; *d* Sep. '88) Pianist, bandleader, composer, A&R man, producer; a fine soloist, emphasis on the melodic in improvisation. From Puerto Rican family, grew up in the Bronx; studied piano at Juilliard; worked '40s-50s with Pupi Campo, Rafael Muñoz, Xavier CUGAT, Tito PUENTE, Tito RODRIGUEZ; also recorded with Latin-jazz group (compiled on *El Fantastico – Charlie Palmieri con su Conjunto* on Tropical). He formed Charanga Duboney late '59 with four violins, Johnny PACHECO on flute: Gilberto Valdes was unsuccessful early '50s in charanga format, but Duboney debut at a New Year's Eve dance launched a craze; they became so popular that they played several dances a night. Pacheco left to form his own group; Duboney LP debut was *Pachanga At The Caravana Club* on Alegre, followed by *Viva Palmieri* and *Salsa Na' Ma' Vol. 3*. Contributed tracks to *Las Charangas – Pacheco, Palmieri, Fajardo*; his *Echoes Of An Era* was on West Side Latino label, with vocalist Vitin Aviles. Became mus. dir. c.'60 for series of studio descarga (Latin jam session) LPs: four vols. by Alegre All Stars, inspired by the legendary *Cuban Jam Session* albums (*see* Israel 'Cachao' LOPEZ), in turn launching similar LPs by Pacheco as well as Tico, CESTA and Fania All Stars (he played piano on Tico and CESTA sessions). In the mid-'60s he joined Latin NY's 'swing to brass' and dropped violins and flute for three trumpets and two trombones; the New Duboney Orchestra incl. Bobby VALENTIN on trumpet, singer Victor Velazquez, made LP *Tengo Maquina y Voy a 60*, followed by *Hay Que Estar en Algo* and *El Hermanisimo* on Alegre; *Latin Bugalu '68* on Atlantic was prod. by Herbie MANN; apart from cashing in on BOOGALOO craze incl. Palmieri's classic composition 'Mambo Show'. Early '70s he recorded with horn section of two trumpets and Bobby Nelson doubling on sax and flute; he played organ as well as piano; best LPs were probably *El Gigante del Teclado '72*, *Vuelve el Gigante '73*, *Adelante, Gigante '75*, all on Alegre with lead singer Aviles; with his regular outfit he played organ only on *Electro Duro '74* on Coco: the organ lent an unfortunate quality of kitsch to some of his work. As prod./A&R he worked with Celia CRUZ, Puente, Rafael Cortijo, Ismael Rivera; played piano on LPs by Cruz, Ismael Quintana, Aviles, others incl. Cal TJADER (*Primo '74*), Cachao (*Dos '77*), Mongo SANTAMARIA (*Red Hot '79*); played on some of Eddie's albums. To mark 17th anniversary of Alegre All Stars '77, eight veterans of the original studio descargas plus Louie RAMIREZ on vibes, young virtuoso flautist/clarinettist/saxist Bobby Rodriguez and members of his 'up & flying' band La Compañia were assembled under Palmieri's leadership for *Perdido* (*Vol. 5 or 6?*). In '79 he was featured in Jeremy Marre's TV film *Salsa*, teaching Latin music and culture in a South Bronx school and playing electric piano with Puente. He went to Puerto Rico early '80, formed successful band but did not record; suffered heart attack and stroke which left him half-paralysed; despite gloomy medical prognosis he recovered, returned to NYC '84, made Latin jazz LP *A Giant Step* with piano, bass, timbales, conga, bongo. He was leading Combo Gigante in NYC '86 incl. two trumpets, trombone (Lewis Kahn doubling on violin), Dick Mesa on sax and flute, Nicky Marrero on timbales, former Joe CUBA vocalists Jimmy Sabater and Willie Torres. Played piano on *El Sabor del Conjunto Candela/86* on Laslos, led by bongo/güiro player Ralphy Marzan.

PALMIERI, Eddie (*b* c.'36, NYC) Pianist, bandleader, composer, arranger, producer; a charismatic figure in Latin music, one of salsa's most innovative artists, noted for fiery piano solos. From Puerto Rican family; formed Latin dance band at age 14, during '50s worked with bands of Johnny Segui, Vincentico Valdes, Tito RODRIGUEZ; left the security of Rodriguez to form his own Conjunto La Perfecta. He had met NYC trombonist Barry Rogers mid-'61, who was infl. by Kai WINDING, J. J. JOHNSON, also embraced Latin music. The craze then was violins and flute sound of charanga, but Palmieri initially formed a trumpet-led conjunto, then with Rogers developed two-trombone and flute sound which brother Charlie PALMIERI christened 'trombanga'. Debut LP *Eddie Palmieri And His Conjunto La Perfecta '62* featured trumpets, but trombanga tracks proved the most popular; other key members of band were NYC-born Puerto Rican Manny Oquendo on timbales and bongos, vocalist Ismael 'Pat' Quintana (*b* Ponce, Puerto Rico; grew up in the Bronx). *Vol. II – El Molestoso* dropped trumpets. Palmieri admired Bill EVANS, Thelonious MONK; *Lo Que Traigo Es Sabroso* incl. major hit 'Muñeca': his 'modal opening, reminiscent of McCoy TYNER, to a piano solo that developed in classically Cuban patterns; above all the strangely ambiguous brass sound, at once driving and despairing, were all hints of what was to come' (John Storm Roberts). Brazilian trombonist José Rodrigues joined '63, stayed with Palmieri into '80s. Band switched from Alegre to Tico for *Echando Pa'lante (Straight Ahead)* and *Azucar Pa' Ti (Sugar For You)* (both with hits written by Palmieri), *Mozambique* and *Molasses* mid-'60s; these were the last purely trombanga LPs, eight-piece lineup incl. George Castro on flute, Tommy Lopez on conga, bassist Dave Perez (later worked with Ray BARRETTO, TIPICA 73). La Perfecta made two LPs with Cal TJADER: *El Sonido Nuevo/The New Soul Sound* '66 on Verve, *Bamboleate* on Tico (reissued '77), the first augmented with two trombones, the second regarded by many as among Tjader's best, La Perfecta lending harder edge to his usual work. La Perfecta disbanded '68; *Champagne* '68 coincided with BOOGALOO craze, incl. 'Ay Que Rico', sung by Cheo FELICIANO; the band incl. Rogers, Israel 'Cachao' LOPEZ on bass, Alfredo 'Chocolate' ARMENTEROS on trumpet on some tracks; other vocalists were Quintana and Cynthia Ellis (who also wrote 'The African Twist'). His *Justicia* '69 reflected the mood of the civil rights era: instrumental 'Verdict On Judge Street', ironic vocal on Leonard BERNSTEIN's 'Somewhere' by electric guitarist Bob Bianco, and a rare vocal from Palmieri himself on 'Everything Is Everything'. *Superimposition* had one side of experimental Latin instrumentals, followed by his last studio LP on Tico, *Vamonos Pa'l Monte* c.'71, introducing Ronnie Cuber on sax, Palmieri on electric piano, brother Charlie guesting on organ. A fusion experiment with black R&B group Harlem River Drive was heard on 'Azucar (Part 2 and 3)' from *Live At Sing-Sing* '72; *Live At Sing-Sing Vol-2* '74 had Charlie on organ; compilations on Tico '74-7 were *Lo Mejor de Eddie Palmieri*, *The History Of Eddie Palmieri*, *Eddie's Concerto*, *The Music Man*. He switched to Coco for *Sentido* '73, the last with Quintana in '70s (Quintana made solo LPs incl. *Punto y Aparte* late '60s on UA; *Ismael Quintana* '74 on Vaya incl. Palmieri sidemen Rogers and Lewis Kahn on trombones, Nicky Marrero on timbales, plus Papo Lucca, Bobby VALENTIN, others; he performed and recorded with Fania All Stars, contributed tracks to Tito PUENTE *Homenaje a Beny* LPs '78-9, did his own *Lo Que Estoy Viviendo* '76, *Amor, Vida y Sentimiento/Love, Life and Feelings* '77, *Ismael Quintana con Ricardo Marrero and the Group – Jessica* '79, *Quintana y Papo – Mucho Talento* '83, all on Vaya). 2-disc *Eddie Palmieri & Friends In Concert Live At The University Of Puerto Rico* '73 was a '71 recording made on non-professional equipment, polished in the stu-

dio, incl. remakes of many hits. His idiosyncratic amalgam of raw salsa and experimentalism brought continued success, incl. the first Grammy for a Latin LP for *Sun Of Latin Music* '74, mixing dance hits arr. by René Hernandez with avant-garde arr. by Rogers; this band had Rogers and Rodrigues on trombone, two trumpets (Victor Paz on lead), baritone sax and flute, young Puerto Rican Lalo Rodriguez singing lead, Alfredo de la Fé on violin. *Unfinished Masterpiece* '76 mixed Cuban rhythms, descarga (Latin jam session) and jazz; compilations were *Gold 1973-76* and *Exploration* '78 on Coco, *Timeless – Live Recording* '81 (mid-'60s trombanga). He went to Epic label with *Lucumi Macumba Voodoo* '78, theme of African-derived religions of Cuba, Brazil, Haiti mixed with R&B elements and diverse instrumentation: unsuccessful commercially, perhaps because of Epic's and the Latin market's unfamiliarity with each other. *Eddie Palmieri* '81 on Barbaro (label part of Musica Latina International Inc., incl. Fania) reunited Palmieri, Feliciano, Quintana, was dedicated to arr. Hernandez, who had died recently; *Palo Pa' Rumba* '84 incl. all Puerto Rican musicians, with three trumpets, three trombones, Charlie on percussion; with *Solito* '85 it incl. older hits reworked; both won Grammies. Palmieri also played on three vols. of Tico All Stars' *Descargas At The Village Gate – Live* '66, two of FANIA ALL STARS' *Live At The Red Garter* '68; made London debut '86. *La Verdad/The Truth* '87 on Fania was made in Puerto Rico: side one features vocalist Tony Vega, side two instrumentals.

PARAMOR, Norrie (*b* '14, England; *d* 9 Sep. '79) Conductor, composer, arranger, A&R man, producer. Left school at 15, worked as office boy, soon playing accompaniment for Gracie FIELDS, then top dance bands; mus. dir. for Ralph Reader Gang shows during WWII; teamed post-war with tenor saxist Harry Gold in Pieces of Eight, writing some of the material (with Geoff Love, who later sold many records under his own name, and pseudonym Manuel and the Music of the Mountains). Gold and the current Eight are still active, toured UK '85 in Bing CROSBY biographical show. Through '50s to '68 Paramor was A&R manager for

EMI Columbia, guiding record careers of Cliff RICHARD, Frank IFIELD, the SHADOWS, Sacha DISTEL, Helen SHAPIRO, many more; top 20 with instrumental Big Ben Banjo Band mid-'50s, under his own name with 'Theme From Summer Place', 'Theme From Z Cars' (then-innovative UK TV cop show) early '60s; also scored several British films; mus. dir. of BBC Midland Radio Orchestra from '72. Mood music *In London In Love* '56 charted in USA.

PARKER, Charlie (*b* Charles Christopher Parker Jr, 29 Aug. '20, Kansas City, Kansas; *d* 12 Mar. '55, NYC) Alto sax, composer, bandleader. Grew up in Kansas City, Missouri; later nicknamed 'Yardbird' (for chicken), 'Bird' for short. Father was an entertainer in small-time black vaudeville, a father figure of the imagination but rarely present; his mother effectively spoiled him. He began on alto c.'31, played baritone horn in school band; left school at 15, soon became a drug addict. Treated with derision by older musicians (on one occasion Jo JONES was said to have thrown a cymbal at him) he practised (perhaps not knowing that he only needed a few chords to play in a band) until he could modulate from any key to any other key; returning from an out-of-town gig his technique was suddenly greatly improved. First influenced by local musicians Buster SMITH and Lester YOUNG, he became a key creator of bop: though the musical ideas were in the air, and others incl. Dizzy GILLESPIE were doing much the same thing, his technique and greatness as a composer combined to make Parker one of the greatest troubadors in history, able to improvise endlessly, continuously inventing melody: he is the most infl. and imitated soloist in 20th-century music after Louis ARMSTRONG. Worked for Jay MCSHANN and Harlan LEONARD '37-9, meeting Tadd DAMERON in Leonard's band, also soon acquiring reputation for unreliability; first went to NYC '39, washed dishes for three months at a club where Art TATUM was playing. Playing 'Cherokee' during a gig in Harlem, he first improvised on the upper intervals of the chords instead of the lower: the new line required new harmonic resolutions and he heard the music he'd been hearing in his head. Returned to K.C. for his father's funeral; back

in NYC he first recorded, with McShann's band '41 (now on MCA USA/Affinity UK; recordings made at a radio station in Wichita, Kansas have also been issued as *Early Bird* on Spotlite UK); left McShann and stayed in NYC, jamming at Minton's, playing in bands of Noble SISSLE (on clarinet as well as alto), Earl HINES (on tenor; band also incl. Gillespie), Cootie WILLIAMS, Andy KIRK, Billy ECKSTINE; made first small-group sides late '44 with Tiny GRIMES, early '45 in quintet with Gillespie (now on complete Savoy sessions in five vols. UK; 2-disc selection in USA). He was already a hero among musicians, but critics' record of opposition to anything new in jazz was not spoiled. To Billy Berg's club in Los Angeles late '45 with band incl. Gillespie, Milt JACKSON, Al HAIG, Ray BROWN, drummer Stan Levey (*b* 4 Apr. '25): both club and group integrated; Parker's and Gillespie's reputations had preceded them, but the West Coast audience for the new music was small. He recorded for Dial, had a complete breakdown, was arrested, sent to Camarillo State Hospital for six months from July '46: soft regime, decent food helped him to recover; he made some of the best sides of his career for Dial early '47, one session incl. Erroll Garner, vocalist Earl Coleman; another Howard MCGHEE and Wardell GRAY (complete Dial sessions now on Spotlite UK). Back to NYC he led racially integrated quintet, sidemen variously incl. Red RODNEY, Kenny DORHAM, Miles DAVIS on trumpets, pianists Haig, Duke JORDAN; Tommy Potter on bass (*b* Charles Thomas Potter, 21 Sep. '18, Philadelphia Pa.; worked in civil service '70s, continued freelancing); drummers Max ROACH, Roy HAYNES; Lucky THOMPSON often a guest. Worshipful followers like Dean Benedetti made bootleg recordings on a portable recording machine (e.g. *Bird On 52nd Street* '48, *Bird At St Nicks* '50, now on Fantasy or in Prestige 2-disc set. Benedetti's lost recordings have been rediscovered and are to be issued on Mosaic.) Parker played with Norman GRANZ' JATP, recorded for Mercury, Verve incl. Afro-Cuban jazz with MACHITO (though Gillespie was more attuned to this music than Parker; *see* CUBOP) and with strings and woodwinds from '50 he was proud of the records with strings, as though they lent legitimacy to his music (complete *Bird On Verve* on eight vols.). Other sessions incl. Miles Davis date at Prestige, Bird playing tenor (as 'Charlie Chan' because of Mercury contract) and famous concert at Toronto's Massey Hall in May '53 with Gillespie, Roach, Charles MINGUS, Bud POWELL issued on Mingus/Roach Debut label (now on Fantasy, or 2-disc Prestige set with Powell trio from same concert); *One Night In Washington DC* is a remarkably successful big-band set '53 not issued for 25 years, now on Elektra. Every scrap and alternate take of Parker has been issued on record; an important document is *Birth Of The Bebop – Bird On Tenor: 1943* on Stash, made in a hotel room with Gillespie and Eckstine on trumpets at a pivotal time in the music; airchecks incl. five LPs from the Royal Roost '48-9 (with announcer Sidney Torin, aka Symphony Sid, *b* 25 Nov. '09 NYC, *d* 14 Sep. '84 Florida: a champion of bop for whom 'Jumpin' With Symphony Sid' was created); *Charlie Parker At Storyville* '53 from Boston club was only released '85 on Blue Note, with Haynes, Red GARLAND, Kenny CLARKE, Sir Charles THOMPSON, local trumpeter/bandleader Herb Pomeroy and others. The tunes he originated, such as 'Now's The Time' (aka R&B hit 'The Hucklebuck'), 'Confirmation', 'Yardbird Suite', 'Relaxin' At Camarillo', 'Billie's Bounce', 'Ornithology', 'Scrapple From The Apple', 'Parker's Mood', 'Marmaduke', 'Steeplechase' and many more, became modern jazz standards; Mingus said that the full title of Mingus's 'Gunslinging Bird' was 'If Charlie Parker were a gunslinger, there'd be a whole lot of dead copycats.' Some so-called jazz fans never accepted the new music, which Parker represented more than any other individual, but Parker himself was not doctrinaire: 'It's either one thing or the other – either good music or otherwise. Call it swing, bebop or dixieland. If it's good music, it will be heard.' He begged his imitators not to imitate him in his drug habit, but many of them didn't listen; the heroin plague that hit Harlem in those years was not the fault of a man who picked up the habit as an obscure teenager in the Midwest. He was also a heavy drinker for years, especially when he was trying to stay off drugs, yet his bad habits rarely affected his playing. When he died in the flat of jazz patroness Baroness Pannonica DeKoenigswarter, he was in such poor condition that an attending doctor estimated his age as between 50 and 60. It is all very well to write, as one jazz historian recently did, that Parker had less 'character' than Gillespie, on the grounds that they were the same age, both black, both geniuses on their respective instruments, but Parker was difficult, unreliable and died young, while Gillespie is still active. But Gillespie had a firm but loving father until he was 12 years old: the fractured family life of Afro-Americans has been a result of 300 years of slavery and racism. As Gary Giddins wrote recently, 'Racist and philistine societies are all alike; every artist is unique.' Parker knew his own worth; by the time he was earning a good living his influence was complete, despite opposition from many critics, but his personal life and physical condition were already hopeless. Yet when he visited Scandinavia '50, greeted by jazz fans as a conquering hero and with a complete absence of racism, he was the soul of generosity, submitting to adulation and requests for interviews with humility and graciousness. His weird personal act was self-protection, costly but successful: he survived long enough to do what he had come to do; his friends valued his sense of humour and did not give up on him despite his difficult behaviour: they knew that such rare genius, described by George RUSSELL as a 'huge conceptual stick', is not to be measured in terms of manners. Within days of his death the graffito 'Bird lives!' appeared in New York. Books *Bird: The Legend Of Charlie Parker* '62 by Robert Reisner, *Bird Lives!* by Ross Russell '72 are valuable but controversial, because each participant in the events of Parker's life has a different version; Giddins' *Celebrating Bird: The Triumph Of Charlie Parker* '87 is well illustrated, the best book on Parker until Stanley CROUCH finishes his. *Jazz Style In Kansas City And The Southwest* '71, also by Russell (who ran Dial Records) has valuable background as well as basic information on Parker; *Jazz Masters Of The 40s* '66, *Swing To Bop* '85 by Ira Gitler are oral histories with many recollections of Parker; *Jazz West Coast* '86 by Robert Gordon has an account of the Dial sessions and late '40s scene. Biopic *Bird* '88 dir. by Clint Eastwood, starring Forest Whitaker and with technical tour-de-force in soundtrack supervised by Lennie NIEHAUS, is said to be worthy of its subject. *See also* BOP, JAZZ, KANSAS CITY.

PARKER, Graham (*b* '50, East London) UK rock singer. Scuffed as hippie, petrol pump assistant, writing songs in spare time; Stiff Records' Dave Robinson put him in touch with pub-rock bands Ducks Deluxe and BRINSLEY SCHWARZ, resulting in forming of the Rumour. Parker appeared on Charlie Gillett's infl. *Honk Tonk* radio show '75 (the show that gave early exposure to DIRE STRAITS and Elvis COSTELLO), he performed haunting 'Between You & Me' and was snapped up for a record deal: *Howlin' Wind* was a crucial album, intense R&B bridging the gap between pub-rock and punk, his vocal style compared to Van MORRISON and Bob DYLAN; *Heat Treatment* assured his stature; *Live At Marble Arch* was 'official bootleg' record of what was already one of the UK's top live acts, all in '76; they stole a tour from headliners SOUTHSIDE JOHNNY & THE ASBURY JUKES '77; EP *The Pink Parker* '77 made good chart showing: his songs were a breath of the fresh in foetid UK music scene of the era, 'Back To Schooldays' covered by Dave EDMUNDS and Rick NELSON, 'Hey Lord, Don't Ask Me Questions' top 40 UK '78. *Stick To Me* '77 kept momentum going but three-sided live *The Parkerilla* '78 was judged a disappointment; *Squeezing Out Sparks* '79, prod. by Jack NITZSCHE, was his best to date, with jagged intensity of 'Discovering Japan', 'Local Girls' and epic 'Passion Is No Ordinary Word'. *The Best Of Graham Parker & The Rumour* '80 is essential, a brilliant distillation of their best work. *The Up Escalator* '80 was made in NYC with guest Bruce SPRINGSTEEN, 'Stupefaction' and 'The Beating Of Another Heart' still displaying his edge; the Rumour released *Max* '77 (a pun on best-selling FLEETWOOD MAC LP *Rumours*), *Frogs, Sprouts, Clogs & Krauts* '79, *Purity Of Essence* '80 separately while Parker went solo with *Another Grey Area* '82, *The Real Macaw* '83, *Steady Nerves* '85, only the last displaying some of the old power. Devout UK following dwindled with his relative lack of excitement in the '80s, hoped for a return to form with *The Mona Lisa's Sister* '88 on

RCA: stripped-down rejection of high-tech production might well pull it off.

PARKER, John W. 'Knocky' (*b* 8 Aug. '18, Palmer, Texas; *d* 3 Sep. '86, Cal.) Pianist. A more than competent traditionalist, of particular interest because he came out of the jazz element of Western Swing: recorded with the Wanderers in Texas '35, with the Light Crust Doughboys '37-9. After WWII switched to jazz, working with New Orleans clarinettist Albert Nicholas and drummer Zutty Singleton; later in trio with Omer SIMEON and drummer Arthur Herbert (*b* 28 May '07, Brooklyn), with Doc EVANS '60. Also English teacher, lecturer in jazz; played at New Orleans Jazz Festival '83. LPs on Jazzology, GHB, Euphonic.

PARKER, Little Junior (*b* Herman Parker, 3 Mar. '27, Clarksdale, Ms.; *d* 18 Nov. '71, Blue Island, Ill.) Blues singer, harmonica player. Sang in gospel groups as a child, in the street for tips; worked clubs late '40s-50s throughout South; with B. B. KING's Beale Streeters in Memphis early '50s, formed own Blue Flames and recorded on Modern and Sun '52-3 in Memphis. Wrote 'Mystery Train' '53, later Elvis PRESLEY's first no. 1 hit (on country chart). With Bobby 'Blue' BLAND in touring Johnny ACE Revue '54-61, recorded for Duke in Houston, Texas; for Mercury, UA etc. late '60s-71. Died of brain tumour. R&B hits on Duke '57-66 incl. top tens 'Next Time You See Me', 'Driving Wheel', 'In The Dark', 'Annie Get Your Yo-Yo'; others on Mercury/Blue Rock, Minit, Capitol '67-71. Compilations: *The Legendary Sun Performers* on Charly UK; *I Wanna Ramble* on Ace USA, Duke sides now on MCA/USA: *Best Of, Driving Wheel, Barefoot/Got Me* with Bland.

PARKS, Van Dyke (*b* 3 Jan '41, Ms.) USA singer/songwriter. Worked as child actor in Hollywood, studied piano, signed to MGM as songwriter for Walt Disney soundtracks, made a couple of solo singles, wrote songs incl. 'High Coin' for Bobby VEE, prod. local acts Mojo Men, HARPERS BIZARRE. Co-wrote songs with BEACH BOYS' Brian Wilson for abortive album *Smile* e.g. 'Heroes And Villains' which appeared on other albums/singles; also *Smiley Smile* '67. His own *Song Cycle* '68 took four years to complete with lavish arrangements, unusual vocal treatments, it was hailed as the first 'art-rock' LP by some, still a masterpiece for many. He prod. *Randy Newman* '68, also work by Arlo GUTHRIE, Ry COODER, Phil OCHS; sessioned on piano with Tim BUCKLEY, LITTLE FEAT, Judy COLLINS, the BYRDS; was dir. of Warner Bros audio/visual services '70, left '71; immersed himself in Caribbean musics, prod. Esso Trinidadian Steel Band which also appeared on his *Discover America* '72, also calypso king Mighty SPARROW (*Hot And Sweet* '74). Third album was straightforward *The Clang Of The Yankee Reaper* '75, then long gap to *Jump!* '84, sleeve carrying illustrations for Joel Chandler Harris's *Tales Of Uncle Remus*: he may have been thinking in terms of a Broadway show. He contributed to Robert Altman film *Popeye* '80; operates on fringe of popular music, with low profile, many credits, layered sounds, eccentric image. First three LPs reissued on Edsel UK '86 to unexpected critical acclaim. Toured with Cooder '88.

PARLAN, Horace (*b* 19 Jan. '31, Philadelphia, Pa.) Pianist. Discovered by Charles MINGUS, came to fame playing and recording with him late '50s; then with others incl. Lockjaw DAVIS-Johnny GRIFFIN quintet, Booker ERVIN, Tubby HAYES, Slide HAMPTON, Dexter GORDON, Roland KIRK '63-6. Own LPs on Blue Note incl. trio LPs *Movin' And Groovin'* with Sam JONES, Al Harewood on drums (*b* 3 June '23, NYC); then *Us Three* with George Tucker (*b* 10 Dec. '27, Palatka, Fla.; *d* 10 Oct. '65, NYC) replacing Jones on bass, *Headin' South* adding Ray BARRETTO, *Speakin' My Piece* and *On The Spur Of The Moment* with Tommy and Stanley TURRENTINE, all '60-1. *Up And Down* '61 incl. Booker Ervin, Grant Green on guitar; *Back From The Gig* '63 had Ervin, Green, Johnny COLES, Billy HIGGINS, bassist Butch Warren (*b* 9 Aug. '39, Washington DC; with Thelonious MONK '63-4): this album was issued in 2-disc set with another Ervin album under Ervin's name as *Back From The Gig*, under Parlan's name as *Happy Frame Of Mind* '86. Parlan moved to Copenhagen '73, made fine series of LPs on that city's Steeplechase label with various local sidemen, visiting Americans incl.

trio/quintet *Arrival* '73 with Idrees Sulieman on trumpet (*b* 7 Aug. '23, St Petersburg, Fla.; also recorded with Gordon on Steeplechase, played in CLARKE/BOLAND BIG BAND), solo sets *The Maestro* and *Musically Yours* '79; trios *No Blues* '75, *Hi-Fly* and *Blue Parlan* '78, *Like Someone In Love* '83; quintet *Glad I Found You* '84 with Eddie HARRIS, Thad JONES. Also on Enja: trio *Pannonica*, another LP with Lockjaw Davis live in Munich '81. *Joe Meets The Rhythm Section* '86 on Timeless features Joe Enkhuizen on tenor.

PARLIAMENT/FUNKADELIC Complex of R&B groups presided over by George Clinton (*b* 22 July '40, Kannapolis, N.C.). He formed vocal quintet the Parliaments '55; they scuffled for some years, signed with Motown '64 (records not released), finally had hits on Revilot incl. '(I Wanna) Testify' '67 (no. 3 R&B, top 20 pop); recorded *Osmium* '70 for HOLLAND-DOZIER-HOLLAND's Invictus label before Motown insisted on keeping rights to name Parliaments. Clinton then shifted into high gear, renamed himself Dr Funkenstein (aka Maggot Overlord), recorded with backup group now called Funkadelic: infl. by '60s rock bands, SLY & THE FAMILY STONE etc. he created black dance music with a black wit (in both senses) at a time when the word FUNK still meant something, before everything was subsumed by the high-tech of DISCO. On Detroit's Westbound label, *Funkadelic* '70 reached top 200 pop albums; with one of the best LP titles ever, *Free Your Mind And Your Ass Will Follow* '70 reached the top 100. Like KC AND THE SUNSHINE BAND a large group, making a big danceable sound without too much help from sterile studio technology, it variously incl. Eddie Hazel, Lucius Ross, Gary Shider, Mike Hampton on guitars; Bernard 'Woo' Worrell or Walter 'Junie' Morrison on keyboards, Ramon Fullwood on drums, vocalist Ray Davis, later bassist William 'Bootsy' Collins and Maceo Parker and Fred Wesley on horns, the last three from James BROWN's backing group; further albums promoted by superbly zany stage act were *Maggot Brain* '71, 2-disc *America Eats Its Young* '72, *Cosmic Slop* '73, *Standing On The Verge Of Getting It On* '74, *Let's Take It To The Stage* '75, *Tales Of Kidd Funkadelic*

'76; switched to WB with *Hardcore Jollies* '76, *One Nation Under A Groove* '78, *Uncle Jam Wants You* '79 (the last two top 20 LPs), *The Electric Spanking Of War Babies* '81 (with Sly Stone guesting, along with Jimi HENDRIX one of Clinton's main influences). Meanwhile he recovered the rights to the name of his own group from Berry Gordy's empire, dropped the 's' and recorded as Parliament on Casablanca with Funkadelic as backing group, albums incl. *Up For The Down Stroke* '74, *Chocolate City* '75 (surrounded by 'vanilla suburbs'), *Mothership Connection* '76 (incl. top 15 single 'Tear The Roof Off The Sucker (Give Up The Funk)'), *The Clones Of Dr Funkenstein* '76, *Parliament Live/P. Funk Earth Tour* '77, *Funkentelechy Vs. The Placebo Syndrome* '77, *Motor-Booty Affair* '78 (the last five top 30 LPs), *Gloryhallastoopid (Or Pin The Tail On The Funky)* '79, *Trombipulation* '81. *The George Clinton Band Arrives* '74 also appeared, on ABC. Clinton obtained an unusual degree of control, forming his own Uncle Jam label to license the output; meanwhile the spinoffs began: Parker/Wesley had recorded as Maceo and the King's Men (*Doin' Their Own Thing* '71 on House), as Maceo and the Macks and as the JBs on People (six albums '72-5), later as Fred Wesley and the Horny Horns on Atlantic (*A Blow For Me, A Toot For You* '77); Hazel issued *Games, Dames, And Other Things* '77 on WB, Worrell *All The Woo In The World* '79 on Arista, Morrison three LPs on Westbound '75-6 and two on Columbia '80-1. Bootsy's Rubber Band released *Stretchin' Out* '76, *Ahh . . . The Name Is Bootsy, Baby!* '77, *Bootsy? Player Of The Year* '78, *This Boot Is Made For Funkin'* '79 on WB. The band's vocal chorus split into Parlet for three LPs on Casablanca, Brides Of Funkenstein for *Funk Or Walk* '78 and *Never Buy Texas From A Cowboy* '80 on Atlantic. In the late '70s he was donating a portion of ticket prices to the United Negro College Fund. As the empire got too big it began to fray around the edges, multiplicity of labels and contracts leading to tangles; there was trouble with WB over issue of *War Babies*, which Clinton intended to be a 2-disc set; latter-day drummer Jerome Brailey formed Mutiny, which made an album criticising the Mamaship; ex-members made *Connec-*

tions And Disconnections '81 on Lax (with sleeve sticker declaring that Clinton was not involved), *Zapp* '80 on WB was fronted by Collins; Rubber Band members made *The Sweat Band* '80 on Uncle Jam. Clinton made singles on a Hump label, switched to Capitol with P-Funk sidemen under his own name for *Computer Games* '82 (incl. hit 'Atomic Dog'), *You Shouldn't-Nuf Bit Fish* '84, *Some Of My Best Jokes Are Friends* '85, *R&B Skeletons In The Closet* and mini-LP *The Mothership Connection Live From Houston Texas* '86.

PARSONS, Gram (*b* Cecil Ingram Connor, 5 Nov. '46, Winterhaven, Fla.; *d* 19 Sep. '73, Joshua Tree, Cal.) Singer, songwriter, bandleader; played guitar, keyboards. A primary inventor of country rock. Grew up in Waycross, Ga.; his mother's family were wealthy; father was Coon Dog Connor, a ranch-hand, singer-songwriter (committed suicide when Parsons was 13); his mother married a man named Parsons and died of alcoholism on the day Parsons graduated from high school. Sang in folk trio with Jim Stafford and Kent Lavoie (*see* LOBO); first pro group was quartet the Shilos (later *Gram Parsons: The Early Years 1963-65* on Sierra). Entered Harvard as divinity student ('I think I was there about four hours and fifteen minutes'), formed the International Submarine Band in Cambridge to make 'Cosmic American Music': album *Safe At Home* '67 prod. by Lee HAZLEWOOD (later *Gram Parsons* on Shilo) with sleeve notes by Duane EDDY, Glen CAMPBELL, Phil EVERLY (who called it the first classic of 'white soul'). I.S.B. contributed a song to soundtrack of film *The Russians Are Coming*. Parsons asked to join the BYRDS but quit after three months, refusing to tour South Africa: helped them make history as the first rock band to play the Grand Ole Opry and with their most important LP *Sweetheart Of The Rodeo* '68, a signpost to the impending fusion; he also infl. the EAGLES, POCO, the 'outlaw' movement incl. Waylon JENNINGS, Willie NELSON (*see* COUNTRY MUSIC). With ex-Byrd Chris Hillman he formed the Flying Burrito Brothers, his LPs with their finest moments: *The Gilded Palace Of Sin* '69, *Burrito Deluxe* '70; posthumous albums *Close Up The Honky Tonks* '74 and *Sleepless*

Nights '76 also incl. Parsons material. (They carried on without him: *Last Of The Red Hot Burritos* '71 was impressive; future editions of the group released *Flying Again* and *Live In Amsterdam* '75, *Airborne* '76, *Hearts On The Line* '80, and *Live In Tokyo* '85.) He hung around with the ROLLING STONES, infl. on Jagger/Richards' songwriting heard on 'Dead Flowers' and 'Wild Horses' from *Sticky Fingers* '71, and 'Sweet Virginia' from *Exile On Main Street* '72 (sang backup). Parsons quarrelled with Jagger over songwriting credits; a Richards/Parsons LP was mooted, but didn't happen. His own *GP* '73 featured duets with Emmylou HARRIS (who'd been rediscovered by Parsons/Hillman), also James BURTON, Rick GRECH, Glen D. Hardin on piano, Parsons songs 'She', 'How Much I've Lied', 'The New Soft Shoe'. He was an alcoholic, estranged from his wife and his house had burned down when he was recording second LP with Harris; he died in a motel of heart failure caused by burning the candle at both ends. He did not get along with his family, had expressed a wish to be cremated and his ashes strewn at Cap Rock, a nearby natural monument; his road manager Phil Kaufman with friend Michael Martin stole the body and carried out these wishes; they were fined $750. *The Return Of The Grievous Angel* '74 incl. Parsons songs 'Grievous Angel', 'Hickory Wind', 'Las Vegas', 'In My Hour Of Darkness', others by Tom T. HALL, the LOUVIN Bros, Everly Bros. *Gram Parsons & The Fallen Angels Live 1973* was released '82. Harris said, 'There's something in my voice that just wasn't there until I sang with Gram'; she went on to become the Queen of country rock, making albums that are utterly timeless. Tributes to Parsons incl. her 'Boulder To Birmingham' on her debut *Pieces Of The Sky* '75, Bernie Leadon's 'My Man' (on the Eagles' *On The Border* '74), Richie Furay's 'Crazy Eyes' (title track of '73 Poco LP). Linda RONSTADT, Tom PETTY, Dwight YOAKUM, Elvis COSTELLO all admitted influence; Costello wrote sleeve note for *The Best Of Gram Parsons* '82, incl. Parsons songs in his *Almost Blue* '81. Book *Gram Parsons: A Music Biography* by Syd Griffin (of the Long Ryders) tells the story; Parson's example led directly to today's healthy country rock scene. (Quotes

in this entry from Tom Russell's article in *Omaha Rainbow*, summer '82.)

PARTCH, Harry (*b* 24 June. '01, Oakland, Cal.; *d* 3 Sep. '74, San Diego) Composer of complete originality. Parents were musical, ex-missionaries in China; he began composing at 14, in '30 tore up everything he'd written: with natural simplicity and lack of disillusion he built his own instruments for just intonation in a 43-tone scale, incl. elongated violas and guitars, a kithera (ancient Greek lyre) with 72 strings, boos (giant bamboo reeds), the massive 'marimba eroica', etc. He travelled the USA as a hobo '35-43, drew inspiration from ordinary sights and sounds; he rejected the adage that an artist should reflect his time, preferred to transcend it. His combination of music and ritual has warmth and variety of timbre rare in the 20th century, the instruments mostly made of natural materials and needing no electricity. Published book *Genesis Of A Music* '49. *The World Of Harry Partch* incl. 'Eight Hitchiker Inscriptions From A Highway Railing At Barstow, California'; also 2-disc *Delusion Of The Fury: A Ritual of Dream And Delusion,* both on CBS; a single LP incl. 'Cloud Chamber Music' (chimes made of bell-jars) and 2-disc dance satire *The Bewitched* are both on CRI (Composers Recordings Inc.).

PARTON, Dolly (*b* 19 Jan. '46, Sevier County, Tenn.) Country singer, songwriter, actress; the best-known female country star of the late '70s-80s. Appeared as a child star on Cas Walker's TV show in Knoxville '56-9, recorded for Gold Band Records '59-61, graduated from high school '64, moved to Nashville, wrote songs with her uncle Bill Owen incl. hits for Bill Phillips ('Put It Off Till Tomorrow' '66), Hank WILLIAMS Jr ('I'm In No Condition' '67). Married building contractor Carl Dean '66, signed with Monument, had minor country hits 'Dumb Blonde' and 'Something Fishy' '67, but was promoted as a pop singer: her greatness would lie in attracting crossover attention from a country direction with excellent songs. Joined syndicated Porter WAGONER TV show '67, replacing NORMA JEAN; signed to RCA same year, had minor hits 'Just Because I'm A Woman' and 'Daddy' '68-9, made breakthrough with 'Mule Skinner Blues' '70, no. 1 country hit 'Joshua' '71. More than 20 Parton/Porter duet hits '67-74 incl. 'We'll Get Ahead Someday', 'Just Someone I Used To Know' '68-9, 'If Teardrops Were Pennies' '73, 'Please Don't Stop Loving Me' '74; among the duet albums, *Just The Two Of Us* and *Always, Always* '69, *Porter Wayne And Dolly Rebecca* and *Once More* '70, *Two Of A Kind* '71 made top 200 pop LPs. They toured together; he prod. her solo hits incl. autobiographical 'Coat Of Many Colors' '71, 'Touch Your Woman' '72, international hit 'Jolene' '74. She felt he was holding her back, left TV show '74, but he retained contract to produce her records incl. more hits 'I Will Always Love You' and 'Love Is Like A Butterfly' '74, 'The Bargain Store' and 'The Seeker' '75, but she wanted to reach a wider audience: her last album to reach the pop LP chart had been *Joshua* '71; split with Wagoner was acrimonious '76, she relocated to West Coast and forged fresh direction with LP *New Harvest . . . First Gathering* '77, her first LP to crack top 100 pop LPs; single 'Light Of A Clear Morning' failed to reach country top 10 but made pop Hot 100; *Here You Come Again* '78 was top 20 pop LP with title track at no. 1 country, no. 3 pop, followed by consecutive country no. 3 hits 'Two Doors Down', 'Heartbreaker', 'Baby I'm Burnin'' '78, all in pop top 40. She was ACM's Entertainer of the Year '77, CMA's '78; in demand for TV shows for her personality, figure-hugging outfits, blonde wigs, delightful knack for kidding herself. Made film debut in *9 To 5* '80 (title song no. 1 pop hit), co-starred with Burt Reynolds in *The Best Little Whorehouse In Texas* '82 (incl. new version of 'I Will Always Love You'), Sylvester Stallone in *Rhinestone* '84. More hits incl. 'You're The Only One' '79, 'Old Flames (Can't Hold A Candle To You)' '80, 'But You Know I Love You' '81, 'Potential New Boy Friend' '83, 'Downtown' '84; teamed with Kenny ROGERS for tours, TV specials, millionseller 'Islands In The Stream' '84, written and prod. by the BEE GEES. A shrewd business lady, Dolly Parton rather than somebody else is doing well from all her talents. Albums (to name just the rest of the crossovers to the pop chart) incl. *My Blue Ridge Mountain Boy* '69, *A Real Live Dolly* '70 (recorded at Sevier County High School,

with Wagoner on four tracks), *Heartbreaker* '78, *Great Balls Of Fire* '79, *Dolly Dolly Dolly* and *9 To 5 And Other Odd Jobs* '80, *Heartbreak Express* and *Greatest Hits* '82, *Burlap & Satin* '83, *The Great Pretender* '84 (covers of '50s-60s pop hits), *Rhinestone* soundtrack and *Once Upon A Christmas* (with Rogers) '84, all on RCA. *Real Love* '85 was top 10 country LP; 2-disc sets on Pair label are *Just The Way I Am* and *Portrait* '86. Long-awaited harmony project *Trio* '87 on WB shared honours with Linda RONSTADT, Emmylou HARRIS, incl. 'The Pain Of Loving You', co-written by Parton and Wagoner, as well as her beautiful 'Wildflowers'. *Rainbow* '87 on Columbia was described as straight pop by *Country Music People* UK, got one star: only one song on it was hers, and it sounded country despite synths.

PARTON, Stella (*b* 4 May '49, Sevier County, Tenn.) Country singer, songwriter. Younger sister of Dolly PARTON made radio debut with her '55, but achieved her own success. Sang in local clubs '66, moved to Washington DC, Texas, then Nashville '72, recorded for small labels Royal American and Music City without much success; toured with gospel group Stella Carroll and the Gospel Carrolls; came back to country music with her own song 'Ode To Olivia' '75, in defence of Olivia NEWTON-JOHN, who had won CMA awards amid protests that she wasn't country. Recorded for Country, Soul & Blues label, had country hits 'I Want To Hold You In My Heart' '75, 'I Want To Hold You In My Dreams Tonight' '76; switched to Elektra, stayed top 20 with 'Danger Of A Stranger' and 'Standard Lie Number One' '77, 'Four Little Words' and 'Stormy Weather' '78, 'Steady As The Rain' '79; then worked on TV, theatre. LPs incl. *Country Sweet* '77, *Love Ya* '78, *Best Of* '79 on Elektra, *So Far So Good* '82 on Town House. Other Parton clan members who've recorded incl. Randy Parton, Rachel Dennison.

PASS, Joe (*b* Joseph Anthony Passalaqua, 13 Jan. '29, New Brunswick, N.J.) Guitarist. Worked with Tony PASTOR while still in school, served a year in the Marine Corps, entered Synanon Foundation in Santa Monica, Cal. for drug problem '61, played on *Sounds Of Synanon* LP on Pacific Jazz '62, won *Downbeat* new star award '63, soon the most influential guitar player since Wes MONTGOMERY for lovely technique, sound: able to swing like a whole group as a solo artist. Six LPs on Pacific Jazz/World Pacific '63-7 incl. quartets *Catch Me*, *For Django*; two others with larger groups arr./cond. by Bob Florence; also *Intercontinental* '70 on MPS/Pausa; *The Living Legends* '69, *Guitar Interludes* '77 on Discovery; he also played with Les McCANN, Gerald WILSON, Julie LONDON, others; toured with George SHEARING mid-'60s, Benny GOODMAN '73. On Norman GRANZ's Pablo label from '73 he became world-famous as sideman on countless albums with Oscar PETERSON, Count BASIE, Ella FITZGERALD, Duke ELLINGTON, others, as well as nearly 20 albums of his own, incl. solos *Virtuoso* '73, *Virtuoso No. 2* '76, *Virtuoso 3* '77, *Live At Montreux* '77, *I Remember Charlie Parker* '79, *Live At Long Beach City College* '84, *University Of Akron Concert* '86; duets with Niels-Henning Ørsted Pedersen on bass *Chops* '78, *Northsea Nights* '79, *Digital III At Montreux* '79; *Eximious* '82 added Ronnie SCOTT's drummer Martin Drew; duet with Jimmy ROWLES *Checkmate* '81, with J. J. JOHNSON *We'll Be Together Again* c.'84; *Oscar Peterson & Joe Pass à Salle Pleyel* '75 incl. solos, duets; other trios/small group sets: *Portraits Of Duke Ellington* '74 with Ray BROWN, Bobby Durham on drums; *Quadrant* '77, *Quadrant Plays Duke Ellington: All Too Soon* '80 with Brown, Milt JACKSON, Mickey Roker on drums (*b* 3 Sep. '32, Miami, Fla.; toured with Dizzy GILLESPIE late '70s); also *Tudo Bem!* '78, *Ira, George And Joe/Joe Pass Loves Gershwin* '81. Played on the first two LPs on the CONCORD JAZZ label, *Jazz/Concord* and *Seven Come Eleven*, quartet incl. Brown, Herb ELLIS, drummer Jake Hanna.

PASTOR, Tony (*b* Antonio Pestritto, '07, Middletown, Conn.; *d* 31 Oct. '69, New London, Conn.) Tenor sax, vocalist, bandleader. Began on C-melody sax; worked for Irving AARONSON late '20s, own band in Hartford, Conn. early '30s, with Smith BALLEW '35, Joe VENUTI, Vincent Lopez, then Artie SHAW '36-40, incl. solos on many hits, zany vocals e.g. on 'Indian Love Call' '38. Led own popular band '40-59, hits every year '41-9 incl. his own novelty vocals on 'Dance With A Dolly (With A Hole In Her Stocking)' '44 (which was adapted from 1844 song 'Buffalo Gals'), Ruth McCullough on no. 2 hit 'Bell-Bottom Trousers' '45; vocal trio the CLOONEY sisters late '40s incl. Rosemary's first recorded solos on 'You Started Something', 'Grieving For You' etc. Good musicianship with arr. late '40s by Walter Fuller, Ralph FLANAGAN, Budd JOHNSON kept band going until '59; later had club act with sons Guy, John, Tony Jr (LP on Roulette *A Guy And His Dad*), also *Plays And Sings Shaw* on Everest, others out of print.

PASTORIUS, Jaco (*b* John Francis, 1 Dec. '51, Morristown, Pa.; *d* 22 Sept. '87, Fort Lauderdale, Fla.) Bassist, composer. Father was drummer, singer; wanted to play drums but injured his arm at 13 and did not get it sorted out until 17, when he took up bass; had also played piano, sax, guitar. Family had moved to Fort Lauderdale where he played in clubs with stars such as the SUPREMES, TEMPTATIONS, Nancy WILSON; also played country music, worked on cruise ships in the Caribbean: acquired unselfconscious eclecticism which stood him in good stead. He preceded Gary PEACOCK, Eberhard Weber in Europe, in redefining the bass in contemporary music, bringing to it the qualities of amplified acoustic instruments, using harmonics and perfect articulation to create a new solo voice, in his case with a delightful Caribbean influence along with R&B and jazz. Played with BLOOD, SWEAT & TEARS '75, drummer Bobby Colomby helped arrange for first LP *Jaco Pastorius* '75 on Epic. Others incl. *Word Of Mouth* '81 and *Invitation* '83 on WB; he also recorded with Ira SULLIVAN, Paul BLEY, Joni MITCHELL, Pat METHENY (*Bright Size Life* '76 on ECM), Bireli LAGRENE. As a member of WEATHER REPORT he played on their best LPs. He suffered from manic depression made worse by alcohol, was destitute in later years, died of injuries ten days after trying to enter a club from which he'd been banned; the club manager was arrested for assault.

PATTON, Charley (*b* 1887, Edwards, Ms.; *d* 28 Apr. '34, Indianola, Ms.) Blues singer, guitarist, composer. He was a half-brother to the Chatmon family of Delta musicians, whose best-known members were singers/ multi-instrumentalists Sam (*b* 10 Jan. 1897, Bolton, Ms.) and Armentier 'Bo' (*b* 21 Mar. 1893, Bolton; *d* 21 Sep. '64, Memphis, Tenn.; aka Bo Carter), both of whom made records and sometimes spelled their name Chatman. He was one of the most important, influential and inventive of Delta bluesmen, aka 'The Masked Marvel', 'Charley Peters'; he altered accents and lengths of verses, recorded blues ballads, ragtime songs and religious songs as well as pure blues, no doubt considering himself an entertainer rather than a blues singer; Son HOUSE disapproved of his 'clowning'. He was popular with white people at a time when racism was not as bitter as it later became in the area. He worked with Tommy JOHNSON and others; recorded 42 sides for Paramount '29-30, some with Henry Sims on violin (and second voice on one side), four with Willie Brown on second guitar; and 26 sides for Vocalion '34, of which only ten were issued at the time; several of the Vocalion sides were as 'Patton and Lee' with vocalist Bertha Lee; he also accompanied Sims and Lee on a few sides of their own. On some issues of religious sides he was 'Elder J. J. Hadley' or 'Rev. J. M. Gates'. His best-known composition was 'Pony Blues'; he also recorded 'Frankie And Albert' and 'Going To Move To Alabama' (variants of 'Frankie And Johnny' and 'Kansas City Blues'), 'Some Of These Days I'll Be Gone' (melody and chords infl. by white country music), much else: his guitar work is fascinating and his work as a whole an excellent example of interplay between voice and guitar that marks a master in the genre. 2-disc *Founder Of The Delta Blues* on Yazoo incl. 28 tracks; John FAHEY contributed to extensive notes, also published musical analysis *Charley Patton* '70, incl. biographical research which was done in the nick of time. *Bottleneck Guitar Pioneer* on Herwin is another selection.

PAUL, Les (*b* Lester Polfus, 9 June '15, Waukesha, Wis.) Guitarist and inventor. Learnt harmonica, guitar and banjo at an early age, began on radio in Racine, then Milwaukee early '30s; a regular on WLS in Chicago, then leader of WJJD house band '34, played country music as Hot Rod Red,

Rhubarb Red. Formed Les Paul Trio '36, moved to NYC; combo became regulars on Fred WARING NBC radio show through '41. He was already building his own electric guitars and moved towards jazz as he worked for Chicago and Los Angeles radio stations; worked for Armed Forces Radio and became NBC staff musician in L.A. upon discharge; recorded for Decca with Bing CROSBY and others: trio's 'Blue Skies' was regarded as seminal by those who linked Paul's name with that of Charlie CHRISTIAN (now on *Guitar Genius* compilation on Charly UK, with tracks by Hank Garland, Grady MARTIN); 'Rumours Are Flying' '46 with the ANDREWS SISTERS was a hit '46; LP *Feed Back* on Circle compiles '44-5 trio. He toured, recorded with JATP; recorded with Clancy HAYES on Mercury. His experimental side moved into high gear: he took the first solid-body electric guitar to Gibson '46, they called it a 'broomstick', relented '47 but would not put their name on it: the Les Paul model became one of the most famous guitars in the world. 'Lover'/'Brazil' '48 was two-sided hit on Capitol, overdubbed until it sounded like six guitars; he broke his right elbow in a car crash and had it reset at an angle so he could still play; the instrumental hits continued through '53 incl. 'Nola' (piano novelty from '16, Paul playing both Spanish and steel guitar), 'Whispering', 'Meet Mr Callaghan', 'Lady Of Spain' all top 10. Meanwhile he met country singer Mary Ford (*b* Colleen Summer, 7 July '28; *d* 30 Sep. '77); they were married '49, separated '63; Les Paul & Mary Ford were among biggest hitmakers of the early '50s, 28 hits '50-7 on Capitol incl. 'Mockin' Bird Hill', 'The World Is Waiting For The Sunrise', 'Tiger Rag' at no. 2, 'How High The Moon' and 'Vaya con Dios' at no. 1, the latter for 11 weeks '53 and it still holds up better than many pop hits of the period. Almost all were recorded in Paul's own studio using an 8-track deck of his design, both his guitar and her voice overdubbed, his equipment and techniques years ahead of their time. They had more top 40 hits on Columbia '58, '61; he retired from active music-making to concentrate on inventing except for LP *Les Paul Now* '68 on London; became active again mid-'70s performing, promoting guitars for Gibson; moved full circle back to country picking, with old friend Chet ATKINS on *Chester And Lester* '77 (won Grammy), *Guitar Monsters* '78. Retired again; subject of TV documentary *The Wizard Of Waukesha* '80; began weekly gigs at Fat Tuesday's in NYC Oct. '84, was still there three years later. Compilations incl. 2-disc *All-Time Greatest Hits* from EMI Holland incl. instrumental hits, others with Ford; in USA *Early Les Paul* and *The World Is Still Waiting For The Sunrise* on Capitol.

PAXTON, Tom (*b* 31 Oct. '37, Chicago) Singer/songwriter, guitarist with large loyal following since '60s. Moved with family to Oklahoma, learned guitar and was infl. by Woody GUTHRIE, the WEAVERS and Burl IVES; went to Greenwich Village after military service '60, fell in with Bob DYLAN, Phil OCHS, PETER, PAUL & MARY; Pete SEEGER was an early champion and helped popularise 'Ramblin' Boy'. Album of that title on Elektra '65 was standard folk LP of the era, Paxton a more mature lyricist than most: 'I Can't Help But Wonder Where I'm Bound', 'The Last Thing On My Mind', children's song 'Goin' To The Zoo' are among his best-known songs; *Ain't That News* '65 added political acerbity for topical wit that still marks his work, incl. 'The Willing Conscript', 'Lyndon Johnson Told The Nation'. *Outward Bound* '66 incl. exemplary title track, 'Leaving London', 'All The Way Home'; he was established as a major concert act, and while never matching Dylan's eclecticism has accumulated a substantial body of work: *Morning Again* '68 is notable for stirring title track; *The Things I Notice Now* '69 was released at the time of the second Isle Of Wight Festival, where he nearly stole the show from Dylan; *The Compleat Tom Paxton* '71 is definitive 2-disc live set made at the Bitter End, with some of his best-known songs, engaging links: wry humour ('Is This Any Way To Run An Airline?', 'Talking Vietnam Pot-Luck Blues'), social comment (anti-war 'Jimmy Newman', 'Forest Lawn' on the American way of death); 'Jennifer's Rabbit' another fine children's song. Switched to Reprise: *How Come The Sun, Peace Will Come* and *New Songs For Old Friends*. At some point he formed his own label, leased output: LPs appearing on Private Stock, Flying Fish,

Mountain Railroad incl. *Something In My Life* '75, *New Songs From The Briar Patch* '77 (incl. 'White Bones Of Allende', 'Born On The Fourth Of July'); *The Paxton Report* '81, *Even A Gray Day* '83, *Up And Up, In The Orchard* '85, *One Million Lawyers . . . And Other Disasters* '86, *And Loving You* '87. Concerts are looked-for events; songs were covered by Peter, Paul & Mary, John DENVER, the KINGSTON TRIO, many others.

PAYCHECK, Johnny (*b* Donald Lytle, 31 May '41, Greenfield, Ohio) An abrasive country vocalist who did very well in the mid-'60s, faded and came back mid-'70s bigger than ever. Began as sideman, playing bass in Porter WAGONER's backing group the Wagonmasters '58, then Faron YOUNG's Country Deputies '59-60, Ray PRICE's Cherokee Cowboys '60-2; recorded as Donnie Young, rockabilly on Decca '59, country on Mercury '60-1; became front man for George JONES' Jones Boys '62-6, playing bass and singing tenor harmony; signed to Hilltop '64 using name of prize fighter Johnny Paycheck, had solo hits 'A-11' and 'Heartbreak Tennessee' '65-6; he was also songwriting seriously, and provided Tammy WYNETTE with her first hit, 'Apartment No. 9' and Price with top 5 'Touch My Heart' '66. Teamed with Aubrey Mayhew to form Little Darlin' Records '66, scored top 10 with 'The Lovin' Machine'; he developed fast-paced honky-tonk style with Lloyd Green's steel guitar and had more hits 'Motel Time Again', 'Jukebox Charlie', 'The Cave'; left Mayhew, went to West Coast and hit bottom owing to self-confessed alcoholism: ace Nashville prod. Billy SHERRILL brought him back '71 and signed him to Epic; first release 'She's All I Got' went to no. 2, starting string of his biggest hits: 'Someone To Give My Love To', 'Mr Lovemaker', 'Song And Dance Man' '72-3, 'For A Minute There' '75, 'Slide Off Your Satin Sheets' '77 and no. 1 hit 'Take This Job And Shove It', David Allan COE's anthem for downtrodden working people (which also inspired a comedy film '81). He still drank heavily and was often close to bankruptcy; his reckless lifestyle mirrored in songs like 'Me And The I.R.S.', 'Drinkin' & Drivin', '(Stay Away From) The Cocaine Train'; duet LP with George Jones '78 incl. hits 'Maybellene', 'You Can Have Her'; solo hits continued incl. 'Friend, Lover, Wife', 'The Outlaw's Prayer', 'D.O.A. (Drunk On Arrival)' '78-80. Acclaimed live LP *New York Town* and tribute to Merle HAGGARD *Mr Hag Told My Story* '81 kept him in the limelight, but Epic dropped him; came back on Mercury with *Modern Times* '87, incl. no. 21 single 'Old Violin'. Sentenced to nine years for a shooting, he was out on appeal early '87. Other LPs: *At Carnegie Hall* '67 on Little Darlin'; *Somebody Love Me* '73, *11 Months & 29 Days* '76, *Take This Job & Shove It* '78, *Armed And Crazy* '78, *Everybody's Got A Family – Meet Mine* '80, *Lovers And Losers* '82, *Biggest Hits* '83, all on Epic.

PAYNE, Cecil (*b* 14 Dec. '22, Brooklyn, NYC) Baritone sax, also alto sax and flute. With Pepper ADAMS, Serge CHALOFF, Gerry MULLIGAN and Leo Parker, one of the few baritones of his generation in modern jazz and an underrated talent: the baritone just doesn't get that much attention. Record debut on alto at J. J. JOHNSON session '46 for Savoy; with Dizzy GILLESPIE '47-8 incl. European tour, freelanced with James MOODY, Tadd DAMERON, others; with Illinois JACQUET '52-4; worked outside music, with Randy WESTON late '50s; acted and played in *The Connection* '61; with Lionel HAMPTON, MACHITO, Weston again, Woody HERMAN '60s; lived in Europe for a year; formed Jazz Zodiac Quartet, joined NY Jazz Repertory Orchestra '74, worked shows and tours incl. with vocalist sister Cavril Payne late '74 (LP with her: *Teasin' Tan*); played at Carnegie Hall mid-'80. Played on Dameron's lovely *Fontainebleau* '56, added dark colour and weight to John COLTRANE's *Dakar* '57 (with Coltrane, Adams, Payne and rhythm: no brass), many other sessions. Own albums, all small-group sets with fine sidemen, five with Duke JORDAN: *Patterns Of Jazz* and *Bird's Night* '56-7 on Savoy, *Cool Blues* and *The Connection* '61-2 on Charlie Parker (the latter also in French Vogue 2-disc set *Movie Music* with a Jordan album), *Brookfield Andante* '66 on Spotlite (made in Manchester with UK rhythm), *Zodiac* c.'69 on Strata-East (quintet with Kenny DORHAM), *Brooklyn Brothers* '73 on Muse (Jordan the other brother),

Bird Gets The Worm '76 on Muse, *Bright Moments* '79 on Spotlite, made in London.

PAYNE, Freda (*b* 19 Sep. '45, Detroit, Mich.) Jazz and soul singer. Studied music in Detroit with sister Scherrie (who later joined the SUPREMES after Diana ROSS left); went to NYC '63, toured in that decade with Quincy JONES, Duke ELLINGTON; recorded with little success for MGM. Big moment came when HOLLAND-DOZIER-HOLLAND left Motown and started their own Invictus label: Payne was one of their first signings and her first record was the unforgettable 'Band Of Gold' '70, no. 3 pop/top 20 soul USA, no. 1 UK. Other hits incl. 'Deeper And Deeper' same year (top 40 USA/UK), 'Cherish What Is Dear To You (While It's Near To You)' (last UK hit), 'Bring The Boys Home' (top 20 USA pop, no. 3 R&B). Invictus closed down; she recorded with less chart success for ABC and Capitol, reverted to earlier jazz style, hosted a USA TV show and remained a popular club attraction.

PAYNE, Leon (*b* 14 June '17, Alba, Texas; *d* 11 Sep. '69) Smooth-voiced country singer, multi-instrumentalist; greatest success as songwriter. Blind since childhood, learned to play guitar, keyboards, trombone at Texas State School for the Blind at Austin '24-35, worked with various Texas bands incl. Bob WILLS on Radio KWET in Palestine, Texas '35-6. Began recording for Bluebird, had hits 'Ten Thousand Tomorrows' '40, 'Cry Baby Heart' '44, 'Cheaters Never Win' '45, 'Lifetime To Regret' '48; began writing early and created country classics 'Lost Highway', 'They'll Never Take Her Love', 'I Heard My Heart Break Last Night', 'The Blue Side Of Lonesome' and 'I Love You Because', his biggest hit: no. 4 country chart '49 on Capitol, recorded '54 by Elvis PRESLEY for Sun, revived '63 for hits by Jim REEVES, Al MARTINO. A member of Jack Rhodes Rhythm Boys '48-9, worked the *Louisiana Hayride*; after the big hit formed his own Lone Star Buddies, joined Grand Ole Opry. Recorded for MGM, Bullet, Capitol, Decca labels '50s, toured the South, based mainly in San Antonio; recorded for Starday early '60s, suffered heart attack '65 and had to quit performing, but carried on writing: with

George JONES co-wrote hits 'Take Me', 'Things Have Gone To Pieces'. LPs incl. *Living Legend* '64 on Starday.

PEACOCK, Annette (*b* 8 Jan.) Singer, composer who has moved from jazz to jazz/rock fusion to free form, always from a position of feminist integrity. Eloped with bassist Gary PEACOCK at 19 to NYC; JCOA first performed her compositions; she met Paul BLEY, succeeded Carla BLEY as his chief composer: his trio album *Ballads* '67 on ECM used her themes entirely and helped set the style of the new label; he has recorded about 35 of her songs, and they were among the first to use the synthesiser, in concert with Han Bennink, others (Bley LPs *Improvise* on America, *Dual Unity* on Freedom '71); she also invented a way to sing through the synth. Her own first LP *Revenge* '72 on Polydor incl. Bley, Gary, Barry ALTSCHUL; *I'm The One* '72 on RCA was reissued '86; *X Dreams* '78 on Aura has jazz-rock jams incl. Bill BRUFORD (she sessioned on Bruford's *Feels Good To Me* same year); funky *The Perfect Release* '79 was made with members of a Jeff BECK band; her '78-9 albums incl. socio-sexual rap, both style and content again ahead of their time. *The Collection* '82 was also on Aura; first LP for her own Ironic label, *Skyskating* '82, was live concert recordings, on which she played all the instruments (acoustic, electric, synth, percussion) in material about sensuality, exploring the danger but not the anger, her free form accessible, sympathetic; studio set *I Have No Feelings* '86 was musically similar; *Been In The Streets Too Long* '83 compiled improvisations from '74-83 in a variety of settings. She once turned down a contract with United Artists, later chances to tour and/or record with David BOWIE, Brian ENO: insists on control over her own work. Band called I Belong To A World That's Destroying Itself '87 toured Europe, incl. 18-year-old daughter Solo; Annette released new album *Abstract Contact* '88.

PEACOCK, Gary (*b* 12 May '35, Barley, Idaho) Bassist, composer, teacher. Studied piano in school, played piano in USA Army band late '50s; began playing bass in Germany after military service; to West Coast USA '58, played with Paul HORN, Shorty ROGERS; to NYC '62, worked with Paul BLEY, Bill EVANS, Jimmy GIUFFRE, Roland KIRK, Steve LACY, Roswell RUDD, George RUSSELL; toured Europe with Albert AYLER, Don CHERRY; briefly played with Miles DAVIS, was less active from late '60s to mid-'70s when he rejoined Bley and began recording for ECM as sideman and own LPs: with beautiful tone and complete technique he is at home in any style, an important infl. in contemporary music. Many LPs as sideman incl. *Spiritual Unity* '64 on ESP with Ayler, albums by Keith JARRETT and Bley on ECM; his own as leader: *Tales Of Another* '77 (with Jarrett, Jack DEJOHNETTE), *December Poems* '79, *Shift In The Wind* '80, *Voices From The Past – Paradigm* '82, *Guamba* '87 with Palle MIKKELBORG, Jan Garbarek, Peter Erskine on drums and drum computer.

PEARL, Minnie (*b* Sarah Orphelia Colley, 25 Oct. '12, Centerville, Tenn.) The leading comedienne in country music for more than 40 years, with her flower-bedecked hat, long country dresses, high-pitched 'Howdee!' and patter about 'ketchin' a feller'. Dancing and acting were first loves; she studied stage technique at college in Nashville, directed amateur plays in schools, developed comedy routines, joined Grand Ole Opry c.'40. She has toured with most of the big country stars, incl. Carnegie Hall '47; appeared on Dean MARTIN, Carol Burnett, Mike Douglas, Joey Bishop TV shows etc. She made the odd record on Everest, RCA, Starday; but her comedy is partly visual in impact. She was named Nashville's Woman of the Year '65, to CMA Hall of Fame '75.

PEARSON, Duke (*b* Columbus Calvin Jr, 17 Aug. '32, Atlanta, Ga.; *d* 4 Aug. '80) Pianist, composer, bandleader in lyrical, unpretentious post-bop style. Had tunes recorded by Cannonball ADDERLEY, moved to NYC and joined Art FARMER – Benny GOLSON Jazztet '60, became assistant producer at Blue Note '63-70, led part-time big band in NYC; accompanied singers Nancy WILSON, Dakota STATON, Carmen MCRAE, Joe WILLIAMS. Own LPs: sextet *Dedication* '61 on Prestige with Pepper ADAMS and Freddie HUBBARD, two on Polydor '61-2, two on Atlantic '65-6, others on Blue Note: trio sets *Profile* and *Tender Feelin's* '59; big band

Introducing Duke Pearson's Big Band '67, *Now Hear This!* '68 both with Adams, Randy BRECKER, Frank Foster, Mickey Roker, Bob Cranshaw on bass, ten others; small-group sets: *Wahoo* '64, *Sweet Honey Bee* '66, *The Right Touch* '67, *The Phantom* '68, *How Insensitive* '69 (with solo title track, AIRTO and Flora PURIM on some tracks), *It Could Only Happen With You* '70, plus Xmas LP *Merry Ole Soul* '69.

PEARSON, Johnny (*b* 18 June '25, Plaistow, London) UK pianist, arranger, bandleader. Child prodigy on piano, winning scholarship to London Academy of Music at age 9, playing recital at 12; formed group the Rhythm Makers, played drums and piano in Royal Artillery Band, after military service worked in TV audition studios, was founder member of Malcolm Mitchell Trio '48-54; radio and session work incl. touring and recording with Lena HORNE, Shirley BASSEY, Connie FRANCIS, Cilla BLACK, many others. Led Sounds Orchestral, making popular instrumental LPs and transatlantic top 10 hit single '64-5 with Vince Guaraldi's 'Cast Your Fate To The Winds' (also top 10 UK hit 'Sleepy Shores' '71 under his own name). Last Sounds Orchestral LP was *On Golden Pond* '82; *Dreams, Golden Hour* still listed in UK catalogues on PRT. TV work incl. music for hit series *All Creatures Great And Small* about a veterinary surgeon.

PEEL, John (*b* John Ravenscroft, 30 Aug. '39, Merseyside) The most influential DJ in the UK by a long way. Dave Cousins of the STRAWBS said that with the BEATLES and Lonnie DONEGAN Peel has been the most formative influence on UK pop music. Childhood ambition was to be DJ; began broadcasting in USA early '60s; by '65 with Beatlemania at its height his Liverpool accent was an advantage. Worked in San Francisco '67, heard first hand the GRATEFUL DEAD, JEFFERSON AIRPLANE, Country Joe (McDONALD) and the Fish; moved to Radio London, the best of the UK pirate radio stations, turned the British on to CAPTAIN BEEFHEART, Frank ZAPPA's Mothers of Invention. To BBC Radio 1, cultivated home-grown talent Marc BOLAN, PINK FLOYD, SOFT MACHINE, JETHRO TULL, etc. Formed own Dandelion label early '70s, did

his best for Bridget St John, Principal Edwards Magis Theatre, Medicine Head, etc. List of artists who made debut on Peel's show is a history of UK rock: the FACES, LED ZEPPELIN, David BOWIE, the NICE, TEN YEARS AFTER; championing underdogs, he was discouraged by mid-'70s, seeing bands he'd promoted become rich and distant: embraced the punk explosion of '76, converted to the primal power of the RAMONES, the DAMNED; in a year Led Zep's 'Stairway To Heaven' had been replaced by the SEX PISTOLS' 'Anarchy In The UK' as listeners' favourite record. His eclecticism has been his only enemy; he has sometimes given airtime to bands so obviously derivative they didn't deserve it: but apart from his beloved Liverpool Football Club, music is his only interest, and his ears are open, the very model of a pop DJ to whom every A&R man in the UK owes a great debt. *The Peel Sessions* EPs began '86 with items by the Damned, New Order, Stiff Little Fingers. He'll never give up: raved mid-'88 about thrash band Extreme Noise Terror

PEER, Ralph Sylvester (*b* 22 May 1892, Independence, Mo.; *d* 19 Jan. '60, Hollywood, Cal.) Talent scout, record producer; with luck, instinct and enlightened self-interest created music publishing empire. Of all the pioneers in early 'hillbilly' and 'race' music, incl. Lester MELROSE and British-born Art SATHERLEY, Peer became the best known and most successful. His father sold sewing machines, Columbia phonographs and records; Ralph ordered records and parts for phonographs, went to work for Columbia in Kansas City, was hired away to Okeh and worked for Fred Hagar, who was responsible for the first blues record (Mamie SMITH's 'Crazy Blues' '20); Peer coined the term 'race' records (less limiting than 'Negro'). He recorded harmonica player Henry Whittier early '23 but thought nothing of it; was sent to Atlanta in June, where furniture dealer Polk Brockman wanted to record Fiddlin' John Carson: 'The Little Old Log Cabin In The Lane'/'Old Hen Cackled And The Rooster's Going To Crow' was the first genuine country record, but Peer didn't like it and refused to give it an Okeh catalogue number; Brockman soon sold out the initial pressing and history was made. Peer made more field trips, recorded Pop STONEMAN, a string band from Virginia called the Hill Billies (naming the music); he soon realised the value of copyrights, pressed artists for 'new' songs, but also knew it was foolish to cheat the composers, offering royalties from the beginning. He left Okeh late '25, could not find another job, so offered to record free for Victor in exchange for copyrights. Time and again he was in the right place at the right time: he chose Bristol, Tennessee because it seemed a good spot, first week in August '27 recorded the first sessions of Jimmie RODGERS and the CARTER FAMILY; also made the most famous sides by bluesmen Tommy JOHNSON and Ishman Bracey in Memphis '28 (his contact in this case was music shop owner H. C. Speir in Jackson, Ms. (*b* 1895), who made test recordings and sent them to Peer). Formed Southern Music '28, owned by Victor with the understanding that Victor would throw pop copyrights his way; Victor did not honour this agreement, Peer picking up scraps (Hoagy CARMICHAEL's 'Lazy Bones', Don REDMAN's 'Cherry'), but RCA's David Sarnoff sold Southern Music with all its copyrights to Peer '32 to avoid anti-trust problems. Affiliated with ASCAP since '28, he formed Peer International '40, among first important BMI affiliates, 40 years later still the biggest; became an expert on international copyright law, set up the first overseas offices for country music. He also grew camellias, receiving a medal from the Royal Horticultural Society in London for research. His widow continued to support the Country Music Association (CMA; *see* COUNTRY MUSIC) especially in international aspects; son Ralph Peer Jr held CMA offices.

PENDERGRASS, Teddy (*b* '50, Philadelphia, Pa.) Sweet soul singer and sex symbol, aka Teddy Bear. Sang in church, accompanied his mother to the night club where she worked, was a capable drummer at 13; joined local group the Cadillacs, who became the backing group for Harold Melvin and the Blue Notes '69; Melvin re-formed that group with Pendergrass as lead singer and signed with Gamble & Huff's Philadelphia International '70; he went solo '76. His singles did not cross over to the pop chart so

well because by then the singles market was dominated by disco's number-of-beats-to-the-minute, but his albums charted strongly: *Teddy Pendergrass* '77, *Life Is A Song Worth Singing* '78, *Teddy* '79 (at no. 5 his best showing), 2-disc *Teddy Live! Coast To Coast* '79 (with three live sides, one of interview and studio recordings), *TP* '80, *It's Time For Love* '81, *This One's For You* '82. His first UK tour was postponed because he was having an affair with the wife of Marvin GAYE, who was touring there for the same promoter; in March '82, a few weeks after his UK tour, he was paralysed from the neck down in a car accident. He came back '84 with *Heaven Only Knows* on Philadelphia International, which charted much less well; returned to the top 40 LPs on Asylum with *Love Language* '84, followed by *Workin' It Back* late '85, *Joy* '88. He also had top 40 duet hit 'Two Hearts' '81 with Stephanie Mills (*b* '57, Brooklyn; starred four years in Broadway hit *The Wiz*, the black version of *Wizard Of Oz*, but Diana ROSS starred in the film because Berry Gordy bought the rights; Mills' hits incl. no. 6 'Never Knew Love Like This Before' '80) and recorded 'Hold Me' with young Whitney HOUSTON '84, leading up to her solo success.

PENGUIN CAFÉ ORCHESTRA UK group formed late '70s by multi-instrumentalist, composer Simon Jeffes (*b* '48). He studied music in London late '60s, visited Japan '72; a friend gave him a tape of African music '73; he rejected experimental music because after a concert of it he still wanted to hear some music. Along the way he arr. strings for Sid Vicious's 'My Way', tutored Adam ANT on Burundi drumming, etc. He says the PCO is for 'people capable of enjoying Wilson Pickett, Beethoven, the Rolling Stones, choral music from West Africa, Bach, Stravinsky, Irish bagpipe music and even Abba on the odd occasion'. LPs on EG label, originally by way of Brian ENO's Obscure label: *Music From The Penguin Café*, *Penguin Café Orchestra* '81, *Broadcasting From Home* '84 (incl. 'Music For A Found Harmonium', used in UK TV advert for new national daily paper *The Independent* '86), *Signs Of Life* '87. The music sounds 'roughly like a string quartet letting its hair down at some mysteriously-located barn dance of the future', wrote Robert Sandall in the *Sunday Times*; it is a string band of up to seven people incl. Helen Liebmann on cello, Gavyn Wright, Elizabeth Perry, Bob Loveday on violins; Steve Nye on keyboards, Neil Rennie on cuatro, ukelele; Jeffes playing everything incl. tape, plus other guests on percussion, etc. Occasionally one wishes that a track led to something more, like a hot fiddle solo by Vassar CLEMENTS, but it is gently insidious, often foot-tapping music.

PENGUINS, The Black USA doo-wop group, one of the first R&B groups to crack the top 10 of the pop chart: lead singer Cleveland Duncan (*b* 23 July '35) and Curtis Williams, Bruce Tate, Dexter Tisby, all *b* '35. They formed on leaving high school in L.A. and named themselves after the Penguin on Kool cigarettes, recorded 'Earth Angel (Will You Be Mine)', no. 1 R&B, no. 8 late '54, selling four million copies on DooTone. Despite their historic success, the era of white covers was not yet over, and the CREW-CUTS beat them to no. 3 in '55 with the song (written by Jesse BELVIN; also revived '69 by the Vogues on Reprise). Manager Buck Ram went on to greater success with the PLATTERS; Penguins recorded for Mercury, Atlantic, Sun State, never had another hit; Duncan reformed the group several times for oldies shows.

PENNY, Hank (*b* Herbert Clayton Penny, 18 Aug. '18, Birmingham, Ala.) Country music bandleader, vocalist: writer Ken Griffis described him as 'The Original Outlaw' in '82. He worked at WWL in New Orleans and on the *Midwestern Hayride* on WLW in Cincinnati, Ohio, but was bowled over by what he called 'Texas fiddle music' and formed band the Radio Cowboys in the jazz-oriented Western Swing style, modelled after Milton Brown's Musical Brownies. He first recorded for Art SATHERLEY on Okeh Records '38 in Atlanta, Ga. and popularised the style in the Southeast, his early sidemen incl. Boudleaux BRYANT on fiddle, steel guitarists Noel Boggs and Eddie Duncan, all influenced by jazzmen. Signature song was 'Won't You Ride In My Little Red Wagon'; his biggest hit was probably 'Bloodshot Eyes' on King; he also recorded for

Columbia, Decca and RCA: Bear Family LP UK has RCA tracks from the early '50s, with several vocals by Jaye P. MORGAN. In the '70s he had reverted to his other skill as a comedian in California.

PENTANGLE British folk group. Original lineup: Terry Cox, drums; Bert Jansch, guitar, vocals; Jacqui McShee, vocals; John Renbourn, guitar, vocals, sitar; Danny Thompson, bass. Their formation sent out ripples in the folk scene, because of the standing of Jansch and Renbourn and their teaming with musicians of the others' quality, but perhaps they never lived up to expectations. They played an innovative mixture of folk and jazz, though remembered as a folk band; Jansch and Renbourn had had strong jazz inflections in their earlier *Bert And John*. Debuted with *The Pentangle* '68, earning acclaim from critics as well as fellow musicians; 2-disc *Sweet Child* '68 was also well-received; *Basket Of Light* '69 was boosted to no. 5 in UK album chart by incl. of theme music from BBC TV drama *Take Three Girls*. They could not maintain the impetus: *Cruel Sister* '70, *Reflections* '71 (all on Transatlantic) and *Solomon's Seal* '72 (on Reprise) were not as highly regarded. Much of this work was repackaged after they split up; Jansch and Renbourn continued as solo artists, Cox and Thompson returned to session work. A reunion in the early '80s was ill-fated; e.g. *Open The Door* '84 on Spindrift united four of them with Mike Piggott replacing Renbourn, but legends are often best left alone. Thompson, best known for partnership with John MARTYN in intervening years, surfaced as a bandleader with *Whatever* '87 on Hannibal, a successful blend of jazz and ethnic shadings.

PEPPER, Art (*b* Arthur Edward Pepper, 1 Sep. '25, Gardena, Cal.; *d* 15 June '82) Alto sax; also tenor and clarinet, composer. Played as a teenager with Gus ARNHEIM, then black groups on Central Avenue in L.A. incl. Lee Young (Lester's drummer brother, an unrecorded but highly praised band), then Stan KENTON; served in US Army, rejoined Kenton, freelanced in L.A. but was off the scene intermittently because of narcotics. Played with Buddy RICH '68-9. Always highly regarded, he had incorporated the melodic side of Lester YOUNG, elements of Zoot SIMS and Benny CARTER as well as Charlie PARKER into his own unique style; later he was infl. by John COLTRANE during an unrecorded period, which left additional toughness rather than a direct stylistic resemblance. Recorded with Shelly MANNE, Shorty ROGERS, Mel TORMÉ, Carl PERKINS, Chet BAKER (*Playboys* on Boplicity), others; among his own albums are some of the era's most beautiful: mostly quartet sessions began with *Popo* '51 (with Rogers), *The Late Show* and *The Early Show* '52 with Hampton HAWES, all on Xanadu; more tracks with Hawes '52, others '52-4 on *Discoveries*, alternate takes on *Rediscoveries*, all on Savoy; others with pianists Sonny CLARK, Russ Freeman, Marty Paich on Straight Ahead Jazz, Jazz West, Tampa '53-6; quintet *The Way It Was* '56 with Warne MARSH, then *Meets the Rhythm Section* '57 on Contemporary: he often rose to the challenge no matter what condition he was in; he later wrote that for the date with Miles DAVIS' rhythm section (Red GARLAND, Paul CHAMBERS, Philly Joe JONES) he was completely unprepared, yet the LP was his first fully-realised masterpiece. Pacific Jazz tracks '57 were released in that label's most slapdash way; tracks with Perkins '58 on Liberty/Blue Note (*Omega Alpha*) and for Apollo (later issued on Onyx, Japanese Trio); then *Modern Jazz Classics: Art Pepper Plus Eleven* '59, arr. by Paich, highly praised by Robert Gordon in book *Jazz West Coast* '86 (Paich said that when word got out he was besieged with calls from musicians who wanted to play on a Pepper session), in '60 *Gettin' Together* (with a new Davis rhythm section, this time Chambers, Jimmy COBB, Wynton KELLY, and Conte CANDOLI on some tracks), quartets *Smack Up* and *Intensity* (both with Frank Butler on drums) all on Contemporary: no more Pepper albums until '73. Repeatedly arrested for narcotics violations, finally entered Synanon Foundation '69-71, played with groups there, began slow comeback with big band LP on Japanese Atco label with Mike Vax (trumpet, leader); by the time he died he had been welcomed back by fans old and new around the world and made many more fine LPs, (quartet sessions except where noted): aptly titled *Living Legend* with Hawes, Manne, Charlie HADEN was followed by *The Trip*, *No Limit* and *Live At*

The Village Vanguard with pianist George Cables, his most frequent latterday collaborator, also Elvin JONES, others, all '75-7 on Contemporary. Four vols. of *The Art Pepper Memorial Sessions* '75-8 on Trio were made in California, Japan; *Among Friends* '78 on Interplay had Butler, Freeman, bassist Bob Magnusson. *Landscape – Live In Tokyo* and *Besame Mucho* '79 were on JVC; *Darn That Dream* '82 on Real Time added Joe Farrell on tenor; *The Gauntlet* '77 on WB is soundtrack of a Clint Eastwood movie ('Buried under a ton of sound effects is a glorious music score by Jerry Fielding . . . with more than a nod towards *Sketches Of Spain*' – David Meeker). The rest of his later LPs are on Galaxy: *Art Pepper Today* '78, *So In Love* (with Hank JONES, Ron CARTER, drummer Frank Foster); *Artworks*, *New York Album*, *Straight Life*, all '79; *One September Afternoon*, *Art Lives*, *Road Games* '80-1, *Winter Moon* '80 with strings, more. Last albums were duets with Cables, *Tête-à-Tête* and *Goin' Home* '82: he must be playing in heaven, because he'd already been to hell and back, documented in *Straight Life* '79, written with his wife Laurie, among the hardest hitting of music autobiographies; he was also subject of film *Notes From A Jazz Survivor* '81 (dir. by Don McGlynn).

PERKINS, Bill (*b* William Reese Perkins, 22 July '24, San Francisco, Cal.) Reeds. Spent part of childhood in Chile; studied music under GI bill, turned pro '50; played with Stan KENTON, Woody HERMAN '50s; worked as engineer at World Pacific Records, then in studios; later played in *Tonight* show band, with SUPERSAX during its first year; much studio work. Played on albums with Art PEPPER, Tal FARLOW, Bud SHANK, Victor FELDMAN, Marty Paich, Paul CHAMBERS, Toshiko AKIYOSHI '74-5, Nat PIERCE, others. Specialised in woodwinds incl. piccolo in studios; main instrument is tenor sax on records, also plays baritone, flute, occasionally bass clarinet. Several LPs on Pacific Jazz/World Pacific '50s incl. *Grand Encounter* '56 with John LEWIS; *Tenors Head-On* '56 co-led by Richie Kamuca; *Bossa Nova With Strings* '63 on Liberty, quintet/quartet LPs *Quietly There* '66 on Riverside, *Plays Lester Young* '78 on Yupiteru, *Confluence* '78 on Interplay,

Many Ways To Go '80 on Sea Breeze, *Journey To The East* '84, also *Serious Swingers* with Shank '86, both on Contemporary.

PERKINS, Carl (*b* 16 Aug. '28, Indianapolis, Ind.; *d* 17 Mar. '58) Very fine and infl. West Coast modern jazz pianist, whose short life was cursed with narcotics. Left hand was slightly handicapped by polio, which perhaps led to more blues inflection than in the work of Hampton HAWES. Played with Tiny BRADSHAW, Big Jay McNeely; settled on West Coast, played with early edition of Max ROACH-Clifford BROWN quintet, was key member of Curtis COUNCE quintet; played and recorded with Harold LAND, Art PEPPER, Chet BAKER, Jim HALL, others. His own albums were too few: Savoy tracks '49, *Introducing Carl Perkins* '56 on DooTone (now on Boplicity in UK) with Leroy Vinnegar, Lawrence Marable on drums (another album may have been recorded and never released), a Pacific Jazz LP '57 with Hall and bassist Red Mitchell, a drummer later dubbed on some tracks. His tune 'Grooveyard' from a '58 Land LP became a standard.

PERKINS, Carl (*b* Carl Lee Perkings, 9 Apr. '32, Tiptonville, Tenn.) Singer, guitarist, songwriter: the quintessential rockabilly, infl. a generation of rock'n'rollers incl. the BEATLES. Grew up listening to black blues, country and gospel music; learned guitar at an early age, won local talent contest playing and singing his own 'Movie Magg' at 13. Formed group the Perkins Brothers with Jay (*d* '58) and Clayton (*d* '74), played at local honky tonk the El Rancho Club '47-8, appeared on radio WDXT in Jackson, Tenn. '50-2; worked days in a bakery for years. Signed to SUN subsidiary Flip in Memphis '54; first release 'Movie Magg' '55, then 'Let The Juke Box Keep Playing', 'Gone, Gone, Gone'; hit jackpot with 'Blue Suede Shoes' '56, suggested by a remark overheard at a dance. It was no. 2 in Billboard pop and country charts (no. 1 in Cashbox), but on the way to NYC to appear on Ed Sullivan, Perry COMO TV shows a car crash hospitalised him; Elvis PRESLEY covered 'Blue Suede Shoes' and Perkins' career never recovered its pop momentum. 'Boppin' The Blues', 'Your True Love', 'Dixie Fried' were top 10 country hits '56-7,

the first two minor pop hits. Presley's early records were classic rock'n'roll, tougher and with a suggestion of a snarl, but Perkins was a truer rockabilly, never losing the flavour of the Saturday-night country dance: 'Blue Suede Shoes' was accepted as a novelty, but Perkins' country boy knows he will be back behind the plough on Monday: the shoes are all he's got, he's not complaining; just don't step on 'em. 'Honey Don't' was intended to be the A-side of the big hit; many a middle-class American teenager found it very strange indeed, flipping the record over; by the time it was covered by the Beatles (along with 'Matchbox' and 'Everybody's Trying To Be My Baby') the contribution of country boys (and blacks, both urban and country) was entering the mainstream. He switched to Columbia '58 for minor pop hits 'Pink Pedal Pushers' and 'Pointed Toe Shoes' '58-9; went back to country music, signing with Dollie '63 for minor country hits 'Country Boy's Dream' and 'Shine, Shine' '66-7, joined the Johnny CASH road show '65-75, lending his guitar wizardry, doing his own solo spots and providing Cash with big hit 'Daddy Sang Bass' '68, the year he returned to Columbia for country hits 'Restless', 'Cotton Top', 'High On Love' '69-72, then to Mercury with remake of 'Dixie Fried' '73. He gained a whole new following mid-'70s in UK with appearances at the Wembley Festival, TV-advertised album *Old Blue Suede Shoes Is Back* '77 on Jet. In the USA he works with a five-piece band incl. sons Gregg and Stan, records for his own appropriately named Suede label. Reissues of early material on Sun in USA; better editions from Charly UK incl. *The Original Carl Perkins* (with 16 tracks) and 3-disc complete box of *The Sun Years*, also *The Million Dollar Quartet* (long a bootleg, with Perkins, Cash, Presley and Jerry Lee LEWIS), *The Trio Plus* (with Lewis, Charlie RICH and friends). Many other albums incl. *Whole Lotta Shakin'* '59, *On Top* '71, *The Man Behind Johnny Cash* '73, *The Survivors* '82 (with Cash and Lewis), all on Columbia (CBS); *My Kind Of Country* '74 on Mercury; *Live At Austin City Limits* '82 on Suede, *That Rockin' Guitar Man Today* '83 and *Goin' Back To Memphis* '86 on Magnum Force, *Class Of '55* '86 on America/Smash (with Cash, Lewis, Roy ORBISON).

PERRY, Richard (*b* 18 June '42, Brooklyn, NY) Record producer with notable success in '70s. From musical family; played in local groups during high school years, studied music at U. of Michigan; interested in musical theatre, went to NYC to do some (bass) singing and dancing, but began to write songs with Kenny Vance of JAY AND THE AMERICANS. His early group was the Legends, who changed their name to the Escorts, recorded for Coral, gigged at Peppermint Lounge etc. (lead singer Goldie Zelkowitz later became Genya RAVAN). Turned from performing to production late '60s, oversaw several obscure singles, got to know bosses at Red Bird Records (LEIBER & STOLLER and George Goldner, whose daughter Linda he married). Moved to L.A.; first notable project was seminal *Safe As Milk* LP by CAPTAIN BEEFHEART; worked for WB/Reprise, prod. TINY TIM (an amusing fluke of the early '70s, whom Perry had discovered in NYC), also Fats DOMINO (*Fats Is Back*), Ella FITZGERALD, ANDERS & PONCIA, Theodore BIKEL; three LPs for all-girl group Fanny. Subsequent freelance work incl. three LPs for Barbra STREISAND (incl. *Stoney End*, with Fanny backing), Harry NILSSON's two best-sellers *Nilsson Schmilsson* and *Son Of Schmilsson* (incl. no. 1 single 'Without You'), three LPs for Carly SIMON (incl. *No Secrets*, with no. 1 hit 'You're So Vain'), Andy WILLIAMS' last hit LP *Solitaire*, two for Ringo STARR '73-4 (*Ringo* and *Goodnight Vienna*, incl. no. 1 hits 'Photographs' and 'You're Sixteen'). Admittedly the '70s were a boring decade, but Perry prod. some of its most memorable work, carrying on with highly regarded (if not huge selling) debut solo LP for Martha REEVES '74, top 10 Art GARFUNKEL *Breakaway* '75, MANHATTAN TRANSFER's *Coming Out* '77 (no. 1 UK hit 'Chanson d'Amour'), disappointing Diana ROSS LP *Baby It's You* '77. Back in the charts '76-8 with three Leo SAYER LPs incl. two more no. 1 USA singles 'You Make Me Feel Like Dancing' and 'Long Tall Glasses', making six Perry-prod. no. ones. Formed own Planet label '78; best act was the POINTER SISTERS, incl. top 3 singles 'Fire', 'He's So Shy', 'Slow Hand', 'Jump (For My Love)'; sold Planet to RCA. He is a master of the studio, but a reaction against too much production now looms.

PETER AND GORDON UK pop duo formed '64: Peter ASHER and Gordon Waller (*b* 4 June '45, Braemar, Scotland), vocals, guitars. School friends modelled duo on EVERLY Bros, were nothing if not well-connected: Asher's sister Jane was Paul MCCARTNEY's girl friend; gift of a BEATLE song ensured no. 1 UK/USA with first release, 'World Without Love' '64. Further top 40s incl. McCartney's 'Nobody I Know', 'Woman' (pseudonymous, but word got out); also Buddy HOLLY's 'True Love Ways', Phil SPECTOR's 'To Know You Is To Love You'. As with CHAD & JEREMY, success lasted longer in the USA, where they seemed archetypical fresh-faced English boys; last hit was 'Sunday For Tea' (by Carter-Lewis, pseudonym for John Shakespeare/Kenneth Hawker). They split '68; Waller made news with Elvis PRESLEY impersonation while playing Judas in *Joseph And The Amazing Technicolor Dreamcoat* '70s. Asher drew prod. job at Beatles' Apple label, met James TAYLOR; prod. and managed him in USA, went on to more success.

PETER, PAUL & MARY Folk-protest trio formed '61 NYC: Peter Yarrow (*b* 31 May '38, NYC) and Paul Stookey (*b* 30 Nov. '37, Baltimore, Md.), guitars and vocals; Mary Travers (*b* 7 Nov. '37, Louisville, Ky.), vocals. Travers had been off-Broadway actress, Yarrow a solo folksinger, Stookey a stand-up comic and sometime singer; they were put together by Albert Grossman (before he managed Bob DYLAN), were immediately successful (one critic described them as 'the KINGSTON TRIO with sex appeal'). Intensive rehearsals saw them in the right place at the right time, in forefront of protest music and champions of Dylan's songs. *Peter, Paul & Mary* '62, *Moving* and *In The Wind* '63 were definitive LPs of their type; appearances at Newport Folk Festivals were instant legends. They allied themselves to civil rights and anti-war movements, encouraged Gordon LIGHTFOOT and John DENVER as well as Dylan; *In Concert* '65 remains a good example of their appeal. In halcyon days of '62-3 their hit singles incl. Pete SEEGER's 'If I Had A Hammer' (no. 10), Dylan's 'Blowin' In The Wind' (no. 3), 'Puff The Magic Dragon' (no. 2; the last still a popular children's song, though at the time some thought it was a drug song). As Dylan began to write more elusive lyrics, they remained faithful to pure folk in LPs *A Song Will Rise* '65, *The Peter, Paul & Mary Album* '66; *Album 1700* '67 was transitional, incl. quirky 'I Dig Rock'n'Roll Music'; *Late Again* '68 kept fans happy; *Peter, Paul & Mommy* '69 was a whole album of children's songs. 'Leavin' On A Jet Plane' was a surprise no. 1 '69, but their impact had now dulled; Stookey was converted to Christianity, changed name to Noel Paul Stookey. *10 Years Together* '69 was a compilation. They split, reunited for George McGovern benefit '72, in '78 after an anti-nuclear benefit, now do 50 concerts a year. *Reunion* '78 was not very strong; *Such Is Love* '82 incl. Phil OCHS' 'There But For Fortune'. Stookey released *Paul & . . .* '71, *Band & Body Works* '80, three sets of biblical songs; Yarrow did highly praised *That's Enough For Me* '73 (incl. an unreleased Paul SIMON song), also wrote hit 'Torn Between Two Lovers' '71 for Mary McGregor (no. 1 USA, 4 UK). Mary did three solo LPs. Trio's *No Easy Walk To Freedom* '86 still slick but sincere, incl. songs about El Salvador. If Mary ever felt self-important, that ended, she says, when she tried to play one of their gold albums out of curiosity: it was a gold-coloured Dean MARTIN record. She is active on behalf of Soviet Jews, does solo gigs: 'There are always new songs . . . but the inherent content of what I'm singing remains the same.'

PETERSON, Oscar (*b* Oscar Emmanuel Peterson, 15 Aug. '25, Montreal, Canada) Piano; also composer. Began playing at age 6; won talent contest at 14, soon played on radio; long a popular Canadian artist (recorded for RCA in Canada '45-9), he had USA offers and came to NYC '49 to Carnegie Hall with Norman GRANZ's JATP. He led trio '50s with Ray BROWN on bass; Irving Ashby on guitar (*b* 29 Dec. '20, Somerville, Mass.; *d* 22 Apr. '87, Perris, Cal.) succeeded by Barney KESSEL, Herb ELLIS; in '58 drums replaced guitar: Ed Thigpen (*b* 28 Dec. '30, Chicago; father Ben played with Andy KIRK in turn replaced '65 by Louis Hayes (*b* 31 May '37, Detroit; with Horace SILVER late '50s); Brown left '66, replaced by Sam JONES.

Peterson played solo recitals c.'72, but soon resumed trio format and has made very few solo records; latterday sidemen incl. drummers Bobby Durham, Ray Price; Joe PASS on guitar, George Mraz, Niels-Henning Ørsted Pedersen on bass; he went to the USSR '74 with the latter, Jake Hanna on drums, but cut tour short in disagreement with Soviet authorities over conditions. He also recorded with Louie BELLSON on drums, had reunions with Ellis, Brown; also played the organ (clavichord '76 in duo with Pass on *Porgy & Bess*) and sang occasionally from '53, resumed singing after some years on LP *With Respect To Nat* '65 on Limelight. He is a serious, hard-working man, intent on doing a good job, and became one of the most popular jazz musicians in the world. His first NYC recordings were duets with Brown or Major Holley on bass '50 on Verve; he recorded with Billie HOLIDAY, Lester YOUNG, Louis ARMSTRONG, Coleman HAWKINS, Fred ASTAIRE, Ella FITZGERALD, Benny CARTER, Roy ELDRIDGE, Clark TERRY, Stan GETZ, Buddy DE FRANCO, Nelson RIDDLE, Milt JACKSON, many more plus nearly 60 LPs of his own, mostly on Granz-associated labels Verve, Clef, Norgan and Mercury '50s-60s; also on MPS/BASF late '60s-early '70s, rejoined Granz on his Pablo label and made over 30 more. Initially he was infl. by Teddy WILSON, Erroll GARNER, Nat COLE, George SHEARING, admitted admiration of Art TATUM and continued to grow as a musician infl. by Tatum, especially harmonically, but it is wrong to assume direct influence of Tatum's style: Tatum and Peterson have common roots in classical music; Peterson's phenomenal technique was already apparent as a teenager and he has been described as the Liszt of jazz (Bill EVANS being the Chopin). With jazz roots deep in the mainstream, he is also a masterful accompanist. He is not an innovator, except in the sense that he has brought immense formal skill to the playing of jazz, and orthodoxy has it that technical skill is supposed to be kept hidden: because he has been among the most commercially successful in jazz since Dave BRUBECK without advancing the frontier of the avant-garde, some critics and musicians have taken him for granted (though sooner or later most admit admiration); some have even said that he does not swing: in fact musicians who play with him discover that his powerful brand of swing dominates the proceedings. His few solo LPs incl. *My Favourite Instrument* '68 and *Tracks* '70 on MPS (now on Pausa and Verve respectively in USA), *Terry's Tune* '74 (made in Tokyo), live tracks from USSR '74, *At Salle Pleyel* '75 on Pablo; these are so fine that fans wish he would record more solo. Duet LPs incl. *Two Of The Few* '83 with Jackson; *Digital At Montreux* '79 with Ørsted Pedersen; with Gillespie in London, Eldridge and Harry EDISON in L.A. '74. *Bursting Out With The All Star Big Band*, trio *Affinity* made Billboard's top 200 pop LPs '63, *Trio + One* '64 (with Terry) no. 81. Other highlights incl. *Jazz Portrait Of Frank Sinatra*, songbook LPs of Cole PORTER, George GERSHWIN, Duke ELLINGTON, Jerome KERN, Richard RODGERS, Harry WARREN & Vincent YOUMANS, Harold ARLEN and Jimmy McHUGH, all '59; his own *Canadian Suite* '64 (all these with Brown and Thigpen) and *Royal Wedding Suite* '81 (orchestra led by Russ Garcia); piano duets with Count BASIE (and rhythm) *Satch And Josh* '74, *Again* '77; *Oscar Peterson Jam* '77 at Montreux with Gillespie, Terry, Lockjaw DAVIS, Durham, Ørsted Pedersen; *The Silent Partner* '79 with Carter, Terry, Jackson, Zoot SIMS, John Heard on bass, drummer Grady Tate; many other combinations plus the many trio LPs. His recording schedule has eased in the last few years, and no wonder: he was exhaustively recorded by Granz, and with so many records to choose from his fans need a long shelf. Biography *Oscar Peterson: The Will To Swing* '88 by Gene Lees.

PETRILLO, James Caesar (*d* 23 Oct. '84 at age 92). Pianist, bandleader from Chicago who was president of the American Federation of Musicians and perpetrated disaster upon it. Record labels bore the legend 'unlicensed for public broadcasting', which was ignored; Supreme Court Judge Learned Hand had ruled '40 that copyright was not infringed by the playing of a record on the radio. The suit had been brought by RCA and the decision was wrong, the opposite of the decision preceding the formation of ASCAP (*which see*), but the record companies were also foolish: broadcasting helped to sell records. Petrillo led the national union

from mid-'40; a combative little man who refused to shake hands for fear of germs, he commissioned bandleader Ben Selvin, experienced in both recording and radio, to determine whether records were putting musicians out of live work: Selvin reported to an AFM convention '41 that record labels paid millions of dollars to musicians and that union action was not the answer to problems caused by mechanisation of music, and got a standing ovation: the membership and the major bandleaders agreed with him, but Petrillo demanded that record companies refuse to allow records to be played on the radio and juke boxes, though they'd already tried that; then he ordered musicians to stop recording on 1 Aug. '42. DECCA caved in Sep. '43, CAPITOL a month later; RCA and COLUMBIA in Nov. '44; the union got a tax on recording dates to pay for free concerts so that the best professional musicians subsidised the mediocre (according to a War Labor Board report, two thirds of the union's rank-and-file membership did not depend on music for a living anyway). Along with many other factors, the strike was a death blow for the BIG BAND ERA (*which see*): many rising bands, as well as established bands in interesting formative periods, could not record (Alvino REY, Earl HINES, Billy ECKSTINE, Boyd RAEBURN, Woody HERMAN, etc.); but vocalists, not allowed to belong to the union, became stars: records made during the strike, many with choral backing, are now mostly forgotten, but that they were cheaper to make (later with studio musicians on salary) than records by name bands was not lost on the record companies. Just in case he hadn't done enough damage, Petrillo called a second recording ban in '48, when many bands had folded. He lasted through the '50s; many veteran musicians raised a glass when he died. Red CALLENDER's autobiography *Unfinished Dream* '85 tells good stories: it wasn't the union who integrated white and black locals, but the musicians themselves; and they had to sue their own union to get money they had earned out of one of Petrillo's trust funds.

PETRUCCIANI, Michel (*b* 28 Dec. '62, Orange, France) Pianist, composer. Mother French, father Sicilian; father and two brothers are also musicians. Suffers from calcium deficiency osteogenesis imperfecta ('glass bones'), has to be carried to and from the piano. He is one of the most exciting young musicians to emerge in recent years, infl. especially by Bill EVANS, Lennie TRISTANO; he played with touring Clark TERRY, etc. at about 15; left home at 17, worked with Kenny CLARKE in Paris; to USA West Coast, established friendship with Charles LLOYD; back to USA '80 and worked in NYC with bassist brother Louis. Still a young man, he is already evolving from the keyboard wunderkind who had to play everything to more imaginative improvising, tough and original. First LP *Flash* '80 on Bingo (French label) with Louis, Aldo Romano on drums, Mike Zwerin guesting on some tracks; *Michel Petrucciani* '81 on Owl with Romano, Jean-François Jenny-Clark on bass; *Estate* '82 on Riviera, made in Rome with Romano, Furio Di Castri on drums; *Toot Sweet* '82 on Owl with Lee KONITZ; solo *Oracle Destiny* '82 on Owl, *100 Hearts* '83 on Concord, *Note 'n' Notes* '84 on Owl, with two tracks overdubbed à la Evans' *Conversations With Myself*; 2-disc *Live At The Village Vanguard* '84 on Concord, with Palle Danielsson, bass, ex-Evans Eliot Zigmund on drums; *Cold Blues* '85 on Owl with bassist Ron McClure; trio *Pianism* '86 and *Power Of Three* on Blue Note, live at Montreux '86 with Jim HALL, guest Wayne SHORTER on some tracks. Trio *Michel Plays Petrucciani* '88 also on Blue Note. Also on Lloyd LPs *Montreux '82* on Elektra with Danielsson, 'Sonship' Theus on percussion; *A Night In Copenhagen* on Blue Note; also track on *One Night With Blue Note*.

PETTIFORD, Oscar (*b* 30 Sep. '22, Okmulgee, Okla. on Indian reservation; *d* 8 Sep. '60, Copenhagen) Bassist, also cello; composer. His father, Harry 'Doc' Pettiford, was a veterinary surgeon, mother a music teacher; they formed family band with ten musical siblings (brothers trumpeter Ira, trombonist Alonzo both played with Jay MCSHANN). The band was successful all over the Midwest; he was raised in Minnesota, hired by Charlie BARNET c.'42-3, got off in NYC, played at Minton's, very soon was the premier bassist, taking up in jazz where Jimmy BLANTON had left off, play-

ing solo lines with astonishing power, time and intonation. Made important recording dates in early modern jazz with Coleman HAWKINS, Ben WEBSTER, Earl HINES '43-4, co-led quintet with Dizzy GILLESPIE '44 etc.; played with Duke ELLINGTON '45-8, lending that band his special sound on broadcast records (during musicians' union strike against record companies). Joined Woody HERMAN '49, broke his arm playing baseball and while recuperating experimented with the cello, becoming the first to play that instrument like a bass. Led own groups (big band mid-'50s), recorded with Thelonious MONK, Art BLAKEY '55-7; went to Europe, settled in Copenhagen, worked with Stan GETZ, Bud POWELL. A heavy drinker and a volatile man, especially when drinking; the most infl. bassist between Blanton and Charles MINGUS. Own records incl. tracks later on Xanadu by Oscar Pettiford Big Band '45; small group tracks on Mercer '50-1 with Ellington, on Roost '52 and *The New Sextet* '53 (now on Fantasy) with Mingus, Pettiford on cello; *The Oscar Pettiford Memorial Album* '54 on Prestige (Pettiford on cello, bass multitracked), three Bethlehem LPs '54-5 incl. *Bohemia After Dark*, now on Affinity; *Oscar Pettiford Orchestra In HiFi* '56, big band on ABC, now on Jasmine; *The Legendary Oscar Pettiford* '59 and *Blue Brothers* '60 on Black Lion, made in Europe.

PETTY, Norman (*b* '27, Clovis, N.M.; *d* 15 Aug. '84, Lubbock, Texas) Pianist, record producer. Played piano from an early age; played on local radio, moved to Texas '48, became part-time recording engineer, led Norman Petty Trio playing organ, with wife Violet Ann on piano (*b* 17 Sep. '28, Clovis) and guitarist Jack Vaughn; moved back to Clovis, established own studio '54; trio recorded Duke ELLINGTON's 'Mood Indigo' for own NorVaJak label, leased it to RCA subsidiary 'X' for a top 20 hit '54, followed by top 40 'On The Alamo', lesser hits: used income to improve the studio. He recorded Buddy KNOX's 'Party Doll', Jimmy Bowen's 'I'm Stickin' With You' '56, leased them to Roulette and they each sold a million; he invited more outside musicians to use the studio; Buddy HOLLY and the CRICKETS turned up. Petty learned to record rock'n'roll drums, while Holly was an innovator to his fingertips: Petty managed them, helping and encouraging Holly's experiments, probably helped with arrangements, took co-credit as composer on some songs (a time-honoured practice in music business; he said he wrote lyrics, but his own hits were instrumentals). Vi played piano (on 'Think It Over'; also co-wrote 'Someone, Someone' with Edwin Greines Cohen, recorded by the Crickets, later a hit by Brian POOLE and the Tremeloes). Holly split from Petty '58; Petty acquired rights to unreleased tracks after Holly's death, overdubbed parts for release: this was criticised, but he made commercial hits from rough demos. Continued recording Crickets briefly; later success with Jimmy Gilmer and the Fireballs ('Sugar Shack' no. 1 '63, 'Daisy Petal Pickin' ' no. 15 '64) and instrumental group the Stringa-Longs ('Wheels' no. 3, 'Brass Buttons' top 40 '61). He sold rights to Holly songs to Paul MCCARTNEY early '70s, continued to run studio until his death.

PETTY, Tom, and the Heartbreakers USA rock group formed '75 in L.A. by Tom Petty (*b* 20 Oct. '53, Gainesville, Fla.), who'd been inspired by seeing Elvis PRESLEY filming on location in Fla. early '60s. Apprenticeship in school surfing bands, graduating to semi-pro Epics playing covers of ANIMALS, James BROWN, SAM & DAVE, instilling catholic taste he retains today. Returned to school to beat draft, joined Mudcrutch, top local band incl. Mike Campbell on guitar, Benmont Tench on keyboards; they moved to L.A. but broke up; Petty's plans to record solo for Shelter came to nothing; Campbell, Tench recruited local rhythm section of Stan Lynch, drums, Ron Blair on bass; Petty wrote them into Shelter plans, got booked supporting Nils LOFGREN on UK tour, taking *Tom Petty And The Heartbreakers* '76 to UK charts, a crisp debut LP borrowing from all areas of USA pop: as with TALKING HEADS, BLONDIE, TELEVISION, UK success preceded home acclaim. Top 40 hits UK/USA were derivative but delivered with panache; got seal of approval when ex-BYRD Roger McGuinn covered 'American Girl', toured with Petty. *You're Gonna Get It* '78 was disappointingly two-dimensional; his muse benefited from enforced layoff as MCA

bought Shelter and legal wrangles ensued; *Damn The Torpedoes* '79 on Backstreet (MCA associate) was better, no. 2 LP USA boosting him into Bruce SPRINGSTEEN/Bob SEGER 'blue collar hero' bracket, incl. top 10 'Don't Do Me Like That'.Follow-up tour cancelled because of tonsillitis; they played *No Nukes* concert (but scratched from film as he considered performance substandard); *Hard Promises* '81 again caused controversy as he refused to sell it for more than $0638.98 (its original title): he won, celebrated in sleeve photo, posing in front of stack of marked-down records. *Long After Dark* '82 was more of the same, Blair replaced by ex-John HIATT sideman Howie Epstein. Side projects incl. backing FLEETWOOD MAC's Stevie Nicks on solo *Bella Donna* '81 (incl. hit 'Stop Draggin' My Heart Around'), Del SHANNON comeback *Drop Down And Get Me* '81 (Petty produced). Top 20 hits finally followed by *Southern Accents* '85, bitty LP with several songs co-written by EURYTHMICS' Dave Stewart (incl. effective hit 'Don't Come Around Here No More'): some ideas worked better than others, but it was first real variation of sound since early days, bringing in some electronics; 2-disc live *Pack Up The Plantation* '85 was overblown, familiar groove of covers, hits; *Let Me Up (I've Had Enough)* '87 had 11 new songs incl. 'Jammin' Me', co-written with Bob DYLAN: few surprises but no clichés either. He can continue on stadium circuit but it would be a shame if he stagnated creatively. They toured Australia backing Dylan (video '87), some members played on Dylan's *Knocked Out Loaded*, all on single/title track of film *Band Of The Hand* (prod. by Petty). Tench backed Elvis COSTELLO live '87; Petty made solo album *Songs From The Garage* '88.

PHILLIPS, Esther (*b* Esther Mae Jones, 23 Dec. '35, Galveston, Texas; *d* 7 Aug. '84, L.A.) Singer, pianist. Moved with mother to Watts, L.A.; won amateur contest '49, then another at Johnny Otis's Barrelhouse Club: joined Otis's band as Little Esther, cut no. 1 R&B hit 'Double Crossing Blues' with Otis and vocal group the Charms for Savoy at about age 14. Probably the best early-teen singer of all time, handling blues with complete conviction, phrasing ballads, uptempo material in manner reminiscent of Dinah

WASHINGTON, to whom she came second in national deejay poll '50 to find best jazz/R&B artist of the year. Other '50 hits: 'Wedding Boogie', 'Far Away Christmas Blues', 'Deceivin' Blues', 'Mistrusting Blues', 'Cupid's Boogie', all top 10, all duets with Mel Walker backed by Otis, all except the last charting under Otis's name. Late '50 went solo, made 32 sides for Federal, only one top 10 R&B ('Ring-A-Ding-A-Doo' with Walker). Back to Savoy '53, to Decca '54; already suffering from drug problem, settled in Houston, inactive until late '50s, recording for Warwick '60. Comeback '62 with country song 'Release Me' on Lenox, no. 8 pop chart, LP of same name. To Atlantic '63; LPs *And I Love Him* (superb version of LENNON-McCARTNEY title song no. '54 pop '65); flown to UK by the BEATLES for TV special *Esther* '65. Newport Jazz Festival '66, then entered Synanon Drug Treatment Center at Santa Monica; out of music till '69: second comeback on Roulette label, appearances on Johnny Carson TV show, and Monterey Jazz Festival; on Atlantic again '70 for a live LP *Burnin' – Live at Freddie Jett's Pied Piper LA*: Carmen McCRAE wrote in sleeve note, 'If it weren't too late for me, I'd be happy to take lessons from Esther.' Album incl. 'Cry Me A River Blues', brilliant amalgam of every cliché in blues lyrics, became part of stage act; another portion of live recording issued on *Confessin' The Blues* '76. Active on world jazz circuit early '70s; recorded for Creed Taylor's Kudu label: albums *From A Whisper To A Scream*, *Alone Again Naturally* '72; *Black-Eyed Blues* '73, *Performance* '74, *Esther Phillips With Beck* '75, *Capricorn Princess* '76. Disco-oriented version of earlier Washington hit 'What A Diff'rence A Day Makes' world wide hit '75. On *Dinah Shore Show* '76, continued touring, no more record success: albums on Mercury *You've Come A Long Way Baby* '77, *All About Esther* '78, *Here's Esther* '79, *Good Black Is Hard To Crack* '81 seemed patchy, with unsuitable songs, settings. Death was from liver ailment. Leonard Feather remembered in *L.A. Times*: 'In 1973 she was nominated for a Grammy as best female R&B vocalist. She lost to Aretha FRANKLIN but Franklin promptly turned over her trophy to Miss Phillips, who she said should have won.'

PHILLIPS, Flip (*b* Joseph Edward Phillips, 26 Feb. '15, Brooklyn, NYC) Tenor sax. Played locally, then with Frankie Newton early '40s on clarinet, switched to tenor, with Benny GOODMAN '42, Wingy MANONE and Red NORVO in '43, Woody HERMAN '44-6; toured with JATP '46-56, moved to Florida, gigging locally with Bill Harris, etc.; working day job. Moved back to NYC and made comeback '75; toured Europe '82. During his JATP years he did a lot of honking crowd-pleasing work, but like Illinois JACQUET his talent was always wider than that; his own albums were always welcome and his comeback has been a welcome surprise to some ageing critics. Nice Signature sides '44-5, mostly with Herman sidemen, now on *A Melody From The Sky* on Doctor Jazz; seven LPs on Clef or Verve of '49-52 material, then with Oscar PETERSON, Herb ELLIS, Ray BROWN, Buddy RICH '54, all long out of print. Then he played bass clarinet as well as tenor on quartets *Flip In Florida* '63 on Sue or Onyx, *Phillips' Head* '75 on Choice; *Together* '78 on Century with Herman band; quartet *Flipenstein* '81 on Progressive, quintet *And His Swedish Friends* '82 on Swedish PHM, *A Sound Investment* '87 on Concord Jazz with Scott Hamilton Quartet. He was recorded at the Colorado Jazz Festival '71 by MPS/BASF.

PIAF, Edith (*b* Edith Giovanna Gassion, '15, Paris; *d* 11 Oct. '63) French cabaret singer. She was born almost in the street, blind from age 3 to 7 (probably psychosomatic), toured with her father's acrobatic act but became a street singer at 15. First employer Louis Leplee named her 'la môme Piaf' ('the waif sparrow') '35; the gig ended when he was murdered (killers never caught), but within six months she was playing the best vaudeville theatres. First sang on radio '36. Her songs about death, drugs, sex etc. make the most degenerate rock songs of today sound like nursery rhymes, because there was no self-pity: her husky, powerful, slightly melancholy voice, emotionally naked delivery, identification with her audience made her the best-loved singer in France, incl. several films. Biggest stardom was '45-early '50s; she first toured the USA '47; never wrote any songs but acquired songwriters intuitively. 'Le Vie en Rose' became an international standard; those best-known in USA/UK (where her more characteristic material did not translate well and could not be played on the radio, even in French) incl. 'What Can I Do?' (English words by Harold Rome; as 'Mais Qu'est-ce que J'ai' identified with her, Yves Montand); 'I'll Remember Today' (English words by William Engvick; hit in USA by Patti PAGE '56), 'If You Love Me (Really Love Me)' ('Hymne à l'Amour', English words by Geoffrey Parsons; hit in USA for Kay STARR '54). She started the careers of Montand, Charles AZNAVOUR, others; one of her many lovers was world middleweight boxing champion Marcel Cerdan (d '49 in plane crash). She toured USA 10 times, with vocal nonet Les Compagnons de la Chanson '47, whose 'Les Trois Cloches' became a hit for her late '40s (as 'The Three Bells' or 'The Jimmy Brown Song', a no. 1 hit for the BROWNS '59); her last hit was 'Milord' '60. Two vols. of memoirs were published in Paris '58, '64. Many compilations in France and UK on EMI incl. *The Complete Piaf* '83 on 14 discs. *Edith et Marcel* c.'83 was autobiographical film, 2-disc soundtrack.

PIANO RED (*b* William Lee Perryman, 19 Oct. '11, Hampton, Ga.; *d* 1 Aug. '85, Atlanta, Ga.) Singer, pianist, songwriter. One of 16 children; brother Rufus was SPECKLED RED; family moved to Atlanta '19; worked as upholsterer, played piano in church but soon moved on to rent parties, clubs. Nickname from complexion (he was an albino; also partly blind). Recorded with Blind Willie MCTELL '36; signed with RCA '50; had two-sided hit 'Rockin' With Red'/'Red's Boogie': first side charted '50, the other '51, sold a million: one of those records sometimes called first rock'n'roll record. Top 10 R&B hits '51: 'The Wrong Yo Yo', 'Just Right Bounce', 'Layin' The Boogie'. Often used sidemen such as Budd JOHNSON, Al Sears on records; was a regular on WAOK Atlanta, toured South, dropped by RCA '58; went to Jax, Chess, then Okeh '61: 'Dr Feelgood' a success; changed name of act, rocking band to Dr Feelgood And The Interns for LP of that name, played college circuit for a while. Was Piano Red again by early '70s; recorded live at Muhlenbrink's Saloon by Underground Atlanta; album *Happiness Is Piano Red* on King; appeared

in TV movie *The Catchers* '72; toured overseas, festivals; made LPs *Ain't Gonna Be Your Lowdown Dog No More* on Black Lion UK, *Dr Feelgood All Alone* aka *Wm Perryman (Alone With Piano)* on Arhoolie, both '75. Saw Europe again late '70s; suffered long illness. Compilation LPs: 20 RCA tracks on *Jumping The Boogie* (Oldie Blues), 16 Okeh tracks on *What's Up Doc?* (Edsel).

PIAZZOLA, Astor (*b* '21, Mar del Plata, Argentina) Arranger, bandleader. Grew up in NYC; encouraged by his father, learned to play bandoneon (an Argentine accordion), studied music. First heard proper tangos at 13 when Carlos GARDEL performed in NYC; Piazzola auditioned and played for Gardel in one of his Paramount films; returned to Argentina at 16 and from '39 played in all the current tango bands, also arranging for them; formed own tango orchestra '46. Was disenchanted with restricting genre; went to Paris, worked at formal composition, won awards; studied with Nadia Boulanger, who persuaded him to take a new look at tango. From mid-'50s he turned it upside down, injecting new rhythms and harmonies, called it the 'new' tango; though welcomed in concert halls in NY and Europe, danced by the world's leading ballet companies, it has never been accepted in Buenos Aires. He has written over 750 compositions incl. concertos, operas, film, theatre scores, made over 70 records incl. *Revolution In Tango 1965* on Polydor, *Live In Wien* on Spalax with quintet, *Tango: Zero Hour* '86 on American Clave with New Tango Quintet. *Astor Piazzola: Live* on American Clave was recorded in Austria and may be the same as the Spalax record. *The New Tango* on Atlantic with Gary BURTON was made at Montreux.

PICKETT, Wilson (*b* 18 Mar. '41, Prattville, Ala.) One of the great '60s soul singers, aka 'Wicked' Pickett. Family moved to Detroit '50s; he formed a vocal group that sang in churches, was recruited by local R&B group the Falcons, went solo and had R&B hits on Lloyd PRICE's Double-'L label ('If You Need Me', 'It's Too Late' '63), signed to Atlantic. After two flop singles Jerry Wexler sent him to Memphis to record at Stax with

915

BOOKER T AND THE MGs: 'In The Midnight Hour' '65 was no. 1 R&B co-written with Steve Cropper, '634-5789' did it again '66 (by Cropper and Eddie Floyd; later covered by Ry COODER); both crossed over strongly to the pop chart. He continued recording in Memphis, Muscle Shoals, Miami; had 30 Top 40 R&B/soul hits '63-71 (not counting '64, when Billboard's R&B chart was not published, it was so similar to the pop chart); other no. ones incl. 'Land Of 1000 Dances' '66, 'Funky Broadway' '67 (both top 10 pop), 'Don't Knock My Love' '71 (no. 13 pop); he never made it to the topof the pop chart, but had 38 entries in the Hot 100, 16 in top 40. Among highlights were two-sided hits 'You Can't Stand Alone'/'Soul Dance Number 3' and 'Stag-O-Lee'/'I'm In Love' '67, 'Jealous Love'/'I've Come A Long Way' '68, also 'Mustang Sally', 'Engine No. 9', 'Hey Jude', and many more. He switched to RCA '73, recorded for UA/EMI America (*I Want You* '79, *The Right Track* '81). Had 14 albums in the top 200 '65-73; the hits compilations will never go out of print.

PIERCE, Nat (*b* 16 July '25, Somerville, Mass.) By own admission one of the finest rhythm pianists in jazz. Worked for Woody HERMAN early '50s, again early '60s, eight years altogether as chief organiser, arr. as well as pianist; also played and/or arr. for Count BASIE, Louie BELLSON, others; depped for Claude THORNHILL, Stan KENTON, Basie when they were ill; also led own big bands on and off (*Big Band At The Savoy Ballroom* '57 on RCA); also did many jazz festivals, worked in music education and played on superb mainstream small-group albums (e.g. *Jo Jones Special*, *Ruby Braff Special* on Vanguard, Basie reunions on Prestige mid-to-late '50s). His style when leading or comping at the piano is hard to tell from Basie's in its economy and swing; any record he plays on is the better for it. He co-leads the big band CAPP-PIERCE JUG-GERNAUT (*which see*). His own LPs incl. *Boston Bustout* on Hep UK and *1948-1950* on Zim USA, different but complementary sets from '48-50 with Charlie MARIANO, Serge CHALOFF, Ralph BURNS, singer Teddi King making her record debut (*b* 18 Sep. '29, Boston, Mass.): sides from long-defunct Motif label, unreleased material

etc. Also reissue *The Nat Pierce – Dick Collins Nonet/Charlie Mariano Sextet* on Fantasy; *Ballad Of Jazz Street* '61 on Zim USA/Hep UK (incl. Paul QUINICHETTE, Paul GONSALVES, Clark TERRY, etc.; three-part title composition), *5400 North* '78 on Hep, live recording with trumpeter Collins (*b* 19 July '24, Seattle, Wash.), Bill PERKINS, Frankie Capp, Mary Ann McCall's vocals.

PIERCE, Webb (*b* 8 Aug. '26, West Monroe, La.) Flamboyant country singer, one of the biggest stars of the '50s-60s. Sold shoes at Sears & Roebuck, joined US Army '44, worked on local radio and clubs late '40s, joined Louisiana Hayride in Shreveport and soon became a star. Contract with Four Star Records led to Decca label, country chart hits every year '52-72, incl. 'Wondering', 'That Heart Belongs To Me', 'Back Street Affair', all '52; 'It's Been So Long' and 'There Stands The Glass' '53; 'Slowly', 'Even Tho' and 'More And More' '54 (latter crossing over to pop chart according to *Pop Memories*); two-sided no. ones '55: 'In The Jailhouse Now' (by Jimmie RODGERS)/'I'm Gonna Fall Out Of Love With You', 'I Don't Care'/'Your Good For Nothing Heart', 'Love Love Love'/'If You Were Me'; many more. His band the Wandering Boys was the start of many careers, incl. those of Faron YOUNG, the WILBURN Bros, Floyd CRAMER, others. Left Hayride and moved to Nashville '54 and with Red SOVINE joined the Grand Ole Opry; they had duet hits incl. 'Why Baby Why?', 'Little Rosa' '55-6. He was more than a star, also pro-foundly influential: 'Back Street Affair' and 'There Stands The Glass' treated adultery and alcoholism as serious subjects rather than comedy; he established the honky-tonk genre permanently, following trail blazed by Hank WILLIAMS, and was one of the first to use electric guitar and steel guitar in big mainstream country hits. Writing or co-writing many of his hits, he helped other writers like Mel TILLIS; with Jim DENNY he formed giant Cedarwood Publishing. Dabbled with rock'n'roll and rockabilly ('Teenage Boogie', 'Bye Bye Love' '56-7, both top 10). He had 45 top 10 hits, eight at no. 1, other notable successes incl. 'Honky Tonk Song' '57, 'Tupelo County Jail' '58, 'I Ain't Never' '59, 'Walking The Streets' '61, 'Cow Town' '62, 'Memory No. 1' '64, 'Fool,

Fool, Fool' '67. Became a larger-than-life personality, with custom-built cars and a guitar-shaped swimming pool at his home in Curtiswood Lane, Nashville, now a tourist attraction. One of the first to be offered a lifetime contract by USA Decca, with change to MCA '72 and falling sales he was dropped after all; moved to Plantation and scored minor hits with 'The Good Lord Giveth', 'I've Got Leaving On My Mind' '75-6; teamed with Willie NELSON '82 for duet album in the old style, incl. hit remake of 'Jailhouse'. LPs incl. *The Wondering Boy* '56, *Bow Thy Head* '58, *Webb With A Beat* '59, *Hideaway Heart* '62, *Fool, Fool, Fool* '67, *Merry-Go-Round World* '70, many more on Decca; compilations *Golden Hits 1 & 2* on Plantation/Philips; *Great Songs Of Webb Pierce* on Bulldog and *I Ain't Never* on Charly UK, others MCA USA.

PILLOW, Ray (*b* 4 July '37, Lynchburg, Va.) Veteran country singer, regularly scored in charts '60s. Joined US Navy, earned high school diploma '58; attended Lynchburg College, sang lead in college rock'n'roll band. Worked on local club circuit and was runner-up in Pet Milk contest on WSM '61; quit job with trucking firm and moved to Nashville, initially working as songwriter; signed with Capitol '64 and reached charts with 'Take Your Hands Off My Heart' '65, 'Thank You Ma'am' and 'Volkswagen' '66, 'I Just Want To Be Alone' and 'Gone With The Wine' '67; teamed with Jean SHEPARD for top 10 duet 'I'll Take The Dog' '66. Joined Grand Ole Opry '66, appeared as regular on BBC TV's *Swinging Country* '66-8. Recorded for other labels incl. Hilltop '78, MCA '79-81, still has many fans. LPs incl. *Presenting, Even When It's Bad It's Good* and *I'll Take The Dog* (with Shepard) '66-7 on Capitol; *Sings* '68 on ABC, *People Music* '69 on Plantation, *Slippin' Around* '73 on Mega, *Countrified* '74 on Dot, *One Too Many Memories* on Allegiance.

PINE, Courtney (*b* 18 Mar. '64, London) Tenor, soprano sax, bass clarinet; composer and bandleader. Jamaican parents; worked in reggae bands, etc. decided to do something about the situation: in the UK 'if you can improvise a bit you get sucked into a funk or a reggae band. You go up and down the M1 [motorway] and you're lost.' Found-

er member of TAJA (The Abiba Jazz Arts) and 21-piece big band the Jazz Warriors '85: gigged at the Fridge in Brixton, fine black musicians of all ages whose combined experience incl. Elvin JONES, Art BLAKEY, ULTRAVOX, WORKING WEEK, Hazel O'CONNOR, Desmond DEKKER, Mike WESTBROOK, Billy OCEAN, many more. Pine's debut quartet LP *Journey To The Urge Within* '86 on Island was prod. by Michael CUSCUNA; tape and CD editions incl. eight of his own tunes incl. 'Miss Interpret', one each by Wayne SHORTER, Horace SILVER, John COLTRANE (also 'Children Of The Ghetto', with vocal by Susaye Greene, a good singer; but the track is an entirely different production, released as a single, and doesn't belong on the album). Quartet incl. Gary Crosby on bass, Mark Mondesir on drums, Julian Joseph on piano; helped by vocalist Cleveland Watkiss, others. The big band's *Out Of Many, One People* '87 had Pine's name alphabetically with the rest, with three Pine tunes, one each by trumpeter Harry Beckett and by Fayyez Virgi (*see* CAYENNE). The Jazz Warriors incl. Philip Bent (*b* 16 Sep. '64; plays full-toned, confident flute instead of the usual twittering), Crosby, Mondesir, Adrian Reid on keyboards (toured with quartet '86), the impressive Watkiss (scatting, vocalising instrumental lines as well as more conventional singing on stage). Also Claude Deppa (*b* South Africa), Kevin Robinson on trumpets; Mamadi Kamara on percussion (*b* Sierra Leone), Orphy Robinson on vibes, Ray Carless on tenor, Alan Weekes on guitar, Brian Edwards on alto, seven more. Pine was subjected to media hype which will have no effect: he's too bright and too talented. He also leads smaller group The World's First Saxophone Posse, contributed to *Angel Heart* film soundtrack on Antilles with Trevor Jones on synth, and to Bryan Ferry LP '87. '87 gigs saw him playing duo with Mondesir; second LP first called *Light At The End Of The Tunnel*, finally *Destiny's Song (& The Image Of Pursuance)*, prod. by Delfeayo Marsalis for early '88 release, incl. tenor solo track 'Round Midnight', said to be a leaner, tougher album. As he comes to terms with the powerful ghosts of earlier giants, it is too soon to know where he will go, but he knows where he's coming from: 'One thing's for sure, I'm not going to spend my life playing "Stella by Starlight" in some wine bar.' (Quoted by Dave Gelly.) Kamara and Orphy Robinson also play with Andy SHEPPARD; Steve Williamson (*b* 28 June '64) is another talented young reedman who has played with Jazz Warriors in the past and who will sign a recording contract '87; Bent will be recording under his own name sooner or later.

PINK FLOYD UK psychedelic band formed c.'65, became top rock act: Syd BARRETT, vocals, guitar, replaced by David Gilmour (*b* 6 Mar. '44, Cambridge), guitar; Roger Waters (*b* 6 Sep. '44, Cambridge), bass, vocals; Nick Mason (*b* 27 Jan. '45, Birmingham), drums; Richard Wright (*b* 28 July '45, London), keyboards. Barrett and Waters knew each other from home town; Waters played in vaguely jazz-rock Architectural Abdabs with Mason and Wright while he was studying in London; Barrett joined, renamed them Pink Floyd Sound after bluesmen Pink Anderson (*b* 12 Feb. 1900, Laurens, S.C.; *d* 12 Oct. '74, Spartanburg; recorded for Riverside '50, Prestige '60-2) and Floyd Council (*b* 2 Sep. '11, Chapel Hill, N.C.; *d* c. June '76, Sanford; aka 'Dipper boy', 'Devil's Daddy-In-Law'; sides for ARC '37); Barrett also provided their early repertoire, direction, with unique mixture of nursery rhymes, blues, music hall and psychedelia. They played benefit at Alexandra Palace '67 for underground paper *International Times* (IT), first UK band to use light shows, project slides as they played; debut single was Barrett's typically quirky 'Arnold Layne', about a transvestite, prod. by Joe BOYD, banned by the BBC; debut LP *The Piper At The Gates Of Dawn* '67 took title from a chapter in *The Wind In The Willows*, with 10 of the 11 songs Barrett's; but by early '68 he struggled to cope, some said because of LSD. Gilmour joined; quintet struggled on for a few weeks before Barrett quit for hospitalisation, followed by erratic solo career, cult fame. *A Saucerful Of Secrets* '68 marked Waters' ascendance, with only one Barrett song, 'Jugband Blues'. 'See Emily Play' also had chart success '67, but losing Barrett's skill at slices of single-length psychedelia, to say nothing of his sense of humour, the second LP concentrated on hallmark lengthy, spacey epics such as title track, 'Let

There Be More Light'. *More* '69 was soundtrack, a direction they wanted to take; their ambition was to score Kubrick's *2001: A Space Odyssey*, instead they contributed to Antonioni's *Zabriskie Point* '70. *Ummagumma* '69 was patchy 2-disc set, half live and half solo work from all four; Waters collaborated on soundtrack for *The Body* '70 with Ron Geesin, who worked with Floyd on *Atom Heart Mother* '70, title track with John Aldiss Choir taking an entire side, experiments with brass and stereo effects: their first no. 1 LP UK, no. 55 USA. *Meddle* '71 had 'Echoes' again occupying an entire side; *Obscured By Clouds* '72 was music from French film *The Valley* (Robert Christgau wrote, 'The movie got buried, now skip the soundtrack'). They still lacked focus, but latched onto doom with *Dark Side Of The Moon* '73, one of the bleakest of all rock albums, no. 2 UK, 1 USA and still in the top 200 USA LPs '85 after 566 weeks (broke the previous record '80, set by Carole KING's *Tapestry*). They spent most of '74 in the studio, trying to make a 'non-musical album' without orthodox instruments (some thought that's what they were already doing); sessions were scrapped and they switched to Columbia (CBS) from EMI's Harvest label with *Wish You Were Here* '75, with unusually lyrical Waters title track, guest vocalist Roy HARPER on 'Have A Cigar' (rare example of Floyd humour), marathon 'Shine On You Crazy Diamond' for Barrett, which some interpreted as Floyd's own lack of direction: their second no. 1 LP both USA/UK. By *Animals* '77 they were a backing band for Waters; another bleak LP sold well despite being totally out of sync during punk era (top 3 both UK/USA); they went into hiatus: Gilmour made eponymous solo LP, Wright made *Wet Dream* '78; Mason prod. albums for the DAMNED, GONG, Robert WYATT while Waters steered them to 2-disc *The Wall* '79, depicting rock star crackup: no. 3 UK; no. 1 USA for 15 weeks (though nobody knew anyone who bought it) incl. no. 1 USA/UK single 'Another Brick In The Wall (Part II)'; it equalled *Dark Side Of The Moon* in sales. Tour promoting it saw band performing only 'The Wall', with a real brick wall built between them and audience during performance, the ultimate 'fuck you'; it was filmed '82 with Bob Geldof giving a better acting performance than it deserved; Floyd did not appear in the film and there were rumours of conflict between Waters and dir. Alan Parker. Wright left, worked with bassist Dee Harris of Fashion in Zee (LP *Identity* '84). *The Final Cut* '83 was a Waters solo LP in all but name, damned by critics as another long whine from a rich, jaded rock star, it still made no. 3 USA, no. 1 UK; for all his pomposity and technical whizzardry, he had makings of a songwriter, but evidence was totally lacking in solo *The Pros & Cons Of Hitch Hiking* '84, with guest Eric CLAPTON, castigated for misogyny of sleeve and sprawling 'concept'. He toured to promote it; it was no. 13 UK, top 40 USA. He contributed to soundtrack of animated antinuke *Where The Wind Blows* '86 with David BOWIE, Paul Hardcastle. At their best, Pink Floyd married acute lyrics with technical innovations; at their worst they were merely pompous. *A Nice Pair* '73 was reissue of first two LPs; *Relics* '71 incl. otherwise unavailable 'Biding My Time'; *A Collection Of Great Dance Songs* '81 and *Works* '83 were also compilations. *Dark Side Of The Moon* was still in USA charts '87, sold 19 million copies, CD edition a USA best-seller; Wright released *Identity* '84; Mason did *Profiles* '85; Waters *Radio KAOS* '87; Mason, Gilmour and Wright made old-fashioned, ponderous *A Momentary Lapse Of Reason* '87 as Pink Floyd, Waters trying unsuccessfully to stop them.

PITNEY, Gene (*b* 17 Feb. '41, Hartford, Conn.) USA pop balladeer, songwriter: 16 top 40 hits '61-8, marked by soaring tenor with distinctive edge. Spotted by Burt BACHARACH/Hal David, who wrote his biggest hits: 'The Man Who Shot Liberty Valance' (inspired by the John Wayne Western movie) and 'Only Love Can Break A Heart', both top 5 '62. Though most of his hits were others' songs, Pitney was an accomplished writer of hits for Rick NELSON ('Hello Mary Lou'), the CRYSTALS ('He's A Rebel'), Roy ORBISON, others. Shared publicist Andrew Loog Oldham with ROLLING STONES; recorded Jagger/Richards' 'That Girl Belongs To Yesterday' (UK no. 7); played maracas on 'Not Fade Away', piano on B-side 'Little By Little'. A distinctive talent, more popular in UK than at home, where he had top 40 hits through '74; later turned to country music, even recording in Italian. *Anthology* on Rhino in either 2-disc or single editions.

PLANXTY Irish folk group, the most infl. with the CHIEFTAINS. Original lineup: Andy Irvine, vocals, mandolin, bouzouki; Donal Lunny, guitar, bouzouki, synthesiser; Christy MOORE, vocals, guitar, bodhrán; Liam Og O'Flynn, Uileann pipes, whistle. They demonstrated incestuousness of Irish folk scene through various formations, having direct or indirect links with nearly every other major act; Lunny had played in shortlived but infl. Bothy Band, others went on in to play in Chieftains, MOVING HEARTS etc. Arose from Moore's album *Prosperous* '72 on Tara (with all four on it); became well-known for use of bouzouki and early embracing of Balkan music in repertoire. *Planxty* and *The Well Below The Valley* '73 and *Cold Blow & The Rainy Night* '74 on Polydor/Shanachie were an impressive if at times uneven body of material; Lunny left after two LPs, replaced by Johnny Moynihan, who left to join De Dahann; Moore left, replaced by Paul BRADY, but no commercial recordings by this lineup came out. With energy spent they broke up; *The Planxty Collection* '76 was a good compilation. Reunited late '70s with Matt Molloy, who went on to Chieftains; released *After The Break* '79, *The Woman I Loved So Well* '80 on Tara, appeared on *Nyon Folk Festival 1979* on Cat, anthology *The High Kings Of Tara* '80. Suite *Timedance* was commissioned for intermission in Eurovision Song Contest '81, an unusual feature in that context. Next phase prod. arguably their best work, *Words & Music* '83 on WEA Ireland, blend of Bob DYLAN ('I Pity The Poor Immigrant'), Si Kahn ('Aragon Mill'), trad. ballad 'Lord Baker' illustrated their ease with folk music in the wider sense; 'Lord Baker', like 'The Well Below The Valley', 'Raggle Taggle Gypsy' before it, acknowledged debt to the traveller John Reilly (*b* c.'26, Shannon; *d* '69, Boyle), whose *The Bonny Green Tree* '78 on Topic is a testament to his unique talents. Compilation *Ansi!* '84 on Polydor was of minor worth. *The Best Of Planxty Live* featured the original quartet plus Nollaig Ni Cathasaigh and Bill Whelan; apparently recorded live at the Olympia Theatre, it appeared '87 with no label: by then they had returned to other careers, for Planxty had not been their sole occupation at any stage.

PLATTERS, The USA vocal group of '50s created by vocal coach Buck Ram (*b* Samuel Ram, 21 Nov. '07, Chicago, Ill.): graduated from law school, never practised; worked for Mills Music as arranger, toured with bands, wrote songs, managed the THREE SUNS, etc. Formed talent agency in L.A. '54; his protégés the PENGUINS scored no. 8 USA hit 'Earth Angel' '55; he took over Platters from Ralph BASS, added them to roster, took both groups to Mercury Records. Platters lineup: lead singer Tony Williams (*b* 5 Apr. '28, Elizabeth, N.J.), second tenor David Lynch (*b* '29, *d* 2 Jan. '81), Alex Hodge, Herbert Reed. Ram added L.A. native Zola Taylor (from another of his acts, Shirley Gunther and the Queens), baritone Paul Robi replaced Hodge; they cut Ram song 'Only You', previously recorded for Federal; this time it reached no. 1 R&B, no. 5 pop chart '55 despite white cover by the HILLTOPPERS; their next, Ram's 'The Great Pretender', topped both charts same year (satirised by Stan FREBERG for the slow, soft kling-kling-kling piano; revived in affectionate impressionist title track of Lester BOWIE LP '81; big UK hit for Freddie Mercury of QUEEN '87); both hits incl. in Alan FREED film *Rock Around The Clock*. Williams' church-influenced lead, string backing and novelty factor of Taylor (women were rare in doo-wop groups) made for the best smooch records of the decade for slow dancing at parties; the group were the first black act of the era to reach no. 1 on the pop chart, helped smash the industry's monopoly though white covers. 35 pop hits on Mercury through '62 incl. 'My Prayer', '39 (song previously recorded by Vera LYNN, Sammy KAYE); adapted from a violin composition by Georges Boulenger; Ram hired ace Sammy Lowe (ex-Erskine HAWKINS band) to arrange it 'because he wanted an arranger who didn't ridicule what his singers were doing' (quoted by Stanley Dance); it went no. 1 pop/2 R&B. 'Twilight Time' (no. 1 both charts, with words by Ram: '38 hit for the Three Suns), 'Smoke Gets In Your Eyes' (Jerome KERN classic; no. 1 pop, 3 R&B), 'Harbor Lights' (no. 8 pop, 15 R&B; '37 song a hit for Kaye '50), also

standards 'I'll Never Smile Again', 'To Each His Own', 'If I Didn't Care', etc. They kept cleancut image even after members arraigned on vice charges '59 (acquitted). Williams left '61, but they came back on Musicor '66-7 with Sonny Turner singing lead, hits incl. 'I Love You 1000 Times', 'With This Ring', both co-written by Luther Dixon. Group members fell out; there were rival groups led by Reed and others, leading to lawsuits and injunctions; Ram had tried to prevent the INK SPOTS syndrome, set up The Five Platters Inc. '56, with members of the group owning shares but not allowed to use the name when they left, but it didn't work. Compilations are sometimes not the original recordings, which sold 50,000,000 records; safest ones are on Mercury, or 2-disc *Anthology* on Rhino.

PLAXICO, Lonnie (*b* 4 Sep. '60, Chicago, Ill.) Bass. First pro gig at age 16; worked with Sonny STITT, Von FREEMAN, etc. With Art BLAKEY's Jazz Messengers from '84, providing big flavourful tone: Blakey LPs incl. *New York Scene* '84; has also recorded with Dizzy GILLESPIE, David MURRAY; with Benny GOLSON, Wynton MARSALIS on *Live In Japan* '83; with Terence BLANCHARD/Donald HARRISON on *New York Second Line* '84. Toured and recorded with Jack DeJOHNETTE; gigged in London '88 with Chico and Von Freeman.

POCO Country-rock band formed '68 in L.A.; BUFFALO SPRINGFIELD survivors Richie Furay, Jim Messina recruited steel guitarist Rusty Young (*b* 23 Feb. '46, Long Beach, Cal.), who'd played on last Springfield LP, recommended drummer George Grantham and bassist Randy Meisner, from Colorado groups Boenzee Cryque and the Poor respectively. First called Pogo, after comic strip, but creator sued; auditioned for Apple, then Epic: after first LP *Pickin' Up The Pieces* '69 Meisner quit to join Rick NELSON, replaced by Tim Schmit (*b* 30 Oct. '47, Sacramento); Messina quit after *Poco* '70 (with long instrumental on one side), live *Deliverin' The Goods* '71, replaced by ex-Illinois Speed Press vocalist/guitarist Paul Cotton (*b* 26 Feb. '43): this was the most creative lineup, both Cotton and Furay prolific songwriters. *From The Inside* '71 followed by acclaimed *A Good Feelin' To*

Know '73, joyous title track being minor hit single. Furay quit after *Crazy Eyes* '73 to join ill-fated supergroup Souther Hillman Furay (*see* J. D.. SOUTHER). Vocal blend especially good (Schmit sessioned, backing vocals with STEELY DAN, etc.); with Furay gone, Young's steel came more to the fore like an extra voice; *Seven* and *Cantamos* followed in '74; against the odds they increased sales in lucrative West Coast country rock market with *Head Over Heels* '75 on ABC, no. 43 LP USA, incl. almost *a cappella* 'Keep On Tryin' '. Epic released *Live* (recorded '74); *Rose Of Cimarron* '76 and *Indian Summer* '77 followed; departure of Schmit (who replaced Meisner again, this time in EAGLES), roadweary Grantham still didn't sink them, replaced by Englishmen Steve Chapman on drums, bassist Charlie Harrison, both ex-Al STEWART and Leo SAYER, Kim Bullard (from Atlanta, Ga.) added on keyboards; *Legend* '78 was their best-seller at no. 14, incl. top 20 singles 'Crazy Love', 'Heart Of The Night'. On parent MCA for *Under The Gun, Blue And Gray, Cowboys And Englishmen* '80-2; *Ghost Town* '82 and '84 reunion *Inamorata* (with Furay, Grantham, Cotton, Schmit, Young) on Atlantic just made top 200 LPs: with demise of Eagles they were undisputed country-rock veterans, but slipped into MOR vein like Eagles before them. Furay had turned from solo career to religion before joining reunion.

POGUES, The UK/Irish folk-rock band formed '82, first called Poguemahone (Gaelic for 'kiss my arse'): vocalist/songwriter Shane MacGowan (*b* 25 Dec. '57, London); Philip Chevron (*b* Philip Ryan, 17 June '57, Dublin), guitar; James Fearnley (*b* 10 Oct. '54, Manchester), accordion; Andrew Ranken (*b* 13 Nov. '53, London), drums; Jem Finer (*b* Jeremy Max Finer, 29 July '55, Dublin), banjo; Spider Stacy (*b* Peter Richard Stacy, 14 Dec. '58, Eastbourne), tin whistle; Cait O'Riordan, bass. MacGowan had been in cult punk band the Nipple Erectors; he and Stacy busked in north London, played set of Irish rebel songs at Richard Strange's club '82. Pogues' debut single was 'Dark Streets Of London' '84; another early single was widely praised cover of Eric BOGLE's 'The Band Played Waltzing Matilda'. They were big-

gest shot in the arm for UK folk scene since '60s, though their anarchic approach upset traditionalists. LP *Red Roses For Me* '84 captured ramshackle appeal and revealed MacGowan as a writer of promise with 'Transmetropolitan' and 'Streams Of Whiskey'; Elvis COSTELLO was an early fan, prod. their *Rum, Sodomy & The Lash* '85, incl. UK hits 'Dirty Old Town', 'Sally Maclennane', 'A Pair Of Brown Eyes'. Costello married bassist O'Riordan, who was replaced by Darryl Hunt (*b* 4 May '50, Bournemouth); Terry Woods was founder member of influential Sweeney's Men and STEELEYE SPAN, joined Pogues '86. Record company problems delayed third LP; they contributed to film soundtracks *Sid And Nancy* '86, *Straight To Hell* '87, starring in latter; remained critical favourites and major live attraction, had UK top 20 hit early '87 with the Dubliners on trad. 'Irish Rover'. Album *If I Should Fall From Grace With God* released early '88.

POINTER SISTERS Harmony group formed Oakland, Cal. by sisters Ruth (*b* '46), Anita ('48), Bonnie ('50) and June ('54) Pointer, all from Oakland. They sang in church, backed Dave MASON and Elvin BISHOP, made two singles for Atlantic; gig at L.A. Troubadour Club '73 launched them as vocal nostalgia act in MANHATTAN TRANSFER vein: signing with ABC/Blue Thumb, guided by San Francisco prod. David Rubinson, they merged originals with hand-picked period pieces to show off close harmony scat-singing. *The Pointer Sisters* '73 launched them in style, incl. covers of Allen TOUSSAINT ('Yes We Can Can'), Willie DIXON ('Wang Wang Doodle'); Anita and Bonnie's 'Fairy Tale' was a country crossover '74, won Grammy and they became first black female act to appear on Grand Ole Opry. Had no. 20 pop hit '75 with hard-nosed 'How Long (Betcha Got A Chick On The Side)', but nostalgia act was becoming restrictive (if lucrative: they worked Las Vegas). After albums *That's A Plenty* and *Live At The Opera House* '74, *Steppin* '75, *Having A Party* '77 Bonnie went solo; trio signed with Richard PERRY's Planet label, groomed as crossover act; scored street-credible no. 2 with Bruce SPRINGSTEEN's 'Fire' '79; eight more top 40 hits '78-84 were mostly predictable as well as fun, and profitable (many charting in UK too). LPs (some now on RCA) incl. *Energy* '78 (incl. 'Fire'), *Priority* '79, *Special Things* '80 ('He's So Shy'), *Black And White* '81 ('Slow Hand'), *So Excited!* '82, *Break Out* '83: their best seller at no. 8, incl. top 10 singles 'Jump (For My Love)', 'Automatic', 'Neutron Dance', 'I'm So Excited' (originally on the '82 LP); then *Contact* '85 (incl. 'Dare Me'), *Hot Together* '86, *Serious Slammin'* '88. June made solo *Baby Sister* '83; Bonnie made LPs both called *Bonnie Pointer* on Motown '78-9, had two top 40 singles; switched to Private Stock (Epic in UK) for *If The Price Is Right* '84.

POLICE UK pop trio: Sting (*b* Gordon Sumner, 2 Oct. '51, Wallsend, Northumberland), bass and vocals; Stewart Copeland (*b* 16 July '52, Alexandria, Va.), drums; Andy Summers (*b* 31 Dec. '42, Blackpool, Lancs.), guitar. Formed in London '76 after Copeland quit Curved Air (on-again, off-again UK art-rock group, first formed '70 with synthesiser, electric violin); his father worked for the CIA, had him educated in UK. He spotted Sting playing jazz bass with ex-Newcastle Last Exit; with Corsican guitarist Henry Padovani they backed USA punk singer Cherry Vanilla; released debut single 'Fall Out' on brother Miles Copeland's Illegal label (drummer playing lead guitar, Padovani's technique was so limited), sold about 2000 copies. Copeland recruited Summers, who had strong pedigree, having played with Eric BURDON, Zoot MONEY, Kevin AYERS; rehearsed as a quartet until Padovani quit to join Wayne County. Trio got nowhere at first, had little real sympathy with punks; did TV commercials, image formed by having hair dyed blonde for chewing gum advert. Sting emerged as songwriter, replacing Copeland; with growing interest of manager Miles, 'Can't Stand Losing You' (suicide threat) was top 50 hit '78, album *Outlandos d'Amour* incl. 'Roxanne', love song to a prostitute. They did USA tour on a shoestring. Sting did films *Quadrophenia* and *Radio On* '79, 'Roxanne' and 'Can't Stand Losing You' were belated hits, LP *Regatta du Blanc* (patois for 'white reggae') incl. no. 1 UK hits 'Message In A Bottle', 'Walking On The Moon'; world tour '80 got media interest, first six singles reissued as 'Six

Pack' (no. 17 on UK chart) and *Zanyatta Mondatta* incl. no. 1 UK single 'Don't Stand So Close To Me', but LP was rushed and group were quick to disown it. Disowned by real punks, they had more talent than that, made it into pop market; appeal was across the board: kids loved their looks, critics liked 'white reggae' style, Sting's acting career ensured media attention. *Ghost In The Machine* '81 boasted their best songs to date, prod. by Hugh Padgham (Phil COLLINS), replacing Nigel Gray (who'd helped shape their sound), incl. no. 1 'Every Little Thing She Does Is Magic', and 'Invisible Sun', Sting's comment on Northern Ireland, banned by the BBC. They took '82 off: Sting acted in Dennis Potter's *Brimstone And Treacle* (surprise hit with '29 song 'Spread A Little Happiness'); Summers published *Throb!* book of photographs, collaborated on less accessible instrumental album *I Advance Masked* with Robert Fripp; Copeland released alter ego LP *Klark Kent* on IRS (changed to 'Klerk Kant' when Marvel Comics sued), worked on soundtrack of Francis Ford Coppola's *Rumblefish*. *Synchronicity* '83 put them back on top, with 'Every Breath You Take' no. 1 both USA/UK, other hits; third LP in a row to enter UK chart at no. 1 also scattered soundalikes like MEN AT WORK who'd prospered during their time off. At NYC's Shea Stadium they were the biggest draw since the BEATLES. Since then they've been in hiatus, though all three say they will work together again. They contributed nothing original, but craftsmanship and good songs had big impact on boring scene, string of fine pop singles incl. a tension which may have been caused by acknowledged antipathies in group. Miles Copeland's astute management meant touring thriftily, recording cheaply, higher royalties instead of big advances: they are among wealthiest of '80s rock stars. Summers collaborated with Frith again for *Bewitched* '84, contributed to soundtracks of *2010* and *Down & Out In Beverly Hills* '85; Copeland's ambitious album/video *The Rhythmatist* '85 acknowledged debt to African music, he appeared on Peter GABRIEL's *So* and Stanley CLARKE's *Hideaway* '86; Sting's *The Dream Of The Blue Turtles* '85 harked back to Last Exit with jazz pianist Kenny Kirkland, drummer Omar Hakim, bassist Darryl

Jones, Branford MARSALIS, backup singers (LP incl. obvious lift from Prokofiev in 'Russians', was also commercial enough to yield hit singles), band did tour/2-disc album *Bring On The Night* '86, then 2-disc *... Nothing Like The Sun* '87 with Marsalis, guests Mark Knopfler, Eric CLAPTON, others; was backed by Gil EVANS band on Jimi HENDRIX song 'Little Wing'. He also starred in heavily panned film of S.F. cult classic *Dune*, also *The Bride, Plenty*; guested on LP tribute to Kurt WEILL *Lost In The Stars* '85, duetted with Mark Knopfler on DIRE STRAITS' 'Money For Nothing', appeared at Live Aid, Anti-Apartheid, Amnesty International charity shows (contributed cover of Billie HOLIDAY's 'Strange Fruit' to Amnesty's *Conspiracy Of Hope*) '85-6. Success of Police allowed Miles Copeland to expand his IRS label, which gave early breaks to R.E.M., the ALARM; he still threatens to sue anyone who says Police have split for good, though reunion after Amnesty benefit was scrapped, resulted only in new (inferior) 'Don't Stand So Close To Me', released as single, on belated compilation *Every Breath You Take: The Singles* '86, UK no. 1 LP. Stewart Copeland's *The Equalizer & Other Cliffhangers* '88 celebrated TV themes in IRS's 'No Speak' series of new age rock albums.

POLLACK, Ben (*b* 22 June '03, Chicago, Ill.; *d* 7 June '71, Palm Springs, Cal.) Drummer, vocalist, bandleader. Played drums in high school, later with Friars' Inn Orchestra (New Orleans Rhythm Kings; *see* JAZZ). He was going to work in the family fur business, but changed his mind and led his own jazz-oriented dance band '24-34. First records '26 on Victor had 11 pieces incl. Glenn MILLER and Benny GOODMAN, Gil Rodin on reeds; Jimmy McPARTLAND, Charlie and Jack TEAGARDEN, Charlie SPIVAK, many others passed through; while playing in the pit in Broadway show *Hello Daddy* '28 he began fronting and conducting, Ray Bauduc hired on drums. The band had 10 big hits '28-34, was admired by musicians and critics and many other records with Goodman solos became classics. Pollack was no dictator, but the younger musicians made fun of his singing and Goodman was never a man to let anyone tell him what to do; Pollack lost some of his stars but

built up the band again until on records in late '33 it was essentially the Bob CROSBY band to come. In '34 the band wasn't working much because Pollack was promoting the career of his singer/girlfriend Doris Robbins: the band jumped ship, hired Bing's brother to front them, and the rest is history: the Bob Crosby band was more successful than Pollack had been, Goodman became the King of Swing in '35, and Miller the number one band in the world '39-40: the Swing Era passed Pollack by (*see* BIG BAND ERA). He made more records, in '36 with Miller, Spivak, Irving Fazola, Harry JAMES, Freddie SLACK, his Pick-A-Rib boys '37 with Muggsy SPANIER, in '38 a musicianly band with no stars at all: his glory days were over. He started hopeless lawsuits against other bandleaders, led a band on radio for comic Joe Penner '38-9, organised a theatre band for Chico Marx '42, opened talent agency in Hollywood '43, led dixieland combos on West Coast early '50s, later ran a restaurant where some former sidemen sometimes gigged. Played himself in *The Benny Goodman Story* '56; his band was a hit at a Disneyland dixieland festival '64, but depressed about heart trouble, he hanged himself. Compilation from '26-33 on Sunbeam.

POLYGRAM Record division of the Dutch multinational Philips Gloeilampenfabrieken, formed '62 by merger of Phonogram, Philips' record division, and Polydor/Deutsche Grammophon. Its history goes back to the early European record industry: in 1898 Emile Berliner (*see* RECORDED SOUND) sold the European and British Empire rights to his gramophone record to Britain's Gramophone Company (*see* HMV); that year with his brothers Joseph and Jacob he formed the Deutsche Grammophon Gesellschaft (German Record Company) to make records for the Gramophone Company at their telephone factory in Hanover. After some dispute between London and Hanover about who owned what, the Gramophone Company took control of Deutsche Grammophon late 1899. In '13 HMV moved most of the German masters to their new record factory in Hayes, Middlesex; for most of WWI HMV kept a tenuous control over their German affiliate, often with the help of their USA affiliate Victor; but by '17 the USA was in the war and Germany was desperate: the German government wanted to melt down DGG's metal stampers for the war effort, but HMV objected, so the Germans offered not to do that if Britain would arrange to send an equivalent amount of metal to Germany. HMV considered this but the British government forbad it. The Germans did not melt the stampers, but seized DGG as enemy property and sold it at auction '17 to Polyphon Musikwerke. Between the wars there was continuing dispute about the ownership of trademarks, matrices; HMV gave up attempts to reassert control in '26, hiring DGG's general manager to set up Electrola. As a result of these disputes DGG, unable to use its trademarks outside Germany, set up Polydor for exports. DGG produced classical records licensed to Brunswick in the USA, Decca in UK; was purchased by the Munich-based electrical firm of Siemens und Halske '40. It used the HMV label for classical music until EMI retrieved the trademark after WWII; in '52 it was reorganised, the DGG label created for classical music, Archiv for historical/early music, Polydor for popular. In '62 Philips and Siemens merged their record company interests, with Phonogram and DGG retaining autonomy; a unified management was created under the PolyGram name in '72. Polydor was slow to establish itself in international pop, though it launched the BEE GEES (on Atco in the USA), also had SLADE, the JAM, the New SEEKERS. Philips had been founded by record shop owner H. van Zoelen, who had been with Dutch Decca; he sold his shares to Philips Gloeilampenfabrieken of Eindhoven in '46. Philips built up an international chain of companies '50s helped by a licensing deal with CBS which gave them access to the best American product: in '56 Philips enjoyed a 22-week run at no. 1 in the UK, with only four of those weeks secured by a British act. In '61 Philips signed an exchange agreement with Mercury, and subsequently bought the company, with jazz subsidiary EmArcy (Mercury was formed in Chicago '46, had the first no. 1 USA pop hit by a black R&B act '55: 'The Great Pretender' by the PLATTERS). DGG and Philips had deserved high reputations for classical discs, incl. pressing quality; on the pop side

in the '60s Philips scored with the Springfields, then Dusty SPRINGFIELD solo; The WALKER BROTHERS and the Spencer DAVIS Group (on Fontana) were big sellers; so at first were Jane Birkin and Serge Gainsbourg, whose sexually suggestive 'Je T'Aime . . . Moi Non Plus' was the first record banned by all broadcasters to reach no. 1 in the UK: a furore arose over the French words and heavy breathing; Philips dropped the record as it climbed the charts (picked up by Major Minor); Philips talked about morality, took out USA adverts about the disc's notoriety in Britain: there was less outcry in the USA and it barely reached the top 60. PolyGram bought interests in Casablanca (Donna SUMMER) and Robert Stigwood's RSO label, which had a no. 1 USA album in soundtrack to *Saturday Night Fever* '77, and enormous success with the Bee Gees, who had six USA no. ones in a row '77-9, the first three from *Fever*; RSO set a record, holding the no. 1 slot in the USA pop chart for 23 weeks '77-8 with six singles: four from *Fever* incl. Yvonne ELLIMAN's 'If I Can't Have You'; a solo by Bee Gee Andy Gibb and 'Baby Come Back' by Player (L.A. pop group, hits written by vocalists/guitarists Peter Beckett, John Cowley). In the '80s Mercury became PolyGram's main pop label, with Philips for classical; Mercury had DEXY'S MIDNIGHT RUNNERS, John Cougar MELLENCAMP, DEF LEPPARD and Bon Jovi, the adolescents' favourite of '86 (*Slippery When Wet* was a no. 1 LP, two no. 1 singles); Mercury signed Robert CRAY in '86. PolyGram took over DECCA in '80 (*which see*); other labels in the group incl. MGM and Verve: MGM was an offshoot of the film studio, formed in '46, had many valuable soundtracks, plus Hank WILLIAMS, Conway TWITTY, Connie FRANCIS; picked up SAM THE SHAM in '60s, and the ANIMALS and HERMAN'S HERMITS from EMI-Columbia, passed over by Capitol. Jazz label Verve was formed '49 by Norman GRANZ in Hollywood; the extremely valuable catalogue incl. Ella FITZGERALD, Oscar PETERSON, was sold to MGM '58: in '60s Verve had the RIGHTEOUS BROTHERS, the VELVET UNDERGROUND and the Mothers of Invention (*see* Frank ZAPPA) PolyGram is one of five major labels operating subsidiaries on all six continents; with companies in 18 countries, behind only

EMI and CBS in this regard. The Hanover factory had been the European home of gramophone technology in the 1890s and was also the birthplace of the compact disc in the 1980s, developed by Philips with Sony: Hanover had the first CD factory outside Japan.

POMUS, Doc, & Mort Shuman Songwriters Jerome 'Doc' Pomus (*b* '25) and Mort Shuman (*b* 12 Nov. '38) were the most successful songwriting team in R&B/rock after LEIBER & STOLLER, peaking in the '60s. Though handicapped by polio, Pomus worked as a blues singer in the Mose ALLISON mode; also wrote or co-wrote songs such as 'Boogie-Woogie Country Girl' for Joe TURNER, 'Lonely Avenue' for Ray CHARLES; he helped Leiber & Stoller on 'Young Blood' for the COASTERS. The first Pomus/Shuman hit was 'A Teenager In Love' (DION & THE BELMONTS, no. 5 '59); they infl. others in the BRILL BUILDING, writing 'Hound Dog Man', 'I'm A Man' and 'Turn Me Loose' for FABIAN, but wrote for much better artists: 'Can't Get Used To Losing You' and 'Wrong For Each Other' for Andy WILLIAMS, 'No One' for Charles, 'Plain Jane' for Bobby DARIN, 'Go Jimmy Go' for Jimmy CLANTON, 'Seven Day Weekend' for Gary 'US' BONDS and 'Spanish Lace' for Gene MCDANIELS. Pomus's label had recorded the Crowns before they became the DRIFTERS, and Pomus & Shuman wrote 'Save The Last Dance For Me' (no. 1 '60), 'Sweets For My Sweet', 'I Count The Tears' and 'This Magic Moment' for them (the last also recorded by JAY & THE AMERICANS), then collaborated together and separately with Leiber & Stoller on several songs for Ben E. KING after he left the group. They wrote 'Surrender', 'She's Not For You', 'Viva Las Vegas', 'Little Sister', 'His Latest Flame', 'A Mess O' Blues', 'Kiss Me Quick' and 'Suspicion' for Elvis PRESLEY; Pomus co-wrote 'She's Not You' for Presley with Leiber & Stoller, also co-wrote songs with others for Chubby CHECKER, Andy Williams, Roger WILLIAMS; Shuman co-wrote 'Little Children' for Billy J. KRAMER with J. Leslie McFarland; Jerry Ragavoy (*b* 4 Sep. '30, Philadelphia) co-wrote 'Piece Of My Heart' with Bert BERNS for Erma Franklin, Janis JOPLIN; then 'Get It While You Can' for

Joplin, 'What's It Gonna Be' for Dusty SPRINGFIELD, 'Look At Granny Run, Run' for Howard Tate with Shuman. Pomus later collaborated with MINK DEVILLE, co-wrote B. B. KING LP *There Must Be A Better World Somewhere* with Mac REBENNACK; Shuman co-wrote 'If We/You Only Have Love' (recorded by Johnny MATHIS, Dionne WARWICK), others with Eric Blau for show *Jacques Brel Is Alive And Well And Living In Paris* '68, relocated to Paris himself.

PONCE, Daniel (*b* 21 July '53, Havana, Cuba) Conga, bata drums; composer, bandleader. Played in street gatherings, annual carnival, tourist hotels; occasionally joined singer Carlos Embale in shows and on record; turned full-time pro after leaving Cuba (forcibly) '80: to NYC July, joined Afro-Cuban jam sessions led by Andy and Jerry Gonzalez (*see* Conjunto LIBRE) in scene at loft Soundscape incl. ex-Irakere saxophonist Paquito D'Rivera, Cuban drummer Ignacio Berroa, Argentine pianist Jorge Dalto; in weekly sessions initially as Inter-American Jazz Quartet led by Andy, later billed as 'Afro-Cuban Nights', they turned their backs on salsa's obsession with dance music, resurrected time-honoured love of all-night jam sessions, Ponce contributing formidable powers on congas, also using bata drum: once a sacred instrument, now increasingly a part of Latin percussion armoury. As congocero (conga player) he used five or six waist-high, differently pitched drums, driving the other musicians; from these sessions Jerry's album *Ya Yo Me Curé* '80 on American Clavé had already emerged; Ponce played on Kip Hanrahan's *Coup de Tête* '81 on that label; also Paquito's *Blowin'* '81, *Mariel* '82 (named after boat taken by Cuban exiles '80), *Live At Keystone Korner* '82; also played in NYC tribute concert to Chano POZO and on McCoy TYNER LP *La Leyenda de la Hora* (The Legend Of The Hour) '81, with Eddie PALMIERI in Puerto Rico '83. Rising maverick producer Bill LASWELL saw Ponce at Soundscape, used him on Herbie HANCOCK 12″ single 'Rockit', album *Future Shock* '83: complexities of Cuban drumming helped knit together Laswell's blend of electronic percussion and synths as bedrock and as a tangible hook. Ponce appeared in productions with Jamaican toaster Yellowman and on Laurie

ANDERSON's 'Mr Heartbreak', wrote track 'Karabali' for Hancock's *Sound System*, played on Nona Hendryx's *Art Of Defence* and Mick Jagger's *She's The Boss*; all '84; in '85 on new Ginger BAKER comeback LP on Celluloid, Sly & Robbie's annual electro-reggae LP, Yoko ONO's *Starpiece* and with avant-garde rock group Golden Palaminos, each time standing out in the mesh of diverse sonic output. Maintained Cuban links: his solo album *New York Now* '83 conceded little overall to the dance crowd: bravely spare in places, resurrecting Cuban ballad style called 'feeling', leaving Paquito to unravel/remake Ernesto LECUONA's classic 'Siboney'. He received the CAPS (Creative Artists Public Service) award for composition, went to Berlin Jazz Festival '83, went to Tokyo with Nona Hendryx and appeared on Caimán LP *Super All Star* '84 (on Globe Style in UK '87), worked with Celia CRUZ in show *Yoruba Fantasy* '85 and visited London, playing with local salsa outfit El Sonido de Londres; appeared on *Afro-Cuban Jazz* '86 on Caimán with Mario BAUZA, Graciela. His *Arawe* '87 on Antilles incl. Tito PUENTE, others.

PONTY, Jean-Luc (*b* 29 Sep. '42, Arranches, Normandy, France) Violin, violectra (a baritone violin); also keyboards, composer. Both parents were music teachers; left school at 13 to practise for hours every day, played in Lamoureux Symphony Orchestra late '50s, turned to jazz. Used amplifier from the beginning, soon exploring electronic possibilities, finding that they helped him to overcome his formal training. Stuff SMITH compared him to John COLTRANE in early '60s; he played at Antibes Jazz Festival '64, violin workshop at Monterey Festival '67, played/recorded in USA '69 with Frank ZAPPA, George DUKE; emigrated '73, worked with Zappa; with John McLAUGHLIN (Mahavishnu Orchestra) '74. Own albums: European LPs on Palm '63 (*The Beginning*), Philips '64, Saba/Pausa '66 (*Sunday Walk*), Electrola '68 (*Lyrics Or The Baroque*), Palm '68; then three albums '69 on Pacific Jazz, all with Duke: *Electric Connection* with Gerald WILSON big band; *King Kong* with Zappa, Buell NEIDLINGER on bass, others cond. by Wilson, and *Experience* '69 with George Duke Trio: the last two also on Blue Note

as *Cantaloupe Island*, the last on Pausa as *The Jean-Luc Experience*. *Live At Dante's* '69 on Blue Note with Duke Trio, *Open Strings* '71 on MPS/BASF (quintet with Philip Catherine, guitar), *Experience* '72 from Montreux Festival on several labels incl. Inner City and Affinity, then series on Atlantic: *Upon The Wings Of Music* and *Aurora* '75, *Imaginary Voyage* '76, *Enigmatic Ocean* '77, *Cosmic Messenger* '78, *A Taste For Passion* '79, *Jean-Luc Ponty Live* '79, *Civilised Evil* '80, *Mystical Adventures* '81, *Individual Choice* '83 (solo tracks, duets, trios), *Open Mind* '84 (solos, duets with George BENSON, Chick COREA, percussionists), quartet *Fables* '85. Other titles: *Critics Choice* on Prestige, *Meets Gaslini* on Pausa, *Violin Summit* on Verve with Stuff Smith, Svend ASMUSSEN, Stephane GRAPPELLI.

POOLE, Brian, & the Tremeloes UK beat group formed '59 in Dagenham, Essex by vocalist Brian Poole, with Ricky West (*b* Richard Westwood, '43), lead guitar; Alan Blakely (*b* '42), rhythm guitar; Dave Munden (*b* '43), drums; Alan Howard, bass. Poole modelled himself on Buddy HOLLY incl. spectacles; they appeared on BBC radio's *Saturday Club* '61, Decca signed them '62 (in preference to BEATLES, it's rumoured); first LP *Big Hits Of '62* was budget album of covers, first hit single (no. 4) was cover of ISLEY BROS 'Twist & Shout' mid-'63, better known as Beatle track from *Please Please Me*. Next cover (of Contours' 'Do You Love Me') went to no. 1: Poole's gravelly vocal made it a dance classic; by then he'd abandoned specs for contact lenses for a better image; hits through '65 incl. no. 2 with CRICKETS' 'Someone, Someone': also cracked Hot 100 in USA. But beat mania was subsiding; Poole and Tremeloes split '66; basically a shy man, he could not get another hit, retired to family butcher shop. Tremeloes moved to CBS, replacing Howard with new front man in bassist/vocalist Len 'Chips' Hawkes (*b* '46) and had 13 top 40 hits '67-71, covers incl. 'Silence Is Golden' (no. 1 UK '67; no. 11 USA on Epic). They publicly renounced goodtime pop for more 'progressive' stance (LP *Masters* '70); this lost them old fans and gained no new ones. Westwood left for two years, came back when Hawkes quit '74 and went to Nashville; Blakely left '75;

Westwood, Munden, Aaron Woolley and Bob Benham carried on in cabaret.

POOLE, Charlie (*b* 22 Mar. 1892, Almance Co., N.C.; *d* 21 May '31, N.C.) Vocalist, banjo player, leader of North Carolina Ramblers, popular and infl. string band of the '20s. Worked in textile mill; because of childhood injury had deformed fingers on right hand, developed a unique three-fingered picking style on banjo; teamed with fiddle player Posey Rorer (*b* 1881, Franklin Co. Va.; *d* '36), married Posey's sister Lou Emma '22; with guitarist Norman Woodlieff they played square dances, corn huskings etc.; then schoolhouses, barns and theatres in North Carolina, Virginia and West Virginia. Rorer and Woodlieff moved to NYC in search of a record deal, working in factories there; auditioned by Frank Walker at Columbia they recorded 'Don't Let Your Deal Go Down' mid-'25: it sold over 100,000 copies, one of the top selling hillbilly records of the time; they made a full-time living from music and in five years sold over a million records. Bill C. Malone says they sometimes used a piano or an extra fiddle, but that the trio format was their most popular. Bill Harvey (*b* 1892, Beckley, West Va.; *d* '58) replaced Woodlieff '26; Lonnie Austin replaced Posey '28, himself replaced by Odell Smith. Poole's accent and sound identified him regionally, but they played vaudeville and ragtime tunes as well as rural material, and Poole's idol was Al JOLSON. The Depression ended their success; Poole became a heavy drinker and died after an all-night party with old friends; the records are still highly regarded, compiled on *Charlie Poole And The North Carolina Ramblers Vols. 1-3* on County; *Charlie Poole* on Historical, *Charlie Poole & The Highlanders* on Arbor, all issued '71-4.

PORTER, Cole (*b* 9 June 1891, Peru, Indiana; *d* 15 Oct. '64, Santa Monica, Cal.) Perhaps the greatest songwriter of the century; of all the great ones from the Golden Age, he was almost the only one who wasn't Jewish, and the only one apart from Irving BERLIN who wrote both music and lyrics: he was RODGERS & HART in one. From wealthy background; piano and violin lessons from an early age, studied law, music

at Harvard; his grandfather (J. O. Cole, source of the money) tried to stop him being a composer and did not accept it even when he was obviously a success. He served in the French army as an American citizen in WWI, married a wealthy woman '19 and spent the '20s in Paris. First big hit 'I'm In Love Again' '24 (not a hit until '29); shows began with *Paris* '28 (incl. 'Let's Do It'), *Fifty Million Frenchmen* '29 ('You Do Something To Me'). Songs were suggested by everyday events ('It's De-Lovely' by a sunrise in Rio), or written for singers of limited range ('Miss Otis Regrets' for his friend, comic actor Monty Woolley; 'Night And Day' for Fred ASTAIRE); 'Don't Fence Me In', written as a send-up, became the best Hollywood cowboy ballad of all, because he could not write bad lyrics. Moved back to NYC early '30s, but never got Paris out of his blood. Both legs were shattered '37 when a horse fell on him; the immensely sophisticated world traveller was semi-invalid for the rest of his life and suffered countless operations to save the legs. Some of the shows/songs: *Wake Up And Dream* '29 (incl. 'What Is This Thing Called Love?'), *The New Yorkers* '30 ('Love For Sale'), *The Gay Divorce* '32 ('Night And Day'; filmed as *The Gay Divorcée* '34), *Anything Goes* '34 ('Anything Goes', 'I Get A Kick Out Of You', 'All Through The Night', 'You're The Top': Porter's record of the last, accompanying himself on the piano, was a top 10 hit); *Jubilee* '35 ('Just One Of Those Things', 'Begin The Beguine'), *Leave It To Me* '38 ('Get Out Of Town'; 'My Heart Belongs To Daddy' was introduced by Mary MARTIN), *Mexican Hayride* '44 ('Count Your Blessings'), *Seven Lively Arts* '44 ('Ev'ry Time We Say Goodbye'), *Kiss Me Kate* '48 ('So In Love', 'I'm Always True To You In My Fashion', 'Too Darn Hot'; show filmed '53), *Out Of This World* '50 ('From This Moment On'), *Can-Can* '53 ('C'est Magnifique', 'I Love Paris', 'It's All Right With Me'; film '60), *Silk Stockings* '55 (musical version of Garbo film *Ninotchka* '39, dir. by Ernst Lubitsch; itself filmed '57). Other film projects incl. *Born To Dance* '36 ('Easy To Love', 'I Get A Kick Out Of You'), *Rosalie* '37 ('In The Still Of The Night'), *Broadway Melody Of 1940* ('I Concentrate On You'; also reintroduced 'Begin The Beguine' after Artie SHAW's hit rec-

ord), *Something To Shout About* '43 ('You'd
Be So Nice To Come Home To'), *High
Society* '56: glittering cast incl. Frank
SINATRA, Louis ARMSTRONG, Bing CROS-
BY, Grace KELLY; lesser songs the silly
'Now You Has Jazz', syrupy 'True Love';
duet on latter by Crosby and Kelly gave
Porter a no. 3 pop hit '56; 'Well, Did You
Evah!' was revived from '39 show *Du Barry
Was A Lady*, which also incl. 'Do I Love
You?' and was filmed '43. Film *Les Girls*
disappointed '57. *Night And Day* '46 was a
biopic with Cary Grant. Porter's wife died
'54, his right leg was amputated '58, he
became even more reclusive; but the songs,
as they say, will live forever. There are
many biographies; *The Unpublished Cole
Porter*, *The Complete Lyrics Of Cole Porter*
and *Cole* edited by Robert Kimball.

POWELL, Bud (*b* Earl Powell, 27 Sep. '24,
NYC; *d* there 31 July '66) Pianist, composer; the most important pianist in BOP, and
one of the most influential musicians in the
history of jazz. He was influenced by Teddy
WILSON and Nat King COLE, but especially
by Art TATUM and Billy Kyle (*b* 14 July '14,
Philadelphia, Pa.; *d* 23 Feb. '66, Youngstown, Ohio): the urbane Kyle was an underrated pianist who played with Lucky
MILLINDER '36-8, John KIRBY '42, served in
WWII, joined Kirby again, led own small
groups '47-8, played two years in the Broadway show *Guys And Dolls*, did studio work,
then found secure berth with Louis
ARMSTRONG's All-Stars '53-66. Powell witnessed and became part of the birth of modern jazz in NYC; encouraged by Thelonious
MONK, he recorded with Cootie WILLIAMS'
band and sextet '43-4: Williams said that
Powell got in some kind of trouble after a
gig in Philadelphia and was beaten so badly
by law enforcement officers (Williams said
the F.B.I.) that he had to go to Bellevue
mental hospital (quoted in Stanley Dance's
The World Of Duke Ellington). Powell also
used drugs and alcohol; in any case paranoia set in and dogged him for the rest of
his life: his whole life was music. He could
hear the sounds even when there was no
instrument; spent '48 and other periods in
hospital, where he was given electroshock
therapy to make him 'normal'. In a famous
incident at a reunion gig early '55 Powell
had to be helped from the stand, incapable;

Charlie PARKER's behaviour was bizarre and
Charles MINGUS announced 'Ladies and
gentlemen, please don't associate me with
any of this. This is not jazz. These are sick
people.' Mingus added years later,
'Thelonious Monk went over to Bird and to
Bud and said, "I told you guys to act crazy,
but I didn't tell you to fall in love with the
act. You're really crazy now" ' (quoted by
Nat Hentoff in *Village Voice* '78 and in
Brian Priestley's fine *Mingus* '82). A week
later Parker was dead. Powell lived in Paris
'59-64, was hospitalised for suspected TB
'62-3, went to NYC for a gig but did not
return to Paris as planned. Not only were
his harmony, rhythm and compositions
central to bop, but his sparkling and percussive right hand, like Parker's playing, encouraged more imitators than geniuses: this
may have been at the expense of the left
hand in modern jazz piano, but that's not
Powell's fault. He recorded as a leader on
Roost '47 with Max ROACH, Curley Russell
on bass (*b* 19 Mar. '20, NYC; played with
Parker, Dizzy GILLESPIE, etc.); '53 with
George Duvivier and Art Taylor: these now
combined on PRT/UK. Quintet date on
Blue Note '49 incl. Fats NAVARRO, Sonny
ROLLINS, Roy HAYNES, bassist Tommy Potter, further Blue Note dates with trios '51,
'53, '57 (Curtis Fuller's trombone on some
tracks), '58 on various Blue Note LPs, or
complete in limited edition 5-disc set *The
Complete Bud Powell Blue Note Recordings*
on Mosaic with an excellent booklet.
Clef/Verve/Norgran recordings now on two
2-disc sets in USA: '49-51 incl. solo set from
'51; '54-5 set all trios. The famous Massey
Hall concert May '53 incl. a Powell trio set
with Roach and Mingus as well as a quintet
with Gillespie, Parker; now on separate
Fantasy LPs or Prestige 2-disc set. In Paris
Powell played in a trio with Pierre Michelot
and Kenny CLARKE; they backed Dexter
GORDON on *Our Man In Paris* '63, made
trio LP *Bud In Paris* '59-60 on Xanadu (two
tracks are duets with Powell and Johnny
GRIFFIN), others on Black Lion/Freedom
and ESP/Fontana, also *A Portrait Of
Thelonious* on CBS (now on Odyssey USA),
all '61; *Bud Powell In Concert* '60 on Polydor
had Oscar PETTIFORD instead of Michelot,
Coleman HAWKINS on two tracks; Michelot
returned for *Memorial Oscar Pettiford* later
the same year on Vogue, a month after

Oscar's death. With other rhythm sections, five vols. of *Live At The Golden Circle* on Steeplechase were made in Copenhagen '62, unreleased for almost 20 years; Fontana LPs incl. tapes made at home by Powell's friend Francis Paudras (the character played by Gordon in film *Round Midnight* '86 is based on Powell; another character is based on Paudras). There are many airchecks and bootlegs on Italian and other labels; last records were made in NYC on Roulette, ESP (unissued). His playing was sometimes handicapped by his personal problems; the mid-'50s seems to have been one of his worst periods: two RCA trio albums '56-7 are among the weaker Powell LPs; the production lacked imagination, and he was sometimes heavily tranquillised. But his seminal accomplishment was complete by then.

POWELL, Mel (*b* 12 Feb. '23, NYC) Pianist, arranger, composer, teacher. Led dixieland sextet at 12; joined Benny GOODMAN '41, Raymond SCOTT CBS band '42, Glenn MILLER AAF band '43, quit film and studio work to study composition at Yale with Paul Hindemith. Wrote 'The Earl', 'Mission To Moscow' for Goodman (latter no. 12 hit '42), won five *Downbeat* polls: he could play anything on the piano; his first stint with Goodman was one of the musical highlights of Goodman's career, comparable to the addition of Charlie CHRISTIAN and Cootie WILLIAMS to Goodman's sextet. He played with Goodman again late '40s, '54, '57; occasionally sat in with Bobby HACKETT in Connecticut mid-'60s, but concentrated on composition, incl. electronic music. He taught at Queens College NYC, then at Yale '54-69, was Dean of Music at Cal. Institute of Arts in Valencia from '69, fellow since '76; many pieces incl. a concerto for harpsichord. He played on the SS *Norway*'s Floating Jazz Festival out of Miami '86, jamming with Ruby BRAFF, Mel LEWIS, Bob WILBER, Warren Vaché, Svend ASMUSSEN, others; now partly disabled by a muscular disease in his legs, but there's nothing wrong with his hands: Wilber said, 'What astounds me is that it's like he never stopped playing – it's all there.' LPs: *The World Is Waiting* with Joe BUSHKIN on Commodore Classics, *The Unavailable Mel Powell* from late '40s on Pausa, trio LP

Bouquet on French Vogue; *Thingamajig* '54 with Ruby BRAFF, drummer Bobby Donaldson, and *Trio* with Paul QUINICHETTE on Vanguard.

POZO, Chano (*b* Luciano Pozo y Gonzales, 7 Jan. '15, Havana, Cuba; *d* 2 Dec. '48, NYC) Bongo and conga drummer; dancer, singer, composer. Steeped in West African rhythms from childhood; belonged to Afro-Cuban religious cult, came to USA '47 and altered the history of jazz. Introduced to Dizzy GILLESPIE by Mario BAUZA; performed in Gillespie's Carnegie Hall concert of Sep. '47, toured Europe with him '48. Made Latin percussion records for Gabriel Oller's SMC label (formed '45); in Dec. '47 played on eight Gillespie studio tracks incl. co-written 'Manteca', 'Cubana Be, Cubana Bop' now on 2-disc *Dizzy Gillespie Vol. 1/2 (1946-49)* on French RCA; also 'Afro-Cuban Suite'; extended playing on concert records incl. Salle Pleyel Feb. '48 now on French Vogue, Prestige USA; Aug. '48 L.A. concert on GNP. Began tour of Southern USA with Gillespie, quit mid-way because of theft of his congas; recorded four tracks with James MOODY late '48 (on Blue Note, incl. Pozo vocal on 'Tin Tin Deo', co-written with Gil Fuller). He could play in one rhythm, sing in another, dance in a third: 'I never knew how he could do that,' said Gillespie. 'Three people wrote ['Cubana Be, Cubana Bop'], not only that but three people wrote it as one person. George RUSSELL wrote the introduction; I wrote the middle part; and Chano and I did that *montuno* thing. It was just perfect . . .' 'You'd better believe everyone received the proper credit for these compositions because none of us was a pushover. Chano personally was a roughneck.' Taught the band multi-rhythms: 'On the bus, he'd give me a drum, Al McKibbon a drum, and he'd take a drum. Another guy would have a cowbell, and he'd give everybody a rhythm . . . we'd sing and play all down the highway' (Dizzy's quotes from Ira Gitler's *Swing To Bop* '85, autobiography *To Be Or Not To Bop* '80). Pozo was shot to death in a Harlem bar. *See also* BAUZA, GILLESPIE, CUBOP, AFRO-CUBAN MUSIC.

PRADO, Perez (*b* 13 Nov. '18, Mantanzas, Cuba; *d* 4 Dec. '83) Pianist, organist, bandleader, arranger, composer. Played organ in cinemas in Cuba, joined Orquesta Casino de la Playa as pianist; developed mambo from as early as '42, formed own mambo band '48. Unsuccessful in Cuba, went to Mexico, thence to the USA; he recorded for Seeco, UA, Epic and other labels, but mostly for RCA. His best-known mambos were numbered: 'Mambo No. 5', 'Mambo No. 8'. The mambo gradually became a craze in various Latin countries and a national fad in the USA '54. In the USA Latin community the three mambo kings were MACHITO, Tito PUENTE and Tito RODRIGUEZ; although the last two also recorded for RCA, Prado became the best known of them all because he had the biggest crossover hit: 'Cherry Pink And Apple Blossom White' '55. 'Cerisier Rose et Pommier Blanc' was published in Paris '50, recorded by Prado '51, again '55 for use in film *Underwater* with Jane Russell: it was a superb recording technically for the time, with juke box bass that could rattle the windows; the arr. had a slower tempo than Prado's authentic mambos and a spectacular trumpet solo by Billy Regis; it was no. 1 in the USA for ten weeks, two weeks in the UK. *Pop Memories* lists 'Anna' (film theme) and 'Skokian' (South African tune also recorded by Louis ARMSTRONG, Johnny HODGES, Ralph MARTERIE, the FOUR LADS, Bulawayo Sweet Rhythm Boys, etc.) as Prado hits '53-4; had second no. one '58 with 'Patricia', a bouncy organ-led jazzish chachacha. Cuban singer (later bandleader) Beny MORÉ, Johnny PACHECO (on percussion), Mongo SANTAMARIA and reedman (later bandleader) Rene Bloch were among those who passed through Prado's band. Compilations incl. *The Fabulous Perez Prado* on Italian RCA, *Los Grandes Exitos* on RCA International.

PREFAB SPROUT UK new wave pop group formed in Newcastle '78 by singer/songwriter, guitarist Paddy (Patrick) McAloon (*b* 7 June '57), inspired to start playing by Marc BOLAN and David BOWIE, then-prevalent teen idols; with brother Martin on drums (*b* 4 Jan. '62), and second vocalist Wendy Smith. Name came from phrase 'pepper sprout' in Nancy SINATRA's 'Jackson', misheard by McAloon. Initials of first self-financed single 'Lions In My Own

Garden (Exit Someone)' spelled Limoges, where his girlfriend had gone to study, pointing up tendency to Elvis COSTELLO-type wordplay (also parallel with AZTEC CAMERA's Roddy Frame); single helped get signing to local Kitchenware label; *Swoon* '84 distributed through CBS, incl. more such fragile jewels; polarised critics (intriguing to some, contrived to others), sold moderately. *Steve McQueen* '85 (retitled *Two Wheels Good* for USA after run-in with star's widow) was glossier, thanks to prod./keyboardist Thomas DOLBY; single 'When Love Breaks Down' their first real hit, while 'Faron Young' mixed wordplay with metaphor on British habit of adapting American/artificial views as their own (though many trendies in the UK pretend to be anti-American). 'When The Angels' was Marvin GAYE tribute (without mentioning his name). McAloon is critics' darling and promising composer in Costello mode; like Costello he often puts melody second, and may remain a cult figure on that account, though *From Langley Park To Memphis* '88 veered towards MOR.

PRESLEY, Elvis (*b* Elvis Aron Presley, 8 Jan. '35, Tupelo, Ms.; *d* 16 Aug. '77, Memphis, Tenn.) Singer, aka 'the King', among the biggest stars of the 20th century, for sociological as well as musical reasons. An only child from a poor family (twin brother Jessie Garon was born dead); the doctor spelled 'Aaron' correctly on the birth certificate but Elvis later had the change made legal; 'Elvis', his father's middle name, is uncommon in the USA except among poor white Southerners, the most direct descendants of English/Scottish emigrants: it was spelled 'Helwiss' or 'Helwys' in 17th-century England. His father served two years on Parchman Farm c.'38-40 for forging cheque, then worked only sporadically. Elvis attended Pentecostal churches, heard impassioned singing; also heard country music and black blues on the radio; won a talent contest singing Red FOLEY's sentimental set-piece 'Old Shep' '45, received a guitar for his birthday. As a teenager he may have known black Memphis clubs, hearing B. B. KING, others; after high school he worked as a truck driver, recorded himself at Memphis Recording Service to hear what he sounded like, came to the attention of proprietor Sam Phillips (*see* SUN Records) and on 6 July '54 made his first commercial records, with Bill BLACK on bass, guitarist Scotty Moore (*b* Winfield Scott Moore, 27 Dec. '31, Gadsden, Tenn.: album *The Guitar That Changed The World* '64 on Epic). He tried to sing ballads, country songs; style that made him famous was discovered while fooling around in the studio: cover of Arthur 'Big Boy' CRUDUP's 'That's All Right (Mama)' backed with Bill MONROE's 'Blue Moon Of Kentucky' created local sensation. Though Presley's idol was Dean MARTIN, he was the greatest of the rockabillies: he brought more black content than others to the combination of blues and country music (*see* ROCK'N'ROLL) and he pushed the beat, adding an exciting urgency to the music. Phillips had looked for a white who could sing like a black; a radio interview was hastily arranged, the name of the high school Presley had attended establishing that he was white. Sun singles continued to combine a blues backed with a country song, strategy paying off when 'Baby Let's Play House' (song by Arthur Gunter, *b* 23 May '26, Nashville; *d* 16 Mar. '76, Port Huron, Mich.; recorded for Excello '54-61) was top 10 country hit, followed by two-sided no. 1: 'Mystery Train' (by Junior PARKER) backed with 'I Forgot To Remember To Forget' (by Stanley Kesler and Charlie FEATHERS), all '55. By then D. J. Fontana was added on drums, and the first great rock'n'roll records were being made. Presley's only appearance on Grand Ole Opry was a flop (they allegedly advised him to go back to driving a truck); became regular on Shreveport's *Louisiana Hayride*; appearances on tour were sensational. Moore was his first manager, Memphis DJ Bob Neal his second; Tom Parker became his third and last as RCA bought his contract and masters from Sun Nov. '55 for the then unheard-of sum of $35,000; Elvis got an advance of $5000, spent it on a pink Cadillac; Hill and Range got publishing of Presley songs (through BMI's Presley Music, ASCAP's Gladys Music, named after his mother): not that he wrote songs, but Parker wanted rights to songs he recorded, which would severely restrict quality of his material in future, but did not do so immediately: first RCA session Jan. '56 in Nashville added Chet ATKINS on rhythm

guitar, pianist Floyd CRAMER; incl. rockaballads 'I Was The One', 'I'm Counting On You', Mae Axton's blues 'Heartbreak Hotel', all accompanied by vocal trio led by Gordon Stoker; covers of Ray CHARLES' 'I Got A Woman', Jesse Stone's 'Money Honey'. 'Heartbreak Hotel'/'I Was The One' was his first no. 1 pop hit (for eight weeks; also no. 1 R&B, no. 5 C&W), helped by Cramer's piano, but not by the appalling recording quality (it would be wonderful now to know what it would have sounded like if it had not been recorded in a breadbox). Next two sessions, in NYC, with better recording quality, Shorty Long on piano, no vocal backing, were the peak of his career, incl. classic covers of Carl PERKINS' 'Blue Suede Shoes', LITTLE RICHARD's 'Tutti Frutti', Crudup's 'My Baby Left Me' and 'So Glad You're Mine', Lloyd PRICE's 'Lawdy Miss Clawdy', also 'I'm Gonna Sit Right Down And Cry Over You', 'Shake, Rattle & Roll' (R&B hit by Joe TURNER, pop hit by Bill HALEY). RCA released an unprecedented six singles with sequential numbers, and Presley's first album was an instant rock classic (12 tracks, five from Sun vaults). Fourth date (in Nashville, with Atkins, pianist Marvin Hughes, echo and vocal trio) was syrupy ballad 'I Want You, I Need You, I Love You', second no. 1; then (in NYC) 'Hound Dog'/'Don't Be Cruel', both sides reaching no. 1, significantly both songs by pop tunesmiths: the first (a blues) by LEIBER & STOLLER, previously done (very differently) by Big Mama THORNTON, spoiled in Presley's recording by incessant handclaps and the inappropriate caterwauling of the JORDANAIRES (quartet led by Stoker);the other a catchy pop song by Otis BLACKWELL (its prettiness more evident in the JUDDS' version '86). No one who'd listened to both R&B and country music could have been astonished by Elvis Presley, but that did not apply to most Americans: parents and clergymen hated him; a petrol station in Texas gave away Presley 78s so that motorists could enjoy smashing them; yet his unbridled (for the time) sexuality was to him completely natural, while offstage he was polite and worshipped his mother. He appeared on the Milton Berle and DORSEY Bros. TV shows (the camera not showing his swivelling hips; he was called 'Elvis the

Pelvis'); Ed Sullivan swore he would never have Presley on his top-rated Sunday night variety show, but changed his mind when Steve ALLEN had him on the other channel, reducing Sullivan to 15% of the viewers. His three Sullivan appearances incl. debut of title song from first film, *Love Me Tender*; rock'n'roll fans groaned: a non-song based on a folksong, it was his fifth no. 1. His second album had more country content (incl. 'Old Shep'); even as a warm review appeared in the *New York Times* by John S. Wilson, he was already a phenomenon which had to do with an upheaval in popular culture more than with music: his voice matured into a rich instrument and he became a stage-wise entertainer, but little of his subsequent output was as exciting as the first three years; yet he had come from nowhere to strike it rich and was a folk hero: the phenomenon ultimately led to the absurdity of people giving their children plastic surgery so they would look like him. No. 1 hits '57-8 incl. Blackwell's 'All Shook Up' (his hits with Blackwell's songs established a pattern: he apparently copied style and all from Blackwell's demo records), 'Teddy Bear' (a Tin Pan Alley product from second film *Loving You*); 'Jailhouse Rock' (title theme of Presley's third and best film) and 'Don't' (both by Leiber & Stoller); 'Hard Headed Woman' (from *King Creole*, one of the less bad films); 'One Night' '58 (co-written by Dave BARTHOLOMEW for Smiley LEWIS) reached no. 4, was close to the earlier excitement, but Dean Martin infl. began to tell. By the time Presley was drafted early '58 his influence on pop music was complete. He later described his mother's death that year as the greatest tragedy of his life. He spent two years in Germany driving tanks; no. 1 hits '60-2 were 'A Big Hunk O' Love', 'Are You Lonesome Tonight?' (written '26), 'Surrender' (adapted from 'Come Back To Sorrento'), 'It's Now Or Never' (from 'O Sole Mio'), 'Good Luck Charm'. Two-sided hit 'Little Sister'/ '(Marie's The Name) His Latest Flame' (by Doc POMUS, Mort Shuman), 'Return To Sender' (by Blackwell and 'Winfield Scott') were excellent and exciting pop records, all top 5; he had only one more no. 1 hit ('Suspicious Minds' in '69). He wanted to be a movie star; spent the '60s making increasingly dreary films; unlike Martin, he showed little sign of having his tongue in his cheek as he cranked out trash like *G.I. Blues* and *Flaming Star* '60; *Wild In The Country* and *Blue Hawaii* '61; *Kid Galahad*, *Girls Girls Girls* and *Follow That Dream* '62; *Fun In Acapulco* and *It Happened At The World's Fair* '63; *Kissin' Cousins*, *Viva Las Vegas* and *Roustabout* '64; *Girl Happy*, *Tickle Me* and *Harem Scarem* '65; *Frankie And Johnny*, *Paradise Hawaiian Style* and *Spinout* '66; *Easy Come Easy Go* and *Double Trouble* '67; *Stay Away Joe*, *Speedway*, *Clambake* and *Live A Little, Love A Little* '68; *Charro* '69; *Change Of Habit* and *The Trouble With Girls* '70. His fanatically adoring public saw to it that the films made a profit and the soundtrack albums were hits; the money continued to pour in, partly because the songs were written to order and owned by Presley, but never was more skill wasted on such dross, such as a song about how to do the hula in a sports car. He taped a TV special mid-'68 which was surprisingly powerful, showing what he could still do; portions were taped without an audience but some of it was his first public appearance in more than seven years; Scotty Moore and D. J. Fontana were there, and exciting out-takes were rumoured to exist, but when these were issued in a six record set of scraps from old TV shows etc. (*Elvis – A Golden Celebration* '84) they proved less than compelling. The LP from the special went top 10; in '69 he recorded 23 songs in Memphis, first time there since Sun days and perhaps the best material of his later career: *From Elvis In Memphis* '69 was no. 13 LP, 2-disc *The Memphis Record* '87 contained it all, incl. 'In The Ghetto', 'Suspicious Minds'. Also in '69 he began performing in Las Vegas, with excellent backing incl. James BURTON on guitar, Glen D. Hardin on keyboards. *Aloha From Hawaii By Satellite* '73 was his ninth and last no. 1 album. He worked hard, touring the USA and putting on many a good show in Las Vegas, but was often overweight, collapsed on stage at least once. He lived in a garish mansion in Memphis called Graceland (the title song on Paul SIMON's *Graceland* '86 LP captures the feeling of the Presley tragedy without referring to him directly). He married Priscilla Beaulieu, army officer's daughter he met in Germany when she was a child, on 1 May

'67; daughter Lisa Marie was born 1 Feb. '68; they divorced '73. He showered acolytes (the 'Memphis Mafia') with gifts, became increasingly reclusive while eating and pilling himself to death; his doctor encouraged him to misuse barbiturates, but he never drank and scorned recreational drugs. Honorary Col. Tom Parker (*b* 26 June '09, probably in Holland) had been a carnival huckster and a dog-catcher, former manager of Gene AUSTIN in his later years, then of Eddy ARNOLD; he saw to it that Presley always paid the maximum in income tax, never toured outside the USA except for three dates in Canada '57, probably because he was an illegal immigrant and wanted to avoid anything to do with the government; during Presley's Las Vegas era Parker lived there gambling at Presley's expense. Worthwhile interviews with Presley do not exist because Parker would have charged any journalist a fortune for the privilege, and in any case did not want any sharp questions to rock the boat. He was finally divested of most of his interest in Presley in court in '83, long after it was too late. Presley helped to keep RCA's record division afloat for 30 years; we will never know whether lack of sense, taste or self-confidence allowed him largely to waste his talent. Phillips later recalled of the early years, 'He tried not to show it, but he felt so *inferior* . . . All he did was set with his guitar on the side of his bed at home. I don't think he even played on the front porch.' He became the cabaret entertainer he always wanted to be, 'The King' of rock'n'roll only in the way that Paul WHITEMAN was the 'King of Jazz', Benny GOODMAN the 'King of Swing'; yet his singing remained influential even through the bad material. Most of the songs that made him famous '54-6 were written by blacks, and the records sold better in black neighbourhoods than Nat King COLE's did, yet Greil Marcus could dismiss as 'nonsense' the obvious truth (in *Mystery Train: Images of America In Rock'n'Roll Music* '76) that it was the black infl. that gave Presley's rock'n'roll what value it had. Documentary films of tours are *Elvis: That's The Way It Is* '70 and *Elvis On Tour* '72; also 'docu-drama' *This Is Elvis* '82. He had 149 hits in Billboard Hot 100 '56-82, 92 albums in the top 200 LPs '56-85, nearly 50 still listed in the USA Schwann catalogue

'87; recommended albums incl. *The Sun Collection* and *The '56 Sessions Vol. 1* (UK); fans can pick and choose from the rest: five vols. of *Elvis' Golden Records*, compilations *Reconsider Baby (Elvis Sings The Blues)*, 4-disc *Return Of The Rocker* ('60-3), gospel LPs *His Hand In Mine* and *How Great Thou Art*, etc. His bibliography is easily the largest in rock, most of it inevitably junk given the mystery of his introverted personality; Dave Hebler, Red and Sonny West (formerly of the Memphis Mafia) published *Elvis – What Happened?* days before his death, raising the lid on the pill-popping; Albert Goldman's massive, controversial and well-written biography *Elvis* '82 is disfigured by disgust but seems unfortunately all too true.

PRESTON, Billy (*b* 9 Sep. '46, Houston, Texas) Singer, keyboardist. Raised in L.A.; played organ for gospel queen Mahalia JACKSON before playing W. C. HANDY as a boy in *St Louis Blues* '58 (Nat COLE played him as a grown-up). Touring Europe with LITTLE RICHARD and Sam COOKE (recorded for Cooke's SAR label, among others), he first met the BEATLES; spotted as backing musician on UK TV's *Shindig* by Ray CHARLES entourage; toured USA/Europe with Charles as catchy organ instrumentals ('Billy's Bag', etc.) attracted attention. George HARRISON bought out his recording contract, prod. LPs *That's The Way God Planned It* '69 (title track no. 11 UK hit), *Encouraging Words* '70 on Apple; played as sideman on Beatles' 'Get Back', 'Let It Be'. Bailed out of Apple, had hits on A&M '72-8 incl. USA top 40s '72-4 'Outa-Space' (no. 2), 'Will It Go Round In Circles' (no. 1), 'Space Race' (no. 4), 'Nothing From Nothing' (no. 1), 'Struttin' ' (no. 22): first, third and fifth instrumentals. Continued as star sessioneer: appeared at Bangla Desh concert '71, backed Harrison '74, ROLLING STONES '75; came back '79 with no. 4 duet with Syreeta Wright 'With You I'm Born Again', from film *Fastbreak*. With cheery, engaging sound and like Nicky HOPKINS, Rick GRECH, etc. a superstar '70s sideman; unlike some of the others had his own hits as well.

PRETENDERS, The UK new wave group formed '78 by expatriate Chrissie Hynde (*b*

933

7 Sep. '51, Akron, Ohio), rhythm guitar, singer, songwriter. She attended Kent State, played with Akron band Saturday, Sunday, matinees, went to London, wrote for the *New Musical Express*; returned to USA to sing with R&B band Jack Rabbit, to France to sing with Frenchies, back to London. Rehearsed with Mick Jones, but he co-formed CLASH; she sang in Malcolm McClaren's Masters of the Backside, which later became the DAMNED; with Steve Strange in shortlived (fortunately) Moors Murderers (one single, lots of space in tabloids); he co-formed VISAGE. She signed with new Real label, met bassist Pete Farndon (*b* '53, Hereford; *d* 14 Apr. '83), who introduced ex-Cheeks guitarist James Honeyman-Scott (*b* 4 Nov. '57, Hereford; *d* 16 June '82); with drummer Gerry Mackleduff they cut top 40 cover of old Ray Davies song 'Stop Your Sobbin' ', her 'The Wait' on reverse. With ex-Cheeks drummer Martin Chambers (*b* 4 Sep. '51, Hereford) they made classic no. 1 LP *Pretenders* '80; by its release 'Kid' had gone top 40, 'Brass In Pocket' was no. 1. The album showed Hynde's variety of pace, from full-tilt rock-'n'roll with aggressive punk overtones ('Precious') to reggae ('Private Life') to ballads ('Lovers Of Today'); soul rhythm guitar meshed with Honeyman-Scott's lead, but second LP *Pretenders II* '81 reflected heavier stage act, his almost metallic guitar drowning out her subtlety. Atypical cover, delicate Sandie SHAW soundalike treatment of another Ray Davies song 'I Go To Sleep' was no. 7, other hits: 'Talk Of The Town', 'Message Of Love'. Incessant touring and personal antipathies took toll: Farndon was sacked mid-'82; two days later Honeyman-Scott died of drink/drugs (a few months later Farndon died of 'heart attack'). Hynde and Chambers recruited ex-Rockpile guitar Billy Bremner, BIG COUNTRY's bassist Tony Butler for jangling one-off 'Back On The Chain Gang' (top 20 '82), while Hynde was romantically involved with Davies. *Learning To Crawl* '84 used guest musicians; ex-Night guitarist Robbie McIntosh, Foster Bros bassist Malcolm Foster made up permanent members; Xmas hit '2000 Miles' (no. 15 '83). A schizophrenic band, much heavier live than first LP suggested; like others, they found it hard to come up with ideas once they were on the album/tour/album treadmill. As sole singer/songwriter Hynde was under special pressure. In Jan. '83 she had a baby; she took time off '85 to have another, by new husband Jim Kerr (SIMPLE MINDS); 'I Got You Babe' was no. 1 UK '85, Hynde with popular band UB40. She is an undoubted talent who will probably be back. *The Singles* '87 is good compilation incl. 'I Got You Babe'.

PRETTY THINGS, The UK R&B band formed at Sidcup art college in Kent '63 by original ROLLING STONES bassist Dick Taylor, singer Phil May (*b* 11 Sep. '44, Kent). Taylor switched to lead to accommodate bassist John Stax; rhythm guitarist Brian Pendleton, drummers Peter Kitley, Viv Andrews, then Viv Prince completed lineup. Very much in Stones mould, from image to covers of USA R&B material (name from BO DIDDLEY lyric). Had top 40 hits, near misses; after three LPs drummer since '65 Skip Alan (*b* Alan Skipper, 11 June '48, London) was replaced by John 'Twink' Adler, Wally Allen replaced Stax on bass and John Povey (*b* 20 Aug. '44, London) replaced Pendleton on keyboards; they switched from Fontana to progressive new EMI Harvest label with *SF Sorrow* '68, a concept LP written by May and Taylor, now seen as the first rock opera, inspired Pete Townshend's more successful *Tommy* for the WHO. Taylor left; Alan returned to form two-drummer arr. with Twink; more changes followed. *Parachute* '69 was acclaimed by *Rolling Stone*, but a commercial failure; *Freeway Madness* '72 incl. new members Pete Tolson on guitar (*b* 10 Sep. '51, Bishop's Stortford), Gordon Edwards on keyboards (*b* 26 Dec. '46, Southport). Signed to LED ZEPPELIN Swan Song label for polished AOR albums *Silk Torpedo*, *Savage Eye* '74-5, the only ones to chart in USA, but May's departure '76 was the end. He formed Fallen Angels with Alan; others formed Metropolis with ex-T-Rex bassist Jack Green (*b* 12 Mar. '51, Glasgow), who'd sung on last LP, but they split again, Edwards joining the KINKS. In '85 May was playing pubs with young musicians as Pretty Things; Taylor played with former Leeds punks the Mekons. First two LPs *The Pretty Things* and *Get The Picture* reissued by Fontana/Holland; *Let Me Hear The Choir*

Sing '84 on Edsel anthologised early singles; *Closed Restaurant Blues* '85 on Bam Caruso portrayed them emerging from blues period, lent weight to the theory that they were several bands, with May as only constant factor; *Cries From The Midnight Circus* '86 on Harvest incl. tracks from *SF Sorrow* and *Parachute*; other compilations: *1967-1971* on See For Miles, *Cross Talk* on WB, two as 'Electric Banana' on Butt. Highly regarded in rock history, but constant change kept them from breakthrough.

PREVIN, André (*b* André Prewin, 6 Apr. '29, Berlin) Jazz pianist, accompanist, jet-set conductor. Began piano lessons, showed promise, enrolled at Berlin High School for Music at 6; kicked out of Conservatory '38 because he was Jewish; family immediately went to Paris to await visas, then to Los Angeles. He thought jazz was 'men in funny hats playing in a hotel band', then he heard an Art TATUM record; played on the radio; played jazz piano on film soundtrack for José Iturbi (who couldn't), scored it as well, at age 16. His music education was on the job: he accompanied violinist Joseph Szigeti at his home in contemporary music and classics, worked at MGM until '50 (first assignment a Lassie film: 'a lot of barks and a few songs'), was drafted, stationed in San Francisco, studied conducting with Pierre Monteux, also played jazz; went back to Hollywood '53, still playing all kinds of music; once impulsively rang Dmitri Shostakovich in the USSR with a musical question. Occasionally composed: 40-minute sequence for Gene KELLY ballet film *Invitation To The Dance* '54, music for *The Subterraneans* '60 (film of Jack Kerouac book) played by all-star big band; scored many films through '71, incl. *It's Always Fair Weather* '55 (music by Adolph Green, Betty Comden), Oscars for *Gigi* '58 (Alan Jay LERNER), *Porgy And Bess* '59 (GERSHWIN), *Irma La Douce* '63 (themes by studio composers), *My Fair Lady* '64 (Lerner); later wrote Broadway play *Coco* with Lerner. Meanwhile he made c.60 LPs in various combinations, many under his own name: about 20 mostly trio tracks on small labels '45-7, some now on Black Lion (*Previn At Sunset*); recorded for RCA '47-53; *Plays Fats Waller* '53 with Buddy CLARK and Shelly MANNE (now on PRT/UK as

The Genius Of Fats Waller); two LPs for Decca '55-6; trio *Shelly Manne And His Friends* '56 on Contemporary, with ace session bassist Leroy Vinnegar (*b* 13 July '28, Indianapolis, Ind.), then same trio did jazz version of *My Fair Lady* same year: hit LP started fad for jazzing Broadway scores. They did *Bells Are Ringing* '58 with Red Mitchell on bass; under Previn's name *Li'l Abner* with Vinnegar; *Pal Joey* '57, *Gigi* '58, *West Side Story* '59 with Mitchell. Other Previn LPs on Contemporary incl. solo piano *Plays Songs By Vernon Duke, Plays Songs By Jerome Kern, Plays Harold Arlen* '58-60. He made an LP of his film music on MGM, also *Secret Songs For Young Lovers* '59, first Previn LP to make pop LP chart (top 20); Columbia LPs '60-4 incl. solo *Like Love* (top 25 '60); *A Touch Of Elegance* '61 (music of Duke ELLINGTON), *André Previn In Hollywood* '63 (both with orchestra) and trio remake of *My Fair Lady* '64 all made top 200 LPs; other trio sets incl. *Give My Regards To Broadway, The Light Fantastic Tribute To Fred Astaire*, others with J. J. JOHNSON or Herb ELLIS added, etc. He realised that he wanted to be a conductor, and overcame the prejudice against anyone who had worked in Hollywood: first classical recording for CBS early '60s with the St Louis S.O. incl. Aaron Copland's film score *The Red Pony* and Benjamin Britten's *Sinfonia da Requiem* (Britten's reaction: 'Who is this fellow André Previn? That's the best performance I've ever heard'). He conducted the Houston S.O. '67-9, London S.O. '68-79 (so popular he also did TV adverts for consumer goods; recordings of Vaughan Williams, William Walton, Shostakovich especially praised). Succeeded William Steinberg as conductor of Pittsburgh S.O. '76; formed trio '79 with violinist Herbert Greenberg, cellist Anne Martindale Williams in Pittsburgh to play chamber music. Resigned '86 as mus. dir. of London Philharmonic in protest at 'unimportant' quality of guest soloists/conductors, was still principal conductor '87, dividing time between LPO, Los Angeles Philharmonic. Played benefit '82 with Manne and bassist Monty Budwig (*b* 26 Dec. '29, Pender, Neb.), raised $75,000 for Rehabilitation Institute of Pittsburgh; made LP of Scott Joplin rags with violinist Itzhak Perlman on EMI, then *A Different Kind Of*

Blues with Perlman, Mitchell, Manne and Jim HALL (made top 200 LPs again '81 after 16 years) followed by same cast on *It's A Breeze* '81, all tunes on both LPs written by Previn; also *Nice Work If You Can Get It* '83 on Pablo, duo with Ella FITZGERALD, with bassist Niels-Henning Ørsted Pedersen on some tracks. He was married to jazz singer Betty Bennett, accompanied her; then lyricist Dory Langdon (they collaborated on film work, made LP; *see* Dory PREVIN, below); then actress Mia Farrow; now married again after some deliberation. Other works incl. music for *Every Good Boy Deserves Favour* with playwright Tom Stoppard about inmates in Soviet insane asylum: remarkably successful for a one-off project, with 300 performances around the world, both authors banned from the USSR. Also piano concerto played by Vladimir Ashkenazy, Emmanuel Ax, André Watts; a violin sonata, *Matthew's Piano Book* (for his son), *Peaches For Trumpet*, much else; was writing cello concerto for Yo Yo Ma '87. He no doubt agrees with Ellington that there are only two kinds of music: good and bad; may be one of the great conductors of the century. (Quotes from *New Yorker* profile by Helen Drees Ruttencutter.)

PREVIN, Dory (*b* Dory Langdon, 22 Oct., Woodbridge, N.J.) Lyricist; became singer/songwriter in uncompromising feminist/confessional mode. She sang and danced in night clubs as a child, left home at age of 16 to study acting but toured in chorus lines; original songs led to work at MGM, then UA; she wrote TV music, married André PREVIN: they made album *Dory & André Previn* '57 on DRG with Kenny BURRELL, collaborated on film work. She was nominated for Oscars for film songs 'The Faraway Part Of Town' (with Previn, for *Pepe* '60; sung by Judy GARLAND), 'Come Saturday Morning' (with Fred Karlin, for *The Sterile Cuckoo* '69, sung by the Sandpipers behind the credits and on top 20 hit; also sung by Liza MINNELLI); also 'A Second Chance' from *Seesaw*. She also wrote (with Previn) 'You're Gonna Hear From Me', sung by Jackie Ward in soundtrack of *Inside Daisy Clover* '65, also recorded by Andy WILLIAMS; songs for *Valley Of The Dolls* '67 incl. 'It's Impossible', 'I'll Plant My Own Tree', title theme (no. 2 hit '68 by Dionne

WARWICK); also title song for *Last Tango In Paris* '73 with Gato BARBIERI, many others. Meanwhile the marriage failed and she was hospitalised c.'65, came back as performer of tough, cathartic material, rewarding for those who can take it: albums *Mythical Kings And Iguanas*, *Reflections In A Mud Puddle*, *Mary C. Brown* '72 (full title of stage musical *Mary C. Brown And The Hollywood Sign*), *On My Way To Where* (also the title of a collection of lyrics and poems), *Live At Carnegie Hall* '73 on UA; *Dory Previn* '74, *Children Of Coincidence* '77 on WB; *One A.M. Phone Calls* '77 on UA again. Also wrote shows *The Flight Of The Gooney Bird*, and screenplay/music for TV movie *Third Girl From The Left*.

PRICE, Kenny (*b* 27 May '31, Covington, Ky.; *d* 4 Aug. '87, Florence, Ky.) Country singer, known as 'The Round Mound of Sound' owing to his size. Played guitar as teenager on WZIP Radio, Cincinnati '45-8; joined US Army, performed with Horace HEIDT USO show in Korea; attended Cincinnati Conservatory of Music, appearing weekends on WLW's Midwestern Hayride, joined accordionist Buddy Ross's Hometowners '57 as lead singer and became Hayride regular. Moved to Nashville early '60s, signed with new Boone label '65, had hits 'Walking On New Grass', 'Happy Tracks', 'Grass Won't Grow On A Busy Street', 'My Goal For Today' '66-7; became regular on *Hee-Haw* TV show. Moved to RCA '69; Boone LP *Happy Tracks* '67 reissued on RCA; returned to top 10 with 'Northeast Arkansas Mississippi County Bootlegger', 'Biloxi', 'The Sheriff Of Boone County' '70-1, stayed in top 40 '72-4, but RCA dropped him '76; joined MRC label and had minor chart comeback with 'Afraid You'd Come Back' '78, then Dimension Records '80 but no hits. LPs: *Heavyweight* '69, *Super Sideman* '72, *You Almost Slipped My Mind* '73, *The Red Foley Songbook* '75, all RCA.

PRICE, Lloyd (*b* 9 Mar. '33, New Orleans) Singer/songwriter, major voice in early rock'n'roll via New Orleans R&B. Wrote 'Lawdy Miss Clawdy' '52 for an advert on a local radio station, had no. 1 R&B hit with New Orleans studio sound by Dave

BARTHOLOMEW and a pianist that might have been Fats DOMINO; he had three more top 10 R&B hits on Specialty; the big one was covered by Elvis PRESLEY '56 (and by Gary Stites '60, the Buckinghams '69 for top 50 hits). After military service he started his own record company, recorded 'Just Because' and leased it to ABC for no. 4 R&B, top 20 pop hit; signed directly to ABC he had no. 1 both R&B and pop with 'Stagger Lee' (reworking of trad. 'Stagolee'), turned more towards a big studio pop sound with 'Personality', one of the most delightful hits of '59, then 'I'm Gonna Get Married', both no. 1 R&B, top 3 pop; several more hits through '60. In '60s he operated a club called the Turntable, labels Double L and Turntable, had a few minor hits; LP *To The Roots And Back* '72 on GSF. Compilations/reissues on Specialty, MCA (ABC stuff), Specialty, Ace; also Charly in UK.

PRICE, Ray (*b* Ray Noble Price, 12 Jan. '26, Perryville, Texas) Country music singer, one of the biggest, with more than 50 top 10 country hits since '52, 11 crossing over to pop Hot 100. Grew up in Dallas, but favoured the rural way of life. Served in US Army; studied at North Texas Agricultural College '46-9 intending to be a vet, but made radio debut as guitarist/singer on KRBC's *Hillbilly Circus* in Abilene '48, became regular on *Big D Jamboree* on KRLD Dallas. Signed with Bullet, first release his own song 'Jealous Lies' '50. He was a friend of Hank WILLIAMS, formed band the Cherokee Cowboys '53 from Hank's DRIFTING COWBOYS. By then he recorded for Columbia and was a member of Grand Ole Opry, big hits incl. 'Don't Let The Stars Get In Your Eyes' at no. 4 '52 (a huge pop hit by Perry COMO, it was published by Acuff-Rose and had four hit versions in the country charts, incl. Red FOLEY at no. 8, Skeets McDonald and co-writer Slim Willet both at no. 2). His first no. 1 was 'Crazy Arms' '56, 45 weeks in country chart and his first crossover; others incl. 'My Shoes Keep Walking Back To You' (no. 3) and 'City Lights' (his second country no. 1) '57-8. This was his classic period, heavily steeped in honky tonk, incl. 'Under Your Spell Again', 'Make The World Go Away', many more; he changed styles, performed in a dress suit, dropped fiddle and steel

guitar for strings: 'Danny Boy' '67 was made with a 47-piece orchestra (top 10 country, his only top 40 pop hit at no. 11), bringing criticism from purists, but hits incl. 'For The Good Times' and 'I Won't Mention It Again' both no. 1 '70-1. He provided breaks for Johnny PAYCHECK, Willie NELSON, others; was first to record a Roger MILLER song ('Invitation To The Blues', top 20 '58). A peerless interpreter of good songs, switched to gospel label Myrrh at his peak, country hits continued: 'Like Old Times Again' and 'Roses And Love Songs' '74; switched again to ABC-Dot '75 but went into temporary retirement, more than happy to breed horses on his Texas ranch; still the hits kept coming: 'Farthest Thing From My Mind', 'A Mansion On The Hill', 'Born To Love Me', the last on both Columbia and ABC-Dot '77. Moved to Monument for top 20 hits 'Feet' and 'That's The Only Way To Say Good Morning' '78-9; teamed with Nelson for *San Antonio Rose* duet LP incl. hit 'Faded Love' '80; top 10 on Dimension with 'It Don't Hurt Me Half So Bad' and 'Diamonds In The Stars' '81; to WB, then Viva and return to old style, records by Ray Price & The Cherokee Cowboys. Despite long and successful career, received only one CMA award for *I Won't Mention It Again* (Album of the Year '71), Grammy for album *For The Good Times* '70 (in charts nearly four years, sold a million). Other LPs: *Sings Heart Songs* '57, *Faith* '60, *Night Life* '63, *Burning Memories* '64, *Western Strings* '66, *Sweetheart Of The Year* '68, *Lonesomest Lonesome* '72, *Tribute To Willie & Kris*, all on Columbia; *This Time Lord* '74 on Myrrh, *Precious Memories* '77 and *How Great Thou Art* on Word; *Rainbows And Tears* '76, *Reunited* '77, *Hank'n'Me* '78, all on ABC-Dot; *Diamonds In The Stars* '80 on Dimension; compilations on Columbia in USA plus *The Honky Tonk Years* '51-6 on Rounder, two 2-disc sets on Pair: *Happens To Be The Best* and *Priceless*.

PRIDE, Charley (*b* 18 Mar. '38, Sledge, Ms.) The most successful black country singer, with more than 50 top 10 hits incl. 29 at no. 1, 10 crossovers to pop chart '69-74. Picked cotton as a child; sidetracked from music by baseball: played for Memphis Red Sox '54, served in US Army, tried out for California Angels and NY Mets '62; played semi-pro in Pioneer League while working in zinc works near Great Falls, Montana but also singing; appeared in local show '63 with Red FOLEY and Red SOVINE who urged him to go to Nashville. A demo reached Chet ATKINS; signed with RCA '65, debut 'Snakes Crawl At Night' with sparse publicity and no photos got airplay; second 'Just Between You And Me' made country top 10 '66; first no. 1 was 'All I Have To Offer You Is Me' '69. One of the few country stars who has never written a song, became a hit machine with his superb voice, appearing at the end on TV shows because nobody wanted to follow him: some said he sang Hank WILLIAMS better than Hank. Began in straight country but turned smoother, one of RCA's best sellers, 17 LPs crossing over to pop album chart '68-81, eight in top 50 USA LPs incl. two compilations. More country no. ones: 'Is Anybody Goin' To San Antone' '70, 'She's Too Good To Be True' '72, 'A Shoulder To Cry On' and 'Amazing Love' '73, 'Then Who Am I' and 'Hope You're Feelin' Me' '75, 'My Eyes Can Only See As Far As You' '76, 'She's Just An Old Love Turned Memory' and 'I'll Be Leaving Alone' '77, 'Someone Loves You Honey' '78, 'Where Do I Put Her Memory' and 'You're My Jamaica' '79 (last recorded in London). Realised childhood dream joining Opry '67, was CMA Entertainer of the Year '71, Male Vocalist '71-2. Took Ronnie MILSAP, Janie FRICKE, others on tours, helped their careers. Good businessman, interests in cattle, oil, music publishing, banking etc. Back to trad. country briefly '80 with *There's A Little Bit Of Hank In Me*, tribute set incl. no. 1 hits 'Honky Tonk Blues' and 'You Win Again'; further no. ones were 'Never Been So Loved (In All My Life)', 'Why Baby Why' and 'Night Games' '81-3. He asked for a release from his RCA contract '86, saying they were no longer promoting his records properly in favour of younger acts; *I'm Gonna Love Her On The Radio* '88 came out on his 16th Avenue Label LPs incl. *The Country Way* '68, live *In Person* (at Panther Hall, Fort Worth) '69, *Sensational* '69, *Just Plain Charley* and *10th Album* '70; *From Me To You, Did You Think To Pray, I'm Just Me, Sings Heart Songs* (incl. 'Kiss An Angel Good Mornin' ', no. 1 country, 21 pop), all '71, all in pop LP chart; then *A Sunshine Day* '72;

The Incomparable, Songs Of Love, Sweet Country '73; *Country Feeling* '75, *Sunday Morning With* '76, *Burgers And Fries* '79, *Roll On Mississippi* '81, *Sings Everybody's Choice* '82, *Country Classics* '83, *Live* '83.

PRIMA, Louis (*b* 7 Dec. '11, New Orleans; *d* there 24 Aug. '78) Trumpet, singer, bandleader. Older brother (*b* '07) well-known trumpeter Leon Prima. First studied violin, but took up trumpet on brother's spare instrument c.'25 while Leon was in Texas with Peck KELLEY. Led local combos, moved to Cleveland, Ohio '32 playing with Red NICHOLS. Recorded in Chicago '33 with David ROSE (piano), Norman Gast (violin) as The Hotcha Trio; formed 17-piece band Louis Prima And His New Orleans Gang NYC '34, signed recording contract and played at the Famous Door in 52nd street. On West Coast '36; appeared in films *Swing It* and *Rhythm On The Range*, first of many such parts. Wrote 'Sing, Sing, Sing', interpolated by Benny GOODMAN in '37 with 'Christopher Columbus' making Swing Era 'killer diller'. (Other well-known comps. are 'It's The Rhythm In Me' and 'Sunday Kind Of Love'.) Appeared with band in *Manhattan Merry-Go-Round* and *You Can't Have Everything* '37, *Start Cheering* '38; back to NYC with his Gleeby Rhythm Orchestra, singing an entertaining, almost nonsensical mixture of jivespeak, Neapolitan slang and plain bad English which, with solid trumpet playing, resulted in hit records through the '40s: his own 'Robin Hood' '44, 'Bell-Bottom Trousers' '45 (no. 10), 'Civilization' '47 (no. 8), 'Oh Babe' '50 (no. 16), each on different labels. Married fourth wife Keely SMITH '52, signed to Capitol with combo featuring tenor sax Sam Butera, dispensing mixture of novelty, R&B and pop; they soon became hot attraction in Las Vegas: Smith sang in clear, straight jazz style, pokerfaced and with a Tonto hair-do, while he perpetrated familiar ebullient nonsense. LP *Las Vegas – Prima Style* was no. 12 '58; interpolation of 'I Ain't Got Nobody'/'Just A Gigolo' hit on EP (copied by David Lee Roth for single hit '85); 'That Old Black Magic' reached no. 18 that year; 'I've Got You Under My Skin' charted '59. They made films *Hey Boy! Hey Girl!* (soundtrack LP charted), *Senior Prom*, both '59. Switched to

Dot label; hits incl. *Louis And Keely!* LP, 'Bei Mir Bist Du Schön' single '59, Prima solo hit 'Wonderland By Night' '60 (his LP of that title made top 10 LPs '61). The marriage failed; Prima worked on in Vegas and Lake Tahoe; provided voice of cartoon orang-utan in Disney film *Jungle Book* '69. Fell into a coma '75, lingered for three years in a nursing home.

PRINCE (*b* Prince Roger Nelson, 7 June '58, Minneapolis, Minn.) Soul singer, composer. Father a black/Italian jazz pianist (Prince Rogers Trio, hence name); mother a singer. Self-taught on piano, guitar and drums; band Grand Central, later called Champagne, with Andre Anderson, bass; Linda Anderson, keyboards; Morris Day on drums; made demos under patronage of local studio owner, was signed by WB while still in teens. Played all the instruments on *For You* '78, incl. top 20 soul/Hot 100 pop hit 'Soft And Wet': album dedicated to 'God' a strange mix of religious and sexual/secular; reached top 200 pop LPs. *Prince* '79 incl. no. 1 soul/11 pop hit 'I Wanna Be Your Lover', made no. 22 pop LP chart, confirmed penchant for X-certificate lyrics that created outcry on *Dirty Mind* '80, with songs about oral sex, incest: together with outrageous stage gear (black lace underwear, provocative female backing trio Vanity 6), no. 45 LP brought more fame. Aptly-named *Controversy* '81 made no. 21 (title track incl. chanted Lord's Prayer), but 2-disc *1999* '82 (initially issued as single LP in UK) confirmed reputation by incl. hard-nosed commercial soul tracks that *could* be broadcast: 'Little Red Corvette', 'Delirious' and title track all big hits, '1999' reaching top 25 in UK. *Purple Rain* album/film '84 shot him into rock's first division, though film (co-starring Patty 'Apollonia' Kotero, member of Vanity 6) was only rescued by scenes of Prince indulging Hendrix fixation in concert; heavily synthesised 'When Doves Cry' was no. 1 single USA, no. 4 UK; 'Let's Go Crazy' also no. 1 USA; title track no. 2 USA/8 UK; the album (billed as 'Prince & the Revolution') kept Bruce SPRINGSTEEN's *Born In The USA* out of no. 1 spot in USA for more than 20 weeks. *Around The World In A Day* '85 was inevitably an anticlimax; first mooted without a single, the plan changed as sales

slumped (relatively): the LP (no. 1 for three weeks USA), new custom label Paisley Park, no. 2 hit (USA) 'Raspberry Beret' all had psychedelic overtones; 'Pop Life' also a hit single. *Parade* '86 saw return to harder funk roots, hit 'Kiss' while he was writing music for another film, *Under A Cherry Moon*. 2-disc *Sign Of The Times* '87 was well-reviewed; *Lovesexi* '88 had him nude on cover. No live album yet but 2-cassette video *Double Live* released early '86. He is a genuine enigma: attended '85 BPI awards with monster bodyguards to say a half-dozen words (offended UK pop press dubbed him 'a toothpick in a purple doily'; Hee Bee Gee Bees parodied him with 'Purple Pain' by 'Ponce'); he was rehearsing in Birmingham for a tour '87 and hadn't told his record company he was in the country. He has threatened to retire as many times as David BOWIE. He has also written/prod. songs for Vanity 6, the Time (incl. Morris Day), Sheena EASTON, the BANGLES, Sheila E, Chaka KHAN, often under pseudonyms Alexander Nevermind, Jamie Starr and Christopher). Though original followers say he's sold out (the invariable claim against real, unpredictable originality), he's the only act comparable to Springsteen in sales terms, probably more influential: he has broken the colour bar on MTV and has it in him to be the SLY STONE of the '80s, not only taking black music to the rock audience but extending its boundaries in other directions as well. Former leader of Vanity 6 Denise Matthews made LPs as Vanity on Motown: *Wild Animal* '84, *Skin On Skin* '86 made top 70 LPs; trio Apollonia 6 with Kotero did as well eponymously on WB '84; Prince sidekicks Wendy Melvoin and Lisa Coleman made *Wendy And Lisa* '87 on Virgin.

PRINE, John (*b* 10 Oct. '46, Maywood, Ill.) Singer/songwriter; began on guitar at 14; spent some childhood time in Kentucky, where his grandparents came from (song 'Paradise' is about strip-mining). Sang in Chicago clubs in preference to walking a postal beat; received early boost from Kris KRISTOFFERSON, who championed him alongside Steve GOODMAN. Performed in NYC, signed with Atlantic: *John Prine* '71 incl. harrowing Vietnam vet saga 'Sam Stone', probably his best-known song; also saw him lumbered with the 'new DYLAN' tag, shared with Goodman, Loudon WAINWRIGHT III, Bruce SPRINGSTEEN, etc.; comparison stretched as Dylan appeared on stage with him early '70s. His songs examined white proletarian USA with keen but not unsympathetic eye; *Diamonds In The Rough* '72, *Sweet Revenge* '73 were strong albums, enhancing reputation; *Common Sense* '75 was harder rock, *Prime Prine* '76 an Atlantic compilation; move sideways to Elektra/Asylum led to *Bruised Orange* '78, a return to folk roots prod. by Goodman. *Pink Cadillac* '79 had rockabilly flavour, made at Sam Phillips studio in Memphis (*see* SUN); *Storm Windows* '80 was his last on Asylum. Goodman played on all the LPs from *Diamonds* to *Orange*; Jethro Burns on *Orange* as well; backup singers on various LPs incl. Bonnie RAITT, Jackson BROWNE, J. D. SOUTHER; songs have been covered by Joan BAEZ, Bette MIDLER, the EVERLY Bros; all albums made Billboard top 200 LPs, only *Common Sense* the top 100. Critical acclaim and loyal following are not enough for major label combines: he joined Goodman, John STEWART, many others in putting out his own records; *Aimless Love* '86 said to be his best in years, made in Nashville with John Sebastian and Jennifer Warnes on Oh Boy USA/Demon UK, as is *German Afternoons*, with country roots showing. His live solo act is spellbinding, for those who like his songs; his pulse is such that if the listener's foot does not tap a doctor should be called.

PROBY, P. J. (*b* James Marcus Smith, 6 Nov. '38, Houston, Texas) USA rock singer with hits in UK. Made a living late '50s-early '60s cutting demos for Elvis PRESLEY had vocal similarity, playing bit parts in Western movies, touring as 'Jet Powers'. Discovered by UK TV prod. Jack GOOD, wowed viewers of '64 BEATLES TV special with flamboyant image: pony tail, frilled shirts, tight trousers (apt to split later in career, accidentally or not). Frantic revival of pre-war ballad 'Hold Me' prod. by Good made no. 3 UK; 'Together', 'Somewhere' and 'Maria' (both from *West Side Story*) also top 10, lesser hits through '68; LP *Somewhere* '65 reissued '85 in UK. 'Niki Hoeky' '67 did not chart in UK but was his only top 40 in USA; by that time his trouser-splitting

gimmick, habit of demanding payment before performing did not endear him to theatre managers on tour with Cilla BLACK; bans resulted, though material ranging from R&B to show tunes pointed to a certain lack of direction. At one point he challenged Tom JONES to a singing contest (it didn't happen); went bankrupt '68 owing to extravagant life style; Good threw him a lifeline, casting him as Iago in *Catch My Soul* (rock version of *Othello*) in London '71; he re-emerged from cabaret to play Presley in *Elvis On Stage* '78; personal/domestic problems made UK news now and then; LP *Focus con Proby* '78 with Dutch band Focus (*see* Jan AKKERMAN); one-off singles incl. curious choice of JOY DIVISION's doom-laden new wave anthem 'Love Will Tear Us Apart' '85. *Somewhere* '65 reissued on Liberty UK '85. Two vols. of *At His Very Best* on See For Miles '86 were generous compilations.

PROCOL HARUM UK rock band, began as the Paramounts early '60s, playing R&B covers in Southend (singles collected on *Whiter Shades Of R&B* '83 on Edsel): Gary Brooker (*b* 29 May '45), piano, vocals; Robin TROWER on guitar; Barrie (B. J.) Wilson (*b* 18 Mar. '47), drums; Chris Copping (*b* 29 Aug. '45), bass. Brooker had bluesy, Ray CHARLES-infl. voice and a tune from J. S. Bach; Keith Reid (*b* 10 Oct. '46) provided mysterious words; with Matthew Fisher (*b* 7 Mar. '46, London) on organ, David Knights on bass (*b* 28 June '45), Ray Royer on guitar, Bobby Harrison on drums, they recorded 'Whiter Shade Of Pale', at no. 1 UK/5 USA, and with the BEATLES' 'All You Need Is Love', Scott MCKENZIE's 'San Francisco', one of *the* singles of the 'Summer of Love' '67, on Decca's Deram label. Some thought follow-up 'Homburg' was a better record (on venerable Regal Zonophone label, A&M in USA); Royer and Harrison quit; they recruited Trower, Wilson to finish *Procol Harum* '67 (Latin for 'beyond these things', or perhaps the name of somebody's cat). The first edition of the LP bravely did not incl. the big hit (but did in the USA), but they were infl. for their two-keyboard approach; *Shine On Brightly* '68 and *Salty Dog* '69 were '60s classics, with Reid's lyrics, Wilson's unusually free drumming, members doubling on celeste, recorder, marimba etc. though the hit was so big they were regarded as one-hit wonders, especially in the UK. Fisher went solo '69 (*Journey's End* '73, *I'll Be There* '74, *Matthew Fisher* '80, *Strange Days* '81; ran his own studio in South London); Copping replaced Knights on bass, doubled on organ; albums *Home* '70, *Broken Barricades* '71 were patchy, Trower's Jimi HENDRIX fixation taking over; he went solo, replaced by Dave Ball (*b* 30 Mar. '50); Copping switched to organ full time, Alan Cartwright (*b* 10 Oct. '45) joined on bass; *Procol Harum: In Concert With The Edmonton Symphony Orchestra* '72 was their biggest hit LP in USA at no. 5, incl. surprise hit 'Conquistador' (the original a track on the first album). Mick Grabham (ex-Cochise) replaced Ball on *Grand Hotel* '73; *Exotic Birds & Fruit* '74 was strong rock, B. J. Cole guesting on steel guitar; last two didn't chart in UK, but *Procol's Ninth* did '75, perhaps because it was prod. by LEIBER & STOLLER. *Something Magic* '77 was their last LP, centred on ambitious, flawed 18-minute 'Worm & The Tree'. Reid went into management; Brooker pursued solo career with LP *No More Fear Of Flying* '79, guested on Eric CLAPTON's *August* '86, etc. Trower's solo career was successful (see his entry). Harum are still remembered for the first hit, but each LP had something of merit. An edition of *A Salty Dog* on Music For Pleasure '72 had different tracks; first four LPs issued in 2-disc sets '72; reissues, compilations abound.

PROCOPE, Russell (*b* 11 Aug. '08, NYC; *d* there 21 Jan. '81) Clarinet, alto sax. Began on violin at six (both parents were musicians, strictly classical). Went from classical to military band music, then heard Fletcher HENDERSON with Louis ARMSTRONG, Coleman HAWKINS, began learning jazz from scratch. Infl. by Buster Bailey; worked/recorded with Jelly Roll MORTON '28 and infl. by Omer SIMEON; worked for childhood friend Benny CARTER '29, Chick WEBB '29-31, Henderson '31-4 (very occasionally played violin when Edgar SAMPSON was in the band, but preferred other people's jazz violin). With Tiny BRADSHAW '34-5; Teddy HILL incl. tour of Europe '36-7; John KIRBY Sextet '38-43 (with Bailey on clarinet), again after military service; joined Duke ELLINGTON '46 until Duke's death. Always believed that there were more voices in the clarinet than the saxophone; he played a lot of alto with Ellington, but was best known for the wooden horn. Among many solo moments of beauty: played the melody on the '52 remake of 'The Mooche' against Jimmy HAMILTON's obbligato. He can be heard on Kirby compilations as well as many Ellington records.

PROFESSOR LONGHAIR (*b* Henry Roeland 'Roy' Byrd, 19 Dec. '18, Bogalusa, La.; *d* 30 Jan. '80) Pianist, composer; aka 'Fess': master of New Orleans rock'n'roll; undoubtedly the biggest single infl. on Huey SMITH, Fats DOMINO, Mac REBENNACK: innovatory style replete with rumba and Spanish tinges; described by Allen TOUSSAINT as 'the Bach of rock'n'roll'. He was infl. by Isadore 'Tuts' Washington Jr (*b* 24 Jan. '07, New Orleans), who did not record until '83 (*New Orleans Piano Professor* on Rounder); Tuts was in turn infl. by Joseph Louis 'Red' Cayou (*b* c. '05), who had heard Jelly Roll MORTON as a child. Fess was hired by Dave BARTHOLOMEW '49; formed own combo called the Four Hairs, took name Professor Longhair; made four sides in local club for Dallas-based Star Talent label as Professor Longhair and his Shuffling Hungarians, incl. 'She Ain't Got No Hair', remade as 'Bald Head' '50 on Mercury (as Roy Byrd) for no. 5 R&B hit. Recorded for Atlantic '50, Federal '54 ('Gone So Long'), Atlantic again '53 (incl. classic 'Tipitina'), Atlantic tracks compiled on *New Orleans Piano* '72. Records on other obscure labels '50s, early '60s; on Watch '63-4: 'Big Chief', 'Third House From The Left' have vocals by guitarist/singer Earl KING. Almost forgotten, he played at New Orleans Jazz & Heritage Festival '71, began comeback but only demos resulted: *Houseparty New Orleans Style: The Lost Sessions 1971-72* on Rounder compiles them, incl. Snooks EAGLIN on guitar plus bass and drums, 53 minutes of delightful mid-period Longhair. Several tunes were covered by Mac Rebennack ('Dr John') on various LPs. Other LPs: *Mardi Gras In New Orleans* '49-57 on Nighthawk; *Rock'n'Roll Gumbo* '74 on Dancing Cat, live *Mardi Gras In New Orleans* '75 on Krazy Kat, 2-disc *The Last Mardi Gras* on Atlantic, *Live On The Queen Mary* '78 on Harvest,

Crawfish Fiesta '80 on Alligator; *The London Concert* on JSP issued in UK '84.

PROPHET, Ronnie (*b* 26 Dec. '37, Calumet, Quebec, Canada) Singer, comedian, guitarist who made his name in Nashville late '60s, became international star with Wembley debut '78. Played local square dances in teens, moved to Toronto early '60s, gained reputation as guitarist: a natural comic, incorporated sketches and impersonations into club act. To Nashville '69, gaining residency at Carousel Club, venue soon renamed Ronnie Prophet's Carousel Club. Very much a visual act, never made much impression on record, though recording regularly from mid-'60s; made USA country chart with 'Sanctuary' '75, lesser hits. Zany stage act made him a star, resulted in BBC TV series '79, top billing on national UK tours. LPs incl. *Ronnie Prophet Country* '76, *Ronnie Prophet* '77 on RCA; *Faces And Phases* '80 on Westwood, *Audiograph Live* '83 and *I'm Gonna Love Him Out Of You* '83 on Audiograph; three LPs in USA on Art label.

PRT Precision Records and Tapes, UK record label tracing itself back through Pye to Nixa and Polygon. Latter small independent was founded by Alan Freeman '49; first and biggest signing was Petula CLARK, then a 16-year-old film star with Rank; first release '50. Polygon also launched Jimmy YOUNG and were one of the first to cater to West Indian immigrants with calypso on the Lyragon label. Nixa was an import/export company run by New Zealander Hilton Nixon; in '50 they were asked to acquire rights to a European label for Australia, approached Pacific in France; when the Australian deal failed Nixa went into the record business. First releases '51 incl. 'Autumn Leaves', by French female singer Dany Dauberson, their first no. 1. Nixa concentrated on Continental and off-beat product, and moved into classical music via licensing deal with USA indie Westminster; having a pressing deal with DECCA, Nixa were among the first to issue long-playing records in UK. Success meant they needed capital for expansion; Nixa approached Thorn Electric, then Pye of Cambridge; in '53 Pye bought 51% of Nixa, acquired Polygon '55 and merged the two. Lonnie

DONEGAN was the biggest Pye artist of the '50s: 'Cumberland Gap' gave the new company its first no. 1; 'My Old Man's A Dustman' was the first hit by a UK artist to enter the charts at no. 1. The UK market was dominated by USA artists and Pye needed access; it was the licensee for Mercury for two years, but when this went to EMI Pye launched Pye International '58. The '60s were Pye's golden age, beginning with Clark, Donegan, Emile Ford and the Marcels, with Kenny BALL on Pye Jazz; the SEARCHERS had 14 hits, three at no. 1; the KINKS, Sandie SHAW, Long John BALDRY and the FOUNDATIONS all had chart toppers. STATUS QUO had their first hits on Pye '68; Pye International had a strong R&B roster headed by Chuck BERRY. Pye was innovative: they were the first in UK to release a stereo record, the first to advertise records on billboards and among first to use TV; with the Golden Guinea label they were the first to issue budget albums of new material, with Golden Hour the first to put 60 minutes on an LP. They pioneered the use of USA logos for licensed material, which other majors hated doing: WB, A&M, Cameo-Parkway, Dot, Reprise, Red Bird (the SHANGRI-LAS) and Chess were some of the first USA labels to appear with their own UK logo, on Pye. Pye formed Piccadilly in the early '60s for UK material, Dawn at the end of the decade. In the '70s they launched Elton JOHN via DJM and had Donna SUMMER on Casablanca; MUNGO JERRY (on Dawn), Carl Douglas and the Brotherhood of Man all gave Pye chart toppers in '70s; Lina Martell's 'One Day At A Time' '79 was the last. Unlike EMI, Philips and others, Pye made no attempt to set up overseas affiliates, with the exception of a joint venture with GRT in Janus Records in the USA, which failed. Pye had good links with Vogue in France, Durium in Italy and Festival in Australia, whence they obtained Olivia NEWTON-JOHN; but the '80s saw Pye in decline. Half the company had been sold to ATV in '59 and Pye of Cambridge sold the other half '66 (C. O. Stanley was a board member of ATV as well as chairman of the Pye group). The sale allowed the use of the Pye name until '80, when a new name had to be found; hence PRT. That was also the year of negotiations for merger with RCA which failed. Debilitating uncertainty was worsened when ATV (renamed ACC) was sold to Australian businessman Robert Holmes A'Court's Bell group '82: ATV had been enthusiastic about the music side; Bell (controlled from Perth) was not. PRT had a valuable back catalogue and was an important distributor of independent labels (e.g. Bob THIELE's Dr Jazz); it issued a fine edition of Thelonious MONK's 1953 Paris solo date on its Jazz Reactivation label; it rescued the fine mono master of Count BASIE's *The Atomic Mr Basie*, made in NYC '57 by Roulette, etc. Bell sold it to Ray Richards early '87; he put daughter Kim in as MD; in early '88 PRT bought a compact disc factory in Sweden, relaunched Nixa as a classical line (first release a set of Verdi arias by USA soprano Carol Furness). With the right spirit behind it, PRT will once again have a full range of facilities.

PRUETT, Jeanne (*b* 30 Jan., Pell City, Okla.) Country singer-songwriter who made initial impact as writer, hits for Marty ROBBINS ('Count Me Out'), others. Sang with brothers and sisters; married Jack Pruett '53, went to Nashville where he became Robbins' lead guitarist for nearly 20 years. For a while she was busy with the children, but Robbins not only recorded about a dozen of her songs but signed her to his publishing company, helped get her RCA contract '63: six titles but no hits; for some years she concentrated on writing, signed with Decca '69 and made chart debut with 'Hold On To My Unchanging Love' '71, further hits incl. no. 1 'Satin Sheets' '73. Moved to Mercury, but luck changed; to small IBC Records and major chart comeback with 'Back To Back' and 'Temporarily Yours' '80, 'It's Too Late' '81. Continued touring regularly and built up following in UK with regular Wembley appearances. LPs: *Love Me* '72 on Decca; *Satin Sheets* '73, *Welcome To The Sunshine* '75 on MCA; *Encore* '80 on IBC/RCA, *Audiograph Live* '83.

PRYSOCK, Arthur (*b* 2 Jan '29, Spartanburg N.C.) Deep baritone jazz and blues singer, compared to Billy ECKSTINE, whose albums charted in the '60s. He came to fame with the Buddy Johnson blues band '44-52 (e.g. 'They All Say I'm The Biggest Fool'; Johnson *b* Woodrow Wilson Johnson, 10 Jan. '15,

Darlington, S.C.; R&B hits on Decca and Mercury '49-56, some with vocals by sister Ella Johnson); Decca Prysock/Johnson compilation *Songs That Made Him Famous* '50s. Recorded for Verve, King, then Sam and Hy Weiss's Old Town label (sold to MGM, now Polydor); known for romantic ballads like Ray NOBLE's 'The Very Thought Of You', but also covered Roy BROWN's 'Good Rockin' Tonight', etc. After years of neglect, suddenly albums *A Rockin' Good Way* '85, *This Guy's In Love With You* '86 on Milestone, accompanied by reissues: *Best Of*, *This Is My Beloved* and *Prysock & Basie* on Verve, 2-disc *Best Of* on Polydor: he's back, not before time. He was always popular in clubs, often working with his brother, saxophonist Wilbert 'Red' Prysock (who worked for Tiny BRADSHAW, then had instrumental juke-box hits on Mercury '55-6).

PSYCHEDELIC FURS, The UK new wave group formed in London '77 by Richard 'Butler Rep' Butler, vocals; brother Tim Butler, bass; Duncan Kilburn, sax; Roger 'Dog' Morris, guitar: name inspired by VELVET UNDERGROUND's 'Venus In Furs'; but the witfully unfashionable adjective cost drummerless band lots of gigs. Picked up ex-Photons John Ashton, guitar, and Vince Ely, drums, '79; by then session for John PEEL's BBC show had brought notoriety, deal with CBS. Steve Lillywhite-prod. *Psychedelic Furs* '80 and more melodic *Talk Talk Talk* '81 were top 30 LPs; Butler's monotone aligned him with John Rotten/Lydon, music owed debt to Velvets, other '60s sources. Singles like their first 'We Love You' entertaining but commercially unsuccessful. Butler streamlined band, shedding Kilburn and Morris: *Forever Now* '82 prod. by Todd RUNDGREN in USA, spawned near-hit 'Love My Way' which together with (temporary) name-change to Furs suggested commercialisation of act, with overdubbed brass, strings. Ex-Birthday Party drummer Phil Calvert joined on *Mirror Moves* '84, prod. by Keith Forsey, incl. long-awaited top 30 (UK) hit 'Heaven', with Euro-disco infl. suggested new horizons for band; *Midnight To Midnight* '86 incl. rerecording of hit film theme 'Pretty In Pink': now just Butler/Butler/Ashton and session players, stylised in BOWIE mould.

PSYCHEDELIC ROCK Pop music phenomenon of the '60s. See ACID ROCK.

PUBLIC IMAGE LTD UK new wave act, aka P.I.L.; now a concept, not a group; formed by John Lydon (reverting to his real name) after demise of SEX PISTOLS; eponymous first single was top 10 UK in post-split publicity, featured bizarre guitar of Keith Levene Jr (an original member of CLASH), bassist Jah Wobble (John Wordle), Canadian drummer Jim Walker (ex-Furies). LP *Public Image Ltd* '78 named the business manager, etc. true to corporate image (same approach used by Sigue Sigue Sputnik more recently), obvious parallel with Malcolm McLaren film *The Great Rock'n'Roll Swindle*. After two singles '79, *Metal Box* '79 (later reissued as 2-disc *Second Edition*) came as three 12″ singles in a metal box, music as wilfully obscure as packaging, bombastic sound featuring new drummer Martin Atkins (*b* 3 Aug. '59, Coventry), who'd replaced ex-101er Richard Dudanski. *Paris Au Printemps* '80, live LP made in Paris, released to beat bootlegs, contained few new ideas; Wobble and Atkins left, reducing ideas quotient still further (Wobble's reggae-inspired playing a main ingredient of sound; he made solo LPs, EP with members of CAN; Atkins went solo but sessioned with Lydon). *Flowers Of Romance* '81 had no. 24 title track hit, group down to Lydon, Lee, Levene (and Atkins); 'Flowers Of Romance' was name of Sex Pistols' Sid Vicious' first group. 'This Is Not A Love Song' was no. 5 hit '83; 2-disc *Live In Tokyo* was a self-indulgence: Lydon swore he'd never play live again after '81 NYC riot when bottles etc. thrown at P.I.L. playing behind screen to tapes. Levene left, Atkins retired as writing partner; after *This Is What You Want This Is What You Get* '84 Lydon used pick-up musicians on tours, even playing Pistols' 'greatest hit' 'Anarchy In The UK'; residence in USA also contrary to everything he didn't stand for. Switched to Elektra from Virgin for *Album* '86 (aka *Cassette* or *Compact Disc* as the case may be); P.I.L. now the creation of producer Bill LASWELL, who calls Lydon 'the Ornette COLEMAN of new wave singers'. Despite voice that Bill Milkowski described in *Downbeat* as 'snotty, annoying, venomous sounds' from 'the snarling gap' of 'the quin-

tessential Johnny One-Note', he gave it three stars: sleeve carries no credits, but backing incl. Ginger BAKER or Tony WILLIAMS, drums; Steve Vai for guitar aficionados, L. SHANKAR on violin, Ryuichi Sakamoto of Yellow Magic Orchestra on keyboards, acoustic bass by Malachi Favors on one track. The sight of Lydon miming on *Top Of The Pops* was unforgettable, as if punk had never been; the lad who once wanted to destroy music may leave a positive mark if he does as he's told. He toured to promote *Album* with former punks Lu Edmonds (DAMNED), John McGeoch (Magazine, Banshees) on guitars, Bruce Smith (ex-Rip Rig and Panic), drums, Allan Dias on bass; they made *Happy?* '87. Now a movie star (in Harvey Keitel's *Cop Killer*) he can wheel out a group whenever he feels like it.

PUB ROCK UK phenomenon of early '70s centred around public houses of London, where music around country, blues roots developed in reaction to 'pomp rock' (YES, EMERSON, LAKE & PALMER, etc.) prevalent in charts and stadia. Posthumously acclaimed pioneers were USA band Eggs Over Easy: residency at North London Tally Ho pub was followed by Bees Make Honey, BRINSLEY SCHWARZ, Quiver, Uncle Dog, others; Eggs returned to USA '72, released *Good'n'Cheap* on A&M same year (reissued '86 on Edsel). UK record labels attempted to cash in, usually with little reward owing to lack of originality in the music and unwillingness of participants to 'dress the part'; indeed Schwarz, whose earlier career had been blighted by hype, revelled in anonymity. Only groups with freak hit (like Ace's 'How Long') could hope to pull a crowd outside capital venues like the Hope and Anchor, Nashville Rooms and the Kensington. Two factors put pub rock in the history books: first was 'Naughty Rhythms' package tour '75 of DR FEELGOOD, CHILLI WILLI and Kokomo, which laid groundwork for Feelgood's no. 1 live LP *Stupidity* '76; second was tour's manager Jake Riviera, who formed Stiff Records, helped Ian DURY (ex-Kilburn and the High Roads), Nick LOWE (ex-Brinsley Schwarz), Elvis COSTELLO (as Declan McManus of Flip City) to stardom. PUNK owed much to pub rock, with Joe Strummer of the Clash and Nick Cash (Keith Lucas) of 999 having served apprenticeships in 101ers, Kilburns respectively. Definitive tome *Music Every Night* was due, by John Eichler (sometime Hope and Anchor landlord) and musician Deke Leonard; Edsel were to release more records to tie in with book.

PUCKETT, Gary, and the Union Gap USA pop band formed as Outcasts '67, bar band playing covers in San Diego; switched names and adopted Civil War gear late that year to attract success with no. 4 hit 'Woman Woman': vocalist Puckett (*b* 17 Oct. '42, Hibbing, Minn.), Dwight Bement (*b* Dec. '45, San Diego), tenor sax; Kerry Chater (*b* 7 Aug. '45, Vancouver), bass; Gary Withem (*b* 22 Aug. '46, San Diego), keyboards; Paul Wheatbread (*b* 8 Feb. '46, San Diego), drums. Latter had previous experience on TV show *Where The Action Is*, had backed big names. 'Young Girl' and 'Lady Willpower' both no. 2 USA '68, 1 and 5 in UK; former no. 6 on reissue '74; both written by prod. Jerry Fuller: catchy songs and Puckett's boyish, yearning quality was their high point. They disbanded '71 when Puckett went into acting after three more top 40 hits USA (no more in UK), no fewer than six LPs. Puckett later recorded unsuccessfully solo and with brother David; Chater wrote MOR songs for Cass Elliot, Bobby DARIN, others; also recorded solo.

PUCKETT, Riley (*b* George Riley Puckett, 7 May 1884, Alpharetta, Ga.; *d* 13 July '46, East Point, Ga.) Guitarist and the first country singing star. Teamed with fiddler James Gideon Tanner (*b* 6 June 1885, Thomas Bridge, near Monroe, Ga.; *d* 13 May '60, Winder, Ga.) for national fiddle contest '16 (begun by Georgia Old Time Fiddlers' Association '13); went north '24 to record old-time and vaudeville tunes. Columbia A&R man Frank Walker combined them with fiddler Clayton 'Pappy' McMichen (*b* 26 Jan. 1900, Allatoona, Ga.; *d* 3 Jan. '70, Battletown, Ky.), banjo player Fate (or Fayte) Norris as Gid Tanner and his Skillet Lickers (some of them had been involved in a Lick the Skillet Band for competitions). McMichen had worked as an auto mechanic, was also songwriter (e.g. 'Peach Pickin' Time Down In Georgia' '33,

co-written and recorded by Jimmie RODGERS). All sang, but Puckett's smooth baritone sold the group; accidentally blinded as an infant, he first recorded '24, thought to be first to yodel on a record ('Rock All Our Babies To Sleep', backed with 'Little Old Log Cabin In The Lane'); his 'My Carolina Home' was a top 10 hit '27. His guitar runs were experimental and he would take a song where he found it, while McMichen was infl. by jazz, Tanner strictly old-time: individually they were influential, but as an unlikely group their hotter, rougher sound established the string band, outsold the others (cf. North Carolina Ramblers, etc.; *see* Charlie POOLE). The original lineup made about 80 sides before splitting '31; 'Turkey In The Straw' and 'John Henry' '26-7 were the equivalent of top 20 hits (according to *Pop Memories*) but they made their living from touring: Ralph PEER, not Walker, was one of the first A&R men in trad. music to pay his artists royalties. Skillets' comedy incl. many versions of 'A Corn Likker Still In Georgia'; McMichen helped with this work, always resenting being typed as hillbilly; while Tanner, Uncle Dave MACON, Fiddlin' John Carson, many others were considered comedians as much as musicians in that era. Group sometimes augmented in the studio, up to four fiddles perhaps infl. later Western Swing; Tanner's younger brother Arthur played banjo and guitar '26-9. Tanner made more than 500 records, had top 10 hit 'Down Yonder' 34 on Bluebird with a later edition of Skillet Lickers incl. his son Gordon on fiddle. Puckett joined McMichen's Georgia Wildcats for a while (formed '32, later incl. at various times Merle TRAVIS, Lester FLATT), had own tent show etc.; his 'Ragged But Right' was a duo with a mandolin; he was always innovative and influential but did not have lasting commercial success as Rodgers did. He was singing with the Stone Mountain Boys on Atlanta's WACA when he died. McMichen tried fusions of popular forms, playing variety incl. bluegrass, rock'n'roll, dixieland on radio incl. WLW's Boone County Jamboree. National Fiddling Champion each year '34-49; retired '54, occasionally seen on WAVE TV in Louisville, Ky.; Tanner returned to chicken farm, was National Fiddle Champion '56. Skillets compilations *A Corn*

Likker Still In Georgia on Voyager, *Skillet Lickers* on County, *Hear These New Southern Records* and *Kickapoo Medicine Show* on Rounder.

PUENTE, Tito (*b* 20 Apr. '23, Ernesto Antonio Puente Jr, NYC) Bandleader, virtuoso timbales player, multi-instrumentalist incl. vibes, piano, sax, bongos, conga; composer, producer, showman. Called Ernestito for short stature, shortened to Tito; aka 'El Rey' ('The King'). Intended to be a dancer, but tore ankle tendon in accident; served in WWII aboard USS *Santee* where he met bandleader Charlie SPIVAK, who taught him some big band composition, arranging; studied at Juilliard under G. I. Bill. Worked in orchestras of Noro MORALES, MACHITO, Pupi Campo; formed the Piccadilly Boys '47, soon became the Tito Puente Orchestra. First lead vocalist was Vincentico Valdes. Record debut was on Seeco 78s; eight tracks on first 10″ LP later reissued with tracks by Tito Rivera as 12″ *Tito Puente And Friend* on Tropical. He signed with new Tico label (formed '48) for a series of 10″ LPs incl. *Puente On Vibes* and five volumes of mambos, some of these later issued on 12″; with Machito and Tito RODRIGUEZ, Puente was leader of the big band mambo style during '50s: 'Abaniquito' was one of the first crossover mambo hits with assistance of English-language DJ Dick 'Ricardo' Sugar. His big band had 'an intense and nervous quality that was pure New York ... his arranging, like his timbales playing, was fast, tight, jumpy, bravura' (John Storm Roberts). He left Tico for RCA for a while in the '50s, some LPs reissued on Cariño, e.g. *Cuban Carnival* '56 incl. 'Para los Rumberos' (covered by SANTANA on their third LP '71, re-recorded by Puente as title track of new LP '72 on Tico), and *Dance Mania* '58, introducing Puerto Rican lead singer Santos Colon. Puente was also prominent during the chachacha craze late '50s on RCA, transcribing some original Cuban chachacha hits from the violin-and-flute charanga format to the brass and reeds frontline of his big band, such as Orquesta Aragon's 'Pare Cochero'; as the chachacha fad subsided his RCA LPs incl. a variety of rhythms: LPs incl. *Ti Mon Bo, La Epoca de Oro de Tito Puente, Best Of, The Many Moods Of, More*

Dance Mania, etc. Among those who played in band '50s were Johnny PACHECO, Mongo SANTAMARIA, Charlie PALMIERI, Ray Barretto, Willie BOBO, Manny Oquendo (*see* Conjunto LIBRE). Recorded for Roulette in crossover vein: *My Fair Lady Goes Latin* and *Bossa Nova By Puente*; *Exciting Band In Hollywood* '61 on GNP was reissued as *Puente Now!*; but he had returned to Tico; on that label into '80s, over 40 LPs incl. classic *Puente In Percussion* with Bobo, Santamaria, Carlos 'Patato' Valdez (reissued '78) and *The Latin World Of Tito Puente* '64, a compilation also issued on EMI/Columbia UK, incl. the original of Puente's composition 'Oye Como Va', covered note-for-note by Santana on their biggest hit LP *Abraxas* '70. *Tito Puente In Puerto Rico Recorded Live* was not a concert, but had on-the-spot immediacy; *De Mi Para Ti (From Me To You)* highlighted vocalist Santos Colon (Colon made solo LPs on Tico and Fania through '75, hits compilations *Exitos de Santos Colon: Imagenes* on Tico (incl. tracks with Puente) and *Siempre Santitos* '76 on Fania; also performed and recorded with Tico All Stars, FANIA ALL STARS, etc.). Puente backed many singers: Manny Roman on *Eras* on Decca, Rolando Le Serie on *Pachanga In New York* on Gema, Valdes on *Puente Swings, Valdes Sings* on Tico, Myrta Silva on *Puerto Rico Canta y Baila* on Musicor; from mid-'60s he backed a number of women on Tico: with La Lupe on *Tito Puente Swings – The Exciting Lupe Sings, Tu y Yo, Homenaje a Rafael Hernandez, El Rey y Yo*; Noraida on *Tito Puente Presenta Noraida* and *Me Voy a Desquitar*; Celia CRUZ on *Cuba y Puerto Rico Son* '66, *Quimbo Quimbumbia* c.'69, *Alma con Alma* c.'71, *Celia Cruz y Tito Puente en España, Algo Especial* '72. Puente and band had won the Golden Cup first prize in Venezuelan carnivals '64-5; *Carnaval en Harlem* c.'65 mixed Latin rhythms with pop/jazz standards like 'Bluesette', 'Jumpin' With Symphony Sid'. *20th Anniversary* c.'67 was a celebration; *The King Tito Puente* c.'68 incl. boogaloo and other styles, vocalists Andy Senatore and Rudy Calzado along with Colon; *Tito Puente en el Puente/On The Bridge* c.'69 incl. 'Congo Mulense', co-written and sung by Machito; also pop-oriented 'Fancy Feet'. *The Legend* '77 incl. title track 'La

Leyenda' written by Rubén Blades; two vols. of *Homenaje a Beny* '78-9 on Tico paid tribute to Cuban singer/bandleader Beny MORÉ, with vocalists Colon, Cruz, Cheo FELICIANO, Hector LAVOE, Ismael Quintana, Ismael Miranda, Adalberto Santiago, Pete 'El Conde' Rodriguez, more; Vol. III '85 on Vaya incl. Cruz, Santiago, Lavoe, El Conde plus Justo BETANCOURT and Hector Casanova. Among his last big band LPs were *Dancemania 80's* '80 and *Ce' Magnifique* '81, with Panamanian-born vocalist Camilo Azuquita (Camilo Luis Argumedez), who also wrote some of the LP (had worked with TIPICA 73, led band Melao in Paris, moved to California). Puente was seen in action in the South Bronx in Jeremy Marre's TV film *Salsa* '79, toured Europe that year with the Latin Percussion Jazz Ensemble (LPJE), a quintet with 'Patato' Valdez, Columbian pianist Eddie Martinez; expanded to sextet for LP *Just Like Magic* '79; LPJE's third European tour incl. *LPJE Live At The Montreux Jazz Festival 1980*, incl. 'Oye Como Va', 'Pare Cochero', with Cuban violinist Alfredo de la Fé, Argentine pianist Jorge Dalto (1948-87: died of cancer). Group became octet Latin Ensemble, recorded *Tito Puente And His Latin Ensemble On Broadway* '83 for Concord Jazz's Picante Latin series and won Grammy, with stalwarts from the big band incl. Jimmy Frisaura (trombone, trumpet, flugelhorn), Bobby Rodriguez on bass, Mario Rivera on saxes and flute, plus Johnny Rodriguez on percussion (*see* TIPICA 73); further LPs on Picante are *El Rey* '84 (live at the Great American Music Hall in San Francisco), *Mambo Diablo* '85 (another Grammy, incl. George SHEARING on his famous 'Lullaby Of Birdland', Sonny Bravo on piano for the rest), *Sensación* '86; *Un Poco Loco* '87 incl. both Latin Ensemble and big band. He also played with the Tico All Stars on their *Descargas At The Village Gate – Live* '66 (three vols. on Tico), with Fania All Stars *Live At The Red Garter* '68 (two vols. on Fania), with *Tico Alegre All Stars Live At Carnegie Hall* '74, also on Cal TJADER LP *Primo* on Fantasy '74, Ray BARRETTO's 2-disc *Tomorrow* '76 on Atlantic, *La Cuna* '81 on CTI; jazz singer Dianne REEVES stopped the show at Monterey Jazz Festival '84 with 'Be My Husband', backed by Puente, a living legend who's still at it.

Puente played timbales, vibes, arr. his 'Ban-Con-Tim' on *Super All Star* '84 on Caimán (issued in UK on Globe Style '87). Classic *Dance Mania* '58, compilation *Los Grandes Exitos de Tito Puente* from '50s issued early '80s by RCA International.

PUKWANA, Dudu (*b* Dudu Mtutuzel Pukwana, 18 July '38, Port Elizabeth, South Africa) Alto and soprano saxes, composer, leader. His parents were musical but he was largely self-taught, taking up sax '56; won prize as best saxophonist at Johannesburg Jazz Festival '62: white pianist Chris MacGregor formed the Blue Notes from the best at the festival, incl. bassist Johnny Dyani (*b* 30 Nov. '45, East London, S.A.; *d* late '86), but interracial group was illegal, so went to Europe '64, played at Antibes, then at Ronnie SCOTT's in London, where Dudu settled. Since then he has played everything from reggae to free jazz (with drummer Han Bennink, *b* 17 Apr. '42, Zaandam, Netherlands, pianist Misha Mengelberg on *Yi Yo Le* '78 on Instant Composers Pool label); he sessioned with the INCREDIBLE STRING BAND and with Keith TIPPETT's Centipede (on *Septober Energy* '71 on RCA Neon), much else. He recorded with the Blue Notes '63 on Gallotone (*The African Sound*), '68 on Polydor (*Very Urgent*), also *For Mongesi* '76 and *In Concert* '78 on Ogun; with MacGregor in big band Brotherhood Of Breath in '71 and '72 on RCA Neon, also *Live At Willisau* '74 and *Procession* '78 on Ogun, soundtrack for Wole Soyinka film *Harvest*. With Dyani on his Steeplechase LPs *Witchdoctor's Son* '78 (sextet with John Tchicai), *Song For Biko* '79 (quartet with Don CHERRY), quartet *Mbizo* '81; Dyani also recorded with Steve LACY '68 and with Abdullah IBRAHIM, like the latter stayed close to African roots: as leader also made two vols. of *Music For Xaba* '72 on Sonet with trio, mostly solo *African Bass* on Italian Red Records, *Backwards And Forwards* on Impetus UK with John STEVENS, septet *Afrika* '83 and quartet *Angolan Cry* c.'85 on Steeplechase. Dudu's other LPs: with bands Assagai '71, '72 on Vertigo, kwela group Spear '73, '74 on Caroline (Spear played at Festac in Lagos '78; album *In The Townships* reissued '87 on Earthworks/Virgin under Dudu's name); with Hugh MASEKELA and trombonist

Jonas Gwangwa as African Explosion on *Who (Ngubani)* '69 for Ahmad Jamal Productions; on Masekela's *Home Is Where The Music Is* '72 on Island; also with Jabula '79, Gavin Povey '81, etc. In '78 he formed combo Zila, made *Diamond Express* '78 on Freedom; *Sondela* as Atte and Zila '79 on Irish label Ceirnini Cladag; formed own Jika Records and made *Zila Sounds* '81, *Life In Bracknell & Willisau* '83, *Zila '86*: Zila's driving African-inspired jazz/dance music is a popular act, personnel variously incl. veteran UK jazzmen Harry Beckett on trumpet/flugelhorn and Phil Steriopulos on bass, plus South Africans Lucky Ranku on guitar, Fats Ramoba Mogoboya on congas, Churchill Jalobe on drums, Mervyn Africa on keyboards, powerful vocalist Miss Pinise Saul; last two LPs have Django Bates on keyboards (*see* LOOSE TUBES). Dudu's *They Shoot To Kill* '87 on Affinity is duo with Stevens, dedicated to Dyani; also trio *Blue Notes For Johnny* an Orgum. Chris McGregor (*b* 24 Dec '36, South Africa) formed larger band Brotherhood of Breath '70, revived it '88 to critical praise.

PULLEN, Don (*b* 25 Dec. '44, Roanoke, Va.) Pianist, leader, composer. Led own group late '60s. A fine pianist who can play 'inside' or 'outside', a musician/composer whose every gig is worth attending. First jazz recordings in quartet of Giuseppe Logan (reedman; *b* 22 May '35, Philadelphia) were also the first for bassist Eddie Gomez (later with Bill EVANS) and Milford Graves (*b* 20 Aug. '41, Jamaica, NY; worked with Hugh MASEKELA, Miriam MAKEBA early '60s; one of the earliest and most influential of 'free jazz' percussionists), '64-5. Also duo records with Graves '64 on ESP; '66 at Yale University, now on SRP. Led own group late '60s; worked with Nina SIMONE, then Charles MINGUS (LPs on Atlantic '74-5); septet LP led by Dannie RICHMOND with George ADAMS, Jack Walrath (trumpet, composer; *b* 5 May '46, Stuart, Fla.): *Jazz a Confronto* '75, made in Rome on Horo; co-led quartet with George Adams (see his entry); among the earliest LPs by this quartet, with Richmond, bassist David Williams (*b* 17 Sep. '46, Trinidad) were two on Horo '75, one under Adams' name, one under Pullen's. Recorded '85 with new quintet: Fred Hopkins on bass, Bobby Battle on drums, Olu Dara on

trumpet, Donald HARRISON: *The Sixth Sense* on Black Saint. Also wrote music commissioned by Baltimore Dance Theatre. Other LPs incl. solo piano sets *Solo Piano Album* '74 on Sackville, *Five To Go* '76 on Horo, *Healing Force* '76 and *Evidence Of Things Unseen* '83 on Black Saint; duo *Milano Strut* '78 with Don Moye (Pullen also playing organ), trio *The Magic Triangle* '79 with Moye, Joseph JARMAN; quartets *Capricorn Rising* '75 with Battle, Sam RIVERS, Alex Blake on bass, *Warriors* '78 with Chico FREEMAN, Battle, Hopkins, all these on Black Saint. Also *Tomorrow's Promises* '76 with 10 pieces, quintet *Montreux Concert* '77, both on Atlantic.

PUNK ROCK Term originally given to garage-band USA rock early-to-mid '60s (Standells, SHADOWS OF KNIGHT, groups collected on *Nuggets*, Lenny Kaye's seminal compilation), later to UK music of '76 onwards played by groups such as SEX PISTOLS, CLASH and Buzzcocks, derived directly from Richard HELL, Patti SMITH, RAMONES, Tom PETTY and the Heartbreakers, others playing in NYC in the preceding couple of years, themselves infl. by the VELVET UNDERGROUND and the NEW YORK DOLLS. NYC iconoclasts had played free in a back room at club CBGB's ('Country, BlueGrass and Blues') which became an important nightspot. Hell, with torn safety-pinned jeans, was a big influence: Malcolm McLaren had briefly managed Dolls in their decline, could not talk Hell into coming to UK, formed Pistols in his image. London's equivalent of CBGB's was the Roxy Club, opened Dec. '76 in Covent Garden, but it was the punk festival at the 100 Club in Soho's Wardour Street that notified arrival. If PUB ROCK (*see above*) had been a reaction to stadia superstars, trying to make rock'n'roll fun again, punk attempted to make it 'dangerous' again, and was more fun for the tabloid media. Fashion with torn clothing, spikey hairdos, safety pins, bondage etc. tried to be as iconoclastic as the music, with aggressive, anti-establishment lyrics, basic guitar rock'n'roll played at breakneck speed (some bragged that they couldn't play). Designer Jamie Reid put a safety pin through the Queen's face on sleeve of Pistols' 'God Save The Queen'; most punk sleeves featured clipped-out newsprint, blackmail-style lettering; Nazi chic was the least attractive facet. As major groups signed to major labels, fashion too was commercialised (McLaren's shop Sex had done it first, then the chain stores joined in); the movement burned itself out, surviving into '80s with anarchists Crass; but spate of fanzines, independent labels and street activity was all but over by '80. Energy survived in NEW WAVE, which found greater market in USA than original punks; lasting influences were two: more women in music (SIOUXSIE, Poly Styrene, the Slits, many more infiltrated widely; Chrissie Hynde came from a proto-punk scene in Ohio to form new wave PRETENDERS in UK) and Rock Against Racism had rock and reggae bands on same bill for the first time: punk interaction with reggae survived in new wave with POLICE, Wang Chung. Latest manifestation of USA garage-band trad. is called 'hard core', wildly distorting electric guitars allied with tunes that try to be pretty: West Coast SST label records bands called Gone, Dinosaur, Meat Puppets.

PURIM, Flora (*b* 6 Mar. '42, Rio de Janeiro) Vocalist; also guitar, percussion. From musical family; studied percussion with AIRTO Moreira, married him. Worked with Airto and Hermeto Pascoal in Quarteto Novo (composer Pascoal, *b* 22 June '36, Lagôa da Canoa, plays keyboards, many other instruments; he inspired Airto, Purim, Milton Nascimento, many other Brazilian musicians; under his tutelage Purim doubled her vocal range. He has recorded with Miles DAVIS, others; his own LPs have appeared on Muse, Atlantic, WB; also *Hermeto Pascoal & Grupo* '82 on Som Dagente). Purim and Airto went to USA late '60s, performed with Chick COREA's Return To Forever (eponymous LP on ECM '72; also *Light As A Feather* on Polydor); formed their own group '73, foremost perpetrators of unique mixture of pop, jazz, Brazilian music, with her remarkable fluent vocal style and distinctive vibrato. *Love Reborn* on Milestone has tracks from '73-6, some with Ron CARTER; she appears on Airto's *Fingers* '73 on CTI; she served a jail term '74-5 for a drug charge which was not proven, resumed her career. Their other LPs together incl. *Humble People* '85 on George Wein/Concord, with Joe Farrell, David SANBORN; *The Magicians* '86 on Crossover/Concord with a big band; *Latin/Aqui Se Puede* '86 on Sobocode; also Mickey Hart LP *Däfos* '85 on Reference. Her LPs as leader on Milestone through '78 incl. Airto on all of them, Carter on most, others variously incl. Stanley CLARKE, George DUKE, Oscar Brashear, Joe Henderson, etc.: *Butterfly Dreams, Stories To Tell* (with Earl KLUGH, Carlos SANTANA), *Open Your Eyes You Can Fly* (with Pascoal), *500 Miles High* (with Nascimento), *Encounter* (with Pascoal), *That's What She Said*.

Q

QUARTERFLASH USA AOR group formed in Portland, Oregon '80. Lineup: Rindy Ross, vocals and sax; Marv Ross and Jack Charles, guitars and vocals; Rick Gooch, bass; Rick DiGiallonardo, keyboards; David Willis, drums. Rosses husband and wife; quit teaching '77 and recruited ex-members of Pilot (not the UK group) to form Seafood Mama; new name from Australian colloquialism. Held-over Seafood number 'Harden My Heart' was first hit (no. 3 USA; no. 1 in Japan, Australia, Italy, France) on newly formed Geffen label. Sound dead ringer for FLEETWOOD MAC given added sheen by prod. John Boylan (Little River Band, ASSOCIATION, Linda RONSTADT) with Ross's keeping vocals over jogalong backing. 'Find Another Fool', also from eponymous '81 debut LP, made no. 16; while *Take Another Picture* '83 yielded 'Take Me To Heart', no. 14 hit. *Back Into Blue* '85 was prod. in France by Culture Club prod. Steve Levine. Band now slimmed down to Rosses, Gooch and Willis; retains gleaming sanitised technologically enhanced sound that sparkles, lacks passion. A favourite on MTV video channel (trademark image is Rindy Ross and saxophone).

QUATRES ÉTOILES One of the first African supergroups, formed Paris '83 by bassist Bopol, guitarist Syran, vocalists Nyboma and Wuta May (*b* Blaise Pasco Wuta May), having established themselves as leading Zairean musicians: LPs *Enfant Bamileke* '84, *Dance* '85. All became stars in Africa '70s: Wuta May had solo albums *Tshitsha*, *Le Beach*, *Tout Mal Se Paie Ici Bas*. Nyboma began with Orchestre Baby National '69, then Negro Success, others; formed Les Kamales '73, had hit 'Kamale' in Zaire; to Togo '79, joined Sam MANGWANA and the African All Stars; to Abidjan '81, hit 'Double Double', LP of same name '83; to Paris '82, second solo LP *Bandona* '84. Bopol played with Afrisa International, others; made own LPs *Manuela*, *Deception Motema*,

Marriage Force, *Samedi Soir*, *Ça C'est Quoi*. Syran is sought-after session guitarist, played with African All Stars (solo on Mangwana's 'Maria Tebbo'), solo LPs *Kouame*, *Ilanga*.

QUATRO, Suzi (*b* 3 June '50, Detroit, Mich.) Singer, bassist. Father Art semi-pro jazz musician, encouraged daughters to play; duo Pleasure Seekers with elder sister Patti on guitar played Detroit clubs '64; single 'Never Thought You'd Leave Me' issued on local Hideout label. Not short of bookings playing top 40 covers, but turned to progressive rock '68, renamed Cradle, brought in younger sister Nancy on vocals; spotted '71 by Mickie MOST who was touring with Jeff BECK, offered Suzi solo deal (Patti turned up later in FANNY). First single flopped: 'Rolling Stone' co-written by Errol Brown (HOT CHOCOLATE); but live work supporting SLADE with Len Tuckey, guitar; Keith Hodge, drums; Alastair McKenzie, keyboards, tightened up music and image. Quatro donned leather, screamed'n'hollered with neanderthal band giving muscular support; what was missing was material, soon supplied by bubble-gum kings CHINN & CHAPMAN: seven top 40 hits incl. chart-toppers 'Can The Can' '73, 'Devil Gate Drive' '74, all nonsense lyrics delivered hysterically over relentless thumping. Rise of punk rendered Suzi, SIOUXSIE, Poly Styrene, even BLONDIE suddenly less interesting: Quatro shrewdly changed image, appeared on USA children's TV show *Happy Days* as Leather Tuscadero, played roles in *Minder* and *Dempsey & Makepeace* on TV; songs became more reflective: 'Stumblin' In', a singalong strummer with Smokie's Chris Norman, significantly her only USA hit at no. 4 '79; three more top 40 hits in UK incl. 'If You Can't Give Me Love', no. 4 '78. Married to Tuckey, with two children; played Annie Oakley in Andrew LLOYD WEBBER prod. of *Annie Get Your Gun*. Having blazed pre-punk trail for women, she may well be around for a while.

QUEBEC, Ike (*b* 17 Aug. '18, Newark, N.J.; *d* 16 Jan. '63, NYC) Tenor sax. Played piano professionally '41-2; debut on tenor '42 established him as master of late Swing Era style. Co-wrote 'Mop Mop' with Kenny CLARKE, recorded later by Coleman HAWKINS on one of the first bop recording sessions; worked in NYC, Chicago etc. with Hawkins, Benny CARTER, many others; joined Cab CALLOWAY and recorded as leader for Blue Note '44. Big bands were dying; 'swingtet' dates allowed 'streamlined septets of three horns and four rhythm that could cleverly deliver the sound and feel of modern swing and still allow room for some of the innovations of the day' (M. CUSCUNA); Blue Note issued only four albums on 78 (with cover artwork, photos, etc.); one was Quebec's. He made a session for Savoy (now on 2-disc *Tenor Sax* compilation), five Blue Note sessions '44-6 of which first incl. 'Blue Harlem', one of the biggest Blue Note hits of the era. A few records with Calloway, Lucky MILLINDER, backing vocalists '49-53; but didn't record again until '59 for several reasons: little work available, personal struggle with heroin addiction, and Quebec himself had helped to change music business: as close personal friend of Alfred Lion (*see* BLUE NOTE), Ike urged him to listen to Thelonious MONK, Bud POWELL, etc. (wrote 'Suburban Eyes' for Monk's first Blue Note date), helping Blue Note to become premier jazz label of '50s-60s. Fortunately came back to play on 10 Blue Note LPs '59-62: dates with Sonny CLARK, vocalist Dodo Green, Jimmy SMITH, and his own albums: *With A Song In My Heart, Congo Lament, Heavy Soul, Blue And Sentimental* (reissued '84 by EMI; also plays piano on two tracks), *It Might As Well Be Spring, Soul Samba; Easy Living* '62 was finally issued '87 in its intended form, bluesy set with Stanley TURRENTINE on second tenor, Clark on piano, Bennie Green, Milt Hinton, Art Blakey. He died of lung cancer. Limited editions on Mosaic compile *Complete Blue Note Forties Recordings Of Ike Quebec And John Hardee* on four discs; *Complete Blue Note 45 Sessions* on three (26 quartet tracks '59-62 nearly all issued on

singles for juke boxes, with organists incl. Sir Charles THOMPSON, Earl Vandyke, Edwin Swanson).

QUEEN UK rock band, lineup unchanged since '71: Freddie Mercury (*b* Frederick Bulsara, 5 Sep. '46, Zanzibar), vocals; Brian May (*b* 19 July '47, Hampton, Middlesex), guitar; John Deacon (*b* 19 Aug. '51, Leicester), bass; Roger Taylor (*b* Roger Meadows-Taylor, 26 July '49, Norfolk). One of UK's most enduring bands despite entrenched critical hostility was formed '71 after demise of Smile, which featured May and Taylor: Mercury came from Wreckage on recommendation of Smile vocalist Tim Staffel; Deacon was recruited by an advert in music press. Unlike many contemporaries, they opted not to go on thankless pub and club circuit, started out on showcase gigs, leading to early record contract. First LP *Queen* '73 smacked of hyperbole, earned enmity of music press, but MOTT THE HOOPLE gave them valuable exposure on tours of UK/USA. *Queen II* '74 incl. needed hit single, ambitious 'Seven Seas Of Rhye'; *Sheer Heart Attack* '74 incl. 'Killer Queen'. They plugged gap in pre-punk UK pop scene, built following with Mercury obvious centrepiece, May as guitar hero, Deacon and Taylor contributing hit songs. Breakthrough came with *A Night At The Opera* '75, believed most expensive UK LP production since BEATLES' *Sergeant Pepper* '67; its hit 'Bohemian Rhapsody' was 6-minute magnum opus with balladry, hard rock, heavy metal: something for everybody made longest running UK no. 1 for 20 years (no. 9 USA), helped inaugurate video age with promo regarded as seminal. *A Day At The Races* '76 followed up well with USA/UK hits 'You're My Best Friend', 'Somebody To Love'; *News Of The World* '77 and *Jazz* '78 continued to demonstrate versatility. *Live Killers* '79 was live 2-disc set; that year they appeared as one of the few 'old guard' outfits at charity concerts for Kampuchea (later issued on *Concerts For The People of Kampuchea* '81, the same year they attracted adverse criticism by appearing in South Africa's Sun City). *The Game* '80 incl. Deacon's 'Another One Bites The Dust', no. 1 USA, while Mercury's 'Crazy Little Thing Called Love' was infectious in rockabilly style. With soundtrack to *Flash Gordon* '80 they became first band to score a major film; *Greatest Hits* '81 has remained in UK album charts for several years; *Hot Space* '82 incl. a tribute to John LENNON and duet with David BOWIE 'Under Pressure', UK no. 1. *The Works* '84 was hard-edged set incl. world-wide no. 1 in Taylor's 'Radio Ga-Ga', several other hits; *A Kind Of Magic* '86 by contrast was disjointed, featuring band's songs from film *Highlander*, as well as more hits. *Live Magic* '86 recorded during Queen's European tour, seen by 500,000 fans at a time in UK. Taylor made solo LPs *Fun In Space* '82, *Strange Frontier* '84, prod. hits for Jimmy Nail, Feargal SHARKEY; May made *Starfleet Project* '84; Mercury *Mr Nice Guy* '85, contributed to films *Metropolis*, *Electric Dreams* '85, London show *Time* '86; had solo UK hit '87 with PLATTERS' classic 'The Great Pretender'.

? AND THE MYSTERIANS US rock band: ? (*b* Rudy Martinez, '45), vocals; Robert Martinez, drums; Larry Borjas, guitar; Frank Rodriguez Jnr (*b* 9 Mar. '51, Crystal City, Texas), keyboards; Francisco Hernandez Lugo (*b* 15 Mar. '47, Weslaco, Texas), bass. Originally called XYZ with ?, played their first gig in Adrian, Michigan c.'64. Recorded '96 Tears' as Mysterians for manager's Pa-Go-Go label, pressing only 750 copies '66; became most requested record on WTAC Flint, KCLW Detroit leading to deal with Cameo, million-selling American pop classic of the period. Band all claimed to be Mexican-born, kept up air of mystery; Rudy Martinez always wore sunglasses during interviews, photo sessions, legally changed name to ?. Note on sleeve of LP (*96 Tears* '66) revealed that Robert Martinez and Borjas had been drafted, replaced by Robert Lee 'Bobby' Balderrama (*b* 27 Feb. '50, O'Donnell, Texas) and Eduardo Delgardo 'Eddie' Serrato (*b* 5 Dec. '45, Encial, Texas). Second single 'I Need Somebody' charted (no. 22 '67), but three further singles on Cameo, next LP *Action*, one-off singles on Chicory, Capitol, Super did little; by '68 band had folded. Garland JEFFREYS covered '96 Tears' for minor hit '80; new edition of ? And The Mysterians formed that year, with ? only original member. During '81 interview in *Goldmine* he revealed that band had used a Vox organ; legend had maintained that sound had been

due to use of a Farfisa. Bar band sound of that hit still causes rush of nostalgia for those of a certain age.

QUICKSILVER MESSENGER SERVICE USA rock band formed in San Francisco '65 by John Cipollina (*b* 24 Aug. '43, Berkeley) and Gary Duncan (*b* 4 Sep. '46, San Diego), guitars, with Greg Elmore (*b* 4 Sep. '46, San Diego), drums; David Freiberg (*b* 24 Aug. '38, Boston), bass; Jim Murray, harmonica. After contributing to *Revolution* soundtrack Murray left '66 to study sitar. Dino Valenti (*b* 7 Nov. '43, NYC) supposed to be vocalist (he'd written 'Hey Joe' and the YOUNGBLOODS' 'Get Together' as Chester A. Powers), but was jailed on drug charges, didn't join until '70. QMS were one of the last bands to be signed in rush to Bay Area by record companies. Eponymous first LP '68 incl. 'Dino's Song' (by Valenti) and with *Happy Trails* '69 contains best work: latter contained side-long improvisations on Bo DIDDLEY's 'Who Do You Love', taking up where first LP's 12 minutes of interwoven guitars on 'The Fool' left off, instrumental LPs reflecting absence of singer. Duncan left to join newly-freed Valenti in the Outlaws (not more famous '70s group of that name); Nicky HOPKINS filled in on keyboards for *Shady Grove* '69, which disappointed; Valenti and Duncan returned for *Just For Love* '70 and *What About Me* '71, for which Mark Naftalin replaced Hopkins, but band fell apart. Guitar legend Cipollina's distinctive vibrato style was relegated to support role as group became song-oriented; he left to form Copperheads with Murray, guested with Welsh progressives Man on live *Maximum Darkness* '75; Freiberg left, resurfaced with Jefferson Starship; survivors made *Quicksilver* and *Comin' Through*, which disappointed, as did reunion of 'original' quartet plus Valenti for *Solid Silver* '75. First two LPs are a good example of best of San Francisco era; classic anthology *The Ultimate Journey* on See For Miles UK.

QUIET RIOT USA heavy rock band formed in L.A. '75 by Kevin DuBrow, vocals, with Randy Rhoads, guitar; Rudy Sarzo, bass; Frankie Banali, drums. Won reputation as hard-rocking live act on West Coast concert circuit; claimed affinity with STATUS QUO, whose Rick Parfitt suggested name. Made LPs *Quiet Riot* and *Quiet Riot II* '77-8 for Japan-only release; they're now collectors' items, though band have since disowned them. Disillusioned Rhoads left to join Ozzy Osbourne '79; Sarzo left to join Angel, rejoined, left again to join Rhoads with Osbourne. Surviving duo changed name to BuBrow, were signed by prod. Spencer Proffer to his Pasha label. Added guitarist Carlos Cavazo, commenced recording *Metal Health* '83 (had changed name back to Quiet Riot late '82); Sarzo rejoined again during sessions; roadwork with ZZ TOP, IRON MAIDEN, BLACK SABBATH etc. brought album to brink of charts; incl. single 'Cum On Feel The Noize' reached no. 5 USA/45 UK (cover of SLADE song ideal for Noddy Holder soundalike DuBrow); title track 'Bang Your Head (Metal Health)' made no. 31 USA early '84. Unlike many HM bands Riot took readily to video, one featuring DuBrow jumping out of skyscraper with parachute harness. *Condition Critical* '84 incl. another Slade cover in 'Skweeze Me Pleeze Me'. DuBrow and Cavazo are a potent live combination reminiscent of CHEAP TRICK; on record perhaps they lack originality. Album *QRIII* '86 had

new bassist Chuck Wright; *Wild, Young And Crazee* '87 was on Raw Power label.

QUINICHETTE, Paul (*b* 17 May '16, Denver, Colo.; *d* 2 June '83, NYC) Tenor sax. Studied alto, clarinet as a child; played with Jay McSHANN, Johnny OTIS, Benny CARTER, Sid CATLETT, Louis JORDAN, Lucky MILLINDER etc. then with Count BASIE '51-3. Known as 'Vice Pres' because of tonal and stylistic resemblance to Lester YOUNG, but was no copycat: had own laid-back swinging style. Delightful work on Basie's small-group Verve/Clef LP *The Swinging Count*, recorded late '52. Led own combos; own LPs incl. *On The Sunny Side* mid-'50s, now on Fantasy; played with Benny GOODMAN octet '55; on Prestige Basie reunion LPs '57-8 (with Nat PIERCE on piano); recorded with Bob BROOKMEYER, Billie HOLIDAY, Woody HERMAN, Dinah WASHINGTON, LaVern BAKER, etc.; left music '60s, worked in electronics; returned '73 and worked in NYC with pianist Brooks Kerr, others incl. group called Two Tenor Boogie '74 with Buddy TATE or Harold Ashby. Later LPs incl. *Prevue* on Famous Door with Kerr, Tate quintet *The Texas Twister* '75 on Master Jazz.

R

RABBITT, Eddie (*b* 27 Nov. '44, Brooklyn, NY) Pop/country vocalist, songwriter with great success since late '70s. Worked as truck driver, soda jerk, fruit picker etc.; released single 'Six Nites & Seven Days' on 20th Century Fox '64; performed '67-8 on WRGB Radio in Albany, NY, then WWVA *Jamboree* '68 in Wheeling, West Va.; signed with Columbia and released flop records of own songs 'The Bed & Holdin' On', 'Bottles' and 'I Just Don't Care Any More'. Had first success as a writer with Roy DRUSKY version of his 'Working My Way Up From The Bottom' and Bobby Lewis's top 20 'Love Me And Make It All Better', both '67. Songs continued to be covered and he finally hit big with 'Kentucky Rain' by Elvis PRESLEY '70, top 20 pop hit and worldwide million-seller: Presley recorded more Rabbitt songs; Mel STREET went top 10 country with 'Livin' On Borrowed Time' and Ronnie MILSAP scored his first no. 1 country hit with Eddie's 'Pure Love' '74. Jack GREENE, Roy CLARK, Willie NELSON all recorded his songs, leading to signing with WB/Elektra '74, minor hit with 'You Get To Me' '74, top 20 hits 'Forgive And Forget', 'I Should Have Married You' '75, no. 1 'Drinkin' My Baby (Off My Mind)' and top 10 hits 'Rocky Mountain Music' (crossed over to pop Hot 100) and 'Two Dollars In The Jukebox' '76. Hits often co-written with prod. David Malloy, long-time friend Even Stevens. Further hits incl. 'I Can't Help Myself', 'You Don't Love Me Anymore', 'I Just Want To Love You', 'Every Which Way But Loose' and 'Suspicions' '77-9, several country no. ones and all pop crossovers; 'I Love A Rainy Day' no. 1 pop, also made UK chart. More country no. ones: 'Gone Too Far' and 'Drivin' My Life Away' '80, 'Step By Step' and 'Someone Could Lose A Heart Tonight' '81, duet 'You And I' '82 with Crystal GAYLE (also top 10 pop), more solo hits '83-5. Switched to RCA '85 with new prod. Richard Landis, Phil Ramone for more up-to-date contem-porary styling; 'Gotta Have You' '87 made country top 10. Never nominated for a CMA award, though he was biggest-selling country artist '80-2. LPs: *Rocky Mountain Music* '77, *Variations* '78, *Love Line* '79, *Horizon* '80, *Step By Step* '81, *Radio Romance* '82, all on WB; *Rabbitt Trax* '86 on RCA: a WB compilation in USA '85 consisted entirely of country no. 1 hits. He was inactive in music while a baby son was dying; *I Wanna Dance With You* '88 reverted to purer country style.

RAEBURN, Boyd (*b* Boyd Albert Raeburn, 27 Oct. '13, near Faith, South Dakota; *d* 2 Aug. '66, Lafayette, Ind.) Saxophonist, composer, leader. Attended U. of Chicago, where he led a campus band; turned pro and played straight 'sweet' style, gradually turned towards swing; came to NYC '44 and built new jazz-oriented band, entering the history books: from '44 to '47 Raeburn's and Woody HERMAN's bands were the ones full of young boppers. Sidemen variously incl. Sonny BERMAN, Al COHN, Oscar PETTIFORD, pianist Dodo Marmarosa, drummer Don Lamond, Trummy Young and future arr. Johnny Mandel on trombones, trumpeter Benny Harris (*b* 23 Apr. '19, NYC; co-wrote 'Ornithology' with Charlie PARKER), and others. Dizzy GILLESPIE occasionally sat in, incl. records; Dizzy and Budd JOHNSON wrote for the band, as did Ed Finckel in the early days, then pianist George Handy (*b* George Joseph Hendelman, 17 Jan. '20, Brooklyn), George Dale 'The Fox' Williams (*b* 5 Nov. '17, New Orleans) and Tadd DAMERON; vocalists were David ALLYN, Ginny Powell (married Raeburn); later the band had Buddy DeFRANCO, arr. by Johnny Richards. In Aug. '44 the band's book was destroyed by fire; Duke ELLINGTON helped with arr., money. Raeburn recorded for small labels (Guild/Musicraft, Jewel) and during musicians' union strike against record companies could not record at all.

Raeburn disbanded '47, re-formed '48-50, sometimes gigged and recorded in NYC until late '50s when he left music, moved to the Bahamas. Reissues: *Experiments In Big Band Jazz* on Musicraft, *Man With The Horns* and 2-disc *Jewels* on Savoy, *Memphis In June* and two vols. of *On The Air* on Hep UK; also on Circle, Aircheck, First Heard, Golden Era.

RAFFERTY, Gerry (*b* 16 Apr. '47, Paisley, Scotland) Folk-rock singer/songwriter and guitarist. Worked with future comedian Billy Connolly in the Humblebums (*Humblebums* and *Open The Door* '69-70); on split made LP *Can I Have My Money Back* '71 (some say still his best), then formed Stealer's Wheel with folksinger Rab Noakes, who soon bowed out; the act centred around Rafferty and vocalist/keyboardist/co-writer Joe Egan. *Stealer's Wheel* '73 incl. their best-known song 'Stuck In The Middle With You' (no. 6 UK, 2 USA), *Ferguslie Park* '74 incl. 'Star' (top 30 USA), both prod. by LEIBER & STOLLER. They had no regular band, which inhibited touring; there was friction with producers and *Right Or Wrong* '75 came out after they'd split. He stayed at home in Scotland sorting out legal problems, went solo with *City To City* '78, which critics like to pan, but the public made a no. 1 LP USA, 'Baker Street' a no. 2 single (sax solo by Raphael Ravenscroft). *Night Owl* '79 was top 30, *Snakes And Ladders* '80 did less well, *Sleepwalking* '82 did not chart. He prod. LP for Richard and Linda THOMPSON '82 (not released), sang on one track on Mark Knopfler's *Local Hero* '83. First album in five years *North & South* '88 on London UK, with long-time colleague Jerry Donahue on guitar, Irish piper Davy Spillane, Alan Clark (from DIRE STRAITS) on piano.

RAGTIME The first internationally popular genre in popular music, sweeping the world c.1897-1920: syncopated melodies set against a march-type ('oompah') bass line. In retrospect ragtime is regarded as solo piano music, but that was only its most highly developed (and most enduring) manifestation; ragtime songs, music for small combos and brass bands, and ragtime waltzes were important, as was banjo music:

ragtime may have begun with attempts to imitate the banjo on the keyboard. Seminal West African roots feature additive rhythms; ragtime was the first indigenously American music, and the first Afro-American music (but not the last) to influence world popular music. Concert pianist and composer Louis Moreau Gottschalk (*b* 8 May 1829, New Orleans; *d* 1869, Rio de Janeiro) was lionised in his day, wrote syncopated piano pieces (incl. 'The Banjo') and might have been America's Glinka (the great Russian nationalist) if he had lived longer; he infl. ragtime, which seemed to emerge in the Midwest, chiefly in Chicago, St Louis, Louisville, but like jazz later, it probably happened in many places at once, and certainly spread rapidly. The dancing in Congo Square, New Orleans was described as in 'ragged' time in 1886; a banjo player in Nebraska wrote in 1888 to a music magazine requesting music in 'broken time' like the 'ear-players' played (but none had been printed yet); the World's Fair of 1893 in Chicago attracted pianists who were already playing the style; the first compositions using the words 'rag' or 'ragtime' were published in 1897. Non-ragtime songs, incl. classical instrumental and operatic pieces, were 'ragged' (played in a syncopated way) but both banjo music and true ragtime songs came from MINSTRELSY (*which see*), songs through 'coon songs', soon seen as racist but popular in the 1890s: most notorious of these, 'All Coons Look Alike To Me', was written by Ernest Hogan, who was black; it was not racial in intent (though he later regretted writing it) but about a woman rejecting her lover for another man with more money: a huge hit, the first published song (1896) to incl. optional 'Negro "Rag" Accompaniment'. The term ragtime like the words jazz and rock in later years was applied to music that was merely rhythmic; Irving BERLIN was the most famous composer of 'ragtime', but 'Alexander's Ragtime Band' (1911) was not ragtime at all. About 2-3000 instrumental rags and a similar number of ragtime songs were published, about 100 ragtime waltzes. Most of the songs are forgotten (though some, like Ben Harney's 'You've Been A Good Old Wagon But You've Done Broke Down', made a transition to other genres); many instrumental rags are miniature masterpieces as fine as piano pieces of Chopin: the greatest composer of these was undoubtedly Scott JOPLIN ('Maple Leaf Rag' was the best-known in the genre, and he wrote the best waltzes: 'Bethena', 'Pleasant Moments'); others were James Scott (*b* 1886, Neosho, Mo.; *d* 30 Aug. '38, Kansas City, Kansas), Tom Turpin (*b* 1873, Savannah, Ga.; *d* '22), Eubie BLAKE and Luckey ROBERTS, all black; Joseph Lamb (*b* 6 Dec. 1887, Montclair, N.J.; *d* 3 Sep. '60, Brooklyn, NY), Charles L. Johnson (*b* 3 Dec. 1876, Kansas City, Kansas; *d* 28 Dec. '50, Kansas City, Mo.), George Botsford (*b* 24 Feb. 1874, Sioux Falls, S. Dakota; *d* 11 Feb. '49, NYC), and Percy Wenrich (*b* 23 Jan. 1887, Joplin, Mo.; *d* 17 Mar. '52, NYC), who were white. Women also wrote fine rags; the most prolific May Aufderheide (*b* 21 May 1890, Indianapolis, Ind.; *d* 1 Sep. '72, Pasadena, Cal.) and Irene Giblin (1888-1974), both white. Banjo players incl. Vess L. Ossman (1868-1923), an international celebrity, and Fred Van Eps (father of jazz guitarist George VAN EPS); among the famous ragtime singers were Al JOLSON, Sophie TUCKER, Dolly Connolly (1888-1965; Mrs Percy Wenrich) Bert Williams (1874-1922; also a dancer, immortalised by Duke ELLINGTON in 'Portrait Of Bert Williams'), and Billy Murray (*b* 25 May 1877, Philadelphia, Pa.; *d* 17 Aug. '54), one of the biggest stars in the history of RECORDED SOUND, with more than 160 big hits 1903-27, plus a great many others as a member of various groups: his 'The Grand Old Rag' (actually 'You're A Grand Old Flag', by George M. COHAN) in '06 was said to be the biggest hit in Victor's first decade. Ragtime's heyday was between 1910-20 in watered-down, ricky-tick style; Joplin found it necessary to print on his music that 'Ragtime should never be played fast'. Controversial in its day, seen as a racial threat by some, it allowed commercial success for some blacks even as racism was being institutionalised in the USA, and encouraged questions about what American music was and could be. It led to novelty piano music (LP by Lincoln Mayorga on Town Hall Records incl. pieces by Zez CONFREY; Felix Arndt's 'Nola' and Gus Chandler's 'Canadian Capers' (both '15); also impressionistic 'In A Mist' by Bix BEIDERBECKE, 'The Moth' by Lee Sims, who infl. Art TATUM;

etc.). Most importantly ragtime infl. Jazz, which succeeded it, but ragtime never went away: it was part of the revival of early jazz which began c.'40; it was kept alive in the '50s by Dick HYMAN (as Knuckles O'Toole), Lou BUSCH (as Joe 'Fingers' Carr), in novelties by Fritz Schulz-Reichel in Germany and Johnny Maddox in USA (*see* CRAZY OTTO), Winifred ATWELL in UK. Max MORATH, Bill BOLCOM, Joshua RIFKIN, Gunther SCHULLER played it properly on LPs '60s-70s; film soundtrack *The Sting* '73 gave it its biggest boost in 50 years. *They All Played Ragtime* '50 by Rudi Blesh and Harriet Janis was seminal book; *Ragtime: A Musical And Cultural History* '80 by Edward A. Berlin is accurately titled; *Ragtime: Its History, Composers And Music* '85 ed. by John Edward Hasse incl. essays by Morath, Schuller, Berlin, many others.

RAINEY, Ma (*b* Gertrude Pridgett, 26 Apr. 1886, Columbus, Ga.; *d* there 22 Dec. '39) Blues singer. Born into family of minstrel troupers, she married William 'Pa' Rainey of Rabbit Foot Minstrels; they formed song and dance team, worked throughout the South, sometimes with Bessie SMITH. Ma and Bessie began recording the same year, and brought to the blues the authentic sound of the black working-class South at a time when the newly discovered genre was in danger of being 'citified' by artists like Lucille Hegamin (*b* 29 Nov. 1894, Macon, Ga.; *d* 1 Mar. '70, NYC) and Edith Wilson (*b* 2 Sep. 1896, Louisville, Ky.; *d* 30 Mar. '81, Chicago), who were fine entertainers, but not the real country stuff. Ma made about 90 sides for Paramount '23-9, at first with Lovie AUSTIN Blue Serenaders, then with her own groups/accompaniment; she made the best-known recording of trad. 'See See Rider' (aka 'Easy Rider'). Collections: *Complete Recordings* Vol. 1 released '79 on VJM/UK, Vol. 2 '86; *Ma Rainey's Black Bottom* on Yazoo '86.

RAINWATER, Marvin (*b* Marvin Percy, 2 July '25, Wichita, Kansas) Country singer, songwriter. Studied veterinary surgery, served in US Navy as pharmacist's mate; half American Indian, he turned to music, took mother's name and paraded as full-blooded Cherokee in regalia. Joined Red FOLEY's Ozark Jubilee show '46, wrote songs covered by Teresa BREWER, Justin TUBB, Connie FRANCIS; appeared on Arthur GODFREY talent show with own song, 'Gonna Find Me A Bluebird'; won a week on Godfrey's morning radio show and signed with MGM. 'Bluebird' was top 20 pop, no. 3 country hit '57; subsequent hits were 'Whole Lotta Woman' and 'Half-Breed' '58-9, plus minor duet 'Majesty Of Love' with Francis. Surgery on vocal chords took him out of circulation; with brother Ray he founded glossy country magazine *Trail* which failed; recorded '60s on WB, UA, his own Brave label; toured UK '71 for the first time in 12 years and found new fans, made LP with London-based Country Fever (Albert Lee on guitar). Other LPs incl. *Especially For You* '77 on Westwood.

RAITT, Bonnie (*b* 8 Nov. '49, Burbank, Cal.) White blues singer, songwriter, guitarist, often with country rock feel. Father John Raitt (*b* 19 Jan. '17, Santa Ana, Cal.) starred in first production of RODGERS & HAMMERSTEIN's *Carousel* '45; on stage in *Pajama Game* '54, film '57, etc. She left college '69 to play the blues in East Coast clubs, touring as acoustic duo with Freebo on tuba/fretless bass, who later played on some of her albums; joined ex-LITTLE FEAT Paul Barrere in Bluesbusters. Her success in Boston, Philadelphia led to signing by Dick Waterman, who had her sharing bills with Sippie WALLACE, Fred McDOWELL, Son HOUSE (all abiding influences); gravelly, emotionally mature voice belied her years, while fine guitar technique (especially on slide) marked her as one to watch. *Bonnie Raitt* '71 was blues, ballads, sidemen incl. Chicago bluesmen Junior WELLS, A. C. Reed on tenor sax; *Give It Up* '72 prod. by Michael CUSCUNA, incl. Woodstock musicians; *Takin' My Time* '73 prod. by John Hall, *Streetlights* '74 by Jerry Ragavoy, *Home Plate* '75 and *Sweet Forgiveness* '77 by Paul Rothchild: the latter incl. cover of Del SHANNON's '61 hit 'Runaway', her nearest to a hit single in top 50 USA, but her albums all did well, going as high as top 25. *The Glow* '79 was prod. by Peter ASHER, incl. sexy slowed-down sex-change treatment of LITTLE RICHARD hit 'The Boy Can't Help It' (written by Bobby Troup), but the LP's gloss didn't suit (she is not another Linda RONSTADT), was deliberately

missing from *Green Light* '82 (incl. Ian McLaughlin on keyboards). Each LP incl. good things: she wrote songs herself, chose others by Allen TOUSSAINT, James TAYLOR, Sippie Wallace, Isaac HAYES & David Porter, J. D. SOUTHER, Eric Kaz, etc.; she helped blues friends by hiring them as support, was active in MUSE anti-nuclear campaign with Jackson BROWNE. Her singing was intimate and knowledgeable, but she changed producers too often, as though unsure of her niche; after a long hiatus, on *Nine Lives* '86 she'd completely lost it: overproduced, unswinging music, undistinguished songs were totally unlike her best work.

RAMBLERS DANCE BAND Highlife band led by tenor sax player Jerry Hansen, formed in golden era of '60s highlife in Ghana, the 15-piece dance band lasting for over two decades, popular throughout West Africa long after the highlife boom was over (though their repertoire, like that of all the great highlife bands, was also infl. by jazz, calypso, soul, etc.). Hits in '60s incl. 'Scholarship', 'Auntie Christie', 'Eka Wo Ekoa'; LPs *The Fabulous Ramblers*, *Ramblers Encores*; in the '70s *Dancing With The Ramblers*, *Doin' Our Own Thing*; their biggest hit album, still widely available, *The Hit Sounds Of The Ramblers Dance Band*. They took up lengthy residency mid-'70s at Accra's Ambassador, one of the best hotels; in '74 Hansen was elected first president of the Musicians' Union of Ghana.

RAMIREZ, Louie Plays timbales, vibes, keyboards; bandleader, composer; one of NY salsa's most successful and imaginative arrangers and producers. Played timbales on Sabu Martinez LP *Sabu's Jazz Espagnole* c.'60 on Alegre, on *Latin Jazz Quintet* LP on UA. *Introducing Louie Ramirez* on Remo, *Latin Au Go Go* on Atco were followed by *Good News* c.'66 on the new Fania label; he led a group called Conjunto Chango and played vibes on *Vibes Galore* on Alegre incl. singer Willie Torres; a disappointing LP on Mercury was meant to cash in on the boogaloo fad '66-8. In the early '70s *Louie Ramirez y Tito Rodriguez: En Algo Nuevo* featured the great singer and bandleader on his own TR label; *Tipico* '74 on UA featured singer Victor Velazquez,

Papo Pepin on conga (became long-term Ramirez associate). LPs on Cotique were seminal experiments: crossover oriented *A Different Shade Of Black* '76; *Louie Ramirez y sus Amigos* '78 incl. Latin-jazz 'Salsa Vibes', BEATLES songs incl. 'Because' (arr. as a Cuban danzon by Sonny Bravo), major hit 'Paula C' composed/sung by Rubén BLADES, other lead singers Azuquita, Adalberto Santiago; *Salsa Progresiva* '79 incl. 'Latin New York', Jimmy Sabater lead singer on Barry White's song 'Sha-La Means I Love You' (Angela Bofill singing backup), Tito Allen and Ismael Quintana singing lead on others; *Salsero* '80 incl. Santiago, pianist/arr./prod. Isidro Infante. *Super Cañonalos con Louie Ramirez* '83 on Gigi was tipico salsa with three trumpets, alto, baritone sax and flute, incl. Infante on piano, impressive voice of Ray de la Paz. Ramirez and Infante had sessioned together from late '70s; Ramirez and de la Paz now co-led a band with horn section of four trumpets and featuring Infante and Pepin: *Con Caché!* '84 on new Caimán label was slickly prod. salsa that charted high in Billboard's Latin list, incl. 'Solo Tu y Yo', salsa version of Bill Withers' 'Just The Two Of Us'. *Alegres y Romanticos* '85 and *Sabor con Clase!* '86 stayed in successful groove. Meanwhile Ramirez has played on and/or contributed production, arrangements to LPs by scores of important Latin artists since the '70s, incl. many of those named above plus Larry HARLOW, Willie COLON, Celia CRUZ & Tito PUENTE, the FANIA ALL STARS, Johnny PACHECO, Cheo FELICIANO, many more. He has complained of the limitations of tipico Cuban format: 'Everybody who hires me wants two trumpets or two trumpets and one trombone. I say, why don't we use an oboe? . . . Aretha Franklin's drummer told me, "You know, in the '50s and '60s you guys were doing some heavy things. Now you're kind of like calypso bands!" ' (quoted by John Storm Roberts). As in other genres, success in salsa brought with it pressure against change; when something new happens, it may be Ramirez who breaks out. *A Tribute To Cal Tjader* '87 on Caimán by Louie Ramirez and his Latin Jazz Ensemble incl. Paquito D'Rivera on alto, Mario Rivera on flute, tenor and soprano saxes; José Fajardo on flute, all taking solos, and many musicians appearing on

Ramirez-Ray de la Paz y su Orquesta LPs; Ramirez produced, played vibes, timbales, synthesiser; composed three tracks, co-arr. with pianist Infante. They split '87 for own LPs: de la Paz fronted sessionmen on *Estoy Como Nunca* on BC Records with Infante; Ramirez made *Louie Ramirez y Super Banda* on Faisan, with lead vocalists Tony Vega and Jorge Maldonado.

RAMONES, The NYC punk band, formed '74 with Joey (*b* Jeffrey Hyman) on vocals, Johnny (John Cummings) on guitar, bassist Dee Dee (Douglas Colvin), drummer Tommy (Tom Erdelyi; *b* Budapest), all *b* '52. Their blitzkrieg brand of non-stop two-minute riffing infl. punk in UK, especially after headline gig at London's Roundhouse '76 with FLAMIN' GROOVIES. Contemporary at NYC's CBGBs club with Patti SMITH, BLONDIE, TELEVISION; *Ramones* '76 remains archetypal LP, with 'Beat On The Brat' and 'Now I Wanna Sniff Some Glue'. Critics liked cartoon vision of rock'n'roll; no-nonsense, hard-edged approach seemed antidote to flaccid '70s scene. *Leave Home* '77 was more of the same, *Rocket To Russia* '77 broadened sound; live shows were good value, with 13 songs crammed into half-hour sets. Tommy quit '77, replaced by Marky (Mark Bell). *Road To Ruin* carried on the joke, by then wearing thin; 2-disc live *It's Alive* incl. 28 Ramones standards; they appeared in trashy exploitation film *Rock & Roll High School* '79, ideally suiting their image. To everyone's surprise, Phil SPECTOR prod. *End Of The Century* '80, their best-sounding LP, with affectionate 'Do You Remember Rock'n'Roll Radio?' and cover of RONETTES 'Baby I Love You'. *Pleasant Dreams* '81 prod. by Graham Gouldman, incl. anthemic 'We Want The Airwaves' and 'The KKK Took My Baby'; by *Subterranean Jungle* '83 their appeal had diminished. *Too Tough To Die* '85 was an improvement, incl. 'Howling At The Moon', prod. by EURYTHMICS' Dave Stewart. *Animal Boy* '86 prod. by Jean Bouvier, ex-bassist with Steve VAN ZANDT's Disciples Of Soul. They retain devoted cult following; time will tell whether they represented everything that went wrong in '70s music or were a crucial element in saving it. Still a popular live act, true to legend with *Halfway To Sanity* '88.

RANDOLPH, Boots (*b* Homer Louis Randolph III, c.'25, Paducah, Ky.) Saxophonist; Nashville session player who also had own hits. Switched from trombone to sax in high school band in Evansville, Ind. because it was easier to play while marching. Played in local combos early '40s-late '50s; wrote 'Yakety Sax' with James 'Spider' Rich, signed to RCA by Chet ATKINS, switched to Monument '61: 'Yakety Sax' was top 40 pop hit '63, novelty instrumental with country and rock elements (also no. 4 country hit '65 for Atkins as 'Yakety Axe'). 13 albums in top 200 '63-72 incl. *Boots Randolph's Yakety Sax* '63, *Boots With Strings* '67 (top 40), gospel LP *Sunday Sax* '68, etc.

RAP Dance fad beginning mid-'70s among black and Hispanic teenagers in NYC's outer boroughs, combining disco beat with breakdancing, graffiti art and rap. Disco became boring to kids in the street who couldn't afford to dance in swanky clubs anyway; they played with harder, funky black pop music that disco had come from, cutting back and forth between copies of the same record (such as James BROWN's 'Get On The Good Foot'), making their own 'mixes' of the music, inspiring dancers to greater inventiveness leading to breaking, soon called breakdancing. When MCs added rapping over the music (chanted street poetry which was improvised at first, from trendy '60s word for conversation), it became rap, also called hip-hop (Lovebug Starsky used the words 'To the hip, hop, hippedy hop'). 'Rapper's Delight' '79 was a freak hit on Sugar Hill by a Bronx group called the Sugar Hill Gang (Sylvia Vanderpool had her ear to the ground; she had also issued one of the first disco hits: *see* MICKEY & SYLVIA). 'The Breaks' '80 on Mercury was also a novelty; there were a few more. Afrika Bambaataa and his Soul Sonic Force released influential 'Planet Rock' '82, then 'Renegades of Funk', duet with Brown 'Unity' '84, etc. Grandmaster Flash (*b* Joseph Saddler) was among the first to montage records, add sound effects and produce rhythmic fills (by 'scratching' the stylus in the groove); after LP *The Message* '82 lead rapper Melle Mel left and Flash released *The Source*, staying close to street credibility rather than straying from

roots. DJ Cheese is a turntable wizard plus mouth; Mantronix are Mantronik (DJ) and Tricky Tee (rapper). The Real Roxanne (*b* c.'67, Brooklyn) was one of Roxanne 'answers' spawned by UTFO hit 'Roxanne, Roxanne'; her 'Bang Zoom Let's Go' '86 is glamorous and slick; rival Roxanne Shante has a cult following for more aggressive if squeaky style. Run DMC are a trio from Queens NY (all *b* c.'65) whose third LP *Raising Hell* '86 was first in genre to go platinum: with a drum machine, Run (Joe Simmons), Darryl Mac (McDaniels, or DMC) using microphones, Jam Master Jay (Jason Mizell) scratching on double-deck turntable they filled Madison Square Garden '86. Lyrics are heavy on social statements; some listeners seek violence but Run says 'Our fans know that we don't want this illin'.' Disappearance of genre, predicted for years, hasn't happened yet: ghetto people not served by music business created their own form of communication which is still spreading; London's Posse went to NYC to record 12″ single 'London Posse' '87, with black Cockney accent on one side, reggae-style version on the other. But rap is a social phenomenon, not a musical one, now used in advertising, which is a ridiculous irony: musically it is equivalent to junk food, yet is not the usual pap; those who don't like it will switch off. The Beastie Boys are a trio of middle-class white kids (one arrested in Liverpool '87, then acquitted on charge of injuring a female fan); 4 million copies of their *Licensed To Ill* '87 were sold to 13-year-olds who don't know any better, giving new credence to the question 'do you spell rap with a big or a small c?'

RARE EARTH Detroit soul-rock band: Gil Bridges on reeds, John Persh on bass and trombone, Pete Rivera on drums played and sang in Detroit bars; recommended to Motown by white session guitarist Dennis Coffey, added three members, signed to Motown '69, one of the few white acts on the label, with own Rare Earth imprint; original three were the only constant factor as they had six top 40 hits '70-8, seven LPs in top 100 on Rare Earth, two more in top 200 on Prodigal. Much of their material co-created by prod. Norman Whitfield at Motown; first LP *Get Ready* charted at no. 12

late '69 with 21.5 minute version of title track, cover of a TEMPTATIONS hit, edited for no. 4 single. Other LPs steadily slipped down chart: *Ecology* '70, *One World* '71, *Rare Earth In Concert* and *Willie Remembers* '72, *Ma* '73, *Back To Earth* '75, *Rare Earth* and *Band Together* on Prodigal '77-8.

RASCALS, YOUNG RASCALS White soul quartet formed '65 NYC by three refugees from Joey DEE and the Starliters: Felix Cavaliere (*b* 29 Nov. '44, NYC) on keyboards, Eddie Brigati (*b* 22 Oct. '46, NYC), vocalist; Gene Cornish (*b* 14 May '45, Ottawa) on guitar; plus drummer Dino Danelli (*b* 23 July '45, NYC). Named after TV comedy; played in N.J. clubs and were soon signed by Ahmet Ertegun to Atlantic (competing with Phil SPECTOR, etc.); had 13 USA top 40 singles '66-9. First LP *The Young Rascals* '66 no. 15 incl. no. 1 single 'Good Lovin' ' with Cavaliere lead vocal; *Collections* '67 reached one notch higher with no top 10 hit; *Groovin'* was no. 5 LP with no. 1 title hit (top 10 UK): with LOVIN' SPOONFUL's 'Summer In The City' the era's premier summer listening track; album also incl. top 10 'A Girl Like You' (their only other UK hit, in top 40), no. 4 'How Can I Be Sure', rivalling ASSOCIATION for lush harmony, covered by David Cassidy. Dropped 'Young' from their name '67; all had been experienced sessioneers, Dinelli playing with Lionel HAMPTON as a teenager; *Groovin'* already showed move towards jazz: as they found room on LPs for sidemen Ron CARTER, Hubert LAWS, Joe Farrell, Joe NEWMAN etc. their beautiful 'blue-eyed soul' vocal blend was obscured; they adopted increasing anti-racist stance, refused to play without a black act on the bill, playing a Martin Luther King benefit, but the times had changed and the golden age of soul was over. Top 20 2-disc *Freedom Suite* '70 incl. no. 1 hit 'People Got To Be Free', instrumental LP called 'Music Music'; *Search And Nearness* '71 barely made top 200. Brigati, Cornish left as they switched to Columbia, replaced by guitarist Buzzy Feiten (ex-Paul BUTTERFIELD), vocalist Ann Sutton, bassist Robert 'Pops' Popwell; *Peaceful World* and *The Island Of Real* '71-2 did not make top 100. Ahead of their time: in competition with HALL & OATES (white act topping black chart early

'80s) they'd have been superstars. Cavaliere made eponymous solo album '74, *Destiny* '75 on Bearsville, *Treasure* '76 and *Castle In The Air* '80 on Epic, to critical praise, poor sales; Cornish and Danelli formed Bulldog; in '80s Cavaliere prod. and Danelli drummed for Steve VAN ZANDT's Disciples Of Soul; Popwell played with CRUSADERS.

RASCOE, Moses (*b* 27 July '17, Windsor, N.C.) Country blues singer, guitarist. Bought first guitar at 13 from mail-order catalogue, left home at 15, drove truck for Allied Van Lines 1946-83, singing for free drinks or amusement at truck stops. 'You're supposed to let the guitar talk to you. You sing to it.' After retirement sang in local clubs in York, Pa.; discovered by manager Harriet Kyriakos, first pro performance '86 opening for Dave VAN RONK, then for Michael Bromberg, Koko TAYLOR; he had never heard of any of them, but got ovations and found out what an encore was. Plays six- and 12-string, act described as a 'dignified and elegant rendition of American heritage'; first LP was due on Flying Fish late '87. 'I knew I could play guitar, but being great, I never thought about it. I don't even think about it now.' (Quoted by UPI feature writer Ken Franckling.)

RASPBERRIES, The USA pop group formed in Cleveland '70 by classically trained Eric Carmen (*b* 11 Aug. '49, Cleveland), guitar; Wally Bryson (*b* 18 July '49, Gastonia, N.C.) and Dave Smalley (*b* 10 July '49, Oil City, Pa.), guitars; Jim Bonfanti (*b* 17 Dec. '48, Windber, Pa.), drums. Ex-Cyrus Erie singer Carmen doubled on bass, keyboards; others were members of the Choir; Bonfanti had drummed on 'Time Won't Let Me' by hitmakers the Outsiders (no. 5 '66, with lead singer Sonny Geraci), only Cleveland group except JAMES GANG to reach national charts in '60s. Rasps shared enthusiasm for sound of British Invasion (the Choir known as the Mods at one point). Demos attracted Jimmy Ienner who signed them to Capitol, prod. eponymous first LP '72, incl. no. 5 single 'Go All The Way'. Carmen wrote this and majority of hits; had teen-appeal looks, and lyrics devoted to romance came close to pin-up pop, but band's skill and musical muscle kept them in with more than a shout of rock credibility. 'I Wanna Be With You' made top 20, 'Let's Pretend' top 40 from *Fresh* '72, BEACH BOY harmonies guaranteeing radio play. After *Side 3* '73 Smalley and Bonfanti left to form Dynamite with two ex-Freeport Cleveland musicians, replaced by Mike McBride (ex-Cyrus Erie drummer) and bassist Scott McCarl: latter was in because he 'played like Paul MCCARTNEY and looked like Todd RUNDGREN', said Carmen. This lineup made suitably titled *Starting Over* '74, incl. top 20 5.5 minute 'Overnight Sensation (Hit Record)', then were lost in AM/FM radio divide and split early '75. They were never original but never less than entertaining; balance of Carmen's teen-dream appeal, band's playing, Ienner's prod. ideas (tranny radio sound on 'Overnight Sensation') could not be maintained without them. Carmen signed with Arista, had five top 40 hits, two incl. themes from Rachmaninov incl. no. 2 'All By Myself' '76 (no. 12 UK); resurfaced on Geffen '84 with *Eric Carmen*, collaborating with lyricist Dean Pitchford on these songs and 'Almost Paradise' from film *Footloose* '84. He wrote hits 'That's Rock'n'Roll', 'Hey Deanie' for teen-throb Shaun Cassidy; other songs covered by Frankie Valli, Olivia NEWTON-JOHN, BAY CITY ROLLERS.

RATTLESNAKE ANNIE (*b* Annie McGowan, 26 Dec. '41, Paris, Tenn.) Country singer and songwriter, long highly regarded by stars like Merle HAGGARD, Willie NELSON; David Allan COE recorded her 'Texas Lullaby'. First LP was *Rattlesnakes And Rusty Water* '79 on her own Rattlesnake label (incl. 'Good Old Country Music', covered by Patsy MONTANA); then *Rattlesnake Annie And The Last Cowboy* '83 made in Czechoslovakia for Supraphon, *Country Livin'* '85 on Rattlesnake, incl. duet 'Long Black Limousine' with Nelson. Several tracks from this (incl. the duet) incl. on *Rattlesnake Annie* '87 on CBS: LP and single 'Callin' Your Bluff' reached country charts in USA. About half the songs on her LPs are her own; she is at last receiving long-overdue wider recognition.

RAVAN, Genya (*b* Goldie Zelkowitz, late '30s, Poland) Singer, harmonica, producer. Family escaped Hitler to USA; she began singing in Brooklyn. Sang in Richard

PERRY group; formed Goldie And The Gingerbreads, all-girl group '60s that had more success in UK than USA; highly regarded for skill by UK musicians, they scored no. 25 UK '65 with 'Can't You Hear My Heart Beat', also remembered for 'That's The Way I Love You'. Regulars on package tours with ROLLING STONES etc., folded '69. Remainder of group formed nucleus of all-girl Isis (lineup: Carol MacDonald, guitar, vocals; Ginger Bianco, drums; Stella Bass, bass; Liberty Mata, percussion; Jeannie Feinberg and Lauren Draper, horns; Lollie Bienenfeld and Suzi Ghezzi, guitars; later Jean Millington of Fanny): LPs *Isis* '74, *Ain't No Backin' Up Now* '75. Goldie/Genya went on to front Ten Wheel Drive, otherwise all-male 10-piece jazz/rock ensemble, recording *Construction No. 1* '69, *Brief Replies* '70, *Peculiar Friends* '71 for Polydor before leaving. Flitted between egos during '70s, recording five LPs for four labels: *Genya Ravan With Baby* '72, *They Love Me/They Love Me Not* '73, *Goldie Zelkowitz* '74, *Urban Desire* '78, *And I Mean It* '79. Meanwhile became one of the first female producers; also sessioned, proving raunchy vocals had lost none of their bite: notably on Lou REED's *Street Hassle* '78, BLUE OYSTER CULT's *Mirrors* '79, with a classic vocal on 'Dr Music' with Ellen Foley. Prod. credits incl. DEAD BOYS' *Young And Loud And Snotty* '77, Ronnie Spector's *Siren* '80. Had own Polish label, based in NYC.

RAVEN, Eddy (*b* 19 Aug. '44, Lafayette, La.) Country singer, songwriter with strong Cajun connection; made impact as performer after years as successful writer. Began as rock'n'roller, first band '57; moved to Georgia '60, had own radio show, gained local hit on Cosmo label; back to La. '64 singing and recording country blues with Bobby CHARLES; also worked with Edgar and Johnny WINTER. Moved to country music; Jimmy C. NEWMAN helped get writer's contract with Acuff-Rose; first success was 'Country Green', top 5 hit by Don GIBSON '71: other songs placed with Jeannie C. RILEY, Roy ACUFF, Roy CLARK, ORBISON; also Connie SMITH, Moe BANDY, Conway TWITTY. Began recording '73 with ABC, Monument '78, Dimension '80, slowly climbing up charts to top 10 on Elektra '81-

2, whereupon Elektra dropped him: joined RCA and made top slot with 'I Got Mexico' '84, many more top tens since then. LPs incl. *The Cajun Country Sound* '73 on La Louisianne, *This Is Eddy Raven* '76 on ABC-Dot, *Eyes* '80 on Dimension, *Desperate Dreams* '82 on Elektra; *I Could Use Another Of You* '84, *Love And Other Hard Times* '85, *Right Hand Man* '87 on RCA; compilations incl. *Thank God For Kids* on MCA.

RAWLS, Lou (*b* 1 Dec. '35, Chicago) Singer, actor with soulful voice; initially popular in black charts but commercial delivery soon crossed over; successful in MOR since mid-'60s. With Pilgrim Travelers gospel group until military service '56; later toured with Sam COOKE (they were in a car crash '58, Rawls almost killed; recorded duet 'Bring It On Home To Me' '62). He signed with Capitol '62; LP *Black And Blue* '63 made pop chart; then *Lou Rawls Live!* and *Lou Rawls Soulin'* were both top 10 albums '66, single 'Love Is A Hurtin' Thing' was no. 1 R&B, 13 pop same year. 'Dead End Street' '67 was top 30 pop, no. 3 R&B, mixed singing with monologue and won a Grammy. *Lou Rawls Carryin' On!*, *Too Much* both top 20, *That's Lou* top 30, all '67; single 'Your Good Thing Is About To End' '69 was top 20, but chart placings of LPs slipped (nevertheless, seven albums in top 200 in three years, incl. 2-disc reissue of first two, is not bad going). Switched to MGM '71-2, had top 20 Grammy winner 'A Natural Man', faded, came back with prod. Gamble and Huff on their Philadelphia International label '76 with *All Things In Time*, no. 7 LP with no. 2 hit 'You'll Never Find Another Love Like Mine'. Altogether had six top 40 singles '66-78, 23 chart LPs '63-83; switched to Epic for *Close Company*, then *Love All Your Blues Away* '86. 13 LPs still in print mid-'87 witness steady long-term popularity.

RAY, Johnnie (*b* 10 Jan. '27, Rosebud, Oregon) Pop singer. Partially deaf since childhood; became huge star in early '50s, still popular in UK decades later. It all began '51: LaVern BAKER and her manager Al Green (no relation to the soul singer) helped him with his music; he was signed by Okeh, 'Whiskey And Gin' (written by Ray) was a minor hit; then 'Cry'/'The Little White Cloud That Cried' with the FOUR LADS backing, prod. by Mitch MILLER charted late that year, was no. 1 for 11 weeks, his emotional delivery becoming staple for stand-up comics/mimics. Lots of people hated the record, and there was no better indicator of the death of the BIG BAND ERA, but the emotionalism derived from R&B was something largely lacking in the pop music of the period: that the pop business was then busy shooting itself in the foot was not Ray's fault (*see* ROCK). ('Cry' was written by Churchill Kohlman, later revived by Ray CHARLES '65, Ronnie Dove '66, Lynn ANDERSON '72; 'Cloud' was written by Ray.) He was switched to parent Columbia label and hit with good old songs: 'Please, Mr Sun'/'Here Am I – Brokenhearted' '52 saw both sides in top 10, still with the Four Lads (the latter was written '27 by DeSYLVA, BROWN & HENDERSON); 'Walkin' My Baby Back Home' was jolly no. 4 the same year ('30 song by Fred E. AHLERT and Roy Turk; sung by Donald O'Conner in *Singing In The Rain* '50, also recorded by Nat COLE); 'Somebody Stole My Gal' top 10 '53 ('18 song by Leo Wood, also recorded by Fats WALLER '35); top 20 'Candy Lips' that year was duet with Doris DAY; 'Such A Night' '54 was top 20 (written by Lincoln Chase, also a hit for the DRIFTERS '54, recorded by Elvis PRESLEY '60). Ray had a good role in Irving BERLIN musical film *There's No Business Like Show Business* '54; his delivery of 'Alexander's Ragtime Band' was the best part of long, bizarre production number based on the one song, but his acting was outclassed by the rest of the cast. Of 25 top 30 hits '51-7 the other top tens were 'Just Walking In The Rain' and 'You Don't Owe Me A Thing' '56-7. His only chart LP was top 20 *The Big Beat* '57. Of many hits in UK, duet 'Good Evening Friends'/'Up Above My Head' with Frankie LAINE was top 30 '57, last hit 'I'll Never Fall In Love Again' top 30 '58. Never noted for swing, but a certain power, rasping clarity of voice guaranteed fans.

RAYE, Susan (*b* 8 Oct. '44, Eugene, Ore.) Country singer who became one of the most successful female stars '70s. Sang in high school rock band; auditioned as country vocalist at KWAY Portland, leading to live morning show, afternoon DJ spot, local bookings and regular spot on *Hoedown* TV show. Spotted by Jack McFadden, manager of Buck OWENS, joined Owens' touring show; Capitol contract led to hits, reaching top 10 '70 with 'Willie Jones', many more top 10 hits incl. duets with Owens '70-5. She was also a regular on national TV *Hee-Haw* show. When Owens left Capitol for WB she was without a contract; joined UA and had minor hits, recorded for other smaller labels but faded from charts. Relocated to Texas; LP *Then And Now* '86 on Westexas.

RAZAF, Andy (*b* Andrea Paul Razafkeriefo, 16 Dec. 1895, Washington DC; *d* 3 Feb. '73, North Hollywood, Cal.) Lyricist, descended from royal family of Madagascar. Wrote lyrics for shows *Keep Shufflin'* '28, *Hot Chocolates* '29, *Blackbirds Of 1930*, many other revues and night club floor shows. Most successful collaboration was with Fats WALLER ('Honeysuckle Rose', 'Keepin' Out Of Mischief Now', 'Ain't Misbehavin'', 'Blue, Turning Grey Over You', 'How Can You Face Me', 'The Joint Is Jumpin'', many others), also Don REDMAN ('Gee, Baby, Ain't I Good To You?'), Paul Denniker ('S'posin''), James P. JOHNSON ('A Porter's Love Song To A Chambermaid'), Eubie BLAKE ('Memories Of You'), William Weldon ('I'm Gonna Move To The Outskirts Of Town'). Wrote both words and music for 'That's What I Like About The South', huge novelty hit for Phil HARRIS; also added words to many Swing Era hits/instrumentals incl. 'Reefer Man' '32 (recorded by Redman), 'Knock Me A Kiss' (hit for Gene KRUPA '42), 'Christopher Columbus' (hilarious recording by Waller '36), etc. Recorded as vocalist, often using pseudonyms: with Luis RUSSELL, Fletcher HENDERSON, Rex STEWART, a few records of his own: as Tommy Thompson recorded 'Back In Your Own Back Yard', 'Nobody Knows How Much I Love You' '28 with another singer, a violin and Waller on piano. Had a stroke, was an invalid many years.

RCA International major record label. The Radio Corporation of America entered the record business '29, buying the Victor Talking Machine Company from bankers Seligman & Spayer, later called it RCA Victor, then RCA. Victor was formed '01 by Emile Berliner (inventor of the gramophone; *see* RECORDED SOUND) and engineer Eldridge R. Johnson (who invented a practical springwound motor for home record players, later helped Berliner perfect his gramophone). To pay for expensive patent war with Columbia and Zonophone, Berliner sold the rights to his invention outside the USA to English investors, who formed Gramophone Co. Ltd; for 50 years there were close links between HMV and Victor, which owned part of HMV '20-35. The patent battle was settled by agreeing to pool patents; Columbia began selling discs in USA '01, but Victor soon overtook it as the most important American record company, its Red Seal label (copied from label of HMV's Russian subsidiary) bringing high-class music into many homes: German contralto Ernestine Schumann-Heink, Italian baritone Antonio Scotti, conductor Arturo Toscanini, Philadelphia Orchestra/ Leopold Stokowski all had top 10 hits in the first 20 years of this century, Stokowski until '25; greatest of all was tenor Enrico Caruso: 'Vesti La Giubba' (from *I Pagliacci*), made in Milan by HMV '04, was the first million-seller; he later signed with Victor direct and had more than 40 top 10 hits through '21. Victor also recorded USA presidents from Theodore Roosevelt to Harding, issued the first jazz records (by the ORIGINAL DIXIELAND JAZZ BAND) and was one of the first to record country music and blues (*see* Ralph PEER, Lester MELROSE, etc.). Popular acts incl. Al JOLSON, Gene AUSTIN, Paul WHITEMAN, Fats WALLER. Johnson sold out to bankers '26; with Depression, record sales plummeted; the Camden N.J. factory mostly converted to making radios; Victor dispensed with most of its artists (though many found their way back to the label through the relationship with HMV). After RCA took over, Victor and Bluebird subsidiary dominated the Swing Era, with Waller's greatest fame from '34, as well as Benny GOODMAN, Artie SHAW, Charlie BARNET, Glenn MILLER, Tommy DORSEY (with Frank SINATRA), and from '40-2 covering Duke ELLINGTON's greatest period. To its eternal credit it recorded Dizzy GILLESPIE's big band late '40s; by then pop singers were taking over: Victor had Perry COMO, Vaughn MONROE, Dinah SHORE, adding

Eddie FISHER, Mario LANZA in '50s. But Columbia recovered its early lead; RCA Victor floundered in the '50s, even its technical work appalling (new classical recordings by Toscanini were dreadful compared to the work that was done in Europe, e.g. by Decca). The label had the good fortune to gamble on Elvis PRESLEY late '55, who carried it for many years. In the late '50s RCA was among first to issue stereo records, made good recordings early '60s but fluffed again with 'Dynagroove' sound, designed for its department-store record players at a time when components were becoming big business. The company was lucky to have hits '70s-80s by John DENVER, Rick SPRINGFIELD, Dolly PARTON, HALL & OATES, from the UK SWEET, David BOWIE, EURYTHMICS. RCA still sold country music, was lucky to have Don ROBERTSON, Jim REEVES; but its Nashville slickness (dubbed 'countrypolitan') eventually lost favour in that market. Meanwhile Columbia Pictures (which had nothing to do with Columbia Records/CBS) formed Colpix in NYC, late '60s took over the Bell/Amy/Mala group formed by Larry Utall '64: had success with David Cassidy, the BOX TOPS, Gary GLITTER, BAY CITY ROLLERS; former Columbia (CBS Records) boss Clive DAVIS brought in to run Bell, label name changed to Arista '75; continued hits with Barry MANILOW; Arista acquired '80 by Ariola/Eurodisc subsidiary of Bertelsmann, who had operated in Germany since after WWII. RCA had slipped near the bottom of the global majors (the others being CBS, EMI, WEA, MCA and Polydor), attempted to rectify this by acquiring Ariola/Arista '85 but was then itself taken over by General Electric, who had no use for the record division; EMI tried to buy it from GE but Bertelsmann owned some of it, got control of the rest. RCA was one of the major labels complaining for decades that classical music and jazz don't sell, but whose parent company also owned a nationwide radio/TV network (NBC), which broadcast very little of either, disbanding the NBC Symphony Orchestra as soon as Toscanini retired '55. In previous decades broadcasting was far more varied and far more healthy. As Gene LEES has been writing in his *Jazzletter*, maybe the best thing that could happen to some of the majors would be to become independent

and forced to do some adequate market research. For more details on Victor worldwide and the famous dog and gramophone trademark, *see* HMV.

REBENNACK, Mac (*b* Malcolm Rebennack, 21 Nov. '41, New Orleans, La.) Guitarist, pianist, singer, composer, producer, aka Dr John. Brought up on country music in his father's record shop, took up guitar and became session player on local Ace, Rex, Ebb labels; played on records with Joe TEX, Huey SMITH, PROFESSOR LONGHAIR, Frankie Ford, others; wrote 'Lights Out' for Jerry Byrne, legendary local hit with Art Neville on piano; 'What's Goin' On' for Neville, 'Lady Luck' for Lloyd PRICE (no. 14 pop hit '60), 'Losing Battle' for Johnny Adams (top 30 R&B hit '62 on Ric). Cut instrumental 'Storm Warning' for Rex '59, subsequently recording as Morgus and the Three Ghouls, with Ronnie Barron as Drits and Dravy as well as under his own name, but career suffered from Crow Jim (he was the only white on the circuit). Went to L.A., linked with former employer Harold Battiste, now MD for SONNY & CHER; prod. Jesse Hill, Shirley Goodman (of SHIRLEY & LEE); worked with Hill as the Zu Zu Blues Band on A&M. Signed to Atlantic/Atco as Dr John Creaux the Night Tripper (after Professor Longhair, BEATLES' 'Day Tripper'), recorded mix of voodoo, tongue-in-cheek mumbo jumbo: *Gris Gris* '68 (made on Sonny & Cher studio time) incl. 'Walk On Gilded Splinters', covered by Marsha Hunt, Johnny Jenkins, Humble Pie; *Babylon* '69, *Remedies* '70, *Sun, Moon And Herbs* '71 ploughed similar furrow: Mick Jagger and Eric CLAPTON guested on the last, which made top 200 LPs. *Dr John's Gumbo* '72 (reissued '86 on Alligator's new Rockback series) returned to straight R&B oldies approach, incl. minor hit 'Iko Iko' (covered by Belle Stars, etc.), covers of Longhair, Huey Smith, with all-star N.O. cast incl. Lee ALLEN and Battiste on reeds, Goodman in the chorus, many others. He then linked with Allen TOUSSAINT, backing group the Meters to prod. *In The Right Place* '73 (top 25 LP with no. 9 hit 'Right Place Wrong Time') and *Desitively Bonaroo* '74, anthologised as *I Been Hoodood* '84 on Edsel UK. Also made eponymous LP with shortlived *Triumvirate* '73 on CBS, trio with Mike BLOOMFIELD, John HAMMOND Jr. Left Atlantic, continued to tour and record sporadically; contributed to Van MORRISON's *Period Of Transition* '77, guested on the BAND's film/concert/album *The Last Waltz* '78. Albums on Clean Cuts *Dr John Plays Mac Rebennack* '81 (solo piano) and *The Brightest Smile In Town* (with more vocals) both on Demon/Fiend UK. From flowing robes and makeup as Dr John to tweed jacket and beret, he is a New Orleans legend whatever hat he's wearing.

RECORDED SOUND, history of Sound may have been recorded in 1857 by Léon Scott in France, on a cylinder blackened with smoke, but there was no way to play it back. Thomas Alva Edison (*b* 11 Feb. 1847, Milan, Ohio; *d* 18 Oct. '31, West Orange, N.J.) invented the phonograph in 1877: wrapping tinfoil round a cylinder, he spoke 'Mary had a little lamb' into a diaphragm which caused a stylus to cut a groove of varying depth on the tinfoil (the 'hill and dale' method of recording); a separate stylus and diaphragm was used for playback. Copies could not easily be made; Alexander Graham Bell (*b* 3 Mar. 1847, Edinburgh, Scotland; *d* 2 Aug. '22, Baddeck, Nova Scotia) built a machine which recorded in wax, called the graphophone. Edison thought the machines would be useful for dictation, not thinking of entertainment, but a graphophone company became the world's biggest record label before 1900 (*see* CO-LUMBIA). Émile Berliner (*b* 20 May 1851, Hannover, Germany; *d* 2 Aug. '29, Washington DC) built his gramophone 1887, cutting a laterally modulating groove spiral on a flat record, more practical for mass production and storage of records; it immediately began to overtake Edison's cylinder. (Americans continued to use the word 'phonograph' to describe either kind of record player.) Much research was done into acoustic recording, which required horns of decreasing diameter for recording or increasing diameter for playback, and a stylus/diaphragm assembly (or soundbox) at each end; some remarkable results were obtained, especially with the human voice (a Caruso record was the first millionseller; *see* HMV) but the recording of large ensembles and difficult instruments such as the piano (with all its overtones) was problematic.

Record speeds varied, so that later reissues by famous opera singers were sometimes transferred at the wrong speed, but 78.26 rpm became standard. Sentimental and novelty songs were huge hits: Billy Murray (*b* 25 May 1877, Philadelphia; *d* 17 Aug. '54) had more than 160 hits 1903-26 incl. 'Meet Me In St Louis, Louis' and 'Come Take A Trip In My Air-Ship' '04-5, 'Take Me Out To The Ball Game' '08; he also recorded definitive versions of hit songs by George M. COHAN. Ada Jones (*b* 1 June 1873, Lancashire, UK; *d* 22 May '22) was the most popular female vocalist of the pre-'20 era; she had over 60 solo hits and 44 hit duets with Murray ('Come, Josephine, In My Flying Machine' '11, backed by a quartet); vocal groups were also big, the Peerless and Haydn Quartets both having hits with 'Sweet Adeline' '04. Jones also did duets with Len Spencer (*b* 12 Feb. 1867, Washington DC; *d* 15 Dec. '14), whose solo hits incl. 'All Coons Look Alike To Me' (not as racist as it sounds: *see* RAGTIME). All these were among the top 100 best-selling artists of 1890-1954 (so says *Pop Memories* '86; *see* CHARTS): Bing CROSBY was no. 1, but Murray was no. 5, Jones 33. The first blues record was made '20 by Mamie SMITH, the first COUNTRY MUSIC '22-3 by old-time fiddlers, and the first JAZZ was recorded '17 by the ORIGINAL DIXIELAND JAZZ BAND, but more importantly by King OLIVER '23. Guglielmo Marconi (*b* 25 Apr. 1874, Bologna, Italy; *d* 20 July '37, Rome) patented wireless telegraphy in 1900; Lee De Forest (*b* 26 Aug. 1873, Council Bluffs, Iowa; *d* 30 June '61, Hollywood) invented the triode '06, which could amplify a weak signal: vacuum tubes made broadcasting possible (called valves in UK, because that's what they are: allowing alternating current in one direction, but not the other); when music was broadcast, musicians spoke of 'De Forest's prime evil'; but he also invented the soundtrack method used in talking films, creating much work for musicians. Attempts to develop electrical methods of recording using telephone and broadcasting technology began c.'15, interrupted by WWI; in '24 the Western Electric method was successful, adopted '25 by virtually all record labels: a microphone converted the sound to an electric signal which drove the recording stylus; Louis ARMSTRONG and his

Hot Five recorded this way and Crosby soon used the microphone in a style that seemed personal to each individual listener, and modern pop music began. Many home record players were still acoustic, but yielding better sound with electrical recordings. Edison made flat discs with hill-and-dale grooves from '13; some gramophones had changeable soundboxes for the two types of flat disc; Edison made both discs and cylinders until '29 for owners of his machines. Early electric playback pickups (cartridges) were magnetic and very heavy, wire wrapped around an armature converting the groove's squiggle to an electrical signal; lighter ceramic pick-ups became standard: the piezo-electric effect causes certain materials to become electrically polarised under pressure; ceramic cartridges are still used today in cheap record players (the principle is also used in cigarette lighters). Records made of powdered slate mixed with shellac wore out quickly under heavy tracking pressures; most 'needles' were made of steel and had to be changed often; cactus or bamboo styli were kinder to discs but gave a weaker sound and had to be sharpened after every play. Before WWII smaller, lighter magnetic cartridges were made by the Germans, who also developed tape recording. Valdemar Poulson (*b* 23 Nov. 1869, Copenhagen; *d* '42) made the first magnetic recordings on wire in 1898; steel tape was also used but by the mid-'30s the first modern magnetic tape of plastic coated with iron oxide was made in Germany: pre-war tapes of complete opera performances were later transferred to LP. The first 'binaural' recordings were made '33 by EMI, using separate tracks on the record, a two-headed tone-arm playing both at once; they were not commercially issued. Meanwhile some record companies had cut two 78 masters of each recording in case one went wrong, and HMV and Victor for some reason used separate microphones as early as '29; in '84 collectors discovered that two versions of the same take when combined yielded stereo: LP *Reflections In Ellington* on Everybodys (USA) incl. stereo medleys by the Duke ELLINGTON band from '32. Edison had made cylinders with the grooves closer together (easily done with hill-and-dale grooves), an early 'long-playing' record; the Ellington medleys were examples of a Vic-

tor long-playing record which failed commercially because it was essentially a 78 slowed down to 33 rpm: the doubled playing time did not compensate for higher surface noise. After WWII Dr Peter GOLD-MARK of CBS Labs perfected the modern long-playing microgroove disc made of PVC (polyvinylchloride) while RCA introduced the microgroove 45, and the 'battle of the speeds' began; 78s became obsolete (BEATLE 78s were made in India as late as '66). Wartime research in electronics meant great advances in sound quality; record companies switched to tape for master recordings, also making editing of recordings possible for the first time; it was soon apparent that there was better sound on the record than home record players were capable of reproducing: for one thing, records sounded better over the radio because broadcasters could afford studio-quality playback gear. Veterans trained in electronics began to build their own, and 'high fidelity' was born. Good sound was measured three ways: dynamic range (soft to loud), frequency range (about 20 to 20,000 cycles per second defined as hi-fi) and definition (ability to distinguish among sounds). But there were no guidelines in consumer goods, and a lot of department-store junk was labelled as hi-fi. Modern magnetic cartridges were essential to good sound, but the signal (though higher in quality) was weaker than that from a ceramic pick-up, requiring a pre-amp stage in the playback system. Edgar Villchur invented the acoustic suspension loudspeaker in the early '50s, in which the speakers are sealed in an airtight cabinet, the cushion of air behind them making low-frequency reproduction possible in a 'bookshelf' speaker system: record players had never included much in the way of wide-range tone controls because there was no point; solid bass had been available only from speakers in very large tuned cabinets for which most people simply didn't have room. Recording characteristics were standardised in the '50s: low frequencies are attenuated in manufacturing records because the grooves cannot store them and they are restored in playback, called compensation, or equalisation; each record industry did this differently until the RIAA (Record Industry Association of America) standard made things easier for designers of quality amplifiers. But hi-fi remained an expensive luxury until the solid-state era and the rise of the Japanese electronics industry provided quality record-playing equipment that most people could afford. Crystals had converted alternating current to direct current in early radios, but De Forest's vacuum tube was better at the time; then it was discovered that germanium crystals containing certain impurities were better still: transisters were invented at Bell Labs '48; they lasted longer than tubes and did not generate as much heat; they won a Nobel Prize for their inventors in '56; by then all-transister radios were available in the USA (for about $50) and transisters were being rapidly improved. Pre-recorded four-track stereo tapes were issued commercially by EMI in the mid-'50s; attempts to develop stereo records included combining lateral and hill-and-dale motion in the same groove, but this would have meant mono records could not be played by the new pick-ups. A Westrex 45/45 system engraved separate stereo information on each wall of a standard groove; stereo records were introduced '58, successful even though they required a new cartridge, the equivalent of two amplifiers and another speaker. Mono recording had reached a very high standard; engineers now had to learn how to do it all over again for stereo, and the public at large did not understand that a good mono recording was better than two low-fi stereo channels: the Count BASIE LP *The Atomic Mr Basie*, made in Oct. '57 in NYC, was an exceptionally fine mono record, but the wretched experimental stereo edition was the only one available for years until PRT UK reissued the mono in '84. Ersatz 'electronic' stereo reissues of older records became common; a stereo illusion could be created by dividing the frequency range across the stereo channels, but most record companies did it by adding distortion to the original master in the form of echo or out-of-phase elements. In '63 the Philips four-track tape cassette was introduced, the Lear 8-track continuous-loop cartridge in '65 was less successful. Recording technology gained from research into lower signal-to-noise ratios for cassettes, a milestone being the Dolby process: first used on master tapes, then in cassette decks, this was a new kind of compensation, raising the volume of

quiet high-frequency passages during recording, then lowering them during playback, reducing tape hiss. (Sales of cassettes passed that of LPs in '83 in the USA, in '87 in the UK.) Quadrophonic sound was introduced early '70s, the idea being that speakers placed behind the listener would reproduce the ambience of the room in which the recording was made; it failed dismally. In the late '60s-70s recording technology was over-used, with too many microphones and too much mixing of master tapes often resulting in grossly unrealistic recordings in both classical and popular genres; digital recording and the compact disc (introduced by Sony and Philips '82) means that producers have to be more careful, and renders dolby and similar processes redundant. For various reasons, the analogue recording process incl. a certain minimum of distortion; in digital recording the signal is broken into billions of tiny bits which represent only the music: playback by means of a laser beam bypasses most sources of distortion, mercilessly revealing any gimmickry in recording technique. Reissue of vintage material in the past was often badly done, but standards are very high now: RCA's LPV reissue series of vintage pop and jazz in the '60s was a model of its kind. John R. T. Davies, a musician who worked for EMI for many years, has overseen many fine reissues incl. classic jazz on the UK Hep label, dubbing only clean copies of original 78s onto master tape. (Hep's reissue series of Don REDMAN has been held up for want of a good copy of one of the records.) Among the best analogue reissues are those by Mosaic Records, who have gone back to Blue Note originals as early as '39. Digital reissue of analogue masters, both classical and popular, is being done well, and often uses the extended playing time of CDs by adding extra tracks from original tapes: Lester Koenig's classic Sonny ROLLINS album *Way Out West* on Contemporary, made in '57, is on CD as *Way Out West Plus*: 70 minutes of prime Rollins, sounding better than ever. Recordings for Blue Note and Prestige made since the '50s by Rudy Van Gelder have come up fresh as paint on CD (they were made without any mixing or editing in most cases, giving the lie to studio gimmickry endemic today), as have EMI's restoration of classic Capitol albums by Frank

SINATRA, Nat COLE etc.; CD reissues of Beatle and ROLLING STONES albums were immediately hits, all this giving a needed shot in the arm to the industry. Direct-cut 78s can be greatly improved by the digital process, which is an incredibly efficient filtering device; English-born Australian engineer Robert Parker issues compilations of early jazz on CD (in UK on BBC Records), dubbing original 78s directly onto digital tape; much of his work is astonishing ('Someday Sweetheart' '26 by King OLIVER; 'Stompy Jones' and 'Live And Love Tonight' '34 by Ellington), but he added phoney stereo ambience to the original sound, often resulting in echo (distortion). Dennis Ferrante and Edward Rich remastered 'American Patrol' '42 by Glenn MILLER for Woody Allen's *Radio Days* soundtrack (on RCA's Novus label): the rhythm guitar, the reed section's baritone sax etc. can be clearly heard for the first time. RCA issued vintage material (Miller, Ellington) on CD, got off to a shaky start: initial transfers were botched, sounding no better than the 20-year-old Vintage series; it was being done again '87 in Germany. RCA's CD '87 of Toscanini's Beethoven Ninth Symphony (made in '52) was a triumph. The industry was suspicious of CD at first, remembering the quad fiasco; the first CD factory outside Japan (Sony) and Hamburg (Philips) was built in the UK by Nimbus, an independent classical company tired of quality-control problems with LPs; they improved the laser mastering process, cut pressing time by more than half and won a Queen's Award for Technology; they stopped making LPs '85. The market was difficult in '87 for small independents who could not afford to issue CDs, but CD was a spectacular success: worldwide production shortfall ended, prices were expected to come down; few new classical records were being issued on LP in USA. USA record companies shipped eight million CDs in '83, 53 million in '86; other figures (net after returns): in '76 USA industry shipped 190m singles, 273m LPs/EPs, 21.8m cassettes and 106m 8-track cartridges; in '86 100m singles, 125m LPs/EPs, 344.5m cassettes, 1.7m cartridges (RIAA statistics). New products '87 incl. DAT (digital audio tape) and new CD formats (singles smaller in diameter and discs combining music and video).

RECTOR, Red (*b* William Eugene Rector, 15 Dec. '29, Marshall, N.C.) One of country music's top mandolin players, in demand for sessions and on bluegrass circuit. School in Asheville, N.C.; worked as dental lab technician, door-to-door salesman; appeared on WWNC Radio in Asheville '45-6, then WPTF in Raleigh, where he met Chet ATKINS and JOHNNIE & JACK: sessions for RCA followed; he joined Johnnie & Jack full-time, worked on WNOX Knoxville and MCYB Bristol (Va.). Played with such bluegrass outfits as Charlie Monroe's Kentucky Pardners, Bill Clifton, FLATT & Scruggs; played on hundreds of recording sessions '50s-60s. By the early '70s he took centre stage at many a bluegrass or folk festival. LPs incl. *Are You From Dixie* '77 on Bear Family (with Clifton), *Red Rector . . . And Friends* '79 on Revonah.

REDBONE Rock band formed c.'68 in L.A. by four American Indians: brothers/vocalists Lolly (guitar), Pat Vegas (bass), Anthony Bellamy on rhythm guitar, and Peter De Poe (aka Last Walking Bear) on drums. De Poe had been a ceremonial drummer on a reservation in Washington state; he was replaced '74 by Butch Rillera. The others had all done session work; the Lollys wrote 'Niki Hoeky', top 30 hit '67 by P. J. PROBY. The name of the group was from 'rehbon', Cajun slang for half-breed; their style of soulful rock resembled that of CREEDENCE CLEARWATER; they were better songwriters than vocalists, had three top 40 hits: 'Maggie' '70, 'The Witch Queen Of New Orleans' '71, top 5 'Come And Get Your Love' '74 (their most successful vocal). LPs on Epic began with *Redbone*; then *Potlatch* '70, *Message From A Drum* '72, *Woyoka* '74, *Beaded Dreams Through Turquoise Eyes* '74 all charted; *Come And Get Your Redbone* was best-of; *Cycles* '78 was flop comeback on RCA.

REDBONE, Leon Singer; a gruff-voiced true urban folkie, specialising in vintage pop songs that have entered the collective consciousness, effectively becoming 'folk' songs. Always described as 'mysterious' (perhaps he gives no interviews). He looks like Groucho Marx; if impelled, he will impersonate a tuba. Began in Toronto c.'70; Bonnie RAITT and Maria MULDAUR championed him; Bob DYLAN said mid-'70s that Redbone would be first signing to Dylan's new Ashes & Sand label (which didn't happen). Album *On The Track* '76 featured Don McLEAN on banjo, incl. 'Polly Wolly Doodle' (minstrel song from 1883), Fats WALLER's 'Ain't Misbehavin' ', Hoagy CARMICHAEL's 'Lazybones'; *Double Time* '77 incl. 'Winin' Boy Blues' by Jelly Roll MORTON, 'Nobody's Sweetheart', etc.; *Champagne Charlie* '78 was more of the same. Switched from WB to Atco/Emerald City for *From Branch To Branch* '81, incl. Hank WILLIAMS' 'Your Cheatin' Heart', Jiminy Cricket's 'When You Wish Upon A Star'. Some critics liked first LP, then decided it was all a joke; nevertheless all charted, the second reaching top 40: there is something about repertory music that confuses pop/rock critics, always looking for something new; listeners can decide for themselves. *Red To Blue* '86 on August label incl. guests the Roches, Mac REBENNACK, Hank WILLIAMS Jr; *No Regrets* '88 is on Sugar Hill.

REDDING, Otis (*b* 9 Sep. '41, Dawson, Ga.; *d* 10 Dec. '67, Madison, Wis.) Soul singer; perhaps the greatest of male soul singers, the most popular black act of his time except for James BROWN, and a fine songwriter as well. Infl. by LITTLE RICHARD and Sam COOKE; early record 'Shout Bamalama' was in Richard style; worked in band Johnny Jenkins and the Pinetoppers in Macon (Richard's home town), drove Jenkins to recording session at then-new Stax label in Memphis: in one of those happy accidents that made the Stax label and sparked off Southern soul, the session did not go well and Redding was recorded at the tail end of it: first release was his own 'These Arms Of Mine', top 20 R&B hit '63: had 15 R&B hits during his lifetime, most in the top 10; the first record also reached the pop Hot 100 and he continued to cross over, but rarely into the top 40. He had hits with the ROLLING STONES' 'Satisfaction' '66, Cooke's 'Shake' '67; co-wrote own hits incl. 'Mr Pitiful' '65 (with Stax guitarist Steve Cropper), 'I've Been Loving You Too Long (To Stop Now)' (with Jerry BUTLER); wrote 'Respect' '65, an even bigger hit by Aretha FRANKLIN '67. His appearance at the Monterey Pop Festival '67 was an in-

tense experience for largely white audience, captured on film, in LP *Otis Redding/Jimi Hendrix Experience* on Reprise; festival inspired the beautiful '(Sittin' On The) Dock Of The Bay' (co-written with Cropper), which reached no. 1 early '68 in both pop/R&B charts, but on the way to a gig his plane had crashed in the icy waters of one of Madison's lakes, also killing four members of his backing group the Bar-Kays. Albums incl. *Pain In My Heart* on Atco, *Otis Blue* on Volt '65; *Dictionary Of Soul* '66, *King And Queen* (duets with Carla THOMAS incl. hit 'Tramp'), *The Soul Album* and *Live In Europe* '67, all on Stax; 2-disc *Best Of* on Atlantic, *Recorded Live* released '82 on Atlantic, 2-disc *The Legend Of* '86 on Pair.

REDDY, Helen (*b* 25 Oct. '42, Melbourne, Australia) Singer. A favourite on FM radio while pop music went through sedate period, she had 14 top 40 hits in USA '71-7. From show business family, made stage debut at 4, left school at 15; work with travelling show led to TV series; won talent contest '66 and prize was trip to USA. Met booking agent Jerry Wald NYC, married him; had TV exposure; first top 20 hit was 'I Don't Know How To Love Him' from *Jesus Christ Superstar*. Her own composition 'I Am Woman' made no. 1 '72 (was adopted by burgeoning women's movement); other chart-toppers were 'Delta Dawn' '73, 'Angie Baby' '74. Made top 20 LPs *I Am Woman* '72, *Long Hard Climb* '73, *Love Song For Jeffrey* and *Free And Easy* '74, *No Way To Treat A Lady* and *Greatest Hits* '75, *Music, Music* '76. LP *Ear Candy* '77 might have been named after FM programming she was (perhaps unfairly) identified with; only made no. 75. As big hits stopped she also worked as TV actress. Heard on film soundtrack *Pete's Dragon* '77.

REDMAN, Dewey (*b* 17 May '31, Fort Worth, Texas) Reeds, composer, teacher. Played in high school marching band with Ornette COLEMAN, Charles Moffett, Prince LASHA. Plays mostly tenor and alto saxes; the master of his instruments, he can play 'inside' or 'outside', uses ethnic elements incl. playing Arabian double-reed musette. Degree in Education '59; went to West

Coast, worked with Pharoah SANDERS, Wes MONTGOMERY, others; to NYC '67, played in Coleman's group until '74. Records with Coleman, Charlie HADEN's Liberation Music Orchestra, Carla BLEY, Roswell RUDD, Keith JARRETT (incl. *The Survivors' Suite* '77 on ECM); with Haden, Don CHERRY, Ed BLACKWELL as Old And New Dreams on ECM. His own records incl. *Look For The Black Star* '66 on Freedom/Arista, *Tarik* '69 on Byg/Affinity, an unissued '69 Blue Note session, *The Ear Of The Behearer* '73 and *Coincide* '74 on Impulse, *Musics* and *Soundsigns* '78 on Galaxy, *Red And Black In Willisau* '80 on Black Saint with Blackwell, *The Struggle Continues* '82 on ECM.

REDMAN, Don (*b* Donald Matthew Redman, 29 July 1900, Piedmont, W. Va.; *d* 30 Nov. '64, NYC) Reeds, vocals, bandleader, arranger, composer. Son of a music teacher; could play any wind instrument by age 12. Studied at conservatories; to NYC '23, joined Fletcher HENDERSON as arr., saxophonist. Invented jazz writing for the big band, not only writing separate parts for reed and brass 'choirs', leaving room for hot solos, but putting sections in opposition: solved the problems of the new style, showing everyone else how to do it. He wrote virtually all of Henderson's arrangements as it became the band to beat. Hoagy CARMICHAEL was an admirer; legend has it that Redman gave Carmichael advice, and may have written the lovely introduction to 'Stardust': he was certainly among the first to record it, two years before it had lyrics. Left Henderson '27 to be mus. dir. of MCKINNEY'S COTTON PICKERS, made it the most popular band in the Midwest; recorded his own pretty tune 'Cherry' twice in '28, once with Cotton Pickers (vocal by Jean Napier) and without vocal with pick-up group incl. T. & J. DORSEY, Jack TEAGARDEN and other stars; led two Chocolate Dandies freelance record sessions '28 (incl. 'Stardust') and '29. On Nov. '29 Cotton Pickers dates he used Henderson sidemen, sang his own 'Gee Baby, Ain't I Good To You?', slyly intimate, half conversational vocals also on 'Miss Hannah', 'Wherever There's A Will, Baby' (with fine solo by Coleman HAWKINS) and 'The Way I Feel Today' (exceptionally fine Fats WALLER

comping behind vocal). Formed own band '31, taking several Cotton Pickers and taking over a Horace HENDERSON group for a gig (early records labelled 'Harlan LATTIMORE and his Connie's Inn Orchestra'. Often had fine soloists: Benny MORTON, Harold BAKER; always Bob Ysaguirre on tuba, then bass (*b* 1897, British Honduras; *d* '82, NYC), but emphasis was on writing, as in Cotton Pickers: he wrote difficult stuff, was good teacher; tricky passages became well known among musicians (cf. reed chorus in 'Tea For Two', trombone in 'I Got Rhythm'). Recorded his theme 'Chant Of The Weed' '31, '40 (and later arranged it for Duke ELLINGTON). In '31 he was the only black bandleader to have his own radio show, sponsored by a soap maker. Invented the 'swing choir': the band sang paraphrase of the words to a counter-melody, often with soloist playing straight melody, using this device '37 on 'Exactly Like You' and 'Sunny Side Of The Street', several years before Sy OLIVER's similar version of 'Street' for T. Dorsey. Redman did as much as anyone to bring about the Swing Era (*see* BIG BAND ERA); with hot tunes ('Nagasaki', 'Hot and Anxious'); novelties and patter vocals ('I Heard', 'Reefer Man', later 'I Got Ya', 'About Rip Van Winkle') made some of the most charming records of '30s under own name. Gave up band '40; fronted other bands (Jay MCSHANN '42). Toured Europe '46 with band incl. Don BYAS, Billy TAYLOR, effectively introducing post-war style to Europe (2-disc concert set *For Europeans Only* on Steeplechase). Wrote freelance (e.g. 'Just An Old Manuscript' for BASIE, '49). From '51 mus. dir. for Pearl BAILEY; played policeman in Harold ARLEN show *House Of Flowers* '54. Made two LPs of big band sides in July '57, some with Hawkins. Happily married to Peetney for more than 30 years. Redman's records and broadcasts provided Gil EVANS with his first lessons in arranging; later he showed Robert FARNON how to lay out a score: his influence is impossible to exaggerate. Compilations of classic sides incl. *Don Redman* '32-7 on CBS UK; *Don Redman – Master Of The Big Band* in RCA Vintage series, 8 tracks by Cotton Pickers '28-30, 8 by '38-40 band: both albums out of print; French RCA complete Cotton Pickers has a lot of

Redman; new series on UK Hep label has complete Redman sides from '31 with good transfers by John R. T. Davies, notes by Frank Driggs: lovely period pop as well as jazz classics.

REDPATH, Jean (*b* 28 Apr. '37, Edinburgh, Scotland) Traditional folksinger, who does children's songs, English and Scottish ballads, bluegrass, etc. Emigrated to USA '61, played at Gerde's Folk City NYC, got good review in *New York Times*; was teaching at Wesleyan U. late '70s. Albums incl. *Skipping Barefoot Through The Heather* on Prestige International; *Scottish Ballad Book*, *Songs Of Love, Lilt And Laughter* and *Laddie Lie Near Me*, all on Elektra; then *Frae My Ain Country* '73 on Folk Legacy. To Philo label: *Jean Redpath* '75 followed by *Shout For Joy* with Lisa Neustadt; five vols. of songs by Robert Burns; *Father Adam*, *Lowlands* and *Lady Nairne* '86, all with Abby Newton. Also *Angels Hovering 'Round* (with the Angel Band), *Anywhere Is Home* on Fretless, both with Neustadt. Keeps many fans happy by remaining faithful to what she does best.

RED RIVER DAVE (*b* Dave McEnery, 15 Dec. '14, San Antonio, Texas) Cowboy singer. Worked Texas rodeo circuit; took up singing and landed radio shows on WPHR (Petersburg, Va.) '35-6, WQAM (Miami) '36-7 and WOR (NYC) '38-41. Led group the Swift Cowboys, recorded for Decca, Savoy, Music-Craft, Sonora, Continental. During the war he scored with patriotic ditties 'I'd Like To Give My Dog To Uncle Sam' and 'It's For God And Country And You Mom'. To Hollywood; became singing cowboy in such films as *Swing In The Saddle* '48, *Hidden Valley Days* and *Echo Ranch* '49, plus more than 20 film shorts. Back to Texas late '40s, appeared on WOAI-TV San Antonio for ten years. Tempted out of retirement early '60s to record for Bluebonnet, also appeared on Radio KBER San Antonio '66-7. LPs incl. *Red River Dave* '52 on Continental, *Red River Dave* Vols. 1 & 2 on Bluebonnet '67-8.

REECE, Dizzy (*b* Alphonso Son Reece, 5 Jan. '31, Kingston, Jamaica) Trumpet. Father played piano for silent films. Began on baritone horn at 11; to Europe '48, London

'54, USA '59. English quintet recordings on Tempo '55-8 with Ronnie SCOTT, Tubby HAYES, etc. Blue Note LPs: *Blues In Trinity* '58, made in London with Hayes, Donald BYRD; *Star Bright* '59 with Hank MOBLEY, quartet *Soundin' Off* '60 made in NYC. *Asia Minor* '62 on Prestige `with Joe Farrell, Cecil PAYNE; *From In To Out* '70 on Futura with John Gilmore (made in Paris); sextet *Possession, Exorcism, Peace* mid-'70s on Honey Dew, *Manhattan Project* '78 on Bee Hive with Clifford JORDAN and *Blowin' Away* with Ted CURSON on Interplay, both '78, latter on Discovery as *Moose The Mooche*. A post-bop stylist with unique voice, admired by Dizzy GILLESPIE: played in Gillespie big band '68, Paris Reunion Band '85; on Duke JORDAN Blue Note LP *Flight To Jordan* '60, etc.

REED, Jerry (*b* Jerry Hubbard, 20 Mar. '37, Atlanta, Ga.) Nashville session guitarist, singer, songwriter. Played in country bands from teens, worked in cotton mills, played at night in Atlanta honky tonks; discovered by prod. Bill Lowery, recorded for Capitol '55, wrote 'Crazy Legs' (recorded by Gene VINCENT), others recorded by Brenda LEE ('That's All You Gotta Do' '60), eventually had 18 BMI awards for songs. After US Army service '59-61 moved to Nashville, recorded for Columbia, became session player, signed with RCA '65: first country hit 'Guitar Man' '67 became his nickname, covered by Elvis PRESLEY '68 (top 20 UK), who had top 30 USA hit same year with Reed's 'U.S. Male'. Reed was regular on Glen CAMPBELL's TV show '70-1, also on *Hee-Haw*, others, revealing a gift for comedy; made films with Burt Reynolds *W.W. And The Dixie Dance Kings* '74, *Gator* '76, *Smokey And The Bandit* '77, *Bandit II* '80; starred with Claude Atkins in TV series *Nashville 99*; moved into film and video production, directed *What Comes Around* '84, made in Nashville. Meanwhile LPs crossed to pop chart: *Cookin'* '70 made pop top 200, *Georgia Sunshine* '71 almost made top 100 (title track and 'Amos Moses' both top 20 country hits, the latter top 10 pop), then *When You're Hot, You're Hot* no. 45 LP, title track no. 1 country, top 10 pop. Lesser chart LPs '71-3 were *KoKo Joe*, *Smell The Flowers, Best Of Jerry Reed, Lord, Mr Ford* (title track another country no. 1).

Duet LP *Me And Jerry* '71 with Chet AT-KINS won a Grammy, followed by *Me And Chet* '72. Other RCA LPs: *Alabama Wild Man* '68, *Better Things In Life* '69, *Hot A' Mighty* '73, *The Uptown Poker Club* '74, *Mind Your Love* '75, *Red Hot Picker* '76, *Sings Jim Croce* '80, *Dixie Dreams* '81, many more incl. *The Bird, East Bound, Texas Bound And Flyin'*; *Lookin' At You* on Capitol '86. Hits and film career have obscured his excellent playing; early tracks such as 'Georgia On My Mind' show jazz infl. often found in the best country pickers.

REED, Jimmy (*b* Mathis James Reed, 6 Sep. '25, Dunleith, Ms.; *d* 29 Aug. '76, Oakland, Cal.) Blues singer, songwriter; played guitar and harmonica. Signed with Vee Jay in Chicago, had 13 infl. R&B hits '55-61 (12 crossovers to pop Hot 100, '57-63) incl. 'Baby, What You Want Me To Do' (covered by Elvis PRESLEY) and 'Honest I Do' (covered by Aretha FRANKLIN, ROLLING STONES), both top 40 pop; came back to R&B chart '66 on Exodus with 'Knocking At Your Door'. An influential stylist whose laid-back work avoided the menace and dread of some other bluesmen, he was one of the first to use a neck mount so that he could play harp and guitar at the same time. His wife Mary Lee 'Mama' Reed wrote many of his songs. LPs incl. *I'm Jimmy Reed* '57, also *Rockin' With Reed, Now Appearing, Best Of* and *Live At Carnegie Hall* (last two combined in 2-disc set and on one Suite Beat CD), compilation *The Legend, The Man* ('53-64 tracks), all on Vee Jay. Also *Compact Command Performances* on a Motown CD, *Cold Chills* on Antilles ('67-70 tracks, on Krazy Kat in K), *Jimmy Reed* on Archive Of Folk and *Wailin' The Blues* on Tradition; in UK: *Boogie In The Dark* on Blue Moon, *Shame Shame Shame* on Krazy Kat, *I'm The Man (Down There)* and *Upside Your Head* on Charly, latter with the R&B hits. Steve MILLER LP *Living In The 20th Century* '86 is partly a tribute to Reed. He had suffered from epilepsy since '57 and died in his sleep.

REED, Lou (*b* Louis Firbank, 2 Mar. '44, NYC) Singer, songwriter, guitarist; came to fame as founder member of the VELVET UNDERGROUND '65-70 after studying poetry and journalism at Syracuse (NY) U. De-parture from Velvets during sessions for *Loaded* was acrimonious; after a period of hibernation he distanced himself from NYC scene which until then had fuelled his writing muse; went to England to make *Lou Reed* '72: UK sessionmen Steve Howe, Rick Wakeman (both YES), others too smooth to be convincing; Reed's customary venom lost. *Transformer* '72 made up in feeling what it lacked in slick playing: prod. by David BOWIE and his guitarist Mick Ronson, both longtime fans, it had decadence written all over it: ode to transexual pleasure 'Walk On The Wild Side' was a shock no. 10 UK/16 USA hit, despite line about 'giving head' that the censors missed; back cover saw female image staring back at Reed out of a mirror, while 'Make Up' struck a chord with growing gay lib movement. *Berlin* '73 prod. by ALICE COOPER's Bob Ezrin bore signs of Cooper's over-the-top shock rock: totally lacking self-mocking humour of *Transformer*, concept LP about ill-fated relationship of two drug addicts, failed to sell, is now seen as lost masterpiece. Disillusioned by critical/public non-acceptance of *Berlin*, Reed went heavy metal for live *Rock'n'Roll Animal* '74 (revamped versions of old hits sold well) and disco-fied *Sally Can't Dance* '74. After *Lou Reed Live* '75, concert set of similar vintage to *Animal*, he made perverse 2-disc set of white noise called *Metal Machine Music* '75: contender for least listenable to album ever won release from RCA contract after surprisingly warm *Coney Island Baby* '76 (stand-out tracks incl. title song, 'Charley's Girl'). LPs for Arista lacked originality (*Rock And Roll Heart* '76, live *Take No Prisoners* and *Street Hassle* '78, *The Bells* '79) with the exception of title track 'Street Hassle', tale of drug OD victim later covered by Simple Minds. Second marriage '80 revitalised the muse: collaborated with keyboardist Michael Fonfara on *Growing Up In Public* '80; *Blue Mask* '81 saw return of lyrical edge; *Legendary Hearts* '83 brought Richard HELL and ex-Voidoids guitarist Robert Quine on board; he resumed touring, released fine slice of '80s rock in *New Sensations* '84 that spawned deserved hit single in 'I Love You Suzanne'. *Mistral* '86 was not reviewed as enthusiastically. He lost credibility by advertising Honda motorcycles (sponsored by Honda on tour), but looked better than any once drug-obsessed '60s survivor deserved to. Admirers incl. Bowie, SPRINGSTEEN, etc.; at its best his narrative songwriting is harrowing, and certainly unique.

REESE, Della (*b* Dellareese Taliaferro, 6 July '31, Detroit, Mich.) Pop/soul singer with big beautiful voice who began in her teens as a gospel singer with Mahalia JACKSON troupe. Recorded for Jubilee, had no. 12 hit 'And That Reminds Me' '57, further Hot 100 entry with 'Sermonette' (Cannonball ADDERLEY tune with words by Jon HENDRICKS); switched to RCA, hit with 'Don't You Know' (no. 2), 'Not One Minute More' (no. 16), both '59; several more lesser hits through '61. Chart LPs on RCA were *Della* '60 (top 40), *Special Delivery* '61, best-of *Classic Della* '62; came back to charts on ABC '65-6 with minor hit singles, LP *Della Reese Live* with Bill DOGGETT, Shelly MANNE. She was well-liked, influential; said to be Martha REEVES' favourite singer; continued popular in clubs. Other LPs: *Della* on Déjà Vu; *Della By Starlight* on RCA International; *Della Della Cha Cha Cha* on RCA reissued '87 in UK; *I Like It Like Dat* on Jasmine, *Sure Like Lovin' You* on President, *Something Cool* on Allegiance; tracks from an LP on Applause c.'82 reissued on Dunhill CD *Jazzy Ladies* '87 (other tracks by Carmen MCRAE, Lena HORNE).

REEVES, Del (*b* Franklin Delano Reeves, 14 July '33, Sparta, N.C.) Country singer, songwriter, entertainer and multi-instrumentalist with big success '65 through '70s. A child star on local radio '45-7, attended Appalachian State College in Boone, served in WSAF, worked at radio WTOP in Galax, Va. '56, moved to West Coast and became regular on Chester Smith TV show in Sacramento, Cal. '58-61. Moved to Nashville and signed with Decca; had top 10 hit 'Be Quiet Mind'; had lesser hits as the first country singer on Frank SINATRA's Reprise label, then Columbia; meanwhile he also wrote hits for Roy DRUSKY, Sheb WOOLEY, Carl SMITH; switched to UA and reached no. 1 with his first release, 'The Girl On The Billboard' '65. Other top 10 hits incl. 'Looking At The World Through A Windshield' and

'Goodtime Charlies' '68, 'Be Glad' '69. He had become a superb showman, touring more than 230 days a year, always giving an audience a good show; named his band the Goodtime Charlies. Joined the GRAND OLE OPRY '66, appeared in films such as *Second Fiddle To A Steel Guitar* '66, *Forty Acre Feud* '67; had syndicated TV show *Del Reeves' Country Carnival*; 'The Philadelphia Phillies' went top 10 '71 and he continued charting, but less strongly; also had duet hits with Bobby GOLDSBORO '68-9, Penny DeHaven '70-1, Billie Jo SPEARS '76; left UA '79 when his hits dried up. Among many LPs there were about seven in '65-8 alone, all now out of print; followed by *Greatest Hits* '80 on Starday, *Del Reeves* '81 on Koala incl. late hit 'Slow Hand' '81.

REEVES, Dianne (*b* '56, Detroit, Mich.) Jazz singer with lovely contralto, 3.5 octave range. Grew up in Denver, sang 'That's All' at 16 with Gene HARRIS, discovered at 17 by Clark TERRY, sang with his band; worked with Colorado Symphony, studied at U. of Colorado, moved to L.A., worked with Sergio MENDEZ, Harry BELAFONTE, others; sensation at Monterey Jazz Festival backed by Tito PUENTE; recorded with Stanley TURRENTINE, George DUKE etc. LPs *For Every Heart* and *Welcome To My Love* on Palo Alto; Blue Note debut *Dianne Reeves* '87 incl. Jerome KERN standard 'Yesterdays', 'I Got It Bad And That Ain't Good' by Duke ELLINGTON, uptempo 'That's All' with scat choruses (written '52 by Alan Brandt and Bob Haymes; recorded by Nat COLE); new tunes incl. 'Chan's Song (Never Said)' by Herbie HANCOCK and Stevie WONDER and her own co-written 'Better Days' and 'Sky Islands'. With her regular trio of Billy Childs on piano, Tony Dumas on bass, Ralph Penland on drums, many guests incl. Stanley CLARKE, Freddie HUBBARD, Hancock, Duke, Tony WILLIAMS; almost overproduced by Duke (synclavier strings on two tracks), an auspicious major label debut by a fine voice.

REEVES, Jim (*b* 20 Aug. '24, Galloway, Texas; *d* 31 July '64, Tenn.) The first big country crossover artist, and one of the most popular of all time. He removed the sound of steel guitar and fiddles from his music and created a pop-country style which scored international hits. Played baseball at U. of Texas, then with St Louis Cardinals, but leg injury stopped sports career; became DJ and newsreader at KGRI, Henderson, Texas; recorded for Macy in Houston, moved to Shreveport, La., became announcer at KWKH and soon a performer on *Louisiana Hayride*. Signed with Abbott and scored no. 1 country hit with second release, 'Mexican Joe' '53, followed by no. 2 'Bimbo'; RCA bought his Abbott contract incl. 36 Abbott masters; he scored more than 40 top 10 hits in country chart altogether, 25 hits in pop Hot 100. First RCA hit with his own 'Yonder Comes A Sucker' '55; top 10 hits incl. his own 'Am I Losing You?' and 'Four Walls' '57 (latter written by Marvin Moore & George Campbell; his biggest pop hit at no. 2 in both country and pop charts); 'Billy Bayou' '58 (no. 1 country), 'He'll Have To Go' '59 (no. 1), his own 'I'm Getting Better' '60 (no. 3); 'Losing Your Love' '61, 'Adios Amigo' and 'I'm Gonna Change Everything' '62, 'Welcome To My World' '64, all at no. 2; 'I Guess I'm Crazy' '64 (no. 1). After USAF tours to Europe '57, '59 he had over two dozen pop hits in UK, often different from the USA ones. His single-engined Beechcraft private plane crashed in a heavy rainstorm near Nashville, followed by no. 1 hits 'This Is It', 'Is It Really Over?', 'Distant Drums', 'Blue Side Of Lonesome', 'I Won't Come In While He's There' '64-7. He also had duet hits with Ginny Wright ('I Love You' '54 on Fabor) and Dottie West ('Love Is No Excuse' '64); he was elected to Country Music Hall of Fame '67, continued to have hits through '70s, many records given new updated backing tracks; Deborah Allen duetted with Reeves record for top 10 hit 'Take Me In Your Arms And Hold Me' '80; Owen BRADLEY created duets by superstars Reeves and Patsy CLINE, who never recorded together when they were alive, incl. top 10 'Have You Ever Been Lonely?' '81. Countless Reeves compilations etc. incl. several *Best Of* sets, 2-disc sets *The Country Side Of Jim Reeves* and *Roomful Of Roses* '86 on Pair, *Greatest Hits* with Cline.

REEVES, Martha, & the Vandellas USA female soul/R&B vocal group formed '61 in Detroit, Mich. by lead singer Martha Reeves (*b* 18 July '41) with Rosalind Ash-

ford (*b* 2 Sep. '43), Annette Sterling, all from Detroit. A more aggressive, more soulful alternative to labelmates the SUPREMES, with 23 Hot 100 entries '63-71, though they passed their peak '67. Martha was secretary to Motown's A&R chief William 'Mickey' Stevenson; with Ashford, Annette Sterling, lead singer Gloria Williams she'd recorded as the Del-Phis on a subsidiary of Chess; at Motown she made demos to test comprehensibility of lyrics; also sang backup on early hits, especially with Marvin GAYE, whose 'Stubborn Kind Of Fellow' '62 credited the Vandellas, named after Van Dyke Street in Detroit, Martha's favourite singer Della REESE. Mary WELLS' unused studio time gave them their chance: after a flop as the Vels on Mel-O-Dy label Williams retired; second release as Vandellas on Gordy was first hit 'Come And Get These Memories' (top 30 pop, no. 6 R&B), then 'Heat Wave' (4/1) and 'Quicksand' (top 10 pop) same year; Sterling had been replaced by Betty Kelly (*b* 16 Sep. '44). 'Live Wire' '64 (42 pop), 'Nowhere To Run' '65 (8/4), 'I'm Ready For Love' and 'Jimmy Mack' '66-7 (both top 10 pop, top 2 R&B) made seven hits written for them by HOLLAND-DOZIER-HOLLAND, but biggest was 'Dancing In The Street' (no. 2 pop '64), one of the era's anthems, written by Gaye and Stevenson: as it was climbing the chart the riots of the 'long hot summer' of '64 were taking place; on a UK tour someone accused Martha of being a militant: 'My Lord, it was a *party* song,' she recalled on Dinah SHORE talk show late '70s; in fact the great party song/dance classic hit precisely when there was no R&B chart in Billboard because white and black kids were buying the same records. 'Love Bug Leave My Heart Alone' and 'Honey Chile' (both by Richard Morris/Sylvia Moy) were their last top 40 hits '67; the personnel was changing and their name was changed from Martha and the Vandellas to Martha Reeves and the Vandellas (echoing change to Diana Ross & Supremes); Martha's previous experience had made her valuable as Stevenson's secretary, but also made her independent: she queried label boss Berry Gordy about this and that; he liked pliable artists, lost interest in her and the group. They broke up '71; she left Motown '72 for solo work: *Martha Reeves* '74 on MCA ('Power Of Love' made

Hot 100), *The Rest Of My Life* '77 on Arista, *We Meet Again* '78 on Fantasy. She is a much-loved attraction on oldies tours; Motown anthologies compile the hits. Profile in Gerri Hirshey's *Nowhere To Run: The Story Of Soul Music* '84.

REGGAE The Jamaican popular music style, emerging in the '70s as an important infl. on world musics, but suffering from the early death of its only superstar, Bob MARLEY. Sound systems (primitive discos) began late '40s; recording of mento, the island's raggedy calypso style, began early '50s (Stanley Motta was a pioneer producer), but went into hiatus during the '50s as USA R&B was tremendously popular; the USA scene turned arid as Elvis PRESLEY was drafted and LITTLE RICHARD left music; in late '50s-early '60s Jamaica invented ska, a shuffling hybrid of R&B and mento, the name coming from the chopped guitar or piano sound on the second and fourth beats. Chinese-born Leslie Kong and Edward Seaga (later prominent Jamaican politician) were early producers, Kong's Beverly's label remaining important until his sudden death of a heart attack '70. Clement Seymour 'Sir Coxsone' Dodd ran Downbeat, a leading dance hall sound system, began recording late '50s, at first to have his own exclusive music; then it became obvious the records would sell: his Studio One was the most important; most of the artists subsequently making a mark in Jamaican music recorded there: singers Delroy Wilson, Bob Andy, Ken Boothe, Alton Ellis, John Holt, Dennis Brown, Sugar Minott, Burning Spear, Freddie MacGregor, Johnny Osbourne; groups such as the Maytals, Wailers, Ethiopians, Heptones, Skatalites, many more. Dodd and the others adopted rough-and-tumble methods in order to survive in the cut-throat Jamaican record scene and didn't pay their artists much, but an atmosphere of informal creativity resulted in rhythms that still dominate the dancehall scene in the '80s. Dodd is still working and reportedly has a wealth of unreleased material, but his output in recent years has slowed. Lee Perry began with Dodd, later went into competition with him and made some of the best records by Marley and the Wailers, as well as many others (compilation *Lee Perry And Friends* on Trojan '88 had tracks

from '70-3). The Skatalites were the island's best house band: Don Drummond on trombone, Roland ALPHONSO and Tommy McCook on tenor saxophones, Lester Sterling on alto, Johnny Moore and Leonard Dillon on trumpets, Jah Jerry on guitar, Jackie Mittoo on piano, Lloyd Brevitte on bass, Lloyd Nibbs on drums. Recording sessions had important effects on Jamaican politics, because the personnel knitted together various slums, and the hit records were the voice of the people, although they were not played on Jamaican radio stations, dominated by the island's aristocracy, who hired foreigners to run them. Ska slowed down and became heavier, influenced by USA rock, and was called 'rude boy' music '64-7 after the street anarchists who followed the music; hits like Prince Buster's 'Judge Dread' and the Slickers' 'Johnny Too Bad' and 'Shanty Town' emphasised the injustices which the rudies thumbed their noses at, while 'Rudy, A Message To You' blamed them for making trouble. The music slowed down still more and became more sensual: late '60s it was called 'rock steady', after the Alton Ellis hit 'Get Ready To Rock Steady'. Meanwhile white Jamaican entrepreneur Chris Blackwell (*b* '37, London) formed Island Records in London and had a world-wide hit with the first Jamaican export, the ska-infl. 'My Boy Lollipop' by Millie Small (no. 2 USA '64). Island did not remain primarily a Jamaican label, but issued Marley's best-known albums as well as LPs by Aswad, the ABYSSINIANS, etc. Under Blackwell's astute leadership it signed many profitable acts (such as TRAFFIC) and celebrated its 25th anniversary, still a vigorous independent, in '87 (latest signings incl. Courtney PINE). The next international Jamaican hit was Desmond DEKKER's 'Israelites' '68, recorded by Kong. Then Jamaican music slowed still still further: reggae perhaps came from patois 'streggae' (rudeness) or 'regge-regge' (quarrel); Toots (Frederick) Hibbert, who wrote 'Do The Reggay', said it was descriptive, meaning simply 'regular'. Its hypnotic, bass-dominated sound was capable of menacing power, but retained the ska chop on the offbeat; it was infl. by ganja (marijuana) and Rastafarianism. The Rastas were infl. by Marcus Mosiah Garvey (1887-1940), a Jamaican-born preacher who gave up on the idea of racial harmony and decided blacks should return to Africa; he started a steamship line, sold shares for a dollar each, went bankrupt and was jailed '25 in USA, sentence commuted by President Calvin Coolidge; he ended up in London without ever seeing Africa, but in Kingston '27 he said, 'Look to Africa, where a black king shall be crowned.' An Ethiopian warlord, Ras Tafari Makonnen, was crowned emperor '30 and took several titles incl. Haile Selassie I, Conquering Lion of the Tribe of Judah, etc., which seemed to fit biblical prophecies. Another preacher, Leonard Howell, sold pictures of Selassie to poor people as passports to Africa, and was locked up in a lunatic asylum; released '40, he founded a Rastafarian commune in the mountains near Kingston, closed by police '54. The Rastas became an alternative cult to the rude boys in Kingston; ascetic, vegetarian and peaceful, they smoked the island's powerful weed as an aid to meditation; they regarded the world and all its works as Babylon. Hitler had been the biblical Beast and Mussolini the false prophet; Ethiopia was the Greek name for Africa, and all the prophecies seemed to be coming true. The sect of the Twelve Tribes, founded in Kingston in '68, decided that the Second Coming had already happened, and that Haile Selassie was God on Earth. The Jamaican establishment feared and despised the Rastas, but given its violence and corruption, the establishment was lucky that Marley and many others were deeply influenced by it, turning away from the rudies. On the face of it, Selassie was an ineffectual little man who lived too long and left his country a mess; today's Rastas would not be welcomed by the insane and criminal regime in Ethiopia. But Selassie never started any wars, and the image of the world as Babylon is hard to resist; Marley became reggae's superstar because of his musicianship and his powerful moral authority at a time when the horror of the Vietnam war was fresh, and Jamaica itself seemed close to civil war. An important lift for Jamaican music was Perry Henzell's film *Hard Road To Travel* '67, in which Jimmy Cliff played a Jamaican gunman who in real life was killed by police late '40s: the soundtrack LP (on Blackwell's Mango label) had tracks by Cliff, Dekker, the Maytals and the Melodians. Cliff (*b* James Chambers, '48) recorded for Island, had worldwide hit '69 with 'Wonderful World, Beautiful People', lesser hit '70 with 'Vietnam'; also recorded for EMI '70s. Other important reggae acts incl. Hibbert and his Maytals, formed '62 as the Vikings (recorded for Dodd, Prince Buster, Byron Lee, Kong and Lee again); their best LPs were said to be *Funky Kingston* and *Reggae Got Soul* on Island; still going in early '80s. Aswad was formed '76 by Angus Gaye and Brinsley Forde, with bass guitar George Oban, Donald Griffiths on lead guitar, Courtney Hemmings on keyboards; Island LPs incl. *Aswad* '76, then on CBS incl. *New Chapter*; *Distant Thunder* '88 back on Island was at last a deserved big hit. The rhythm section of Sly & Robbie (drummer Sly Dunbar, bassist Robbie Shakespeare) became stars in their own right: they first got together on Cliff's *Follow My Mind* '75, recorded with many of the best Jamaican artists and were in demand for sessions all over the world, with Grace JONES, Joe COCKER, Ian DURY, Bob DYLAN, others. *See also* BURNING SPEAR, Bob ANDY, Horace ANDY, Ken BOOTHE, Junior BYLES, Cornell CAMPBELL, CARLTON AND THE SHOES. Toasting emerged late '50s as sound system DJs heard black USA DJs rapping over the records; they dropped the vocals and used the microphone for satirical street poetry: U-Roy was the first prominent toaster, then Dennis ALCAPONE early '70s, swept away by Rasta-infl. BIG YOUTH, who was succeeded by BRIGADIER JERRY. The dub is the Jamaican DJ's raw material, the rhythm track; Perry, whose nickname was 'Scratch', innovated technically, remixing the rhythm tracks for instrumental versions on B sides of records which often became hits. Augustus Pablo plays melodica, a plastic keyboard-wind instrument; he got weird beauty from it on a few Wailers tracks, became one of the first dub artists with *King Tubby Meets The Rockers Uptown* '74, recorded by Perry. The dub poet reads written verse to reggae backing tapes; Linton Kwesi Johnson, of Brixton, South London, is the best known.

REICH, Steve (*b* 3 Oct. '36, NYC) Composer. From musical family; studied philosophy at Cornell; music at Juilliard, then at Mills College in Cal., with Darius Milhaud and Luciano Berio. Formed his own ensemble '66, studied drumming in Ghana '70, Balinese gamelon '73. He deliberately rejected the increasing complexity of contemporary 'serious' music in favour of a reduced vocabulary, searching in ethnic and ancient musics for ideas; his style often involves repetition, such as a chord changing one note at a time, and has been described as minimalist, modular, phase music and pulse music. It is both modern and elemental; the latest edition of *Baker's Biographical Dictionary Of Musicians* (ed. Nicolas Slonimsky) came up with the word 'hypnopompic' to describe it. By thumbing his nose at the academics and causing some critics to question his seriousness, he came to the attention of the avant-gardists in popular music, whom he has influenced. Three albums on Nonesuch are *The Desert Music, Drumming* (for eight small tuned drums, three marimbas, three glockenspiels, two female voices, whistling and a piccolo), and a collection including tape music and 'Clapping Music' (two musicians clapping their hands in an interlocking rhythmic pattern). Two ECM records compile music for ensembles, incl. 'Violin Phase' for violin and tape; also one each on Angel (EMI's classical label in USA) and DGG (Polydor); other pieces on Hungaroton and Philips.

REINHARDT, Django (*b* Jean Baptiste Reinhardt, 23 Jan. '10, Liverchies, Belgium; *d* 16 May '53, Fontainebleau, France) Guitar, composer; the first European musician to infl. USA jazz. Wandered in Belgium and France as a Gypsy, playing guitar, violin, banjo; injured in a fire in his caravan '28 which partially paralysed his left hand; developed new technique to overcome it. He was already an adult professional musician when he discovered jazz, immediately understood it and incorporated it into the Gypsy guitar tradition, infl. by Eddie LANG; worked with singer Jean Sablon (playing Lang to Sablon's Bing CROSBY), formed the Quintet of the Hot Club Of France '34 with Stephane GRAPPELLI on violin (then spelled 'Grappelly'), brother Joseph Reinhardt and Roger Chaput, guitars, Louis Vola on bass (other musicians passing through incl. guitarists Pierre Ferret, Eugène Vées; basses Emmanuel Soudieux, Roger Grasset). They made more than 200 sides and became internationally famous, on account not only of Django's technique and swing but his lyricism and lyrical interplay with the violin. He recorded with Coleman HAWKINS, Benny CARTER and Dicky WELLS '37, Carter '38, Rex STEWART and Barney BIGARD '39 (compiled on Prestige USA, Giants Of Jazz in Italy); quintet recorded in London '38-9. During the war he became a superstar, people whistling his lovely 'Nuages' in the street: Grappelli was in England; Django experimented with big band, formed quintet with clarinettist Hubert Rostaing; during Occupation Nazis outlawed jazz and murdered half a million Gypsies: a Gypsy jazz musician was twice an outlaw; Django not only survived but lived in a sumptuous flat, ate and gambled in the poshest places. (The ban on jazz didn't work too well either; *see* Mike Zwerin's *La Tristesse de St Louis*.) The quintet was re-created on record '46 in London with Jack Llewellyn, Alan Hodgkiss on guitars, Coleridge Goode on bass. During the war he had worked on 'serious' music (a Mass for organ, a symphony, etc.); some of this music was used in film soundtrack *La Village de la Colère* '46; late that year he went to USA to tour with Duke ELLINGTON: owing to his tendency to wander off, tour was not a success. Began to play electric guitar; infl. by bop, which may not have been congenial with his personal lyricism; occasionally reunited with Grappelli; died of a stroke. His compositions incl. 'Love's Melody', 'Improvisation', 'Belleville', others; co-wrote with Grappelli: 'H.Q.C. Strut', 'Daphne', 'Souvenirs', 'Stomping At Decca', 'My Sweet', 'Djangology', 'Appel Direct', 'Nocturne', many more. Compilations: seven vols. on GNP, with USA Air Transport Command Band on Vee Jay, others on Archive of Folk in USA; 20 *Djangologie* LPs on French EMI, 2-disc *The Indispensable* on French RCA, *Together* on Pathé Marconi (with Eddie SOUTH as well as Grappelli), 2-disc *Struttin' Out* on Decca UK (36 tracks), many others on Swaggie, CBS, Polydor, etc. A bargain-priced 8-disc box *Django* '87 (on Swing label in USA, Affinity in UK) has 144 tracks, good examples of everything he did. His heirs incl. Birel LAGRENE, Fapy Lafertin in Belgium, Elios Ferre and the brothers Boulou in Paris, his son Babik Reinhardt.

REISMAN, Leo (*b* 1897, Boston, Mass.; *d* 18 Dec. '61, Miami, Fla.) Bandleader. Studied violin, attended New England Conservatory of Music; led band at Boston's Brunswick Hotel '19, first records '21. Ran several bands to be able to play several gigs at once. Played Central Park date '21, became well-known in NYC. 'Puttin' On The Ritz' '30 incl. Bubber MILEY, trumpet; Cole PORTER song 'What Is This Thing Called Love', recorded same date, became band's theme. During '30s played swank hotel dates, many broadcasts and records, some with Fred ASTAIRE, Lee WILEY etc. To West Coast '38; soon returned to NYC; hotel dates continued through '40s; in early '50s led small group in Beverly Hills.

R.E.M. Rock group formed '80 in Athens, Ga.: Michael Stipe, vocals (*b* 4 Jan. '60), Peter Buck, guitar (*b* 6 Dec. '56), Michael Mills, bass (*b* 17 Dec. '58), Bill Berry, drums (*b* 31 July '58). Name said to come from random sequence of letters, though matched 'rapid eye movement', the state of sleep in which dreaming takes place. Independent single 'Radio Free Europe' '81 followed by EP *Chronic Town* '82, LP *Murmur* '83 incl. 'Radio Free Europe', 'Talk About The Passion'; became critics' favourites, in vanguard of roots revival: early sound reminiscent of BYRDS; band acknowledged influences, enriched by Stipe's mysterious lyrics, Buck's eclectic guitar. *Reckoning* '84 confirmed promise, with 'So Central Rain', '(Don't Go Back To) Rockville', 'Seven Chinese Brothers'. *Fables Of The Reconstruction/Reconstruction Of The Fables* '85 prod. by Joe BOYD; *Life's Rich Pageant* '86 was a stronger and less dreamy-sounding album; *Dead Letter Office* collected B sides, live tracks, covers, then *Number 5: Document* '87 was also more outward looking. They were at centre of flourishing Athens scene incl. Don Dixon, Let's Active; Stipe sang backup on JASON & THE SCORCHERS' *Fever* '83, worked with Warren ZEVON '86; Buck guested on Dream Academy debut LP, worked with Robbie Robertson '86.

REMBETIKA Accompanied song style built on long Byzantine, Turkish, Greek tradition, emerging in urban Greece '20s. After Turko-Greek war ended '22, Turks living in Greece and Greeks in Asia Minor were re-patriated; returning Greeks lived in seaport towns like Piraeus, regarded as low-caste, unwelcome outsiders (called 'mages', 'rembetes' because of distinctive style of dress and behaviour): they lived on the fringe in a life of petty crime, and brought a Turkish culture of music, dance and hashish. Accompanied by baglama (small bouzouki), jail songs mixed with established café aman style ('aman' meaning improvisation) and incoming more decorative Turkish or smyrna style; lyrics marked by contempt for the world at large and for authority, a sensual response to the moment, disregard for the future: aided by hashish the singer sought to transcend his circumstances in a mood of 'meraki'. Themes incl. comradeship, release from pain and trouble via the narghile (hookah pipe), familiarity with and indifference to death. Accompaniment of baglama or bouzouki later increased to band of several bouzoukis; audience danced dances called hasapiko, tsifteteli, zembekiko. Flourished '30-40s (records made '30s in USA); became bland in '50s; revived late '70s as young Greeks turned to their own popular culture with the end of the Junta. Important singers/writers were Vassilis Tsitsanis, Markos Vamvakaris, Rosa Eskenazi, Sotiria Bellou. Six LPs *The History Of Rembetika* on Columbia/EMI.

RENAISSANCE UK rock band of '70s. Original group formed '69 by YARDBIRDS vocalist Keith Relf (*b* 22 Mar. '43, Richmond; *d* 14 May '76) and drummer Jim McCarty (*b* 25 July '43, Liverpool), recruiting bassist Louis Cennamo, ex-NASHVILLE TEENS keyboardist John Hawken and Relf's vocalist sister Jane to make eponymous folky LP for Island '69. Ex-Yardbirds left; by the time of *Prologue* '72 personnel was entirely new: Annie Haslam, vocals; Jon Camp, bass; John Tout, keyboards; Rob Hendry, guitar; Terry Sullivan, drums. Hendry was replaced by Mick Dunford, who rarely used electric guitar, preferring acoustic; corresponding with one Betty Thatcher by post, he set her words for *Ashes Are Burning* and *Turn Of The Cards* '73-4, which charted in UK; *Scheherezade And Other Stories* '75 heavily orchestrated 'contemporary version' of Rimsky-Korsakov classic, top 50 LP USA

'75, where they went for two years: at home they were stuck on college circuit, 2-disc *Live At Carnegie Hall* '76 (with NY Philharmonic) emphasising difference. Sound based on Tout's keyboards, Haslam's 'classical rock' wailing. After *Novella*, *A Song For All Seasons* and *Azure d'Or* '77-9, Peter Gosling and Peter Barron replaced Tout, Sullivan; they carried on bucking fashion with *Camera Camera* and *Time Line* in '80s. Haslam made solo *Annie In Wonderland* '78; Relf, Cennamo and Hawken from first band formed Illusion (two LPs '77-8) but Relf was electrocuted. Like fellow pomprockers BARCLAY JAMES HARVEST, they can hardly be said to have influenced anybody; sole UK hit was top 10 single 'Northern Lights' '78.

RENDELL, Don (*b* 4 Mar. '26) UK jazz reedman, arranger; also active in music education. Played in dance bands, then in early UK bop clubs with Ronnie SCOTT, etc.; in original Johnny DANKWORTH Seven, co-led combo with Ian CARR '60s; another group employed Graham BOND. Played with Ted HEATH; toured Europe with Stan KENTON '56, Woody HERMAN '59; led group accompanying Billie HOLIDAY on UK tour; leads own groups. On teaching panel of the Inner London Education Authority and the annual Jazz and Rock School in the City of London. Own favourites among his LPs incl. *Dusk Fire* '66 (with Carr) on Columbia/EMI; other LPs incl. *Live At The Avgarde Gallery Manchester* '73 with Joe Palin Trio, guest Pete Martin on trumpet; *Just Music* '74 by the Don Rendell Five with Barbara THOMPSON; *Earth Music* by the Don Rendell Nine and *Set Two* by Five '79 on Spotlite, live concert celebrating 35 years in music.

RENT PARTY UK jump band formed '82 at seaside resort of Southend. Lineup: Jackson Sloane, vocals; John Willmott, tenor sax; sister Chris Willmott, alto; Laurence Parry, trumpet; Steve Weston, piano; Andy Stevens, guitar; Tony Wilsonham, bass; Neil Robinson, drums; all *b* c.'60-7, all former students or blue-collar workers. Another young group searching back behind disco for some good music: wearing zoot-suits with wide ties, describe their stuff as '50s R&B/jazz dance music, infl. by Count BASIE, Louis JORDAN, Big Joe TURNER. Hit at Cork Jazz Festival '84, played Kool Jazz Festival and gigs at the Lone Star NYC '85. UK singles incl. 'Walk That Mess', 'Honey Bee' '84; mini-LP *Honk That Saxophone* '85 incl. title track, 'Honey Bee', 'Big Ten Inch', 'One Off The Riff', two more. Single cover of Fats WALLER's 'Ain't Misbehavin'' '86. They were still going in '88, more popular live than on record.

REO SPEEDWAGON USA rock group formed '67 in Champagne, Ill.; named after make of fire engine. Founder-members were U. of I. students Alan Gratzer (*b* 9 Nov. '48, Syracuse, NY), drums, and Neal Doughty (*b* 29 July '46, Evanston, Ill.), keyboards; plus Gary Richrath (*b* 10 Oct '49, Peoria, Ill.), guitar; Terry Luttrell, vocals, Gregg Philbin, bass. After eponymous LP debut '71 Luttrell was replaced by Kevin Cronin, himself replaced after *R.E.O. T.W.O.* '72 by Mike Murphy. They played long tours on stadium circuit with Ted NUGENT, Bob SEGER, KANSAS; seen as a bar band who might make it, wished well by critics; they made it eventually without getting better. Managed until '77 by EAGLES boss Irv Azoff. Crept slowly up charts with *Ridin' The Storm Out*, *Lost In A Dream*, *This Time We Mean It* '74-5 to top 75 LPs; then Cronin returned, his country-tinged singing giving Richrath's songs a little more distinction, yet *R.E.O.* '76 slipped back below no. 150. 2-disc *Live/You Get What You Pay For* did better; *You Can Tune A Piano, But You Can't Tuna Fish* '78 was top 30 LP, perhaps because of its silly title; they prod. *Nine Lives* '79 themselves; after 2-disc compilation *A Decade Of Rock And Roll 1970 To 1980*, *Hi Infidelity* '80 was no. 1 for 15 weeks, incl. no. 1 'Keep On Lovin' You', soundalike top 5 'Take It On The Run' (also UK hits), two others, their first top 40 entries: they struck it rich as USA radio became completely spineless, making major-label money-spinners of faceless bands like REO, Kansas, JOURNEY, STYX who could graft an occasional hook onto otherwise unmemorable songs. Later LPs less frequent: *Good Trouble* '82 (with no. 7 'Keep The Fire Burnin' '), *Wheels Are Turnin'* '84 (with no. 1 'Can't Fight This Feeling') were both no. 7 LPs, followed by compilation *Best Foot Forward* '85, *Life As We Know It* '87.

REVERE, Paul, & the Raiders USA pop group formed '59 in Boise, Idaho as the Downbeats by organist Paul Revere (his real name; *b* '42, Boise), saxist/vocalist Mark Lindsay (*b* 9 Mar. '42, Cambridge, Idaho). They recorded three instrumentals for Gardena; 'Like, Long Hair' reached top 40 '61 but they couldn't follow up; duo ditched backing group and moved to Portland, Ore.; recruited Mike 'Smitty' Smith, drums; Philip 'Fang' Volk, bass; Drake 'The Kid' Levin, guitar. Columbia signed them on strength of a demo of 'Louie Louie' made by DJ Roger Hart; their version did not reach Hot 100: local competition the KINGSMEN beat them to classic hit. 'Steppin' Out' '65 made top 50; Dick CLARK signed them for *Where The Action Is*, TV show designed to counteract the BRITISH INVASION: 18th century costumes with jackets and breeches carried American image, 'Just Like Me' was no. 11 '65 (cover of local group Rick Dey and the Knights that owed much to the KINKS). TV show caused realignment of style after Barry MANN/Cynthia WEIL's 'Hungry' (no. 4), 'Kicks' (6): Lindsay was projected as sex-symbol frontman, while group members took on writing; Lindsay and prod. Terry MELCHER co-wrote 'The Great Airplane Strike' (no. 20), 'Good Thing' (4), all '66. 'Him Or Me – What's It Gonna Be?' at no. 5 '67 was classic pop single; *Just Like Us!*, *Midnight Ride*, *The Spirit Of '67* were top 10 LPs '67, but further efforts less successful; four top 20 hits through '69 as they tended towards progressive rock, where credibility was limited owing to unashamedly commercial origins. Original backing musicians formed Brotherhood '67 (flop LPs on RCA), replaced by Freddy Weller on guitar (*b* 9 Sep. '47, Ga).), Charlie Coe on bass (*b* 19 Nov. '44), Joe Correro Jr on drums (*b* 19 Nov. '46, Greenwood, Ms.); shortened name to Raiders for renaissance with John D. LOUDERMILK's 'Indian Reservation', subtitled 'The Lament Of A Cherokee Reservation Indian', their only no. 1 hit '71 (LP of same title top 20); they had one more top 40 hit, slipped from the charts. Lindsay made solo LPs *Arizona* '70 (top 40, top 10 title single), *Silverbird* and *You've Got A Friend*, but teen idol genre had died. Duo continue on oldies circuit with pickup Raiders; Lindsay doubles as country act; *Kicks* is a compilation of hits on Edsel UK made in '83.

REY, Alvino (*b* Alvin McBurney, 1 July '11, Oakland, Cal.) Guitarist, bandleader. Began as sideman with Phil Spitalny (*b* 7 Nov. 1890, Odessa, Russia; *d* 11 Oct. '70; best known for all-girl band '30s-40s), then with Russ MORGAN, Freddy MARTIN; came to prominence with Horace HEIDT '34-9, changed name; formed band '39, took King Sisters vocal group from Heidt (incl. Rey's wife Louise); band worked on West Coast radio station as house unit. Rey gained respect for guitar work, often playing Hawaiian steel guitar in non-corny manner; opening theme 'Blue Rey' unique for multiple-voice gimmick. Played one-night gigs across USA; big hit at Hotel Biltmore, NYC; at Rustic Cabin, scene of a fire in which Rey's contract was burned up; and at Meadowbrook, N.J. '42. Formed excellent band that year using arr. by Ray CONNIFF, Johnny Mandell, Billy MAY, Neal HEFTI, but met recording ban (musicians' union strike). Band had 10 brass; six saxes at one time incl. Al COHN, Zoot SIMS, Herbie Steward (later 3/4 of Woody HERMAN's famous 'Four Brothers'); musical chairs behind drum kit employed Don Lamond, Nick Fatool, Mel LEWIS, Dave TOUGH etc.: one of the most interesting white bands of era. Made films *Sing Your Worries Away* '42, *Larceny With Music* '43; Rey seen without band in *Syncopation* '42. Worked in L.A. aircraft factory '43, ran band in own time (mainly broadcasts); joined US Navy '44, formed service band, resumed civilian bandleading '46. Recorded for RCA Bluebird (top 10 '42: 'Deep In The Heart Of Texas', 'I Said No', 'Strip Polka'); then on Capitol ('Cement Mixer' '46, 'Near You' '47). Had smaller line-up early '50s but carried on to mid-'60s with *King Family Show* on TV; later sporadic reunions, TV shows; he took up classical guitar. *Alvino Rey And His Orchestra 1946* with great lineup issued by Hindsight '78.

REYNOLDS, Malvina (*b* 23 Aug. 1900, San Francisco; *d* 17 Mar. '78, Berkeley, Cal.) Songwriter, singer who wrote topical and children's songs. Married Bud Reynolds '34, a labour organiser; wrote 'Bury Me In My Overalls' to cheer him up as he recovered from heart attack '56. She co-wrote 'Sally, Don't You Grieve' with Woody GUTHRIE, many songs with Pete SEEGER, who recorded her 'Little Boxes': the LIMELITERS, KINGSTON TRIO etc. refused to cover it because they wanted Seeger to have it; it was his only hit single after years of blacklisting. He recorded five of her songs on *God Bless The Grass* '66, incl. title song, 'The Faucets Are Dripping', 'Cement Octopus', 'From Way Up Here'. Her best-known song is 'What Have They Done To The Rain', recorded by Joan BAEZ and by the SEEKERS, who also covered 'Morningtown Ride'. 'It Isn't Nice' about demonstrations was rewritten by Barbara Dane, recorded by Judy COLLINS. Reynolds wrote for *Sesame Street* children's TV show; published her own collections incl. *Cheerful Tunes For Lutes And Spoons, Tweedles And Foodles For Young Noodles*; Oak published *Little Boxes And Other Handmade Songs, The Muse Of Parker Street*. LPs incl. *Artichokes, Griddlecakes, Etc.* and *Funnybugs, Giggleworms, Etc.* on Pacific Cascades; *Malvina Reynolds Sings The Truth* on Columbia; *Another Country Heard From* on Folkways; *Malvina, Malvina Held Over, Mama Lion* and *Magical Songs* on her own Cassandra Records.

RHYTHM & BLUES Genre of black popular music emerging '40s, the most important element in rock'n'roll and still informing white pop today. In earlier decades black music incl. jazz, country blues of Bessie SMITH, Charley PATTON, Blind Lemon JEFFERSON, many others; also vaudeville 'hokum' (*double-entendre* lyrics of Georgia Tom, etc.), songs of Big Bill BROONZY, others. The blues of Leroy CARR ('In The Evening When The Sun Goes Down') already had a smoother urban style '30s. The great black bands of Duke ELLINGTON, Fletcher HENDERSON, others were enormously popular: the 'Swing Era' really began in the black community, called the BIG BAND ERA only after it also dominated white pop from '35. As that era decayed, both black and white acts got smaller; vocalists took over in white pop and two strands of blues and pop came together in the black: the history of the Lucky MILLINDER band illustrates the process. Louis JORDAN typified the emergence of the jump band '40s, rocking small band playing party

music with humorous lyrics; both Jordan, Jack McVEA had one of the biggest hits of the era with 'Open The Door, Richard' in '47 (written by McVea). Bill DOGGETT, Earl BOSTIC, Jimmy FORREST, many other jazzmen led popular combos; Dexter GORDON accompanied Etta JAMES, the 'Swingtets' that recorded for Blue Note were influential (*see* Illinois JACQUET). As in white pop the vocalists began to take over; as the jazz element decreased the electric guitar made inroads and the drummer's backbeat became stronger, but saxophone remained important, showmanship element emphasised by Big Jay McNEELY; rocking solos on hits were played by Hank CRAWFORD, David NEWMAN, Lee ALLEN, Plas JOHNSON, KING CURTIS, Red Tyler, Noble 'Thin Man' Watts (whose first album was *Return Of The Thin Man* '87 on Bedrock), others. Blues were electrified and urbanised by Elmore JAMES, B. B. KING, Muddy WATERS, many others, but still with a strong trad. element; on the West Coast small combos led by Amos MILBURN, Roy BROWN, others sang a smoother bar-room style; Roy MILTON gave smoothness to white audiences, a different style in black clubs (as did Sam COOKE later). Vocal groups were important: the Ravens, the Crows etc. sang doo-wop with the accent on soulful singing, often no drums at all. Independent R&B labels sprang up late '40s, many operated by Jews who had grown up in black neighbourhoods or at least lived in them: King in Cincinnati; Chess in Chicago; Savoy in New Jersey; Excello in Nashville; Modern/RPM, Specialty and Aladdin in Los Angeles; a few labels were black-owned: United and States labels were run by Lew Simpkins and Leonard Allen '51-4; shortlived owing to Simpkins' death, the labels recorded Forrest, Tab SMITH, MEMPHIS SLIM, Roosevelt SYKES, Walter HORTON, guitarist Robert Nighthawk, vocal group the Four Blazes etc. in excellent sound which is still fresh. Other black-owned labels were Vee Jay in Chicago, Duke/Peacock in Houston, later (most successful of all) Motown in Detroit; there were small labels that never achieved national distribution but had local hits, e.g. in New Orleans. Influential producers and bandleaders incl. Ralph BASS, Dave BARTHOLOMEW, Johnny OTIS, Paul GAY-

TEN, Allen TOUSSAINT, Bumps BLACKWELL and others. *Billboard* changed designation of 'Race Records' chart to 'Rhythm & Blues' '49 (*see* CHARTS). In early '50s R&B lyrics were often more fun (and more honest) than in white pop; it was also danceable, and white kids began to buy black hits, which threatened to cross over to the pop chart, and finally did when rock'n-'roll exploded. For the rest of that story and more on R&B, *see* ROCK. Some of the best R&B never crossed over: Bo DIDDLEY had only one top 40 hit, novelty 'Say Man' '59; urban blues never made the pop chart, but UK bands gave new meaning to the word 'cover' in the '60s, mining the mother lode with affection: great black artists like Waters, PROFESSOR LONGHAIR, B. B. King, Albert KING, John Lee HOOKER, Lightnin' HOPKINS, many others became international stars '60s-70s thanks largely to homage paid them by British rockers. As dominant genre in black pop, R&B was succeeded by SOUL '60s, which became the new name of the *Billboard* black chart '69, but R&B is still happening: veterans Earl KING, Johnny COPELAND, Albert COLLINS sell albums internationally, while new stars like Robert CRAY make it fresh as today, and any self-respecting bar band still needs roots in R&B after 30 years. Good books incl. *Rhythm & Blues In New Orleans* '74 by John Broven (aka *Walking To New Orleans*), *Honkers And Shouters: The Golden Years Of Rhythm & Blues* '78 by Arnold Shaw.

RICE, Bobby (*b* 11 July '44, Boscobel, Wis.) Country/pop singer with solo success late '70s following many years as member of family group. Began in rock'n'roll but had been raised on a farm, with four sisters and a brother formed group running dance hall programme called Circle D, by mid-'50s had own show on WRCO Richmond, Va. Two sisters married '64; Bobby teamed with Lorraine in duo, went solo '68, forming Bobby Rice band, signing with Royal American Records '69: first chart hit was 'Sugar Shack' '70, followed by several more through '70s incl. top 5 'You Lay So Easy On My Mind' '73, then on GRT label, then Republic for minor hits '78-9, the Sunbird and Charts labels, but never returned to top 10. LPs incl. *You Lay So Easy On My Mind* '73 on Metromedia; *She Sure Laid The Lonelies On Me, Write Me A Letter, Instant Rice, Best Of* '74-7 all on GRT.

RICH, Buddy (*b* Bernard Rich, 30 Sept. '17, Brooklyn, NY; *d* 2 Apr. '87) Drummer, bandleader. Apparently a natural performer from birth, worked with parents on stage at 18 months, played drums as Baby Traps, danced and drummed on Broadway at 4 and led band on stage at 11. Played in bands of Joe Marsala '37-8 (clarinettist; *b* 4 Jan. '07, Chicago; *d* 4 Mar. '78, Santa Barbara, Cal.), then Bunny BERIGAN, Harry JAMES, Artie SHAW, Tommy DORSEY '39-42, Benny CARTER '42. Opinionated and with a flint-hard intelligence, he did not get along with Dorsey (nor with Frank SINATRA, though they somehow remained friends). Military service '42-4, rejoined Dorsey '44-5. One of the best white drummers of the BIG BAND ERA, with more tendency towards showmanship than Dave TOUGH or Don Lamond, but never losing sight of musical values. Formed own band '45, lasted two years; joined JATP '47 (*see* Norman GRANZ), played with Les BROWN late '49, member of Big 4 '51 with Charlie VENTURA, Chubby Jackson, pianist Marty Napoleon (*b* 2 June '21, Brooklyn). During '50s he played with James and Dorsey again, led combos, was also a good singer. LPs as sideman incl. *Flip Phillips Quintet*, others with Dizzy GILLESPIE, Lester YOUNG, Lionel HAMPTON, Gene KRUPA, Harry EDISON, trio with Art TATUM and Hampton, *This One's For Basie* '56, *Rich Versus Roach* '59 with Max, *Sings Johnny Mercer, Just Sings, In Miami* etc. almost all on Granz's labels. Contemplated giving up playing for singing and acting but always came back to drums. Had first heart attack '59, came back with keep-fit regimen, acquired black belt at karate. Worked for James again from '61, formed own big band '66: some thought he was crazy, but demanding boss and hard worker had international success with brilliant band, arr. by Bill Holman, Don Sebesky (*b* 10 Dec. '37, Perth Amboy, N.J.), John La Barbera (*b* 10 Nov. '45, Warsaw, NY), Bill Reddie (arr. of 'West Side Story' medley incl. tour-de-force drum solo), others. Art PEPPER played in band briefly '60s; La Barbera played trumpet, brother Pat reeds (*b* Pascel La Barbera, 7 Apr. '44, Mt Morris, NY). With fine young talent, roaring arr. of contemporary pop incl. BEATLES songs, Paul SIMON etc. he toured the world, had first TV show '68. Led small group '74, lent name to club Buddy's Place; re-formed big band '75. After heart by-pass surgery '83, ignored doctors and was back at work in two months, at first with combo; toured nine months a year '85-6, incl. concerts with Sinatra. Albums made pop charts: *Swingin' New Big Band, Big Swing Face, Mercy, Mercy, Buddy & Soul* '66-9 on World Pacific/Pacific Jazz (the last now on Pausa); *Rich In London* '72 on RCA (live at Ronnie SCOTT's). Many more incl. *Big Band Machine, Roar Of '74* on Groove Merchant; *Stick It* and *Different Drummer* on RCA; *Keep The Customer Satisfied* on Liberty; *Hampton Presents* '77 on Who's Who, etc. Rich's personality and flashy showmanship saw to it that many of his fans were the kind of people who talk through the music on the bandstand, but musicians were in awe of his skill; on *The Swinging Count* '52 with Basie small group he was certainly in evidence, but every accent was appropriate and in exactly the right place. 3-disc *Live At King Street* compiles tracks from Pacific Jazz label on Café.

RICH, Charlie (*b* 14 Dec. '32, Colt, Ark.) Country singer with pop crossover success, aka the 'Silver Fox' (hair turned prematurely white at age 23). A gifted keyboardist, while in USAF he formed jazz-blues band the Velvetones with wife Margaret doing vocals; moved back to home state and worked part-time as a farmer, but pull of music was too strong: moved to Memphis, landed residency at the Sharecropper Club. Bill JUSTIS saw him there, took him to Sun Records where he worked as session player, began recording '58 but had only isolated pop success 'Lonely Weekends' '60 (no. 21 on Sam Phillips' subsidiary Phillips label). He followed Justice to RCA subsidiary Groove, where he made two highly praised LPs '63-4; went to Mercury's Smash, had hit 'Mohair Sam' '65 (no. 11); recorded for Memphis label Hi '67, then reunited with Billy SHERRILL, whom he knew from Sun: signed with Epic in Nashville and was groomed by Sherrill in the early days of countrypolitan, an easy-listening country style that would appeal to the middle-of-the-road market: minor country hits '68-9; scraped into pop chart '70 with 'July 12, 1939'; 'Behind Closed Doors' was his first country no. 1, reached no. 15 pop, won a Grammy and led to three CMA awards '73 for Best Male Vocalist, Best Single and Best Album; 'The Most Beautiful Girl' same year was no. 1 in both country and pop charts, reached top 10 in UK. Groove tracks reissued on RCA incl. three no. 1 country hits: 'There Won't Be Anymore' (top 20 pop), 'I Don't See Me In Your Eyes Anymore' and 'She Called Me Baby' (both top 50 pop); his fourth no. 1 country hit in a row was 'I Love My Friend' on Epic (top 25 pop); a Mercury issue of 'Field Of Yellow Daisies' went top 30 country, all in '74; he was named CMA Entertainer of the Year. 'My Elusive Dreams' and 'Every Time You Touch Me (I Get High)' were top 5 country '75, also reached pop chart; he lost credibility with country fans that year by turning up drunk to present the CMA Awards show, and chart success waned; 'Since I Fell For You' '76 was country top 10, his last Hot 100 pop entry; a couple of singles failed to make the country top 20 but 'Rollin' With The Flow' swept back to no. 1 (and no. 101 on Billboard's Bubbling Under pop chart). He switched to UA '78 and had only one top 10 country hit ('Puttin' In Overtime At Home' '78) while 'Beautiful Woman' did better and 'On My Knees' (a duet with Janie FRICKE) reached no. 1, both on Epic; in '79 four UA singles failed to reach the country top 20, while 'I'll Wake You Up When I Get Home' on Elektra was top 3 and 'Spanish Eyes' on Epic top 20. In recent years he has faded from the chart completely with few new recordings. Early Sun tracks on 2-disc *Original Hits And Midnight Demos* on Charly UK; other albums incl. *Charlie Rich* on Groove '63, *Mohair Sam* and *The Best Years* on Smash, *Sings Country & Western* on Hi '67 (reissued as *Charlie Rich Sings The Songs Of Hank Williams And Others* '74, reached top 200 pop LPs), *There Won't Be Anymore* and *She Called Me Baby* '74 on RCA, many more compilations. Among many Epic LPs best-sellers were *Behind Closed Doors, Very Special Love Songs* and *The Silver Fox* '73-4; *Silver Linings* '76 was a gospel LP which made top 200. *Greatest Hits/Best Of Charlie Rich* is a double-play cassette on CBS. UA LPs: *I Still Believe In Love*, *The Fool Strikes Again* '78-9; *Nobody But You* '80; *Once A Drifter* '81 on Elektra.

RICHARD, Cliff (*b* Harry Roger Webb, 14 Oct. '40, Lucknow, India) UK pop singer. To UK age 8; sang in school group the Quintones, saw Bill HALEY in '57 UK tour, played SKIFFLE with Dick Teague Group, left with drummer Terry Smart; formed Drifters '58 with Ken Pavey on guitar, replaced by Ian Samwell after gig at 2 I's coffee bar in Soho, cradle of UK rock'n'roll. Changed name on advice of agent, signed to EMI Columbia: first single was cover of Bobby Helms' 'Schoolboy Crush', flipped to reveal 'Move It', the most exciting UK R&R disc so far, no. 2 hit '58. Drifters renamed to avoid confusion with USA R&B group, new personnel recruited for tours turned out to be the SHADOWS (*which see*). Initially an Elvis PRESLEY imitator, but clearly in a class above others like Tommy STEELE, as 'High Class Baby' showed (no. 7 '58); first no. 1 was 'Livin' Doll' '59, written by Lionel BART, used in soundtrack of *Serious Charge*; first LP *Cliff* '59 made in studio with an audience; first film starring role *Expresso Bongo* '60, followed by string of family film musicals *The Young Ones* '61, *Summer Holiday* '62, *Wonderful Life* '64 that brought him into musical middle-of-the-road. He had 93 chart hits in UK '58-86 not counting re-entries, incl. *Expresso Bongo* EP, and 42 hit LPs. Other no. 1 singles were 'Travellin' Light' '59, 'Please Don't Tease' and 'I Love You' '60, 'The Young Ones' and 'The Next Time'/'Bachelor Boy' '61, 'Summer Holiday' '62, 'The Minute You're Gone' '65, 'Congratulations' '68 (also runner-up in EUROVISION contest). Five no. 1 LPs incl. *21 Today* '61, two film soundtracks, 2-disc *40 Golden Greats* '77, *Love Songs* '81. 'Power To All Our Friends' '73 reached no. 4, was also a Eurovision entry. The Shadows had many successful records of their own, broke up late '60s; Richard ignored changes in music during '60s, only a cover of Jagger/Richard's 'Blue Turns To Grey' (no. 15 '66 with the Shadows) showing any interest in current trends, perhaps because of well-publicised conversion to Christianity; disavowed cover of 'Honky Tonk Angel' when someone told him it referred to a prostitute. Despite cleancut image (remains a bachelor today) he regained some rock credibility with 'Devil Woman', good soul/rock treatment that made no. 9 UK '76, no. 6 USA, only his third hit there, from LP *I'm Nearly Famous*, no. 5 LP and his best LP in USA at no. 76, prod. by ex-Shadow Bruce Welch, who also prod. *We Don't Talk Anymore* '79, no. 7 LP UK, top 100 USA; title track was his first UK no. 1 in 15 years. No. 4 LP *I'm No Hero* '80 also made top 100 USA, incl. 'Dreamin'' (top 10 single UK/USA); *Wired For Sound* '81 was no. 4 UK, last chart entry USA at no. 132. Alan Tarney wrote 'We Don't Talk Anymore', took over from Welch as producer, succeeded by Craig Pruess; subsequent work saw him less adventurous. Charity remake of 'Living Doll' with comedy team the Young Ones '86 was no. 1; duet 'All I Ask Of You' same year with Sarah Brightman (Andrew LLOYD WEBBER's wife) was top 3. He also made inspirational LP *Walking In The Light* '85 for Word; also recorded with Olivia NEWTON-JOHN, Phil EVERLY, ex-Shadow Hank Marvin; appeared in first stage musical *Time* '85, had two hits from it, left '87 (*see* Dave CLARK). Remains an abiding figure in UK pop, live shows good value for fans.

RICHIE, Lionel (*b* 20 June '49, Ala.) Soul singer, songwriter, producer. Founder member of the COMMODORES, vocal/instrumental act successful on Motown from '74; he played tenor sax, then his lead vocals and songwriting made the group even bigger; he went solo c.'81 and became the biggest black crossover artist of the '80s with fine ballads, smooth voice. Nine top 10 hits '82-5 incl. no. ones 'Truly' '82, 'All Night Long (All Night)' '83, 'Hello' '84, 'Say You, Say Me' '85 (heard in film but not soundtrack LP *White Nights*). His song 'Three Times A Lady' (hit for the Commodores and nominated for a Grammy '78) won ASCAP Nashville Country Songwriter Award, making crossover success complete. Albums cluttered with hits incl. *Lionel Richie* '82, *Can't Slow Down* '83, *Dancing On The Ceiling*, retitled *Say You, Say Me* '86 to milk the hit. Also video *The Making Of Dancing On The Ceiling* '87; CD compilation *The Composer: Great Love Songs* incl. tracks with the Commodores and duets with Diana Ross.

RICHMAN, Jonathan (*b* May '51, Boston, Mass.) Singer, songwriter, leader of the Modern Lovers, USA new wave act with cult following, better known in UK than at home; described as naive genius. Heard the VELVET UNDERGROUND at 15, emulated them; it was said that he went to more of their gigs than they did. Kim FOWLEY claimed he discovered Richman and band '72 in Boston; Richman disputed this in sleeve note to *The Original Modern Lovers* '81, compiled early demos incl. 'Road Runner', 'She Cracked', 'Hospital'; an early champion was Jack NITZSCHE; the demos were hawked around record companies who were not interested at a time when singer/songwriters James TAYLOR, Joni MITCHELL were the rage, Richman's dark and brooding rock was out of step: some critics claimed that if they'd been released then the records would have changed what came after. But they weren't. Early lineup of band incl. TALKING HEADS Jerry Harrison on keyboards, CARS David Robinson on drums. Debut LP was prod. by John CALE, who did Richman's 'Pablo Picasso' in concert, but LP was rejected by WB, not released until *The Modern Lovers* '76, by which time the climate was more receptive, but Richman's style had changed to tweeness: *Jonathan Richman & The Modern Lovers* '76 incl. 'Here Come The Martian Martians' and 'Hey There Insect'; *Rock & Roll With The Modern Lovers* '77 incl. unlikely UK hit 'Egyptian Reggae' (no. 5 '77); *The Modern Lovers Live* '77 had Richman emphatically refusing to play 'Roadrunner'; *Back In Your Life* '79 took tweeness further with 'Abdul & Cleopatra' and 'I'm Nature's Mosquito'. 'Roadrunner' was no. 11 UK '77, 'Morning Of Our Lives' '78 top 30; no hits in USA. Albums on Rhino in USA, Berserkly in UK.

RICHMOND, Dannie (*b* Charles D. Richmond, 15 Dec. '35, NYC; *d* 15 Mar. '88) Drummer, one of the best. Also played tenor sax as teenager. Joined Charles MINGUS Workshop '56 and was Mingus's drummer of choice for the rest of his life: 'He's a musician, not just a timekeeper, one of the most versatile and creative drummers I've ever heard.' First recordings were Mingus dates for Atlantic early '57, then trio with Hampton HAWES on Jubilee, classic *Tijuana Moods* on RCA same year, scores more. Between Mingus dates he recorded with Chet BAKER on Riverside, Jimmy KNEPPER and Herbie NICHOLS on Bethlehem, also worked with Mark-Almond band (LP on CBS), Joe COCKER, Elton JOHN, soul singer Johnny Taylor; gave drum clinics when not on tour, published method book in Germany '65. With Chico FREEMAN quartet '80. His versatility is still under-recognised; inspired by Philly Joe JONES and Max ROACH, he himself should have been better known. Mostly carried on working with other Mingus alumni: LPs *Live At Montreux* '81 on Atlantic, *Reincarnation* '82 on Soul Note as mus. dir. of Mingus Dynasty; founder member of George ADAMS/Don PULLEN quintet for many LPs; own albums as leader: *'In' Jazz For The Culture Set* '65 on Impulse, trio with Jaki BYARD, Cecil MCBEE, guests; *Jazz a Confronto* '75 on Horo with Adams, Jack Walrath; *Ode To Mingus* '79 on Soul Note with Bill Saxton on tenor sax, Danny Mixon on piano (*b* 19 Aug. '49, NYC), Mike Richmond on bass; *The Last Mingus Band Plays Charles Mingus* on Timeless '80 (also sings), *Dannie Richmond Quintet* on Gatemouth '80, *Dionysius* '83 on Italian Red label, all with Walrath, Ricky Ford, Cameron BROWN, Bob Neloms on piano. Co-led George Adams/Dannie Richmond Quintet for *Hand To Hand* '80, *Gentleman's Agreement* '83 on Soul Note, with Knepper, Hugh Lawson on piano (*b* 12 Mar. '35, NYC), Mike Richmond. Mike is not related; busy freelance with own LPs *Dream Waves* '77 on Inner City (trio with drummer Billy Hart), duo *For Us* '78 on Steeplechase, both with keyboardist Andy Laverne.

RIDDLE, Nelson (*b* 1 June '21, Oradell, N.J.; *d* 6 Oct. '85, L.A.) Arranger, conductor, composer. Played trombone and arr. for Charlie SPIVAK '40, then Jerry Wald, Tommy DORSEY; after WWII Bob CROSBY, Dorsey again; staff arr. for NBC radio. From c.'50 with Capitol records, arr. and cond. for Judy GARLAND, Jimmy WAKELY, Betty HUTTON, Margaret WHITING, Ella Mae MORSE, Dean MARTIN, Peggy LEE, others; arr. on Nat COLE hits 'Mona Lisa', 'Too Young' '50-1, but became best-known arr. in Hollywood with Frank SINATRA from Apr. '53: used first-class sidemen such as Harry EDISON; wit and swing generated by use of bass clarinet or trombone as springboard for rhythmic phrases, knowledge of precisely when to bring in rhythm section after introduction to song, when to allow an explosion of brass. Work brought generous tribute from Sinatra: 'Nelson had a fresh approach to orchestration and I made myself fit into what he was doing.' (For rundown of hit singles and albums, see Sinatra entry.) Had own no. 1 hit 'Lisbon Antigua' '55, instrumental with wordless chorus (not his own composition), other minor hits; own LPs in '50s incl. *Hey, Let Yourself Go, Joy Of Living, Cross-Country Suite* (on Dot label, it featured Buddy DEFRANCO, and won Grammy '58). Worked freelance with Oscar PETERSON, Ella FITZGERALD (*Swings Brightly With Nelson, George Gershwin Songbook*) on Verve; on Sinatra's Reprise label with him, Rosemary CLOONEY (LP *Love*); also worked with Johnny MATHIS, others. Film work in various capacities often incl. soundtrack albums: *Pal Joey* and *The Pajama Game* '57, *St Louis Blues* '58, *Li'l Abner* '59, *Can-Can* '60, *Harlow* '65, *Camelot* '67, *Paint Your Wagon* '69, *The Great Gatsby* '74 (Academy Award); many others incl. Sinatra movies; TV theme music incl. *The Untouchables*, *Route 66* (one of the first TV themes to be hit single, no. 30 USA '62). Mus. dir. Julie ANDREWS TV show '72-3. Retired with ill health, but came back to arr. and cond. Linda RONSTADT LPs *What's New* '83 (another Grammy for Riddle), *Lush Life* '84, *For Sentimental Reasons* '86, all hits; also arranged *Blue Skies* '85 for opera singer Kiri Te Kanawa.

RIFKIN, Joshua (*b* 22 Apr. '44, NYC) Pianist, arranger, conductor. Studied at Juilliard, composition with Karlheinz Stockhausen in Germany. Early folk experience with Even Dozen Jug Band; later arr./cond. Judy COLLINS' *Wildflowers* LP on Elektra, her biggest hit (no. 5 '68 incl. top 10 'Both Sides Now'). *The Baroque Beatles Book* '65 on Elektra, classical-style variations on Beatle songs, Rifkin cond. the 'Baroque Ensemble Of The Merseyside Kammermusikgesellschaft', made top 100 LPs USA; then was instrumental in ragtime revival with three LPs of *Piano Rags By Scott Joplin*, which began coming out '70, won

Billboard and *Stereo Review* records of the year awards, charted '74 (the year of the film *The Sting*, whose soundtrack was no. 1 LP), were the best-selling records in Nonesuch's history. Worked, toured, appeared on TV in UK; made classical LPs on Nonesuch with English ensembles; remade digital recordings of rags on EMI; conducted Bach on L'Oiseau-Lyre/Florilegium mid-'80s.

RIGHTEOUS BROTHERS, The White soul duo formed '62: Bobby Hatfield (*b* 10 Aug. '40, Beaver Dam, Wis.) with soaring gospel-style voice, bass Bill Medley (*b* 19 Sep. '40, L.A.). Signed by Moonglow Records as the Paramours, sound dubbed 'blue-eyed soul' and 'righteous' by black fans; changed name and had minor hits (dance-craze 'Little Latin Lupe Lu' made top 50), spotted by Jack GOOD and appeared on *Shindig*, signed by Phil SPECTOR to his Philles label '64 and had no. 1 USA/UK 'You've Lost That Lovin' Feelin' ', co-written by Spector, Barry MANN and Cynthia Weil, one of the biggest, most fondly remembered hits of the era. Formula repeated with 'Just Once In My Life' (top 10 USA), then switched to doo-wop standards 'Unchained Melody', 'Ebb Tide' (both top 5); switched to Verve label for '(You Are My) Soul And Inspiration' (no. 1 USA, 15 UK); album of same title also incl. top 20 'He'. Six LPs on Verve incl. *Standards* '68 on which they each sang a side; they split that year: Hatfield recruited Jimmy Walker as bogus brother for Verve LP *Re-birth* '70; Medley went solo for five MGM LPs (two reached top 200 LPs USA), two each on A&M and Liberty through '80. They reunited '74-5 on Haven label, had surprise necrological hit 'Rock And Roll Heaven' (no. 3 '74). 21 Hot 100 singles altogether '63-74; three top 10 LPs (two on Philles, one on Verve); *Greatest Hits* on Verve '67 incl. hits from Moonglow and Philles. Deserved credit for blue-eyed soul, but spent beautiful voices on mostly mediocre material.

RILEY, Billy Lee (*b* c.'33, Pocahontas, Ark.) Rockabilly singer and multi-instrumentalist, playing guitar, bass, harmonica, drums. First release on Sun 'Rock With Me Baby' was recorded by Jack CLEMENT at WMPS Radio in Memphis, Riley's guitar, bass and drums overdubbed, one of the few Sun discs of the era that had so much production in it; it was Clement's entrée to Sun as well as Riley's. Never had any big hits despite good looks and powerful rock'n'roll, said Riley, because Sun put out too many records in those years: '. . . when there was a Perkins release, a Cash release and later Jerry Lee Lewis, the deejays didn't want to be bothered with the rest . . . The public could only afford so many at one time, anyway.' His influence on the Sun sound was great: Lewis played piano on his regional hit 'Flying Saucers Rock'n'Roll' '57; his band incl. guitarist Roland Janes, drummer Jimmy Van Eaton, became Sun house band. He added sax to rockabilly (Martin Willis, then Ace Cannon, who both also worked for Bill BLACK); he also recorded pop, soul, funky country; had own Rita label, but never made national charts. 2-disc *Red Hot Riley* on Charly UK.

RILEY, Jeannie C. (*b* Jeannie Stephenson, 19 Oct. '45, Anson, Texas) Country singer who made one of the biggest hits of all time. Sang in local talent shows; married childhood sweetheart Mickey Riley '64; encouraged by him she moved to Nashville '67, worked as secretary on Music Row, made demo tapes, signed with Shelby Singleton's Plantation Records: debut single of Tom T. HALL's 'Harper Valley P.T.A.' was no. 1 on country and pop charts, a worldwide hit. She was packaged with a sexy image (knee-length boots, mini-skirt), won Grammy for Best Female Country Vocal Performance '68, scored more hits incl. top tens 'The Girl Most Likely', 'There Never Was A Time', 'Country Girl', 'Oh Singer', 'Good Enough To Be Your Wife' '68-71, all reaching pop charts. Constant touring led to divorce '70; she became a born-again Christian '72, turned to gospel music, was reunited with Mickey. Moved to MGM '71, had minor hits; to Mercury '74 and left charts; briefly returned with 'The Best I've Ever Had' '76 on WB. Published autobiography *From Harper Valley P.T.A. To The Mountain Top* '77. LPs: *Harper Valley P.T.A.* '68, *Yearbooks And Yesterdays* '68, *Generation Gap* '69, *Jeannie* '70, all on Plantation; *Give Myself A Party* '72, *When Love Has Gone Away* '73 on MGM; *Sunday After Church* '75 on Hilltop, *Wings To Fly*

'79 on Cross Country, *The Girl From Texas* '81 on President; *Tears, Joys & Memories* on Allegiance; *Total Woman* '87 on Magnum/ Sundown. *Best Of* on Charly.

RILEY, Terry (*b* 24 June '35, Colfax, Cal.) Composer; like Steve Reich and Philip Glass a 'minimalist' who has influenced the avant-garde. Degree in music '61 at Berkeley, Cal.; played piano and sax in cabarets in Europe, studied with North Indian singer Pandit Pran Nath. His Music appeals to the New Age brigade. *In C* for orchestra is a fragment to be played any number of times (with occasional F sharp); it is so hypnotically repetitious that you can see the pattern of it on the grooved surface of the CBS record. *Rainbow In Curved Air* and *Shri Camel* are also on CBS; there are two albums on Kukuck and a 2-disc set on Celestial Harmonies (*The Harp Of New Albion*, for solo piano). Many of these are solo albums, with Riley playing keyboards, tape etc.; he vocalises on one of the Kukucks, recorded live in Munich '82. String quartet music ('Cadenza On The Night Plain', 'Sunrise Of The Planetary Dream Collector', two more) is played by the Kronos Quartet on a 2-disc set on Gramavision/ Gravity.

RIPERTON, Minnie (*b* 8 Nov. '48, Chicago; *d* 12 July '79, L.A.) Soul singer with operatic training, five-octave range. Joined girl-group the Gems, worked as receptionist at Chess; group sang backing for Fontella BASS, Etta JAMES, etc.; she sang lead with group Rotary Connection, who had two hit LPs '68; recorded solo as Andrea Davis. Solo LP as herself *Come To My Garden* was critically praised. Toured with Roberta FLACK, Quincy JONES etc.; did studio work; signed with Epic for *Perfect Angel*, prod. by Stevie WONDER: no. 4 hit LP incl. no. 1 USA/2 UK single 'Lovin' You' '74 (co-written with husband Dicky Rudolph), whereupon first LP charted on Janus. *Adventure In Paradise* '75 was top 20, *Stay In Love* '77 did well; switched to Capitol for *Minnie* '79 (top 30 LP), but died of cancer. *Love Lives Forever* '80 made top 40 LPs, '78 tracks with new backing dubbed.

RITCHIE, Jean (*b* 8 Dec.'22, Viper, Ky.) Trad. folksinger. One of 14 children, whose parents collected songs and were visited by English folklorist Cecil SHARP '17 and recorded '30s by John and Alan LOMAX. She learned to play dulcimer at home, went to college, taught in school, recorded '46 for Alan's Library of Congress Archive; gigged with WEAVERS, Woody GUTHRIE, Oscar BRAND; first LP *Jean Ritchie Singing Traditional Songs Of Her Mountain Family* '52 on 10″ Elektra. Appeared on TV, recorded for Tradition, Riverside, Prestige, other labels; began building dulcimers with her husband; was one of the original board of directors of the Newport Folk Festival. Among albums: *The Appalachian Dulcimer* '63 on Folkways, *A Time For Singing* on WB, *Clear Waters Remembered* on Sire (reissued on Geordie), *None But One* on Sire issued '79 in UK. Published *Singing Family Of The Cumberlands* '55, *Jean Ritchie's Dulcimer People* '75. The Trio (*see* Emmylou HARRIS) covered her 'My Dear Companion' '87. Her sister also recorded; album *Edna Ritchie* on Folk-Legacy. Jean continues to record on her own Greenhays label, distributed by Flying Fish.

RITENOUR, Lee (*b* 1 Nov. '52, Hollywood, Cal.) Guitarist; also banjo, mandolin etc. Has recorded with Sergio MENDES, Herbie HANCOCK, Gato BARBIERI, Peggy LEE, Oliver NELSON, Carly SIMON, many others; taught classical guitar at USC; ace studio musician makes albums fusing Latin, jazz and soul. Began with *Guitar Player* '76 on MCA Coral; *Gentle Thought, Sugar Loaf Express, Lee Ritenour Friendship* '77-8 on Japanese JVC, all by group called Gentle Thoughts; *First Course* on Epic followed by first chart entry *Captain Fingers* '77; switched to Elektra for *The Captain's Journey* '78, *Feel The Night* '79, *Rit* '81 (helped to no. 26 slot by top 15 single 'Is It You', with vocal by Eric Tagg), all acoustic *Rio* '82, *Rit/2* '82, *On The Line* '83 (did not make pop chart), *Banded Together* '84. *Harlequin* '85 on GRP was co-led with Dave Grusin (*b* 26 June '34), who played on many of the others, incl. two Portuguese songs sung by Brazilian Ivan Lins. *Rio* is now also on GRP; other titles incl. *Earth Run*, soundtrack *American Flyers* on GRP.

RITTER, Tex (*b* Woodward Maurice Ritter, 12 Jan. '05, Panola County, Texas; *d* 2 Jan.

'74, Nashville) Singer, actor. Raised on ranch; attended U. of Texas, Northwestern law school, but switched to music. On radio in Chicago, Houston late '20s, then to Broadway; five plays incl. *Green Grow The Rushes* '30. On radio as actor in *Cowboy Tom's Round-Up*, also co-hosted WHN Barn Dance. First records for ARC '34; movies '36, appearing in more than 50 in about 10 years, mostly as singing cowboy. Unsuccessful on Decca '35-9; first country singer to sign with Capitol '42, scored with 'Rock And Rye Rag' '48, 'Daddy's Last Letter' '50; 'High Noon' '52 made no. 12 pop chart (Oscar-winning song from Gary Cooper movie). Constantly toured after acting career slowed up; co-hosted *Town Hall Party* on radio with Johnny BOND '53-60. Other pop crossovers were 'The Wayward Wind' and co-written 'I Dreamed Of A Hillbilly Heaven' '61; nine entries in country charts '60-71. Moved to Nashville from West Coast '65, joined Grand Ole Opry, hosted late-night radio show on WSM. Ran for US Senate '73 but lost, incurring heavy debts. Helped set up Country Music Foundation and Hall of Fame (elected '64); work carried on after his death by wife Dorothy. LPs incl. *Blood On The Saddle, Songs Of The Golden West* on Capitol; compilation *High Noon* on Bear Family label incl. previously unissued 'Dark Day In Dallas', about JFK assassination. First Capitol LP was *Songs From The Western Screen* '58, reissued on Stetson '87.

RIVERA, Ismael (*b* Santurce, Puerto Rico; *d* 12 May '87, San Juan) Singer, bandleader, composer, producer, percussionist. Magnificent husky voice and distinctive improvisational vocal style earned him title 'El Sonero Mayor' – 'The Best Latin Singer'. Was star of Rafael CORTIJO combo in Puerto Rico; recorded on Ansonia with Orquesta Panamericana; to NYC c.'62 and was reunited with Cortijo on two Tico LPs c. '66-7: wrote seven of 12 tracks on *Bienvenido!/Welcome!*, also headlined on *Con Todos los Hierros (Everything But The Kitchen Sink!)* (*see* Cortijo's entry). Fronted own 9-piece band Cachimbos on *De Colores* c.'68, *Controversia* c.'69; made *Lo Ultimo en la Avenida* c.'71 with Kako & his Band; *Esto Fué lo Que Trajo El Barco* and *Vengo por la Maceta* '72-3 with Cachimbos, incl.

veteran Cuban pianist/arr. Javier Vázquez. *Traigo de Todo* '74 incl. Alfredo 'Chocolate' ARMENTEROS on trumpet as well as Vázquez. Reunited with Cortijo y su Combo on Coco '74; LP reissued '82 as *Ismael Rivera Sonero No. 1*. Ismael Rivera y sus Cachimbos performed 'Sale el Sol (Dormi Contingo)' at Carnegie Hall '74, incl. on *Tico-Alegre All Stars Live At Carnegie Hall Vol. 1* on Tico, which was absorbed by Fania/Vaya mid-'70s; Rivera switched to Vaya for *Soy Feliz* '75; best-of *Eclipse Total* on Tico same year as well as Xmas LP *Feliz Navidad*, prod. by Louie RAMIREZ. *De Todas Maneras Rosas* '77, *Esto Si Es lo Mío* '78 were on Tico with Vázquez; Rivera duetted with Celia CRUZ on *Fania All Stars Live* '78; *Oro* '79 on Tico was a compilation; last LP with Cachimbos was *Maelo* '80, prod. by Rivera. He sang on FAS LP *Latin Connection* '81; *Legend* '84 was a compilation.

RIVERS, Johnny (*b* John Ramistella, 7 Nov. '42, NYC) Versatile pop/rock singer with many hits. Grew up in Louisiana; on trip to NYC met Alan FREED, who suggested name change, helped get record deal with Gone late '50s. To West Coast '60, by '63 a headliner at the Whisky A Go Go, performing covers with catchy arrangements similar to those used by Trini LOPEZ in similar surroundings. *Johnny Rivers Live At The Whisky A Go Go* '64 on Imperial was no. 12 LP incl. no. 2 single 'Memphis', cover of Chuck BERRY hit; he had 25 Hot 100 singles '64-73 on Imperial/United Artists (now EMI), most in top 40, eight altogether in top 10; also 14 LPs in top 200. At the time rock'n'roll was turning into rock; its classics were enough to be revisited as juke box hits by entertainers like Rivers and Lopez (along with folk-protest songs; Rivers had top 30 hit with Pete SEEGER's 'Where Have All The Flowers Gone' '65). His biggest hit and only no. 1 was 'Poor Side Of Town' '66. LP *Realization* '68 was change of direction, with more thoughtful work, his best-selling LP at no. 5, incl. top 15 'Summer Rain', written by James Hendricks, who'd signed to Rivers' Soul City Records, along with the FIFTH DIMENSION, who cashed in with songs by Jimmy WEBB. Rivers' LPs *Slim Slo Slider* '70, *Home Grown* '71 were critically praised as an advance for him, but didn't

chart as well as earlier ones; *L.A. Reggae* '72 got back up to no. 78 with help of no. 6 hit cover of 'Rockin' Pneumonia', '57 R&B hit by Huey SMITH. *Blue Suede Shoes* '73 did not chart, but Carl PERKINS title cover went top 40; this was also the period when the singles market was being abandoned to kids, while baby-boomers buying LPs wanted something more serious. He switched to Atlantic for live *Last Boogie In Paris* and *Road* '74, which didn't chart; surfaced on Epic with *New Lovers And Old Friends* '75, which did: incl. 'Help Me Rhonda', USA top 30 hit with backing vocal by Brian Wilson of the BEACH BOYS (LP retitled for UK but it didn't work: he had no hits at all there). Then to Soul City for *Outside Help* '78 (on Big Tree in USA, Polydor in UK), his last chart entry, with top 10 single 'Swayin' To The Music (Slow Dancin')'. *Not A Through Street* '83 was an inspirational LP on CBS; hits compilations now on Liberty.

RIVERS, Sam (*b* Samuel Carthorne Rivers, 25 Sep. '30, El Reno, Okla.) Tenor sax, composer; also other instruments. Father was a member of Fisk Jubilee Singers, Silvertone Quartet. Attended Boston Conservatory, high reputation among musicians began with local gigs with Herb Pomeroy, Jaki BYARD, Gigi GRYCE; worked with Miles DAVIS mid-'64 incl. tour of Japan. Taught in Harlem; played/recorded with Cecil TAYLOR late '70s; opened Studio RivBea '71 in Manhattan with his wife Bea, played there with own group, guests incl. Clifford JORDAN, Dewey REDMAN, Frank LOWE, Charles TYLER, others; became highly rated composer/leader in 'free jazz'. Began recording on Blue Note, with Bobby HUTCHERSON, Tony WILLIAMS, others; plus own albums: quartets *Fuchsia Swing Song* and *A New Conception*, quintet *Contours*, 2-disc set *Involution*: sextet led by Rivers on one record, quartet led by Andrew HILL (incl. Rivers) on the other, all on Blue Note '64-7 (also *Dimensions And Extensions*, not released until '86). *Hues* and *Streams* incl. live trio tracks made '71-3 with Cecil McBEE, percussion (now *Live Trio* on MCA), *Crystals* '74 was a big band set, *Sizzle* '75 a quintet, all on Impulse. Two vols. of duo *Sam Rivers/Dave Holland* on Improvising Artists, trio *The Quest* with

Holland, Barry ALTSCHUL on Red/Pausa, contribution to *Wildfowers* Festival with different trio (*see* JAZZ), several vols. of *Black Africa* on Horo with another trio, Joe Daley on trombone/euphonium, plus *The Essence* on Circle by The Tuba Trio with Daley on tuba (various parts of the piece on several LPs), all '76. *Paragon* on Fluid made in Paris with Holland, Altschul; *Rendezvous* on Red made in Milan adding Mario Schiano on alto, both '77; *Waves* '78 on ill-fated Tomato label with Holland, Daley, Thurman Barker; *Contrasts* '79 with George LEWIS, Holland, Barker; quartet *Crosscurrent* '81 on Blue Marge made in Paris; *Colours* '82 on Black Saint by 11-piece Winds Of Manhattan incl. Bobby WATSON.

ROACH, Max (*b* Maxwell Roach, 10 Jan. '24, New Land, N.C.) Drummer, composer, leader. Grew up in NYC; given drum kit at age 12. Worked with Charlie PARKER as a teenager at Clarke Monroe's Uptown House, deeply infl. by Kenny CLARKE at Minton's; depped briefly with Duke ELLINGTON, replaced George RUSSELL in Benny CARTER band, recorded with Coleman HAWKINS, all mid-'40s; soon a key member of the bop movement, since then one of the giants of modern jazz, his legato rhythmic feeling perhaps the most widely influential of all. Worked and recorded with Miles DAVIS, many others; to Paris with Parker '49, recorded there with others incl. Kenny DORHAM; to Europe again with JATP '52, at Howard RUMSEY's Lighthouse '54; soon co-led quintet with Clifford BROWN, becoming the most popular jazz combo in the country when Brown, pianist Richie Powell (Bud's brother) were killed in a car crash (for LPs *see* Brown entry). Carried on with Dorham, Sonny ROLLINS (*Max Roach + 4* '56, *Jazz In 3/4 Time* '57 on EmArcy); with Lighthouse All Stars *Drummin' The Blues* on Liberty, quartet *Max Plays Charlie Parker* '57-8 on EmArcy, quintet *Max* '58 on Argo adding Ramsey LEWIS (now in *Percussion Discussion* on Chess, set with LP by Art BLAKEY; that title also used for duo track on Charles MINGUS LP '55: he was partner in Mingus's Debut label, played at Massey Hall concert '53 with Mingus, Parker, Gillespie, Bud POWELL). Changing personnel incl. Coleman, Booker LITTLE, Julian Priester

on trombone: Max Roach + 4 *On The Chicago Scene* and *At Newport Jazz Festival* (now on Japanese import Fontana), Max and Boston Percussion Ensemble at Lenox Music Inn (he taught at Lenox, Mass. School Of Jazz each summer), all '58 originally on EmArcy; *Deeds, Not Words* on Riverside; *Sessions, Live* on Calliope, all '58. *The Many Sides Of Max Roach* on Mercury, *Award-Winning Drummer* on Time/Bainbridge '59; *Quiet As It's Kept* and *Parisian Sketches* on Mercury, *Drum Conversation* on Enja, then one of his best-known records: *Freedom Now Suite* on Candid (also known as *We Insist – Freedom Now!*; made into award-winning film by Gianni Amici '66), followed by *Moon-Faced And Starry-Eyed* on Mercury, all '60, last two with singer Abbey LINCOLN (they were married '62-70). *Percussion Bitter Suite, It's Time* '60-1 on Impulse, *Max Roach – Again* now on Affinity (live from Paris '60, c.'62-3), all with Lincoln. *Speak, Brother, Speak* on America/Fantasy '62, then the duo *The Legendary Hasaan* '64 on Atlantic, with the pianist Hasaan Ibn Ali (*b* 6 May '31, Philadelphia: well-known locally, encouraged by Elmo HOPE when he was young, recorded his own tunes with Roach in NYC incl. 'Hope So Elmo', with Art Davis on bass on some tracks). Sextet *Drums Unlimited* '65-6 on Atlantic incl. solo 'For Big Sid', title track; *Sounds As A Roach* '68 on Lotus made in Oslo with Lincoln, Steve LACY. *Members Don't Git Weary* '68 on Atlantic with quintet, Andy Bey vocals; *Lift Every Voice And Sing* '71 with 22-voice J. C. White Singers on Atlantic, dedicated to Paul ROBESON, Malcolm X, Martin Luther King, Medgar Evers (politician murdered in Mississippi), Patrice Lumumba (murdered in Africa), etc.; also performed at Newport that year. Quartet with Cecil Bridgewater on trumpet made *Live In Tokyo* on Denon, *The Lodestar* on Horo in Rome, *Live In Amsterdam* on Baystate, all '77; *Confirmation* '78 in Paris on Fluid, *Pictures In A Frame* '79 in Milan on Soul Note, *Chattahoochie Red* '81 in NYC on CBS, *In The Light* '82 and *Scott Free* '84 on Soul Note in Milan, and with added string quartet *Live At Vielharmonie Munich* '83, *Easy Winners* '85, *Survivors* '84, *Bright Moments* '87, all with strings, all on Soul Note, the last three octets called 'double quartet'. *Long As You're Living* on Enja is quintet with TURRENTINES. Roach *Solos '77* on Baystate; duos with Archie SHEPP: *Force - Sweet Mao - Suid Afrika '76* in Paris on French Uniteledis, *The Long March '79* at Willisau on Hat Hut; with Anthony BRAXTON: *Birth And Rebirth '78* in Milan on Soul Note, *One In Two - Two In One* at Willisau on 2-disc Hat Hut; with Cecil TAYLOR: *Historic Concerts '79* on Soul Note, live in NYC. Also *Rich Versus Roach '59*, a battle of the bands on Mercury; trio with Sonny CLARK, George DUVIVIER on Bainbridge. He was involved from '72 with percussion ensemble M'Boom: LPs *Re: Percussion '73* on Baystate, *M'Boom '79* on CBS and *Collage '84* on Soul Note, with remarkably consistent personnel incl. Ray Mantilla, Joe Chambers, Fred Waits, up to six more on marimba, xylophone, tympani, woodblocks, orchestral bells, gongs, etc. He taught at Yale, other schools; is Professor of Music at U. of Mass. at Amherst. An infl. in turn on Elvin JONES, many others.

ROBBINS, Marty (*b* Martin Robertson, 26 Sep. '25, Glendale, Ariz.; *d* 8 Dec. '82) One of the most versatile vocalists in country music and one of the all-time most successful; he moved effortlessly through rock'n'-roll, Hawaiian, teenage pop, cowboy ballads, evergreen standards, folk songs and his own compositions. Grew up in the desert, served in US Navy, worked as truck driver, ranch hand etc.; turned to music: had radio show on KTYL in Mesa '48 and played in local clubs; had own TV show *Western Caravan '51* on KPHO Phoenix; with help from Little Jimmy DICKENS, signed to Columbia and hit with his third single, own song 'I'll Go On Alone' '53: joined the GRAND OLE OPRY that year and starred there nearly 30 years, the last performer in the old Ryman Auditorium and the first in the new Opryland complex. Further hits in early '50s led to 'Mr Teardrop' nickname due to his catch-in-the-voice style, but a sign of versatility was 'That's All Right' '54: top 10 country hit with cover of Arthur CRUDUP song, same year it was also Elvis PRESLEY's first release. He had no hits in '55, as though consolidating new influences; then both Robbins and Guy MITCHELL recorded 'Singing The Blues' for Columbia '56 (comp. '54 by Melvin Endsley); Mitchell had the bigger pop hit but Robbins' made the top 20 and was his first no. 1 country hit; 'A White Sport Coat (And A Pink Carnation)' was another no. 1 country and pop no. 2; he had crossovers to the pop Hot 100 every year through '63, incl. his own 'El Paso' '60, a story-song that was no. 1 on both charts and won a Grammy. Meanwhile he appeared regularly on Ed Sullivan TV show, formed own Robbins Records '57, discovered Tompall & the Glaser Brothers; appeared in several films from *Buffalo Guns '57* to *Road To Nashville '67*; he was also a stock car driver, working the circuits whenever the music allowed. Albums of cowboy ballads gained him a fresh country audience; for a while he was absent from the pop charts but had several country hits every year; he starred in TV series *The Drifter*, returned to the pop chart with 'I Walk Alone' '68. He was stopped '69 by major heart surgery and was hospitalised several months; the hits continued and when he returned to work he wrote a song about his wife Marizona, 'My Woman, My Woman, My Wife', which was a country no. 1, won him a second Grammy '70 and was his last Hot 100 hit. He ignored doctors' orders and enjoyed life to the full, touring and racing and having hits every year. Switched to Decca/MCA '72 and prod. his own records, had more hits, not as big as on Columbia; returned there and had country no. 1 with 'El Paso City' '76, stayed in top 10 with 'Among My Souvenirs' ('27 song, *see* Lawrence WRIGHT), 'Adios Amigo' (written by Ralph Freed and Jerry Livingston, a hit for Jim REEVES '62), 'I Don't Know Why (I Just Do)' ('31 hit by Fred AHLERT and Roy Turk), others. In the mid-'70s he first visited UK, found a new audience, returned regularly and saw TV-advertised hits compilation high in the UK charts. He was elected to the Country Music Hall of Fame in Oct. '82 and died of a massive heart attack less than two months later. He had 50 top 10 country hits, 14 at no. 1, 24 crossing over to pop, the feat bettered only by Johnny CASH, Kenny ROGERS and Glen CAMPBELL. Albums incl. *Song Of Robbins '57*, *Song Of The Islands '58*, *Gunfighter Ballads '59*, *A Little Sentimental '60*, *More Gunfighter Ballads '61*, *Devil Woman '62*, *Hawaii's Calling Me* and *Turn The Lights Down Low '63*, *R.F.D. '64*, *What God Has Done '65*, *The Drifter '67*,

Tonight Carmen '67, *It's A Sin* '68, *Country* '69, *My Woman, My Woman, My Wife* '70, all on Columbia; *This Much A Man* '72 on Decca, *Have I Told You Lately* '73 on Columbia, *Good'n'Country* '74 on MCA; *El Paso City* '76, *Adios Amigo* '77, *Don't Let Me Touch You* '78, *All Around Cowboy* and *The Performer* '79, *With Love* '80, *Everything I've Always Wanted* and *The Legend* '81, *Come Back To Me* and *Some Memories Just Won't Die* '82, *Long Long Ago* '85, all on Columbia; *The Master's Call* '83 on Word; *Rockin' Rollin' Robbins* '83, *Pieces Of Your Heart* and *In The Wild West* Parts 1-5 on Columbia/Bear Family '85.

ROBERTS, Luckey (*b* Charles Luckeyeth Roberts, 7 Aug. 1887, Philadelphia, Pa.; *d* 5 Feb. '68, NYC) Piano, composer. Sang and danced in vaudeville aged 5. 'Junk Man Rag' was hit in '13, also wrote 'Pork And Beans', 'Railroad Blues', many more; 'Ripples On The Nile' recorded with words as 'Moonlight Cocktail', big hit for Glenn MILLER '42. Wrote more than a dozen Broadway shows, beginning with *My People* '11. Led society orchestra for decades, counting Franklin D. Roosevelt and the Duke of Windsor among his fans. Had radio show; operated Rendezvous Club in Harlem '42-54. Prodigious keyboard technique woefully under-recorded; best of very few sessions was for one side of '58 LP on Good Time Jazz (other side by Willie 'The Lion' SMITH). Used wide dynamic range, trademark inverted chords, furious decoration in right hand, always with strong pulse: like all the best New York 'ticklers', used piano like a whole orchestra.

ROBERTSON, Don (*b* 5 Dec. '22, Peking, China) Singer, pianist, songwriter. Son of head of dept. of medicine at Peking Union Medical College; family returned to Chicago '27; mother taught him piano. Befriended by poet/folk-singer Carl Sandburg at an early age; studied medicine and music in Chicago; worked in radio, becoming arr. at WGN. To L.A. mid-'40s, making demos for publishers; became rehearsal pianist at Capitol. Moved into songwriting; first hit 'I Really Don't Want To Know' for Eddy ARNOLD '54; then 'I Don't Hurt Anymore' for Hank SNOW same year (with lyricist Jack Rollins); own hit 'The Happy Whistler' '56

(no. 6 USA pop chart '56). Provided more songs for Snow, Les PAUL & Mary Ford, Carl SMITH, Faron YOUNG, Kitty WELLS, Skeeter DAVIS, Nancy WILSON; Hank LOCKLIN's 'Please Help Me I'm Fallin' ' '60 multi-million seller, reached top 10 UK pop chart: Robertson's demo incl. device of using a whole tone as grace note instead of customary half-tone; 'slip note' hallmark of Nashville piano style also practised by Floyd CRAMER (turned up same year on his hit 'Last Date'). Al Martino had a top 10 hit '64 with 'I Love You More And More Each Day'. Also wrote songs for Elvis PRESLEY movies '61-3. Nashville Songwriters Association Hall of Fame '72.

ROBESON, Paul (*b* 9 Apr. 1898, Princeton, N.J.; *d* 23 Jan. '76) Singer of operatic quality, a bass, but often billed as a baritone; also actor. Played football in college, attended Columbia Law School, sang spirituals and became interested in the theatre. Played title role Brutus Jones in Eugene O'Neill's *The Emperor Jones*, in London with it '25, film version '33 (made in a week; it was also Billie HOLIDAY's first film, as an extra in a crowd scene). Played *Othello* in London '30; revival of Jerome KERN's *Show Boat* '32, film version '36; other films: *King Solomon's Mines* '37, *The Song Of Freedom, Dark Sands* and *Jericho* '38; *The Proud Valley* '41, *Native Land* and *Tales Of Manhattan* '42. Began recording for Victor '25; later on Columbia; recorded a great many spirituals, work songs; 'Ballad For Americans' in four parts on two Victor 78s was political in nature; 'King Joe' with Count BASIE on Okeh was also in two parts. His career faltered '40-50s because he was a Communist sympathiser: he had given up hope of amelioration of racism in the USA from any other direction, and he was not alone in those days. Gave concerts in Europe late '50s, early '60s; was president of the Pete Seeger Committee in London early '60s; retired to Harlem '63 in ill health. Many compilations have come and gone, incl. *Songs Of My People* on RCA/UK; in mid-'80s only *The Essential Paul Robeson* on Vanguard in USA, in UK also *Lonesome Road* on ASV, *Songs Of Free Men* on CBS; *Sings 'Ol' Man River' And Other Favourites, The Golden Age Of Paul Robeson, The Best Of Paul Robeson* on EMI labels.

ROBINSON, Smokey (*b* William Robinson Jr, 19 Feb. '40, Detroit) Lead singer of the Miracles, songwriter, producer; became vice-president of Motown '72. Group called the Matadors in high school; other founder members: Ronnie White (*b* 5 Apr. '39), Bobby Rogers (*b* 19 Feb. '40), Pete Moore (*b* Warren Moore, 19 Nov. '39), Claudette Rogers (Bobby's sister, *b* '42), all from Detroit. They knew Berry Gordy when he was writing songs for Jackie WILSON, hadn't formed label yet; were among the first signings when he did, although their first records appeared on other labels: 'Got A Job' on End, 'Bad Girl' on Chess (reached the Hot 100). The Miracles had 46 Hot 100 hits '59-75, 29 in top 40, all but the first on Motown, all but the last four with Smokey, incl. 'Shop Around' (no. 2 '61), 'You've Really Got A Hold On Me' (8 '62, covered by the BEATLES), also 'That's What Love Is Made Of' '64, 'Ooo Baby Baby' and 'The Tracks Of My Tears' '65; Claudette and Smokey had married '59; after a while she stopped touring; they were known as Smokey Robinson and the Miracles from '67, 'I Second That Emotion' no. 4 that year and their first UK top 30; then 'If You Can Want', 'Yester Love', 'Special Occasion', 'Baby, Baby Don't Cry' (no. 8 '69), 'The Tears Of A Clown' (no. 1 '70, both USA/UK), 'Satisfaction' '71 (not the ROLLING STONES song), many more all written/co-written by Smokey. Also 'Mickey's Monkey' '63, 'Come 'Round Here (I'm The One You Need)' '66 written by HOLLAND-DOZIER-HOLLAND, his only rivals for total number of Motown hits; guitarist Marvin Tarplin not only played the classic riffs on the hits but co-wrote 'I Like It Like That', 'My Girl Has Gone', etc., became regular member of the group; other co-writers incl. Ronnie White and Bobby Rogers; Al Cleveland came up with the title of 'I Second That Emotion' while they were Xmas shopping (and later co-wrote 'What's Goin' On' for Marvin GAYE). Gordy, not only an old friend but seasoned spotter of talent, soon assigned other work to Smokey, who wrote 'My Guy' for Mary WELLS, 'I'll Be Doggone' and 'Ain't That Peculiar' for Gaye, hits for the Marvelettes and above all for the TEMPTATIONS: 'My Girl', 'Get Ready', 'The Way You Do The Things You Do', many others as well as classic LP *The Temptations Sing Smokey* '65. He went solo '72 to spend more time with his family and on other Motown duties; they had a few more hits incl. no. 1 'Love Machine' '75, left Motown and had no more success; Smokey had Hot 100 hits, 7 in top 40: with 'Cruisin' ' (no. 4 '79), 'Being With You' (no. 1 UK/2 USA '81), he became one of the few in the rock era to have hits in four decades: his memorable tunes, unique falsetto, way with a metaphor were probably helped by his strong marriage (two children named Berry and Tamla). His songs were covered by Linda RONSTADT, Johnny RIVERS, many others; Bob DYLAN called him the greatest living poet in America. David Morse wrote that his voice 'recognizes no distinction between speech and song; it uncoils from a breathy intimate whisper into a clear, bright, continuously intense verbal pressure . . . While other singers land heavily on the beat, Smokey Robinson maintains a subtle continuous contact with it, a kind of prehensile touching.' (Quoted by Nelson George in his excellent *Where Did Our Love Go? The Rise And Fall Of The Motown Sound* '85.) 3-disc *Anthology* by the Miracles is a priceless document; 15 chart solo albums incl. solo LPs incl. *Smokey* '73, *A Quiet Storm* '75, *Where There's Smoke* '79 (incl. 'Cruisin' '), *Being With You* '81, *Essar* '84, *Smoke Signals* '86.

ROBINSON, Sugar Chile (*b* Frank Robinson, '40, Detroit, Mich.) Pianist, singer. A child prodigy who could play Erskine HAWKINS's 'Tuxedo Junction' age 2. Aided by bandleader Frankie CARLE, made first record age 6, appeared in Van Johnson movie *No Leave, No Love* same year. Played at party for President Truman; signed by Capitol, had hits 'Numbers Boogie', 'Caldonia', 'Christmas Boogie' '49; TV appearances *This Is Show Business* and *The Milton Berle Show*; toured UK incl. London Palladium; made short films *The Negro In Entertainment*, *With Billie Holiday And Count Basie Sextet*, *Jazz Cocktail* '50-1; played dates with Lionel HAMPTON; slipped into obscurity.

ROBINSON, Tom (*b* '50, Cambridge) Singer, songwriter, bandleader, gay activist. Studied oboe, clarinet, bass as a teenager; after nervous breakdown, entered therapeutic community, met guitarist Danny Kustow, formed Café Society '73: trio was early signing to KINKS' label; eponymous LP sold about 600 copies; they left acrimoniously. Formed Tom Robinson Band with Kustow, drummer 'Dolphin' Taylor and keyboardist Mark Ambler; within months they were the talk of London: committed political activist Robinson was older and more articulate than most punks, soon the darling of the critics. Played safe with single 'Motorway' (top 10 '77); live *Rising Free* EP incl. anthemic 'Glad To Be Gay'. *Power In The Darkness* '78 was an essential punk LP, like debuts of CLASH and SEX PISTOLS, to understanding political/musical mood of UK late '70s, incl. strident 'Up Against The Wall', epic 'Winter Of '79'. TRB live were always good value, but *TRB II* '79 was TRB by numbers, acute lyrics largely replaced by sloganeering (prod. by Todd RUNDGREN). They split that year; Robinson collaborated on songs with Elton JOHN (tongue-in-cheek gay single 'Never Gonna Fall In Love'), Peter GABRIEL; formed Sector 27 (flaccid eponymous LP '80). He moved to East Germany. Solo *North By Northwest* '82 made in Hamburg was return to form, with 'Now Martin's Gone', early version of 'Atmospherics' (co-written with Gabriel). *Tom Robinson Band* '81 was definitive compilation. Returned to UK '82, worked in cabaret and fringe theatre (*Cabaret 79* '82). 'War Baby' and 'Atmospherics: Listen To The Radio' were hits '83; *Hope & Glory* '84 incl. them plus impressive cover of STEELY DAN's 'Rikki Don't Lose That Number'. *Still Loving You* '86 incl. anti-cocaine 'The Real Thing'; *Midnight At The Fringe* '87 made at Edinburgh Festival '83.

ROBISON, Carson J. (*b* 4 Aug. 1890, Chetopa, Kansas; *d* 24 Mar. '57, Pleasant Valley, N.Y.) USA singer, songwriter, early country music star. Sang professionally in Midwest age 15; by '24 recording for Victor NYC, mainly as a whistler; worked with Vernon DALHART four years, then Frank Luther (*b* Francis Luther Crowe, 4 Aug. '05, Kansas; freelance pop, hillbilly records; later composed and recorded children's songs; dir. of children's radio NYC mid-'40s; recording executive, lecturer, author of *Americans And Their Songs*). Formed group the Buckaroos '32, later Carson

Robison Trio, then Pleasant Valley Boys. Co-wrote 'Barnacle Bill The Sailor' '29 with Luther, also 'Way Out West In Kansas', 'My Blue Ridge Mountain Home', 'Carry Me Back To The Lone Prairie', many others; his own recitative 'Life Gets Tee-Jus, Don't It' was no. 14 pop hit '48. Even dabbled with rock'n' roll: 'Rockin' And Rollin' With Grandmaw' made in '56 a few months before he died.

ROCK, ROCK'N'ROLL, ROCKABILLY Rock-'n'roll began with white people playing rhythm & blues in the mid-'50s; the part of it infl. by country music was called rockabilly; it all came to be called 'rock' in the '60s when it grew up: rock has dominated popular music internationally for 30 years, twice as long as Jazz did in the Big Band Era. At the end of that era pop singers took over, following the lead of Bing CROSBY; many of these were much-loved stars and fine musicians such as Frank SINATRA, Dinah SHORE, Jo STAFFORD, Rosemary CLOONEY, Perry COMO; new stars Tony BENNETT, Vic DAMONE came forward; Kay STARR, Patti PAGE, Georgia GIBBS etc. had good voices and many hits. But the quality of new songs seemed to slump badly as the golden age of Broadway and American popular song faded, mainly because the rise of television meant that radio broadcasting was abandoned to the marketplace, where the easiest way to make money was to play a limited number of hit records by vocalists singing songs which in many cases were no more than jingles. Good albums were being made which are still selling today, but the rise of the radio 'playlist' was the worst thing ever to happen to popular music, and is still a curse decades later; some people stopped listening to the radio when 'How Much Is That Doggie In The Window' was no. 1 for 8 weeks '53, and a new generation was growing up hearing fewer good songs and little jazz of any kind. Another problem was that few of the hits were dance music; demographics played a part as it would continue to do in the following decades: in late '40s-early '50s as baby-boomers were being born, their parents had to rely on a smaller generation born during the Depression for baby-sitters and that problem became a standard sit-com joke; parents often stayed at home watching TV instead of going out to the few clubs and dance-halls that were left. As jazz had dominated pop music in the Swing Era, so black music once again came to the rescue: *see* RHYTHM & BLUES. A few young whites discovered urban blues, for example on radio from the south side of Chicago, but the full impact of that was not felt for some years; the dance/party strand of R&B crossed over to the pop charts: lyrics were more fun and true to life; novelties had a danceable beat; the era of covers began: Lloyd PRICE's 'Lawdy Miss Clawdy' '52, Joe TURNER's 'Shake, Rattle And Roll' '54 were huge R&B hits that found white fans; Ray CHARLES had regional R&B hits in a smooth style from '49, from '54 brought gospel fervour to them; Buddy MORROW covered Jimmy FORREST's R&B hits; Bill HALEY covered 'Shake, Rattle & Roll' '54. Black vocal groups were of great import (*see* DOO-WOP); the Orioles' 'Crying In The Chapel' '53 was covered by white acts, biggest version by June Valli (*b* 30 June '30, NYC; Arthur GODFREY talent show winner had six RCA hits '52-4, married Chicago DJ Howard Miller). The McGUIRE Sisters had no. 1 hit '55 with 'Sincerely', co-written by Harvey FUQUA for his Moonglows (who had no. 2 R&B hit); the Chords lost their R&B novelty 'Sh-Boom' to the CREW-CUTS, whose indomitably white version was no. 1 in the pop chart, and who took the Penguins' 'Earth Angel' to no. 3 '55, also covered Gene & Eunice's 'Ko Ko Mo' '55 (but Perry Como had the no. 2 pop hit). Georgia Gibbs took 'Tweedle Dee' (from LaVern BAKER) to no. 2, then 'Roll With Me Henry' to no. 1 '55 (changed to 'Dance With Me Henry'; *see* Hank BALLARD). Black songwriters got royalties from white hits (when not cheated by publishers), but handwriting was on the wall: 'Sh-Boom' was described as the first rock'n'roll record: it was not, but it was the first no. 1 rock'n'roll hit. The BOSWELL Sisters had sung 'Rock And Roll' '34 (hit from film *Transatlantic Merry-Go-Round*); the black sexual euphemism was now borrowed by white DJ Alan FREED, among the first to perceive the new trend, to avoid the obvious racial connotation of 'rhythm & blues'. The first R&B act to cross over to no. 1 on the pop chart was the PLATTERS (with 'The Great Pretender' '55); Chuck BERRY stormed the pop chart from the same year, songs about cars, girls and high school appealing to white and black kids equally, with emphasis on electric guitar; the New Orleans scene exploded with pop hits by Fats DOMINO '55, LITTLE RICHARD '56, Huey SMITH '57, all incl. rocking sax solos. SHIRLEY & LEE with 'Let The Good Times Roll', Thurston Harris with 'Little Bitty Pretty One' crossed over '56-7. Covers by Pat BOONE, Gale STORM etc. continued for a while, but soon abated. Meanwhile country boogie came from honky tonk (*see* COUNTRY MUSIC), infl. by Hank WILLIAMS and by hits like 'Freight Train Boogie' by The DELMORE Brothers late '40s (especially Alton's guitar playing), Arthur SMITH's 'Guitar Boogie' '48, Ernie FORD's 'Shot Gun Boogie' '51, and by the long career of Sidney Louie 'Hardrock' Gunter (*b* 18 Sep. '18, Birmingham, Ala.): Gunter growled 'We're gonna rock'n'roll' on 'Gonna Dance All Night' '50 on the Bama label; recorded for Bullet, Decca, MGM, King, own labels; but not even his worst records could hit ('Hillbilly Twist' on Starday '62); he gave up, joined insurance business (compilation *Boogie Woogie On Saturday Night* on Charly UK). In '54 he had leased a new version of 'Gonna Dance All Night' to Sun Records in Memphis; months later Sun released Elvis PRESLEY's first record: the fusion of country music and R&B called rockabilly made Presley the most successful rocker of all, indeed a phenomenon beyond the merits of his undoubted talent; he brought the clearest infusion of black blues to the new genre, covering songs by Price, Turner, Charles, Arthur CRUDUP, others. Rockabilly also incl. Carl PERKINS, Jerry Lee LEWIS and Roy ORBISON, who all began on Sun; local boys Dorsey and Johnny BURNETTE were turned down by Sun; from Texas came Buddy HOLLY and Buddy KNOX; Eddie COCHRAN and Gene VINCENT were also young white hopes. Surf music began on the West Coast (*see* JAN & DEAN, the BEACH BOYS); its harmonies, adolescent values led to the soft rock of today's MOR radio, but for the most part rock'n'roll was simple, 12-bar music with a good beat, unashamedly sensual (the best songs of earlier decades had been sensual in a more lyrical way, but a new generation knew nothing of that and had no way of knowing). The music business hated rock'n'roll, not aware that its own sleazy greed had made it inevitable; Count BASIE took the reasonable view that anything that got kids dancing again couldn't be all bad; in any case the excitement abated as there was a terrible toll among the stars: Presley sold out to Hollywood, Perkins was sidetracked by a car crash when he should have been touring to promote his hit 'Blue Suede Shoes', Lewis disappeared from the charts when he married his 13-year-old cousin without divorcing his wife, Berry was hampered by a racist arrest under the outmoded Mann Act, Holly and Cochran died in accidents, Vincent drank too much and Little Richard quit to get religion. Racism and payola continued to affect what was played on the radio, yet rock'n'roll also had influence: before long every TV studio band played an unnecessary backbeat, and songwriters jumped on the gravy train; Starr had hit 'The Rock And Roll Waltz' as early as '56, 3/4 time with kling-kling-kling piano: the business soon embraced the distasteful as it smelt money. New rock'n'roll entrepreneurs found teen idols like FABIAN; clever producers like Phil SPECTOR (a millionaire at 21) invented instant nostalgia (his studio technique sounded like a transister radio even if it was heard over a 12″ woofer). Off-the-peg songs from the BRILL BUILDING were the best part of USA pop early '60s; then rock'n'roll was rescued by the British Invasion: Skiffle had got British kids playing guitars in the '50s; black R&B artists and bluesmen were more honoured in Europe than in USA, many playing in London; Alexis KORNER and Cyril DAVIES opened a blues club '55, and Long John BALDRY, Jack Bruce, Ginger BAKER, Graham BOND, future ROLLING STONES drummer Charlie Watts played in their band Blues Incorporated, succeeded by John MAYALL's Bluesbreakers, the YARDBIRDS and the Stones. In Liverpool young people heard USA rock'n'roll as merchant seamen brought home the latest records and on Continental radio (Cochran, Vincent, Holly were more popular in the UK in their lifetimes than in the USA); the Merseyside scene threw up rock'n'roll bands incl. the BEATLES, who took the USA by storm '64 and set the music business on its ear for the rest of the decade. Many reasons for the emergence of rock'n'roll came to a head: the '50s had been a decade of boring hypoc-

risy, seen by a Washington journalist as 'the age of the slob', when the average American seemed interested only in the crabgrass in his lawn, while Britain suffered from postwar drabness as rationing was extended far longer than necessary. Demography meant that post-war baby-boomers became the largest group of consumers, whose economic clout meant the ability to dominate popular culture (and willingness of commercial interests to allow them to do so); people who grew up in the '50s overthrew that decade's values with vengeance. The name of the music was shortened to 'rock' c.'67 to differentiate it from manufactured pop that had briefly subverted rock'n'roll, became 'progressive' rock as the Beatles, Stones, KINKS, and WHO in UK, Beach Boys, BYRDS, BUFFALO SPRINGFIELD etc. in USA wrote their own songs for their generation, producing an unwise attitude on the part of critics that everybody should write their own songs, lowering the average quality still further. (Artists who wrote their own hits were able to keep more of the money, and before long managers and producers got into the act: the economics of music publishing is another factor that has helped lower the quality of the average popular song.) Progressive rock was a contradiction in terms, and soon began to decay as the MOODY BLUES and PINK FLOYD invented the banal equivalent of Mahler symphonies for rock band, and as YES, QUEEN, KISS, GONG, King Crimson, others made pomp-rock, art-rock, classical rock etc., bestowing a weight that a form based on the blues could never carry. (In the UK mid-'80s, Marillion was a new 'progressive' success, the act the same from one year to the next.) Paul BUTTERFIELD played electric blues at Newport '65, while SOUL music replaced R&B as the dominant black genre, bringing good songs and gorgeous singing to the charts; acid rock and psychedelic rock began in San Francisco during the hippie/flower-power era, infl. by ingested chemicals. SOFT MACHINE in UK, CHICAGO USA made early attempts to invent jazz-rock. Baker, Bruce, guitarist Eric CLAPTON formed blues-based power trio CREAM, bestowing long, loud, improvised solos on a form that again could not bear them; LED ZEPPELIN carried the grandiose further towards HEAVY METAL, an absurd antithesis of the blues. Jimi HENDRIX, Janis JOPLIN, Jim Morrison (of the DOORS) were culture heroes, but died young; Hendrix was a hugely influential guitarist who might have gone on to forge a new direction. Durable work came from UK folkrockers (FAIRPORT CONVENTION, etc.); in the USA Frank ZAPPA, CAPTAIN BEEFHEART, the VELVET UNDERGROUND (with Lou REED) had individual voices; the BAND, CREEDENCE CLEARWATER, Neil YOUNG, LITTLE FEAT, a few others created classic rock, effectively white rhythm & blues and infl. by country music, neither pretentious nor imitative. Gram Parsons came up through the Byrds and the Burrito Brothers to pioneer country rock, of great importance for the future; singer/songwriters had their day in the charts, the best incl. Joni MITCHELL, Van MORRISON and Bob DYLAN, rock's best writer, who knew he was no hero but was wilfully misunderstood. Others such as John PRINE, Tom PAXTON, Loudon WAINWRIGHT III, Steve GOODMAN, Bob GIBSON, Tom RUSH, Spider John KOERNER and John STEWART came from folk/country musics: the singer/songwriters were the true art-rockers, but would not have accepted the label. By the early '70s most of rock's stars had done their best work, some not surviving its excesses, and rock had become diffuse, lost its impact and was in fact exhausted: it had become a socio-cultural phenomenon having little to do with musical values, a bad omen for the future, the rock concert established as ritual; as the '70s were marked by politics as usual, terrorism and the floundering of the world economy, the idealism of the '60s went underground and popular music floundered too: Elton JOHN was a big star of the new decade, rock's LIBERACE; the lounge-lizard cabaret style of Bryan Ferry was an attempt at chic rock; Gary GLITTER invented glitter-rock; David BOWIE was responsible for glam-rock and several other images: a clever *poseur*, or expertly catching the narcissism of the era, or simply determined to be a star, or all three. The promo video began to have undue influence, leading to the complaint 'nice video, shame about the song'. DISCO soon went sour, its electronics over-used and production too elaborate; critics complained that disco was the worst thing that ever

happened to rock, not realising that rock itself had nowhere to go. Boring '70s rock brought reaction: PUB ROCK bands in London played R&B-based music in local venues; PUNK ROCK tried to lead a revolt but was merely revolting, its new broom's worn-out bristles followed by NEW WAVE pop, whose willingness to experiment mostly proved to be ephemeral: the 'new romantics' (e.g. Boy George) were frank about simply having a good time. New teen idols came and went (DURAN DURAN, WHAM!). Mid-'80s big trad. rock acts were U2, Bruce SPRINGSTEEN, Bob SEGER, having in common sincerety, complete identification with fans, little musical progress. Technology has resulted in little more than ephemeral pop after a decade, much of it merely noise; the best rock rhythm sections had always learned from rhythm & blues, while machines do not and cannot swing, yet drum machines and electronic drums are used by people who should know better and there are studio engineers who do not know how to record live drummers (digitalised noise makers are now fitted with a device providing a random element: a 'humaniser'). Rock is now repertory, like all popular music, but rock fans have grown up to control advertising and TV music with little musical judgement: the inappropriate backbeat, irritating in film scores and TV adverts, reached an apotheosis in 'Little Rootie Tootie' on the Thelonious MONK tribute LP *That's The Way I Feel Now* '84, and the debut LP by UK saxophone quartet Sticky Fingers '87: what incessant, loud, unswinging rock drumming has to do with jazz is hard to fathom. After 30 years neither the MOR radio rock of HEART, JOURNEY, FOREIGNER etc. nor the adolescent angst of the SMITHS, THOMPSON TWINS, Pet Shop Boys etc. are much advance on 'Doggie In The Window': pop music is a fusion of image and sound, a pastime, and there is nothing wrong with that, but music lovers cannot take it seriously. The major record labels were caught flat-footed when the bubble burst: the baby-boomers were getting older and buying fewer records as the music got worse; with the oil crises of the mid-'70s the majors could no longer get money for old rope, and a decade later had not got over the shock, but wrung their hands and asked for a tax on blank tape. Ironically there is more good music around than ever, interesting things happening under the noses of the accountants, while continuing reissue of the best music of the century (jazz, rock, folk, country and all) made more good records available than ever, many of them leased from the major labels, who regarded their vaults as hindering the search for a new megabuck: the availability of everything may mean that there will never again be domination of popular music by one genre. What is needed now is the abolition of the playlist (by law if necessary), forcing broadcasters to hire people who like music to play the records. Recent revival bands such as the STRAY CATS, LOS LOBOS, BLASTERS etc., unlike earlier revival acts such as SHOWADDYWADDY, SHA NA NA, are not mere imitators, but the quality of revival in rock will be more limited than in jazz, where musical values are higher: the Stray Cats soon tired of the limitation of it, while the lead vocalist of USA quartet the Del Fuegos sounds like a tired mixture of Dylan, Mick Jagger and Randy NEWMAN. 'Third world' music always threatens to achieve a higher profile (that is, music heretofore ignored by the rest of us) (from Africans, Puerto Ricans, others; *see also* TEX-MEX, CAJUN, ZYDECO). Country 'outlaws' like Willie NELSON, Waylon JENNINGS, Joe ELY and others combined rock and country values to give the whole business a shot in the arm (*see* COUNTRY MUSIC); country-rock artists like Emmylou HARRIS, Butch HANCOCK, Terry ALLEN, Richard DOBSON, Guy CLARK, others have led some of the best bands and written some of the best songs in years; some of these, along with many singer/songwriters of yesteryear, ignore the big business entirely, marketing their own records for their fans, who may never hear them on the radio, while younger ones like Lyle LOVETT, Nanci GRIFFITH, Robert Earl KEEN, Darden SMITH and Steve EARLE have been signed by major labels, one of the best signs in the late '80s: their work brings the values of country music to rock, good songs coming first. Continuing black input is hopeful, newcomers like Stan Campbell, Robert CRAY, Whitney HOUSTON steeped in soul and blues (though even critics have noticed that many of Houston's songs are hackneyed, written by producers to make

money). Jazz-based music refuses to go away; Linda RONSTADT's LPs of old standards (dire as they are) and the wide popularity of LOOSE TUBES, Wynton MARSALIS, SADE, Courtney PINE etc. indicated boredom with simple-minded pop/rock. Lack of taste and imagination on the part of the industry, not rock'n'roll itself, is to blame for the apparently dismal state of popular music today: as the song has always had it, 'It's Only Rock'n'Roll'; while pop/rock drowned in noise, many a bar band played basic music with roots in R&B but without studio toys or too much production (*see* ROCKIN' JIMMY; also ALLIGATOR label). Carl Belz' *The Story Of Rock* '69 was an early book; see also Charlie Gillett's excellent *The Sound Of The City* '70 (new edition '83); *Rock'n'Roll Is Here To Pay* '77 by Steve Chapple and Reebee Garofalo is useful on the history/politics of the rock industry, except for naive flower-power sentiments in the last chapter. *The Rolling Stone Illustrated History Of Rock & Roll* '81 (ed. Jim Miller) has 83 essays on artists/genres. *Rock Of Ages: The Rolling Stone History Of Rock And Roll* '86 by Ed Ward, Geoffrey Stokes and Ken Tucker is very good, though Ward on the '50s takes a familiar attitude that the whole history of music was only a prelude to rock. The narcissism of rock's stars, fans and critics has resulted in a huge bibliography; despite its title, *Popular Music Since 1955: A Critical Guide To The Literature* '85 by Paul Taylor is a valuable guide to rock writing, excluding jazz etc. but incl. some folk and country.

ROCKIN' DOPSIE (*b* Alton Jay Rubin, 10 Feb. '32, Carencro, La.) ZYDECO accordionist and vocalist, bandleader; also spelled 'Dupsee' in the past. Plays hot dance music style steeped in R&B. Played local venues in Lafayette from '55, covered R&B hits zydeco style; first records '69 for Bon Temps, then Blues Unlimited labels; after New Orleans Jazz And Heritage Festival '76 signed with Swedish-based Sonet label for Europe: with energetic promotion, critical acclaim, first toured Europe '79 with his group the Twisters, his novelty assisting him: with Clifton CHENIER and Queen Ida among first in Louisiana genres to tour there. Guested on Paul SIMON hit LP *Graceland* '86. LPs: *Doing The Zydeco* '78,

Zy-De-Blue '78, *Hold On* '79, *Big Bad Zydeco* '80, *French Style* '82, all on Sonet, some on GNP USA; also *Rockin' Dopsie & The Twisters* on Rounder USA; *Crowned Prince Of Zydeco* '87 on Maison de Soul/Sonet incl. originals and R&B interpretations, vocal by guitarist Sherman Robertson on 'Something On Your Mind', Dopsie's sons Alton Rubin Jr on drums and David on rub-board, John Hart on sax, Paul Senegal on guitar, Alonzo Johnson on bass.

ROCKIN' JIMMY & THE BROTHERS OF THE NIGHT Tulsa, Oklahoma bar band with deserved cult following. Oklahoma is home base for J. J. CALE, Elvin BISHOP, Leon RUSSELL; Eric CLAPTON recruited sidemen there incl. Jamie Oldaker on drums, covered 'Little Rachel' by Jimmy Byfield (*b* 7 Feb. '49, Tulsa) on *There's One In Every Crowd* '74, had top 30 USA hit 'Tulsa Time' '80. Ex-Joe COCKER roadie Peter Nicholls from UK was engineer for Russell's Shelter label, formed Pilgrim label in Tulsa, recorded local acts: Tulsa clique turned out 2-disc sampler unreleased commercially, edited to single LP *The Tulsa Sampler* '77 (incl. track by Guava, band fronted by Byfield); another sampler *The Green Album* '78 incl. 'Little Rachel', others by Jim Byfield And His Band; then *By The Light Of The Moon* '81 by Rockin' Jimmy And The Brothers Of The Night: Byfield on vocals, Steve Hickerson on guitar, Chuck DeWalt on drums, Gary Gilmore on bass, Walt Richmond on keyboards, backing singers Jim Sweney and Debbie Campbell, horns (electronic?) on some tracks, subtle and appropriate. Gilmore had played with Cale, Taj MAHAL; Richmond with Bonnie RAITT, Rick Danko, others; Campbell (from Fort Worth, Texas) was lead singer with L.A. group Buckwheat, toured with Raitt. Gilmore was replaced by Gary Cundiff on second album *Rockin' Jimmy & The Brothers Of The Night* '82 (quintet only): it should have been called *Rockin' All Night* after the first track. All songs (except Ray CHARLES cover 'Leave My Woman Alone' on first LP) written or co-written by Byfield, co-writers incl. Nicholls, on second LP Hickerson, Richmond, Cundiff. Distribution problems of all small labels prevailed; Byfield, a family man, did not want to tour widely; the band is now history but the LPs

live, on Sonet in UK: fine songs, Byfield's soulful tenor, rhythm section rooted in R&B (laid-back yet tense) made music with space, time, loneliness, roadhouse optimism in it, proving that there's nothing wrong with rock no matter what's on the radio. Fans treasure the LPs, feel a shock of recognition upon meeting one another, and wonder how many more great bands there are out there not recording at all. The band also played on Sweney's *Didn't I Blow Your Mind?* '79 (on Pilgrim), Campbell's *Two Hearts* c.'82 (on Tulsa's Churchill label).

RODGERS, Jimmie (*b* James Charles Rodgers, 8 Sep. 1897, Meridian, Miss.; *d* 26 May '33 NYC) Singer/songwriter, guitarist; first country music star of lasting importance. Worked on railroads, learned music from workmates, hoboes, black and white. First recorded for Ralph PEER in Bristol, Tenn. Aug. '27 (the day Peer first recorded the CARTER family). He made 110 sides in less than five years, the last two days before death from TB. Worked vaudeville, tent show circuits; made *The Singing Brakeman* short film '29; did benefit concerts for dust bowl farmers with humorist Will Rogers '31; had radio show on KMAC (San Antonio, Texas) '32-3. Emmett Miller (who recorded 'Lovesick Blues' '20s, big hit for Hank WILLIAMS '49) was said to have introduced yodelling to country music, others said it was Riley PUCKETT; calling himself a 'popular entertainer', Rodgers combined yodelling with 12-bar blues; recorded sometimes solo, often with a small band, often with Hawaiian guitar: the guitar had been imported to Hawaii with Spanish and Portuguese cowboys mid-19th century; Hawaiians invented slack tuning (called *ki ho alu*), also open-chord tunings; Joseph Kekeku was the first to fret the guitar with a comb instead of his fingers, inventing slide guitar; by '30s hot Hawaiian guitar had been popular in vaudeville and restaurants for a decade (King Bennie Nawahi played jazz and blues as well as hulas; compilation on Yazoo). By incl. it in his act (played by Joe Kaipo e.g. on 'Everybody Does It In Hawaii', 'Tuck Away My Lonesome Blues') Rodgers set the stage for the soon-ubiquitous steel guitar; in fact he defined the content of country music for decades to come, many songs co-written with sister-in-law Elsie McWilliams: repertoire incl. sentimental ballads ('Daddy And Home', 'My Old Pal'); hard times ('Waiting For A Train', 'TB Blues'); love ('Looking For A New Mama' and 'My Little Lady'); bravado, double entendre ('Pistol Packin' Papa'). 'In the Jailhouse Now' no. 1 hit for Webb PIERCE '55; 'Muleskinner Blues', others have been covered many times. He recorded 13 Blue Yodels, the first ('T for Texas') a million-seller; many simply numbered, some also titled: 'Blue Yodel No. 4 (California Blues)'. 'Blue Yodel No. 9' made in Hollywood on 16 July '30 had Louis ARMSTRONG among the sidemen. He was not a good guitar player; his quirky sense of time caused trouble for others (Louis plays beautifully on 'Blue Yodel No. 9', but with unusual caution). Total sales probably about 12 million by '50, but were phenomenal for Depression era: poor people felt he was one of them, bought his records with other necessities. All have been reissued on haphazard series of RCA LPs and in Japanese boxed set. Among first elected to Country Music Hall of Fame '61; original talent infl. Gene AUTRY, Ernest TUBB, Lefty FRIZZELL, Hank SNOW, many more. Definitive biography *Jimmie Rodgers* by Nolan Porterfield '79.

RODGERS, Jimmie (*b* James Frederick Rodgers, 18 Sep. '33, Camas, Wash.) Folk/pop singer, no relation to the Jimmie RODGERS above, though perhaps named after him as many boys were in the early '30s. Taught music by his mother, won on Arthur GODFREY talent show, signed by Hugo Peretti and Luigi Creatore, producers who had left RCA to form new Roulette label. 'Honeycomb' ('54 song by Bob Merrill) was no. 1 hit '57, followed by 'Kisses Sweeter Than Wine' (revival of '51 WEAVERS hit), 'Oh-Oh, I'm Falling In Love Again', 'Secretly', 'Are You Really Mine', all top 10 '57-8; string of lesser hits, on Dot '62-6, then A&M for 25 Hot 100 entries altogether. He suffered a serious skull fracture in a mysterious assault late '67; LPs *It's Over* '66 on Dot, *Child Of Clay* '68 (title track was last chart entry) and *Windmills Of Your Mind* '69 on A&M made album chart. Others incl. *Jimmie Rodgers, This Is Jimmie Rodgers* '87 on RCA. *Honeycomb & Other Hits* now on Accord.

RODGERS, Richard (*b* 28 June '02, Arverne, Long Island, NY; *d* 30 Dec. '79, NYC) Composer, songwriter; one of the most successful of all on Broadway and in films; half of two great songwriting teams, first with Lorenz Hart (*b* 2 May 1895, NYC; *d* 22 Nov. '43, NYC), then with Oscar Hammerstein II (*b* 12 July 1895, NYC; *d* 23 Aug. '60, Doylestown, Pa.). Rodgers first wrote songs at 11, then saw Jerome KERN's *Very Good Eddie* at 14: Kern virtually invented the American musical show, taking it out of the genre of European operetta (*see* Rudolph FRIML, Sigmund ROMBERG, Victor HERBERT, etc.); Rodgers subsequently said that 'Life began for me at 2:30', curtain time for Saturday matinees. Punctual, well-groomed Rodgers met bohemian Hart '18, who was adapting and translating German and Viennese operettas for the Schuberts, who owned theatres; adaptation of Ferenc Molnar's novel/play *Liliom* was a success, but Hart, on salary, received little credit. Rodgers & Hart had little success until previously written 'Manhattan' was put into *The Garrick Gaities* '25 (also 'Mountain Greenery'); they were signed by a publisher and with five shows running '26 were making $1000 a week each. Rodgers used unusual chords, would write a 32-bar verse with a 16-bar chorus instead of the other way round; Hart was hard to get to work but when he wrote he did it quickly, creating love songs with wit: the results are among the best-loved songs of the century, equalled (if at all) only by those of Cole PORTER. 80 crates of lost music was discovered in a Warner Brothers warehouse in Secaucus, N.J. '82 by Robert Kimball, incl. work by all of those named above plus the GERSHWINS, Vincent YOUMANS, etc.; Kimball published fine edition of *The Complete Lyrics Of Lorenz Hart* '87. Some of the shows/songs: *The Girl Friend* '26 ('The Blue Room'), *A Connecticut Yankee* '27 ('My Heart Stood Still'), *Present Arms* '28 ('You Took Advantage Of Me'), *Spring Is Here* ('With A Song In My Heart'), *Simple Simon* '30 ('Ten Cents A Dance'), *Evergreen* '30 ('Dancing On The Ceiling'), *Jumbo* '35 ('Little Girl Blue', 'The Most Beautiful Girl In The World'), *On Your Toes* '36 ('There's A Small Hotel'), *Babes In Arms* '37 ('Where Or When', 'The Lady Is A Tramp', 'My Funny Valentine', 'I Wish I Were In Love

Again', latter with perhaps the best-known of Hart lyrics: 'When Love congeals/It soon reveals/The faint aroma of performing seals/The doublecrossing of a pair of heels/I wish I were in love again'), *Pal Joey* '40 ('I Could Write A Book', 'Bewitched, Bothered And Bewildered'). Film work early '30s was not too successful except for *Love Me Tonight* '32 (with Maurice CHEVALIER: 'Mimi', 'Isn't It Romantic'). 'Blue Room' never made it into a play or a film, still became a classic. Hammerstein, like Hart, attended Columbia U., turned to theatre: wrote and acted in Columbia Varsity shows; began as stage manager for impresario grandfather (hence 'II' to avoid confusion); his father William managed one of Oscar I's theatres. He wrote with Friml, Romberg, Youmans, Herbert Stothart, Arthur SCHWARTZ, Otto HARBACH, George GERSHWIN, Harold ARLEN; unlike Hart, he was asleep by midnight, had to work hard on his lyrics; like Hart, he achieved apparent spontaneity in his words, and was floundering in the early '40s. Hart was small of stature, an alcoholic, unlucky in love (hence perhaps the bittersweet humour of his work); died of pneumonia a few weeks after attending the premiere of Rodgers & Hammerstein's *Oklahoma!* '43: Rodgers & Hart's are greater songs, but Rodgers & Hammerstein's shows marked an advance on Kern in musical theatre: in *Oklahoma!*, book as well as songs written by Hammerstein (based on play *Green Grow The Rushes* by Lynn Riggs), songs advanced the action rather than distracting the audience from a soon-to-be-forgotten plot: with 'Oh What A Beautiful Morning', 'People Will Say We're In Love', 'Surrey With The Fringe On Top' etc., one of the biggest Broadway hits of all time. *Carousel* '45 was ironically based on *Liliom*, incl. 'If I Loved You', 'You'll Never Walk Alone', etc.; *South Pacific* '49 another smash to match *Oklahoma!*, based on stories by James A. Michener, with 'Some Enchanted Evening', 'Bali Ha'i', 'Younger Than Springtime', 'I'm In Love With A Wonderful Guy', several more; *The King And I* '51 (based on *Anna And The King Of Siam* by Margaret Landon) with 'Hello Young Lovers', 'I Have Dreamed', others. These four shows accounted for more than 6300 performances in original productions, made spectacular films, Yul Brynner successful

until the end of his life as the King of Siam. They wrote for film *State Fair* '45 ('It Might As Well Be Spring'), formed prod. company that mounted Irving BERLIN's *Annie Get Your Gun* '46; also wrote shows *Allegro* '47 ('The Gentleman Is A Dope'), *Pipe Dream* '55, *Flower Drum Song* '58 ('I Enjoy Being A Girl'). Rodgers also scored documentary film series *Victory At Sea* (about WWII in the Pacific; music orchestrated, like many of the shows, by Robert Russell Bennett), turned one of its themes into 'No Other Love' for *Me And Juliet* '53 (a relative flop: it only ran for a year; song was hit for Perry COMO). Hammerstein also adapted Bizet's *Carmen* into musical/film '54 *Carmen Jones*. The sentimentality of their work (compared to that with Hart) reached an apotheosis with *Sound Of Music* '59, made into one of the most successful musical films of all time '65, with Julie ANDREWS. Hammerstein died of cancer; Rodgers wrote his own lyrics for *No Strings* '62, worked with Stephen SONDHEIM on *Do I Hear A Waltz?* '65, with Martin Charnin on *Two By Two* '70.

RODNEY, Red (*b* Robert Roland Chudnick, 27 Sep. '27, Philadelphia, Pa.) Trumpet. At Mastbaum music school classmates incl. John COLTRANE, Buddy DeFRANCO. Pro at 15, worked for Jimmy DORSEY, other good white dance bands, then Georgie AULD, Claude THORNHILL, Gene KRUPA, Woody HERMAN, then an offer from Charlie PARKER: Rodney protested that there were more qualified people, 'And Bird said, "Hey, let me be the judge of that. I want you . . ." I was really frightened. I didn't think I belonged. And he made me feel like I belonged.' (Quoted in Ira Gitler's *Swing To Bop* '85.) Became drug addict (against Parker's advice); with Parker '49-50, Charlie VENTURA '50-1, others; beaten by cops occasionally, jailed for narcotics; led own combos in Philadelphia; records: as Red Rodney's Be-Boppers recorded for Mercury, EmArcy, Keynote '46-7; quintet LP *The New Sounds* '51 on Prestige; singles on Okeh '52 with vocalist Morton Perry; *Modern Music From Chicago* '55 on Fantasy (aka *Encores*) with Ira SULLIVAN; Signal sessions '56 on Savoy as *Fiery*, also on Onyx, also with Sullivan and incl. 'The Red Arrow'; an LP on Cadet made '58 in Philadelphia. Did well playing dance music, weddings late '50s in home town: left jazz as business was bad (and rising black pride resulted in Crow Jim), his place as one of the first bop trumpeters after Dizzy GILLESPIE and Miles DAVIS almost forgotten. Sold band business, went to West Coast, played in Las Vegas, thought of a scam: got his own back for a while by dressing as USAF general, cashing forged paychecks on military bases. Served 27 months for that, kicked heroin, acquired college degree; studied law, came second in class in three years instead of four but not allowed to take bar exam in California. Suffered stroke early '70s; recovered, but hospital took all his money; realising that the good earnings playing Mickey Mouse music hadn't been worth it, he returned to jazz with *Bird Lives!* '73 quintet with Charles MCPHERSON on alto, Sam JONES on bass; *Superbop* '74 with Ray BROWN, Shelly MANNE, pianist Dolo Coker (*b* Charles Mitchell Coker, 16 Nov. '27, Hartford, Conn.; *d* 13 Apr. '83, L.A.) with guest soloists, both on Muse. *Red Rodney & The Bebop Preservation Society* on Spotlite was made in London; *And The Danish Jazzarmy* on Storyville in Copenhagen, both '75; *Yard's Pad* '76 on Sonet in Stockholm; other Muse LPs: *Red, White And Blues* '76, *Home Free* '77, *The Three R's* '79 with Richie Cole on alto, the last also with Roland Hanna on piano, Ricky Ford's tenor on two tracks; *High Jinks At The Vanguard* and *Live At The Village Vanguard* '80, *Night And Day* '81 all with Sullivan; *Spirit Within* '81 and *Sprint* '82 on Elektra Musician also with Sullivan. In '87 he toured with James Morrison, an Australian who plays trumpet, trombone, baritone horn and euphonium.

RODRIGUEZ, Arsenio (*b* 30 Aug. '11, Güira de Macurije, Matanzas Province, Cuba; *d* '70, NYC) Virtuoso tres player, also bass, conga and other percussion; bandleader, vocalist, composer/arranger; known as 'El Ciego Maravilloso' ('The Marvellous Blind Man'). His grandfather came from the Congo; he was fourth in family of 18 children; lost sight at age 7; said to have begun playing professionally at 8 in Guateques, Cuba, on African-derived bass instruments incl. the marímbula (wooden box with metal prongs sounding different bass notes when plucked) and botija (a clay jug, blown

into to give a booming bass note); became an expert in toques, standard percussive rhythmic phrases derived from African religious drumming; turned to the tres (six- or nine-stringed Cuban guitar), became acknowledged master. Began composing '27, boleros at first, then other rhythms. He strengthened the African elements of the Cuban son '30s, which had been toned down by earlier bands; founded the Cuban conjunto style by adding a cowbell, conga, second and third trumpets and piano to the trad. sexteto or septeto of trumpet, tres, guitar, maracas, bass and bongo; introduced soloing section (montuno) to the son, the new form then called son montuno. Some credit him with introducing the MAMBO rhythm from Congolese-derived religious groups into Cuban dance halls '37. In the NYC Cuban tipico revivals of late '60s, early '70s, again early '80s, Arsenio's conjunto style and many of his compositions were interpreted by many salsa artists. René Alvarez joined Arsenio's conjunto as featured singer early '40s, became famous for smooth interpretations e.g. 'El Reloj de Pastora' '46; he left '48, and with the legendary tres player Niño Rivera and trumpeter Juanito Roger from Arsenio's band formed Conjunto Los Astros: *Dejame Tranquilo* '74 on Cariño collected 10 tracks by this conjunto recorded by RCA in Havana '48-50; *El Sentimiento de Arsenio* '74 on Cariño was an anthology of Arsenio's own RCA records. Arsenio's *Sabroso y Caliente* on Puchito incl. 'Hay Fuego en el 23'; *Exitos de Arsenio Rodriguez y su Conjunto* on Tropical was a hits collection. He moved to NYC '50, leaving his band with Félix Chapottin (*d* '82), an exponent of the distinctively ornate septeto trumpet style who had also played with Sexteto Habanero; *Cumbanchando con Arsenio (Fiesta en Harlem)* was made in NYC by Gabriel Oller for his SMC label (formed '48): Arsenio wrote all the tracks and sang on 'Guaguanco en el Remeneo'; the band incl. Sabu Martinez on percussion, Arsenio appearing on Sabu's *Palo Conga* '57 on Blue Note. He wrote all the tracks on *La Pachanga* c.'63, his debut on Tico. *Quindembo/Afro Magic/La Magia de Arsenio Rodriguez* '63 on Epic was the first LP on which he played tres as the featured instrument; he called the music quindembo, a

Congolese word for a mixture of many things: instrumentation incl. bass, drums and two saxes; as well as playing tres he wrote and sang on all the tracks, incl. 'Bruca Manigua', which won a prize at a music festival in Milan. He played tres on *Patato & Totico* on Verve (reissued in MGM Latino series), by Afro-Cuban conga player Carlos 'Patato' Valdez and percussionist/ singer Totico (Eugenio Arango). His debut on Ansonia was *Arsenio Rodriguez y su Conjunto*; used trumpet, sax and tres combination on *Vol. 2* on Ansonia, *Arsenio Dice . . ./Arsenio Says . . .* on Tico c.'68; among the singers on *Vol. 2* was Dominican Santiago Ceron, who made successful solo LPs early '80s with Luis 'Perico' ORTIZ. Sonora Ponceña (*see* Papo LUCCA) had hits with covers of 'Hay Fuego en el 23' and 'Hachero pa' un Palo' c.'68-9; Larry HARLOW made *Tribute To Arsenio Rodriguez* '71 on Fania; Tito PUENTE paid homage with song 'Guaguanco Arsenio' on his *Ce' Magnifique* '81 on Tico, sung by Camilo Azuquita.

RODRIGUEZ, Tito (*b* 4 Jan. '23, San Juan, Puerto Rico; *d* 28 Feb. '73) Singer, bandleader; played timbales and vibes; also arranger, composer. At 13 he recorded in Puerto Rico with Conjunto Tipico Lali, also worked with guitar group Cuarteto Mayari. After finishing high school went to live with his brother Johnny in East Harlem, NYC. (Popular vocalist Johnny sang with many bands, favoured smaller outfits; led his own trio, toured South America, spent much time in Puerto Rico.) Tito worked with Enric MADRIGUERA, Xavier CUGAT; then five years with Noro MORALES; recruited by José Curbelo '46, formed own Mambo Devils (one of NYC's first conjuntos) and made first record on Tico (formed '48): 'Hay Craneo' (in Spanish)/ 'Ardent Night' (in English). He soon enlarged his group to a big band, which he led until '65. Tracks on 10" LPs for Tico later compiled, e.g. on *Nostalgia* '72, *Uptempo* '78 (SonoDisc in France). Switched to RCA in the '50s (compilations *The Best Of Tito Rodriguez* '65; *La Epoca de Oro de Tito Rodriguez (1953-1955)*, the latter reissued '72). Regular resident at Palladium Ballroom NYC '49-64 (made two live LPs there on UA), one of the best-loved leaders on Latin scene, with Tito PUENTE, MACHITO one of the kings of the mambo in the '50s. Other UA LPs incl. *West Side Beat* and *Back Home In Puerto Rico* '62 (latter made in P.R.: his visit was marked by government receptions and media buzz); also *Live At Birdland* '63 (featuring Zoot SIMS, Al COHN, Bob BROOKMEYER, Clark TERRY etc.; reissued '86); also smoochy bolero LPs with strings incl. *From Tito Rodriguez With Love* on UA, and *En Escenario* on Musicor. The band was usually anonymous on the record sleeves of the time; on lead track on *Big Band Latino* on Musicor, 'Esta Es Mi Orquesta', he introduced band incl. Israel 'Cachao' LOPEZ, trumpeter Victor Paz, pianist/arr. René Hernandez, saxist Mario Rivera; Charlie and Eddie PALMIERI also passed through. The band made about 50 LPs for RCA, Decca, Tico, mostly on UA and Musicor. Cachao's Latin jam session (descarga) infl. was reflected on 'Descarga Cachao' on *Tito Tito Tito* on UA; he returned to P.R. for a while '60s, made *El Doctor* there on UA. 2-disc *Tito Rodriguez Superpak* on WS Latino, French SonoDisc is recommended compilation of hits from UA. He also backed others, e.g. prod./ conducted on *A Latin In America* mid-'60s on Musicor for Colombian singer Nelson Pinedo. He also appeared as a singer with bands incl. La Playa Sextet, Louie RAMIREZ, and Machito, giving his last performance with Machito at Madison Square Garden shortly before he died of leukaemia.

ROE, Tommy (*b* 9 May '42, Atlanta, Ga.) Pop singer, producer. Formed the Satins while still in high school, recorded for local Judd label; signed to ABC and recorded 'Save Your Kisses', backed with uptempo self-composed song first recorded for Judd: DJs flipped the record and plugged 'Sheila' to USA no. 1/UK 2 '62. 22 Hot 100 entries in USA '62-73, only occasionally reaching top 10: Robin Luke's 'Susie Darlin'' '62 made top 40 USA/UK '62; 'The Folk Singer' flopped in USA, made no. 4 UK; 'Everybody' was no. 3 USA/9 UK '63. He became even more poppy, the oldest of the bubblegum blowers in the heyday of the MONKEES, Archies etc., reaching top 10 USA with 'Sweet Pea' and 'Hooray For Hazel' '66, transatlantic no. 1 with infuriating 'Dizzy' '69, top 10 USA with 'Jam Up

Jelly Tight' same year, a few other top 40s. Like many bubblegum/pop contemporaries (Paul REVERE's Mark Lindsay, etc.) turned to country music, occasionally toured as an oldie. Prod. Felton Jarvis, later Elvis PRESLEY.

ROENA, Roberto Puerto Rican bongo player, bandleader, producer, dancer who has been prominent in salsa since late '60s, as a bandleader, also one of the genre's premier bongo players, aka 'El Gran Bailarin' (The Great Dancer). Played with (Rafael) CORTIJO y su Combo, EL GRAN COMBO; left the latter '69: LP *Se Pone Bueno/It Gets Better* with his Megatones in Puerto Rico (on Alegre, now on Tico), then formed Apollo Sound with 2-3 trumpets, trombone, tenor sax/flute, 23 vocalists, chorus, piano, bass and piano. Ten vols. of *Roberto Roena y su Apollo Sound* c.'69-78 on Fania International and International, the first incl. cover of BLOOD, SWEAT & TEARS' 'Spinning Wheel' and 'Tu Loco Loco, y Yo Tranquilo', by LP's mus. dir. Catalino 'Tite' Curet Alonso; *Lucky 7* '76 incl. big hit 'Mi Desengaño', arr. and co-written by virtuoso trombonist Julio (Gunda) Merced, a member '73-8 (he formed Salsa Fever, which made LPs on Top Hits and Sonotone, incl. *Gunda Merced y su Salsa Fever y algo Máa!* '87 on Sonotone). *Pa' Fuera* '74 was a hits compilation; Vol. 10 *El Progreso* '78 was one of Apollo Sound's best, made in Puerto Rico, incl. Louis Garcia's inventive arr. of 'Regaño al Corazón', part of which turned up on Trinidadian soca record 'Pump' '81 by Brother Idi on the now-defunct Semp label: Semp's co-owner was Stan Chaman, now owner of Hitman Records, leading London specialist shop for Latin-American discs. Arrangers, composers etc. contributing to the Apollo Sound LPs incl. Bobby VALENTIN, trumpeters Elias Lopés and Mario Ortiz, Luis 'Perico' ORTIZ, Papo LUCCA, Rubén BLADES; vocalists incl. Piro Mantilla, Tito Cruz, Sammy Gonzalez, Papo Sanchez, Mario Cora, Carlos Santos. *Que Suerte He Tenido de Nacer* (with Roena lead vocal on a track), *Looking Out For 'Numero Uno'* and compilation *Gold* all came out on Fania '80; *Super Apollo 47:50* '82 with vocalist Adalberto Santiago. Fania LPs were as Roberto Roena; billing Roberto Roena y su Apollo Sound used again on

Pa'lante label for *Afuera y Contento* '85 ('Out And Contented'; with sleeve depicting Roena in a prison suit, may have referred to release from Fania); made in Puerto Rico, LP incl. an example of Puerto Rican dance fad zuky, which is essentially a derivation of soca, 'Apollo Zuky' a version of 'Soca Rhumba' '81 by Monserrat's soca/calypsonian Arrow (Alphonsus 'Phonsie' Cassell). Roena also played on LPs by FANIA ALL STARS '71-84 incl. soundtrack *Our Latin Thing* '72; Charlie PALMIERI's *Electro Duro* '74, LPs by Cheo FELICIANO '76-82. *Cortijo y su Combo Original con Ismael Rivera* '74 on Coco was a Cortijo reunion, reissued '82 as *Ismael Rivera Sonero No. 1*; he also appeared on *El Combo del Ayer* '82 on Ten Top Hits, which reunited some of original members who had left El Gran Combo. Roena moved to new Up label for *Roberto Roena Apollo Sound Regreso* '87.

ROGERS, Jimmy (*b* 3 June '24, Ruleville, Ms.) Blues singer; plays guitar, harmonica, piano. Raised in Atlanta, Ga., then Memphis, Tenn., other places; one of ten children; self-taught on home-made guitar from c. '35; worked in East St Louis late '30s, Chicago from '41; became one of the most important sidemen in Chicago blues, performing and recording with Muddy Waters, Howlin' Wolf, Sonny Boy Williamson (Rice Miller), Sunnyland Slim, many others. Worked outside music; recorded with Bob Riedy's Blues band on Rounder '75 and with Waters on Blue Sky '77. His records as a leader began on Regal '49; he recorded for Chess through '50s. Compilations incl. 2-disc set in Chess Masters series, *Feelin' Good* on Murray Brothers (USA) and three sets on JSP (London) with Left Hand Frank.

ROGERS, Kenny (*b* Kenneth Donald Rogers, 21 Aug. '38, Houston, Texas) Country singer and superstar, with several crossover pop hits every year since '76. Began playing rock'n'roll in the Scholars, a high school band; they had regional hit 'Crazy Feeling' '57. Studied at U. of Houston; joined jazz combo the Bobby Doyle Trio, harmony quartet the Lively Ones; after a stint with the NEW CHRISTY MINSTRELS '64-6 left with Mike Settle, others to form the First Edition, signed with Reprise and scored top

5 pop hit with Mickey NEWBURY song 'Just Dropped In (To See What My Condition Was In)' '68. Billing was changed to Kenny Rogers & The First Edition; 10 hits total through '72 saw many co-prod. by Rogers. His grainy vocals were perfectly suited to their country-rock sound; they had albums *Tell It All Brother* and *Transition* '70-1 and TV series *Rollin'* '72, split up when hits fell off. He signed solo with UA in Nashville '75, prod. by Larry Butler; first single, gospel-styled 'Love Lifted Me', reached country top 10 and scraped into pop Hot 100; fourth single 'Lucille' was a country no. 1, no. 5 pop, won a Grammy and several CMA awards. He soon developed a slick MOR sound that had moved some way from pure country, but it didn't seem to matter: fans just loved that voice, reportedly made him the highest paid entertainer in the world. Country hits incl. duets with Dottie West, four of them in '78-9 alone; he crossed over with total of 29 Hot 100 pop entries through '85: three top 10 pop hits in '79 ('She Believes In Me', 'You Decorated My Life', 'Coward Of The Country'), top 5 duet with Kim CARNES 'Don't Fall In Love With A Dreamer' '80; switch to Liberty imprint began with no. 1 pop hit 'Lady', written/prod. by Lionel RICHIE, no. 3 'I Don't Need You' and several others prod. by Richie; duet 'We've Got Tonight' with Sheena EASTON '83 was top 10 pop, no. 1 country; RCA reportedly paid a record fee to secure his contract and were rewarded with what was said to be the biggest-selling single in their history: duet 'Islands In The Stream' with Dolly PARTON was no. 1 both country/pop, written by the BEE GEES, from album prod. by them called *Eyes That See In The Dark* with more hits incl. title track. Liberty released new hits from the vault incl. another duet with West ('Together Again' '84). Country hits incl. 'Morning Desire' and 'Tomb Of The Unknown Love' at no. 1, 'Twenty Years Ago' no. 2 '86; 'They Don't Make Them Like They Used To' and duet 'The Pride Is Back' with Nickie Ryder were country entries also listed in Billboard 'Hot Adult Contemporary' chart. Albums incl. *Love Lifted Me* '76, *Daytime Friends* '77, *Love Or Something Like It* '78, duets with West *Everytime Two Fools Collide* and *Classics* '78-9, *The Gambler* '79, *Kenny*, *Gideon* and *Singles Album* '80, all on UA;

Lady and *Share Your Love* '81, *We've Got Tonight* '83, *Short Stories* '86 on Liberty; *The Heart Of The Matter* '85, *They Don't Make Them Like They Used To* '87 on RCA.

ROGERS, Roy (*b* Leonard Slye, 5 Nov. '11, Cincinnati, Ohio) Singing cowboy, actor. One of the greatest Western movie stars of '30s-40s, the only real rival of Gene AUTRY as the Saturday matinee cowboy idol, billed as 'the King of the Cowboys'. His father made mandolins and guitars; he grew up on a farm, worked in a shoe factory, performed locally '20s; to California '30, worked picking peaches, driving a truck; formed band International Cowboys; as Dick Weston led Pioneer Trio: it appeared in Western sci-fi serial *The Phantom Empire* '34, name changed to the SONS OF THE PIONEERS. He remained in Pioneers until '37-8, had bit parts in Columbia Westerns, signed with Republic and had first starring role in *Under Western Skies* '38, which may have been the one which was a fairly realistic portrait of the Pony Express postal service. With palomino horse Trigger (1932-65; now stuffed and mounted at his California home) made about 100 films. Dale Evans (*b* Frances Octavia Smith, 31 Oct. '12, Uvalde, Texas) sang with Anson WEEKS, other bands; with first husband pianist Dale Butts co-wrote a few songs; sang on Chicago radio with Caesar PETRILLO band; starred with Rogers in *The Cowboy And The Senorita* '44; they married '47. His late '40s films, often with the Pioneers, with Republic's peculiarly sunsettish colour process, are redolent of nostalgia for millions; he also appeared as guest in variety films like *Hollywood Canteen* '44; together they had radio show *Saturday Night Roundup* mid-'40s. In *Son Of Paleface* '52 (with Bob Hope, Jane Russell) he came close to sending himself up. They had popular TV series '51-6; he came back with film *Mackintosh And Tʃ* '75 (soundtrack LP). Hits 'Hi-Yo, Silver' on Vocalion '38, 'Think Of Me' on Decca '43, recorded for RCA many years; theme was 'Happy Trails To You' (co-written by Evans). With Pioneers made 'Pecos Bill' (by Johnny Lange and Eliot Daniel) for Disney cartoon *Melody Time* '48; later country hits on Capitol 'Money Can't Buy Love', 'Lovenworth', 'Happy Anniversary' '70-1; 'Hoppy, Gene And Me' '74 on 20th Century, 'Ride Concrete Cowboy Ride' '80 on MCA with the Pioneers. They were popular guests on TV shows, had own show again '62, did charity work, adopted children. She wrote book *Angel Unaware* about her retarded child, several other books; wrote song 'The Bible Tells Me So' '55, co-wrote 'I Wish I Had Never Met Sunshine' '45 (with Autry, Oakley Haldeman); he wrote or co-wrote 'Dusty', 'My Heart Went Thataway', others. His compilations incl. an album in Columbia Historical Edition series, *Melody Of The Plains* on MCA, *King Of The Cowboys* and *Roll On Texas Moon* on Bear Family; together they made *Good Life* on Word and *Sweet Hour Of Prayer* on RCA; she made *Get To Know The Lord* on Capitol.

ROGERS, Shorty (*b* Milton Michael Rajonsky, 14 Apr. '24, Great Barrington, Mass.) Trumpet, bandleader, arranger, composer. Played with Will BRADLEY, Red NORVO, Woody HERMAN late '40s (wrote 'Keen And Peachy'), Stan KENTON '50-1; recorded on West Coast: small group *Modern Sounds* '51 on Capitol with Art PEPPER, Hampton HAWES, Jimmy GIUFFRE, Shelly MANNE, Gene Englund on tuba, John Graas on French horn (*b* 14 Oct. '24, Debuque, Iowa; *d* 13 Apr. '62, Van Nuys, Cal.), the last two from Kenton's Neophonic Orchestra, Don Bagley on bass (*b* 18 July '27, Salt Lake City, Utah); with Lighthouse All Stars '51 on Xanadu (*Popo* with Pepper), '53 on Contemporary; then on RCA: *Shorty Rogers And His Giants* with similar lineup to the first LP and big band *Cool And Crazy* with some of those above plus Bud SHANK, Bob COOPER, Maynard FERGUSON, etc. were 10″ LPs; *Shorty Rogers Courts The Count* '54 was 12″ set of BASIE covers with Harry EDISON, Zoot SIMS, etc. There was also a 45 EP called *The Wild One* '53 for big band. The nonet album was reissued in 12″ format with quintet tracks made '54; *Cool And Crazy* reissued as *The Big Shorty Rogers Express* with additional tracks made '56. Went to Atlantic for *The Swinging Mr Rogers* '55 with Manne, Giuffre, Curtis COUNCE: hit track 'Martians Come Back' led to LP *Martians Go Home!* same year. There were more RCA LPs, all big band except *Wherever The Five Winds Blow*; he gave up playing after *Jazz Waltz* '62, big band with

Shank, Bob Cooper, Mel LEWIS, also *Return To Rio*, both on Discovery, as jazz suffered from increasing studio work (he wrote music for show *That Certain Girl*, visited London '66). The music was rooted in swing era yet infl. by Miles DAVIS Birth of the Cool sessions; his style as arranger was influential. Reissues on Pausa, Atlantic, French RCA; also *Live From The Rendezvous Ballroom '53* on Scarecrow with Ferguson. It has been fashionable for years to denigrate the early records, which were very popular at the time, but 2-disc *Short Stops* on RCA has eight sessions digitally remastered from '53-4, compiling two original 10″ LPs, the EP and *Courts The Count* complete: eight nonet tracks and 24 big band; the music comes up fresh as paint and is lots of fun, with delightful touches like four baritone saxes on 'Sweetheart Of Sigmund Freud'. Came back '82 after UK tour with National Youth Jazz Orchestra: *Yesterday, Today And Forever* '83 on Concord Jazz (quintet with Shank), *Back Again – Live At The Concord Club* '85 on Concept with Shank, UK big band led by Vic Lewis (veteran trombonist, guitarist, *b* 29 July '19, London).

ROLLING STONES, The UK rock band, self-styled 'Greatest rock'n'roll band in the world': Mick Jagger, vocalist (*b* Michael Philip Jagger, 26 July '43, Dartford, Kent); Keith Richards, guitar (*b* 18 Dec. '43, Dartford); Bill Wyman, bass (*b* William Perks, 23 Oct. '36, Penge, SE London); Charlie Watts, drums (*b* 2 June '41, Neasden, N London); Brian Jones, rhythm guitar, other instruments (*b* Lewis Brian Hopkin-Jones, 28 Feb. '42, Cheltenham, Glos.; *d* 3 July '69), replaced by Mick Taylor (*b* 17 Jan. '48, Herts.), who was succeeded by Ron Wood (*b* 1 June '47, Hillingdon, Middx.); plus Ian Stewart, keyboards (*b* '38, *d* 12 Dec. '85). Jagger and Richards attended primary school together, met on a train as teenagers and discovered they were both rhythm & blues fans; Jagger attended London School of Economics, Richards was in same art school as guitarist Dick Taylor, who played in the same R&B band as Jagger (with fame Keith dropped the 's', calling himself Richard, until reconciled with his father years later); Jones followed a similar enthusiasm a hundred miles away, travelled to

London to visit Korner's club, where Jagger was the second-string vocalist after Long John BALDRY, and where he met Watts and Stewart; nucleus of Jones, Jagger and Richards began to rehearse together, with Watts or with Mick Amory (later drummer with the KINKS), Dick Taylor on bass, and Stewart. Drummer Tony Chapman also passed through; Wyman replaced Taylor '62 (who then formed the PRETTY THINGS); Watts was persuaded to quit his job in advertising '63. European blues enthusiast Giorgio Gomelsky booked them a weekly slot at the Railway Hotel in Richmond, Surrey, acted as unofficial manager until they attracted a following, when hustling publicist Andrew Loog Oldham turned up (b '44): he'd worked for designer Mary Quant, then for BEATLES' manager Brian EPSTEIN; moulded the Stones into a saleable commodity as a rebellious London answer to the relatively goody-goody northern Beatles; he demoted Stewart, who did not fit slim-hipped image (Stewart became tour manager, trusted confidant, frequent keyboard player on tours/records; had 'Boogie With Stu' dedicated to him on LED ZEPPELIN's *Physical Graffiti* LP '75; played pub blues with Watts early '80s in Rocket 88). Contract with Decca was easily obtained, as that label was kicking itself for turning down the Beatles; first record '63 was cover of Chuck BERRY's 'Come On', minor UK hit. Oldham asked the Beatles for an original song; Stones' version of 'I Wanna Be Your Man' was top 20 UK (where the song was not a Beatle single); they toured UK winter '63 at the bottom of a bill with EVERLY Bros and LITTLE RICHARD; cover of Buddy HOLLY's 'Not Fade Away' (to which they added Bo DIDDLEY's beat) was no. 3 '64, also reaching USA top 50. Eponymous debut LP was no. 1 UK, with Phil SPECTOR, Gene PITNEY helping; 'Tell Me' from it made USA top 30, as did their first UK no. 1, cover of the Valentino's 'It's All Over Now' (by Bobby WOMACK). EP *Five By Five* was made in Chicago during their first USA tour '64; Willie DIXON's 'Little Red Rooster' from it was a UK no. 1, while Jerry Ragavoy's 'Time Is On My Side' was their first USA top 10. *Rolling Stones No. 2* was second UK no. 1 LP; USA counterparts *12 × 5* and *The Rolling Stones Now!* both reached top 5 '64-5. They exploited their opposite image to

the Beatles, refusing to wave bye-bye on a UK pop TV programme; while the Beatles collected MBEs from the Queen, the Stones were arrested for urinating on a garage forecourt. They were popular in the USA but had no no. 1 hits there, where it seemed slightly peculiar to have five English kids copying Chuck Berry and the rest; Oldham '65 pushed them to write songs of their own. *Out Of Our Heads* '65 was a roots LP in UK, only no. 2; a different LP of the same title in USA incl. first Jagger/Richards songs 'The Last Time' (no. 1 UK, top 10 USA) and '(I Can't Get No) Satisfaction', their first transatlantic no. 1; 'Get Off Of My Cloud' was their second, same year (on USA LP *December's Children (And Everybody's)*. They helped Jagger's then girlfriend Marianne FAITHFULL to four consecutive top 10 hits '64-5. Compilation *Big Hits (High Tide And Green Grass)* and *Aftermath* '66, *Between The Buttons* '67 all in different editions on each side of the pond, as well as *got Live if you want it* '66 (made at Albert Hall: exciting souvenir EP in UK, stretched to a dubious LP in USA); *Flowers* '67 not issued in UK at all. Their early 'Under-Assistant West Coast Promo Man' had sent up the record business; big hits in both UK/USA incl. '19th Nervous Breakdown', 'Paint It, Black', 'Mother's Little Helper' (song about housewives' tranquillisers, years before the problem of 'legal' pills was widely recognised), 'Have You Seen Your Mother, Baby, Standing In The Shadow?'. 'Sittin' On A Fence' (on *Flowers*) was an acoustic lament for an innocence everyone was losing in those years: in the songs at least, they had no illusions about their own or anyone else's generation. *Aftermath* was their most cohesive LP to date, yet still too poppish; overshadowed by Beatles' *Revolver*, Bob DYLAN's *Blonde On Blonde*, the BEACH BOYS' *Pet Sounds*, all the same year. In '67 they faltered badly: *Their Satanic Majesties Request* late in the year achieved record advance orders and was the biggest disappointment of the decade, a dreadful attempt at psychedelia. Meanwhile Jagger, Richards, Jones had been arrested on drugs charges, the law clumsily making it obvious that it wanted to arrest outlaw Stones rather than Beatles; prison terms were quashed after a famous *Times* leader asked, quoting William Blake, 'Who Breaks

A Butterfly Upon A Wheel?'. Their only single '67 was the limp 'We Love You', accompanied by a film with Jagger dressed as Oscar Wilde, Marianne as Lord Alfred Douglas, Richards as the Marquess of Queensberry. They were also growing distant from prod. Glyn JOHNS, and from Oldham (they had entered the clutches of Allen Klein, who would soon add to the list of lawsuits pending against him the one with Oldham over the Stones' money). There may be a sense in which they wanted *Majesties* to fail: £15,000 was spent on an opulent 3-D cover for the LP, also a flop. But in '68 they pulled it all together and reached their peak: 'Jumpin' Jack Flash' (no. 1 UK, 3 USA) was classic, exciting rock'n'roll, dispelling notions of studio or electronic wizardry for the Stones: while the Beatles no longer toured at all, the Stones *had* to tour, because they really were the world's greatest rock'n'roll band. It was also the year that flower-power began obviously to fail, a year of riots and the emergence of terrorism; after a squabble with Decca over the sleeve, by the time *Beggars Banquet* came out at the end of the year the Stones were almost bored with it, but it was their first masterpiece, with knowing 'Sympathy For The Devil' (title of Jean-Luc Godard's film of the sessions), 'Street Fighting Man', 'Salt Of The Earth'; low-down dirty 'Parachute Woman', 'Stray Cat Blues', etc. The sleeve thanked Nicky HOPKINS and 'many friends', believed to incl. Eric CLAPTON and Steve WINWOOD. Jagger made film *Performance* '68, playing a jaded, faded rock star: not a happy pop Beatle film but a risky portrait of psychopaths, with Edward Fox and Anita Pallenberg, communal Stones' girlfriend; soundtrack music was by Jack NITZSCHE, Lowell George; Jagger's only song was 'Memo From Turner', one of his best tracks, recorded with members of TRAFFIC incl. Winwood. Out-takes of Pallenberg and Jagger won a prize at a pornographic film festival in Amsterdam. TV film *Rolling Stones Rock And Roll Circus* was made in December, with the WHO, JETHRO TULL, John LENNON, Clapton, others, but never shown; Jagger thought he had been outshone by the Who. Brian Jones was far more than a rhythm guitarist; he had been the musical centre of the group many times, his slide guitar on 'No Expectations' e.g. an

attraction of *Beggars Banquet*. They might not have accomplished anything without him, but he was now unreliable and drug-sodden; he could not get another visa for touring in the USA. In May '69 the unhappy, asthmatic, alcoholic woman-beater, his liver and heart already badly damaged, was eased out of the group; in July he drowned in his swimming pool in Sussex (having purchased the former home of A. A. Milne, the 'House at Pooh Corner'), amid the usual rumours of foul play. (His last project issued '72 as *Brian Jones Presents The Pipes Of Pan In Joujouka*, Moroccan trad. music.) A free concert in Hyde Park two days later with Mick Taylor (ex-John MAYALL's Bluesbreakers) went on as scheduled; in tribute to Jones boxes of butterflies were released, many of them also dead; the band gave one of its worst performances ever. Jagger and Marianne then flew to Australia; he played legendary outlaw in flop film *Ned Kelly*, soundtrack with Waylon JENNINGS, Kris KRISTOFFERSON (one song by Jagger). She took an overdose of pills while they were there and Jagger saved her life, but the days of the affair were numbered. 'Honky Tonk Woman' was no. 1 USA/UK mid-'69, one of their best (video saw them in drag); *Through The Past Darkly (Big Hits Vol. 2)* '69 was dedicated to Jones; *Let It Bleed* '69 was their second masterpiece in a row, with cover of Robert JOHNSON's 'Love In Vain', 'Country Honk' (a different version of 'Honky Tonk Woman'), strutting title track, orchestrated 'You Can't Always Get What You Want', etc. incl. guests Leon RUSSELL, Ry COODER, Al KOOPER. Flower-power was well and truly over after another free concert at Altamont, disused racetrack in northern California, Dec. '69: bad organization with 'security' provided by Hell's Angels, who hacked and stomped to death Meredith Hunter, an 18-year-old black man foolishly waving a pistol, captured in film *Gimme Shelter*. *Get Your Ya-Yas Out* '70 was their best live LP, made during USA tour, and marked end of Decca contract: they formed Rolling Stones label. *Sticky Fingers* '71 incl. 'Brown Sugar' (no. 1 USA, 2 UK), 'Wild Horses' and 'Sister Morphine' (infl. by Gram PARSONS, who fell out with Jagger over composer credits). Klein had their money tied up tight, but meanwhile their taxes hadn't been paid: they moved to

France. Jagger married model/socialite Bianca Pérez Mora Macías (the marriage didn't last, but she was a more substantial person than anyone knew at the time, later working for her native Nicaragua and other troubled countries). 2-disc *Exile On Main Street* '72 incl. 'Sweet Virginia', 'Sweet Black Angel', top 10 single 'Tumbling Dice' (revived for top 40 USA hit '78 by Linda RONSTADT): it was criticised at the time as sprawling, in retrospect is definitive and the end of their peak: henceforth they would coast through a boring musical decade with fans complaining about their work but buying it anyway. *Jamming With Edward* '72 really did sprawl, jam with Jagger, Wyman, Watts, Hopkins. Jagger sang on Carly SIMON's no. 1 'You're So Vain' '72. *Goat's Head Soup* '73 made it obvious that their peak was past, but incl. 'Angie', no. 1 USA/5 UK; *It's Only Rock & Roll* '74 had good title track, cover of the TEMPTATIONS' 'Ain't Too Proud To Beg'; Taylor quit (running for life: heroin came too close; he worked with Mike OLDFIELD, Bob DYLAN, made expensive flop *Mick Taylor* '79), replaced by ex-FACES Wood on *Black & Blue* '76, notable only for Jagger & Richards' interest in reggae (he sang with Peter Tosh on 'Don't Look Back', both were on Tosh LP *Bush Doctor* '78). 2-disc *Love You Live* '77 had one side recorded in a small Canadian club, showing some of the old vigour; *Some Girls* '78 was their best in years, perhaps pushed by competition with punk rock, incl. discoish 'Miss You' (their last no. 1 single); feminists were outraged by title track, as though surprised by Stone-age chauvinism. *Emotional Rescue* '80 pursued sloppy disco; *Tattoo You* '81 was an improvement; *Still Life* '82 was shoddy souvenir of '81 USA tour, reportedly the highest grossing tour in rock history (tour film *Let's Spend The Night Together* was surprisingly effective). *Undercover* '83 had some driving tracks; *Dirty Work* '86 saw them in best form since *Some Girls*. Jagger made solo *She's The Boss* '85 with Pete Townshend, Jeff BECK; 'Just Another Night' was a standout track, but LP disappointed Stones fans, as did *Primitive Cool* '87. He did duo 'Dancing In The Street' '85 with David BOWIE for Band Aid (no. 1 hit), made video 'Running Out Of Luck' '87. Richards made one-off cover of Berry's 'Run Rudolph Run' '79, had never

made a solo LP (joint project with Parsons was mooted early '70s, never happened) but was rehearsing mid-'87 in NYC with drummer Steve Jordan, bassist Charlie Drayton, guitarist Waddy Wachtel for tour and LP. Richards and Pallenberg were heroin addicts for many years, finally split up; indestructible Richards said that 'When I was on heroin, I learned to ski and I made *Exile On Main Street*': he could always beat Jagger, a fitness freak, at tennis. Long known as the 'Glimmer Twins', Jagger and Richards are said to be not speaking; they may never play together again, though the Stones came together for a benefit for Stewart '86. Jagger and Wyman are said to be working on autobiographies; Wyman has made solo LPs *Monkey Grip* '74, *Stone Alone* '76, soundtrack *Green Ice* and *Bill Wyman* '81 (with engaging top 20 UK single '(Si, Si) Je Suis Un Rock Star'); formed Willie & The Poor Boys '85 (name from CREEDENCE CLEARWATER track) for eponymous LP/video to aid Faces' Ronnie Lane (MS victim) with Watts, Wood, Chris Rea, Ringo STARR. Wood's solo work incl. *I've Got My Own Album To Do* '74, *Now Look* '75, *Gimme Some Neck* '79, *1,2,3,4* '81; he collaborated with Lane on LP *Mahoney's Last Stand* '76, formed short-lived New Barbarians with Richards '79. Oldham formed Immediate label c.'67, became bright independent with the NICE, SMALL FACES, HUMBLE PIE, FLEETWOOD MAC, NICO, Chris FARLOWE, Amen Corner on roster; folded '70; unsuccessful relaunch '76. He moved to NYC, worked as producer, oversaw reissue of Stones albums on CD '87. Watts was always the quiet one, always a jazz fan; he played with Stewart in Rocket 88, bankrolled the Charlie Watts Big Band for gig at Ronnie SCOTT club late '85, with John STEVENS and 31 others (arr. by Alan Cohen); unexpectedly successful venture toured USA: LP *The Charlie Watts Orchestra Live At Fulham Town Hall* on CBS was made 'after we'd played together only a week, and we're much better than that now'. The Rolling Stones at their best expertly reflected the times that they played through, transcending the farce and melodrama of their story; many books incl. Barbara Charone's biography of Richards, Philip Norman's *The Stones* '84, Stanley Booth's memoirish *The True Adventures Of*

The Rolling Stones '86. Incredibly, there were rumours of a Stones tour in '89.

ROLLINI, Adrian (*b* 28 June '04, NYC; *d* 15 May '56, Homestead, Fla.) Bass sax; also vibes, goofus, hot fountain pen, etc. An influential and underrated jazzman, one of the few masters of the cumbersome bass sax (admired by Coleman HAWKINS, Budd JOHNSON, Harry CARNEY), playing vibes with four mallets remarkably like Gary BURTON decades later, also fooling with novelty instruments. He was a child prodigy on piano; his brother Arthur played tenor, clarinet (*b* 13 Feb. '12, NYC; with Benny GOODMAN classic '34-9 band, later Will BRADLEY); both of them played in the California Ramblers, managed by sometime vocalist/banjoist Ed Kirkeby (*b* Wallace Theodore Kirkeby, 10 Oct. 1891, Brooklyn; *d* 12 June '78, Mineola, Long Island; later Fats WALLER's manager); the Ramblers were the most prolifically recorded dance band of the era '21-37 incl. under many pseudonyms; Glenn MILLER, both DORSEY brothers, vocalists Vernon DALHART, Smith BALLEW, countless others appeared on the records; the last couple of sessions used Tommy Dorsey, Charlie BARNET bands; it was Kirkeby who suggested bass sax to Adrian. He played in London '27-9; freelance on countless record dates '20s-early '30s, opened Adrian's Tap Room '35 at the Hotel President NYC (Eddie CONDON was regular), led own small groups for long hotel gigs; he opened his own hotel in Florida early '50s. He recorded with Bix BEIDERBECKE, Red NICHOLS, Frankie TRUMBAUER, Joe VENUTI, Louisiana Rhythm Kings, Miff Mole etc. Own records '30-40 began and ended with trio sessions; Adrian Rollini and his Orchestra '33 incl. Arthur, Goodman, Bunny BERIGAN; Barnet, Jack TEAGARDEN, Bud FREEMAN '34; Adrian and his Tap Room Gang '35 incl. Wingy MANONE; quintet '38 incl. Bobby HACKETT, Buddy RICH. Quintet, trio sessions on Swedish Tax; '33-4 orchestra on Sunbeam; many other compilations have come and gone.

ROLLINS, Sonny (*b* Theodore Walter Rollins, 7 Sep. '29, NYC) Tenor saxophone, composer. The most infl. tenor saxophonist between Coleman HAWKINS and John COLTRANE; his infl. continues and may in the end be as great as Coltrane's. Had piano lessons at 9, gave it up; took up alto '44 inspired by Louis JORDAN, soon infl. by Charlie PARKER; switched to tenor '46 infl. by Sonny STITT, Dexter GORDON. First records '48 with Babs GONZALES. Worked with J. J. JOHNSON (who recorded first Rollins tune 'Audubon'); Thelonious MONK, Art BLAKEY, Bud POWELL, Tadd DAMERON '49-50, Miles DAVIS '51, freelanced, joined Clifford BROWN – Max Roach quintet '55-7, led own combos ever since, with sabbaticals late '50s, late '60s. One of the most vocal of jazz musicians, complaining about having to play in saloons; abandoned them completely for concert halls '80s. Sabbaticals were times of examination and woodshedding as well as dissatisfaction with the jazz scene; he practised late '50s on the Williamsburg Bridge over the East River. His tone is uncompromising, harmonic ideas unique; he can do more with the bare bones of a tune than some composers with a whole orchestra: the way he improvises on the melody rather than jumping around in the chords means that he cannot hide from the musically literate listener; he walks a tightrope, skill and ideas always fully in view, and has been described as extending the possibilities of the solo more than anyone since Louis ARMSTRONG. His many recordings with Max Roach '50s (some under each name) generated the excitement of two masters tossing rhythmic challenges to each other. Best-known tunes are 'Oleo' and 'Airegin'; wrote score for *Alfie* '66 incl. 'Alfie's Tune' (not the BACHARACH-David title song). Davis LP *Collectors Items* on Prestige has '53 tracks with both Rollins and Parker (as 'Charlie Chan'). Tracks from Rollins' own Prestige LPs were compiled in 2-disc sets; some LPs now in original formats on Fantasy's OJC series (Original Jazz Classics): 2-disc *Vintage Sessions* incl. six '51-4 dates (incl. MODERN JAZZ QUARTET, Monk), from earlier LPs *First Recordings*, *Movin' Out*, *Sonny And The Stars*, etc. 2-disc *Saxophone Colossus And More* incl. '56 tracks from *Plus Four* (with Brown), *Plays For Bird* and *Saxophone Colossus* (all with Roach). Other 2-disc sets are *Taking Care Of Business* (incl. *Tenor Madness* '56 with Coltrane on title track, Davis's rhythm section) and survey *Sonny Rollins* (with tracks from almost all these except Monk). Other single Prestige LPs are *Worktime, Plays For Bird, Tour de Force* '55-6, all with Roach. *Way Out West* '57 on Contemporary, trio with Ray BROWN and Shelly MANNE, was a landmark LP, with famous sleeve photo of Rollins with cowboy hat in the desert; also *Sonny Rollins And The Contemporary Leaders* '58, with Manne, Hampton HAWES, Barney KESSEL, Leroy Vinnegar on bass, Victor FELDMAN playing vibes on one track; *Alternate Takes* from both dates released '86 on LP, tracks added to CD editions of the original LPs. On Blue Note: *Sonny Rollins* '56 is a quintet LP incl. 'How Are Things In Glocca Morra?' (from Yip HARBURG/ Burton Lane show *Finian's Rainbow*), an unusual vehicle for a jazzman, typically lovely ballad playing from Rollins; *Vol. 2* '57 is quintet with Monk on two tracks; quartet *Newk's Time* '57; trios with bass, drums on *A Night At The Village Vanguard* and *More From The Vanguard* '57. On Riverside: *The Sound Of Sonny* '57 is quartet with Sonny CLARK; famous *The Freedom Suite* '58 is trio with Oscar PETTIFORD and Roach, title composition recorded in two sessions, with four other tracks (LP aka *Shadow Waltz* on Jazzland; all Riverside tracks also in 2-disc *Freedom Suite Plus* on Milestone). Also on Abbey LINCOLN LP *That's Him!* on Riverside. Sessions for Metrojazz '58 incl. one each with big band, Modern Jazz Quartet, compiled on *Tenor Titan* on Verve. Toured with trio, tracks from broadcasts/clubs '59 issued in Sweden. He visited Japan and India, came back from sabbatical on RCA with epochal *The Bridge* '62, pianoless quartet with young Jim HALL on guitar; other quartet tracks with Hall from *What's New?* '62, *The Standard Sonny Rollins* '64, all compiled '86 in 2-disc Bluebird set. Balance of quartet, trio and quintet tracks from the last two LPs, some with Hall, Herbie HANCOCK, others, mostly issued in 2-disc *Alternative Sonny Rollins* on French RCA. *Our Man In Jazz* '62 was made live at Village Gate NYC, quartet incl. Don CHERRY, Billy Higgins on drums, Bob Cranshaw on bass (*Live In Europe* of unknown date on Jazz Horizons has Henry Grimes instead of Cranshaw), and *Sonny Meets Hawk!* '63 has quintet with two tenor giants, Paul BLEY, Cranshaw, Roy

McCurdy on drums. French RCA also issued *The Bridge* and *Sonny Meets Hawk* in a set. On Impulse '65-6: *Sonny Rollins On Impulse!, There Will Never Be Another You* (live at Modern Art Museum), *Sonny Rollins Plays Alfie* (nine pieces with Roger KELLAWAY, J. J. JOHNSON, Phil WOODS, Kenny BURRELL, arr. by Oliver Jackson), *East Broadway Run Down* '66, some of this on Jasmine in UK, 2-disc compilation *Great Moments* on MCA USA. Returning from his next layoff he did not much care whether he recorded, but trusted Orrin Keepnews' well-deserved reputation, went with his Milestone label: *Next Album* '72, *The Cutting Edge* '74 (from Montreux), *Nucleus* '75, *The Way I Feel* '76, *Easy Living* '77 (two tenors overdubbed), *Don't Stop The Carnival* '78 (live in San Francisco), *Milestone Jazzstars* '78 (recorded live with McCoy TYNER, Ron CARTER, Al Foster on drums, Rollins on soprano on one track), *Don't Ask* '79, *Love At First Sight* '80, *No Problem* '81, *Reel Life* '82, *Sunny Days, Starry Nights* '84, various personnel incl. Mark Soskin on keyboards, Bobby Broom on guitar, George DUKE, Stanley CLARKE, others; then *The Solo Album* '85 (composition 'Soloscope', made at Museum of Modern Art NYC), *Plays G-Man* '86 with Cranshaw, Soskin, Marvin Smith on drums, Clifton Anderson on trombone; *Dancing In The Dark*' 87 with Jerome Harris on electric bass replacing Cranshaw. Also *Sonny Rollins In Japan* '73 on JVC, *Island Lady* mid-'70s on Joker, Lotus. Awarded Guggenheim Fellowship '72; *Concerto For Saxophone And Orchestra* premiered in Japan '86, featured in film *Saxophone Colossus* (as was music from *G-Man* LP).

ROMBERG, Sigmund (*b* 29 July 1887, Hungary; *d* 9 Nov. '51, NYC) Composer of about 50 Broadway shows in operetta style, packed with songs and nearly all hit shows; many of the songs have survived on their sheer charm. Many early songs were heard in others' shows; the Schubert Bros. (theatre owners) seemed to regard Romberg as a hack, but a string of hits converted them. First show *Whirl Of The World* '14; hits incl. *Maytime* '17 (filmed '37), *Blossom Time* '21, *The Student Prince* '24 (filmed '54 with Mario LANZA), *The Desert Song* '26 (filmed '29, '44, '53), *The New Moon* '28 (filmed '31,

'40), *May Wine* '35, *Up In Central Park* '45 (filmed '48). *The Girl In Pink Tights* '54 was staged after his death. He was a founder member of ASCAP; conducted orchestra on radio and on tour, recording for Victor (LP in RCA LPV series '60s). Biography *Deep In My Heart* by Elliot Arnold; biopic of same name '54 starred José Ferrer. Collaborating lyricists incl. Otto HARBACH, Oscar Hammerstein II, Dorothy Fields, Gus Kahn, many others; best songs incl. 'When Hearts Are Young', 'Deep In My Heart, Dear', 'Golden Days', 'Lover, Come Back To Me', 'Softly, As In A Morning Sunrise', 'When I Grow Too Old To Dream', 'Close As Pages In A Book', many others.

RONETTES, The USA girl group, vocal trio formed in NYC '59: sisters Veronica (*b* 10 Aug. '43) and Estelle Bennett (*b* 22 July '44), their cousin Nedra Talley (*b* 27 Jan. '46). Began as dance act the Dolly Sisters; early singles as Ronnie and the Relatives on Col-Pix failed; they were resident dancers at the Peppermint Lounge and appeared with DJ Clay Cole in *Twist Around The Clock* '61; when the twist died out they were spotted by Phil SPECTOR, signed to Philles '63: first single and biggest hit 'Be My Baby' was no. 2 USA/4 UK, with Spector's everything-but-the-kitchen-sink prod. style incl. castanets, strings, etc. They alternated between aching teen ballads and uptempo boomers like the first; 'Baby I Love You' was no. 24 USA/11 UK '63; 'Do I Love You' top 40 both USA/UK, '(The Best Part Of) Breaking Up' and 'Walking In The Rain' top 40 USA '64. Topped UK package bill with ROLLING STONES '64, but star waned: two singles '65 did not make top 40, last chart entry '66 (turned over to prod. Jeff Barry) barely made Hot 100, despite good songs from ANDERS/PONCIA, Barry MANN/Cynthia Weil. Recorded for A&M and Buddah with different lineups before Ronnie went solo. She was married to Spector '68-74. Despite connections with George HARRISON (covered his 'Try Some Buy Some'), SOUTHSIDE JOHNNY and the Asbury Jukes (sang live with them and on first LP '76) and Bruce SPRINGSTEEN's E Street Band (covered Billy JOEL's 'Say Goodbye To Hollywood' '77) she could never translate respect of fellow artists into record sales.

RONSON, Mick (*b* Hull) Guitarist. Played in local band the Rats, joined David BOWIE's Spider From Mars (with fellow rat Woody Woodmansey) to play key part in LPs *The Man Who Sold The World* '70, *Hunky Dory* '71; his riffy playing was linchpin of power trio approach effective on *Ziggy Stardust* '72 and *Aladdin Sane* '73; he was also credited as co-arranger on these and *Pin-Ups* '73. Bowie's retirement that year left Ronson with solo career for which he wasn't ready; tour and LP *Slaughter On 10th Avenue* '74 were derided; he returned to sideman role with MOTT THE HOOPLE, forming partnership with singer Ian Hunter after that band split late '74; made *Play Don't Worry* '75 with Hunter's help but RCA dropped him. Split with Hunter, based himself in USA, joined Bob DYLAN's Rolling Thunder tour where he met ex-BYRD Roger McGuinn: played on and prod. his highly praised *Cardiff Rose* '76, leading to further prod. credits: Dead Fingers Talk, David Johansen, Rich Kids, Houserockers '78-80, others. With Hunter prod. ex-MEATLOAF vocalist Ellen Foley on first LP *Night Out* '79, appeared on three Hunter LPs '79-81; prod. and played with folky protégée Sandy Dillen.

RONSTADT, Linda Marie (*b* 15 July '46, Tucson, Arizona) C&W/pop singer. To L.A. '64; three LPs on Capitol with Stone Poneys '66-8 (trio with Bob Kimmel, Ken Edwards on guitars and vocals, backing musicians on disc): second *Evergreen* made top 100 LPs late '67 with top 20 track 'Different Drum'; first was reissued '75, made top 200. Solo albums on Capitol established country rock status: *Hand Sown, Home Grown* did not chart; *Silk Purse* '70 incl. single hit 'Long Long Time'; *Linda Ronstadt* '72 incl. backing by all four original EAGLES. Changed labels to Asylum with producer Peter ASHER; *Don't Cry Now* '73 made top 50 LPs without a big hit single; *Heart Like A Wheel* appeared on Capitol, hit no. 1 late '74 with top 2 singles 'You're No Good' and 'When Will I Be Loved'. Top 5 LPs *Prisoner In Disguise*, *Hasten Down The Wind* '75-6 continued successful formula of well-chosen material carefully produced; *Simple Dreams* and *Living In The USA* '77-8 were no. 1 albums; *Mad Love* '80 no. 3; *Get Closer* '82 slipped to no. 31. Total of 18 hit singles by end of '82 incl. no. 3 cover of Roy ORBISON's 'Blue Bayou' (three singles, five LPs hits in UK). Relationship with then Governor Jerry Brown of California in news late '70s. Her appearance on stage in GILBERT & SULLIVAN's *Pirates Of Penzance* was praised: perhaps showing an intelligent refusal, rare in pop, to showcase new songs just because they are new, she switched to songs from the Golden Age for *What's New* '83, mostly lesser-known items by George GERSHWIN, Irving BERLIN, etc., arr./cond. by Nelson RIDDLE: unfortunately the sort of phrasing necessary in this genre was conspicuously absent. *What's New* sold well, as did *Lush Life* '84, incl. Billy STRAYHORN title song, *For Sentimental Reasons* '86, also with Riddle, benefiting from better-known songs (it takes a Betty CARTER or a Bobby SHORT to revive lesser-known ones); three LPs were boxed for Christmas set '86. She also sang on Philip GLASS LP *Songs From Liquid Days* '85 on CBS; joined Dolly PARTON and Emmylou HARRIS in long-awaited *Trio* '87 on WEA: singing lead on Linda THOMPSON's beautiful 'Telling Me Lies', her gorgeous gospel-quality voice tumbles down the song in exactly the right way: when she sticks to what she does best she has few peers. She went back to roots and to part of her true identity with *Canciones de Mi Padre* '88, sung in Spanish and prod. by Ruen Fuentes, a godfather of Mexican music.

ROOMFUL OF BLUES Nine-piece blues band based in Providence, R.I., now making international waves after 20 years: formed '67 by pianist Al Copley, guitarist Duke Robillard. Current lineup: Greg Piccolo, vocals, tenor sax (*b* 10 May '51, Westerly, R.I.); Rich Lataille, alto and tenor sax (*b* 29 Oct. '52, Westerly); Doug James, baritone (*b* 21 Aug. '53, Turlock, Cal.); Porky Cohen, trombone (*b* 2 June '24, Springfield, Mass.); Bob Enos, trumpet and vocals (*b* 4 July '47, Boston, Mass.); Ronnie Earl, guitar (*b* 10 Mar. '53, NYC); Paul Tomasello, bass and vocals (*b* 17 Nov. '51, Boston); John Rossi, drums (*b* 13 Nov. '42, Providence); Junior Brantley, keyboards (*b* Carthage, Ms.). They broke up briefly '70, re-formed with Piccolo and Lataille; Rossi replaced Frannie Christina (went to FABULOUS THUNDER-BIRDS) and James joined '71. They gigged

with Sil AUSTIN, Red Prysock, Eddie 'Cleanhead' VINSON, B. B. KING, Maria MULDAUR '73 (gave her 'It Ain't The Meat'), played Ann Arbor Blues Festival, first long residencies at Brandy's in Boston, Knickerbocker Café in Westerly. First gigs with Count BASIE '74, who paid them high compliments, came to see them whenever possible; their 'swing era' began as they met critics Helen and Stanley Dance, who introduced them to Helen HUMES, who came out of retirement to sing with them. Played Roseland ballroom with Basie '77. Doc POMUS helped get record deal: first LP *Roomful Of Blues* on Island. Opened for PROFESSOR LONGHAIR '78 at New Orleans Jazz Festival; LP *Let's Have A Party* '79 on Antilles; Robillard left (formed trio the Pleasure Kings for two LPs on Rounder, then *Swing* '87 with Scott HAMILTON); Earl and Cohen joined: Cohen had played with Tony PASTOR '42, then Charlie BARNET, CASA LOMA band, Barnet again '46 (*Town Hall Jazz Concert*), worked with Boyd RAEBURN, others, then with Lucky MILLINDER (incl. tour of South as one of three white sidemen), also Tommy DORSEY, Artie SHAW '49-50, with Max KAMINSKY, Bob WILBER, etc.; played dixieland in Providence '55-79: since joining Roomful he has played in almost every state in the Union. Lou Ann Barton sang with Roomful '79-80; Piccolo took over vocals; band backed Lou RAWLS on a track for *Shades Of Blue* '81; LP *Hot Little Mama* '81 on Blue Flame voted among top 10 blues albums in W. C. Handy Awards. Brought Roy BROWN to East Coast for tour; Enos joined; first national tours began; played San Francisco Bread & Roses Festival '82 with Etta JAMES and Tracy NELSON; club gigs with Jimmy McCRACKLIN, Cleanhead, Big Joe TURNER led to LPs *Eddie 'Cleanhead' Vinson & Roomful Of Blues* '82, *Blues Train* '83 with Turner (and guest Mac REBENNACK) '83, both on Muse; Turner LP nominated for Grammy '84, named among top LPs in W. C. Handy Awards. Keith Dunn hired to sing as Piccolo had throat surgery, replaced by Curtis Salgado (played on first Robert CRAY LP); bassist Randy Simmons replaced Preston Hubbard (went to Thunderbirds); Copley replaced by Ron Levy, who also played organ, sang. LP *Dressed Up To Get Messed Up* on Rounder's

Varrick subsidiary. In Texas '85 Billy Gibbons (ZZ TOP) followed the band, gave Earl a custom-made guitar. First European tour incl. London, Scandinavia; Rory MacLeod replaced Simmons. *Hot Little Mama* reissued on Varrick '86 as band backed Earl KING on *Glased*, recorded own *Live At Lupo's Heartbreak Hotel* in Providence, with members of LOS LOBOS guesting. Salgado left as Piccolo resumed singing; Tomasello joined early '87, then Brantley, who had worked in Milwaukee, Wis., recorded with Short Stuff, joined Thunderbirds '85. Gigs '87 incl. West Coast date with Charlie Watts Big Band. Horn section backed Stevie Ray VAUGHAN and Double Trouble at Carnegie Hall debut '84, recorded with Thunderbirds (*Butt Rockin'*), The Legendary Blues Band (*Red, Hot'n'Blue* on Rounder), J. B. HUTTO (*Slippin' And Slidin'* on Varrick), John Mooney (*Telephone King* on Blind Pig). Band sponsored by Miller Beer '87 along with Delbert MCCLINTON, Maines Brothers Band, 18 other regional acts; European tour mid-'87.

ROS, Edmundo (*b* 7 Dec. '10, Venezuela) UK drummer, vocalist, bandleader. As a jazz drummer he recorded with Fats WALLER in London '38; then his society Latin-American band was extremely popular, said to be Princess Margaret's favourite. His 'Wedding Samba' '49 sold three million copies worldwide, was top 20 USA (song written '40 in Yiddish; covered in USA by Carmen MIRANDA with the ANDREWS SISTERS); his tours of Japan were sellout affairs; *Rhythms Of The South* '57 was a hit LP. Compilations on Decca UK.

ROSARIO, Willie (*b* Puerto Rico) Bandleader, composer, producer; virtuoso timbales player (timbalero), also bongos. Led own band El Conjunto Coamex in home town of Coamo at 16; moved to NYC still in his teens, worked with Noro MORALES, Aldemaro Romero, Johnny Segui, Herbie MANN. Formed own band '58 and made *El Bravo Soy Yo* c.'62 on Alegre (reissued '78 on Inca) with lead singer Frankie Figueroa, the band regarded as one of the best on the scene. Other '60s LPs were *Too Too Much* on Musicor (with Figueroa) and *Boogaloo y Guaguanco* on Atco (he did not approve of boogaloo, calling it 'American

music played with Latin percussion', according to John Storm Roberts). He played percussion on some of legendary series of '60s descarga LPs by the Alegre All Stars (*see* Charlie PALMIERI) and CESTA All Stars; he added a baritone sax '67 to his frontline of four trumpets, moved back to Puerto Rico, on Inca label with *El Bravo de Siempre* c.'69, *Mr Ritmo* c.'71, *Mas Ritmo* '72 with lead singer Chamaco Rivera, *Infinito* '73 with Junior Toledo (Figueroa in the chorus), *Otra Vez* '75 with Toledo (Louie Ramirez, mus. dir./arr.), *Gracias Mundo* '77 with vocals by Bobby Concepción and Guillo Rivera (prod. by Bobby VALENTIN), best-of *Campanero Rumbero* '78. To the Florida-based Top Hits (TH) for *From The Depth Of My Brain* '78 and *El Rey del Ritmo* '79 (both with Toledo and Guillo); celebrated 20th anniversary with *El de a 20 de Willie* (lead singers Tony Vega and Concepción). *The Portrait Of A Salsa Man* '81 had Vega and Concepción joined by Gilberto Santa Rosa on lead vocals; *Atizame el Fogón* '82 and *The Salsa Machine* '83 were the last on TH, latter the last with Concepción. Joined Valentin's Puerto Rican Bronco label with hit *Nuevos Horizontes* '84; TH issued hits compilation *15 Exitos de . . . Willie Rosario y su Orquesta* '85; 25th anniversary was marked by *Afincando/25 Aniversario* on Bronco; *Nueva Cosecha* '86 had lead singers Vega and Santa Rosa joined by Tony (Pupy Cantor) Torres from NYC-based Manny Oquendo y su Conjunto Libre (*see* LIBRE), incl. remake of Willie's 'Dame Tu Amor Morenita' from *El Bravo Soy Yo*: this was Vega and Santa Rosa's last with Willie; latter formed own band, made hit *Good Vibrations* on Combo '86, co-prod. by Mario Ortiz, Rafael Ithier (*see* EL GRAN COMBO); Santa Rosa's followup was *Keeping Cool!* on Combo. Willie's *A Man Of Music* '87 featured Pupy Cantor with new singer Josué Rosado.

ROSE, Billy (*b* 6 Sep. 1899, NYC; *d* 10 Feb. '66, Jamaica, West Indies) Lyricist, producer, showman. Owned two theatres in NYC, opened Billy Rose's Music Hall '34, hired Benny GOODMAN's first band for long gig; opened the Diamond Horseshoe '38 and it was a premier night spot for many years. He was also broadcaster, syndicated columnist. His lyrics were always of their time, and still fine period pieces, from novelties like 'Barney Google' and 'Does The Spearmint Lose Its Flavor On The Bedpost Overnight' (early '20s) to flapper-era good-time tunes such as 'Don't Bring Lulu' ('25, with Brown and Henderson; *see* DESYLVA), 'Me And My Shadow', 'Back In Your Own Back Yard', 'There's A Rainbow 'Round My Shoulder' (all '27-8 with Al JOLSON, Dave Dreyer), and fine ballads 'Without A Song' and 'More Than You Know' ('29, with Edward Eliscu and Vincent YOUMANS for show *Great Day*), 'It Happened In Monterey' ('30, with Mabel Wayne for film *King Of Jazz*), 'I Found A Million Dollar Baby (In A Five And Ten Cent Store)' ('31, with Harry WARREN and Mort Dixon for show *Billy Rose's Crazy Quilt*), 'It's Only A Paper Moon' ('32, with Yip HARBURG and Harold ARLEN, at first 'If You Believed In Me' in show *The Great Magoo*), also 'Got The Jitters' (recorded by Don REDMAN), 'Have A Little Dream On Me' and 'The Girl I Left Behind Me' (both recorded by Fats WALLER, many more). From c.'40 the times he loved best were receding; he quit show business '50s and played the stock market.

ROSE, Calypso (*b* McCartha Lewis, 27 Apr. '40, Bethel, Tobago: her 'official' birthdate) Calypsonian and soca artist. Father led his own Spiritual Baptist Church; she was sent to Trinidad to live with an aunt at age 10; her first calypso was called 'Glass Tief' (thief) and her first calypso name was Crusoe Kid when she was still in her teens. Her father and aunt opposed her wish to sing calypso, then still considered dishonourable and in any case completely dominated by male artists; she returned to Tobago at 16 because her aunt had gone to London. Promoters gave her the name Calypso Rose; she turned pro '63 with Lord KITCHENER's calypso tent; won crowns for the Virgin Islands and Tobago with 'Cooperation', which she recorded. Moved to Mighty SPARROW's tent '67; that year 'Fire, Fire' was a contender for the Road March: initially prevented by discrimination from recording it, but Sparrow heard it and made the appointment at the recording studio; it was one of her biggest hits. Early LPs incl. *Calypso Queen Of The World*, *Sexy Hot Pants* and *Splish Splash*. Another Road March contender was 'Do Dem Back' '75

(it's said that she lost to Kitchener by only one point) and that year she won third prize in the Calypso Monarch contest: competition still for a Calypso *King*, but that year there were two other women (Singing Francine and Singing Diane) in the seven finalists. She won the Road March with 'More Tempo' '77 (on LP *Action Is Tight*); won both Road March (with 'Soca Jam') and Calypso Monarch of Trinidad and Tobago '78 ('Her Majesty' and 'I Thank Thee', the first and only time a woman has won it (winning selections on *Her Majesty*). '79 LP was *Mas Fever*; became a regular in Mighty SHADOW's tent ('Masters Den') '80, issued *We Rocking For Carnival* (last four LPs all on Charlies). *Ah Can't Wait* '81 on 2000AD Records was made in Hollywood, not well received at home; *Mass In California* '82 on Strakers saw her back on form, incl. 'Balance Wheel'; *Rose Goes Soca Unlimited* '83, *Trouble* '84, *Pan In Town* '85, *Stepping Out* '86, *Leh We Punta* '87 are all on Strakers; in '86-7 she led her own Rose's Superstar tent in Tobago. She has lost some favour since her peak; based in USA she is criticised for losing touch. But she took on the establishment in a male-dominated (and chauvinist) genre and beat the rest convincingly: she must get some credit for the fact that there is now an annual Calypso Queen contest.

ROSE, David (*b* 15 June '10, London) Composer, conductor. Two sources agree on birth date; ASCAP says 3 June '15. To USA age 4, grew up in Chicago. Worked with Jack HYLTON in USA '36, arr. Benny GOODMAN hit 'It's Been So Long' that year; arr. and radio work took him to Hollywood studios. Big hit '43 on Victor with his own 'Holiday For Strings'; 'Poinciana (Song Of The Tree)' '44 not his own (probably recorded earlier, became a hit during musicians' strike when records were not being made). Was married '38-41 to the actress/comedienne/singer Martha Raye (*b* Martha Reed, 27 Aug. '16, Butte, Montana), backed her on her only hit record 'Melancholy Mood' '39; he was also married to Judy GARLAND '41-3. Composer and conductor of AAF show *Winged Victory*, on Broadway and filmed '43-4. Lesser instrumental hits on MGM '55-8 incl. 'Calypso Melody', written by Larry CLINTON; also with André

PREVIN on Previn's 'Like Young' '59; then no. 1 hit with 'The Stripper' '62, a brilliant piece of work: only written c.'61, now impossible to imagine strippers without it. Other tunes incl. 'Dance Of The Spanish Onion'; also 32 piano solos collectively called Music For Moderns. Radio and TV work with Tony MARTIN, comedian Red Skelton etc.; much incidental music for films; backed Connie FRANCIS etc. on hits.

ROSE, Fred (*b* 24 Aug. 1897, Evansville, Ind.; *d* 1 Dec. '54, Nashville, Tenn.) Vocalist, songwriter, publisher. Played the piano and sang in Chicago, recorded piano rolls, with Paul WHITEMAN briefly, formed duo with whistler Elmo Tanner. His 'Deep Henderson' was recorded by King OLIVER, COON-SANDERS Nighthawks; he wrote/co-wrote ' 'Deed I Do', 'Red Hot Mama', 'Honestly And Truly' for Sophie TUCKER; had radio show Fred Rose's Song Shop, on which he wrote songs on the spot. Toured with trio the Vagabonds, played piano on WSM in Nashville and got into country music by accident: wrote/co-wrote songs for Gene AUTRY incl. 'Be Honest With Me' (Oscar nomination '41, from film *Ridin' On A Rainbow*), for Roy ACUFF incl. 'Fireball Mail', 'Pins And Needles', 'No One Will Ever Know'; 'Texarkana Baby' for Eddy ARNOLD '48. He didn't like country music at first, but came to admire its strengths; he had joined ASCAP '28, but formed Acuff-Rose Music '42, the first all-country publishing company, and affiliated with BMI. Turning publishing over to son Wesley '45, he worked with artists and plugged songs; Hank WILLIAMS walked in one day without an appointment '46 and was signed as a writer. Rose's work is of the greatest importance in post-war popular music: he knew it would not be easy to sell country songs in the pop market, but when crossover hits began they were Acuff-Rose songs, especially those by Pee Wee KING and Redd Stewart ('Slow Poke', 'Bonaparte's Retreat', the biggest of all 'Tennessee Waltz', no. 1 for 13 weeks '50 by Patti PAGE), then Williams: great as Hank was, he was also almost illiterate; Rose helped to polish many of his hits, still popular and influential today, but took co-writing credit on only a few, incl. 'Take These Chains From My Heart', 'Setting The Woods On Fire', 'Kaw-Liga'.

ROSS, Diana Pop/soul vocalist, superstar: famous as lead singer of the SUPREMES (*which see*); became centrepiece late '60s when trio's name changed to Diana Ross and the Supremes; long-predicted solo move took place '70, for 33 Hot 100 hits in the USA through '85. First solo hit 'Reach Out And Touch' made USA top 20 and charted in UK; second 'Ain't No Mountain High Enough' (new arrangement of Tammi Terrell/Marvin GAYE hit of '67) was no. 1 USA/top 10 UK; she had three top 40s USA '71, but 'I'm Still Waiting' (no. 63 USA) was her first UK no. 1. She had always been the favourite of Berry Gordy, who saw her as the ultimate Motown superstar; he obtained her first film role for her in *Lady Sings The Blues* '72; as a biopic of Billie HOLIDAY it was panned, but commercially successful, soundtrack LP no. 1 USA; Ross nominated for an Oscar. 'Touch Me In The Morning' was no. 1 USA '73, top 10 UK; another project was duet LP with her male Motown equivalent, Marvin GAYE: they charted with two singles in USA, two different ones in UK. Second film *Mahogany* '75 not very well received: there is something sad about the necessity for Gordy to direct and Ross to star in a Joan Crawford type of vehicle, but it had a no. 1 USA/top 5 UK single in 'Theme From Mahogany (Do You Know Where You're Going)'. *Diana Ross* '76 incl. no. 1 'Love Hangover' (top 10 UK), no. 5 LP USA also incl. the film theme. She played Dorothy character in the *The Wiz* '78 (black remake of *Wizard Of Oz*, with pre-immortal Michael JACKSON in the cast), unusually bad casting spoiling what could have been a good movie. LP *Baby It's Me* '77 was prod. by Richard PERRY (also prod. of Carly SIMON and Barbra STREISAND); result disappointed some fans. She returned to Motown production for a less ambitious LP *The Boss* '79 (top 20 title single USA), then *Diana* '80, no. 2 LP incl. 'Upside Down' (no. 1 USA) and 'I'm Coming Out' (no. 5), 'My Old Piano' (top 10 UK), still considered by many her best album, but there was much stress with prod. team of Nile Rogers and Bernard Edwards of CHIC. She cut a huge hit single duet with Lionel RICHIE: 'Endless Love' was no. 1 for nine weeks in USA '81, but then left Motown for RCA (USA), Capitol (UK). Prod. her own *Why Do Fools*

Fall In Love '81, no. 15 LP with two top 10 singles USA; got involved in fitness syndrome '82 with 'Muscles' (top 10 USA), 'Work That Body' (top 10 UK); routine LP *Ross* '83 used outside producers; then she prod. improved *Swept Away* '84, with guest stars Jeff BECK, Daryl HALL, Richie, Julio IGLESIAS, Rogers and Edwards, previous quarrels swept away. *Eaten Alive* '85 co-prod. and largely written by BEE GEE Barry Gibb: 'Missing You' was dedicated to Gaye; 'Chain Reaction' was a huge hit in UK, very much in Motown mould. *Red Hot Rhythm Plus Blues* '87 prod. by Tom DOWD. Her work is uneven whenever she tries to step out of the style that made her famous, but the star quality that Gordy spotted 25 years ago is still there. Other albums incl. *Diana Ross Live At Caesar's Palace* '74, 2-disc *An Evening With Diana Ross* '77 live in L.A. theatre; many compilations.

ROSSELSON, Leon (*b* 22 June '34, London) UK folk-revival singer, and an important political, often polemical songwriter. Wrote songs for BBC-TV's *That Was The Week That Was* early '60s, made EP *Songs For City Squares* '62 on Topic; also a member of the Galliards on LPs *Scottish Choice* and *A-Roving* '62 on Decca, *The Galliards* '63 on EMI (work also appeared on Monitor in USA). Worked with Roy Bailey, Martin CARTHY, others in 3 City 4, whose *The Three City Four* on Decca and *Smoke & Dust* '64-5 mixed songs by Rosselson (some co-written with poet Adrian Mitchell), Bob DYLAN, Pete SEEGER, Sydney Carter. First solo LP was *Songs For Sceptical Circles* '67 on Bounty (reissued '70 on Acorn); *A Laugh, A Song And A Hand-Grenade* '68 on Transatlantic continued association with Mitchell. *The Word Is – Hugga Mugga Chugga Lugga Humbugga Boom Chit* '71 on Trailer (co-credited to Carthy and Bailey) followed by *That's Not The Way It's Got To Be* '75, incl. his 'The World Turned Upside Down', covered by Billy BRAGG, Dick Gaughan; *Palaces Of Gold* '75 (remakes of older songs), both on Acorn. Rosselson and Bailey's *Love, Loneliness, Laundry* '77 on Acorn incl. controversial 'Stand Up For Judas'. *If I Knew Who The Enemy Was . . .* '79 on Acorn was followed by *For The Good Of The Nation* '81, *Temporary Loss Of Vision* '83 (with Carthy, Simon Nicol, mem-

bers of HOME SERVICE), *Bringing The News From Nowhere* '86, all on Fuse. 'Ballad Of A Spycatcher' '87 on Upside Down Records incl. Bragg and the Oyster Band, addressed issues spotlit by Peter Wright's second-rate book *Spycatcher* and Campaign for Press and Broadcasting Freedom in UK, where bureaucratic secrecy is a virulent, ridiculous disease.

ROUSE, Charlie (*b* 6 Apr. '24, Washington DC; *d* Dec. '88) Tenor sax. Inspired by band that rehearsed nearby. Played with Billy ECKSTINE, then Dizzy GILLESPIE big bands '44-5, Tadd DAMERON and Fats NAVARRO late '40s, with Duke ELLINGTON '49-50. Freelanced through '50s, co-formed Les Jazz Modes with French hornist Julius Watkins (*b* 10 Oct. '21, Detroit; *d* 4 Apr. '77), LPs on Seeco, Atlantic; also recorded with Paul QUINICHETTE (*The Chase Is On* on Bethlehem), etc. Joined Thelonious MONK quartet '59-70. His quirky rhythmic style was compatible with Monk's tunes and he could play them the way Monk wanted: 'He thought if you practiced the changes themselves, you'd play the chords as such and he didn't want to hear that. He wanted you to experiment.' Critics who earlier failed to understand Monk also tended to underrate Rouse, whose sly high spirits are always recognisable and entertaining, as Monk's were. Worked with Mal WALDRON early '80s, then co-operative band Sphere: Buster Williams on bass, Kenny Barron, Monk alumnus Ben Riley on drums: plays Monk's tunes among others, but is more than a Monk repertory band. LPs *Four In One* and *Flight Path* on Elektra, *On Tour* '85 on Red Records, *Four For All* '87 on Verve, *Live At Umbria Jazz* on Red. Own albums as leader: quintet *Takin' Care Of Business* on Jazzland and quartet LP on Epic '60; *Bossa Nova Bacchanal* '62 on Blue Note, *Two Is One* '74 on Strata East, *Cinnamon Flower* '76 on Casablanca, all with Latin flavour; quartet *Moment's Notice* '77 on Storyville; *The Upper Manhattan Jazz Society* '81 on Enja, with Williams, Al Dailey on piano, Benny BAILEY, Keith COPELAND; *Social Call* '84 on Uptown, with Dailey, Red RODNEY, Cecil McBEE, Kenny Washington on drums; *Playin' In The Yard* '87 on Steam with UK quartet incl. Clark and Stan TRACEY.

ROUSSOS, Demis (*b* 15 June '47, Alexandria, Egypt) Greek crooner. Member of successful trio APHRODITE'S CHILD; then solo career, singing in several languages with highpitched voice and considerable girth; he then lost considerable weight (perhaps tired of the jokes). Sold a lot of records in Europe on Polydor labels, not much in USA; UK hits '75-7 in the strange pop calm before punk rock incl. 'Happy To Be On An Island In The Sun' at no. 5, EP *The Roussos Phenomenon* at no. 1 (the first EP to top all the UK singles charts), 'When Forever Has Gone' at no. 2; then forever went, as far as charts were concerned.

ROWLES, Jimmy (*b* James Charles Rowles, 19 Aug. '18, Washington DC) Pianist, composer; long famed as accompanist with an amazing memory, said to be the favourite of every singer he has backed, incl. Peggy LEE, Julie LONDON, Billie HOLIDAY, Carmen MCRAE, Sarah VAUGHAN etc.; also did much studio work (e.g. boogie-woogie calliope on Henry MANCINI's 'Elephant Walk') and has uniquely witty solo style, coming to the fore since mid-'70s but always highly regarded by musicians. Jess STACY told Whitney Balliett '75 that it still made him laugh that Benny GOODMAN (who often didn't get along with people) fired Rowles '42 to rehire Stacey. Moved to West Coast '40, worked with Slim GAILLARD, Lester YOUNG, others incl. big bands; recorded with Buddy DeFRANCO, Barney KESSEL, Bob BROOKMEYER, Benny CARTER (LP *BBB & Co.*), with Zoot SIMS (*If I'm Lucky*, *Warm Tenor* on Pablo; *Zoot Sims Party* on Choice); Joe PASS (*Checkmate* on Pablo). Own LPs incl. *Special Magic* '74 on Halcyon, *Paws That Refresh* and *Grandpaws* '76 on Choice, *Plays Duke Ellington And Billy Strayhorn* '77 on CBS; *We Could Make Such Beautiful Music Together* '78 on Xanadu, *Music's The Only Thing That's On My Mind* on Progressive and *Isfahan* on Soñet, all '78-80 with bassist George Mraz. Duo with Red Mitchell '85 on Contemporary; his daughter Tracey (*b* 11 Sep. '55) plays fine trumpet on small-group LPs *Tell It Like It Is* '84 on Concord, *Trio* '86 on Contemporary with Mitchell. Solo *Ellington by Rowles* on Cymbol (cassette only) is 64-minute bargain. Also duets with Joe NEWMAN on that UK Label.

ROXY MUSIC UK rock band of '70s: original lineup incl. Bryan Ferry, vocals, keyboards and songwriter (*b* 26 Sep. '45, Co. Durham); Brian ENO, synths, composer; Phil Manzanera, guitar (*b* Philip Targett-Adams, 31 Jan. '51, London); Paul Thompson, drums (*b* 13 May '51, Jarrow, Newcastle); Andy Mackay, sax (*b* 23 July '46). Ferry studied art in Newcastle '64, worked in local R&B bands the Banshees, the Gas Board; moved to London late '60s, auditioned unsuccessfully for King Crimson, recruited Mackay and Eno for fledgling Roxy. First guitarist was ex-NICE David O'List, soon replaced by Roxy roadie Manzanera; they had a different bassist on every album. Roxy's rise was meteoric, glamorous image and beguiling musical hybrid championed by DJ John PEEL and *Melody Maker*'s Richard Williams, only David BOWIE having anything like as much stylistic infl. in early '70s. Debut LP *Roxy Music* '72 drew on BEATLES infl. with Ferry's love of '50s rock'n'roll and Eno's experimentalism, one of the distinctive debuts of the decade, enhanced by piledriving single 'Virginia Plain' (no. 4 UK), follow-up 'Pyjamarama' (no. 10 '73). *For Your Pleasure* '73 was extravagant, exotic follow-up, with clutch of Ferry classics: 'Do The Strand', 'Editions Of You', 'In Every Dream A Heartache'. Eno and Ferry clashed over band's direction, Eno left late '73; *Stranded* '73 introduced multi-instrumentalist Eddie Jobson (ex-art rock band Curved Air; *b* 28 Apr. '55), incl. hit single 'Street Life' (Ferry's policy of keeping singles off LPs lasting only through the first two), more originals; his parallel solo career also began with *These Foolish Things* '73, incl. cover of Bob DYLAN's 'A Hard Rain's A-Gonna Fall' (top 10 UK) also covers of Beatles, Smokey ROBINSON, ROLLING STONES, LEIBER & STOLLER and title song (excellent British cabaret standard c.'36). *Another Time, Another Place* '74 completed image as cabaret rock'n'roller and sartorial lounge lizard, with his own masterly title track, more covers (Kris KRISTOFFERSON, Joe SOUTH, Willie NELSON). Roxy's *Country Life* '74 was their first top 40 LP in USA, with 'All I Want Is You' and 'Out Of The Blue'; *Siren* '75 saw cracks appear in the façade, their weakest album to date, with soulless 'Love Is The Drug'. By then Roxy were effectively Ferry, Manzanera and Mackay; as band waned, all pursued solo projects; with Ferry's *Let's Stick Together* '76 his albums as showcases for others' songs also wore thin, despite no. 4 hit title track. They had made their stylistic point; Ferry's mannered delivery was not enough to maintain what was essentially a repertory act. Live *Viva Roxy Music* seemed to administer their last rites; Ferry's *In Your Mind* '77 did not restore his flagging reputation; model Jerry Hall chose the moment to cuckold him with Mick JAGGER, who is another relentlessly unswinging singer. *The Bride Stripped Bare* '78 should have revived his credibility, but didn't receive due attention at the time: Ferry's originals were again strong and imaginative covers incl. trad. Irish 'Carrickfergus', J. J. CALE's 'Same Old Blues'. Roxy's first four LPs had been tours-de-force, elevating them far above contemporaries; like many pop acts they suffered from fickle taste: the idea of chic rock'n'roll was anathema to a public distracted by spitting punks. Having nosedived, Ferry convened Manzanera and Mackay again for *Manifesto* '79, with disco-infl. 'Dance Away' and 'Angel Eyes', both hits; LP was pale shadow of earliest innovative work, but *Flesh & Blood* '80 was an improvement; tribute to John LENNON, a cover of his 'Jealous Guy' '80, was their only UK no. 1 single. *Avalon* '82 was smooth and empty, though Ferry's hit 'More Than This' was refreshing; *The High Road* '83 was a mini-album and Roxy's last except for live *Musique/The High Road*, made in Glasgow and released '83. Ferry's *Boys And Girls* '85 was his first solo LP in seven years; made in several different studios with guests Mark Knopfler, Dave Gilmour, Nile Rogers, it was lacklustre despite a couple of hit singles. He remains one of the distinctive rock voices; 2-disc *Street Life* '86 was a package of Ferry and Roxy hits, a surprise no. 1 album in UK. Manzanera re-formed his early group Quiet Sun for one-off *Mainstream* '75, then did solo *Diamond Head* '75, *Listen Now* '77, *K-Scope* '78, *Primitive Guitars* '81; Mackay released well-received *In Search Of Eddie Riff* '74 and *Resolving Contradictions* '78, supplied music for TV shows *Rock Follies* '76 and *Rock Follies 77*, appeared on Paul MCCARTNEY's *Pipes Of Peace* '83, joined Manzanera in the Explor-

ers '84; Ferry appearanced at Live Aid '86; released LP *Bête Noire* '87, with three 60-year-old tango musicians on title track, other guests incl. Courtney PINE, Gilmour, Johnny Marr (from the SMITHS).

ROY C. (*b* Roy Charles Hammond, '43, NYC) Soul singer. Became Roy C. to avoid confusion with Ray CHARLES, Roy HAMILTON. Lead singer with The Genies early '60s; solo when group broke up; immediate hit with 'Shotgun Wedding', R&B chart only USA but no. 6 pop hit UK '66, re-entered at no. 8 '72. Switched labels from Black Hawk to Shout; started own Alaga label '69; series of singles about sex: 'Divorce Court', 'I Found A Man In My Bed', etc. Best-seller 'Gotta Get Enough' '71. Wrote, produced Mark IV's hit 'Honey I Still Love You' for Mercury '72; signed to that label '73; repackaged own Alaga cuts in LP *Sex And Soul*, also moderately successful singles, LPs (e.g. *More Sex And Soul* '77). 'Shotgun Wedding' single reissued UK '82, again '83.

ROYAL, Billy Joe (*b* '45, Valdosta, Ga.) Pop/country singer, grew up near Atlanta. Eight pop hits '65-7, had five of them written and prod. by close friend Joe SOUTH, incl. the biggest, 'Down In The Boondocks'. He made top 15 '69 with 'Cherry Hill Park', came back to Hot 100 '71 with 'Tulsa', switched to Private Stock label to reach Hot 100 again '78 with 'Under The Boardwalk'; went country: 'Burned Like A Rocket' on Atlantic America reached the country top 10 '85; album *Looking Ahead* spent more than a year on the country chart, reaching no. 21; *The Royal Treatment* '87 was in the top 30 and climbing, incl. 'Members Only' (duet with Donna FARGO), 'I'll Pin A Note On My Pillow'.

RUDD, Roswell (*b* Roswell Hopkins Rudd Jr, 17 Nov. '35, Sharon, Conn.) Trombone, composer. Studied French horn as a child, played trad. jazz in NYC late '50s, began playing with the avant-garde early '60s incl. Herbie NICHOLS, Steve LACY (who also had dixieland background), then New York Art Quartet with John Tchicai, Reggie Workman, Milford Graves (recorded for Fontana, toured Europe), also played at Newport with Jazz Composers Orchestra incl. Archie SHEPP, Jimmy LYONS, Steve SWALLOW etc. (LP *Communication* on Fontana; also seminal 2-disc set on JCOA '68); toured, recorded with Shepp, Charlie HADEN, etc. In early '60s he also began studying ethnic music, having noticed that vocal traditions thought unique to jazz were in fact common around the world: graduated from Yale, taught at Bard College, U. of Maine; worked as musicologist with Alan LOMAX, etc. His compositions fuse jazz tradition, ethnic music and classical technique. Own LPs incl. *Roswell Rudd Quartet* '65 on America with Tchicai, sextet *Everywhere* '66 on Impulse with Haden, then *Numatik Swing Band* '73 on JCOA, 24 pieces incl. Haden, Dewey REDMAN, vocal by Sheila JORDAN on one track. Also quintet *Flexible Flyer* '74 on Arista incl. Barry ALTSCHUL, Jordan; septet *Blown-bone* '76 on Japanese Philips incl. Lacy, Paul MOTIAN, Jordan; quintet *Inside Job* '76 on Arista incl. Dave BURRELL; quartet *Maxine* '76 on Dutch Bv Haast label, made in Amsterdam; duo *Sharing* '78 with pianist Giorgio Gaslini on Dischi della Quercia, made in Milan; overdubbed *The Definitive Roswell Rudd* '79 on Horo, made in Rome with Rudd playing trombone, piano, drums, percussion, vocals on two tracks; quintet *Regeneration* '82 on Soul Note, with Lacy, Misha Mengelberg on piano, Han Bennink on drums, Kent Carter on bass.

RUDDER, David (*b* Michael David Rudder, '53, Belmont, Port of Spain, Trinidad) Calypso artist, composer, painter, sculptor. Son of a chauffeur, eldest of five children; began singing '65 with the Solutions, imitating the Motown sound, 'the only black music we knew that really had symbolic force . . .' Performed solo '70 with own songs and pop songs of the period; turned to calypso late '70s, worked with KITCHENER, joined band Charlies Roots '80 as temporary replacement for lead vocalist Chris 'Tambu' Herbert (aka Corporal Christopher Herbert of the Trinidad & Tobago Police Band since '73). Charlies Roots was formed '77; Tambu joined same year after death of original vocalist Maestro (Cecil Hume); since Rudder joined Herbert has been somewhat overshadowed. Brass bands (as they are known in Trinidad) like Charlies Roots, Ed Watson & his Brass Circle, Sound Revolution, Fireflight etc. perform at public fetes (pay party/dances) during carnival season and are hired by mas (masquerade) bands to provide music for revellers during the two-day parade of costume bands at the climax of carnival; customarily they covered the season's popular calypsos, but increasingly they play their own material. Charlies Roots have longstanding association with controversial mas band leader and designer Peter Minshall and performed theme for his mas band Golden Calabash: 'Calabash' was arr. and sung by Rudder, a remake of 'In A Calabash' '50 by Mighty Killer (Cephas Alexander); it came third in the Road March contest '85, was incl. with 'Jump Up' (written by Rudder and Roots' mus. dir., arr. and keyboardist Pelham Goodard) on LP *The Golden Calabash* '85 on Charlies Records, made in Rawlston 'Charlie' Charles' Rawlston Recording Studio in Brooklyn, NY, prod. by Goodard with Rudder on lead vocals. He performed in a calypso tent (Spektakula tent) for first time '86 and swept the board, winning young King and Calypso Monarch titles, his songs 'Bahia Gyal' (Girl) and 'The Hammer' coming first and second in the Road March, 'The Hammer' also played by the winner of the National Panorama title (steel orchestra contest), the Catelli Trinidad All Stars. 'The Hammer' was co-written with Goodard; both incl. in Roots' LP *The Hammer* '86 on Charlies, made at Coral Studio, Trinidad, Rudder sharing lead and background vocals with Tambu. He was not the first calypso artist to come from a pop/soul background: e.g. Errol Asche with Watson's Brass Circle and Ellsworth James (late '60s soul/R&B singer) preceded him; nor the first to eschew a calypso sobriquet (although Mighty SPARROW called him King David) but he was the most successful. Traditionalists incl. Kitch were critical, but Rudder himself was challenging the norms, making a distinction as 'calypso artist' as opposed to 'calypsonian'. Singles were issued on London Records in UK incl. remixes by Eddy GRANT; winning '86 songs incl. in London compilation *This Is Soca 2* '86. He made UK debut on BBC 2 Arena programme *Caribbean Nights* mid-'86, followed by many UK appearances '86-7 and considerable media hype. He returned to the Spektakula tent '87 (Tambu entered in the same tent); as the previous year's winner he was automatically entitled to be incl. in finals; two-way battle with '86 runner-up Mighty STALIN (who had support of capacity Dimanche Gras Show crowd) saw him dethroned into second place. His 'Madness' placed second in the Road March, together with 'Calypso Music', 'Dedication (A Praise Song)' and Tambu's 'Yes Darling' were incl. in Roots' *Calypso Music/Tenth Anniversary Album* '87 on Lypsoland, made at Coral; the LP incl. guests Ralph McDonald on percussion (an American of Trinidadian descent, prominent in USA jazz/fusion scene) and virtuoso steel pianist Robert Greenidge (played with Taj MAHAL, Grover WASHINGTON, John LENNON); most of these tracks (plus 'Bahia' again) were incl. in 2-disc *This Is Soca With David Rudder And Charlies Roots* '87 (the second disc incl. Stalin's winner 'Burn Dem'). In May '87 Stalin and Rudder appeared together at the New Orleans Jazz & Heritage Festival, in August at London's Town & Country Club. As an artist Rudder has exhibited in Trinidad; he works as an accounts clerk with PTSC, T&T's public bus company. Calypso purists criticising his music forget that SOCA was fuelled by a new international consciousness and was itself criticised before becoming today's dominant calypso form: 'When people hear soca they'll say, I'm hearing jazz in there, I'm hearing reggae, samba, blues. In fact . . . they're hearing Africa . . . the reason I've crossed over is because I've crossed back.' (Interview with Tony Heatherington in the *Wire*.) Tambu made a comeback '88; won Road March and got into Monarch competition. Rudder didn't compete.

RÜEGG, Mathias (*b* 8 Dec '52, Zurich) Pianist, composer. Gigged in Graz and Vienna while studying '70s, formed Vienna Art Orchestra '77, big band which plays his arrangements of others' music as well as his own: eclectic, amusing, theatrical music is compared to that of Mike WESTBROOK; played with thrilling precision and bristling with solos (e.g. by Herbert Joos, trumpeter, composer, *b* 21 Mar. '40, Germany). LPs on Hat Art: *Concerto Piccolo* '80 (one LP, one EP), 2-disc sets *From No Time To Rag Time* '82 (his adaptations of Charles MINGUS, Jelly Roll MORTON, Scott JOPLIN, Bud

POWELL, Anthony BRAXTON, Roswell RUDD, others), live *Suite For The Green Eighties* '81 (all his own music), *Minimalism Of Eric Satie* '83-4, *Perpetuum Mobile* '85 (mostly his own; two tunes by Thelonious MONK, Bhumibol Adolaydej).

RUFFIN, David and Jimmy Soul vocalists, David (*b* 18 Jan. '41) and Jimmy (*b* 7 May '39) from Meridian, Ms. originally, where their father was a Baptist preacher. David sang gospel with the Dixie Nightingales, worked as a jockey in Arkansas where he met Anna Gordy, who was planning to start her own Anna label, which became part of the Motown empire of her brother Berry; David joined the TEMPTATIONS, alternating as lead vocalist '64-8 on many hits. Jimmy worked in a factory in Detroit; a co-worker who was a member of the Contours introduced him to Gordy, who signed him as a solo artist to subsidiary Miracle label (he turned down offer to join the Temptations). Jimmy hit top 10 USA and UK '66 with 'What Becomes Of The Brokenhearted' on Soul (another Motown label), six more Hot 100 entries by mid-'71 and three top 10 UK hits '70, then 'Hold On To My Love' '80 on RSO for transatlantic top 10; 'There Will Never Be Another You' '85 on EMI reached UK chart; 'The Foolish Thing To Do' '86 with blue-eyed Heaven 17 was UK soul hit on Virgin. David's solo career incl. 'My Whole World Ended (The Moment You Left Me)' '69, 'Walk Away From Love' '75 (both top 10 USA); other Hot 100 entries incl. duet with Jimmy 'Stand By Me' '70; recorded for WB late '70s-early '80s; appeared with HALL & OATES at Live Aid, made LP with them *Live At The Apollo With David Ruffin & Eddie Kendricks* '85. Fine voices deserved more hits.

RUIZ, Hilton (*b* 29 May '52, NYC) Pianist, composer, leader. Studied classical, played in solo recital at Carnegie Hall age 8; became prominent in NYC post-bop and Latin jazz: played/recorded with Ismael Rivera, Frank Foster, Charles MINGUS, Roland KIRK, Roy Brooks (*Ethnic Expression* on Im Hotep: drummer Brooks *b* 3 Sep. '38, Detroit; with Horace SILVER '59-64, played with M'Boom, Dollar Brand, many others; formed own group Artistic Truth). Own LPs incl. *Fantasia* on Denon; trio LPs

Piano Man '75; *New York Hilton, Excitation* (adding Foster on reeds, Richard Williams on trumpet), *Steppin' Into Beauty* '77, all on Steeplechase; *Crosscurrents* '84 on Stash (trio and quintet). Gig at Village Gate '87 with Papo LUCCA, Eddie PALMIERI celebrated first LP on major label, octet *Something Grand* on RCA Novus, incl. Sam RIVERS; followed by *El Camino*.

RUMBA A group of African-derived Cuban instrumental, vocal and dance forms, e.g. columbia, guaguancó, yambú, evolved during slavery. Interlocking rhythms are produced using three conga drums, claves (two short sticks struck together) and palitos (two sticks struck on a hard, resonant surface). The term rumba or rumbón also refers to a community social activity, a party. Danilo Orozco in the BBC2 *Arena* film *What's Cuba Playing At?* '84 said that all Cuban music was made up of one or more of four forms: rumba, canción (song), danzón and son; John Storm Roberts in *The Latin Tinge* says that rumba, son, son montuno and guaracha are all separate forms; one thing everyone agrees on is that the ballroom dance Americans call rumba or rhumba is actually a SON (*which see*).

RUMSEY, Howard (*b* 7 Nov. '17, Brawley, Cal.) Began on piano, then drums; worked in Vido Musso band where pianist was Stan KENTON, founder member of Kenton's first band, featured on 'Concerto For Doghouse' '42. Freelanced with various bands on West Coast; began jam sessions at the Lighthouse in Hermosa Beach, Cal. '49, the Lighthouse All Stars or guests sitting in a roll call of '50s jazz: Shelly MANNE, Shorty ROGERS, Bob COOPER, Jimmy GIUFFRE, Victor FELDMAN, Max ROACH, Hampton HAWES, Bud SHANK, Barney KESSEL, Conte CANDOLI, Frank Rosolino, Sonny CLARK, Lennie NIEHAUS, Maynard FERGUSON, drummer Stan Levey, bassist Monty Budwig, pianist Marty Paich (later famous studio arranger), many more. Many LPs on Contemporary '52-7 began with 10″ LPs, half a dozen 12″ LPs incl. *Music For Lighthouse Keeping* '57. *At Last! Miles Davis And The Lighthouse All Stars* '53 on Boplicity UK '86, with Shank, Roach, Lorraine Geller on piano, Rolf Erickson on trumpet. *Howard Rumsey Lighthouse All Stars &*

Charlie Persip's Jazz Statesmen '57 on Liberty had Rumsey in the control room, incl. Candoli, Rosolino, Cooper, Lee MORGAN; two different rhythm sections on various tracks, pianist Dick Shreve, Levey, bassist Wilfred Middlebrooks (*b* 17 July '33, Chattanooga, Tenn.) alternating with Wynton KELLY, drummer Persip and Red Mitchell: said to be one of the forgotten gems of the era. *Jazz Rolls Royce* '57 was 16-piece edition of All Stars recorded live, issued on Lighthouse, Omega, Fresh Sound labels. Last All Stars album on Philips, recorded '61-2; as co-owner, manager, mus. dir. Rumsey had big-name combos, big bands from c.'62, still playing with house combo several nights a week; expanded to plusher Concerts By The Sea in Redondo Beach '72. With Village Vanguard in NYC (opened '35 by Max Gordon) the Lighthouse was one of the longest-running jazz venues in USA.

RUNDGREN, Todd (*b* 22 June '48, Philadelphia, Pa.) Singer, songwriter, producer, multi-instrumentalist. Inspired by BRITISH INVASION and earlier groups like the VENTURES, acquired guitar and formed Woody's Truckstop; left within a year to display burgeoning talents in the Nazz, named from a Lord BUCKLEY routine, incl. bassist Carson Van Osten (*b* 24 Sep. '46, N.J.), singer Robert 'Stewkey' Antoni (*b* 17 Nov. '47, R.I.), drummer Thom Mooney (*b* 5 Jan. '48, Pa.). First LP *Nazz* '68 prod. by Michael Friedman; Rundgren was introduced to the studio by remixing it; prod. and recorded *Nazz Nazz* '69, left after *Nazz III* '70 to specialise in production (LPs sold poorly at the time, third didn't chart; all now on Rhino, they are regarded as classic USA pop). Albert Grossman hired him as prod./eng. at his Bearsville studio near Woodstock, NY; label called Ampex then, since renamed after studio; prod. American Dream, IAN & SYLVIA, engineered for the BAND, Paul BUTTERFIELD, released own first solo *Runt* (incl. top 20 'We Gotta Get You A Woman', all '70. *The Ballad Of Todd Rundgren* '71 also finely crafted pop with harmonies aplenty; he played everything except drums as well as producing. Prod. Jesse WINCHESTER, BADFINGER, Sparks (then called Halfnelson); own stunningly varied 2-disc *Something/Anything?*

'72 incl. soul, heavy metal, pop, again almost all played by himself: top 30 LP USA incl. hit singles 'Hello It's Me' (no. 5; an old Nazz song no. 66 '69) and 'I Saw The Light' (top 20 USA, 40 UK). *A Wizard/A True Star* '73 slipped, with perennial Rundgren problem of too many songs and ideas for one album. Prod. NEW YORK DOLLS, GRAND FUNK, FANNY '73; own 2-disc *Todd* '74 accompanied by formation of Utopia for heavier sounds, chance to be guitar hero, with keyboardists 'Moogy' Klingman, Roger Powell and Ralph Shuckett, with John Siegler on bass, John Wilcox on drums, Kevin Elliman, percussion; by '77 only Powell and Wilcox remained, with Kasim Sulton on bass; LPs *Todd Rundgren's Utopia* '74, *Another Live* '75, *RA* and *Oops! Wrong Planet* '77 indulged HM leanings with bombastic production to boot, also used on first MEATLOAF solo LP *Bat Out Of Hell* '79: marshalling of personnel from Utopia and Bruce SPRINGSTEEN band with Loaf's colossal voice and grandiose sound won platinum status worldwide. Also prod. GONG guitarist Steve Hillage, Tom ROBINSON, the Tubes, Patti SMITH. Further Utopia LPs were *Adventures In Utopia* '80, *Deface The Music* '80 (BEATLES sendup), *Swing To The Right* and *Utopia* '82 (latter with 5-track 'bonus' LP), *Oblivion* '84, *POV* '85, *Trivia* '86. Solo LPs were *Initiation* '75, aptly titled but pointless *Faithful* '76 (incl. re-creations of Beatles, YARDBIRDS and BEACH BOYS hits), *Hermit Of Pink Hollow* '78 (name referring to his studio habitat) was the best since '72, almost an album of classic demos, with 'Can We Still Be Friends' (covered by Robert PALMER), 'You Cried Wolf' (covered by Night, etc.). Also 2-disc live *Back To The Bars* '81, *The Ever Popular Tortured Artist Effect* '83; on most solo albums he still played almost everything himself, but on *A Cappella* '85 he re-created sounds of instruments by feeding his voice through a synthesiser: startling results arguably the most adventurous use of vocals since Brian ENO/David Byrne's 'found' voices on *My Life In The Bush Of Ghosts* '81. Toured with 11-piece group to promote *A Cappella*. Continued prod. Shaun Cassidy, PSYCHEDELIC FURS, Meatloaf collaborator Jim Steinman, Rubinoos, CHEAP TRICK, Jules Shear, others; video-making also restricted live performance

('Time Heals' a notable video). Work too fragmented for superstar status, yet every LP has charted; one of USA pop's enigmatic all-rounders.

RUSH Canadian heavy metal trio formed in Sarnia, Ontario '69 by bassist/vocalist Geddy Lee (*b* 29 July '53, Willowdale), guitarist Alex Lifeson (*b* 27 Aug. '53, Fernie, B.C.), drummer John Rutsey as school group playing CREAM, IRON BUTTERFLY covers. Supported NEW YORK DOLLS in Toronto '73, decided to record: *Rush* '74 on manager's Moon label picked up by Mercury, who'd signed Canadian high-flyers BACHMAN-TURNER OVERDRIVE. Rutsey's departure due to ill health introduced Neil Peart (*b* 12 Sep. '52, Hamilton), itinerant drummer with lyric-writing skills; *Fly By Night* '75 incl. mythological themes in 'Rivendell' (from *Lord Of The Rings*) and 'By-Tor And The Snow Dog'; latter story continued on *Caress Of Steel* '75 by 'Necromancer'; whole side taken up by 'The Fountain Of Lamneth'. *2112* '76 based on right-wing novelist Ayn Rand's *Anthem* (title of Peart track on *Fly By Night*) which led to 'crypto-fascist' jibe, enhanced by logo of man fighting a red star (and by rock critics who think that if you're not a marxist you must be a fascist). *2112* and live *All The World's A Stage* '76 sold well in USA and on import in UK; encouraged, band recorded *A Farewell To Kings* '77 at Rockfield in Wales. Mix of Lee's banshee vocals and Peart's thunderous Keith Moon-inspired drumming leavened by more modern influences, even reggae: *Hemispheres* '78, *Permanent Waves* '80, *Moving Pictures* '81, second live set *Exit Stage Left* '81, *Signals* '82 all showed some progress; *Grace Under Pressure* '84 saw new co-producer Peter Henderson take over from long-time collaborator Terry Brown, bring more influences: 'Distant Early Warning' an example of lyrics more intelligent than usual in genre. *Power Windows* '85, *Hold Your Fire* '87 from rare HM band that's moved with the times.

RUSH, Otis (*b* 29 Apr. '34, Philadelphia, Ms.) Blues singer, plays harmonica, guitar, drums. Raised on farm, self-taught on guitar from age 8; to Chicago '48, worked outside music at first, formed group as Little Otis for gigs, soon at forefront of Chicago blues scene. Recorded for Cobra '56-8 (album *The Classic Recordings* now on Charly UK), Chess '60, Duke '62, Vanguard '65 (Vol. 2 of Chicago blues compilations). Own LPs *This One's A Good Un* '68 and *Otis Rush* '72 on Blue Horizon, *Mourning In The Morning* '69 on Cotillion/Atco, *Right Place, Wrong Time* '71 on Capitol/Bullfrog (reissued '86 on Hightone), *Screaming & Crying* '74 on French Black & Blue, *Cold Day In Hell* '76 and *So Many Roads* '78 on Delmark; also recorded with Jimmy DAWKINS on Delmark '71. Also at Ann Arbor Blues Festival '72, tracks on Atlantic; Japanese tour '74-5 recorded and partly issued as *Blues Live* on Trio; concert in Sweden '77 on Sonet LP *Troubles, Troubles*. Compilations incl. one side each of *The Final Takes And Others* on Flyright UK, *Door To Door* on Chess.

RUSH, Tom (*b* 8 Feb. '41, Portsmouth, N.H.) Folksinger. Father was a teacher; he attended Groton, then Harvard. Self-taught on guitar; played rock'n'roll after school, then discovered folk in Cambridge, Mass., with Greenwich Village in NYC a hotbed of the folk revival of early '60s. First LPs for Prestige/Folklore: *Got A Mind To Ramble* '63, *Blues/Songs/Ballads* '65 (later 2-disc *Tom Rush* on Fantasy), switched to Elektra for *Tom Rush* '65, played electric guitar on *Take A Little Walk With Me* '66; single of Joni MITCHELL song 'Urge For Going' was mild hit, incl. in *Circle Game* '68. To Columbia for *Tom Rush* '70, *Wrong End Of The Rainbow*, *Merrimack County*, *Ladies Love Outlaws*. He continued to tour '70s, lived on farm in New Hampshire. Album *Late Night Radio* '85 on Nightlight label.

RUSHING, Jimmy (*b* James Andrew Rushing, 26 Aug. '02, Oklahoma City, Okla.; *d* 8 June '72, NYC) Blues singer, 'Mr Five By Five' on account of his generous girth; his powerful voice, happy spirit, unsurpassable swing inseparable from the classic Count BASIE band of the late '30s. Parents were both musicians; studied music theory in high school; attended Wilberforce U. in Ohio but dropped out, moved to West Coast, worked outside music but occasionally with Jelly Roll MORTON at house parties etc. and as singing pianist in clubs; toured with Walter PAGE '25, returned to Oklaho-ma City to work in his father's café but left with Page's Blue Devils '28-9, first records with them '29 on Vocalion. Toured with Bennie MOTEN '29-35 (recorded '31), then with Basie from '35: Basie later said it was Rushing's optimism that kept him going when the road was rough. Sang at 'Jones-Smith Inc.' session '36: classic Basie small-group session was Lester YOUNG's first, prod. by John HAMMOND; 'Boogie-Woogie' (aka 'I May Be Wrong'), 'Evenin'' were Rushing classics forever after. Basie records on Decca with Rushing vocals incl. 'The Blues I Love To Hear', 'Do You Wanna Jump Children', 'Good Morning Blues', 'Sent For You Yesterday And Here You Come Today' (last two co-written by Rushing, Basie, Eddie DURHAM), also the occasional ballad in swinging style ('Exactly Like You'), many others '37-8, more on Columbia, then RCA '47-50 ('After You've Gone', 'Brand New Wagon', novelty 'Did You Ever See Jackie Robinson Hit That Ball', others). Airchecks of 'Dinah', 'Flat Foot Floogie' '37 are widely available. He tried to retire to South Carolina after Basie broke up his first band '50, but 'I knew the first time I heard a band come through town I'd be finished. It happened and one night I told my wife we were packing our bags and going to New York.' He led his own band briefly; 10" Vanguard LP *Jimmy Rushing Sings The Blues* '54 re-created classics incl. 'Goin' To Chicago' (then also being sung by Joe WILLIAMS with Basie), sidemen incl. Page, Jo JONES, Buddy TATE; 12" LPs incl. *Listen To The Blues, Goin' To Chicago, If This Ain't The Blues* (Vanguard material compiled on 2-disc *The Essential Jimmy Rushing*, now on French Vogue); Columbia LPs prod. by John Hammond began with *Cat Meets Chick*, continued into stereo era: *The Jazz Odyssey Of James Rushing Esq.* incl. 'Tricks Ain't Walkin'' No More', accompanying himself on the piano (with Page, Jones) as he did in K.C.; also *Rushing Lullabies, Jimmy Rushing And The Big Brass, The Smith Girls* (songs associated with Bessie, Clara, Mamie and Trixie), all with appropriate backing by studio band led by Buck CLAYTON, incl. Basie alumni and other mainstream veterans. Also recorded with Dave BRUBECK. Reunited with Basie, Young and Jones at Newport Jazz Festival '57, tracks released on Verve; again '62 on film. Other LPs: *Blues And Things* '67 with the Earl HINES Quartet, Budd JOHNSON guesting; *Gee Baby, Ain't I Good To You?* and *Who Was It Sang That Song?* with Jones, Clayton, Dicky WELLS, Julian Dash on tenor, Gene Ramey on bass and Sir Charles THOMPSON, all '67 on Master Jazz; also *The You And Me That Used To Be* on RCA; it was overproduced and he sounded lost in its slickness. He appeared in films with Basie incl. soundies *Take Me Back Baby, Air Mail Special* '41, short *Choo Choo Swing*, feature *Funzapoppin'* '43 (aka *Crazy House*); was also in TV special *The Sound Of Jazz* '57, sixth segment of 13-part series *The Subject Is Jazz* '58; film *Monterey Jazz* '73 (film of '70 festival); acting/singing role in *The Learning Tree* '69. Asked which singers he admired, he allegedly replied, 'Oh, I like Perry Como, Bing Crosby . . .' The interviewer obviously puzzled, he added, 'You see, I love music.'

RUSSELL, George Allan (*b* 23 June '23, Cincinnati, Ohio) Composer. Played drums in Boy Scouts; won scholarship to Wilberforce University High School (followed Fletcher HENDERSON, Benny CARTER, Ben WEBSTER in playing in band Wilberforce Collegians; Ernie Wilkins was a classmate; Frank Foster followed). Joined Carter's band on drums; not surprised to be replaced by Max ROACH, he turned to composing/arranging: sold first big band arr. 'New World' to both Carter and Dizzy GILLESPIE '45. Wrote for shows in Chicago, for Earl HINES; to NYC inspired by Monk's 'Round Midnight'; asked by Charlie Parker to play drums in his quintet, but became ill; spent time in hospital formulating tonal principles at a time when jazz was undergoing profound changes, inspired by Miles DAVIS, who'd remarked that he wanted to be able 'to play all the changes'. Wrote 'Cubana Be, Cubana Bop' for Dizzy Gillespie, based on a theme provided by Diz and premiered in Carnegie Hall '47 by big band with Chano POZO, who shared composer credit with Diz and Russell. 'A Bird In Igor's Yard' '49 recorded by Buddy DeFranco big band (not released until '60s Capitol import *Crosscurrents*); wrote for Charlie Ventura, Artie Shaw, Claude Thornhill; small-group pieces 'Odjenar' and 'Ezz-thetic' for Lee Konitz (on Prestige).

Published *The Lydian Concept of Tonal Organisation* '53 (revised '64; Concept Publishing Company). Original work commissioned by Brandeis U. '57 from Jimmy GIUFFRE, Charles MINGUS and Russell, who wrote 'All About Rosie'. Taught at School of Jazz, Lenox, Mass. '59-60; formed and led sextet '60-5; played at Washington DC Jazz Festival '62, landmark event in short presidency of John Kennedy. Sextet briefly incl. Eric DOLPHY, also Russell's students such as Don ELLIS, Steve SWALLOW, Dave Baker (*b* 21 Dec. '31, Indianapolis, Ind.; outstanding trombonist later played other instruments, became prominent in music education; books incl. *A History Of Jazz, Contemporary Black Music*); played structured compositions with a 'freely swinging modality' and a 'hymnic tone' that was also being developed by Davis, reaching 'larger audience only years later through John Coltrane's *A Love Supreme*' (J. Berendt). From '64 Russell spent much time in Europe, especially Scandinavia; Sabu Martinez (*b* Luis Martinez, 14 July '30, NYC; *d* c.'80) played with the Radio Jazz Group of Stockholm, later re-created Chano Pozo's Cuban drumming on new recording of 'Cubana Be, Cubana Bop'. Russell returned to USA and faculty at New England Conservatory of Music '69; has taught at many other schools both USA and Europe, many festivals and broadcasts, especially in Europe. Jazz musicians had been improvising on the chord structures of songs for decades, whereas the emphasis in modal composition is more linear (like a melody) rather than vertical (chordal); Russell's theory unites the Lydian (one of several ancient modes, which is 'the scale of unity for the tonic major chord') with a modern use of chromaticism, so that instead of a key signature limiting the musician's choice of notes, the tonal centre of a piece of music is its centre of gravity: the harmonic chordal richness is still available, but the choice of notes becomes wider. Jazz had always intimated that it had a theory of its own; the greatest jazz musicians were never afraid to break the formal rules: Russell's work is described by John LEWIS, Art FARMER, Ornette COLEMAN, many others as the single most important advance in jazz theory. Russell describes it as 'a way to think about music which . . . lends a disciplined

freedom to the composer and/or improviser
... The final component – involvement of
the human being on an emotional
level – can make it complete.' Russell's hu-
manism is evident in the wit, accessibility
and emotional power of his music. His own
albums began with sextet sets: *George Russell – The Jazz Workshop* '56 on RCA has
Farmer, Bill EVANS, Milt HINTON, Hal
McKusick on alto sax (*b* 1 June '24,
Medford, Mass.; became CBS staff musician), Barry Galbraith on guitar (*b* 18 Dec.
'19, Pittsburgh; concentrated on studio
work and music education), Osie Johnson
and Paul MOTIAN alternating on drums. On
Decca (MCA): *New York, New York* '59
with Hinton, Farmer, Roach, Coleman,
lyricist/vocalist Jon HENDRICKS; *Music In
The Space Age* '60; also *The George Russell
Sextet At The Five Spot, In Kansas City*
(both studio sets). On Riverside: *Strato-
sphunk, Ezz-thetics, The Outer View, The
Stratus Seekers* '60-2; 2-disc Milestone compilation of these *Outer Thoughts* incl. superb
Dolphy on a legendary version of 'Round
Midnight', two pieces by Carla BLEY (then
Russell's composition student), sentimental
country song 'You Are My Sunshine' (becomes scathing yet sympathetic jazz with
beautiful vocal by Russell discovery Sheila
JORDAN, for whom Bley later wrote *Escalator Over The Hill*). *At Beethoven Hall* c.'65
on MPS made live in Europe with Don
CHERRY; except for *Living Time* '72 on
Columbia with Bill Evans, most of Russell's
later records, many recorded in Sweden, are
now on Soul Note: 2-disc *The Essence of
George Russell* '66-7 incl. first (big band)
version of *Electronic Sonata For Souls Loved
By Nature* and a concerto for unaccompanied guitar, others; *Othello Ballet
Suite/Electronic Organ Sonata No. 1* '67-8
(the latter a solo by Russell turned into
musique concrète on tape); smaller-group
version of *Electronic Sonata* '68 incl. European cast with Jan Garbarek, others who
later became stars in roster of European
ECM label. LP *Trip To Prillarguri* '73 recorded in Stockholm, as was *Listen To The
Silence (A Mass For Our Time)* '74; *New
York Big Band At The Village Vanguard* '78
followed by *Vertical Forms VI* '79, second
small-group recording of *Electronic Sonata*
'80, recorded in Milan with Keith
COPELAND on drums; then back to the Vil-

lage Vanguard for *Live In An American
Time Spiral* '82. *The African Game* made '83
in Boston, one of the first records to be
issued on the resuscitated Blue Note label
'85, with Copeland, Bill Urmson (*b* 12 June
'61, Hartford, Conn.) on electric bass; it is
about the African origin of the human race,
and is another example of 'vertical form',
organising polyrhythmic complexity as
heard in African drum choirs. Russell made
first UK tour early '86 with band incl.
Copeland, Urmson, Brad Hatfield (keyboards, *b* 15 May '56, Columbus, Ohio),
Courtney PINE, Kenny WHEELER, Palle
MIKKELBORG, two members of LOOSE
TUBES, six other British musicians; he came
back for festivals '87-8.

RUSSELL, Hal (*b* 28 Aug. '26, Detroit,
Mich.) Composer, multi-instrumentalist,
leader of NRG Ensemble. Moved to Chicago as a teenager, majored in trumpet at U.
of Illinois, though his primary instruments
were drums and vibes. Played with Woody
HERMAN, Boyd RAEBURN '40s, sat in with
Duke ELLINGTON, Benny GOODMAN small
groups, played with Miles DAVIS, Stan
GETZ, Sonny ROLLINS etc. in Chicago
clubs, in band led by Joe Daley (tenor sax; *b*
30 July '18, Salem, Ohio); was involved with
drugs, fired for nodding out, cleaned up,
turned to free-form jazz early '60s, rejoined
Daley in trio with composer/bassist Russell
Thorne (*Joe Daley Trio At Newport* '63 on
RCA); now feels that he found his own
voice c.'71: led experimental groups in Chicago incl. Hal Russell's Chemical Feast,
usually with saxophonist Mars Williams
(later with the Waitresses, Psychedelic
Furs); took up C-melody sax '77 to be able
to show sidemen what he wanted and because he found a C-melody cheap; soon
acquired a tenor and found his true love.
After a long career teaching, playing in
everything from dixieland to show bands,
finally assembled the NRG Ensemble '78-
80: Chuck Burdelik (*b* 16 Aug. '58, Chicago;
studied sax with Daley '74-5), bassist Curt
Bley (*b* 27 Feb. '57, Lombard, Ill.), Steve
Hunt on percussion (*b* 9 Aug. '54, Geneva,
Ill.), Brian Sandstrom on trumpet, guitar,
bass etc. (*b* 11 July '55, Rockford, Ill.).
Quintet sounds bigger than it is: played a
dozen instruments in various combinations
plus percussion on first LP *Hal Russell*

NRG Ensemble '81 on Nessa, four Russell tunes incl. 'Linda Jazz Princess'; next LP *Conserving NRG* on Principally Jazz '84 prod. by Linda Prince had seven tunes incl. contributions from Bley, Hunt and Sandstrom (two extra tunes on CD): 'Blue Over You' and 'OJN' are tributes to Ellington and his sidemen, Sandstrom's 'Pontiac' suggested by Sonny Boy WILLIAMSON's 'Pontiac Blues' becomes one of the ultimate car/train tunes of jazz/R&B history. The music is bright, biting, witty; it demands attention as serious work but also entertains, with layers and colours and the precision that only a working band can achieve. *Eftsoons* '81 on Nessa is a duo with Russell on drums, vibes, C-melody, cornet, toy horns etc. and Williams on tenor, bells, slide whistle and what not, a free communion in surrealistic sounds; an album to come from Nessa (on Chief label in Europe) has Charles TYLER with NRG Ensemble.

RUSSELL, Leon (*b* 2 Apr. '41, Lawton, Okla.) Singer, songwriter, pianist, guitarist, bandleader, producer. Studied classical piano from age 3 to 13, took up trumpet, formed own band as teenager; played with Ronnie HAWKINS, Jerry Lee LEWIS; moved to West Coast '59, studied guitar with James BURTON, became one of the busiest session musicians of the era, playing on most Phil SPECTOR hits, also in studios with Frank SINATRA, Gary LEWIS, Paul REVERE, Bobby DARIN, the BYRDS, Herb ALPERT, many others. Worked with Delaney and Bonnie BRAMLETT in the New Electric Horn Band; formed the Asylum Choir '68 with Marc Benno (*b* 1 July '47, Dallas, Texas), first LP *Look Inside The Asylum Choir* '68 on Mercury subsidiary Smash flopped despite critical praise; second *Asylum Choir II* '69 not released until '71 on Shelter: Benno later made *Marc Benno, Minnows, Ambush* '70-2 on A&M, came back with *Lost In Austin* '79 featuring Eric CLAPTON, but never made stardom despite superior songwriting, songs covered by Rita COOLIDGE, others. Russell helped Delaney and Bonnie with their debut *Original – Accept No Substitute* LP and Joe COCKER with his second album, co-formed Shelter Records with UK producer Denny Cordell, released his own eponymous debut '70 (no. 60 LP USA incl. classic Russell songs 'Delta Lady', 'Hummingbird',

'A Song For You'; Clapton, George HARRISON, Ringo STARR, Stevie WINWOOD among sidemen). He organised Cocker's *Mad Dogs And Englishmen* tour, swiping most of Delaney and Bonnie's band for it. The tour/2-disc set were huge success '70, Russell and Coolidge stealing a lot of the spotlight. He helped Clapton with his debut solo album; *Leon Russell And The Shelter People* '71 used four sets of backing musicians, was top 20 LP without a hit single; *Asylum Choir II* was released on Shelter and made no. 70; *Carney* '72 was no. 2 LP incl. hit 'Tight Rope', also 'This Masquerade', a hit for George BENSON '76. 3-disc *Leon Live* '73 was top 10 LP; C&W collection *Hank Wilson's Back, Volume I, Stop All That Jazz, Will O' The Wisp* '73-5 were all top 35 LPs. Left Shelter for WB with own Paradise label, recorded with wife, vocalist Mary McCreary (she'd made solo LPs *Butterflies In Heaven* '73 on MCA, *Jezebel* '74 on Shelter); now Leon And Mary Russell had top 40 LP *Wedding Album* '76, but *Make Love To The Music* '77 slipped. She made *Heart Of Fire*, he made *Americana, Live And Love* '78-9. 2-disc set *One For The Road* by Willie (NELSON) And Leon was top 25 LP '79 on Columbia; *The Live Album* '81 with New Grass Revival bluegrass band and *Hank Wilson Volume II* '84 followed. There was also something called *Looking Back* '74 on Olympic which did not chart, perhaps early tapes from somebody's vaults. Many other activities incl. prod. Bob DYLAN singles 'Watching The River Flow' and 'George Jackson', appearance at Harrison's charity concert for Bangla Desh '71; he played fine piano on B. B. KING LP *Indianola* '70 (which incl. cover of 'Hummingbird'); indeed he is probably one of the last giants in rock, helping to restore piano and horn section to their rightful place, never forgetting with his gospelish piano, gritty vocals and fine songs that the best rock is essentially white rhythm and blues.

RUSSELL, Luis Carl (*b* 6 Aug. '02, Careening Clay, an island off Panama; *d* 11 Dec. '63, NYC) Pianist, composer, bandleader. Had a winning lottery ticket, used the money to bring himself, mother and sister to New Orleans. Played with King OLIVER in NYC, other bands; formed own band and cut four sides in Chicago '26 as sextet Heebie Jeebie Stompers with Darnell Howard, Barney BIGARD on reeds; went to the Saratoga Club in Harlem with Henry ALLEN, Bill COLEMAN on trumpets, Albert Nicholas, Charlie Holmes on reeds, Paul Barbarin on drums, later J. C. HIGGINBOTHAM, Dicky WELLS, Teddy Hill on tenor etc. and was one of the best young black bands in the land when it recorded more than 30 sides for various labels '29-34, incl. backing Louis ARMSTRONG on 'Song Of The Islands' '30 with violins added. They backed Armstrong for two days at the Savoy '35; subsequently Joe Glaser took them over as Louis's permanent backing band and they lost their identity, Russell mus. dir. for Louis until '43. He led other bands mid-'40s but styles had passed him by; he ran a candy shop, gift shop, worked as a chauffeur and piano teacher. *Luis Russell And His Orchestra 1926-30, 1930-4* on VJM UK are the best compilations ever of some of the era's most delightful music, incl. 'Call Of The Freaks', 'Saratoga Shout', 'Jersey Lightning', etc.; vocal on 'On Revival Day' by songwriter Andy RAZAF.

RUSSELL, Pee Wee (*b* Charles Ellsworth Russell, 27 Mar. '06, Maple Wood, Mo.; *d* 15 Feb. '69, Alexandria, Va.) Reeds, mainly clarinet; a unique stylist who managed to play progressive even though mostly stuck in dixieland contexts. Playing all over the Midwest and East with Red NICHOLS, Bix BEIDERBECKE, Ben POLLACK and many others, he had phenomenal technique, which lessened (he always drank heavily), but his playing became more interesting harmonically, his ability to structure a logical solo (incl. cliffhanging element) never wavering. From '37 he located in NYC, mostly playing with Eddie CONDON, his deeply lined and sadly comical face distracting from his music in the context of dixieland for businessmen. *Pee Wee Russell And His Rhythmakers* was limited edition octet session made in '38, with Max KAMINSKY, James P. JOHNSON, now on Fantasy with Jack TEAGARDEN session on the other side; he shone in Bud FREEMAN's Summa Cum Laude records '39 ('I've Found A New Baby', 'China Boy'), with Condon, Kaminsky. In '62 he broke out with a pianoless quartet incl. Marshall Brown on

trombone (*b* 21 Dec. '20, Framingham, Mass.), also recorded with Oliver NELSON, duet with Jimmy GIUFFRE (in Columbia LP *The Sound Of Jazz*), soon toured, recorded with Condon again, Bobby HACKETT, UK trad bands, his playing never less than memorable. Also recorded with Ruby BRAFF, Wild Bill DAVISON etc. LPs as leader: obscure *Portrait Of Pee Wee* on Counterpoint, *Pee Wee Plays Pee Wee* on Stere-O-Craft; then *New Groove* on Columbia; *Ask Me Now, College Concert, Spirit Of '67* on Impulse (2-disc *Salute To Newport* now on MCA); also *Jam Session In Swingville* and *Memorial Album* on Prestige, *Pee Wee Russell* on Archive Of Folk; Commodore small group sides (incl. Three Deuces with Joe SULLIVAN, Zutty Singleton '41) on Columbia Special Products with alternate takes.

RYAN, Paul & Barry (*b* 24 Oct. '48) UK vocal duo, twins. Had eight hits '65-7, three in top 20, ranging from 'Don't Bring Me Your Heartaches' (first hit, no. 13) to 'Claire' (last at no. 47). Barry then went solo for six hits of his own '68-72; the only big one was 'Eloise', no. 2 '68, revived by the DAMNED early '86. Paul continued writing songs, spent 10 years on USA West Coast, moved back to London '85, opened chain of hairdressing salons.

RYDELL, Bobby (*b* Bobby Ridarelli, 26 Apr. '42, Philadelphia, Pa.) USA teen idol of early '60s. Encouraged by his parents to sing in restaurants, etc.; at age 9 made it to TV with Paul WHITEMAN, who suggested name change; impersonating e.g. Milton Berle and Louis PRIMA, his appeal faded; he turned to rock'n'roll as singer/drummer with Rocco and the Saints, incl. Frankie AVALON; cut flop singles for Chancellor. Dukes bassist Frankie Day spotted him '58, took over management, formed Vekko label, but 'Fatty Fatty' failed to lift off; had him signed to local Cameo, who invested in singing and dancing lessons; result was no. 11 hit with third release 'Kissin' Time' '59. 26 Hot 100 entries through '64 incl. top 10s 'We Got Love', 'Wild One' (at no. 2 his biggest), 'Swingin' School' (from film *Because They're Young*), 'Volare' (a million-seller '58 by Domenico Modugno and Dean MARTIN), all '59-60; then 'The Cha-Cha-

Cha' '62, 'Forget Him' '64. Some lesser hits were rocked-up standards like 'That Old Black Magic' ('42 song by Johnny MERCER/Harold ARLEN); also scored Xmas 'Jingle Bell Rock' duet with Chubby CHECKER. He co-starred with ANN-MARGRET in *Bye Bye Birdie* '63, switched to Capitol and had two more singles scrape into Hot 100 '64-5, but was washed away with the rest of the teen idols by the British Invasion, though he had a fresher voice than most. Toured revival circuit, remade '60 hit 'Sway' '76 in disco style.

RYDER, Mitch, & the Detroit Wheels USA group of '60s formed by Mitch Ryder (*b* William Levise, '45, Hamtramack, Mich.), who'd been brought up in Detroit on black music, sang in black quartet the Peps until harassment drove him out. After sojourn in L.A., returned to form Billy Lee and the Rivieras, with himself as vocalist Lee, Jim McCarty on guitar, Earl Elliott on bass, John Badanjek on drums, adding Joe Cubert on rhythm guitar from Levise's high school group the Tempest (all *b* '47-8). Changed name at behest of NY prod. Bob Crewe; after flop 'I Need Help', second single on New Voice label made top 10 '66: 'Jenny Take A Ride!' was effectively a medley of 'See See Rider' and LITTLE RICHARD's 'Jenny Jenny', making up in energy what it lacked in originality. Five top 40 hits incl. 'Devil With A Blue Dress On & Good Golly Miss Molly', 'Little Latin Lupe Lu' with torrid voice and wailing organ, 'Sock It To Me Baby' with brass-laden James BROWN style. Under Crewe's infl. he was persuaded to go solo, but 'What Now My Love' on Crewe's DynoVoice label was the only top 30 to show: disillusion and lawsuits followed. Came back on Dot with *The Detroit-Memphis Experience* '69, backed by BOOKER T AND THE MGs, but it didn't sell; he formed Detroit with Badanjek, five others for an eponymous LP; submerged to write songs with his wife Kimberley, paint, write a novel. Badanjek and McCarty (now ex-Cactus) formed Rockets '77; Ryder surfaced '78 on local label with *How I Spent My Vacation*: released in Europe on Line label, it led to a tour. John MELLENCAMP prod. well-received *Never Kick A Sleeping Dog* '83; Bruce SPRINGSTEEN used hits in show-closing 'Detroit Medley', keeping Ryder name alive.

S

SADE (*b* Helen Folasade Adu, 16 Jan. '59, Ibadan, Nigeria) UK singer. Mother British, father Nigerian; he taught at Ibadan U.; Sade came to UK '63. Always interested in music; as a teenager searched bargain bins for LPs by Peggy LEE, Julie LONDON, Nina SIMONE, Astrud Gilberto; studied fashion design at St Martin's School of Art, opened boutique, but 'To be a good designer, you have to be a good businesswoman, which I am not.' Sang harmony with Latin-funk group Ariva '81; group evolved into Pride, hired saxophonist Stuart Matthewman (*b* '61), who recruited bassist Paul Denman (*b* '58); Pride changed its name to Sade (name of both singer and group, pron. Shah-day, abbreviation of Folasade), added pianist Andrew Hale (*b* '63); other regulars on tours incl. Matthewman's brother Gordon. Signed with Epic Jan. '84: label wanted just the singer, but she insisted band came with her; she appeared on cover of trendy mag *The Face* April '84; the band attracted the smart set in London clubs; featured in *Vogue, Cosmopolitan, Elle*; when she made the cover of *Time* (6 April '86) she was the Queen of Cool; two LPs had sold 12m worldwide: *Diamond Life* '84, *Promise* '85. She travelled, took her time writing songs; then *Stronger Than Pride* '88 further refined the style. Not in a hurry to record too much, she may have staying power.

SAGER, Carole Bayer (*b* '47, NYC) Singer, songwriter. Began writing at 15 while in high school, a teacher helping to obtain contract with Don Kirshner's Screen Gems; first demo 'Groovy Kind Of Love' co-written with Tony Wein became no. 2 hit USA/UK by the Mindbenders '66. She wrote with other Screen Gems inmates incl. Neil SEDAKA, but had more success in the following decade. She was the youngest lyricist to write a Broadway musical with *Georgy* '70, but it closed after five nights; she spotted backup singer Melissa MANCHESTER (with Bette MIDLER); they co-

wrote 'Midnight Blue' '75 (top 10 hit), 'Better Days' (aka 'Looks As Though We're Doing Something Right') '76, 'Come In From The Rain' '76 (hit by CAPTAIN AND TENNILLE). Sager wrote with Peter Allen: 'Quiet Please, There's A Lady On Stage' '75 (written for Allen's one-time mother-in-law Judy GARLAND), 'I'd Rather Leave While I'm In Love' '77 (hit for Rita COOLIDGE), 'Don't Cry Out Loud' '78 (hit by Manchester); with Albert Hammond: 'When I Need You' '77 (hit for Leo SAYER); with Bruce Roberts: 'You're The Only One' '79 (hit for Dolly PARTON); 'You're Moving Out Today' '77 with Roberts and Midler, recorded by both Midler and Sager, incl. in Sager's eponymous debut solo LP on Elektra. With David Wolfert: 'Heartbreaker' '77 (hit for Parton); with film composer Marvin Hamlisch (*b* 2 June '44, NYC): 'Break It To Me Gently' '77 (hit by Aretha FRANKLIN), 'Better Than Ever' '79 (sung by Candice Bergen in film *Starting Over*), 'If You Remember Me' '79 (film *The Champ*), 'Looking Through The Eyes Of Love' '78 (performed by Manchester in film *Ice Castles*, song nominated for an Oscar), James Bond theme 'Nobody Does It Better' (*The Spy Who Loved Me*). She made her second LP *Too* '78 for Elektra; wrote songs with Hamlisch for Neil Simon musical *They're Playing Our Song* '79, said to be loosely based on their relationship. Co-wrote Oscar-winning theme for film *Arthur* '81 with Allen, Christopher CROSS, Burt BACHARACH; married Bacharach '82; they collaborated with Neil DIAMOND on several songs for his *Heartlight* LP '82, wrote 'That's What Friends Are For' '85 for team of Dionne WARWICK, Elton JOHN, Gladys KNIGHT and Stevie WONDER, proceeds to AIDS research. Her songs were recorded by Frank SINATRA, Gene PITNEY, Eydie GORME, Steve LAWRENCE, Astrud Gilberto, Patti LABELLE, etc. Bacharach collaborated on third LP *Sometimes Late At Night* '81 on

Boardwalk incl. top 30 hit 'Stronger Than Before'.

SAHM, Doug (*b* 6 Nov. '42, San Antonio, Texas) Singer, bandleader. Began with garage band the Sir Douglas Quintet, hits incl. own songs 'She's About A Mover' '65, 'Mendicino' '69 (LP *Mendicino* on Smash/Oval). By the time of this last hit he was moving on to roots music, bringing Tex-Mex, blues, country to his act; after a few years in San Francisco he relocated to Austin, Texas and was among prime movers in 'outlaw' movement in country music there. Albums incl. *Texas Rock For Country Rollers* '76 on ABC, *Groovers Paradise* '75 on WB (tribute to Austin), *Hell Of A Spell* '80 on Takoma. He moved to Canada; as Sir Douglas Quintet released *Border Wave* on Takama; also *Live* and *Best Of* '87.

SAILOR Keyboard-based pop quartet formed '74 by guitarist-vocalist Georg Kajanus (real name Georg Hultgren), former member of Australian folk-rockers Eclection, whose eponymous Elektra LP '68 incl. vocalist Kerrilee Hale, guitarist Trevor Lucas (later with FAIRPORT CONVENTION). Kajanus recruited Phil Pickett initially for guitar-keyboard duo, but acquired Henry Marsh (keyboards), Grant Serpell (drums) for unusual group with no bass or electric guitar (Kajanus played acoustic). *Sailor* '74 was inventive concept LP based on seafarer's life, flopped in UK but did well in Europe, as did single 'Traffic Jam'. Stage act featured nickelodeon, double keyboard like two pianos back-to-back, with red-light district backdrop, lamp post on street corner; songs often accordion-led, high on nostalgia ('Josephine BAKER'). *Trouble* '75 was more lively, with Kajanus affecting a Bryan Ferry drawl. 'Glass Of Champagne' was no. 2 single UK, 'Girls Girls Girls' no. 7 '76. *The Third Step*, *Checkpoint*, *Greatest Hits* '76-8 sold well, with one more top 40 hit in 'One Drink Too Many' '77; but punk boom hurt UK success and Kajanus left. Marsh and Pickett carried on as Sailor with *Dressed To Drown* '81 before splitting. Pickett resurfaced as keyboardist/songwriter with Culture Club (co-wrote megahit 'Karma Chameleon' '83); Kajanus formed duo Data with Frankie Boulter with less success.

SAINTE-MARIE, Buffy (*b* 20 Feb. '41, Canada) Singer/songwriter, guitarist; perceived as a folksinger but performing original material. Grew up in New England, studied oriental philosophy at U. of Mass., intended to be a teacher but went to Greenwich Village for a weekend and soon signed with Vanguard. Best-known song, 'Universal Soldier', was a hit by DONOVAN, recorded by Glen CAMPBELL, the Highwaymen, etc.; some thought that Donovan had written it: she was self-effacing about her authorship. Folksinger and instrument maker Patrick Sky (*b* 2 Oct. '40, near Atlanta, Ga.) appeared on her first album (made two of his own on Vanguard, others on Verve/Forecast and Adelphi), taught her to play the Indian mouth bow; her part-Indian ancestry was honoured in songs like 'My Country 'Tis Of Thy People You're Dying' and 'Now That The Buffalo's Gone'. She stopped to rest '63 because of ill health, became addicted to codeine and wrote 'Cod'ine' about it. She performed at Carnegie Hall with Johnny CASH and Chuck BERRY, toured North America, then the world. Her song 'Until It's Time For You To Go' was recorded by Bobby DARIN, 'Piney Wood Hills' by Bobby BARE; had Hot 100 singles '71-2 with 'I'm Gonna Be A Country Girl Again', 'Mister Can't You See' (top 40), 'He's An Indian Cowboy In The Rodeo'. Vanguard albums (in chronological order) incl. *It's My Way!*, *Many A Mile*, *Little Wheel/Spin And Spin* '66, *Fire, Fleet, Candlelight* '67, *I'm Gonna Be A Country Girl Again* '68 (made in Nashville; incl. 'Tall Trees In Georgia'), *Illuminations* '69 (incl. 'God Is Alive, Magic Is Afoot', co-written with Leonard COHEN), *She Used To Wanna Be A Ballerina* '71 (with Ry COODER, Neil YOUNG and Crazy Horse), *Moonshot* '72 (moving towards mainstream rock), *Quiet Places, Native North American Child: An Odyssey*, plus best-of sets (incl. 2-disc set on PRT UK). Six albums charted, most are still in print. More recent MCA LPs: *Buffy*, *Changing Woman*.

SALSA Word meaning 'sauce', used by Cuban musicians in the sense of 'spice'; began to be used early '70s to describe NYC's hot and uptempo Latin music. A classic Cuban son of the late '20s by Ignacio Piñeiro was called 'Echale Salsita' ('Swing

It!'); Pupi LEGARRETA's '62 debut LP *Salsa Nova* ('New Spice') was made in NYC; a '66 album by Venezuelan band Federico y su Combo Latino was called *Llegó la Salsa* ('Salsa Has Arrived'), etc; Izzy Sanabria, immodest MC, designer, editor/publisher of *Latin NY* magazine (now defunct), claimed to have originated it; by '75 the term was firmly established as the title of the Fania film *Salsa*. Salsa is mainly derived from Cuban music, which contributed trad. Latin percussion (i.e. timbales, congas, bongos), types of ensemble (conjuntos of trumpets and percussion, charangas with flute and violins, brass- and sax-led big bands), clave (the basic rhythmic pattern) and numerous dance forms: son, son montuno, rumba, guaguanco, mambo, chachacha, bolero, guajira, guaracha. Salsa also embraces an international range of musics incl. Puerto Rican bomba and plena, Colombian cumbia, etc.; also fusion experiments with rock, jazz, soul. Salsa used to incl. Dominican merengue, but this became a major force of its own '80s. Arrangers are important, among the most successful Louie RAMIREZ and Luis 'Perico' ORTIZ. At the time the word was adopted, the music had returned to its roots, the tipico (typical) Cuban conjunto sound, after the Latin/R&B fusion called boogalo late '60s; the music had always lacked a suitable tag and 'salsa' assisted marketing. Central to NYC salsa was the Fania label, formed '64 by Johnny PACHECO and Jerry Masucci, their roster incl. Pacheco, Larry HARLOW, Bobby VALENTIN, Ray BARRETTO, Willie COLON (and his lead vocalist Hector LAVOE), Roberto ROENA and the house band, FANIA ALL STARS. Fania also had stablemate Vaya and Inca labels, absorbed most rival NYC labels (incl. Cotique, and the older Tico and Alegre labels), creating a virtual monopoly; one of the few outside the empire was Salsoul, which recorded the jazzy LIBRE and Grupo Folklorico (*see* LIBRE), and the descargas (Latin jam sessions) of Israel 'Cachao' LOPEZ, through to the progressive tipico of Saoco (*see* Henry FIOL) and the Cuban purism of Roberto TORRES. Another independent and avant-garde force was Angel CANALES, with his own Selanac label. These and others created a salsa boom which peaked in the mid-'70s, just as it was being discovered by non-Latin fans who thought it was something new. (Mario BAUZA, quoted by John Storm Roberts in *The Latin Tinge*, was probably talking about Latino kids: 'When Cuban music was really in demand the kids didn't go for it. Now they call it salsa and they think it belongs to them.') In the second half of the '70s there was a charanga explosion within salsa as an alternative to the brass-led sounds; veterans re-emerged (Legarreta, José FAJARDO; *see also* CHARANGA); new bands emerged; NYC salsa bands did well in the Latin Caribbean (except Cuba) and the Caribbean coasts of South America, as did local salsa bands and leaders such as P.R.-based Willie Rosario and Tommy Olivencia, others; at the end of the '70s salsa was tending towards overproduction, as in the successful (but heavily produced) Colon LP *Solo '79* on Fania. In the early '80s it swung back to its roots again, the tipico revival led by Torres and his SAR label. Fania declined and merengue enjoyed its massive boom, stealing the limelight from salsa. By the mid-'80s Miami, Puerto Rico, Colombia and Venezuela were centres of salsa; what *Billboard* calls the tropical salsa market was represented by EL GRAN COMBO, its former vocalist Andy Montañez, vocalist Frankie Ruiz (ex-Olivencia), Rosario, Mario Ortiz, GRUPO NICHE and Oscar D'LEON. An El Gran Combo concert in Madison Square Garden Sep. '87, celebrating its 25th anniversary, was sold out two weeks in advance; the bill incl. a reunion with Montañez as well as Celia CRUZ, Cheo FELICIANO, Lavoe, D'Leon and the currently hitmaking bands of Ruiz and Eddie Santiago: many saw it as marking the resurgence of salsa and the ebbing of merengue fever.

SAM AND DAVE Soul vocal duo: Sam Moore (*b* 12 Oct. '35, Miami, Fla.), Dave Prater (*b* 9 May '37, Ocilla, Ga.) Sam sang with gospel group the Melonaires, went solo to secular music, was joined onstage by Dave in Miami '58: audience response was good. Morris Levy signed them to Roulette '60; they made good records prod. by Henry Glover, but no hits. Switched to Atlantic '65; Jerry Wexler sent them to Stax to record songs by Isaac HAYES and David Porter with the Memphis Horns: some of the best-loved hits of the soul era resulted, 13 entries each in soul and pop charts being almost the same, incl. 'Hold On! I'm A Comin' ' '66 (no. 1 soul, 21 pop): with Sam's gospel-flavoured call and Dave's earthier response, 'Hold On' was Stax's biggest impact on the pop chart since Carla THOMAS's 'Gee Whiz' '61. Then came 'Soul Man' '67 (no. 1 soul, 2 pop), 'I Thank You' (no. 4 soul, 7 pop). When Stax was sold '68 they switched to parent Atlantic, had more hits incl. 'Soul Sister, Brown Sugar' (no. 18 soul, 41 pop), split up '70, reunited '71 on UA but had no more hits. Compilation *Best Of* on Atlantic.

SAMBA Brazilian rhythm, dominating that country's popular music by the '40s and becoming internationally popular. The word is probably African, the rhythm from an Afro-Brazilian ring dance. Ethno-musicologist Oneida Alvarenga (quoted by John Storm Roberts in *The Latin Tinge*) said that 'the European polka gave it its movement, the Cuban habanera its rhythm, and Afro-Brazilian music added its syncopations.' Of the many samba rhythms, the earliest is the maxixe, a well-known example being 'Os Quindins de Yaya', used in Walt Disney film *The Three Caballeros*. Ary Barroso (who wrote 'Brazil', several times a hit in the USA) was the most prolific composer of sambas, incl. the samba jongo 'Na Baixa do Sapateiro', better known as 'Baia' (also the name of the old capital of Brazil). The Banda Do Lua (later accompanying Carmen MIRANDA) was among the popular Brazilian groups playing sambas; her biggest hit, 'Mama Eu Queiro', was a marcha, a carnival samba (march) rhythm; she also recorded 'Rebola a Bola', an embolada ('rolling ball' in Portuguese), a fast samba that gathers speed. The batuque is a slow samba, batucada a carnival rhythm, sambaiao a cross between a samba and a baiao, samba cancao a slow samba for backing ballads; there are other variations. The bossa nova is a cross between a samba and 'cool jazz', but was a self-conscious creation rather than arising in the streets and dance halls like the others.

SAMPSON, Edgar (*b* 31 Aug. '07, NYC; *d* 16 Jan. '73, Englewood, N.J.) Violinist, also reeds; one of the great composer/arrangers of the Swing Era. Played with Duke ELLINGTON '27, Fletcher HENDERSON '31-3 (violin solo on 'House Of David Blues'),

Chick WEBB '33-7; played baritone sax on Lionel HAMPTON record date '38 ('Ring Dem Bells'). His arrangements were the equal of Henderson's, though he was not as prolific: he wrote 'Stompin' At The Savoy', 'Don't Be That Way', 'Blue Minor' and 'If Dreams Come True' (words by Irving MILLS), all '34; 'Blue Lou' '35, 'Lullaby In Rhythm' '38, others, most recorded by Webb, later big hits for Benny GOODMAN, the first two among the era's classics. 'Blue Lou' also had a fine recording by the RCA Victor All-Stars '39, with Goodman, Tommy DORSEY, Bunny BERIGAN, Jack TEAGARDEN, etc. Sampson led own band '49-51, played with Tito PUENTE, Tito Rodriguez, other Latin bands; he led his own combos in the '60s.

SAM THE SHAM AND THE PHARAOHS Texas rock'n'roll group with hits '65-7, led by Sam the Sham (Domingo Samudio, *b* Dallas), with Ray Stinnet, guitar; David Martin, bass; Jerry Patterson, drums. Recorded in Memphis early '60s; covered novelty 'Haunted House', then 'Wooly Bully' on Memphis Pen label was first and biggest hit (no. 1 USA), leased to MGM; they scored with top 30 'Ju Ju Hand', 'Lil Red Riding Hood' (top 3), 'The Hair On My Chinny Chin Chin'. Butch Gibson augmented the group on sax. Like so many other novelty regional groups they didn't last long on the charts. Samudio went solo on Atlantic with LP *Sam, Hard And Heavy* '70, contributed Spanish-language songs to Ry COODER's soundtrack for *The Border* '81.

SANBORN, David (*b* David William Sanborn, 30 July '45, Tampa, Fla.) Alto sax, flute. Proficient and emotive reedman regarded by many as the white Junior WALKER because of feeling for rhythm & blues. Had polio as a child, spent time in iron lung, took up wind playing as physical therapy. Raised in St Louis; at 14 played with Albert KING, LITTLE MILTON at youth centres, also in high school groups; to Chicago area early '60s, studied at U. of Iowa '65-7, then to West Coast; joined Paul BUTTERFIELD Blues Band, worked with that unit on and off '67-72. Worked with Stevie WONDER '72-3; Gil EVANS, David BOWIE '74, BRECKER Bros, Paul SIMON '75, also debut LP *Taking Off* '75 for Warner

Brothers. Further own albums *Sanborn* '76, *David Sanborn Band* '77, *Heart To Heart* '78, *Hideaway* '80, *Voyeur* '81 (won Grammy), *As We Speak* '82, *Backstreet* '83, *Straight To The Heart* '84, *Love And Happiness* '84, all since *Hideaway* selling more than 250,000. Still sessioned '80s with Bowie, Roger Waters, Michael FRANKS, etc. Toured Europe '84 playing support to Al JARREAU; scored TV movie *Finnegan Begin Again*. In Leonard FEATHER'S blinfold test in *Downbeat* '88 James MOODY said 'I'm a romanticist; I love David's sound.'

SANDERS, Pharoah (*b* Farrell Sanders, 13 Oct. '40, Little Rock, Ark.) Reeds, leader. Studied piano, drums, clarinet; turned to sax and flute at 16; played with R&B bands; to West Coast '59 on music scholarship, played with Dewey REDMAN, others; to NYC '62, worked with SUN RA, Rashied ALI; infl. by Albert AYLER. Made quintet album on ESP, sextet on Impulse '64; played with John COLTRANE '66-7, then Alice Coltrane; formed own band '69 incl. vocalist/lyricist Leon Thomas (*b* Amos Leon Thomas Jr, 4 Oct. '37, East St Louis, Ill.; changed spelling to 'Leone' '76), keyboardist/composer Lonnie Liston Smith (*b* 28 Dec. '40, Richmond, Va.). Sanders pursued Coltrane's spiritual quest at a somewhat more accessible level of intensity than where Coltrane had left off, improvising with romantic lyricism over a three-octave range; Thomas had sung with Count BASIE, now used scat devices and also an evocative yodelling technique which he had learned from Central African trad. music. Album *Izipho Zam (My Gifts)* '69 on Strata-East incl. Cecil MCBEE, guitarist Sonny Sharrock, Chief Bey on African drums and three other percussionists, multi-instrumentalist Howard Lewis Johnson on tuba (*b* 7 Aug. '41, Montgomery, Ala.), Sonny Fortune on additional reeds; *Karma* '69 on Impulse used a more conventional nine-piece group, incl. 'The Creator Has A Master Plan', with lyrics by Thomas, made top 200 pop LPs. Another Impulse LP with Thomas followed before he left the group; Smith had left before the fourth Impulse LP, sextet *Thembi* '71, was the second to make the pop chart. *Black Unity* and *Live At The East* '71, *Wisdom Through Music* and *Village Of The Pharoahs* '72, *Elevation* and

Love Is In Us All '73 were all on Impulse with changing personnel, much material now on MCA/USA incl. 2-disc *Best Of*. *Harvest Time* '76 on India Navigation was a small-group set; *Love Will Find A Way* '77 on Arista was third chart entry with the largest group yet: 23 pieces incl. three keyboardists, plus singers. *Beyond A Dream* '78 on Arista was live at Montreux; *Journey To The One* '80 (with Bobby MCFERRIN among vocalists, 17 pieces incl. tabla, synth, koto, sitar, harmonium, etc.) and *Rejoice* '81 (septet with Bobby HUTCHERSON, Elvin JONES) are 2-disc sets, *Live* and *The Heart Is A Melody* '82 single LPs, all on Theresa. *Quartet Africa* '87 is on Timeless. Thomas also recorded with Mary Lou WILLIAMS, Roland KIRK, Oliver NELSON, SANTANA, others; Smith made LPs *Dreams Of Tomorrow*, *Silhouettes*, *Rejuvenation* '85 on Dr Jazz, prod. by Bob THIELE; *Oh Lord, Let Me Do No Wrong* with Thomas released '87 on Thiele's Dr Jazz.

SANDII AND THE SUNSETZ Japanese rock band: vocalist Sandii (*b* Sandy O'Neale, 27 Dec. '51, Tokyo), Makoto Kubota on guitar, keyboards, percussion; guitarist Keni Inoue, bassist King Champ Onzo, Hideo Inoura on drums. All sing except Inoura. Sandii and Kubota formed Makoto Kubota And The Sunset Orchestra '77; her first solo LP was *Eating Pleasure* '80 on Alfa, prod. by Haruomi Hosono of the YELLOW MAGIC ORCHESTRA; she guested on Y.M.O.'s *Xoo Multiples* on A&M same year; Sandii And The Sunsetz' *Heat Scale* '81 on Alpha was followed by more successful *Immigrants* '82 on Alpha, by which time they had fused Western rock and techno-pop with Japanese and Okinawan trad. elements, also trading on striking looks of lead vocalist. *Viva Lava Liva* '84 on Sire was a compilation; next was *Banzai Baby* '86; also 12" single 'Babes In The Wood' on Eastworld, 'Sticky Music' (in French) on a Yen anthology '85; she duetted with Stephen Duffy on 'Something Special' '86 from film *Knights And Emeralds* on 10 Records.

SANDS, Tommy (*b* 27 Aug. '37, Chicago, Ill.) Pop singer, actor. Was a DJ at 12 in Houston, Texas; pursued acting in school; later appeared on Ted LEWIS and Ernie FORD TV shows; played singing sensation in TV play *The Singing Idol* early '57 and became one: signed with Capitol, first hit was no. 2 'Teen-Age Crush': he mined that lode for 11 Hot 100 entries '57-60. *Steady Date With Tommy Sands* '57 was no. 4 LP '57; played singer in film *Sing Boy Sing* for top 20 soundtrack album '58, continued in films: *Love In A Goldfish Bowl* '59, *Babes In Toyland* '60, *The Longest Day* '62, *None But The Brave* '65, etc. Married to Nancy SINATRA '60-5.

SANTAMARIA, Mongo (*b* Ramon Santamaria, 7 Apr. '22, Havana, Cuba) Latin percussionist (primarily conga drums), bandleader, composer. His grandfather was born in Africa; always called Mongo, he later learned that the word means 'chief of the tribe' in Senegalese. Studied violin, but first love was drums, inspired by Chano POZO. Dropped out of school to play congas; spent five years in opulent clubs of pre-Castro Havana and went to Mexico City '48 with cousin Armando Peraza; they arrived in NYC c.'50, billed as the Black Cuban Diamonds; within months Mongo joined Perez PRADO for three years, later seven years with Tito PUENTE; meanwhile made LPs of music derived from Afro-Cuban religious cults: *Tambores Afro Cubanos* on SMC and *Chango* '53 on Tico (reissued '78 on Vaya as *Drums And Chants*). Played Latin-jazz with George SHEARING '53 on congas, with Peraza on bongos, Willie BOBO on timbales, Cal TJADER on vibes; joined Tjader's group '58 for three years with Bobo (LPs on Fantasy, Prestige); also played with Dizzy GILLESPIE, Jack McDUFF, etc. Own LPs on Fantasy: *Yambu* and *Mongo* '58-9 later combined in 2-disc *Afro Roots* '72 on Prestige; also *Our Man In Havana*; *Bembe, Mongo In Havana*; *Sabroso*; *Pachanga con Joe Loco*; *Arriba! La Pachanga*; *Mas Sabroso*; *Viva Mongo*; *Mighty Mongo*; *Mongo y La Lupe* (with vocalist La Lupe). *Mongo's Greatest Hits* on Fantasy '87 incl. 'Afro Blue' (became jazz standard); compilations of Fantasy material on Ace '87 were *Mongo's Groove* and *Cal's Pals*. He recorded fusions of Latin, R&B, jazz, soul, hiring musicians like Chick COREA, Hubert LAWS; had top 10 hit with Herbie HANCOCK tune 'Watermelon Man' '63 on Battle label: album *Watermelon Man* incl. single's B side 'Don't Bother Me

No More', also 'Yeh Yeh', covered for UK chart hit by Georgie FAME; packaged with *Mongo At The Village Gate* on Battle plus 'Para Ti' (recorded at the Village Gate, from Riverside LP *Mongo Explodes*) to make 2-disc *The Watermelon Man* '73 on Milestone; five Riverside LPs altogether early '60s also surveyed on 2-disc *Skins*, with Nat ADDERLEY on some tracks. Success led to Columbia (CBS) contract, LPs *El Pussy Cat, La Bamba, Hey! Let's Party, Mongo Mania* (incl. 'Mongo's Boogaloo'), *Explodes At The Village Gate, Soul Bag, Stone Soul, Workin' On A Groovy Thing* (incl. top 40 cover '69 of 'Cloud Nine', hit by the TEMPTATIONS), *All Strung Out* '65-70: most of these made USA pop LP chart, making Mongo the most successful Latin musician of the '60s. Switched to Atlantic for *Feelin' Alright* and *Mongo* '70, which also charted; *Mongo's Way* '71 incl. Israel 'Cachao' LOPEZ on bass, also incl. Peraza, as did *Mongo At Montreux* '71; *Up From The Roots* '72 had one side of Afro-Cuban music, other conjunto. To Vaya label for *Fuego* '73, *Mongo Santamaria Live At Yankee Stadium* '73 (on same bill as Fania All Stars, with whom he also guested), *Afro-Indio* '75, *Mongo & Justo 'Ubane'* '76 with Justo Betancourt, *Sofrito*, then *Dawn (Amanecer)* '77, *A La Carte* '78; *Mongo Mongo* '78 was a compilation on Vaya, *Red Hot* '79 on CBS UK. *Images* '80 back on Vaya; *Summertime* '81 on Pablo was made live at Montreux with Gillespie, Toots THIELEMANS; *Mongo Magic* '83 appeared on Roulette; *Free Spirit* '85 on Tropical Buddah (label went broke). Gigs with FAS incl. *Live At Yankee Stadium Vol. 2* '75, film footage incl. in *Salsa* (also 2-disc soundtrack album). *Soy Yo* '87 on Concord Picante has guest Charlie Palmieri on 'Mayeya', Yoruban religious chant co-written by Santamaria.

SANTANA Latin/rock group led by guitarist Carlos Santana (*b* 20 July '47, Autlan de Novarra, Mexico). To San Francisco '62 with his father, a mariachi musician; emerged during SF's musical heyday. First recorded appearance jamming onstage in *Live Adventures Of Mike Bloomfield And Al Kooper* '69; that year Santana Bluesband incl. David Brown, bass; Gregg Rolie, organ and vocals; Marcus Malone, Mike Carabello and Jose 'Chepito' Areas, percussion. Mike

Shrieve replaced imprisoned Malone on debut LP *Santana* '69, dropping Bluesband suffix, concentrating on Afro-Cuban rhythms allied to Carlos's sweet, flowing rock guitar; no. 4 LP incl. 'Soul Sacrifice' (played at Woodstock). *Abraxas* '70 incl. instrumental tour-de-force 'Samba Pa Ti' (top 30 hit single in UK) plus guitar-laced version of Peter Green's 'Black Magic Woman', already a hit in UK by FLEET-WOOD MAC but USA no. 4 by Santana. These were his most enduring work, and spawned further USA singles in top 10 'Evil Ways' and Tito PUENTE's 'Oye Como Va' (no. 13). Percussion (placed left-right in stereo image) and leader's guitar were highlights; vocals less important, often merely chants. *Santana III* '71 incl. no. 12 'Everybody's Everything', with *Caravanserai* '72 added second guitarist Neal Schon, Coke Escovedo on percussion, but by the time of the latter's recording, showing jazz-rock fusion that watered down original appeal, the band had split. Santana became Devadip, disciple of guru Sri Chinmoy; re-formed group around Shrieve and Areas; personnel fluctuated, *Welcome* '73 introduced vocalist Leon Thomas (*see* Pharoah SANDERS); *Borboletta* '74 was top 20 LP but *Amigos* '76 returned to top 10 LPs USA with percussive Latin-rock format. He recorded live jamming with Buddy MILES '72, again in studio with John MCLAUGHLIN (fellow Chinmoy disciple) in appallingly self-indulgent *Love Devotion Surrender* '73; *Illuminations* '74 with Alice Coltrane. Band's *Festival* '77 was top 30; *Moonflower* '77 top 10 again (incl. poppy hit cover of ZOMBIES' 'She's Not There'); by this time Rolie and Schon had formed successful JOURNEY, Shrieve formed Automatic Man. He continued to tour and record; *Inner Secrets* and *Marathon* '78-9 were a disco phase; *Zebop!* '81 returned to top 10 with the tested formula and top 20 single 'Winning', *Shango* '82 top 25 with no. 15 'Hold On'; *Beyond Appearances* '85 reached no. 50, followed by *Freedom* '87. His solo albums incl. *Oneness/Silver Dreams – Golden Reality* '79, *The Swing Of Delight* '80 with Herbie HANCOCK, Wayne SHORTER, and Ron CARTER; *Havana Moon* '83 with Willie NELSON, BOOKER T, FABULOUS THUNDERBIRDS. His influence is permanent; best albums still selling after nearly 20 years.

SANTO & JOHNNY Guitar duo: Santo Farina (*b* 24 Oct. '37, Brooklyn, NY) on steel guitar, brother Johnny (*b* 30 Apr. '41) on rhythm wrote 'Sleep Walk' '59, leased disc to Canadian American Records, had nice no. 1 instrumental hit, followed by five lesser entries '59-64. Hit albums were *Santo & Johnny* '60, *Encore* '60, *Hawaii* '61.

SATHERLEY, Art (*b* Arthur Edward Satherley, 19 Oct. 1889, Bristol, Engand; *d* 10 June '86, Fountain Valley, Cal.) Talent scout, producer, A&R man. Went to USA '13, worked in a Wisconsin factory that made cabinets for Edison's phonographs, got into the record industry promoting Ma RAINEY and Blind Lemon JEFFERSON records on Paramount. By 1930 he worked for ARC (*see* COLUMBIA), and after Ralph PEER was the most important A&R man in country music. He recorded Gene AUTRY from '29, Bob WILLS from '35, Hank Penny from '38; but his favourite was Roy ACUFF (from '36): Satherley was quite right in regarding any music of rural origin, whether white or black, as country music, but he was a traditionalist, and Acuff never became a 'singing cowboy' (*see also* Wills' entry). Satherley and colleague Don Law regarded Molly O'Day as the greatest female country singer of all (*b* LaVerne Williamson, '23, Pike County, Ky.; *d* 5 Dec. '87, Huntington, W. Va.; the female equivalent of Acuff, O'Day's style resembled that of Wilma Lee COOPER, probably infl. Kitty WELLS; she recorded Hank WILLIAMS' first published compositions incl. 'When God Comes And Gathers His Jewels' '46, left music for religion). Satherley worked for Columbia after '38, retired '52, having helped careers of Lefty FRIZZELL, Carl SMITH, Marty ROBBINS, many others.

SAUTER, Eddie (*b* Edward Ernest Sauter, 2 Dec. '14, Brooklyn, NY; *d* 21 Apr. '81, NYC) Arranger, composer. First played drums, then trumpet. Worked in bands on Atlantic liners, studied at Juilliard, worked for Archie BLEYER '32, Charlie BARNET '35, played trumpet and mellophone for Red NORVO '35, wrote virtually all the arr. for Red and Mildred BAILEY '35-9, then for Benny GOODMAN: 'Superman', 'Benny Rides Again', 'All The Cats Join In', 'Clarinet A La King' etc. plus arr. of pop tunes.

Worked for Artie SHAW ('The Maid With The Flaccid Air', etc.), Tommy DORSEY, Ray MCKINLEY in '40s. An album of his arr. for Goodman was among the first 12″ pop LPs on Columbia mid-'50s. He led band backing Bailey on Majestic, later Stan GETZ on MGM. Formed SAUTER-FINEGAN Orchestra '52 with ex-Glenn MILLER arr. Bill Finegan (*see below*). His *Concerto For Jazz Band And Orchestra* was recorded for RCA. Sauter went to work for German radio '57-9, later scored Broadway shows, film *Mickey One* '65, etc. 2-disc set *Eddie Sauter In Germany* on Big Band International in UK '80.

SAUTER-FINEGAN ORCHESTRA Concert band led '52-7 by arrangers Eddie SAUTER and Bill Finegan for studio work, then gigs: it was not a jazz band, though incl. top sidemen such as ex-Glenn MILLER saxist Al Kirk, Ralph BURNS, Kai WINDING, etc., but arrangements used unusual voicings with muted horns, recorders, bass clarinet, piccolo, oboe, English horn, tuneable drums, etc., the work of two fine Swing Era arrangers still sounding up-to-date. Delightfully twee 'Yankee Doodletown' was based on 'Yankee Doodle', 'Doodletown Fifers' (no. 12 hit) on a civil war song, 'Midnight Sleighride' on Prokofiev (top 30 hit), 'Now That I'm In Love' on Rossini (with vocal by Sally Sweetland); 'Nina Never Knew' (vocal by Joe Mooney) and film theme 'The Moon Is Blue' (with Sweetland) were top 20 hits '52-3. Albums incl. 10″ LPs *Inside Sauter-Finegan*, *The Sons Of Sauter-Finegan*, *The Sound Of The Sauter-Finegan Orchestra*, *Concert Jazz*; 12″ *New Directions In Music*, *Adventure In Time*, *Under Analysis*, *Memories Of Goodman And Miller*, all on RCA. The band broke up when Sauter went to work in Germany, but re-made tracks in stereo for *The Return Of The Doodletown Fifers* (reissued '85 on Liberty in UK); Finegan has revived it and played a gig early '87 in NYC with Jim HALL, others.

SAVITT, Jan (*b* 4 Sep. '13, St Petersburg, Russia; *d* 4 Oct. '48, Sacramento, Cal.) One source gives more realistic birth date '08. Violinist, singer, arranger, leader, songwriter. Father played in Tsar Nicholas II's Imperial Regiment Band. Family to USA '14. A child prodigy on violin, Savitt studied at Curtis Institute, was invited to join Philadelphia orchestra at age 15; studied in Europe, formed string quartet which broadcast nationwide; offered jobs as mus. dir. radio stations, formed dance band Top Hatters for radio '37, began touring late '38. Now underrated band was well-drilled outfit with superb ensemble sound; first theme was modernistic 'Quaker City Jazz', then '720 In The Books', so called because that was its number in band's book: top 20 hit '39 was as typical of the Swing Era as 'One O'Clock Jump'. Vocalists incl. Bon Bon (real name George Tunnell, one of the first blacks to work with a white band; later led vocal trio The Three Keys); 'It's A Wonderful World' with Bon Bon became new theme; hits incl. 'Meadowbrook Shuffle', all composed by Savitt; other hits incl. cover of 'Tuxedo Junction', 'Make Believe Island' no. 8 '40. Records on Bluebird '37-8; best hits on Decca; switched to Victor mid-'41; recorded pop versions of Chopin, Liszt etc. on Decca early '41, two-part Debussy's 'Afternoon Of A Faun' on Victor added strings '42; expanded band for theatre tour '44 (Savitt cond. for Frank SINATRA), later forced to reduce it. Made low-budget films '46-7; died suddenly while on tour.

SAVOY BROWN Hard-working British blues-rock quintet with constantly changing personnel that was more popular in USA than at home. Originally Savoy Brown Blues Band, formed '66 by guitarist/vocalist/harmonica Kim Simmonds, the only constant factor. First albums were *Shake Down* and *Getting To The Point* '67-8 followed by *Blue Matter* and *A Step Further* '69, each with one live side and the first two to chart in the USA; by this time nine musicians had already passed through. *Raw Sienna* was followed by *Looking In*, both '70, *Street Corner Talking* '71 and *Hellbound Train* '72, the latter their second, last and best top 40 seller at no. 34. Dave Peverett, Roger Earl, and Tone Stevens had left '71 to form another blues-boogie band, Foghat; Simmonds carried on, picking up sidemen from CHICKEN SHACK, Keef HARTLEY. *Lion's Share*, *Jack The Toad*, *Boogie Brothers* and *Wire Fire* '72-5 were the last to chart in the USA; *Savage Return* and *Blues Roots* '78 were still on Decca UK labels; *Rock'n'Roll Warrior* '81 on Town House (Capitol) returned to the USA top 200 LPs. According to Terry Houndsome's *Rock Record*, over 50 musicians and vocalists took part in all this recording.

SAVOY SULTANS, The House band at NYC's Savoy Ballroom '37-46, the name revived 30 years later. First band led by reedman Al Cooper (*b* Lofton Alphonso Cooper, 1911-81), incl. his half-brother Rudy Williams on reeds (*b* '09, Newark, N.J.; *d* Sep. '54: played with Hot Lips PAGE, Luis RUSSELL, John KIRBY, etc.), Grachan Moncur on bass (*b* '15). They were capable of raising the roof; visiting bigger names had tough competition. Compilations incl. *Jump Steady* on Affinity UK, similar *Jumpin' At The Savoy* on MCA USA. Freelance drummer David A. 'Panama' Francis (*b* 21 Dec. '18, Miami, Fla.) had played with Roy ELDRIDGE, Lucky MILLINDER, Tony BENNETT, Dinah SHORE, Ray CHARLES, Sy OLIVER, many others; worked in L.A. '68-73; was mus. dir. '75 for Carnegie Hall show re-creating Savoy era, formed new Sultans: fine LPs *Grooving* c.'80 and *Everything Swings* '83 on Stash. Albums listed in catalogues under Cooper or Francis.

SAXON Heavy metal band formed '77 in Yorkshire, England: Peter 'Biff' Byford, vocals (*b* 5 Jan. '51); Paul Quinn, Graham Oliver, guitars; Steve Dawson, bass; Pete Gill, drums. Created following with live work, established themselves in New Wave of British Heavy Metal with IRON MAIDEN, DEF LEPPARD, etc. *Saxon* '79 showed lyrical ability not restricted to sex and well-worn sword-and-sorcery themes beloved of HM axegrinders. *Wheels Of Steel* '80 provided top 20 hit with title track, took LP to no. 5; no. 11 LP *Strong Arm Of The Law* '80 incl. 'Dallas 1pm', about presidential assassination, no. 13 single '747 (Strangers In The Night)', tale of a near-miss in the air. *Denim And Leather* incl. 'Princess Of The Night', about steam trains, Nigel Glockler (ex-TOYAH) replacing Gill, who later joined MOTORHEAD. 'And The Bands Played On' and 'Never Surrender' were hit singles '81; *The Eagle Has Landed* '83 was an accurate record of impressive stage act; *Power & The Glory* '83 was best studio set to date, with top 40 title track, first to make top 200 LPs in USA, but *Crusader* '84 disappointed. Dis-

pute with Carrere label kept them out of studio for a while, then *Innocence Is No Excuse* '85 and reissue of back catalogue on EMI/Parlophone: with endearingly brash North Country image and sound, they have not reaped the rewards of slicker bands named above; major label exposure may help. On lyrical imagination alone they rate highly in a field not noted for it. *Rock The Nations* '86 had Elton JOHN guesting on piano, followed by *Destiny* early '88, with single 'Ride Like The Wind'.

SAYER, Leo (*b* Gerard Hugh Sayer, 21 May '48, Shoreham-by-Sea, Sussex) Pop singer, songwriter. Encouraged to sing in church choir by his father; formed band Terraplane Blues at Worthing Art College; moved to London to work as designer, also busked in the street with Lol COXHILL, others; formed band Patches with songwriting partner David Courtney: they got record contract with help of Adam FAITH and Keith Moon of the WHO, but LP on WB flopped. He went solo, took name Leo at Faith's wife's suggestion. Began recording debut solo album at Roger Daltrey's Sussex studio; the Who's vocalist was impressed and began making his own debut solo LP with Sayer-Courtney material, having no. 1 hit with 'Giving It All Away'. Sleeve of Sayer's *Silverbird* '73 depicted him as Pierrot, guise in live act getting media attention; LP charted immediately incl. no. 2 single 'The Show Must Go On' for first of ten UK top 10 hits '73-82. Discarded clown gear for *Just A Boy* '74; of top 10 singles, exuberant 'One Man Band' recalled busking days, dented USA chart slightly, while 'Long Tall Glasses (I Can Dance)' also made top 10 USA; after *Another Year* '75 he made *Endless Flight* '76 in USA, prod. by Richard PERRY, who also prod. *Thunder In My Heart* '77, *Leo Sayer* '78. Ten USA Hot 100 entries '75-81 saw 'You Make Me Feel Like Dancing' and 'When I Need You' '76-7 both at no. 1, three more top 40 hits '77, but he made *Here* '79 in UK, expressing disillusion with USA in title track. *Living In A Fantasy* '80 incl. cover of Bobby VEE's 'More Than I Can Say' (no. 2 UK/USA), *World Radio* '82 continued move into smoother, less lyrically acute pop. TV-advertised *Have You Ever Been In Love* '83 did well, title track was top 10 UK hit; *Leo* on Music For Pleasure '84 is bargain priced hits compilation.

SCAGGS, Boz (*b* William Ross Scaggs, 8 June '44, Ohio) Rock singer. Grew up in Texas, joined schoolmate Steve MILLER's band the Marksmen as vocalist, joined him again in the Ardells at the U. of Wisconsin in Madison, but quit, returned to Texas to play R&B with the Wigs '63. They relocated to Europe, broke up (remnants Bob Arthur, bass; John Andrews, guitar, became Mother Earth); he stayed on to tour as folksinger, made LP *Boz* in Stockholm '65 for Polydor. Returned to San Francisco to rejoin Miller, but quit after two LPs, now a more than competent songwriter/guitarist; one band couldn't hold them both. *Boz Scaggs* '69 appeared on Atlantic thanks to patronage of *Rolling Stone* editor Jann Wenner: Duane ALLMAN's solo on lengthy 'Loan Me A Dime' was acclaimed, but Muscle Shoals sidemen played important parts. Switched to Columbia/CBS for *Moments* and *Boz Scaggs And His Band*, both prod. '72 by Glyn JOHNS, the former much more impressive. *My Time* '72 introduced Muscle Shoals sidemen once more alongside his band – drummer George Rains (ex-Mother Earth), bassist David Brown, Joachim Young on keyboards; *Slow Dancer* '74 was prod. by Motown's Johnny Bristol, showed heavy soul influence; Bristol's 'I Got Your Number' a perennial stage staple from this set. *Silk Degrees* '76 refined the approach, was commercial apogee at no. 2 USA LP chart; 'Lowdown', 'What Can I Say', 'Lido Shuffle' were all hits USA/UK, beautiful 'We're All Alone' was a big hit for Rita COOLIDGE, who'd sung backing vocals on the first two CBS LPs. Smooth *Two Down Then Left* '77 was poor imitation, but *Middle Man* '80 was back in top 10 LPs, made singles chart USA with 'Breakdown Dead Ahead', 'Jojo', 'Miss Sun', 'Look What You've Done To Me'. Same year saw hits compilation, contribution to *Urban Cowboy* soundtrack.

SCHICKELE, Peter (*b* 17 July '35, Ames, Iowa) Composer, arranger. Studied at Juilliard, was on faculty there '61-5; among freelance composing, arranging, conducting (tracks on early Joan BAEZ LPs) he is best known for musical jokes using persona

of P. D. Q. Bach, affectionately sending up the sudden '60s popularity of baroque music (itself helped by excellent budget-priced records on Nonesuch and other labels) and admired by musicians for the consummate skill with which they were done: concerts were well attended; several LPs on Vanguard incl. *An Evening With P. D. Q. Bach*, *Portrait Of P. D. Q. Bach*, *An Hysteric Return*, etc.; also opera/ballet *The Stoned Guest* (title pun on *Don Juan* story, e.g. Dargomizhsky opera based on Pushkin poem *The Stone Guest*).

SCHIFRIN, Lalo (*b* Boris Schifrin, 21 June '32, Buenos Aires, Argentina) Pianist, composer, arranger. Father played in Buenos Aires Philharmonic; studied music, law, went to Paris on scholarship, represented Argentina at International Jazz Festival at Salle Pleyel '55. Formed 16-piece band in Argentina; encouraged by Dizzy GILLESPIE on a visit '56. Began composing, went to USA '58, worked with Gillespie '60-2, then for Quincy JONES; soon busy at jazz festivals and writing TV and film music. Own LPs on Roulette, pop chart hits with *Bossa Nova – New Brazilian Jazz* '62 on Audio Fidelity, Grammy-winning *Music From Mission: Impossible* '67 on Dot. He wrote *Dialogues For Jazz Quintet And Orchestra* for Cannonball ADDERLEY, *Jazz Suite On The Mass Text* for Paul HORN, LPs *Sweet Sass* for Sarah VAUGHAN, *Reflections* for Stan GETZ, *The Cat* for Jimmy SMITH; like Gunther SCHULLER (below) he hoped for 'third stream' fusion of jazz and formal music which hasn't happened. His film scores incl. *Cincinnati Kid* '65, *Bullitt* '68, *Dirty Harry* '71, many more.

SCHOEBEL, Elmer (*b* 8 Sep. 1896, East St Louis, Ill.; *d* 14 Dec. '70, Miami, Fla.) Pianist, composer, arranger. Played in silent cinemas, in vaudeville; with Friars Society Orchestra in Chicago (*see* JAZZ), later became the New Orleans Rhythm Kings; led own bands; with Isham JONES; wrote arrangements for Ina Ray HUTTON, '35; chief arr. for Warner Brothers music publishing in NYC '35-45. He invented and manufactured a 'tunematic' radio in the early '30s, but mainly he was one of the first composers/arrangers in jazz, preparing the works of King OLIVER, Louis ARMSTRONG,

Jelly Roll MORTON for publication, writing or co-writing classics 'Farewell Blues', 'Bugle Call Rag', 'Prince Of Wails', 'Nobody's Sweetheart', 'House Of David Blues', others.

SCHULLER, Gunther (*b* 11 Nov. '25, Jackson Heights, NY) French horn; composer, conductor, author, teacher. Played with Miles DAVIS '49-50; played in Cincinnati Symphony, Metropolitan Opera Orchestra NYC; plugged away for 'third stream' classical jazz fusion without much reward, recording on Columbia and Verve '50s, his *Conversations* performed '59 by the MODERN JAZZ QUARTET and the Beaux Arts String Quartet, recorded with other pieces on Atlantic LPs '60s. Fusions can't be forced; they happen by themselves when no one is looking. His ballet *Variants* was choreographed '61 by George Balanchine. He took part in Monterey Jazz Festivals '59, '61; was an instructor at the School of Jazz at Lenox, Mass.; presented the first jazz concert at Tanglewood, Mass. '63; he toured East Europe lecturing for the State Department; published *Early Jazz* '68, the most important and exhaustive history-analysis of the subject. President of the New England Conservatory in Boston, he formed the New England Conservatory Ragtime Ensemble, arr. JOPLIN rags and made hit LP of them: *Scott Joplin: The Red Back Book* was no. 65 pop LP '73 on Angel (EMI's USA classical label); the arrangements were used in the film *The Sting* (for some reason Marvin Hamlisch got an Oscar). He formed the New England Conservatory Jazz Repertory Orchestra to play classic arrangements of Duke ELLINGTON, MCKINNEY'S COTTON PICKERS, etc.: albums *Happy Feet: Tribute To Paul Whiteman*, *The Road From Rags To Jazz* on Golden Crest. He has continued composing, his works available on more than a dozen labels listed in the classical section of the Schwann catalogue.

SCHWANN RECORD & TAPE GUIDE USA record catalogue with world's largest circulation. William Joseph Schwann (*b* 13 May '13, Salem, Ill.) was clergyman's son, lived all over Midwest; became organist, dir. choirs, gave broadcasts, recitals, taught in Louisville, Ky. '32-5; studied at Harvard music dept grad school '37-9; carried on with music in Boston, owned The Record Shop in Cambridge, Mass. '39-53, associated with Technichord label. Published first long-playing record catalogue in any country: 26-page list of 674 LPs '49. Called *Schwann Record & Tape Guide* since '71, monthly catalogue listed all classical records plus new releases in other categories, cumulative bumper issue once a year. Over 150,000 out-of-print records passed through about 34 million copies since '49; editorial staff grew from two to three '77. Also Artists Issue (classical listing by artist), Basic Record Library (list of 750 classical records). Began monthly Schwann Compact Disc Catalog May '86, now listing all CDs in print plus each month's new releases in all formats; with Dec. '86 issue, main Schwann became quarterly super Schwann listing everything, with features on record labels, etc.: Fall '87 issue had over 500 pages, 78,000 listings in many categories incl. international folk, spoken word, religious etc. Available in record shops or by subscription. Schwann is trustee/board member of Marlboro Music School, Cambridge Society of Early Music, etc.; honorary doctorates in music from U. of Louisville '69, New England Conservatory '82; many awards, citations incl. honorary gold record from Recording Industry Association of America (RIAA). In UK *Gramophone* magazine publishes catalogues; Music Master service for popular music provides hefty annual, monthly updates for shops, also lists singles. In Germany, handsome paperback Bielefelder Katalog of jazz has cross-references even incl. song titles.

SCHWARTZ, Arthur (*b* 25 Nov. 1900, Brooklyn, NY) Songwriter. With several college degrees, father a successful lawyer, turned to music. Wrote 'I Love To Lie Awake In Bed' with Lorenz Hart for a summer camp show c.'22, met Howard Dietz '27 who wrote new lyrics for it: 'I Guess I'll Have To Change My Plan' was their first hit, for *The Little Show* '29. *The Band Wagon* '31 incl. 'Dancing In The Dark', their biggest hit; *Flying Colors* '32 incl. 'Louisiana Hayride', 'Alone Together'; flop *Revenge With Music* '34 (based on Spanish novel *The Three-Cornered Hat*) incl. 'You And The Night And The Music'; *At Home Abroad* '35 incl. 'Love Is A Dancing Thing' (hit in UK by Jessie Matthews), 'Got A Bran' New Suit' (recorded by Fats WALLER, who also had a top 10 hit '34 with 'Then I'll Be Tired Of You', by Schwartz with Yip HARBURG). After a flop show Schwartz and Dietz split up '37; Schwartz worked with Dorothy Fields, went to Hollywood '39-46 where he prod. *Cover Girl* (music by George GERSHWIN, Jerome KERN) and Cole PORTER biopic *Night And Day*. Teamed with Dietz again for *Inside USA* '46 on Broadway, two more flops; with Fields for more successful *A Tree Grows In Brooklyn* '51, *By The Beautiful Sea* '54. Wrote 'That's Entertainment' with Dietz for '53 film of *The Band Wagon*, retired to England late '60s, made LP singing his own songs '75. Dietz (*b* 8 Sep. 1896, NYC; *d* '84) was a journalist who worked as a publicist for MGM, invented the Leo the Lion trademark, stayed 30 years and became a director of Loews Inc. while writing songs on the side; he also wrote with Kern, Gershwin, Vernon DUKE, Sammy FAIN. He was a director of ASCAP '59-61; ASCAP gave him a prize for his autobiography *Dancing In The Dark, Words By Howard Dietz* '74; *Song By Song By Howard Dietz* '80 was a TV special. One of his songs was called 'Why Did I Leave Wisconsin? Kenosha Wisconsin': he must have liked the syllables; Orson Welles, who was born there, said Kenosha was a terrible place.

SCOBEY, Bob (*b* 9 Dec. '16, Tucumcari, N.M.; *d* 12 June '63, Montreal, Canada) Trumpet, bandleader. Studied cornet at 9, trumpet at 14, turned pro at 20. In at the beginning of the revival period in jazz (*see* JAZZ), a founder member with Lu WATTERS of the Yerba Buena Band late '30s, subsequently led his own Bob Scobey's 'Frisco Band '50s, with banjo and vocals by Clancy HAYES, playing a less faithful but still charming good-timey music, intended to recreate turn-of-the-century West Coast rather than New Orleans. Five LPs on Good Time Jazz: two compilations of '50-3 tracks incl. Watters alumni Wally Rose on piano, Dick Lammi on bass ('Silver Dollar'/'Ace In The Hole' was a single that got some airplay '53); three albums '55-6, still with Hayes. Moved to Chicago early '60s, toured Europe with Harlem Globetrotters '63; died of cancer.

SCOFIELD, John (*b* 26 Dec. '51, Ohio) Guitar. Grew up in Connecticut, took up guitar in high school, attended Berklee '70-3; recorded live at Carnegie Hall with Gerry MULLIGAN/Chet BAKER '74; played in Billy COBHAM band two years. Recorded with Charles MINGUS '77, joined Gary BURTON, led own quartet, played in Dave Liebman quintet late '70s-early '80s, then with Miles DAVIS (*Decoy, Star People, You're Under Arrest*). Also recorded with Jay McSHANN on Atlantic, Paul BLEY, George ADAMS/Don PULLEN Quartet, others. Own albums began with *Live* and *Rough House* '77-8 on Enja, *Who's Who* on Arista/Novus; then with trio incl. bassist Steve SWALLOW, drummer Adam Nussbaum: *Bar Talk* on Arista/Novus, *Shinola* and *Out Like A Light* on Enja. Switched to Gramavision for *Electric Outlet* while he was still playing with Miles, then *Still Warm* (with drummer Omar Hakim, bassist Darryl Jones, Don Grolnick on keyboards), *Blue Matter* '86: always infl. by the blues, resolved contradiction with fusion deciding that there needn't be any; new rhythm section incl. drummer Dennis Chambers (10 years with the PARLIAMENT/FUNKADELIC circus), Gary Grainger (ex-Pockets) on bass: *Pick Hits* (live in Japan) and *Loud Jazz* '87. With lots of fans among guitarists, he is one of the people who has to decide what jazz-rock fusion should be.

SCORPIONS German heavy metal band formed in Hanover '70 by brothers Michael and Rudolf Schenker (*b* 31 Aug. '52), guitars; Klaus Meine, vocals; Lothar Heimberg, bass; Wolfgang Dziony, drums. Euro-rock or 'kraut rock' was in vogue, with TANGERINE DREAM, Amon Duul and CAN in their heyday, but Scorpions chose HM genre. Rudy had led Copernicus since '65, Michael had played with Cry. *Lonesome Crow* '72 sold well in Germany, led to film score *The Cold Paradise*, but Michael quit '73 to join UFO after their guitarist Bernie Marsden quit on tour which Scorpions were supporting; Rudy broke up band, re-formed same year with Meine and Ulrich Roth, guitar; Francis Buchholz, bass; Jorgen Rosenthal, drums. *Fly To The Rainbow* '74 saw HENDRIX-infl. Roth much in evidence. Toured UK after *In Trance* '75 with new drummer Rudy Lenners; after *Virgin Kill-*

ers '76 Herman Rarebell (*b* 18 Nov. '53) replaced him for *Taken By Force* '77. Tour of Japan elevated them to major status there: 2-disc *Tokyo Tapes* '78 was live souvenir. Roth left to form Electric Sun; Matthias Jabs (*b* 25 Oct. '56) replaced him with gutsier, less lyrical style on *Lovedrive* '79, top 40 UK, no. 55 USA. Now headlining in UK, in USA they supported Ted NUGENT, Rainbow, Sammy HAGAR; *Animal Magnetism* '80 made no. 52 USA, 23 UK. Michael returned to oust Jabs briefly; left to form another group, Jabs returning. Break for Meine to have surgery on vocal chords did not hinder *Blackout* '82: no. 11 both USA/UK; they played second to VAN HALEN at US Festival. *Love At First Sting* '84 was no. 6 USA, 2-disc *World Wide Live* no. 14. Perhaps the biggest band sales-wise to come out of Germany, but arguably less distinctive than lesser-selling acts in their genre.

SCOTT, Bobby (*b* 29 Jan. '37, Mt Pleasant, NY) Pianist, vocalist, composer, teacher; also plays vibes, accordion, other instruments, but as a performer best known as a fine jazz pianist who also sang. First teacher was Dorothea Anderson LaFollette, who taught the legendary William Kapell; studied composition with Edvard Moritz, a pupil of Debussy. Scott worked with Louis PRIMA, Tony SCOTT (no relation), Gene KRUPA while still a teenager; recorded with Krupa on Verve. Had own no. 13 hit 'Chain Gang' '56 on ABC-Paramount (not his own song and not the same as the later Sam COOKE hit). Albums: '53 tracks on *The Jazz Keyboards* on Savoy (others by Marian MCPARTLAND, Joe BUSHKIN, Lennie TRISTANO); trio, sextet, septet LPs on Bethlehem '54-5; trio and quintet LPs on ABC '55-6; two trio LPs on Verve '57-8; two LPs on Atlantic '60: one with big band and vocals, another a smaller group playing Scott's incidental music for NYC play *A Taste Of Honey* (filmed in UK '61). The theme tune was first recorded by Victor FELDMAN Quartet '62; other hit versions incl. Martin DENNY '62, Tony BENNETT '64 (words by Ric Marlow; BEATLES covered it on their first LP). It won a Grammy for Best Instrumental Theme '62 and three more Grammies '65 when Herb ALPERT revived it for a top 10 hit. Scott was mus. dir. for

Dick HAYMES early '60s, wrote LPs *The City* and *Legends* for Larry ELGART on MGM; made a quartet LP '64, quintet LP '65 on Mercury; played on several tracks on a Chet BAKER LP on Limelight '65; made two big band LPs '61-2 with Quincy JONES, subsequently played piano on nearly all of Jones's Mercury LPs and two on A&M, accompanied Tatia Vega and John Lee HOOKER on Jones's soundtrack for *The Colour Purple* '86. Meanwhile he prod. pop sessions at Mercury, Columbia (incl. Aretha FRANKLIN), tracks by Marvin GAYE recently released on CBS; discovered/recorded guitarist/vocalist Perry Miller, changing his name to Jesse Colin Young '64 (*see* YOUNGBLOODS). Took singer/songwriter Bobby Hebb back to Mercury after Hebb's contract there had run out; Scott then left Mercury but Hebb recorded international hit 'Sunny' '66. (Hebb, *b* 26 July '41 in Nashville, was one of the first blacks to appear on Grand Ole Opry, at age 12; wrote more than 1000 published songs incl. Grammy winner 'A Natural Man', hit by Lou RAWLS '71.) Scott worked for Bobby DARIN, Sarah VAUGHAN, Harry BELAFONTE etc.; songs incl. 'He Ain't Heavy . . . He's My Brother' (hit by the HOLLIES '70), 'Where Are You Going' (sung by Jerry BUTLER in soundtrack of film *Joe* '70), 'Slaves (Don't You Know My Name?)' (sung by Dionne WARWICK in film *Slaves* '69), incidental music for play *Dinny And The Witches*; compositions for harp, two string trios (one called The Giacometti Variations, because part used in radio advert for Giacometti exhibition at Museum of Modern Art), etc.; writing for guitar incl. gorgeous *Solitude Book* and *The Book Of Hours* for piano and guitar; the former has been digitally recorded with Carlos Barbosa-Lima on guitar, but USA record companies don't want to know.

SCOTT, Hazel (*b* Hazel Dorothy Scott, 11 June '20, Port of Spain, Trinidad) Pianist, composer, singer. To USA at 4, a piano prodigy at 8, worked with mother's American Creolians all girl band; studied at Juilliard. Had own radio series '36; appeared in Broadway musical *Sing Out The News* '38 (played and sang 'F. D. R. Jones'), revue *Priorities Of 1942*, films *I Dood It*, *The Heat's On*, *Something To Shout About*

'43, *Broadway Rhythm* '44, *Rhapsody In Blue* '45. Wrote 'Love Comes Softly', 'Nightmare Blues'. She recorded for Signature, Decca (compilation *'Round Midnight*), Columbia (10" LPs), had her own show on early TV, was married to NYC Congressman Adam Clayton Powell, divorced; made album *Relaxed Piano Moods* '55 for Charles MINGUS's Debut label, a 10" limited edition with Mingus on bass and drummer Max ROACH, reissued '85 on Fantasy; also *Afterthoughts* '80 on Tioch.

SCOTT, Jack (*b* Jack Scafone Jr, 24 Jan. '36) Rock'n'roll/country singer, songwriter. Father was a guitarist, gave Jack a guitar at age 8. Moved to a Detroit suburb at 10, heard Hank WILLIAMS and Roy ACUFF on the radio; later performed himself on radio and formed band the Southern Drifters. Signed with ABC-Paramount '57 for two flop singles; Joe Carleton left ABC to form his own Carleton label and took Jack with him; Jack's song about an imprisoned friend, 'Leroy', was a rocker backed by a funereal ballad, 'My True Love'; his deep baritone laced with humour, excellent recording quality took each side to the top 20 '58, the ballad making no. 3; next release backed rocker 'Geraldine' (just made Hot 100) with mournful 'With Your Love' (top 30). Several more hits '59 incl. 'Goodbye Baby' (top 10), 'The Way I Walk' (top 40); joined short-lived Top Rank label and had seven Hot 100 entries '60 incl. 'Burning Bridges' (no. 3) and 'What In The World's Come Over You' (no. 5); moved to Capitol '61 and brought total to 19 Hot 100 hits in less than 3.5 years. On RCA subsidiary Groove '63 he veered towards country music as chart interest in pure rock'n'roll was waning. He also recorded with ABC (again), Jubilee, GRT, Dot and his own Ponie label (on which his greatest hits LP was issued); visited Europe '77 in all-star rock'n'roll package that incl. Buddy KNOX, Charlie FEATHERS, Warren Smith. Hits remain listenable to today, but hard to find.

SCOTT, Raymond (*b* Harry Warnow, 10 Sep. '10, NYC) Pianist, arranger, composer, bandleader. Studied at Juilliard, played piano in brother Mark's band, joined staff at CBS radio, appeared in and wrote music for films '35-8. Formed Quintette (six pieces),

made many records, clever novelty arr. requiring good playing: best known was 'In An Eighteenth-Century Drawing Room', cribbed from Mozart. Theme was 'The Toy Trumpet' (a hit twice: '37-8), other titles incl. 'Twilight In Turkey', 'Dinner Music For A Pack Of Hungry Cannibals'. Records on Master, reissued on Brunswick; as mus. dir. at CBS radio recorded for Columbia, then Decca with big band incl. Cozy COLE, Coleman HAWKINS, Benny MORTON, Charlie SHAVERS, other top jazzmen, though Scott himself was never a jazz musician; sides incl. 'When Cootie Left The Duke' (when Cootie WILLIAMS left Duke ELLINGTON to join Benny GOODMAN). Discovered Dorothy Collins (*b* Marjorie Chandler in Canada) in Chicago '40s, hired her to sing with band; meanwhile *Your Hit Parade* had started on radio '35; Scott took over as conductor when brother Mark died '49, took it to TV '50, stayed until it died with the advent of rock'n'roll; Collins sang theme for cigarette sponsor ('Be Happy! Go Lucky!'), soon became regular on programme, along with Snooky Lanson (*b* Memphis, Tenn.; sang with Francis CRAIG, Ray NOBLE). Scott and Collins married '53, divorced later. He also scored Broadway musical *Lute Song* '46 ('Mountain High, Valley Low'), had own Audivox label, was mus. dir. for Everest; later manufactured electronic musical instruments.

SCOTT, Ronnie (*b* Ronald Schatt, 28 Jan. '27, London) Tenor sax, leader; operator with Peter King of venerable eponymous London jazz club, said to employ bouncers to throw people *in*. Father was bandleader Jock Scott; Ronnie played with Ted HEATH '46, soaked up bop in NYC, working back and forth on the *Queen Mary* ('Geraldo's Navy': bandleader GERALDO booked the bands on the boat), hung out with first generation of UK modern jazzmen at cooperative Soho Club Eleven (raided '50 due to odour of unusual cigarillos). Formed own combo '53; own club '59 in Gerrard Street; moved to Frith Street late '65; 20th anniversary album on PRT incl. tracks by Scott quintet, Count BASIE, Stan GETZ, Sonny STITT, Roland KIRK, Zoot SIMS and Al COHN, Kenny CLARKE/BOLAND Big Band, Woody HERMAN, Buddy RICH; celebrated 25 years with club issue of 2-disc set with tracks by Sims, Rich, George COLEMAN, Sarah VAUGHAN, Gil EVANS, Clarke/Boland, others incl. own trio and generous measure of famous rotten jokes (greets audiences with 'This is the first time I've seen dead people smoke'). Many records on Esquire '49-55 with King, Phil Seamen, jazzman turned journalist Benny Green on baritone, Victor FELDMAN, etc.; *Battle Royal* '51-2 has been reissued on PRT: one side has Kenny Graham, second tenor; the other Scott's quintet of the period. Other LPs on Tempo, Philips, Fontana, RCA, CBS, with Stan TRACEY, many others, out of print, but *Serious Gold* '77 is also on PRT, with Ron Mathewson, bass; Martin Drew, drums; Louis Stewart, guitar; John Taylor, keyboards. Modest about his own playing, the only records he will mention with approval are not his own but those with Clarke/Boland, because he loved the band; but some fans say he was a better jazzman than the still-loved Tubby HAYES. Leads house quintet with John CRITCHENSON, piano; Dick Pearce, flugelhorn, trumpet; Mathewson and Drew. Biography *Let's All Join Hands And Contact The Living* '85 by John Fordham.

SCOTT, Shirley (*b* 14 Mar. '34, Philadelphia, Pa.) Organ. Played trumpet in high school, piano in father's club; took up organ '55, worked with Eddie Lockjaw DAVIS '56-60, formed trio, worked with Stanley TURRENTINE, married him, recorded with him on Blue Note; they separated '71; she formed a new group '74 with saxophonist Harold Vick (*b* 3 Apr. '36, Rocky Mount, N.C.; also teacher, composer, actor; LPs on StrataEast, Muse, RCA, Blue Note). She often appeared on NYC and Philadelphia TV, a very popular, swinging blues-oriented player. LPs with Davis incl. *Cookbook* on Prestige; of about 20 LPs with own trio on Prestige '58-64 *Soul Sister* '60, *Satin Doll* '61, *Sweet Soul* are still in print. She also recorded prolifically for Impulse '64-7 (sometimes with larger groups, once with strings), sessions with Turrentine now on MCA; on Atlantic '68-70 (with Turrentine '68) incl. *Shirley Scott And The Soul Saxes* with Hank CRAWFORD, Fathead NEWMAN, KING CURTIS; on Cadet '71-2, *One For Me* '74 on StrataEast with Vick, Billy HIGGINS.

SCOTT, Tony (*b* Anthony Sciacca, 17 June '21, Morristown, N.J.) Clarinet. From musical family, studied at Juilliard, played in the Army '42-5; played with Tommy DORSEY, Charlie VENTURA, Claude THORNHILL, Earl BOSTIC, etc. Own combos from '49, also arr. for and accompanied singers Billie HOLIDAY, Carmen McRAE, Sarah VAUGHAN, etc.; also played piano and saxophones, gigged with Latin bands; mus. dir. for Harry BELAFONTE '55, international tours '57, from '59-65 studying ethnic music in the Orient. With a modern, facile style, not as warm-toned as Buddy DeFRANCO, but like him more or less ignored in modern jazz, playing an instrument inexplicably out of fashion. Concert of Indian-infl. modern jazz at Museum of Modern Art NYC '67, toured with pianist Romano Mussolini '72. Records as leader: on Gotham '46 with Vaughan, all-star septet incl. B. Bopstein (Dizzy GILLESPIE), with quartet and big band on Brunswick '53 (backed Jackie Paris vocal on Coral), on RCA: EP '54, LPs *Scott's Fling* '55 with septet incl. Milt HINTON, Osie Johnson on drums; quartet *Both Sides Of Tony Scott*; *The Touch Of Tony Scott* and *The Complete Tony Scott* with some quartet tracks, all-star big band featuring Hinton, Johnson, guitarists Barry Galbraith, Freddie GREEN, Mundell LOWE, all '56; *The Modern Art Of Jazz* '57 on Seeco; tracks on ABC-Paramount, Dot, Coral '58; *Tony Scott Quartet* on Signature with Lowe, Jimmy Garrison on bass, Pete La Roca on drums, *Golden Moments* and *I'll Remember* on Muse with Bill EVANS instead of Lowe, all '59. *Sung Heroes* '59 issued on Sunnyside '87 with Evans, Scott LA FARO, guitarist Juan Sastre on one track, Scott also playing baritone, piano, guitar on various tracks. *Music For Zen Meditation* '64, *Music For Yoga Meditation* '67, *Tony Scott* '69-70, all on Verve; with Indonesian All Stars on MPS '67; octet on Sonet '74, recorded in Sweden; *Prism* '77 on Polydor with Jan AKKERMAN quartet; big band *Boomerang*, trio *Conversation* '77-8 on Czech Supraphon; *African Bird – Come Back! Mother Africa* '81 on Soul Note, also various small groups recorded in England and Milan.

SCOTT-HERON, Gil (*b* 1 Apr. '49, Chicago, Ill.) Attended Lincoln and Johns Hopkins

U., MA '72; published novels *The Vulture, The Nigger Factory*. Began collaborating with Brian Robert Jackson on music so as to get message across, half-spoken, half-sung; has large cult audience. *Small Talk At 125th Street And Lenox* '72 was a mostly verbal rendition of his book of poems, followed by *Free Will, Pieces Of A Man, The Revolution Will Not Be Televised* '72-5 (latter title track covered by LaBELLE), all on Flying Dutchman; *Winter In America* '75 on StrataEast; he was then an early and successful signing to new Arista label: *The First Minute Of A New Day* and *From South Africa To South Carolina* '75, *It's Your World* '76, *Bridges* '77, *Secrets* and *The Mind Of Gil Scott-Heron* '78, *1980* and *Real Eyes* '80, *Reflections* '81, *Moving Target* '82.

SEALS AND CROFTS Soft-rock vocal and instrumental duo: Jim Seals (guitar, sax, fiddle) and Dash Crofts (drums, mandolin, keyboards) both *b* '40 in Texas; Seals won a fiddle championship at age 9, later played on 'Tequila!', phenomenal novelty Latin rock'n'roll hit '68 by the Champs; Crofts joined the Champs, who carried on till mid-'60s; they formed the Dawnbreakers and the entire group adopted the Bah'ai faith; they emerged as a duo '70, sentiments (and sentimentality) perhaps replacing the inactive SIMON & GARFUNKEL among college audiences as pop music hurled itself onto MOR radio. Signed with WB and had eight top 40 singles '72-8 incl. 'Summer Breeze', 'Diamond Girl' and 'Get Closer', all no. 6, latter with Carolyn Willis (ex-BOBB B SOXX, Honey Cone). Chart LPs '71-8 incl. *Year Of Sunday* '71; *Summer Breeze, Diamond Girl, Unborn Child* '72-4, all gold LPs; 2-disc *Seals And Crofts I And II*, a reissue of their first two on TA label; *I'll Play For You* and *Greatest Hits* '75, *Get Closer* and *Sudan Village* '76 (both with Willis), *One On One* '77 (a soundtrack), *Takin' It Easy* '78.

SEALS, Son (*b* Frank Seals, 13 Aug. '42, Osceola, Ark.) Blues singer, guitarist; also plays drums. Father was Jim 'Son' Seals, who played with Rabbit Foot Minstrels, owned club in Osceola, from '53 taught Frank, who sat in at the club with touring bluesmen, worked with Earl HOOKER in Little Rock, toured with Albert KING, settled in Chicago '71, recorded for Alligator,

played many clubs, festivals, toured Europe (with B. B. KING '77 in London). Albums incl. *Blues Band* '73, *Midnight Son* '76, *Live & Burning* '78, *Chicago Fire* '80, all on Sonet UK.

SEALS, Troy (*b* 16 Nov. '38, Big Hill, Ky.) Successful country songwriter, sometime vocalist and session guitarist. Began on guitar in teens, formed combo, toured in Dick CLARK review late '50s with pop singer Jo Ann Campbell; they married early '60s, signed as duo to Atlantic, had top 40 R&B hit 'I Found A Love, Oh What A Love' '64. Left music business, worked in construction in Indianapolis, made some demos and took them to Nashville, got writer's contract late '60s; sessioned with Ray STEVENS, Waylon JENNINGS etc., wrote with Donnie Fritts ('We Had It All'), Don Goodman, Will Jennings. 'Feelin's' (written with Goodman and Jennings) was a hit duet by Conway TWITTY and Loretta LYNN; Twitty recorded 'There's A Honky Tonk Angel Who'll Take Me Back In' '74, 'Don't Take It Away' '79. His songs have been recorded by Lonnie MACK, Dobie GRAY, Percy SLEDGE ('Stop The World Tonight'), Ronnie MILSAP, George JONES, Rod STEWART, OAK RIDGE BOYS, etc. His records on Monument, Polydor, Atlantic (*Now Presenting Troy Seals* '73), Columbia (*Troy Seals* '76), Elektra '80, RCA '83 have not been successful despite critical praise.

SEARCHERS, The UK pop quartet, one of the first and best to emerge from Liverpool early '60s: lead guitar John McNally (*b* 30 Aug. '41), rhythm guitar Mike Pender (*b* Michael Pendergast, 3 Mar. '42), bassist Tony Jackson (*b* 16 July '40), drummer Chris Curtis the only one not originally from Liverpool (*b* Christopher Crumney, 16 Aug. '41, Oldham, Lancs.). They named themselves after the John Wayne film (Wayne's catchphrase in the film 'That'll be the day!' also providing the title of Buddy HOLLY's first hit). Their imaginative harmonies and distinctive guitar sound were an infl. on the BYRDS. Like the BEATLES, they played at the Cavern and in Hamburg '61-2; had three no. 1 UK hits '63-4 with 'Sweets For My Sweet', 'Needles & Pins', 'Don't Throw Your Love Away' (last two top 20 USA); *Meet The Searchers* '63 was astonishingly strong debut at the time, when LPs usually meant one or two hits and much dross: incl. standard Merseybeat fare 'Money', 'Twist And Shout', etc. but also Pete SEEGER's 'Where Have All The Flowers Gone'. They had top 5 hits with Jackie DeSHANNON's 'When You Walk Into The Room' '64, 'Goodbye My Love' '65, other lesser hits through '66; total of 13 Hot 100 entries in USA through '66 incl. no. 3 with revival of Clovers' '59 hit 'Love Potion No. 9' '64 (from *Hear! Hear!* on Mercury in USA, recorded live in Hamburg). Unlike the Beatles, they did not progress; as rock'n'roll turned into rock and became 'progressive', the Beatles and others took time over recording, while the Searchers' albums *Sugar & Spice, It's The Searchers, Sounds Like The Searchers* '63-4 (slightly different LPs in the USA) did not improve on the first. Jackson quit '64 at height of success, replaced by Frank Allen (ex-Cliff BENNETT); Curtis was replaced '66 by Johnny Blunt, in turn replaced by Billy Adamson '69, this lineup touring/recording well into '80s, though fading from charts to cabaret circuit; there was some renewed interest as Bruce SPRINGSTEEN incl. 'When You Walk Into The Room' in concert, lead track on his *The River* '80 ('The Ties That Bind') recalled the sound. *The Searchers* '80 charted briefly on Sire in USA; *Play For Today* '81 incl. songs by John Fogerty, KURSAAL FLYERS, Chris Kenner; they also released *Love Melodies* '81, but new look Searchers didn't catch on. *Greatest Hits* '85 on Rhino still sound good.

SEDAKA, Neil (*b* 13 Mar. '39, NYC) Singer/ songwriter who had early candyfloss success and stayed the course. Parents played piano (grandmother to concert standard); began writing in high school, enlisting schoolmate Howard Greenfield as lyricist. 'While I Dream' demo issued on Melba '56, written for the Tokens but not recorded by them; local success encouraged him; combined scholarship to Juilliard with writing, also recorded for Decca, Guyden labels. Wrote with Greenfield '58 for Don Kirshner's Aldon Music (*see* BRILL BUILDING), their songs recorded by LaVern BAKER, Clyde McPHATTER, Connie FRANCIS ('Stupid Cupid' no. 14 hit '58, 'Frankie' top 10 '59); signed to RCA late '58, immediate success

was big: only Elvis PRESLEY outsold him for five years. Thirteen top 40 hits '59-63 from 'The Diary' to 'Bad Girl' incl. top tens 'Oh! Carol' (for Carole KING), 'Stairway To Heaven', 'Calendar Girl', 'Happy Birthday, Sweet Sixteen', 'Breaking Up Is Hard To Do' (no. 1 '62), 'Next Door To An Angel'. All were cute pop songs, his light tenor double-tracked, Latinesque backing and his pounding piano added to simple sound. British Invasion washed him away; Sedaka/Greenfield turned to MOR, writing through '60s for Peggy LEE, Johnny MATHIS, FIFTH DIMENSION, etc. Brill contemporary King brought singer/songwriters back and he enjoyed a second chart career '70s: after LP *Emergence* '71 he worked with 10CC on *The Tra-La Days Are Over* (incl. 'That's Where The Music Takes Me', top 20 UK hit '73, top 30 USA '75); 'Laughter In The Rain' '74 was his second USA no. 1, twelve years after the first; he did it again '75 with 'Bad Blood' (harmony vocal by Elton JOHN, on whose Rocket label his records appeared in USA), had top 10 '76 with slow remake of 'Breaking Up Is Hard To Do'. He wrote with Greenfield, Phil Cody and daughter Dara (they scored top 20 USA '80 with 'Should've Never Let You Go'). Quality pop was also recorded by CAPTAIN AND TENNILLE, the Partridge Family, many others; popular in UK, where top 40 hits total 15. *Laughter And Tears* '76 was good compilation of later work; early RCA hits much anthologised; Elton John is just one piano player who owes a lot to Sedaka.

SEEDS, The Garage band turned psychedelic outfit formed by famed L.A. hippie Sky Saxon (*b* Richard Marsh), who'd led groups incl. Amoebas. Lineup was Daryl Hooper, keyboards; Jan Savage, guitar; Rick Andridge, drums. Signed to GNP Crescendo; first single 'Can't Seem To Make You Mine' with CAPTAIN BEEFHEART-style howling by Saxon, almost made top 40 '67 after the second, 'Pushin' Too Hard', went top 40 '66, championed by local radio a year after release; 'Try To Understand' flopped. All incl. on *The Seeds* '66 (reissued as *Legendary Master Recordings* '78 on Sonet) but failed to emulate success of local rivals LOVE. They recycled ROLLING STONES, Bo DIDDLEY, Merseyside sounds (solo on

'Pushin' Too Hard' cribbed from Billy J. KRAMER's 'Bad To Me'); originality lay in Saxon's rambling word-association patterns. *Web Of Sound* '66 with Harvey Sharpe added on bass was more polished but had less charm; 'Mr Farmer', 'A Thousand Shadows' were Hot 100 entries '67; *Future* '67 reflected flower-power; *Full Spoon Of Seedy Blues* '67 was made only to fulfil contract, despite sleeve note by Diddley. Struggled on through patchy live LP, split mid-'71. Saxon retired to Hawaii, where he released *Sky Saxon And The Stars New Seeds Band*. 'Pushin' Too Hard' remains classic of '60s USA punk rock; the BANGLES play it live. Recent issues incl. *A Groovy Thing* on French New Rose label, *Retrospective* on German Line, *Destiny's Children* on PVC (with psychedelic revival guests incl. Mars Bonfire), all '86.

SEEGER, Mike (*b* 15 Aug. '33, NYC) Folksinger, instrumentalist, producer. Parents were musicologist Charles and composer (turned song editor and piano teacher) Ruth Crawford Seeger (her *String Quartet* '31 particularly fine, recorded by Nonesuch '73). Sister Peggy, half-brother Pete (*see below*). Played autoharp at 12, got serious at 18, taking up a dozen stringed instruments. Played with Peggy in square dance bands; worked in Baltimore hospital as conscientious objector '54, discovering country and bluegrass; formed New Lost City Ramblers '58 with John Cohen, Tom Paley, to recreate traditional music, began recording for Folkways; made field recordings for the label by the STONEMAN FAMILY, Libba COTTEN, MCGEE brothers, etc.; the Ramblers performed at the first Newport Folk Festival; Tracy Schwartz joined '62 and Paley left; the group played more country music. Formed Strange Creek Singers late '60s with Alice Gerrard (married her '70), Hazel Dickens, Lamar Grier and Tracy (LP on Arhoolie). He was a trustee of Newport Folk Festival '63-71, on board of directors of National Folk Festival, Washington DC, and Southern Folk Revival Cultural Project, Atlanta, Ga.; etc.; by the late '70s he had made nearly 50 albums, incl. five with Peggy; 15 in print by the Ramblers on Folkways incl. collections *The Depression, Moonshine And Prohibition, Rural Delivery No. 1*, etc., and 2-disc *20 Years: Concert Perfor-*

mances on Flying Fish; solo albums *Old Time Country Music* on Folkways, *Music From The True Vine* and *Second Annual Farewell Reunion* mid-'70s on Mercury with many friends incl. Pete. Others on Argo, Rounder, Vanguard; *Old Time Music Dance Party* '87 on Flying Fish is by A. Robic & The Exertions.

SEEGER, Peggy (*b* Margaret Seeger, 17 June '35, NYC) Folksinger, music editor; brother is Mike Seeger (*see above*), half-brother is Pete (*see below*); she married Scottish folksinger Ewan MACCOLL. Played piano, took up guitar at 10, other instruments; helped mother with transcriptions while growing up in Maryland. Studied music at Radcliffe and began performing in public; studied Russian in Holland '55, travelled widely, incl. Russia and China; went to England '56 to act in Granada TV prod. of folk musical *Dark Side Of The Moon* '56. Joined the Ramblers, incl. MacColl; she settled in Britain, recorded and wrote music for films and TV with MacColl, as well as making more than 30 solo albums, also recording with MacColl, Tom Paley, her sisters Penny and Barbara, and publishing anthologies such as *Folk Songs Of Peggy Seeger* '64, wherein she thanks her brothers, and MacColl, saying that he showed her 'who "the folk" really are'. Whereas Pete Seeger likes to get crowds singing and Mike prefers to teach trad. music to small groups, Peggy has specialised in ballads, often from feminist point of view; her solo LPs incl. *Different Therefore Equal* and *From Where I Stand* on Folkways, also *Penelope Isn't Waiting Any More* on Rounder, *Who's Going To Shoe Your Pretty Little Foot?* with Paley on Topic, many more; others with MacColl.

SEEGER, Pete (*b* 3 May '19, NYC) Folksinger, banjo player, songwriter, spark plug: he is called 'America's tuning fork', though at times some doubted whether America deserved him. His parents were musicologist Charles Louis Seeger and his first wife, violin teacher Constance de Clyver (Edson). As a child he played with musical instruments but refused to study, practise, learn to read music; he attended private schools, university; decided to be a painter, then a journalist, but there were no jobs; he soon realised that music was all he could do, and that he had to stop playing so many instruments and learn one well: he had taken up 4-string banjo at school, now tackled the more difficult 5-string, eventually designing his own model, writing a manual on how to play it. He had witnessed his father's involvement in the Composers' Collective, a well-meaning attempt to write radical folk-songs according to political and musical theory, and rejected it: folk music is built on work that already exists. He assisted Alan LOMAX '39-40, appeared on Lomax's radio show; worked with a Vagabond Puppets music and theatre show mid-'39, performing for union meetings and radical groups, often narrowly escaping violence; formed Almanac Singers '40 with Lee Hays, Woody GUTHRIE, Millard Lampell; they toured to initial derision, then applause as they got meetings singing 'Which Side Are You On?', etc. Seeger was a member of the Communist Party, attended a few meetings, a premature anti-fascist like many others. He hated injustice and knew only one way to fight it; he sang for Communists because 'They were the hardest-working people.' He meant ordinary union members, not Party bosses, who were busy doing flip-flops: during the Hitler-Stalin pact of '39-40, pro-union, anti-fascist songs were suddenly not wanted. Seeger's politics were naive but honest; he quit the Party c.'51. The Almanacs recorded for Folkways but could not support themselves; WWII broke them up as Seeger went into the Army, Guthrie to the merchant marine. He was director of People's Songs Inc. '46, called concerts hootenannies, a word Seeger and Guthrie had discovered in Seattle before the war; supported Henry A. Wallace for President '48, went bankrupt '49; formed People's Artists late '49 with Lomax, Paul ROBESON, Irwin Silber (*b* 17 Oct. '25, NYC), others; it began publishing *Sing Out!* magazine '50. He formed a new quartet, the WEAVERS '48: a sudden huge success, with million-selling hits on Decca, but gigs vanished, Decca contract was not renewed as McCarthyism got under way: anonymous right-wing publications attacked them; informer Harvey Matusow called three of them Communists (Hays had 'quit'). Years later Matusow admitted making it all up, wrote book *False Witness*, got five years for perjury. Seeger, whose ancestors had fought injustice at Valley Forge, refused to testify before the House Un-American Activities Committee '55, using the Fifth Amendment; he was indicted for contempt and the case was thrown out by the United States Court of Appeals May '62; but the court merely instructed the government to prepare better documents in future and went out of its way to insult Seeger, who did not appear on network TV for 17 years, incl. ABC-TV *Hootenanny* show beginning early '63: it was like Birdland without Charlie PARKER as Joan BAEZ, Bob DYLAN, PETER, PAUL & MARY, many others refused to appear (the show also tried to turn down the Tarriers, an interracial group, but pressure was brought to bear; Seeger depped at their club gig so they could take time off for the show). Meanwhile the Weavers temporarily split up; Seeger recorded for Folkways from '53, sang in colleges and schools, on local radio and TV, slipping in and out of town before local witch-hunters found out, calling it 'cultural guerilla tactics'. He toured Britain for the second time '61; a Pete Seeger Committee there listed Ewan MACCOLL (Seeger's brother-in-law), Benjamin Britten, Doris Lessing and Sean O'Casey among its sponsors; eventually he toured the world: his great talent was getting people singing and feeling good about it, the Johnny Appleseed of music: in Moscow he got 10,000 non-English-speaking people doing four-part harmony to 'Michael, Row The Boat Ashore'. He signed with Columbia Records (CBS/USA) '61, though still not welcome on CBS-TV; promotion/distribution of the CBS records was not very good, though some are still selling; cover of Malvina REYNOLDS's 'Little Boxes' made Hot 100 '64, Billboard calling it a 'novelty'. He co-founded *Broadside* magazine '62 with Sis Cunningham (who had sung with the Almanacs); it published songs by Dylan, Phil OCHS, Tom PAXTON, Eric ANDERSEN, many more. He marched for civil rights at Selma, Ala. '65, same year neighbours in New York state tried to stop him singing at a local high school. Brokenhearted and angry when electric music was first played at a Newport Folk Festival '65 (by Paul BUTTERFIELD, Dylan), a year later he recorded *Waist Deep In The Big Muddy* backed by Danny Kalb's Blues Project. A long-time contributor to *Sing Out!*, he broke with Silber '67: against commercialism in folk music, Silber was co-owner of the largest folk-music publishing house, Oak Publications; he sold the magazine to its editorial board without mentioning its debts; when he criticised the Newport Festival '67, Seeger had had enough. He launched sloop *Clearwater* '69, built by volunteers to raise money to help clean up the filthy Hudson River; even the *Reader's Digest* donated. In '81 he sang at a benefit for the banned Polish trade union Solidarity, his first (long overdue) anti-Stalinist act. By then a whole generation had grown up with Pete Seeger as its music teacher. He co-wrote 'If I Had A Hammer' c.'49 with Hays, no publisher would then touch it; it was a top 10 hit by Peter, Paul & Mary '62, no. 3 by Trini LOPEZ '63, recorded by Perry COMO, Aretha FRANKLIN, Ray BARRETTO etc., is now heard on the muzak in the supermarket. He wrote or co-wrote 'Where Have All The Flowers Gone?' '56 (words from wartime Russian novel *And Quiet Flows The Don*), a hit by the KINGSTON TRIO '62, who copyrighted it at first because they didn't know who'd written it; 'Bells Of Rhymney' '59 (about Welsh coal towns, words by Idris Davies); 'Turn! Turn! Turn! (To Everything There Is A Season)' '62, words from *Ecclesiastes*, a hit by the BYRDS '65-6; 'Waist Deep In The Big Muddy' '69, entered the language as a reference to Vietnam; he discovered/adapted/popularised 'On Top Of Old Smokey', 'We Shall Overcome' (from Baptist hymn, '01), 'Guantanamera', 'Gotta Travel On', African songs 'Wimoweh' (aka 'The Lion Sleeps Tonight'), 'Abiyoyo'; much more. Good biography *How Can I Keep From Singing* '81 by David King Dunaway. More than 30 LPs on Folkways incl. instrumental *Goofing Off Suite*, five vols. of *American Favorite Ballads*, two of *At The Village Gate*, *American Industrial Ballads*, *Champlain Valley Songs*, *Sings Guthrie*, *Sings Leadbelly*, *Talking Union* (with Almanacs), *With Sonny Terry*, *Folk & Blues* with Big Bill BROONZY, etc. Columbia LPs incl. *The Bitter And The Sweet*, *We Shall Overcome* (live at Carnegie Hall; no. 42 hit album), *Children's Concert At Town Hall*, all '63; *Strangers And Cousins* and *I Can See A New Day* '65, *God Bless The Grass* and *Dangerous Songs!?* '66, *Waist Deep In*

The Big Muddy '67, *Pete Seeger Now* '68, *Young vs. Old* '71, *Rainbow Race* '73, 2-disc compilation *The World Of Pete Seeger* (incl. most of the songs mentioned above, others by Woody Guthrie, Dylan, Joni MITCHELL). Live 2-disc set with Arlo Guthrie *Together In Concert* '75 on Reprise. *See also* the WEAVERS.

SEEKERS, NEW SEEKERS Vocal, instrumental folk/pop group first formed in Australia by bassist Athol Guy (*b* 5 Jan. '40, Melbourne), guitarists Keith Potger (*b* 2 Mar. '41, Ceylon) and Bruce Woodley (*b* 25 July '42, Melbourne), lead singer Judith Durham (*b* 7 July '43). They went to England '64, gigged at Palladium in London with Dusty SPRINGFIELD, who wrote 'I'll Never Find Another You', no. 1 UK/4 USA '65. Other hits incl. 'A World Of Our Own', film theme 'Georgy Girl'; they split up '68. Potger re-formed as the New Seekers '69 with Eve Graham (*b* 13 Apr. '43, Perth, Scotland), Lyn Paul (*b* 16 Feb. '49) and Peter Doyle (*b* 28 July '49), both from Melbourne, plus Paul Layton (*b* 4 Aug. '47, Beaconsfield, England), Marty Kristian (*b* 27 May '47, Leipzig, Germany); they had hits '70-3 incl. Delaney Bramlett's 'Never Ending Song Of Love' (no. 2 UK), 'Look What They've Done To My Song, Ma' (aka 'What Have They ...') written by MELANIE Safka (top 50 UK, top 20 USA), 'I'd Like To Teach The World To Sing (In Perfect Harmony)' no. 1 UK/7 USA (Roger Cook/Roger Greenaway song), medley 'Pinball Wizard/See Me Feel Me' from the WHO's *Tommy*, UK hits continuing to '78.

SEELY, Jeannie (*b* Jeanne Marylin Seally, 6 July '40, Titusville, Pa.) Country singer, songwriter. Made debut on local radio in Meanville '51, later on Midwest Hayride '56; studied banking '59-61, but moved to West Coast, got writer's contract with Four Star Music '62, recorded for Challenge '63, appeared on Country Music Time TV in L.A. '63-5. Married songwriter Hank COCHRAN, moved to Nashville '66, recorded for Monument, wrote for Tree International Music; had no. 2 hit '66 and won Grammy with Cochran song 'Don't Touch Me', more top 20 hits 'It's Only Love', 'A Wanderin' Man', 'I'll Love You More' '66-7; linked with singer Jack GREENE '69, joined his show for almost ten years, switched to Decca and had duet hits with him incl. 'Wish I Didn't Have To Miss You' (no. 2 '69), others. She had top 10 solo hits with 'Can I Sleep In Your Arms' '73, 'Lucky Ladies' '74, 'He Can Be Mine' '75; recorded for Columbia '77 with less success, remained moderately successful as songwriter. LPs incl. *Little Things* and *Thanks Hank* '68 on Monument, *Jeannie Seely* '70 and *Please Be My New Love* '71 on Decca, *Two For The Show* '74 on MCA and *Live At The Grand Ole Opry* '78 on Pinnacle with Greene.

SEGER, Bob (*b* 6 May '45, Ann Arbor, Mich.) Rock singer, songwriter, bandleader. Played Detroit from '61, a local hero who could not make national breakthrough; he formed band the Last Heard '64 and 'Heavy Music' on Cameo-Parkway almost reached the Hot 100 '67 as the label folded. 'Ramblin' Gamblin' Man' '68 made top 20 on Capitol; he made LPs *Ramblin' Gamblin' Man, Noah, Mongrel, Brand New Morning* '69-71, quit to go to college, came back the same year with duo Teegarden and Van Winkle (Skip Knape and Dave Van Winkle) on their third LP *On Our Way*; they played on his *Smokin' O.P.s* '72, first of three on Palladium label (later reissued on Capitol). Seger's road band of this period (Dick Sims, keyboards; Jamie Oldaker, drums; Marcy Levy, vocals) went on to Eric CLAPTON. *Back In '72* '73, *Seven* '74 did little, though the former, partly made in Muscle Shoals and with J. J. CALE on some tracks, made top 200 LPs and critics loved it, latter yielded 'Get Out Of Denver', later covered by Dave EDMUNDS and EDDIE & THE HOT RODS; blistering 'Need Ya' pointed up vocal similarity to Rod STEWART at his rockiest. Back on Capitol for *Beautiful Loser* '75, incl. most of the musicians who'd worked on *Seven*, soon to be known as the Silver Bullet Band: Chris Campbell, bass; Drew Abbott, guitar; Charlie Allen Martin, drums; Rick Manasa on keyboards (replaced by Robyn Robbins), Alto Reed, sax. *Loser* had these on uptempo tracks, Muscle Shoals men on ballads. 2-disc *Live Bullet* '76, made in Detroit's Cobo Hall, made breakthrough into top 40 LPs, stayed in charts for 140 weeks, eventually selling a million, as have all subsequent albums. *Night Moves* '76 was

top 10 LP, title track a typical ballad and top 5 single, also stressing traditionalism in 'Rock And Roll Never Forgets', first of many songs extolling blue-collar rock: Bruce SPRINGSTEEN's contemporary breakthrough helped Seger's as they brought working-class rock to the masses. Martin was paralysed in a car crash, replaced by Teegarden. *Stranger In Town* '78 yielded ballad hit 'Still The Same' (top 5) and rockier 'Hollywood Nights' (no. 12); 'We've Got Tonight' (13) became MOR standard, covered by Sheena EASTON, Kenny ROGERS, etc. *Against The Wind* '80 saw EAGLES on backing vocals, critical praise (almost predictably) turn to charges of formulism as album went to no. 1, title track to no. 5, 'Fire Lake' to no. 6. GRAND FUNK keyboardist Craig Frost replaced Robbins; second live 2-disc set *Nine Tonight* '81 took title from his contribution to *Urban Cowboy* soundtrack '80, incl. no. 5 single 'Tryin' To Live My Life Without You'. *The Distance* '82 saw drop in ballad content, still no. 5 LP with no. 2 single in Rodney CROWELL's 'Shame On The Moon'; seasoned session players Waddy Wachtel on guitar, drummer Russ Kunkel took part as did Springsteen keyboardist Roy Bittan, while Grand Funk's Don Brewer joined the Bullet Band on drums. Seger came back after a long break with *Like A Rock* '86, backing vocals by the Weather Girls; for the first time he shared writing chores, with Frost. He has been remarkably consistent, success coming as the public caught up to him, rather than the reverse; surprisingly, after 14 top 40 singles in the USA '76-84, he hasn't had one in the UK, though that probably doesn't cause him to lose sleep.

SERENDIPITY SINGERS Vocal/folk outfit briefly popular in the wake of the similar NEW CHRISTY MINSTRELS, with a wide repertoire of folk, pop and show tunes, formed by U. of Colorado students Mike Brovsky, Brooks Hatch, Bryan Sennet, with guitarists Jon Arbenz and John Madden, bassist Bob Young, vocalists/musicians Diane Decker, Tommy Tieman, Lynne Weintraub. They were featured on TV's *Hootenanny*, had LPs on Philips '64-5 of which the first (eponymous) set reached no. 11, incl. top 10 hit 'Don't Let The Rain Come Down (Crooked Little Man)', a folk song written in '64.

SESSIONS, Ronnie (*b* 7 Dec. '48, Henrietta, Okla.) Country-rock singer. Grew up in Bakersfield, Cal. making first recordings for small Pike label '57, novelty rock'n'roll versions of 'Keep A'Knocking' and 'My Last Night In Town'. He was a regular on the Herb Henson *Trading Post* TV show for six years, continued on TV after high school on such shows as *The Melody Ranch*. He studied veterinary surgery, but began recording for small labels like Starview and Mosrite, gained regional hits with 'The Life Of Riley' and 'More Than Satisfied' on Gene AUTRY's Republic label '68. Moved to Nashville, signed as a writer with Tree Publishing '72, recorded for MGM, charted with 'Never Been To Spain' '72, minor hits 'Tossin' And Turnin' ' and 'She Feels So Good I Hate To Put Her Down' '72-3; switched to MCA for major hit 'Wiggle Wiggle' '76, followed by Bobby GOLDSBORO's 'Me And Millie', 'Ambush', last big hit 'Juliet And Romeo' '77-8. Dropped by MCA '80 and has hardly recorded since, but still recognised as a rewarding live act. LP *Ronnie Sessions* '77 MCA.

SEVERINSEN, Doc (*b* Carl H. Severinsen, 7 July '27, Arlington, Ore.) Trumpet. Began on cornet, won contests; turned pro as a teenager. Played with Charlie BARNET, Sam DONAHUE, Tommy DORSEY late '40s; an excellent technician and soloist, his studio work kept him from winning major fame: at NBC he was seen and heard on Steve ALLEN, other TV shows; worked for Skitch HENDERSON, then Milton DeLugg on the *Tonight* show with Johnny Carson, finally took over that studio band late '67. He moved to the West Coast May '72 with the Carson show, led a band in the '70s that often incl. Snooky Young (*b* 3 Feb. '19, Dayton, Ohio; played trumpet with Jimmie LUNCEFORD, Count BASIE '40s; Thad JONES-Mel LEWIS band '60s), Conte CANDOLI, Louie BELLSON, etc. He played as guest with symphony orchestras, was a brass clinician and consultant, played on big band LPs led by Stan GETZ, Bob BROOKMEYER, Gerry MULLIGAN, also raised quarter horses. His own LPs were poppish, several charting on Enoch LIGHT's Command label (*Best Of* now on MCA), on RCA with Henry MANCINI; also *Night*

Journey '76 on Epic. Long-awaited first *Tonight Show Band* album '86 on Amherst won a Grammy, followed by Vol. 2 '87 with Candoli, Bill PERKINS, Ernie Watts etc. Favourite horn player of many horn players, runs trumpet factory on West Coast, perhaps inspired by Chicago horn-maker Dave Monette (*see* Bobby SHEW).

SEVILLE, David (Ross Bagdasarian, *b* 27 Jan. '19, Fresno, Cal.; *d* 16 Jan. '72, Beverly Hills, Cal.) Composer, author, actor. A cousin of playwright William Saroyan, acted in his *The Time Of Your Life* for two years; they co-wrote 'Come On-A My House' while driving across New Mexico '39, used it in off-Broadway play *The Son* '50; it was first recorded by Kay Armen, then a big hit by Rosemary CLOONEY '51. He acted in films incl. Alfred Hitchcock's *Rear Window* '54; changed his name for work in recording studios: he composed and recorded minor hits, instrumental 'Armen's Theme' '56, novelties 'Gotta Get To Your House' and 'The Bird On My Head' '57-8; had no. 1 hit 'Witch Doctor' '58, suggested by book *Duel With The Witch Doctor*, created by recording at half speed, playing tape back at full speed. He next did it with voices: the Chipmunks, Alvin, Simon and Theodore, were named after chiefs at Liberty Records; Christmas novelty 'The Chipmunk Song' late '58 sold 3.5 million copies in five weeks. There were more hits, mostly seasonal; total Chipmunk sales in '70 were more than 30 million; there were four chart LPs '59-64 incl. *The Chipmunks Sing The Beatles Hits*; Bagdasarian's son revived the idea for more hit LPs '80-2 incl. *Chipmunk Punk*.

SEX PISTOLS UK punk band formed '75. Lineup: Johnny Rotten (*b* John Lydon, 31 Jan. '56), vocals; Steve Jones (*b* 3 May '55), guitar; Glen Matlock (*b* 27 Aug. '56), bass; Paul Cook (*b* 27 July '56), drums. Matlock was replaced '77 by Sid Vicious (*b* John Simon Ritchie, 10 May '57; *d* 2 Feb. '79 NYC of a heroin overdose). Formed by boutique owner and entrepreneur Malcolm McLaren. Cook, Matlock and Jones were customers/employees at boutique, formed even more primitive informal group called Swankers with various vocalists; McLaren agreed to manage them; Rotten recruited with no experience for ability to sneer and pose. Made no bones about musical shortcomings; object was to make rock'n'roll dangerous again. Built a following; signed with EMI, planned to headline punk UK tour; obnoxious on TV interview show (though provoked) and tour dates were cancelled amid extensive media coverage; first single 'Anarchy In The UK' a hit late '76 but EMI cancelled contract; A&M signed them but cancelled contract in a week owing to more obnoxious behaviour; signed by Virgin. 'God Save The Queen' released week of Queen Elizabeth II's Silver Jubilee celebrations June '77, banned by BBC, made no. 2 in charts. Six more made top 10 incl. 'Pretty Vacant' and 'Holidays In The Sun' both '77; debut album *Never Mind The Bollocks – Here's The Sex Pistols* topped UK chart late '77. Worked on film *The Great Rock'n'Roll Swindle* '78; on USA tour Rotten (disagreeing violently with McLaren) left, changed name back to Lydon and formed PUBLIC IMAGE LTD. Trio completed film, recorded new material with Vicious as vocalist ('My Way', 'Something Else', 'C'mon Everybody', 'Silly Thing' – all UK top 10 hits), also recorded track and additional film footage with Ronnie Biggs, escaped train robber (*No One is Innocent*). Recruited new singers (Jimmy Pursey, Tenpole Tudor) but group collapsed. Paved the way for CLASH, the DAMNED; compilation albums and film soundtrack also released.

SEXTON, Charlie (*b* '68, San Antonio, Texas) USA guitarist, keyboards, vocalist, prodigy of mid-'80s. Allegedly played first professional gig at age 11, then deputised for guitarist in Joe ELY band at 13, subsequently recording with Bob DYLAN, Don Henley (LP *Building The Perfect Beast*), ROLLING STONES Keith Richards and Ron Wood (on film soundtrack *Easy Street*). Signed to MCA; debut LP *Pictures For Pleasure* late '85 made top 20 LPs '86. Bringing to mind melange of Tom PETTY, Bruce SPRINGSTEEN, John MELLENCAMP, with his talent seems destined for major stardom if he survives hype of genesis.

SHADOW, Mighty (*b* Winston Bailey, late '30s) Calypsonian and soca artist, usually referred to as Shadow. Grew up on grand-father's farm, began composing at 9, at 16 joined group Fire Sticks that provided backing vocals at Mighty SPARROW tent, appeared solo there '70 but forgot his lines. Debut '71 at Victory tent led by Lord Blaikie (Carlton Joseph), recorded 'The Threat' that year (directed at Sparrow and Lord KITCHENER); moved '73 to Kitchener's tent for three seasons. He has a propensity for the eccentric with a touch of eeriness; in early performances he wore dark clothing with broad-brimmed hat and regal cape, but no longer adheres rigidly to that image; his calypsoes tell of bizarre, sometimes violent events in an unmistakable raspy voice, interspersed with tremulous humming. Two of his calypsoes, 'Obeah Ma Man' and 'Run Du-Du', were incl. in album *Calypso In Rage* '73 on Strakers. He won first and second places in the Road March contest '74 (*see* CALYPSO) with 'Bass Man' and 'Ah Come Out To Play', breaking the stranglehold on the title held for 11 years by Kitchener and Sparrow (both incl. in LP *Bass Man* '74 on Strakers), as well as autobiographical 'Winston'. He reached Calypso Monarch final '74, but despite having the crowd eating out of his hand with 'Bass Man', was pipped by Sparrow. 'King From Hell' and 'Rap To Me' from *King From Hell* '75 got him into Calypso Monarch final; moved to Sparrow's tent '76 and released *Constant Jammin'*: title track and 'Shift Yuh Carcass' got him into Monarch final again; LP also incl. 'Pressure'. During the off-season (i.e., after carnival) he released *The Flipside Of Shadow*; in '77 *Dreadness*, incl. 'Jump, Judges, Jump' an attack on the judges of the Calypso Monarch contest, concluding that they had 'degrees in stupidity'. In '77 off-season came 12" single 'Shadow Thing' on Charlies. He moved to the Kingdom of the Wizards calypso tent '78; *De Zessman* incl. road march contender 'Sugar Plum'. He appeared with Calypso ROSE in *Bacchanal Time* '78, composing and performing title track in film, soundtrack LP and a single. From '79 he headed his own Masters Den tent; *If I Coulda, I Woulda, I Shoulda* '79 is probably his best album, incl. 'Dat Soca Boat' (about encounter with a calypsonian who challenged his reputation, threatened him with violence), 'Through The Mirror' (about his self-image), 'Jumbies', 'Dread

Wizard'. Off-season '79 brought single 'Evolution – Part One And Two'. Title track *Doh Mess Wid Meh Head* '80 expressed feeling that he was rejected by Calypso Monarch judges and others in authority because he came from the ghetto; off-season album *Shadow Wake Up* '80 incl. hit 'Charlane' also incl. on *Music Fever* '81, the top selling LP during carnival season that year; also issued 12″ single 'Yesterday Was Yesterday'/'Freedom Street'. *Return Of The Shadow* '82 ended years on Charlies; he went back to Strakers with *Going Off* '83, incl. 'Ah Come Out To Party'; in film of '83 carnival commissioned by UK's Channel 4 he performed title track and 'Pirates'. *Return Of De Bassman* '84 incl. 'Snakes', about Trinidad's ruling party; made UK debut '84. His next two LPs dropped horns from the instrumentation: *Sweet Sweet Dreams* '84 off-season on Kalico and *Mystical Roots* '85 on MRS (one of his poorest sellers). He was featured in TV film *Kaiso* '85, also from Channel 4; *Better Than Ever* '86 on Charlies had him back on form, with horns on most tracks. Despite his popularity he never did win Monarch, and no longer competes; did not head a tent '86 but performed with Spektakula tent; appeared at Socalypso '86 in London. Belatedly organised Master's Den tent '87, but it closed before the end of carnival season because of poor business; '87 LP was *Raw Energy* on B's Records, incl. 'Janette' and 'Ah Hearing Pan'.

SHADOWS, The UK instrumental rock group. Original lineup: Hank Marvin (*b* Brian Rankin, 28 Oct. '41, Newcastle), lead guitar; Bruce Welch (*b* 2 Nov. '41, Newcastle), rhythm guitar; Jet Harris (*b* Terry Harris, 6 July '39, London), bass; Tony Meehan (*b* 2 Mar. '43, London), drums. The most influential UK group of its kind late '50s-early '60s, turning a whole generation onto homegrown rock'n'roll; trademarks were gleaming red Fender Stratocasters and the 'Shadows Step', a silly three-step onstage movement; worldwide admirers incl. teenaged Neil YOUNG in Toronto. Marvin and Welch came to London '58, played as duo at legendary Two I's coffee bar in Soho, formed the Drifters with Ian Samwell, who wrote Cliff RICHARD's first hit, 'Move It', to accompany Richard on his first tour; soon changed name to avoid confusion with the famous vocal group. On the tour, Mickie MOST was singing in the Most Brothers; Morris and Meehan quit his backing group to join Shadows. They made three flop singles, no. 1 hit 'Apache' '60 (Danish guitarist Jorgen Ingmann had the no. 2 hit USA '62; the Shadows had no USA hits because room for instrumentals in rock'n'roll was always limited: USA had the VENTURES, Duane EDDY); they had four UK no. ones '61-3 ('Kon Tiki', 'Wonderful Land', 'Dance On', 'Foot Tapper'), plus seven other top 10 hits. Meehan quit '61, replaced by Brian Bennett (worked with Marty WILDE, Joe BROWN); Harris quit '62, had solo hit 'The Man With The Golden Arm', teamed with Meehan for duo hit 'Diamonds' (no. 1 '63), top 5 hits same year. Brian 'Liquorice' Locking joined '62-3, replaced by John Rostill. They backed Richard on all his hits, appeared with him in films *The Young Ones, Summer Holiday, Wonderful Life* '62-4; albums incl. *The Shadows, Out Of The Shadows, Dance With The Shadows, The Sound Of The Shadows* '62-5. After the BEATLES the Shadows seemed anachronistic, split '68. Marvin, Welch and bassist John Farrar released *Marvin, Welch & Farrar* '71; Welch worked with protégée Olivia NEWTON-JOHN. Harris was badly injured in car crash '65; comeback attempts incl. *Remembering* '76; he was seen in rock'n'roll revival shows in London '86. The Shadows came back with *Rockin' With Curly Leads* '73, incl. covers of hits by the WHO and the BEACH BOYS; they were UK entrants in Eurovision Song Contest '75, uncharacteristically singing 'Let Me Be The One', incl. on *Specs Appeal*. TV-promoted *The Shadows: 20 Golden Greats* '77 was surprise no. 1 LP; tours delighted with the Shadows Step, note-for-note renditions of hits; they had top 5 hits '78-9 'Don't Cry For Me Argentina', theme from film *The Deer Hunter*; *String Of Hits* '79 was no. 1, *Another String Of Hits* '80 top 20; *Change Of Address, Hits Right Up Your Street* '80-1 top 20; *Live In The Jungle/Live At Abbey Road* and *XXV* did less well; *Guardian Angel* just made top 100 LPs; *Moonlight Shadows* '86 went top 10 more than 25 years after first hit; *Out Of The Shadows* '87 was compilation from early '70s. UK catalogues still list a page of albums. Marvin also sang occasionally, incl. duets with Richard;

played in Paul MCCARTNEY's Rockestra. *The Shadows* by Mike Read tells their story.

SHADOWS OF KNIGHT Garage/punk band formed '66 in Chicago: Jim Sohns, vocals; Joe Kelley, lead guitar; Jerry McGeorge, rhythm guitar; Warren Rogers, bass; Tom Schiffour, drums; studio guest 'The Hawk' on keyboards were among the most endearing of the genre: amateurs who rehearsed in garages, mostly sacrificing finesse for volume. They signed to Dunwich (Atlantic subsidiary), had four Hot 100 entries '66: 'Gloria' was no. 10 copy of Van MORRISON's now-classic B-side with Them; 'Oh Yeah' made the top 40; by '68 they were on the Kasenetz-Katz subsidiary Team label for top 50 'Shake', though Sohns was the only original member. Reissues are on UK Radar and Edsel labels.

SHA NA NA Rock'n'roll revival group formed '69 at Columbia U., led by John 'Bowzer' Baumann (piano); previous incarnations were known as Eddie and the Evergreens, the Dirty Dozen. Vocalists were Scott Powell, Johnny Contardo, Frederick Dennis Greene, Don York, Rich Joffe; guitarists Chris Donald, Elliot Cahn; bassist Bruce Clarke, second piano Screamin' Scott Simon, drummer Jocko Marcellino, Lennie Baker on sax (their link to the Golden Age: he played with DANNY AND THE JUNIORS). They stole the show at Woodstock '69, featured in film; live act with humour and choreography was more popular than records. Seven LPs charted on Kama Sutra '69-75; first *Rock & Roll Is Here To Stay!* incl. some originals; from then on they concentrated on oldies, aping Elvis PRESLEY, Eddie COCHRAN, Gene VINCENT styles and songs or crooning together in Marcels vocal group style. Live *The Golden Age Of Rock'n'Roll* '73 was far the best seller, reaching top 40 LPs USA (a K-Tel TV album in UK). Vinnie Taylor replaced Donald '70, died of heroin Apr. '74, replaced by Elliott Randall; Cahn and Joffe left; Chico Ryan replaced Clarke; guitarist Henry Gross passed through en route to solo career; they had TV show from '77; their goodtime UK counterparts were SHOWADDYWADDY. Simon had solo LP *Transmissions From Outer Space* '82; Gross made seven LPs '72-81 incl. *Plug Me Into*

Something '75 on A&M, *Release* '76 on Lifesong (incl. no. 6 hit 'Shannon').

SHANGRI-LAS, The Female vocal quartet with 11 hits '64-6, a milestone in pop both for musical content and visual presentation: lead vocalist Betty Weiss, sister Mary Weiss, twins Marge and Mary Ann Ganser. Only three tended to appear at gigs, the identity of the missing member changing from time to time, allegedly due to bad habits; their image combined cheerleaders with biker's molls, a not-so-virgin queen with streetwise ladies-in-waiting: a vocal style still being parodied two decades later was combined with the imagination of renegade producer George 'Shadow' MORTON. He conceived 'Remember (Walkin' In The Sand)' when the girls were still in high school in Queens, NY; took demo to Artie Ripp of Kama Sutra Productions, who played it for Jeff BARRY and Ellie Greenwich, who helped Morton with the production, which was leased to LEIBER & STOLLER's Red Bird Records, complete with dubbed seagulls crying: it was no. 5 hit '64 (top 20 UK), followed by no. 1 'Leader Of The Pack', with dubbed-in revving motorcycles and a horrific crash at the end; it charted four times in UK: top 20 '65, top 3 '72, top 10 twice in '76 (and was sent up as 'Leader of the Laundramat' by the Detergents in USA '64). No more hits in UK; top 20 'Give Him A Great Big Kiss' had smooching noise, 'Give Us Your Blessing' was more sedate in top 30, 'I Can Never Go Home Anymore' '65 was their last top 10, 'Long Live Our Love' the last top 40. 'Past, Present And Future' was top 60 '66, described as 'spoken word' by Billboard, 'one of the most mysterious and moving tracks in all of pop' by critic Richard Williams, as one of his favourite ten discs by Pete Townshend. Red Bird label folded; the girls drifted to Mercury but had no more hits; rumours persist that they made 'What's Wrong With Ringo?' as the Bon Bons, 'Wishing Well' on obscure Spokane label as the Shangri-Las, Morton-produced 'Only Seventeen' as the Beatlettes on Jubilee. Nothing came of '70s reunion rumours.

SHANK, Bud (*b* Clifford Everett Shank Jr, 27 May '26, Dayton, Ohio) Alto sax, flute; also baritone sax, composer. Began on clarinet at 10, attended U. of N.C., went to West Coast '47 and studied with Shorty ROGERS. Played with Charlie BARNET, Alvino REY, Art MOONEY, Stan KENTON etc.; became a regular at Howard RUMSEY's Lighthouse in Hermosa Beach and a mainstay of '50s West Coast jazz. Toured Europe with Bob COOPER '50s, recorded as sideman with Lighthouse All Stars, Kenton, Cooper, Rogers, Jimmy GIUFFRE, Shelly MANNE, Chet BAKER, Laurindo ALMEIDA, Gerry MULLIGAN, Gerald WILSON, Julie LONDON, and many more; moved into studio work '60s incl. film scores *Slippery When Wet* '59, *Barefoot Adventure* '61, *War Hunt* '62; played solo spots in soundtracks incl. *Assault On A Queen* '66, *The Thomas Crown Affair* '68, *Summer Of '42* '71, etc. Played concerts and clinics at colleges. He led quartet in L.A. clubs '50s: *Live At The Haig* '56 on Choice, Bainbridge, Concept labels with pianist Claude Williamson (*b* 18 Nov. '26, Brattleboro, Vt.) on piano was an early stereo recording; he continued to gig alongside studio work; nearly 30 albums as leader on World Pacific/Pacific Jazz '54-70 were mostly small-group sets, always with excellent sidemen, incl. LPs of pop songs '66-7: *Michelle*, with Baker on flugelhorn, arr. by Bob Florence was no. 56 in pop LP chart. He also made *Brazil* '65 on Capitol with Sergio MENDES. With studio work to keep him busy and presumably bored with playing pop songs and film themes, he took a break from prolific recording until the small-group scene revived, then co-formed L.A. Four '74 with Manne, Almeida and Ray BROWN (LPs on Concord Jazz, some with Jeff Hamilton on drums), began recording again as leader, all but abandoning the flute and re-emerging as the first-class player he was all along, but with a more powerful and personal style. *Sunshine Express* '76, *Heritage* '78, *Crystal Comments* '79, *Explorations 1980* on Concord Jazz, all except the first with pianist/composer Bill Mays, the last a duo with Shank and Mays playing Mays's suite for flute and piano, also pieces by Bach, Ravel, Debussy, Scriabin; *Brazilville* '81 on Concord with Charlie BYRD; *Shades Of Dring* '81 on Cambria, chamber jazz arr. by Lennie NIEHAUS played by Manne, Brown, Leigh Kaplan on piano, second reedman Bill PERKINS; *This Bud's For You* '84 on Muse,

with Ron CARTER, Kenny Barron, Al Foster on drums; *California Concert* '85 (quintet set with Rogers), *At Jazz Alley* '86 a quartet, both on Contemporary.

SHANKAR, Lakshminarayana (*b* 26 Apr. '50, Madras, India) Violinist. Began singing ragas at age 2; violin lessons from his father (a noted musician) at 5. Went to the USA '69 to study and to pursue a pan-cultural synthesis; took Ph.D. in ethnomusicology at Wesleyan U.; from '73 he and John McLAUGHLIN studied each other's music, co-founding Shakti and co-writing for it (*see* entry for McLaughlin) '75-8. He plays a ten-string, double-necked violin of his own design; plays part of the year in India, where he is a best-selling classical musician; has recorded with Frank ZAPPA, Peter GABRIEL, Phil COLLINS. Albums incl. *Touch Me There* '79 on Philips; *Who's To Know* '80 (Indian classical quartet), *Vision* '83 with Jan Garbarek and Palle MIKKELBORG, *Song For Everyone* '84 with Garbarek, *The Epidemics* '86 with Caroline, all on ECM.

SHANKAR, Ravi (*b* '20, Benares, India) Sitar, composer/player of Indian classical music, a best-selling artist in India. He worked in Indian radio '49-56, went to the USA and was res. lecturer at U. of Cal. '64, City College of NY '67; when BEATLE George HARRISON played sitar on 'Norwegian Wood' '65, his teacher had been Shankar. The sitar became a fad in rock; Shankar played at Woodstock '69 (not in film), at George Harrison's *Concert For Bangla Desh* '71; as the sitar in rock became associated with drugs in the public mind, Shankar gracefully withdrew from that scene. Albums incl. *The Sounds Of India* and *The Genius Of Ravi Shankar* on Columbia USA; *Live At Monterey* '67 on Bainbridge; 2-disc *Ragas* on Fantasy with Ali Akbar Khan.

SHANNON, Del (*b* Charles Westover, 30 Dec. '39, Coopersville, Mich.) Rock'n'roll singer/songwriter infl. by Hank WILLIAMS. Played and sang in local clubs, working in a carpet store days; falsetto first came to notice on 'Runaway' (no. 1 USA/UK '61), aided by a nagging riff on the Musitron (forerunner of the synthesiser): it was one of the most distinctive records of its era. His only other top tens were 'Hats Off To Larry' the same year, 'Keep Searchin' (We'll Follow The Sun)' '64, but he had 16 Hot 100 chart entries '61-6; he was influential and also popular in UK, where he had eight top tens. On a UK tour '63 he met the BEATLES and was the first USA artist to cover a Beatle song ('From Me To You'). *Little Town Flirt* '63 was no. 12 LP, an above average pop album of the period; he displayed his musical roots in *Del Shannon Sings Hank Williams* '65. He was one of the few of his era to write and record his own songs, collecting royalties on 200 cover versions of 'Runaway'. He made an album in London '67 with Andrew Loog Oldham, never released; oversaw his friend Brian HYLAND's comeback, prod. 'Gypsy Woman', a USA no. 3; *Del Shannon Live In England* '72 is a fine live set, demonstrates inimitable yodel. He worked with ELECTRIC LIGHT ORCHESTRA's Jeff Lynne '73, made single 'And The Music Plays On' '74 with Dave EDMUNDS and Nick LOWE; album *Drop Down And Get Me* '83 prod. by Tom PETTY reached LP chart in USA, single 'Sea Of Love' made top 40; also incl. cover of ROLLING STONES' 'Out Of Time' and his own 'Sucker For Your Love'. *Runaway Hits* '83 was definitive compilation; *I Go To Pieces* '86 collected his rarest work from the '60s, incl. title track which had been covered by PETER & GORDON, Nils LOFGREN.

SHAPIRO, Helen (*b* 28 Sept. '46, Bethnal Green, London) Singer, actress. Called 'Foghorn' at school because of masculine voice, she took singing lessons from a onetime big-band drummer, made debut single for EMI at 14, went straight into top 10 with 'Please Don't Treat Me Like A Child', then no. 1 hits 'You Don't Know', 'Walkin' Back To Happiness', no. 2 'Tell Me What He Said', top 10 'Little Miss Lonely' (all '61-3): a bouffant-haired teen queen of pop, she starred in Richard Lester film *It's Trad, Dad* and Michael Winner's *Play It Cool* '62, but it soon ended: 'Fever' '64 was last top 40. She label-hopped; records pleased fans but found not enough buyers. She worked clubs; on verge of retirement '78 was asked to appear in show *The French Have A Song For It*, then a prod. of *How To Succeed In Business Without Really Trying*, then to critical acclaim in revival of Lionel BART's *Oliver!*, playing Nancy; has since mixed club dates, concerts, stage work. Album of evergreens *Straighten Up And Fly Right* on Oval '83, same year EMI reissued set of earlier albums, *Tops With Me* and *Helen Hits Out*. Moved increasingly towards jazz, gigging with Humphrey LYTTELTON, George MELLY; LP *The Quality Of Mercer* '87 produced by Lyttelton on his Calligraph label, songs of Johnny MERCER.

SHARKEY, Feargal (*b* 13 Aug. '58, Londonderry, Northern Ireland) Rock singer. Began with pop band the Undertones, formed in Derry '77 with John and Damian O'Neill on guitars, Michael Bradley on bass, drummer Billy Doherty. John PEEL championed them in UK, helped make 'Teenage Kicks' a minor hit '78: appeal was their ingenuousness and naivety; during punks' overtly political, nihilistic thrust they were quintessential pop band. Album *The Undertones* '79 incl. 'Jimmy Jimmy' and 'Here Comes The Summer', emphasising O'Neills' songwriting and Sharkey's appealing, quavery vocals; *Hypnotised* '80 incl. biggest hit, 'My Perfect Cousin' (no. 9 UK), threatened to typecast forever-young image; *Positive Touch* '81 displayed more maturity with 'Julie Ocean', 'Forever Paradise', 'It's Going To Happen', but fans/critics seemed to want them to remain perpetual teenagers. *The Sin Of Pride* '83 was confident, but dissension in band, disillusion with UK music scene saw them split '83; *All Wrapped Up* '83 was a good compilation; '79 radio *Peel Session* issued on 12" single '86. Sharkey worked with Vince CLARKE in Assembly (no. 4 UK hit '83 with 'Never Never'), had solo top 30 hit '84 with funky 'Listen To Your Father'; debut solo LP *Feargal Sharkey* '85 on Virgin sold two million copies around the world (compared to total Undertones sales of perhaps 250,000), incl. no. 1 UK hit with Lone Justice song 'A Good Heart', effective cover of Percy SLEDGE's 'When A Man Loves A Woman'. He worked with Dave Stewart of the EURYTHMICS, appeared in Bob DYLAN videos '85; he has one of rock's identifiable voices: second LP *Wish* recorded '87 for early '88 release incl. single 'More Love' with guest Keith Richards on guitar. The

O'Neills formed That Petrol Emotion, made singles 'Keen' and 'V2' '85, energetic and well-received *Manic Pop Thrill* '86.

SHARP, Cecil James (*b* 22 Nov. 1859, London; *d* there 28 June '24) English folk music collector, editor. Educated at Cambridge, worked in Australia; taught in England 1892-6, principal of Hampstead Conservatory '96-05. Saw the Headington Morris dancers acc. by William Kimber Jr on concertina '99; heard vicarage gardener John England sing 'The Seeds Of Love' '03; began collecting with missionary zeal: first publication was *Folk Songs From Somerset* in five parts '04-9, first three co-credited to Charles Marsh; *Songs Of The West* '05 and *English Folk-Songs For Schools* co-edited with Rev. Sabine Baring-Gould. He was prime mover in founding of English Folk Dance and Song Society '11, successor of Folk Song Society of 1898; EFDSS HQ in Regent's Park is called Cecil Sharp House. He contributed songs and dances to Granville Barker's London prod. of *Midsummer Night's Dream* '14; visited USA several times collecting Anglo-American ballads; he was accompanied '16-18 by amanuensis Maud Karpeles (*b* 12 Nov. 1885, London; *d* there 1 Oct. '76); she'd met him '09 in Stratford-on-Avon, where he taught at a summer school; she also accompanied Barker to NYC for prod. of *Midsummer*. His *English Folk Song: Some Conclusions* '07 was the first major treatise on the subject; she edited fourth edition '65. Work based on field trips incl. *English Folk Songs From The Southern Appalachians* and *Nursery Songs From The Appalachian Mountains* '17-23. Unlike Francis James CHILD and other early ballad collectors, Sharp was the first to write down the tunes as well as the words. Hearing about Appalachia from Oliver Campbell, an American who began collecting '08, he thought that some of the songs he and Karpeles collected were earlier, more authentic versions of those he'd found in England; but whereas the dying Lord Randall bequeathed to his father his lands and houses, Jimmy Randall left his mules and wagons. They had become the songs of the hillbillies ('our contemporary ancestors', as the *Atlantic Monthly* called them in 1899; see also COUNTRY MUSIC). An example of continuity in folk is the Ritchie family:

Sharp collected songs from them '17; John and Alan LOMAX recorded them '30s for the LoC; Jean RITCHIE, unborn at the time of Sharp's visit, became leading figure in postwar USA folk revival. Sharp worked more and more in education, which he regarded as vital; collaborated with illustrator A. P. Oppé on *The Dance: An Historical Survey Of Dancing In Europe*, published after his death. Karpeles worked with Ralph Vaughan Williams as adviser to Douglas Kennedy, dir. of EFDSS; wrote biography *Cecil Sharp* '33 with A. H. Fox Strangways (revised edition '67 under her name alone). *The Crystal Spring: English Folk Songs Collected By Cecil Sharp* '87 from Oxford U. Press was edited by her. His significance lies not only in research but in impetus he gave to wider appreciation of folk music; his disquisition also lived on in the work of Vaughan Williams, Gustav Holst, Percy Grainger and George Butterworth, who tapped a rich vein of trad. music as English composers of formal music developed their 20th-century style.

SHAVER, Billy Joe (*b* 15 Sep. '41, Corsicana, Texas) Country singer/songwriter. Family moved to Waco, Texas '53; he worked as a bronc buster, in a sawmill (losing two fingers in an accident), served in US Navy, made his first trip to Nashville with songs early '60s: several trips later he signed as a writer with Bobby BARE's Return Music; Kris KRISTOFFERSON recorded his 'Good Christian Soldier' '71; soon had other songs recorded by Tom T. HALL, Jan HOWARD, Dottie WEST, Jerry Lee LEWIS. He recorded for Mercury '72, then Monument (Kristofferson prod. album *Old Five And Dimers Like Me* '74), Capricorn (*When I Get My Wings* '76, *Gypsy Boy* '77), CBS (*I'm Just An Old Chunk Of Coal* '81): his coarse, grating voice was ideal for his songs, but not for smooth country radio, which didn't play his records, although he achieved some prominence in the Outlaw movement mid-'70s with discerning fans, and is regarded by many as one of the best songwriters working today. In recent years other songs were recorded by Johnny CASH, Conway TWITTY, George JONES; title track of the Columbia album was a no. 1 hit for John ANDERSON. *Salt Of The Earth* '87 on CBS could be a compilation of unreleased tracks, but all his own songs: fans will be pleased.

SHAVERS, Charlie (*b* Charles James Shavers, 3 Aug. '17, NYC; *d* 8 July '71, NYC) Trumpet, composer. Father played trumpet; he was a distant relative of Fats NAVARRO, began on piano and banjo; played with Tiny BRADSHAW, Lucky MILLINDER; became famous with the John KIRBY sextet '37-44 as an ideally pretty and imaginative voice in 'the biggest little band in the land' and as composer of 'Pastel Blue', 'Undecided' (with words by Sid Robin, the latter a hit by Ella FITZGERALD with Chick WEBB '39, the AMES Bros. '51, Benny GOODMAN Sextet version early '50s, etc.). One of the most popular and original stylists of the Swing Era, he later played with Tommy DORSEY, co-led a sextet with Terry Gibbs and Louie BELLSON, toured with JATP, with Dorsey ghost band dir. by Sam DONAHUE, stayed with it and was featured as a vocalist on world tours when its name changed to the Frank SINATRA Jr Show. Also recorded with Coleman HAWKINS on Prestige, Bellson, Goodman, Georgie AULD, Charlie VENTURA, Lionel HAMPTON, many others; own LPs '50s on MGM, Bethlehem (*The Complete Charlie Shavers*), Capitol (*Excitement Unlimited*).

SHAW, Artie (*b* Arthur Arshawsky, 23 May '10, NYC) Clarinettist, bandleader, composer. Worked for Irving AARONSON, Red NICHOLS, Vincent Lopez, Roger Wolfe KAHN; was among the most successful freelancers in the business, quit music, came back mid-'35 playing one of his own compositions with a string quartet at a swing concert; formed short-lived band with brass, rhythm, only one saxophone (Tony PASTOR); then another with conventional swing era instrumentation: after half a dozen top 20 hits came 'Indian Love Call' (with novelty vocal by Pastor) backed with Cole PORTER's 'Begin The Beguine' '38; the first was a top 10 hit, 'Beguine' intended to be the B side, but it was no. 1 for six weeks, made him world famous (the Billy COTTON record in the UK copied the Jerry Gray arrangement). From then on there were fierce arguments between fans of Shaw and Benny GOODMAN over which was King of Swing: Shaw had a woody, prettier tone,

more musical flexibility and curiosity; who was the better jazz soloist is still an argument better left unopened. Georgie AULD and Buddy RICH joined '39; mercurial, strong-minded and critical of the music business, Shaw quit at the height of success late '39, not for the last time; went to Mexico but came back '40-1, new band recorded Mexican song 'Frenesi', arr. by composer William Grant Still (*b* 11 May 1895, Woodville, Ms.; *d* 3 Dec. '78, L.A., Cal.), used conventional 15-piece band plus French horn, oboe, bass clarinet, 13 strings: it was no. 1 for 13 weeks '41. Band-within-a-band the Gramercy Five had Billy BUTTERFIELD on trumpet (later Roy ELDRIDGE), Nick Fatool on drums, Johnny GUARNIERI on harpsichord: 'Summit Ridge Drive' was top 10 '41. He led a US Navy band '43-4; revived the small group early '50s (last chart hit with 'My Little Nest Of Heavenly Blue' '52 with Connee BOSWELL on Decca). He made good oft-repeated threat to quit music entirely: was a farmer, moved to Spain and became translator, became a theatrical producer, published novel *I Love You, I Hate You, Drop Dead!* '65; formed new 16-piece band '83, fronting it at NYC's Blue Note, not playing himself. Married eight times, wives incl. Lana Turner, Ava Gardner, Kathleen Winsor (novelist famous for bodice-ripper *Forever Amber*); he wrote in his autobiography *The Trouble With Cinderella* that he married often because in those days 'we weren't allowed to shack up'. Over 50 hits '36-52 incl. reissues during musicians' union strikes '42-4; '38-9 hits incl. famous instrumentals 'Back Bay Shuffle' and 'Traffic Jam' (featuring Rich); 'Nightmare' (band's theme, a Shaw composition); 'The Blues' from Still's *Lenox Avenue Suite*; 'They Say' and 'Thanks For Ev'rything' (vocals by Helen Forrest), both no. 1; an Artie Shaw album of four 78s (none of the eight sides also single hits) was no. 12 in singles market (says *Pop Memories*; see CHARTS). '41-2 saw hits 'Stardust' (arr. by Lennie HAYTON; opened with a solo by Butterfield, had solos by Shaw, trombonist Jack Jenny), 'Dancing In The Dark' and 'Concerto For Clarinet' (top 10 hits, the latter a Shaw composition on a two-sided 12" 78), 'Blues In The Night' and 'St James' Infirmary' had vocals, trumpet by Hot Lips PAGE. '45-6 hits incl. 'Accent-tchu-ate The

Positive' (Oscar-winning Johnny MERCER tune had Eldridge on trumpet, Barney KESSEL on guitar, vocal by Imogene Lynn), 'I Got The Sun In The Morning' (vocal by Mel TORMÉ), 'My Heart Belongs To Daddy' (Kitty KALLEN). Shaw also had top 10 hit playing 'I'm Forever Blowing Bubbles' '50 with Gordon JENKINS. With Goodman he was one of the first white bandleaders to hire blacks; Billie HOLIDAY toured with him and recorded 'Any Old Time' at the same session that recorded 'Begin The Beguine': it was issued but had to be withdrawn because she was under contract to another label. In a Billboard DJ poll '56, Shaw's 'Stardust' was named all-time favourite record (Glenn MILLER's was no. 4), 'Begin The Beguine' no. 3, 'Summit Ridge Drive' no. 8, 'Frenesi' no. 15, 'Dancing In The Dark' no. 25. Six 2-disc sets on Bluebird (RCA) in USA have the complete Artie Shaw '38-45, another is a selection from those years; other compilations on RCA, MCA, Musicraft, Hindsight, Sunbeam etc. The Gramercy Five tracks were compiled on a budget CD in '88.

SHAW, Robert (*b* '16, Red Bluff, Cal.) Conductor; advanced the art of choral singing in the USA, agreeing with composer Paul Hindemith that the highest degree of musical expression was *a cappella* singing in 15th-16th centuries. His mother was gospel singer Nellie Lawson; he was dir. of Fred WARING Glee Clubs '38-45, conducted premiere of cantata *The Prairie* '44 by Lukas Foss with his Collegiate Singers, formed Robert Shaw Chorale '48: choral music by Poulenc, Ravel, Debussy was almost unknown in the USA; now it is sung in high schools. Worked with conductors Koussevitsky, Toscanini (legendary recording of Beethoven's Ninth), George Szell; recorded for RCA: Xmas LP '57, *Deep River And Other Spirituals* '59, *This Is My Country* '63 were pop hits; *Sea Shanties*, *Yours Is My Heart Alone* etc. still in print mid-'80s. Commissioned music by Bartók, Copland, Britten, Milhaud, others; folded Chorale '67 when he became mus. dir. of the Atlanta Symphony Orchestra and Chorus, raising obscure band to major secondrank status; left '87 for academia. Plans to start music festival and art school in south of France.

SHAW, Sandie (*b* Sandra Goodrich, 26 Feb. '47, Dagenham, Essex) Pop singer. A longtime fan of Adam FAITH, she approached him backstage at a local show, kicked off her shoes and sang for him: he helped her become one of the UK's leading female singers '64-6, epitomising the cool London 'Swinging '60s' girl: 'There's Always Something There To Remind Me' '64, 'Long Live Love' '65 were no. 1, 'Girl Don't Come' and 'Message Understood' top 10, thanks partly to intuitive pop tunesmith Chris ANDREWS. She was '67 UK entrant to Eurovision Song Contest: 'Puppet On A String' was another no. 1, giving rise to years of derivative Eurovision imitations. Marriage to fashion designer Jeff Banks, motherhood kept her out of the spotlight, then she came back guesting on HEAVEN 17 LP *Music Of Quality & Distinction* '81, doing 'Anyone Who Had A Heart', her rival Cilla BLACK's '60s hit; Morrissey of the SMITHS was a fan, and she had minor hit with their 'Hand In Glove' '84; another '86 with Lloyd COLE's 'Are You Ready To Be Heartbroken?'. London concerts in '86 were well-received.

SHAW, Woody (*b* 24 Dec. '44, Laurinburg, N.C.) Trumpet and flugelhorn, composer, bandleader. Grew up in Newark, N.J.; his father sang with gospel group the Diamond Jubilee Singers; began on bugle, then trumpet at 11. First important gig with Willie BOBO in band that incl. Chick COREA, Joe Farrell; then with Eric DOLPHY until his death; gigged in Europe with expatriates Bud POWELL, Johnny GRIFFIN, Kenny CLARKE etc.; played/recorded with Horace SILVER, Corea (*Inner Space*), Art BLAKEY, others; during the '70s the infl. of Dolphy came out and the stylistic resemblance to Freddie HUBBARD lessened: as he made his own albums as leader he became more his own man and a leader/composer to be reckoned with. LPs incl. *Blackstone Legacy* '70, *Song Of Songs* '72 on Contemporary, *Moontrane* and *Love Dance* '75, *Little Red's Fantasy* '78 on Muse; CBS signed him at the suggestion of Miles DAVIS: *Stepping Stones* and *Rosewood* '78, *Woody III* '79 appeared on that label, are now out of print while earlier LPs are still available, plus *Live Berliner Jazztage*, *The Iron Men* (with Anthony BRAXTON, Arthur BLYTHE) and

Setting Standards (with Cedar WALTON), as well as '65 recordings *In The Beginning*, with Herbie HANCOCK, Joe HENDERSON, Ron CARTER, Paul CHAMBERS, etc., all on Muse; other albums incl. *Time Is Right* on Red Records (live in Europe), *Lotus Flower* '82 on Enja, *Night Music* on Elektra, *With Tone Jansa Quartet* on Timeless '85; quintet *Imagination* '87 on Muse.

SHAY, Dorothy (*b* '23) Singer popular in '40s cabaret with gimmick of singing hillbilly songs in sophisticated setting as 'the Park Avenue Hillbilly'; recorded for Columbia. 'Feudin' And Fightin' ' was a hit '47 (from Broadway musical *Laffing Room Only*). She appeared in Abbott & Costello film *Comin' Round The Mountain* '51.

SHEARING, George (*b* 13 Aug. '19, London, England) Pianist, blind from birth. Studied classical piano at a school for the blind, learned jazz from records; toured with a band of blind musicians, played with AMBROSE, on BBC radio, etc. Began recording '36; won UK polls '39-46; to USA c.'48 with help of Leonard FEATHER, played in Oscar PETTIFORD Trio (replacing Erroll GARNER), led quartet with Buddy DeFRANCO '48; in '49 formed own quintet, originally with Marge Hyams on vibes, Chuck Wayne on guitar, John Levy on bass, Denzil BEST on drums; became world-famous and popular, playing rich block chords ('locked hands' style popularised by Milt BUCKNER), guitar and vibes blending prettily in unison. He mined this vein to exhaustion, but was cheerful about it, remarking (about another blind pianist) that 'Lennie (TRISTANO) would never be happy compromising as I'm doing' (quoted by Ira Gitler in *Jazz Masters Of The 40s*); but it was a uniquely pretty sound, and kept him working and in the charts for decades. He occasionally worked solo, led trio, once led a big band, mostly quintet format through '70s; Cal TJADER, Toots THIELEMANS, Gary BURTON, Joe PASS, others passed through. He wrote many tunes, the best-known being 'Lullaby Of Birdland'; Bud POWELL thought well enough of 'Conception' and 'Consternation' to play them. Recorded for Decca UK, Discovery and Savoy in USA (*So Rare* reissues from '47-9 on Savoy), then MGM '49-55 (2-disc compila-

tion on Verve: *Lullaby Of Broadway*). 'September In The Rain' '49 (film song by Harry Warren, Al Dubin) was an international hit, sold a million. *You're Hearing George Shearing* was chart album '50; other LPs: *An Evening With Shearing, A Shearing Caravan, Touch Of Genius*. Switched to Capitol till early '70s for chart LPs *Velvet Carpet* '56, *Black Satin* '57, *Burnished Brass* '58, *White Satin* '60, *Satin Affair* '61; others incl. *Deep Velvet, Latin Escapade, Here And Now!, New Look!*, many more incl. *Beauty And The Beat* with Peggy LEE, *In The Night* with Dakota STATON, *The Swinging's Mutual* with Nancy WILSON, *Nat King Cole Sings/George Shearing Plays, On Target* '79-80 with Robert FARNON orchestra, *The Reunion* '76 with Stephane GRAPPELLI, others reissued on Pausa USA; also recorded '61 with the MONTGOMERY Bros, now on Fantasy. Formed Sheba label for *Music To Hear, The Heart And Soul Of Joe Williams And George Shearing*; *The Young George Shearing* compiled early tracks. A whole new career with less compromising began on Concord Jazz, delighting old fans: duos *Blues Alley Jazz* '79 and *On A Clear Day* '80 with bassist Brian Torff, *Two For The Road* accompanying Carmen McRAE, *First Edition* with Jim HALL and *Alone Together* with Marian McPARTLAND '81, four albums with Mel TORMÉ '83-5 incl. Grammy-winning *Top Drawer* '83 with Don Thompson on bass, then *A Vintage Year* '87; duo with Thompson *Live At The Cafe Carlyle* '84; trio *Breakin' Out* '87 with Ray BROWN, Marvin 'Smitty' Smith on drums; also solos *Grand Piano, More Grand Piano*.

SHELTON, Anne (*b* 10 Nov. '27, Dulwich, London, England) Singer, performed on BBC at age 12, auditioned for AMBROSE and went to work for him rather than being evacuated with other children from WWII London. She was under contract to Ambrose for years, but managed to do seven shows with Glenn MILLER in the UK: he'd asked for her, told her as he left for France that he wanted to bring her to the USA after the war, but he never made it to France. She worked with Bing CROSBY '44 (again at his request); a successful USA tour '50 incl. work with Percy FAITH on radio. She was the first to sing the English words to 'Lili Marlene' (it was already her theme;

she'd hummed it on the air). She had many hits before UK charts began; 'Be Mine' and 'Galway Bay' charted in USA top 30 '49; no. 1 UK hit with 'Lay Down Your Arms' '56; last chart hit was top 10 with 'Sailor' '61; sang 'I'll Be Seeing You' for film *Yanks* '79; sang 'You'll Never Know' for the Queen Mother on her 80th birthday '80 (her favourite song); sang with ghost Miller band on UK TV '84, the 40th anniversary of D-Day. With Vera LYNN one of the UK's favourite singers of her era. Compilations in UK on Decca, EMI, President.

SHEPARD, Jean (*b* 21 Nov. '33, Paul's Valley, Okla.) Country singer. Eleven children in family; moved to West Coast '46, formed all-girl Western Swing outfit the Melody Ranch Girls with sisters, played on same bill as Hank THOMPSON and he helped her to get Capitol contract '52: duet with Ferlin HUSKY 'Dear John Letter' was no. 1 country hit '53 (mercilessly satirised by Stan FREBERG on the same label). Follow-up was 'Forgive Me John'. Had hits 'Satisfied Mind', 'Beautiful Lies' '55, worked on Red FOLEY Ozark Jubilee Show '55-7, then Grand Ole Opry, more hits. Her '56 LP *Songs Of A Love Affair* (reissued '87 on Stetson) was an early concept album, one side with songs from a single woman's point of view, the other from the wife's. She was married to Hawkshaw HAWKINS, lost him in plane crash '63 that also killed Patsy CLINE, Cowboy COPAS. She came back with more hits late '60s and through the '70s incl. duets with Ray PILLOW '66-7; she was one of the first artists to be prod. by Larry Butler '69, who later made crossover hits with Kenny ROGERS: her 'Slippin' Away' '73 crossed over to the pop Hot 100, by which time she had switched to UA, retaining association with Butler. Despite that association she soon became vociferous champion of trad. country music, criticising such acts as John DENVER and Olivia NEWTON-JOHN; since appearances at Wembley late '70s her trad. style is now more popular in the UK than at home. Many LPs on Capitol '50s to '72; compilations on Power USA, EMI labels UK; on UA: *Slippin' Away, Poor Sweet Baby, Mercy, Ain't Love Good, The Good Shepard* '74-7; *I'll Do Anything It Takes* '78 on Sunset; also recorded on Scorpion '78, Starday-Gusto '81.

SHEPP, Archie (*b* 24 May '37, Ft Lauderdale, Fla.) Saxophones, composer, leader; also playwright, poet. Grew up in Philadelphia; studied piano, clarinet, alto sax, switched to tenor as a child, later played soprano as well. Worked in R&B bands, obtained drama degree (plays prod. in NYC incl. *The Communist* '65; musical with trumpeter/composer Cal Massey *Lady Day: A Musical Tragedy* '72; also *Junebug Graduates Tonight*, etc.). He worked with Cecil TAYLOR '60 (incl. performing in prod. of *The Connection*), co-led groups: with Bill DIXON and New York Contemporary Five with John Tchicai and Don CHERRY (LPs on Savoy USA, Storyville UK), worked, recorded with John COLTRANE '65, has toured the world and led own groups, also teaching at U. of Mass. '75, other places. He is a romantic and an eclectic traditionalist, infl. by Ben WEBSTER, Sonny ROLLINS etc., trying to incl. everything; eclecticism meant that he confused some critics, but his technical ability as a player and his emotional sincerity as a composer result in a body of work that has to be reckoned with, though some say that his latest work lacks the 'operatic rush and dark ambience that made him a '60s guru' (*Cadence* magazine). Albums incl. many on Impulse: *Four For Trane* '64 with Tchicai and Roswell RUDD, *Fire, New Thing At Newport* '65 with Coltrane, *On This Night* '66, *Mama Too Tight* '67 (octet LP with infl. of Duke ELLINGTON, R&B, parodies of pop evergreens, avant-garde freakouts), *Magic Of Ju-Ju*, several more, some now on Jasmine in UK. *Blasé, Yasmina: A Black Woman* and *Live At The Pan-African Festival* (attempt at African fusion '69; probably a failure) were made for French Byg, later on Affinity UK. Other albums: 2-disc *Montreux One/Two* '75 and *There's A Trumpet In My Soul* '76 on Arista/Freedom; *A Sea Of Faces* '75 on Black Saint; *Hi Fly* '76 on Phonogram with vocalist Karin Krog; *Goin' Home* '77 and *Trouble In Mind* '80 (duets with Horace PARLAN), *Looking At Bird* '80 with Niels-Henning Ørsted Pedersen, *Mama Rose* '82, all on Steeplechase; *Ballads For Trane*, quartet *On Green Dolphin Street* and *Duet* (with Abdullah IBRAHIM) on Denon; *Soul Song* and *Steam* on Enja, *Attica Blues* '81 (arr./cond. by Ray COPELAND) on Impulse, *Down Home New York* '84 and *Little Red*

Moon '85 both on Soul Note. He made many other records.

SHEPPARD, Andy (*b* 20 Jan. '57, Bristol, UK) Tenor and soprano saxophones, composer, leader. One of several young UK jazzmen suddenly making a stir mid-'80s (he says there's more around who haven't got a break yet). Was a choirboy as a child, discovered perfect pitch, later taught himself to read music from books, to play flute by ear; then infl. by John COLTRANE, Steve LACY, Charles Brackeen. 'I played my first gig three weeks after I got the tenor. I learnt jazz the old way: on the stand alongside better players.' Played and recorded with UK band Sphere, worked and recorded in Paris with 19-piece Lumière; also recorded with rock band Freur, later called Underworld. Took part early '87 in BBC-2 Young Jazz Band of the Year competition; Joe ZAWINUL (a judge) described him as world-class; debut *Andy Sheppard* '87 on Antilles prod. by Steve SWALLOW features quartet with Dave Buxton on piano (and synth on two tracks), Pete Maxfield on bass, Simon Gore on drums, assisted on various tracks by Randy BRECKER or Dave De Fries, trumpets; Mamadi Kamara on percussion, Orphy Robinson on vibes (plays with Jazz Warriors; *see* Courtney PINE), others; Kamara joined quartet on tour. Wants to play totally improvised music on some future albums; eight original tunes (on CD) make the mainstream debut one of the brightest of the decade.

SHEPPARD, T. G. (*b* William Bowder, 20 July '44, Humboldt, Tenn.) Pop-country singer, one of the most successful of the '80s. Mother was a piano teacher; he was an accomplished pianist as a teenager, but joined the Travis Wammack band as singer/guitarist in Memphis '60. Recorded for Atlantic c.'62 as Brian Stacy; 'High School Days' was a regional hit. By '65 he had married, quit performing to do promotional work, for RCA in Memphis, then for his own company, Umbrella Productions. Among demos he received was 'The Devil In A Bottle', a song by Bobby David; he could interest no record company in it so recorded it himself as T. G. Sheppard; on Motown Melodyland label it was a no. 1 country hit '75, followed by no. 1 same year

with his own song 'Trying To Beat The Morning Home' (both crossed over to pop Hot 100). After further top 10 hits Motown had become Hitsville, but then closed down in Nashville; he switched to WB for more hits incl. no. ones with 'Last Cheater's Waltz' '79, 'I'll Be Coming Back For More', 'Smooth Sailin' ' and 'Do You Wanna Go To Heaven' '80. His sensual, half-whispered style was aimed squarely at females; many hits incl. 'I Loved 'Em Every One' (top 40 pop '81), duets 'Faking Love' with Karen Brooks, 'Make My Day' with Clint Eastwood (no. 1 country, Hot 100 pop); switched to Columbia '85 and carried on. Albums incl. *Nashville Hitmaker* '76 on Hitsville; *T.G.* and *Daylight* '78, *3/4 Lonely* '79, *Smooth Sailin'* '80, *I Love 'Em All* '81, *Finally* and *Perfect Stranger* '82, *Slow Burn* '83, *One Owner Heart* '84, all on WB; *Livin' On The Edge* '85, *One For The Money* '87 on Columbia.

SHERMAN, Bobby (*b* '44, Santa Monica, Cal.) Pop singer. A teen idol of the late '60s, discovered at a party by actor Sal Mineo, widely exposed on TV shows *Shindig* '65-6, then sitcom *Here Come The Brides*. He had four top 10 hits '69-70, faded.

SHERRILL, Billy (*b* 5 Nov. '36, Phil Campbell, Ala.) Country music producer, songwriter, talent scout. Played piano as a child at father's evangelist meetings, played sax in local rock'n'roll bands incl. the Fairlanes with Rick Hall; in Memphis late '50s engineered records by Jerry Lee LEWIS, Charlie RICH at Sun Records, back to Alabama and worked in studio with Hall, Tom Stafford, recorded local hits: Dan Penn's 'Crazy Over You', his own sax instrumental 'Tipsy' c.'60. To Nashville '63 as prod. at Epic; breakthrough 'Almost Persuaded' was written and prod. for David HOUSTON, no. 1 country hit '66. He discovered hairdresser Tammy WYNETTE, co-wrote songs with her, prod. her records; she became the biggest female star of the era. He was promoted to Vice-President and Executive Producer of CBS Nashville, discovered 13-year-old Tanya TUCKER, Janie FRICKE and Lacy J. DALTON; brought Johnny PAYCHECK back to the limelight '71; worked with Rich, George JONES, Marty ROBBINS, Barbara MANDRELL; carried on slick 'countrypolitan' style invented by Chet ATKINS and Owen BRADLEY in the early '60s for better or worse, turning country music into MOR, acceptable to people who'd never listened to it before. Left CBS '80, worked freelance with Elvis COSTELLO, David Allan COE, Ray CHARLES, etc.

SHEW, Bobby (*b* 4 Mar. '41, Albuquerque, N.M.) Trumpet. Began at 13 with a few lessons, but largely self-taught; turned pro after playing in NORAD band at Colorado Springs; played in Tommy DORSEY ghost band '64, then Woody HERMAN, Benny GOODMAN, Buddy RICH, settled in Las Vegas as long as he could stand it, moved to West Coast and divided his time for seven years between Toshiko AKIYOSHI and Louie BELLSON bands. A teacher and clinician, with all the studio work he wants, he also plays flugelhorn and shewhorn, a trumpet with two bells, one open and one muted, with a fourth valve to control air flow; plays call-and-response and 'trades fours' with himself, but is careful not to use it so much it becomes a gimmick. 'Someday, somebody is going to lock themselves into a room for a while and do some real stylistic innovations on it' (quoted by UPI's Ken Franckling). The shewhorn was designed and built by Chicago's David Monette, who hand-makes and tunes horns for Art FARMER, Wynton MARSALIS, concert artist Maurice André, etc. Shew LPs: *Round Midnight* on MoPro, *Shewhorn* '82-3 and *Breakfast Wine* '85 on Pausa, *Trumpets No End* '83 on Delos with Chuck Findley.

SHILKRET, Nathaniel (*b* 25 Dec. 1896, NYC) Composer, conductor. Played clarinet in symphony orchestras, for Arthur Pryor and John Philip SOUSA; as conductor had over 50 hits '24-32 on Victor, biggest being 'Dancing With Tears In My Eyes', no. 1 '30 with vocal by Lewis James. He was mainly infl. as dir. of light music for Victor '15-45, backing many Victor artists. His best-known song is 'The Lonesome Road', co-written with Gene AUSTIN; most of his songs were sentimental, but Frank SINATRA made definitive version of this one mid-'50s.

SHINES, Johnny (*b* 26 Apr. '15, Frayser, Tenn.) Blues singer, guitarist; aka 'Little

Wolf'. Father was a farmer, mother played guitar; he worked in the street for tips with other children, often worked outside music; hoboed playing and singing with Robert JOHNSON mid-'30s; appeared with Johnson on radio in Detroit '37; based in Memphis late '30s, in Chicago from '41, made first recordings '46 (for Columbia) not released until many years later on a blues compilation. He recorded for Chess and JOB '50s but did not hit the big time like Muddy WATERS and Howlin' WOLF: with his strong, clear tenor, excellent bottleneck guitar, original compositions and thrilling recreations of Johnson's songs, he was as good as the best, but perhaps too country for the R&B market. He quit music '58-65, bought a camera and took pictures in the clubs; rediscovered in mid-'60s he worked many blues festivals, clubs, tours incl. overseas: he was just as good as ever, but got tired of being asked about Johnson. Recordings for Vanguard '65 in 'Blues Today' series incl. 'Dynaflow Blues' on Johnson's classic 'Terraplane Blues'; other excellent albums incl. *Last Night's Dream* '68 on Blues Horizon (with Walter HORTON, Willie DIXON, drummer Clifton James; Otis SPANN on one track), solo *Sitting On Top Of The World* '72 (incl. 'Dynaflow' and remake of 'Ramblin' Blues', legendary '51 JOB track itself based on Johnson's 'Walkin' Blues'), then with Dave Bromberg Band, both on Biograph; *Country Blues* '74 on Transatlantic/Xtra, made in Canada with harmonica, second guitar and bass. Also *Johnny Shines* '66 with Horton, *Masters Of Modern Blues Vol. 1* '69, *Crossroads* '70, all on Testament; *Hay-Ba-Ba-Re-Bop* on Rounder.

SHIRELLES, The Female vocal quartet of the early '60s, one of the most successful, yet allied neither to Phil SPECTOR nor Motown. Original lineup formed in Passaic, N.J. '58: lead singer Shirley Owens (*b* 10 June '41), Addie 'Micki' Harris (*b* 22 Jan. '40), Beverly Lee (*b* 3 Aug. '41), Doris Kenner (*b* 2 Aug. '41). Schoolmate Mary Jane Greenberg's mother Florence signed the group (then known as the Pequellos or the Honeytones) to her little Tiara label, recorded their self-penned 'I Met Him On A Sunday'; it sold so well it was picked up for distribution by Decca, reached USA top 50 '58, regarded by many as the first hit in the 'girl group' genre: Greenberg formed new Sceptor label; update of 'Dedicated To The One I Love' (written '57 by Lowman Pauling of the '5' Royales, with Ralph BASS also getting credit; revived '67 by the MAMAS AND THE PAPAS) made the Hot 100 '59 without major label distribution, a feat unheard of then, especially by a black group. They made top 40 with 'Tonight's The Night', then no. 1 with definitive version of Gerry GOFFIN/Carole KING's 'Will You Love Me Tomorrow?' '60 (their biggest UK hit at no. 4); Sceptor reissued 'Dedicated' which this time made no. 3. 'Mama Said' '61 was their third top 5 hit in a row; then they recorded 'Baby It's You', a song by Burt BACHARACH, lyricist Mack David (nominated eight times for Oscars; brother Hal teamed with Bacharach); it was top 10 late '61, and somewhat over-sentimental 'Soldier Boy' was no. 1 early '62. Luther Dixon (wrote 'Mama Said' and 'Soldier Boy') left Sceptor for another label; 'Foolish Little Girl' (by Howard Greenfield/Helen Miller) reached top 5 '63, the year the BEATLES covered both 'Baby It's You' and 'Boys' (a Dixon song that flopped) on their first album, acknowledging Shirelles' influences. They had another top 40 hit that year, a few more lesser hits, but faded from the charts late '67. They re-formed '70s for oldies shows; Kenner married, became Doris Coley; Owens became Shirley Alston, had successful solo career: her album *With A Little Help From My Friends* '75 featured the Flamingos, the DRIFTERS, Shep & the Limelights, the FIVE SATINS, DANNY & THE JUNIORS and Lala Brooks of the CRYSTALS, helping her re-create some of Shirelles' best moments. Micki Harris died, replaced by Louie Bethune; they re-formed '80s to sing backup on a Dionne WARWICK record. 2-disc Shirelles anthology on Rhino incl. all the hits except the first.

SHIRLEY & LEE R&B duo, Shirley Pixley Goodman (*b* '37), Leonard Lee (*b* '35). Several top 5 R&B hits began with 'I'm Gone' '52 on Aladdin, written by Lee and Dave BARTHOLOMEW; they pretended to be sweethearts through series 'Shirley Come Back To Me' etc., leaning on contrast of his big voice with her smaller, higher one. The other big hits incl. 'Feel So Good' '55 and 'I Feel Good' '56, but 'Let The Good Times

Roll' (no. 2 R&B, 20 pop '56) was the teenage party record with a black sound that no one will ever forget, banned by some white DJs who thought it was suggestive. They split up '63; Lee recorded for Imperial; Shirley teamed with Jesse Hill as Shirley & Jesse, worked in New Orleans with Mac REBENNACK, others; recorded 'Shame Shame Shame' as Shirley (And Company), one of the first disco hits '76, prod. and co-written by Sylvia Robinson (*see* MICKEY & SYLVIA). *The Best Of Shirley & Lee* compiles the hits on Ace.

SHIRLEY, Don (*b* 27 Jan. '27, Kingston, Jamaica) Piano, composer. From academically brilliant family, invited to Leningrad Conservatory, has doctorates in psychology, liturgical art; his classical technique praised by Stravinsky, he was encouraged to play jazz by George SHEARING and Duke ELLINGTON, made highly praised albums, but remained a classical musician. On his first three LPs '54-6 his accompanist was bassist Richard Davis; *Tonal Expressions* incl. pop songs ('Secret Love'), several evergreens and a medley from show *New Faces*; it made top 15 albums '55. Six more LPs '57-61 incl. three solo sets and three with bass and cello; another trio record was on Audio Fidelity, all the others on Archie BLEYER's Cadence label. Three Columbia LPs '65-8 incl. *In Concert* (live at Carnegie Hall); he played organ and piano on an Atlantic LP '74, with long-time associates Kenneth Fricker on drums, Juri Taht on cello, James Bond on second cello, incl. a Gershwin medley, pop songs: 'Bridge Over Troubled Water', 'By The Time I Get To Phoenix'.

SHOCKED, Michelle (*b* c. '62) Singer, songwriter. She does not reveal her real name. From a strict Mormon family in Texas; infl. by Woody GUTHRIE, ran away from home at 16, drifted in USA and Europe. Discovered singing at a campfire during Kerrville Folk Festival by Englishman Pete Lawrence; he recorded her on a portable cassette player, released *Texas Campfire Tapes* on his Cooking Vinyl label '87, in LA she made *Short Sharp Shocked* '88. Like other new artists of integrity, she will accept stardom, if it happens, only on her own terms. Emergence of singer-songwriters in each generation is a welcome and necessary antidote to the too familiar pop-star syndrome and its sound-alike songs.

SHORE, Dinah (*b* Frances Rose Shore, 1 Mar. '17, Winchester, Tenn.) Began on Nashville radio; adopted '25 song 'Dinah' as theme, changed her name; auditions with Benny GOODMAN, Tommy and Jimmy DORSEY, others not successful: her voice was perhaps too soft to sing with a big band, and she became one of the first of a new breed: the pop singer as star in her own right. Recorded with Xavier CUGAT: hits with him were 'Quierme Mucho (Yours)' (recorded '39, a hit '41), 'The Breeze And I', two-sided hit 'Whatever Happened To You?'/'The Rumba-Cardi', all '40. She was a regular on the CHAMBER MUSIC SOCIETY OF LOWER BASIN STREET radio show '40, Eddie CANTOR show '41; by then one of the singing stars of the decade. Appeared occasionally on radio's *Your Hit Parade* early '40s; in films *Thank Your Lucky Stars* '43, *Up In Arms* and *Belle Of The Yukon* '44, *Till The Clouds Roll By* and *Fun And Fancy Free* '47, *Aaron Slick From Punkin Crick* '52; sang on soundtrack of *Make Mine Music* '46; entertained troops during WWII. 75 hit records '40-54 on Bluebird, Victor, then Columbia '46-50, then RCA, incl. first big hit 'Yes My Darling Daughter' '40; no. 1 hits: 'I'll Walk Alone' '44, 'The Gypsy' '46, 'Anniversary Song' '47, 'Buttons And Bows' '48 (with the Happy Valley Boys, song from film *Paleface*). 'Blues In The Night' '42 was no. 4, eventually sold a million; other hits: 'Doin' What Comes Natur'lly' '46 with Spade COOLEY, 'Baby, It's Cold Outside' '49 one of several duets with Buddy CLARK: Oscar-winning song by Frank LOESSER was sung by Esther Williams and Ricardo Montalban in *Neptune's Daughter*, revived '60 by Ray CHARLES/Betty CARTER. Also 'In Your Arms' '51 (duet with Tony MARTIN), even top 30 vocal version of hit instrumental 'Delicado' '52 (Percy FAITH had no. 1). Fame even greater thanks to TV: variety show sponsored by Chevrolet was top-rated mid-'50s to early '60s; she hosted specials, came back early '70s with non-musical morning show *Dinah's Place*. Albums incl. 10″ LP *S' Wonderful* on Columbia (duets with Clark), *Holding Hands At Midnight* and *Moments Like These* on RCA (latter reissued in UK '87); *Sings Cole Porter And*

Richard Rodgers and *Love Songs* on Harmony (Columbia compilations), *Dinah, Yes Indeed!* and *Dinah Sings, Previn Plays* with André PREVIN on Capitol, all '50s; later *Songs For Sometime Losers* on Project, *Oh Lonesome Me* on Seagull, *Once Upon A Summertime* on Bainbridge; also radio shows with Crosby compiled on Sunbeam.

SHORT, Bobby (*b* Robert Waltrip Short, 15 Sep. '26, Danville, Ill.) Pianist, cabaret singer. The ninth of ten children ('There were never more than seven of us alive at any one time'); father was a coal miner, died c.'35; Short left home age 11 with mother's permission to perform in Chicago, then briefly NYC ('I became the colored counterpart of Bobby Breen'), went home and finished high school (but did not graduate: he flunked typing). Infl. by Bing CROSBY, Ivie ANDERSON, Fats WALLER on the radio as a child; met/worked opposite Nat COLE and Art TATUM in places like Omaha, Nebraska; then infl. by Hildegarde's act in Milwaukee early '40s, met Mabel MERCER, pianist Cy Walter; people kept bringing him obscure songs: with a tremulous baritone subject to laryngitis and a slight rhythmic insecurity at the piano lending urgency and bounce, he became a walking Smithsonian of the golden age of American popular song, a nonpareil discoverer and interpreter of lesser known works of RODGERS & HART, Cole PORTER, Vernon DUKE and the rest. Worked at the Blue Angel in NYC for four weeks as opening act, then to West Coast at the Haig, then chic Café Gala '48-54; then back to NYC with help from columnist Dorothy Kilgallen, record contract with Atlantic. Wider fame came with regular appearances on the first Playboy TV series c.'60: people tuned in hoping to see lots of Bunnies, instead got then-new comedy from Phyllis Diller and a generous set of forgotten masterpieces with great lyrics from Short. The bottom dropped out of the night-club business mid-'60s and he didn't work much; then replaced pianist George Feyer at NYC's Café Carlyle (recommended by Atlantic's Ertegun Bros.) and worked there eight months a year from '68. He often made best-dressed lists; has also modelled, worked with Gloria Vanderbilt early '80s when she went into designer clothes. Atlantic LPs incl. *Mad About Noel Coward,*

The Mad Twenties; with Mercer *At Town Hall, Second Town Hall Concert*; 2-disc sets *Bobby Short Loves Cole Porter* (made top 200 albums '72), *Celebrates Rodgers & Hart, Krazy For Gershwin, Live At Café Carlyle*. Autobiography *Black And White Baby* '71 about his first 17 years.

SHORT, J. D. (*b* 26 Dec. '02, Port Gibson, Ms.; *d* 21 Oct. '62, St Louis, Mo.) Blues singer; played several instruments incl. guitar and harmonica. His first names were only initials. He learned piano and guitar, worked parties etc.; recorded for Paramount '30 as Jaydee Short, for Vocalion '32 as Jelly Jaw Short (owing to the way he produced his unusual vocal vibrato); it is also thought that he recorded duets with Peetie WHEATSTRAW '30 as 'Neckbones'. Joined the Army '42 at age 40, was injured in an obstacle course and had a disability pension; it slowed him down for the rest of his life; finally his circulation suffered. He lived in St Louis for 30 years but retained the Delta style. Recorded for Delmark '58, Sonet '62: *Legacy Of The Blues Vol. 8* on GNP/Sonet recorded and produced by Sam Charters, who also filmed him for documentary *The Blues*, released '63. A speciality was 'Sliding Delta', about a train 'so slow it almost slid, like a turtle'. *Early Recordings 1930-33* on Wolf (Austria).

SHORTER, Wayne (*b* 25 Aug. '33, Newark, N.J.) Tenor and soprano saxophones; composer, leader. Served in US Army '56-8, worked with Horace SILVER, to NYC '58, played in Maynard FERGUSON band, joined Art BLAKEY '59-63 and was obviously a newcomer to watch: played in epochal Miles DAVIS quintet '64-70, took up soprano; formed WEATHER REPORT with Joe ZAWINUL '70-85, but carried on parallel career as a solo artist, composing almost all his own music as well as works recorded with Davis and Weather Report. He won the *Downbeat* poll on soprano nearly every year after '69 and has many fans who will listen to him in any context; also writes and paints. First recorded as a leader on Vee Jay (albums *Second Genesis, Blues A La Carte, Wayning Moments* now on Affinity); then on Blue Note for series of albums all with top sidemen, many from Davis's group: *Night Dreamer, Juju, Speak No Evil* '64;

The Soothsayer, Etcetera, The All Seeing Eye '65, *Adam's Apple* '66, *Schizophrenia* '67; he moved away from pure jazz and showed a Latin infl. with *Super Nova* '69 featuring guitarists John McLAUGHLIN, Sonny Sharrock; also Miroslav Vitous, Chick COREA (playing vibes), Jack DeJOHNETTE, AIRTO; *Odyssey Of Iska* '70 incl. vibes, three percussionists, bassists Ron CARTER and Cecil McBEE, Gene BERTONCINI on guitar; *Moto Grosso Feio* '70 incl. McLaughlin, Carter, Dave HOLLAND on bass, Corea playing marimba, Michelin Prell on drums. He was busy with Weather Report, then *Native Dancer* '74 on Columbia reached the top 200 albums, with Brazilian vocalist Milton Nascimento, Airto, Herbie HANCOCK on variously recorded tracks. *Atlantis* '85 (aka *Endangered Species*) on CBS incl. six musicians plus vocal septet; was described as 'faceless' and a 'shaky' start to new solo career. He has also recorded with Joni MITCHELL, STEELY DAN, Hancock's VSOP outfit; formed own group '86. Fans will listen to whatever he plays, but he stayed too long with Weather Report: he made fine contributions on both tenor and soprano to the *Round Midnight* soundtrack '86 and *Power Of Three* by Michel PETRUCCIANI with Jim HALL, guested on one track of a Bobby McFERRIN LP; critics wait to see what his new direction will be, one grousing about 'mewling synthesisers' in '86. Live gigs in London in '87 were judged superior to album *Phantom Navigator* '86 (probably over-produced, with four keyboards, clutter of drum machines); quintet incl. keyboardist Jim Beard (*b* 26 Aug. '60), Shorter's highly praised discovery Terri Lyne Carrington on drums (*b* 4 Aug. '65), plus bassist Carl James (*b* 20 Aug. '64), Marilyn Mazur (*b* 18 Jan. '55) on percussion. *Joy Ryder* came out '88.

SHOWADDYWADDY UK rock'n'roll revival group formed '73 from merger of Leicester groups Choice and Hammers: Dave Bartram and Buddy Gask, vocals; Russ Field and Trevor Oakes, guitars; Al James and Rod Deas, bass; Malcolm Allured, Romeo Challenger on drums. Signed with Bell, had 22 top 40 singles '74-81 (label taken over by Arista mid-'70s). 'Hey Rock And Roll' at no. 2 first of three hits '74, but after originals did less well they switched to covers: Eddie COCHRAN's 'Three Steps To Heaven' was no. 2 '75; seven more in top 10 '76-8. Like USA counterparts SHA NA NA they were a popular live act, with period costumes, over-the-top stage show, but unlike them did not get additional exposure on TV. Still popular in cabaret.

SIBERRY, Jean (*b* '56, Canada) Singer/songwriter, experimental pop: more romantic than Laurie ANDERSON, less autobiographical than Joni MITCHELL. LPs on Duke Street label: debut *No Borders Here* '85 (on Open Air in USA), then *The Speckless Sky* late '85 (released '87 in UK), incl. 'One More Colour', hit single in Canada. Some of her vocal mannerisms resemble Mitchell's, while her light voice is in some danger of being lost in the activity. *The Walking* '88 on Reprise was said to be more sparsely produced.

SIDRAN, Ben (*b* 14 Aug. '43, Chicago, Ill.) Pianist, vocalist. Grew up in Racine, Wis.; played piano age 7, played in local bands in high school, went to U. of Wis./Madison at 17, met Steve MILLER and Boz SCAGGS, was member of early Steve Miller Band mixing blues, rock. Attended U. of Sussex in England, turning PhD thesis into highly rated book *Black Talk* '71; met Eric CLAPTON, Peter FRAMPTON, ROLLING STONES; Frampton and Charlie Watts guested on his debut LP *Feel Your Groove* '71 on Capitol. *I Lead A Life* '72, *Puttin' In Time On Planet Earth* '73 on Blue Thumb were jazz-funk, the last with ex-Stan KENTON sidemen Bill PERKINS and Frank Rosolino in backing; *Don't Let Go* '74 incl. 'She's Funny That Way' rendered Mose ALLISON-style. To Arista label for *Free In America* '76, with slight nudge towards the commercial; back to jazz with *The Doctor Is In* '77, covers of 'Goodbye Pork Pie Hat' (by Charles MINGUS), 'Silver's Serenade' (Horace SILVER). Bop-infl. jazz remained at the centre of LPs *A Little Kiss In The Night* '78 (with Blue MITCHELL, Phil WOODS, vocal version of Charlie PARKER's 'Moose The Mooche' by Sidran and Jon HENDRICKS), *Old Songs For The New Depression* '82, *Bop City* '83 (collection of jazz themes e.g. 'Monk's Mood', 'Nardis' by Miles DAVIS, 'Big Nick' by John COLTRANE, etc., the last two on Antilles).

He prod. jazz TV shows, wrote magazine articles, became resident jazz critic of national public radio; he was moving away from bop repertory towards fusion; after *Cat In The Hat* for Horizon (A&M) he moved to Magenta label, division of Windham Hill: *On The Cool Side* '85 incl. Miller, Mac REBENNACK; *On The Live Side* '86 Miller, Woods, Sidran on piano and Ricky Peterson on synth, bass and drums; both made in Minnesota. He has written much of his own material; compilation of Arista stuff on Bluebeard CD '88 called *That's Life I Guess* incl. Randy NEWMAN, BRECKER Brothers, others; duo *Live At The Elvehjem Art Museum* '83 with bassist Richard Davis is on French Madrigal label.

SIEGEL-SCHWALL BLUES BAND Blues-rock band formed mid-'60s in Chicago by Corky Siegel (vocals, harmonica, keyboards) and Jim Schwall (guitar) (both *b* c.'42) who met at Roosevelt U., with Rollow Radford on bass (later toured with SUN RA) and drummer Shelley Plotkin. Unlike the Paul BUTTERFIELD Blues Band, the 'other' Chicago blues band leaned in the direction of psychedelia. Of 11 LPs for Vanguard and RCA/Woode Nickel the first three were probably the best: *Siegel Schwall Band, Say Siegel-Schwall*, and *Shake!*. Arguably the worst was the last, *Three Pieces For Blues Band And Orchestra* '73, written by Bill Russo (ex-Stan KENTON), with Seiji Ozawa and San Francisco Symphony on DGG (music from Leonard BERNSTEIN's *West Side Story* on the other side): it was the only one that reached top 200 LPs USA. They split early '74, reunited '87 for 15th anniversary party for WXRT in Chicago (Sam Lay on drums).

SILHOUETTES, The Vocal quartet formed '55 in Philadelphia, Pa. as gospel group the Gospel Tornados; they sang R&B as the Thunderbirds, then lead singer Billy Horton (*b* 25 Dec. '29) plus tenor Richard Lewis (*b* 2 Sep. '33), baritone Earl Beal (*b* 18 July '24), bass Raymond Edwards (*b* 27 Sep. '22), all from Philadelphia, Pa. became the Silhouettes. They had only one hit but it was a monster: 'Get A Job' was no. 1 both R&B and pop charts '58, co-written by Lewis, arranger Howard Biggs; its doo-wop lyrics provided the name for the rock'n'roll revival group SHA NA NA in the '70s. They re-formed early '80s for oldies shows.

SILVER, Horace (*b* 2 Sep. '28, Norwalk, Conn.) Pianist, composer, bandleader, sometime vocalist. Father was Portuguese, from Cape Verde Islands. First important job with Stan GETZ quintet '50-1; with Art BLAKEY '51-6: Blue Note LPs by Horace Silver Trio had Gene Ramey, Curley Russell, Percy Heath on bass, Blakey on drums; then with Blakey's Jazz Messengers on several Blue Note LPs '53-6, formed own quintet '56: his blues-drenched piano garnished with amusing quotes and his compositions set the tone for the early Messengers, and then even more for the label itself. 10" LPs *Horace Silver Quintet Vols. 1 & 2* '54-5 combined on 12" *Horace Silver And The Jazz Messengers*, incl. 'Doodlin' ' (covered by Ray CHARLES), 'The Preacher'. *Silver's Blue* '56 appeared on Epic; about 20 Blue Note quintet LPs '56-72 mined vein thoroughly, defining much of the post-bop mainstream. Those passing through incl. Kenny DORHAM, Hank MOBLEY, Art FARMER, Clifford JORDAN, Blue MITCHELL, Woody SHAW, Joe Henderson, the BRECKER Bros, George COLEMAN, bassist Doug Watkins, Carmell Jones on trumpet (*b* '36, Kansas City; moved to Germany '65), Junior Cook on tenor (*b* 22 July '34, Pensacola, Fla.; played with Silver '58-64, then with similar Blue Mitchell quintet '64-9; own LPs on Muse), many more; *Six Pieces Of Silver* '56 incl. 'Señor Blues'; title tunes '59-63 incl. *Finger-Poppin', Blowin' The Blues Away, Horace-Scope* (incl. 'Nica's Dream'), *Silver's Serenade*. In '60s Lee MORGAN ('Sidewinder'), Herbie HANCOCK ('Watermelon Man', 'Maiden Voyage') built on what Silver had begun, also on Blue Note: he was the most important originator of what is now called funk, which had more soul when he was doing it. LPs *Song For My Father* '65 and *Cape Verdean Blues* '66 made pop top 200 albums. In '70s compositions and albums were more ambitious; *The United States Of Mind* was a trilogy: *That Healin' Feelin', Total Response, All* '70-2 incl. electric bass, vocalists Andy Bey, Salome Bey, Jackie Verdel, Gail Nelson on various tracks; *Silver 'n Brass* '75 had 14 pieces, *Silver 'n Wood* four-part suites called 'Tranquilizer', 'Process Of Creation'; *Silver*

'n Voices '76 had quintet plus six voices; *Silver 'n Percussion* had OLATUNJI and Camara (African percussion) on one side, Omar Clay (American Indian) on the other; *Silver 'n Strings Play The Music Of The Spheres* '78-9 had quintet plus strings, voices recorded in four sessions. Formed own Silveto label ('Self Help – Holistic Metaphysical Music') for *Guides To Growing Up* '81, *Spiritualising The Senses* and *There's No Need To Struggle* '83, quintet incl. Eddie HARRIS, voices on first and third, Bill Cosby speaking on *Guides*. On tour '86 with vocalist Bey, no trumpet, his music remained potent, according to Larry Kart in *The Chicago Tribune*, but lyrics in 'moral-uplift bag' (by Steve ALLEN, Weaver Copeland etc.) are wanting, described by Bob Blumenthal as 'surprisingly inoffensive'. Silveto subsidiary Emerald established for reissues, began with *Horace Silver – Live 1964* with Henderson, Jones, previously unissued versions of 'Señor Blues', 'Filthy McNasty', 'Skinney Minnie', others.

SILVERSTEIN, Shel (*b* '32, Chicago) Songwriter, poet, author, cartoonist. Formed Red Onion Jazz Band '61 (LP *Hairy Jazz*); worked as cartoonist, supplying social commentary in drawings to *Playboy, The Village Voice* etc. for nearly 20 years. Also wrote comic verse for children (*Where The Sidewalk Ends* '74, *A Light In The Attic* '81), stories *The Giving Tree* etc., illustrated with his unmistakable drawings, and songs: 'A Boy Named Sue' by Johnny CASH was no. 1 '69 both country and pop, no. 3 UK, won two Grammies; 'Here I Am Again' and 'One's On The Way' were recorded by Loretta LYNN, the latter a no. 1 country hit '71; 'Sylvia's Mother' by DR HOOK was no. 5 USA, 2 UK '72 (they recorded other Silverstein songs); also Hank SNOW ('I'm Still Moving On'), Tompall GLASER (*Songs Of Shel Silverstein* '76 on MGM), Bobby BARE (many hits, incl. LPs *Lullabies, Legends And Lies* '75 on RCA, *Bare* '81 on CBS). His own albums have a cult following, incl. *Freaking At The Freaker's Ball* '69 on Columbia/Embassy (incl. 'I Got Stoned And I Missed It', 'Don't Give A Dose To The One You Love Most'), *Songs And Stories* '72 on Parachute, *The Great Conch Train Robbery* '81 on Flying Fish, *Where The Sidewalk Ends* on Columbia.

SILVESTER, Victor (*b* Victor Marlborough Silvester, 25 Feb. 1900, England; *d* 14 Aug. '78, France) Bandleader, composer. Named after a Boer War victory, middle name from an Archbishop. Repeatedly ran away from school (to London from Sussex at age 9), finally joined the army before he was 15. After WWI attended Sandhurst intending to become an army officer, became professional ballroom dancer instead: won World Ballroom Dancing Championship '22, operated dancing school '24, opened a larger one in London's Bond Street '27 (celebrities such as Gracie FIELDS and actress Merle Oberon taking lessons); wrote *Modern Ballroom Dancing* '28. Finding most records unsuitable for his sort of dancing, he produced sides by pianist Gerry Moore '34, led own orchestra '35: the records sold well and he was soon given a radio series, leading to complaints from other leaders that he wasn't a real bandleader. Radio series incl. *BBC Dancing Club* '41; he led a 'Jive Band' at one point with the best UK jazzmen, but mostly stuck to 'strict tempo', Strings for Dancing orchestra as well as a conventional dance band; radio show went to TV '48; after many years with Parlophone he switched to Pye '70 and continued making more records than any other bandleader in the world, his son Victor Jr carrying on since his death. Compilations: *Quick, Quick Slow, Dancing Club No. 1, Celebration Party Dances (For Every Occasion), Waltzes, Tangos And Modern Beat*, many more.

SIMEON, Omer (*b* 21 July '02, New Orleans, La.; *d* 17 Sep. '59, NYC) Clarinet; also saxes. Family moved to Chicago '14. Of all the clarinet players from the classic New Orleans period, his playing (on records with Jelly Roll MORTON '26-8, King OLIVER's Dixie Syncopators '27-8) was the most soulful and beautifully liquid. He played and/or recorded with Earl HINES '31-41 (except for brief periods with Fletcher HENDERSON), Coleman HAWKINS '41, Jimmie LUNCEFORD '42-7 (staying with band under Eddie Wilcox's leadership until '50), Wilbur DE PARIS '51-7. There was also a recording date '44 with Kid ORY, etc. Among his best sessions: Morton trio date '28 with Tommy BENFORD (two takes of 'Shreveport Stomp'); the Carnival Three (with James P. JOHNSON, Pops Foster) made for disc early '45.

SIMON & GARFUNKEL Vocal duo: Paul Simon (*b* 5 Nov. '41, Newark, N.J.) and Art Garfunkel (*b* 13 Oct. '42, Forest Hills, NY). Came together as childhood friends, singing at parties etc., strongly infl. by EVERLY Bros; as Tom & Jerry they scored minor USA hit '57 with 'Hey Schoolgirl' (Tom & Jerry material reissued as *Simon & Garfunkel* '67 at height of later fame and to their displeasure). *Wednesday Morning 3 a.m.* '64 on CBS was their first proper LP, incl. 'The Sound Of Silence', promising 'Bleecker Street', with 'Sparrow' and 'Benedictus' emphasising precision, clarity of harmony singing. Such was the vogue for Bob DYLAN's pioneering folk-rock fusion that producer Tom Wilson added electric backing to 'Sound Of Silence' without their knowledge; it was a no. 1 hit early '65: Simon was touring UK folk clubs as a solo as the single raced up the chart and they found themselves on the rock merry-go-round. *Sounds Of Silence* '65 was rushed, largely rocked-up versions of songs from *The Paul Simon Songbook* (see his entry, below), but his articulate lyrics and their beguiling harmonies made them international stars, 'I Am A Rock' and 'Homeward Bound' top 5 hits, both still heard in pubs all over the world. They were perfectionists in recording (and Simon as a writer, so subsequent releases were few); *Parsely, Sage, Rosemary & Thyme* '66 was the first they had control over and arguably their best: 'The Dangling Conversation' about isolation; 'A Poem On The Underground Wall', 'Patterns' about urban alienation; '59th Street Bridge Song (Feelin' Groovy)' on the light side. They released singles 'Fakin' It', 'A Hazy Shade Of Winter', 'At The Zoo'; immaculately crafted and too good for the top 40, their appeal was largely collegiate. Another breakthrough occurred with film *The Graduate* '68 (dir. by Mike Nicholls), one of the first major films to use rock in the soundtrack, using Simon songs, giving them huge worldwide hit with 'Mrs Robinson'. *Bookends* '68 incl. singles mentioned above plus caustic 'Save The Life Of My Child', poignant 'America', 'Old Friends'; steamrolling success continued with *Bridge Over Troubled Water* '70: fragmented, it incl. anthemic (if syrupy) title song, now a standard; 'The Boxer' (some say their best ever); breezy pop of 'Cecilia',

'Keep The Customer Satisfied'; it won a record six Grammies, sold over 11 million copies, was first simultaneously to top USA and UK album and singles charts; then they split up, still friends but no longer able to work together: Simon's 'The Only Living Boy In New York' on *Bridge* was allegedly a commentary on Garfunkel's acting debut in *Catch 22* '70, itself allegedly part of the reason for the split. *Greatest Hits* '72 collected four otherwise unavailable live tracks; they re-formed for a benefit for Senator George McGovern '72; Simon wrote 'My Little Town' for Garfunkel '75 (it appeared on both their solo albums of the period); they re-formed for NYC concert and 2-disc album *The Concert In Central Park* '82, incl. new performances of hits, solo work, revisited roots in songs by Everlys, Chuck BERRY. But subsequent reunion studio LP didn't work, became Simon's solo *Hearts & Bones*; *The Simon & Garfunkel Collection* '81 collected 19 of their best tracks. *Paul Simon: Then And Now* by Spencer Leigh and *Bookends: The Simon & Garfunkel Story* by Patrick Humphries are recommended. *See also* their individual entries

SIMON, Carly (*b* 25 June '45, NYC) Singer/songwriter. Father co-founder of publishers Simon & Schuster; with sister Lucy as Simon Sisters had minor hit 'Winken, Blinken And Nod' '64 on Kapp; solo LP to be prod. for Columbia by Bob DYLAN's manager Albert Grossman aborted '66; wrote much of proper debut *Carly Simon* '71 on Elektra with Jacob Brackman, film critic of *Esquire* magazine: more knowing, less confessional than others in genre, 'That's The Way I've Always Heard It Should Be' a top 10 hit. *Anticipation* '71 was recorded in London with ex-YARDBIRD Paul Samwell-Smith; title track no. 13 USA single, while 'A Legend In Your Own Time' displayed humorous cynicism that gave her no. 1 USA/3 UK hit '72 with 'You're So Vain' (candidates for identity of portrait incl. James TAYLOR, Mick Jagger, Warren Beatty, but she wasn't talking), from album *No Secrets* '72, prod. by Richard PERRY and perhaps her best (also incl. top 20 USA/UK 'The Right Thing To Do'). Further LPs incl. *Hotcakes* '73, *Playing Possum* '74; marriage to Taylor seemed to

blunt both their muses: they had hit duet with carbon copy of Inez and Charlie Foxx's 'Mockingbird' '74, their solo outings being similarly cheery singalongs. She switched to DOOBIE Bros. prod. Ted Templeman for *Another Passenger* '76 chasing MOR appeal, returned to Perry for transatlantic smash hit with James Bond theme 'Nobody Does It Better' '77, which had no edge at all. LPs *Boys In The Trees* '78 (incl. top 10 hit 'You Belong To Me'), *Spy* '79, *Come Upstairs* '80 (on WB, incl. 'Jesse'); with marriage to Taylor on the rocks she took more chances: *Torch* '81 resurrected evergreens 'Body And Soul', 'I Get Along Without You Very Well' etc. arr. by Mike Manieri, while one-off disco single with CHIC 'Why' (from film *Dinner For One*) was UK no. 10 '82. *Hello Big Man* '83 was followed by switch from WEA group to Epic for *Spoiled Girl* '85. Hit 'Coming Round Again' '86 is title song from her score for Streep/Nicholson film *Heartburn*, based on Nora Ephron novel; album of same name on Arista. She was writing a novel '86. She recruits men to play in her videos in an impromptu fashion: they incl. actors Jeremy Irons, Al Corley (from TV's *Dynasty*), and a garage mechanic named Carl, fished out from under a car for temporary stardom. Her father had taken her to so many Brooklyn Dodgers games that she became team mascot; years later she said 'If I was to see myself as anyone, it would be Pee Wee Reese . . . A shortstop is not quite in the infield and not quite in the outfield.'

SIMON, Paul Singer, songwriter, guitarist; half of SIMON & GARFUNKEL (see above), but his solo career began before that: worked with Carole KING '58, had minor hits as Tico & The Triumphs ('Motorcycle' '62), as Jerry Landis ('The Lone Teen Ranger' '63); his debut solo LP *The Paul Simon Song Book* '65 preceded success of Simon & Garfunkel by a matter of months, and formed the basis of their repertoire for some time, with such standards as 'The Sound Of Silence', 'I Am A Rock', 'Kathy's Song'. He enjoyed attention as a fledgling folksinger type in UK (also prod. LP by Jackson C. FRANK '65) when 'folk-rock' studio job on duo version of 'Silence' changed that; international stardom began. When they split he took songwriting classes in

NYC, poured energy into *Paul Simon* '72, a diverse collection from reggae ('Mother And Child Reunion') to jazz ('Hobo's Blues' with Stephane GRAPPELLI), Latin ('Me & Julio'). Notable for narrative flair and further South American infl. was 'Duncan'. *There Goes Rhymin' Simon* '73 was more straightforward, 'Kodachrome' and 'Take Me To The Mardi Gras' being hit singles, 'American Tune' lushly produced with beautiful singing, haunting lyric. 'Was A Sunny Day' incl. the Roches, while 'St Judy's Comet' was a lullaby. He prod. LP by Urubamba '73; his *Live Rhymin'* '74 incl. remakes of S&G hits (with extra verse in 'The Boxer', gospel-flavoured 'Bridge Over Troubled Water'), as well as his own new material; *Still Crazy After All These Years* '75 incl. deft '50 Ways To Leave Your Lover', reunion with Garfunkel on 'My Little Town'. It was his last album for five years; he worked on the soundtrack of the film *Shampoo* '75, did cameo in Woody Allen's *Annie Hall* '77, joined Garfunkel and James TAYLOR in USA top 20 hit cover of Sam COOKE's 'Wonderful World' '78; *Greatest Hits Etc.* '77 incl. otherwise unavailable singles 'Slip Slidin' Away', 'Stranded In A Limousine'. *One Trick Pony* '80 was soundtrack of ambitious film depicting decline of once-famous rock star (played by Simon) obsessed with Elvis PRESLEY; it matched his scrupulous standard, but disappointed by film's reception (panned, perhaps unfairly) he spent three years on *Hearts And Bones* '83 (switching from Columbia to WB amid lawsuits): it was intended to be a studio reunion with Garfunkel following their 2-disc live set from Central Park '82, but latter's contributions were scrapped: 'The Late Great Johnny Ace', orchestrated by Philip GLASS, was a tribute to both Johnny ACE, John LENNON; also notable were title track, wistful 'Train In The Distance'. He duetted with Randy NEWMAN on single 'The Blues' '83, appeared on USA For Africa's 'We Are The World' '85, Glass album *Songs For Liquid Days* '86. Then *Graceland* '86 was an album of the decade, full of beauty and joy and haunting lyrics, one track each featuring ROCKIN' DOPSIE and LOS LOBOS, the rest with Africans, incl. Senegalese singer Youssou N'DOUR, South African choral group LADYSMITH BLACK MAMBAZO, many others; hit singles incl. 'You Can Call Me Al' (pennywhistle solo by Morris Goldberg, a white South African living in NYC), 'Boy In The Bubble'; the title track was successfully pan-cultural between Africa and USA country music, with guitar solo by Ray Phiri. Some tracks were made in South Africa; single-issue fanatics attacked him for offending United Nations resolution, as though the UN could/should embargo music, but Hugh MASEKELA and Miriam MAKEBA, themselves exiled from their own country, toured with him '87; anyway Simon had already described critics and others in 'You Can Call Me Al', itself about mistaken identity: 'A man walks down the street/It's a street in a strange world/Maybe it's the Third World/Maybe it's his first time around/He doesn't speak the language . . .' *Collected Works* is a five-disc compilation on CBS of one of our best lyricists. Biography *The Boy In The Bubble* '88 by Patrick Humphries.

SIMONE, Nina (*b* Eunice Waymon, 21 Feb. '33, Tryon, N.C.) Cabaret singer, songwriter, pianist; an interpreter of unique emotional power with a world-wide audience. Parents were both Methodist clergy; one of eight children, all musical; her brother Samuel, the youngest, was her manager in '84. To Philadelphia at 17, then to NYC; studied at Juilliard, accompanied singers, began to sing herself. Debut on Bethlehem incl. top 20 single 'I Loves You Porgy' '59 (LP now on Charly as *My Baby Just Cares For Me*); her material and her career has defied category, with equal amounts of blues, jazz, folk, gospel, show tunes, adding up to love and protest. Renounced the USA late '60s, went to Barbados, then Liberia (Miriam MAKEBA is a close friend), then France; her career has been dogged by personal problems leading to unreliability: engagement at Ronnie SCOTT's in London '84 was standing-room only at premium prices; she was booked to return a few weeks later and didn't turn up. Her best-known composition is 'To Be Young, Gifted And Black' '69; her own single on RCA reached Hot 100 and the song often covered (incl. Aretha FRANKLIN '72). Albums incl. *Here Comes The Sun, Sings The Blues, The Artistry Of Nina Simone, Pure Gold, Black Soul* in various RCA editions; *Fine And Mellow* and *Nina Simone* from PRT UK; *I Loves You Porgy* on CBS UK incl. Willard Robison song 'Don't Smoke In Bed' (a hit by Peggy LEE '48) and her own powerful 'Mississippi Goddam' and 'Central Park Blues'. Also *Cry Before I Go* and *I Want A Little Sugar In My Bowl* on Manhattan; *A Very Rare Evening With Nina Simone* on PM; *Baltimore* '78 on CTI; *Fodder On My Wings* '82 on Polygram, a concept LP partly in French about rejection of the USA. Other French sets incl. 2-disc *A Portrait* on Musidisc and *Our Love* on Barclay; *Music For The Millions* on Philips is a compilation; other titles are *Little Girl Blue* on SalSoul, *Best Of* sets on RCA and Philips, all in USA. Bethlehem track 'My Baby Just Cares For Me' was used in TV adverts for Chanel No. 5 perfume '87; as a single it sold 175,000 copies in the first week and reached no. 5 on UK chart; Charly, having licensed the material from American owners, was not required to pay her anything but offered $20,000 royalties.

SIMPLE MINDS Scottish new wave group formed '77 as punks Johnny and the Self Abusers, who released single 'Saints And Sinners' on Chiswick, split on day of issue: vocalist Jim Kerr, guitarist Charlie Burchill, Brian McGee on drums re-formed early '78 with bassist Derek Forbes, Mick McNeil on keyboards, second guitarist Duncan Barnwell ousted before recording of their first LP *Life In A Day* '79 for local Zoom label: edgy and full of ideas, it brought them a following and made UK top 30. *Real To Real Cacophony* late '79 again prod. by John Leckie, this time for Arista, who'd taken over Zoom; McNeil's keyboards more to the fore, Burchill's Banshee-style guitar motifs showing promise on 'Changeling', 'Premonition'; influences at this time were European art-rock: KRAFTWERK, Edgar Froese. *Empires And Dance* '80 added dance-floor appeal *à la* Giorgio Moroder (e.g. 'I Travel'). Kerr had come into his own, vocals atop carefully layered music in a far more distinctive sound; success in Europe and among new romantics led to problem with record label, switch to Virgin for 2-disc *Sons And Fascination/Sister Feelings Call* '81 prod. with ex-GONG guitarist Steve Hillage; LP reached top 20 UK; warmer sound and longer tracks led to singles success in vari-

ous countries (but not yet UK or USA) with 'The American', 'Love Song' (latter top 10 Australia). *New Gold Dream* '82 was first LP without McGee (tired of touring), replaced by Kenny Hyslop (ex-Skids, Zones), then Mel Gaynor (ex-Central Line); three top 40 singles in UK gave their bombastic music a commercial edge; *Sparkle In The Rain* '84 entered chart at no. 1, prod. by Steve Lillywhite with three more top 30 hits, spacious, vast sound ideal for USA stadia: breakthrough there came with single 'Don't You (Forget About Me)' (no. 1 '85) from soundtrack of *The Breakfast Club*, not their own song but written by Keith Forsey (Billy IDOL, etc.). Forbes quit (later toured with Propaganda), replaced by John Giblin (ex-Kate BUSH, Brand X), whose background of sessions, jazz-rock emphasised musicianship that set Minds apart from punks. *Once Upon A Time* '85 prod. by Stadium-rock experts Jimmy Iovine (Tom PETTY, Bruce SPRINGSTEEN) and Bob Clearmountain (Bryan ADAMS, HALL & OATES); sound now homogenised, but fans of guitar bands (U2, BIG COUNTRY) lapped it up. Kerr married Chrissie Hynde '84, his group having supported PRETENDERS in USA; they're unlikely to play support in future. They did benefits for Amnesty; 2-disc live *In The City Of The Light* reflected success, raised question whether Simple Minds sound like U2 or vice-versa.

SIMPLY RED UK pop band formed '85 in Manchester by vocalist/songwriter Mick Hucknall (*b* 8 June), who had fronted punk band the Frantic Elevators, with three former members of Durutti Column: bassist Tony Bowers (*b* 31 Oct.), drummer Chris Joyce (*b* 11 Oct.), Tim Kellet (*b* 23 July) on brass; plus Fritz McIntyre (*b* 2 Sep.) on keyboards, Sylvan Richardson on guitar. Signed to Elektra, supported James BROWN on UK tour; first LP *Picture Book* '85 incl. UK hits 'Money's Too Tight To Mention' (top 15), 'Holding Back The Years' (no. 2 '86); second *Men And Women* '87 with hit 'The Right Thing', two other songs co-written by Hucknall with Lamont Dozier. They became headliners '87: live show is good value; Hucknall has a singing voice and uses old standards in the act (Cole PORTER's 'Ev'ry Time We Say Goodbye'), setting them apart from other bands, another sign that pop as we have known it since '60s is increasingly to be regarded as bubblegum.

SIMS, Zoot (*b* John Haley Sims, 29 Oct. '25, Inglewood, Cal.; *d* 23 Mar. '85) Reeds, mainly tenor sax. Played with Bobby Sherwood '42-3 (trumpet, guitar, bandleader, *b* 30 May '14, Indianapolis, Ind; *d* 23 Jan. '80; records on Capitol incl. 'The Elk's Parade', hit 'Sherwood's Forest' '46), then Benny GOODMAN, others; served in US Army '44-6, recorded with Bill Harris group under Joe BUSHKIN's name on Commodore '46, became famous as one of the Four Brothers sax section in Woody HERMAN band '47-9. He freelanced, toured with Goodman, Stan KENTON, Gerry MULLIGAN; first teamed with Al COHN '52, later often made two-tenor gigs; toured USSR with Goodman '62; sometimes rejoined Herman. He played with John COLTRANE, Sonny ROLLINS, Coleman HAWKINS at Titans of the Tenor concert NYC '66: with Cohn, Stan GETZ and a handful of others, he was one of the few white players of his generation who belonged in that company; infl. by Lester YOUNG, developing his own beautiful tone and ideas, never failing to swing, he was also one of the most popular. In the late '70s he occasionally played soprano. First own recordings in Europe '50 now on Prestige *First Recordings!*, many with Kenny CLARKE, bassist Pierre Michelot, Gerald Wiggins on piano (*b* 12 May '22, NYC; his son Gerald, *b* 15 Apr. '56, L.A. plays bass, trombone, joined Mercer ELLINGTON '74). More tracks '50-4 on Prestige 2-disc *Zootcase*, incl. first session with Cohn '52, also with Kai WINDING, Percy HEATH, Art BLAKEY, George Wallington on piano. Sims/Bob BROOKMEYER Quintet tracks from '56 released on five different labels incl. Biograph (*One To Blow On*), from '58 on UA; quintet *Zoot!* '56 on Riverside. He was multi-tracked on ABC-Paramount LPs, playing three horns '56, four altos '57 (now on Impulse in USA); Sims Quartet *Down Home* '60 now on Affinity. Sets with three saxes on UA '59 (Cohn, Phil WOODS; Mose ALLISON, Paul MOTIAN, bassist Knobby Totah), on Pumpkin '65 (*Suitably Zoot* with Cohn, Richie Kamuca, Dave FRISHBERG, Tommy Potter, Mel LEWIS); on Sonet '74 made in Sweden with Horace PARLAN. With orchestra on Impulse '66, made in

London (arr. by Gary MCFARLAND, leader Jack Parnell); more LPs on Argo, RCA, Pacific Jazz, Colpix, Famous Door, Choice; duos with guitarist Bucky Pizzarelli on Groove Merchant '77, Ahead '76. On Norman GRANZ's Pablo label '75-84 incl. quartet *Soprano Sax* and 10-piece *Hawthorne Nights* (arr. and cond. by Bill Holman), both '76; big band *Passion Flower/Plays Duke Ellington* '80 (arr. and cond. by Benny CARTER), duo (with Joe PASS) *Blues For Two* '82, 11 more quartet/quintet LPs incl. excellent *Basie & Zoot* also *If I'm Lucky* and *I Wish I Were Twins* quartet sets with Jimmy ROWLES. Last date was trio *In A Sentimental Mood* '84 on Sonet, made in Sweden with bassist Red MITCHELL, guitarist Rune Gustafsson.

SINATRA, Frank (*b* Francis Albert Sinatra, 12 Dec. '15, Hoboken, N.J.) Singer, actor, superstar. Infl. by Billie HOLIDAY and Bing CROSBY, he was the second popular singer after Crosby (who pioneered the modern use of the microphone) to transform the art: he lived a stormy and often painful emotional life, putting it into the way he phrased the songs: together with his attractive and instantly recognisable baritone, this made him not a jazz singer but the greatest male interpreter of America's best songs. Quit school at 16 to sing at weddings, the local Union Club, for anyone who would have him; on *Major Bowes Amateur Hour* talent show on radio with three others as the Hoboken Four '35 (they won, toured with Bowes, were filmed in blackface as minstrels); sang '37-9 at the Rustic Cabin, roadhouse near Englewood, N.J. where he doubled as head waiter, keeping the job because the place had a radio wire. Married sweetheart Nancy early '39; singing (for free) on WNEW radio *Dance Parade*, heard by Harry JAMES, who had just left Benny GOODMAN to start his own band: first sang with James mid-'39 after refusing to change his name; first press notice (in *Metronome*) commended his 'easy phrasing'. First record (uncredited) with James July '39 sold 8000 copies; 'All Or Nothing At All' in Sep. became no. 1 hit when reissued '43. A CBS executive advised Tommy DORSEY to 'Go listen to the skinny kid who's singing with Harry's band'; Dorsey made an offer and James, one of the nicest people in show business, let him go without a murmur. Recorded with Dorsey early '40 as a member of the Pied Pipers, vocal quintet with Jo STAFFORD, Connie Haines (see Dorsey entry), arr. by Axel STORDAHL; made first film with the band Las Vegas Nights '40, by mid-'41 named in Billboard survey of colleges as outstanding male band vocalist, displaced Crosby in Downbeat poll late '41, although usually uncredited on records. First hit with Dorsey was 'Polka Dots And Moonbeams', no. 1 hits incl. 'I'll Never Smile Again' '40, 'Delores' '41, 'There Are Such Things' '42, 'In The Blue Of The Evening' '43. 'I'll Be Seeing You' recorded '40, was no. 4 '44 after he'd left Dorsey: Sep. '42 he bought out his contract, hearing that Bob Eberly was leaving Jimmy DORSEY; he wanted to be the first since Crosby to make it on his own. From 30 Dec. '42 appeared for four weeks at Paramount theatre with Goodman, booked for four more, drove bobby-soxers wild: it is said that some girls were hired to scream, but many more screamed for free, and modern pop hysteria was born; he was dubbed 'The Sultan Of Swoon', 'The Voice That Thrills Millions', then 'The Voice'. On return engagement at the Paramount 12 Oct. '44 ('The Columbus Day Riot') 25,000 teenagers blocked the streets. He explained it later: 'It was the war years, and there was a great loneliness. And I was the boy in every corner drug-store . . . who'd gone off, drafted to the war. That was all.' But it was more than that; pop singers were a new phenomenon, taking over as the Big Band Era wound down, and he was the best of the lot; he gave Dorsey credit for lessons in breath control and phrasing; many critics and musicians knew he was a better than average singer, even then making a song his own by phrasing it in such a way as to make the listener feel that he or she was being sung to personally, yet never lachrymose or idiosyncratic, always in the service of the song. Jazz musicians appreciated him for this, although he did not recompose a song to suit himself, as the best jazz singers have done. He took over top spot in Your Hit Parade '43-5, popular network show since '35 (having to sing 'The Woody Woodpecker Song' several weeks); first solo discs for Columbia June '43 arr. by Stordahl, who'd left Dorsey with him; 86 hits on Columbia '43-52 (not count-

ing 'All Or Nothing At All') incl. 33 in top 10: 'Oh! What It Seemed To Be', 'Five Minutes More', 'Mam'selle', all no. 1 '46-7; 'You'll Never Know' '43, 'Saturday Night Is The Loneliest Night Of The Week' '45 (first record after year-long musicians' union recording ban), 'They Say It's Wonderful' '46, all at no. 2; accompanied mostly by Stordahl but also Page Cavanaugh Trio ('That's How Much I Love You' '47), James ('Castle Rock' '51), Mitch MILLER ('Goodnight Irene' '50); sidemen/soloists over the years incl. Ziggy Elman, Chris Griffin, Bobby HACKETT, Billy BUTTERFIELD on trumpets; Will BRADLEY, Si Zentner, Buddy MORROW on trombones; Tony Mottola, Dave BARBOUR on guitar; Herbie Haymer, Babe Russin on tenor sax. Films incl. Reveille With Beverly and Higher And Higher '43, Step Lively '44, Till The Clouds Roll By '46 (cameo in Jerome KERN biopic), It Happened In Brooklyn '47 with Jimmy DURANTE; others incl. those with Gene KELLY: Anchors Aweigh '45, Take Me Out To The Ball Game and On The Town '49. He supported Franklin D. Roosevelt for President (naming his son after him), made short film The House I Live In '45 (dir. Mervyn Le Roy) on behalf of religious/racial tolerance (received Special Oscar '46), visited Cuba '47; was accused of Communism, Mafia links. He left Nancy '50, married actress Ava Gardner '51, co-wrote, recorded 'I'm A Fool To Want You', described by critic George T. Simon as 'the most moving song Sinatra has ever recorded'. It was public knowledge that the new marriage was stormy; he had been too successful, too outspoken for too long: the gossip columnists turned against him; hits fell off, partly because of the junk forced on him, probably by Miller (novelty 'Mama Will Bark' '51 with busty actress Dagmar); career faltered. But he turned it round '53: he fought for part of Maggio in film of James Jones novel From Here To Eternity (won Oscar '54), switched to Capitol label, then the most innovative in the USA: first Capitol session was last with Stordahl ('Lean Baby' was top 15 hit), second was first with Nelson RIDDLE, incl. 'I've Got The World On A String' (by Ted Koehler and Harold ARLEN '32), 'South Of The Border' (written by Englishmen Jimmy Kennedy and Michael Carr '39, first sung that year by Gene AUTRY on UK tour; the Sinatra record was not arr. by Billy MAY, but purposely in his style), 'Don't Worry 'Bout Me' (by Koehler and Rube Bloom '39): the first two were hits at a time when the pop chart was descending into slop like 'How Much Is That Doggie In The Window'; when he sang 'I've Got The World On A String', everybody knew he had: good songs, Riddle's arr., fine recording technology put him back on top for good. He had more single hits, but sold albums to grown-ups: 13 brilliant Capitol 12″ LPs were top 5 LPs '54-61, nearly all with Riddle: some with eight tunes on each side, compiled from 10″ LPs, an example of Capitol's fearlessness in those days: these LPs cost more because of the publisher's royalties to be paid on additional songs, but the public bought them anyway. *Swing Easy* '54 had accompaniment in chamber-jazz style; *In The Wee Small Hours* '55 is often called the first concept album in pop, songs of aching love at time of separation from Gardner; *Songs For Swingin' Lovers* '56 used big band with tasteful strings, sidemen like Harry EDISON on muted trumpet; incl. Cole PORTER's 'I've Got You Under My Skin' (voted by thousands of his fans '80 as all-time favourite), also 'You Make Me Feel So Young', 'It Happened In Monterey', 'You're Getting To Be A Habit With Me'; perhaps Sinatra's peak and Riddle's best work. Further albums were *Close To You*, *A Swingin' Affair* (incl. RODGERS & HART's 'I Wish I Were In Love Again'), *Where Are You* (arr. by Gordon JENKINS), all '57; *Come Fly With Me* (arr. by May) and *Only The Lonely* (arr. by Jenkins, cond. by Felix Slatkin) '58 (both no. 1 LPs); *Come Dance With Me* '59 (May) and *No One Cares* (Jenkins) '59; *Nice 'N' Easy* '60 (no. 1 album), *Sinatra's Swingin' Session* '60, *All The Way* '61 all with Riddle. *Come Swing With Me* '61 was no. 8 LP with May; *Point Of No Return* '62 (top 20) was reunion with Stordahl. Sinatra formed his own Reprise label (merged with WEA '63 in a deal that made him a lot of money), had 36 more hit albums '61-81, almost all in the top 40 LPs, incl. *Ring-A-Ding-Ding!* '61 (arr. by Johnny Mandel), *Sinatra Swings* (arr. by May), *I Remember Tommy* (remakes of Dorsey hits arr. by Sy OLIVER), all '61; *Sinatra And Strings* (arr. by Don COSTA), *Sinatra And Swingin' Brass* (arr. by Neal HEFTI) and *All*

Alone (Jenkins), all '62; albums with Count BASIE: *Sinatra-Basie* '63 (Hefti), *It Might As Well Be Swing* '64, 2-disc live *Sinatra At The Sands* '66 (both arr. by Quincy JONES). Set of Oscar-winning songs '64 arr. by Riddle; *September Of My Years* '65 by Jenkins was thoughtful concept set by a man now turning 50. *Francis Albert Sinatra & Antonio Carlos Jobim* '67 was bossa nova, arr. by Claus Ogerman; *Sinatra & Company* by Eumir DEODATO used Jobim on one side. *Great Songs From Great Britain* '62 with Robert FARNON was issued in UK and Italy, never in USA: he was in tired voice, having just completed a world tour, but the LP became a collector's item anyway, reissued in Japan '85. Quality of his material sometimes slipped; he made an album of songs by poet Rod McKuen, LPs *Cycles* and *My Way* (sets of contemporary pop) all with Costa; one of his hit singles was 'Strangers In The Night' (no. 1 '66), song adapted from film theme by Bert Kaempfert whose success is a complete mystery. He announced his retirement, but *Ol' Blue Eyes Is Back* '73 with Jenkins was top 15 LP; *Sinatra – The Main Event* '74 top 40, live from various concerts with Woody HERMAN, arr. by Riddle, Costa, May, 'The Lady Is A Tramp' by Billy Byers. His recording slowed up; *Trilogy: Past, Present, Future* '80 was a top 20 3-disc set with arr. by May, Costa, Riddle, Jenkins; *L.A. Is My Lady* '84 arr. by Quincy Jones on Jones's Qwest label. Over 70 Hot 100 entries '54-75 incl. duets with Crosby, Keely SMITH, Sammy DAVIS Jr, Nancy SINATRA; 'Three Coins In The Fountain' (no. 4 '54), 'Learnin' The Blues' (no. 1 '55), 'Hey! Jealous Lover' (no. 3 '56), 'All The Way' (no. 2 '57), 'Witchcraft' (no. 6 '58), 'That's Life' (no. 4 '66). He cannot keep away from the charts: even '75 was not the end of the hit singles; 'Theme From New York, New York' made top 40 '80; 'L.A. Is My Lady' '85 made Billboard's 'adult contemporary' list. *The Voice 1943-1952* on CBS '86 incl. 72 tracks; *Dorsey/Sinatra Sessions* have been reissued on three 2-disc sets by RCA, the original Capitol albums digitally remastered. He had conquered radio in the '40s, TV from '50; he made more than 40 films after *From Here To Eternity*, most non-musical, some less than masterpieces: best straight roles incl. *Suddenly* '54 (psychopathic would-be killer), *Not As A Stranger* '55 (as doctor chum of Robert Mitchum in hospital soap opera), *The Man With The Golden Arm* '55 (drug addict), thriller *The Manchurian Candidate* '62. There were 'rat pack' romps with buddies Dean MARTIN, Sammy DAVIS Jr, Peter Lawford, Joey Bishop; later played detective Tony Rome. In '60 he wanted to film *The Execution Of Private Slovik*, the true story of the only USA soldier executed for desertion during WWII, but scriptwriter Albert Maltz had been blacklisted and USA wasn't ready for it: post-Vietnam soul-searching still around the corner. He made debut as dir. with war movie *None But The Brave* '64, narrowly escaped drowning in the Pacific, pulled from the surf by actor Brad Dexter. Musical films incl. *Young At Heart* (title song was no. 2 hit) and *The Tender Trap* (no. 7 hit), both '55; classics *Guys And Dolls* (Frank LOESSER songs; Sinatra played the operator of 'The Oldest Established Permanent Floating Crap Game In New York'), *High Society* (Cole Porter score, Crosby co-star), *Pal Joey* (songs by Rodgers & Hart; Sinatra played gilt-edged heel Joey Evans, Kim Novak's voice dubbed by Trudy Erwin; author John O'Hara said 'I don't have to see Sinatra. I invented him'); *The Joker Is Wild* (played comedian Joe E. Lewis in true story of a singer who turned comic after his throat was slashed by gangsters), all '55-7. Good songs written for Sinatra films by Sammy CAHN/Jimmy Van Heusen incl. 'The Tender Trap', 'Love And Marriage' (no. 5 '55, from TV prod. of Thornton Wilder's *Our Town*), 'High Hopes' (from *A Hole In The Head* '59) and 'Come Blow Your Horn' (title song '62). In '57 he attacked rock'n'roll as 'degenerate', but modified his views, welcomed Elvis PRESLEY home from the army on TV spectacular '60. Briefly engaged to dancer Juliet Prowse '62, married Mia Farrow '66, then Barbara Marx (Zeppo's widow) '76 (Ronald Reagan among the guests). He is noted for private generosity to friends and strangers in need; he has continuously been accused of having shady friends, as though one could be the biggest headliner in Las Vegas while avoiding the people who run it; his private life has been stormy, but that no doubt helped to make the singer-as-interpreter one of the best-loved of the century. Illustrated, un-

critical *The Frank Sinatra Scrapbook* by Richard Peters '82 is jammed with facts incl. filmography, complete discography '39-82 by Ed O'Brien and Scott P. Sayers; *His Way: The Unauthorised Biography* '86 by Kitty Kelley has dirt for those who want it.

SINATRA, Frank, Jr (*b* Franklin Wayne Sinatra, 10 Jan. '44, Jersey City, N.J.) Became cabaret singer after his father's style and was doing well with many fans when he was kidnapped Dec. '63 for ransom; money was paid and kidnappers caught. At the trial the defence suggested it had all been publicity stunt (media loved it; Frank Sr said 'This family needs publicity like it needs peritonitis'). Jury threw out hoax theory, sent three men to prison, but Frank Jr's career hurt: audiences heckled him. Album *It's All Right* on Churchill label.

SINATRA, Nancy (*b* Nancy Sandra Sinatra, 8 June '40, Jersey City, N.J.) Frank Sinatra's daughter's career as a pop singer began '65, the year she divorced Tommy SANDS. She was helped by prod. Lee HAZLEWOOD, had six top 40 hits '66-7, incl. huge no. 1 'These Boots Are Made For Walkin' '. Sang title theme for father's movie *Tony Rome* '67; also had no. 1 hit '67 in duet with him: 'Somethin' Stupid'; made duets with Hazlewood. Nine albums charted '66-9 incl. top 40 *Movin' With Nancy* (TV soundtrack with her father, Dean MARTIN, Hazlewood), no. 13 LP *Nancy & Lee* '68. Later had duet country hit with Mel TILLIS.

SINGLETON, Shelby (*b* 16 Dec. '31, Waskom, Texas) Producer, publisher, label owner. Began in record promotion, worked with artists on Shreveport's *Louisiana Hayride* '50s; guided wife Margaret to country hits (Margie Singleton, *b* 5 Oct. '35, Coushatta, La.; scored with 'Eyes Of Love' '60, 'Old Records' '63 as she moved through Starday, Mercury and 'D' Records; split with Shelby, teamed with Leon Ashley on their Ashley label for duet hits '67-8). He worked for Mercury in NYC and Nashville, as product manager, then producer working with Brook BENTON '60; on Smash subsidiary label with Bruce Channel ('Hey Baby', no. 1 '62), Jerry Lee LEWIS, Roger MILLER, Charlie RICH. Left and formed own SSS

International '68, formed Plantation label, prod. Jeannie C. RILEY's 'Harper Valley PTA', sold five million copies in USA/Canada alone. Became a household name in some circles when he purchased Sun Records '69, acquiring vault full of Rich, Lewis, Carl PERKINS, Johnny CASH, much else (see SUN). Shelby Singleton Music signed writers such as Ben Peters, Vivian Keith, Naomi Martin, Royce Clark.

SIOUXSIE & THE BANSHEES UK post-punk punk band. Vocalist Siouxsie Sioux (b Susan Janet Dallion, 27 May '57, London) met bassist Steve Severin (b Steve Bailey, '55, London) at a SEX PISTOLS gig '75; with Billy IDOL, they were part of infamous 'Bromley contingent' of Pistols fans. With Marco Pirroni (later with Adam ANT) and Sid Vicious (soon joined Pistols) they made an inauspicious debut at 100 Club Punk Festival '76 with 20-minute version of 'The Lord's Prayer', which incl. bits of 'Twist & Shout', 'Rebel, Rebel' and 'Knockin' On Heaven's Door'. Guitarist John McKay, Kenny Morris on drums, Severin and Sioux were first proper Banshee lineup, with strong live following by the time they got record deal; *The Scream* '78 incl. manic version of the BEATLES' 'Helter-Skelter'; they were criticised for Nazi infatuation (lyric 'Too many Jews for my liking'; Siouxsie flaunted swastika), tried to atone with 'Israel' single '80, but stigma remained. *Join Hands* '79 incl. abbreviated 'Lord's Prayer'; on its release McKay and Morris quit, the CURE's Robert Smith was drafted in and Budgie (b Peter Clarke, 21 Aug. '57, St Helens, Lancs.) joined on drums. *Kaleidoscope* '80 incl. minor hits 'Christine' and 'Happy House'; Smith went back to Cure; John McGeoch (b '55, Greenock, Scotland; ex-Magazine) joined on guitar. *Juju* '81 saw them descend into their own psychedelic maelstrom; *Once Upon A Time: The Singles* '81 was premature 'Best Of'. *A Kiss In The Dreamhouse* '82 was McGeoch's last; he was sacked and went to work with PUBLIC IMAGE LTD; Smith came back. Siouxsie and Budgie branched off as The Creatures, whose *Feast* '83 incl. hit singles 'Right Now' and 'Miss The Girl'; Severin and Smith as The Glove released *Blue Sunshine* '83. 2-disc live *Nocturne* '83 was a success, but *Hyaena* '84 was so dismal that Smith quit;

Tinderbox '86 delighted fans, but their gloomy gothic rock now seems less relevant. They were the first UK group to visit Argentina after the Falklands War. *Through The Looking Glass* '87 incl. covers of hits by Tom Verlaine, IGGY POP, the DOORS, ROXY MUSIC; comes seriously unstuck on Billie HOLIDAY's 'Strange Fruit'. Cover of Bob DYLAN's 'This Wheel's On Fire' issued on a single. *Peepshow* '88 had only two original members remaining.

SISSLE, Noble (b 10 July 1899, Indianapolis, Ind.; d 17 Dec. '75, Tampa, Fla.) Bandleader, vocalist, composer. To Baltimore '15, worked in a band with Eubie BLAKE, sometimes Luckey ROBERTS on piano; within days Sissle/Blake auditioned their first hit 'It's All Your Fault' for Sophie TUCKER, who sang it in her act. He joined Jim EUROPE as guitarist-vocalist, with him in US Army '16 and until his death incl. tours of Europe. Formed duo with Blake, writing and prod. shows *Shuffle Along*, *Chocolate Dandies* etc. (see entry for Blake). Sissle recorded over 30 vocals '21-7, most accompanied by Blake; 'Arkansas' and 'Down-Hearted Blues' were hits '22-3. Continued leading bands, often in Europe: split up with Blake because he wanted to stay in England while Blake was homesick; was pals with Cole PORTER, Fred WARING; in Dec. '30 the Prince of Wales sat in on drums. Returned to USA '31, broadcast from Park Central Hotel NYC (breaking colour bar there); show *Shuffle Along Of 1933* flopped (allegedly among the cast was Nat 'King' COLE). Lena HORNE sang with band mid-'30s, conducted when Sissle had been in car crash. He employed Buster Bailey, Tommy LADNIER, other greats: hit 'Got The Bench, Got The Park' '31 incl. Sidney BECHET. At Billy Rose's Diamond Horseshoe club '38-50, except for USO tours WWII; succeeded Bill 'Bojangles' Robinson as honorary mayor of Harlem '50, played at Eisenhower inaugural '53, guests incl. Blake and W. C. HANDY; he was the first black DJ at radio WMGM NYC '60s; ran publishing company, club Noble's; retired to Tampa to live with Noble Jr after he'd been mugged several times. He appeared in film shorts with Blake c.'30; compilation on *Classic Jazz Masters* '86 incl. tracks by Noble Sissle & His Sizzling Syncopators.

Book *Reminiscing With Sissle And Blake* by Kimball and Balcom '73.

SKAGGS, Ricky (*b* 18 July '54, Cordell, Ky.) Country singer and musician with trad. orientation who has dominated USA country charts in the '80s, also has large European following. A prodigy, both religion and music playing vital parts in early life; played mandolin at 5 and since learned banjo, fiddle and guitars. Performed with family at church socials etc. and played 'Ruby' at Bill MONROE gig '59; appeared on Lester FLATT & Earl Scruggs TV show '61, joined Ralph Stanley & The Clinch Mountain Boys '70 as vocalist-mandolinist. Left music '73 but came back on fiddle with the Country Gentlemen '74, meeting young musicians who were cross-breeding country and bluegrass with jazz and folk. Replaced Rodney CROWELL in Emmylou HARRIS's Hot Band '77, playing guitar, fiddle and mandolin, singing harmony vocals; wrote arr. for highly praised *Roses In The Snow* album '80, went solo on the small North Carolina label Sugar Hill with *Sweet Temptation*, Emmylou, Jerry Douglas, Bobby Hicks, Albert Lee all featured; also *Skaggs & Rice* with Tony Rice on Sugar Hill, *Family & Friends* on Rounder; switched to Epic '81 and made country chart debut with 'Don't Get Above Your Raising', then no. 1 hits 'Crying My Heart Out Over You' and 'I Don't Care', won awards such as CMA Male Vocalist of the Year, ACM New Male Vocalist, *Music City News* Bluegrass Act of the Year; he had further no. 1 hits 'Heartbroke' '82, 'I Wouldn't Change You If I Could', 'Highway 40 Blues', 'Don't Cheat In Our Home Town', all '83; 'Honey (Open That Door)' and 'Uncle Pen' '84, 'Country Boy' and 'You Make Me Feel Like A Man' '85. He married Sharon White of The Whites '81 and has prod. their records as well as his own; his band won CMA Instrumental Group of the Year '83-4-5, he was Entertainer of the Year '85 and won Grammy for Best Instrumental ('Wheel Hoss' from *Country Boy*). He toured UK, appeared on Terry Wogan TV show, made 5-part series *Hit It Boys* for BBC2 '86. Hit albums incl. *Waitin' For The Sun To Shine* '81, *Highways And Heartaches* '82, *Don't Cheat In Our Hometown* '83, *Country Boy* '84, *Favourite Country Songs* '85, *Live In London* '85, *Love's Gonna Get Ya!* '86, all on Epic.

SKIDS, The Scottish new wave group formed in Dunfermline '77 from hard rockers Tattoo, whose guitarist Stuart Adamson, bassist Bill Simpson linked with drummer Tom Kellichan, singer Richard Jobson to ride punk wave, made single 'Charles' on own No Bad Label '78, signed with Virgin for *Scared To Dance* '79, with hit singles 'Into The Valley', 'Masquerade'. Added ex-Visage drummer Rusty Egan on *Days Of Europa* '79, prod. Bill (BE-BOP DELUXE) Nelson, befitting Nelson's axe-hero past, Adamson's bagpipe-like guitar chords a trademark; hits 'Charade', 'Working For The Yankee Dollar' incl. in double-single pack with cover of MOTT THE HOOPLE's 'All The Young Dudes', showing glam infl. of David BOWIE, T-Rex. After acrimonious tour Jobson and Adamson picked up new rhythm section, Russell Webb from Zones and Mike Baillie from Insect Bites; *The Absolute Game* '80 was top 10 LP; Zones drummer Kenny Hyslop replaced Baillie. But only 'Circus Games' of next four singles made top 40; freshness had gone out of band: Adamson departed to form BIG COUNTRY, further developing his distinctive guitar sound and reflecting frustration at Jobson's second career as media darling: he became actor, recorded poetry *The Ballad Of Etiquette* '81 for Nelson's Cocteau label. Webb and Jobson made folky *Joy* '81 as Skids, then split; later attempted comeback as The Armoury Show with ex-SIOUXSIE guitarist John McGeoch (LP *Waiting For The Floods* '85) without much success. Skids were refreshing regional variation on guitar-based post-punk new wave music; critics of Big Country point to banal lyrics, suggesting that Adamson's guitar, Jobson's poetic licence went well together.

SKIFFLE A word used in the USA to describe music played by those too poor to buy musical instruments and who used washboards, jugs etc. (blues medley 'Hometown Skiffle' issued '29 on Paramount, incl. Blind Lemon JEFFERSON, the Hokum Boys, others: one of the first samplers). The term became better known describing a late '50s British pop genre important as a bridge between the trad. jazz fad (*see* DIXIELAND) and

SLADE

UK R&B of the '60s, growing out of rhythm sections of bands like those of Chris BARBER and Ken COLYER; Lonnie DONEGAN was the undisputed king, sparking off a movement that took on craze proportions: 'A strange bedlam was taking over which had nothing to do with anything we had previously known' (quoted in Iain Chambers' *Urban Rhythms: Pop Music And Popular Culture* '85); Donegan's first hit 'Rock Island Line' (recorded '54) was regarded as a novelty, but backed with 'John Henry' '56 it was no. 6 UK, no. 10 USA (satirised there by Stan FREBERG, a sure sign of something or other). The VIPERS had several hits; Chas McDevitt & Nancy Whiskey made no. 10 (top 40 USA) with Libba COTTEN'S 'Freight Train'. Skiffle's big hits relied on USA folk songs by Woody GUTHRIE, LEADBELLY, Big Bill BROONZY, etc. It appealed to amateurs because of its relative simplicity, with acoustic guitars, washboards, bass often of tea chest and single-string-with-broomstick type; it was a training ground for musicians such as the SHADOWS, Cyril DAVIES, Alexis KORNER, Tommy STEELE, John LENNON, Paul McCARTNEY and many more. It was washed away suddenly: Donegan lasted longest, vanished from the top 10 in '62 with the advent of UK pop music that conquered the world: the British Invasion, hence all subsequent pop owed a lot to skiffle. Brian Bird's *Skiffle: The Story Of Folksong With A Jazz Beat* '58 is a good book, but over-emphasises the jazz input and offers little analysis, being too close to events.

SLACK, Freddie (*b* 7 Aug. '10, LaCrosse, Wis.; *d* 10 Aug. '65, Hollywood, Cal.) Pianist, bandleader, composer. Studied at American Conservatory in Chicago, played with Ben POLLACK, '35-6, Jimmy DORSEY '36-9, Will BRADLEY '39-41, fame during boogie-woogie fad: 'Beat Me, Daddy, Eight To The Bar' (no. 2 '40), named in 'Down The Road A Piece' (no. 10 '40): 'You remember Doc, and ol' "Beat Me Daddy" Slack.' On Capitol he backed T-Bone WALKER on 'I Got A Break, Baby', Johnny MERCER on 'I Lost My Sugar In Salt Lake City'; ten own hits '42-6 incl. four with Ella Mae MORSE, two with Margaret WHITING, instrumentals 'Cuban Sugar Mill', 'Riffette'.

He was seen in films *Reveille With Beverly* (incl. 'Cow Cow Boogie' with Morse) and *The Sky's The Limit* '43, *Babes On Swing Street* and *Follow The Boys* '44. Played in piano duo or led trio in '50s, '60s. Wrote or co-wrote 'Stange Cargo' (sometime Bradley theme), 'House Of Blue Lights' (hit with Morse; hit for Chuck Miller '55).

SLADE UK pop quartet formed as Ambrose Slade '68: Noddy Holder (guitar, vocals; *b* Neville Holder, 15 June '50, Walsall, Staffordshire), Jim Lea (bass, vocals, piano; *b* 14 June '52, Wolverhampton), Dave Hill (guitar; *b* 4 Apr. '52, Devon), Don Powell (drums; *b* 10 Sep. '50, Bilston, Staffs.) capitalised on skinhead image, though skins alleged fondness was for reggae, while Slade delivered pile-driving rock'n'roll. Former ANIMALS bassist Chas Chandler, who'd helped discover Jimi HENDRIX, managed them through greatest success. *Ambrose Slade* and *Ballzy* '69 were unrepresentative; from *Play It Loud* '70 they were unstoppable, with Gary GLITTER and Marc BOLAN providing UK with some of its most fondly-remembered pop of the era, Holder & Lea writing classic singles. 'Get Down And Get With It' scraped into top 20 '71; then 13 top 10 hits '71-5 incl. no. 1 'Coz I Love You', 'Mama Weer All Crazee Now', 'Cum On Feel The Noize', 'Skweeze Me, Pleeze Me', 'Merry Xmas Everybody' '73, the mis-spellings part of football-terrace appeal. Holder's aggressive vocals at times sounded uncannily like John LENNON's (e.g. on 'Merry Xmas'). *Slade Alive* '72 captured live appeal; *Slayed* '72, *Sladest* '73, *Old New Borrowed Blue* '74 were quintessential pop albums of the period; *Slade In Flame* was soundtrack for film which hoped to do for them what *A Hard Day's Night* had done for the BEATLES a decade before; they tried to broaden appeal and aimed at USA market, lost home fans; *Whatever Happened To Slade* '77 was apposite title: the punk explosion of that year was largely a working-class movement, taking away their fans. They refused to go away, still popular on club/college circuits; persistence was rewarded with *We'll Bring The House Down* '81 (title track back in top 10), followed by *Till Death Do Us Part* '81, *Slade On Stage* '82, *Amazing Kamikazi Syndrome* '83 (incl. no. 2 hit, sentimental 'My Oh

My'). 'Run Run Away' was no. 7 '84; *Rogues Gallery* '85 still found fans; *You Boyz Make Big Noize* '87 prod. by Roy Thomas Baker, better known for work with CARS, QUEEN. *Slade Smashes* '80 is 20-track compilation of the biggest hits of the early '70s.

SLEDD, Patsy (*b* Patsy Randolph, 29 Jan. '44, Falcon, Mo.) Country singer, one of the best back-up singers in Nashville. Began in family group, The Randolph Sisters backing Nashville stars appearing on the Ozark Opry; married Dale Sledd, guitarist with the OSBORNE Bros; moved to Nashville '65, worked as backing vocalist, joined Roy ACUFF show; recorded solo for UA '68, Epic '71, then had hits on small Mega label: 'Nothing Can Stop My Love' '72, 'Chip Chip' '74 (albums *Chip Chip* '74, *Yours Sincerely* '75). She toured as back-up vocalist with George JONES and Tammy WYNETTE, then just with Tammy, providing harmonies on record and concert dates; continues busy on Nashville sessions.

SLEDGE, Percy (*b* '41, Leighton, Ala.) Soul singer. Began singing as a teenager; became a nurse after high school, singing in local churches and in group the Esquires Combo. Encouraged by DJ/producer Quin Ivy in Sheffield, Ala. and another local entrepreneur, Phil Walden, who advised Atlantic to release the first single: 'When A Man Loves A Woman' was no. 1 in both pop and soul charts, top 5 in UK. He had ten more soul hits '66-9 incl. 'Warm And Tender Love', 'It Tears Me Up', 'Take Time To Know Her'; several crossed over to pop top 40. He recorded for Walden's Capricorn label, had minor hit 'I'll Be Your Everything' '74; but that first single has never been long off the radio. *Best Of* on Atlantic USA; *Any Day Now* on Charly UK compiled hits; when the big hit was used in UK TV advert '87, Atlantic rushed out new compilation *When A Man Loves A Woman*.

SLY AND THE FAMILY STONE USA rock group that fused pop, soul and rock to make first-class dance music with a political edge. Sly Stone (*b* Sylvester Stewart, 15 Mar. '44, Dallas, Texas) sang gospel music as a child, moved with his family to the San Francisco area '50s, had local hit 'Long Time Away' at age 16, formed various groups and studied

music formally; he became a DJ on KSOL, then KDIA, and worked as a producer for Autumn records with the BEAU BRUMMELS, Bobby FREEMAN, the Great Society (*see* JEFFERSON AIRPLANE), others. He formed The Stoners '66 with Cynthia Robinson (*b* 12 Jan. '46, Sacramento) on trumpet, then Sly and the Family Stone, singing, playing guitar and organ, with Robinson, brother Fred (as Freddie Stone; *b* 5 June '46, Dallas) on guitar and vocals, Larry GRAHAM on bass (important contribution led to later solo success), Greg Errico (*b* 1 Sep. '46, S.F.) on drums, Rosie Stone (*b* 21 Mar. '45, Vallejo, Cal.) on piano, Jerry Martini (*b* 1 Oct. '43, Col.) on sax. First album on Epic *A Whole New Thing* '67 sank without a trace, but *Dance To The Music* '68 was more coherent: while curiously reaching only no. 142 in the pop LP chart, it incl. a top 10 title track, the music transcending musical boundaries as the group ignored racial and sexual ones: they were the first to fuse an R&B beat with jazz-oriented horns, psychedelic guitar work, lyrics with a social message. *Life* '68 did less well; *Stand!* '69 was a no. 13 LP incl. 'Everyday People' (no. 1 both soul and pop charts), also '(I Want To Take You) Higher', 'Don't Call Me Nigger, Whitey', 'Somebody's Watching You', 'Sex Machine'; the album stayed in the charts for nearly two years. Exciting versions of 'Higher' and 'Dance To The Music' were heard in Woodstock Festival film/LP '69; *Greatest Hits* '70 was a no. 2 LP incl. singles 'Hot Fun In The Summertime' (no. 2), 'Thank You (Falettinme Be Mice Elf Agin)' (no. 1), which despite its silly title was not only a slice of ghetto life but a profound infl. for Graham's percussive, popping bass line. *There's A Riot Goin' On* '71 changed the pace, variously described as violent and controversially militant, or as having a softer, more personal feel: incl. 'Family Affair', no. 1 hit marking one of the first uses of a drum machine, since thought by many to be the most disastrous innovation in pop music. By this time he'd acquired a reputation for unreliability due to a drug problem; Graham left to form Graham Central Station, Andy Newmark replaced Errico and Pat Rizzo was added on sax. *Fresh* '73 was a top 10 album; Sly got married in concert at Madison Square Garden '74; *Small Talk* '74 slipped to no. 15; his solo *High On You* '75 did not reach the top 40 LPs. The group's *Heard Ya Missed Me, Well, I'm Back* '76 did not make the top 200 LPs. *Back On The Right Track* '79 reached no. 152 on WB; *Ten Years Too Soon* '79 had Epic re-editing tapes, laying disco backing on the hits; *Anthology* '81 was 2-disc compilation. Stone also toured and worked with George Clinton's PARLIAMENT/FUNKADELIC family, which he had deeply influenced.

SMALL FACES One of the best pop bands of '65-8, all from London's East End: Steve Marriott (*b* 30 Jan. '47), guitar and vocals; Ronnie Lane (*b* 1 Apr. '46), bass and vocals; Kenny Jones (*b* 16 Sep. '48) on drums; Ian McLagen (*b* 12 May '45) on keyboards. Jones and Lane were in the Outcasts and the Pioneers late '50s; Marriott was a child actor, like Phil COLLINS playing the Artful Dodger in Lionel BART show *Oliver!*; first Small Faces lineup incl. Jimmy Winston on organ, who'd played in the Moments with Marriott, was replaced by McLagen. Along with the WHO, Smalls were an archetypal Mod band (ROLLING STONES were Rockers; BEATLES transcended category); indeed some say Smalls' Mod credibility was greater than Who's. Managed by UK music business mogul Don Arden, they were soon in the charts, 'Watcha Gonna Do?' top 20 '65. Marriott and Lane soon made an effective songwriting partnership, scoring top 10 hits with 'Hey Girl', 'All Or Nothing' (no. 1) and 'My Mind's Eye'. At the height of 'Swinging London' they were enormously popular with teenage audiences; quickly tiring of being pretty faces, they went psychedelic: their hits of the period are not only still listenable to but an accurate picture of it, 'Itchycoo Park' for innovative use of electronic phasing, 'Tin Soldier' also ambitious. *Small Faces* '66 packaged singles for no. 3 LP UK; *Ogden's Nut Gone Flake* '68 was no. 1, lavish and effective, its circular sleeve a landmark in the period's pop art, tracks linked by linguistic comedian Stanley Unwin. 'Lazy Sunday' '68 was excellent marriage of hard rock and music hall, a strong contender behind Beatles and KINKS as epitomising the year. Marriott's growing disenchantment heard on 'The Universal', recorded in his garden on a mono cassette machine; *The Autumn Stone* '68 was a collection of live tracks, alternate takes; *From*

The Beginning '67 on Decca incl. early stuff (other discs were on Immediate). Marriott left to form HUMBLE PIE, Lane, Jones, Rod STEWART formed new group Faces (*see* Stewart's entry). 'Itchycoo Park' was top 10 on reissue '75; hits were later covered by the SEX PISTOLS, the Enid and the Tempest. They re-formed minus Lane for *Playmates* and *78 In The Shade* '77-8, but magic was gone. *Small Faces Big Hits* '80 is definitive compilation on Virgin. Marriott is still gigging in London pubs with his Packet of Three; Jones worked with the Who; McLagen made solo LPs *Troublemaker* '79, *Bump In The Night* '81 and played with Bob DYLAN '84; Lane enjoyed success with his Slim Chance, recording *Anymore For Evermore* '74, *Slim Chance* '75, *One For The Road* '76, *See Me* '79, as well as *Rough Mix* '77 with Pete Townshend. He was a victim of multiple sclerosis; in '83 the Stones, Jimmy Page, Steve WINWOOD and Eric CLAPTON played MS benefits on his behalf in USA and UK.

SMITH, Arthur (*b* 1 Apr. '21, Clinton, S.C.) Country guitarist, bandleader, songwriter. He worked in a textile factory, as semi-pro baseball player; formed the Crackerjacks '38 and worked on local radio in South and North Carolina; recorded for RCA '37-8, Super-Disc from '45: 'Guitar Boogie' was a mysterious hit, not appearing in charts then, either because nobody knew what chart to put it in or because it took some years to sell a million. It was picked up by MGM (Smith recorded for that label until '59); Joseph Murrells' *Million Selling Records* puts it in '46, while *Pop Memories* calls it a no. 25 hit '48: a jaunty country instrumental with a laid-back, implied backbeat, it's often cited as prequel to rock'n'roll. He also co-wrote 'Beautiful Brown Eyes' ('51 Rosemary CLOONEY hit), wrote 'Feuding Banjos', later called 'Duelling Banjos', played in soundtrack of *Deliverance* '72 by Eric Weissberg and Steve Mandel (no. 2 USA hit '73). He hosted his own syndicated TV show from Charlotte, N.C., guested on Kate SMITH, Bill ANDERSON shows; led the Crossroads Quartet, wrote gospel songs recorded by Johnny CASH, Ernie FORD, George HAMILTON IV; was regular at Singin' On The Mountain religious fests at Grandfather Mountain. LPs incl. *Battlin'*

Banjos '69 on Monument, *Singin' On The Mountain* '73 on RCA with Hamilton, *Original Guitar Boogie* '74 on Rediffusion, *Feudin' Again* '78 on CMH with Don Reno. Acoustic *Jumpin' Guitar* '87 on Relaxed Rabbit label compiles '45 tracks.

SMITH, Bessie (*b* 15 Apr. 1894, Chattanooga, Tenn.; *d* 26 Sep. '37, Clarkedale, Ms.) The greatest of all blues singers, 'Empress of the Blues'. She was one of seven children, orphaned c. age 7; sang in the streets for pennies. Worked with Ma RAINEY '12, as chorus girl c.'12; toured with Rainey '15 in Rabbits Foot Minstrels; had her own *Liberty Belles* revue in Atlanta '18-19. She may have recorded for Swan/Emerson '21; some sources say a record was issued under the name of Rosa Henderson, but blues discographies give Henderson's first record date as '23. There may have been a test record for Okeh '23, now lost; she recorded for Columbia '23-33; 160 sides survive. She was paid $250 a side in her heyday; her records are said to have saved Columbia from bankruptcy. 36 tracks were reissued on three LPs early '50s (*The Bessie Smith Story*); all 160 in five 2-disc sets '70. She was a headliner in mid-to-late '20s; *Pop Memories* '86 calculates that 15 of her records were best-sellers, beginning with 'Downhearted Blues' (no. 1 '23, selling 780,000 in six months), accompanied (as on several others) by Clarence WILLIAMS; on three '25 hits incl. 'St Louis Blues' she was accompanied by Louis ARMSTRONG, but he sounds uncharacteristically restrained: he was becoming a star and she didn't like competition. Other hits incl. accompaniment by Fletcher HENDERSON and Buster Bailey ('After You've Gone'), Coleman HAWKINS (on clarinet); legendary trombonist Charlie Green (then with Henderson) played on many records; two '23 sides were duets with Clara SMITH; prophetically, 'Nobody Knows You When You're Down And Out' '29 was her last big seller. She made short film *St Louis Blues* '29, the soundtrack issued on several labels incl. Biograph (with band incl. James P. JOHNSON, Hall-Johnson Choir). The Depression wrecked her career and Columbia dropped her '31. John HAMMOND brought her back into the studio Nov. '33; she refused to record blues, wanted to do something more modern: she was

paid $50 a side for four sides with a band led by Buck Washington incl. Chu BERRY, Jack TEAGARDEN, Frankie Newton (on trumpet: *b* 4 Jan. '06, Emory, Va.; *d* 11 Mar. '54, NYC: a 52nd Street regular, with John KIRBY '37, Lucky MILLINDER, led own bands) and a barely audible Benny GOODMAN on 'Gimme A Pigfoot'. She was considered old-fashioned by then; even the black community saw her as washed-up vaudevillian: Hammond prod. Billie HOLIDAY's first recording session the following month; an era had ended and another began. Badly injured in a car crash and lost too much blood before help was obtained; Chris Albertson found in researching biography *Bessie: Empress Of The Blues* '72 that the legend that she was refused hospital admittance because she was black was not true. There was pain enough in her life without that, but there was also a powerful dignity and a sense of humour along with irony, resignation: she is one of the all-time great stars of the gramophone record, her big, beautiful voice and emotionally naked interpretations resulting in records that will never stop selling. Not related to Clara, Mamie or Trixie SMITH, or Bessie Mae Smith, who recorded for Okeh, Paramount and Vocalion '27-30, also probably under other names.

SMITH, Buster (*b* Henry Smith, 26 Aug. '04, Ellis County, Texas) Alto sax, other instruments; arranger, leader. Began on piano and organ, switched to clarinet in teens; began on alto c.'22; played in local bands; to Oklahoma City '25, joined Blue Devils led by trombonist Emir Coleman, stayed under new leader Walter PAGE. Co-led Barons of Rhythm with Count BASIE briefly; led own band, played with Claude HOPKINS in Iowa '36, back to Basie as staff arranger. He did not want to go to NYC with Basie; worked with Andy KIRK, led own bands in Kansas City, went to NYC to work as arr. with Gene KRUPA, Hot Lips PAGE; led own band in Virginia, worked with Don REDMAN, Eddie DURHAM, Snub Moseley, returned to K.C. '42, had residencies there, worked in Southwest. As an arranger he worked with the best; on alto sax he was a profound influence on Lester YOUNG and Charlie PARKER. One LP under his own name made '59 for Atlantic in Fort Worth, Texas;

he was still playing gigs on bass guitar, leading a band in Dallas in '88.

SMITH, Cal (*b* Calvin Grant Shofner, 7 Apr. '32, Gans, Okla.) Deep-voiced country singer who had hits with compelling country yarns set to music. Grew up in Oakland, Cal.; turned pro early '50s in San José, became regular on *California Hayride* TV show; was DJ on Radio KEEN '58-61, joined Ernest TUBB's Texas Troubadours as frontman and vocalist '63-70: the move to Nashville led to contract with Kapp, minor solo hits '67-70; switched to Decca. Scored first top 10 hit with 'I've Found Someone Of My Own' '72, then no. 1 with 'The Lord Knows I've Been Drinking' '73. Further no. 1 hits with 'Country Bumpkin' (CMA Song of the Year), 'It's Time To Pay The Fiddler', both '74, while 'Between Lust And Watching TV' made top 10 despite being banned from the radio. 'She Talked A Lot About Texas' and 'Jason's Farm' were big hits, then top 40 'Thunderstorms' '76, top 15 'I Just Came Home To Count The Memories' '77, faded from the charts. LPs on MCA; recorded for Soundwave, then Step One (LP *Stories Of Life* '86).

SMITH, Carl (*b* 15 Mar. '27, Maynardsville, Tenn.) One of the most successful country singers of the post-war decades, with about 75 hits in 20 years. Began on guitar in his teens, turned pro following US Navy service, working on Radio WROL Knoxville '48, WWNC Asheville, N.C. '49; moved to Nashville and joined Grand Ole Opry '50, signing with Columbia and having his first hit with 'Let's Live A Little' '51 (no. 3); 'Let Old Mother Nature Have Her Way' '51, 'Hey Joe' '53, 'Loose Talk' '54 at no. 1. Other hits: 'Trademark' and 'Satisfaction Guaranteed' '53; two-sided hits 'There She Goes'/'Old Lonesome Times', 'You're Free To Go'/'I Feel Like Cryin' ' '55; also 'Kisses Don't Lie' '55, 'You Are The One' '56, 'You Can't Hurt Me Anymore' '57. 'Ten Thousand Drums' '59 crossed over to the pop chart but was his last top 10 hit except for 'Deep Water' '67. The first year he failed to make the charts was '74; he recorded for Hickory '75-8. He married June Carter (of the CARTER FAMILY) '52; their daughter Carlene CARTER has since become a country-rock star; married Goldie Hill '57

(*b* 11 Jan. '33, Karnes City, Texas), who had top 5 hit with 'I Let The Stars Get In My Eyes' '53 (an answer to 'Don't Let The Stars Get In Your Eyes', one of the biggest hits of the year: no. 1 for Perry COMO in the pop chart, no fewer than four country hits incl. Red FOLEY). Goldie semi-retired to their 600-acre ranch near Franklin, Tenn. to raise a family. Carl appeared in films *The Badge Of Marshall Brennan* '57, *Buffalo Guns* '62; had *Carl Smith's Country Music Hall* TV show in Canada '60s, syndicated to USA stations; retired late '70s, but he recorded hits for successful TV-advertised LP *Greatest Hits Volume One* '81 on Gusto/Starday. Many Columbia LPs incl. *Sunday Down South* '54, *Smith's The Name* '57, *Easy To Please* '63, *Sings Bluegrass* '71; also *A Way With Words* '77 on Hickory.

SMITH, Clara (*b* c.1894, Spartanburg, S.C.; *d* 3 Feb. '35, Detroit, Mich.) Blues singer. She worked in black southern vaudeville from c.'10, in NYC from '25-31 in many shows, revues incl. her own *Black Bottom*, *Clara Smith Revue* '27, all-black Western musical *Trouble At The Ranch* '31 in Philadelphia; worked in Cleveland, Ohio, then back in NYC for *Harlem Madness* '33. She recorded for Columbia '23-32, with Fletcher HENDERSON accompanying her at first; with her own Triflin' Trio; often with Porter Grainger on kazoo or piano and also with pianists Lem Fowler, James P. JOHNSON; on one '24 date her Jazz Band incl. Henderson, Don REDMAN, Charlie Green (according to *Pop Memories*, 'Chicago Blues' was no. 15 hit), on a '25 date Henderson with Louis ARMSTRONG, on a '30 date guitar and vocal duet by Lonnie JOHNSON. Her duets with Bessie SMITH '23 were 'Far Away Blues' and 'I'm Going Back To My Used To Be'. Bessie did not normally tolerate competition; on record her more powerful voice outclasses Clara's thinner one, but Clara was highly regarded, more versatile than Bessie, doing novelties and pop songs ('When My Sugar Walks Down The Street', '25). Three vols. of collected tracks on Vintage Jazz Mart label (VJM).

SMITH, Connie (*b* 14 Aug. '41, Elkhart, Ind.) Country singer. One of 14 children; sang in high school; worked on radio in West Va., switched to *Saturday Jamboree* on

WSAZ TV, got married and quit music but encouraged by husband (Jack Watkins) she won a talent show '63, spotted by Bill ANDERSON; moved to Nashville and signed with RCA '64; first single 'Once A Day' (written by Anderson) was no. 1 country hit, won CMA Song of the Year. Made TV debut on Jimmy DEAN show; notched up more than 30 hits, 14 more in top 10; switched to Columbia '74, Monument '77; meanwhile joined Grand Ole Opry '65, appeared on other TV shows, films *Road To Nashville, Las Vegas Hillbillies, Second Fiddle To An Old Guitar*; by the late '70s the hits were fading and she confined herself to gospel music, Opry appearances; announced intention to retire c.'80 but came back (minor hit 'A Far Cry From You' '85 on Epic). Many LPs on RCA in '60s plus *I Never Once Stopped Loving You, Where's My Castle, If It Ain't Love* '70-2; Columbia LPs incl. *God Is Abundant, That's The Way Love Goes, I Never Knew What That Song Meant Before, Sings Hank Williams Gospel, Joy To The World, I Got A Lot Of Hurting Done Today, I Don't Want To Talk About It Anymore, Songs We Fell In Love To; Pure Connie Smith* on Monument.

SMITH, Darden (*b* 11 Mar. '62, Brenham, Texas) Country singer, songwriter. Grew up in Houston; parents named him after a small-time rodeo rider, but he will soon be more famous than that: with Lyle LOVETT, Nanci GRIFFITH, Robert Earl KEEN one of the up-and-coming new Texas stars. Played with garage bands in high school, then moved to Austin at 19 and began appearing in clubs; leads own band and has evolved honky-tonk style owing nothing to the neo-hillbilly of Dwight YOAKUM: excellent lyrics earned him honours at '85 Kerrville Folk Festival, invited back as feature artist '86; his yarn-spinning imagery makes characters come alive, like that of Guy CLARK. First LP *Native Soil* on his own RediMix label had Griffith and Lovett singing backup, guests such as Ponty Bone; next release *Darden Smith* '88 on Epic prod. by Ray Stevens of ASLEEP AT THE WHEEL.

SMITH, Ethel (*b* 22 Nov. '10, Pittsburgh, Pa.) Organist popular in films, radio, records '40s. She played with symphony orchestras, made films *Bathing Beauty* '44,

George White's Scandals Of 1945, Easy To Wed '46, *Melody Time* '48; 'Tico Tico' with Bando Carioca no. 14 hit '44. She wrote or co-wrote songs 'Cuban Pete', 'Melody Time', others. She had a publishing company; wrote book *Hammond Organ Method*. LPs on Decca incl. *Latin From Manhattan, Miss Smith Goes To Paris, Lady Fingers, On Broadway*.

SMITH, Huey 'Piano' (*b* 26 Jan. '34, New Orleans, La.) R&B star of the '50s, with piano style infl. by PROFESSOR LONGHAIR. He sessioned with Guitar Slim '49, Earl KING ('Those Lonely, Lonely Nights'), Smiley LEWIS ('I Hear You Knocking'), Lloyd PRICE, LITTLE RICHARD; hits on Ace '57-8 with the Clowns incl. Bobby Marchan, lead singer; Charles Williams, drums; both Lee ALLEN and Red Tyler on saxes: '(I Got The) Rocking Pneumonia & The Boogie Woogie Flu' (top 10 R&B, no. 52 pop), 2-sided million-seller 'Don't You Just Know It'/'High Blood Pressure' (no. 4 R&B, 9 pop), 'Don't You Know Yockomo'; switched to Imperial label, back to Ace with last chart entry 'Pop-Eye' '62. Good compilation was *Rocking Pneumonia & The Boogie Woogie Flu* on Ace; *Somewhere There's Honey For The Grizzly Bear* on same label has more inspired nonsense; *The Imperial Sides 1960-1* from French EMI, *Rockin' And Jivin'* on Charly, *Serious Clownin'* on Rhino USA. The '60s tracks incl. vocalists Gerri Hall, Curley Moore (replacing Marchan); Hall had single 'I'm The One' on Ace, duet 'I Think You Jivin' Me' on Vin as Huey and Jerry; she also sang with Ray CHARLES's Raelets. Moore had local hit '66 'Soul Train' on Hotline '66. *Twas The Night Before Christmas* '62 on Ace had R&B versions of 'Jingle Bells', 'White Christmas'; public reaction was poor but LP reissued in UK '79. They toured USA, were even better live, best of all at home in New Orleans. As success declined Huey became a Jehovah's Witness.

SMITH, Jabbo (*b* Cladys Smith, 24 Dec. '08, Pembroke, Ga.) Trumpet, trombone, vocals. Legendary freelancer/bandleader went to Jenkins Orphanage age 6, played with orphanage band at age 10. Ran away several times, finally for good at 16 and stayed independent: worked in Atlantic City, N.J.;

NYC '25-8 (recorded with Duke ELLINGTON '27); toured with James P. JOHNSON in *Keep Shufflin'* '28; show folded in Chicago and he worked there, in Detroit, Milwaukee; joined Claude HOPKINS on tour in Milwaukee '36, back to NYC; led own band, worked with Sidney BECHET; long residency in Newark, N.J.; back to Milwaukee late '40s. European tours '70s; suffered from ill health early '80s but recovered to play in Europe again '83. Jabbo Smith and his Rhythm Aces '29 on Brunswick incl. Omer SIMEON, Ikey Robinson on banjo, Hayes Alvis on bass (later with Ellington); four sides with octet on Decca '38. Two discs of his best work on Melodeon '65; also *Ace Of Rhythm* on MCA, *Jazz Ace Of The Twenties* on Biograph (two vols. same as the Melodeons); most recent compilation of '29 sides *Sweet & Lowdown* on Affinity UK. *Hidden Treasure Vol. 1* on Jazz Art USA has newly discovered rehearsal tapes of early '60s combo.

SMITH, Jack (*b* c.1899; *d* May '51) aka 'Whispering Jack'. Singer who used influential half-whispering style because of injury from gas in WWI. He had a dozen big hits '26-8 incl. no. ones 'Gimme A Lil' Kiss, Will Ya, Huh?', 'Me And My Shadow'; no. 3 'There Ain't No Maybe In My Baby's Eyes'. He was also very popular in the UK.

SMITH, Jack (*b* c.'18) Singer; a tenor who was popular '40s. Part of trio The Three Ambassadors with Gus ARNHEIM '33 at Coconut Grove in L.A.; trio went with Phil HARRIS, later worked with Kate SMITH, split '39. Sang in chorus on *Your Hit Parade*, own radio shows late '40s; sang, acted, emcee'd on TV early '50s. Appeared in film *On Moonlight Bay* '51. Hit records on Capitol '47-9 incl. novelties, Clark Sisters backup singing; biggest was no. 3 'Cruising Down The River' '49, one of several hit versions.

SMITH, Jimmy (*b* James Oscar Smith, 8 Dec. '25, Norristown, Pa.) Jazz organist, with Wild Bill DAVIS probably the most popular and influential on the instrument. Both parents played piano; he worked with his father in clubs '42; studied music formally late '40s, turned pro '52, formed own trio '55 and was immediately successful, inventing modern jazz on the organ as Charlie Christian had done on the guitar: within a few years imitators of his trio format with guitar and drums were legion. Eddie McFadden played guitar '56-7, then Kenny BURRELL, then Quentin Warren for most of the '60s; regular drummer through Blue Note years was Donald Bailey (*b* 26 Mar. '34, Philadelphia; settled on West Coast freelancing in clubs; also recorded with Hampton HAWES, etc.). Smith had 12 Hot 100 singles in Billboard's pop chart '62-8; 22 albums '62-70 also crossed over to the pop LP chart. About 20 albums for Blue Note '56-63, many now being reissued, many with guests Lou DONALDSON, Stanley TURRENTINE, Tina BROOKS, Jackie McLEAN, Ike QUEBEC, George COLEMAN etc. incl. *Plays Pretty Just For You* '57, *House Party* and *The Sermon* '57-8, *Home Cookin'* '58, *Crazy Baby*, *Open House* and *Back At The Chicken Shack* '60, *Plays Fats Waller* '62. LPs on Verve '62-73 began with his biggest seller, first of several with big band arr. and cond. by Oliver NELSON: *Bashin'* '62 was top 10 LP with no. 21 single 'Walk On The Wild Side'; others with Nelson incl. *Hobo Flats* '63, *Who's Afraid Of Virginia Woolf* '64, *Monster* '65, *Hoochie Coochie Man* and *Peter And The Wolf* '66 (latter had finale called 'Peter Plays Some Blues'), *Livin' It Up* '68. LPs with Wes MONTGOMERY '66 (*The Dynamic Duo* and *The Further Adventures Of Jimmy And Wes*) also had tracks with Nelson, as did *Got My Mojo Workin'* '65 (Smith's debut as singer on title track). *The Cat* '64 was a no. 12 LP, arr. and cond. by Lalo SCHIFRIN, won a Grammy. There were also plenty of fine small-group sets, incl. *Organ Grinder Swing* '65, with Burrell, Grady Tate on drums (*b* 14 Jan. '32, Durham, N.C.; ace sideman began with Quincy JONES, later with Peggy LEE, began singing; played in *Tonight* show band '68-74), *Respect* '67, *The Boss* '69 with George BENSON, etc. Other albums on MGM, Mercury, Pride, Mojo, Milan labels '74-80. *Off The Top* '82 incl. Tate, Turrentine, Benson, Ron CARTER, Smith playing some synthesiser; *Keep On Comin'* '83, live at Atlanta jazz festival, had Johnny GRIFFIN, Burrell, Mike Baker on drums, Smith on piano as well as organ; both on Elektra. Johnny 'Hammond' Smith (*b* John Robert Smith, 16 Dec. '33, Louisville, Ky.), also a popular organist, made LPs on Prestige '59-71; guitarist Johnny Smith (*b* John Henry Smith, 25 June '22, Birmingham, Ala.) recorded for Roost '52-63 (successful with 'Moonlight In Vermont' '52 with Stan GETZ), Verve '67-8; Jimmie Smith (*b* James Howard Smith, 27 Jan. '38, Newark N.J.) is a drummer who has worked and recorded with Erroll GARNER, B. B. KING, Richard 'Groove' HOLMES, Jimmy FORREST, O. C. SMITH, many others. None of these is related.

SMITH, Joe (*b* 28 June '02, Ripley, Ohio; *d* 2 Dec. '37, NYC) Trumpet. His father led a big brass band in Cincinnati, Ohio; six brothers also played trumpet, several professionally. Played with Fletcher HENDERSON off and on from c.'21 (with Black Swan Masters), '25-8 full time, again in '30, '33; also with Mamie SMITH's Jazz Hounds, Noble SISSLE-Eubie BLAKE show *Chocolate Dandies* '24, recorded with Bessie SMITH, worked with MCKINNEY'S COTTON PICKERS '29-30, again '31-2; lived in Kansas City and probably worked with Bennie MOTEN, but suffered from ill health. Like Tommy LADNIER one of the greatest of his era who died too young; many fine solos survive on records. On Henderson's 'The Stampede' '26 there are two trumpet solos; Smith's is sweeter, melodic, almost laconic; then Rex STEWART takes the arrangement out with a more urgent, almost angry statement: two very different styles, but both with plenty of swing.

SMITH, Kate (*b* 1 May '07, Greenville, Ala.; *d* June '86, Raleigh, N.C.) Singer with good soprano voice, popular from mid-'20s into '70s. Was training as a nurse, but quit to sing; known as 'The Songbird of the South', worked her way to NYC in vaudeville, Broadway musical *Honeymoon Lane* '26; first hit was 'One Sweet Letter From You' '27 with Red NICHOLS, then began 15-minute radio show several nights a week and became an institution '31: second hit 'When The Moon Comes Over The Mountain' that year became her theme, eventually said to have sold 19 million copies; second no. 1 was 'River, Stay 'Way From My Door' '32 (with Guy LOMBARDO, as was top 10 'Too Late' same year). Radio greeting 'Hello everybody!' and closing 'Thanks for

listenin'' were famous; she appeared in film *The Big Broadcast* '32, starred in *Hello, Everybody!* '33. Her voice and personality were a comfort and a source of optimism during the Great Depression; later she raised money for GIs during WWII. Various radio shows through '30s; late in decade she gave boost to Abbott & Costello comedy team. 24 hits '27-46 were almost all on Columbia, but she happened to be recording for Victor when she sang 'God Bless America' on the radio: Irving BERLIN wrote it for a patriotic show '18, decided it was over the top, gave it to her '38, within a year it was unofficial national anthem: Victor record with 'Star Spangled Banner' on the other side was no. 10 '39, no. 4 '40 (before Pearl Harbor!), no. 25 '42. She had sole performing rights to it, but song royalties went to the Boy Scouts. Appeared in film *This Is The Army* '43 (co-star Ronald Reagan); recorded for MGM from late '40s, had afternoon TV show '51-4. Ted Collins was her manager since '31; when he died '54 she retired, but came back for guest spots, had her own show again for a while. Always a large lady, she suffered from diabetes in later life. LPs incl. *At Carnegie Hall, Just A Closer Walk, Here And Now, Songs Of The New Generation* all on RCA; *When The Moon Comes Over The Mountain* was a compilation on CBS/Harmony; some radio broadcasts issued on Sunbeam.

SMITH, Keely (*b* 9 Mar. '32, Norfolk, Va.) Jazz-oriented pop singer with excellent clear voice; first came to wide fame with husband Louis PRIMA mid-'50s in combo, hot attraction in Las Vegas with mixture of comedy, jazz and pop: she sang in a straight jazz style, poker-faced and with a Tonto hairdo, while he perpetrated familiar ebullient nonsense. For their LPs, films etc. together, see his entry. The marriage failed; she had charted in '58 duet with Frank SINATRA 'How Are Ya Fixed For Love?' and LPs of her own: *Swingin' Pretty* '59 (digitally remastered and reissued '85 by EMI UK), *Be My Love* '60. LP of BEATLE songs '64; worked in UK '65, 'You're Breakin' My Heart' on Sinatra's Reprise label, no. 14 on UK chart that year. Returned with *I'm In Love Again* '85 on Fantasy, with excellent backing by Bud SHANK, Bob COOPER, etc.

SMITH, Leo (*b* 18 Dec. '41, Leland, Ms.) Trumpet, composer; also other instruments incl. flugelhorn, flutes, koto, keyboards, etc. Stepfather was Alex 'Little Bill' Wallace, blues singer and guitarist on radio '50s; studied blues with him, played in high school band and organised own group for improvisation. Studied music formally at US Army School of Music, other schools, incl. ethnic musics of Africa, Asia; meanwhile joined AACM in Chicago '67. Worked with ensembles Creative Construction Company with Muhal Richard ABRAMS, Anthony BRAXTON (two LPs on Muse), Integral with Henry THREADGILL, Creative Improvisation Ensemble with Marion BROWN in Germany: seen in German documentary film with Brown *See The Music* '70. Recorded with Abrams and Maurice McIntyre on Delmark, with Braxton on Freedom and Affinity, with Brown on Impulse, Arista; settled in Connecticut to compose and published own albums on Kabell: *Creative Music 1* '71 (solo), *Reflectativity* '74, *Song Of Humanity* '76; also booklets *Notes*, *Rhythm*. As a composer he works in 'rhythm units'; in this method and in his playing the infl. of the blues is evident; he is also infl. by the purity in Miles DAVIS: the result should be called neoclassical, the silence as important as the music. *Spirit Catcher* '79 on Nessa incl. 'The Burning Of Stones' with three harps, whose music is notated while Smith improvises with a mute, its sheer beauty as contemporary music transcending category; 'Images' and side-long title track have quintet playing reeds and flutes, vibes, bass, drums as well as Smith's brass. Other albums incl. *Go In Numbers* on Black Saint; *Divine Love* '79 on ECM, *Human Rights* '82-5 on Kabell (in association with Icelandic Gramm label): the latter has Thurman Barker and several others in music with lyrics sympathetic to Jah Rastafari, using marimba, koto, synthesiser, guitars and other instruments: 'Human Rights World Music' is a side-long free improvisation, four other tracks attempt more accessibility with African, reggae, rock flavours. Lovely *Procession Of The Great Ancestry* '83 released on Nessa '88 (on Chief in UK) has Bobby Naughton again on vibes, Kahil El Zabar on various percussion, Joe Fonda on bass and others on various tracks.

SMITH, Lonnie Liston (*b* 28 Dec. '40, Richmond, Va.) Piano, composer; also tuba, trumpet. Father sang with gospel group the Harmonising Four for decades; two brothers are singers. Played with Betty CARTER '63-4, Roland KIRK '65 (LPs on Atlantic and Verve), Art BLAKEY '66-7, Joe WILLIAMS '67-8, Pharoah SANDERS, Leon Thomas, Gato BARBIERI '69-73 (LPs on Flying Dutchman and Impulse; wrote Sanders' album *Jewels Of Thought*), with Miles DAVIS '73-4. Own LPs incl. *Visions Of A New World, Cosmic Funk, Astral Traveling, Expansions* on Flying Dutchman; *Dreams Of Tomorrow, Silhouettes, Rejuvenation* '85 on Doctor Jazz.

SMITH, Mamie (*b* 26 May 1883, Cincinnati, Ohio; *d* 30 Oct. '46, NYC) (dates are unconfirmed) Blues singer, with Bessie, Clara and Trixie SMITH (all unrelated) one of the most famous, although less purely a blues artist than the others. Working in theatres 1893, in NYC '13; in many shows and revues incl. *Fireworks Of 1930* with Fats WALLER – Jimmie Johnson Syncopators; also short films *Jailhouse Blues* '29, soundie *Because I Love You* '43 with Lucky MILLINDER; also films *Paradise In Harlem* '39 (singing 'Harlem Blues', with Millinder's band), *Mystery In Swing* '40, *Murder On Lenox Avenue* '41 and *Sunday Sinners* '41. She also worked theatres in Europe c.'36. A high-class entertainer with a wide repertoire, she allegedly made a Victor test record early '20 accompanying herself at the piano, now lost; then sides for Okeh, probably accompanied by a white band: 'That Thing Called Love', 'You Can't Keep A Good Man Down'; then it fell to her to make the first blues record, because Sophie TUCKER (not a blues singer at all) was not available: with her Jazz Hounds (incl. Willie 'The Lion' SMITH on piano, no relation), 'Crazy Blues' (Aug. '20) was runaway bestseller, no. 3 national hit (according to *Pop Memories*). She had seven more big hits '21-3, incl. a reissue of 'You Can't Keep A Good Man Down', others with sidemen such as Buster Bailey, Bubber MILEY, Coleman HAWKINS (who began his big-time career with her). Recorded for Okeh through '31, also on Ajax '24 (Jazz Hounds incl. Elmer SNOWDEN), Victor '26. Victor sides were later issued in the compilation

Women Of The Blues in RCA Vintage series '60s.

SMITH, Margo (*b* 9 Apr. '42, Dayton, Ohio) Teacher turned country singer who writes most of her own material. Demo brought record deal on Chart label in Nashville but nothing happened; switched to 20th Century '75, hits incl. top 5 with first single 'There, I Said It'. To WB for big hits incl. 'Don't Break The Heart That Loves You' and 'It Only Hurts For A Little While' at no. 1, no. 2 'Little Things Mean A Lot' '78; three consecutive top 10 hits '79; she also sang duets with prod. Norro Wilson on WB; lesser hits on Moonshine, Bermuda Dunes labels '83-5 incl. 'Every Day People', duet with Tom Grant. She called her band Love's Explosion. LPs incl. *Margo Smith, Song Bird, Happiness, Don't Break The Heart That Loves You, A Woman, Just Margo* on WB, all good sellers; *Margo Smith* '86 on Dot.

SMITH, O. C. (*b* Ocie Lee Smith, 21 June '32, Mansfield, La.) Pop/soul singer. To West Coast as a child; served in USAF early '50s as an entertainer, touring with Horace HEIDT; sang with Sy OLIVER, appeared on Arthur GODFREY's talent show and got a contract with Cadence label. First single was 'Lighthouse', slow rock'n'roll ballad with dubbed-in seagulls; he also made a vocal version of 'Slow Walk', Sil AUSTIN hit of the period. Recorded with LEIBER & STOLLER on Big Top and Broadway; succeeded Joe WILLIAMS as vocalist with Count BASIE '61. Versatile entertainer changed his name to O.C. and had successful chart career '68-74: 10 hits in pop/soul charts incl. top 40 version of Dallas FRAZIER's 'The Son Of Hickory Holler's Tramp', no. 2 with Bobby Russell's Grammy-winning song 'Little Green Apples', both '68. Four albums plus *Greatest Hits* set charted: *Hickory Holler Revisited* (incl. 'Apples'), *For Once In My Life, O.C. At Home* '68-9, then *Help Me Make It Through The Night* '71 reached top 200. UK hits were 'Tramp' (no. 2) and 'Together' on Caribou, top 30 '77.

SMITH, Patti (*b* 30 Dec. '46, Chicago, Ill.) New wave singer/poet. Grew up in New Jersey, infl. by Arthur Rimbaud, Bob DYLAN for lyrics, Elvis PRESLEY for performance. She wrote play *Cowboy Mouth* '71 with actor/playwright Sam Shepard, read poetry to Lenny Kaye's guitar accompaniment at St Mark's Church in the Bowery; rock critic Kaye encouraged her to write for *Creem* and *Rolling Stone*; published volumes of poems. Into rock through boyfriend Allen Lanier of BLUE OYSTER CULT: contributed lyrics to some of their songs, notably 'Career Of Evil' '74. Her single 'Piss Factory' '74 with Kaye and Richard Sohl's piano, his florid keyboard forming suitable background for Smith's nihilistic ramblings about industrial life. Signed to Arista '75; completed band with Ivan Kral, bass; Jay Dee Daugherty, drums; *Horses* '76 prod. by John CALE, frightening and influential on new wave females, incl. passionate cover of Them's 'Gloria'. *Radio Ethiopia* '76 was a flop, partly owing to unsympathetic prod. Jack (AEROSMITH) Douglas; she broke her neck '77, wrote *Babel* (poems) while recuperating. *Easter* '78 incl. single 'Because The Night' (no. 13 USA/5 UK), powerful yet commercial song co-written with Bruce SPRINGSTEEN: connection was producer Jimmy Iovine. *Waves* '79 disappointed, aside from cover of BYRDS 'So You Wanna Be A Rock'n'Roll Star'; band split. She married ex-MC5 Fred 'Sonic' Smith, retired until *Dream Of Life* '88 on Arista.

SMITH, Pine Top (*b* Clarence Smith, 11 June '04, Troy, Alabama; *d* 15 Mar. '29, Chicago) Boogie-woogie pianist. Not the first to record in this blues genre, but first to use 'boogie woogie' in song title. Grew up in Birmingham, worked on Pittsburgh club circuit, toured on TOBA circuit (Theatre Owners Booking Association, aka 'Tough On Black Asses'); worked with Ma RAINEY, BUTTERBEANS AND SUSIE. Settled in Chicago late '20s; recorded 'Pine Top's Boogie Woogie', 'Pine Top's Blues' late '28, on first side shouting instructions for dancing boogie. Six more sides for Vocalion label Jan. '29 incl. 'I'm Sober Now', 'Jump Steady Blues'; then hit by stray bullet in dance-hall shoot-out. Scores of artists have recorded 'Pine Top's Boogie Woogie', often known as just 'Boogie Woogie'; most successful was smash Tommy DORSEY hit for Victor, recorded '38, reissued '43 during recording ban; Clark Sisters did harmony vocal version for Dot in '58, based on the Dorsey arrangement by Dean Kincaide.

SMITH, Sammi (*b* 5 Aug. '43, Orange, Cal.) Country singer with husky voice, poignant phrasing; highly regarded by iconoclastic 'outlaw' elements in Nashville, incl. Billy Joe SHAVER, Willie NELSON, Waylon JENNINGS (joined the last two in their show at '73 DJ convention). Grew up in Oklahoma, sang from age 12; Marshall Grant and Luther Perkins (with Johnny CASH show) encouraged her, Cash helped to get Columbia contract '68-9 and she had minor country hits there ('So Long Charlie Brown') but also met janitor Kris KRISTOFFERSON: switched to new Mega label and had top 10 pop hit (no. 1 country) with his 'Help Me Make It Through The Night' '71 (her version used in film soundtrack *Fat City*; won her a Grammy). Had more hits late '70s, joining Elektra '76-9, back in country charts with 'What A Lie' '79 on Cyclone. Like other outlaws, making the charts is not her only priority; active on behalf of American Indians, gave benefit concerts for scholarships helping to keep the Apache language alive. LPs incl. *He's Everywhere* (retitled *Help Me Make It Through The Night*), *Rainbow In Daddy's Eyes*, *Something Old, Something New, Lonesome, I've Got To Have You, Today I Started Loving You Again*, all on Mega; *As Long As There's A Sunday, New Winds, All Quadrants* and *Mixed Emotions* on Elektra; *Girl Hero* on Cyclone. Minor hit 'You Just Hurt My Last Feeling' '85 on Step One.

SMITH, Stuff (*b* Hezekiah Leroy Gordon Smith, 14 Aug. '09, Portsmouth, Ohio; *d* 25 Sep. '67, Munich, Germany) Violinist, composer, leader, vocalist. One of the few jazz violinists and the most influential; an underrated leader; played the instrument in an unorthodox manner, having learned how best to make it swing; Fritz Kreisler was a fan. Worked with Alphonse Trent in Dallas; to Buffalo with Trent and formed own group there c.'30; took sextet to Onyx Club late '35, began to play amplified violin; group's forte was comedy and singing as well as good music (as Trent's was): they recorded speciality 'I'se A Muggin' ' on two Vocalion sides '36 and 15 more sides with Jonah JONES on trumpet, most with Cozy

COLE on drums, incl. 'You'se A Viper', with Jones vocal. Five more sides on Decca '37 were also by 'Stuff Smith And His Onyx Club Boys' adding Buster Bailey, with Clyde Hart on piano (*b* '10, Baltimore, Md.; *d* 19 Mar. '45, NYC), eight more on Varsity '39-40 by 'Stuff Smith And His Orchestra'. Continued leading small groups through the '50s, toured Europe '57, recorded with Nat COLE on Capitol, Dizzy GILLESPIE on Savoy and Verve, Ella FITZGERALD on Verve; duos with Stephane GRAPPELLI and Svend ASMUSSEN (also *Violin Summit* on MPS); his own albums were *Black Violin* on MPS; *Desert Sands* (with Oscar PETERSON Trio), *Have Violin, Will Swing* and *Stuff Smith* on Verve; *Swingin'* and *Stuff* on EmArcy. Compilations: *Memorial Album* on Prestige, *The Varsity Sessions* on Danish Storyville (other tracks apparently airchecks from the period), another LP on American Storyville. Good long interview in Stanley Dance's *The World Of Swing*.

SMITH, Tab (*b* Talmadge Smith, 11 Jan. '09, Kingston, N.C.; *d* 17 Aug. '71, St Louis) Saxophonist. Began on C-melody, then alto. St Louis gigs '30s incl. Fate MARABLE; then Mills Blue Rhythm Band led by Lucky MILLINDER '36-9; Frankie Newton, Teddy WILSON big band, then Count BASIE. Wrote arrangements e.g. 'Blow Top' (cut on his first Basie recording session, Mar. '40), 'Harvard Blues' '41; left Basie mid-'42, back with Millinder; freelance activities incl. Coleman HAWKINS and his Sax Ensemble date on Keynote '44: Hawkins and Don BYAS on tenors, Smith on alto, Harry CARNEY on baritone, plus Johnny GUARNIERI, Sid CATLETT and bassist Al Lucas: 12″ 78s were made with exquisite results. He formed his own small band '44; car crash set-back killed singer-guitarist Trevor Bacon, also ex-Millinder star; band recorded for more than a dozen labels '44-50, finally hit with Chicago-based United '51: first record 'Because Of You', lush instrumental version of Tony BENNETT hit, made no. 25 in pop chart in a year that was kind to alto men: Earl BOSTIC ('Flamingo'), Johnny HODGES ('Castle Rock') also scored. Cut more than 50 sides for United till '57, mostly dance-oriented; then for Argo, Checker, King '58-60; then moved back to

St Louis, went into real estate, taught and played occasional gigs. Compilations incl. *Because Of You* on Delmark; *Joy At The Savoy* and *I Don't Want To Play In The Kitchen* on Saxophonograph incl. mostly '44-5 stuff with Bacon.

SMITH, Trixie (*b* 1895, Atlanta, Ga.; *d* 21 Sep. '43, NYC) Blues singer, one of the famous Smiths, unrelated to Bessie, Clara, Mamie. Attended Selma U. but went to NYC and worked there in theatres from '15, at Reisenweber's Restaurant '22, many shows and revues incl. non-singing dramatic roles incl. with Mae West in *The Constant Sinner* '31, film *The Black King* '32. She recorded for Black Swan '22-3, records also appearing on Paramount, then Paramount '24-6; eight sides on Decca '38 (one unissued) with band incl. Charlie SHAVERS, Sidney BECHET. In '24-5 her Down Home Syncopators were Fletcher HENDERSON's band, sometimes so called, incl. variously Henderson, Louis ARMSTRONG, Charlie Green, Buster Bailey; on an early '25 date the Original Memphis Five, a white band with Phil Napoleon (*b* Fillipo Napoli, 2 Sep. '01, Boston, Mass.) and Miff Mole. No reissues listed.

SMITH, Willie (*b* William McLeish Smith, 25 Nov. '10, Charleston, S.C.; *d* 7 Mar. '67, L.A.) Alto sax, also clarinet, vocalist, arranger. One of the most important assets of the popular Jimmie LUNCEFORD band '29-42 as arranger, leader of excellent reed section, singing in the band's vocal trio; with Charlie SPIVAK '42-3, US Navy '43-4, then Harry JAMES nearly 20 years except for '51-3 with Duke ELLINGTON (after Duke's 'Great James Raid'), Billy MAY. Freelance work incl. JATP, records with Nat COLE, with Charlie BARNET '67; worked with Johnny RIVERS in Las Vegas. One of the all-time crowd-pleasers of the alto sax.

SMITH, Willie 'The Lion' (*b* William Henry Joseph Bonaparte Bertholoff Smith, 25 Nov. 1897, Goshen, NY; *d* 18 Apr. '73, NYC) Pianist, composer; sometime vocalist. His mother played piano and organ; he began in ragtime, like Luckey ROBERTS and Eubie BLAKE; then with Fats WALLER and James P. JOHNSON one of the all-time great artists in the NYC style of stride piano: as

with Roberts, the ragtime heritage bestowed upon The Lion a fondness for arabesques and distinctive harmonies. Stories about origin of his nickname incl. 'Lion of Judea' (one of his parents was Jewish), ferocity as a soldier in WWI ('It was a tough war, and I'm proud and happy that I won it'). He worked almost his whole life in NYC ('I would rather be a fly on a lamp post in Harlem than a millionaire anywhere else'); played on the first blues record (Mamie SMITH's 'Crazy Blues' '20), toured Europe and North Africa '49-50. Passed judgement on the young Waller, helped Duke ELLINGTON (who wrote 'Portrait Of The Lion'); other pupils incl. Mel POWELL, Joe BUSHKIN, Artie SHAW, many others. With his derby and ever-present cigar, only Waller rivalled him as the archetypal tickler. Autobiography *Music On My Mind* '65 with George Hoefer is a delight (foreword by Ellington). More than 70 compositions incl. 'Contrary Motion', 'Echo Of Spring', 'Portrait Of The Duke', 'Rippling Waters'; songs like 'The Stuff Is Here And It's Mellow' with lyrics by Walter Bishop, Andy RAZAF; 'Sweeter Than The Sweetest' '41 (words by Jack Lawrence) recorded by Glenn MILLER. Recorded '20s-30s with many small groups: led by Mezz MEZZROW '34-6; septet Willie Smith and his Cubs on Decca '35-7; with organist Milt Herth (*b* Kenosha, Wis.; *d* 18 June '69) and drummer O'Neill Spencer '37-9 on Decca; duos and trios (Smith on celeste) with Bushkin and Jess STACY '38, piano solos '39 on Commodore. With Sidney BECHET '41 on Victor, Max KAMINSKY '44 on Brunswick; solo LP *Musical Compositions Of James P. Johnson* '53 on Blue Circle; playing, singing, talking on *Reminiscing The Piano Greats* '49 on Dial USA (Vogue in France), *The Lion Roars* '57 on Dot, *The Legend Of Willie (The Lion) Smith* '58 on Grand Award, 2-disc *Memoirs Of Willie The Lion Smith* on RCA. With three others backed blues singer Lucille Hegamin (*b* Lucille Nelson, 29 Nov. 1894, Macon, Ga.; *d* 1 Mar. '70, NYC) on *Songs We Taught Your Mother* '61 on Prestige. Also solos on one side of *Luckey & The Lion* '58 on Good Time Jazz (Roberts overside); *Grand Piano* duets with Don EWELL '67, now on Sackville, *A Legend* on Mainstream, solo *Pork & Beans* '66 on Black Lion, *Live At Blues Alley* and *Relaxing* '70 on Chiaroscuro, tracks now on PRT/UK. The album *The Original 14 Plus Two* on Teldec in Germany, and the Columbia Collectors Series in the USA reissues the Commodore sides.

SMITHS, The UK vocal/instrumental quartet formed in Manchester '82: singer Morrissey (*b* Steven Morrissey, 22 May '59), guitarist Johnny Marr (*b* 31 Oct. '63), both from Manchester, also songwriting partners; plus Andy Rourke, bass; Mike Joyce, drums. Very independent: the name was chosen for anonymity, never made a promo video, remained on indie Rough Trade despite offers from major labels. Early sessions prod. by Troy Tate (ex-TEARDROP EXPLODES); distinctive debut single 'Hand In Glove' '83 followed by 'This Charming Man', 'What Difference Does It Make', 'Heaven Knows I'm Miserable Now' and 'William, It Was Really Nothing', all top 30 hits '83-4. *The Smiths* '84 incl. 'Hand In Glove' (later a hit for Sandie SHAW), majestic 'Reel Around The Fountain', sombre 'Suffer Little Children'. Marr's lavish BYRDS-style guitar, Morrissey's enigmatic lyrics, delivery were centre of their appeal. *Meat Is Murder* '85 regarded as less substantial; *Hatful Of Hollow* '85 was sessions culled from John PEEL radio show. Attracted cult following in USA; Morrissey, a devoted fan of Johnnie RAY and Billy FURY, was rarely out of the rock press, leading to '86 single 'Bigmouth Strikes Again'. Singles 'That Joke Isn't Funny Anymore', 'Shakespeare's Sister' and 'Boy With The Thorn In His Side' regarded as disappointing, but top 20 'Panic' '86 was return to form, as was *The Queen Is Dead* '86, with remarkable title track, music-hall 'Frankly Mr Shankly' and 'Cemetry Gates' (sic). Marr was 'Duane Tremelo' on Billy BRAGG single 'Levi Stubbs' Tears' '86. Craig Gannon (ex-AZTEC CAMERA) played with them last eight months of '86; they donated track to charity LP *Animal Liberation* '87; *Shoplifters Of The World Unite* compiled recent hits, alternate takes, *The World Won't Listen* other rare tracks, and *Strangeways, Here We Come* was their last new record. They split mid-'87 after Marr went to USA to record with Talking Heads; Rough Trade said Morrissey would look for a new guitarist; he released *Viva Hate* '88 on Sire.

SMOKIE UK pop group of '70s, first called Kindness, then Smokey; changed spelling to avoid confusion with Smokey ROBINSON: Chris Norman, vocals, guitar, keyboards; Alan Silson, lead guitar; Peter Spencer, drums, sax; Terry Uttley, bass. Signed to UK bubblegum label Rak, affected notions of progressive EAGLES, CSN&Y pop with *Pass It Around* '75 (title track banned by BBC for drug reference), soon emerged as singles act. 'If You Think You Know How To Love Me', 'Don't Play Your Rock'n'Roll To Me' (both top 10 '75) revealed class popsters in vein of early '70s harmony hitmakers New World (who were discredited after allegations of vote-rigging on TV talent show). Ten more top 40 hits to '80 incl. update of New World's 'Living Next Door To Alice'; all showcased growling, gravelly vocals of Norman, whose '78 duet with Suzi QUATRO 'Stumblin' In' was no. 4 USA '79 (Smokie as a group hit in USA only with 'Alice' at no. 25). On albums the group moved away from songs of producers CHINN & CHAPMAN which had brought them hits; by *The Montreux Album* '78, their last collaboration, they were taking much more credit, but found success waning correspondingly, as did Mud, SWEET, other Chinnichap acts who broke away. It was too late to return to first LP's attempt at 'credibility' and they split early '80s.

SNOW, Hank (*b* Clarence Eugene Snow, 9 May '14, Liverpool, Nova Scotia, Canada) Country singer, guitarist, songwriter; one of the all-time greats of the post-war era, called 'The Singing Ranger'; had a record-breaking association with the same label (RCA) for 45 years '34-79. From a poor family; left home at 12 as cabin boy in Merchant Marine, where he first thought to become a singer. Influenced like so many others by Jimmie RODGERS, sang in local clubs and on radio in Halifax as Clarence Snow and his guitar; shortened name and became known as The Yodelling Ranger. Signed to Victor in Montreal '34, recording with own guitar accompaniment; within ten years he was among Canada's leading country performers. To USA mid-'40s, working at WWVA radio in Wheeling, West Va. '45, moved to Hollywood '46 with a show incl. his performing horse, Shawnee; returned to Canada '47 heavily in debt. Further trips south saw him on KRLD in Dallas, Texas '48; by now his records were being issued by RCA in the USA; he moved to Nashville, appeared on Grand Ole Opry '49, made USA country chart debut with 'Marriage Vow'; next disc, his own song 'I'm Movin' On', was nearly a year on Billboard's country chart, 18 weeks at no. 1 '50, crossed to pop chart (says *Pop Memories*); revived '60s by Ray CHARLES. He made the country charts every year through '79, the year he was elected to the Country Music Hall of Fame; 35 top 10 hits incl. 'Golden Rocket' and 'Rhumba Boogie' (both no. 1), 'Music Makin' Mama From Memphis' (no. 6), all his own songs '50-1; plus no. 4 'A Fool Such As I' '52 (song by Bill Trader, also pop hit by Jo STAFFORD, revived '59 by Elvis PRESLEY); other no. 1 hits were 'I Don't Hurt Anymore' '54 (by Don ROBERTSON and Jack Rollins, also crossed to pop chart, also a hit by Dinah WASHINGTON), top 10 'Millers Cave' '60 (by Jack CLEMENT), 'I've Been Everywhere' '62 (road song made of place names), 'Hello Love' '74; plus 'Gal Who Invented Kissing', 'Spanish Fire Ball', 'When Mexican Joe Met Jole Blon' (by Sheb WOOLEY), 'The Last Ride' (co-written by Ted DAFFAN). He was one of the first to record duets with Chet ATKINS; he won five BMI songwriter awards; member of Nashville Songwriters' Hall of Fame; still appears on Opry. His son Jimmie Rodgers Snow was a country performer and became an evangelist clergyman. Over 100 albums incl. *Railroad Man* '64, *Hits Covered By Snow* and *Sings Jimmie Rodgers* '69, *Award Winners* '71, *Opry Favourites* and *Hello Love* '74, *No. 104* and *Still Movin' On* (title song by Shel SILVERSTEIN) '77, *The Mysterious Lady* '79; *20 Of The Best* on RCA International. 2-disc *I'm Movin' On* on Pair '86 in USA.

SNOW, Phoebe (*b* Phoebe Laub, 17 July '52, Teaneck, N.J.) Singer, guitarist, songwriter with jazz-infl. melismatic style, flexible contralto voice. Studied piano as a child, guitar at 15; began writing poems and setting them to music. First LP on Leon RUSSELL's Shelter label *Phoebe Snow* '74 went gold, incl. no. 5 hit 'Poetry Man'; 'Harpo's Blues' incl. Stan GETZ and Teddy WILSON in backing. Switched to Columbia, toured with Paul SIMON and had no. 23 hit

duet 'Gone At Last' '75; second album *Second Childhood* '76 also gold, with some backing from Ron CARTER, drummer Grady Tate, Jerome Richardson (reeds and flute; *b* 25 Dec. '20, Oakland, Cal.; played with Thad JONES/Mel LEWIS band late '60s, on hit Quincy JONES LPs '70s). *It Looks Like Snow* '76 was still top 30 album; *Never Letting Go* '77 slipped, *Against The Grain* '78 made top 100; she came back on Mirage label with *Rock Away* '81 at no. 51 in album chart. All were still in print '87, the sure sign of a loyal following.

SNOWDEN, Elmer (*b* 9 Oct. 1900, Baltimore, Md.; *d* 14 May '73, Philadelphia, Pa.) Banjo, guitar, saxes, leader. Played banjo and guitar from childhood; worked for Eubie BLAKE '15, Claude HOPKINS '21, formed own band and began to play reeds. To NYC '23 (combo incl. Sonny Greer, Toby Hardwicke) hoping that Fats WALLER would join; he didn't, they sent for Duke ELLINGTON, became the Washingtonians, made Victor test records (as Snowden's Novelty Orchestra); Snowden rejoined '24 after Ellington had taken over. Ran several bands NYC late '20s-early '30s; short films incl. *Smash Your Baggage* '32; his popular bands incl. variously many of the best jazzmen of the era, recorded for various labels, e.g. as Jungle Town Stompers (with Luis RUSSELL and Louis Metcalf), Musical Stevedores (with Metcalf, Freddy Jenkins), also backed blues singers such as Bessie SMITH; finally got in trouble with musicians' union, went to Philadelphia, continued leading small bands (dispute eventually settled with help of John HAMMOND). Worked on West Coast '60s (also played with Turk MURPHY). Toured Europe '67, moved back to Philadelphia.

SOCA A Trinidadian genre, claimed by its opponents to be a decadent form of CALYPSO, by supporters to be just another dimension of it, by outsiders as a fusion of soul and calypso; Lord Shorty said 'It's the nucleus of calypso, the soul' (*Trinidad Carnival* magazine, '79). Originators were Shorty (*b* Garfield Blackman, 5 Oct. '41, Trinidad; now calls himself Ras Shorty I), calypsonians Maestro (Cecil Hume, *b* '45, *d* '78 in car crash) and SHADOW, arrangers Ed Watson and Pelham Goddard. Shadow acknowledged Shorty, while Maestro did not record soca until 'Savage' '76 on Kalinda label (arr. was by Goddard, keyboardist with backing band Charlie's Roots); this was three years after Shorty, who was raised in Lengua village in South Trinidad, a community largely of East Indian descent. He arranged for steel bands late '50s, began singing calypso '62 with East Indian infl.: songs 'Long Mango' (greeted with derision), 'Sixteen Commandments' '63 (more successful), 'Indian Singers' '66 (better still). Turned to calypso full time '67 (fired from job as a joiner). 'Indranee' was a hit '72. He developed a sexual image as 'Shorty – The Love Man', was charged with obscenity for presentation of 'Lesson In Love' '73; early LPs incl. *Gone, Gone, Gone, Love Man, Love In The Caribbean*. Concerned that reggae would eclipse calypso in popularity, he turned to soca to revitalise it, recorded his first soca song 'Soul Calypso Music' '73 (in Toronto, Canada), incl. in *Endless Vibrations* '74 on his own Shorty label, co-arranged by Watson, followed by *Sweet Music* '76, adding Earl Rodney to arrangers. Then he went bankrupt, but came back with *Sokah, Soul of Calypso* '77 on Semp, arr. by Shorty and Frankie Callender (spelling 'sokah' reflected East Indian influence). Shocked by Maestro's death, he rejected a self-confessed five-year orgy of the flesh '78, reinterpreted 'love man' to more universal image. *Soca Explosion* '79 on Charlies incl. 'Soca Fever', 'Shanti Om' (a Hindu prayer in soca), political commentary 'Money Eh No Problem'. Hits '79 incl. 'Young And Moving On', sung by 14-year-old daughter Abbi Blackman, 'Don't Stop Dancing', by 11-year-old O. C. Blackman; *We Have Love* '79 on Soca Productions was family album by Shorty and his Home Circle. 'Plant De Land' and 'Soca Man Scrunt' were 12″ single '80; he became a rastafarian, changed his name, took his children out of school, went bankrupt '81: Ras Shorty I and his Home Circle appeared at Kingdom of the Wizards calypso tent '81, then moved to a remote part of Trinidad, developed slow soca/reggae/gospel fusion he called jamoo; returned to public performing '84 with his Love Circle, LP *Jamoo – The Gospel Of Soca*. In general soca is faster and has more bass than calypso, the singer accompanied by trumpets, trombones, tenor and alto

saxes, bass, guitar, keyboards incl. synthesisers, drums, congas, chorus and percussion. Soca lyrics initially treated the same sort of topics as calypso, but there is a tendency towards blandness aimed at crossover success. Soca exponents also incl. BLUE BOY, KITCHENER, SPARROW, David RUDDER, Arrow, Becket, Crazy, Explainer, Merchant, Penguin, Scrunter, Singing Francine, Swallow, Baron, Bally, Duke, Rootsman. A lot of soca was recorded by Semp Studios (now closed); co-owner Stan Chaman co-owns Hitman Records, a leading London shop for Latin, soca and calypso discs.

SOFT MACHINE Avant-garde UK jazz-rock outfit, came from Wilde Flowers, '61 group with nucleus from a Canterbury school and which also incl. members of CARAVAN, Kevin AYERS, Daevid Allen. Named from William Burroughs novel; first flop single prod. by Kim FOWLEY with Jimi HENDRIX on rhythm guitar, later supported him on tour in USA; made first (trio) LP there (without Allen, who had been refused re-entry to UK, stayed on Continent and formed GONG), prod. by Tom Wilson, disbanded; re-formed in UK with members of Keith TIPPETT group, carried on, personnel fluctuating constantly, often incl. Karl Jenkins on reeds, keyboards; Mike Ratledge, keyboards; Robert WYATT, then John Marshall on drums; Roy Babbington, bass; John Ethridge, guitar; Allan Wakeman on reeds, others. Influential at the time (especially first four albums) with jazz-infl. voicings, free-form improvisations. LPs: *The Soft Machine* (made USA LP chart '68) and *Volume Two* '69 on Probe; *Third* '70 and *Fourth* '71 (both charted in UK), plus *Fifth, Sixth, Seventh*, all on CBS; then *Bundles* '75, *Softs* '76, *Alive And Well In Paris* '78 on Harvest, *Land Of Cockayne* '81 on EMI. Compilations incl. *At The Beginning* on Charly; they also played on *Faces & Places* and *Rock Generation* albums on French Byg: had cult following in France as did Gong. Jenkins and Ratledge went into jingles, using rock in TV advertising: Jack Bruce singing 'I Feel Free' to sell cars, Kate Robbins (cousin of Paul McCARTNEY) imitating Grace JONES to sell hair conditioner, 'I Heard It Through The Grapevine' for Levi jeans, etc.

SOILEAU, Leo (*b* 19 Jan. '04, Ville Platte, La.; *d* there 2 Aug. '80) Cajun fiddler, vocalist, bandleader; one of the most important pioneers of the genre. Duetted with accordionists '28-9, notably Mayuse LaFleur and Moise Robin. When market picked up after the Depression he raised his sights, formed a series of small combos as Leo Soileau's Three Aces or Four Aces; '35 sessions incl. drums, new in Cajun. Repertoire incl. trad. and pop songs of the day, sung mostly in French but also in English. Fronted band called the Rhythm Boys late '30s, probably to cash in on boom in Western swing. Apart from radio transcriptions, he last recorded in '37, but continued playing until the '50s, when he gave up full-time music, worked in oil industry, then as janitor. Compilation *Leo Soileau And His Four Aces* on Old Timey.

SOLAL, Martial (*b* 23 Aug. '27, Algiers) Jazz pianist in Paris since '40s, often playing with visiting Americans; led own trios; solo concerts and teaching since '70s; has also done film work, several visits to USA. Recorded with Lee KONITZ on Milestone, Hampton HAWES on Byg; own LPs on Pathé late '60s, French RCA early '70s; *Live* 4-disc set issued on Stefanotis '85: '59-85 material incl. solos, duos with Konitz, John LEWIS, Stephane GRAPPELLI, others; trios, composition *Suite In D Flat* by quartet incl. trumpeter Roger Guerin, big band pieces. Highly regarded by critics but underrated in general because he is not an American, much of his work was done before jazz became an international language with an international record industry.

SON One of Cuba's main popular music forms, a fusion of African and Spanish-derived elements. Began with the changui in Oriente province in 19th century, brought to Havana c.1900 and spread through working class, capable of incorporating African-derived elements such as rumba, Spanish-descended such as the guajira (rural form, often with nostalgic lyrics); by the '20s appealed to Cubans at all levels. Spread to Puerto Rico '30s; continuing migration to NYC took it to USA (though by then it was a ballroom fad which Americans mistakenly called the rumba or rhumba). Three bands represented development of son in Cuba: by '18 Sexteto Habanero had developed basic conjunto son style, with vocal trio, bass, trumpet, guitar, tres (similar to a guitar, with six or nine strings), bongos, maracas and claves (sticks struck together); by late '20s Septeto Nacional, formed by Ignacio Piñeiro (1888-1969), used tighter harmonies with more melodic range, faster tempo, more trumpet ornamentation but less rhythmic improvisation and complexity; then in late '30s Arsenio Rodriguez brought in more directly African styles that had until then been only an influence, particularly the guaguancó style of rumba, adding more trumpets, piano, conga and cowbell, and incorporating tumbao (repeated, interlocking rhythms played by bass and conga). Inserted a montuno section, for solos with rhythmic backing, forming son montuno. Compilations incl. *Hot Dance Music From Cuba* (tracks from '09-37, on Harlequin in UK '86) and *Colección de Oro* (12 tracks by Sexteto Habanero); *El Septeto Nacional de Ignacio Piñeiro* '58 on WS Latino was made in Cuba at studios of Radio Progreso.

SONDHEIM, Stephen (*b* Stephen Joshua Sondheim, 22 Mar. '30, NYC) Composer and lyricist. Lessons as a child from family friend Oscar Hammerstein II which incl. full-length experimental musicals; studied with composer Milton Babbitt (*b* 10 May '16, Philadelphia, Pa.), wrote musicals while in college; wrote incidental music for Broadway shows *Twigs*, *Girls Of Summer*, *Invitation To A March*; some lyrics for a revival of Leonard BERNSTEIN's *Candide* '56, then lyrics for his *West Side Story* '58; *Gypsy* '59 might have been the first Sondheim musical, but star Ethel MERMAN insisted on a 'name' composer, so he worked with Jule Styne ('62 film without Merman was less successful). Wrote words/music for *A Funny Thing Happened On The Way To The Forum* '62 (film '66, dir. by Richard Lester, photographed by Nicholas Roeg, with Phil Silvers, Zero Mostel, Michael Crawford, Jack Gilford, Michael Hordern, Buster Keaton: Pauline Kael called it 'coitus interruptus going on forever'; many of the songs had been dropped): original cast LP on Capitol, soundtrack on United Artists. The next few OC LPs were on Columbia: *Anyone Can*

Whistle '64 flopped, was recorded the day after it closed: record companies seemed to understand the importance of recording Sondheim shows; at Columbia (CBS) the albums were produced by Goddard Leiberson, then by Thomas Z. Shepard, who went to RCA '76 and produced them there (and went to MCA '86). Sondheim collaborated with Richard RODGERS on flop *Do I Hear A Waltz?* '65 (Rodgers was difficult/past his prime, perhaps knew it). *Evening Primrose* '66 was a television play by James Goldman, with Anthony Perkins and four songs by Sondheim, followed by *Company* '70 on the stage, almost plotless, with witty cynical lyrics and internal rhymes which are his trademark. *Follies* '71, set in show business, looked back to heyday of Broadway with cynicism about romance, but also better melodies, incl. clever parodies of Irving BERLIN, George GERSHWIN etc.; it collected seven Tonies and ran 522 performances but lost money (Capitol OC LP was a disaster, mangling the songs to make it fit on one LP; 2-disc Lincoln Center concert performance '85 on RCA was done properly). *A Little Night Music* '73 was written mostly in 3/4 time (USA OC LP on Columbia, UK '75 on London); it incl. his only hit song 'Send In The Clowns' (top 40 '75, top 20 '77 by Judy COLLINS); further evidence that he wrote a new kind of show, it contained his usual gloom (especially about marriage: his parents were divorced when he was 10), also ever more graceful wit: first commercial hit (filmed '77 with Hermione Gingold, Elizabeth Taylor, soundtrack on Columbia; a poorly-planned film generally regarded as a disaster). 2-disc *Sondheim: A Musical Tribute* '73 on WB was a benefit, with 33 performers and 42 songs, one of the first events of its kind to be recorded. *Pacific Overtures* '76 did not do well (OC LP on RCA); *Sweeney Todd (The Demon Barber Of Fleet Street)* '79 began with a blank verse play by Christopher Bond, itself a version of an 1847 original, rewritten many times; the touring production was videotaped in L.A. (OC on RCA in both complete 2-disc and single LP abridgement). The last five shows all won NY Drama Critics' Circle Awards and all but *Pacific Overtures* won Tonies, in spite of the fact that some were flops and important NYC critics disliked nearly all of them. The purpose of his songs is to advance the plot; they have been called 'unhummable', but in fact they are not reprised until the audience remembers them, as in many shows: there is no reprise without a dramatic reason for it. *Side By Side By Sondheim* '76 was compiled of his songs, dir. by Ned Sherrin (also one of the four performers); a hit in London, went to Broadway, totalled 384 performances (2-disc album on RCA). He also wrote film music (*Stavisky* '74, *The Seven Percent Solution* '77, *Reds* c.'80), co-wrote script with Perkins for non-musical Hollywood in-joke/whodunnit *The Last Of Sheila* '73, which began with a murder game he invented (which also inspired Anthony Shaffer to write smash play/film *Sleuth*). He also acted in TV revival '74 of play *June Moon*, same year wrote score for adaptation of Aristophanes' *The Frogs*, staged in Yale's swimming pool during its repertory season. *Marry Me A Little* '80 was a one-hour late-night entertainment using unpublished and unperformed songs, a hit off-Broadway; flopped when moved to a theatre where its intimacy was lost (LP on RCA). *Merrily We Roll Along* '81 was a flop, again recorded the morning after, incl. derisive lyric about 'humma-mamumma-mamummable melodies' (LP on RCA; show revived '85 on West Coast). *Sunday In The Park With George* '84, on Georges Seurat with suitably pointillist music, received awards, as had *Sweeney*, was also taped for TV; *Time*'s Richard Corliss described it as 'a cool unblinking object. Only a closer look reveals it as a shapely work of art' (album on CD is a triumph). *Into The Woods* opened on Broadway late '87, combining characters from fairy tales, more affirmative than anything he has written, haunting ballad 'No One Is Alone' compared to 'Clowns'. *Follies* finally reached London '87 and *Pacific Overture* was revived by the English National Opera, combining Kabuki and Broadway, demanding more from performer and listener than Broadway is used to. A revival of an old idea for a show called *Pray By Blecht* with Bernstein was being mooted. His songs and lyrics were recorded by Johnny MATHIS, Frank SINATRA, Carly SIMON; he worked with Barbra STREISAND on her *Broadway Album* '85: Columbia didn't want her to do an album of show songs; half the songs were Sondheim's; the LP was no. 1 in USA for three weeks. (Cleo LAINE released new album of Sondheim songs '88.) Many other bits and pieces incl. crossword puzzles for *New York* magazine '68 described as diabolical, two songs (with Styne's music) for Tony BENNETT ('Come Over Here' and 'Home Is The Place'), other incidental music, lyrics. *A Stephen Sondheim Evening* '83 at the Whitney Museum was recorded by Shepard (2-disc set on RCA), some of it incl. in Shepard's 4-disc *A Collector's Sondheim*, other bits not previously issued; 3-disc *Sondheim* '83 from Book Of The Month Club was a new set supervised by Sondheim, incl. 27-minute arr. of dances from *Pacific Overtures*, song 'Goodbye For Now' (theme from *Reds*). Composer-lyricist Jerry Herman (*b* 10 July '33, NYC; wrote *Hello, Dolly* and *La Cage aux Folles*) said 'We would all agree that Steve is the genius of the group, the only one who keeps on taking the musical theatre to new places' (quoted in *Time*). Illustrated *Sondheim & Co.* '87 by Craig Zaden is definitive, with commentary from principals incl. prod./dir. Hal Prince, stars of the shows, award-winning orchestrator Jonathan Tunick, many others; also valuable appendices.

SONNY & CHER USA vocal duo formed '63 by Sonny Bono (*b* Salvatore Bono, 16 Feb. '35, Detroit) and Cher (*b* Cherilyn Lapiere, 20 May '46, El Centro, Cal.). Sonny worked in A&R for Specialty, graduating to house producer of acts like Don And Dewey, Roddy Jackson. Wrote songs incl. 'High School Dance', 'You Bug Me Baby', 'She Said Yeah' for Larry WILLIAMS, the latter covered by ROLLING STONES; co-wrote with Jack NITZSCHE incl. SEARCHERS hit 'Needles And Pins'. Worked with Nitzsche again for Phil SPECTOR, playing percussion and helping with arrangements; also formed shortlived Rush label. Met Cher in restaurant; they married '64; she got work backing CRYSTALS and RONETTES; as Caesar and Cleo they recorded 'The Letter' for Vault, 'Love Is Strange' for Reprise; she made novelty 'Ringo We Love You' prod. by Spector. First release as Sonny & Cher 'Baby Don't Go' won them contract as duo with Atco/Atlantic, solo for Cher with Reprise; 'I Got You Babe' was their first hit, innocent yet rebellious, catchy, impeccably arranged (with nagging oboe in chorus) by

Harold Battiste: it was no. 1 both USA/UK. Cher's cover of Bob DYLAN's 'All I Really Want To Do' was no. 15 USA, 'Baby Don't Go' was transatlantic hit on re-release, Sonny had solo hit with gruff 'Laugh At Me'; duo's 'Just You' was top 20 USA, hookless 'But You're Mine', 'What Now My Love', 'Little Man', 'The Beat Goes On' were USA/UK hits through '67, but then they faded, folk-rock/harmony scene giving way to 'progressive' sounds: they seemed out of touch, impression reinforced in that hippie time by their appearance in government anti-drug film. Their films together *Good Times* '66, *Chastity* '68 (named after their daughter) sank without trace; TV brought them back to top 10 with 'All I Ever Need Is You', 'A Cowboy's Work Is Never Done' '71-2; she modelled for *Vogue*, had no. ones 'Gypsys, Tramps And Thieves', 'Half Breed', 'Dark Lady' '71-4; they split personally/professionally '74; his TV show flopped, hers was a success: she sent herself up in dated hippie togs, a figure of fun with belly-button showing, but laid-back persona won favour. She recorded in a variety of styles, from Jim WEBB-prod. pop (*Stars* '75) to Southern rock (*Allman And Woman: Two The Hard Way* '77 with short-term husband Gregg ALLMAN), even hard-rock band (*Black Rose* '80 with lover Les Dudek, guitar); she made cameo on MEATLOAF's 'Dead Ringer' '81 as female lead. Her acting was highly praised in play/film *Come Back To The Five And Dime, Jimmy Dean Jimmy Dean*, films *Silkwood* and *Mask*; won Oscar for *Moonstruck* '88. The duo is history, but no one who was there can forget the big hit.

SONS OF THE PIONEERS Country & Western vocal group formed '33 by Roy ROGERS, Bob Nolan (*b* Robert Charles Nobles, 1 Apr. '08, New Brunswick, Canada; *d* 15 June '80, L.A.) and Tim Spencer (*b* 13 July '08, Webb City, Mo.; *d* 26 Apr. '74) as the Pioneer Trio, becoming the Sons of the Pioneers when Hugh Farr (*b* 6 Dec. '03; *d* 17 Mar. '80) and Karl Farr (*b* 29 Apr. '09; *d* 20 Sep. '61) joined: two real cowboys from Texas, who went on to appear in cowboy movies with Rogers. The group's gentle close harmony perfectly suited 'singing cowboy' genre; they sang on the radio, appeared in such films as *Rhythm On The Range* '36 with Bing CROSBY. Nolan and Spencer were exceptional songwriters: Nolan wrote 'Tumbling Tumbleweeds' '27 (a hit for the Pioneers '34 and for Crosby '40 on Decca; sung by Gene AUTRY in films *Tumbling Tumbleweeds* '35 and *Don't Fence Me In* '45, by Rogers in *Silver Spurs* '43), 'Cool Water' '36 (hit for the Pioneers on Decca '41; a hit again when they recorded it with Vaughn MONROE '48); Nolan and Spencer co-wrote 'Blue Prairie' '36; Spencer wrote 'The Timber Trail' '42, 'Cowboy Camp Meetin' ' '46, 'Cigareetes, Whusky and Wild, Wild Women' and 'The Everlasting Hills Of Oklahoma' '47, 'Careless Kisses' '49 (hit by Eddy HOWARD), 'Roomful Of Roses' '49 (a hit for the Pioneers, Howard, Sammy KAYE with Don CORNELL, Dick HAYMES and George MORGAN, all in '49; sung by Autry in *Mule Train* '50; revived by Mickey GILLEY '74). Spencer co-wrote 'Roses' with Glenn Spencer '50 (another hit for Kaye). The Pioneers recorded for Decca, Columbia, Victor; Lloyd Perryman (*b* 29 Jan. '17; *d* 3 May '77) joined '36, Rogers left '38; they appeared in films *Hollywood Canteen* '44, *Gay Rancheros* '44, *Melody Time* '48 (Disney cartoon compilation: they sang 'Pecos Bill' with Rogers). Spencer, Nolan left '50: Ken Curtis, Ken Carson, Doyle O'Dell, Dale Warren, Tommy Doss, Rusty Richards and Shug Fisher were all Pioneers in later years; albums incl. *Favourite Cowboy Songs* '56, *Wagons West* '58, *Lure Of The West* '59, *Down Memory Trail* '61, *Campfire Favourites* '63, *South Of The Border* '66, all on RCA. The original six members were elected to the Country Music Hall of Fame '80; historical compilations incl. *Sons Of The Pioneers* in Columbia Historical Series; *Empty Saddles, Tumbleweed Trails, Tumbling Tumbleweeds* (with Rogers) on MCA; others available from the Country Music Hall of Fame in Nashville incl. radio transcriptions '40 and *Way Out West*; in UK *Cowboy Country* on Bear Family (with Ken Curtis) and historical *20 Of The Best* on RCA International.

SOUKOUS Genre emerging in Congo/Zaire but now widely played throughout Africa, known as Lingala music in East Africa, Congo music in Anglophone West Africa. Developed in work camps of European companies 1900-30 where mix of cultures led to new forms; originally performed on likembe (sanza), guitar and bottle, early innovators such as Wendo and Djhimmy giving it a more modern feel; early infl. incl. highlife and Cuban rumba, but the abiding strength of the style lay in the adaptation of indigenous traditions. In '40s the development of a radio network and the opening of studios helped in its diffusion; in '50s foreign instruments, especially electric guitars, began to give it its modern sound. Early exponents incl. Joseph Kabaselle, O.K. Jazz, Dr NICO, Les Bantous de la Capitale. The first 'orchestres' appeared '50s with guitars, double bass, congas, clips and male vocals; later the 'mi-solo', a third guitar line between lead and rhythm, was introduced, along with brass and woodwinds. Kazadi ('73) identified eight stages in the evolution of soukous, but by the'70s two distinct styles were identifiable, differentiated by the vocal presentation of melodic material and its reproduction on lead guitar. By this time it had spread to East Africa, while also playing a formative role in the development of Francophone West African music. Today a basic lineup incl. three or four guitars, bass, drums, brass and vocals, with top orchestres having over 20 musicians, lyrics usually in Lingala. It flourished '60s with heavy rumba overtones evident in recordings of orchestres Kamale, Kiam, Lipua-Lipua, Bella Bella and Veve; towards decade's end a new, rougher version appeared, associated with Stukas, Zaiko Langa Langa and Empire Bukuba; a new generation of '80 soukous stars incl. Souzy KASSEYA, KANDA BONGO MAN, Fidele Zizi, Victoria, Theo Blaise, Orchestre Virunga.

SOUL music A genre in black American popular music which, with the black pop of Motown, dominated both pop and R&B charts to the extent that Billboard's R&B chart was abolished for 14 months from late '63 to early '65; for the first and only time blacks and whites were buying the same records. (From 23 Aug. '69 the black chart was called the soul chart, after the golden age of soul was over.) Ray CHARLES was the first soul artist, bringing the passion and vocal techniques of black gospel music (especially the vocal ornamentation called melisma) to rhythm & blues: he sang secular songs in a 'sanctified' manner, considered scandalous in some circles. Black rockers such as LITTLE RICHARD did the same thing with more frenzy, which was an exciting novelty to white teenagers, unfamiliar with black gospel music. Sam COOKE was the first pop star to come directly from black gospel music (had many fans as lead singer of the Soul Stirrers); his 'You Send Me' (no. 1 pop hit '57) is the real beginning of the soul era, an excellent example of melisma, but subsequent hits saw his style watered down in the studio: black audiences knew who he really was. James BROWN on King in Cincinnati was unique, began crossing over to the pop chart '58. The Satellite label was formed in Memphis '60 to record local talent by Jim Stewart, his sister Estelle Axton; first hits were by Rufus THOMAS and his daughter Carla '60 (but Otis REDDING was their biggest home-grown success); the name changed to Stax because there was already a Satellite label on the West Coast; they soon made distribution deal with Atlantic, and Fame in Muscle Shoals soon followed, with Jerry Wexler sending Atlantic artists south to record. The Stax house band began when the Royal Spades, a local white R&B group, became the Mar-Keys, then BOOKER T AND THE MGs, plus the Memphis Horns (Packy Axton, Wayne Jackson and Don Nix); Chips Moman was a young producer who soon started his own studio; Isaac HAYES, David Porter soon wrote songs for SAM & DAVE. Muscle Shoals is reclaimed land, across the river from Florence, Alabama; Fame Music was started in a room above a drugstore by local eccentric/visionary Tom Stafford, with young producers Rick Hall (built Fame Studio) and Billy SHERRILL, keyboardist Spooner Oldham, vocalist Dan Penn (a white kid who sang more black than Elvis PRESLEY ever did), songwriter Donnie Fritts all hanging around: among their first hits were Arthur ALEXANDER's. The phenomenon that actually caused the soul explosion was black artists like those named above plus Aretha FRANKLIN, Wilson PICKETT, Joe TEX, Percy SLEDGE, Ben E. KING, William BELL, Solomon BURKE, many others recording in these small studios run by white amateurs, backed by integrated groups of young Southern musicians of great talent who were steeped in the appropriate style: at a time when

singers and musicians still could not eat lunch together in local restaurants they created a fusion (by accident, the only way true fusions in music ever happen) which captured the hearts of a whole generation. The golden age of soul is generally agreed to have ended on 4 Apr. '68, when Martin Luther King was murdered: there was unmistakable hostility in black neighbourhoods all over the USA and Stax had to close for a while because the staff couldn't go to work; at the '68 convention in Atlanta of the National Association of Radio and Television Announcers (NARTA), Wexler was hanged in effigy, and several people were beaten up and others were said to be carrying guns. The truth was that despite the complete triumph of black input into the pop charts, black artists and businessmen (with the unusual exception of Berry Gordy at Motown) still did not have the personal success they deserved, having to curry favour with the white establishment. (This had not changed in the '80s, when black artists said of the major labels that 'If you're not Lionel RICHIE, they don't want to know,' which is why the jazz community has taken matters into its own hands; *see* JAZZ, AACM, etc.) The Civil Rights era at the same time as the golden age of soul music saw the end of *de facto* segregation, but it will take a lot longer than 20 or 30 years to undo the effects of 300 years of racial oppression. Meanwhile the participants in the glorious accident that had occurred at Stax and Fame went their various ways, but the classics that were recorded are still selling and still tingle the spine of the listener. Arnold Shaw in his *Black Popular Music In America* '86 pursues the theory that rhythm & blues was the thesis, soul and Motown pop the antithesis, and their absorption by the white music business the synthesis: 'blue-eyed soul' is the name given to the music of whites such as the RIGHTEOUS BROTHERS who successfully learned the lessons of soul: Steve WINWOOD's success at the Grammy awards '87 is another fruit of the soul era. 'Northern soul' is a brand of white pop from northern England which takes some cues from the great black music of the recent past rather than from the sterile posturing that takes place in London TV studios, while dance floors in British clubs are dominated by black music, with its heavy inheritance of soul. Soul carried on: Al GREEN came from the church to become one of the great artists of the '70s (on Memphis's Hi label), then went back to it; 'sweet soul' is the term applied to the gorgeous singing of black romantics like Peabo BRYSON; Al JARREAU's albums are overproduced, like many albums in the '80s, but he has soul in his voice. The generation that runs the advertising, film and record industries is between 30 and 40 in mid-'80s; they know how great the soul classics are: a revival has been marked by reissues such as seven 2-disc sets on Atlantic, and by use of the original recordings in TV adverts: soul is a trademark of good taste, except when the term is used carelessly. *See* entry for ATLANTIC. Peter Guralnick's book *Sweet Soul Music* '86 is a masterpiece.

SOUSA, John Philip (*b* 6 Nov. 1854, Washington DC; *d* 6 Mar. '32, Reading, Pa.) Bandleader, composer. He played violin in symphony orchestras, led USMC Band 1880-92, brass concert band for the rest of his life, the best-loved act of its kind: he hired first-class musicians and paid them well, even had a good word for jazz: he did not quite know what it was, but understood its value and tried to use its flavour in his concerts. He inspired untold numbers of kids to take up instruments; composed 'Stars And Stripes Forever', 'King Cotton', 'El Capitan' (title theme of his comic opera), 'Semper Fidelis' (Marine Corp hymn written at request of President Chester A. Arthur), 'The Thunderer', 'Washington Post March', many others. He disapproved of 'canned music'; about two dozen of his records were big hits 1895-1918, most cond. by trombonist Arthur Pryor (*b* 22 Sep. 1870, St Joseph, Mo.; *d* 18 June '42, West Long Beach, N.J.), who had a similar number of hits of his own.

SOUTH, Eddie (*b* 27 Nov. '04, Louisiana, Mo.; *d* 25 Apr. '62, Chicago, Ill.) Jazz violinist. To Chicago as a baby; a child prodigy on the violin, later coached in jazz by Darnell Howard, who played violin as well as reeds (*see* Kid ORY). South spent most of his life in Chicago, except for tours of Europe '28-30 (with own group, the Alabamians, recorded two sides for HMV in Paris; studied music in Budapest), '37-8 (recorded with

Django REINHARDT, Stephane GRAPPELLI '37, quintet with Tommy BENFORD '38), also work on West Coast '32, later occasional residencies in NYC, Hollywood, etc. Led small groups, usually a quartet, sometimes a big band '40s-50s, on Chicago radio '40s, TV '50s. He was billed as 'the Dark Angel of the Violin'; never played an amplified instrument. European tracks reissued on Swing label '85; other records for Victor '27-33 in Chicago, Columbia and Okeh '40-1 in NYC; later album *The Distinguished Violin Of Eddie South* on Mercury. He was very highly rated by those in the know, but playing the violin in jazz and staying in Chicago he remained relatively obscure.

SOUTH, Joe (*b* Joe Souter, 28 Feb. '42, Atlanta, Ga.) Guitarist, singer, songwriter. Played country music on the radio at age 12, later in Pete Drake band, made singles (his novelty 'The Purple People Eater Meets The Witch Doctor' almost made the top 40 '58); did sessions at Nashville and Muscle Shoals backing Marty ROBBINS, Eddy ARNOLD, Bob DYLAN, others; wrote songs and prod. hits for Billy Joe ROYAL incl. 'Down In The Boondocks' '65. South album *Introspect* '68 on Capitol reissued as *Games People Play* when people began covering that song; his single was no. 12 '69; song won a Grammy. Other albums were *Don't It Make You Want To Go Home* '69 (title single almost top 40), *So The Seeds Are Growing* '71 (no. 12 hit 'Walk A Mile In My Shoes'); *Midnight Rainbows* '75 on Island.

SOUTHER, J. D. (*b* c.'46, Texas) Singer/songwriter. Raised in Amarillo, played in obscure groups: Longbranch Pennywhistle duo with future EAGLE Glenn Frey made eponymous LP for Amos '70. Own first LP *John David Souther* '72 on David GEFFEN's Asylum label (released first Eagles album same year); he prod. Linda RONSTADT's *Don't Cry Now* '73, then was tempted into Souther-Hillman-Furay Band, label's attempt at megabuck supergroup in CSN&Y mould: Chris Hillman ex-BYRDS, Burrito Brothers, Stephen STILLS's Manassas; Richie Furay newly solo ex-lead singer of POCO. First eponymous album '74 had six faces on cover, incl. pianist Paul Harris, Al Perkins on steel guitar (both ex-Manassas), drummer Jim Gordon (ex-Derek & The

Dominos). Album went gold on expectations but lacked any consistency; Furay's 'Fallin' In Love' was the classiest track, while Hillman exhumed 'Safe At Home' from International Submarine Band repertoire. *Trouble In Paradise* '75 was rightly named as egos got out of hand; despite several Eagles sitting in, it flopped. Gordon left to session, replaced by Ron Grinel; three principals split '76, all making solo LPs for Asylum: Souther's *Black Rose* (prod. by Peter ASHER) had all-star cast of Ronstadt, Joe WALSH, Lowell George; songs typically lovelorn singer/songwriter stuff. His songs were recorded by Bonnie RAITT, Ronstadt (title track of *Prisoner In Disguise*). *You're Only Lonely* '79 on CBS incl. more Eagles, attempt to break out of mould with shot at reggae; continued in '80s with songwriting, singing background for Warren ZEVON, Christopher CROSS, etc.; album *Home By Dawn* '84 on Full Moon/Asylum.

SOUTHERN, Jeri (*b* Genevieve Hering, 5 Aug. '26, Royal, Nebr.) Singer. Graduated from Notre Dame Academy, Omaha; studied piano; worked at Omaha's Blackstone Hotel. Toured with US Navy recruiting show; began to sing and played important dates in Chicago incl. Hi Note Club '49 supporting Anita O'DAY; gained nightly TV spot. Signed to Decca; 'You Better Go Now', 'When I Fall In Love' successful '52, especially in UK where the latter beat Doris DAY version. LPs on Decca incl. *Warm Intimate Songs, The Southern Style, You Better Go Now, When Your Heart's On Fire, Jeri Jumps Gently, Southern Hospitality*; UK hit '57 with 'Fire Down Below', tune from Rita Hayworth movie. Capitol LPs incl. *Jeri Southern Sings Cole Porter*, with witty arr. by Billy MAY; also *Southern Breeze* on Roulette. To West Coast early '60s, quit to teach singing; later was the companion of film composer Hugo FRIEDHOFER, orchestrated some of his work. Intriguing detached sultriness still has many fans: 'You'll listen in vain for the manufactured lump in the throat or any bogus jollity' (Peter Clayton). 16-track reissue *When I Fall In Love* '84 UK compiled and with notes by Colin Butler, incl. songs named above; some of his carefully compiled discographical data was garbled by MCA.

SOUTHSIDE JOHNNY & THE ASBURY JUKES Rock band formed '75 by vocalist and harmonica player Southside Johnny (*b* John Lyons, 4 Dec. '48, N.J.), a contemporary of Bruce SPRINGSTEEN, forever in The Boss's shadow, despite a series of soulful albums. First band was in '67; band called the Blackberry Booze Band became the Jukes when horns were added, played in Asbury Park clubs incl. legendary Stone Poney; original lineup (with nearly everybody helping on vocals) incl. Miami Steve VAN ZANDT (for a few months until he joined Springsteen later in '75), Billy Rush, guitar; Kenny Pentifallo, drums; Alan Berger, bass; Kevin Kavanaugh, keyboards; Carlo Novi, sax; Ricki Gazda and Tony Palligrosi, trumpets and Richie 'La Bamba' Rosenberg on trombone, who also worked with Diana ROSS and Van Zandt's Disciples of Soul. Rumoured early LP *Live At The Bottom Line* '76 on Epic (probably a promo); then proper debut *I Don't Wanna Go Home* same year, with classic title track written by Van Zandt, effusive sleeve note by Springsteen and duets with Lee DORSEY, Ronnie Spector; also Lyons' version of Bruce's widely bootlegged 'The Fever'. *This Time It's For Real* '77 incl. Lyons' own title track, Springsteen/Van Zandt songs 'Love On The Wrong Side Of Town' and 'When You Dance'; in trad. of Asbury Park band acknowledging its roots, also incl. guest contributions from the DRIFTERS, COASTERS, FIVE SATINS. Most highly rated album is *Hearts Of Stone* '78, a good companion to Springsteen's *Darkness On The Edge Of Town* same year: indeed, title track of *Hearts* was scheduled for the latter. In spite or because of Springsteen's championing, Lyons never reached mass audience, but retained cult following in USA and Europe; *Having A Party With Southside Johnny And The Asbury Jukes* '79 was effective Best Of from the three albums prod. by Van Zandt (who played on *Hearts*) with one new track; switched to Mercury for *The Jukes* '79 and *Love Is A Sacrifice* '80, lacking punch of earlier work; 2-disc *Reach Up And Touch The Sky* was definitive live set, incl. best-known material as well as a Sam COOKE medley. *Trash It Up!* '83 and *In The Heat* '84 came out on Mirage, *At Least We Got Shoes* '86 on Atlantic was better, incl. cover of 'Walk Away Renee'. Lyons was also behind the Jersey Artists For Mankind single '86.

SOVINE, Red (*b* Woodrow Wilson Sovine, 17 July '18, Charleston, W. Va.; *d* 4 Apr. '80, Nashville, Tenn.) Country singer, songwriter who finally achieved world-wide fame with truck-driving songs. Worked in hosiery mills in Charleston, singing part-time with Jim Pike's Carolina Tar Heels on Radio WCHS '35; turned full-time pro when the group moved to WWVA *Jamboree*, Wheeling, W.Va.; formed own Echo Valley Boys and returned to WCHS '47, replaced Hank WILLIAMS on *Louisiana Hayride*, Shreveport '49, also taking over Hank's daily Johnny Fair Syrup Show stint, acquiring nickname The Old Syrup Sopper. Teamed with Goldie Hill for duet hit 'Are You Mine?' '55, then no. 1 hit duet with Webb PIERCE 'Why Baby Why' same year, 'Little Rosa' '56; moved to Nashville, joined Grand Ole Opry, signed with Decca but had no hits of his own, though he was popular on stage and made a mark as songwriter with 'Missing You' '57 (two-sided Pierce top 10 country hit had 'Bye Bye Love' on the other side), other lesser hits. Joined Starday '63, had own hit 'Dream House For Sale', followed by no. 1 'Giddyup Go', his first truck-drivin' song; he had 13 hits on Starday through '70, but his only other top 10 was 'Phantom 309', the ultimate truck drivin' ghost story. Moved to Chart label, top 10 with 'It'll Come Back' '74; back to reactivated Starday and scored with a new version of 'Phantom 309' '75, then no. 1 country hit (top 40 pop) with 'Teddy Bear', about a crippled boy, a teddy bear and trucks (it was no. 5 in UK on reissue '81). Maintained a steady stream of respectable hits until his death. Albums incl. *Country Music Time* '57 on Decca; *Town And Country Action* '66, *I Didn't Jump The Fence* '67, *I Know You're Married* '70, *Woodrow Wilson Sovine* '77, all on Starday; *16 New Gospel Songs* '80 and *Phantom 309* '81 on Starday/Gusto.

SPACE MUSIC Mood music genre, crossing over into new age music, but differing from that mostly acoustic genre in that space music began as a California FM radio phenomenon, composed by Californians and Japanese to be played by synthesisers, e.g.

the music of Kitaro, whose many LPs (on six different labels in the USA) some critics profess to be unable to tell apart. In its purest manifestation space music is ultimate mood music: not music at all but soothing noise, wallpaper for the ears. Hearts Of Space in San Francisco offers records, tapes and compact discs on its own label and others through the post; about 100 artists and composers represented incl. Stomu Yamashta, Vangelis, Brian ENO (*Music For Airports*, etc.) and guitarist Steven Halpern (*Eastern Promise*), blamed by some for inventing new age. The company feels compelled to warn fans that Kitaro's album *Asia* is loud. New age artists such as Will Ackerman, George Winston are listed as well as film composer Jean Michel Jarre, etc.; more interesting offerings reveal some of the sources of the genre, such as the Majnun Symphony by the prolific composer Alan Hovhaness (*b* 8 Mar. '11, Somerville, Mass.); half Armenian, he has specialised in synthesis of music of East and West (his *The Mysterious Mountain* was beautifully recorded by Fritz Reiner and the Chicago S.O.). Minimalist composer Terry RILEY appeals (*Rainbow In Curved Air*); as do LPs by Paul HORN (*Inside The Taj Mahal* '68, etc.) and Tony SCOTT (*Music For Zen Meditation* '64, with traditional Japanese musicians). Hearts Of Space also offers sets of cassettes called *Beyond The Blahs*, *Mobile Serenity*, *The Sonic Martini*, etc. with harps, zithers, synthesisers, wordless choruses. There is sacred space music for digital orchestra, choral voices, electronics, composed by Constance Demby, who plays metal instruments of her design called the whale sail and the space bass. Videos are offered, e.g. *White Nights* by Tadayoshi Arai, electronic art with slowly changing abstract patterns in colour, as well as T-shirts, space tubes (a sort of magic wand) and stars which glow in the dark and can be pasted on your ceiling.

SPANDAU BALLET UK 'new romantics' band formed '79 by guitarist/songwriter Gary Kemp (*b* 16 Oct. '60, London), like his friends a habitué of London club scene based around black funk music and gaudy sartorial backlash against punk. Had played with schoolmates in youthful ensemble the Makers with Tony Hadley (*b* 2 June '59), vocalist; John Keeble (*b* 6 July '59), drums; Steve Norman (*b* 25 Mar. '60), rhythm guitar; recruited brother Martin Kemp (*b* 10 Oct. '61) as bassist (brothers also had experience in children's theatre). Initial gigs were invitation only at unconventional venues (e.g. HMS *Belfast* on the Thames); branded as escapist by press, but stance very much anti-rock'n'roll. Manager Steve Dagger signed them to Chrysalis, who gave them their own Reformation label. Early hits were 'experimental' electro-funk: 'To Cut A Long Story Short', 'The Freeze', chanting, Slavonic 'Musclebound' '80-1. Pioneered different mixes for 7″ and 12″ singles, a practice taken from black music. First LP *Journeys To Glory* '81. 'Chant No. 1' was brassy African-sounding single, but second LP *Diamond* '82 pale by comparison, prod. like first by Richard James Burgess (ex-Landscape), one side commercial singles and one of JAPAN-like 'experimental' music; also released as four 12″ singles (parallel with MOBY GRAPE's five 7-inchers in '60s): first two of these flopped, but Trevor Horn remixed 'Instinction' for face-saving no. 10 hit. Changed Burgess for Jolly/Swain, pop/soul prod. team behind Imagination, Bananarama: *True* '83 dropped experimental pretence for white soul in HALL & OATES mould: hits incl. 'True' (no. 1), 'Gold' (2) attested to consumer satisfaction, with Norman's newly acquired saxophone adding icing to the cake. *Parade* '84 incl. more pop hits incl. 'Only When You Leave' (3) but dispute with label caused damaging year's hiatus, broken only by best-selling *The Singles Collection*, released against band's wishes. They blanded out to become shamelessly populist group that appeared '85 in Live Aid; Kemp appeared solo on Labour Party Red Wedge tour '86, surprising as their success was based on conspicuous consumption. *Through The Barricades* '86 on CBS/Reformation was judged superior to *Parade*, but still tired; title song (about Northern Ireland) was first Kemp political song to make it into band's repertoire.

SPANIER, Muggsy (*b* Francis Joseph Spanier, 9 Nov. '06, Chicago, Ill.; *d* 12 Feb. '67, Sausalito, Cal.) Cornet, leader. One of ten children; nicknamed after a baseball manager; began on drums, switched to cornet at 13. Played in many bands, joined Ted

LEWIS '29-36 incl. European tour, Ben POLLACK '36-8, ill-health took him to the Touro clinic in New Orleans; formed Ragtimers for gigs at Sherman Hotel in Chicago, Nick's in NYC: band lasted less than eight months but made sixteen 78 sides reissued many times since, their prewar charm in neo-New Orleans style showing why the revival movement in jazz began at about that time. Four octet sides were made in Chicago in July, the rest by a septet (*sans* guitar) at the end of the year, all for Victor; all incl. George Clarence Brunies on trombone (*b* 6 Feb. '02, N.O.; *d* 19 Nov. '74, Chicago; later spelled his name Georg Brunis) and George Frederick 'Rod' Cless on clarinet (*b* 20 May '07, Lennox, Iowa; *d* 8 Dec. '44, NYC); Joe BUSHKIN played piano in NYC. Blues 'Relaxin' At The Touro' was an original; of the chestnuts they revived, their 'Livery Stable Blues' was probably the sweetest version ever made. He rejoined Lewis, then with Bob CROSBY '40-1; led big band '41-3 styled after Crosby's which recorded eight sides for Decca '42, 'Two O'Clock Jump' something of a hit; 'Hesitating Blues' was a 'Ragtimers' (band-within-a-band) side with Vernon Brown on trombone, Irving Fazola on clarinet. Played with Lewis again '44; led small groups, worked in '50s with Earl HINES in San Francisco.

SPANKY & OUR GANG Vocal/instrumental group formed '66 in Chicago. Lineup: vocalist Elaine 'Spanky' McFarlane (*b* 19 June '42, Peoria, Ill.), guitarist/vocalist Martin Hale (*b* 17 May '41, Butte, Mont.; *d* '68), rhythm guitarist Nigel Pickering (*b* 15 June '29, Pontiac, Mich.), drummer John Seiter (*b* 17 Aug. '44, St Louis, Mo.), bassist Kenny Hodges from Jacksonville, Fla., Lefty Baker (real name Eustace Britchforth, from Roanoke, Va.) on guitar and banjo. Folk-rock/pop style was similar to that of the MAMAS & THE PAPAS, whom they replaced in the charts late '60s; comparison further underlined by Spanky's non-sylphlike similarity to Mama Cass. She and Mama had met early '60s; Spanky joined folk/cabaret act New Wine Singers; formed quartet with Hodges, Pickering and Baker, taking the name from the short comedy films made beginning mid-'20s by Hal Roach (later star was George Emmett

Spanky McFarland (b '28); shown on TV the kid stars were called *Little Rascals*), Hale and Seiter joining after they signed with Mercury. Of nine Hot 100 entries '67-9, biggest was the first, 'Sunday Will Never Be The Same', top 10 and still with a certain charm. Albums were *Spanky And Our Gang* '67, *Like To Get To Know You* (top 20 title single) and *Without Rhyme Or Reason* '68, a live LP and Greatest Hits collection '70. Hale died of cirrhosis during making of third album. Spanky and Pickering reformed and made *Change* '75 for Epic with Marc McClure on guitar, Bill Plummer on bass, Jim Moon on drums, incl. cover of Larry Norman's 'I Wish We'd All Been Ready' which was highly praised; toured in Texas until '80, sang on Roger McGuinn's debut solo LP, joined re-formed Mamas/Papas '82.

SPANN, Otis (b 21 Mar. '30, Jackson, Ms.; d 24 Apr. '70, Chicago, Ill.) Pianist, also singer; played organ, harmonica. With Muddy WATERS and LITTLE WALTER, one of the greatest of the originators of post-war Chicago blues. Began on piano age 7; attended junior college, played football and was a boxer, also worked in blues clubs. Served in US Army '46-51, then to Chicago, working mostly outside music at first, almost continuously with Waters from '53, also recording with Howlin' WOLF and Bo DIDDLEY '54-5, as Chess house pianist. Own records on Chess/Checker '55-63. Albums incl. *Otis Spann Is The Blues* '60 on Candid (Candid sessions issued on Crosscut in UK incl. Vol. 2, *And His Piano*); *Good Morning Blues* '63 on Storyville (made in Copenhagen); *Chicago Blues* on Testament '64-5; *Blues Never Die* '65 on Prestige; *Crying Time* '66 on Vanguard (now on PRT UK); *Nobody Knows Chicago Like I Do* '66 (live with Waters on BluesWay, now on Charly UK). Also recorded with Wolf again '60 on Chess; with Johnny Young on Arhoolie '65, Blue Horizon '69; with Johnny SHINES on Testament '66, with Buddy GUY on Vanguard '68, Junior WELLS/Guy on Delmark c. early '70. Died of cancer.

SPARROW, Mighty (b Slinger Francisco, '35, Grenada) Calypso King of the World, soca artist. Moved to Port of Spain as an infant and grew up in poverty; sang for extra milk at New Town Boys School, also as an acolyte at St Patrick's R.C. Church; formed steel band with other boys. Inspired by radio adverts sung in calypso style, heard calypsonians at local Spike Club where he worked at the control board; turned pro, first recorded '55 (nicknamed when somebody said he jumped around the stage like a sparrow). The late Dr Eric Williams won elections '56 and his People's National Movement ruled Trinidad & Tobago until '86; 'Jean And Dinah' won both Road March and Calypso Monarch (*see* CALYPSO), commenting on USA presence in Trinidad; calypsonians had been without social standing but took on celebratory rather than protesting role with nationalist government: for ten years his political calypsoes supported the PNM, e.g. 'William The Conqueror' '57 on the Balisier label (named after a plant, emblem of the PNM); that year he prod. the first calypso LP *King Sparrow's Calypso Carnival* for '58 season (incl. 'Pay As You Earn', supporting new income tax law). In '57-9 he did not enter Monarch contest in protest against small prizes, bad conditions. *Sparrow In Hi-Fi* '59 was followed by Road March and Monarch wins with 'May May' '60; his other entry that year 'Ten To One Is Murder' was public defence against charge of wounding with intent (he was acquitted). *Sparrow: Calypso King* '61 on RCA incl. 'Princess And The Cameraman' (bewildered that Princess Margaret could marry a mere cameraman), 'Madam Dracula', attacking his then-rival Lord Melody (Fitzroy Alexander). He won Road March '61 with 'Royal Jail' (*Sparrow The Conqueror* on RCA); first UK appearance/UK LP debut *The Calypso King Of Trinidad* '61, incl. 'May May', 'Royal Jail'. Won '62 Monarch with songs incl. in *Sparrow Come Back*; *Sparrow At The Sheraton* incl. concert versions of 'Ten To One Is Murder', 'Dan Is The Man' (one of his '63 entries, satire on primary education: used theatrical disguise in live act for the first time in calypso). *True Stories Of Passion, People And Politics* on Mace USA incl. 'The Slave' '63, which he still performs; *Congo Man* '65 on Hilary (aka *Trinidad Heat Wave* on Mace) incl. 'Solomon Out' and 'Get To Hell Outa Here', the first about cabinet minister who resigned, accused of using his office to free his stepson from police detention, the other quoting Williams's advice to those criticising his handling of the incident: disappointment with Williams marked one of Sparrow's last political calypsoes until the '80s. He retired from Monarch competition '65-71. *Genius* '66 on Hilary incl. Road March winner 'Obeah Wedding (Melda)'; *Sparrow Meets The Dragon* '67 on SpaLee, made with Jamaican bandleader Byron Lee, and *Sparrow Calypso Carnival* '68 followed by *More Sparrow More* '69, regarded as one of his best; *Calypso Time, Many Moods Of Sparrow* '70-1 were followed by response to challenge '72 from the Mighty Duke (Kelvin Pope), who won Calypso Monarch four consecutive times: Sparrow re-entered and beat Duke into last place with 'Rope' and 'Drunk And Disorderly' (latter also won Road March), incl. in *Hotter Than Ever* '72; then won Monarch three years in a row; albums were *Calypso Spectacular* '73, *Knock Dem Down Sparrow* and *Peace Pipe* (by his backing band, Calypso Troubadours), both '74; *Calypso Maestro* '75. He re-made some of his earlier calypsoes in Miami for *Hot And Sweet* '74 on WB. From '75 he withdrew from the Monarch contest, still eligible for the Road March. *Sparrow vs. The Rest* was made in Jamaica; *Sparrow Dragon* was reunion with Byron Lee, both '76 on Dynamic. *Boogie Beat* '77 on Semp was a flop; *NYC Black Out* '78 on Charlies was better; ballad 'Only A Fool Breaks His Own Heart' was no. 1 hit in Holland, in charts there for 20 weeks; LP *Only A Fool* '78 on Trojan sold two million copies in Common Market. By '79 he had embraced soca: *Pussy Cat Party* incl. 'Rip Off'; *25th Anniversary* '80 was first 2-disc calypso album; *Sanford* '81 revived political comment, 'Karl Say' hinting support for Organisation for National Reconstruction party opposing PNM (now part of National Alliance for Reconstruction, which won a landslide late '86); next year *Sweeter Than Ever* incl. 'We Like It So (Steel Beam)', on political conservatism of Trinidadians. *The Greatest* '83 incl. 'Capitalism Gone Mad', 'Philip My Dear', the latter an irreverent treatment of the entry of Michael Fagin into Queen Elizabeth II's Buckingham Palace bedroom. *King Of The World* '84 incl. Road March winner 'Don't Back Back', 'Grenada' (comment on USA's invasion); *Venessa* '85 incl. 'Soca Pressure', *A Touch Of*

Class '86 incl. 'Invade South Africa'. He won the King of Kings contest '85, beating current and former calypso title winners, live performances incl. in LPs on B's Records. Trinidad company Imprint published booklet *Sparrow, The Legend* incl. lyrics of 100 of his calypsoes; he was featured in TV film *Kaiso* '85 on UK Channel 4. He set a record of seven Calypso Monarch and eight Road March wins, second only to Lord KITCHENER in Road March wins; he is the only artist to win both Monarch and Road March in the same year three times. He raised calypso's status and did well out of it, building Sparrow's Hideaway, a sports and cultural complex outside Port of Spain; for many years he has led his own calypso tent, the Original Young Brigades. His '87 LP was delayed by contractual problems; for the carnival he promoted *Sparrow's Party Classics* on Charlies, soca-ised versions of earlier hits, also prod. and wrote two songs for *Introducing Miss Natasha Wilson* on M&M, debut LP by 11-year-old former Junior Calypso Monarch '85: she performed in his tent and he tutored her to Monarch finals. U. of West Indies announced his honorary Doctor of Letters degree; LP *One Love, One Heart* finally appeared on B's, incl. title track comment on '86 election, revival of calypso humour 'Lying Excuses'.

SPEARS, Billie Jo (*b* 14 Jan. '37, Beaumont, Texas) Country singer with bluesy voice and downhome personality, especially popular in UK. A child prodigy, appearing on *Louisiana Hayride* '51-2; made novelty 'Too Old For Toys, Too Young For Boys' '53 on Abbott. Worked at various jobs after high school, singing in clubs at night; songwriter Jack Rhodes persuaded her to come to Nashville, where she signed with UA, made some singles and became session singer; signed with Capitol, had first hit 'He's Got More Love In His Little Finger' '68. 'Mr Walker, It's All Over' '69 was top 5 hit (very much in 'Harper Valley P.T.A.' mode; *see* Jeannie C. RILEY), led to European tour with Capitol Caravan. She had hits '69-71, faded from scene owing to throat problem that prevented her from singing for a year. Back on UA she did update of Bobby GOLDSBORO's 'See The Funny Little Clown' '74, then 'Blanket On The Ground' was no. 1 country hit USA, also no. 6 in UK pop chart. More USA hits '75-8, 'Sing Me An Old Fashioned Song', 'What I've Got In Mind', 'I Will Survive' all making UK pop chart; her LPs sold well in UK while in the USA she could not get a contract with a major label; came back with minor hit 'Midnight Blue' '84 on Parliament. LPs: *Voice, Miss Sincerity, Country Girl* on Capitol '67-9; *Blanket On The Ground* '75, *What I've Got In Mind* '76, *Everytime I Sing A Love Song* '77, *Lonely Hearts Club* '78, *Singles Album* '79, *Standing Tall* '80 on UA; *Special Songs* '81 on Liberty, *We Just Came Apart At The Dreams* '84 on Premier, *At The Country Store* '85 on Starblend.

SPECIALS, The UK rock group formed in Coventry '77: Jerry Dammers, keyboards and songwriter (*b* 22 Apr. '54); Terry Hall, vocals (*b* 19 Mar. '59); Lynval Golding, rhythm guitar (*b* 24 July '51), all from Coventry; vocalist Neville Staples, Roddy Radiation on guitar, Sir Horace Gentleman on bass, drummer John Bradbury. They inaugurated integrated 2-Tone label and movement, brainchild of Dammers; the movement re-popularised ska and acted as a blanket organisation for groups who resented colour prejudice in UK; it was the most potent contribution to post-punk UK scene. By '78 movement incl. MADNESS, the BEAT, the Selector and the Bodysnatchers (later Belle Stars). Celebrated in belated film *Dance Craze* '81, album *This Are 2-Tone* '83. Specials were quintessential; championed by the CLASH '78; debut single 'Gangsters' was tirade against staid UK music scene, originally limited edition on indie label, no. 6 hit '79; LP *Specials* '79 was striking debut, prod. by Elvis COSTELLO (another fan), incl. hits 'A Message To You Rudy' and 'Too Much Too Young' (no. 1 '80). *More Specials* '80 was less effective, still a chart hit. They tried to crack USA market supporting the POLICE, but appeal was home-based. Finest hour was single 'Ghost Town' (no. 1 '81), chilling after riots in Brixton and Liverpool, remaining one of UK rock's most apposite statements. They fell apart soon after from internal friction and riots at gigs, which attracted oafish right-wing elements. Hall, Golding and Staples quit '81 objecting to what they saw as Dammers' high-handed approach; they formed Fun Boy Three, had hit albums *Fun Boy Three* and *Waiting* '82-3; Hall later went to Colour Field; Golding returned to Coventry and supervised new ska band After Tonight. Dammers/Bradbury forged on as The Special AKA: Dammers' songs became more overtly political and were mostly commercial flops: 'The Boiler' '82 (with singer Rhoda Dakar) was about rape, 'War Crimes' about Israeli provocation in the Lebanon, and 'Racist Friend' castigated UK's cosy attitude to colour problem; but 'Nelson Mandela', again prod. by Costello, with vocal by Stan Campbell, was top 20 hit '83, became anthem of anti-apartheid movement. Dammers' perfectionism led to delays in ironically titled *In The Studio* '84, collecting singles as well as light-hearted 'The Girlfriend'. He teamed with Robert WYATT for 'Wind Of Change' single '85, organised anti-apartheid concert in London mid-'86; proved that political message could combine with infectious dance music: it would be hard to overestimate his influence in the superficial world of UK pop. He appeared at Mandela's 70th birthday party at Wembley '88.

SPECKLED RED (*b* Rufus G. Perryman, 23 Oct. 1892, Monroe, La.; *d* 2 Jan. '73, St Louis, Mo.) Blues singer, pianist; also played organ; aka 'Detroit Red'. One of 16 children; brother William was PIANO RED; they got nicknames from complexion (they were both albinos). Lived in Detroit as a child, back to Hampton, Ga.; played organ in church, lived in Atlanta early '20s; back to Detroit and worked outside music, also rent parties etc. mid-'20s. Hoboed through South, often working with guitarist/singer Jim Jackson (c.1890-1937); recorded ten sides for Brunswick '29-30, two unissued; ten more on Bluebird '38. Settled in St Louis '41; played at World's Fair Bar there, recorded for Tone/Delmark labels mid-'50s; toured Europe late '50s, recorded in Copenhagen '61. 'The Dirty Dozens' '29 in his barrelhouse lumber-camp style adapted a mnemonic song for teaching biblical stories to young people into an erotic vehicle for insult; though cleaned up on early records it was said to have given currency to the word 'motherfucker', the twelfth category of abuse. Recorded 'The Dirty Dozens No. 2' '30. Albums: *1929-1938* on Wolf USA,

Speckled Red In London 1960 on VJM UK, *The Dirty Dozen* '61 on Storyville.

SPECTOR, Phil (*b* 26 Dec. '40, Bronx, NYC) Producer. To L.A. as a child; formed vocal group the Teddy Bears in high school; had smash hit with own song 'To Know Him Is To Love Him' '58 inspired by his late father. Worked with Lee HAZLEWOOD and Lester Sill in Phoenix, LEIBER & STOLLER in NYC '60: co-wrote Ben E. KING hit 'Spanish Harlem' with Leiber. Formed Philles label with Sill '61; began to develop 'wall of sound' style by packing musicians into small studio, using echo, tape loops etc., made hit after hit by Darlene LOVE, BOB B SOXX AND THE BLUEJEANS, RONETTES, CRYSTALS, others. Bought out Sill, became youngest record company head and millionaire age 21, dubbed Tycoon of Teen. Style dominated period between rockabilly and British Invasion, celebrated teen idol genre but transcended it, using good songs, first class arr. and sidemen; low output but high success rate was good business. Xmas album featuring Spector artists released same weekend JFK was shot, not shipped then; reissued '67 and sells annually ever since. RIGHTEOUS BROS hit 'You've Lost That Lovin' Feelin'' was high point '65; Ike & Tina TURNER's 'River Deep – Mountain High' was a flop in USA '66 (but has charted twice in UK); story that sound was too black for white DJs, too white for black didn't ring true: Righteous Bros sounded black and Spector style was infl. on black pop. Spector incensed by what he saw as industry jealousy; retired for some years. Did cameo part in film *Easy Rider* '69; prod. John LENNON disc 'Instant Karma' and doctored tapes of final BEATLES LP *Let It Be* '70; prod. *Plastic Ono Band* for Lennon '71, *All Things Must Pass* and *Bangladesh* LPs for Geo. HARRISON '70-1; financed Kung Fu film *Enter The Dragon* '73, worked with Cher, DION, others. Place in pop history assured; classic hits issued in *Greatest Hits* compilation.

SPENCE, Joseph (*b* 3 Aug. '10, Andros, the Bahamas; *d* 18 Mar. '84) Guitarist, singer; played hymns, anthems, island songs with a jazz musician's sense of time, interaction of voice and guitar like that of the best bluesmen. Infl. Ry COODER, Taj MAHAL, many others. Recorded from '58: *Happy All The Time* on Elektra (now on Carthage in UK); *Music Of The Bahamas* and *Folk Guitar* (with John Roberts and Frederick McQueen), both on Folkways; *Good Morning Mr Walker* on Arhoolie and *On The Hallelujah Side* on Rounder; also heard on 2 vols. of *The Real Bahamas* '65 on Nonesuch.

SPIRIT USA psychedelic rock group formed '67: Randy California (*b* Randy Wolfe, 20 Feb. '51, L.A.), guitar and vocals; stepfather Ed Cassidy (*b* 4 May '31, Chicago), drums; Mark Andes (*b* 19 Feb. '48, Philadelphia, Pa.), bass; vocalist Jay Ferguson (*b* John Ferguson, 10 May '47, Burbank, Cal.) had played together '65 as Red Roosters, recruited John Locke (*b* 25 Sep. '53, L.A.) on keyboards. Andes played on Bobby 'Boris' Pickett's dance novelty 'Monster Mash' (no. 1 '62), also with CANNED HEAT; Cassidy had gigged on West Coast with Cannonball ADDERLEY, Gerry MULLIGAN etc. '50s, formed New Jazz Trio incl. Locke, later played with Taj MAHAL. California was inspired by Jimi HENDRIX, whose backing group he'd joined in NYC '66; Spirit was first called Spirits Rebellious, after Kahlil Gibran novel. Jazz-rock fusion new at the time attracted Ode label's Lou ADLER, LP *Spirit* (writing dominated by Ferguson), *The Family That Plays Together* (with their only hit single, California's 'I Got A Line On You'), *Clear Spirit* '68-9. Switched to Epic for *The Twelve Dreams Of Dr Sardonicus* '70, regarded as best: David Briggs prod. suitably hallucinogenic, incl. 'Nature's Way', their best-known track. Ferguson, disappointed at his waning influence, took Andes to form straightahead rockers Jo Jo GUNNE; California quit too, made bizarre *Kaptain Kopter And The Fabulous Twirlybirds* '72; remaining two members made *Feedback* '72 with brothers Chris and Al Staehely from Texas on guitar and bass, but Cassidy and Locke left and a bogus Spirit toured. California re-formed band with Cassidy, Barry Keene on bass, for 2-disc *Spirit Of '76* '75, a strange collage of TV science fiction, Hendrix tributes and originals; Locke rejoined for *Son Of Spirit* '76 and Andes (with brother Matt on guitar) for *Farther Along* '76, the last three on Mercury. All except *Son* made top 200 USA albums; the first three re-entered charts when reissued on Epic. California solos incl. *Shattered Dreams* '83 on Line, *Spirit Of '84* (called *The Thirteenth Dream* in the UK); Edsel reissued *Kopter* '86; rumours of re-formation of Spirit in '87.

SPIVAK, Charlie (*b* 17 Feb. '06, Kiev, Ukraine; *d* 1 Mar. '82, Greenville, N.C.) Trumpet, bandleader. Excellent sideman and lead trumpet with Ben POLLACK '31-4, DORSEY Brothers '34, Ray NOBLE and Glenn MILLER '35; did much radio work, also played with Bob CROSBY, Tommy DORSEY, Jack TEAGARDEN late '30s. Formed own band '40 with backing from Miller, had hits through the decade, many in top 10, biggest was 'My Devotion' '42. Vocal group the Stardusters incl. June Hutton; Willie SMITH and Dave TOUGH played in the band; arr. by Sonny Burke, Jimmy MUNDY, Nelson RIDDLE. Airchecks etc. on Circle, Hindsight, Insight.

SPIVEY, Victoria (*b* 15 Oct. '06, Houston, Texas; *d* 3 Oct. '76, NYC) Blues singer, pianist. Grew up in Dallas, played piano locally at age 12; recorded prolifically for Okeh '26-9, Victor '29-30, Vocalion '31, Decca '36, Vocalion '36-7; accompanists incl. Lonnie JOHNSON, Thomas A. DORSEY (Georgia Tom), Clarence WILLIAMS' Blue 5 with King OLIVER, Louis ARMSTRONG, Henry ALLEN Jr and his New York Orchestra, her own Hunter's Serenaders (with Lloyd Hunter on trumpet; 11-piece band '31 incl. Jo JONES on drums). Her sisters Addie 'Sweet Pease' Spivey (1910-43) and Elton Island Spivey (1900-71; 'The Zu Zu Girl') were also recording artists. She appeared in the first all-black musical film *Hallelujah!* '29, toured with Olsen & Johnson in *Hellzapoppin* c.'40, etc. Left music '50s but came back, formed Queen Vee label '61, recorded on Bluesway '61 (with Johnson, Buster Bailey), on Folkways '62; formed Spivey label c.'61 and frequently recorded until '76, on GHB with the Easy Rider Jazz Band '66 etc. as well as on her own label, where she also recorded young talent. Spivey records were available once again '87, incl. *The Recorded Legacy Of Victoria Spivey* '27-37; *Basket Of Blues* with Victoria, Lucille Hegamin, Hannah

Sylvester; two vols. of *Three Kings And The Queen* '61, with Victoria, Big Joe WILLIAMS, Roosevelt SYKES, Lonnie Johnson, guest Bob DYLAN (he played harmonica as 'Big Joe's Buddy'; a photo of Dylan with her appeared on the back of his *New Morning* '70); about 30 more incl. blues compilations, etc.

SPOOKY TOOTH UK progressive rock group formed '67 with keyboardists/vocalists Gary Wright (*b* 26 Apr. '45, Englewood, N.J.) and Mike Harrison (*b* 3 Sep. '45, Carlisle), with Greg Ridley (*b* 23 Oct. '41, Cumberland) on bass, Mike Kellie (*b* 24 Mar. '47, Birmingham) on drums and Luther Grosvenor (*b* 23 Dec. '49, Worcester), lead guitar. All except Wright (a student in Berlin) had played in VIPs, who cut singles on Island and became Art for LP *Supernatural Fairytales*, all '66-7 on Island. Spooky Tooth's *It's All About* and *Spooky Two* '68-9 were well received, prod. by Jimmy Miller (TRAFFIC, ROLLING STONES, etc.), appeal lying in contrast between styles of Wright and Harrison; none of their albums charted in the UK, but second and subsequent did well in USA (mostly on A&M). *Ceremony* '70 used overdubs by French electronics pioneer Pierre Henry, uneven experiment instigated by Wright, who soon left to form Wonderwheel. Chris Stainton and Alan Spenner replaced Wright and recent bassist Andy Leigh, guitarist Andy McCulloch also added (all ex-Grease Band); disbanded after *The Last Puff* (incl. their best-known track, ultra-heavy version of BEATLES' 'I Am A Walrus'). Harrison's and Wright's solo careers successful, they re-formed with Kellie, guitarist Mick Jones (ex-Wonderwheel), Chris Stewart on bass, made *You Broke My Heart So I Busted Your Jaw*, *Witness*, *The Mirror* '73-4, latter with vocalist Mike Patto replacing Harrison, Val Burke on bass. Final split '75; Wright went on to successful *Dream Weaver* '76, keyboard-generated sounds yielding two USA no. 2 singles in title track, 'My Love Is Alive'; Grosvenor played with MOTT THE HOOPLE, Kellie with the ONLY ONES, Jones formed FOREIGNER.

SPRINGFIELD, Dusty (*b* Mary O'Brien, 16 Apr. '39, Hampstead, London) UK pop singer, still reckoned one of the best of her generation. Sang with the Lana Sisters, then with brother Tom and Mike Hurst in folk trio the Springfields early '60s (UK hits 'Island Of Dreams', 'Say I Won't Be There'; USA top 20 'Silver Threads And Golden Needles'); solo career began well with 'I Only Want To Be With You' (no. 4 UK, 12 USA '63; later hit for pre-EURYTHMICS Tourists '79); 'Wishin' And Hopin' ' was USA no. 6 '64. Biggest hit was 'You Don't Have To Say You Love Me' '66 (no. 1 UK, 4 USA); 'Son Of A Preacher Man' was top 10 both countries '68; her original version of GOFFIN & KING's 'Goin' Back' was top 10 UK '66, song later covered by the BYRDS, Nils LOFGREN, Bruce SPRINGSTEEN; she was a keen advocate of Motown and one of the few white singers who could sound convincingly black; she exercised immaculate choice of material while UK competitors Cilla BLACK, Sandie SHAW were content with production-line pop songs. Albums *A Girl Called Dusty, Everything Is Coming Up Dusty* '64-5 were representative; she switched from Philips to Atlantic for *Dusty In Memphis* '69, perhaps her best, prod. by Jerry Wexler (incl. 'Preacher Man'); *The Very Best Of* '81 on K-Tel is good compilation. She moved to the USA early '70s, her career there not a success; *Cameo* '73 incl. strong cover of Van MORRISON's 'Tupelo Honey', but long-awaited comeback *It Begins Again* '78 was overproduced. She remained in USA and was active on behalf of animal welfare; *Whiteheat* '82 was flop comeback album; '86 comeback backed by London nightclub boss Peter Stringfellow also unsuccessful. Elton JOHN, Elvis COSTELLO among many have sung her praises; cult status was enhanced when '60s *Ready Steady Go* TV shows were released on video. Fans still hope she will find sympathetic producer, the right songs. Sang as well as ever on title track of *What Have I Done To Deserve This* '87, second hit LP by UK act the Pet Shop Boys (Chris Lowe, Neil Tennant), whose music is described as pop's ideal mixture of lush and tacky (she duetted with Tennant).

SPRINGFIELD, Rick (*b* 23 Aug. '49, Sydney) Australian actor/singer based in USA. Of military family, grew up in Australia, UK; first band was ROLLING STONES-inspired Jordy Boys; later Rock House played covers to troops in Vietnam. Joined future Little River Band star Beeb Birtles in Zoot (also incl. Darryl Cotton); 'Speak To The Sky' Aus. no. 1, but Springfield dissatisfied, remade it for LP *Beginnings* '72 on Capitol for no. 14 USA hit. Switched labels to CBS for *Comic Book Heroes* '74, but work permit and management problems caused three-year break in recording, so he studied acting; *Wait For The Night* '76 preceded Chelsea label's demise; he abandoned music for TV episodes of *Rockford Files, Wonder Woman, Six Million Dollar Man, Incredible Hulk*, etc. Returned to music '80; *Working Class Dog* '81 on RCA spawned no. 1 'Jessie's Girl', powerful John MELLEN-CAMP/Bruce SPRINGSTEEN-style rocker, helped by role of Dr Noah Drake on prime-time soap opera *General Hospital*. Eleven more USA top 10 hits through '84, LPs *Success Hasn't Spoiled Me Yet* '82 (no. 2), *Living In Oz* '83 (top 20), *Tao* '85 (no. 21), then *Rock Of Life* '88. *Beautiful Feelings* '84 on Mercury has '78 vocals with new backing added. Film *Hard To Hold* '84 yielded hit singles; MTV gives him showcase for acting to promote records. Capable of rocking out or bland pop; when youthful looks fade his (mainly teen) fans may leave him with lucrative sideline to acting career.

SPRINGSTEEN, Bruce (*b* Bruce Frederick Joseph Springsteen, 23 Sep. '49, Freehold, N.J.) Rock singer, songwriter, guitarist, bandleader; first a cult figure, by '85 the biggest white rock star on the planet, aka 'The Boss'. Scrupulous attention to recording and performance, generous live sets, obvious loyalty to and identification with audience gets fanatical loyalty from them: he may be the last true rock star. The only son of a working-class family living in and around Asbury Park, N.J., he worked in a number of local bands: the Castiles, Earth And Child; Steel Mill from '69-71 saw firm relationship established with guitarist 'Miami' Steve VAN ZANDT; foundations of E Street Band were formed by '72; brought to the attention of John HAMMOND, who signed him to CBS: *Greetings From Asbury Park N.J.* '73 was brash, invigorating debut, with eye-catching postcard-art cover, but almost swamped by press's effort to make him the new Bob DYLAN, as it had tried to do to Steve GOODMAN, John PRINE, Loudon

WAINWRIGHT III, others. A stint opening for CHICAGO was chastening; he began honing stagecraft. *The Wild, The Innocent & The E Street Shuffle* '74 was more mature effort, with showstopper 'Rosalita', jazzy 'New York Street Serenade', epic 'Incident On 57th Street', beguiling 'Sandy (Asbury Park, 4th Of July)'. Critic Jon Landau, later his manager, saw Springsteen gig '74 and proclaimed him 'the future of rock'n'roll'. He agonised over *Born To Run* '75, hailed as instant classic, a key album of the decade: *Time* and *Newsweek* put him on their covers the same week; hype affected his European tour dates '75 (he did not play there again for five years). In '75 first two LPs finally charted, with *Born To Run* at no. 3: title track, 'Thunder Road', 'Jungleland', 'Night' were classic rock songs in an era desperately short of them. Management problems saw him forbidden to enter a recording studio for three years; heavy touring made legendary shows, started process which saw him become most widely bootlegged of artists: in three- and four-hour marathon concerts he carried flame for rock'n'roll with loving covers of Chuck BERRY, Buddy HOLLY, Mitch RYDER, Gary 'U.S.' BONDS and the SEARCHERS as well as his own originals; unable to record, he saw to it that others had hits with 'Because The Night' (Patti SMITH), 'The Fever' (SOUTHSIDE JOHNNY); wrote 'Fire' for Elvis PRESLEY, who did not live to record it; Robert PALMER and the POINTER SISTERS did. *Darkness On The Edge Of Town* '78 was starker, more sombre album, which did not diminish its success: no. 5 was in charts for 83 weeks; title track, 'Badlands', 'The Promised Land' already concert favourites. As favour to Jackson BROWNE he guested on 3-disc anti-nuclear *No Nukes* '79, no doubt its highlight. 2-disc *The River* '80 was his first no. 1 album, demonstrated his mastery so far as fans were concerned; 20 tracks incl. 'Hungry Heart', his first top 10 single. World tour '80-1 saw international bandwagon gathering steam, joined onstage by Pete Townshend, Link WRAY, performing songs by Woody GUTHRIE, John Fogerty. To everyone's consternation, *Nebraska* '82 was solo acoustic LP made at home on a cassette deck, a pensive consideration of the state of the nation (obliquely, not overtly political) in the spirit of Guthrie and Hank WIL-LIAMS; it reached no. 3, stayed only 29 weeks in chart, a function of his determination to do as he thinks necessary, in turn part of his populist appeal. Johnny CASH covered 'Johnny 99' and 'Highway Patrolman'; Ronald Reagan quoted from the LP on the campaign trail, to Springsteen's disgust, but he was too smart to react negatively. *Born In The USA* '84 was no. 1 for seven weeks; though not his best, incl. four hit singles, 'Dancing In The Dark' at no. 2 one of his best; it also saw him the darling of the year (along with MADONNA) in the world's media; despite his success, he still popped up in Asbury Park to sit in with local bands like Cats On A Smooth Surface. He has helped promote Southside Johnny, prod. Gary Bonds LPs (excellent *Dedication* '81, not-so-good *Back On The Line* '82); his songs have been recorded by Donna SUMMER, Warren ZEVON, BIG DADDY, Dave EDMUNDS, Emmylou HARRIS, many others; he guested on USA For Africa's 'We Are The World' single '85. E Street Band were in demand for sessions: pianist Roy Bittan played on LPs by DIRE STRAITS, David BOWIE, Bob SEGER, MEATLOAF; saxophonist Clarence Clemons with Joan ARMATRADING and Carlene CARTER; Clemons and his Red Bank Rockers made *Rescue* '83, then Clemons solo *Hero* '87 was slicker, hit vocal duet with Browne on single 'You're A Friend Of Mine' (also known as the Big Man, Clemons also acts on TV). Springsteen's long-overdue live set turned out to be the five-disc retrospective *Bruce Springsteen & The E Street Band: Live, 1975-1985*, incl. Springsteen songs not commercially released before, as well as live versions of his best-known work, cover of Edwin Starr's 'War', world-wide hit single '86: song by Norman Whitfield and Barrett Strong was no. 1 '70 for soul star Starr (*b* Charles Hatcher, 21 Jan. '42, Nashville). It must be the only five-disc set to enter charts at no. 1 on day of release, earning him perhaps $10 million; later it suddenly ran out of steam as fans all had copies and dealers were left with many on shelves. *Tunnel Of Love* '87 moved away from stadium-filling hard rock sound of *USA* back to homemade simplicity and the concerns of ordinary lives, incl. single 'Brilliant Disguise'. His '88 tour incl. backing vocalist Patti Sciafa, horn section from N.J. band

La Bamba & the Hubcaps. In the contradictory position of superstar with populist appeal, innate honesty allows him to handle it without fumbling; best books on Springsteen are *Born To Run* by Dave Marsh, *Blinded By The Light* by Patrick Humphries and Chris Hunt, fuller *Glory Days* '87 by Marsh.

SQUEEZE UK pop band formed '75 in Deptford, London: guitarists/vocalists/songwriters Glenn Tilbrook (*b* 31 Aug. '57) and Chris Difford (*b* 11 Apr. '54) with Jools Holland (*b* 24 Jan. '58) on keyboards, replaced by Paul Carrack (*b* Apr. '51, Sheffield); John Bentley on bass (*b* 16 Apr. '51), Gilson Lavis on drums (*b* 27 June '51). Difford and Tilbrook had been writing together since '73; with Holland they made EP *Packet Of Three* '77; LP *Squeeze* '78 prod. by John CALE; *Cool For Cats* '79 by John Wood (FAIRPORT CONVENTION, Nick DRAKE) displayed Difford & Tilbrook's idiosyncratic writing, concentrating on specifically London points of reference, incl. 'Goodbye Girl', 'Up The Junction' and title track, latter two no. 2 UK hits. Critics compared them to LENNON & MCCARTNEY, though they were closer in style to KINKS' Ray Davies. After *Argybargy* '80 Holland quit, released boogie album *Jools Holland & The Millionaires* '81 (later fronted pop show *The Tube* on UK TV), replaced by pianist Carrack (ex-Ace, with London guitarists King and Phil Harris: three LPs, first incl. 'How Long', UK/USA hit). *East Side Story* '81 regarded as their masterpiece, prod. by fan Elvis COSTELLO; *Sweets From A Stranger* '82 had backing vocals from Costello, Paul YOUNG. Carrack quit '81, went on to work with Nick LOWE, Carlene CARTER, Mike Rutherford (ex-GENESIS); made solo albums *Paul Carrack* '80, *Suburban Voodoo* '82. He was briefly replaced by Don Snow before Squeeze split '82; *Singles, 45s & Under* '82 was impressive collection; on split all attention focused on Difford & Tilbrook, who wrote musical *Labelled With Love*, prod. at Deptford Albany '83, album *Difford & Tilbrook* '84. Holland and Lavis occasionally played one-off gigs together, joined at one by Tilbrook late '84; Squeeze reunion led to *Cosi Fan Tutti Frutti* '85: they had lost none of their charm, but the LP's averageness was followed by return to better

form in *Babylon And On* '87. They had 14 hit singles in UK '78-85.

SQUIER, Billy (*b* 12 May '50, Wellesley Hills, Mass.) Heavy metal singer/guitarist. Formed Sidewinders while still at school; then Piper (with Alan Laine Nolan and Tommy Gunn, guitars; Danny McGary, bass; Richie Fontana, drums) for albums *Piper* and *Can't Wait* c.'77; went solo. *Tale Of The Tape* '80 prod. by Eddy Offord (ex-YES); *Don't Say No* '81 co-prod. by Squier with Mack (Reinholdt Mack, German prod. of ELO, QUEEN, etc.) saw more direct approach pay off with three hit singles, no. 5 LP. *Emotions In Motion* '82 repeated formula but Squier dissatisfied, remixed it and collapsed with overwork. Admits Anglophile leanings and has vocal similarity to Robert Plant, but has done little in UK; pursued more American path, writing/performing on soundtrack to *Fast Times At Ridgemont High* '83, which celebrated high school lifestyles; engaged MEATLOAF collaborator Jim Steinman to add stamp to *Signs Of Life* '84.

STACY, Jess (*b* Jess Alexandria Stacy, 11 Aug. '04, Merge Point, Mo.) Pianist, bandleader. His home town is not there any more: washed into the Mississippi River. Began playing dixieland and steam calliope on a steamboat, not quite 16 years old: Bix BEIDERBECKE sat in on piano; Stacy heard what he wanted to play. Played in many small groups, occasionally leading; joined Benny GOODMAN '35-9, went down in history playing lovely unscheduled solo on Carnegie Hall performance of 'Sing Sing Sing' Jan. '38. Worked for Bob CROSBY '39-42, Goodman again, Horace HEIDT; married to Lee WILEY '43-c.'46; led own band with her singing, recorded for Victor (classy 'It's Only A Paper Moon' '45). With Goodman again '46-7; went to West Coast and played in piano bars until '60. Left music, came back '74 to record for Chiaroscuro, play at Carnegie Hall (Newport Jazz Festival/NYC). Compilations incl. *Blue Notion* ('41 tracks) on Jazzology, broadcasts of '44-5 band on Aircheck, *Piano Solos* '35-56 on Australian Swaggie, also *Two Good Men*: one side of LP (Teddy WILSON overside) on Esquire has '44 trio tracks with Bob Casey on bass, drummer George Wettling. *Jess*

Stacy & Friends is Commodore tracks '38-44 incl. solos, with Wiley, etc. on Columbia Special Products USA (German Teldec edition incl. CD had transfers at wrong speed, Wiley sounding like Minnie Mouse). Chiaroscuro albums are *Stacy Still Swings* '74, *Stacy's Still Swinging* '77.

STAFFORD, Jo (*b* 12 Nov. '20, Coalinga, Cal.) Pop singer, one of the best: described by lyricist Gene Lees as a highly educated folk singer. Her 'relative pitch' is so good that it may as well be perfect; she puts a song across with honesty and warm vocal colour but without stylistic excess; she was a favourite singer of American soldiers in WWII, who called her 'G.I. Jo'. Studied classical voice in high school, formed vocal trio with sisters Pauline and Christine, then joined octet the Pied Pipers, who sang like a whole band, sang on Tommy DORSEY radio programme '38, joined his band as a quartet, backing Frank SINATRA on 'Star Dust', 'I Guess I'll Have To Dream The Rest', 'There Are Such Things' (no. 1 hit '42), many others; Jo's first solo record was 'Little Man With A Candy Cigar'; solo hits with Dorsey incl. 'Manhattan Serenade' and 'You Took My Love' '42-3; she sang with arranger Sy OLIVER on 'Yes, Indeed!' '41. Pipers left Dorsey late '42, worked on radio, recorded for Capitol, had a dozen hits '44-8 incl. no. 1 'Dream' '45; Jo went solo mid-'44, helped by ex-Dorsey arr. Paul WESTON. Musicians knew that she had great technical skill; some critics (unbelievably) called her 'cold': chart success with excellent beat, phrasing was swift: among nearly 50 hits on Capitol '44-50 were first-class show songs 'Long Ago And Far Away', 'I Love You', 'No Other Love'; no. 1 hit 'Candy' '45 with Johnny MERCER and the Pipers. She was the first pop singer to record folk songs, as early as '46; also novelties, playing hillbilly on cover of Dorothy SHAY's 'Feudin' And Fightin' ', also 'I'm My Own Grandmaw'. Ten duet hits with Gordon MACRAE incl. 'My Darling, My Darling'; 'Whispering Hope' (song from 1868) sold a million in Bible Belt. As Cinderella Stump she recorded 'Timtayshun' '47, hilarious novelty sending up country music on which she purposely sang slightly off key, an impressive technical trick. Switched to Columbia with Weston (married him '52) for 30 more hits

'50-7 incl. cover of Hank WILLIAMS' 'Hey Good Lookin' ' (top ten duet with Frankie LAINE), no. 1 hits 'You Belong To Me' '51 (co-written by Pee Wee KING; also a big hit in UK) and 'Make Love To Me!' '54 ('Tin Roof Blues' '23 with new lyrics). Sang off-key as Darlene Edwards, with pianist Weston (as Jonathan Edwards) playing wrong notes, too many beats in the bar (Jonathan claimed that he played better stride piano than Fats WALLER; Darlene added, 'Well, actually, a 5/4 bar gives you an extra stride'). Sessions for *The Piano Artistry Of Jonathan Edwards* '57 incl. drummer Jack Sperling, who had to quit because he couldn't stop laughing; LP was followed by several more. She never craved stardom, gave up public performance '59, stopped recording mid-'60s (Darlene carried on until *Darlene Remembers Duke* '82). Joel Whitburn calculated on the basis of weeks in Billboard charts she was one of the top five artists '40-55. LPs on Capitol incl. *Memory Songs* with MacRae, on Columbia *Sings Broadway's Best, Ski Trails, Swingin' Down Broadway, Ballad Of The Blues, Jo Plus Jazz*; many of these and more (incl. hits compilations, Jonathan and Darlene) now on their Corinthian label.

STALIN, Black (*b* Leroy Calliste, 24 Sep. '41, San Fernando, Trinidad) Calypsonian. Name bestowed '58 by veteran Lord Blaikie (Carlton Joseph). One of the dying breed who adhere to calypso as a trad. vehicle for social and political commentary, seen as direct descendant of ATILLA and a didactic poet of the first order, with legendary onstage charisma; a Rastafarian, firmly aligned with the black masses; has never shown any interest in winning the Road March (*see* CALYPSO). Long and fruitful relationship with Lord KITCHENER since '67 led to valuable experience as MC etc. in Kitchener's Calypso Revue tent '68-76; he was still performing there '83 through '87. 'The Message Of Martin Luther King' '69 was his reaction to the assassination (a new live recording '85 incl. in *King Of Kings – Live! Vol. 1* on B's Records); 'New Portrait Of Trinidad' '72 listed harsh realities (as opposed to Mighty Sniper's 'Portrait Of Trinidad' '65, which painted rosy picture); 'Pan Gone' '74 told how nearly everybody benefits from the steel band except the panman; other noteworthy calypsoes: 'De Ole Talk', 'Nothing Ent Strange', 'Piece Of The Action' '74-6. Withdrew from competition '76-8, returned and won Calypso Monarch '79 with 'Play One' and 'Caribbean Unity', both incl. in his first LP *Caribbean Man* '79 on Makossa, now regarded as a classic: defined Caribbean unity in black nationalist terms, controversial in Trinidad & Tobago, which has a rich racial mix; the calypso was discussed by Prime Minister Eric Williams at the ruling party's annual convention. He performed at Carifesta in Cuba, and in Granada after the New Jewel Movement came to power; in T&T he won both North and South Calypso King titles and awards for best composition ('Caribbean Unity') and best performing artist; he performed with Brother Valentino in show *Blood Brothers*, all in '79. In '80 he defended his Monarch title with 'When The Well Run Dry' and 'Money', came sixth; 'Money' was incl. in *Just For Openers*, set of two disco singles also incl. 'Breakdown Party', a comment on the ruling party in T&T. 'Vampire Year' and 'Run De Head' (from LP *In Ah Earlier Time* '81 on Hula) took him to third place in Monarch contest; 'Nothing Come Easy' and 'Man Is Boo' (on 12″ single *Black Stalin 1982*) to sixth; 'That Is Head' and 'Better Days' to second in '83, latter incl. in *You Ask For It* . . . '84 on Kalico. He won in '85 with 'Wait Dorothy Wait' and 'Ism Schism' (12″ single on Charlies), former a commentary on social injustice incl. a clever repudiation of smut; in '85 also he came close second in King Of Kings contest to Mighty SPARROW. Booklet *Black Stalin, The Caribbean Man* by Louis Regis published '86 in Trinidad. 'No Part Time Lover' and 'More Come' brought him to second in '86 (incl. on *Sing For The Land* on B's), beaten by David RUDDER; in '87 he dethroned Rudder with 'Burn Dem' and 'Mr Pan Maker' (LP *1 Time* on B's); 'Burn Dem' offering St Peter advice on judgement day about oppressors of black people. In May '87 Stalin and Rudder performed together at the New Orleans Jazz & Heritage Festival.

STAMPLEY, Joe (*b* 6 June '43, Springhill, La.) Honky-tonk country singer. Infl. early by Hank WILLIAMS, but turned to rock'n'-roll on Imperial and Chess late '50s-early '60s without success; formed band the Uniques for minor pop hits '64-6. By this time he was writing songs; signed with Al Gallico Music in Nashville, Dot label as solo singer: country chart debut was 'Take Time To Know Her' '71, first top 10 was 'If You Touch Me (You've Got To Love Me)' '72, first no. 1 'Soul Song' '73 (also made top 40 pop). He has scored 17 country top 10 hits incl. four no. ones; in '76 he had eight in the charts: four on Dot and four on his new label, Epic. Duets with Moe BANDY began after a visit to England's annual Wembley Festival '79; their no. ones incl. 'Just Good Ole Boys' '79, 'Where's The Dress' '84 (a send-up of both Boy George and Wendy's hamburger commercials); other duet hits incl. 'Holding The Bag' '80, 'Honky Tonk Queen' '81; they were named top vocal duo by ACM '79, CMA '80. He carried on with his own solo hits, incl. 'There's Another Woman' '80, 'Whiskey Chasin'' '81, 'Back Slidin'' '82, 'Double Shot Of My Baby's Love' '83; encouraged his son Tony, who emerged writing hits for his father and others incl. Hank WILLIAMS Jr. Albums incl. *Soul Song* '74, *I'm Still Loving You* '74, *Take Me Home To Somewhere* '75 on Dot (Ember in UK); *Red Wine And Blue Memories* '78, *I Don't Lie* '79, *I'm Goin' Hurtin'* '82, *I'll Still Be Loving You* '85 on Epic.

STANLEY BROTHERS Carter Glen Stanley, lead guitar and vocals (*b* 27 Aug. '25, McClure, Va.; *d* 1 Dec. '66, Bristol, Va.) and Ralph Edmund Stanley, banjo and vocals (*b* 25 Feb. '27, Stratton, Va.). Leaders of the infl. bluegrass group Clinch Mountain Boys, the Stanleys created some of the most beautiful harmonies in country music, specialising in religious material, much of it self-written and reflecting their early days in the Shenandoah Valley region. After US Army service they formed The Stanley Brothers and the Clinch Mountain Boys '46, worked on radio WCYB in Bristol, first records for Rich-R-Tone label '48, by that time infl. by Bill MONROE; move to Columbia '49 gave them wider exposure, though like other bluegrass artists they were never part of the mainstream, their infl. having to wait 20 years to come out in the '70s-80s. In '50s-60s they recorded for Mercury, Starday and King, their sole top 20 country hit being 'How Far To Little Rock' '60 on King. Ralph continued to lead the group after Carter's death, appearing at bluegrass festivals and recording extensively on Rebel; their songs have been covered by John CONLEE, Emmylou HARRIS, Dan FOGELBERG, others. LPs incl. *Columbia Sessions Vols. 1&2* on Rounder, *Hymns From The Cross* '62 on King, *The Stanley Brothers From Virginia* '69 and *Uncloudy Day* '71 on County, *Old Country Church* '72 and *Ralph Stanley – Child Of The King* '83 on Rebel.

STAPLE SINGERS Family gospel group with soul hits. Roebuck 'Pop' Staples (*b* 28 Dec. '15, Winona, Ms.) played blues guitar, was converted at 15, sang in church, toured with Golden Trumpets group; settled in Chicago with wife Oceola, worked outside music to support growing family. Sang in a Chicago Baptist church '50 (brother Chester was pastor) with son Pervis, daughters Cleo, Mavis; young Yvonne later replaced Pervis; made single on United '53 (more were made, but leased to smaller labels: United wanted them to do rock'n'roll, held them to two-year contract); on Vee Jay '55-9: 'Uncloudy Day' 'sold like rock'n'roll', said Pops later; Vee Jay records are gospel classics, with his understated guitar, Mavis's beautiful voice, incl. 'Stand By Me' (secularised for Ben E. KING) and 'This May Be The Last Time' (made money for the ROLLING STONES with different lyric), 'Will The Circle Be Unbroken', 'Amazing Grace', etc. Recorded for Riverside '60-4; on Epic in '67 'Why? (Am I Treated So Bad)' and 'For What It's Worth' made pop Hot 100. In the spirit of the Soul era '60s they still did some of the same material they had done since the beginning, but also message songs with a heavier beat; after they'd refused to do rock'n'roll on United, almost 20 years later the church rejected them. To Stax/Volt '68, hits with prod. Al Bell: did some secular songs (Mavis had hit 'I Have Learned To Do Without You' '70), but mostly message songs; a dozen crossing over to pop chart '70-6 incl. 'Respect Yourself' (no. 12), 'I'll Take You There' (no. 1 pop and soul charts '72), 'If You're Ready (Come Go With Me)' (top 10 pop, no. 1 soul), Percy MAYFIELD movie theme 'Let's Do It Again' on his Curtom label (no. 1 '75

both charts). They appeared in films *Soul To Soul* '71 (made in Ghana) and *Wattstax* '73, in finale of the BAND's final concert/film/album *Last Waltz* '78. Albums incl. *Pray On* on Charly UK (Vee Jay classics), *Great Day* on Milestone (Riverside era); *The Staple Singers* '71, *Bealtitude: Respect Yourself* '72, *Be What You Are* '73, *City In The Sky* '74, also *This Time Around*, *Chronicle*, *Mavis Staples*, instrumental *Jammed Together* (with Pop, Albert KING, studio sideman Steve Cropper), all on Stax; *Let's Do It Again* '75 on Curtom was very short weight; *Pass It On, Family Tree, Unlock Your Mind* '76-8 on WB; *Hold On To Your Dream* '81 on 20th Century; *Turning Point* '84 (on Epic in UK) and *The Staple Singers* '85 on Private I; *At Their Best* is Stax hits compilation from RCA UK.

STAPLETON, Cyril (*b* '14, Nottingham; *d* 25 Feb. '74) UK violinist, bandleader, producer. Worked in theatre pit bands, then top dance bands Henry HALL, Jack Payne; conducted RAF S.O. at Potsdam during WWII; own band '46 for Bond Street restaurant in London, BBC broadcasts, records on Decca (vocalist was Dick JAMES). BBC Showband was all-star outfit '52-3, had more airtime than any other bandleader; accompanied visiting USA stars Rosemary CLOONEY, Frank SINATRA, etc. A few chart entries late '50s; came back as executive, producer with Pye (Singalong series with Max BYGRAVES); toured early '70s with new Showband.

STARDUST, Alvin (*b* Bernard William Jewry, 27 Sep. '42, Muswell Hill, London) Pop singer, stage debut in panto age 4. Road manager, occasional singer with Johnny Theakston and the Tremeloes; they submitted tape to BBC as Shane Fenton & the Fentones; Theakston died and Jewry became Fenton, had top 40 entries '61-2, appeared in films; quit recording '64 to work in management. Came back '73 with prod./composer Peter Shelley, name changed to Alvin Stardust, image to black leather incl. gloves, stuck-on sideburns, dyed black hair; success with singles and albums (*The Untouchable Alvin Stardust* no. 4 UK '74). Late '70s, early '80s appeared on Jack GOOD TV shows *Oh Boy* and *Let's Rock*; record comeback '81 with revival of

'53 Nat COLE hit 'Pretend' on Stiff, followed by 'I Feel Like Buddy Holly' (written by Mike BATT). Appeared regularly on BBC TV *Rock Gospel Show sans* black leather. Albums: Fenton stuff on *I'm A Moody Guy* on See For Miles; Stardust *Greatest Hits* on Music For Pleasure; *I Feel Like . . . Alvin Stardust* on Chrysalis.

STARR, Kay (*b* Katherine Starks, 21 July '22, Dougherty, Oklahoma) Pop singer. Began as country singer; sang with Bob CROSBY, Charlie BARNET; solo pop star on Capitol from '48 with big accurate voice, lots of personality: 30 hits incl. 'Bonaparte's Retreat' '50, 'Wheel of Fortune' '52 (no. 1 for ten weeks), 'Side By Side' (double-tracked duets with herself particularly effective on delightful '27 chestnut). Switched to RCA '55-7 for more hits incl. 'Rock And Roll Waltz' '55 (no. 1 for six weeks, also a hit in UK), 'My Heart Reminds Me' (top 10 '57), back to Capitol, covered Jim REEVES hit 'Four Walls' '62. Albums: *Back To The Roots* and *Country* on GNP; *1947* on Hindsight with studio orchestra; RCA LP *Blue Starr* reissued '87 in UK.

STARR, Kenny (*b* 21 Sep. '53, Topeka, Kansas) Country singer, guitarist, songwriter. Grew up in Burlingame, Kansas; led own band at age 9, as teenager played clubs and college dances as Kenny and the Imperials; moved to country music '69, won talent contest in Wichita, promoter Hap Peebles put him on a Loretta LYNN – Conway TWITTY show and they hired him as guitarist and singer. Hits on MCA '73-7 incl. no. 1 '75 with 'The Blind Man In The Bleachers', then he faded.

STARR, Ringo Drummer, singer, actor. Played with Rory Storm and the Hurricanes; picked to replace Pete BEST in the BEATLES and became world-famous, but the least well equipped of the four for solo success. He sang solo on a few Beatle numbers ('With A Little Help From My Friends', 'Octopus's Garden') but was never taken seriously in that role. First solo album *Sentimental Journey* '70 was mawkish collection of evergreens to which he was hopelessly unsuited; said he did it for his mother. *Beaucoups Of Blues* '71 was passable, made

in Nashville with first-class pickers; one-off singles were hits '71-2, rockers made with George HARRISON 'It Don't Come Easy' and 'Back Off Boogaloo' re-established his stock. For *Ringo* '73 prod. Richard PERRY brought together George and John Lennon (in USA) and Paul McCARTNEY (in UK) on same LP; it made no. 2 USA and deserved to: hits on Harrison's 'Photograph', Johnny BURNETTE's 'You're Sixteen', his own 'Oh My My', eminently listenable to with Billy PRESTON, Marc BOLAN, Harry NILSSON also in the cast. He'd played a cameo in film of *Candy* '67; continued filming with *The Magic Christian* '69, Frank ZAPPA's *200 Motels* '71 and *Blindman* '72, *That'll Be The Day* '73 (his best, as an ageing Ted, co-starring with David ESSEX), *Lisztomania* and *Stardust* (with Essex again) '75; also produced *Son Of Dracula*, prod./dir. Bolan biopic *Born To Boogie*, both '72. Musically it was downhill from there. *Goodnight Vienna* '74 had two hits; his label Ring O'Records failed; continued to make occasional LPs (*Blast From Your Past* '75, *Rotogravure* '76, *Ringo The Fourth* '77, *Bad Boy* '78, *Stop And Smell The Roses* '81). Divorced from Maureen, met second wife Barbara Bach making film *Cave Man* '81; now avuncular showbiz figure with interests in UK cable TV, etc. Guest spot on Carl PERKINS TV special '86 demonstrated unimpaired backbeat. Son Zak is budding rock drummer, played with Ringo on Artists Against Apartheid 'Sun City' single and with WHO's Roger Daltrey on Keith Moon tribute 'Under A Raging Moon', both '85.

STATLER BROTHERS, The Country vocal quartet: Philip Balsley (*b* 8 Aug. '39), Don Reid (*b* 5 June '45), Harold Reid (*b* 21 Aug. '39), Lew DeWitt (*b* 8 Mar. '38); Jimmy Fortune replaced DeWitt '82, retired owing to ill health. They are the most successful vocal group in country music, with four-part harmony, their own songs and some corny humour. Harold, Lew and Phil began in Lyndhurst Methodist Church in Staunton, Va. '55; worked as gospel trio the Kingsmen until Don joined '60; took new name '63 from a box of tissues to avoid confusion with pop group, passed audition and joined Johnny CASH show '64, signed with Columbia. Sales of their records were nil for 18 months, label executives so dis-

STEELE

gusted they would not advance more studio
time; Cash let them sneak into one of his
sessions when he went to lunch and they
recorded 'Flowers On The Wall' '65: smash
hit sold two million copies, won them two
Grammies, reached no. 2 country, no. 4
pop. More hits on Columbia incl. 'You
Can't Have Your Kate And Edith', but their
career there was strained; they switched to
Mercury and scored with 'Bed Of Roses' '71
and have had a steady stream of hits ever
since; won another Grammy for 'Class Of
'57' '72. An extension of their act was their
alter egos, Lester 'Roadhog' Moran & The
Cadillac Cowboys, who won a plywood disc
for selling 1,250 copies of their LP *Live At
Johnny Mack Brown High School*. The
Statlers were named CMA Vocal Group of
the Year every year from '72 to '80 except
one; their Old-Fashioned Fourth Of July
Celebration in Staunton brings 60,000 peo-
ple, the largest annual country music festi-
val anywhere. Albums incl. *Flowers On The
Wall*, *Big Hits* and *Oh Happy Day* '66-9 on
CBS; *Country Music Then And Now* '72,
Symphonies In E Major '73, *Carry Me Back*
'74, *Entertainers On And Off Record* '78,
The Originals '79, 2-disc *The Holy
Bible – The New And Old Testaments* '79,
10th Anniversary '80, *Years Ago* '81, *The
Legend Lives On* '82, *Today* '83, *Atlanta
Blue* '84, *Pardners In Rhyme* '85, *Four For
The Show* and *Radio Gospel Favorites* '86,
Maple Street Memories '87, etc. all on Mer-
cury.

STATON, Dakota (*b* Aliyah Rabia, 3 June
'31, Pittsburgh, Pa.) Jazz-oriented singer
who won *Downbeat* poll '55 as most promis-
ing newcomer, soon recorded for Capitol:
The Late, Late Show, *Dynamic!*, *Crazy He
Calls Me*, *Time To Swing* were chart hits in
USA '58-9; she also made an album with
George SHEARING. Top 5 first LP, with one
of the earliest recordings of Erroll GAR-
NER's 'Misty', reissued '84 by EMI UK; *No
Man Is Going To Change Me* released '85 on
GP (Glenn Productions, NYC).

STATUS QUO UK rock group popular for
25 years and still going. Lineup: Francis
Rossi (*b* 29 April '49) and Richard Parfitt (*b*
12 Oct. '48), guitars and vocals; Alan Lancaster (*b* 7 Feb. '49) on bass, John Coghlan
(*b* 19 Sep. '46) on drums, all Londoners.

Began as the Spectres in school, made singles; then as Traffic Jam, then abandoned
harmony pop and boogied into the charts as
Status Quo; toured USA but far more successful at home. More than 30 hits in UK,
over half in top 10; about 30 albums plus
compilations, of which first was *Picturesque
Matchstickable* '68; first to chart was
Piledriver '73 (no. 5); *Hello* '73, *On The
Level* '75, *Blue For You* '76, *1982* were all
no. 1. There is always something to be said
for status quo music.

STEAGALL, Red (*b* Russell Steagall, 22
Dec., Gainesville, Texas) Rodeo rider,
country singer-songwriter. Learned to play
guitar and mandolin recuperating from
polio; played in coffee houses while studying animal husbandry at West Texas State
U. Worked as soil chemist for oil company;
switched to full-time music, forming a band
and working ski resort clubs in the Rockies
'63-4. To West Coast '65, writer's contract
with Tree Publishing; co-wrote 'Here We
Go Again' with Don Lanier (top 20 hit for
Ray CHARLES). More of his songs were recorded; he recorded for Dot '69, then Capitol; first chart hits were 'Party Dolls And
Wine' and 'Somewhere My Love' '72. Hits
through '70s incl. his biggest (back on Dot),
'Lone Star Beer And Bob Wills' Music' '76;
last was 'Good Time Charlie's Got The
Blues' '79. He is an in-demand performer
on the rodeo circuit, recording for small
labels; he discovered Reba MCENTIRE,
whom he saw working a rodeo in Oklahoma. Albums incl. *Party Dolls And Wine* '72
on Capitol, *For All Our Cowboy Friends* and
Lone Star Beer And Bob Wills' Music '77 on
ABC-Dot, *Cowboy Favorites* '85 on Delta.

STEELE, Tommy (*b* Thomas Hicks, 17 Dec.
'36, Bermondsey, London) UK entertainer,
touted as the British Elvis PRESLEY late '50s
but like other UK entertainers turned out to
be an all-rounder with roots in music hall.
Spent four years at sea in a variety of jobs;
spotted on leave at Two I's coffee bar in
Soho by Fleet Street photographer John
Kennedy, soon his manager; signed with
Decca and first release was top 20 'Rock
With The Caveman' '56: the following
month his 'Singin' The Blues' replaced
Guy MITCHELL original at no. 1. 18 hits
through '61 incl. 'Butterfingers', 'Water,

Water', 'Nairobi', 'Little White Bull'; ended with 'Writing On The Wall' as initial phase of British rock'n'roll ran out of steam; he had ridden the wave with BBC TV's trail-blazing pop show *6.5 Special*, films *The Tommy Steele Story*, *The Duke Wore Jeans*, *Tommy The Toreador*; revealing an appetite for a challenge he played Tony Lumpkin in Oliver Goldsmith's 18th-century comedy *She Stoops To Conquer* '62 at the Old Vic; then musical *Half A Sixpence* '63 (by David Heneker and Beverley Cross, based on H. G. Wells novel *Kipps*), which went to Broadway '65 and to film '67 (Hollywood knocking the charm out of it); he also appeared in *The Happiest Millionaire* '67 (Disney's last film and one of his worst), *Finian's Rainbow* '68 (whimsical '47 fantasy by Yip HARBURG/Burton Lane did not transfer well to big screen, despite Fred ASTAIRE, Petula CLARK, Steele's leprechaun). TV specials, Frank LOESSER's *Hans Christian Andersen* at London Palladium in '70s topped by record 60-week run in one-man show at the Prince of Wales '79; starred in and dir. stage version of classic film *Singin' In The Rain* '83-5: mixed reviews, family coachloads attending. A natural performer, still with permanent grin; awarded OBE '79. *Greatest Hits* on Spot.

STEELEYE SPAN UK folk-rock group. Original lineup: Tim Hart, guitar, dulcimer, vocals; Ashley Hutchings, bass; Maddy Prior and Gay Woods, vocals; Terry Woods, guitar, mandolin, vocals. Hutchings was disappointed with FAIRPORT CONVENTION after *Leige & Lief* '68; he came together with Hart and Prior (who had worked as a duo) and the Woods (ex-Sweeney's Men); group's name (suggested by Martin CARTHY) after character in trad. song 'Horkston Grange'. Once described as 'the folk supergroup', they became the most commercially successful of their type. The lineup broke up after *Hark The Village Wait* '70 on RCA without ever having performed live; for *Please To See The King* on B&C and *Ten Man Mop* on Pegasus (both '70) Carthy on electric guitar and vocals replaced the Woods, Peter Knight joined on fiddle. (The Woods worked as duo and in the Woods Band, albums on Polydor and Rockburgh, separately in Auto da Fé and the POGUES.) Hutchings left, worked in the ALBION

BAND and in theatre (had worked with Steeleye in Keith Dewhurst's play *Corunna*); Steeleye lineup settled as Prior, Hart, Knight, Rick Kemp on bass, Bob Johnson on guitar, later Nigel Pegrum on drum and flute; albums *Below The Salt* '72, *Parcel Of Rogues* '73, *Now We Are Six* '74 (incl. rare guest appearance by David BOWIE), *Commoners Crown* '75 were successful; Chrysalis funded solo projects while the group released *All Around My Hat* '75 and *Rocket Cottage* '76; by the time of *Storm Force Ten* '77 and *Live At Last* '78, Carthy and John Kirkpatrick were with them (later worked as duo, on Kirkpatrick's *Plain Capers* on Free Reed, in trio BRASS MONKEY). Later work incl. *Sails Of Silver* '80 (all these on Chrysalis) was less successful commercially, but they still drew enthusiastic audiences without trading on nostalgia; on *Back In Line* '86 on Flutterby they were Johnson, Kemp, Knight and Prior, followed by *Where Would You Rather Be Tonight?* '87 on Sunrise with various others. Compilations *Individually & Collectively* and *Almanack* '72-3, *Original Masters* '77 were succeeded by more representative 2-disc *Best Of* '84 on Chrysalis. Tim Hart released solo album '79; Johnson and Knight did *The King Of Elfland's Daughter* '77; Maddy Prior's incl. *The Silly Sisters* '76 (with June TABOR), *Woman In The Wings* '78 and *Changing Winds*, all Chrysalis; *Nyon Folk Festival 1979* on Cat; *Hooked On Winning* '82 on Plant Life, *Going For Glory* '83 on Spindrift; *A Tapestry Of Carols* '87 on Saydisc (with the Carnival Band); *Silly Sisters Vol. 2* '88 on Topic with Tabor.

STEELY DAN USA jazz-influenced pop band, renowned for meticulous production on records and cryptic lyrics; named after a dildo in William Burroughs' *Naked Lunch*. Basically a duo of songwriters/vocalists Walter Becker (bass, guitar) and Donald Fagen (keyboards; both *b* c.'50-1) who met at college in New York State; actor Chevy Chase played drums in one of their early groups. They wrote soundtrack for film *You Gotta Walk It Like You Talk It* 71, prod. by Kenny Vance of JAY AND THE AMERICANS (whose backing group they played in). Went with prod. Gary Katz to ABC Records as songwriters, began making own albums: *Can't Buy A Thrill* '72 with vocalist David Palmer, *Countdown To Ecstacy* '73, *Pretzel Logic* '74 with future DOOBIE Michael McDonald on backing vocals, *Katy Lied* '75, *The Royal Scam* '76, *Aja* '77 (with Jim Keltner on drums), *Gaucho* '80 with Patti AUSTIN, Mark Knopfler, the BRECKER Bros, David SANBORN. They disliked touring, largely ignored singles market; all LPs charted in USA with *Aja* at no. 3; last two LPs won Grammies for engineering. Guitarist Denny Dias played on all albums, Victor FELDMAN on most; sidemen on various tracks/albums incl. Ray BROWN, Wilton Felder, Larry Carlton, Phil WOODS, Plas JOHNSON. Compilations etc. incl. Fagen and Becker's *The Early Years*. Fagen made *The Nightfly* '82 on WB with Carlton, Rick DERRINGER, Randy Brecker, Hugh McCracken, many others; he composes at the keyboard but lacks confidence in his playing: tries to get someone else to play on recordings, then has to do it himself because no one else can play it the way they want it; got together with Becker to play on *Zazu* '87, debut LP by model Rosie Vela (*b* c.'54; had sung and written songs since childhood); they began working on new Steely Dan album.

STEPPENWOLF Heavy metal band formed in California '67, briefly regarded with IRON BUTTERFLY and VANILLA FUDGE as rock's great white hopes. Guitarist/vocalist John Kay (*b* Joachim Krauledat, 12 Apr. '44, East Germany), drummer Jerry Edmonton (*b* 24 Oct. '46), Goldy McJohn (*b* 2 May '45) on keyboards had played in Canadian band Sparrow; new group named after Hermann Hesse novel incl. John Russell Morgan on bass, Michael Monarch on guitar. *Steppenwolf* '68 incl. biker's anthem 'Born To Be Wild' (no. 2 hit, heard in film *Easy Rider*) and 'The Pusher'; *The Second* '68 incl. 'Magic Carpet Ride' (no. 3 hit); but they turned out to be as conservative as any MOR group, compared e.g. to revolutionary MC5. Personnel changes weakened appeal as they churned out *At Your Birthday Party* (top 10 'Rock Me') and *Monster* '69, 2-disc *Live* and *Steppenwolf 7* '70, *For Ladies Only* '71; *Early Steppenwolf* '69 was a Sparrow LP made '67, with 21-minute version of 'The Pusher' on side 2. They split up; Kay made solo LPs, Edmonton and McJohn were also unsuccessful as duo Manbeast; re-formed for *Slow Flux* '74; Wayne Cook replaced McJohn for *Hour Of The Wolf* '75.

STEVENS, Cat (*b* Steven Demitri Georgiou, 21 July '47, London) Singer/songwriter. Prod. Mike Hurst (ex-Springfields) helped get contract with Deram; *Matthew & Son* and *New Masters* '67-8 were both above-average pop albums of the period from an able songwriter who was always uncomfortable as a pop idol (one package tour put him on the same bill with Jimi HENDRIX and Engelbert HUMPERDINCK). The albums yielded a couple of hit singles and his songs were covered by others; he then spent some time in a TB clinic, came back on Island UK, A&M USA with *Mona Bona Jakon* '70, an introspective set incl. no. 2 hit 'Lady D'Arbanville'. *Tea For The Tillerman* '71 broke him in USA, where it went top 10 with hit 'Wild World', later a hit for Jimmy Cliff; *Teaser & The Firecat* reached no. 2 USA with hits 'Peace Train', 'Morning Has Broken'. *Very Young And Early Songs* '72 was a compilation; *Catch Bull At Four* '72 was no. 1 with no hit singles, but *Foreigner* '73 dropped to no. 3, ill-conceived 'Foreigner Suite' taking up side 2. *Buddha And The Chocolate Box* '74 was no. 2 USA; *Numbers* '75 and *Izitso* '77 did well; *Back To Earth* '78 was still top 40 but his disenchantment with the music business was growing: by '79 he had converted to Islam, changed his name to Yusif Islam, since teaches in London's Islamic community. Songs still covered, still heard on radio.

STEVENS, John (*b* 10 June '40, Brentford, Middlesex) UK drummer, composer; also plays mini-trumpet. Studied in RAF School of Music; began in skiffle and trad. bands, gigged with Tubby HAYES, Joe HARRIOTT, Ronnie SCOTT; played in group with John MCLAUGHLIN and Ian Carr; formed own Spontaneous Music Ensemble late '60s which was at the centre of free music in UK. Drew back from complete abstraction, experimenting with various groups, rhythms etc.; albums by Freebop and Folkus were on Affinity. Albums with Trevor Watts on tenor incl. two vols. of *Spontaneous Music Ensemble With Bobby Bradford* '71 on Nessa, also *Application Interaction* and *No Fear* on Spotlite; *Longest*

Night '76 (two vols.) on Ogun has Evan Parker. Mus. dir. of Outreach Community Music Project since '83. Toured '88 with quintet Fast Colour, incl. Dudu PUKWANA, Harry Beckett on trumpet (*b* 30 May '35, Barbados), Annie Whitehead on trombone (*b* 16 July '55, Oldham, Lancashire; played in Ivy Benson band at 16), Nick Stephens on bass. His son Ritchie, also a drummer, was half of pop duo Red Well '87 with vocalist Lorenzo Hall.

STEVENS, Ray (*b* 24 Jan. '41, Clarkdale, Ga.) Entertainer who began with a smash novelty hit and turned out to have a long shelf-life. Was a DJ at 15, studied music at Georgia State U., made singles incl. 'Jeremiah Peabody's Poly Unsaturated Quick Dissolving Fast Acting Pleasant Tasting Green & Purple Pills' (top 40 '61), then to no. 5 with wacky 'Ahab The Arab' '62 (album *1,837 Seconds Of Humour*). More minor hits and work in Nashville studios with Dolly PARTON, Waylon JENNINGS etc. followed by switch from Mercury to Monument, top 10 'Gitarzan' '69, then no. 1 hits on Andy WILLIAMS' Barnaby label with 'Everything Is Beautiful' '70 (also country hit), topical humour of 'The Streak' '74 (album *Boogity Boogity*). Long string of hits big and small incl. 'Turn Your Radio On' '72 (title track of album of inspirational songs), country adaptation of Erroll GARNER's 'Misty' '75 (won Grammy), 'I Need Your Help Barry Manilow' '79 on WB; a fine straight vocalist, but novelties just won't stop: 'Shriner's Convention' '80 (LP on RCA), 'Mississippi Squirrel Revival' '84, 'It's Me Again, Margaret' '85 (about nuisance phone calls). Other LPs incl. *Just For The Record* '76 on WB; *I Have Returned* and *He Thinks He's Ray Stevens* '85, *Surely You Joust* '86 on MCA.

STEVENS, Shakin' (*b* Michael Barratt, 4 Mar. '48, Ely, Wales) UK rock'n'roll revivalist with the style down pat. Began as frontman with Sunsets, revival band formed '69 who were big live attraction; *A Legend* '70 prod. by Dave EDMUNDS for EMI (reissued '78) was first of albums of classics by the Sunsets. PRESLEY soundalike voice won him part in *Elvis* musical in London, starring alongside P. J. PROBY; made debut solo LP for Track, moved to Epic, starred on

Jack GOOD's revived *Oh Boy* TV show. With prod. Stuart Colman, made singles which cleverly avoided self-conscious revivalism while paying dues to roots: 'Hot Dog' first hit (top 25), 'Marie Marie' written by then-unknown Dave Alvin of the BLASTERS top 20, both '80; first no. 1 was 'This Ole House' '81, huge '54 USA hit by its writer Stuart HAMBLEN in country chart, Rosemary CLOONEY in pop. 11 more top 10 hits '81-4 incl. 'Green Door' (no. 1 USA hit by DJ Jim Lowe '56), 'Oh Julie' (USA hit by the Crescendos '57), both no. 1 for Stevens. Returned to Edmunds for prod. of LP *Lipstick Powder And Paint* '85. He uses video constructively for hip-swivelling appeal; happy hits owe much to former prod. Colman, sidemen such as Edmunds, guitarist Billy Bremner, etc.

STEVENSON, B. W. (*b* Louis C. Stevenson, 5 Oct. '49, Dallas, Texas) Singer/songwriter. Began to find success in a sort of hard folk-rock category and was influential in the Austin, Texas 'redneck rock' phenomenon of the '70s, but was subsequently misplaced by the music business. Played in rock bands as a teenager, went solo, was spotted in Dallas '72 by an RCA promo man: albums *B. W. Stevenson* and *Lead Free* were regional hits; single 'Shambala' written by Daniel Moore began to climb chart but cover by THREE DOG NIGHT eclipsed Stevenson's; 'My Maria' (co-written with Moore) reached top 10, pulling RCA LP of that title to no. 45 '73, but *Calabasas* '74 on RCA, *We Be Sailin'* '75, *Lost Feeling* '77 on WB, *Lifeline* '80 on MCA did little.

STEWART, Al (*b* 5 Sep. '45, Glasgow, Scotland) Folk-rock singer/songwriter. Began in rock bands in Bournemouth; influenced by Bob DYLAN, signed to EMI Columbia for *Bedsitter Images* '67, *Love Chronicles* '69 (with Jimmy Page and members of FAIRPORT CONVENTION; voted folk LP of the year by UK critics, issued on Epic in USA): title track was epic 18-minute confessional, also notable for first use of the word 'fucking' on record. *Zero She Flies* '70 was better, many thought, with historic 'Manuscript', rocking 'Electric Los Angeles Sunset'. After *Orange* '72 he emphasised historical sagas in *Past, Present & Future* '74 (on Janus label in USA), with QUEEN's

Roger Taylor, Rick Wakeman; standout was 10-minute 'Nostradamus'. *Year Of The Cat* '76 was on RCA in UK, Janus in USA, then Arista after lawsuit caused by label switch; title single went top 10 and album top 5 in USA. Both LP and title single *Time Passages* '78 were top 10; *24 Carrots* '80 still top 40; 2-disc *Live/Indian Summer* '81 had three live sides, one of new material; *Russians & Americans* '84 incl. 'Accident On 3rd Street'. Several albums charted in UK, three in top 40 LPs. He was accumulating a wine cellar in Calif.; released *The Last Days Of The Century* '88 on Earthworks/ Virgin.

STEWART, Gary (*b* 28 May '45, Letcher County, Ky.) Honky-tonk country singer, one of the best, but apart from a short period mid-'70s commercial success eluded him. Raised in Florida; to Nashville and teamed with policeman Bill Eldridge as songwriter; songs recorded by Nat STUCKEY, Hank SNOW, Billy WALKER, Jack GREENE, Warner MACK resulted in Kapp record contract, but no hits. He returned to Florida disillusioned, but was called back by prod. Roy Dea and signed to RCA: first single, a stunning remake of the ALLMAN BROTHERS' 'Ramblin' Man', was minor hit '73; 'Drinkin' Thing' and 'Out Of Hand' '74 made top 10: he opened shows for Charley PRIDE, his rocking honky-tonk a complete contrast; no. 1 hit with 'She's Actin' Single (I'm Drinkin' Doubles)' '75 led to MCA (new owners of Kapp) reissuing singles: 'You're Not The Woman You Used To Be' went top 20, better than current RCA single 'Flat Natural Born Good-Timin' Man'. Held in high esteem by other artists, Emmylou HARRIS, Waylon JENNINGS, Rodney CROWELL guesting on records; he continued to chart '76-8 but slipped: he stuck to honky-tonk clubs where he felt at home but records did not get much airtime. Team with songwriter Dean Dillon led to classic honky-tonk, but only 'Brotherly Love' and 'Smokin' In The Rockies' '82-3 were minor hits; Dillon went on to more Nashville success, but Stewart remained in relative obscurity. Albums incl. *Out Of Hand* '75, *Steppin' Out* '76, *Your Place Or Mine* '77, *Little Junior* '78, *Gary* '79, *Brotherly Love* and *Those Were The Days* '82-3 with Dillon; *20 Of The Best* in UK, compilations *Collector's Series* and

Greatest Hits USA, all on RCA. He may yet be discovered by the mainstream.

STEWART, John (*b* 5 Sep. '39) Singer, songwriter, guitarist. Made 16 albums on seven different labels in 20 years, concentrating mostly on Americana and love songs with little commercial reward; formed own Homecoming label and carried on, with many loyal fans around the world. Led the Cumberland Three on Roulette '60, making LPs *Folk Scene* and two vols. of Civil War songs, one for the North, one for the South: an imaginative idea for the record business of that time, or any time. He was a member of the KINGSTON TRIO '61-7; wrote 'Daydream Believer' for the MONKEES '67. A proposed group with Scott MCKENZIE, John Phillips didn't come off; *John Stewart And Buffy Ford* '68 (reissued as *Signals Through The Glass*), solo *California Bloodlines* '69 (regarded as a classic by many), *Willard* '70 were all on Capitol; the underrated *The Lonesome Picker Rides Again* '71 and *Sunstorm* '72 on WB; *Cannons In The Rain* '73, 2-disc *The Phoenix Concerts* '74, *Wingless Angels* '75 and *In Concert* '80 on RCA. *Fire In The Wind* '77 was the first on RSO, fifth of solo LPs to make the lower reaches of the charts; he picked up an electric guitar and made hit singles '(Turning Music Into) Gold' (no. 5) and 'Midnight Wind' (no. 28) with Stevie Nicks and Lindsay Buckingham, pushing *Bombs Away Dream Babies* '79 to no. 10 in USA LP chart; third RSO album *Dream Babies Go Hollywood* '80 was still in the top 100 LPs. *Blondes* '82 was on Allegiance (a different version on Polydor in Sweden), *Revenge Of The Budgie* was a mini-LP on Takoma with Nick Reynolds from Kingston Trio days; they were combined on a Takoma CD. Good songs still pouring out of him prolifically, he tired of deals with others' labels and joined ranks of roots artists forming their own: sampler *The Gathering* (with tracks by Stewart, guitarist Bruce Abrams, girl duo Heriza & Buffy incl. Buffy Ford, now his wife), Stewart's *Trancos* and instrumental *Centennial* all came out on Homecoming '84; in '85 one of his best (say the fans) *The Last Campaign*, incl. songs from his period campaigning for Robert Kennedy in '68. Also cassette-only *The Secret Tapes* '85 (an 'official bootleg') and *The*

Trio Years '86, new versions of songs written and performed during the Kingston Trio period, again with Reynolds participating. In UK Sunstorm reissued Stewart albums; See For Miles reissued *California Bloodlines* '87 with 17 songs (some from *Willard*). *Punch The Big Guy* '87 on Cypress incl. duets with Nanci GRIFFITH and Rosanne CASH, who covered his 'Runaway Train' on her *King's Record Shop* '87; he duetted with Griffith on her album *Little Love Affairs* '88 (on his 'Sweet Dreams Will Come').

STEWART, Rex (*b* Rex William Stewart, 22 Feb. '07, Philadelphia, Pa.; *d* 7 Sep. '67, L.A., Cal.) Cornet. Family moved to Washington DC '14; he played on Potomac riverboats, went to Philadelphia, then NYC '21. Worked with Elmer SNOWDEN '25, with Fletcher and Horace HENDERSON '26-31, MCKINNEY'S COTTON PICKERS briefly '31-2, Fletcher again; led own band, worked with Luis RUSSELL, then a star in the Duke ELLINGTON band '34-45 except for brief absences. Led own Rextet combos, toured Europe/Australia '47-51; settled in New Jersey to run a farm '51-6, also worked in local radio and TV, also led own band in Boston and worked as a DJ in Albany, NY, say various sources. He helped organise and lead Henderson reunion band '57-8 and recorded with it. At Eddie Condon's Club NYC '58-9; moved to West Coast, worked as DJ and began writing and lecturing on jazz history: his book *Jazz Masters Of The 30s* published posthumously '72. He specialised in a half-valve effect, notably on 'Boy Meets Horn' '38; apart from other solos on Ellington records, Ellington small-group recording sessions were issued under his name on various labels '36-41, usually compiled under Ellington's name; the most famous of these are eight tracks '40-1 with septet incl. Jimmy BLANTON, Ben WEBSTER etc. as Rex Stewart and his Orchestra on Bluebird: on 'Menelik (The Lion Of Judah)' he growled like a fey lion through his mute; 'Subtle Slough (Just Squeeze Me)' is particularly fine. A different collection from '40 as by Rex Stewart & The Ellingtonians on Hot Record Society label (limited edition at the time) is now on Fantasy. Also *Memorial Album* and *Trumpet Jive* (with Wingy MANONE) on Prestige, the

delightful Henderson reunion band LP on Hall of Fame, *Porgy & Bess Revisited* '58 now on Swing (instrumental, with Cootie WILLIAMS, Lawrence BROWN etc. playing parts), *The Irrepressible Rex Stewart* '71 on Jazzology.

STEWART, Rod (*b* 10 Jan. '45, London) Singer, songwriter; one of the biggest rock stars of the '70s, Sam COOKE was profound influence. Bummed around Europe as a teenager; worked in UK with Long John BALDRY, singles '64; founder member of Steampacket '66 with Baldry, Brian AUGER, Julie Driscoll (*First Of The Supergroups* '77); moved on to Shotgun Express, with Mick Fleetwood. Joined Jeff BECK for *Truth* and *Beck-O-La* '68-9, by now a recognised and distinctive singer; one-off single 'In A Broken Dream' with Australian instrumental group Python Lee Jackson was reissued '72 for a no. 3 UK hit. Solo career commenced with *An Old Raincoat Won't Ever Let You Down* '69, *Gasoline Alley* '70, well-liked by critics, but public still not sure. Joined reconstituted SMALL FACES with Ronnie Lane, Ron Wood, Ian MacLagen and Kenny Jones; called the Faces they were one of the best-loved bands of the early '70s while Stewart worked parallel solo career. *First Step* '71 displayed Faces potential; *Long Player* and *A Nod's As Good As A Wink To A Blind Horse* '71-2 were their best good-time UK rock'n'roll; Stewart's solo career caused some friction, but one of the world's top live acts never realised its potential on record: *Ooh La La* '73 and shoddy live *Overtures & Beginners* '74 disappointed fans; *Best Of The Faces* '77 was acceptable compilation. Meanwhile Stewart's *Every Picture Tells A Story* '71 was his best solo work to date, incl. 'Maggie May'; album and single were simultaneous no. ones both UK and USA. *Never A Dull Moment* '72 yielded UK no. 1 in 'You Wear It Well'. *Sing It Again Rod* '73 was premature Greatest Hits; *Smiler* '74 boasted good clutch of covers of Cooke and Bob DYLAN; he quit Faces '75. By *Atlantic Crossing* '75 he was a bona-fide superstar: romance with Britt Ekland found him in gossip columns; album incl. Dobie GRAY's 'Drift Away', the ISLEY Bros. 'This Old Heart Of Mine'; but the Sutherland Bros 'Sailing' gave him another UK no. 1, became his anthem (and theme of BBC TV's *Sailor*). Appositely titled *A Night On The Town* '76 revealed how much jetsetting had affected his art, though it incl. fine cover of Cat STEVENS' 'The First Cut Is The Deepest'; his own 'The Killing Of Georgie' was a big USA/UK hit. *Foot Loose & Fancy Free* '77 saw switch to lucrative disco market with hit 'Hot Legs'; *Blondes Have More Fun* '78 was huge success: 'Do Ya Think I'm Sexy?' was USA/UK no. 1, but smelled of self-parody. *Greatest Hits Volumes I And II* '79 filled a gap, incl. such '70s hits as Jimi HENDRIX's 'Angel', Carole KING's 'Oh No, Not My Baby' and 'I Don't Want To Talk About It'. *Foolish Behaviour* '80 seemed further proof of decline, though 'Passion' was big hit. *Tonight I'm Yours* '81 and 2-disc *Absolutely Live* were predictable, his own writing seemed to have deteriorated; but *Body Wishes* '83 was an encouraging fillip, with his own 'Sweet Surrender' and 'Baby Jane', a surprise no. 1 in UK. His '83 concerts in UK were a triumph: he had lost none of his charm as a live performer. *Camouflage* did little to recover his reputation with critics; *Every Beat of My Heart* '86 had effective cover of the BEATLES' 'In My Life', while his own title track easily recalled 'Sailing'. In mid-'86 he re-formed Faces for one-off London gig as a benefit for Ronnie Lane, a victim of multiple sclerosis, with DURAN DURAN's Andy Taylor standing in on bass. His creativity may have nose-dived, or perhaps his gravelly voice and 'Jack the Lad' persona haven't changed as much as his critics have. They carped about *Out Of Order* '88 on WB.

STEWART, Slam (*b* Leroy Stewart, 21 Sep. '14, Englewood, N.J.; *d* 10 Dec. '87, Binghamton, NY) Bassist, vocalist. Met Slim GAILLARD in Harlem '37; teamed as Slim & Slam, had hits mostly written by Gaillard: 'Flat Foot Floogie', 'Tutti Frutti', 'Jump Session', 'Laughing In Rhythm', 'Buck Dance Rhythm' '38-9. Seen in film *Stormy Weather* '43 with Fats WALLER; toured and recorded with Art TATUM, Benny GOODMAN '43-5; formed own trio with Billy TAYLOR, then Beryl Brooker on piano (*b* c.'24, *d* '80; recorded with Don BYAS, had several record dates of her own, all prod. by Leonard FEATHER, but remained obscure), Johnny Collins on guitar

(later with Nat COLE). Stewart practised one of the most distinctive and delightful gimmicks in jazz, bowing a bass solo and humming in unison an octave above; one of his best-known recording sessions was late '43 with Lester YOUNG quartet incl. Johnny GUARNIERI, Sid CATLETT. He worked in '50s with Tatum, Brooker; toured late '50s-60s with pianist/vocalist Rose Murphy (*b* '13, Xenia, Ohio; billed as 'the Chee-Chee Girl', had hit 'I Can't Give You Anything But Love' '47 on Majestic; was still working NYC clubs '80s). He toured with Goodman '70s, with his own quartet; taught at NY State U. at Binghamton; played *La Rêve Symphonique pour Slam* by Jack Martin with Indianapolis S.O. '70; gigged in London with Illinois JACQUET c.'82, etc. Own LPs on Savoy, UA; *Shut Yo' Mouth* '81 on PM with Major Holley has two fine bassists humming and scatting, with Oliver Jackson on drums (Dick HYMAN on one track); *Dialogue* with guitarist Bucky Pizzarelli (*b* 9 Jan. '26, Patterson, N.J.) is on Stash (Pizzarelli and son John Jr have Stash LPs incl. duos on seven-string guitars, Bucky's trio plus Red NORVO, etc.).

STEWART, Wynn (*b* 7 June '34, Morrisville, Mo.; *d* 17 July '85, Hendersonville, Tenn.) Country singer/songwriter. Began on Radio KWTO in Springfield '47; family moved to California '48; he first recorded '49, worked club circuit, recorded for Capitol '50s without much success. Move to Jackpot subsidiary of Challenge label led to first chart hit, 'Wishful Thinking' '58 in top 10. A popular act on the Las Vegas circuit, he had his own Nashville-Nevada Club and his own weekly TV show; he renamed his band the Tourists and toured the Southwest, at one time with Merle HAGGARD as front man. He moved back to Capitol '64; hits incl. 'It's Such A Pretty World Today' '67, no. 1 country hit in charts almost six months. He continued to make the charts, but songs are commercially underrated. He recorded for RCA '73, Atlantic '74, Playboy '75-7 (back in country top 10 with 'After The Storm' '76), more small labels. Albums incl. *Songs* '65, *In Love* '68, *Let The Whole World Sing It With Me* '69, *Yours Forever* '70, *It's A Beautiful Day* '71, all on Capitol; *Above And Beyond* '68 on Hilltop, *After The Storm* '76 on Playboy.

STILLS, Stephen (*b* 3 Jan. '45, Dallas, Texas) Singer, guitarist, songwriter. Left U. of Florida to work NYC folk circuit with little success; met Richie Furay during spell with Au Go Go Singers and formed BUFFA-LO SPRINGFIELD with him, having first flown to L.A. to form abortive band with Van Dyke PARKS. (He also auditioned for the MONKEES; story is that his teeth weren't pretty enough: Mike NESMITH got the part.) He wrote many of Buffalo's songs, the most famous 'For What It's Worth'. When they split '68 he made *Supersession* with Al KOOPER and Mike BLOOMFIELD, which sparked a rash of collaborative LPs by big stars (e.g. Triumvirate, etc.), in retrospect very loose jam sessions. He sessioned with Judy COLLINS (and fell in love), also Jimi HENDRIX, Joni MITCHELL; then joined CROSBY, STILLS & NASH, with ex-BYRD David Crosby, ex-HOLLIE Graham Nash, soon joined by ex-Buffalo Neil YOUNG to make CSN&Y. It was one of the most successful groups of the era in both critical and commercial terms; as it ended he made his first (eponymous) solo LP, released '70: it was a creative tour-de-force and incl. hit single 'Love The One You're With' (no. 14 USA, 37 UK '70-1): even the presence of superstar friends Hendrix, John Sebastian, Eric CLAPTON didn't intrude. *Stephen Stills 2* '71 disappointed by comparison, indicated a need for collaborators after all, to bounce ideas off. He formed Manassas, with Calvin 'Fuzzy' Samuels, bass; Dallas Taylor, drums; Paul Harris, keyboards; Al Perkins, steel guitar; Joe Lala, percussion; Chris Hillman (ex-BYRDS, Burrito Bros) on guitar: though *Manassas* and *Down The Road* '72-3 have not worn well, the mix of rock, Latin, country and blues was considered innovative at the time. Hillman was a major talent to have in the band, but he left to form Souther-Hillman-Furay Band '73, taking Perkins and Harris with him (another much-vaunted supergroup which folded after two disappointing LPs). Stills reformed CSN&Y: concerts helped the bank balance but there were no recordings. He switched to Columbia from Atlantic for *Stills* '75, the debut of his new right-hand man, guitarist Donnie Decus (later joined CHICAGO). But songwriting freshness had been lost, though his guitar was still impressive (he could also play bass, drums and keyboards). *Illegal Stills* '76 was better, but he linked with Young once more for *Long May You Run* '76, which began as a CSN&Y LP, but Crosby's and Nash's contributions were erased after altercations, then Young walked out of subsequent tour: they never worked together again. CS&N regrouped, released albums; Stills solos continued with *Throughfare Gap* '78 but remained uninspired. Underestimated as a guitarist (described as the best wahwah player since Hendrix), his best chance for solo stardom would have been to cash in on CSN&Y's phenomenal popularity and carry on writing love songs; as it is he has taken part in some of the best West Coast pop of all time.

STITT, Sonny (*b* Edward Stitt, 2 Feb. '24, Boston, Mass.; *d* 22 July '82) Saxophones. From musical family; played mostly alto at first, was both inspired and admired by Charlie PARKER: not as inventive as Parker but with plenty of fire and a voice of its own, his modernist style may not have owed everything to Parker's: the ideas were in the air. Became one of the best-loved during the golden age of the sax, on tenor in the late '40s-early '50s, with more than a hint of Lester YOUNG; played more alto after Parker died, but mainly known as a tenorist. Played in Dizzy GILLESPIE band '45-6, co-led band with Gene AMMONS '49-50, toured with JATP, own groups; rejoined Gillespie briefly '58, replaced John COLTRANE in Miles DAVIS quintet for most of '60 incl. UK visit; played at many festivals. Giants of Jazz world tour '72, with Gillespie, Thelonious MONK, Art BLAKEY, others. Albums: with Ammons on Prestige; *Sonny Stitt/Bud Powell/J. J. Johnson* '49-50, *Kaleidoscope* '50-1 on Fantasy, many own LPs on Prestige from '50s on incl. *'Nuther Fu'ther* '63 with Jack McDUFF, *Primitivo Soul* '64, *Shangri-La* and *Soul People* '65, *Stitt's Bits* and *Soul Electricity* '68. Also *Stitt And Top Brass* '62, *Stitt Plays Bird* '65 on Atlantic; *Blues For Duke* '75, *The Bubba's Sessions* and an album with Harry EDISON and Eddie DAVIS, both '81, on Who's Who In Jazz; *My Buddy: Stitt Plays For Gene Ammons* '75, *Sonny's Back* '80, *In Style* '81, *Last Stitt Sessions* '82, several others, all on Muse; *In Walked Sonny* with Blakey on Sonet, many more.

STONE, Cliffie (*b* Clifford Gilpin Snyder, 1 March '17, Burbank, Cal.) Country music producer, bandleader, songwriter, music publisher, label boss. Father was banjo player/comedian called Herman the Hermit. Worked in the house band at the Pasadena Community Playhouse, joined Ken Murray's Hollywood Blackouts, worked with bands of Anson WEEKS, Freddie SLACK; meanwhile he became country DJ and comedian at age 17 on KFVD's *Covered Wagon Jubilee*, by mid-'40s emceed more than two dozen country music shows a week, incl. daily variety show on KXLA '45 called *The Dinner Bell Roundup* (became the *Hometown Jamboree* '49); by then he'd joined Capitol Records in charge of country music '46, was a big influence in West Coast country, signing Tex WILLIAMS, Tennessee Ernie FORD, Jimmy WAKELY, Hank THOMPSON, Merle TRAVIS, many others. Own LPs incl. *Original Country Sing-A-Long* '56, *Square Dance USA* '57, *The Party's On Me* '58, *Don Stewart & Cliffie Stone* '67; left Capitol in mid-'60s to concentrate on his business interests (such as Central Songs, sold to Capitol '69); formed own Granite Records '74; later retired.

STONE, Lew (*b* c.1900; *d* 13 Feb. '69) Popular UK bandleader on radio, playing in clubs and restaurants; accompanying musicals such as Jack Hulbert's *Under Your Hat* '39, later *Annie Get Your Gun* at the Coliseum. In his heyday in the mid-'30s his band played 'hot' as often as possible, with the Louis ARMSTRONG-inspired trumpet of Nat Gonella (*b* 7 Mar. '08, London); other stars incl. reedman Joe Crossman, young vocalist Al BOWLLY.

STONEMAN FAMILY The longest continuously performing family act in country music, the Stonemans revolved around Ernest V. 'Pop' Stoneman (*b* 25 May 1893, Monarat, Carroll Co., Va.; *d* 14 June '68, Nashville), who played banjo, autoharp, harmonica and jaw harp in his teens, then gained an audition with Ralph PEER at Okeh Records: his 'The Titanic' was a national no. 3 hit in '25, according to *Pop Memories*. He made over 200 titles with Okeh, Paramount, Gennett and Victor, recorded with Riley PUCKETT and Uncle Dave MACON; went back to work as a carpenter (in a naval gun factory in Washington DC) during the Depression. In the late '40s he formed a family band, playing in the DC area; they recorded *The Stoneman Family* '57 on Folkways, became popular on college and folk club circuits, appeared on Grand Ole Opry '62 and began recording for Starday. They guested on Jimmy DEAN's TV show '64, signed with MGM and landed their own TV series *Those Stonemans* '66; had several minor country hits, made top 20 with 'Five Little Johnson Girls' '66, won CMA award for Best Vocal Group '67. The band consisted of Pop on guitar and autoharp, Scotty on fiddle, Jim on bass, Van on guitar, Donna on mandolin and Roni on banjo. After Pop's death they carried on, updating their material and stage act, recorded for RCA. Patsy joined; Scotty dropped out early '70s, by then an indemand session musician; Roni, a naturally funny lady, became a regular on TV's *Hee-Haw*; and Gene and Dean gigged as the Stoneman Brothers. The Stonemans were still working as a unit mid-'80s and the whole family sometimes got together for special shows. Albums incl. *White Lightning* '63 on Starday; *Those Singin', Swingin', Stompin', Sensational Stonemans* '66, *It's All In The Family* '67 and *Tribute To Pop Stoneman* '68 on MGM; *Dawn Of The Stoneman's Age* '69, *In All Honesty* '70 on RCA; *Country Hospitality* '78 on Meteor, *Scotty Stoneman Live In L.A. With The Kentucky Colonels* '79 on Sierra Briar, *The First Family Of Country Music* '82 on CMH.

STORDAHL, Axel (*b* 8 Aug. '13, Staten Island, NY; *d* 30 Aug. '63, Encino, Cal.) Conductor, arranger, composer. Trombonist and arr. '34-5, joined Tommy DORSEY '36, became singer with vocal group, lead arranger. Conducted on Frank SINATRA's first sessions for RCA '42, became his regular arr.-cond. '43-9, with him on *Hit Parade* radio shows '47-9, cond. his first Capitol session '53. Also worked with Bing CROSBY, Dean MARTIN, Eddie FISHER, Dinah SHORE, Doris DAY, etc.; LPs on Capitol with wife, singer June Hutton; own LPs on Capitol, Decca, Dot incl. *Lure* '59, *Jasmine And Jade* '60, *The Magic Islands Revisited* '61, *Guitars Around The World* '63. Good songwriter: 'I Should Care' '45, 'Day By Day' '46 (Sinatra hit).

STORM, Gale (*b* Josephine Cottle, '22, Texas) Actress, singer. Won Gateway to Hollywood contest, went to Hollywood '40, appeared in Roy ROGERS movies, etc.; success in hit TV series *My Little Margie* '52 (with venerable actor Charles Farrell) helped record sales on Dot '55-7, covers of 'I Hear You Knocking' (Smiley LEWIS), 'Why Do Fools Fall In Love' (Frankie LYMON), etc. until blacks broke through to pop chart, washed away cover merchants. Compilations on Ace, MCA.

STRAIT, George (*b* 18 May '52, Poteet, Texas) Honky-tonk country singer, the most successful of the '80s. Father was a cattle rancher; he eloped with his girl friend, then joined the US Army. Became fulltime Army entertainer; recorded briefly for Pappy Daily's 'D' Records in Houston '76, went to Nashville and signed with MCA; hit country top 10 with first single 'Unwound' '81 and stayed there, nine no. 1 hits incl. 'Fool Hearted Memory' and 'Amarillo By Morning' '82, 'Does Fort Worth Ever Cross Your Mind?' '84 and 'The Chair' '86. He was rated the fourth most popular live act in the USA '85, above celebrated heavy metal acts and even above Willie NELSON; named CMA Male Vocalist of the Year '85 and '86. Infl. by Bob WILLS, Hank WILLIAMS, George JONES and Merle HAGGARD, he avoids much of the slickness of Nashville product. Albums incl. *Strait Country* '81, *Strait From The Heart* '82, *Right Or Wrong* '83, *Something Special* '85, *Does Fort Worth Ever Cross Your Mind?* '84 (CMA Album of the Year '85), *Greatest Hits* '85, *Number 7* '86, *Ocean Front Property* '87, *If You Ain't Lovin' You Ain't Livin'* '88. With all his hits, he hasn't given up his day job: farms ranch in San Marcos, Texas (degree in agriculture from South West Texas State U.) and leads his Ace In The Hole Band by night.

STRANGLERS, The UK rock band which came to fame during the punk era, but had played the London pub circuit two years before, their gloomy DOORS-style music attracting attention; they have outlasted most of the punks. Guitarist/vocalist Hugh Cornwell (*b* 28 Aug. '49), bassist/vocalist Jean Jacques Burnel, Dave Greenfield on keyboards and drummer Jet Black began as the Guildford Stranglers '75, were older than punk contemporaries. Album *Rattus Norvegicus* '77 incl. hits 'Grip' and 'Peaches', the latter notable for overt misogyny, which they have retained. *No More Heroes* '77 was better, title track a UK hit; *Black & White* '78 competent, *Live X-Cert* '79 merely workmanlike: they seemed set to follow the course of '60s progressive bands they despised. Sneering cover of Dionne WARWICK's 'Walk On By' was top 30; *The Raven, Meninblack* and *La Folie* '79-81 brought further comparisons with '60s music; hit singles were gathered in *The Collection* '82. 'Golden Brown' '82 was their biggest hit at no. 2, Cornwell's song about heroin (he was imprisoned '80 on drug offences). A long silence was followed by a switch of labels, return with *Feline* '83 and *Aural Sculpture* '84, latter with fetching 'Skin Deep', no. 15 UK hit. Their antipathy towards the press has seen them consistently reviled by critics, but the public pays little attention; *Dreamtime* '86 incl. top 20 'Nice In Nice'. *Off The Beaten Track* '86 was compiled by the band, collecting rare tracks. Burnel's solo *Euroman Cometh* '79 was interesting; Cornwell and Robert Williams collaborated on *Nosferatu* '79; Greenfield and Burnel worked together on *Fire & Water* '83; Cornwell contributed song to anti-nuclear animated film *When The Wind Blows* '86, was preparing next solo LP.

STRAWBERRY ALARM CLOCK USA West Coast psychedelic band which had one massive hit and faded. Guitarist/vocalist Ed King later worked with LYNYRD SKYNYRD, then a gospel group; with Randy Seol on drums (reportedly played bongos with his hands on fire), Mark Weitz on keyboards and two bassists (Gary Lovetro and Lee Freeman, who also played guitar, horns etc.), they had no. 1 hit with flower-power anthem 'Incense And Peppermints' '67, pulling album of that title to no. 11; several other albums with changing personnel quickly sank.

STRAWBS UK folkrock group formed '67, originally Strawberry Hill Boys, from that London neighbourhood. Singer/songwriter Dave Cousins, Tony Hooper on guitar, Ron Chesterman on bass and Sandy DENNY recorded *All Our Own Work* '68, incl. early version of her 'Who Knows Where The Time Goes'; before it was released Denny left to go to FAIRPORT CONVENTION. *Stawbs* '69 was made with the help of LED ZEPPELIN's John Paul Jones, Nicky HOPKINS; 'Man Who Calls Himself Jesus' and epic 'The Battle' marked Cousins as a songwriter of promise: though *Dragonfly* '70 was disappointing, his 'Josephine For Better Or Worse' was standout track. Chesterman left; Richard Hudson on bass and John Ford on drums were recruited; whizzkid keyboardist Rick Wakeman joined for exemplary live *Just A Collection Of Antiques And Curios* '70; *From The Witchwood* '71 brought Wakeman to the fore, incl. 'The Hangman And The Papist'; Wakeman left for YES and Blue Weaver from Amen Corner was drafted in; *Grave New World* '72 was highly acclaimed, but marked by Hooper's departure. *Bursting At The Seams* '73 incl. their first real single hit, 'Lay Down', soon eclipsed by Hudson-Ford song 'Part Of The Union', no. 2 '73 (they left to capitalise on this success, had hits '73-4; albums *Nickelodeon, Free Spirit, Worlds Collide* and *Daylight* '73-7; as the Monks a surprise hit with punkish 'Nice Legs, Shame About The Face' '79). Cousins persevered with Strawbs: *Hero & Heroine* '74 was flawed; *Ghosts* '75, *Nomadness* '75, *Deep Cuts* '76 had some good tracks; they declined with *Burning For You* '77, *Deadlines* '78, split. Cousins had released solo *Two Weeks Last Summer* '72; his *Old School Songs* '80 incl. live versions of Strawbs favourites; 2-disc *Best Of The Strawbs* '78 remains.

STRAY CATS USA rockabilly revival trio: vocalist/songwriter/guitarist Brian Setzer (*b* 10 Apr. '60, NYC), Lee Rocker (*b* Lee Drucher) on bass, drummer Slim Jim Phantom (*b* James McDonell) teamed '79 NYC, went to UK, where musical climate favoured them; Setzer previously played with Bloodless Pharoahs, who played on New Wave sampler *Marty Thau Presents 2×5*, prod. by BLONDIE's Jimmy Destri. Cats' visual approach soon made headlines in scene looking for the next big thing after punk: Setzer's quiff, Rocker's twirling standup bass, Phantom's one-snare/one-cymbal kit played standing up were unusual to say the least. Signed by Arista; Dave EDMUNDS

prod. 'Runaway Boys', 'Stray Cat Strut', 'Rock This Town' UK hits '80-1: authentic-sounding rockabilly with New Wave edge. They backed Edmunds on 'The Race Is On', single from his *Twangin'* LP '81; opened for ROLLING STONES on USA tour; returned with heads held high: eponymous '81 LP was top 10 UK, sold well on import in USA; self-produced *Gonna Ball* '82 missed Edmunds' painstaking touch; compilation of these as *Built For Speed* '82 made no. 2 USA; with MTV help, 'Rock This Town' was top 10 there, 'Stray Cat Strut' no. 3. *Rant'n'Rave* '83 saw Edmunds back in prod. chair, but novelty had worn off, Setzer was unhappy with limitation of gimmick: they split; Rocker and Phantom stayed together, though Phantom's wedding with Britt Ekland made more headlines than link with ex-David BOWIE guitarist Earl Slick as Phantom, Rocker & Slick (eponymous LP '85). Setzer's *The Knife Feels Like Justice* '86 had 11 of his songs, incl. 'Aztec', 'Maria', co-written with Mike Campbell (of Tom PETTY's Heartbreakers), Steve VAN ZANDT respectively; band incl. guitarist Tommy Byrnes, Kenny Aaronson on bass, John MELLENCAMP drummer Kenny Aronoff. The trio released *Cover Girl* '86; Rocker and Setzer appeared in TV tribute to Carl PERKINS with George HARRISON; Setzer released *Live Nude Guitar* '88 on EMI.

STRAYHORN, Billy (*b* 29 Nov. '15, Dayton, Ohio; *d* 31 May '67, NYC) Pianist, composer, lyricist, arranger; aka 'Swee'Pea', 'Strays'. Played classics with school orchestra in Pittsburgh; met Duke ELLINGTON '38, hoping to write lyrics for him; early '39 Duke made his first recording of a Strayhorn song, 'Something To Live For' (vocal by Jean Eldridge). During one of the most important Ellington periods ('40-2) Strayhorn contributed 'Take The "A" Train' (soon the band's theme), 'Clementine', 'Chelsea Bridge', 'After All', 'Day Dream', 'Raincheck', 'Johnny Come Lately'; 'Midriff' in '44, 'Smada' and 'Boo'Dah' in Duke's CBS period late '40s-early '50s; perhaps 200 pieces in all. He became Duke's amanuensis and collaborator until, often, neither of them could remember which had done this or that, and nobody else could tell either. He arr. many of the pop songs Duke occasionally incl. in LPs in the '50s-60s, also helped with more ambitious works, from *The Perfume Suite* mid-'40s through *Suite Thursday, A Drum Is A Woman, Such Sweet Thunder*, adaptations of Tchaikovsky's *Nutcracker*, Grieg's *Peer Gynt* in '50s; some critics think Strays may have been entirely responsible for some of the suites which carried both names. He dir. the band in Duke's *My People* '63; often arr. the small group sessions for Johnny HODGES, Barney BIGARD; played piano with Duke's small groups and big band but rarely appeared with him in public. He wrote particularly beautiful things for Hodges' sensuous alto, such as 'Passion Flower', 'A Flower Is A Lovesome Thing' (aka 'Passion'); recorded piano duets with Duke (now on Prestige), led Hodges and Jimmy Grissom in a trio '58; *Cue For Saxophone* '59 (septet with Hodges) on Felsted, Master Jazz issued on Affinity UK '86; *Live!* was on Roulette, *The Peaceful Side* '61 on United Artists (made in Paris with bassist Michel Goudret, voices and strings on some tracks). One of his first compositions was 'Lush Life' (words and music) '38 (first recorded by Nat COLE '49, became cabaret standard); last was 'Blood Count', sent to the band from the hospital where he died of cancer. His melodic and harmonic contribution to the development of jazz composition must be reckoned almost as great as Duke's; beautiful Ellington album . . . *And His Mother Called Him Bill* '67 on RCA was made in tribute, incl. beautiful 'Lotus Blossom' (played solo at the end of a session as musicians packed up; previously known as 'Charlotte Russe', recorded by a Hodges small group '47). Tributes incl. Art FARMER album *Something To Live For* on Contemporary, *Marian McPartland Plays The Music Of Billy Strayhorn* on Concord Jazz, both '87.

STREET, Mel (*b* 21 Oct. '33, Grundy, West Va.; *d* 21 Oct. '78, Hendersonville, Tenn.) Honky-tonk country singer, songwriter who had hits through the '70s. Began on local radio early '50s, moved to Niagara Falls, NY to work in construction; sang in local night club, moved back to West Va. to local clubs there. First records on small Tandem label incl. his own 'Borrowed Angel' '70, picked up by Royal American Records in

Nashville, made top 10 country chart '72; recorded for Metromedia, GRT, finally Polydor with hits along the way, but despite growing fame, depression due to personal problems led him to shoot himself on his 45th birthday. He scored posthumous hit with 'The One Thing My Lady Never Puts Into Words' '79. Albums incl. *Smokey Mountain Memories* '75 on GRT, *Country Soul* '78 on Polydor, *The Many Moods Of Mel Street* '80 on Sunbird.

STREISAND, Barbra (*b* Barbara Joan Streisand, 24 Apr. '42, Brooklyn, NY) Singer, actress, screenwriter, film director; one of the biggest stars of the era: association with Columbia records for more than 20 years except for original cast album of *Funny Girl* '64 on Capitol and soundtrack of *Hello, Dolly!* '69 on 20th Century (now on Casablanca). 37 albums charted in Billboard '63-84 incl. these and other soundtracks; 30 singles '63-82 plus duets with Neil DIAMOND (no. 1 hit 'You Don't Bring Me Flowers' '78), Donna SUMMER (no. 1 hit 'No More Tears (Enough Is Enough)' '79), Barry Gibb (top 10 'Guilty', 'What Kind Of Fool' '80-1). Many hits in UK too, but nothing like as many: her complete show-business talent and personality are indubitably American. She began in amateur productions, then off-Broadway in *Another Evening With Harry Stoons*, on Broadway as Miss Marmelstein in *I Can Get It For You Wholesale* '62 (where she met first husband Elliott Gould); was chosen to play Fanny BRICE in *Funny Girl* (also in film version '68). First LP *The Barbra Streisand Album* was top 10 album, incl. showstopping version of hoop-de-do '29 song 'Happy Days Are Here Again', performed as a slow ballad for the first time. Her next seven albums were all top 5: *Second* and *Third* '63-4, *People* '64 with top 5 title single (song from *Funny Girl* by Bob Merrill and Jule Styne; single won Grammy for arrangement by Peter Maltz and for Best Female Vocal Performance), *My Name Is Barbra* and *My Name Is Barbra, Two* '65, *Color Me Barbra* and *Je m'appelle Barbra* '66; the *Funny Girl* original cast LP was also top 5; other '60s album all big hits: *Simply Streisand, Funny Girl* soundtrack, *A Happening In Central Park, What About Today?*, *Hello, Dolly!* film soundtrack (show starred

Carol CHANNING on Broadway '64). Biggest hits among later albums were *Stoney End* '71 (no. 6 title single), *Barbra Joan Streisand* '71, *Live Concert At The Forum* '72, *The Way We Were* '74 (no. 1 album was not film soundtrack but incl. no. 1 hit single of film theme), *Butterfly* '74, *Funny Lady* '75 (soundtrack of sequel to *Funny Girl*), *Lazy Afternoon* '75, *A Star Is Born* '76 (with Kris KRISTOFFERSON, her then boyfriend: soundtrack of second remake of '37 film *Evergreen*, but *see* Judy GARLAND), *Streisand Superman* '77 (incl. no. 4 hit 'My Heart Belongs To Me'), *Songbird* '78, *Barbra Streisand's Greatest Hits Vol. 2* (no. 1 LP, no. 1 in UK also, incl. the big duet with Diamond), *The Main Event* '79 (soundtrack incl. hit title single, others by various artists), *Wet* '79 (incl. duet with Summer), compilation *Memories* '81. Her other films incl. musical *On A Clear Day You Can See Forever* '70, non-singing roles in *The Owl And The Pussycat* '71 with George Segal, *What's Up Doc?* '72 with Ryan O'Neal and Madeline Kahn (attempt to re-create '30s 'screwball comedy' genre, dir. by Peter Bogdanovich). In '83 she became the first woman to write, produce, direct and star in title role of her own film *Yentl*; story was an unlikely one of a girl masquerading as a boy in an orthodox Jewish setting, and made an uneasy musical; the film was panned but soundtrack LP went top 10. LP *Emotion* '84 went top 20, *The Broadway Album* '85 no. 1 (*see* Stephen SONDHEIM). Duet single 'Make No Mistake, He's Mine' '85 with Kim CARNES was in Hot 100 for 10 weeks that year. Fear of performing in public has kept her off the stage for 20 years (except for a couple of political rallies) but her larger-than-life persona and unquenchable exuberance keep her at the top. She also contributed to *Harold Sings Arlen (With Friend)*, now on Columbia Special Products. When *One Voice* '87 went gold she had 30 gold albums, more than any other artist; her magic seems imperishable.

STRINGBEAN (*b* David Akeman, 17 June '15, Annville, Ky.; *d* 10 Nov. '73, Nashville, Tenn.) One of country music's best-loved comedians and instrumentalists. Son of a fine banjo player; worked on a farm, played with various bands in his spare time; joined Cy Rogers' Lonesome Pine Fiddlers on Radio WLAP, Lexington, Ky. '35-8 and began working on comic routines, called Stringbean on account of lanky appearance and ability to play almost any stringed instrument. Joined Charlie Monroe's Kentucky Pardners on Radio WBIG, Greenville, N.C. '39-41; moved to Nashville and appeared on Grand Ole Opry with Bill MONROE '42-5; then formed his own band, Stringbean and his Kentucky Wonders, specialising in banjo playing in the trad. style of Uncle Dave MACON. A regular on the Opry for almost 30 years; also appeared on WSM's *Prince Albert Show*, *Ozark Jubilee* '55, with Merv Griffin '66, Porter WAGONER '67-8, FLATT & SCRUGGS and *Hee-Haw* '69-73. He and his wife were murdered on returning home from the Opry by burglars surprised in their house. LPs incl. *Old Time Banjo Picking And Singing* '60, *Salute To Uncle Dave Macon* '66, *Back In The Hills Of Kentucky* '68 on Starday; *Me And My Old Crow* '70 on Nugget.

STUART, Rory (*b* 9 Jan. '56, Brooklyn, NY) Guitarist, composer, leader. Began on drums, switched to guitar and began buying jazz records at about 13, thanks to school outing at the Village Vanguard (matinee with Roland KIRK), Jaki BYARD teaching at the school, etc. Studied classical guitar for two years, then heard Wes MONTGOMERY, George BENSON; spent seven years living in Colorado except for tour with Jack McDUFF and a season in Paris; returned to NYC '81, mostly self-taught and formed quartet; first LP *Nightwork* '83 on Cadence made live at Seventh Avenue South with pianist Armen Donelian, Calvin Hill on bass, Keith COPELAND on drums incl. four Stuart tunes, intimate and intelligent music which repays repeated listenings; second *Hurricane* '86 on Sunnyside (Anthony Cox replacing Hill) has four originals plus one tune each by Thelonious MONK and Donelian. Stuart is a new voice to look out for in post-bop eclecticism; there's more on tape at Sunnyside. Donelian (*b* 1 Dec. '50, Queens, NY) worked with Sonny ROLLINS, Ted CURSON, singer Anne Marie Moss, others; he lived next door to Charles MINGUS, sent tapes of Mingus's work-in-progress to Joni MITCHELL helping to inspire her Mingus LP; his solo LP on Sunnyside '84 is *A Reverie*. Stuart and Donelian have been interviewed at length in CADENCE magazine.

STUCKEY, Nat (*b* Nathan Wright Stuckey, 17 Dec. '37, Cass Co., Texas) Underrated country singer and songwriter. Obtained college degree in radio, TV and speech, worked as radio announcer, playing in local bands weekends incl. a jazz group '57-8 and his own country outfit the Corn Huskers '58-9. Led studio band on Shreveport's *Louisiana Hayride* '62-6, leading to record contract with Paula Records and self-penned hits 'Sweet Thang' and 'Oh Woman' '66-7. Buck OWENS took his 'Waitin' In Your Welfare Line' to no. 1 '66; he formed his own touring band the Sweet Thangs. Signed with RCA in Nashville and had top 10 hits 'Plastic Saddle', 'Joe And Mabel's 12th Street Bar And Grill', 'Sweet Thang And Cisco', 'Young Love' (duet with Connie SMITH), 'She Wakes Me Every Morning With A Kiss', 'Got Leaving On Her Mind', all '68-73. Hits slipped; he moved to MCA and came back with 'Sun Comin' Up' '76, 'Days Of Sand And Shovels' '78; since then recorded for small labels like Stargem, toured on the basis of old hits. Albums incl. *Nat Stuckey Sings* '67 on Paula; *Keep 'Em Country* '69, *New Country Roads* '70, *Only A Woman Like You* '71, *Is It Any Wonder That I Love You* '73, all on RCA; *Independence* '76 on MCA.

STYLE COUNCIL UK pop band. Following dissolution of the JAM '82, Paul Weller's first appearance onstage was with jazzy EVERYTHING BUT THE GIRL '83, indicating new direction to be taken with Style Council: duo with Mick Talbot (*b* 11 Sep. '59) on keyboards (ex-'New Mod' band Merton Parkas '79, briefly DEXY'S MIDNIGHT RUNNERS). Debut single was funky 'Speak Like A Child' (no. 4 UK '80) which followed in direction Jam was pursuing with last single 'The Beat Surrender', itself a step away from former militance. Through '84 Weller and Talbot served up a tasty array of singles: 'Money Go Round', 'Solid Bond In Your Heart', 'Long Hot Summer', displaying former's writing ability and picking up following from Jam days. *Café Bleu* '84 was successful LP debut, bossa nova mixture with hits 'My Ever Changing Moods', 'You're The Best Thing'. Some tracks were instrumentals, showing off Talbot's skill; guest vocalists incl. Tracey Thorn, D. C. Lee. *My Favourite Shop* '85 incl. 'Welcome To Milton Keynes' and 'Walls Came Tumbling Down'. Weller appeared on Band Aid singles '85, other charity records for striking miners and victims of sickle cell anaemia. Style Council contributed to soundtrack of *Absolute Beginners* '86; live album and video *Home & Abroad* '86 was effective souvenir; *The Cost Of Living* '87 featured Curtis MAYFIELD; they made short film *Jerusalem* '87. He'd vanquished ghost of Jam, though Style Council may not have same impact or durability.

STYLISTICS, The Soul vocal quintet formed in Philadelphia '68: Russell Thompkins Jr, lead singer, with Airrion Love, James Smith, Herbie Murrell, James Dunn. They had big pop/R&B hits '71-3, some co-written by Thom BELL with Linda Creed (incl. oft-covered 'I'm Stone In Love With You'); in their heyday they were prod. by Bell and were typical of the mid-'70s Philadelphia sound. Ten albums charted in Billboard '71-80, of which the biggest was *Let's Put It All Together* '74 at no. 14, their only top 40 LP. Compilations now on Amherst label in USA. They remained popular in Europe; album *Some Things Never Change* on Virgin UK '85.

STYX USA AOR group formed by brothers Chuck (bass) and John Panozzo (drums), who's met Dennis De Young (keyboards, vocals) in Chicago '63; adding guitarists John Curulewski and James 'JY' Young '68 they became Tradewinds; changed to Styx '70, signed to Wooden Nickle and made *Styx I*, *Styx II*. *The Serpent Is Rising* and *Man Of Miracles* '73-4 were recycled into *Rock Galaxy* by RCA after they broke big; 'Lady' from *Styx II* was first hit single (no. 6 '75). *Equinox* '75 on A&M incl. 'Suite Madame Blue', pointing to symphonic pretensions; replacement of Curulewski by Tommy Shaw for *Crystal Ball* '76 even more significant. *The Grand Illusion* '77 made breakthrough, with no. 8 single 'Come Sail Away', stage favourites 'Miss America', 'Castle Walls', 'Superstars'. Having found platinum formula of harmonies, keyboards and pomp aplenty, they stuck to it with *Pieces Of Eight* '78, *Cornerstone* '79,

USA hits 'Renegade' (no. 16), syrupy ballad 'Babe' (no. 1; 6 UK). *Paradise Theatre* '80 was concept album around Chicago playhouse that fell down: parallel with USA of late '70s, incl. hits 'The Best Of Times', 'Too Much Time On My Hands'. Stage show for *Kilroy Was Here* '83 preceded by 11-minute film: rush-like telling of totalitarian state where rock is outlawed; 'Mr Roboto' no. 7 hit. But solo projects from De Young (*Desert Moon* '84) and Young (*Girls With Guns* '84) indicated dissatisfaction with rut, however profitable; Young's much more rock'n'roll oriented, while De Young's effort could have been a Styx album. Future was uncertain, but they've made a lot of money without influencing anything.

SUICIDE USA electronic/new wave duo formed '71: vocalist Alan Vega (*b* '48), Marty Rev, keyboards (ex-jazz band organist). Mixture of Vega's rockabilly and Rev's relentless keyboards came from same scene as NEW YORK DOLLS ('Rocket USA' appeared on seminal *Max's Kansas City* showcase '76); uncompromising live act inspired love or hate (like Dolls) but remained unsigned until punk era. Craig Leon (RAMONES) and Marty Thau prod. *Suicide* '77 on Thau's Red Star label (now on Demon UK), it and *24 Minutes Over Brussels* '78 found few takers. They were bottled off the stage supporting CLASH in UK '77, too much even for punks. Patronage of CARS' Ric Ocasek led to pop crossover; he used as Cars tour support, featured them on *Midnight Special* (Cars TV show), prod. *Alan Vega And Martin Rev* '79 for Ze label. They went for solo careers, put Suicide on hold (track 'Hey Lord' on Ze's *A Christmas Album* '81 served notice they'd be back). NYC tape label ROIR released *Half Alive* '81 on cassette only. Vega's eponymous solo LP '81 incl. European hit single 'Juke Box Baby' (top 5 in France, Benelux): much more vocal oriented than Suicide. He continued with career as sculptor, with one-man show in NYC's Barbara Gladstone Gallery '82, again '83, in Amsterdam '83. *Collision Drive* '82 returned more to Suicide's metallic drone, was followed by live dates with surprisingly conventional rock band (Mark Kuch, guitar; Larry Chaplan, bass; Sesu Coleman, drums). Ocasek-prod.

Sunset Strip '83 updated 'Juke Box Baby' to 'Video Babe' and had a track in French for Europe ('Je T'Adore'), plus rockabilly-based 'American Dreamer' and 'Wipe Out Beat', off-the-wall cover of HOT CHOCOLATE's 'Every 1's A Winner'. *Just A Million Dreams* '85 prod. by Chris Lord-Alge, Arthur BAKER associate and disco producer, acclaimed as best yet, also denigrated for commercialism, ironic since duo were being recognised as founding fathers of European synth pop and new wave; they'd had their influence on Soft Cell, DEPECHE MODE, DAF, Birthday Party, Sisters of Mercy, others right up to Sigue Sigue Sputnik, using only a rhythm machine, a cheap Farfisa keyboard and heavily-echoed Vega neo-PRESLEY vocals. Rev had done solo LPs *Martin Rev* '79 and *Clouds Of Glory* on French New Rose label. They re-formed '86 for gigs, new LP. Early tracks 'Frankie Teardrop' and 'Viet Vet' are unlikely to be bettered by future releases, which might be better received now that the rest have caught up. Asked to explain the group's name, Vega said, 'If I'd called it "Life", no one would have come.'

SULLIVAN, Ira (*b* 1 May '31, Washington DC) Trumpet, saxophones. Worked at the Bee Hive in Chicago early '50s with visiting stars incl. Charlie PARKER; also played with Art BLAKEY '56 (recorded on Columbia), mostly worked in Chicago until moving to Florida in the '60s. Recorded with J. R. Monterose on Blue Note, Red RODNEY on Fantasy, Roland KIRK on Cadet, Eddie HARRIS on Atlantic (*Come On Down*); own albums: *Nicky's Tune* and *Ira Sullivan Quartet* on Delmark, *The Incredible Ira Sullivan* on Stash, *Ira Sullivan* on Flying Fish, reunited with Rodney on *Spirit Within* on Elektra '82; reissue *Bird Lives*, Chicago quintet on Affinity.

SULLIVAN, Joe (*b* Joseph Michael Sullivan, 4 Nov. '06, Chicago; *d* 14 Oct. '71, San Francisco) Pianist, composer. Studied at Chicago Conservatory, worked in vaudeville circuit, then in Chicago through '20s with much radio work, many records as sideman in heyday of Chicago style (*see* JAZZ), worked with bands of Enoch LIGHT, COON-SANDERS, many others. To NYC late '20s, played with Red NICHOLS, Roger

Wolfe KAHN, Red MCKENZIE, Ozzie NELSON, Russ COLUMBO; to West Coast, worked as Bing CROSBY's accompanist (incl. three films); back to NYC '36 and joined Bob CROSBY band, but had to leave for 10 months in a sanatorium with lung trouble: a benefit for him in Chicago '37 incl. Bob Crosby band, Roy ELDRIDGE, Johnny and Baby DODDS, etc. He rejoined Bob Crosby '39, led own groups at NYC venues, worked with Bobby HACKETT, on West Coast, back to NYC at Nick's; lived and worked mostly on West Coast from '50, with long residencies at the Hangover in S.F., etc. Bob Crosby band reunited for a TV tribute to him '55, he played Monterey Jazz Festival '63. Film work incl. leading sextet recording music for *Fight For Life* '40. Under his own name he recorded piano solos for Columbia '33, Brunswick '35, Commodore '41; eight sides for Vocalion/Okeh '40 with octet Joe Sullivan and his Café Society Orchestra; a solo Riverside LP mid-'50s incl. his best-known tunes 'Gin Mill Blues', 'Little Rock Getaway' (both cut '33), others. On small Shoestring label: *And The All Stars* '50 (live concert with small group incl. Hackett), *At The Piano* '44 (AFRS transcription solos).

SULLIVAN, Maxine (*b* Marietta Williams, 13 May '11, Homestead, Pa.; *d* 7 April '87, NYC) Singer. Subtle phrasing and swing; strong on lyric interpretation, not given to elaborate display; perennially popular. Sang in Pittsburgh clubs and on radio; Claude THORNHILL, mus. dir. of band at Onyx Club NYC, arranged hit disc 'Loch Lomand' '37 which typed her: recorded folkish songs with swing arrangements, sang 'Cockles And Mussels', 'If I Had A Ribbon Bow' on radio with Onyx-based sextet of then-husband John KIRBY '37-8, her voice and that band's chamber-jazz style well suited: coast-to-coast on CBS radio Sunday afternoons, *Flow Gently Sweet Rhythm* was the only black show networked at the time. She appeared in films *Goin' Places*, *St Louis Blues*; on stage in *Swingin' The Dream* '39 (played Titania in flop treatment of *Midsummer Night's Dream*, with Louis ARMSTRONG as Bottom, Benny GOODMAN sextet as strolling players, Eddie CONDON gang in a box). Toured with Benny CARTER '41; temporarily retired '42; comeback in mid-'40s. To UK '48, '54; on stage again in *Take A Giant Step* '53; went into nursing, came back to music '58 not only singing but playing brass instruments, esp. valve trombone. Played jazz festivals, dates with World's Greatest Jazz Band '69-71; LPs incl. *With Earl Hines At The Overseas Press Club*; *Maxine* '75; with Ike Isaacs trio '79; *Close As Pages In A Book* with Bob WILBER and Dick HYMAN's settings of Shakespeare, both c.'78; *The Queen* '81; *Great Songs From The Cotton Club* '84 (written by Harold ARLEN and Ted Koehler for '30-4 productions). Release of *Uptown* '86 (with Scott HAMILTON quartet) on Concord Jazz accompanied by short UK tour, one date recorded by BBC. *Together* '87 on Atlantic (songs of Jule Styne) was her last studio album. Married '50 to pianist Cliff Jackson until his death (*b* 19 July '02, Washington DC; *d* 23 May '70, NYC). She was nominated for a Grammy three times, but never won. Reissues on Audiophile incl. *We Just Couldn't Say Goodbye, It Was Great Fun* etc.

SUMAC, Yma (*b* c.'28) Singer with amazing range of four octaves; phenomenon of early '50s popular music. She was said to have been born in the Peruvian Andes, descendant of Inca kings, real name Zoila Imperatriz Charrari Sumac del Castillo; she went to the USA '47, sang at Carnegie Hall and with Toronto, Montreal, Hollywood Bowl Symphony Orchestras. Some said she was a housewife named Amy Camus. Capitol 10″ LP *Voice Of The Xtabay* was a no. 1 album '50; strange compositions/arrangements by her husband Moises Vivianco (with Conjunto Folklorico Peruano), said to be based on Inca legends, highlighted her unusual vocal ability. Next LP *Inca Taqui*, these later combined on 12″ LP with title of the first. Other LPs: *Legend Of The Sun Virgin* (no. 5 '52; reissued in Australia '85), *Fuego del Ande* (various Latin rhythms), *Mambo, Miracles*, the latter with arr. by Les BAXTER. Sleeves of LPs took advantage of voluptuous figure, strange costumes; she also appeared in low-budget films. She retired c.'62, but played three-week gig in NYC early '87.

SUMMER, Donna (*b* LaDonna Adrian Gaines, 31 Dec. '48, Boston, Mass.) USA pop singer. Sang in church as a child;

turned pro at Boston club the Psychedelic Supermarket and got role in German prod. of *Hair* '67; married actor Helmut Sommer (divorced '74), sang in Vienna Folk Opera prod. of *Porgy And Bess*; sang backup in German studios, met budding disco prod. Giorgio Moroder, had European hits; then 'Love To Love You Baby' made USA pop chart end '75: no. 2 hit used Moroder's thumpa-thumpa disco beat with 17 minutes of Summer's orgasmic sound effects; one of the first disco hits pulled an album of that title to no. 11. She turned out to have more talent than that, however; *A Love Trilogy* and *Four Seasons Of Love* '76 did well; *I Remember Yesterday* '77 went top 20 with clever synth juke-box single 'I Feel Love' at no. 6; 2-disc concept *Once Upon A Time* '77 with lyrics mostly by Summer was again top 30; then eight top 5 singles '78-80 (three at no. 1 plus duet 'No More Tears' with Barbra STREISAND), three 2-disc no. 1 albums: *Live And More* '78 incl. Jimmy WEBB's 'MacArthur Park' (no. 1) and 'Heaven Knows'; *Bad Girls* '79 incl. no. ones 'Hot Stuff' and 'Bad Girls', no. 2 'Dim All The Lights'; *On The Radio – Greatest Hits* '79 incl. 'Last Dance' (from a film; single won two Grammies, 2-disc soundtrack *Thank God It's Friday* was top 10), 'On The Radio' (no. 5 hit written by Moroder/Summer, covered by Emmylou HARRIS), duet with Streisand. Lawsuit with Casablanca label run by Neil Bogart (1943-82) freed her to switch to David GEFFEN's new Geffen label; sales slipped but were still good: *The Wanderer* '80 incl. no. 3 title single, also material with a born-again Christian message (she no longer wanted the gay following which came with being a disco queen). *Donna Summer* '82 was prod. by Quincy JONES; *She Works Hard For The Money* '83 on Mercury was back in top 10 with no. 3 hit title single; *Cats Without Claws* '84 reached top 40. 'Highway Runner' (from LP prod. by Moroder, rejected by Geffen) was heard in film/soundtrack album *Fast Times At Ridgemount High* '82. With 25 Hot 100 singles '75-84 and 13 hit LPs, Summer has lasted longer than most who came from disco and deserved to, a hard-working pro with excellent vocal equipment who has won four Grammies: 'Last Dance' '78 (R&B), 'Hot Stuff' '79 (rock), 'He's A Rebel' '83 and 'Forgive Me' '84 (inspirational). She

recorded Gene LEES' song 'Let It Live' for a video on the life of Pope John Paul II '87, arr. by H. B. BARNUM; she was playing Lake Tahoe, sisters Dara and Mary singing backup; hit single 'Dinner With Gershwin' from LP *All Systems Go* '87.

SUN, Joe (*b* James Paulson, 25 Sep. '43, Rochester, Minn.) Underrated country-blues singer. Grew up on a farm and was initially interested in rock'n'roll, working at various jobs incl. DJ work in Minnesota, Madison, Wisconsin and Florida. He sang as Jack Daniels in Chicago clubs with semi-pro bands but had no confidence in his guitar playing; inspired by a Mickey NEWBURY record he changed direction, went to Nashville, started his own graphic company called the Sun Shop, became a well-known promo man, finally recording almost accidentally for Ovation Records '79: first single 'Old Flames (Can't Hold A Candle To You)' went top 20 '79, followed by hits 'I Came On Business', 'I'd Rather Go On Hurtin' ' '79-80. Ovation closed down its record division; he switched to Elektra but failed to make top 20; since '83 he has enjoyed success in Europe, touring with his band the Solar System and recording for Swedish-based Sonet. Albums incl. *Old Flames* '78, *Out Of Your Mind* '79, *Livin' On Honky Tonk Time* '80 on Ovation; *Storms Of Life* '81 on Intercord, *I Ain't Honky Tonkin' No More* '82 on Elektra, *The Sun Never Sets* '84 on Sonet.

SUN RA (*b* on Saturn; Zodiac sign Gemini; arrival zone USA; aka Le Sony'r Ra) Keyboards, other instruments; composer, bandleader. In another incarnation he closely resembled Herman 'Sonny' Blount, *b* c. May '14, Birmingham, Alabama; played piano and wrote arr. for Fletcher HENDERSON band at Chicago's Club DeLisa '46-7. Formed trio, built it into a rehearsal band, soon to become the Arkestra. He played piano with Eugene Wright and his Dukes of Swing on the Chess brothers' Aristocrat label '48; the group incl. Hobart Dotson on trumpet, Yusef LATEEF, vocal group the Dozier Boys; on Chess '54 with Red Saunders, also possibly with Wynonie Harris on Route 66; meanwhile first known records as leader early '50s with Stuff SMITH, later issued on

Deep Purple (aka *Dreams Come True*) on his own Saturn label. *Sun Song* '56 and *Sound Of Joy* '58 on Delmark were seminal; the first, originally on Transition, incl. 'Call For All Demons', 'Brainville', etc. as idiosyncratic and witty as the contemporary work of Thelonious MONK, advancing the colours of big band jazz in the manner of Duke ELLINGTON, others; e.g. 'Possession' is a lovely ballad in the Tadd DAMERON mould. They already used unusual instrumentation for the time: electric guitar, tympani; also Julian Priester on trombone (*b* '35, Chicago; later with Ellington), John Gilmore on tenor (*b* '31, Summit, Ms.; also worked and/or recorded with Art BLAKEY, McCoy TYNER, Freddie HUBBARD, Elmo HOPE, Andrew HILL), Pat Patrick on baritone (*b* Laurdine Patrick, Nov. '29; also worked with James MOODY, Quincy JONES, Ellington, Latin bands incl. Mongo SANTAMARIA); Von FREEMAN had also played with the band. They left Chicago '60 for Montreal gig where the club owner expected a rock'n'roll band, their costumes and lighting assuming other-world aspects; they ended up in NYC with no money. For the next 25 years they were seen as weird: 'I'm actually painting pictures of infinity with my music, and that's why a lot of people can't understand it,' said Ra, who told his soloists to play 'free' years before the experimental era of the late '60s; the band stayed together because it regarded the big band still an important mode of contemporary black music and even though Ra is a hard-driving leader ('I tell my Arkestra that all humanity is some kind of restricted limitation, but they're in the Ra jail, and it's the best in the world'). They were sometimes known as the Solar Arkestra, the Band From Outer Space, the Astro-Intergalactic-Infinity Arkestra. Gilmore, Patrick and Marshall Allen on reeds incl. oboe (*b* 25 May '24, Louisville, Ky.), Ronnie Boykins on electric bass (through '66), others took other gigs to eat, helped the band record on Saturn: LPs available at the band's gigs or at a few shops, in plain sleeves and with no discographical information. Sun Ra has influenced many; some say that it was meeting him that helped John COLTRANE to find his path and kick his drug habit. His music is no longer considered weird, the rest of the world having

caught up with his long-distance vision; the band still come from Saturn, but their Halloween costumes now have a strong African flavour; Ra plays keyboards incl. synths, and most members of the band also play percussion instruments; the act incl. exciting bouts of African-style drumming, furious duels among the reedmen (playing superbly even while chasing one another round the platform), dancing and singing: they may stop playing to march round chanting 'Space is the place!' until the listener would fly with them wherever they want to go; they might pause in the middle of all this to play Ellington's 'Lightnin' ', Jimmie LUNCEFORD's 'Yeah Man!', both from '32, or Henderson's 'Big John Special' '34: they carry with them the whole history of black music. Saturn LPs *Jazz In Silhouette*, *The Nubians Of Plutonia*, *The Magic City*, *Astro-Black*, *Atlantis*, *Angels & Demons At Play*, *Planet Earth*, *Bad And Beautiful*, several others recorded between '55 and '72 once available on Impulse; many other Saturns listed in discography by Tilman Stahl (Freudenberg, W. Germany) with such details as can be puzzled out. 2-disc *The Heliocentric Worlds Of Sun Ra* '65 was made for ESP, appeared on several other labels. Other LPs incl. '60s compilation *We Are The Future* on Savoy, *Picture Of Infinity* '68 on Black Lion, *It's After The End Of The World* '70 on MPS, two discs of *The Solar-Myth Approach* '70-1 first on Byg, now on Affinity; *Space Is The Place* '72 on Blue Thumb, *Live At The Gibus* '73 on Atlantic in France, *Cosmos* '76 on Cobra, *Live At Montreux* '76 on Inner City, *Unity* '77 and *Other Voices, Other Blues/Featuring John Gilmore* '78 on Horo, *Lanquidity* '78 and *On Mythic Worlds* '79 on Philly Jazz, *The Other Side Of The Sun* '78-9 on Sweet Earth, 2-disc *Sunrise In Different Dimensions* '80 on Hat Art (live from Willisau) incl. Henderson and Ellington tunes; *Strange Celestial Road* c.'80 on Rounder/Virgin, *Sun Ra Arkestra Meets Salah Ragab In Egypt* '83 on Praxis (Greece), made in Cairo; also *Love In Outer Space* '83 on Leo; *A Night In East Berlin* released '87 on Leo captures act as well as any. Ra played piano and celeste in Walt Dickerson Quartet '66 on MGM, made piano and vibes duo LP *Visions* '78 on Steeplechase with Dickerson; there are also two LPs of piano solos '71 on Improvising

Artists. *Reflections In Blue* '86 on Black Saint, made in Milan, is a joyous tribute to the Swing Era, original compositions (some by Patrick) in the style of the big bands of yore.

SUN Records Label formed '52 in Memphis, Tenn. by former DJ Sam Phillips (*b* 5 Jan. '23, Florence, Ala.), who bought studio at 706 Union Ave. '50 for Memphis Recording Service, for weddings etc., noticed that he had the only convenient studio for many local black artists, began prod. hits for Chess, RPM, Duke etc. with B. B. KING, Bobby 'Blue' BLAND, Howlin' WOLF, Earl HOOKER, Walter HORTON, Rosco Gordon (local musician who helped launch King, Bland, Johnny ACE; had R&B hits '52, came back '60 with 'Just A Little Bit': compilations on Ace USA). 'Rocket 88' by Jackie BRENSTON (Ike TURNER band) was R&B no. 1 '51. First hit on Sun was raw, rowdy 'Bear Cat' by Rufus THOMAS '53; others incl. sides by Junior PARKER, Billy 'The Kid' Emerson (*b* 21 Dec. '29, Tarpon Springs, Fla.; compilation *Crazy 'Bout Automobiles* on Charly UK) and the Prisonaires (guests at Tennessee State Pen.). His greatest success was Elvis PRESLEY, a white kid who sang like a black: his first record was made in July '54; Phillips sold his masters and contract to RCA late '55 and always maintained he'd done the right thing: trying to hold on to Presley would have meant dealing with his manager, the odious Col. Tom Parker, and Phillips used the money to develop his other white kids. Carl PERKINS' rockabilly classic 'Blue Suede Shoes' was Sun's first national pop hit (no. 2 '56 in Billboard's country, R&B, pop charts; no. 1 in *Cashbox*); Johnny CASH's 'I Walk The Line' '55 pared down the Sun sound to a country edge (no. 2 country, top 20 pop '55); Roy ORBISON cut 'Ooby Dooby' at Sun, went on to greater success elsewhere; Jerry Lee LEWIS merged rockabilly with his inimitable piano pounding on 'Whole Lotta Shakin' Goin' On', the first of three top 10 hits '57-8. There were other legendary rockabillies, less successful at the time: Mack Self, Malcolm Yelvington, Warren Smith, Billy Riley; original Sun singles have spiralled in value although almost everything has been reissued on LP. Charlie RICH and Bill JUSTIS were among studio

talents at Sun who also had solo careers. The '50s was Sun's golden decade: with the phenomenon of rockabilly itself and Sun's raw sound, untreated except for a tape delay echo, a new era had been introduced; recording continued through the '60s, but Phillips (by now a millionaire) followed other interests in hotels, mining, radio; he sold Sun '69 to Shelby SINGLETON. Memphis remained a musical hotbed, but it was left to Stax and Hi labels to discover SOUL music. Sun reissues are marketed by Singleton's SSS in USA, on Charly in UK (incl. superb boxed sets, anthologies). The old studio had been sold; leased early '87 by local musician Gary Hardy for recording, public tours: no changes except for 14-track console in control room.

SUNNYLAND SLIM (*b* Albert Luandrew, 5 Sep. '07, Vance, Ms.) Blues singer, pianist. Self-taught as a child; toured/hoboed through the South, settled in Memphis late '20s, Chicago from '42; first recorded on Specialty, Aristocrat, Apollo, other labels late '40s with Jump Jackson, Muddy WATERS, others; established '50s as leading blues pianist. Toured with Otis RUSH '63, with American Blues Festival '64 incl. Europe, USSR; with Chicago All Stars '69, Ann Arbor Blues Festival '70, etc. Recorded for many small labels in the '50s, Prestige/Bluesville '60 (*Slim's Shout*, with KING CURTIS), Storyville in Copenhagen '64 (*Portraits In Blues* Vol. 9), Jewel '71 (*Sad & Lonesome*), Sonet '73 in Sweden (*Legacy Of The Blues* series); many more: on Delmark '63, again with J. B. HUTTO '68; on Blue Horizon '68 with Walter HORTON, Johnny SHINES; on Adelphi '69, his own Airway label '74, others incl. solo *Sunnyland Train* '83, combo *Chicago Jump* '85 on Chicago-based Red Beans label. *Old Friends: Together For The First Time* '80 on Earwig incl. Horton, Kansas City Red, Floyd Honeyboy Edwards, Floyd Jones (*b* 21 July '17, Marianna, Ark.; recorded for Chess, Vee Jay).

SUPERSAX Band formed by Med Flory and Buddy CLARK that played Charlie PARKER's solos in unison, reached unexpectedly wide audience: made debut '72; first album *Supersax Plays Bird* won Grammy '73. Reedman/arr. Meredith 'Med' Flory (*b* 27

Aug. '26, Logansport, Ind.) had left music after studio work in NYC, then West Coast; was acting, writing TV scripts, when he conceived Supersax with bassist Clark (who left '75). Other LPs: *Salt Peanuts (Supersax Plays Bird Vol. 2)*, *Supersax Plays Bird With Strings*, *Chasin' The Bird*, *Dynamite!* '78; three LPs with The L.A. Voices on CBS incl. *Embraceable You* '84, *Straighten Up And Fly Right* '86. Lou Levy on piano (*b* 5 Mar. '28, Chicago) was a member from end '73 to '80s; also records with Chubby Jackson (*Bebop Revisited* on Xanadu), as accompanist for Peggy LEE, Nancy WILSON, Frank SINATRA (*My Way* on Reprise) etc. Many musicians who've toured with Supersax incl. reedman Jack Nimitz (*b* 11 Jan. '30, Washington DC), bassist Frank De La Rosa (*b* 26 Dec. '33, El Paso, Texas), Conte CANDOLI; Warne MARSH was with them in Chicago '76 when he took time off to make *All Music* on Nessa, with Levy, drummer Jake Hanna, bassist Fred Atwood.

SUPERTRAMP UK rock group formed in London '69 by keyboardist/vocalist Rick Davies, who enlisted support of Dutch millionaire Sam Miesegaes for group Joint. When they split he recruited Roger Hodgson (vocals, guitar) and formed Daddy, which became Supertramp with addition of Dave Winthrop, sax, Bob Miller, drums; Richard Palmer, guitar; Hodgson doubled on bass. *Supertramp* '70 on A&M flopped (not released in USA); Miller was replaced by Kevin Currie, Frank Farrell added on bass; *Indelibly Stamped* '71 didn't sell; all but Davies/Hodgson left, incl. the millionaire. Regrouped with former Alan Bown Set players Dougie Thomson on bass, John Helliwell, sax; Bob C. Benberg (*b* Robert Siebenberg, USA) joined from pub-rockers Bees Make Honey; they spent a year rehearsing/writing before *Crime Of The Century* '74 prod. by Ken Scott (ex-David BOWIE): concept LP contrasted vocal styles of writers Davies and Hodgson. Electric piano and sax were trademarks, but band remained faceless (a tiny picture appeared on back of sleeve). Nevertheless, quiet catchy pop found them audience in stagnant mid-'70s pop scene: 'Dreamer' was first hit single at no. 13 UK '75, 'Bloody Well Right' top 40 USA; *Crime* a no. 4 LP UK, top 40 USA. Quality of songs assured

by year's stockpile; albums *Crisis? What Crisis?* '76, *Even In The Quietest Moments* '77 (self-prod., without Scott), *Breakfast In America* '79 scored: the last was their biggest, at no. 3 UK, 1 USA (even the first album, finally issued USA '78, reached top 200 albums). They were too well ordered: 2-disc live *Paris* '80 incl. version of hit 'Dreamer' (no. 15 USA) indistinguishable from the studio one. Heavy tour to promote 16m sales of *Breakfast* worsened differences between Davies/Hodgson; . . . *famous last words* . . . '82 saw these come to a head, with Davies' bluesier approach next to Hodgson's neat, ordered pop: latter left after '83 tour to go solo as 'It's Raining Again' charted USA/UK. Supertramp made *Brother Where You Bound* '85 with guest Dave Gilmour; compilation *Autobiography* '86; Hodgson made well-received *In The Eye Of The Storm* '84 (top 50 USA).

SUPREMES, The USA female vocal group from Detroit: the undisputed first among girl groups, queens of charts and airwaves in the '60s. Classic lineup: Florence Ballard (*b* 30 June '43; *d* 21 Feb. '76); Diana Ross (*b* Diane Earle, 26 Mar. '44); Mary Wilson (*b* 6 Mar. '44), all from a Detroit housing project. Began working together late '50s, met the TEMPTATIONS, then called the Primes; called themselves the Primettes. Went to MOTOWN '61 after Ballard (then seen as group's leader) suggested name change to Supremes; Berry Gordy saw more in them than in his other girl groups (Marvelettes, Vandellas): they would become his ultimate crossover group, and indeed it was in their heyday that the Billboard R&B chart was abolished for a year, black/white charts being virtually identical. Special attention was paid to their education in the Motown 'finishing school', where they were taught movement and deportment; some early releases were flops; first hit was 'When The Lovelight Starts Shining Through His Eyes' (USA top 30 '63), but when HOLLAND-DOZIER-HOLLAND began prod. and writing their material it was megahit time: three no. 1 hits in a row in '64 were 'Where Did Our Love Go', 'Baby Love', 'Come See About Me'; in '65 'Stop! In The Name Of Love', 'Back In My Arms Again', 'I Hear A Symphony' were all no. 1, 'Nothing But Heartaches' in top 20; in '66 'You

Can't Hurry Love' and 'You Keep Me Hanging On' were no. 1, plus 'My World Is Empty Without You' and 'Love Is Like An Itching In My Heart' in top 10. Most of these charted high in UK too, incl. two no. ones; but storm clouds were already forming: it was clear that Ross was seen as the group's leader, because she was Gordy's favourite, but also – to be fair – because the Motown education probably did her the most good: she was the star material, but all of this was to Ballard's discomfort. After two more no. ones in early '67, 'Love Is Here And Now You're Gone' and 'The Happening' (the latter show-type tune departing from the soulful, danceable formula for the first time among the hits, though not in the stage act), Ballard left, an event forever in the 'did she jump or was she pushed' category, replaced by Cindy Birdsong (*b* 15 Dec. '39, New Jersey), a fine singer from Patti LaBelle's Blue Belles. The group was then known as Diana Ross & The Supremes for more hits incl. 'Reflections' (no. 2), 'In And Out Of Love' (no. 9) '67; 'Forever Came Today' (top 30; their last collaboration with H-D-H), 'Love Child' (no. 1) '68, 'I'm Livin' In Shame' (no. 10) and 'Someday We'll Be Together' (no. 1) '69. They recorded with the Temptations, octet hits '68-9 incl. 'I'm Gonna Make You Love Me' (no. 2); Ross left, replaced by Jean Terrell (*b* c.'44, Texas); they recorded with the Four Tops '70-1 incl. 'River Deep – Mountain High' (top 15) but there were no more chart toppers; Birdsong left '72, replaced by Lynda Lawrence; hits had virtually dried up. Terrell left '73 replaced by Scherrie Payne (*b* 14 Nov. '44); later replacements incl. Karen Jackson and Susaye Greene, but by end of '70s they had all quit. Ballard had received a financial settlement from Motown which was soon spent; her solo career began with a signing to ABC, but her first single flopped: she was not allowed to mention her Supremes background in press releases and the single did not even get publicity in Detroit owing to a newspaper strike; she died penniless, having tried unsuccessfully to sue Motown and her former partners. Wilson later led a group billed as Mary Wilson and the Supremes; Ross has had showbiz solo success; the hit musical *Dreamgirls* '81 was based on their story and brought back the painful back-

stage machinations; Wilson published a book about her life as a dreamgirl '87 and the story is well-covered in Nelson George's excellent *Where Did Our Love Go?* '85, a history of Motown. Their splendid 19 top 10 hits '64-70, 12 at no. 1, are as remarkable in their way as Glenn Miller's hits of '39-43 as souvenirs of their era. Compilations incl. 3-disc *Anthology*, vols. of *Greatest Hits* (two on one CD).

SURMAN, John (*b* John Douglas Surman, 30 Aug. '44, Tavistock, Devon, UK) Baritone and soprano saxophones, bass clarinet, synthesisers. From music family; studied in London '60s, meanwhile playing with Alexis Korner, Mike Westbrook; has become world famous soloist and composer, innovating by extending the upper range of the baritone, but like Albert Mangelsdorff in Germany choosing to remain in Europe. Played on John McLaughlin LP *Extrapolation* '69, on LPs with Westbrook, trombonist/pianist/composer Mike Gibbs (*b* 25 Sep. '37, Salisbury, now Zimbabwe), bassist Miroslav Vitous (toured in quartet '79-82); formed trio SOS '73 with reedmen Mike Osborne (*b* 28 Sep. '41, Hereford), Alan Skidmore (*b* 21 Apr. 42, London), LP on Ogun '75 incl. synth, Osborne and Skidmore doubling on percussion to make sound of larger group. His musical roots incl. folk, ethnic and church music as well as jazz; his commissions incl. church and ballet music. Own LPs incl. *The Trio* '70 on Pye (Barre Phillips, bass; Stu Martin, drums); solo *Westering Home* '72 and *Morning Glory* '73 (with Terje Rypdal), both on Island; duos with Stan Tracey (*Sonatinas*) and vocalist Karin Krog (*Cloudline Blue*) '78, solo *Upon Reflection* '79, award-winning *The Amazing Adventures Of Simon Simon* '81 (with Jack DeJohnette), *Such Winters Of Memory* (with Krog and drummer Pierre Favre) '83, solo *Withholding Pattern* '85, all on ECM. (Karin Krog Bergh, *b* 15 May '37, Oslo, is one of Europe's finest vocalists; also made *Two Of A Kind* and *A Song For You* with pianist Bengt Hallberg, *Hi-Fly* with Archie Shepp, *I Remember You* with Warne Marsh, Red Mitchell.)

SURVIVOR USA AOR band formed '78, Chicago: Jim Peterik (keyboards, guitar),

Frankie Sullivan (lead guitar): Peterik, from Ides of March (whose 'Vehicle' was no. 2 '70) had done solo *Don't Fight That Feeling* '76; Sullivan from local group Mariah. With vocalist David Bickler and a rhythm section they signed to Scotti Brothers label for eponymous LP debut '79; *Premonition* '81 was more heavy-metal oriented, yielding top 40 single 'Poor Man's Son'; actor/dir. Sylvester Stallone sent them the first 10 minutes of *Rocky III* and their response was 'Eye Of The Tiger', a USA/UK no. 1, title track of their next LP, the biggest selling single of '82: topped charts in half a dozen other countries and won Grammy for best rock vocal. Follow-up 'American Heartbeat' made only top 20 USA but was title track of compilation LP and theme of USA football programme on UK TV. After *Caught In The Game* '83, Bickler (with voice problems after heavy touring) was replaced by Jimi Jamison, who inspired band on *Vital Signs* '84, incl. hit 'I Can't Hold Back', prod. (like first LP) by Ron Nevison, with JEFFERSON STARSHIP singer Mickey Thomas and keyboardist Peter Wolf sitting in. Tried film music again with 'The Moment Of Truth' from *The Karate Kid* '84, but 'Burning Heart', 'Eye Of The Tiger' soundalike for *Rocky IV* put them back in USA/UK charts, also brought criticism of limited approach which they will have to vary before Rocky XXV. This isn't impossible, as Peterik/Sulllivan also wrote 'Rockin' Into The Night' for .38 SPECIAL, title song for film *Heavy Metal*. Album *When Seconds Count* '86.

SUTCH, David (*b* Harrow, Middlesex, '42) British rock'n'roll singer. As Screamin' Lord Sutch formed band the Savages '58, took cues from Screamin' Jay HAWKINS, old horror movies: he imitated Jack The Ripper on stage and was carried on in a coffin; wore a toilet seat for a hat. Never had any hits; Atlantic album *Lord Sutch And Heavy Friends* '70 incl. ex-Savages Nicky HOPKINS, Jeff BECK, Jimmy Page but availed him nought, ditto *Hands Of Jack The Ripper* '72. He also tried running a pirate radio station. He's run for Parliament several times as the Raving Loony Party: he never gets many votes, despite the fact that he often looks better than some of the other candidates. Compilations on Ace in UK.

SUTTON, Ralph (*b* 4 Nov. '22, Hamburg, Mo.) Pianist in NYC stride style, inspired by Fats WALLER and James P. JOHNSON, playing it very well indeed. Began in St Louis mid-'30s; with Jack TEAGARDEN band before and after US Army service; to NYC late '40s and was well known playing intermissions at Eddie CONDON's; to West Coast, replacing Earl HINES at San Francisco's Hangover Club while Hines toured '57; played at jazz festivals, etc.; to Aspen, Col. '64, worked in a supper club; played from '65 in Denver with Ten Giants of Jazz, soon called World's Greatest Jazz Band, on many albums with them; also *The Compleat Bud Freeman*, own LPs: *Bix Beiderbecke Suite And Piano Portraits* '50 on Commodore, & *The All-Stars* '54 (from the Hangover) on Jazz Archives, solos *Off The Cuff* '76 on Audiophile, *Quartet* '77 on Storyville USA, *Live* '79 on Flyright UK; also with Jess STACY on Ace Of Hearts, with Ruby BRAFF on Blue Angel Jazz Club, others.

SWALLOW, Steve (*b* 4 Oct. '40, NYC) Bassist, composer. Began on piano and trumpet, switched to bass at 18; played and recorded with George RUSSELL, Jimmy GIUFFRE, Stan GETZ; with Gary BURTON late '60s. Lived on West Coast, played more and more fusion, switched to electric bass c.'70 and became a master of it, not trying to play it like an amplified upright instrument as most do in jazz but with a pick and using guitar-type fingering. Often rejoined Burton from '73. Played on several Carla BLEY albums since '78; also often worked with UK keyboardist, composer-arranger Mike Gibbs. As leader: *Home* '80 on ECM (Swallow's settings of poems of Robert Creeley); *Carla* '87 on XtraWatt/ECM with Bley.

SWAMP DOGG (*b* Jerry Williams Jr, 12 July '42, Portsmouth, Va.) Singer, songwriter, producer. Began as Little Jerry Williams: first single 'Weenie Roast' for Mechanic label at age 12. R&B no. 32 hit 'Baby You're My Everything' '66 on Calla label; dropped 'Little' tag and became prod. at Atlantic, working with DRIFTERS, Wilson PICKETT, others; to Wally Roker's Canyon label '70, there encouraged to commence career as Swamp Dogg: ahead-of-its-time LP *Total Destruction To Your Mind* linked funk and nuttiness in manner later perpetrated by George Clinton, Bootsy Collins (*see* PARLIAMENT/FUNKADELIC). Canyon collapsed; moved on to Elektra for *Rat On* '71, to Cream for *Cuffed Collared And Tagged* '72 (incl. mini-hit version of John PRINE's 'Sam Stone'). *Gag A Maggot* '73, *Swamp Dogg's Greatest Hits* '76 on Stone Dogg label; *Have You Heard This Story* '74 on Island incl. 'Did I Stay Away Too Long', about a man who comes home to find wife in bed with another woman; *I'm Not Selling Out I'm Buying In* '81 on Tacoma incl. duet with Esther PHILLIPS on 'The Love We Got Ain't Worth Two Dead Flies'. Wrote Gene PITNEY '68 hit 'She's A Heartbreaker'; also songs for Freddie North, Z.Z. Hill, Irma THOMAS, Johnny PAYCHECK, etc. Ever outrageous, says he married very young because 'of the imperfections of the condoms of that period'.

SWAN, Billy (*b* 12 May '43, Cape Girardeau, Mo.) Country-rock singer, songwriter, studio musician, producer. Moved to Memphis '60, recorded under the guidance of Bill BLACK as a member of Milt Mirley and the Rhythm Steppers; one of the songs was Swan's 'Lover Please', later covered by Clyde MCPHATTER for a big hit '62: using the money he made, moved to Nashville '63 intending to write more but had no luck, working odd jobs around studios, publishing houses. Friendship with Tony Joe WHITE led to prod. his records, incl. million-selling 'Polk Salad Annie' '69. Worked in studio and band with Kris KRISTOFFERSON, appearing at Isle of White Festival '70; contract with Monument led to 'I Can Help' '74: his own song, simple production with Swan's swirling organ, neo-rockabilly style with irresistible melody was one of the biggest hits ever made in Nashville, no. 1 pop and country USA and charting in 18 countries. Spasmodic chart success since with 'Don't Be Cruel' (in the UK) and 'I'm Her Fool' '75, 'Just Want To Taste Your Wine' '76, 'Hello, Remember Me' '78; he remained a long-time member of Kristofferson's band and teamed with Randy Meisner, Jimmy Griffin and Robb Royer to form country-rock band Black Tie '86. Had healthy albums sales as he moved through Columbia '76-7, A&M '78-80, Epic '81-2; albums incl. *I Can Help* '74, *Rock'n'-*

Roll Moon '75, *At His Best* '76 on Monument; *I'm Into Lovin' You* '81 on Epic; incredibly, no albums listed as available in '88. With Black Tie: *When The Night Falls* '86 on Bench Records.

SWEET, The UK bubblegum pop group formed '68 from remains of Wainwright's Gentleman, pop covers band incl. drummer Mick Tucker, vocalist Brian Connolly; with bassist Steve Priest and Frank Torpey on guitar they became Sweetshop, shortened to Sweet as Andy Scott replaced Torpey. After four flop singles they linked with prod. Phil Wainman, young writers CHINN & CHAPMAN '70 for long string of bubblegum hits in the mould of USA's Archies, Ohio Express, etc. with same silly titles ('Funny Funny', 'Co-Co' '71) and catchy tunes, the band willing to risk ridicule, dressing up in character. 'Little Willy' and 'Wig Wam Bam' '72 (the last requiring headdresses) followed by somewhat heavier fare: 'Blockbuster', 'Hell Raiser', 'Ballroom Blitz', 'Teenage Rampage' '73 (all these except the first top 5 UK). In the androgynous heyday of David BOWIE, Sweet were not left out: Connolly's blond locks appealed to boys and girls, while Priest affected camp. Live act was rather more powerful (they composed their own rockier B sides); tiring of manipulation they split from producers, for a time made passable imitation of Chinnichap pop ('Fox On The Run' was no. 2 UK and their third top 5 in USA), but as HM edge took over their hits faded, falling between two stools: they lacked rock credibility while forsaking pop that made them. Connolly left '79; album *Identity Crisis* '81 was not even issued in UK. Scott recorded solo on Statik and Priest became USA-based session player; Connolly fronted New Sweet mid-'80s.

SWEET HONEY IN THE ROCK Unaccompanied gospel and black music vocal group formed '73 in Washington DC by Bernice Johnson Reagon, as part of the workshop of the Black Repertory Theatre Company. She had been active in the civil rights movement in Albany, Alabama; from '62 sang as a member of Freedom Singers of SNCC (Student Nonviolent Co-ordinating Committee); against this backdrop collected source material from urban and rural blacks, later worked as dir. of black culture at Smithsonian Institution in Washington; also sang with the Harambree Singers late '60s, an all-black female group and precurser of Sweet Honey, recorded *Give Your Hands To Struggle* '75 on Paredon, subtitled 'the evolution of a freedom fighter'. Debut *Sweet Honey In The Rock* '76 on Flying Fish owed much to political struggle, but primary focus is on greater humanity, a hallmark of their work against racism, sexism, destruction of the environment and kindred issues. Debut incl. Evelyn Harris, Patricia Johnson, Carol Lynne Maillard, Louise Robinson and Reagon. 'A Woman' from *B'lieve I'll Run On . . . See What The End's Gonna Be* on Redwood (*see* Holly NEAR) also appeared on 3-disc *No Nukes* set on Asylum '79, though they were not in film; *B'lieve* was named best women's album of '79 by USA's National Association of Independent Record Distributors. *Good News* '81 incl. Reagon's 'Chile Your Waters Run Red Through Soweto', later performed by Billy BRAGG. From '77 they experimented with concerts being signed for those with impaired hearing; this had such positive reaction that it became permanent feature, 'signers' using ASL (American Sign Language) and accorded equal status with singers; since late '70s this has been Shirley Childress Johnson. Subject of documentary *Gotta Make This Journey* (Eye of the Storm Productions) '83; *We All . . . Everyone Of Us* '83 incl. standard 'Study War No More', incl. with tracks by Pete SEEGER, Near, Dick GAUGHAN etc. on 'songs for survival' album *Out Of The Darkness* on Fire On The Mountain. *Feel Something Drawing On Me* and *The Other Side* '85 drew on religious and political foundations; by this time the group incl. Reagon, Harris, Ysaye Barnwell, Aisha Kahill and Yasmeen Bheti Williams. Reagon was a consultant on TV documentary series *Eyes On The Prize* '86 on civil rights movement; released solo album *River Of Life, Harmony: One* '87. All albums on Flying Fish, except as noted; some also on Spindrift in UK; *Breaths* (a compilation) and *Live At Carnegie Hall* appeared on both Flying Fish and on Cooking Vinyl in UK. Apart from their musical achievement they provide an authentic voice for those carrying on the civil rights struggle while staying close to their black gospel roots.

SWEET TALKS, The Highlife band formed in Ghana '73, became one of the most popular, playing uptempo, modern style. Began under joint leadership of Smart Nkansah and A. B. Crentsil as resident band at The Talk Of The Town hotel in Tema, with series of hit albums incl. *Kusum Beat* '75; Smart left to form the Black Hustlers '76, replaced by Eric Agyeman: band with Agyeman on guitar, vocalist Crentsil, J. Y. Thorty on drums, Prince Nana Afful on keyboards, plus horns and percussionists, was renamed Super Sweet Talks, recorded *Adam And Eve* '77, then to Los Angeles for highlife classic *Hollywood Party*, incl. hits 'Nawa To Be Husband', 'Only Your Voice Juliana', 'Angelina'. By '80 faced with uncertain economic climate and declining record industry, they split to pursue separate careers: Crentsil re-formed the band as the Super Sweet Talks International for earthy, even risqué LPs *Mewo Road*, *Moses* and *Tantie Alaba*, also impressive *Masters* '85 with Thorty; Agyeman was even more successful with his Kokoroko Band, albums *Wonko Menko*, *Highlife Safari* and *Kona Kohwe*, the last with Crentsil and Thomas Frempong (drummer, vocalist who also did highlife hit *Aye Yi* '85). Agyeman also sessioned with Crentsil, Atakora Manu, Nana Tuffuor; featured prominently with Crentsil and Frempong on *Pete Pete* '83 by Highlife Stars One, joining with members of OSIBISA to make Ghana's first supergroup.

SWING in music The manipulation of time in performance, according to the performer's skill and personality, the mood he/she is in, the nature of the song or tune being played or sung, many other factors: part of the essence of jazz and blues, hence infl. on all pop music. The first great master of swing was Louis ARMSTRONG, who placed a note slightly before the beat or behind it, stretched phrases or notes across the beat, sometimes seemed to ignore bar lines altogether; this is why his records beginning '25 astonished everyone: others were doing it, but none with such mastery. First solos recorded by Lester YOUNG ('Shoe Shine Boy', 'Lady Be Good' '36) are perfect examples of swing. For bigger bands, the best arrangers – Don REDMAN and Fletcher HENDERSON (who were turned on by Armstrong), Benny CARTER, Sy OLIVER, etc. – wrote 'charts' that could swing if the right musicians were playing them; a great deal depended on lead players in each section (*see* BIG BAND ERA). Duke ELLINGTON and Jimmie LUNCEFORD were also reliable for swing in '30s, Count BASIE from '36; then in '40 Ellington's bassist Jimmy BLANTON revised the playing of that instrument with his own definition of swing. By then the word was common: earlier musicians spoke of it as 'getting off' or 'taking a Boston', and a swinging ensemble was 'in the groove': sometimes it happened, sometimes not; the band had to be in the mood. In the Big Band Era from '35 jazz-oriented dance bands suddenly became big, hence 'swing era'. There are many stories about Fats WALLER (usually, or Armstrong) being asked what swing was, replying 'If you don't know what it is, don't mess with it', or 'If you gotta ask, you'll never know.' Danceable medium tempo is best for swinging, *pace* popular conception of loud, fast 'killer diller'. Billie HOLIDAY, the greatest of jazz singers, always sang after the beat, the last word of a phrase fractionally late, the essence of languor: passionate, resigned or humorous, depending on the song (e.g. 'Back In Your Own Back Yard', 'On The Sentimental Side', both recorded same day in '38). Thelonious MONK was his own rhythm section; his tunes had swing built in: one of the best recorded illustrations of what swings and what doesn't is take one of 'Hackensack', made in London '71 for Black Lion by Monk, Art BLAKEY, Al McKibbon, issued in complete set '85 on Mosaic: Monk re-enters in the wrong place, intentionally or not, after Blakey's solo, and stays there: the rest of the take without Monk's unique beat is recognisably his tune, yet sounds like something a cocktail pianist might invent. The original home of rhythmic subtlety was in jazz and blues; blacks were thought to have 'natural rhythm' in former times, but the truth is more interesting than racism: blacks kept the aspect of music as a means of social intercourse as well as of self-expression from Africa, aspects which had been played down in European music; Mozart, Beethoven, Chopin were great improvisors, but today's concert pianists can't do it at all. (But classical music can 'swing' when orchestra and conductor are 'in the groove': Wilhelm Furtwängler was a terrible con-

ductor technically, but he was improvising on the podium; when the band could figure out what he wanted, magic happened. Hence his record of Schumann's Fourth Symphony is a great soaring arc of song.) Blacks had less to lose from self-expression, while hundreds of years of European protestantism on top of 3000 years of Aristotelian consciousness left whites uptight. Slaves in America were not allowed to learn to read in most of the South; dependent upon the spoken word for communication, they were forced to live in the 'now', which is where you have to be to manipulate time, while whites felt guilty about the past or anxious about the future, rarely living in the present. (Hence Bix BEIDERBECKE was the first great white jazz musician, but his Midwestern, middle-class family didn't even listen to the records.) Further, rhythm is at the centre of African music (harmony in European music): the performer who is swinging is commenting on the beat, which is somewhere else; hence to some extent swing is a polyrhythmic phenomenon. Whites learned quickly; Jews and Italians were especially prominent among white jazz musicians from the '20s; in the UK a significant number of good jazz musicians have been Scottish: Benny CARTER, whose UK band in the '30s contained many Scots, said it was because 'Wherever they are, there's happiness.' The first European jazz musician of consequence was Django REINHARDT, a Gypsy; among white singers who swung, Connie BOSWELL was from New Orleans and Mildred BAILEY was part Indian. There were many good white jazz musicians from New Orleans (many playing with Bob CROSBY), then others who learned by listening and practising. Country music (bluegrass, honky tonk, western swing) often showed rhythmic swagger. Much was learned post-WWII: white rhythm sections improved and Frank SINATRA made songs his own partly by phrasing past the beat, but many pop singers remained tied to the ground beat. Neither Shirley BASSEY nor Joan BAEZ are known for their swing, while critical reservations about Linda RONSTADT versions of Sinatra's type of songs are wholly justified (which does not mean that she does not bring other virtues to more suitable material). Rock is based on the blues, where melodic/rhythmic elements are set against each other more subtly than in jazz; blues-drenched Van MORRISON in his 'Into The Mystic' '70 has each line of the lyric beginning after the beat and ending before it, while the bass figure seems to ignore it: a gentle rocking results. A good rhythm section in any genre doesn't play precisely on the beat, hitting the listener on the head with it; classic Elvis PRESLEY of early '56 imparted urgency by rushing the beat, while ROLLING STONES drummer Charlie Watts was once criticised for consistently playing behind the beat, perhaps the essence of the best rock: the Stones swung on their best albums (but Mick Jagger never did); Morrison's bands nearly always swing, as did those of Ry COODER, LITTLE FEAT, Bob DYLAN (at least through *Street Legal*), other classic rock, much of country rock: on Emmylou HARRIS LPs the musicians listen to one another rather than to the beat; *Save The World* by Richard DOBSON and *Smokin' The Dummy* by Terry ALLEN have fine backing bands. In all genres, live gigs can be better than studio dates; an audience helps, as dancers did in the Swing Era, but jumping up and down is not dancing. Much pop today has been sterilised by the infl. of disco's drum machine and other studio toys. A good musician can swing *against* a metronome, but a collection of metronomes does not swing, and musicians learning to play by imitating a metronome can never swing. Too many records today are overproduced: Bonnie RAITT albums often had rhythmic swagger, but *Nine Lives* '86 does not. Production and technology are easily overdone; in a wall of sound there is no swing because there is no space and the music cannot breathe: Phil SPECTOR and MOTOWN were not good models in the long run. Rhythm & blues had a rhythmic looseness which led to rock'n'roll; where R&B roots are alive good music results, as in ROCKIN' JIMMY AND THE BROTHERS OF THE NIGHT, an excellent bar band recorded as such; but rock has dominated popular music for too long thanks to the stupidity and greed of broadcasters and record companies, so that each generation of young people is now more familiar with studio technology than with its own musical roots. A reaction may be on the way: some fans are now looking for swing, whether they know it or not.

SWINGING BLUE JEANS UK beat group formed '57 in Liverpool as skifflers the Swinging Bluegenes: guitarist Ray Ennis (*b* 26 May '42), Les Braid (*b* 15 Sep. '41) on bass, Norman Kuhlke (*b* 17 June '42) on drums, Paul Moss on banjo replaced '60 by Ralph Ellis (*b* 8 Mar. '42). Played in Hamburg and at the Cavern, where their guest nights billed SEARCHERS, BEATLES, GERRY AND THE PACEMAKERS, etc. They had hits on HMV of which biggest was cover of USA hit 'Hippy Hippy Shake' (no. 2 '64), but like many contemporaries they suffered from lack of original material and (fans say) never adequately captured live act on record. They continued into the mid-'80s as a cabaret act, Braid moving to organ to make room for Mike Gregory on bass '67, Ellis replaced by Terry Sylvester '68 (both newcomers ex-Escorts), Gregory replaced '70 by Billy Kinsley (ex-Merseybeats); Sylvester went on to Manchester's HOLLIES and further changes ensued, Braid and Ennis enduring. *Shake! The Best Of The Swinging Blue Jeans* '86 is good 20-track compilation for fans.

SWINGLE SINGERS, The Vocal group formed by singer/arranger Ward Lamar Swingle (*b* 21 Sep. '27, Mobile, Ala.), who also played piano and alto sax. He gigged locally, got master's degree in music '51, Fulbright scholarship same year, studying piano in Paris with Walter Gieseking; taught in Iowa but moved to Paris permanently '56. Worked as arranger, accompanist, pianist; with vocal groups the Blue Stars, then Double Six Of Paris with Christiane Legrand (sister of Michel); they formed group to improve sightreading etc. singing Bach fugues etc. wordlessly, added bass and drums and had surprise hit LPs with light music of impressive quality: *Bach's Greatest Hits* '63 was top 15 USA; similar *Jazz Sebastian Bach* year in UK '64 (with Pierre Michelot on bass, drummer Guz Wallez), plus *Going Baroque* '64, *Anyone For Mozart?* '65, *Place Vendôme* with the MODERN JAZZ QUARTET '65; later on CBS with *Love Songs For Madrigals And Madriguys*, others.

SYKES, Roosevelt (*b* 31 Jan. '06, Elmar, Ark; *d* 17 July '83, New Orleans) Blues singer, songwriter and one of the greatest of all blues pianists. His brother Walter Sykes also played piano and sang; Roosevelt accompanied blues singers incl. Mary Johnson (Lonnie JOHNSON's wife until '32) as Sykes & Johnson on Champion '32, his sister Isabel on Bluebird '33; own records prolifically for Okeh, Paramount, Victor, Melotone, Columbia, Decca '33-43, often under names of Easy Papa Johnson, Dobby Bragg, Willie Kelly; on Decca as Rosy Sykes, The Honeydripper (from reputation as lady's man). On Specialty c.46 with Jump Jackson; on Victor again '45-9; worked club dates in Chicago with Lonnie Johnson c.'50. Appeared in films *Roosevelt Sykes: The Honeydripper* '61 (made in Belgium), *Roosevelt Sykes* '71, *Blues Under The Skin* '72 (France), documentary *The Devil's Music* '76 (BBC TV), etc. LPs: *The Honeydripper* on Prestige '60, *Blues* '61 on Folkways, *Roosevelt Sykes: Portraits In Blues Vol. 11* '66 on Storyville (made in Copenhagen); on Delmark '63-73: *Feel Like Blowin' My Horn, In Europe, Hard Drivin' Blues* with Homesick James (singer, played bass, guitar, harmonica; *b* John William Henderson, 30 Apr. '10, Somerville, Tenn.). Also *Blues & Ribald* '71 on Southland, *Blues From The Bottoms* '71 on 77 with Robert Pete Williams (singer, played guitar, harmonica; *b* 14 Mar. '14, Zachary, La.; *d* 31 Dec. '80, L.A.), *The Honeydripper's Duke's Mixture* c.'71 on French Barclay; also *Country Blues Piano Ace* on Yazoo, *Meet Roosevelt Sykes* on Jewel, *Urban Blues* on Fantasy with Little Brother MONTGOMERY, *Original Honeydripper* on Blind Pig. *Raining In My Heart* on Delmark collects United combo sides '51-3, some with Remo Biondi on violin.

SYLVIA (*b* Sylvia Kirby Allen, '57, Kokomo, Ind.) Pop-styled country singer with hits from '79 that sometimes crossed over to pop chart; also an artist: she made pencil portraits of visiting stars at the Little Nashville Opry in Indiana. Moved to Nashville after high school, worked as secretary in publishing offices, graduated from singing on demo tapes to back-up on records by Ronnie MILSAP, Charley PRIDE, Barbara MANDRELL; signed with RCA '79 and chart debut was 'You Don't Miss A Thing' '79. More hits incl. 'The Drifter' and 'The Matador', both no. 1 '81, top 5 hits 'Heart On The Mend' '81, 'Sweet Yesterday' and 'Nobody' '82 (last crossed over and sold a million). Albums incl. *Drifter* '81, *Sweet Yesterday* '82, *One Step Closer* '85 on RCA.

SZABO, Gabor (*b* 8 Mar. '36, Budapest, Hungary) Guitarist, composer. To USA '56; played with Chico HAMILTON, Gary McFARLAND, Charles LLOYD. Formed group with Cal TJADER and McFarland '68-9, recorded for Skye incl. an album with Lena HORNE; led quartets on West Coast, formed eclectic group Perfect Circle '75. Albums on Blue Thumb, CTI; on Impulse (now 2-disc *Greatest Hits* on MCA); also *Nightflight* '76 on Mercury, *Femme Fatale* on Pepita with Chick COREA.

SZYMCZYK, Bill (*b* 13 Feb. '43, Muskegon, Mich.) USA producer. Naval radar training led to interest in electronics, part-time job in recording studio while waiting to start student course: he never took it. Apprenticeship from '64 led to first prod. job *How To Play Electric Bass* '67 by Harvey Brooks; joined ABC as staff producer and prod. albums by B. B. KING incl. *Completely Well* and *Indianola, Mississippi*; prod. first two LPs for the JAMES GANG, continued with Joe WALSH solo (linking again when Walsh joined the EAGLES at his suggestion '75-6). Also with J. GEILS Band for *The Morning After* '71 and their next five LPs; went freelance. Always linked with trad. guitar rock; made name with 'heavier' acts but took over prod. Eagles when Glyn JOHNS left halfway through *On The Border* '74. Continued with them through '80, also (on the heavier side) Rick DERRINGER and Jo Jo GUNNE '73, WISHBONE ASH, REO SPEEDWAGON '75, Outlaws '77, Elvin BISHOP '75-6. Co-prod. with engineer Allen Blazek on several projects, while reverting to his own former role as engineer for Walsh's prod. of Dan FOGELBERG's *Souvenirs* '74. With demise of Eagles, broadened scope with tracks for Bob SEGER's *Against The Wind* '80, also the WHO's *Face Dances* '81, LPs for SANTANA '82.

T

TABOR, June (*b* 31 Dec. '47, Warwick, England) Folksinger, infl. by trad. and revivalist acts such as Anne BRIGGS, CLANCY Bros., Blairs of Blairgowie; hailed by people as diverse as Steve WINWOOD, Mike OLDFIELD, Elvis COSTELLO. Sang sessions, etc.; break came with *Silly Sisters* '76 on Chrysalis UK (Takoma, then Shanachie in USA), collaboration with Maddy Prior and Prior's extramural project from STEELEYE SPAN, with Martin CARTHY, Nic JONES etc. in backing group. Solo debut *Airs And Graces* on Topic same year made reputation, partly for stunning singing and for Eric Bogle's 'The Band That Played Waltzing Matilda', later found in many repertoires. Guested on Peter BELLAMY LP *The Transports* that year. *Ashes And Diamonds* '77 on Topic was later complemented by *The John Peel Sessions* on Strange Fruit, a radio broadcast from that year. She did not work full-time and her output is not prolific; *A Cut Above* '80 on Topic is an extremely successful collaboration with guitarist Martin Simpson (*b* 5 May '53, Scunthorpe); her finest to date was *Abyssinians* '83 on Topic/Shanachie, her formidable talent in both trad. and contemporary material fully realised. Sang sessions with Bill Caddick, whose songwriting she championed, Andy Cronshaw, Flowers & Frolics, Ashley Hutchings; performed in ALBION BAND theatre projects *The Passion* '79, *The Nativity* '80, *The Albion River Hymn* '81; sang theme songs for TV programmes *Spy Ship*, *Whale Music*. Guested with FAIRPORT CONVENTION '87. Sang solo 'Our Captain Cried' on Cronshaw's *Till The Beast's Returning* '88 on Topic. Tabor's solo *Aqaba* said to be her finest yet; reunion with Prior for second Silly Sisters album *No More To The Dance* also '88.

TABU LEY (*b* Tabu Pascal, '40, Bandundu, Zaire) Singer, composer, bandleader, aka Rochereau; an African superstar, having written over 2000 songs, released over 150 albums, leading developing of Congo music from the 78 era to the present. Began early, assimilating indigenous styles and the music of the Catholic church; wrote 'Besame Muchacha' at 14, a hit recorded by Kabaselle; joined Kabaselle and African Jazz '59, wrote hit 'Kelia'; became known as Rochereau, left '63 to form African Fiesta with Dr NICO (prolific singles compiled on LPs *Authenticitie*, two vols.), *Succès d'Hier*. Left Nico '65 to form own African Fiesta National, innovating ever since with new instrumentation, elements of salsa, soul, disco etc. within basic rumba framework. In late '60s he toured Africa and continued prodigious recorded output; for many fans the pristine beauty of his recordings of this era remain unequalled: *La Musique Congolaise de Variétés* (two vols.), *L'Afrique Danse* (vol. 4), *Tango Ya Ba Vieux Kalle No. 2*. Renamed band Afrisa International '70, performed at Olympia Theatre in Paris, *À l'Olympia* (two vols.) reflecting relaxed and lilting classic congo dance music. On return to Zaire he was feted as a national hero; Afrisa began to become a training ground for a new generation incl. Sam MANGWANA and Mbilia BEL; two vols. of *Afrisa International* from this period are still available. He retired temporarily '75 to look after business affairs, returned triumphant at the Nigerian festival (2-disc *FESTAC 77*). By mid-'80s he had established his own production company, Genidia, and was poised on the brink of international fame, touring USA, Japan, Europe. LPs alternating driving dance beat with slower haunting ballads: *En Amour y'a pas de Calcul* and *Maze* '82, *Femmes d'Autrui* and 2-disc *Loyenghe* '83, *In America* and *Sarah* '84, *African Selection* '85: Sterns in London had more than 30 albums available mid-'88 incl. some with vocalists Bel, Abbe Imana, Faya Tess.

TALKING HEADS New wave group formed '74 in NYC by design-school grads David Byrne (*b* 14 May '52, Dumbarton, Scotland), vocals, guitar; drummer Chris Frantz (*b* 8 May '51, Fort Campbell, Ky.) and his girlfriend Martina 'Tina' Weymouth (*b* 22 Nov. '50, Coronado, Cal.) on bass. Frantz and Byrne had played together in the Artistics, now played celebrated gig at CBGB's, where trio with acoustic guitar backing Byrne's quirky high-pitched voice marked them down with Jonathan RICHMAN as one of USA new wave's more unusual sounds. Keyboardist Jerry Harrison (*b* 21 Feb. '49, Milwaukee, Wis.) came from Richman's Modern Lovers, doubling on guitar and adding new textures. First single 'Love Goes To Building On Fire' established yearning, wistful quality reinforced by *Talking Heads 77*, delicate pop LP with occasional uneasy edge (as on 'Psycho Killer', an early single choice); second LP *More Songs About Buildings And Food* '78 parodied Byrne's obsessions in its title (as 'Psycho Killer' had been parodied by the Fools as 'Psycho Chicken'): LP smoothed out quirkily rough edges, brought in Harrison's keyboards as integral part of sound (e.g. his organ on 'Take Me To The River', top 30 cover of Al GREEN song, first showing their interest in black sound). *Fear Of Music* '79 like its predecessor was prod. by Brian ENO, brought African sounds to tracks like 'I Zimbra', whose nonsense lyrics derived from a poem by Hugo Ball; intense, paranoiac 'Life During Wartime' continued Byrne's lyrical acuity. *Fear* had featured session musicians (African drummers and guitarist Robert FRIPP); *Remain In Light* '80 went further, with BOWIE guitarist Adrian Belew, Nona Hendryx guesting on vocals, requiring nine pieces to play the music on stage incl. Belew, Busta Cherry Jones (bass, ex-Sharks), Bernie Worrell (keyboards, ex-Parliament), Dollette MacDonald, vocals; Steven Scales, percussion: their best synthesis yet of black and white pop. Eno/Byrne collaboration *My Life In The Bush Of Ghosts* '81 was dominated by 'found' voices from radio, etc.: American evangelist preacher vying with Islamic chants to hypnotic and disturbing effect. Harrison made solo *The Red And The Black* '81; Frantz and Weymouth formed spin-off Tom Tom Club with Tina's sisters Loric, Lani and Laura, their light, summery music recorded at Compass Sound in the Bahamas rewarded by eponymous LP reaching USA chart and

no. 7 single 'Wordy Rappinghood': they opened for Heads on later tours. Byrne prod. B-52s and Fun Boy Three; Heads returned from sabbatical to embrace former pop style: *Speaking In Tongues* '83 stripped down to basics, fascination with black sounds lessening with Eno's departure and exorcised by live stopgap *The Name Of This Band Is Talking Heads*, one of whose two discs showcases expanded band. Songs of this era very influential, covered by SIMPLY RED, Decoys, STAPLE SINGERS (last giving black music credibility). Unusually, another live LP followed, *Stop Making Sense* accompanied by acclaimed video of same name, now on new EMI America label (previously on Sire). *Little Creatures* '85 took them once more in pop direction, impressive hit singles incl. 'Road To Nowhere' with award-winning video and 'And She Was'. Byrne did *The Catherine Wheel* '82, composed for Twyla Tharp ballet co.; now *Music For The Knee Plays* '85. Byrne film *True Stories* '86 accompanied by album of that name, versions of film songs sung by different artists (soundtrack was also issued); tale of USA musics in Ry COODER mould acclaimed, ranging from Tex-Mex ('Radio Head') to gospel ('Hey Now'); Byrne predicted as cinematographer of the future. Heads album *Naked* '88 said to be their most exuberant. They were influential in bringing naive, acoustic pop back into fashion after punk (cf. Orange Juice, etc.), having taken VELVET UNDERGROUND etc. as model; then tribal rhythms created another set of fans; they may well spring more stylistic surprises in future. Harrison prod. second LP by up-and-coming USA band BoDeans (*Outside Looking In* on Reprise/Slash '87).

TANGERINE DREAM Electro/techno West Berlin band led by Edgar Froese (guitar, bass, organ, mellotron, electronics); began '70 with delayed '60s ambience of psychedelic nightmare, developed into meticulous electronic music. Froese's friendship with Salvador Dali was an influence. Debut LP *Electronic Meditations* delivered free improvisation of feedback, distortion *à la* Jimi HENDRIX, and impressions of Stockhausen; *Alpha Centauri* '71 settled down a bit, used synthesiser (played by Christopher Franke); 2-disc *Zeit* '72 allowed still more breathing space, used cello quartet: sound solidified around Froese, Franke and Peter Baumann (keyboards, flute, electronics). *Atem '73* allowed interplay of droning synths with shimmering backgrounds and glissando effects; *Green Desert '73* is a side-long track, the LP filled with other bits and not issued until '86 (all these in a 6-disc set . . . *In The Beginning* on a Relativity label). Subsequent LPs on Virgin International: *Phaedra '74, Rubycon '75, Ricochet '75, Stratosfear '76, Live – Encore '77, Cyclone '78, Force Majeure '79, Tangerine Dream '80, Exit '81, Logos Live At The Dominion, London 1982, White Eagle '82* follow development to *Hyperborea '83,* which is listed in the Hearts Of Space catalogue USA (*see* SPACE MUSIC): the angstridden feedback of the early years has become middle-aged, like the politics of the Berlin Wall. Other LPs incl. film soundtracks on MCA with cooperation of Virgin: *Sorcerer '82, Firestarter '84*; also *Poland '84* on Jive Electro/Zomba label. *Alpha Centauri/Atem* are available in a set on Virgin UK; *Exit* is on Elektra in USA.

TANGO Dance, then song form emerging in Buenos Aires, Argentina c.1880, in brothels of the new suburbs, in which crowding of European immigrants engendered poverty and violence. Men danced the milonga (infl. by the Cuban habanera), transformed into the tango by the gestures of knife fights and sexual stimulation: the corte (sudden halt), quebrada (twist) and refalada (glide). Accompanied by guitar, violin and flute, the early tango was an aggressive and even violent dance, praised by writers such as Borges as the real tango and its milieu compared to that of New Orleans. By '25 it had become a popular song form and was romanticised; larger bands had added a bandoneon (a German accordion) and another violin; it had been exported to Europe/USA and become the rage as an outrageously suggestive dance in this diluted form; exhibition dancers Vernon and Irene CASTLE led the USA cult from c.'13. It continued as a song form in Argentina with composers such as Ernesto Discepolo, found its star in Carlos GARDEL; by late '30s returned to B.A. in its orchestrated dance form: '40s saw large tango orchestras in B.A., galaxy of musicians/composers/arrangers: Anibal Troilo, Rob-

erto Firpo, Astor PIAZZOLA; more recent revival in Paris has groups like Quarteto Cedron (LP *Faubourgs Sauvages* on Messidor) and Valeria Munariz (*Tango* and *Je te Chanterai un Tango* on Le Chant du Monde) re-creating the '40s style, while Piazzola continues updating it.

TARABU African musical style popular along East African coast, of indeterminate origin but combining African, Indian and Arabic elements to prod. a music somehow identifiably African. Developed in coastal cities from Somalia to Mozambique, reflecting the cosmopolitan outlook of multiracial peoples, its major centres incl. Mombasa and the Island of Zanzibar; by combining Arabic and Indian melodies and drumming with Swahili, a classical culture, maintains links with Swahili literature. During '30s the instrumentation was mainly Arabic, incl. lute, pottery drums, zither, fiddle, tambourine and rattle; guitar-like gambuz was also used. Performed mainly on ceremonial occasions, tarabu survived the generations and remained a popular recreational music; a modern selection on LP *Songs The Swahili Sing* is both amplified and augmented by the tabla from India, Western instruments guitar, accordion, violin. By the '60s the invasion of the Zairean rumba became universal, resulting in a Latin infl. in tabaru; meanwhile, more mainstream Kenyan pop was infl. by the arrival of dozens of Zairean musicians in East Africa: even today such bands as Orchestre Virunga, Orchestre Makassy and Super Mazembe are composed mainly of Zaire nationals. Towards the end of the '70s specifically East African styles began to emerge, such as benga, a fusion of Luo trad. music and the rumba.

TATE, Buddy (*b* George Holmes Tate, 22 Feb. '13, Sherman, Texas) Tenor sax in the line of Coleman HAWKINS and Herschel Evans. Played in territory bands; replaced Evans in Count BASIE band '39 for nine years; worked for Lucky MILLINDER, Hot Lips PAGE, Jimmy RUSHING; then resident at Celebrity Club in Harlem for 21 years, finally pushed out by rock music. Recorded regularly all that time, e.g. with Buck CLAYTON, Rushing on Columbia (CBS) and Vanguard in '50s, own LP *Unbroken* with Celebrity Club band now on Pausa; has toured Europe and festivals ever since, cheerful and welcome past master of swing wherever he goes. Had duo with trombonist Al Grey, co-led band with drummer Bobby Rosengarden at the Rainbow Room, etc. More LPs: with Nancy Harrow on *Wild Women Don't Get The Blues* c.'60 on Candid; with Al HIBBLER, Hank JONES, Milt HINTON etc. on *For Sentimental Reasons* '82 on Open Sky; *& Muse Allstars* and *Hard Blowin'* '78, both *Live At Sandy's* on Muse; *The Great Buddy Tate* (also plays baritone, clarinet) and *Scott's Buddy* (with Scott HAMILTON) '81 on Concord Jazz; *The Ballad Artistry Of Buddy Tate* '81 on Sackville; also *Swinging Like Tate* '58 (with Clayton, Dicky WELLS, Jo JONES) and with Jay MCSHANN on *Going To Kansas City* '72, both on MJR (former also on Felsted); *And His Buddies* '73 (with Roy ELDRIDGE, Illinois JACQUET, Milt Hinton, Mary Lou WILLIAMS, drummer Gus Johnson) and *Meets Dollar Brand* '77 on Chiaroscuro; *Kansas City Woman* '74 with Humphrey LYTTELTON on Black Lion; *Quartet* and *Sherman Shuffle* on Sackville late '70s; *Kansas City Joys* on Sonet UK, *Play The Thing* '62 on Columbia by Marlowe Morris (*b* 16 May '15, NYC; *d* there c.'77: keyboardist's only LP won a French prize); others on Prestige-Swingville, etc.

TATUM, Art (*b* 13 Oct. '09, Toledo, Ohio; *d* 5 Nov. '56, L.A.) Pianist, without doubt the greatest in the history of jazz, his astonishing technique admired by everyone else who played the instrument, including Vladimir Horowitz. Virtually blind from birth; attended special schools in Columbus and Toledo; began gigging as a teenager; toured with Adelaide HALL '32-3, made first solo records '33, recorded exclusively for Decca well into '40s incl. with combo '37 and '41 ('Body And Soul' by Art Tatum & His Swingsters '37, solo 'Tea For Two' '39 were top 20 hits according to *Pop Memories*); formed trio '43 with Slam STEWART, Tiny Grimes on guitar, later Everett Barksdale; he was neglected late '40s, went two years without any commercial recordings, but also recorded with trio on Dial and Capitol, then recorded extensively for Norman GRANZ in '50s until he died of uraemia. He was probably infl. by the harmonic richness

of Duke ELLINGTON's music; admitted infl. of Fats WALLER, who announced in a club with Tatum present, 'Ladies and gentlemen, I play piano, but tonight God is in the house.' Like all the greatest musicians since Bach he summarised everything that had gone before, adding such rich rhythmic and harmonic invention that he immediately infl. horn players (such as young Coleman HAWKINS), ultimately the whole bop generation and beyond. He did not write songs, but embroidered standards, seeming to paint himself into a corner harmonically speaking and then continuing to improvise until his ideas fit the context after all: this was often over the heads of lay listeners, who complained that he played too many notes; but after-hours recordings made '40-1 by jazz buff Jerry Newman are relaxed, sheer beauty (LP *God Is In The House* '73 on Polydor), showing ability to adapt to out-of-tune pianos and quote Mozart as he did it (also a rare, amusing vocal on 'Knockin' Myself Out'). Compilations of early work incl. 2-disc *Masterpieces* on MCA USA, *Pure Genius* on Affinity UK; also *Radio Broadcasts* '32-45 on Aircheck, *Keystone Session* (transcriptions from '38-9) on Varèse (also *Get Happy* on Black Lion), *The V-Discs* (solo, quartet, trio '44-6) on Black Lion, *The Genius* and *Song Of The Vagabonds* '44-5 on Black Lion have some tracks in common. *At The Crescendo* (two vols. on GNP) is not a live concert but has audience noise dubbed in; two solo LPs well-recorded at a private party c.'55 have been available on World Records, 20th-Century Fox, etc. The Granz recordings comprise 12 LPs now on Pablo as *Solo Masterpieces* and nine volumes of *Group Masterpieces*: trio sets with Lionel HAMPTON/Buddy RICH, Red CALLENDER/ Jo JONES, Benny CARTER/Louie BELLSON; a sextet set with Hampton, Rich, Callender, Harry EDISON, Barney KESSEL; and quartet sets: with Roy ELDRIDGE, John Simmons on bass, Alvin Stoller on drums; with Buddy DEFRANCO, Callender and drummer Bill Douglass; with Ben WEBSTER, Callender, Douglass: the last, made weeks before Tatum died, is one of the most beautiful jazz records of all time.

TAYLOR, Billy (*b* 24 July '21, Greenville, N.C.) A fine jazz pianist who has become better known as a writer, broadcaster and

teacher. Degree in music, to NYC, played
with Ben WEBSTER, Dizzy GILLESPIE, in
Chicago with Stuff SMITH, Eddie SOUTH;
went to Europe with Don REDMAN '46; led
own quartet '49-50, fronted by Artie SHAW
late '50 as his Gramercy Five; led own trios
since '52. LPs on Argo, Atlantic, Capitol,
Mercury, Savoy, ABC-Paramount (incl.
Introduces Ira Sullivan), others incl. *Billy
Taylor Trio* '54 with CANDIDO now in Fantasy OJC series; also *Touch Of Taylor* on
Prestige, *Sleeping Bee* '69 on Pausa,
Where've You Been '80 on Concord Jazz
(with Keith COPELAND, Victor Gaskin on
bass, Joe Kennedy on violin). Co-founder of
Jazzmobile '65 which gives free concerts in
the street; was mus. dir. of the David Frost
TV talk show, the first black to hold such a
position (many years later he is still the only
one). Published *Jazz Piano* '82, based on
radio series; does jazz segment once a
month or so on Charles Kuralt's CBS-TV
Sunday Morning show.

TAYLOR, Cecil (*b* Cecil Percival Taylor, 15
Mar. '30, NYC) Pianist, composer, leader.
One of the most important musicians to
emerge from jazz roots since WWII, he has
been described as a 'Bartók in reverse', taking what he wants from European music
without ever compromising his blues roots;
treating piano as percussion instrument: '88
tuned drums'; opens new doors every couple of years. With his complete command of
the instrument he is the successor to Art
TATUM, but he admired Fats WALLER more
'for the depth of his single notes'; also infl.
by the thick chord clusters of Dave
BRUBECK. 'Taylor and Ornette COLEMAN
are the nominal heads of the jazz avant-
garde, but they are very different. Coleman
refuses to record or play in public unless he
is paid handsomely. Taylor until recent
years often played for pennies – when he
was asked to play at all. Coleman's music is
accessible, but he is loath to share it;
Taylor's music is difficult, and he is delighted to share it . . . The American aesthetic
landscape is littered with idiosyncratic marvels – Walt Whitman, Charles Ives, D. W.
Griffith, Duke Ellington, Jackson
Pollock – and Taylor belongs with them'
(Whitney Balliett in the *New Yorker*).
Formed group with Steve LACY, bassist
Buell NEIDLINGER, drummer Dennis

Charles (*b* 4 Dec. '33, St Croix, Virgin Islands; records with Gil EVANS '59, calypsoes
with Sonny ROLLINS '62, etc.; with Jazz
Doctors incl. Frank LOWE: *Intensive Care*
'83 on Cadillac). Quartet LP *Jazz Advance*
late '56 on Transition, made in Boston,
poorly recorded by prod. Tom Wilson (then
a beginner) is not as startling now as then
but already showed Taylor's unique approach to standards. Quartet found its style
playing six weeks at the Five Spot '56, transformed it from a neighbourhood bar into a
premier jazz spot, but Taylor was never
popular with club owners because he insists
on a properly tuned piano and is then very
hard on it; also, his music is meant to be
listened to: as Neidlinger put it, you would
not say to Igor Stravinsky, 'Stop it, Igor!
Like, we want to sell a few drinks!' Next
Cecil Taylor Quartet At Newport '57 on
Verve (already regarded as avant-gardist at
Newport); *Looking Ahead!* '58 on Contemporary was all Taylor tunes, with Earl
Griffith on vibes (*b* 1 May '26, Brooklyn),
Charles, Neidlinger. An album with John
COLTRANE on United Artists '58 was called
Stereo Drive, then *Hard Driving Jazz*, then
Coltrane Time; now on Boplicity, it is usual-
ly described as unsuccessful but it makes
fascinating listening. His own LP *Love For
Sale* '59 on UA with Ted CURSON, Bill
Barron on tenor, Rudy Collins on drums (*b*
24 July '34, NYC); Neidlinger says he
played on released LP; discography says
Chris White. (*Jazz Advance* and *Love For
Sale* reissued in 2-disc *In Transition* on Blue
Note '75.) Short-lived Candid label made
The World Of Cecil Taylor '60 with Charles,
Neidlinger, Archie SHEPP (on two tracks)
(this lineup appeared in Jack Gebler's play
The Connection), Neidlinger session *New
York City R&B* (not released for 11 years),
and *Jumpin' Punkins*, with two Ellington
tunes incl. title track, one original each by
Cecil and Buell with Shepp, Lacy, Charles,
Roswell RUDD, Clark TERRY (it was sup-
posed to be Don CHERRY), Billy HIGGINS
on the Ellingtons: unreleased outside Japan
until '87. (Boxed set of complete Taylor on
Candid to come from Mosaic in USA.) With
Gil EVANS on *Into The Hot* on Impulse
(showcase for Taylor and arranger Johnny
Carisi), also *The New Breed* '61; Jimmy
LYONS and Sunny MURRAY played Taylor's
music on *Into The Hot*, trio became the

Cecil Taylor Unit, went to Europe and made *At The Café Montmartre '62* (aka *Nefertite – Beautiful One* on Freedom); Albert AYLER played with trio in Europe. Taylor's impact on the new music was overshadowed by Coleman's; like Thelonious MONK earlier he was neglected; worked outside music, practising hours every day. Often in the early years he had gently, often humorously pointed out the distance between himself and sidemen while he was recomposing standards; by now he played only his own music. As it became apparent that contemporary black music was no longer willing to help sell booze he became an international concert artist, phenomenal energy and technique allowing two and three hour sets. He was involved in abortive Jazz Composers Guild with Bill DIXON, others (*see* JAZZ); his music reached its abstract maturity on *Conquistador!* '65 (with Andrew CYRILLE, Dixon, Lyons, Henry Grimes and Alan Sylva on basses), and *Unit Structures* '66 (Eddie Gale Stevens Jr replacing Dixon, adding Ken McIntyre on reeds), both on Blue Note, among the most beautiful and coherent LPs of the new era. Returned to Europe; 2-disc *Student Studies* '66 with Lyons, Sylva, Cyrille was preserved by French radio (on Freedom in Japan, also other labels), 3-disc *The Great Concert Of Cecil Taylor* on Prestige (aka *Nuits de la Fondation* on Shandar); recorded with Jazz Composers Orchestra '68, in huge orchestral setting by Mike Mantler; joined academia: taught black music and led Black Music Ensemble at U. of Wis./Madison '70-1; a story which made the rounds had a member of Madison's piano faculty overheard after a Taylor recital: 'What do I *think* of it? I wish I could *play* it.' He failed most of the students, quit when the university passed them over his head; also taught at Antioch (Ohio), where Lyons and Cyrille joined him; he wrote for student big bands, but music not documented; also Glassboro State (N.J.). Sam RIVERS often played with his group '69-73; Tokyo visit '73 yielded 2-disc *Akisakila* concert; *Spring Of 2 Blue-Js* on Unit Core '73 incl. bassist Sirone (*b* Norris Jones, 28 Sep. '40, Atlanta), making the Unit a quartet; *Silent Tongues* (live at Montreux '74) on Freedom is over 50 minutes of solo piano, the querulous, amusing sort of figures heard in his comping on the Coltrane LP grown into compositions alternately delicate and bursting with power, always full of energy, still never far from the blues, the keyboard become an 88-piece orchestra. *Innovations* and *Indent* c.'74-6 also on Freedom; *Dark To Themselves, Air Above Mountains (Buildings Within)* '76 on Enja; two-piano concert at Carnegie Hall '77 with Mary Lou WILLIAMS was her brave idea; *Live In The Black Forest* '78 on MPS; 3-disc *One Too Many Salty Swift And Not Goodbye* '78 on Hat Art (live in Stuttgart) has sextet incl. Lyons, Sirone, Raphe Malik (on trumpet, Taylor student from Antioch), Ramsey Ameen on violin, drummer Ronald Shannon Jackson. More albums: *Unit* '78 and *3 Phasis* '79 on New World, 2-disc *Historic Concerts* late '79 on Soul Note (duo at Columbia U. with Max ROACH), solo *Fly! Fly! Fly! Fly! Fly! Fly!* '80 on Pausa, 2-disc solo *Garden* '81 on Hat Art (digitally made in Basle on a Bosendorfer piano); 2-disc solo *Praxis* '84 on Praxis, *Winged Serpent (Sliding Quadrants)* '84 on Soul Note with 'Segments II (Orchestra Of Two Continents)' and *What's New?* '85 on Black Lion; solo *For Olim* '86 on Soul Note, his sixth official solo LP and according to *Cadence* magazine one of the best; then 2-disc *Live In Bologne*, single *Chinampus* '87, both on Leo: latter is another dimension, with no piano but words and percussion. This fairly complete list of prolific recordings is in/out of print in various countries. He was a subject in A. B. Spellman's *Black Music: Four Lives* (originally *Four Lives In The BeBop Business* '68), still a valuable book; received Guggenheim fellowship '73, played at Carter's White House '79, has worked with dramatists, ballet companies; now has the world fame he deserves. John Litweiler's chapter on the music in *The Freedom Principle* '84 is first-rate.

TAYLOR, Hound Dog (*b* Theodore Roosevelt Taylor, 12 Apr. '17, Natchez, Ms.; *d* 17 Dec. '75, Chicago, Ill.) Blues singer; also guitar, piano. Ran away from home before he was 10; worked in juke joints, picnics etc. through South, with Elmore JAMES, others; with Sonny Boy WILLIAMSON on King Biscuit Time radio show in Ark. c.'42, went to Chicago. Recorded for Firma '62, formed House Rockers trio with Brewer Phillips' rhythm guitar also serving as a bass line, Ted Harvey on drums: Bruce Iglauer managed them, drove their equipment, recorded them for his new Alligator label. Hound Dog played slide on a 'supercheap' Japanese guitar, using a brass-lined piece of steel chair leg; he told awful (often incomprehensible) jokes, called his intense good-time music rock'n'roll, though purists called it blues. Worked every Sunday afternoon for ten years at Florence's club; other clubs and festivals incl. European tour '67, also Australia. Albums, also on Sonet UK: *Hound Dog Taylor & The HouseRockers* '71, *Natural Boogie*, *Beware Of The Dog* '74 (made at live gigs for radio broadcasts); *Genuine Houserocking Music* has tracks from '71, 73. 'When I die, they'll say, "he couldn't play shit, but he sure made it sound good!" ' Also tracks on *King Of The Slide Guitar* on JSP with Johnny Littlejohn (*b* 16 Apr. '31, Lake, Ms.)

TAYLOR, James (*b* 12 Mar. '48, Boston, Mass.) Singer/songwriter. From large musical family; siblings Livingstone, Alex, Kate all recorded following his success. Worked in various teenage bands incl. the Fabulous Corsairs with Alex; met guitarist Danny Kortchmar '63, they formed the Flying Machine '67 (*James Taylor & The Flying Machine* issued '71 to capitalise on success). He had admitted himself to a psychiatric hospital suffering from acute depression; by age 20 he was heroin addict, went to London to get away from the habit; Kortchmar had backed PETER & GORDON mid-'60s, suggested that Taylor contact Peter ASHER, then dir. of A&R for BEATLES' Apple label: result was *James Taylor* '68 with guests George HARRISON, Paul MCCARTNEY: patchy LP incl. excellent Taylor songs 'Carolina In My Mind', 'Something In The Way She Moves'; sales were not massive. Returned to USA, now managed by Asher, who got contract with WB; *Sweet Baby James* '70 was one of those albums that effortlessly epitomises an era: with '60s ideals in disarray and as an antidote to bombast of LED ZEPPELIN and CHICAGO, his moody and introspective work coincided with success of Joni MITCHELL, Carole KING, Neil YOUNG to create singer/ songwriter 'genre' that has always existed and always will. Despite hyperbole, the LP remains remarkable for title track,

'Fire & Rain', 'Country Road'; but lugubrious voice, incessantly self-centred lyrics could never maintain that peak. Elvis PRESLEY covered 'Steamroller', Taylor's tongue-in-cheek blues; *Mud Slide Slim & The Blue Horizon* '71 was inevitably weaker, but at the time sold even better (both LPs top 3 USA); 'You've Got A Friend' (King's song) was no. 1 single USA; 'Hey Mister, That's Me Up On The Juke Box' was comment on his own success. He made cover of *Time* '71 (often a bad sign) and starred with BEACH BOY Dennis Wilson in cult movie *Two Lane Blacktop*. *One Man Dog* '72 was no. 4 LP but *Walking Man* '74 slipped to 13, both seen as disappointing; *Gorilla* was back up to no. 6, redeemed him somewhat incl. top 5 cover of Marvin GAYE hit 'How Sweet It Is'; he had married Carly SIMON '72; they were a big item in the rock aristocracy. *In My Pocket* '76 was followed by switch to Columbia; *JT* '77 was no. 4 LP with no. 4 hit 'Handy Man' (song by Otis BLACKWELL and Jimmy Jones); *Flag* '79 and *Dad Loves His Work* '81 were both no. 10 LPs, latter with no. 11 duet hit on 'Her Town Too' with J. D. SOUTHER; with Carly had hits with Inezz & Charlie Foxx's 'Mockingbird' '74 and the EVERLY Bros.' 'Devoted To You' '78; joined SIMON & GARFUNKEL '78 on cover of Sam COOKE's 'What A Wonderful World' '78; appeared with Bruce SPRINGSTEEN and Jackson BROWNE live '79. Ironically in view of his own good songs, biggest hits were all covers. Divorced from Simon '82; returned with *That's Why I'm Here* '86, successful UK and USA tours proving that fans were still there. New CBS album *Never Die Young* '88 was to be followed by two-hour concert broadcast on PBS.

TAYLOR, Koko (*b* Cora Walton, 28 Sep. '35, Memphis, Tenn.) Blues singer in the great female line of Bessie SMITH, Victoria SPIVEY etc. but also very much Chicago style, with more than a dash of Muddy WATERS. Sang in church choir as teenager; moved to Chicago, married Robert Taylor '53; occasional club dates with Buddy GUY, Junior WELLS; recorded with J. B. LENOIR '63 on USA ('Honkey Tonkey'), for Spivey '64, Checker '64-73 (took Willie DIXON's 'Wang Wang Doodle' to no. 4 in soul chart '66, top 60 pop), then on Alligator. Appeared in film *The Blues Is Alive And Well*

In Chicago '70; festivals incl. Ann Arbor (on Atlantic) and Montreux with Waters (on Chess), both '72. Fine Checker tracks prod. and mostly written by Dixon reissued '87; LPs on Alligator/Sonet: *I Got What It Takes, The Earthshaker, From The Heart Of A Woman, Queen Of The Blues* '85, *Live From Chicago – An Audience With The Queen* '87. In '87 her band the Blues Machine incl. Michael 'Mr Dynamite' Robinson and Eddie King, guitars; Jerry Murphey, bass; Clyde 'Youngblood' Tyler, drums.

TEAGARDEN, Jack (*b* Weldon Leo Teagarden, 29 Aug. '05, Vernon, Texas; *d* 15 Jan. '64, New Orleans, La.) Trombone; also vocalist, bandleader; one of the all-time greats in the history of jazz. Vic DICKENSON, himself a great jazz trombonist, described the tail-gate bass-line New Orleans-style trombone as sounding like 'a dying cow in a thunderstorm'; with Jimmy Harrison and Miff Mole in the North, Teagarden invented the jazz trombone, but single-handedly in the Southwest, and more completely than anyone else, his style described as doing the difficult thing at the last moment and making it sound easy: yet his laid-back drawl marked both horn and blues singing. Father was an engineer; he became an auto mechanic (later rebuilt Stanley Steamers) and approached the trombone like a machine: he'd played peck horn (which has valves) and developed trombone technique so that he didn't have to move the slide more than 18 inches, redesigning mouthpiece, mutes etc. Virtually a pop-star too, charming singing on 'I Ain't Lazy, I'm Just Dreaming', 'I Gotta Right To Sing The Blues', 'Meet Me Where They Play The Blues', many others. Sister Norma played piano (*b* 28 Apr. '11, Vernon; played with Jack '44-6, '52-5; also with Ben POLLACK, Pete DAILY, etc.), brother Cub was drummer (*b* Clois Lee Teagarden, 16 Dec. '15, Vernon; *d* '69) and Charlie was well-known trumpet player (*b* 19 July '13, Vernon; often with Jack, Pollack, etc.). Jack started on piano at 5, baritone horn at 7, trombone at 10, turned pro at about 15; played with Peck KELLEY's Bad Boys, other territory bands; first recorded '27, from then on prolific session work, often leading own pickup band on records while with Pollack '28-33, Paul WHITEMAN '33-8 (re-corded, gigged '36 in NYC with Frankie TRUMBAUER, Charlie as the Three T's: 'I'se A Muggin' ' on Victor); led own band '39-46 with musical but little commercial success; also appeared in films incl. *Birth Of The Blues* '41. Led sextet, joined Louis ARMSTRONG's All Stars '47-51, formed own All Stars and led own group except periods with Pollack '56, Earl HINES '57. Sides with Eddie CONDON '29 are jazz classics: 'That's An Awful Serious Thing' and 'I'm Gonna Stomp Mr Henry Lee', with solos and vocals by Teagarden, solos on the latter by Joe SULLIVAN on piano, and Happy Cauldwell, who tried jazz tenor sax before it was invented by Coleman HAWKINS. Of many freelance records under Teagarden's name, most featuring Charlie as well, highlights incl. 'You Rascal You', 'That's What I Like About You' and 'Chances Are' '31, incl. comedy with Fats WALLER on the first two as well as good singing and blowing; 'Someone Stole Gabriel's Horn' '33, 'Ive Got "It" ' '34 were hits, all on Columbia; 'The Sheik Of Araby', 'Cinderella, Stay In My Arms' '39 on Brunswick were hits, with Charlie SPIVAK. Having done well over the years leading bands on the side he tried it full time when contract with Whiteman ran out, backed Hoagy CARMICHAEL in his eponymous short film '39 (with Cub on drums), played at Roseland in Boston with airtime exposure but luck ran out: at prime big band venues the Meadowbrook (N.J.), Black Hawk Hotel (Chicago), war news cut them off the air while they lost money: he ended $50,000 in debt, but nice music was made. 16 *Varsity Sides* early '40 reissued on Savoy '86, vocals by Kitty KALLEN, 17-year-old David ALLYN as well as Jack and Marianne Dunne. Band recorded for Decca; in '41 lovely ballad 'A Hundred Years From Today' (by Victor YOUNG, Ned Washington, Joe Young '33) became associated with Jack; novelty 'The Waiter And The Porter And The Upstairs Maid' was a hit, vocal by Bing CROSBY, Mary MARTIN and Jack. Armstrong's '47 Town Hall concert (2-disc set on French RCA) incl. classic vocal duet on 'Rockin' Chair'; records on RCA, then Decca with Armstrong's All Stars are highly prized (series of 2-disc reissues began on RCA '87). Later Teagarden LPs: *Jazz Original* (Bethlehem, now on Affinity), *Mis'ry Of The Blues* on Verve, *Jazz*

Maverick on Roulette; on Capitol: *This Is Teagarden* (with studio big band) and *Shades Of Night*, also with Bobby HACKETT: *Coast Concert* '55 (now on Pausa), made in Hollywood with Hackett on cornet, Bob CROSBY alumni Matty Matlock on clarinet, Nappy Lamare, guitar; Abe Lincoln on second trombone (*b* 29 Mar. '07, Lancaster, Pa.; replaced Tommy DORSEY in California Ramblers '26, later with Roger Wolfe KAHN, Paul WHITEMAN, Ozzie NELSON, then studio work), Don Owens on piano, Phil Stephens on bass and tuba, Nick Fatool on drums, incl. Teagarden's classic vocal and 'tram-bone coda' on 'Basin Street Blues'; Chicago-style *Jazz Ultimate* '57 in NYC is slicker, but with many fine moments (reissued '85 France/UK): Hackett switches to trumpet, with Ernie Caceres on baritone, Peanuts Hucko on tenor, both also on clarinet; Billy Bauer on guitar, Condonites Jack Lesberg on bass (*b* 14 Feb. '20, Boston), Gene Schroeder on piano (*b* 5 Feb. '15, Madison, Wis.; *d* there 16 Feb. '75), Benjamin 'Buzzy' Drootin on drums (*b* c.'20 in Russia; grew up in Boston). Compilations incl. 3-disc *King Of The Blues Trombone* '28-40 now from Columbia Special Products USA, two vols. of Standard transcriptions from '41-5 on Storyville, *Jack & Max* (KAMINSKY) on Hall of Fame Jazz (Commodore tracks), two LPs with Trumbauer on Aircheck (one also has Whiteman tracks), *In San Francisco* '53-4 on Rarities, *Hollywood Bowl Concert* '63 with Hackett on Shoestring, various Queen-Disc imports incl. V-discs with Armstrong, Hot Lips PAGE, also tracks by Jack McVEA, big band broadcasts and soundtrack from the Carmichael short. V-discs also on Pumpkin; *Jack Teagarden & His Big Eight* was limited edition in '40, now on Fantasy with Rex STEWART, Barney BIGARD, Ben WEBSTER, Pee Wee RUSSELL etc. Other big band LPs on Aircheck, Archive of Folk, *Golden Horn* '44-50 on MCA in phoney stereo, etc. Books incl. *Jack Teagarden's Music* by Howard J. Waters (incl. films), biography *Jack Teagarden* by Jay D. Smith and Len Guttridge '60; see also Humphrey LYTTELTON on Big T in *The Best Of Jazz Vol. 2: Enter The Giants* (Charlie was 'Little T') and Whitney Balliett in his *American Musicians: 56 Portraits In Jazz*, a priceless collection of *New Yorker* pieces.

TEARDROP EXPLODES UK new wave group formed '78 in Liverpool. Original lineup: vocalist/bassist Julian Cope (*b* 21 Oct. '57, Bargoed, Wales), Mick Finkler, guitar; Paul Simpson, organ; Gary Dwyer, drums. Cope had been member of Crucial Three with seminal Liverpool characters Pete Wylie (later leader of WAH!), Ian McCulloch (ditto ECHO AND THE BUNNYMEN), then Nova Mob and A Shallow Madness; took name of new group from Marvel comic caption. Finkler had replaced Pete Johnson at an early stage. First gig at Eric's late '78 on bill with Bunnymen, like them signed to local Zoo label; first single 'Sleeping Gas'. Dave Balfe (Zoo co-founder with Bill Drummond; both from influential Big In Japan) replaced Simpson mid-'79; 'Bouncing Babies' another acclaimed single. Balfe's keyboards were an important element of sound, which veered towards '60s USA style of LOVE, etc. Finkler left during recording of *Kilimanjaro* '80, by which time they'd signed to Mercury, replaced by Alan Gill (ex-Dalek I Love You); Cope began to dominate band, leading to departure of Gill (back to Dalek) and Balfe after non-album single 'Reward', no. 6 UK hit with fine brass arrangement. Cope switched to guitar and brought in bassist Alfie Agius (*b* Malta; ex-Interview), Jeff Hammer, keyboards; Troy Tate (ex-Shake), guitar: this lineup made *Wilder* '81, looser and more self-indulgent than first LP; reissued 'Treason' from first LP made no. 18 UK, but band failed to make impact; Cope called Balfe back for last-chance single 'You Disappear From View', but disbanded late '82: solo career started brightly with typically titled *World Shut Your Mouth* '84, but faltered with *Fried* '85. Recorded one-off single 'Competition' under pseudonym Rabbi Joseph Gordan for indie Bam Caruso label, returned on Island with hit 'World Shut Your Mouth' '86 (no relation to LP); album *St Julian* '87 sacrificed his love for the '60s. His vocal style had resembled that of hero Scott Engel (*see* WALKER BROS) for populist approach, pounding rock backing.

TEARS FOR FEARS UK new wave duo formed by Curt Smith (*b* 24 June '61), bass and vocals, with Roland Orzabal (*b* 22 Aug. '61), guitar and vocals, refugees from mod-revival band Graduate (LP *Acting My Age*

'80 with Steve Buck on keyboards, John Baker on guitar, Andy Marsden, drums). Aimed for self-consciously new wave approach with single 'Suffer The Children' on indie label Idea before signing with Phonogram. Third single 'Mad World' made no. 3, 'Change' no. 4, re-recorded second single 'Pale Shelter' no. 5, all '82-3. Though from Bath, they fitted Liverpool bracket of pop production (China Crisis, Pale Fountains etc.). LP *The Hurting* '83 sold almost a million, but music gained strength through recruitment of two supernumerary group members: drummer Manny Elias (ex-Interview) played on first LP; keyboardist Ian Stanley (*b* 28 Feb. '57, High Wycombe) was local musician whose home studio was venue for recording of *Songs From The Big Chair* '85, with more muscular sound exemplified by hits 'Shout' and 'Mothers Talk', stronger electro-dance material; but LP also incl. more usual TFF fare, e.g. 'I Believe', dedicated to ex-SOFT MACHINE vocalist Robert WYATT, with his 'Sea Song' on flip. Set out to conquer USA with aptly titled Orzabal/Stanley song 'Everybody Wants To Rule The World', written with prod. Chris Hughes (ex-Adam ANT): no. 1 in USA/2 UK; 'Shout' also no. 1 USA; 'Head Over Heels' made five hits from LP at no. 12 UK/3 USA. Strange partnership: Orzabal writes most of the songs, though duo share lead vocals; they are not attractive in the usual pop way, both openly and happily married, yet gain wide audience from teens upward of both sexes. Though they claim LPs inspired by intellectual concepts (*Hurting* by Janov's primal scream therapy, *Chair* by USA film *Sybil* about a girl with 16 personalities who retreats to psychiatrist's chair) teen audience bought them because they're catchy. Lyrical concern, premium set on musicianship etc. set them in '70s, yet songs and image not dated. They took '86 off and apparently didn't come back. Mancrab was a splinter group of band members.

TEEN IDOL There have been many teen idols, or heart-throbs, such as Frank SINATRA and Perry COMO in earlier times, but the term usually describes the pop phenomenon of late '50s-early '60s of good-looking teenage boys discovered on their front porches (especially in Philadelphia) and turned into stars. The apparent bursting of the rock'n'roll balloon (which turned out to be a lull, *see* ROCK) left a vacuum filled by entrepreneurs who made stars out of not very promising material, often with the help of clean-cut Dick CLARK and his *Bandstand Matinee* TV dance show (broadcast after school, like *Howdy Doody* for younger kids). The whole thing was exquisitely sent up by Stan FREBERG, who had the kid saying, 'Who, me? But I can't sing,' to which the entrepreneur replies, 'Believe me, kid, that doesn't matter' (quoted from memory). Girls who got the treatment incl. Sandra Dee (star of beach movies), Shelley Fabares (Nanette Fabray's niece; huge hit '62 with 'Johnny Angel'). To be fair, some of these (e.g. Frankie AVALON) had previous show business experience, but that didn't make them singers. There have been many teen idols since (OSMONDS, David CASSIDY, JACKSONS etc.) but some had talent, in any case were no longer a phenomenon.

TELEVISION Punk group formed in NYC '74: Tom Verlaine (*b* Tom Miller, 13 Dec. '49), guitar, vocals; Fred Smith on bass, Billy Ficca, drums; Richard Lloyd, guitar. Got break at CBGBs club alongside BLONDIE, TALKING HEADS, RAMONES. Verlaine had moved to NYC from Delaware '68, was in shortlived band the Neon Boys with Ficca and Richard Hell, who was original bassist (fired '75). Independent single 'Little Johnny Jewel' '75 led to *Marquee Moon* '77, seen as one of the era's more interesting debut LPs. They were hardly punk, but almost pre-new wave, christened 'Ice Kings of Rock', describing clinical style of Verlaine; nevertheless musically superior to many contemporaries. Debut incl. chilling classic 'Venus', 'Torn Curtain'. UK tour '77 with Blondie created interest, but *Adventure* '78 was a nosedive, critics comparing Verlaine's lengthy solos to officially despised GRATEFUL DEAD. They split '78, attention focused on Verlaine, though Lloyd's *Alchemy* '79 was well-received; *Tom Verlaine* '79 was highly praised, *Dreamtime* '81, *Words From The Front* '82 and *Cover* less so. Reputation still rests on the debut.

TEMPERANCE SEVEN, The UK band formed at Royal College of Art mid-'50s, playing semi-hot dance music in late-'20s style, members (usually nine) dressed accordingly, vocals by 'Whispering' Paul McDowell delivered through a megaphone. Trombonist was jazz buff John R. T. Davies using pseudonym Sheik Wadi El Yadounir, wearing a fez; others incl. Cephas Howard (trumpet), John Watson (banjo and spoons), Brian Innes (percussion). Appeared on TV's *Juke Box Jury* '61 playing 'You're Driving Me Crazy', which shot to no. 1 UK; same year had chart hits 'Pasadena', 'Hard-Hearted Hannah', 'Charleston'; made three LPs. They did it all straight but appeared hilarious; in film *It's Trad Dad* '62 upstaging serious jazzers; they also appeared in film *Take Me Over* and play *The Bed Sitting Room* with Spike Milligan, were regulars on TV series headed by comedian Arthur Haines, but began to fall apart, McDowell leaving (replaced by Alan Mitchell), then sousaphone ace Martin Fry. Split '68; drummer Dave Mills later leased the name, but a new edition disappeared after a trip to Hong Kong: they had to hitch-hike home as Mills had failed to negotiate their passage. Another version played odd gigs mid-'80s, original members occasionally sitting in.

TEMPTATIONS, The USA male soul vocal group formed c.'62 in Detroit. Original lineup: bass Melvin Franklin (*b* David English, 12 Oct. '42, Montgomery, Ala.), lead singer Eddie Kendricks (*b* 17 Dec. '39, Birmingham, Ala.); Otis Williams (*b* Otis Miles, 30 Oct. '41, Texarkana, Texas), Paul Williams (*b* 2 July '39, Birmingham; *d* 17 Aug. '73) and Eldridge Bryant. Arguably the longest-running group still active, the much-loved Temptations were the result of two groups merging: Otis Williams and Bryant, with James Crawford, Bernard Plain and Arthur Walton, sang in classic doo-wop early soul style, known as the Questions, the Elegants then the Distants; by '59 Crawford, Walton, Plain had been replaced by Melvin Franklin, Albert Harrell and Richard Street (*b* 5 Oct. '42, Detroit) and the group had located in Detroit; the Primes (Paul Williams, Eddie Kendricks and C. L. Osborne) had moved there from Birmingham. They decided to merge, with Harrell, Osborne and Street leaving; signed with Berry Gordy's Miracle label as the Elgins (a 'sister act', the Primettes, later became the SUPREMES), switched to the Temptations on the Gordy label. A few early singles were unsuccessful; Bryant left, replaced by David RUFFIN, sharing lead duties with Kendricks; early '64 they scored first of nearly 40 USA top 40 hits with 'The Way You Do The Things You Do', written and prod. by Smokey ROBINSON; early '65 had first no. 1 USA with his 'My Girl', still a masterpiece. Smokey worked with them into '66; his songs such as 'It's Growing', 'Get Ready', though now regarded as classics, did not reach top 10; Norman Whitfield was assigned to the group: worked with Brian HOLLAND initially, but soon on his own induced top 10 hits '66-7 incl. 'Beauty Is Only Skin Deep', '(I Know) I'm Losing You', 'You're My Everything', 'All I Need'. Ruffin went solo '67, citing insufficient reward for their success, replacement Dennis Edwards (ex-Contours; *b* 3 Feb. '43, Birmingham) fitted in perfectly, 'I Wish It Would Rain' top 5 '68. But hits became smaller; Whitfield began writing in more psychedelic soul style perpetrated by SLY Stone, and they went into orbit again: 'Cloud Nine' and 'Runaway Child, Running Wild' were top 10, 'I Can't Get Next To You' their second no. 1, all '68-9; '70 saw more top 10 hits plus third no. 1 'Just My Imagination' early '71, a by now untypical balled. By then Kendricks had left to go solo, replaced by Damon Harris (*b* 3 July '50, Baltimore); Paul Williams, suffering from poor health, was replaced by stand-in Street, who meanwhile had worked in admin for Motown and in minor group the Monitors. Brilliant fourth no. 1 was 'Papa Was A Rolling Stone' '72, but after 'Masquerade' same year there were no more top 10 hits, though lesser entries incl. six top 40s continued through '84, along with personnel changes: Harris was replaced '75 by Glenn Leonard (*b* '48, Washington DC), Edwards '77 by Louis Price (*b* '53, Chicago). There were no hits '77-9 as they left Motown (though one of two Atlantic LPs *Hear To Tempt You* '77 reached top 200 LPs); they returned to Motown '79 with Edwards returning in place of Price. In '82 *Reunion* with Kendricks, Ruffin was top 40 LP; Leonard was replaced by Ron Tyson, in '84 Edwards by Ali-Ollie Woodson. Through it all Franklin's amazing deep voice and co-founder Williams have been present; *The Temptations 25th Anniversary Album* '86 was around their 50th, incl. collaborations with the Supremes '69-70 (top 3 single 'I'm Gonna Make You Love Me'). Many LPs in print; 3-disc *Anthology* (2 CDs) is a great compilation. Kendricks' solo career has moved slowly; he broke through '73 with no. 1 'Keep On Truckin' ', top 3 'Boogie Down'; switched to Arista '77 but had no luck; received boost from reunion '82, Live Aid appearance and LP '85 with Ruffin, HALL & OATES.

10CC UK pop group formed c.'70 as Hotlegs. Graham Gouldman, vocalist, bassist, keyboardist (*b* 10 May '46, Manchester), had met vocalist/guitarist Eric Stewart in a late edition of Wayne FONTANA's Mindbenders, had written top 10 hits for the YARDBIRDS, HOLLIES, HERMAN'S HERMITS; worked with Kasenetz-KATZ in NYC, made *The Graham Gouldman Thing* late '60s, formed Hotlegs in UK with fellow Mancunians Stewart, guitarist/vocalist Lol Creme (*b* 19 Sep. '47), drummer/vocalist Kevin Godley (*b* 7 Oct. '45), had no. 2 UK hit 'Neanderthal Man' '70; made demo of Godley-Creme song 'Donna'; Jonathan KING claimed to rename them 10cc after the average male ejaculation, which sounds like him: 'Donna' was no. 2 hit '72, followed by 10 more top 10 hits '73-8 incl. 'Rubber Bullets' '73, 'I'm Not In Love' '75 at no. 1; latter (with 256 vocal overdubs) was no. 2 USA; 'The Things We Do For Love' no. 5 '77 (6 UK); their pop was seen as witty, above-average stuff. All writers, enjoying studio work, they refused to tour; Godley and Creme left, promoted their Gizmo (an electronic sustaining device for guitars), made a good living prod. promo videos for other groups, had top 10 UK hit 'Wedding Bells' '82, LPs *Consequences* '77, *L* '78, *Ismism* '81. Stewart and Gouldman carried on with more hits, recruited Rick Fenn, Duncan MacKay, Tony O'Malley and Stuart Tosh; had third no. 1 'Dreadlock Holiday' '78, from top 3 LP *Bloody Tourists*; then suddenly nose-dived for no very evident reason. Their other top 10 LPs UK were *Sheet Music* '74, *The Original Soundtrack* '75, *How Dare You?* '76, *Deceptive Bends* '77; several more did less well; *10 Out Of Ten* '81 did not chart and *Windows In The Jungle* '83 reached no. 70. Went out

of fashion, but had good innings. Andrew GOLD contributed to the '81 LP; Gouldman and Gold teamed as Wax '85.

TEN YEARS AFTER UK progressive rock group formed '67 by Alvin Lee (*b* 19 Dec. '44, Nottingham) and Leo Lyons (*b* 30 Nov. '43, Bedfordshire), who'd formed blues trio, played in Hamburg after BEATLES; became Jaybirds with Ric Lee on drums (*b* 20 Oct. '45, Staffordshire); became Ten Years After with Chick Churchill on keyboards (*b* 2 Jan '49, Mold, Flintshire, Wales). Signed to Decca's progressive Deram label, made eponymous blues-based LP '67: unusually, no single was issued, setting trend for such groups. Promoter Bill GRAHAM brought them to Fillmores East and West, establishing USA following, reputation based on Alvin Lee's speed and dexterity in post-CLAPTON 'axe hero' period, confirmed by 11-minute 'I'm Going Home' at Woodstock, which made them superstars, followed by *Undead* '68, *Stonehenge* and *Sssh* '69, *Cricklewood Green* and *Watt* '70: guitar overkill resulted. One-off hit single was 'Love Like A Man' (top 10 '70 UK); lesser hits in USA. Switched to Columbia USA for *A Space In Time* '71 (top 20 LP certified gold), *Rock & Roll Music To The World* '73, *Positive Vibration* '74. Intent of living down image as fleet-figured guitar hero, Lee made *On The Road To Freedom* '73 with gospel singer Myron LeFevre, *Alvin Lee & Company* '74 with 9-piece band, 2-disc *In Flight* '74, *Pump Iron* '75. Toured and recorded as Ten Years Later, with Tom Compton on bass, drummer Mick Hawksworth, LPs *Rocket Fuel* and *Ride On* '78-9; *Free Fall* and *RX5* '80-1 appeared on Atlantic; *Detroit Diesel* '86 reunited him with Lyons, guest George HARRISON.

TERRY, Clark (*b* 14 Dec. '20, St Louis, Mo.) Trumpet, flugelhorn. Played in local bands, Navy band with Willie SMITH during WWII, then with Lionel HAMPTON, Charlie BARNET, Count BASIE postwar; Duke ELLINGTON '51-9. Worked with Quincy JONES, then recommended by Ray COPELAND (who had to turn down the job) for *Tonight* show TV band '60-72 led by Doc SEVERINSEN, leading to wide and deserved public popularity. Mainstream style out of Charlie SHAVERS, Rex STEWART, infl. by modernists, but with personality all its own; one of the first to adopt mellower flugelhorn as second instrument; also has amusing mumbling real style. Co-led quintet with Bob BROOKMEYER (LP '65 on Mainstream), occasional big band (*Big B-A-D Band Live At Buddy's Place* on Vanguard, *Live On 57th Street* on Big Bear); also with Thelonious MONK on European tour '67 (and LPs *In Orbit* on Riverside, 2-disc *Cruising* on Milestone. Other LPs: *Serenade To A Bus Seat* '57 on Riverside, *Paris 1960* with Kenny CLARKE and Martial SOLAL on Swing, with Oscar PETERSON Trio '64 on Mercury (with Oscar again later on Pablo), *It's What's Happenin'* '67 on Impulse (now on MCA), *Funk Dumplin's* '78 on Matrix (made in Copenhagen with Kenny Drew, Ed Thigpen, Red Mitchell); also *& His Jolly Giants* on Vanguard, *The Happy Horns Of* on Jasmine UK; on BASF/MPS late '70s: *Clark After Dark* and *Wham* (live at Jazz House, Hamburg; also on Pausa). On Pablo: *Ain't Misbehavin'*, *Memories Of Duke*, *Yes The Blues*, *Mother-Mother* with Zoot SIMS, *Alternate Blues* with Oscar, Freddie HUBBARD, Dizzy GILLESPIE.

TERRY, Sonny (*b* Saunders Terrell, 24 Oct. '11, Greensboro, N.C.; *d* 11 Mar. '86) Blues singer, harmonica player. Sang at Baptist tent meetings as a child; lost sight '20s one eye at a time in accidents; often worked and recorded with Blind Boy FULLER '34-8 on Vocalion, ARC group; for Library of Congress '38, again '42; John HAMMOND's Spirituals To Swing concerts '38-9 at Carnegie Hall (tracks with Bull City Red on washboard on Vanguard), with Fuller and Oh Red (same Red; real name George Washington) '40 on Okeh. Worked almost continuously with Brownie MCGHEE from '39 as duo, incl. '42 LoC records; first records together '41 on Okeh. Many of the early bluesmen who were rediscovered in '60s after years of neglect (Bukka WHITE, Skip JAMES etc.) had lost none of their earthy strength; the delicate Piedmont style of Sonny Terry & Brownie McGhee suffered somewhat in authenticity over the years because they were successful right the way through: nevertheless they were a popular and well-loved act. He also worked with LEADBELLY, Woody GUTHRIE, recorded

with Stick McGhee (*see* Brownie's entry) on Atlantic '50, with jook band in NYC '52, solo and duo recordings on a great many labels, mostly out of print. They made three LPs on Storyville in Copenhagen '71: one as duo and one each solo; *Sonny's Story*, *Brownie's Blues*, *Sonny Is King!*, *At The Second Fret* on Prestige; *At Sugar Hill*, *Back To New Orleans*, *Midnight Special* and *California Blues* on Fantasy; *Walk On* on Bulldog or Astan in UK is the duo; *Whoopin'!* on Alligator has Terry, Johnny WINTER, Willie DIXON, etc.; others on Folkways, Stinson, Archive Of Folk, etc.

TESCHEMACHER, Frank (*b* 13 Mar. '06, Kansas City, Mo.; *d* 1 Mar. '32, Chicago) Clarinet; very influential out of proportion to the number and quality of recordings: allegedly disliked recording. He also played alto sax and violin with the original Austin High Gang (*see* JAZZ); to NYC '28 and achieved considerable reputation, worked for Ben POLLACK, bandleader/contractor Sam Lanin, was back in Chicago late '28. Only one side survives under his own name: Frank Teschemacher's Chicagoans made 'Jazz Me Blues' '28 in Chicago, with Eddie CONDON, Joe SULLIVAN, Mezz MEZZROW, Gene KRUPA, two others. Also recorded with Chicago Rhythm Kings, McKenzie-Condon Chicagoans, Elmer Schoebel, etc. He was working for Wild Bill DAVISON and was killed in a car crash while Davison was driving; for some years some of the musicians blamed Davison, who must have felt bad enough as it was.

TEX, Joe (*b* Joseph Arrington, 8 Aug. '33, Rogers, Texas; *d* 12 Aug. '82, Navasota, Texas) (Peter Guralnick says birth date was '35) Soul singer. While still in high school won talent show in Houston, appeared at the Apollo amateur show and won that. Recorded for King '55-7, Ace '58-60, also Anna, Parrot, Checker without chart success but developed popular stage show; James BROWN covered his 'Baby You're Right' '61; recorded for manager Buddy Killen's Dial label in Nashville: UK records on Atlantic, who sent him to Muscle Shoals to record (*see* SOUL). 26 Hot 100 hits '64-72 incl. 8 in top 40, 'Hold What You've Got' '64 at no. 5, 'Skinny Legs And All' no. 10 '67, 'I Gotcha' '72 at no. 2 his biggest. Nine hits were top 10 in soul chart; he thought the first hit (after 10 years of trying) was a terrible record and had been promised it wouldn't be released; with the money he bought his grandmother a house. Left Atlantic, recorded for various labels, became a Muslim and was known as Joseph Hazziez; came back with novelty 'Ain't Gonna Bump No More (With No Big Fat Woman)' (no. 12 '77 on Epic).

TEX-MEX A dance music played by tejanos (Texan-Mexicans), a simple definition blurred by easy confusion with music norteña (on the USA-Mexico border), CONJUNTO and even MARIACHI and CAJUN, much of this summed up as musica chicana (Texan term for anyone of Mexican descent). In general Tex-Mex may be said to revolve around the accordion, important in most of these genres since the mid-19th century, the accordion ensemble being forged during the years '28-60 (Manuel Peña in his *The Texas-Mexican Conjunto* '85, U. of Texas Press). Recorded history parallels that of black folk music ('race' music), Jewish KLEZMER etc. in that a market was identified and then exploited by record labels, a measure of diversity reflected in long series of anthologies *Una Historia de la Musica de la Frontera* on Folklyric, drawing on original recordings made of dozens of regional acts by local labels refreshing the parts Bluebird, Okeh, Decca, Vocalion etc. couldn't reach, incl. accordionists Santiago JIMENEZ Sr, Narcisco MARTINEZ and Bruno Villareal; ensembles Los Alegres de Teran (named after town in Mexico: Eugenio Abrego on accordion, Tomas Ortiz, bajo sexto) and Conjunto Bernal (led by Paulino Bernal, *b* 21 June '39 in Rio Grande valley), with albums on Falcón, others on Mexican Columbia reissued on Caytronics/Caliente; also Los Hermanos Chavarria, Lydia MENDOZA y Familia, Pedro Rocha y Lupe Martinez. Some had considerable local success, usually not approaching much commercial reward. In post-war years the community became more aware of its own cultural roots, and became attractive to chicano and anglo audiences alike; artists such as Mendoza, Flaco JIMENEZ, Steve JORDAN, SAM THE SHAM, Doug SAHM, LOS LOBOS had success with the music or were

infl. by it; similarly, acts like Freddy FENDER, Ry COODER, SANTANA, Peter Rowan and David Byrne (of TALKING HEADS) have drawn upon it; films *Chulas Fronteras* and *Del Mero Corazon* captured it (soundtrack music on Arhoolie); non-documentary films *True Stories* (from Byrne) and *The Border* used the music to great atmospheric effect; a spin-off of the Ritchie VALENS biopic *La Bamba* was a curiosity about the music's roots. It may have come of age, yet as Jeremy Marre and Hannah Charlton point out in a TV documentary in their *Beats Of The Heart* series, in the '80s it still immortalised tales of smuggling, outlaws and derring-do in newly created corridos: its roots run deep. *Texas-Mexican Border Music* series on Folklyric incl. *The First Recordings, Early Corridos, Vol. 14: The Chicano Experience, Vol. 17: The First Women Duets, Vol. 19: The Chavarria Brothers*, etc.; on Arhoolie: *The Texas-Mexican Conjunto, Del Mero Corazon*. See also entries for individuals. Books incl. Américo Paredes' *A Texas-Mexican Cancionera* '76, Marre/Charlton's *Beats Of The Heart* '85.

THARPE, Sister Rosetta (*b* Rosetta Nubin, '15, Cotton Plant, Ark.; *d* 9 Oct. '73, Philadelphia, Pa.) Singer, and guitarist whose licks anticipated those of Chuck BERRY, other rockers. Daughter of Kate Nubin Bell, travelling gospel-bringer, old-time shouter, pianist and mandolinist; raised in Chicago, trad. of Holiness Church; played acoustic guitar, switched to electric; became vocalist with Cab CALLOWAY Revue, recorded 'Pickin' The Cabbage' '40; more fame with Lucky MILLINDER '41-2: 'Rock Me', 'Trouble In Mind', 'I Want A Tall Skinny Papa', 'Rock Daniel', 'Shout Sister Shout', tour-de-force 'That's All', with guitar solo years ahead of its time. Solo career in cabaret, appeared at chic Café Society; resumed pure gospel career '44: classics of genre on Decca incl. duets with Marie Knight 'Didn't It Rain', 'Up Above My Head' (latter covered by Frankie LAINE and Johnny RAY '57; duet hit in UK). Accompaniment often incl. Sammy Price on piano, Pops Foster on bass, Kenny CLARKE on drums. Originally married to a pastor named Thorpe in '34 (changed spelling), she married Russell Morrison (ex-INK SPOTS manager) '51: they had outdoor wedding with 25,000 paying guests. She up-staged Rev. Jimmy CLEVELAND at the Apollo '60, stormed Newport Jazz Festival '67, made LPs for Savoy, gained Grammy nomination; suffered stroke during European tour '70: speech impaired and leg eventually amputated, but toured again '72 on crutches. Planned first LP in four years for Savoy, but had final stroke on day of proposed first session. LPs incl. *Apollo Jump* with Millinder (Affinity UK), *Gospel Train* MCA, *Best Of* Savoy.

THEODORAKIS, Mikis (*b* c.'26) Greek composer, most famous for soundtrack of *Zorba The Greek* '64. He was unalterably opposed to the regime of fascist colonels in Greece '60s-70s; many LPs were international sellers, keeping hope alive among Greeks everywhere. Communist MP in Greece '76-86; gave up seat because he despaired of hoped-for political change. Series of 20 concerts in West Germany '86.

THIELE, Bob (*b* 27 July '22, Brooklyn, NYC) Producer, label boss, songwriter. Announcer on jazz radio shows '36-44, he led 14-piece dance band on clarinet, editor/publisher of *Jazz Magazine* '39-41; formed Signature label '39-48: first to record Erroll GARNER; many priceless sessions now on his Dr Jazz label incl. *Classic Tenors* compilations (two vols. with Coleman HAWKINS, Lester YOUNG, Eddie DAVIS, Julian DASH), *A Melody From The Sky* by Flip PHILLIPS, *Hi Ho Trailus Boot Whip* by Anita O'DAY. Joined Decca '52 on Coral/Brunswick labels, prod. Teresa BREWER, Pearl BAILEY, McGUIRE Sisters, BURNETTE Bros, Lawrence WELK; made cult LPs of Al 'Jazzbeaux' Collins' hip versions of fairy tales; signed Buddy HOLLY after he'd been turned down by Decca; among first to spot talent of Eydie GORME, Steve LAWRENCE, Henry MANCINI, Jackie WILSON. To Dot label '59; prod. Pat BOONE, MILLS Bros; edited soundtrack of Red NICHOLS biopic; recorded Clara Ward Singers live at the Apollo (*see* GOSPEL MUSIC); made album with poet Jack Kerouac, Steve ALLEN on piano: label boss Randy Wood refused to release it, so Thiele quit, took LP with him, with Allen formed Hanover-Signature label, made another LP with Kerouac adding Zoot SIMS, Al COHN;

also had novelty hit by the Nutty Squirrels (Don Elliot, Sascha Burland), recorded Ray BRYANT (R&B hit 'Little Susie' '60). Went to Roulette, recorded LPs of Louis ARMSTRONG playing Duke ELLINGTON, with Duke on piano. To ABC-Impulse '61-9: Creed Taylor had signed John COLTRANE and prod. *Africa Brass;* Thiele took over and recorded more than 100 classic and influential sets by Coltrane, Charles MINGUS, Archie SHEPP, Pharoah SANDERS, Johnny HODGES, Oliver NELSON, Quincy JONES, Earl HINES, Albert AYLER, Count BASIE, Charlie HADEN's Liberation Music Orchestra, incl. two of the most beautiful LPs of the decade: *Duke Ellington Meets Coleman Hawkins* and *Duke Ellington & John Coltrane,* successful far beyond the usual all-star efforts; also prod. sessions for parent ABC incl. Frankie LAINE, Della REESE, etc.; instituted BluesWay label which recorded T-Bone WALKER, B. B. KING, John Lee HOOKER etc. Formed Flying Dutchman/BluesTime/Amsterdam labels '69-77, made albums by Otis SPANN, Joe TURNER, Eddie VINSON, Gil SCOTT-HERON, Gato BARBIERI, Nelson, Hodges, Basie, Armstrong (three sessions for *Louis Armstrong And His Friends* on Amsterdam were Louis's last; song 'What A Wonderful World' co-written by Thiele). Went freelance again with Mysterious Flying Orchestra on RCA with Larry CORYELL, Lonnie Liston SMITH; took Smith to CBS, where he also recorded Arthur BLYTHE. He had married Brewer '72, recorded her with Basie, Ellington, Hines, etc.; formed Teresa Gramophone Co. Ltd '82 with Dr Jazz and Signature labels: recorded Brewer with Stephane GRAPPELLI, Oily Rags (*see* CHAS & DAVE); Smith again, composer/saxophonist Arnie Lawrence (*b* 10 July '38, Brooklyn); previously unreleased Ellington (two 2-disc sets of *All Star Road Band*), Basie's *Afrique* etc. as well as reissuing classic Signature stuff. Other compositions incl. words for 'Duke's Place' (tune of 'C-Jam Blues'), also 'Bean's Place', 'Dear John C', others; own LP *The 20s Score Again* with the New Happy Times Orchestra. There can be few behind-the-scenes careers with so many high spots.

THIELEMANS, Toots (*b* Jean Baptiste Thielemans, 29 Apr. '22, Brussels) Jazz harmonica, guitar; composer; also whistles. Played accordion as a child; studied maths at college; took up harmonica as teenager, then guitar inspired by Django REINHARDT. Infl. by bop after WWII; shared bill with Charlie PARKER in Paris '49; first visited USA '47, toured Europe with Benny GOODMAN '50, resident in USA since '51. Worked with George SHEARING '53-9; has led own groups, visited Europe many times, done much studio work; with Quincy JONES incl. hit LPs '69-71; film soundtrack work incl. *Midnight Cowboy* '69; best-known tune 'Bluesette' has at least 100 recordings. Records as sideman incl. *Big Six Live At Montreux* '75 on Pablo with Oscar PETERSON, also with Zoot SIMS, J. J. JOHNSON, etc. Own LPs: *Man Bites Harmonica* '57 on Riverside, *Captured Alive* '74 on Choice (with Cecil MCBEE), *Live* '75 on Polydor, *Sun Games* '82 on Timeless, *Apple Dimple* '86 on Denon, *Aquerela do Brazil* '87 on Verve; also *When I See You* on Jeton with Bill Ramsey, *Autumn Leaves* on Soul Note, 2 disc *The Silver Collection* on Verve, *Harmonica Jazz* on CBS, *Music For The Millions* on Polydor, *Toots & Svend* (ASMUSSEN) on A&M, *Your Precious Love* on Sonet, *Live In The Netherlands* on Pablo with Joe PASS, Niels-Henning Ørsted Pedersen.

THIN LIZZY Irish HM group formed '69 by Phil Lynott (*b* 20 Aug. '51, Dublin; *d* Jan. '86), half-caste Irishman who'd sung with Black Eagles, Orphanage, learned bass in Skid Row; drummer Brian Downey (*b* 27 Jan. '51) played with Lynott in the first two; guitarist Eric Bell (*b* 3 Sep. '47, Belfast) played in various groups incl. (briefly) Them, showband Dreams (which he left to join Lizzy). Signed to Decca, relied on heavy rock for stage act; Hendrix-lookalike Lynott featured two of Hendrix's songs on stage, but *Thin Lizzy* and *Tales From A Blue Orphanage* '71-2 reflected folk, blues and lyrical imagery of Lynott, who was also a poet of sorts (published book of verse later in '70s). Freak hit single with non-LP track, rocked-up version of trad. Irish 'Whiskey In The Jar', UK no. 6 '73; but singles flopped, as did *Vagabonds Of The Western World* '73 (incl. 'The Rocker' but retained Lynott's lyrical gentleness in songs like 'Little Girl In Bloom'). Bell left; replacements Gary

Moore (ex-Skid Row), Andy Gee and John Cann came and went; eventual choices were Brian Robertson (*b* 12 Sep. '56, Glasgow) and Scott Gorham (*b* 17 Mar. '51, Santa Monica, Cal.; ex-Fast Buck). Signed to Vertigo '74; *Nightlife* and *Fighting* '74-5 flopped; *Jailbreak* '76 hit: first chart LP in USA reached top 20 (on Mercury; their best hit there) with double lead sound *à la* WISHBONE ASH, Downey's hard and heavy double drumkit, Lynott's sneering vocals, but his tongue-in-cheek humour still in evidence. It was unusual: hard rock with a lyrical, romantic twist. *Johnny The Fox* '77 did well; Lynott's hepatitis, Robertson's hand injured in a brawl caused touring problems. Robertson left, leaving trio for *Bad Reputation* '77; rejoined for *Live And Dangerous* '78 (possibly their finest hour, with standout 'Still In Love With You'); left to form Wild Horses. Moore rejoined for *Black Rose* '79 at commercial peak: LP topped UK chart with four hit singles; deftness of touch that ensured pop acceptance rivalled only by Rainbow among HM bands. But Moore departed acrimoniously; ULTRAVOX's Midge Ure filled in before PINK FLOYD stage sideman Snowy White joined, but White didn't gell; *Chinatown* and *Renegade* '80-1 disappointed. John Sykes (ex-Tygers of Pan Tang) provided more of required attack; group incl. Darren Wharton on keyboards for *Thunder And Lightning* '83, then Lynott disbanded, claiming rightly that format had become cliché. Live 2-disc *Life* was epitaph. He'd begun solo career with *Solo In Soho* '80 and *The Philip Lynott Album* '82, giving free rein to romantic side in 'Sarah' (for baby daughter) and 'Yellow Pearl' (co-written with Ure), which became *Top Of The Pops* theme tune; but group venture Grand Slam with Downey and others remained unsigned (too many Lizzy songs in repertoire didn't help). He began solo career proper with single 'Nineteen' on Polydor, died of drugs. His combination of bubbling personality and rebel stance helped Lizzy win over even punks (formed group with SEX PISTOLS Cook and Jones called Greedy Bastards for Xmas single '78); an outstanding writer in genre whose talents could not be summed up by singles collection *Adventures Of Thin Lizzy* '82. When band made top 10 with 'Killer On The Loose' '80 during hunt for the Yorkshire Ripper, one had to believe it was foolishness rather than opportunism.

13th FLOOR ELEVATORS Psychedelic/R&B group formed '66 in Austin, Texas. Lineup: Roky Erickson, vocals; Stacy Sutherland, guitar; Tommy Hall, jug; Benny Thurman, bass and violin; John Ike Walton or Ronnie Leatherman, drums. LPs: *The Psychedelic Sounds Of The Thirteenth Floor Elevators* '66 (predated the first GRATEFUL DEAD LP in psychedelic stakes), *Easter Everywhere* (with Erickson, Sutherland, Hall, Dan Galindo on bass, Danny Thomas on drums) and *Thirteenth Floor Elevators Live* '68, *Bull Of The Woods* '69, first two issued on short-lived Radar label UK. Erickson played guitar in the Spades, Austin R&B group; Sutherland, Thurman and Walton were the Lingsmen (with vocalist Max Rainey), recruited Erickson, who introduced Hall, whose jug-blowing was a bizarre sound complementing psychedelic lyrics often written by Erickson. They changed name, signed with local International Artists label (Lelan Rogers, related to superstar Kenny ROGERS, was an executive); 'You're Gonna Miss Me' from the first LP was their closest thing to a hit, not quite reaching top 50: they might have been forgotten had it not been incl. in *Nuggets* compilation of psychedelia on Rhino. The LPs immediately became collectors' items, incl. in 13-disc complete edition of International Artists output. (Even more obscure is Spades' original version of 'You're Gonna Miss Me'.) They disbanded '69; Erickson published *Openers* volume of poetry; was hospitalised several times, unique world view diagnosed as a mental problem; made singles on Mars and Rhino; worked with group called Bleib Alien; in the Explosives with drummer Fred Krc; Elevators reissues led CBS to sign his group the Aliens of the period, whose '80 LP (title appears to be in Arabic) was prod. by Stu Cook (ex-CREEDENCE), with Duane Alaksen, guitar; Bill Miller, autoharp; Steve Burgess, bass; Fuzzy Furioso, drums, semi-classic track 'Two Headed Dog'. CBS did not renew its option.

.38 SPECIAL USA southern rock band formed '75 in Jacksonville, Fla. by vocalist Donnie Van Zant, younger brother of LYNYRD SKYNYRD's Ronnie: like that band plays guitar rock loud and proud. Other members: Don Barnes, vocals, guitar; Jeff Carlisi, guitar; Jack Grondin and Steve Brookins, drums; Larry Jungstrom, bass (replaced Ken Lyons '78). *.38 Special* '77 on A&M featured guest Dan Hartman on vocals (ex-Edgar WINTER bassist); *Special Delivery* and *Rocking Into The Night* '78-9 moved away from straight R&R towards song-oriented AOR, cemented by *Wild-Eyed Southern Boys* '81 incl. hits 'Hold On Loosely' (no. 27), 'Fantasy Girl' (52). *Special Forces* '82 continued rise with top 10 'Caught Up In You', top 40 'You Keep Runnin' Away'; *Tour De Force* made three million-selling LPs in a row. More hit singles '83-4; long-awaited LP *Strength In Numbers* '86. Always open to outside influences, increasingly inviting non-members' contributions to songwriting; established with MOLLY HATCHET and Blackfoot as leading southern rockers, eclipsing Lynyrd Skynyrd survivors Roosington/Collins Band. Have never toured Europe; live act said to be good value.

THOMAS, Chris (*b* 13 Jan. '47, Perivale, Middlesex) UK producer. Student at Royal Academy of Music; played in semi-pro groups such as Second Thoughts, with Patrick Campbell-Lyons (later NIRVANA), Tony Duhig (Jade Warrior), John 'Speedy' Keen (THUNDERCLAP NEWMAN). 'I'm Finding It Rough', co-written by Thomas and Campbell-Lyons, recorded by the EVERLY Bros '67. Joined George MARTIN's AIR London studios as office boy, began prod. with CLIMAX BLUES BAND (first four LPs), then PROCOL HARUM, whose quasi-classical sound fitted in with Thomas's background: success of their *Live With Edmonton Symphony Orchestra* '71, which required much studio editing, made his name and he went freelance '72. Helped mix PINK FLOYD's *Dark Side Of The Moon* '73, prod. *For Your Pleasure* '73 and next four for ROXY MUSIC, as well as BADFINGER. Returned to the road with John CALE, playing keyboards; continued prod. Bryan Ferry after Roxy split, also co-writing material with him. Prod. tracks on SEX PISTOLS' *Anarchy In The UK* '77 incl. the first three historic singles, continuing new wave affiliations with Tom ROBIN-

SON's *Power In The Darkness* '78. First involved with BEATLES at AIR (*White Album* period); organised Paul MCCARTNEY's *Wings Over America* soundtrack/album, then his *Back To The Egg* '79. Met Chrissie Hynde when she sang backup on a Chris Spedding LP; prod. *Pretenders* '80, his second chart-topping new wave LP, continued with more PRETENDERS LPs, consolidating with Pete Townshend and Elton JOHN, diversifying into electro-pop with HUMAN LEAGUE's *Hysteria* '84, co-prod. with Hugh Padgham.

THOMAS, Irma (*b* 18 Feb. '41, Ponchatoula, La.) Blues, R&B, soul vocalist; veteran of New Orleans scene, infl. by Etta JAMES and an important performer in that great line. Had R&B hit 'Don't Mess With My Man' '60 on Ron; recorded for Minit (distributed by Lew Chudd's Imperial label; *see* Allen TOUSSAINT), had four Hot 100 entries '64 (top 20 'Wish Someone Would Care') on Imperial; also recorded for Bert BERNS' Shout label; R&B hit 'Good To Me' '68 on Chess. Continuing popularity evidenced by many compilations, etc.: *Irma Thomas Sings* on Bandy (Joe Banashak's New Orleans Minit/Bandy tracks '59-63), *Time Is On My Side* on Kent (Minit/Imperial tracks incl. 'Ruler Of My Heart', covered '63 by Otis REDDING as 'Pain In My Heart'), *In Between Tears* (from early '70s, originally on Fungus USA) and *Hip Shakin' Mama* (live, mid-'70s) on Charly UK, *Soul Queen Of New Orleans* on Maison de Soul (late '70s). *The New Rules* '85 on Rounder followed by *The Way I Feel* '88; *To The Power Of Three* on Geffen. *Best Of: Break-Away* issued on EMI American '86.

THOMAS, Rufus and Carla Soul stars of the '60s whose hits helped get Stax label off the ground, sparking off a golden age of popular music. Rufus (*b* 26 Mar. '17, Casey, Ms.) describes himself as 'the world's oldest teenager'; was in high school in Memphis, Tenn. when he joined a teacher as second banana in a comedy act at a local theatre; worked in show business until he married '40, continued part-time as theatre MC, DJ on WDIA, where B. B. KING was another DJ, Jim Stewart (later co-founder of Stax) played fiddle in a country band. Rufus's 'Bear Cat' was no. 3 R&B hit '53: answer to

Big Mama THORNTON's 'Hound Dog' was first national hit for Sun, but Elvis PRESLEY soon changed label's direction. Daughter Carla (*b* '42, Memphis) had years of experience in local Teen Town Singers, was about to enter college when they recorded uptempo duet 'Cause I Love You' '60 for Satellite, backed by Carla's brother Marvell on organ, BOOKER T on baritone sax, Steve Cropper on guitar, Robert Talley on piano: local hit was noticed by Atlantic, who made distribution deal with Satellite, which became Stax after Carla's 'Gee Whiz (Look At His Eyes)' made top 10 pop, top 5 R&B '61. Carla had 15 Hot 100 entries '61-9 (first six on Atlantic), almost identical list on R&B chart; 'B-A-B-Y' '66 was top 15 pop, no. 3 R&B. Rufus re-entered R&B chart 10 years after his first hit, had ten more there and nine in Hot 100 '63-71, all dance novelties: 'Walking The Dog' was top 10 pop '63, followed by 'Can Your Monkey Do The Dog' ('Do The Monkey' was KING CURTIS dance hit '63), 'Do The Funky Chicken', the 'Push And Pull', 'The Breakdown', 'Do The Funky Penguin'. When Stax went broke they did not bother label-hopping, but remained popular in local clubs; *Chronical* on Stax (now from Fantasy) compiles tracks by both; Carla's *Memphis Queen* was reissued. Rufus has compilation *Jump Back* on Edsel UK, EP of Sun material on Charly.

THOMAS, Sam Fan (*b* '52, Bafoussam, Cameroon) Singer, composer, guitarist, arranger; achieved international success '80s, blending several African rhythms with makossa for dance floor action. Joined Black Tigers, led by blind André Marie Tala, as guitarist '68; stayed for eight years as Tala developed his tchamasi rhythm, recorded in Paris, toured Senegal, played on soundtrack of film *Pousse Pousse* and had several hit singles. Went solo; *Funky New Bel* on Satel label in Cotonou; third LP incl. hit 'Rikiatou'. Recorded *Makassi* in Paris '83 incl. track 'African Typic Collection', massive hit '84-5 in Africa, crossing to Europe and West Indies; *Neng Makassi* '85, also on Tamwo label, featured many of Cameroon's leading session musicians.

THOMPSON, Barbara (*b* 27 July '44, Oxford) UK saxophonist, composer; plays alto, tenor and soprano saxes, flutes, other instruments. Studied at Royal College of Music; recorded with Howard Riley Trio (*Angle* on CBS), joined New Jazz Orchestra and met future husband, drummer Jon Hiseman (played with Graham BOND, Georgie FAME; *see also* John MAYALL, COLOSSEUM); NJO albums are *Western Reunion* on Decca UK, *Le Déjeuner sur l'Herbe* on MGM. She led various groups, worked with Don RENDELL, John DANKWORTH, MANFRED MANN, others; founder member with Hiseman of United Jazz & Rock Ensemble '75 (five LPs on Mood incl. *Highlights* on CD), formed her fusion group Paraphernalia '75 (Hiseman joined '79). Pieces for 20-piece orchestra were recorded by the BBC; other session work incl. LLOYD WEBBER's *Variations, Cats, Requiem*. She played at Adolphe Sax centenary celebrations in Brussels, wrote 'Blues For Adolphe' (incl. in *Just Music* by the Don Rendell Five, BBC tapes from '74 issued '76 on Spotlite). Her LPs incl. *Barbara Thompson's Jubiaba* '78 on MCA, with 10-11 piece band; *Ghosts* '83 on MCA and *Shadowshow* '84 on TM both with Rod ARGENT vocals; Paraphernalia quartet with keyboards, bass, drums on *Paraphernalia* '78, *Wilde Tales* '79 (incl. musical treatment of Oscar Wilde's *The Selfish Giant*), *Live In Concert* '80 on MCA. She and Hiseman have four children, made BBC documentary *Jazz, Rock And Marriage* '79 about being busy musicians/parents; opened their own studio at home '82 and made records on TM: on *Mother Earth* '83 Paraphernalia is Thompson, Hiseman, Dill Katz on bass, Colin Dudman on keyboards, Anthony Oldridge added on violin (three-part 'Mother Earth Suite' incl. 'Country Dance', used by London's Capitol Radio as a signature tune, this version featuring Oldridge). *Pure Fantasy* '84 is largely based on Sri Lankan folk tunes, has Bill Worrall on keyboards, Dave Ball on bass, Rod Dorothy on violin. (CD edition adds 'Suite' for over an hour's music.) Her jazz-rock fusion has memorable tunes with excellent playing and production throughout, rhythmically compelling with the composer's playing usually front and centre. *Heavenly Bodies* '86 is an LP of Thompson compositions; she plays eight instruments incl. keyboards and clarinet with latest members of Paraphernalia (Hiseman,

Ball, Peter Lemer on keyboards, Paul Dunne on guitar), 10 others incl. string quartet on some tracks; cassette-only compilation *Barbara Thompson's Special Edition* incl. live tracks. Bassist Phil Mulford replaced Ball on '87 UK tour; live 2-disc *A Cry From The Heart* was recorded. Her *Concert For Saxophone And Orchestra* was premiered in West Germany mid-'88. Hiseman still plays with UJ&RE, made own *A Night In The Sun* '82 in Rio de Janeiro (on Kuckuck label); *About Time Too!* '86 is drum solo album on TM. Wanting her music to be published properly, Hiseman bought a publishing company that had gone broke: their Temple Music owns UK/Eire rights to music by · Cecil TAYLOR, Gil EVANS, Mal WALDRON, Benny GOLSON, Dexter GORDON, many others incl. many South Americans like AZYMUTH; some of these people are now receiving money from this market for the first time in years.

THOMPSON, Charles, Sir (*b* Charles Phillip Thompson, 21 Mar. '18, Springfield, Ohio) Piano, organ; composer, arranger. Worked in territory bands; for Lionel HAMPTON '40, Coleman HAWKINS incl. famous Capitol *Hollywood Stampede* sessions '45, Illinois JACQUET '47-8: composed 'Robbins Nest', tribute to DJ Fred Robbins, hit for Jacquet and a jazz standard. (Vocal version 'Just When We're Falling In Love' has words by Bob Russell.) Recorded as leader on Apollo late '40s; often with Buck CLAYTON '50s incl. famous Jam Sessions series of Columbia LPs (first one had 'Robbins Nest' as side-long vehicle '53); four dates as leader on Vanguard '53-4 prod. by John HAMMOND incl. octet date with Hawkins, Emmett BERRY, Benny MORTON, Earle Warren; also recorded as sideman on Vanguard with Clayton, Jimmy RUSHING. Toured Europe with Clayton '61; gigged solo and with trio all over USA, Canada, Puerto Rico; had long residency in Pennsylvania club early '70s; suffered from ill health mid-'70s but came back. Also had own Columbia LP, *Hey There* on Black And Blue, *Kansas City Nights* with Clayton and Buddy TATE on Prestige, tracks on *Master Jazz Piano Vol. 2* on Master Jazz. Nickname no doubt from elegant lightness with substance; like Nat PIERCE, capable of sounding remarkably like Count BASIE.

THOMPSON, Eddie (*b* Edgar Charles Thompson, 31 May '25, London; *d* 6 Nov. '86) UK jazz pianist, eclectic and much-loved. Attended same school for the blind as George SHEARING; house pianist at Ronnie SCOTT's '59-60, lived in USA '62-72, duo gigs with Roger KELLAWAY in NYC '85. LPs: *By Myself* '82 on 77; *Some Strings, Some Skins And A Bunch Of Keys* '79 on Hobo; others on Hep: *Ain't She Sweet* '81, *With Roy Williams* '82 (trombonist, *b* 7 Mar. '37, Bolton, Lancs.), *Memories Of You* '84, *At Chesters* '85.

THOMPSON, Hank (*b* Henry William Thompson, 3 Sep. '25, Waco, Texas) Country singer and bandleader, the most successful exponent of western swing from late '40s to today. Served as radio technician in US Navy, attended universities '45-6. Appeared on radio '42-3 on WACO; had own show as 'Hank The Hired Hand' on KWTX Waco '46-7. Record debut on Globe with his own 'Whoa Sailor' '46 led to contract with Capitol '47-65, top 10 hit with remake of 'Whoa Sailor' '49. To Nashville to join *Smokey Mountain Hayride* '48, formed band the Brazos Valley Boys, toured heavily and had hits almost every year from '52, picking up every award possible in the genre. To name the top 5 hits: 'Wild Side Of Life' '52 (no. 1), 'Waiting In The Lobby Of Your Heart' '52, 'Rub-A-Dub-Dub' and 'Wake Up Irene' '53, 'Don't Take It Out On Me' '55, 'Squaws Along The Yukon' '58; later top tens were 'A Six Pack To Go' and 'Oklahoma Hills' '60-1. No hits in '65; switched to WB and came back to top 20 '66-7, to Dot and top 10 with 'On Tap, In The Can Or In The Bottle' and 'Smokey The Bar' '68, lesser hits '69-76 incl. 'The Older The Violin, The Sweeter The Music', 'Asphalt Cowboy'. Dot taken over by MCA, records on that label; he switched to Churchill and carried on with remake of '57 hit 'Rockin' In The Congo', contemporary 'Cocaine Blues', 'Once In A Blue Moon' '81-3. A prolific album seller, he was the first country artist to record in stereo. Albums incl. *Songs Of The Brazos Valley* '50, *North Of The Rio Grande* '53, *Dance Ranch* '56, *At The Golden Nugget* '58, *No. 1 Country & Western Band* '59, *Breakin' In Another Heart* '60, *Songs For Rounders* and *A Six Pack To Go* '61, *Breakin' The Rules* '62, *Best* '63, all on Capitol; *On Tap, In The Can Or In The Bottle* '68, *Smokey The Bar* '69, *Salutes Oklahoma* '70, *Next Time I Fall In Love (I Won't)* '71, *25th Anniversary Album* '73, *Back In The Swing Of Things* '76, *The Thompson Touch* '77, *Doin' My Thing* '78, all on Dot; *Brand New Hank* '79 and *Take Me Back To Tulsa* '80 on MCA, *Best Of The Best* '80 on Gusto, *20 Golden Pieces* '85 on Bulldog; two vols. of remade *Greatest Hits* and new *Here's To Country Music* '87 on Step One.

THOMPSON, Lucky (*b* Eli Thompson, 16 June '24, Detroit) Tenor sax; also soprano later. A unique stylist: disciple of Don BYAS with softer tone and personal sense of time. Worked for Lionel HAMPTON, Don REDMAN '44, Count BASIE '44-5; recorded for Dial on West Coast '46 with Dizzy GILLESPIE and Charlie PARKER in Dizzy's Tempo Jazzmen, also with Parker septet; played with Boyd RAEBURN; led band at Savoy Ballroom; worked in R&B recording, songwriting, publishing; came back to jazz mid-'50s: played on Miles DAVIS classic 'Walkin' ' session Apr. '54, on *Jo Jones Special* on Vanguard c.'55, joined Milt JACKSON on tracks for *Ballads And Blues* on Atlantic, *The Jazz Skyline* on Savoy with Hank JONES, Kenny CLARKE, Wendell Marshall on bass, both early '56; left for Europe the next month: *Paris 1956* on Swing, *Brown Rose* in Paris with Martial Solal on Xanadu; back to USA, with Jackson on Atlantic again on *Plenty, Plenty Soul* '57; returned to Europe until '62, taking up soprano late '50s. Three LPs on Prestige incl. *Lucky Strikes!* '63 with Hank Jones, Richard Davis, Connie Kay; also two LPs on Rivoli; back to Europe '68-71, recorded for MPS. *Body & Soul* '70 on Nessa with Tete MONTOLIU trio made in Barcelona is almost retrospective, 'Blue N Boogie' reprised from the Davis session, 'What's New?' from the Savoy/Jackson session, but this time on soprano, etc. Taught at Dartmouth '73-4 and made two LPs on Groove Merchant; inactive on record since then. Other LPs incl. *Lucky Thompson Featuring Oscar Pettiford* c.'56 now on Jasmine, two albums on ABC-Paramount reissued on Impulse incl. *Dancing Sunbeam* with Jimmy Cleveland, Pettiford. The list isn't long enough for his many fans.

THOMPSON, Richard and Linda Reigning stars of UK folk-rock, long the country's best-kept secret. Richard (*b* 3 Apr. '49, London) left FAIRPORT CONVENTION '71 with high reputation as guitarist and songwriter; he sessioned with Nick DRAKE, John MARTYN, Sandy Dennis, others; appeared on Fairport alumni LP *The Bunch: Rock On* and pioneering ALBION BAND LP *Morris On* '72. Solo debut was *Henry The Human Fly* '72, crucially underrated on release, still an impressive testament, with wife Linda (*b* Linda Peters, Glasgow) singing backup. Together they released *I Want To See The Bright Lights Tonight* '74 on Island: championed by John PEEL it was better received, crystallised ideal of English rock; Julie COVINGTON covered title track, Martin CARTHY featured 'The Great Valerio', Elvis COSTELLO covered two songs. *Hokey Pokey* '74 was less introspective, with jaunty title track; 'Georgie On A Spree' described by critics as nearest thing in UK to the BAND: like most of these LPs it was prod. by Joe BOYD, now on his Hannibal label. *Pour Down Like Silver* '75 was stark and demanding, reflecting their recent conversion to Sufi religion; 'Night Comes In' was live favourite because of his solo space, while good songs, her soaring voice kept quality high. *Guitar, Vocal* '76 collected his unreleased material; their *First Light* '78 was excellent comeback incl. 'Don't Let A Thief Steal Into Your Heart', covered by POINTER SISTERS. *Sunny Vista* '79 was quirky and uncommercial, with guests Gerry RAFFERTY, MCGARRIGLE SISTERS; he sessioned with John CALE, Ralph MCTELL, others; *Strict Tempo* '81 was solo instrumental; *Shoot Out The Lights* '82 was last LP with Linda, incl. classic title track, 'Wall Of Death'; well-received in USA, it led to his first tour there in nearly 10 years, but the marriage was breaking up. *Hand Of Kindness* '83 was a classic even by his high standards, full of good songs; solo acoustic *Small Town Romance* '84 was made live in NYC, featuring much of their best work, and classic Fairport material. He prod. work by Loudon WAINWRIGHT, guested on LPs by Any Trouble, J. J. CALE and T-Bone BURNETT '84-6; his first major label LP in 10 years was *Across A Crowded Room* '85 on Polydor, disappointing compared to Linda's long-overdue solo: *One Clear Moment* '85 on

WB had her singing as well as ever on mostly her own fine songs, incl. 'Telling Me Lies' (co-written with Betsy Cook), soon covered by the Trio (*see* Linda RONSTADT); she also sang with the HOME SERVICE in their production of the medieval mystery plays. *Doom & Gloom From The Tomb* was USA cassette-only release, effectively tidying up his back catalogue: few can compile such a collection from scraps; *Daring Adventure* '86 saw him back on form, with Cajun-like 'Valerie', other good songs. French, Frith, Kaiser, Thompson made experimental LP for Rhino '87 called *Live, Love, Larf And Loaf* (CAPTAIN BEEFHEART drummer John French, avant-garde guitarists Henry Kaiser and Fred Frith). Hailed as an infl. by such diverse artists as the SMITHS, LOS LOBOS, R.E.M. and Mark Knopfler, his LPs have charted in USA since '83: not even his self-effacement could keep him a secret forever.

THOMPSON TWINS UK new wave group formed in Sheffield '77 by Tom Bailey (*b* 18 Jan '56, Halifax), vocals and bass; Chris Bell, drums; Peter Dodd and John Roog, guitars. DEVO-esque quartet evolved into seven pieces and tribal rhythms on *A Product Of* '81: fluctuating cast incl. Jane Shorter, sax; Joe Leeway (*b* 15 Nov. '57, London), percussion; Alannah Currie (*b* 28 Sep. '57, Auckland, N.Z.), sax; name derived from characters in Hergés Tintin cartoons. Four flop singles, cult following; *Set* '82 incl. ex-Soft Boys bassist Matthew Seligman: Bailey had come stage centre as vocalist; Shorter had left; Currie became permanent member, took over lyric writing. First two singles from LP flopped but 'In The Name Of The Law', disco-infl. synthesised throwaway written by Bailey to fill LP, hit top of Billboard dance chart: Bailey, Currie and Leeway shed the others, evolved synth/percussion-based sound. 'Lies' from *Quick Step And Side Kick* '83 (prod. by Alex Sadkin at Compass Point) reached USA top 30 before audience at home caught on; two more made top 10 UK, another top 40. Distinctive image (one white man, one black, one woman) was popular on MTV, which boosted 'Hold Me Now' to no. 3 USA '84, from *Into The Gap* '84 (co-prod. by Bailey and Sadkin); three singles from the LP charted in USA, five in UK. *Here's To*

Future Days '85 lacked this potency; Bailey (now sole prod.) collapsed and CHIC's Nile Rodgers was brought in to finish the job: facile anti-heroin 'Don't Mess With Doctor Dream' followed by 'King For One Day'; appalling cover of BEATLES' 'Revolution' didn't chart at all. Popular on dance floor (cassettes and 12″ singles all had different mixes), glossy pop was ultimately meaningless, and Howard JONES (for one) was doing it better. Despite participation in Live Aid, CND affiliation, they'd sacrificed credibility for success. Leeway left '86; Currie and Bailey released *Close To The Bone* '87, but moment was gone with earlier idiosyncrasy.

THORNHILL, Claude (*b* 10 Aug. '09, Terre Haute, Ind.; *d* 1 July '65, NYC) Pianist, arranger, bandleader. After formal studies played in territory bands, worked for Paul WHITEMAN and Benny GOODMAN '34, Ray NOBLE '35-6. Session work incl. arr. of 'Loch Lomond' for Maxine SULLIVAN; toured with her and began recording under his own name '37; took over Gil EVANS group '38 fronted by Skinnay ENNIS (incl. Bob Hope radio show), began touring. A dance band rather than a jazz band, but '37-41 employed such Swing Era stars as trumpets Charlie SPIVAK, Manny Klein, Conrad Gozzo (*b* 6 Feb. '22, New Britain, Conn.; *d* 10 Oct. '64, L.A.; later played with Woody HERMAN, Boyd RAEBURN); reedmen Babe Russin, Toots Mondello (*b* Nuncio Mondello, '12, Boston, Mass.), Nick Fatool or Dave Tough on drums, Barry Galbraith on guitar, etc.; soon earned great respect among musicians as well as hits with forward-sounding arrangements, such as his own 'Portrait Of A Guinea Farm'. Six-piece reed section '41-2 incl. clarinettist Irving Fazola, later Danny Polo (*b* '01, Clinto, Ind.; *d* 11 July '49, Chicago), others also doubling on clarinet; two French horns added '42 (John Graas and Vincent Jacobs, later Mike Glass) and some unusual sounds were made, with Evans, later Gerry MULLIGAN arranging. He played in Artie SHAW Navy band, reorganised after WWII. Hits did not make Billboard chart, but according to *Pop Memories* at least 16 sides deserved top 30 status '37-53, incl. theme 'Snowfall' '41 (written by Thornhill: not just a fox trot but a lovely tone poem), 'A Sunday Kind Of Love' '46 with vocal by Fran

Warren (*b* 4 Mar. '26, Brooklyn; sang with Randy BROOKS, Art MOONEY, Charlie BARNET, later on Broadway), 'Love For Love' '47, solo by Lee KONITZ. In '48 Evans, Mulligan, Konitz took part in Thornhill-infl. Miles DAVIS 'Birth of the Cool' sessions, which also incl. French horn, Mike Zwerin on trombone. Thornhill's band played arr. of jazz standards 'Robbins' Nest', 'Anthropology', Charlie PARKER tunes, but also standards and straight stuff: Addinsell's 'Warsaw Concerto', 'Coquette' (written by Carmen, Guy LOMBARDO's brother); his own piano was often ornate, but with the sense that he was sending up cocktail piano: his musical sense of humour may have kept him from greater commercial success, but his music still holds up today. He wrote 'I Wish I Had You', 'Buster's Last Stand', others; was mus. dir. for Tony BENNETT mid-'50s; led smaller band; Zwerin toured with him '58 when salad days were over, recalled humour of adversity in autobiography *Close Enough For Jazz* '83. 2-disc *Tapestries* on Affinity has 32 tracks from heyday, 17 arranged by Evans.

THORNTON, Willie Mae 'Big Mama' (*b* 11 Dec. '26, Montgomery, Ala.; *d* 25 July '84, L.A.) Blues singer; also played harmonica, drums. Toured South from '41, settled in Houston, Texas '48, recorded for Peacock '50s (no. 1 R&B hit 'Hound Dog' '53, later covered by Elvis PRESLEY: LEIBER & STOLLER are famous for writing it, but some thought Thornton should have got a credit). Toured with Johnny OTIS '52, Junior PARKER/Johnny ACE '53-4, Clarence BROWN '56, then settled in L.A. '57, often worked with Roy MILTON. Recorded for small labels incl. Kent, then Arhoolie '65-6, '68; Mercury '69, Vanguard '75. Various appearances incl. Monterey Jazz Festival '66, Dick Cavett TV show '71, state prisons '75. She was a legendary figure and popular in West Coast clubs until she died. LPs: *Ball & Chain*, *& Chicago Blues Band*, *In Europe* on Arhoolie; *Jail* on Vanguard (aka *Mama's Pride* in UK); portions of concerts once on Fontana etc.

THREADGILL, Henry (*b* 15 Feb. '44, Chicago, Ill.) Reeds, composer, leader. Had formal studies; played with gospel and blues groups; joined Richard ABRAMS' Experimental band and became founder member of AACM, trio AIR. His Sextett is six pieces plus Threadgill; LPs *When Was That?*, *Just The Facts And Pass The Bucket* and *Subject To Change* on About Time label; *You Know The Number* '86 on new RCA Novus imprint, with Deidre Murray on cello, Frank Lacy on trombone, Rasul Sadik on trumpet, Fred Hopkins on bass, Pheeroan akLaff, Reggie Nicholson on drums. Hopkins and akLaff from New Air; several playing in Oliver LAKE combo as well. Debut was followed by *Easily Slip Into Another World* '88. Threadgill's contemporary music uses classical harmonies, gospel voicings and the earliest jazz principle, of collective improvisation; his group is tightly drilled yet at ease.

THREE DEGREES, The USA black vocal trio from Philadelphia: Fayette Pinkney, Linda Turner, Shirley Porter, last two replaced '65 by Sheila Ferguson, Valerie Holiday. Minor hits on Swan '65-6; recorded for WB, Metromedia, Neptune (GAMBLE & HUFF), then Roulette: George Goldner's 'Maybe' prod. by Richard Barrett (who'd prod. it for a hit by the Chantels '58) reached top 30 '70; switched to Gamble & Huff's Philadelphia International label and had smash 'When Will I See You Again', no. 2 USA '74 and said to be biggest-selling single of the year in UK. Also backed group MFSB on no. 1 USA hit 'TSOP (The Sound Of Philadelphia)' '74; never had any more single hits of their own in USA, but LPs charted: *The Three Degrees* '74 (top 30), *International* '75, *Live* and *New Dimensions* (on Ariola) '76; singles continued to chart in UK, where they were said to be Prince Charles' favourite act, performed at his 30th birthday party: 12 UK hits '74-9 incl. top tens 'Take Good Care Of Yourself' (LP of that title charted), 'Woman In Love' (no. 3), 'My Simple Heart'; came back '85 with 'The Heaven I Need' on Supreme label.

THREE DOG NIGHT Pop group formed '68, name from Australian expression referring to temperature and canine comfort: vocalist Daniel Anthony Hutton (*b* 10 Sep. '42, Buncrana, Ireland) had worked for many record labels, recorded voices for Hanna-Barbera cartoons; recruited former Enemies vocalist Cory Julius Wells (*b* 5 Feb. '42,

Buffalo, N.Y.) and Charles (Chuck) William Negron (*b* 8 June '42, NYC) to head new group with three featured singers; hired Jim Greenspoon (*b* 7 Feb. '48, L.A.) on organ, Floyd Chester Sneed (*b* 22 Nov. '43, Calgary, Alberta) on drums, Mike Allsup (*b* 8 Mar. '47, Modesto, Cal.) on guitar, Joe Schermie (*b* 12 Feb. '48, Madison, Wis.) on bass. They recorded for Dunhill and had 21 hit singles '69-75, 11 in top 10; they were derided for sticking to covers, but gave early breaks to little-known songwriters. First eponymous LP reached no. 11 with top 30 'Try A Little Tenderness' (hit by Otis REDDING), top 5 with 'One' (by Harry NILSSON), *Suitable For Framing* also '69 was no. 16 LP with no. 4 hit 'Easy To Be Hard' (from *Hair*), top 10 with 'Eli's Coming' (by Laura NYRO), also incl. 'Lady Samantha' (by Elton JOHN). Live *Captured At The Forum* '69 and *It Ain't Easy* '70 were top 10 LPs, latter with first no. 1, Randy NEWMAN's 'Mama Told Me (Not To Come)' (no. 3 in UK, almost their only hit there); *Naturally* '71 slipped to no. 16 with Russ Ballard's 'Liar' (no. 7) and no. 1 with 'Joy To The World' by Hoyt AXTON. Compilation *Golden Bisquits* and *Harmony* '71 (latter with ten top 5 hits), *Seven Separate Fools* '71 with no. 1 'Black & White' (Greyhound's reggae hit, suitable for multi-racial group, written '55 by David Arkin/Earl Robinson to celebrate end of legal segregation). Other hit LPs were live *Around The World* '73, *Cyan* '73 (with no. 3 hit 'Shambalaya' by B. W. STEVENSON); another hit was 'The Show Must Go On' (no. 14, by Leo SAYER). *Coming Down Your Way* slipped to no. 70, *American Pastime* out of top 100. Schermie left '73, replaced by Jack Ryland (*b* 7 June '49); keyboardist Skip Konte (ex-Blues Image) was added; Hutton left '76, replaced by Jay Gruska and three ex-members of Rufus (*see* Chaka KHAN) joined as band left the charts. Sneed, Ryland and Allsup left to form S.S. Fools; Hutton, Negron and Wells re-formed '81 to relive golden era.

THREE SUNS, The Popular USA trio formed '39, played hotel and radio gigs: Artie Dunn on organ and vocals, Marty Nevins on accordion, Al Nevins on guitar. Hits on Hit, Majestic and RCA '44-54 with ballads incl. no. 14 '44 with 'Twilight Time'

(co-written by trio with Buck Ram; see the PLATTERS), later on RCA and eventually sold a million; also no. 1 '47 for four weeks with 'Peg O' My Heart' (HARMONICATS version was even bigger). LPs on RCA '50s; Al Nevins was replaced '50s by Johnny Buck, Joe Negri; Dunn re-formed '57 with Johnny Romano (guitar), Tony Lovello (accordion). Album on Circle has '39-57 tracks. Al Nevins formed Aldon Music with Don Kirshner; see BRILL BUILDING.

THUNDERCLAP NEWMAN UK pop group formed late '60s by singer/drummer John 'Speedy' Keen, ex-Post Office engineer and jazz pianist Andy Newman. Latter had met Pete Townshend at art school; Keen had persuaded WHO to record his 'Armenia City In The Sky' on their *Sell Out* LP '67. Townshend put them together, played bass and added the guitar prodigy Jimmy McCulloch (*b* 13 Aug. '53, Glasgow; *d* 27 Sep. '79, London); first single 'Something In The Air' for Who's Track label was surprise no. 1 '69, perfect for post-psychedelic era, with wistful Keen vocal and sympathetic piano. TV showed them visually unlikely pop stars and live gigs failed to take off too, with Jim Avory on bass, Jimmy's younger brother Jack on drums (to let Keen out in front); 'Accidents' just missed top 40; Townshend prod. slice of psychedelia *Hollywood Dream* '70; then they faded. Newman made solo *Rainbow* '71, still on Track with wide array of strange instruments; Keen made *Previous Convictions* '71 on Track, *Y'Know Wot I Mean* '75 on Island, both standard singer/songwriter material; McCulloch became journeyman guitarist with John MAYALL, Stone The Crows, Blue, Wings, Dukes; died of suspected OD. Underrated group with necessarily short life.

TIGER, Growling (*b* Neville Marcano, Siparia, Trinidad) Calypsonian. Boxer at 14; the 'Siparia Tiger' became flyweight champion of Trinidad '29. Worked in aerated water and sugar factories; unemployed early '34, given food and writing materials by Mr Mentor (a shopkeeper who thought he was a calypsonian) to write a calypso about water scheme workers striking for more pay; he performed it that evening for an audience. Mentor showed him newspaper

story about ATILLA THE HUN and Roaring Lion (Raphael de Leon) going to NYC to record; he decided he wanted to go there and that becoming a top calypsonian was the only way to get there. Entered competition in San Fernando a few months later to write and sing a calypso about the death of noted athlete/aviator Mikey Cipriani in air crash, tied with Atilla for second place; in second contest in Port of Spain he won with the same calypso, calling himself Growling Tiger. Sang at Salada Millionaires calypso tent in Nelson Street, Port of Spain during '35 season, had big success with 'Money Is King'. Businessman Edward Sa Gomes sent him with Atilla and Lord Beginner (Egbert Moore) to NYC to record for Decca; as Keskidee Trio they made 'Dingo Lay' and 'Don't Let Me Mother Know', Tiger recorded 'Money Is King'; returned '36 with Lion and King Radio (Norman Spann) to record 'Ask No Questions' and 'Monkey' with them, also his own 'The Gold In Africa' about Italian invasion of Ethiopia (most of these records issued in UK '38 on Brunswick). He won the first National Calypso King competition in Trinidad '39 with 'Try And Join A Labour Union'. Appeared at Newport Folk Festival '66, gave up public performing but remained active as songwriter; made LP *Growling Tiger – Knockdown Calypsoes* '79 for Rounder, re-creating the instrumentation and style of '30s-40s, incl. 'Water Scheme Labourers Strike' and 'Money Is King', with backing largely of NYC Latin musicians: nominated for a Grammy in Best Ethnic and Traditional category. Original recordings of 'Money Is King' and 'Gold In Africa' in Folkways collections *The Real Calypso* and *Send Your Children To The Orphan Home: The Real Calypso Vol. 2.*

TILLIS, Mel (*b* 8 Aug. '32, Pahokee, Fla.) Prolific country songwriter, first-class country vocalist, comedy star (based on life-long stammer) and actor. Was drummer in high school band, studied violin and was keen on football. Served in USAF, worked on railroads, went to Nashville with suitcase full of songs and immediately placed hits with Webb PIERCE: 'I'm Tired', 'Tupelo County Jail', 'I Ain't Never' '57-9, other hits recorded by Carl SMITH, Brenda LEE, Stonewall JACKSON, Ray PRICE; contract with Columbia saw first own hit 'The Violet And A Rose' '58, two more top 30 hits '59, but songwriting overshadowed singing for a while yet. Duet with Bill Phillips 'Georgia Town Blues' was no. 24 '60; with Pierce 'How Come Your Dog Don't Bite Nobody But Me' no. 25 '63; 'Wine' '65 was Tillis's first top 20 entry, on Ric; he moved to Kapp and a consistent run of hits '65-70, only 'Who's Julie' reaching top 10; moved to MGM and had several top 10 hits in a row, incl. 'The Arms Of A Fool' in top 5, and duets with Sherry Bryce, then no. 1 solo 'I Ain't Never' '72; more hits incl. more duets with Bryce incl. 'Let's Go All The Way Tonight' '73. Meanwhile with band the Statesiders had one of the hottest acts on the country circuit. He switched to MCA, had no. 1 'Good Woman Blues' and was named Entertainer of the Year by CMA, followed by no. ones 'Heart Healer' '77, 'I Believe In You' '78, 'Coca Cola Cowboy' '79 as well as other hits incl. no. 2 'Send Me Down To Tucson'. Moved to Elektra for several hits '79-82 incl. rather twee duets with Nancy SINATRA; back to MCA for some more hits for a total of 38 top tens and six no. ones. He switched to RCA, where his first album was *California Road* '85: title track charted and 'You Done Me Wrong' reached top 40. He also had 23 BMI songwriting awards, for such songs as 'Detroit City' (hit for Bobby BARE '63), 'Ruby, Don't Take Your Love To Town' (Kenny ROGERS '69), 'Heart Over Mind' (his own country no. 2 '70). He has been a regular on TV's *Hee-Haw*, made films incl. *Cotton Pickin' Chicken Pickers* and *W. W. And The Dixie Dance Kings* '75 and *Uphill All The Way* '85, was frequent guest on chat shows. Albums incl. *Stateside* '65, *Life Turned Her That Way* and *Mr Mel* '67, *Let Me Talk To You* and *Something Special* '68, *Who's Julie* and *Old Faithful* '69, *She'll Be Hanging 'Round Somewhere* '70, *Mel Tillis & Bob Wills In Person* '71, all on Kapp; *One More Time* '70, *The Arms Of A Fool/Commercial Affection* '71, *Live At The Sam Houston Coliseum* '71, *Living And Learning* (with Bryce) '72, *Would You Want The World To End* '72, *I Ain't Never* and *Sawmill* '73, *Let's Go All The Way Tonight* and *Stomp Them Grapes* '74, *M-M-Mel* and *Welcome To Mel Tillis Country* '76, all on MGM; *Love Revival* '76, *Heart Healer* and *Love's Trou-*

bled Waters '77, *I Believe In You* '78, *Are You Sincere?* and *Mr Entertainer* '79, *M-M-Mel Live* '80, all on MCA; *Me And Pepper* '79, *Your Body Is An Outlaw* '80, *Southern Rain* '81, *Mel & Nancy* '81, *It's A Long Way To Daytona* '82, all on Elektra; *After All This Time* '83, *New Patches* '84 on MCA.

TILLMAN, Floyd (*b* 8 Dec. '14, Ryan, Okla.) Country singer, guitarist; justly famous as writer of classic country songs. Western Union Messenger at age 13; worked with Blue Ridge Playboys, others; recorded own song 'I'll Keep On Loving You' on Victor '39; hit with 'It Makes No Difference Now' on Decca same year, recorded 'Each Night At Nine' and 'G.I. Blues' '44; 'I Love You So Much It Hurts' '48 for Columbia (hit covers by Jimmy WAKELY, the MILLS Bros); 'I Gotta Have My Baby Back' on Columbia '49; made top 10 of country chart that year with 'Slippin' Around' (among earliest cheatin' songs), answer 'I'll Never Slip Around Again', both big pop crossover duet hits by Wakely and Margaret WHITING ('Slippin' Around' no. 2). Tillman came back to C&W chart '60 with top 30 'It Just Tears Me Up' on Liberty. LP on Columbia Historic Edition compiles '46-50 tracks.

TILLOTSON, Johnny (*b* 20 Apr. '39, Jacksonville, Fla.) Country/pop singer. Discovered at Nashville talent show by Cadence, EVERLY Bros. label; followed them into charts with popped-up versions of country songs: over 25 Hot 100 entries '58-66, 14 in top 40. 'Poetry In Motion' '60 was biggest at no. 2, though 'It Keeps Right On A-Hurtin'' '61 ran close at no. 3. 'Without You' '61 and 'Talk Back Trembling Lips' '63 were both no. 7. 'Poetry' was no. 1 UK; he continued in USA country chart '67-8 on MGM.

TIMBUCK 3 USA duo plus cassette machine. Pat McDonald (*b* 6 Aug. '52, Green Bay, Wis.), wife Barbara K (for Kooyman; *b* 4 Oct. '57, Wausau, Wis.; grew up in San Antonio) began in Madison, Wis. separately (McDonald's rock band the Essentials; Barbara K and the Cat's Away); she joined the Essentials, which made an album on Mountain Railroad label, split up early '84; they became street singers, now tour out of Austin, Texas with pre-recorded bass and drum machine programmed by McDonald. They trade guitar and lead vocals, both play harmonica; she plays violin and mandolin. Became regulars at Austin's Hole in the Wall, made *Cutting Edge* (MTV showcase) prod. by Carl Grasso, vice-president of Miles Copeland's IRS label; signed with IRS, released *Greetings From Timbuk 3* '86 to raves in the press: bluesy send-up of yuppie culture 'The Future's So Bright, I Gotta Wear Shades' went top 20 USA; they also did Xmas single '87 'All I Want For Christmas', proceeds to War Resisters League; second album *Eden Alley* '88. They travel light, but their mixture of country, reggae, folk, funk and everything else will probably lead to live backing when their JVC jambox wears out.

TIMMONS, Bobby (*b* Robert Henry Timmons, 19 Dec. '35, Philadelphia, Pa.; *d* 1 Mar. '74, NYC) Piano, composer. Infl. by bop, but strongest infl. was perhaps gospel music. One of the instigators of funk, following Horace SILVER into Art BLAKEY's Jazz Messengers '58, where he wrote 'Moanin'' '; with Cannonball ADDERLEY '59-60, where he wrote 'Dis Here' and 'Dat Dere'. Rejoined Blakey briefly '60, led own trios, began playing vibes as well c.'66. Died of cirrhosis of the liver. Own LPs on Riverside (*This Here Is Bobby Timmons* '60), on Prestige (*Soulman, Chicken & Dumplins, ChunKing, Little Barefoot Soul, Soul Food, Workin' Out*), on Milestone (*Moanin', Got To Get It, Do You Know The Way*).

TIN PAN ALLEY By 1900 most of the biggest USA song publishers had offices in Manhattan's 28th Street, a rabbit-warren of small rooms with pianos where writers and pluggers of songs worked: the windows would have been open in the summer, before air conditioning; hence 'Tin Pan Alley' (the equivalent in London was Denmark Street). Many songwriters became publishers because they made more money that way (not a phenomenon of the rock era); one of the first was Charles K. Harris (*b* 1 May 1867, NYC; *d* there 22 Dec. '30), who received a royalty payment of 85 cents for a hit in 1892, formed his own company and was soon raking in $25,000 a week for 'After The Ball'. Others were Paul Dresser (*b* 21 Apr. 1857, NYC; *d* 30 Jan. '06; brother of novelist Theodore Dreiser; he wrote 'My Gal Sal', 'On The Banks Of The Wabash'), Harry Von Tilzer (*b* 8 July 1872, Detroit; *d* 10 Jan. '46, NYC: 'Wait Till The Sun Shines, Nellie', 'A Bird In A Gilded Cage', 'I Want A Girl Just Like The Girl That Married Dear Old Dad'), Kerry Mills (*b* Frederick Allen Mills, 1 Feb. 1869, Philadelphia; *d* 5 Dec. '48, Hawthorne, Cal.: 'At A Georgia Camp Meeting', 'Red Wing', 'Meet Me In St Louis, Louis'), etc. The sentimental easy-to-sing songs gave way to more sophisticated fare under the infl. of the great composers of Broadway shows, but the way to get a hit was always to persuade a prominent artist to sing the song, hence the pluggers; the biggest names got the best songs, down to the blacks, who got the worst; hence the incandescent series of pop records made in 1933 by Henry Red ALLEN and Coleman HAWKINS were mostly songs forgotten today, transmuted into gold by their talent (though 'The Day You Came Along' was a hit for Bing CROSBY); Al JOLSON, a huge star, was cheerfully given co-writing credit (and royalties) just for singing the song. The golden age of Tin Pan Alley lasted until WWII, when music began to change (*see* BMI, ASCAP) though there was a last gasp in the BRILL BUILDING, which was just around the corner. *See also* VAUDEVILLE.

TINY TIM (*b* Herbert Khaury, 12 Apr. '30, NYC) Vocalist; an entertainer who never pretended to be anything else. Worked as Darry Dover, Larry Love in Greenwich Village for some years; fame began with dotty versions of 'Be My Baby', 'Sonny Boy' in film *You Are What You Eat* '68; further breakthrough on TV's *Laugh In*, also thought bizarre at the time. Cultivated weird appearance: tall and toothy with dirty-looking long hair and loud clothes he was instantly funny at the height of hippiedom; falsetto version of 'Tiptoe Through The Tulips' went top 20 '68; two more reached Hot 100 and three LPs '68-9: *God Bless Tiny Tim, Second Album* and *For All My Friends*. Last splash was marriage to 'Miss Vicky' (Victoria May Budinger) on TV Dec. '69; they had daughter Tulip, split up '77. WB dropped him '71; he was touring with a circus mid-'80s, tried comeback with country style on Tenn.-based NLT label '88.

TIPICA 73 Salsa band formed '73, its history the story of mid-'70s salsa boom. Original lineup split from Ray BARRETTO band at height of its popularity: Adalberto Santiago, lead singer; Orestes Vilato on timbales, doubling on bongos; bongo player Johnny Rodriguez, now moving to congas; trumpeter Rene Lopez, bassist Dave Perez, joined by pianist Sonny Bravo (from José FAJARDO), trombonist Leopoldo Pineda (from Larry HARLOW), trumpeter Joe Mannozzi (from Orquesta Flamboyan). They played tipico (typical) Latin music in contemporary style on *Tipica 73* on Inca, prod. by Johnny PACHECO; joined by tres player Nelson Gonzalez for self-prod. *Tipica 73* '74, *La Candela* '75 (title track cover of Cuban hit by its composer Juan Formell with his band Los Van Van). Santiago, Vilato, Mannozzi, Gonzalez left '76 to form Los Kimbos; Tipica 73 continued with *Rumba Caliente* '76, joined by young Cuban violinist Alfredo de la Fé from Eddie PALMIERI's band, others. *The Two Sides Of Tipica 73* '77 referred to dance and concert sides, with experimentation and fusion one of salsa's most interesting LPs, with lead vocalist Camilo Azuquita on this and on half of *Salsa Encendida* '78, which introduced Dominican singer José Alberto on the rest. Most of the band appeared on *Dandy's Dandy, A Latin Affair . . .* '79 on Latin Percussion Ventures Inc. label (maker of Latin percussion instruments; 'Dandy' is Johnny Rodriguez's nickname). They switched to Fania; *Tipica 73 en Cuba: Intercambio Cultural* '79 was made in Havana, adding Mario Rivera on soprano and baritone sax; *Charangueando con la Tipica 73* '80 was followed by *Into The 80's* '81 with guests Mario BAUZA (on alto sax), Rafael CORTIJO on congas and Yomo Toro on cuatro. Los Kimbos was a gutsy club band on eponymous LP '76 on Cotique, Mannozzi switching to piano and with trumpeter, mus. dir. Roberto Rodriguez from Barretto's band; on second LP they were *The Big Kimbos With Adalberto Santiago* '77, whereupon Santiago went solo with one of salsa's best voices and the band split into Vilato y Los Kimbos and Nelson Gonzalez & his Orchestra, all making LPs '78. Santiago has widely sessioned as a chorus singer and lead on various tracks, with Barretto, Tito PUENTE, Louie RAMIREZ, Roberto ROENA, Celia CRUZ, FANIA ALL STARS; his solo LPs incl. *Adalberto* '78 prod. by Barretto, *Adalberto Featuring Popeye El Marino* '79, *Feliz Me Siento* '80 (in tandem with Santiago/Barretto collaboration *Rican/Struction* with many of the same musicians), *Adalberto Santiago* '81 (a return to roots, prod. by pianist Javier Vázquez), *Calidad* '82 (return to slick salsa), all on Fania; also *Cosas del Alma* '84 on WS Latino, *Mas Sabroso* '85 on Tropical Buddah. Sonny Bravo and Mario Rivera have widely sessioned and both worked in Puente's Latin Ensemble (LPs on Concord Picante). De la Fé studied classical violin in Havana, grew up in NYC, has played with many big names in Latin music; solo LPs incl. *Alfredo* '79 (mélange of styles incl. jazz-classical fusion 'My Favorite Things'), *Para Africa con Amor – Alfredo de la Fé y su Charanga Afro-Cubana* '79 on Ivory Coast's Sacodis label; *Triunfo* '82 on Toboga, a basic charanga set co-prod. by Roberto TORRES; he emigrated to Bogota: LP *Made In Colombia* on Mercurio '84, then *Vallenata* '86, embracing Colombia's popular accordion-based vallenata style. Also played electric violin with Puente's *Latin Percussion Jazz Ensemble Live At The Montreux Jazz Festival 1980* on Latin Percussion Ventures Inc., appeared in London with Puente's Latin Septet '81.

TIPPETT, Keith (*b* Keith Tippetts, 25 Aug. '47, Bristol, England) Pianist, composer. Led sextet '60s; wrote *Septober Energy*, performed by 50-piece orchestra '70 called Centipede; turned to free improvisation '72 with smaller group Ovary Lodge incl. his wife Julie (*née* Driscoll: see Brian AUGER; *Ovary Lodge* '75 on Ogun); wrote *Frames – Music For An Imaginary Film* for the Ark, 22-piece international group (LP '77 on Ogun). Touring '80s with septet. Piano duos with Stan TRACEY *T'N'T* '74 on Steam, Howard Riley (*b* 16 Feb. '43, Huddersfield, Yorkshire) *In Focus* '84 on Affinity; with cornettist Marc Charig on *Pipedream* '78, with Louis Moholo (drummer, vocalist; *b* 10 Mar. '40, Capetown) on *No Gossip* '80, also *Tern* '83, solo *Mujician* '81, all on FMP. With Julie in duo *Couple In Spirit* '88 on EG, with her voice overdubbed; she also recorded '71 with John STEVENS and Bobby BRADFORD.

TJADER, Cal (*b* Callen Radcliffe Tjader Jr, 16 July '25, St Louis, Mo.; *d* 5 May '82, the Philippines) Vibes, piano, percussion, composer, leader. Mother was a pianist; played with Dave BRUBECK '48-51, experimenting with time signatures; joined George SHEARING '53-4 and met bassist Al McKibbon, who'd worked with Dizzy GILLESPIE/Chano Pozo in heyday of cubop, and encouraged Tjader's interest in Latin music. He led a group on West Coast; over two dozen LPs on Fantasy began in the early '50s, incl. *Mambo With Tjader*, then *Ritmo Caliente* '54, quintet with McKibbon on bass, Richard Wyands (*b* 2 July '28, Oakland) on piano at one recording session, Eddie Cano (*b* 6 June '27, L.A.) at the other; sessions for *Mas Ritmo Caliente* '57 incl. McKibbon, Eugene Wright (Brubeck bassist), violinist/saxist José 'Chombo' Silva, bassist Bobby Rodriguez, pianist Vince Guaraldi (*b* 17 July '28, San Francisco; *d* 6 Feb. '76, Menlo Park; won Grammy for 'Cast Your Fate To The Winds' '62, wrote and played music for *Peanuts* TV cartoons from '63), Mongo SANTAMARIA and Willie BOBO on percussion (with Tjader the rest of the decade, incl. *Concert By The Sea* LPs '59, combined in 2-disc *Monterey Concerts* on Prestige); *Demasiado Caliente* '62 incl. big band arr. by Cano. Albums on Verve incl. *Several Shades Of Jade* '63 with Lalo SCHIFRIN, *Soul Sauce* '65 with Bobo, Donald BYRD, Kenny BURRELL (these made top 100 pop LPs); *El Sonido Nuevo/New Soul Sound* on Verve and *Bamboleate* on Tico incl. Eddie PALMIERI; *Primo!* on Fantasy incl. Charlie PALMIERI; he continued recording on Fantasy through the '70s incl. LPs with Stan GETZ, Charlie BYRD; often Latin style, often straight jazz. *Guarabe* '77 on Fantasy followed by *Breathe Easy* '77 with Hank JONES and *Here* '79 with Clare Fischer on keyboards, incl. Fischer's Latin-jazz standard 'Morning', both on Galaxy. Like many others Tjader received a new impetus of enthusiasm on new Concord Jazz label late '70s-80s: *The Shining Sea* is straight jazz, with Jones, Scott HAMILTON, bassist Dean Reilly, drummer Vince Lateano; *Heat Wave* incl. vocals by Carmen MCRAE, trombone, piano, bass, drums, Latin percussion; Concord's Latin Picante series incl. *La Onda Va Bien* '80 (won a Grammy), *Gozame! Pero Ya* '80, *A Fuego Vivo* '82 and his last, *Good*

Vibes '82. 44 LPs still in print in USA '87 testifies to large number of loyal fans.

TOKENS, The USA vocal/instrumental group. Lineup: lead singer Jay Siegel (*b* 20 Oct. '39), tenors Hank Medress (*b* 19 Nov. '38) and Mitchell Margo (*b* 25 May '47), baritone Philip Margo (*b* 1 Apr. '42). Sang in school with Neil SEDAKA, then stayed together. Had no. 15 hit 'Tonight I Fell In Love' '61 on Warwick, switched to RCA and had no. 1 smash 'The Lion Sleeps Tonight' same year (revival of the WEAVERS' 'Wimoweh'); had 9 more Hot 100 entries in Billboard '62-70, only two in top 40. As Bright Tunes Productions they prod. hits for the CHIFFONS, others; Medress prod. new version of 'Lion' for Robert John (Bobby Pedrick Jr) which was no. 3 hit '72; Siegel and the Margos formed Cross Country, made eponymous LP on Atlantic prod. by Medress and Dave Appell (incl. top 30 hit 'In The Midnight Hour' '73), who also prod. Frankie Valli, others. Re-formed for Radio City Music Hall doo-wop revival show Oct. '81.

TOLLIVER, Charles (*b* 6 Mar. '42, Jacksonville, Fla.) Trumpet; composer, leader. Self-taught; infl. by Clifford BROWN, later Freddie HUBBARD; came to prominence with Jackie McLEAN (whose LP *It's Time* incl. Tolliver tunes). With Art BLAKEY briefly '65; also gigs and records with Gerald WILSON, Booker ERVIN, Roy AYERS, Horace SILVER, Max ROACH, McCoy TYNER. Formed group Music Inc. '69; co-founder of Strata-East label '71, owned by artists. His *Collection Suite* played by New York Jazz Repertory Orchestra in Carnegie Hall '74. Own LPs incl. several on Polydor, *Paper Man* on Arista; on StrataEast: *Compassion*, two vols. of *Live At Slugs'*, *Live At Loosdrecht Jazz Festival*, *Live In Tokyo*, *Music Inc.*, many with pianist/composer Stanley Cowell (*b* 5 May '41, Toledo, Ohio; own LPs on Polydor, Byg, ECM; solo *Musa/Ancestral Dreams* on StrataEast; with own sextet *Brilliant Circles* on Arista; more with Clifford JORDAN, Bobby HUTCHERSON, Jack DeJOHNETTE, etc.).

TOMORROW UK psychedelic group: vocalist Keith West, bassist John 'Junior' Wood, guitarist Steve Howe all played in the In

Crowd (minor UK hit '65 with 'That's How Strong My Love Is'), became Tomorrow adding drummer Twink (John Alder; ex-Fairies). Strong stage act confirmed promise with single 'My White Bicycle' (prod. by Pete Townshend; revived by NAZARETH); eponymous LP '68 (reissued on Decal/Charly UK '86) incl. cover of 'Strawberry Fields Forever', quirky 'Real Life Permanent Dream', 'Auntie Mary's Dress Shop'. Producer/keyboardist Mark Wirtz encouraged West to record 'An Excerpt From A Teenage Opera', no. 2 '67; group then billed as 'featuring Keith West' although psychedelic rock was a long way from poppy single; West's solo follow-up 'Sam' made top 40, group cover of BEATLES' 'Revolution' did not; they split '68. Twink joined Pretty Things; Howe formed Bodast, made it big with YES; Wood was briefly with Jeff BECK, West went into production, came back with Howe's ex-Bodast bassist Bruce Thomas, drummer Chico Greenwood and ex-FAMILY, ex-ANIMALS guitarist John Weider in short-lived popsters Moonrider (LP '75).

TORMÉ, Mel (*b* Melvin Howard Tormé, 13 Sep. '25, Chicago, Ill.) Singer, composer; also producer, pianist, drummer, writer, actor. One of the great jazz singers, reputation for quality mainstream work unsullied by decades of ups and downs of music business. Sang on radio with COON-SANDERS band at age 4, acted in radio soap operas at 9; toured with band fronted by Chico Marx '42-3; formed group the Mel-Tones, recording under that name and with Artie SHAW '45-6 on Majestic; went solo. Hits on Decca with Mel-Tones and Eugenie Baird on 'I Fall In Love Too Easily' (band singer Baird worked with Tony PASTOR, CASA LOMA band, on radio; early album on Design of Duke ELLINGTON songs), with Bing CROSBY on 'Day By Day' '45-6; Mel-Tones own 'It's Dreamtime' '47 on Majestic; Tormé solo hits on Capitol '49-52 incl. no. 1 'Careless Hands' '49, top tens 'Bewitched' (with band led by Stan KENTON arranger Pete Rugolo) and duet 'The Old Master Painter' with Peggy LEE '50. Known as 'The Velvet Fog' during Mel-Tones period, but he opened up c.'55 recording for Bethlehem and sang the way he really wanted to sing: his range increased about an octave, his art

well suited to a golden age of mid-'50s, when he and others made albums backed by arrangers like Marty Paich (*b* 23 Jan. '25, Oaklands, Cal.), but never got near the charts at a time when USA radio broadcast only jingles (incl. pop songs resembling the jingles so closely that there was little difference); since that time for many years he has done his own arrangements. He began writing songs at 15: 'Lament To Love' was a hit by Les BROWN, top 10 by Harry JAMES '41; also 'A Stranger In Town' '44 (by Martha Tilton on Capitol '45), 'Christmas Song' '46 ('Chestnuts Roasting On An Open Fire'; hit record by Nat COLE), 'Born To Be Blue' '47, 'County Fair' '48 (in Disney's *So Dear To My Heart*), last three co-written with Robert Wells (Robert Wells Levinson, *b* Raymond, Wash.; also collaborated with Cy COLEMAN, Henry MANCINI, others), also 'Born To Be Blue', others. Acted in more than a dozen mostly pleasant and forgettable films '43-60 (e.g. *Junior Miss*, *Let's Go Steady* '45); did TV show with Lee '51, got his own half-hour talk show that lasted until '58; nominated for Emmy '56 as best supporting actor in Playhouse 90's *The Comedian*. LPs incl. Majestic reissues *Gone With The Wind* ('46-7 tracks), *It Happened In Monterey* with Mel-Tones; composition *California Suite* on Capitol '49 with Mel-Tones now on Discovery; *Right Now* and *That's All* from Columbia Special Products; *Songs About Love* '58 on Audiophile; LPs now on Affinity UK from Bethlehem '50s: *Lulu's Back In Town* and *Sings Fred Astaire* (both with Paich), *It's A Blue World*, 2-disc *Live At The Crescendo*; also *Prelude To A Kiss* on Tops; *My Kind Of Music*, *Duke Ellington-Count Basie Songbooks*, *Tormé* (with Frank Rosolino), *Back In Town* (with Mel-Tones), all on Verve; Atlantic LPs '60s: *Live At The Maisonette* (Gershwin arrangements nominated for Grammy), *At The Red Hill*, *Comin' Home Baby* (title track a top 40 hit '62), *Sunday In New York* (title track from soundtrack of film). Latest career on Concord Jazz: *An Evening With George Shearing And Mel Tormé* '82 won Grammy; *Top Drawer* and *An Evening At Charlie's* '83, *An Elegant Evening* '85 also with Shearing; also big band set *Mel Tormé With Rob McConnell And The Boss Brass* '86. Others: *Mel Tormé* and *Easy To Remember* on Glendale, *Velvet Fog* on Vocalion. Autobiography to be published soon.

TORNADOS UK session group formed '61 by prod. Joe MEEK as house band: Roger Lavern (*b* Roger Jackson, 11 Nov. '38), keyboards; Alan Caddy (*b* 2 Feb. '40), lead guitar; George Bellamy (*b* 8 Oct '41), rhythm guitar; Clem Cattini (*b* 28 Aug. '39), drums; Heinz Burt (*b* July '42) on bass, second keyboardist Norman Hale. Caddy and Cattini were ex-Pirates (*see* Johnny KIDD); after backing Billy FURY live, Don Charles and John Leyton on disc, they were unleashed: one single flopped; second was 'Telstar': keyboard-led futuristic instrumental was no. 1 UK/USA '62, first USA no. 1 by a UK group. Hale left; 'Globetrotter' was no. 5 UK '63; after a few lesser hits they disappeared in Mersey flood: there was room for only one SHADOWS. LP *Away From It All* '63; split '65. Heinz went solo '63, had no. 5 hit with Eddie COCHRAN tribute 'Just Like Eddie', three more top 40s; reappeared as TV actor '70s, revival shows '80s. Tornado split '65, after changing personnel incl. Heinz's replacement Tab Martin, founder of jazz/pop Peddlers. Cattini became top-class session player, with LULU, MARMALADE, KINKS, Cliff RICHARD, etc.

TORRES, Roberto (*b* Guines, Cuba) Singer, bandleader, percussionist (maracas, güiro, clave), composer, producer, label boss. He formed the cooperative charanga Orquesta Broadway in NYC early '60s (*see* CHARANGA), left early '70s and made solo albums incl. *Roberto Torres de Nuevo* '76, *y su Caminantes* '77 on Salsoul; 15 tracks '73-8 compiled on best-of *Lo Mejor de 'El Caminante'* (his nickname, 'the Traveller') on TVO. Launched NYC-based SAR label '79 with his own *El Rey del Montuno*; over the next three years prod. LPs on SAR and allied Guajiro, Toboga and Neon labels for veteran Afro-Cuban singer/percussionist/composer Papaito (Mario Muñoz Salazar), singer/composer Linda Leida, Alfredo 'Chocolate' ARMENTEROS, Henry FIOL, Charanga Casino, Cuban singer La India de Oriente (Luisa Maria Hernández), Peruvian singer Lita Branda, Charanga De La 4, Cuban pianist/arranger Alfredo Valdés Jr and his father, veteran singer Alfredo Valdés, many others. The senior Valdés was vocalist with Septeto Nacional, formed in Cuba '20s by Ignacio Piñeiro; in '81 Valdés Jr was pianist/arr. on father's LP *Alfredo Valdés Interpreta Sus Exitos con el Septeto Nacional*, prod. by Torres: six conjunto arr. of songs originally written by Piñeiro for septeto format. Torres headed an early '80s revival of tipico (typical, traditional) Cuban music which was not simply imitation of the orthodox; with African market in mind he went for a 'rootsy' sound, extended tracks: millions of albums were sold. Using many of the same NYC-based musicians on various sessions, he formed SAR All Stars, incl. Chocolate, Leopoldo Pineda on trombone, Zervigón bros. from Orquesta Broadway, Valdés Jr and many others; All Stars made LP debut with live descarga (Latin jam session) LPs *SAR All Stars Recorded Live In Club Ochentas* (two vols.), with e.g. one side of second LP devoted mostly to an exceptional extended version of the Cuban classic 'El Manisero' (The Peanut Vendor), with lead vocals by Papaito; also *SAR All Stars Interpretan a Rafael Hernández*: versions of songs by the Puerto Rican composer incl. moving Torres' vocal on 'Lamento Borincano' '29, about émigré's nostalgia for his home. SAR group's output fell off after '82; many stars switched to Caimán Records, formed '83, whose co-executive prod. Sergio Bofill had come from SAR; others moved to Laslos Records, formed '84; Valdés Jr recorded for Ivory Coast's Sacodisc label. Torres' albums incl. *Recuerda a Portabales* (songs associated with the Cuban singer/composer Guillermo Portabales), *Presenta: Ritmo de Estrellas* (an all-star charanga, arr. by Pupi LEGARRETA), *Recuerda al Trio Matamoros* (songs from repertoire of Cuban trio), *Charanga Colonial* (another all-star lineup), all '79-81; also three LPs by his Charanga Vallenata '80-2, fusing Cuban charanga and conjunto elements with Colombian vallenata accordion played by Jesus Hernández; *Corazón de Pueblo* '84; *Elegantemente Criollo* '86, made in Miami (where SAR had relocated) with Israel 'Cachao' LOPEZ, others (appeared frequently in Billboard salsa chart). Torres produced six LPs by Charanga De La 4 '79-87; *Se Pegó . . . !* was top 10 hit in salsa chart mid-'87. La India de Oriente was born in Cuba, did radio, recording, TV work there; lived in Miami '60-3, went to NYC for 10 years and made two LPs on Gema; returned to Miami and made three more on Guajiro '80-2 prod. by Torres (recorded in NYC) with Valdés Jr arr. and playing piano; switched to Caimán for *Le Reina de la Guajira* '85, made in Miami. Papaito was born in Cuba, worked with chachacha creator Enrique Jorrin, others; made films in Mexico and joined Sonora Matancera there; left Cuba for good c.'60. Papaito's first solo LP was *Robert Torres Presenta a su Amigo: Papaito* '79 on SAR; *Papaito* '80 incl. memorable version of Cuban classic 'Aprietala en el Rincon', both these with trumpet/tres-led conjunto: *Papaito Rinde Homenaje a Abelardo Barroso* '80 used a charanga augmented by tres, was tribute to Cuban vocalist Barroso; it is regarded as one of his best. Switched back to conjunto for *Papaito* '82, *Para Mis Amigos* '84; he also appeared with various artists on *El Canonazo de la SAR!* '84.

TOTO USA AOR group formed in L.A. '78 by top session musicians whose credits incl. Aretha FRANKLIN, Boz SCAGGS, STEELY DAN, Jackson BROWNE, SONNY & CHER, EARTH WIND & FIRE, countless others: drummer Jeff Porcaro (*b* '54), keyboardist brother Steve (sons of jazz percussionist), keyboardist David Paich (son of Marty), David Hungate on bass, Steve Lukather on guitar, vocalist Bobby Kimball: name from Kimball's real name (Toteaux) and/or name of dog in *Wizard Of Oz*. Eponymous '78 debut predictably slick, top 10 LP in USA; 'Hold The Line' top 5 USA (14 UK), two others top 50 USA; *Hydra* had top 30 '99' but slumped in chart, as did *Turn Back* '81; but *Toto IV* '82 was no. 4 LP with seven Grammy nominations, top 30 'Make Believe', no. 2 'Rosanna' (no. 12 UK), no. 1 'Africa' (3 UK), last unusual in being keyboard-based rather than guitar riff-rock, showing mellower outlook. Third Porcaro, Mike, replaced Hungate '82, but defection of rasp-voiced Kimball was more serious (later turned up in Frank Farian's studio-HM band for Corporation cover of 'Stairway To Heaven' '85), replaced in Toto by Dennis 'Fergie' Frederiksen; *Isolation* '84 found them in doldrums again, after contribution to soundtrack of widely panned SF film *Dune* same year. Members continue

session careers in tandem; Lukather wrote top 5 'Turn Your Love Around' for George BENSON. Despite sell-out status in Japan they rarely venture outside studio; this often shows in clinical quality of music. Despite ups and downs, long relationships involved (schoolboy band Rural Life) will keep them going. *Fahrenheit* '86 incl. new singer Joseph Williams; *The Seventh One* '88 was still on CBS.

TOUGH, Dave (*b* David Jarvis, 26 Apr. '08, Oak Park, Ill.; *d* 6 Dec. '48, Newark, N.J.) Drummer, easily the best white drummer of his generation, the only one to be compared to Chick WEBB, Sid CATLETT, Jimmy CRAWFORD. Parents were Scottish immigrants; left high school to play with Austin High Gang (*see* JAZZ); with Eddie CONDON late '20s, went to Europe with clarinettist Danny Polo, then with big bands: Tommy DORSEY '36-7 (played on some of the biggest hits of the era incl. 'Marie', 'Song Of India'); improved Benny GOODMAN band when he replaced Gene KRUPA, also played with Bunny BERIGAN, Bud FREEMAN, and some of Goodman's excellent sextet sides on Columbia; with Artie SHAW's US Navy band, then with Woody HERMAN '44-5: with Chubby Jackson made one of the most exciting rhythm sections in jazz on 'Northwest Passage', etc. A master of the cymbals; though a small man he could drive a band with the brushes; played on the beat yet gave the impression he was lying back, his unique mastery of time precursing Elvin JONES; had the ability to give each soloist the most appropriate support, but refused to play drum solos. 'He said that human beings weren't metronomes, and drummers shouldn't be, either' (Jackson, quoted by Whitney Balliett in the *New Yorker*: users of drum machines please note). Wrote an advice column for drummers in *Metronome*, alternately hilarious (a survey of chewing gum) and of great value. He admired Max ROACH, followed bop, thought (certainly wrongly) that its intricacies were beyond him; he played all kinds of jazz equally well (with Charlie VENTURA/Bill Harris combo, Condon, Muggsy SPANIER, Jackson on Keynote, all '40s), he took too seriously the rivalry between boppers and the old guard, now almost forgotten. An alcoholic who had already been a derelict early '30s, he spent his last few months in a veterans' hospital; died as an outpatient from skull fracture caused by a fall.

TOURE KUNDA African 10-piece fusion band from Senegal, formed '75 by eldest brother Amadou Tile (*d* '83), with Sixu, Ismaila and Ousmane; born in Casamance region of Soninke parents, the four had trad. Catholic mission education, became singing/percussion troupe playing dance music known as djabadong, a Senegalese rhythm with strong reggae resonance; moved to Paris '79 and began to experiment with fusions. At first tending to acoustic in live performance with voices, percussion, balaphon and kora, in time they adopted electric guitar and synth, also French, Antillean and Cameroonian musicians. Sixu and Ismaila made a record '77 in Paris, but Amadou's arrival there '79 sparked off creativity; they played regularly in Paris environs, released LP *Emma Africa* '80, *Turu* '81. Amadou's death seemed to concentrate their vision; memorial *Amadou Tile* same year followed by West African tour, return to Paris, acoustic LP *Casamance au Clair de Lune*; film of tour was seen on French TV and increasing popularity was marked by live shows in France and UK, 2-disc *Live, Paris-Zinguinchor*; in '85 EP *Emma*, 12″ single *Toure Kunda*, LPs *Natalie* and *Live*.

TOUSSAINT, Allen (*b* 14 Jan. '38, New Orleans, La.) Pianist, singer, composer, producer, partner in SeaSaint studio. Grew up in Gert Town neighbourhood (originally Gehrke, after a German immigrant grocer), where in '02 Buddy BOLDEN played in Lincoln Park. Began playing sister's piano at age 7, later infl. by PROFESSOR LONGHAIR, whom he dubbed 'the Bach of Rock'. Formed schoolboy band the Flamingoes (with Snooks EAGLIN); dropped out of school to tour with SHIRLEY & LEE (replacing Huey SMITH); was regular at legendary Dew Drop Inn but felt pull to the studio: Dave BARTHOLOMEW hired him for session work at Cosimo Matassa's; he played backing tracks for Fats DOMINO (e.g. 'I Want You To Know', 'Young School Girl'); found talent for arranging on the spot, took hold of Lee ALLEN session that resulted in

chart hit 'Walking For Mr Lee' '58. Made LP *The Wild Sounds Of New Orleans* '58 (on RCA as 'Al Tousan') in two days, incl. 'Java' (no. 4 hit for Al HIRT '63). Worked for new Minit label ('Take a Minit and listen to it'), formed by Joe Banashak and Larry McKinley, who announced audition '60: Irma THOMAS, Larry WILLIAMS, NEVILLE Bros, others showed up, but Toussaint, who'd come to accompany a singer, was given responsibility for Minit's music at the age of 22, oversaw Jesse Hill's 'Ooo Poo Pah Do' (no. 3 R&B, top 30 pop '60); on Ernie K-Doe's 'Mother-In-Law' '61 (no. 1 R&B/pop '61) he plucked Benny Spellman from ringsiders to sing the low notes: he wrote arrangements that fitted the voices and incl. jazz infl. lyrical trombone solo on Spellman's 'Lipstick Traces' (top 30 R&B, Hot 100 pop '62), tail-gate trombone on 'I Done Got Over' (written by K-Doe for Thomas). When Banashak felt neglected by Imperial's Lew Chudd, who distributed the records, he founded Instant and again put Toussaint in charge; he prod. Chris Kenner's 'I Like It Like That' (no. 2 R&B/pop '61), 'Land Of A Thousand Dances' (Hot 100 '63; covered by Cannibal and the Headhunters (no. 30 '65), Wilson PICKETT (no. 6 '66), Patti SMITH). (Alcoholic, erratic songwriter Kenner *b* '29 near New Orleans; *d* 25 Jan. '76.) Toussaint was drafted '63. Marshall Sehorn worked for Bobby Robinson's NYC's Fire/Fury labels; he signed Wilbert Harrison (*b* 6 Jan. '29, Charlotte, N.C., also Sehorn's home town): his 'Kansas City' had been no. 1 R&B/pop '59; signe Lee Dorsey (*b* 24 Dec. '26, New Orleans); 'Yah Yah' was no. 1 R&B, 7 pop '61, prod. by Toussaint, who returned from the US Army '65, was courted by several labels, formed a partnership with Sehorn, Sansu Enterprises opening SeaSaint studios '72. Carried on into modern New Orleans era with more Dorsey hits, then the Meters, Neville Bros; prod. Mac REBENNACK, LABELLE, Joe COCKER, many others; did horn tracks for the BAND's 'Life Is A Carnival', arr. for Paul SIMON album *Rhymin' Simon*; own LPs *Toussaint* '71 on Tiffany, *Life, Love And Faith* '72 and *Southern Nights* '75 (title track a country hit for Glen CAMPBELL) on Reprise, *Motion* '78 on WB. His songs have been covered by the OAK RIDGE BOYS, DEVO, LITTLE FEAT, the

Band, Boz SCAGGS, Bonnie RAITT, Lawrence WELK, many more.

TOUSSAINT, Jean (*b* 27 July '57, island of Aruba) Tenor sax. Played in calypso band in high school, exploring all the West Indian styles; attended Berles School of Music in Boston '77-80, joined in local R&B band the Energetics (later renamed Plant Patrol), formed quintet with Wallace Roney (ex-Messengers trumpeter). Recommended by Billy PIERCE (teacher at Berklee) to replace him in Art Blakey group from '82 to '86, became mus. dir. and played on Blakey albums on Concord Jazz, Japanese King, Timeless and Delos, as well as CD-video *Live At Ronnie Scott's* released '87. Taught at Guildhall School of Music in London, gigged in duo with bassist Ike Leo, quartet with Mike Carr; led quartet with Jason Rebello on piano (*b* '70), Mark Taylor on drums, Alec Dankworth on bass. Played on *Kirk 'n Marcus* on Crisscross (Kirk Lightsey and Marcus Belgrave), on one track on a Nathan Davis album for Mole Jazz; own CD *Impressions Of Coltrane* on September, with Rebello, Ray Drummond on bass, Kenny Washington on drums.

TOYAH (*b* Toyah Willcox, 18 May '58, Birmingham) UK new wave singer/actress. Graduated from drama school and made first TV appearance '76; appeared in films, notably musicals *Jubilee* '78, *Quadrophenia* '79; first single 'Victims Of The Riddle' '79 on indie Safari label, 6-track EP *Sheep Farming In Barnet*. Diminutive stature, lisp and flame-red hair marked her out as an individual to follow SIOUXSIE, Lene Lovich and Poly Styrene (X-Ray Specs) as colourful new wave female character. *The Blue Meaning* '80 was top 40 LP; timely TV documentary *Toyah! Toyah! Toyah!* yielded soundtrack which made no. 22. Revamped her band '81, retaining guitarist Joel Bogen, recruiting Original Mirrors bassist Phil Spalding, plus keyboardist Adrian Lee, drummer Nigel Glockler; hits 'Thunder In The Mountains', 'I Want To Be Free' (both top 10), EP *Four From Toyah* (no. 4), *Four More* (14), accent on the anthemic, with scope for theatrics; third LP suitably titled *Anthem*, all '81. *The Changeling* and *Warrior Rock – Toyah On Tour* '82, two top 30 singles; return to acting '83 in Clare

Luckham's wrestling play *Trafford Tanzi*, impressive for physical effort involved (BLONDIE's Debbie Harry did it on Broadway). LP *Love Is The Law* '83 ventured into electronic sphere, new keyboardist Simon Darlow writing with Willcox and Bogen. Signed with CBS/Portrait '85 for single 'Don't Fall In Love (I Said)', LP *Minx*, looking to major label to boost music career to another level; LP *The Lady And The Tiger* '87 on Editions EG with consort Robert Fripp; continued on stage in London revival of *Cabaret* '87, shut down by behaviour of musicians in pit: they were sacked and it ran for a few nights as first musical in history without accompaniment.

TRACEY, Stan (*b* 30 Dec. '26, London) Pianist, composer, leader; also played vibes, accordion. Turned pro at 16, played with many groups incl. Kenny Baker, Ronnie SCOTT; with Ted HEATH band '57-9, became house pianist at Scott's club '60-7, backed and recorded with Zoot SIMS, Ben WEBSTER, etc.; recorded with Sonny ROLLINS on his soundtrack for *Alfie* '66. Infl. by Duke ELLINGTON, Thelonious MONK, developed idiosyncratic and challenging keyboard style and became highly regarded composer: formed own quartet '64, has gigged all over Europe with groups up to tentet and larger bands, also solo. Best-known composition is *Under Milk Wood*, inspired by Dylan Thomas's play; recorded '65 by quartet incl. Bobby Wellins on tenor (*b* 24 Jan. '36, Glasgow) and in '76 at Wigmore Hall, narrated by Donald Houston, Art Themen on tenor (*b* 26 Nov. '39, UK). Other albums incl. solo *Alone (At Wigmore Hall 1974)* and *Hello, Old Adversary* '79; duos *T'N'T* '79 (with Keith TIPPETT); *Sonatinas* (with John SURMAN), also quartet LPs *Captain Adventure* '75 (live at 100 Club), *The Poet's Suite* '84; octet *Salisbury Suite* '78 (live at Royal Festival Hall, with Wellins, Themen, Art Daly on alto), *The Bracknell Connection* '76 (live at 100 Club with Wellins, Themen, Pete King on alto); *Live At Ronnie Scott's* '86 by his Hexad, all on his own Steam label; also duos *Original* '74 on Cadillac, *Tandem* '77 on Ogun with Mike Osborne on alto. Suite for big band *Genesis* on Steam Records, solo *Plays Duke Ellington* on Mole '87. His son, drummer Clark Tracey (*b* 5 Feb. '61, London), has worked with Stan, backed James MOODY, Art FARMER, Charlie ROUSE etc.; formed own quartet: *Suddenly Last Tuesday* '86 on Cadillac, *Stiperstones* '88 on SJ; Stan Tracey quartet with Clark and guest Rouse made *Playin' In The Yard* on Steam.

TRAFFIC Versatile UK rock group formed mid-'60s: Steve WINWOOD, vocals, keyboards, guitar, percussion, bass; Dave MASON, vocals, keyboards, guitar, sitar, tambura, bass; Jim Capaldi (*b* 8 Feb. '44), vocals, drums, percussion; Chris Wood (*b* 24 June '44; *d* 12 July '83), vocals, sax, flute, keyboards. Winwood had been the star of the Spencer DAVIS group with his keyboards and bluesy voice; the new band found a communal retreat in a cottage in Aston Tirrold, reflected in songs like 'Berkshire Poppies', 'House For Everyone', 'Little Woman'. Signed to Island and had single hits in UK and USA beginning with 'Paper Sun' '67; played in soundtrack of *Here We Go Round The Mulberry Bush* '67 (title song was a hit in UK); first LP *Mr Fantasy* '67; different edition in USA was first titled *Heaven Is In Your Mind* on United Artists, and garbled in order to incl. the hit. Traffic epitomised psychedelia, with sound effects, the obligatory sitar, unusual lyric twists. Mason contributed to *Traffic* and *Last Exit* '68 (top 20 LPs in USA), then left. Winwood recorded with the abortive supergroup BLIND FAITH; group Mason, Capaldi, Wood & Frog ('Frog' being Mick Weaver) was in a sense an answer to that; Traffic re-formed to work on *John Barleycorn Must Die* '70, which began as a Winwood solo LP, its title track a ritual allegory inspired by trad. *Fire And Frost* (the WATERSONS): at no. 5 it was their best chart entry in USA; unable to reproduce its sound on stage the trio was augmented with bassist Rick GRECH, drummer Jim Gordon, Anthony 'Reebop' Kwaku Baah on percussion, sometimes Mason; this lineup made lacklustre live *Welcome To The Canteen*, more successful *Low Spark Of High Heeled Boys* '71. Grech worked on Capaldi's first solo LP *Oh How We Danced* at Muscle Shoals, whose musicians Barry Beckett (keyboards), Dave Hood (bass), Roger Hawkins (drums) joined on Traffic's *Shoot Out At The Fantasy Factory* '73. *On The Road* '73 was 2-disc set of German tour

recordings; *When The Eagle Flies* '74 a mostly doleful swansong and their fourth top 10 USA LP, incl. 'Dream Gerrard', in which lay the seed of future Winwood work with ex-BONZO Viv Stanshall. Traffic were more successful in the USA than at home; albums were more successful than live act, where desire to innovate sometimes led to meandering solos. Capaldi went on to successful solo career; his *Whale Meat Again* and *Short Cut Draw Blood* '74-6 on Island made USA top 200 LPs, *Fierce Heart* '83 on Atlantic made first 100, with rare guest appearance from Van MORRISON, and reunited him with Winwood; *see also* entries for Grech, Mason, Winwood.

TRAPP, Baroness Maria von (*b* Maria Augusta Kutschera, 26 Jan. '05, Vienna; *d* 28 Mar. '87, USA) Author of *The Story Of The Trapp Family Singers* '48. An orphan, she left a convent to serve as governess in the household of widowed, anti-Nazi Baron Georg von Trapp (*d* '47); they married, had three children (making 10 altogether), fled Nazis '38 to USA, settled in Vermont, made a living giving concerts. She sold rights to her book to a German company for $1500; RODGERS & HAMMERSTEIN made hit musical *The Sound Of Music* of it; '65 film version is one of the top-grossing films of all time: she received not a penny from either.

TRAVIS, Merle (*b* 29 Nov. '17, Rosewood, Ky.; *d* 20 Oct. '83, Tahlequah, Okla.) Country singer, guitarist, songwriter, actor. Father was tobacco farmer, coal-miner. Learnt guitar from Mose Rager, Ike Everly's mentor; became one of the best guitarists in country music and one of the most influential. Joined Tennessee Tomcats, Clayton McMichen's Georgia Wildcats, Brown's Ferry Four; with US Marines in WWII. First recorded for King with Grandpa JONES as the Sheppard Brothers. Moved to West Coast, appeared in many minor film roles, worked with bands led by Cliffie STONE, Jimmy WAKELY, Tex RITTER etc. Signed to Capitol, hits in '40s incl. 'Divorce Me C.O.D.', 'So Round, So Firm, So Fully Packed' '46-7. Asked to make album of folk songs, he wrote some: set of 78s *Folk Songs From The Hills* incl. 'Nine-Pound Hammer', 'I Am A Pilgrim', 'Dark As A Dungeon', 'Sixteen Tons'; latter later one of the biggest hits of all time for Ernie FORD '55. Co-wrote 'No Vacancy' with Stone, 'Smoke! Smoke! Smoke! (That Cigarette)' with Tex WILLIAMS, whose recording sold over two million '47; more songs incl. 'Petal From A Faded Rose', 'Cincinnati Lou', 'Information Please', many more. A regular on Pasadena's Hometown Jamboree Town Hall Party show; backstage in late '40s got an idea, drew a diagram on the back of a programme, had the first solid-body guitar built, reasoning that with an electric pickup the hollow body wasn't necessary, since sustainability would be better. Memorable film role singing 'Re-enlistment Blues' in *From Here To Eternity* '53; continued in films through *Honky Tonk Man* '82. His only hit single in later years was 'John Henry Jr' '66; LPs late '50s-early '60s incl. *Back Home*, *Walkin' The Strings*, *Travis!*, *Songs Of The Coal Miners*. He never lost his attachment to the coal-mining country where he grew up: *Back Home* incl. lovely version of 'Barbara Allen', as well as description and imitation of the coal-miners' cage coming above ground at the end of the day. In '70s appeared on NITTY GRITTY DIRT BAND set *Will The Circle Be Unbroken*; teamed with Chet ATKINS (whom he greatly influenced) on *The Atkins-Travis Travelling Show*. LPs now on Country Music Heritage: *Travis Pickin'* and *Light Singin' & Heavy Pickin'*, 2-disc sets *Guitar Standards*, *Merle Travis Story*, *Country Guitar Giants* with Joe Maphis, *Merle & Grandpa's Farm & Home Hour* with Jones.

TRAVIS, Randy (*b* 4 May '59, Marshville, N.C.) Young country singer with sepulchral voice and ballad style. He moved to Nashville in 1981; his debut album *Storms Of Life* on WB was a spectacular no. 1 country hit in the USA '86, with four top 10 country singles incl. 'On The Other Hand' and 'Diggin' Up Bones' at no. 1. Second *Always And Forever* '87 was also no. 1, as was title track in singles chart. There are two kinds of 'new country' artists: story-telling singer-songwriters like Lyle LOVETT and Nanci GRIFFITH, who served apprenticeships in the boondocks before recording for major labels, and others like Travis, whose appeal to the country audience lies in its essentially conservative taste. *Old 8 × 10* '88 another hit; also signed to make CBS TV movie.

TRENET, Charles (*b* '13, Narbonne, France) Singer, songwriter. Published first poems at age 15; intended to be a painter, met Johnny Hess, teamed as vocal duet Charles et Johnny, successful until both drafted; worked solo after WWII, internationally popular. His poems made natural lyrics; he wrote over 500 songs, words and music for most of them, of which the best-known is 'La Mer' '38 ('Beyond The Sea' '47, English words by Jack Lawrence; lovely instrumental arr. by Percy FAITH c.'49); 'Boum!!' won Grand Prix du Disque '38 ('When Our Hearts Go Boom!); also 'Vous Qui Passez Sans Me Voir' '36 (co-written with Hess; 'Why Do You Pass Me By' '36 with words by Desmond Carter, 'Passing By' '47 with words by Lawrence); 'L'Âme des Poètes' ('At Last! At Last!' '51, sung by Tony Martin, English words by Florence Miles; more literally 'The Poet's Dream' '59 by Mal Peters); 'Que Reste-t-il de Nos Amours' '46 ('I Wish You Love' '55, words by Albert A. Beach aka Lee Wilson, sung by Keely SMITH and Felicia Saunders; USA top 30 hit '64 by Gloria Lynne). Trenet compilations from EMI France incl. *Disque d'Or*, 2-disc sets *Charles Trenet*, *J'ai Ta Main*.

TRISTANO, Lennie (*b* Leonard Joseph Tristano, 19 Mar. '19, Chicago; *d* 18 Nov. '78) Pianist, composer. Born in the middle of a measles epidemic, he was blind by age 11. Also played reeds; played in dixieland and rumba bands, absorbing everything. Recorded with trombonist Earl Swope (*b* 4 Aug. '22, Hagerstown, Md.; *d* 3 Jan. '68, Washington DC), *The Lost Session* '45 originally on Marlor in USA, then Nostalgia or Phontastic; went to NYC '46 and became a legend for advanced ideas; rarely performed in public but concentrated on teaching, students incl. Warne MARSH, Lee KONITZ, guitarist Billy Bauer from Woody HERMAN band. His harmonic thinking was similar to bop, rhythmically and melodically he was his own man; the way he put it all together was unique: he tried to get hornmen to play uninflected so that the result would depend on musical construction rather than emotion; his music sounded cold to some but fascinated others (especially musicians). He did a V-disc date '46; then Lennie Tristano Trio incl. Bauer recorded for KEYNOTE '46 with Clyde Lombardi on bass, '47 with Bob Leininger: total of 19 tracks incl. eleven alternate takes (six of these different versions of 'Interlude', aka 'Night In Tunisia'), plus an untitled fast blues almost four minutes long, all incl. in *The Complete Keynote Collection* on Japanese Phonogram (*see* KEYNOTE); complete on a Mercury CD '87. Capitol Records had an intensive jazz programme '49-50; Lennie Tristano Sextet with Konitz, Marsh, Bauer, Arnold Fishkin on bass, drummers Harold Granowsky at one session and Denzil BEST at another in March '49: seven tracks incl. 'Intuition' and 'Digression', in which players were told to start playing without a key, chord structure or melody, reading each others' minds many years before 'free jazz' became a buzz phrase: Capitol was outraged and tried to refuse to pay for the date. (*Crosscurrents* session now on *Lennie Tristano/Tadd Dameron* on Affinity.) Similar lineup without Bauer recorded for Prestige as Lee Konitz Quintet '49; some sources said Tristano played piano, discographies say it was acolyte Sal Mosca (*b* 27 Apr. '27, Mt Vernon, NY; UK bassist Peter Ind was another Tristano follower who often played with Konitz).Tristano recorded for Atlantic '55 (first edition had no title, later ones called *Lines*, *Requiem*; with quartet incl. Konitz, Gene Ramey on bass, Art Taylor on drums), solo '62 (*The New Lennie Tristano*); now compiled on 2-disc sets *Lennie Tristano Quartet* and *Requiem*. The '55 date incl. weird sound; experiments incl. solo blues 'Requiem' (for Charlie PARKER) allegedly recorded at half speed so it would have an undefinable strangeness when played back. Other LPs: *Manhattan* on Elektra Musician (aka *New York Improvisations* in UK); broadcast airchecks with Bill Harris All Stars etc. (*Cool In A Jam, New Sounds Of The Forties* '47 on Jazz Live); *Solo In Europe* '60s on Unique Jazz with Konitz sessions; items on Jazz Records incl. a concert from Toronto with Konitz c. '52.

TROGGS, The UK pop group formed by Reg Ball (*b* 12 June '43), bricklayer turned singer, with co-worker Ronnie Bond (*b* 4 May '43) on drums, bassist Pete Staples (*b* 3 May '44), all from Andover, Hants., and guitarist Chris Britton (*b* 21 June '45, Watford). Ball and Bond first played in Ten

Foot Five with Tony Mansfield and Dave Wright on guitar and bass, re-formed as the Trogglodytes, signed by KINKS manager Larry Page thanks to their basic rendition of Kinks' 'You Really Got Me'; when Ball's 'Lost Girl' failed to sell on CBS Page signed them to Fontana as the Troggs; with USA writer Chip Taylor's 'Wild Thing' had no. 1 hit USA, 2 UK '66. Basic in the extreme with an incongruous ocarina solo in the middle, it flew in the face of fashion, was later covered by Jimi HENDRIX. Ball had been renamed Reg Presley by Page in a flash of iconoclastic vision parallel to christening of Elvis COSTELLO later. Presley wrote 'With A Girl Like You' ('Wild Thing' clone) for no. 1 UK, top 30 USA; with his 'I Can't Control Myself' they switched to Page's Page 1 label, reached no. 2 UK despite airplay ban (because of line 'Your slacks are low and your hips are showing'), missed top 40 in USA, where last two singles were on both Fontana and Atco labels. Taylor's 'Any Way That You Want Me' ended '66 with top 10 UK hit; Presley's 'Give It To Me' became a football chant as well as no. 12 hit '67; 'Night Of The Long Grass' slid to no. 17, 'Hi Hi Hazel' missed top 40; they went psychedelic with Presley's 'Love Is All Around', no. 5 UK '67 (7 USA '68 for fourth and last chart entry there); 'Little Girl' was top 40 UK and they faded to cabaret, college circuit. Legend nurtured early '70s with *Troggs Tapes*, bootleg of studio sessions incl. instrumental incompetence, mutual recrimination and much foul language. Reunited with Page '76 to record LP cheekily called *The Troggs Tapes*, with Britton and Staples replaced by Richard Moore and Tony Murray, rhythm guitarist Colin Fletcher added; brief flash of fame late '70s when punk adopted them (X covered 'Wild Things', Beirut City Rollers 'I Want You'); Presley was arguably the first of punk's non-vocalists, Wreckless Eric (whom Fletcher went on to record) a prime example (perhaps also an example of how novelties get out of hand and become genres).

TROUP, Bobby (*b* Robert William Troup Jr, 18 Oct. '18, Harrisburg, Pa.) Songwriter, pianist, vocalist. Staff songwriter with Tommy DORSEY: '(You're A) Snootie Little Cutie' written for Frank SINATRA, Connie

Haines and the Pied Pipers '42; wrote, prod. and dir. service musicals during WWII; '(Get Your Kicks On) Route 66!' and 'Baby, Baby All The Time' hits for Nat COLE Trio '46; settled in Hollywood, played piano/sang in clubs, formed trio, recorded for Capitol, RCA, Liberty, Bethlehem (*Bobby Troup Plays Johnny Mercer* '55 reissued on Affinity '87, incl. 'I'm With You', co-written with Mercer), Decca, Interlude, Mode; other reissues on Pausa from '52, Audiophile from '58. Married Julie LONDON, prod. her LPs on Liberty, wrote songs for her. Also acted on TV (NBC's *Emergency* '71-6) and films (*The High Cost Of Loving* '58, *The Five Pennies* and *The Gene Krupa Story* '59 etc.); wrote film songs incl. 'Daddy' for *Two Latins From Manhattan* '41 (hit record by Sammy KAYE), title songs for *Rock Pretty Baby* and *The Girl Can't Help It* '56, 'The Meaning Of The Blues' for *The Great Man* '57 (sung by London); many other songs.

TROWER, Robin (*b* 9 Mar. '45, London) UK HM guitarist. After career with PROCOL HARUM until '71, vying with Gary Brooker and Matthew Fisher for songwriting credits, he contemplated supergroup Jude with Scots singer Frankie Miller, ex-Stone The Crows bassist Jim Dewar, ex-JETHRO TULL drummer Clive Bunker, but it fell through; retained Dewar (whose gravelly vocals not dissimilar to Miller's), recruited Reg Isadore on drums for power-trio LPs beginning with *Twice Removed From Yesterday* '73; from *Bridge Of Sighs* '74 they did well in USA charts (that title track a mainstay of stage act into '80s); ex-SLY Stone drummer Bill Lordan replaced Isadore on *For Earth Below* '75, *Live!* and *Long Misty Days* '76; Sly bassist Rusty Allen joined for *In City Dreams* '77, *Caravan To Midnight* '78, allowing Dewar to concentrate on vocals. After *Victims Of The Fury* '80, Jack Bruce joined Lordan and Trower in *B.L.T.* '81; *Truce* '82 had Bruce and returning Isador; with *Back It Up* '83, all these were on Chrysalis; *Beyond The Mist* '85 on UK indie Music For Nations (Passport in USA) had Southend buddies Dave Bronze on bass and vocals, drummer Bob Clouter. Made Atlantic debut '88 *with Take What You Need.*

TRUMBAUER, Frankie (*b* 30 May '01, Carbondale, Ill.; *d* 11 June '56, Kansas City,

Mo.) C-melody sax; also vocals, other instruments; aka 'Tram'. The best white saxist of the '20s, a great technician who could play hot, also liked to play pretty, infl. Lester YOUNG, Benny CARTER, Buddy TATE, many others. Worked with Bix BEIDERBECKE in Jean GOLDKETTE band (where Tram was mus. dir.) and on their classic small-group sides '27 incl. 'Singin' The Blues', the finest white jazz of the day; with Adrian ROLLINI; then in Paul WHITEMAN band, where Tram stayed '27-32, '33-6. Also co-led the Three Ts '36 with the TEAGARDEN bros, then a band with trumpeter Manny Klein '38. Led own bands in '33, '38 (used name 'Trombar'). He was also a pilot; first left full-time music '39, during and after WWII working for Civil Aeronautics Administration, also some musical studio work after '45. Played at a Bix tribute '52, but neglected giant was out of fashion.

TSHIBAYI, Bibi Dens (*b* '54, Luebo, Zaire) African singer-composer, taught to sing by his mother, Protestant missionary and choir mistress; sang and composed while still in primary school in academic group SavioFiesta, for more elaborate amateur group Lisango at secondary school in Kananga; to Kinshasa '72, sang with Thu Zahina using equipment provided by FRANCO; also took B.S. degree '75, worked as reporter on local newspaper, turned to music full-time with The Best '79 at the Kinshasa International, but took up computer studies to please his parents; when group was offered contract at Abidjan Intercontinental '82 he returned to music, released his first LP *The Best Ambience* '83: title single on Earthworks in UK, LP on Rounder USA '84. Second album *Sensible* confirmed fast-maturing talent.

TUBB, Ernest (*b* Ernest Dale Tubb, 9 Feb. '14, Crisp, Texas; *d* 6 Sep. '84, Nashville) Country singer, guitarist; one of the all-time kings of country music. Consumed by a passion for Jimmie RODGERS as a boy, he went to see Rodgers' widow, still living in San Antonio '35 (where Tubb got his first radio dates on KONO); she was impressed with his sincerity, convinced him he didn't sound a bit like Rodgers, gave him Rodgers' guitar and helped arrange for two Victor sides ('The Passing Of Jimmie Rodgers' and Jimmie Rodgers' Last Thoughts') which went nowhere. He worked digging ditches for the WPA (Depression-era Works Progress Administration), played nights for oilfield workers in bars; signed with Decca late '39 and promoted Gold Chain Flour on KGKO Fort Worth, becoming the Gold Chain Troubador; became more famous as the Texas Troubador after massive '42 hit 'I'm Walkin' The Floor Over You'. Joined the Grand Ole Opry and became an innovator, taking honky tonk music to that already hallowed institution, a fusion of rough country vocals with the swagger of WESTERN SWING, also one of the first to establish the electric guitar in country music and headlined the first country music show at Carnegie Hall '47 (said to have looked around and observed, 'This place sure could hold a lot of hay'). Appeared in cowboy movies *Fighting Buckaroo* and *Ridin' West* '42 (with Charles Starrett as the Durango Kid), also *Jamboree* '43 and *Hollywood Barn Dance* '47, opening his famous record shop same year near the Opry's Ryman Auditorium in Nashville, also *Midnight Jamboree* show on WSM, plugging the record shop and up-and-coming country stars. Bing CROSBY had covered 'Walkin' The Floor Over You'; Tubb's country hits incl. duets with the ANDREWS SISTERS ('Don't Rob Another Man's Castle') backed with his own 'I'm Bitin' My Fingernails And Thinking Of You' '49), Red FOLEY (top 10 hits '49-53: 'Tennessee Border No. 2' at no. 2, 'Goodnight Irene' at no. 1, 'Too Old To Cut The Mustard', 'No Help Wanted'), the WILBURN BROTHERS ('Hey Mr Bluebird' '58), Loretta LYNN (incl. 'Mr And Mrs Used To Be' '64, 'Who's Gonna Take The Garbage Out' '69). Solo hits nearly every year, with a gap '53 when a Far East tour on top of his normal two or three hundred nights a year left him exhausted and forced him to rest, incl. 'Slippin' Around' and 'Blue Christmas' '49, 'I Love You Because' plus his own 'Letters Have No Arms' and 'Throw Your Love My Way' '50, 'Missing In Action' '52, 'Thanks A Lot' '63, all top 5. Producer Pete DRAKE (steel guitarist and alumnus of Tubb's Texas Troubadors) made surprise tribute album on Tubb's 65th birthday: 2-disc *Ernest Tubb: The Legend And The Legacy* on Cachet label had original Tubb tracks overdubbed with additional vocals by Lynn, son Justin (see below), Waylon JENNINGS, Conway TWITTY, Charlie RICH, Merle HAGGARD, Johnny PAYCHECK, Marty ROBBINS, George JONES, Ferlin HUSKY and others; 'Waltz Across Texas' (a '65 hit) issued as a single with Ernest, Willie NELSON, Charlie DANIELS. He made over 200 singles altogether over the years; compilation LPs in print '87 incl. *Honky Tonk Classics* on Rounder, more on MCA.

TUBB, Justin (*b* 20 Aug. '35, San Antonio, Texas) Country singer and songwriter, eldest son of Ernest TUBB. His father recorded one of his songs '52; he had begun performing in high school, then at U. of Texas; left school to become DJ at WHIN in Gellatin, Tenn.; signed with Decca and had duet hits 'Looking Back To See' and 'Sure Fire Kisses' with Goldie Hill; became Opry regular. Recorded for Challenge and Starday late '50s; hit 'Take A Letter Miss Gray' on RCA subsidiary Groove '63 led to stay on parent label, duet hits with Lorene Mann 'Hurry, Mister Peters' and 'We've Gone Too Far Again', minor solo entry 'But Wait There's More' '67; recorded for Paramount incl. LP *Things I Still Remember*. A popular entertainer, he toured hard, incl. Vietnam; continued to appear on Opry; his country style was based on his father's honky tonk, which in its day was innovative, but ironically received less radio time in '60s-70s: it had become traditional. His songs did well; Hawkshaw HAWKINS had no. 1 hit '63 with 'Lonesome 7-7203', Jim REEVES/Dottie WEST duet on 'Love Is No Excuse', Faron YOUNG/Margie Singleton with 'Keeping Up With The Joneses' both went top 10 '64. He settled down to run publishing company and manage his father's live radio show from the record shop in Nashville.

TUCKER, Mickey (*b* 28 Apr. '41, Durham, N.C.) Piano, composer; other instruments. Raised in Pittsburgh, back to Durham at 13; now lives in East Orange, N.J. Taught high school in Florida, college in Mississippi; played with Damita Jo, LITTLE ANTHONY AND THE IMPERIALS, James Moody, Thad Jones-Mel LEWIS band, Cecil PAYNE; with singer Joe Lee Wilson (*b* 22 Dec. '35, Bristow, Okla.) at International Jazz Festival

(Singapore '83). LPs with Roland KIRK, James Moody, Jake Hanna, many others. His own albums since '75 incl. *Triplicity, Sojourn, Sweet Lotus Lips* and *Theme For A Woogie Boogie* on Xanadu and/or Denon, as well as *Mister Mysterious* on Muse. He has roots in Fats WALLER and Earl HINES with technique to match: solos full of pleasant surprises, often furious energy; at Ronnie SCOTT's club '85 with Benny GOLSON quartet, playing Golson's fine tunes as well as his own lovely waltz 'I Should Have Known'. Also played with re-formed Golson/Art FARMER Jazztet mid-'80s. Recent compositions incl. *Rhapsody For Alto Flute And Strings*, played by New Jersey Chamber Music Society '81; *Trilogy For Piano And Orchestra* to be premiered by André Watts and Chicago Symphony Orchestra.

TUCKER, Orrin (*b* '11, St Louis, Mo.) Bandleader, vocalist. Formed dance band '36; 16 hits '39-42 incl. smash hit 'Oh, Johnny, Oh, Johnny, Oh!' '39 for Columbia (just purchased by CBS; hit helped put new red label in the black): song from '16 musical *Follow Me* had precious vocal by Wee Bonnie Baker (*b* Evelyn Nelson, Orange, Texas) adding period effect. Tommy Tucker (no relation; *b* '08) was another sweet bandleader (and pianist) who had hits at the same time and on the same label group (incl. Okeh and Vocalion), his records and broadcasts labelled 'Tommy Tucker Time'.

TUCKER, Sophie (*b* Sophie Kalish-Abuza, 13 Jan. 1884, on the move between Russia and Poland; *d* 9 Feb. '66, NYC) Cabaret singer. Her father changed his name from Kalish to Abuza when emigrating to USA; she reached there age 3; sang at 10 in parents' café in Hartford, Conn.; went to NYC '06. Plain and plump, she was persuaded to work blackface, became popular 'coonshouter' (*see* RAGTIME); added 'er' to first husband's name to make Tucker. Small role in *Ziegfeld Follies Of 1909*; headliner by '11, dropped blackface, played Chicago that year, heard 'Some Of These Days' played by its composer, pianist Sheldon Brooks (*b* 4 May 1886, Amesburg, Ontario; *d* 6 Sep. '75, L.A.; also wrote 'Darktown Strutters' Ball', 'If I Were A Bee And You Were A Red, Red Rose', more), recorded it several times,

adopted it as her theme (and title of autobiography): it sold a million copies in sheet music alone; '11 recording on Edison was no. 2 national hit according to *Pop Memories*; '26 version with Ted LEWIS on Columbia sold a million, one of over 20 big Tucker hits '10-37. During jazz fad of WWI she formed Sophie Tucker and her Five Kings of Syncopation; disbanded '21 and hired Ted Shapiro as her pianist (*b* 31 Oct. 1899, NYC): he stayed until the end. ('After You've Gone'/'I Ain't Got Nobody' were made with Miff Mole's Molers: influential trombonist Mole, Shapiro, Jimmy DORSEY, Red NICHOLS, Eddie LANG.) Shapiro wrote some of the special Tucker material, often with Jack Yellen (*b* 6 July 1892, Poland), often extremely blue and unbroadcastable. London debut '22 in revue *Round In Fifty* with comic George Robey at the Hippodrome; the morals watchdog Lord Chamberlain objected to her references to the Prince of Wales. In '25 Yellen and Lew Pollack (*b* 16 June 1895, Chicago; *d* 18 Jan. '46, Hollywood) wrote 'My Yiddishe Mama' for her; recorded in English on one side, Yiddish on reverse; it was top 5 hit '28, sold another million (they also wrote 'Cheatin' On Me' recorded by Tucker, later hit for Jimmie LUNCEFORD; Yellen also co-wrote 'Ain't She Sweet', 'Happy Days Are Here Again', 'Are You From Dixie?', many more). She introduced 'When The Red Red Robin Goes Bob Bob Bobbin' Along' '27 (before Al JOLSON) in revue *La Maire's Affairs*. Film debut '29 as night club singer in *Honky Tonk*; sang 'I Never Want To Get Thin' and 'I'm The Last Of The Red Hot Mamas', latter her billing for the rest of her life. Always popular in London at Kit Kat Club, music halls; first of several Royal Command Performances '34: she greeted George V with 'Hiya, King!'. Played owner of boarding houses in films *Broadway Melody Of 1938* and *Thoroughbreds Don't Cry*, both with Judy GARLAND; she played wife of U.S. Ambassador to Soviet Union (ironic in view of her origins) in Cole PORTER musical *Leave It To Me* (also Broadway debuts of Mary MARTIN, who stole the show with 'My Heart Belongs To Daddy', and Gene KELLY; Tucker sang 'Most Gentlemen Don't Like Love (They Just Like To Kick It Around)'. Film *Follow The Boys* '44 followed by *Sensations Of 1945*, with Cab

CALLOWAY, Woody HERMAN, W. C. Fields. Described as 'a battleship with a voice like 70 trombones', she handed out advice to ladies in half-sung, half-spoken style; marked later decades with 'Life Begins At 40', 'I'm Having More Fun Now I'm Fifty', 'I'm Having More Fun Since I'm Sixty', 'I'm Starting All Over Again'. She still worked continuously in clubs, TV '50s (especially Ed Sullivan show); had cameo role in *The Joker Is Wild* '57, with Frank SINATRA; last Royal Command show '62, last performances '63 at NYC's Latin Quarter. *Greatest Hits* on MCA, others on CBS Cameo, World Records, Monmouth, Golden Age; *Vintage Show Biz Greats* on Folkways with Jimmy DURANTE, Tallulah Bankhead.

TURNER, Big Joe (*b* 18 May '11, Kansas City, Mo.; *d* 23 Nov. '85, Inglewood, Cal.) Blues singer. Tending bar and singing at 14 in K.C.; teamed with pianist Pete JOHNSON: they worked together through '40s incl. John HAMMOND's *Spirituals To Swing* concert '38, records on Vocalion (incl. Turner's own song 'Cherry Red'), reunion later on EmArcy/Mercury; recorded with Joe SULLIVAN on Vocalion, Benny CARTER on Okeh, Art TATUM on Decca (incl. 'Corrine, Corrina' and his own 'Wee Baby Blues'), under his own name on Decca, National, Aladdin, then Atlantic: first R&B chart hit listed as 'Still In The Dark' on Freedom '50, then 'Chains Of Love' and 'Sweet Sixteen' '51-2 with Van 'Piano Man' Walls (who co-wrote 'Chains' with Ahmet Ertegun, revived '69 by Bobby 'Blue' BLAND), 'Honey Hush' '53, several more '54-6 incl. 'T.V. Mama' (with Elmore JAMES band), 'Shake, Rattle And Roll', two-sided hit 'Corrine, Corrina'/'Lipstick, Powder And Paint': these made him a rock'n'roll giant; 'Shake, Rattle And Roll' written by Charles Calhoun, with Atlanic bosses Ertegun and Jerr Wexler singing backups on Turner's record, was covered by Bill HALEY, Elvis PRESLEY (by Arthur Conley '67); 'Chains' by Pat Boone; 'Corrina' was his biggest pop hit, almost making top 40 (adapted from trad. song by Bo Chatmon and J. Mayo Williams c.'29; covered by Bob DYLAN on his first LP, also a top 10 hit in USA by Ray Peterson '60); 'Honey Hush' made top 60 when reissued '59. But he didn't try to be-

come a rock'n'roll star; he was too big, too black, too old and too strong, a blues shouter in the classic mould, and anyway closer to jazz, demonstrated by Atlantic LP *Boss Of The Blues* '56, with sidemen incl. Johnson, Lawrence Brown (from Duke ELLINGTON band), Pete Brown on sax (*b* James Ostend Brown, 9 Nov. '06; had played with John KIRBY, Jimmie NOONE, etc.; with Coleman HAWKINS '57 at Newport, on record). Turner appeared at Newport, Monterey and Ann Arbor festivals, in films *Shake, Rattle And Roll* '56, *Last Of The Blue Devils* '74 (documentary about K.C. with Count BASIE, Jay McSHANN, others). Atlantic LPs or compilations incl. *Joe Turner, Rockin' The Blues, Big Joe Is Here*; also *Singing The Blues* on Impulse, *Roll 'Em* on Bluesway ('Roll 'Em, Pete' was co-written by Johnson and Turner, covered by Basie and Joe WILLIAMS '55), *Big Joe Turner Turns On The Blues* on Kent; on Papa John Creach's *Filthy* on Grunt; to Pablo label for LPs incl. *The Bosses* with Basie, *The Trumpet Kings Meet Joe Turner, Every Day I Have The Blues* with Sonny STITT, *Kansas City Shout, Kansas City, Here I Come* (with Basie and Eddie VINSON), *In The Evening, Things That I Used To Do, Patcha Patcha* (with Jimmy WITHERSPOON), etc. Also *Blues Train* '83 on Muse with ROOMFUL OF BLUES and Mac REBENNACK. Reissues, compilations incl. *Early Big Joe* on MCA ('40-4 tracks), *Jumpin' Blues* with Johnson on Arhoolie, *Blues'll Make You Happy, Too!* and 2-disc *Have No Fear, Big Joe Is Here!* in Roots of Rock'n'Roll series, both on Savoy; *Jumpin' With Joe* on Charly (Atlantic hits).

TURNER, Ike & Tina USA soul/R&B vocal-instrumental duo. Ike Turner (*b* 5 Nov. '31, Clarksdale, Ms.) was a prodigy on piano, accompanied Sonny Boy WILLIAMSON and Robert Nighthawk before he reached his teens. Formed first band Kings Of Rhythm while still in high school; they made 'Rocket 88' at Sun in Memphis, released under vocalist Jackie Brenston's name on Chess, no. 1 R&B hit '51; Brenston went solo, soon faded. He recorded country music as Icky Renrut, also recorded with first wife Bonnie; played fine guitar on many tracks with B. B. KING, Howlin' WOLF, Johnny ACE, others. In a St Louis night club, regular customer Annie Mae Bullock sang with the band '56; Ike added her to lineup, they were married by '58 and her name changed to Tina Turner; initially she did not record with the band, but depped for absent vocalist on the Sue label; 'A Fool In Love' was top 30 pop single '60, concentrating his mind wonderfully: act became the Ike & Tina Turner Revue, female backing singers the Ikettes added (ever-changing personnel incl. Merry Clayton, Venetta Fields, P. P. Arnold and Bonnie Bramlett); they reached top 20 '61 with 'It's Gonna Work Out Fine', took 'Poor Fool' and 'Tra La La La' into top 50 '61-2 (all these plus 'I Idolize You' were top 10 R&B hits); recorded for Kent with no hits, returned to R&B chart on Loma, Modern, Innis '65-8; meanwhile got involved with Phil SPECTOR, who wanted to record with Tina alone, contractually barring Ike from the studio (though a photograph of all three appeared on the resulting LP sleeve): *River Deep – Mountain High* '66 had Spector/Tina productions incl. title track (no. 3 UK, 88 USA), 'A Love Like Yours' (16 UK, did not chart in USA); was filled up like a best-of, incl. two big '60-1 hits; album reached top 30 UK album chart, did not chart in USA until '69 on A&M, when it did not make top 100 LPs, USA failure popularly supposed to be the reason for Spector's withdrawal from production for some years. Meanwhile Ike & Tina's LPs incl. *Live!* on WB '65; *Outta Season* (top 100 LPs) and *The Hunter* on Blue Thumb, live *In Person* on Minit, all '69; *Come Together* and *Workin' Together* '70 on Liberty, the latter a top 25 LP incl. no. 4 single 'Proud Mary'; they switched to United Artists for 2-disc *Live At Carnegie Hall/What You Hear Is What You Get* '71 (also top 25), *'Nuff Said* '71, *Feel Good* '72, *Nutbush City Limits* '73 (infectious title track no. 5 UK, top 30 USA). He prod. her solo *Acid Queen* '75, named after her memorable part in the WHO film *Tommy*. She left; they were divorced '76; owning his own studio by then, he retired to it; after some floundering she became one of the biggest stars of the '80s (*see below*). *Ike Turner & The Kings Of Rhythm* eponymous compilations on Ace and Flyright (latter has Cobra and Artistic tracks '58-9), also *I'm Tore Up* and 2-disc *Hey Hey* on Red Lightnin'; despite Ike & Tina's patchy commercial success the duo was a hot act whose reissues/compilations continue to sell, incl. *It's Gonna Work Out Fine* on EMI America, *The Soul Of Ike & Tina* on Kent, *Nice And Rough* and *Tough Enough* on EMI/Liberty in UK (with all the hits), *Her Man . . . His Woman* (from '70) on EMI Stateside, *Rock Me Baby* on Charly, others on Audio Fidelity, Crown, Striped Horse, Bulldog, Musidisc, German Platinum and Happy Bird labels, etc.

TURNER, Joe (*b* 3 Nov. '07, Baltimore, Md.) Pianist, vocalist in stride style with blues feeling. To NYC c.'25, worked with Benny CARTER, Louis ARMSTRONG, others; accompanied Adelaide HALL from mid-'30s, to Europe with her; served in US Army band directed by Sy OLIVER, returned to Europe c.'48. Based in Paris, toured the world incl. USA. LPs incl. *Another Epoch Stride Piano* on Pablo, *Joe Turner Trio* with Slam STEWART, Jo JONES on Black & Blue, *Stride By Stride* and *Smashing Thirds* on MPS.

TURNER, Tina (*b* Annie Mae Bullock, 26 Nov. '38, Nutbush, Tenn.) Rock/soul singer, one of the biggest stars of the '80s. When she left her Svengali Ike Turner (*see above*) she also left his financial management and organisation; like many other USA artists since the early days of rock'n'roll she was more appreciated in UK than at home; *Love Explosion* and *Rough* '79-81 on UA had not set the world on fire and label seemed to be losing interest; she was asked to be one of several vocalists on *Music Of Quality And Distinction* '82 on Virgin, a concept LP organised by synth players Martyn Ware and Ian Craig Marsh as British Electric Foundation (*see also* HUMAN LEAGUE and HEAVEN 17); she sang 'Ball Of Confusion'; they prod. cover of Al GREEN's 'Let's Stay Together' for UK top 10 late '83, USA top 40 '84. Cover of BEATLES' 'Help' a minor UK hit '84, prod. in USA by the CRUSADERS; the other nine tracks on *Private Dancer* all prod. in UK, incl. 'What's Love Got To Do With It', written by Terry Britten and Graham Lyle, prod. by Britten: UK top 3 hit, no. 1 for three weeks in USA, won Grammies for Record of the Year, Song of the Year, Female Pop Performance and Female Rock Vocal of the Year: Tina was back. 'Better Be Good To Me' was USA top 5, minor UK hit; LP's title track top 30 UK: all these except 'Ball Of Confusion' on *Private Dancer*, no. 3 LP USA '84. She starred in SF fantasy *Mad Max Beyond Thunderdrome*, won plaudits for acting and sang 'We Don't Need Another Hero', also major hit; duetted with Mick Jagger in Live Aid concert mid-'85; follow-up LP on Capitol was *Break Every Rule* '86 (prod. incl. Britten, Mark Knopfler) as well as reissue of '75 *Acid Queen* on Fame, video cassettes of *Nice And Rough* and *Private Dancer Concert Tour*; there's also mini-LP *Mini* on Fantasy USA. She sang on one track of Eric CLAPTON's *August* '86.

TURRENTINE, Stanley (*b* Stanley William Turrentine, 5 Apr. '34, Philadelphia, Pa.) Tenor sax. Began on tenor '47, played with Ray CHARLES '52, then Earl BOSTIC; Max ROACH '59-60, formed own group, married organist Shirley SCOTT, worked with her through '60s, also making own LPs on Blue Note, mostly with combo (but *Joy Ride* had a big band). Split with Scott '71; turned to pop/soul vein on CTI, then Fantasy, always with funky, blues-tinged feeling which always attracted fans. Albums reaching pop 200 LPs in USA incl. *Rough 'N' Tumble* and *The Look Of Love* '67-8 on Blue Note; *Sugar* '71 on CTI, then compilations *The Baddest Turrentine* and *The Sugar Man* on that label; *Pieces Of Dreams* '74, *In The Pocket* and *Have You Ever Seen The Rain* '75, *Everybody Come On Out* and *The Man With The Sad Face* '76, *Nightwings* '77, *West Side Highway* and *What About You!* '78, all on Fantasy; *Tender Togetherness* '81 on Elektra. *Use The Stairs* on Fantasy incl. Cedar WALTON, Ron CARTER. Blue Note reissues incl. *Blue Hour, Straight Ahead, That's Where It's At* with Les McCANN Trio; *Jubilee Shout* from early '60s was previously unissued. Back on Blue Note with *Wonderland* '87 (tunes by Stevie WONDER). His brother Tommy (*b* 22 Apr. '28, Philadelphia) was a popular trumpeter who played on Blue Note LPs, made album as Leader '60 on Time/Bainbridge with Stanley, Roach, Julian Priester, Horace PARLAN, Bob Boswell on bass.

TURTLES, The USA vocal/pop group formed in L.A. '65 with Howard Kaylan (*b* Howard Kaplan, 22 June '47, NYC) and Mark Volman (*b* 19 Apr. '47, L.A.): began as Nightriders '61 with bassist Chuck Portz, guitarist Al Nichol (*b* 31 Mar. '45); added drummer Don Murray and became the Crossfires, made singles, added rhythm guitarist Jim Tucker but split '65. Incited to reform by new White Whale label, changed name to Tyrtles, then Turtles; updated ecstatic harmonies of early '60s surf music and rode folk-rock boom, starting with cover of Bob DYLAN's 'It Ain't Me Babe' (top 10 '65); more hits with P. F. Sloan songs 'Let Me Be' and 'You Baby' (turned down his 'Eve Of Destruction', one of the biggest hits of '65); 'Happy Together' was no. 1 '67, their best, written by Gary Bonner and Alan Gordon from unknowns the Magicians, who then wrote similar no. 3 'She'd Rather Be With Me'; more hits '67-9 were pop gems with classic production incl. 'Elenore' and 'You Showed Me', both top 6 from overloaded concept LP *Battle Of The Bands* '68: they were never satisfied to be a pop band, dabbled in psychedelia, lost touch. Personnel changes meant that only Nichols, Kaylan, Volman were founders left at the end: John Barbata replaced Murray before the big hit; Chip Douglas replaced Portz, himself replaced by Jim Pons; John Seiter (ex-SPANKY) replaced Barbata, who went to CROSBY STILLS NASH & YOUNG, later JEFFERSON Starship. *Turtle Soup* '69 was prod. by KINKS' Ray Davies; they split '70, their last hit ironically 'Eve Of Destruction' after all (it barely made Hot 100 '70). Pons, Volman and Kaylan went to Frank ZAPPA, the last two as vocal duo Phlorescent Leech and Eddie, then Flo and Eddie (pseudonyms forced on them by White Whale's lawyers); became noted back-up singers for Marc BOLAN, Keith Moon, Bruce SPRINGSTEEN, the Knack, PSYCHEDELIC FURS; also prod. DMZ, Good Rats, etc.; released *Rock Steady With Flo & Eddie* '81 with reggae pick-up band incl. Augustus Pablo (issued on CD '87).

TWILLEY, Dwight (*b* 6 June '51, Tulsa, Okla.) USA singer, songwriter, keyboardist; formed Dwight Twilley Band with drummer Phil Seymour, who doubled on bass and sang second lead vocals on hit 'I'm On Fire' '75, incl. in *Sincerely* '76. With photogenic looks and high, breathy harmonies, they were tipped for the top by critics, but pipped by labelmates Tom PETTY and the Heartbreakers, hindered by Shelter label's uncertain future; they followed up with less successful *Twilley Don't Mind* '77, split. Twilley made third eponymous solo LP on Arista, but unlike Petty, who consolidated success on MCA, he fell out with new label: from extrovert rock'n'roll pastiche of *Sincerely* he'd discovered MCCARTNEY-esque introspective pop and failed to generate sales. Turned to EMI America for *Scuba Divers* '82 and *Jungle* '84, latter incl. second USA hit 'Girls', top 20 entry helped by X-rated video which almost but not quite recaptured excitement. Seymour sessioned on Moon Martin's first LP, made promising solo *Phil Seymour* '80 incl. no. 22 hit 'Precious To Me', patchy *Phil Seymour 2* '82; '85 saw him drumming with Textones. Twilley pursued parallel career as artist, exhibited in L.A. '82; they reunited for *Mad Dog* '86 on CBS, new label did not revive fortunes greatly.

TWISTED SISTER USA heavy rock band formed NYC '76 by Dee Snider (*b* 15 Mar. '55), vocals; Jay Jay French, guitar (ex-Wicked Lester), joined by Mark 'The Animal' Mendoza (ex-Dictators) on bass '78, drummer J. J. Pero '82. Temporarily based in UK, where metal/glam rock audience received them with more enthusiasm (in USA they were seen as KISS imitators; members of Kiss had also come from Wicked Lester). UFO bassist Pete Way prod. *Under The Blade* '82 for Secret label, but appearance on live TV (*The Tube*) got them signed to Atlantic for vastly superior *You Can't Stop Rock'n'Roll* '83; proved they could sell to pop audience with top 20 UK hit 'I Am (I'm Me)' from LP, followed by no. 32 'The Kids Are Back'. *Stay Hungry* '84 was the first LP made in USA and noticeably more polished, followed by *Come Out And Play* '85, *Love Is For Suckers* '87. Live show still raw rock, Snider particularly outrageous.

TWITTY, Conway (*b* Harold Jenkins, 1 Sep. '33, Friars Point, Ms.) Country singer. Grew up in Helena, Arkansas; took his stage name from towns in Arkansas and Texas, in late '50s was a singer of pop rockaballads, turned to country '65 and in 20 years had 61 top 10 hits incl. 31 no. ones. Following an initial interest in baseball he recorded for Sun under his real name, but no sides were released; he moved to Mercury, had a minor pop hit with 'I Need Your Lovin' ' '57, moved to MGM and made no. 1 with 'It's Only Make Believe' '58, 13 more hits through '62 incl. top tens 'Danny Boy' and 'Lonely Boy Blue' '59. He already dabbled with country, writing 'Walk Me To The Door', top 10 country hit for Ray PRICE early '63, and incl. country songs on his albums (in '70-1 MGM recycled tracks in album *You Can't Take The Country Out Of Conway*, reached country chart with two singles incl. '60 hit 'What Am I Living For'). He moved to Nashville '65, signed with Decca and the hit machine started slowly, climbed to the top 5, then no. 1 with 'Next In Line' '68. He teamed with Loretta LYNN for a series of duet hits '71-5; he won a Grammy for their 'After The Fire Is Gone' '71 and they were CMA's Duo of the Year each year '72-5. His no. ones incl. 'Hello Darlin' ' and '15 Years Ago', which also crossed to the pop chart '70, as did the Grammy-winning duet. 'You've Never Been This Far Before' '73 was his biggest crossover, almost making pop top 20. 'Don't Cry Joni' '75 reached top pop Hot 100, featuring his daughter; he was named CMA Male Vocalist that year. He runs a booking agency with Lynn, several music publishing companies, burger chain Twitty Burgers and a theme park called Twitty City in Hendersonville, Tenn., where you have to go through the gift shop to get out. The hits haven't stopped, too many to list here; he switched to Elektra c.'82 and had three chart-toppers, went to WB '83 and carried on, moved back to MCA for '87 hits. Many albums incl. *Look Into My Teardrops* '66, *Country* and *Here's Conway Twitty* '67, *Next In Line* '68, *I Love You More Today* '69, *Hello Darlin'* and *15 Years Ago* '70, *We Only Make Believe* (with Lynn) and *I Wonder What She'll Think About Me Leaving* '71, *I Can't Stop Loving You* '72, *Never Been This Far Before* '73, *Clinging To A Saving Hand* '74, *Linda On My Mind* '75, *United Talent* and *Never Ending Song Of Love* (both with Lynn) '76, *Now And Then* '76, *Play Guitar Play* '77, *Georgia Keeps Pulling On My Ring* '78, *Crosswinds* '79, *Rest Your Love On Me* '80, *Two's A Party* (with Lynn) '81, *Mr T.* '81, all on MCA; *Southern Comfort* and *Dream Maker* '82 on

Elektra; *Lost In The Feeling* and *Chasin' Rainbows* '83-5 on WB; *Borderline* back on MCA '87. Compilation *The Beat Goes On* on Charly has the earliest hits.

TYLER, Bonnie (*b* 8 June '53, Skewen, South Wales) UK female vocalist. Infl. by Motown music of her youth, entered talent contest at 17, won, turned pro; club background led to wide-ranging style apparent in later work; sang with local soul group Mumbles before songwriter/producers Ronnie Scott and Steve Wolfe signed her up. Surgery for troublesome throat nodules '76 left her with distinctive husky sound apparent on that year's 'Lost In France', UK no. 9, followed with similar 'More Than A Lover' (top 30), 'It's A Heartache' (no. 4 UK, USA no. 3), all ballads in gentle country-rock mode; seven flops in a row persuaded her to change direction in '81, approaching MEATLOAF prod./writer Jim Steinman, who assembled crack session players, e.g. Rick Derringer, E Street Band's Max Weinberg, Roy Bittan, etc. to record *Faster Than The Speed Of Night* '83, with material from CREEDENCE, BLUE OYS-TER CULT as well as his own (title track derived from his soundtrack music for *Small Circle Of Friends*). Steinman employed same neo-SPECTOR wall-of-sound approach that Todd RUNDGREN had used for Meatloaf, down to the male-female counterpoint on 'Total Eclipse Of The Heart' (USA/UK no. 1 '83; male voice Meatloaf sideman Rory Dodd); Steinman and Tyler repeated success with 'Holding Out For A Hero' (no. 2 UK '85); she had duetted with Shakin' STEVENS '84 on old Dinah WASHINGTON/Brook BENTON hit 'A Rockin' Good Way' (no. 5), now with Rundgren on 'Loving You's A Dirty Job But Somebody's Gotta Do It' late '85. Second LP with Steinman *Secret Dreams And Forbidden Fire* '86 faint clone of former glory, confirmed by rushed-out *Greatest Hits* same year. In two careers her distinctive voice has done others' bidding; despite alluring husky tones (similar to Kim CAR-NES') she may need a mind of her own.

TYLER, Charles (*b* Charles Lacy Tyler, '41, Cadiz, Ky.) Alto and baritone saxophones, composer, leader. Grew up in Indianapolis, Ind.; played clarinet as a child, alto sax in

early teens, baritone in US Army late '50s. First met Albert AYLER in Indiana; moved to Cleveland, Ohio after Army service and met Ayler again; they commuted to NYC, jammed with Ornette COLEMAN, Sunny MURRAY, others. Tyler played on Ayler's *Bells* and *Spirits Rejoice* on ESP; played C-melody sax on a bootleg album unique for incl. Ayler with Coleman on trumpet. He also gigged in R&B groups, remained his own man and soon emerged as a unique composer. His own first LP on ESP was followed by study on scholarship at Indiana U. '66-8, then *Eastern Man Alone* on ESP with Dave Baker on cello (former trombon-ist with George RUSSELL), two bassists. To U. of California at Berkeley; played on Stanley CROUCH LP '73 incl. Tyler tune 'Youngster's Eyes'; played with Arthur BLYTHE, David MURRAY, Bobby BRADFORD etc.; returned to NYC and organised group with Earl Cross on trumpet, Ronnie Boykins or John Ore on bass, Steve Reid on drums, occasionally Blythe; *Voyage From Jericho* was issued on Tyler's Ak-Ba label; tour with Boykins, Reid and Mel Smith on guitar yielded *Live In Europe* '75 on Ak-Ba. *Saga Of The Outlaws* '76 on Nessa is a tone poem inspired by western movies, in con-temporary idiom, like all his music also in-formed by studies of western music going back to the 16th century: with Tyler on alto, Boykins and Ore on basses, Cross and Reid, the 'polyphonic sonic tale of the old & new West' was made at the Wildflowers Festival (*see* JAZZ). *Sixty Minute Man* '79 on Adelphi is solo Tyler; *Folk And Mystery Stories* '80 on Sonet was made in NYC with Tyler on alto and baritone, with Reid, Baker on cello, Richard Dunbar on French horn, Ore and Wilbur Morris on basses; two vols. of *Defi-nites* '81 on Storyville live in Stockholm have Cross, Reid, bassist Kevin Ross. He also played on Reid's *Odyssey Of The Ob-long Square* on Reid's Mustevic label. He moved to Europe, lived in Stockholm; guests on a new album by Hal RUSSELL's NRG Ensemble, due '88 on Nessa in USA, Chief in Europe.

TYLER, T. Texas (*b* David Luke Myrick, 20 June '16, Mena, Ark.; *d* 28 Jan. '72, Spring-field, Mo.) Country singer with growl in his voice. Grew up in Texas, performed on *Louisiana Hayride*, served in WWII, had hit with his own talking-song 'Deck Of Cards' '48 on West Coast 4 Star Records, about a soldier playing cards in church because the 52 cards represent the weeks in the year, 12 in suit the Apostles etc., the deck being almanac and bible: *Pop Memories* reckoned it sold well enough almost to make the pop top 20; it was also a hit by Tex RITTER, by Wink Martindale on Dot '59, comic Max Bygraves in UK '73. Co-written 'Daddy Gave My Dog Away' was another hit; appeared in movie *Horseman Of The Sierras* '49; 'Bumming Around' '53 was no. 5 country hit on Decca; ran popular and influential T. Texas Western Dance Band for some years; had L.A. TV show *Range Roundup*. Gave up performing and became clergyman late '60s, made religious albums, died of cancer. LPs on King, Starday, Capitol in honky tonk style did well '60s; *His Great Hits* on Hilltop incl. his theme 'Remember Me'; also album *Old Corrals & Sagebrush* on Columbia.

TYNER, McCoy (*b* McCoy Alfred Tyner, 11 Dec. '38, Philadelphia, Pa.) Pianist, composer; recognised as an important part of the epochal John COLTRANE Quartet '60-5, then became a master in his own right. Has taken Islamic name Sulaimon Saud. His mother played piano; he was infl. by Richie and Bud POWELL, who were neighbours; first met Coltrane '59 in Philadelphia, played with Art FARMER – Benny GOLSON Jazztet, then joined Coltrane. Led own trio '66, then quartet (also worked with Ike & Tina TURNER, Jimmy WITHERSPOON, etc.); LPs on Impulse now compiled on MCA 2-disc sets as *Early Trios, Great Moments, Reevaluation: The Impulse Years*; *The Real McCoy* '67 for Blue Note, with Joe HENDERSON, Ron CARTER, Elvin JONES, was hailed as a significant and beautiful album. Other Blue Notes incl. *Tender Moments* '68, *Expansions, It's About Time* (with Jackie McLEAN). Long series on Milestone incl. *Sahara* '72, *Sama Lucaya, Song For My Lady, Song For The New World*, solo *Echoes Of A Friend* (dedicated to Coltrane), 2-disc sets *Enlightenment* '73 (at Montreux) and *Atlantis*, many of these with Azar Lawrence on reeds (*b* 3 Nov. '53, L.A.; own LPs on Prestige), adding John Blake on violin c.'73. Also *Trident* (with Jones, Carter), *Fly With The Wind* '76 (with Hubert LAWS, Billy COBHAM, Carter), *Focal Point* '76, *Inner Voices, Greeting* '78, *Together, Passion Dance* '78 (live in Tokyo), *Horizon* '79, *13th House* and 2-disc *4X4* (with Cecil McBEE) '80; 2-disc compilations *Supertrios* and *Reflections*. On other labels: *Time For Tyner* '69 with Bobby HUTCHERSON, now on Pausa; *Leyenda de la Hora (The Legend Of The Hour)* and *Looking Out* on CBS; *Dimensions* on Elektra; *Reunited* '82 on Blackhawk with Jones, Pharoah SANDERS; *Just Feelin'* '85 on Palo Alto. Tyner is a master of structure, using it in his improvising like a composer, and of tension and release; he rarely plays 'free' but stretches rhythms and tonalities to their limit with unerring judgement; his sound is bright, exultant, affirmative: life-enhancing. Back on Blue Note for *Double Trios* '87 (CD on Denon in USA), incl. standards such as 'Lover Man', played as no one else could play them.

U

UB40 Integrated UK band formed '78 in Birmingham, where they were all born/raised; took their name from British unemployment benefit form: guitarist/lead vocalist Alistair (Ali) Campbell (*b* 15 Feb. '59), guitarist Robin Campbell (*b* 25 Dec. '54), Jim Brown on drums (*b* 20 Nov. '57), saxophonist Brian Travers (*b* 7 Feb. '59), Earl Falconer on bass (*b* 23 Jan. '59), Norman Hassan on percussion (*b* 26 Jan. '58), Mickey Virtue on keyboards (*b* 19 Jan. '57), Astro (*b* 24 June '57), the 'toaster' (*see* REGGAE). First pro gig early '79; invited to support PRETENDERS tour late '79; first three singles all two-sided hits '80 on Graduate, first to make national top 10 without promotion from major label: 'King'/'Food For Thought', 'My Way Of Thinking'/'I Think It's Going To Rain', 'Dream A Lie'/'The Earth Dies Screaming'; first LP *Signing Off* '80 reached no. 2; formed own label Dep International, distributed by Virgin; eight top 10 LPs and 17 top 20 singles followed. 'Food For Thought' was about hungry children in Africa; 'If It Happens Again' (top 10 '84) disguised criticism of Margaret Thatcher in a love song, but they are far more than a political band: music informed by the sprung rhythms of Jamaican music is excellent rock, listenable and danceable to, with singing and lyrics of integrity. LPs incl. *Present Arms* and *Present Arms In Dub* '81, *UB44* '82, *UB40 Live* and *Labour Of Love* (no. 1 LP incl. cover of Neil DIAMOND's 'Red Red Wine', no. 1 single) '83, *Geffery Morgan* '84 (strongly political), *Baggariddim* '85: featuring dub and toasting, reached only no. 14 UK but incl. no. 1 hit duet by Ali and Pretender's Chrissie Hynde on 'I Got You Babe' (international hit '65 by SONNY & CHER), and their own haunting no. 2 hit 'Don't Break My Heart'. *Rat In The Kitchen* '86 has 'sweet' tunes, but also political: '. . . personal confusion and personal ideas for every member of the band, so when you read the lyrics you'll read eight different people talking to you,' said Brown.

Rat incl. single 'Sing Our Own Song', incorporating African chant 'Amandla Awethu' ('Power Is Ours'), with female backing vocal trio of Mo Birch, Jaki Graham, Ruby Turner; guest Herb ALPERT on trumpet. *The Singles Album* was on Graduate '82; *Best Of UB40 Vol. 1* '87 is good value with 14 hits (four extra tracks on CD); 2-disc *The UB40 File* '86 compiles Graduate output. Travers makes videos for them, also prod. short film *Labour Of Love* (dir. by Bernard Rose), partly based on their real life adventures; Ali invented 'Orchestral Dub', his tune of that name orchestrated by Lewis Clarkin of ELECTRIC LIGHT ORCHESTRA for benefit record for Birmingham's children's hospice, with City of Birmingham Symphony Orchestra (Robin described it as 'like something out of *Seven Brides For Seven Brothers*'). They sponsor rally driver James Prochowski (a Pole from Glasgow) and his Nissan, with UB40-DEP markings. Two of their hits made USA top 40 '84-5 on A&M; they sold out a USA tour and *Rat In The Kitchen* was in top 60 USA LPs '86: they may conquer the world yet.

UFO UK heavy metal band formed '69 by Phil Mogg (*b* '51, London), vocals; Pete Wray, bass; Mick Bolton, guitar: all ex-Hocus Pocus, they recruited Andy Parker, drums. First two albums for Beacon label *UFO 1* '70 and *Flying* '71 were unremarkable examples of genre, but found popularity in Germany and (especially) Japan: *UFO: Landed In Japan* '71 was recorded live exclusively for that country. In '72 Bolton left to join Pink Fairies, replaced by Larry Wallis (ex-Blodwyn Pig); and Bernie Marsden replaced Wallis, but left for Wild Turkey during their '73 German tour: the band picked up Michael Schenker, lead axeman for support group Scorpions: his unpredictable style would be a major asset. Signed with Chrysalis: *Phenomenon* '74 sold well in UK and USA with perennial live staples 'Doctor Doctor' and 'Rock Bottom' among tracks. Added second guitarist Paul Chapman (ex-Skid Row), Danny Peyronel on keyboards, but neither stayed long: *No Heavy Petting* marked Peyronel's only appearance on the records, while *Force It* '75 is quartet album. Paul Chapman (ex-CHICKEN SHACK), doubling on guitar and keyboards, proved a more permanent addition; this lineup recorded the most commercially successful LPs. *Lights Out* '77 incl. 'Love To Love' and title track, both live favourites, and made no. 23 USA LP chart. *Obsession* '78 broached UK top 30 while live *Strangers In The Night* '78 reflected confident stage show and made no. 7 UK, where audience was undiminished despite rise of punk: live single 'Doctor Doctor' made no. 35 UK. Schenker departed '78 to rejoin Scorpions, later form own band; Chapman returned from stint with Lone Star; some excitement lost. *No Place To Run* '80 prod. by George MARTIN lacked edge (though 'Young Blood' no. 36); Paul Raymond's departure to Michael Schenker Group didn't help; Neil Carter (ex-Wild Horses, Gilbert O'SULLIVAN sideman) replaced him for *The Wild, The Willing And The Innocent* '81, but when founder member Way left after *Mechanix* '82 to form Fastway with ex-MOTORHEAD guitarist Eddie Clarke, band began to disintegrate. Ex-Hot Rods, DAMNED bassist Paul Gray filled in for *Making Contact* '83 but Mogg's collapse onstage in Athens that year preceded announcement of disbandment, with well-assembled 2-disc *Headstone* a suitable epitaph. Surprisingly, Mogg resurrected name '85, with Wray, Jim Simpson (drums) and Atomik Tommy M (guitar) for LP *Misdemeanour* '85. Former members Wray and Chapman still active in less successful Waysted. Long running metallurgists never became legends, surviving on loyal following for workmanlike HM, with Schenker providing most of the inspired moments.

UKWU, Celestine (*b* Celestine Obiakor, '42, east Nigeria; *d* '79) Singer-composer, guitarist. First played with Mike Ejeagha's Paradise Rhythm Orchestra in Enugu '62; formed own band the Music Royals in Onitsha '66, but civil war started '67; relaunched career '70 with band the Philosophers National, went on to dominate highlife style until his early death. Popular

early LPs incl. *True Philosophy, Ejim Nk'onye, Tomorrow Is So Uncertain,* all on Philips; style was a softer, gently paced highlife, blending keyboards into genre, with heavily accented percussion and occasional use of pedal steel. Became 11-piece band with lyrics about social evils, need for peace and unity, etc. Other LPs incl. *Ilo Abu Chi* and *Ndu Ka Aku* '74; *Igede Fantasia* '76 incl. hit 'Money Palaver'. *Uru Gini* and *His Philosophies* reissued by Polydor after '79.

ULLMAN, Tracey (*b* 30 Dec. '59, Buckinghamshire) UK pop singer. Attended stage school from age 12; appeared with Shakin' STEVENS in London stage show *Elvis,* also appeared in productions of *Grease* and *Rocky Horror Show;* starred in BBC TV series *Three Of A Kind* early '80s and launched singing career after meeting wife of Stiff label boss at the hairdresser's. Three top 10 hits '83 with covers of others' hits: Jackie DESHANNON's 'Breakaway', Kirsty MACCOLL's 'They Don't Know', Doris DAY's 'Move Over Darling'; 'They Don't Know' reached Hot 100 USA '84. Guests in her promo videos incl. Paul MCCARTNEY, Labour Party leader Neil Kinnock. *You Broke My Heart In 17 Places* '83 incl. all her hits, plus more covers. She appeared in McCartney's panned *Give My Regards To Broad Street* '84, had further hit with MADNESS's 'My Guy's Mad At Me'. She concentrated on acting, appearing in *Plenty* with POLICE's Sting, then relocating to the USA. Sitcom *The Tracey Ullman Show* began on Rupert Murdoch's Fox TV network in USA, appeared on UK TV '88.

ULMER, James 'Blood' (*b* 2 Feb. '42, St Matthews, S.C.) Guitarist, vocalist; also plays flute; composer. An uncategorisable musician, a sort of avant-garde bluesman full of pent-up passion. Sang gospel music, learned guitar as a child; moved to Philadelphia as pro c.'60, worked with organ funk groups; to Detroit, studying and practising in a quintet late '60s; to NYC '71 and steady gig at Minton's for several months. Worked with Art BLAKEY, Paul BLEY, others; studied with Ornette COLEMAN '74, appeared with him at Ann Arbor Jazz And Blues Festival, tours late '70s. Played on LPs by Joe Henderson, others; with Arthur

BLYTHE, another fine talent who hasn't found his niche, on *Lenox Avenue Breakdown* and *Illusions* '79-80; first LP as leader *Tales Of Captain Black* '78 on Artists House (with COLEMAN in group), then *Are You Glad To Be In America?* '80 on Rough Trade, *Freelancing*, *Black Rock* and *Odyssey* on CBS, *Part Time* '84 on Rough Trade, *Live At The Caravan Of Dreams* '87 on C of D label, and *America – Do You Remember The Love?* '87 on Blue Note, co-prod. by Bill LASWELL, who also plays bass, with Ronald Shannon Jackson on drums, Nicky Skopelitis on 12-string guitar and banjo: a low-key but passionate question about the nature of the USA, with plenty of bent notes and fine, subtle R&B-infl. playing from everyone.

ULTRAVOX UK new romantic/new wave group formed '75 by vocalist John Foxx (*b* Dennis Leigh, Chorley, Lancs.), bassist Chris Cross (*b* Chris Allen, 14 July '52), who met when Cross moved from London to join Preston-based Stoned Rose. Infl. by ROXY MUSIC they formed Tiger Lily with drummer Warren Cann (*b* 20 May '52, Canada), guitarist Steve Shears, and keyboard/violinist Billy Currie (*b* 1 Apr. '52). After arty cover of Fats WALLER's 'Ain't Misbehavin' ' (used as theme for porn movie) band slipped through several names (Innocents, Fire Of London, London Soundtrack, the Zips) before signing with Island as Ultravox! (exclamation later dropped). *Ultravox!* '77 co-prod. by Roxy hero Brian ENO; like him used keyboards in unorthodox manner behind Foxx's half-spoken vocals to court interest: it didn't sell, along with *Ha! Ha! Ha!* '77, despite being hailed by Gary NUMAN and others as infl. on the coming wave of synth music. On stage they were an uncomfortable mixture of old (glam-rock) and new (punk), sneering in plastic macs. Shears replaced by Robin Simon for *Systems Of Romance* '78, made with German prod. Conny Plank, but band still ahead of its time: Simon and Foxx left and Island dropped them (later compiled *Three Into One* '80 to cash in). Currie moonlighted with Numan (who still plugged band in interviews) and VISAGE, where he met Midge Ure (*b* James Ure, 10 Oct. '53, Glasgow; ex-Slik, Rich Kids): Ure joined Ultravox and resuscitated it, now a quartet with Cross, Ure's vocals/guitar, Cann, Currie. Signed with Chrysalis, hit with title track from *Vienna* '80, made with Plank, quasi-classical ballad with haunting violin solo from Currie, magical video (dir. Russell Mulcahy), bravura vocal from Ure: no. 2 UK, followed by no. 8 'All Stood Still'; band since established as top-selling LP and single act in UK and Europe (though not yet in USA). *Rage In Eden* '81 yielded 'The Thin Wall' and 'The Voice' as '81 top 20 hits, while seeming a trifle self-important; *Quartet* '82 was prod. by George MARTIN, incl. 'Reap The Wild Wind', 'Hymn', 'Visions In Blue', all top 15. Group diversified, Ure and Cross directing own videos from 'The Voice' onward, prod. for other artists; Cann meanwhile linked with ex-Buggle Hans Zimmer to record as Helden; Ure commenced solo career, made no. 9 with cover of WALKER Bros 'No Regrets' '82, top 40 duet with Mick Karn 'After A Fashion' '83, solo LP *The Gift* '85 which yielded no. 1 single 'If I Was': co-wrote most songs with Danny Mitchell, half of former Ultravox tour support the Messengers (he also played in Ure's live band that toured to promote LP). Ultravox continued, at sparing pace; live mini-LP *Monument* '83 suggested that ideas for group framework were lacking, confirmed by release of Ureera compilation *The Collection* after studio LP *Lament*, both '84, and several more hit singles. Ultravox parallel Roxy Music in having had one career as innovators and another with smoother, more commercial blend. Foxx did well with chart LPs of his own (*Metametix* '80, *The Garden* '81), but thenceforth recorded less; Ure found worldwide fame as co-writer of Band Aid anthem 'Do They Know It's Christmas' '84, world's fastest selling single, with Bob Geldof; with Geldof he is now part of rock establishment, paradoxically making it harder to do anything radically new. Cann left '86, disagreeing with machines; album *U-Vox* that year used them less, one track featuring Irish folk band CHIEFTAINS.

UNIT 4+2 UK pop group of '60s: folk group Unit Four (lineup: Peter Moules, vocals, Tommy Moeller, Howard Lubin, David Meilke, all guitars and vocals) moved into pop with addition of bass (Bob Garwood) and drums (Hugh Halliday) in '64. First shot 'The Green Fields' scraped top 50, but '65 saw them hit no. 1 with 'Concrete And Clay', written by Moeller with former member Brian Parker, who provided many of their lyrics. Rhythmic invention and drive carried it to no. 28 in USA; cover by Eddie Rambeau made no. 35 USA; Randy Edelman revived it more than 10 years later. Success was shortlived: after 'You've Never Been In Love Like This Before' (no. 14) nothing else troubled top 40. *First Album* '65 was last. Former Roulettes Bob Henrit (drums) and Russ Ballard (guitar and vocals) passed through before the end; later found greater success with ARGENT.

URIAH HEEP UK heavy metal group formed '69 by guitarist Mick Box (*b* 8 June '47, London) and vocalist David Byron (*b* 29 Jan. '47, Essex; *d* 28 Feb. '85), both ex-Stalkers and Spice. Lineup named after unctuous Dickens character was completed by drummer Alex Napier and Ken Hensley (*b* 24 Aug. '45), multi-talented guitarist, keyboardist, writer who'd played in the Gods with Mick Taylor and ex-Spice bassist Paul Newton: joined straight from unsuccessful Toefat. *'Very 'Eavy Very 'Umble* '70 featured Hensley's keyboards and Box's extrovert guitar leads, with Byron's high-register vocals enhanced by harmonies that took them out of standard HM rut. 'Gypsy' a perennial favourite. *Salisbury* '71 featured new drummer Keith Baker and unusual, heavily orchestrated 16-minute title track. *Look At Yourself* '71 had Iain Clarke on drums, incl. best-known track 'July Morning' (with Manfred Mann on Moog): sold well but not as well as *Demons And Wizards* '72, with stable rhythm section (at last) of drummer Lee Kerslake (ex-Gods) and bassist Gary Thain (ex-Keef HARTLEY; *b* N.Z.; *d* 19 Mar. '76). *Magician's Birthday* '72 continued sword and sorcery image; these together with tour-de-force 2-disc *Uriah Heep Live* '73 went gold in USA and UK: single 'Easy Livin' ' made no. 39 USA '72. But it was downhill from there: *Wonderworld* '74 was unexceptional; Thain had an electrical accident onstage, arguments over that, personal problems led to his leaving early '75 and he was found dead of drug accident; John Wetton (ex-King Crimson, FAMILY) filled in for aimless *Return To Fantasy* and *High And Mighty* '75-6; in '76 Byron was

replaced by John Lawton (ex-Lucifer's Friend) who had made solo LP *Take No Prisoners* '75 and soon departed to form Rough Diamond with Clem Clempson (ex-HUMBLE PIE); Wetton left, replaced by Trevor Bolder (ex-David BOWIE sideman). Music continued to disappoint even loyal fans and departure of Hensley left Box without lieutenant, co-composer; *Firefly*, *Innocent Victim*, *Fallen Angel* and *Conquest* '77-80 were all poor: Box dissolved band and formed another: new Heep with Box, John Sinclair (keyboards; ex-Heavy Metal Kids), Pete Goalby (vocals; ex-Trapeze), bassist Bob Daisley (ex-Rainbow) and Kerslake (who'd left to join Ozzy Osbourne) made LPs *Abominog* and *Head First* '82-3, both returns to form. Daisley quit '83, replaced by returning Bolder, while band acrimoniously split from one-time producer Gerry Bron's Bronze label to release *Equator* '85 on CBS/Epic. Like BLACK SABBATH's Tony Iommi, Mick Box has striven for standard expected by fans despite personnel changes; most serious loss was Hensley, who'd written most of the material (he made solo LPs *Proud Words On A Dusty Shelf* '73, *Eager To Please* '75, *Free Spirit* '80; spent much of early '80s with USA southern rockers Blackfoot). Renewed USA success with decidedly AOR-tinged HM may mean life for a few more years. *Anthology* '85 of Bronze stuff recommended for fans.

U2 Pop band formed in Dublin '77 by schoolfriends heavily infl. by punk: vocalist Bono (*b* Paul Hewson, 10 May '60), guitarist The Edge (*b* David Evans, 8 Aug. '61), drummer Larry Mullen (*b* 31 Oct. '61), bassist Adam Clayton (*b* 13 Mar. '60). Debut was an EP '79; 'Another Day' and 'Stories For Boys' were singles in Ireland only; London debut '79 was disaster, '80 visit more successful, landing record deal. *Boy* '80 prod. by Steve Lillywhite, incl. anthemic 'I Will Follow'; *October* '81 incl. minor UK hits 'Fire' and 'Gloria' and they made USA debut same year; *War* '83 incl. 'New Year's Day' (top 10 UK) and political 'Sunday Bloody Sunday'. By then they numbered Bruce SPRINGSTEEN and Pete Townshend among fans; growing confidence saw them regarded as one of the best of new rock bands for the '80s: ideologically sound, devoted Christians, they communicated care and loyalty to their audience; their sweeping, epic-style rock'n'roll found favour in USA, especially with release of live mini-LP *Under A Blood Red Sky* '83, largely recorded in USA. An outstanding live band, with Bono a charismatic front man and The Edge on his way to guitar-hero status. Brian ENO prod. *The Unforgettable Fire* '84, their second no. 1 LP in UK after *War*; 'Pride (In The Name Of Love)' was global hit '84, their first USA top 40. EP *Wide Awake In America* '85 was stop-gap. Bono and Clayton appeared on BAND AID record '84, were Live Aid highlight '85; Bono appeared with Bob DYLAN at his '84 Dublin concert, guested on *Sun City* '85 with Keith Richard and Ron Wood on 'Silver & Gold', sang with CLANNAD on *Macalla* '85; The Edge supplied soundtrack to film *Captive* '86. Their hit *The Joshua Tree* '87 was described as more mature, focusing on feelings as much as issues; but perhaps 'mature' in this context means 'smooth', as in MOR radio fodder. Nine people turned up to see them at the Hope And Anchor in London '79; the album and single 'With You Or Without You' were no. 1 USA May '87, their sincerity and audience identification compared to that of Bruce Springsteen. Dublin-based Mother label has helped other Irish bands such as Tua Nua, Cactus World News (U2 records are on Island elsewhere).

UWAIFO, Sir Victor (*b* '41 Benin City, Nigeria) Singer-composer, leader; plays guitar, flute, keyboards etc. Former amateur wrestler 'Sir' Victor adapted 'palm wine' style of mid-west Nigeria, sings in Edo and Pidgin, developed new rhythms and dance styles with facility that maintained popularity for two decades. To Lagos late '50s to complete education; led school bands, joined Victor OLAIYA All-Stars; won scholarship to technical college '62, played in spare time with E. C. Arinze. Joined Nigerian TV service '64, saving money to buy instruments; formed the Melody Maestros '65, made singles: 'Joromi' a huge hit all over West Africa. More than 100 singles and eight LPs in next decade; with 16-piece band representing Nigeria at Black Arts Festival in Algeria '69, toured USA and Japan '70; opened Joromi Hotel in Benin City '71; toured USSR and Europe '73, many tours of West Africa. Best-selling albums incl. *Roots, At The Crossroads, Jackpot, Laugh And Cry*. Over 50 graduates of band have own careers, e.g. Sonny OKOSUN, etc. Established own TV studio '80s with weekly national half-hour show; LPs in '80s incl. *Uwaifo '84, No Palava*.

V

VALE, Jerry (*b* Genaro Louis Vitaliano, 8 July '32, Bronx, NY) Pop crooner who worked as shoeshine boy in high school, then in a factory while he sang part-time; won a talent contest and was regular at Club del Rio for more than a year, changed his name and was discovered by Guy MITCHELL and Mitch MILLER, signed with CBS/Columbia: four hits '56-8 incl. 'You Don't Know Me' at no. 14; pleasant Italian light baritone came back '64-6 with four more. He sold LPs, 20 of them charting '62-72; five compilations still in print '87 incl. *17 Most Requested Hits*, 2-disc *Italian Hits*.

VALENS, Ritchie (*b* Richie Valenzuela, 13 May '41, Pacoima, Cal.; *d* 3 Feb. '59, Iowa) First Chicano rock star and the only one until SANTANA, then LOS LOBOS. Recorded 'Come On, Let's Go' for Bob Keene's Del-Fi label; it almost made top 40 '58. Then smoochie rockaballad 'Donna' (written for his girl friend) was smash no. 2, with trad. Latin party song 'La Bamba' on flip: DJs made B side a no. 22 hit, much the more influential. 'That's My Little Susie' and 'Little Girl' made Hot 100 '59; he was killed in same plane crash as Buddy HOLLY and the BIG BOPPER. Rhino records have somehow spun out short career into three compilations incl. 3-disc set with booklet. Hit film biopic *La Bamba* '87 incl. original music by Carlos Santana and Miles Goodman; Los Lobos on screen and soundtrack made 'La Bamba' a no. 1 hit this time.

VALENTE, Caterina Pop singer born in Paris of Italian parents. Impressive voice led to top 10 hit '55 USA (top 5 UK) 'The Breeze And I' (from *Andalucia – Suite Espagnole* by Ernesto LECUONA '28, English words by Al Stillman, no. 1 hit '40 for J. DORSEY). She remained a popular concert star in Europe. Among many albums, Teldec CD compiles '60-73 tracks on *Around The World*; original *Greatest Hits* on Jasmine UK concentrates on the Latin songs: 'La Paloma', 'My Shawl', 'Malagueña', etc.

VALENTIN, Bobby (*b* Puerto Rico) Salsa bandleader, bassist (also played trumpet), producer, arranger, label boss. He came to USA at 17; played trumpet with Charlie PALMIERI mid-'60s; made his debut as leader on LP *Ritmo Pa Goza* on Fonseca label; signed to Fania and made LPs *Young Man With A Horn – Best In Bugaloo, Bad Breath, Let's Turn On, Se La Comio, Algo Nuevo/Something New* c.'66-70, the latter featuring lead singer Frankie Hernandez (incl. hit 'Huracan'). Valentin's further LPs incl. *Rompacabezas* c.'72; *Soy Boricua* ('I Am Puerto Rican') '73 became something of a classic, incl. major hits such as title track and 'Pirata de la Mar'; incl. lead singer Marvin Santiago. *Rey del Bajo* and *In Motion* '74 incl. both Santiago and Hernandez lead vocals, with Santiago on standout tracks (Santiago's vocals were compiled on *Marvin Santiago & Bobby Valentin* '80). Valentin played trumpet on FANIA ALL STARS' debut albums *Live At The Red Garter* '68; also with FAS he played bass and arranged on *Live At The Cheetah* '71, in film/soundtrack album *Our Latin Thing (Nuestra Cosa)* '72, *Latin-Soul-Rock* '74, *Live At Yankee Stadium* '75 (arr. tracks with Hector LAVOE, Celia CRUZ), film/soundtrack LP *Salsa* '76, *Tribute To Tito Rodriguez* '76, *Live* '78, *California Jam* '80, *Viva la Charanga* '86, all for Fania; also on less well regarded *Delicate & Jumpy* '76 on CBS (Island in UK, Fania in Europe through SonoDisc). He also played bass and arranged on Larry HARLOW LP *Orchestra Harlow Presenta a Ismael Miranda* '68 on Fania; on Vaya he played bass and co-arranged (with Nick Jimenez) on *Cheo* '72 (debut Cheo FELICIANO LP), played and wrote the arrangements on Cheo's *With A Little Help From My Friend* '73, arr. two tracks each on *Celia & Johnny* (Cruz and PACHECO) '74 (incl. her major hit 'Toro

Mata') and their second collaboration *Tremendo Caché* '75, played/arranged on eponymous *Ismael Quintana* '74. That year he formed his own Bronco label in Puerto Rico; first releases were two vols. of *Va a la Cárcel* '75, made at State Penitentiary of Puerto Rico, Santiago and Hernandez again lead singers (Santiago left '76, went solo; recent LP was *Oficial! y Ahora . . . con Tremenda Pinta!* '86 on Top Hits). Valentin's Bronco LPs incl. *Bobby Valentin* '83, *Algo Excepcional* '85, *Bobby Valentin* '86 (incl. salsa version by Tite Curet Alonso of Stevie WONDER's 'Part Time Lover'). His band still has front line of two trumpets, trombone, alto and baritone saxes; lead singers are Rafael (Rafu) Warner, Juan (Johnny) Vázquez and Angel Luis Carrion. Bronco's roster also incl. top Puerto Rican bands Willie Rosario, Mulenze, and Ralphy Leavitt y su Orquesta La Selecta.

VALENTINE, Dickie (*b* Richard Brice, 4 Nov. '29, London; *d* 6 May '71, Wales in road crash) UK pop singer. Film debut at age 3 in farce *Jack's The Boy* '32, with Cicely COURTNEIDGE. Was page boy at Manchester Palace, then London Palladium; encouraged by musical comedy star Bill O'Connor, who paid for singing lessons (against medical advice; Valentine had chronic asthma). Spotted at London's Blue Angel club by music publisher Sid Green; recommended to bandleader Ted HEATH, joined Heath's Sunday night Swing Sessions at the Palladium '49. Initially sang only one song per evening early in the show, then sat on stage: once asked by latecomer if he was the band's mascot. Left Heath to go solo '54, having become teenage idol; played to SRO business at first solo show in Blackpool, despite Nat COLE appearing 200 yards down the road. Developed fast, humorous act with lots of impressions: Mario LANZA, Billy DANIELS, Johnny RAY; at a time when American stars dominated the Palladium so that it was called the 49th state, Valentine was the first British singer to headline there in five years '55; in '57 he hired the Royal Albert Hall for fan club's annual party. 12 top 20 UK hits '53-9 incl. no. ones 'Broken Wing', 'Finger Of Suspicion', 'Christmas Alphabet'; cover of Frankie AVALON's 'Venus' re-entered chart four times '59 (he was a much better singer than Avalon).

Continued very popular in cabaret. Hits compilation on Decca *The Very Best Of Dickie Valentine* incl. previously unissued track 'That Lovely Weekend', song written '42 by Heath and his wife Moira.

VALLEE, Rudy (*b* Hubert Prior Vallee, 28 July '01, Island Pond, Vt.; *d* 3 July '86, Cal.) Singer, actor, composer, publisher. Grew up in Westbrook, Maine; self-taught on drums and reeds; first pro job playing sax in a theatre in Maine. Went to Yale and formed Yale Collegians; played in England with band '24-5; sang in pre-CROSBY crooner style, assisted by a megaphone. He was enormously popular, perhaps the first pop idol: 'I never had much of a voice . . . one reason for the success was that I was the first articulate singer – people could understand the words.' Said to have predicted the demise of his own style with the rise of Bing Crosby, who possessed a microphone technique unnecessary when Vallee began. He graduated from Yale '27; big break at NYC's Heigh-Ho Club '28, billed as Rudy Vallee and his Connecticut Yankees, featured novelty, college numbers: 'Heigh-ho, everybody' was the famous greeting; show was carried by four radio stations. First film *The Vagabond Lover* '29; sang own co-written title song 'I'm Just A Vagabond Lover'; same year began weekly radio show *The Fleischmann Hour* for yeast company: show ran 10 years (theme 'My Time Is Your Time'), promoted careers of Eddie CANTOR, Edgar Bergen & Charlie McCarthy, George Burns & Gracie Allen, and especially singer Alice Faye (*see* Phil HARRIS). Collaborated '31 on big hit 'Betty Co-Ed'; lyrics incl. list of USA colleges. Broadway debut *George White's Scandals* '31, with Faye in chorus; also *Scandals* of '36, film version '34 with Jimmy DURANTE in blackface. No. 2 hit USA '43 with Herman Hupfield's 'As Time Goes By'. Late '30s-early '40s changed movie image from romantic to wealthy stuffed-shirt type who never got the girl; became good comic actor: singing waned from early '50s in favour of comedy on TV talk and talent shows; played hilarious role '61 as caricature of old college type J. B. Biggley in Frank LOESSER show *How To Succeed In Business Without Really Trying*; repeated role in film '67 and in a San Francisco revival at the age of 74. Narrated and sang title song '68 in burlesque movie *The Night They Raided Minsky's*. Other hits, many co-written (mostly before charts began): 'Life Is Just A Bowl Of Cherries', 'Dancing With Tears In My Eyes', 'The Whiffenpoof Song', 'Say It Isn't So', 'Vieni, Vieni' (Come, Come), etc. Ran two publishing companies, wrote three autobiographies, had four wives. Compilation *Heigh-Ho, Everybody, This Is Rudy Vallee* on ASV.

VAN DER GRAAF GENERATOR UK art-rock band formed '67 in Manchester, whose constant factor was guitarist/keyboardist/composer/ vocalist Peter Joseph Andrew Hammill (*b* 5 Nov. '48, London). Named after a generator of high-voltage electrostatic energy built at M.I.T. '31 by Dr Robert Jemison Van Der Graaf (1901-67), name suggested by foundermember and first drummer Chris Judge Smith. They broke up; Hammill began making a solo album which turned out to be *The Aerosol Grey Machine* '68 on Fontana/Mercury, the first Van Der Graaf LP, with Keith Ellis on bass, Hugh Banton on keyboards, Guy Evans on drums, others. *The Least We Can Do Is Wave To Each Other* '69 on new Charisma label was their only chart LP (top 50 UK), with Nic Potter replacing Ellis, David Jackson added on sax; *H To He Who Am The Only One* '70 was almost a pop album, with a sweet sound and guest Robert FRIPP, title referring to thermonuclear reaction in stars, 'the prime energy source in the universe'; *Pawn Hearts* '71 (without Potter) was oddly unfocused, transitional in retrospect; they broke up again and Hammill's solo career began with *Fools Mate* with Fripp sitting in (Hammill guested on Fripp's *Exposure*), followed by *Chameleon In The Shadows Of The Night*, both '72, and *The Silent Corner And The Empty Stage* (guest Randy California on guitar) and *In Camera* '74. He created alter ego Rikki Nadir for *Nadir's Big Chance* '75, presaging punk rock; Van Der Graaf re-formed for *Godbluff*, *Still Life* and *World Record* '75-6, their peak of creativity (especially 'Still Life' title track), Hammill's bleak, existential lyrics, Banton's gothic organ and Evans's virtuoso drumming making sound paintings as good as anything art rock ever came up with: they were already mellowing by the time of *World Record*, and broke up again; Hammill released *Over* and

The Future Now '77-8; they re-formed once more for 2-disc *Vital/Live* '78, made live at the Marquee Club: Potter had returned, while Charles Dickie on cello, electric piano and synth, Graham Smith on violin added new sound. Other Van Der Graaf compilations etc. incl. *68-71* (released '72), *The Long Hello* '73, *The Quiet Zone* '77 (all on Charisma) and *Time Vaults* '85 on Charly's Demi-Monde label. Punk rockers cited Van Der Graaf as an inspiration, but they weren't that bad. Hammill carried on, with loyal cult fans: *pH7* '79 on Charisma, *A Black Box* '80 on S-Type Records, *Sitting Targets* '81 on Virgin, *Enter K* '82 and *Patience* '83 on Naive, *Skin* '85 on Foundry, *And Close As This* '86 on Virgin. Sofa Sound offered by post *The Love Songs*, *Loops And Reels*, 2-disc *The Margin*, series *The Long Hello* by various ex-Generators, Potter's *Mountain Music*, an Ellis single, badges, T-shirts, newsletter. Published collections of lyrics etc. were *Killers, Angels, Refugees* '66-73, *Mirrors, Dreams & Miracles* '74-80.

VANDROSS, Luther (*b* 20 Apr. '51, NYC) Soul singer. Began singing commercial jingles; became top session vocalist and arranger, backing stars such as David BOWIE, Bette MIDLER, Carly SIMON, Chaka KHAN, Barbra STREISAND, Donna SUMMER; worked with Quincy JONES and with Italian disco band Change; contributed to films *The Wiz* and *Bustin' Loose*, finally busted loose as solo artist to wide acclaim. LPs *Never Too Much* '81, *Forever, For Always, For Love* '82 (released '87 in UK), *Busy Body* '83, *The Night I Fell In Love* '85, *Give Me The Reason* '86 on Epic have all charted well in USA; 10 singles hits incl. duet with Dionne WARWICK on 'How Many Times Can We Say Goodbye' from *Busy Body*. LPs began charting in UK with *Busy Body*; LP *Luther Vandross* '81 in UK was some sort of compilation from his first two LPs: UK labels like to do that for some reason.

VAN EPS, George (*b* 7 Aug. '13, Plainfield, N.J.) Guitarist. Father was Fred Van Eps, ragtime banjo player who began recording on cylinders in 1897, made an LP 60 years later. George played banjo, switched to guitar early '30s; played with many bands incl. Smith BALLEW, Freddy MARTIN, Benny GOODMAN '34-5; Ray NOBLE '35-6, again

'39-41; also much radio and studio work. Did research into sound technology early '40s with his father. After WWII much studio work, especially with Paul WESTON (solos on LPs); heard in excellent studio dixieland band led by trumpeter Dick Cathcart (*b* 6 Nov. '24, Michigan City, Ind.; also singer) for film *Pete Kelly's Blues* '55 (and later TV series); on LPs in a similar vein with Rampart Street Paraders (Matty Matlock, etc.) on Columbia early '50s. He invented a seven-string guitar with an extra bass string, accompanying his own solos; always playing acoustic, among the most highly regarded by other guitarists. Very few solo records incl. 78s on a Jump label, a George Van Eps Ensemble session on Columbia USA; eight tracks from '51-3 on compilation *Stacy'n'Sutton* on Affinity (pianists Jess STACY and Ralph SUTTON); later LPs: *Mellow Guitar* on Columbia; *Soliloquy, My Guitar* and *Seven Strings* on Capitol, latter in stereo. Toured UK '86.

VAN HALEN Hard rock/heavy metal quartet formed USA '74: David Lee Roth, vocals; Edward Van Halen, guitar; Michael Anthony, bass; Alex Van Halen, drums. Van Halen brothers born in Holland, emigrated with parents to Cal.; joined Roth and Anthony in group loosely based on FREE; first called the new group Mammoth, but name was being used by another group. Energy-packed act gained early following, with Roth's overtly sexual image (world's tightest trousers?) and Van Halen's highly rated guitar; promoted own gigs and eventually signed by WB. Debut eponymous LP '78 made USA top 20; each album charted higher: *Van Halen II* '79, *Women And Children First* '80, *Fair Warning* '81; *Diver Down* '82 all reaching top 10 in USA, also charting in UK. Hit singles less frequent, but 'Dance The Night Away' '79, '(Oh) Pretty Woman' '82 (old Roy ORBISON song) made USA top 20 ('Runnin' With The Devil' charted UK '80). Big live attraction domestically, less so in Europe; records all produced by Ted Templeman. *1984 (MCMLXXXIV)* '84 was no. 2 LP USA, incl. hits 'Jump', 'I'll Wait', 'Panama'; Roth left, replaced by Sammy Hagar; LP *5150* '86. Roth hit with old BEACH BOYS' 'California Girl' '85; planned film *Crazy From The Heat*, material released in solo LP of

that name followed by *Eat 'Em And Smile* '86, *Skyscraper* '87.

VANILLA FUDGE USA heavy metal band formed '67 as the Pigeons: Vince Martell (*b* 11 Nov. '45, NYC), vocals and guitar; Mark Stein (*b* 11 Mar. '47, N.J.), keyboards; Tim Bogert (*b* 27 Aug. '44), bass; Carmine Appice (*b* 15 Dec. '46, Staten Island, NY), drums. Stein and Bogert had played together in the Showmen, picked up Appice, then Martell. Stein had first recorded for Cameo in a high school band '59. Played first date '67, down bill under the BYRDS; signed by Atlantic, quickly made eponymous 2-disc set that relied on cover versions ('People Get Ready', 'Ticket To Ride', 'Bang Bang' etc.): gimmick was playing them very slowly, imitating time-distorting effect of drugs, also quasi-gospel harmonies, classical keyboards and elaborate production: in an age of innovation this passed for progress. Cover of SUPREMES' 'You Keep Me Hangin' On' demonstrated formula well, became sleeper hit (no. 6 USA/18 UK) a year after release; 'Take Me For A Little While' no. 38 followup. Others followed: *Renaissance, The Beat Goes On* (about the history of the world), *Near The Beginning, Rock'n'Roll* '68-70, plus *Star Collection* '73, but DEEP PURPLE, LED ZEPPELIN etc. had taken up the torch; Fudge split '70. Stein formed unsuccessful Boomerang; Bogert and Appice went to Cactus, then Jeff BECK. With IRON BUTTERFLY and others, Fudge laid foundation of heavy metal genre when record companies thought that 'underground' music was the wave of the future; stress of technique over songwriting and originality brought temporary success which soon faded.

VAN RONK, Dave (*b* 30 June '36, Brooklyn, N.Y.) Folk/blues singer, guitarist. Played in trad. jazz bands mid-'50s, became fixture in Greenwich Village folk scene with Jack ELLIOTT, Phil OCHS, Bob DYLAN etc. Played Newport Folk Festival '63; formed Ragtime Jug Stompers '63, recorded with them '64 on Mercury. Big, raspy voice, sometimes bawdy material and excellent guitar playing owed much to country blues; he also wrote songs and many fans thought he would become a big star, but he remained popular on college/club circuit.

Also played Carnegie Hall, had own NYC radio show '66, etc. Recorded for Lyrichord and Folkways late '50s, Prestige '63-4, Verve-Folkways '67-8, Fantasy early '70s, Philo '76. LPs: *Blues, Black Mountain Blues, Sings Earthy Ballads And Blues* on Folkways; 2-disc *Dave Van Ronk* on Fantasy; *Folksinger, In The Tradition* and *Sings Dave Van Ronk* on Prestige; *Somebody Else, Not Me* and *Sunday Street* on Philo.

VAN STRATEN, Alfred 'Alf' (*b* 20 Sep. '05, London) Saxes, leader. Youngest society bandleader in England when he opened at fashionable West End restaurant Quaglino's '31, stayed there till '41, then to Embassy Club. Best shops advertised by giving free clothes to 'The Debonair Bandleader'. Publishers would not then allow new show tunes to be played before shows had opened in London; Van Straten and others copied them from USA broadcasts, running a taxi/library service so they could play requests. Was mus. dir. after WWII for several hotels; then thought of quitting, but bookings would not stop for weddings and debutante parties. Still a booking agent and gifted raconteur, instead of retiring he decided to stay young.

VAN ZANDT, Steve 'Miami' (*b* c.'51, Boston, Mass.) Guitarist, songwriter, vocalist, leader. Gigged in bar bands in New Jersey incl. Steel Mill, where he met Bruce SPRINGSTEEN. Joined Asbury Jukes on its formation in '75, later that year joined Springsteen's E Street Band, but remained close to the highly rated band that had become SOUTHSIDE JOHNNY AND THE ASBURY JUKES. He was the bedrock of the E Street Band, vocal harmonies and long friendship with Springsteen making perfect partnership, but inevitably he stood in the Boss's shadow. E Streets were on hold '82 as Springsteen prepared solo LP *Nebraska*; he adopted sobriquet Little Steven & the Disciples of Soul for 12-piece band, played one-off gig at London Marquee that year to critical acclaim: band incl. Jukes horn section, ex-Plasmatics bassist Jean Beauvoir; debut album *Men Without Women* '82 was impressive, his voice not a strong one, but band's sound awesome. He prod. two LPs for Gary 'US' BONDS, left Springsteen (replaced by Nils LOFGREN) '84; he'd called

himself Sugar Miami Steve on a Southside Johnny album, had also written songs for Jukes and Bonds, now turned to Disciples full time: second album *Voice Of America* '84 was a good follow-up, overtly political incl. title track, 'Solidarity' (covered by reggae trio Black Uhuru), 'Los Desaparecidos'. Went on fact-finding trip to South Africa mid-'85; result was powerful *Sun City* album/concert '85, anti-apartheid project with Springsteen, Bob DYLAN, Arthur BAKER, Gil SCOTT-HERON, Stevie WONDER which raised over $400,000. He guested on some Springsteen tour dates '85, co-prod. LONE JUSTICE LP *Shelter* '86; new Disciples set *Freedom – No Compromise* '87, still on EMI/America, Manhattan Records.

VAN ZANDT, Townes (*b* Fort Worth, Texas) Elusive, highly regarded Texas singer/songwriter and guitarist whose best-known work is 'Pancho And Lefty', recorded by Willie NELSON and Merle HAGGARD (no. 1 country hit), also by Emmylou HARRIS. Emmylou and Don WILLIAMS both covered his 'If I Needed You'. First infl. was Elvis PRESLEY: 'There were stars before him but they had sort of round edges.' Among later infl. was Lightnin' HOPKINS; learned to finger-pick from a Hoyt AXTON record. Lived and chummed with Richard DOBSON, Guy and Susanna CLARK; joined the Peace Corps for a while; began writing 'funny bar room type [songs] just to get the audience'; first serious song was 'Waitin' Around To Die', incl. on first LP *For The Sake Of A Song* '68, followed by *Our Mother The Mountain* '69, *Townes Van Zandt* '70, *Delta Mama Blues* '71: title song refers to a cough syrup (drug-store high) called Delta Mama, co-written while working in trio Delta Mama Boys; he normally cannot write with others. Then *High, Low And In Between* and, *The Late, Great Townes Van Zandt* '73 (incl. 'Pancho And Lefty'), another not then released, all on Poppy label with poor distribution; then 2-disc *Live At The Old Quarter, Houston, Texas* '77 on Tomato: some Poppies were to be reissued on Tomato, which soon went broke anyway. *Live And Obscure* on Heartland was made live in Nashville '85; *At My Window* '87 on Sugar Hill his 'first studio album' in nine years, prod. by Jack CLEMENT and Jim Rooney. Songbook *For The Sake Of A Song*;

feature film *The New Country* with Townes, Clark, Charlie DANIELS, David Allan COE, others late '70s. Poppy albums are being reissued on Charly.

VAUDEVILLE The American theatrical circuit, the equivalent of the British MUSIC HALL. The term *Chanson du vau de Vire* (song of the Vale of Vire) originated from a valley in Calvados, France, which was famous for satirical songs; this was corrupted to 'vau de ville', which came to mean any satirical song or light entertainment. The rise of vaudeville coincided with the end of the era of MINSTRELSY; while the entire minstrel troupe had been on stage the whole time, the vaudeville theatre presented a variety show, complete with jugglers and dog acts as well as comedy and music. The songs carried on from the 'coon' songs (*see also* RAGTIME) and sentimental songs, though many of them still had tear-jerking tragedy in the verse (the words of the lovely 'In The Shade Of The Old Apple Tree, written c. '05 and recorded instrumentally by Duke ELLINGTON in the early '30s, turn out to be about a grave). Tony Pastor (1837-1908) had worked in minstrel shows, opened his Opera House in the Bowery in 1865 and another theatre in 1881, presenting the most popular entertainers of the time; he also hired talented newcomers (who were also cheaper) and before long every town in the USA had its own vaudeville theatre. Sophie TUCKER in her autobiography (*Some Of These Days*) is very good on the tribulations of the artist: she was responsible for her own transport, lodging, costumes, songs, arrangements and so on, collected her wages from the theatre manager and paid a commission to her booking agent; the manager decided where on the bill she was presented. It was sheer talent rather than hype or TV exposure that got an artist to the top, and up-and-comers were soon the targets of the songpluggers (*see* TIN PAN ALLEY). It was the aim of the more ambitious acts to get to the 'legitimate' theatre (i.e. Broadway shows) where few jugglers were to be seen. The principal booking agency for black theatres was TOBA (Theatre Owners Booking Agency, aka 'Tough On Black Asses'). In Britain the music hall was more truly family entertainment, while vaudeville and theatre people

were sneered at by snobs in the USA; paradoxically the theatre owners tried to keep the acts fairly wholesome, and many towns also had burlesque houses where the more daring material (incl. strippers) was presented. As the quality of the music got better under the infl. of jazz and Broadway composers, vaudeville was already under increasing competition from records and radio and was past its peak by WWII; the dance halls took over during the Swing Era and TV was the ultimate death blow. The most popular radio and screen comedy acts (the Three Stooges, Jack Benny, W. C. Fields, George Burns and Gracie Allen and many others) had served their time on the vaudeville stage, and TV shows like Broadway columnist Ed Sullivan's kept the tradition going: these were in fact essentially weekly vaudeville shows, even incl. the occasional dog act.

VAUGHAN, Frankie (*b* Frank Abelson, 3 Feb. '28, Liverpool) UK pop singer. Attended Leeds College of Art, intending to teach; spotted in college revue by BBC prod. Barney Colehan. First pro job in variety at Kingston Empire made immediate impression '50. Advised by veteran music hall star Hetty King. Began recording '53, from '54-68 chart entries every year except '66; 29 altogether incl. no. ones 'Garden Of Eden', 'Tower Of Strength'; also no. 2 'Green Door' '56 (cover of USA no. 1 by DJ Jim Lowe, *b* 7 May '27, Springfield, Mo.; novelty written by Marvin Moore and Bob Davie was inspired by young men hanging around outside a club, unable to enter because they had no union cards; Lowe wrote 'Gambler's Guitar', hit for Rusty DRAPER). USA chart entry '58 with 'Judy' (no. 22). Film *Those Dangerous Years* '57 was first of four LP *Frankie Vaughan Live At The London Palladium* '59 with Kaye Sisters, King Brothers; also had two top 10 UK entries with the Kayes. Made film *Let's Make Love* '60 with Marilyn Monroe, Yves Montand. Active through '70s in concert and cabaret; surprise choice '85 to replace James Laurenson in London cast of *42nd Street*. Famous theme 'Give Me The Moonlight', song from '18 by Albert Von Tilzer and Lew Brown, now always associated with stylish performer, major British star. Consistent worker with youth projects; proceeds of

'Green Door' and much else went to National Association of Boys' Clubs; awarded OBE '65. Compilations in '80s: *Greatest Hits* on Spot, *Low Hits And High Kicks* on Creole, *Music Maestro Please* on Flashback, several more.

VAUGHAN, Sarah (*b* Sarah Lois Vaughan, 27 Mar. '24, Newark, N.J.) Singer, also plays piano; aka 'Sassy', 'The Divine One'. As with Ella FITZGERALD, there is argument about whether she is a jazz singer; as with Ella, the argument is academic: with her effortless swing, wide vocal range, rare but excellent scatting, apparently perfect pitch and a vocal colour that has become warmer than Ella's over the years, she is one of the great vocalists of the century. Sang in church, studied piano as a child; won amateur night at the Apollo theatre, joined Earl HINES band '44-5; when Billy ECKSTINE left to form his own band she was a founder member (*see* Eckstine's entry for tracks with Sarah); then she recorded under her own name, often duetting with Eckstine. Compilations of early tracks are *The Man I Love* and *Lover Man* '45-8 on Musicraft, *Summertime* '49-51 on CBS UK; *After Hours, Sarah Vaughan In HiFi* ('55, with Miles DAVIS) and *Linger Awhile* (top 20 LP '56) are from Columbia Special Products in USA. She usually toured with a piano trio, often with symphony orchestras in '80s; most of her records incl. a cast of first-class jazzmen, most made for the EmArcy/Mercury/Verve labels, all now belonging to Polydor: many of these are available separately round the world, but *The Complete Sarah Vaughan On Mercury* has been issued in USA: Vol. 1 is 6-disc *Great Jazz Years* '54-6, with Clifford BROWN, Cannonball ADDERLEY, others; Vol. 2 5-disc *Sings Great American Songs* '56-7 with Eckstine, others; Vol. 3 6-disc *Great Show On Stage* '54-6; Vol. 4 Part 1 4-disc *Live In Europe*, Part 2 5-disc *Sassy Swings Again* with Freddie HUBBARD, Benny GOLSON etc. also available as set of six compact discs. Also on CD is *Irving Berlin Songbook* with Eckstine on Mercury; EmArcy has been revived as CD label incl. classics *Sarah Vaughan* '54, *Rodgers & Hart Songbook* '54-8, *In The Land Of Hi-Fi* '55 with Ernie Wilkins, *No Count Sarah* with Thad Jones. Other LPs incl. *Songs Of The Beatles* on

Atlantic, *A Foggy Day* and *Tenderly* on Astan in UK, *O, Som Brazileiro De* on RCA/Brazil; sets on Vogue/Pye/PRT (some in UK) are probably all from Roulette late '50s: *With Count Basie And Benny Carter*, *Sarah Vaughan* with Barney KESSEL, others. Like so many other great artists she turned to Norman GRANZ' Pablo label in the '70s, incl. *Duke Ellington Songbook* (2 vols., with Duke), *Send In The Clowns* with Basie, *How Long Has This Been Going On* with Oscar PETERSON, *Copacabana*. *Gershwin Live!* on CBS was made c.'82 with the Los Angeles Philharmonic, cond. Michael Tilson Thomas. *Live At Ronnie Scott's* on Pye in UK did not incl. breathtaking 'Things Must Change', lovely song written by Bernard Ighner, later incl. on a 2-disc compilation sold at the club. *The Planet Is Alive . . . Let It Live!* '85 on Gene LEES' Jazzletter label is subtitled *Sarah Vaughan Sings Pope John Paul II*: the Pope's poems adapted by Lees to music by Tito Fontana and Sante Palumbo; Ighner sang one song; Lees wrote 'Toward The Light' (with Francy Boland; *see* Kenny CLARKE) and 'Let It Live' (with Lalo SCHIFRIN); album made live in Düsseldorf, prod. by Gigi Campi, arr. by Boland; orch. cond. by Schifrin incl. Benny BAILEY, Art FARMER, Tony COE, Sahib Shihab, 30 others plus strings. (Reedman Shihab, *b* Edmund Gregory, 23 June '25, Savannah, Ga., is one of USA's best-kept secrets; teaches at New England Conservatory.) Sassy also sang in London studio recording of *South Pacific* '86 on CBS, with Kiri Te Kanawa, José Carreras in leading roles. Other pop hit LPs were *Sassy* '56 on EmArcy, 2-disc sets *Great Songs From Hit Shows* and *Sings Gershwin* '57 on Mercury, *Sarah Vaughan/Michel Legrand* '72 on Mainstream; 20 hit singles '54-66 incl. duet with Eckstine 'Passing Strangers' '57, top tens 'Make Yourself Comfortable' and 'Whatever Lola Wants' '54-5, 'Broken-Hearted Melody' '59, all on Mercury.

VAUGHAN, Stevie Ray (*b* c.'56, Dallas, Texas) Blues guitarist. Younger brother of FABULOUS THUNDERBIRDS' Jimmie; absorbed his brother's collection of B. B. KING, Lonnie MACK, Albert COLLINS records; by age 8 played with the Chantones, later CREAM-infl. group Blackbird.

Dropped out of school to join the Nightcrawlers (cut LP in L.A., never released); played with locally renowned Cobras '75-7 before forming own Triple Threat Revue with W. C. Clark, guitar and Lou Ann Burton, vocals. Formed Double Trouble '81, named after Otis RUSH song: bassist Tommy Shannon (ex-Johnny WINTER), drummer Chris 'Whipper' Layton (ex-Greazy Brothers). Offered free studio time by Jackson BROWNE; came in for attention from CBS prod. John HAMMOND; after rave reviews from Montreux Jazz Festival Apr. '82, used studio time to make *Texas Flood* '83 with Hammond. Had attracted more big-time fans: played private audition in NYC for ROLLING STONES Apr. '82, while David BOWIE asked him to play lead on his *Let's Dance* '83. His own *Couldn't Stand The Weather* '84, again prod. by Hammond, paid homage to Jimi HENDRIX with cover of 'Voodoo Chile', also incl. Jimmy REED's 'Tin Pan Alley', four originals. *Soul To Soul* continued pattern, this time with Willie DIXON's 'You'll Be Mine', but addition of Reese Wynons on keyboards gave music a more modern edge, which purist critics seemed surprisingly happy with. 2-disc stage set *Live Alive* '86 was acclaimed; he has played with Johnny COPELAND, prod. Mack and Albert KING; with reverence for established blues legends, he is the Johnny WINTER of the '80s, will go further if he continues widening scope: worked with composer Tom Newman on *Gung Ho* soundtrack '85, was scoring film *Judgement Day*, said to be contributing to second LP by eclectic percussionist Brian Slawson (*b* c.'57; debut on Columbia *Bach On Wood*).

VEE, Bobby (*b* Robert Velline, 30 Apr. '43, Fargo, N.D.) Pop singer whose first break came as result of Buddy HOLLY's death: Velline's group the Shadows depped at dance in Mason City, Iowa in '59 when Holly didn't make it. Local hit 'Suzie Baby' picked up by prod. Snuff GARRETT, who groomed Vee for stardom in Holly vein; ironically covered Adam FAITH Holly imitation 'What Do You Want' for USA market (without success). 'Devil Or Angel' made no. 6 '60, as did his infectious 'Rubber Ball' (also first UK hit at no. 4). Continued to score both sides of the Atlantic with best

Brill Building bullets – the kind of innocent pop BEATLES soon destroyed forever: 11 USA top 40 hits to '63; biggest in '61 'Take Good Care Of My Baby' (no. 1), 'Run To Him' (no. 2), with '63's 'The Night Has A Thousand Eyes' (no. 3) later becoming an MOR staple. Equally popular in UK with 10 hits '61-3. His appeal was not all manufactured: *Bobby Vee Meets The Crickets* '62 was much acclaimed by purists, established the Holly connection once more. Had massive comeback 'Come Back When You Grow Up' (no. 3 '67) with the Strangers, two more top 40 entries '67-8; LP *Nothin' Like A Sunny Day* '72 under real name failed; plays revival shows to much affection.

VEE JAY label Formed in Chicago c.'52-3 by Vivian and James Bracken and Calvin Carter; began as a gospel label with Maceo Smith (steady album seller) and the STAPLE singers; among the few black-owned labels between Don Robey's Peacock in Houston and Berry Gordy's MOTOWN in Detroit and almost became a giant, but foundered '65 amid rumours of mismanagement, staff dishonesty. Biggest seller was probably Jimmy REED, but also had hits with seminal vocal groups the Spaniels, El Dorados and the Dells (later also big on Cadet); Gladys KNIGHT and the Pips had one of their first big hits, sold to Vee Jay by tiny Huntom Records; meanwhile the group had been signed by Fury who sued Vee Jay and won, then went broke: both Vee Jay and the Pips lost out. John Lee HOOKER, Jerry BUTLER, Dee CLARK and the FOUR SEASONS all had Vee Jay hits, but as the company got bigger it also got more expensive to run: there was dead weight on the staff, no forward planning. Ironically their biggest success probably helped to put them under: Capitol having turned down the BEATLES, they were first released in the USA on Vee Jay; if a small-to-middling company has a huge hit, it has to buy a lot of pressings in a hurry, and the money is slow to come back from distributors.

VEGA, Suzanne Singer, songwriter, guitarist. Emerged from USA East Coast folk circuit; debut *Suzanne Vega* '85 on A&M reached top 100 pop LPs in USA, top 20 UK, incl. 'Marlene On The Wall', 'Small

Blue Thing': comparisons with Joni Mitchell and Laura Nyro were inevitable, but some heard a little Lou REED and Dory PREVIN as well. Six-track *Live In London* '86 not as widely released; second LP *Solitude Standing* '87 built on style of debut, light arr. incl. synth, guitar, drums, electric bass; songs incl. 'Calypso', 'Tom's Diner', 'Luka'. Video *Live At The Royal Albert Hall* '87 was representative of her act.

VELVET UNDERGROUND USA rock band '66-70 whose profound influence wasn't recognised until after they'd split up. Vocalist, songwriter Lou REED recruited classically trained bassist Sterling Morrison, drummer Maureen Tucker for various groups; John CALE joined '66, they became the Velvets and were taken up by Andy Warhol for his multi-media organisation The Factory, tour the Exploding Plastic Inevitable; NICO joined from the Factory, Warhol was nominal prod. of first LP *The Velvet Underground & Nico* '67 on Verve, with Warhol's famous banana sleeve art: with drug songs 'Heroin' and 'I'm Waiting For The Man', 'Venus In Furs' (sadomasochist), Nico vocal on 'I'll Be Your Mirror', it did not get a lot of airplay. Nico left; Warhol lost interest and second LP *White Light/White Heat* '68 barely made top 200 LPs, despite 17-minute horror classic 'Sister Ray'. Cale left, replaced by Doug Yule; after *The Velvet Underground* '69 on MGM, Tucker was replaced by brother Billy Yule; *Loaded* '70 appeared on Cotillion, as did *Live At Max's Kansas City* (from '70 residency, released '72); Reed left and the Yule brothers carried on through '72. 2-disc *1969 Velvet Underground Live* first appeared '74 on Mercury. Compilations on MGM, Mercury, Pride; their dark urban vision had its effect on a generation until *VU* appeared '85 on Verve (previously unreleased tracks from '68-9): reached top 100 LPs in USA; *Another View* '86 on Verve incl. more unreleased tracks with Reed and Cale. See entries for individuals.

VENTURA, Charlie (*b* 2 Dec. '16, Philadelphia, Pa.) Tenor sax, other reeds. Showman with a touch of vulgarity who was very popular with several Gene KRUPA bands from '42, in between leading own bands/combos. Late '40s-early '50s combos were infl. by jump bands of Illinois JACQUET and Louis JORDAN, but also by modern jazz, though Ventura himself was not a bopper; quartet '51 incl. Buddy RICH. LPs: *Charlie Boy* '46 on Phoenix, made in L.A. with Barney BIGARD, Red CALLENDER, etc.; *In Chicago 1947* on Zim, with Kai WINDING, Shelly MANNE; *Bop For The People* '49-53 on Affinity, 2-disc *Euphoria* '45-8 on Savoy (with Winding, Charlie SHAVERS, Buck CLAYTON etc.) both feature JACKIE & ROY, excellent hip vocal duo; *Charlie Ventura Quintet In Hi-Fi* '56 on Harlequin; *Chazz* '77 on Famous Door, others. Still active '80s.

VENTURES, The USA instrumental rock'n' roll group formed '59: Don Wilson (*b* 10 Feb. '37) and Bob Bogle (*b* 16 Jan. '37), guitars; Nokie Edwards (*b* 9 May '39), bass; Howie Johnson, drums. Based in Seattle. First called Versatones, pressed copies of infectious 'Walk Don't Run' on own Blue Horizon label and mailed it to radio stations; picked up by Dolton, made no. 2 USA/8 UK '60. Clean, bright sound and bags of tremolo was distinctively different from prevalent raunchy instrumental sound (cf. JOHNNY AND THE HURRICANES), was copied by countless other groups incl. the SHADOWS in UK. Wilson and Bogel gave up building work for full-time music. 'Perfidia', cover of Latin tune c.'39 by Alberto Dominguez, made no. 15 USA/4 UK, but band gave up singles for albums: only two more single hits: remake of 'Walk Don't Run' '64, theme from TV show 'Hawaii Five-O' '69; but more than 50 albums by the end of '73. Major popularity in Japan, as instrumental music transcended language barrier; albums of covers of hits of the day kept them afloat through '60s and British Invasion. Many LPs for Japan only, where they were made first foreign members of Conservatory of Music in recognition of 40m-plus sales. Johnson was carcrash casualty, replaced by Mel Taylor '63, while Edwards and Bogle swapped instruments; guest and session players in '60s incl. Harvey Mandel, Leon RUSSELL, David Gates; Edwards was replaced by seasoned sessioneer Jerry McGee (EVERLY BROS, etc.), who pushed them in R&B direction, but returned '72. Evidently they will rock till they drop.

VENUTI, Joe (*b* Giuseppe Venuti, 16 Sep. '03, Philadelphia; *d* 14 Aug. '78, Seattle, Wash.) Jazz violinist and legendary practical joker, eclipsed '60s by alcoholism but came back for second career. Countless stories had him pushing a piano out of a hotel room window, pouring Jello into Bix BEIDERBECKE's bath water, etc. Claimed to have been born on a boat coming over from Italy. Boyhood friends with Eddie LANG, often worked with him, legendary records incl. duos '26-7, Blue Four sides from '27 well into '30s, '29 sides incl. Frankie TRUMBAUER, Lennie HAYTON, Lang and Venuti. They co-led an all-star band which recorded '31 with Charlie and Jack TEAGARDEN and Benny GOODMAN; recorded with J. DORSEY, Adrian ROLLINI, etc.; also leaders Jean GOLDKETTE, Red MCKENZIE, Roger Wolfe KAHN, Paul WHITEMAN (in film *King Of Jazz* '30; allegedly poured flour in the tuba during filming); visited Europe '35; formed own unsuccessful band with young vocalist Kay STARR; got drafted during WWII. With Bing CROSBY on radio '50s; made comeback '67 at Dick Gibson's Colorado Jazz Party, remained a star until he wore out, fighting cancer during '70s. LPs incl. classics with Lang compiled on *Violin Jazz* on Yazoo, 2-disc *Stringing The Blues* '27-32 from Columbia Special Products, *Doin' Things* '28-33 on Decca UK; *Great Original Performances 1926-1933* on BBC Records UK (digital remastering by Robert Parker is excellent). Later LPs incl. *The Mad Fiddler From Philly* on Shoestring (Crosby show airchecks from '52-3), *Sliding By* '77 on Sonet, *Joe In Chicago* '78 on Flying Fish, *Plays Jerome Kern* and *George Gershwin* on Golden Crest with Ellis Larkins, two albums on Concord Jazz with George Barnes, one with Marian MCPARTLAND on Halcyon; *The Daddy Of The Violin* on MPS; *Venupelli Blues* with Stephane GRAPPELLI on Byg, *Nightwings* with guitarist Bucky Pizzarelli on Flying Dutchman, etc. Several on lamented Chiaroscuro label incl. duo *Hot Sonatas* with Earl HINES, two with Zoot SIMS combined in *Joe & Zoot* on Vanguard UK.

VERCKYS (*b* Kiamuangana Maleta, '44, Zaire) Singer-composer, saxophonist, bandleader, producer, studio owner. Played in FRANCO band, left to form own Orchestre Veve, one of most popular Zaire bands '70s-80s. Early hit with Franco was 'Nakomituna', about struggle against cultural alienation. Band featured on compilation *Bankoko Baboyi* '69; own LP *Dynamite* '70; mid-'70s sound captured on two vols. of *Verckys et l'Orchestre Veve*. Established own prod. company '76, released classic 9-disc series *Les Grands Succès des Éditions Veve*: as the boss, Verckys picked the best, with volumes by Kamele, Lipua-Lipua, Veve, Kiam, ZAIKO, etc. Re-organised own ensemble and added *Papy Baluti* '78 to series. Became one of the most influential prod. in Zaire; by the '80s own EVVI label had issued classic LPs, incl. two vols. of *Verckys et L'Immortel Veve*.

VINCENT, Gene (*b* Vincent Eugene Craddock, 11 Feb. '35, Norfolk, Va.; *d* 12 Oct. '71, L.A.) USA rock'n'roller of '50s; turned out of US Navy after breaking leg (subsequently wore a brace), turned to music. Local DJ Bill 'Sheriff Tex' Davis cut Vincent demo of 'Be-Bop-A-Lula', basic rocker based on 'Money Honey', got contract with Capitol; semi-pro group christened Blue Caps (Cliff Gallup, Willie Williams, guitars; Jack Neal, bass; Dickie Harrell, drums) re-cut track in Nashville; slated as B-side to Vincent's own 'Woman Love' but DJs flipped disc and sent 'Be-Bop-A-Lula' (co-credited to wily Davis) to no. 7 USA '56. Followups 'Race With The Devil' and 'Bluejean Bop' failed, though they played hit in film *The Girl Can't Help It* '56; 'Lotta Lovin' ' brought him back to USA chart '57 (no. 13), and revamped Blue Caps with Johnny Meeks on lead guitar were big live attraction. Band split '58; Vincent's refusal to conform, Capitol's refusal to pay payola, persecution by tax people led to emigration to UK '59. Last USA top 40 hit was 'Dance To The Bop' (no. 23 '58); UK pop impresario Jack GOOD encouraged rebel image, dressed him in leather. Had eight UK top 40 hits '56-61; more importantly, was rock'n'roll's biggest live draw. Constant touring proved strain; car crash that killed Eddie COCHRAN injured leg again '60, drinking problem didn't help. Returned to USA '65, cut some country tracks for Challenge; returned to UK '69 and '71, a bloated parody of himself. Died of ulcers.

Temperamental and unpredictable, he was unfortunate to find his best form during an era when teen dreams like Ricky NELSON held sway in USA and Elvis PRESLEY was going soft; never appreciated there as supercharged rocker that he was.

VINSON, Eddie 'Cleanhead' (*b* 19 Dec. '17, Houston, Texas; *d* 2 July '88). Alto sax, blues singer, bandleader: an R&B stalwart also highly regarded in jazz circles; nickname from bald head. Worked with Big Bill BROONZY early '40S; joined Cootie WILLIAMS band '42-5, recorded with it on Okeh, Hit, Capitol and regarded as one of the best big band vocalists of the decade; formed own band '45, recorded for Mercury '45-7, for King '49-52; rejoined Williams for tours '54; recorded for Bethlehem '57; with Cannonball ADDERLEY on Riverside '61; worked with Arnett COBB '66; recorded for BluesWay '67, Black & Blue '68 (in France while touring with Jay MCSHANN), BluesTime '69; often worked with Johnny OTIS from '70 incl. Monterey Jazz Festival; appeared at many festivals incl. Ann Arbor, Montreux etc., live portions released on Epic, Flying Dutchman, Buddah, Black Lion. Worked with Count BASIE in Europe '72. Powerful singer, influenced by bluesmen and jazz musicians alike; LPs incl. *Cherry* on King and *Back In Town* on Charly ('50s tracks); *And The Muse All Stars Live At Sandy's* and *Hold It Right There* (also live at Sandy's, incl. Cobb, Buddy TATE) and *The Clean Machine* (incl. Lloyd Glenn, Rashied ALI) all '78 on Muse; with ROOMFUL OF BLUES '82 and *Sings The Blues* with Cobb, Tate, Roomful on Muse; *Kansas City Shout* with Big Joe TURNER and Basie and *I Want A Little Girl* on Pablo; also *Mr Cleanhead Steps Out* on Saxophonograph (Sweden), *Fun In London* and *Mr Cleanhead's Back In Town* on JSP UK. Also *The Late Show* on Fantasy with Etta JAMES. Among best-known tunes is 'Kidney Stew Blues', incl. in Charly LP; led to *Kidney Stew Is Fine* on Delmark, *Kidney Stew* '83 on Circle.

VINTON, Bobby (*b* Stanley Robert Vinton, 16 Apr. '35, Canonsburg, Pa.) Singer, bandleader from same home town as Perry COMO. Played clarinet, other instruments in high school band; after US Army discharge '61 turned to bandleading, dance LPs for Epic *Dancing At The Hop*, *Bobby Vinton Plays For His Li'l Darlin's*. Early '62 began making purely vocal records aimed at teen market: USA no. 1 with 'Roses Are Red' later that year: total of 30 top 40 hits '62-75 incl. more at no. 1: 'Blue Velvet' '63, 'There, I Said It Again' '63, 'Mr Lonely' '65. Switched to ABC late '72, back up to no. 3 'My Melody Of Love'. 24 LPs also charted in Billboard top 200 incl. *All-Time Greatest Hits* '72, *The Golden Decade Of Love* '75 (songs from '50s), both 2-disc sets on Epic; last top 20 LP was *Mr Lonely* '65 until surprise *Melodies Of Love* '74 on ABC. Also had syndicated TV series '75-8, LP *The Bobby Vinton Show* '75.

VIPERS, The UK skiffle group formed '56 with various personnel incl. Jet Harris, Hank B. Marvin, Tony Meehan, Wally Whyton and Tommy STEELE. They grew out of the London coffee-bar scene, in time centred on Soho's 21s, considered to be a guaranteed springboard to success: Whyton told Pete Frame (*Rock Family Trees* '79): 'I remember Adam FAITH complaining to me that he'd been singing at the 21s for about two months but still wasn't nationally famous yet.' If Lonnie DONEGAN was king of skiffle, the Vipers were the crown princes; they scored with infl. singles 'Pick A Bale Of Cotton', 'Don't You Rock Me Daddy-O', 'Cumberland Gap', 'Maggie May', 'Streamline Train' '56-7; made strides in musicianship led by Whyton, turning to amplifiers '58, later becoming Cliff RICHARD's backing group the SHADOWS. Whyton became a folk and country singer, worked in TV (hosted children's show *5 O'Clock Club*), now works in radio, hosting folk and country music programmes. *Coffee Bar Session* '86 on Roller Coaster label is good Vipers compilation.

VISAGE UK pop/dance band formed by Steve Strange (*b* Steve Harrington, 28 May '59, Wales), who was prime mover in New Romantics movement of early '80s. Had roadied for Generation X after moving to London, then formed Moors Murderers with future PRETENDER Chrissie Hynde (late '77-early '78), then the Photons, who played one gig, then started elitist Billy's Club with former Rich Kids drummer

Rusty Egan '79. Club in London's Soho played ULTRAVOX, HUMAN LEAGUE, KRAFTWERK and other electrodance music with Egan at turntable, Strange vetting clientele's wardrobes. Transferred to Blitz Club in Covent Garden and floated musical project Visage, with Strange's vocals, Egan on drums, Midge Ure (ex-Rich Kids) and John McGeoch on guitars, Dave Formula on keyboards, Barry Adamson on bass (last three moonlighting from Magazine), Billy Currie (ditto Ultravox). Ure and Strange wrote material, others contributed. After demos (incl. cover of Zager/Evans's 'In The Year 2525'), single 'Tar' '79 on Radar, LP *Visage* '80 released with synths on top of monotonous Eurodisco beat, much in line with club's policy and equally popular: hit singles 'Fade To Grey', 'Mind Of A Toy', 'Visage'; but group was vinyl-only proposition; other members too busy to tour, and Ure's meeting Currie led to his becoming vocalist with Ultravox, further limiting work with Visage. *The Anvil* '82 yielded hits 'Damned Don't Cry' and 'Night Train'; a couple of failures persuaded Strange to quit while ahead; hits collected on *Fade To Grey* '84. Strange and Egan opened Camden Palace, London equivalent of Studio 54 in NYC; Strange relinquished control of that mid-'80s, turned back to music as frontman of Strange Cruise with Wendy Cruise (ex-Photos singer Wendy Wu) but hard-bitten public was not beguiled a second time by half-baked disco dressed as trendy pop.

VISCONTI, Tony (*b* 24 Apr. '44, NYC) Producer based in UK. Played guitar in schoolboy bands; picked up double bass, backing acts like Tony BENNETT, Milton Berle; cut demos with wife as Tony and Sigrid and RCA put out harmony pop singles, but he became A&R man. He arranged a Georgie FAME session for Denny Cordell, came to England to arr. and prod. for him; worked with the MOVE, PROCOL HARUM, Joe COCKER. First 'solo' prod. was Tyrannosaurus Rex; through that met David BOWIE, prod. Bowie tracks that only saw light on later anthologies, plus LPs *Space Oddity* (except title track), *The Man Who Sold The World*; oversaw development of Rex to electric rockers T-Rex, and relationship with Marc BOLAN was compared to that of George MARTIN with the BEATLES. Had prod. folk-rockers the STRAWBS; prod. of Paul McCARTNEY protégée Mary HOPKIN led to second marriage. Folk artists Tom PAXTON, Ralph McTELL came to Visconti for clear, simple sound. Reputation for handling unusual, temperamental acts led him to Afro-rockers OSIBISA, progressives Gentle Giant. Shortlived label Good Earth (named after studio) incl. his own (unreleased) LP, artists like Hopkin, Judy Tzuke. Linked again with Bowie from *Diamond Dogs* onwards; other acts incl. heavy metal (THIN LIZZY) to new wave (BOOMTOWN RATS, Hazel O'CONNOR, Photos, STRANGLERS). Own LP *Visconti's Inventory* '77.

W

WADE, Adam (*b* 17 Mar. '37, Pittsburgh, Pa.) Singer, actor. Worked as lab assistant after college; later part of Dr Jonas Salk's polio research team. Infl. by Nat King COLE, Jesse BELVIN, went to NYC '60; soon signed to Co-Ed Records; within six months opened at Copacabana. Vocally similar to Johnny MATHIS; four minor hits '60 followed by greater success: 'Take Good Care Of Her', 'The Writing On The Wall', 'As If I Didn't Know' all top 10 '61; LPs incl. *And Then Came Adam, Adam And Evening*. Signed to Epic '65 to replace Mathis, who was leaving CBS; LPs incl. *One Is A Lonely Number, What Kind Of Fool Am I, A Very Good Year For Girls*, but only one minor hit ('Crying In The Chapel' no. 88 '65); without recording contract by '69. Became TV actor; first black entertainer to host network show (*Musical Chairs*) '76; resumed recording '77 with funkier *Adam Wade* for Kirshner Records (incl. 'Alexander's Soul Time Band'); played six months in all-black cast of *Guys And Dolls* Las Vegas '78. Still turns up in film and TV parts.

WAGONER, Porter (*b* 12 Aug. '30, West Plains, Mo.) Country singer, guitarist, songwriter; some sources give '27 birth date. Grew up listening to country music; took up heavy farm duties at an early age because of father's arthritis; later worked in grocery shop, picking and singing when things were slow, leading to local radio spot promoting the shop: got his own show on KWTO in Springfield '51, was discovered by Red FOLEY, who asked him to join his Ozark Jamboree, staying for four years until it was on national TV. Signed with RCA, soon had top 10 hits 'Satisfied Mind', 'Eat, Drink, And Be Merry', 'What Would You Do If Jesus Came To Your House?' '55-6; joined Grand Ole Opry '57 but had no more hits until starting own syndicated TV show '60 which became the most popular of all: stream of hits incl. 'Misery Loves Company' '62 (no. 1), 'I've Enjoyed As Much Of This

As I Can Stand' '62 (no. 7), 'Sorrow On The Rocks' '64, 'Green, Green Grass Of Home' and 'Skid Row Joe' '65, 'The Cold Hard Facts Of Life' '67, 'The Carroll County Accident' and 'Big Wind' '68-9, all top 5. His act was among the most popular touring the country, incl. his band the Wagonmasters and NORMA JEAN singing solo and duet from mid-'60s, then Dolly PARTON from late '60s: they had eight top 10 duet hits '67-71 and carried on through '70s, both also good writers: their 'Say Forever You'll Be Mine' '75 was Parton's song, 'Is Forever Longer Than Always' '76 was his, both top 10; his solo hit 'Carolina Moonshine' '75 was her song; hits with his own songs '70s incl. 'Tore Down', 'I Haven't Learned A Thing', 'Ole Slew Foot', several more. His many LPs incl. *Duets With Skeeter Davis* '62, *Sings His Own Songs* '71; he made gospel LPs with the BLACKWOOD BROTHERS that won Grammies: *Grand Ole Gospel* '66, *More Grand Ole Gospel* '67, *In Gospel Country* '69. Duet LPs with Parton incl. *Always, Always* '69, *Porter Wayne And Dolly Rebecca* '70, *Once More* and *Two Of A Kind* '71, *Right Combination/Burning The Midnight Oil* '72. He performed honky tonk, bluegrass and other styles; Buck Trent first played electric banjo on his show and he was involved in some of Parton's early innovative work, but himself remained within country genres; he prod. her records and she began to feel constrained: she left late '70s despite lawsuits; RCA continued to have hits with their stuff into the '80s. Compilation LPs of his solos and duets with Parton still on RCA, as well as *Down Home Country* on Accord, *Porter Wagoner* '86 on Dot.

WAH UK new wave group formed as Wah! Heat in Liverpool '79 by guitarist/vocalist Pete Wylie (*b* 22 Mar. '58), who'd been a member of Crucial Three '77 with Julian Cope and Ian McCulloch, who founded TEARDROP EXPLODES and ECHO AND THE

BUNNYMEN respectively. Wylie was last to make his move, having played in short-lived local groups incl. Nova Mob and A Shallow Madness (both with Cope) and Crash Course with drummer Rob Jones, who followed him into trio Wah! Heat, completed by Colin Williams, then Pete Younger (ex-Those Naughty Lumps) on bass. First single 'Better Screams' for local Inevitable label had B-side 'Joe' on *Hicks From The Sticks* '80 compilation of post-punk regional bands. Carl Washington replaced Younger and became Wylie's right-hand man; 'Seven Minutes To Midnight' edged towards HM where 'Scream' had been supercharged BYRDS; LP *Nah Poo – The Art Of Bliff* '81 on WB (with own custom Eternal label) confirmed this heavier approach and didn't sell well (trio augmented by part-time members Colm Redmond on guitar, King (Ken) Bluff on keyboards). Returned to form with one-off single 'Remember' '82 (billed as Shambeko! Say Wah, after Bavarian Nazifighters), with a muscular Washington bassline providing backbone where LP had flown off on torrents of guitar and wailing vocals. Revamped group to become keyboard-based new wave, with Washington, Jay Naughton on piano, Chris Joyce on drums, Charlie Griffiths on synths, plus the Sapphires vocal trio, scoring neo-SPECTOR 'Story Of The Blues' (no. 3 UK); cover of the THREE DEGREES' 'Year Of Decision' would have made good followup, but weak 'Hope' reached top 40 with 'Decision' on 12″ flip. Argument with WB led to Eternal linking with Beggars Banquet; once again mercurial Wylie flattered to deceive with anthemic 'Come Back' (no. 20 '84) from bombastic, disappointing *A Word To The Wise Guy*, billed on single and LP as The Mighty Wah!. Disbanded when followups failed to emulate success of 'Come Back'; Wylie formed group Oedipus Wrecks, made single 'Sinful' for no. 13 hit on Eternal through MDM/Virgin; again couldn't follow up; it was rumoured he'd replace Holly Johnson in FRANKIE.

WAINWRIGHT, Loudon, III (*b* 5 Sep. '46, Chapel Hill, N.C.) Singer/songwriter with devoted cult following after two decades. Hitched to San Francisco '67, began writing songs '68, landed record deal in NYC '69; *Album I* and *Album II* '70-1 on Atlantic

characterised early appeal: solo, acoustic, stark, confessional work saw him one of many branded as the new DYLAN; songs like 'When I Was Young' and 'Be Careful There's A Baby In The House' had sly humour which some of his contemporaries lacked. Switched to CBS for *Album III*, which almost made pop top 100 LPs '73 helped by 'Dead Skunk', a song he wrote in 15 minutes which became a no. 16 single. *Attempted Mustache* '73 went for humour and lacked the slyness, but incl. Kate McGarrigle's 'Come A Long Way' and his 'Swimming Song', covered by the McGARRIGLE Sisters; *Unrequited* '75 and *T-Shirt* '76 (the last on Arista) were back on form, made top 200 LPs USA, *Final Exam* '78 also well-received by fans; last two incl. backing by five-piece Slow Train, harmony on 'Golfin' Blues' by the Roches (sisters Maggie and Terre, LP *Seductive Reasoning* c.'72 on CBS; joined by Suzzy, eclectic vocal trio made *The Roches* '79, *Nurds* '80, *Keep On Doing* '82 on WB; all three charted in USA, first and third prod. by Robert FRIPP). Described '75 as the last true solo performer (by Jon Landau), his live act is funny as well as personal, captured on *A Live One* '80 on Rounder (on Radar, then Edsel in UK, which also reissued *Album III*). *Fame And Wealth* '83 incl. autobiographical 'Westchester County'; like the rest of his Rounder LPs was issued on Demon UK: *I'm Alright* '85 and *More Love Songs* '86 were prod. by Richard THOMPSON, the latter incl. 'Unhappy Anniversary'. Also acted on TV (*M.A.S.H.*), on stage (*Pump Boys And Dinettes*). Marriage to Kate ended '77; had child with Suzzy Roche '82.

WAITRESSES, The USA new wave group formed in Cleveland, Ohio by Chris Butler, guitar (ex-Tin Huey, 15-16-75, the Stereos): confederates were drummer Billy Ficca (ex-TELEVISION), vocalist Patty Donahue, bassist Tracy Wormworth (ex-Gwen McCrae band), Daniel Klayman on keyboards, Mars Williams, sax (ex-Fred Frith, GONG; see also Hal RUSSELL). Appearance on *The Akron Compilation* '78 on Stiff led to some fame; when they moved to NYC their zany new wave material attracted Ze Records, who released *Wasn't Tomorrow Wonderful* '81, Butler writing songs for Donahue. 'I Know What Boys Like' was a cult hit in

UK, went top 10 in Australia; 'Christmas Wrapping' (from Ze's *A Christmas Record*) made no. 45 UK '82, but despite exposure on TV series *Square Pegs* failed to click at home. *Bruiseology* '83 flopped; Donahue was replaced by Holly Beth Vincent (ex-Holly and the Italians, UK-based new wave band); when Butler left only Ficca remained of original group, doing Butler's songs. Broke up soon after: unsung but had some good material.

WAITS, Tom (*b* 7 Dec. '49, Pomona, Cal.) Singer, songwriter with whispery tobacco-stained voice; began with interest in '50s beatniks, claimed to have slept through the '60s, specialised in off-beat portraits of the flotsam and jetsam of bars and motels, slowly rose from cabaret cult to stardom without working too hard at it. Began accompanying himself at the piano in L.A. '69, signed by Frank ZAPPA's manager '72, first LP *Closing Time* '73 incl. 'Ol' 55', covered by the EAGLES. *The Heart Of Saturday Night* '74 was more assured, with archetypal Waits vignettes 'Shiver Me Timbers', 'Diamonds On My Windshield', title track. 2-disc live *Nighthawks At The Diner* '76 was exemplary souvenir of Waits as raconteur with jazz roots. *Small Change* '76 regarded as his best yet, with wry 'The Piano Has Been Drinking', wistful title track, majestic 'Tom Traubert's Blues'; *Foreign Affairs* '77 incl. duet with Bette MIDLER on 'I Never Talk To Strangers', also epics 'Burma Shave', 'Potter's Field'. By now he was in danger of becoming articulate anachronism, success taking him out of the milieu he portrayed, but humour and apparent lack of pretence saves him. *Blue Valentine* '78 was lacklustre by his standards; *Heartattack & Vine* '80 was back on form, incl. 'Jersey Girl', covered by Bruce SPRINGSTEEN. *Bounced Checks* '81 was adequate best-of, incl. some alternate takes. He had acted in Sylvester Stallone's *Paradise Alley* '78; Francis Ford Coppola heard the duet with Midler, cast him in *One From The Heart* '82: Midler wasn't available and his highly praised soundtrack saw him duetting successfully with the apparently incongruous Crystal GAYLE, good songs incl. 'Little Boy Blue', 'Old Boyfriends', 'Broken Bicycles'. *The Asylum Years* '84 was an excellent compilation in UK; single-disc *Anthology* on Elektra in USA; he'd switched

to Island for *Swordfishtrombone* '83, a staccato work full of experiments, but also vintage 'In The Neighborhood' and 'Soldier's Things', which was covered by Paul YOUNG; *Rain Dogs* '85 was a further bold step, featuring Keith Richards. Coppola cast him in *Rumblefish* and *The Cotton Club*; first major role in *Down By Law* '86; meanwhile he co-wrote his first play with his wife Kathleen Brennan: *Frank's Wild Years*, from song of that title on *Swordfishtrombone*, with a dozen new songs was premiered mid-'86 in Chicago; it was about a failed entertainer on a park bench ('Remember me? I ordered the blonde, the Firebird . . . Somebody's made a terrible mistake'), album on Island '87. Starring in film *Ironweed* '87 with Jack Nicholson: '30s atmosphere of novel by William Kennedy should suit them both.

WAKELY, Jimmy (*b* 16 Feb. '14, Mineola, Ark.; *d* 23 Sep. '82) Country & Western/pop singer, a major star of late '40s-50s. Grew up in Oklahoma, worked as sharecropper, journalist etc.; teamed with Johnny BOND and Scotty Harrell as the Jimmy Wakely Trio '37 on WKY radio in Oklahoma City; heard by Gene AUTRY who recruited them for *Melody Ranch* CBS radio show in Hollywood. Wakely made a good impression and soon appeared in over 50 films incl. *Heart Of The Rio Grande* and *Twilight On The Trail* '41, *Cowboy In The Clouds* '43, *Song Of The Range*, *Springtime In Texas* '45. By the time he was named fourth most popular Western film actor '48 he was also a big-name recording artist, band incl. Spade COOLEY, Cliffie STONE, Merle TRAVIS and Wesley Tuttle (who had one of several '46 country hits with 'Detour', written by Paul Westmoreland and a pop hit for Patti PAGE '51). Signed first to Decca, Wakely hit with 'Too Late', 'Cimmaron', 'Cattle Call', 'There's A Star-Spangled Banner Waving Somewhere' '43 (Elton BRITT version was one of the biggest-selling country records ever). Joined Capitol, whose West Coast roster was of great importance to country music. 'I Wish I Had A Nickel' was a country hit '49; all his other hits crossed over to pop (according to *Pop Memories*; see CHARTS): 15 hits '43-'56 incl. seven duos with Margaret WHITING: 'Slippin' Around' was a no. 1 country hit '49; *Billboard* ranked it a no. 2 pop hit, but *Pop Memories* ignores genres, says it was a no. 1 national hit for three weeks; apart from being a good song (by Floyd TILLMAN, who had his own no. 5 country hit) it was one of the first cheatin' songs, dealing realistically with the subject of adultery. 'Wedding Bells' on the flip was also a hit. A late Wakely hit was a duet with Karen Chandler, 'Tonight You Belong To Me' '56 on Decca (Chandler had sung with Benny GOODMAN '46 as Eve Young; was married to Jack Pleis, whose band backed her on Decca). Wakely had a CBS network radio show until '60, remained popular in clubs and was still recording on his own Shasta label mid-'70s. Albums incl. *I'll Never Slip Around Again* on Hilltop (with Whiting); *Heartaches* '61, *Please Don't Hurt Me Anymore* '63 on Decca; *Slipping Around* '67 on Dot, *Jimmy Wakely Country* '75 on Shasta.

WALDRON, Mal (b Earl Malcolm Waldron, 16 Aug. '26, NYC) Pianist, composer. Began on alto sax; BA in music from Queens College; worked with Ike QUEBEC late '40s, Della REESE, R&B sessions, then with Charles MINGUS '54-7 (Debut LPs now on Fantasy), Gigi GRYCE '56, accompanied Billie HOLIDAY '57-9, etc. Became virtually house pianist on Prestige/Status labels; work of great value resulted, inimitable compositions infl. by those of Thelonious MONK: LPs incl. *Mal 1* '56 with Gryce, *Mal 2* '57 with Jackie MCLEAN, Sahib Shihab, John COLTRANE; also *Impressions*, trio *Mal 4* (CD only '87); *The Quest* '61 with Eric DOLPHY, Booker LITTLE reissued as Dolphy LP, now restored to original format: with Ron CARTER on cello, Joe Benjamin on bass, Charles Persip on drums, seven fine Waldron tunes, it is one of the most beautiful masterpieces of what was then called 'the new music'. He played with co-led Dolphy-Little combo at the Five Spot '61 (Richard Davis on bass, Ed Blackwell on drums), three live albums another landmark of the era, compiled as *The Great Concert Of Eric Dolphy*; also on Carter's *Where?* '61 with Dolphy, others; Coltrane's *Dakar* and *The Dealers – Mal Waldron With John Coltrane* '57, others, most now in various 2-disc sets, always with fine Waldron tunes. He had written ballet music earlier, did film scores *The Cool*

World '63, *Three Bedrooms In Manhattan* and *Sweet Love Bitter* '65 and incidental music for plays by LeRoi Jones; went to Europe on film work, relocated there, with frequent visits to Japan. Trio *Free At Last* was one of the first LPs on the new ECM label; *The Call* '79 was on Japo/ECM; series on Enja (based in Munich) incl. trio sets *Black Glory*, *Up Popped The Devil*, *A Touch Of The Blues*; *One-upmanship* and *Hard Talk* (quartets with Steve LACY), *Moods* (sextet with Lacy, Cameron BROWN); solo tracks), solo *Mingus Lives*; *What It Is* '81 had quartet with Clifford JORDAN, Cecil McBee, Dannie RICHMOND. Also *Blues For Lady Day* on Black Lion; trio *Set Me Free* with Philly Joe JONES on Affinity (released '85); *Signals* on Freedom; *One Entrance, Many Exits* on Palo Alto; *Encounters* on Muse; *You And The Night And The Music* '86 on ProJazz with frequent associates Reggie Workman and Blackwell; live in Paris with Lacy in duets *Herbe de l'Oubli*, *Snake-Out* '81 on Hat Art, *The Git Go: Live At The Village Vanguard* '86 on Soul Note with Woody SHAW, Charlie ROUSE, Workman, Blackwell.

WALKER, Billy (b 14 Jan. '29, Ralls, Texas) Country singer popular for 40 years. Won amateur contest as a teenager, gaining own radio show on KICA in Clovis, New Mexico. Joined Big D Jamboree in Dallas '49 with gimmick of masked singer; had first chart hit 'Thank You For Calling' '54 on Columbia; appeared on Louisiana Hayride '52-5, Ozark Jubilee '56-60, Grand Ole Opry '60. Hits every year in '60s incl. 'Charlie's Shoes' (no. 1 '62), switching to Monument, then MGM for more top 10 hits; then to RCA for top 10 'Word Games' '75, smaller hits. Recorded for MRC, Scorpion, Caprice, Dimension, his own Tall Texan Records; came back with duet hits '80 with Barbara FAIRCHILD. Like many other veterans, built following in UK with regular visits to country music festivals. LPs incl. *Greatest Hits* and *The Gun, The Gold & The Girl* '62-4 on Columbia; *A Million And One, I Taught Her Everything She Knows, Salutes The Music Hall Of Fame* and *How Big Is God* '66-8 on Monument; *When A Man Loves A Woman* '70 and *Fine As Wine* '74 on MGM; *Alone Again* '76 on RCA; *Star Of The Grand Ole Opry* '79 on First Generation, *It Takes Two* with Fairchild '80 on Paid, *Waking Up To Sunshine* '83 on Golden Melodies, *Billy Walker* '86 on Dot, *For My Friends* '87 on Bulldog.

WALKER BROTHERS Vocal and instrumental trio formed on West Coast '64: bassist Scott Engel (*b* 9 Jan. '44, Hamilton, Ohio), John Maus (*b* 12 Nov. '43, NYC) on bass, drummer Gary Leeds (*b* 3 Sep. '44, Glendale, Cal.). Leeds had toured UK with P. J. PROBY and suggested they try their luck there; they had two top 20 singles in USA '65-6, but were seen as a British import: much greater success in UK with nine top 30 singles '65-7 incl. 'My Ship Is Coming In' at no. 3, 'Make It Easy On Yourself' and 'The Sun Ain't Gonna Shine Anymore' both at no. 1; four top 10 LPs incl. *Take It Easy*, *Portrait* and *Images*, plus a compilation. Dramatic ballads with epic prod. style borrowed from Phil SPECTOR, their brooding good looks were a hit, with Engel singled out as a teen idol, but withdrawn nature and nervous disposition ill-fitted him for it. Pressure split them '67; all three pursued solo careers, but only Engel (as Scott Walker) had any success: three eponymous solo LPs '65-7 were top 3 LPs UK, brought Jacques BREL songs to a wider audience; three hit singles incl. top 10 UK with 'Joanna'. 'Brothers' reunited for *Lines* '76, *Night Flights* '78, former giving them a last UK top 10 with cover of Tom RUSH's 'No Regrets'. Engel's enigmatic, withdrawn image, doomed romantic ballad mould had infl. on Julian Cope (TEARDROP EXPLODES), Marc ALMOND and young David BOWIE. He returned with *Climate Of The Hunter* '84 on Virgin (earlier work on Philips/Smash), reached top 60 LPs UK. There are various compilations of the Brothers; Scott's Brel songs were compiled and Cope compiled *Fire Escape In The Sky: The God-Like Genius Of Scott Walker* '81 on Zoo, title perhaps slightly over the top.

WALKER, Jerry Jeff (*b* Paul Crosby, 16 Mar. '42, Oneonta, NY) Country rock singer, songwriter, guitarist. Family played and sang trad. music; sang with high school group the Pizzerinos, went on the road and landed in Texas, formed Circus Maximus '66 with bassist Gary White, incl. Bob Bruno on lead guitar and keyboards, Peter

Troutner on guitar, David Scherstrom on drums; all sang except drummer: they made LPs *Circus Maximus* and *Neverland Revisited* c.'67-8 on Vanguard, disbanded; Walker made *Drifting Way Of Life* on Vanguard '69, switched to Atco for three LPs: *Mr Bojangles* (incl. his own title song, Hot 100 hit '68), *Five Years Gone* and *Bein' Free* '70. Took a break, settled in Texas; signed with MCA and made *Jerry Jeff Walker* '72 with the Four-Man Deaf Cowboy Band; cover of Guy CLARK's 'L.A. Freeway' became juke box hit, reached pop Hot 100 '73. *Viva Terlingua!* '73 with the Lost Gonzo Band reached top 200 LPs USA, recorded live in Luckenbach, Texas, later made famous by a Waylon JENNINGS song; by now he hobnobbed with Clark, Townes VAN ZANDT etc., found niche as an unlikely 'outlaw'; rough-edged voice and unpredictable humour in stage act, well-chosen songs incl. his own provided loyal following. Good covers incl. Clark's 'Desperadoes Waiting For A Train', Butch HANCOCK's 'Standin' At The Big Hotel', John D. LOUDERMILK's 'Bad News', Rodney CROWELL's 'Banks Of The Old Bandera'. MCA LPs incl. *Walker's Collectibles* '74, *Ridin' High* '75, *It's A Good Night For Singing* '76, 2-disc *A Man Must Carry On* '77 (his best showing, at no. 60 in LP chart); *Contrary To Ordinary* '78. MCA released *Best Of* '80; meanwhile he split with Gonzos; *Jerry Jeff* '78 (aka *Comfort And Crazy*, title song by Clark) appeared on Elektra/Asylum (also incl. Walker's 'Good Loving Grace') followed by *Too Old To Change* '79 with his Bandito band; *Reunion* on his South Coast label was distributed by MCA; *Cowjazz* '82 was not. Almost all his LPs charted, but he joked 'Sometimes the music business is so bad, I'm glad I'm not in it,' recorded 24-song cassette *Gypsy Songman* '86 available from his Tried And True Music incl. 'Bojangles', 'My Old Man', 'Hill Country Rain', 'Charlie Dunn', but many songs not previously available, first album he could retain control over (also now on CD or 2-disc LP). Whether he gigs solo or (as he did in '87) with orchestra cond. by David AMRAM (pal from Greenwich Village days), he makes fans feel as though 'none of us was ever gonna die, and when we did, he'd be there too' (Earl Casey).

WALKER, Junior (*b* Autry DeWalt Jr, '42, Blytheville, Ark.) R&B alto sax; bandleader. Early infl. incl. Illinois JACQUET, Earl BOSTIC; played in local Jumping Jacks, later Stix Nix; by early '60s he lived in Battle Creek, Mich., formed the All Stars (a minor exaggeration) with Vic Thomas on keyboards, Willie Woods on guitar, James Graves on drums; Johnny Bristol recommended them to Harvey FUQUA, then running his own Harvey label but soon absorbed by MOTOWN; Junior Walker and the All Stars were issued on subsidiary Soul in USA, had 21 Hot 100 entries in USA charts '65-72, many instrumentals (though Junior also sang). Biggest were the first, 'Shotgun', and 'What Does It Take (To Win Your Love)' '69, both no. 4; also 'How Sweet It Is' and 'Road Runner' '66, 'These Eyes' '69, all top 20; also six top 40 hits in UK on Tamla/Motown. The good-time music was an echo of the jump bands of the late '40s and made many a packed house happy; later hits were often ballads, sometimes with strings. Ten hit LPs in USA incl. *Soul Session* '66, entirely instrumental; *Greatest Hits* '69 reached top 50. He still toured in '80s, sometimes with son Autry DeWalt III on drums.

WALKER, T-Bone (*b* Aaron Thibeaux Walker, 28 May '10, Linden, Texas; *d* 16 Mar. '75, L.A.) Blues singer, songwriter, guitarist. Teenage friends with Charlie CHRISTIAN (they had same teacher for a time, Chuck Richardson); Christian was profound infl. on jazz guitar, Walker was more of a showman and was similar infl. in blues, on B. B. KING, Chuck BERRY, Lowell FULSON, Freddie KING, many others, responsible for a generation taking up electric guitar. Won Cab CALLOWAY amateur contest '30, toured heavily, recorded with Jack McVEA on Black & White '46, etc.; first own records on Capitol late '40s; recorded for Atlantic '55-9, with MEMPHIS SLIM on Polydor '62 in Germany, with Jimmy WITHERSPOON '63 on Prestige, on Modern '64, Jet Stream label in Texas '66, on BluesWay '67-8, French Black & Blue '68, BluesTime in NYC '69, Reprise '73. Toured with JATP '66; played at Monterey Jazz Festival '67 (filmed). Among many songs, 'Call It Stormy Monday' was covered by the ALLMAN Bros. Recorded several

times for Polydor in Europe; *Good Feelin'* '68 made in Paris with Manu DIBANGO won Grammy '70. Other LPs: *Original '45-50 Performances* on French Capitol; *Hot Leftovers* and *I Get So Weary* on Pathé Marconi; *The Natural Blues* (18 tracks from '46-8), *T-Bone Jumps, Stormy Monday Blues, Plain Ole Blues* all on Charly UK. Also *I Want A Little Girl* on Delmark, 2-disc *Classics* in USA. Biography *Stormy Monday* '87 by Helen Oakley Dance.

WALLACE, Jerry (*b* 15 Dec. '28, Kansas City, Mo.) Pop/country singer with string of hits '58-64; birth date used to be given as '38 but it's said he first recorded for Allied in '51. Hits were on Challenge, formed in Hollywood '56 by Gene AUTRY, Joe Johnson; the label also had the huge rock'n'roll instrumental hit 'Tequila', by the Champs (no. 1 '58). Wallace's mainstream pop incl. movie songs 'A Touch Of Pink' '59 (from *The Wild And The Innocent*) to remake of 'Swinging Down The Lane' ('23 hit by Isham JONES; more famous version by Frank SINATRA); his only top 10 was 'Primrose Lane', with backing group the Jewels. He switched to Mercury for one minor pop hit, then Liberty; came back to top 40 on Decca and on TV '72: 'If You Leave Me I'll Cry' ('The Tune in Dan's Café') from *Night Gallery*; acted on TV incl. series *Hec Ramsey*. MCA LP *Do You Know What It's Like To Be Lonesome?* made top 200 '73; others (still in print '87) incl. *Primrose Lane, I Wonder, Wives And Lovers*. Left Decca, continued into '80s with minor country hits on small labels.

WALLACE, Sippie (*b* Beulah Thomas, 1 Nov. 1898, Houston, Texas; *d* 1 Nov. '86) Blues singer; played organ, piano. One of 13 children; brother George W. Thomas Jr was composer/publisher/musician (*d* '36), niece Hociel Thomas was well-known blues singer (*b* 10 July '04, Houston; *d* 22 Aug. '52, Oakland, Cal.; recorded with Louis ARMSTRONG '25-6, on Circle and Riverside labels '46). Sippie recorded with Eddie Heywood, Clarence WILLIAMS, Sidney BECHET, King OLIVER, Perry BRADFORD, Armstrong '23-7, all on Okeh, incl. Williams Blue Five session with Armstrong and Bechet '24. Recorded for Victor '29; she worked outside music, did not record again until '45 on

Mercury with Albert AMMONS. Began playing festivals etc. '60s, live tracks on various labels; also with Jim Kweskin Jug Band '67 on Reprise, recorded for Spivey '70; also *Sippie Wallace Sings The Blues* '66 on Storyville, made in Copenhagen.

WALLER, Fats (*b* Thomas Wright Waller, 21 May '04 , NYC; *d* on a train near Kansas City, 15 Dec '43) Piano, organ, composer, leader. A great master of the New York 'stride' piano style and a prolific composer of shows and hit songs, incl. 'Keepin' Out Of Mischief Now', 'Ain't Misbehavin' (written while in jail for non-payment of alimony), 'Black And Blue', 'I've Got A Feelin' I'm Fallin' ', 'I'm Crazy 'Bout My Baby' and 'Honeysuckle Rose' (which began as a piano variation on 'Tea For Two'). He sold many hits outright and regretted it later; he apparently wrote the melodies of 'On The Sunny Side Of The Street' and 'I Can't Give You Anything But Love' and sold them to Jimmy McHUGH, but he also obtained advances when he needed cash, selling songs and lead sheets (some never finished) to more than one publisher. Though a great jazz musician it was his singing and irrepressible humour that made him an internationally popular star. Began playing at 6, won a talent contest as a teenager with James P. JOHNSON's 'Carolina Shout', later had lessons from Johnson. Began making piano rolls in c.'20, records in '22 (piano solos 'Muscle Shoals Blues', 'Birmingham Blues'); accomp. blues singers Sara Martin (*b* 18 June 1884, Louisville, Ky.; *d* there 24 May '55), Rosa Henderson (as Mamie Harris; *b* 24 Nov. 1896, Henderson Co., Ky.; *d* 6 Apr. '68, NYC; used many other names), others; played rent parties, piano and organ in silent movie houses (giving informal lessons to Bill BASIE). Collaborated with lyricist Andy RAZAF; shows incl. *Keep Shufflin'* '28, *Hot Chocolates* '29, *Early To Bed* '43. Recorded with Fletcher HENDERSON ('Henderson Stomp' '26 and other arrangements were sold to Henderson and Don REDMAN for the price of some hamburgers); McKINNEY'S COTTON PICKERS (his accomp. behind Redman's vocal on 'The Way I Feel Today' '29 is a masterpiece of delicacy), Jack TEAGARDEN (singing and repartee on 'You Rascal You' and 'That's What I Like About You' '31). His records

for Victor '26-9 began with pipe organ solos made in a disused church in Camden, N.J.: the piano was the instrument of his stomach, the organ of his heart; and his ability to make the pipe organ swing has never been equalled: titles incl. W. C. HANDY's 'St Louis Blues', 'Loveless Love' (aka 'Careless Love'), but 'Soothin' Syrup Stomp', 'Sloppy Water Blues', 'Rusty Pail' etc. are a beautiful series of original improvisations; issued complete on French RCA incl. alternate takes, they have a unique and timeless beauty. There were also vocals by Alberta HUNTER with pipe organ (e.g. 'Sugar', 'I'm Goin' To See My Ma'); sides by Fats Waller and his Buddies incl. historic '29 quintet date organised by Eddie CONDON on which the titles (made up on the spot) were reversed, so that 'Harlem Fuss' is a slow blues, 'Minor Drag' an uptempo romp. He also recorded piano solos and the first of two dates with his friend and admirer Gene AUSTIN (the other in '39). The Depression brought a temporary halt to his own recording; he played with Elmer SNOWDEN and others, led his own band, had popular radio shows '32-4, but in '34 began the small-group series for Victor – 'Fats Waller and his Rhythm' – that made his fame. Sextet usually incl. Al CASEY, guitar, Eugene 'Honey Bear' Sedric (*b* 17 June '07, St Louis, Mo.; *d* 3 Apr. '63, NYC), reeds; and Herman Autrey (*b* 4 Dec. '04, Evergreen, Ala.; *d* 14 June '80, NYC), trumpet; Charles Turner on bass, drummers Yank Porter (*b* c.1895, Norfolk, Va.; *d* 22 Mar. '44, NYC) or Harry Dial (*b* 17 Feb. '07, Birmingham, Ala.; autobiography *All This Jazz About Jazz* '85). They could take almost any song Victor pushed at them and turn it into gold: if Waller liked the song he might do it fairly straight, but made hilarious fun of second-rate material, often blurting out salacious tag-lines ('No, Lady, we can't haul your ashes for twenty-five cents. That'd be bad business'). They made scores of records, and towards the end some of the songs were so bad that nothing could save them, but there is a very large number of masterpieces: 'I'm Gonna Sit Right Down And Write Myself A Letter', 'Lulu's Back In Town', 'What's The Reason (I'm Not Pleasin' You)', 'Your Feet's Too Big' – the list could go on for a page; *Pop Memories* '86 lists 63 of them as hits, incl. 'Truckin' ', 'A Little Bit Independent', 'All My Life', 'It's A Sin To Tell A Lie' '35-6, 'Smarty' '37, 'Two Sleepy People' '38 all at no. 1. He recorded more piano solos '34, '37, '41, toured with a big band ('Fat And Greasy' was never officially issued and might be considered offensive today, but remains a fine performance). He went to Europe twice ('32, '38), recording the last time in London with a pick-up group incl. Edmundo ROS, George CHISHOLM; also pipe organ solos and his *London Suite*, six piano impressions (masters were lost in WWII; test pressings were later found and issued). He appeared in several films (*Hooray For Love* and *King Of Burlesque*, '35; *Stormy Weather*, '43), gave a Carnegie Hall recital '42 (he was almost too drunk to play). He also loved Bach; he tired of the role of clown, but his success and his life-style would not let him stop. He ate, drank and partied without stinting; he developed pneumonia and his body gave up the struggle. His last records were V-discs, solos for the armed forces incl. 'The Reefer Song' ('I dreamed about a reefer five feet long . . .'). All his records have been reissued, mostly in France; Nat Hentoff compiled good selections late '50s (*Handful Of Keys* and *One Never Knows, Do One?*); series of 2-disc sets on RCA USA incl. *Piano Solos* '29-38, *Complete* '34-6 in three sets. *Live At The Yacht Club, Live Vol. 2* on Giants Of Jazz in UK; '27-34 tracks compiled, digitally remastered by Robert Parker on BBC Records. Books incl. one by his manager Ed Kirkeby, and *Fats Waller* '77, by his son Maurice with Anthony Calabrese.

WALSH, Joe (*b* 20 Nov. '47, Wichita, Ks.) Guitarist, vocalist, songwriter; came to fame as one-third of the JAMES GANG. On going solo retained services of prod. Bill SZYMCZYK for *Barnstorm* '72, surprisingly restrained debut backed by bassist Kenny Passarelli, drummer Joe Vitale. Added Rocke Grace on keyboards (making band Barnstorm) for *The Smoker You Drink, The Player You Get* '73, starting fad for silly titles (many years later he is still asked what it means), incl. hard-rock masterpiece 'Rocky Montain Way' (top 30 USA, top 40 UK) showcasing slide guitar and trademark 'mouth bag' style of channelling guitar sound from amp into mouth enabling voic-

ing of sounds, later popularised by Peter FRAMPTON. *So What* '74 saw him in aviator goggles (after biplane of *Smoker* sleeve); with Vitale, Passarelli, bassist Bryan Garofalo, others helping on various tracks incl. protégé Dan FOGELBERG, J. D. SOUTHER, EAGLES on vocals, 'Time Out' and other tracks hold up well, neither more nor less than they should be, making much later pop sound the poorer, but synthesised Ravel and jokey 'All Night Laundry Mat Blues' suggested paucity of material confirmed on flaccid live *You Can't Argue With A Sick Mind* '75. Joined Eagles in time for *Hotel California* '76, adding guts to predictable sound on one of their best LPs, his 'Life In The Fast Lane' one of its best tracks; solo work took up-turn with *But Seriously Folks* '76: deadly ironic account of rock'n'roll lifestyle in 'Life's Been Good' made top 15 hit USA/UK; *There Goes The Neighborhood* '81 incl. top 40 'A Life Of Illusion', followed by *You Bought It You Name It* '83, *The Confessor* '85, *Got Any Gum?* '87. He prod. LPs for Fogelberg, Jay Ferguson (ex-SPIRIT), Ringo STARR, Fools Gold (Fogelberg backing band); contribution to *Urban Cowboy* soundtrack ('All Night Long' top 20 hit '80). Also ran for President of USA '79: rock'n'roller with a sense of humour as well as a highly rated guitarist.

WALTON, Cedar (*b* 17 Jan. '34, Dallas, Texas) Pianist, composer. Worked with J. J. JOHNSON, '59-60, Benny GOLSON – Art FARMER Jazztet '60-1, Art BLAKEY '61-4, '73; a highly-rated sideman and accompanist on many Blue Note and Prestige records (own *Cedar!*, *Spectrum*, *Soul Cycle* on Prestige, etc.); also recorded with Freddie HUBBARD, Eddie HARRIS; spent much time in Europe since '70. Own LPs incl. *Breakthrough* '72 with Hank MOBLEY, Sam JONES, Billy HIGGINS on drums, Charles Davis on baritone and soprano; *A Night At Boomer's* '73 (2 vols.) with Clifford JORDAN, Jones, Louis Hayes on drums; trio *Firm Roots* '74 with Jones and Hayes; *Eastern Rebellion* '75 with George COLEMAN, Jones and Higgins, *The Maestro* '80 with Abbey LINCOLN, all on Muse; three more vols. of *Eastern Rebellion* '77-9 on Timeless, with Jones and Higgins, Bob Berg on reeds (*b* '51, Brooklyn), Curtis FULLER ('79); quartet sets *First Set, Second Set* '77 on Steeple-chase with Berg, Jones, Higgins; *Third Set* also issued. Also *Piano Solos* on Clean Cuts, *Mobius* on RCA, *Animation* on CBS, duo *Heart & Soul* on Timeless with Ron CART-ER; *The Trio* '85 with David Williams and Higgins, *Vol. 2*, then *Cedar's Blues* '86 adding Berg and Fuller, all on Red Records. With new J. J. Johnson quintet '87.

WAR Latin-rock fusion band formed in Long Beach, Cal. '59: Lonnie Jordan, keyboards (*b* 21 Nov. '48, San Diego); Harold Brown, drums (*b* 17 Mar. '46, Long Beach); Howard Scott, guitar (*b* 15 Mar. '46, San Pedro); Peter Rosen on bass (*d* '69), replaced by Morris 'B. B.' Dickerson (*b* 3 Aug. '49, Torrence), replaced later by Luther Rabb; Charles Miller, sax and flute (*b* 2 June '39, Olathe, Kansas); 'Papa Dee' Allen, percussion (*b* 18 July '31, Wilmington, Del.). They gigged locally, were discovered by producer Jerry Goldstein, who put them up for job as Eric BURDON backing band; Lee Oskar came with Burdon, joined on harmonica (*b* 24 Mar. '46, Copenhagen); they were successful with Burdon, left him to make 15 hit LPs, singles incl. six in top 10 '72-6 on United Artists, '77 on MCA, '82 on RCA, all prod. by Goldstein. Big hit LPs *All Day Music* '71, no. 1 *The World Is A Ghetto* '72, *Why Can't We Be Friends?* '75 still available on Lax; also *Galaxy, The Music Band*, several more on MCA.

WARD, Billy, and the Dominoes R&B vocal group with classic hits in '50s and famous for some of its graduates. Arranger/pianist Ward did not often sing; group incl. Joe Lamont, baritone; Clyde MCPHATTER, lead tenor, replaced by Jackie WILSON '53, who was succeeded by Eugene Mumford '57; second tenor Charlie White and bass Bill Brown, replaced '52 by James Van Loan and David McNeil. Big Dominoes hits '51-2 incl. no. 1 'Sixty-Minute Man', featuring Brown's bass (no. 23 on pop chart); 'Have Mercy Baby' also written by Ward. Billing changed to Billy Ward and his Dominoes for more hits '53 on Federal and King; 'St Therese Of The Roses' was a top 20 pop hit on Decca '56 with Wilson's lead; switched to Liberty for '57 top 20s 'Stardust' and 'Deep Purple'. Compilations: *Have Mercy Baby* on Charly; others on King in USA.

WARINER, Steve (*b* 25 Dec. '54, Ky.) Country singer, guitarist and songwriter. Began in family combo run by his father and uncle; served apprenticeship in road bands of Dottie WEST, Bob LUMAN; signed with RCA and had minor hits with 'I'm Already Taken' (his own song, later a no. 1 for Conway TWITTY), climbed the charts until no. 1 'All Roads Lead To You' '82. Further hits incl. 'Midnight Fire' and 'Lonely Women Make Good Lovers' '83, 'What I Didn't Do' '84, all in top 5; he switched to MCA for more control over his product: hits incl. no. ones 'Some Fools Never Learn' '85, 'You Can Dream Of Me', 'Starting Over Again', 'Small Town Girl' all '86; also duets with Nicolette Larson ('That's How You Know') and Glen CAMPBELL ('The Hand That Rocks The Cradle'). Albums incl. *Midnight Fire* '83, *Down In Tennessee* '86 on RCA; *One Good Night Deserves Another* and *Life's Highway* '85, *It's A Crazy World* '87, *I Should Be With You* '88 on MCA.

WARING, Fred (*b* 9 June 1900, Tyrone, Pa.; *d* 29 July '84, State College, Pa.) Bandleader; also songwriter, arranger, played violin, banjo. He attended Penn State U., led banjo-based dance band age 18; later formed Fred Waring's Collegians, became Pennsylvanians, based in Detroit. Recorded for Victor in '20s, mostly very commercial but some jazz-infl. records: 'Farewell Blues', 'Down Home Blues'; in early '30s covers of Don REDMAN's 'I Heard', 'How'm I Doin'?'. Band incl. singing trumpeter Johnny 'Scat' Davis; drummer Poley McClintock (did vocals styled after Popeye the Sailor); McFarland twins Arthur and George, handsome blonds who both played reeds, had own corny band late '30s, suddenly became more modern c.'42, but never hit big time. Brother Tom Waring (*b* 12 Feb. '02, Tyrone; *d* 29 Dec. '60, Shawnee, Pa.) played piano, also well-known songwriter. Both brothers sang in early days, later had many singers. Irving AARONSON was chief rival, having band on Broadway in *Paris* while Waring's appeared in *Hello, Yourself* '28. Made film *Syncopation* '29, show *The New Yorkers* '30. Made fewer records after '32, afraid that others were copying arrangements; also became even more commercial, aimed at family audience with glee club style. Much radio work '30s-40s, made film with Dick Powell *Varsity Show* '37, at New York World's Fair '40, on Broadway in *Laffing Room Only* '45, cartoon film *Melody Time* '48; hits with Bing CROSBY 'Whiffenpoof Song' '47, brother Tom's song 'Way Back Home' '49; first band to have own TV show '49. Less touring and recording '50-70, had business interests: workshop for glee club directors, published band and choral arrangements, monthly *Music Journal*, 600-acre Shawnee Inn, Waring Corp. (made Waringblender Fred invented '37). Made absolutely no mark on music history, but knew what middle-America wanted: said in '66 'We don't sing music, we sing songs.' Last public appearance '81 Reagan inauguration. LPs. incl *Fred Waring In Hi Fi* c.'55 on Capitol, *America I Hear You Singing* and *White Christmas* '64 on Reprise with Crosby, Frank SINATRA, *The Memorial Album* on Stash (compilation of 20s stuff).

WARREN, Guy (*b* '23, Accra, Ghana) Drummer, composer; recently aka Kofi Ghanaba. Studied traditional drums and jazz from an early age; played in Accra Rhythmic Orchestra, visited USA '39, played in various groups in Accra for servicemen passing through en route to Middle East during WWII, joined Tempos dance band '47 playing mixture of ballroom and highlife music; went to UK and played with Kenny Graham (*b* 19 July '24, London; played reeds, formed Afro-Cubists early '50s, gave up performing for arranging). Warren returned to Tempos with new ideas and Cuban percussion. Also worked as journalist favouring Nationalist cause of Nkrumah; visited Lagos and Liberia, working in local radio and on Afro-jazz fusion: to USA c.'55, met and played with his idols Dizzy GILLESPIE, Lester YOUNG in Chicago, to NYC '57 and led trio at the African Room. LPs incl. *African Rhythms* and *Africa Speaks, Africa Answers* on Decca, *Themes For African Drums* on RCA. Returned to Accra '59, worked as lecturer and broadcaster on music, so far ahead of his time in African terms that he became a virtual recluse in his hideaway in Achimota, amassing a library of music and preparing his autobiography '70s (still unpublished). Regarded as the spiritual father of Afro-beat,

inspiring a generation to make greater use of indigenous music.

WARREN, Harry (*b* Salvatore Guaragna, 24 Dec. 1893, Brooklyn, NY; *d* 22 Dec. '81, L.A.) Composer; one of the great ones, especially successful in films. Parents Italian immigrants; 11th of 12 children; learned to play his father's accordion, sang in church choir, left school to play drums in carnival, used earnings to buy second-hand piano, taught himself to play and worked at Vitagraph studios playing mood music for silent screen actors. US Navy service WWI; worked as pianist/songplugger for Stark and Cowan, who issued his first published song, 'Rose Of The Rio Grande', co-written with Ross Gorman and Edgar Leslie, which was later a crowd-pleaser for years by Duke ELLINGTON with Lawrence Brown and Ivie ANDERSON. 'I Love My Baby (My Baby Loves Me)' and 'Home In Pasadena' followed '22; he worked with Billy ROSE from his first production: revue *Sweet And Low* '30 was originally titled *Corned Beef And Roses*, incl. 'Cheerful Little Earful' by Warren, Rose and Ira GERSHWIN, 'Would You Like To Take A Walk?' by Warren, Rose and Mort Dixon; when the show's title changed yet again to *Crazy Quilt* one of Warren's all-timers was added: 'I Found A Million Dollar Baby (In A Five And Ten Cent Store)' sung by Rose's wife Fanny BRICE in top hat and tails. *The Laugh Parade* '31 incl. 'Ooh That Kiss' and 'You're My Everything' by Warren, Dixon, Joe Young. Briefly to Hollywood for minor films, back there to work with Al Dubin on Warner Brothers' first big musical *42nd Street* '33 with all-star cast, Busby Berkeley choreography, songs incl. 'Shuffle Off To Buffalo', 'You're Getting To Be A Habit With Me'. The *Gold Diggers* series with Dubin incl. 'Pettin' In The Park', 'We're In The Money', 'Shadow Waltz' '33 (latter sequence used violins edged with neon, one of its first uses on film); 'Lullaby Of Broadway' (Warren's first Oscar and Berkeley's favourite production number) and 'The Words Are In My Heart' (with 56 pianos shoved around by 56 very small men underneath them) '35; last in series incl. 'All's Fair In Love And War' and 'With Plenty Of Money And You' '37. *Roman Scandals* (with Eddie CANTOR) incl. 'Keep Young

And Beautiful', *Dames* 'I Only Have Eyes For You', both '33; *Moulin Rouge* incl. 'Boulevard Of Broken Dreams', *20 Million Sweethearts* 'I'll String Along With You' (sung by Dick Powell; the film was also Ginger Rogers' first big role), both '34; *Go Into Your Dance* '35 had Al JOLSON and his then-wife Ruby Keeler, songs 'About A Quarter To Nine' and 'A Latin From Manhattan' (*Wonder Bar* '34 was a WB low point, with Jolson in blackface singing 'Going To Heaven On A Mule' to 200 children dressed as black angels). Warren teamed with Johnny MERCER '38 in *Goin' Places* (Louis ARMSTRONG and Maxine SULLIVAN sang 'Jeepers Creepers') and *Hard To Get* (Dick HAYMES with 'You Must Have Been A Beautiful Baby'). To 20th Century Fox '39-45, collaborating with Mack Gordon: *Springtime In The Rockies* ('I Had The Craziest Dream'), *Sweet Rosie O'Grady* ('My Heart Tells Me') both had Betty Grable singing; films with Glenn MILLER were *Sun Valley Serenade* and *Orchestra Wives*, Warren songs 'Chattanooga Choo Choo', 'I Know Why', 'I've Got A Gal In Kalamazoo', 'At Last', 'Serenade In Blue'; Rose's *Diamond Horseshoe* had Phil Silvers in one of his best roles, Haymes singing 'I Wish I Knew', 'The More I See You'; *Hello Frisco Hello* had Alice Faye singing Warren's second Oscar winner 'You'll Never Know'; for Faye's last film Warren worked with Leo Robin: *The Gang's All Here* incl. 'No Love, No Nothin' ', 'Journey To A Star', also 'The Lady In The Tutti-Frutti Hat' for Carmen MIRANDA. To MGM '45 with ace prod./lyricist Arthur Freed on Fred ASTAIRE film *Yolande And The Thief* ('Coffee Time') and multi-star *Ziegfeld Follies* ('This Heart Of Mine'); third Oscar with Mercer for 'On The Atcheson, Topeka And The Sante Fe' from *The Harvey Girls* with Judy GARLAND (Warren said to Harold ARLEN, 'From now on, you walk two Oscars behind me'). Last Astaire/Rogers film *The Barkleys Of Broadway* '49 with Gershwin incl. 'You'd Be Hard To Replace', 'My One And Only Highland Fling', 'Shoes With Wings On' (with Hermes Pan choreography); *Summer Stock* '50 incl. Gene KELLY dancing with a squeaky floorboard and a piece of newspaper to 'You, Wonderful You'; last Warren songs for MGM in *Belle Of The Ball* '52:

Astaire with Vera Ellen and 'Seeing's Believing', 'Baby Doll'. At Paramount with Robin '52 for *Just For You*, with Bing CROSBY and 'Zing A Little Zong'. Last big pop hit was 'That's Amore', with Jack Brooks for Martin & Lewis film *The Caddy* '53, sold millions for Dean MARTIN. Movie musicals were now usually transfers from Broadway; Warren wrote title themes for dramatic films *Marty* '55, *An Affair To Remember* '57 (score by Hugo FRIEDHOFER), *Separate Tables* '58. Earliest hits were revived '80s following Broadway version of *42nd Street*; elected to Songwriters Hall of Fame on his 80th birthday. Other Warren hits were 'Nagasaki' '28 (Swing Era hit recorded by Paul Mares' Friars' Society Orchestra, Don REDMAN, Benny GOODMAN etc.; sung in *My Dream Is Yours* '49 by Doris DAY), also 'September In The Rain', 'Remember Me', 'There Will Never Be Another You', 'I Wish I Knew', 'Lulu's Back In Town', many more. Lyricist Al Dubin (*b* 10 June 1891, Zurich; *d* 11 Feb. '45, NYC) was songwriter for early sound films; wrote 'Indian Summer' (with Victor HERBERT), 'Anniversary Waltz' (with Dave Franklin), 'Tiptoe Through The Tulips' and 'Dancing With Tears In My Eyes' (with Joe Burke), also with Rose, Meyer, Irving Mills, Jimmy McHUGH etc. Leo Robin (*b* 6 Apr. 1900, Philadelphia) worked with all the best composers, co-wrote Billie HOLIDAY hit 'Miss Brown To You', scores more. Mack Gordon (*b* 21 June '04, Warsaw, Poland; *d* 1 Mar. '59, NYC) also worked with Jimmy Van Heusen, Vincent YOUMANS and Ray Henderson; co-wrote 'Did You Ever See A Dream Walking?', 'The More I See You', 'It Happens Every Spring', many more.

WARWICK, Dionne (*b* 12 Dec. '40, East Orange, N.J.) Pop singer, with more than 50 hit singles, 30 hit albums since '62. From family bursting with vocal talent incl. sister Dee Dee (*b* '45), aunts Cissy and Thelma HOUSTON, niece Whitney HOUSTON. Sang in Gospelaires with Dee Dee and Cissy; did studio work; was discovered by Burt BACHARACH and Hal David, the ideal voice and stylist for their exceptionally successful songs: they placed her with Sceptre label (*see* SHIRELLES); of her first 37 hits all but four were written and all but two prod. by them. She added 'e' to 'Warwicke' for luck, whereupon Bacharach/David team lost steam, her chart run was broken '72; she worked with HOLLAND-DOZIER-HOLLAND, Jerry Ragavoy; went to WEA, was teamed with the Spinners for freak no. 1 smash 'There Came You' '74 (her first no. 1); live 2-disc LP *A Man And A Woman* with Isaac HAYES on HBS was top 50 album '77; having dropped the 'e' she went to Arista, had big hit LPs and singles prod. by Barry MANILOW, no. 12 LP *Dionne* incl. 'I'll Never Love This Way Again' and 'Déjà Vu'. More hits on Arista incl. *Friends In Love* '82 incl. title duet with Johnny Mathis, *Heartbreaker* '82; prod. by Barry Gibb, who sang back-up on top 10 title track; *How Many Times Can We Say Goodbye* '83, prod. and co-sung by Luther VANDROSS. She sang in hit soundtracks *Love Machine* '72, Stevie WONDER's *Woman In Red* '84; her second no. 1 was AIDS aid single 'That's What Friends Are For' by 'Dionne & Friends' incl. Wonder, Elton JOHN, Gladys KNIGHT. Throughout the rock era she has continued to sell albums with big-time show-biz glamour; recently teamed again with Bacharach: see his entry.

WASHINGTON, Dinah (*b* Ruth Lee Jones, 29 Aug. '24, Tuscaloosa, Ala.; *d* 14 Dec. '63, Detroit) Singer whose gutsy style, unique phrasing, gospel background and feeling for the blues transcended category. Won talent contest at the Regal theatre, toured with Sallie Martin Gospel Singers, changed her name and sang with Lionel HAMPTON band '43-6; first session under her own name was prod. by Leonard FEATHER for Keynote label late '43 with Hampton sidemen incl. Arnett COBB, Milt BUCKNER, incl. Feather's 'Evil Man', 'Salty Papa'; Hampton turned up and played a little piano and drums, but his manager (Joe Glaser), record label (Decca) and wife (Gladys) made no end of trouble, though Decca was never interested in Washington. She subsequently recorded for Mercury, nearly 30 R&B hits '49-61 beginning with Feather's 'Baby, Get Lost' a no. 1 hit (Decca's Milt Gabler had Billie HOLIDAY record a cover). Her only other no. 1 was 'This Bitter Earth' '60, but more than half the hits were in the top 10; over 20 singles making pop chart on Mercury incl. good songs going back to '34: 'What A Diff'rence A Day Makes', 'It Could Happen

To You', 'Our Love Is Here To Stay', 'For All We Know', others: unlike today's pop stars she could make a good song mean something new instead of recording soundalike ditties written in the studio. Duets with Brook BENTON were top 10: 'Baby (You've Got What It Takes)', 'A Rockin' Good Way (To Mess Around And Fall In Love)', both '60. She switched to Roulette '62, had a few more hits; she was married seven times; died of a common show-business accident, mixing alcohol and pills. Albums incl. *The Best In Blues* (reissues of early hits), 2-disc *The Dinah Washington Story* (incl. remakes of early hits, with Quincy JONES); chart LPs were *What A Diff'rence A Day Makes* '60, *Unforgettable* and *September In The Rain* '61 (all three with hit title singles, unique revivals of hit songs by the DORSEY Bros. '34, Nat COLE '51, Guy LOMBARDO '37 respectively), *I Wanna Be Loved* '62 (title track charted, revival of her own first pop hit '50), all on Mercury; also *Dinah '62*, *Drinking Again*, *Back To The Blues* and *A Stranger On Earth* '62-4 on Roulette. Many compilations and reissues in various countries incl. albums with Benton, *The Fats Waller Songbook* '57, 2-disc *The Jazz Sides* '54-8 incl. tracks with Jones, others from Newport Jazz Festival '58, *The Bessie Smith Songbook* '57-8, *In The Land Of Hi-Fi* '56, 2-disc *Slick Chick (On The Mellow Side)* '43-54, many others on Polygram labels; *With Arnett Cobb And His Mob* on Phoenix, recorded live in '52.

WASHINGTON, Geno Soul singer from Indiana who came to UK as serviceman and had chart success there. Began by leaping onto the stage of a club in East Anglia; went to London and sat in at Flamingo Club, a G.I. hangout. Left Air Force to sing full time; guitarist Pete Gage chose him to front his white Ram Jam Band (formed '65) incl. Jeff Wright, organ; John Roberts, bass; Herb Prestidge, drums; Bud Beadle, baritone sax; Lionel Kingham, tenor. Gained audience by cloning Stax sound (*see* SOUL), emulating SAM & DAVE, Wilson PICKETT, Otis REDDING, etc. After flop singles 'Water' and 'Hi Hi Hazel' they took obvious step of recording live LP: *Hand Clappin' – Foot Stompin' – Funky Butt – Live!* was top 5 LP late '66 without a hit single to help it; *Hipsters, Flipsters, And Finger-*

Poppin' Daddies made top 10 a year later, but Stax heyday ended: they couldn't replace covers with original material, went out of fashion overnight. *Sisters, Shifters, Finger-Clickin' Mamas* '68 didn't sell. He went to USA, learned guitar, bravely came back late '70s with rock trio: riding disco wave which revived some fading soul stars would have been more logical at the time, but he did reach no. 1 UK as subject of DEXY'S MIDNIGHT RUNNERS' tribute 'Geno' '80, in style he'd helped popularise in UK. Gage formed Vinegar Joe; Beadle sessioned, joined CAYENNE.

WASHINGTON, Grover, Jr (*b* 12 Dec. '43, Buffalo, N.Y.) Saxophonist, playing all the reeds; began in jazz which became lighter until it has almost become Muzak, with much commercial success. Worked with organ trios, rock bands; played on Randy WESTON LP *Blue Moses* on CTI; own LPs on Kudu label began to chart '72 with *Inner City Blues*, suddenly reached top 10 albums with *Mister Magic* and *Feels So Good* '75; 2-disc *Live At The Bijou* '78 was no. 11; switched to Motown, then Elektra: biggest hit was *Winelight*, no. 5 LP incl. smooth vocals by Bill Withers ('Just The Two Of Us' no. 2 hit '81).

WAS (NOT WAS) Studio wizards Don and David Was are not related, not called Was; record industry will not say who they really are. They make a slick, affectionate pastiche of black pop. First album *Was (Not Was)* '81 on Ze had vocalists Harry Bowens (sweet doo-wop) and Sweet Pea Atkinson (more R&B-ish) plus 11 backing singers; quirkily amusing *Born To Laugh At Tornadoes* '83 on Geffen had guest vocalists Mitch RYDER, Ozzy Osbourne, Mel TORMÉ; single 'Spy In The House Of Love' '87 was typically cluttered, noisy piece of neo-disco, or what is nowadays described as black 'dance' music, albeit skilfully done followed by album *What Up Dog?* 88. Live act said to be good value.

WATERS, Ethel (*b* 31 Oct. 1900, Chester, Pa.; *d* 1 Sept. '77, L.A.) Vocalist, actress. Began typed as blues singer, but became one of the most highly regarded pop singers of the '30s, infl. Lena HORNE, many others; in '40s worked as cabaret artist and more

often as a film actress. Worked as a maid, won a talent contest, worked theatres and was called 'Sweet Mama Stringbean' because she was tall and slim; moved to NYC and had hit records on Black Swan early '20s, recording and touring with Fletcher HENDERSON; then on Columbia and ARC labels. 25 hits '21-34 incl. many show songs; always associated with no. 1 hit 'Stormy Weather' '33, featured at COTTON CLUB. Recorded with Duke ELLINGTON '32, Benny GOODMAN '33 (hit 'A Hundred Years From Today' incl. Jack TEAGARDEN; Goodman played on several of her hits). 'Come Up And See Me Sometime' (from Mae West film) incl. Bunny BERIGAN on trumpet. Recorded for Decca later in '30s; toured with own show '35-9, accompanied by husband/bandleader Eddie Mallory; toured '48-9 with Henderson on piano. On stage: *Hello, 1919!*, *Africana* '27, *Blackbirds Of 1930*, *Rhapsody In Black* '31, *As Thousands Cheer* '33, *At Home Abroad* '35, *Cabin In The Sky* '40 (filmed '43), *Laugh Time* '43; non-singing roles: *Mamba's Daughters* '39, *Member Of The Wedding* '50 (New York Drama Critics Award for Best Actress; filmed '52); other films: *On With The Show* '29, *Check And Double Check* '30 (with Amos 'n'Andy, Ellington), *Gift Of Gab* '34, *Tales Of Manhattan* and *Cairo* '40, *Stage Door Canteen* '43, *Pinky* '49 (nominated for Oscar, Best Supporting Actress), *The Sound And The Fury* '59. On TV one season in title role of sit-com *Beulah* as a maid (role also played by Hattie McDANIEL). She was said to be the first black woman to star in network radio show '33, to appear on TV '39. Autobiography *His Eye Is On The Sparrow* '51 was best-seller (gospel LP on Word of the same title); *To Me It's Wonderful* '72 was also autobiography. LPs: *On Stage & Screen* '25-40 from Columbia Special Products, *Oh Daddy* '21-4 and *Jazzin' Babies Blues* on Biograph, *Ethel Waters* '46-7 on Glendale, *Miss Ethel Waters* on Monmouth-Evergreen, *On The Air* on Totem.

WATERS, Muddy (*b* McKinley Morganfield, 4 Apr. '15, Rolling Fork, Ms.; *d* 30 Apr. '83, Chicago) Blues singer, guitarist, composer; the greatest artist in the genre between the classic era of Robert JOHNSON, Tommy JOHNSON, Charley PATTON, and later success of B. B. KING. Nickname from playing in a muddy creek; learned to play harmonica at 13, guitar at 17 infl. by Son HOUSE, Robert Johnson; recorded by John LOMAX (*Stovall's Plantation* '41-2 on Testament). To Chicago '43, already a master of slide guitar; switched to electric guitar '44, played clubs and parties nights, worked in paper mill, then drove truck days. Recorded for Okeh '46 (unreleased until anthology *Okeh Chicago Blues* '81), for Aristocrat '46, which became CHESS '48: first Chess records reissued on *Best Of*, later called *Sail On*, then half of 2-disc *Chess Masters* from PRT/ UK: 'I Can't Be Satisfied' '48; 'Rollin' Stone' '50; 'Honey Bee', 'She Moves Me', 'Long Distance Call', 'Louisiana Blues' '51, 'Hoochie Coochie Man' and 'I'm Ready' '54; others: all R&B hits, all profoundly influential. Urban blues took up the electric guitar in order to be heard in noisy clubs, but in Waters' hands the urgency of country blues, its aching sexuality, homesickness for the South, touches of country superstition (black cat bone, mojo tooth) were undiluted. 'I Can't Be Satisfied' did not have drums on it, and the bass sound (probably Big Crawford) was similar to that of Marshall Grant, with Johnny CASH some years later: the infl. of white and black musics, country and urban musics can never be fully sorted out. From '50 Waters' band incl. LITTLE WALTER on harmonica, then Elgar Edmonds or Elgin Evans on drums, Jimmy ROGERS on second guitar, Otis SPANN on piano; among others passing through were arranger/producer/songwriter Willie DIXON or Luther Tucker on bass, Fred Below or Francis Clay on drums; then Walter HORTON, James COTTON, Buddy GUY, Junior WELLS, nearly all the stars of Chicago blues. White kids heard these strange records on the radio from the South Side and were enchanted by a mysterious world they could never hope to enter; English kids would be bolder. 'I Love The Life I Live' (covered by Mose ALLISON), 'Rock Me', 'Got My Mojo Working', 'She's Got It', 'She's Nineteen Years Old' all came in '57, 'Baby Please Don't Go' in '58, but none charted; Waters' last R&B chart hit was 'Close To You' '58 as younger black record buyers wanted the sweeter voices of people like Sam COOKE and Waters' classic work was done, but on his first UK tour '58 he discovered that his audience was interna-tional: when the music of the USA black community once again revitalised popular music in the '60s, no one was more influential than Waters. He played concert tours and festivals all over the world; the ROLLING STONES named themselves after the '50 hit, and Waters said, 'They stole my music, but they gave me my name.' Waters' LPs on Chess incl. *Electric Mud*, which was widely considered to have been a disaster; 2-disc *Fathers And Sons* '69 (one disc live, one studio) was much better, with Spann, Sam Lay on drums, young white acolytes Paul BUTTERFIELD, Michael BLOOMFIELD, Donald 'Duck' Dunn on bass, others guesting on various tracks. *Mud In Your Ear* '67 on Muse incl. classic lineup; *Live At Newport 1960*, *Live At Mr Kelly's* are on French Vogue; *They Call Me Muddy Waters* '71 won first of several Grammies; *The London Muddy Waters Sessions* '72 was highly rated, now on Chess/PRT in UK, as is compilation *Rare And Unissued*, tracks from '47-60. After *Can't Get No Grindin'* '73, Waters left Chess (sued them for back royalties), recorded for Blue Sky, *Hard Again* '77 and *I'm Ready* '78 prod. by Johnny WINTER, with Cotton and Rodgers; also *Live* '80 and *King Bee* on that label. He was one of the most important guests in the valedictory concert/film of the BAND, *The Last Waltz* '76, with 'I'm A Man'. As Chess masters were kicked around for years, reissue series stopping and starting, Syndicate Chapter attempted to rescue classics in UK (2-disc *Back In The Early Days*, *Good News*, also *We Three Kings* with Little Walter and Waters' main rival, Howlin' WOLF); now the classics have been digitally remastered: no fewer than six CD compilations were listed in Schwann '88 on Chess, Vogue, Blue Sky.

WATERSONS, The UK unaccompanied folk vocal group: Michael (*b* 16 Jan. '41), Lal (Elaine; *b* 15 Feb. '43) and Norma Christine Waterson (*b* 15 Aug. '39), all from Hull, Yorkshire, and their cousin John Harrison. Formed a group called the Mariners, then the Folksons before settling on family name and abandoning skiffle for trad. music; they infl. acts as diverse as Christy MOORE, Anne BRIGGS and TRAFFIC, as well as scores of subsequent folk groups. Debuted on *New Voices* anthology '64 on Topic, along with Harry Boardman (*d* 20 Dec. '87) and Mareen Craik, with songs like 'The Greenland Whale Fisheries' and 'Three Score And Ten'; sang 'The Ploughboy' on HMV LP *Folksongs Of Britain* '65, stayed with Topic: *Frost & Fire* '65 was 'a calendar of ceremonial folksongs', ritual songs incl. suggestions of A. L. LLOYD and drew upon pre-Christian trads. of British Isles: Traffic openly acknowledged debt to it, title track directly inspiring their title track *John Barleycorn Must Die* '70. They made *The Watersons* and *A Yorkshire Garland* '66, split '68 when Harrison moved to London; re-formed '72 with Bernie Vickers, then Martin CARTHY replacing him: *For Pence And Spicy Ale* '75 was *Melody Maker* folk LP of the year; *Sound Sound Your Instruments Of Joy* '77 explored the British hymnal trad. neglected since the Victorian era; *Green Fields* '81 dealt with rural customs and crafts. Guested on Richard and Linda THOMPSON's *Shoot Out The Lights* '82. Lal and Mike also made *Bright Phoebus* '72 on Trailer, a seminal record of original songs in contemporary folk style, followed by *Mike Waterson* and *A True Hearted Girl* (Lal and Norma), both on Topic. Carthy pursued concurrent celebrated solo career; the group expanded '85 to incl. Mike's daughter Rachel (*b* 3 Apr. '66, Hull). Members of Swan Arcade and the Watersons combined '87 to form offshoot Blue Murder.

WATSON, Bobby (*b* 23 Aug. '53, Lawrence, Kansas) Alto and soprano sax, other instruments; composer/arranger. Began arranging for high school concert band, organised dance band and wrote all the music; played with and was mus. dir. for Art BLAKEY '77-81; a very popular and personable soloist he was not in a big hurry to make solo LPs, but worked with Philly Joe JONES' Dameronia, George COLEMAN Octet, the SAVOY SULTANS etc. Working with Max ROACH, arr. the award-winning music for off-Broadway Sam Shepard play *Shepard Sets* '84; plays in 29th Street Saxophone Quartet with Ed Jackson (alto), Rich Rothenberg (tenor), Jim Hartog (baritone): *Watch Your Step* '85 on New Note. Own LPs began coming, incl. *Perpetual Groove* '84 (live in Italy), and *Appointment In Milano* '85 with Italian sidemen, which were both on Red Records; *Beatitudes* '84 on Newnote/Hep,

Gumbo '85 on Amigo; quartet *Love Remains* '87 was on Red, with Marvin 'Smitty' Smith.

WATSON, Doc (*b* Arthel Watson, 2 Mar. '23, Deep Gap, N.C.) Guitarist: one of the best flat-pickers of all. Father was a farmer who sang in local Baptist church, taught his blind son that he could pull his own weight around the farm despite handicap. Learned harmonica as a child, later banjo, then guitar; played 'Mule Skinner Blues' at a fiddlers' convention, from then on played at local functions, joined a group at age 18 which occasionally played on the radio. From '54 played in a small band for dances, mixture of rock'n'roll, country, square dance tunes, pop standards; continued to play trad. music at home, learned from the Skillet Lickers (*see* Riley PUCKETT), CARTER FAMILY, DELMORE Brothers, Bill MONROE. Ralph Rinzler came to the area to record Clarence 'Tom' Ashley for Folkways; *Old Time Music At Clarence Ashley's* (2 vols.) was Watson's record debut at nearly 40 years of age. Further LPs on Folkways were *The Doc Watson Family* (2 vols.), *Jean And Doc At Folk City* with Jean RITCHIE and *Progressive Bluegrass And Other Instrumentals*; switched to Vanguard for *Doc Watson* '64; *Doc Watson & Son* '65 incl. Merle Watson (*b* 8 Feb. '49; *d* 23 Oct. '85 in tractor accident), whose speciality was slide guitar but who learned to flat pick almost as well as Doc. LPs *Southbound* '66, *Home Again* '67, several others followed incl. collections of various folk artists; concert recordings incl. 2-disc sets *Old Timey Music* '67 and *Doc Watson On Stage, Featuring Merle Watson*. Switched to Popp label for *Then And Now* and *Two Days In November*, which won Grammies '73 and '74 for Best Ethnic or Traditional Recording; *Elementary Doctor Watson* was also on Poppy; Doc played on CBS LPs *Strictly Instrumental* with FLATT & Scruggs, *Earl Scruggs, Family And Friends*; Doc and Merle played on NITTY GRITTY DIRT BAND's *Will The Circle Be Unbroken*; then into '80s on UA, incl. *Doc Watson/Memories, Lonesome Road, Look Away!*, other material now on Liberty USA. Doc made bluegrass LP *Ridin' The Midnight Train* '86 on Sugar Hill; Doc and Merle also made *Down South* on Sugar Hill; *Guitar Album* (with other artists), *Pickin'*

The Blues and *Red Rocking Chair* on Flying Fish.

WATSON, Gene (*b* 11 Oct. '43, Palestine, Texas) Smooth honky tonk singer with more than 20 top 10 hits since mid-'70s, mostly sad country love ballads. Worked out of Houston, recording for local labels Resco, Wide World late '60s-early '70s; regional hit with 'Love In The Hot Afternoon' led to signing with Capitol, who made it a top 5 hit '75, followed by a long list of quality hits. Led, toured and often recorded with his own Farewell Party Band; switched to MCA '80, Epic '85, continuing with top 10 hits. LPs incl. *Love In The Hot Afternoon* '75, *Because You Believed In Me* '76, *Beautiful Country* '77, *Reflections* '78, *Should I Come Home* '80, *No One Will Ever Know* '81, all on Capitol; *Old Loves Never Die* '81, *Sometimes I Get Lucky* '82, *Little By Little* '84 (top 35 country LP), *Heartaches, Love & Stuff* '84 (no. 21 LP), all on MCA; *Memories To Burn* '85, *Starting New Memories* '86, *Honky Tonk Crazy* '87 on Epic all hits. Sang with Tammy WYNETTE on her *Higher Ground* '87.

WATSON, Johnny 'Guitar' (*b* 3 Feb. '35, Houston, Texas) Guitarist, vocalist; also plays piano: influenced (like everyone else) by T-Bone WALKER, he infl. Jimi HENDRIX and others in turn. To West Coast '50, worked with Big Jay MCNEELY, Bumps BLACKWELL, Amos MILBURN, others; first recorded as Young John Watson '53-4 on Federal; also for small local labels, then King '61; had top 10 R&B hit 'Cuttin' In' '62. Toured with Larry WILLIAMS (Watson/Williams hit 'Mercy, Mercy, Mercy' made Hot 100 '67 on Okeh); made LPs *Bad* '66, *Two For The Price Of One* '67, *In The Fats Bag* '68 on Okeh; *Gangster Of Love* '73 on Fantasy (now on Power), 'I Don't Want To Be A Lone Ranger' made Hot 100 '75, LP *I Don't Want To Be Alone, Stranger* '76; more success with funk on DJM: LPs *Ain't That A Bitch* '76, *A Real Mother For Ya* (title track almost made top 40) and *Funk Beyond The Call Of Duty* '77, *Giant* '78, *What The Hell Is This* '79, *Love Jones* '80, *Johnny 'Guitar' Watson And The Family Clone* '81 (played all instruments himself): almost all reached top 200 LPs; later work on A&M (e.g. *That's What Time*

It Is '82) did not. *Strike On Computers* '86 from Sound Service in Switzerland licensed for UK by Polygram, incl. Percy MAYFIELD song 'Please Send Me Someone To Love'. Compilations of later stuff on MCA, Fantasy; *The Gangster Is Back* on UK's Red Lightnin' has '50s-60s tracks; also *I Heard That!* on Charly has Federal King-tracks (prod. by Johnny OTIS). *Hit The Highway* on Ace has tracks from Modern, RPM mid-'50s incl. two vocals by Cordella De Milo, and CD-only *Three Hours Past Midnight* adds two tracks from Class ('The Bear' and 'Just One Kiss') and 'Motorhead Baby' from Combo (by Chuck Higgins band with Watson).

WATTERS, Lu (*b* Lucious Watters, 19 Dec. '11, Santa Cruz, Cal.) Trumpet, bandleader. Formed first band '25, larger bands until '39 residency at the Dawn Club launched the jazz 'revival', re-creating classic New Orleans style. By '40 the band had been named the Yerba Buena Jazz Band; recorded and played at the Dawn Club through '50 (except '42-5; Watters in US Navy leading 20-piece band in Hawaii). By then key sidemen Bob SCOBEY and Turk MURPHY had left; Watters had surgery, studied geology, reformed a new band briefly, left music. Of LPs on Good Time Jazz *Dawn Club Favourites*, *Originals & Ragtime*, *Stomps & The Blues* (the first three 12″ LPs on that label), all tracks were made '46 with Watters, Scobey, Murphy, Bob Helm on clarinet, Wally Rose on piano, Harry Mordecai on banjo, Dick Lammi on tuba, Bill Dart on drums; *Yerba Buena Days* ('42-9 tracks) and *The '50s Recordings* (2 vols.) were issued on Dawn Club; *Bunk Johnson & Lu Watters* on Good Time Jazz incl. '41 and '44 tracks with two different Watters lineups, one with Burt Bales on piano, Clancy HAYES on drums.

WEA Warner-Elektra-Atlantic, the biggest record group in the USA and internationally third behind EMI and CBS. USA film company Warner Brothers first entered music '30 when they bought Brunswick Records; they also bought four leading music publishers for $28m. Partly because of the Depression and because they knew nothing about the music business, these ventures failed and were sold off. (In '82, 80 crates of priceless manuscript by George GERSHWIN, Cole PORTER, Jerome KERN, Richard RODGERS etc. were found in a WB warehouse in New Jersey, dating from that period.) WB entered the record business again '58 with its own Warner Brothers label, relying at first on movie stars like Tab HUNTER; they signed the EVERLY BROTHERS, whose first WB release was the first on WB's own logo in the UK: 'Cathy's Clown' was the biggest Everly hit, spending five weeks at no. 1 in the USA, seven in UK; WB also signed PETER, PAUL & MARY and were well on the way to success marked by amalgamations: WB bought Reprise from Frank SINATRA '63 and were themselves taken over by the film production company Seven Arts '66; Atlantic/Atco/Cotillion were added '67 (see ATLANTIC); WB-Seven Arts were taken over by the Kinney Corporation '69 and purchased Elektra/Asylum '70, becoming WEA. The British Invasion of the '60s had done little for the company though Reprise licensed Petula CLARK and the KINKS from Pye (see PRT). But Warner-Reprise in the late '60s was a more artist-oriented company than some others and signed artists of lasting quality: WB had Van MORRISON, James TAYLOR and the ASSOCIATION, and took a chance on Ry COODER, who had never made an album; Reprise had Joni MITCHELL, Neil YOUNG and Kenny ROGERS; the group also did interesting and creative offbeat things, e.g. with Van Dyke PARKS and CAPTAIN BEEFHEART. Its UK subsidiary paid for itself by signing FLEETWOOD MAC. In the '70s-80s WEA slowly grew; an attempt to buy PolyGram was thwarted by other labels on anti-trust grounds, though it did acquire the UK music publisher Chappells, once owned by PolyGram. VAN HALEN, the CARS, links with Sire Records (MADONNA) and Paisley Park (PRINCE) kept WEA at the top; creativity continued with Laurie ANDERSON. WEA UK had one of the best press offices of any record company in London, released Stan CAMPBELL's first solo album and picked up Mary COUGHLAN in the mid-'80s. While becoming a giant WEA somehow managed to remain artist-oriented: as country music became more important than ever, releases by Emmylou HARRIS, Hank WILLIAMS Jr, the FORESTER SISTERS, Dwight YOAKUM, Randy TRAVIS etc. had

integrity in their production that was almost a company trademark.

WEATHERFORD, Teddy (*b* 11 Oct. '03, Bluefield, W.Va.; *d* 25 Apr. '45, Calcutta) Pianist. To Chicago '21 from New Orleans; recorded as a sideman with Jimmy Wade's Moulin Rouge Orchestra '23-4, Erskine Tate's Vendome Orchestra '26 (with Louis ARMSTRONG; two tracks on *Young Louis The Sideman* on MCA), left USA '26 for Asia. Worked in Shanghai '29, recruited Buck CLAYTON band for a season there '34; worked in Singapore etc. and India, where he died of cholera. Seven solos made during Paris visit to 1937 International Exhibition (five on *Piano And Swing 1935-8* on Pathé; four on *Jazz Piano à Paris 1937-39* on EMI) reveal swing resembling James P. JOHNSON, treble voicing that may have influenced Earl HINES. He also made eight tracks for EMI/Columbia in India '42, four with bass and drums, four in an octet, Weatherford vocals on six.

WEATHER REPORT Fusion band co-led by Joe ZAWINUL and Wayne SHORTER, formed '71 after Zawinul had worked with Cannonball ADDERLEY, Shorter with Art BLAKEY, both with Miles DAVIS. All of their 15 albums charted in top 200 LPs USA, making them the most successful electric jazz group of all; but their sales had an arc from the first LP (at no. 191) up to the top 40 to the last (no. 195); their time-scape had less and less to do with jazz, as though they were experiencing it from a distance; the composer/keyboardist Zawinul eventually eclipsed the jazzman Shorter and the idea seemed to be to make as much as possible of very little: though some of their work shimmered and twinkled impressively, it may have been very much of its time. The group ranged in size from five to nine; there were sometimes two bassists, on *Mr Gone* three drummers incl. Tony WILLIAMS, Steve GADD. First four LPs incl. Miroslav Vitous on bass: *Weather Report* '71, *I Sing The Body Electric* '72 (one side live in Japan, where 2-disc live set was released) were poorly mixed, came out of Davis's late '60s style, but with more prettiness; *Sweetnighter* '73 and *Mysterious Traveller* '74 saw the weather becoming more purple. On *Tale Spinnin'* '75 Zawinul used a monophonic Arp synthesiser, on *Black Market* '76 an Oberheim polyphonic (with Jaco PASTORIUS on two tracks) and the weather became *Heavy Weather* '77, their biggest seller at no. 30, with Pastorius taking over on bass: his undoubted genius was indulged too much in a setting that was really about a quasi-orchestral sound rather than solos; his solos (and Shorter's) were longer on stage. *Mr Gone* '78 was followed by 2-disc *8:30* (three sides live), *Night Passage* '80, *Weather Report* '82, *Procession* '83, *Domino Theory* '84 (incl. 'The Peasant', their best swansong, according to Richard Cook in the *Wire*), *Sportin' Life* '85 and *This Is This* '86. By that time both Zawinul and Shorter each needed to do something else; to judge from reviews of Shorter's records and gigs, he needed time to come down from the meteorological balloon.

WEAVERS, The Folk quartet formed '48 by Pete SEEGER, Lee Hays (*b* '14, Little Rock, Ark.; *d* 26 Aug. '81, New York State), Fred Hellerman (*b* 13 May '27, NYC), Ronnie Gilbert: 'two low baritones, one brilliant alto and a split tenor', in Seeger's words. Seeger and Hays had sung together since '40 in various groups incl. Almanac Singers; Hays was capable of a sepulchral bass. Ronnie was a voice student whose voice changed when she discovered folk music; Fred was a student with receding hair. They sang informally, campaigned for left-wing political candidates, recorded for Charter and Hootenanny labels (incl. Seeger/Hays' 'The Hammer Song'; became pop hit '62-3 as 'If I Had A Hammer'); signed for two weeks at Village Vanguard at Christmas '49, which might have been a farewell gig: that year the Seeger family had escaped serious injury by a right-wing mob (with local cops helping) in the Peekskills after a gig; he felt discouraged, did not want to risk others' lives, was also ambivalent about seeking commercial success. The two-week gig lasted six months; Carl Sandburg heard them, was quoted in papers: '. . . when I hear America singing, the Weavers are there.' Harold Lowenthal heard them, became their manager (was Seeger's manager for over 25 years). Gordon JENKINS wanted to record them; Dave Kapp at Decca didn't, but Gordon got his way. First record 'Tzena Tzena Tzena' made in Hebrew (written '41 by Issacher Miron, then a Palestinian, later an Israeli; rewritten '47 by Julius Grossman); it caused a stir and was remade by Gordon Jenkins and his Orchestra with the Weavers, English words by Jenkins; DJs flipped this record and found 'Goodnight Irene': using a song by a black ex-convict (LEADBELLY) was itself almost a political statement then. 'Irene' was no. 1 for 13 weeks '50, sold two million copies ('answer' song 'Say Goodnight To The Guy, Irene' was written); 'Tzena' reached no. 2. The Weavers had no competition: their unusual lineup, close harmony could have been country music (it echoed the sound of the CARTER Family and of the CHUCK WAGON GANG); Jenkins' arr. of 'Irene' opened with a violin solo, imparting a front-porch quality. Ten hits through '52 incl. no. 2 'On Top Of Old Smokey' (adding Terry GILKYSON vocal), Woody GUTHRIE's 'So Long (It's Been Good To Know Ya)', 'Kisses Sweeter Than Wine' (Irish folksong adapted by Leadbelly and Weavers, revived '57 by Jimmie RODGERS), 'Wimoweh' (Zulu song was no. 1 hit '61 by the Tokens as 'The Lion Sleeps Tonight'), Leadbelly's 'Midnight Special' and (fluke '54 hit) 'Sylvie'. They also recorded Guthrie's 'Hard Ain't It Hard', slavery-era 'Follow The Drinking Gourd', a Christmas LP, etc. On some non-hit and album tracks they accompanied themselves, as on 10″ LP *Folksongs Of America And Other Lands*. Not all hits were listed in *Billboard* (but now in *Pop Memories*; see CHARTS): their chart run was spoiled by liars during McCarthy-era blacklisting (*see* Seeger's entry): 'First we took a sabbatical,' said Hays later. 'Then we took a mondical and a tuesdical.' (Musical establishment helped scupper folk music for the time being, then was outraged two years later when rock'n'roll relieved the monotony of pop.) Seeger carried on solo activities; when NYC's Town Hall would not accept the Weavers, they sang at Carnegie Hall instead on New Year's Eve '55; concert was issued on Vanguard (formed in NYC c.'48 by Maynard and Seymour Solomon); other Vanguard LPs incl. *At Carnegie Hall* '60 (2 vols.), *Reunion At Carnegie Hall* '63 (*Part 2* '65), studio sets *At Home* '58, *Travelling On* '60, *Almanac* '62, *Songbag* '67, compilations. Members also recorded as the Babysitters for children. Seeger left '58 but appeared with them occasionally; replacements incl. Frank Hamilton, Bernie Krause, Erik DAR-LING. Disbanded late '63; re-formed for final Carnegie Hall gig '81, the irrepressible Hays in a wheelchair; preparations and concert filmed as *Wasn't That A Time*. When Hays died his friends placed his ashes on his compost heap at his request. The Weavers were a profound influence, e.g. on children who always love folk music and who were angry on discovering years later why the Weavers suddenly disappeared from the airwaves and juke boxes; Holly NEAR (appeared in *Wasn't That A Time*) was among those inspired by the Weavers, especially by Gilbert, who has appeared with her; Gilbert and Hellerman have been active in theatre projects, etc.

WEBB, Chick (*b* William Henry Webb, 10 Feb. '09, Baltimore, Md.; *d* 16 June '39) Drummer, bandleader; one of the greatest of all jazz drummers, despite a hunchback; died of TB of the spine. Buddy RICH said of him, 'Every beat was like a bell.' To NYC '24, formed band '26, first record '27 not issued; '31 band incl. Hilton Jefferson in reed section, Jimmy HARRISON on trombone, John Trueheart on guitar, Benny CARTER; he was always swapping musicians with Fletcher HENDERSON. The late '33 band incl. Trueheart, trumpeters Mario BAUZA, Taft Jordan (later with Duke ELLINGTON), Sandy WILLIAMS on trombone, John KIRBY on bass and Edgar SAMPSON, who wrote 'Let's Get Together', an arr. with an unusual amount of dynamic variation it it. He had written 'Stompin' At The Savoy' earlier, with Rex STEWART band; it was a top 10 hit for Webb '34. Harlem's Savoy Ballroom had been built on the site of old car barns; 20,000 people attended grand opening of 'The World's Most Beautiful Ballroom' '26 (it was torn down '58 for a housing project); Webb moved in '31, and from then on every visiting band had to do battle. In '34 trumpeter Bobby Stark, Wayman CARVER on reeds/flute, Claude Jones on trombone were added; the band switched to new Decca label from ARC labels '34; Louis JORDAN joined '36; Carter played with the band on record '38 and Jefferson came back; Chick Webb and his Little Chicks was a quintet, made three

sides '37. But in '35 he'd discovered Ella FITZGERALD: her first record with the band was 'I'll Chase The Blues Away'; 11 of the band's 18 hits '34-9 were Ella's, incl. no. 1 'A-Tisket, A-Tasket' '38, 'MacPherson Is Rehearsin' To Swing', 'Undecided'. Benny GOODMAN had a hit with 'Stompin' At The Savoy' '36, but was blown away in honest combat at the Savoy a few months before Webb's death: 20,000 people were allegedly turned away that night; Gene Krupa said 'I have never been beaten by anybody who was so strong.' The records are wonderful, but do not do Webb justice; by the time studio engineers had learned to cope with a drummer who could drive a big band, he was terminally ill. Ella sang 'My Buddy' at his funeral (he had adopted her when her mother died); she led the band for two more years. *In The Groove* on Affinity UK incl. Sampson's 'Don't Be That Way', 'Blue Lou', Ella's hits; in USA *Ella Swings The Band* '36-9, *Legend*, 2-disc *Best Of* on MCA; *Featuring Ella* '39 on Folkways, *Stompin' At The Savoy* '36 on Circle.

WEBB, Jimmy (*b* 5 Aug.'46, Elk City, Okla.) Songwriter, singer. Started jingle company before major success as writer; millionaire by age 21. Wrote for Motown's Jobete Music, but first successes '67-8 for FIFTH DIMENSION ('Up, Up And Away'), Glen CAMPBELL ('By The Time I Get To Phoenix', 'Wichita Lineman', 'Galveston'), Richard HARRIS ('MacArthur Park'). Webb was one of the first to write, arr., prod. complete albums for other artists: Fifth Dimension's *Magic Garden*, Thelma HOUSTON's *Sunshower*, Harris's *A Tramp Shining*, *The Yard Went On Forever*. Own singing first recorded '67 on Strawberry Children's 'Love Years Coming'. Continued to be associated with others (Campbell, Art GARFUNKEL, Joe COCKER, the SUPREMES) but began to make own albums as well: voice not remarkable but sensitive interpreter of own songs, with excellent West Coast backing musicians: *Letters* '72 on Reprise, *El Mirage* '77 on Atlantic are his most consistent LPs. Songs covered by diverse artists: Frank SINATRA, Waylon JENNINGS, Judy COLLINS, Donna SUMMER, Arlo GUTHRIE, Lowell George; simple and direct in commercial material ('Didn't We', 'The Moon's A Harsh Mistress'), more adventurous in both words and music in songs like 'MacArthur Park', 'Watermark', 'Requiem'. Other LPs are *Jim Webb Sings Jim Webb* '68 (CBS), *Words And Music* '70, *And So: On* '71 (Reprise), *Land's End* '74 (Asylum), *Angel Heart* '82 (CBS/Lorimer). Fine talent in some danger of bogging down in bland AOR mould, but in mid-'85 Webb's writing had comeback in charts with no. 1 'Highwayman', originally written for Campbell, now title cut from LP by Johnny CASH, Jennings, Willie NELSON, Kris KRISTOFFERSON.

WEBSTER, Ben (*b* Benjamin Francis Webster, 27 Mar. '09, Kansas City, Mo.; *d* 20 Sep. '73, Amsterdam) Tenor sax; also piano. The greatest tenor of the Swing Era after Coleman HAWKINS, whom he always called 'the old man' though there was little difference in their ages. He began on violin as a child, learned piano from Pete JOHNSON and played in silent cinemas; he was infl. by Frankie TRUMBAUER solo on 'Singin' The Blues', learned a scale from Budd JOHNSON and soon played in the YOUNG family band alongside Lester. Played with Jap Allen, Blanche Calloway; Bennie MOTEN '31; then Andy KIRK, Fletcher HENDERSON, Benny CARTER, Cab Calloway, Teddy WILSON; joined Duke ELLINGTON '40-2: his solos on 'Cotton Tail', 'All Too Soon', many others are classics; he played 'Stardust' at a dance date in Fargo, N.D. '40, never recorded commercially, perhaps in response to Hawkins' 'Body And Soul' '39, but he was no Hawkins acolyte: combined powerful, brusque swing with a breathy sensuality on ballads, like that of Johnny HODGES on alto, straightforwardly mainstream compared to Hawkins' more scientific approach. He freelanced, came back to Ellington '48-9 (despite having cut one of Duke's best suits to ribbons earlier); lived on West Coast '50s to be near his family, toured with JATP; moved to Copenhagen '64 and spent most of his time in Europe. Recorded with Sid CATLETT '44 on Commodore; *Tribute* compiles rare tracks with various bands '36-45, *Ben And The Boys* from mid-'40s, both on Jazz Archive; *Ben Webster – Rare Live Performance* on Jazz Anthology is dated '62, but sounds years earlier, with at least 3/4 of MODERN JAZZ QUARTET incl. Kenny CLARKE; 2-disc *The Complete Ben Webster*

On EmArcy '51-3 was a prize-winning reissue '86; 2-disc *Ballads* '54-5 on Verve; *Ben Webster And Friends* '59 on Verve (aka *And Associates*) incl. Hawk, Johnson, Roy ELDRIDGE; quartet *See You At The Fair* '64 on Jasmine has Hank JONES or Roger KELLAWAY on piano; *Ben Webster Meets Don Byas* '68 on MPS was made in Germany, *Did You Call?* '72 on Nessa in Spain, both with Tete MONTOLIU on piano. *No Fool, No Fun* '70 on Spotlite has rehearsal with Denmark Radio Big Band. Also on Verve: *Meets Gerry Mulligan*, *Meets Oscar Peterson* (trio), *The Kid And The Brute* with Illinois JACQUET; on Enja: *Live At Pio's* with Junior MANCE, Bob Cranshaw on bass, Mickey Roker on drums; more LPs on Black Lion, others.

WEEDON, Bert (*b* 10 May '20, East Ham, London) UK guitarist. Studied music at 9, took up guitar at 13; studied classical music but played with local dance bands; first broadcast '40. Played with Stephane GRAPPELLI, Django REINHARDT; with Ted HEATH early '50s, Cyril STAPLETON BBC Show Band '56; sessioned with Cliff RICHARD, Dickie VALENTINE, Frank SINATRA, Judy GARLAND, Nat COLE; 10 top 50 hits '59-61 began with top 10 'Guitar Boogie Shuffle'; 'Mr Guitar' '61 was written and dedicated to him by the SHADOWS. Gold and platinum discs for no. 1 compilation *22 Golden Guitar Greats* '76. Though his dance-band oriented style was soon considered old-fashioned by the younger audience, he had great infl. on UK rock with teach-yourself books *Play In A Day* and sequel *Play Every Day*, translated into many languages and sold over a million copies. LPs incl. top 20 *King Size Guitar* '60 on Top Rank, more recently *Bert Weedon And His Dancing Guitars* on Danson; *Blue Echoes* and *16 Country Guitar Greats* on Polydor, 2-disc hits compilation *Mr Guitar* on Music For Pleasure, others.

WEEKS, Anson (*b* 14 Feb. 1896, Oakland, Cal.; *d* 7 Feb. '69, Sacramento) Pianist, bandleader. Led highly successful hotel dance band, dispensing strict tempo fare. First band at U. of Cal. '24; first pro date at Hotel Oakland, then Sacramento, Lake Tahoe, then residency at San Francisco Mark Hopkins Hotel '27-34. National fame with *Lucky Strike Magic Carpet* radio show early '30s; then tours of most major USA cities, also appearing in films. Band's vocalists incl. Tony MARTIN, Bob CROSBY, Dale Evans; recorded with Bing. Wrote own theme 'I'm Writing You This Little Melody', other songs. Less active after injury in '41 bus crash; made film *Rhythm Inn* '51, returned with 7-piece lineup late '50s, played same hotel circuit he'd been king of 25 years earlier. Residencies in San Francisco '56, Sacramento Inn mid-'60s; *Dancin' With Anson* LPs on Fantasy. Compilation of '32 tracks on Hindsight *Anson Weeks And His Orchestra*.

WEEMS, Ted (*b* Wilfred Theodore Weymes, 26 Sep. '01, Pitcairn, Pa.; *d* 6 May '63, Tulsa, Okla.) Bandleader. Led popular dance band with occasional semi-hot style and novelties. Played trombone in band at U. of Pa.; formed first band c.'22, resident in Philadelphia café for a year; early hit was 'Somebody Stole My Gal' c.'23. Toured, mostly midwest from '29; radio exposure and novelty hit 'Piccolo Pete'; vocalists incl. Elmo Tanner (*b* 8 Aug. '04, Nashville), more famous for whistling on band's theme 'Out Of The Night', hit 'Heartaches' '33. Other hits incl. 'Oh, Monah', 'The Martins And The Coys', 'The One Man Band' (wrote or co-wrote last two). On radio '32-3 with Jack Benny, later with Fibber McGee & Molly; young baritone Perry COMO joined '36; *Beat The Band* radio show '40-1 with MC Garry Moore. Merchant marine WWII, formed new band '45; three top 10 hits in Billboard charts '47: 'Heartaches' no. 1 with reissues on Victor ('Piccolo Pete' on flip) and Decca ('Oh, Monah'); 'I Wonder Who's Kissing Her Now' on Victor with Como, 'Mickey' on Mercury. DJ in Memphis mid-'50s. Compilations incl. 3 vols. on Grannyphone label; Vol. 3 is '28-30 stuff: period 'hot dance band'.

WEILL, Kurt (*b* 2 Mar. 1900, Dessau, Germany; *d* 3 Apr. '50, NYC) Composer. Third son of Cantor of Dessau synagogue; his family traced its roots in Baden back to 13th century. Studied piano; he began composing/conducting '16, studied in Berlin '18, became vocal coach at Dessau Opera '18, conductor '20. Returned to Berlin '20; his music first performed '23 incl.

string quartet and *Sinfonia Sacra*; met expressionist playwright Georg Kaiser (1878-1945) and through him Austrian actress/singer Lotte Lenya (*b* Caroline Blamauer, 18 Oct. 1900; *d* 27 Nov. '81, NYC: they married '26, were divorced '33, remarried '37). *Zaubernacht* ('Magic Night') dance pantomime for children, successful in Berlin '22, was his first USA production at Xmas '25 in NYC. Weill-Kaiser one-act operas *Der Protagonist* '26 and *Der Zar Lässt sich Photographieren* '28 made him one of the most important composers of his generation. Began working with playwright Bertolt Brecht on opera *Aufstieg und Fall der Stadt Mahagonny*, from which a *songspiel* was performed '27; mid-'28 their *Die Dreigroschenoper* was premiered in Berlin: 'The Threepenny Opera' immediately successful, based on Elizabeth Hauptmann translation of John Gay's *The Beggar's Opera* (popular in England since 1728, music by J. C. Pepusch); complete *Mahagonny* premiered '30 in Leipzig, '31 in Berlin, was considered scandalous in its almost amoral commentary on 20th-century attitudes; also 'school opera' *Der Jasager* ('The Yes-sayer'). Three-act opera *Die Bürgschaft* '32 with libretto by Caspar Neher and Weill was his most ambitious work to date, mounted by the State Opera in Berlin and a rallying point for liberal art policies as Germany slid into chaos; a semi-staged performance of *Der Jasager* and *songspiel* from *Mahagonny* was a fashionable success in Paris; the second performance of 'Wintermärchen' *Der Silbersee* (with Kaiser) early '33 disrupted by Nazi demonstrations. Weill went to Paris after the Reichstag fire; finished his second symphony '34; worked on *Der Weg der Verheissung* ('The Road Of Promise') about Jewish history; went to NYC '35; musical play *Johnny Johnson* with Paul Green a moderate success '36; 'Promise' finally put on at Manhattan Opera House as *The Eternal Road* '37, a critical and public success but with running costs too high: it was considered the most expensive failure in history at the time. Worked in Hollywood (incl. score for Fritz Lang film *You And Me*); in mid-'38 he wrote, orchestrated music for Maxwell Anderson's book/lyrics for *Knickerbocker Holiday*, which opened in October: his first Broadway hit, incl. 'It Never Was You' (sung by

Judy GARLAND in film *I Could Go On Singing* '63), 'September Song' (recorded by Bing CROSBY, Frank SINATRA, many others; hit for Stan KENTON and LIBERACE '51-2, sung by Maurice CHEVALIER in film *Pepe* '60). Music for pageant *Railroads On Parade* at '39 World's Fair was a hit; *Lady In The Dark* '41 with Moss Hart and Gershwin, *One Touch Of Venus* '43 with book by S. J. Perelman and Ogden Nash both hits (*Lady* with patter song 'Tchaikovsky': names of 49 Russian composers delivered by Danny KAYE; *Venus* incl. 'Speak Low', hit for Guy LOMBARDO '44); musical film *Where Do We Go From Here?* followed by operetta *The Firebrand Of Florence* (play by E. J. Meyer about Cellini, Lenya in a leading role), both with Ira GERSHWIN; latter was his only Broadway flop. 'Broadway opera' *Street Scene* based on Elmer Rice play was critical and public hit '47 (lyrics by Langston Hughes) but had high running costs; Weill was angry because it closed too soon. His unpublished ballad opera *Down In The Valley* (written for radio '45) was premiered to acclaim at U. of Indiana in Bloomington '48. *Love Life* with Alan Jay LERNER was a moderate success on Broadway; *Lost In The Stars* '49 with Anderson was a hit (adapted from Alan Paton's *Cry The Beloved Country*). He was working on a musical adaptation of *Huckleberry Finn* when he died (patched together and performed on Austrian TV '64, lyrics by Anderson). He wrote a great deal of music, some of which is still being rediscovered; he was a lifelong democrat, caring little for posterity, but Brecht, like many committed left-wing artists, had his eye on his posthumous reputation and nothing good to say about collaborators, especially his most famous one: Brecht even hinted that he wrote some of the tunes from their collaboration, but the only evidence is Brecht's draft of 'Seeräuberjenny' ('Pirate Jenny', from *Threepenny*), re-composed by Weill, whose reputation continues slowly to rise: the English adaptation by Marc Blitzstein '52 of *Threepenny* was among the longest-running shows in Broadway history, with Lenya re-creating her role, incl. 'Mack The Knife', among biggest hits of the century: seven hit versions '56 incl. instrumentals as 'Moritat' ('Die Moritat vom Mackie Messer' was original title), top 20 vocal by

Louis ARMSTRONG; no. 1 hit by Bobby DARIN '59, another hit '60 by Ella FITZGERALD; 'Bilbao Song' (from flop *Happy End* '29 with Brecht, Hauptmann) added to *Threepenny* by Blitzstein for '56 London production as 'Bide-awee In Soho'; as 'Bilbao Song' with new lyrics by Johnny MERCER it was a hit for Andy WILLIAMS '61). *The Rise And Fall Of The City Of Mahagonny* was revived by Sadler's Wells (now English National Opera) in London '63, then at La Scala and in USA; its metaphor of the moral confusion in the Weimar Republic will be of permanent value, made more pointed by tension between Brecht's didacticism and Weill's sympathy. *Lost In The Stars* was revived on Broadway '72; among filmed Weill shows are *Die Dreigroschenoper* '31 (with Lenya, dir. by G. W. Pabst, who adapted it for NYC stage in '33) and English/German prod. '64 with Sammy DAVIS Jr and Hildegarde Neff (Kurt Muehlhardt dubbed in German version for Davis, Martha Schlamme in English for Neff); *Knickerbocker Holiday* '44 (with Charles Coburn singing 'September Song'), *Lady In The Dark* '44 (most of the songs cut), *One Touch Of Venus* '48 (watered down). Lenya became an international star as his interpreter: her recordings incl. songs from *Threepenny* and *Mahagonny* '28-30, now on Teldec; for CBS '56-60 she recorded *September Song And Other American Theatre Songs*, *Berlin Theatre Songs* now in 2-disc set with complete *Dreigroschenoper*, complete 3-disc *Mahagonny*, *Happy End* (incl. 'Surabaya Johnny', 'Bilbao'), *Seven Deadly Sins* (ballet with music written in Paris '33). Original cast of USA *Threepenny* '54 was once available on MGM. (Her film roles incl. SMERSH agent in James Bond film *From Russia With Love* '63, with poisoned blades in shoe tips.) An RCA LPV (Vintage series) LP '60s compiled *Lady In The Dark* on one side, *Down In The Valley* on the other; other Weill works/collections (by Teresa Stratas on Nonesuch, etc.) listed in classical sections of record catalogues. Weill scholar David Drew has helped with countless Weill projects/revivals; his *Kurt Weill: A Handbook* '87 has long been needed, will be followed by a full-scale biography. Tribute LP *Lost In The Stars: The Music Of Kurt Weill* on A&M incl. Marianne FAITHFULL, Van Dyke PARKS,

Lou REED, Carla BLEY, Phil WOODS, Tom WAITS, Todd RUNDGREN, Charlie HADEN, others.

WELK, Lawrence (*b* 11 Mar. '03, Strasburg, N.D.) Accordionist, bandleader. Began leading polka/sweet dance bands '20s; had about 20 hits with 'champagne music' incl. 'Bubbles In The Wine' '39 (band's theme); others were no. 2 'Don't Sweetheart Me' '44 (vocal by Wayne Marsh) backed with top 20 'Mairzy Doats' (vocal by Bobby Beers), a nonsense song that had five hit versions that year, and 'Shame On You' '45, vocal by Red FOLEY (last hit until '53). Welk had a regional TV show from '51, went national mid-'55 and stayed until '70s, becoming one of the biggest things on the tube with musical variety. He was a figure of fun for his corny music and for what appeared to be a Czech accent, but when ABC-TV cancelled the show '71 he prod. it himself and was carried by more stations than before. He was in fact a shrewd hard-working musician whose highly competent band could and did play anything; the secret of the programme was constant music, unrelieved by chat or celebrity egos. Myron Floren was featured accordionist; singers incl. the Lennon Sisters, Joe Feeney, Norma Zimmer, Alice Lon, Larry Hooper (with sepulchral voice: cover of Don HOWARD's 'Oh Happy Day' was Welk's return to national charts). Jazzmen playing with the band incl. Dick Cathcart on trumpet, Pete Fountain and Peanuts Hucko on clarinet, Mahlon Clark on reeds; later recorded with Johnny HODGES on Dot. 20 more hit singles '56-65 incl. no. 1 instrumental 'Calcutta' '60, with Frank Scott on harpsichord. He sold albums: 42 in top 200 '56; having recorded for Vocalion, Okeh and Decca on 78s (two 2-disc compilations now on MCA), he reached his fame on Coral, switched to Dot '60 and had several top 10 LPs incl. *Last Date, Calcutta, Moon River* and *Yellow Bird* '60-2 and several top 40 entries '63-4, many still in print on Ranwood (label formed by Randy Wood, who had formed Dot; *see* HILLTOPPERS): 40 albums on that label '87 incl. several 2-disc sets plus several polka sets with Floren, and they're still coming: *Dance To The Big Band Sounds* came out '87 on CD. The sound on the programmes and records was always excellent; there are a lot of people out there who like simple music played well. Best-selling autobiography *Wunnerful, Wunnerful*.

WELLS, Dicky (*b* William Wells, 10 June '07, Centerville, Tenn.; *d* 12 Nov. '85, NYC) Trombonist, composer; aka Dickie. Together with Jack TEAGARDEN, J. C. HIGGINBOTHAM, Jimmy HARRISON, among the most influential trombonists in the decades before J. J. JOHNSON. Like the saxophone until Coleman HAWKINS' time, the trombone was meant for comedy, playing a 'tailgate' role in New Orleans jazz, until technicians like these showed what could be done with it; Wells bravely put the comedy back in, but on a sophisticated level, always doing the unexpected. Invented his own 'pepperpot' mute. Humphrey LYTTELTON calls him best of all in an excellent chapter in Humphrey's *Enter The Giants*. Wells worked with many bands incl. Fletcher HENDERSON; starred on the Spike HUGHES sessions, made in NYC '33 when he was 23; another important LP is *Dicky Wells In Paris 1937* on Prestige; became famous with Count BASIE '38-'45: for Basie he wrote 'After Theatre Jump', several others; but the famous 'Dickie's Dream' was written for him by Lester YOUNG. With Sy OLIVER '46-7, Basie again '47-50, Jimmy RUSHING early '50s, toured Europe with Buck CLAYTON '59, '61; played with Ray CHARLES '61-3; freelanced but worked as bank messenger in Wall Street from '67. Mugged at least twice, suffered from alcoholism, but kept sense of humour, evident in autobiography *The Night People* '71, as told to Stanley Dance. Later '50s sessions incl. *Swinging The Blues* with Buck Clayton All Stars; *Trombone Four-In-Hand* and *Bones For The King*, now on Affinity UK; *Lonesome Road* '81 on Uptown with Buddy TATE.

WELLS, Junior (*b* Amos Blackmore, 9 Dec. '34, Memphis, Tenn.) Blues singer, plays harmonica; often works with guitarist/vocalist Buddy GUY. Taught himself harmonica, worked in streets for tips; to Chicago c.'46, worked outside music; from the late '40s worked in various groups called the Little Boys, the Three Deuces, the Three Aces; worked with Muddy WATERS (replacing LITTLE WALTER '52-3), MEMPHIS SLIM;

recorded with the Eagle Rockers on States '53-4, with Waters on Chess; toured USA clubs late '50s, worked with Guy '58 and frequently thereafter. Recorded on small labels Shad, Profile, Chief; with Guy on Chess '60-1; recorded for Vanguard mid-'60s (LPs *Comin' At You*, *It's My Life, Baby*; tracks on one volume of *Chicago/The Blues/Today*); toured Africa for US State Dept '67-8 and Far East '69; recorded with Guy on Atlantic '68; toured with CANNED HEAT incl. Bath, England, toured Europe with ROLLING STONES '70, recording for Barclay with Memphis Slim in France; appeared in UK film *Chicago Blues* '70, French films *Blues Under The Skin, Out Of The Blacks Into The Blues* '72; worked many jazz, blues and folk festivals: had become one of the most highly regarded Chicago bluesmen of his generation: recorded for Delmark; LP *Hoodoo Man Blues* '66 won a prize from *Jazz* magazine as best blues LP of the year, with 'Friendly Chap' on guitar, Jack Myers on bass, Billy Warren on drums, Wells' own tunes 'Snatch It Back And Hold It', 'In The Wee Wee Hours', 'Hoodoo Man Blues', fine version of classic 'Good Morning Schoolgirl', etc. Other Delmark LPs are *Southside Blues Jam, On Tap, Blues Hit The Big Town* (latter with Waters, etc.); portion of Tokyo concert '75 released on Bourbon label; States sides compiled on *Universal Rock* on Flyright; other LPs: *Chiefly Wells* on Flyright, *In My Younger Days* on Red Lightnin'* (compilation of tracks with Earl Hooker, etc.) and with Guy: *Original Blues Brothers – Live* on Blue Moon, *Drinking TNT And Smoking Dynamite* '74 on Sonet, with Bill Wyman on bass, Pinetop Perkins on piano, Dallas Taylor on drums.

WELLS, Kitty (*b* Muriel Deason, 30 Aug. '18, Nashville, Tenn.) Country singer. Sang in church as a child, began playing guitar at 14; sang on WXIX Dixie Early Birds show '36; married Johnny Wright '38; he suggested name change (from CARTER FAMILY's 'I'm A'Goin' To Marry Kitty Wells'). She raised a family, appeared on Grand Ole Opry '47, recorded for RCA, switched labels and joined Opry '52 when her first Decca record was first no. 1 country hit by a female artist since *Billboard* charts began: 'It Wasn't God Who Made Honky Tonk Angels' '52 was an answer song (to Hank

THOMPSON's 'Wild Side Of Life') but a good one (by J. B. Miller), eventually sold a million (it was also early evidence of feminism, though the bra-burners probably never heard of it). 'I Don't Want Your Money, I Want Your Time' was also an answer, to hit by Lefty FRIZZELL 'If You've Got The Money I've Got The Time'. There was little chance of Wells crossing over to a pop audience: infl. by Molly O'Day (*see* Art SATHERLEY) she sang in her Tennessee accent with an untrained country vibrato, but integrity, sincerity and choice of good songs led to over 50 country hits in '50s-60s (25 in top 10), over 450 singles and 40 albums released by '73: the acknowledged Queen of Country Music. 'Paying For That Back Street Affair' '53 was probably an answer to the Webb PIERCE hit; 'Makin' Believe' '55 was no. 2 (song by Jimmy Work, who had his own hit version on Dot '54, covered by Emmylou HARRIS '77), backed with 'Whose Shoulder Will You Cry On', co-written by Wells/Billy Wallace; 'Searching' '56 was no. 4, song by Pee Wee Maddux, backed by 'I'd Rather Stay Home', by Felice & Boudleaux BRYANT: her B sides were always worth a listen; several hits were two-sided: 'Lonely Side Of Town'/'I've Kissed You For The Last Time' '55; 'Repenting' (by Gary Walker) backed with Don ROBERTSON's 'I'm Counting On You' '56; 'She's No Angel' backed with Don GIBSON's 'I Can't Stop Loving You'. 'Jealousy' '58 made pop Hot 100; 'Amigo's Guitar' '59 co-written with John LOUDERMILK; 'Heartbreak U.S.A.' was no. 1 country hit '61. She had hit duets with Pierce, Red FOLEY (four in country top 10 '54-6), Roy DRUSKY and Wright ('We'll Stick Together' '68, the year of their 30th wedding anniversary). She was part of the Johnnie & Jack show until Jack's death ended that successful duo; the *Johnnie Wright-Kitty Wells Family Show* was syndicated on TV. She appeared on TV's *Ozark Jamboree*, Carl SMITH's *Country Music Hall*, Jimmy DEAN's show, Johnny Carson's *Tonight* show, many others; also film *Second Fiddle To A Steel Guitar*. Despite having signed 'lifetime' contract with Decca '59, she left MCA mid-'70s, made LP *Forever Young* '74 (title track written by Bob DYLAN). She was elected to Country Music Hall of Fame '76. Son Bobby Wright became singer, actor; *see also* JOHNNIE & JACK.

LPs and compilations on MCA, Vocalion incl. *Dust On The Bible* '59; also *The Golden Years* on Rounder; 5-disc *The Golden Years (1949-1957)* on German-based Bear Family label '87 incl. RCA tracks, with bonus EP nearly 100 selections.

WELLS, Mary (*b* 13 May '43, Detroit, Mich.) Soul singer: one of the first Motown stars and still many people's favourite. Began singing at age 10, sang in local clubs and talent contests. In Motown's early days the label held open auditions; she walked in hoping to sell a song; Berry Gordy bought song and singer at a time when Smokey ROBINSON was virtually the only other artist under contract: 'Bye Bye Baby' went top 50, first of 11 Hot 100 entries on Motown '61-4, incl. top tens 'The One Who Really Loves You', 'You Beat Me To The Punch' and 'Two Lovers', culminating with no. 1 classic 'My Guy', all written for her by Smokey: 'My Guy' was the first Tamla/Motown record to reach no. 1 in UK; admired by the BEATLES, she toured with them ('John Lennon was funny but always gentle to me, always respectful. I have a *hard* time with the fact that some fool murdered the man'). Lured by empty promise of a film contract she switched to 20th Century Fox (able to leave Motown because she'd been under age when she signed there); she had five hits on that label '64-5 but only 'Use Your Head' reached the top 20. Two minor hits on Atlantic/Atco '66 and one on Jubilee '68 saw her leave the pop chart, though she had two more top 40 hits '69 on Jubilee in the black chart (which in that year belatedly changed its name from Rhythm & Blues to Soul). She also recorded for Reprise and Epic; married Cecil Womack and raised three children; they were divorced and manager/companion became Curtis, another member of the WOMACK clan; years after her biggest success, playing oldies ('but goodies') shows, she realised fans' love for her would never die. Excellent profile in Gerri Hirshey's *Nowhere To Run: The Story Of Soul Music* '84; see also *Where Did Our Love Go?* '85, Motown story by Nelson George.

WELLSTOOD, Dick (*b* Richard MacQueen Wellstood, 25 Nov. '27, Greenwich, Conn.; *d* 24 July '87, Palo Alto, Cal.) Pianist in trad. style derived from James P. JOHNSON, etc. Also a good writer (e.g. of sleeve notes) and a qualified attorney. Came to fame playing in a band with Bob WILBER '46, played with Sidney BECHET in Chicago '47, played with Rex STEWART, Charlie SHAVERS etc.; at Nick's in NYC. Toured with World's Greatest Jazz Band; toured '80s in the Blue Three with Kenny Davern, drummer Bobby Rosengarden. Made many albums as sideman with Wilber, etc.; solo *From Ragtime On* '71, *At The Cookery* '75; *Dick Wellstood And His Famous Orchestra Featuring Kenny Davern* '74 (duo, Davern on soprano), *Ain't Misbehavin'* by sextet The Friends Of Fats '78 with Herman Autrey, Tommy BENFORD, all on Chiaroscuro; also solo *Alone* on Jazzology, sextet *Live Hot Jazz* '86 on Statiris with drummer Chuck Riggs (known for work with Scott HAMILTON) and Davern.

WEMBA, Papa (*b* Shungu Wembadia, '50s, Zaire) African singer, composer. First came to notice as leader and singer with 'new wave' outfit Orchestre Viva La Musica early '70s (compilation *L'Afrique Danse*) alongside other new bands such as ZAIKO and Les Trois Frères; as one of the strongest guardians of Zaire's musical traditions (despite eccentric appearance) he became a champion of the 'authenticité' movement of cultural identity; hit 'Analengo' incl. on *Papa Wemba et l'Orchestre Viva La Musica*. By the '80s he had left the band and recorded in Paris with the cream of Zaire's expatriate musicians: *Papa Wemba et les Djamukets de Paris* on Pass, *Firenze* '84 with Strervos Niarcos, then with Lita Bemba (ex-Stukas) in new Zaire super-group *La Guerre des Stars* on Tchika.

WEST, Dottie (*b* Dorothy Marie Marsh, 11 Oct. '32, McMinnville, Tenn.) Country/pop singer, songwriter. Raised on farm, oldest of 10 children; sang soprano in church choir; obtained degree in music, moved to Ohio, appeared as duo on local TV with first husband steel guitarist Bill West; recorded for Starday, Atlantic; success came on RCA, after song/jam sessions with Patsy CLINE, others; she learned from Roger MILLER, Willie NELSON, others; Jim Reeves recorded her 'Is This Me?' for no. 3 hit '63; her first hit 'Let Me Off At The Corner' was top 30 same year; duets with Jim Reeves incl. top 10 with Justin TUBB's 'Love Is No Excuse' '64 (she made an album with Reeves but he didn't want to tour; ironically, he was killed that year in a plane crash). Top 10 solo 'Here Comes My Baby' '64 was co-written with Bill, covered by Perry COMO, earned her a Grammy. She joined the Grand Ole Opry '64, had many hits incl. 'Would You Hold It Against Me' '66, 'Paper Mansions' '67, both top 10; 'Mommy, Can I Still Call Him Daddy?' was top 25 '66 as she and Bill divorced (she later married drummer Bryon Metcalf). Hit duets with Don GIBSON '69-70 incl. 'Rings Of Gold' (no. 2), 'There's A Story Goin' Round' '69 (no. 7). 'Country Girl' '68 was no. 15 hit, turned into Coca-Cola TV advert '70 that won awards, showing her tending a garden which turned out to be atop a skyscraper: her good looks, solid professional training paid off in crossover success; 'Country Sunshine' '73 was another Coke advert and reached top 50 of pop chart. Toured Europe, popular in UK; switched to United Artists '76, had big hit 'When It's Just You And Me'; duets with Kenny ROGERS incl. LPs *Classics* '79 and *Every Time Two Fools Collide* '81 (both crossed to pop chart; latter was no. 1 country LP), duet single 'What Are We Doin' In Love' went top 15 pop; her solo LP *Wild West* '81 made top 200 pop LPs; by now on Liberty, her *New Horizons* charted, single 'Tulsa Ballroom' reaching country top 40 '83; duet *Together Again* with Rogers was top 15 country hit '84; her singles came out on Permian and charted '84-5, but peak seemed to be past.

WESTBROOK, Mike (*b* Michael John David Westbrook, 21 Mar. '36, High Wycombe, Buckinghamshire, UK) Bandleader, composer, arranger; plays piano, tuba. Mainly self-taught. Heard jazz records at school; infl. by ELLINGTON, MONK, MINGUS etc. determined to become composer, has combined poetry, theatre etc. with jazz inspiration in large-scale works. Formed jazz workshop at Plymouth Art Centre '60; octet incl. John SURMAN, who became world-famous playing with Westbrook's Concert Band (formed '66), won Best Soloist award at Montreux '69. Co-led multi-media group Cosmic Circus '70-2; formed rock-oriented Solid Gold Cadillac '71-4, Brass Band '73

for cabaret on TV and in theatre. Kate Westbrook (*b* Katharine Jane Bernard, Guildford, Surrey) joined Brass Band '74; plays tenor horn, other instruments; also vocalist, adapting and singing texts in several languages. He formed Mike Westbrook Orchestra '79, she joined '81; they formed trio '82 (album *A Little Westbrook Music* '83 on Westbrook) with Chris Biscoe on reeds (*b* 5 Feb. '47, East Barnet, Herts.); formed Westbrook Theatre Music '84. Their various projects have involved from 10 to upwards of more than 26 pieces; 3-disc *The Cortege* '82 on Original won Montreux Grand Prix du Disque '82, texts adapted by Kate from Hesse, Lorca, Rimbaud, Blake etc. Other albums: *Celebration* '67, *Release* '68, *Marching Song* '69, all on Deram (latter incl. writing and arranging by Surman); *Metropolis* '71 and *Citadel/Room 315* '75 on RCA; *Mama Chicago* '79 on Teldec/RCA; solo *Mike Westbrook Piano* '78 and *The Westbrook Blake* '80 on Original; 2-disc *The Paris Album* '81 on Polydor (settings of Brecht-Weill, Blake etc.); *On Duke's Birthday* '85 on Hat Art; *Pier Rides* '86 with Kate speaking (uses Pierides, Greek name for muses, as title of set of chamber music dances, 'end-of-pier turns'); 2-disc *Westbrook Rossini* '87 on Hat Art uses concert band incl. two tubas, sopranino sax to play *William Tell Overture*, etc.

WESTERN SWING Country music genre infl. by jazz and often employing a large band, popular from mid-'30s to early '50s, itself still infl. today. Relationships between white and black rural musics and between country music and jazz is usually under emphasised: hot solos and improvisation have always been present in country music. Bob WILLS was the most important artist in Western Swing, enormously popular all over the Southwest from early '30s, partly as a result of radio sponsorship by flour mills, mineral water (Crazy Water Crystals), etc. Wills' fiddling transcended category and his band often resembled the typical swing band of the era; he wrote million-seller 'New San Antonio Rose' '40. Hank Penny, Milton Brown and his Musical Brownies were also popular; Spade COOLEY filled dance halls during WWII; in '50s Hank THOMPSON, later Buck OWENS led largish groups which were infl. by Western Swing, but it was wrecked by the same forces that put an end to the BIG BAND ERA: wartime entertainment tax, closure of ballrooms (in WWII because of petrol rationing, later because of competition from TV) and the economics of the road: it became impossible to keep a big band together permanently. ASLEEP AT THE WHEEL has kept the flame burning with a fine series of LPs; many musicians in country music can swing with the best. Compilations on Texas Rose label in '87 incl. *Milton Brown* ('34 tracks), *Light Crust Doughboys* ('36-9), *Bob Wills* ('32-41), *Cliff Bruner's Texas Wanderers* ('37-44). *See also* Wills' entry.

WESTON, Paul (*b* Paul Wetstein, 12 Mar. '12, Springfield, Mass.) Arranger, conductor, composer. Played piano and led dance band at Dartmouth College; arranged for Rudy VALLEE, Phil HARRIS, Joe Haymes; stayed with Tommy DORSEY '35-40 when Dorsey took over Haymes band; worked for Bob CROSBY '41-2, Dinah SHORE '42-3, joined new Capitol label '43 on staff, A&R dir. '44-50, Columbia Records (CBS/USA) '50-7, Capitol again '58. Mus. dir. on Johnny MERCER radio show '43, Chesterfield Supper Club show mid-'40s, also Duffy's Tavern, Paul Weston Show, etc.; mus. dir. on TV shows '60s-70s incl. Danny KAYE, many others. Accompanied Shore on Bluebird; Andy Russell, Jo STAFFORD, Dean MARTIN on Capitol; Doris DAY, Frankie LAINE on Columbia, others; married Stafford '52. Own hits on Capitol incl. show tunes, vocals by Margaret WHITING, Matt Dennis, others; also made albums of instrumentals; hits on Columbia '50-1 with the Norman Luboff Choir incl. no. 2 'Nevertheless (I'm In Love With You)'. Late hit was instrumental film theme 'Shane' '53. From '54 he collaborated with Stafford in comedy duo Jonathan & Darlene Edwards (*see* her entry); they now operate Corinthian label, keeping Stafford and Edwards LPs in print. He wrote 'I Should Care' ('45 hit for Dorsey), 'Shrimp Boats' ('51 hit for Stafford), others. His instrumental records on Columbia were masterpieces of their kind in the golden era of USA 'light music' (*see* MOOD MUSIC): rooted in the Swing Era and less orchestral than those of Percy FAITH, lightly swinging singles like 'Anna' (film theme), LPs like *Caribbean Cruise* were im-

peccably arranged, played and recorded for listening or dancing; others were *Mood Music By Paul Weston*, *Music For A Rainy Night*, *Moonlight Becomes You*. *Mood For 12* (12 tracks with first-class jazz soloists incl. Eddie Miller, George VAN EPS), similar *Solo Mood – Hi-Fi From Hollywood*. When he used strings he softened the rest of the band so as not to drown them out instead of amplifying the strings; the result was a chamber-music quality. Capitol work remade for stereo late '50s incl. *Carefree*, with refreshing sound of four flugelhorns, four trombones, four French horns, no reeds or strings. More ambitious work incl. *Crescent City* (now on Corinthian, with compilations *Easy Jazz*, *Cinema Cameos*). 2-disc *Columbia Album Of Jerome Kern* still on Columbia Special Products.

WESTON, Randy (*b* 6 Apr. '26, Brooklyn, NY) Pianist, composer, teacher with unique voice, infl. by Thelonious MONK, interest in African and West Indian music. Greatly underrated. Best-known tunes incl. 'Saucer Eyes', 'Hi-Fly', 'Little Niles', 'Babe's Blues', 'Cry Me Not', 'African Cook Book'. Worked with Art BLAKEY late '40s, others; led own trios-quartets since '55, playing many colleges, museums, festivals; visited Nigeria '61, '63; ran a club in Tangiers '70, back in USA '72. Recorded for UA, Jubilee, Dawn, Roulette, own Bakton label; Riverside LPs mid-'50s: *Get Happy*, *With These Hands*, *Jazz à la Bohemia*; *Zulu* was a 2-disc compilation on Milestone, sidemen incl. Blakey, Cecil PAYNE. Later LPs incl. *Blues '67* on Trip with Ray COPELAND, others; *Carnival* (made at Montreux with quintet; also solo 'Tribute To Ellington'), solo *Blues To Africa* on Arista/Freedom; *Tanjah* and *African Rhythms* on Polydor; *Blue Moses* on CTI; *African Cookbook* on Atlantic; solo *African Night* '75 on Owl/Inner City (also on Enja with two tracks missing).

WHAM! UK pop vocal duo: George Michael (*b* Yorgos Kyriatou Panayiotou, 25 June '63, Finchley, N. London) and Andrew Ridgeley (*b* 26 Jan. '63, Bushey, Herts.). Ridgeley also played guitar; Michael was the mastermind and songwriter; they became the acceptable face of conservative '80s UK pop: slick, debonair and massively successful. They came together in the Executives '79; demos incl. 'Careless Whisper' led to recording contract which turned out to be a nightmare when they hit big. 'Wham! Rap (Enjoy What You Do)' attracted attention; breakthrough came with 'Young Guns (Go For It)' at no. 3 '82, 'Bad Boys' at no. 2; LP *Fantastic* '83 displayed Motown-influenced white soul, escapist fantasies such as 'Club Tropicana' (no. 4 '83); just behind DURAN DURAN and SPANDAU BALLET in popularity, soon became the pin-ups of the decade with 'Wake Me Up Before You Go-Go', no. 1 both USA/UK '84; 'Freedom' and 'Last Christmas' were both UK no. ones; second album *Make It Big* '84 was mega-success. Michael's solo 'Careless Whisper' was USA/UK no. 1 and he was lead voice on the BAND AID single '84; in '85 he received the Ivor Novello Songwriter of the Year award, duetted with Elton JOHN at Live Aid. They were the first Western pop group to perform in China, leading to contentious video *Under Foreign Skies*. Tabloid press couldn't get enough; Michael seemed unhappy with incessant interest but Ridgeley was ideal fodder, crashing racing cars and squiring series of pretty girls. Michael was also unhappy with management company's South African links, announced Wham! split early '86: farewell show was at Wembley mid-'86; 'I'm Your Man' and 'The Edge Of Heaven' were both no. 1, as was Michael's solo 'A Different Corner'; 2-disc best-of *The Final* was predictable success. Ridgeley concentrated on acting and racing career; Michael duetted with Aretha FRANKLIN on her LP *Aretha*; first solo LP *Faith* '87 incl. hit 'I Want Your Sex' '87, partially banned despite plea that it was paean to monogamy. Critical opinion was divided on whether he was a pop genius or a pretty flash in the pan; time will tell: commercially he was one of the biggest acts in the world in '88.

WHEATSTRAW, Peetie (*b* William Bunch, 21 Dec. '02, Ripley, Tenn.; *d* 21 Dec. '41, East St Louis, Ill.) Blues singer; played guitar, piano; aka 'The Devil's Son-In-Law', 'High Sheriff From Hell'. Hoboed through South late '20s; teamed with Big Joe WILLIAMS to operate a club in St Louis c.'39; killed in car crash. Recorded for Vocalion '30-1, Bluebird '31, Vocalion again '32, '34; Decca '34, mostly Decca to Nov. '41: more

than 160 sides altogether, usually playing piano and accompanied by a guitarist, incl. Charlie McCoy, Kokomo ARNOLD, Lonnie JOHNSON, '40-1 by Lil ARMSTRONG on piano plus (on a '40 date) Jonah JONES and Big Sid CATLETT. Recorded every year straight through the Depression except '37: the records must have sold fairly well, yet reissues have been rare; 16 tracks '30-6 appeared on a Flyright LP '74 in UK.

WHEELER, Doc Front man for cooperative band the Sunset Royals, for tour of USA south with INK SPOTS. Doc Wheeler's Sunset Royal Serenaders cut Tommy DORSEY '36 in Philadelphia theatre (according to Nov. '37 review in *Metronome*); Dorsey traded eight arrangements for 'Marie'; recorded it Jan. '37 and had one of the biggest hits of the Swing Era. Band later incl. Cat ANDERSON '38-41, whose 'How 'Bout That Mess' it recorded for Bluebird '41. (Cat changed title to 'Swinging The Cat' for record with own band '47.) Later Wheeler became MC at the Apollo theatre, top gospel and R&B disc jockey in New York.

WHEELER, Kenny (*b* 14 Jan. '30, Toronto, Canada) Trumpet, cornet, flugelhorn; composer. Grew up in same small town (St Catharines) as Gene LEES; from musical family; began on cornet at 12, studied at Toronto Conservatory; to UK '52, played in big bands of Roy Fox, Vic Lewis, then with John DANKWORTH '59-65; began composing and arranging. Studied with British composer Richard Rodney Bennett; played with Ronnie SCOTT, Joe HARRIOTT, Tubby HAYES, CLARKE-BOLAND BIG BAND. With complete mastery over trumpet range and turning to 'free' jazz, worked with John STEVENS' Spontaneous Music Ensemble, Globe Unity Orchestra, Anthony BRAXTON Quartet, other groups; co-founder of trio AZIMUTH '77, joined United Jazz And Rock Ensemble '79, played in Dave HOLLAND Quintet since '83; toured UK with international George RUSSELL band '85. Composes for groups of all sizes, incl. Rome, Helsinki, Stockholm radio orchestras; also active as educator. Own LPs incl. big band *The Windmill Tilter* '68 on Fontana; *Song For Someone* '73 on Incus; *Gnu High* '76 (quartet with Keith JARRETT, Jack DeJOHNETTE, Holland), *Deer Wan* '78 (with Jan Garbarek,

Holland, John Abercrombie, DeJohnette), *Around Six* '80 (sextet), *Double, Double You* '84 (quintet with Mike BRECKER, John Taylor, Holland, DeJohnette), all on ECM. Pianist Taylor, Stan Sulzmann on reeds made lovely duo LP of Wheeler compositions *Everybody's Song But My Own* '87 on Loose Tubes; Wheeler quintet with Holland, Taylor, Sulzman, drummer Billy Elgart made *Flutter By, Butterfly* on Soul Note. *See also* AZIMUTH, Dave HOLLAND.

WHITE, Andrew (*b* Andrew Nathaniel White III, 6 Sep. '42, Washington DC) Alto and tenor saxes, oboe, English horn, electric bass; composer, lecturer. Much formal study followed by scholarly work incl. transcription of over 200 John COLTRANE solos for publication. Played double reed instruments with American Ballet Theatre Orchestra of New York; played and/or recorded with Kenny CLARKE (in Paris), Stanley TURRENTINE, Otis REDDING, Stevie WONDER, McCoy TYNER (*Asante* on Blue Note), many others. More than 25 LPs on his own Andrew's Music label in Washington DC incl. six- and nine-disc sets; wind quintet, concerto for 16 instruments etc. listed in Schwann's classical section. Runs zany adverts e.g. in *Cadence* magazine, but did not answer a postal query, so it's impossible to know who else is on the LPs or anything about them except what can be gleaned from the Schwann catalogue and his adverts: two vols. of *Live In New York* said to be the only recordings made during the 'loft war' of mid-'77, at the Ladies' Fort Jazz Loft, with Donald Waters, piano; Steve Novosel, bass; Bernard Sweeney, drums.

WHITE, Barry (*b* 12 Sep. '44, Galveston, Texas) Pop/soul singer, voice described as sounding like chocolate cake tastes; also keyboardist, producer, arranger. Grew up in L.A. Recorded on Lummtone '60 with Upfronts vocal group; A&R man for Mustang/Bronco '66-7; formed girl trio Love Unlimited '69 incl. his future wife Glodean James, with her sister Linda and Diana Taylor; they had no. 14 hit '72 'Walkin' In The Rain With The One I Love', with his voice on telephone; their no. 3 LP *Under The Influence Of . . .* '73 still in print (another LP was called *In Heat*). 40-piece Love Unlimited Orchestra had instru-

mental no. 1 hit '73 'Love's Theme' from orchestra's *Rhapsody In White* (top 10 LP '74). Under his own name he used unusual voice in romantic chat, e.g. 'Can't Get Enough Of Your Love, Babe' '74, at no. 1 the biggest of six top 10 singles '73-7 in USA, from no. 1 LP *Can't Get Enough*; 12 other LPs charted '73-82. Most of this was written/produced by White on 20th Century Fox; his *Beware* is on Unlimited Gold; two vols. of his *Greatest Hits* on Casablanca. Came back with *The Right Now Barry White* '87, more slick studio product.

WHITE, Bukka (*b* Booker T. Washington White, 12 Nov. '06, Houston, Ms.; *d* 26 Feb. '77, Memphis, Tenn.) Blues singer, guitarist; also played piano, harmonica. Learned guitar from his father, then piano as a child. Worked in and outside music, in St Louis early '20s, hoboed through South; made 14 sides for Victor '30 as Washington White (only four issued then) with Napoleon Hairiston on second guitar, 'Miss Minnie' second vocalist. Worked as professional boxer and baseball player mid-'30s; made two sides for Vocalion '37: 'Pinebluff, Arkansas' and 'Shake 'Em On Down', latter henceforth a classic with many variants ('Ride 'Em On Down', etc.). Sentenced to Parchman Farm for assault, recorded by John LOMAX there '39 for Library of Congress (offered no money, he refused to make more than two sides); after release he made 12 more sides '40 with Washboard Sam for Okeh and Vocalion incl. 'Parchman Farm Blues', 'Where Can I Change My Clothes' (protest at prison garb), 'District Attorney Blues', etc. His rough-hewn voice, passionate but not overstated style, driving and rhythmically inexorable guitar made some of the most beautiful and emotionally powerful music in the genre, 14 tracks compiled on *Parchman Farm/Bukka White* by Columbia USA c.'70, unbelievably out of print '87. This was at the end of classic period of country blues; he was rediscovered '63 with much power intact by John FAHEY and Ed Denson, who recorded him that year in Memphis: *Legacy Of The Blues Vol. 1* on GNP USA, Sonet in Europe, playing piano on 'Drunk Man Blues' and remembering Charley PATTON in conversation. Other LPs: two vols. of *Sky Songs* on Arhoolie, *Mississippi Blues* on

Takoma, *Big Daddy* '70s on Biograph USA, Blue Moon UK. Washboard Sam (*b* Robert Brown, 15 July '10, Walnut Ridge, Ark.; *d* 13 Nov. '66, Chicago) was prolific sideman and recording artist; '41-2 tracks with his Washboard Band (incl. Big Bill BROONZY and MEMPHIS SLIM) issued '71 in RCA Vintage Series; '53 tracks with Broonzy, Slim and others issued on Chess '87. 'Miss Minnie' was probably Memphis Minnie, who recorded the same day (*b* Lizzie Douglas, 3 June 1897, Algiers, La.; *d* 6 Aug. '73, Memphis); acknowledged by contemporaries as one of the greatest female blues singers, she recorded prolifically, incl. with husbands Charlie McCoy and Little Son Joe (*b* Ernest Lawlers, 18 May 1900, Hughes, Ark.; *d* 14 Nov. '61, Memphis), but reissues have been few: *World Of Trouble* on Flyright from Chicago in early '50s.

WHITE, Josh (*b* Joshua Daniel White, 11 Feb. '08, Greenville, Ms.; *d* 5 Sep. '69, Manhasset, NY) Blues/folk singer, guitarist. Some sources give year of birth as '14 or '15. Father was Baptist clergyman; left home working as eyes for blind street singers incl. Blind Lemon JEFFERSON. To NYC c.'30; played Jefferson in play *John Henry* (starring Paul ROBESON), recorded for ARC labels (chiefly Banner) '32-6, secular material as Pinewood Tom (or Tippy Barton) to avoid offending his family, spirituals as Joshua White (The Singing Christian). Dixon and Godrich's *Blues & Gospel Records 1902-1943* says that 'From this point Josh White's recordings become increasingly inclined to commercialism, and are only included for completeness.' This means that his experience, his self-confidence and his diction allowed him to transcend his social condition as a black and to become a top cabaret artist. He made two 12" 78 sides for Blue Note '40 as the Josh White Trio, with Sidney BECHET on clarinet, Wilson Myers on bass; spirituals for Columbia as Josh White and his Carolinians (with Bayard Rustin, first tenor); sang with the Golden Gate Quartet (concert in Coolidge Auditorium, Washington DC partly recorded by Library of Congress; tour of Mexico '41), had NBC radio show with group the Southernaires; stayed three years at Café Society Uptown club in NYC and sang at Franklin Roosevelt's White House; in mid-'40s broadcast for the Office of War Information and had show on WNEW New York. Recorded for Keynote '41, on one side with the Almanac Singers incl. Pete SEEGER, Woody GUTHRIE; other tracks incl. 'Bad Housing Blues', 'Jim Crow Train', 'Southern Exposure', 'Uncle Sam Says', 'Defence Factory Blues' etc. Having associated with all these leftwingers and recorded songs overtly about being black in the USA he was not much liked by the professional anti-communist brigade in Congress postwar, but as a black cabaret artist he was not likely to have any top 10 hits anyway. Recorded for Decca (2-disc *Legendary* now on MCA), Stinson (2-disc *Sings The Blues*), Tradition (issued *In Memoriam* after he died), Mercury (*Live At Town Hall*), Period (with Big Bill BROONZY), ABC-Paramount (two vols. of *The Josh White Story* etc.) but longest association was with Elektra: albums *Josh At Midnight* and *Josh* late '50s incl. songs like Cole PORTER's 'Miss Otis Regrets'; 'One Meat Ball' (by Hy Zaret and Lou Singer '44) which White did with pantomimist Jimmy Savo, about a down-and-out who's only got a dime and is loudly told 'You gets no bread with one meat ball'; affecting song about a man who wakes up at night to find his wife's not there, but she's just 'Turnin' The Children In The Bed'. Other Elektra LPs were *Chain Gang Songs* '59, *Spirituals And Blues* '61, *The House I Live In* '62, others. His folk music was slick but it had kept the flame alive in the '50s; he remained popular (appeared on TV's *Hootenanny*), was badly injured in a car crash, died three years later during open-heart surgery. His son Josh White Jr (*b* Joshua Donald White, '40) received award as Best Child Actor on Broadway in *How Long Till Summer?* '47; more plays, appearances on TV as singer and straight dramatic roles in TV plays; wrote music for documentary *The Freedom Train* '67; LPs *Josh White Jr* '78 on Vanguard, *Sing A Rainbow* on Mountain Railroad, *Jazz, Ballads & Blues (A Tribute To Josh White Sr)* '87 on Rykodisc.

WHITE, Tony Joe (*b* 23 July '43, Oak Grove, La.) Singer/songwriter, one of the few authentic practitioners of the short-lived swamp-rock genre. Played in Tony & the Mojos in teen years, moved to Texas and led Tony & the Twilights, worked solo for some years, signed with Monument in Nashville '68 and was prod. by Billy SWAN: debut *Black And White* '69 incl. White's originals 'Polk Salad Annie', top 10 hit later covered by Elvis PRESLEY, 'Willie And Laura Mae Jones', covered by Dusty SPRINGFIELD, and several covers . . . *Continued* also charted '69; this time all the tunes were originals incl. 'Rainy Night In Georgia', covered by Brook BENTON. *Tony Joe* '70 incl. seven originals (of 11 songs), top 30 UK hit 'Groupy Girl' but failed to make top 200 LPs in USA; he switched to WB, where *Tony Joe White* '71 was prod. by Peter ASHER, briefly charted; *The Train I'm On* '72 prod. by Jerry Wexler and Tom DOWD incl. well-known 'I've Got A Thing About You Baby'; *Home Made Ice Cream* '73, prod. by Dowd and White himself, was full of collaborative songs. *Eyes* '77 appeared on 20th Century, *Real Thing* '80 on Casablanca, *Dangerous* '83 on CBS, *Roosevelt & Ira Lee* c.'84 on Astan.

WHITEMAN, Paul (*b* 28 Mar. 1890, Denver, Col.; *d* 29 Dec. '67, Doylestown, Pa.) Bandleader. Played violin and viola in Denver and San Francisco symphony orchestras, served in WWI, formed band '19 with arr./pianist Ferde Grofe, Henry BUSSE on trumpet and had well over 200 hits through to '36, mostly on Victor: the two-sided 'Whispering'/'Japanese Sandman' sold over two million, 'Wang Wang Blues' featuring Busse sold another, all three titles no. 1 '20. Easily the most popular bandleader before the Big Band Era, he saw the end of the sentimental songs and corny comedy that had dominated the recording industry until then, while Grofe helped to invent the big dance band. According to *Pop Memories* (see CHARTS) he had 28 no. 1 records '20-34, incl. 'Hot Lips' '22 (with Busse), 'Three O'Clock In The Morning' '22, 'My Blue Heaven' '27 (with Red NICHOLS on trumpet, vocal quintet incl. Bing CROSBY), 'Ol' Man River' '28 (Crosby solo vocal), 'All Of Me' '32 (with Mildred BAILEY), 'Smoke Gets In Your Eyes' '33 (with Bunny BERIGAN). Whiteman was called the King of Jazz, which he was not, but hired great sidemen while pianist/arr. Bill Challis (joined '28) left space for hot solos: 'San' '28 is a small-group side with J. DORSEY, Bix

BEIDERBECKE, Frankie TRUMBAUER, Challis, six more. Sidemen who passed through incl. Jack TEAGARDEN, Tommy DORSEY, Joe VENUTI, Eddie LANG, Red McKENZIE, Miff Mole, later vocalist Johnny MERCER. Most hits '34-8 incl. Teagarden, such as 'I'm Comin' Virginia' '38 (on Decca); 'Trav'lin' Light' '42 incl. Billie HOLIDAY (as 'Lady Day') and 'The Old Music Master' '43 had vocal duo of Mercer and Teagarden, last hits (on Capitol) until remake of 'Whispering' '54 (on Coral) made top 30. Whiteman commissioned George GERSHWIN's *Rhapsody In Blue* and conducted the sensational premiere '24, orchestrated by Grofe: acoustic recording '24, electrical remake '27 (cond. by Nat SHILKRET) were both top 10 hits on 12" 78s. Rhythm Boys vocal trio late '20s incl. Crosby, Barry Harris, Al Rinker (Mildred Bailey's brother). The band appeared in Broadway musicals *George White's Scandals Of 1922* (had no. 1 hit with 'I'll Build A Stairway To Paradise'), *Lucky* '27, *Jumbo* '35; films *King Of Jazz* '30, *Thanks A Million* '35, *Strike Up The Band* '40, *Atlantic City* '44, *Rhapsody In Blue* '45. Had *Paul Whiteman's Teenagers* TV show early '50s; hosted Jackie GLEASON summer replacement TV show '55, presenting other bands. Co-wrote songs 'Wonderful One' '22, 'Charlestonette' '25, 'My Fantasy' '40 (based on A. Borodin), etc.; had radio shows with Al JOLSON '33-4, Kraft Music Hall '34-5; own *Music Varieties* show '36, etc. In *Pop Memories*' calculation he was the second best-selling recording artist of 1890-1954 after Crosby. Compilation LPs *Concert 1927-32* on Sunbeam, *Tribute To Gershwin 1936* on Mark 56, *With Bing Crosby* on Columbia ('28-31); many others out of print. His style became old-fashioned because superseded by the big band jazz of Don REDMAN, Fletcher HENDERSON and others; but Whiteman prepared the ground and will always be remembered by tracks on Beiderbecke compilations: he kept Bix's chair open until Bix's death.

WHITESNAKE UK heavy metal group formed '78 by ex-DEEP PURPLE vocalist David Coverdale. On demise of Purple '78 he made solo LPs *White Snake* and *North Winds* '77-8, despite being prohibited contractually from playing live; when this constraint was removed he formed band named after first LP and led by guitarist Mick Moody (ex-Snafu, Juicy Lucy) who'd met Coverdale at art school years before in Middlesbrough. Other members were guitarist Bernie Marsden (ex-UFO, Wild Turkey, Babe Ruth), drummer Dave 'Duck' Dowle on drums and Brian Johnson on keyboards (both ex-Streetwalkers) and bassist Neil Murray (ex-Colosseum II and National Health). Pete Solly depped for Johnson; Coverdale left Purple's label for UA; ex-Purple Jon Lord played keyboards on bluesy *Trouble* '78; ex-Purple Ian Paice replaced Dowle soon after. EP *Snake Bite* '78, LP *Love Hunter* '79 continued mining blues-rock vein that existed long before Purple; *Ready An' Willing* '80 made no. 6 UK LP chart with top 20 'Fool For Your Loving'; as titles and sleeve artwork showed, Coverdale had no compunction about playing HM's macho role to the hilt. *Live . . . In The Heart Of The City* '80 captured impressive live act from '78-80 shows; *Come An' Get It* '81 incl. second top 20 in 'Don't Break My Heart Again'; *Saints And Sinners* '82 (top 10 LP) was last from this lineup. Murray was replaced by ex-Back Door bassist Colin Hodgkinson, Paice by Cozy Powell (from Rainbow, another Purple spinoff); Mel Galley (*b* 8 Mar. '48; ex-Trapeze) replaced Marsden, who formed own group Alaska but shared writing credits with Coverdale for *Slide It In* '84; Murray retired '82, replaced early '84 by ex-THIN LIZZY axeman John Sykes (*b* 29 July '59), while Murray rejoined; all this led to re-recording of parts of *Slide It In* for USA release, and two versions of the same LP played by different lineups. Lord's departure for re-formed Purple reduced them to a quartet; Powell's leaving to join EMERSON, LAKE & Powell necessitated rethink. Coverdale made eponymous solo LP, had hit 'In The Heat Of The Night'. There had been four more top 40 Whitesnake singles in UK, but following was maintained by heavy touring and band made little impact in USA; Coverdale's vocal skill is unquestioned, but blues-rock seam may be petering out.

WHITFIELD, David (*b* 2 Feb. '25, Hull, England; *d* 16 Jan. '80, Sydney, Australia) Pop singer, a tenor with operatic quality voice. Entertained in Royal Navy; began record-

ing for Decca '53, made UK top 10 with 'Bridge Of Sighs', written towards the end of a long career by Billy Reid, who also wrote 'I'm Walking Beside You', 'It's A Pity To Say Good Night', etc. Also had UK no. 1 '53 with German song 'Answer Me' (Frankie LAINE topped UK chart at the same time with the same song). About 20 UK hits incl. second no. 1 'Cara Mia' '54, written by Lee Lange and Tulio Trapino, pseudonyms for MANTOVANI (who conducted on the record) and Bunny Lewis, Whitfield's recording manager; it was the first hit by a British male singer to reach no. 1 in USA. A couple of others also charted in USA, but hits dried up '60; *My Heart And I* '61 was a light classical album; he turned to an operatic career '63; his voice made him welcome world-wide: when he died he was working on cruise ships around Australia.

WHITING, Margaret (*b* 22 July '24, Detroit, Mich.) Superior pop singer of '40s-early '50s. Daughter of songwriter Richard Whiting (*b* 12 Nov. 1891, Peoria, Ill.; *d* 10 Feb. '38, Beverly Hills, Cal.), who wrote 'Till We Meet Again', 'Sleepytime Gal', 'Miss Brown To You', 'She's Funny That Way', many others; worked with Johnny MERCER, Gus Kahn, etc. She sang on the radio '41 with Mercer, had hits with bands of Freddie SLACK ('That Old Black Magic'), Billy BUTTERFIELD ('Moonlight In Vermont'), Paul WESTON ('It Might As Well Be Spring'); her own string of more than 40 hits '46-54 on Capitol, the last of which was a remake of 'Moonlight'. Biggest hits incl. 'Now Is The Hour', 'A Tree In The Meadow', 'Far Away Places', all no. 1 or 2 '48; then teamed with Jimmy WAKELY for smash hit with Floyd TILLMAN song 'Slippin' Around', no. 1 '49; the other side 'Wedding Bells Will Soon Be Ringing' was also top 30; they had other duet hits (see his entry). She toured '72-4 with Cavalcade of Bands, incl. Freddy MARTIN, Bob CROSBY, Frankie CARLE.

WHITMAN, Slim (*b* Otis Dewey Whitman Jr, 20 Jan. '24, Tampa, Fla.) Country singer with yodelling style; one of the first cross-over artists and an international star, bigger in UK than he is at home. Played pro baseball, worked in a shipyard and as a mailman, making regular appearances on radio

(WDAE and WHBU in Tampa '47). Signed with RCA but had no hits; appeared on *Louisiana Hayride* in Shreveport, signed with Imperial and had no. 2 country, no. 10 pop hit '52 with 'Indian Love Call' (written by Rudolph FRIML for operetta *Rose-Marie* '24, words by Otto HARBACH and Oscar Hammerstein II). Further top 10 country hits incl. 'Keep It A Secret', 'North Wind', 'Secret Love', 'Rose Marie' '52-4; title song from the operetta was no. 1 for a record-breaking 11 weeks in UK '55 and *Pop Memories* (see CHARTS) says it deserved a top 25 spot in the USA. 'The Cattle Call' '55 was a top 10 country hit suiting his yodel (other hit versions by Jimmy WAKELY '42, Eddy ARNOLD '55); on tour of UK he played to packed theatres for a year and his career suffered at home: he had no more country hits until '61, though charming version of 'I'll Take You Home Again Kathleen' (by Will Oakland, '12) reached top pop Hot 100 '57, backed with 'Lovesick Blues' (reminiscent of the big Hank WIL-LIAMS hit); at about the same time he recorded 'Careless Love' ('Loveless Love', by W. C. HANDY), with male harmony backing and a dixielandish muted trumpet, a sort of restrained rollick. 'Indian Love Call' and 'China Doll' were issued in UK '55 and both hit; other hits '56-7 incl. 'Kathleen'; he had no more chart singles in UK except 'Happy Anniversary' '74, but returned to the USA country chart and was a steady seller for years, rarely in the top 10; often recorded standards and pop songs such as 'Twelfth Of Never', 'My Happiness', 'It's A Sin To Tell A Lie', 'It's All In The Game'. By this time Imperial had been taken over by United Artists. In late '70s he was popular in UK all over again, found TV-advertised albums selling well in both UK and USA; signed new contract with Epic/Cleveland. Many reissues and compilations incl. boxed set *The Slim Whitman Story* on World in UK '81, 2-disc *One Of A Kind* '86 on Pair, others on Liberty, Hallmark etc.

WHITTAKER, Roger (*b* 22 Mar. '36, Nairobi, Kenya) Singer, songwriter, guitarist, whistler. Born of British parents, studied medicine in Capetown, S.A., then marine biology at Bangor, Wales '59-62; performed in Kenya between terms, had minor hit 'Steel Man' and switched to music. After 25 years of sellout tours in Europe and North America he might be the most popular singer in the world currently working, although many people have never heard of him: dubbed 'king of the middle-of-the-road' by one critic. Represented Britain at Knokke Festival in Belgium '67 and won; entries 'Mexican Whistler' and 'If I Were A Rich Man' went top 3 in Europe, did nothing anywhere else; then 'Durham Town (The Leavin')' was no. 12 UK and he was on his way. Writes most of his own material; lives in England but retains ties to Africa, singing 'Save The Rhino' on tour '87. Seven chart LPs in UK '70-81 mostly on EMI/Columbia incl. compilations, *Best Of* '75 reaching no. 5; six chart LPs in USA '75-81 incl. *The Last Farewell And Other Hits* '75, 2-disc *Live In Concert* '81 at no. 177, all on RCA. Also had UK top 10 hit duet 'The Skye Boat Song' '86 with TV entertainer Des O'Conner, also so middle-of-the-road he blends with the woodwork.

WHO, The The most prominent UK rock band of the '60s after the BEATLES and ROLLING STONES: vocalist Roger Daltrey (*b* 1 Mar. '44); vocalist, guitarist, songwriter Pete Townshend (*b* 19 May '45), John Entwistle (*b* 9 Oct. '44), bass and French horn; Keith Moon (*b* 23 Aug. '47; *d* 7 Sep. '78) on drums, replaced by Kenny Jones (ex-SMALL FACES). All the original members were from London; Entwistle and Daltrey were schoolfriends, played in the Detours '60, joined by Townshend '63 from art school; name changed to the High Numbers after which Moon joined. They made one coveted single 'I'm The Face', which established them. Managers Chris Stamp and Kit Lambert (son of Constant Lambert, composer and critic who published *Music Ho! A Study Of Music In Decline* '34) changed their name to the Who; Lambert encouraged Townshend to become their chief writer, though Daltrey remained lead vocalist and focal point. They were the archetypal Mod band; early stage set consisted of R&B covers; singles 'I Can't Explain' and 'Anyway, Anyhow, Anywhere' appealed; breakthrough came with Townshend's anthemic 'My Generation' (no. 2 UK '65), LP of that title capturing live act. Helped by spots on TV's *Ready,*

Steady, Go and legendary auto-destructive live shows they became prime Pop Art band, helped by hits like acerbic 'Substitute', 'I'm A Boy', 'Happy Jack' (latter top 25 USA). With the KINKS' Ray Davies, Townshend became UK's leading pop writer, proved by *A Quick One* '66, with mini-opera of title, plaintive 'So Sad About Us'. *The Who Sell Out* '67 was best to date, with psychedelic 'Armenia City In The Sky' and 'Real'; innovative use of adverts between tracks to give feel of pirate Radio London predated Sigue Sigue Sputnik by 20 years. Explosive appearance at Monterey Pop Festival '67 established them in USA and they toured heavily incl. stunning set at Woodstock '69. Townshend's magnum opus and rock's first opera was *Tommy* '69, which soon became a millstone; its strengths were 'Pinball Wizard' and 'See Me, Feel Me' (it become orchestrated LP '72 with London Symphony Orchestra, Rod STEWART, Sandy DENNY, Steve WINWOOD; was filmed by Ken Russell '75). He couldn't top it, watched derivative rock operas follow it, abandoned 'Lifehouse' project, returned to elementary strengths with *Live At Leeds* '70, still one of rock's best live LPs, salvaged some songs from 'Lifehouse' for *Who's Next* '71, which many regard as their best, incl. 'Baba O'Riley', 'Behind Blue Eyes', 'Won't Get Fooled Again'. 2-disc *Quadrophenia* '73 was further concept, more down to earth than *Tommy*, a retrospective on the ideology fuelling the Mod movement. With hiatus in group, Entwistle compiled *Odds And Sods* '74, an 'authorised bootleg' cull of back catalogue incl. rare first single. *The Who By Numbers* '75 was patchy, 2-disc *Story Of The Who* '76 a good compilation; *Who Are You* '78 pulled band back together, notable for title track and 'Love Is Coming Down'. Moon had released idiosyncratic solo *Two Sides Of The Moon*; he died of overdose of a drug he was taking to control alcoholism; Kenny Jones joined but Townshend admitted later they should have quit. 2-disc *The Kids Are Alright* '79 was soundtrack of film history: media-conscious from the beginning, they had seen to it that much film footage survived. 2-disc *Quadrophenia* '79 was soundtrack of film of '73 album, which gave early acting role to Sting (POLICE). During USA tour '79 11 fans were killed in crush outside Cincinnati stadium. The Who were one of the few bands who escaped punk backlash of late '70s, named as influence by SEX PISTOLS, CLASH, the JAM. *Face Dances* '81 had hit single 'You Better You Bet', also 'Don't Let Go The Coat'; *It's Hard* '82 was spirited final album with surprisingly strong selection of material; always determined unlike the Beatles to be a working band, they went out with an exhaustive USA tour that year. Other good compilations are *Meaty, Beaty, Big & Bouncy* '71, *The Who: Singles LP* '84; best book is *Before I Get Old* '83 by Dave Marsh. Entwistle made solo *Smash Your Head Against The Wall* '71, *Whistle Rhymes* '72, *Rigor Mortis* '73, *Mad Dog* '75 and *Too Late The Hero* '81; Daltrey had solo no. 5 UK hit 'Giving It All Away' '73 (written by Leo SAYER), made LPs *Ride A Rock Horse* '75, *One Of The Boys* '77, *After The Fire* '85, *Can't Wait To See The Movie* '87; acted in Russell's *Lisztomania* '75, TV Shakespeare, film *McVicar* '80 (soundtrack single 'Free Me' went top 40). Townshend's songs have been covered by David BOWIE, Tina TURNER, Elton JOHN, Billy FURY, many others; after *Happy Birthday* '70 and *I Am* '72, privately made for followers of guru Meher Baba, his first proper solo was *Who Came First* '72, incl. 'Let's See Action' (first official example of a Townshend demo for the Who), cover of Jim REEVES' 'There's A Heartache Following Me', Baba's favourite song. He oversaw Eric CLAPTON's comeback show in London '73, played own solo shows '74; *Rough Mix* '77 was collaboration with FACES' Ronnie Lane, also Baba follower. He joined Paul McCARTNEY onstage for Kampuchean benefit '79, also appeared at charity shows for AMNESTY INTERNATIONAL, Rock Against Racism and the Princes Trust; founded Magic Bus bookshop in Richmond, Surrey '78, leading to Eel Pie publishing imprint. *Empty Glass* '80 was considerable solo work, improvement on the Who's work of the period, incl. 'Rough Boys' and 'Let My Love Open The Door' (USA top 10). He kicked heroin habit, went into alcoholic stupor, pulled himself together and made *(All The Best Cowboys Have) Chinese Eyes* '82, with BIG COUNTRY's rhythm section, fine originals incl. bouncy 'Uniforms', vitriolic 'Exquisitely Bored', poignant 'The Sea Refuses No River'. 2-disc *Scoop* '83 featured legendary demos for the Who, works in progress, instrumental bits, songs culled from 20 years. Joined Faber & Faber (T. S. Eliot's old firm) as commissioning editor, himself published *Horse's Neck* '85, a collection of short prose. *White City* '85 was ambitious album and video project. He worked with his Double-O anti-drug charity, worked with band Deep End incl. Ian Gilmour; *Deep End Live* '86 incl. 'Behind Blue Eyes', 'Pinball Wizard'; *Another Scoop* '87 was further collection of demos. Edgily over 40, he remains venerated by rock fans for polymath energies.

WILBER, Bob (*b* Robert Sage Wilber, 15 Mar. '28, NYC) Clarinet, saxophones, leader. Played with Dick WELLSTOOD while still in school; studied with both Sidney BECHET and Lennie TRISTANO, setting a pattern: first-class musician who refuses to be limited to this or that genre, feeling strongly that the proper home of jazz is in mainstream of popular music. He played dixieland (*Bob Wilber And His Famous Jazz Band Featuring Sidney Bechet* recorded '50s, now on Jazzology); formed cooperative group The Six '54-6, an attempt to create a music neither old-fashioned nor self-consciously modern; toured UK with Eddie CONDON, played with Bobby HACKETT (doubling on vibes); freelanced with Ruby BRAFF, Bud FREEMAN, Benny GOODMAN, others. Yank Lawson, Bob Haggart (*see* Bob CROSBY) had formed Lawson – Haggart Jazz Band for records in '50s; Dick Gibson promoted it from his Colorado Jazz Parties as the World's Greatest Jazz Band from '68, of which Wilber was founder member: some thought it was badly named but it was named in a proud earlier tradition ('Original Dixieland Jazz Band', 'New Orleans Rhythm Kings', etc.); music resembled that of the Crosby band, drew on material from dixieland classics to mainstream standards, show tunes: LPs on Enoch LIGHT's Project 3 label, Monmouth-Evergreen, others (later LPs without Wilber issued or reissued on World Jazz incl. *Century Plaza, At Carnegie Hall, At Massey Hall, On Tour* (with Maxine SULLIVAN), songbooks *Plays Gershwin, Cole Porter, Rodgers & Hart, Ellington*, etc., sidemen variously incl. Lawson and Haggart, Billy BUTTERFIELD, Eddie MILLER, Roger KELLAWAY, Ralph SUTTON, Peanuts

Hucko, Carl Fontana, Al Klink, drummers Nick Fatool, Gus Johnson, Bobby Rosengarden). Wilber left WGJB '73 and formed Soprano Summit with Kenny Davern, Marty Grosz on banjo and guitar, George Duvivier on bass, various drummers: LPs on World Jazz, Chiaroscuro (*Crazy Rhythm, Chalumeau Blue*), also *Live At Big Horn Jazzfest* '76 on Jazzology, *In Concert* '76 (with Jake Hanna, Ray BROWN) and *Live At Concord* '77 on Concord Jazz. He toured in trio with his wife, vocalist Joanne Horton, Dave McKENNA on piano: *Origina Wilber* and *Groovin' At The Grunewald* on Swedish Phontastic label; transcribed Jelly Roll MORTON tunes for performance; formed Bechet Legacy '81: septet LPs (incl. Horton) made live at Bechet's NYC (one with guest Vic DICKENSON) on Jazzology, *On The Road* on Bodeswell (Wilber's label). Transcribed King OLIVER for Bob Wilber's Jazz Repertory Orchestra: *The Music Of King Oliver Vol. 1* on Bodeswell; re-created Duke ELLINGTON Washingtonians of '27 for soundtrack of *The Cotton Club* '84; formed Goodman tribute band with British musicians, toured '85-6. Other LPs: *Reflections* with 'The Bodeswell Strings', Wilber playing all five reed parts, and sextet *Dizzyfingers* on Bodeswell (*Reflections* from Circle in USA); *Vital Wilber, Swingin' For The King* (Goodman tribute with Horton, eight Swedes), sextet *Rapturous Reeds* (no brass), septet *In The Mood For Swing* (with Klink, Hank JONES, Frank Wess, Bucky Pizzarelli), all on Phontastic. Out-of-print albums incl. *Music Of Hoagy Carmichael* with Sullivan on Monmouth, LP with Scott HAMILTON on Chiaroscuro, many more. On 19 Jan. '88 he re-created Goodman's famous Carnegie Hall concert on its 50th anniversary. He has survived decades of critical lusting after the new to become one of the most popular musicians in the present age of repertory music, as has Davern (*b* John Kenneth Davern, *b* 7 Jan. '35, Long Island, NY), who had worked with Clara Ward, Wild Bill DAVISON, Jackie GLEASON, Braff and many others; after Soprano Summit Davern returned to clarinet, on which he is very highly regarded; own LPs incl. *El Rado Scuffle: A Tribute To Jimmy Noone* '82 on Kenneth with Scandinavian band; *The Very Thought Of You* '84; *Live*

Hot Jazz '84 on Statiris with Wellstood, Chuck Riggs.

WILBURN BROTHERS Loyle (*b* 7 July '30, Hardy, Mo.) and Teddy Wilburn (*b* 30 Nov. '31, Hardy), a vocal duo and one of the most popular in country music. Began as part of the Wilburn Family act, touring the South and joining Grand Ole Opry '41. Family act split late '40s, Teddy and two older brothers Leslie and Lester joining Webb PIERCE's Southern Valley Boys '51; when the brothers were drafted into US Army Lester joined the JOHNNIE & JACK band '52, Doyle and Teddy joined Faron YOUNG '53-5, also began working as a duo, recording for Decca from '54 and making country chart debut with 'Which One Is To Blame' '59. They joined the Opry and had a first-class touring show; in early '60s they had a syndicated TV show, helped up-and-comers like Loretta LYNN, formed Surefire Music, one of Nashville's leading independents. They recorded for Decca/MCA until the mid-'70s, have not made the charts for some years, but still appear on the Opry and recorded for First Generation Records '80s.

WILDE, Marty (*b* Reginald Smith, 15 Apr. '39, Blackheath, London) UK pop star and sex idol who had 14 hits '58-62 with covers of USA rock songs: 'Endless Sleep' (Jody Reynolds in USA, revived by Hank WILLIAMS Jr '64), 'Donna' (Ritchie VALENS), 'Rubber Ball' (Bobby VEE), etc. 'Bad Boy' was his only USA chart entry (top 50 '60). In '70s with Mickie MOST he tried to launch his son Ricky as successor; had more luck with good-looking blonde daughter Kim (*b* Nov. '60, London): Ricky prod. hits, mother Joyce managed her; increasingly Marty and Ricky wrote the songs. LPs on EMI/Rak: *Kim Wilde* '81, *Select* '82, *Catch As Catch Can* '83; switched to MCA '84 with *Teases And Dares* '84, *Serenade* and *Another Step* '86. First hit 'Kids In America' '81 was no. 2 UK; her singles soon slid out of the top 40; then 'Rage To Love' made the top 20 '85 (remixed by Dave EDMUNDS) '85, 'You Keep Me Hangin' On' '86 back up to no. 2. Two singles and two LPs were minor chart entries in the USA. She will ultimately have no more influence than her father.

WILDER, Alec (*b* Alexander LaFayette Chew Wilder, 16 Feb. '07, Rochester, N.Y.; *d* 23 Dec. '80, Gainesville, Fla.) Composer. Studied at Eastman School of Music, Rochester; collaborated with Howard Dietz and Edward Brandt on 'All The King's Horses' for hit revue *Three's A Crowd* '30 (also incl. Johnny GREEN's 'Body And Soul'). Wrote several hundred popular, descriptive jazz, classical works, etc. incl. standards 'I'll Be Around' '43 (used in film *The Joe Louis Story*, recorded by the MILLS Bros, Mildred BAILEY; by Frank SINATRA on LP *In The Wee Small Hours*, many others), 'While We're Young', 'It's So Peaceful In The Country', 'Who Can I Turn To?', 'April Age', 'Summer Is A-Comin' In', many more. Co-wrote 'J. P. Dooley III', recorded by Harry JAMES '42 with vocal quartet (incl. James); also words for Eddie SAUTER's 'All The Cats Join In', played by Benny Goodman in Walt Disney's *Make Mine Music* '45; six Wilder instrumentals conducted by Sinatra for V-discs late '45. Songs for minor movie *Open The Door (And See All The People)* were 'Mimosa And Me' and 'Such A Lovely Girl' (sung by JACKIE & ROY on album *Lovesick*), also 'I See It Now' (by Mabel MERCER on her *Second Town Hall Concert*, with Bobby SHORT). Unorthodox work, sometimes with unusual titles, often recorded by his octet: 'Neurotic Goldfish', 'Sea Fugue Mama', 'A Debutante's Diary'. Last songs were written for Sinatra: 'The Long Night' and 'One More Road'. Books: *American Popular Song: The Great Innovators* '72 with James T. Maher (and National Public Radio series '76), *Letters I Never Mailed* '75 (insights into people and music). Lived for over 50 years at NYC's Algonquin Hotel and the Sheraton in Rochester. LP *Elaine Sings Wilder* '66 by Elaine Delmar (*b* 13 Sep. '39, Harpenden, Herts.; several appearances on London stage incl. *No Strings* '61, *Bubbling Brown Sugar* '77; also Ken Russell film *Mahler*; other LPs on Polydor, World).

WILDER, Joe (*b* Joseph Benjamin Wilder, 22 Feb. '22, Colwyn, Pa.) Trumpet, flugelhorn. Has combined classical training with jazz in low-profile career; highly regarded by other musicians. Played with Les HITE, Lionel HAMPTON, Jimmie LUNCEFORD etc.; settled in NYC '47; featured on Count

BASIE LP *Softly With Feeling* '54; worked with Noble SISSLE, in Broadway pit bands; studied with Joseph Alessi, first trumpet in Toscanini's NBC Symphony, played Bach under cond. Jonel Perlea, etc. Played in film soundtrack *The Wild Party* '56; ABC network staff musician '57-73 (played in bands on Jack Paar, Dick Cavett shows), then back to Broadway. First chair with Symphony of the New World '65-71; played at Colorado Jazz Party from '72. Sessioned in concerts and/or records with New York Philharmonic, Benny GOODMAN (incl. USSR tour '62), big band recording sessions with Ralph BURNS, Jimmy GIUFFRE; also Tony BENNETT, Lena HORNE, Roberta FLACK, Charles MINGUS (LP *Let My People Hear Music*), etc. Golden Crest LP '63 incl. Alec WILDER's *Sonata For Trumpet And Piano*, written for Joe (no relation). Solos with immaculate tone, selection of notes (never too many: 'You try not to trample on a nice melody'). Own records on Savoy, Columbia long out of print; plays on *Benny Carter: A Gentleman And His Music*, co-led quintet LP *Hangin' Out* with Joe NEWMAN and Hank JONES, both on Concord Jazz.

WILEY, Lee (*b* 9 Oct. '15, Port Gibson, Okla.; *d* 11 Dec. '75, NYC) Jazz singer with breathy, little-girl sound, distinctive vibrato: intimate warmth with great respect for lyrics. Sang with bands of Johnny GREEN, Green's pianist Leo REISMAN (big hit 'Time On My Hands' '31), Victor YOUNG; worked with Eddie CONDON and associates late '30s; married to pianist Jess STACY, toured with his band (fine version of 'It's Only A Paper Moon' '45 once incl. on '50s RCA jazz compilation LP *String Of Swingin' Pearls*). In the days of 78s she made albums of classic songs; she was also a lyricist, e.g. adding words to Young's music for 'Got The South In My Soul' and 'Anytime, Anyday, Anywhere' (revived for no. 1 R&B hit '50 by trumpeter/bandleader Joe Morris on Atlantic with vocalist Laurie Tate). Made album *Night In Manhattan* for Columbia early '50s, with Bobby HACKETT, pianists Stan Freeman, Cy Walter, Joe BUSHKIN, now on Columbia Special Products; *A Touch Of Blues* '58 on RCA, with band led by Billy BUTTERFIELD, arr. by Al COHN, Bill Finegan, reissued '87 in UK. She was more or less retired until *Back*

Home Again '71 on Monmouth-Evergreen, which also reissued tracks now on Audiophile: original Liberty Music Shop records *Sings Ira & George Gershwin And Cole Porter* '39-40, *Sings Richard Rodgers & Lorenz Hart And Harold Arlen* '40-3, accompanied by Condon, Bushkin, Max KAMINSKY, Bunny BERIGAN, Bud FREEMAN, Pee Wee RUSSELL etc.; solo organ by Fats WALLER on 'Someone To Watch Over Me'. Also two vols. of *On The Air* on Totem, tracks on *Eddie Condon Town Hall Concerts With Lee Wiley* on Chiaroscuro ('44-5 AFRS broadcasts), *You Leave Me Breathless* on Jass (broadcasts etc.). *Sweet And Lowdown* on Halcyon UK has some '39-40 tracks (there are two Halcyons: one in UK and Marian McPARTLAND's in USA, both using the same numbering system); also on Storyville USA (there are at least two Storyville labels).

WILLIAMS, Andy (*b* Howard Andrew, 3 Dec.'30, Wall Lake, Iowa) USA pop singer with enormous success '50s-60s (various sources give birth date as early as '27). Began in church choir with three brothers; they worked on radio in Cincinnati and Chicago, backed Bing CROSBY on no. 1 hit 'Swinging On A Star' '44, appeared in film about music publishing industry *Kansas City Kitty* same year; formed act with headliner Kay Thompson for night clubs '47-8 (Thompson *b* 9 Nov. '13, St Louis; married to trombonist Jack Jenny; appeared in film *Funny Face* '56; also wrote *Eloise* books for children). One of the all-time film mysteries is the persisting story that Andy Williams dubbed Lauren Bacall's singing voice in *To Have And Have Not* '45. He went solo '52, was regular on Steve ALLEN's *Tonight* TV show, signed to Archie BLEYER's Cadence label: 15 hits '56-61 incl. no. 1 'Butterfly' '57 (million-seller for Charlie GRACIE too), top tens 'Canadian Sunset', 'I Like Your Kind Of Love' (duet with Peggy Powers), 'Are You Sincere', 'Lonely Street', 'In The Village Of St Bernadette'. Began on TV as summer replacement '57, music/variety show was an institution until '71: he was hard-working and exacting professional but came across as relaxed and amusing host; format similar to successful Perry COMO TV show. He was American Variety Club's Personality of the

Year '59, won Emmy for Best Variety Show '62; the show inflicted the OSMONDS on the nation. As a recording artist his romantic ballads were sung with great control; he was ineffective up-tempo. Switched to Columbia '61, by then a major artist; 29 Hot 100 singles through '72 incl. only two top tens: 'Can't Get Used To Losing You' (by Doc POMUS and Mort Shuman, no. 2 '63) and '(Where Do I Begin) Love Story' (no. 9 '71, theme from smash weepie film). Over 30 hit albums incl. 12 in top 10 of LP chart: no. 1 *Days Of Wine And Roses* '63 incl. no. 26 title hit (by Henry MANCINI) as well as the no. 2 hit; *Moon River And Other Great Movie Themes* '62 reached no. 3: in retrospect it is surprising that he had no single hit with Mancini's 'Moon River' in that pre-BEATLE era, so widely was he identified with it, but he toured, appeared on TV with Mancini. LP *Love Story* '73 also reached no. 3. Appeared in film *I'd Rather Be Rich* '64 with Sandra Dee, Robert GOULET and Maurice CHEVALIER (remake of *It Started With Eve* '42); song 'Almost There' from film was minor USA hit but no. 2 in UK, where he had eight top 10 hits. Record success was very much connected with TV popularity, soon dried up when show ended; last minor hit was 'Tell It Like It Is' '76. *Close Enough For Love* '87 reprised Mancini songs, others. There was still a remote connection with Bleyer mid-'70s: his twin nephews Andy and David had minor hit 'What's Your Name' '74 on his Barnaby label, which also briefly reissued fine LPs by Charles MINGUS, etc. originally on Bleyer's Candid subsidiary.

WILLIAMS, Billy (*b* 28 Dec. '16, Waco, Texas; *d* 17 Oct. '72, Chicago) Led black vocal group with several well-deserved hits in '50s. Studied to be Methodist minister at Wilberforce College in Ohio, formed quartet Charioteers and broadcast on WLW in Cincinnati, WOR in NYC, worked on Bing CROSBY show on West Coast; hit 'My Adobe Hacienda' '47 on RCA; he formed own Billy Williams Quartet with Eugene Dixon, Claude Riddick and John Ball '50: had a few hits on MGM, on Mercury '53, became regulars on Sid Caesar's *Show Of Shows* on TV. Of ten hits on Coral '54-9, by far the biggest was cover of 'I'm Gonna Sit Right Down And Write Myself A Letter' (big hit

'35 by Fats WALLER). He later worked as a social worker in Chicago.

WILLIAMS, Clarence (*b* 8 Oct. 1898, Plaquemine, La.; *d* 6 Nov. '65, Queens, NYC) Composer, pianist, record producer, music publisher, also sometime vocalist. Other birth dates are mentioned; some scholars favour 1893 as most logical, but his widow and death certificate give 1898. He was part Creole Negro, part Choctaw; worked in a hotel and sang in a band in the streets as a child; ran away from home at 12 to work in a minstrel show, becoming MC and singer; returned to N.O. and studied piano infl. by Tony Jackson; said he was the first to 'write up north' for the new hit songs. Managed a cabaret '13; later danced in vaudeville; with bandleader/violinist/-composer Armand John Piron (*b* 16 Aug. 1888, N.O.; *d* there 17 Feb. '43) he formed publishing company (called Piron 'the Paul Whiteman of New Orleans'; Piron was credited with writing 'I Wish I Could Shimmy Like My Sister Kate', which Louis ARMSTRONG claims to have written as 'Get Off Katie's Head'). Clarence's first song was 'You Missed A Good Woman When You Picked All Over Me'; he claimed to be the first to use the word 'jazz' on a piece of sheet music. Toured with Piron c.'17 with W. C. HANDY. He moved to Chicago, then to NYC c.'20; Willie 'The Lion' SMITH said Williams was the first New Orleans musician to infl. jazz in NYC and first publisher to help black songwriters ('. . . nobody on Broadway would') incl. Smith, James P. JOHNSON, Fats WALLER. First record in Oct. '21 as vocalist accompanied by white band; he also made piano rolls. He acted as 'race records' A&R dir. (for Okeh '23-8); his countless recording projects helped the careers of Armstrong, Sidney BECHET, Buster Bailey; he employed King OLIVER, Don REDMAN, Coleman HAWKINS, Lonnie JOHNSON, Bubber MILEY, Tommy LADNIER, and Jimmy HARRISON; worked with vocalists BUTTERBEANS & SUSIE, Sara Martin, Sippie WALLACE, Eva Taylor (his wife from '21), many others; played on Bessie SMITH sessions and she recorded many of his songs; he wrote words and/or music for 'Baby Won't You Please Come Home', 'Royal Garden Blues', 'Cake Walking Babies From Home', 'Gulf Coast

Blues', 'Michigan Water Blues', 'Swing Brother Swing', 'The Stuff Is Here (And It's Mellow)', 'Wild Cat Blues', 'West End Blues', 'West Indies Blues', many more; often shared credit with Spencer WILLIAMS (no relation). Wrote music for flop Broadway show *Bottomland* '27; from late '30s concentrated on writing; sold his catalogue to Decca '43. He later ran shops in Harlem, went blind after being knocked down by a taxi '56 but continued working. Nearly 300 sides under his own name '21-38 incl. those issued by Clarence Williams and his Blue Five '23-6, and his Stompers, and his Orchestra, Blue Seven, Jazz Kings, Washboard Band, Bottomland Orchestra, Swing Band ('37), etc. A last Blue Five session on Bluebird '41 had both Williams and James P. on pianos, Wellman BRAUD on bass, Taylor singing (duet with Clarence on one side). Almost all the records were for ARC labels, now the property of CBS. Compilations incl. two vols. of '27-9 tracks on Biograph, *Music Man* on MCA, others on VJM, CJM, Jazz Unlimited, Rhapsody in UK, Swaggie in Australia. *Clarence Williams* by Tom Lord '76 is exhaustive bio-discography, virtually a history of NYC race music, with rare photos from Eva's collection.

WILLIAMS, Cootie (*b* Charles Melvin Williams, 24 July '08, Mobile, Ala.; *d* 15 Sep. '85, Long Island, NY) Trumpet, bandleader. Played in school band, with Young Family Band one summer at 14, incl. Lester YOUNG; went to Florida with Ed HALL and worked in Eagle Eye Shields' band, then to NYC with Alonzo Ross's Deluxe Syncopators; worked briefly with Chick WEBB, Fletcher HENDERSON; replaced Bubber MILEY in Duke ELLINGTON band '29, soon learned how to growl: distinctive, important sound in that band with both muted, open horn, featured on 'Echoes Of Harlem' '36, 'Concerto For Cootie' '40 (later 'Do Nothing Till You Hear From Me'), many more. He played on Ellington small-group sessions led by Barney BIGARD, Johnny HODGES; also led his own Ellington small-group dates and made four sides as Gotham Stompers (ten men from Ellington and Webb bands plus Ivie ANDERSON vocals) '37-40, all compiled on Swedish Tax label as *Cootie And His Rug Cutters, And The Boys From Harlem*, some

on Australian Swaggie; also freelance small-group dates with Lionel HAMPTON, Teddy WILSON ('37 track 'Carelessly' with Billie HOLIDAY has typically wonderful muted solo). Left Duke '40 to go with Benny GOODMAN (Raymond SCOTT wrote 'When Cootie Left The Duke'): he loved playing with Goodman's sextet and Goodman could pay more; played on 'Wholly Cats', 'Royal Garden Blues', 'Breakfast Feud', 'On The Alamo', 'Gilly (Gone With What Draft)' etc. with Charlie CHRISTIAN, often Count BASIE on piano; also with big band ('Superman', etc.); left Goodman after a year to form his own big band until late '40s: it made wonderful music but was only moderately successful; years later in an interview apropos problem drinkers in Duke's band he remarked that he had never been a drinker until leading his own band drove him to it. His band occasionally incl. Charlie PARKER, Bud POWELL, Eddie DAVIS, drummer Ben Thigpen; 'Epistrophy', written by Thelonious MONK, Kenny CLARKE, Cootie taking co-credit, was first called 'Fly Right', recorded '42 but not issued until 3-disc anthology *The Sound Of Harlem* on CBS. On big band and sextet records '44 for Majestic/Hit labels, Cootie again took a credit on Monk's ' 'Round Midnight' (aka ' 'Round About Midnight'), remade 'Echoes Of Harlem', and the band had its biggest hits: 'Tess' Torch Song' (vocal by Pearl BAILEY) and 'Cherry Red Blues' (vocal by Eddie 'Cleanhead' VINSON); these sides (all with Powell) compiled as *Echoes Of Harlem* on Affinity UK, *Cootie Williams Sextet And Orchestra* on Phoenix, Storyville. From late '40s he toured with combos, sometimes just rhythm; rejoined Duke '62. From the early '70s he rarely played in section but as featured soloist, sometimes absent owing to ill health (high blood pressure); stayed with Mercer ELLINGTON after Duke's death and can be heard as late as *Teresa Brewer At Carnegie Hall* '78. Other LPs: *Typhoon* on Swingtime, *Memorial* on RCA, *Big Challenge* with Rex STEWART on Hall of Fame Jazz.

WILLIAMS, Don (*b* 27 May '39, Floydada, Texas) Country singer, dubbed The Gentle Giant of Country Music for laid-back style. Keen music fan as a teenager, liked rock'n'-roll and R&B but tended towards country in is own playing; following military service ormed Pozo Seco Singers with Susan 'aylor and Lofton Kline, also from Texas; ing lead on six folkish Hot 100 entries on olumbia '66-7; he wanted the group to nd more to country, but it split '71. He loved to Nashville, landed contract as ongwriter with Jack's Music (Jack CLEM-NT), made demos, then own records, made ebut on country chart with 'The Shelter of Your Eyes' '72 on JMI: first album *Don 'illiams Vol. 1* '73 was acclaimed for set-ing new direction; in fact it was a basic, ncluttered prod. allowing his deep vocals nd lyrics to shine. More hits followed; by ne time JMI closed and he went to ABC-Iot, taking his recordings with him, he had nade major breakthrough with his records egularly in the top 10 and his songs were corded by Johnny Russell, Jim and ompall GLASER, Lefty FRIZZELL, Jeanne RUETT, Dickey LEE, Kenny ROGERS. He oon made a UK breakthrough, visit to Jembley Festival '76 among the most nemorable: he took five places at once in K country album chart, incl. first four, for our weeks; 'I Recall A Gypsy Woman' crossing into pop (not even a single in USA) nd album *Visions* going gold on day of elease. In USA he was Male Vocalist of the ear '78 and carried on with stream of hits, witching to parent MCA label '79, to Capi-ol mid-'80s. 15 no. 1 country hits '86, with Believe In You' in pop Hot 100 '80; ap-eared in films *W.W. And The Dixie Jancekings, Smokey & The Bandit II*. His acking group, the Scratch Band, led by Janny Flowers, have also made records of neir own. Albums incl. *Volume One* '73, *olume Two* '74, *You're My Best Friend* '75, *Iarmony* '76, *Visions* '77, *Expressions* '78, *'ortrait* '79, *Especially For You* '81, *Listen 'o The Radio* '82, *Yellow Moon* '83, *Café 'arolina* '84, all on ABC/Dot/MCA; *Love tories* '85 on K-Tel, *New Moves* '86 and *'races* '87 on Capitol.

VILLIAMS, Hank (*b* Hiram Hank Williams, 7 Sept. '23, near Georgiana, Alabama; *d* 1 an. '53 in back seat of chauffered Cadillac, omewhere in Virginia) Singer/songwriter; iggest star in history of country music. nfl. by black street singer Tee-Tot (Rufe 'ayne); started band while still in school, ang on KSFA radio (Montgomery) age 13

and served long, hard apprenticeship in honky tonks ('blood buckets'). Took songs to Acuff-Rose, Nashville; first records for Stirling label '46; booked on Louisiana Hayride; changed to MGM label '47. Sensational guest spot on Grand Ole Opry singing hit 'Lovesick Blues' '49 (ironically a song older than he was) led to contract despite reputation for unreliability and lingering dislike of honky tonk genre on Opry. Often bought lyrics from others (common practice in country music); always had pocket full of scraps of paper with ideas and lines jotted down. Fred ROSE produced recording sessions, co-wrote some songs and hawked them around to pop A&R men: Mitch MILLER at Columbia assigned 'Cold, Cold Heart' to Tony BENNETT, made no. 1 pop chart '51; many more songs became crossovers: 'Half As Much' (Rosemary CLOONEY), 'Jambalaya' (Jo STAFFORD), 'Your Cheatin' Heart' (Frankie LAINE, Joni JAMES), 'Kawliga' (Dolores GRAY, Champ Butler), 'There'll Be No Teardrops Tonight' (Bennett), 'Hey Good Lookin' (Laine and Stafford) were pop hits while Williams's own recordings made country chart (27 top 10 hits '49-53). Among his others: 'I'm So Lonesome I Could Die', 'Baby We're Really In Love', 'Settin' The Woods On Fire', 'I'll Never Get Out Of This World Alive' (which climbed the charts after he died). Insisted on using own band on recording sessions, not usual then; generous to sidemen in allowing them to shine (*see* the DRIFTING COWBOYS). In many ways precursor of Elvis PRESLEY as culture hero: perfect singer for genre; had evident unforced sympathy for the predicament of his fans (mostly poor white southerners), considerable effect on women (causing many a fist-fight in early days); also funky in performance: e.g. in 'I Won't Be Home No More', each group of words seems to be sung to a triplet, but number of syllables is always more than three; in centre of a line, three words may be sung on two different notes, but apparently on same beat; in solos fiddler Jerry Rivers and steel guitarist Don Helms float over beat: it has insouciant swagger which suits bravado of lyrics. Although he never read anything but comics and weekly hits charts, his memorable (if sometimes interchangeable) tunes and simple rhyming lyrics added up to folk-poetry; he was one of the great modern troubadors. Wrote about 125 songs, incl. religious songs he called 'hymns'; also sentimental/moralising monologues under name of Luke the Drifter. Alcoholic, addicted to painkillers (probably due to painful untreated birth defect *spina bifida*); much material (happy and sad) came out of stormy eight-year marriage to Audrey, who wanted to be a star herself (without much talent, though they recorded duets). Divorced, remarried (to Billie Jean Jones, later married Johnny HORTON) and fired from the Opry, all in '52; his last few months were hell: returned to Hayride, intended comeback but never made it. Songs and records are still selling; uncountable number of covers from Elvis COSTELLO to CARPENTERS; infl. on country music incalculable. Bob DYLAN, Elvin BISHOP and Bruce SPRINGSTEEN among many pop, rock people to pay tribute. In '76, 'Jambalaya' charted in Europe, live recording from Opry stage ('Why Don't You Love Me') also hit in the USA, 23 years after his death. Many compilations issued; *The Immortal Hank Williams* is complete recordings in 10-disc boxed set from Japan; Polydor is issuing the complete series on 2-disc sets in the West; *On The Air* '86 is a set of airchecks '49-52, on Polydor but compiled by the Country Music Foundation. Biographies: *From Life To Legend* '64 by Jerry Rivers; *Sing A Sad Song* '70 by Roger M. Williams (anecdotes, interviews with people who knew Hank; '80 edition incl. discography by Bob Pinson); *Hank Williams* '79 by Jay Caress; *Your Cheatin' Heart* '81 by Chet Flippo (impressionistic treatment very well done, with much recent research).

WILLIAMS, Hank, Jr (*b* Randall Hank Williams, 26 May '49, Shreveport, La.) Country singer, guitarist, songwriter; grew up in Nashville; the son of country music's greatest superstar, who nicknamed him Bocephus. During high school he excelled in sports and became a health fanatic; toured with his mother Audrey in her Caravan of Stars show '62-4 and signed a contract with MGM, moulded by the elder statesman of Nashville as a second Hank Williams; sang Hank's songs incl. in soundtrack of biopic *Your Cheatin' Heart* '65 and crossing to the pop chart with 'Long Gone

Lonesome Blues' '64. He began writing hi own songs and scored minor hits, but the public demanded endless replays of Han Sr's songs; he finally made the top 20 sever al times late '60s and no. 1 '70 with 'All Fo The Love Of Sunshine'. Also recorded nar rations in his father's style using the same name of Luke the Drifter '69-70. He place many singles in the top 5, also duetted with Lois Johnson for series of hits incl. 'So Sa (To Watch Good Love Go Bad)', 'Send M Some Lovin' '. He broke from the Nash ville elite '74, moved to Alabama; with the help of old friend James R. Smith bega work on a sound of his own: recorded ac claimed *Hank Williams Jr And Friends* with country-rock musicians incl. Charlie DAN IELS, Toy Caldwell of the Marshall Tucke Band, ex-ALLMAN BROS Chuck Leavell just before its release he literally fell down mountain on a hunting trip, suffered appal ling head injuries, and was almost two year on the mend. 'Stoned At The Jukebox' '7 from the new album just made top 20, 'Liv ing Proof' '76 made top 40. He joined WB had only minor hits at first and slowl climbed the charts on his own terms with gritty, rock-based country sound, returnin to top 20 with 'I Fought The Law' '78 moved to Elektra, made top 5 with 'Famil Tradition' and 'Whiskey Bent And Hel Bound' '79 and hasn't looked back: teame with Waylon JENNINGS for 'The Conversa tion' '80, had no. 1 hits 'Women I've Neve Had' and 'Old Habits' '80, 'Texas Woman and 'All My Rowdy Friends' '81, 'A Countr Boy Can Survive' and 'Honky Tonkin' ' '82 'Leave Them Boys Alone' and 'Queen O My Heart' '83, and had eight albums in th Billboard chart at once. Duetted with Ra CHARLES on 'Two Old Cats Like Us' '85 had solo hits 'Are You Sure Hank Done l This Way' and 'Ain't Misbehavin' ' '86 'Mind Your Own Business' '87; album *Hank Live* '87 sold half a million copie without a single to help it; after selling 13n albums he was named Entertainer of th Year by the CMA '87, said 'This is the on old Bocephus has been looking for.' Othe albums: *Songs Of Hank Williams* '64, *You Cheatin' Heart* and *Ballads Of The Hill And Plains* '65, *Blues Is My Name* an *Standing In The Shadows* '66, *My Own Wa '67, My Songs* '68, *Luke The Drifter Jr* an *Live At Cobo Hall* '69, *Songs Of Johnn*

Cash and *Removing The Shadow* (with Johnson) '70, *Eleven Roses* '72, *Just Picking* '73, *Bocephus* '75 and *And Friends* '75, all on MGM; *The New South* '78 on WB; *Family Tradition* and *Whiskey Bent & Hell Bound* '79, *Habits Old & New* '80, *Rowdy* and *The Pressure Is On* '81, *High Notes* '82, *Strong Stuff* and *Man Of Steel* '83, all on Elektra; *Are You Sure Hank Done It This Way* and *Five-O* '85, *Born To Boogie* and *Hank Live* '87 on WB.

WILLIAMS, Big Joe (*b* 16 Oct. '03, Crawford, Ms.; *d* 17 Dec. '82) Blues singer, guitarist; aka Po' Joe Williams; not to be confused with the jazz singer Joe WILLIAMS (below); there were two or three more blues singers named Joe Williams, one recording before WWII, at least two younger men who recorded after the war. Big Joe had a distinctive sound on a nine-string guitar. One of 16 children; made himself a one-string instrument, began singing as a small child; worked in railroad gangs, lumber camps; recorded for Bluebird '35-41, compiled on *Baby Please Don't Go* on Charly UK; later LPs incl. *Nine String Guitar Blues* and *Pineywood Blues* on Delmark, *Tough Times* and *Thinking Of What They Did* on Arhoolie, *Legacy Of The Blues Vol. 6* '72 on Sonet.

WILLIAMS, Joe (*b* Joseph Goreed, 12 Dec. '18, Cordele, Ga.) Jazz singer, now very popular for over 30 years, with big voice even deeper than that of Billy ECKSTINE; first famous for sophisticated blues, but equally at home in ballads. Sang in Chicago clubs with Jimmie NOONE late '30s, then Coleman HAWKINS and Lionel HAMPTON bands; first recorded with Andy KIRK late '40s, then '50 with Hot Lips PAGE. Worked with Count BASIE septet '50, recorded 'Every Day (I Have The Blues)' c.'51 (by Peter Chatman; *see* MEMPHIS SLIM) with King Kolax R&B band; joined Basie '54-60, becoming a star and helping that band to its last great peak: *Count Basie Swings, Joe Williams Sings* '55 on Verve incl. 'Every Day', much else (*see* entry for Basie). Another treat is 'Party Blues' c.'56, joyous swinging scat duet with Ella FITZGERALD, Basie. He toured solo, expanding repertoire to incl. all kinds of good songs, with Harry EDISON quintet early '60s, then own trios with Chi-

cago pianists Junior MANCE, then Norman Simmons. Other LPs with Basie incl. *The Greatest* on Verve; 2-disc set on French Vogue compiles Roulette tracks incl. marvellous re-creation of Jimmy RUSHING classic 'Goin' To Chicago' with Lambert, Hendricks & Ross (*see* Jon HENDRICKS); RCA LPs '60s incl. *Jump For Joy, Me And The Blues, The Song Is You, The Exciting Joe Williams; Having The Blues Under European Skies* early '70s on Denon; *Live!* with Nat and Cannonball ADDERLEY on Fantasy; *Live At The Century Plaza* with the CAPP – PIERCE Juggernaut (big band) on Concord Jazz. *Nothin' But The Blues* '83 on Delos with Jack McDuff, Eddie VINSON, Ray BROWN etc. got rave reviews; *Every Night* '87 on Verve made live at Vine Street Bar & Grill in Hollywood with Simmons quartet. Other LPs incl. *Every Day I Have The Blues* on Savoy ('51-3 tracks), *Chains Of Love* on Jass (Stash) from early '60s, *Worth Waiting For* on Pausa. Plays the star's father-in-law on *The Bill Cosby Show* with presence as big as his voice.

WILLIAMS, John (*b* John Towner Williams, 8 Feb. '32, Flushing, NY) Conductor, composer of film music. Father Johnny Williams played drums with Raymond SCOTT late '30s. Played jazz piano, recorded for Kapp, RCA, Bethlehem; studio work led to movies: themes from soundtracks for *Jaws* '75, *Star Wars* and *Close Encounters Of The Third Kind* '77, *Superman* '79 have been hits. Succeeded Arthur Fiedler as conductor of the Boston Pops '80 (Fiedler *d* '79 at age 83; 18 chart LPs '59-79 incl. those with Al HIRT, Peter NERO, Chet ATKINS, *The Duke At Tanglewood* '66 with Duke ELLINGTON). Williams' Boston Pops slipped into top 200 with *Pops In Space* '80. He should not be confused with pianist John Williams (*b* 28 Jan. '29, Windsor, Vt.), who recorded '50s with Stan GETZ, Cannonball ADDERLEY etc.

WILLIAMS, John (*b* 24 Apr. '41, Melbourne, Australia) Classical guitarist who has often reached the pop charts. *John Williams Plays Spanish Music* '70 on CBS reached UK top 50 followed by *Travelling* '78 on Cube; his recording of Rodrigo's *Concerto de Aranjuez* with English Chamber Orchestra cond. by Daniel Barenboim '76 on CBS reached top

20; *Bridges* '79 on Lotus/K-Tel was no. 5 and *Cavatina* '79 on Cube/Electric also charted. He formed fusion group Sky, with Steve Gray on keyboards, Herbie Flowers on electric bass, Kevin Peek on guitars, Tristan Fry on tuned percussion; their instrumental skill was amazing but for many pop listeners they lacked soul. Two LPs charted in USA but all did well in UK: *Sky* '79, *Sky 2* '80 (no. 1), *Sky 3* '81, *Sky Forthcoming* '82; 2-disc *Sky Five Live* '83 was recorded on Australian tour; *Cadmium* '83 was also on Ariola/Arista. *Masterpieces* '83 was Telstar compilation; the first three were issued in boxed set. Williams left the group early '84 (others carried on as quartet: *The Great Balloon Race* '85 on CBS, *Mozart* '87 on Mercury with orch. conducted by Neville Marriner). Other LPs: *Portrait Of John Williams* '82, *The Guitar Is The Song* '83, *Let The Music Take You* '83 with Cleo LAINE, Paul Hart's *Concerto For Guitar And Jazz Orchestra* '87, all on CBS; new LP on the way with Chilean folk group Inti-Illinali; also reissues and compilations on Discovery, PRT, Sierra.

WILLIAMS, Larry (*b* 10 May '35, New Orleans; *d* 7 Jan. '80) R&B, rock'n'roll singer, songwriter, pianist. Learned to play piano on West Coast; worked in bands of Lloyd PRICE, Roy BROWN, Percy MAYFIELD; according to one story was working as Price's valet when he first recorded for Specialty: 'Short Fat Fannie' was a great party record, frenetic rocker in the LITTLE RICHARD mould: no. 1 R&B, 5 pop hit, followed by 'Bony Maronie'/'You Bug Me, Baby', all '57, 'Dizzy Miss Lizzy' '58 (later covered by the BEATLES). A good entertainer; had not much more luck in the charts. Narcotics conviction '60 didn't help. '58-9 sessions incl. 'Heeby Jeebies': he whistled the bridge taken by sax solo on Little Richard hit; band incl. Gerald WILSON, trumpet; Plas JOHNSON, tenor; Alvin 'Red' Tyler, baritone; Earl Palmer, drums; Ernie Freeman, piano (sometimes Williams), Barney KESSEL, guitar. Came back '62 with band incl. Johnny 'Guitar' WATSON; *The Larry Williams Show* '62 was recorded on tour in UK; *On Stage* '87 on Starclub is reissue of LP originally on Sue UK. He had minor hits on Okeh '67-8 with Watson incl. 'Mercy, Mercy, Mercy'; made unsuccessful disco-style comeback attempt '78; he shot himself. Compilations incl. *Here's Larry Williams* on Specialty, *Dizzy Miss Lizzy* and *Alacazam* ('87) on Ace.

WILLIAMS, Mary Lou (*b* Mary Elfrieda Scruggs, 8 May '10, Atlanta, Ga.; *d* 28 May '81) Pianist, composer. Grew up in Pittsburgh; played by ear in public at 6, worked in carnival and vaudeville at 13. Married reedman John Williams (*b* 13 Apr. '05, Memphis) from the carnival; she played in his band '27; he left to join Terrence Holder band, she hired Jimmie LUNCEFORD to replace him, joined him in Holder's band '29: by then Andy KIRK had been elected to run it; she wrote arr. 'Froggy Bottom', 'Walkin' And Swingin' ', 'Little Joe From Chicago' etc. for Kirk, also played piano with the band '31-42. Williams played with Cootie WILLIAMS, Earl HINES '40s; Mary Lou wrote 'Camel Hop', 'Roll 'Em' '37 for Benny GOODMAN, had own small band '42 with second husband Harold BAKER; work for Duke ELLINGTON incl. 'Trumpets No End'; played her own *Zodiac Suite* at NY Town Hall '45 (New York Philharmonic played it '46). Always an individual stylist, she was infl. late '40s by Dizzy GILLESPIE, Bud POWELL; co-wrote, recorded 'In The Land Of Oo-Bla-Dee' '49 on King (vocal by Pancho Hagood; Gillespie later recorded it), 'Satchel-Mouth Baby' '47 on Asch (became 'Pretty Eyed Baby', hit for Frankie LAINE and Jo STAFFORD '51). Played briefly for Goodman '48; spent '52-4 in Europe; left music for a while: entered Catholic Church; formed foundation for helping musicians with personal problems. Returned to play at Newport with Gillespie '57 (LP on Verve); played *St Martin de Porres* for trio and voices at Monterey '65, recorded it for her own Mary Records; *Praise The Lord In Many Voices* performed at Carnegie Hall '67 (LP on Avant Garde); the Vatican commissioned her third mass '69 as *Music For Peace*; recorded on Mary as *Mary Lou's Mass*, also re-written for Alvin Ailey Dance Theatre. Always innovative, among the most consistent of swingers. LPs incl. Kirk compilation *Walkin' And Swingin'* '36-42 on Affinity; 2-disc *Asch Recordings* '44-7, later *Zodiac Suite*, others on Folkways; *Mary Lou Williams* '44-6 on Stinson; *First Lady Of Piano* on Giants Of

Jazz with Coleman HAWKINS, Don BYAS, etc.; *Black Christ Of The Andes* and *Zoning* '74 on Mary; trio *Free Spirits* '75 on Steeplechase with Buster Williams on bass, Mickey Roker on drums; duo *Embraced* '77 with Cecil TAYLOR, *My Mama Pinned A Rose On Me*, *Montreux Jazz Festival 1978* on Pablo; LPs on Chiaroscuro incl. *Buddy Tate And His Buddies*, duo *Live At The Cookery* with Brian Torff on bass, solo *From The Heart* (also on Storyville).

WILLIAMS, Maurice, and the Zodiacs Vocal quartet first known as the Royal Charms: lead singer/songwriter Williams, Earl Gainey, William Massey, Willie Jones, Norman Wade won talent contest in Lancaster, S.C., recorded for Excello in Nashville as the Gladiolas: Williams' 'Little Darlin' ' was top 50 hit '57, taken to no. 2 by the DIAMONDS. Changed name to Excellos, then Zodiacs '59, re-formed '60 with Williams, Wiley Bennett, Henry Gaston, Albert Hill, Charles Thomas, Little Willie Morrow: next Williams classic 'Stay' was no. 1 hit '60 on Herald, covered by the HOLLIES, the FOUR SEASONS '64, Jackson BROWNE '78 for more hits. Soundalike followups 'I Remember' and 'Come Along' were minor hits; Williams recorded solo for Atco and Scepter. *Best Of* on Relic has early '60s tracks.

WILLIAMS, Otis, and the Charms R&B vocal group: Williams, Richard Parker, Donald Peak, Joe Penn, Rolland Bradley had classic early rock'n'roll hit 'Hearts Of Stone' '54 (no. 1 R&B, no. 15 pop), covered by the Fontane Sisters on Dot, Red FOLEY on Decca; several other hits as the Charms; as Otis Williams and the Charms scored big again with ballad 'Ivory Tower' '56 (top 10 R&B, no. 11 pop), taken to no. 2 by Cathy Carr (*b* 28 June '36, the Bronx, NYC). Still favourite period stuff. LP *16 Hits* on King.

WILLIAMS, Roger (*b* Louis Weertz, '25, Omaha, Neb.) Pianist. Son of a music teacher; played piano at age 3, later studied at Juilliard and with Lennie TRISTANO and Teddy WILSON; a winner on Arthur GODFREY Talent Scouts programme, signed with Kapp, had hits with cleanly-played schlock instrumentals: 'Autumn Leaves' no. 1 for four weeks '55 (a French

song from '47). Of 22 more hits through '69, top tens 'Near You' revived Francis CRAIG '47 hit, 'Born Free' '66 was film theme. 'Two Different Worlds' '56 had vocal by Jane MORGAN. He had an incredible 38 LPs in USA top 200 '56-72, was still recording for Bainbridge, MCA mid-'80s.

WILLIAMS, Sandy (*b* Alexander Balos Williams, 24 Oct. '06, Somerville, S.C.) Highly regarded Swing Era trombonist. Moved to Washington DC as a child, played in school bands, with Claude HOPKINS, Horace and Fletcher HENDERSON etc. then with Chick WEBB '33-40. Fine solos on 'Dipsy Doodle', 'One O'Clock Jump', 'Sugar Foot Stomp', etc. Took Webb's death in '39 very hard; worked for band fronted by Ella FITZGERALD but his spark was gone; alcohol problem appeared. Played with many bands – Duke ELLINGTON mid-'43 – visited Europe with Rex STEWART '48-9; had complete breakdown c.'50. Recovered and has remained teetotal; worked as lift operator; resumed playing late '50s despite dental and other problems.

WILLIAMS, Spencer (*b* 14 Oct. c.1889, New Orleans, La.; *d* 14 July '65, Flushing, NYC) Pianist, composer, vocalist. Lived in famous brothel Mahogany Hall, owned by his aunt, after his mother died; played and sang in Chicago '07; wrote or co-wrote many jazz and pop classics: 'Squeeze Me' with Fats WALLER; 'Royal Garden Blues', 'West Indies Blues', others with Clarence WILLIAMS (no relation); 'I've Found A New Baby' and 'Everybody Loves My Baby (But My Baby Don't Love Nobody But Me)' with Jack Palmer, both first recorded by Clarence Williams' Blue Five; 'Basin Street Blues', recorded by Louis ARMSTRONG, but strongly associated with Jack TEAGARDEN; 'Ticket Agent, Ease Your Window Down', recorded by Bessie SMITH; 'When Lights Are Low' with Benny CARTER '36, recorded in England (vocal by Elizabeth Welch), later in famous instrumental small-group versions by Carter, Lionel HAMPTON. (Not to be confused with song of the same name written '23 by Gus Kahn, Ted Koehler, bandleader/composer Ted Fiorito, who had hits in '30s). Also 'Shim-Me-Sha-Wobble', 'Mahogany Hall Stomp', many more. Went to Paris '25 to write for Josephine BAKER;

returned '32 on holiday with Waller, was involved in a murder case, acquitted; lived in England until '52, Scandinavia until '57; returned to USA in poor health. He made a few obscure records, none under his own name.

WILLIAMS, Tex (*b* Sol Williams, 23 Aug. '17, Ramsey, Ill.; *d* 11 Oct. '85, Newhall, Cal.) Singing cowboy who began as one-man band on local radio at 13, playing banjo, harmonica and singing. Joined Spade COOLEY band '46, sang on huge hit 'Shame On You'; formed his own 12-piece Western Caravan, recorded for Capitol: first release 'The Rose Of The Alamo' said to have sold 250,000 copies, but record of Tex RITTER-Merle TRAVIS song 'Smoke! Smoke! Smoke! (That Cigarette)' was no. 1 pop hit '47, said to be Capitol's first million-seller. More hits same year incl. 'Don't Telephone, Don't Telegraph, Tell A Woman'; 'Bluebird On Your Windowsill' was no. 12 country hit '49: band remained popular act, appeared with stars like Dinah SHORE, Jo STAFFORD; he returned to country charts on Boone label with hits '65-8, biggest of which was top 20 'Bottom Of A Mountain' '66; two more on Monument incl. 'It Ain't No Big Thing' and 'The Night Miss Nancy Ann's Hotel For Single Girls Burned Down' '70-1. He appeared in scores of Western films '35-55 with Ritter, Buster Crabbe, Charles Starrett. *Smoke! Smoke! Smoke!* on Capitol '60 (reissued on Stetson '87) incl. remake of the big hit, but prod. was typical of the period, with too much brass.

WILLIAMS, Tony (*b* 12 Dec. '45, Chicago, Ill.) Drummer, composer. From musical family; grew up in Boston, went to NYC late '62, joined Miles DAVIS '63. The Davis rhythm section of that period, with Herbie HANCOCK on piano and Ron CARTER on bass, is regarded as one of the most important; Williams with Elvin JONES was among the most influential of the decade. He played on Davis LPs through *In A Silent Way* '69, playing either 'inside' or 'outside' with phenomenal facility; also played with other groups and made own LPs beginning with *Life Time* '65 on Blue Note; left Davis to form jazz-rock fusion group Lifetime with John MCLAUGHLIN, Jack Bruce, Larry Young on organ; it suffered many person-

nel changes and was never as successful commercially as it was influential: its free playing over a rock beat etc. soon became clichés. LPs incl. *Emergency* '69, *Turn It Over* '70, *Ego* '71, *The Old Bum's Rush* '72 (with David Horowitz on keyboards); completely reformed for *Believe It* and *Million Dollar Legs* on Columbia with Allen Holdsworth on tenor (ex-GONG, SOFT MACHINE); under Williams' own name *The Joy Of Flying* '79 on Columbia incl. fusionists Hancock, George BENSON, Jan HAMMER, also a duet with Cecil TAYLOR, reached no. 113 on USA LP chart. He also toured and recorded with V.S.O.P.: *The Quintet* '77 recreated the Davis group, with Hancock, Carter, Wayne SHORTER and Freddie HUBBARD replacing Davis. 2-disc *Once In A Lifetime* compiles fusion tracks; recent LPs incl. *Foreign Intrigue* and *Civilization* on Blue Note, the last released '86 with Billy Pierce, Mulgrew MILLER, Wallace Roney and Charnett Moffett. Trio *Third Plane* with Carter and Hancock issued on French Carrere CD '87.

WILLIAMSON, John Lee 'Sonny Boy' (*b* 30 Mar. '14, Jackson, Tenn.; *d* 1 June '48, Chicago, Ill.) Blues singer, harmonica player; the original Sonny Boy Williamson. Taught himself harmonica as a child; hoboed with Sleepy John ESTES '20s-30s; worked with SUNNYLAND SLIM early '30s; settled in Chicago '34; recorded about 120 sides for Bluebird/Victor from '37, accompanists on various dates incl. Big Bill BROONZY, Big Joe WILLIAMS, SPECKLED RED, others; for Columbia backing Williams '47. Worked in Chicago with Broonzy, Williams, Muddy WATERS; his songs, such as 'Good Morning Little Schoolgirl', many more became blues standards; his harmonica was a direct infl. on LITTLE WALTER, Big Walter HORTON, etc. He was becoming a legend in his own lifetime when he was murdered by muggers. Compilations incl. *Bluebird Blues* on Charly, several vols. on Blues Classics (from Arhoolie) incl. tracks with Williams.

WILLIAMSON, Sonny Boy (*b* Aleck Ford, 5 Dec. 1899, Glendora, Ms.; *d* 25 May '65, Helena, Ark.) Blues singer, harmonica player. Known as Rice Miller, from childhood nickname and stepfather's surname. Hoboed through South, worked as 'Little

Boy Blue'; according to Sheldon Harris's *Blues Who's Who* both Miller and John Lee Williamson (*see above*) worked with Sunnyland Slim early '30s; Miller later worked with Elmore JAMES, Big Boy CRUDUP, Robert JOHNSON, Howlin' WOLF; appeared on radio show *King Biscuit Time* '41-5, billed as Sonny Boy Williamson. After the original Sonny Boy Williamson was murdered he claimed to be the original; his talent justified the arrogance. He recorded on small labels in Arkansas and Mississippi early '50s, then for Checker and Chess in Chicago '55-63, had R&B hits 'Don't Start Me Talkin' ', 'Keep It To Yourself' '55-6, came back to that chart '63 with 'Help Me'. Recorded for Mercury '63 in Chicago, in Europe with Victoria SPIVEY for her label, with Otis SPANN on Fontana, both in Germany '63-4; toured with Chris BARBER trad. band '64 (concert on Black Lion), with MEMPHIS SLIM in Paris (live tracks on Vogue/GNP), made *A Portrait In Blues* '63 on Storyville in Denmark with Memphis Slim on two tracks; he was one of the most direct influences on UK R&B, recording with ANIMALS and YARDBIRDS '63, Brian AUGER '65 (LPs now on Charly: *Jam Session* with Auger and Jimmy Page, *Newcastle December 1963* with Animals; see entry for Yardbirds). Other LPs: Chess reissues, *King Biscuit Time* on Arhoolie.

WILLS, Chuck (*b* 31 Jan. '28, Atlanta, Ga.; *d* 10 Apr. '58) R&B singer. Attracted local notice, lead singer with Red McAllister band, taken to Columbia Records by Atlanta DJ 'Daddy' Sears, signed to subsidiary Okeh '52; five hits in R&B chart. More success after move to Atlantic '56: top 40 pop hits with 'C.C. Rider', 'Betty And Dupree'; two-sided hit 'What Am I Living For'/'Hang Up My Rock And Roll Shoes' in the month of his death following surgery. 'My Life' charted August '58. Known in final years as 'Sheik of the Stroll' because of stage costume incl. turban, minor hit record of dance craze. Compilations: *Be Good Or Be Gone* on Edsel (Okeh tracks), *Keep A Drivin'* on Charly.

WILLS, Bob (*b* James Robert Wills, 6 Mar. '05, on a farm near Kosse, Texas; *d* 13 May '75, Fort Worth, Texas) Fiddler, bandleader, composer; the King of WESTERN SWING. The fiddle had been a favourite instrument of the American frontier; his grandfathers, father and most of his uncles were good fiddlers. The family was poor, did not own land; picked cotton alongside blacks, where he heard the blues first hand, played on horns and guitars; he made music his career with no prejudices against horns, drums or any other instruments and demanded a good dance beat from his band, because he began playing rhythm, served apprenticeship at farmhouse dances; played first dance at 15 when his father didn't show up, played them for 55 years, still breaking attendance records in California '69. His fiddle style broke with tradition, incl. both frontier style and more modern dance music; at first his sound was unique, but blues feeling was later much imitated. He encouraged, indeed insisted on hot solos and improvisation; the violin had been used in early jazz, but was being abandoned by the time Western Swing came along: his music could have been called western jazz, but by the time it had a label the Swing Era had come (*see* BIG BAND ERA). Almost all his records were made in Texas until '41; first sides for Brunswick '29 were unissued duos with Herman Arnspiger on guitar. Won fiddling contest on radio '30, already best-known fiddler in Texas; quartet broadcast for Aladdin Lamp Company '30 as the Aladdin Laddies, then for Burrus Mills and Elevator Company's Light Crust Flour as Light Crust Doughboys '31 on KFJZ, Fort Worth: Burrus president Wilbert Lee 'Pappy' O'DANIEL, future governor of Texas and United States Senator, hated their music at first, paid them as little as possible; when he realised how popular they were, he bought them a car to tour in, appeared regularly on the show and wrote songs for them, promoting himself along with the band. Vocalist Milton Brown wrote and sang Victor sides '32 billed as the Light Crust Doughboys; O'Daniel tried to stop them playing dances, where they could make more money; Brown quit, partly because he also wanted to run the band (took his brother Durwood Brown from Wills on rhythm guitar, hired Jesse Ashlock on fiddle, also hired a banjo, bass and piano, successful as Milton Brown and his Musical Brownies until killed in car crash '36, friends with Wills until the end; recorded over 100 sides; the Victors were later sold in Montgomery Ward mail-order catalogue as Brownies records; Brownies compilations on Rambler, String/Topic and Charly in UK. After '36 Durwood carried on with Brownies; younger brother Roy Lee Brown formed his own Music Brownies '40s). The Doughboys were carried over other Texas stations, became the most popular radio attraction in the Southwest; Wills hired Tommy Duncan to replace Brown, played few dances and worked at the mill, knuckling under to O'Daniel, but was fired because of his drinking; half the band left with him. The Doughboys were established: with changing personnel lasted into '50s on TV, but were not as popular without Wills; having fired Wills, O'Daniel sued him for $10,000 (at a time when the band didn't have $40 between them) for advertising his band as 'formerly the Light Crust Doughboys', making Texas case law by taking it all the way to the state supreme court, which refused to hear it. Wills called the band the Playboys, with Duncan on vocals and piano, Kermit Whalin on steel guitar and bass, brother Johnnie Lee Wills on tenor banjo, June Whalin, rhythm guitar; broadcast in Waco, then went to KVOO in Tulsa, Okla.; always an innovator, Wills bought half an hour of prime mid-day time, sold it to a sponsor himself, probably the first to do so: talked a miller into making Play Boy flour, paying a royalty on every barrel; Bob or Johnnie Lee broadcast for General Mills six days a week for 23 years. In Sep. 35 Bob Wills and his Texas Playboys were playing packed dancehalls six nights a week, began recording for Brunswick/ARC/Columbia through '47, over 250 sides still being reissued: first records with Duncan, Arnspiger and C. G. 'Sleepy' Johnson on guitars, Ashlock on fiddle, Art Haines doubling on fiddle/trombone, Robert 'Zeb' McNalley on sax, Son Lansford on bass, Al Stricklin on piano, William E. 'Smokey' Dacus on drums and Leon McAuliffe on steel guitar (*b* 3 Jan. '17, Houston, Texas): hired away from Doughboys, McAuliffe's 'Steel Guitar Rag' was a huge infl. on steel playing; he later had a long career as solo artist and champion of 'Western' as opposed to 'Country' music; his 'Panhandle Rag' was top 10 country hit '49 and he made the chart several times in early '60s, incl. 'Shape Up Or Ship Out' and 'I Don't Love Nobody' '64 on Capitol. The great Wills records were mostly prod. by Art SATHERLEY, who was a traditionalist: he told Wills 'We do not want any horns,' and was shocked when Wills threatened not to make any records at all. Wills also had a holler ('Ah-haa!') which would erupt when the band's swing was particularly hot; he would shout 'Take it away, Jesse!' etc. during a recording; Satherley was shocked by all this but got used to it: years later he asked, 'Where's your "Ah-haa", Bob?' Western music did not count for much in NYC where sales were calculated, but relatively poor people bought huge numbers of Wills records; *Pop Memories* (see CHARTS) calculates national hits for the band '39-46, incl. Wills' song 'San Antonio Rose' '39: re-made '40 as 'New San Antonio Rose' with 18-piece band incl. two trumpets, four or five reeds, it was a certified million-seller. Leon Huff was added on vocals and guitar '42 and the band began recording in Hollywood; they made two musical shorts and 13 feature films '40-6 (incl. *Take Me Back To Oklahoma* with Tex RITTER, *Go West Young Lady* with Glen Ford and Ann Miller). They recorded jazz, blues, rags, stomps as well as the usual ballads and sentimental songs; the largest band was 21-piece mid-'44 tour band that never recorded. Transcription records were made for the AFRS (Armed Forces Radio Service) '43-4; Tiffany Music 16″ transcription discs '45-7 were sold to radio stations, totalled 220 selections, the whole breadth and versatility of Wills' repertoire; the Antones was fan club label, issued 78s, two 10″ LPs. The band recorded for MGM '47-51, early personnel incl. Luke and Billy Jack Wills in rhythm section, Johnny Gimble on fiddle and mandolin; the war had wrecked the original band and the Big Band Era was over: the last MGM session was with only eight pieces. Transcriptions for Snader '51; records for Decca '55-7, mostly with no horns; Decca version of 'San Antonio Rose' heard on juke boxes from '55 had vocal by guitarist Kenny Lowrey with Wills' interjections. Recorded for Liberty '60-3, often with Duncan returning; for Longhorn '64 with Stricklin, C. G. Johnson on some sessions; on Kapp '65-9 with larger groups incl. horns again, sidemen incl. Harold BRADLEY on guitar, Hargus 'Pig'

Robbins on piano, Vassar CLEMENTS or Buddy Spicher on fiddle, Pete DRAKE on steel. Merle HAGGARD made album *A Tribute To The Best Damn Fiddle Player In The World* '70, using many original Wills sidemen; unissued tracks were made at Haggard's home '71, with Gimble, Hag and Joe Holley on fiddles, also Dacus, McAuliffe, Stricklin, Johnnie Lee and Luke Wills, Alex Brashear on trumpet, several others; Tommy Duncan had died '67 and his brother Glyn filled in: Wills had suffered a stroke and could not play, but he was still the leader. Similar group recorded 2-disc *For The Last Time* '73 on UA, instrumentals with Hag's fiddle on some tracks. Liberty and UA tracks now belong to EMI, Decca and Kapp to MCA, MGM to Polydor; eight compilation LPs on MCA USA are mostly in phoney stereo; 2-disc *24 Greatest Hits* on Polydor; *The Tiffany Transcriptions* fill several volumes on Kaleidoscope; *Keepsake Album* is on Longhorn. Original '30s-40s 78s are compiled on *Bob Wills*, 2-disc *Anthology* (24 tracks), 2-disc *The Golden Years* (32 tracks). *San Antonio Rose: The Life And Music Of Bob Wills* '76 by Charles R. Townsend is an excellent biography with full discography and filmography. Johnnie Lee Wills' *Tulsa Swing* is on Rounder, *Reunion* on Flying Fish; *High Voltage Gal* on Bear Family reissues 20 tracks by Luke Wills and his Rhythmbusters from '47.

WILLSON, Meredith (*b* Mason City, Iowa, 18 May '02) Composer, flautist. Played flute in John Philip SOUSA band, then New York Philharmonic; was Major in Armed Forces Radio Service during WWII; mus. dir. of KFRC radio in San Francisco, later also host on various radio and TV shows. Wrote music for films and TV, Broadway shows *Here's Love*, *The Music Man* and *The Unsinkable Molly Brown* (latter two filmed early '60s), drawing upon his own small-town background for smash hit *Music Man*, which ran for 1375 performances on Broadway. Robert Preston (*b* Robert Preston Meservy, 8 June '18, Newton Highlands, Mass.; *d* 21 Mar. '87, Santa Barbara, Cal.) starred in *Music Man* on stage and in '61 film; also in *Mame* '73; of his many films from '48, among best roles was non-musical *Dark At The Top Of The Stairs* '60, from William Inge play.

WILSON, Garland (*b* 13 June '09, Martinsburg, W.Va.; *d* 31 May '54, Paris, France) Pianist, infl. by Earl HINES and highly regarded in the blues. To NYC '30; Europe '32 with vocalist Nina Mae McKinney; back to USA '39, back to Paris after the war. He recorded piano solos (sang on one track) in NYC '31-2; in Paris '32 (two vocals by McKinney), London '36, Paris '38; very little post-war. '38 tracks incl. on EMI anthologies of jazz piano in Paris; *The Way I Feel* on Collectors Items incl. Nat Gonella, McKinney.

WILSON, Gerald (*b* 4 Sep. '18, Shelby, Ms.) Trumpet, bandleader, composer. A highly rated all-round musician who deserves more fame; excellent trumpet player who rarely solos. Played in clubs and went on the road late '30s; replaced Sy OLIVER in Jimmie LUNCEFORD band '39-42 (wrote 'Hi Spook'; co-wrote 'Yard Dog Mazurka'); settled on West Coast; worked for Les HITE, Benny CARTER, Willie SMITH; led own big band in L.A. mid-'40s; with Count BASIE and Dizzy GILLESPIE late '40s (his wife Melba Liston also played with Gillespie; Wilson wrote 'Katy', 'Dizzier & Dizzier' for Gillespie); left music but returned '52, led band in San Francisco; wrote for Duke ELLINGTON ('Smile' and 'If I Give My Heart To You' on Capitol). Studio work incl. Larry WILLIAMS session on Specialty. At least eight LPs of his own on Pacific Jazz, then World Pacific incl. *The Golden Sword*, now on Discovery; used sidemen like Joe PASS, Harold LAND, etc.; led big rehearsal/workshop band. Arr. albums *Man Of Many Parts* for Buddy COLLETTE on Contemporary, *Unforgettable* for Johnny HARTMAN on ABC-Paramount, *Yesterday's Love Songs* for Nancy WILSON on Capitol, *Things Ain't What They Used To Be* for Ella FITZGERALD on Reprise, *Al Hirt Live At Carnegie Hall* on RCA, others for Al HIBBLER, Bobby DARIN, Julie LONDON. Ella sang his 'Imagine My Frustration' on LP *Ella At Duke's Place* with Ellington on Verve. He played trumpet solos on *Leroy Walks!* by bassist Leroy Vinnegar on Contemporary; also did film work, wrote for symphony orchestra, had popular radio interview show on KBCA L.A., etc. Interested in the bullfight: his 'Viva Tirado' recorded by L.A. band El Chicano for a top

30 hit '70. Own LPs incl. *Lomelin* '81 on Discovery; *Jessica* '84, *Calafia* '86 on Trend by Gerald Wilson's Orchestra Of The '80s on Trend (with Land, others).

WILSON, Jackie (*b* 9 June '34, Detroit, Mich.; *d* 21 Jan. '84) Singer, songwriter; one of the most prodigiously talented and best-loved of all pop/soul singers, with about 35 R&B hits '58-71, nearly half in top 10; over 50 Hot 100 pop singles '57-72. He suffered a heart attack on stage at the Latin Casino in Camden, N.J. on 25 Sep. '75, spent the rest of his life in a coma. Discovered by Johnny OTIS '51, worked solo, replaced Clyde McPHATTER as lead singer in Billy WARD's Dominoes '53; his first six solo hits were co-written by Berry Gordy and Tyran Carlo: first 'Reet Petite' '57 on Brunswick; it was regarded as a novelty and reached only no. 67 in USA (but no. 6 in UK); despite a big band arrangement and recording balance which now seem dated, his extraordinary high spirits and unbelievable range of vocal sounds made it irresistible, huge hit '87 on reissue. 'Lonely Teardrops' '58 was no. 1 R&B, no. 7 pop; ninth/tenth hits were 'Night' (throbbing, operatic performance based on 'My Heart At Thy Sweet Voice' from Saint-Saëns' *Sampson and Delilah*) and its flip side, 'Doggin' Around' (more R&B flavour). 'Alone At Last' '60 had tune from Tchaikovsky's Piano Concerto No. 1. Among songs he co-wrote was duet with Linda Hopkins 'I Found Love' '62; 'Think Twice' '66 was duet with LaVern BAKER. His unbelievable virtuosity was overshadowed during the golden era of soul music; he had 29 more hits '62-72 but only seven in top 40 (incl. 'Baby Workout' '63 and 'Higher And Higher' '67, both top 10). Several chart LPs incl. live *Jackie Wilson At The Copa* '62, *Baby Workout* '63 (reached top 40 LPs with the big hit), *Manufacturers Of Soul* '68 with Count BASIE (incl. hits 'For Your Precious Love', 'Chain Gang'). During his years of unconsciousness he was recognised as a great artist; said to have infl. Elvis PRESLEY in stage act; Van MORRISON claimed him for an infl. and wrote 'Jackie Wilson Said (I'm In Heaven When You Smile)' (covered by DEXY'S MIDNIGHT RUNNERS for no. 5 UK hit '82); the COMMODORES had transatlantic no. 3 '85 with 'Nightshift', a tribute to both

Wilson and Marvin GAYE; Rita COOLIDGE, Shakin' STEVENS, many others covered hits. Compilations on Kent, Epic, Columbia Special Products; *Reet Petite* on Ace incl. Hopkins.

WILSON, Nancy (*b* 20 Feb. '37, Chillicothe, Ohio) Perennially popular pop singer handling all kinds of material with strong jazz qualities of phrasing, feeling, good intonation. Toured with Rusty Bryant band '56-8, first recorded for Dot '56. To NYC '59; signed with Capitol, began making fine LPs like *The Swingin's Mutual* with George SHEARING. 29 chart LPs '62-71 incl. top 10 albums *Yesterday's Love Songs, Today's Blues* (arr. by Gerald WILSON, no relation), *Today, Tomorrow, Forever, How Glad I Am, Today – My Way* '64-5; other hit LPs were *Nancy Wilson/Cannonball Adderley* '62, *The Nancy Wilson Show!* (live at the Coconut Grove) '65; *Lush Life* '67 had arr. by Billy MAY, Oliver NELSON, Sid Feller; reissued as *The Right To Love* '71, charted again in USA, then under first title in UK '84; *Nancy – Naturally* '67 arr. by May reissued '85 on Pausa. She had nine Hot 100 singles '63-71, only '(You Don't Know) How Glad I Am' '64 reaching top 40 (no. 11). No chart albums '72-4; remained popular club and cabaret artist; came back to top 200 LPs each year '74-7, left Capitol and charted again '84 with *The Two Of Us* with Ramsey LEWIS on CBS; *Keep You Satisfied* '86 was also on CBS, CD edition on Denon, which also issued *I'll Be A Song, Godsend* and *Yaksa* (with Toots THIELEMANS).

WILSON, Teddy (*b* 24 Nov. '12, Austin, Texas; *d* 31 July '86, New Britain, Conn.) Studied piano and violin at Tuskegee Institute; to Detroit '29, Chicago '31; played with Louis ARMSTRONG, Jimmie NOONE, joined Benny CARTER, played on his Chocolate Dandies dates '33; recorded with Benny GOODMAN and Gene KRUPA '35, went on tour with Goodman in trio (quartet when Lionel HAMPTON joined), helping to make history as the Swing Era's first integrated group. By this time his style of single-note lines, infl. by Earl HINES and Art TATUM but immensely sophisticated in its understated way, made him the most infl. pianist since Hines; but eschewing obvious flash caused him later to be underrated. He led scores of small-group record dates '35-42 for Brunswick labels, incl. instrumentals, famous vocals by Billie HOLIDAY (some issued under his name on Brunswick, others hers on Vocalion), but also vocalists Lena HORNE, Helen Ward, Thelma Carpenter, Sally Gooding, Nan Wynn, Jean Eldridge, others *(see below)*: made cheaply for juke boxes, using the best sidemen in town for each date, the records employ nearly all the best jazzmen alive at the time; about 50 were hits '35-8, some listed under both his and Holiday's names in *Pop Memories*. Among biggest hits were 'Carelessly', many others with Holiday; 'Where The Lazy River Goes By' (vocal by Midge Williams), 'My Melancholy Baby' (Ella Fitzgerald), 'Remember Me?' (Boots Castle). Nearly all were made in NYC, but L.A. dates '37 yielded no. 1 instrumental 'You Can't Stop Me From Dreaming', several vocals by Francis Hunt, unusual quartet session with Wilson, Red NORVO on xylophone, Harry JAMES on trumpet, John Simmons on bass: 'Just A Mood' (two sides), 'Honeysuckle Rose' and top 10 'Ain't Misbehavin' '. Left Goodman '39, led own fine big band for a year which was not recorded, writing some arrangements himself; played in NYC with a sextet '40-4; lived there the rest of his life, teaching (each summer at Juilliard '45-52), broadcasting, occasionally recording, playing in clubs, touring overseas. Rejoined Goodman occasionally (*Seven Lively Arts* on Broadway '45, film *The Benny Goodman Story*, quartet reunion LP on RCA '63, etc.), had his own radio show and worked on staff at CBS mid-'50s. 19 piano solos '38-9 were recorded as Teddy Wilson School For Pianists, reissued '88 by Mosaic USA as part of massive complete Commodore project. 2-disc *Teddy Wilson And His All-Stars* on CBS incl. 32 tracks '36-40, mostly instrumentals incl. those mentioned above; *Too Hot For Words* on Hep UK has excellent transfers of the first 16 issued small-group sides from '35, *Warmin' Up* covers '36. *See also* Holiday compilations on CBS/Columbia. Later LPs incl. *Gypsy* and *Mr Wilson & Mr Gershwin* on Columbia; *For Quiet Lovers, I Got Rhythm, Impeccable Mr Wilson, Intimate Listening*, all on Verve, as is 2-disc *Prez & Teddy* '56, with Lester Young, Vic DICKENSON, Roy ELDRIDGE, Freddie GREEN, Jo JONES, bassist Gene Ramey, virtually re-creating the '30s small groups. Others: sextet compilations from '44-7 with Charlie SHAVERS etc. on various labels incl. *And His All Stars* (vocals by Maxine SULLIVAN), *As Time Goes By* (Kay Penton), *Time After Time* (Sarah VAUGHAN), solo piano *Sunny Morning*, all on Musicraft; *Dutch College Swing Band Meets Teddy Wilson* on Timeless; *With Billie In Mind* on Chiaroscuro; *Elegant Piano* with Marian McPARTLAND on her Halcyon label; *Trio In Europe '68* on Fantasy; *Lionel Hampton Presents* '77 on Who's Who In Jazz; on Black Lion: *Striding After Fats, Runnin' Wild, Cole Porter Classics, Moonglow*; on Storyville: *Inez Cavanaugh With Teddy Wilson's Trio: An Evening At Timme's Club, The Delicate Swing Of Teddy Wilson* (Standard transcriptions '45), *The Noble Art Of* (with bassist Niels-Henning Ørsted Pedersen), *Revisits The Goodman Years, Masters Of Jazz Vol. 11*, etc. A French CBS compilation of piano solos incl. his very first from '34, rejected at the time as 'too monotonous'.

WINCHESTER, Jesse (*b* 17 May '44, Shreveport, La.) USA singer/songwriter. Son of a USA serviceman, he was studying in Munich when Vietnam draft papers arrived; made home in Canada, became Canadian citizen '73. Eponymous debut LP '70 prod. by Robbie Robertson, who played on it along with Levon Helm; like the best work of the BAND emphasis was on a bygone America: 'Yankee Lady' and 'Brand New Tennessee Waltz' were covered widely. *Third Down, 110 To Go* '72 (referring to Canadian football) was prod. by Todd RUNDGREN (all LPs on Ampex/Bearsville, where Rundgren is house producer); semi-*a cappella Learn To Love It* '74 found him in mellower mood, with a gospel touch carried over into *Let The Rough Side Drag* '76. *Nothin' But A Breeze* '77, *A Touch On The Rainy Side* '78 were well-crafted country rock, with Emmylou HARRIS, Anne MURRAY helping on vocals; he was pardoned in President Carter's amnesty for Vietnam, toured USA; *Talk Memphis* '81 was prod. by Willie Mitchell (Al GREEN, Hi Records, etc.) and added R&B bite to thoughtful lyrics: incl. 'Say What', his first top 40 single. Songs have been covered by EVERLY Bros,

Tim HARDIN, Joan BAEZ, Elvis COSTELLO, many others.

WINDING, Kai (*b* Kai Chresten Winding, 18 May '22, Aarhus, Denmark; *d* 6 May '83) Trombone. To USA at age 12; worked with Stan KENTON, Charlie VENTURA, Tadd DAMERON late '40s; played on Miles DAVIS *Birth Of The Cool* session '48; co-led quintet with J. J. JOHNSON '54-6 which was one of the most popular jazz acts of the '50s, helping to restore the trombone to its rightful place after some neglect in early modern jazz. Led four-trombone sextet '56-61 (*Brass Fever* and *Incredible Trombones* on Impulse); mus. dir. of Playboy Clubs '60s; toured with Dizzy GILLESPIE, Thelonious MONK etc. in Giants Of Jazz early '70s, was semi-retired in Spain. Toured with Lionel HAMPTON '79, two-trombone group with Curtis FULLER (*Bones 80* on Black & Blue). Other LPs: *Solo*, *Dirty Dog*, *Rainy Day*, *More Brass* on Verve; Verve single 'More' (theme from film *Mondo Cane*) was top 10 pop hit '63. With Sonny STITT on *Early Modern* on Hall Of Fame Jazz; reunions with Johnson on *Israel*, *Betwixt And Between*, *Stonebones* on A&M; *Jazz Showcase '77* on Gateway; *Caravan* and *Danish Blue* on Glendale, *Lionel Hampton Presents* on Who's Who, all with Frank Strazzeri (*b* 24 Apr. '30, Rochester, NY; pianist/composer, also plays vibes, reeds, etc.), others on MPS, Cobblestone.

WINGFIELD, Pete (*b* 7 May '48) UK singer, pianist, producer. Formed blues band Jellybread while studying at Sussex U. late '60s: Paul Butler, guitar; John Best, bass; Chris Waters, drums; made *First Slice* and *65 Parkway* '69-70, left, made name as session musician, credits incl. Freddie KING, Maggie BELL, BLOODSTONE, mostly under augis of Blue Horizon's prod. Mike Vernon. Played in Colin BLUNSTONE band, wrote three songs for him; backed Van MORRISON live '74; signed with Island for solo *Breakfast Special* '75, collection of white soul and R&B that revealed unsuspected vocal talent incl. stunning falsetto; continued to front band with Joe Jammer (Joseph Wright) on guitar, Glen LeFleur on drums, Delisle Harper on bass, George Chandler vocals; had three minor UK hits with them. Retired to produce, notably DEXY'S MIDNIGHT

RUNNERS' *Searching For The Young Soul Rebels* '80 with no. 1 hit 'Geno' (the band hijacked the master tape to secure a better deal for themselves); also Dexy's spinoff *The Bureau* '81, new romantics Blue Ronde A La Turk, Polish group LGT, Newcastle soulsters the Kane Gang, soul group Second Image; as sideline created session group Bands Of Gold whose medley of soul hits 'Love Songs Are Back Again' was top 25 hit in '84.

WINTER, Edgar (*b* 28 Dec. '46, Beaumont, Texas) Singer, keyboardist, saxophonist, bandleader; brother of Johnny (*see below*) and like him an albino. They played together in Black Plague, split to go solo; Edgar played on several of Johnny's LPs incl. the first, which helped him to gain solo contract with CBS: debut *Entrance* '70 saw him playing almost all the instruments, but sold poorly; he formed band White Trash with Jerry Lacroix, lead vocals and sax; John Smith on sax, Mike McClellan on vocals and trumpet, George Sheck on bass, Bobby Ramirez on drums, Floyd Radford on guitar; *White Trash* '71, live 2-disc *Road Work* '72; these did better, *Road Work* reaching top 25 LPs in USA, but he disbanded and formed the Edgar Winter Group with Ronnie Montrose, lead guitar; Dan Hartman on bass, drummer Chuck Ruff; B-side to first single 'Hangin' Around', moog-led instrumental 'Frankenstein', made no. 1 USA, top 20 UK and boosted *They Only Come Out At Night* '72 to no. 3; 'Free Ride' was top 15 USA. Prod. Rick DERRINGER had played on two or three LPs, toured with group that recorded *Shock Treatment* '74 and *With Rick Derringer* '75, hard rock LPs interspersed with Winter's solo, jazzy *Jasmine Nightdreams*; Derringer and Hartman struck out solo '76, Winter rejoined Johnny (who'd also played on several Edgar LPs) for live/oldies set *Together*. He issued *The Edgar Winter Album* '79, *Standing On Rock* '81; *Recycled* '77 was compilation of Trash. Sessioned widely, on Johnny's LPs, also with Bette MIDLER, MEATLOAF, Montrose, etc.

WINTER, Johnny (*b* 22 Feb. '44, Leland, Ms.) Blues guitarist. Grew up in Texas with younger brother Edgar (*above*). Brought up on Howlin' WOLF, Muddy WATERS etc.;

first record at 15: 'Schoolday Blues' by Johnny and the Jammers on Dart (with Edgar on piano). Moved to Chicago, playing with many obscure groups: Gene Taylor and the Down Beats, It and Them (aka Black Plague, with Edgar); early work released on Imperial as *Progressive Blues Experiment*, on GRT as *The Johnny Winter Experiment* at same time as proper debut *Johnny Winter* '69 on Columbia, which despite the competition reached top 25 LPs USA, with *Second Winter* '70 featuring Tommy Shannon on bass, John 'Red' Turner on drums, who'd played with him since '68, plus Edgar. Club owner Steve Paul signed him to management contract, linked him with McCoys (of pop hit 'Hang On Sloopy' fame) for *Johnny Winter And* '71, which took him towards rambling acid rock. Guitarist Rick Derringer, Randy Hobbs on bass were joined by Bobby Caldwell on drums for *Live/Johnny Winter And* '71, covering Chuck BERRY, ROLLING STONES, others in good-time rock vein. After drug-imposed period of retirement, emerged with *Still Alive And Well* '73; thenceforth returned to hard blues, prod. Waters' popular *Hard Again*, toured with him. *Saints And Sinners* and *John Dawson Winter III* '74, *Captured Live* and *Together* (with Edgar) '76, *Nothin' But The Blues* '77, *Red Hot And Blue* '79 worked the same ground; he sparked briefly with *Raisin' Cain* '80, trio with Jon Paris on bass and harmonica, Bobby Torello, drums. Most of the later LPs were on custom Blue Sky label, most went out of print while the earliest LPs were still selling. Signed with Chicago's Alligator label, with unpretentious policy of ladling out the straight stuff for fans: no horns, no background singers, no synthesisers; *Guitar Slinger* '84 returned him to charts, backed by labelmates; *Serious Business* kept him there, with Casey Jones on drums, Johnny B. Gayden on bass, Ken Saydack on piano; *Third Degree* '86 added guests Mac REBENNACK on two tracks, old comrades Turner and Shannon on three.

WINTERHALTER, Hugo (*b* 15 Aug '09, Wilkes-Barre, Penn.; *d* 17 Sep. '73, Greenwich, Conn.) Arranger, conductor. Studied at New England Conservatory, wrote arr. for Benny GOODMAN, Count BASIE, Claude THORNHILL, Will BRADLEY, others. Mus. dir. at MGM '48-9, Columbia '49-50, RCA '50-63, and Kapp. At RCA he wrote arr. for Eddie FISHER, Dinah SHORE, AMES Bros, others; his record of 'Canadian Sunset' (with its comp. Eddie HEYWOOD on piano) was no. 2 million-seller '56. His recording of George GERSHWIN's *Rhapsody In Blue* early '50s (the excellent Byron Janis on piano) touched up the Ferde Grofé arrangement, swung more than most.

WINWOOD, Steve (*b* 12 May '48, Birmingham, UK) Singer, multi-instrumentalist, songwriter. Became a star in Spencer DAVIS group with keyboards and bluesy voice, formed TRAFFIC, made one LP with supergroup BLIND FAITH; intended to start solo career with album to be called *Mad Shadows* which became Traffic LP *John Barleycorn Must Die*; 2-disc *Winwood* '71 on United Artists UK was compilation from all this. He worked as a session musician for several years on LPs by people as diverse as Jim Capaldi (of Traffic), Sandy DENNY, the FANIA ALL STARS, George HARRISON, John MARTYN, Toots and the Maytals, with ex-BONZO Viv Stanshall on his *Men Opening Umbrellas Ahead* and *Sir Henry At Rawlinson's End*, Japanese percussionist Stomu Yamashta and his ambitious Go group (two LPs charted in USA '76-7, both with Al DiMEOLA). Debuted with *Steve Winwood* '77 on Island, then big hit *Arc Of A Diver* '80, songs co-written with Will Jennings, George Fleming and Stanshall: it was self-produced like latter-day Traffic work and early work with the Habits (now on Charly compilation *Sixties Lost And Found*), incl. top 10 hit 'While You See A Chance', showed evidence of his greater aptitude in the recording studio than on stage. Mooted collaboration as producer with June TABOR was cancelled when Island foresaw it holding up his next album still further; he worked as session player, arguably at the expense of solo career, on Capaldi's *Fierce Heart*, Marianne FAITHFULL album *Broken English*, with Julie COVINGTON, with Stanshall on *Teddy Boys Don't Knit*. *Talking Back To The Night* '82 was top 30 LP USA, showing complete mastery of studio tools; he carried on sessioning: on Talk Talk's *The Colour Of Spring*, Billy JOEL's *The Bridge*, soundtrack for Delon's *They Call That An Accident*;

emerged '86 with his glossiest and most commercial record *Back In The High Life*, overproduced compared to the last one, but loaded with that unmistakable voice: it reached no. 3 in USA, copped several Grammy nominations, incl. no. 1 USA hit 'Higher Love' (with Chaka KHAN and strong video), top 10 'The Finer Things'. *Chronicles* '87 on Island compiled tracks from solo career; switched to Virgin for *Roll With It* '88.

WISEMAN, Mac (*b* 23 Mar. '25, Crimoa, Va.) Bluegrass guitarist, singer. Played in a country band in high school, joined Molly O'Day as lead singer (*see* Art SATHERLEY), then with Lester FLATT and Earl Scruggs, then Bill MONROE; went solo, recorded for Dot and became label's country A&R man; bluegrass began to be picked up by folkies, especially on college campuses; cover of CARTER FAMILY song 'Jimmy Brown, The Newsboy' was a top 5 country hit '59. Switched to Capitol: first Capitol LP *Bluegrass Favourites* '62 reissued on Stetson '87; 'Your Best Friend And Me' was '63 hit. Starred on WWVA *Jamboree* in Wheeling West Va. (also appeared on Louisiana Hayride, Grand Ole Opry, various radio barn dances around the country); had own radio show *Mac Wiseman's Record Shop*. Recorded for MGM ('Got Leavin' On Her Mind' '68); to RCA '69: 'Johnny's Cash & Charley's Pride' was top 40 hit that year; he reunited with Flatt for two LPs *Lester 'n' Mac, On The Southbound*. Also ran annual bluegrass festival in Renfro Valley, Ky. Not only a fine guitarist but one of the half-dozen best singers in the genre; other LPs incl. *16 Great Performances* on MCA, *Mac Wiseman* on MCA/Dot, *Early Dot Recordings* on County, two vols. of *New Traditions* on Vetco; also *Greatest Bluegrass Hits, Sings Gordon Lightfoot*, 2-disc sets *Mac Wiseman Story* and *Songs That Made Juke Box Play*, all on Country Music Heritage.

WISHBONE ASH Progressive rock band formed in Torquay, England '69 by brothers Glen (lead guitar) and Martin Turner (bass and vocals; *b* 10 Jan. '47), drummer Steve Upton (*b* 24 May '46). After local success rhythm section relocated to London, auditioned lead guitarists, hired both Andy Powell (*b* 8 Feb. '50) and Ted Turner

(*b* David Turner, 8 Feb. '50; no relation). Unique twin-lead guitar lineup gave blues-based progressive rock its trademark. *Wishbone Ash* '70 recorded after much touring; manager was future POLICE Svengali Miles Copeland; stage favourite 'Phoenix' helped LP to top 40 UK. *Pilgrimage* '71 reached top 15 (and Ted sessioned on John LENNON's *Imagine*); *Argus* '72 saw them hit creative and commercial peak: helmeted soldier and UFO on sleeve set tone for quasi-mystical titles ('Warrior', 'The King Will Come', etc.) but tracks ignited by dueling guitars ALLMAN-style that enlivened breaks and fades. *Wishbone Four* '73 disappointed owing to their determination not to duplicate *Argus*, but reached top 50 USA; Ted got religion and left after 2-disc *Live Dates* '73, replaced by Laurie Wisefield (ex-Home). Now successful in USA, recorded *There's The Rub* '74 in Miami with Bill SZYMCZYK, their last top 20 LP in UK; recorded with Tom DOWD on *Locked In* '76 (thus this and next LP were on Atlantic in USA instead of MCA); decided to stay in USA since Copeland's Star Trucking world tour, designed to break them big, collapsed when Lou REED pulled out; *New England* '76 was their best since *Argus* but did not recapture commercial ground. *Front Page News* '77, *No Smoke Without Fire* '78, *Just Testing* '79 all disappointed: they'd become clichéd. Martin Turner departed for career in production; bassist John Wetton (ex-King Crimson, FAMILY) played on *Number The Brave* '81, Trevor Bolder (ex-BOWIE, URIAH HEEP) on *Twin Barrels Burning* '82, both prod. by Nigel Gray (ex-Police) and sound was revamped at last. '70s folksinger Clare Hamill sang for a while but didn't record with them. Bolder rejoined Heep, replaced by Mervyn Spence (ex-Trapeze); *Raw To The Bone* '85 on Neat carried on once influential twin-guitar sound. Original lineup made instrumental *Nouveau Calls* '88, said to be one of the best in IRS label's 'No Speak' series of new age rock albums.

WITHERS, Bill (*b* 4 July '38, Slab Fork, West Va.) Sweet soul singer, songwriter; youngest of six children. Worked as bricklayer, spent nine years in US Navy, etc.; moved to West Coast '67, made demo records of his songs; began recording for Sussex label '70, first pro appearance in public in mid-'71 at age

33: late start because of shyness and a stammer, both cured by the Navy, the latter partly by speech therapy. 'Ain't No Sunshine' was no. 3 pop hit '71 and won a Grammy, from top 40 LP *Just As I Am*, prod. by Booker T. Jones; *Still Bill* '72 was no. 4 LP incl. 'Lean On Me' (no. 1 hit), 'Use Me' (no. 2). Eleven hit singles through '77 were all written by Withers except one. Hit LPs incl. 2-disc *Live At Carnegie Hall* '73, *'Justments* '74; switched to Columbia for *Making Music* '75, *Naked & Warm* '76, top 40 *Menagerie* '77, *'Bout Love* '79. Sang on Grover WASHINGTON LP *Winelight* '81 incl. co-written 'Just The Two Of Us', no. 2 hit with Washington on sax (single on Elektra, incl. in *Best Of* on Columbia). *Watching You Watching Me* '85 was another top 200 LP.

WITHERSPOON, Jimmy (*b* 8 Aug. '23, Gurdon, Ark.) Singer with big deep beautiful voice, characterised as blues singer but with all-round skills. While in Merchant Marine early '40s sang with Teddy WEATHERFORD band on stop in Calcutta; replaced Walter Brown in Jay MCSHANN band '44-8; R&B hits began with no. 1 'Ain't Nobody's Business' '49, more '49-52 on Supreme and Modern labels. Began making LPs '58; appeared at Monterey Jazz Festival '59 (live on HiFiJazz label) and recorded for RCA, Atlantic, World Pacific, Reprise. Visited prisons regularly '60s to sing for inmates, toured Europe once a year; sang at Monterey in Jon HENDRICKS' *Evolution Of The Blues Song* and in Columbia LP of it. Prestige LPs incl. *Blues Around The Clock* and *Blue Spoon*, with keyboard and three rhythm; *Some Of My Best Friends Are The Blues* with horns, strings arr./cond. by Benny GOLSON: title track released as single and flip side, soulful medium-tempo ballad 'You're Next', was Hot 100 hit '65; further Prestige LPs were *Blues For Easy Livers* (with Pepper ADAMS, Roger KELLAWAY, others), *Best Of* and *Mean Old Frisco* (with 12 pieces). *Spoon In London* probably incl. in 2-disc *Spoon Concerts* on Fantasy (incl. Monterey Jazz Festival recording with Ben WEBSTER, Coleman HAWKINS, Roy ELDRIDGE, etc.). Others: *Spoonful* on Blue Note; *Love Is A Five Letter Word* on Capitol (top 200 LP '75), *Handbags & Gladrags* on ABC; also record-ed with Gerry MULLIGAN (now on Joker); *Sings The Blues* '80 with Panama Francis's SAVOY SULTANS on Muse. Also: *Cry The Blues* with Richard 'Groove' HOLMES now on Bulldog, *Live In Paris* with Buck CLAYTON on Vogue, *Big Blues* on JSP (made in London '81), *Ain't Nobody's Business* on Black Lion, *Live* with Robben Ford on MCA, *(Evenin') Blues* on Fanstasy with T-Bone WALKER, compilation of early tracks *Who's Been Jivin' You* on Ace.

WOLF, Howlin' (*b* Chester Arthur Burnett, 10 June '10, West Point, Ms.; *d* 10 Jan. '76, Hines, Ill.) Blues singer, guitarist, played harmonica; became a legend with his compulsively powerful performance, named after a howl of frustration and bitterness. Spent most of his time working as a farmer until '48, but also performed at Juke Joints etc. with Charley PATTON, Robert JOHNSON, Alger ALEXANDER; learned harmonica from Sonny Boy WILLIAMSON (Rice Miller). Formed band with Junior PARKER, James COTTON, others in West Memphis '48, worked at station KWEM; Ike TURNER took him to Sam Phillips at Sun Records (first tracks leased to Chess), then to RPM label; moved to Chicago '52 and stayed with Chess. Muddy WATERS helped him to get work there, but their rivalry later became legendary (Wolf allegedly tried to stretch out his segment at the Ann Arbor Blues Festival '69 so that Waters would not get on). Had several heart attacks but would not stop working; died of cancer. By the time he began recording he was too raw, too powerful for the R&B charts; the only hits he had were 'How Many More Years' '51, 'Smoke Stack Lightning' '56, 'Evil' '69 (first record-ed '54), all incl. in compilation *Evil* mid-'60s on Chess, also in first of three 2-disc sets of *Chess Masters* series early '80s in UK. *Moanin' In The Moonlight* '51-9 tracks on Chess USA; compilations on other labels incl. Sun tracks from Charly UK, e.g. on *Sam's Blues*, with LITTLE WALTER tracks; *Ridin' In The Moonlight* on Ace, etc. Good profile in Peter Guralnick's *Feel Like Going Home*.

WOLF, Kate (*b* 27 Jan. '42; *d* 10 Dec. '86) Country singer-songwriter. One of the best in mould of Nanci GRIFFITH, Guy CLARK etc.; she died of leukaemia just as her fame was growing. LPs on Kaleidoscope label: *Back Roads* with the Wildwood Flower, *Lines On The Paper* adding the Cache Valley Drifters, *Safe At Anchor, Close To You, Poet's Heart*, 2-disc live *Give Yourself To Love*, 2-disc compilation *Gold In California* (compiled by Wolf when she knew she would be unable to record again, with one new song). She also contributed to *Out Of The Darkness – Songs For Survival* on Fire On The Mountain label, with Holly NEAR, Pete SEEGER, Jesse Colin Young, others.

WOMACK, Bobby (*b* 4 Mar. '44, Cleveland, Ohio) Singer, songwriter, guitarist. Formed gospel group with brothers Cecil, Curtis, Harry and Friendly. They toured with Sam COOKE; he signed them to his Sar label when they went secular; as the Valentinos they made legendary R&B tracks 'It's All Over Now' (written by Bobby & Shirley Womack; covered by the ROLLING STONES) and 'Lookin' For A Love' (by James Alexander and Zelda Samuels; no. 8 R&B '62; covered by J. GEILS Band). Also recorded as the Lovers, split up when Cooke died; Bobby became a session guitarist, worked for Wilson PICKETT, wrote big Pickett hits 'I'm A Midnight Mover' and 'I'm In Love'; he went solo, had nine chart LPs and single hits on Minit, Liberty, then United Artists, where he did better in soul chart, also made pop top 40 with 'That's The Way I Feel About 'Cha', 'Harry Hippie', 'Nobody Wants You When You're Down And Out' '71-3; revived 'Lookin' For A Love' for top 10 hit '74; had less luck on Columbia and Arista; came back to soul chart with no. 1 LP *The Poet* on Beverly Glen label incl. no. 3 soul hit 'If You Think You're Lonely Now' '81, also sequel *The Poet 2* '84, incl. first UK hit 'Tell Me Why', also 'Love Has Finally Come At Last', duet with Patti LABELLE, Hot 100 in USA. He also sang on Wilton Felder hits (*see* CRUSADERS) 'Inherit The Wind' '80, '(No Matter How High I Get) I'll Still Be Looking Up To You' '85, both top 3 in what is now called the black chart. Bobby was married for a while to Cooke's widow, Barbara; Cecil Womack to Mary WELLS. Cecil and Mary divorced; he married Cooke's daughter Linda and Mary married Curtis. Harry was shot dead by a jealous girlfriend who found a woman's clothes in his closet; they belonged to Bob-

by's girlfriend. Cecil and Linda as Womack And Womack wrote hits for Teddy PENDERGRASS, George BENSON, etc.; their own 'Love Wars' was top 20 hit UK '84, title track of Elektra LP; after differences with prod. Stuart Levine in London they recorded for Manhattan. Bobby's LPs incl. *So Many Rivers* '85, *Womagic* '86, *The Last Soul Man* '87 (three tracks remixed from *Womagic*), all on MCA; others incl. *Soul Survivor* '87 on EMI America, compilations *Somebody Special* and *Understanding* on Liberty UK, Valentinos tracks on Chess Masters in UK.

WONDER, Stevie (*b* 13 May '50, Saginaw, Mich.) Singer, songwriter, multi-instrumentalist. Real name sometimes given as Steveland Judkins; ASCAP biographical dictionary gives it as Stevland Morris. A premature baby, he was made permanently blind by receiving too much oxygen in an incubator; was named Little Stevie Wonder by Berry Gordy, who signed him to Motown '61 after the Miracles' Ronnie White heard him play harmonica at age 10. Much was made of his blindness; in additional comparison to Ray CHARLES his live first LP was called *Little Stevie Wonder/The 12 Year Old Genius*; both LP and single 'Fingertips' were no. 1 hits: two singles had flopped but he was a hit in Motown's touring show and 'Fingertips' was finished showpiece by the time of recording at Chicago's Regal theatre. He's had 56 hit singles '63-86 (27 in top 10, nine at no. 1) and 21 hit albums. As his voice deepened so did his repertoire; he had hits with Bob DYLAN's 'Blowing In The Wind' (top 10), his co-written 'I Was Made To Love Her', and 'For Once In My Life' (previously recorded by Tony BENNETT), last two at no. 2. He appeared in films *Bikini Beach* and *Muscle Beach Party*, continued having hits; co-wrote 'Tears Of A Clown' for the Miracles, their first no. 1 pop hit '70 (also no. 1 in soul chart); he prod. his own LP *Where I'm Coming From* '71 himself: it was uneven, reached only no. 62 in pop LP chart but incl. top 10 hit 'If You Really Love Me'. At Motown he was a prankster, insatiably curious, prodigiously talented; the company had looked after his schooling, royalties; when he turned 21 his contract ran out and he came into a million dollars: he formed production company Taurus, publishing company Black Bull, moved with his wife to NYC (at a time when Motown was moving to L.A.). (Syreeta Wright is from Pittsburgh; the marriage was brief and he has not married again; he masterminded LPs *Syreeta* '72 and *Stevie Wonder Presents Syreeta Wright* '74; she continued to record for Motown, co-wrote songs on several of his albums during this significant period, later had hit duet with Billy PRESTON, top 5 'With You I'm Born Again' '80.) He stayed with Motown, but on his own terms, the first Motown artist to obtain complete control over his own work. He was enchanted by *Zero Time*, by Tonto's Expanding Head Band (Tonto: The Original New Timbral Orchestra, a group of synthesisers), recruited Tonto's Malcolm Cecil and Robert Margouleff as guides and plunged into the technology, master of it ever since and doing more things well than anybody else: one of the few who can do it all himself without rhythmically stiff results. *Music Of My Mind* '72 was his 12th album, incl. two *Greatest Hits* sets; it reached no. 2. Toured that year with the ROLLING STONES, gaining exposure to white audience; subsequent new albums all reached top 5. *Talking Book* '72 incl. no. 1 hits 'Superstition' and 'You Are The Sunshine Of My Life'; *Innervisions* '73 incl. two top 10 hits; in mid-'73 he survived a near fatal car crash. *Fulfillingness' First Finale* '74 incl. no. 1 'You Haven't Done Nothing' (with JACKSON 5 on background vocal), no. 3 'Boogie On Reggae Woman'; 2-disc *Songs In The Key Of Life* incl. a bonus 7″ EP with four tracks, also no. 1 hits 'I Wish' and tribute to Duke ELLINGTON 'Sir Duke' (last two both no. 1 albums). *Looking Back* '77 was another compilation, a top 40 3-disc set; he resumed his career with 2-disc *Journey Through The Secret Life Of Plants* '79: took three years to make, a largely instrumental soundtrack to a film that was never made, it still reached no. 4. *Hotter Than July* '80 was followed by 2-disc *Stevie Wonder's Original Musiquarium 1*, compilation of '72-82 hits at no. 4; *The Woman In Red* '84 was a soundtrack LP, with no. 1 hit 'I Just Called To Say I Love You' (won an Oscar), Dionne WARWICK on three songs; *In Square Circle* '85 incl. no. 1 hit 'Part-Time Lover', also 'It's Wrong (Apartheid)', with chorus in

Xhosa dialect sung by South African exiles. He accepts the challenges of new genres such as reggae, rap (as in 'Master Blaster (Jammin')', top 5 pop hit and no. 1 in black chart from *Hotter Than July*; his 'Happy Birthday' from same LP was tribute to Martin Luther King; he led the movement to make King's birthday a national holiday. Songs like 'You Ain't Done Nothing' and 'Living For The City' (top 10 '73) incl. social commentary; he has devoted much time and energy to causes such as research into cancer and AIDS, campaign against drunken driving; his duet with Paul MCCARTNEY 'Ebony And Ivory' was a no. 1 '82 (on CBS; the only hit that did not appear on Tamla/Motown); he contributed to USA For Africa's charity record 'We Are The World' '85, and brought two Ethiopian women into the recording session at 4 a.m., perpetrating the emotional highlight of it. He has won 16 Grammies. Some feel that his ballads are sometimes undistinguished, such as 'I Just Called To Say I Love You' and 'Part-Time Lover', but songs like 'My Cherie Amour' ('69), 'You Are The Sunshine Of My Life', 'Isn't She Lovely' (from *Songs In The Key Of Life*) are regarded by many as among the era's most enduring love songs: basically he can do no wrong, perhaps USA's best-loved recording artist. *Characters* '87 incl. duet with Michael JACKSON on 'Get It'; a few meandering ballads, but also sprightly funk; an example of a completely different album on CD, with two important tracks adding 12 minutes' playing time.

WOOD, Del (*b* Adelaide Hazelwood, 22 Feb. '20) Pianist, vocalist. A secretary for the state of Tennessee, she recorded a spirited ragtimey version of the old fiddle tune 'Down Yonder' ('34 hit by Gid Tanner and his Skillet Lickers) which was a top 10 hit '51 on the national USA pop chart. She had to sue the Tennessee label for royalties; had a sizeable hit with 'Elmer's Tune' '53 on Republic, recorded for many other labels and remained a regular on the Grand Ole Opry. LP *Tavern In The Town* on Vocalion.

WOOD, Roy (*b* Ulysses Adrian Wood, 8 Nov. '46, Birmingham, England) Producer, singer, songwriter, multi-instrumentalist. Played in local groups incl. Mike Sheridan and the Nightriders, then Falcons, Lawmen, Gerry Levene and the Avengers; made name in MOVE. Tiring of pop formula he formed ELECTRIC LIGHT ORCHESTRA around Move's drummer Bev Bevan, multi-instrumentalist Jeff Lynne (ex-Idle Race); first LP incl. hit '10538 Overture', Lynne's composition. It set tone for group; Wood left to form Wizzard with guitarist Rick Price (ex-Move) and cellist Hugh McDowell (ex-ELO), others. Cloned Phil SPECTOR wall of sound prod. style for series of upbeat pop hits incl. two no. ones ('See My Baby Jive' and 'Angel Fingers' '73). Wood promoted hits in flamboyant makeup, weird hairpieces etc. but they lacked variety of his solo LP *Boulders* '73, which had quite contrasting hits in BEATLE-ish 'Dear Elaine' (top 20), BEACH-BOYS style 'Forever' (top 10). Solo *Mustard* '75 continued showing off instrumental and prod. technique. Wizzard ran its course; he floated short-lived groups Wizzo '70s, Helicopters '80s; prod. Darts and Annie Haslam (from RENAISSANCE) but little of his own work except a Wizzo LP and solo *On The Road Again* '79. Signed to indie Legacy mid-'80s, was building home studio for next phase; *Starting Up* '87 incl. collaboration with Dr & The Medics on 'Waterloo', showing affection younger generation has for him.

WOODING, Sam (*b* 17 June 1895, Philadelphia, Pa; *d* 1 Aug. '85) Pianist, arranger, bandleader. Served in US Army during WWI, playing tenor horn in service band; in '25 already a prominent bandleader, he went to Europe leading band accompanying revue *Chocolate Kiddies*, left revue and continued touring, playing in Eastern Europe incl. Russia, UK, Italy etc., then South America before returning home mid-'27; returned to Europe again '28-31 for extensive touring. Led a band until '35, then studied music formally, led Southland Spiritual Choir on tours, worked as full-time teacher, led a vocal group that sang at Carnegie Hall '49, taught and ran Ding-Dong record label '50s, toured the world in duo with vocalist Rae Harrison '60s, went to Japan '67, lived in Germany '68, still touring '70s. One of the first to take black music to Europe, he created a sensation, played top venues with sidemen like Tommy LADNIER, Doc CHEATHAM, Gene Sedric;

but it was at the expense of fame at home: when he returned to the USA to stay early '30s, he had been overtaken by Fletcher HENDERSON in hot music, soon by the big-name white bands of the Swing Era. *Sam Wooding's Chocolate Kiddies* on Biograph has '25-9 tracks made in Europe.

WOODS, Phil (*b* Phillip Wells Woods, 2 Nov. '31, Springfield, Mass.) Alto sax, clarinet, leader. He toured with big bands, worked with small groups; was married to Chan Richardson (Charlie PARKER's consort at the time of his death); played with Dizzy GILLESPIE big band '56, co-led two-alto combo with Gene Quill (*b* Daniel Eugene Quill, 15 Dec. '27, Atlantic City, N.J.; recorded with Gerry MULLIGAN, many others); played in Buddy RICH Quintet '58-9, became founder member of Quincy JONES big band '59. Along with Cannonball ADDERLEY he was one of the most influential alto players of the post-bop era, deepening the style with a full tone and blues inflections, becoming a jazzman of internationally high regard. Recorded with George RUSSELL (on Decca), others in '50s; with T. MONK big bands on Riverside and Columbia in '60s, others. Own albums incl. *Woodlore, Pairing Off, Phil & Quill* '55-7 on Prestige (compilation 2-disc *Altology*); *Phil Talks With Quill* '57 on Epic (now on budget Odyssey label); *Rights Of Swing* '60 on Candid (his own extended composition); played concerts with Michel LEGRAND, contributed to film soundtracks *The Hustler* '61, *Blow Up* '66; recorded with Oliver NELSON, Joe Morello, on *Further Definitions* '61 by Benny CARTER, etc., lived in Europe '68-72, formed European Rhythm Machine (*At The Frankfurt Jazz Festival* '70 on Atlantic). More LPs: *Musique du Bois* on Muse, *New Music* on Testament, 2-disc *Live From Showboat* '76 on RCA, *'More' Live* '79 on Adelphi, *Quartet* '79 on Clean Cut, 3-disc *Macerata Concert* '80 on Philology, *Birds Of A Feather* '81 and *At The Vanguard* '82 on Antilles, *Live From New York* '82 on Palo Alto, *European Tour Live* and *Integrity* '84 on Red Record. *Heaven* '84 on Blackhawk and *Gratitude* '86 on Denon feature his quintet incl. Tom Harrell on trumpet (since '84): Harrell has played with Horace SILVER, Mel LEWIS; a victim of schizophrenia, he has taken powerful tranquillisers since

'67 to enable him to concentrate; his playing incl. the whole history of jazz trumpet: vocalist Helen MERRILL said, 'He plays from such a wonderfully deep place . . . When he plays a ballad, he can bring tears.' Woods is also heard on *Old Acquaintance* '85 on Pausa with Conte CANDOLI, with Lew Tabackin '80 on Omnisound, with Chris Swanson on Sea Breeze (*Crazy Horse* '79, *Piper At The Gates Of Dawn* '84).

WOOLEY, Sheb (*b* 10 Apr. '21, Erick, Okla.) Country singer, songwriter, actor. Raised on farm; formed band in high school, worked in oil field and decided music must be better. Recorded for Bullet in Nashville, guested on radio shows; landed radio show in Fort Worth, Texas advertising Calument Baking Powder '46, singing, writing the adverts, creating character the Chief from company's logo. To West Coast late '40s, studied acting, signed with MGM; began writing parodies of hits: 'When Mexican Joe Met Jolie Blon' was hit for Hank SNOW '53. Played in more than 40 films, best-known role in *High Noon* '52 as the baddie trying to gun down Gary Cooper; working on the set of *Giant* he wrote 'Are You Satisfied?' and had minor hit '55 but cover by Rusty DRAPER was bigger; wrote and recorded novelty 'The Purple People Eater', no. 1 pop hit for six weeks '58. 'That's My Pa' '62 made the pop chart but was a no. 1 country hit; he had sporadic hits in that chart for the rest of the decade. Acted in several TV shows incl. role of Pete Nolan in *Rawhide* with Clint Eastwood for five years late '50s-early '60s. As Ben Colder he made LPs and singles of parodies such as 'Detroit City No. 2' '63, 'Almost Persuaded No. 2' '66, 'Harper Valley P.T.A. (Later That Same Day)' '68; named comic of the year by CMA '68. Seen on every major country TV show, several times on Grand Ole Opry; was a regular on *Hee Haw* and still entertaining in the '80s including film *Hoosiers* with Gene Hackman.

WORKING WEEK UK soul-jazz dance band: Julie Roberts (*b* 11 Jan. '62), guitarist Simon Booth (*b* 12 Mar. '56), Larry Stabbins (*b* 9 Sep. '49) on soprano and tenor saxes, flute; augmented with percussion, lots of horns etc. Search for jazz roots of disco results from boredom with soundalike mid-'80s

pop. Booth worked at Mole Jazz, London shop/label, formed band Weekend: single 'The View From Her Room' had pastel shades; group evolved into hard-blowing percussion-based dance band with Stabbins, who had played in '60s soul bands, also worked with Keith TIPPETT, others. Broke up '83 after two LPs on Rough Trade label; new band formed in response to dancing scene at Electric Ballroom. Debut single Latin-based 'Venceremos', political tribute to Chilean people, sung by vocal trio Robert Wyatt, Tracey Thorn, Claudia Figueroa; second single 'Storm Of Light' featured Mike Carr on organ, voice of Julie Tippett (Keith's wife, née Driscoll; *see* Brian AUGER). Booth and Stabbins wanted a band to play their songs, recruited excellent big-voiced Roberts (also appears on stage with Jazz Warriors; *see* Courtney PINE) for cover of Marvin GAYE's 'Inner City Blues' (12″ version labelled 'urbane guerilla mix'). Album *Working Nights* '85 produced by Robin Millar (EVERYTHING BUT THE GIRL, SADE) incl. all Booth-Stabbins comps. except Gaye cover; good features incl. Roberts's singing, trombone solo by Annie Whitehead on instrumental 'No Cure, No Pay'. LP parcel also incl. fourth single 'Stella Marina', with Tippett, rap by Jalal of The Last Poets. Band also did *Lygmalion* soundtrack, Arena BBC1 TV special Easter '85. Mindless beat for modern dancers and busy arrangements precluded much swing, but they were a step in an interesting direction for pop.

WORLD SAXOPHONE QUARTET USA saxophonists Hamiet BLUIETT, Julius HEMPHILL, Oliver LAKE and David MURRAY (replaced in '86 by John Stubblefield). LPs: *Point Of No Return* '77 on Moers Music; *World Saxophone Quartet* '78, *Steppin'* '79, *Revue* '80, *Live In Zurich* '81, *Live At Brooklyn Academy Of Music* '85, all on Black Saint; *Plays Duke Ellington* '86, *Dances And Ballads* '87 on Nonesuch. See entries for individuals.

WRAY, Link (*b* 2 May '35, Fort Bragg, N.C.) Guitarist, composer. Some sources give birth date as '30. Served in Korea; played with brothers Vernon and Doug in the Ranch Gang Band in Norfolk, Va.; TB caused him to lose a lung '55, but he continued in music; on DJ Milt Grant's TV show he was asked to play an instrumental and came up with 'Rumble', one of the most influential of rock'n'roll records: he punched a hole in amplifier speaker with a pencil, inventing fuzz-tone; the slow, menacing record (by Link Wray and his Wray Men) reached top 20 on Cadence '58 and was banned from NYC radio because of gang warfare connotations. Flip side 'The Swag' was another gloriously simple rock riff, at a faster tempo; both list Grant and Wray as co-writers, as does 'Raw-Hide', top 25 hit on Epic '59 (he switched labels because Cadence boss Archie BLEYER wanted him to go country, emulating Bleyer's big hit act the EVERLY Bros). Minor hit 'Jack The Ripper' '62 appeared on Swan. He played in bars and recorded for pleasure at home; home-made tapes released '71 as *Link Wray* as generation of rock-star guitarists incl. Jeff BECK, Pete Townshend, Marc BOLAN, Bob DYLAN, Dave Davies etc. named him as an influence. Albums: *Early Recordings* and *Good Rockin' Tonight* on Ace incl. Swan material; *There's Good Rockin' Tonight* on Red Lightnin' and *Rock'n'Roll Rumble* on Charly UK are the same LP; and *Link Wray And The Raymen* on Edsel has Epic tracks. *Growling Guitar* to be released on Ace has '60s tracks from Vermilion label; later LPs incl. *Beans And Fatback* '73, *Bullshot* '79 on Charisma, *Live At The Paradiso* '80 (on Magnum Force/PRT in UK), *Live In* '85 on Big Beat USA, Ace UK (made at Scandinavian concerts).

WRIGHT, Lawrence (*b* 15 Feb. 1888, Leicester, England; *d* 19 May '64, London) Composer, publisher, arranger, UK pop music pioneer: father ran music shop; he began selling songs from a market stall; first published hit was 'Don't Go Down The Mines, Daddy' '10 by William Geddes and Robert Donnelly; went to London's Denmark Street '11 and it became UK equivalent of TIN PAN ALLEY: house journal *Melody Maker* formed '22 is still in print in very different form. He had UK rights to USA hits by Hoagy CARMICHAEL, others; specialised in comedy ('Burlington Bertie From Bow'; 'Yes, We Have No Bananas'); famous for promotional stunts: for 'Sahara' '24 he rode a camel round Piccadilly Circus; for 'Me And Jane In A Plane' '27 he

flew Jack HYLTON and his band round Blackpool Tower, dropping sheet music. At Blackpool (UK seaside resort) his production of *On With The Show* ran 32 years. He adopted name Horatio Nicholls for his own writing; best known of more than 500 songs was 'Among My Souvenirs' '27 (words by American Edgar Leslie, his best-known collaborator), introduced by Hylton in UK, Paul WHITEMAN in USA; sung by Carmichael in film *The Best Years Of Our Lives* '46, hit for Connie FRANCIS '59, revived '76 by Marty ROBBINS, etc. Won Ivor Novello award '62 for Outstanding Services to British Popular Music. After he died Lawrence Wright Music was sold to Dick JAMES, then to ATV, then to Michael JACKSON.

WRIGHT, O. V. (*b* Overton Ellis Wright, 9 Oct. '39, Memphis, Tenn.; *d* 16 Nov. '80) Soul singer, songwriter; highly regarded for powerful, moody style, but never had as much personal success as he deserved. Sang with gospel groups Sunset Travellers, Spirit Of Memphis, Highway QCs; recorded his own 'That's How Strong My Love Is' but Otis REDDING had the hit '65; Wright had R&B hits and crossed over to pop Hot 100 with 'You're Gonna Make Me Cry' '65, 'Eight Men, Four Women' '67, chilling 'Ace Of Spade' '70 on Duke/Peacock subsidiary Back Beat; later recorded for Hi. Hits compilation *Gone For Good* on Charly UK.

WULOMEI African neo-trad. percussion group formed '73 in Ghana. Spearheaded Ghanaian folk revival with updated music and cultural shows. Formed by Nii Ashitey (ex-Tempos, Police band, Brigade Band No. 2) and Sake Acquaye (composer and impresario), with three female singers supported by acoustic guitar, three male vocalists, bamboo flutes and substantial percussion section of drums, labash, clips, gong and giant frame gombe drum; sang in Ga but mixture of sea shanties, street songs, highlife, pachanga had appeal beyond Ga-speaking Ghanaians. First LP *Mibi Shi Dinn* '74 followed by *Walatu Walasa* same year (incl. several hits); LP *Drum Conference* and 45-day tour of USA '75. Further LPs on Polydor encouraged other bands: Dzadzaloi (*Two Paddies Follow One Girl*

'78, *Napoliata* '81), Abladei (*Abladei BII* '75), also Suku Troupe, Agbafoi, Blemabii, Bokoor.

WYATT, Robert (*b* 28 Jan. '45, Bristol, England) Singer, songwriter. Co-founded, arranged and played drums with SOFT MACHINE '66-71, then Matching Mole (a pun on the French for 'soft machine'), LPs *Matching Mole* '72 and *Matching Mole's Little Red Record* '73 on CBS. Began playing keyboards on Soft Machine's 'Moon In June' and first solo album *The End Of An Ear* '71 on CBS; he broke his back in a fall '73, concentrated more on keyboards on *Rock Bottom* and *Ruth Is Stranger Than Richard* '74-5 on Virgin; had surprise top 30 UK hit '74 with cover of MONKEES' 'I'm A Believer'. Increasingly political and unconcerned with usual career moves, he receded from the music business until a series of singles for Rough Trade, compiled on *Nothing Can Stop Us*, incl. 'Strange Fruit' (with Ernest Mothle on double bass), Cuban 'Caimanera' (with Harry Beckett on flugelhorn), 'The Red Flag', 'Stalin Wasn't Stallin' ' (first recorded '43 by the Golden Gate Quartet), his own 'Born Again Cretin'. Then albums on Rough Trade: *The Animals Soundtrack* '82 for Victor Schonfield's film about abuse of animals; 12″ EP *Work In Progress* '83 incl. 'Amber And The Amberines' (with Hugh Hopper), covers of 'Biko', 'Yolanda' and 'Te Recuerdo' (by Peter GABRIEL, Pablo Milanes and Victor Jara respectively); *Old Rotten Hat* '85 incl. material such as 'The United States Of Amnesia', 'Alliance' and 'Gharbzadegi'. His minimalist style and delivery tackle issues head-on without succumbing to sloganising. More singles incl. 'Shipbuilding' '83 (which reached the UK top 40; song by Elvis COSTELLO and Clive Langer is comment on Falklands war), Jackson Kaujeua's 'The Wind Of Change' '85 (with Jerry Dammers and the S.W.A.P.O. Singers, addressing apartheid), 'The Last Nightingale' '84 on Recommended, a collaboration to raise money for the miners' strike of '84-5. 12″ EP *Robert Wyatt* '87 on Strange Fruit is one of series from John PEEL radio shows, four solo tracks incl. live version of 'I'm A Believer' from '74 and the sound of the BBC's piano, Hammond organ and marimbas.

WYNETTE, Tammy (*b* Virginia Wynette Pugh, 5 May '42, Tupelo, Ms.) Country singer; one of the most successful of all time. Her father died when she was a baby; raised by her mother and grandparents in Birmingham, Ala. she was married at 17, soon had three children and left her young husband before the third was born. Worked long hours as a beautician to pay bills incurred by her youngest child's ill health; took up music to earn more money, working in local clubs and landing a spot on WBRC's *Country Boy Eddy Show* '63-4; appearances on Porter WAGONER syndicated TV show and endless rounds of Nashville record companies led to signing with Epic Records; joined Billy SHERRILL for one of the most successful artist-producer teams in the history of country music. Debut 'Apartment No. 9' was minor hit late '66; then 'Your Good Girl's Gonna Go Bad' was no. 3; 'I Don't Wanna Play House', 'Take Me To Your World', 'D-I-V-O-R-C-E', 'Stand By Your Man' (co-written with Sherrill), 'Singing My Song', 'The Ways To Love A Man', 'He Loves Me All The Way', 'Run Woman Run', 'Good Lovin' Makes It Right' were all no. 1 '67-71. *Tammy's Greatest Hits* was the best-selling album ever by a female country artist, reached top 40 of pop LP chart '69; she also had duet hits with David HOUSTON ('My Elusive Dreams', 'It's All Over' '67-8); marriage to country superstar George JONES '69 only consolidated her success. Jones changed labels to Epic; they toured together, had duet hits 'Take Me', 'The Ceremony', 'We're Gonna Hold On', '(We're Not) The Jet Set', 'We Love It Away' '71-4. His drinking and unprofessional behaviour ('No Show Jones') did not go down well, her earlier financial insecurity causing her to put her career first; it was a stormy, violent marriage which ended '75. They continued to record together, initially to fulfil contractual obligations, more hits followed by reunion session '80. Meanwhile she continued to dominate the country charts with ever more personal hits, to which her audience could relate completely: 'Woman To Woman', '(You Make Me Want To Be) A Mother', 'I Still Believe In Fairytales', 'Til I Can Make It On My Own', 'You And Me' '74-6; she made a UK breakthrough when 'Stand By Your Man' (reissued for the sixth time) became a no. 1

pop hit '75; success continued at home: she has had 20 no. 1 country hits, more than any other female, and survived it all: disastrous marriages, ill health due to stress and other problems, and even a kidnapping. She had well-publicised affairs incl. with actor Burt Reynolds and Rudy Gatlin; finally settled down and married longtime friend, songwriter and producer George Richey '78. In the '80s she moved away from Sherrill and worked with others; has not dominated the charts the way she did earlier, but still had big hits such as 'Starting Over' '80, 'Crying In The Rain' '81, 'I Heard A Heart Break' '83, no. 1 duet with Mark Gray 'Sometimes When We Touch' '85. Biography *Stand By Your Man* became a successful film '82; she made artistic comeback '87 with album *Higher Ground* '87, which began as concept idea to be called *Out With The Boys*, incl. the GATLIN BROTHERS, the O'KANES, duets with Ricky SKAGGS, Gene WATSON, Emmylou HARRIS, Vince Gill. LPs incl. *Your Good Girl's Gonna Go Bad* and *Take Me To Your World* '67, *Inspiration* '68, *The First Lady* '70, *We Sure Can Love Each Other* '71, *Bedtime Story* '72, *Another Lonely Song* '73, *Woman To Woman* '74, *Til I Can Make It On My Own* '75, *You And Me* '76, *One Of A Kind* '77, *Just Tammy* '79, *You Brought Me Back* '81, *Soft Touch* '82, *Even The Strong Get Lonely* '83; with Jones: *We Go Together* '71, *We Love To Sing About Jesus* '72, *We're Gonna Hold On* '73, *George, Tammy & Tina* '74, *Golden Ring* '76, *Together Again* '80.

X

X USA punk rock band formed L.A. '77 by pseudonymous John Doe (*b* '54, Decatur, Ill.) on bass and Billy Zoom on guitar, who had simultaneously advertised in classifieds. John met Exene (Christine) Cervenka at poetry workshop; D. J. Bonebrake spotted in L.A. club. Zoom's rockabilly infl. (claims to have backed Gene VINCENT) and Doe's new wave affiliation make fascinating if uneasy listening. First single was 'Adult Books'/'We're Desperate' on Dangerhouse label. Spotted by former DOORS keyboardist Ray Manzarek '79; he prod. debut LP *Los Angeles* '80 on Slash. Doe and Cervenka married; their vocal duets and discordant harmonies were compared to JEFFERSON AIRPLANE, though Cervenka more reminiscent latterly of SIOUXSIE, like her becoming more accomplished singer as time went by. *Wild Gift* also prod. by Manzarek, covered Doors' 'Soul Kitchen' (at punk tempo). Like most of USA new wave, X were chasing tail of UK punk, but lyrics by Doe and Cervenka a cut above. Signed to Elektra for *Under The Big Black Sun* '82 and *More Fun In The New World* '83 (latter incl. cover of Jerry Lee LEWIS's 'Breathless'); in '82 Cervenka published poetry with Lydia Lunch in *Adulterers Anonymous*. X's songs autobiographical, confronting American dream (e.g. *Black Sun*'s 'Riding With Mary', antidote to all those American car songs, about Exene's sister, who died in a car crash). *Ain't Love Grand* '85 changed producers from Manzarek to Michael Wegener, shot through with irony, songs dealing with break-up of Doe/Cervenka relationship; it wasn't Doe but Zoom who split that year, replaced by the BLASTERS' Dave Alvin, with whom Doe, Cervenka and Bonebrake had been collaborating as the Knitters, country-rock ensemble recording part-time for Slash (*Poor Little Critter On The Road* '85). X mixed hard-to-listen-to originals, idiosyncratic covers: TROGGS' 'Wild Thing', SMALL FACES' 'All Or Nothing', etc.; also showed interest in multi-media presentations and appeared in films. *Ain't Love Grand* incl. single 'Burning House Of Love', which got radio play, but band promised to return to harder-edged stuff. Semi-documentary film *The Unheard Music* '86 by writer/dir. W. T. Morgan five years in the making, portraying band in L.A. context since release of first LP. Alvin returned to Blasters temporarily on death of his replacement, Hollywood Fats. *See How We Are* '87 saw them mellowing somewhat again, with new member Tony Gilkyson.

XTC UK new wave band formed '76: Andy Partridge, guitar (*b* 11 Dec. '53); Colin Ivor Moulding, bass (*b* 17 Aug. '55); Terry Chambers, drums (*b* 18 July '55); all from Swindon, Wiltshire; formed part of local band Star Park, then glitzy Helium Kidz '73, then XTC with addition of keyboardist John Perkins, replaced by Barry Andrews (*b* 12 Sep. '56, West Norwood, London). Partridge and Moulding are the vocalists and songwriters. Debut on Virgin with EP *XTC* '77 followed by LP *White Music* early '78, Euro-tour with TALKING HEADS, 35-date headlining tour of UK. LP *Go 2* '78 critically acclaimed but hit single failed to arrive until after departure of Andrews to join League of Gentlemen; then 'Making Plans For Nigel' reached top 20 '79; third LP same year *Drums And Wires* followed by Partridge solo *Takeaway/The Lure Of Salvage*; he also appeared on *Miniatures*, oddball album fashioned by ex-MOTT THE HOOPLE keyboardist Morgan Fisher, involving multitude of one-minute tracks by various celebrities, Partridge using his minute to illustrate the whole history of pop. Next XTC LP was *Black Sea* '80 followed by top 20 singles 'Sgt Rock (Is Going To Help Me)' '81, 'Senses Working Overtime' '82; fifth LP, 2-disc *English Settlement*, was change of direction towards folk sound, 'like PENTANGLE on mescaline', according to Partridge. *Mummer* '83 followed this path, but *The Big Express* '84 was another change: collection about obsolescence, traditions and growing old (since Partridge was turning 30). The band hasn't toured since '82; now operates as trio of Partridge, Moulding and guitarist Dave Gregory, who replaced Chambers, who left for Australia when XTC became Swindonbound. Mock psychedelic LP *25 O'Clock* '85 made under pseudonym the Dukes of Stratosphear and released on April Fool's Day; they kept the new name for *Psonic Psunspot* and *Chips From The Chocolate Fireball*. Partridge was prod. records for other acts.

Y

YANCEY, Jimmy (*b* James Edwards Yancey, 20 Feb. 1898, Chicago; *d* there 17 Sep. '51) Pianist, singer, composer in boogie-woogie style: not the fast, commercially successful style but the original keyboard blues idiom: wrote 'Yancey Stomp', 'State Street Special', '35th & Dearborn', many more blues tunes enhanced by variations in bass line. He toured incl. Europe before WWI but was inactive in music from c.'25; groundskeeper at Comiskey (White Sox baseball) Park for years. Rediscovered during boogie-woogie fad; Meade Lux LEWIS dedicated 'Yancey Special' to him (recorded by Bob CROSBY band with Bob Zurke). Yancey made his first records '39 for SoloArt (*Yancey's Getaway* later appeared on Riverside, then Jazzology); with his wife, blues singer Estella 'Mama' Yancey (*b* 1 Jan. 1896, Cairo, Ill.; *d* 19 Apr. '86, Chicago) at Carnegie Hall '48 (she appeared there again '81); she also wrote songs; they recorded together for Atlantic '51 (LP *Pure Blues*); also recorded for RCA. Storyville LPs *The Yancey-Lofton Sessions* (2 vols.) incl. '43 tracks by Yancey, others by Chicago pianist/blues singer Cripple Clarence Lofton (*b* 28 Mar. 1887, Kingsport, Texas; *d* 9 Jan. '57, Chicago; also recorded for ARC labels '35, Yazoo '37, SoloArt '39, etc.).

YANKOVIC, Frankie (*b* Davis, W.V.) Accordionist, bandleader. Self-taught, was playing professionally at 15; led the best-known of all polka bands. His recording of a lovely Czech tune 'Blue Skirt Waltz' was a national hit in '49 for 23 weeks. Album *Greatest Hits* on Columbia.

YANKOVIC, Weird Al USA accordionist, parodist. Qualified architect became DJ on radio; bored with songs and began parodying them; studio tape of 'Another One Rides The Bus' (sending up QUEEN hit 'Another One Bites The Dust') almost made Hot 100 '81. Followed this with 'My Bologna' (from Knack's 'My Sharona'); fell in with guitarist Rick DERRINGER; did 'I Love Rocky Road' (from Joan Jett's 'I Love Rock-'n'Roll'), again just missed Hot 100 '83; eponymous LP made Billboard LP chart '83. 'Eat It', spoof of Michael JACKSON's 'Beat It', had hilarious video of teenagers pulling apart plastic chicken, on theme of recalcitrant child refusing to eat dinner (Jackson loved it); Derringer cloned Eddie VAN HALEN solo on original for no. 12 hit USA '84. Other chart entries that year: 'King Of Suede' (from POLICE hit 'King Of Pain'), 'I Lost On Jeopardy' (from Greg Kihn's 'Jeopardy'); second album *In 3-D* was no. 17 LP '84: incl. 'Polkas On 45' (pop hits done polka style), MEN WITHOUT HATS parody 'The Brady Bunch' (to tune of 'The Safety Dance'). Also sent up Sylvester Stallone, MADONNA ('Like A Surgeon') etc. Third LP *Dare To Be Stupid* '85, then *Even Worse* '88, all on Rock'n'Roll label in USA. Brings back memories of Stan FREBERG.

YARDBIRDS, The UK R&B/rock band formed '63 by Keith Relf (*b* 22 Mar. '43, Richmond, Surrey; *d* 14 May '76, electrocuted), harmonica, vocals; Paul Samwell-Smith (*b* 8 May '43, Twickenham, Middlesex), bass; Chris Dreja (*b* 11 Nov. '46, Surbiton, Surrey), rhythm guitar; Tony 'Top' Topham, lead guitar. Relf and Samwell-Smith originally in Metropolitan Blues Quartet; became Yardbirds, adding Jim McCarty (*b* 25 July '43) later in '63. Topham stayed on at art school, replaced by Eric CLAPTON (ex-Roosters), already fine blues guitarist. Resident at Richmond's Crawdaddy Club; its manager Giorgio Gomelsky signed them to Columbia (EMI); version of Billy Boy ARNOLD's 'I Wish You Would' flopped; poppier 'Good Morning Little Schoolgirl' (by Sonny Boy WILLIAMSON) almost made top 40 and illustrated dichotomy between pop and blues that led Clapton to leave for John MAYALL after Graham Gouldman's blatantly commercial 'For Your Love' reached no. 3

UK/6 USA '65. Though single's hook relied on Brian AUGER's harpsichord, Clapton's guitar was evident in *Five Live Yardbirds* '64 that showcased R&B stage act. Jeff BECK (ex-Tridents) took job Jimmy Page declined; 'Heart Full Of Soul' '65 (UK no. 2/USA 9) represented new direction; 'Evil Hearted You', third Gouldman-penned single, had Gregorian chant-infl. B-side 'Still I'm Sad', written by McCarty and Samwell-Smith: 2-sided hit no. 3 UK '65. 'I'm A Man' was USA-only hit (no. 17); transatlantic '66 hits 'Shapes Of Things' and 'Over Under Sideways Down' had psychedelic and Indian sounds respectively, Beck's guitar sounding more like sitar. But anarchic stage act (featured in Antonioni's 'Swinging London' film *Blow-Up* '66) led to Samwell-Smith leaving (to prod. Cat STEVENS, etc.); Page now accepted standing invitation, first as bassist, then as twin lead with Beck, Dreja switching instruments. Hit 'Happenings Ten Years Time Ago' saw Beck daringly using feedback on record, but he departed under a cloud after illness and reported eccentricities; remaining quartet's alliance with Mickie MOST led to recording of unsuitably poppy material: they split '68. LP of Most sessions *Little Games* '67 remains unsatisfactory; only official studio LP was *Yardbirds* '65, also known as *Roger The Engineer* and reissued under that title by Edsel. Relf and McCarty formed folk duo Together, then founded Renaissance (aka Illusion); later joined Medicine Head, Shoot respectively. Page formed LED ZEPPELIN. McCarty, Dreja, Samwell-Smith and ex-Medicine Head vocalist John Fiddler became Box Of Frogs; made eponymous LP '84 with help of Beck, etc. trading on Yardbirds past: predictably bigger in USA (no. 45 LP) than in UK; second LP *Strange Land* '86 with guests on various tracks: Page, Rory GALLAGHER, Ian DURY, etc. Yardbirds were famous for axe heroes Clapton, Beck, Page; also crucially important group emerging from blues boom to infl. 'progressive' music of the '70s. Output mostly singles, adding to mystique; others incl. one track on *Blow-Up* soundtrack (*see* Herbie HANCOCK) and *Sonny Boy Williamson And The Yardbirds* (recorded '65 with visiting bluesman). 2-disc *Compleat* compilation on Compleat label in USA; in UK Charly label offers *Five Live Yardbirds*, *The Yardbirds Single Hits*, *Our Own Sound*, *Featuring Jeff Beck*, *Featuring Eric Clapton*, and for real fanatics, 7-disc boxed set *Shapes Of Things*, incl. LP with Sonny Boy and *Odds And Sods* from the studio floor: backing tracks of hits, etc.

YELLOW MAGIC ORCHESTRA Japanese technopop band, purveying synthesised sound similar to KRAFTWERK, CAN, TANGERINE DREAM, etc. Very big in Japan but unable to get export sales. Leader keyboardist Ryuichi Sakamoto is a serious, experienced musician, predicted for a world tour '80 that 'The 1980s will be strong on anxiety feelings ... Music will work as a cleaning filter to dissolve distorted satisfactions.' But the tour was not a great success and it is difficult to see why anyone should turn to electronic music to allay anxieties, though the techniques are used by Michael JACKSON, PRINCE, many others. LPs mostly distributed by CBS incl. *Yellow Magic Orchestra* '78, *Solid State Survivor* '79, *Multiplies* '80 (incl. 'Computer Game (Theme From "The Invader")', top 20 UK hit '80; YMO had four LPs in Japanese top 20 that year); *People With Nice Smiles* '83 had guest Bill Nelson (BE-BOP DELUXE); *After Service* was distributed on Alpha by Rough Trade in the UK '84; *Neo Geo* '87 on CBS was prod. by Bill LASWELL, combining Western/Eastern elements, mostly fabricated by a Fairlight CMI but incl. contributions from Sly Dunbar, IGGY POP. Meanwhile Sakamoto has diversified, collaborating with David Sylvian (leader of JAPAN), writing scores for and acting in films: *Merry Christmas, Mr Lawrence* with David BOWIE, Nagisa Oshima's *Furyo* and Bernardo Bertolucci's *The Last Emperor* (shot in China). Recorded on Denon incl. *Tokyo Joe* with guitarist Kazumi Watanabi (*b* 14 Oct. '53, Tokyo), solo *The Thousand Knives of Ryuichi Sakamoto*, *The End Of Asia* with Danceries.

YES UK rock band formed '68. Along with EMERSON, LAKE & PALMER and others of that ilk, and with several classically-trained members, they combined instrumental fluency with electronics and thick vocal harmonies to make 'classical rock', a commercial success but critically regarded as pretentious and empty. Vocalist Jon Anderson (*b* 25 Oct. '44, Lancashire), bassist Chris Squire (*b* 4 Mar. '48, London) recruited guitarist Peter Banks (who'd previously played with Squire in Syn), Tony Kaye on keyboards, Bill BRUFORD on drums; began gigging in London and opened for CREAM farewell concerts late '68. LPs on Atlantic began with *Yes* and *Time And A Word* '69-70; Banks left (released *The Two Sides Of Peter Banks* on Capitol '73), replaced by Steve Howe; with Anderson as primary composer and Kaye introducing synthesiser *The Yes Album* '71 scraped into top 40 LPs in the USA. Kaye left, was replaced by composer/keyboardist Rick Wakeman (*b* 18 May '49, London) ex-STRAWB and experienced session player: he played mellotron, harpsichord, clavinet etc. as well as standard keyboards; *Fragile* '72 was a top 5 LP in USA incl. hit 'Roundabouts' (edited for length). *Close To The Edge* '72 reached no. 3 in USA, their best showing; Bruford left to join King Crimson, replaced by Alan White (had played with John LENNON's Plastic Ono Band, others) for live 3-disc *Yessongs* '73, 2-disc *Tales From Topographic Oceans* '74 (with lyrics by Howe and Anderson based on Shastric scriptures). Wakeman had already begun making solo albums, left, replaced by Patrick Moraz for *Relayer* '74; Wakeman returned for *Going For The One* '77 and *Tormato* '78; all these except *Yessongs* were top 10 LPs. Wakeman and Anderson left, replaced by team of Geoff Downes and vocalist Trevor HORN for *Drama* '80. Anderson, White, Kaye, Squire re-formed with Trevor Rabin on guitar to make *90125* '83 (prod. by Horn), top 5 LP incl. USA no. 1 hit 'Owner Of A Lonely Heart'. *9012Live* '86 recorded on tour in Canada and West Germany; *Big Generator* came out '87. Compilations incl. *Yesterdays* '75, *Classic Yes* '82, *Best Of*. Moraz made *Refugee* '74, '*i*' '76, *Patrick Moraz* '79; Howe made *Beginnings* '75, *Steve Howe Album* '80; Squire made *Fish Out Of Water* '75, White *Ramshackled* '76. Anderson solo LPs were *Olias Of Sunhollow* '76, *Song Of Seven* '80; teamed with Vangelis as Jon And Vangelis '80-1 (*see* APHRODITE'S CHILD); Horn and Downes had success in UK as Buggles '80 (*see* Trevor HORN). Wakeman's instrumental LPs were on A&M were commercially successful, incl. *The Six Wives Of Henry VIII* '73, *Journey To The Centre Of*

The Earth '74 (based on Jules Verne, made live with the London Symphony Orchestra and narrated by actor David Hemmings), *Myths And Legends Of King Arthur And The Knights Of The Round Table* '75 (ice pageant with huge forces), soundtrack to Ken Russell film *Lisztomania* '75 (with Roger Daltrey), *No Earthly Connection* '76 with scaled-down English Rock Ensemble, soundtrack *White Rock* '77 (about Innsbruck Winter Games), *Criminal Record* '77 (with Squire, White), *Rhapsodies* '79; his *Country Airs* was the biggest seller on the UK new age Coda label '88.

YOAKUM, Dwight (*b* 23 Oct. '54, Pikesville, Ky.) Country singer, songwriter with allegiance to pure honky tonk: result is a little like early Elvis PRESLEY but with less gospel influence and with a nasal vocal quality typical of honky tonk. He is immobile onstage, totally unlike Presley. From religious background: sang hillbilly hymns three times a week in church. The name Yoakum, which has hillbilly overtones in the USA thanks to the Al Capp comic strip *Li'l Abner* (Yokum), is a corruption of German Joachim: he can trace ancestors back 200 years. Unrecorded song 'Readin', Ritin' And Route 23' is about his parents' efforts at self-improvement and the road out of Kentucky. Ignored by Nashville, he went to L.A., fell in with burgeoning LOS LOBOS/BLASTERS talent pool; made sizzling EP on Oak label *Guitars, Cadillacs, Etc., Etc.* '85 with Jeff Donovan (drums), J. D. Foster (bass), Pete Anderson (guitar), Brantley Kearns (fiddle; has recorded with David Bromberg, etc.), also help from Glen D. Hardin, Blasters' Gene Taylor on keyboards, J. D. Maness on pedal steel, David Mansfield (Alpha Band, etc.) on mandolin and dobro. Own song 'I'll Be Gone' also incl. on 'new country' LP *A Town South Of Bakersfield* on Enigma label (others anthologised incl. Billy SWAN, Albert Lee). Yoakum was snapped up by WB, *Guitars Etc.* reissued with same sleeve, four more tracks. Covers of Johnny CASH's 'Ring Of Fire', Ray PRICE's 'Heartaches By The Number', Johnny HORTON's 'Honky Tonk Man' (released as single) are adequate homage; promising originals incl. 'Bury Me' (duet with LONE JUSTICE's Maria McKee), 'Minor's Prayer' (for his grandfather),

'South Of Cincinnati': it was a no. 1 USA country album '86, followed by *Hillbilly Deluxe* '87 and *Buenos Noches From A Lonely Room* '88, also huge sellers. So much for Nashville, where (Yoakum points out) 'their music always starts in offices and trickles down to the streets'.

YOUMANS, Vincent (*b* Vincent Miller Youmans, 27 Sep. 1898, NYC; *d* 5 Apr. '46, Denver, Col.) Composer, producer; nicknamed 'Millie'. Worked in Wall Street, became song-plugger, served in US Navy WWI, then plugged songs again alongside George GERSHWIN; became rehearsal pianist for Victor HERBERT. Small output of extremely high quality: many of his shows had short runs or flopped, but incl. great songs; he was not a good producer and a poor businessman, trying to do too much instead of delegating to professionals. He also changed lyricists more often than any of the other great songwriters. *No, No, Nanette* '25 was a big hit (with Otto HARBACH and Oscar Hammerstein II), incl. 'I Want To Be Happy', 'Tea For Two'; *Oh, Please* '26 was a flop, but incl. 'I Know That You Know' (with Harbach); *Hit The Deck* '27 was a hit, incl. 'Halleluja' (first written as a march while he was in the Navy), 'Sometimes I'm Happy' (Irving Caesar lyric); *Great Day!* '29 ran only 36 performances; originally called *Horse Shoes*, it was modelled after Jerome KERN's *Showboat* and called for a black band: Duke ELLINGTON was supposed to take part, but backed out; Fletcher HENDERSON did it instead and producer Youmans allowed the white conductor to fire Henderson's men one by one until there were almost none left; it was one of the worst disasters of Henderson's career and the show flopped, but incl. songs 'More Than You Know' and 'Without A Song' (with Billy ROSE). *Smiles* '30 was prod. by Florenz Ziegfeld but ran only 63 nights, incl. 'Time On My Hands' (with Harold Adamson, Mack Gordon); he contributed 'Rise 'n' Shine' to *Take A Chance* '32 by Richard Whiting and Nacio Herb BROWN, a hit, but he gave up on Broadway and went to Hollywood, where *Flying Down To Rio* '33 (first film teaming Fred ASTAIRE, Ginger Rogers) was a big success, incl. title song, 'The Carioca', 'Orchids In The Moonlight' (with Gus Kahn).

Several other films were not as successful; *Hit The Deck* was filmed '30, again '55; *Nanette* in '41. His publishing company went broke, he himself went bankrupt '35; had TB, ignored doctors' orders; big project *The Vincent Youmans Ballet Revue* '44 was a disaster. *Nanette* was revived on stage early '70s, one of the all-time great shows.

YOUNGBLOODS, The USA folk-rock group formed in Boston '65 by Jesse Colin Young (*b* Perry Miller, 11 Nov. '44, NYC), vocals, guitar, bass; and Jerry Corbitt (*b* Tifton, Ga.). Young was discovered, renamed and produced by Bobby SCOTT, made solo LPs *Soul Of A City Boy* '64 and *Young Blood* '65 on Capitol; duo took name from latter, recruited Joe Bauer (*b* 26 Sep. '41, Memphis) on drums and multi-instrumentalist Lowell 'Banana' Levinger (*b* '46, Cambridge, Mass.). Eclectic music was infl. by bluegrass, harmony singing and British Invasion, not unlike that of LOVIN' SPOONFUL. Group worked as house band at Café A Go Go NYC '66; first sessions released '70 as *Two Trips*, but debut LP was *The Youngbloods* '67 (reissued '88 on Edsel) incl. single 'Get Together' (written by Dino Valenti of QUICKSILVER MESSENGER SERVICE), no. 62 on first release, became anthem of flower-power era, a hit again on reissue after exposure in TV advert. Co-vocalist Corbitt went solo after *Earth Music* '67; *Elephant Mountain* '69 was made on West Coast as a trio, Banana's piano/guitar work becoming distinctive feature along with Young's melifluous vocals. *Rock Festival* '70 and *Ride The Wind* '71 made for own Raccoon label, but latter disappointed and marked start of decline. Added bassist Michael Kane for *Good And Dusty* '71, *High On A Ridgetop* '72; split '73. Bauer and Banana cut LPs, linked with Kane in Noggin (*Crab Tunes* '72); Young had solo career with *Together* '72 on Raccoon, series of hit LPs on WB: *Song For Juli*, *Light Shine*, *Songbird*, live *On The Road*, *Love On The Wing* '73-7 averaged no. 30 in LP chart; *American Dreams* '78 on Elektra marked chart decline.

YOUNG, Faron (*b* 25 Feb. '32, Shreveport, La.) Country singer, songwriter; one of the top 10 most successful of all time. Formed band still in high school, joined Shreveport's important Louisiana Hayride radio show, then Webb PIERCE travelling show; signed with Capitol '51; his first records were favourably received, he was drafted during the Korean War, came back with first top 10 hit: his own song 'Goin' Steady' '53; went to Grand Ole Opry. There was hardly a week when one of his records was not found in the Billboard country chart for 20 years, and he was still going strong for another decade. First no. 1 hit was 'Country Girl' '59; second was 'Hello Walls' '61 (also no. 12 pop hit and a big break for its author, Willie NELSON); he helped a bellhop named Roger MILLER, hiring him to play drums although Miller had never played drums in his life. He switched to Mercury '63, had duet hits with Margie Singleton '64, eight top 10 hits in a row '69-71 incl. remake of 'Goin' Steady' and huge international hit with no. 1 'It's Four In The Morning' (made pop Hot 100, top 30 in UK). Among his own compositions in country top 10 were 'All Right' '55, 'I Miss You Already' '57, 'Alone With You' '58 (also made pop chart), 'Your Old Used To Be' '60, 'Backtrack' '61 (also pop hit), 'Three Days' '62, 'Wine Me Up' '69. Also a good businessman, interests incl. Nashville magazine *Music City News* for many years, also publishing, recording studio, commercials (for Ford, BC Headache Powders, etc.), films (*Country Music Holiday*, with Ferlin HUSKY and Zsa Zsa Gabor), TV (*Daniel Boone*), and one of the best-loved attractions on the state/county fair circuit. Switched to MCA late '70s. Far too many LPs to list here incl. *Step Aside, Leavin' And Sayin' Goodbye, Four In The Morning, This Little Girl Of Mine, This Time The Hurtin's On Me*, all on Mercury; *Chapter Two* and *Free & Easy* on MCA; *The Sheriff* on Allegiance.

YOUNG, Jimmy (*b* 21 Sep. c.'23, Cinderford, Glos.) UK singer, broadcaster. Son of a miner; keen sportsman in younger days; joined RAF '39, teacher post-war. First pro singing job '49 in variety; spotted by BBC prod. George Innes (who later created long-running TV series *The Black And White Minstrel Show*). First records for Polygon '51; UK version of international hit 'Too Young' picked up by DJ Jack Jackson; minor hit on Decca with Charlie Chaplin's

'Eternally' ('Terry's Theme' from *Limelight* '53); no. 1 hits with more movie themes '55: 'Unchained Melody', 'The Man From Laramie'. Played London's Dominion Theatre '57 with Sophie TUCKER; conventional DJ work with BBC from '60s; top 20 '63 with 'Miss You' (song from '29). Straightforward crooner, not noted for subtle phrasing; broadcasting came along just in time: precipitated by BBC upheaval in face of competition from offshore pirates, from '67 developed revolutionary radio format mixing records with dispensing information on consumer relations and current affairs, interviews with politicians incl. Prime Ministers; popular programme still running.

YOUNG, Lester (*b* Lester Willis Young, 27 Aug. '09, Woodville, Ms.; *d* 15 Mar. '59, NYC) Tenor sax; one of the most infl. jazzmen of the century. Played drums in family's touring band but quit in Phoenix, refusing to tour the South (brother Lee, *b* 7 Mar. '17, New Orleans, also a drummer; later played on records with Nat COLE, Lionel HAMPTON, etc.; became record company executive for Vee Jay, Motown). Lester took up tenor late '20s, later alto as well: he carried a portable record player with him, and said he was infl. by Frankie TRUMBAUER's C-melody sax on Bix BEIDERBECKE's records. He played in territory bands all over the midwest; joined the Blue Devils '32, left with several others to join Bennie MOTEN; worked for Count BASIE '34 but left to join Fletcher HENDERSON, replacing Coleman HAWKINS: he already had an unusual tone on the tenor, sounding almost like an alto, very different from Hawkins, with more swing, playing slightly behind the beat rather than pushing it, in improvisation concentrating on the melody rather than the chords: his coolness (as opposed to Hawkins's fat richness) became an alternative tenor style and a major contribution to post-war music, but Henderson's wife, by all accounts a terrible nag, didn't like it: she made him listen to Hawkins's records and demanded that he sound like someone he wasn't. Lasted less than five months, then played with Andy KIRK, others; auditioned for Earl HINES '36, but rejoined Basie and made his first records Oct. that year in Chicago. The effortless, innocent joy of the small-group sides made at that session (see Basie's entry) are among the century's most beautiful: of 'Shoe Shine Boy', Michael Brooks (prod. of the 2-disc Basie compilation *Super Chief*) wrote that 'his genius forever banishes the image of that Uncle Tom . . .'; Jo JONES described 'Lady Be Good' as 'the best solo Lester ever recorded'. From Jan. '37 to Dec. '40 Young was a star of the Basie band on Decca, then Columbia; on Decca the band also incl. Herschel Evans (*d* early '39), a tenorist more in the Hawkins style: they were rivals, complementing each other; both are heard on 'Every Tub', 'Doggin' Around', 'Jumpin' At The Woodside' (Evans on clarinet); Young is featured on 'Honeysuckle Rose' and 'Time Out'; Evans plays tenor and Young clarinet on 'Texas Shuffle', etc. (all on Decca); among best-known Young solos on CBS are 'Taxi War Dance', 'Rock-A-Bye Basie', 'Lester Leaps In' (a septet 'head' allegedly created when he walked in during a take). He was nick-named 'Prez' (for President) by Billie HOLI-DAY; he played on many of her small-group sessions with Teddy WILSON: he claimed to be thinking of the words when improvising on a ballad, and they were obvious soulmates, both personally and musically. He guested at Benny GOODMAN's Carnegie Hall Concert '38; played both clarinet and tenor on a wonderful Commodore session '38 with Buck CLAYTON, Eddie DURHAM, Basie's rhythm section of Freddie GREEN, Walter PAGE and Jones. A Goodman session of Oct. '40 (now on Jazz Archives) with Charlie CHRISTIAN, Clayton, Basie and his rhythm, was a rehearsal for a session that took place a few days later with other personnel, but has a lovely Young solo on 'I Never Knew'. He co-led a band with Lee '41-3, worked with Al Sears, Basie, Dizzy GILLESPIE, rejoined Basie late '43 until he was drafted Sep. '44. During '43-4 there were small-group records for Commodore, Bob THIELE's Signature label (*Classic Tenors*, now on Doctor Jazz), Keynote (*At His Very Best* on Mercury, now in complete Keynote compilation, incl. 4.5 minute version of 'Lester Leaps Again'). He was featured in a famous short film, *Jammin' The Blues* '44, by Gjon Mili and Norman GRANZ. A shy, sensitive, superstitious man, he was a master of the put-on, foreshadowing the bop era not only in his playing but

in inventing his own cryptic language, as much to hide his feelings as to express them; an unlikely soldier, he found racism a terrible burden: he spent less than a year in the US Army, much of it in a stockade in Georgia, and emerged after suffering his earliest bouts of poor health. He made small-group sides '45-8 for Aladdin (later prod. for reissue on Blue Note by Michael CUSCUNA), also for Savoy; toured with JATP; spent the rest of his life as a freelance soloist surrounded by imitators: hearing a younger player on a bandstand he allegedly said, 'You're not you, you're me!' Lived in NYC hotel room, drinking excessively, listening to Frank SINATRA and Billie Holiday records and watching old western movies on TV; appeared with Holiday and others on the CBS TV show *Sound Of Jazz* '57; he played in Paris early '59, died within 24 hours of returning. Holiday thought that she would soon join him; she lived only months longer. Other records issued incl. four discs on Pablo made at a Washington DC club; Verve set with Wilson, Vic DICKENSON, Roy ELDRIDGE and Kansas City rhythm section of Green, Jones and Gene Ramey on bass, all made in '56; *The President Plays* with Oscar PETERSON trio plus Barney KESSEL incl. Young vocal on 'It Takes Two To Tango'. He received composer credit for tunes incl. 'Jumpin' With Symphony Sid' (named after a disc jockey). Orthodox critical opinion was that Young's post-war playing was second-rate; Lewis Porter refutes this using musical analysis in his book *Lester Young* '86: the real world may have broken his heart, but Prez knew what he was doing on his horn until the end.

YOUNG, Neil (*b* 12 Nov. '45, Toronto, Canada) USA-based singer/songwriter. Had diabetes, epilepsy and polio as a child; music gave him a goal. Met Stephen STILLS in high school group the Squires, but couldn't get work permit to join him in USA; joined Mynah Birds, whose lead singer (Motown soul star Rick James, then known as Ricky James Matthews) had to return to US Navy; Young made it to L.A. and joined BUFFALO SPRINGFIELD, leaving before their demise and signing to Reprise as solo act. Debut *Neil Young* '68 was disturbing folk-style album, with stage favourite 'The Loner' and 9.5 minute 'The Last Trip To Tulsa' noteworthy. But songs and plaintive singer needed a band: he recruited Crazy Horse (originally the Rockets: Danny Whitten, guitar; Ralph Molina, drums; Billy Talbot, bass); basic band proved its worth on *Everybody Knows This Is Nowhere* '69: manic, passionate 'Down By The River' had singer and band on the edge, while they could equally deal with pop picking on whimsical 'Cinnamon Girl'. Sales of *After The Goldrush* '70 profited from Young's stint with CROSBY, STILLS & NASH '69: no. 8 LP incl. 'Only Love Can Break Your Heart' (no. 33 hit), 'Southern Man' (inexorable warning for Alabama Gov. George Wallace in style of CSN&Y protest song 'Ohio'); plaintive title track told of spaceships and surrealistic images (revived by Preludes for top 30 UK/USA hit '74, did it again on reissue in UK '82). *Harvest* '72 was no. 1 LP USA and best seller to date, despite pretentious inclusion of London Symphony Orchestra on two tracks; standout numbers incl. 'Heart Of Gold' (no. 1 single USA), 'Old Man' (no. 31), 'Are You Ready For The Country' and anti-drug 'The Needle And The Damage Done', recorded live after Whitten's death from a heroin overdose; backing incl. Stray Gators with Nashville drummer Kenny Buttrey, CS&N, others on vocals. Patchy 2-disc soundtrack *Journey Through The Past* '72 incl. remakes of Buffalo and CSN&Y hits; live *Time Fades Away* '73 incl. Crosby and Nash; *On The Beach* '74 laughed in adversity's face, while *Tonight's The Night* '75, actually recorded first, wallowed in misery: observations of drug culture were dedicated to Whitten. As on *Goldrush*, Nils LOFGREN helped out on guitar. By *Zuma* '75 he had worked it out, and created another lengthy classic in 'Cortez The Killer', a guitar tour-de-force about Spanish imperialism in South America. *Long May You Run* '76 was credited as 'Stills – Young Band'; *American Stars'n'Bars* '77 had guests Linda RONSTADT and Emmylou HARRIS, and was mostly unchallenging except for stage favourite 'Like A Hurricane'; *Comes A Time* '78 was all acoustic guitars, with Crazy Horse playing bit parts; softest LP since *Harvest* incl. cover of IAN & SYLVIA's 'Four Strong Winds'. Crazy Horse back in evidence on *Rust Never Sleeps* '79, fusing attack of *Tonight's The Night* with punkish lyric on 'Hey Hey My My (Into The Black)' and 2-disc concert *Live Rust* '79. *Hawks And Doves* '80 was loose country; *Re-ac-tor* '81 was R&B; he switched to Geffen label for *Trans* '83, a synthesiser LP using vocoder for remake of Buffalo's 'Mr Soul', mixing Crazy Horse, Lofgren, drum machines in set that amused some, alienated others. *Everybody's Rockin'* '83 was rock'n-'roll (by 'Neil & The Shocking Pinks'); *Old Ways* '85 a return to country followed by *Landing On Water* '86: unpredictable as ever, he made a full-length video of the entire *Landing On Water* LP, financing it himself, playing a variety of visual parts, not aimed at MTV: 'He doesn't want to be associated with that rubbish and neither do I,' said director Tim Pope; but the LP was MOR rock with studio musicians, not one of his best; the last two albums suffered from modern fashion of being recorded at different times and places with different lineups. Young has created a powerful body of work (3-disc compilation *Decade* '77); his guitar style has echoes in work of new wave artists like Tom Verlaine; despite experiments he remains the darling of the Woodstock generation: every LP charted except the first, averaging no. 23 in Billboard. *This Note's For You* '88 with the Bluenotes.

YOUNG, Paul (*b* 17 Jan. '56, Luton, Bedfordshire) UK pop singer. Had one-off hit with Streetband's 'Toast', UK no. 18 '78; then fronted band Q-Tips '78-82, popular with critics but releasing only *Q-Tips* '80. On their split he signed solo deal, released excellent *No Parlez* '83, a big success incl. no. 1 single with Marvin GAYE's 'Wherever I Lay My Hat', top fives 'Come Back And Stay', 'Love Of The Common People'. Recording of JOY DIVISION's 'Love Will Tear Us Apart' found little favour with that band's cult following, but proved imaginative and soulful interpretation. Strain on voice due to hard touring forced delay in follow-up; *The Secret Of Association* '85 was workmanlike, building on vocal strengths, but lacked variety of debut, still incl. no. 1 USA cover of Daryl HALL's 'Everytime You Go Away', other hits. He duetted with Alison MOYET at Live Aid '85; *Between Two Fires* '86 incl. engaging 'Wonderland'; he remains one of pop's best discoveries of the decade. Q-Tips *Live* '85 on Hallmark in UK; 2-disc *Streetband* incl. 'Toast' on Cambra in UK, as *London Dilemma* on Compleat in USA.

YOUNG, Steve (*b* 12 July '42, Ala.) Country singer, guitarist, songwriter. Apprenticeship in Southern bars and honky tonks; went to L.A. First LP was *Rock Salt & Nails* on A&M, now on Edsel UK, with original version of 'Seven Bridges Road', with James BURTON on guitar and dobro, guests Gram PARSONS and Gene CLARK, etc. Album called *Seven Bridges Road* '72 on Reprise has been reissued/recycled on Blue Canyon and Rounder/Sonet; latter edition has five original tracks remixed, four previously unreleased with Ry COODER, Pete DRAKE, members of AREA CODE 615. He moved to Nashville, made *Renegade Picker* '76, *No Place To Fall* '77 on RCA; *Honky Tonk Man* '76 on Mountain Railroad, now on Rounder; *To Satisfy You* '81 on Rounder, *Old Memories* on Country Roads, *Look Homeward, Angel* on Mill. Both *Renegade Picker, Seven Bridges Road* incl. 'Lonesome Orn'ry And Mean', covered for title track of Waylon JENNINGS' '73 album: Jennings calls him 'the second best country singer' after George JONES. The EAGLES covered 'Seven Bridges Road' for a pop hit '80; Young remains underrated.

YOUNG TRADITION, The UK folk group of '60s: Peter BELLAMY, Heather Wood, Royston Wood. Formed '65, taking name from a club (which was originally called The Grand Tradition) and to avoid being called the Scottish Hoose Singers, name proposed by organiser Bruce Dunnet. Infl. by the COPPER FAMILY, but also trad. Balkan singing, the American sacred harp style, acts like Ewan MACCOLL, Peggy SEEGER, Pennywhistlers, Frankie Armstrong, Louis Killen, Cyril Tawney; a bit later than the other major unaccompanied folk act, the WATERSONS, their own infl. (on Home Bru, Swan Arcade) continued to grow after they broke up. Debut LP *The Young Tradition* '66 incl. dynamic versions of 'Byker Hill', 'Lyke Wake Dirge', 'The Innocent Hare'; their dress and long hair placed them in the era of pop/rock acts like the BEATLES, Jimi HENDRIX, INCREDIBLE STRING BAND, a revelation to the folk

world, but distracted unduly from their act. *So Cheerfully Round* and EP *Chicken On A Raft* of sea chanties '67 were followed by *Galleries* '68, an attempt to blend infl. from early music, trad. folk, spoof Delta blues, with guests Dolly COLLINS, Sandy DENNY, Dave Swarbrick, David Munrow, went off at half cock (reissued as *Galleries Revisited*, like all their records on Transatlantic). Final LP *The Holly Bears The Crown* '69, collaboration with Shirley & Dolly Collins, never released (by Argo), though some tracks did find their way out. They also sessioned for Judy COLLINS, Dolly Collins, Matt McGinn, Tony Rose; Bellamy had already begun solo career; the Woods called duo LP *No Relation* '77, to silence question they had heard too often.

YOUNG, Victor (*b* 8 Aug. 1900, Chicago; *d* 11 Nov. '56, Palm Springs, Cal.) Violinist, arranger, conductor, composer. To Warsaw, Poland '10, studied at conservatory there, played in Warsaw Philharmonic; toured USA as concert violinist early '20s; worked in theatre orchestras as concert master, leading to playing and composing popular music in top dance bands such as Ted Fio Rito, Isham JONES: featured violin solo in Jones recording of Hoagy CARMICHAEL song 'Stardust' '31, establishing it as a ballad (had been a 'hot' tune). Conducted on radio early '30s; on records and film as well from '35, becoming top film composer: over 300 film scores/themes incl. *Wells Fargo* '37, *Raffles* '40, *The Glass Key* '42, *For Whom The Bell Tolls* '43, *The Blue Dahlia* '46, *The Quiet Man* '52, *Shane* '53; posthumous Oscar for *Around The World In Eighty Days* '56; also wrote 'Blue Star' '55 (theme for TV's *Medic*). Eight chart entries '50-7 all on Decca incl. 'Mona Lisa' (no. 10 '50), 'The High And The Mighty' (no. 6 '54), 'Around The World In Eighty Days' (no. 13 '57; flip side had a Bing CROSBY vocal version with Harry Adamson's words; soundtrack LP was no. 1 for 10 weeks). He led orchestra on Judy GARLAND hit 'Over The Rainbow' '39, Crosby gold discs 'Too-Ra-Loo-Ra-Loo-Ral (That's An Irish Lullaby)' '44, 'Galway Bay' '48, many more. He worked with lyricist Will J. Harris on 'Sweet Sue' '28, several people incl. Wayne KING on 'Beautiful Love' '31, with Sam M. Lewis on 'Street Of Dreams' '33, Edward Heyman on 'When I

Fall In Love' '51 (recorded by Doris DAY, Nat COLE), many others, but his most successful collaborator was Ned Washington (*b* 15 Aug. '01, Scranton, Pa.; *d* 20 Dec. '76, Beverly Hills): they wrote 'Can't We Talk It Over' '32, 'A Hundred Years From Today' (for *Blackbirds Of 1933*; later sung by Jack TEAGARDEN), 'I Don't Stand A Ghost Of A Chance With You' '33 (Crosby got a co-credit), 'Stella By Starlight' '46, 'My Foolish Heart' '49 (film theme), many more. Washington also wrote with George Bassman ('I'm Getting Sentimental Over You' '32; later became Tommy DORSEY theme song), Carmichael ('The Nearness Of You' '40), Bronislaw Kaper ('On Green Dolphin Street' '47), etc. With Leigh Harline he scored Disney's *Pinocchio* '40, winning Oscars for best score and best song ('When You Wish Upon A Star'); with Dmitri Tiomkin wrote the theme for *High Noon* '52 ('Do Not Forsake Me, Oh My Darling') for another Oscar; won a Golden Globe award '65 for *Circus World* score; also TV title song *Rawhide*.

YURO, Timi (*b* Rosemarie Yuro, 4 Aug. '40, Chicago) Singer. To L.A. as a child, sang in family's Italian restaurant, finding a blues infl. to add to Mediterranean heritage so that some thought she was black. Signed to Liberty and had 11 mostly minor Hot 100 entries '61-5 with writer/producer Clyde Otis, the biggest being the first, the throbbing ballad 'Hurt'. 'What's A Matter Baby (Is It Hurting You)', 'Gotta Travel On' and 'Down In The Valley' (which didn't chart) also evinced a soulful sound compared to that of Brenda LEE, but her later work lacked it. Singles on Mercury ('64-6) and Playboy ('75) missed the Hot 100; she had a hit in Holland in '80.

Z

ZABACH, Florian (*b* 15 Aug. '21, Chicago) Violinist, composer. A concert artist at 12, then soloist on radio with Percy FAITH, others; recorded for Decca. 'Hot Canary', a jazzed-up version of a European tune, used harmonic overtones produced by touching the strings lightly instead of pressing them firmly: it was no. 13 '50, sold a million eventually on Decca. He recorded the trad. fiddle tune 'Turkey In The Straw' (originally 'Zip Coon', c.1834), Leroy ANDERSON's 'Plink, Plank, Plunk', etc. Fine technique and showmanship made him a hit in clubs; he had a TV series '55 and a minor hit 'When The White Lilacs Bloom Again' on Mercury '56, but the version by German conductor/violinist Helmut Zacharias sold better.

ZAIKO LANGA LANGA African guitar band, formed Kinshasa '69; in forefront of new wave in Congolese music with a rougher, simpler soukous style. Founded by drummer Bakunde Ilo Pablo, Zaiko acted as catalyst for younger bands emerging early '70s: Empire Bakuba, Viva La Musica, Stukas etc.; features three guitars, strong front line of four vocalists (first lineup Likinga, LengiLengi, Bim Ombale and N'yoko Longo). Series of frenzied soukous hits incl. '74-8 items compiled on *Oldies And Goldies*; from same period is Vol. 6 of *Les Grands Succès des Éditions Veve* (*see* VERCKYS). By '80s one of the most prolific African recording bands, with dozens of albums on many labels; best sellers incl. *Sarah Djenni, Le Tout Neige, Tout Choc – Anti Choc, Kekete Zekete, Crois-Moi, On Gagne le Procès, Mère Tity, De Paris à Brazzaville, En Europe.* Fairly vigorous turnover in personnel caused by members leaving to form other top bands: Viva La Musica '74 (indirectly Victoria '82), Grand Zaiko Wa-Wa '80, Langa Langa Stars '81, Choc Stars '83; in turn, sparkling LPs by new groups incl. four vols. by Langa Langa Stars on Verckys' EVVI label, the last incl. Choc Stars; Choc Stars on their own label with *À Paris*; new supergroup with Bozi Boziana, Tchipaka Roxy and Esperant: together the heart of Zaire pop.

ZAPPA, Frank (*b* Francis Vincent Zappa Jr, 21 Dec. '40, Baltimore, Md.) Guitar, other instruments; leader, composer. To West Coast with family age 9, to Mohave Desert area '56; listened to R&B and to composers like Edgar Varèse; led combo in high school called the Blackouts. Played in cocktail lounges; wrote B film music (*The World's Greatest Sinner, Run Home Slow*); used money to buy 3-track studio in Cucamonga; recorded CAPTAIN BEEFHEART. Made sex tape for money, spent 10 days in jail (becoming draft-exempt), raised bail for the girl involved by co-writing 'Memories Of El Monte' for the PENGUINS with Ray Collins. Joined group the Soul Giants, renamed the Mothers (later renamed Mothers of Invention by MGM); heard by producer Tom Wilson (Bob DYLAN, VELVET UNDERGROUND), signed to Verve (by then a subsidiary of MGM): lineup with Elliot Ingber, Roy Estrada on guitars; Jimmy Carl Black, drums, Collins on vocals, began sessions resulting in rock's first 2-disc set *Freak-Out!* '66 (specially priced at the time), also one of the first concept LPs, incl. '50s parodies ('You Didn't Try To Call Me', etc.), social commentary ('Trouble Every Day', 'Who Are The Brain Police'), also autobiography/rock-opera: 'The Return Of The Son Of Monster Magnet', 'Hungry Freaks, Daddy', 'Help, I'm A Rock', 'Susie Creamcheese'. The album reached Billboard's top 200 LPs, established the group as an 'underground' attraction and Zappa as an important figure: surprisingly, the savage satire of the Mothers period has not dated, perhaps because America never really changes. *Absolutely Free* '67 carried on the reaction against boredom, hypocrisy in post-war USA which was gathering steam in the counter-culture ('Brown Shoes Don't

Make It', 'Plastic People', 'America Drinks And Goes Home'); *We're Only In It For The Money* '67 was satire of BEATLES' *Sergeant Pepper* and an ominous send-up of the hippie era; *Cruising With Ruben And The Jets* was a send-up of '50s rock'n'roll, though with an affection that even Zappa could not deny. Verve subsequently issued compilation LPs, of which only *Mothermania* was assembled by Zappa. On Mercury *For Real* and *Con Safos* were issued '73 as by Ruben and the Jets. He formed labels Straight, Bizarre; former issued ALICE COOPER debut LP and Beefheart's *Trout Mask Replica*, perhaps Zappa's most memorable production; he also prod. *Permanent Damage* by the GTOs (groupie collective Girls Together Outrageous), *An Evening With Wild Man Fischer* (L.A. street entertainer), etc. Bizarre issued 2-disc *Uncle Meat* '69 (score for unmade film, with Beefheart, Jean-Luc PONTY on violin), and *Weasels Ripped My Flesh* '70; *Burnt Weenie Sandwich* '70 was on Reprise. By this time the Mothers no longer toured; Ingber had left to join Fraternity of Man (he wrote 'Don't Bogart That Joint', heard in soundtrack of *Easy Rider* '69), later Beefheart; drummers Black, Billi Mundi, Art Tripp (also to Beefheart) all came and went, as did Lowell George (formed LITTLE FEAT with Estrada). Zappa made solo LPs *Lumpy Gravy* '68 with 50 pieces, Mothers on vocals; *Hot Rats* '69, often called his best, with synthesisers, vocal by Beefheart on 'Willie The Pimp'; *Chunga's Revenge* '70, with Don 'Sugarcane' Harris on violin; also wrote *King Kong: Jean-Luc Ponty Plays The Music Of Frank Zappa* (played uncredited guitar). Formed new Mothers with keyboardists Ian Underwood and George DUKE, drummer Aynsley DUNBAR; bassist Jim Pons, vocalists Mark Volman and Howard Kaylan (last two ex-TURTLES, billed as 'Phlorescent Leech and Eddie' then 'Flo and Eddie'), Ruth Underwood on percussion, etc. This group toured; live material issued on John and Yoko LENNON's *Sometime In New York City*, also *Fillmore East, June 1971* on Reprise, *Just Another Band From L.A.* '72 on Bizarre (then distributed by Reprise). 2-disc score *200 Motels* '71 was critical success, film (cameos by Ringo STARR, Keith Moon) got mixed reviews. (He played score '70 at a sold-out

concert with Zubin Mehta, L.A. Philharmonic.) A tour of Europe was a disaster: equipment destroyed in a fire and Zappa injured when shoved from the stage in London. LP *Waka Jawaka – Hot Rats* with horn section, side-long 'Big Swifty' was billed as solo LP; same group as Mothers made *The Grand Wazoo*; with changing lineups the Mothers were retired with *Over-Nite Sensation* (went gold), 2-disc *Roxy And Elsewhere* (incl. instrumental 'Don't You Ever Wash That Thing'), *One Size Fits All*, all on his DiscReet label. Zappa solo *Apostrophe (')* '74 (reissued as *A-Pos-Tro-Phe*) certified gold; incl. 'Don't Eat The Yellow Snow', first single in Hot 100 (no. 86); LP made no. 10 in Billboard LP chart, best showing of 32 albums charted '67-83. *Bongo Fury* '75 was made live in Austin with Beefheart and various Mothers; *Zoot Allures* '76 (issued on WB) was last LP from WB/Reprise/DiscReet (but previously unissued material came out in '78-9: 2-disc *Zappa In New York*, *Studio Tan*, *Sleep Dirt*, *Orchestral Favorites*). Zappa/Mercury/Phonogram deal yielded 2-disc *Sheik Yerbouti* '79 (title was a pun on KC AND THE SUNSHINE BAND's 'Shake Your Booty': no. 21 LP incl. no. 45 hit disco send-up 'Dancin' Fool', 'Jewish Princess' resulting in an Anti-Defamation League complaint to the FCC, also Peter FRAMPTON send-up 'I Have Been In You'); *Joe's Garage* '79, intended as a 3-disc set: *Act 1* was well-received as a single LP (incl. 'Catholic Girls'), 2-disc *Acts 2 & 3* was a critical flop, still made no. 53 in Billboard. When Mercury would not issue single 'I Don't Wanna Get Drafted' he left, formed Barking Pumpkin and distribution deal with CBS; *Tinsel Town Rebellion* and *You Are What You Is* '81 were 2-disc sets; *Ship Arriving Too Late To Save A Drowning Witch* '82 reached no. 23, helped by no. 32 single 'Valley Girl', with brilliant monologue improvised by his daughter, Moon Unit. 3-disc *Shut Up'n Play Yer Guitar* '81 sold through the post as single LPs in USA, issued as set in Europe late that year, the next year as set in USA. *The Man From Utopia* '83 charted; *Them Or Us*, *Thing Fish*, *Francesco* have appeared on Barking Pumpkin. Despite the apparent anarchy, Zappa's music has always been ambitious (he used to tell audiences, 'You wouldn't know good music if it bit you on the ass!'; defined rock journalism as 'people who can't write interviewing people who can't talk for people who can't read'). His mastery of prod. technology is complete; output is regarded as variable in quality and some of its success is due to deliberate bad taste (an endless stream of titles like 'Broken Hearts Are Assholes', 'Why Does It Hurt When I Pee', 'Shove It Right In', etc.). Some regard him as a great composer; his electronic rock has already made its mark, but *The Perfect Stranger And Other Works* '85 on (MI/Angel in USA) is impressive (no. 7 '84 in Billboard classical chart): three dances are played by Pierre Boulez and his Ensemble Intercontemporain, others by the Barking Pumpkin Digital Gratification Consort. Typically, Zappa says the title tune, commissioned by Boulez's IRCAM in Paris, is about a vacuum-cleaner salesman and a slovenly housewife. *London Symphony Orchestra Vol. 22* '87 was on Barking Pumpkin; son Dweezil released *Havin' A Bad Day* '87.

ZAWINUL, Joe (*b* 7 July '32, Vienna) Keyboards, composer. To USA '59; accompanied Dinah WASHINGTON; joined Cannonball ADDERLEY '61 and was a key member of that popular group: wrote arrangements for the Adderley album with Nancy WILSON, wrote 'Mercy, Mercy, Mercy', Adderley's biggest hit and a Grammy winner, etc. Also recorded with Ben WEBSTER (*Soulmates* on Riverside), many others. He began playing electronic keyboards and miscellaneous instruments; made important LPs with Miles DAVIS '69-70, incl. *In A Silent Way* (wrote title tune) and *Bitches Brew*; recorded *Concerto For Two Pianos And Orchestra* with Friedrich Gulda on Preiser; founded WEATHER REPORT '71 with Wayne SHORTER, which they co-led until '85, parting to pursue their own projects for a while. Zawinul's own LPs incl. *Money In The Pocket* and *Rise And Fall Of The Third Stream* on Atlantic; *Dialects* '86 on CBS is a solo disc, all synthesisers with no overdubbing. In mid-'86 he formed a quintet with guitarist John SCOFIELD and three Weather Report veterans.

ZEITLIN, Denny (*b* Dennis Jay Zeitlin, 10 Apr. '38, Chicago) Composer, keyboards, bass; has parallel career in psychiatry. Stud-

ied harmony with George RUSSELL; began recording with Jeremy Steig trio on Columbia '63 (flautist Steig *b* 23 Sep. '42, NYC; LPs on Atlantic, Reprise, Blue Note; with Bill EVANS on *What's New*, etc.). Zeitlin LPs incl. *Carnival*, *Zeitgeist* (latter now available from Columbia Special Products); appeared at Monterey and Newport jazz festivals; retired '68 to study electronics, keyboards, possibilities of fusion while maintaining private psychiatric practice. Formed own record company Double Helix '73 (LPs *Expansion* '73, solo piano *Soundings*, also *Syzygy*; now on label called 1750 Arch). Other LPs incl. *Time Remembers One Time Once* '81 on ECM with Charlie HADEN, *Tidal Wave* '83 on Palo Alto, *Homecoming* '86 on Living Music.

ZEVON, Warren (*b* 24 Jan. '47, Chicago) Singer/songwriter with view on the dark side. Of Russian ancestry; grew up in West USA; wrote 'She Quit Me Man', heard in soundtrack of *Midnight Cowboy* '69; debut LP *Wanted – Dead Or Alive* '69 on Imperial was a flop. He wrote jingles, played piano for the EVERLY Bros; Linda RONSTADT covered 'Hasten Down The Wind', title track of no. 3 hit LP '76, two more on *Simple Dreams* ('Poor Poor Pitiful Me' made top 40 as a single); on his return from Spain, Jackson BROWNE prod. *Warren Zevon* '76 (incl. members of EAGLES and FLEETWOOD MAC, critical hit just making Billboard LP chart) and *Excitable Boy* '78, helped to no. 8 by no. 21 single 'Werewolves Of London'; also with 'Roland The Headless Thompson Gunner'. He took time off to deal with alcoholism; then *Bad Luck Streak In Dancing School* '80, *Stand In The Fire* '81, *The Envoy* '82 (title track about diplomat Philip Habib in Middle East) were all successful, though the last was regarded as uneven; he admits that he tinkered with it too long: '. . . the songs that come well in the early takes usually work better in the long run'. He suffered a writing block and concentrated on touring; he predicted that new works will be 'more realistic songs with "Gee, I'm lonely, gee I'm working hard" kind of themes,' but maintaining the sardonic edge. *A Quiet, Normal Life: The Best Of Warren Zevon* '86 is useful compilation; *Sentimental Hygiene* '87 on Virgin his first new work in five years, with 'Springsteenian beat, the bass line pushing home the message that somewhere down in the male rock psyche lies something very grim' (Simon Frith).

ZIGLIBITHY African music style developed in Ivory Coast during '70s. Francophone Africa was dominated by sound of music of Zaire; apart from a variety of trad. styles Ivory Coast had not developed a distinctive national style until Ernesto Djedje (*b* '48, Tahiraguhe; *d* '83) combined local elements with Congolese rhythms to make Ivorian sound since known as ziglibithy: slightly slower than Makossa, with a curious jerky character, ziglibithy is now considered to be national music of the Ivory Coast. He made pro debut '63, two years later formed first band; to Paris '68, recorded 'Anoma' '70, returned home '72 to launch new style: classic LPs *Ziglibithy* and *Zibote* '77. By '82 he was one of the most influential musicians in the country, scored with huge hit 'Taxi Sognon'; honoured by President Houphouët-Boigny for contribution to national culture, but died suddenly. Younger stars maintained appeal of style, incl. J. B. Zibodi on LP *Wazie Meo*, Blissi Tebil on hit *Ziglibithy la Continue: Homage à Ernesto Djedje*, singer Luckson Padaud on *Bithye* '82, *AgnonNouke, Homage à Ernesto Djedje*; now there are hundreds: the style seems secure.

ZOMBIES UK pop group formed '63 by Hertfordshire schoolboys Rod ARGENT, keyboards; Colin BLUNSTONE, vocals; Paul Atkinson (*b* 19 Mar. '46, Cuffley), guitar; Hugh Grundy (*b* 6 Mar. '45, Winchester), drums; Paul Arnold on bass, replaced same year by Chris White (*b* 7 Mar. '43, Barnet). Band won talent contest, auditioned for Decca, were signed on strength of Argent/White songs like 'She's Not There' and 'You Make Me Feel Good' along with ubiquitous R&B covers. Argent's second-ever composition, 'She's Not There', made no. 12 UK: classic pop song built around breathy Blunstone vocal, his rolling piano; both Argent and White became reliable writers. Followup 'Leave Me Be' flopped, but 'She's Not There' reached no. 2 USA, where band became a cult. 'Tell Her No' was no. 6 USA, only 42 UK; further USA Hot 100 entries were 'She's Coming Home'

and 'I Want You Back Again'; their polite yet potent pop infl. the TURTLES, CRITTERS, ASSOCIATION, even SIMON & GARFUNKEL. Album *Begin Here* '65 mixed originals with R&B covers but was poorly received; they moved to CBS hoping to become album band; *Odessey And Oracle* (sic) '68 was underrated result (reissued on Rock Machine UK), incl. USA no. 3 hit 'Time Of The Seasons' (promoted by BLOOD, SWEAT & TEARS' Al KOOPER), but by that time disillusioned band had split. Argent formed eponymous progressive band, for which White co-wrote with him; Atkinson and Grundy became CBS A&R men. Like MANFRED MANN, Zombies could have done more than hit singles, but public preconceptions and rise of 'progressive' rock forced the direction of pop music. Their jazzy, classy pop has lasted well. *She's Not There* '82 is Decca compilation.

ZORN, John (*b* '53, NYC) Avant-garde composer of aural works of art compared to the paintings of Jackson Pollock, a chameleon crawling through a paint box or an elephant trapped in barbed wire, but no description does it justice: influenced by Stockhausen, Anthony BRAXTON and Bugs Bunny, like all good music it is about filling the soundspace, but not filling it too full. Plays alto, soprano saxes, clarinet, keyboards, duck calls; has been known to place toy footballs in the bell of the sax or blow the mouthpiece under water. Own LPs: *Locus Solus* on Rift (two 12″ EPs, four pieces with four different trios); 2-disc sets *Pool* and *Archery* on Parachute, *Cobra* '86 on Hat Art (two versions, live and studio, of molecular system for 13 players cued by Zorn, who does not play). Plays solo with overdubbing on *A Classic Guide To Strategy* '87 on Lumina; an earlier solo LP on Lumina already out of print. Signed to Nonesuch: *The Big Gundown* '87 (premiere '86 at Brooklyn Academy of Music) treats music of film composer Ennio Morricone (*b* '28; scored 300 movies, spaghetti Westerns brought fame), followed by *Spillane* '88. Plays on pianist Wayne Horvitz's *Simple Facts* on Theatre For Your Mother label; with rock group *The Golden Paliminos*, Derek BAILEY and George LEWIS on *Yankees* on OAO; a duo with drummer David Moss on *Full House* and plays in his *Dense*

Band, both on Moers Music. Duets with percussionist Charles K. Noyes on *The World And The Raw People* on Zoar, with trombonist Jim Staley on one side of *OTB* and with reedman Ned Rotherberg on *Trespass*, both on Lumina; and with Michihiro Sato (playing the Japanese classical-style shamisen, a guitar/banjo-like instrument) on *Ganryu Island* on Yukon. Also contributed tracks to 2-disc sets *That's The Way I Feel Now* '83 (tribute to Thelonious MONK), *Lost in The Stars* '84 (Kurt WEILL), both on A&M; in group Alterations (on Nato label); plays hard-edged alto in Sonny Clark Memorial Quartet (*Voodoo* '87 on Black Saint, with Horvitz, Bobby Previte on drums, Ray Drummond on bass), tribute to late pianist. Among perpetrators on various discs are KRONOS QUARTET, guitarist Fred Frith, violinist Polly Bradfield, Bill LASWELL; Zorn is known to admire Mars Williams (*see* Hal RUSSELL). Zorn's *News For Lulu* '87 on HatArt is a trio with Lewis and guitarist Bill Frisell; he also plays on Frith's *The Technology Of Tears* on SST.

ZYDECO Black USA genre, indigenous to southwest Louisiana and West Texas, equivalent of white CAJUN, often very similar to it. 'La La' (*la musique Créole*) was a dance music created from meeting with Cajun, old French, Afro-American and Afro-Caribbean idioms from mid-19th century onwards; the tightly-knit community was upended by conscription during WWII and urban and country blues crept in, making zydeco (aka zodico); it had a two-way impact, infl. appearing in the work of LEADBELLY and Lightnin' HOPKINS. The term is believed to come from a creolised pronunciation of *les haricots*, from the one-step 'Les Haricots Sont Pas Salés' ('the snap beans aren't salted'); versions of this incl. those of Clifton CHENIER (*Louisiana Blues And Zydeco*) and Albert Chevallier (*Zydeco* compilation, both on Arhoolie); a children's version appears on *Songs Of Childhood* (Library of Congress Recorded Library). Zydeco is characterised by syncopated, driving rhythms; the piano accordion replaced Cajun's diatonic instrument; saxophone tended to oust the fiddle, one of the best saxists in genre being John Hart in ROCKIN' DOPSIE. Rub- or wash-board (*frittoir*, worn like a metal vest) adds a percussive element,

as it did in skiffle. Amplification and rhythm sections of drums and electric bass have further coloured the music. Rockin' Sidney (*b* Sidney Simien, 9 Apr. '38, Lebeau, La.) is best known for 'My Toot Toot'; four LPs incl. *My Zydeco Shoes Got The Zydeco Blues* '84 on Maison de Soul, also *Hotsteppin'* '87 on JSP. Queen Ida (*b* Ida Lewis, Lake Charles, La., now based on West Coast) billed as the Queen of Zydeco, appeared with her Bon Temps Zydeco Band in Francis Ford Coppola film *Rumble Fish*; LPs on GNP/Sonet. Accordionist Stanley 'Buckwheat' Dural Jr played keyboards in R&B bands, joined Chenier for three years, formed Buckwheat Zydeco and the Ils Sont Partis Band '79, using many elements 'like good jambalaya'; appeared in film *The Big Easy*; his *On A Night Like This* '87 is the first zydeco on 'major' label (Island).

ZZ TOP USA blues/rock trio formed '69 in Texas: Billy Gibbons, guitar, vocals; Dusty Hill, bass, vocals; Frank Beard, drums. Gibbons had supported Jimi HENDRIX '68 in Moving Sidewalks ('99th Floor' was regional hit); recruited Beard from American Blues, where he'd played with Hill. Released single 'Salt Lick' on manager/prod. Bill Ham's Scat label, made first LP privately, issued on London as *ZZ Top's First Album*, reflected straightforward blues infl. (John Lee HOOKER, B. B. KING etc.); *Rio Grande Mud* '72 almost reached top 100 LPs USA; *Tres Hombres* '73 climaxed first stage of career, no. 8 LP USA: incl. stage favourites 'Jesus Just Left Chicago', 'La Grange', latter tale of Texas bordello becoming first USA single hit at no. 41. Having achieved the big time, they peppered material with in-jokes for fans. *Fandango* '75 was half live, half studio, incl. much-covered heavy metal classic 'Tush', while *Tejas* '76 accompanied Worldwide Texas Tour '76-7 that sold 1.2m tickets and incl. (in USA) $140,000 worth of Texas livestock to set the scene: *Newsweek* reported ticket sales exceeded Elvis PRESLEY's, attendance exceeded LED ZEPPELIN, record sales beat ROLLING STONES. Drained, took three-year break (Gibbons studied synthesiser music in Europe), switched to WB, released *Deguello* '79, with nods to the past in covers of Elmore JAMES's 'Dust My Broom' and SAM & DAVE's 'I Thank You'. Now bearded and in boiler suits, they settled into two-year pattern, releasing *El Loco* '81, *Eliminator* '83: latter a new commercial breakthrough and peak of second stage, merged heavy metal with disco and pop hooks but retained blues base, stormed charts with hits 'Gimme All Your Lovin' ' (no. 37 USA/10 UK), 'Legs' (8 USA), 'Sharp Dressed Man' (56/45), all backed by videos, distinctive hot-rod car pictured on sleeve, translating group's well-known sexist/macho sense of humour: all in all, they could move with the times and simultaneously buck fashion. An-other two-year break (during which Hill nearly killed in firearms accident); then *Afterburner* '85 (car had become spaceship), almost cut-for-cut remake of *Eliminator*: no. 4 LP USA incl. top ten 'Sleeping Bag', but for the time being European success at least had been temporary. They surmount limitation of trio format by using backing tapes in live act (which draws criticism), but fans are loyal; if they do not wait too long to better *Afterburner*, critics may be surprised again. Compilations: London *Best Of* '77; WB *Best Of* '83.

APPENDIX

Finding a record is often difficult; this list of distributors and do-it-yourselfers is meant to make it easier. We welcome information in this area for the next edition of the book.

ALLEN, Terry
Fate Records
215 W. Superior Street
Chicago, Ill. 60610 USA

Austin Record Distributors
Box 132
Austin, Texas 78767 USA
*R&B, rock, country, folk,
jazz, Tex-Mex, Cajun, Western
Swing, etc.*

CADENCE
Cadence Building
Redwood, NY 13679 USA
*See main entry: as well as the
magazine and the label, an incredible
mail-order source for jazz records
(huge list in each issue), also
wholesaler to shops (as North Country
Distributors).*

Canadian River Music
4106 Tyler Street
Amarillo, Texas 79110 USA
*Dozens of artist-owned and small-label
albums.*

Canadisc
P.O. Box 142
Saulnierville
Nova Scotia
CANADA B0W 2Z0
*Hundreds of albums on small Canadian
labels in 16 categories incl. rock, folk,
ethnic, country, jazz, electronic etc.*

CHAPMAN, Marshall
Tall Girl Records
900 19th Ave South, Ste. 803
Nashville, Tenn. 37212 USA

CLARK, Guy newletter:
Friends of Guy Clark
P.O. Box 147
Fall River MIlls, Cal. 96028 USA

Delmark Records
4243 North Lincoln
Chicago, Ill. 60618 USA
*One of the small labels we all know and
love; see main entry.*

DOBSON, Richard
RJD Records
P.O. Box 120042
Nashville, Tenn. 37212 USA

Down Home Music Inc.
10341 San Pablo Avenue
El Cerrito, Cal. 94530 USA
Blues, folk, contry, vintage rock'n'roll, etc.

EAR Magazine of New Music
325 Spring Street Roon 208
New York, NY 10013 USA
*for people fed up with MTV and the trash
in the charts, or for music lovers in
general. See New Music Distribution
Service below.*

Folk Era/Kingston Korner
6 So. 230 Cohasset Road
Naperville, Ill. 60540 USA
American folk music.

GIBSON, Bob
BiG Records
1812 West Hood
Chicago, Ill. 60660 USA

GOODMAN, Steve
Red Pajamas Records
P.O. Box 233
Seal Beach, Cal. 90740 USA

HANCOCK, Butch
Rainlight Records
403 E. 7th Street
Austin, Texas 78701 USA

Jazzletter
P.O. Box 1305
Oak View, Cal. 93022 USA
*Unique, influential, often hilarious
monthly newsletter about mainstream and
jazz-oriented popular music, with
scathing attitude towards music business.
See Gene* LEES.

McGHEE, Wes
TRP Records
28 Gondar Gardens
West Hampstead
LONDON NW6 1HG
ENGLAND

MAINES BROTHERS BAND
Texas Soul Records
1214 Avenue Q
Lubbock, Texas 79401 USA

Mike's Country Music Room
18 Hilton Avenue
Aberdeen AB2 3RE
SCOTLAND
*The largest stock of bluegrass/acoustic and
contemporary country music in the UK.*

Mosaic Records
197 Strawberry Hill Avenue
Stamford, Conn. 06902-2510 USA
*Priceless limited-edition boxed
compilations of the complete Thelonious
Monk, Herbie Nichols, Tina Brooks from
Blue Note, Paul Desmond/Jim Hall from
RCA, etc. Not to be confused with Graham
Collier's UK Mosaic label.*

Music Master
John Humphries (Publishing) Ltd
Music House
1 De Cham Avenue
Hastings, Suxsex TN37 6HE
ENGLAND
*Unique British record catalogue for shops,
researchers.*

N'DOUR, Youssou
Saprom
B.P. 1310
40 Ave Malick Sy
Dakar, Senegal
Many cassettes available. Write in French.

New Music Distribution Service
500 Broadway
New York, NY 10012 USA
*Affiliated with Jazz Composers Orchestra
Association; distributes hundreds of
albums by John Zorn, Carla Bley, many
more; hard-to-find labels like Nessa,
American Clave, Celluloid, many others
you never heard of. Among the most
important enterprises of its kind. See also
EAR magazine, above.*

Omaha Rainbow
10 Lesley Court
Harcourt Road
Wallington, Surrey SM6 8AZ
ENGLAND
*Periodical published and edited by Peter
O'Brien since 1973 and now up to its 40th
issue. Named after a song by John
Stewart, who is featured in every issue
along with a host of singers and
songwriters, long interviews carefully and
fully transcribed: Guy Clark, David
Lindley, Ian Tyson, Albert Lee, Phil
Everly, Hal Blaine etc.*

Original Music
R.D. 1 Box 190, Lasher Road
Tivoli, NY USA
*Records, videos and books on music from
around the world, making no artificial
distinctions between ethnic, popular and
classical musics, but mostly eschewing
revivalism.*

PRINE, John
Oh Boy Records
P.O. Box 67800-5333
Los Angeles, Cal. 90067 USA

Projection Records
1 Leigh Hill, Old Town
Leigh-On-Sea, Essex
ENGLAND
*Comprehensive mail-order service for folk,
blues, ethnic, bluegrass, jazz.*

Recommended Records
387 Wandsworth Road
LONDON SW8
ENGLAND
Small label; distributor of many hard-to-find records; Henry Cow, Kalahari Surfers, Annette Peacock, other strange, wonderful stuff. Send a quid for the catalogue; if you go there, take bottles of wine.

Record Information Services
74 Brockley Rise
Forest Hill
LONDON SE23 1LR
ENGLAND
Discographical compilations mainly of UK labels/singles, incl. e.g. Complete British Directory of Popular 78/45 rpm Singles 1950-80 in several volumes; but also Blues Records 1943 to 1970 in two volumes, an update of the Mike Leadbitter – Neil Slaven classic; much else.

Record Research
P.O. Box 200
Menomenie Falls, Wisconsin 53051 USA
Unique reference books from Billboard charts (see entry for CHARTS)

Red Lick Records
P.O. Box 3
Porthmadog, Gwynedd, WALES
Blues, R&B, zydeco, gospel, old-timey etc.

RUSH, Tom
Night Life Recordings
Box 16
Hillsboro, N.H. 03244 USA

Schwann Record & Tape Guide
535 Boylston Street
Boston, Mass. 02116 USA
The most important USA general catalogue; see main entry.

SILVER, Horace
Silveto Records
P.O. Box 700-306
Rancho Palos Verdes, Cal. 90274 USA

STEWART, John
Homecoming Records
P.O. Box 2050
Malibu, Cal. 90265-7050 USA
Storyville Magazine
66 Fairview Drive
Chigwell, Essex IG7 6HS
ENGLAND
Traditional jazz reviews, intervies, good bookshelf.

TYSON, Ian
See IAN & SYLVIA
Eastern Slope Records
Box 820, High River, Alberta
CANADATOL 1BO

WALKER, Jerry Jeff
Tried & True Music
P.O. Box 39
Austin, Texas 78767 USA

WHITE, Andrew
Andrew's Music
4830 S. Dakota Avenue NE
Washington DVC 20017 USA
He didn't answer a postal query from us, but he advertises in Cadence; *presumably if you wave money at him, he responds.*

WOLF, Kate
Kaleidoscope Records
P.O. Box 0
El Cerrito, Cal. 94530 USA

YOUNG, Steve
2712 Westwood Avenue
Nashville, Tenn. 37212 USA

INDEX

Reference to certain well-known artists, such as Elvis Presley and Duke Ellington, are so numerous that to list them all would be of little help to the reader. In such cases the page number of the main entry is given, followed by the word <u>passim</u>.

CHARLES, Bobby 225, 961
Charles, Dennis 678, 1146
Charles, Don 1171
Charles, Jack 950
Charles, Jacques 64
Charles, Rawlston 'Charlie' 123, 663, 1020
CHARLES, Ray 225 and passim
CHARLES, Ray (arranger) 225, 354
Charlot, Andre 174
Charlton, Hannah 1155
Charlton, Manny 843
CHARLY/AFFINITY labels 226
Charmers, Lloyd 138
Charms 1247
Charnin, Martin 1001
Charo 307
Charone, Barbara 1009
Charters, Sam 128, 147, 392, 595, 620, 1066
CHARTS 227
CHAS & DAVE 156, 228, 845, 1156
Chase, Barrie 47
CHASE, Bill 228, 541
Chase, Chevy 1116
Chase, Lincoln 386, 962
Chater, Kerry 945
Chatham label 467
Chatman, Peter see MEMPHIS SLIM
Chatman, Sam 790
Chatmon, Armentier 'Bo' 900, 1181
Chatmon, Sam 900
Chatterton, Simon 523
Chatterton-Dew, Nick 88
Chavarria, Los Hermanos 1155
CHEAP TRICK 126, 228, 814, 1023
CHEATHAM, Doc 229, 604, 664, 743, 1260
CHEATHAM, Jimmy & Jeannie 229, 346, 862
CHECKER, Chubby 66, 71, 230, 329, 710, 745, 804, 925, 1029
Cheese, DJ 959
Cheetham, Richard 153
Chekasin, Vladimir 449
Chen, Phil 89
CHENIER, Clifton 36, 230, 444, 723, 998, 1280
Chequered Past 121, 889
Cher 21, 27, 580, 586, 787, 1096, 1106; see also SONNY & CHER
Cherry Bombz 512
CHERRY, Don 17, 55, 70, 114, 119, 231, 260, 261, 268, 275, 345, 374, 499, 531, 577, 603, 678, 725, 760, 762, 797, 839, 840, 903, 947, 970, 1011, 1026, 1061, 1146
CHERRY, Don (vocalist) 231
Cherry Keys 291
Chescoe, Laurie 796
CHESS 231
Chess, Leonard 103, 594
Chess, Marshall 232
Chester, Pete 829
Chesterman, Ron 1124, 1125
CHEVALIER, Maurice 55, 232, 375, 399, 504, 1001, 1225, 1241

Chevallier, Albert 1280
Chevron, Philip 835, 921
Chew-it, Brian 59
CHIC 50, 121, 232, 344, 582, 1016, 1070
CHICAGO 122, 227, 233, 318, 358, 445, 1109, 1148
Chicago Rhythm Kings 69, 1154
Chicago, Roy 99, 544, 689
Chicago Transit Authority 233
CHICKEN SHACK 233, 420, 494, 657, 1037, 1188
Chiefs Of Relief 145
CHIEFTAINS 234, 370, 822, 919, 1189
CHIFFONS 234, 491, 520, 655, 1169
CHILD, Francis James 153, 234, 423, 858, 1057
CHILDRE, Lew 235
Childs, Billy 973
CHI-LITES 171, 235, 591
CHILLI WILLI AND THE RED HOT PEPPERS 235, 285, 944
Chilton, Alex 145, 295
CHILTON, John 41, 88, 235, 302, 553, 747, 789
Chimes, Terry 578
Chin, Leonard 32
China Crisis 218, 568, 1151
CHINN & CHAPMAN 80, 236, 830, 950, 1091, 1137
Chinn, Nicky 236; see also CHINN & CHAPMAN
Chipmunks 1051
CHISHOLM, George 24, 236, 1211
Chitsvatsva, Kenny 106
CHITTISON, Herman 236
Chkiantz, George 614
CHOATES, Harry 65, 192, 236
Chocolate Dandies 102, 205, 209, 217, 525, 544, 617, 625, 747, 802, 873, 970, 1252
CHOCOLATE WATCH BAND 5, 237
Choc Stars 1276
Choice, Damon 726
Chong, Tommy 537
CHORDETTES 120, 237, 343, 518, 743
CHORDS 237, 298, 355
Chosen Few 418, 708
Chouinard, Bobby 823
Christensen, Jon 598
Christgau, Robert 122, 304, 442, 737, 918
CHRISTIAN, Charlie 51, 125, 139, 237, 407, 410, 475, 489, 503, 508, 545, 581, 602, 641, 698, 819, 900, 1209, 1242, 1272
Christian, Jodie 812
Christian, Neil 113
Christie Brothers Stompers 270
Christie, Keith 270
CHRISTIE, Lou 238, 477
Christina, Fran 46, 398, 1013
Christmas, Keith 153
Christopher, Gretchen 496
Christy, Edwin P. 808
CHRISTY, June 238, 276, 279, 411,

647, 868
Christy Minstrels 808, 852
Chrome, Cheetah 326
CHUCK WAGON GANG 238, 1221
Chudd, Lew 579, 1159, 1173
Church, Bill 500
Churchill, Chick 1153
Churchill, Winston 293, 549
Ciambotti, John 700
Ciccone, Don 430
Cindi, Abe 60
Ciner, Al 25
Cipollina, John 952
Cipollina, Mario 701
Cipriani, Mikey 1165
Cipriano, Gene 844
Circle 153, 282, 553
Circus Maximus 1208
Cisko Kid 859
Cissoko, Souldiou 668
Cita, Raoul J. 355
City 655
CLANCY BROTHERS & TOMMY MAKEM 110, 130, 239, 1142
Clancy, Liam 239
Clancy, Pat 239
Clancy, Tom 239
CLANNAD 239, 429
CLANTON, Jimmy 239, 925
CLAPTON, Eric 240 and passim
Clare, Kenny 244
Clarinet Family 128
Clark, Alan 343, 955
Clark, Andrew 88
CLARK, Buddy (singer) 240, 299, 307, 325, 402, 658, 717, 837, 861, 935, 1065
CLARK, Buddy (bass, arranger) 241, 466, 1133
CLARK, Charles E. 1, 43, 241
CLARK, Dave 241, 325, 559, 716, 814
CLARK, Dee 114, 241, 491, 1199
CLARK, Dick 66, 72, 103, 168, 230, 233, 242, 314, 340, 341, 374, 398, 495, 530, 534, 610, 649, 980, 1045, 1151
CLARK, Gene 187, 188, 242, 341, 546, 1274
Clark, Glen 735
CLARK, Guy 72, 242, 291, 292, 304, 347, 424, 465, 725, 998, 1196, 1208, 1257
Clark, John 171
Clark, June 521
Clark, Mahlon 1226
Clark, Nicky 355
Clark, Nobby 82
Clark, Papa 190
Clark, Pete 391
CLARK, Petula 243, 356, 523, 566, 942, 1116, 1220
Clark, Ray 163
CLARK, Roy 29, 156, 243, 249, 590, 884, 954, 961
Clark, Royce 1077
Clark, Samford 530
Clark, Shellie 553

CRAWFORD, Hank (cont.)
981, 1044
Crawford, James 1152
CRAWFORD, Jesse 295
CRAWFORD, Jimmy 295, 728
Crawford, Joan 47, 1016
CRAWFORD, Johnny 295
Crawford, Michael 715, 1094
CRAWFORD, Randy 295, 304
Crawford, Ray 592
Crawford, Sugar Boy 849
CRAY, Robert 20, 127, 227, 240,
262, 263, 281, 292, 296, 512,
924, 982, 998
Crazy 663
Crazy Horse 717, 861, 1273
CRAZY OTTO 296
Crazy Tennesseans 5
Creach, Papa John 249, 605, 606,
1181
CREAM 63, 112, 120, 133, 166, 233,
240, 296, 317, 326, 436, 532,
595, 620, 690, 783, 834, 996,
1023, 1269
Creamer, Henry 617
Creath, Charles 617
Creative Construction Company
153, 1087
Creative Improvisation Ensemble
1087
Creative World label 647
Creatore, Luigi 1, 94, 278, 583, 1000
Creatures, The 1077
Creed, Linda 94, 1128
CREEDENCE CLEARWATER RE-
VIVAL 297, 331, 406, 496, 512,
526, 527, 705, 997, 1009
Cregan, Jim 405, 448
Creme, Lol 1153
CRENSHAW, Marshall 298, 723
Crentsil, A. B. 1138
Creole Jazz Band 873
Creole Sunshine Orchestra 862
Crespo, Jimmy 11
Creswell-Davis, Andy 670
CREW-CUTS 96, 166, 237, 298, 906,
995
Crewe, Bob 200, 430, 477, 1029
Crewes, Felton 322
Crewsdon, Roy 436
Cribbins, Bernard 777
Cricket, Jiminy 969
CRICKETS 171, 299, 488, 555, 608,
666, 786, 843, 912, 913, 926
Crill, Charles Chester 708
Crill, Connie 708
Crimes, Tory 246
Criner, Clyde 438
Criss, Peter 662
CRISS, Sonny 299, 324, 355, 408
Cristancho, Nicolas 494
CRITCHENSON, John 299, 1044
Crittendon, Ronnie 238
CRITTERS 300, 1279
Croce, Ingrid 300
CROCE, Jim 300
Crocker, Frankie 81
Crofts, Dash 1045

Crombie, Tony 208, 411
Cromwell, Rodney 1208
Cronin, Kevin 979
Cronshaw, Andy 1142
Crook Brothers 483, 741
Crooker, Earle 698
Crooks, Sydney 16
Cropper, Sammy 44
Cropper, Steve 136, 137, 174, 181,
296, 654, 770, 789, 916, 969,
1113, 1159
CROSBY, Bing 300 and passim
CROSBY, Bob 107, 141, 183, 236,
275, 301, 318, 325, 336, 357,
533, 746, 767, 798, 827, 985,
1102, 1107, 1110, 1114, 1130,
1139, 1150, 1224, 1230, 1235,
1267
Crosby, David 176, 187, 302, 546,
605, 781, 1122
Crosby, Gary 917
Crosby, Israel 474, 503, 592, 672,
828, 862
Crosby, Stills & Nash 158, 168, 302,
455, 554, 810, 813, 1122
CROSBY, STILLS, NASH & YOUNG
50, 176, 302, 481, 1273
Cross, Beverley 1116
Cross, Chris 1189
CROSS, Christopher 58, 303, 1030,
1100
Cross Country 1169
Cross, David 440
Cross, Earl 1185
Cross, Tim 10
Crossley, Payton 593
Crossman, Joe 24, 1123
CROSSOVER records 303
Crotty, Ron 169
CROUCH, Andrae Edward 303
Crouch, Nicky 814
CROUCH, Stanley 129, 303, 775,
839, 893, 1185
Crow, Alvin 510
Crow, Bill 694
Crowder, Robert 43
CROWELL, Rodney 72, 210, 216,
242, 243, 291, 292, 303, 347,
518, 608, 1050, 1078, 1119
Crowns 655
CROWS 248, 304, 355, 981
Crucial Three 373, 1204
CRUDUP, Arthur 'Big Boy' 104, 304,
790, 931, 991, 995, 1249
Cruikshank, John 494
Cruikshank, Pete 494
Cruise, Wendy 1203
Cruisers 104
Crum, Simon 572
Crumb, Robert 630
Crump, Bruce 814
Crumwell, Martha 524
CRUSADERS 74, 162, 255, 295, 303,
304, 336, 435, 688, 733, 826,
1182
CRUZ, Celia 11, 75, 105, 132, 266,
274, 304, 405, 515, 687, 727,
824, 878, 887, 890, 926, 946,

947, 958, 989, 1032, 1168, 1192
Cruz, Colin 406
Cruz, Tito 1004
CRYAN' SHAMES 305
CRYSTALS 130, 305, 329, 345, 491,
705, 724, 765, 919, 1064, 1096,
1106
Cuba, Joe 115, 305, 411, 890
Cuber, Ronnie 447, 891
Cubert, Joe 1029
CUBOP 306
Cuddly Duddly 651
Cuffee, Ed 747
Cuffley, John 250
CUGAT, Xavier 11, 41, 81, 91, 132,
241, 306, 416, 474, 690, 743,
754, 793, 809, 823, 886, 889,
1003, 1065
Culley, Wendell 79
Culshaw, Robert 329
CULT 307
Culture Club 34, 83, 125, 147, 227,
312, 327, 625, 854, 1031
Cumberland Ridge Runners 422
Cumin, Cy 418
Cummings, Burton 495, 496
Cummings, George 348
Cundiff, Gary 999
Cunningham, Billy 145
Cunningham, Blair 542
Cunningham, Merce 190
Cunningham, Sis 1048
Curb, Mike 138
Curbelo, José, 73, 219, 706, 793,
1003
CURE 307, 496
Curl, Langston 107, 747
CURLESS, Dick 308
Curnin, Cy 417
Currie, Alannah 1162, 1163
Currie, Billy 864, 1189, 1203
Currie, George 316
Currie, Kevin 1134
Currie, Steve 131
Curry, Mickey 503
CURSON, Ted 116, 281, 308, 350,
391, 545, 806, 838, 840, 971,
1127, 1146
Curtis, Alan 363
Curtis, Barry 659
Curtis, Chris 330, 1045, 1046
Curtis, Clem 428
Curtis, Eddie 220
Curtis, Ian 491, 634
Curtis, Jamie 587
Curtis, Ken 1097
Curtis, King see KING CURTIS
Curtis, Phil 330
Curtis, Sonny 246, 299, 443, 555
Curulewski, John 1128
CURVED AIR 308, 922
CUSCUNA, Michael 1, 43, 125, 153,
170, 222, 269, 282, 308, 476,
603, 917, 951, 957, 1272
Cutler, Chris 539
CYRILLE, Andrew 3, 166, 212, 245,
309, 499, 603, 732, 815, 1147
Czukay, Holger 198, 393

DODDS, Baby (cont.)
  790, 873, 1130
DODDS, Johnny 39, 88, 89, **349**,
  618, 648, 829, 873, 879, 1130
Dodge, Joe 169
Dodgion, Jerry 704
Dodou, Lee 316
Doe, John 119, 1265
Doerge, Craig 539
Dogget, Steve 708
DOGGETT, Bill 6, 140, 161, 227,
  340, **349**, 447, 570, 590, 653,
  802, 869, 973, 981
Doherty, Billy 1056
Doherty, Dennis 757, 758
DOLBY, Thomas **349**, 426, 721, 811,
  930
Doldinger, Klaus 762
Dolenz, Mickey 146, 816, 817
DOLLAR, Johnny 350
Dolphins 554
DOLPHY, Eric 98, 114, 133, 185, 212,
  222, 260, 268, 308, **350**, 376,
  406, 505, 510, 517, 545, 573,
  602, 682, 685, 710, 714, 806,
  845, 1025, 1059, 1207
Domanico, Chuck 650
Domingo, Placido 334, 715
Dominguez, Alberto 1200
Dominions 405
DOMINO, Fats 18, 76, 136, 138, 156,
  225, 230, 292, 303, 344, **351**,
  363, 370, 435, 527, 579, 637,
  702, 704, 770, 845, 909, 937,
  995, 1173
Domino, Floyd 46
Dominoes 80
Donahue, Jerry 334, 401, 955
Donahue, Patty 1205, 1206
DONAHUE, Sam 15, 34, **351**, 427,
  1051, 1058
Donahue, Tom 87, 225, 437, 605
Donald, Chris 1054
Donald, Keith 835
Donaldson, Bobby 929
DONALDSON, Lou 20, 73, 116, 125,
  218, 222, **352**, 355, 371, 519,
  560, 813, 1085
Donaldson, Pat 815
Donaldson, Stan 620
Donaldson, Walter 201
Don & Dewey 1096
Don & Juan 610
DONEGAN, Dorothy 352, 366
DONEGAN, Lonnie 228, 270, 310,
  329, **352**, 401, 448, 473, 523,
  665, 689, 723, 787, 942, 1079,
  1202
Donelian, Armen 1127
Donen, Stanley 102
Donkor, Eddie 11
Donnelly, Ben 581
Donnelly, Dorothy 683
Donnelly, Phillip 347
Donnelly, Robert 1262
Donnelly, Ted 'Muttonleg' 661
DONNER, Ral 352
DONOVAN 89, 263, 318, 319, **353**,

586, 690, 733, 779, 829, 1031
Donovan, Jeff 1269
DOOBIE BROTHERS 303, **353**, 359,
  516, 700, 710, 718, 813, 1070
Doody, Tom 'Toad' 305
DOONICAN, Val 169, 225, 272, **354**,
  779
DOORS 27, 314, **354**, 373, 412, 538,
  582, 665, 756, 857, 997, 1077,
  1265
DOO-WOP 355
Dopsie, Rockin' *see* ROCKIN'
  DOPSIE
Dopyera, John 124
DORHAM, Kenny 116, 260, **355**,
  361, 373, 682, 706, 805, 892,
  902, 990, 1068
Dorman, Lee 111, 582
Dorothy, Rod 1160
Dorough, Bob 831
Dorset, Ray 838
Dorsey, Alan 672
Dorsey Brothers 96, 141, 177, 205,
  217, 301, 356, 548, 683, 746,
  798, 802, 825, 931, 970, 1010,
  1065, 1107, 1215
DORSEY, Jimmy 34, 41, 91, 107,
  196, 217, 221, 262, 306, **356**,
  376, 386, 460, 466, 468, 470,
  533, 638, 640, 683, 690, 704,
  720, 786, 792, 798, 827, 857,
  862, 1001, 1074, 1079, 1180,
  1192, 1201, 1234; *see also*
  Dorsey Brothers
DORSEY, Lee 356, 849, 1100, 1173
Dorsey, Milton 220
DORSEY, Thomas A. 114, 249, **356**,
  478, 479, 1107
DORSEY, Tommy 357 and *passim;*
  see also **Dorsey Brothers**
Doss, Tommy 1097
Dot label 546
Dotson, Hobart 1131
Dotson, Ward 496
DOTTSY 169, **358**
Double Six of Paris 16, 695, 1140
Doucet, Michael 193
Doughty, Neal 979
Douglas, Alan 351, 538
Douglas, Carl 942
Douglas, Charlie 361
Douglas, Chip 1183
Douglas, Clifford 'Boots' 138
DOUGLAS, Craig 343, **358**
Douglas, George 229
Douglas, Graeme 374, 673
Douglas, Jack 1088
Douglas, Jerry 786, 1078
Douglas, Kirk 325, 595
Douglas, Lew 595
Douglas, Mike 339, 675, 903
Douglas, Steve 374
Douglas, Walter 196
Douglass, Bill 194, 1145
Douglass, Greg 652
Douglass, Jimmy 449
Dove, Ronnie 962
Dovells 76, 878

Dovey, Gary 753
DOWD, Tom 358, 434, 727, 1017,
  1234, 1256
Dowell, Saxie 646
Dowle, Dave 'Duck' 94, 1235
Downes, Geoff 45, 562, 1269
Downes, Sean 396
Downey, Brian 822, 1157
Downey, Rick 126
Downie, Tyrone 771, 772, 773
Downing, K. K. (Kenneth) 635
Doyle, Bobby 122, 1004
Doyle, Peter 1049
D'Oyly Carte, Richard 462
Dozier Boys 1131
Dozier, Lamont 148, 430, 553, 835,
  1072; *see also* HOLLAND-
  DOZIER-HOLLAND
Draffen, Willis, Jr 122
Dragon, Carmen 83, 202
Dragon, Daryl 83, 202
Dragon, Dennis 83
DRAKE, Alfred 358, 382, 644, 698
Drake, Bill 359
Drake, Hamid Hank 29, 760
Drake, Jack 359
Drake, John 863
Drake, Laverne 190
DRAKE, Nick 147, **358**, 780, 1110,
  1162
DRAKE, Pete 359, 514, 646, 759,
  819, 824, 885, 1099, 1179, 1251,
  1274
Drake, Rob 232
Draper, Gary 664
Draper, Lauren 961
Draper, Paul 9
DRAPER, Rusty **359**, 425, 1197,
  1261
Drayton, Charlie 1009
Dread, Mikey 246
Dream Academy 359, 978
Dream Police 53
Dreams 155, 1157
DREGS 359
Dreiser, Theodore 1167
Dreja, Chris 1267, 1268
Dresden, Martin 13
Dress, Paul 1167
Dressler, Len 547
Drew, David 1225
Drew, Kenny 1154
Drew, Martin 167, 300, 568, 899,
  1044
Dreyer, Dave 1015
DRIFTERS 49, 97, 101, 329, 343,
  355, 358, **359**, 386, 481, 556,
  599, 611, 628, 655, 656, 696,
  750, 765, 770, 865, 925, 962,
  1064, 1100, 1136
Drifters (English) 984, 1053
DRIFTING COWBOYS 360, 937
DRIFTWOOD, Jimmy 360, 516, 563
Driggs, Frank 971
Drinkard, Carl 552
Drinkard Singers 565
Driscoll, Gary 113, 342
Driscoll, Julie 5, 50, 51, 353, 1120;

531, 544; *see also* **HEATH BROTHERS**
Heath, Percy 260, 320, 337, 394, 495, 529, 531, 589, 703, 813, 816, 1068, 1073; *see also* **HEATH BROTHERS**
HEATH, Ted 24, 108, 218, 238, 314, 409, 517, **531**, 574, 979, 1043, 1174, 1193, 1223
Heatherington, Tony 1021
Heatwave 272, 484
HEAVEN 17, 47, **532**, 569, 1059
HEAVY METAL 5, **532**
Heavy Metal Kids 1190
Heavy Pettin' 393
Hebb, Bobby 134, 1042
Hebler, Dave 933
Hechavarria, Francisco 'Paquito' 722
Heckman, Don 633
Heckstall-Smith, Dick 133, 266, 267, 783
Hedge, Christopher 561
Hedgecock, Ryan 720
Hedgehoppers Anonymous 657
Heffington, Don 720
HEFTI, Neal 51, 73, 78, 107, 163, 179, 410, **533**, 536, 540, 541, 595, 629, 650, 822, 980, 1075
Hegamin, Lucille 956, 1090, 1107
Hegarty, Den 316
HEIDT, Horace 204, 338, 362, 364, 499, **533**, 548, 658, 936, 980, 1088, 1110
Heidt, Horace, Jr 533
Heilbut, Tony 149, 480
Heimberg, Lothar 1041
Heinz 113, 347
Held, Zeus B. 327
Helium Kidz 1265
HELL, Richard 285, 480, **533**, 948, 972, 1151
Hellerman, Fred 1221, 1222
Hellions 781
Helliwell, John 1134
Helm, Bob 839, 1219
Helm, Levon 66, 67, 137, 184, 527, 1253
Helman, Lillian 102
Helmer, Jim 502
HELMS, Bobby **534**, 778, 984
Helms, Don 360, 1243
Hemmings, Courtney 976
Hemmings, David 1269
HEMPHILL, Julius 23, 120, 128, 129, 143, **534**, 603, 795, 1261
Hemphill, Sheldon 803
Henderson, Chick 91, 723
Henderson, Dougie 773
HENDERSON, Fletcher **535** and *passim*
Henderson, Herbert 552
HENDERSON, Horace 104, 106, 150, 209, 377, 438, 528, **536**, 547, 552, 562, 614, 616, 626, 767, 799, 970, 1120
Henderson, Jimmy 111
Henderson, Joe 148, 245, 568, 573,

651, 825, 949, 1060, 1068, 1186, 1188
Henderson, Joe (UK composer) 852
Henderson, Katherine 873
Henderson, Louis 20
Henderson, Peter 1023
Henderson, Ray 337, 622, 1214; *see also* **DeSYLVA, BROWN & HENDERSON**
Henderson, Rosa 1082, 1210
HENDERSON, Skitch 19, 104, 281, **536**, 1051
Henderson, Wayne 55, 112, 304, 682, 755, 781
Hendler, Herb 419
Hendricks, Belford 99
Hendricks, John 757
HENDRICKS, Jon 404, **536**, 740, 763, 816, 973, 1026, 1067, 1257
HENDRIX, Jimi 5, 33, 54, 103, 120, 147, 154, 262, 296, 307, 315, 330, 367, 387, 508, 532, **537**, 559, 583, 593, 633, 634, 657, 669, 672, 712, 755, 781, 804, 896, 923, 997, 1079, 1093, 1106, 1117, 1121, 1122, 1177, 1199, 1219, 1280
Hendry, Rob 978
Hendryx, Nona 677, 686, 926, 1143
Heneker, David 1116
Henke, Bob 'Willard' 348
Henley, Don 370, 415, 455, 811, 1052
Henning, Doug 372
Henrit, Robert 36, 782, 1190
HENRY, Clarence 'Frogman' 231, 225, 455, **539**
HENRY COW 280, 294, **539**
Henry, Ernie 645
Henry, Pierre 1107
HENSKE, Judy **539**
Hensley, Ken 97, 1190
Henson, Denny 422
Henson, Herb 1051
Hentoff, Nat 120, 260, 366, 604, 805, 807, 928, 1211
Henzell, Perry 976
Hepburn, Audrey 31, 256, 470
Hepburn, Katherine 110
Heptones 975
Herbal Mixture 494
Herbert, Arthur 894
Herbert, Chris 'Tambu' 1020, 1021
Herbert, Gregory 703
HERBERT, Victor 44, 337, 375, **540**, 642, 825, 1214, 1270
Herd 431, 566
Herendez, Rene 886
Herion, Trevor 350
Herman, Bonnie 547
Herman, Gus 'Hot Lips' 59
Herman, Ian 638
Herman, Jerry 223, 1096
Herman, Ron 149
HERMAN, Woody **540** and *passim*
HERMAN'S HERMITS 128, 159, 165, 318, 389, **541**, 564, 655, 661, 829, 924, 1153

Hernandez, Almacenas 706
Hernandez, Coco 203
Hernandez, Frankie 1192
Hernandez, Gene 878
Hernández, Jesus 1171
Hernandez, Oscar 74, 75, 695, 706, 879
Hernandez, Patrick 754
Hernandez, Rafael 706
Hernandez, Ray 651
Hernandez, René, 891, 1003
Herndon, Mark Joel 14
Heron, Mike 264, 580
Herren, John 378
Herrit, Robert 37
Herst, Jerry 41
Herth, Milt 1090
Hervey, Irene 625
Hess, Johnny 1176
Hesse, Hermann 1117
HESTER, Carolyn 290, 508, **542**
Hewitt, Paolo 592
Hewlett, John 613
Heyman, Edward 1274
Heyward, DuBose 458
HEYWARD, Nick 401, **542**
HEYWOOD, Eddie 29, 229, 340, **542**, 571, 851, 1209, 1255
Heywood, Eddie, Sr 542
HIATT, John 216, 277, 285, 348, **543**, 726, 846, 913
Hiatus 584
Hibbert, Jimmy 15
Hibbert, Toots (Frederick) 889, 975, 976
HIBBLER, Al 230, 382, 383, 506, **543**, 662, 751, 1145, 1251
Hickerson, Steve 999
Hickman, Art 106, 458
Hicks, Bert 502
Hicks, Bobby 1078
HICKS, Dan 224, 225, 350, 490, **543**
Hicks, John 129, 210
Hicks, Tony 554, 555
Hidalgo, David 119, 179, 286, 723
HIGGINBOTHAM, J. C. 18, 125, 259, 535, **543**, 795, 802, 828, 1028, 1226
HIGGINS, Billy 114, 119, 177, 185, 231, 259, 260, 261, 268, 376, 409, 499, 531, **544**, 573, 629, 632, 682, 813, 820, 825, 895, 1011, 1044, 1146, 1211, 1212
Higgins, Chuck 1219
Higgs, Dave 374
Higgs, Joe 770
High Level Ranters 28, 454
HIGHLIFE 98, **544**
Highlife Stars One 1138
Hightower, Rosetta 878
Highway QCs 278, 480, 1262
Hildegarde 698, 720, 1065
HI-LIFE INTERNATIONAL **544**
Hill 408
Hill, Albert 1247
HILL, Andrew (pianist) 308, 438, **545**, 573, 631, 989, 1132
Hill, Andy 175, 176

Meyers, Toby 789
MEZZROW, Mezz 349, 549, 679, 795, 1090, 1154
Miall, Terry Lee 34
Micahnik, Irving 613
Michael, George 68, 216, 434, 612, 1230, 1231
Michelino 433
Michelot, Pierre 185, 245, 324, 464, 476, 501, 524, 928, 1073, 1140
Michener, James A. 1001
Mickens, Robert 668
MICKEY & SYLVIA 464, 795
Middlebrooks, Wilfred 1022
Middleton, Hunt 557
Middleton, Max 89
Middleton, Ray 794
Middleton, Tony 684
Middleton, Velma 40
MIDLER, Bette 32, 50, 72, 80, 271, 336, 437, 500, 631, 759, 764, 796, 850, 940, 1030, 1194, 1206, 1254
Midnight, Charlie 164
Midnight Flyer 94
Midnighters 66, 593
MIDNITE FOLLIES ORCHESTRA 796
Miesegaes, Sam 1134
Mighty Baby 5, 235
Mighty Clouds Of Joy 434, 480
Mihm, Danny 418, 419
MIKKELBORG, Palle 217, 797, 903, 1026, 1055
Milanes, Pablo 1263
Milano, Fred 343
MILBURN, Amos 14, 18, 161, 559, 695, 784, 797, 832, 981, 1219
Miles, Barry 342
Miles, Buddy 122, 158, 538, 747, 1036
Miles, Butch 182, 507
Miles, Florence 1176
Miles, Garry 523
Miles, John 556
Miles, Lizzie 700, 873
Miles, Otis 1152
Miles-Kingston, Paul 715
MILEY, Bubber 205, 380, 601, 797, 802, 874, 978, 1087, 1241, 1242
Milford, Kim 89
Milhaud, Darius 9, 169
Mili, Gjon 485, 1272
Milito, Helcio 812
Milkowski, Bill 686, 944
Millan, William 415
Millar, Chris 312
Millar, Robin 396, 1261
Millennium 300
Miller, Ann 1250
Miller, Arthur 869
Miller, Bill 474, 1158
Miller, Bob 1134
Miller, Charles 1212
Miller, Chuck 1079
Miller, Daniel 336
MILLER, Eddie 301, 437, 548, 601, 767, 798, 1230, 1238

Miller, Emmett 999
Miller, Frank 463, 776
MILLER, Frankie 158, 798, 1178
MILLER, Glenn 798 and passim
Miller, Helen 1064
Miller, Henry 738
Miller, Herb 799
Miller, Howard 995
Miller, Jerry 813
Miller, Jim 998
Miller, Jimmy 324, 831, 1107
MILLER, Jody 799
Miller, Johnny 258
Miller, Marcus 322, 464
Miller, Max 185, 868
MILLER, Mitch 1, 218, 508, 681, 799, 810, 962, 1074, 1192, 1243
MILLER, Mulgrew 117, 186, 492, 573, 685, 774, 800, 1248
MILLER, Ned 800
Miller, Perry 1042
Miller, Robin 791
MILLER, Roger 390, 490, 584, 671, 799, 800, 803, 847, 852, 937, 1076, 1228, 1271
MILLER, Steve 271, 559, 560, 614, 652, 801, 972, 1039, 1067
Miller, Steve (keyboardist) 203, 294
Miller, Steven (organist) 110
Miller, Tom 533
Milliams, Martin 816
Milligan, Spike 1152
MILLINDER, Lucky 18, 167, 185, 259, 318, 349, 365, 375, 463, 503, 506, 520, 528, 544, 614, 653, 661, 686, 728, 802, 803, 815, 928, 951, 953, 981, 1013, 1038, 1058, 1082, 1087, 1089, 1144, 1155
Millington, Jean 406, 961
Millington, June 406
Mills Blue Rhythm Band 177, 802, 1089
MILLS BROTHERS 40, 41, 79, 171, 191, 328, 355, 447, 690, 802, 1156, 1166, 1239
Mills, Dave 1152
Mills, Denise 553
Mills, Don 666
Mills, Florence 116, 380, 616
Mills, Garry 523
Mills, Gordon 335, 570, 630, 881
MILLS, Irving 69, 177, 380, 381, 399, 729, 744, 798, 802, 1033, 1214
Mills, Kerry 1167
Mills, Michael 978
Mills, Stephan 316
Mills, Stephanie 905
Mills, Ted 125
Millward, Mike 429
Milne, A. A. 1008
MILSAP, Ronnie 69, 426, 803, 938, 954, 1045, 1141
MILTON, Roy 136, 352, 711, 803, 981, 1163
MIMMS, Garnet 804
Mindbenders 425
Mineo, Sal 673, 1062

Minevich, Borrah 515
Ming 327
MINGUS, Charles 804 and passim
Mingus Dynasty 985
Mingus, Susan 806, 807
Minhinnit, Ray 798
MINK DeVILLE 807, 855, 861, 925
Minnear, Kerry 457
MINNELLI, Liza 451, 807, 936
Minnelli, Vincente 807
Minor, Dan 78, 830
Minor, David 605
Minott, Sugar 975
Minshall, Peter 1020
MINSTRELSY 808
Miracles 73, 993
MIRANDA, Carmen 32, 272, 809, 1014, 1033, 1214
Miranda, Freddy 379
Miranda, Ismael 115, 266, 514, 515, 878, 947
Mirley, Milt 1137
Miron, Issacher 1221
Missal, Steve 578
Missourians 194
Misty in Roots 68
MISUNDERSTOOD 809
Mitchell, Adrian 1017
Mitchell, Alan 1152
Mitchell, Billy 252
MITCHELL, Blue 96, 282, 312, 452, 577, 645, 682, 809, 812, 853, 1067, 1068
Mitchell, Bruce 15
MITCHELL, Chad, Trio 187, 334, 810
Mitchell, Charles 610
Mitchell, Chuck 810
Mitchell, Danny 1189
Mitchell, Dwike 812
MITCHELL, Guy 218, 251, 275, 389, 402, 567, 800, 810, 888, 991, 1115, 1192
Mitchell, Harold 866
Mitchell, Haskell 238
Mitchell, Ian 26
Mitchell, John 'Mitch' 387, 404, 538
MITCHELL, Joni 67, 257, 263, 302, 350, 368, 400, 412, 455, 506, 511, 518, 620, 628, 644, 699, 782, 810, 843, 899, 985, 997, 1024, 1049, 1066, 1122, 1127, 1220
Mitchell, Julian 660
Mitchell, Liz 134
Mitchell, Malcolm 904
Mitchell, Mike 658, 659
Mitchell, Mitch 387, 404, 538
Mitchell, Murray 496
Mitchell, Phil 348
Mitchell, Priscilla 360
MITCHELL, Red 260, 419, 524, 645, 650, 668, 682, 766, 775, 811, 837, 862, 908, 935, 1018, 1022, 1073, 1135, 1154
Mitchell, Richard 202
MITCHELL, Roscoe 1, 43, 72, 143, 153, 154, 180, 241, 333, 598,

MITCHELL, Roscoe (cont.) 700, **811**, 815, 840, 848
Mitchell, Whitey 811
Mitchell, Willie 489, 1253
Mitchelle, Jimmy 526
MITCHELL-RUFF DUO 812
Mitchum, Robert 1076
Mitropoulos, Dmitri 102
Mittoo, Jackie 975
Mixon, Danny 985
MIZE, Billy 812
MOBLEY, Hank 116, 180, 186, 243, 244, 268, 321, 355, 492, 544, 560, 568, 602, 622, **812**, 825, 971, 1068, 1211
MOBY GRAPE 353, 605, **813**, 1102
Modeliste, Joseph 'Zigaboo' 849
Modernaires 777
MODERN JAZZ QUARTET 21, 50, 86, 245, 320, 337, 344, 531, 588, 702, **813**, 1010, 1011, 1040, 1140, 1223
Modern Lovers 855, 985
Modugno, Domenico 1028
Moe, Big 97
Moe, Rick 809
Moeller, Lucky 333
Moeller, Tommy 1189, 1190
Moerlen, Pierre 472
Moffett, Charles 119, 685, 969
Moffett, Charnett 685, 726, 774, 800, 1248
Mogg, Phil 1187, 1188
Mogoboya, Fats Ramoba 948
Mogul Thrash 45, 53
Moholo, Louis 1168
Mojo Men 894
MOJOS 814
Mole, John 267
Mole, Miff 91, 376, 499, 638, 857, 1010, 1090, 1149, 1180, 1234
Molina, Ralph 1273
Molinaro, Edouard 117
Molland, Joey 59, 569
Molloy, Matt 919
MOLLY HATCHET 732, **814**
Moloney, Mick 620
Moloney, Paddy 234, 822
Moman, Chips 94, 145, 770, 803, 1098
Mona, Eugene 189
Monaghan, Walt 578
Monarch, Michael 1117
MONCUR, Grachan 166, 180, 309, 437, 726, 733, **814**, 840, 1038
Mondane Willis Singers 163
Mondello, Toots 1163
Mondesir, Mark 917
Mondo Cane 404
Mondo, Ray 307
Mondragon, Joe 837
Monette, David 1051, 1063
MONEY, Zoot 54, 177, 267, 339, 517, **815**, 922
Monge, César 346
Mongrel 835
Monguito 887
Monica, Santa 469

MONK, Thelonious 815 and *passim*
Monk, Thelonious, Jr 816
Monk, William Henry 816
MONKEES 79, 146, 173, 216, 252, 339, 473, 538, 640, 790, **816**, 848, 859, 861, 1119, 1122, 1263
Monkman, Francis 308
Monks 1125
Monotones 231
MONRO, Matt 56, 491, **817**, 852
MONROE, Bill 124, 249, 288, 289, 347, 371, 419, 483, 493, 610, 675, 741, 749, 753, 778, **817**, 821, 860, 880, 931, 1078, 1112, 1127, 1218, 1256
Monroe, Birch 817
Monroe, Charlie 419, 817, 968, 1127
Monroe, Clarke 990
Monroe, James 552, 818
Monroe, Marilyn 178, 754, 1197
Monroe, Mike 512
MONROE, Vaughn 284, **818**, 963, 1097
Monsborough, 'Lazy' Ade 93
Montalban, Ricardo 1065
MONTANA, Patsy **818**, 961
Montana, Vince 125
Montand, Yves 915, 1197
Montañez, Andy 346, 379, 727, 1032
Montañez, Ricardo 198
Monte, Tony 522
Monterose, J. R. 805, 1129
Monteux, Pierre 935
MONTEZ, Chris **818**, 876
Montgomery, Bob 62, 299, 439, 555, 666, 716
Montgomery Brothers 819, 1060
MONTGOMERY, Little Brother 136, 455, **819**, 1141
MONTGOMERY, Melba 148, 623, 724, **819**
Montgomery, Monk 780
MONTGOMERY, Wes 8, 99, 154, 231, 253, 406, 419, 492, 511, 568, 589, 633, 645, 682, 795, **819**, 970, 1085, 1127
MONTOLIU, Tete 185, 259, 477, 518, **820**, 1161, 1223
Montrose, Ronnie 500, 1254
Monty Python 135, 393, 521
MOOD MUSIC 820
MOODY BLUES 71, 161, 329, 430, 457, 780, **820**, 996
MOODY, Clyde 821
MOODY, James 261, 443, 463, 473, 477, 529, 537, 591, 606, 622, 688, **821**, 886, 902, 929, 1034, 1132, 1175, 1179, 1180
Moody, Mick 1235
Moody, Ron 76
Moog, Dr Robert A. 204
Moon, Doug 202, 203
Moon, Jim 1103
Moon, Keith 312, 392, 399, 406, 690, 1038, 1114, 1183, 1236, 1237, 1277
MOONDOG 821

MOONEY, Art 318, 646, **822**, 1055, 1163
Mooney, Joe 1037
Mooney, John 1014
Mooney, Malcolm 198
Mooney, Ralph 608
Mooney, Thom 1022
Moonglows 231, 643, 784
Moonlighters 444
Moore, Alan 635
Moore, Anthony 539
Moore, Billy 729
Moore, Bob 813
Moore, Brew 244, 306
MOORE, Christy 150, 157, **822**, 835, 919, 1217
Moore, Curley 1084
Moore, Daniel 1118
Moore, Dannie 259
Moore, Don 345
Moore, Dudley 303, 780
Moore, Garry, (USA radio TV) 364, 460, 1224
MOORE, Gary 234, 267, 783, **822**, 1157
Moore, George 382
Moore, Gerry 1069
Moore, Johnny 162, 360, 571, 655, 975
Moore, Marvin 974, 1197
Moore, Michael 104, 507
Moore, Oscar 258
Moore, Pete 993
Moore, Pop 133
Moore, Ralph 568
Moore, Richard 1177
Moore, Sam 1032
Moore, Scotty 111, 181, 353, 846, 931, 932
Moore, Tim 502
Moore, Warren 993
Moorehead, Agnes 249
Moorshead, John 362
Moors Murderers 934, 1202
MOR 823
Mora, Pepe 403, 722, 824
Morais, Vinisius de 140
Morales, Edgardo 379
Morales, Esy 823
Morales, Humberto 823
Morales, Noro 306, 515, 743, 793, 823, 946, 1003, 1014
Morales, Obdulio 823
MORALES, Orquesta Hermanos 823
Moran, Gayle 283, 459
Moran, Mike 335
Moran, Pat 679
Moran, Robert 467
MORATH, Max 132, 631, **823**, 956
Moray Eels 557
Moraz, Patrick 171, 821, 1269
Mordecai, Harry 1219
Morder, Doug 16
MORÉ, Beny 38, 199, 305, 415, 758, **824**, 930, 947
Morello, Joe 169, 1260
Moreno, Rita 439

MUNDY, Jimmy 78, 349, 474, 475, 547, **838**, 1107
MUNGO JERRY **838**
Muñoz, Rafael 889
Munro, John 130
Munrow, David 264, 1274
Murad, Jerry 515
Murcia, Billy 855
Murdoch, Rupert 1188
Murphey, Elliott 642
Murphey, Jerry 1149
Murphy, Gregg 353
Murphy, John 46
Murphy, Kevin 25, 650
MURPHY, Mark 259, 644, **838**
Murphy, Mike 979
Murphy, Peter 597
Murphy, Rose 1121
MURPHY,Turk 397, 528, **838**, 1092, 1219
Murphy, Walter, & The Big Apple Band 232
Murphy, Willie 667
Murray, Alex 829
MURRAY, Anne 198, 206, 718, 723, **839**, 1253
Murray, Arthur 168, 249
Murray, Bill (UK bass) 822, 823
Murray, Billy (US singer) 956, 965
Murray, Bobby 296
Murray, Dave (UK bass) 582
MURRAY, David (US reeds) 212, 332, 350, 506, 523, 603, 732, 774, **839**, 840, 920, 1185, 1261
Murray, Dee 324, 611, 612
Murray, Deidre 1164
Murray, Don 1183
Murray, Jim 952
Murray, Kel 474
Murray, Ken 1123
Murray, Martin 558, 559
Murray, Mitch 109, 330, 436, 457
Murray, Neil 267, 1235
Murray, Pauline 875
MURRAY, Sunny 55, 180, 449, 523, 603, 732, **840**, 1146, 1185
Murray, Tony 1177
Murrell, Herbie 1128
Murrells, Joseph 1081
Murvin, Junior 246
Muscle Shoals 1098
Muse, David 415
Music Explosion 173
MUSIC HALL genre **840**
Music Master Catalogue 1040
Musica Electronica Viva 25
Musica Internacional 224
Musker, Joe 327
MUSSELWHITE, Charlie 122, 759, **840**
Musso, Vido 646, 647, 1022
Mussolini, Romano 1044
Mussulli, Boots 221
Muybridge, Eadweard 467
Mwana, Master 833
Myddle Class 655
Mydland, Brent 486, 487
Myers, Alan 337

Myers, Amina Claudine 3, 129, 726
Myers, Jack 1227
Myers, Wilson 1233
Myrick, Weldon 36
Mystery Girls 327
Mystics 599

N

Nadir, Rikki 1194
Naftalin, Mark 183, 952
Nagle, Ron 861
Naikim, Lou 559
Nail, Jimmy 952
Nails, Jimmy 21
Nancarrow, Colin 672
Nance, Ray 46, 185, 380, 381, 382, 383, 473, 485, 547
Nanton, Joe 'Tricky Sam' 165, 380, 381, 382
Napier, Alex 1190
Napier, Jean 970
Napier-Bell, Simon 131, 597, 613
Napoleon, Marty 982
Napoleon, Phil 1090
Narvaez, Jesus Chuito 347
Nascimento, Milton 56, 173, 949, 1066
Nash, Brian 433
Nash, Graham 302, 554, 555, 709, 781, 810, 1122
NASH, Johnny 506, 511, 771, **842**
Nash, Ogden 487, 1225
Nash, Paul 314
Nashville Brass 318
Nashville Grass 420
NASHVILLE TEENS 33, 723, **842**
Nasser, Jamil 501
Nathan, Syd 653
NATIONAL BARN DANCE 842
National Health 170, 197, 267, 1235
National Youth Jazz Orchestra 108, 604, 835, 1006
Natural Gas 569
Naughton, Bobby **1087**
Naughton, Jay 1205
Nauseef, Mark 823
Naux 534
Navarro, Esther 190
NAVARRO, Fats 132, 139, 163, 312, 373, 501, 661, 741, 806, **843**, 928, 1017, 1058
Nawahi, King Bernie 999
NAYLOR, Jerry **843**
NAZARETH 523, 711, 810, **843**, 1170
N'DOUR, Youssou 668, 784, **843**, 1071
Neagle, Anna 165, 458
Neal, Bob 931
Neal, Jack 1201
Near 1138
NEAR, Holly **843**, 1222, 1258
Needham, Margie 237
Neff, Hildegarde 1225
Negri, Joe 1165
Negron, Charles (Chuck) William 1164
Negroni, Joe 730

Neher, Caspar 1224
NEIDLINGER, Buell 277, 678, 816, **844**, 926, 1146
Neighbor, Jeff 635
Neil, Chris 372
NEIL, Fred 175, **844**, 859
Neil, Vince 512, 831
Neilsen, Rick 229
Neilson, Shaun 467
Neloms, Bob 985
Nelson, Bill 88, 245, 421, 597, 864, 1078, 1268
Nelson, Bobby 890
Nelson, Dave 486, 874
Nelson, Earl 325
Nelson, Evelyn 1180
Nelson, Gail 1068
Nelson, Gene 325
Nelson, Harrison 14
Nelson, Ian 88
Nelson, Ken 595
Nelson, Nate 418
NELSON, Oliver 79, 199, 281, 352, 394, 408, 427, 510, 561, 625, 644, 816, **844**, 988, 1028, 1034, 1085, 1156, 1252, 1260
NELSON, Ozzie 310, 798, **845**, 1130, 1150
NELSON, Rick 76, 179, 181, 216, 297, 329, 351, 398, 543, 579, 768, 786, **845**, 884, 894, 919, 920
NELSON, Sandy 431, 580, 596, **846**
Nelson, Skip 720
NELSON, Tracy **846**, 847, 1013
Nelson, Wayne 713
NELSON, Willie **846** and passim
Nemzo, Lisa 416
Neon Boys 533, 1151
NERO, Peter **848**, 1245
Nesbitt, John 747
NESMITH, Mike 146, 177, 442, 514, 782, 816, 817, **848**, 1122
NESSA label **848**
Nessa, Ann 811
Nessa, Chuck 19, 42, 848
Nestico, Sam 79
Nestor, Pam 37
Neubergh, Patrick 50
Neustadt, Lisa 971
Nevarez, Edgar 495
NEVILLE Brothers **849**, 850, 964, 1173
Nevins, Al 157, 877, 1164
Nevins, Marty 1164
Nevison, Ron 1136
NEW AGE **850**
New Air 1164
New Animals 177, 815
New Barbarians 245
NEWBORN, Phineas, Jr 94, 529, **851**
NEWBURY, Mickey 529, **851**, 1005, 1131
NEW CHRISTY MINSTRELS 187, 206, 242, 546, 743, **852**, 1004
New Church 670
Newell, Nick 815

SWAN, Billy 179, **1137**, 1234, 1269
Swan Silvertones 479
Swanson, Chris 1261
Swanson, Edwin 951
Swarbrick, Dave 95, 213, 282, 400,
    401, 714, 1274
Swartz, Harvie 633
Sweatman, Wilbur 560, 728
Sweeney, Bernard 1232
Sweeney's Men 921, 1116
SWEET 236, 964, **1137**
Sweet, Darrel 843
SWEET HONEY IN THE ROCK 844,
    1137
Sweet Inspirations 99, 801, 565
Sweet Savage 342
Sweet Sensation 523
SWEET TALKS 44, 544, **1138**
Sweetland, Sally 1037
Sweney, Jim 999
Swenson, John 533
Swift Jewel Cowboys 192
Swing Era see BIG BAND ERA
SWING in music 997, **1138**
SWINGING BLUE JEANS 391, 395,
    554, **1140**
SWINGLE SINGERS 695, 814, **1140**
Swingle Sisters 459
Swingle, Ward Lamar 1140
Swinney, Warrick 638
Switch 587
Swope, Earl 1176
Sykes, John 1157, 1235
SYKES, Roosevelt 127, 136, 333,
    618, 790, 981, 1107, **1140**, 1141
Sylva, Alan 1147
Sylvain, Sylvain 855, 856
Sylvester 655
Sylvester, Andy 233
Sylvester, Hannah 1107
Sylvester, Terry 154, 391, 554, 1140
SYLVIA 1141
Sylvia, Margo 455
Sylvian, David 597, 1268
Symphonic Slam 113
Symphony Sid 893
Syn 1269
Syran 950
SZABO, Gabor 505, 562, 714, **1141**
Szell, George 1059
Szigeti, Joseph 935
SZYMCZYK, Bill 262, 655, **1141**,
    1211, 1256

T

Tabackin, Lew 13, 568, 1261
Tabane, Philip 60
Tabbal, Tani 812
TABOR, June 95, 130, 157, 214,
    558, 627, 1116, **1142**, 1255
TABU LEY 92, 433, 638, 639, 833,
    1142
Tackett, Fred 711
Tacuma, Jamaaladeen 171, 261
Tagg, Eric 988
Taht, Juri 1064
Tailgate style (trombone) 879

Tait, Philip Goodhand 197
Takase, Aki 633
Taking Chances 665
Takoma label 399
Tala, André Marie 1159
Talas, Grigory 449
Talazo Fuji Commanders 75
Talbot, Billy 1273
Talbot, Mick 1128
TALKING HEADS 80, 326, 391, 440,
    445, 449, 855, 985, 1091, **1142**,
    1265
Talley, Gary 145
Talley, Nedra 1012
Talley, Robert 1159
Talmadge, Art 705
Talmy, Shel 372, 560, 787
Tampa Red 356, 599
Tams, John 15, 558
Tana, Akira 504, 531
Tanas, Anday 112
Tandy, Richard 460, 780
TANGERINE DREAM 5, 671, 1041,
    1143
TANGO **1144**
Tanner, Elmo 1016, 1224
Tanner, Gid 288, 945, 1259
Tan Nightingale 7
Tapia, Antonio 198
TARABU **1144**
Tarasov, Vladimir 449
Tarlton, Jimmie 315
Tarney, Alan 984
Tarnopol, Nat 171
Tarplin, Marvin 993
Tate, Bruce 906
TATE, Buddy 78, 172, 175, 248,
    257, 273, 324, 448, 507, 570,
    626, 732, 733, 751, 953, 1024,
    1144, 1160, 1178, 1202, 1226
Tate, Erskine 365, 648, 873, 1220
Tate, Fran 711
Tate, Grady 427, 459, 838, 911,
    1085, 1092
Tate, Houston 443
Tate, Howard 925
Tate, Laurie 1240
Tate, Troy 1091, 1150
TATUM, Art 139, 194, 201, 209, 236,
    331, 485, 493, 525, 536, 547,
    617, 624, 682, 786, 892, 910,
    928, 956, 982, 1065, 1121, **1145**,
    1181, 1252
Taupin, Bernie 5, 17, 593, 611
Taupin, Dick 612
Tavares 502
Tavernier, Bertrand 477
Tawney, Cyril 1274
Taylor, Andy 363, 889, 1121
Taylor, Art 186, 268, 312, 356, 408,
    471, 489, 492, 748, 928, 1177
TAYLOR, Billy 199, 253, 281, 473,
    513, 522, 775, 970, 1121, **1145**
Taylor, Bobby 537
TAYLOR, Cecil 55, 98, 120, 125, 308,
    309, 345, 355, 395, 523, 603,
    678, 725, 732, 815, 839, 840,
    844, 989, 991, 1061, **1146**, 1247,

    1248
Taylor, Chip 1177
Taylor, Clive 24
Taylor, Creed 99, 914, 1156
Taylor, Dallas 302, 1122, 1227
Taylor, Deems 44
Taylor, Diana 1232
Taylor, Dick 934, 1007
Taylor, 'Dolphin' 994
Taylor, Don 772, 773
Taylor, Drew 145
Taylor, Eddie 593
Taylor, Elizabeth 416, 1095
Taylor, Eva 601, 873, 1241, 1242
Taylor, Eve 175
Taylor, Frank C. 571
Taylor, Gary 431
Taylor, Gene 119, 508, 1255, 1269
Taylor, Graeme 15, 557, 558
TAYLOR, Hound Dog 19, 110, 127,
    1147
Taylor, Ian 229
Taylor, Jack 818
TAYLOR, James 44, 86, 98, 155,
    168, 257, 370, 451, 481, 810,
    909, 957, 985, 1070, 1071,
    1148, 1220
Taylor, James 'JT' 669
Taylor, Joe 591
Taylor, John (piano) 55, 722, 1044,
    1232
Taylor, John (guitar) 363, 889
Taylor, Johnny 985
TAYLOR, Koko 20, 93, 232, 960,
    1148
Taylor, Larry 200
Taylor, Lynne 316
Taylor, Mark 1174
Taylor, Mary 799
Taylor, Mel 1200
Taylor, Mick 89, 561, 657, 760, 766,
    783, 1006, 1008, 1009, 1190
Taylor, Myra 698
Taylor, Paul 998
Taylor, Phil 'Philthy Animal' 831
Taylor, Richard 763
Taylor, Roger 363, 864, 951, 952,
    1119
Taylor, Sam 'The Man' 2, 555
Taylor, Susan 1243
Taylor, Vinnie 1054
Taylor, Zola 730, 920
Tchicai, John 55, 98, 231, 269, 345,
    947, 1019, 1020, 1061
Tchico 70
Tchoupitoulas 849
Teachy, John 270
Teagarden, Charlie 857, 923, 1149,
    1178, 1201
Teagarden, Cub (Clois) 1149
TEAGARDEN, Jack **1149** and pas-
    sim
Teagarden, Norma 1149
Teague, Dick 984
TEARDROP EXPLODES 327, 373,
    418, 568, 577, 1091, **1150**, 1204
Tear Gas 522
TEARS FOR FEARS 60, 619, 670,

NOTES

NOTES

NOTES

NOTES

NOTES